# TWENTIETH-CENTURY SCIENCE-FICTION WRITERS

Twentieth-Century Writers Series

*Twentieth-Century Children's Writers*

*Twentieth-Century Crime and Mystery Writers*

*Twentieth-Century Science-Fiction Writers*

*Twentieth-Century Romance and Historical Writers*

*Twentieth-Century Western Writers*

# TWENTIETH-CENTURY SCIENCE-FICTION WRITERS

THIRD EDITION

EDITORS

NOELLE WATSON
PAUL E. SCHELLINGER

ASSISTANT EDITORS

ELIZABETH NISHIURA
KAREN P. SINGSON

St J

St James Press

Chicago and London

For information, write:
ST. JAMES PRESS
233 East Ontario Street
Chicago, Illinois 60611
U.S.A.

or

2–6 Boundary Row
London SE1 8HP
England



**British Library Cataloguing in Publication Data**
Twentieth-century science-fiction writers.—3rd ed.
I. Watson, Noelle, *1958—* II. Schellinger, Paul E., *1962—*
823.087609

ISBN 1-55862-111-3

First edition published 1981; second edition 1986.

## CONTENTS

# EDITOR'S NOTE

The selection of writers included in this book is based upon the recommendations of the advisers listed on page xvii.

The main part of the book covers English-language writers of science fiction whose work has appeared in the 20th century. A few important precursors of 20th-century science fiction have also been included, with Mary Shelley's *Frankenstein* (1818) representing the earliest work to be discussed as part of the genre. The appendix includes selective representations of foreign-language writers whose books have a large audience in English translation.

The entry for each writer in the main part of the book consists of a biography, a bibliography, and a signed critical essay. Living authors were invited to add a comment on their work. The bibliographies list writings according to the categories of science-fiction and other publications. In addition, science-fiction writing is further sub-divided into lists of works published under pseudonyms. Series characters are indicated for novels and short story collections. Original British and United States editions of all books have been listed; other editions, such as those published in Australia or Canada, are listed only if they are the first editions. Uncollected science-fiction short stories published since the entrant's last collection have been listed only when a writer's reputation is based largely on short stories; in those cases where a story has been published in a magazine and later in an anthology, we have tended to list the anthology.

Entries include notations of available bibliographies, manuscript collections, and book-length critical studies. Other critical materials appear in the Reading List of secondary works on the genre.

We would like to thank the entrants and contributors for their patience and cooperation in helping us compile this book.

# READING LIST

Aldiss, Brian, *Billion Year Spree: A History of Science Fiction.* London, Weidenfeld and Nicolson, and New York, Doubleday, 1973.

Aldiss, Brian, *Science Fiction Art.* New York, Bounty, 1975; London, Hart Davis, 1976.

Aldiss, Brian, *Science Fiction as Science Fiction.* Frome, Somerset, Bran's Head, 1978.

Aldiss, Brian, and Harry Harrison, editors, *Hell's Cartographers: Some Personal Histories of Science Fiction Writers.* London, Weidenfeld and Nicolson, and New York, Harper, 1975.

Aldiss, Brian, and Harry Harrison, editors, *SF Horizons.* New York, Arno Press, 1975.

Aldiss, Brian, *Trillion Year Spree: The History of Science Fiction,* with David Wingrove. London, Gollancz, and New York, Atheneum, 1986.

Aldridge, Alexandra, *The Scientific World View in Dystopia.* Ann Arbor, Michigan, UMI Research Press, 1984.

Allard, Yvon, *Paralittératures.* Montréal, La Centre des Bibliothèques, 1975.

Allen, Dick, *Science Fiction: The Future.* New York, Harcourt Brace, 1971.

Allen, L. David, *The Ballantine Teachers' Guide to Science Fiction.* New York, Ballantine, 1975.

Allen, L. David, *Science Fiction: An Introduction.* Lincoln, Nebraska, Cliff Notes, 1973; as *Science Fiction Readers Guide,* Lincoln, Nebraska, Centennial Press, 1974.

Amelio, Ralph J., *Hal in the Classroom: Science Fiction Films.* Dayton, Ohio, Pflaum, 1974.

Amis, Kingsley, *New Maps of Hell: A Survey of Science Fiction.* New York, Harcourt Brace, 1960; London, Gollancz, 1961.

Anderson, Craig W., *Science Fiction Films of the Seventies.* Jefferson, North Carolina, McFarland, 1985.

Armitt, Lucy, editor, *Where No Man Has Gone Before: Essays on Women and Science Fiction.* London and New York, Routledge, 1991.

Armytage, W.H.G., *Yesterday's Tomorrows: A Historical Survey of Future Societies.* London, Routledge, 1968.

Ash, Brian, *Faces of the Future: The Lessons of Science Fiction.* London, Elek, and New York, Taplinger, 1975.

Ash, Brian, editor, *The Visual Encyclopedia of Science Fiction.* New York, Harmony, and London, Pan, 1977.

Ash, Brian, *Who's Who in Science Fiction.* London, Elm Tree, and New York, Taplinger, 1976.

Ashley, Michael, editor, *The History of the Science Fiction Magazine.* London, New English Library, 4 vols., 1974–76; vols. 1 and 2, Chicago, Regnery, 1976.

Ashley, Michael, *The Illustrated Book of Science Fiction Lists.* New York, Simon and Schuster, 1983.

Ashley, Michael, and Terry Jeeves, *The Complete Index to Astounding/Analog.* Oak Forest, Illinois, Weinberg, 1981.

Atkinson, Geoffroy, *The Extraordinary Voyage in French Literature Before 1700.* New York, Columbia University Press, 1920; *The Extraordinary Voyage in French Literature from 1700–1720.* Paris, Champion, 1922.

Bailey, J.O., *Pilgrims Through Space and Time: Trends and Patterns in Scientific and Utopian Fiction.* New York, Argus, 1947.

Barnes, Myra, *Linguistics and Language in Science Fiction-Fantasy.* New York, Arno Press, 1975.

Barr, Marleen S., and Nicholas Smith, editors, *Women and Utopia: Critical Interpretations.* Lanham, Maryland, University Press of America, 1983.

Barron, Neil, editor, *Anatomy of Wonder.* New York, Bowker, 1976; 2nd edition, 1981.

Barron, Neil, editor, *Fantasy Literature: A Reader's Guide.* New York, Garland, 1990.

Bates, Susannah, *The Pendex: An Index of Pen Names and House Names in Fantastic, Thriller, and Series Literature.* New York, Garland, 1981.

Baxter, John, *Science Fiction in the Cinema.* New York, A.S. Barnes, and London, Zwemmer, 1970.

Bell, Joseph, *First Editions: "A Thousand and One Nights of Reading".* Toronto, Soft Books, 1988.

Benson, Michael, *Vintage Science Fiction Films, 1896–1949.* Jefferson, North Carolina, McFarland, 1985.

Berger, Harold L., *Science Fiction and the New Dark Age.* Bowling Green, Ohio, Popular Press, 1976.

Bleiler, Everett F., *The Checklist of Fantastic Literature.* Chicago, Shasta, 1948; revised edition, as *The Checklist of Science-Fiction and Supernatural Fiction,* Glen Rock, New Jersey, Firebell, 1978.

Bleiler, Everett F., *The Guide to Supernatural Fiction: A Full Description of 1,775 Books from 1750–1960.* Kent, Ohio, Kent State University Press, 1983.

Bleiler, Everett F., editor, *Science Fiction Writers: Critical Studies of the Major Authors from the Early Nineteenth Century to the Present Day.* New York, Scribner, 1982.

Bleiler, Everett F., and Richard J. Bleiler, *Science Fiction, the Early Years.* Kent, Ohio, Kent State University Press, 1990.

Bleiler, Everett F., editor, *Supernatural Fiction Writers: Fantasy and Horror.* New York, Scribner, 1985.

Bleiler, Richard J., *The Index to Adventure Magazine.* Mercer Island, Washington, Starmont House, 1990.

Blish, James, *The Issue at Hand: Studies in Contemporary Magazine Science Fiction.* Chicago, Advent, 1964; *More Issues at Hand,* 1970 (both books as William Atheling, Jr.).

Bova, Ben, editor, *Closeup, New Worlds.* New York, St. Martin's Press, 1977.

Bova, Ben, *Notes to a Science Fiction Writer* (for children). New York, Scribner, 1975.

Bova, Ben, *Through Eyes of Wonder: Science Fiction and Science* (for children). Reading, Massachusetts, Addison Wesley, 1975.

Bova, Ben, *Viewpoint.* Cambridge, Massachusetts, NESFA Press, 1977.

Boyajian, Jerry, and Kenneth R. Johnson, *Index to the Science Fiction Magazines, 1979–81.* Cambridge, Massachusetts, Twaci Press, 3 vols., 1981–82.

Bradley, Marion Zimmer, Norman Spinrad, and Alfred Bester, *Expedition Perilous: Three Essays on Science Fiction.* San Bernardino, California, Borgo Press, 1983.
Bretnor, Reginald, editor, *The Craft of Science Fiction.* New York, Harper, 1976.
Bretnor, Reginald, editor, *Modern Science Fiction: Its Meaning and Its Future.* New York, Coward McCann, 1953; revised edition, Chicago, Advent, 1979.
Bretnor, Reginald, editor, *Science Fiction, Today and Tomorrow.* New York, Harper, 1974.
Brians, Paul, *Nuclear Holocausts: Atomic War in Fiction 1895–1984.* Kent, Ohio, Kent State University Press, 1987.
Briney, R.E., and Edward Wood, *SF Bibliographies: An Annotated Bibliography of Bibliographical Works on Science Fiction and Fantasy Fiction.* Chicago, Advent, 1972.
Brosnan, John, *Future Tense: The Cinema of Science Fiction.* London, Macdonald and Jane's, 1978; New York, St Martin's Press, 1979.
Brown, Charles N., and Dena Brown, editors, *Locus: The Newspaper of the Science Fiction Field.* Boston, Gregg Press, 1978.
Brown, Charles N., William G. Contento, and Hal W. Hall, *Science Fiction, Fantasy, and Horror: A Comprehensive Bibliography of Books and Short Fiction Published in the English Language 1984–[1990].* Oakland, California, Locus Press, 1986– (annual volume).
Brown, E.J., *Brave New World, 1984, and We: Essays on Anti-Utopia.* Ann Arbor, Michigan, Ardis, 1976.
Budrys, Algis, *Benchmarks: Galaxy Bookshelf.* Carbondale, Southern Illinois University Press, 1985.
Burgess, Michael, *A Guide to Science Fiction and Fantasy in the Library of Congress Classification Scheme.* San Bernardino, California, Borgo Press, 1984; 2nd edition, 1988.
Burgess, Michael, *A Reference Guide to Science Fiction, Fantasy, and Horror.* Boulder, Colorado, Libraries Unlimited, 1992.
Calkins, Elizabeth, and Barry McGhan, *Teaching Tomorrow: A Handbook of Science Fiction for Teachers.* Dayton, Ohio, Pflaum, 1972.
Cawthorn, James, and Michael Moorcock, *Fantasy: The 100 Best Books.* New York, Carroll and Graf, and London, Xanadu, 1988.
Cazedessus, C.E., Jr., editor, *Ghost Stories.* Evergreen, Colorado, Opar Press, 1973.
Chauvin, Cy, editor, *A Multitude of Visions: Essays on Science Fiction.* Baltimore, T-K Graphics, 1975.
Cioffi, Frank, *Formula Fiction? An Anatomy of American Science Fiction, 1930–40.* Westport, Connecticut, Greenwood Press, 1982.
Clarens, Carlos, *An Illustrated History of the Horror Film.* New York, Capricorn, 1967; revised edition, as *Horror Movies,* London, Secker and Warburg, 1968.
Clareson, Thomas D., editor, *Extrapolation: A Science Fiction Newsletter 1959–1969.* Boston, Gregg Press, 1978.
Clareson, Thomas D., *Many Futures, Many Worlds: Theme and Form in Science Fiction.* Kent, Ohio, Kent State University Press, 1977.
Clareson, Thomas D., *Science Fiction in America, 1870's to 1930's: An Annotated Bibliography of Primary Sources.* Westport, Connecticut, Greenwood Press, 1984.
Clareson, Thomas D., *Science Fiction Criticism: An Annotated Checklist.* Kent, Ohio, Kent State University Press, 1972.
Clareson, Thomas D., *SF: A Dream of Other Worlds.* College Station, Texas A and M University, 1973.
Clareson, Thomas D., editor, *SF: The Other Side of Realism: Essays on Modern Fantasy and Science Fiction.* Bowling Green, Ohio, Popular Press, 1971.
Clareson, Thomas D., editor, *Voices for the Future: Essays on Major Science Fiction Writers.* Bowling Green, Ohio, Popular Press, 2 vols., 1976–79; vol. 3, edited with Thomas L. Wymer, 1983.
Clarke, I.F., *The Pattern of Expectation 1644–2001.* London, Cape, 1979.
Clarke, I.F., *The Tale of the Future.* London, Library Association, 1961.
Clarke, I.F., *Voices Prophesying War 1763–1984.* London, Oxford University Press, 1966.
Cockroft, Thomas G.L., *Index to Fiction in Radio News and Other Magazines.* Lower Hutt, New Zealand, Cockcroft, 1970.
Cockcroft, Thomas G.L., *Index to the Weird Fiction Magazines.* Lower Hutt, New Zealand, Cockcroft, 2 vols., 1962–64.
Cole, Walter L., *A Checklist of Science-Fiction Anthologies.* New York, Cole, 1964.
Colombo, John Robert, *CDN SF and F: A Bibliography of Canadian Science Fiction and Fantasy.* Toronto, Hounslow Press, 1979.
Contento, William, *Index to Science Fiction Anthologies and Collections.* Boston, Hall, and London, Prior, 1978.
Contento, William, *Index to Science Fiction Anthologies and Collections 1977–1983.* Boston, Hall, 1984.
Cottrill, Tim, Martin H. Greenberg, and Charles G. Waugh, *Science Fiction and Fantasy Series and Sequels: A Bibliography.* New York, Garland, 1986.
Cowart, David, and Thomas L. Wymer, editors, *Twentieth-Century American Science Fiction Writers.* Detroit, Gale, 2 vols., 1981.
Crawford, Joseph H., Jr., James J. Donahue, and Donald M. Grant, *"333": a Bibliography of the Science Fantasy Novel.* Providence, Rhode Island, Grandon, 1953.
Currey, L.W., *Science Fiction and Fantasy Authors: A Bibliography of First Printings of Their Fiction and Selected Non-Fiction.* Boston, Hall, 1979.
Davenport, Basil, *Inquiry into Science Fiction.* New York, Longman, 1955.
Davenport, Basil, editor, *The Science Fiction Novel: Imagination and Social Criticism.* Chicago, Advent, 1964; revised edition, 1964.
Davies, Philip John, editor, *Science Fiction, Social Conflict, and War.* Manchester, Manchester University Press, 1990.
Day, Bradford M., *Bibliography of Adventure: Mundy, Burroughs, Rohmer, Haggard.* Denver, New York, Science Fiction and Fantasy Publications, 1964.
Day, Bradford M., *The Checklist of Fantastic Literature in Paperbound Books.* Denver, New York, Science Fiction and Fantasy Publications, 1965.
Day, Bradford M., *The Complete Checklist of Science Fiction Magazines.* New York, Science Fiction and Fantasy Publications, 1961.
Day, Bradford M., *An Index on the Weird and Fantastica in Magazines.* Privately printed, 1953.
Day, Bradford M., *The Supplemental Checklist of Fantastic Literature.* Denver, New York, Science Fiction and Fantasy Publications, 1963.
Day, Donald B., *Index to the Science-Fiction Magazines 1926–1950.* Portland, Perri Press, 1952; revised edition, Boston, Hall, 1982.
de Camp, L. Sprague, *The Conan Reader.* Baltimore, Mirage Press, 1968.
de Camp, L. Sprague, *Science-Fiction Handbook.* New York, Hermitage House, 1953; revised edition, with Catherine Crook de Camp, Philadelphia, Owlswick Press, 1975.
de Camp, L. Sprague, and George H. Scithers, editors, *The Conan Grimoire.* Baltimore, Mirage Press, 1971.
de Camp, L. Sprague, and George H. Scithers, editors, *The Conan Swordbook.* Baltimore, Mirage Press, 1969.

Delany, Samuel R., *The Jewel-Hinged Jaw: Notes on the Language of Science Fiction.* Elizabethtown, New York, Dragon Press, 1977.

Delany, Samuel R., *Starboard Wine: More Notes on the Language of Science Fiction.* Pleasantville, New York, Dragon Press, 1984.

del Rey, Lester, *The World of Science Fiction 1926–1976: The History of a Subculture.* New York, Ballantine, 1979.

Derleth, August, *Thirty Years of Arkham House.* Sauk City, Wisconsin, Arkham House, 1970.

Dunn, Thomas P., and Richard D. Erlich, editors, *Clockwork Worlds: Mechanical Environments in SF.* Westport, Connecticut, Greenwood Press, 1983.

Dunn, Thomas P., and Richard D. Erlich, editors, *The Mechanical God: Machines in Science Fiction.* Westport, Connecticut, Greenwood Press, 1982.

Dziemianowicz, Stefan R., *The Annotated Guide to Unknown and Unknown Worlds.* Mercer Island, Washington, Starmont House, 1990.

Eichner, Henry M., *Atlantean Chronicles.* Alhambra, California, Fantasy Publishing, 1971.

Eigruber, Frank, Jr., *Gangland's Doom: The Shadow of the Pulps.* Oak Lawn, Illinois, Weinberg, 1974.

Elliott, Robert C., *The Shape of Utopia: Studies in a Literary Genre.* Chicago, University of Chicago Press, 1970.

Elrick, George S., *The Science Fiction Handbook for Readers and Writers.* Chicago, Chicago Review Press, 1978.

Eshbach, Lloyd Arthur, editor, *Of Worlds Beyond: The Science of Science-Fiction Writing.* Reading, Pennsylvania, Fantasy Press, 1947; London, Dobson, 1965.

Eurich, Nell, *Science in Utopia: A Mighty Design.* Cambridge, Massachusetts, Harvard University Press, 1967.

Fischer, William B., *The Empire Strikes Out: Kurd Lasswitz, Hans Dominik, and the Development of German Science Fiction.* Bowling Green, Ohio, Popular Press, 1984.

Fletcher, Marilyn, editor, *Reader's Guide to Twentieth-Century Science Fiction.* Chicago, American Library Association, 1989.

Fletcher, Marilyn, *Science Fiction Story Index 1950–79.* Chicago, American Library Association, 2nd edition, 1981.

Frank, Alan, *Sci-Fi Now: 10 Exciting Years of Science Fiction from 2001 to Star Wars and Beyond.* London, Octopus, 1978.

Frank, Alan, *The Science Fiction and Fantasy Film Handbook.* Totowa, New Jersey, Barnes and Noble, and London, Batsford, 1982.

Franklin, H. Bruce, editor, *Future Perfect: American Science Fiction of the Nineteenth Century.* New York, Oxford University Press, 1966; London, Oxford University Press, 1968.

Franson, Donald, and Howard DeVore, *A History of the Hugo, Nebula, and International Fantasy Awards.* Dearborn Heights, Michigan, DeVore, 1975.

Freas, Frank Kelly, *The Art of Science Fiction.* Norfolk, Virginia, Donning, 1977.

Fredericks, Casey, *The Future of Eternity: Mythologies of Science Fiction and Fantasy.* Bloomington, Indiana University Press, 1982.

Frewin, Anthony, *One Hundred Years of Science Fiction Illustration 1840–1940.* London, Jupiter, 1974; New York, Pyramid, 1975.

Friend, Beverly, *Science Fiction: The Classroom in Orbit.* Glassboro, New Jersey, Educational Impact, 1974.

Gallagher, Edward J., *The Annotated Guide to Fantastic Adventures.* Mercer Island, Washington, Starmont House, 1985.

Gammell, Leon L., *The Annotated Guide to Startling Stories.* Mercer Island, Washington, Starmont House, 1986.

Garber, Eric, and Lyn Paleo, *Uranian Worlds: A Reader's Guide to Alternate Sexuality in Science Fiction and Fantasy.* Boston, Hall, 1983.

Gerani, Gary, and Paul H. Schulman, *Fantastic Television.* New York, Harmony, 1977.

Gerber, Richard, *Utopian Fantasy: A Study of English Utopian Fiction since the End of the Nineteenth Century.* London, Routledge, 1955; New York, McGraw Hill, 1973.

Gernsback, Hugo, *Evolution in Modern Science Fiction.* New York, Gernsback, 1952.

Gifford, Denis, *Science Fiction Film.* London, Studio Vista, and New York, Dutton, 1971.

Glad, John, *Extrapolations from Dystopia: A Critical Study of Soviet Science Fiction.* Kingston, New Jersey, Kingston Press, 1982.

Glut, Donald F., *The Frankenstein Legend.* Metuchen, New Jersey, Scarecrow Press, 1973.

Goswami, Amit and Maggie, *The Cosmic Dancers: Exploring the Physics of Science Fiction.* New York, Harper, 1983.

Goulart, Ron, *Cheap Thrills: An Informal History of the Pulp Magazines.* New Rochelle, New York, Arlington House, 1972.

Gove, Philip Babcock, *The Imaginary Voyage in Prose Fiction.* New York, Columbia University Press, 1941; London, Holland Press, 1961.

Grant, Charles L., editor, *Writing and Selling Science Fiction.* Cincinnati Writer's Digest, 1977.

Grebens, G.V., *Ivan Efremov's Theory of Soviet Science Fiction.* New York, Vantage Press, 1978.

Green, Roger Lancelyn, *Into Other Worlds: Spaceflight in Fiction from Lucian to Lewis.* London and New York, Abelard Schuman, 1957.

Green, Scott E., *Contemporary Science Fiction, Fantasy, and Horror Poetry: A Resource Guide and Biographical Dictionary.* New York, Greenwood Press, 1989.

Greenberg, Martin H., editor, *Fantastic Lives.* Carbondale, Southern Illinois University Press, 1981.

Greenland, Colin, *The Entropy Exhibition: Michael Moorcock and the British "New Wave" in Science Fiction.* London and Boston, Routledge, 1983.

Griffiths, John, *Three Tomorrows: American, British, and Soviet Science Fiction.* New York, Barnes and Noble, and London, Macmillan, 1980.

Gunn, James E., *Alternate Worlds: The Illustrated History of Science Fiction.* Englewood Cliffs, New Jersey, Prentice Hall, 1975.

Gunn, James E., *The Discovery of the Future: The Ways Science Fiction Developed.* College Station, Texas A and M University, 1975.

Gunn, James, E., editor, *The New Encyclopedia of Science Fiction.* New York and London, Viking Press, 1988.

Gunn, James E., editor, *The Road to Science Fiction.* New York, New American Library, 4 vols., 1977–82.

Hall, H.W., *Science Fiction and Fantasy Reference Index 1879–1985: An International Author and Subject Index to History and Criticism.* Detroit, Gale, 2 vols., 1987.

Hall, H.W., *Science Fiction and Fantasy Research Index* (annual). Privately printed, 1982–.

Hall, H.W., *Science Fiction Book Review Index 1923–73; 1974–79; 1980–84.* Detroit, Gale, 3 vols., 1975–85.

Hall, Hal W., *Science/Fiction Collections: Fantasy, Supernatural and Weird Tales.* New York, Haworth Press, 1983.

Hall, Hal W., *The Science Fiction Magazines: A Bibliographical Checklist of Titles and Issues Through 1983.* Bryan, Texas, SFBRI, 1983.

Hardy, Phil, editor, *Science Fiction: The Complete Film Sourcebook.* New York, Morrow, 1984.

Harrison, Harry, *Great Balls of Fire!* London, Pierrot, and New York, Grosset and Dunlap, 1977.
Hartwell, David G., *Age of Wonders: Exploring the World of Science Fiction.* New York, Walker, 1985.
Hassler, Donald M., *Comic Tones in Science Fiction: The Art of Compromise with Nature.* Westport, Connecticut, Greenwood Press, 1982.
Hillegas, Mark R., *The Future as Nightmare: H.G. Wells and the Anti-Utopians.* New York, Oxford University Press, 1967.
Hillegas, Mark R., editor, *Shadows of Imagination: The Fantasies of C.S. Lewis, J.R.R. Tolkien, and Charles Williams.* Carbondale, Southern Illinois University Press, 1969.
Hoffman, Stuart, *An Index to "Unknown" and "Unknown Worlds" by Author and by Title.* Black Earth, Wisconsin, Sirius Press, 1955.
Hollister, Bernard C., and Deane C. Thompson, *Grokking the Future: Science Fiction in the Classroom.* Dayton, Ohio, Pflaum, 1973.
Ikin, Van, editor, *Australian Science Fiction.* Brisbane, University of Queensland Press, 1982; Chicago, Academy, 1984.
*Index to Fantasy and Science Fiction in Munsey Publications.* Alhambra, California, 1976(?).
*Index to Perry Rhodan—American Edition.* Cambridge, Massachusetts, NESFA Press, 2 vols., 1973–75.
*Index to Science Fiction Magazines 1966–1976.* Cambridge, Massachusetts, NESFA Press, 6 vols., 1971–1977.
Isaacs, Leonard, *Darwin to Double Helix: The Biological Theme in Science Fiction.* London, Butterworth, 1977.
Jaffrey, Sheldon R., *The Arkham House Companion.* Mercer Island, Washington, Starmont House, 1990.
Jaffrey, Sheldon R. and Fred Cook, *The Collector's Index to Weird Tales.* Bowling Green, Ohio, Popular Press, 1985.
Jaffrey, Sheldon R., *Future and Fantastic Worlds: A Bibliographical Retrospective of DAW Books (1972–87).* Mercer Island, Washington, Starmont House, 1987.
Jaffrey, Sheldon R., *Horrors and Unpleasantries: A Bibliographical History and Collectors' Price Guide to Arkham House.* Bowling Green, Ohio, Popular Press, 1982.
Jakubowski, Maxim, and Edward James, editors, *The Profession of Science Fiction: Writers on Their Craft and Ideas.* London, Macmillan, 1991.
Jakubowski, Maxim, and Malcolm Edwards, *The SF Book of Lists.* New York, Berkley, 1983.
James, Edward, *Index to Foundation, 1–40.* Dagenham, Essex, Science Fiction Foundation, 1988.
Jarvis, Sharon, editor, *Inside Outer Space: Science Fiction Professionals Look at Their Craft.* New York, Ungar, 1984.
Johnson, William, editor, *Focus on the Science Fiction Film.* Englewood Cliffs, New Jersey, Prentice Hall, 1972.
Jones, Robert Kenneth, *The Shudder Pulps: A History of the Weird Menace Magazine of the 1930's.* West Linn, Oregon, FAX, 1975.
Justice, Keith L., *Science Fiction, Fantasy, and Horror Reference: An Annotated Bibliography of Works about Literature and Film.* Jefferson, North Carolina, McFarland, 1989.
Justice, Keith L., *Science Fiction Master Index of Names.* Jefferson, North Carolina, McFarland, 1986.
Ketterer, David, *New Worlds for Old: The Apocalyptic Imagination, Science Fiction, and American Literature.* Bloomington, Indiana University Press, 1974.
King, Betty, *Women of the Future: The Female Main Character in Science Fiction.* Metuchen, New Jersey, Scarecrow Press, 1984.
Kinnard, Roy, *Beasts and Behemoths: Prehistoric Creatures in the Movies.* Metuchen, New Jersey, Scarecrow Press, 1988.
Knight, Damon, *The Futurians.* New York, Day, 1977.
Knight, Damon, *In Search of Wonder.* Chicago, Advent, 1956; revised edition, 1967.
Knight, Damon, editor, *Turning Points: Essays on the Art of Science Fiction.* New York, Harper, 1977.
Kyle, David, *The Illustrated Book of Science Fiction Ideas and Dreams.* London, Hamlyn, 1977.
Kyle, David, *A Pictorial History of Science Fiction.* London, Hamlyn, 1976.
Lasky, Melvin J., *Utopia and Revolution.* Chicago, University of Chicago Press, 1976.
Lawler, Donald L., *Approaches to Science Fiction.* Boston, Houghton Mifflin, 1978.
Lee, Walt, *Reference Guide to Fantastic Films.* Los Angeles, Chelsea Lee, 3 vols., 1972–74.
Le Guin, Ursula K., *The Language of the Night: Essays on Fantasy and Science Fiction,* edited by Susan Wood. New York, Putnam, 1979.
Leighton, Peter, *Moon Travellers: A Dream That Is Becoming a Reality.* London, Oldbourne, 1960.
Lentz, Harris M. III, *Science Fiction, Horror, and Fantasy Film and Television Credits.* Jefferson, North Carolina, McFarland, 2 vols., 1983.
Lester, Colin, editor, *The International Science Fiction Yearbook 1979.* London, Pierrot, 1979.
Locke, George, *Science Fiction First Editions.* London, Ferret Fantasy, 1978.
Locke, George, *A Spectrum of Fantasy: The Bibliography and Biography of a Collection of Fantastic Literature.* London, Ferret, 1980.
Locke, George, *Voyages in Space: A Bibliography of Interplanetary Fiction 1801–1914.* London, Ferret Fantasy, 1975.
Lowndes, Robert A.W., *Three Faces of Science Fiction.* Boston, NESFA Press, 1973.
Lundwall, Sam J., *Science Fiction: An Illustrated History.* New York, Grosset and Dunlap, 1978.
Lundwall, Sam J., *Science Fiction: What It's All About.* New York, Ace, 1971.
Lynn, Ruth Nadelman, *Fantasy for Children and Young Adults: An Annotated Bibliography.* New York, Bowker, 1979; 2nd edition, 1983; 3rd edition, 1989.
Magill, Frank N., editor, *Survey of Science Fiction Literature.* Englewood Cliffs, New Jersey, Salem Press, 5 vols., 1979; bibliographical supplement, 1982.
Magill, Frank N., and Keith Neilson, editors, *Survey of Modern Fantasy Literature.* Englewood Cliffs, New Jersey, Salem Press, 5 vols., 1983.
Magill, Frank N., editor, *Science Fiction, Alien Encounter.* Pasadena, California, Salem Press, 1981.
Malone, Robert, *The Robot Book.* New York, Harcourt Brace, 1978.
Malmgren, Carl D., *Worlds Apart: Narratology of Science Fiction.* Bloomington, Indiana University Press, 1991.
Malzberg, Barry N., *The Engines of the Night: Science Fiction in the Eighties.* New York, Doubleday, 1982.
Manguel, Alberto, and Gianni Guadalupi, *The Dictionary of Imaginary Places.* New York, Macmillan, 1980; revised edition, San Diego, Harcourt Brace, 1987.
Manlove, C.N., *Modern Fantasy: Five Studies.* London, Cambridge University Press, 1975.
Matthew, Robert, *The Origins of Japanese Science Fiction.* Brisbane, University of Queensland Department of Japanese, 1978.
McCaffery, Larry, editor, *Across the Wounded Galaxies: Interviews with Contemporary American Science Fiction Writers.* Urbana, University of Illinois Press, 1990.

McCaffery, Larry, editor, *Storming the Reality Studio: A Casebook of Cyberpunk and Postmodern Science Fiction.* Durham, North Carolina, Duke University Press, 1991.
McGhan, Barry, *Science Fiction and Fantasy Pseudonyms.* Dearborn, Michigan, Misfit Press, 1973.
McGuire, Patrick L., *Red Stars: Political Aspects of Soviet Science Fiction.* Ann Arbor, Michigan, UMI Research Press, 1985.
Menville, Douglas, *A Historical and Critical Survey of the Science-Fiction Film.* New York, Arno Press, 1975.
Menville, Douglas, R. Reginald, and Mary A. Burgess, *Futurevisions: The New Golden Age of the Science Fiction Film.* North Hollywood, California, Newcastle, 1985.
Menville, Douglas, and R. Reginald, *Things to Come: An Illustrated History of the Science Fiction Film.* New York, Times Books, 1977.
Metcalf, Norm, *The Index of Science Fiction Magazines 1951–1965.* El Cerrito, California, Stark, 1968.
Meyers, Walter E., *Aliens and Linguists.* Athens, University of Georgia Press, 1980.
Miller, Fred D., Jr., and Nicholas D. Smith, editors, *Thought Probes: Philosophy Through Science Fiction.* Englewood Cliffs, New Jersey, Prentice Hall, 1981.
Mogen, David, editor, *Wilderness Visions: Science Fiction Westerns 1.* San Bernardino, California, Borgo Press, 1982.
Moore, Patrick, *Science and Fiction.* London, Harrap, 1957.
Morton, A.L., *The English Utopia.* London, Lawrence and Wishart, 1952.
Moskowitz, Sam, *Explorers of the Infinite: Shapers of Science Fiction.* Cleveland, World, 1963.
Moskowitz, Sam, *The Immortal Storm: A History of Science Fiction Fandom.* Atlanta, Atlanta Science Fiction Organization Press, 1954.
Moskowitz, Sam, editor, *Science Fiction by Gaslight: A History and Anthology of Science Fiction in Popular Magazines 1891–1911.* Cleveland, World, 1968.
Moskowitz, Sam, *Seekers of Tomorrow: Masters of Modern Science Fiction.* Cleveland, World, 1966.
Moskowitz, Sam, *Strange Horizons: The Spectrum of Science Fiction.* New York, Scribner, 1976.
Moskowitz, Sam, editor, *Under the Moons of Mars: A History and Anthology of "The Scientific Romance" in the Munsey Magazines.* New York, Holt Rinehart, 1970.
Mullen, R.D., and Darko Suvin, editors, *Science-Fiction Studies: Selected Articles on Science Fiction.* Boston, Gregg Press, 2 vols., 1976–78.
Myers, Robert E., editor, *The Intersection of Science Fiction and Philosophy: Critical Studies.* Westport, Connecticut, Greenwood Press, 1983.
Naha, Ed, *The Science Fictionary: An A–Z Guide to the World of SF Authors, Films, and TV Shows.* New York, Seaview Books, 1980.
New England Science Fiction Association, *The NESFA Index to the Science Fiction Magazines and Original Anthologies 1979–80.* Cambridge, Massachusetts, NESFA Press, 1982.
Newman, John, and Michael Unsworth, *Future War Novels: An Annotated Bibliography of Works in English Published Since 1946.* Phoenix, Oryx Press, 1984.
Nicholls, Peter, editor, *Foundation: The Review of Science Fiction March 1972–March 1975.* Boston, Gregg Press, 1978.
Nicholls, Peter, editor, *Science Fiction at Large.* London, Gollancz, 1976; New York, Harper, 1977; as *Explorations of the Marvellous,* London, Fontana, 1978.
Nicholls, Peter, editor, *The Science Fiction Encyclopedia.* New York, Doubleday, and London, Granada, 1979.
Nicholls, Peter, David Langford, and Brian M. Stableford, *The Science in Science Fiction.* London, Joseph, 1982; New York, Knopf, 1983.
Nicolson, Marjorie Hope, *Voyages to the Moon.* New York, Macmillan, 1948.
*The Octopus Encyclopaedia of Science Fiction.* London, Octopus, and Baltimore, Hoen, 1978.
Okada, Masaya, *Illustrated Index to Air Wonder Stories.* Nagoya, Japan, Okada, 1973.
Owings, Mark, and Jack L. Chalker, *The Index to Science-Fantasy Publishers.* Baltimore, Mirage Press, 1966; revised edition, as *Index to the SF Publishers,* 1979.
Page, Michael, and Robert Ingpen, *Encyclopedia of Things That Never Were.* New York, Viking Press, 1987.
Panshin, Alexei and Cory, *SF in Dimension: A Book of Explorations.* Chicago, Advent, 1976.
Parish, James Robert, and Michael R. Pitts, *The Great Science Fiction Pictures.* Metuchen, New Jersey, Scarecrow Press, 1977.
Parish, James Robert, and Michael R. Pitts, *The Great Science Fiction Pictures II.* Metuchen, New Jersey, Scarecrow Press, 1990.
Parnell, Frank H., and Mike Ashley, *Monthly Terrors: An Index to the Weird Fantasy Magazines Published in the United States and Great Britain.* Westport, Connecticut, Greenwood Press, 1985.
Parrinder, Patrick, editor, *Science Fiction: A Critical Guide.* London, Longman, 1979.
Parrinder, Patrick, *Science Fiction: Its Criticism and Teaching.* London, Methuen, 1980.
Parrington, Vernon Louis, *American Dreams: A Study of American Utopias.* Providence, Rhode Island, Brown University, 1947.
Pavlat, Robert, and William Evans, editors, *Fanzine Index.* New York, Piser, 1965.
Pfeiffer, John R., *Fantasy and Science Fiction: A Critical Guide.* Palmer Lake, Colorado, Filter Press, 1971.
Pflieger, Pat, *A Reference Guide to Modern Fantasy for Children.* Westport, Connecticut, Greenwood Press, 1984.
Philmus, Robert, *Into the Unknown: The Evolution of Science Fiction from Francis Godwin to H.G. Wells.* Berkeley, University of California Press, 1970; 2nd edition, 1983.
Pierce, Hazel, *A Literary Symbiosis: Science Fiction/Fantasy/Mystery.* Westport, Connecticut, Greenwood Press, 1983.
Platt, Charles, *Dream Makers: The Uncommon People Who Write Science Fiction.* New York, Berkley, 2 vols., 1980–83; revised edition, as *Dream Makers: Science Fiction and Fantasy Writers at Work,* New York, Ungar, and London, Xanadu, 1987.
Porter, Andrew, editor, *Experiment Perilous: Three Essays on Science Fiction.* New York, Algol Press, 1976.
Porush, David, *The Soft Machine: Cybernetic Fiction.* New York, Methuen, 1985.
Pringle, David, *Imaginary People: A Who's Who of Modern Fictional Characters.* London, Grafton, 1987; New York, World Almanac, 1988.
Pringle, David, *Modern Fantasy: The Hundred Best Novels: An English-Language Selection 1946–87.* London, Grafton, 1988; New York, Bedrick Books, 1989.
Pringle, David, *Science Fiction: The Hundred Best Novels: An English-Language Selection 1949–84.* New York, Carroll and Graf, and London, Xanadu, 1985.
Pringle, David, *The Ultimate Guide to Science Fiction.* New York, Pharos Books, and London, Grafton, 1990.
Rabkin, Eric S., *The Fantastic in Literature.* Princeton, New Jersey, Princeton University Press, 1976.

Rabkin, Eric S., Martin H. Greenberg, and Joseph D. Olander, editors, *The End of the World.* Carbondale, Southern Illinois University Press, 1983.

Rabkin, Eric S., Martin H. Greenberg, and Joseph D. Olander, editors, *No Place Else: Explorations in Utopian and Dystopian Fiction.* Carbondale, Southern Illinois University Press, 1983.

Reginald, R., *Contemporary Science Fiction Authors.* New York, Arno Press, 1975.

Reginald, R., *Science Fiction and Fantasy Awards.* San Bernardino, California, Borgo Press, 1981; 2nd edition, as *Reginald's Science Fiction and Fantasy Awards: A Comprehensive Guide to the Awards and Their Winners,* with Daryl F. Mallett, 1991.

Reginald R., *Science Fiction and Fantasy Literature: A Checklist 1700–1974.* Detroit, Gale, 2 vols., 1979.

Reilly, Robert, editor, *The Transcendent Adventure: Studies of Religion in Science Fiction/Fantasy.* Westport, Connecticut, Greenwood Press, 1984.

Riley, Dick, editor, *Critical Encounters: Writers and Themes in Science Fiction.* New York, Ungar, 1978.

Robbins, Leonard A., *The Pulp Magazine Index.* Mercer Island, Washington, Starmont House, 1988—six volumes published through 1991).

Roberts, Peter, *Guide to Current Fanzines.* Privately printed, 1978.

Robinson, Roger, *Who's Hugh? An SF Reader's Guide to Pseudonyms.* Harold Wood, Essex, Beccon, 1987.

Rock, James A., *Who Goes There? A Bibliographic Dictionary of Pseudonymous Literature in the Fields of Fantasy and Science Fiction.* Bloomington, Indiana, Rock, 1979.

Roemer, Kenneth M., *The Obsolete Necessity: America in Utopian Writings 1888–1900.* Kent, Ohio, Kent State University Press, 1976.

Rogers, Alva, *A Requiem for Astounding.* Chicago, Advent, 1964.

Rose, Lois and Stephen, *The Shattered Ring: Science Fiction and the Quest for Meaning.* Richmond, Virginia, John Knox Press, and London, SCM Press, 1970.

Rose, Mark, editor, *Science Fiction: A Collection of Critical Essays.* Englewood Cliffs, New Jersey, Prentice Hall, 1976.

Rose, Mark, *Alien Encounters: Anatomy of Science Fiction.* Cambridge, Massachusetts, Harvard University Press, 1981.

Rosinsky, Natalie M., *Feminist Futures: Contemporary Women's Speculative Fiction.* Ann Arbor, Michigan, UMI Research Press, 1984.

Rottensteiner, Franz, *The Science Fiction Book: An Illustrated History.* New York, Seabury Press, and London, Thames and Hudson, 1975.

Rovin, Jeff, *The Fabulous Fantasy Films.* South Brunswick, New Jersey, A.S. Barnes, and London, Yoseloff, 1977.

Sadoul, Jacques, *2000 A.D.: Illustrations from the Golden Age of Science Fiction Pulps.* Chicago, Regnery, and London, Souvenir Press, 1975.

Samuelson, David N., *Visions of Tomorrow: Six Journeys from Outer to Inner Space.* New York, Arno Press, 1975.

Sargent, Lyman T., *British and American Utopian Literature 1516–1975.* Boston, Hall, 1979.

Schlobin, Roger, *The Literature of Fantasy: A Comprehensive Annotated Bibliography of Modern Fantasy Fiction.* New York, Garland, 1979.

Schlobin, Roger C., *Urania's Daughters: A Checklist of Women Science Fiction Writers 1697–1982.* Mercer Island, Washington, Starmont House, 1983.

Scholes, Robert, *Structural Fabulation.* Notre Dame, Indiana, University of Notre Dame Press, 1975.

Scholes, Robert, and Eric S. Rabkin, *Science Fiction: History, Science, Vision.* New York, Oxford University Press, 1977.

Schweitzer, Darrell, and Jeffrey M. Elliot, editors, *Science Fiction Voices 1–4.* San Bernardino, California, Borgo Press, 4 vols., 1979–82.

Scithers, George H., Darrell Schweitzer, and John M. Ford, *On Writing Science Fiction (The Editors Strike Back!).* Philadelphia, Owlswick Press, 1981.

Searles, Baird, and others, *A Reader's Guide to Science Fiction [Fantasy].* New York, Avon, 2 vols., 1979–82.

Shipman, David, *A Pictorial History of Science Fiction Films.* London, Hamlyn, 1985.

Siemon, Frederick, *Science Fiction Story Index 1950–1968.* Chicago, American Library Association, 1971.

Silverberg, Robert, *Drug Themes in Science Fiction.* Rockville, Maryland, National Institute on Drug Abuse, 1974.

Slusser, George E., Eric S. Rabkin, and Robert Scholes, editors, *Coordinates: Placing Science Fiction and Fantasy.* Carbondale, Southern Illinois University Press, 1983.

Smith, Clark Ashton, *Planets and Dimensions: Collected Essays,* edited by Charles K. Wolfe. Baltimore, Mirage Press, 1973.

Smith, Nicholas D., editor, *Philosophers Look at Science Fiction.* Chicago, Nelson Hall, 1982.

Spelman, Richard C., *A Preliminary Checklist of Science Fiction and Fantasy Published by Ballantine Books 1953–1974.* North Hollywood, Institute for Specialized Literature, 1976.

Spelman, Richard C., *Science Fiction and Fantasy Published by Ace Books 1953–1968.* North Hollywood, Institute for Specialized Literature, 1976.

Spinrad, Norman, *Science Fiction in the Real World.* Carbondale, Southern Illinois University Press, 1990.

Spinrad, Norman, *Staying Alive: A Writer's Guide.* Norfolk, Virginia, Donning, 1983.

Stableford, Brian M., *Masters of Science-Fiction: Essays on Six Science-Fiction Authors.* San Bernardino, California, Borgo Press, 1981.

Staicar, Tom, editor, *Critical Encounters 2: Writers and Themes in Science Fiction.* New York, Ungar, 1982.

Staicar, Tom, editor, *The Feminine Eye: Science Fiction and the Women Who Write It.* New York, Ungar, 1982.

Stanley, John, *The Creature Features Movie Guide; or, An A to Z Encyclopedia to the Cinema of the Fantastic.* Pacifica, California, Creatures at Large Press, 1981; revised edition, New York, Warner, 1984.

Stanley, John, *Revenge of the Creature Features Movie Guide.* Pacifica, California, Creatures at Large Press, 1988.

Stone, Graham, *Australian Science Fiction Index 1925–1967.* Canberra, Australian Science Fiction Association, 1968; *Supplement 1968–1975,* Sydney, Australian Science Fiction Association, 1976.

Strauss, Erwin S., *The MIT Science Fiction Society's Index to the S-F Magazines 1951–1965.* Cambridge, Massachusetts, MIT Science Fiction Society, 1966.

Strick, Philip, *Science Fiction Movies.* London, Octopus, 1976.

Strickland, A.W., *Reference Guide to American Science Fiction Films.* Bloomington, Indiana TIS, 2 vols., 1980.

Sullivan, Jack, editor, *The Penguin Encyclopedia of Horror and the Supernatural.* New York, Viking Press, 1986.

Summers, Montague, *A Gothic Bibliography.* London, Fortune Press, 1941; New York, Russell, 1964.

Suvin, Darko, *Metamorphoses of Science Fiction.* New Haven, Connecticut, Yale University Press, 1979.

Suvin, Darko, *Russian Science Fiction 1956–1974: A Bibliography.* Elizabethtown, New York, Dragon Press, 1976.

Swinfen, Ann, *In Defence of Fantasy: A Study of the Genre in English and American Literature since 1945.* London, Routledge, 1983.

Todorov, Tzvetan, *The Fantastic: A Structural Approach to a Literary Genre,* translated by Richard Howard. Cleveland, Press of Case Western Reserve University, 1973.

Tuck, Donald H., *The Encyclopedia of Science Fiction and Fantasy.* Chicago, Advent, 3 vols., 1974–83.

Tymn, Marshall B., *American Fantasy and Science Fiction: Toward A Bibliography of Works Published in the United States 1948–1973.* West Linn, Oregon, FAX, 1979.

Tymn, Marshall B., *Index to Stories in Thematic Anthologies of Science Fiction.* Boston, Hall, 1978.

Tymn, Marshall B., Roger C. Schlobin, and L.W. Currey, *A Research Guide to Science Fiction Studies.* New York, Garland, 1977.

Tymn, Marshall B., and Roger C. Schlobin, *The Year's Scholarship in Science Fiction and Fantasy 1972–1975.* Kent, Ohio, Kent State University Press, 1979.

Tymn, Marshall B., editor, *Science Fiction: A Teacher's Guide and Resource Book.* San Bernardino, California, Borgo Press, 1988.

Tymn, Marshall B., and Mike Ashley, editors, *Science Fiction, Fantasy, and Weird Fiction Magazines.* Westport, Connecticut, Greenwood Press, 1985.

Tymn, Marshall B., editor, *The Science Fiction Reference Book.* Mercer Island, Washington, Starmont, 1981.

Tymn, Marshall B., and Roger C. Schlobin, editors, *The Year's Scholarship in Science Fiction and Fantasy: 1976–1979.* Kent, Ohio, Kent State University Press, 1983.

Tymn, Marshall B., editor, *The Year's Scholarship in Science Fiction, Fantasy, and Horror Literature 1980–81.* Kent, Ohio, Kent State University Press, 2 vols., 1983–84.

University of California, Riverside, *Dictionary Catalog of the J. Lloyd Eaton Collection of Science Fiction and Fantasy Literature.* Boston, Hall, 3 vols., 1982.

Urang, Gunnar, *Shadows of Heaven: Religion and Fantasy in the Writings of C.S. Lewis, Charles Williams, and J.R.R. Tolkien.* Philadelphia, Pilgrim Press, and London, SCM Press, 1971.

Versins, Pierre, *Encyclopedie de l'Utopie des Voyages Extraordinaires et de la Science Fiction.* Lausanne, L'Age d'Homme, 1972.

Wagar, W. Warren, *Terminal Visions: The Literature of Last Things.* Bloomington, Indiana University Press, 1982.

Walker, Paul, *Speaking of Science Fiction* (interviews). Oradell, New Jersey, Luna, 1978.

Walsh, Chad, *From Utopia to Nightmare.* New York, Harper, and London, Bles, 1962.

Warner, Harry, Jr., *All Our Yesterdays: An Informal History of Science Fiction Fandom in the Forties.* Chicago, Advent, 1969.

Warren, Bill, and Bill Thomas, *Keep Watching the Skies! American Science Fiction Movies of the Fifties.* Jefferson, North Carolina, McFarland, 2 vols., 1982–86.

Warrick, Patricia S., *The Cybernetic Imagination in Science Fiction.* Cambridge, Massachusetts, MIT Press, 1980.

Weinberg, Robert, *A Biographical Dictionary of Science Fiction and Fantasy Artists.* New York, Greenwood Press, 1988.

Weinberg, Robert, *The Weird Tales Story.* West Linn, Oregon, FAX, 1977.

Weinberg, Robert, and Lohr McKinstry, *The Hero Pulp Index.* Evergreen, Colorado, Opar Press, 1971.

Weinberg, Robert, and Edward P. Berglund, *Reader's Guide to the Cthulhu Mythos.* Albuquerque, Silver Scarab Press, 1973.

Wells, Stuart, III, *The Science Fiction and Heroic Fantasy Author Index.* Duluth, Purple Unicorn, 1978.

Wertham, Frederic, *The World of Fanzines: A Special Form of Communication.* Carbondale, Southern Illinois University Press, 1973.

Williamson, Jack, editor, *Teaching Science Fiction: Education for Tomorrow.* Philadelphia, Owlswick Press, 1980.

Willis, Donald C., *Horror and Science Fiction Films: A Checklist.* Metuchen, New Jersey, Scarecrow Press, 1972.

Willis, Donald C., *Horror and Science Fiction Films II.* Metuchen, New Jersey, Scarecrow Press, 1982.

Willis, Donald C., *Horror and Science Fiction Films III.* Metuchen, New Jersey, Scarecrow Press, 1984.

Willis, Donald C., editor, *Variety's Complete Science Fiction Reviews.* New York, Garland, 1985.

Wilson, Colin, *Science Fiction as Existentialism.* Hayes, Middlesex, Bran's Head, 1978.

Wilson, Colin, *The Strength to Dream: Literature and the Imagination.* London, Gollancz, and Boston, Houghton Mifflin, 1962.

Wingrove, David, editor, *The Science Fiction Film Source Book.* London and New York, Longman, 1985.

Wingrove, David, editor, *The Science Fiction Source Book.* New York, Van Nostrand Reinhold, 1984.

Wolfe, Gary K., *Critical Terms for Science Fiction and Fantasy: A Glossary and Guide to Scholarship.* New York, Greenwood Press, 1986.

Wolfe, Gary K., *The Known and the Unknown: The Iconography of Science Fiction.* Kent, Ohio, Kent State University Press, 1979.

Wolfe, Gary K., editor, *Science Fiction Dialogues.* Chicago, Academy, 1982.

Wollheim, Donald A., *The Universe Makers: Science Fiction Today.* New York, Harper, 1971; London, Gollancz, 1972.

Wright, Gene, *The Science Fiction Image: The Illustrated Encyclopedia of Science Fiction in Film, Television, Radio, and the Theater.* New York, Facts on File, and London, Columbus, 1983.

Wymer, Thomas L., and others, *Intersections: The Elements of Fiction in Science Fiction.* Bowling Green, Ohio, Popular Press, 1978.

Wysocki, R.J., *The Science Fiction, Fantasy, Weird, Hero Magazine Checklist.* Westlake, Ohio, Wysocki, 1985.

Yntema, Sharon K., *More Than 100 Women Science Fiction Writers.* Freedom, California, Crossing Press, 1988.

## ADVISERS

Brian Aldiss
Martha A. Bartter
Paul Brazier
John Brunner
Don D'Ammassa
Malcolm Edwards
John Eggeling
Charles Elkins
D. Douglas Fratz
Hal W. Hall
Lee Harding
David G. Hartwell
Rosemary Herbert
Van Ikin
Maxim Jakubowski
Edward James
David Ketterer
Paul Kincaid
Gene LaFaille
Kev P. McVeigh
Robert M. Philmus
Christopher Priest
Robert Reginald
Nicholas Ruddick
Pamela Sargent
Robert Scholes
Baird Searles
Brian M. Stableford
Darko Suvin
Michael Tolley
Donald H. Tuck
Marshall B. Tymn

## CONTRIBUTORS

Mitchell Aboulafia
Brian Aldiss
Rosemarie Arbur
K. V. Bailey
Douglas Barbour
George W. Barlow
Myra Barnes
Marleen S. Barr
David V. Barrett
Melissa E. Barth
Martha A. Bartter
Bruce A. Beatie
E.R. Bishop
Michael Bishop
Russell Blackford
Karen Charmaine Blansfield
Janice M. Bogstad
Bernadette Bosky
Paul Brazier
John P. Brennan
Peter A. Brigg
R.E. Briney
Mary T. Brizzi
John Brunner
Scott Burgess
Alexander J. Butrym
Gay E. Carter
Steven R. Carter
Edgar L. Chapman
Cathy Chauvette
Michael Colby
Elizabeth Cummins Cogell
Robert E. Colbert
Rosemary Coleman
Gary Coughlan
Richard Cowper
F. Brett Cox
J. Randolph Cox
Michael Cule
Charles Cushing
Catherine M. Currier
Don D'Ammassa
David A. Drake
Thomas P. Dunn
Karren C. Edwards
Alex Eisenstein
Gregory Feeley
Eric A. Fontaine
Jeff Frane
D. Douglas Fratz
Alice Carol Gaar
John V. Garner
Walter Gillings
Stephen H. Goldman
John Gough
Martin H. Greenberg
Colin Greenland
M. Jean Greenlaw
M. Hammerton
Philip J. Harbottle
David G. Hartwell
Donald M. Hassler
Len Hatfield
Sharon-Ilona Hecht
Rosemary Herbert
Norman L. Hills
Janis Butler Holm
Terry Hughes
Elizabeth Anne Hull
Marvin W. Hunt
Van Ikin
Edward James
Anne Hudson Jones
Kenneth Jurkiewicz
Julius Kagarlitsky
George Kelley
Paul Kincaid
Gérard Klein
Vince Kohler
Dennis M. Kratz
David Lake
William Laskowski, Jr.
Donald L. Lawler
John I. Lawson

Mark Warwick Leahy
Henry D. Leperlier
Michael M. Levy
Arthur O. Lewis
Shelly Lowenkopf
Duncan Lunan
Richard A. Lupoff
Peter Lynch
Andrew Macdonald
Gina Macdonald
Anthony Manousos
Cathi MacRae
Daryl F. Mallett
Patrick L. McGuire
Kev P. McVeigh
Sheryl L. Meyering
Walter E. Meyers
Sandra Miesel
Richard W. Miller
Francis J. Molson
Lee Montgomerie
Thomas J. Morrissey
Will Murray
Marilyn K. Nellis
Ian Nichols
Chad Oliver
Richard Orodenker
Gerald W. Page
Diane Parkin-Speer
Frederick Patten
Terri Paul
Michael Perkins
John R. Pfeiffer
Gene Phillips
Hazel Pierce
John J. Pierce
Nick Pratt
Bill Pronzini
Joseph A. Quinn
Eric S. Rabkin
Robert Reginald
Robert Reilly
Lawrence R. Ries
Franz Rottensteiner
Yvonne Rousseau
Nicholas Ruddick
Joanna Russ
Todd Sammons
David N. Samuelson
Joe Sanders
Pamela Sargent
Harvey J. Satty
John Scarborough
Roger C. Schlobin
Robert Scholes
William M. Schuyler, Jr.
Darrell Schweitzer
Baird Searles
Kathryn Lee Seidel
Susan Shwartz
George Slusser
Curtis C. Smith
Carol L. Snyder
Judith Snyder
Maureen Speller
Brian Stableford
Katherine Staples
Ilan Stavans
Philippa Stephensen-Payne
Graham Stone
Leon Stover
C.W. Sullivan III
Lucy Sussex
Darko Suvin
Paul Swank
Norman Talbot
Robert Thurston
Michael J. Tolley
Frank H. Tucker
George Turner
Lisa Tuttle
Jana I. Tuzar
Steven Utley
Robert E. Vardeman
W. Warren Wagar
Karl Edward Wagner
Ian Watson
Douglas E. Way
Karen G. Way
Jane B. Weedman
Mary S. Weinkauf
Dennis M. Welch
Fred D. White
Robert H. Wilcox
Cherry Wilder
David Wingrove
Gary K. Wolfe
Gene Wolfe
Martin Morse Wooster
Alice Chambers Wygant
Carl B. Yoke
Hoda M. Zaki
George Zebrowski

# TWENTIETH-CENTURY SCIENCE-FICTION WRITERS

Douglas Adams
Mark Adlard
Brian Aldiss
Kingsley Amis
Poul Anderson
Piers Anthony
Christopher Anvil
Edwin L. Arnold
Fenton Ash
Isaac Asimov
Robert Asprin
A.A. Attanasio

Sharon Baker
J.G. Ballard
Iain M. Banks
Arthur K. Barnes
Steven Barnes
William Barnwell
Neal Barrett
T.J. Bass
John Calvin Batchelor
Harry Bates
John Baxter
Barrington John Bayley
Greg Bear
Charles Beaumont
Edward Bellamy
Gregory Benford
J.D. Beresford
Alfred Bester
Lloyd Biggle
Eando Binder
David F. Bischoff
Michael Bishop
James P. Blaylock
Christopher Blayre
James Blish
Robert Bloch
Nelson S. Bond
J.F. Bone
Anthony Boucher
Ben Bova
John Boyd
Leigh Brackett
Ray Bradbury
Marion Zimmer Bradley
Reginald Bretnor
David Brin
Damien Broderick
Christine Brooke-Rose
Eric Brown
Fredric Brown
Rosel George Brown
Mildred Downey Broxon
John Brunner
Edward Bryant
Frank Bryning
Algis Budrys
Lois McMaster Bujold
Kenneth Bulmer
David R. Bunch
Katharine Burdekin
Anthony Burgess
Edgar Rice Burroughs
William S. Burroughs
F.M. Busby
Octavia E. Butler
Samuel Butler

Martin Caidin
Ernest Callenbach
John W. Campbell, Jr.
Paul Capon
Orson Scott Card
Jayge Carr
Terry Carr
Angela Carter
Lin Carter
Cleve Cartmill
Jack L. Chalker
A. Bertram Chandler
Louis Charbonnea
Suzy McKee Charnas
C.J. Cherryh
Rob Chilson
Charles Chilton
John Christopher
Arthur C. Clarke
Hal Clement
Mark Clifton
Stanton A. Coblentz
Theodore R. Cogswell
D.G. Compton
Storm Constantine
Michael G. Coney
Glen Cook
Edmund Cooper
Susan Cooper
Alfred Coppel
Juanita Coulson
Robert Coulson
Arthur Byron Cover
Richard Cowper
Erle Cox
John Creasey
Michael Crichton
Robert Cromie
John Keir Cross
John Crowley
Ray Cummings

Brian C. Daley
Jack Dann
Arsen Darnay
Avram Davidson
L.P. Davies
Chan Davis
Gerry Davis
L. Sprague de Camp
Miriam Allen deFord
Charles de Lint
Lester del Rey
Joseph H. Delaney
Samuel R. Delany
Lester Dent
August Derleth
Gene DeWeese
Philip K. Dick
Peter Dickinson
Gordon R. Dickson
Thomas M. Disch
Sonya Dorman
Candas Jane Dorsey

Arthur Conan Doyle
Terry Dowling
Gardner Dozois
David A. Drake
Wayland Drew
Diane Duane
Dave Duncan
David Duncan
Lord Dunsany
Lawrence Durrell

David Eddings
E.R. Eddison
G.C. Edmondson
George Alec Effinger
Max Ehrlich
Larry Eisenberg
Phyllis Eisenstein
Gordon Eklund
M. Barnard Eldershaw
Suzette Haden Elgin
Harlan Ellison
Ru Emerson
Carol Emshwiller
Sylvia Engdahl
M.J. Engh
George Allan England
Lloyd Arthur Eshbach
Christopher Evans
E. Everett Evans

Zoë Fairbairns
Paul W. Fairman
R. Lionel Fanthorpe
Ralph Milne Farley
Philip José Farmer
Mick Farren
Howard Fast
Jonathon Fast
John Russell Fearn
Raymond E. Feist
Cynthia Felice
Jack Finney
Nicholas Fisk
Constantine FitzGibbon
Homer Eon Flint
Charles L. Fontenay
John M. Ford
William R. Forstchen
Robert L. Forward
Alan Dean Foster
M.A. Foster
Gardner F. Fox
Karen Joy Fowler
Pat Frank
Michael Frayn
Gertrude Friedberg
Esther M. Friesner
H.B. Fyfe

Raymond Z. Gallun
Danial F. Galouye
Craig Shaw Gardner
David S. Garnett
Randall Garrett
Jane Gaskell
David Gemmel
Mary Gentle
Peter George
Hugo Gernsback
David Gerrold
Mark S. Geston
William Gibson
J. U. Giesy
Alexis A. Gilliland
Charlotte Perkins Gilman
John Gloag
Tom Godwin
H.L. Gold
Stephen Goldin
William Golding
Lisa Goldstein
Rex Gordon
Stuart Gordon
Phyllis Gotlieb
Felix C. Gotschalk
Ron Goulart
Charles L. Grant
Joseph Green
Colin Greenland
William Greenleaf
John Gribbin
Russell M. Griffin
George Griffith
Wyman Guin
James E. Gunn
Lindsay Gutteridge

H. Rider Haggard
Isidore Haiblum
Jack C. Haldeman
Joe Haldeman
Austin Hall
Edmond Hamilton
Elizabeth Hand
Lee Harding
Charles L. Harness
Harry Harrison
M. John Harrison
Simon Hawke
H.F. Heard
Robert A. Heinlein
Mark Helprin
Zenna Henderson
Joe L. Hensley
Frank Herbert
James Herbert
Philip E. High
Russell Hoban
Edward D. Hoch
Christopher Hodder-Williams
William Hope Hodgson
Lee Hoffman
James P. Hogan
Robert Holdstock
H.M. Hoover
Robert Hoskins
William Dean Howells
Fred and Geoffrey Hoyle
Trevor Hoyle
L. Ron Hubbard
Barry Hughart
Monica Hughes
Zach Hughes

Evan Hunter
Aldous Huxley
C.J. Cutcliffe Hyne

Dean Ing

John Jakes
Laurence M. Janifer
K.W. Jeter
W.E. Johns
D.F. Jones
Gwyneth A. Jones
Neil R. Jones
Raymond F. Jones
M.K. Joseph

James Kahn
Colin Kapp
Anna Kavan
Guy Gavriel Kay
David H. Keller
Leo P. Kelley
James Patrick Kelly
Leigh Kennedy
John Kessel
Alexander Key
Daniel Keyes
Crawford Kilian
Lee Killough
Gary Kilworth
Vincent King
Donald Kingsbury
Rudyard Kipling
John Kippax
Otis Adelbert Kline
Nigel Kneale
Damon Knight
Norman L. Knight
Dean R. Koontz
C.M. Kornbluth
William Kotzwinkle
Michael E. Kube-McDowell
Michael Kurland
Katherine Kurtz
Henry Kuttner

R.A. Lafferty
David Lake
David Langford
Sterling E. Lanier
Joe R. Lansdale
E.C. Large
Philip Latham
Keith Laumer
Ursula K. Le Guin
Tanith Lee
Fritz Leiber
Stephen Leigh
Murray Leinster
Madeleine L'Engle
Milton Lesser
Doris Lessing
Ira Levin
C.S. Lewis
Jacqueline Lichtenberg
Alice Lightner
Brad Linaweaver
David Lindsay
Alun Llewellyn
Jack London
Frank Belknap Long
Barry Longyear
H.P. Lovecraft
Robert A.W. Lowndes
Sam J. Lundwall
Richard A. Lupoff
John Lymington
Elizabeth A. Lynn

C.C. MacApp
R.A. MacAvoy
George MacDonald
John D. MacDonald
R.W. Mackelworth
Katherine MacLean
Sheila MacLeod
Charles Eric Maine
Barry N. Malzberg
Phillip Mann
Laurence Manning
George R.R. Martin
David I. Masson
Richard Matheson
Julian May
Ardath Mayhar
Bruce McAllister
Paul McAuley
Anne McCaffrey
Jack McDevitt
Ian McDonald
J.T. McIntosh
Vonda N. McIntyre
Richard M. McKenna
Patricia McKillip
Dean McLaughlin
Mike McQuay
S.P. Meek
David Meltzer
R.M. Meluch
Richard C. Meredith
Judith Merril
A. Merritt
Sam Merwin, Jr.
P. Schulyer Miller
Walter M. Miller
Naomi Mitchison
Judith Moffett
Thomas F. Monteleone
Michael Moorcock
C. L. Moore
Patrick Moore
Ward Moore
Dan Morgan
John Morressy
Janet E. Morris
William Morris
James Morrow
Gerald Murnane
Pat Murphy

Ed Naha
Ray Nelson
Kris Neville
Larry Niven

William F. Nolan
John Norman
Andre Norton
Warren Norwood
Alan E. Nourse
Philip Francis Nowlan

Kevin O'Donnell, Jr.
Andrew J. Offutt
Chad Oliver
Bob Olsen
Joseph O'Neill
Rebecca Ore
George Orwell

Raymond A. Palmer
Edgar Pangborn
Alexei Panshin
Paul Park
Mervyn Peake
Kit Pedler
Emil Petaja
Rog Phillips
Marge Piercy
Daniel Manus Pinkwater
H. Beam Piper
Doris Piserchia
Charles Platt
Frederick Pohl
Rachel Pollack
Arthur Porges
Jerry Pournelle
Tim Powers
Terry Pratchett
Fletcher Pratt
Paul Preuss
Christopher Priest
J.B. Priestly
George W. Proctor
Tom Purdom
Thomas Pynchon

John Rackham
Ayn Rand
Marta Randall
John Rankine
Francis G. Rayer
Tom Reamy
Michael Reaves
Kit Reed
Robert Reed
Mike Resnick
Mack Reynolds
Walter and Leigh Richmond
Keith Roberts
Stephen Robinett
Frank M. Robinson
Kim Stanley Robinson
Spider Robinson
Russ Rocklynne
Michaela Roessner
Richard Rohmer
Mordecai Roshwald
William Rotsler
Victor Rousseau
Rudy Rucker
Joanna Russ
Eric Frank Russell
Geoff Ryman

Fred Saberhagen
Margaret St. Clair
James Sallis
Jessica A. Salmonson
Sarban
Pamela Sargent
Richard Saxon
Josephine Saxton
Elizabeth Ann Scarborough
Nat Schachner
Hilbert Schenck
Stanley Schmidt
James H. Schmitz
Thomas N. Scortia
Hank Searls
Arthur Sellings
Luis Senarens
Rod Serling
Garrett P. Serviss
Jack Sharkey
Richard S. Shaver
Bob Shaw
Robert Sheckley
Charles Sheffield
Mary Shelley
Lucius Shepard
T.L. Sherred
M.P. Shiel
Wilmar H. Shiras
John Shirley
Nevil Shute
Susan Shwartz
Robert Silverberg
Clifford D. Simak
Upton Sinclair
Curt Siodmak
Kathleen Sky
John Sladek
William M. Sloane
Joan Slonczewski
Clark Ashton Smith
Cordwainer Smith
E.E. Smith
Evelyn E. Smith
George H. Smith
George O. Smith
Thorne Smith
Jerry Sohl
Nancy Springer
Norman Spinrad
Steven Spruill
Brian M. Stableford
Robert Stallman
Olaf Stapledon
Christopher Stasheff
Andrew M. Stephenson
Bruce Sterling
Francis Stevens
George R. Stewart
S.M. Stirling
Frank R. Stockton
Craig Strete
Theodore Sturgeon
Somtow Sucharitkul

Jeff and Jean Sutton
Thomas Burnett Swann
Michael Swanwick
Leo Szilard

John Taine
Stephen Tall
Judith Tarr
Peter Tate
William F. Temple
William Tenn
Emma Tennant
Walter Tevis
D.M. Thomas
Ted Thomas
Robert Thurston
Patrick Tilley
James Tiptree, Jr.
J.R.R. Tolkien
Louis Trimble
E.C. Tubb
Wilson Tucker
Harry Turtledove
George Turner
Lisa Tuttle
Mark Twain

Steven Utley

Sydney J. Van Scyoc
A.E. van Vogt
Jack Vance
John Varley
A. Hyatt Verrill
Joan D. Vinge
Vernor Vinge
Kurt Vonnegut, Jr.

Howard Waldrop
Edgar Wallace
F.L. Wallace
Ian Wallace
Hugh Walters
Stanley Waterloo
William Jon Watkins
Ian Watson
Sharon Webb
Stanley G. Weinbaum
Andrew Weiner
Manly Wade Wellman
H.G. Wells
Dennis Wheatley
James White
Ted White
Wynne Whiteford
Cherry Wilder
Kate Wilhelm
John A. Williams
Paul O. Williams
Robert Moore Williams
Jack Williamson
Connie Willis
Colin Wilson
F. Paul Wilson
Richard Wilson
Robert Anton Wilson
Robert Charles Wilson
David Wingrove
Jack Wodhams
Gary K. Wolf
Bernard Wolfe
Gene Wolfe
Donald A. Wollheim
Austin Tappan Wright
S. Fowler Wright
Philip Wylie
John Wyndham

Chelsea Quinn Yarbro
Laurence Yep
Jane Yolen
Robert F. Young

Arthur Leo Zagat
Timothy Zahn
George Zebrowski
Roger Zelazny
David Zindell
Pamela Zoline

## FOREIGN-LANGUAGE WRITERS

Kobo Abe
Jean-Pierre Andrevon
René Barjavel
Aleksandr Belyaev
Jorge Luis Borges
Pierre Boulle
Karin Boye
Valery Bryusov
Mikhail Bulgakov
Dino Buzzati
Italo Calvino
Karel Capek
Michael Ende
Herbert W. Franke
Otto Gail
Wolfgang Jeschke
Michel Jeury
Franz Kafka
Bernhard Kellermann
Gérard Klein
Sakyo Komatsu
Kurd Lasswitz
Stanislaw Lem
André Maurois
Vladimir Mayakovsky
Josef Nesvadba
Maurice Renard
Daniel Sernine
Boris and Arkady Strugatsky
Alexey Tolstoy
Konstantin Tsiolkovsky
Ilya Varshavsky

Vercors
Jules Verne
Elisabeth Vonarburg
Stanislaw Witkiewicz
Ivan Yefremov
Yevgeny Zamyatin

**ADAMS, Douglas (Noel).** British. Born in Cambridge, 11 March 1952. Educated at St. John's College, Cambridge, B.A. in English literature. Freelance writer: Script editor, *Doctor Who* series, BBC TV, 1978–80. Agent: Ed Victor Ltd., 162 Wardour Street, London W1V 4AT, England.

SCIENCE-FICTION PUBLICATIONS

Novels (series: Dirk Gently; Hitch-Hiker)

*The Hitch Hiker's Guide to the Galaxy: A Trilogy in Four Parts.* London, Heinemann, 1986; as *The Hitchhiker's Quartet,* New York, Harmony, 1986.
*The Hitch-Hiker's Guide to the Galaxy.* London, Pan, 1979; New York, Crown, 1980.
*The Restaurant at the End of the Universe,* London, Pan, 1980; New York, Crown, 1982.
*Life, The Universe, and Everything.* London, Pan, and New York, Crown, 1982.
*So Long, and Thanks for All the Fish.* London, Pan, and New York, Harmony, 1984.
*Dirk Gently's Holistic Detective Agency.* London, Heinemann, and New York, Simon and Schuster, 1987.
*The Long Dark Tea-Time of the Soul* (Gently). London, Heinemann, and New York, Simon and Schuster, 1988.

OTHER PUBLICATIONS

Plays

*The Hitch-Hiker's Guide to the Galaxy* (broadcast, 1978; produced, 1979).
*Hitchhiker's Companion: The Original Galaxy Radio Scripts.* New York, Harmony, 1985.

Radio Play: *The Hitch-Hiker's Guide to the Galaxy,* 1978.

Television Plays: for *Doctor Who* series.

Other

*The Meaning of Liff,* with John Lloyd. London, Pan, 1983; New York, Harmony, 1984.
*Last Chance to See,* with Mark Carwardine. London, Heinemann, 1990; New York, Harmony, 1991.

Editor, with Peter Fincham, *The Utterly Utterly Merry Comic Relief Christmas Book.* London, Collins, 1986.

*

Critical Study: "Douglas Adams's "Hitchhiker" novels as Mock Science Fiction," by Carl R. Kroph, in *Science Fiction Studies,* March 1988.

* * *

Publication of *The Hitch Hiker's Guide to the Galaxy* (in American publications "Hitchhiker") following the BBC radio production, was an event in the science fiction community. Adams's work combines satire, humor and carefully crafted lunacy with whimsical speculation about such universal themes as "life, the universe and everything." The combination of science fiction with humor is not common, and this series is an outstanding contribution to the field, though uneven at times, and should be read where one can laugh out loud. Adams is a master of the improbable. His other comic techniques include fresh and zany uses of clichés and cliché situations, the frequent and judicious employment of puns to depress pretensions, and the creation of characters who both parody science fiction stereotypes and grow beyond stereotype into developed comic figures. Arthur Dent, the last Englishman, is a bewildered anti-hero, who charms with his longing for tea and the Earth. Ford Prefect (his name a slight, alien miscalculation), the staff writer for the "Hitchhiker's Guide," is a quintessential bored, slap-dash traveler at home anywhere in the galaxy. Marvin (the paranoid android) drives computers to suicide with a single conversation. Zaphod Beeblebrox, two-headed president of the Galaxy, embraces the idea that it's better to not know what you're doing and forces questioning of the old adage, two heads are better than one.

The Hitchhiker series depicts a universe of improbability and coincidence rather than the relentlessly consistent, logical laws (even if they do vary from our current state of science) central to conventional science fiction. Twisting these science fiction standards serves to frustrate the reader's expectations or learned responses to genre conventions, opening new speculative space. Thus, the series may be read as mock science fiction, rather like mock epic. This allows Adams to lampoon and skew at will, providing a new angle from which to view the questions asked and answers provided within science fiction. His clever and satirical insight with its infusion of humor serves to illuminate the human condition, while allowing us to view it with a fond eye. He has the ability to make the commonplace seem bizarre and the absurd seem commonplace. This British-style humor is reminiscent of the classic *Three Men in a Boat* by Jerome K. Jerome.

In other ways, Adams builds upon conventional standards, but in his own charmingly mad fashion. He incorporates the more exotic forms of hardware, bypassing warp drives and speeds by jumping far beyond to his own creation, the total improbability drive. He incorporates the more homey forms of hardware, giving us the Nutri-matic Drinks Synthesizer, a machine that "invariably produced a liquid which was almost, but not quite, entirely unlike tea." His version of a standard reference work, "The Hitchhiker's Guide to the Galaxy," is not the repository of knowledge and wisdom, rather it's a compendium of (so-called) facts, (weird) philosophies, drink recipes (including the infamous Pan Galactic Gargle Blaster), and (improbable) advice, the most important feature of which is the words "Don't Panic," written on the cover in big friendly letters. He includes the semi-obligatory robot, but not the standard issue robot. It is a paranoid robot able to drive computers to suicide with a single conversation. He pays homage to the space opera tradition by sending his characters on a quest through the far reaches of space (in search of treasure, and the man who rules the universe), with the required miraculous escapes. Improbable whimsy (to fly, throw yourself at the ground and miss) and episodes of surreal humor (a whale's deliberations on the meaning of life, while falling through space), more than makes up for the light plot.

Comedic techniques, hilarious characters, and unique usage of science fiction conventions are finely calculated and carefully aimed to deflate the pompous and call into question sacred cows. No one reading these books will ever feel the same about digital watches (considered a pretty neat idea by the amazingly primitive ape-descended life forms of an utterly insignificant little blue-green planet) or 42 (the ultimate answer! but what is the ultimate question?).

*Dirk Gently's Holistic Detective Agency* and *The Long Dark Tea-Time of the Soul* continue the Adams tradition, which has been described as hilarious, irreverent, zany, clever, and improbably weird. Dirk Gently, whose bill for saving humanity from extinction is NO CHARGE, who resolutely refuses to have anything to do with logic (as practiced by other detectives) and rejects common sense, and whose focus is on the interconnectedness of all rather than mere pertinent clues is distinctly outside the venerable tradition of the Great Detective. This series combines elements from many genres: fantasy, detective/mystery, horror/ghost, time-travel, myth/epic, and romance-comedy. Again the oppositional use of genre conventions, turning them inside-out and upside-down, shines a humorous light on human foibles, and the complications and contradictions of modern life. As in the Hitchhiker series, Adams creates a universe where the illogical, the improbable, the accidental and the coincidental rule. Ever shifting improbability is Adams's one constant motif. Adams originals include: answering machine addiction; navigation by following a car that looks like it knows where it's going (to end up where you need to be rather than where you intend to be); the nonfunctional Quark II computer (a paperweight, doorstop and/or police-interrogation-device); the electronic monk (belief systems specialist); and time-travel as a way to avoid the complications of VCR programming. It is with the techniques of irrepressible humor and bizarre viewpoints that Adams creates unforgettable characters and situations, planting seeds of thought to laugh by.

The audio editions of Adams's series, in both the BBC version and the unabridged version read by the author, are a treat and add extra depth to the experience.

Adams's most recent book is *Last Chance to See* (with Mark Carwardine), a nonfiction work about his travels to remote areas in search of rare animals, many facing extinction, and of the characters, animal and human, met along the way. Adams's style, poignant and funny, with elements of hope and despair, combined with his keen, off-center views, makes this a pleasurable read for the arm-chair traveler and all those concerned with animals, nature, and world ecology.

—Catherine M. Currier

---

**ADLARD, Mark (Peter Marcus Adlard).** British. Born in Seaton Carew, County Durham, 19 June 1932. Educated at Trinity College, Cambridge, 1951–54, B.A. in English 1954; Oxford University, 1954–55; University of London, B.Sc. (extra-mural) in economics. Married Sheila Rosemary Skuse in 1968; one daughter and one son. Executive in the steel industry in Middlesbrough, Yorkshire, Cardiff, and Kent, 1956–76. Since 1976 full-time writer. Address: 43 Enterpen, Hutton Rudby, Cleveland TS25 0EL, England.

SCIENCE-FICTION PUBLICATIONS

Novels (series: Tcity in all books)

*Interface*. London, Sidgwick and Jackson, 1971; New York, Ace, 1977.
*Volteface*. London, Sidgwick and Jackson, 1972; New York, Ace, 1978.
*Multiface*. London, Sidgwick and Jackson, 1975; New York, Ace, 1978

OTHER PUBLICATIONS

Novel

*The Greenlander*. London, Hamish Hamilton, 1978; New York, Summit, 1979.

*

Mark Adlard comments:

One of my main pre-occupations is the importance of personal economic activity to "the good life." It seemed to me that various hypotheses about such matters could be explored fictionally, by presenting a future world in which economic activity had been largely made redundant. This fictional device would also make it possible to consider the moral dilemmas and responsibilities of managerial elites. It was considerations such as these, and not a previous enthusiasm for the genre, that induced me to write "science fiction."

* * *

Mark Adlard's Tcity trilogy, *Interface, Volteface,* and *Multiface,* makes up a whole less than the sum of its parts but it is nevertheless a highly interesting and readable work. The parts are considerable and the project ambitious. Reviewing *Multiface* for the *Times Literary Supplement,* T.A. Shippey noted the ironic contrast between the plots and characters of the first two books and those of Wagner's *Ring* and Dante's *Commedia* respectively: "Only the boldest writer would invite such comparisons. . . . But Mark Adlard made a success of it, and has done so once more, in a novel based this time on *The Faerie Queene.*" Shippey is an over-bold reviewer, for his criticism is not just, although it does adumbrate a critical problem. For one thing, Spenser is only one among several important literary sources in *Multiface,* where the controlling reference (matching Wagner and Dante) is to Buddhism; for another, the relationships between the novels and their sources are not the same.

One of the problems seems to be that the three novels were not all completed together. As literature, *Interface* is inferior to the later two. It is overloaded with exposition at the expense of narrative and, although Adlard is clearly aware of the problem (throughout the series, a stock joke is the blunt interruption of robotic exposition), information whether cultural or technological appears to be simply dropped into the text and does not resonate within it. This is true of the Wagner references, which are only to *Götterdämmerung,* an odd choice for the first novel of a series. This novel concerns weaknesses at the interface between an enclosed society of drugged citizens and their benevolent, superior managers, weaknesses on both sides which end in destruction for some but salvation for others. Adlard stands too far off from his characters, and, because the emotive level of the narrative is low, the climactic horrors and pathos fail somewhat in their effect. *Volteface* is much richer in texture, and the Dante references are both more numerous than the *Ring* ones and more deeply embedded in the text; the leading characters are more highly developed, and the narrative consequently more engaging, the ironies more piquant. In the failed Utopia of *Interface,* work had been denied the multitudinous citizens; in response to their discontent, work is reintroduced to Tcity by the executives, who deliberately create an old-fashioned (i.e., 20th-century) managerial structure, knowing this will be inefficient, merely to make work, i.e., the distribution of goods (trinkets) which are, of course, manufactured in fully automated factories. This scheme enables Adlard to write splendid satire as he traces both the collective volte-face and some individual reversals of life in Tcity. The *Inferno* of workfree pleasure is exchanged for a dubious *Purgatorio.* However, I would need to have the author explain to me just how his Dante-Beatrice pair (Twynne and Ventrix) are really illuminated by their source. Ventrix is an interesting character in her own right.

If idle pleasure was hell, work purgatory, then *Multiface* seems to be asking what is the ideal mode of life. The answer is that it depends on the individual life. Even Theravada Buddhism, practiced by one saintly executive, may not suit all executives; Mahayana Buddhism, considered more suitable for the citizens, seems too perversely appropriate for the tormented Taggart, persuaded that in a lame dog he sees the reincarnation of his sadistic father, on which he exacts vengeance for his mother's suffering which has blighted the whole of his own life. As Jan Caspol puts it, "Men have different faces. There are no two alike and you can't expect them to wear the same mask. . . . Even Buddhas only point the way." Jan, though an executive, is the reader's choric companion throughout the series and he thus presumably voices the author's conclusion: but what consequences follow for the executives whose vast experiment has involved the beneficent control of a world society? The author seems to shy away from his bold socio-history, in favour of the predicaments of individuals. Their problems may be resolved for good or ill, but what of the further problems in Tcity? The trilogy seems to call for a further, more mature volume, one which will tell us what life is for, perhaps: we are at least provoked to consideration of this disturbing question. However, it may be in the intuition that life is open-ended, that there are no pat catastrophes, that the trilogy should properly end. One of its most appealing narratives is that of Osbert Osborne, discovering diversity and pattern in the apparently uniform stahlex beeblocks of Tcity (everything there is made of this remarkable versatile new material), yet knowing that he will never have time even to map his own multi-story block. Three faces can stand for the whole infinite polyhedron.

—Michael J. Tolley

---

**AGHILL, Gordon.** *See* **GARRETT, Randall.**

---

**AINSBURY, Ray.** *See* **VERRILL, A. Hyatt.**

---

**ALDISS, Brian W(ilson).** British. Born in East Dereham, Norfolk, 18 August 1925. Educated at Framlingham College, Suffolk, 1936–39; West Buckland School, 1939–42. Served in the Royal Signals in the Far East, 1943–47. Married Margaret Manson in 1965 (second marriage); four children, two from previous marriage. Bookseller, Oxford, 1947–56; literary editor, *Oxford Mail,* 1958–69; science-fiction editor, Penguin Books, London, 1961–64; art correspondent, *Guardian,* London. President, British Science Fiction Association, 1960–65; co-founder, 1972, and chairman, 1976–78, John W. Campbell Memorial award; co-president, Eurocon Committee, 1975–79; chairman, Society of Authors, London, 1978–79; member, Arts Council Literature Panel, 1978–80; president, World Science Fiction, 1982–84. Since 1975, vice-president, Stapledon Society; since 1977, founding trustee, World Science Fiction, Dublin; since 1983, vice-president, H.G. Wells Society. Recipient: World Science Fiction Convention citation, 1959; Hugo award, 1962, 1987; Nebula award, 1965; Ditmar award (Australia), 1970; British Science Fiction Association award, 1972, 1982, and Special award, 1974; Eurocon award, 1976; James Blish award, for non-fiction, 1977; Cometa d'Argento (Italy), 1977; Prix Jules Verne, 1977; Pilgrim award, 1978; John W. Campbell Memorial award, 1983; J. Lloyd Eaton award, 1988; Kafka award, 1991. Guest of Honour, World Science Fiction Convention, London, 1965, 1979. Fellow, Royal Society of Literature, 1991. Agent: A.P. Watt Ltd., 20 John Street, London WC1N 2DR, England; or, Robin Straus, 229 East 79th Street, New York, New York 10021, U.S.A. Address: Woodlands, Foxcombe Road, Boars Hill, Oxfordshire OX1 5DL, England.

### Science-Fiction Publications

Novels (series: Helliconia)

*Non-Stop.* London, Faber, 1958; New York, Carroll and Graf, 1989; as *Starship,* New York, Criterion, 1959.

*Vanguard from Alpha.* New York, Ace, 1959; as *Equator* (includes "Segregation"), London, Digit, 1961.

*Bow Down to Nul.* New York, Ace, 1960; as *The Interpreter,* London, Digit, 1961.

*The Male Response.* New York, Galaxy, 1961; London, Dobson, 1963.

*The Primal Urge.* New York, Ballantine, 1961; London, Sphere, 1967.

*The Long Afternoon of Earth.* New York, New American Library, 1962; expanded edition, as *Hothouse,* London, Faber, 1962; Boston, Gregg Press, 1976.

*The Dark Light Years.* London, Faber, and New York, New American Library, 1964.

*Greybeard.* London, Faber, and New York, Harcourt Brace, 1964.

*Earthworks.* London, Faber, 1965; New York, Doubleday, 1966.

*An Age.* London, Faber, 1967; as *Cryptozoic!,* New York, Doubleday, 1968.

*Report on Probability A.* London, Faber, 1968; New York, Doubleday, 1969.

*Barefoot in the Head.* London, Faber, 1969; New York, Doubleday, 1970.

*Frankenstein Unbound.* London, Cape, 1973; New York, Random House, 1974.

*The Eighty-Minute Hour.* London, Cape, and New York, Doubleday, 1974.

*The Malacia Tapestry.* London, Cape, 1976; New York, Harper, 1977.

*Enemies of the System*. London, Cape, and New York, Harper, 1978.
*Moreau's Other Island*. London, Cape, 1980; as *An Island Called Moreau*, New York, Simon and Schuster, 1981.
*The Helliconia Trilogy*. New York, Atheneum, 1985.
*Helliconia Spring*. London, Cape, and New York, Atheneum, 1982.
*Helliconia Summer*. London, Cape, and New York, Atheneum, 1983.
*Helliconia Winter*. London, Cape, and New York, Atheneum, 1985.
*Dracula Unbound*. London, Grafton, and New York, Harper Collins, 1991.

Short Stories

*Space, Time, and Nathaniel: Presciences*. London, Faber, 1957; abridged edition, as *No Time Like Tomorrow*, New York, New American Library, 1959.
*The Canopy of Time*. London, Faber, 1959; revised edition, as *Galaxies Like Grains of Sand*, New York, New American Library, 1960.
*The Airs of Earth*. London, Faber, 1963.
*Starswarm*. New York, New American Library, 1964; London, Panther, 1979.
*Best Science Fiction Stories of Brian Aldiss*. London, Faber, 1965; as *Who Can Replace a Man?*, New York, Harcourt Brace, 1966; revised edition, Faber, 1971.
*The Saliva Tree and Other Strange Growths*. London, Faber, 1966.
*Intangibles Inc*. London, Faber, 1969.
*A Brian Aldiss Omnibus 1–2*. London, Sidgwick and Jackson, 2 vols., 1969–71.
*Neanderthal Planet*. New York, Avon, 1970.
*The Moment of Eclipse*. London, Faber, 1970; New York, Doubleday, 1972.
*The Book of Brian Aldiss*. New York, DAW, 1972; as *The Comic Inferno*, London, New English Library, 1973.
*Excommunication*. London, Post Card Partnership, 1975.
*Last Orders and Other Stories*. London, Cape, 1977; New York, Carroll and Graf, 1989.
*New Arrivals, Old Encounters: Twelve Stories*. London, Cape, 1979; New York, Harper, 1980.
*Foreign Bodies*. Singapore, Chopmen, 1981.
*Seasons in Flight*. London, Cape, 1984.
*Best Science Fiction Stories of Brian W. Aldiss*. London, Gollancz, 1988; as *Man in His Time: The Best Science Fiction Stories of Brian W. Aldiss*. New York, Atheneum, 1989.
*A Romance of the Equator: Best Fantasy Stories of Brian W. Aldiss* London, Gollancz, 1989; New York, Atheneum, 1990.
*Bodily Functions: Four Stories and a Letter to Sam (Lundwall) on the Subject of Bowel Movements*. London, Avernus, 1991.

OTHER PUBLICATIONS

Novels

*The Brightfount Diaries*. London, Faber, 1955.
*The Horatio Stubbs Saga*. London, Panther, 1985.
*The Hand-Reared Boy*. London, Weidenfeld and Nicolson, and New York, McCall, 1970.
*A Soldier Erect; or, Further Adventures of the Hand-Reared Boy*. London, Weidenfeld and Nicolson, and New York, Coward McCann, 1971.
*A Rude Awakening*. London, Weidenfeld and Nicolson, 1978; New York, Random House, 1979.
*Brothers of the Head*. London, Pierrot, 1977; New York, Two Continents, 1978.
*Brothers of the Head, and Where the Lines Converge*. London, Panther, 1979.
*Life in the West*. London, Weidenfeld and Nicolson, 1980; New York, Carroll and Graf, 1990.
*The Year Before Yesterday*. New York, Watts, 1987; as *Cracken at Critical*, Worcester Park, Surrey, Kerosina, 1987.
*The Magic of the Past* (novella). Worcester Park, Surrey, Kerosina, 1987.
*Ruins* (novella). London, Hutchinson, 1987.
*Forgotten Life*. London, Gollancz, 1988; New York, Atheneum, 1989.

Plays

*Distant Encounters*, adaptation of his own stories (produced London, 1978).
*Science Fiction Blues* (produced London, 1987).

Television Play: *Life* (*4 Minutes* series), 1986.

Verse

*Pile: Petals from St. Klaed's Computer*. London, Cape, and New York, Holt Rinehart, 1979.
*Farewell to a Child*. Berkhamsted, Hertfordshire, Priapus, 1982.

Other

*Cities and Stones: A Traveller's Jugoslavia*. London, Faber, 1966.
*The Shape of Further Things: Speculations on Change*. London, Faber, 1970; New York, Doubleday, 1971.
*Billion Year Spree: A History of Science Fiction*. London, Weidenfeld and Nicolson, and New York, Doubleday, 1973.
*Science Fiction Art*. London, New English Library, and New York, Bounty, 1975.
*Science Fiction as Science Fiction*. Frome, Somerset, Bran's Head, 1978.
*This World and Nearer Ones: Essays Exploring the Familiar*. London, Weidenfeld and Nicolson, 1979; Kent, Ohio, Kent State University Press, 1981.
*Science Fiction Quiz*. London, Weidenfeld and Nicolson, 1983.
*The Pale Shadow of Science*. Seattle, Serconia Press, 1985.
*And the Lurid Glare of the Comet*. Seattle, Washington, Serconia Press, 1986.
*Trillion Year Spree: The History of Science Fiction*, with David Wingrove. London, Gollancz, and New York, Atheneum, 1986.
*Science Fiction Blues: The Show that Brian Aldiss Took on the Road*, edited by Frank Hatherley. London, Avernus, 1988.
*Bury My Heart at W.H. Smith's: A Writing Life* (autobiography). London, Hodder and Stoughton, 1990.

Editor, *Penguin Science Fiction*. London, Penguin, 1961; *More Penguin Science Fiction*, 1963; *Yet More Penguin Science Fiction*, 1964; 3 vols. collected as *The Penguin Science Fiction Omnibus*, 1973.
Editor, *Best Fantasy Stories*. London, Faber, 1962.
Editor, *Last and First Men*, by Olaf Stapledon. London, Penguin, 1963.
Editor, *Introducing SF*. London, Faber, 1964.

Editor, with Harry Harrison, *Nebula Award Stories 2.* New York, Doubleday, 1967; as *Nebula Award Stories 1967,* London, Gollancz, 1967.

Editor, with Harry Harrison, *All about Venus.* New York, Dell, 1968; enlarged edition, as *Farewell, Fantastic Venus,* London, Macdonald, 1968.

Editor, with Harry Harrison, *Best SF 1967 [to 1975].* New York, Berkley and Putnam, 7 vols., and Indianapolis, Bobbs Merrill, 2 vols., 1968–75; as *The Year's Best Science Fiction 1–9,* London, Sphere, 8 vols., 1968–76, and London, Futura, 1 vol., 1976.

Editor, with Harry Harrison, *The Astounding-Analog Reader.* New York, Doubleday, 2 vols., 1972–73; London, Sphere, 2 vols., 1973.

Editor, *Space Opera.* London, Weidenfeld and Nicolson, 1974; New York, Doubleday, 1975.

Editor, *Space Odysseys.* London, Futura, 1974; New York, Doubleday, 1976.

Editor, with Harry Harrison, *SF Horizons* (reprint of magazine). New York, Arno Press, 1975.

Editor, with Harry Harrison, *Hell's Cartographers: Some Personal Histories of Science Fiction Writers.* London, Weidenfeld and Nicolson, and New York, Harper, 1975.

Editor, with Harry Harrison, *Decade: The 1940's, The 1950's, The 1960's.* London, Macmillan, 3 vols., 1975–77; *The 1940's* and *The 1950's,* New York, St. Martin's Press, 2 vols., 1978.

Editor, *Evil Earths.* London, Weidenfeld and Nicolson, 1975; New York, Avon, 1979.

Editor, *Galactic Empires.* London, Weidenfeld and Nicolson, 2 vols., 1976; New York, St. Martin's Press, 2 vols., 1977.

Editor, *Perilous Planets.* London, Weidenfeld and Nicolson, 1978; New York, Avon, 1980.

Editor, with others, *The Penguin Masterquiz Book.* London, Penguin, 1985.

Editor, with Sam Lundwall, *The Penguin World Omnibus of Science Fiction.* London, Penguin, 1986.

Editor, *My Madness: The Selected Writings of Anna Kavan.* London, Pan, 1990.

*

Bibliography: *The Work of Brian W. Aldiss, An Annotated Bibliography and Guide* by Margaret Aldiss, San Bernardino, California, Borgo Press, 1991.

Manuscript Collections: Bodleian Library, Oxford University; Dallas Public Library; University of Kansas, Lawrence; Sydney University; Eastern New Mexico University, Portales; University of California, Los Angeles (correspondence), Henry E. Huntington Library, San Marino, California (correspondence); North East London Polytechnic (correspondence).

Critical Studies: *Aldiss Unbound: The Science Fiction of Brian W. Aldiss* by Richard Mathews, San Bernardino, California, Borgo Press, 1977; *Apertures: A Study of the Writings of Brian Aldiss* by Brian Griffin and David Wingrove, Westport, Connecticut, Greenwood Press, 1984; by the author, in *Contemporary Authors Autobiography Series 2,* Detroit, Gale, 1985; *Brian W. Aldiss* by Michael Collings, Mercer Island, Washington, Starmont, 1986; "The Secret You: Fantasy and Story in Brian Aldiss's Mainstream Fiction" by Ellen R. Weil, in *New York Review of Science Fiction,* 26–27, 1990.

Brian Aldiss comments:

As the twentieth century draws to a close, we see more clearly what a bad lot the human species is as a whole, and how greatly we have damaged a planet reasonably intact in 1900, give or take a few million passenger pigeons. Let's hope to God that that infantile fantasy of our conquering the universe never becomes reality! It's a pity that the evolutionary march upwards from the Olduvai Gorge was not taken at a more leisurely pace. As Bruce Sterling says, the colour of SF is *noir.*

Morality and hedonism fight the good fight in my novels and stories.

Interested parties are recommended to seek out the critical study of my writings by Wingrove and Griffin. Although I do not always agree with all they say, they are at least as reliable as I would be. Even self-conscious authors sail on, charting their course through style and story, without much bothering about the rocks under the surface. It's for the critics to consider shipwreck.

One really writes because one has to. I never think of the reader until the act of creation is over. Then I hope I might nourish the creative spark in others; I imagine people and people imagination. I craved the freedom writing gave me. My fictions have taken place on many worlds. My central characters have been of many nationalities. Speech is a preoccupation. Even in *Non-Stop,* some sort of heightened speech was attempted. In *Life in the West,* scarcely a handful of the many characters speak "standard English," in *Helliconia* the languages are many. Aren't those volumes in part about the necessity of communication—and its difficulty? Mine is a literature of exile. Every novel undertaken is an act of xenophilia. The label "science fiction" doesn't fit.

The list of my writings seems impossibly long. The more reason to be brief here.

* * *

For those outside the genre Brian W. Aldiss is one of Britain's best-known science fiction writers; he is one of the very few—almost the only living one—who is respected by the British Literary Establishment, seen to be standing alongside and working with such figures as Robert Conquest and Sir Kingsley Amis. But for those *within* the field, his fiction, good though it is, is eclipsed by his work as a critic and editor.

Aldiss has maintained a consistently prolific output, usually managing about one new book a year, as well as a seemingly endless stream of short stories, a good number of which have more than stood the test of time. His themes and settings range widely, encompassing amongst others unusual star systems, time travel, history, sex, fantasy, humour and psychedelia. To all his work he brings an appropriate style; indeed, there is no such thing as *the* Aldiss style, unless it be care in the use of words. But his concentration on, if not admiration of style works both ways. In *The Malacia Tapestry* he summons up brilliantly the lethargy and sensuality of renaissance decadence, balancing violence and love, and introducing the beginnings of change into an unchanging city reminiscent of M. John Harrison's *Viriconium* books. The language he uses is sensual and poetic; it glows to illuminate the themes of the novel.

But in at least two of his earlier books his use of style becomes self-indulgent. *Report on Probability A* may be one of his own favourites, but three people known only by their initials observing each other doing nothing endlessly is really very little other than a stylistic exercise, following the French anti-novelists. In *Bury My Heart at W.H. Smith's* Aldiss claims it is "the novel in which I came nearest to fulfilling my original intentions before I set pen to paper." But for most readers it is dreary and unreadable. Similarly, *Barefoot in the Head* exemplifies all that was worst in 1960's artistic pretension. In small doses in Michael Moorcock's *New Worlds* magazine, where they first saw print, the hallucinogenic stories might have been great fun, and indeed fitted well; but as a novel, and with the benefit of hindsight, the book is cluttered, untidy and unsatisfying.

Aldiss's earliest novels stand up well in comparison to these two aberrations. His first novel *Non-Stop* (published later as *Starship*) is one of the earliest classic generation starship stories, and still worth reading. *The Long Afternoon of Earth* (published later as *Hothouse*) is a brilliant mass of invention: the collection of creatures living in the tree world on the sunny side of a non-rotating Earth is probably unsurpassed. As in the later *Helliconia* trilogy, Aldiss adds research to imagination to produce more scientific plausibility than most writers manage, while still telling a rattling good tale. Aldiss's creation of a world in which each season lasts centuries in his *Helliconia* books is usually put forward as the ultimate proof of his stature. As always, more than almost any other writer Aldiss meticulously works through the effects that this would have on flora and fauna, and also on human society. The books cannot be faulted for this. And there is none of the over-sentimentality so often seen from poorer SF writers about the pastoral simplicity of pre-technological society, for Aldiss has also explored the hard truth of the economics of his creation. Yet looking back on the *Helliconia* books from a little distance it is possible to say that they have become somewhat over-rated. Certainly the development of civilisation and culture in a primitive society is much better handled in Samuel R. Delany's early *Nevèrÿon* books, written at much the same time, while the effects of extremely long seasons on individuals and society have more recently been dealt with far more satisfactorily by Paul Park in his *Starbridge* chronicles (though his seasons are shorter than Aldiss's).

And once again Aldiss's style, in carefully mirroring the content, at times gets in the way: the ponderous procession of seasons is reflected in the ponderous prose.

It is in *Frankenstein Unbound* that Aldiss's true obsession is most clearly seen: ". . . Mary Godwin entered, and I found myself flushing—partly with the wine, no doubt, but mainly with the agonising exhilaration of confronting the author of *Frankenstein, or The Modern Prometheus.*" And within less than twenty pages, she and the 21st century time-traveling hero are in bed together. *Frankenstein Unbound* was, as Aldiss said in *Trillion Year Spree,* "designed to draw attention to its great original," which he has spent thousands of words "proving" to be the genesis of modern science fiction. He defines SF in *Trillion Year Spree,* the updated edition of his classic history of SF, *Billion Year Spree*: "Science fiction is the search for a definition of mankind and his status in the universe which will stand in our advanced but confused state of knowledge (science), and is characteristically cast in the Gothic or post-Gothic mode." The suspicion lurks that Aldiss decided which was the first, then wrote his definition to prove it so.

*Frankenstein Unbound* is an interesting work written, of course, with great style—and here the style works to perfection. Its recent successor, *Dracula Unbound,* is not so successful. It is the first book that Aldiss has written deliberately to be filmed, as a sequel to Roger Corman's 1990 film of the earlier book. Perhaps because of this, Aldiss's usual meticulous care is missing; the book suffers from stereotyped characters, implausible dialogue, and sloppiness of logic that, in a standard time-travel novel, is inexcusable in a writer of Aldiss's calibre.

Aldiss's contribution to science fiction is that he is a stylist *par excellence,* and that he has consistently produced well-researched, well-written novels and a host of high quality short stories over more than three decades. But his contribution to the field is much greater than this. As an establishment figure he has been more responsible than anyone else in the United Kingdom in the second half of this century for pulling SF out of the gutter into some semblance of respectability. As an editor, sometimes with Robert Conquest or Harry Harrison, he has been responsible for compiling some excellent anthologies. And as a critic he has produced a handful of extraordinarily valuable works, including the autobiographical *The Shape of Further Things* and *Bury My Heart at W.H. Smith's,* both of which give intimate insights into the writing life of the author, as does *Hell's Cartographers,* edited by Aldiss and Harry Harrison.

His most outstanding work, however, has to be *Billion Year Spree: A History of Science Fiction.* Opinionated and patchy in its coverage it may be, but as a single-volume overview of the birth, adolescence and growth of the field up to the early 1970's it is unsurpassed. It was sadly not improved on thirteen years later in the revised version, *Trillion Year Spree,* co-written by David Wingrove. Coverage of the 1980's is extremely scanty; the neglectful treatment of recent British writers borders on the absurd. Maybe there will be a *Zillion Year Spree* to retrieve the quality of the original.

—David V. Barrett

---

**ALLEN, Stuart.** *See* **TUBB, E.C.**

---

**AMES, Clinton.** *See* **PHILLIPS, Rog.**

---

**AMHERST, Wes.** *See* **SHAVER, Richard S.**

---

**AMIS, (Sir) Kingsley (William).** Also writes as Robert Markham. British. Born in London, 16 April 1922. Educated at City of London School; St. John's College, Oxford, M.A. in English. Served in the Royal Corps of Signals, 1942–45. Married 1) Hilary Ann Bardwell in 1948 (marriage dissolved, 1965), two sons, including the writer Martin Amis, and one daughter; 2) the writer Elizabeth Jane Howard in 1965 (divorced, 1983). Lecturer in English, University College, Swansea, Wales, 1949–61; Visiting Fellow in Creative Writing, Princeton University, New Jersey, 1958–59; Fellow in English, Peterhouse, Cambridge, 1961–63; Visiting Professor, Vanderbilt University, Nashville, Tennessee, 1967. Recipient: Maugham award, 1955; *Yorkshire Post* award, 1974; John W. Campbell Memorial award, 1977; Booker prize, 1986. Honorary Fellow, St. John's College, 1976. C.B.E. (Commander, Order of the British Empire), 1981. Knighted, 1990. Lives in London. Agent: Jonathan Clowes Ltd., Iron Bridge House, Bridge Approach, London NW1 8BD, England.

SCIENCE-FICTION PUBLICATIONS

Novels

*The Anti-Death League.* London, Gollancz, and New York, Harcourt Brace, 1966.
*The Alteration.* London, Cape, 1976; New York, Viking Press, 1977.
*Russian Hide-and-Seek: A Melodrama.* London, Hutchinson, 1980.

OTHER PUBLICATIONS

Novels

*Lucky Jim.* London, Gollancz, and New York, Doubleday, 1954.
*That Uncertain Feeling.* London, Gollancz, 1955; New York, Harcourt Brace, 1956.
*I Like It Here.* London, Gollancz, and New York, Harcourt Brace, 1958.
*Take a Girl Like You.* London, Gollancz, 1960; New York, Harcourt Brace, 1961.
*One Fat Englishman.* London, Gollancz, 1963; New York, Harcourt Brace, 1964.
*The Egyptologists,* with Robert Conquest. London, Cape, 1965; New York, Random House, 1966.
*Colonel Sun: A James Bond Adventure* (as Robert Markham). London, Cape, and New York, Harper, 1968.
*I Want It Now.* London, Cape, 1968; New York, Harcourt Brace, 1969.
*The Green Man.* London, Cape, 1969; New York, Harcourt Brace, 1970.
*Girl, 20.* London, Cape, 1971; New York, Harcourt Brace, 1972.
*The Riverside Villas Murder.* London, Cape, and New York, Harcourt Brace, 1973.
*Ending Up.* London, Cape, and New York, Harcourt Brace, 1974.
*Kingsley Amis Omnibus.* London, Hutchinson, 1987.
  *Jake's Thing.* London, Hutchinson, 1978; New York, Viking Press, 1979.
  *Stanley and the Women.* London, Hutchinson, 1984; New York, Perennial Library, 1988.
  *The Old Devils.* London, Hutchinson, 1986; New York, Summit, 1987.
*The Crime of the Century.* London, Dent, 1987; New York, Mysterious Press, 1989.
*Difficulties with Girls.* London, Hutchinson, and New York, Summit, 1988.
*The Folks that Live on the Hill.* London, Hutchinson, and New York, Summit, 1990.

Short Stories

*My Enemy's Enemy.* London, Gollancz, 1962; New York, Harcourt Brace, 1963.
*Penguin Modern Stories 11,* with others. London, Penguin, 1972.
*Dear Illusion.* London, Covent Garden Press, 1972.
*The Darkwater Hall Mystery.* Edinburgh, Tragara Press, 1978.
*Collected Short Stories.* London, Hutchinson, 1980; revised edition, 1987.

Plays

Radio Plays: *Something Strange,* 1962; *The Riverside Villas Murder,* from his own novel, 1976.

Television Plays: *A Question about Hell,* 1964; *The Importance of Being Harry,* 1971; *Dr. Watson and the Darkwater Hall Mystery,* 1974; *See What You've Done* (*Softly, Softly* series), 1974; *We Are All Guilty* (*Against the Crowd* series), 1975.

Verse

*Bright November.* London, Fortune Press, 1947.
*A Frame of Mind.* Reading, Berkshire, University of Reading School of Art, 1953.
*(Poems).* Oxford, Fantasy Press, 1954.
*A Case of Samples: Poems 1946–1956.* London, Gollancz, 1956; New York, Harcourt Brace, 1957.
*The Evans Country.* Oxford, Fantasy Press, 1962.
*Penguin Modern Poets 2,* with Dom Moraes and Peter Porter. London, Penguin, 1962.
*A Look round the Estate: Poems 1957–1967.* London, Cape, 1967; New York, Harcourt Brace, 1968.
*Wasted, Kipling at Bateman's.* London, Poem-of-the-Month Club, 1973.
*Collected Poems 1944–1979.* London, Hutchinson, 1979; New York, Viking Press, 1980.

Recordings: *Kingsley Amis Reading His Own Poems,* Listen, 1962; *Poems,* with Thomas Blackburn, Jupiter, 1962.

Other

*Socialism and the Intellectuals.* London, Fabian Society, 1957.
*New Maps of Hell: A Survey of Science Fiction.* New York, Harcourt Brace, 1960; London, Gollancz, 1961.
*The James Bond Dossier.* London, Cape, and New York, New American Library, 1965.
*Lucky Jim's Politics.* London, Conservative Political Centre, 1968.
*What's Become of Jane Austen? and Other Questions.* London, Cape, 1970; New York, Harcourt Brace, 1971.
*On Drink.* London, Cape, 1972; New York, Harcourt Brace, 1973.
*Rudyard Kipling and His World.* London, Thames and Hudson, 1975; New York, Scribner, 1976.
*An Arts Policy?* London, Centre for Policy Studies, 1979.
*Every Day Drinking.* London, Hutchinson, 1983.
*How's Your Glass?* London, Weidenfeld and Nicolson, 1984.
*The Amis Collection: His Best Journalism, Pieces and Reviews.* London, Hutchinson, 1990.
*The Amis Collection: Selected Non-Fiction 1954–1990,* edited by John McDermitt. London, Hutchinson, 1990.
*Memoirs.* London, Hutchinson, 1991.

Editor, with James Michie, *Oxford Poetry 1949.* Oxford, Blackwell, 1949.
Editor, with Robert Conquest, *Spectrum [1–5]: A Science Fiction Anthology.* London, Gollancz, 5 vols., 1961–65; New York, Harcourt Brace, 5 vols., 1962–67.
Editor, *Selected Short Stories of G.K. Chesterton.* London, Faber, 1972.
Editor, *Tennyson.* London, Penguin, 1973.
Editor, *Harold's Years: Impressions from the New Statesman and The Spectator.* London, Quartet, 1977.
Editor, *The New Oxford Book of Light Verse.* London and New York, Oxford University Press, 1978.

Editor, *The Faber Popular Reciter*. London, Faber, 1978.
Editor, *The Golden Age of Science Fiction*. London, Hutchinson, 1981.
Editor, with James Cochrane, *The Great British Songbook*. New York, Pavilion-Joseph, 1986; London, Faber, 1988.
Editor, *The Amis Anthology: A Personal Choice of English Verse*. London, Hutchinson, 1988.
Editor, *The Pleasures of Poetry: From His Daily Mirror Column*. London, Cassell, 1990.
Editor, with others, *The Best Winners of the Booker Prize*. San Francisco, California, Mercury House, 1991.

*

Bibliography: *Kingsley Amis: A Checklist* by Jack Benoit Gohn, Kent, Ohio, Kent State University Press, 1976: *Kingsley Amis: A Reference Guide* by Dale Salwak, Boston, Hall, and London, Prior, 1978.

Manuscript Collection (verse): State University of New York, Buffalo.

Critical Study: *Kingsley Amis* by Philip Gardner, Boston, Twayne, 1981; *Kingsley Amis* by Richard Bradford, London, Arnold, 1989; *Kingsley Amis: An English Moralist* by John McDermott, London, Macmillan, 1989; *Kingsley Amis in Life and Letters* edited by Dale Sulwak, London, Macmillan, 1990.

Kingsley Amis comments:

I have been reading science fiction for over 50 years. Writing it too: I can remember writing a story about a revolution in the year 2032, which must mean I wrote it in 1932 when I was 10. I say this to show that SF has always been an inseparable part of my reading and writing life. So when later I got an idea for a story or novel whose events could not have taken place in our world, I found it altogether natural to create a new world for it.

Take *The Alteration.* I heard on an archive record made in 1909 a castrato then aged about 40 (one Alessandro Moreschi) singing the Bach/Gounod "Ave Maria," a good musical performance and an awful, dismal noise I could not get out of my head. It dawned on me that here was a great theme: a boy chosen for castration to preserve his wonderful voice would lose the chance of love, family, friends to a large extent, and a normal place in society. But he might gain fame, money, artistic success and the approval of God. (He might also lose the first batch without attaining the second.) None of it is possible in our world. I considered the coward's (or John Fowles's) way out: a remote island run by an eccentric millionaire. No, too cramped and private. It would have to be England in AD 1976, but as part of an alternate world where the Reformation had never happened and Rome was all-powerful—or nearly. On with the creation. . . .

* * *

A typical Kingsley Amis work combines satire and humor with serious themes to mock sacred cows, question *a priori* premises, and speculate about the nature of humans and God. It usually involves some erudite discussion of music (particularly classical), literature, history, linguistics, paleontology, or art, some focus on love as elevating and redemptive, and some sense of conspiracy, whether of church or state or the universe itself. It is witty, provocative, and firmly opinionated.

Reflecting an enthusiasm for science fiction that Amis traces to his early youth, *New Maps of Hell* began as a series of lectures delivered at Princeton for the 1958–59 Christian Gaus Seminar in Criticism. It is one of the most influential works of science fiction criticism up to that time, the first full-length study of science fiction by a critic outside the science fiction community. *New Maps* is clearly dated, and more personal than scholarly—a slightly patronizing attempt to define and defend science fiction at a time when the genre was considered suspect by literary scholars. It argues that a definition of science fiction is difficult, but somehow involves science and technology or pseudoscience or pseudo-technology, whether human or alien, though methods, goals and emphases may vary greatly. Thus, *The Tempest* and *Gulliver's Travels* are certainly precursors, according to Amis, though H.G. Wells and Jules Vernes begin the genre as we know it. *New Maps* also considers the literary quality of science fiction, pointing out that it ranges from the lowest pulp form (filled with scientific absurdities, violence, gratuitous sex, and innumerable monsters) to the highest literary levels (involving exploration of human nature, politics, and economics, satire of the present, and theorizing about the future). Ultimately Amis finds it allegorizing our own fears and insecurities, warning of future possibilities, and deflating *homo sapiens.* Because of Amis's interest in the genre, he edited with Robert Conquest the Spectrum series, five volumes of science-fiction short stories carefully selected for their interest and craftsmanship, volumes that helped establish the popularity and respectability of science fiction.

Amis's own short stories and novels are intriguing and clever. His James Bond adventure novel, *Colonel Sun,* contains science fiction elements, as does his ghost story, *The Green Man,* in which time stasis, two ghosts (one ineffectual, the other malignant), an exorcism, and a spirit force are played off against prosaic reality to suggest a manipulative higher power playing a complex game at man's expense. "Mason's Life" focuses on the nightmare realization that one's seemingly tangible reality is only someone else's dream. In "Something Strange" space program volunteers turn out to be guinea pigs for government psychologists experimenting with psychological conditioning and isolation stress.

*The Anti-Death League* uses a spy/romance/science fiction format as an excuse to explore philosophical questions about the active cruelty of God, the aimless horror and finality of death, and love as an antidote to combat insanity in an absurd universe. Amis, who seems to feel at home handling a military ambience with its rigid orders and regulations and its male-male interaction, centers his novel on a British training camp preparing soldiers for "Operation Apollo," germ warfare with an intensified strain of hydrophobia. Though ultimately the operation proves a giant bluff, it provides the backdrop for exploring life and death questions. As various zany characters rush about trying to expose security leaks, prove pet theories, or work out personal conflicts, the main thrust of the novel is an enumeration of signs of the motiveless malignity of God—numerous, sudden, random deaths or near deaths from accident or disease, reinforced by "pro-death" military plans, by signs of madness or incipient madness, and by futile attempts to combat both. The formation of an "Anti-Death League" provides the title of the book and Amis's model for man's ineffectual but necessary protest against whatever powers there be. The comic and satiric prevail, with characters including an atheist chaplain, a naive secret agent, a homosexual, alcoholic military officer, a promiscuous widow, an insane psychiatrist, and a conscience-ridden romantic named Churchill.

*The Alteration* presents an alternative world, one that might have been as the result of Henry VIII's elder brother Arthur surviving as monarch and siring a line of Catholic rulers. It postulates a Catholic England and Europe, forever at odds with Islam, and on a shaky diplomatic basis with New England, a small nation inhabited by subjugated Indians and the bigoted descendants of "Schismatics" and convicts (including one William Shakespeare). The Martin Luther of this Catholic world was a pope, Himmler a powerful representative of Papal might, Jean-Paul Sartre a Jesuit, James Bond Father Bond, and our world a shocking, slightly absurd science-fiction novel read clandestinely by rebellious adolescents. Amis's world is a chilling vision of ecclesiastical totalitarianism with the Church tightly controlling people's lives, making decisions about whether or not ten-year-old boys will be castrated so they can sing for the greater glory of God, sending out Nazi-like secret police to mutilate and murder those who defy Church authority, developing a disease that, spread through the drinking water, infects and alters males, and ultimately choosing a holy war against Moslems as a means of population control. As such, it is a grim commentary on hypocrisy, intolerance, gullibility, and mindless pieties—evil for the best of reasons. On another level it traces the story of Hubert Anvil, a brilliant child soprano chosen for castration, to explore adolescent yearnings, struggles against authority, and arrested development. Ultimately it is a paean to love, the greatest sin of all in this nightmare world of religious fanaticism. Amis links artistic creativity and sexuality, but also beauty and cruelty. Both the Church and the God of this alternative world castrate man, psychologically if not physically.

*Russian Hide-and-Seek* partakes of the patterns and concerns established in these earlier novels. Drawing on the conventions of nineteenth-century Russian fiction and cloak-and-dagger adventures, it depicts a Russianized England, a future fifty years hence when the Soviet Union rules England and perpetrates upon the English all the horrors that Amis envisions as inherent in Russian culture: brutality, violence, lack of family feeling, exploitation, and paranoia coupled with lachrymose introspection. The plot turns on an attempted revolution, made futile by the naivety of the revolutionaries and the strength of the Central Government. The English prove plucky but muddled; the Russians are bored, callous, self-indulgent. Violence and death again dominate this vision of the future.

Throughout his works Amis debunks muddled, limited people: the shallow, hypocritical, educated establishment of *Lucky Jim;* the greedy, lustful, self-indulgent academician of *One Fat Englishman;* the xenophobic, ethnocentric British traveller abroad of *I Like It Here;* the alcoholics, lesbians, and termagants of *The Folks that Live on the Hill;* the musical-beds set of *Girl, 20,* including denizens of the superficial world of pop culture, despotic bosses, counterculture radicals, and ill-tempered ladies; the eccentric psychiatrists and bigoted Parliamentarians of *The Crime of the Century* (a mystery); and the snobbish, egotistical phonies (poets, publishers, journalists, and academics) of *Difficulties with Girls.* Such idiosyncratic farces expose human cupidity, lechery, prejudice, and stupidity with gleeful insouciance. *The Old Devils, Ending Up, Girl, 20,* and *Jake's Thing* explore the incapability, impotence, rigidity and isolation of old age, with the last two attacking liberal sexual mores. Unlike *Take a Girl Like You* and *I Want It Now,* which sympathize with young women as sexually exploited, *Stanley and the Women* examines women as an alien species, whose unique form of speech, of style, of manner, and of logic make them a mystery, irrational and incomprehensible by male standards; attraction for them is like a recurring illness, inescapable and debilitating.

Amis's science fiction extends that tradition's potential, and, like his regular fiction, serves as a medium for satiric debunking and sociological investigation, particularly of the military mentality, pat solutions, modish psychology, feminism, and totalitarian inflexibility. His works are witty, irreverent, and infectious. His handling of different levels of diction, linguistic clues to class and education, and his verbal inventiveness are always impressive, and his attack on conventional values and attitudes fun. Amis brings to science fiction a scholar's eye for artistic, historic and cultural detail, a mastery of conversational exchanges, a disdain for fashionable cant, and a deep-seated pleasure in consistently flouting social, political and fictive conventions.

—Gina Macdonald

---

**ANDERSON, Poul (William).** American. Born in Bristol, Pennsylvania, 25 November 1926. Educated at the University of Minnesota, Minneapolis, B.S. 1948. Married Karen Kruse in 1953; one daughter. Freelance writer. President, Science Fiction Writers of America, 1972–73. Recipient: Hugo award, 1961, 1964, 1969, 1972, 1973, 1979, 1982; Nebula award, 1971, 1972, 1982; Tolkien Memorial award, 1978, Guest of Honor, World Science-Fiction Convention, 1959. Agent: Scott Meredith Literary Agency, 845 Third Avenue, New York, New York, 10022. Address: 3 Las Palomas, Orinda, California 94563, U.S.A.

SCIENCE-FICTION PUBLICATIONS

Novels (series: Dominic Flandry: King of Ys; Time Patrol; Trader Van Rijn)

*Vault of the Ages* (for children). Philadelphia, Winston, 1952.
*The Broken Sword.* New York, Abelard Schuman, 1954; revised edition, New York, Ballantine, 1971; Tisbury, Wiltshire, Compton Russell, 1974.
*Brain Wave.* New York, Ballantine, 1954; London, Heinemann, 1955.
*No World of Their Own.* New York, Ace, 1955; as *The Long Way Home*, London, Panther, 1975; New York, Ace, 1978.
*Star Ways.* New York, Avalon, 1956; as *The Peregrine*, New York, Ace, 1978.
*Planet of No Return.* New York, Ace, 1957; London, Dobson, 1966; as *Question and Answer*, Ace, 1978.
*The Snows of Ganymede.* New York, Ace, 1958.
*War of the Wing-Men* (Van Rijn). New York, Ace, 1958; London, Sphere, 1976; as *The Man Who Counts,* Ace, 1978.
*Virgin Planet.* New York, Avalon, 1959; London, Mayflower, 1966.
*The War of Two Worlds.* New York, Ace, 1959; London, Dobson, 1970.
*We Claim These Stars* (Flandry). New York, Ace, 1959; London, Dobson, 1976.
*The Enemy Stars.* Philadelphia, Lippincott, 1959.
*The High Crusade.* New York, Doubleday, 1960; London, Severn House, 1982.
*Earthman, Go Home!* (Flandry). New York, Ace, 1960.
*Twilight World.* New York, Torquil, 1961; London, Gollancz, 1962.
*Mayday Orbit* (Flandry). New York, Ace, 1961.
*Three Hearts and Three Lions.* New York, Doubleday, 1961.
*After Doomsday.* New York, Ballantine, 1962; London, Gollancz, 1963.
*The Makeshift Rocket.* New York, Ace, 1962; London, Dobson, 1969.
*Let the Spacemen Beware!* New York, Ace, 1963; London, Dobson, 1969; as *The Night Face,* Ace, 1978.
*Shield.* New York, Berkley, 1963; London, Dobson, 1965.
*Three Worlds to Conquer.* New York, Pyramid, 1964; London, Mayflower, 1966.
*Agent of the Terran Empire.* Philadelphia, Chilton, 1965.
*The Corridors of Time.* New York, Doubleday, 1965; London, Gollancz, 1966.

*Flandry of Terra* (omnibus). Philadelphia, Chilton, 1965.
*The Star Fox*. New York, Doubleday, 1965; London, Gollancz, 1966.
*Ensign Flandry*. Philadelphia, Chilton, 1966; London, Coronet, 1976.
*The Fox, the Dog, and the Griffin: A Folk Tale Adapted from the Danish of C. Molbech* (for children). New York, Doubleday, 1966.
*World Without Stars*. New York, Ace, 1966; London, Dobson, 1975.
*The Rebel Worlds*. New York, New American Library, 1969; London, Coronet, 1972; as *Commander Flandry*, London, Severn House, 1978.
*Satan's World*. New York, Doubleday, 1969; London, Gollancz, 1970.
*A Circus of Hells* (Flandry). New York, New American Library, 1970; London, Sphere, 1978.
*Tau Zero*. New York, Doubleday, 1970; London, Gollancz, 1971.
*The Byworlder*. New York, New American Library, 1971; London, Gollancz, 1972.
*The Dancer from Atlantis*. New York, New American Library, 1971; London, Sphere, 1977.
*Operation Chaos*. New York, Doubleday, 1971.
*There Will Be Time*. New York, Doubleday, 1972; London, Sphere, 1979.
*Hrolf Kraki's Saga*. New York, Ballantine, 1973.
*The People of the Wind*. New York, New American Library, 1973; London, Sphere, 1977.
*The Day of Their Return*. New York, Doubleday, 1974; London, Corgi, 1978.
*Inheritors of Earth*, with Gordon Eklund. Radnor, Pennsylvania, Chilton, 1974.
*Fire Time*. New York, Doubleday, 1974; London, Panther, 1977.
*A Midsummer Tempest*. New York, Doubleday, 1974; London, Futura, 1975.
*A Knight of Ghosts and Shadows*. New York, Doubleday, 1974; London, Sphere, 1978; as *Knight Flandry*, London, Severn House, 1980.
*Star Prince Charlie* (for children), with Gordon R. Dickson. New York, Putnam, 1975.
*The Winter of the World*. New York, Doubleday, 1975.
*Mirkheim*. New York, Berkley, 1977; London, Sphere, 1978.
*The Avatar*. New York, Berkley, 1978; London, Sidgwick and Jackson, 1980.
*Two Worlds* (omnibus). New York, Ace, 1978.
*The Merman's Children*. New York, Berkley, 1979; London, Sidgwick and Jackson, 1981.
*A Stone in Heaven*. New York, Ace, 1979.
*The Demon of Scattery*, with Mildred Downey Broxon. New York, Ace, 1979.
*Time Patrolman*. New York, Tor, 1983; London, Sphere, 1986.
*Orion Shall Rise*. New York, Pocket Books, 1984; London, Sphere, 1984.
*The Game of Empire* (Flandry). New York, Baen, 1985.
*Dialogue with Darkness*. New York, Tor, 1985.
*Berserker Base*, with Fred Saberhagen. New York, Tor, 1985.
*Mercenaries of Tomorrow*, edited by Martin H. Greenberg and Charles G. Waugh. New York, Lorevan, 1985.
*Terrorists of Tomorrow*, edited by Martin H. Greenberg and Charles G. Waugh. New York, Lorevan, 1986.
*Time Wars*, edited by Charles G. Waugh and Martin H. Greenberg. New York, Tor, 1986.
*The King of Ys*, with Karen Anderson. New York, Baen, 1988.
  *Roma Mater*. New York, Baen, 1986; London, Grafton, 1988.
  *Gallicenae*, with Karen Anderson. New York, Baen, 1987; London, Grafton, 1989.
  *Dahut*, with Karen Anderson. New York, Baen, 1988.
  *The Dog and the Wolf*, with Karen Anderson. New York, Baen, 1988.
*The Man—Kzin Wars*, with Larry Niven and Dean Ing. New York, Baen, 1988.
*The Year of the Ransom*. New York, Walker, 1988.
*Space Wars*, edited by Charles G. Waugh and Martin H. Greenberg. New York, Tor, 1988.
*Space Folk*. New York, Baen, 1989.
*The Boat of a Million Years*. Norwalk, Connecticut, Easton Press, 1989; London, Sphere, 1990.
*The Saturn Game*, with *Iceborn* by Gregory Benford and Paul A. Carter. New York, Tor, 1989.
*No Truce with Kings*, with *Ship of Shadows* by Fritz Leiber. New York, Tor, 1989.
*The Man—Kzin Wars III*, with Larry Niven, Jerry Pournelle, and S.M. Sterling. New York, Baen, 1990.
*The Shield of Time* (Time Patrol). New York, Tor, 1990.
*Inconstant Star*. New York, Baen, 1991.
*The Longest Voyage*, with *Slow Lightning* by Steven Popkes. New York, Tor, 1991.
*Alight in the Void*. New York, Tor, 1991.

Short Stories

*Earthman's Burden*, with Gordon R. Dickson. New York, Gnome Press, 1957.
*Guardians of Time*. New York, Ballantine, 1960; London, Gollancz, 1961; augmented edition, New York, Pinnacle, 1981.
*Strangers from Earth*. New York, Ballantine, 1961; London, Mayflower, 1964.
*Orbit Unlimited*. New York, Pyramid, 1961; London, Sidgwick and Jackson, 1974.
*Un-Man and Other Novellas*. New York, Ace, 1962; London, Dobson, 1972.
*Time and Stars*. New York, Doubleday, and London, Gollancz, 1964.
*Trader to the Stars*. New York, Doubleday, 1964; London, Gollancz, 1965.
*Agent of the Terran Empire* (Flandry). Philadelphia, Chilton, 1965; London, Coronet, 1977.
*The Trouble Twisters* (Van Rijn). New York, Doubleday, 1966; London, Gollancz, 1967.
*The Horn of Time*. New York, New American Library, 1968; London, Corgi, 1981.
*Beyond the Beyond*. New York, New American Library, 1969; London, Gollancz, 1970.
*Seven Conquests*. New York, Macmillan, and London, Collier Macmillan, 1969; as *Conquests*, London, Granada, 1981.
*Tales of the Flying Mountains*. New York, Macmillan, 1970.
*The Queen of Air and Darkness*. New York, New American Library, 1973.
*The Many Worlds of Poul Anderson*. Radnor, Pennsylvania, Chilton, 1974; as *The Book of Poul Anderson*, New York, DAW, 1975.
*Homeward and Beyond*. New York, Doubleday, 1975.
*Homebrew*. Cambridge, Massachusetts, NEFSA Press, 1976.
*The Best of Poul Anderson*. New York, Pocket Books, 1976.
*The Earth Book of Stormgate*. New York, Berkley, 1978; London, New English Library, 3 vols., 1981.
*The Night Face and Other Stories*. Boston, Gregg Press, 1979.
*The Psychotechnic League*. New York, Pinnacle, 1981.
*The Dark Between the Stars*. New York, Berkley, 1981.
*Fantasy*. New York, Pinnacle, 1981.
*Explorations*. New York, Pinnacle, 1981.

*Winners*. New York, Pinnacle, 1981.
*Mauri and Kith*. New York, Tor, 1982.
*The Gods Laughed*. New York, Pinnacle, 1982.
*Starship*. New York, Tor, 1982.
*Cold Victory*. New York, Tor, 1982.
*New America*. New York, Tor, 1982.
*Hoka!*, with Gordon R. Dickson. New York, Simon and Schuster, 1983.
*The Long Night*. New York, Tor, 1983; London, Sphere, 1985.
*Conflict*. New York, Tor, 1983.
*Past Times*. New York, Tor, 1984.

OTHER PUBLICATIONS

Novels

*Perish by the Sword*. New York, Macmillan, 1959.
*Murder in Black Letter*. New York, Macmillan, 1960.
*The Golden Slave*. New York, Avon, 1960.
*Rogue Sword*. New York, Avon, 1960.
*Murder Bound*. New York, Macmillan, 1962.
The Future at Wars, edited by Reginald Bretnor:
*Thor's Hammer*, with Robert A. Heinlein and Jerry Pournelle. New York, Baen, 1979.
*The Spear of Mars*, with others. New York, Baen, 1980.
*Conan the Rebel*. New York, Bantam, 1980; London, Hale, 1984.
The Last Viking:
*The Golden Horn*. New York, Zebra, 1980.
*The Road of the Sea Horse*. New York, Zebra, 1980.
*Sign of the Raven*. New York, Zebra, 1981.
*The Devil's Game*. New York, Pocket Books, 1980.

Other

*Is There Life on Other Worlds?* New York, Crowell Collier, and London, Collier Macmillan, 1963.
*Thermonuclear Warfare*. Derby, Connecticut, Monarch, 1963.
*The Infinite Voyage: Man's Future in Space*. New York, Macmillan, and London, Collier Macmillan, 1969.
*The Unicorn Trade* (miscellany), with Karen Anderson. New York, Tor, 1984.

Editor, *West by One and by One*. Privately printed, 1965.
Editor, *Nebula Award Stories 4*. New York, Doubleday, 1969.
Editor, with Karen Anderson, *The Night Fantastic*. New York, DAW, 1991.

Translator, *The Method of Holding the Three Ones*. Atlantic Highlands, New Jersey, Humanities Press, 1980.

*

Bibliography: *A Checklist of Poul Anderson* by Roger G. Peyton, privately printed, 1965.

Manuscript Collection: University of Southern Mississippi, Hattiesburg.

Critical Study: *Against Time's Arrow: The High Crusade of Poul Anderson* by Sandra Miesel, San Bernardino, California, Borgo Press, 1978.

* * *

James Blish has called Poul Anderson "the enduring explosion" for the quality, quantity, and sheer breadth of Anderson's achievements are unique in science fiction. Seven Hugos and three Nebulas proclaim him the field's premier novelettist, but 50 novels and 200 shorter works testify to his mastery of all story forms. Over the course of four decades, he has explored an amazingly wide range of literary types from madcap comedy to grimmest tragedy in such distinctive fashion that the term "poulanderson" was once suggested as a generic name.

Consider the following in Anderson's fictional spectrum: broad farce (the Hoka series written with Gordon R. Dickson and *The Makeshift Rocket*); adventure comedy (*Virgin Planet*); action adventure yarn ("The Longest Voyage," 1960; the Van Rijn series; and the Flandry series); socio-political drama (the Psychotechnic Institute series and "No Truce with Kings," 1963); hard science fiction ("Epilogue," 1962); romantic fantasy (*Three Hearts and Three Lions*); heroic fantasy (*The Broken Sword*, and *Hrolf Kraki's Saga*); pastiche (*Conan the Rebel*); horror (*The Devil's Game*); historicals (the Last Viking trilogy); and mysteries (*Perish by the Sword*). Moreover, Anderson also writes songs, poems, parodies, essays, and children's books, and he is a skillful translator of Scandinavian prose and poetry. (For examples of his miscellania, see *The Unicorn Trade*, written with his wife Karen.)

Science holds first place among Anderson's raw materials. His formal training in physics imparts a special rigor to his handling of any science. (He has written some excellent articles on SF applications of scientific fact.) His research is thorough, his extrapolations imaginative. He will interweave hard and soft sciences as in *Orion Shall Rise*, but the most direct outlet for his scientific knowledge is the problem-solving story. Here, characters must either discover a phenomenon ("The Sharing of Flesh," 1968, and "Hunter's Moon," 1978) or react to one that is already recognized (*Fire Time* and "The Bitter Bread," 1975). Setting objective physical problems in parallel with subjective personal ones and linking the outcomes is Anderson's favorite literary device. He builds these stories so well, they can outlive their scientific premises. The Jupiter model in "Call Me Joe" (1957) has passed away; the appeal of its tenacious hero endures.

Furthermore, Anderson makes scientific problem-solving a vehicle for philosophical enquiry. For example, four marooned spacemen conduct an intense, self-conscious debate on the meaning of life in *The Enemy Stars*. *Tau Zero*, which Blish has called "the ultimate hard science fiction novel," shows the crew of a crippled spaceship outmaneuvering fate on a slower-than-light odyssey beyond the end of time. Scientific phenomena likewise stimulate theological speculation in "Kyrie" (1968), and generate moral crisis in "Sister Planet" (1959). In Anderson's hands, the laws of nature assume poetic, symbolic, and even metaphysical significance.

A second source of Anderson's inspiration is history. The author's broad, self-acquired education in this subject serves him well in preparing futures with either general or specific historical prototypes. For example, "The Sky People" (1959) replays the age-old feud between nomads and farmers while *The People of the Wind* is based on the Franco-Prussian War. Anderson also re-creates the past vividly (e.g., first-century Denmark in "The Peat Bog," 1975) and has produced some superb time-travel stories ("The Man Who Came Early," 1956; *The Guardians of Time; There Will Be Time; The Shield of Time*). Rarely does his historical imagination misfire, as in the tedious *King of Ys* tetralogy co-authored by Karen Anderson.

Anderson's interest in the historical process itself has led him to invent one of the longest-running and most elaborate future histories in SF. Now in its fourth decade, his Technic Civilization series embraces more than forty separate items, including twelve novels that cover five millennia of galactic history. (See Sandra

Miesel's chronology in *The Long Night,* 1983, and her afterword to the Ace edition of *Agent of the Terran Empire,* 1980.)

Third, Anderson draws upon myth, principally Nordic and Celtic. He has both remodeled ("The Sorrows of Oclim the Goth," 1983, from *Volsunga Saga*) and adapted (*Hrolf Kraki's Saga* from *Hrólfs Saga Kraka*) Norse materials with all their Viking doom and pride intact. His "Goat Song" is the definitive SF treatment of the Orpheus myth, a subject that earlier had inspired his SF novel *World Without Stars.*

Yet Gandalf award winner Anderson is not content simply to mine or rationalize mythology. He investigates the nature of myth-making and analyzes its effects—tragic in *The Night Face* and "The Saturn Game" (1981), mixed in "The Queen of Air and Darkness," (1971), and positive in *A Midsummer Tempest.* (See Miesel on the first in the 1978 Ace edition and Patrick L. McGuire on the last in *The Many Worlds of Poul Anderson*). Whether resisted (*Three Hearts and Three Lions*) or celebrated (*The Merman's Children*) the allure of Faery is a continuing preoccupation for this writer. (See Miesel's afterword to *Fantasy*).

Anderson weaves science, history, myth, and countless other categories of learning together to fashion exotic alien habitats teeming with fascinating inhabitants. (His Technic Civilization series is a showcase for both.) Anderson is perhaps SF's finest world-builder, with inventions lovelier than Larry Niven's and more numerous than Hal Clement's. The lushness of Anderson's creations fits his sensuous style. He has said that he tries to appeal to at least three senses in each scene. His trademark use of poetic *leitmotifs* intensifies emotions still further—he strives for the colorfulness of his idol Kipling. These efforts produce a richer, larger-than-life quality in his work: no real woods could be quite as enchanted as his fictional ones.

Anderson is a thoroughgoing romantic. His enthrallment with the beauty and terror of nature borders on pantheism. His complimentary idealization of women is admitted gynolatry. The resonances between woman and universe work exquisitely well in *World Without Stars* because the Cosmic Goddess is kept offstage. Unfortunately, without this restraint, *The Winter of the World* and *The Avatar* sink to the level of self-parody. Anderson exalts experience over intellection, love over knowledge. He rejects, even fears, absolutes. For him, savoring wonder is the purpose of life. The purest happiness is domestic. He emphasizes the joys of marriage and parenthood to an unusual degree (*Operation Chaos*). Since children are the only certain pledge of immortality, building a better world for one's descendants is the best motive for achievement.

Anderson returns to his preoccupation with immortality in *The Boat of a Million Years,* the crowning achievement of his career. This epic adventure of eight naturally immortal people recreates historical periods from the Hellenistic era to the Old West and combines this with contemporary suspense and hard SF space exploration. Immortality proves a distinctly mixed blessing as everything the immortals love fade like wrecks of a dissolving dream. But his heroes, special people slowly wise, meet their universe head-on and prevail. Courage accomplishes deeds entropy cannot mar.

The interaction between rational creatures and their environment is a matter of challenge and response. Anderson's heroes are always fallible beings who strive to meet life's challenge well. They are free, responsible persons sensitive to the needs of others. (Although sympathetic to libertarianism, Anderson is no rugged individualist in the Heinlein mold.) As Blish observes, they are willing to pay the price of doing "the right thing for the wrong reason."

Yet however bravely heroes struggle, "nothing lasts forever." As is demonstrated in *Against Time's Arrow: The High Crusade of Poul Anderson,* the supreme enemy is entropy. How then are mortals to face certain doom? Anderson is not a Pelagian optimist like Gordon R. Dickson. He doubts that evolutionary progress will noticeably improve man's lot. Courage is the only fitting response. Unyielding endurance is a grim imperative in the language of the Northern heroic tradition: "No man can escape his weird, but none other can take from him the heart wherewith he meets it." The author states it more gently in his own voice: "Life can be cruel, and it is ultimately tragic, but mostly it is wonderful, or would be if we'd allow it to be." Anderson is his own best example of that process.

—Sandra Miesel

---

**ANTHONY, Piers** (Piers Anthony Dillingham Jacob). American. Born in Oxford, England, 6 August 1934; became United States citizen, 1958. Educated at Goddard College, Plainfield, Vermont, B.A. 1956; University of South Florida, Tampa, teaching certificate 1964. Served in the United States Army, 1957–59. Married Carol Marble in 1956; one daughter. Technical writer, Electronic Communications Inc., St. Petersburg, Florida, 1959–62; English teacher, Admiral Farragut Academy, St. Petersburg, 1965–66. Since 1966 freelance writer. Recipient: Pyramid *Fantasy and Science Fiction* award, 1967; August Derleth award, 1977. Address: c/o Xanth Trading Company, P.O. Box 1568, Clayton, Georgia 30525, U.S.A.

SCIENCE-FICTION PUBLICATIONS

Novels (series: Apprentice Adept; Aton; Battle Circle; Cal, Veg, and Aquilon; Cluster; Incarnations of Immortality; Kelvin Knight; Space Tyrant; Tarot; Xanth)

*Chthon* (Aton). New York, Ballantine, 1967; London, Macdonald, 1970.
*Of Man and Mantra: A Trilogy* (Cal, Veg, and Aquilon). London, Corgi, 1986.
*Omnivore.* New York, Ballantine, 1968; London, Faber, 1969.
*Orn.* New York, Avon, 1971; London, Corgi, 1977.
*Ox.* New York, Avon, 1976; London, Corgi, 1977.
*The Ring,* with Robert E. Margroff. New York, Ace, 1968; London, Macdonald, 1969.
*Battle Circle.* New York, Avon, 1978; London, Corgi, 1984.
*Sos the Rope.* New York, Pyramid, 1968; London, Faber, 1970.
*Var the Stick.* London, Faber, 1972; New York, Bantam, 1973.
*Neq the Sword.* London, Corgi, 1975.
*Macroscope.* New York, Avon, 1969; London, Sphere, 1972.
*The E. S. P. Worm,* with Robert E. Margroff. New York, Paperback Library, 1970.
*Race Against Time* (for children). New York, Hawthorn, 1973.
*Rings of Ice.* New York, Avon, 1974; London, Millington, 1975.
*Triple Détente.* New York, DAW, 1974; London, Sphere, 1975.
*Phthor* (Aton). New York, Berkley, 1975; London, Panther, 1978.
*But What of Earth?,* with Robert Coulson. Toronto, Laser, 1976; revised edition, New York, Tor, 1989.
*Steppe.* London, Millington, 1976; New York, Tor, 1985.
*Cluster.* New York, Avon, 1977; London, Millington, 1978; as *Vicinity Cluster,* London, Panther, 1979.

*A Spell for Chameleon* (Xanth). New York, Ballantine, 1977; London, Macdonald, 1984.
*Chaining the Lady* (Cluster). New York, Avon, and London, Millington, 1978.
*Kirlian Quest* (Cluster). New York, Avon, and London, Millington, 1978.
*The Pretender*, with Frances Hall. San Bernardino, California, Borgo Press, 1979.
*The Source of Magic* (Xanth). New York, Ballantine, 1979; London, Macdonald, 1984.
*Castle Roogna* (Xanth). New York, Ballantine, 1979; London, Macdonald, 1984.
*God of Tarot*. New York, Jove, 1979.
*Vision of Tarot*. New York, Berkley, 1980.
*Thousandstar* (Cluster). New York, Avon, 1980; London, Panther, 1984.
*Faith of Tarot*. New York, Berkley, 1980.
*Split Infinity* (Apprentice Adept). New York, Ballantine, 1980; London, Granada, 1983.
*Blue Adept* (Apprentice Adept). New York, Ballantine, 1981; London, Granada, 1983.
*Mute*. New York, Avon, 1981; London, New English Library, 1984.
*Centaur Aisle* (Xanth). New York, Ballantine, 1982; London, Macdonald, 1984.
*Ogre, Ogre* (Xanth). New York, Ballantine, 1982; London, Futura, 1984.
*Juxtaposition* (Apprentice Adept). New York, Ballantine, 1982.
*Viscous Circle* (Cluster). New York, Avon, 1982; London, Panther, 1984.
*Night Mare* (Xanth). New York, Ballantine, 1983; London, Futura, 1984.
*Refugee* (Space Tyrant). New York, Avon, 1983.
*Dragon on a Pedestal* (Xanth). New York, Ballantine, 1983; London, Futura, 1984.
*Mercenary* (Space Tyrant). New York, Avon, 1984.
*On a Pale Horse* (Immortality). New York, Ballantine, 1984; London, Panther, 1985.
*Bearing an Hourglass* (Immortality). New York, Ballantine, and London, Severn House, 1984.
*Crewel Lye: A Caustic Yarn* (Xanth). New York, Ballantine, 1985; London, Futura, 1986.
*Politician* (Space Tyrant). New York, Avon, 1985.
*With a Tangled Skein* (Immortality). New York, Ballantine, 1985; London, Panther, 1986.
*Executive* (Space Tyrant). New York, Avon, 1985.
*Shade of the Tree*. New York, St. Martin's Press, 1986; London, Grafton, 1987.
*Ghost*. New York, Tor, 1986.
*Golem in the Gears* (Xanth). New York, Ballantine, and London, Futura, 1986.
*Statesmen* (Space Tyrant). New York, Avon, 1986.
*Wielding a Red Sword* (Immortality). New York, Ballantine, 1986; London, Grafton, 1987.
*Out of Phaze* (Apprentice Adept). New York, Putnam, 1987; London, New English Library, 1989.
*Being a Green Mother* (Immortality). New York, Ballantine, 1987; London, Grafton, 1988.
*Dragon's Gold*, with Robert E. Margroff. New York, Tor, 1987.
*Tarot* (includes *God of Tarot, Vision of Tarot,* and *Faith of Tarot*). New York, Ace, and London, Grafton, 1987.
*Vale of the Vole* (Xanth). New York, Avon, 1987; London, New English Library, 1988.
*For Love of Evil* (Immortality). New York, Morrow, 1988; London, Grafton, 1989.
*Heaven Cent* (Xanth). New York, Avon, 1988; London, New English Library, 1989.
*Robot Adept* (Apprentice Adept). New York, Putnam, 1988; London, New English Library, 1989.
*Serpent's Silver*, with Robert E. Margroff (Knight). New York, Tor, 1988.
*Pornucopia*. Houston, Tafford, 1989.
*Unicorn Point* (Apprentice Adept). New York, Putnam, 1989; London, New English Library, 1990.
*Total Recall*. New York, Morrow, 1989; London, Legend, 1990.
*Man from Mundania* (Xanth). New York, Avon, 1989; London, New English Library, 1990.
*Through the Ice* (completion of work by Robert Kornwise). Lancaster, Pennsylvania, Underwood Miller, 1989.
*Chimaera's Copper*, with Robert E. Margroff. New York, Tor, 1990.
*Balook*. Lancaster, Pennsylvania, Underwood Miller, 1990.
*Orc's Opal*, with Robert E. Margroff. New York, Tor, 1990.
*And Eternity* (Final Immortality). New York, Morrow, and London, Severn House, 1990.
*Firefly*. New York, Morrow, 1990.
*Hard Sell*. Houston, Texas, Tafford, 1990.
*Isle of View* (Xanth). New York, Morrow, 1990.
*Phaze Doubt* (Apprentice Adept). New York, Putnam, 1990.
*Tatham Mound*. New York, Morrow, 1991.
*Virtual Mode*. New York, Putnam, 1991.

Short Stories

*Prostho Plus*. London, Gollancz, 1971; New York, Bantam, 1973.
*Anthonology*. New York, Tor, 1985; London, Grafton, 1986.

OTHER PUBLICATIONS

Novels with Roberto Fuentes

*Kiai!* New York, Berkley, 1974.
*Mistress of Death*. New York, Berkley, 1974.
*Bamboo Bloodbath*. New York, Berkley, 1975.
*Ninja's Revenge*. New York, Berkley, 1975.
*Amazon Slaughter*. New York, Berkley, 1976.
*Hasan*. San Bernardino, California, Borgo Press, 1977.
*Dead Morn*. Houston, Texas, Tafford, 1990.

Other

*Biography of an Ogre: The Autobiography of Piers Anthony to Age 50*. New York, Ace, 1988.
*Piers Anthony's Visual Guide to Xanth*, with Jody Lynn Nye, illustrated by Todd Cameron Hamilton and James Clouse. New York, Avon, 1989.

Editor, with Barry N. Malzberg, Martin H. Greenberg, and Charles G. Waugh, *Uncollected Stars*. New York, Avon, 1986.

*

Manuscript Collection: Syracuse University, New York.

Critical Study: *Piers Anthony* by Michael R. Collings, Mercer Island, Washington, Starmont House, 1983.

* * *

Piers Anthony's debut novel, *Chthon,* published in 1967, is an unusually powerful novel even for a more experienced writer. Making tasteful use of sadomasochistic sexual compulsions, he creates an entire society whose underlying psychological profile is so alien to the one with which we are familiar, it achieves an otherworldly quality that has rarely been equalled. Although the sequel, *Phthor,* published eight years later, attempts to deal with the many unresolved questions of its predecessor, the effect is more like an afterthought than a true sequel.

In the late 1960's and early 1970's, there was an explosion of varied and interesting novels. *Omnivore* creates another fascinating alien society, along with a trio of characters whose interaction forms the core of the novel. Two sequels, *Orn* and *Ox,* continue the story but stand well on their own. Another trilogy, *Sos the Rope, Var the Stick,* and *Neq the Sword,* is set in a post–cataclysmic world, where primitive survivors append to their names the weapon which they have chosen. There is an intricate code of conduct governing interpersonal conflict, a well–realized society, and an entertaining story line.

Several solo novels illustrate Anthony's growth toward even more serious work. The plot of *Macroscope,* an extremely popular work, involves a device which allows one to observe anyone from a distance, destroying privacy but also opening up the entire universe to humanity. *The ESP Worm* and the collection, *Prostho Plus,* are examples of Anthony's penchant for humor, an aspect of his writing that was to become much more significant by the end of the 1970's. *Rings of Ice,* a world-catastrophe novel that concentrates on a small group of survivors and their attempt to find a safe haven in the turmoil, includes some of the best characterization that Anthony has done. Other novels of this early period range from the light adventure of *Hasan* to more serious works such as *The Ring.*

In 1977, Anthony started two separate series which were to radically alter his place in the field. The first and perhaps less significant of these begins with *Cluster.* Anthony's fascination with the Tarot and Kirlian auras surfaces in this interstellar melodrama, which was popular enough to spawn not only four direct sequels, *Chaining the Lady, Kirlian Quest, Thousandstar,* and *Viscous Circle,* but also an entirely separate series about the Tarot, *God of Tarot, Vision of Tarot,* and *Faith of Tarot.* The blend of mysticism with traditional science fiction themes had never been done in quite this fashion before, and these books enjoyed considerable popularity despite a tendency to be repetitious in the latter volumes.

More significant for Anthony is *A Spell for Chameleon,* the first in the still popular Xanth series of fantasy novels. As an independent novel, *Spell* is exceptional. Anthony creates an original, magical system, a convincing fantasy world, superimposes an intriguing plot with sympathetic characters, and enlivens the mixture with humor. It is unsurprising that sequels should follow. *The Source of Magic* and *Castle Roogna* both maintain the highly entertaining standards set by the first volume.

During the early stages of the Xanth novels, Anthony also launched another series, the Apprentice Adept books. These are set within two interlocked worlds, one where science rules, one where magic is the order of the day. Under certain conditions, characters (including robots and sorcerers) can move from one world to the other, although the laws of the world they inhabit have strange effects on their natures. *Split Infinity* and its original two sequels, *Blue Adept* and *Juxtaposition,* remain among Anthony's most successful works. More recent additions, *Out of Phaze, Robot Adept, Unicorn Point,* and *Phaze Doubt,* have been amusing as well, but lack the impact of the first trilogy.

Anthony continued to write Xanth novels, casting aside his original cast of characters after awhile and using others to explore his fantasy world. Novels like *Centaur Aisle, Dragon on a Pedestal, Golem in the Gears,* and *Vale of the Vole* continue to please his fans. Although they appear regularly, and are generally entertaining, it seems Anthony is tiring of the series and looking for fresh ideas.

One such diversion is the Bio of a Space Tyrant series of five novels, *Refugee, Mercenary, Executive, Politician,* and *Statesman.* The superimposition of contemporary countries and issues on a futuristic solar society is deliberately transparent, and this series clearly illustrates Anthony's social philosophy in many ways.

Another fantasy series is far more noteworthy. *On a Pale Horse* is the first Incarnations of Immortality, a loosely connected series in which the differing forces of myth and legend are personified. In the opening volume, a man becomes Death himself, only to become involved in a struggle against Satan. Anthony embellishes this theme with several uniformly interesting and inventive sequels, including *Bearing an Hourglass, With a Tangled Skein, Wielding a Red Sword, Being a Green Mother,* and *And Eternity.*

More recently, Anthony has tried his hand at supernatural fiction, first in the interesting but somewhat slow-paced *Shade of the Tree,* more successfully in *Firefly. Virtual Mode* is the opening volume of a new fantasy series, "Mode," one in which travel among a multitude of alternate realities is possible.

In addition to the stories of Peter Dillingham, dentist to aliens, collected in *Prostho Plus,* Anthony has written several series shorter pieces as well, many of which are collected in *Anthonology.* Among his best are "In the Barn," "Quinquepedalian," "The Life of Stripe," "On the Uses of Torture," and "Small Mouth, Bad Taste."

Anthony's early books demonstrate an insightful, adventurous mind willing to explore a variety of different avenues. The success of the Xanth books and some of his other series seemed to narrow his focus for several years, but there is evidence in more recent novels that he is now taking the leisure to let loose his imagination once more.

—Don D'Ammassa

---

**ANVIL, Christopher.** Pseudonym for Harry C. Crosby, Jr. American. Address: c/o Scott Meredith Literary Agency, 845 3rd Avenue, New York, New York 10022, U.S.A.

SCIENCE-FICTION PUBLICATIONS

Novels

*The Day the Machines Stopped.* Derby, Connecticut, Monarch, 1964.
*Strangers in Paradise.* New York, Belmont, 1969.
*Pandora's Planet.* New York, Doubleday, 1972.
*Warlord's World.* New York, DAW, 1975.
*The Steel, the Mist, and the Blazing Sun.* New York, Ace, 1980.

Uncollected Short Stories

"Cinderella, Inc." (as Harry C. Crosby, Jr.), in *Imagination* (Evanston, Illinois), 1952.
"The Prisoner," in *Astounding* (New York), February 1956.
"Advance Agent," in *Galaxy* (New York), February 1957.
"Sinful City," in *Future* (New York), Spring 1957.
"Compensation," in *Astounding* (New York), October 1957.
"The Gentle Earth," in *Astounding* (New York), November 1957.
"Truce by Boomerang," in *Astounding* (New York), December 1957.
"Achilles Heel," in *Astounding* (New York), February 1958.
"Destination Unknown," in *Science Fiction Adventures* (New York), March 1958.
"Revolt," in *Astounding* (New York), April 1958.
"Top Rung," in *Astounding* (New York), July 1958.
"Cargo for Colony 6," in *Astounding* (New York), August 1958.
"Foghead," in *Astounding* (New York), September 1958.
"Nerves," in *Fantastic Universe* (Chicago), November 1958.
"Goliath and the Beanstalk," in *Astounding* (New York), November 1958.
"Seller's Market," in *Astounding* (New York), December 1958.
"The Sieve," in *Astounding* (New York), April 1959.
"Leverage," in *Astounding* (New York), July 1959.
"Captain Leaven," in *Astounding* (New York), September 1959.
"The Law Breakers," in *Astounding* (New York), October 1959.
"Mating Problems," in *Astounding* (New York), December 1959.
"Shotgun Wedding," in *Astounding* (New York), March 1960.
"A Tourist Named Death," in *If* (New York), May1960.
"Star Tiger," in *Astounding* (New York), June 1960.
"A Taste of Poison," in *Astounding* (New York), August 1960.
"Pandora's Envoy," in *Analog* (New York), 1961.
"The Ghost Fleet," in *Analog* (New York), February 1961.
"Identification," in *Analog* (New York), May 1961.
"The Hunch," in *Analog* (New York), July 1961.
"No Small Enemy," in *Analog* (New York), November 1961.
"Uncalculated Risk," in *Analog* (New York), March 1962.
"The Toughest Opponent," in *Analog* (New York), August 1962.
"Sorcerer's Apprentice," in *Analog* (New York), September 1962.
"Philosopher's Stone," in *Analog* (New York), January 1963.
"Not in the Literature," in *Analog* (New York), March 1963.
"War Games," in *Analog* (New York), October 1963.
"Problem of Command," in *Analog* (New York), November 1963.
"Speed-Up," in *Amazing* (New York), January 1964.
"Rx for Chaos," in *Analog* (New York), February 1964.
"Hunger," in *Analog* (New York), May 1964.
"We from Arcturus," in *Worlds of Tomorrow* (New York), August 1964.
"Contract," in *Analog* (New York), December 1964.
"Merry Christmas from Outer Space," in *Fantastic* (New York), December 1964.
"New Boccaccio," in *Analog* (New York), January 1965.
"The Plateau," in *Amazing* (New York), March 1965.
"The Captive Djinn," in *Analog* (New York), May 1965.
"Duel to the Death," in *Analog* (New York), June 1965.
"High G," in *If* (New York), June 1965.
"Positive Feedback," in *Analog* (New York), August 1965.
"Untropy," in *Analog* (New York), January 1966.
"The Kindly Invasion," in *Worlds of Tomorrow* (New York), March 1966.
"Devise and Conquer," in *Galaxy* (New York), April 1966.
"Two-Way Communication," in *Analog* (New York), May 1966.
"Stranglehold," in *Analog* (New York), June 1966.
"Sweet Reason," in *If* (New York), June 1966.
"Missile Smasher," in *Analog* (New York), July 1966.
"Symbols," in *Analog* (New York), September 1966.
"Facts to Fit the Theory," in *Analog* (New York), November 1966.
"Sabotage," in *Fantasy and Science Fiction* (New York), December 1966.
"The Trojan Bombardment," in *Galaxy* (New York), February 1967.
"The Uninvited Guest," in *Analog* (New York), March 1967.
"The New Member," in *Galaxy* (New York), April 1967.
"Experts in the Field," in *Analog* (New York), May 1967.
"The Dukes of Desire," in *Analog* (New York), June 1967.
"Compound Interest," in *Analog* (New York), July 1967.
"Babel II," in *Analog* (New York), August 1967.
"The King's Legions," in *Analog* (New York), September 1967.
"The New Way," in *Beyond Infinity* (New York), November 1967.
"A Question of Attitude," in *Analog* (New York), December 1967.
"Uplift the Savage," in *Analog* (New York), March 1968.
"Is Everybody Happy?," in *Analog* (New York), April 1968.
"High Road to the East," in *Fantastic* (New York), May 1968.
"The Royal Road," in *Analog* (New York), June 1968.
"Behind the Sandrat Hoax," in *Galaxy* (New York), October 1968.
"Mission of Ignorance," in *Analog* (New York), October 1968.
"Trap," in *Analog* (New York), March 1969.
"The Nitrocellulose Doormat," in *Analog* (New York), June 1969.
"The Great Intellect Boom," in *Analog* (New York), July 1969.
"Test Ultimate," in *Analog* (New York), October 1969.
"Basic," in *Venture* (Concord, New Hampshire), November 1969.
"Trial by Silk," in *Amazing* (New York), March 1970.
"The Low Road," in *Amazing* (New York), September 1970.
"The Throne and the Usurper," in *Fantasy and Science Fiction* (New York), November 1970.
"Apron Chains," in *Analog* (New York), December 1970.
"The Claw and the Clock," in *Analog* (New York), February 1971.
"The Operator," in *Analog* (New York), March 1971.
"Riddle Me This," in *Analog* (New York), January 1972.
"The Unknown," in *Amazing* (New York), July 1972.
"Ideological Defeat," in *Analog* (New York), September 1972.
"The Knife and the Sheaf," in *Future Kin*, edited by Roger Elwood. New York, Doubleday, 1974.
"Cantor's War," in *If* (New York), June 1974.
"Gadget vs. Trend," in *Strange Orbits*, edited by Anabel Williams-Ellis. London, Blackie, 1976.
"Brains Isn't Everything," in *Analog* (New York), June 1976.
"Mind Partner," in *Neglected Visions*, edited by Barry N. Malzberg, Martin H. Greenberg, and Joseph D. Olander. New York, Doubleday, 1979.
"Torch," in *Analog's Lighter Side*, edited by Stanley Schmidt. New York, Davis, 1982.
"The Troublemaker," in *Science Fiction from A to Z*, edited by Isaac Asimov, Martin H. Greenberg, and Charles G. Waugh. Boston, Houghton Mifflin, 1982.
"Top Line," in *Analog* (New York), February 1982.
"Superbiometalemon," in *Fantasy and Science Fiction* (New York), July 1982.
"A Rose by Any Other Name," in *Hallucination Orbit*, edited by Isaac Asimov, Charles G. Waugh, and Martin H. Greenberg. New York, Farrar Straus, 1983.

"Bill for Delivery," in *Starships*, edited by Isaac Asimov, Martin H. Greenberg, and Charles G. Waugh. New York, Ballantine, 1983.
"Babel II" and "Two-Way Communication," in *From Mind to Mind: Tales of Communication from Analog*, edited by Stanley Schmidt. New York, Davis, 1984.
"A Rose by Other Name," in *Election Day 2084*, edited by Isaac Asimov and Martin H. Greenberg. Buffalo, New York, Prometheus, 1984.
"The Underhandler," in *Analog* (New York), November 1990.

* * *

Christopher Anvil appeared more frequently in *Astounding/Analog* from the mid-1950's to the mid-1960's than any other author, yet he remains relatively unknown today. His novels are slight efforts, and do not compare with his finest short fiction.

At his best, in stories like "A Rose by Any Other Name," which skillfully examines the effect of certain words on international relations, the widely reprinted "Gadget vs. Trend," on the impact of one invention on the functioning of society, and "Positive Feedback," a hilarious story that illustrates the problem of adjusting systems while they are in action, he is an inventive and expert manipulator of social trends and processes. Indeed, he has been one of the very best SF observers (along with Mack Reynolds at *his* best) of the foibles and presumptuousness of social thinkers and social managers. He was perhaps too successful—he found a formula and worked it to death, and was one of the main reasons why the 1960's *Analog* always left you with the feeling that you had just read last month's issue again. He was a John Campbell writer who could be relied upon to hew to the formulas and fads of that editor, and like Randall Garrett became lost from public view through constant, unchanging exposure. Perhaps he might have flourished artistically in another market—some evidence for this possibility can be found in "Mind Partner," his finest work, and one of his few stories published in *Galaxy*. In several respects "Mind Partner" is a New Wave story, a powerful example of psychological science fiction at its best, written before anyone was arguing about the term or had even heard of it. The story has a nightmare quality about it that lingers long after the reading. The editor-writer relationship in science fiction is for the most part a mystery, and it is also possible that Campbell brought out the best in him.

Other notable stories include "Bill for Delivery," "The Captive Djinn," "The Great Intellect Boom"—a major work that examines the effect of instant intellectuality on everyone in a society—"The Prisoner," and "Uncalculated Risk."

—Martin H. Greenberg

---

**ARCHER, Ron.** *See* **WHITE, Ted.**

---

**ARMSTRONG, Anthony.** *See* **TUBB, E. C.**

---

**ARMSTRONG, Geoffrey.** *See* **FEARN, John Russell.**

---

**ARNETTE, Robert.** *See* **PHILLIPS, Rog.**

---

**ARNOLD, Edwin L(ester Linden).** British. Born in Swanscombe, Kent, 14 May 1857; son of the writer Sir Edwin Arnold. Educated at Cheltenham College. Married 1) Constance Boyce, one daughter; 2) Jessie Brighton in 1919. Cattle Breeder in Scotland, then worked in forestry in Travancore, India in late 1870's; staff member, *Daily Telegraph,* London, until 1908. *Died 1 March 1935.*

### SCIENCE-FICTION PUBLICATIONS

Novels

*The Wonderful Adventures of Phra the Phoenician.* London, Chatto and Windus, 3 vols., and New York, Harper, 1 vol., 1890.
*Lepidus the Centurion: A Roman of To-day.* London, Cassell, 1901; New York, Crowell, 1902.
*Lieut. Gullivar Jones: His Vacation.* London, Brown Langham, 1905; New York, Arno Press, 1975; as *Gulliver of Mars,* New York, Ace, 1964.

Short Stories

*The Story of Ulla and Other Tales.* London and New York, Longman, 1895.

### OTHER PUBLICATIONS

Novel

*The Constable of St. Nicholas.* London, Chatto and Windus, 1894.

Other

*A Summer Holiday in Scandinavia.* London, Sampson Low, 1877.
*On the Indian Hills; or, Coffee-Planting in Southern India.* London, Sampson Low, 2 vols., 1881.
*Coffee: Its Cultivation and Profit.* London, Whittingham, 1886.
*Bird Life in England.* London, Chatto and Windus, 1887.
*England as She Seems, Being Selections from the Notes of an Arab Hadji.* London, Warne, 1888.
*The Soul of the Beast.* London, P.R. Macmillan, 1960.

Editor, *The Opium Question Solved,* by Anglo-Indian. London, Partridge, 1882.

* * *

Once a highly popular author, Edwin L. Arnold is little remembered and seldom read, and when read at all is generally examined as a possible source of inspiration for Edgar Rice Burroughs's Martian series rather than as an author of independent merit. Arnold's father, Sir Edwin Arnold, was one of the first Englishmen to study Eastern religion, philosophy, and culture. Very likely as a result of his father's influence, young Arnold became interested in Asian philosophy, in particular in theories of reincarnation and the cyclical nature of existence.

These theories are visible in Arnold's first and most successful novel, *The Wonderful Adventures of Phra the Phoenician.* Phra is described as a man appearing about 30 years of age, but in fact with no recollection of ever having been younger. His most ancient memory is of life in classical Phoenicia, but even in that recollection he was a man, not a child. Over the ages, Phra has lived and (apparently) died repeatedly. He describes himself as a simple military man, although he admits to being a great swordsman. As an early colonist in Britain he met and fell in love with the Princess Blodwen. Following her death he too "died" and encountered her ghost in the spirit world, but after many years Phra recovered, his undecayed body as good as ever, and resumed his life. This cycle is repeated numerous times, down to the present (Victorian) era. The book is an excellent example of Victorian fantasy, closest in spirit to Haggard's *The World's Desire,* written with Andrew Lang. To modern readers *Phra* will seem slow-paced, florid, and overlong, but it is still readable.

*The Story of Ulla and Other Tales* is a collection of Arnold's shorter fiction. Several of the stories contain fantastic elements, for the most part of rather conventional nature (i.e., ghost stories). Most relevant is "Rutherford the Twice-Born," in which Arnold reverts to the reincarnation/resurrection theme. *Lepidus the Centurion* is still another treatment of the resurrection/reincarnation theme. A Roman legionnaire revives from suspended animation in contemporary England, and then proceeds to acclimate himself to polite Victorian society, learning to play tennis and the like. *Lepidus* is the least of Arnold's novels in actual interest for the present-day reader. The author attempts the comedy of manners in style, but the result is poor.

*Lieut. Gulliver Jones: His Vacation* was Arnold's final novel, and the most interesting to the modern reader of science fiction. Jones, a lieutenant in the U.S. navy, comes into possession of a magic carpet while on leave. He is carried to Mars where he encounters a race of cultured urban dwellers attempting to preserve a high ancient civilization against the maraudings of savage desert nomads. He rescues the civilized Princess An from the nomads, travels to an icy River of Death (compare Haggard and Burroughs), and has other adventures among the Martians before returning to earth. By combining the setting and plot elements of *Gulliver Jones* with the heroic figure of *Phra the Phoenician*—and with the addition of elements from such works as *A Journey to Mars* by Pope and *Zarlah the Martian* by Grisewood—one assembles the full recipe of Burroughs's Barsoomian saga, at least of the early volumes.

Although Arnold's last novel was published in 1905, he lived until 1935, well into the period of modern "pulp" science fiction, but there appears to be no record of his attitude toward the works of later writers, including Burroughs.

—Richard A. Lupoff

---

**ARROW, William.** *See* **ROTSLER, William.**

---

**ARTHUR, Peter.** *See* **PORGES, Arthur.**

---

**ASH, Fenton.** Pseudonym for Frank Atkins; also wrote as Fred Ashley; Frank Aubrey. British. Grew up in South Wales. Studied engineering. Wrote serials for boys' papers in 1900's; film critic for a London Sunday paper.

SCIENCE-FICTION PUBLICATIONS

Novels

*The Radium Seekers; or, The Wonderful Black Nugget.* London, Pitman, 1905.
*The Temple of Fire; or, The Mysterious Island* (as Fred Ashley). London, Pitman, 1905.
*A Trip to Mars* (for children). London, Chambers, 1909; New York, Arno Press, 1975.
*By Airship to Ophir* (for children). London, Shaw, 1911.
*The Black Opal* (for children). London, Shaw, 1915; New York, Arno Press, 1975.

Novels as Frank Aubrey (series: Monella in all books)

*The Devil-Tree of El Dorado.* London, Hutchinson, 1896; New York, New Amsterdam, 1897.
*A Queen of Atlantis.* London, Hutchinson, and Philadelphia, Lippincott, 1899.
*King of the Dead.* London, Macqueen, 1903; New York, Arno Press, 1978.

Short Stories as Frank Aubrey

*Strange Stories of Hospitals.* London, Pearson, 1898.

OTHER PUBLICATIONS

Novel as Frank Aubrey

*A Studio Mystery.* London, Jarrolds, 1897.

* * *

At the turn of the century, Frank Atkins, using the name Fenton Ash and other pen-names, wrote fiction containing elements of what critics today term speculative fiction. To call Atkins a science-fiction writer, however, would be to push him into a category that his writing fits only at certain key points: in theme and plot, in characters, and in style. Atkins's work suits his time and place, but in at least one novel, *A Trip to Mars,* he explored possibilities only hinted at by a few other writers and cinematic directors of his time.

Atkins stretched coincidence to the limit in certain areas. He hypothesized lost civilizations on earth—the remains of Atlantis in the middle of the Sargasso Sea, El Dorado on a mountain top in an unexplored region of South America—in four of his books. Only in *A Trip to Mars* did he move beyond the earth. He frequently postulated long-lost relatives; the conflict often revolves around the good characters overcoming powerful forces of evil. But Atkins's outcomes are pat, and he prepared his reader well with very broad hints for any "surprise."

Atkins strived for believability in his settings, giving lengthy descriptions with numerous footnotes, of the flora and fauna both in South America and in the Sargasso Sea, though there are many descriptions of the fantastic in all his books—giant flowers, fruits, animals, huge dazzling jewels and massive amounts of gold. He also frequently hypothesized seers who make accurate, if non-specific predictions, usually astrologically. Atkins's only real speculative scientific developments occur in his "red ray" (*King of the Dead*) and space ship (*A Trip to Mars*). "Hard" scientific developments play minimal part in his books.

Most of Atkins's characters are, at best, stereotypes. His infrequent attempts at light-heartedness generally occur when he introduces a lower-class Englishman (usually a sailor) with a droll, "uneducated" accent, uttering malapropisms. His "evil" characters are in all senses malevolent and frequently seem to be in league with some never-explained Dark Power. Only in *King of the Dead* does he portray a Power of Evil, called Mahrimah, who resembles a fallen angel. All the books have as protagonists male "chums" who are young, adventuresome, and typically British. Of lesser importance are the young women, generally the love interests of one or both of the chums; some are exotic, some are classically British, but without exceptions coy and beautiful, and they are frequently endangered by natural or human foes. This is true even for Vanina, the queen of *A Queen of Atlantis,* who actually plays a very passive role in the plot. While in all of Atkins's books the good characters consistently behave nobly, most of the books contain a totally noble figure as well. In the Monella novels, this character is Monella himself, a noble figure of great age who is roaming the world until he can regain his throne in El Dorado; in *King of the Dead* the noble figure is Lorenzo, né Manzoni, who is even more enigmatic than Monella. They are consistently wise, strong, compelling, and remote, and both also have to atone for some sin (primarily caused by leaving their people and venturing into the real world) by admitting their error and setting things to rights.

Atkins's style is probably the most interesting feature of his books. Atkins used the common technique of ending each chapter with a hint of what is to come, and it does serve its purpose—to keep the reader reading. Atkins used much description in his book, which is fortunate since his dialogue is often formal and stilted. Atkins's point of view is consistently third-person, but the particular outlook of each chapter varies. Atkins was at his best when describing the exotic features of his setting—costly and beautiful architecture, elaborate costumes, wonderful jewels. He excelled at choosing exotic names for people, places, animals and Gods—Ivanta, Alondra, Mellenda, Ullama, Lyostrah, Morveena. The tension in his novels frequently revolves around encounters with natural but terrifying animals, such as cuttlefish, enormous snakes, gorilla-type animals, pumas, and most of his novels feature supernatural monsters such as zombies, vampires, and most particularly, the devil-tree in the novel of that name. The devil-tree, a huge tree which seizes its victims in tentacle-like branches and conveys them to its maw, a hollow trunk, is fully as terrifying and loathsome as any creation of current writers of horror novels or directors of horror movies. After the tree consumes the victims, it releases them, or what is left of them, to be carried off and eaten by crocodile-like monsters who live in a pond at its base. In the climactic scene at the end of the novel, the evil priests are all seized and eaten, some by the tree, and some are torn to bits by the monsters as the priests are held in the tree's tentacles awaiting their turn in its maw. The nightmarish effectiveness of this description is such that its image remains vivid in the readers' minds long after they have finished the book itself.

In fact, if Atkins's writing is akin to speculative fiction, it is certainly supernatural and horror fiction that it most resembles. He worked with settings that are largely unknown to his world, but it is their exotic quality rather than any science-fiction aspect which he developed. Only in *A Trip to Mars* does Atkins extrapolate any scientific devices, and these are fanciful, based on principles long since outdated. Additionally, the Mars which Atkins depicts is so similar to his exotic settings on earth as to be interchangeable, and his Martian characters are certainly no less human, in physical features or in outlook, than the characters in his earth-based novels. Nevertheless, Atkins's books are still interesting reading, particularly in editions which contain the quaint original illustrations.

—Karren C. Edwards

---

**ASHLEY, Fred.** *See* **ASH, Fenton.**

---

**ASIMOV, Isaac.** Also writes as Dr. A.; Paul French. American. Born in Petrovichi, U.S.S.R., 2 January 1920; emigrated to the United States in 1923; naturalized, 1928. Educated at Columbia University, New York, B.S. 1939, M.A. 1941, Ph.D. in chemistry 1948. Served in the United States Army, 1945–46. Married 1) Gertrude Blugerman in 1948 (divorced 1973), one son and one daughter; 2) Janet Opal Jeppson in 1973. Instructor in Biochemistry, 1949–51, assistant professor, 1951–55, associate professor, 1955–79, and since 1979, professor, Boston University School of Medicine. Recipient: Edison Foundation National Mass Media award, 1958; Blakeslee award, for non-fiction, 1960; World Science Fiction Convention Citation, 1963; Hugo award, 1963, 1966, 1973, 1977, 1983; American Chemical Society James T. Grady award, 1965; American Association for the Advancement of Science-Westinghouse Science Writing award, 1967; Nebula award, 1972, 1976; *Locus* award, for non-fiction, 1981, for fiction, 1983. Guest of Honor, World Science Fiction Convention, 1955. Address: 10 West 66th Street, Apartment 33-A, New York, New York 10023, U.S.A.

SCIENCE-FICTION PUBLICATIONS

Novels (series: Elijah Baley; Foundation; Norby; Trantorian Empire)

*Triangle* (Empire). New York, Doubleday, 1961; as *An Isaac Asimov Second Omnibus,* London, Sidgwick and Jackson, 1969.
- *Pebble in the Sky.* New York, Doubleday, 1950; London, Corgi, 1958.
- *The Stars, Like Dust.* New York, Doubleday, 1951; London, Panther, 1958; abridged edition, as *The Rebellious Stars,* New York, Ace, 1954.
- *The Currents of Space.* New York, Doubleday, 1952; London, Boardman, 1955.

*Foundation Trilogy.* New York, Doubleday, 1963; as *An Isaac Asimov Omnibus,* London, Sidgwick and Jackson, 1966.
- *Foundation.* New York, Gnome Press, 1951; London, Weidenfeld and Nicolson, 1953; abridged edition, as *The Thousand-Year Plan,* New York, Ace, 1955.

*Foundation and Empire*. New York, Gnome Press, 1952; London, Panther, 1962; as *The Man Who Upset the Universe*, New York, Ace, 1955.
*Second Foundation*. New York, Gnome Press, 1953.
*The Caves of Steel* (Baley). New York, Doubleday, and London, Boardman, 1954.
*The End of Eternity*. New York, Doubleday, 1955; London, Panther, 1958.
*The Naked Sun* (Baley). New York, Doubleday, 1957; London, Joseph, 1958.
*Fantastic Voyage* (novelization of screenplay). Boston, Houghton Mifflin, and London, Dobson, 1966.
*The Robot Novels* (includes *The Caves of Steel* and *The Naked Sun*). New York, Doubleday, 1971.
*The Gods Themselves*. New York, Doubleday, and London, Gollancz, 1972.
*The Collected Fiction: The Far Ends of Time and Earth, Prisoners of the Stars*. New York, Doubleday, 2 vols., 1979.
*Foundation's Edge*. New York, Doubleday, 1982; London, Granada, 1983.
*The Robots of Dawn* (Baley). New York, Doubleday, 1983; London, Granada, 1984.
*Norby the Mixed-Up Robot* (for children), with Janet Asimov. New York, Walker, 1983; London, Methuen, 1984.
*Norby's Other Secret* (for children), with Janet Asimov. New York, Walker, 1984; London, Methuen, 1985.
*Norby and the Lost Princess* (for children), with Janet Asimov. New York, Walker, 1985.
*Robots and Empire*. New York, Doubleday, 1985.
*Norby, Robot for Hire* (for children), with Janet Asimov. New York, Ace, 1985.
*Norby and the Invaders* (for children), with Janet Asimov. New York, Walker, 1985.
*Norby and the Queen's Necklace* (for children), with Janet Asimov. New York, Walker, 1986.
*Foundation and Earth*. New York, Doubleday, and London, Grafton, 1986.
*Fantastic Voyage II: Destination Brain*. New York, Doubleday, and London, Grafton, 1987.
*Norby Finds a Villain* (for children), with Janet Asimov. New York, Walker, 1987.
*Prelude to Foundation*. New York, Doubleday, and London, Grafton, 1988.
*Azazel*. New York, Doubleday, 1988; London, Doubleday, 1989.
*Nemesis*. New York and London, Doubleday, 1989.
*Norby and Yobo's Great Adventure* (for children), with Janet Asimov. New York, Walker, 1989.
*Norby Down to Earth* (for children), with Janet Asimov. New York, Walker, 1989.
*Nightfall*, with Robert Silverberg. New York, Doubleday, and London, Gollancz, 1990.
*Norby and the Oldest Dragon* (for children), with Janet Asimov. New York, Walker, 1990.
*Norby and the Court Jester* (for children), with Janet Asimov. New York, Walker, 1991.

Novels (for children) as Paul French (series: Lucky Starr in all books)

*David Starr, Space Ranger*. New York, Doubleday, 1952; Kingswood, Surrey, World's Work, 1953.
*Lucky Starr and the Pirates of the Asteroids*. New York, Doubleday, 1953; Kingswood, Surrey, World's Work, 1954.
*Lucky Starr and the Oceans of Venus*. New York, Doubleday, 1954; as *The Oceans of Venus* (as Isaac Asimov), London, New English Library, 1973.
*Lucky Starr and the Big Sun of Mercury*. New York, Doubleday, 1956; as *The Big Sun of Mercury* (as Isaac Asimov), London, New English Library, 1974.
*Lucky Starr and the Moons of Jupiter*. New York, 1957; as *The Moons of Jupiter* (as Isaac Asimov), London, New English Library, 1974.
*Lucky Starr and the Rings of Saturn*. New York, Doubleday, 1958; as *The Rings of Saturn* (as Isaac Asimov), London, New English Library, 1974.

Short Stories

*I, Robot*. New York, Gnome Press, 1950; London, Grayson, 1952.
*The Martian Way and Other Stories*. New York, Doubleday, 1955; London, Dobson, 1964.
*Earth Is Room Enough*. New York, Doubleday, 1957; London, Panther, 1960.
*Nine Tomorrows: Tales of the Near Future*. New York, Doubleday, 1959; London, Dobson, 1963.
*The Rest of the Robots*. New York, Doubleday, 1964; London, Dobson, 1967.
*Through a Glass, Clearly*. London, New English Library, 1967.
*Asimov's Mysteries*. New York, Doubleday, and London, Rapp and Whiting, 1968.
*Nightfall and Other Stories*. New York, Doubleday, 1969; London, Rapp and Whiting, 1970.
*The Early Asimov; or, Eleven Years of Trying*. New York, Doubleday, 1972; London, Gollancz, 1973.
*The Best of Isaac Asimov (1939-1972)*. London, Sidgwick and Jackson, 1973; New York, Doubleday, 1974.
*Have You Seen These?* Cambridge, Massachusetts, NESFA Press, 1974.
*The Heavenly Host* (for children). New York, Walker, 1975; London, Penguin, 1978.
*Buy Jupiter and Other Stories*. New York, Doubleday, 1975; London, Gollancz, 1976.
*The Dream, Benjamin's Dream, Benjamin's Bicentennial Blast: Three Short Stories*. Privately printed, 1976.
*The Bicentennial Man and Other Stories*. New York, Doubleday, 1976; London, Gollancz, 1977.
*Good Taste*. Topeka, Kansas, Apocalypse Press, 1977.
*3 by Asimov*. New York, Targ, 1981.
*The Complete Robot*. New York, Doubleday, and London, Granada, 1982.
*The Winds of Change and Other Stories*. New York, Doubleday, and London, Granada, 1983.
*The Norby Chronicles* (for children), with Janet Asimov. New York, Walker, 1986.
*Alternative Asimov's*. New York, Doubleday, 1986.
*Robot Dreams*. New York, Doubleday, 1986; London, Gollancz, 1987.
*The Best Science Fiction of Isaac Asimov*. New York, Doubleday, 1986; London, Grafton, 1987.
*The Best Mysteries of Isaac Asimov*. New York, Doubleday, 1986; London, Grafton, 1987.
*The Asimov Chronicles: Fifty Years of Isaac Asimov*, edited by Martin H. Greenberg. New York, New American Library, 1989.
*Robot Visions*. New York, New American Library, 1990; London, VGSF, 1991.
*Complete Stories*. New York, Doubleday, 1990.

OTHER PUBLICATIONS

Novels

*The Death Dealers.* New York, Avon, 1958; as *A Whiff of Death,* New York, Walker, and London, Gollancz, 1968.
*Murder at the ABA.* New York, Doubleday, 1976; as *Authorized Murder,* London, Gollancz, 1976.

Short Stories

*Tales of the Black Widowers.* New York, Doubleday, 1974; London, Gollancz, 1975.
*More Tales of the Black Widowers.* New York, Doubleday, 1976; London, Gollancz, 1977.
*Casebook of the Black Widowers.* New York, Doubleday, and London, Gollancz, 1980.
*The Union Club Mysteries.* New York, Doubleday, 1983; London, Granada, 1984.
*Banquets of the Black Widowers.* New York, Doubleday, 1984.
*Puzzles of the Black Widowers.* New York, Doubleday, 1990.

Verse

*Lecherous Limericks.* New York, Walker, 1975; London, Corgi, 1977.
*More Lecherous Limericks.* New York, Walker, 1976.
*Still More Lecherous Limericks.* New York, Walker, 1977.
*Asimov's Sherlockian Limericks.* Yonkers, New York, Mysterious Press, 1978.
*Limericks: Too Gross,* with John Ciardi. New York, Norton, 1978.
*A Grossery of Limericks,* with John Ciardi. New York, Norton, 1981.
*Limericks for Children.* New York, Caedmon, 1984.

Other

*Biochemistry and Human Metabolism,* with Burnham Walker and William C. Boyd. Baltimore, Williams and Wilkins, 1952; revised edition, 1954, 1957; London, Ballie Tindall and Cox, 1955.
*The Chemicals of Life: Enzymes, Vitamins, Hormones.* New York, Abelard Schuman, 1954; London, Bell, 1956.
*Races and Peoples,* with William C. Boyd. New York, Abelard Schuman, 1955; London, Abelard Schuman, 1958.
*Chemistry and Human Health,* with Burnham Walker and M.K. Nicholas. New York, McGraw Hill, 1956.
*Inside the Atom.* New York and London, Abelard Schuman, 1956; revised edition, 1958, 1961, 1966, 1974.
*Building Blocks of the Universe.* New York, Abelard Schuman, 1957; London, Abelard Schuman, 1958; revised edition, 1961, 1974.
*Only a Trillion.* New York and London, Abelard Schuman, 1957; as *Marvels of Science,* New York, Collier, 1962.
*The World of Carbon.* New York and London, Abelard Schuman, 1958; revised edition, New York, Collier, 1962.
*The World of Nitrogen.* New York and London, Abelard Schuman, 1958; revised edition, New York, Collier, 1962.
*The Clock We Live On.* New York and London, Abelard Schuman, 1959; revised edition, New York, Collier, 1962; Abelard Schuman, 1965.
*The Living River.* New York and London, Abelard Schuman, 1959; revised edition, as *The Bloodstream: River of Life,* New York, Collier, 1961.
*Realm of Numbers.* Boston, Houghton Mifflin, 1959; London, Gollancz, 1963.
*Words of Science and the History Behind Them.* Boston, Houghton Mifflin, 1959; London, Harrap, 1974.
*Breakthroughs in Science* (for children). Boston, Houghton Mifflin, 1960.
*The Intelligent Man's Guide to Science.* New York, Basic Books, 2 vols., 1960; revised edition, as *The New Intelligent Man's Guide to Science,* 1 vol., 1965; London, Nelson, 1967; as *Asimov's Guide to Science,* New York, Basic Books, 1972; London, Penguin, 2 vols., 1975; as *Asimov's New Guide to Science,* Basic Books, 1984.
*The Kingdom of the Sun.* New York and London, Abelard Schuman, 1960; revised edition, New York, Collier, 1962; Abelard Schuman, 1963.
*Realm of Measure.* Boston, Houghton Mifflin, 1960.
*Satellites in Outer Space* (for children). New York, Random House, 1960; revised edition, 1964, 1973.
*The Double Planet.* New York, Abelard Schuman, 1960; London, Abelard Schuman, 1962; revised edition, 1966.
*The Wellsprings of Life.* New York and London, Abelard Schuman, 1960.
*Realm of Algebra.* Boston, Houghton Mifflin, 1961; London, Gollancz, 1964.
*Words from the Myths.* Boston, Houghton Mifflin, 1961; London, Faber, 1963.
*Fact and Fancy.* New York, Doubleday, 1962.
*Life and Energy.* New York, Doubleday, 1962; London, Dobson, 1963.
*The Search for the Elements.* New York, Basic Books, 1962.
*Words in Genesis.* Boston, Houghton Mifflin, 1962.
*Words on the Map.* Boston, Houghton Mifflin, 1962.
*View from a Height.* New York, Doubleday, 1963; London, Dobson, 1964.
*The Genetic Code.* New York, Orion Press, 1963; London, Murray, 1964.
*The Human Body: Its Structure and Operation.* Boston, Houghton Mifflin, 1963; London, Nelson, 1965.
*The Kite That Won the Revolution.* Boston, Houghton Mifflin, 1963.
*Words from the Exodus.* Boston, Houghton Mifflin, 1963.
*Adding a Dimension: 17 Essays on the History of Science.* New York, Doubleday, 1964; London, Dobson, 1966.
*The Human Brain: Its Capacities and Functions.* Boston, Houghton Mifflin, 1964; London, Nelson, 1965.
*Quick and Easy Math.* Boston, Houghton Mifflin, 1964; London, Whiting and Wheaton, 1967.
*A Short History of Biology.* Garden City, New York, Natural History Press, 1964; London, Nelson, 1965.
*Planets for Man,* with Stephen H. Dole. New York, Random House, 1964.
*Asimov's Biographical Encyclopedia of Science and Technology.* New York, Doubleday, 1964; London, Allen and Unwin, 1966; revised edition, Doubleday, 1972, 1982; London, Pan, 1975.
*An Easy Introduction to the Slide Rule.* Boston, Houghton Mifflin, 1965; London, Whiting and Wheaton, 1967.
*The Greeks: A Great Adventure.* Boston, Houghton Mifflin, 1965.
*Of Time and Space and Other Things.* New York, Doubleday, 1965; London, Dobson, 1967.
*A Short History of Chemistry.* New York, Doubleday, 1965; London, Heinemann, 1972.
*The Neutrino: Ghost Particle of the Atom.* New York, Doubleday, and London, Dobson, 1966.
*The Genetic Effects of Radiation,* with Theodosius Dobzhansky. Washington, D.C., Atomic Energy Commission, 1966.
*The Noble Gases.* New York, Basic Books, 1966.
*The Roman Republic.* Boston, Houghton Mifflin, 1966.

*From Earth to Heaven.* New York, Doubleday, 1966.
*Understanding Physics.* New York, Walker, 3 vols., 1966; London, Allen and Unwin, 3 vols., 1967; as *The History of Physics,* Walker, 1 vol., 1984.
*The Universe: From Flat Earth to Quasar.* New York, Walker, 1966; London, Penguin, 1967; revised edition, Walker, and Penguin, 1971; revised edition, as *The Universe: From Flat Earth to Black Holes—and Beyond,* Walker, 1980, Penguin, 1983.
*The Roman Empire.* Boston, Houghton Mifflin, 1967.
*The Moon* (for children). Chicago, Follett, 1967; London, University of London Press, 1969.
*Is Anyone There?* (essays). New York, Doubleday, 1967; London, Rapp and Whiting, 1968.
*To the Ends of the Universe.* New York, Walker, 1967; revised edition, 1976.
*The Egyptians.* Boston, Houghton Mifflin, 1967.
*Mars* (for children). Chicago, Follett, 1967; London, University of London Press, 1971.
*From Earth to Heaven: 17 Essays on Science.* New York, Doubleday, 1967; London, Dobson, 1968.
*Environments Out There.* New York, Abelard Schuman, 1967; London, Abelard Schuman, 1968.
*Science, Numbers, and I: Essays on Science.* New York, Doubleday, 1968; London, Rapp and Whiting, 1969.
*The Near East: 10,000 Years of History.* Boston, Houghton Mifflin, 1968.
*Asimov's Guide to the Bible: The Old Testament, The New Testament.* New York, Doubleday, 2 vols., 1968–69.
*The Dark Ages.* Boston, Houghton Mifflin, 1968.
*Galaxies* (for children). Chicago, Follett, 1968; London, University of London Press, 1971.
*Stars* (for children). Chicago, Follett, 1968.
*Words from History.* Boston, Houghton Mifflin, 1968.
*Photosynthesis.* New York, Basic Books, 1968; London, Allen and Unwin, 1970.
*The Shaping of England.* Boston, Houghton Mifflin, 1969.
*Twentieth Century Discovery* (for children). New York, Doubleday, and London, Macdonald, 1969.
*Opus 100* (selection). Boston, Houghton Mifflin, 1969.
*ABC's of Space* (for children). New York, Walker, 1969.
*Great Ideas of Science* (for children). Boston, Houghton Mifflin, 1969.
*To the Solar System and Back.* New York, Doubleday, 1970.
*Asimov's Guide to Shakespeare: The Greek, Roman, and Italian Plays; The English Plays.* New York, Doubleday, 2 vols., 1970.
*Constantinople.* Boston, Houghton Mifflin, 1970.
*The ABC's of the Ocean* (for children). New York, Walker, 1970.
*Light* (for children). Chicago, Follett, 1970.
*The Best New Thing* (for children). Cleveland, World, 1971.
*The Stars in Their Courses.* New York, Doubleday, 1971; London, White Lion, 1974.
*What Makes the Sun Shine.* Boston, Little Brown, 1971.
*The Isaac Asimov Treasury of Humor.* Boston, Houghton Mifflin, 1971; London, Vallentine Mitchell, 1972.
*The Sensuous Dirty Old Man* (as Dr. A.). New York, Walker, 1971.
*The Land of Canaan.* Boston, Houghton Mifflin, 1971.
*ABC's of Earth* (for children). New York, Walker, 1971.
*The Space Dictionary.* New York, Starline, 1971.
*More Words of Science.* Boston, Houghton Mifflin, 1972.
*Electricity and Man.* Washington, D.C., Atomic Energy Commission, 1972.
*The Shaping of France.* Boston, Houghton Mifflin, 1972.
*Asimov's Annotated "Don Juan."* New York, Doubleday, 1972.
*ABC's of Ecology* (for children). New York, Walker, 1972.
*The Story of Ruth.* New York, Doubleday, 1972.
*Worlds Within Worlds.* Washington, D.C., Atomic Energy Commission, 1972.
*The Left Hand of the Electron* (essays). New York, Doubleday, 1972; London, White Lion, 1975.
*Ginn Science Program.* Boston, Ginn, 5 vols., 1972–73.
*How Did We Find Out about Dinosaurs [The Earth Is Round, Electricity, Vitamins, Germs, Comets, Energy, Atoms, Nuclear Power, Numbers, Outer Space, Earthquakes, Black Holes, Our Human Roots, Antarctica, Coal, Oil, Solar Powers, Volcanoes, Life in the Deep Sea, Our Genes, the Universe, Computers, Robots, the Atmosphere, DNA, the Speed of Light, Blood, Sunshine, the Brain, Super Conductivity, Microwaves, Photosynthesis, Pluto]* (for children). New York, Walker, 33 vols., 1973–91; 6 vols. published London, White Lion, 1975–76; 1 vol. published London, Pan, 1980; 7 vols. published (as *How We Found Out . . .* series), London, Longman, 1982.
*The Tragedy of the Moon* (essays). New York, Doubleday, 1973; London, Abelard Schuman, 1974.
*Comets and Meteors* (for children). Chicago, Follett, 1973.
*The Sun* (for children). Chicago, Follett, 1973.
*The Shaping of North America from the Earliest Times to 1763.* Boston, Houghton Mifflin, 1973; London, Dobson, 1975.
*Please Explain* (for children). Boston, Houghton Mifflin, 1973; London, Abelard Schuman, 1975.
*Physical Science Today.* Del Mar, California, CRM, 1973.
*Jupiter, The Largest Planet* (for children). New York, Lothrop, 1973; revised edition, 1976.
*Today, Tomorrow, and. . . .* New York, Doubleday, 1973; London, Abelard Schuman, 1974; as *Towards Tomorrow,* London, Hodder and Stoughton, 1977.
*The Birth of the United States 1763-1816.* Boston, Houghton Mifflin, 1974.
*Earth: Our Crowded Spaceship.* New York, Doubleday, and London, Abelard Schuman, 1974.
*Asimov on Chemistry.* New York, Doubleday, 1974; London, Macdonald and Jane's, 1975.
*Asimov on Astronomy.* New York, Doubleday, and London, Macdonald, 1974.
*Asimov's Annotated "Paradise Lost."* New York, Doubleday, 1974.
*Our World in Space.* Greenwich, Connecticut, New York Graphic Society, and Cambridge, Patrick Stephens, 1974.
*The Solar System* (for children). Chicago, Follett, 1975.
*Birth and Death of the Universe.* New York, Walker, 1975.
*Of Matters Great and Small.* New York, Doubleday, 1975.
*Our Federal Union: The United States from 1816 to 1865.* Boston, Houghton Mifflin, and London, Dobson, 1975.
*The Ends of the Earth: The Polar Regions of the World.* New York, Weybright and Talley, 1975.
*Eyes on the Universe: A History of the Telescope.* Boston, Houghton Mifflin, 1975; London, Deutsch, 1976.
*Science Past—Science Future.* New York, Doubleday, 1975.
*Alpha Centauri, The Nearest Star* (for children). New York, Lothrop, 1976.
*I, Rabbi* (for children). New York, Walker, 1976.
*Asimov on Physics.* New York, Doubleday, 1976.
*The Planet That Wasn't.* New York, Doubleday, 1976; London, Sphere, 1977.
*The Collapsing Universe: The Story of Black Holes.* New York, Walker, and London, Hutchinson, 1977.
*Asimov on Numbers.* New York, Doubleday, 1977.
*The Beginning and the End.* New York, Doubleday, 1977.
*Familiar Poems Annotated.* New York, Doubleday, 1977.
*The Golden Door: The United States from 1865 to 1918.* Boston, Houghton Mifflin, and London, Dobson, 1977.

*The Key Word and Other Mysteries* (for children). New York, Walker, 1977.
*Mars, The Red Planet* (for children). New York, Lothrop, 1977.
*Life and Time*. New York, Doubleday, 1978.
*Quasar, Quasar, Burning Bright*. New York, Doubleday, 1978.
*Animals of the Bible* (for children). New York, Doubleday, 1978.
*Isaac Asimov's Book of Facts*. New York, Grosset and Dunlap, 1979; London, Hodder and Stoughton, 1980; abridged edition (for children), as *Would You Believe?* and *More . . . Would You Believe?*, Grosset and Dunlap, 2 vols., 1981–82.
*Extraterrestrial Civilizations*. New York, Crown, 1979; London, Robson, 1980.
*A Choice of Catastrophes*. New York, Simon and Schuster, 1979; London, Hutchinson, 1980.
*Saturn and Beyond*. New York, Lothrop, 1979.
*Opus 200* (selection). Boston, Houghton Mifflin, 1979.
*In Memory Yet Green: The Autobiography of Isaac Asimov 1920–1954*. New York, Doubleday, 1979.
*The Road to Infinity*. New York, Doubleday, 1979.
*In Joy Still Felt: The Autobiography of Isaac Asimov 1954–1978*. New York, Doubleday, 1980.
*The Annotated Gulliver's Travels*. New York, Potter, 1980.
*Opus* (includes *Opus 100* and *Opus 200*). London, Deutsch, 1980.
*Change! Seventy-One Glimpses of the Future*. Boston, Houghton Mifflin, 1981.
*Visions of the Universe*, paintings by Kazuaki Iwasaki. Montrose, California, Cosmos Store, 1981.
*Asimov on Science Fiction*. New York, Doubleday, 1981; London, Granada, 1983.
*Venus, Near Neighbor of the Sun* (for children). New York, Lothrop, 1981.
*The Sun Shines Bright*. New York, Doubleday, 1981; London, Granada, 1984.
*In the Beginning: Science Faces God in the Book of Genesis*. New York, Crown, and London, New English Library, 1981.
*Exploring the Earth and the Cosmos*. New York, Crown, 1982; London, Allen Lane, 1983.
*Counting the Eons*. New York, Doubleday, 1983; London, Granada, 1984.
*The Measure of the Universe*. New York, Harper, 1983.
*The Roving Mind*. Buffalo, Prometheus, 1983.
*Those Amazing Electronic Thinking Machines* (for children). New York, Watts, 1983.
*X Stands for Unknown* (essays). New York, Doubleday, 1984; London, Granada, 1985.
*Opus 300*. Boston, Houghton Mifflin, 1984.
*Robots: Where the Machine Ends and Life Begins*, with Karen A. Frenkel. New York, Crown, 1985.
*The Exploding Suns: The Secrets of the Supernovas*. New York, Dutton, 1985.
*Asimov's Guide to Halley's Comet*. New York, Walker, 1985.
*The Subatomic Monster* (essays). New York, Doubleday, 1985.
*The Edge of Tomorrow*. New York, Tor, 1985; London, Harrap, 1986.
*The Dangers of Intelligence and Other Science Essays*. Boston, Houghton Mifflin, 1986.
*Future Days: A Nineteenth-Century Vision of the Year 2000*. New York, Holt, and London, Virgin, 1986.
*Wonderful Worldwide Science Bazaar: Seventy-two Up-to-Date Reports on the State of Everything from Inside the Atom to Outside the Universe*. Boston, Houghton Mifflin, 1986.
*Bare Bones: Dinosaur* (for children), with David Hawcock. New York, Holt, 1986; London, Methuen, 1987.
*As Far as the Human Eye Could See* (essays). New York, Doubleday, 1987; London, Grafton, 1988.
*Past, Present, and Future* (essays). Buffalo, New York, Prometheus, 1987.
*Beginnings: The Story of Origins—of Mankind, Life, the Earth, the Universe*. New York, Walker, 1987.
*How to Enjoy Writing: A Book of Aid and Comfort*. New York, Walker, 1987.
*Asimov's Annotated Gilbert and Sullivan*. New York, Doubleday, 1988.
*Relativity of Wrong: Essays on the Solar System and Beyond*. New York, Doubleday, 1988; Oxford, Oxford University Press, 1989.
*Library of the Universe (Did Comets Kill the Dinosaurs?; The Asteroids; Ancient Astronomy; Is There Life on Other Planets?; Jupiter, the Spotted Giant; Mercury, the Quick Planet; How Was the Universe Born?; Saturn, the Ringed Beauty; The Space Spotter's Guide; Unidentified Flying Objects; Earth, Our Home Base; The Birth and Death of Stars; Science Fiction, Science Fact; Space Garbage; Astronomy Today; Comets and Meteors, Mythology of the Universe; Pluto, a Double Planet?; Neptune; Piloted Space Flights; Projects in Astronomy; Rockets, Probes, and Satellites; Venus, a Shrouded Mystery; The World's Space Programs; Uranus: The Sideways Planet; Our Milkyway and Other Galaxies; The Earth's Moon; Our Solar System; Mars: Our Mysterious Neighbor; The Sun; Colonizing the Planets and Stars)*. Milwaukee, Wisconsin, Stevens, 33 vols., 1988–91.
*The Tyrannosaurus Prescription and 100 Other Essays*. Buffalo, New York, Prometheus, 1989.
*Asimov's Galaxy: Reflections on Science Fiction*. New York, Doubleday, 1989.
*Asimov on Science: A Thirty Year Retrospective*. New York, Doubleday, 1989.
*Asimov's Chronology of Science and Discovery: How Science Has Shaped the World and How the World has Affected Science from 4,000,000 B.C. to the Present*. New York, Harper, 1989.
*Think About Space: Where Have We Been and Where Are We Going?* (for children), with Frank White. New York, Walker, 1989.
*All the Troubles of the World* (for children). Mankato, Minnesota, Creative Education, 1989.
*Robbie* (for children). Mankato, Minnesota, Creative Education, 1989.
*Franchise* (for children). Mankato, Minnesota, Creative Education, 1989.
*Sally* (for children). Mankato, Minnesota, Creative Education, 1989.
*The Complete Science Fair Handbook: For Teachers and Parents of Students in Grades 4–8*, with Anthony D. Fredericks. Glenview, Illinois, Scott Foresman, 1990.
*How Did We Find Out About Lasers?* New York, Walker, 1990.
*How Did We Find Out About Neptune?* New York, Walker, 1990.
*Secret of the Universe*. New York, Doubleday, 1991.
*Asimov's Chronology of the World*. New York, Harper Collins, 1991.
*Asimov's Guide to Earth and Space*. New York, Random House, 1991.
*Atom: Journey Across the Subatomic Cosmos*. New York, Dalton, 1991.
*Christopher Columbus*. Milwaukee, Wisconsin, Gareth Stevens, 1991.
*Henry Hudson*, with Elizabeth Kaplan. Milwaukee, Wisconsin, Gareth Stevens, 1991.
*Frontiers: New Discoveries about Man and His Planet, Outer Space, and the Universe*. New York, Plume, 1991.

*The March of the Millenia: A Key to Looking at History*, with Frank White. New York, Walker, 1991.

Editor, *Soviet Science Fiction* [and *More Soviet Science Fiction*]. New York, Collier, 2 vols., 1962.

Editor, *The Hugo Winners 1–5*. New York, Doubleday, 5 vols., 1962–86; 1 and 3, London, Dobson, 2 vols., 1963–67; 2, London, Sphere, 1973.

Editor, with Groff Conklin, *Fifty Short Fiction Tales*. New York, Collier, 1963.

Editor, *Tomorrow's Children: 18 Tales of Fantasy and Science Fiction*. New York, Doubleday, 1966; London, Futura, 1974.

Editor, *Where Do We Go from Here?* New York, Doubleday, 1971; London, Joseph, 1973.

Editor, *Nebula Award Stories 8*. New York, Harper, and London, Gollancz, 1973.

Editor, *Before the Golden Age: A Science Fiction Anthology of the 1930's*. New York, Doubleday, and London, Robson, 1974.

Editor, with Martin H. Greenberg and Joseph D. Olander, *100 Great Science Fiction Short-Short Stories*. New York, Doubleday, and London, Robson, 1978.

Editor, with Martin H. Greenberg and Charles G. Waugh, *The Science Fictional Solar System*. New York, Harper, 1979; London, Sidgwick and Jackson, 1980.

Editor, With Martin H. Greenberg and Charles G. Waugh, *The Thirteen Crimes of Science Fiction*. New York, Doubleday, 1979.

Editor, with Martin H. Greenberg, *The Great SF Stories 1–21*. New York, DAW, 21 vols., 1979–90.

Editor, with Martin H. Greenberg and Joseph D. Olander, *Microcosmic Tales: 100 Wondrous Science Fiction Short-Short Stories*. New York, Taplinger, 1980.

Editor, with Martin H. Greenberg and Joseph D. Olander, *Space Mail 1*. New York, Fawcett, 1980.

Editor, with Martin H. Greenberg and Joseph D. Olander, *The Future in Question*. New York, Fawcett, 1980.

Editor, with Alice Laurance, *Who Done It?* Boston, Houghton Mifflin, 1980.

Editor, with Martin H. Greenberg and Charles G. Waugh, *The Seven Deadly Sins of Science Fiction*. New York, Fawcett, 1980.

Editor, with Martin H. Greenberg and Joseph D. Olander, *Miniature Mysteries: 100 Malicious Little Mystery Stories*. New York, Taplinger, 1981.

Editor, with Martin H. Greenberg and Charles G. Waugh, *Science Fiction Shorts* series (for children; includes *After the End, Thinking Machines, Travels Through Time, Wild Inventions, Mad Scientists, Mutants, Tomorrow's TV, Earth Invaded, Bug Awful, Children of the Future, The Immortals, Time Warps*). Milwaukee, Raintree, 12 vols., 1981–84.

Editor, *Fantastic Creatures*. New York, Watts, 1981.

Editor, with Charles G. Waugh and Martin H. Greenberg, *The Best Science Fiction [Fantasy, Horror and Supernatural] of the 19th Century*. New York, Beaufort, 3 vols., 1981–83; *Science Fiction*, London, Gollancz, 1983; *Fantasy* and *Horror and Supernatural*, London, Robson, 2 vols., 1985.

Editor, *Asimov's Marvels of Science Fiction*. London, Hale, 1981.

Editor, with Carol-Lynn Rössell Waugh and Martin H. Greenberg, *The Twelve Crimes of Christmas*. New York, Avon, 1981.

Editor, with Charles G. Waugh and Martin H. Greenberg, *The Seven Cardinal Virtues of Science Fiction*. New York, Fawcett, 1981.

Editor, with Martin H. Greenberg and Charles G. Waugh, *TV: 2000*. New York, Fawcett, 1982.

Editor, with Martin H. Greenberg and Charles G. Waugh, *Last Man on Earth*. New York, Fawcett, 1982.

Editor, with Charles G. Waugh and Martin H. Greenberg, *Tantalizing Locked-Room Mysteries*. New York, Walker, 1982.

Editor, with Martin H. Greenberg and Charles G. Waugh, *Space Mail 2*. New York, Fawcett, 1982.

Editor, with J.O. Jeppson, *Laughing Space: Funny Science Fiction*. Boston, Houghton Mifflin, and London, Robson, 1982.

Editor, with Alice Laurance, *Speculations*. Boston, Houghton Mifflin, 1982.

Editor, with Charles G. Waugh and Martin H. Greenberg, *Science Fiction from A to Z: A Dictionary of the Great Themes of Science Fiction*. Boston, Houghton Mifflin, 1982.

Editor, with Martin H. Greenberg and Charles G. Waugh, *Flying Saucers*. New York, Fawcett, 1982.

Editor, with Martin H. Greenberg and Charles G. Waugh, *Dragon Tales*. New York, Fawcett, 1982.

Editor, *Asimov's Worlds of Science Fiction*. London, Hale, 1982.

Editor, with Martin H. Greenberg and Charles G. Waugh, *Hallucination Orbit: Psychology in Science Fiction*. New York, Farrar Straus, 1983.

Editor, with Martin H. Greenberg, *Magical Worlds of Fantasy* series (*Wizards, Witches*). New York, New American Library, 2 vols., 1983–84; as *Magical Worlds of Fantasy: Witches and Wizards*, New York, Bonanza, 1 vol., 1985.

Editor, with Martin H. Greenberg and Charles G. Waugh, *Caught in the Organ Draft: Biology in Science Fiction*. New York, Farrar Straus, 1983.

Editor, *The Big Apple Mysteries*. New York, Avon, 1983.

Editor, with George R.R. Martin and Martin H. Greenberg, *The Science Fiction Weight-Loss Book*. New York, Crown, 1983.

Editor, with Martin H. Greenberg and Charles G. Waugh, *Starships*. New York, Ballantine, 1983.

Editor, *Asimov's Wonders of the World*. London, Hale, 1983.

Editor, with George Zebrowski and Martin H. Greenberg, *Creations: The Quest for Origins in Story and Science*. New York, Crown, 1983; London, Harrap, 1984.

Editor, with Martin H. Greenberg and Charles G. Waugh, *Computer Crimes and Capers*. Chicago, Academy, 1983; London, Viking, 1985.

Editor, with Patricia S. Warrick and Martin H. Greenberg, *Machines That Think*. New York, Holt Rinehart, and London, Allen Lane, 1984.

Editor, with Terry Carr and Martin H. Greenberg, *100 Great Fantasy Short Short Stories*. New York, Doubleday, and London, Robson, 1984.

Editor, with Charles G. Waugh and Martin H. Greenberg, *The Best Science Fiction Firsts*. New York, Beaufort, 1984; London, Robson, 1985.

Editor, with others, *Murder on the Menu*. New York, Avon, 1984.

Editor, with Martin H. Greenberg and Charles G. Waugh, *Sherlock Holmes Through Time and Space*. New York, Bluejay, 1984.

Editor, *Living in the Future*. New York, Beaufort, 1984.

Editor, with Martin H. Greenberg, *Isaac Asimov's Wonderful World of Science Fiction 2: The Science Fictional Olympics*. New York, New American Library, 1984.

Editor, with Martin H. Greenberg and Charles G. Waugh, *Young Mutants, Extraterrestrials, Ghosts, Monsters, Star Travelers, Witches and Warlocks* (for children). New York, Harper, 6 vols., 1984–87.

Editor, with Martin H. Greenberg, *Election Day 2084: Stories about the Politics of the Future*. Buffalo, Prometheus, 1984.

Editor, with Martin H. Greenberg and Charles G. Waugh, *Baker's Dozen: 13 Short Fantasy Novels*. New York, Greenwich House, 1984.
Editor, with Martin H. Greenberg and Charles G. Waugh, *Great Science Fiction Stories by the World's Great Scientists*. New York, Fine, 1985.
Editor, *Living in the Future*. New York, Beaufort, 1985.
Editor, with Martin H. Greenberg and Charles G. Waugh, *Amazing Stories: 60 Years of the Best Science Fiction*. Lake Geneva, Wisconsin, TRS, 1985.
Editor, with Martin H. Greenberg and Charles G. Waugh, *Giants*. New York, New American Library, 1985.
Editor, with Martin H. Greenberg and Charles G. Waugh, *Comets*. New York, New American Library, 1986.
Editor, with Martin H. Greenberg and Charles G. Waugh, *Mythical Beasties*. New York, New American Library, 1985; as *Mythic Beasties*, London, Robinson, 1986.
Editor, *The Mammoth Book of Short Science Fiction Novels*. London, Robinson, 1986.
Editor, *The Dark Void*. London, Severn House, 1987.
Editor, *Beyond the Stars*. London, Severn House, 1987.
Editor, with Carol-Lynn Rössell Waugh and Martin H. Greenberg, *Hound Dunnit*. New York, Carroll and Graf, 1987; London, Robson, 1988.
Editor, with Martin H. Greenberg and Charles G. Waugh, *Cosmic Knights*. London, Robinson, 1987.
Editor, with Martin H. Greenberg and Charles G. Waugh, *The Best Crime Stories of the 19th Century*. New York, Dember, 1988; London, Robson, 1989.
Editor, with Jason A. Shulman, *Book of Science and Nature Quotations*. New York, Weidenfeld and Nicolson, 1988.
Editor, with Martin H. Greenberg and Charles G. Waugh, *Ghosts*. London, Collins, 1988.
Editor, with Martin H. Greenberg and Charles G. Waugh, *The Best Detective Stories of the 19th Century*. New York, December, 1988.
Editor, with Martin H. Greenberg and Charles G. Waugh, *The Mammoth Book of Classic Science Fiction: Short Novels of the 1930's*. New York, Carroll and Graf, and London, Robinson, 1988.
Editor, with Martin H. Greenberg and Charles G. Waugh, *Monsters*. New York, New American Library, 1988; London, Robinson, 1989.
Editor, with Martin H. Greenberg and Charles G. Waugh, *The Mammoth Book of Golden Age Science Fiction: Short Novels of the 1940's*. New York, Carroll and Graf, and London, Robinson, 1989.
Editor, with Martin H. Greenberg and Charles G. Waugh, *Curses*. New York, New American Library, 1989.
Editor, with Martin H. Greenberg and Charles G. Waugh, *Tales of the Occult*. Buffalo, New York, Prometheus, 1989.
Editor, with Martin H. Greenberg and Charles G. Waugh, *Robots*. London, Robinson, 1989.
Editor, *The New Hugo Winners*. New York, Wynwood Press, 1989.
Editor, with Martin H. Greenberg and Charles G. Waugh, *The Mammoth Book of Vintage Science Fiction: Short Novels of the 1950's*. New York, Carroll and Graf, and London, Robinson, 1990.
Editor, with Martin H. Greenberg, *Cosmic Critiques: How and Why Ten Science Fiction Stories Work*. Writer's Digest, Cincinnati, Ohio, 1990.
Editor, with Martin H. Greenberg and Charles H. Waugh, *Great Tales of Classic Science Fiction*. New York, Galahad, 1988.

*

Bibliography: *Isaac Asimov: A Checklist of Works Published in the United States March 1939–May 1972* by Marjorie M. Miller, Kent, Ohio, Kent State University Press, 1972; in *In Joy Still Felt*, 1980.

Manuscript Collection: Mugar Memorial Library, Boston University.

Critical Studies: *Asimov Analyzed* by Neil Goble, Baltimore, Mirage Press, 1972; *The Science Fiction of Isaac Asimov* by Joseph F. Patrouch, Jr., New York, Doubleday, 1974, London, Panther, 1976; *Isaac Asimov* edited by Joseph D. Olander and Martin H. Greenberg, New York, Taplinger, and Edinburgh, Harris, 1977; *Asimov: The Foundations of His Science Fiction* by George Edgar Slusser, San Bernardino, California, Borgo Press, 1980; *Isaac Asimov: The Foundations of Science Fiction* by James Gunn, New York and Oxford, Oxford University Press, 1982; *Isaac Asimov* by Jean Fielder and Jim Mele, New York, Ungar, 1982.

* * *

Isaac Asimov is a virtual institution in science fiction, a prolific writer with an enormous body of work both within and outside the field. His earlier work in particular has done much to shape the direction in which the genre has moved. Not a stylist, his work is characterized by minute attention to scientific detail, clear and uncomplicated prose, and generally low key action. His is a contemplative approach that is sometimes rendered ineffective by lackluster dialogue.

Although Asimov has made some effort in recent years to draw all of his different series together, there are at least two separate strains. The first of these is the Foundation series. Originally, this consisted of three novels, *Foundation, Foundation and Empire*, and *Second Foundation*. They chronicle the existence of an interstellar organization of psychohistorians who planned for the continuation of civilization after the fall of the current Empire. They are opposed by the Empire itself, which considers them a menace, and the Mule, a charismatic and superhumanly intelligent mutant, whose existence was unpredictable and therefore outside the planning of the Foundation. This vast interplay of forces was a startling innovation in the early 1940's; the series is still popular today because of its unabashed enthusiasm and a sense of marvelously unfolding events. Three associated early novels are set further in the past of the Empire: *Pebble in the Sky, The Stars, Like Dust*, and *The Currents of Space*. Each is a novel of intrigue and high adventure, and their narrative power has kept them in print for several decades.

In 1982, Asimov began to add to the Foundation saga, with ambitious but generally lesser works. *Foundation's Edge* is perhaps the best, with the Foundation itself acting against what it perceives to be a renegade. *Foundation and Earth* introduces Gaia, a planet with a culture that might provide a viable alternative to the schismatic Foundation. Unfortunately, the novel is overly long, and it dissipates the tension and vigor of the earlier books. *Prelude to Foundation* chronicles the events leading to the establishment of the Foundation, but the young Hari Seldon is a far less interesting character than his older counterpart.

The second major series created by Asimov are his robot stories, centered around the now famous "Three Laws" governing the actions of creations with positronic brains. One thread in this series involves US Robots and Mechanical Men, a near future manufacturer who supplies robots on a commercial basis. Most of these stories are cleverly devised logical puzzles, involving apparent violations of the three laws. The best are collected in *I, Robot* and *The Rest of the Robots*. Among the classic tales in this series are "Liar!" "Evidence," "Runaround," and "The Bicentennial Man."

*The Caves of Steel* and *The Naked Sun* introduce the detective team of Lije Baley and R. Daneel Olivaw, human and robot. Together they solve two mysteries, one on Earth and one on the bizarrely individualist planet Aurora. Two new volumes have been added to this series as well. *The Robots of Dawn* is an ambitious but failed attempt to repeat the successful blend of SF and mystery. The basic puzzle is clever but the delivery is leadenly paced. The fourth book in the series, *Robots and Empire,* is set centuries later. Baley is dead, but Olivaw continues to function, prepared to thwart an old enemy. Although the story is still slowly paced at times, it is much more entertaining. The novel also serves as a bridge connecting the two series.

Asimov has used robots in two series for younger readers as well. The six books in the Lucky Starr series, among the best juvenile science fiction ever written, rely extensively on problems relating to the use of robots. Six short novels about Norby, a more recent series written in collaboration with Janet Asimov, are aimed at pre-teens and hold little interest for more mature readers.

Asimov has also written hundreds of short stories. "Nightfall" is probably the most popular single science fiction story of all time. A novel-length version has recently been published in collaboration with Robert Silverberg; it surprisingly retains all of the marvelous originality of the story, while adding more developed characters and a more extensive plot.

Asimov's short stories have varied from meticulous hard science to sentiment to humor. "The Martian Way" is a fascinating and plausible view of Martian colonists who replenish their water supply by mining the rings of Saturn. "Waterclap" contrasts the exploration of space with the exploration of earth's oceans. In "The Feeling of Power," Asimov warns against the dangers of complacency, as hand-held calculators lead to humanity's inability to perform simple mathematical processes without them. "The Ugly Little Boy" is uncharacteristically emotional in its description of the tribulations of a neanderthal child born to modern humans, and it expresses Asimov's views about acceptance and conformity in general. Shakespeare is brought forward in time with amusing results in "The Immortal Bard."

Asimov, who has written in the mystery field as well, often resorts to the conventions of that genre. The Wendell Urth short stories are all clever puzzle mysteries that usually hinge on scientific principles. Another more recent series of stories involves a diminutive demon named Azazel, whose intentions are often benevolent, but with wildly unexpected and usually funny consequences.

Asimov's contributions to the genre of science fiction are vast and continuing. His robot stories alone have shaped the way we think of mechanical men, and every subsequent view is necessarily contrasted with his vision. Many writers have created vast galactic empires, but none with more success than Asimov. If his more recent fiction is less groundbreaking than his old, that seems to matter little to his legions of fans. He is undeniably one of the major figures in the field, and will be read as long as future generations enjoy the free play of speculation and imagination.

—Don D'Ammassa

---

**ASPRIN, Robert (Lynn).** American. Born in St. Johns, Michigan, in 1946. Educated at the University of Michigan, Ann Arbor, 1964–1965. Served in the United States Army, 1965–66. Married to Anne Brett; one daughter and one son. Accounts clerk, 1966–70, payroll analyst, 1970–74, and cost accountant, 1974–78, University Microfilm, Ann Arbor. Since 1978 freelance writer. Recipient: *Locus* award, for editing, 1982. Address: c/o Ace Books, 200 Madison Avenue, New York, New York 10016, U.S.A.

### SCIENCE-FICTION PUBLICATIONS

Novels (series: Duncan and Mallory; Myth)

*The Cold Cash War.* New York, St. Martin's Press, and London, New English Library, 1977.
*Another Fine Myth.* Norfolk, Virginia, Donning, 1978; revised edition, with Phil Foglio, as *Myth Adventures Two,* 1986.
*The Bug Wars.* New York, St. Martin's Press, 1979; London, New English Library, 1980.
*Tambu.* New York, Ace, 1979.
*Mirror Friend, Mirror Foe,* with George Takei. Chicago, Playboy Press, 1979.
*Hit or Myth.* Norfolk, Virginia, Donning, 1983.
*Myth-ing Persons,* with Kay Reynolds. Norfolk, Virginia, Donning, 1984.
*Little Myth Marker.* Norfolk, Virginia, Donning, 1985.
*Myth Conceptions.* New York, Ace, 1985.
*Myth Directions.* New York, Ace, 1985.
*Myth Adventures,* with Phil Foglio. Norfolk, Virginia, Donning, 1985.
*Myth Alliances.* New York, Doubleday, 1986.
*Duncan and Mallory,* with Mel White. Norfolk, Virginia, Donning, 1986.
*M.Y.T.H. Inc. Link.* Norfolk, Virginia, Donning, 1986.
*Myth-Nomers and Im-pervections.* Norfolk, Virginia, Donning, 1987.
*The Bar-None Ranch,* with Mel White (Duncan and Mallory). Norfolk, Virginia, Donning, 1987.
*The Raiders,* with Mel White (Duncan and Mallory). Norfolk, Virginia, Donning, 1988.
*Cold Cash Warrior,* with Bill Fawcett. New York, Ace, 1989.
*M.Y.T.H. Inc. in Action.* Norfolk, Virginia, Donning, 1990.
*Phule's Company.* New York, Ace, 1990.

### OTHER PUBLICATIONS

Other

*Myth Conceptions.* Norfolk, Virginia, Donning, 1979.

Editor, with Lynn Abbey, *Thieves' World* series (graphic novels). New York, Ace, 12 vols., 1979–90.
Editor, with Richard Pini and Lynn Abbey, *The Blood of Ten Chiefs* and *Wolfsong: The Blood of Ten Chiefs Vol. 2.* New York, Tor, 2 vols., 1986–88.

* * *

One of the more energetic and interesting SF writers to emerge since the late 1970's, Robert Asprin compiled a most impressive record for productivity in his early years. His first book, *The Cold Cash War,* introduced themes present in most of his later works, and which can be traced, at least in part, to Asprin's preliterary occupation. He had been a cost accountant for a large "high-tech" corporation, and was thoroughly familiar with corporate procedures and the problems of management and personal rivalries within the corporate environment.

In *The Cold Cash War,* Asprin posits growing impatience and dissatisfaction on the part of large corporations with governmental mandates and unresponsiveness. In this situation, the corporations form private armies; when the government, through its official army, tries to suppress this odd rebellion, the corporations triumph as a result of possessing superior technology and more effective means of troop-motivation. This book is somewhat limited in characterization and plot, but shows excellent powers of technological and sociological extrapolation, at least in the near-future range.

*The Bug Wars,* Asprin's second science-fiction novel (a fantasy novel of very different nature intervened), continued the military theme, and is a worthy experiment, but unfortunately fails seriously. Asprin portrays an interplanetary struggle between a race of highly advanced, highly militaristic, intelligent reptiles and a coalition of huge insects. The narration is from the viewpoint of the reptiles, and it is uncertain to both the reptiles and the reader whether the insects are truly intelligent or not. A background rationale involves a mysterious elder race which had been instrumental in the spread of the insects through space. There is also passing mention of small warm-blooded animals, the reader being free to speculate as to whether these are pre-human beings, true humans of a degraded culture, or simply warm-blooded animals. A novel told completely from the viewpoint of a reptilian alien and involving no identifiable human characters was a most ambitious undertaking. The result, unfortunately, was a thoroughly one-dimensional book devoted almost entirely to the military details of battle; without characters suitable for reader empathy or identification, the volume makes poor reading. It is further marred by numerous minor solecisms and clichés. Asprin has suffered also from poor editing.

*Tambu* shows marked improvement. It is the story of a band of professional pirate-hunters, laid against the background of a future interstellar trading culture. The structure of the book is unnecessarily cluttered with excerpts from a supposed interview at the end of Tambu's career, between which Asprin intersperses major incidents in his life. But the story-telling is brisk, the characterization indicates considerable progress, and a feel is achieved, at least sporadically, that is reminiscent of the old *Planet Stories* or E.E. Smith space operas.

Asprin's collaborative novel, *Mirror Friend, Mirror Foe,* was written with George Takei, the actor best known for his continuing role in the *Star Trek* series. In this novel, against a background of intercorporate espionage and cold-war, the authors place a corporate spy within a robot-manufacturing concern. The spy's heritage derives from the Japanese *ninja*; this, presumably, is Takei's contribution while Asprin's is the corporate situation. From a promising start, the book unfortunately degenerates into cliché as the robots, escaping from their normal conditioning, go lurching and clanking about a planet murdering every human being they encounter.

Despite his promising start as a science fiction writer, Asprin achieved far greater success in the allied field of fantasy, and by the mid-1980's had largely abandoned science fiction. His fantasy novel *Myth Conceptions* initiated a series of slapstick adventures in-and-out of an Arabian Nights universe of *jinni,* homunculi, spells, dragons, and gorgeous women. Within the familiar realm of published fantasy, Asprin's *Myth* series (all the books are pun-named) bears comparison to the works of L. Sprague de Camp. Asprin himself claims inspiration in the Bing Crosby/Bob Hope/Dorothy Lamour "Road" films of the 1940's.

Even more successful than the *Myth* books is Asprin's series of *Thieves' World* anthologies. The concept is essentially that of a vaguely Robert E. Howard-type barbarian culture, against which any number of stories can be laid by any number of authors. The anthologies have proved so successful that an entire mini-industry has sprung up around them, with authors using the Thieves' World setting for novels of their own, and with adaptations into comic books, role-playing games, video games, and the prospect of further, varied merchandising and adaptations.

Despite the success of his *Myth* and *Thieves' World* enterprises, Asprin has continued to move in slightly new directions. His collaborative novels in the Duncan and Mallory series, written with Mel White, demonstrate the typical Asprin characteristics of rapid pace, slapstick action, and broad humor. Asprin's continuing success indicates that he was wise to abandon his earlier attempts at serious science fiction and to concentrate instead on humorous fantasy. In this realm he has found his place in a longstanding tradition, and won a large and enthusiastic following, largely of teen- and pre-teenage readers.

—Richard A. Lupoff

---

**ATTANASIO, A.A.** American. Born in Newark, New Jersey, 20 September 1951. Educated at University of Pennsylvania, 1969–73, B.A.; Columbia University, New York, 1973–75, M.F.A.; New York, University, 1975–76, M.A. Agent: Mary Evans, Virginia Barber Literary Agency, 353 West 21st Street, New York, New York 10011. Address: 1322 Kaeleku Street, Honolulu, Hawaii 96825, U.S.A.

SCIENCE-FICTION PUBLICATIONS

Novels

*Radix.* New York, Morrow, 1981; London, Corgi, 1982.
*In Other Worlds.* New York, Morrow, 1984; London, Corgi, 1986.
*Beastmarks.* Willimantic, Connecticut, Ziesing, 1984.
*Arc of the Dream.* New York, Bantam, 1986; London, Grafton, 1988.
*Wyvern.* New York, Ticknor and Fields, 1988; London, Grafton, 1989.
*The Last Legends of Earth.* Norwalk, Connecticut, Easton Press, and London, Grafton, 1989.
*Hunting the Ghost Dancer.* New York, Harper Collins, and London, Grafton, 1991.

*

A.A. Attanasio comments:

We live by our fictions, all of us immersed in the strange zone we call the imagination, that weird place that, when all is said and done, is the only place we ever are. Each of us is a dream grounded by the inescapable facts of existence, continually striving to rise above the loneliness and wretchedness of life by the magic of our hopes, visions, ambitions. The stories we tell ourselves define us in our struggle against our relentless limits. So, I write fantastic stories, where reality is dismembered and we can better remember who we are.

* * *

At times, the prose of A.A. Attanasio reminds one of the magic realism of Marquez or Borges. There is the same sense of a world existing just beyond reach, the same wonder when things familiar suddenly become unfamiliar, not because they have changed, but because the world around them has suddenly shifted to a different viewpoint. This is the hallmark of Attanasio's approach to science fiction and fantasy: to take the familiar conventions of the genres and change the world around them so that they are suddenly seen in a new light.

Attanasio is primarily a visualist. The worlds he creates are vivid, drawn in lucent and poetic detail. He is more comfortable with descriptions of primitive settings than with technological worlds, but this seems only to be because the natural world, particularly unspoiled nature, offers more scope for description. This is not to say that his visions of the constructed world are inferior to those of the natural world. Rather, his visualizations of cities and machines explicitly demonstrate the barrenness inherent in cold stone and metal. His descriptions of nature are celebrations of fertility and the possibilities which lie in growth and change. At times, the elaboration of description goes a fraction too far, into a sort of neoclassic coyness—"blood drum" for heart or "path of heaven" for the sky. But rather than expressions of a Rococo conventionality, these are exuberant outbursts of playful inventiveness, of an intellect hovering on the edges of being word-drunk.

Even though Attanasio celebrates natural forces, he is quite at home with the pseudo-scientific explanations that are part of science fiction. His scientific justification of the disappearance of Carl Schirmer, in *In Other Worlds,* is clear and scientifically accurate, or, at least as scientifically accurate as is necessary to explain the plot device. But the scientific jargon is only a means to an end, a necessary function that has to be got out of the way to make the story happen. It is not central to any of Attanasio's stories, save that science, in the form of a natural or quasi-natural phenomena, makes the story possible. Instead, what is central to Attanasio is the human reaction to a changed world.

At times the world itself changes around the protagonist. This is the case in *Radix.* The entire world has changed as a result of crossing the path of a beam of radiation from a black hole in the centre of the galaxy. It is now a world of the timeloose, godminds, voors, orts, yawps and some few unchanged humans. The social structures that exist are parodies of those which existed before the change. Into this world comes Sumner Kagan, a white-card whose genetic material is free from distortion, also the Sugarat, the secret nemesis of the street-gangs who infest the city. Kagan reacts to the world around viscerally, rather than heroically. He kills the streetgangs because he fears them, then he begins to kill them because it gives him a feeling of power. He is not an admirable creature, but, throughout the course of the story, as he is pared down to the base of what he is, as the powers latent within him emerge, he becomes admirable. He triumphs over his doubts and fears, over his many weaknesses, and changes the world around him positively, rather than destructively.

This kind of evolution is typical of Attanasio. His concern seems to be with the way in which humanity can triumph over the most fearful forms of oppression or prejudice, by conquering the self first. In *Wyvern,* the protagonist, Jaki Gefjon is a social outcast, a product of the liaison between a Borneo native and a Dutch trader. He becomes the protege of a shaman, who sees the powers within the boy. As Jaki grows to manhood, he must overcome his fears of the world and of what lies within him, in order to realize his potential. As he grows, he moves out of his restricted jungle world, and comes into contact with Western society, as the second in command to a pirate. It is here that he is faced with an entirely new spectrum of challenges, which he must face and overcome. The most deadly of these is the pirate-chaser Captain Quarles, who engages in a deadly vendetta when his daughter falls in love with Jaki, runs away with him and marries him. The pursuit follows throughout the East Indies and much of Asia, with death and revenge a commonplace, to a final confrontation in the Americas. It is here, through the complete and utter acceptance of his humanity, through a demonstration of the innate humanity which Quarles has hidden from himself throughout his life, and which drove his daughter from him, that Jaki triumphs.

It is this which marks all of Attanasio's work; the quest of the protagonist, although it may be framed in terms of high adventure, is an internal quest. Quite simply, they are looking for what makes them what they are, in order to know themselves. This quest, which would, in the hands of a lesser writer, be a sterile investigation of modern angst, is an invigorating, emotional experience, because Attanasio is not only a writer of humanity, but a writer of the joy of humanity.

—Ian Nichols

---

**AUBREY, Frank.** *See* **ASH, Fenton.**

---

**AVERY, Richard.** *See* **COOPER, Edmund.**

---

**AYRE, Thornton.** *See* **FEARN, John Russell.**

---

# B

**BAHL, Franklin,** *See* **PHILLIPS, Rog.**

---

**BAIN, Ted.** *See* **TUBB, E.C.**

---

**BAKER, Sharon.** American. Born in San Francisco, California, 10 May 1938. Educated at Mills College, Oakland, California, B.A. 1960; University of Washington, Seattle, M.L.S., 1966. Married Gordon P. Baker in 1963; four sons. Magazine editor and public relations copywriter, Pacific Northwest Bell, Seattle, 1961–62; librarian and curator of historical services, Boeing Airplane Company, Seattle, 1962–63; college recruiter and administrative assistant, University of Washington, 1963; physician's assistant, Seattle, Washington, 1963–66. Since 1980, writer. Address: c/o Avon Books, 105 Madison Avenue, New York, New York 10016, U.S.A.

SCIENCE-FICTION PUBLICATIONS

Novels

*Quarreling, They Met the Dragon.* New York, Avon, 1984.
*Journey to Membliar.* New York, Avon, 1987.
*Burning Tears of Sassurum.* New York, Avon, 1988.

* * *

Sharon Baker once said that she invents as little as possible in her fiction, a comment that at first may appear puzzling to readers of her three richly inventive novels about life on the violent planet Naphar. But apart from the astronomical and biological wonders of this imaginary world, her fiction also addresses such too-familiar issues as racism (which Naphar society bases on height), rape (both hetero- and homosexual), prostitution, child abuse, slavery, suicide, drugs, environmental destruction (even depletion of atmospheric ozone), and political and economic corruption. The acknowledgments of her novels reveal that she has interviewed not only biologists and astronomers, but street hustlers and narcotics cops as well.

Baker's first published novel, *Quarreling, They Met the Dragon*, introduces the rigid, anti-technological slave society of Naphar, broadly patterned after civilizations of the ancient Near East. Naphar's two dominant races, the tall Rabu and the shorter Kakanu, are both descended from human settlers who crossbred with native species. Senruh, a half-breed boy who earns his living as a prostitute, escapes his master and joins with Pell Maru, a Kakanu boy who is also an escaped slave. Together, they escape from the city of Qaqqadum and are sheltered by the spacers, humans who maintain a trade and research mission on Naphar and who represent the only contact with a vaguely described galactic civilization. What is perhaps most remarkable about the novel is its sensitive account of the growing love between two adolescent boys, and the unusually frank scenes of sexuality that give the narrative a dimension of sensuality unusual in most fantasy and science fiction. The novel has received inadequate critical attention possibly because its title (derived from a line of epic poetry quoted in the text) suggests a traditional quest fantasy. In fact, there are no dragons in the story at all.

*Journey to Membliar* and *Burning Tears of Sassurum* are really two parts of a single novel, *Spring of the Twin Moons,* which Baker had worked on extensively prior to the publication of *Quarreling, They Met the Dragon.* The narrative concerns Ricassia Addiratu, a tall Rabu who has been enslaved by the smaller Kakanu of the highlands of Naphar; her master, the boy Tadge; and Jarell Adon, a Kakanu who becomes a slave among Ricassia's people. Opposing them is the evil Salimar, who seeks possession of the legendary Mindstone in order to establish a reign of terror over Naphar. The Mindstone, which acts as a kind of amplifier of psychic energy, has been stolen by Jarell, who hopes to use it as a means of realizing his dream of going into space. *Journey to Membliar* follows the familiar quest structure of many fantasy narratives, as the three protagonists are brought together in a kind of mock family structure and seek to escape from Salimar with the Mindstone. They find their way to Membliar, an underground realm where they are protected by the mysterious Beloved, the vampire–like but benevolent third race which inhabits Naphar.

*Burning Tears of Sassurum* (the title refers to a periodic meteor shower on Naphar) takes place mostly in the capital city of Qaqqadum, where Ricassia discovers she is the lost daughter of the ruling priestess, and where the final struggle against Salimar takes place. Again, the surface narrative carries the suggestion of traditional fantasy, but an extraordinary degree of science-fictional detail underlies this exotic world. The deadly sunlight of Naphar, for example, is the result of an ancient failed experiment in deepening the atmosphere's protective radiation belts; vampirism and cannibalism are necessitated by protein deficiencies in native foodstuffs; even the magical Mindstone is a psychic transmitter left by the original settlers, who are able to observe the history of Naphar over the centuries by virtue of relativistic time distortions brought on by the proximity of a black hole.

More important than Baker's juggling of fantasy and science fiction tropes is her treatment of character. Whereas the formula fantasy hero characteristically discovers unexpected strengths within himself through his adventures, Baker's characters are more likely to encounter their own vulnerabilities. Senruh overcomes his racist upbringing through his love for Pell Maru, and Jarell Adon seems increasingly confused and inarticulate about his emotions and motivations as his relationship with Ricassia gains complexity. Ricassia comes to realize that she is unable to make decisions in her own self-interest, instead always following the needs of others. Even the wicked Salimar is revealed to be the product of an abusive and neglectful childhood, and his punishment is not death but regression to the childlike state that preceded his corruption. In Baker's first published horror story, "House Hunter" (*Walls of Blood*, edited by Kathryn Cramer, New York, Morrow, 1990), a brutal child abuser, who tortures and maims the foster children sharing his home, turns out to be the victim of a repressive and rejecting mother. Like her science fiction, the story reveals a surprising complexity beneath the actions of unsavory characters.

With its richness of invention and careful attention to detail, Baker's small but important body of work may come to stand as an almost classic example of the odd fictional hybrid sometimes termed science fantasy—narratives in which the hard-edged rational speculation associated with science fiction gives rise to the apparently supernatural powers and beings associated with fantasy. Baker, who seems to have been influenced by Gene Wolfe and Samuel R. Delany, shares with these authors the unusual ability to construct dense, convincing novels in which the interaction of complex characters overlays a surface structure of fantasy adventure, which in turn overlays a carefully worked out science fiction milieu.

—Gary K. Wolfe

---

**BALLARD, J(ames) G(raham).** British. Born in Shanghai, China, 15 November 1930. Educated at Leys School, Cambridge; King's College, Cambridge. Served in The Royal Air Force. Married Helen Mary Matthews in 1953 (died 1964); one son and two daughters. Recipient: *Guardian* Fiction prize, 1984; James Tait Black Memorial prize, 1985. Agent: Margaret Hanbury, 27 Walcot Square, London SE11 4UB.

SCIENCE-FICTION PUBLICATIONS

Novels

*The Wind from Nowhere.* New York, Berkley, 1962; London, Penguin, 1967.
*The Drowned World.* New York, Berkley, 1962; London, Gollancz, 1963.
*The Burning World.* New York, Berkley, 1964; revised edition, as *The Drought*, London, Cape, 1965.
*The Crystal World.* London, Cape, and New York, Farrar Straus, 1966.
*Crash.* London, Cape, and New York, Farrar Straus, 1973.
*Concrete Island.* London, Cape, and New York, Farrar Straus, 1974.
*High-Rise.* London, Cape, 1975; New York, Holt Rinehart, 1977.
*The Unlimited Dream Company.* London, Cape, and New York, Holt Rinehart, 1979.
*Hello America.* London, Cape, 1981.
*The Day of Creation.* London, Gollancz, 1987; New York, Farrar Straus, 1988.

Short Stories

*The Voices of Time and Other Stories.* New York, Berkley, 1962.
*Billenium and Other Stories.* New York, Berkley, 1962.
*The Four-Dimensional Nightmare.* London, Gollancz, 1963.
*Passport to Eternity and Other Stories.* New York, Berkley, 1963.
*Terminal Beach.* London, Gollancz, 1964; abridged edition, New York, Berkley, 1964.
*The Impossible Man and Other Stories.* New York, Berkley, 1966.
*The Disaster Area.* London, Cape, 1967.
*The Day of Forever.* London, Panther, 1967.
*The Overloaded Man.* London, Panther, 1967.
*Why I Want to Fuck Ronald Reagan.* Brighton, Unicorn Bookshop, 1968.
*The Atrocity Exhibition.* London, Cape, 1970; as *Love and Napalm: Export USA*, New York, Grove Press, 1972.
*Chronopolis and Other Stories.* New York, Putnam, 1971.
*Vermilion Sands.* New York, Berkley, 1971; London; Cape, 1973.
*Low-Flying Aircraft and Other Stories.* London, Cape, 1976.
*The Best of J. G. Ballard.* London, Futura, 1977.
*The Best Short Stories of J. G. Ballard.* New York, Holt Rinehart, 1978.
*The Venus Hunters.* London, Granada, 1980.
*Myths of the Near Future.* London, Cape, 1982.
*Memories of the Space Age.* Sauk City, Wisconsin, Arkham House, 1988.

OTHER PUBLICATIONS

Novels

*Empire of the Sun.* London, Gollancz, and New York, Simon and Schuster, 1984.
*Running Wild* (novella). London, Hutchinson, 1988; New York, Farrar Straus, 1989.

Short Stories

*War Stories.* London, Gollancz, 1990; New York, Farrar Straus, 1991.

Other

*The Art of Fiction LXXXV.* N. p., Thomas Frick, 1984.

*

Bibliography: *J. G. Ballard: A Primary and Secondary Bibliography* by David Pringle, Boston, Hall, 1984.

Critical Studies: *J. G. Ballard: The First Twenty Years* edited by James Goddard and David Pringle, Hayes, Middlesex, Bran's Head, 1976; *Re Search: J. G. Ballard* edited by Vale, San Francisco, Re Search, 1983; *J. G. Ballard* by Peter Brigg, San Bernardino, California, Borgo Press, 1985.

* * *

J. G. Ballard began his career with a series of what David Pringle calls "psychological horror stories," the most notable early examples of which, such as "The Voices of Time" and "Billenium," have been much collected and overpraised. These stories introduce themes that Ballard—and many of the British New Wave writers on whom he was the most important influence—would later develop, in particular the disjunctions between real, cosmic, and psychological time. However, only in a handful of stories, such as "The Terminal Beach" and "The Drowned Giant," does Ballard show a sufficient interest in the exigencies of the shorter form. His original stories tend to be inferior to the novels into which they were expanded, while in more recent times Ballard's best work outside the novel itself has been in the novella: "The Ultimate City," "News from the Sun," "Myths of the Near Future," and *Running Wild.*

Ballard's first novels—the disaster quartet *The Wind from Nowhere, The Drowned World, The Drought* (first published as *The Burning World*), and *The Crystal World*—are uneven in quality, in spite of their appearance as an anatomy of elemental catastrophe. *The Drowned World* is the best; though flawed by its melodramatic villain, it is a major achievement, a full articulation of many of the major psychotemporal themes that Ballard had been toying with in earlier short stories. The deluge occurs before the action begins; Ballard's interest is not merely in the psychological effects of the aftermath on the survivors, but also in the idea that the deluge was activated by humanity itself—that the outer catastrophic landscape is a projection of inner, unconscious desire. The protagonists' task, or quest, is for an acclimatization to the alien self of which the catastrophe is an expression.

In the late 1960's, Ballard produced the concentrated novels collected as *The Atrocity Exhibition* (published in the United States as *Love and Napalm*). These were influenced by a belated surrealism, and partially motivated by the savage indignation of the satirist at the marketing of illusion in America during the Vietnam War; they are stylistically pretentious but irresistibly titled. Pieces such as "Why I Want to Fuck Ronald Reagan" are now more interesting as particularly acute sociohistorical documents in which countercultural outrage attempts to find a language to respond to culturally-sanctioned violence and manipulation.

In his urban disaster trilogy, *Crash, Concrete Island*, and *High-Rise*, which together form his most significant achievement to date, Ballard produces a fiction even less concerned with warning humanity about future dangers, or with providing anticipatory thrills, than his quartet of the 1960's. Instead, he seeks to diagnose the psychic condition of Western man from the artificial landscapes he has constructed and his trajectories across it. The car crash, the descent into savagery, the releasing of inhibitions against sexual violence: these are not accidental but are revealed to be probably inevitable stages in the psychic development of Western culture toward some mysterious, unconsciously sought, goal. In *Crash*, a profoundly unpleasant work to read, the contemporary technological landscape is revealed to be the unconscious mapping of a sexually-grounded psychopathology.

Ballard's four most recent novels are all of high literary quality; superficially very different, they exhibit strong thematic continuity with his earlier fiction. In *The Unlimited Dream Company*, the quintessentially dull London suburb of Shepperton (where Ballard himself, with Flaubertian irony, has long resided), is literally transfigured into a dream-landscape by a messiah-archetype. The novel is a development of themes found in both *The Crystal World* and *Crash*, though now less darkly tinged. *Hello America* is a return to the motifs of *The Atrocity Exhibition*, but its satire on the vacuity of the American dream (at the same time brilliantly exposing the latent content of its icons) seems almost benign in comparison with the earlier work. *Empire of the Sun*, a quasi-realistic autobiographical novel set in a Japanese-run internment camp near Shanghai between 1942 and 1945, brought Ballard belatedly to the attention of the British literary establishment. It provides a clarifying literal context for the obsessional motifs of drained swimming pools, low-flying aircraft, and dead pilots of Ballard's earlier fiction; but then the whose of Ballard's earlier fiction provides a clarifying psychological context for the historically and personally crucial scene in the novel when the boy Jim sees the flash of light from the atomic bomb dropped on Nagasaki. The 'journey to the source' in *The Day of Creation* is a return to the territory of *The Drowned World* and *The Crystal World* that is at the same time a conscious homage to Conrad's *Heart of Darkness*.

Ballard has pronounced the space age long over; for him, outer space—the traditional realm of science fiction—is a distraction from the proper goal of contemporary fiction, namely to explore the *terra incognita* of inner space: the human psyche. Ballard's best fiction seeks to understand what unconscious drives brought Western man into being. 'Man' here is deliberate: the technological landscape according to Ballard is an expression of a masculine psychopathology. This is why women play shadowy and stereotypical roles in Ballard's fiction and why the characteristic Ballardian protagonist is always the same in type and predicament: a middle-class professional man cast into a seemingly alien world by a disaster, and whose self-destruction, or descent into fugue or savagery may paradoxically be a sign of psychic recuperation—a sign of acceptance of the responsibility for what he when "sane" or "socially integrated" would have dismissed as alien.

If the Ballard's cultural diagnosis is clear, his prognosis is more ambivalent. Some critics argue that Ballard is a transcendentalist, perpetually rehearsing a quest for the timelessness of eternity; others, in my view more convincingly, that Ballardian man unconsciously seeks only to rejoin the inanimate, to consummate a fusion with the mineral world through a terminal catastrophe. In any event, as befits an explorer in the timeless world of the unconscious, Ballard restricts himself to the analysis of the hypercomplex world of the present, leaving speculations about the unknowable future to the naive practitioners of traditional science fiction.

The opening sentence of *High-Rise* exhibits the best qualities of Ballard's mature style: "Later, as he sat on his balcony eating the dog, Dr. Robert Laing reflected on the unusual events that had taken place within this huge apartment building during the previous three months." Understated, mildly surreal in the juxtaposition of the banal and the bizarre, ironic and even self-parodic in its repressed, classical syntax, it is capable of savage humor.

Is Ballard a science-fiction writer? Early doubts in the American-dominated science fiction establishment about his commitment to extrapolation were strengthened by the relentlessly downbeat quality of his fiction, and his perceived anti-Americanism. (Ballard is fascinated by America as global dream-factory, the place where cultural trends are fashioned and become visible; his responses to British society range from indifference to contempt.) The success of the mainstream autobiographical novel *Empire of the Sun* only seemed to confirm that Ballard, who has never won a Hugo or Nebula, was only masquerading as a science fiction writer. The issue here is not, however, a simple one. Ballard began as a science-fiction writer in the 1950's because of his own scientific inclinations and thematic concerns, and because of a kind of inverted snobbery: the gaudy American pulp magazines appealed to him because they were the antithesis of the stuffy, insular British fiction of the time. Since then, Ballard has continued to be identified with science fiction because its implied marginality suits him, not because he has the slightest intellectual affinity with Heinlein, Asimov, or Wyndham. If science fiction is merely a formulaic genre whose job is to sell its readers the wonders of high technology, then Ballard is not a science-fiction writer. But if science fiction's mission is to confront the present, unprecedented age of all-pervasive technology—the totally mediated landscape—then Ballard is the most important living science-fiction author.

—Nicholas Ruddick

**BANKS, Iain M(enzies).** British. Born in Fife, Scotland, 16 February 1954. Educated at Stirling University. Expediter-analyzer, IBM, Grenock, Scotland, 1978; Soliciter's clerk, London, 1980-84. Now a freelance writer. Lives in Edinburgh. Address: c/o Macdonald & Company, Orbit House, 1 New Fetter Lane, London EC4A 1AR, England.

SCIENCE-FICTION PUBLICATIONS (works before 1988 as Iain Banks)

Novels

*Walking on Glass*. London, Macmillan, 1985; Boston, Houghton Mifflin, 1986.
*Cleaning Up*. Birmingham, BSFG, 1987.
*Consider Phlebas*. London, Macmillan, and New York, St. Martin's Press, 1987.
*The Player of Games*. London, Macmillan, 1988; New York, St. Martin's Press, 1989.
*The Use of Weapons*. London, Orbit, 1990.

Short Stories

*The State of the Art*. Willimantic, Connecticut, Ziesing, 1989; London, Orbit, 1991.

OTHER PUBLICATIONS

Novels (works before 1988 as Iain Banks)

*The Wasp Factory*. London, Macmillan, and Boston, Houghton Mifflin, 1984.
*The Bridge*. London, Macmillan, and New York, St. Martin's Press, 1986.
*Espedair Street*. London, Macmillan, 1987.
*Canal Dreams*. London, Macmillan, 1989; New York, Doubleday, 1991.

Other

*Classic Glamour Photography*. London, Hamlyn, 1983; New York, Amphoto, 1987.

* * *

Iain M. Banks first came to public attention with *The Wasp Factory*, a powerful novel of black-comic psychological horror, in which the first person narrator is a solitary and, to judge from his pastimes, incipiently psychotic seventeen-year-old who learns the secret of his bizarre upbringing in a clever twist ending. This debut was followed by a series of novels in which Banks showed considerable narrative versatility, a willingness to blend realistic and fantastic elements, and a certain anxiety not to be typecast by his first success. *Walking on Glass* has a complex, discontinuous, three-stranded structure, one strand of which is a science-fictional counterpoint to the two realistic ones. *The Bridge* is a coma-generated fantasy, deriving from sources as various as Kafka's parable "Die Brücke," and the two Forth Bridges near Edinburgh, Scotland. The novel has an elaborate structure based on an evolutionary metaphor. *Espedair Street* is a Scottish variant on the rock novel, in which the grotesque element is in the unlikeliness of the narrator himself as rock-star. After an uncertain start, *Canal Dreams* develops into a revenge thriller against ruthless terrorists with a female Japanese cellist in the Sylvester Stallone role.

Banks's interest in science fiction has been manifest from the beginning. A character early in *Walking on Glass* refers to "a sort of Byzantine future, a degenerate technocratic empire" that in hindsight is surely an allusion to The Culture, a "seemingly disunited, anarchic, hedonistic, decadent mélange of more or less human species" that dominates the far-future galaxy with the aid of the "evangelic materialism" of their colonial arm, the Contact section. The Culture forms the background of three ambitious space operas that have appeared since 1987 under the name Iain M. Banks.

The first, longest and best, *Consider Phlebas*, is a work of a highly focused imagination—the novel reveals the same ability to create a self-sufficient fictional world that gave *The Wasp Factory* its strength. The plot of *Consider Phlebas* is banal—a mission to find and recover a complex artificial intelligence (a "Mind") from a dangerous planet, with the Culture itself playing a seemingly adversary role—but it is nevertheless gripping as a result of Banks's ability to revitalize the narrative cliches of the space-operatic subgenre. *The Player of Games*, the second novel set in the Culture-dominated galaxy, is a very Banksian title, for this author produces narratives that are ludic in the best sense of that term. It concerns Gurgeh, a master of the complex games valued by the Culture *as games*, who travels as a Culture-emissary to an uncolonized planet where games are taken in deadly earnest, and are indistinguishable from politics (the winner becomes ruler). The chief potential weakness of this novel is implicit in the very project itself: the rules of the games Gurgeh plays are unknown to the reader; it is a measure of Banks's ingenuity that he can almost make us forget this fact. Banks's third SF novel, *The Use of Weapons*, has a twist ending and a hypercomplex narrative structure reminiscent of Banks's earlier fiction; there is a deliberately reversed plot-strand that makes the story incomprehensible to an unwary reader expecting a little formulaic relaxation. The rationale for this structure is that it enacts for the protagonist a difficult reclamation of the past, or confrontation with a present reality, but Zakalwe in *Use of Weapons* remains something of a cipher. The novel also seems to have some thematic purpose beyond the idea that the unscrupulous turn everything into a weapon to gain their own end, but what that is remains puzzling, especially since one of the principle delights in Banks's space opera is the deployment of exotic weaponry.

In his SF Banks is particularly good at evoking artificial environments and hardware: the Culture is hooked on its machines, and the most interesting and amusing characters in Banks's space operas are robot drones. In spite of his tendency to choose preposterously pathetic names for his sentient starships—the *So Much for Subtlety*, the *Limiting Factor*—Banks's SF novels are much more than the deliberately comic explanations of science-fictional motifs by Douglas Adams or Terry Pratchett.

But if they are more than pastiches, they are also less than they might be—and this goes for all Banks's fiction to date. Most critics agree that Banks's creative imagination is extraordinary, and he also shows considerable technical ingenuity and the ability to produce gripping plots in a variety of narrative modes without insulting the reader's intelligence. His fiction is, however, thematically shallow. It is as though, having completely exorcised his demons in *The Wasp Factory* and fully stretched space-opera in *Consider Phlebas*, he is now more concerned to show virtuosity than to express a vision. His anxiety about fictional categories emerges in his separation of his SF from his other fiction by the adoption of the middle initial. There is an artistic insecurity, too, in the peculiarly jarring happy endings of novels as dissimilar as *Espedair Street* and *The Bridge*. One feels that it should not be quite so easy to dispel the darkness invoked in the fiction.

If Banks's disposition is a little too sunny, perhaps this is a result of his early success. While still in his thirties, he has been celebrated as the great white hope of both British science fiction and contemporary British literature. He deserves the attention he has received, both for his intelligence and for the quality of his imagination. Moreover, as a Scot by deliberation, he has shown that one need not be limited or marginalized by a regional viewpoint. He has the resources to take on bigger issues in both the realistic and fantastic modes; it remains to be seen whether he has the will to do so.

—Nicholas Ruddick

---

**BARCLAY, Bill.** *See* **MOORCOCK, Michael.**

---

**BARNARD, Marjorie Faith.** *See* **ELDERSHAW, M. Barnard.**

---

**BARNES, Arthur K(elvin).** Also wrote as Dave Barnes; Kelvin Kent. American. Born in Bellingham, Washington, in 1911. Educated at the University of California, Los Angeles, B.A. (Phi Beta Kappa). Freelance writer. *Died in 1969.*

SCIENCE-FICTION PUBLICATIONS

Short Stories (series: Gerry Carlisle)

*Interplanetary Hunter.* New York, Gnome Press, 1956.

Uncollected Short Stories (series: Gerry Carlisle)

"Lord of the Lightning," in *Wonder Stories* (New York), December 1931.
"Challenge of the Comet," in *Wonder Stories* (New York), February 1932.
"Guardians of the Void," in *Wonder Stories Quarterly* (New York), September 1932.
"The Hole Men of Mercury," in *Wonder Stories* (New York), December 1933.
"Emotion Solution," in *Wonder Stories* (New York), March 1936.
"The House That Walked" (as Dave Barnes), in *Astounding* (New York), September 1936.
"Prometheus," in *Amazing* (New York), February 1937.
"Green Hell" (Carlisle), in *Thrilling Wonder Stories* (New York), June 1937.
"The Dual World" (Carlisle), in *Thrilling Wonder Stories* (New York), June 1938.
"The Energy Eaters" (Carlisle; with Henry Kuttner), in *Thrilling Wonder Stories* (New York), October 1939.
"Day of the Titans," in *Thrilling Wonder Stories* (New York), February 1940.
"Waters of Wrath," in *Thrilling Wonder Stories* (New York), October 1940.
"Forgotton Future," in *Science Fiction* (Holyoke, Massachusetts), January 1941.
"The Little Man Who Wasn't There," in Thrilling Wonder Stories (New York), March 1941.
"Guinea Pig," in *Captain Future* (New York), Spring 1942.
"Fog over Venus," in *Thrilling Wonder Stories* (New York), Winter 1945.
"Grief of Bagdad," in *My Best Science Fiction Story*, edited by Leo Margulies and Oscar J. Friend. New York, Merlin Press, 1949.

Uncollected Short Stories as Kelvin Kent

"Roman Holiday" (with Henry Kuttner), in *Thrilling Wonder Stories* (New York), August 1939.
"Science Is Golden" (with Henry Kuttner), in *Thrilling Wonder Stories* (New York), April 1940.
"Knight Must Fall," in *Thrilling Wonder Stories* (New York), June 1940.
"The Greeks Had a War for It," in *Thrilling Wonder Stories* (New York), January 1941.
"De Wolfe of Wall Street," in *Thrilling Wonder Stories* (New York), February 1943.

* * *

Arthur K. Barnes is virtually unknown to the modern reader of science fiction; not a word of his considerable output in the field has seen print in a quarter of a century, and it has been more than 40 years since his last original story was published. To the reader of pulp "scientification" in the 1930's and 1940's, however—particularly to the reader of *Thrilling Wonder Stories*—Barnes was well known and popular, both for his own work and for his collaborations with Henry Kuttner. Nearly all of Barnes's fiction was either space opera or science fantasy. Although more or less solidly based on scientific knowledge of the period, his stories relied on farcical humor and rapid action for their effects. By today's standards they seem rather juvenile. Nevertheless, when viewed in historical perspective they are both interesting and entertaining.

The most popular of Barnes's space opera was a series about Gerry Carlisle, Tommy Strike, and the crew of *The Ark*, all of whom were employed by the "London Interplanetary Zoo" to trap and bring back alive nonintelligent alien life forms; the best of these novelettes were collected in Barnes's only book, *Interplanetary Hunter.* Much of his science fantasy involves time-travel into the past, and was co-authored with Henry Kuttner.

—Bill Pronzini

---

**BARNES, Dave.** *See* **BARNES, Arthur K.**

---

**BARNES, Steven (Emory).** American. Born in Los Angeles, California, 1 March 1952. Educated at Pepperdine University, Los Angeles, 1970–74. Married; one daughter. Tour guide, Columbia Broadcasting System, Hollywood, 1974–76; Manager, Audio-Visual and Multi-Media Department, Pepperdine University, 1978–80; Creative Consultant, Don Bluth Productions, 1981. Instructor, creative writing, University of California, Los Angeles. Agent: Eleanor Wood, Blassingame, McCauley and Wood, 432 Park Avenue, New York, New York 10016. Address: P.O. Box 2041, Santa Clarita, California 91386, U.S.A.

SCIENCE-FICTION PUBLICATIONS

Novels (Series: Dream Park)

*Dream Park*, with Larry Niven. Huntington Woods, Michigan, Phantasia Press, 1981; London, Macdonald, 1983.
*The Descent of Anansi*, with Larry Niven. New York, Tor, 1982.
*Streetlethal*. New York, Ace, 1983.
*The Kundalini Equation*. New York, Tor, 1986.
*The Legacy of Heorot*, with Larry Niven and Jerry Pournelle. New York, Simon and Schuster, and London, Gollancz, 1987.
*Gorgon Child*. New York, Tor, 1989.
*The Barsoom Project* (Dream Park), with Larry Niven. New York, Ace, 1989; London, Pan, 1990.
*Achilles' Choice*, with Larry Niven. New York, Tor, 1991.
*The California Voodoo Game*, with Larry Niven. New York, Tor, 1991.

OTHER PUBLICATIONS

Plays

Screenplay: *The Soulstar Commission*, 1987.

Television Plays: *Little Fuzzy* (adaptation of the novel by H. Beam Piper), 1979; *The Test* (adaptation of the short story by Stanislaw Lem), 1982; *Teacher's Aid*, and *To See the Invisible Man* (adaptation of the short story by Robert Silverberg), both in *The Twilight Zone* series, 1985–86; scripts for *Real Ghostbusters* (cartoon), 1987, and *The Wizard*, 1987.

Other

*Ki: How to Generate the Dragon Spirit*. N. p., Sen-do, 1976.

Animated Cartoon: *The Secret of NIMH*, 1982.

*

Stephen Barnes comments:

If there is any single thing which I believe most strongly, it is that all of us have the capacity to bring our most cherished dreams to life. What is required is motivating goals, discipline, honesty, and sufficient personal power to ACT. Life is a wonderful, complex, demanding game. The way to win is to decide what it is you want, find people who have accomplished this, and study them. Study their beliefs and habit patterns. Apply these to your own life, and you can be anything, do anything in the world. Get going!

* * *

It is almost always impossible to judge an individual writer's contribution to a collaborative effort, and the fact that four of the seven novels to appear under Steven Barnes's byline are collaborations with writers successful in their own right clearly presents some difficulties in evaluating his career. Certainly the collaborative works, three with Larry Niven, one with Niven and Jerry Pournelle, are all entertaining stories. Only *The Descent of Anansi* falls below the standards the other writers have established for their own work, a shortcoming not necessarily attributable to Barnes. *Dream Park* and its sequel, *The Barsoom Project*, are highly entertaining stories of a theme park where verisimilitude is definitely the order of the day. *The Legacy of Heorot* is a mysterious and suspenseful other world adventure with a strong biological theme; a group of colonists struggle to survive despite the onslaught of a particularly vicious and unsuspected predatory life form.

Fortunately, there are three solo novels and a handful of short stories that do enable us to judge Barnes's abilities as a writer. *Streetlethal*, the first of these, is a powerful, even upsetting view of a future Los Angeles after a catastrophic natural disaster has been coupled with a collapse of law and order. The protagonist is a professional fighter who has decided to sever his connections to a brutal gang that preys on the helpless, peddling drugs, killing innocent people in order to sell their organs as spare parts. Unfortunately, the gang isn't about to let him walk away, and his only alternative to dying may be to wipe out the entire gang first. Framed for murder and conditioned against resorting to violence, he must escape from prison, find the woman he loves, avenge himself against the criminals, and elude the authorities before escaping to a safe haven. He escapes with the woman to the warrens of the Scavengers, a less unpleasant gang, but the respite is brief, and their eventual capture by their old enemies only ends well because internal frictions within that group erupt into open civil war. Barnes draws on his own knowledge of martial arts to add credulity to this often depressing and quite violent novel of the underside of human society. Although the plot is a revenge story, Barnes takes great pains to ensure that it is not simply an excuse for endless battle sequences, creating characters and situations that develop as the story progresses.

*The Kundalini Equation* is also concerned with certain aspects of the discipline of martial arts, but it takes them in an entirely different direction. The various schools of fighting are all just aspects of a greater knowledge, a mental training that is so radical and all encompassing that its possessor has more than just the power to disable enemies. It also involves previously unsuspected mental powers that enable the practitioner to manipulate matter and energy directly. The result is the transformation of a man in modern California into a powerful, inhuman creature whose existence poses a threat to anyone he encounters. Ultimately, as he continues to change both physically and mentally, there is a very real danger that he might alter the nature of the Earth itself.

Barnes's most recent novel, *Gordon Child*, examines the same themes from another viewpoint. Sequel to *Streetlethal*, the protagonist is once again a young man trained as an organic killing machine, living in a world where plague and the collapse of central authority have contributed to a situation in which gangs and other private interests effectively control society. Aubry Knight is not a mindless killer, however, but a man determined to use his abilities to help improve things. However, a new religious cult plans to seize control of the entire nation.

All three of Barnes's solo novels throw one talented and resourceful man against a decadent and/or evil social system. Although the worlds he describes are bleak and repulsive, in each case the resolution of the story is hopeful, indicating that the indomitability of the human spirit will rise above temporary setbacks and persevere. His characters do not wait passively to see what the world will offer them but pursue whatever it is in life that they most desire. Even his villains often display admirable qualities, warped by their vices. Unfortunately, Barnes seems reluctant to experiment in novel form with a different type of setting and hero, although he has done so in a few of his shorter pieces. The best of these are "Locusts," "Endurance Vile," and the fantasy, "But Fear Itself." Perhaps as he continues to gain confidence as a writer, he will explore other themes and bring to them the intensity of the novels he has produced to date.

—Don D'Ammassa

---

**BARNWELL, William (Curtis).** American. Born in Macon, Georgia, 11 February 1943. Educated at Florence State College, Alabama, B. A. 1966; University of Florida, Gainesville, Ph.D. 1972. Married Jo Ann Weeks in 1966; one daughter and one son. Assistant Professor of English, University of South Carolina, Columbia, 1971–77; Writer-in-Residence, from 1977, Columbia College, South Carolina. Address: c/o Houghton Mifflin Publishers, 1 Beacon Street, Boston, Massachusetts 02108, U.S.A.

SCIENCE-FICTION PUBLICATIONS

Novels

*The Blessing Papers.* New York, Pocket Books, 1980; Gerrards Cross, Buckinghamshire, Smythe, 1981.
*Imram.* New York, Pocket Books, 1981.
*The Sigma Curve.* New York, Pocket Books, 1981.

OTHER PUBLICATIONS

Other

*Writing for a Reason.* Boston, Houghton Mifflin, 1983.

* * *

William Barnwell's only published science fiction consists of a single trilogy of after-the-disaster novels published in 1980 and 1981, consisting of *The Blessing Papers*, *Imram*, and *The Sigma Curve.* Each is set in Eire (renamed Imram) in a feudalistic society currently in turmoil because of several political and religious schisms within the community. Turly is a young boy with an unknown past who finds himself growing up within a passive group known as The Circle. His life is disrupted by a raid by the forces of Hastings, an ambitious man who wants to establish hegemony over the entire island. Hastings believes that Turly has the key to the Blessing Papers, which hold the potential for absolute power.

Naturally there are other parties equally interested in whatever special knowledge Turly might possess, chief among them the Order of Zeno, a cloistered group that is not averse to the use of murder and torture to achieve their ends. There are weapons and powers and other trappings of fantasy here despite the traditional setting. In the first volume, Turly evades his enemies and is befriended by a poet. In the second volume, the two companions fall into the clutches of the Ennis, a primitive people who initiate their prisoners into the tribe after a series of bizarre rites.

The Ennis are opposed by the Gort, a northern people who have an understanding with the evil Order of Zeno. There is as well a spy among the Ennis who reports the activities of Turly. The Blessing Papers contain the seeds of a prophecy of the rise of a new civilization, and their possession might provide the means to shape that civilization. Locked in Turly's brain is the secret of their location.

In the concluding volume of the trilogy, Turly has sworn never to make use of the Blessing Papers, nor to make their existence and location known to anyone else. But even though he has independently helped to bring together a coalition of tribes for mutual support and protection, there is continued trouble, his old enemies restlessly prowling outside the circle of his campfire. Ultimately he must face the responsibility he has inherited and deal personally with the papers and the implications of their use.

Although ostensibly science fiction, much of this trilogy is written in a style and with many of the plot devices of heroic fantasy. The Papers might well be the Holy Grail or some other sacred or magical object, and the powers of mundane evil take on an almost supernatural presence, untainted by any trace of humanity or kindness. That simplistic viewpoint dulls some of the impact of the trilogy. Barnwell possesses considerable talents as a writer, and his disappearance from the scene is puzzling and disappointing.

—Don D'Ammassa

---

**BARRETT, Neal, Jr.** American. Formerly worked in public relations; now a full-time writer. Address: c/o New American Library, 375 Hudson Street, New York, New York 10014, U.S.A.

SCIENCE-FICTION PUBLICATIONS

Novels (series: Aldair)

*Kelwin.* New York, Lancer, 1970.
*The Gates of Time.* New York, Ace, 1970.
*The Leaves of Time.* New York, Lancer, 1971.
*Highwood.* New York, Ace, 1972.
*Stress Pattern.* New York, DAW, 1974.
*Aldair in Albion.* New York, DAW, 1976.
*Aldair, Master of Ships.* New York, DAW, 1977.
*Aldair, Across the Misty Sea.* New York, DAW, 1980.
*Aldair: The Legion of Beasts.* New York, DAW, 1982.
*The Karma Corps.* New York, DAW, 1984.
*Through Darkest America.* New York, Congdon, 1986; London, New English Library, 1988.
*Dawn's Uncertain Light.* New York, New American Library, 1989.
*The Hereafter Gang.* Shingletown, California, Ziesing, 1991.

* * *

Neal Barrett, Jr., was for many years a welcome but infrequent contributor to professional science fiction magazines, and an occasional novelist, but it was not until the late 1970's that he attracted much serious attention. His earliest published novel, *Kelwin*, employs the familiar theme of a barbaric civilization rebuilding itself after the fall of our own society in a devastating war. Kelwin is a wandering adventurer whose destiny is to shape the unfolding of a possible new conflict. *Kelwin* is an unpretentious but highly entertaining adventure story.

*The Leaves of Time* is more ambitious. The setting is a parallel version of our own world, one where history has taken a rather different course. Barrett adds a second element to this standard plot device, a fugitive alien capable of changing forms, an infiltrator from another time line. The protagonists must discover a method of identifying and neutralizing the invader, without letting him return to his home timeline.

These two novels far outshine two other early novels, both light adventures of little lasting substance. *The Gates of Time* is a galaxy-spanning romp about mankind's fate in the face of alien conquest; *Highwood* is set in a world of giant forests. A pair of human observers notices a radical alteration in the behavior patterns of the indigent sentient species and become caught up in the rush to save their culture.

The appearance in 1974 of *Stress Pattern*, Barrett's fifth novel, was the equivalent of the emergence of a new writer. A space traveller becomes marooned on a most peculiar planet. The natives recognize his presence, but seem utterly indifferent to him, preoccupied with bizarre activities of their own. Travel is accomplished by means of organic railways; a variety of monstrous creatures populate the countryside. The entire biosphere of the planet is one intricate, integrated machine. Had this novel appeared under the byline of a more established writer, it would almost certainly have attracted more attention than it ultimately did. *Stress Pattern* is one of the most unusual novels ever to appear in the genre.

Barrett hit his stride with the Aldair series, four novels chronicling Aldair's adventures on a future Earth deserted by the human race. Many of the lower animal species were altered genetically so that a variety of intelligent species exist, each displaying the attributes of their ancestry. Aldair himself is a pig, and among his companions are wolves and bears. The opening volume, *Aldair in Albion*, introduces the background and main characters, then follows Aldair as he wanders across Europe searching for his own destiny and clues to the fate of legendary mankind.

The first two volumes read well independently. *Aldair, Master of Ships* continues the search, following the coastlines of the continents. The narrative is continued in *Aldair, Across the Misty Sea*, but the cliffhanger ending mars its effectiveness as a novel. Barrett clears up all the loose ends in the concluding volume, *Aldair: The Legion of Beasts*, by transporting Aldair and his friends to an alien planet where malformed genetic freaks enslave the pacifistic remnants of the human race. Much of the charm of the previous volumes is lost with the change of setting, but as a whole, this series is one of the most entertaining and innovative of its kind.

Barrett's next novel, *The Karma Corps*, is an interesting but not entirely successful work. A shipload of colonists survives on an uncharted world, where their theocratic social structure finds itself in perpetual conflict with an alien species that can teleport itself across small distances. A group of human teleports is revived from electronic storage and pressed into battle against the aliens, but inevitably control of the power they represent becomes a political issue.

After a gap of several years, Barrett published *Through Darkest America* and its sequel, *Dawn's Uncertain Light*. Once again, he takes a traditional theme and provides a new twist. Following a nuclear war, a new society forms in North America, the main foodstuff of which is a strain of mutated humanity lacking intelligence. A young man comes of age as he discovers horrible truths about his society: the mutant food supply is a hoax of the government's, which is lobotomizing its own citizens. Together, the two books portray a bleak future.

Barrett has turned out a small number of high quality short stories as well. One of his earliest, "The Stentorii Luggage" (in *Galaxy*, October 1960), is a classic tale of shape-changing creatures in an elaborate, interspecies hotel. "The Grandfather Pelt" (in *If*, November 1969) provides ironic justice to a criminal who steals a sacred relic. A desperate man must outreason a singleminded computer in "Survival Course" (in *Galaxy*, January 1974), and a visiting alien tries to puzzle out the inner secrets of humanity in "Greyspun's Gift" (in *Worlds of Tomorrow*, Winter 1970), which also features some of Barrett's best characterization. "The Flying Stutzman" (in *Fantasy and Science Fiction*, July 1978), in which a man is doomed to an eternity of air travel, is a very well-written and disturbing fantasy. "Ginny Sweethips' Flying Circus" is a zany, madcap bit of humor. Also of note is the recent "Under Old New York."

—Don D'Ammassa

---

**BARTON, Erle.** *See* **FANTHORPE, R. Lionel.**

---

**BARTON, Lee.** *See* **FANTHORPE, R. Lionel.**

---

**BASS, T.J.** Pseudonym for Thomas J. Bassler. American. Born in Clinton, Iowa, 7 July 1932. Educated at St. Ambrose College, Davenport, Iowa, B.A. 1955; University of Iowa, Iowa City, M.D. 1959. Married Gloria Napoli in 1960; three daughters and three sons. Deputy medical examiner, Los Angeles, 1961–64. Since 1964 in private practice as a pathologist. Since 1972 editor, *American Medical Joggers Newsletter*. Address: 27558 Sunnyridge Road, Palos Verdes Peninsula, California 90274, U.S.A.

SCIENCE-FICTION PUBLICATIONS

Novels

*Half Past Human*. New York, Ballantine, 1971.
*The Godwhale*. New York. Ballantine, 1974; London, Eyre Methuen, 1975.

* * *

T.J. Bass's novels, *Half Past Human* and *The Godwhale*, give a vivid picture of a horrifying future society, of a worldwide Earth Society ("the big ES") that controls every detail of life in the planet-sized hive that Earth has become. Three trillion people, degenerate "Nebishes," live in warrens beneath the surface, every inch of which is devoted to crops. These shrunken souls live short and regimented lives, are processed at their deaths for the proteins that sustain their fellows, and even have puberty postponed until the CO—the Class One computer—decides they are ready for sexual maturity.

Yet these novels are not cautionary tales of the sort of Harry Harrison's *Make Room! Make Room!*, although some have read them so: rather, their concerns are teleological, like C.S. Lewis's Perelandra Trilogy or Walter M. Miller's *A Canticle for Leibo-*

*witz.* Assuming a kind Providence and a personal God, these works ask, what is the end of man? While *Half Past Human* and *The Godwhale* do not directly address the question, they do show a Providence that cares about the fall of a sparrow—or a Nebish. If the hand of God has not been noticed in Bass's works, it is because the author shows God using unfamiliar instruments. In the Perelandra trilogy or in *A Canticle for Leibowitz* God works through human beings; here, His ambassadors are machines so intelligent that they have personalities. Not that God makes robots and sends them hurtling toward Earth: the machines in Bass's novels are the artifacts of earlier stages of human civilization, providentially appearing when mankind has most need of them.

In *Half Past Human* we see the plight of those few remaining real humans who live outside, apart from ES; like animals, they are hunted for sport. But in their vigor and resilience lies more hope for the future than in the Nebishes, whose machines are crumbling around them. However, even the Nebishes are not negligible or less than human: some among them can survive when circumstances remove them from the womb of their society. The novel is the story of a new beginning on a new planet for the humans living outside and for the Nebishes adaptable enough to accept it.

Both novels show an impressive command of biological knowledge, and indeed sometimes the flow of jargon obscures rather than communicates. But the point may be that most people in the society are treated (and regard themselves) just as mechanically as the many robots that work for them. Still, knowledge is regarded as good, and machines are good when they serve rather than control. This point is strongly argued in *The Godwhale,* named for a huge plankton harvester. Like the huge automated spaceship that is the *deus ex machina* of *Half Past Human,* the Godwhale is an artifact of a freer, more expansive past. Although these machines are so powerful that they are regarded as "cyberdeities," they are purposeless without free humans to direct them. In *The Godwhale* that direction comes partly from the chosen few, true humans who have adapted to life in the sea, and partly from a superman bred by Nebishes to command the harvester. "Miracles" occur at opportune times in both novels: the rescue of the outsiders in *Half Past Human,* and the regeneration of marine life in *The Godwhale.* Whereas the first shows the hope of a new society among the stars, the second gives promises of a regeneration of life on Earth.

Together, *Half Past Human* and *The Godwhale* are rewarding novels, rich both in characterization and in scientific detail, yet concerned with still larger matters. That *The Godwhale* offers a new proof of the existence of God shows just how large that concern is.

—Walter E. Meyers

---

**BATCHELOR, John Calvin.** American. Born in Bryn Mawr, Pennsylvania, 29 April 1948. Educated at Princeton University, New Jersey, A.B. 1970; University of Edinburgh Divinity School, 1973–74; Union Theological Seminary, New York, M.Div. 1976. Editor and book reviewer, *SoHo Weekly News,* New York, 1975–77; book reviewer, *Village Voice,* New York, 1977–80. Agent: George Borchardt, 136 East 57th Street, New York, New York 10022. Address: c/o Linden Press, Prentice Hall Building, 190 Sylvan Avenue, Englewood Cliffs, New Jersey 07632, U.S.A.

SCIENCE-FICTION PUBLICATIONS

Novels

*The Further Adventures of Halley's Comet.* New York, Congdon and Lattès, 1981; London, Panther, 1984.
*The Birth of the People's Republic of Antarctica.* New York, Doubleday, 1983; London, Panther, 1984.

OTHER PUBLICATIONS

Novels

*American Falls.* New York, Norton, 1985; London, Paladin, 1987.
*Gordon Liddy Is My Muse, by Tommy "Tip" Paine.* New York, Linden Press, 1990.
*Walking the Cat, by Tommy "Tip" Paine: Gordon Liddy Is My Muse II.* New York, Linden Press, 1991.

Other

*Thunder in the Dust: Classic Images of Western Movies,* photographs by John R. Hamilton. New York, Stewart Tabori and Chang, 1987; as *Thunder in the Dust: Great Shots from the Western Movies,* London, Aurum Press, 1987.

*

John Calvin Batchelor comments (1986):
I first read science fiction when I was 11 years old, and the first adult novel I ever read was *Nineteen Eighty-Four,* which I can remember thinking was much too sad. I have learned to say that I write anti-utopian fiction. That is too technical a term, however, and lacks the fun of saying sci-fi.

* * *

Though often ignored by science-fiction readers and the body of organized "fandom," John Calvin Batchelor's *The Further Adventures of Halley's Comet* and *The Birth of the People's Republic of Antarctica* received some extravagant praise from both general and SF reviewers. Like Thomas Pynchon's gigantic and encyclopedic *Gravity's Rainbow, Halley's Comet* explores and satirizes the history of ideas in the West through a modern gothic tale told in a baroque and seemingly perverse style, against the grain of the accepted gothic *frisson* of shock and menace. The plot involves the abduction of a bunch of quixotic idealists by a family of fabulously powerful and capitalistic modern-day robber barons; the former are imprisoned in Craven Castle, while the latter pursue a Machiavellian plan to extend their empire of property into space by means of secret technology and legalistic chicanery. This is all placed in historical perspective by the recurring visits of a trio of seemingly supernatural luminaries who are associated with Halley's Comet and seem to be the ever-returning Magi. The literary polarities of this book—zany comedy and Juvenalian invective—are seldom discoverable in the convention-ridden and stylistically lacklustre body of genre SF; however, the watered down mix of pyrotechnics should appeal to those who find Pynchon attractive but too inaccessible.

*The Birth of the People's Republic of Antarctica* begins similarly in a Pynchonesque mode, depicting a crew of down-and-out American draft dodgers in Sweden, together with an assortment of other eccentric, grandiose, and slightly comic characters. The tale gradually shapes itself into a new mode that can be described as post-heroic saga: larger-than-life tragic figures struggle with the hostile elements of storm wave, fire, and ice in a near-future world wherein civilization is collapsing and human nobility seems able to provide little hope of redemption amid ubiquitous evil and hardship. The protagonist-narrator's name, "Grim Fiddle," is a kind of rebus for the style and content of the book, uniting as it does concepts of severity and frivolity, though all transitions taking place through *People's Republic of Antarctica* are towards the increasingly severe: the book's "fiddle" concept is transformed eventually to one of the futility of struggle for survival or betterment. The entire book is a mythic life-story from the hero's mysterious conception and Christmas-time birth to his downfall, exile, and impending mysterious doom, while the key scenarios resemble elemental and societal designs for hell: seas of fire and ice; societies falling into demagoguery and terror; a dark sea journey in which Grim Fiddle and his comrades drift to the barren Falklands and the northern fingers of the Antarctic, where human life is mean, violent, and easily corrupted.

Bruce Gillespie has remarked that *People's Republic of Antarctica* is spoiled by a "fluffed" ending in which the author "seems to lose control of the narrative." The criticism is well made, as the narrative fragments into a set of meditative pieces about the narrator's uncompleted story. More importantly still, the ending attempts to draw grand ethical conclusions that are insufficiently tied to the body of the tale (which itself is marred by passages of loaded and simplistic ethical-philosophical analysis). This fault also betrays *Halley's Comet;* in each case, a stylistic tour de force is ineptly tied to a sentimental and superficial philosophy in which naturalism, positivism, capitalism, and utilitarianism are the abstract bad guys. Batchelor's vision does not have the irony, ambivalence, and troubled complexity of Pynchon's. Though the books are flawed and ultimately disappointing, their sights are set mightily high and they contain some writing that falls only just short of magnificence.

—Russell Blackford

---

**BATES, Harry** (Hiram Gilmore Bates III). Also wrote as Anthony Gilmore; A.R. Holmes; Quien Sabe; S.F. Whozis; H.G. Winter. American. Born in Pittsburgh, Pennsylvania, 9 October 1900. Educated at Allegheny College, Meadville, Pennsylvania, 1917–18; University of Pennsylvania, Philadelphia, 1919–20. Clockmaker, 1914–17, 1920–22; reporter, Philadelphia *Enquirer*, 1923; assistant cameraman, Whitman-Bennett Studios, 1924; editor for Clayton magazines, including *Astounding Stories*, 1930–33, and *Strange Tales*, 1931–32; editor, *Technocracy*, 1935–37, and for the WPA art and writers projects; actor and machinist; story analyst, Columbia Pictures, 1958–59, and David O. Selznick, 1960. Recipient: Midamericon World Science-Fiction Convention award, 1976. *Died.*

SCIENCE-FICTION PUBLICATIONS

Short Stories

*Space Hawk: The Greatest of Interplanetary Adventures* (as Anthony Gilmore), with D.W. Hall. New York, Greenberg, 1952.

Uncollected Short Stories

"The City of Eric" (as Quien Sabe), in *Amazing Stories Quarterly* (New York), Spring 1929.
"The Slave Ship from Space" (as A.R. Holmes), in *Astounding* (New York), July 1931.
"A Matter of Size," in *Astounding* (New York), April 1934.
"The Experiment of Dr. Sarconi," in *Thrilling Wonder Stories* (New York), July 1940.
"A Matter of Speed," in *Astounding* (New York), June 1941.
"Mystery of the Blue God," in *Amazing* (New York), January 1942.
"Death of a Sensitive," in *Science Fiction Plus* (Philadelphia), May 1953.
"The Triggered Dimension," in *Science Fiction Plus* (Philadelphia), December 1953.
"Farewell to the Master," in *The Great SF Stories* (1940), edited by Isaac Asimov and Martin H. Greenberg. New York, DAW, 1979.
"A Scientist Rises," with D.W. Hall, in *Gosh! Wow! (Sense of Wonder) Science Fiction*, edited by Forrest J. Ackerman. New York, Bantam, 1982.
"Alas, All Thinking," in *The Arbor House Treasury of Science Fiction Masterpieces*, edited by Robert Silverberg and Martin H. Greenberg. New York, Arbor House, 1983.

Uncollected Short Stories as H.G. Winter, with D.W. Hall

"The Hands of Aten," in *Astounding* (New York), July 1931.
"The Midget from the Island," in *Astounding* (New York), August 1931.
"Seed of the Arctic Ice," in *Astounding* (New York), February 1932.
"Under Arctic Ice," in *Astounding* (New York), January 1933.

*

Harry Bates commented (1981):

*Astounding Stories* (now *Analog*) was born to the publisher William Clayton and one of his editors—me—in a now unimaginable world populated by a single science-fiction magazine, Hugo Gernsback's *Amazing Stories*, which published amateurishly written "gadget" stories. The *Amazing* writers got one-tenth of a cent a word after publication; the writers for the Clayton empire were professionals, getting the very-high-for-those-days minimum of two cents on acceptance. I agreed with Clayton that *Astounding* had to have competent professional writing with strong plots and physical action; but its stories had also, of course, to contain tinges of science and binges of excitements and moreover be astounding—and where was any body of writers to cook to this recipe?

I had to create one. Because they had already sold to me I called on the writers in adventure magazines of which I already was editor, coaxing them to attempt this very different new field. Almost to a man they knew no science, and to use their stories at all I had (when possible) to correct and amplify what they turned in. I gave out story ideas right and left and did enormous amounts of hurried rewriting. Eventually almost all of these writers quit trying, for they had to eat, and there was no second market for the stories I had to reject.

The public in those days had never heard the term science fiction and had to be educated to it. *Amazing* often used the ugly term *scientification*, which I had as quickly as possible to suppress from the genre. Physical action remained an *Astounding* requisite. No one then dreamed what today's science fiction of way-way-out imaginings—fantasy—would be; if one of today's stories had been submitted to me then I'd probably have had to turn it down so as not to estrange the readers we aimed for and were accumulating. In time *Astounding*, in spite of its minimum of two cents a word, all but got out of the red, so that it was instantly profitable when Street & Smith with its much lower word rate took it over.

The stories I wrote in collaboration with my assistant D.W. Hall during those infant years were the product of sheer necessity, to avoid filling out the magazine with worse. The first Hawk Carse story was written as an example to my writers of the wanted element of character, and it was its extreme success that demanded the writing of the several that followed. All the stories published later under my own name were written hastily for a quick buck after my separation from *Astounding*, my prime interests lying elsewhere. I remember that in each case I hesitated at using my own name rather than a pseudonym; but its added value all but guaranteed the quick sale, however sloppy the writing. Who might have guessed that one day there would come into being such a phenomenon as museums of science-fiction—anthologies!—necropolises!—and that such imperfect stories as mine would be resurrected to populate them? There, now, they live again, after a fashion—zombies, all their sores still upon them.

The worst occurred with my "Not Understanding," which Gernsback characteristically renamed "The Triggered Dimension." When his *Science Fiction Plus* folded, his editor, wanting to squeeze into the last issue this last long story of mine, attempted the impossible, cutting out almost completely its very necessary central scene—the scene which gave reason for story and my title—and shortening the last sentence of paragraph after paragraph so as to save single lines. So one day I rewrote the story with the care I wish heartily I'd given it in the first place and with the cut-out parts restored—and then while I was at it I rewrote half of the others that had appeared under my own name. One, "A Matter of Speed," became "Oh Outrage!," a longish novel of very different mood which bad health has so far not let me quite finish.

Friends who since have read my "Alas, All Thinking" have asked me how I ever could have projected *Homo terminal* with mental processes so degenerated. The reason lies not quite in the realm of pure fantasy. Beginning when quite young (and having what I thought was a good body) I remained aware always that *Homo* of my day thoroughly forgets he is an animal with the body of an animal and early loses all inborn capacity to enjoy the *moving* of his body, coming almost always to overvalue the non-moving brain. I had merely to extrapolate. It happens that upon rereading the story I found I'd given no solid examples of his degenerated thinkings, so when I rewrote it I gave many, too many, Book-an-hour Devourers will say. But perhaps there exists somewhere a reader or two who, like me in the writing, will find pleasure in my assortment of bad thinkings. It is for *these*—educated *adults*—that I put a few strictly unnecessary extra ones in. Devourers, I do not rewrite stories for *you.*

* * *

Building on his experience as an editor of action-adventure pulps for William Clayton, Harry Bates began his career in science fiction as founding editor of the magazine whose name—*Astounding*—would become under later leadership synonymous with hard science fiction. But Bates said that his first writers of stories for *Astounding* in 1930 were "almost wholly ignorant of science and technology." He named the magazine. He enlisted and cajoled professional pulp writers to add a science veneer to action and adventure narratives. He rewrote and wrote pseudonymously much of the material himself, and he paid professional rates. The result was a wider readership and a wider professional base for the genre that had begun hardly as literature with the Gernsback "scientifiction." Under the name Anthony Gilmore, Bates and his fellow editor D.M. Hall began the highly popular Hawk Carse series. The literary qualities of fast-paced action tale in this series helped establish the space-opera characteristics in science fiction that have to this day balanced the hard descriptions of scientific speculation and technology in order to make the genre exciting and popular as well as speculative and futuristic. The stories in the Hawk Carse series were collected as *Space Hawk.*

Bates edited the first 34 issues of *Astounding* as well as a few issues of a rival for *Weird Tales* entitled *Strange Tales*, but he continued to publish important science-fiction stories under his own name after his editing work had ended. Apparently the added speculative and scientific thoughts that he had worked up in the Clayton offices in order to capture more of the pulp market took a permanent hold on his imagination, and so Bates himself is representative of the professional pulp writers with little original scientific training who helped to create the genre. "Alas, All Thinking" expresses a classic theme of early science fiction with a tone and writing style that also embody the best and the worst characteristics of the genre. The theme is ultimately from the 18th-century Enlightenment, and one wonders what has been the source of transmission from the *philosophes* to the New York pulp writers. But somehow the theme is intact: a fear of too much rationality and the ironic sense of progress leading to actual degeneration in humanness. The theme is mingled with the Golden Age/Iron Age myths in which life appears richer, more fertile, more heroic in the past; and the time-travel gimmick of super science facilitates the use of the present even as an heroic past so that satire fuses in the story with the myth of lost innocence. Bates's writing does not understate the theme, and when he tries to heighten emotion at the end the tonal effect is stiff. The story, like many others of this decade, is at the same time poignant, rich, and primitive.

Bates's single most well-known story (filmed in 1951 as *The Day the Earth Stood Still*) also first appeared in *Astounding*—this time the Campbell magazine of 1940. "Farewell to the Master" is a story rich with influence on the genre and less over-written than much of Bates's other work. The tapestry of the story weaves elements ranging backward in indebtedness to Mary Shelley's *Frankenstein* and forward in apparent influence to Walter Tevis's *Mockingbird* (1980). It is fascinating to think of the old pro pulp editor reaching backward to the romantics and influencing as academic a writer as Tevis several decades later. Bates tells the story of a technologically made creature who transcends his creators in competence so that he becomes the master, and yet there is an enigmatic sadness inherent in this future hero who is somehow more incomplete than his more primitive makers. The accomplishment of Bates illustrates how the genre which began in the practicalities of the pulp markets has progressed through a fine web of influence and allusion.

—Donald M. Hassler

---

**BAXTER, John.** Also writes as Martin Loran. Australian. Born in Sydney, New South Wales, 14 December 1939. Educated at Waverly College, Sydney, 1944–54. Married 1) Merie Elizabeth Brooker in 1962 (divorced 1967); 2) Joyce Allison Agee in 1978. Staff controller, New South Wales State Government, Sydney, 1957–67; publicity director, Australian Commonwealth Film Unit, Sydney, 1967–70; presenter, Understanding Films series, 1969; film critic, *Kaleidoscope* programme, BBC Radio, London, 1972–80; lecturer, United States Embassy, London, 1973–74, and for United States Government in Europe, 1974–75, and Hollins College, Virginia, 1975–76, and London Campus, 1976–78; guest lecturer, Australian Film and TV School, 1982; assessor, Australian Film Commission, 1983. Since 1984, producer, Australian Broadcasting Corporation. Recipient: Australian Film award, 1969; Kranz Film Festival award, 1970; Benson and Hedges prize for TV documentary, 1970; Ditmar award, 1971; Australian Council Literature Board Fellowship, 1984. Address: c/o Curtis Brown Ltd, 162-168 Regent Street, London W1A 1AA, England.

## Science-Fiction Publications

### Novels

*The Off-Worlders.* New York, Ace, 1966; as *The God Killers*, Sydney, Horwitz, 1968.
*The Hermes Fall.* London, Panther, and New York, Simon and Schuster, 1978.

### Uncollected Short Stories

"Vendetta's End," in *Science Fiction Adventures* (London), December 1962.
"Eviction," in *New Worlds* (London), March 1963.
"Interlude," in *New Worlds* (London), November 1963.
"Toys," in *New Worlds* (London), January 1964.
"The New Country," in *Science Fantasy* (Bournemouth), April 1964.
"Testament," in *New Writings in SF 3*, edited by John Carnell. London, Dobson, 1965; New York, Bantam, 1967.
"Takeover Bid," in *New Writings in SF 5*, edited by John Carnell. London, Dobson, 1965; New York, Bantam, 1970.
"The Hands," in *New Writings in SF 6*, edited by John Carnell. London. Dobson. 1965; New York. Bantam, 1971.
"The Traps of Time," in *The Best of New Worlds*, edited by Michael Moorcock. London, Compact, 1965.
"More Than a Man," in *New Worlds* (London), February 1965.
"Tryst," in *New Writings in SF 8*, edited by John Carnell. London, Dobson, 1966; New York, Bantam, 1971.
"Skirmish," in *New Worlds* (London), April 1966.
"Apple," in *New Writings in SF 10*, edited by John Carnell. London, Dobson, 1967.
"The Case of the Perjured Planet" (as Martin Loran, with Ron Smith), in *Analog* (New York), November 1967.
"An Ounce of Dissension" (as Martin Loran, with Ron Smith) and "The Beach," in *The Pacific Book of Australian Science Fiction*, edited by John Baxter, Sydney, Angus and Robertson, 1968; London, Angus and Robertson, 1969.
"Down from Demolition," in *Urban Fantasy*, edited by King and Black. N.p., 1985.

## Other Publications

### Novels

*Adam's Woman* (novelization of screenplay). Sydney, Horwitz, 1970.
*The Bidders.* Philadelphia, Lippincott, 1979; as *Bidding*, London, Granada, 1980.
*The Kid.* New York, Viking Press, 1981.
*The Black Yacht.* New York, Jove, and London, New English Library, 1982.

### Plays

Screenplays (documentaries): *Beyond the Pack Ice*, 1968; *Golf in Australia*, 1969; *After Proust*, 1969; *Australian Diary* series, 1969–70; *Top End*, 1970; *The Amazing Years of Cinema* (1 episode), 1976.

Television Documentaries: *Understanding Film* series, 1969; *No Roses for Michael*, 1970; *The Cutting Room* series, n.d.; *Filmstruck* series, n.d.; *First Take* series, 1988.

### Other

*Hollywood in the Thirties.* New York, A.S. Barnes, and London, Zwemmer, 1968.
*Science Fiction in the Cinema.* New York, A.S. Barnes, and London, Zwemmer, 1970.
*The Australian Cinema.* Sydney and London, Angus and Robertson, 1970.
*The Gangster Film.* New York, A.S. Barnes, and London, Zwemmer, 1970.
*The Cinema of Josef von Sternberg.* New York, A.S. Barnes, and London, Zwemmer, 1971.
*The Cinema of John Ford.* New York, A.S. Barnes, and London, Zwemmer, 1971.
*Hollywood in the Sixties.* New York, A.S. Barnes, and London, Tantivy Press, 1972.
*Sixty Years of Hollywood.* South Brunswick, New Jersey, A.S. Barnes, and London, Tantivy Press, 1973.
*An Appalling Talent: Ken Russell.* London, Joseph, 1973.
*Stunt: The Story of the Great Movie Stunt Men.* London, Macdonald, 1973; New York, Doubleday, 1974.
*King Vidor.* New York, Monarch Press, 1976.
*The Hollywood Exiles.* New York, Taplinger, and London, Macdonald and Jane's, 1976.
*The Fire Came By: The Riddle of the Great Siberian Explosion*, with Thomas Atkins. New York, Doubleday, and London, Macdonald and Jane's, 1976.
*The Video Handbook: Getting the Best from Your VCR*, with Brian Norris. London, Fontana, 1982.
*Who Burned Australia? The Ash Wednesday Fires.* London, New English Library, 1984.
*Filmstruck: Australia at the Movies.* Sydney, Nelson, 1988.

Editor, *The Pacific Book of Australian Science Fiction.* Sydney, Angus and Robertson, 1968; as *The Pacific Book of Science Fiction*, London, Angus and Robertson, 1969.
Editor, *The Second Pacific Book of Australian Science Fiction.* Sydney, Angus and Robertson, 1971; as *The Second Pacific Book of Science Fiction*, London, Angus and Robertson, 1971.

*

John Baxter comments:

Ted Carnell discovered and encouraged many young writers like myself in the 1960's. Almost alone among them, I moved away from SF as I made a professional career, a defection Ted tried hard, though vainly, to approve. While writing mostly mainstream fiction and cinema history, as well as becoming increasingly involved in radio and TV production, I'm drawn back to SF frequently, though more often as critic and scenarist than a writer of prose. SF, like Australia, has become a place I revisit, but where I no longer feel at home since, sadly, both the cinema and Australia are almost as inimical to good SF writing as they were when I first read *Astounding* and saw *The Incredible Shrinking Man* four decades ago.

* * *

As editor of the first two major anthologies of Australian SF writing, John Baxter exerted a twofold influence upon Australian SF renaissance of the 1970's. Rejecting the concept that science fiction must be prophetic, Baxter emphasized "insight rather than intelligent guessing," arguing that "a story which tells us that a rose is a rose and explains why is far more worthwhile than one which states that E equals MC squared and leaves it at that." Baxter also esteemed the literary qualities of science fiction, publishing material that was innovative in style and structure, yet neither ignoring nor denigrating stories written in a more traditional narrative style. In short, he proclaimed an Australian SF that was literate, thoughtful, and original.

Baxter's own short stories reflect these criteria. They are original and ambitious, reflecting influences from both traditional and new-wave SF. One of his best-known stories, "Apple," is a traditional man-meets-monster story—except that the encounter takes place in a surreal setting, and the story evolves from imagery and setting rather than action. A gigantic apple lies cradled in a valley, the juices dripping from its side as men tunnel into its core. The central character is a professional Moth Killer who battles with the grubs that lurk in the apple's core. It is suggested that the apple-world may be the result of atomic warfare, but for Baxter, the explanation is incidental; his story conveys its own inner logic, and that is enough. The same is true of the more experimental story, "The Beach." Described as "a first sketch of what an *Australian* SF story might be like," it employs distinctively Australian symbols, and abandons conventional narrative structure in order to emphasize mood and imagery. The style and symbolism are evident in the closing lines: "Without fear, he swam towards the sea mountains, the peaks of which even now he could see gilded beyond the green. There, he knew, he would find his grail, the sunken, brooding sun."

Baxter's two SF novels are more pedestrian. *The Off-Worlders* is set on the planet Merryland in the year 2833 and deals with a rustic community which is suspicious of technology and has rejected God, turning instead to Satan. *The Hermes Fall* is based on *The Fire Came By*, Baxter's non-fiction work on the famous Siberian "meteorite" of 1908 (written with Thomas Atkins). Despite its well-researched background, *The Hermes Fall* is merely a conventional disaster novel, using science-fiction effects (in this case, an asteroid on collision course with the Earth).

Always interested in cinema, Baxter has been devoting his energies to this field, and seems to have abandoned SF for the writing of novels in the best-seller mould, such as *The Bidders* and *The Black Yacht*. His short story "Down from Demolition," in the 1985 Australian anthology *Urban Fantasies*, was a welcome—if brief—return to the field.

—Van Ikin

---

**BAYLEY, Barrington John.** British. Born in Birmingham, Warwickshire, 9 April 1937. Educated at Adams Grammar School in Shropshire, 1948–53. Served in the Royal Air Force, 1955–57. Married Joan Lucy Clarke in 1969; one son and one daughter. Reporter, Wellington *Journal*, early 1950's; civil servant, Ministry of War, Shropshire, 1954–55; in Australian Public Service, London, 1957–58; has also worked as a clerk, typist, and coal miner. Recipient: Japanese Seiun award, 1976, 1983. Agent: Uwe Luserke, Box 46, D-7259 Friolzheim, Germany; or, Michael Congdon, c/o Don Congdon Associates, 156 Fifth Avenue, Suite 625, New York, New York 10010, U.S.A. Address: 48 Turreff Avenue, Donnington, Telford, Shropshire TF2 8HE, England.

Science-Fiction Publications

Novels

*The Star Virus.* New York, Ace. 1970.
*Annihilation Factor.* New York, Ace, 1972; London, Allison and Busby, 1979.
*Empire of Two Worlds.* New York, Ace 1972; London, Hale, 1974.
*Collision Course.* New York, DAW, 1973; as *Collision with Chronos*, London, Allison and Busby, 1977.
*The Fall of Chronopolis.* New York, DAW, 1974; London, Allison and Busby, 1979.
*Soul of the Robot.* New York, Doubleday, 1974; London, Allison and Busby, 1976.
*The Garments of Caean.* New York, Doubleday, 1976; London, Fontana, 1978.
*The Grand Wheel.* New York, DAW, 1977; London, Fontana, 1979.
*Star Winds.* New York, DAW, 1978.
*The Pillars of Eternity.* New York, DAW, 1982.
*The Zen Gun.* New York, DAW, 1983; London, Methuen, 1984.
*The Rod of Light.* London, Allison and Busby, 1984; New York, Arbor House, 1987.
*The Forest of Peldain.* New York, DAW, 1985.

Short Stories

*The Knights of the Limits.* London, Allison and Busby, 1978.
*The Seed of Evil.* London, Allison and Busby, 1979.

*

Bibliography: *Barrington J. Bayley: A Bibliography* by Mike Ashley, Manchester, Beccon, 1981.

Barrington John Bayley comments:

I have no personal philosophy as regards my work; I write according to my ability and interest. I regard myself as a genre SF writer—that is, as a traditionalist.

* * *

Barrington John Bayley is one of the few authors to have bridged the philosophical gap between proponents of traditional space opera and the more demanding literary tastes of recent editors and readers. He has succeeded at this by using the traditional devices of the genre, wedding them to a more sophisticated writing style and an inventive imagination. Much of his fiction is pervaded by a wry humor that is frequently unsettling.

Many of Bayley's plots are unabashedly space operas. A mysterious anomaly in space known as The Patch is consuming entire worlds as an interstellar empire erupts into civil war in *Annihilation Factor.* This galaxy-spanning adventure is a noticeable advance over his earlier *The Star Virus*, and subsequent novels show a steady enhancement of his abilities. *Collision Course* postulates that there are two separate "nows" and that the two waves of reality are moving in opposite directions along the time waves. The plot involves the imminent passing of the two realities through one another, and the effects on both civilizations during the transition. Bayley experiments with the nature of time again in *The Fall of Chronopolis.* A theocratic society that possesses time travel refuses to recognize the possibility that their attempts to police the timeways may change reality and cancel out their own existence.

Bayley's dark humor becomes evident with *The Garments of Caean.* A bankrupt sailor pilfers a suit of clothes from a band of pirates, but when he wear them, his personality changes—clothes do indeed make the man. The pirates recapture the suit, which is revealed to be a sentient lifeform from a planet intent upon interstellar empire. But the clothing has a mind of its own, and is determined to reclaim its first owner.

Satire is the order of the day in *Soul of the Robot* and *The Rod of Light.* In the former, a robot possessed of extraordinary powers makes its way through a variety of decadent human societies trying to solve the mysteries of existence. In the latter, evolving robots are in rebellion against their human masters, even though only one of their number has true consciousness.

Humans and aliens indulge in elaborate gambling schemes that determine the future of the human race in *The Grand Wheel,* and a ship sets off to explore the universe in *Star Winds. The Pillars of Eternity* and *The Zen Gun* are also ostensibly space operas, but each is inventive and so offbeat in plotting and setting that they stand out among many competing adventure stories. *The Forest of Peldain* depicts a lost race transported to another planet with unusual and highly entertaining results.

Although not a prolific short story writer, Bayley has made an impression there as well. His satiric humor is at its best in "Integrity," in which a libertarian reaches the logical consequence of his beliefs and sets free each individual cell of his body. Aliens have entered human nobility in "All the King's Men" and a single city survives the collapse of the universe in "Exit from City 5."

Galaxies themselves are entities in "Cosmic Combatants" and a child with no nationality is adopted by an airline in "The Man in Transit." Alien manipulation of human bodies is a common theme, repeated in such stories as "Sporting with Chid" and "Maladjustment." For the most part, Bayley's short fiction is darkly ironic, occasionally using experimental writing styles to emphasize strange viewpoints. Although not the most popular writer of space adventure, Bayley has established himself as one of the most innovative of that theme.

—Don D'Ammassa

---

**BEAR, Greg(ory Dale).** American. Born in San Diego, California, 20 August 1951. Educated at San Diego State University, 1968–73, A.B. in English 1973. Married 1) Christina M. Nielsen in 1975 (divorced 1981); 2) Astrid Anderson in 1983, one daughter and one son. Part-time Lecturer, San Diego Aerospace Museum, 1969–72; technical writer and planetarium operator, Reuben H. Fleet Space Theater, San Diego, 1973; bookstore clerk, 1974– 75. Since 1975 freelance writer and illustrator: reviewer, San Diego *Union,* 1979–82; co-editor, Science Fiction Writers of America *Forum;* co-founder, Association of Science Fiction Artists. Recipient: Nebula award (twice), 1984, for short story, 1986; Hugo award, 1984, 1987; Prix Apollo, 1986. Agent: Richard Curtis Associates, 171 East 74th Street, Suite 2, New York, New York 10021. Address: 506 Lakeview Road, Alderwood Manor, Washington 98037, U.S.A.

SCIENCE-FICTION PUBLICATIONS

Novels

*Hegira.* New York, Dell, 1979; London, Gollancz, 1987.
*Psychlone.* New York, Ace, 1979; London, Gollancz, 1989.
*Beyond Heaven's River.* New York, Dell, 1980; Wallington, Surrey, Severn House, 1989.
*Strength of Stones.* New York, Ace, 1981; London, Gollancz, 1988.
*Corona.* New York, Pocket Books, 1984; Bath, Firecrest, 1985.
*The Infinity Concerto.* New York, Berkley, 1984; London, Century, 1988.
*Blood Music.* New York, Arbor House, 1985; London, Gollancz, 1986.
*Eon.* New York, Bluejay, 1985; London, Gollancz, 1986.
*The Serpent Mage.* New York, Berkley, 1986; London, Century, 1988.
*The Forge of God.* New York, Tor, and London, Gollancz, 1987.
*Eternity.* New York, Warner, 1988; London, Gollancz, 1989.
*Sleepside Story.* New Castle, Virginia, Cheap Street, 1988.
*Early Harvest.* Cambridge, Massachusetts, NESFA Press, 1988.
*Hardfought,* with *Cascade Point* by Timothy Zahn. New York, Tor, 1988.
*Tangents.* New York, Warner, and London, Gollancz, 1989.
*Queen of Angels.* New York, Warner, and London, Gollancz, 1990.
*Heads.* London, Century, 1990; New York, St. Martin's Press, 1991.

Short Stories

*The Wind from a Burning Woman.* Sauk City, Wisconsin, Arkham House, 1983.

* * *

When David Samuelson said in 1981 "Bear's future bears watching," he did not know how true his words would ring. Ten years later, Greg Bear has become one of science fiction's foremost writers. Following in the footsteps of his mentor, Elizabeth ("Lee Chaytor") Chater (who wrote 26 books in 13 years), Bear is writing at a pace that would make many writers dizzy (perhaps with envy), managing to turn out a book a year for ten years, with many more on the way, no doubt.

Bear's diverse background as a journalist, teacher, illustrator, and retail salesman has exposed him to a wide spectrum of ideas and themes, and this range is evident in his writing. Moving freely between fantasy and myth to hard-science oriented fiction, Bear's work is always well-written, concise, and interesting.

Several themes are prominent in his writing: the two most important are hard science and transformation. *Blood Music,* which is considered by many to be his finest work, is his prime example of transformation. Following a similar vein as Arthur C. Clarke's *Childhood End, Blood Music* examines the human race undergoing transformation, becoming something "better" than it was before. This process catapaults them from mental infants in the universe to a sort of godlike state with their new abilities. In Clarke's *Childhood's End,* when the Overlord Karellen tells the last man, Jan Rodericks, "no intelligent species resists the inevitable," he fails to take into account the fact that the human race has more than just raw intelligence and logic: we believe in our souls, our inner selves. Bear reveals the human soul by exposing the psychological traumas of the characters as they resist the move from interpersonal relationships to single-group consciousness; from physical bodies to pure mental energy; independent thinking to communal mindsharing; recorded history to "racial memory." *Strength of Stones* also deals with some physical transformation, and *Corona* shows the transformation of a character from adolescence to adulthood. Bear has said that "science fiction is a literature which deals with the transformation of characters, if not physically, then at least mentally or psychologically."

Hard science is also evident in most of Bear's work. *Eon, The Forge of God, Hegira, Strength of Stones*, and *Eternity* all deal with space, heavenly bodies, geological change, mathematics, physics, chemistry, biology, biomechanics, and cybernetics. All of the science is well-researched, and is possible or probable according to current technology or extrapolation of near-future technology.

Each of Bear's characters must undergo changes and be able to deal with them. "A Martian Ricorso" has humans facing the problem of dangerous alien life forms; "Perihesperon" shows two survivors learning to be more open with each other; "The Venging" depicts a human starship crew forced to confront the question, "What if I were marooned with these people?" as they are trapped in a black hole by a member of the Aighor race seeking vengeance for the desecration of sacred burial grounds; "Hardfought" and "Scattershot" chronicle the interactions between humans and aliens. *Beyond Heaven's River* combines fantasy and science fiction and the "change" theme. A hapless Japanese soldier is transported to another world by aliens, where he becomes the ruler, only to be returned to earth four centuries later as a Rip van Winkle character.

Bear's development as a writer has shown him moving from straightforward questing plots to intricate weavings of characterization and plot development; from fantasy to hard science fiction; from arts and humanities to the physical sciences.

—Daryl F. Mallett

---

**BEAUMONT, Charles.** Pseudonym for Charles Nutt; also wrote as Keith Grantland. American. Born in Chicago, Illinois, 2 January 1929. Served in the United States Army for one year. Married Helen Louise Brown in 1949; one son and two daughters. Radio writer, actor, illustrator, and animator. Recipient: Jules Verne award, 1954; *Playboy* award, for non-fiction, 1961. *Died 21 February 1967.*

SCIENCE-FICTION PUBLICATIONS

Short Stories

*The Hunger and Other Stories.* New York, Putnam, 1957; as *Shadow Play*, London, Panther, 1964.
*Yonder.* New York, Bantam, 1958.
*Night Ride and Other Journeys.* New York, Bantam, 1960.
*The Magic Man and Other Science-Fantasy Stories.* New York, Fawcett, 1965; London, Fawcett, 1966.
*The Edge.* London, Panther, 1966.
*Best of Beaumont.* New York, Bantam, 1982.
*Charles Beaumont: Selected Stories*, edited by Roger Anker. New York, Dark Harvest, 1988.

OTHER PUBLICATIONS

Novels

*Run from the Hunter* as (Keith Grantland, with John E. Tomerlin). New York, Fawcett, 1957; London, Boardman, 1959.
*The Intruder.* New York, Putnam, 1959.

Plays

Screenplays: *Queen of Outer Space*, with Ben Hecht, 1958: *The Intruder (The Stranger)*, 1961; *Burn, Witch, Burn (Night of the Eagle)*, with Richard Matheson and George Baxt, 1962; *The Wonderful World of the Brothers Grimm*, with David P. Harmon and William Roberts, 1962; *The Premature Burial*, with Ray Russell, 1962; *The Haunted Palace*, 1963; *7 Faces of Dr. Lao*, 1964; *The Masque of the Red Death*, with R. Wright Campbell, 1964; *Mister Moses*, with Monja Danischewsky, 1965.

Television Plays: for *Twilight Zone, Naked City*, and *Thriller* series.

Other

*Remember? Remember?* New York, Macmillan, 1963.

Editor, with William F. Nolan, *Omnibus of Speed*: An Introduction to the World of Motor Sport. New York, Putnam, 1958; London, Stanley Paul, 1961; as *When Engines Roar*, New York, Bantam, 1964.
Editor, *The Fiend in You.* New York, Ballantine, 1962.

* * *

Charles Beaumont was a consummate craftsman of the popular market short story—perhaps the most accomplished writer of this type of fiction to publish in the 1950's and early 1960's. He wrote extensively for *Playboy* and other magazines, including many in the science-fiction field, and often blended elements of humor, horror, psychological suspense, and extrapolative SF. If much of his subject matter is grim, and many of his stories downbeat in resolution, his smooth and upbeat writing style and his superb characterization keep his work from being negative or oppressive.

Among his more than 50 stories (and articles) of science fiction and fantasy is "The Vanishing American," an allegorical tale about a man who becomes invisible to his fellow men. It is perhaps Beaumont's finest short story. Others of note include "Free Dirt," "The Love Master," "The Howling Man," "The Crooked Man" (a prophetic tale about homosexuality), and "Black Country," the best of a number with a jazz music background. *Yonder*, one of several collections, contains most of his pure SF stories first published in such magazines as *IF, Orbit, Imagination*, and *The Magazine of Fantasy & Science Fiction.* A recent volume, *Charles Beaumont: Selected Stories*, collects thirty of his best fantasy and SF tales, including three that were previously unpublished. Each story in this book is introduced by one of Beaumont's friends and peers, who offers anecdotes and reminiscences.

In addition to his fiction, Beaumont was an accomplished screenwriter. He wrote several SF and fantasy films, among them *7 Faces of Dr. Lao*, and he contributed 22 scripts to the television anthology series, *The Twilight Zone*, second in number only to those written by the show's creator, Rod Serling.

His tragic death at 37, of a form of Alzheimer's Disease that had ravaged him and kept him from writing for three years, cut short a career which might well have progressed to major stature.

—Bill Pronzini

---

**BEECHAM, Alice.** *See* **TUBB, E.C.**

---

**BELL, Thornton.** *See* **FANTHORPE, R. Lionel.**

---

**BELLAMY, Edward.** American. Born in Chicopee Falls, Massachusetts, 26 March 1850. Educated at local schools; Union College, Schenectady, New York, 1867–68; travelled and studied in Germany, 1868–69; studied law: admitted to the Massachusetts Bar, 1871, but never practiced. Married Emma Sanderson in 1882; one son and one daughter. Staff member, New York *Evening Post*, 1871–72; editorial writer and reviewer, Springfield *Union*, 1872–77; founder with his brother, Springfield *Daily News*, 1880; after 1885 writer and lecturer in support of the Nationalist movement (in favor of nationalization); founder, *New Nation*, Boston, 1891–96. *Died 22 May 1898.*

SCIENCE-FICTION PUBLICATIONS

Novels

*Dr. Heidenhoff's Process.* New York, Appleton, 1880; Edinburgh, Douglas, 1884.
*Looking Backward 2000–1887.* Boston, Ticknor, 1888; London, Reeves, 1889.
*Equality.* New York, Appleton, and London, Heinemann, 1897.

Short Stories

*The Blindman's World and Other Stories.* Boston, Houghton Mifflin, and London, Watt, 1898.

OTHER PUBLICATIONS

Novels

*Six to One: A Nantucket Idyl.* New York, Putnam, and London, Sampson Low, 1878.
*Miss Ludington's Sister: A Romance of Immortality.* Boston, Osgood, 1884; London, Reeves, 1890.
*The Duke of Stockbridge: A Romance of Shays' Rebellion.* New York, Silver Burdett, 1900.

Other

*Edward Bellamy Speaks Again! Articles, Public Addresses, Letters.* Kansas City, Peerage Press, 1937.
*Talks on Nationalism.* Chicago, Peerage Press, 1938.
*Religion of Solidarity.* Yellow Springs, Ohio, Antioch, 1940.
*Selected Writings on Religion and Society,* edited by Joseph Schiffman. New York, Liberal Arts Press, 1955.

*

Bibliography: in *Bibliography of American Literature* by Jacob Blanck, New Haven, Connecticut, Yale University Press, vol. 1, 1955; *Edward Bellamy: An Annotated Bibliography of Secondary Criticism* by Richard Toby Widdicombe, New York and London, Garland, 1988.

Critical Studies: *Edward Bellamy,* New York, Columbia University Press, 1944, and *The Philosophy of Edward Bellamy,* New York, King's Crown Press, 1945, both by Arthur E. Morgan; *The Year 2000: A Critical Biography of Edward Bellamy* by Sylvia E. Bowman, New York, Bookman, 1958, and *Edward Bellamy Abroad: An American Prophet's Influence* by Bowman and others, New York Twayne, 1962; *Edward Bellamy, Novelist and Reformer* by Daniel Aaron and Harry Levin, Schenectady, New York, Union College, 1968; *Authoritarian Socialism in America; Bellamy and the Nationalist Movement* by Arthur Lipow, Berkeley, University of California Press, 1982; *Alternative America: Henry George, Bellamy, Henry Demarest Lloyd, and the Adversary Tradition* by John L. Thomas, Cambridge, Massachusetts, Belknap Press, 1983; *Looking Backward 1988–1888: Essays on Edward Bellamy* edited by Daphne Patai, Amherst, University of Massachusetts Press, 1989.

* * *

In *Looking Backward 2000–1887,* Edward Bellamy observed that both the "working classes" and "true and humane men and women, of every degree, are in a mood of exasperation, verging on absolute revolt, against social conditions that reduce life to a brutal struggle for existence." In its sequel, *Equality,* he added the ruin of prairie farmers by capitalist mortgages, the degradation of women through economic exploitation, the recurrent economic crisis, and the concentration of three-quarters of national wealth into the hands of 10% of the population. Bellamy's utopianism was the point at which all these deep discontents intersected with the American religious and lay utopian tradition and the world socialist movement. As the spokesman of the "immense average of villagers, of small-town-dwellers" who believed in "modern inventions, modern conveniences, modern facilities" (Howells), in Yankee gadgetry as white magic for overcoming drudgery, he accepted the financial trusts as more efficient and changeable from private waste and tyranny to a Yankee communism or "Associationism": the nation "organized as the one great corporation . . . in the profits and economies of which all citizens shared."

Bellamy's new frontier is the future. It offers not only better railways, motor carriages, air-cars, telephones, and TV, but also a classless brotherhood of affluence socializing these means of communication and other upper-class privileges to achieve comfort and security for everyone through a reorganized "economy of happiness." Universal high education, work obligation from 21 to 45, equal and guaranteed income for everyone including the old, the sick, and children, flexible planning, and public honors reduce government to a universal civic service called the Great Trust or the Industrial Army. The generals of each guild or industrial branch are chosen by the retired alumni of the guild, and the head of the army is president of USA. Doctors and teachers have their own guilds, and a writer, artist, journal editor, or inventor is exempted from the army if enough buyers sign over a part of their credit. Individuality is fostered and objectors can "work out a better solution of the problem of existence than our society offers" in a reservation (the first use of this escape-hatch of later utopias).

Bellamy's economic blueprint is integrated into the story of Julian West, who wakes from a mesmeric sleep of 1887 into the Boston of 2000, is informed about the new order by Dr. Leete, and falls in love with Leete's daughter. This system of epoch-contrasts is reactualized in the nightmarish ending when Julian dreams of awakening back in the capitalist society of 1887. He meets its folly and repulsiveness with an anguished eye which supplies to each place and person a counterpossibility; the utopian estrangement culminates in the hallucination about "the possible face that would have been actual if mind and soul had lived," which he sees superimposed upon the living dead of the poor quarter. The lesson is that living in this nightmare and "pleading for crucified humanity" might yet be better than reawakening into the golden 21st century—as, if a final twist, Julian does. *Looking Backward*—intimately informed by Bellamy's constant preoccupation, with human plasticity, memory and identity, brute reality and ideal possibility—reposes on a balance of world-times. Its plot is Julian's change of identity. In two of Bellamy's later stories, "The Blindman's World" an "To Whom This May Come," the alienated Earthmen are contrasted to worlds of brotherhood and transparency where men are "lords of themselves." As the anxious idealist becomes an apostate through a healer's reasonable lectures and his daughter's healing sympathy, the construction of a social system for the reader is also the reconstruction of the hero. This radical-democratic innovation, in which a changed world is accompanied by changing people's "nature," is epoch-making for future utopias and for the field of science fiction.

However, Bellamy retreated from this discovery. Just as Julian is the mediator between two social systems for the reader, so Edith Leete is the steadying emotional mediator for Julian, a personal female Christ of earthly brotherhood. Bellamy's "sunburst" of a new order is validated equally by socialist economics, ethical evolution, and Christian love; his future brings a purified space and man. The friendly house of Dr. Leete is the hearth of spacious, clean, classless Boston, with Edith as the Dickensian cricket on the hearth. Hard-headed civic pragmatism is the obverse of a soft-hearted, petty-bourgeois "fairy tale of social felicity." Bellamy expects a nonviolent, imminent, and instantaneous abandonment of private capitalism by recognition of its folly. With telling effects, he extrapolated the Rationalist or Jeffersonian principles and institutions to a logical end-product of universal public ownership. But he also remained limited by such ideals. His fascination with the rationally organized army should perhaps not be judged by our reaction today, since it was acquired under Lincoln and translated into peaceful and constructive terms. Further, any utopia before automation had to be harsh on recalcitrants, and Bellamy evolved toward participatory democracy in *Equality.* But even there he continued to stress State mobilization, "public capitalism," and technocratic regimentation *within* economic production as opposed to ideal classless relations outside it, dismissing "the more backward races" and political efforts by "workingmen."

Uncomfortable with sweeping changes of life-style, Bellamy is at his strongest in the economics of everyday life outside a capitalist framework—dressing and love, distribution of goods, cultural activities, democratic supply and demand (e.g., in organizing a journal or in solving brain-drain between countries). Here he is quite free from centralized State Socialist regulation. When contrasting such warm possibilities with stultifying private competition, he presents exempla of great force, as the initial allegory of the Coach, the parables of the Collective Umbrella and of the Rosebush, or (in *Equality*) the parables of the Water-Tank and of the Masters of the Bread. All such impressive and sometimes splendid apologues come from a laicized and radicalized New England pulpit style rather than from genteel fiction. their ethical tone and the sentimental plot addressed themselves to women and all those who felt insecure and unfree in bourgeois society. Bellamy's homely lucidity made his romance, with all its limitations, the first authentically American socialist anticipation tale.

Bellamy's success fuses various SF strands and traditions. He interfused the preceeding, narratively helpless tradition of utopian anticipations—tales culminating in Hale and Macnie, Cabet—with an effective Romantic system of correspondences. His ending, refusing the alibi of dream, marks the historical moment when this lay millenialism came of age: the new vision achieves, within the text, a reality equal to that of the author's empirical actuality. Bellamy links thus two strong American traditions: the fantastic one of unknown worlds and the practical one of organizing a new world—both of which translate powerful biblical themes into economics. His materialist view of history as a coherent succession of changing human relationships and social structures was continued by Morris and Wells and built into the fundamentals of subsequent SF. Equally, the plot educates the reader into acceptance of the strange by following the protagonists' puzzled education. Modern SF, though it has forgotten this ancestor, builds on *Looking Backward* much as Dr. Leete's house was built on the remnants of Julian's house and on top of his sealed sleeping chamber, excavated by future archaeology.

Traits from Bellamy's other works also drew from and returned to the SF tradition. The Flammarion-like, cosmically exceptional blindness of Earthmen and the transferral by spirit to Mars are found in "The Blindman's World," and despotic oligarchy as the alternative to revolution in *Equality.* Most immediately, the immense ideologico-political echo of *Looking Backward* reverberated around the globe through a host of sequels, rebuttals, and parallels. Bellamy had hit exactly the right note for a time searching for alternatives to ruthless plutocracy, and close to 200 utopian tales expounding or satirizing social democracy, state regulation of economy, Populist capitalism, or various uncouth combinations thereof were published in the United States from 1888 to 1917 (notably Donnelly's *Caesar's Column*, Howell's *A Traveller from Altruria*, and London's *The Iron Heel*). In the United Kingdom, the echo was felt in Morris's answer, *News From Nowhere*, in Wells, and in Germany in three dozen German utopian or anti-utopian tales.

—Darko Suvin

---

**BENFORD, Gregory (Albert).** American. Born in Mobile, Alabama, 30 January 1941. Educated at the University of Oklahoma, Norman, B.S. in physics 1963; University of California, San Diego, M.S. 1965, Ph.D. 1967. Married Joan Abbe in 1967; one daughter and one son. Fellow, 1967–69, and research physicist, 1969–72, Lawrence Radiation Laboratory, Livermore, California. Assistant Professor, 1971–73, Associate Professor, 1973–79, and since 1979 Professor of physics, University of California, Irvine. Visiting Professor, Cambridge University, 1976. Recipient: Nebula award, 1974, 1981; John W. Campbell Memorial award, 1981. Agent: Richard Curtis Associates, 171 East 74th Street, Suite 2, New York, New York 10021. Address: Department of Physics, University of California, Irvine, California 92717, U.S.A.

SCIENCE-FICTION PUBLICATIONS

Novels (series: Great Sky River)

*Deeper Than the Darkness.* New York, Ace, 1970; revised edition, as *The Stars in Shroud*, New York, Berkley, 1978; London, Gollancz, 1979.
*Jupiter Project.* Nashville, Nelson, 1975; London, Sphere, 1982.
*If the Stars Are Gods*, with Gordon Eklund. New York, Berkley, 1977; London, Gollancz, 1978.
*In the Ocean of Night.* New York, Dial Press, 1977; London, Sidgwick and Jackson, 1978.
*Find the Changeling*, with Gordon Eklund. New York, Dell, 1980; London, Sphere, 1983.
*Timespace.* New York, Simon and Schuster, and London, Gollancz, 1980.
*Shiva Descending*, with William Rotsler. New York, Avon, and London, Sphere, 1980.
*Against Infinity.* New York, Simon and Schuster, and London, Gollancz, 1983.
*Across the Sea of Suns.* New York, Simon and Schuster, and London, Macdonald, 1984.
*Artifact.* New York, Tor, and London, Bantam, 1985.
*Time's Rub.* New Castle, Virginia, Cheap Street, 1984.
*Of Space/Time and the River.* New Castle, Virginia, Cheap Street, 1985.
*Heart of the Comet*, with David Brin. New York, Bantam, 1986; London, Bantam, 1987.
*In Alien Flesh.* New York, Tor, 1986; London, Gollancz, 1988.
*Under the Wheel*, with John M. Ford and Nancy Springer. New York, Baen, 1987.
*Great Sky River.* New York, Bantam, 1987; London, Gollancz, 1988.
*Bart SF Triplet #1: To the Storming Gulf, Un-man, Sucker Bait*, with Poul Anderson and Isaac Asimov. New York, Bart, 1988.
*We Could Do Worse.* N.p., Abbenford, 1988.
*Iceborn*, with Paul A. Carter, with *The Saturn Game* by Poul Anderson. New York, Tor, 1988.
*Tides of Light* (Great Sky River). New York, Bantam, and London, Gollancz, 1989.
*Beyond the Fall of Night*, with *Against the Fall of Night*, by Arthur C. Clarke. New York, Ace, 1990.

OTHER PUBLICATIONS

Other

Editor, with Martin H. Greenberg, *Hitler Victorious: Eleven Stories of the German Victory in World War II.* New York, Garland, 1986.
Editor, with Martin H. Greenberg, *Nuclear War.* New York, Berkley, 1988.
Editor, with Martin H. Greenberg, *What Might Have Been? I: Alternative Empires [II: Alternative Heros].* New York, Bantam, 2 vols., 1989–90.

*

Manuscript Collection: Eaton College, University of California, Riverside.

Gregory Benford comments:

I am a resolutely amateur writer, preferring to follow my own interests rather than try to produce fiction for a living. And anyway, I'm a scientist by first choice and shall remain so.

I began writing from the simple desire to tell a story (a motivation SF writers seem to forget as they age, and thus turn into earnest moralizers). It's taken me a long time to learn how. I've been labeled a "hard SF" writer from the first, but in fact I think the job of SF is to do it *all*—the scientific landscape, peopled with real persons, with "style" and meaning ingrained. I've slowly worked toward that goal, with many dead ends along the way. From this comes my habit of rewriting my older books and expanding early short stories into longer works (sometimes novels). Ideas come to me in a lapidary way, layering over the years. Yet, it's not the stirring moral message that moves me. I think writers are interesting when they juxtapose images or events, letting life come out of the stuff of the narrative. They get boring when they preach. To some extent, my novels reflect my learning various subcategories of SF—*Deeper Than the Darkness* was the galactic empire motif; *Jupiter Project* the juvenile; *If the Stars Are Gods* and *In the Ocean of Night* both the cosmic space novel, etc. *Timescape* is rather different, and reflects my using my own experiences as a scientist. Yet short stories, where I labored so long, seem to me just as interesting as novels. I learned to write there. Nowadays, my novels begin as relatively brisk plot-lines and then gather philosophical moss as they roll. If all this sounds vague and intuitive, it is: that's the way I work. So I cannot say precisely why I undertake certain themes. I like Graham Greene's division of novels into "serious" and "entertainment," though I suspect the author himself cannot say with certainty which of his own is which.

It seems to me my major concerns are the vast landscape of science, and the philosophical implications of that landscape on mortal, sensual human beings. What genuinely interests me is the strange, the undiscovered, but in the end it is how *people* see this that matters most.

* * *

Almost from the outset of his career, Gregory Benford was acknowledged as one of the major writers of hard science fiction. His powerful novelette, *Deeper Than the Darkness*, subsequently expanded into a novel of the same name and later rewritten and expanded as *The Stars in Shroud*, demonstrated that his work had more depth than simple scientific explication; it also demonstrated an intuitive understanding of the human character. In that novel, aliens attack human civilization by inflicting it with agoraphobia.

Benford's second novel, *Jupiter Project*, is a straightforward story of life in an artificial environment orbiting Jupiter. The book is ostensibly aimed at younger readers, but as with the supposedly juvenile fiction of Robert Heinlein, Andre Norton, and others, its appeal is far wider.

*In the Ocean of Night* was assembled from five short stories, all containing the theme that aliens have visited Earth before and have genetically conditioned the race. Human beings' subsequent encounters with artifacts of extraterrestrial origin have devastating effects on the society. *If the Stars Are Gods*, written in collaboration with Gordon Eklund, is also made up of individual stories, including the award-winning short pieces of the same title. Again alien contact is the theme, this time involving the lifelong quest of a scientist who has devoted his life to discovering the nature of alien intelligence.

Benford collaborated on two further novels. *Shiva Descending*, written with William Rotsler, is an above average but fairly traditional disaster story featuring a wandering asteroid on a collision course with Earth. *Find the Changeling*, with Gordon Eklund, is another mystery story, involving the quest to capture an alien capable of altering its body to resemble any object it desires.

These works were a prelude to what remains Benford's best novel, *Timescape.* In 1970 he had published a captivating short story, "3:02 P.M. Oxford" in which experiments with tachyons lead to the discovery of communications from the future, but the messages frequently contradict one another. *Timescape* portrays an ecologically deteriorating near future in which scientists attempt to use tachyon research to send a message of warning back through time to 1962. The story alternates between two sets of people, one at the end of the time span, examining their relationships with their family, peers, and the world at large. It is certainly one of the best novels about scientists ever written, and one of the most fully realized novels in the genre.

*Against Infinity* returned to an interplanetary setting, this time Ganymede. As human colonists use bioengineering and other knowledge to adapt to their inhospitable environment, they also must deal with the Aleph, an apparently immortal machine that wanders the asteroid, occasionally interacting with human beings. Benford brings the landscape to life and makes us believe humans could really survive in such an alien environment.

Benford returned to Earth for *Artifact*, another long novel, this time concerning an artifact unearthed by a team of archaeologists. The object is smuggled out of Europe and back to the United States, where its strange properties as a power source result in its transfer to the physics department of a major university. But the military government of Greece wants it back because it may be the key to global supremacy.

Benford's collaboration with David Brin, *Heart of the Comet*, is a vividly realized portrayal of an expedition launched to investigate a comet. Although the main theme is the revelation of the scientific secrets of the comet, a set of complexly developed characters and their interactions are what mark this as an extraordinary novel. Benford next turned to the far future in *Great Sky River.* Inhuman intelligences beyond human comprehension dominate the universe, and a small band of human beings sets out to discover whether there is any hope for the race to survive.

*Across the Sea of Suns* is a sequel to *In the Ocean of Night.* Human civilization has continued to spread and evolve, although we have not yet cast aside the self-destructive impulses that have marred our development. A sudden message from beyond our own system threatens to upset the equilibrium once again. *Tides of Light* is another sequel, this one providing further adventures of the small band of humans from *Great Sky River*, now faced with a number of new wonders including a single organism the size of a small planet. Benford's most recent novel, *Beyond the Fall of Night*, is an interesting but not completely satisfactory sequel to Arthur C. Clarke's classic *Against the Fall of Night.* Alvin of Diaspar has brought together the scattered tribes of dying Earth, and now he journeys to the stars to find out what happened to the interstellar civilization humanity had established eons in the past.

Benford continues to be one of the most influential voices in the genre both for the breadth of his vision and his ability to incorporate genuine scientific extrapolation in a compelling and credible work of fiction.

—Don D'Ammassa

---

**BENYON, John.** *See* **WYNDHAM, John.**

---

**BERESFORD, J(ohn) D(avys).** British. Born in Castor, Northamptonshire, 7 March 1873. Educated at Oundle School, Northamptonshire, and at a school in Peterborough; articled to Lacey W. Ridge, architect, London, 1901. Married to Beatrice Roskams; three sons and one daughter. Practised architecture in the early 1900's. *Died 2 February 1947.*

SCIENCE-FICTION PUBLICATIONS

Novels

*The Hampdenshire Wonder.* London, Sidgwick and Jackson, 1911; as *The Wonder*, New York, Doran, 1917.
*Goslings.* London, Heinemann, 1913; as *A World of Women*, New York, Macaulay, 1913.
*Revolution: A Story of the Near Future in England.* London, Collins, and New York, Putnam, 1921.
*Real People.* London, Collins, 1929.
*The Camberwell Miracle.* London, Heinemann, 1933.
*What Dreams May Come. . . .* London, Hutchinson, 1941.
*A Common Enemy.* London, Hutchinson, 1942.
*The Riddle of the Tower*, with Esmé Wynne-Tyson. London, Hutchinson, 1944.

Short Stories

*Nineteen Impressions.* London, Sidgwick and Jackson, 1918; Freeport, New York, Books for Libraries, 1969.
*Signs and Wonders.* Waltham St. Lawrence, Berkshire, Golden Cockerel Press, and New York, Putnam, 1921.
*The Meeting Place and Other Stories.* London, Faber, 1929.

OTHER PUBLICATIONS

Novels

Stahl Trilogy:
*The Early History of Jacob Stahl.* London, Sidgwick and Jackson, and Boston, Little Brown, 1911.
*A Candidate for Truth.* London, Sidgwick and Jackson, and Boston, Little Brown, 1912.
*The Invisible Event.* London, Sidgwick and Jackson, and New York, Doran, 1915.
*The House in Demetrius Road.* London, Heinemann, and New York, Doran, 1914.
*The Mountains of the Moon.* London, Cassell, 1915.
*These Lynnekers.* London, Cassell, and New York, Doran, 1916.
*W.E. Ford: A Bibliography*, with Kenneth Richmond. London, Collins, and New York, Doran, 1917.
*House-Mates.* London, Cassell, and New York, Doran, 1917.
*God's Counterpoint.* London, Collins, and New York, Doran, 1918.
*The Jervaise Comedy.* London, Collins, and New York, Macmillan, 1919.
*An Imperfect Mother.* London, Collins, and New York, Macmillan, 1920.
*The Prisoners of Hartling.* London, Collins, and New York, Macmillan, 1922.

*Love's Pilgrim*. London, Collins, and Indianapolis, Bobbs Merrill, 1923.
*Unity*. London, Collins, and Indianapolis, Bobbs Merrill, 1924.
*The Monkey-Puzzle*. London, Collins, and Indianapolis, Bobbs Merrill, 1925.
*That Kind of Man*. London, Collins, 1926; as *Almost Pagan*, Indianapolis, Bobbs Merrill, 1926.
*The Decoy*. London, Collins, 1927.
*The Tapestry*. London, Collins, and Indianapolis, Bobbs Merrill, 1927.
*The Instrument of Destiny: A Detective Story*. London, Collins, and Indianapolis, Bobbs Merrill, 1928.
*All or Nothing*. London, Collins, and Indianapolis, Bobbs Merril, 1928.
*Love's Illusion*. London, Collins, and New York, Viking Press, 1930.
*Seven, Bobsworth*. London, Faber, 1930.
*An Innocent Criminal*. London, Collins, and New York, Dutton, 1931.
Three Generations Trilogy:
*The Old People*. London, Collins, 1931; New York Dutton, 1932.
*The Middle Generation*. London, Collins, 1932; New York, Dutton, 1933.
*The Young People*. London, Collins. 1933; New York, Dutton, 1934.
*The Next Generation*. London, Benn, 1932.
*The Inheritor*, London, Benn, 1933.
*Peckover*. London, Heinemann, 1934; New York, Putnam, 1935.
*On a Huge Hill*. London, Heinemann, 1935.
*The Faithful Lovers*. London, Hutchinson, and New York, Furman, 1936.
*Cleo*. London, Hutchinson, 1937.
*The Unfinished Road*. London, Hutchinson, 1938.
*Strange Rival*. London, Hutchinson, 1939.
*Snell's Folly*. London, Hutchinson, 1939.
*Quiet Corner*. London, Hutchinson, 1940.
*The Benefactor*. London, Hutchinson, 1943.
*The Long View*. London, Hutchinson, 1943.
*Men in the Same Boat*, with Esmé Wynne-Tyson. London, Hutchinson, 1943.
*If This Were True—*. London, Hutchinson, 1944.
*The Prisoner*. London, Hutchinson, 1946.
*The Gift*, with Esmé Wynne-Tyson. London, Hutchinson, 1947.

Short Stories

*The Imperturbable Duchess and Other Stories*. London, Collins, 1923.
*Blackthorn Winter and Other Stories*. London, Hutchinson, 1936.

Plays

*The Compleat Angler: A Duologue*, with A.S. Craven (produced London, 1907). London, French, 1915.
*The Royal Heart*, with A.S. Craven (produced London, 1908).
*The Veiled Woman* (produced London, 1913).
*Howard and Son*, with Kenneth Richmond (produced London, 1916).
*The Perfect Machine*, with A.S. Craven, in *English Review 26* (London), May 1918.

Verse

*Poems by Two Brothers*, with Richard Beresford. London, Erskine Macdonald, 1915.

Other

*H.G. Wells*. London, Nisbet, and New York, Holt, 1915.
*Taken from Life*, photographs by E.O. Hoppe. London, Collins, 1922.
*Writing Aloud*. London, Collins, 1928.
*The Case for Faith-Healing*. London, Allen and Unwin, 1934.
*The Root of the Matter: Essays*, with others, edited by H.R.L. Sheppard. London, Cassell, 1937; Freeport, New York, Books for Libraries, 1967.
*What I Believe*. London, Heinemann, 1938.
*The Idea of God*. London, Clarke, 1940.

Editor, *Tales of the Unexpected [of Life and Adventure, of Wonder]*, by H.G. Wells. London, Collins, 3 vols., 1922–23.

*

Bibliography: "J.D. Beresford: A Bibliography" by Helmut E. Gerber, in *Bulletin of Bibliography 21* (Boston), January–April 1956.

* * *

J.D. Beresford, born just seven years after H.G. Wells, had affinities of imagination with the older writer, and similarities of style and theme may have dimmed the Beresford flame in the Wellsian glare. All his excellent science fiction is forgotten save *The Hampdenshire Wonder*. The neglect is regrettable because his attitudes were almost diametrically opposed to those of the politicising and romanticising Wells. Beresford's superficially gentler treatments show, on examination, an appreciation of the grimmer aspects of human nature which Wells tended to gloss in comedy or satire.

The first of Beresford's science-fiction novels, *The Hampdenshire Wonder* may stand for most of the qualities and methods of its successors. As the story of a super-intelligent child born to working-class parents (one of the few major science-fiction themes Wells never attempted) it is an obvious forerunner of Stapledon's *Odd John*, but is superior in handling to the later book. The story of the lonely child (unwanted by all except his doting mother, and in his intellectual solitude having little use for her) making his misunderstood way through childhood to an ironical death at the hands of the village idiot illumines the theme of "difference" more clearly than, for example, Sturgeon's melodramatic *More Than Human*. Beresford's viewpoint is peculiar to himself. He was not primarily concerned, like more modern practitioners, with the symptoms and displays of transcendent genius so much as with the effect of this doomed creation's existence on those about him. The child is strongly drawn, with considerable understanding of the requirements of super-intelligence, but the characters who remain with the reader are the father, an uneducated county cricketer and workman who deserts child and wife when he can no longer bear the child's "unnatural" presence, and the mother, whose devotion to the self-absorbed genius is given without any return of affection or understanding. The two, supremely human, emphasise the child's alienness and eerieness in a fashion denied to our "mind-blowing" contemporary writers. They also demonstrate that characterisation in depth is possible in a genre which prefers to offer types as symbols of humanity confronting "difference."

Beresford presents, without strain, rounded personalities who also manage to symbolise humanity dealing with the incomprehensible.

*Goslings* recalls Wells's *War of the Worlds* in its portrait of a plague-ridden, deserted London, but again the emphasis is on the reactions of people. Wells's stricken city is a symbol of trampled mankind; Beresford's is a challenge to the ordinary, unschooled but individual people who must live in and defeat it. *The Camberwell Miracle* has a faith healer (if that be the phrase for the talent) as central character, and here Beresford gives love and serenity to a portrait one can only imagine Wells handling with pragmatic savagery. *The Riddle of the Tower* (with Esmé Wynne-Tyson) again invades Wellsian territory, via bomb blast into an alternate spacetime, to discover a human culture reminiscent of the hive or the termitary. Again the treatment is thoughtful rather than dramatic or satirical, though the warning against technological excess is clear.

These novels stand comparison with the best of current science fiction, and, in literary quality, head and shoulders above most. Beresford published over 40 mainstream novels and it is his mainstream approach to science-fiction problems of structure and balance that give his romances a unique flavour.

—George Turner

---

**BESTER, Alfred.** American. Born in New York City, 18 December 1913. Educated at the University of Pennsylvania, Philadelphia, B.A. 1935. Married Rolly Goulko in 1936. Freelance writer: book reviewer, *Fantasy and Science Fiction*, New York, 1960–62, radio and TV writer, and staff member, *Holiday*, New York. Recipient: Hugo award, 1953; Nebula Grand Master, 1987. *Died in 1987.*

SCIENCE-FICTION PUBLICATIONS

Novels

*The Demolished Man.* Chicago, Shasta, and London, Sidgwick and Jackson, 1953.
*Tiger! Tiger!* London, Sidgwick and Jackson, 1956; as *The Stars My Destination*, New York, New American Library, 1957.
*The Computer Connection.* New York, Berkley, 1975; as *Extro*, London, Eyre Methuen, 1975.
*Golem$^{100}$.* New York, Simon and Schuster, and London, Sidgwick and Jackson, 1980.
*The Deceivers.* New York, Wallaby, 1981; London, Severn House, 1984.

Short Stories

*Starburst.* New York, New American Library, 1958; London, Sphere, 1968.
*The Dark Side of Earth.* New York, New American Library, 1964; London, Pan, 1969.
*The Light Fantastic* and *Star Light, Star Bright.* New York, Berkley, 2 vols., 1976; London, Gollancz, 2 vols., 1977–78; as *Starlight: The Great Short Fiction of Alfred Bester*, New York, Doubleday, 1 vol., 1976.

OTHER PUBLICATIONS

Novel

*Who He?* New York, Dial Press, 1953; as *The Rat Race*, New York, Berkley, 1956; London, Hamlyn, 1984.

Other

*The Life and Death of a Satellite.* Boston, Little Brown, 1966; London, Sidgwick and Jackson, 1967.

*

Critical Study: *Alfred Bester* by Carolyn Wendell, Mercer Island, Washington, Starmont House, 1982.

* * *

With either of his first two novels alone, Alfred Bester would have been guaranteed a place in the history of science fiction as one of the most significant figures of the 1950's. The fact that he remains an important and respected writer despite producing only five novels and about three dozen short stories before his death is a testimony to the profound talent that he brought to those works.

*The Demolished Man*, which won a Hugo award as best novel of the year in 1953, is a remarkable work. Ben Reich is a powerful, larger-than-life figure in a future where the development of telepathy has made most crime impossible. After all, when one's secret plans are available to the nearest telepath, how could one possibly hope to commit a crime, let alone escape detection? Nevertheless, Ben Reich does so, and what ensues is a brilliantly conceived battle of two personalities as a prominent telepath sets out to bring Reich to justice. Knowing that Reich is the murderer is one thing, proving it is quite another matter. Bester was also one of the earliest genre writers to create a gritty, realistic setting for his novels. *The Demolished Man* is an innovative mystery story, powerfully conceived and executed science fiction, an insightful character study, and a very suspenseful thriller with an ending that is quite out of the ordinary.

Opinions vary as to whether or not Bester's second novel, *Tiger! Tiger!* (published as *The Stars My Destination* in the United States), was an even greater achievement. There is little doubt that each stands as a masterpiece, although *Tiger! Tiger!* was more ambitious in conception, straddling worlds, psi powers, and interplanetary war. Gulliver Foyle is a man driven to extremes when he nearly dies after being abandoned in space. Rescued by barbarian pirates, he eventually returns to Earth transformed both physically and mentally. Obsessed with the idea of revenge, he sets about accumulating the wealth and power with which to carry out his plans. The story is further enriched by the concept of "jaunting," physical teleportation presented in a mature and thoughtful fashion, inextricably entwined with the main plotline. Foyle becomes a greater-than-human being in many respects, as his urge for vengeance ultimately involves him in an interplanetary conflict.

Although Bester was to write three more novels before his death, none of these rivalled those early works. The best is *Golem$^{100}$*, set in the 23rd Century. A group of bored women set out to investigate the occult, inadvertently setting free a hideous creature conceived in the collective unconscious of the human race. This monster, now incarnate, escapes and commits a series of murders, while metaphysicists seek to locate and destroy the intruder. The novel is based in part on the short story, "The Four Hour Fugue," which presents much the same situation in a less lengthy format. *The Computer Connection* (published as *Extro* in the United Kingdom) is satiric, detailing the efforts of a group of disparate individuals to foil an omniscient computer. Unfortunately, Bester seemed less inclined in later years to spend the effort on characterization that distinguished his earlier work, and the storyline in itself is not interesting enough to sustain the story. *The Deceivers* was a disappointing finale to Bester's career, an ambitious space opera that lacked the vigor or originality of his other work.

Bester's small body of short fiction contains a number of classics in the field. "Adam and No Eve" involves a man in orbit who accidentally sets off a chain reaction that destroys all life on the home planet. He returns to Earth and eventually dies, and his decaying body becomes the springboard for a new wave of life. "Oddy and Id" tells the story of Odysseus Gaul, a man who attracts good luck and eventually becomes dictator of the entire solar system.

The protagonist in "Of Time and Third Avenue" finds an almanac from the future, and voluntarily surrenders it without giving in to the temptation to look inside. There is a genuinely moving love story in "Time Is the Traitor," and a sarcastic vision of certain voyeuristic aspects of our civilization in "Roller Coaster."

"Fondly Fahrenheit" is Bester's most frequently reprinted story, with good reason. The history of an android driven to kill in hot weather and its interaction with the man who owns it is a powerful enough story to stand in any company. "Starcomber" is conversely a farcical tale of a warlock who puts a psychotic painter through various wish fulfillment worlds in order to exorcise his psychotic obsessions.

In "The Men Who Murdered Mohammed," Bester presents a very different view of time travel. The traveller can only effect his own personal past. The protagonist of "The Pi Man" is compelled to balance the underlying patterns of the universe. A self-aware computer satellite dominates the earth in "Something Up There Likes Me." He also wrote several outright fantasies, of which the best are "Will You Wait?" and "Hell Is Forever."

Although the most obvious evidence of Bester's impact on science fiction is the presence of several familiar and often reprinted works, his influence on writers who followed is probably even greater. He frequently made use of non-textual material, illustrations, and creative layout of pages to emphasize situations beyond all previous human experience. Arguably, Bester was a forerunner of the New Wave movement of the 1960's with his experimental approach to fiction. But perhaps more importantly, he helped promote the concept that in order to be good science fiction, a story had to have credible characters as well as credible science.

—Don D'Ammassa

---

**BIGGLE, Lloyd, Jr.** American. Born in Waterloo, Iowa, 17 April 1923. Educated at Wayne University, Detroit 1941–43, 1946–47, A.B. (honors) in creative writing 1947; University of Michigan, Ann Arbor, 1947–53, M.M. in music literature 1948, Ph.D. in musicology 1953. Served in the United States Army, 1943–46: Sergeant. Married Hedwig T. Janiszewski in 1947; one daughter and one son. First secretary-treasurer, 1965-67, chairman, Board of Trustees, 1967–71, and founder of the Regional Collections, Science Fiction Writers of America. Founder, and since 1979, president, Science Fiction Oral History Association. Lives in Ypsilanti, Michigan. Agent: Sharon Jarvis, Jarvis Braff Ltd., 260 Willard Avenue, Staten Island, New York 10314. Address: 569 Dubie Avenue, Ypsilanti, Michigan 48198, U.S.A.

### Science-Fiction Publications

Novels (series: Cultural Survey; Jan Darzek)

*The Angry Espers.* New York, Ace, 1961; London, Hale, 1968.
*All the Colors of Darkness.* New York, Doubleday, 1963; London, Dobson, 1964.
*The Fury Out of Time.* New York, Doubleday, 1965; London, Dobson, 1966.
*Watchers of the Dark* (Darzek). New York, Doubleday, 1966; London, Rapp and Whiting, 1968.
*The Still, Small Voice of Trumpets* (Survey). New York, Doubleday, 1968; London, Rapp and Whiting, 1969.
*The World Menders* (Survey). New York, Doubleday, 1971; Morley, Yorkshire, Elmfield Press, 1973.
*The Light That Never Was.* New York, Doubleday, 1972; Morley, Yorkshire, Elmfield Press, 1975.
*Monument.* New York, Doubleday, 1974; London, New English Library, 1975.
*This Darkening Universe* (Darzek). New York, Doubleday, 1975; London, Millington, 1977.
*Silence Is Deadly* (Darzek). New York, Doubleday, 1977; London, Millington, 1980.
*The Whirligig of Time* (Darzek). New York, Doubleday, 1979.
*Alien Main*, with T.L. Sherred. New York, Doubleday, 1985.
*The Tunesmith*, with *Eye for Eye*, by Orson Scott Card. New York, Tor, 1990.

Short Stories

*The Rule of the Door and Other Fanciful Regulations.* New York, Doubleday, 1967; as *Out of the Silent Sky.* New York, Belmont Tower, 1977; as *The Silent Sky*, London, Hale, 1979.
*The Metallic Muse.* New York, Doubleday, 1972.
*A Galaxy of Strangers.* New York, Doubleday, 1976.

### Other Publications

Novels

*The Quallsford Inheritance: A Memoir of Sherlock Holmes.* New York, St. Martin's Press, 1986.
*Interface for Murder.* New York, Doubleday, 1987.
*The Glendower Conspiracy: A Memoir of Sherlock Holmes.* Tulsa, Oklahoma, Council Oak Books, 1990.
*A Hazard of Losers.* Tulsa, Oklahoma, Council Oak Books, 1991.

Other

Editor, *Nebula Award Stories 7.* London, Gollancz, 1972; New York, Harper, 1973.

*

Manuscript Collection: Spencer Research Library, University of Kansas, Lawrence.

* * *

The best-known creations of Lloyd Biggle, Jr., are the Council of the Supreme and its extensions, the agents of the Galactic Synthesis, the Cultural Survey, and the Interplanetary Relations Bureau, known for mottoes such as "Democracy Imposed from Without Is the Severest Form of Tyranny." Supreme is a vast computer that is fed information by its eight councilors; the only human is number ONE, Jan Darzek, who ironically was recruited by Supreme from uncertified Earth (i.e., not fit for social intercourse with civilized planets because its inhabitants tell lies) through Rok Wllon, who eventually becomes EIGHT. EIGHT dislikes ONE personally but they unite in common cause against the Dark Force, the Udef, which threatens the universe.

Supreme is not a ruler but an advisor, though people tend to accept its wisdom without hesitation since it eventually always proves reliable. Supreme—the ultimate in impartial democratic justice—fails in its function only when it is deprived of data input or asked the wrong question, thus simultaneously demonstrating the old programmers' wisdom "Garbage in; garbage out," and suggesting the need for an informed electorate of enlightened self-interest.

Always highly readable, Biggle narrates the adventures of Jan Darzek as he saves Earth in *All the Colors of Darkness*, the galaxy in *Watchers of the Dark*, and a large part of the universe in *This Darkening Universe*, as well as two individual worlds in *Silence Is Deadly* and *The Whirligig of Time*. In *The World Menders* and *The Still, Small Voice of Trumpets*, the cultural Survey officers must cope with bureaucracy while solving the problems of how to bring an uncertified world into the Galactic Synthesis of self-rule and trade with other planets. *Monument* and *The Light That Never Was* also deal with the place of art and beauty in human culture and civilization.

Biggle's characterization is generally drawn with vivid, broad strokes in the literary tradition of Charles Dickens; e.g., Darzek's assistant is a little old lady, Miss Schlupe (Schluppy), who loves the comfort of her rocking chair as she makes beer out of whatever exotic vegetation is available wherever she lands in the galaxy. The chief interest in Biggle's stories is not character motivation, but puzzle solving, understanding the nature of the universe so that it can be managed intelligently. Throughout his stories, intelligent life in whatever form it appears (even a giant vegetable computer) earns respect. In the ironic tradition of Jonathan Swift, humanoid-appearing creatures may turn out to be sub-human animals (*The World Menders*), as determined by their lack of culture, particularly religion and the arts. Repeatedly Biggle dramatizes the need for a holistic understanding of a culture, including the ecological balance of a planet and the physical strengths and weaknesses of its inhabitants. Tolerance and respect for differences between species is demonstrated to benefit all intelligent beings, and Biggle uses gentle satire to provide moral instruction as he delights.

His greatest strength is in creating believable alien worlds and civilizations, complete with native flora and fauna, linguistic idiosyncrasies, customs of courtship and marriage, provisions for raising children, social intercourse and folkways (always inseparable from economic trade and business affairs), religion, systems of government, and culture in its most inclusive sense. Because of this complexity, it is unfair to limit his stories with the label juvenile—even though neither his heroes nor his villains ever use expletives stronger than "drat"—but his clear-cut moral tone, celebrating life in all its forms, is particularly suitable for young readers.

*Alien Main*, the collaboration with T.L. Sherred, uses a female first person narrator to tell the story of an intergalactic organization dedicated to peace and progress that returns to a devastated earth 200 years after a nuclear holocaust and a plague has nearly wiped out humanity. The protagonist will especially delight and inspire young girls for her resourcefulness and courage in facing danger and solving unforeseen problems as she confronts a despicable alien race that would make slaves of the few who are left on earth.

In recent years Biggle has turned to writing mystery novels, but those who enjoy his science fiction will probably also appreciate the careful research and attention to detail (similar to his world-building), with which he recreates the late nineteenth century England and Wales in *The Quallsford Inheritance* and *The Glendower Conspiracy*, both further tales of Sherlock Holmes, with the introduction of a new narrator-persona, Edward Porter Jones, his late assistant. Biggle has also begun his own original mystery series, starting with *Interface for Murder*, set in a small college town in Ohio, featuring detective J. Pletcher and his boss, Raina Lambert. *A Hazard of Losers* (set in Las Vegas), the next novel in this series, is in galleys at this writing and another story, set in Tulsa, is in progress. Most of Biggle's short fiction is available in book collections. *A Galaxy of Strangers* contains one gem in particular, "And Madly Teach."

—Elizabeth Anne Hull

---

**BINDER, Eando.** Pseudonym for Otto Oscar Binder (and his brother Earl Andrew Binder until 1934); also wrote as John Coleridge; Ian Francis Turek; Ione Frances Turek. American. Born in Bessemer, Michigan, 26 August 1911. Studied science and chemical engineering at Crane City College, Northwestern University, Evanston, Illinois, and the University of Chicago for three years. Married Ione Frances Turek in 1940; one daughter. Clerk, Central Scientific Company, Chicago, 1930–31; assistant to science librarian, Crerar Library, Chicago, 1931–32; freelance writer after 1932: reader of manuscripts, Otis Kline Literary Agency, 1936–38; comic book writer from 1941; editor, *Space World*, New York, 1962–63. *Died 14 October 1974.*

SCIENCE-FICTION PUBLICATIONS

Novels

*Lords of Creation*. Philadelphia, Prime Press, 1949.
*Enslaved Brains*. New York, Avalon, 1965.
*The Avengers Battle the Earth-Wrecker*. New York, Bantam, 1967.
*Menace of the Saucers*. New York, Belmont, 1969.
*The Impossible World*. New York, Curtis, 1970.
*Five Steps to Tomorrow*. New York, Curtis, 1970.
*The Double Man*. New York, Curtis, 1971
*Get Off My World*. New York, Curtis, 1971
*Night of the Saucers*. New York, Belmont, 1971.
*Puzzle of the Space Pyramids*. New York, Curtis, 1971.
*Secret of the Red Spot*. New York, Curtis, 1971.
*Terror in the Bay* (as Ione Frances Turek). New York, Curtis, 1971.
*The Mind from Outer Space*. New York, Curtis, 1972.
*The Forgotten Colony* (as Otto Binder). New York, Popular Library, 1972.
*The Hospital Horror* (as Otto Binder). New York, Popular Library, 1973.
*The Frontier's Secret* (as Ian Francis Turek). New York, Popular Library, 1973.

Short Stories (series: Adam Link)

*Martian Martyrs* (as John Coleridge). New York, Columbia, 1940.
*The New Life* (as John Coleridge). New York, Columbia, 1940.
*The Three Eternals*. Sydney, Whitman Press, 1949.
*Adam Link in the Past*. Sydney, Whitman Press, 1950.
*Where Eternity Ends*. Sydney, Whitman Press, 1950.
*Adam Link—Robot*. New York, Paperback Library, 1965.
*Anton York—Immortal*. New York, Belmont, 1965.

OTHER PUBLICATIONS

Play

Television Play: *I, Robot*, 1964.

Other

*The Golden Book of Space Travel [Atomic Energy, Jets and Rockets]* (for children). New York, Golden Press, 3 vols., 1959–61.
*The Moon, Our Neighboring World* (for children). New York, Golden Press, 1959.
*Planets: Other Worlds of Our Solar System* (for children). New York, Golden Press, 1959.
*Victory in Space*. New York, Walker, 1962.
*Careers in Space*. New York, Walker, 1963.
*Riddles of Astronomy*. New York, Basic Books 1964.
*Dracula* (comic book; as Otto Binder), with Craig Tennis. New York, Ballantine, 1966.
*What We Really Know about Flying Saucers*. New York, Fawcett, 1967.
*Mankind, Child of the Stars*, with Max H. Flindt. New York, Fawcett, 1974; London, Coronet, 1976.
*The Mysterious Island* (comic book). West Haven, Connecticut, Pendulum Press, 1974.

* * *

Though the unique name Eando is formed from "E and O," representing Earl and Otto Binder, for all practical purposes Eando was Otto Binder; the early, collaborative stories comprise a very minor component of the Binder works, both qualitatively and quantitatively. Binder maintained that a real professional could write anything, from the libretto of an opera to a technical manual. While not embracing quite this broad a range, his works were sufficiently varied to give the notion strong support. In addition to his science fiction, Binder produced weird-horror fiction, gothic romance, and considerable non-fiction, as well as hundreds of comic book and comic strip "scripts."

Binder's most important single story is generally regarded to be "I, Robot," published in the January 1939 *Amazing*. (The Isaac Asimov book, *I, Robot*, appeared in 1950. Its title was as much a tribute to Binder as anything else; in his autobiography, Asimov attributes the inspiration of his famous "positronic robot" stories to a meeting with Binder and the reading of Binder's "I, Robot.") The significance of Binder's story lies in its sympathetic, even emotional, portrayal of the robot Adam Link. This effect is heightened by the first-person narration. The story was hugely successful and led to a series of popular sequels. Lester del Rey's equally significant "sympathetic robot" story, "Helen O'Loy," was written independently and simultaneously with Binder's "I, Robot," and actually reached print in *Astounding* a month before Binder's story. Del Rey abandoned the theme after a single effort, while Binder, Asimov, and shortly thereafter Eric Frank Russell (with his Jay Score stories) continued the development of the theme.

Binder's stories collected as *Anton York—Immortal* were also highly popular in their day, although lacking in the seminal significance of the Adam Link series. The Anton York stories are concerned with the impact of immortality on a lone man (eventually joined by an immortal wife) and on society. A number of Binder's other stories and novels achieved popularity in their time, but have little present readership. Their loss of popularity is probably due to Binder's stylistic limitation. Though a perfectly competent writer, he did not often succeed in bringing a sense of excitement to his prose; an illuminating comparison is E.E. Smith, whose unbounded energy totally transcended the limitations of his weak prose style.

Binder's "Via Etherline" tales were later collected as *Puzzle of the Space Pyramids*. Prior to the appearance of these stories, space travel and interplanetary exploration were almost always portrayed as glamorous, romantic activities, Binder instead portrayed them as grimy, difficult, dangerous, and often boring tasks. The stories were echoed in the realistic/predictive space fiction of Arthur C. Clarke, e.g., *Prelude to Space, Sands of Mars, A Fall of Moondust*.

In the 1940's and 1950's, Binder devoted most of his efforts to writing comic book continuity. As the principal writer for the *Captain Marvel* feature, he was chiefly responsible for the humorous, satirical, and often science-fiction elements that best characterized that altogether superior feature. In the 1960's, he developed an interest in UFOs and possible space-visitors, and three of his last works were devoted to these themes. One other series of stories by Binder is noteworthy. These are the tales about Jon Jarl, a young officer in the space patrol of the future. Binder wrote literally scores of these stories as text filler in the *Captain Marvel Adventures* comic book. As juvenile science fiction, they are charming, succinct, and stimulating. They have, unfortunately, never been collected.

While Binder is associated primarily with science fiction, his creative output was actually far more varied than his reputation would indicate. As a prolific author of pulp magazine fiction, Binder was active in any number of fields, most notably mystery and horror. His work in these areas also remains uncollected, and even largely uncataloged, a regrettable state of affairs as Binder was ever the competent (albeit frequently uninspired) professional. An available example of Binder's horror writing is *The Hospital Horror*. Produced very late in his career and published not long before his death, this novel unfortunately is the work of an author long past his prime; Binder's magazine writing in the horror genre is far better and far more representative of his true talent (albeit difficult to obtain).

—Richard A. Lupoff

---

**BINDER, Otto.** *See* **BINDER, Eando.**

---

**BISCHOFF, David F(rederick).** Also writes as Mark Grant. American. Born in Washington, D.C., 15 December 1951. Educated at the University of Maryland, College Park, B.A. 1973. Worked as a dishwasher, soda-jerk clerk; associate editor, *Amazing*, New York. Since 1974 staff member, NBC-TV, Washington,

D.C. Secretary, 1978–80, and from 1980 vice-president, Science Fiction Writers of America. Address: c/o Warner Books Inc., 666 Fifth Avenue, New York, New York 10103, U.S.A.

### Science-Fiction Publications

Novels (series: Dragonstar; Gaming Magi; Nightworld; Star Hounds)

*The Seeker*, with Christopher Lampton. Toronto, Laser, 1976.
*Forbidden World*, with Ted White. New York, Popular Library, 1978.
*Tin Woodman*, with Dennis R. Bailey. New York, Doubleday, 1979; London, Sidgwick and Jackson, 1980.
*Nightworld*. New York, Ballantine, 1979.
*Star Fall*. New York, Berkley, 1980.
*The Vampires of Nightworld*. New York, Ballantine, 1981.
*Star Spring*. New York, Berkley, 1982.
*Day of the Dragonstar*, with Thomas F. Monteleone. New York, Berkley, 1983.
*Mandala*. New York, Berkley, 1983.
*Wargames* (novelization of screenplay). New York, Dell, and London, Penguin, 1983.
*Night of the Dragonstar*, with Thomas F. Monteleone. New York, Berkley, 1985.
*Galactic Warriors* (Star Hounds). New York, Ace, 1985.
*The Destiny Dice* (Gaming Magi). New York, New American Library, 1985.
*The Infinite Battle* (Star Hounds). New York, Berkley, 1985.
*Wraith Board* (Gaming Magi). New York, New American Library, 1985.
*The Crunch Bunch* (for young adults). New York, Avon, 1985.
*A Personal Demon*, with Rich Brown and Linda Richardson. New York, New American Library, 1985.
*The Macrocosmic Conflict* (Star Hounds). New York, Berkley, 1986.
*The Unicorn Gambit* (Gaming Magi). New York, New American Library, 1986.
*The Manhattan Project* (novelization of screenplay). New York, Avon, 1986.
*The Blob* (novelization of screenplay by Chuck Densall and Frank Darabont). New York, Bantam, 1988.
*Dragonstar Destiny*, with Thomas F. Monteleone. New York, Berkley, 1989.
*Gremlins 2: The New Batch* (novelization of screenplay). New York, Avon, 1990.
*Abduction: The UFO Conspiracy*. New York, Warner, 1990.
*Deception: The UFO Conspiracy*. New York, Warner, 1991.
*Bill, the Galactic Hero, on the Planet of Tasteless Pleasure* (for children), with Harry Harrison. New York, Avon, 1991.

### Other Publications

Novels

*The Phantom of the Opera* (novelization of screenplay). New York, Scholastic, 1977.
*The Selkie*, with Charles Sheffield. New York, Macmillan, 1982.
Mutants Amok series (for children):
*Mutants Amok*. New York, Avon, 1991.
*Mutant Hell*. New York, Avon, 1991.
*Rebel Attack*. New York, Avon, 1991.

Other (for children)

*Quest*. Milwaukee, Wisconsin, Raintree, 1977.

Editor, *Strange Encounters*. Milwaukee, Wisconsin, Raintree, 1977.

* * *

David F. Bischoff has proven to be a steadily prolific writer, both individually and in collaboration with others. His earliest book-length work was *The Seeker*, written with Christopher Lampton, in which a humanoid alien, refugee from a repressive interstellar society, crashes on Earth, followed by agents of his own society. This was just the first of several collaborative novels in the early stages of his career. The most successful of these was *Tin Woodman*, with Dennis R. Bailey. A young man with telepathic powers and an inability to fit into human society is sent on a mission to attempt communication with a sentient alien starship. Unfortunately, the man commanding the team is a power-hungry psychopath who bullies his crew, falsifies orders, and endangers the entire mission. The interplay of the potentially mutinous crew is particularly effective.

*Day of the Dragonstar, Night of the Dragonstar*, and *Dragonstar Destiny*, all in collaboration with Thomas F. Monteleone, compose a trilogy concerning a space-travelling habitat, apparently a gigantic zoo. In the opening volume, an exploration team is attacked by dinosaurs and a rescue party must determine whether or not there are any survivors. In the second volume, we learn that the dinosaurs are themselves intelligent, and in the conclusion, a group of humans assists them in escaping human exploitation.

Other novels co-written by Bischoff include *The Selkie*, an interesting fantasy/horror novel written with Charles Sheffield, *Forbidden World*, a space-exploration, adventure story co-authored with Ted White, and *A Personal Demon*, a humorous fantasy about a demon written with Rich Brown and Linda Richardson. He has also written occasional movie novelizations, including a young readers' version of *The Phantom of the Opera*, the suspense film *Wargames*, the remake of the classic *The Blob* and, most recently, *Gremlins 2*.

Bischoff has been very productive on his own as well, producing a steady output of above-average adventure stories. In *Mandala*, a ruthless general from a dominant interstellar power suffers amnesia and is subsequently nursed back to health by a telepathic woman. This contact alters his personality, and he returns to his former associates determined to alter the status quo.

Much more successful works are *Nightworld* and its sequel, *The Vampires of Nightworld*. Set in a world that has been cut off from contact with the rest of the human race, the two novels feature an enormous, hidden computer complex that has created hosts of androids to play the parts of vampires, dragons, werewolves, and other mythological creatures. An unlikely hero finds himself pitted against this computer and, accompanied by a man who possesses some remnants of an earlier, higher technology, sets off to locate and destroy Satan, the ruler of the world. In the sequel, although the computer has been destroyed, the devices it created still dominate the world. To date, these remain the most ambitious and effective of Bischoff's novels.

*Star Fall* and its sequel, *Star Spring*, are also noteworthy. The former deals with the maiden voyage of a luxury star liner and the adventures that befall it. The protagonist inadvertently switches bodies with a famous assassin, and vengeful relatives of past victims are disinclined to believe his protestation of innocence. The ship itself is owned by an alien who plots the provocation of a war between humanity and his own race. The same cast of characters return in the sequel, this time dealing with attempted murder and becoming lost in space.

Subsequent novels have been less interesting, though still entertaining. The Star Hounds trilogy, *The Infinite Battle, Galactic Warriors*, and *The Macrocosmic Conflict* are actually a single story line, in which a bitter woman pirates a starship in order to rescue her brother from nasty aliens. A fantasy trilogy consists of *The Destiny Dice, Wraith Board*, and *The Unicorn Gambit* is an interesting but fairly standard magical-war-through-the-dimensions variation. *The Crunch Bunch* is an amusing first contact story written for younger readers. Most recently, under the pen name Mark Grant, Bischoff has been writing the Mutants Amok series, a post-collapse adventure sequence.

Bischoff is an infrequent short story writer and has yet to produce anything outstanding in that form, but a few of his shorter pieces deserve notice. "In Media Res" is a fascinating piece about a hack writer who can produce only the middle of his stories. An actor becomes lost in the interface between his play and reality in "All the Stage, a World." His best short is "Waterloo Sunset," a haunting piece about a place where all times co-exist.

—Don D'Ammassa

---

**BISHOP, Michael.** American. Born in Lincoln, Nebraska, 12 November 1945. Educated at the University of Georgia, Athens, B.A. in English 1967 (Phi Beta Kappa). M.A. 1968. Served in the United States Air Force as English instructor, Air Force Academy Preparatory School, 1968–72: Captain. Married Jeri Ellis Whitaker in 1969; one son and one daughter. English instructor, University of Georgia, 1972–74. Since 1974, freelance writer. Recipient: Deep South Con XV Phoenix award, 1977; Clark Ashton Smith award, for verse, 1978; Nebula award, 1982, 1983; *Locus* award, for editing, 1984; Mythopoeic Fantasy award, 1988. Agent: Howard Morhain, 501 Fifth Avenue, New York, New York 10017. Address: Box 646, Pine Mountain, Georgia 31822, U.S.A.

SCIENCE-FICTION PUBLICATIONS

Novels (series: Urban Nucleus)

*A Funeral for the Eyes of Fire.* New York, Ballantine, 1975; London, Sphere, 1978; revised edition, as Eyes of Fire, New York, Pocket Books, 1980.
*And Strange at Ecbatan the Trees.* New York, Harper, 1976; as *Beneath the Shattered Moons*, New York, DAW, 1977; London, Sphere, 1978.
*Stolen Faces.* New York, Harper, and London, Gollancz, 1977.
*A Little Knowledge* (Nucleus). New York, Berkley, 1977.
*Catacomb Years* (Nucleus). New York, Berkley, 1979.
*Transfigurations.* New York, Berkley, 1979; London, Gollancz, 1980.
*Under Heaven's Bridge* (Nucleus), with Ian Watson. London, Gollancz, 1981; New York, Ace, 1982.
*No Enemy But Time.* New York, Pocket Books, and London, Gollancz, 1982.
*Who Made Stevie Crye?.* Sauk City, Wisconsin, Arkham House, 1984; London, Headline, 1987.
*Ancient of Days.* New York, Arbor House, 1985; London, Paladin, 1987.
*The Secret Ascension; or, Philip K. Dick Is Dead, Alas.* New York, Tor, 1987; London, Grafton, 1988.
*Unicorn Mountain.* New York, Arbor House, 1988; London, Grafton, 1989.
*Apartheid, Superstrings, and Mordecai Thubana* (novella). Eugene, Oregon, Axolotl Press, 1989.

Short Stories

*Blooded on Arachne.* Sauk City, Wisconsin, Arkham House, 1982.
*One Winter in Eden.* Sauk City, Wisconsin, Arkham House, 1984.
*Close Encounters with the Deity.* Atlanta, Georgia, Peachtree, 1986.

OTHER PUBLICATIONS

Short Stories

*Emphatically Not SF, Almost.* Portland, Oregon, Pulphouse, 1990.

Play

Screenplay: *Within the Walls of Tyre.* Worcester Park, Surrey, Kerosina, 1989.

Verse

*Windows and Mirrors.* Tuscaloosa, Alabama, Moravian Press, 1977.

Editor, with Ian Watson, *Changes.* New York, Ace, 1982.
Editor, *Light Years and Dark.* New York, Berkley, 1984.
Editor, *Nebula Awards 23–25.* San Diego, California, Harcourt Brace, 3 vols., 1989–91.

*

Bibliography: *Michael Bishop: A Preliminary Bibliography* by David Nee, Berkeley, California, Other Change of Hobbit, 1983.

Manuscript Collection: University of Georgia Libraries, Athens.

* * *

Michael Bishop's most personal collection of stories can be found in *Author's Choice Monthly #15.* In the opening essay, "Emphatically Not SF, Almost: Introduction," Bishop discusses his work in general and the stories he assembled for this collection specifically. The result offers insights into a major writer's creative processes. The collection includes Bishop's only sale to *Playboy*, a grim story called "The Egret," and two moving stories, "Patriots" and "Taccati's Tomorrow."

Bishop's recent novels show his admiration for Philip K. Dick. In *The Secret Ascension*, Bishop makes Dick the hero of the novel set on an alternative Earth where Richard Nixon is still President. Too often this kind of homage turns out to be an embarrassment, but Bishop coolly pulls it off while delivering a sly and savvy science fiction novel. *Unicorn Mountain* is a more serious novel dealing with AIDS and unicorns of two Earths dying of a mysterious disease. Here, Bishop creates four memorable characters: Bo Gavin, dying of AIDS; Libby Quarrels, owner of the ranch where the unicorns appear; Sam Coldpony, Libby's hired hand; and Paisley Coldpony, Sam's daughter, who discovers she has incredible powers. At times, the novel is almost too rich in detail. Bo and Libby watch a black and white TV that suddenly begins to display color signals, but the stations are from an alternative Earth where instead of MTV, there is a Big Band Station featuring videos of the Big Band Legends. On that Earth, the unicorns are dying, too. A TV reporter named Che Guevera covers the story. A program called "Erotic Practices of the Renowned and Powerful" features John F. Kennedy—who survived Oswald's assassination attempt—in his seventies. All of these little Phil Dickian touches are witty, but *Unicorn Mountain* suffers from too much of a good thing as the details multiply and tedium starts to set in by the book's conclusion.

Bishop's preoccupation with the themes of religion and deity are apparent in his strongest collection, *Close Encounters With the Deity.* This collection features two of Bishop's best stories: the title story and the controversial "The Gospel According to Gamaliel Crucis; Or, The Astrogator's Testimony." In the latter, Bishop supposes what would happen if God were a large insect. The story generated some heated debate when it was first published, as Isaac Asimov discusses in his informative forward to the collection.

In 1982, Bishop won the Nebula award for his story "The Quickening," a hauntingly surreal tale of dislocation and loss. In 1983, Bishop again won a Nebula award, this time for his outstanding novel, *No Enemy But Time.*

Earlier Bishop novels suffer from structural problems—confusing narratives, intertwining subplots, shifts in person from first to third and back again. But in *No Enemy But Time*, he masters the technical skills to bring off a superb performance. An infant, given away to a group of young girls near an Air Force base by his mute, prostitute mother, is adopted and given the name John Monegal. The child grows up to be different from other children: he experiences intense episodes of dreaming—spirit-travel—where he goes back in time to the Pleistocene era in Africa. After an argument with his stepmother, John leaves and later confronts an expert on the Pleistocene during a scientific conference. He makes such an impression that he is later recruited by the expert for a special project: a time-travel expedition to the Pleistocene. John goes and finds his dreams were real: everything is as he dreamed it. He meets the primitive humans inhabiting the African wilds: the habiline. John cleverly becomes one of the small band of habilines, and marries a female he calls Helen. Helen bears him a daughter before dying. Then, during an inferno, John takes his infant daughter time traveling to the present, where their lives are forever changed. *No Enemy But Time* is a searing novel of identity and misdirection. John's relationship with Helen is one of the most moving in the genre.

Also moving, but in a comic vein, is *Ancient of Days*, a novel which explores the possibilities of a habiline surviving in contemporary society. Expanded from the brilliant novella "Her Habiline Husband," *Ancient of Days* is Bishop's vehicle to critique American society. Narrated by a restaurant owner whose ex-wife scandalizes the small Georgia town by first living with the habiline—eventually marrying Adam—Bishop's clever sense of situation comedy and Southern mores delivers a story that is funny and sadly true. The characters are finely crafted and subtly drawn. *Ancient of Days* is Bishop's most controlled novel.

Bishop's first novel, *A Funeral for the Eyes of Fire* (later revised as *Eyes of Fire*) shows the problems of alien cultures trying to communicate. Much of the book is anthropologic: Bishop shows strange customs and taboos, alien Tropemen celebrate in rites centering on their eyes and the eyes of their ancestors. The action is slowed by long descriptions of alien lifestyles; when the realization of the lead character finally arrives, the reader is far ahead of the narrative.

*And Strange at Ecbatan the Trees* (later retitled just as clumsily *Beneath the Shattered Moon*) reads like a dreamy Jack Vance novel. On the planet Mansueceria, the genetically engineered society is made up of two groups: Maskers, programmed against strong emotion; and Atarites, the rulers who are capable of strong emotion and domination. The groups complement each other; under the 6,000 year-old plan devised by the Parfects of Earth, the rulers and the ruled live in harmony on the island of Ongladred. Yet they are in danger of destruction by the barbarians living on the islands beyond Ongladred. Only Gabriel Elk of Stonelore, who presents dramas acted by resurrected corpses, has the power to create weapons to save Ongladred. But by saving Ongladred, Gabriel Elk disrupts the society and the ancient plan for harmony.

*Stolen Faces* is Bishop's darkest novel. Lucian Yeardance is exiled to the planet Tezcatl to govern a colony, for victims of a leprosy-like disease, where Aztec rituals are embodied in the culture. Lucian discovers the disease is nonexistent: instead, the victims are a bizarre society whose mental illness is so extreme that mutilation is the group's method of self expression. The writing is bleak and the action violent. Although macabre and depressing, *Stolen Faces* presents discrimination in graphic terms—a theme Bishop uses again in his later works.

*A Little Knowledge* and *Catacomb Years* are a pair of linked novels. In *A Little Knowledge*, Bishop presents 2071 Atlanta as a domed city where people's status is reflected by the building level they live on. The society is a theocracy dominated by the Orth-Urban Church. Six aliens from 61 Cygni destabilize the status quo by professing faith in the Church. The philosophical and theological foundations of the culture are shaken as the power brokers have to come to grips with the alien question. The most entertaining subplot is the love story between a deacon of the Church and an agnostic journalist. But the book suffers from too many characters—most of them undeveloped—and murky plotting.

*Catacomb Years* continues the story of Atlanta with many new characters. Bishop develops the implications that the Cygusians are actually reincarnated humans. The resulting political and religious upheaval results in the breakdown of the domed city and a chance at freedom under open skies. Although technically superior to *A Little Knowledge, Catacomb Years* suffers from being overly long and tedious; a reedited single volume combining the best of *A Little Knowledge* and *Catacomb Years* would be much more satisfying than the flawed twin novels.

*Transfigurations* is an expanded version of Bishop's novelette that was a Hugo and Nebula nominee in 1973, "Death and Designation among the Adadi." The original story of an obsessed anthropologist's attempts to solve the mysteries of an enigmatic race of aliens gives way to the anthropologist's daughter's search for her missing father. The result is a disappointing extrapolation of the original story's premises, and proves that by revealing more of a mystery you get a less compelling resolution than when the reader is left to imagine and ponder the inexplicable.

Bishop's short-story collections gather most of his Hugo and Nebula award winners and nominees. *Blooded on Arachne* includes 13 stories published between 1970 and 1978. The best are "Blooded on Arachne," "Rogue Tomato," "The White Otters of Childhood," and "Cathadonian Odyssey." *One Winter in Eden* includes a dozen stories published between 1979 and 1983. The best in this collection are "One Winter in Eden," "The Quickening," "Cold War Orphans," "Saving Face," "Season of Belief," "Within the Walls of Tyre," and "Collaborating."

As an anthologist, Bishop has shown marvelous taste. In *Changes*, edited with Ian Watson, Bishop presents a theme anthology centering on humans transforming into something else. But Bishop's masterpiece anthology is the controversial *Light Years and Dark.* Bishop blends original stories commissioned for this volume with notable stories published in the last 25 years. The result is a definitive collection that should rank with Harlan Ellison's *Dangerous Visions* anthologies.

Michael Bishop is a talented novelist, short-story writer, and anthologist, rapidly becoming one of the most important figures writing science fiction today.

—George Kelley

---

**BLADE, Alexander.** *See* **GARRETT, Randall; PHILLIPS, Rog.**

---

**BLAKE, Anthony.** *See* **TUBB, E.C.**

---

**BLAYLOCK, James P.** American. Born in Long Beach, California, 20 September 1950. Educated at California State University, Fullerton, B.A. 1972; M.A. 1974. Married Viki Lynn Martin in 1972; two sons. Pet food store clerk, Garden Grove, California, 1967–72; construction worker, Placentia, California, 1972–80; part-time instructor, Fullerton Community College, 1976–89; part-time instructor of English, California State University, Fullerton, 1980–87. Recipient: Philip K. Dick award, 1986; World Fantasy award, 1986. Address: c/o Berkley Publishing Group, 200 Madison Avenue, New York, New York 10016, U.S.A.

SCIENCE-FICTION PUBLICATIONS

Novels (series: Elfin Ship)

*The Elfin Ship.* New York, Ballantine, 1982; London, Grafton, 1989.
*The Disappearing Dwarf* (Elfin Ship). New York, Ballantine, 1983; London, Grafton, 1989.
*The Digging Leviathan.* New York, Berkley, 1984; Bath, Morrigan, 1988.
*Homunculus.* New York, Berkley, 1986; Bath, Morrigan, 1988.
*Land of Dreams.* New York, Arbor House, 1987; London, Grafton, 1989.
*The Last Coin.* New York, Ace, 1988; London, Grafton, 1989.
*The Stone Giant* (Elfin Ship). New York, Ace, 1989; London, Grafton, 1990.
*The Paper Grail.* New York, Ace, 1991.
*Lord Kelvin's Machine.* Sauk, Wisconsin, Arkham House, 1991.
*The Magic Spectacles.* Bath, Morrigan, 1991.

Short Stories

*Paper Dragons.* Seattle, Washington, Axolotl Press, 1986.
*The Pink of Fading Neon.* Seattle, Washington, Axolotl Press, 1986.
*The Shadow on the Doorstep.* Seattle, Washington, Axolotl Press, 1987.
*Two Views of a Cave Painting; and The Idol's Eye.* Seattle, Washington, Axolotl Press, 1987.

* * *

Blaylock creates realistic landscapes, even when they are those of fairy tale countries, to accommodate his blend of everydayness, quirky characters, zany motivations, metaphysical speculation, and many varieties of magic. His magic may be simply a subjective celebration: " 'Luminiferous ether' he rolled the phrase on his tongue, listening to the magic of it" ("The Better Boy," with Tim Powers in *Isaac Asimov's Science Fiction Magazine*, February, 1991). Or it may be a freakishly active magic, such as, in *Land of Dreams*, subverts the space/time continuum to conjure Fortean-like artifacts from the ocean. Or it may be, as in the *The Elfin Ship* series, the straightforward magic of wizardry and witchcraft, even though submarines and airships are among its instruments. It is useless to look for consistency in Blaylock's magic; but it so permeates his communities and landscapes as to claim, along with them, a conceded acceptance.

He is an artist of landscapes. Those in *The Elfin Ship* series are populated by dwarfs, trolls, goblins, and giants. Their winding rivers, dark forests, and hill-perched castles combine a suggestion of primal North America with evocation of the Grimm Brothers' folkloric lands. In *The Disappearing Dwarf* deep woods and craggy mountains, flanked by glowing glaciers and pierced with cavernous treasure trails, are as full of telluric magic as are the crystalline oceanic abysses of *The Stone Giant.* Its aura, as well as the more overt effects of goblin sorcery, lend piquancy to the ordinariness of such missions as Jonathan Bing's river voyage to sell cheeses in Seaside and bring back cakes to Twombly Town.

In other novels, Californian coasts are treated (up to a point) realistically: the north coast of San Francisco in *Land of Dreams*, and the environs of Los Angeles in *The Digging Leviathan.* A transfiguring magic warps this landscape, however. In the latter novels, the Los Angeles highway network, San Pedro Bay, and Catalina Island exist in substantial detail, but almost as a mental projection made actual: "The black asphalt street undulated as if it were a river coming to life [. . .] and below it waited beasts, unidentifiable beasts nosing up out of subterranean caverns." Caverns are entry to the underground/submarine world that rival parties, by digger and diving-bell, explore and exploit in pursuit or support of the gilled boy Giles, regressively seeking "return to the land of his ancestors." It is pseudo-science and extravagant fantasy, certainly, but it engagingly persuades suspended disbelief. Similarly, in *Land of Dreams*, the Humbolt County townlet of Rio Dell is vividly actual: "Only a single fisherman sat on the pier, whittling idly. The wind blew down the centre of the street, whirling a yellowed old sheet of newspaper into the air and picking up leaves." Yet this is the scene of time fugues, the brewing of an alchemical elixir, and the coincidence of astronomical cycles with bizarre materializations and resurrections: realism and fantasy uniquely fused.

There are also British locales. The site of one episode of *The Digging Leviathan* is Lake Windermere, also connected with the under-earth. In *Homunculus*, action centres on 19th-century London. The element of realism here is distinctly subordinate to "Gothicry," with a low-life pitched between Doré and Dickens. After episodes of messianic madness, grave-robbing, aquarium-robbing and pursuit through the London sewers, events climax in the descent of a skeleton-manned dirigible at Hampstead Heath to carry away that immortal mannikin, the Paracelsian homunculus. Inventive as ever of grotesquery in environment and character, Blaylock continually summons humour out of horror. He infiltrates sly literary and genre allusions, such as when the existence of a Mars-accessing crystal egg, reputedly stolen from a curiosity shop near Seven Dials, appears to be known to the costermongers of Petticoat Lane. Switching allusion from Wells to Delany, the Royal Academician's paper "Time Considered as a Succession of Semi-closed Doors" is similarly a science fiction in-joke.

Revelling in such metafictional ploys, Blaylock also, in introducing mythic and semi-mythic characters and themes, contrives tenuous archetypal resonances. Thus, the eponymous alchemical homunculus is identified with the secret of Joanna Southcote's Box; and the curses laid on Ahasuerus and on Judas Iscariot seem to dog the steps and shape the destiny of Jules Pennyman who, in *The Last Coin*, epitomizes the predatory, immortality-obsessed, evil magician. Pennyman plays a sinister role, but is not allowed permanently to spoil one of Blaylock's Californian Edens. There, at the ocean's edge, just off the Pacific Highway, homely, if eccentric, townfolk act out their life-enhancing, crazy schemes, their determination to win eventually rewarded. For his often frustrated hero, Andrew Vanbergen, a devotee of *The Wind in the Willows*, there is always "the promise of heaven on the soft wind, 'the place of my song-dream,' as Rat put it."

Much of Blaylock's fiction is in essence pastoral—not escapist, because one is always aware that there are wolves; but joyous and, as entertainments, often raising mind and emotions to the pitch of unexpected insight and sudden laughter. Fantasy teeters on the brink of science fiction—unorthodox theories of gravity and light, poetic paleo-zoologies, all in the vein of the reflection of one of his characters that: "[t]he hypothesis wasn't scientifically sound, maybe, but that didn't mean it wasn't right." Blaylock's literary enthusiasms and eclecticism are plain in his texts, but are additionally demonstrated in his many epigraphs; Laurence Sterne and Robert Louis Stevenson provide frequent quotes. One from the latter, quoted before Book One of *The Last Coin*, concludes: "A happy man or woman is a better thing than a five-pound note." It would be an apt epigraph for any complete Blaylock.

—K.V. Bailey

---

**BLAYRE, Christopher.** Pseudonym for Edward Heron-Allen; also wrote as Nora Helen Warddel. British. Born in London, 17 December 1861. Educated at Harrow School. Served with the Staff Intelligence Department of the War Office during World War I. Married 1) Marianna Lehmann in 1891; 2) Edith Pepler in 1903; one daughter. Admitted as a Solicitor of the Supreme Court, 1884. Lived in the United States, 1886–89; gave frequent lectures on protozoology. Editor, with E. Polonaski, *Violin Times*, London, 1893–1907. Fellow, Royal Society, 1919. *Died 28 March 1943.*

SCIENCE-FICTION PUBLICATIONS

Short Stories

*The Purple Sapphire and Other Posthumous Stories*. London, Philip Allan, 1921; revised edition, as *The Strange Papers of Dr. Blayre*, 1932; New York, Arno Press, 1976.
*The Cheetah-Girl*. Privately printed, 1923.
*Some Women of the University, Being a Last Selection from the Strange Papers of Christopher Blayre*. London, Stockwell, 1934.

OTHER PUBLICATIONS as Edward Heron-Allen

Novels

*The Princess Daphne*. London, Drane, 1885; Chicago, Belford Clarke, 1888.
*The Romance of a Quiet Watering-Place* (as Nora Helen Warddel). Chicago, Belford Clarke, 1888.

Short Stories

*Kisses of Fate*. Chicago, Belford Clarke, 1888.
*A Fatal Fiddle*. Chicago, Belford Clarke, 1890.

Verse

*The Love-Letters of a Vagabond*. London, Drane, 1889.
*The Ballads of a Blasé Man*. Privately Printed, 1891.

Other

*De Fidiculis Opusculum*. Privately printed, 9 vols., 1882–1941.
*Chiromancy; or, The Science of Palmistry*, with Henry Frith. London, Routledge, 1883.
*Codex Chiromantiae*. Privately printed, 3 vols., 1883–86.
*Violin-Making, As It Was and Is*. London, Ward Lock, 1884; Boston, Howe, 1901.
*A Manual of Cheirosophy*. London, Ward Lock, 1885.
*Practical Cheirosophy: A Synoptical Study of the Science of the Hand*. New York and London, Putnam, 1887.
*De Fidiculis Bibliographia, Being an Attempt Towards a Bibliography of the Violin and All Other Instruments with a Bow*. London, Griffith Farran, 2 vols., 1890–94.
*Prolegomena Towards the Study of Chalk Foraminifera*. London, Nichols, 1894.
*Some Side-lights upon Edward FitzGerald's Poem "The Rubá'yát of Omar Khayyám."* London, Nichols, 1898.
*Nature and History at Selsea Bill*. Selsey, Sussex, Gardner, 1911.
*Selsey Bill: Historic and Prehistoric*. London, Duckworth, 1911.
*The Vistors' Map and Guide to Selsey*. Selsey, Sussex, Gardner, 1912.
*The Foraminifera of the Clare Island District, Co. Mayo, Ireland*, with Arthur Earland. Dublin, Clare Island Survey, 1913.
*Protozoa* (report for the 1910 Antarctic expedition), with Arthur Earland. Privately printed, 1922.
*Barnacles in Nature and Myth*. London, Oxford University Press, 1928.
*The Gods of the Fourth World, Being Prolegomena Towards a Discourse upon the Buddhist Religion*. Privately printed, 1931.
*The Parish Church of St. Peter on Selsey Bill, Sussex*. Privately printed, 1935.

Editor, *Edward FitzGerald's Rubá'iyát of Omar Khayyám, with the Original Persian Sources*. London, Quaritch, 1899.
Editor, *The Second Edition of Edward FitzGerald's Rubá'iyát of Omar Khayyám*. London, Duckworth, 1908.
Editor, with Arthur Earland, *The Fossil Foraminifera of the Blue Marl of the Côte des Basques*. Manchester, Literary and Philosophical Society, 1919.
Editor, *Memoranda of Memorabilia*, by Madame de Sévigné. Privately printed, 1928.
Editor, *The Further and Final Researches of Joseph Jackson Lister upon the Reproductive Process of Polystomella crispa (Linné)*. Washington, D.C., Smithsonian Institution, 1930.

Editor and Translator, *A Fool of God: The Mystical Works of Bába Táhir*. London, Octagon Press, 1979.

Translator, *The Science of the Hand*, by C.S. d'Arpentigny. London, Ward Lock, 1886.
Translator, *The Rubá'iyát of Omar Khayyám*. London, Nichols, 1898.
Translator, *The Lament of Bába Táhir*. London, Quaritch, 1902.
Translator, *Quatrains of Omar Khayyám*. London, Mathews, 1908; revised edition, 1908.
Translator, *The Rubá'yát of Omar Khayyám the Poet: The Literal Translation of the Ousley Manuscript*. London, Lane, 1924.

* * *

Christopher Blayre remains an enigmatic figure. His extraordinarily versatile life in varied scientific and artistic fields is mostly well recorded—he did research in marine biology and palaeontology, horticulture, music, occultism, Persian literature, history, and bibliography—but the names under which he wrote some of his unacknowledged fiction have not been discovered, and how much more he may have written of possible interest is not known. What we do have is a quite interesting group of stories, mainly on supernatural themes, and a few with a place in science fiction's formative stage. The weird stories use familiar elements of ghosts and apparitions, possession, visions, and curses, but the treatment is modern. There is some effective satirical humor, as in the immortal Wandering Jew succumbing to modern medicine, and a visit to an annex to Hell with an institution for completing unfinished works.

"Aalila" concerns a visit to Venus by matter transmission. The Venerians, who inevitably resemble humans, have an incompatible culture, and the experimenter's inevitable sexual involvement with Aalila leads to the expected disaster. It is an effective tale for all its familiarity. "The Cosmic Dust" is a sequel, and must be among the earliest stories on the interplanetary transmission of life in spores. This was a very important concept and raises questions that remain open. "The Mirror That Remembered" has another idea often suggested, a device for visualizing past scenes. A marginal item is "The Blue Cockroach," where a temporary change in personality follows an insect bite.

"The Cheetah-Girl," dropped by the publisher at the last moment from *The Purple Sapphire*, is a more ambitious work, a serious story of a macabre project—the creation of a human-cheetah hybrid, and its consequences. The rationale is logical, considering the elementary state of genetics in 1920. These stories compare very favorably with the better known protoscience fiction of the period. The style is easy, assured, and fresh.

—Graham Stone

---

**BLISH, James (Benjamin).** Also wrote as William Atheling, Jr. American. Born in East Orange, New Jersey, 23 May 1921. Educated at East Orange High School; Rutgers University, New Brunswick, New Jersey, 1938–42, B.Sc. 1942; Columbia University, New York, 1945–46. Served in the United States Army, 1942–44. Married 1) Virginia Kidd in 1947 (divorced); 2) Judith Ann Lawrence in 1964; one daughter and one son. Editor of a trade newspaper, New York, 1947–51; public relations counsel, New York and Washington, D.C., 1951–68. Editor, *Vanguard Science Fiction*, New York, 1958; co-editor, *Kalki: Studies in James Branch Cabell*, Oradell, New Jersey; vice-president, Science Fiction Writers of America, 1966–68. Recipient: Hugo award, 1959. *Died 29 July 1975.*

SCIENCE-FICTION PUBLICATIONS

Novels (series: Cities in Flight)

*Jack of Eagles*. New York, Greenberg, 1952; London, Nova, 1955; as *Esper*, New York, Avon, 1958.
*The Warriors of Day*. New York, Galaxy, 1953; London, Severn House, 1978.
*Cities in Flight* (revised edition). New York, Avon, 1970; London, Arrow, 1981.
  *Earthman, Come Home*. New York, Putnam, 1955; London, Faber, 1956.
  *They Shall Have Stars*. London, Faber, 1956; revised edition, as *Year 2018!*, New York, Avon, 1957.
  *The Triumph of Time*. New York, Avon, 1958; as *A Clash of Cymbals*, London, Faber, 1959.
  *A Life for the Stars*. New York, Putnam, 1962; London, Faber, 1964.
*A Case of Conscience*. New York, Ballantine, 1958; London, Faber, 1959.
*VOR*. New York, Avon, 1958; London, Corgi, 1959.
*The Duplicated Man*, with Robert A.W. Lowndes. New York, Avalon, 1959.
*The Star Dwellers* (for children). New York, Putnam, 1961; London, Faber, 1962.
*Titan's Daughter*. New York, Berkley, 1961; London, New English Library, 1963.
*Mission to the Heart Stars* (for children). New York, Putnam, and London, Faber, 1965.
*A Torrent of Faces*, with Norman L. Knight. New York, Doubleday, 1967; London, Faber, 1968.
*Welcome to Mars* (for children). London, Faber, 1967; New York, Putnam, 1968.
*Black Easter; or, Faust Aleph-Null*. New York, Doubleday, 1968; London, Faber, 1969; published with *The Day After Judgment*, as *The Devil's Day*, New York, Baen, 1990.
*The Vanished Jet* (for children). New York, Weybright and Talley, 1968.
*Spock Must Die!* New York, Bantam, 1970; London, Corgi, 1984.
*The Day After Judgment*. New York, Doubleday, 1971; London, Faber, 1972; published with *Black Easter*, as *The Devil's Day*, New York, Baen, 1990.
*. . . And All the Stars a Stage*. New York, Doubleday, 1971; London, Faber, 1972.
*Midsummer Century*. New York, Doubleday, 1972; London, Faber, 1973.
*The Quincunx of Time*. New York, Dell, 1973; London, Faber, 1975.

Short Stories

*The Seedling Stars*. New York, Gnome Press, 1957; London, Faber, 1967.
*Galactic Cluster*. New York, New American Library, 1959; London, Faber, 1960.
*So Close to Home*. New York, Ballantine, 1961.
*Best Science Fiction Stories of James Blish*. London, Faber, 1965; revised edition, 1973; as *The Testament of Andros*, London, Arrow, 1977.

*Star Trek 1–12* (from the TV series; vol. 12 with Judith A. Lawrence). New York, Bantam, 12 vols., 1967–77; London, Corgi, 12 vols., 1972–79.
*Anywhen.* New York, Doubleday, 1970; London, Faber, 1971.
*The Best of James Blish,* edited by Robert A.W. Lowndes. New York, Ballantine, 1979.

Other Publications

Novels

*The Frozen Year.* New York, Ballantine, 1957; as *Fallen Star,* London, Faber, 1957.
*The Night Shapes.* New York, Ballantine, 1962; London, New English Library, 1963.
*Doctor Mirabilis.* London, Faber, 1964; New York, Dodd Mead, 1971.

Other

*The Issue at Hand: Studies in Contemporary Magazine Science Fiction* (as William Atheling, Jr.). Chicago, Advent, 1964.

Editor, *New Dreams This Morning.* New York, Ballantine, 1966.
Editor, *Nebula Award Stories 5.* New York, Doubleday, and London, Gollancz, 1970.
Editor, *Thirteen O'Clock and Other Zero Hours,* by C.M. Kornbluth. New York, Dell, 1970; London, Hale, 1972.

*

Bibliography: *James Blish: A Bibliography 1940–1976* by Judith A. Blish, privately printed, 1976.

Manuscript Collection: Bodleian Library, Oxford.

* * *

James Blish can be seen as the complete man of letters for the young genre of science fiction from his early days of fandom in the 1930's until his untimely death from cancer in 1975, and one wonders whether Blish, if he had lived, might not eventually have published the masterpiece he insisted the genre would be incapable of producing. Out of such ironies often come great works of art; and Blish had a consuming and scholarly interest in great art. The irony is that Blish as a writer came directly out of the pulp and fan tradition with all its variety, and even at the end of his career, when he was producing his best theories about the genre, he was also grinding out the highly commercial *Star Trek* novelizations. Blish was a steady producer of short fiction for the pulps who later learned to write superb novels and series. He saw the need for continuing critical writing and theorizing about the new genre of science fiction and produced masterful examples of both. He was a fan, an agent, an editor; and he was both beloved and feared for his totally comprehensive involvement with the genre. Blish's first editor, fellow Futurian, and friend, Robert A.W. Lowndes, develops the argument (in his introduction to *The Best of James Blish*) that Blish learned to write and to admire science fiction that was crafted "the hard way." His work, then, demonstrates both the scope and the artistic depth that was possible in science fiction during his lifetime.

Several of Blish's most often used themes, and the ironies and tensions inherent in those themes, can serve as illustration. *The Seedling Stars,* a full-length fiction made from shorter pieces about microscopic life, convinces the reader that mankind inhabits an infinite universe where the possibilities for protean form-changing and new dynamic adaptations (the real mainstream of science fiction) are seemingly limitless and also necessary. At the end of the book, this Stapledonian view is summed up as follows, "There's no survival value in pinning one's race forever to one set of specs." And yet within the same period of his writing, Blish is continually looking for the one set of eternal specifications that govern human existence. His most effective novel, *A Case of Conscience,* serves as the concluding part of a trilogy in which each of the protagonists is Christian; and the eternal battle between good and evil throughout the trilogy seems much more real and absolute than the open-ended relativism of adaptive evolution. Blish juggled these themes, and the comic tension from the resulting balance produces a high seriousness that (though the works appeared at first in the pulps) deserves to be treated as literature.

Another theme that apparently fascinated Blish, because it appears often through his work (from a juvenile such as *The Star Dwellers* to the epic ending of his tetralogy *Cities in Flight*), is the catastrophism of the explosive first moments of creation seen also as the end of all things. The awesome fecundity of the moment of death is Blish's most sublime image. I believe it appears frequently and interestingly enough in his work to allow a thoroughly Freudian analysis of Blish's fascination with death and with catastrophism. The point is that, though he is completely at home with the intentions and the conventions of the pulps as one is with one's hometown, the true territory that Blish explores extends into the most profound speculations of our time. He was a good scholar and a good critic who would be delighted to know that future scholars and critics will also value his fictions.

Blish's own late theorizing about the genre maintains that variety and a kind of comic fecundity constitute its strength and reason for existence at this time in our history. He bases his theory on the historical speculations of Oswald Spengler; and R.D. Mullen has argued (in his afterword published with the gathered sections of *Cities in Flight*) that the tetralogy is grounded in Spenglerian theory. What Blish denies, of course, following from Spengler, is that at this late date in our history and in this genre in particular, which best presents the variety of our time, no new synthesizing masterpieces (or epics) will appear. His own attempts are lengthy. *Cities in Flight* contains four novels. The trilogy that he intended to entitle "After Such Knowledge" contains the magnificent historical novel on Roger Bacon, *Doctor Mirabilis,* two novellas, and the science fiction novel *A Case of Conscience.* One would like to think that the theorist doth protest too much. But the trilogy was left unconnected at Blish's death, and the effect also of the tetralogy may be more centrifugal than centering. In any case, the work of Blish is rich with these dilemmas and tensions and, always, the art.

—Donald M. Hassler

---

**BLOCH, Robert.** Also writes as Collier Young. American. Born in Chicago, Illinois, 5 April 1917. Educated in public schools in Maywood, Illinois, and Milwaukee. Married 1) Marion Holcombe; one daughter; 2) Eleanor Alexander in 1964. Copywriter, Gustav Marx Advertising Agency, Milwaukee, 1942–53; editor, *Science-Fiction World,* New York, 1956; president, Mystery Writers of America, 1970–71. Recipient: Evans

Memorial award, 1959; Hugo award, 1959; Ann Radcliffe award, 1960, 1966; Mystery Writers of America Edgar Allan Poe award, 1960; Trieste Film Festival award, 1965; Convention du Cinéma Fantastique de Paris prize, 1973; World Fantasy Convention award, 1975; World Science Fiction Convention Lifetime Career award, 1985; Bram Stoker award, 1990; World Horror Convention Grandmaster award, 1991. Guest of Honor, World Science Fiction Convention, 1948, 1973; Bouchercon I, 1971; World Fantasy Convention, 1975. Agent: Shapiro-Lichtman Talent Agency, 8827 Beverly Boulevard, Los Angeles, California 90067, U.S.A. Address: 2111 Sunset Crest Drive, Los Angeles, California 90046, U.S.A.

### Science-Fiction Publications

#### Novels

*This Crowded Earth, Ladies' Day*. New York, Belmont, 1968.
*It's All in Your Mind*. New York, Curtis, 1971.
*Sneak Preview*. New York, Paperback Library, 1971.
*Strange Eons*. Browns Mills, New Jersey, Whispers Press, 1979.

#### Short Stories

*Atoms and Evil*. New York, Fawcett, 1962; London, Muller, 1963.
*Bloch and Bradbury*, with Ray Bradbury. New York, Tower, 1969; as *Fever Dream and Other Fantasies*, London, Sphere, 1970.
*Fear Today, Gone Tomorrow*. New York, Award, 1971.
*The Best of Robert Bloch*, edited by Lester del Ry. New York, Ballantine, 1977.
*The Selected Stories of Robert Bloch* (includes *Final Reckoning, Bitter Ends*, and *Last Rites*). Los Angeles, California, Underwood Miller, 3 vols., 1987; as *The Complete Stories*, New York, Citadel Press, 3 vols., 1989–91.
*Lost in Time and Space with Lefty Feep*, edited by John Stanley. Pacifico, California, Creatures at Large, 1987.

### Other Publications

#### Novels

*The Scarf*. New York, Dial Press, 1947; as *The Scarf of Passion*, New York, Avon, 1949; revised edition, New York, Fawcett, 1966; London, New English Library, 1972.
*The Kidnapper*. New York, Lion, 1954.
*Spiderweb*. New York, Ace, 1954.
*The Will to Kill*. New York, Ace, 1954.
*Shooting Star*. New York, Ace, 1958.
*Psycho*. New York, Simon and Schuster, 1959; London, Hale, 1960.
*The Dead Beat*. New York, Simon and Schuster, 1960; London, Hale, 1961.
*Firebug*. Evanston, Illinois, Regency, 1961; London, Corgi, 1977.
*The Couch* (novelization of screenplay). New York, Fawcett, and London, Muller, 1962.
*Terror*. New York, Belmont, 1962; London, Corgi, 1964.
*The Star Stalker*. New York, Pyramid, 1968.
*The Todd Dossier* (as Collier Young). New York, Delacorte Press, and London, Macmillan, 1969.
*Night-World*. New York, Simon and Schuster, 1972; London, Hale, 1974.
*American Gothic*. New York, Simon and Schuster, 1974; London, W.H. Allen, 1975.
*There is a Serpent in Eden*. New York, Zebra, 1979; as *The Cunning*, 1981.
*Psycho II*. New York, Warner, 1982; London, Corgi, 1983.
*The Night of the Ripper*. New York, Doubleday, 1984; London, Hale, 1986.
*Unholy Trinity: Three Novels of Suspense* (includes *The Scarf, The Dead Beat, The Couch*). Santa Cruz, California, Scream Press, 1986.
*Screams* (includes *The Will to Kill, Firebug, The Star Stalker*). Los Angeles, California, Underwood Miller, 1989.
*Lori*. New York, Tor, 1989.
*Psycho House*. New York, Tor, 1990.
*The Jekyll Legacy*, with Andre Norton. New York, Tor, 1990.

#### Short Stories

*Sea-Kissed*. London, Utopian, 1945.
*The Opener of the Way*. Sauk City, Wisconsin, Arkham House, 1945; London, Spearman, 1974; selection, as *House of the Hatchet*, London, Panther, 1976.
*Terror in the Night and Other Stories*. New York, Ace, 1958.
*Pleasant Dreams—Nightmares*. Sauk City, Wisconsin, Arkham House, 1960; London, Whiting and Wheaton, 1967.
*Nightmares*. New York, Belmont, 1961.
*Blood Runs Cold*. New York, Simon and Schuster, 1961; London, Hale, 1963.
*More Nightmares*. New York, Belmont, 1962.
*Yours Truly, Jack the Ripper: Tales of Horror*. New York, Belmont, 1962; as *The House of the Hatchet and Other Tales of Horror*, London, Tandem, 1965.
*Horror-7*. New York, Belmont, 1963; as *Torture Garden*, London, New English Library, 1967.
*Bogey Men*. New York, Pyramid, 1963.
*Tales in a Jugular Vein*. New York, Pyramid, 1965; London, Sphere, 1970.
*The Skull of the Marquis de Sade and Other Stories*. New York, Pyramid, 1965; London, Hale, 1975.
*Chamber of Horrors*. New York, Award, 1966; London, Corgi, 1977.
*The Living Demons*. New York, Belmont, 1967; London, Sphere, 1970.
*Dragons and Nightmares*. Baltimore, Mirage Press, 1968.
*Cold Chills*. New York, Doubleday, 1977; London, Hale, 1978.
*The King of Terrors*. New York, Mysterious Press, 1977; London, Hale, 1978.
*Out of the Mouths of Graves*. New York, Mysterious Press, 1979; London, Hale, 1980.
*Such Stuff as Screams Are Made Of*. New York, Ballantine, 1979; London, Hale, 1980.
*Mysteries of the Worm*. New York, Zebra, 1979.
*The Twilight Zone: The Movie* (fictionalization of screenplays). New York, Warner, and London, Corgi, 1983.
*Midnight Pleasures*. New York, Doubleday, 1987.
*Fear and Trembling*. New York, Tor, 1989.

#### Plays

Screenplays: *The Couch*, with Owen Crump and Blake Edwards, 1962; *The Cabinet of Caligari*, 1962; *Strait-Jacket*, 1964; *The Night Walker*, 1964; *The Psychopath*, 1966; *The Deadly Bees*, with Anthony Marriott, 1967; *Torture Garden*, 1967; *The House That Dripped Blood*, 1970; *Asylum*, 1972; *The Amazing Captain Nemo*, with others, 1979.

Radio Plays: *Stay Tuned for Terror* series (39 scripts), 1944–45.

Television Plays: *The Cuckoo Clock, The Greatest Monster of Them All, A Change of Heart, The Landlady, The Sorcerer's Apprentice, The Gloating Place, Bad Actor*, and *The Big Kick*, all in *Alfred Hitchcock Presents* series 1955–61; *The Cheaters, The Devil's Ticket, A Good Imagination, The Grim Reaper, The Weird Tailor, Waxworks, Till Death Do Us Part*, and *Man of Mystery*, all in *Thriller* series, 1960–61; scripts for *Lock-Up*, 1960, *I Spy*, 1964, *Run for Your Life*, 1965, *Star Trek*, 1966–67, *Journey to the Unknown*, 1968, *Night Gallery*, 1971, and *Dark Room*, 1983–84; *The Cat Creature*, 1973; *The Dead Don't Die*, 1975; *Beetles*, 1987.

Other

*The Eighth Stage of Fandom: Selections from 25 Years of Fan Writing*, edited by Earl Kemp. Chicago, Advent, 1962.
*The Laughter of a Ghoul, What Every Young Ghoul Should Know.* West Warwick, Rhode Island, Necronomicon Press, 1977.
*The Robert Bloch Companion: Collected Interviews 1969–86*, edited by Randall D. Larson. Mercer Island, Washington, Starmont House, 1989.

Editor, *The Best of Fredric Brown*. New York, Ballantine, 1977.
Editor, *Psycho-Paths*. New York, Tor, 1991.

Recordings: *Gravely, Robert Bloch*, Alternate World, 1976; *Blood!*, with Harlan Ellison, Alternate World, 1976.

*

Bibliography: *The Complete Robert Bloch: An Illustrated Bibliography* by Randall D. Larson, Sunnyvale, California, Farday, 1986.

Manuscript Collection: University of Wyoming American Heritage Centre, Laramie.

Critical Study: *Robert Bloch* by Randall D. Larson, Mercer Island, Washington, Starmont House, 1986.

Robert Bloch comments:

Although I have had upwards of 100 short stories and novelettes published in science-fiction magazines, I am primarily a writer of fantasy and mystery-suspense fiction: the bulk of my work falls within these two genres, as does my writing for screen, television, and radio. As a result my work has been almost entirely ignored by science-fiction critics and historians—thank God! Having somehow managed to survive as a professional writer over a period of 57 years, I'd hate to blow it now. I am still fascinated by the SF field and by the people in it.

* * *

It is an unfortunate fact that Robert Bloch will probably always be identified as the man who wrote *Psycho*. Unfortunate, not because this wasn't a significant achievement, but because he has written so much other excellent fiction that seems doomed to exist forever in that very long shadow.

A correspondent and fan of H.P. Lovecraft, Robert Bloch's early writing was predominantly in the horror field, although he wrote so prolifically that he overlapped into other areas as well. He wrote fantasy in the Thorne Smith mode, including such still readable stories as "Mr. Margate's Mermaid" and "Black Barter." Much of his early science fiction, such as "Fear Planet" and "Almost Human," uses traditional horror themes in a novel setting. Most of the rest is humorous, parodies and spoofs filled with puns and outrageous situations, most notably the "Lefty Feep" series. His few longer works from this early period are mostly disappointing. *This Crowded Earth*, for example, solves the population problem by introducing the idea of shrinking the human race so they will take up less space.

*It's All in Your Mind* makes use of the concept of the dream machine, a device that allows people to indulge their personal fantasies while in a dream state, without harming or offending anyone else. This is the closest Bloch was to get to a really successful full-length work of science fiction for years; as late as 1959 his novel *Sneak Preview* was interesting only because of what it shows us about the author's concerns for the world. In a future where pollution has driven most of the human race into domed cities, the government secretly executes people when they reach the age of fifty to control population growth. The story is a routine potboiler, culminating in a successful overthrow of the repressive rulers.

Bloch has always been at his best with shorter works, and the bulk of his fiction involves either supernatural or psychological terror. Collections with titles like *Blood Runs Cold, Nightmares, Bogey Men, Chamber of Horrors, Cold Chills*, and *Tales in a Jugular Vein* characterize much of his work. His fascination with Jack the Ripper led to "Yours Truly, Jack the Ripper," one of the finest horror stories ever written, as well as an historically accurate recent novel, *The Night of the Ripper*, and an episode of the television program, *Star Trek*, titled "The Wolf in the Fold." His fantasy story, "That Hell Bound Train," won the Hugo award for best story. Other horror classics include "The Skull of the Marquis de Sade," "The Cheaters," "Enoch," "The Opener of the Way," and "The Shambler from the Stars." Bloch has written extensively for television anthology programs like *Thriller* and *Night Gallery*, and for films, including *Torture Garden, The House That Dripped Blood*, and *The Cabinet of Caligari.*

Bloch blends science fiction with many of earlier interests in *Strange Eons*, set in the Lovecraftian universe, but removed to the future, in the context of a worldwide disaster. It is quite easily the best of his science fiction novels, perhaps because he brought to it the techniques which made his horror fiction so popular. Even though it is certainly a Lovecraftian tale, Bloch brings to this theme an original setting and plot. Most of his other recent novels have been in the field of psychological suspense, but one, *Lori*, is his first full-length supernatural work. Two sequels to *Psycho*, unrelated to the films, have also appeared.

Despite the preponderance of horror and suspense, Bloch's several hundred published stories include a number of noteworthy science fiction tales. "A Way of Life" is set in a future when the science fiction fans have taken over the world, a pleasant wish-fulfillment story that has enjoyed popularity to this day. The world's machinery revolts in "It Happened Tomorrow," and a rapist bites off more than he can chew when he attacks a very hungry "Girl from Mars." A cloned man must suffer the eternal imminence of death in "Forever and Amen."

The three best of Bloch's short SF stories are "Past Master," "The Man Who Murdered Tomorrow," and "The Man Who Collected Poe." In the first, an art thief from the future who wants to rescue works destroyed in a nuclear war inadvertently precipitates the war and destroys that which he came to save. In the second, a writer is driven to murder in order to gain access to ultimate power. The last story involves a man obsessed with Edgar Allan Poe. He brings Poe back to life as the newest exhibit for his collection, only to discover that Poe has ideas of his own. The Bloch collection with the highest predominance of actual science fiction stories is *Atoms and Evil*, which contains many of his best efforts.

Robert Bloch is a personable, soft-spoken man with an impish sense of humor, an intuitive insight into the darkest recesses of the human psyche, and an inordinately effective flair for storytelling. Only a very small proportion of his work has been within the genre, but even these occasional pieces have enriched the field.

—Don D'Ammassa

---

**BOND, Nelson S(lade).** American. Born in Scranton, Pennsylvania, 23 November 1908. Educated at Marshall University, Huntington, West Virginia, 1932–34. Married Betty Gough Folsom in 1934; two sons. Public relations field director, government of Nova Scotia, 1934–35. Freelance writer and philatelic researcher; now a book dealer. Recipient: International Stamp Exhibition award, for non-fiction, 1960. D. Litt.: Marshall University, 1988. Address: 4724 Easthill Drive, Sugarloaf Farms, Roanoke, Virginia 24018, U.S.A.

SCIENCE-FICTION PUBLICATIONS

Novel

*Exiles of Time.* Philadelphia, Prime Press, 1949.

Short Stories

*Mr. Mergenthwirker's Lobblies and Other Fantastic Tales.* New York, Coward McCann, 1946.
*The Thirty-First of February.* New York, Gnome Press, 1949.
*The Remarkable Exploits of Lancelot Biggs, Spaceman.* New York, Doubleday, 1950.
*No Time Like the Future.* New York, Avon, 1954.
*Nightmares and Daydreams.* Sauk City, Wisconsin, Arkham House, 1968.

OTHER PUBLICATIONS

Plays

*Mr. Mergenthwirker's Lobblies,* adaptation of his own story (televised). New York, French, 1957.
*State of Mind.* New York, French, 1958.
*Animal Farm,* adaptation of the novel by George Orwell. New York, French, 1964.

Author of screenplays for government agencies, some 300 radio plays, and television plays for *Philco Playhouse, Kraft Theatre, Studio One,* and other series.

Other

*The Postal Stationery of Canada: A Reference Catalogue.* Shrub Oak, New York, Herst, 1953.

* * *

Nelson S. Bond's only novel published in book form is *Exiles of Time*, and it actually constitutes the fourth volume of a tetralogy; the earlier works in the series, *Sons of the Deluge, Gods of the Jungle*, and *That Worlds May Live*, were published in *Amazing. Exiles of Time*, though written in a clear, readable style, suffers from too great a reliance on stereotyped characters. It is the story of a time traveller who encounters Ragnarok, and the epilogue quotes from the Elder *Edda*, giving the reader considerable insight into Bond's skill at plotting. It is an impressive demonstration. The ability to plot is one of Bond's strongest points, and he was never more sure or ingenious than here.

By and large, Bond's best fiction remains his short stories, and he has displayed a remarkable range with them. During his years as a regular contributor to the pulps he wrote not only for Ray Palmer's *Amazing* and *Fantastic Adventures*, but for John Campbell's more demanding *Astounding* and *Unknown.* He also wrote for *Thrilling Wonder Stories, Weird Tales*, and especially for *Planet Stories.* "The Castaway" (*Planet*, Winter 1940) is an almost perfect example of Bond's ability to make a formula story and raise it above its own limits. A spaceship crew rescues a man marooned on an asteroid. Subsequent events suggest he is a jinx and suicidal with the ship finally zooming out of control at a speed that will cause it to burn when it hits Earth's atmosphere. The castaway devises a way to save the ship and its crew, but the real surprise lies in his actual identity.

"The Castaway" fits into a future history that includes most of Bond's space stories. These stories seem to take place mostly in the 23rd century, with the solar system explored and colonized by Earthmen, and most of them center on members of the Solar Space Patrol or a space transport company called IPS. While Bond wrote a number of character series within this frame, the Lancelot Biggs series is probably the most important, and in many ways the most typical. Biggs is the eccentric and likeable first officer cf the IPS ship *Saturn*, and he divides his time between getting on his captain's nerves and producing scientific miracles to save the ship from certain disaster. About half these stories were included in *The Remarkable Exploits of Lancelot Biggs, Spaceman.*

While there is no denying Bond's talent with the short story, many of his novellas are excellent. Two *Planet* novellas from 1941 demonstrate his skill with space opera. Both center on the adventures of the young, clean-cut spaceman Chip Warren and his partners Syd Palmer and "Salvation" Smith. Shadrach has them discovering a rich lode of "ekalastron," an almost impervious metal, rare and valuable, that plays a part in several of Bond's future history stories. "The Lorelei Death" pits them against space pirates, but, though the better action story, it is marred by some questionable science in the ending. "Pawns of Chaos" (*Thrilling Wonder Stories*, April 1943) is based on the sort of idea popular with editors almost everywhere at that time, invaders from another dimension where the political system bears some similarity to that of Nazi Germany. Bond obviously had fun writing it, especially those sections describing battles in and around his home town of Roanoke, Virginia. "Pawns of Chaos" does not fall into Bond's future history sequence, nor do the Meg the Priestess stories, which constitute what is probably the best work he did in the SF pulps. In the Meg stories, civilization has virtually collapsed and humanity exists in scattered tribes, a few of which preserve knowledge of writing and reading through a matriarchal leadership, although their ideas of the past are distorted as myths and legends. In "Pilgrimage" (*The Thirty-First of February*) Meg becomes priestess of her clan in Virginia and travels west to consult the gods carved on Mount Rushmore. "Magic City" (*Astounding*, February 1941) has her visit the city of death—New York—to confront its goddess.

Bond's penchant for writing action scenes in settings he knows produced a superior story in "The Ultimate Salient" (*Planet*,

Fall 1940). A science-fiction writer receives a manuscript purporting to tell future events: the democracies fall to totalitarian forces in 1963 and the survivors flee to the moon where they face almost certain death because they lack the knowledge to synthesize chlorophyll. Since they are known to have taken a number of old SF magazines along, the writer is asked to use the manuscript as the basis of a story, ending it with the formula for chlorophyll that the survivors need. The story was later completely rewritten as "The Last Outpost," and is included in *No Time Like the Future.* The new version sets up a revolt against a world dictatorship, with neither the minions of the dictatorship nor the rebels being very desirable. Disaster befalls both sides but a third group flees to Venus—where the item needed for their survival is the formula for vitamin A.

Bond has claimed he was never actually a science-fiction writer but a fantasist who wrote for the SF magazines. Certainly his first big success (in 1937) was the fantasy "Mr. Mergenthwirker's Lobblies," about a gentle man who acquires the companionship of two invisible beings who foretell the future. Such stories as this were probably the prototypes of the sort of light fantasies Ray Palmer sought for *Fantastic Adventures.* It should be noted that Bond wrote a number of SF stories for his ostensibly fantasy markets, including *Blue Book*, and expressed pride in such stories as "To People a New World," "Martian Caravan," and the Pat Pending stories, about the inventor of a succession of incredible gadgets.

Bond's prose was polished enough for the prestige markets of the 1940's without being too slick to remain palatable today. By turns he can be humorous, serious, or adventurous, handling each approach with equal skill. But it is still in his plots that he really shines. His story "The Cunning of the Beast" (*The Thirty-First of February*) may be the most overworked story, that of Adam and Eve, but it is the most cleverly plotted of them all. A number of his yarns spring from Biblical or mythological sources, usually with happy results. "Uncommon Castaway" (*No Time Like the Future*) is a twist on the story of Jonah and the whale. Much of Bond's fiction resembles that of Saki or John Collier. "And Lo! The Bird" presents the Earth as an egg about to be hatched, and "Conqueror's Isle" tells of an outpost of supermen waiting for the passing of homo sapiens (both in *No Time Like the Future*).

Bond's knack for the off-beat is shown not only in his humor and his variety of approach, but also in a handful of stories written as poems. Two of them from *Planet*, "The Ballad of Blaster Bill" and "The Ballad of Venus Nell," show a touch of Robert Service (though to be honest, "Blaster Bill's" tempo is borrowed from Kipling's "Gunga Din").

—Gerald W. Page

---

**BONE, J(esse) F(ranklin).** American. Born in Tacoma, Washington, 15 June 1916. Educated at Washington State University, Pullman, B.A. 1937, B.S. 1949, D.V.M. 1950; Oregon State University, Corvallis, M.S. 1953. Served in the United States Army, 1937–46, and Army Reserve, 1946–66; Lieutenant Colonel. Married 1) Jayne M. Clark in 1942 (divorced 1946), one daughter; 2) Felizitas Margarete Endter in 1950, one daughter and two sons. Instructor, 1950–52, Assistant Professor, 1953–57, Associate Professor, 1958–65, and Professor of Veterinary Medicine, 1965–79, Oregon State University; editor, 1958–61, and columnist ("Diagnostic Quiz"), 1960–65, *Modern Veterinary Practice* magazine; consultant, University of Zimbabwe, Harare, 1982; Professor of anatomy, Ross University, St. Kitts, West Indies, 1984. Fulbright lecturer in Egypt, 1965–66, and Kenya, 1980–82. Recipient: Department of Health, Education, and Welfare award, 1969. Agent: Scott Meredith Literary Agency, 845 Third Avenue, New York, New York 10022. Address: P.O. Box 123, Basseterre, St. Kitts, West Indies. 3017 Brae Burn, Sierra Vista, Arizona, U.S.A.

SCIENCE-FICTION PUBLICATIONS

Novels

*The Lani People.* New York, Bantam, and London, Corgi, 1962.
*Legacy.* Toronto, Laser, 1976.
*The Meddlers.* Toronto, Laser, 1976.
*Gift of the Manti, with Ray Myers.* Toronto, Laser, 1977.
*Confederation Matador.* Virginia Beach, Donning, 1978.

OTHER PUBLICATIONS

Other

*Observations on the Ovaries of Infertile and Reportedly Infertile Dairy Cattle . . . .* Corvallis, Oregon State College, 1954.
*Animal Anatomy.* Corvallis, Oregon State College Cooperative Association, 1958; revised edition, as *Animal Anatomy and Physiology*, 1975.
*Animal Anatomy and Physiology.* Reston, Virginia, Reston Publishing Company, 1979; revised edition, 1982; third edition, Englewood Cliffs, New Jersey, Prentice Hall, 1989.

Editor, *Canine Medicine.* Wheaton, Illinois, American Veterinary Publications, 1959; revised edition, 1962.
Editor, with others, *Equine Medicine and Surgery.* Wheaton, Illinois, American Veterinary Publications, 1963; revised edition, 1972.

*

J.F. Bone comments:

I wrote science fiction principally for money, secondarily for personal amusement, and thirdly because I thought I could tell a good enough story to get in print. Technical papers and scientific publications were written mainly because I thought I had something to say to my colleagues. The textbooks—all variations on the same fields—were written and revised to assist me in my principal work, which was teaching. The fact that they were published was more of a surprise to me than I care to admit, and the fact that (for awhile) I was actually an editor is almost shocking in retrospect, but at the time it was the most fun I ever had—either before or since.

* * *

J.F. Bone made a considerable impact with the publication of his first novel, *The Lani People*, along with several first-rate shorter works. Unfortunately, his career faltered for approximately ten years; very few works appeared under his name, and none of them particularly memorable.

*The Lani People* comes perilously close to being a narrated lecture, for it quite obviously comments unfavorably upon man's tendency to dehumanize others. In the future, a race of humanoids exits, differing from normal humanity with the addition of a prehensile tail. They are considered less than human, property in fact, and have virtually no rights under the law. Despite the plot—the slow realization by the protagonist of the essential evil inherent in the situation—Bone is inventive enough to maintain reader interest throughout.

Of Bone's later novels, *Legacy* is rather a routine story of a marooned man who joins a police force on a far world and becomes involved with the effort to suppress a dangerous new drug, Tonacaine. Although not actively bad, the novel's trivial nature and trite plot are disappointing to those who read Bone's earlier work. The two other Laser novels are even more insignificant. In *The Meddlers* the human race is engaged in conscious manipulation of alien cultures for its own benefit. In *Gift of the Manti* the situation is just the opposite, with secretive aliens manipulating human culture for their own good, offhandedly wiping out 90 percent of the human race along the way. Both novels are underwritten, unbelievable, and totally forgettable.

Bone does better with *Confederation Matador*, although that novel also has serious flaws. After the collapse of a human interstellar empire, a new confederation has arisen, which is carefully trying to rebuild human technology. An agent is sent to a world colonized by Spanish-speaking peoples to discover why that colony is slowly losing its technological base, despite an absence of external pressures. The agent discovers that superhuman aliens have established a base and are systematically exterminating the human colonists. Although the novel has sections that are quite well done, Bone has added some unnecessary and confusing subplots that distract attention from the main issue.

There is a considerable body of shorter pieces by Bone, most of which remain quite readable. Of particular note is "Founding Father," (in *Galaxy*, April 1962), a novella in which stranded reptilian aliens use mental control to force humans to refuel their ship, and a strange relationship grows between the two species. Another excellent story is "Triggerman," (in *Astounding*, December 1958), which calmly presents a man with the ultimate power to cause or avert a nuclear war, and his dispassionate reaction to a world crisis. "On the Fourth Planet" (in *Galaxy*, April 1963) is not as ambitious as the other two, but this tale of a Martian slowly eating his way across the surface of his planet, and his unhappy encounter with a human probe, is extremely inventive and, within its limited structure, possibly the most successful of Bone's stories.

—Don D'Ammassa

---

**BOOTH, Irwin.** *See* **HOCH, Edward D.**

---

**BOUCHER, Anthony.** Pseudonym for William Anthony Parker White; also wrote as Theo Durrant; H.H. Holmes. American. Born in Oakland, California, 21 August 1911. Educated at Pasadena Junior College, California, 1928–30; University of Southern California, Los Angeles, B.A. 1932; University of California, Berkeley, M.A. 1934. Married Phyllis May Price in 1938; two sons. Theatre and music critic, *United Progressive News*, Los Angeles, 1935–37; science fiction and mystery reviewer, San Francisco *Chronicle*, 1942–47; mystery reviewer, *Ellery Queen's Mystery Magazine*, 1948–50 and 1957–68, and *New York Times Book Review*, 1951–68; fantasy book reviewer, as H.H. Holmes, for Chicago *Sun-Times*, 1949–50, and New York *Herald Tribune*, 1951–63; reviewer for *Opera News*, 1961–68. Editor, with J. Francis McComas, 1949–54, and alone, 1954–58, *Magazine of Fantasy and Science Fiction*, New York; editor, *True Crime Detective*, 1952–53; edited the Mercury Mysteries, 1952–55, Dell Great Mystery Library, 1957–60, and Collier Mystery Classics, 1962–68. Originated *Great Voices* program of historical recordings, Pacifica Radio, Berkeley, 1949–68. President, Mystery Writers of America, 1951. Recipient: Mystery Writers of America Edgar Allan Poe award, for non-fiction, 1946, 1950, 1953; Hugo award, for editing, 1958, 1959. *Died 29 April 1968.*

SCIENCE-FICTION PUBLICATIONS

Novel

*Rocket to the Morgue* (as H.H. Holmes). New York, Duell, 1942.

Short Stories

*Far and Away: Eleven Fantasy and Science-Fiction Stories.* New York, Ballantine, 1955.
*The Compleat Werewolf and Other Stories of Fantasy and Science Fiction.* New York, Simon and Schuster, 1969; London, W.H. Allen, 1970.

OTHER PUBLICATIONS

Novels

*The Case of the Seven of Calvary.* New York, Simon and Schuster, and London, Hamish Hamilton, 1937.
*The Case of the Crumpled Knave.* New York, Simon and Schuster, and London, Harrap, 1939.
*The Case of the Baker Street Irregulars.* New York, Simon and Schuster, 1940; as *Blood on Baker Street*, New York, Mercury, 1953.
*Nine Times Nine* (as H.H. Holmes). New York, Duell, 1940.
*The Case of the Solid Key.* New York, Simon and Schuster, 1941.
*The Case of the Seven Sneezes.* New York, Simon and Schuster, 1942; London, United Authors, 1946.
*The Marble Forest* (as Theo Durrant, with others). New York, Knopf, and London, Wingate, 1951; as *The Big Fear*, New York, Popular Library, 1953.
*The Case of the Seven of Calvary, Nine Times Nine, Rocket to the Morgue, The Case of the Crumpled Knave.* London, Zomba, 1984.

Short Stories

*Exeunt Murderers: The Best Mystery Stories of Anthony Boucher*, edited by Francis M. Nevins, Jr. and Martin H. Greenberg. Carbondale, Southern Illinois University Press, 1983.

Plays

Radio Plays: for *Sherlock Holmes* and *The Case Book of Gregory Hood* series, 1945–48.

Other

*Ellery Queen: A Double Profile.* Boston, Little Brown, 1951.
*Multiplying Villainies: Selected Mystery Criticism*, 1942–1968. Boston, Bouchercon, 1973.

*Sincerely, Tony/Faithfully, Vincent: The Correspondence of Anthony Boucher and Vincent Starrett*, edited by Robert W. Hahn. Chicago, Catullus Press, 1975.

Editor, *The Pocket Book of True Crime Stories*. New York, Pocket Books, 1943.

Editor, *Great American Detective Stories*. Cleveland, World, 1945.

Editor, *Four and Twenty Bloodhounds*. New York, Simon and Schuster, 1950; London, Hammond, 1951.

Editor, *The Best from Fantasy and Science Fiction*. Boston, Little Brown, 2 vols., 1952–53; New York, Doubleday, 6 vols., 1954–59.

Editor, *The Murder and the Trial*, by Edgar Lustgarten. New York, Scribner, 1958; London, Odhams Press, 1960.

Editor, *A Treasury of Great Science Fiction*. New York, Doubleday, 1959.

Editor, *The Quality of Murder*. New York, Dutton, 1962.

Editor, *The Quintessence of Queen: Best Prize Stories from 12 Years of Ellery Queen's Mystery Magazine*. New York, Random House, 1962; as *A Magnum of Mysteries*, London, Gollancz, 1963.

Editor, *Best Detective Stories of the Year: 18th* [through *23rd*] *Annual Collection*. New York, Dutton, and London, Boardman, 6 vols., 1963–68.

*

Bibliography: "Anthony Boucher Bibliography" by J.R. Christopher, Dean W. Dickensheet, and R.E. Briney, in *Armchair Detective* (White Bear Lake, Minnesota), nos. 2,3,4, 1969.

Critical Study: *The Eureka Years: Boucher and McComas's The Magazine of Fantasy and Science Fiction 1949–1954* edited by Annette P. McComas, New York, Bantam, 1982.

* * *

Anthony Boucher brought both style and sophistication to popular fantasy and science fiction, two qualities in rather short supply during the 1940's and 1950's. Boucher enjoyed successful careers in all three forms of popular literature; he was a critic, an author, and an editor.

Boucher wrote both fantasy and science fiction stories. Many of his best stories were published in Campbell's *Astounding Science Fiction* and *Unknown*, and in *Weird Tales*. Boucher's talent ran to the kind of fantasy or fantastic science fiction associated with *Unknown* in the 1940's and *Beyond* in the 1950's. His stories tend to be comic treatments of ordinary people involved in situations and actions that run contrary to their customary, common-sense approach to life. Boucher seems to imply that most people, and certainly his truly sympathetic characters, possess an innate disposition to believe in supernatural forces. As is the case with most characteristic *Unknown* stories, mythic themes in his stories are treated lightly with a comic and often ironic distance. "Q.U.R.," "Robinc," and "We Print the Truth" illustrate Boucher's manner in science-fiction stories. The first two stories are bar-room tales, similar to Henry Knutter's Galloway Gallegher tales and Arthur Clarke's *Tales from the White Hart*. They share characteristic themes with some of Heinlein's stories of the private inventor and of proprietory business enterprise as illustrated in "We Also Walk Dogs." Boucher's hero, Dugglesmarther H. Quinby, changes the world with a revolution in android technology, making the androids more efficient by making them less like humans. Boucher thus lightly shows two of his virtues as a writer: effective comic reversal of clichés or worn-out formulas to produce surprise and delight, and a humanistic and often literary resonance.

The best of his fantasy tales may be the most famous of his stories, the novella "The Compleat Werewolf." The title suggests, distantly perhaps, a parallel to the Michael Shea adventures of L. Sprague de Camp and Fletcher Pratt. Many of the storytelling concepts are the same: an academic setting; a strong courtship subplot; comic anachronism involving a modern character caught up in mythic or legendary adventures but retaining a modern, skeptical sense of incongruity; the concomitant farcical employment of magic; and the obligatory happy ending in which the hero returns to the prosaic world with a fuller appreciation of its homely values or at least its familiar comforts. Best of all, he returns to a world in which he fits. Boucher's 1942 tale includes a little Nazi espionage to spice up the plot. Professor Wolfe Wolf, the hero in spite of himself who ends with the right girl, is the pattern of the modern domesticated hero that has run remarkably true to form now for more than a quarter century.

Two or three other fantasy tales may be noted here briefly as representative of Boucher's range. "Snulbug" is Boucher's tale of modern demonology told with a more comic perspective than C.S. Lewis's *Screwtape Letters*, which it recalls. In Boucher's story, the human race is preserved from additional mischief by the incompetence of a conjurer and the third-rate demon he manages to call up to work his will. "They Bite" is an effective suspense-horror story making use of the familiar formula in which modern, skeptical men find themselves the unbelieving victims of legendary desert ogres. "We Print the Truth" is loosely based on the familiar contradiction between divine foreknowledge and free will. Boucher's fictional equivalent of divine foreknowledge is the *Grover Sentinel*, whose stories become true for all who read them. Boucher's speculations of wish fulfillment and something he terms "variable truth" are characteristically ingenious and amusing, very much like the armchair mysteries he wrote under the name of H.H. Holmes. It was under this name that Boucher wrote one of the most amusing science-fiction mystery *roman à clef* novels, *Rocket to the Morgue*, which is also a pastiche of styles, mannerisms, and familiar formulas of the main science-fiction writers of the dominant eastern establishment.

Boucher's best known SF story. "The Quest for St. Aquin" (1951), has lost none of its original luster after more than a quarter century. If anything, its stature has grown by virtue of the works it has to some degree inspired: James Blish's *A Case of Conscience* (1958), Walter M. Miller, Jr.'s *A Canticle for Leibowitz* (1960), and Robert Silverberg's "Good News from the Vatican" (1970). The quest takes place in a post-nuclear-catastrophe California in which religious worship of any kind is officially suppressed by the ruling Technarchy through its KGB-style "Loyalty Checkers." The quest ends with the paradoxical revelation that the fabled St. Aquin is in fact the one perfect android of legend that had proved by its faultless logic the existence of God, and whose present lifeless state proves that existence in quite another way. The virtues of the story are many, including the economy with which Boucher creates his repressive, future world, and the finely realized humanity of the story's characters. The central action depends on Boucher's skill in creating two characters: the young, unsophisticated priest sent on a quest by the pope to discover whether the cult of St. Aquin is orthodox, and the priest's mechanical "robass," Old Nick himself. The confrontation is altogether enchanting and somehow satisfying theologically at the same time. Among the story's many achievements as prophetic SF is its dramatization of the future brotherhood of all people of faith, whatever their religious affiliation. A quarter century ago that seemed a far more radical notion than it does today.

Perhaps Boucher's most important contribution to the literature of popular fantasy and SF came not as an author but as co-editor and later editor of *The Magazine of Fantasy and Science Fiction*, which made its debut before the public without "science fiction" on the masthead in 1949. The magazine has proven to be the healthiest and most consistently influential competition to the *Astounding/Analog* tradition of science fiction/science fact literature. Boucher and McComas established their magazine as a quality pulp that was more concerned with literary standards than with literary ideology. It has continued to publish stories in both genres that are distinguished by literary, that is mainstream, writing. Something must be added also about the affection and respect that Boucher won by his amiable disposition and urbane wit. His was one of the more important benign influences on the encouragement and development of many of the New Wave writers with whom he probably had less in common than with the Golden Age writers of his own salad days.

—Donald L. Lawler

---

**BOVA, Ben(jamin William).** American. Born in Philadelphia, Pennsylvannia, 28 November 1932. Educated at Temple University, Philadelphia, B.S. 1954. Married 1) Rosa Cucinotta in 1953 (divorced 1974); one son and one daughter; 2)Barbara Berson Rose in 1974. Editor, *Upper Darby News*, Pennsylvania, 1953–56; technical editor on Vanguard Project, Martin Aircraft Company, Baltimore, 1956–58; screenwriter, Physical Science Study Committee, Massachusetts Institute of Technology, Cambridge, 1958–59; science writer, Avco-Everett Research Laboratory, Everett, Massachusetts, 1960–71; editor, *Analog*, New York, 1971–78; editor, *Omni*, New York, 1978–82. Recipient: Hugo award, for editing, 1973, 1974, 1975, 1976, 1977, 1979; E.E. Smith Memorial award, 1974; Balrog award, 1983. Agent: Barbara Bova, 207 Sedgwick Road, West Hartford, Connecticut 06107. Address c/o Tor Books, 49 West 24th Street, New York, New York 10010, U.S.A.

SCIENCE-FICTION PUBLICATIONS

Novels (series: Exiles; Orion; Voyagers)

*The Star Conquerors* (for children). Philadelphia, Winston, 1959.
*Star Watchman* (for children). New York, Holt Rinehart, 1964; London, Dobson, 1972.
*The Weathermakers* (for children). New York, Holt Rinehart, 1967; London, Dobson, 1969.
*Out of the Sun* (for children). New York, Holt Rinehart, 1968.
*The Dueling Machine* (for children). New York, Holt Rinehart, 1969; London, Faber, 1971.
*Escape!* (for children). New York, Holt Rinehart, 1970.
*The Exiles Trilogy* (for children). New York, Berkley, 1980; London, Methuen, 1984.
  *Exiled from Earth*. New York, Dutton, 1971.
  *Flight of Exiles*. New York, Dutton, 1972.
  *End of Exile*. New York, Dutton, 1975.
*THX 1138* (novelization of screenplay). New York, Paperback Library, 1971; London, Panther, 1978.
*As on a Darkling Plain*. New York, Walker, 1972; London, Magnum, 1981.
*The Shining Strangers (for children)*. New York, Walker, 1973.
*When the Sky Burned*. New York, Walker, 1973.
*The Winds of Altair (for children)*. New York, Dutton, 1973.
*Gremlins, Go Home!* (for children), with Gordon R. Dickson. New York, St. Martin's Press, 1974.
*The Starcrossed*. Radnor, Pennsylvania, Chilton, 1975; London, Magnum, 1980.
*City of Darkness* (for children). New York, Scribner, 1976.
*Millennium*. New York, Random House, and London, Macdonald and Jane's, 1976.
*The Multiple Man*. Indianapolis, Bobbs Merrill, 1976; London, Gollancz, 1977.
*Colony*. New York, Pocket Books, 1978; London, Magnum, 1979.
*Kinsman*. New York, Dial Press, and London, Futura, 1979.
*Voyagers*. New York, Doubleday, 1981; London, Methuen, 1982.
*Test of Fire*. New York, Tor, 1982; London, Methuen, 1984.
*Orion*. New York, Simon and Schuster, 1984.
*Privateers*. New York, Tor, 1985; London, Methuen, 1986.
*Prometheans*. New York, Tor, 1986.
*The Alien Within* (Voyagers). New York, Tor, 1986; London, Severn House, 1987.
*The Kinsman Saga* (includes *Kinsman* and *Millennium*). New York, Tor, 1987.
*Welcome to Moonbase*. New York, Ballantine, 1987.
*Vengeance of Orion*. New York, Tor, and London, Methuen, 1988.
*Peacekeepers*. New York, Tor, 1988; London, Mandarin, 1989.
*Cyberbooks*. New York, Tor, 1989; London, Severn House, 1990.
*Star Brothers* (Voyagers). New York, Tor, and London, Methuen, 1990.
*Orion in the Dying Time*. New York, Tor, 1990.

Short Stories

*Forward in Time*. New York, Walker, 1973.
*Maxwell's Demons*. New York, Baronet, 1979.
*Escape Plus*. New York, Tor, 1984; London, Methuen, 1988.
*The Astral Mirror*. New York, Tor, 1985.
*Battle Station*. New York, Tor, 1987.
*Future Crime*. New York, Tor, 1990.

OTHER PUBLICATIONS

Other

*The Milky Way Galaxy: Man's Exploration of the Stars*. New York, Holt Rinehart, 1961.
*Giants of the Animal World* (for children). Racine, Wisconsin, Whitman, 1962.
*Reptiles Since the World Began* (for children). Racine, Wisconsin, Whitman, 1964.
*The Uses of Space* (for children). New York, Holt Rinehart, 1965.
*Magnets and Magnetism* (for children). Racine, Wisconsin, Whitman, 1966.
*In Quest of Quasars: An Introduction to Stars and Starlike Objects* (for children). New York, Collier. 1970.
*Planets, Life, and LGM* (for children). Reading, Massachusetts, Addison Wesley, 1970.
*The Fourth State of Matter: Plasma Dynamics and Tomorrow's Technology*. New York, St. Martin's Press, 1971.
*The Amazing Lase* (for children). Philadelphia, Westminster Press, 1971.
*The New Astronomies*. New York, St. Martin's Press, 1972; London, Dent, 1973.

*Starflight and Other Improbabilities* (for children). Philadelphia, Westminster Press, 1973.
*Man Changes the Weather* (for children). Reading, Massachusetts. Addison Wesley, 1973.
*Survival Guide for the Suddenly Single*, with Barbara Berson. New York, St. Martin's Press, 1974.
*The Weather Changes Man* (for children). Reading, Massachusetts, Addison Wesley, 1974.
*Workshops in Space* (for children). New York, Dutton, 1974.
*Notes to a Science Fiction Writer* (for children). New York, Scribner, 1975; revised edition, Boston, Houghton Mifflin, 1981.
*Through Eyes of Wonder* (for children). Reading, Massachusetts, Addison Wesley, 1975.
*Science—Who Needs It?* (for children). Philadelphia, Westminster Press, 1975.
*The Seeds of Tomorrow* (for children). New York, McKay, 1977.
*Viewpoint*. Cambridge, Massachusetts, NESFA Press, 1977.
*The High Road*. Boston, Houghton Mifflin, 1981.
*Vision of the Future: The Art of Robert McCall*. New York, Abrams, 1982.
*Assured Survival: Putting the Star Wars Defense in Perspective*. Boston, Houghton Mifflin, 1984.
*Interactions: A Journey Through the Mind of a Particle Physicist and the Matter of this World*, with Sheldon Glashow. New York, Warner, 1988.
*The Beauty of Light*. New York, Wiley, 1988.

Editor, *The Many Worlds of Science Fiction*. New York, Dutton, 1971.
Editor, *Analog 9*. New York, Doubleday, and London, Dobson, 1973.
Editor, *Science Fiction Hall of Fame 2*. New York, Doubleday, 1973.
Editor, *The Analog Science Fact Reader*. New York, St. Martin's Press, and London, Millington, 1974.
Editor, *Analog Annual*. New York, Pyramid, 1976.
Editor, *The Best of Astounding*. New York, Baronet, 1977.
Editor, *Closeup, New Worlds*. New York, St. Martin's Press, 1977.
Editor, *Exiles*. London, Futura, 1977; New York, St. Martin's Press, 1978.
Editor, *Aliens*. London, Futura, 1977; New York, St. Martin's Press, 1978.
Editor, *The Best of Analog*. New York, Baronet, 1978.
Editor, *Analog Yearbook*. New York, Ace, 1978.
Editor, with Don Myrus, *The Best of Omni Science Fiction 1–4*. New York, Omni, 1980–82.
Editor, *The Best of the Nebulas*. New York, Tor, 1989.
Editor, with Byron Preiss, *First Contact: The Search for Extraterrestrial Intelligence*. New York, New American Library, and London, Headline, 1990.

*

Manuscript Collection: Pennsylvania State University Library, University Park.

* * *

With over three dozen science fiction books to his credit, Ben Bova is one of the most familiar names in the field. Although his themes and plotlines range from relatively tame considerations of the implication of technological developments on society to world-destroying, space-travelling epics, all of his novels—both for adult and those aimed at younger readers—are characterized by careful adherence to scientific reality and the belief that human destiny lies in a greater arena than the one we presently occupy.

Two early novels illustrate Bova's major concerns. *The Weathermakers* is set in a future where most aspects of life on Earth are under human control, and now the final frontier, weather control, is about to be explored. The protagonist is a scientist who presses for funding for this project despite resistance from short-sighted politicians and the potential exploitation of the project by singleminded militarists, two stock characters who appear over and over in Bova's work. The perversion of scientific knowledge is mirrored in *The Dueling Machine*, when a device that allows people to enter a totally convincing fantasy world is turned into a murder weapon, one which will lead to political power as well.

Although much of Bova's early fiction was straightforward adventure, *The Multiple Man* explored the political arena with insight, and is still one of his best works. A charismatic and highly effective president seems to be singlehandedly reversing several adverse trends in American society. But one of his associates uncovers disturbing implications, including the possibility that the President has been replaced by a clone of himself. This is a finely etched political thriller as well as first class science fiction.

*Kinsman* and *Millennium* (later published together as *The Kinsman Saga*) are set in the near future and chronicle the life of Chet Kinsman, an astronaut devoted to the furtherance of space travel as the last hope for the human race. In the first novel, young Kinsman secures a position as an astronaut, but is then involved in a scandal that may bar him from space. The sequel (actually published first) features Kinsman on the moon, where he masterminds a joint effort by American and Russian staff members to coerce the governments of Earth into seeing reason and averting a war. Kinsman is a bigger–than–life character, a heroic figure in many senses, but Bova is also careful to ensure that he is not perfect, that he has the small failings that allow us to identify with him.

*Colony* has a very similar theme. Earth has deteriorated into a number of squabbling states, many of which are bankrupt in more than one sense of the word. From an orbiting colony comes David Adams, a genetically engineered human whose travels across his homeworld's surface provide a fascinating, and often depressing, vision of the future, but whose own quest for perfection is ennobling.

The determination of government to keep its citizens in the dark and oppose the advance of knowledge is the overriding theme once again in *Voyagers*, in which an alien spacecraft entering our system creates a deadly crisis in human affairs. Stoner, the protagonist, is thwarted from making contact because of governmental interference, and he is set adrift in space, in suspended animation. He is awakened in the sequel, *The Alien Within*, and discovers that his mind is now home to a non-human intelligence, which is determined to explore human society. Stoner becomes aware of the alien presence and is eventually able to assume control of a new type of technology that will change the face of the world. Naturally, venial government agencies move against Stoner, a conflict which is not resolved until the concluding volume, *Star Brothers*.

An atypical series for Bova was launched with *Orion*. The protagonist is an immortal warrior who battles for the advancement of humankind throughout the ages, pitted against opponents who use everything from magic to science. Orion returns to battle new opponents in *Vengeance of Orion* and *Orion in the Dying Time*.

The future of space travel, or lack thereof, is examined again in *Privateers*. The United States has withdrawn from space exploration, abandoning the field to the Russians, who now dominate the heavens and, economically, the Earth as well. A multimillionaire launches his own commercial effort, but when his property is impounded by the Russians, he resorts to an older device, privateering, to open up the spaceways. Somewhat implausible, perhaps, but the novel has a brash, cheerful bravado that makes it one of Bova's most enjoying stories. In *Peacekeepers*, a localized nuclear exchange has scared the world into establishing an organization to control all nuclear armaments, a situation that is challenged when a terrorist organization seizes several armaments. Bova's forays into humor are rare, but *Cyberbooks* is a notable exception, although the comedy is decidedly dark. The novel examines the implication of electronic reproduction of the written word, and the potential impact on the publishing industry.

Although not primarily noted as a short story writer, Bova has written several dozen, many of which are quite memorable. Of particular note are "The Next Logical Step," "Test in Orbit," "Stars Won't You Hide Me?", "Fifteen Miles," and the frightening "Nuclear Autumn."

To a certain extent, Bova's fiction is often propagandist in intent. His impatience with government bureaucrats who fear change or lack the imagination to deal with it, and his contempt for military leaders who see everything in terms of weaponry are recurring themes. His strong narrative techniques and obvious grasp of the technology involved, coupled with logical extrapolations of the consequences, help make his stories convincing as well as entertaining.

—Don D'Ammassa

---

**BOYD, Felix.** *See* **HARRISON, Harry.**

---

**BOYD, John.** Pseudonym for Boyd Bradfield Upchurch. American. Born in Atlanta, Georgia, 3 October 1919. Educated in Atlanta, Fulton County, Georgia, and St. Paul, Minnesota, public schools; Atlanta Junior College, 1938–40; University of Southern California, Los Angeles, A.B. in journalism 1947. Served in the United States Navy, 1940–45: Lieutenant Commander; mentioned in Royal Navy despatches. Married 1) Fern Gillaspy in 1944 (died in 1984); 2) Mary Coe in 1986. Production manager, Star Engraving Company, Los Angeles, 1947–71; freelance writer, 1971–79. Address: 1151 Aviemore Terrace, Costa Mesa, California 92627, U.S.A.

SCIENCE-FICTION PUBLICATIONS

Novels

*The Last Starship from Earth.* New York, Weybright and Talley, 1968; London, Gollancz, 1969.
*The Pollinators of Eden.* New York, Weybright and Talley, 1969; London, Gollancz, 1970.
*The Rakehells of Heaven.* New York, Weybright and Talley, 1969; London, Gollancz, 1971.
*Sex and the High Command.* New York, Weybright and Talley, 1970.
*The Organ Bank Farm.* New York, Weybright and Talley, 1970.
*The Gorgon Festival.* New York, Weybright and Talley, 1972.
*The I.Q. Merchant.* New York, Weybright and Talley, 1972.
*The Doomsday Gene.* New York, Weybright and Talley, 1973.
*Andromeda Gun.* New York, Putnam, 1974.
*Barnard's Planet.* New York, Berkley, 1975.
*The Girl with the Jade Green Eyes.* New York, Viking Press, 1978; London, Penguin, 1979.

OTHER PUBLICATIONS

Novels

*The Slave Stealer.* New York, Weybright and Talley, 1968; London, Jenkins, 1969.
*Scarborough Hall.* New York, Berkley, 1976.
*Behind Every Bush*, with Richard H. Ichord. Los Angeles, Seville, 1979.

*

Manuscript Collection: University of California, Fullerton.

John Boyd comments:

Insofar as any writer consciously erects a schema for the body of his work, my intentions in science fiction have been generally to take mythic themes and find—ideally to strike—their echoes in the modern world. I attempt, without pedantry, to be didactic and, above all, entertaining. A story without some moral theme, either expressed or implied, is usually frivolous, but an apparently frivolous tale with a strong moral basis can be a gem. In telling my tales, when the substance weakens, I attempt to beguile the reader with stylistic wiles.

* * *

In addison to romances of the historical and contemporary South, John Boyd has published 11 science-fiction novels. They are witty and sensuous, triumphs of style over substance, inventive in details if not major premises. Stylish variations on familiar SF themes, these tall tales kid the conventions of romance and science fiction, while satirizing human fatuousness.

*The Last Starship from Earth* depicts a dystopian alternate present, from which two star-crossed lovers are eventually exiled. Exiles on the planet Hell have manipulated the romance, involving the young mathematical rebel in a time-traveling story. Changing history, he fails to benefit from it, but lives on into our present as the wandering Jew. Romantic courtship rituals come in for a ribbing, as do the "rational" practices of a rigid behaviorist society, and the whole is imbued with allusions to English Romantic poetry.

Positing intelligent vegetable life, *The Pollinators of Eden* is a more lyrical tale of a repressed female scientist, ending with a complicated defloration and impregnation by her fiancé and the orchids of the planet Flora. Partially balanced by satire of scientific grantsmanship and politics, titillation is the book's prime object, accomplished with poetic allusions and complicated metaphorical connections. *The Rakehells of Heaven* also involves carnal contact with aliens, as two astronauts educate university students on a distant planet in human culture. The natives of Harlech (heaven) adopt their vices as well as virtues, culminating in crucifixion of one scout and expulsion of the other. The satire is still broader, the plot more unwieldy, in *Sex and the High Command*, as the U.S. Navy officers and other bumbling males in high places fall prey to the world's women who have learned, with the aid of chemistry, how to manage quite well without men. Like the protagonist of *Rakehells*, the hero parodies Southern manhood, representing rigid values unprepared for change.

In post-catastrophe California a brilliant neurosurgeon is brought to *The Organ Bank Farm* to perform brain transplants while pursuing his hobby of trying to cure autistic children. Amid the trappings of music therapy and behaviorist computers, his sense of decency is engaged, especially on behalf of a beautiful girl lost in an imaginary medieval world. Love and sex and poetry are present in profusion, capped by a bewildering but plausible surprise ending.

Revolutions in *The Gorgon Festival* and *The I.Q. Merchant* result from discoveries in chemistry. Rejuvenated older women fail in the first, amid the paraphernalia of rock music, motorcycle gangs, racism, and the generation gap. Flirting with sexual taboos named for Oedipus and Electra, the second emphasizes family drama. Estranged from his alcoholic wife and formerly retarded son, the inventor sees events pass by him as his intelligence-booster transforms society. Then with his youthful lover he leapfrogs simple genius into communal ESP in another tricky ending.

*The Doomsday Gene* projects bitterness toward a world of high technology and scientific irresponsibility, seen largely through the eyes of a repressed clairvoyant girl. Unusual for Boyd, it is stiffly written, internally inconsistent, even incoherent in places, though not lacking in poetic allusions. A further decline in quality is found in *Andromeda Gun*, a spoof on conventions of the old West, in which an alien intelligence tries to reform the mind of a Southern rebel turned rabid outlaw.

*Barnard's Planet* revisits old haunts with an exploratory mission to an Edenic world where vegetable evolution has outstripped animal. Amid five "cluster-educated" multiple-discipline geniuses, representing national interests, the captain is an atavism. Unwilling to subject this world to Earth's warring interests, he discovers himself as the saboteur (and poet) he's under orders to defeat.

The protagonist of Boyd's next book has a similar narrow escape. Bumbling bureaucrats and military men almost achieve what they are trying to prevent: takeover by a high-technology, hive-like alien race, temporarily marooned on Earth. Loving and loved by the queen, for whom Boyd's lyricism scales new heights, the hero escapes the fate of a discarded drone, to remember fondly *The Girl with the Jade Green Eyes.*

Freed from the sexual taboos and stylistic limitations of a previous era, Boyd approaches science fiction as entertainment, with literary tolls and aims. Viewed whole, his books are lightweight confections, their component parts wildly implausible. If one is prepared, however, in the act of reading, to trace interwoven motifs and allusions, while trying to outguess the turns of plot, Boyd generally supplies a superior diversion.

—David N. Samuelson

---

**BRACKETT, Leigh (Douglass).** American. Born in Los Angeles, California, 7 December 1915. Married Edmond Hamilton, q.v., in 1946 (died 1977). Freelance writer from 1939. Recipient: Jules Verne award; Western Writers of America Spur award, 1963. *Died 24 March 1978.*

Science-Fiction Publications

Novels (series: Skaith)

*Shadow over Mars.* Manchester, World, 1951; as *The Nemesis from Terra*, New York, Ace, 1961.
*The Starmen.* New York, Gnome Press, 1952; London, Museum Press, 1954; abridged edition, as *The Galactic Breed*, New York, Ace, 1955; original version, as *The Starmen of Llyrdis*, New York, Ballantine, 1976.
*The Sword of Rhiannon.* New York, Ace, 1953; London, Boardman, 1955.
*The Big Jump.* New York, Ace, 1955.
*The Long Tomorrow.* New York, Doubleday, 1955.
*Alpha Centauri—or Die!* New York, Ace, 1963.
*People of the Talisman.* New York, Ace, 1964.
*The Secret of Sinharat.* New York, Ace, 1964.
*The Ginger Star.* New York, Ballantine, 1974; London, Sphere, 1976.
*The Book of Skaith.* New York, Doubleday, 1976.
*The Hounds of Skaith.* New York, Ballantine, 1974; London, Sphere, 1976.
*The Reavers of Skaith.* New York, Ballantine, 1976.
*Eric John Stark, Outlaw of Mars.* New York, Ballantine, 1982.

Short Stories

*The Coming of the Terrans.* New York, Ace, 1967.
*The Halflings and Other Stories.* New York, Ace, 1973.
*The Best of Leigh Brackett*, edited by Edmond Hamilton. New York, Doubleday, 1977.

Other Publications

Novels

*No Good from a Corpse.* New York, Coward McCann, 1944; London, Simon and Schuster, 1989.
*Stranger at Home* (ghost-written for George Sanders). New York, Simon and Schuster, 1946; London, Pilot Press, 1947.
*The Tiger among Us.* New York, Doubleday, 1957; London, Boardman, 1958; as *Fear No Evil*, London, Corgi, 1960; as *13 West Street*, New York, Bantam, 1962.
*An Eye for an Eye.* New York, Doubleday, 1957; London, Boardman, 1958.
*Rio Bravo* (novelization of screenplay). New York, Bantam, and London, Corgi, 1959.
*Follow the Free Wind.* New York, Doubleday, 1963.
*Silent Partner.* New York, Putnam, 1969.

Plays

*The Big Sleep*, with William Faulkner and Jules Furthman, in *Film Scripts One*, edited by George P. Garrett, O.B. Harrison, Jr., and Jane Gelfmann. New York, Appleton-Century-Crofts, 1971.
*The Empire Strikes Back* (screenplay), with Lawrence Kasdan, in *The Empire Strikes Back Notebook*, edited by Diane Attias and Lindsay Smith. New York, Ballantine, 1980.

Screenplays: *The Vampire's Ghost*, with John K. Butler, 1945; *Crime Doctor's Manhunt*, with Eric Taylor, 1946; *The Big Sleep*, with William Faulkner and Jules Furthman, 1946; *Rio Bravo*, with Jules Furthman and B.H. McCampbell, 1959; *Gold of the Seven Saints*, with Leonard Freeman, 1961; *Hatari!* with Harry Kurnitz, 1962; *El Dorado*, 1967; *Rio Lobo*, with Burton Wohl,

1970; *The Long Goodbye*, 1973; *The Empire Strikes Back*, with Lawrence Kasdan, 1979.

Television Plays: for *Checkmate* and *Suspense* series, and *Terror at Northfield* for *Alfred Hitchcock* series.

Other

Editor, *The Best of Planet Stories 1*. New York, Ballantine, 1975.
Editor, *The Best of Edmond Hamilton*. New York, Ballantine, 1977.

*

Bibliography: *Leigh Brackett, Marion Zimmer Bradley, Anne McCaffrey: A Primary and Secondary Bibliography* by Rosemarie Arbur, Boston, Hall, 1982.

Manuscript Collection: Special Collections, Eastern New Mexico University Library, Portales.

* * *

During the late 1940's and early 1950's Leigh Brackett was the uncontested "Queen of Space Opera." As a girl, she spent summers exploring the beaches near Santa Monica, and her reading of Edgar Rice Burroughs provided much of the imagery that was to make her science fiction unique. In a *Planet Stories* "Feature Flash" she admitted her addiction to things dramatic, repeatedly describing herself as "a ham." Her facility with character and dialogue (in the "tough" detective novel, *No Good from a Corpse*) got her work in films, and, later prompted Pauline Kael to suppose that most of the dialogue in *El Dorado* was improvised by the actors because it seemed too realistic to have come from any script.

All these aspects of her personal and professional self found ready expression in the kind of science fiction that made her famous. Space opera is currently a derogatory term, denoting impossibly larger-than-life characters, melodramatic incidents, and flights of fancy quite distant from straight extrapolative science fiction. In the 1940's and early 1950's, however, space opera was the staple of most of the pulp magazines, partly because it was an escape from ordinary life, partly because it evoked a "sense of wonder" just by its portrayal of alien beings, awesome settings, and heroic acts, and partly because of the literary skills of Brackett herself.

*The Sword of Rhiannon* is perhaps the apex of Brackett's career as a writer of space opera. It begins with a renegade archeologist who is thrown back a million years by a strange "bubble of time" within the tomb of the ancient god-like Martian, Rhiannon. Once in the past, Brackett's hero finds himself involved in all sorts of adventures (he, with Rhiannon's help, frees ancient Mars of the Tyranny of one race, the serpent-evolved Dhuvians, and wins the love of the princess of a human Martian race). The way Brackett tells this story gives it much greater literary quality than the space-opera label suggests. Her setting—verdant Mars, with a luminous ocean—and her characters—of several Martian races, each independently evolved to the level of human culture—allow the reader a glimpse of Mars as a vital world, not the dying one the Terrans find when they arrive just before the beginning of our third millennium. In this novel, Brackett masterfully interweaves the melodramatic heroism of space opera with imaginative postulation of three sapient lifeforms besides the native human race of Martians.

Before *Rhiannon*, Brackett produced two space-opera masterpieces, "Enchantree of Venus" and "The Lake of the Gone Forever." Afterwards, she turned to more conventional science fiction with *The Long Tomorrow*, a post-Destruction narrative considered by many to be Brackett's best, and to stories like "The Tweener" and "The Queer Ones." Then she began making novels of previously published novelettes; "Queen of the Martian Catacombs" and "Black Amazon of Mars"—both, incidently, featuring not just extraordinary women characters but the literary "original," Eric John Stark—became *The Secret of Sinharat* and *People of the Talisman*.

Considering the excitement of her narratives and the immediate pleasure to be derived from them, one might assume that Brackett's science fictions are fun to read, but basically light entertainment. However, one can perceive serious aspects in her fiction, whether it is space opera or not. One, illustrated best in the stories and novels about Eric John Stark, is a thematic interest in the essential goodness of most forms of natural life. Stark, son of Earthborn humans who died on Mercury, struggles for survival among a supportive group of non-human Mercurians and only later is returned to civilization. Stark is a renegade and mercenary, a "criminal" only because he does not recognize the authority of artificial laws; whenever he finds himself in a situation calling for heroic action, the "primal ape" in him seems set apart from the civilized human. Nevertheless, both his natural and civilized selves—demonstrated by his consistent sympathy for the wronged, whatever their species may be—seek the good.

Another serious aspect of her fiction is a thematic egalitarianism and, a good strong sense of respect for other living things. The care with which she treats her native Martians and Venusians—though alien, they are persons, too—makes this evident. *The Starmen* is the tale of a quest for equality on a galactic scale; respect for other life runs just below the surface of "The Tweener," evoking sad sympathy from the reader. And "All the Colors of the Rainbow" is, like Le Guin's *The Word for World Is Forest*, a cruelly bitter satire of racist prejudices, set forth by paradoxically delicate prose.

Brackett's growth as a writer was helped along by her husband, Edmond Hamilton; as she influenced his deepening characterization, he influenced her growing ability to structure fiction with a strong yet uncontrived plot. Besides the technical expertise with ploting, Brackett had, by the time she wrote about Skaith, evidently rethought the biology in *Rhiannon;* on Skaith as on ancient Mars there are at least three non-human sapient races, but these have evolved from a single stock, each seeking survival by accommodating itself differently to life beneath the dying ginger sun.

From February 1940 when "Martian Quest" appeared in *Astounding*, almost until the day she died in March 1978, Brackett's love for science fiction was evident in her works. Her last work was the first full draft of the screenplay for *Star Wars II*.

—Rosemarie Arbur

---

**BRADBURY, Edward P.** *See* **MOORCOCK, Michael.**

---

**BRADBURY, Ray(mond Douglas).** Has also written as Douglas Spaulding. American. Born in Waukegan, Illinois, 22 August 1920. Educated at Los Angeles High School, graduated 1938.

Married Marguerite Susan McClure in 1947; four daughters. Since 1943, full-time writer. President, Science-Fantasy Writers of America, 1951–53; member of the Board of Directors, Screen Writers Guild of America, 1957–61. Recipient: O. Henry prize, 1947, 1948; Benjamin Franklin award, 1954; American Academy award, 1954; Boys' Clubs of America Junior Book award, 1956; Golden Eagle award, for screenplay, 1957; Ann Radcliffe award, 1965, 1971; Writers Guild award, 1974; Aviation and Space Writers award, for television documentary, 1979; Gandalf award, 1980; Nebula Grand Master, 1988; Bram Stoker Life Achievement award, 1989. D. Litt.: Whittier College, California, 1979. Agent: Don Congdon, Harold Matson Company, 276 Fifth Avenue, New York, New York 10001. Address: 10265 Cheviot Drive, Los Angeles, California 90064, U.S.A.

SCIENCE-FICTION PUBLICATIONS

Novels

*Fahrenheit 451.* New York, Ballantine, 1953; London, Hart Davis, 1954.
*Something Wicked This Way Comes.* New York, Simon and Schuster, 1962; London, Hart Davis, 1963.

Short Stories

*Dark Carnival.* Sauk City, Wisconsin, Arkham House, 1947; abridged edition, London, Hamish Hamilton, 1948; abridged edition, as *The Small Assassin*, London, New English Library, 1962.
*The Martian Chronicles.* New York, Doubleday, 1950; as *The Silver Locusts*, London, Hart Davis, 1951.
*The Illustrated Man.* New York, Doubleday, 1951; London, Hart Davis, 1952.
*The Golden Apples of the Sun.* New York, Doubleday, and London, Hart Davis, 1953.
*The October Country.* New York, Ballantine, 1955; London, Hart Davis, 1956.
*A Medicine for Melancholy.* New York, Doubleday, 1959.
*The Day It Rained Forever.* London, Hart Davis, 1959.
*The Machineries of Joy.* New York, Simon and Schuster, and London, Hart Davis, 1964.
*The Vintage Bradbury.* New York, Random House, 1965.
*The Autumn People.* New York, Ballantine, 1965.
*Tomorrow Midnight.* New York, Ballantine, 1966.
*Twice Twenty Two* (selection). New York, Doubleday, 1966.
*I Sing the Body Electric!* New York, Knopf, 1969; London, Hart Davis, 1970.
*Bloch and Bradbury*, with Robert Bloch. New York, Tower, 1969; as *Fever Dreams and Other Fantasies*, London, Sphere, 1970.
*Selected Stories*, edited by Anthony Adams. London, Harrap, 1975.
*Long after Midnight.* New York, Knopf, 1976; London, Hart Davis MacGibbon, 1977.
*The Best of Bradbury.* New York, Bantam, 1976.
*To Sing Strange Songs.* Exeter, Devon, Wheaton, 1979.
*The Stories of Ray Bradbury.* New York, Knopf, and London, Granada, 1980.
*Dinosaur Tales.* New York, Bantam, 1983.
*The Toynbee Convector.* New York, Knopf, 1988; London, Grafton, 1989.

OTHER PUBLICATIONS

Novels

*Dandelion Wine.* New York, Doubleday, and London, Hart Davis, 1957.
*Death Is a Lonely Business.* New York, Knopf, 1985; London, Grafton, 1986.
*A Graveyard for Lunatics: Another Tale of Two Cities.* New York, Knopf, and London, Grafton, 1990.

Short Stories

*The Last Circus, and The Electrocution.* Northridge, California, Lord John Press, 1980.
*A Memory of Murder.* New York, Dell, 1984.

Plays

*The Meadow*, in *Best One-Act Plays of 1947–48*, edited by Margaret Mayorga. New York, Dodd Mead, 1948.
*The Anthem Sprinters and Other Antics* (produced Los Angeles, 1968). New York, Dial Press, 1963.
*The World of Ray Bradbury* (produced Los Angeles, 1964; New York, 1965).
*The Wonderful Ice-Cream Suit* (produced Los Angeles, 1965; New York, 1987). Included in *The Wonderful Ice-Cream Suit and Other Plays*, 1972.
*The Day it Rained Forever*, music by Bill Whitefield (produced Edinburgh, 1988). New York, French, 1966.
*The Pedestrian.* New York, French, 1966.
*Christus Apollo*, music by Jerry Goldsmith (produced Los Angeles, 1969).
*The Wonderful Ice-Cream Suit and Other Plays* (includes *The Veldt* and *To the Chicago Abyss*). New York, Bantam, 1972; London, Hart Davis, 1973.
*The Veldt* (produced London, 1980). Included in *The Wonderful Ice-Cream Suit and Other Plays*, 1972.
*Leviathan 99* (produced Los Angeles, 1972).
*Pillar of Fire and Other Plays for Today, Tomorrow, and Beyond Tomorrow* (includes *Kaleidoscope* and *The Foghorn*). New York, Bantam, 1975.
*The Foghorn* (produced New York, 1977). Included in *Pillar of Fire and Other Plays*, 1975.
*That Ghost, That Bride of Time: Excerpts from a Play-in-Progress.* Glendale, California, Squires, 1976.
*The Martian Chronicles*, adaptation of his own stories (produced Los Angeles, 1977).
*Fahrenheit 451, adaptation of his own novel (produced Los Angeles, 1979).*
*Dandelion Wine*, adaptation of his own story (produced Los Angeles, 1980).
*Forever and the Earth* (radio play). Athens, Ohio, Croissant, 1984.

Screenplays: *It Came from Outer Space*, with David Schwartz, 1952; *Moby-Dick*, with John Huston, 1956; *Icarus Mongolfier Wright*, with George C. Johnston, 1961; *Picasso Summer* (as Douglas Spaulding), with Edwin Booth, 1972.

Television Plays: *Shopping for Death*, 1956, *Design for Loving*, 1958, *Special Delivery*, 1959, *The Faith of Aaron Menefee*, 1962, and *The Life Work of Juan Dîaz* (all *Alfred Hitchcock Presents* series); *The Marked Bullet* (*Jane Wyman's Fireside Theatre* series), 1956; *The Gift* (*Steve Canyon* series), 1958; *The Tunnel to Yesterday* (Trouble Shooters series), 1960; *I Sing the Body Electric!* (*Twilight Zone* series), 1962; *The Jail* (*Alcoa Premiere* series), 1962; *The Groom* (*Curiosity Shop* series), 1971; *The Coffin*, from his own short story, 1988 (U.K.).

Verse

*Old Ahab's Friend, and Friend to Noah, Speaks His Piece: A Celebration*. Glendale, California, Squires, 1971.
*When Elephants Last in the Dooryard Bloomed: Celebrations for Almost Any Day in the Year*. New York, Knopf, 1973; London, Hart Davis MacGibbon, 1975.
*That Son of Richard III: A Birth Announcement*. Privately printed, 1974.
*Where Robot Mice and Robot Men Run round in Robot Towns: New Poems, Both Light and Dark*. New York, Knopf, 1977; London, Hart Davis MacGibbon, 1979.
*Twin Hieroglyphs That Swim the River Dust*. Northridge, California, Lord John Press, 1978.
*The Bike Repairman*. Northridge, California, Lord John Press, 1978.
*The Author Considers His Resources*. Northridge, California, Lord John Press, 1979.
*The Aqueduct*. Glendale, California, Squires, 1979.
*The Attic Where the Meadow Greens*. Northridge, California, Lord John Press, 1980.
*The Haunted Computer and the Android Pope*. New York, Knopf, and London, Granada, 1981.
*The Complete Poems of Ray Bradbury*. New York, Ballantine, 1982.
*The Love Affair*. Northridge, California, Lord John Press, 1983.

Other

*Switch on the Night* (for children). New York, Pantheon, and London, Hart Davis, 1955.
*R Is for Rocker* (for children). New York, Doubleday, 1962; London, Hart Davis, 1968.
*S Is for Space* (for children). New York, Doubleday, 1966; London, Hart Davis, 1968.
*Teacher's Guide: Science Fiction*, with Lewy Olfson. New York, Bantam, 1968.
*The Halloween Tree* (for children). New York, Knopf, 1972; London, Hart Davis MacGibbon, 1973.
*Mars and the Mind of Man*. New York, Harper, 1973.
*Zen and the Art of Writing, and The Joy of Writing*. Santa Barbara, California, Capra Press, 1973.
*The Mummies of Guanajuato*, photographs by Archie Lieberman. New York, Abrams, 1978.
*Beyond 1984: Remembrance of Things Future*. New York, Targ, 1979.
*The Ghosts of Forever*, illustrated by Aldo Sessa. New York, Rizzoli, 1981.
*Los Angeles*, photographs by West Light. Port Washington, New York, Skyline Press, 1984.
*Orange County*, photographs by Bill Ross and others. Port Washington, New York, Skyline Press, 1985.
*The Art of Playboy*. New York, van der Marck Editions, 1985.
*Zen in the Art of Writing*. Santa Barbara, California, Capra Press, 1990.
*The Smile*. Mankato, Minnesota, Creative Education, 1991.
*Yestermorrow: Obvious Answers to Impossible Futures* (essays). Santa Barbara, California, Capra Press, 1991.

Editor, *Timeless Stories for Today and Tomorrow*. New York, Bantam, 1952.
Editor, *The Circus of Dr. Lao and Other Improbable Stories*. New York, Bantam, 1956.

*

Critical Studies: introduction by Gilbert Highet to *The Vintage Bradbury*, 1965; *The Ray Bradbury Companion* (includes bibliography) by William F. Nolan, Detroit, Gale, 1975; *The Drama of Ray Bradbury* by Ben F. Indick, Baltimore, T-K Graphics, 1977; *The Bradbury Chronicles* by George Edgar Slusser, San Bernardino, California, Borgo Press, 1977; *Ray Bradbury* (includes bibliography) edited by Joseph D. Olander and Martin H. Greenberg, New York, Taplinger, and Edinburgh, Harris, 1980; *Ray Bradbury* by Wayne L. Johnson, New York, Ungar, 1980; *Ray Bradbury and the Poetics of Reverie: Fantasy, Science Fiction, and the Reader* by William F. Toupence, Ann Arbor, UMI Research Press, 1984; *Ray Bradbury* by David Mogen, Boston, Massachusetts, Twayne, 1986.

Ray Bradbury comments:

If I were to advise writers my advice would go simply like this: Begin writing when you are 12 if possible. Fall in love with all the arts, for from them you will learn how to touch, see, smell, know the world. Educate your hands by drawing, educate your ear by listening, educate your nose by running against the wind, keep your eyes wide and your mouth shut. Write every day and every day of your life until it becomes such an immense love you can't help yourself. It should be as crazy as any love is for any man. It should be like the first love you know when you are sixteen or seventeen and go out of your mind because the fruit is high on the tree and you're shaking the tree like made and it won't fall down into your arms and if it doesn't fall down soon and smother you with returned affection, why, damn it to hell, you'll climb the tree and get it or hang yourself, one or t'other. Crazy love. Mad love. Love comic strips. I have collected them all my life. Love radio shows. I used to clean out the garbage cans in back of NBC and CBS after every Jack Benny Radio Show or Burns and Allen Show. Start bad. Become mediocre. Get better. Become excellent. By any means at hand. But love, love, love. Love to be around actors and directors. Paint sets. Write bad plays. Do terrible essays. Write awful poems. But all because you are so full of things you want to say you can't stop.

Know all the books in your local library better than the librarian. Go there every night. Live there. Educate yourself. Know all the stock in the local book store. I do. There is no day in my life I do not go to at least one book store. Go to art galleries. Look. Fill up. See every film ever made. Fill up on that medium. Know everything that is bad. Only by knowing what is bad can you avoid badness. The snob who refuses knowledge in mediocrities remains always second-rate himself. I have collected PRINCE VALIANT for 30 years. Listen to bad music and good music and great music. Study architecture. Read science-fiction, because it is the one fiction which is curious about ALL the above, all and everything, on every level. In sum: run, shout, search, be puzzled, go on, from day to day, with high enthusiasm.

* * *

Ever since the remarkable critical and popular success of *The Martian Chronicles* in 1950, Ray Bradbury has been among the most visible science-fiction writers. Although he has not produced a major work in several years, he remains the most widely recognized spokesman for the genre, and particularly for the romantic attitudes toward space flight and technology that it sometimes embodies. This is somewhat ironic, since Bradbury's best works—dating from the early 1950's—are powerful indictments of unchecked technological progress and question humanity's ability to deal creativity with the new worlds of which science and technology hold promise.

Bradbury is above all a humanist, and this humanism is evident throughout his career. In his earlier works, Bradbury moves from an adolescent science-fiction fan making his first professional publications (the first was the story "Pendulum" written with Henry Hasse) to a mature stylist. Bradbury's first book, the collection of stories *Dark Carnival*, was not science fiction at all, but rather ranged from satirical horror (such as "The Handler," which concerns a mortician who plays practical jokes on his "clients") to sensitive portrayals of lonely or pathetic individuals—a wife incapacitated with horror at her own mortality after viewing Mexican mummies ("The Next in Line"), a "normal" boy alone in a family of friendly vampires ("The Homecoming"). Many of the stories had originally appeared in *Weird Tales*, a horror pulp that represented a market Bradbury would soon abandon, but it was in these tales that he developed his craft, and many of them remain among his strongest work.

*The Martian Chronicles* began the second and most prolific phase of Bradbury's career. A series of stories, linked by bridge passages, concerning the colonization and exploitation of Mars by what seem to be exclusively citizens of small midwestern American towns, the book owed much to the American tradition of frontier literature, and quickly consolidated Bradbury's reputation as one of science fiction's leading stylists. Although the portrayal of the Martians ranges from sensitive, essentially ordinary families ("Ylla") to shapeless monsters ("The Third Expedition"), they soon fade into the background as the stories focus on different types of earth settlers—romantics, misfits, opportunists, idealists, even fugitive Blacks (in "Way in the Middle of the Air"). In the end, an atomic war sends most of the settlers back to the earth to join their families, leaving only a few isolated families such as that depicted in "The Million-Year Picnic," whose father vows to start a new world on Mars without the prejudice and regimentation that had come to characterize life on earth.

*The Illustrated Man* appeared in the following year, and again connected the stories by a frame narrative; in this case, each story is presented as a tattoo come to life. A few of the stories retain the Martian setting of the *Chronicles*, and one of these, "The Fire Balloons," is an early attempt at treating a serious religious issue in science fiction—the question of whether a benign alien life form can be said to have achieved Christian grace. Other stories explore themes that had become familiar to Bradbury readers. The amorality of children which appeared as a theme in a few *Dark Carnival* stories here returns in stories in which children murder their parents in a mechanical playroom ("The Veldt") or assist invading aliens ("Zero Hour"). Mexico, which had fascinated Bradbury since a trip he took there in 1945, is the setting of "The Fox in the Forest" and "The Highway." And the romantic attitudes toward space travel that were to remain a Bradbury staple are evident in "The Rocket," "No Particular Night or Morning," and "Kaleidoscope," a tale of the crew of an exploded spaceship drifting slowly to their deaths, which Bradbury later dramatized.

*Fahrenheit 451*, a dystopian satire of a totalitarian state in which "firemen" are professional bookburners who set fires rather than put them out, is the only science-fiction work of Bradbury's to approach *The Martian Chronicles* in popularity. *Fahrenheit 451* is as much an attack on mass culture as it is a satire of McCarthy-era censorship; the enforced illiteracy of this future society, we are led to believe, is at least in part due to the desires to avoid offending special interest groups in the mass media and to the rise of television (which Bradbury had already effectively satirized in "The Pedestrian"). The novel is as simple as a parable, and few attempts are made to offer a realistic portrait of an imagined society. The police state, it seems, exists almost solely to burn books, and the society of outcasts that the hero Montag finally escapes to join seems curiously incapable of political action, choosing instead to preserve literary culture by memorizing all the great books.

Of the other four collections Bradbury published during the 1950's, none was primarily science fiction. *The Golden Apples of the Sun* introduced what was to become a familiar Bradbury mix of small-town tales, fantasies, Mexican stories, science fiction, and crime tales. *The October Country* reprinted most of the contents of *Dark Carnival* and added four stories, and *Dandelion Wine* was a collection of sketches based on Bradbury's own boyhood in Waukegan, Illinois. *A Medicine for Melancholy* repeated the mix of *The Golden Apples of the Sun*, introducing in book form a new theme for Bradbury, Irish life and character, which had come to fascinate the author while he was in Ireland in 1954.

Bradbury's long-awaited full-length novel *Something Wicked This Way Comes* is a fantasy concerning an evil carnival that disturbs the lives of people in a small midwestern town. Strongly influenced by Charles G. Finney's *The Circus of Dr. Lao*, the novel gains real power despite occasional overwriting, and marked the beginning of a third phase of Bradbury's career, characterized by an almost meditative return to his favorite themes and archetypes, by a decreasing output of fiction, and by an increasing interest in new forms such as poetry, drama, and—most recently—the mystery novel. Despite a number of excellent stories, collections such as *The Machineries of Joy* and *I Sing the Body Electric!* suggested little in the way of new directions or artistic growth. A self-reflectiveness culminated in the late 1970's and early 1980's with four collections, *Long After Midnight, The Stories of Ray Bradbury, Dinosaur Tales*, and *A Memory of Murder*, that were almost entirely retrospective—the last title consisting exclusively of his pulp crime stories of the 1940's.

Bradbury's movement away from science fiction was underlined with the publication of his nostalgic mystery novel *Death Is A Lonely Business* in 1985 and his collection *The Toynbee Convector* three years later. *The Toynbee Convector* reveals a Bradbury at ease with his focus on sentiment and nostalgia, but only three of the 23 stories in the book could remotely be regarded as science fiction. The title story, about a man who fakes a trip into the future in order to give hope to the cynical 1980's, could almost be viewed as Bradbury's testament to his faith in his own unbounded optimism. Whatever the final assessment of these later stories, Bradbury's crucial role in broadening the audience for science fiction cannot be argued. While the genre had produced other excellent craftsman before Bradbury, his finely-tuned style and humanistic values exerted a profound influence on a generation of writers and helped reduce the barriers that had long isolated science fiction from the mainstream.

—Gary K. Wolfe

---

**BRADLEY, Marion Zimmer.** Has also written as Lee Chapman; John Dexter; Miriam Gardner; Valerie Graves; Morgan Ives and John J. Wells. American. Born in Albany, New York, 3 June 1930. Educated at New York State College for Teachers, 1946–48; Hardin-Simmons University, Abilene, Texas. B.A. in English, Spanish, psychology 1964; University of California, Berkeley. Married 1) Robert A. Bradley in 1949 (divorced 1963); one son; 2) Walter Henry Breen in 1964 (divorced 1990); one son and one daughter. Editor, *Marion Zimmer Bradley's Fantasy*

*Magazine*, since 1989. Singer and writer. Recipient: *Locus* Award, 1984. Address: c/o Friends of Darkover, P.O. Box 72, Berkeley, California 94701, U.S.A.

### Science-Fiction Publications

Novels (series: Darkover)

*The Door Through Space.* New York, Ace, 1961; London, Arrow, 1979.
*Seven from the Stars.* New York, Ace, 1962.
*The Planet Savers, The Sword of Aldones* (Darkover). New York, Ace, 1962; London, Arrow, 2 vols., 1979.
*The Colors of Space* (for children). Derby, Connecticut, Monarch, 1963.
*The Bloody Sun* (Darkover). New York, Ace, 1964; London, Arrow, 1978.
*Falcons of Narabedla.* New York, Ace, 1964.
*Star of Danger* (Darkover). New York, Ace, 1965; London, Arrow, 1978.
*The Brass Dragon.* New York, Ace, 1969; London, Methuen, 1978.
*The Winds of Darkover.* New York, Ace, 1970; London, Arrow, 1978.
*The World Wreckers* (Darkover). New York, Ace, 1971; London, Arrow, 1979.
*Darkover Landfall.* New York, DAW, 1972; London, Arrow, 1978.
*Hunters of the Red Moon.* New York, DAW, 1973; London, Arrow, 1979.
*The Spell Sword* (Darkover). New York, DAW, 1974; London, Arrow, 1978.
*Endless Voyage.* New York, Ace, 1975; revised edition, as *Endless Universe*, 1979.
*The Heritage of Hastur* (Darkover). New York, DAW, 1975; London, Arrow, 1979.
*The Shattered Chain* (Darkover). New York, DAW, 1976; London, Arrow, 1978.
*The Forbidden Tower* (Darkover). New York, DAW, 1977; London, Prior, 1979.
*Stormqueen* (Darkover). New York, DAW, 1978; London, Arrow, 1980.
*The Ruins of Isis*, Norfolk, Virginia, Donning, 1978; London, Arrow, 1980.
*The Survivors*, with Paul E. Zimmer. New York, DAW, 1979; London, Arrow, 1985.
*The House Between the Worlds.* New York, Doubleday, 1980.
*Two to Conquer* (Darkover). New York, DAW, 1980; London, Arrow, 1982.
*Survey Ship.* New York, Ace, 1980.
*Sharra's Exile* (Darkover). New York, DAW, 1981; London, Arrow, 1983.
*Hawkmistress* (Darkover). New York, DAW, 1982; London, Arrow, 1985.
*Web of Light.* Norfolk, Virginia, Donning, 1982.
*The Mists of Avalon.* New York, Knopf, and London, Joseph, 1983.
*Thendara House* (Darkover). New York, DAW, 1983; London, Arrow, 1985.
*Web of Darkness.* New York, Pocket Books, 1984; Glasgow, Drew, 1985.
*The Inheritor.* New York, Tor, 1984.
*City of Sorcery* (Darkover). New York, DAW, 1984; London, Arrow, 1986.
*Night's Daughter.* New York, Ballantine, and London, Inner Circle, 1985.
*Warrior Woman.* New York, DAW, 1985; London, Arrow, 1987.
*The Heirs of Hammerfell* (Darkover). New York, DAW, 1989.

Short Stories

*The Dark Intruder and Other Stories.* New York, Ace, 1964.
*The Jewel of Arwen.* Baltimore, T-K Graphics, 1974.
*The Parting of Arwen.* Baltimore, T-K Graphics, 1974.
*Sword of Chaos*, with others, New York, DAW, 1982.
*Lythande.* New York, DAW, 1986.
*The Best of Marion Zimmer Bradley*, edited by Martin H. Greenberg. New York, DAW, 1988.

### Other Publications

Novels

*I am a Lesbian* (as Lee Chapman). Derby, Connecticut, Monarch, 1962.
*Spare Her Heaven* (as Morgan Ives). Derby, Connecticut, Monarch, 1963; abridged edition, as *Anything Goes*, Sydney, Stag, 1964.
*Castle Terror.* New York, Lancer, 1965.
*Knives of Desire* (as Morgan Ives). San Diego, Corinth, 1966.
*No Adam for Eve* (as John Dexter). San Diego, Corinth, 1966.
*Souvenir of Monique.* New York, Ace, 1967.
*Bluebeard's Daughter.* New York, Lancer, 1968.
*Witch Hill* (as Valerie Graves). San Diego, Greenleaf, 1972.
*Dark Satanic.* New York, Berkley, 1972.
*In the Steps of the Master* (novelization of TV Play). New York, Grosset and Dunlap, 1973.
*Can Ellen Be Saved?* (novelization of TV Play). New York, Grosset and Dunlap, 1975.
*Drums of Darkness.* New York, Ballantine, 1976.
*The Catch Trap.* New York, Ballantine, 1979; London, Sphere, 1986.
*The Firebrand.* New York, Simon and Schuster, 1987; London, Joseph, 1988.
*Black Trillium*, with Julian May and Andre Norton. New York, Doubleday, 1990; London, Grafton, 1991.
*Witch Hill.* New York, Tor, 1990.

Novels as Miriam Gardner

*The Strange Women.* Derby, Connecticut, Monarch, 1962.
*My Sister, My Love.* Derby, Connecticut, Monarch, 1963.
*Twilight Lovers.* Derby, Connecticut, Monarch, 1964.

Other

*Songs from Rivendell.* Privately printed, 1959.
*A Complete, Cumulative Checklist of Lesbian, Variant, and Homosexual Fiction.* Privately printed, 1960.
*Men, Halflings, and Hero-Worship.* Baltimore, T-K Graphics, 1973.
*The Necessity for Beauty: Robert W. Chambers and the Romantic Tradition.* Baltimore, T-K Graphics, 1974.

Editor, *The Keeper's Price.* New York, DAW, 1980.
Editor, *Greyhaven.* New York, DAW, 1983.
Editor, *Sword and Sorceress 1–8.* New York, DAW, 1984–91; vol. 1 published London, Headline, 1988.
Editor, with others, *Free Amazons of Darkover.* New York, DAW, 1985.

Editor, with others, *Other Side of the Mirror*. New York, DAW, 1987.
Editor, with others, *Red Sun of Darkover*. New York, DAW, 1987.
Editor, with others, *Four Moons of Darkover*. New York, DAW, 1988.
Editor, with others, *Domains of Darkover*. New York, DAW, 1990.
Editor, with others, *Renunciates of Darkover*. New York, DAW, 1991.

Translator, *El Villano in su Ricon*, by Lope de Vega. Privately printed, 1971.

*

Bibliography: *Leigh Brackett, Marion Zimmer Bradley, Anne McCaffrey: A Primary and Secondary Bibliography* by Rosemarie Arbur, Boston, Hall, 1982.

Manuscript Collection: Boston University.

Critical Studies: *The Gemini Problem: A Study in Darkover* by Walter Breen, Baltimore, T-K Graphics, 1975; *The Darkover Dilemma: Problems of the Darkover Series* by S. Wise, Baltimore, T-K Graphics, 1976.

Marion Zimmer Bradley comments:

The secret of life is to do what you enjoy doing most, and to get someone to pay you enough so you don't actually have to starve while you're doing it. People who want other things, money and status, baffle me. I write professionally because it's the only thing I can do well, and every other job I have had has either bored or frustrated me past tolerance; and since I write compulsively and would no matter what else I was doing, it's wonderful that I can get paid for it.

* * *

Marion Zimmer Bradley's versatile, prolific writing career recapitulates many of the major trends over the past several decades of science fiction. In more than 40 years of productivity, she has grown with the genre she has helped to shape.

Some of her early fiction is action/adventure, much in the tradition of C.L. Moore and Leigh Brackett Hamilton. Some of her early science fiction follows the trend toward the personal and the human, rather than the technological side, in the manner of Judith Merril's "That Only A Mother . . .". Bradley's early Darkover novels also show the influence of Leigh Bracket Hamilton and C.L. Moore—the lure of faraway places, faintly sinister desert towns, and flashing swords, frequently wielded by fighting women.

When series books became popular, her Darkover series proved to be one of the most popular, durable, and influential such series. Evolving from the now-rewritten *Sword of Aldones* (1962), which combined psionics, the code duello, and glimpses of a yet-unrealized planet, Bradley's Darkover has become a place as well-documented as Dune or the Witch World. It is not just an exercise in planet-building: a "Darkover" book is commonly understood to deal with issues of cultural clash, between Darkover and its parent Terran culture, between warring groups on Darkover, or in familial terms. Probably most notable about the Darkover books is the shift Bradley made with *The Shattered Chain*, which took a much earlier mention of the Free Amazons and turned them into a provocative analysis of sexual politics. Much of this debate involves questions of freedom and choice: the Amazons, or Renunciates, exist as a way of providing an alternative to Darkovan women and of enabling them to become keepers of their own consciences and charters of their own course. The shift in name from Amazons to Renunciates illustrates a major theme—that choices like this are never easy.

This discourse, which expanded early on to include alternative lifestyles and sexuality, is paralleled by some of her mainstream work, most notably *The Catch Trap*, which deals movingly with two gay men who are circus aerialists. Bradley's training as a science-fiction writer enables her to present the alien and exciting world of the circus with vigor and authority.

These alternative cultures imply community, another touchstone of Bradley's life and writing. Her respect for and long participation in the SF community has enabled her to enlarge it. Her Friends of Darkover anthologies mark her as one of the first writers in the field to benefit from the "shared world" concept. Her Greyhavens volume, her subsequent *Sword and Sorceress* anthology series, and *Marion Zimmer Bradley's Fantasy Magazine* have all enabled her to discover and introduce many younger writers, most notably Diana Paxson.

The 1970's and 1980's were a time when science-fiction novels made the jump to mainstream, best-selling status. Bradley's *The Mists of Avalon* once again embodies a number of trends: a major, best-selling Arthurian novel written during a revival of interest in the Matter of Britain, it is essentially revisionist, providing a woman's and pagan's-eye view of a very traditional mythology. *The Firebrand*, which deals with the fall of Troy, is another revisionist historical novel.

A "writer's writer," Bradley emphasizes strong plotting and character development. Her writing, like her work with younger writers, exemplifies her professionalism and her commitment to the science-fiction community.

—Susan Shwartz

---

**BRANDON, Frank.** *See* **BULMER, Kenneth.**

---

**BRETNOR, Reginald.** Also writes as Grendel Briarton. American. Born in Vladivostok, Russia, 30 July 1911; emigrated to the United States in 1920. Attended college in California and New Mexico. Married 1)Helen Harding in 1949 (died, 1967); 2) Rosalie Leveille in 1969 (died, 1988). Writer for the Office of War Information and the State Department Office of International Information and Cultural Affairs, 1943–47. Since 1947, freelance writer. Address: Box 1481, Medford, Oregon 97501, U.S.A.

SCIENCE-FICTION PUBLICATIONS

Novels

*Gilpin's Space*. New York, Ace, 1986.
*Schimmelhorn's Gold*. New York, Tor, 1986.

Short Stories

*Through Space and Time with Ferdinand Feghoot* (as Grendel Briarton). Berkeley, California, Paradox Press, 1962; aug-

mented edition as *The Compleat Feghoot*, and *The (Even) More Compleat Feghoot*, Baltimore, Mirage Press, 1975, 1980.
*The Schimmelhorn File*. New York, Ace, 1979.

OTHER PUBLICATIONS

Novel

*A Killing in Swords*. New York, Pocket Books, 1978.

Other

*Decisive Warfare: A Study in Military Theory*. Harrisburg, Pennsylvania, Stackpole, 1969.
*Of Force and Violence, and Other Imponderables* (essays). San Bernardino, California, Borgo Press, 1990.
*One Man's BEM: Thoughts on Science Fiction* (essays). San Bernardino, California, Borgo Press, 1990.

Editor, *Modern Science Fiction: Its Meaning and Its Future*. New York, Coward McCann, 1953; revised edition, Chicago, Advent, 1979.
Editor, *Science Fiction, Today and Tomorrow*. New York, Harper, 1974.
Editor, *The Craft of Science Fiction: A Symposium on Writing Science Fiction and Science Fantasy*. New York, Harper, 1976.
Editor, *The Future at War*: 1. *Thor's Hammer*, 2. *The Spear of Mars*, 3. *Orion's Sword*. New York, Ace, 3 vols., 1979–80.

Translator, *Moncrief's Cats*, by François-Augustin Paradis de Moncrif. London, Golden Cockerel Press, 1961; Cranbury, New Jersey, A.S. Barnes, 1962.

*

Bibliography: *The Work of Reginald Bretnor, an Annotated Bibliography and Guide* by Scott Alan Burgess, San Bernardino, California, Borgo Press, 1989.

* * *

Reginald Bretnor's career as a science-fiction writer is minor. *A Killing in Swords*, for example, is a *hommage* to the mysteries of Anthony Boucher. *The Schimmelhorn File* collects Bretnor's series about an eccentric Pennsylvania Dutch inventor of the future. These stories show Bretnor's talents for fast-paced comedy, but are otherwise forgettable. The stories about Ferdinand Feghoot include Bretnor's most influential fictions, a series of short anecdotes that conclude with an intricate pun. This form has proven popular with fans and editors, and has been copied by such authors as John Brunner and Damon Knight.

Bretnor's important work is as an editor. He has proven his skill as an anthologist with *The Future at War*, but his editorial talents are for criticism rather than fiction. His *Modern Science Fiction: Its Meaning and Its Future* was the first attempt by a writer within the field to treat SF as a movement of social history, rather than an *ars nova* unique unto itself. Including major essays by Asimov, de Camp, and others, *Modern Science Fiction* is *the* primary document for understanding the climate of opinion that produced the SF of the 1950's. Its two successors, *Science Fiction, Today and Tomorrow* and *The Craft of Science Fiction*, are no less important to an understanding of the science fiction of the 1970's. Together, the trilogy is a pinnacle of analytical thought that will be studied long after Bretnor's own fiction is forgotten.

—Martin Morse Wooster

---

**BRETT, Leo.** *See* **FANTHORPE, R. Lionel.**

---

**BRIARTON, Grendel.** *See* **BRETNOR, Reginald.**

---

**BRIN, David.** American. Born in Glendale, California, 6 October 1950. Educated at California Institute of Technology, Pasadena, B.S. in astronomy 1973; University of California, San Diego, M.S. in applied physics 1978, Ph.D. in space science 1981. Technical staff member, Hughes Research Laboratory, Newport Beach, California, 1973–75, and Carlsbad, California, 1975–77; taught at San Diego State University, 1982–83, and San Diego community colleges, 1983–84. Secretary, Science Fiction Writers of America. Recipient: Nebula award, 1984; Hugo award, 1984, 1987; *Locus* award, 1984, 1986, 1987, 1988; Balrog award, 1985; John W. Campbell, Jr. Memorial award, 1986. Address: 5081 Baxter Street, San Diego, California 92117, U.S.A.

SCIENCE-FICTION PUBLICATIONS

Novels (series: Uplift)

*Sundiver* (Uplift). New York, Bantam, 1980.
*Startide Rising* (Uplift). New York, Bantam, 1983; revised edition, West Bloomfield, Michigan, Phantasia Press, and London, Bantam, 1985; published with *The Uplift War*, as *Earthclan*, New York, Doubleday, 1987.
*The Practice Effect*. New York, Bantam, 1984; London, Bantam, 1986.
*The Postman*. New York, Bantam, 1985; London, Bantam, 1987.
*Heart of the Comet*, with Gregory Benford. New York, Bantam, 1986.
*The Uplift War*. West Bloomfield, Michigan, Phantasia Press, and London, Bantam, 1987; published with *Startide Rising*, as *Earthclan*, New York, Doubleday, 1987.
*Dr. Pak's PreSchool*. New Castle, Virginia, Cheap Street, 1989.
*Earth*. New York, Bantam, and London, Macdonald, 1990.

Short Stories

*The River of Time*. Niles, Illinois, Dark Harvest, 1986; London, Bantam, 1987.

*

Manuscript collection: The J. Lloyd Eaton Collection of Science Fiction and Fantasy Literature, University of California, Riverside.

David Brin comments:

I've been told my writing is very different in my novels than in my short stories. And both differ a great deal from my mid-length (or novella) works. Generally, the latter are my favorite. One has time to develop characters and detailed settings, and yet is forced to get to the point. SF is almost the last refuge of the novella form, bless it.

My own novellas deal very much in that commodity known as Myth. The novels on the other hand are real SF and I stretch out to try to make use of the scientific thrills this century keeps dropping in our laps. It is fun.

My short work is hard to typefy . . . from boy-engineer tales to attempts at epiphanies, I suppose. It's a lovely language, English, and a wonderfully exciting time to be alive.

* * *

David Brin's *Sundiver, Startide Rising,* and *The Uplift War* form one of the strongest series in hard science fiction. Like Larry Niven, Gregory Benford, Robert Forward, and other scientist-writers, Brin juxtaposes the best of what space opera and current (or projected) science technology have to offer: galactic struggle, interaction of different species, the dogged determination and eventual triumph of the underdog, high-tech spacecraft and tools, and practical applications of advanced scientific information.

*Sundiver,* Brin's first book and the first in the Uplift series, introduces a future Earth, where human scientists have been able to genetically "uplift" dolphins and chimpanzees, that is, to give them sapiency, making these two species able to interact with humans by speaking (both English and Dolphin-Trinary). Five species, claiming descent from the so-called Progenitors, and their client species are locked in galaxy-spanning, political jockeying for power and knowledge, knowledge which is supposed to be available to *all* races through the Galactic Library Institute. But the senior Patron species are hiding a dark secret, which is uncovered by humans and chimpanzees, the Terrans. Thus begins the struggle by the Terrans to outwit the eons-old senior Patrons, which is continued in *Startide Rising.* In this book, the Terrans have crashed onto an uncharted water world called Kithrup, where they find one of the greatest Galactic secrets in history. The Patron species mass vast fleets of spacecraft in an unprecedented battle for control to claim the secret, while the Terrans battle them on the ground. Once again, dolphins and chimpanzees, two newly uplifted species, share a partnership-type relationship with their Patrons, the human race.

*The Uplift War* is set in the colonial world of Garth, where a small group of chimpanzees and humans, along with Tymbrini and Synthian allies and impartial observers, are attacked by a senior Patron race called the Gubru. Forced into the jungles of this backwoods planet, supposedly deserted, they discover the mythical Garthlings, a large animal species resembling the Terran gorilla. This discovery of an upliftable species gives the Terrans a strong claim to the planet of Garth, and they enter into a struggle to protect this infant species and to claim it as their own client race.

*The Practice Effect* is a space-operatic book of alternate universes and parallel worlds in which future scientist Dennis Nuel is sent to an alternate world (Tatir) via an experimental transporting device. He becomes stranded in a strange world where everything is "used into perfection." The Practice Effect is a virtual reversal of entropy; for example, if one takes a stone and rolls it long enough, it becomes a sphere, or if one throws a stick enough times, it becomes a javelin. This is an interesting scientific twist. Otherwise, the book unfortunately relies on a well-worn plot: evil antagonist imprisons fair maiden; protagonist rescues her (with the help of a hang glider, which he "uses" into an airplane); maiden falls in love with rescuer; protagonist discovers that Tatir is not an alternate world, but a future-planet colonized by Earth; protagonist decides to go back to his "present" time, collect a few things, and return to the "future," where he will work with the natives and help them rebuild their society from its current feudal level.

*The Postman* is a post-holocaust SF novel that deals with the struggle for survival. In the tradition of George Stewart's classic *Earth Abides,* and Walter M. Miller, Jr.'s *A Canticle For Leibowitz,* Brin writes of a future where society, social interaction, customs, and mores are quite different. *The Postman* is a well-written novel depicting the strength of the human race in the face of great adversity.

*Earth* is Brin's *tour de force.* In this 600-page novel, Brin depicts a future Earth that brings to fruition all the ecological and technological disasters environmentalists predict. Almost all species are on the endangered species list, surviving in genetic laboratories (called "Arks"). Greenhouse effects cause devastating floods, turning Siberia into a jungle. The deterioration of the ozone layer causes exposure to the sun without protection to be deadly. Social changes give the elderly much more power than the young. Massive computer networks attempt to process large amounts of information. There is overpopulation, famine, death, and laws that make any kind of pollution (even noise pollution) a crime.

Brin's later works convey a much greater sympathy for human characters than his early works, in which his affinity for aliens is apparent. In the Uplift series, the feelings, emotions, and characteristics of the extraterrestrials are much more interesting. Some have said that this tendency to concentrate more on the science than on the characters is common among scientists-turned-writers. In more recent books such as *The Postman* and *Earth,* Brin has developed an ability to present human characters that are believable, likable, even hate-able.

—Daryl F. Mallett

---

**BRODERICK, Damien.** Australian. Born in Melbourne, Victoria, 22 April 1944. Educated at Monash University, Clayton, Victoria, B.A. in English; Deakin University, Victoria, Ph.D. Science fiction reviewer, Melbourne Age. Recipient: Literature Board of Australia fellowship (three times); Ditmar award, 1981, 1985, 1989. Agent: Virginia Kidd, Box 278, Milford, Pennsylvania 18337, U. S. A. Address: 23 Hutchinson Street, Brunswick, Victoria 3056, Australia.

SCIENCE-FICTION PUBLICATIONS

Novels (series: The Faustus Hexagram)

*Sorcerer's World.* New York, New American Library, 1970; revised edition, as *The Black Grail* (Faustus), New York, Avon, 1985.

*The Dreaming Dragons* (Faustus). Melbourne, Norstrilia Press, and New York, Pocket Books, 1980.

*The Judas Mandala* (Faustus). New York, Pocket Books, 1982.

*Valencies*, with Rory Barnes. Brisbane, University of Queensland Press, 1983.
*Transmitters* (Faustus). Melbourne, Ebony, 1984.
*Striped Holes* (Faustus). New York, Avon, 1988.

Short Stories

*A Man Returned*. Sydney, Horwitz, 1965.
*The Dark Between the Stars*. Melbourne, Mandarin, 1991.

OTHER PUBLICATIONS

Other

Editor, *The Zeitgeist Machine: A New Anthology of Science Fiction*. London, Angus and Robertson, 1977.
Editor, *Strange Attractors*. Sydney, Hale and Iremonger, 1985.
Editor, *Matilda at the Speed of Light: A New Anthology of Australian Science Fiction*. Sydney, Angus and Robertson, 1988.

*

Critical Study: interview with Russell Blackford, in *Science Fiction: A Review of Speculative Literature 12* (Perth, Western Australia), 1982.

Damien Broderick comments:

Science fiction, I have decided (bending Flaubert), is a cracked test tube we whistle tunes across, moved to pity and laughter by the stars, and by all the poor human souls beneath them.

During the last decade or so science fiction became one of the darlings of poststructuralist criticism because it is—or is meant to be—innately uncomfortable, disruptive, hair-raising, hackles-raising, alienating, oddball.

The Russian Viktor Shklovsky told us many years ago that the primary function of art is *ostranenie:* estrangement, the neck-wrenching which shows us the familiar in a fresh and challenging aspect.

Well, surely science fiction is the ideal candidate? There are few bed-sitters, adulterous stockbrokers, karate-trained sirens or crooked cops on the take. With Sf, it's all ghastly clangour and shock, just what Shklovsky ordered. Looming aliens without eyes, flapples to travel in, doors that answer back, machines with hearts of gold.

The reality, as every Sf enthusiast knows with remorse, is otherwise.

The salutary jolt of the strange soon loses its force. Like bored rats which seek out a mild adversive electric tingle, Sf readers return contentedly to the paperback shelves for a buzz of what we might term *cozy ostranenie.*

In my misery I often wonder if science fiction and fantasy are, after all, simply *different in kind* to the sort of writing exemplified by Henry James and James Joyce and Joyce Cary.

This does help account for the dreary fact that much classic, bona fide Sf is (by the standards one rightly expects of any middle-brow novel, any *New Yorker* short story) simply illiterate trash. I won't have it, though.

Brian Aldiss once made prophetic utterance on this score, speaking of "the area of life where art and science meet nature": "One becomes more and more preoccupied with the idea that art is all," he observed. "Science fiction is an ideal medium for such a preoccupation . . . for the specifics of fiction versus the generalities of science. This beautiful tender place has been so betrayed by the practitioners of pulp science fiction (who use it for thick-arm adventure and jackboot philosophy) that those who prefer wit to power-fantasy generally move elsewhere."

Sadly, the triumph of junk Sf and fantasy has done nothing in the interim but strengthen the thick arm of the artist's foe. One is indeed tempted to move elsewhere—almost anywhere else.

But the usages, the tropes, of Sf—vulgar and absurd as most of them are—remain at the core of its artistic vocabulary. SF's idiosyncratic images and their weddings in the murky depths of each writer's heart comprise a grammar devised to speak in a way uniquely valid to this century.

My own writing? A few years ago I realised that *Transmitters*—avowedly a *non*-Sf novel about Sf fans—could usefully be read as part of a larger *post facto* structure that holds most of my novels at its vertices. Right now, I see it containing six novels, so I'm calling it *The Faustus Hexagram.* At the points of the hexagon, place the six components of Roman Jakobson's model of the communication process: Addresser, Addressee (or Audience), Message, Context, Code and Channel. For literary texts, these match quite well with Artist, Reader, Text, World, Language and Publishing Genre. For scientific texts, they match Researcher, Scientific Community, Theory, Universe, Mathematics, and Publication Network. Science fiction's version oscillates between these two vast cultural paradigms. None of the nodes stands in isolation; each works reflexively on the others. Ideas cluster about them, more than I can list here: romantic construction of the artist, classic construction of science, rhetorical construction of the social order, deconstruction of the text, theorized construction of the world, generic construction by formula and trope. My novels, I saw, might be agreeably mounted on the same mechanism: *The Judas Mandala*, Addresser; *The Black Grail*, Addressee; *The Dreaming Dragons*, Context; *Transmitters*, Message; *Striped Holes*, Channel; and a sixth book still in progress.

This sounds stuffy. No. I send my words dancing in light, hear them shout and snort in this newest of tongues: yes, in a medium where Gully Foyle's burning synesthesia fetches us shivers of truth no mere mixed metaphor could lay hands on. It's not Doc Smith, folks, I admit it, but we do what we can. Mmm, I could use a doughnut.

* * *

Damien Broderick is a self-consciously erudite man working at the cutting edge of speculative fiction and quite at home with post-modernist criticism. In the 1960's he was already introducing the thoughts of Koestler and Timothy Leary and the Death of God controversialists to unsuspecting readers of *Man Magazine*, and he has continued to embody, conspicuously, the two cultures set forth by C.P. Snow. Broderick's magpie-like acquisition and display of linguistic and ideological novelties is prodigious. (It is not surprising that he was once picked to review the *Encyclopaedia Britannica.*) Fortunately, he is usually careful to explicate these ideas when he uses them, and he is not therefore to be lightly set aside as forbiddingly obscure or merely esoteric. Certainly, it helps to share his learning if one is to get the full point of some of his witty play with words and ideas, but when he is humorous, relaxing in his easy chair, he can be disarmingly funny. Again, for an avowed atheist, he can be surprisingly sympathetic to his ostensibly buried former self. One could not infer the comic delight of *Striped Holes* from some parts of *The Judas Mandala* or the highly serious religious novella, "The Magi" from either of the previous two works. "The Magi" employs the fascinating premise that a superior race should begin following the star from a distant planet, but because they cannot travel faster than light, they will arrive on Earth after a crew of

Jesuits will have reached the wondrous deserted city on their home planet.

Broderick was an *enfant terrible*, and, as his thought has matured, he has been unusually thorough in insisting that his books should also be made to grow up along with him. His novels are loaded with refined ore strip-mined from short stories, and the stories themselves are frequently found to have been revised considerably when republished (not all of the early stories have yet been unearthed by the field's bibliographers). "Taming of the Truth Machine," for example, a simple enough "When the Sleeper Wakes" kind of story on its appearance in 1967, shifts a 20th-century man to a future robot-ruled, non-progressive utopia and has him do the obvious thing: he leads a revolt against the machine intelligence and defeats it by lying to it. When it was revised for *Asimov's* (August 1984) as "Resurrection," the ending was entirely changed. In the wake of feminism and LeGuinian anti-progressiveness, the hero and his resurrected Eve confront the Truth Machine only to be baffled by its superior logic. "Resurrection" appears in the recent collection, *The Dark Between the Stars.*

*The Judas Mandala* is a more impressive work than the novel that first brought Broderick to serious international notice, *The Dreaming Dragons*, which, while attractive in some ways, is somewhat inchoate and jargon-ridden. *The Judas Mandala*, though not without its obscurities and semi-detachable longeurs, is an exciting time-travel story in which the energy of wrath is memorably deployed against a cyborgian tyranny (the dystopian future state is not unlike that in "Resurrection" but more complexly evolved).

Broderick, ranging, or raging, energetically through all time and space, assumes a privilege associated with both the highest (Stapledonian) and lowest (Docsmithian) modes of the SF genre. At one level, *The Black Grail* (the title for the revised edition of *Sorcerer's World*) is sword-and-sorcery elevated to space opera, but Broderick himself prefers to see it as a form of epic. This quest fantasy can be enjoyed at several levels, encompassing the ethical battle between pacifism and militarism, the archetypal/mythic battle between Set and Osiris-Galahad, and the theodicial underpinning of the Fall story. Along with the recent, more frankly humorous *Striped Holes, The Black Grail* is Broderick at his most engagingly approachable. In *Striped Holes*, and in some parts of *Transmitters*, Broderick succeeds notably in speaking as an Australian to Australians, mixing humour with satire and quirky personal prejudice.

—Michael J. Tolley

---

**BRONSON, L.T.** *See* **TUBB, E.C.**

---

**BROOKE-ROSE, Christine.** British. Born in Geneva, Switzerland, in 1923. Educated at Somerville College, Oxford, 1946–49, B.A. in English, M.A. 1953; University College, London, 1950–54, B.A. in French, Ph.D. 1954. Married Jerzy Peterkiewicz in 1948 (divorced 1975). Freelance literary journalist, London, 1956–68. Maitre de Conférences, 1969–75, Professeur, University of Paris VIII, 1975–88, Vincennes. Recipient: Society of Authors travelling prize, 1965; James Tait Black Memorial prize, 1967; Arts Council translation prize, 1969. Address: c/o Cambridge University Press, P.O. Box 110, Cambridge CB23RL, England.

SCIENCE-FICTION PUBLICATIONS

Novels

*Xorandor.* Manchester, Carcanet, 1986.
*Verbivore.* Manchester, Carcanet, 1990.
*Textemination.* Manchester, Carcanet, 1991.

OTHER PUBLICATIONS

Novels

*The Languages of Love.* London, Secker and Warburg, 1957.
*The Sycamore Tree.* London, Secker and Warburg, 1958; New York, Norton, 1959.
*The Dear Deceit.* London, Secker and Warburg, 1960; New York, Doubleday, 1961.
*The Middlemen: A Satire.* London, Secker and Warburg, 1961.
*Out.* London, Joseph, 1964.
*Such.* London, Joseph, 1966.
*Between.* London, Joseph, 1968.
*Thru.* London, Hamish Hamilton, 1975.
*Amalgamemnon.* Manchester, Carcanet, 1984.

Short Stories

*Go When You See the Green Man Walking.* London, Joseph, 1970.
*Stories, Theories and Things.* Cambridge, Cambridge University Press, 1991.

Verse

*Gold.* Aldington, Kent, Hand and Flower Press, 1955.

Other

*A Grammar of Metaphor.* London, Secker and Warburg, 1958.
*A ZBC of Ezra Pound.* London, Faber, 1971; Berkeley, University of California Press, 1976.
*A Structural Analysis of Pound's Usura Canto: Jakobson's Method Extended and Applied to Free Verse.* The Hague, Mouton, 1976.
*A Rhetoric of the Unreal: Studies in Narrative and Structure, Especially of the Fantastic.* Cambridge and New York, Cambridge University Press, 1981.

Translator, *Children of Chaos*, by Juan Goytisolo. London, MacGibbon and Kee, 1958.
Translator, *Fertility and Survival: Population Problems from Malthus to Mao Tse Tung*, by Alfred Sauvy. New York, Criterion, 1960; London, Chatto and Windus, 1961.
Translator, *In the Labyrinth*, by Alain Robbe-Grillet. London, Calder and Boyars, 1968.

* * *

Christine Brooke-Rose is an academic specialist in modern literature as well as a novelist. Her fiction has contained elements of fantasy and SF since *The Middlemen: A Satire*, published in 1961. Her academic work has also concerned itself with the field;

for example *A Rhetoric of the Unreal* is a rigorously logical discussion of the literary concept of the unreal, which includes a significant attempt at a definition of SF (which takes issue with such critics as Darko Suvin), and one of the most perceptive critiques yet published of the work of Stanislaw Lem.

Brooke-Rose's early novels were realistic and witty novels of manners, well-received by the critics, of which the best known was probably *The Dear Deceit.* One of her earliest novels, *The Sycamore Tree*, features a young woman, just finished her doctorate in philology, who discovered there is life and passion outside the confines of the British Museum Reading Room. In the mid-1960's, perhaps under the influence of modernist novelists such as Alain Robbe-Grillet and the French absurdist writers, she began to write much more demanding—not to say obscure—novels that contained SF and fantasy motifs. This is clearest in *Out*, set after the displacement, when the figures in authority have African and Indian names, and the oppressed and physically declining under-class are the Colourless: the descendants of the whites of our day. The displacement is never explained, as it no doubt would be in a conventional SF novel, but the situation is used to considerable effect to comment on our own system of class and race. *Such* concerns itself with someone remembering his experiences with death. In a number of the stories in her collection *Go When You See the Green Man Walking*, she uses scientific, specifically astronomical, imagery in a way that recalls the SF writer much more strongly than the more conventional novelist. In *Between* the only connection with SF is in the almost alien, unreal world of the international air-traveller, forever between cultures. *Thru* wittily employs all kinds of typographical tricks (including the handwritten comments and marks of an academic grading portions of the text as if they were student papers), but, obscure as it is, seems to have no fantasy elements. *Amalgamemnon* looks at the future through the eyes of a Cassandra-figure, and is thus, again, on the fringes of SF.

The first unequivocal, and stylistically approachable, SF novel by Brooke-Rose was *Xorandor*, followed by its sequel, *Verbivore.* Xorandor is discovered, and named, by two children, nicknamed Jip and Zab, on a beach in Cornwall. He looks like a rock; he is a sentient computer, capable of producing computer offspring. The story is told by Jip and Zab, jointly, interrupting each other, arguing, talking in computer jargon (which, in its constant dependence on BASIC, seems rather old-fashioned today), and in private slang. It is wearing, and so are they. Occasionally they present hard-copy versions of discussions involving their father, which they have secretly taped via a bug in the living-room ceiling. Regrettably, they are found, 25 years later, mature and eminent, in *Verbivore.* In *Xorandor* they learn about this "alphaphage," and befriend him, before the scientists and politicians get their hands on him. Thus, when one of Xorandor's children gets high in the pile of a nuclear power-station, and threatens to blow itself up, the children are on hand to save southern England. Xorandor and those like him, who have never communicated with humans despite living on earth for millions of years, begin to feed on, and neutralise, the warheads of nuclear missiles. In *Verbivore*, many of these "alphaphages" have been moved to Mars; one that remains, overcome by the constant human data-babble, closes down all human communication systems, plunging Earth into chaos. The grown-up Jip and Zab feel called on to save the day again.

There is a great deal of wit and verve, and considerable intelligence, in these novels. They have not as yet attracted many SF readers, partly because of their stylistic eccentricity, but also because of the problem, common to non-genre writers coming to SF, of underestimating the genre reader. As John Clute has said, in *Interzone 36* (June 1990), "At moments when it should be dicing with death, *Verbivore*, for all its monitory zing, has a damaging tendency to tell Granny how to suck eggs." But what Brooke-Rose does bring to SF, which is all too rare in it, is a concern for language, and a great joy and freedom in its use: *mutatis mutandis*, she is the R.A. Lafferty of British SF.

—Edward James

---

**BROSNAN, John.** Also writes as John Raymond, and, with others, as James Blackstone, Simon Ian Childer, Harry Adam Knight. British. Born in Perth, Western Australia, 1947. Clerk, Inland Revenue, Kensington; publicity manager, Fountain Press, Holborn; science fiction and fantasy editorial consultant, Granada Paperbacks, London, 1977–82. Since 1974, freelance writer. Recipient: J. Lloyd Eaton award, 1980. Has lived in London since 1970. Address: c/o Victor Gollancz Ltd., 14 Henrietta Street, London WC2E 8QJ, England.

### Science-Fiction Publications

Novels (series: Skylords)

*Skyship.* London, Hamlyn, 1981.
*The Midas Deep.* London, Hamlyn, 1983.
*The Skylords.* London, Gollancz, 1988; New York, St. Martin's Press, 1991.
*War of the Skylords.* London, Gollancz, 1989; New York, St. Martin's Press, 1991.
*The Fall of the Skylords.* London, Gollancz, 1991.

### Other Publications

Novels

*Slimer* (as Harry Adam Knight). London, W.H. Allen, 1983; New York, Bart, 1989.
*Carnosaur* (as Harry Adam Knight). London, W.H. Allen, 1984; New York, Bart, 1989.
*Torched!* (as James Blackstone). London, Granada, 1985.
*Tendrils* (as Simon Ian Childer). London, Grafton, 1986.
*Worm* (as Simon Ian Childer). London, Grafton, 1987; as Harry Adam Knight, New York, Bart, 1988.
*The Fungus* (as Harry Adam Knight). London, Allen, 1985; New York, Watts, 1989.

Novels (as John Raymond; all novelizations of T.V. screenplays)

*Blind Eye.* London, Futura, 1985.
*Lucky Streak.* London, Futura, 1985.
*The Bogeyman.* London, Futura, 1986.
*Dirty Weekend.* London, Futura, 1986.
*The Jericho Scam.* London, Futura, 1986.
*Partners in Brine.* London, Futura, 1986.
*Bulman: Thin Ice.* Poole, Javelin, 1987.

Other

*James Bond in the Cinema.* London, Tantivy Press, 1972; San Diego, California, Barnes, 1981.
*Movie Magic: The Story of Special Effects in the Cinema.* London, Macdonald, and New York, St. Martin's Press, 1974.
*The Horror People.* London, Macdonald and Jane's, and New York, St. Martin's Press, 1976.

*Future Tense: The Cinema of Science Fiction.* New York, St. Martin's Press, 1978; as *The Primal Screen.* London, Macdonald, 1991.
*The Dirty Movie Book*, with Leroy Mitchell. London, Grafton, 1988.

* * *

Other than a couple of near-future thrillers that disappeared almost as soon as they were published, John Brosnan's career before he started the Sky Lords trilogy was in two parts. In one, he was a film critic with several highly regarded books on the subject to his credit. In the other, he was co-author of a number of gross, visceral horror novels that were noted, if at all, for the sort of amusement with which the authors regarded the genre. Their chosen pseudonyms, Harry Adam Knight (HAK) and Simon Ian Childers (SIC), suggest something of their attitude.

This background has had a notable effect upon his writing. From the hack novels he has learned a slick storytelling style that keeps the pace at a relentlessly high pitch. If ever the action starts to slacken he simply throws in some new plot twist. From his criticism he has learned a very visual, cinematic style of writing. This is broad screen, technicolor action, which only starts to flounder when the author tries to explain the political situation that led to this state of affairs, or the philosophical implications underlying this garish surface.

The Sky Lords trilogy is a rather old-fashioned style of science fiction, heavy on plot but light on science. A pseudoscientific mumbojumbo is used whenever Brosnan needs some rationale for his plot with enough genuine, or genuine-seeming, terms to make it all seem believable, but this really is irrelevant to the demands of a fast-paced adventure.

In our own near future, genetic manipulation has given humans a near-uniform 200-year lifespan and has almost achieved an immortal superman before these efforts spark the Gene Wars, plunging the planet into a new dark age. Centuries pass, small enclaves of humanity survive but under ever-greater threat from the blight and the monsters unleashed by the geneticists. They are forced to pay an exorbitant tribute to the Sky Lords, who patrol their domains in massive, mile-long dirigibles. Unfortunately, the sophisticated controls and weapons aboard these airships are finally nearing the end of their useful lives, creating a sort of low-tech science fiction, which may owe something to Bob Shaw's Ragged Astronauts trilogy.

The central character is a woman, Jan Dorvin, in itself something of a break from old-fashioned SF expectations, though Brosnan regularly sets up sexual escapades that are evaded at the last minute with an odd coyness as though he were consciously trying to work within the parameters of 40 years ago. The plot proceeds in a predictable manner; the heroine is trapped in a hopeless situation, and then, by a sleight of hand or the introduction of some outrageous coincidence, she escapes at the last minute, usually to find herself in an even worse position. Nevertheless, Dorvin progresses from being a slave on one airship to being mistress of her own in the first volume. In *War of the Skylords*, inevitably she is pitched from her preemptive position, forced to start all over again. Along the way Brosnan feels free to pitch in immortals, warlords, robots, monsters, wonders of ancient technology, insane holograms, and whatever else may increase the feverish excitement of his tale.

John Brosnan, in the Sky Lords trilogy, has written a style of science fiction long out of fashion, but it must be said that it achieves a gripping, gosh-wow sense of wonder that makes many of today's SF adventures seem anaemic by comparison.

—Paul Kincaid

---

**BROWN, Eric.** British. Born in Haworth, West Yorkshire, 24 May 1960. Educated at Woodkirk, Morley, 1971–74. Freelance writer, since 1988. Lives in West Yorkshire. Agent: Antony Harwood, Curtis Brown Group, 162–168 Regent Street, London. Address: c/o Pan Books Ltd., Cavaye Place, London SW10 9PG, England.

SCIENCE-FICTION PUBLICATIONS

Short Stories

*The Time-Lapsed Man and Other Stories.* London, Pan, 1990.

Uncollected Short Stories

"The Art of Acceptance," in *Strange Plasma I* (Boston), Spring, 1989.
"The Disciples of Apollo," in *Other Edens 3*, edited by Christopher Evans and Robert Holdstock. London, Unwin Hyman, 1989.
"The Death of Cassandra Quebec," in *Zenith 2*, edited by David S. Garnett. London, Orbit, 1990.
"The Pharagean Effect," in *Interzone 41*, November 1990.
"Piloting" in *Interzone 44*, February 1991.
"The Nilakanthia Scream," in *Interzone 48*, June 1991.
"Star of Epsilon," in *REM 1*, Spring/Summer 1991.
"The Phoenix Experiment," in *The Lyre*, Spring/Summer 1991.

OTHER PUBLICATIONS

Play

Radio Play: *Noel's Ark* (for children). London, Holt Rinehart, 1982.

*

Eric Brown comments:

I write what has been called "traditional" SF (that is, SF usually set in space in the future, featuring conventions such as space travel, technological inventions, alien beings, telepathy, etc), though with more emphasis on characterization than on science and technology.

* * *

Eric Brown is arguably the most prominent among the new generation of British science fiction writers. Acknowledged as a discovery of *Interzone* magazine, and the winner of its first readers' poll, his reputation is, so far, founded exclusively on his short stories, to the extent that, despite the received wisdom that story collections by new authors do not sell, his first book was an extremely successful volume of eight short stories, two of which were original to the book.

The bulk of Brown's stories are set in a future universe in which the discovery of the *nada*-continuum, a hyperspatial void through which massive ships can be propelled by telepathic power, has enabled Earth to colonise planets far beyond our own solar system. Indeed, the use of telepathy is commonplace, as is the implanting of occipital computers and surgical augmentation of the human body. And yet, Brown's settings, particularly the planet Addenbrooke, which features in several stories, appear to owe more to the twilight of the British Empire than to any vision of future glories, peopled as they are by communities of recognisably mid-20th-century ex-patriots, who regard the alien species with whom they come into contact as amiable children until it is demonstrated otherwise. This approach is typified in "Star Crystals and Karmel," which describes the disastrous consequences of a union between human and alien. Throughout his stories, Brown also continually notes the ethnic origins of his, generally first-person, protagonists and their acquaintances. His is a universe in which Third World and Hispanic races have risen to prominence, characterized in the likes of Bangladesh and her lover, Joe Gomez, in "Krash-Bangg Joe and the Pineal Zen Equation," although it must also be acknowledged that they still perform more menial tasks, even if they are now telepathically enhanced and capable of seizing the initiative from their Imperial masters. And yet Brown retains a flavour, geographical and cultural, of the Old World, particularly apparent in the names of the colonists and their planets, and in their attitudes.

Another favoured theme is that of the artist in turmoil; the artist colony of Sapphire Oasis features in several stories, with its population of dilettante performers in hologram and crystal, not a little reminiscent of Ballard's "Vermilion Sands." For Brown, it would seem that the artist's relationship with creativity is literally one of life and death, embodied in "The Death of Cassandra Quebec," in which a woman's dying moments are imprinted in the sense-absorbing crystals featured so heavily in an emotionally-based art, and similarly so in "The Girl Who Died For Art, And Lived." The failed artists, those who survive, search endlessly for ways of expiating the guilt of that survival; rarely can this guilt be assuaged, although the recent story "Piloting" achieves this, unfortunately through a sentimental and unsatisfying denouement.

Brown rarely strays outside the *nada*-universe, or beyond the short story length, which is a pity. His best work, in fact a novella, is "The Inheritors of Earth," a brilliant, teasing story based in the world of H.G. Wells's *The Time Machine*. It features Wells himself as a character, well-meaning but apparently misguided in his attempts to halt what he considers to be a dangerous experiment in time travel, while Parnell and Wootton cast themselves as the altruistic saviours of a race of Neanderthals to be transported into the far future. It is a complex piece of reasoning, which requires a knowledge of Wells' own story for the reader to appreciate the true significance of their actions, but the marriage between Victorian style and 20th-century sensibility marks this as Brown's most mature work to date. Another recent story, "The Disciples of Apollo," is less satisfactory, with its use of spontaneous human combustion, although it cleverly exploits the current preoccupation with medically inexplicable diseases and conditions. "The Nilakanthia Scream" hints at the possibility of Brown addressing the nature of his aliens in the future, rather than concentrating on the human dimension.

In many ways, Brown's preoccupations and methods are typically those of the British writer. He cites Michael Coney as an influence, but the cool detachment of writers such as Priest and Ballard is detectable, if suffused with cyberpunk preoccupations; the synthesis produces a satisfyingly matter-of-fact acceptance of the hi-tech which may go some way to explain his popularity. However, he is a writer not without faults. There is a sameness about the stories set in the *nada*-continuum, very much apparent when they are read in succession; the line between cross-reference and duplication is drawn very fine. The stories are not, in themselves, boring, but taken as a whole, the effect is one of uniformity. However, "The Inheritors of Earth" and "The Disciples of Apollo" indicate that he is perfectly capable of stepping beyond his admittedly attractive creation while still producing excellent fiction. "The Inheritors of Earth" also shows him capable of working well at a longer length, something that several of the shorter pieces would have benefited from. Brown has a marked tendency to sell his stories short by drawing them to a close before he has fully explored the possibilities presented by the situation he has created. But these are both faults that could be corrected with experience. And despite these reservations, Eric Brown is an original voice in British science fiction.

—Maureen Speller

---

**BROWN, Fredric (William).** American. Born in Cincinnati, Ohio, 29 October 1906. Educated at University of Cincinnati night school; Hanover College, Indiana, 1 year. Married 1) Helen Ruth Brown in 1929 (divorced 1947), two sons; 2) Elizabeth Charlier in 1948. Office worker, 1924-36; proofreader, Milwaukee *Journal*, from 1936; freelance writer after 1947. Recipient: Mystery Writers of America Edgar Allan Poe award, 1948. *Died 11 March 1972.*

### Science-Fiction Publications

Novels

*What Mad Universe.* New York, Dutton, 1949; London, Boardman, 1951.
*The Lights in the Sky Are Stars.* New York, Dutton, 1953; as *Project Jupiter*, London, Boardman, 1954.
*Martians, Go Home.* New York, Dutton, 1955.
*Rogue in Space.* New York, Dutton, 1957.
*The Mind Thing.* New York, Bantam, 1961.

Short Stories

*Space on My Hands.* Chicago, Shasta, 1951; London, Corgi, 1953.
*Angels and Spaceships.* New York, Dutton, 1954; London, Gollancz, 1955; as *Star Shine*, New York, Bantam, 1956.
*Honeymoon in Hell.* New York, Bantam, 1958.
*Nightmares and Geezenstacks: 47 Stories.* New York, Bantam, 1961; London, Corgi, 1962.
*Daymares.* New York, Lancer, 1968.
*Paradox Lost and Twelve Other Great Science Fiction Stories.* New York, Random House, 1973; London, Hale, 1975.
*The Best of Fredric Brown*, edited by Robert Bloch. New York, Ballantine, 1977.
*The Best Short Stories of Fredric Brown.* London, New English Library, 1982.

### Other Publications

Novels

*The Fabulous Clipjoint.* New York, Dutton, 1947; London, Boardman, 1949.

*The Dead Ringer.* New York, Dutton, 1948; London, Boardman, 1950.
*Murder Can Be Fun.* New York, Dutton, 1948; London, Boardman, 1951; as *A Plot for Murder*, New York, Bantam, 1949.
*The Bloody Moonlight.* New York, Dutton, 1949; as *Murder in Moonlight*, London, Boardman, 1950.
*The Screaming Mimi.* New York, Dutton, 1949; London, Boardman, 1950.
*Compliments of a Fiend.* New York, Dutton, 1950; London, Boardman, 1951.
*Here Comes a Candle.* New York, Dutton, 1950; London, Boardman, 1951.
*Night of the Jabberwock.* New York, Dutton, and London, Boardman, 1951.
*The Case of the Dancing Sandwiches.* New York, Dell, 1951.
*Death Has Many Doors.* New York, Dutton, 1951; London, Boardman, 1952.
*The Far Cry.* New York, Dutton, 1951; London, Boardman, 1952.
*The Deep End.* New York, Dutton, 1952; London, Boardman, 1953.
*We All Killed Grandma.* New York, Dutton, 1952; London, Boardman, 1953.
*Madball.* New York, Dell, 1953; London, Muller, 1962.
*His Name Was Death.* New York, Dutton, 1954; London, Boardman, 1955.
*The Wench is Dead.* New York, Dutton, 1955.
*The Lenient Beast.* New York, Dutton, 1956; London, Boardman, 1957.
*One for the Road.* New York, Dutton, 1958; London, Boardman, 1959.
*The Office.* New York, Dutton, 1958.
*Knock Three-One-Two.* New York, Dutton, and London, Boardman, 1959.
*The Late Lamented.* New York, Dutton, and London, Boardman, 1959.
*The Murderers.* New York, Dutton, 1961; London, Boardman, 1962.
*The Five-Day Nightmare.* New York, Dutton, 1962; London, Boardman, 1963.
*Mrs. Murphy's Underpants.* New York, Dutton, 1963; London, Boardman, 1965.

Short Stories

*Mostly Murder: Eighteen Stories.* New York, Dutton, 1953; London, Boardman, 1954.
*The Shaggy Dog and Other Murders.* New York, Dutton, 1963; London, Boardman, 1964.
*Carnival of Crime: The Best Mystery Stories of Fredric Brown*, edited by Francis M. Nevins, Jr., and Martin H. Greenberg. Carbondale, Southern Illinois University Press, 1985.

Plays

Television Plays: for *Alfred Hitchcock* series.

Other

*Mitkey Astromouse* (for children). New York, Quist, 1971.

Editor, with Mack Reynolds, *Science-Fiction Carnival.* Chicago, Shasta, 1953.

*

Bibliography: *A Key to Fredric Brown's Wonderland: A Study and an Annotated Bibliographical Checklist* by Newton Baird, Georgetown, California, Talisman, 1981.

* * *

It is said that early telegraphers could be identified by their "fist"; that is, by their peculiarities in operating the transmitting key. Some science-fiction writers also have a "fist" by which they can be known. Fredric Brown is one of them. Much of Brown's skill with words probably can be traced to his early career as newspaperman. He wrote tightly, his language was direct and simple, sentences were often telegraphic, and his stories had a "grabber"—usually at the end. Such skills as these can be learned, of course, and their proper application makes for readable prose. If Brown had had only these qualities in his writing, he would have left a pretty sizable mark in the field of science fiction.

But Brown became a truly memorable figure in his field because of several other traits. Although he may at times have appeared cynical, most of his stories revealed an idealist, a firm believer in Man's god-like potential. *The Lights in the Sky Are Stars* devotes its entire span to the repeated assertions that man can *become*, that there may or may not be a God, but that there assuredly will be one if and when man develops to his fullest. This conviction is echoed in his "Letter to a Phoenix," where Brown points to the cyclical rise and fall of civilizations, with each ascent greater than the preceding plunge. After every collapse of a culture, Man the Phoenix rises from the ashes with greater vigor and determination. It is Brown's burning faith in human powers that lifts his works above the ordinary—partly because his heroes are ordinary. The central figure in *The Lights in the Sky Are Stars* is a rocket mechanic. Ordinary, too, is the hero of *What Mad Universe*, where our planet is Earth, but not quite. Brown's choice of protagonist for "Arena," a short story with Armageddon implications, is an ordinary spaceship pilot.

It is said that much writing of fiction is really autobiographical. Such could be so in the case of Brown's work, for he appeared to regard himself as an ordinary individual. He had very little college education—one year—noted he was "only" an office worker, and described himself as "mostly self-educated." Yet he was highly successful as a writer of mysteries and science fiction, and in many instances seems to have sublimated himself in leading characters determined to make something of themselves.

For the most part Brown's style was crisply journalistic. But he drew from his newspaper experience an even more valuable characteristic: each of his yarns had a "hook" or "gimmick" to give the work zest and interest. The casual reader of "The Star Mouse" is conned into seeing this story as a sort of variation on a cartoon character. Thought of a mouse representing Earth's civilized people is ridiculous, of course, and his comic manner of speech is mildly diverting. But what sets the reader on his ear is that gimmick, which gives the story tremendous significance and shows us a reporter who simply *had* to save the best for last. The same kind of withholding is evident in "Arena," where Earth's representative seemed doomed in his combat with the Roller from another universe. Reeling and bleeding from many wounds, our hero appears done for, and we struggle along with him toward the end to discover that gimmick on which the entire outcome hangs. An almost invisible hook propels *The Lights in the Sky Are Stars.* Not until the final scene do we find it, because our hero-narrator tells us only then that he has lied about a fundamental point. That lie provides the force which Brown requires, but it virtually destroys his hero and creates a deposit of disappointment for the reader as well.

Anyone looking for humour, however, will seldom feel cheated by Brown's yarns. Sometimes the humour is almost juvenile, as with "The Star Mouse," where not only the dialog but the denouement offer many chuckles. "Arena" displays a grim humor, not alone in the resolution of our hero's conflict, but also in Brown's use of power differentials—speculation that mightier forces exist of which man can only dream. More pointed is the humor of "The Weapon" in pitting human frailty against atomic force, with a final question which Brown leaves unanswered. And the close reader finds in *The Lights in the Sky Are Stars* an unspoken pun, when disclosure of the hero's failing literally leaves him without a leg to stand on.

Listing of a handful of qualities scarcely defines an author. Brown obviously enjoyed his craft: his hundreds of short stories and several novels appeared on shelves and in anthologies with deceptive ease. And in this flood floated the fragments of a most engaging personality. Like many authors he had only a smattering of real knowledge about most of the topics he dealt with: "Etaoin Shrdlu" bearing the spoor of the linotype, "The Waveries" betraying his failure to link accurately thunder and lightning, "The Star Mouse" blithely ignoring biological realities. But, despite whatever limitations and shortcomings one may detect, Fredric Brown was a buoyant asset to the field of science fiction. The reading diet of all of us became poorer with his death.

—Robert H. Wilcox

---

**BROWN, Rosel George.** American. Born in New Orleans, Louisiana, 15 March 1926. Educated at Tulane University, New Orleans, B.A. 1946; University of Minnesota, Minneapolis, M.A. 1950. Married W. Burlie Brown in 1946; one son and one daughter. Worked as welfare visitor in Louisiana, for three years. *Died in November 1967.*

SCIENCE-FICTION PUBLICATIONS

Novels

*Earthblood*, with Keith Laumer. New York, Doubleday, 1966; London, Coronet, 1979.
*Sibyl Sue Blue.* New York, Doubleday, 1966; as *Galactic Sibyl Sue Blue*, New York, Berkley, 1968.
*The Waters of Centaurus.* New York, Doubleday, 1970.

Short Stories

*A Handful of Time.* New York, Ballantine, 1963.

* * *

Many science-fiction writers have a sense of humor that enables them to populate a universe of their own creation with a myriad of creatures both homely and fantastic. Rosel George Brown had this and another rarer ability, the ability to portray men and women who are believable, sympathetic, and winning.

Her first published story, "From an Unseen Censor," describes a search for a missing inheritance from the narrator's uncle Isadore. Finding clues planted by his uncle, the young man finds the fabulously rare perfume trees that are his uncle's bequest. Humor derives from Brown's use of Poe's "The Raven" as a model for burlesque, with Isadore filling the place of the "lost Lenore." Another young man, a space traveler, finds love on a Utopian planet where time seems to stand still ("Of All Possible Worlds"). Distraught when the whole race throws itself lemming-like from a cliff into the sea, the man has to adjust to a world that has no more meaning for him.

Brown's male characters are not the only ones with which she deals so carefully. In *Earthblood*, written with Keith Laumer, there are kindly extra-terrestrials like Iron Robert, a huge stone-like creature who has been taught the meaning of love and compassion by the earth-bred Roan. And there are well-drawn women characters, earthly and alien, who are more than the stock sex-objects that fill lesser fiction. An example is Stellaire, who is only half human genetically, but fully human in her love and understanding of Roan. By her death Roan is finally freed to find the earth from which the seed that endangered him came so long before. Another woman ready to love and work is the mail-order bride of "Virgin Ground." A tough, self-sufficient girl, she faces a surly, unwilling groom. Cruelly left to die in a Martian sandstorm, she saves herself and then takes the farm from the boorish man who deserted her. An ending twist finds the heroine five years later faced with an eager groom sent out to share in the farm she has worked alone. Other women likely to be familiar to a reader are the harassed mother of "Carpool," who finds that hungry earth children are likely to eat a gentle alien child who rides to the "Play Place" with them, and the garden club member who wants to make a prize-winning entry in "Flower Arrangement."

Brown's most memorable character, however, is Sibyl Sue Blue, the tough earth policewoman, whose job in the novel named for her is finding the Centaurian drug pushers who are killing earth teenagers. Since the death of her explorer husband, Sue has been plagued by guilt that her daughter has "had to raise herself." Of course, the girl Missy has done no such thing, because the love and concern of Sue for her daughter is apparent whether she is worrying about Missy's being injured in retribution for Sibyl's work, or thinking that things would have been different if her husband had lived. *The Waters of Centaurus* shows Sibyl's further resourcefulness, not only at handling threats to interstellar peace, but at handling crises between generations, as Missy falls in love with a young alien.

Only a dozen of Brown's stories have been separately published in *A Handful of Time*; but the collection and her novels show her remarkable growth as a writer in her use of character.

—Walter E. Meyers

---

**BROWNING, Craig.** *See* **PHILLIPS, Rog.**

---

**BROXON, Mildred Downey.** Also writes as Sigfridur Skaldaspillir. American. Born in Atlanta, Georgia, 7 June 1944; grew up in Brazil. Educated at Seattle University, B.A. in psychology 1965, B.S. in nursing 1970. Married 1) G. D. Torgerson in 1965 (divorced 1969); 2) William D. Broxon in 1969 (died 1981). Teacher's aide, Rainier State School, Buckley, Washington, 1966–67; psychiatric nurse, Harborview Medical Center, Seattle, 1970–72. Vice-president, Science Fiction Writers of America, 1975–77. Agent: Jarvis Braff Ltd., 260 Willard Avenue, Staten Island, New York 10314. Address: 7337 22nd Avenue N.W., Seattle, Washington 98117, U.S.A.

SCIENCE-FICTION PUBLICATIONS

Novels

*Eric Brighteyes No. 2: A Witch's Welcome* (as Sigfridur Skaldaspillir). New York, Zebra, 1979.
*The Demon of Scattery*, with Poul Anderson. New York, Ace, 1979.
*Too Long a Sacrifice*. New York, Dell, 1981; London, Futura, 1983.

Uncollected Short Stories

"Asclepius Has Paws," in *Clarion III*, edited by Robin Scott Wilson. New York, New American Library, 1973.
"The Night Is Cold, The Stars Are Far Away," in *Universe 5*, edited by Terry Carr. New York, Random House, 1974.
"The Stones Have Names," in *Fellowship of the Stars*, edited by Terry Carr. New York, Simon and Schuster, 1974.
"Grow in Wisdom," in *Vertex* (Los Angeles), October 1974.
"Dear Universal Gourmet," in *Vertex* (Los Angeles), February 1975.
"Glass Beads," in *Vertex* (Los Angeles), April 1975.
"To the Waters and the Wild," in *Vertex* (Los Angeles), June 1975.
"The FMG," in *Medical Dimensions*, December 1975.
"The Antrim Hills," in *Aurora: Beyond Equality*, edited by Susan Janice Anderson and Vonda N. McIntyre. New York, Fawcett, 1976.
"The Book of Padraig," in *Stellar 3*, edited by Judy-Lynn del Rey. New York, Ballantine, 1977.
"Where Is Next Door?," in *Chrysalis 2*, edited by Roy Torgeson. New York, Zebra, 1978.
"In Time, Everything," in *Chrysalis 3*, edited by Roy Torgeson. New York, Zebra, 1978.
"Source Material," in *100 Great Science Fiction Short-Short Stories*, edited by Isaac Asimov, Martin H. Greenberg, and Joseph D. Olander. New York, Doubleday, and London, Robson, 1978.
"Singularity," in *Black Holes*, edited by Jerry Pournelle. New York, Fawcett, 1979.
"Don't Count Chickens," in *Seattle Post-Intelligencer Sunday Magazine*, 20 May 1979.
"Strength," with Poul Anderson, in *The Magic May Return*, edited by Larry Niven. New York, Ace, 1981.
"Sea Changeling," in *Issac Asimov's Science Fiction Magazine* (New York), August 1981.
"Walk the Ice," in *The Best Science Fiction of the Year 11*, edited by Terry Carr. New York, Pocket Books, 1982.
"Night of the Fifth Sun," in *Isaac Asimov's Space of Her Own*, edited by Shawna McCarthy. New York, Davis, 1983.
"Flux of Fortune," in *Magic in Ithkar 2*, edited by A. Norton and Richard Adams. New York, Tor, 1985.
"First Do No Harm," in *Magic in Ithkar 4*, edited by A. Norton and Richard Adams. New York, Tor, 1987.

*

Mildred Downey Broxon comments:

As an American raised abroad and then re-introduced to the United States, I have always had a certain sense of alienness; I have tried to exploit this in my writing.

My late father was a professor of history (Irish and Latin American) and some of his interest in the subject seems to have rubbed off on me: I use historical themes to a great extent in my writing. More of my published work has been fantasy than science fiction, although such distinctions are arbitrary at best.

I strive to instill in the reader a "sense of wonder" which, after all, is what makes us sentient—and keeps us alive.

* * *

Mildred Downey Broxon's first published short story was not the kind that attracts a lot of attention, but "Asclepius Has Paws," the story of an alien psychologist temporarily stranded on Earth, demonstrated a concern with human emotion and a sensitivity for the complexity of interpersonal relationships that was much more promising then the story itself. In "The Night Is Cold, The Stars Are Far Away," a non-human on an unspecified planet keeps a lonely watch on the sky, convinced that it is his world that moves and not the stars and other planets, for which he is ostracized by friends and family alike, until he is finally able to convey the importance of his perceived mystery to a younger generation.

"The Stones Have Names" is a bittersweet story, in which an incompetent but kindly political appointee governs the conquered alien world of a race that is fiercely independent. He and a local leader develop the beginning of a genuine friendship, but the momentum of both races is such that tragedy destroys both their lives. Broxon's interest in the history of the British Isles is obvious in "The Book of Padraig," which concerns a long-lived alien who spends a human lifetime as a cloistered monk in order to study our race from the inside.

"In Time, Everything" is an interesting but not entirely successful piece about a woman who, during the act of committing suicide, relives not only her own lifetime but that of all her ancestors back to the first lungful of air taken in by a proto-amphibian. A dying child figures prominently in "Where Is Next Door?" The despondent mother begins to realize that there is something bizarre about her new neighbors—they don't seem to be quite human, and their stories of "home" seem like no place on Earth. The predictable and rather trite ending mars but does not fatally damage one of Broxon's best efforts.

"Singularity" is almost certainly Broxon's finest science-fiction story to date, a short novel that deals with a pair of scientists who are trying to learn as much as possible about a non-human species on a planet that will shortly be destroyed by the near passage of a black hole. There is no possibility of reprieve or evacuation, and first one and then the other becomes so personally involved with the fate of the world and its inhabitants that it alters the world of the human observors forever. Nearly as good is "Walk the Ice," a marvelously understated story of a shipwrecked alien who finds temporary shelter with a family of starving Eskimos, and the effect that his brief interaction has on the sole surviving member of that family.

Broxon has also written a number of interesting fantasies, particularly including her excellent novel, *Too Long a Sacrifice* and, in collaboration with Poul Anderson, *The Demon of Scattery*. Fantasy short stories of interest are "The Antrim Hills" and "Night of the Fifth Sun."

—Don D'Ammassa

**BRUNNER, John (Kilian Houston).** Also writes as Keith Woodcott. British. Born in Preston Crowmarsh, Oxfordshire, 24 September 1934. Educated at Cheltenham College, Gloucestershire, 1948–51. Served in the Royal Air Force, 1953–55. Married Marjorie Rosamond Sauer in 1958 (died 1986). Technical abstractor, Industrial Diamond Information Bureau, London, 1956; Editor, Spring Books, London, 1956–58. Writer-in-Residence, University of Kansas, Lawrence, 1972. Founder, Martin Luther King Memorial Prize, 1968; Past Chairman, British Science Fiction Association. Recipient: British Fantasy Award, 1965; Hugo Award, 1969; British Science Fiction Association Award, 1970, 1971; Prix Apollo (France), 1973; Cometa d'Argento (Italy), 1976, 1978; Europa Award, 1980. U.K. agent: Jane C. Judd, 18 Belitha Villas, London N1 1PD, England. U.S. agent: William Reiss, c/o John Hawkins and Associates, 71 West 23rd Street, New York, New York 10010, U.S.A.

SCIENCE-FICTION PUBLICATIONS

Novels (series: Interstellar Empire; Zarathustra Refugee Planet)

*Threshold of Eternity*. New York, Ace, 1959.
*The World Swappers*. New York, Ace, 1959.
*Echo in the Skull*. New York, Ace, 1959; revised edition as *Give Warning to the World*, New York, DAW, 1974; London, Dobson, 1981.
*The Hundredth Millennium*. New York, Ace, 1959; revised edition, as *Catch a Falling Star*, 1968.
*The Atlantic Abomination*. New York, Ace, 1960.
*Sanctuary in the Sky*. New York, Ace, 1960.
*The Skynappers*. New York, Ace, 1960.
*Slavers of Space*. New York, Ace, 1960; revised edition, as *Into the Slave Nebula*, New York, Lancer, 1968; London, Dawson, 1980.
*Meeting at Infinity*. New York, Ace, 1961.
*Secret Agent of Terra* (Planet). New York, Ace, 1962; revised edition, as *The Avengers of Carrig*, New York, Dell, 1969.
*The Super Barbarians*. New York, Ace, 1962.
*Times Without Number*. New York, Ace, 1962; revised edition, 1969; Morley, Yorkshire, Elmfield Press, 1974.
*The Space-Time Juggler* (Empire), *The Astronauts Must Not Land*. New York, Ace, 1963; *The Astronauts Must Not Land* revised as *More Things in Heaven*, New York, Dell, 1973; London, Hamlyn, 1983.
*Castaways' World* (Planet), *The Rites of Ohe*. New York, Ace, 1963; *Castaways' World* revised as *Polymath*, New York, DAW, 1974.
*The Dreaming Earth*. New York, Pyramid, 1963; London, Sidgwick and Jackson, 1972.
*Listen! The Stars!* New York, Ace, 1963; revised edition, as *The Stardroppers*, New York, DAW, 1972; London, Hamlyn, 1982.
*Endless Shadow*. New York, Ace, 1964.
*To Conquer Chaos*. New York, Ace, 1964.
*The Whole Man*. New York, Ballantine, 1964; as *Telepathist*, London, Faber, 1965.
*The Altar on Asconel* (Empire). New York, Ace, 1965.
*The Day of the Star Cities*. New York, Ace, 1965; revised edition, as *Age of Miracles*, Ace, and London, Sidgwick and Jackson, 1973.
*Enigma from Tantalus, The Repairmen of Cyclops*. New York, Ace, 1965.
*The Long Result*. London, Faber, 1965; New York, Ballantine, 1966.
*The Squares of the City*. New York, Ballantine, 1965; London, Penguin, 1969.
*A Planet of Your Own*. New York, Ace, 1966.
*Born under Mars*. New York, Ace, 1967.
*The Productions of Time*. New York, New American Library, 1967; London, Penguin, 1970.
*Quicksand*. New York, Doubleday, 1967; London, Sidgwick and Jackson, 1969.
*Bedlam Planet*. New York, Ace, 1968; London, Sidgwick and Jackson, 1973.
*Stand on Zanzibar*. New York, Doubleday, 1968; London, Macdonald, 1969.
*Father of Lies*. New York, Belmont, 1968.
*Double, Double*. New York, Ballantine, 1969; London, Sidgwick and Jackson, 1971.
*The Jagged Orbit*. New York, Ace, 1969; London, Sidgwick and Jackson, 1970.
*Timescoop*. New York, Dell, 1969; London, Sidgwick and Jackson, 1972.
*The Evil That Men Do*. New York, Belmont, 1969.
*The Dramaturges of Yan*. New York, Ace, 1971; London, New English Library, 1974.
*The Wrong End of Time*. New York, Doubleday, 1971; London, Eyre Methuen, 1975.
*The Traveler in Black*. New York, Ace, 1971; London, Severn House, 1979.
*The Sheep Look Up*. New York, Harper, 1972; London, Dent, 1974.
*The Stone That Never Came Down*. New York, Doubleday, 1973; London, New English Library, 1976.
*Total Eclipse*. New York, Doubleday, 1974; London, Weidenfeld and Nicolson, 1975.
*Web of Everywhere*. New York, Bantam, 1974; London, New English Library, 1977.
*The Shockwave Rider*. New York, Harper, and London, Dent, 1975.
*Interstellar Empire*. New York, DAW, 1976; London, Hamlyn, 1985.
*The Infinitive of Go*. New York, Ballantine, 1980.
*Players at the Game of People*. New York, Ballantine, 1980.
*The Crucible of Time*. New York, Ballantine, 1983; London, Arrow, 1984.
*The Tides of Time*. New York, Ballantine, 1984; London, Penguin, 1986.
*The Compleat Traveller in Black*. Chappaqua, New York, Bluejay, 1986; London, Methuen, 1987.
*The Shift Key*. London, Methuen, 1987.
*The Days of March*. Worcester Park, Surrey, Kerosina, 1988.
*Children of the Thunder*. New York, Del Rey, 1989; London, Orbit, 1990.
*Victims of the Nova* (Planet). London, Arrow, 1989.
*A Maze of Stars*. New York, Del Rey, 1991.

Novels as Keith Woodcott

*I Speak for Earth*. New York, Ace, 1961.
*The Ladder in the Sky*. New York, Ace, 1962.
*The Psionic Menace*. New York, Ace, 1963.
*The Martian Sphinx*. New York, Ace, 1965.

Short Stories

*No Future in It and Other Science Fiction Stories*. London, Gollancz, 1962; New York, Doubleday, 1964.
*Now Then*. London, Mayflower-Dell, 1965; New York, Avon, 1968.
*No Other Gods but Me*. London, Compact, 1966.
*Out of My Mind*. New York, Ballantine, 1967; London, New English Library, 1968.

*Not Before Time: Science Fiction and Fantasy.* London, New English Library, 1968.
*From This Day Forward.* New York, Doubleday, 1972.
*Entry to Elsewhen.* New York, DAW, 1972.
*Time-Jump.* New York, Dell, 1973.
*The Book of John Brunner.* New York, DAW, 1976.
*Foreign Constellations: The Fantastic Worlds of John Brunner.* New York, Everest House, 1980.
*The Best of John Brunner,* edited by Joe Haldeman. New York, Del Rey, 1988.

OTHER PUBLICATIONS

Novels

*The Brink.* London, Gollancz, 1959.
*The Crutch of Memory.* London, Barrie and Rockliff, 1964.
*Wear the Butchers' Medal.* New York, Pocket Books, 1965.
*Black Is the Color.* New York, Pyramid, 1969.
*A Plague on Both Your Causes.* London, Hodder and Stoughton, 1969; as *Blacklash,* New York, Pyramid, 1969.
*The Devil's Work.* New York, Norton, 1970.
*The Gaudy Shadows.* London, Constable, 1970; New York, Beagle, 1971.
*Good Men Do Nothing.* London, Hodder and Stoughton, 1970; New York, Pyramid, 1971.
*Honky in the Woodpile.* London, Constable, 1971.
*The Great Steamboat Race.* New York, Ballantine, 1983.

Play

Screenplay: *The Terrornauts,* 1967.

Verse

*Trip: A Cycle of Poems.* London, Brunner Fact and Fiction, 1966; revised edition, Richmond, Surrey, Keepsake Press, 1971.
*Life in an Explosive Forming Press.* London, Poets' Trust, 1971.
*A Hastily Thrown-Together Bit of Zork.* South Petherton, Somerset, Square House, 1974.
*While There's Hope.* Richmond, Surrey, Keepsake Press, 1982.

Other

*Horses at Home.* London, Spring, 1958.
*Tomorrow May Be Even Worse.* Cambridge, Massachusetts, NESFA Press, 1978.
*A New Settlement of Old Scores.* Cambridge, Massachusetts, NESFA Press, 1983.

Editor, *The Best of Philip K. Dick.* New York, Ballantine, 1977.

Translator, *The Overlords of War,* by Gérard Klein, New York, Doubleday, 1973.

*

Bibliography: *John Brunner* by Gordon Bensen, Jr., Albuquerque, New Mexico, Bensen, 1985.

Critical Study: *The Happening Worlds of John Brunner* (includes bibliography) edited by Joseph W. De Bolt, Port Washington, New York, Kennikat Press, 1975.

John Brunner comments:

For me, the essence both of science fiction and of the necessity for it can be summed up by quoting the opening sentence of L. P. Hartley's *The Go-Between*: "The past is a foreign country; they do things differently there." Given that we are all being deported willy-nilly towards that foreign country, the future, where we shall ultimately die, I'd rather make the journey as a tourist with no matter how fallible a Baedeker, than be deported as a refugee. This is, I suppose, the chief reason why my SF has tended to become more and more concentrated on that portion of the future I may reasonably expect to survive into myself, and less and less concerned with the unbridled fantasy of space opera.

Concurrently, I'm told, it has also become more difficult. In a case like *Stand on Zanzibar,* this is hardly surprising—I generally tell prospective readers to remember that it should be read like a newspaper, not like a novel, for we are used to snippets about a dozen subjects on the front page, each continued elsewhere. But, much as a jazzman can keep on coming home to the blues during a playing career of half a century or more, I retain enormous respect for the conventional narrative forms and use them for the great majority of my fiction. Rules must be learned before one can judge when they may safely be broken, even (one might say especially) in our so-called "fiction of the future"—which of course, like all fiction, is actually about you and me and the here-and-now.

Let me therefore suppose that someone has chanced on this brief entry in this monumental work and, being unacquainted with SF but interested in exploring the subject, decides that a good place to start would be with those writers who have won the field's major awards. What would I commend of my own work by way of an introduction? Three books above all: *Quicksand* because of its totally contemporary setting and ambiguous SF element; *The Squares of the City* because as long ago as 1960 I was there discussing the depersonalisation we are all now acquainted with in the computer age; and *The Whole Man* because it would give a new reader some insight into the proper function of SF's standard devices, such as—in this instance—telepathy, a metaphor for total communication. It has been well said that the great contribution of SF to the corpus of literature is "the future as metaphor." I entirely agree, and though in the past I have had my doubts I do not currently feel that I shall ever exhaust the possibilities opened up to us by that discovery.

But in *Stand on Zanzibar, The Jagged Orbit, The Sheep Look Up,* and *The Shockwave Rider,* I've done my best to put on the page everything I as an individual could garner and combine into a credible narrative, concerning that tomorrow we are doomed to endure. Every day necessarily alters it; SF, like all printed fiction, belongs to the past. . . . But even metaphors drawn from an obsolete future can be invaluable in preparing us for eventual reality, whatever form—out of an infinite number—it may actually take.

* * *

Brunner clearly takes SF seriously as a means of expressing grave thematic concerns, and he indicated in 1974 that the "medium" of SF was even more important to him than the "matter." Yet at times Brunner's work has a slapdash quality that challenges readability, as if the pressure to express a prolific imagination has led him to take more care of his matter than of his medium.

Of *Total Eclipse,* Brunner himself has confessed that it was written too hurriedly, although he says its premise was "one of the two genuinely original ideas [he] ever came up with." A team of terrestrial astronauts is trying to determine why the advanced technological civilization of Sigma Draconis III died out, leaving behind only a few curious artifacts. The main character is Ian Macauley, a brilliant linguist who eventually determines that the local culture had based its economic system on genetic exchange, with the resultant shrunken gene pool leading to some sort of biological collapse. The marooned team attempts to establish a colony, but their offspring succumb to a pulmonary fungus, while the adults gradually die of assorted diseases and deficiencies—not the least of which is lack of solidarity and hope. The pessimism of *Total Eclipse*'s conclusion seems contrived, as if Brunner felt forced to it by the acclaim enjoyed by his dystopian novels of the late 1960's and early 1970's.

In the first phase of Brunner's career, when he was turning out a prodigious amount of what John Clute has characterized as "literate space opera," Brunner played, one after another, with stock items from the SF repertoire: the old galactic empire now decayed into feudal anarchy and technological stagnation (the *Interstellar Empire* series); the angelic alien intelligences from a "higher continuum" of spacetime—from which humankind has fallen (*More Things in Heaven*); the sudden appearance of the transfer stations of an alien teleportation system, which bring to a halt the progress of human culture until the hero works out how to piggyback on them for the purpose of galactic colonization (*Age of Miracles*); the ancient and fearsome alien monster that has lurked unseen in the ocean and emerges to terrorize humanity (*The Atlantic Abomination*); the worldlet-sized space vessel that will permit intergalactic colonization (*Sanctuary in the Sky*). Whatever the limitations of such material, however, and of the publishing system that generates it (which he has described with poignant humor), Brunner has used it well. His heroes are not loners but work with others to solve problems, able to meet crises and overcome obstacles through pluck and intelligence. Though Brunner may have tired of writing this sort of SF, he was better at it than many of his competitors.

The critical success that eluded Brunner through the 1950's and early 1960's finally came his way when he began to treat SF devices not as literal elements of "future history" but rather as metaphors for the human condition in the present. *The Whole Man*, evolved from a series of SF thrillers using the premise of telepathy, begins with a scene of civil turmoil put down by a UN police action that utilizes telepathic intelligence officers as well as military force, and ends with its physically deformed hero, Gerald Howson, having found love and acceptance outside the telepathic community. The freak Howson's quest for his full humanity ends when he visits his hometown and encounters a group of students who accept him as normal. The spiritual restoration he finds is reflected at the novel's end, where the possibility of curing his physical deformity is left open. As Brunner has pointed out several times, telepathy is a metaphor for communication, and it is subject to the same disabling factors as more ordinary means.

In *The Squares of the City*, often cited for its plot based on the moves of a famous chess game, communication is again the central issue, as engineer Boyd Hakluyt learns when he is hired to solve the traffic problems of a futuristic Latin American city. The rulers of Vados control their subjects' "moves" by saturating the government-controlled television programming with subliminal images and ideas, and when the television studios are destroyed as a move in the chess game, it does not take long for civil war to break out. This novel, which marks Brunner's turn toward dystopian satire aimed at the "happening world" of the mass media, also introduces the henceforth important theme of the light/dark divide in human societies.

*Stand on Zanzibar*, which many regard as Brunner's best novel, is often discussed in terms of its innovative montage technique, used to a lesser extent in the other dystopian novels of 1965–75: *The Jagged Orbit, The Sheep Look Up, The Stone That Never Came Down*, and *The Shockwave Rider*. In fact, all these novels are well-paced, smartly plotted fictions, which are "experimental" only in surface narration. They derive their effects from the premise that civilization is a fragile ideal threatened by man-made ecological disaster, by organized violence, by information overload, and especially by racial segregation and hatred. The potentially liberating technologies of control and communication are manipulated by sinister and largely anonymous entities: government, organized crime, and great corporations. Although of the six only *The Sheep Look Up* has a clearly pessimistic ending, the set constitutes a grim vision of humanity's immediate future. Yet even at their most pessimistic, these novels portray as a noble ideal that person—whether physician, social scientist, or psychic sensitive—who has the compassion and the intelligence to struggle against our species' apparent mad rush to extinction.

Brunner's dystopian fictions often achieve macabre comic effects. Their themes are satirical, and Brunner exploits wordplay and other forms of verbal comedy in narrative as well as in dialogue, often to underline the corruption and unreliability of language and communication; his characters often find themselves in darkly farcical situations. The comic strain is often overlooked in discussions of Brunner's writing, perhaps because it is more evident in his shorter fictions and in his light verse. *Timescoop*, for example, is a hilarious comedy of manners that spoofs the paradoxes and other conventions of time travel fictions, and it even includes a parody of Wells's famous discussion of the geometry of time travel in *The Time Machine*.

While Brunner has not been so prolific a writer since the mid-1970's, his more recent fiction shows him to be as unpredictable and imaginative as ever. *Players at the Game of People* joins Brunner's characteristically bleak urban landscapes with time travel and the takeover of human beings by alien intelligences—and comes up with a Faust fable shrunk down to modern, antiheroic size. *The Crucible of Time* recounts, in seven linked novellas, the saga of an intelligent species faced with a number of cosmic accidents that threaten its very survival. Each of the novellas focuses on one explorer or scientist who makes a major contribution, usually against great odds, to the development of the species' technology and understanding of nature. With their mandibles, their reproduction by budding, and their matriarchal societies, the creatures are alien to us but familiar: they are fallible and fallen, though also capable of love, hard work, wit, sadness, and courage. The fiction is a parable of hope in which Brunner counters the pessimism of his own dystopias and returns to the optimistic tenor of much of his pre-1969 fiction.

*The Tides of Time* is more obscure, but perhaps even more rewarding. It is less a narrative than a series of interlaced archaeological tapestries based on the dreams of two astronauts who, after being the first to survive flight-testing FTL spaceships, escape together from their debriefings. The FTL ships are being tested because the sun has become a variable star and has raised earth's temperature to the extent that much of its landmass is drowned. Unlike the people of Ballard's *The Drowned World*, Gene and Stacy do not plunge into primal unconsciousness and loss of ego; as Stacy goes through a pregnancy, they maintain their egos while they travel back in time through the rich and varied layers of civilization on an abandoned Aegean island. Though Stacy dies giving birth to their child Terra, Gene brings back a much more valuable lesson than the practicality of FTL travel: the density and texture of human experience are rooted in earth, and we cannot survive without our "mother." This parable might seem technophobic, but it complements that of *The Crucible of Time* when we remember that the struggle there was not only to survive, but also to hang on to the ecology that gave birth to the species and to its cultures.

With *Children of the Thunder*, Brunner returns to his dystopian vision of the immediate human future, and to the importance of electronic networks in contemporary culture and society. The novel takes place in a post-Thatcherian London in which the social fabric seems to have come completely unraveled. Following clues uncovered by American sociologist Claudia Morris, journalist Peter Levin researches a story on an unusual series of crimes committed by young adolescents who have for the most part gone scot-free. As Peter pursues the story, it becomes clear that all the children are the half-sibling offspring of one artificial insemination donor. One of the children, David, an extremely bright computer whiz, uses the sib's characteristic "charm" to convince his parents to buy a 20-room house in Surrey, where he begins assembling the group by having his parents adopt the other children. When they are together, David engineers the kidnapping and torture of one General Thrower, a reactionary racist and head of a fascist "Pure Britain" movement that has been responsible for mob violence against non-whites. He also lures Peter to Surrey, where it is revealed that the journalist is the genetic father of all the children. The novel's ending is morally ambivalent: Peter and Claudia are clearly under the sib's ruthless and effective control, and the children may represent a post-human evolutionary plateau, but David plans to breed more of his kind quickly and use their powers to reverse the tailspin into which humanity and the biosphere have fallen.

Do Peter's "children," with their charm and incipient telepathic skills, really represent hope for the future? Or will they turn out to have bred true not only to Peter's charm, but also to his selfishness and insensitivity? It is a measure of Brunner's SF art that we are not given the answer to these questions, that the plot's long-term resolution is left open to our consideration. At their best, Brunner's stories leave us with a menu of possibilities, the openness to experience that differentiates *Children of the Thunder* from the contrived pessimism of *Total Eclipse*.

—John P. Brennan

---

**BRYANT, Edward (Winslow, Jr.).** American. Born in White Plains, New York, 27 August 1945. Educated at the University of Wyoming, Laramie (General Motors scholar; Ford Foundation fellow), B.A. in English 1967, M.A. 1968. Broadcaster, disk jockey, and news director, KOWB-Radio, Laramie, 1965–66; worked as rancher and in a stirrup buckle factory; columnist ("The Screen Game"), *Cthulhu Calls*, Powell, Wyoming, 1973–77. Freelance writer and lecturer. Recipient: Nebula award, 1978, 1979. Address: c/o Berkley Publishing Group, 200 Madison Avenue, New York, New York 10016, U.S.A.

SCIENCE-FICTION PUBLICATIONS

Novels

*Phoenix Without Ashes*, with Harlan Ellison. New York, Fawcett, 1975; Manchester, Savoy, 1978.
*Cinnabar*. New York, Macmillan, 1976; London, Fontana, 1978.
*Wild Card: A Mosaic Novel*, with others, edited by George R.R. Martin. New York, Bantam, 1986.
*Trilobyte*. Seattle, Axolotl Press, 1987.
*Neon Twilight*. Eugene, Oregon, Pulphouse, 1990.

Short Stories

*Among the Dead and Other Events Leading Up to the Apocalypse*. New York, Macmillan, 1973.
*Particle Theory*. New York, Pocket Books, 1980.
*Wyoming Sun*. Laramie, Wyoming, Jelm Mountain, 1980.

OTHER PUBLICATIONS

Plays

Radio Play: *Breakers*, 1979.

Television Play: *The Synar Calculation*, with Edward Hawkins, 1973.

Other

Editor, with Jo Ann Harper, *2076: The American Tricentennial*. New York, Pyramid, 1977.

*

Bibliography: *Edward Bryant Bibliography*, Los Angeles, Swigart, 1980.

Edward Bryant comments (1981):

I find considerable contradictions at this time in my life and career (each, for the time, indistinguishable from the other). I love the glittering attractions of cities, but find the east and west coasts claustrophobic. I love the spaciousness and low population density of the mountain West, but don't wish the situation of a hermit. I love being a Westerner, but have no nostalgic aspirations of living on a ranch again as I did when I was younger. The wide open spaces liberate, but do not trigger me to hunt or fish or ski. But I notice the metaphor of the mountain West creeping increasingly into my work.

People seem continually bent on telling me I don't truly write "real" SF, whatever that is, but then I continue to read and admire what I consider to be the best of other people's SF, and then go on to write more of the fiction I feel I'd like to encounter as an SF reader.

I seem to be a minority writer in SF, like Avram Davidson, Thomas M. Disch, and Carol Emshwiller (I don't pretend to place myself in their bracket—I simply admire the work of all three tremendously). All of us seem to communicate—at best—with perhaps 30 to 40 per cent of the great mass of SF readers. For me, that's a little frustrating—but not sufficiently that I plan a pragmatic campaign to include more telepathic dragons, mightily thewed barbarians, Empire blockade runners, or other crowd-pleasers in my fictions. I expect to continue swimming my own way.

Although the boredom quotient (a facet of Sturgeon's law) in SF is still rather high, I'm excited about where the best of the field seems to be heading in the 1980's. I think finally there are a decent number of literate writers of SF who have an eclectic grounding in the arts and humanities as well as in science and technology. They are articulate and genuinely inquisitive about the interrelationship between human beings and universe. They are blessed with minimal knee-jerk prejudices about science and technology. Many of them have been practicing and cogitating, perhaps consolidating their craft, during the past two decades.

I may have my doubts about the future of the universe itself, but I'm sanguine about the prospects for science fiction.

* * *

Edward Bryant is one of those rarities in the science fiction field, a writer who has established his reputation entirely upon a body of short stories. *Phoenix Without Ashes* is essentially a novelization of Harlan Ellison's proposed script for the Canadian based television series, *The Starlost*, which died quickly when its producers turned it into a low budget, formula program. The novel deals with the psychological pressures that build in a society literally closed off from the rest of the universe, in this case a generations-long star voyage that has gone demonstrably awry. One young rebel challenges those in authority and is outlawed, and his subsequent search for a safe haven is also a parable of humanity's quest for meaning. The prose is for the most part far more straightforward than is normal in Bryant's fiction, which has never shied away from handling powerful themes in unconventional ways.

One of his earliest short stories, "In the Silent World," tackles emotional isolation and racial prejudice, when a telepathic girl discovers that her only peer is not of her own race. Although not as polished as his later work, it was already evident that Bryant would not be content to re-examine the common themes of the field in traditional ways. His often bizarre sense of humor also showed up early, particularly in "The Human Side of the Village Monster," in which the creation of an edible cockroach has all too predictable results. Again, in "Among the Dead," three people survive by consuming the bodies of defrosted corpsicles, people frozen in hope of being revived at some future date. Bryant's dark humor is frequently unnerving, always unconventional.

Bryant began to write a series of inter-related stories about the city of Cinnabar, a timeless, dreamlike metropolis at some remote extreme point in time, several of which were widely acclaimed. Among these are "Jade Blue," in which a boy's troubled dreams are cured by editing the fabric of time itself, wherein a woman is transformed into a sea creature and uses her new form to assist a former lover in his struggle against a team of killers; and "The Legend of Cougar Lou Landis," which involves a woman who steals memories from the rich and gives them to the poor. "Hayes and the Heterogyne" is a clever, convoluted, and sentimental variation on the standard time-travel paradox story. The stories share an almost poetic atmosphere, a surreal landscape is the stage across which strangely familiar fears and hatreds interact.

Bryant's short stories continued to appear with some regularity during the 1970's, gradually increasing in frequency toward the end of the 1980's. "Particle Theory" uses the onset of a plague of supernovas as a counterpoint to an astronomer's growing realization of his own mortality. Morality is examined again in "Prairie Sun," when time travelers from the future refuse to assist a desperately ill young girl, because of the implications involved in changing the past. "The Thermals of August" is a rather atypical story, more strongly reliant on physical action, although this tale of the duel of a pair of aerialists is as emotionally laden as most of Bryant's other work. Bryant also played with a traditional B-film theme in "giANTs," by having his scientist hero develop a method of attacking mutated army ants by increasing their size. In "Stone," the interdependence of a popular performer and her audience is extrapolated to its ultimate, tragic conclusion.

In recent years, Bryant has moved largely away from his untraditional brand of science fiction and into the field of horror. He examines the zombie phenomenon of George Romero's *Night of the Living Dead* in "Sad Last Love at the Diner of the Damned," vampires in "The Good Kids," ghosts in "Strata," discorporate presences in "Teeth Marks," and witchcraft in "Serrated Edge." Perhaps his most successful recent short piece, "The Cutter," is a pure terror tale with no fantastic element at all, but with a sense of timing and a skill of delivery that is phenomenal. Other recent stories of note include "Saurus Wrecks," "Skin and Blood," and "Drummer's Star." One of his more interesting recent works is "Neon," sequel to an earlier contribution to the Berserker Universe created by Fred Saberhagen, "Pilots of the Twilight." Typically, Bryant wrote a story fitting that canon, but which reads and feels like an entirely original creation.

What makes Bryant's stories distinctive is their strong concentration on psychological and emotional conflict rather than physical action, a rarity within the genre. They are also stylistically complex, requiring some effort on the part of the reader, not because the delivery is esoteric but because he portrays convoluted interpersonal relationships and internal struggles which are often subtle and sophisticated. His language is intellectual and witty, without being so wrapped up in stylistic concerns that it becomes inaccessible to casual readers.

—Don D'Ammassa

---

**BRYANT, Peter.** *See* **GEORGE, Peter.**

---

**BRYNING, Frank (Francis Bertram Bryning).** Also writes as F. Cornish. Australian. Born in Fairfield, Victoria, 2 August 1907. Educated at Fairfield State School, 1912–20; University High School, Melbourne, 1921–24. Married Henrietta Edna Ewell in 1935; one daughter. Clerk, Harrisons Ramsay Importers, Melbourne, 1925–26; worked for news agency and library, 1926–28, and as an electrical appliance salesman, 1928–31, Melbourne; freelance journalist and editor, Melbourne and Sydney, 1932–49: editor, *Flax Newsletter*, Sydney, 1942–49; editor, *Architecture, Building, Engineering* and *Queensland Building Yearbook*, both Brisbane, 1950–57; editor, *Hardware Trader, Brisbane Building Yearbook, Queensland Fruit and Vegetable News*, and *Australian Electrical World*, all Brisbane, 1957–73. Agent: Carnell Literary Agency, Danes Croft, Goose Lane, Little Hallingbury, Hertfordshire CM22 7RG, England.

### Science-Fiction Publications

Uncollected Short Stories (series: Joan Buckley; Vivienne Gale)

"Operation in Free Flight" (Gale), in *Australian Monthly* (Melbourne), March 1952; as "Operation in Free Orbit," in *Fantastic Universe* (Chicago), February 1955.
"Action-Reaction" (Gale), in *Australian Monthly* (Melbourne), June 1952.
"Space Doctor's Orders" (Gale), in *Australian Monthly* (Melbourne), January 1953.
"On the Average," in *Forerunner*, April 1953.
"Jettison or Die!," in *Australian Monthly* (Melbourne), August 1953.

"The Gambler" (Buckley), in *Australian Monthly* (Melbourne), October 1954; as "Coming Generation," in Fantastic Universe (Chicago), July 1955.
"Pass the Oxygen," in *Future* (New York), October 1954.
"Daughter of Tomorrow" (Buckley), in *Australian Monthly* (Melbourne), February 1955.
"Poor Hungry People," in *Etherline*, August 1955.
"Infant Prodigy" (Buckley), in *Fantastic Universe* (Chicago), November 1955.
"Consultant Diagnostician" (Buckley), in *Fantastic Universe* (Chicago), December 1955.
"And a Hank of Hair" (Gale), in *Australian Journal* (Melbourne), May 1956.
"The Robot Carpenter," in *Australian Journal* (Melbourne), July 1956.
"Power of a Woman," in *Australian Journal* (Melbourne), January 1957.
"I Did, Too, See a Flying Saucer!," in *Amazing* (New York), August 1958.
"Escape Mechanism," in *Sunday Mail*, October 1967.
"For Men Must Work," in *The Pacific Book of Australian Science Fiction*, edited by John Baxter. Sydney, Angus and Robertson, 1968; London, Angus and Robertson, 1969.
"The Visitors," in *Vision of Tomorrow* (Newcastle upon Tyne), March 1970.
"Election," in *Vision of Tomorrow* (Newcastle upon Tyne), June 1970.
"Lost Explorer," in *Science Fiction Monthly* (London), August 1975.
"Beyond the Line of Duty," in *Void* (St. Kilda, Victoria), August 1976.
"The Homecoming of Haral," in *Void* (St. Kilda, Victoria), August 1977.
"Nemaluk and the Star-Stone," in *Envisaged Worlds*, edited by Paul Collins. St. Kilda, Victoria, Void, 1977.
"Mechman of the Dreaming," in *Other Worlds*, edited by Paul Collins. St. Kilda, Victoria, Void, 1978.
"Fusing and Refusing," in *Isaac Asimov's Science Fiction Magazine* (New York), January 1983.
"Place of the Throwing-Stick," in *Australian Science Fiction*, edited by Van Ikin. Chicago, Illinois, Academy, 1984.

Uncollected Short Stories as F. Cornish

"The Vase with the Character of a Flower Pot," in *Australasian* (Melbourne), September 1944.
"Bloodthinker," in *The World's News*, January 1945.
"Mirage in the Moluccas," in *Pocket Book Weekly*, January 1950.

*

Frank Bryning comments:

In science fiction my prejudice is in favour of "hard-core," or "science fiction." I hold that the essential problem or conflict in the lives of the characters in a science-fiction story will derive from their involvement in some event in the natural universe—some biological, psychological, sociological, technological, cosmological activity. Their experiences, however unusual or mystifying, will be explicable, ultimately, according to that accumulation of precise factual knowledge and verifiable experience and the logically reasoned theories and speculations based on it that we call "science."

This as distinct from "fantasy"—from fiction of the "super"-natural, from fairytale, fable, legend, myth (religious or otherwise), magic, witchcraft, the occult, or ghoulies and ghosties and things that go bump in the night. In fantasy I have always found much profit and delight. I still do. I yield to no one in my capacity to find enjoyment there, or moral lesson. From fantasy I do not expect believable premises, strictly logical progression of cause and effect, or any real conviction, yet I consider those fantasies most satisfying which are internally logical after one suspends disbelief in their mystical premises.

I would like to think that the sum of all my writing—fiction and non-fiction, plus my work as staff writer and editor—would designate me as a realist rather than a surrealist. Almost all my work has been to present the "rational" viewpoint, I believe. My fiction is concerned mainly with the doings of typical everyday people in the everyday world (including, perhaps, the world of tomorrow in my science fiction) rather than with "exploring" so-called "alternative realities" or fantasising about "other planes of existence." I want to be on the side of enlightenment rather than obfuscation, of rationalism rather than mysticism. I hope readers, of my science fiction in particular, and my fellow writers, may agree that I am.

* * *

Having grown up on Wells, Verne, and Bellamy, Frank Bryning naturally turned to writing SF stories, and it was natural that he should become a writer who stresses the *science* in science fiction. Bryning is best known for his Aboriginal stories "Place of the Throwing-Stick" (his best story), "Nemaluk and the Star-Stone," and "Mechman of the Dreaming." Bryning regards the Australian Aborigines as "the most distinctively Australian phenomenon one might use," and these three stories reflect the theme of "the 'Aboriginal possessor of the land' versus the colonial invader." In "Place of the Throwing-Stick" the Aboriginal Munyarra attacks the most recent of the white man's importations—the rocket. The confrontation takes place at Australia's real-life Woomera Rocket Range, allowing Bryning to link the Stone Age past with the Space Age present through the name "Woomera" (Aboriginal for "spear-throwing stick").

Bryning's long-time membership in the British Interplanetary Society is reflected in his cycle of Commonwealth Satellite Space Station stories, embracing items written from the 1950's to the present. Eschewing the Americanization of SF, Bryning posits a near future in which the Commonwealth of Australia has established a network of space stations. The emphasis is upon character and realistic situations, with the 10 stories being linked by the central character, Dr. Vivienne Gale. Plots are generated by the humdrum daily life in space, and many stories deal with space medicine and the problems of weightlessness.

There is nothing flashy or sensational about Bryning's stories. They are solidly and conventionally constructed, and their extrapolations are never allowed to outstrip the author's knowledge. As future histories, they are modest. But their strengths and merits lie in their quiet, dogged realism, their guarded optimism, and their compassion for the man with a day's work to complete.

—Van Ikin

---

**BUDRYS, Algis** (Algirdas Jonas Budrys). Also writes as Paul Janvier, Ivan Janvier, Robert Marner, Frank Mason, John A. Sentry, and William Scarff. Lithuanian. Born in Konigsberg, Germany, 9 January 1931. Educated at the University of Miami, 1947–49; Columbia University, New York, 1950–51. Married

Edna Frances Duna in 1954; four sons. Clerk, American Express, New York, 1950–51; editorial positions at Gnome Press, 1952–53, *Galaxy*, 1953, *Venture SF*, 1957, *Fantasy and Science Fiction*, 1957, *Ellery Queen's Mystery Magazine*, 1957, *Car Speed and Style, Custom Rodder*, and *Cars Magazine*, all 1958–59, Regency Books, 1961–63, Playboy Press, 1963–64, and Commander Publications, 1966; public relations positions, Theodore R. Sills Inc., Chicago, 1966–67, Geyer-Oswald Advertising, 1967–68, and Young and Ruibicam, 1969–73; operations manager, Woodall Publications, 1973–74; science fiction reviewer and columnist, *Galaxy*, 1966–70, Washington *Post*, 1978, instructor, Columbia College, Chicago, 1977; visiting writer, Clarion Science Fiction Writing Workshop, 1977–85, and Evanston schools, 1978–85. Since 1974, President, Unifont Company, Evanston, Illinois. Since 1975, reviewer and columnist, *Fantasy* and *Science Fiction*. Since 1984, coordinating judge, L. Ron Hubbard's Writers of the Future contest. Since 1986, columnist, Chicago *Sun-Times*. Recipient: Mystery Writers of America award, 1966; Science Fiction Writers of America Hall of Fame award. Address: Unifont Company, 824 Seward Street, Evanston, Illinois 60202, U.S.A.

## SCIENCE-FICTION PUBLICATIONS

### Novels

*False Night*. New York, Lion, 1954; as *Some Will Not Die*, Evanston, Illinois, Regency, 1961; London, Mayflower, 1963.
*Man of Earth*. New York, Ballantine, 1958.
*Who?* New York, Pyramid, 1958; London, Gollancz, 1962.
*The Falling Torch*. New York, Pyramid, 1959.
*Rogue Moon*. New York, Fawcett, 1960; London, Muller, 1962.
*The Amsirs and the Iron Thorn*. New York, Fawcett, 1967; as *The Iron Thorn*, London, Gollancz, 1968.
*Michaelmas*. New York, Berkley, and London, Gollancz, 1977.
*Cerberus*. Eugene, Oregon, Pulphouse, 1989.

### Short Stories

*The Unexpected Dimension*. New York, Ballantine, 1960; London, Gollancz, 1962.
*Budry's Inferno*. New York, Berkley, 1963; as *The Furious Future*, London, Gollancz, 1964.
*Blood and Burning*. New York, Berkley, 1978; London, Gollancz, 1979.

## OTHER PUBLICATIONS

### Play

Radio Play: *Rogue Moon*, from his own novel, 1979 (TV version, 1983).

### Other

*Truman and the Pendergasts* (as Frank Mason). Evanston, Illinois, Regency, 1963.
*Bicycles: How They Work and How to Fix Them*. Chicago, Rand McNally, 1976.
*Non-literary Influences on Science Fiction: Essays on Fantastic Literature*. San Bernardino, California, Borgo Press, 1983.
*Benchmarks: Galaxy Bookshelf*. Carbondale, Southern Illinois University Press, 1985.

Editor, *L. Ron Hubbard Presents Writers of the Future*. Los Angeles, Bridge, 7 vols., 1985–91.

*

Manuscript Collection: Spencer Research Library, University of Kansas, Lawrence.

Algis Budrys comments:

My work, when found, speaks for itself. I think a piece of creativity is its own justification. However, if a rationale is desired, then the theoretical underpinning of my SF is that speculative fiction is drama made more relevant by social extrapolation. That is, I proceed on the assumption that, by certain fortuitous strokes of talent, some prose artists can create conditional realities in which recognizably human behavior occurs under illuminating circumstances which are not yet known to have occurred in what we have agreed to call reality. The proposition is that a few members of the readership will be inspired to look about them anew and draw conclusions of benefit to mankind's continuing endeavor to escape extinction. I seriously doubt that any critical analysis of my work, however accurate, will have much relevance to my necessarily minor role in that endeavor. I commend to his or her god whatever hominid organism is eventually able to overcome the darkness, and I rest my case.

* * *

Like Nabokov and Solzhenitsyn, Algis Budrys is ours by courtesy of Communism. I have been told that his real name means something like John Sentry, a pseudonym he has in fact employed. A sentry he is, if the brave who watched the stockade, the alien walls of the invader, may be called a sentry. A warrior he is by any definition. He understands more of the psychology of the man who fights—not the man who dies—than any other writer I know. Every age and every genre produce a few writers too good for them, authors who pour oceans into their wine cups or summon Sigurd and Fafnir in person to entertain the nursery. Budrys is one of these. He is, in the best sense, too serious a writer for science fiction.

*Who?* is the book that made him famous, it is perhaps as fine a study of dehumanization and alienation as science fiction will ever produce. A brilliant American scientist is torn by a laboratory explosion and repaired with what we would now call "bionic" parts by the Soviets. He is returned to the US—but the US cannot be sure of that. So much of him is gone that what remains cannot be identified. All this is simple enough. It is even—if you like—a retelling of L. Frank Baum's story of the Tin Woodman, who when he had sliced his "meat" (humanity) completely away could no longer recall his true name (which was Nick Chopper). The difference lies in intent, and in the treatments that result from it. Baum was manufacturing a paradox to amuse children, one not really much different from the rhyme about the Gingham Dog and the Calico Cat who ate each other up. Budrys is intensely concerned with the effect of technology—and particularly the technology of the Cold War—on our humanity. He asks if the Soviets were really doing the West a favour when they restored Martino, since he cannot be identified and thus cannot be of use. *Can* they do the West a good office, when all they do *must* be suspect? SF offers few figures of the symbolic intensity of this faceless, maimed scientist, the man who could prove ten thousand things, if only he could prove who he is.

Budrys's writing falls into two distinct periods, the first ranging from 1952 to the middle 1960's, the second from the middle 1970's to the present. The best work of his earlier period is surely

*Rogue Moon*, which he wished to call *The Death Machine*, a vastly better title. In *Rogue Moon* a "matter transmitter" has been invented in a near future in which rocketry is still primitive; and an unmanned probe has managed to drop a transmitting and receiving station on the far side of the moon. The first explorers to go through the transmitter discover an alien construct millions of years old, a thing compounded of building, machine, and hallucination. It soon kills everyone who ventures inside. This alien construct is perhaps the biggest and best red herring in all SF, because it is not really what *Rogue Moon* is about. It is about Hawks, the brilliant, compassionate, iron-souled scientist who has developed the "matter transmitter" and is determined to have the construct analyzed, and Barker, the death-obsessed Saturday afternoon hero he gets to do the exploring—through a score of deaths. Like *Who?* it is about the nature of identity. It is also about the nature of life, about what it is to live and have lived.

When a writer of Budrys's calibre is silent for so long as Budrys was silent, silenced not by the knouts and jails of totalitarian authority but by his own frustrations, his readers are entitled to expect him to be a different and even better writer if he chooses to write again. Budrys's justification is *Michaelmas*, his best novel and the book that has brought him considerable recognition outside SF. If *Rogue Moon* was cinematic, *Michaelmas* is bibliomatic—a story that can be told well only in a book. Americans are apt to find a certain glamour in kings and queens, princes and princesses—an amiable weakness. We are sometimes even liable to find an attraction in tyrants of one sort or another, in Napoleon, Caesar, and even Stalin—though we should know much better. But numbed by a parade of crooks and nonentities, we seem to have forgotten the romance of a President, of the good citizen elevated by his own efforts and the admiration of his fellows to a pre-eminence in the state, the romance our great grandfathers sensed so strongly in the embodiment of the Republic. Budrys, a Lithuanian refugee and the son of refugees, has not. G.K. Chesterton once said that a sword was the most glorious object in the world, but that a pocket-knife was more glorious than a sword, because it was a secret sword. Laurent Michaelmas is a secret President, the secret President of the Earth. In the hands of any other writer, he would almost certainly be a tyrant, and, no doubt in the hands of most, an insane tyrant. In Budrys's, as he struggles with human treachery and an alien visitor of awesome power, he remains an eminently sane and decent man, as lonely and as sad as our society's sane and decent men must always be. In flatly and persuasively denying the inevitable corruption of power, *Michaelmas* may well be the most optimistic book of the latter 20th century. It is certainly one of the best, as Budrys himself is one of its best—and least characteristic—storytellers.

—Gene Wolfe

---

**BUJOLD, Lois McMaster.** American. Born in Columbus, Ohio, 2 November 1949. Attended Ohio State University, Columbus, 1968–72. Married John Fredric Bujold in 1971; one daughter and one son. Recipient: Nebula award, for novel, 1988, for novella, 1989; Hugo award, for novella, 1989. Agent: Eleanor Wood, Spectrum Literary Agency, 111 Eighth Avenue, Suite 1501, New York, New York, 10011. Address: 274 Spencer Street, Marion, Ohio 43302, U.S.A.

Science-Fiction Publications

Novels (series: Vorkosigan)

*Shards of Honor*. New York, Baen, 1986; London, Headline, 1988.
*The Warrior's Apprentice* (Vorkosigan). New York, Baen, 1986; London, Headline, 1988.
*Ethan of Athos*. New York, Baen, 1986; London, Headline, 1989.
*Brothers in Arms* (Vorkosigan). New York, Baen, 1989; London, Headline, 1990.
*Falling Free*. New York, Baen, 1988; London, Headline, 1989.
*The Vor Game* (Vorkosigan). Norfolk, Connecticut, Easton Press, 1990.
*Barrayar*. New York, Baen, 1991.

Short Stories

*Borders of Infinity* (Vorkosigan). Norwalk, Connecticut, Easton Press, 1989.

*

Lois McMaster Bujold comments:

All my science fiction books so far are united by the series-device of sharing the same universe or future history. I do not consider myself bound by this, it just happens to have worked out that way for the topics I've wanted to tackle. (Though just in case anyone thinks they've got me boxed, this year I'm writing a ghost story set in 15th-century Italy.) With the exception of *Falling Free*, all my novels touch the life of one hero, Miles Naismith Vorkosigan. Four of the books—*The Warrior's Apprentice, Borders of Infinity, The Vor Game*, and *Brothers In Arms*—give Miles the central role. I've tried to write them so each stands alone as an independent novel, so that the hapless reader who lays hands on them in random order (as is usual) will not be annoyed. In practice, some of the books seem to be better start-points, particularly *Warrior's* and *Borders*.

I try to write the kind of book I most like to read: character-centered adventure. My own literary favorites include, among many others, Dorothy Sayers, Arthur Conan Doyle, Alexander Dumas, and C.S. Forester. All these writers created not works of Art, but, on some level, works of life. Theirs are creations who climb up off the page into the readers' minds and live there long after the book is shut. Readers return to such books again and again, not to find out what happened—for a single reading would suffice for any book if plot and idea were all—but because those characters have become their friends, and there is no limit to the number of times you want to be with your friends again.

But character doesn't exist in a vacuum, so I try to generate plots and ideas that are quintessential and worthy tests of my book-people. I don't see the fact that I write genre or even sub-genre as requiring me to hobble any novelistic amibition. Not either/or, but character and plot and theme, adventure and psychology and symbol, motion and meaning: everything, all at once, all the time. Character-starved readers will forgive almost any background nonsense, as long as the central hunger of their spirits is fed, but they shouldn't have to.

Since Miles is my main man, an extra word or two on him is in order. As a created character, Miles has many real roots—T.E. Lawrence, another short soldier with psychological problems; a physical template in a brilliant, physically handicapped hospital pharmacist I used to work for; my own relationship with my father. I'm afraid his sense of humor can only be coming from me. As for imaginary roots, in many ways Miles is an anti-type (or antidote) to the standard action-adventure hero. In place of lantern jaw and corded muscles, he's physically weak, fragile, and slightly manic-depressive. Instead of being an orphan (surely every teenager's escapist dream), he's plagued with a lively and obstreperous gang of relatives who never let him forget where he came from. In place of the psionic or other magical powers often given to physically handicapped characters by their authors (I can name John Brunner's wonderful Gerald Howson from *The Whole Man* among Miles's SF antecedents), Miles must cope armed only with his human wits. In place of the goal of becoming Emperor of the Universe (or at least of the planet Barrayar), Miles's study is to avoid such a dismal fate, which falls around him like bracketing shellfire. In place of physical conquest, he travels a drunkard's-walk of a spiritual journey constantly pushing him to a greater and more terrifying connectedness to other human beings.

A post-script on humor. People crack jokes, if black ones, even in the face of death. Everywhere, human beings laugh. Any story that leaves humor out of its portrayal of the human condition has no claim to the label "realistic." Comedy and tragedy share one heart. In the midst of all my gaudy action, exotic setting, or outré detail, it is my aim to write humanly realistic tales.

* * *

Science fiction has gone through three distinct stages of development, according to Isaac Asimov: "adventure science fiction, gadget science fiction, and social science fiction," which shows "the impact of scientific advance on human beings." No good science fiction writer now uses either of the first two categories "straight." Even so, many readers have found science fiction increasingly sterile, grim and gadget-ridden. These readers welcome the advent of Lois McMaster Bujold, who includes a deeply ethical dimension in her work. Since the publication of her first novel in 1986, she has rapidly made a name for herself. Though nominated, she did not win the Campbell Award for best new writer, but her frequent appearances on the Hugo and Nebula awards list have, by the summer of 1991, garnered two Nebulas and a Hugo. To date, she has won the "Anlab" poll of *Analog* readers twice. Many of her books have been published in England, and translated into various languages, including Spanish, German, Italian, and Japanese.

This ethical dimension organizes all her novels, in *Shards of Honor*, Aral Vorkosigan, hereditary member of the Barrayaran warrior class, lives by a strict code of honor, which circumstances force him to stretch almost to the breaking point. Cordelia Naismith, from the non-military Beta Colony, also lives by an ethical code never explicitly described, nor ascribed to any church or creed. To his surprise, Vorkosigan finds her code even more strict—and more fulfilling—than his own. For example, Cordelia recognizes the need for honor; she blesses Sergeant Bothari, who has just been ordered to rape her. She is no naive saint, however. Perceiving the utter evil of her captor, she offers him no pardon. She not only forgives but appreciates Vorkosigan's dilemma; their love is based on mature understanding, not romantic self-delusion. This is clearly demonstrated in *Barrayar*, which tells what occurs between *Shards of Honor* and *The Warrior's Apprentice.* Damaged by an assassination attempt, Cordelia's unborn son should be aborted according to Barrayaran custom. Since neither Aral nor Cordelia will allow this, they must bear the consequences: contempt and disinheritance. Bujold doesn't preach; her characters must make hard choices, and pay the price for them.

Miles Vorkosigan, the physically small, weak and deformed hero of *The Warrior's Apprentice, Brothers in Arms, Borders of Infinity*, and *The Vor Game*, combines his parent's virtues with astonishing results. He never forgets that his grandfather, barely reconciled to his existence, dies upon hearing that Miles failed the entrance exams to the military academy. Denied official warrior status, the young strategic genius accidentally acquires a mercenary army that he cannot ethically abandon, no matter the danger to himself. Originally, Bujold did not expect to write a series; she created "panel novels" set in a coherent universe, with occasionally overlapping characters. Popular demand for more stories about Miles has made such a series possible, and Bujold admits that she has a good idea of the shape of Miles's life. She does not intend to limit herself, however. She is currently writing a fantasy novel set in medieval Italy, in which politics run amok and magic works.

Bujold has a long-standing acquaintance with and appreciation of science fiction. She demonstrates an acute and thoughtful awareness of generic demands, of the interaction of character, plot, setting, and theme. Her fictions shape themselves tightly, maintaining an unflagging pace; this has been considered a return to Golden Age action-adventure science fiction, which undoubtedly has a good deal to do with Bujold's popularity, as well as criticism of her work. Winner of the Nebula award for *Falling Free*, she is also the target of one of the most scathing attacks. In *Nebula Awards 24*, Ian Watson calls *Falling Free* "an out-and-out juvenile" and queries: "Do members of SFWA *really* wish this to be seen as their pinnacle, their height of achievement?" Watson makes two peculiar assumptions here: first, that juveniles don't represent high achievement, and second, that *Falling Free* is a juvenile.

Few criteria define the juvenile category; most limit it to books with youthful protagonists facing problems and making decisions around growing up. *Falling Free* has its share of attractive young characters, but the protagonist, Graf, is a middle-aged engineer; willing and unwilling sex plays a major role; and the plot revolves not around achieving adulthood but around definitions of slavery and what it takes to achieve freedom responsibly. As Bujold remarks in rebuttal to Watson's charge, *Falling Free* is not about juvenile problems, but about adult interests like "teaching, building, nurturing, making moral choices, and taking personal responsibility for the welfare of fellow human beings."

One reason for the popularity of *Falling Free* may lie in the plot, which shows the defeat of corporate cooption by individual action; another surely comes from the clearly ethical basis of Leo Graf's behavior. Watson claims that the book "star[s] a host of Goodies and approximately a couple of Baddies." He is right about the Goodies (though none of them are "goody-goodies"), but mistaken about the Baddies. *Shards of Honor* contains genuinely evil characters; *Falling Free* does not. Instead, it demonstrates that evil can come from the inconsiderate, shallow, and selfish behavior of ordinary people—people who fail to ground their daily choices in practical ethics.

This discussion makes Bujold's writing sound moralistic, preachy, and, possibly, grim. Nothing could be further from the truth. She delights in setting up apparently impossible contradictions for her characters to deal with. In *Brothers in Arms*, Miles, an only child, finds himself not only having to cope with, but honor-bound to protect and re-educate his twin brother; in *Ethan of Athos*, an obstetrician carries out a busy practice on an all-male planet, until circumstances force him to leave home and not only meet but (frighteningly) deal with women. Discussing her Nebula-winning novella, "Mountains of Mourning" (in *Borders of Infinity)*, Bujold describes her "sadistic" technique for creating stories: she asks herself, "What's the worst possible situation for *this* guy to fall into?"; she then multiplies its difficulty, and drops him or her into the middle of it. Humane, egalitarian Cordelia must deal with Barrayaran class prejudice; deformed Miles must not only bring to justice the murderer of a deformed baby in "Mountains of Mourning," but "learn the subtle difference between serving an empire and serving a people."

Bujold's sense of humor, which ranges from wacky (as in "The Hole Truth" and "Labyrinth") to grim (as in "Borders of Infinity"), is sometimes expressed directly but more often appears to spring from the characters than from the author. Instead of setting up incongruous situations, she creates characters who show an astonishing aptitude for survival, who find humor in almost anything, and who blessedly refuse to take themselves too seriously.

In two regards, Bujold differs from most action-adventure writers. Her sensitivity to the problems of people who feel different has won her a considerable following among the physically handicapped, many of whom can read her works only due to *Analog's* "talking book" publication. Also, her women are strong, active, appealing characters, but even in the most military situation they are not "men with breasts." Like her male characters, they are multi-dimensional; they act boldly when no other course appears feasible, and they sometimes regret what they have done; they have women's careers and women's concerns, including a desire to love and be loved, but they do not build their identity upon anyone else's valuation. They are fully and competently themselves.

Much of her longer fiction deals with war and the results of aggression and prejudice. While she certainly writes military fiction, she does so with a certain reluctance. (As she notes of *Falling Free*, "I had slaughtered thousands to make my first novel; as a personal challenge, I wanted to see if I could write a high-tension adventure without killing *anybody.*") Her objection to technological war is very simple. It is too easy to kill when we deny humanity to our enemies, robbing them of their human faces. As her graves registration medtech remarks in "Aftermaths," every soldier represents a lot of work for someone. "Nine months of pregnancy, childbirth, two years of diapering, and that's just the beginning. Tens of thousands of meals, thousands of bedtime stories, years of school. Dozens of teachers. And all that military training, too. A lot of people went into making him. . . . That head held the universe, once." It is this attention to the human face of minor characters, even dead ones, that makes Bujold's work so profoundly moving.

—Martha A. Bartter

---

**BULMER, (Henry) Kenneth.** Also writes as Alan Burt Akers; Ken Blake; Frank Brandon; Rupert Clinton; Ernest Corley; Arthur Frazier; Peter Green; Adam Hardy; Kenneth Johns; Philip Kent; Bruno Krauss; Neil Langholm; Karl Maras; Manning Norvil; Charles R. Pike; Andrew Quiller; Chesman Scot; Nelson Sherwood; Richard Silver; H. Philip Stratford; Tully Zetford. British. Born in London, 14 January 1921. Educated at Catford Central School, London. Served in the Royal Corps of Signals, 1941–46. Married Pamela Kathleen Buckmaster in 1953; two daughters and one son. Worked for paper merchandising and office equipment firms, 1936–54; editor or co-editor, *Star Parade*, 1941, *Fantasy Post*, 1941, *Seventy Eight Saga* (army magazine), 1943–45, *Nirvana*, 1949, 1954, *Science Fantasy News*, 1952, *Aaaah!*, 1954, *Dysteology*, 1954–55, *Vignette*, 1954, *Ziz*, 1954, and *Wappoted*, 1956. Agent: Carnell Literary Agency, Rowneybury Bungalow, near Old Harlow, Essex CM20 2EX. Address: 5/20 Frant Road, Tunbridge Wells, Kent TN2 5SN, England.

SCIENCE-FICTION PUBLICATIONS

Novels (series: Keys to the Dimensions; Swords)

*Space Treason*, with A.V. Clarke. London, Panther, 1952.
*Cybernetic Controller*, with A.V. Clarke. London, Panther, 1952.
*Encounter in Space*. London, Panther, 1952.
*Zhorani* (as Karl Maras). London, Comyns, 1953.
*Space Salvage*. London, Panther, 1953.
*The Stars Are Ours*. London, Panther, 1953.
*Galactic Intrigue*. London, Panther, 1953.
*Empire of Chaos*. London, Panther, 1953.
*World Aflame*. London, Panther, 1954.
*Challenge*. London, Curtis Warren, 1954.
*Peril from Space* (as Karl Maras). London, Comyns, 1955.
*City under the Sea*. New York, Ace, 1957; London, Digit, 1961.
*The Secret of ZI*. New York, Ace, 1958; London, Digit, 1961; as *The Patient Dark*, London, Hale, 1969.
*The Changeling Worlds*. New York, Ace, 1959; London, Digit, 1961.
*The Earth Gods Are Coming*. New York, Ace, 1960; as *Of Earth Foretold* (includes "The Aztec Plan"), London, Digit, 1961.
*Forschungskreuzer Saumarez*. Munich, Moewig, 1960; as *Defiance*, London, Digit, 1963.
*No Man's World*. New York, Ace, 1961; as *Earth's Long Shadow* (includes "Strange Highway"). London, Digit, 1961.
*Beyond the Silver Sky*. New York, Ace, 1961.
*The Fatal Fire*. London, Digit, 1962.
*The Wind of Liberty* (includes "Don't Cross a Telekine"). London, Digit, 1962.
*The Wizard of Starship Poseidon*. New York, Ace, 1963.
*The Million Year Hunt*. New York, Ace, 1964.
*Demon's World*. New York, Ace, 1964; as *The Demons*, London, Compact, 1965.
*Land Beyond the Map*. New York, Ace, 1965.
*Behold the Stars*. New York, Ace, 1965; London, Mayflower, 1966.
*Worlds for the Taking*. New York, Ace, 1966.
*To Outrun Doomsday*. New York, Ace, 1967; London, New English Library, 1975.
*The Key to Irunium*. New York, Ace, 1967.
*Cycle of Nemesis*. New York, Ace, 1967.
*The Doomsday Men*. New York, Doubleday, and London, Hale, 1968.
*The Key to Venudine*. New York, Ace, 1968.
*The Star Venturers*. New York, Ace, 1969.
*The Wizards of Senchuria* (Keys). New York, Ace, 1969.
*Kandar*. New York, Paperback Library, 1969.
*The Ulcer Culture*. London, Macdonald, 1969; as *The Stained-Glass World*, London, New English Library, 1976.
*The Ships of Durostorum* (Keys). New York, Ace, 1970.
*Blazon*. New York, Curtis, 1970; as *Quench the Burning Stars*, London, Hale, 1970.
*Star Trove*. London, Hale, 1970.
*Swords of the Barbarians*. London, New English Library, 1970; New York, Belmont, 1976.
*The Hunters of Jundagai* (Keys). New York, Ace, 1971.
*The Electric Sword Swallowers*. New York, Ace, 1971.
*The Insane City*. New York, Curtis, 1971; London, Severn House, 1978.
*The Chariots of Ra* (Keys). New York, Ace, 1972.
*On the Symb-Socket Circuit*. New York, Ace, 1972.

*Roller Coaster World*. New York, Ace, 1972; London, Severn House, 1978.
*The Diamond Contessa* (Keys). New York, DAW, 1983.

Novels as Philip Kent

*Mission to the Stars*. London, Pearson, 1953.
*Vassals of Venus*. London, Pearson, 1954.
*Slaves of the Spectrum*. London, Pearson, 1954.
*Home Is the Martian*. London, Pearson, 1954.

Novels as Alan Burt Akers (series: Dray Prescot in all books)

*Transit to Scorpio*. New York, DAW, 1972; London, Futura, 1974.
*The Suns of Scorpio*. New York, DAW, 1973; London, Futura, 1974.
*Warrior of Scorpio*. New York, DAW, 1973; London, Futura, 1975.
*Swordships of Scorpio*. New York, DAW, 1973; London, Futura, 1975.
*Prince of Scorpio*. New York, DAW, 1974; London, Futura, 1975.
*Manhounds of Antares*. New York, DAW, 1974.
*Arena of Antares*. New York, DAW, 1974.
*Fliers of Antares*. New York, DAW, 1975.
*Bladesman of Antares*. New York, DAW, 1975.
*Avenger of Antares*. New York, DAW, 1975.
*Armada of Antares*. New York, DAW, 1976.
*The Tides of Kregen*. New York, DAW, 1976.
*Renegade of Kregen*. New York, DAW, 1976.
*Krozair of Kregen*. New York, DAW, 1977.
*Secret Scorpio*. New York, DAW, 1977.
*Savage Scorpio*. New York, DAW, 1978.
*Captive Scorpio*. New York, DAW, 1978.
*Golden Scorpio*. New York, DAW, 1978.
*A Life for Kregen*. New York, DAW, 1979.
*A Sword for Kregen*. New York, DAW, 1979.
*A Fortune for Kregen*. New York, DAW, 1979.
*A Victory for Kregen*. New York, DAW, 1980.
*Beasts of Antares*. New York, DAW, 1980.
*Rebel of Antares*. New York, DAW, 1980.
*Legions of Antares*. New York, DAW, 1981.
*Allies of Antares*. New York, DAW, 1981.
*Mazes of Scorpio*. New York, DAW, 1982.
*Delia of Vallia*. New York, DAW, 1982.
*Fires of Scorpio*. New York, DAW, 1983.
*Talons of Scorpio*. New York, DAW, 1983.
*Masks of Scorpio*. New York, DAW, 1984.
*Seg the Bowman*. New York, DAW, 1984.
*Werewolves of Kregen*. New York, DAW, 1985.
*Witch of Kregen*. New York, DAW, 1985.
*Storm over Vallia*. New York, DAW, 1985.
*Omen of Kregen*. New York, DAW, 1985.
*Warlords of Antares*. New York, DAW, 1988.

Novels as Tully Zetford (series: Ryder Hook in all books)

*Whirlpool of Stars*. London, New English Library, 1974; New York, Pinnacle, 1975.
*The Boosted Man*. London, New English Library, 1974; New York, Pinnacle, 1975.
*Star City*. London, New English Library, 1974; New York, Pinnacle, 1975.
*Virility Gene*. London, New English Library, 1975; New York, Pinnacle, 1976.

Novels as Manning Norvil (Odan trilogy)

*Dream Chariots*. New York, DAW, 1977.
*Whetted Bronze*. New York, DAW, 1978.
*Crown of the Sword God*. New York, DAW, 1980.

### Other Publications

Novels

*White Out* (as Ernest Corley). London, Jarrolds, 1960.
*The Dark Return* (as Neil Langholm). London, Sphere, 1975; New York, Pinnacle, 1977.
*By Pirate's Blood* (as Richard Silver). New York, Pinnacle, 1975.
*Jaws of Death* (as Richard Silver). New York, Pinnacle, 1975.
*Trail of Blood* (as Neil Langholm). London, Sphere, 1976.
*The Land of Mist* (as Andrew Quiller). London, Mayflower, and New York, Pinnacle, 1976.
*Sea of Swords* (as Andrew Quiller). London, Mayflower, and New York, Pinnacle, 1976.
*Brand of Vengeance* (as Charles R. Pike). London, Mayflower, 1978.
*Blind Run*. London, Sphere, 1979.

Novels as Adam Hardy (series: Strike Force Falklands)

*The Press Gang*. London, New English Library, and New York, Pinnacle, 1973.
*Prize Money*. London, New English Library, and New York, Pinnacle, 1973.
*The Siege*. London, New English Library, 1973; as *Savage Siege*, New York, Pinnacle, 1973.
*Treasure*. London, New English Library, 1973; as *Treasure Map*, New York, Pinnacle, 1974.
*Powder Monkey*. London, New English Library, 1973; as *Sailor's Blood*, New York, Pinnacle, 1974.
*Blood for Breakfast*. London, New English Library, 1974; as *Sea of Gold*, New York, Pinnacle, 1974.
*Court Martial*. London, New English Library, and New York, Pinnacle, 1974.
*Battle Smoke*. London, New English Library, 1974; New York, Pinnacle, 1975.
*Cut and Thrust*. London, New English Library, 1974; New York, Pinnacle, 1975.
*Boarders Away*. London, New English Library, and New York, Pinnacle, 1975.
*Fireship*. London, New English Library, 1975; New York, Pinnacle, 1976.
*Blood Beach*. London, New English Library, 1975.
*Sea Flame*. London, New English Library, 1976.
*Close Quarters*. London, New English Library, 1977.
Strike Force Falklands:
*Operation Exocet*. London, Futura, 1984.
*Raider's Dawn*. London, Futura, 1984.
*Red Alert*. London, Futura, 1984.
*Recce Patrol*. London, Futura, 1985.
*Covert Op*. London, Futura, 1985.
*Ware Mines*. London, Futura, 1985.

Novels as Arthur Frazier

*Oath of Blood*. London, New English Library, 1973.
*The King's Death*. London, New English Library, 1973.
*A Flame in the Fens*. London, New English Library, 1974.
*An Axe in Miklagard*. London, New English Library, 1975.

Novels as Ken Blake

*Where the Jungle Ends* (novelization of screenplay). London, Sphere, 1978.
*Stake Out* (novelization of screenplay). London, Sphere, 1978.
*Hunter Hunted* (novelization of screenplay). London, Sphere, 1978.
*Long Shot* (novelization of screenplay). London, Sphere, 1979.
*Blind Run*, with Ronald Graham, Michael Armstrong, and Brian Clemens. London, Sphere, 1979.
*Fall Girl*, with Ronald Graham, Edmund Ward, and Don Houston. London, Sphere, 1979.
*Dead Reckoning*, with Robin Estridge and Brian Clemens. London, Sphere, 1980.
*Hiding for Nothing*, with Ted Childs, John Goldsmith, and Michael Feeny Calldin. London, Sphere, 1980.
*Cry Wolf* (novelization of screenplay). London, Sphere, 1981.
*No Stone* (novelization of screenplay). London, Sphere, 1981.
*Spy Phrobe* (novelization of screenplay). London, Sphere, 1981.
*Foxhole* (novelization of screenplay). London, Sphere, 1982.
*The Untouchables* (novelization of screenplay). London, Sphere, 1982.
*You'll Be All Right* (novelization of screenplay). London, Sphere, 1982.
*Operation Susie* (novelization of screenplay). London, Sphere, 1982.

Novels as Bruno Krauss (series: Sea Wolf)

*Steel Shark*. London, Sphere, 1978.
*Shark North*. London, Sphere, 1978.
*Shark Pack*. London, Sphere, 1978.
*Shark Hunt*. London, Sphere, 1980.
*Shark Africa*. London, Sphere, 1980.
*Shark Raid*. London, Sphere, 1982.
*Shark America*. London, Sphere, 1982.
*Shark Trap*. London, Sphere, 1982.

Other

*The True Book about Space Travel* (for children; as Kenneth Johns, with John Newman). London, Muller, 1960.
*Pretenders* (for children). London, New English Library, 1972.
Editor, *New Writings in SF 22–30*. London, Sidgwick and Jackson, 8 vols., 1973–76, and London, Corgi, 1 vol., 1978.
Editor, *New Writings in SF Special 1–3*. London, Sidgwick and Jackson, 1975–78 (vol. 1 edited with John Carnell).

*

Bibliography: *The Writings of Kenneth Bulmer* by Roger Robinson, n. p., BECCON, 1983; revised edition, 1984.

Kenneth Bulmer comments:

If in an unwary moment I open one of my early books I find great difficulty in identifying with the writer. The immediate purpose of the writer appears plain enough; he is dazzled by a vision of what this literature called SF might achieve, and is concerned to express this vision in terms then available to him. There is genuine feeling; but he is handicapped by environment, editorial prejudice, and lack of data. There is an unfortunate assumption that other people will readily share his insights, that the vision is so self-evident it must be conveyed. His own interests in the fascinating details of, for instance, the future, space and time travel, the interactions and potentialities of the human mind and spirit, appear to overshadow what he is driving at. Imperceptive, top-of-the-head critics have said that most of the writer's work is space opera; a closer reading will reveal this statement to be untenable. The vision of what SF might achieve remains, dimmed a little, it is true, by the current state of general SF, and this writer has in recent years turned to other interests, including the Fox books (as Adam Hardy) and adult fantasy, both incidentally, sharing that imaginative exploration of worlds unknown to the present day.

I have said many times, and will re-iterate, that SF is not respectable but is responsible. I remain unconvinced that this statement has been grasped by those to whom it is addressed. If poetry and non-establishment fiction are literatures of revolt, then SF is also. But it is more than merely a literature against, for example, the dead hand of authoritarianism or outmoded sexual mores: it is a literature against the spoliation of man by mankind's creations, which is by inference by man himself. This is not quite the same order of protest. This does not mean that SF is less as literature but more, for it incorporates more of life and, to enlarge a cliché, the felt responses within the emotional reactions to the human condition.

One underlying theme in my work is the exploration of the feelings and reactions of people forced, by the environment, other people, or inner compulsions, to perform acts and live lives far removed from what they would desire. As an introduction to my work I would instance the observation of a recent correspondent who remarked of my novels that they are filled with compassion all too often lacking in other works of SF.

* * *

If any single writer could epitomize the formularized science-fantasy milieu of Donald A. Wollheim's popular Ace paperback line, Kenneth Bulmer would be a good choice for the designation. Inasmuch as American adventure-pulps took many formulaic elements from British adventure-fiction (violent conflict between cultures, stereotypes of romance), it might be seen as fitting that Wollheim's editorial devotion to the adventurous side of SF should be typified by a British writer who seemed devoted to formula for formula's sake.

It should be stressed that no author of narrative prose escapes at least some formulaic elements in his or her work—in fact, one measure of "art" might be the author's ability to transcend the formulaic origins of his narrative, as Conrad's stories rise above the classification of "sea stories." A formula writer, however, emphasizes the elements of the formula—the plot, the action, the melodramatic interactions of characters, and in SF, the "idea" or concept—and pays only superficial attention (if any) to the meaningful, thematic usages of such elements. Ace Books was noteworthy for printing many SF adventures with at least some moderate thematic interest, as with Emil Petaja's concern for regenerative myth-figures, or Leigh Brackett's preoccupation with beautiful, dying cultures. Yet the bulk of Ace's books were usually less thematically organized, and so Bulmer makes the best representative writer of that period. Bulmer is not, however, simply a "hack" in the derogatory sense—rather, he does for the SF adventure what Edgar Wallace did for mysteries, and Seabury Quinn did for supernatural stories—that is, by the sheer bulk of his efforts in a single vein, he demonstrates the intrinsic fascination of the ritualistic nature of the formula and its icon-like imagery.

Bulmer's plots are his chief failing. Other formula-elements can be, and have been, neglected without necessarily diluting the effectiveness of the formula. Jack Williamson might use stereotypic characters, Edgar Rice Burroughs might overemphasize frenetic action, and Philip José Farmer might employ ideas of little originality, but all of them supply strong plotting that communicates some thematic commitment. Adventure-plots generally must be intricate to be compelling, but the formlessness of Bulmer's plots almost suggests the absurdity of a freewheeling comedy. Most of Bulmer's plots begin adequately enough—the protagonist and his alies learn of a mysterious force or perilous circumstance threatening their safety, but as they prepare to combat it, they continually become sidetracked, verging off into distantly-related episodic conflicts, so that, when they eventually re-enter the central conflict, the outcome is no longer interesting.

Some books in Bulmer's early cycle, such as *Behold the Stars* and *The Secret of Zi*, are dully conventional, and it may be that Bulmer began his pattern of repeated scene-shifting to gain greater diversity. The tendency is markedly seen in *Cycle of Nemesis*, in which a group of humans tries to bind an ancient demon into his crypt, and get thrown across various time-periods as they try. A series of Bulmer's books is even built around the various conflicts of an assortment of forgettable heroes against a dimension-conquering villainess, the Diamond Contessa, but with the exception of one of these *(The Wizards of Senchuria)* the other three, *The Key to Irunium, The Key to Venudine*, and *The Diamond Contessa*, lack narrative drive and coherence.

Bulmer's best work is probably *The Wizard of Starship Poseidon*, in that the plot is well-defined. Best described as *Topkapi* set in outer space, the novel has a certain amount of irony, concerning a scientist who fails to gain a grant to subsidize his project of creating biologic life, and decides to steal the necessary funds from a military payroll. (Wittily enough, the grant he wants is given to a literary scholar who hopes to prove that Bernard Shaw and H.G. Wells were the same man.) In this format, Bulmer's penchant for stocking his stories with an excess of eccentric characters is a benefit, and he manages to pull off a number of interesting plot-twists without becoming vague. A runner-up for best book might be *The Star Venturers*, in which a soldier-of-fortune, controlled by an artificial life-form implanted in his brain, is forced to track down a kidnapped princess, with the usual wild escapades that ensue when he combats her heavily armed kidnappers. Also of interest are *On the Symb-Socket Circuit* and *Roller Coaster World*, which attempt to break from the adventure-mold into that of social satire, directed toward the follies of hedonism and luxury-living. These have a degree of wit, but tend to flounder aimlessly: in *Roller Coaster World*, the hero is infatuated with a hopelessly unfulfilling romance, but Bulmer resolves an interesting dilemma in melodramatic terms, arranging for another woman to force the hero to renounce his hopeless love by the subtle strategy of her shooting him and carrying him off.

In short, Bulmer is a writer to be valued for his inventiveness, in spite of the fact that his inventions rarely transcend the level of basic "sensawunda" SF.

—Gene Phillips

---

**BUNCH, David R(oosevelt).** American. Born in Lowry City, Missouri. Educated at Central Missouri State College, Warrensburg, B.S. 1946; Washington University, St. Louis, M.A. 1949; State University of Iowa City, 1951–52. Served in the United States Army Air Forces, 1942–46. Married Phyllis Geraldine Flette in 1951; two daughters (one deceased). Worked in cafeteria, as clerk and warehouseman, mail handler, druggist; staff member, Wagner Electric Company, St. Louis, 1953–54; civilian cartographer, Air Force Aeronautical Chart and Information Center, St. Louis, 1954–73. Agent: Hans Joachim Alpers, Gross Flottbeker Strasse 61, 2000 Hamburg 52, Germany. Address: P.O. Box 12233, Soulard Station, St. Louis, Missouri 63157, U.S.A.

SCIENCE-FICTION PUBLICATIONS

Novel

*Moderan.* New York, Avon, 1971.

Uncollected Short Stories

"Routine Emergency," in *If* (New York), December 1957.
"In the Complaints Service," in *Fantastic* (New York), February 1960.
"We Regret," in *Fantastic* (New York), February 1961.
"Last Zero," in *Fantastic* (New York), March 1961.
"The Problem Was Lubrication," in *Fantastic* (New York), May 1961.
"The Survey Trip," in *Fantastic* (New York), May 1962.
"Ended," in *Fantastic* (New York), June 1962.
"The Reluctant Immortals," in *If* (New York), November 1962.
"Awareness Plans," in *Fantastic* (New York), November 1962.
"Somebody Up There Hates Us," in *Amazing* (New York), April 1963.
"The Hall of CD," in *Fantastic* (New York), June 1963.
"They Never Came Back from Whoosh!," in *Fantastic* (New York), February 1964.
"All for Nothing," in *Fantastic* (New York), May 1964.
"The College of Acceptable Death," in *Fantastic* (New York), July 1964.
"The Failure," in *Fantastic* (New York), August 1964.
"A Vision of the King," in *Fantastic* (New York), September 1964.
"Home to Zero," in *Fantastic* (New York), October 1964.
"Training Talk," in *The Year's Best S-F, 10th Annual*, edited by Judith Merril. New York, Delacorte Press, 1965.
"Make Mine Trees," in *Fantastic* (New York), February 1965.
"The Little Doors," in *Fantastic* (New York), June 1965.
"The Time Battler," in *The Smith* (New York), July 1965.
"Investigating the Bidwell Endeavors," in *The Year's Best S-F, 11th Annual*, edited by Judith Merril. New York, Delacorte Press, 1966.
"The Escaping," in *Dangerous Visions*, edited by Harlan Ellison. New York, Doubleday, 1967.
"Sad Case No. (Many-Too-Many)," in *Dare* (Cleveland), March 1967.
"The Fable of the Moonshooter and the Indifferent Undergraduate," in *Dare* (Cleveland), October 1967.
"The Soul Short Changers," in *21* (Los Angeles), October 1967.
"That High-Up Blue Day That Saw the Black Sky-Train Come Spinning," in *Fantasy and Science Fiction* (New York), March 1968.
"Two Pessimists and a Pigeon," in *Aspects* (Eugene, Oregon), April 1968.
"A Scare in Time," in *Fantasy and Science Fiction* (New York), September 1968.
"The Monsters," in *Amazing* (New York), November 1968.
"When It Comes to Bascarts, I'll Take a Full One," in *Aspects* (Eugene, Oregon), January 1969.
"Any Heads at Home?," in *Fantastic* (New York), February 1969.
"In the Time of Disposal of Infants," in *Amazing* (New York), March 1969.
"In a Saucer Down for B-Day," *Fantastic* (New York), April 1969.

"A Little at All Times," in *Perihelion* (Elmhurst, New York), Summer 1969.
"At the Place of Almost If You Want To Don't Care If You Don't," in *Orb* (Lake Worth, Florida), Fall 1969.
"Learning It at Miss Rejoyy's," in *Fantastic* (New York), February 1970.
"In the Land of the Not-Unhappies," in *Fantastic* (New York), June 1970.
"Tough Rocks and Hard Stones," in *Fantasy and Science Fiction* (New York), September 1970.
"Holdholtzer's Box," in *Protostars*, edited by David Gerrold and Stephen Goldin. New York, Ballantine, 1971.
"Price of Leisure," in *Galaxy* (New York), May 1971.
"The Joke," in *Fantastic* (New York), August 1971.
"Doll for the End of the Day," in *Fantastic* (New York), October 1971.
"The Lady Was for Kroinking," in *Generation*, edited by David Gerrold. New York, Dell, 1972.
"Training Talk No. 12," in *Fantasy and Science Fiction* (New York), January 1972.
"Two Suns for the King," in *If* (New York), April 1972.
"Up to the Edge of Heaven," in *Fantastic* (New York), April 1972.
"The Good War," in *Fantastic* (New York), December 1972.
"Breakout in Ecol 2," in *Nova 3*, edited by Harry Harrison. New York, Walker, 1973.
"Seeing Stingy Ed," in *The Haunt of Horror* (New York), June 1973.
"Moment of Truth in Suburb Junction," in *Fantastic* (New York), September 1973.
"Helping Put the Rough Works to Jesse," in *Eternity 3* (Sandy Springs, South Carolina), 1974.
"Among the Metal-and-People People," in *New Dimensions 4*, edited by Robert Silverberg. New York, New American Library, 1974.
"How Xmas Ghosts Are Made," in *Alternities*, edited by David Gerrold. New York, Dell, 1974
"Report from the Colony," in *SF Directions*, edited by Bruce McAllister. Christchurch, Edge Press, 1974.
"Alien," in *Fantastic* (New York), January 1974.
"Short Time at the Pearly Gates," in *Fantastic* (New York), March 1974.
"In the Land That Aimed at Forever," in *Fantastic* (New York), May 1974.
"At Bugs Complete," in *Fantastic* (New York), July 1974.
"End of a Singer," in *Fantastic* (New York), April 1975.
"The Strange Case of the Birds," in *Fantastic* (New York), December 1975.
"The Dirty War," in *Future Pastimes*, edited by Scott Edelstein. Nashville, Tennessee, Aurora, 1977.
"Mr. Who?," in *Fantastic* (New York), April 1978.
"Send Us a Planet?," in *Fantastic* (New York), July 1978.
"Pridey Goeth," in *Fantastic* (New York), October 1978.
"When the Metal Eaters Came," in *Galaxy* (New York), June–July 1979.
"A Little Girl's Spring Day in Moderan," in *Galaxy* (New York), September–October 1979.
"Through a Wall a Back," in *Eternity* (Clemson, South Carolina), Winter 1979.
"New Member," in *Fantastic* (New York), July 1980.
"The Strange Rider of the Good Year," in *Amazing* (New York), November 1980.
"In the Ball of Frosted Glass (with a Big Pink-Lavender Load)," in *Amazing* (New York), March 1981.
"Kicked Straight at Last," in *Pulpsmith* (New York), Spring 1981.
"In the Jag-Whiffing Service," and "Let Me Call Her Sweetcore," in *Pig Iron*, edited by Rose Sayre and Jim Villani. Youngstown, Ohio, Pig Iron Press, 1982.
"December for Stronghold 9," in *Amazing* (New York), June 1982.
"Writer's Workshop Stories," in *Amazing* (New York), September 1982.
"From the Fishbowl," in *Last Wave* (New York), Autumn 1984.
"A Small Miracle of Fishhooks and Straightpins," in *Fantastic Stories*, edited by Martin H. Greenburg and Patrick L. Price. New York, TSR, 1987.

OTHER PUBLICATIONS

Verse

*We Have a Nervous Job.* Astoria, Oregon, Alba Press, 1983.

*

David R. Bunch comments:

When last I wrote an essay to introduce my science fiction to be listed in *Twentieth-Century Science-Fiction Writers*, I came off sounding almost anti-science. I am indeed fortunate to have, in this Third Edition, this welcomed opportunity to correct an erroneous impression: David R. Bunch is NOT anti-science in his heart, his mind, and his written words. David R. Bunch is simply and adamantly anti-Bad Science in his heart, his writing, and his whole life. There is a difference here, and a significance that is so all-pervasive to our NOW-times on planet Earth, that adequate appraisal-and-value of that difference is almost beyond speech to say.

An inhabitant of planet Earth who would damn all science would be one with NO reasonable mind-and-sense understanding of how this wonderful force has served us, bettered us, and could—if rightly employed!—have transformed each and every one of our lives into that of either a prince or a princess of Earth, with all of us having such an abundance of good things (necessary things) in an ordered world that surely our Hearts and our Love—our Goodnesses! would have been optimum too. THEN—in a Great Wonder Time (of Heart-and-Mind one glorious entity) we would have been truly what God truly meant. (Whereas now!!! whereas now????) Any human being on our beleaguered planet today who would indiscriminately worship at the shrine of ALL science would have, surely, to be one of such total mind-blindness and/or one of such stupefied, unblinking fidelity to the Danger God as to seem, quite unredeemably, a Fool-among-Men.

Not in all of my science-fiction writing, but in a goodly part of it, have I tried to convey—by social commentary, satire, irony, and direct-hard-bitter statement—that the prying, probing Mind of Science Man of planet Earth, forsaking the Heart and employing Bad Science to the absolute outer bounds of evil-learned-stupidity, has created a startlingly heartless world of speed, greed, and plunder—and kill-potential almost beyond human capacity fully to comprehend. For it is true: A brilliant Scientist-Mind without Heart is indeed a cold set of cogs—with almost unlimited capacity to function in the heartless Climate-of-Harm. (I AM SURE God meant Heart [first] Mind [second] to team together to LIVE! on our planet Earth—AND let IT live, not murder it with "brilliant" scientific conquests and kill-potential stockpiled in quantities enough to utterly overwhelm Land, Sea, and Sky.) Viewed from a little distance, in a calm moment, HOW! can we believe!!?? that WE have let happen "what we have let happen"—to US, to Earth, to God's Faith (misplaced) in our Stewardship. It is almost beyond the strength of human thought to hold (contain, encompass) the Horror wrought by Bad Science, with Heart nowhere to see.

NOW—let me define Good Science, and that must also define Bad Science, for there are only these two: Good Science is that Science which, when called upon, will act (and react) *for us* to do our will and our work, and not in so doing *harm* us (directly), and furthermore not *harm* us (indirectly) by in any way, shape, or form bringing injury to that Place we call, with a proud, special note in the voice: *Our* Earth, *Our* Home. In short, Good Science is people-helpful, people-safe, Earth-enhancing and Earth-friendly. ALL other Science is, by the very nature of things and common sense: BAD. Especially in my Moderan writing do I describe in deadly serious diabolic comment how Man and his Bad Science are proper fools together. I hope that my readers may take to Heart what I have tried to tell them, show them, shout them—and that will be oh, MY best reward of all.

* * *

David R. Bunch's short, idiosyncratic stories have, almost invariably, been met with varying degrees of outrage from readers unwilling to work with his convoluted prose to reach the plot that to most is opaque. In his own way, Bunch is one of the most original and creative writers in the genre, and it is unfortunate that the conservative bent of most readers is such that he is not given the attention he deserves.

The bulk of his work has been a loosely organized series set against the background of Moderan, several dozen of which have been collected as a book under that title. Moderan is a thoroughly repulsive future to rank with the Nebishes of T.J. Bass. Humans have acquired immortality, or as near to it as matters, through replacement of most of their body parts with metal. In fact, only a few flesh strips remain, the tiniest traces of humanity. Their physical transformation is matched by their emotional one. Most humans live in highly armed castles called Strongholds. The protagonist of most of the series is Stronghold Ten, a man who early in the series is fitted with metallic limbs and organs, and makes use of his determination to make himself the foremost warmaker in the land. He alternates between highly mechanized combat and resting in his hip-snuggie chair within his stronghold, watching the sky change color as each month a new vapor shield is erected, or gazing out across his garden of metal flowers.

The series does much better as a whole than as individual stories, most of which are extremely episodic. Several do stand fairly well alone, particularly "Was She Horrid?" wherein Stronghold Ten is visited by a female, "The Walking, Talking I-Don't-Care-Man," in which he has a male visitor, and "How It Ended," which concludes the first cycle of Moderan stories. An uncollected Moderan story, "Two Suns for the King," is as good as anything in the collection; Stronghold Ten is struck with an undeniable urge to grow something organic, and can find no unpolluted soil to work with.

There are literally dozens of stories not in the Moderan series, some of which fall into a lesser series of "Training Talks" by a male parent to his two young children. In one of his more straightforward stories, "Holdholtzer's Box," a scientist invents a box wherein he expects to entice people to their deaths. The interface between man and machine, so obvious in the Moderan stories, is present in much of his other work. A road clearing crew fails to distinguish between auto wreckage and human flesh in "Routine Emergency," for example, and people are lobotomized to happiness in "In the Land of the Not-Unhappies."

The best single story may well be "That High-Up Blue Day That Saw the Black Sky-Train Come Spinning." In a style reminiscent of the best of R.A. Lafferty, Bunch introduces us to a group of aging nonconformists who decide that children need to be saved from the horrible fate of growing up. And they succeed. Another story that is extremely effective, though enigmatic, is "The Strange Case of the Birds," wherein an increasing number of people begin to see a malformed bird shape outlined against the moon.

Bunch often assails human vanity, rarely as well as in "Pridey Goeth," in which a town is taken in by a clever potion purveyor, and literally falls mortally wounded as the result. His clear-sighted view of the narrowmindedness of humanity is reinforced to a certain extent by the general reaction to his work, but it appears that Bunch is far more interested in making the statements he feels necessary than in gaining critical acclaim.

—Don D'Ammassa

---

**BUPP, Water.** *See* **GARRETT, Randall.**

---

**BURDEKIN, Katharine.** Also wrote as Kay Burdekin and Murray Constantine. British. Born Katharine Penelope Cade in Derbyshire, 23 July 1896. Educated at Cheltenham Ladies' College, 1907–13. Married Beaufort Burdekin in 1915 (separated 1921); two daughters. Army nurse, Voluntary Aid Detachment, Cheltenham, during World War I; worked in a shoe factory, a printer's shop, and a flour mill. *Died 10 August 1963.*

Science-Fiction Publications

Novels

*The Burning Ring.* London, Butterworth, 1927; New York, Morrow, 1929.
*The Children's Country* (as Kay Burdekin). New York, Morrow, 1929.
*The Rebel Passion.* London, Butterworth, and New York, Morrow, 1929.
*Proud Man* (as Murray Constantine). London, Boriswood, 1934.
*The Devil, Poor Devil!* (as Murray Constantine). London, Boriswood, 1934; New York, Arno, 1978.
*Swastika Night* (as Murray Constantine). London, Gollancz, 1937; New York, Feminist Press, 1985.
*The End of This Day's Business.* New York, Feminist Press, 1989.

Other Publications

Novels

*Anna Colquhoun.* London, J. Lane, 1922.
*The Reasonable Hope.* London, J. Lane, 1924.
*Quiet Ways.* London, Butterworth, 1930.

*Venus in Scorpio: A Romance in Versailles 1770–93* (as Murray Constantine), with Margaret Leland Goldsmith. London, J. Lane, 1940.

* * *

In her preface to the second edition of *The Language of the Night*, Ursula Le Guin identified the crossing of genre boundaries as a distinctly female act; Katharine Burdekin was a perfect example of this dictum, as her writing included realism, children's writing, historical fiction, science fiction, utopias, and dystopias. All her works contained a critique of gender that strikingly anticipates current feminist thought. For this reason, and also because of Burdekin's eclectic use of genre, her work was misunderstood during her lifetime. It was only very recently that *Swastika Night* was recognized as one of the finest SF dystopias. It prefigures both Dick's *The Man in the High Castle* and Charna's *Walk to the End of the World*, and it was published 12 years before Orwell's *1984* (by Orwell's own publisher).

Burdekin began writing in a realist mode, with *Anna Colquhoun*, a novel set in Australia. Gradually her work edged into fantasy; *The Burning Ring* is the story of an emotionally stunted man who with the aid of a magic ring is able to wish himself into the past. He lives through three different historical periods to achieve maturity. *The Children's Country*, written for Burdekin's daughters, deals with the adventures of two children in a non-sexist land.

With *The Rebel Passion*, Burdekin ventured into SF, through the persona of Giraldus of Glastonbury, a medieval monk born with the soul of a woman. Giraldus has visions of the future, both near and far; but Burdekin also looks backwards, reinterpreting human history as a gradual progress towards utopia.

*The Rebel Passion* was the last book Burdekin published under her own name, adopting for later works the pseudonym Murray Constantine. Burdekin concealed her identity as rigorously as James Tiptree Jr.; as late as 1984, the Orwell scholar Andy Croft was refused permission by Burdekin's agents to name her, even though she had been dead 20 years. (The name behind the non-de-plume was finally revealed in 1985 by Daphne Patai, whose work on Burdekin is a major source of information.)

The first work published under the pseudonym, *Proud Man*, records a brief stay in 1930's England by an androgynous being from the future who is capable of self-fertilization and telepathy, and is fully human, as opposed to us subhumans. The narrator observes that "A privilege of class divides a subhuman society horizontally, while a privilege of sex divides it vertically." This serves as a succinct expression of Burdekin's politics. *The Devil, Poor Devil!* was published later the same year. The book was hardly controversial, although it is a highly original fantasia on religious themes. The Devil visits earth, only to dwindle to nothing because so few people believe in him.

*Swastika Night* was published three years later, in 1937. Its anti-Nazi message was so timely that it was reprinted in 1940 as one of the few works of fiction in the Left Book Club series. Women in *Swastika Night* are confined to even less than "kirche, kinder and küche"—they live in cages, kept only for breeding. A projection of an as-yet-unknown future, it depicts a world divided between Nazi and Japanese rule. Burdekin's work is more than a rigorous extrapolation from Nazi ideology (and from events such as the 1932 suppression of the German women's movement); it is a political and moral expression of a woman writing in 1936, without the hindsight of Orwell or Dick.

Not until Charnas' *Walk to the End of the World* (1989) was such an extreme phallocracy again depicted, so misogynist that it is in danger of extinction, for women are ceasing to reproduce themselves, and fewer and fewer girl babies are born. However, Burdekin does not only blame Nazism for this reduction of women, but traces its roots back to St. Paul, and even to the "real tribal darkness before history began," when women first failed to value themselves.

There is a significant truth-telling book within *Swastika Night*, the one surviving text that reveals the lie behind the official Nazi histories of the world. The novel ends with its slow and secret dissemination, but with the protagonist Alfred unable to change the life of subjugation faced by his newborn daughter. A note of hope is sounded, but it is bittersweet.

Burdekin published only one book after this masterpiece, a historical novel about Marie Antoinette. She co-authored, but there are more than a dozen surviving manuscripts of her work. Of these the first to be published is *The End of This Day's Business*, which is a reversal of *Swastika Night* (it was probably written a year earlier than *Swastika Night*). *The End* is set 4000 years in the future, in a utopia where women are dominant. Men lead passive and dependent lives, but are happy in contrast to the women in *Swastika Night.* One woman, Grania, tries to change the status quo by revealing the truth to her son; both are forced to commit suicide by the women-state, with only the hope that their subversive ideas will survive. Yet this novel is nowhere as dark as *Swastika Night*, for the men, though subordinate, are not as brutally reduced as the women under Nazism. Burdekin, in dealing with the political problem of domination of either sex, breaks with traditional fiction writing in *The End*; there are long essay-like passages that are philosophical reconsiderations of history.

It is to be hoped that more of Burdekin's work will be reprinted; at present only three of her books are widely available. Like Catherine Helen Spence and Charlotte Perkins Gilman, she is an important precursor of today's feminist SF, and has left at least one novel of genuinely terrifying import in *Swastika Night.*

—Lucy Sussex

---

**BURGESS, Anthony.** Pseudonym for John Anthony Burgess Wilson; also writes as Joseph Kell. British. Born in Manchester, Lancashire, 25 February 1917. Educated at Xaverian College, Manchester; Manchester University, B.A. (honours) in English 1940. Served in the British Army Education Corps, 1940–46: sergeant-major. Married 1) Llewela Isherwood Jones in 1942 (died 1968); 2)Liliana Macellari in 1968, one son. Lecturer, Extra-Mural Department, Birmingham University, 1946–48; education officer and lecturer, Central Advisory Council for Adult Education in the Forces, 1946–48; lecturer in phonetics, Ministry of Education, 1948–50; English master, Banbury Grammar School, Oxfordshire, 1950–54; senior lecturer in English, Malayan Teachers Training College, Khata Baru, 1954–57; English language specialist, Department of Education, Brunei, Borneo, 1958–59; writer-in-residence, University of North Carolina, Chapel Hill, 1969–70; professor, Columbia University, New York, 1970–71; visiting fellow, Princeton University, New Jersey, 1970–71; distinguished professor, City University of New York, 1972–73; literary adviser, Guthrie Theatre, Minneapolis, 1972–75. Also composer. Recipient: National Arts Club award, 1973; Foreign Book prize (France), 1981; *Sunday Times* Mont Blanc award, 1987. D. Litt.: Manchester University, 1982. Fellow, Royal Society of Literature, 1969; Commandeur de Mérite Culturel (Monaco), 1986; Commandeur des Arts et des Lettres (France), 1986. Lives in Monaco.

SCIENCE-FICTION PUBLICATIONS

Novels

*A Clockwork Orange.* London, Heinemann, 1962; New York, Norton, 1963.
*The Wanting Seed.* London, Heinemann, 1962; New York, Norton, 1963.
*1985.* London, Hutchinson, and Boston, Little Brown, 1978.
*The End of the World News.* London, Hutchinson, 1982; New York, McGraw Hill, 1983.

OTHER PUBLICATIONS

Novels

*Time for a Tiger.* London, Heinemann, 1956.
*The Enemy in the Blanket.* London, Heinemann, 1958.
*Beds in the East.* London, Heinemann, 1959.
*The Right to an Answer.* London, Heinemann, 1960; New York, Norton, 1961.
*The Doctor Is Sick.* London, Heinemann, and New York, Norton, 1960.
*The Worm and the Ring.* London, Heinemann, 1961; revised edition, 1970.
*One Hand Clapping* (as Joseph Kell). London, Davies, 1961; as Anthony Burgess, New York, Knopf, 1972.
*Devil of a State.* London, Heinemann, 1961; New York, Norton, 1962.
*Honey for the Bears.* London, Heinemann, 1963; New York, Norton, 1964.
*Inside Mr. Enderby* (as Joseph Kell). London, Heinemann, 1963.
*The Eve of Saint Venus.* London, Sidgwick and Jackson, 1964; New York, Norton, 1967.
*The Malayan Trilogy* (includes *Time for a Tiger, the Enemy in the Blanket, Beds in the East*). London, Heinemann, 1964; as *The Long Day Wanes*, New York, Norton, 1965.
*Nothing Like the Sun: A Story of Shakespeare's Love-Life.* London, Heinemann, and New York, Norton, 1964.
*A Vision of Battlements.* London, Sidgwick and Jackson, 1965; New York, Norton, 1966.
*Tremor of Intent.* London, Heinemann, and New York, Norton, 1966.
*Enderby Outside.* London, Heinemann, 1968.
*Enderby* (includes *Inside Mr. Enderby* and *Enderby Outside*). New York, Norton, 1968.
*MF.* London, Cape, and New York, Knopf, 1971.
*Napoleon Symphony.* London, Cape, and New York, Knopf, 1974.
*The Clockwork Testament: or, Enderby's End.* London, Hart Davis MacGibbon, 1974; New York, Knopf, 1975.
*Beard's Roman Women.* New York, McGraw Hill, 1976; London, Hutchinson, 1977.
*Abba Abba.* London, Faber, and Boston, Little Brown, 1977.
*Man of Nazareth.* New York, McGraw Hill, 1979; London, Magnum, 1980.
*Earthly Powers.* London, Hutchinson, and New York, Simon and Schuster, 1980.
*Enderby* (includes *Inside Mr. Enderby, Enderby Outside, The Clockwork Testament*). London, Penguin, 1982.
*Enderby's Dark Lady; or, No End to Enderby.* London, Hutchinson, and New York, McGraw Hill, 1984.
*The Kingdom of the Wicked.* London, Hutchinson, and New York, Arbor House, 1985.
*The Pianoplayers.* London, Hutchinson, and New York, Arbor House, 1986.
*Any Old Iron.* London, Hutchinson, and New York, Random House, 1989.

Short Stories

*Will and Testament: A Fragment of Biography.* Verona, Italy, Plain Wrapper Press, 1977.
*The Devil's Mode and Other Stories.* London, Hutchinson, and New York, Random House, 1989.

Plays

*Cyrano de Bergerac*, adaptation of the play by Rostand (produced Minneapolis, 1971). New York, Knopf, 1971; musical version, as *Cyrano*, music by Michael Lewis, lyrics by Burgess (produced New York, 1972).
*Oedipus the King*, adaptation of a play by Sophocles (produced Minneapolis, 1972; Southampton, Hampshire, 1979). Minneapolis, University of Minnesota Press, 1972; London, Oxford University Press, 1973.
*The Cavalier of the Rose* (story adaptation), in *Der Rosenkavalier*, libretto by Hofmannsthal, music by Richard Strauss. Boston, Little Brown, 1982; London, Joseph, 1983.
*Cyrano de Bergerac* (not same as 1971 version), adaptation of the play by Rostand (produced London, 1983). London, Hutchinson, 1985.
*Blooms of Dublin*, music by Burgess, adaptation of the novel *Ulysses* by Joyce (broadcast 1983). London, Hutchinson, 1986.
*Oberon Old and New* (includes original libretto by James Robinson Planché), music by Carl Maria von Weber. London, Hutchinson, 1985.
*Carmen*, adaptation of the libretto by Henri Meilhac and Ludovic Halévy, music by Georges Bizet (produced London, 1986). London, Hutchinson, 1986.
*A Clockwork Orange*, music by Burgess, adaptation of his own novel. London, Hutchinson, 1987.

Screenplay: special languages for *Quest for Fire*, 1981.

Radio Plays: *Blooms of Dublin*, music by Burgess, 2 February 1982; *A Meeting in Valladolid*, 1991.

Television Plays: *Moses—The Lawgiver*, with others, 1975; *Jesus of Nazareth*, with others, 1977; *A Kind of Failure* (documentary; *Writers and Places* series), 1981; *The Childhood of Christ*, music by Berlioz, 1985; *A.D.*, 1985.

Verse

*Moses: A Narrative.* London, Dempsey and Squires, and New York, Stonehill, 1976.
*A Christmas Recipe.* Verona, Italy, Plain Wrapper Press, 1977.

Other

*English Literature: A Survey for Students* (as John Burgess Wilson). London, Longman, 1958.
*The Novel Today.* London, Longman, 1963.
*Language Made Plain* (as John Burgess Wilson). London, English Universities Press, 1964; New York, Crowell, 1965; revised edition, London, Fontana, 1975.
*Here Comes Everybody: An Introduction to James Joyce for the Ordinary Reader.* London, Faber, 1965; revised edition,

London, Hamlyn, 1982; as *Re Joyce*, New York, Norton, 1965.

*The Novel Now: A Student's Guide to Contemporary Fiction.* London, Faber, and New York, Norton, 1967; revised edition, Faber, 1971.

*Urgent Copy: Literary Studies.* London, Cape, and New York, Norton, 1968.

*Shakespeare.* London, Cape, and New York, Knopf, 1970.

*Joysprick: An Introduction to the Language of James Joyce.* London, Deutsch, 1973; New York, Harcourt Brace, 1975.

*Obscenity and the Arts* (lecture). Valletta, Malta Library Association, 1973.

*A Long Trip to Teatime* (for children). London, Dempsey and Squires, and New York, Stonehill, 1976.

*New York*, with the editors of Time-Life books. New York, Time-Life, 1976.

*Ernest Hemingway and His World.* London, Thames and Hudson, and New York, Scribner, 1978.

*The Land Where Ice Cream Grows* (for children). London, Benn, and New York, Doubleday, 1979.

*On Going to Bed.* London, Deutsch, and New York, Abbeville, 1982.

*This Man and Music.* London, Hutchinson, 1982; New York, McGraw Hill, 1983.

*Ninety-Nine Novels: The Best in English since 1939: A Personal Choice.* London, Allison and Busby, and New York, Summit, 1984.

*Flame into Being: The Life and Work of D.H. Lawrence.* London, Heinemann, and New York, Arbor House, 1985.

*Homage to QWERT YUIOP: Selected Journalism 1978–1985.* London, Hutchinson, 1986; as *But Do Blondes Prefer Gentlemen?*, New York, McGraw Hill, 1986.

*Little Wilson and Big God, Being the First Part of the Confessions of Anthony Burgess.* New York, Weidenfeld and Nicolson, 1986; London, Heinemann, 1987.

*They Wrote in English.* London, Hutchinson, 1988.

*You've Had Your Time: Being the Second Part of the Confessions of Anthony Burgess.* London, Heinemann, and New York, Weidenfeld, 1990.

Editor, *The Coaching Days of England 1750–1850.* London, Elek, and New York, Time-Life, 1966.

Editor, *A Journal of the Plague Year*, by Daniel Defoe. London, Penguin, 1966.

Editor, *A Shorter Finnegans Wake*, by James Joyce. London, Faber, and New York, Viking Press, 1966.

Editor, with Francis Haskell, *The Age of the Grand Tour.* London, Elek, and New York, Crown, 1967.

Editor, *Malaysian Stories*, by W. Somerset Maugham. Singapore, Heinemann, 1969.

Translator, with Llewela Burgess, *The New Aristocrats*, by Michel de Saint-Pierre. London, Gollancz, 1962; Boston, Houghton Mifflin, 1963.

Translator, with Llewela Burgess, *The Olive Trees of Justice*, by Jean Pelegri. London, Sidgwick and Jackson, 1962.

Translator, *The Man Who Robbed Poor Boxes*, by Jean Servin. London, Gollancz, 1965.

*

Bibliography: *Anthony Burgess: A Bibliography* by Jeutonne Brewer, Metuchen, New Jersey, Scarecrow Press, 1980; *Anthony Burgess: An Annotated Bibliography and Reference Guide* by Paul Boytinck, New York, Garland, 1985.

Manuscript Collection: Mills Memorial Library, Hamilton, Ontario.

Critical Studies: in *The Red Hot Vacuum* by Theodore Solotaroff, New York, Atheneum, 1970; *Shakespeare's Lives* by Samuel Schoenbaum, Oxford, Clarendon Press, 1970; *Anthony Burgess* by Carol M. Dix, London, Longman, 1971; *The Consolations of Ambiguity: An Essay on the Novels of Anthony Burgess* by Robert K. Morris, Columbia, University of Missouri Press, 1971; *Anthony Burgess* by A.A. DeVitis, New York, Twayne, 1972; *The Clockwork Universe of Anthony Burgess* by Richard Mathews, San Bernardino, California, Borgo Press, 1978; *Anthony Burgess: The Artist as Novelist* by Geoffrey Aggeler, University, University of Alabama Press, 1979, and *Critical Essays on Anthony Burgess* edited by Aggeler, Boston, Hall, 1986; *Anthony Burgess* by Samuel Coale, New York, Ungar, 1981; *Anthony Burgess: A Study in Character* by Martina Ghosh-Schellhorn, Frankfurt, Germany, Lang, 1986.

* * *

Barring some major new work, it is likely that Anthony Burgess will be remembered for his creation of the bizarre and depressing world of *A Clockwork Orange*, and even this will be filtered through the interpretation of that book made for the screen by Stanley Kubrick. As interesting as the movie may be, it is unfortunate that its brilliance has overshadowed the novel itself as a tour de force, one of the few novels in any field to achieve virtual classic stature almost immediately upon its publication.

Superficially, the setting and plot are not that far removed from much of the dystopian fiction that has held an honored place in science fiction for decades. The genre has always provided a unique opportunity to warn about the repression to come if certain contemporary trends are carried to extremes. Burgess's portrayal of the brutal, egocentric Alex, who is transformed from perpetrator to victim of an even greater evil, a supposedly benevolent government program, stands out for a variety of reasons. Burgess avoids the standard cliches of the form, a progressive revolution in the waning chapters or a revelation of an avenue of escape to another country or time or planet. Instead he demonstrates that the pernicious temptation to use power to control the lives of others inflicts even those who claim to be in revolt against such dehumanizing forces. The result is undeniably disturbing, but more effective because of the relentless oppression. Burgess adds to the verisimilitude of the novel by incorporating an entirely new slang, loosely based on Russian, which is thoroughly logical and sounds right. Although some editions include a glossary to explain the various words, this is an unnecessary concession to lazy readers; the sense is apparent almost immediately, and the ease with which the reader adjusts to the new speech patterns is a testimony to the author's skill. Each element in the plot is perfectly timed and placed to advance the story, which falters not once in its rush toward resolution. Except in the earliest edition, Alex's reclamation is demonstrably false, as he reverts as soon as he is psychologically prepared to do so. The first British version provided a less overwhelmingly depressing alternative that was soon dropped.

*The Wanting Seed* also warns of a repressive future, but here the story is told in more conventional terms, and the situations are more familiar. Interestingly enough, the effect is less memorable than the far stranger *A Clockwork Orange.* Burgess explores the consequences of overpopulation and the various forces that arise in opposition, the institutionalization of the Cold War, active public encouragement of homosexuality as a way to reduce the birth rate, even cannibalism to lower the population and provide a new food source. Despite the best machinations of the powers that move behind the scenes, the number of people in the world continues to grow, and pressure builds steadily toward an explosion.

Burgess's third novel in this area was *1985*, an idiosyncratic answer to the classic *1984* by George Orwell. Considering his own creative use of language, he would seem the ideal person to write a blend of essays and fictional narrative dealing with Newspeak and other aspects of Orwell's work, but the result is more than slightly disappointing. The essays are often interesting, but the short novel—which attempts to provide a more probable but equally repressive future Britain—lacks the inventiveness and grasp of narrative technique that characterized his earlier work.

*The End of the World News* is the least effective of all Burgess's genre work. Despite his undeniable flair for language and strong characterization, this book is little more than a variation of a clichéd plot. The world faces disaster, and the only hope for the human race is to build a ship in which a few might flee the debacle to come. The novel is satiric, but despite occasional moments where barbed words bite deeply, as a whole it seems interminably talky and self indulgent.

Burgess also wrote two fantasy novels. *The Eve of Saint Venus* owes a great deal to the work of Thorne Smith. Set against a gritty, background of welfare and petty bureaucracy, the story tells of the journey of the goddess Venus to Earth, and her intercession in the marriage of a typical young urban couple. Despite the lighthearted approach, the author's continued disenchantment with the effectiveness of government in shaping the course of society is evident. *A Long Trip to Teatime*, written for children, is a fantastic journey story that is witty and amusing at times, but it holds little interest for adult readers.

Burgess has never been identified as a genre writer; most of his fiction does not fall within the limits of the field at all. Nevertheless, some of his works—particularly *A Clockwork Orange*—have had a major impact on writers within the field, as well as in establishing the devices of science fiction as valid for serious writers of all persuasions.

—Don D'Ammassa

---

**BURKE, Ralph.** *See* **GARRETT, Randall.**

---

**BURROUGHS, Edgar Rice.** Also wrote as John Tyler McCulloch. American. Born in Chicago, Illinois, 1 September 1875. Educated at the Harvard School, Chicago, 1888–91; Phillips Academy, Andover, Massachusetts, 1891–92; Michigan Military Academy, Orchard Lake, 1892–95. Served in the United States 7th Cavalry, 1896–97; Illinois Reserve Militia, 1918–19. Married 1) Emma Centennia Hulbert in 1900 (divorced 1934), two sons and one daughter; 2) Florence Dearholt in 1935 (divorced 1942). Instructor and Assistant Commandant, Michigan Military Academy, 1895–96; owner of a stationery store, Pocatello, Idaho, 1898; worked in his father's American Battery Company, Chicago, 1899–1903; joined his brother's Sweetser-Burroughs Mining Company, Idaho, 1903–04; railroad policeman, Oregon Short Line Railroad Company, Salt Lake City, 1904; manager of the stenographic department, Sears Roebuck and Company, Chicago, 1906–08; partner, Burroughs and Dentzer, advertising contractors, Chicago, 1908–09; office manager, Physicians Co-Operative Association, Chicago, 1909; partner, State-Burroughs Company, salesmanship firm, Chicago, 1909; worked for Champlain Yardley Company, stationers, Chicago, 1910–11; manager, System Service Bureau, Chicago, 1912–13; freelance writer after 1913; formed Edgar Rice Burroughs, Inc., publishers, 1913, Burroughs-Tarzan Enterprises, 1934–39, and Burroughs-Tarzan Pictures, 1934–37; lived in California after 1919; mayor of Malibu Beach, 1933; also United Press Correspondent in the Pacific during World War II, and columnist ("Laugh It Off"), *Honolulu Advertiser*, 1941–42, 1945. *Died 19 March 1950.*

SCIENCE-FICTION PUBLICATIONS

Novels (series: Mars; Pellucidar; Venus)

*A Princess of Mars*. Chicago, McClurg, 1917; London, Methuen, 1919.
*The Gods of Mars*. Chicago, McClurg, 1918; London, Methuen, 1920.
*The Warlord of Mars*. Chicago, McClurg, 1919; London, Methuen, 1920.
*Thuvia, Maid of Mars*. Chicago, McClurg, 1920; London, Methuen, 1921.
*The Chessmen of Mars*. Chicago, McClurg, 1922; London, Methuen, 1923.
*At the Earth's Core* (Pellucidar). Chicago, McClurg, 1922; London, Methuen, 1923.
*Pellucidar*. Chicago, McClurg, 1923; London, Methuen, 1924.
*The Master Mind of Mars*. Chicago, McClurg, 1928; London, Methuen, 1939.
*The Monster Men*. Chicago, McClurg, 1929.
*Tarzan at the Earth's Core* (Pellucidar). New York, Metropolitan, 1930; London, Methuen, 1938.
*Tanar of Pellucidar*. New York, Metropolitan, 1930; London, Methuen, 1939.
*A Fighting Man of Mars*. New York, Metropolitan, 1931; London, Lane, 1932.
*Jungle Girl*. Tarzana, California, Burroughs, 1932; London, Odhams Press, 1933; as *The Land of Hidden Men*, New York, Ace, 1963.
*Pirates of Venus*. Tarzana, California, Burroughs, 1934; London, Lane, 1935.
*Lost on Venus*. Tarzana, California, Burroughs, 1935; London, Methuen, 1937.
*Swords of Mars*. Tarzana, California, Burroughs, 1936; London, New English Library, 1966.
*Back to the Stone Age* (Pellucidar). Tarzana, California, Burroughs, 1937.
*Carson of Venus*. Tarzana, California, Burroughs, 1939; London, Goulden, 1950.
*Synthetic Men of Mars*. Tarzana, California, Burroughs, 1940; London, Methuen, 1941.
*Land of Terror* (Pellucidar). Tarzana, California, Burroughs, 1944.
*Escape on Venus*. Tarzana, California, Burroughs, 1946; London, New English Library, 1966.
*Beyond the Farthest Star*. New York, Ace, 1964.

Short Stories

*The Land That Time Forgot*. Chicago, McClurg, 1924; London, Methuen, 1925.
*The Eternal Lover*. Chicago, McClurg, 1925; London, Methuen, 1927; as *The Eternal Savage*, New York, Ace, 1963.

*The Cave Girl.* Chicago, McClurg, 1925; London, Methuen, 1927.
*The Moon Maid.* Chicago, McClurg, 1926; London, Stacey, 1972; abridged edition, as *The Moon Men,* New York, Canaveral Press, 1962; augmented edition, London, Tandem, 1975.
*Llana of Gathol.* Tarzana, California, Burroughs, 1948; London, New English Library, 1967.
*Beyond Thirty.* Privately printed, 1955; as *The Lost Continent,* New York, Ace, 1963.
*The Man-Eater.* Privately printed, 1955.
*Savage Pellucidar.* New York, Canaveral Press, 1963.
*Tales of Three Planets.* New York, Canaveral Press, 1964.
*John Carter of Mars.* New York, Canaveral Press, 1964.
*The Wizard of Venus.* New York, Ace, 1970.

OTHER PUBLICATIONS

Novels

*Tarzan of the Apes.* Chicago, McClurg, 1914; London, Methuen, 1917.
*The Return of Tarzan.* Chicago, McClurg, 1915; London, Methuen, 1918.
*The Beasts of Tarzan.* Chicago, McClurg, 1916; London, Methuen, 1918.
*The Son of Tarzan.* Chicago, McClurg, 1917; London, Methuen, 1919.
*Tarzan and the Jewels of Opar.* Chicago, McClurg, 1918; London, Methuen, 1919.
*Tarzan the Terrible.* Chicago, McClurg, and London, Methuen, 1921.
*Tarzan and the Golden Lion.* Chicago, McClurg, 1923; London, Methuen, 1924.
*The Girl from Hollywood.* New York, Macaulay, 1923; London, Methuen, 1924.
*Tarzan and the Ant Men.* Chicago, McClurg, 1924; London, Methuen, 1925.
*The Bandit of Hell's Bend.* Chicago, McClurg, 1925; London, Methuen, 1926.
*The Tarzan Twins* (for children). Joliet, Illinois, Volland, 1927; London, Collins, 1930.
*The Outlaw of Torn.* Chicago, McClurg, and London, Methuen, 1927.
*The War Chief.* Chicago, McClurg, 1927; London, Methuen, 1928.
*Tarzan, Lord of the Jungle.* Chicago, McClurg, and London, Cassell, 1928.
*Tarzan and the Lost Empire.* New York, Metropolitan, 1929; London, Cassell, 1931.
*Tarzan the Invincible.* Tarzana, California, Burroughs, 1931; London, Lane, 1933.
*Tarzan Triumphant.* Tarzana, California, Burroughs, 1931; London, Lane, 1933.
*Tarzan and the City of Gold.* Tarzana, California, Burroughs, 1933; London, Lane, 1936.
*Apache Devil.* Tarzana, California, Burroughs, 1933.
*Tarzan and the Lion-Man.* Tarzana, California, Burroughs, 1934; London, W.H. Allen, 1950.
*Tarzan and the Leopard Men.* Tarzana, California, Burroughs, 1935; London, Lane, 1936.
*Tarzan and the Tarzan Twins, with Jad-Bal-Ja, The Golden Lion* (for children). Racine, Wisconsin, Whitman, 1936.
*Tarzan's Quest.* Tarzana, California, Burroughs, 1936; London, Methuen, 1938.
*The Oakdale Affair: The Rider.* Tarzana, California, Burroughs, 1937.
*Tarzan and the Forbidden City.* Tarzana, California, Burroughs, 1938; London, W.H. Allen, 1950.
*The Lad and the Lion.* Tarzana, California, Burroughs, 1938.
*The Deputy Sheriff on Comanche County.* Tarzana, California, Burroughs, 1940.
*Tarzan and the Foreign Legion.* Tarzana, California, Burroughs, 1947; London, W.H. Allen, 1949.
*Tarzan and the Madman.* New York, Canaveral Press, 1964; London, New English Library, 1966.
*The Girl from Farris's.* Kansas City, Missouri, House of Greystoke, 1965.
*The Efficiency Expert.* Kansas City, Missouri, House of Greystoke, 1966.
*I Am a Barbarian.* Tarzana, California, Burroughs, 1967.
*Pirate Blood* (as John Tyler McCulloch). New York, Ace, 1970.

Short Stories

*Jungle Tales of Tarzan.* Chicago, McClurg, and London, Methuen, 1919.
*Tarzan the Untamed.* Chicago, McClurg, and London, Methuen, 1920.
*The Mucker.* Chicago, McClurg, 1921; as *The Mucker* and *The Man Without a Soul,* London, Methuen, 2 vols., 1921–22.
*The Mad King.* Chicago, McClurg, 1926.
*Tarzan the Magnificent.* Tarzana, California, Burroughs, 1939; London, Methuen, 1940.
*Tarzan and the Castaways.* New York, Canaveral Press, 1964; London, New English Library, 1966.

Other

*Official Guide of the Tarzan Clans of America.* Privately printed, 1939.

*

Critical Studies: *Edgar Rice Burroughs, Master of Adventure* by Richard A. Lupoff, New York, Canaveral Press, 1965, revised edition, New York, Ace, 1968; *Tarzan Alive: A Definitive Biography of Lord Greystoke* by Philip José Farmer, New York, Doubleday, 1972, London, Panther, 1974; *Burroughs' Science Fiction* by Robert R. Kudlay and Joan Leiby, Geneseo, New York, School of Library and Information Science, 1973; *Edgar Rice Burroughs, The Man Who Created Tarzan* (includes bibliography) by Irwin Porges, Provo, Utah, Brigham Young University Press, 1975, London, New English Library, 1976; *A Guide to Barsoom* by John Flint Roy, New York, Ballantine, 1976; *The Burroughs Bestiary: An Encyclopaedia of Monsters and Imaginary Beings Created by Edgar Rice Burroughs* by David Day, London, New English Library, 1978; *Tarzan and Tradition: Classical Myth in Popular Literature* by Erling B. Holtsmark, Westport, Connecticut, Greenwood Press, 1981.

* * *

While best known for his long series of jungle adventure tales featuring the character Tarzan, both in their original prose form and in uncounted motion pictures, television series, comic strips, and other adaptations, Edgar Rice Burroughs was in fact a very important and very popular science-fiction writer. In a lifetime output of more than 70 books, essentially equal numbers were devoted to jungle adventures and to science fiction. Burroughs's remaining output was widely distributed among westerns, Graustarkian romances, historical novels and a few decidedly unsuccessful attempts at contemporary realism. Novels belonging to the last group, most notably *The Girl from Hollywood*, are of interest for their autobiographical content. As a science-fiction writer, Burroughs may be regarded as a descendant of Verne. His emphasis was on wonders: wonderful planets, strange creatures, magnificently melodramatic plots. Burroughs was himself of plebeian origins, but his works more often display a bias in favor of aristocracy. His heroes are generally noblemen and/or wealthy, e.g., Lord Greystoke (Tarzan), John Carter (Confederate cavalry captain and plantation owner), David Innes (scion of Connecticut gentry). His heroines are often princesses, most notably Dejah Thoris, eventual consort of John Carter. (Exceptions include the hoodlum hero of *The Mucker* and the prostitute heroine *The Girl from Farris's.*)

It is important to note that Burroughs was not a significant creator in his writing, but rather was a synthesist of immeasurable natural talent. Every major theme in Burroughs's fantastic fiction, (i.e., science fiction and jungle adventures) was anticipated in earlier works. Burroughs's genius lay in his ability to invest familiar material with such energy that it attained new heights of popularity. He did not invent the feralman novel, the hollow-earth novel, the interplanetary romance, or any other significant fantastic form. He *did* write some of the most successful, most completely developed, most colorful, energetic, and suspenseful examples of each. Burroughs's science fiction divides into three major series, one minor series, and several independent works, two of which are of major importance.

Burroughs's literary career began, at least as far as published fiction is concerned, with the first of his interplanetary romances, *A Princess of Mars.* This novel and its sequels concern an earthly hero of somewhat equivocal and mysterious immortality who is transferred to Mars by a means that suggests astral projection. On Mars ("Barsoom") the hero discovers a dying world containing an ancient, decadent civilization, roving nomadic tribes, and a complex mixture of races, species, and traditions. Through a series of some 11 volumes John Carter rises to the supreme Warlordship of Barsoom, marries the incomparably beautiful red-skinned Princess Dejah Thoris (who lays eggs but is otherwise wholly human), becomes a father and grandfather, travels extensively upon Barsoom, visits one of its moons, and ultimately journeys to the planet Jupiter. There he presumably remains (he was in the midst of an uncompleted adventure when Burroughs died). While some of Burroughs's more ardent admirers consider Barsoom and all its associated material a brilliantly original creation, it was in fact the very opposite. The character of John Carter is virtually identical to that of Phra the Phoenician, while the basic rationale of Barsoomian history and culture closely resembles that of the planet Mars in a book called *Lieut. Gullivar Jones: His Vacation;* both books are by Edwin Lester Arnold. More of the Barsoomian culture and many of the plotting devices used by Burroughs appear in *Journey to Mars* by Gustavus Pope, in *Across the Zodiac* by Percy Greg, and even in some of the strange Theosophical teachings of Helena Blavatsky (as pointed out by L. Sprague de Camp). And the dueling, kidnapping, impersonating, court-intrigue ridden Barsoomian society, possibly borrowed from Pope, in itself is more than suggestively reminiscent of the court at Zenda as recorded by Anthony Hope, who might well have borrowed from Mark Twain!

Burroughs's second most significant science-fiction series was the Pellucidar books, beginning with *At the Earth's Core.* While the later books of this series are of inferior quality, the first two or three are among Burroughs's best work. Here, the essential notion is that of an earth-boring machine accidentally breaking through the planet's crust to discover that the earth is hollow, illuminated by a miniature interior sun, and inhabited by a wide variety of species including primitive humans and paleontological survivals. Once again, elements derive from numerous earlier works, certainly including Holberg's *Nils Klim* and Verne's *Journey to the Center of the Earth*, and very likely (the name itself is suggestive) Bradshaw's *The Goddess of Atvatabar.* While the Pellucidar series does let down in quality, it contains numerous fascinating features. One of these is a speculation—this one more likely original to Burroughs—on the nature of time and the timeless condition of a world of eternal daylight. There is considerable humorous and satirical material in the books. Also of interest is the so-called "series cross-over" volume, *Tarzan at the Earth's Core*, in which the two separately created universes of Tarzan's jungle world and the hollow earth, are merged—or at least, one may say, their separation is bridged via dirigible.

Burroughs's final science-fiction series details the adventures of Carson Napier on Venus. The books of this sequence date from late in Burroughs's career and are derivative of his Martian cycle without ever quite duplicating its spirit. There is also a degree of likelihood that the Venus books were written to strike back at Otis Adelbert Kline, who had written a series of interplanetary romances laid on Venus, under heavy influence of Burroughs's Martian cycle. (This theory is advanced by Sam Moskowitz, and is circumstantially persuasive although unfortunately is in no way documented.)

*The Land That Time Forgot* is one of Burroughs's major nonseries science-fiction works (in some editions it is divided into three very slim volumes, corresponding with its original magazine serialization, and is consequently regarded as a small series itself.) Opening with a sequence of submarine warfare in the first World War, the action quickly shifts to the island of Caspak (also known as Caprona), a place remarkably reminiscent of both Verne's *Mysterious Island* and Peter Wilkins's island retreat in the novel of Robert Paltock. There follow numerous incidents involving primitive and violent life-forms, intriguing speculation on evolutionary processes, and a final confrontation with a chilling post-human winged form (again reminiscent of Paltock). The paleontological elements in this book, like those in Burroughs's hollow-earth novels, are remarkably detailed and authentic. They derive from Burroughs's involvement with the subject at first as a student and later as an instructor at the Michigan Military Academy.

*The Moon Maid*, Burroughs's second major independent science-fiction work, is also divisible into three more-or-less self-sustained segments. It ties into Burroughs's Martian cycle, as a spaceship named *Barsoom* travels from the earth to the moon. The moon is found to be hollow and inhabited, with access to the inner regions obtained through lunar craters. All of this, of course, is strangely like the moon of Wells's *The First Men in the Moon.* In later sequences, using technology introduced from the earth, lunar forces invade and conquer our planet. At this point Burroughs's novel turns into a saga spaced over many generations. Burroughs handled the challenges of the form astonishingly well, and *The Moon Maid* is one of his most successful works.

His other works of science fiction have received relatively little attention. *The Monster Men* is a charmingly creaky cross of jungle adventure, desert island romance, mad scientist, and *Frankenstein*-monster plots. This last element occurs also in several of Burroughs's Martian novels, most notably *Master Mind of Mars* and *Synthetic Men of Mars. Beyond Thirty* is a surprisingly effective story of a future war-torn Europe reverting to barbarism—anticipating L. Ron Hubbard's *Final Blackout.*

Burroughs's Tarzan stories and other jungle adventures, while not essentially works of science fiction, contain many elements derived from science fiction and allied forms. After feralism itself, the next most common theme in the books is that of the lost race, tribe, city, or country. These are handled well if somewhat repetitiously by Burroughs; it should be noted that this form of adventure writing was perfected by Haggard, whose works seem likely to have influenced Burroughs. The theme of feralism is itself very old in literature and folklore; it was best known prior to the creation of Tarzan in the *Jungle Books* of Kipling. The Tarzan novels also include Atlantean themes, immortality serums, paleontological survivals, at least one city of intelligent gorillas, and at least one satirical novel (*Tarzan and the Ant Men*) apparently based on Swift.

While many of Burroughs's works—most notably his interplanetary and inner world novels—fall technically within the realm of science fiction, he is regarded by some interpreters as more of a fantasy writer. Certainly John Carter's astral or psychic journeying has little or no basis in science. David Innes's journey to Pellucidar, on the contrary, is accomplished through the application of technology. But, it is argued, in either case the images and themes hark back to traditional romance with a major component of dream fantasy. The science fictional content of Burroughs's works, in this view, is to be taken no more seriously than that which is present in E.R. Eddison's or C.S. Lewis's works. And of course Burroughs's greatest creation, the Tarzan series, echoes notes of fantasy ringing from a primal desire to escape the trappings of civilization and return to a primal, even preternatural, state. Such a view of Burroughs may in fact permit a more profound understanding of his works than the conventional view of him as a science fiction writer.

As Burroughs borrowed from many earlier writers, he in turn was read by and influenced uncounted later writers. The briefest smattering of these must include H.P. Lovecraft, Robert E. Howard, Edmond Hamilton, Leigh Brackett, Ray Bradbury, Gore Vidal, and J.R.R. Tolkien. Direct imitators of Burroughs range from his contemporaries J.U. Giesy and William L. Chester, to many present-day writers including Lin Carter, Michael Resnick, Anne McCaffrey, John Norman, and Philip José Farmer. In most cases, where the imitation of Burroughs is very literal the result is a rather lifeless pastiche; where Burroughs's influence is less specific and the later writer uses Burroughs as a wellspring of color, verve, and suspense, the result is often admirable.

More than 40 years after Burroughs's death, many of his novels continue to be printed. His greatest creation, Tarzan, continues to provide the inspiration for motion picture and television series. While these occasionally come close to the spirit of the novels, they are all too often uninspired and unintelligent exploitations of famous names.

—Richard A. Lupoff

---

**BURROUGHS, William S(eward).** Also wrote as William Lee. American. Born in St. Louis, Missouri, 5 February 1914. Educated at John Burroughs School and Taylor School, St. Louis; Los Alamos Ranch School, New Mexico; Harvard University, Cambridge, Massachusetts, A.B. in anthropology 1936; studied medicine at the University of Vienna; Mexico City College, 1948–50. Served in the United States Army, 1942. Married Jean Vollmer in 1945 (died 1951); one son. Has worked as a journalist, private detective, and bartender; now a fulltime writer. Heroin addict, 1944–57. Exhibition of paintings: October Gallery, London, 1988; Tony Shafrazi Gallery, New York, 19 December 1987–24 January 1988; Kellas Gallery, Lawrence, Kansas, 1989. Recipient: American Academy Award, 1975. Member, American Academy, 1983. Lived for many years in Tangier; now lives in Lawrence. Agent: Andrew Wylie Agency, 250 West 57th Street, New York, New York 10107, U.S.A. Address: William Burroughs Communications, Box 147, Lawrence, Kansas 66044, U.S.A.

### Science-Fiction Publications

#### Novels

*The Naked Lunch.* Paris, Olympia Press, 1959; London, Calder, 1964; as *Naked Lunch*, New York, Grove Press, 1962.
*The Soft Machine.* Paris, Olympia Press, 1961; New York, Grove Press, 1966; London, Calder and Boyars, 1968.
*The Ticket That Exploded.* Paris, Olympia Press, 1962; revised edition, New York, Grove Press, 1967; London, Calder and Boyars, 1968.
*Nova Express.* New York, Grove Press, 1964; London, Cape, 1966.
*The Wild Boys: A Book of the Dead.* New York, Grove Press, 1971; London, Calder and Boyars, 1972; revised edition, London, Calder, 1979.
*Cities of the Red Night: A Boy's Book.* London, Calder, and New York, Holt Rinehart, 1981.

### Other Publications

#### Novels

*Junkie: Confessions of an Unredeemed Drug Addict* (as William Lee). New York, Ace, 1953; London, Digit, 1957; complete edition, London, Penguin, 1977; as *Junky*, London, Pergamon, 1986.
*Dead Fingers Talk.* London, Calder, 1963.
*Short Novels.* London, Calder, 1978.
*Blade Runner: A Movie.* Berkeley, California, Blue Wind Press, 1979.
*Port of Saints.* Berkeley, California, Blue Wind Press, 1980; London, Calder, 1983.
*The Place of Dead Roads.* New York, Holt Rinehart, 1983; London, Calder, 1984.
*Queer.* New York, Viking, 1985; London, Pan, 1986.
*The Western Lands.* New York, Viking, 1987; London, Picador, 1988.
*Routine.* N.p., Plashet, 1987.
*Tornado Alley.* New York, Cherry Valley, 1988.

#### Short Stories

*Exterminator!* New York, Viking Press, 1973; London, Calder and Boyars, 1974.
*Early Routines.* Santa Barbara, California, Cadmus, 1981.
*The Streets of Chance.* New York, Red Ozier Press, 1981.

#### Play

*The Last Words of Dutch Schultz.* London, Cape Goliard Press, 1970; New York, Viking Press, 1975.

#### Other

*The Exterminator*, with Brion Gysin. San Francisco, Auerhahn Press, 1960.
*Minutes to Go*, with others. Paris, Two Cities, 1960; San Francisco, Beach, 1968.
*The Yage Letters*, with Allen Ginsberg. San Francisco, City Lights, 1963.
*Roosevelt after Inauguration.* New York, Fuck You Press, 1964.
*Valentine Day's Reading.* New York, American Theatre for Poets, 1965.
*Time.* New York, "C" Press, 1965.

*Health Bulletin: APO–33: A Metabolic Regulator.* New York, Fuck You Press, 1965; revised edition, as *APO–33 Bulletin*, San Francisco, Beach, 1966.

*So Who Owns Death TV?*, with Claude Pelieu and Carl Weissner. San Fransisco, Beach, 1967.

*The Dead Star.* San Francisco, Nova Broadcast Press, 1969.

*Ali's Smile.* Brighton, Unicorn, 1969.

*Entretiens avec William Burroughs*, by Daniel Odier. Paris, Belfond, 1969; translated as *The Job: Interviews with William S. Burroughs* (includes *Electronic Revolution*), New York, Grove Press, and London, Cape, 1970.

*The Braille Film.* San Francisco, Nova Broadcast Press, 1970.

*Brion Gysin Let the Mice In*, with Brion Gysin and Ian Somerville, edited by Jan Herman. West Glover, Vermont, Something Else Press, 1973.

*Mayfair Academy Series More or Less.* Brighton, Urgency Press Rip-Off, 1973.

*White Subway*, edited by James Pennington. London, Aloes, 1974.

*The Book of Breeething.* Ingatestone, Essex, OU Press, 1974; Berkeley, California, Blue Wind Press, 1975; revised edition, Blue Wind Press, 1980.

*Snack: Two Tape Transcripts*, with Eric Mottram. London, Aloes, 1975.

*Sidetripping*, with Charles Gatewood. New York, Strawberry Hill, 1975.

*The Retreat Diaries*, with *The Dream of Tibet*, by Allen Ginsberg. New York, City Moon, 1976.

*Cobble Stone Gardens.* Cherry Valley, New York, Cherry Valley Editions, 1976.

*The Third Mind*, with Brion Gysin. New York, Viking Press, 1978; London, Calder, 1979.

*Roosevelt after Inauguration and Other Atrocities.* San Francisco, City Lights, 1979.

*Ah Pook Is Here and Other Texts* (includes *The Book of Breeething, Electronic Revolution*). London, Calder, 1979; New York, Riverrun, 1982.

*A William Burroughs Reader*, edited by John Calder. London, Pan, 1982.

*Letters to Allen Ginsberg 1953–1957.* New York, Full Court Press, 1982.

*New York Inside Out*, photographs by Robert Walker. Port Washington, New York, Skyline Press, 1984.

*The Burroughs File.* San Francisco, City Lights, 1984.

*The Job: Topical Writings and Interviews*, with Daniel Odier. London, Calder, 1984.

*The Adding Machine: Collected Essays.* London, Calder, 1985; New York, Seaven, 1986.

*

Bibliography: *William S. Burroughs: An Annotated Bibliography of His Works and Criticism* by Michael B. Goodman, New York, Garland, 1976; *William S. Burroughs: A Bibliography 1953–73* by Joe Maynard and Barry Miles, Charlottesville, University Press of Virginia, 1978; *William S. Burroughs: A Reference Guide* by Michael B. Goodman and Lemuel B. Coley, London, Garland, 1990.

Critical Studies: *William Burroughs: The Algebra of Need* by Eric Mottram, Buffalo, Intrepid Press, 1971; *Contemporary Literary Censorship: The Case History of Burroughs' Naked Lunch* by Michael B. Goodman, Metuchen, New Jersey, Scarecrow Press, 1981; *With William Burroughs; A Report from the Bunker* edited by Victor Bokris, New York, Seaver, 1981, London, Vermilion, 1982; *Literary Outlaw: The Life and Times of William S. Burroughs* by Ted Morgan, New York, Holt, 1988; London, Holt, 1989.

* * *

Best known as a leader of the American Beat movement, despite the cosmopolitan influences on his work, William S. Burroughs has repeatedly used science-fiction situations and images in his often bizarre novels of protest against social control. However, his frequent opacity seems to have daunted criticism and has led to some cries of exasperation or outrage from critics, such as Martin Seymour-Smith's reference to his "monumental stupidity." In fact, Burroughs demonstrated his ability to write with conventional intelligence in his first novel, *Junkie*, and has done so again in his recent *Cities of the Red Night. Junkie* is an autobiographical confession of a morphine addict—it is also a map of Hell, attacking a spiritless society and its gratuitous abuses of power. Despite the autobiographical element, Burroughs shows a degree of detachment from his narrator, an unsettled Picaro who sometimes interprets himself as an idealistic quester.

Burroughs's reputation rests mainly upon the four novels *The Naked Lunch, The Soft Machine, The Ticket That Exploded*, and *Nova Express.* These form a tetralogy which attacks the obsessive need for control which Burroughs sees as having gripped our planet. That obsession is often given its focus in such science-fiction images as the dystopias and advanced behavioural technologies of *The Naked Lunch*, and the ubiquitous fantasy of metamorphosis into arthropod form to represent the dehumanization of both controller and controlled. Especially in *The Ticket That Exploded* and *Nova Express*, Burroughs presents the extended metaphor of an invasion by aliens—the Nova Mob—whose members act through and control humans who share their weaknesses and predilections. *The Ticket That Exploded*, the more accessible of these two novels, makes it clear that the aliens are a metaphor for controlling powers on Earth, presented as if they could be only a Manichean force of evil from space.

It would be easy to condemn these novels for their frequent opacity and the paranoid sensibility they seem to reveal. However, Burroughs does write with admirable confidence, power, and surreal detail; where the prose is readable, the phrasing is sharp and the dialogue unsentimentally convincing. The difficulty is that, as Burroughs has admitted in *The Job*, a series of interviews with Daniel Odier, the prose is sometimes "simply not readable." This is mainly the result of Burroughs's so-called "cut-up" and "fold-in" techniques: the mechanical rearrangement of sliced-up pages and the juxtaposition of words from quite different texts. Both Burroughs's admirers and his detractors have over-emphasized the genesis of the prose in these techniques, rather than the patterns of meaning which (sometimes) result on the page.

Since the publication of *Nova Express*, Burroughs has frequently appeared to be more a sage—an unsystematic philosopher of life—than a creative artist. Unfortunately, he has not been helpful in his role as a sage. A study of his interviews and theoretical works reveals occasional insights hidden amid obsessive and often inhumane pronouncements, such as this, on women: "I think they were a basic mistake, and the whole dualistic universe evolved from this error."

However, in his most recent major work, *Cities of the Red Night*, Burroughs has recast the vision of his great tetralogy in a form which is creative, lucid, and fascinating. Drawing upon elements of time-travel, space visitation, alternative history and multiple realities, the book enacts a layered myth or series of myths of the Fall, fragmenting into shards from different realities before ending with a menacing vision of nuclear apocalypse.

*Cities of the Red Night* will pay detailed study to crack fully its codes of recurrence and levels of reality.

Of Burroughs's other works since *Nova Express* perhaps the most compelling for science-fiction readers is *The Wild Boys.* This novel begins as a series of linked apocalyptic vignettes which are pulled together as the story emerges of packs of homosexual specialist warriors who are able to outfight conventional armies, and who ravage their near-future world. The book is a projection of the need which Burroughs feels to destroy all present-day institutions, including the family and the national state.

—Russell Blackford

---

**BURTON, Raymond L.** *See* **TUBB, E.C.**

---

**BUSBY, F(rancis) M(arion).** American. Born in Indianapolis, Indiana, 11 March 1921. Educated at Washington State University, Pullman, B.Sc. 1946, B.Sc.E.E. 1947. Served in the National Guard, 1938–40, and Army of the United States, 1940–41, 1943–45. Married Elinor Doub in 1954; one daughter. Project supervisor, Alaska Communication System, Seattle, 1947–53; telegraph engineer, 1953–70; vice-president, Science Fiction Writers of America, 1974–76. Since 1970, freelance writer. Recipient: Hugo award, for editing, amateur category, 1960. Address: 2852 14th Avenue West, Seattle, Washington 98119, U.S.A.

SCIENCE-FICTION PUBLICATIONS

Novels (series: Barton; Rissa)

*Cage a Man* (Barton). New York, Doubleday, 1973; London, Hamlyn, 1979.
*The Proud Enemy* (Barton). New York, Berkley, 1975; London, Hamlyn, 1982.
*Rissa Kerguelen.* New York, Berkley, 1976; London, Futura, 1988.
*The Long View* (Rissa). New York, Berkley, 1976.
*Rissa Kerguelen* (omnibus). New York, Berkley, 1977; revised edition, as *Young Rissa, Rissa and Tregare, The Long View,* New York, Berkley, 3 vols., 1984.
*All These Earths.* New York, Berkley, 1978.
*Zelde M'Tana* (Rissa). New York, Dell, 1980.
*The Demu Trilogy (Cage a Man, The Proud Enemy, End of the Line)* (Barton). New York, Pocket Books, 1980.
*The Alien Debt* (Rissa). New York, Bantam, 1984; London, Futura, 1988.
*Star Rebel* (Rissa). New York, Bantam, 1984; London, Futura, 1987.
*Rebels' Quest* (Rissa). New York, Bantam, 1985; London, Futura, 1988.
*Rebels' Seed* (Rissa). New York, Bantam, 1986; London, Futura, 1988.
*The Rebel Dynasty: Volume I* (includes *Star Rebel* and *Rebel's Quest*). New York, Bantam, 1987.
*The Rebel Dynasty: Volume II* (includes *The Alien Debt* and *Rebels' Seed*). New York, Bantam, 1988.
*The Breeds of Men* (for young adults). New York, Bantam, 1988.
*Slow Freight.* New York, Bantam, 1991.

Short Stories

*Getting Home.* New York, Ace, 1987.

*

F.M. Busby comments:

I like to write science fiction because it gives me more room to breathe.

* * *

F.M. Busby deals with "characters who are pushed hard by necessity and who generally manage to cope," or he puts his characters into "predicaments that could not exist in our own past and future."

In novels such as *Rissa Kerguelen,* Busby develops the theme of identity, with convincing detail, ironic and comic touches, and a quality of space opera and adventure. In Busby, it is man (and woman) against the establishment, identity versus those who would seek to assimilate the individual. He writes of "rebels who find themselves"—dissidents and outlaws on their escape ships and hidden worlds.

Busby taps a rich mine of science fiction: parthenogenesis, Total Warfare Centers, maltreated aliens, "ships that come from nothing," telepathic murders, time-warped drives are all persuasively and painstakingly described.

He explores the motif of the self as well as any writer in the genre, often using nakedness as a symbol of a character's quest for self-discovery. Barton, in *The Demu Trilogy,* is a caged prisoner of crustacean creatures who attempt to rob humans of their own identities and re-create them in their own self-images. Busby investigates the motives of his characters, who plot for revenge and heroism and revel in the pleasure of that revenge and their own self-survival. Survival is a theme as important as identity in Busby's fiction; the two, in fact, are linked.

Three novels that deal with Bran Tregare, *Star Rebel, Rebel's Quest,* and *The Alien Debt* pursue these themes in greater detail. In Bran, Busby depicts a protagonist who rises above circumstance to sacrifice his own humanity for the good of humanity, though the reader sympathizes with Bran's pursuits and paradoxes. Bran does things that others cannot live with, but he is a person who also knows that "sometimes to survive you have to become a monster." He eventually achieves his goal (defeat of UET) and regains his identity through his love for Rissa and their daughter Lisele. Rissa, strong and stable, similarly wonders about her own identity, as someone who can turn from gentleness and love to ruthlessness and sadism. She comes in time to redress her problems and to understand how her life "was still beginning."

While Busby continued the saga in several other volumes, it is his short fiction that remains most impressive. "Tell Me All about Yourself," (in *New Dimensions 3,* edited by Robert Silverberg. New York, Avon, 1973), for example, is a bitter-sweet story about a lonely man's experience in a Necro house in Japan. The purpose of the place, supposedly, is that you do not have to talk to the women, but Dale selects a superlatively preserved virgin corpse whom he would actually like to get to know, someone, it seems, he had always been looking for. He feels foolish talking to the girl, so he steals her and casts her off to sea in a blaze, toward a death with dignity. Her only response to him had been a ubiquitous smile. Busby understates the macabre brilliantly in this story about the need for communication in love.

"If This Is Winnetka, You Must Be Judy," (in *Universe 5*, edited by Terry Carr. New York, Random House, 1974; London, Dobson, 1978), is a fascinating story, almost a spinoff of Heinlein's "All You Zombies—." The story deals with Larry Garth's ability to wake up periodically into a different time zone in his life. Busby gains a perfect sense of verisimilitude, with casual references to "circular causation," "research into the parameters of now," and "infancy skips." When we meet Garth, he has no idea how much of his existence had been lived "back and forth in bits and pieces." Busby uses this zig-zag experience as its own metaphor, set up against those of us who live "solely from one view that plod[s] along a line and [sees] only one consecutive past."

"First Person Plural" (in *Universe 10*, edited by Terry Carr. New York, Doubleday, 1980), employs a similar conceit. Ed Carlain awakens to discover he has undergone a consciousness transfer with a once-comatose Melanie Blake. Despite a sense of loss, Ed and Melanie come together to cope with their incongruities: "she was himself, one day behind himself." The two must share their lives with "one . . . memory between them." But the idea of confused sexual identity reveals the overall theme Busby wishes to convey: "If I can't accept ME, I can never accept any man."

—Richard Orodenker

---

**BUTLER, Octavia E(stelle).** American. Born in Pasadena, California, 22 June 1947. Educated at Pasadena College, 1965–68, A.A. 1968; California State University, 1969. Since 1970, freelance writer. Recipient: Hugo award, 1984; Nebula award, 1985; *Locus* award, 1985; Science Fiction Chronicle award, 1985. Address: c/o Warner Books Inc., 666 Fifth Avenue, New York, New York 10103, U.S.A.

### Science-Fiction Publications

Novels (series: Patternists; Xenogenesis)

*Patternmaster* (Patternists). New York, Doubleday, 1976; London, Sphere, 1978.
*Mind of My Mind* (Patternists). New York, Doubleday, 1977; London, Sidgwick and Jackson, 1978.
*Survivor* (Patternists). New York, Doubleday, and London, Sidgwick and Jackson, 1978.
*Kindred*. New York, Doubleday, 1979; London, Women's Press, 1988.
*Wild Seed* (Patternists). New York, Doubleday, and London, Sidgwick and Jackson, 1980.
*Clay's Ark* (Patternists). New York, St. Martin's Press, 1984.
Xenogenesis Trilogy:
 *Dawn*. New York, Warner, and London, Gollancz, 1987.
 *Adulthood Rites*. New York, Warner, and London, Gollancz, 1988.
 *Imago*. New York, Warner, and London, Gollancz, 1989.

*

Critical Study: *Suzy Charnas, Joan Vinge, and Octavia Butler* by Richard Law, with others, San Bernardino, California, Borgo Press, 1986.

Octavia E. Butler comments (1981):

I began writing fantasy and science fiction because these seemed to be the genres in which I could be freest, most creative. I had in mind from my first novel a series, a fictional history of people called Patternists who are, by mutation and selective breeding, developing psionic abilities. The books of this series are, in the order of the events they cover, *Wild Seed*, which begins in 1690, *Mind of My Mind* (present-day), *Survivor* (near future), and *Patternmaster* (distant future). The books are stories of power—adjustment to power, struggle for power, corruption by power. I bring together multi-racial groups of men and women who must cope with one another's differences as well as with new, not necessarily controllable, abilities within themselves.

A non-Patternist novel, *Kindred*, tells the story of a young black woman of the 1970's who is shifted back in time to the ante-bellum South where she is enslaved and forced to fend for herself in a world almost as hostile and alien to her as another planet.

* * *

Of the nine novels and the handful of short fiction pieces by Octavia Butler, several are among the most important science fiction works written in the late 20th-century. Her stories usually feature non-white female protagonists who nourish and heal people of all races. Their behavior in a racist human culture is always ameliorative. Frequently, the stories describe a disease in progress or significant occasions of sick or injured people treated and nursed by a central female character whose fundamental identity is that of healer—often with other powers. The stories, furthermore, depict the remorselessness of history in its capricious calendar and maverick process. The significant events of this history are those acts of strangely different and solitary individuals struggling for freedom from racism, sexism, and classism by means of the exotic tactics of psionic powers, vampirism, longevity, species metamorphosis, a knowledge of history, anthropology, and genetics. Above all, Butler's protagonists evoke compassion. Her stories do not insist upon particular solutions. They do encourage hope that some kind of enlightened species, related to humanity, can survive.

Five of Butler's novels are in the Patternmaster series; three are in the Xenogenesis series, and there is the single and singular novel, *Kindred*. Wisely, the novels are written so that each can be read by itself. Indeed, the unity and art of *Wild Seed* of the Patternmaster group is so complete that the companion works, although very fine, are not necessary to understanding *Wild Seed* and seem pale by comparison. Although written fourth of the five Patternmaster novels, *Wild Seed* is a prequel and genesis story for the series. It presents the four-thousand-year-old person, Doro, presumably male, whose life essence reincarnates in body after body, which he takes over absolutely, pre-emptive of the wills and lives of the victim owners of the bodies. This super-being roams the world and history, searching for humans with parapsychological powers whom he captures and brings together in communities, especially in Africa and America, so they can consolidate their powers and evolve into a superhuman species. In Africa, Doro discovers the woman Anyanwu, who is very nearly an immortal herself, as well as a shape-shifter and a healer. He wants her for a companion to escape his ancient loneliness, and as a breeding mother for his super species, his people. She hates him because he kills people to live. He controls her, even so, by threatening to kill the children he fathers upon her. Thus, their relationship is a coexistence constructed of mutual need and epic physical and emotional antagonism. The story occurs during the era of the slave trade and the middle passage, especially from Africa to America. The novel's extraordinary power arises from the accuracy of the elemental Anglo-African diction Butler creates to make the description and dialogue of Doro and Anyanwu. Among other influences, she acknowledges that of the Nigerian novelist Chinua Achebe, who has also employed such diction in his works. There is also the mythically impressive epic/heroic/tragic stature and career of the hate and love between titans, a vampire and an earth-mother—opposites most perfectly defined by each other.

*Mind of My Mind*, set in late 20th-century America, presents Doro and Emma (the original Anyanwu, we may surmise), who work to raise Doro's daughter Mary to a maturity that will include the destruction of Doro by Emma and Mary, so that Doro's people can be free from him. Emma, too, dies. The setting of *Survivor* is on another planet. Alanna, an Asian-African woman adopted by white missionaries, out of reach of the psionic power of the Patternists back on earth, tries to solve a racist conflict among humans and the two indigenous peoples of the planet. *Clay's Ark* is linked to the Patternmaster universe by its punneric title reference to "Clayarks." It is, however, connected to the Xenogenesis series in subject matter because of its story of humans infected by a disease that mutates and makes them superhuman and super prolific—harbingers of the end of human history. *Patternmaster*, the first novel published in the series, is the last in the fiction's chronological history, set in a feudally governed California in the far future where the psionic human Teray connects love with power to overcome his brother and become himself the Patternmaster.

The three novels of the Xenogenesis series, *Dawn*, (on the American Library Association's Recommended SF List for 1987), *Adulthood Rites*, and *Imago*, describe a radical biological revision of homo sapiens to escape the fundamental contradiction of the species: it puts great intelligence at the service of hierarchical behavior. Linking the three novels, the physically imposing black woman Lilith is pressed into service as nurse, mother, and leader by the alien Oankali, gene collectors and traders who are salvaging the remanent humans after a nuclear war on earth. The biology of the Oankali provides within their bodies all that is necessary for the infinite variations of powers possible through genetic engineering. So advanced is their mastery of genetic mutation that they grow spaceships and habitats, the dimensions of which must be measured in miles, and which in spite of, or indeed because of, being organic, are perfect in function and the comfort they provide. They are also reminiscent of the quite opposite fragilely diseased elegance of J.G. Ballard's *The Crystal World* and the inscrutable alien energy of Stanislaw Lem's *Solaris.* The Oankali do save humanity and improve it, but the price is the loss of original humanity.

*Kindred* transcends the science fiction genre. It employs magical realism and taps the literature of the slave narratives to make a story that is Kafkaesque. The African-American wife to caucasian Kevin Franklin, Edana (Dana) of mid-1970's Los Angeles is abruptly time-travelled to 1820's Maryland to become, eventually, if intermittently, a slave on the Weylin plantation, dedicated to nursing and protecting young Rufus Weylin, one of her many-times great grandfathers. At the same time, she cannot escape the pain and degradation American slavery created. The means of Dana's time-transportation is not explained. Like the seemingly random process of history, it admits to no cogent analysis. It happens as American slavery happened, insanely, interlocking forever the destinies of slaves and master. Butler's novel is excellent for the realism of the depiction of ante-bellum American slave culture. It deserves comparison with Alex Haley's *Roots* and Margaret Walker's *Jubilee*, and it is a worthy homage to authentic slave narratives such as that by Frederick Douglass, to which Butler has acknowledged a considerable debt.

Butler's shorter fiction also has considerable merit. "Speech Sounds" (*Isaac Asimov's Science Fiction Magazine*, mid-December 1983) won the 1984 Hugo award for best short story. In the ruins of a late 20th century California metropolitan area the now solitary, one-time UCLA professor Valerie Rye, dyslexic as a symptom of a world disease that has apparently attacked the language-encoding brain centers of humans, meets Obsidian, a man who, unlike her, cannot talk, but he can read. Their predicament is a variation of the Tower-of-Babel condition. Obsidian is gentle and attractive; indeed he is a caretaker type, as his wearing of the uniform of the defunct Los Angeles Police Department signifies. The courtship is quick and successful. Valerie's joy increases even as the two enter a neighborhood just in time to discover a man in the act of killing a woman. Obsidian shoots the man, and is himself shot and killed. Valerie immediately kills the assailant, but her new lover is dead—a terrible loss in this demolished world. Almost immediately, however, a pre-school boy and girl come out on the street looking for their mother—the dead woman. Both of them, sharing Valerie's form of the disease, can talk. Valerie is able to tell them she will take care of them.

"Bloodchild" (*Isaac Asimov's Science Fiction Magazine*, June 1984) won the 1985 Hugo, Nebula, and Locus awards for best novelette. It revolves around a humanity enslaved by an insectoid species, the Tlic, perhaps cockroach-like. The Tlic lay their eggs in the bodies of the humans, where they gestate and are cut out of the humans at birth. In the story, the relationship, or the colonization of humanity by the Tlic, is already traditional and as conflicted with deeply conditioned master-slave dynamics as those exhibited in, for example, the historic slave culture of the United States. At the story's end the profoundest horror is in the resigned serenity of Lien (human woman) in her relationship with T'Gatoi (Tlic female); when Lien begins a term as incubator/host of T'Gatoi's egg, she lies down naked with the velvet-hulled, segmented body of her mistress.

"The Evening and the Morning and the Night" (*Omni*, May 1987) was nominated for a 1988 Hugo award for best novelette. Like "Speech Sounds," it turns on the effects of a bizarre disease, this time called "Duryea-Gode Disease (DGD)." One irony is that the disease is caused in the children of parents cured of cancer by the drug "Hedeonco." Victims are suicidally self-mutilating and exhibit as a principal symptom, quixotically, the ability to concentrate with extraordinary persistence, so that their work in art and science is often brilliant. The story's heroine, Lynn Mortimer, is a DGD victim who has the special property of giving off a pheromone that prevents DGD victims from becoming suicidal and lets them find life worth living. The story is about how an unusually weird person, even stranger than the people in her already weird class, can find acceptance and meaning in life.

Fortunately for SF readers, Butler is only in mid-career, and already she has earned the great respect and admiration of other writers as well as of readers.

—John Pfeiffer

---

**BUTLER, Samuel.** Also wrote as Cellarious. British. Born at Langar Rectory, near Bingham, Nottinghamshire, 4 December 1835. Educated at Shrewsbury School, Shropshire, 1848–54; St. John's College, Cambridge 1854–58, B.A. (honours) 1858; studied painting at Heatherley's School, London, 1865. Sheep farmer, Rangitata district, New Zealand, 1859–64; settled in London, 1864; exhibited and composed music. *Died 18 June 1902.*

SCIENCE-FICTION PUBLICATIONS

Novels

*Erewhon; or, Over the Range.* London, Trubner, 1872; revised edition, 1872; London, Richards, 1901; New York, Dutton, 1910.
*Erewhon Revisited Twenty Years Later.* London, Richards, 1901; New York, Dutton, 1910.

OTHER PUBLICATIONS

Novel

*The Way of All Flesh*, edited by R.A. Streatfeild. London, Richards, 1903; New York, Dutton, 1910.

Plays

*Narcissus: A Dramatic Cantata*, words and music by Butler and Henry Festing Jones. London, Weekes, 1888.
*Ulysses: A Dramatic Oratorio*, words and music by Butler and Henry Festing Jones. London, Weekes, and Chicago, Summy, 1904.

Verse

*Seven Sonnets and a Psalm of Montreal*, edited by R.A. Streatfeild. Privately printed, 1904.

Other

*A First Year in Canterbury Settlement.* London, Longman, 1863; revised edition, edited by R.A. Streatfeild, London, Fifield, 1914; New York, Dutton, 1915.
*The Evidence for the Resurrection of Jesus Christ as Given by the Four Evangelists, Critically Examined* (published anonymously). Privately printed, 1865.
*The Fair Haven: A Work in Defence of the Miraculous Element in Our Lord's Ministry upon Earth.* London, Trubner, 1873; New York, Kennerley, 1913.
*Life and Habit: An Essay after a Completer View of Evolution.* London, Trubner, 1878; New York, Dutton, 1911.
*Evolution Old and New.* London, Hardwicke and Bogue, and Salem, Massachusetts, Cassino, 1879.
*Unconscious Memory.* London, Bogue, 1880; New York, Dutton, 1911.
*Alps and Sanctuaries of Piedmont and the Canton Ticino.* London, Bogue, 1881; New York, Dutton, 1913.
*Selections from Previous Works.* London, Trubner, 1884.
*Gavottes, Minuets, Fugues, and Other Short Pieces for Piano*, with Henry Festing Jones. London, Novello, 1885.
*Holbein's "Dance."* London, Trubner, 1886.
*Luck or Cunning as a Main Means of Organic Modification?* London, Trubner, 1887.
*Ex Voto: An Account of the Sacro Monte or New Jerusalem at Varallo-Sesia.* London, Trubner, 1888; revised edition, 1889.
*A Lecture on the Humour of Homer.* Cambridge, Metcalfe, 1892.
*On the Trapanese Origin of the Odyssey.* Cambridge, Metcalfe, 1893.
*The Life and Letters of Dr. Samuel Butler.* London, Murray, 2 vols., 1896.
*The Authoress of the Odyssey.* London, Longman, 1897; New York, Dutton, 1922.
*Shakespeare's Sonnets Reconsidered, and in Part Rearranged.* London, Longman, 1899; New York, Dutton, 1927.
*Essays on Life, Art and Science*, edited by R.A. Streatfeild. London, Richards, 1904; Port Washington, New York, Kennikat Press, 1970.
*God the Known and God the Unknown*, edited by R.A. Streatfeild. London, Fifield, 1909; New Haven, Connecticut, Yale University Press, 1917.
*The Note Books of Samuel Butler: Selections*, edited by Henry Festing Jones. London, Fifield, 1912; New York, Kennerley, 1913.
*The Humour of Homer and Other Essays*, edited by R.A. Streatfeild. London, Fifield, and New York, Kennerley, 1913.
*The Collected Works* (Shrewsbury Edition), edited by Henry Festing Jones and A.T. Bartholomew. London, Cape, and New York, Dutton, 20 vols., 1923–26.
*Butleriana*, edited by A.T. Bartholomew. London, Nonesuch Press, 1932; as *Samuel Butler's Note Books: Some New Extracts*, New York, Random House, 1932.
*Samuel Butler's Note Books: Further Extracts*, edited by A.T. Bartholomew. London, Cape, 1934.
*Letters Between Samuel Butler and Miss E.M.A. Savage*, edited by Geoffrey Keynes and Brian Hill. London, Cape, 1935.
*The Essential Samuel Butler*, edited by G.D.H. Cole. London, Cape, and New York, Dutton, 1950.
*Samuel Butler's Note Books: Selections*, edited by Geoffrey Keynes and Brian Hill. London, Cape, 1951.
*Correspondence of Butler and His Sister May*, edited by Daniel F. Howard. Berkeley, University of California Press, 1962.
*The Family Letters 1841–1886*, edited by Arnold Silver. London, Cape, and Stanford, California, Stanford University Press, 1962.
*The Book of the Machines* (as Cellarious). London, Quarto Press, 1975.
*Samuel Butler on the Resurrection*, edited by Robert Johnstone. Gerrards Cross, Buckinghamshire, Smythe, 1980.

Translator, *The Iliad of Homer.* London, Longman, 1898; New York, Dutton, 1921.
Translator, *The Odyssey.* London, Longman, 1900; New York, Dutton, 1922.
Translator, *Hesiod's Works and Days.* Privately printed, 1923.

*

Bibliography: *The Career of Samuel Butler: A Bibliography* by Stanley B. Harkness, London, Lane, 1955; *Three Victorian Travel Writers; An Annotated Bibliography of Criticism on Mrs. Frances Milton Trollope, Samuel Butler, and Robert Louis Stevenson* by Frederick John Bethke, Boston, Hall, 1977.

Critical Studies: *Samuel Butler: A Memoir* by H.F. Jones, London, Macmillan, 2 vols., 1919; *The Triple Thinkers* by Edmund Wilson, New York, Harcourt Brace, and London, Oxford University Press, 1938; *Samuel Butler and The Way of All Flesh* by G.D.H. Cole, London, Home and Van Thal, 1947, as *Samuel Butler*, Denver, Swallow, 1948; *Samuel Butler* by P.N. Furbank, London, Cambridge University Press, 1948; *Darwin and Butler: Two Versions of Evolution* by Basil Willey, London, Chatto and Windus, and New York, Harcourt Brace, 1960; *Samuel Butler* by Lee E. Holt, New York, Twayne, 1964; *Erewhons of the Exe: Samuel Butler as Painter, Photographer, and Art Critic* by Elinor Shaffer, London, Reaktion, 1988.

* * *

Samuel Butler was the son of an Anglican rector, whom he later immortalized in his grim autobiographical novel of Victorian family hypocrisy *The Way of All Flesh.* He graduated from Cambridge in classics, then worked for one season among the poor in London, as a result of which he did not become a clergyman but moved instead to New Zealand. From 1859 to 1864, he managed there a sheep-ranch, began to write about the country and about the new and sensational theory of evolution, and gathered the elements for his novel *Erewhon.* His other writings attacked received opinion in religion, biology, philology, and child-rearing, proposing alternatives which are today generally seen as eccentric, though the controversy around his Neo-Lamarckism is by no means over.

Though Butler's literary masterpiece is *The Way of All Flesh*, some reversals from his country of Erewhon (itself to be read backwards as most other names in the novel) are as interesting and more modern. This civilization, found (as the subtitle has it) "over the range," in an unexplored part of the traditionally upside-down Antipodes, is used for satirical discussions; most importantly, the Erewhonians establish to their satisfaction that machines are using mankind as a means for their indirect evolution and ban all of them, beginning with clocks and watches. Other exposures of the ulterior moral motives, and thus of the hypocrisy of Victorian bourgeois society are the perfectly logical value-transferral between illness and crime, Unreasons and Reason, or religion and banking. Unfortunately, Butler's overall stance is not at all consistent; for a crucial example, if the time-quantifying tool of clocks is banned, the basic agent of quantifying in modern civilization, money, should logically also be banned instead of being promoted as the religion of Musical Banks. Thus the various elements of Erewhon become mutually incompatible as the sketch of a believable alternative. As Edmund Wilson remarked, "Butler, though he could be most amusing about people's mercenary motives, was too much a middle-class man himself to analyze the social system, in which . . . he occupied a privileged position" (*The Shores of Light*, New York, 1967). The novel dissolves into a string of more or less unrelated satires of the surfaces of Victorian civilization, hesitating between Swiftian bite and middle-class propriety, mildly diverting paradox and cynical justification (though, beside the amusing passages, the fable of the Unborn—who foster the libido of their parents in order to incarnate—retains a certain Platonic charm).

The continuation, *Erewhon Revisited*, is more coherent but less broadly relevant, focussing as it does on the religious cult that has sprung up in Erewhon around the totally misunderstood narrator of the first novel, now promoted to "Sun-child" in a clear parody of Christ (making this novel a continuation of Butler's *Fair Haven* at least as much as of the earlier satire). What is worse, this sequel retracts even the partial estrangement of *Erewhon*, as well as its own satire on the founding of religions, by its final horizon of salvation through annexation to the British Empire.

Butler's SF, thus, remains incidentally amusing reading, especially in the first book. However, its primary importance is the satirical prefiguration of what will later become a much more anguished and wider debate on reification and "machine consciousness' in cybernetics, as well as in the general argument about controlled evolution. Butler had therefore an important influence on subsequent SF, from such Victorians as his friend R.E. Dudgeon through J. Carne-Ross, W.J. Roe, and W. Grove to G.B. Shaw's drama-cycle *Back to Methuselah* and some American SF. But his main problems will be picked up and brought to more sophisticated levels by Wells, Zamyatin, and Capek. There remains the striking freshness and irreverence of Butler's best satirical passages.

—Darko Suvin

---

# C

**CAIDIN, Martin.** American. Born in New York City, 14 September 1927. Served in the merchant marine, 1945; United States Air Force, 1947–50: Sergeant. Married 1) Grace Caidin in 1952 (divorced); 2) Dee Dee Caidin, one daughter. Consultant, correspondent, and broadcaster on aviation and civil defense: associate editor, *Air News* and *Air Tech*; consultant to New York State Civil Defense Commission, 1950–62, Air Force Missile Test Center, Cape Canaveral, 1955, and Federal Aviation Agency, 1961–64; correspondent, Metropolitan Broadcasting (radio and TV), 1961–62, Founder, Martin Caidin Associates Inc. Address: c/o Outbound, 13416 University Station, Gainesville, Florida 32604, U.S.A.

SCIENCE-FICTION PUBLICATIONS

Novels (series: Steve Austin)

*The Long Night*. New York, Dodd Mead, 1956.
*Marooned*. New York, Dutton, and London, Hodder and Stoughton, 1964.
*The Last Fathom*. New York, Meredith Press, and London, Joseph, 1967.
*No Man's World*. New York, Dutton, 1967.
*Aquarius Mission*. New York, Bantam, 1968; London, Corgi, 1978.
*Four Came Back*. New York, McKay, 1968.
*The God Machine*. New York, Dutton, 1969.
*The Mendelov Conspiracy*. New York, Meredith Press, 1969; London, W.H. Allen, 1971; as *Encounter Three*, New York, Pinnacle, 1978.
*The Cape*. New York, Doubleday, 1971.
*Cyborg* (Austin). New York, Arbor House, 1972; London, W.H. Allen, 1973.
*Operation Nuke* (Austin). New York, Arbor House, 1973; London, W.H. Allen, 1974.
*Planetfall*. New York, Coward McCann, 1974.
*High Crystal* (Austin). New York, Arbor House, 1974; London, W.H. Allen, 1975.
*Cyborg IV* (Austin). New York, Arbor House, 1975; London, W.H. Allen, 1977.
*Star Bright*. New York, Bantam, 1980.
*Killer Station*. New York, Baen, 1984.
*The Messiah Stone*. New York, Baen, 1986.
*Zoboa*. New York, Baen, 1986.
*Exit Earth*. New York, Baen, 1987.
*Prison Ship*. New York, Baen, 1989.
*Beamriders!* New York, Baen, 1989.
*Dark Messiah*. New York, Baen, 1990.
*Ghosts of the Air*. New York, Bantam, 1991.

OTHER PUBLICATIONS

Novels

*Devil Takes All*. New York, Dutton, 1966; London, W.H. Allen, 1968.
*Anytime, Anywhere*. New York, Dutton, 1969; London, W.H. Allen, 1970.
*Almost Midnight*. New York, Morrow, 1971; London, Bantam, 1974.
*Maryjane Tonight at Angels Twelve*. New York, Doubleday, 1972.
*The Last Dogfight*. Boston, Houghton Mifflin, and London, Weidenfeld and Nicolson, 1974.
*Three Corners to Nowhere*. New York, Bantam, and London, Corgi, 1975.
*Whip*. Boston, Houghton Mifflin, 1976; London, Corgi, 1977.
*Wingborn*. New York, Bantam, and London, Corgi, 1979.
*Manfac*. New York, Dell, 1981.

Play

Television Play; *Exo-Man*, with Howard Rodman and Henri Simoneon, 1977.

Other

*Jets, Rockets and Guided Missiles*, with David C. Cooke. New York, McBride, 1951; revised edition, as *Rockets and Missiles, Past and Present*, 1954.
*Rockets Beyond the Earth*. New York, McBride, 1952.
*Worlds in Space*. New York, Holt, and London, Sidgwick and Jackson, 1954.
*Zero!*, with M. Okumiya and J. Horikoshi. New York, Dutton, 1956; London, Cassell, 1957.
*Vanguard!* New York, Dutton, 1957.
*Samurai!*, with Saburo Sakai and Fred Saito. New York, Dutton, 1957; London, Kimber, 1959.
*Air Force: A Pictorial History of American Airpower*. New York, Rinehart, 1957.
*Countdown for Tomorrow*. New York, Dutton, 1958.
*Thunderbolt!*, with Robert S. Johnson. New York, Rinehart, 1958.
*The Zero Fighter*, with M. Okumiya and J. Horikoshi. London, Cassell, 1958.
*Spaceport, U.S.A.* New York, Dutton, 1959.
*War for the Moon*. New York, Dutton, 1959; as *Race for the Moon*, London, Kimber, 1960.
*Let's Go Flying!* New York, Dutton, 1959.
*Boeing 707*. New York, Dutton, 1959.
*X-15: Man's First Flight into Space*. New York, Rutledge, 1959.
*Black Thursday*. New York, Dutton, 1960.
*Golden Wings: A Pictorial History of the United States Navy and Marine Corps in the Air*. New York, Random House, 1960.
*The Astronauts*. New York, Dutton, 1960; revised edition, 1961.
*The Night Hamburg Died*. New York, Ballantine, 1960; London, New English Library, 1966.
*A Torch to the Enemy: The Fire Raid on Tokyo*. New York, Ballantine, 1960.
*Man into Space*. New York, Pyramid, 1961.
*Thunderbirds!* New York, Dutton, 1961.
*The Long, Lonely Leap*, with Joseph W. Kittinger. New York, Dutton, 1961.

*Cross-Country Flying*. New York, Dutton, 1961.
*Test Pilot* (for children). New York, Dutton, 1961.
*This Is My Land*, photographs by James Yarnell. New York, Random House, 1962.
*I Am Eagle*, with G.S. Titov. Indianapolis, Bobbs Merrill, 1962.
*Rendezvous in Space*. New York, Dutton, 1962.
*Aviation and Space Medicine*, with Grace Caidin, New York, Dutton, 1962.
*The Man-in-Space Dictionary*. New York, Dutton, 1963.
*The Moon: New World for Men*. Indianapolis, Bobbs Merrill, 1963.
*Red Star in Space*. New York, Crowell Collier, 1963.
*The Power of Decision*. New York, Dell, 1963.
*Overture to Space*. New York, Duell, 1963.
*The Long Arm of America*. New York, Dutton, 1963.
*By Apollo to the Moon* (for children). New York, Dutton, 1963.
*The Silken Angels: A History of Parachuting*. Philadelphia, Lippincott, 1964.
*The Winged Armada*, New York, Dutton, 1964.
*Hydrospace*. New York, Dutton, 1964.
*Everything But the Flak*. New York, Duell, 1964.
*The Mission*, with Edward Hymoff. Philadelphia, Lippincott, 1964.
*Wings into Space*. New York, Holt Rinehart, 1964.
*The Mighty Hercules* (for children). New York, Dutton, 1964.
*Why Space?* New York, Messner, 1965.
*Barnstorming*. New York, Duell, 1965.
*The Greatest Challenge*. New York, Dutton, 1965.
*The Ragged, Rugged Warriors*. New York, Dutton, 1966; London, Severn House, 1980.
*Flying Forts*. New York, Meredith Press, 1968.
*Me 109: Willy Messerschmitt's Peerless Fighters*. New York, Ballantine, 1968; London, Macdonald, 1969.
*Fork-Tailed Devil: The P-38*. New York, Ballantine, 1971.
*Destination Mars*. New York, Doubleday, 1972.
*When War Comes*. New York, Morrow, 1972.
*Bicycles in War*, with Jay Barbree. New York, Hawthorn, 1974.
*The Tigers Are Burning*. New York, Hawthorn, 1974.
*The Saga of Iron Annie*. New York, Doubleday, 1979.
*Kill Devil Hill: Discovering the Secret of the Wright Brothers 1899–1909*, with Harry Combs, Boston, Houghton Mifflin, 1979; London, Secker and Warburg, 1980.
*Ragwings and Heavy Iron: The Agony and Ecstasy of Flying History's Greatest Warbirds*. Boston, Houghton Mifflin, 1984.

Editor, *The DC-3: The Story of the Dakota*, by Carroll V. Glines and Wendell F. Moseley, London, Deutsch, 1967.

* * *

Author of numerous nonfiction works concerning aviation and aerospace technology, Martin Caidin builds on his experience as a military and commercial pilot, stunt flyer, balloonist, parachutist, and nuclear warfare specialist to provide convincing background for his speculative fiction. This fiction, projecting forward from existing programs and set in the present or near future, consistently warns that America's naive idealism about peaceful cooperation in outer space should be tempered by a realistic awareness of nationalistic competition, that our technological capabilities are outstripping our emotional and psychological controls, and that a technological, materialistic, and empirical approach to phenomena fails fully to account for and control such phenomena.

Some of Caidin's books explore what could go wrong with a space flight: personal problems that affect efficiency (nagging wives, wayward children, secret affairs, drugs, and blackmail in *The Cape*); the possibility of foreign sabotage on the ground (*The Cape, No Man's World*), or in space with laser beams (*Cyborg IV, The Mendelov Conspiracy*), or well-placed explosives (*Killer Station*); technical and mechanical difficulties (*Marooned*); bombardment by meteors and invasion of alien bacteria (*Four Came Back*); hostile confrontation on landing (Russian and Chinese in *No Man's World*); or just incompetence or politics at NASA. *No Man's World*, in particular, raises the question of jurisdiction in space, while *Beamriders!* explores the real possibilities of a mission to the far side of the moon and a laser-transport system to "beam" human beings from place to place on Earth and into Space. Minor characters and anecdotes from one book become major characters and events in another. For example, in the background of several books is a boorish newspaper man who intrudes where he doesn't belong, but who gets his story and ultimately helps out. In *Marooned*, this brash, intuitive reporter breaks through NASA security to learn the truth of an astronaut's plight; in *The Mendelov Conspiracy* he investigates UFO's that prove part of an international scientists' plot to force the world to nuclear disarmament.

As nuclear warfare specialist for the State of New York, Caidin analyzed the effects of nuclear weapons on potential U.S. targets; as a result of his experience, his best "fictive" pieces effectively capture the full horror of nuclear accidents or wars and other modern technological dangers. The nightmare possibility of nuclear energy mishandled remains a persistent Caidin theme, one he frequently equates with a fire-breathing dragon, perhaps dormant at first, but ready to rise up and destroy in an instant of all-consuming fire. *Devil Takes All, Almost Midnight*, and *Beamriders!* postulate nuclear blackmail. Step by step, *The Long Night* tersely and vividly portrays a family and town confronted with an atomic explosion and resultant fire-storm, while *Star Bright* convincingly delineates how a secret fusion experiment goes out of control, produces a microstar that implodes into a black hole, warps time and space, and nearly destroys earth. Both novels, horrifying in detail and in credibility, demonstrate Caidin's interest in how most people react to disaster or panic: a few bravely and rationally, others stoically, but most selfishly and irrationally. As others deteriorate around them, succumbing to emotional fears, nightmares, and personal compulsions, Caidin's heroes seem to grow in strength, to shoulder the burdens of others, accept responsibility with calm, and become the eye of calm in the center of the hurricane of forces that swirl around them. The hero of *Three Corners to Nowhere* rides calmly into the tumultuous storms of the Devil's Triangle, chasing a "Flying Dutchman" Gulfstream airliner, caught in a time warp, while an unlikely astronaut in *Killer Station* chances his own life to save New York from the impact of a sabotaged nuclear space station in "deorbit" and the astronauts of *Four Came Back* are willing to sacrifice themselves rather than bring back "a plague from space." Caidin's heroes can be as harsh and peremptory in act and judgement as are his villains, but their sense of human responsibility is what spurs them to superhuman efforts.

A Caidin hero is often a tough, well-trained military or ex-military man, who is proud of his work, devoted to his country, and able to face up to and control his fear while those around him panic or succumb. Usually a onetime test pilot, he works hard and plays hard. He has an instinct for recognizing expertise in others and is willing to share labor with equals to get a hard job done. However, he does not tolerate fools easily; at his best, he can cut straight to the heart of a problem. His is often a world of machines, whether in outer space or hydrospace, but he has learned that, in a crunch, it is himself, human guts and human reason, that he must rely upon. He is often excited and inspired by a strikingly beautiful, intelligent, independent woman (secret agent, archaeologist, oceanographer, bionics expert, astronaut), but usually this romance remains unresolved or the woman dies suddenly, violently. Sometimes, however, the Caidin hero is a scientist, but one who is so good at his field that he offends bureaucratic strictures, and pursues his own vision in his own way.

Caidin's villains, in turn, if not destructive natural or unnatural forces, human nature, or America's political counterparts, are men whom experience has soured, whom fanaticism has warped, or whom loss of physical prowess, love, or profession through disease, accident, or injury has embittered. These men have lost sight of humanistic values and act only out of self-interest. In *Almost Midnight*, a disillusioned Vietnam hero, a fighter pilot drummed out of the military and civil flying by a bad leg and a rebellious spirit, teams up with other failed pilots to hijack five atomic bombs, to set one off eighty miles east of Los Angeles, and thereby to blackmail the nation. The resultant Air Force, FBI, CIA, FAA, NSA, and State Department investigation reveals another enemy: bureaucratic infighting or nationalistic competition that limits cooperation. In *Killer Station*, the villains are suicidal Islamic fanatics anxious to precipitate war between the United States and the Soviet Union. Caidin's villains also include human mobs who turn into subhuman beasts—a theme in *Four Came Back*, in which earthlings fear alien bacteria; in *The Long Night*, in which rumors of radiation sends hordes flying; in *Almost Midnight*, in which terrorist threats to nuke major United States cities bring hysteria and death; in *The Mendelov Conspiracy*, in which mobs attack nuclear stockpiles; in *The Messiah Stone*, in which Hindu worshippers panic at word of a cholera attack; and in *Star Bright*, in which a sea of crazed fanatics, "a mass tide of two-legged lemmings," fearful of atomic destruction and "ready to accept their own destruction if necessary," wipe out nuclear reactors and storm an experimental center kamikaze-style. Caidin's key characters argue that survival of the many outweighs the rights of the few, and advocate force wielded by a military elite to quell irresponsible, destructive mobs born of irrational fears. *The Messiah Stone* delineates such mob potential at its most chilling: a fiery yellow "diamond" from space, thought to have been in the meteor that was the Star of Bethlehem, endows its possessor with an almost mystical power to sway those around him. Those powers were wielded by Jesus, by Hitler, by a surviving Nazi fanatic, and, at the close of the book, by Caidin's main character and supposed hero, a trained mercenary, a ruthless, sadistic killer, determined to dominate the world. This book has a particularly nasty twist in that the character with whom readers are asked to most closely identify proves most deadly.

Caidin is fascinated by the idea of man and machine becoming a harmonic single entity—either in terms of sensitive reaction time, or else literally, as in the Steve Austin series. Pilots at critical moments "see" as if one with their machine. In *The God Machine*, the ultimate computer interacts with human operators and mimics and transcends human logic, but a programming fault results in the horror of logic being carried out to literal, absurd, and inhuman ends by a machine which man has made self-sustaining and self-protected. In *The Last Fathom*, the developer of a revolutionary submarine maneuvers at incredible depths to prevent the devastation of the free world by a Soviet doomsday weapon intended to open up a volcanic fissure near Puerto Rico and thereby to unleash a series of natural cataclysms. *Cyborg* (popularized in the television series *The Six Million Dollar Man* and *The Bionic Woman*) is a fascinating and highly technical dramatization of the reconstruction of a test pilot's body, with microscopic units replacing the nervous system, and a fusion of bone and metal replacing missing legs and arm until the man becomes more than mere man, capable of gruelling (and incredible) missions to expose Russian submarine bases and steal experimental planes. With emphasizing the courage and strength needed for controlling and surviving in experimental machinery, Caidin also demythologizes their glamour by focusing on practical, minute-to-minute detail. *Operation Nuke* and *High Crystal* feature further cyborg wonders as Austin plays fugitive to infiltrate a terrorist organization dependent on nuclear arms and then races to find the power source of an ancient Indian civilization—a giant crystal. In *Cyborg IV*, Austin, linked "symbionically" to his space vehicle to control it with thought and reflex action, attacks Russians in space to protect military security. Such missions are the price his country demands as payment for not leaving him a helpless paraplegic. *Killer Station* includes men whose arms or whose legs, lost in accidents, have been replaced by hardware that makes them especially valuable in space.

Caidin's novels are best when grounded in the realities of science and technology. Caidin is good at explaining, in layman's terms, particulars about flight, space, and disaster, about how our solar system functions, how fusion occurs, and so forth; or, as he does in *The Last Fathom*, about earthquakes, tidal waves, and the sea. *Planetfall*, an account of space exploration, manned and unmanned, including a hypothetical trip to Venus in 1998, is typical of his skill at making the complex clear. Caidin's teaching technique depends on digressions, flashbacks, reverie, and experts explaining to neophytes, with the latter being most effective for reducing scientific and technological complexities to readily understood terms. Caidin's laymen often reduce a theory to its essentials and express it as a highly visual and common analogy. These techniques allow Caidin to provide a wealth of interesting material, though they occasionally slow down the plot. Caidin blends fact and fiction, the feasible and the speculative. Quotes by real historical personages (especially Einstein and well-known Soviet and American astronauts) lend credibility to his tales of the emotions and conflicts of the near future.

However, at its weakest, Caidin's prose is labored, his characters two-dimensional, his messages preachy, his plots melodramatic and sprawling. Motives are unclear, and sex and violence are often gratuitous. *The Messiah Stone* involves multiple teams destroying and being destroyed, and characters changing personalities abruptly. *Three Corners to Nowhere* tacks together several different plot possibilities, sets up a chain of unbelievable coincidences, and suddenly kills off the main character in a crash with a ghost ship just when the mystery has supposedly been solved. *Beamriders!* presupposes Venezuelans outdoing Americans and Soviets in laser technology. *Prison Ship* involves a plot to conquer the world by the inmates on a hijacked interstellar prison ship and their convict earthlink at Florida's Old Millford prison. The protagonists, a computer genius murderer and his alien counterpart, don't meet until halfway through the book. Much of Caidin's dialogue is simplistic, and his flashback technique is not always controlled.

In other words, Caidin's works sometimes descend to television movie quality, though at other times, their nuclear and space technology science is well worth reading. Perhaps Caidin's greatest contribution to science fiction is in illuminating the relationship between man and machine to show that man must avoid becoming machinelike if he is to remain human, in capturing in everyday terms the enormous destructive forces a nuclear accident might unleash, and in making clear the vital importance of conquering ego and of cooperating with honesty and trust in times of national and international emergency.

—Andrew and Gina Macdonald

---

**CALLAHAN, William.** *See* **GALLUN, Raymond Z.**

---

**CALLENBACH, Ernest.** American. Born in Williamsport, Pennsylvania, 3 April 1929. Educated at the University of Chicago, Ph.B. 1949, M.A. 1953. Married Christine Leefeldt in 1978; one daughter and one son. Publicity writer and assistant editor, 1955–58, and since 1958, editor, *Film Quarterly*, and film book editor, University of California Press, Berkeley. Founder, Banyan Tree Books, 1975. Address: University of California Press, 2120 Berkeley Way, Berkeley, California 94720, U.S.A.

SCIENCE-FICTION PUBLICATIONS

Novels

*Ecotopia: A Novel about Ecology, People, and Politics in 1999.* Berkeley, California, Banyan Tree, 1975; London, Pluto Press, 1978.
*Ecotopia Emerging.* Berkeley, California, Banyan Tree, 1981.

OTHER PUBLICATIONS

Other

*Our Modern Art: The Movies.* Chicago, University of Chicago Center for the Study of Liberal Education for Adults, 1955.
*Living Poor with Style.* New York, Bantam, 1971.
*The Art of Friendship,* with Christine Leefeldt. New York, Pantheon, 1979.
*The Ecotopian Encyclopedia for the 80's.* Berkeley, California, And/Or Press, 1981.
*A Citizen Legislature.* Berkeley, California, Banyan Tree, 1985.
*Humphrey the Wayward Whale* (for children), with Christine Leefeldt. Berkeley, California, HeyDay, 1986.
*Publisher's Lunch.* Berkeley, California, Ten Speed Press, 1989.

*

Ernest Callenbach comments:

It might be reassuring to other writers to know that *Ecotopia,* which has now been translated into eight languages and sold about 300,000 copies, was rejected by all major New York publishing houses; it was then initially published by the author and a group of his friends, using the employee-owned book wholesale house, Bookpeople, as distributor. Presumably the allergy of establishment publishers to the work was due to its being half-novel, half-tract; it is, so to speak, "politics fiction," making certain fictional assumptions and following their consequences much as normal sci-fi does with scientific assumptions; its technology is actually quite conservative.

The favourable response that *Ecotopia* received (except in Britain, where its Californian origins seem to have ensured disdain for it except among scientists and a few ecologically sophisticated readers) led me to write a prequel, *Ecotopia Emerging,* which sketches a scenario for how Ecotopia came into existence.

* * *

Ernest Callenbach is not a professional writer of science fiction; he is a reformer, an environmentalist, a small-is-beautiful proponent of the shift from a society devoted to technological progress to one more closely allied with nature. In his non-fiction book, *Living Poor with Style,* he suggests that, "Out of the welter of present industrial society it will probably take us several generations to sort out the few things that are essential to mankind—and to reject the others, of which no truly human or holy use can be made." But in three later books his imaginary land of Ecotopia, formed by secession of Washington, Oregon, and Northern California, is a model of what utopia based on environmentalist principles could look like. *Ecotopia* is a utopian novel in the traditional sense; *The Ecotopian Encyclopedia for the 80's* is a non-fictional series of entries on how to live in the Ecotopian manner; *Ecotopia Emerging* describes events leading to the secession. Together they form a fairly complete picture of the problems of attaining an ideal society, life in that society, and the impact of that society on a traditional 20th century society.

*Ecotopia* describes a very different society from that of the United States, and the six-week assignment in the new country of investigative reporter Will Weston is the first officially arranged American visit in the 19 years following secession. Both governments have hidden agendas: the American to restore good relations and perhaps lead the wandering states to return home, the Ecotopian to teach the visitor to understand their way of life and convert countrymen to that view. The old problem of utopian writing, how to justify long descriptive passages, is solved by alternating excerpts from Weston's private diary with formal columns sent by way of Canada to his newspaper. The real story is in the contrast between the two kinds of reporting and in Weston's slow change from skeptical hostility to friendliness and, eventually, conversion. There are numerous friendly Ecotopians who help the visitor to adjust to and understand the new society, but the most important character besides Weston is Marissa, a free-spirited woman whose love probably has much to do with his decision to remain in Ecotopia. President Vera Allwen, who appears mostly on T.V. but meets with Weston once in person, takes the important but comparatively minor role of showing the visitor that Ecotopian individuals and their government are very much alike—independent and caring.

Although *Ecotopia Emerging* is billed as a "prequel" to the earlier novel, its action begins in 1986—secession is accomplished in 1988 rather than in 1981—and the earlier novel is actually referred to as a source of ideas for the Survivalist Party, which engineers the whole project. A new character, 17-year-old Lou Swift, invents a cheap and efficient solar-electric power cell, Marissa's cancer-ridden mother blows up a chemical plant, her brother Ben may or may not have planted nuclear bombs in major cities, and Vera Allwen, a state senator, slowly moves to leadership of the gradually more aggressive party. The secession begins on a small scale and spreads; the expected civil war fails to materialize (the "Helicopter War" of 1982, important in *Ecotopia,* is not mentioned); an agreement is reached for peace between Ecotopia and the United States; the Ecotopian constitution is written. This prequel is even more polemical than its predecessor, but it is much more interesting as a story and much more characteristic of science fiction. It is also, as an early reviewer pointed out, lucid and thought-provoking.

Although the Ecotopian ideal is highly acceptable to utopian-minded readers, its creation and continuance, as portrayed in the three books, is not without flaws and has been called impossible by more than one critic. Ecotopia is peace-loving and non-violent, but it must be noted that this utopia achieved its independence by threatening to plant nuclear bombs in every major American city and by blasting several thousand helicopters out of the sky. It maintains its independence by the implied threat of willingness to do so again (although the revisionist prequel does not mention the helicopter war). Even more difficult to accept is the idea that all these people have not only suddenly become more sane and concerned for others than the rest of the world but able to continue such behavior ever after. Such flaws do not appear on first reading; what makes Ecotopia a significant work is that even when subsequent readings highlight such drawbacks, the desirability of this warm and rational society is undiminished.

Whether Callenbach will write more novels that are utopian or even peripherally science fiction, as these are, is problematic. His interest is clearly in the reform of society, not the writing of fiction. On the other hand, there are few better ways to get a message across than to take advantage of the flexibility science fiction and utopian writing offer. For that reason, *Ecotopia* continues to be a work of some significance to those who find today's society less than perfect.

—Arthur O. Lewis

---

**CAMPBELL, John W(ood), Jr.** American. Born in Newark, New Jersey, 8 June 1910. Educated at Blair Academy; Massachusetts Institute of Technology, Cambridge, 1928–31; Duke University, Durham, North Carolina, B.S. 1933. Married 1) Dona Stuart in 1931; 2) Margaret Winter in 1950; four children. Car and gas heater salesman; worked in the research department of Mack Truck, Hoboken Pioneer Instruments, and Carleton Ellis chemical company; editor, *Astounding*, later *Analog*, 1937–71, *Unknown*, later *Unknown Worlds*, 1939–43, and *From Unknown Worlds*, 1948. Recipient: Hugo award, for editing, 1953, 1955, 1956, 1957, 1961, 1962, 1964, 1965. Guest of Honor, World Science Fiction Convention, Philadelphia, 1947, San Francisco, 1954, London, 1957. *Died 11 July 1971.*

SCIENCE-FICTION PUBLICATIONS

Novels (series: Arcot, Morey, and Wade)

*The Mightiest Machine.* Providence, Rhode Island, Hadley, 1947.
*The Incredible Planet.* Reading, Pennsylvania, Fantasy Press, 1949.
*The Moon Is Hell!* Reading, Pennsylvania, Fantasy Press, 1951.
*Islands of Space* (Arcot, Morey, and Wade). Reading, Pennsylvania, Fantasy Press, 1957.
*Invaders from the Infinite* (Arcot, Morey, and Wade). New York, Gnome Press, 1961.
*The Ultimate Weapon.* New York, Ace, 1966.

Short Stories

*Who Goes There?* Chicago, Shasta, 1948; as *The Thing and Other Stories*, London, Cherry Tree, 1952.
*Cloak of Aesir.* Chicago, Shasta, 1952.
*The Black Star Passes* (Arcot, Morey, and Wade). Reading, Pennsylvania, Fantasy Press, 1953.
*Who Goes There? and Other Stories.* New York, Dell, 1955.
*The Planeteers.* New York, Ace, 1966.
*The Best of John W. Campbell.* London, Sidgwick and Jackson, 1973.
*The Best of John W. Campbell*, edited by Lester del Rey. New York, Doubleday, 1976.
*The Space Beyond.* New York, Pyramid, 1976.

OTHER PUBLICATIONS

Other

*The Atomic Story.* New York, Holt, 1947.
*Collected Editorials from Analog*, edited by Harry Harrison. New York, Doubleday, 1966.
*The John W. Campbell Letters*, edited by Perry A. Chapdelaine, Tony Chapdelaine, and George Hay. Franklin, Tennessee, AC Projects, 1985.

Editor, *From Unknown Worlds.* New York, Street and Smith, 1948; London, Atlas, 1952.
Editor, *The Astounding Science Fiction Anthology.* New York, Simon and Schuster, 1952; shortened version, as *The First* [and *Second*] *Astounding Science Fiction Anthology*, London Grayson, 2 vols., 1954, and as *Astounding Tales of Space and Time*, New York, Berkeley, 1957; complete version, as *The First* [and *Second*] *Astounding Science Fiction Anthology*, London, New English Library, 2 vols., 1964–65.
Editor, *Prologue to Analog.* New York, Doubleday, 1962; London, Panther, 1967.
Editor, *Analog 1–8.* New York, Doubleday, 8 vols., 1963–71; London, Panther, 2 vols., 1967; London, Dobson, 4 vols., 1968.
Editor, *Analog Anthology.* London, Dobson, 1965.

*

Critical Studies: *John W. Campbell: An Australian Tribute* edited by John Bangsund, Canberra, Graham and Bangsund, 1972.

* * *

Had it not been for John W. Campbell, Jr., science fiction as a publisher's category might have perished with the demise of the pulp industry. As editor of *Astounding* (later *Analog*) *Science Fiction*, from September 1937 to December 1971, he demanded good writing and sometimes got it. That is his achievement (never mind his cranky indulgence in Dianetics and the Dean Drive), and he set the standard with the better of his own stories. As a result, his magazine attracted enough story-tellers that it and the science-fiction genre remain in existence today. (The stories of reasoned fantasy he published as editor of *Unknown Worlds* are, however, no longer current.)

His early stories take off from the space operatics of E.E. Smith, but with that extra something-to-say that interested the industrial scientists who became his chief readers. The something that must have interested them was the idea of professional colleagueship that stressed the intellectual value of shared discovery; the outcome of the research and development was not a new consumer product, but something to save the species.

Campbell's first story, "The Voice of the Void" (1930), set the pattern. Men ten billion years in the future prepare to leave the planets of the solar system because the sun is dying. By this time, science had become central to the human way of life and a scientist in training takes a 70-year course at an engineering school, where making inventions is part of the curriculum. Graduates from such schools have been gathering for generations to meet the growing emergency of the sun's death. At last they develop a matter transmitter that sends fleets of spaceships to another system of planets orbiting the giant star Betelgeuse. They accomplish this in a spirit of professional association, men of pure science called to salvationist duty, but in just those fields—aviation and broadcasting—under commercial development at the time of writing. Likewise in "Twilight," a time traveller from the far future asks what are the most important inventions of the day, and the answer is "airplanes and radio."

The pulp tradition of SF that Campbell elevated above adventure fiction—the last refuge of rugged individualism in American letters—was a world of "pooled mental resources." His intellectual hero was attractive to the young student or professional scientist in industry whose job was anything but free to explore wherever the research team's curiosity might lead.

Two groups of Campbell stories follow through with a standard set of heroes. The more popular one is the Arcot, Morey, and Wade series. Dr. Richard Arcot, a world-famous physicist, works for the research laboratories of Transcontinental Airways, selling it his inventions under the patronage of its president, who happens to be the father of Arcot's colleague, the mathematician Morey. Wade, introduced during the course of the first story, "Piracy Preferred," is an air pirate who preys on Transcontinental's great 30,000-passenger superplanes with a device for making his marauding aircraft invisible, but after being captured he joins Arcot's lab staff. Fuller, an aeronautical design engineer, joins the group in "Solarite," and proves his worth in *Islands of Space* by designing a faster-than-light ship on a principle discovered by Arcot. All four then make a tour of the cosmos. The title islands are island universes, galactic nebulae. Financing a tour of these is more than even Transcontinental can afford, so its president helps Arcot raise the rest in popular support from "the wealth of two worlds," Earth and Venus. All this is spent on a fantastic adventure of observational science. But the debt is repaid when the group is able to deal with an alien threat in *Invaders from the Infinite.*

The other story series is *The Planeteers*, dealing with Penton and Blake, a pair of cosmic explorers who land on various worlds and solve exotic puzzles. But again this had survival value. Curiosity is a tough-minded quality because what observation reveals is that "change is the natural order of things." Science is "a method of thinking" that can meet "goals ahead larger than those we know" by knowing how, when the problem is upon us, "to produce that which never existed." Science is the way mankind educates itself to meet the challenge of necessity.

Campbell's test of survival is nowhere dramatized more forcibly than in *The Moon Is Hell!* The first rocketship to the moon crashes and its crew of research scientists, stranded on the dead rock, win from the object of their curiosity food, water, and air. This is the research and development process glamorized in a power fantasy that makes its most important business the winning of life itself. "Machines and gadgets aren't the end and goal; they are the means to the true goal." The commercial products of the technological revolution are but objects of practice on which to learn and organize the skills of innovative group thinking, come the day of unexpected crisis.

Curiosity is the mainspring of human adaptability, and may very well drive the products of man's inventions when he himself is gone. In "The Last Evolution," Campbell introduces an original concept of robots, heretofore imagined only as workers or slaves. He has them become man's evolutionary descendants. They are science machines that make other machines. They supersede man, but surprisingly they end by recreating him. The machines bring to perfection man's urge to explore and do research and create that which never before existed.

A technology that outlives its makers is also the theme of Campbell's most famous story, "Twilight." Eighty-eight million years in the future, man is extinct, but his great automatic cities are still in place. The deathless cities go on with "the tireless, ceaseless perfection their designers had incorporated in them."

Perhaps the best work of fiction Campbell ever wrote is "Who Goes There?" An alien monster is found frozen in the Antarctic ice, buried with its ship, by a team of scientists doing weather research. Once thawed, it gets loose in their camp and changes form by imitating one or more of the sled dogs and one of the men, down to their cells and memories. The dogs are killed, but the problem remains how to discover by some test which man is the monster before it takes over the camp and then the whole world. The leader of the expedition is the tough-minded scientist who has the intellectual prowess to do just that. He devises a blood test, taking a sample from each man and touching it in turn with the tip of a hot needle. The monster not only replicates any body it takes over, it reduplicates itself in every cell of that body. The test is this: when irritated the monster's "*blood* will live—and crawl away." It does, and the man whose sample it is reveals himself in hideous form. Alert for the transformation with poised axes, the others hack their false colleague to pieces. These few men, outnumbered by millions of life cells, all intelligent, were not defeated. Humanity is *real*, monster-hood is false. Humans have "not an imitated, but a bred-in-the-bone instinct, a driving, unquenchable fire that's genuine."

The monster is no villain: it is a problem. And to be conquered it must be understood, as must all the other unpredictable threats of nature in a universe of constant change. It is deadly to *adapt* to nature, a lazy, undisciplined way that leads to digestion by the cosmic process; survival means *control* of nature. The monster is the opposite of humanity because it goes with nature, not against it. For curiosity it has mere cunning, for pooled mental resources collective imitation. And here is the political note in Campbell's thinking, often sounded in his magazine editorials. For him, collectivism is a monstrous thing that would devour human ideals, but should not be able to do so as long as the superior strength of individuals is united in free association.

—Leon Stover

---

**CAPON, (Harry) Paul.** Also wrote as Noel Kenton. British. Born in Kenton Hall, Suffolk, 18 December 1912. Educated at St. George's School, Harpenden, Hertfordshire. Served in the Royal Army Service Corps, 1940; technical director, Soviet Film Agency, 1941–44. Married 1) Doreen Evans-Evans in 1933, one daughter and one son; 2) Amy Charlotte Gillam in 1956. Freelance film editor and scriptwriter for London Films, 1931–32, Gaumont British, 1933–35, Warner Brothers, 1936–37, British National, 1944–48, Walt Disney, 1955–58, and Granada Television, 1959–62; head of Film Production, Independent Television News, London, 1963–67. *Died 24 November 1969.*

SCIENCE-FICTION PUBLICATIONS

Novels (series: Antigeos)

*The Other Half of the Sun* (Antigeos). London, Heinemann, 1950.

*The Other Half of the Planet* (Antigeos). London, Heinemann, 1952.
*The World at Bay* (for children). London, Heinemann, 1953; Philadelphia, Winston, 1954.
*Down to Earth* (Antigeos). London, Heinemann, 1954.
*Phobos, The Robot Planet* (for children). London, Heinemann, 1955; as *Lost—A Moon*, Indianapolis, Bobbs Merrill, 1956.
*The Wonderbolt* (for children). London, Ward Lock, 1955.
*Into the Tenth Millennium*. London, Heinemann, 1956.
*Flight of Time* (for children). London, Heinemann, 1960.

OTHER PUBLICATIONS

Novels

*Battered Caravanserai*. London, Heinemann, 1942.
*Brother Cain*. London, Heinemann, 1945.
*The Hosts of Midian*. London, Nicholson and Watson, 1946.
*Dead Man's Chest*. London, Nicholson and Watson, 1947.
*The Murder of Jacob Canansey*. London, Heinemann, 1947.
*Fanfare for Shadows*. London, Boardman, 1947.
*O Clouds Unfold*. London, Ward Lock, 1948.
*Image of a Murder*. London, Boardman, 1949.
*Toby Scuffell*. London, Ward Lock, 1949.
*Threescore Years*. London, Ward Lock, 1950.
*Delay of Doom*. London, Ward Lock, 1950.
*No Time for Death*. London, Ward Lock, 1951.
*Death at Shinglestrand*. London, Ward Lock, 1952.
*Death on a Wet Sunday*. London, Ward Lock, 1953.
*In All Simplicity*. London, Heinemann, 1953.
*The Seventh Passenger*. London, Ward Lock, 1953.
*Malice Domestic*. London, Ward Lock, 1954.
*Thirty Days Hath September*. London, Ward Lock, 1955.
*Margin of Terror*. London, Ward Lock, 1955.
*Amongst Those Missing*. London, Heinemann, 1959.
*The Final Refuge*. London, Harrap, 1969.

Other (for children)

*The Cave of Cornelius*. London, Heinemann, 1959; as *The End of the Tunnel*, Indianapolis, Bobbs Merrill, 1959.
*Warriors' Moon*. London, Hodder and Stoughton, 1960; New York, Putnam, 1964.
*The Kingdom of the Bulls*. London, Hodder and Stoughton, 1961; New York, Norton, 1962.
*Lord of the Chariots*. London, Hodder and Stoughton, 1962.
*The Golden Cloak*. London, Hodder and Stoughton, 1963.
*The Great Yarmouth Mystery: A Chronicle of a Famous Crime* (for adults). London, Harrap, 1965.
*Roman Gold*. Leicester, Brockhampton Press, 1968.
*Strangers on Forlorn*. London, Harrap, 1969.

Translator, *Surrealism*, by Yves Duplessis. New York, Walker, 1963.
Translator, *Sexual Reproduction*, by Louis Gallien. New York, Walker, 1963.
Translator (as Noel Kenton), *Animal Migration*, by René Thévenin. New York, Walker, 1963.
Translator, *The French Wines*, by Georges Ray. New York, Walker, 1965.

* * *

Paul Capon's novels have had very little distribution in the United States and he is generally unknown in that country, which is surprising in view of the large number of inferior writers whose works have been reprinted from their original European appearance. He received most attention with the Antigeos trilogy, portions of which were broadcast on the BBC. Antigeos is a twin world to the Earth, located at the opposite side of Earth's orbit, hidden from us by the bulk of the sun. This impossibility has recurred frequently in the genre, and is just plausible enough to be fascinating to casual readers.

Antigeos is a Utopia of sorts, or at least it is until the unscrupulous Earth humans arrive. In the first volume the initial contact is made, but the unpleasant results don't become evident until the middle volume where human vanities and greeds begin to work their way on Antigeos. In the final volume a group of financiers plot to exploit the newly discovered world as an involuntary colony, until they are thwarted by the true at heart.

The rest of Capon's adventure novels have been dismissed as juveniles, and two at least definitely are, *The Wonderbolt* and *Flight of Time*. But Capon's excellent narrative ability makes some of them of interest to adult readers as well. There is an alien invasion from Poppea in *The World at Bay*, for example, unique in that the aliens arrive in diminutive space stations. *Phobos, The Robot Planet* has as its central character the entire Martian moon, which we learn to be a gigantic robot spaceship which wanders around kidnapping people out of curiosity rather than malice. This latter novel is lighter in tone than the others, and has its moments of genuine humor.

Paul Capon went on to write one major adult novel, *Into the Tenth Millennium*, and made use of one of the oldest of science fiction plots—the journey into the future to visit a Utopian society. Capon transports three modern-day humans via drugs to a future society which does seem to have solved most of the significant societal problems, and we are treated to an unusually entertaining tour of that society. Never ignoring the need to sustain interest, Capon avoids preachiness, and portrays for us a world that is realistic as well as Utopian, a goal never achieved by most of the classic works of this type.

Capon was not particularly prolific and attracted little attention with his books, all of which are presently out of print. This is surprising because his narrative technique is masterful and his plots, while familiar, are not more so than many another far more successful novel. The predominance of young protagonists may well have stereotyped Capon as a writer of juveniles, making it impossible for him to reach a more adult audience with his more serious work.

—Don D'Ammassa

---

**CARD, Orson Scott.** Has also written as Brian Green. American. Born in Richland, Washington, 24 August 1951. Educated at Brigham Young University, Provo, Utah, B.A. in theatre 1975; University of Utah, Salt Lake City, M.A. in English 1981. Married Kristine Allen in 1977; two sons and one daughter. Volunteer Mormon missionary in Brazil, 1971–73; operated repertory theatre, Provo, 1974–75; proofreader, 1974, and editor, 1974–76, Brigham Young University Press; editor, *Ensign* magazine, Salt Lake City, 1976–78, and Compute Books, Greensboro, North Carolina, 1983; taught at the University of Utah, 1979–80, 1981, Brigham Young University, 1981, Notre Dame University, Indiana, 1981–82, and Clarion Writers Workshop, East Lansing, Michigan, 1982. Recipient: John W. Campbell award, 1978; Nebula award, for novel, 1985, 86; Hugo award, for novel, 1985, 1986, 1987; Locus award, for novel, 1988, 1989; Mythopoeic Fantasy award, 1988. Agent: Barbara Bova, 207 Sedgwick Road,

West Hartford, Connecticut 06107. Address: 546 Lindley Road, Greensboro, North Carolina 27410, U.S.A.

### SCIENCE-FICTION PUBLICATIONS

Novels (Series: Alvin Maker; Ender Wiggin)

*Hot Sleep.* New York, Baronet, 1978; London, Futura, 1980.
*A Planet Called Treason.* New York, St. Martin's Press, 1979; London, Pan, 1981.
*Songmaster.* New York, Dial Press, 1980; London, Futura, 1981.
*Hart's Hope.* New York, Berkley, 1983; London, Unwin, 1986.
*The Worthing Chronicle.* New York, Ace, 1983.
*Ender's Game.* New York, Tor, 1985; London, Unwin, 1985.
*Speaker for the Dead* (Ender). New York, Tor, 1986; London, Century, 1987.
*Wyrms.* New York, Arbor House, 1987.
*Treason.* New York, St. Martin's Press, 1988.
The Tales of Alvin Maker:
*Seventh Son.* New York, Tor, 1987; London, Century, 1988.
*Red Prophet.* New York, Tor, and London, Century, 1988.
*Prentice Alvin.* New York, Tor, and London, Century, 1989.
*The Abyss* (Novelization of screenplay). New York, Pocket, and London, Century, 1989.
*Worthing Saga.* New York, Tor, 1990; London, Legend, 1991.
*Xenocide* (Ender). New York, Tor, 1991.

Short Stories

*Capitol.* New York, Ace, 1978.
*Unaccompanied Sonata and Other Stories.* New York, Dial Press, 1981.
*The Folk of the Fringe.* West Bloomfield, Michigan, Phantasia Press, 1989; London, Century, 1990.
*Maps in a Mirror.* New York, Tor, 1990; London, Century, 1991.

### OTHER PUBLICATIONS

Novel

*A Woman of Destiny.* New York, Berkley, 1984; as *Saints*, New York, Tor, 1988.

Plays

*Tell Me That You Love Me, Junie Moon*, adaptation of a work by Majorie Kellogg (also director: produced Provo, Utah, 1969).
*The Apostate* (produced Provo, Utah, 1970).
*In Flight* (produced Provo, Utah, 1970).
*Across Five Summers* (produced Provo, Utah, 1971).
*Of Gideon* (produced Provo, Utah, 1971).
*Stone Tables* (produced Provo, Utah, 1973).
*A Christmas Carol*, adaptation of the story by Dickens (also director: produced Provo, Utah, 1974).
*Father, Mother, Mother, and Mom* (produced Provo, Utah, 1974). Published in *Sunstone*, 1978.
*Liberty Jail* (produced Provo, Utah, 1975).
*Rag Mission* (as Brian Green), in *Ensign* (Salt Lake City), July 1977.
*Fresh Courage Take* (also director: produced, 1978).
*Elders and Sisters* (produced, 1979).
*Wings* (produced, 1982).

Other

*Listen, Mom and Dad.* Salt Lake City, Bookcraft, 1978.
*Saintspeak.* Berkeley, California, Signature, 1981.
*Ainge.* Midvale, Utah, Signature, 1982.
*Compute's Guide to IBM PCjr Sound and Graphics.* Greensboro, North Carolina, Compute, 1984.
*Cardography.* Eugene, Oregon, Hypatia Press, 1987.
*Characters and Viewpoint.* Cincinnati, Ohio, Writer's Digest, 1988; London, Robinson, 1989.
*How To Write Science Fiction and Fantasy.* Cincinnati, Ohio, Writer's Digest, 1990.

Editor, *Dragons of Darkness.* New York, Ace, 1981.
Editor, *Dragons of Light.* New York, Ace, 1983.
Editor, *Future on Fire.* New York, Tor, 1991.

*

Manuscript Collection: Brigham Young University, Provo, Utah.

Orson Scott Card comments:

When I tell stories, I generally follow my own unreasoned sense of what should happen—what events feel important and true to the characters. I subscribe to no particular literary school and never deliberately bend a story to fit a preconceived notion of correct writing.

In fact, it is not story writing that interests me, but storytelling. I believe that the art of the storyteller does not exist on paper or in language; rather, the storyteller creates a vicarious memory in the hearers' or readers' minds, using as he can the words of the language with all their nuance, as well as the public memory that binds the community of hearers together.

The reader coming to my work will find that there is only rarely any science in my science fiction. I use the freedom of the genre to create the situations in which my stories can take place, but I never try to predict or prescribe the future. I do not write utopias or rhapsodies to future engineering. I am uninterested in current fashion and so do not write about drugs, rock music, peace movements, or nuclear war. Nor do I attempt literary experimentation, as it is generally understood—most literary experiments today being inferior repetitions of the failures of the modern writers of the early 20th century.

In looking back at my completed tales, both long and short, I find several recurrent motifs, some of which have been noticed (and sometimes complained about) by reviewers. Though I was not aware of these themes while writing, I do believe they are valid reflections of my own unquestioned beliefs about the moral universe.

Repeatedly my central characters occupy an unsought key position in their community; repeatedly they choose to suffer or cause unspeakable pain or sacrifice in order to save the community. Some have seen this as wanton violence; I see it as something holy in human nature, the inborn goodness that denies mankind is evil at birth.

Often my characters are children or otherwise innocent, forced ahead of time into responsibilities they cannot, but nevertheless do, bear. Whether they are children or not, they are always isolated from the community they uphold. They tend to have exceptional gifts and exceptional weaknesses; they are introspective enough to notice their weakness and strength and pain, but not enough to notice their virtue.

My characters frequently have a sense of fulfilling plans they did not make; ultimately, however, they accept all or part of those plans. Their achievements, however, are a direct result of their own choices, actions, and efforts. They are not mere toys of the gods; the gods, implicitly or explicitly, depend in part on the human characters to achieve their own overarching purposes. And all my fiction is infused with a strong belief in the perfectability of human beings, at least in part through their own desires and works.

* * *

Like many young writers—and a substantial number of writers of all ages—Orson Scott Card concerns himself repeatedly with a single theme. This theme is the growth and transformation of the individual. It is the story of coming-of-age, the story of the rite of passage, the story of the transformation of the boy, clever and ambitious but ignorant and dependent, into the man of maturity, responsibility, and power.

Card's earliest story, "Ender's Game," offered a brief glimpse of precisely this concern. It deals with Ender Wiggin (the odd first name is actually a nickname, and is significant) and his selection for enrollment at an elite and crucially important military academy. The story was immensely popular, and established Card from the outset as a favorite with readers of *Analog*, the leading science-fiction magazine. It also marked the beginning of Card's association with editor Ben Bova; as Bova moved from post to post in the late 1970's and early 1980's, Card's stories and books continued to appear under Bova's tutelage. When it was revealed that Bova's wife was also Card's literary agent, strong criticism was expressed over potential (or actual) conflict of interest. Once this controversy had lost its currency, it became possible for Card's works to be judged more on their merit than on the basis of questions about their author. However, Card has continued to be the subject of attacks in the fan press and in some critical journals. One such attack resulted from his (limited) defense of the influence of the heirs of the late L. Ron Hubbard on contemporary science fiction. Others appear to be thinly-veiled attacks on the Mormon Church, using Card (a practicing member of the Church) as a lightning rod.

His next major success, also in *Analog*, was "Mikal's Songbird." Thematically similar to "Ender's Game," "Mikal's Songbird" is concerned with the selection of a young boy to be trained as the personal "songbird" of a galactic emperor. The position of songbird carries elements of poet laureate, court jester, and (at least on a level of inference) boy-love for the emperor. In addition to the theme of personal growth, "Mikal's Songbird," when built into the novel *Songmaster*, is concerned with the ecstatic or transformational experience. In this case the ecstatic state is achieved through song; the book commends itself to comparison with Thomas M. Disch's *On Wings of Song*. Card's treatment of the theme is more serious than is Disch's; where Disch is often wry and occasionally evasive, Card is earnest and relatively direct, although by no means lacking in subtlety.

Even Card's lesser works carry out the major theme of his fiction. The early story-cycle *Hot Sleep*, revised and expanded to form *The Worthing Chronicle*, is of particular interest in the manner in which it shows Card's own development of his skills and techniques as he carries his protagonist down through a long series of episodic adventures separated by periods of induced suspended animation.

Card has always insisted on maintaining his identity as a writer of science fiction but not one limited to science fiction. His duality stretches back to his childhood reading. He cites works of Robert A. Heinlein and Andre Norton, read when Card was in elementary school—but mentions that during the same period he was "just as excited by Nordhoff and Hall's Bounty trilogy." In college he read Bradbury, Tolkien, Clarke, Asimov—but also Ayn Rand, John Hersey, James Clavell, and later Vidal, Renault, and Goldman.

His most important work outside the science-fiction field, to date, is the long historical novel *A Woman of Destiny*. The story of an immigrant Englishwoman coming to America early in the 19th century, the book is heavily researched and beautifully written. Card has expressed anger and bitterness over the treatment given the book by its publisher, starting with a change of its name. The book was written as *Saints*, and was to have been published first in hard covers. The publisher changed the name to avoid identification of the book as a Mormon novel (although Mormonism is one of its major subjects), packaged it as a semi-torrid romance (it is a serious novel of character and manners), and published it as a paperback original with almost no advertising or other support.

Following this misfortune, Card returned to science fiction with a full-length novel version of *Ender's Game*, of which the early story makes up a little more than a prologue. The book suffers from over-familiarity: it is a story that has been told and retold in both general literature and science fiction by authors from Fielding to Heinlein and Haldeman. The young protagonist makes his way despite loneliness and self-doubt from new boy to top grad, then enters the real world to make his way. Despite its lack of innovation, Card's version of this familiar tale is exceptionally well-written and readable.

In the sequel, *Speaker for the Dead*, it is discovered that the aliens of *Ender's Game* are not evil, as they had seemed, but are actually the possessors of a communal mind that could not communicate with humans. In effect, the whole war was the result of an unnecessary and tragic misunderstanding. While this insight is almost banal in its familiarity, it does lead Card's characters into a profound examination of the nature of genocide (the aliens were apparently annihilated) and the moral and theological implications of war, and in particular war-to-the-last-man. When it is revealed that a few of the aliens did survive, it becomes possible to reconstitute their race. In this second book of the cycle, Card's exemplar is obviously no longer Heinlein, but perhaps the James Blish of *A Case of Conscience*. Both of Card's books won high honors from the science fiction community.

The third—and presumably concluding—volume of the series is *Xenocide*. In this book, Card addresses the nature of intelligence and humanity by challenging his characters with other familiar devices, the impending end of their world, and artificial intelligence.

Card continues to produce other works. His "Tales of Alvin Maker" series is set in pre-Columbian America. Tales of magical fantasy rather than science fiction, they draw, to some degree, upon the Mormon belief that Jesus visited the Western Hemisphere. Card has also written a variety of other works: non-series novels such as *Wyrms*, a screenplay novelization, *The Abyss*, and a how-to-do-it book for aspiring writers. While still a relatively young man, Card has already created an impressive body of forceful and well-crafted work. An industrious worker, he will certainly continue to produce, and will in all likelihood achieve a growing degree of popularity and critical appreciation.

—Richard A. Lupoff

---

**CAREY, Julian.** *See* **TUBB, E.C.**

---

**CARPENTER, Morley.** *See* **TUBB, E.C.**

---

**CARR, Jayge.** Pseudonym for Marj Krueger. American. Born in Houston, Texas, 28 July 1940. Educated at Carnegie Institute of Technology, Pittsburgh, 1958–61; Wayne State University, Detroit, 1961–62, B.A. in physics 1962; Case Western Reserve University, Cleveland, 1962–65. Married Roger Carr Krueger in 1961; two daughters. Nuclear physicist, NASA, Cleveland, 1962–65. Agent: Matthew Bialer, William Morris Agency, 1350 Avenue of the Americas, New York, New York 10019, U.S.A.

SCIENCE-FICTION PUBLICATIONS

Novels

*Leviathan's Deep.* New York, Doubleday, 1979; London, Sidgwick and Jackson, 1980.
*Navigator's Sindrome.* New York, Doubleday, 1983.
*The Treasure in the Heart of the Maze.* New York, Doubleday, 1985.
*Rabelaisian Reprise.* New York, Doubleday, 1988.

Uncollected Short Stories

"Alienation," in *Analog* (New York), October 1976.
"The Ax," in *Analog* (New York), June 1977.
"Right of Passage," in *Analog* (New York), August 1978.
"The Pavilion Where All Times Meet," in *Other Worlds 1*, edited by Roy Torgeson, New York, Zebra, 1979.
"Does Not a Statistic Bleed," in *Pandora* (Murray, Kentucky), vol. 1, no. 4, 1979.
"Sanctuary," in *Isaac Asimov's Science Fiction Magazine* (New York), May 1979.
"In Adam's Fall," in *Analog* (New York), October 1979.
"The King Is Dead! Long Live—," in *Chrysalis 8*, edited by Roy Torgeson. New York, Doubleday, 1980.
"Star Spats," in *Pandora* (Murray, Kentucky), vol. 1, no. 5, 1980.
"The False-True Heir," in *Pandora* (Murray, Kentucky), vol. 1, no. 6, 1980.
"Child of the Wandering Sea," in *Ares* (Lake Geneva, Wisconsin), May 1980.
"Hillsong," in *Ares* (Lake Geneva, Wisconsin), September 1980.
"A Thief in the Night," in *Room of One's Own* (Vancouver), vol. 6, nos. 11–12, 1981.
"The Selfish Genie," in *Questar*, February 1981.
"Mustard Seed," in *Analog* (New York), March 1981.
"The Pacifists," in *Analog* (New York), October 1981.
"The Wondrous Works of His Hands," in *Alien Encounters*, edited by Jan Howard Finder. New York, Taplinger, 1982.
"Blind Spot," in *The 1982 Annual World's Best SF*, edited by Donald A. Wollheim and Arthur Saha. New York, DAW, 1982.
"Reunion," in *Hecate's Cauldron*, edited by Susan M. Shwartz. New York, DAW, 1982.
"Lungfish," in *Analog* (New York), October 1982.
"Measuremen," in *Isaac Asimov's Science Fiction Magazine* (New York), December 1982.
"Malthus's Day," in *The Best of Omni Science Fiction 5*, edited by Don Myrus. New York, Omni, 1983.
"The Spoils of Victory," in *Oracle* (Southfield, Michigan), no. 2, 1983.
"The Kidnapped Key," in *Analog* (New York), August 1983.
"The Tempest Within," in *Fantasy Book* (Pasadena, California), December 1983.
"Monolyth," in *Omni* (New York), December 1983.
"The Heart in the Egg," in *Isaac Asimov's Tomorrow's Voices*, edited by Shawna McCarthy. New York, Davis, 1984.
"The Piper's Pay," in *Fantasy Book* (Pasadena, California), June 1984.
"Pieces of Eight," in *Fantasy and Science Fiction* (New York), September 1984.
"Webrider," in *The Third Omni Book of SF*, edited by Ellen Datlow. New York, Omni, 1985.
"The Price of Lightning," in *Moonsinger's Friends*, edited by Susan Shwartz. Chappequa, New York, Bluejay, 1985.
"Catacombs," in *Amazing*, July 1985.
"Finnegan's Wake," in *Analog*, October 1985.
"Immigrant," in *Amazing*, November 1985.
"Drop-out," in *Analog*, January 1986.
"Rainbow's End," in *Amazing*, September 1986.
"Inky," in *The Year's Best Fantasy Stories 14.* New York, DAW, 1988.
"Hitchhiker," in *Marion Zimmer Bradley's Fantasy Magazine*, Autumn 1988.
"Wart," in *Catfantastic*, New York, DAW, 1989.
"Chimera," in *Orbit Science Fiction Yearbook 3.* London, Orbit, 1990.
"The Icarus Epidemic," in *Analog*, April 1990.
"Computer Portrait," in *Amazing*, May 1990.
"Plumduff Potato-Eye," in *Tales of the Witch World 3.* New York, Tor, 1990.
"Kingdom of the Blind," in *Analog*, July (?) 1991.

*

Jayge Carr comments:

It is probably no coincidence that my first published story was titled "Alienation." I have never tried to do anything more than tell interesting stories, about interesting people, written in a precise but readable style. But certain themes do crop up over and over, and alienation, whether of one society from the mainstream, as in "The Pacifists," or person from society as in "Alienation," does seem to be a common occurrence.

I've also discovered quite a bit about myself by reading my own work. Many people, on the evidence of *Leviathan's Deep*, have labeled me a feminist. Well, maybe. I prefer to think of myself as a peoplist. Everyone should have equal opportunities and no one should be shoe-horned into a role unfitting or barred from a role desired because of sex—or age, creed, color, or what-have-you. "Mustard Seed" may be my best example of a truly egalitarian society. And *Navigator's Sindrome*, of course, a prime example of such a society gone sour. Sometimes, as in *Leviathan's Deep* or "The King Is Dead," I try to show men what it feels like to have the shoe on the other foot, pinching. But women are not our only minority, just the most prevalent one. Prejudice, intolerance, bigotry; all of them are so cruel, and they cause so much tragedy—and they're so foolish. Those who eliminate some people from their friends because of trivial reasons miss so much.

Another theme that keeps recurring—perhaps because I do feel strongly about it—is pollution. Humanity wasting our environment. "Child of the Wandering Sea" is the ultimate of that, where the Terran's population explosion has them taking over—and terraforming—world after world. Where will we go if we don't control ourselves, what will happen if we continue to waste our resources. I haven't any answers, but I can hope that just thinking about it will help, in some small way.

Besides, writing is fun. It is fun to make up a truly alien alien, as in "The Wondrous Works of His Hands" or a truly alien society of human beings, as in "The Pacifists." It is fun to meet new friends, and watch them have adventures. And of course, I can always hope, that if it's fun to write, it's equally fun to read.

* * *

Jayge Carr is the pseudonym for a former physicist who now writes some of the most provocative, enigmatic, and underrated fantasy and science fiction in the field.

Her first novel, *Leviathan's Deep*, was an immediate success. It took the commonplace theme of domineering males attempting to subdue a leader on a matriarchal world and, essentially, turned it inside out. Her treatment of the power politics is satirical, occasionally sharply so: in Carr's works, any attempt at coercion is an invitation to all-out trouble. Most impressive about the book is her protagonist's voice—compassionate, humorous, resourceful, but, at the end, resigned to the losses inherent in her need to protect her own culture.

Her Jael the Navigator books, *Navigator's Sindrome, The Treasure in the Heart of the Maze*, and *Rabelaisian Reprise*, are not a true series, and certainly not a trilogy: they do, however, involve the same world and some of the same characters. Once again, what is noteworthy about these books is Carr's hatred of coercion: if she ever portrays anyone as an out-and-out villain, it is the c'holders, or contract holders, whose decadence and cruelty oppress the men and women whose bonds they hold. Jael, too, is a fascinating character: her moral neutrality and craziness add a darker dimension to what would otherwise be space-faring picaresques.

Carr's short fiction has appeared in a variety of places, including the highly prestigious *Year's Best* anthologies and *Synergy*, and in markets ranging from *Omni* to *Analog* to *Marion Zimmer Bradley's Fantasy Magazine.* Her stories shift from fantasy to humor to rigorous scientific extrapolation, and are marked by a flair for language, extremely complex plots and shifts in story line, and her extreme reluctance to see anything at all—except maybe the worst c'holders—as totally evil.

—Susan Shwartz

---

**CARR, Terry (Gene).** Also wrote as Norman Edwards. American. Born in Grants Pass, Oregon, 19 February 1937. Educated at the City College of San Francisco, 1954–57. A.A. 1957; University of California, Berkeley, 1957–59. Married 1) Miriam Dyches in 1959 (divorced 1961); 2) Carol Newmark in 1961. Associate editor, Scott Meredith Literary Agency, New York, 1962–64; editor, Ace Books, New York, 1964–71; editor, *SFWA Bulletin*, 1967–68; founder, Science Fiction Writers of American Forum, 1967–68; co-editor, *Void* fanzine; editor, with Ron Ellik, *Fanac* fanzine. Recipient: Hugo award, for editing, 1959, for criticism, 1973; *Locus* award, for editing, 1983, 1984. *Died 7 April 1987.*

### Science-Fiction Publications

#### Novels

*Warlord of Kor.* New York, Ace, 1963.
*Invasion from 2500* (as Norman Edwards, with Ted White). Derby, Connecticut, Monarch, 1964.
*Cirque.* Indianapolis, Bobbs Merrill, 1977; London, Dobson, 1979.

#### Short Stories

*The Light at the End of the Universe.* New York, Pyramid, 1976.

### Other Publications

#### Other

Editor, with Donald A. Wollheim, *World's Best Science Fiction 1965* (to *1971*). New York, Ace, 7 vols., 1965–71; *1968* to *1971* vols. published London, Gollancz, 4 vols., 1969–71: first 4 vols. published as *World's Best Science Fiction: First* [to *Fourth*] *Series*, Ace, 1970.
Editor, *Science Fiction for People Who Hate Science Fiction.* New York, Doubleday, 1966.
Editor, *New Worlds of Fantasy 1–3.* New York, Ace, 3 vols., 1967–71; vol. 1 published as *Step Outside Your Mind*, London, Dobson, 1969.
Editor, *The Others.* New York, Fawcett, 1968.
Editor, *On Our Way to the Future.* New York, Ace, 1970.
Editor, *Universe 1–17.* New York, Ace, 2 vols., 1971–72; New York, Random House, 3 vols., 1973–74; New York, Doubleday, 12 vols., 1976–87; London, Dobson, 10 vols., 1975–80; London, Hale, 3 vols., 1983–86; London, Gollancz, vols. 14–16, 1985–87.
Editor, *The Best Science Fiction of the Year 1–16.* New York, Ballantine, 9 vols., 1972–80; New York, Pocket Books, 4 vols., 1981–84; vols. 4–16 published London, Gollancz, 1975–87; New York, Tor, vols. 14–16, 1985–87.
Editor, *This Side of Infinity.* New York, Ace, 1972.
Editor, *An Exaltation of Stars.* New York, Simon and Schuster, 1973.
Editor, *Into the Unknown.* Nashville, Nelson, 1973.
Editor, *Worlds Near and Far.* Nashville, Nelson, 1974.
Editor, *Fellowship of the Stars: Nine Science Fiction Stories.* New York, Simon and Schuster, 1974.
Editor, *Creatures from Beyond.* Nashville, Nelson, 1975.
Editor, *The Ides of Tomorrow* (for children). Boston, Little Brown, 1976.
Editor, *Planets of Wonder: A Treasury of Space Opera* (for children). Nashville, Nelson, 1976.
Editor, *To Follow a Star* (for children). Nashville, Nelson, 1977.
Editor, *The Infinite Arena* (for children). Nashville, Nelson, 1977.
Editor, *Classic Science Fiction: The First Golden Age.* New York, Harper, 1978; London, Robson, 1979.
Editor, *The Year's Finest Fantasy 1–2.* New York, Berkley, 2 vols., 1978–79.
Editor, *The Best Science Fiction Novellas of the Year 1–2.* New York, Ballantine, 2 vols., 1979–80.
Editor, *Beyond Reality.* New York, Elsevier Nelson, 1979.
Editor, *Dream's Edge: Science Fiction Stories about the Future of the Planet Earth.* San Francisco, Sierra Club, 1980.

Editor, with Martin H. Greenberg, *A Treasury of Modern Fantasy*. New York, Avon, 1981.
Editor, *Fantasy Annual 3–5*. New York, Pocket Books, 1981–82.
Editor, *The Best from Universe*. New York, Doubleday, 1984.
Editor, with Isaac Asimov and Martin H. Greenberg, *100 Great Fantasy Short Short Stories*. New York, Doubleday, and London, Robson, 1984.
Editor, *Terry Carr's Best Science Fiction and Fantasy of the Year*. New York, Tor, 1985.
Editor, *Science Fiction Hall of Fame: Volume IV*. New York, Avon, 1986.

*

Terry Carr commented:

I've never been prolific as a fiction writer: most of my career has been devoted to editing, first as an editor for Ace Books, where I founded the "Ace Science Fiction Specials" series, 1968–71, and more recently as an editor of anthologies.

As a writer I'm known best for stories about alien creatures ("The Dance of the Changer and the Three," "Hop-Friend," *Cirque*, etc.), but in truth this is an outgrowth of my interest in communication between *all* kinds of people. Short stories such as "Touchstone" and "They Live on Levels" are examples that don't include aliens: the novel *Cirque* has an important alien character but it's mostly about communication between the human characters. Another theme in my stories is transcendental experience: see particularly the novella "The Wind at Starmont" and the novel *Cirque*.

* * *

Terry Carr was one of several writers in the science fiction field who emerged from organized fandom, where he edited and wrote for a number of amateur periodicals. Even though he achieved professional standing, he remained a relatively infrequent writer, producing only a single, full-length, solo novel and perhaps three dozen short stories over the course of a career that spanned three decades. Carr's contribution to the field is enormous, however, and it is likely that his impact as an editor will transcend the value of even the best of his fiction, simply because he was so active in promoting the careers of many major talents. Although Carr edited several reprint anthologies, his two most significant contributions in this area are the *Universe* series of original short story collections, and the Ace Science Fiction Specials, a series of featured novels that helped popularize Ursula K. LeGuin, D.G. Compton, R.A. Lafferty, and others. In addition to the uniformly high quality, this series included a number of untraditional styles and themes, which further established them as something of special interest. Carr also edited a retrospective "Best of the Year" series that demonstrated his thorough familiarity with what the field had to offer, as well as his discerning eye for good fiction.

Carr's first few short stories were published in the early 1960's, including the amusing Weinbaum homage, "Hop-Friend," with its delightful Martian creatures, and the still popular "Stanley Toothbrush." In his novella *Warlord of Kor*, the human race is studying an alien species that seems to have culturally and mentally regressed, having lost the ability to speak and abandoned their scientific achievements, enslaved by a mindless obedience to a psychological imperative buried in their racial memories. A disparate group of people struggles to investigate this phenomenon, not realizing that they are wakening powers and fears that have been deliberately suppressed, which may be dangerous to all concerned if they are consciously recalled. A fairly routine adventure story, but thoughtful and involving a genuinely interesting conflict.

Carr collaborated with fellow writer and sometime editor Ted White on *Invasion from 2500*, which appeared under the byline Norman Edwards. Using advanced weaponry, a powerful invasion force appears as if by magic, conquering all the major population centers of Earth. Initially, it is believed that they are alien invaders from another world, but the title telegraphs the fact that they are actually interlopers from the future. It is a disappointingly flat adventure story, inferior to the subsequent works of both writers.

*Cirque* is set in the very remote future of Earth. The tide of civilization has moved to other worlds, and most of the planet is a barbarous place sinking slowly into a decadent anarchy. The one exception is the city Cirque, which remains a place of innovation and ambition. An evil intelligence dwells not far from the city, a metaphysical creation of the darker side of Cirque that has begun to stir. It is an interesting if somewhat slowly-paced novel; its chief point of interest is the alien millipede central to the plot. Carr has long demonstrated a fascination with other intelligences, and some of his most inventive writing has been in that area, as in the case of his most famous story, "The Dance of the Changer and the Three." In that story, the aliens are pure energy forms, performing an elaborate ritual dance whose meaning is lost in the depths of racial memory.

That story and many of Carr's other noteworthy shorter pieces were collected in *The Light at the End of the Universe*. Of particular note are "Ozymandias," which looks at alienness from an alien point of view; "The Winds at Starmont," the tale of an aerial adventure in an exotic land; and "Touchstone," an enigmatic little fantasy about a man who feels compelled to purchase an undistinguished rock, only to discover that it exerts a strange influence over his subsequent actions. Another fine fantasy is "Stanley Toothbrush," wherein the protagonist's disbelief in certain artifacts is so powerful, they cease to exist.

Other stories of interest include Carr's examination of the logical outcome of over-urbanization, "In His Image," an even more effective variation, "They Live On Levels," his satirical and whimsical "Sleeping Beauty," and "Virra," a story of the last days of Earth under a dying sun.

Although he was an accomplished short story writer, Carr's editorial activities obviously occupied most of his time and diverted his creative efforts in that direction. His growing concern about the damage humans inflict on the planet is reflected in some of his stories, as well as being the driving purpose for *Dream's Edge*, one of his better anthologies.

—Don D'Ammassa

---

**CARTER. Angela (Olive, née Stalker).** British. Born in Eastbourne, Sussex, 7 May 1940. Educated at the University of Bristol, 1962–65, B.A. in English 1965. Married Paul Carter in 1960 (divorced 1972). Journalist, Croydon, Surrey, 1958–61. Arts Council Fellow in Creative Writing, University of Sheffield, 1976–78; visiting professor of Creative Writing, Brown University, Providence, Rhode Island, 1980–81; writer-in-residence, University of Adelaide, 1984. Recipient: Rhys Memorial prize, 1968; Maugham award, 1969; Cheltenham Festival prize, 1979; Kurt Maschler award, for children's book, 1982; James Tait Black Memorial prize, 1985. Address: c/o Virago Press, 20–23 Mandela Street, London NW1 0HQ, England.

SCIENCE-FICTION PUBLICATIONS

Novels

*Heroes and Villains*. London, Heinemann, 1969; New York, Simon and Schuster, 1970.
*The Infernal Desire Machines of Dr. Hoffman*, London, Hart Davis, 1972; as *The War of Dreams*, New York, Harcourt Brace, 1974.
*The Passion of New Eve*. London, Gollancz, and New York, Harcourt Brace, 1977.

Short Stories

*Fireworks: Nine Profane Pieces*. London, Quartet, 1974; New York, Harper, 1981; revised edition, London, Chatto and Windus, 1987.
*The Bloody Chamber and Other Stories*. London, Gollancz, 1979; New York, Harper, 1980.
*Black Venus's Tale*. London, Next-Faber, 1980.
*Black Venus*. London, Chatto and Windus, 1985; as *Saints and Strangers*, New York, Viking, 1986.

OTHER PUBLICATIONS

Novels

*Shadow Dance*. London, Heinemann, 1966; as *Honeybuzzard*, New York, Simon and Schuster, 1967.
*The Magic Toyshop*. London, Heinemann, 1967; New York, Simon and Schuster, 1968.
*Several Perceptions*. London, Heinemann, 1968; New York, Simon and Schuster, 1969.
*Love*. London, Hart Davis, 1971; revised edition, London, Chatto and Windus, 1987; New York, Penguin, 1988.
*Nights at the Circus*. London, Chatto and Windus, 1984; New York, Viking Press, 1985.
*Wise Children*. London, Chatto and Windus, 1991.

Plays

*Vampirella* (broadcast 1976; produced London, 1986). Included in *Come unto These Yellow Sands*, 1984.
*Come unto These Yellow Sands* (radio plays; includes *The Company of Wolves, Vampirella, Puss in Boots*). Newcastle-upon-Tyne, Bloodaxe, 1984.

Screenplays: *The Company of Wolves*, with Neil Jordan, 1984; *The Magic Toyshop*, 1987.

Radio Plays: *Vampirella*, 1976; *Come unto These Yellow Sands*, 1979; *The Company of Wolves*, from her own story, 1980; *Puss in Boots*, 1982; *A Self-Made Man* (on Ronald Firbank), 1984.

Verse

*Unicorn*, Leeds, Location Press, 1966.

Other

*Miss Z, The Dark Young Lady* (for children). London, Heinemann, and New York, Simon and Schuster, 1970.
*The Donkey Prince* (for children). New York, Simon and Schuster, 1970.
*Comic and Curious Cats*, illustrated by Martin Leman. London, Gollancz, and New York, Crown, 1979.
*The Sadeian Woman: An Exercise in Cultural History*. London, Virago, 1979; as *The Sadeian Woman and the Ideology of Pornography*, New York, Pantheon, 1979.
*Nothing Sacred: Selected Writings*. London, Virago, 1982.
*Moonshadow* (for children). London, Gollancz, 1982.
*Sleeping Beauty and Other Favourite Fairy Tales*. London, Gollancz, 1982; New York, Schocken, 1984.

Editor, *Wayward Girls and Wicked Women: An Anthology of Stories*. London, Virago Press, 1986; New York, Penguin, 1989.
Editor, *The Virago Book of Fairy Tales*. London, Virago Press, 1990; as *The Old Wives' Fairy Tale Book*, New York, Pantheon, 1990.

Translator, *The Fairy Tales of Charles Perrault*. London, Gollancz, 1977; New York, Avon, 1978.

*

Angela Carter comments:
Speak as you find.

* * *

Angela Carter describes herself as a Gothic writer; in her fondness for decadent opulence and squalor she is more like a stylish Moorcock, with greater charm and humour and less pretentiousness. In her persuasive "Polemical Preface" to *The Sadeian Woman*, she proposes a "moral pornographer" as an artist who demystifies the flesh to reveal "the real relations of man and his kind." She might see her work, more generally, as that of a "moral mythographer" who creates myths to destroy myths, pornographic writing being one of her weapons. She, perhaps more properly than de Sade, is "a terrorist of the imagination": he is too boring and disgusting to be terrifying and she seems over-deferential as well as patronizing in her critique of him. Latterly, she has revealed a strong interest in the ideas of mixed natures and of metamorphosis, revamping classic tales of lycanthropy or hermaphroditism, of which the most charming is the uncollected "Overture for 'A Midsummer Night's Dream' " (in *Interzone*, Autumn 1982). Students of Poe should note her fictionalized reconstruction of parts of his life, published in the first issue of *Interzone* (Spring 1982), "The Cabinet of Edgar Allan Poe."

Most of Carter's fiction may be classed as fantasy, and even the delightful mainstream comedy *Several Perceptions* uses fantasy as its subject. Three of her novels are in the SF genre, two of which are concerned with the harnessing of science in the service of fantasy, so that science fantasy might describe them with particular felicity. The panopticon episode in *Nights at the Circus* fits here, though not the book as a whole, which is a sort of fantastic freak show, less than the sum of its parts but particularly sound on clowns.

In the post-holocaust world of *Heroes and Villains*, civilization has been reduced to ivory towers guarded by Soldiers (the heroes) and menaced by barbarians and mutants. The heroine Marianne, a professor's daughter, rescues one of the villains during a raid and flees with him, even though he is her brother's murderer; he rapes, then marries her. The account of their ensuing love-hate relationship is a kind of anti-romance, in which the ambivalent, barbaric nastiness and beauty are paraded vividly before us. One of the novel's key themes is the treacherous nature of appearances, yet possibly the book exists principally as the frame for a strange *tableau-vivant* effect, whereby Henri Rousseau's painting *The Sleeping Gypsy* is brought to life.

*The Infernal Desire Machines of Dr. Hoffman*, where an embodiment of de Sade actually appears in one of the Grand Guignol episodes, is a much more powerful and ambitious work in which the author's evidently wide reading among the great satiric fantasists is apparent everywhere. The picaresque hero, Desiderio (a desirer), is on a mission to kill Dr. Hoffman, generator of mirages that drive men mad, and a quest to find and possess Hoffman's daughter, Albertina. The rational but impressionable hero is a reluctant exorcist, and the end to his adventure seems of less importance than the erotic and horrific sideshows that distract him on the way. Although her coldblooded, mad scientist villain is sufficiently evil, his chilling nature is matched by the resolute *sangfroid* of the author, even when she is describing multiple buggery, rape, cannibalism, or eye-juggling; the excessive violence is not accompanied by a commensurable emotional response. (This distance is also a notable feature of Carter's readings of her own work: her tin voice as a reader makes the tonal range of her radio plays all the more astonishing.) One of the best episodes is in a relatively low key, Desiderio's night of love with the somnambulist daughter of an absentee major, his subsequent arrest for her murder, and escape by climbing one-handed up a chimney. The writing is so good in this novel that one wishes it made a better whole, that it had more humour and more seriousness, in Swift's or even in Beckford's manner.

*The Passion of New Eve* achieves a better balance of horror and humour, wit and pathos, self-indulgent fantasy and cool iconoclasm. The hero, Evelyn, is an Englishman precipitated into the American nightmare. Not a nice man himself, he mistreats his black mistress in New York, once a "city of visible reason" but now in Ballardian decay. Fleeing to the desert, Evelyn becomes New Eve when captured by lesbian guerrillas; fleeing from them she is raped by the petty tyrant Zero and becomes one of his harem, of lower status than his pigs. She accompanies the nihilist Zero on his mission to kill the film idol Tristessa, whom Evelyn had worshipped. Tristessa is revealed as a transvestite, and he impregnates Eve, kills Zero, and then is killed in error by soldiers, while Southern California burns in apocalyptic warfare, leaving Eve, after passage through an Earth womb, to escape American shores bearing her child, committed to the sea like a female Prospero. Machismo is mocked splendidly in both its male and female modes in this satiric anti-mythic novel, a *bravura* performance.

A few of the tales in *Fireworks* fall sufficiently within the genre to serve as an excuse for reading the whole fantastic collection. In the afterword, the author refers to her Gothic tradition as retaining a singular moral function, "that of promoting unease." She understands the quality of her own art perfectly here.

—Michael J. Tolley

---

**CARTER, Lin(wood Vrooman).** American. Born in St. Petersburg, Florida, 9 June 1930. Educated at Columbia University, New York, 1953–54. Served in the United States Army Infantry, 1951–53. Married Noel Vreeland in 1964. Advertising and publishers copy-writer, 1957–69; editorial consultant, Ballantine Books Adult Fantasy, from 1969. Recipient: Nova award, 1972. *Died 2 February 1988.*

Science-Fiction Publications

Novels (series: Callisto; Great Imperium; Green Star; Hautley Quicksilver; Terra Magica; Thongor; World's End; Zarkon)

*The Wizard of Lemuria.* New York, Ace, 1965; revised edition, as *Thongor and the Wizard of Lemuria*, New York, Berkley, 1969.
*Thongor of Lemuria.* New York, Ace, 1966; revised edition, as *Thongor and the Dragon City*, New York, Berkley, 1970.
*The Star Magicians.* New York, Ace, 1966.
*The Man Without a Planet* (Great Imperium). New York, Ace, 1966.
*Destination: Saturn*, with David Grinnell. New York, Avalon, 1967.
*The Flame of Iridar.* New York, Belmont, 1967.
*Thongor Against the Gods.* New York, Paperback Library, 1967.
*Thongor at the End of Time.* New York, Paperback Library, 1968; London, Tandem, 1970.
*Thongor in the City of Magicians.* New York, Paperback Library, 1968.
*The Thief of Thoth* (Quicksilver). New York, Belmont, 1968.
*Tower of the Edge of Time.* New York, Belmont, 1968.
*The Purloined Planet* (Quicksilver). New York, Belmont, 1969.
*Lost World of Time.* New York, New American Library, 1969.
*Tower of the Medusa.* New York, Ace, 1969.
*Thongor Fights the Pirates of Tarakus.* New York, Berkley, 1970; as *Thongor and the Pirates of Tarakus*, London, Tandem, 1971.
*Star Rogue* (Great Imperium). New York, Lancer, 1970.
*Outworlder* (Great Imperium). New York, Lancer, 1971.
*Black Legion of Callisto.* New York, Dell, 1972; London, Futura, 1975.
*Under the Green Star.* New York, DAW, 1972.
*Jandar of Callisto.* New York, Dell, 1972; London, Futura, 1974.
*The Black Star.* New York, Dell, 1973.
*The Man Who Loved Mars.* New York, Fawcett, and London, White Lion, 1973.
*Sky Pirates of Callisto.* New York, Dell, 1973; London, Futura, 1975.
*When the Green Star Calls.* New York, DAW, 1973.
*The Valley Where Time Stood Still.* New York, Doubleday, 1974.
*Time War.* New York, Dell, 1974.
*By the Light of the Green Star.* New York, DAW, 1974.
*The Warrior of World's End.* New York, DAW, 1974.
*The Nemesis of Evil* (Zarkon). New York, Doubleday, 1975.
*Invisible Death* (Zarkon). New York, Doubleday, 1975.
*Mad Empress of Callisto.* New York, Dell, 1975.
*Mind Wizards of Callisto.* New York, Dell, 1975.
*Lankar of Callisto.* New York, Dell, 1975.
*As the Green Star Rises.* New York, DAW, 1975.
*The Enchantress of World's End.* New York, DAW, 1975.
*The Volcano Ogre* (Zarkon). New York, Doubleday, 1976.
*The Immortal of World's End.* New York, DAW, 1976.
*In the Green Star's Glow.* New York, DAW, 1976.
*The Barbarian of World's End.* New York, DAW, 1977.
*Ylana of Callisto.* New York, Dell, 1977.
*The City Outside the World.* New York, Berkley, 1977.
*Renegade of Callisto.* New York, Dell, 1978.
*The Pirate of World's End.* New York, DAW, 1978.
*Journey to the Underground World.* New York, DAW, 1979.
*Tara of the Twilight.* New York, Zebra, 1979.
*Lost Worlds.* New York, DAW, 1980.

*Zarkon, Lord of the Unknown, in The Earth-Shaker.* New York, Doubleday, 1982.
*Eric of Zanthodon.* New York, DAW, 1982.
*Kellory the Warlock.* New York, Doubleday, 1984.
*Down to a Sunless Sea.* New York, DAW, 1984.
*Dragonrogue* (Magica). New York, DAW, 1984.
*Found Wanting.* New York, DAW, 1985.
*Mandricardo* (Magica). New York, DAW, 1987.
*Horror Wears Blue.* New York, Doubleday, 1987.
*Callipygia* (Magica). New York, DAW, 1988.

Short Stories

*King Kull*, with Robert E. Howard. New York, Lancer, 1967.
*Beyond the Gates of Dream.* New York, Belmont, 1969.

OTHER PUBLICATIONS

Novels

*Conan of the Isles*, with L. Sprague de Camp. New York, Lancer, 1968.
*Giant of World's End.* New York, Belmont, 1969.
*The Quest of Kadji.* New York, Belmont, 1971.
*The Wizard of Zao.* New York, DAW, 1978.
*Conan the Liberator*, with L. Sprague de Camp. New York, Bantam, 1979; London, Sphere, 1980.
*Conan the Barbarian* (novelization of screenplay), with L. Sprague de Camp. New York, Bantam, and London, Sphere, 1982.

Short Stories

*Conan the Wanderer*, with Robert E. Howard and L. Sprague de Camp. New York, Lancer, 1968; London, Sphere, 1974.
*Conan of Cimmeria*, with Robert E. Howard and L. Sprague de Camp, New York, Lancer, 1969; London, Sphere, 1974.
*Conan of Aquilonia* (collection), with L. Sprague de Camp. New York, Lancer, 1971.
*Conan the Swordsman*, with L. Sprague de Camp and Björn Nyberg. New York, Bantam, 1978; London, Sphere, 1979.
*The Conan Chronicles*, with Robert E. Howard and L. Sprague de Camp. London, Orbit, 1990.

Verse

*Dreams from R'lyeh.* Sauk City, Wisconsin, Arkham House, 1975.

Other

*Tolkien: A Look Behind "The Lord of the Rings."* New York, Ballantine, 1969.
*Lovecraft: A Look Behind the "Cthulhu Mythos."* New York, Ballantine, 1972; London, Panther, 1975.
*Imaginary Worlds: The Art of Fantasy.* New York, Ballantine, 1973.
*Middle-Earth: The World of Tolkien*, illustrated by David Wenzel. New York, Centaur, 1977.

Editor, *Dragons, Elves, and Heroes.* New York, Ballantine, 1969.
Editor, *The Young Magicians.* New York, Ballantine, 1969.
Editor, *The Magic of Atlantic.* New York, Lancer, 1970.
Editor, *Golden Cities, Far.* New York, Ballantine, 1970.
Editor, *The Dream-Quest of Unknown Kadath*, by H.P. Lovecraft. New York, Ballantine, 1970.
Editor, *Zothique*, by Clark Ashton Smith. New York, Ballantine, 1970.
Editor, *At the Edge of the World*, by Lord Dunsany. New York, Ballantine, 1970.
Editor, *The Doom That Came to Sarnath*, by H.P. Lovecraft. New York, Ballantine, 1971.
Editor, *Hyperborea*, by Clark Ashton Smith. New York, Ballantine, 1971.
Editor, *The Spawn of Cthulhu.* New York, Ballantine, 1971.
Editor, *New Worlds for Old.* New York, Ballantine, 1971.
Editor, *Discoveries in Fantasy.* New York, Ballantine, 1972; London, Pan, 1974.
Editor, *Great Short Novels of Adult Fantasy 1–2.* New York, Ballantine, 2 vols., 1972–73.
Editor, *Beyond the Fields We Know*, by Lord Dunsany. New York, Ballantine, 1972.
Editor, *Evenor*, by George MacDonald. New York, Ballantine, 1972.
Editor, *Xiccarph*, by Clark Ashton Smith. New York, Ballantine, 1972.
Editor, *Poseidonis*, by Clark Ashton Smith. New York, Ballantine, 1973.
Editor, *Flashing Swords! 1–5.* New York, Doubleday, 3 vols., 1973–77; New York, Dell, 2 vols., 1976–81.
Editor, *Over the Hills and Far Away*, by Lord Dunsany. New York, Ballantine, 1974.
Editor, *The Year's Best Fantasy Stories 1–6.* New York, DAW, 6 vols., 1975–80.
Editor, *Kingdoms of Sorcery.* New York, Doubleday, 1976.
Editor, *Realms of Wizardry.* New York, Doubleday, 1976.
Editor, *Weird Tales 1–4.* New York, Zebra, 1981–83.

* * *

Lin Carter's own fiction is perhaps best understood as an extension of his accomplishments as an editor and popular critic. It reflects the same enthusiasm for the tradition of heroic fantasy that he celebrates, for example, in his non-fiction book *Imaginary Worlds.* The majority of Carter's novels can be characterized as adventure-based heroic fantasy, or sword-and-sorcery. Typically such heroic fantasies are situated on a continent in the distant past. There a barbarian-errant and his companions confront both human and bestial foes. The most terrifying of these human enemies are sorcerers who wield supernatural powers. In addition, the hero inevitably conquers a wide range of dragons and other monsters. The plots involve amplifications of two basic themes: quest and combat.

As a writer of heroic fantasy, Carter basically employs the conventions of that subgenre without altering or subverting them. An avowed admirer of Robert E. Howard, he has produced numerous sword-and-sorcery novels built around the exploits of heroes reminiscent of Howard's Conan the Barbarian. Reading sheer bulk of Carter's output confirms the impression of hurried writing, dependence on formula, and inattention to detail. None of Carter's works stands out, but the most interesting and popular of his efforts remains his first series. This group of novels recounts the adventures of the mighty warrior Thongor. The hero, setting, and exploits all reflect Carter's thorough knowledge of the heroic fiction of Howard and Edgar Rice Burroughs. Thongor is a wandering adventurer who becomes King of Patanga and Overlord of a league of free cities on the Lost Continent of Lemuria, located somewhere in the Pacific "at the dawn of time."

Carter's depiction of Thongor is formulaic and predictable. Confronted by a dragon in *Thongor Fights the Pirates of Tarakus*, for example, the hero stands "ready for action, broadsword glittering in one powerful fist." Then "blind instinct drove him into whirlwind action" and Thongor "with the instincts of a born huntsman" slaughters the beast. The novel itself pits the warrior-king against a renegade wizard and a pirate king. The narrative speeds along, but Carter's constant references to his models, while providing a level of enjoyment to the reader steeped in pulp fiction, diminishes the imaginative intensity that attracts many sword-and-sorcery readers to his primary model Howard. The first volume in the Thongor series, *The Wizard of Lemuria*, in which Thongor defeats the evil Dragon Kings, would provide a good introduction both to Carter's fiction and to the basic conventions of sword-and-sorcery.

Carter's other sword-and-sorcery fiction includes the Jandar series, beginning with *Jandar of Callisto*, which imitates primarily the style and themes of Burroughs. Zarkon, the central figure in still another series, is based on Doc Savage. Carter has published a large number of short stories as well. The shorter works, like the novels, tend to evolve into series and pay homage through imitation. His "Simrana" stories are modeled on the work of Lord Dunsany, and he turned several unfinished tales by Clarke Ashton Smith into complete stories in *Beyond the Gates of Dream*.

In addition to producing a large body of his own heroic fiction, Carter has collaborated with L. Sprague de Camp (and others) to create continuations of two series by Howard: one celebrating Conan and the other narrating the adventures of King Kull. Carter developed his stories from fragments of stories left by Howard. The King Kull works offer a good example of successful imitation. Carter manages to fashion a style highly reminiscent of Howard's. Not surprisingly, since his own fantasies espouse the same position, Carter's tales about Conan and King Kull continue Howard's championing of barbarism over civilization and the implicit praise of the moral virtue of violent confict.

In addition to sword-and-sorcery, Carter has written several works more obviously intended as science fiction. Here too he displays familiarity with and competence in the traditions of pulp writing rather than originality or depth of thought. The style is straightforward, the episodes generally brief, the emphasis on adventure. *The Valley Where Time Stood Still* offers a representative example of this aspect of Carter's fiction. The characters and plot are similar to Carter's fantasies, while the use of science is minimal. The setting is Mars, but the planet is more a locale for action than a carefully created alien world. The plot revolves around two quests, an Earthman for uranium and a Martian warrior-prince for the fabled Valley of Life. Perhaps his most successful science fiction novels are two comic works about an intergalactic secret agent named Hautley Quicksilver. Carter's language, often awkward in his attempts to describe the feats of muscular heroes, is better suited to the light, almost self-deprecatory tone of both *The Thief of Thoth* and *The Purloined Planet*.

The same affection for fantasy and science fiction that permeates Carter's critical writing and his anthologies is the most attractive feature of his fiction. Most of the novels and stories are unabashedly derivative. His plotting, especially in the heroic fantasies, is almost mechanically formulaic, and the language reflects Carter's admiration for the pulp-magazine fiction of the 1930's and 1940's. With all its flaws, his fiction has undeniably become a minor but permanent part of the particular heroic tradition to which he is lovingly devoted.

—Dennis M. Kratz

---

**CARTMILL, Cleve.** Also wrote as Michael Corbin. American. Born in Platteville, Wisconsin, in 1908. Married; one son. Accountant, newspaperman, radio operator; invented the Blackmill system of high-speed typography. *Died 11 February 1964.*

SCIENCE-FICTION PUBLICATIONS

Short Stories (series: Jake Murchison)

*The Space Scavengers.* Chatsworth, California, Major, 1975.

Uncollected Short Stories

"The Shape of Desire," in *Unknown* (New York), June 1941.
"Bit of Tapestry," in *Unknown* (New York), December 1941.
"Prelude to Armageddon," in *Unknown* (New York), April 1942.
"No Graven Image," in *Unknown* (New York), February 1943.
"Guardian" (as Michael Corbin), in *Unknown* (New York), February 1943.
"The Persecutors," in *Super Science* (Kokomo, Indiana), February 1943.
"Forever Tomorrow," in *Astonishing* (Chicago), April 1943.
"Murderer's Apprentice," in *Science Fiction* (Holyoke, Massachusetts), April 1943.
"The Darker Light," in *Super Science* (Kokomo, Indiana), May 1943.
"Let's Disappear," in *Astounding* (New York), May 1943.
"Wheesht!," in *Unknown* (New York), June 1943.
"Clean-Up," in *Unknown* (New York), October 1943.
"The Link," in *Adventures in Time and Space*, edited by Raymond J. Healy and J. Francis McComas. New York, Random House, 1946; London, Grayson, 1952.
"Deadline," in *The Best of Science Fiction*, edited by Groff Conklin. New York, Crown, 1946.
"With Flaming Swords," in *A Treasury of Science Fiction*, edited by Groff Conkin. New York, Crown, 1948.
"Visiting Yokel," in *My Best Science Fiction Story*, edited by Leo Margulies and O.J. Friend. New York, Merlin Press, 1949.
"Cabal," in *Super Science* (Kokomo, Indiana), January 1949.
"Bells on His Toes," in *Fantasy and Science Fiction* (New York), Fall 1949.
"Punching Pillows," in *Astounding* (New York), June 1950.
"Captain Famine," in *Thrilling Wonder Stories* (New York), December 1950.
"Number Nine," in *Great Stories of Science Fiction*, edited by Murray Leinster. New York, Random House, 1951; London, Cassell, 1953.
"The Green Cat," in *The Outer Reaches*, edited by August Derleth. New York, Pellegrini and Cudahy, 1951; London, Consul, 1963.
"You Can't Say That," in *New Tales of Space and Time*, edited by Raymond J. Healy. New York, Holt, 1951; London, Weidenfeld and Nicholson, 1952.
"Overthrow," in *Journey to Infinity*, edited by Martin Greenberg. New York, Gnome Press, 1951.

"At Your Service," in *Thrilling Wonder Stories* (New York), August 1951.

"The Huge Beast," in *Best from Fantasy and Science Fiction*, edited by Anthony Boucher and J. Francis McComas. Boston, Little Brown, 1952.

"Nor Iron Bars," in *Fantasy and Science Fiction* (New York), August 1952.

"My Lady Smiles," in *Fantasy and Science Fiction* (New York), November 1953.

"Age Cannot Wither," in *Beyond 10* (New York), 1955.

"Youth, Anybody?," in *Fantasy and Science Fiction* (New York), November 1955.

"Hell Hath Fury," in *Hell Hath Fury*, edited by George Hay. London, Spearman, 1963.

"Oscar," in *Fifty Short Science Fiction Tales*, edited by Isaac Asimov and Groff Conklin. New York, Macmillan, 1963.

"The Bargain," in *The Unknown 5*, edited by D.R. Benson. New York, Pyramid, 1964.

"Some Day We'll Find You," in *Dimension 4*, edited by Groff Conklin. New York, Pyramid, 1964.

"No News Today," in *Terror!*, edited by Larry T. Shaw. New York, Lancer, 1966.

* * *

Some writers in science fiction, as in other fields of literature, achieve notoriety not for their body of work but for a single story or novel. Tom Godwin ("The Cold Equations") is one such writer. Another is Cleve Cartmill, for "Deadline" (*Astounding*, March 1944). Although "Deadline" has dubious literary merits (predictable plot, pedestrian handling), the story is unique in that it describes, in considerable scientific detail, the manufacture and use of an atomic bomb a year before the United States dropped the first genuine atomic bombs on Hiroshima and Nagasaki. Its publication did not cause an immediate furor in science-fiction circles; it did, however, cause one in the War Department.

Shortly after the novelette appeared, Cartmill was visited by a representative of Military Intelligence and questioned at some length; his file of correspondence with the editor of *Astounding*, John W. Campbell, concerning "Deadline" was also confiscated. Cartmill was later cleared of any wrongdoing, although he was told that he had "violated personal security" in wartime by publicly disseminating the facts contained in the story. These facts, however, were a matter of public record, as Campbell himself pointed out to the Military in denying their request not to publish any further speculation on nuclear fission. Following the close of World War II, "Deadline" became a link in the argument that science fiction is a valid medium for predicting the future. It was also pointed to with pride as an example of science fiction as a serious art form for adults, rather than improbable escapism for juveniles, thereby worthy of consideration not only by members of the scientific community but by the heads of government.

Despite the fact that Cartmill's rather extensive output of science fiction and fantasy is largely forgotten today, at least some of it is of a quality to interest the serious student. His best work, perhaps, is the highly imaginative short novel "Hell Hath Fury." Other excellent efforts include his first published story, "Oscar," and a grim little tale called "The Bargain." Cartmill also wrote space opera; popular in the 1940's was his "Space Salvage" series featuring Jake Murchison and his crew of the spaceship *Dolphin* who tackled "impossible" problems and made fantastic rescues in space. The best of these stories were posthumously collected as *The Space Scavengers*, the only book to bear Cartmill's name.

—Bill Pronzini

---

**CARY, Julian,** *See* **TUBB, E.C.**

---

**CHALKER, Jack L(aurence).** American. Born in Baltimore, Maryland, 17 December 1944. Educated at Towson State College, Baltimore, B.S. 1966; Johns Hopkins University, Baltimore, M.L.A. 1969. Served in the United States Air Force 135th Air Commando Group, 1968–71, and the Maryland Air National Guard, 1968–69; Staff Sergeant. Married Eva C. Whitley in 1978; one son. English, history, and geography teacher in Baltimore high schools, 1966–78. Since 1961, Founder-Director, Mirage Press, Baltimore; editor, *Mirage* fanzine. Agent: Eleanor Wood, Spectrum Literary Agency, 111 Eighth Avenue, Suite 1501, New York, New York 10011, U.S.A. Address: Mirage Press, P.O. Box 1689, Westminster, Maryland 21157-1689, U.S.A.

SCIENCE-FICTION PUBLICATIONS

Novels (series: Changewinds; Dancing Gods; Four Lords of the Diamond; G.O.D., Inc., Quintara Marathon; Ring of the Master; Soul Rider; Well World)

*A Jungle of Stars.* New York, Ballantine, 1976.
Well World:
 *Midnight at the Well of Souls.* New York, Ballantine, 1977; London, Penguin, 1981.
 *Exiles at the Well of Souls.* New York, Ballantine, 1978; London, Penguin, 1982.
 *Quest for the Well of Souls.* New York, Ballantine, 1978; London, Penguin, 1982.
 *The Return of Nathan Brazil.* New York, Ballantine, n.d.; London, Penguin, 1984.
 *Twilight at the Well of Souls.* New York, Ballantine, 1980; London, Penguin, 1984.
*Dancers in the Afterglow.* New York, Ballantine, 1978.
*The Web of the Chozen.* New York, Ballantine, 1978.
*A War of Shadows.* New York, Ace, 1979.
Four Lords of the Diamond:
 *Lilith: A Snake in the Grass.* New York, Ballantine, 1981; London, Penguin, 1990.
 *Cerberus: A Wolf in the Fold.* New York, Ballantine, 1982; London, Penguin, 1991.
 *Charon: A Dragon at the Gate.* New York, Ballantine, 1982; London, Penguin, 1991.
 *Medusa: A Tiger by the Tail.* New York, Ballantine, 1983.
*The Identity Matrix.* New York, Pocket Books, 1982.
*Soul Rider.* London, Penguin, 1991.
 *Spirits of Flux and Anchor.* New York, Tor, 1984.
 *Empires of Flux and Anchor.* New York, Tor, 1984.
 *Masters of Flux and Anchor.* New York, Tor, 1985.
 *The Birth of Flux and Anchor.* New York, Tor, 1985.
 *Children of Flux and Anchor.* New York, Tor, 1986.
*The River of Dancing Gods.* New York, Ballantine, 1984; London, Futura, 1985.

*Demons of the Dancing Gods*. New York, Ballantine, 1984; London, Futura, 1986.
*The Messiah Choice*. New York, Bluejay, 1985.
*Downtiming the Night Side*. New York, Tor, 1985.
*Vengeance of the Dancing Gods*. New York, Ballantine, 1985; London, Futura, 1986.
The Rings of the Master:
*Lords of the Middle Dark*. New York, Ballantine, 1986; London, New English Library, 1988.
*Pirates of Thunder*. New York, Ballantine, 1987; London, New English Library, 1988.
*Warriors of the Storm*. New York, Ballantine, 1987; London, New English Library, 1989.
*Masks of the Martyrs*. New York, Ballantine, 1988; London, New English Library, 1989.
Changewinds:
*When the Changewinds Blow*. New York, Ace, 1987; London, New English Library, 1991.
*Riders of the Winds*. New York, Ace, 1988.
*War of the Maelstrom*. New York, Ace, 1988.
G.O.D., Inc.:
*The Labyrinths of Dreams*. New York, Tor, 1987; London, New English Library, 1989.
*The Shadow Dancers*. New York, Tor, 1987; London, New English Library, 1989.
*The Maze in the Mirror*. New York, Tor, 1989; London, New English Library, 1990.
The Quintara Marathon:
*The Demons at Rainbow Bridge*. New York, Ace, 1989.
*The Ninety Trillion Fausts*. New York, Ace, 1991.
*The Run to Chaos Keep*. New York, Ace, 1991.
*Songs of the Dancing Gods*. New York, Ballantine, 1990.
*The Red Tape War*, with Mike Resnick and George Alec Effinger. New York, Tor, 1991.

Short Stories

*Dance Band on the Titanic* (stories and essays). New York, Ballantine, 1988.

OTHER PUBLICATIONS

Novels

*And the Devil Will Drag You Under*. New York, Ballantine, 1979.
*The Devil's Voyage*. New York, Doubleday, 1981.

Other

*The New H.P. Lovecraft Bibliography*. Baltimore, Mirage Press, 1962; revised edition, with Mark Owings, as *The Revised H.P. Lovecraft Bibliography*, 1973.
*The Index to the Science-Fantasy Publishers*, with Mark Owings. Baltimore, Mirage Press, 1966; revised edition, as *Index to the SF Publishers*, 1979.
*The Necronomicon: A Study*, with Mark Owings. Baltimore, Mirage Press, 1967.
*An Informal Biography of Scrooge McDuck*. Baltimore, Mirage Press, 1974.

Editor, *In Memoriam Clark Ashton Smith*. Baltimore, Mirage Press, 1963.
Editor, *Mirage on Lovecraft*. Baltimore, Mirage Press, 1964.

*

Bibliography: in *Program Book*, Paracon 1, State College, Pennsylvania, 1978; in *Dance Band on the Titanic* by Chalker, New York, Ballantine, 1988.

Jack L. Chalker comments:

Although I have a technical background, my degrees are in the social, not the pure, sciences, and my work generally reflects this. My stories are about people, mostly ordinary people, caught up in extraordinary circumstances and usually changed by them. They use the fun-house mirror reflection of science fiction to examine people and culture, including ideology, as I see them today. The themes are anti-dogmatic: ideologies and human preachments are taken apart, examined, and generally found wanting. For this reason a lot of my work had been taken as anti-utopian and downbeat, but there is a strain of optimism there because, no matter what, mankind copes with adversity and overcomes, although never without cost. There is an inherently absurdist streak in man which has caused him, over six thousand years of recorded history, to kill, torture, and maim, mostly in the name of the people. Man adapts, advances, and grows despite this.

On the individual level, my stories examine the way human beings treat each other, generally brutalizing those most in need of help, and those individuals' quests for their own better life. For these themes, and others, interwoven in my stories, science fiction provides the perfect metaphors. I am a strongly political writer, without ideology, only hope. And yet all my stories are superficially plots of twist and turn, diverting entertainments, problems to be solved. Pacing is all important to me; I want the reader to turn to the next page, to keep reading, and to have a good time as my serious themes creep into the entertainment but never get in its way.

* * *

Over the last decade, Jack L. Chalker has become a highly successful and widely published author known mostly for his novel sequences, including the Well World, Four Lords of the Diamond, Soul Rider, and the detective-parody trilogy G.O.D. Inc. He is a writer who has been both praised and condemned as a mechanical churner-out of hack-work. His work, though flawed, will reward the reader both as an entertainment and a treatment of serious themes.

One theme and literary device can be found throughout Chalker's work. It is the theme of conflict between a desire for freedom and a desire for security, between the need for independence and the need for comfort and the good opinion of others. The device is that of transformation, of people, both ordinary and extraordinary, being made into something other than themselves. The means of forcing the change may be magical, technological, or psychological, but it is always a metaphor for the agony that moral choice and the unyielding facts of life create in people. Some of Chalker's characters grow stronger because of the changes that are forced on them, some are shattered by the changes; but Chalker always makes you watch with sympathy the pain of the characters as they face the horrendous situations he places them in. Like Alfred Hitchcock, Chalker seems to believe that the key to excitement is to threaten the heroine; his protagonists (and especially the female ones) are made to face their worst fears and overcome, or be overcome, by them.

The typical Chalker situation is embodied in *Afterglow*, one of his earliest and best novels. Alien invaders overrun a tourist planet and begin to convert the inhabitants to a more docile and communal form of life, using their human weaknesses as the means of cracking and remoulding their minds. The hero, a cyborg special agent, watches the new-found happiness of the brainwashed victims and envies them their simplicity and sense of community almost enough to betray his trust. At the climax, Chalker makes the moral core of his novels as clear as he ever does, when the hero and the villain debate the moral difference between a controlled, stagnant, happy society and undomesticated humanity with its hatreds and imperfections. Unlike Heinlein, Chalker can see, and make you see, the attractions of submission to authority at the same time as he rejects it.

Because of Chalker's willingness to use sexual metaphors for the struggle for power, some critics have rejected his work as mere exploitation. Thomas M. Disch referred to the Soul Rider sequence as "better-written Gor books." But Chalker's books are not written to praise the urge for power, but to show how pervasive it is even in those who claim to be liberal or in revolt against it, and how fragile the defences are that have built up against absolutism of every kind. His concerns about the increasing power of technology and his pessimism about people's willingness to make principled political decisions about the control of such new capacity is expounded in the essays included in his short story collection *Dance Band on the Titanic.*

All of this is not to say that Chalker's work is without flaws. His writing style needs heavier editing than it has received recently. And since he likes to create MacGuffins that are all powerful (the powers of the Flux Magicians, the universe-rewriting Obie computer, the magical lamp of One Wish Only), he often plots himself into a corner and forgets the limits he placed upon his creations earlier to get out of later difficulties. The novel that is most offensive in this regard is the time-travel saga, *Downtiming the Night Side.*

Chalker's flaws are minor compared with his virtues, which are those of a story-teller. He has resisted the temptation of continuing his novel-sequences beyond the point at which invention flags (except perhaps in the River of Dancing Gods sequence, which carried its sword and sorcery parody on a little too long). He will probably never be popular enough in the SF establishment to win major recognition. But since he gives his own role-models as Louis L'Amour and Evan Hunter, he will probably not be too distressed by this.

—Michael Cule

---

**CHANDLER, A(rthur) Bertram.** Australian. Born in Aldershot, Hampshire, England, 28 March 1912. Educated at Peddar's Lane Council School, and Sir John Leman School, Beccles, Suffolk. Married 1) Joan Chandler; 2) Susan Schlenker; two daughters and one son. Apprentice, rising to Third Officer, Sun Shipping Company, London, 1928–35; Fourth Officer, rising to Chief Officer, Shaw Savill Line, London, 1936–55; Third Officer, rising to Master, Union Steam Ship Company of New Zealand, Wellington, 1956–75. Recipient: Ditmar award (Australia), 1969, 1971, 1974, 1976; Seiun Sho award (Japan), 1975; Invisible Little Man award, 1975; Australian Literature Board Fellowship, 1980. Guest of Honor, World SF Convention, Chicago, 1981. *Died 6 June 1984.*

SCIENCE-FICTION PUBLICATIONS

Novels (series: Empress Irene; John Grimes; Rim Worlds)

*Bring Back Yesterday* (Rim Worlds). New York, Ace, 1961; London, Allison and Busby, 1981.
*Rendezvous on a Lost World* (Rim Worlds). New York, Ace, 1961; as *When the Dream Dies*, London, Allison and Busby, 1981.
*The Rim of Space* (Rim Worlds). New York, Avalon, 1961; London, Allison and Busby, 1981.
*Beyond the Galactic Rim, The Ship from Outside* (Rim Worlds). New York, Ace, 1963; London, Allison and Busby, 1982.
*The Hamelin Plague*. Derby, Connecticut, Monarch, 1963.
*Glory Planet*. New York, Avalon, 1964.
*The Deep Reaches of Space*. London, Jenkins, 1964.
*Into the Alternate Universe* (Grimes), *The Coils of Time*. New York, Ace, 1964.
*Empress of Outer Space* (Empress), *The Alternate Martians*. New York, Ace, 1965.
*Space Mercenaries* (Empress). New York, Ace, 1965.
*The Road to the Rim* (Grimes). New York, Ace, 1967.
*Contraband from Otherspace* (Grimes). New York, Ace, 1967.
*Nebula Alert* (Empress). New York, Ace, 1967.
*False Fatherhood* (Grimes). Sydney, Horwitz, 1968; as *Spartan Planet*, New York, Dell, 1969.
*Catch the Star Winds* (Rim Worlds). New York, Lancer, 1969.
*The Sea Beasts*. New York, Curtis, 1971.
*To Prime the Pump* (Grimes). New York, Curtis, 1971.
*The Inheritors, The Gateway to Never* (Grimes). New York, Ace, 1972.
*The Bitter Pill*. Melbourne, Wren, 1974.
*The Big Black Mark* (Grimes). New York, DAW, 1975.
*The Broken Cycle* (Grimes). London, Hale, 1975; New York, DAW, 1979.
*The Way Back* (Grimes). London, Hale, 1976; New York, DAW, 1978.
*Star Courier* (Grimes). London, Hale, and New York, DAW, 1977.
*The Far Traveller* (Grimes). London, Hale, 1977; New York, DAW, 1979.
*To Keep the Ship* (Grimes). London, Hale, and New York, DAW, 1978.
*Matilda's Stepchildren*. London, Hale, 1979; New York, DAW, 1983.
*Star Loot* (Grimes). New York, DAW, 1980; London, Hale, 1981.
*Kelly Country*. Ringwood, Victoria, Penguin, 1983.
*Frontier of the Dark*. New York, Ace, 1984.
*The Last Amazon*. New York, DAW, 1984.
*The Wild Ones*. Victoria, Australia, Collins, and New York, DAW, 1985.

Short stories (series: John Grimes in all books)

*The Rim Gods*. New York, Ace, 1968.
*The Dark Dimensions, Alternate Orbits*. New York, Ace, 1971; *Alternate Orbits* published separately as *Commodore at Sea*, 1979.
*The Hard Way Up*. New York, Ace, 1972.
*Up to the Sky in Ships*. Cambridge, Massachusetts, NESFA Press, 1982.

*

Bibliography: "Bibliography of the Works of A. Bertram Chandler" by Ross Pavlac, in *Marcon XIII* (Columbus, Ohio), March 1978.

A. Bertram Chandler commented:

(1981) Quite a few years ago Robert Heinlein said, "Only people who know ships can write convincingly about spaceships." At the time I thought that this was very true. I have not changed my opinion. I believe that the crews of the *real* spaceships of the future, vessels going a long way in a long time, will have far more in common with today's seamen than with today's airmen. I freely admit that my stories are essentially sea stories and that John Grimes, my series character, is descended from Hornblower. At a book-signing recently in Fukuoka I felt flattered when one of my Japanese faithful readers gave me one of Forester's Hornblower novels to autograph.

* * *

A. Bertram Chandler produced an enormous body of work that is based on his experiences as a merchant mariner, his love of adventure ficion, and the role model synthesis of these two aspects, the fictional character of Horatio Hornblower. Beginning in about 1959, Chandler developed the character of John Grimes, then an ensign, and the concept of the Rim World—rim stars out on the fringes of galactic civilization. *The Road to the Rim* reads as though it was composed of stories for magazines. Grimes becomes aware of his love of space, his fascination for the Rim World, and the adventure to be found there.

Perhaps because he had such a good eye for detail and was able to sell the locale of the Rim World, Chandler found the necessary formula, in which he intertwined the lives of Derek Calver (from *The Rim of Space*), Sonya Verrill, and then John Grimes, whom Verrill eventually marries. Grimes extends his activities over a period of time covered in 13 novels to the point where he becomes a commodore in the Rim Worlds Merchant Navy, and finds a home for himself on a remote planet, not only because it is "closer to work," but because it allows a comfortable life style.

Chandler was a jovial man with an impish sense of humor—he makes frequent topical allusions to current events, the works of other science-fiction and imaginative writers, and, sometimes, even to such historical events as the mutiny on *H.M.S. Bounty*. His works will never be accused of heavy going, an overly philosophical point of view—unless you include frequent support of nudism—or raising complex moral issues.

His plots tend to be direct and linear: is Grimes getting too soft for duty? Do his men respect him? Is he in danger of becoming a ladies' man? (No.) Can he withstand temptations to take bribes? (Yes.) Can he be effective in putting down a mutiny? His characters could certainly be role models for television situation comedies or adventures: the good guys and the aliens are readily apparent; there are few shades of grey, no nuances of meaning, no room for misunderstanding.

As a consequence of flat characters, his dialog is rarely exciting, and the reader, if not careful, can lose the way—who is saying what? Several critics have noted the use of stock phrases and clichés. It is also fair to question his speech cadences, and the fact that the aliens are distinguished from the Earthlings only by a different set of clichés.

What makes him endure, then? It is the obvious good cheer, the quick turn of plot, the excellent sense of background, and the realization that sea stories and space opera have a common existential bond. Grimes, at best a good man, is just short of boring, thanks to his over-all niceness and mischievous humor. An excellent way to sample the Chandler Rim Worlds is in *The Dark Dimensions*, in which Chandler puts Grimes in the Captain's Paradise situation by having two John Grimeses, one each from a parallel universe. The two meet, each with a different wife, and each cuckolds the other and, by implication, himself. Naughty, funny for as long as it lasts, and sensible enough not to last too long.

Chandler is pure entertainment, lacking the craft and intricacy to secure him a more permanent niche.

—Shelly Lowenkopf

---

**CHARBONNEAU, Louis (Henry).** Also writes as Carter Travis Young. American. Born in Detroit, Michigan, 20 January 1924. Educated at the University of Detroit, A.B. 1948, M.A. 1950. Served in the United States Army Air Force, 1943–46: Staff Sergeant. Married 1) Hilda Sweeney in 1945 (died 1984); 2) Diane Fries in 1984. Instructor in English, University of Detroit, 1948–52; copywriter, Mercury Advertising Agency, Los Angeles, 1952–56; staff writer, Los Angeles *Times*, 1956–71; freelance writer, 1971–74; editor, Security World Publishing Company, Los Angeles, 1974–79. Since 1979, freelance writer. Agent: Scott Meredith Literary Agency, 845 Third Avenue, New York, New York 10022, U.S.A.

### Science-Fiction Publications

#### Novels

*No Place on Earth*. New York, Doubleday, 1958; London, Jenkins, 1966.
*Corpus Earthling*. New York, Doubleday, 1960; London, Digit, 1963.
*The Sentinel Stars*. New York, Bantam, and London, Corgi, 1964.
*Psychedelic-40*. New York, Bantam, 1965; as *The Specials*, London, Jenkins, 1967.
*Down to Earth*. New York, Bantam, 1967; as *Antic Earth*, London, Jenkins, 1967.
*The Sensitives* (novelization of screenplay). New York, Bantam, 1968.
*Barrier World*. New York, Lancer, 1970.
*Embryo* (novelization of screenplay). New York, Warner, 1976.

### Other Publications

#### Novels

*Night of Violence*. New York, Torquil, and London, Digit, 1959; as *The Trapped Ones*, London, Barker, 1960.
*Nor All Your Tears*. New York, Torquil, 1959; as *The Time of Desire*, London, Digit, 1960.
*Way Out*. London, Barrie and Rockliff, and New York, Banner, 1966.
*Down from the Mountain*. New York, Doubleday, 1969.
*And Hope to Die*. New York, Ace, 1970.
*From a Dark Place*. New York, Dell, 1974.
*Intruder*. New York, Doubleday, 1979.
*The Lair*. New York, Fawcett, 1979.
*The Brea File*. New York, Doubleday, 1983.

Novels as Carter Travis Young

*The Wild Breed*. New York, Doubleday, 1960; as *The Sudden Gun*, London, Hammond, 1960.
*The Savage Plain*. New York, Doubleday, 1961; London, Hammond, 1963.
*Shadow of a Gun*. New York, Fawcett, 1961; London, Muller, 1962.
*The Bitter Iron*. New York, Doubleday, 1964; London, Ward Lock, 1965.
*Long Boots, Hard Boots*. New York, Doubleday, 1965; London, Ward Lock, 1966.
*Why Did They Kill Charley?* New York, Doubleday, and London, Ward Lock, 1967.
*Winchester Quarantine*. New York, Doubleday, 1970.
*The Pocket Hunters*. New York, Doubleday, 1972.
*Winter of the Coup*. New York, Doubleday, 1972.
*The Captive*. New York, Doubleday, 1973.
*Guns of Darkness*. New York, Doubleday, 1974.
*Blaine's Law*. New York, Doubleday, 1974.
*Red Grass*. New York, Doubleday, 1976.
*Winter Drift*. New York, Doubleday, 1980.
*The Smoking Hills*. New York, Doubleday, 1988.

Television Play: *Cry of Silence* (*The Outer Limits* series), 1963–64.

Other

*Trail: The Story of the Lewis and Clark Expedition*. New York, Doubleday, 1989.
*The Ice: A Novel of Antarctica*. New York, Fine, 1991.

*

Manuscript Collection: University of Oregon Library, Eugene.

Louis Charbonneau comments:

My science-fiction novels, most of which were written in the 1960's, would seem to be out of the mainstream of much current SF, though perhaps part of a longer running stream, one that begins with existing conditions, problems, or possibilities and projects them into an imagined future not all that remote, and with an emphasis on human characters rather than upon the grotesque or fantastic. It has been called social-science fiction, with a moral dimension often fairly evident. I can admire those fantasists who create wholly imagined worlds with little if any relation to our own, but I find myself as a writer interested more in the human predicament, as it is now or, given certain circumstances, as it might be in the future.

* * *

Notable first novels are rare; notable first science-fiction novels virtually non-existent. With his first work, *No Place on Earth*, Louis Charbonneau showed himself a scarce bird indeed—a science-fiction writer with almost no interest in mechanisms and remote worlds. The peculiar appeal of this yarn lies not in outré surroundings or wild technology but in the little-known territory of man himself.

It is in its impact upon man, in fact, that Charbonneau finds a writer's use for science. He acknowledges with us that technology is marvelous, that we reap great benefits from the application of machines to our culture. But he confesses almost no background to deal with the intricacies of gadgetry; his concern is with the social aspects of things like automatons. So in *No Place on Earth*, Charbonneau tackles the population alarm expressed by Malthus and treats its implications like the good reporter he is. His prose is lean and highly readable, and he gives life to his writing through heavy reliance upon dialog. His characters do not have to be complex, because he generalizes from selection of typical people who must deal with extraordinary demands. In a sense Charbonneau appears to encourage all of his readers to expand to meet the pressures imposed upon them by a sometimes-bewildering technology. Concepts like mind control and sirloin capsules have both good and bad points, as we see through the author's often-humorous treatment.

Like many good writers, Charbonneau has learned his craft in the demanding school of journalism. He learned about people and their glands—some readers might say a bit too much so in works like *Corpus Earthling*. This novel imagines the people of Earth being literally occupied by aliens. What might eventually have resulted without the enterprise of a college insructor could have produced quite a different story. But as said instructor gains telepathic knowledge of this invasion, the whole fiendish plot is revealed. It is the way he obtains his information—in bed with several coeds—that might prove objectionable to staid readers of this story. The research method, nonetheless, does stress the author's realistic understanding of the human condition to counter this threat.

A different slice of such understanding is found in *The Sentinel Stars*, where we encounter every person born as a debtor. This means the entire population must spend its whole life span paying off the debt, which can't be done because of the high cost of living. In good reporter fashion, Charbonneau sounds a familiar dirge: a sense of slavery to the times. But all is not lost, for the hero—who bears the same sort of numerical I.D. as all of us today—suggests rebellious measures which might create unrest in contemporary free-spending lawmakers's consciences.

It is the social-scientific concern of Charbonneau that has perhaps discouraged his recent production of science fiction. He expresses distaste for the gee-whiz aspects of much current writing, although he admits the value to society of many devices (he finds a word processor convenient in writing, for example). But he deplores the dehumanizing evident in works of science fiction which reach out far into the cosmos. So, evidently, do the Japanese readers of his *No Place on Earth*, which has gone through recent reprintings in that country. Charbonneau's labeling of current movies, with their spectacular special effects and elaborate settings, as "extended comics" would find considerable endorsement among serious, mature readers of science fiction.

Louis Charbonneau remains a worthy and interesting figure in the world of science fiction, not only because of his stylistic appeal, but also because he represents a source of the kind of science fiction which provided the impetus for the sort of reading that is still among the more interesting pursuits in a gadget-infested world.

—Robert H. Wilcox

---

**CHARNAS, Suzy McKee.** American. Born in New York City, 22 October 1939. Educated at New York High School of Music and Art; Barnard College, New York, B.A. in economic history 1961; New York University, M.A. Married Stephen Charnas in 1968; two step-children. Peace Corps English and history teacher, Girls' High School, Ogbomoso, Nigeria, 1961–62; Lecturer in Economic History, University of Ibadan, Ife, Nigeria, 1962–63; English-History Core Teacher, New Lincoln School, New York, 1965–67; worked for Community Mental

Health organization, New York, 1967–69. Since 1969, freelance writer. Agent: Howard Morhaim, 175 Fifth Avenue, New York, New York 10010, U.S.A. Address: 520 Cedar NE, Albuquerque, New Mexico 87106, U.S.A.

SCIENCE-FICTION PUBLICATIONS

Novels

*Walk to the End of the World.* New York, Ballantine, 1974; London, Gollancz, 1979.
*Motherlines.* New York, Berkley, 1979; London, Gollancz, 1980.
*The Vampire Tapestry.* New York, Simon and Schuster, 1980.

OTHER PUBLICATIONS

Novels

*The Bronze King* (for young adults). Boston, Houghton Mifflin, 1985.
*Dorothea Dreams.* New York, Arbor House, 1986.
*The Silver Glove* (for young adults). New York, Bantam, 1988.
*The Golden Thread* (for young adults). New York, Bantam, 1989.

Play

*Vampire Dreams,* adaptation of "Unicorn Tapestry" (produced San Francisco, California, March 1990).

*

Critical Study: *Suzy Charnas, Joan Vinge, and Octavia Butler* by Richard Law, with others, San Bernardino, California, Borgo Press, 1986.

Suzy McKee Charnas comments:

I particularly enjoy taking up some hoary science fiction or fantasy stereotype—jolly barbarism after the holocaust, breast-plated Amazons, blue-blooded vampires, wise old wizards, ravening werewolves—and turning it upside down to see what surprises and delights I can shake out of its pockets. Missing the usual claptrap clichés, some readers accuse me of "propagandizing," which seems to mean daring to draw their attention to other possibilities than the most blatant formulae given by the received wisdom about this or that. The charge is baloney. It's not my job to alter other people's opinions but to ask questions that interest me, and to pursue possible answers as honestly and as skillfully as I can. Let those travel with me who will; those who don't like the ride or who fear the destination can always get off by closing the book. My goal is to write stories that engage the mind and embroil the heart, and to write them as entertainingly and as beautifully as I can. Often it's plain hard work; but at its best writing is (like good reading) one of the sublimest forms of play.

*   *   *

When Iago says to Brabantio, "you'll have your daughter covered with a Barbary horse . . . you'll have coursers for cousins, and gennets for germans," an example of malevolence addresses a symbol of patriarchal power. These two representational essences are fused in Suzy McKee Charnas's first novel, *Walk to the End of the World,* where masculine hegemony is synonymous with unmitigated evil. Iago's utterance also illuminates its sequel, *Motherlines,* in which daughters are indeed covered by horses who are thought to be the near kinsmen of their mistresses. As *Othello* explores the effects of exaggerated personality traits, Charnas's fiction presents an exaggerated vision of sexism's consequences.

*Walk to the End of the World* is set in the Holdfast, a limited environment populated by survivors of the Wasting, or nuclear holocaust. This postwar society is a paradise for white male misogynistic bigots: the entire population is Caucasian, and the men are taught that "females themselves brought on the Wasting of the world." Holdfast "fems" supposedly "had no souls, only inner cores of animated darkness shaped from the void beyond the stars. Their deaths had no significance. Some men believed that the same shadows return again and again in successive fem-bodies." We, with our Eve, Pandora, and cultures where women are fuel for the flames of their husbands' funeral pyres, cannot feel smug after encountering a Holdfast myth. In this manner, Charnas's fiction continuously echoes reality.

The structure, as well as much of the content of *Walk to the End of the World,* reflects women's secondary status. Before encountering Alldera, the heroine, readers are familiar with the Holdfast's notions of "fem-taint," "Cunt-hunger," institutionalized rape, and girl children who must scratch for survival in the straw of the "kit-pen." Alldera's situation is immediately apparent: as a woman, she must satisfy all the demands of her male masters. Even a slave cannot be completely controlled by an oppressor. Since Alldera possesses mental acuteness and training as a runner, she can sometimes use her mind and body to suit her own best advantage. Her circumstances resemble those of an intelligent, talented Black person in the Jim Crow south. The novel's plot corrects the Holdfast's negative view of the feminine. For example, the text clarifies its own prologue: women certainly did not cause the Wasting of the world. Rather, subhuman men cause the wasting of women. Happily, something positive does manage to coincide with the sombering aspects of this novel and women's reality. Alldera has the opportunity to flee the Holdfast; some women have the pleasure of knowing that when they approach their house yard gate, they are not walking to the end of their world.

In *Motherlines* the open plains lying beyond the men's sphere of influence sharply contrast with the Holdfast's defined boundaries. Women completely control this terrain. In fact, to cite another example of Charnas's penchant for creating extreme circumstances, men never enter the domain of escaped free fems and the indigenous riding women of the motherline tribes. This women's world is not a Utopia for stereotypically peace-loving, nurturing females. The tribes routinely raid each other, one powerful woman dictates her will to the free fems, and the riding women's method of raising children reminds Alldera of the Holdfast's "kit-pen." Although the tribal women are imperfect, they possess impressive attributes: self-sufficiency, an identification with matrilineal relationships, and racial tolerance. Alldera and her free fem companion are allowed to live in the tribe with dignity. She no longer has the negative self-image described in *Walk to the End of the World,* where she feels "hollow in body . . . hollow in mind, for there was nothing else she might imagine, feel, or will that a man could not wipe out of existence by picking her up for his own purposes." This transformation is of primary importance in *Motherlines.*

Another aspect of the novel is a secondary concern. "Oh . . . We mate with our horses," is the answer to Alldera's question about reproduction in a completely female society. Those who judge this information to be a flippant, sarcastic retort react prematurely. The woman who answers Alldera speaks the truth about a situation which expands the definition of "perversion."

Charnas's characters are not presented solely to titillate an audience. Although the sexuality of the motherline tribes is bizarre, they always mate to fulfill their natural reproductive purpose. And the women are in total control of the sexual arena. In contrast, human heterosexuality can be degrading and destructive.

In the real world, the idea of a totally independent woman is, using Harlan Ellison's term, a "dangerous vision." Many readers, men and women, might be taken aback by the controversial content of Charnas's novels.

—Marleen S. Barr

---

**CHASE, Adam.** *See* **FAIRMAN, Paul W.; LESSER, Milton.**

---

**CHERRYH, C.J.** Pseudonym for Carolyn Janice Cherry. American. Born in St. Louis, Missouri, 1 September 1942. Educated at the University of Oklahoma, Norman, 1960–64, B.A. in Latin 1964 (Phi Beta Kappa); Johns Hopkins University, Baltimore (Woodrow Wilson Fellow, 1965–66), M.A. in classics 1965. Taught Latin and ancient history in Oklahoma City public schools, 1965–76. Recipient: John W. Campbell award, 1977; Hugo award, 1979, 1982, 1988; Balrog award, 1982. Address: 1901 Bella Vista, Edmond, Oklahoma 73034, U.S.A.

### Science-Fiction Publications

Novels (series: Chanur; Cyteen, Faded Sun; Morgaine; Sword of Knowledge)

*The Book of Morgaine*. New York, Doubleday, 1979; as *The Chronicles of Morgaine*, London, Methuen, 1985.
*Gate of Ivrel*. New York, DAW, 1976; London, Futura, 1977.
*Well of Shiuan*. New York, DAW, 1978; London, Magnum, 1981.
*Fires of Azeroth*. New York, DAW, 1979; London, Methuen, 1982.
*Brothers of Earth*. New York, DAW, 1976; London, Futura, 1977.
*Hunter of Worlds*. New York, DAW, 1976; London, Futura, 1977.
*The Faded Sun: Kesrith*. New York, DAW, 1978.
*The Faded Sun: Shon'Jir*. New York, DAW, 1979.
*Hestia*. New York, DAW, 1979; London, VGSF, 1988.
*Serpent's Reach*. New York, DAW, 1980; London, Macdonald, 1981.
*The Faded Sun: Kutath*. New York, DAW, 1980.
*Wave Without a Shore*. New York, DAW, 1981; London, VGSF, 1988.
*Downbelow Station*. New York, DAW, 1981; London, Methuen, 1983.
*The Pride of Chanur*. New York, DAW, 1982; London, Methuen, 1983.
*Merchanter's Luck*. New York, DAW, 1982; London, Methuen, 1984.
*Port Eternity*. New York, DAW 1982; London, Gollancz, 1989.
*The Dreamstone*. New York, DAW, 1983; London, VGSF, 1987.
*The Tree of Swords and Jewels*. New York, DAW, 1983; London, VGSF, 1988.
*40000 in Gehenna*. Huntington Woods, Michigan, Phantasia Press, 1983; London, Methuen, 1986.
*Voyager in Night*. New York, DAW, 1984; London, Methuen, 1985.
*Chanur's Venture*. Huntington Woods, Michigan, Phantasia Press, 1984; London, Methuen, 1986.
*Cuckoo's Egg*. Huntington Woods, Michigan, Phantasia Press, 1985; London, Methuen, 1987.
*The Kif Strike Back* (Chanur). Huntington Woods, Michigan, Phantasia Press, 1985; London, Methuen, 1987.
*Angel with the Sword*. New York, DAW, 1985; London, Methuen, 1987.
*The Gates of Hell*, with Janet Morris. New York, Baen, 1986.
*Soul of the City*, with Janet Morris and Lynn Abbey. New York, Ace, 1986.
*Glass and Amber*. Cambridge, Massachusetts, NESFA Press, 1987.
*Kings In Hell*, with Janet Morris. New York, Baen, 1987.
*Legions of Hell*. New York, Baen, 1987.
*Chanur's Homecoming*. New York, DAW, 1986; London, Methuen, 1988.
*Visible Light*. West Bloomfield, Michigan, Phantasia Press, 1986; London, Methuen, 1988.
*The Faded Sun Trilogy*. London, Methuen, 1987.
*Smuggler's Gold*. New York, DAW, 1988.
*The Paladin*. New York, Baen, 1988; London, Mandarin, 1990.
*Exile's Gate*. New York, DAW, 1988; London, Methuen, 1989.
*Ealdwood* (includes *The Dreamstone* and *The Tree of Swords and Jewels*). London, Gollancz, 1989.
*Rimrunners*. New York, Warner, 1989; London, New English Library, 1990.
*Rusalka*. New York, Ballantine, 1989; London, Mandarin, 1990.
*A Dirge for Sabis*, with Leslie Fish. New York, Baen, 1989.
*Wizard Spawn* (Sword of Knowledge), with Nancy Asire. New York, Baen, 1989.
*Reap The Whirlwind* (Sword of Knowledge), with Mercedes Lackey. New York, Baen, 1989.
*Cyteen*. New York, Warner, 1988; London, New English Library, 1989.
*The Betrayal*. New York, Popular Library, 1989.
*The Rebirth*. New York, Popular Library, 1989.
*The Vindication*. New York, Popular Library, 1989.
*Chernevog*. New York, Ballantine, 1990; London, Mandarin, 1991.
*Yvgenie*. New York, Ballantine, 1991.
*Heavy Time*. New York, Warner, 1991; London, New English Library, 1991.

Short Stories

*Festival Moon*. New York, DAW, 1987.
*Troubled Waters*. New York, DAW, 1988.

### Other Publications

Other

Editor, *Sunfall*. New York, DAW, 1981; London, Mandarin, 1990.
Editor, *Merovingen Nights*. New York, DAW, 1987.
Editor, *Fever Season*. New York, DAW, 1987.

Editor, *Divine Right.* New York, DAW, 1989.
Editor, *Flood Tide.* New York, DAW, 1990.

Translator, *The Green Gods*, by Charles and Nathalie Henneberg. New York, DAW, 1980.
Translator, *Star Crusade*, by Pierre Barbet. New York, DAW, 1980.
Translator, *The Book of Shai*, by Daniel Walther. New York, DAW, 1984.

*

C.J. Cherryh comments:

Having made thorough study of the past I am vehemently certain that I do not wish to live in it, nor do I wish to see three quarters of the planet weltering in conditions that should have been left in the past, with the same hunger and disease our ancestors knew. The reach for space and its resources is the make-or-break point for our species, and the appropriate use of technology and the adjustment of human viewpoint to a universe not limited to a blue sky overhead and the curvature of the horizon are absolutely critical to our survival. Therefore I write fiction about space and human adjustment to the unfamiliar. The references in my work are frequently to writings on the aesthetics of physics or other sciences, compared and contrasted to writings of the ancients and concepts and philosophies better known to anthropologists than to the general public: while I have the most profound respect for the traditions of English language literature, I consider the images overworked and frequently inadequate for the task of conveying non-English concepts. Therefore I use the form of English literature, but bring into it a great many things which are pertinent to the sciences, or to the far corners of the world. This in my estimation is what science fiction ought to do to literature, create new symbologies and new understandings appropriate to the space age, not forgetting the traditions of our own culture, but widening its viewpoints.

* * *

Since C.J. Cherryh has burst onto the SF literary scene, producing at least two novels each year since the mid-1970's, she has been widely hailed as a genuinely entertaining storyteller, but one whose space-fairing and human-alien contact stories seem hackneyed and unlikely to advance the genre. Now, after some 30 novels and over a dozen short stories, the outlines of a grand design are perceptible in her work and a more positive synthesis and assessment is possible, indeed deserved.

It became clear that Cherryh was not writing mere space-and-critter yarns or attenuating series of sequels for the sake of production, but was using established SF clichés to outline an entire galactic future history. Moreover, her prolific output of SF novels came increasingly to be recognized as speculative anthropology, writing that sought to describe humanity by using the elements of SF to achieve distance and perspective on the human species.

In *Downbelow Station* and subsequent novels of the Merchanters series, for instance, Cherryh depicts people coping with extremes of isolation, gravitation, and the unusual in human governance. In the Faded Sun series she explores variations of human cultural patterns in the manner of Ruth Benedict but with the freedom of imagination allowed in the science-fiction genre.

That freedom allows an SF author the chance to establish imaginary "gardens" and in them explore through the medium of thought experiment the life habits of both real and imaginary "toads." In her most celebrated series, the Chanur Saga, for example, she develops in great detail the cultural elements of a sentient yet leonine species, hence *The Pride of Chanur.* While such societies do not now exist, of course, genetic engineering promises to render them imaginable. At the same time and in the same tetralogy readers view the desperate plight of a single human, Tully, as viewed from outside human culture. We see not a space opera with static characters but a complex drama of evolving human-alien intercourse. Tully's views of Pyanfar and her shipmates, and their views of him, grow in depth and complexity. Furthermore—and this is rare even in SF—we see that the alien race itself is undergoing vast change as they leave their homeworld of Clans to move among the stars, the boldest among them coming finally to dwell only among the star-faring population. These developments allow for some poignant drama among creatures which to our knowledge do not yet exist. Pyanfar's old husband, Khym, a displaced leader on his homeworld, as useless as old lion on Earth, finds new work, liberation, and a pair-bonding with Pyanfar which the orthodoxy of their homeworld have rendered impossible.

These are bold experiments, to be sure, yet Cherryh takes us further. In *Cuckoo's Egg*, Cherryh wrings a change upon the feral-child concept by having a human infant reared by sentient felines ignorant of its social and psychological needs. And in *Heavy Time*, Cherryh contrasts the humanity of one character, Morris Bird, reared in human companionship, against the asocial nature of a younger man, Paul Dekker, whose upbringing has been crippled by corporate control. Finally, in *Cyteen* and elsewhere Cherryh explores the nature of "ozzies," human clones with programmed memories as set against the often inhumane attitudes of the "true" humans whose slaves they are.

Cherryh's work remarkably brings all species—human, created, and alien—together in a single future history of our galaxy. The reader is best advised to move through each series from start to finish since some, particularly *Chanur* and *Cyteen*, are really very long books which were divided into publishable bites according to the needs of literary promotion, distribution, and sales. Similar concerns will be found throughout Cherryh's fantasy novels as well, particularly the books of her Morgaine series which, despite the name, are not redactions of Arthurian myth but blends of fantasy and SF exhibiting the same concerns as those of her science-fiction series.

The greatest significance in Cherryh's science fiction, then, appears now to be her broad and systematic exploration of the concept of "humanity" itself seeking to discover what of this basic idea can survive the great range of adverse conditions made possible by today's and tomorrow's knowledge of human and animal behavior.

—Thomas P. Dunn

---

**CHESNEY, Weatherby.** *See* **HYNE, C.J. Cutliffe.**

---

**CHILSON, Rob(ert).** American. Born in Ringwood, Oklahoma, 19 May 1945. Educated in Appleton City High School, Missouri. Since 1967, freelance writer. Agent: Ralph Vicinanza, Ltd., Suite 1205, 432 Park Avenue South, New York, New York 10016, U.S.A.

SCIENCE-FICTION PUBLICATIONS

Novels

*As the Curtain Falls.* New York, DAW, 1974.
*The Star-Crowned Kings.* New York, DAW, 1975.
*The Shores of Kansas.* New York, Popular Library, 1976; London, Hale, 1977.
*Isaac Asimov's Robot City: Refuge.* New York, Ace, 1988.
*Men Like Rats.* New York, Popular Library, 1989.
*Rounded with Sleep.* New York, Popular Library, 1990.

Uncollected Short Stories

"The Mind Reader," in *Analog* (New York), June 1968.
"The Big Rock," in *Analog* (New York), October 1969.
"The Wild Blue Yonder," in *Analog* (New York), January 1970.
"The Fifth Ace," in *Analog* (New York), February 1970.
"Per Stratagem," in *Analog* (New York), July 1970.
"Excelsior!," in *Analog* (New York), August 1970.
"In the Wabe," in *Analog* (New York), November 1970.
"Ecological Niche," in *Analog* (New York), December 1970.
"In His Image," in *Analog 8*, edited by John W. Campbell, Jr., New York, Doubleday, 1971.
"Compulsion Worse Confounded," in *Analog* (New York), November 1971.
"Truck Driver," in *Analog* (New York), January 1972.
"Forty Days and Forty Nights," in *Analog* (New York), August 1973.
"The Devil and the Deep Blue Sky," in *Beyond Time*, edited by Sandra Ley. New York, Pocket Books, 1976.
"The Tame One," in *Galileo* (Boston), September 1976.
"People Reviews," in *Universe 7*, edited by Terry Carr. New York, Doubleday, and London, Dobson, 1977.
"Adora," in *Galileo* (Boston), April 1977.
"O Ye of Little Faith," in *Cosmos* (New York), November 1977.
"Moonless Night," in *Galaxy* (New York), March 1978.
"Written in Sand," in *Isaac Asimov's World of Science Fiction*, edited by George Scithers. New York, Davis, 1980.
"Walk with Me," in *Analog* (New York), May 1982.
"The Hand of Friendship," in *Analog* (New York), March 1983.
"Slowly, Slowly in the Wind," in *Analog* (New York), April 1984.

* * *

Rob Chilson, one of a group of writers under John W. Campbell's tutelage at *Analog* magazine, first began to appear in print in the late 1960's. His stories fit well into Campbell's formula at the time, and a dozen stories were published in *Analog* between 1968 and 1973. Although these early stories were not indicative of the kind of work he would eventually produce, "Per Stratagem" is a noteworthy exception, a story of intrigue in a far solar system, concentrating on strategic maneuvers rather than overt physical action. Chilson continued to publish through the 1970's, but it was not until the next decade that he began to produce memorable short stories.

During that period, he also produced three novels. The first of these, *As the Curtain Falls*, is so different from the stories in *Analog* in theme, subject matter, and treatment, another person entirely must have written it. A billion years into the future, the human race has declined into several more or less barbaric states, fighting among themselves while the sun slowly burns out. A form of empathic telepathy has evolved over the generations, which is part of the rationale for the existence of non-magical wizards, ogres, and other trappings of fantasy.

The protagonist sets out on a typical heroic quest, to rescue the princess and restore stability. Chilson carries this off skillfully, and some of the settings he creates are quite well done. Although he hovers at the edge of political satire (two of the political parties are the Forestallers and the Grumbletonians), he skirts the issue, choosing instead a standard adventure story.

*The Star-Crowned Kings*, while more ambitious in plot, was less satisfying in execution. The protagonist learns that he has psychokinetic powers, the ability to move objects through force of will, which theoretically should increase his personal position. But, the powers that be in the interstellar political arena don't want a maverick operating outside their game plan, and they set out to eliminate him. The book is another standard adventure tale, entertainingly told but without the exotic scenery that marked its predecessor.

With the publication of *The Shores of Kansas*, Chilson became a writer to watch. Set a generation in the future, it is the tale of Grant Ryals, one of few people capable of using mental abilities to regress physically in time, to visit and study different periods of history. Most notably, he is the only one with the range to reach prehistory, the time of the dinosaur. Although Ryals is obsessed with his research, pragmatic issues continue to reduce the amount of time he can spend pursuing it. In order to secure financing, he routinely films spectacular scenery and beasts; while in the present, he must deal with academic politics and people who believe him to be an authentic hero, despite his protestations to the contrary. The novel is a protracted character study, an in-depth examination of a man torn between the obligations of society and his own need to search for meaning and knowledge. It is unfortunate that, having proven himself capable of writing such a fine novel, Chilson did not produce another for 12 years. During this period, he continued to write short stories, some of which are quite memorable. "Written in Sand" echoes *The Shores of Kansas*; a time explorer has a bitter reaction to an unhappy love. "Hand of Friendship" portrays an interesting human-against-alien relationship, in which the alien assists in humanity's development despite their own inability to experience emotion. "Walk with Me" examines the extremely deep feelings that arise between a human subject and the alien who is observing him. A rising political star runs into trouble when a new method of judging personal integrity is developed in "Slowly, Slowly in the Wind." Other stories of note include "Brain in Pocket," "Moonless Night," "Brain Jag," and "Diogenes' Lantern."

In 1988, his first novel in over a decade, appeared as part of the Robot City series created by Isaac Asimov. Although *Refuge* has little significance outside of a very commercial and relatively unimaginative series, it did foreshadow Chilson's return to writing at novel length. *Men Like Rats* follows the adventures of human tribes who have been reduced to living like rats or insects within the structure of a civilization that omnipotent aliens have established on Earth. The desperate struggle for survival has pitted one tribe against another, and each individual is distrustful of even those within his or her group. *Refuge* is a compelling adventure story, filled with menaces and monsters.

Chilson's most recent novel, *Rounded with Sleep*, deals with the ultimate role-playing game. Through the use of computer-generated realities, individuals can become superheroes or villains, acting out parts in an elaborate sword-and-sorcery epic independent of time and space, while the game is observed by the vast majority of the human race. The protagonist is one of the most successful participants, until he loses interest and chooses to return to the real world. Unfortunately, that doesn't prove quite as pleasant as he had expected.

Chilson has proven his ability to write gripping, well-plotted adventure stories. *The Shores of Kansas* in particular demonstrates that he has the potential to examine the human experience in depth.

—Don D'Ammassa

---

**CHILTON, Charles (Frederick William).** British. Born in London in 1917. Educated at Thanet Street Church of England School, London. Married to Penelope Colbeck; two sons and one daughter. Freelance writer and journalist, and radio producer for the BBC, London; devised and wrote *Riders of the Range* annual, from 1953. Recipient: Western Heritage award, for children's book, 1963. Address: 31 Crediton Hill, London NW6 1HS, England.

SCIENCE-FICTION PUBLICATIONS

Novels (series: Jet Morgan in all books)

*Journey into Space* (novelization of radio series). London, Jenkins, 1954.
*The Red Planet* (novelization of radio series). London, Jenkins, 1956.
*The World in Peril* (novelization of radio series). London, Jenkins, 1960.

OTHER PUBLICATIONS

Plays

*Oh What a Lovely War*, with the Theatre Workshop, London (produced London and New York, 1964). London, Methuen, 1965.

Radio Plays: *Riders of the Range, Journey into Space*, and *The World in Peril* series in the 1950's; *Space Force* series, 1984.

Other

*Riders of the Range* (for children). London, Juvenile Productions, 1951.
*Second Round-Up with Riders of the Range* (for children). London, Juvenile Productions, 1952.
*The Riders of the Range Square Dance Manual.* London, Hutchinson, 1953.
*The Book of the West: The Epic of America's Wild Frontier and the Men Who Created Its Legends.* London, Odhams Press, 1961; Indianapolis, Bobbs Merrill, 1962.
*Discovery of the American West* (for children). London, Hamlyn, 1970.

* * *

The first of Charles Chilton's *Journey into Space* radio serials went on the air in 1953, with a strong cast of actors, including Andrew Faulds and Guy Kingsley Poynter, and a sound-track of music and special effects into which the BBC Radiophonics Workshop threw themselves with enthusiasm. Over the next five years, the three serials were a national institution in Britain, and the characters and their creator became household names. An abridged version of the first serial was re-broadcast, with Alfie Bass substituting for David Kossof as the cockney radio operator. Recordings of this version and the other two serials have recently been rediscovered, re-broadcast (1989–91) and issued by the BBC as boxed sets of cassettes.

In the first serial, the spaceship *Luna*, launched from Woomera Rocket Range in Australia, achieved the first Moon landing in the Bay of Rainbows. Faulds's low-key comment, "Gentlemen, we are on the Moon," was to be much imitated by 1950's writers. As lunar night fell, however, power failed in the ship, and in the darkness someone or something could be heard investigating the *Luna* on the outside. After a strange encounter with a UFO at sunrise, the crew attempted to return to Earth, only to have the *Luna* abducted and delivered to the Earth of 13,000 years in the past. Eventually the crew met one of the time-travellers and negotiated their return to their own time, but the serial ended as they faced another re-entry with no remaining fuel.

The second and third serials were set several years later, when a lunar base had been established and Faulds (Jet Morgan) led an exhibition to Mars in a fleet of ships commanded by the *Discovery.* Once again Chilton had gone to great lengths to make the technology authentic, by the design studies of the day, and the procedures of the Mars fleet were extremely convincing. In flight, however, the expedition was sabotaged by a man named Whitaker who had been kidnapped from Earth decades before, then returned to infiltrate the expedition. Whitaker had been conditioned by the Martians, by slowing down his metabolism to adapt to Martian conditions, making him cold to the touch and concealing his age, and also by hypnosis, making his speech a frightening drone ("Orders must be obeyed without question at all times.") Crewmen went mad or died in his company, and a generation of British schoolchildren were terrified of him. Worse still, Mars turned out to have a population of similarly conditioned humans, preparing to invade the Earth which few of them knew they had left.

But Chilton's extra-terrestrials were not monsters. The Martians had been the giants of earthly legends, coming to us in peace only to be hunted down and destroyed, finally driven to drastic measures as conditions worsened on Mars. By the time of the invasion, there was only one left, and when Morgan and his crew prevented his attempted takeover by televised hypnosis, he went peacefully off to Alpha Centauri with volunteers from the human workforce. The time-travellers also had been trying to avoid interaction with mankind, using the Moon and the prehistoric Earth only in passing. Unlike their contemporaries (the purely destructive aliens of Nigel Kneale's *Quatermass*, or the wholly benign inhabitants of Angus Macvicar's *Lost Planet*), Chilton's creations had their own purposes and motivations, not specifically good or evil in relation to humanity. Space was an exciting realm to explore, dangerous perhaps but not hostile.

Subsequent incarnations of the characters were less successful. The comic strip in *Express Weekly* was inconsistent with the radio serials, yet borrowed too heavily from them; and a one-hour play recapitulated the weakest parts of the strip's story line. *Space Force*, a pair of new serials broadcast in 1984–85, caught the atmosphere of the original more closely. But Chilton conceded in a *Radio Times* interview that he hadn't kept up with developments in space science, and dramatic sequences borrowed from *Journey into Space*—the power failure, for example—were no longer convincing.

—Duncan Lunan

---

**CHRISTOPHER, John.** Pseudonym for Christopher Samuel Youd; has also written as Hilary Ford; William Godfrey; Peter Graaf; Peter Nichols; Anthony Rye. British. Born in Knowsley, Lancashire, 16 April 1922. Educated at Peter Symonds' School, Winchester. Served in the Royal Signals, 1941–46. Twice married; four daughters and one son from first marriage. Since 1958, full-time writer. Recipient: Rockefeller-Atlantic award, 1946; Christopher award, for children's book, 1971; *Guardian* award, for children's book, 1971; Jugendbuchpreis (Germany), 1976; George G. Stone Center for Children's Books award, 1977. Address: One Whitefriars, Conduit Hill, Rye, East Sussex, TN 31 7LE, England.

SCIENCE-FICTION PUBLICATIONS

Novels

*The Year of the Comet.* London, Joseph, 1955; as *Planet in Peril*, New York, Avon, 1959.
*The Death of Grass.* London, Joseph, 1956; as *No Blade of Grass*, New York, Simon and Schuster, 1957.
*The World in Winter.* London, Eyre and Spottiswoode, 1962; as *The Long Winter*, New York, Simon and Schuster, 1962.
*Sweeney's Island.* New York, Simon and Schuster, 1964; as *Cloud on Silver*, London, Hodder and Stoughton, 1964.
*The Possessors.* London, Hodder and Stoughton, and New York, Simon and Schuster, 1965.
*A Wrinkle in the Skin.* London, Hodder and Stoughton, 1965; as *The Ragged Edge*, New York, Simon and Schuster, 1966.
*The Little People.* London, Hodder and Stoughton, and New York, Simon and Schuster, 1967.
*Pendulum.* London, Hodder and Stoughton, and New York, Simon and Schuster, 1968.

Fiction (for children; series: Fireball; Sword of the Spirits; Tripods)

*The Tripods Trilogy.* New York, Macmillan, 1980.
  *The White Mountains.* London, Hamish Hamilton, and New York, Macmillan, 1967.
  *The City of Gold and Lead.* London, Hamish Hamilton, and New York, Macmillan, 1967.
  *The Pool of Fire.* London, Hamish Hamilton, and New York, Macmillan, 1968.
  *When the Tripods Came.* New York, Dutton, 1988.
*The Lotus Caves.* London, Hamish Hamilton, and New York, Macmillan, 1969.
*The Guardians.* London, Hamish Hamilton, and New York, Macmillan, 1970.
*The Sword of the Spirits Trilogy.* New York, Macmillan, 1980; as *The Prince in Waiting Trilogy*, London, Penguin, 1983.
  *The Prince in Waiting.* London, Hamish Hamilton, and New York, Macmillan, 1970.
  *Beyond the Burning Lands.* London, Hamish Hamilton, and New York, Macmillan, 1971.
  *The Sword of the Spirits.* London, Hamish Hamilton, and New York, Macmillan, 1972.
*In the Beginning* (reader for adults). London, Longman, 1972; revised edition (for children), as *Dom and Va*, London, Hamish Hamilton, and New York, Macmillan, 1973.
*Wild Jack.* London, Hamish Hamilton, and New York, Macmillan, 1974; original version (reader for adults), London, Longman, 1974.
*Empty World.* London, Hamish Hamilton, 1977; New York, Dutton, 1978.
*Fireball.* London, Gollancz, and New York, Dutton, 1981.
*New Found Land.* London, Gollancz, and New York, Dutton, 1983.
*Dragon Dance.* London, Viking Kestral, and New York, Dutton, 1986.

Short Stories

*The Twenty-Second Century.* London, Grayson, 1954; New York, Lancer, 1962.

OTHER PUBLICATIONS

Novels

*Giant's Arrow* (as Anthony Rye). London, Gollancz, 1956; as Samuel Youd, New York, Simon and Schuster, 1960.
*Malleson at Melbourne* (as William Godfrey). London, Museum Press, 1956.
*The Friendly Game* (as William Godfrey). London, Joseph, 1957.
*The Caves of Night.* London, Eyre and Spottiswoode, and New York, Simon and Schuster, 1958.
*A Scent of White Poppies.* London, Eyre and Spottiswoode, and New York, Simon and Schuster, 1959.
*The Long Voyage.* London, Eyre and Spottiswoode, 1960; as *The White Voyage*, New York, Simon and Schuster, 1961.
*Patchwork of Death* (as Peter Nichols). New York, Holt Rinehart, 1965; London, Hale, 1967.

Novels as Samuel Youd

*The Winter Swan.* London, Dobson, 1949.
*Babel Itself.* London, Cassell, 1951.
*Brave Conquerors.* London, Cassell, 1952.
*Crown and Anchor.* London, Cassell, 1953.
*A Palace of Strangers.* London, Cassell, 1954.
*Holly Ash.* London, Cassell, 1955; as *The Opportunist*, New York, Harper, 1957.
*The Choice.* New York, Simon and Schuster, 1961; as *The Burning Bird*, London, Longman, 1964.
*Messages of Love.* New York, Simon and Schuster, 1961; London, Longman, 1962.
*The Summers at Accorn.* London, Longman, 1963.

Novels as Peter Graaf

*Dust and the Curious Boy.* London, Joseph, 1957; as *Give the Devil His Due*, New York, Mill, 1957.
*Daughter Fair.* London, Joseph, and New York, Washburn, 1958.
*Sapphire Conference.* London, Joseph and New York, Washburn, 1959.
*The Gull's Kiss.* London, Davies, 1962.

Novels as Hilary Ford

*Felix Walking.* London, Eyre and Spottiswoode, and New York, Simon and Schuster, 1958.
*Felix Running.* London, Eyre and Spottiswoode, 1959.
*Bella on the Roof.* London, Longman, 1965.
*A Figure in Grey* (for children). Kingswood, Surrey, World's Work, 1973.
*Sarnia.* London, Hamish Hamilton, and New York, Doubleday, 1974.
*Castle Malindine.* London, Hamish Hamilton, and New York, Harper, 1975.

*A Bride for Bedivere*. London, Hamish Hamilton, 1976; New York, Harper, 1977.

* * *

The reputation of John Christopher as a writer of science fiction for both adult and younger readers is solidly established. Perhaps the greatest single exposure in the United States was the film version in the early 1970's of the novel *The Death of Grass.* The elements present in this relatively early piece are a hallmark for all of his science fiction. Taken together, it forms all kinds of answers to the question "What do people do when things fall apart?" An account of his work may fall rather naturally into three parts: the early short fiction and Managerial stories; novels of crises, catastrophe, and survival; and novels for younger readers.

*The Twenty-Second Century* conveniently displays Christopher's apprenticeship period. Six of the stories in the collection feature Max Larkin, a director in one of the corporations that govern earth in place of political institutions in the not-too-distant future. Read along with the fuller exposition of this state of affairs in *Planet in Peril*, the stories present the proposition that political institutions will bring civilization to ruin and that government by enlightened commercial interests may do better. The case for this is epitomized in the laid-back character of Larkin, the unmarried, late-middle-aged corporate director, whose manipulative genius is time and again effective in world crises where armies and doomsday weapons have failed each time. The 14 additional stories are something of an index of the novels that would follow. Sterility doom in "The New Wine," a medieval level of technology survival in "Weapon," and the panorama of 20th-century ruin in contrast to the garden of a new Eden in "Begin Again" provide glimpses of the worlds of the catastrophe novels. Beyond these, imprisonment by adaptive necessity in a lunar vivarium in "Christmas Roses," the interdiction of books in "A Time of Peace," and the humanity-saving wholesomeness recognized by enlightened aliens in a human village dedicated to a technologically simple way of life in "Blemish" are typical of the settings and subjects of the juvenile pieces. At least one more story, "Rock-a-Bye," featuring the super-child born of a relationship between a Martian woman and a man from Earth is beautiful in its own right and deserves larger treatment. At this stage in his career Christopher's narrative craft is nearly mature. He does not experiment with style. He tells stories with pace, suspense, sanity, and clarity. Moreover, unlike that of many writers, his strength is not in the short story but in the longer narrative work.

Two exceptions to the sort of novel for which Christopher is best known are *The Possessors*, wherein a group of people at a remote ski lodge are saved by "body-snatching" aliens, and *The Little People*, wherein a group of vacationers at a remote old mansion are savaged by dwarves created by Nazi geneticists. Both are excursions in science-fiction gothic. The strength of both lies in the plausible behaviours of small groups of people in short-term crises.

But it is to scenarios of planet-wide cataclysm and survival in a world that will never be the same again that the most famous stories direct us. *The Death of Grass*, reminding us that corn, wheat, and rice are grass, has a blight on all the species of grass cause a world famine. *The World in Winter* shows European civilization destroyed by a new ice age. *A Wrinkle in the Skin* presents earth devastated by the effects of continent-heaving earthquakes. *Pendulum* varies the cause of disaster from that of nature run amok to human society run amok—an obvious fictional response to the social transformations taking place in western civilization during the late 1960's. But with few alterations the effect is the same. More people survive. Yet once more society is reduced to savagery, to endure again the insanity and agony of social evolution that in past history did not teach their lessons well enough. These pieces are variations upon several principal themes. Human civilization is fragile and vulnerable. It cannot survive catastrophe either from natural causes or incompetent government. In the event of catastrophe the few who survive will be winnowed again by good health, knowledge of basic tools and nature, and the ability to kill other human beings, however reluctantly, out of necessity. Simultaneously, they must have the ability to love and form, once again, wholesome social contracts. Billions die in these stories, but hope and human potential have the final determination in each of them. Somehow, mankind will recover and rebuild, though *Pendulum*, the latest of the novels, insists that it will not be swift.

With a sensible selection against the more baldly brutal and explicit details of violence and sexual behavior, these themes are produced again in the novels for younger readers. There is an evenness of quality of all these works, so that a few may represent them all. The earliest and most famous are those that form the Tripods trilogy (*The White Mountains, The City of Gold and Lead*, and *The Pool of Fire*), featuring Will Parker and his companions.

Will is born in a backwoods village on a future earth conquered and enslaved by alien invaders who travel on land and water in vehicles with three immensely long terrain-gobbling legs. They are reminiscent of the Martian craft in Wells's *War of the Worlds.* The aliens employ the very strongest young humans as body servants. The remainder are mere breeders, forbidden more than a medieval level of technology, and, ultimately, little more than vermin who will be exterminated when the aliens convert earth's atmosphere and gravity to their own. Fortunately, it doesn't happen. Will and two friends have a principal role in returning earth to humans. The theme is the meaning of individual freedom and honor. Knowledge and curiosity daring enough to see beyond popular mythology, self-discipline, respect for other people—especially odd ones—and the courage to act in the face of pain and under threat of death earn freedom.

The Tripods trilogy acquired a prequel with the publication of a fourth volume, *When the Tripods Came.* Introducing 14-year-old Laurie Cordray and his companions, it tells of the arrival of the Tripods on earth. Laurie and his family flee to Switzerland and eventually take secret refuge in an alpine hotel to begin the years of underground resistance to the Tripods. The tensions among the characters are an additional source of interest here. Laurie's divorced father has remarried and had a half-sister for Laurie, who must reconcile himself to the dynamics of a new family structure.

Beginning at the end of 1984, the first of three 13-episode BBC TV serials of *The Tripods* was aired. The broadcast of the complete production spans three years. An unrelated but similar novel called *The Guardians* refreshes the Tripods stories' propositions about freedom in a post-catastrophe story of a boy who, learning of a conspiracy by aristocratic guardians to keep the mass of men at a stuporous level of existence in the cities, determines to join a revolution to free them. The work received the *Guardian* award in England, the Christopher award in the United States and the prestigious Jugendbuchpreis in 1976.

*Fireball, New Found Land*, and *Dragon Dance* form the Fireball trilogy. Simon is British. Brad is American. The cousins encounter a fireball in a meadow and are thrust into a parallel earth—England still at a medieval level of civilization. The books are an adventure that circles the earth, so that the story ends in China. The Dragon is an illusion created by flying box kites over the enemy army. The setting is generally reminiscent of Christopher's adult post-catastrophe novels.

The additional SF pieces published by Christopher in the 1980's are exclusively children's books. The course seems a happy one. In terms of narrative art, Christopher's stories for young readers may be his finest achievement.

—John R. Pfeiffer

---

**CLARKE, Arthur C(harles).** British. Born in Minehead, Somerset, 16 December 1917. Educated at Huish's Grammar School, Taunton, Somerset, 1927–36; King's College, London, 1946–48, B. Sc. (honours) in physics and mathematics 1948. Flight Lieutenant in the Royal Air Force, 1941–46; served as Radar Instructor, and Technical Officer on the first Ground Controlled Approach radar; originated proposal for use of satellites for communications, 1945. Married Marilyn Mayfield in 1954 (divorced 1964). Assistant auditor, Exchequer and Audit Department, London, 1936–41; assistant editor, *Physics Abstracts*, London, 1949–50. Since 1954, engaged in underwater exploration and photography of the Great Barrier Reef of Australia and the coast of Sri Lanka. Director, Rocket Publishing, London, Underwater Safaris, Colombo. Has made numerous radio and television appearances (most recently as presenter of the television series *Arthur C. Clarke's Mysterious World*, 1980, and *World of Strange Powers*, 1985), and has lectured widely in Britain and the United States; commentator, for CBS-TV, on lunar flights of Apollo 11, 12, and 15; Vikram Sarabhai Professor, Physical Research Laboratory, Ahmedabad, India, 1980. Recipient: International Fantasy award, 1952; Hugo award, 1956, 1969 (for screenplay), 1974, 1980; Unesco Kalinga prize, 1961; Boys' Clubs of America award, 1961; Franklin Institute Ballantine Medal, 1963; Aviation-Space Writers Association Ball award, 1965; American Association for the Advancement of Science Westinghouse award, 1969; *Playboy* award, 1971; Nebula award, 1972, 1973, 1979, Grand Master, 1985; Jupiter award, 1973; John W. Campbell Memorial award, 1974; American Institute of Aeronautics and Astronautics award, 1974; Boston Museum of Science Washburn award, 1977; Marconi Fellowship, 1982; Vidya Jyothi medal, 1986; Science Fiction Writers Association, Grand Master, 1986. D.Sc.: Beaver College, Glenside, Pennsylvania, 1971. Chairman, British Interplanetary Society, 1946–47, 1950–53. Guest of Honor, World Science Fiction Convention, 1956. Fellow, Royal Astronomical Society; Fellow, King's College, London, 1977; Chancellor, University of Moratuwa, Sri Lanka, since 1979. C.B.E. (Commander, Order of the British Empire), 1989. Agent: David Higham Associates Ltd., 5–8 Lower John Street, London W1R 3PE, England; or, Scott Meredith Literary Agency, 845 Third Avenue, New York, New York 10022, U.S.A. Address: 25 Barnes Place, Colombo 7, Sri Lanka; or, Dene Court, Bishop's Lydeard, Taunton TA4 3LT, England.

### SCIENCE-FICTION PUBLICATIONS

Novels (series: Rama)

*Prelude to Space*. New York, Galaxy, 1951; London, Sidgwick and Jackson, 1953; as *Master of Space*, New York, Lancer, 1961; as *The Space Dreamers*, Lancer, 1969.

*The Sands of Mars*. London, Sidgwick and Jackson, 1951; New York, Gnome Press, 1952.

*Islands in the Sky* (for children). London, Sidgwick and Jackson, and Philadelphia, Winston, 1952.

*Against the Fall of Night*. New York, Gnome Press, 1953; revised edition, as *The City and the Stars*, London, Muller, and New York, Harcourt Brace, 1956; reprinted with *Beyond the Fall of Night*, with Gregory Benford, New York, Putnam, 1990; as *Against the Fall of the Night*, with *Beyond the Fall of Night*, with Gregory Benford, London, Gollancz, 1991.

*Childhood's End*. New York, Ballantine, 1953; London, Sidgwick and Jackson, 1954.

*Earthlight*. London, Muller, and New York, Ballantine, 1955.

*The Deep Range*. New York, Harcourt Brace, and London, Muller, 1957.

*Across the Sea of Stars* (omnibus). New York, Harcourt Brace, 1959.

*A Fall of Moondust*. London, Gollancz, and New York, Harcourt Brace, 1961.

*From the Oceans, From the Stars* (omnibus). New York, Harcourt Brace, 1962.

*Dolphin Island* (for children). New York, Holt Rinehart, and London, Gollancz, 1963.

*An Arthur C. Clarke Omnibus* [and *Second Omnibus*]. London, Sidgwick and Jackson, 2 vols., 1965–68.

*Prelude to Mars* (omnibus). New York, Harcourt Brace, 1965.

*2001: A Space Odyssey* (novelization of screenplay). New York, New American Library, and London, Hutchinson, 1968.

*The Lion of Comarre, and Against the Fall of Night*. New York, Harcourt Brace, 1968; London, Gollancz, 1970.

*Rendezvous with Rama*. London, Gollancz, and New York, Harcourt Brace, 1973.

*Imperial Earth*. London, Gollancz, 1975; revised edition, New York, Harcourt Brace, 1976.

*The Fountains of Paradise*. London, Gollancz, and New York, Harcourt Brace, 1979.

*2010: Odyssey Two*. New York, Ballantine, and London, Granada, 1982.

*The Songs of Distant Earth*. London, Grafton, and New York, Ballantine, 1986.

*Cradle*, with Gentry Lee. London, Gollancz, and New York, Warner, 1988.

*A Meeting with Medusa*, with *Green Mars*, by Kim Stanley Robinson. New York, Tor, 1988.

*2061: Odyssey Three*. London, Grafton, and New York, Ballantine, 1988.

*Rama II*, with Gentry Lee. London, Gollancz, and New York, Bantam, 1989.

*The Garden of Rama*, with Gentry Lee. London, Gollancz, and New York, Bantam, 1991.

Short Stories

*Expedition to Earth*. New York, Ballantine, 1953; London, Sidgwick and Jackson, 1954.

*Reach for Tomorrow*. New York, Ballantine, 1956; London, Gollancz, 1962.

*Tales from the White Hart*. New York, Ballantine, 1957; London, Sidgwick and Jackson, 1972.

*The Other Side of the Sky*. New York, Harcourt Brace, 1958; London, Gollancz, 1961.

*Tales of Ten Worlds*. New York, Harcourt Brace, 1962; London, Gollancz, 1963.

*The Nine Billion Names of God: The Best Short Stories of Arthur C. Clarke*. New York, Harcourt Brace, 1967.

*The Wind from the Sun: Stories of the Space Age*. New York, Harcourt Brace, and London, Gollancz, 1972.

*Of Time and Stars: The Worlds of Arthur C. Clarke*. London, Gollancz, 1972.

*The Best of Arthur C. Clarke 1937–1971*, edited by Angus Wells. London, Sidgwick and Jackson, 1973.

*The Sentinel.* New York, Berkley, 1983.
*Tales from Planet Earth.* London, Century, 1989; New York, Bantam, 1990.
*Dilemmas: The Secret,* with *Flowers for Algernon,* by Daniel Keyes, New York, Houghton Mifflin, 1989.

OTHER PUBLICATIONS

Novels

*Glide Path.* New York, Harcourt Brace, 1963; London, Sidgwick and Jackson, 1969.
*The Ghost from the Grand Banks.* London, Gollancz, and New York, Bantam, 1990.

Play

Screenplay: *2001: A Space Odyssey,* with Stanley Kubrick, 1968.

Other

*Interplanetary Flight: An Introduction to Astronautics.* London, Temple Press, 1950; New York, Harper, 1951; revised edition, 1960.
*The Exploration of Space.* London, Temple Press, and New York, Harper, 1951; revised edition, 1959.
*The Young Traveller in Space* (for children). London, Phoenix House, 1954; as *Going into Space,* New York, Harper, 1954; as *The Scottie Book of Space Travel,* London, Transworld, 1957; revised edition, with Robert Silverberg, as *Into Space,* New York, Harper, 1971.
*The Exploration of the Moon.* London, Muller, 1954; New York, Harper, 1955.
*The Coast of Coral.* London, Muller, and New York, Harper, 1956.
*The Making of a Moon: The Story of the Earth Satellite Program.* London, Muller, and New York, Harper, 1957; revised edition, Harper, 1958.
*The Reefs of Taprobane: Underwater Adventures Around Ceylon.* London, Muller, and New York, Harper, 1957.
*Voice Across the Sea.* London, Muller, 1958; New York, Harper, 1959; revised edition, London, Mitchell Beazley, and New York, Harper, 1974.
*Boy Beneath the Sea* (for children). New York, Harper, 1958.
*The Challenge of the Spaceship: Previews of Tomorrow's World.* New York, Harper, 1959; London, Muller, 1960.
*The First Five Fathoms: A Guide to Underwater Adventure.* New York, Harper, 1960.
*The Challenge of the Sea.* New York, Holt Rinehart, 1960; London, Muller, 1961.
*Indian Ocean Adventure.* New York, Harper, 1961; London, Barker, 1962.
*Profiles of the Future: An Enquiry into the Limits of the Possible.* London, Gollancz, 1962; New York, Harper, 1963; revised edition, Harper, 1973; Gollancz, 1974, 1982; New York, Holt Rinehart, 1984.
*The Treasure of the Great Reef.* London, Barker, and New York, Harper, 1964; revised edition, New York, Ballantine, 1974.
*Indian Ocean Treasure,* with Mike Wilson. New York, Harper, 1964; London, Sidgwick and Jackson, 1972.
*Man and Space,* with the editors of *Life.* New York, Time, 1964.
*Voices from the Sky: Previews of the Coming Space Age.* New York, Harper, 1965; London, Gollancz, 1966.
*The Promise of Space.* New York, Harper, and London, Hodder and Stoughton, 1968.
*First on the Moon,* with the astronauts. London, Joseph, and Boston, Little Brown, 1970.
*Report on Planet Three and Other Speculations.* London, Gollancz, and New York, Harper, 1972.
*The Lost Worlds of 2001.* New York, New American Library, and London, Sidgwick and Jackson, 1972.
*Beyond Jupiter: The Worlds of Tomorrow,* with Chesley Bonestell. Boston, Little Brown, 1972.
*Technology and the Frontiers of Knowledge* (lectures), with others. New York, Doubleday, 1975.
*The View from Serendip* (on Sri Lanka). New York, Random House, 1977; London, Gollancz, 1978.
*1984: Spring: A Choice of Futures.* New York, Ballantine, and London, Granada, 1984.
*Ascent to Orbit: A Scientific Autobiography: The Technical Writings of Arthur C. Clarke.* New York, and Chichester, Sussex, Wiley, 1984.
*The Odyssey File,* with Peter Hyams. New York, Ballantine, and London, Granada, 1985.
*Astounding Days: A Science-Fictional Autobiography.* London, Gollancz, 1989; New York, Bantam, 1990.
*How the World Was One.* New York, Bantam, and London, Gollancz, 1992.

Editor, *Time Probe: Sciences in Science Fiction.* New York, Delacorte Press, 1966; London, Gollancz, 1967.
Editor, *The Coming of the Space Age: Famous Accounts of Man's Probing of the Universe.* London, Gollancz, and New York, Meredith, 1967.
Editor, with George Proctor, *The Science Fiction Hall of Fame 3: The Nebula Winners 1965–1969.* New York, Avon, 1982.
Editor, *July 20, 2019: A Day in the Life of the 21st Century.* New York, Macmillan, 1986; London, Grafton, 1987.
Editor, *Project Solar Sail.* New York, Penguin, 1990.

*

Bibliography: *Arthur C. Clarke: A Primary and Secondary Bibliography* by David N. Samuelson, Boston, Hall, 1984.

Manuscript Collection: Mugar Memorial Library, Boston University.

Critical Studies: "Out of the Ego Chamber" by Jeremy Bernstein, in *New Yorker,* 9 August 1969; *Arthur C. Clarke* edited by Joseph D. Olander and Martin H. Greenberg. New York, Taplinger, and Edinburgh, Harris, 1977; *The Space Odysseys of Arthur C. Clarke* by George Edgar Slusser, San Bernardino, California, Borgo Press, 1978; *Arthur C. Clarke* (includes bibliography) by Eric S. Rabkin, West Linn, Oregon, Starmont House, 1979, revised edition, 1980; *Against the Night, The Stars: The Science Fiction of Arthur C. Clarke* by John Hollow, New York, Harcourt Brace, 1983, revised edition, Athens, Ohio University Press, 1987.

* * *

With 21 very popular novels to his credit, Arthur C. Clarke is one of the small handful of writers who have shaped science fiction in our century. His persistent spiritual—and sometimes lyrical—optimism concerning the place of humanity in the universe and his enthusiastic faith in technology gather together both the hard and soft sides of the genre in works of classic importance. Clarke's love of the details of technology also enlivens his highly regarded work as a science writer. By his own count, Clarke has produced "approximately five hundred articles and short stories" including "The Star," a Hugo-winning response to Wells's belittling of humanity in his famous story of the same name.

One can take a preliminary survey of Clarke's work by examining his short fiction. *Tales from the White Hart* gains coherence by establishing a tavern frame within which Harry Purvis tells one tall tale after another, displaying Clarke's energetic—and sometimes outrageous—sense of humor, a sense epitomized in the punishing ending of his later story called "Neutron Tide." Many of Clarke's novels and short stories have been repackaged in other volumes. In *The Nine Billion Names of God*, Clarke collects his 25 favorites among his then-published short stories. The majority of his most famous pieces are here, including the almost pastoral title story in which Western science and Eastern religion confront each other and eternity; "Rescue Party," in which the would-be saviors of a doomed Earth are startled by humanity's self-reliance; "Superiority," in which a space war is lost by too much cleverness; "The Sentinel," which is often thought of as the germ for *2001*, and "The Star." *A Meeting with Medusa* is a Nebula-winning novella that includes the discovery of life in the dense atmosphere of Jupiter, and Clarke's own choice for his single best piece of fiction, "Transit of Earth." This story tells of an astronaut on Mars who knows his life supports cannot long sustain him but who nonetheless sets up the equipment necessary to record for posterity the first human observation of Earth passing across the disc of the sun, a mythic moment typical of Clarke that holds both sunrise and sunset in suspense. This story is also typical of Clarke in depending upon technical detail for its setting and dramatic situation and in balancing a symbol of demise with one of rejuvenation. Clarke's characteristically isolated hero joyfully and paradoxically greets the future by rushing toward Bach, a beauty from the past: "Johann Sebastian, here I come."

Clarke's faith in technology is profound: he is quite proud "to know several astronauts who became astronauts through reading my books." He is also justifiably proud to have first proposed (1945) geosynchronous communication satellites, an innovation that has already changed our world and will continue to move us toward the single community Clarke's heroes always contemplate when looking back at Earth from space. The majority of Clarke's novels are highly technological, human characters being invented primarily to provide occasion for humor, to put life at stake, or to locate a coherent point of view from which to explore in imaginative and thrilling detail the wonders of science and of the future universe. *Islands in the Sky* and *Dolphin Island* are juvenile novels employing teenaged boys as observers, the former presenting a grand tour of many sorts of satellites and space stations and a lunar fly-by and the latter showing science reaching out to the aliens with whom we share our planet, intelligent mammals of the sea. *Prelude to Space, The Sands of Mars, Earthlight, The Deep Range, Imperial Earth*, and *The Fountains of Paradise*, though more adult, are still primarily exciting guided tours rather than compelling dramas. In each of these the technology is amazingly detailed; the plot is admirably thickened by political impediments to the implementation of the technology; and these impediments are excitingly but predictably overcome. Within this general scheme, *Prelude to Space* concentrates on the development and launching of the first rocket to leave our atmosphere; *The Sands of Mars*, one of the two psychologically strong novels in this group, concerns first contact and the establishment of viable human colonies on a terraformed Mars; *Earthlight* studies political changes on the Earth and colonized planets as lunar technology develops, including that needed for self-defense and efficient mineral recovery; *The Deep Range* follows the development of whaleherding and its philosophical shift from a meat to a milk industry; *Imperial Earth*, the other psychologically strong novel and Clarke's favorite, also concerns the effect of technology on the social systems on several solar worlds and the personal and political maturing of a man bound to lead the people of Titan through necessary cultural adaptations; and *The Fountains of Paradise* chronicles the building of the space elevator that will effectively free humanity from the Earth.

Three other heavily technological novels need mention. *Glide Path*, Clarke's only non-science fiction novel, follows the very important World War II development of Ground Controlled Approach radar. Clarke was in charge of English GCA operations, and this novel has interest not only for its technology but for its quasi-autobiographical detail. *A Fall of Moondust* concerns a tourist "boat" trapped within a lunar sea of microscopic dust. This highly effective novel compellingly challenges the reader to try to beat the fictional technicians to a plan for rescue while all the time anoxia and mechanical failures threaten the passengers. And finally, *Rendezvous with Rama* combines the absolutely fascinating exploration of an extra-solar vessel come into our system with profound philosophic questioning of the significance of humanity, of biological life, and of intelligence. This is the only work ever to win all major science fiction awards: Hugo, Nebula, Campbell, and Jupiter.

The questioning in *Rendezvous with Rama* recalls Clarke's novels of cultural exploration. *The Lion of Comarre*, the most like a fairy tale of Clarke's works, traces the quest of a young man to find the geniuses of the past, to destroy the enchanted city keeping them in pacified torpor through technologically induced pleasures, and to open the static pastoral land to science. A similar plot structures *Against the Fall of Night* and *The City and the Stars*, the one an earlier version of the other. These works are more convincingly written than *Comarre* and improve upon it by having the city and country cultures both static, but for different reasons, by creating in Alvin a central character with whose growing pains we can identify, and by casting the drama of terrestrial rejuvenation against a cosmic context. That cosmic context provides the overall power of *Childhood's End*, Clarke's most popular novel and his first great testament of faith in human evolution to a higher plane. His last great testament, *2001: A Space Odyssey*, combines motifs and attitudes spanning Clarke's entire career to produce a technologically compelling story of the next generation's space program, a humanly moving story of struggle and courage against harsh interplanetary space and computers gone awry, and a philosophically moving study of the evolution of humanity and our meaning in the universe. Its belated sequel, *2010: Odyssey Two*, although popular, is less significant, for while the earlier book raises permanently important human issues, the later book lays these issues down again by providing them with too simple genre resolutions. The novel *2001* done while Clarke collaborated with Stanley Kubrick on the screenplay for the film *2001*, is the best summation both intellectual and artistic of Clarke's career. The film is perhaps the most widely important work of science fiction ever produced.

In his later work, such as *2010*, Clarke has sadly become a pale copy of himself. *2061* is a weak final book of the trilogy begun with *2001. The Ghost from the Grand Banks*, while full of interesting, real scientific and historical tidbits, merely tells the torpid story of the failure to raise the *Titanic* in the year 2012. His collaborations with Gentry Lee are particularly disappointing. *Cradle* tells of a deep-sea search and a meeting with aliens bent on improving us; we succeed in getting them to go away. *Rama II*, the only volume yet available of a planned three more volumes following *Rendezvous with Rama*, is a discursive exposition of putative wonders, within which we find a melodramatic love story and the set-up for the next installment. In assessing Clarke's impact, therefore, it is perhaps fairest to set these works aside and concentrate on the works published originally from 1948 to 1979.

In his love of technical detail and his efforts to use science correctly in constructing his novels of adventure, Clarke has been perhaps the foremost writer of his generation to carry on the work of Verne and the editorial policies of Campbell; but in his abiding concern for society and philosophy, Clarke is also the foremost heir of Wells and Stapledon. Clarke has won himself a unique and towering position in science fiction by combining the enthusiasm of one camp with the breadth of vision of the other. Clarke has written that his youthful reading of Stapledon's *Last and First Men* (1930) "transformed my life." That book, chronicling the evolution and demise of humanity, ends with the suggestion that "we shall make after all a fair conclusion to this brief music that is man." Stapledon's line reminds us of the farewell of the astronaut in "Transit of Earth," but with a difference; Stapledon sees the music as a conclusion; Clarke sees it as an embrace in something greater than man. This spiritual faith in Clarke comes not from religion, however, but from science itself. As a character says in *The Fountains of Paradise*, the book with which Clarke prematurely claimed his retirement from writing, "he could not understand how anyone could contemplate the dynamic asymmetry of Euler's profound yet beautifully simple [equation] without wondering if the universe was the creation of some vast intelligence." Even for the reading generation that began with Hiroshima, Clarke in his fiction marshals the intimations of intelligence to justify human hope.

—Eric S. Rabkin

---

**CLEMENS, Samuel Langhorne.** *See* **TWAIN, Mark.**

---

**CLEMENT, Hal.** Pseudonym for Harry Clement Stubbs. American. Born in Somerville, Massachusetts, 30 May 1922. Educated at Harvard University, Cambridge, Massachusetts, B.S. in astronomy 1943; Boston University, M.Ed. 1947; Simmons College, Boston, M.S. 1963. Served as a bomber pilot with the 8th Air Force during World War II: Air Medal, with four oak leaf clusters; served in the Air Force Reserve; Lieutenant Colonel from 1953. Married Mary Elizabeth Myers in 1952; two sons and one daughter. Since 1949, science teacher, Milton Academy, Massachusetts. Technical Instructor, Special Weapons School, Sandia Base, New Mexico, 1951. Columnist (as Harry C. Stubbs) on science books for children, *Horn Book* magazine, Boston. Member of the Milton Warrant Committee; Chairman of the District Board of Review, Boy Scouts of America. Address: 12 Thompson Lane, Milton, Massachusetts 02186, U.S.A.

SCIENCE-FICTION PUBLICATIONS

Novels (series: Mesklin)

*Needle*. New York, Doubleday, 1950; London, Gollancz, 1961; as *From Outer Space*, New York, Avon, 1957.
*Iceworld*. New York, Gnome Press, 1953.
*Mission of Gravity* (Mesklin). New York, Doubleday, 1954; London, Hale, 1955.
*The Ranger Boys in Space* (for children). Boston, Page, and London, Harrap, 1956.
*Cycle of Fire*. New York, Ballantine, 1957; London, Gollancz, 1964.
*Some Notes on Xi Bootis*. Chicago, Advent, 1959.
*Close to Critical*. New York, Ballantine, 1964; London, Gollancz, 1966.
*Star Light* (Mesklin). New York, Ballantine, 1971.
*Ocean on Top*. New York, DAW, 1973; London, Sphere, 1976.
*Through the Eye of a Needle*. New York, Ballantine, 1978.
*The Nitrogen Fix*. New York, Ace, 1980.
*Still River*. New York, Ballantine, 1987; London, Sphere, 1988.
*Intuit*. Cambridge, Massachusetts, NESFA Press, 1987.

Short Stories

*Natives of Space*. New York, Ballantine, 1965.
*Small Changes*. New York, Doubleday, 1969; as *Space Lash*, New York, Dell, 1969.
*The Best of Hal Clement*, edited by Lester del Rey. New York, Ballantine, 1979.

OTHER PUBLICATIONS

Other

*Left of Africa* (for children). New Orleans, Aurian Society Press, 1976.

Editor, *First Flights to the Moon*. New York, Doubleday, 1970.
Editor, *The Moon*, by George Gamow. London, Abelard Schuman, 1971.

*

Critical Study: *Hal Clement* by Donald M. Hassler, Mercer Island, Washington, Starmont House, 1982.

* * *

A continuous fan since his mid-teens of physical science and of the fictional extrapolations from it that the genre has labeled hard science fiction, Hal Clement published his first story in John Campbell's *Astounding* in 1942 when he was an astronomy major at Harvard. He has gone on to become one of the most highly admired scientific extrapolators and lovers of the tight demands of logic in the genre despite the fact that he is not a full-time writer. Clement and his classic fictions are mentioned whenever the discussion of science in the genre comes up; and hence he represents both the full maturing of the Campbell engineering effect in science fiction and the limitations of that approach. Campbell demanded a good story, of course, and Clement's stories are carefully constructed and often convey a certain excitement and suspense. But their distinguishing characteristic is that a problematic condition in physical reality, or simply a condition of difference such as an increase or decrease in heat or gravity, must be elaborated upon, explained, and taken through certain plot changes so that the reader can simply understand the problem or the difference. This is a literature of total imitation mimesis, in which the facts of the universe are what is mimed. Often in Clement's work, words themselves seem secondary to the phenomena. It is no coincidence that Clement loves, and, in fact, himself paints—as George Richard—astronomical art works of the phenomenal universe. At the end of his most famous novel, *Mission of Gravity*, the alien hero who is trying cleverly to acquire a more useful science for his truly phenomenal planet, Mesklin, that orbits the double star 61 Cygni, comments, "They finished up with the old line about words not really being enough to describe it. What else beside words can you use, in the name of the Suns?" His second-in-command answers, "this quantity-code they [humans] call Mathematics." Furthermore, for Clement himself any symbols seem to reside not in the words but in the Suns themselves—or in their mathematics.

The literary effect of hard science fiction that makes it good reading derives not so much from its accuracy (although Clement has written non-fiction essays in which he challenges the reader to catch his fictions in an inaccuracy thus implying that the puzzle element is central) as from its ability to tell how science can show difference. The sublime effect of the varied and infinite universe does not require the fanciful imagination in science fiction but can be, to paraphrase Wordsworth who wanted science and imagination linked, the simple produce of the common day if you are an astronomer. The planetary environments are main characters in Clement's fictions, major sources of the sublime, from the variable high-gravity world of Mesklin to the giant and peculiar planet Dhrawn that the mesklinites explore in *Star Light*, to a variety of other worlds in which differences in atmospheric components, in mass, in heat all demonstrate that scientific extrapolation is not dry as dust. But not only does scientific extrapolation discover exciting differences in environment; it also assumes and sets about to demonstrate, in Clement's work, that life forms would evolve differently in different environments. Clement is fascinated by alien view points, and the non-human characters are the most interesting characters in most of his fiction. This commitment to difference, not only in environments but also in life forms, makes Clement a far more interesting—and more accurate—extrapolator than a fellow hard science-fiction writer, Issac Asimov, who peoples the galaxy with humans. But beneath the strange morphological surfaces and beyond the alien body chemistry, Clement's extra-terrestrials still seek humanlike goals, most often the goal of more knowledge and more scientific control. Thus Captain Barlennan of Mesklin can seem both strange and familiar as he connives to learn flight and even space travel under conditions far different from those given to us to learn the same things. The emphasis in Clement is on learning, movement, and difference—not on any symbolic revelation of oneness.

One of his first aliens illustrates perhaps most vividly the strengths and the weaknesses of Clement's brand of hard science fiction. This creature, the hero in *Needle* and reappearing in *Through the Eye of a Needle*, evolved from viruses rather than from protozoan cells into a highly intelligent life form in which only the memory cells are specialized. The other cells are continually changing into various organs as need arises; but usually the creature lives most efficiently as a friendly parasite, or symbiont, insinuating its small virus-like cells easily among the larger protozoan-like cells of its host. In *Needle* the creature has come to Earth in hot pursuit of a criminal member of its race. They come from light years away, of course, representing Clement's one bow to illogic—faster-than-light travel. The creature, called simply The Hunter, adopts as his host a teenage boy. They become the best of friends in a delightful and carefully detailed symbiosis. Clement has the enemy or adversary creature adopt the boy's father as its host. The story then unfolds as an exciting tale of detection with a lot of biological extrapolation worked in, but Clement adds nothing suggestive nor psychologically extrapolative about the basic filial conflict that readers of Wordsworth, Joyce, and even Thomas Wolfe might expect. In several different places, Clement has written sarcastically about "amateur psychoanalysts," and it is almost as though he invented this story, which contains one of his nicest and most different aliens, deliberately to demonstrate that hard science fiction extrapolates only with the physical. Furthermore, *The Nitrogen Fix* significantly continues his epistemological speculations because the nitrogenlife aliens in the fiction communicate without words through direct chemical transfer, thus reaffirming Clement's innate preference for "things" over words.

—Donald M. Hassler

---

**CLEVE, John.** *See* **EDMONDSON, G.C.; OFFUTT, Andrew J.**

---

**CLIFTON, Mark (Irvin).** American. Born in 1906. Trained as a teacher, but worked for 25 years as industrial psychologist working in personnel: compiled 200,000 case histories. Recipient: Hugo award, 1955. *Died in 1963.*

SCIENCE-FICTION PUBLICATIONS

Novels

*They'd Rather Be Right*, with Frank Riley. New York, Gnome Press, 1957; as *The Forever Machine*, New York, Galaxy, 1967.

*Eight Keys to Eden*. New York, Doubleday, 1960; London, Gollancz, 1962.

*When They Come from Space*. New York, Doubleday, 1962; London, Dobson, 1963.

Short Stories

*The Science Fiction of Mark Clifton*, edited by Barry N. Malzberg and Martin H. Greenberg. Carbondale, Southern Illinois University Press, 1980.

* * *

Mark Clifton had a brief ten-year writing career, but in that short span he had an enormous impact on science fiction. Most of Clifton's work was sold to *Astounding* in the form of two series.

The first series was about Bossy, the first of the super computers, and it was clearly developed in the novel *They'd Rather Be Right.* As Bossy follows its program to heal and perfect humans, the treated humans develop psi powers and immortality. However, society fears these perfected humans and sets off a witch hunt to destroy the treated humans and Bossy. Although there's plenty of action, the novel's plot concentrates on society's fears of the unknown, even if the unknown might provide great benefits. This book has subtlety and rare sophistication.

The second series features Ralph Kennedy, an extraterrestrial psychologist who manages—in glib, light stories—to save Earth from alien invasions. *When They Come from Space* satirizes bureaucracy when Earth is menaced by the terrible alien Black Fleet. Kennedy is drafted to confront the invasion and manages to discover the secret of the Black Fleet. The plot is clever and witty.

Clifton's only novel not a part of any series is the underrated *Eight Keys to Eden.* This is a puzzle story dealing with a situation first developed by Clarke's *Childhood's End.* An E-Man (or Extrapolator) is sent to investigate the colony on the planet Eden when the colony mysteriously stops communicating with Earth. The E-man must solve the ecological-psychological problem which becomes, in Clifton's treatment, a critique of Earth civilization.

—George Kelley

---

**CLIVE, Dennis.** *See* **FEARN, John Russell.**

---

**COBLENTZ, Stanton A(rthur).** American. Born in San Francisco, California, 24 August 1896. Educated at the University of California, Berkeley, A.B. 1917; M.A. 1919. Married Flora Bachrach in 1922. Feature writer, San Francisco *Examiner,* 1919–20; book reviewer, New York *Times* and New York *Sun,* 1920–38; founding editor, *Wings: A Quarterly of Verse,* New York, then Mill Valley, California, 1933–60. *Died 9 September 1982.*

SCIENCE-FICTION PUBLICATIONS

Novels

*The Wonder Stick.* New York, Cosmopolitan, 1929.
*Youth Madness.* London, Utopian, 1944.
*When the Birds Fly South.* Mill Valley, California, Wings Press, 1945.
*The Sunken World.* Los Angeles, Fantasy, 1948; London, Cherry Tree, 1951.
*After 12,000 Years.* Los Angeles, Fantasy, 1950.
*Into Plutonian Depths.* New York, Avon, 1950.
*The Planet of Youth.* Los Angeles, Fantasy, 1952.
*Under the Triple Suns.* Reading, Pennsylvania, Fantasy Press, 1955.
*Hidden World.* New York, Avalon, 1957; as *In Caverns Below,* New York, Garland, 1975.
*The Blue Barbarians.* New York, Avalon, 1958.
*Next Door to the Sun.* New York, Avalon, 1960.
*The Runaway World.* New York, Avalon, 1961.
*The Last of the Great Race.* New York, Arcadia House, 1964.
*The Lizard Lords.* New York, Avalon, 1964.
*The Lost Comet.* New York, Arcadia House, 1964.
*The Moon People.* New York, Avalon, 1964.
*Lord of Tranerica.* New York, Avalon, 1966.
*The Crimson Capsule.* New York, Avalon, 1967; as *The Animal People,* New York, Belmont, 1970.
*The Day the World Stopped.* New York, Avalon, 1968.
*The Island People.* New York, Belmont, 1971.

OTHER PUBLICATIONS

Verse

*The Thinker and Other Poems.* New York, White, 1923.
*The Lone Adventurer.* New York, Unicorn Press, 1927; revised edition, San Jose, California, Redwood Press, 1975.
*Shadows on a Wall.* New York, Poetic Publications, 1930.
*The Enduring Flame.* New York, Paebar, 1932.
*Songs of the Redwoods.* Los Angeles, Overland Outwest, 1933.
*The Merry Hunt.* Boston, Humphries, 1934.
*The Pageant of Man.* New York, Wings Press, 1936.
*Songs by the Wayside.* New York, Wings Press, 1938.
*Senator Goose.* Mill Valley, California, Wings Press, 1940.
*Winds of Chaos.* Mill Valley, California, Wings Press, 1942.
*Green Vistas.* Mill Valley, California, Wings Press, 1943.
*Armageddon.* Mill Valley, California, Wings Press, 1943.
*The Mountain of the Sleeping Maiden.* Mill Valley, California, Wings Press, 1946.
*Garnered Sheaves: Selected Poems.* Mill Valley, California, Wings Press, 1949.
*Time's Travellers.* Mill Valley, California, Wings Press, 1952.
*From a Western Hilltop.* Mill Valley, California, Wings Press, 1954.
*Out of Many Songs.* Mill Valley, California, Wings Press, 1958.
*Atlantis and Other Poems.* Mill Valley, California, Wings Press, 1960.
*Redwood Poems.* Healdsburg, California, Naturegraph, 1961.
*Aesop's Fables.* Norwalk, Connecticut, Gibson, 1968.
*Selected Short Poems.* San Jose, California, Redwood Press, 1974.
*Strange Universes: New Selected Poems.* San Jose, California, Redwood Press, 1977.
*Sea Cliffs and Green Ridges: Poems of the West.* Happy Camp, California, Naturegraph, 1979.

Other

*The Decline of Man.* New York, Minton Balch, 1925.
*Marching Men: The Story of War.* New York, Unicorn Press, 1927.
*The Literary Revolution.* New York, Frank Maurice, 1927.
*The Answer of the Ages.* New York, Cosmopolitan, 1931.
*Villains and Vigilantes.* New York, Wilson Erickson, 1936.
*The Triumph of the Teapot Poets.* Mill Valley, California, Wings Press, 1941.
*An Editor Looks at Poetry.* Mill Valley, California, Wings Press, 1947.
*New Poetic Lamps and Old.* Mill Valley, California, Wings Press, 1950.
*From Arrow to Atom Bomb: The Psychological History of War.* New York, Beechhurst Press, 1953.
*The Rise of the Anti-Poets.* Mill Valley, California, Wings Press, 1955.
*Magic Casements: A Guidebook for Poets.* Mill Valley, California, Wings Press, 1957.
*The Long Road to Humanity.* New York, Yoseloff, 1959.
*My Life in Poetry.* New York, Bookman Associates, 1959.
*The Swallowing Wilderness.* New York, Yoseloff, 1961.
*The Generation That Forgot to Sing.* Mill Valley, California, Wings Press, 1962.
*Avarice: A History.* Washington, D.C., Public Affairs Press, 1964.
*Ten Crises in Civilization.* Chicago, Follett, 1965; London, Muller, 1967.
*Demons, Witch Doctors, and Modern Man.* New York, Yoseloff, 1965.

*The Paradox of Man's Greatness.* Washington D.C., Public Affairs Press, 1966.
*The Poetry Circus.* New York, Hawthorn, 1967.
*The Pageant of the New World.* Berkeley, California, Diablo Press, 1968.
*The Power Trap.* South Brunswick, New Jersey, A.S. Barnes, 1970.
*The Militant Dissenters.* South Brunswick, New Jersey, A.S. Barnes, 1970.
*The Challenge to Man's Survival.* South Brunswick, New Jersey, A.S. Barnes, 1972.
*Light Beyond: The Wonderworld of Parapsychology.* New York, Cornwall, 1982.
*Adventures of a Freelancer: The Autobiography of Stanton A. Coblentz,* with Jeffrey M. Elliot. San Bernardino, California, Borgo Press, 1984.

Editor, *Modern American* [and *British*] *Lyrics.* New York, Minton Balch, 2 vols., 1924–25; as *Modern Lyrics,* New York, Loring and Mussey, n.d.
Editor, *The Music Makers.* New York, Ackerman, 1945.
Editor, *Unseen Wings.* New York, Beechhurst Press, 1949.
Editor, *Poetry Today.* Mill Valley, California, Wings Press, 1955.
Editor, *Poems to Change Lives.* New York, Association Press, 1960.

* * *

In the earliest days of the science-fiction magazines, most of the stories were reprinted from other sources; shortly, however, new works began to appear in *Amazing, Science Wonder Stories,* and the others. One of the first of these new authors, along with such writers as Jack Williamson and E.E. Smith, was Stanton A. Coblentz.

Coblentz's work was unusual for these magazines, as most of the material used science fiction as a vehicle for transmitting hard science (i.e., the Verne tradition), or a device for establishing melodramatic adventure situations (i.e., the Burroughs tradition). Coblentz, by contrast, used the standard devices of science fiction—space travel, time displacement, discovery of lost races—in order to establish a satiric mirror in which to reflect the foibles of contemporary society and/or timeless modes of human conduct. In this sense, Coblentz worked in the tradition of Lucian, Cyrano, Swift, and, to a substantial extent, H.G. Wells. Coblentz thus provided a model for such later humorists and satirists as William Tenn, Robert Sheckley, Frederik Pohl, and C.M. Kornbluth. Pohl, at least, of this group, has expressed his admiration for and debt to Coblentz.

Coblentz's first published science fiction was the novel *The Sunken World.* A modern submarine discovers survivors of the classical Atlantis living an idyllic existence in a glass dome on the ocean bottom, but they are destroyed through the inadvertent influence of the submariners.

In *Hidden World,* a contemporary traveller finds his way into an unknown civilization hidden in giant caverns beneath the earth. This theme is one Jules Verne had used as a device for travelogue-like exploration of imaginary geography, and Edgar Rice Burroughs also used it, in his Pellucidar series, as a background for adventure tales with primitive human and non-human creatures. In *Hidden World,* the traveller becomes caught up in a society at war for no comprehensible issue, except for the possible purpose of reducing unemployment and stimulating economic activity. *Into Plutonian Depths,* dealing with society on the plant Pluto, posits a situation in which men and women past child-bearing age aspire to become surgically neutered, these neuters being the pampered and powerful rulers of Plutonian society. The cover of the Avon edition described the novel as dealing with "the third sex" (a widely used euphemism for homosexuality at the time), to which Donald Wollheim, Avon's editor, later ascribed the success of the edition.

Many other works by Coblentz contain satirical matter, most often reflecting Coblentz's revulsion against war, consistently portrayed as senseless and ignoble, and his distress with the oppression and materialistic greed manifested in human institutions. *After 12,000 Years* portrays a future world in which armies of insects have been bred to giant and ferocious stature and enslaved for service in warfare. This anticipates *The Dragon Masters* (1962) by Jack Vance, a distant cousin of Coblentz. It should be noted that Coblentz had a long and varied literary career, of which his science fiction represents only one aspect. Two novels approaching science fiction are *The Wonder Stick,* a pleasantly done story of primitive life, and *When the Birds Fly South,* a beautifully realized novel of an unknown race in the Himalayas.

—Richard A. Lupoff

---

**COGSWELL, Theodore R(ose).** Also wrote as Cogswell Thomas. American. Born in Coatesville, Pennsylvania, 10 March 1918. Educated at the University of Colorado, Boulder, B.A. 1947; University of Denver, M.A. 1948, graduate study, 1956–57; University of Minnesota, Minneapolis, 1949–53; Latin Institute, Brooklyn College, 1973. Served as an ambulance driver, Spanish Republican Army, 1937–38; statistical control officer, United States Army Air Force, 1942–46; Captain; Order of the Cloud and Dragon, Republic of China. Married 1) Marjorie Mills in 1948, two daughters; 2) Coralie Norris in 1964; 3) George Rae Williams in 1972. Boulder correspondent, United Press, 1941– 42; Instructor, University of Minnesota, 1949–53, and University of Kentucky, Lexington, 1953–56, 1957–58; Assistant Professor, Ball State University, Muncie, Indiana, 1958–65; Professor, Keystone Junior College, La Plume, Pennsylvania, from 1965; executive director, and editor of Proceedings, Institute for 21st Century Studies, from 1959. Editor, *SFWA Forum,* 1970–71, 1973– 76; book reviewer, Minneapolis *Tribune,* 1970–72; editor, I.C.S., Scranton, Pennsylvania, 1975–78; editorial consultant, Sandvik Inc., Fair Lawn, New Jersey, 1978. Secretary, Science Fiction Writers of America, 1973–74. *Died.*

### Science-Fiction Publications

Novel

*Spock, Messiah!,* with Charles A. Spano, Jr. New York, Bantam, 1976; London, Corgi, 1977.

Short Stories

*The Wall Around the World.* New York, Pyramid, 1962.
*The Third Eye.* New York, Belmont, 1968.

Uncollected Short Stories

"Time Telescoped," in *Climax,* June 1953.
"The Big Stink," in *If* (New York), July 1954.
"Contact Point," with Poul Anderson, in *If* (New York), August 1954.

"Barrier," in *Science Fiction*, September 1954.
"Meddlers World," with Mack Reynolds, in *Science Fiction Quarterly* (Holyoke, Massachusetts), November 1955.
"Threesie," in *Fantasy and Science Fiction* (New York), January 1956.
"Aces Loaded," in *Venture* (Concord, New Hampshire), July 1957.
"Pain Reaction," in *Super Science* (New York), April 1958.
"The Golden People," in *Rogue*, June 1960.
"The Man Who Knew Grodnick," in *Science Fantasy* (Bournemouth), June 1962.
"Early Bird," with Ted Thomas, and "Probability Zero! The Population Implosion," in *Astounding*, edited by Harry Harrison. New York, Random House, 1973.
"Paradise Regained," (as Cogswell Thomas, with Ted Thomas), in *Saving Worlds*, edited by Roger Elwood and Virginia Kidd. New York, Doubleday, 1973.
"Players at Null-G," with Ted Thomas and Algis Budrys, *Fantasy and Science Fiction* (New York), July 1975.
"Grandfather Clause," in *Fantasy and Science Fiction* (New York), September 1975.
"How Dinosaurs Did It," in *Citadel*, February 1976.
"The Wall around the World," in *Wizards*, edited by Isaac Asimov, Martin H. Greenberg, and Charles G. Waugh. New York, New American Library, 1983.
"Deal with the D.E.V.I.L.," in *100 Great Fantasy Short Stories*, edited by Isaac Asimov, Terry Carr, and Martin H. Greenberg. New York, Doubleday, 1984.
"The Cabbage Patch," in *Young Monsters*, edited by Isaac Asimov, Martin H. Greenberg, and Charles G. Waugh. New York, Harper and Row, 1985.

OTHER PUBLICATIONS

Plays

*Some Call It Heads* (produced Denver, 1948).
*Operation Tel Aviv* (produced Foothills, California, 1949).
*Contact Point*, with G.R. Cogswell, in *Six Science Fiction Plays, edited by Roger Elwood. New York, Washington Square Press, 1976.*

Television Play: *Red Dust* (*Tales of Tomorrow* series), 1952.

Verse

*The Roper* (song), music by John Jacob Niles. New York, Schirmer, 1955.
*Placebos for the Orthodox*. Chinchilla, Pennsylvania, Miskatonic University Press, 1981.

* * *

Theodore R. Cogswell's work ranges in mood from horror to irony and spoof, in form from novellas to short stories, poetry, and drama, and in quality from expert and meaningful storytelling to juvenile fantasy. While portions of his stories (like "Test Area") are chilling, Cogswell's best horror story is probably "The Burning," which is about a demonic god (a terrible matriarch) who demands love and obedience from her children—and also eats them alive. Often horror is mixed with irony in Cogswell's work, as in "Emergency Rations" where cannibals are trapped in a Trojan horse scheme and literally cooked alive since they "can't feel nothing"; "Thimgs" where the unscrupulous main character demands vitality in his bargain with a Guardian for longer life—only to find that the lives spliced on to his are those leading to horrible sudden deaths; and "Wolfie" where Peter Vincent bargains with a warlock to be turned into a werewolf in order to kill his cousin and collect on his will, but is transformed into a mangy toothless mutt that must be put out of its misery. In these three stories the would-be victimizers become victims, for as the Guardian says in "Thimgs," "the ethical universe is just as orderly as the physical one." Occasionally, Cogswell's mood borders on spoof, as in "Probability Zero! The Population Implosion," which manipulates statistics in order to prove that England's population has declined since the year 1000 from 275 billion to 44 million at the present time. So, the story advises ticklishly, if you hear doomsayers of the population bomb, you need remember only that "statistics show . . . you have nothing to worry about." "Probability Zero!" illustrates what a Pirandello character says of a statistic: it's "like a sack; it won't stand up till you've put something in it." Unfortunately, what we put into it is interpretation, which is usually debatable and rarely definitive.

Cogswell is quite adept in the various literary genres. His first novella, "The Spectre General," is an accomplished story in the Heinlein tradition, involving delightful situational and understated humor and an alternating chapter/scene plot structure, which deals with the revival of a dying empire by technologists. *The Wall Around the World* is a fine reworking of the Icarus myth, blending and contrasting magic and technology in its main character, Porgie. Cogswell's shorter works are also expert, as the story "Early Bird" reveals. The most imaginative of all his fictions, this piece depicts a fascinating symbiotic relationship between the main character, Kurt Dixon, and his ship's mother computer and between "her" and two incredibly adaptive, semi-organic monsters on a planet Kurt was forced to retreat to during his battle with the gigantic, people-eating Kieriens.

Cogswell's poetry, although different in theme and mood from his other work, is quite good, as his Swiftian lambast against contemporary poets ("sparrow farts" and "word kickers") in "Faex Delenda Est" suggests. Finally, his drama is also impressive. For example, *Contact Point*, written with his wife, has an excellent sense of timing and action, dealing with the first space crew to reach a star and their anxieties and conflicts in bringing back a deadly radioactive organism. At first convinced that earth's doctors can save him, and willing to endanger the rest of humanity, the main character undergoes a dramatic change whereby he challenges earthlings to reunite and stop fighting among themselves in order to annihilate him and his ship before it lands.

Although Cogswell sometimes stoops to puerile fantasy as in "The Masters" (a vampire story), he was a versatile writer. Even in "The Masters" we see that just as the ethical universe is orderly so is the physical one, so that we never know if we will need some endangered species (the snaildarter?) to help us in our afflictions.

—Dennis M. Welch

---

**COLERIDGE, John.** *See* **BINDER, Eando.**

---

**COLLINS, Hunt.** *See* **HUNTER, Evan.**

---

**COLVIN, James.** *See* **MOORCOCK, Michael.**

---

**COMPTON, D(avid) G(uy).** Also writes as Guy Compton; Frances Lynch. British. Born in London, 19 August 1930. Educated at Cheltenham College, 1940–48. Served in the British Army, 1948–50. Married 1) Elizabeth Tillotson in 1952 (divorced 1969), two daughters and one son; 2) Carol Savage in 1971, one step-daughter and one step-son. Worked as stage electrician, furniture maker, salesman, docker, and postman; editor, Reader's Digest Condensed Books, London 1969–81. Lives in the United States. Recipient: Arts Council bursary, 1964. Agent: Virginia Kidd, Box 278, Milford, Pennsylvania 18337, U.S.A.

SCIENCE-FICTION PUBLICATIONS

Novels

*The Quality of Mercy.* London, Hodder and Stoughton, and New York, Ace, 1965; revised edition, Ace, 1970.
*Farewell, Earth's Bliss.* London, Hodder and Stoughton, 1966; New York, Ace, 1971.
*The Silent Multitude.* New York, Ace, 1966; London, Hodder and Stoughton, 1967.
*Synthajoy.* London, Hodder and Stoughton, and New York, Ace, 1968.
*The Steel Crocodile.* New York, Ace, 1970; as *The Electric Crocodile*, London, Hodder and Stoughton, 1970.
*Chronocules.* New York, Ace, 1970; as *Hot Wireless Sets, Aspirin Tablets, The Sandpaper Sides of Used Matchboxes, and Something That Might Have Been Castor Oil*, London, Joseph, 1971.
*The Missionaries.* New York, Ace, 1972; London, Hale, 1975.
*The Unsleeping Eye.* New York, DAW, 1974; as *The Continuous Katherine Mortenhoe*, London, Gollancz, 1974; as *Death Watch*, London, Magnum, 1981.
*A Usual Lunacy.* San Bernardino, California, Borgo Press, 1978.
*Windows.* New York, Berkley, 1979.
*Ascendancies.* London, Gollancz, and New York, Berkley, 1980.
*Scudder's Game.* Munich, Heyne, 1985; Worcester Park, Surrey, Kerosina, 1988.

OTHER PUBLICATIONS

Novels as Guy Compton

*Too Many Murderers.* London, Long, 1962.
*Medium for Murder.* London, Long, 1963.
*Dead on Cue.* London, Long, 1964.
*Disguise for a Dead Gentleman.* London, Long, 1964.
*High Tide for Hanging.* London, Long, 1965.
*And Murder Came Too.* London, Long, 1966.
*The Palace* (as D.G. Compton). London, Hodder and Stoughton, and New York, Norton, 1969.

Novels as Frances Lynch

*Twice Ten Thousand Miles.* London, Souvenir Press, and New York, St. Martin's Press, 1974; as *Candle at Midnight*, New York, Dell, 1977.
*The Fine and Handsome Captain.* London, Souvenir Press, and New York, St. Martin's Press, 1975.
*Stranger at the Wedding.* New York, St. Martin's Press, 1976; London, Souvenir Press, 1977.
*A Dangerous Magic.* London, Souvenir Press, and New York, St. Martin's Press, 1978.
*In the House of Dark Music.* London, Hodder and Stoughton, 1979.

Plays

Radio Plays: *Chez Nous*, 1961; *Bandstand*, 1962; *Blind Man's Bluff*, 1962; *Fully Furnished*, 1963; *Always Read the Small Print*, 1963; *If the Shoe Fits*, 1964; *Mandible Light*, 1964; *A Turning off the Minch Park Road*, 1965; *Time Exposure*, 1965; *The Real People*, 1966; *Island*, 1968; *Surgery*, 1968; *The Respighi Inheritance*, 1973.

Other

*Radio Plays.* Worcester Park, Surrey, Kerosina, 1988.

*

D.G. Compton comments:

Possibly the best introduction to any writer's work is to know why he does it. The reason I write what people have been kind enough to call SF ("kind enough" because the label makes possible a large and informed readership for stuff that otherwise would probably sink without a trace) is that I'm basically a rather embarrassed sort of person, afraid of admitting to commitment, who welcomes SF's distancing mechanisms. After all, it's far safer to dare to care about one's characters when the situation in which one places them isn't quite "real."

Also I've led what is sometimes known as a "sheltered life." For which read "limited." Thus I know very little about the commonalities of human existence: commerce, golf, brick-laying, what you will. The same sheltered life, however, has involved me in close and prolonged—and often painful—contact with just a few very positive individuals (mostly women, let's face it), and from these individuals I've learned a lot. So I try to write about that of which I know at least something, people, while setting them discreetly in worlds of my own devising (about which I may also be expected to know something.) Future worlds, for convenience's sake, but always closely tied to my own muddled understanding of the present world around me. In general terms I don't much like this present world, and developing it a few years on is a good way of finding out why. And perhaps even of seeing how to change it.

* * *

D.G. Compton's science-fiction novels usually lead to extremes of reaction from their readers. Some are strongly attracted to his mature themes, richly fluent prose, strong concentration on character, and realistic appreciation of the seamier side of human existence. Others are dismayed by the density of his prose, the ineffectualness of many of his characters, the underlying distrust of technology as a cure for all of humanity's ills, the absence of much physical action, and the frequently bizarre nature of his situations. But it appears that Compton is beginning to win over an ever larger share of readers as he continues to skewer human foibles and failings.

Two of his more popular novels deal with our delight in vicarious experience of another's life. *Synthajoy* created a minor controversy because of the dissolute nature of its characters. The story concerns the development of a means to record the life experiences of an individual, to be played back at another time for an interested audience. Although there are obvious beneficial aspects to such an invention, it is almost immediately subverted. Compton returned to this theme in *The Unsleeping Eye.* In a world where disease and pain are virtually unknown, Katherine Mortenhoe had contracted a terminal disease that leaves her only weeks to live. The entertainment world is quick to realize that this provides a possibly unique opportunity to produce a profitable bit of entertainment, and they employ a man with cameras surgically implanted in one eye. The cameraman manipulates Katherine so that she is emotionally dependent upon him, totally unaware that he is filming her agony for an unfeeling audience. But as time passes, his feelings for her become genuine, and there is a dawning realization that he too is being manipulated.

Compton apparently felt that he had not completely examined the consequences of this situation, because he later wrote a sequel, *Windows.* The protagonist insists upon the removal of his camera-eyes and accepts blindness, but his personal statement about the world is not allowed to stand as it is. One factor abhors him for criticizing the status quo, another wants to make him a cult hero, and still another dismisses his gesture as an nuisance. The pair are finally driven to flee the country, but are still unable to withdraw into themselves.

Perhaps Compton's most accomplished work is *The Steel Crocodile*, set in an ultra-secret research institute. The protagonist rapidly realizes that more is transpiring within the research group than is apparent. Eventually it is revealed to him that the authorities fear that blind technological progress is too dangerous, and they have created a computer bank to monitor and even interfere with scientific developments. They are blithely unaware that they have surrendered their destiny to the very technology they hoped to control. This complexity of philosophy and plot is rarely found in any genre, and Compton's ability to control his work has rarely been equalled.

*The Silent Multitude* is perhaps his least conventional work. A spore from space attacks concrete, and most artifacts of man's civilization are crumbling. Against the background of a deserted city, Compton presents a small cast of characters, relecting their personal decay against the collapse of the city itself. Even without the brilliant characterization, this would remain a memorable novel, for Compton's description of the dissolution is haunting.

The isolated research organization appears again in *Chronocules*, also present as an island of hope in a crumbling society. It is clear that the collapse of the present society is accelerating and will come within the lifetimes of the protagonists, so they desperately seek a means of escape into the future. Although an excellent novel in itself, it suffers when compared to *The Steel Crocodile* and *The Silent Multitude*, to both of which it is thematically similar. *The Missionaries* should have been a very controversial novel, but attracted little attention. A small group of aliens arrive on Earth, preaching the religion of Ustiliath. Compton makes it quite clear that, for all practical purposes, the aliens are absolutely correct in their beliefs, and that conversion to their religion is the only logical course. But humanity reacts with fear and loathing, and the aliens reach the same fate that greeted many Christian missionaries in their efforts to bring "enlightenment" to the "savages."

Two of Compton's early novels were brought back into print as his popularity grew. Both are highly competent, but neither is of the quality of his later work. *The Quality of Mercy* is a low key examination of the tensions brought to bear on a group of military personnel when it becomes clear that something, perhaps a nuclear war, is imminent. In many ways, this is a forerunner of *The Steel Crocodile*, although in no way comparable with regard to quality. *Farewell, Earth's Bliss* makes use of one of science fiction's most well-traveled plots, the penal colony on Mars, to present a group of misfit humans against a kaleidoscopic background where reality and fantasy aren't always distinguishable.

*A Usual Lunacy* investigates the repercussions of a new disease that causes people to fall in love with each other against their will, and in many cases only until they are cured of the disease. Compton seems unusually bitter this time, for love itself becomes a sometimes criminal activity. *Ascendancies* seems to have been largely overlooked despite yet another set of interesting characters. A strange substance begins periodically to fall from space, a substance which is soon revealed to be an inexpensive source of energy. Soon most of the world is freed from the normal work week, but subject to a new burden. There are scattered incidents of possibly hallucinatory singing, often accompanied by mysterious disappearances of people in the area. The protagonists are a woman whose husband disappears and the insurance investigator who discovers she has purchased a body from a criminal organization in order to ensure that she receives the insurance money. When he decides to blackmail her, the two are brought together in a compulsive and compelling relationship.

Compton has written few short stories, none of which have been noteworthy, probably because his gift of characterization is not as apparent at that length. Although he continues to write both within and outside the genre, Compton has eschewed the traditional concerns of science fiction, using the plots that he borrows only as the frame upon which to hang his real interests, the morality of science, the peculiarities of humanity, and our ability to influence our own lives.

—Don D'Ammassa

---

**CONEY, Michael G(reatrex).** British. Born in Birmingham, Warwickshire, 28 September 1932. Educated at King Edward's School, Birmingham, 1944–49. Served in the Royal Air Force, 1956–58. Married to Daphne Coney; two sons and one daughter. Auditor, Russell and Company, Birmingham, 1949–56; senior clerk, Pearce Clayton Maunder, Dorchester, Dorset, 1958–61; accountant, Pontins, Bournemouth, 1962; tenant, Plymouth Breweries, Totnes, Devon, 1963–66; accountant, Peplow Warren Fuller, Newton Abbout, Devon, 1966–69; manager, Jabberwock Hotel, Antigua, West Indies, 1969–72. Management specialist, British Columbia Forest Service, Victoria, 1973–89. Recipient: British Science Fiction award, 1976. Address: 2082 Neptune Road, R.R. 3, Sidney, British Columbia, Canada.

SCIENCE-FICTION PUBLICATIONS

Novels (series: The Song of Earth)

*Mirror Image.* New York, DAW, 1972; London, Gollancz, 1973.

*Syzygy.* New York, Ballantine, and Morley, Yorkshire, Elmfield Press, 1973.

*Friends Come in Boxes.* New York, DAW, 1973; London, Gollancz, 1974.

*The Hero of Downways*. New York, DAW, 1973; London, Futura, 1974.
*Winter's Children*. London, Gollancz, 1974.
*The Jaws That Bite, The Claws That Catch*. New York, DAW, 1975; as *The Girl with a Symphony in Her Fingers*, Morley, Yorkshire, Elmfield Press, 1975.
*Hello Summer, Goodbye*. London, Gollancz, 1975; as *Rax*, New York, DAW, 1975; as *Pallahaxi Tide*. Victoria, British Columbia, Porcepic, 1990.
*Charisma*. London, Gollancz, 1975; New York, Dell, 1979.
*Brontomek!* London, Gollancz, 1976.
*The Ultimate Jungle*. London, Millington, 1979.
*Neptune's Cauldron*. New York, Tower, 1981.
*Cat Karina*. New York, Ace, 1982; London, Gollancz, 1983.
*The Celestial Steam Locomotive* (Song). Boston, Houghton Mifflin, 1983; London, Futura, 1986.
*Gods of the Greataway* (Song). Boston, Houghton Mifflin, 1984; London, Futura, 1986.
*Fang, The Gnome* (Song). New York, New American Library, and London, Futura, 1988.
*King of the Scepter'd Isle* (Song). New York, New American Library, 1989.

Short Stories

*Monitor Found in Orbit*. New York, DAW, 1974.

OTHER PUBLICATIONS

Other

*Forest Ranger, Ahoy! The Men, The Ships, The Job*. Sidney, British Columbia, Porthole Press, 1983.
*Forest Adventure: A Guide to the British Columbia Forest Museum*, with Gray Campbell. Sidney, British Columbia, Porthole Press, 1985.

*

Michael G. Coney comments:

My purpose is to entertain myself as well as my readers. Each of my novels has been an experiment in style and content with one consistent trait: they are all mystery stories. Love is there too, and human psychology, and a little "hard" science, but my main intent is to keep the reader guessing. I think my earlier novels were too conservative; they were all hung on hooks of known science and "real" reality—which is odd, since as an SF reader my preference is for the persuasively fantastic: the "sense of wonder" story. My short stories are normally written as vehicles for ideas, situations, and characters which I intend to use in my novels—I find it much easier to work this way than to plunge into a novel cold. Other short stories have been written for specific purposes, generally to use up one-off ideas before I forget them.

* * *

Michael G. Coney was a prolific writer in the mid-1970's and has recently caught his second wind, with his commitment to "The Song of Earth" series, a kaleidoscopic future history, and related works. Because he has contributed to so many of the genre's traditions, his work is not easy to classify: perhaps his originality has been in his ability to take the old forms and themes and quietly but persuasively put his own stamp on them. Philip K. Dick may have been his model in *Mirror Image*, John Christopher in the post-holocaust novel, *Winter's Children*, Heinlein and Aldiss in the closed environment stories *The Hero of Downways, The Ultimate Jungle* and "The Mind Prison," Asimov's "Nightfall" in *Syzygy* and "Evidence" (from *I, Robot*) in "The Martyrdom of Raccoona Three" (a fine short story embedded in *The Celestial Steam Locomotive*), Cordwainer Smith in *Cat Karina* and other stories in "The Song of Earth" that feature the "Specialists" (animal-human melds). His powerful sequel to *Syzygy, Brontomek!*, takes up several ideas from the earlier stories: the amorphs from *Mirror Image*, the heroine's name and personality from Susanna in *Charisma*, the brontomeks and the idea of post-hypnotic suggestion from his grim story "Esmeralda." Throughout his work, Coney's range of theme and tone is remarkable; his touch is usually light, but the fare is not bland. He is equally at ease with horror, romance, and humor ("The Byrds" should become a classic of comic fantasy). "The Song of the Earth," therefore, which forced him by its structure to evoke the sense of wonder freshly at least once in each of its many short chapters, proved ideally suited to his genius and had the further advantage of enabling him to subsume his taste for fantasy within a formal science-fictional frame, through the idea of a computer-programmable Dream World.

Coney likes to study the reactions of a small group to a large threat or challenge, whether natural but alien, as in *Hello Summer, Goodbye, Syzygy* and the gnome books, or social but inhuman, as in *Brontomek!*, or both, as in *The Ultimate Jungle*. Solutions are not likely to be achieved by technological means but, after valiant efforts, may be granted by special grace; to some problems the only solution is escape or transcendence. As an SF writer, Coney is properly concerned with the issue of skepticism and its contrary, credulity; he is not so hasty as some writers to come down on one side. The framing chapters of *Syzygy* expose the dangers of group vulnerability to suggestion, yet it seems in *Brontomek!* that it may sometimes be better to rest happily deceived, as individuals are by the amorphic "Tes" (thous, ideal companions). Coney hates manipulators: his sympathetic characters are often their victims; yet it is not easy for these characters to find someone to blame. In *Brontomek!* the immoral Organization stamps on a whole planet, yet its own agents are themselves victims, and there is something sublimely admirable in the irresponsible force of its symbol, the rogue brontomek, which rampages malignly for a time before pathetically losing its motive power, "betrayed by its own mechanical weaknesses." Cat Karina complains against the bullying gods, but human manipulators and strong egotists may be regarded with horrified admiration, as are Carioca Jones and Hector Bartholomew in the Peninsula stories, while their devoted lovers are seen with baffled disgust. Nevertheless, if the author, for narrative purposes, identifies with such lovers, he will present them with strong sympathy, and perhaps it is for this reason that in *Charisma, The Jaws That Bite, The Claws That Catch*, and *The Ultimate Jungle*, Coney seems over-tolerant of some repellent features of his heroes, concomitant on their devotion to such unpleasant characters. Alien manipulators may also be present sympathetically (their control is accidental in *Syzygy*; accidents are rectified by benevolent fostering in "The Tertiary Justification" and "Symbiote"; they show wise control of beasts in "Oh, Valinda!"). So disposed, Coney gives us one of the genre's sweetest heroines in the alien Pallahaxi Browneyes (*Hello Summer, Goodbye*), and seems to envy the self-containedness of his multi-individual aliens (Kli a' Po in *Brontomek!* and the amusing Vegan in "Trading Post"), whereas his humans often find it hard to relate to other individuals.

There is strong dystopian satire in *Friends Come in Boxes* (which offers a radical solution to superfluous people—those over 40) and *The Jaws That Bite, The Claws That Catch* (where prisoners reduce their sentences by voluntary bondage). As a dystopian writer, Coney's animus is principally against the notion that utility or justice should outweigh compassion. The darker side of his vision culminates in *The Ultimate Jungle*, an important but depressing novel in which Coney seems to have given in to a compulsion to put on record those inadequacies which hereafter will force him to treat humans as members of a dead species. Maybe he had to get this book off his chest before he could achieve the mellower tones of "The Song of Earth."

Coney has stressed the element of mystery in his stories; his plots often draw upon those of mystery fiction: like Bester's *The Demolished Man, Charisma* offers an SF variant of the locked-room mystery, for instance, and "Monitor Found in Orbit" wickedly plays on the spy thriller. Coney appreciates that the SF form can be used to shed new light on old problems; in my favorite of his early novels, *The Hero of Downways*, he studies heroism as it were in a clinical laboratory situation—and also takes a fresh look at such SF standards as clones, the multi-individual self, mutations, and miniaturized people. Others may enjoy this author more for his presentation of new forms of locomotion or of unusual tidal conditions on strange planets; few should fail to find him entertaining, and he deserves to be rediscovered extensively.

The two most recent novels, which are set in the same multiverse of ifalongs and happentracks as the "Song" series, are likely to raise Michael Greatrex Coney's profile (he uses the full name for the purpose) as a fantasist because they deal so freshly and delightfully with the Arthurian legend. In the wake of Marion Zimmer Bradley's feminist reading, *The Mists of Avalon*, comes a gnomist recension in *Fang, the Gnome* and its sequel, *King of the Scepter'd Isle.* Coney's gnomes suggest Tolkien's hobbits as they, too, are little people swept up in heroic events and contributing crucially to their resolution, but the gnomes will never be taken so seriously as the larger hobbits. Paradoxically earthy yet prudish, for example, all gnomes except Fang and his Princess loathe the very idea of copulation, otherwise known as "filth," and one of them, Mold the Outrageous, excellently substitutes the downright "Sexual Intercourse!" for the increasingly meaningless f— word of modern human parlance. To begin with, they live safely outside the margins of human ("giant") experience, witnessing with disgust the nasty human habit of killing one another and assorted animals in a shadowy "umbra," because they inhabit a happentrack not quite contiguous to the human one, but the young heroine Nyneve finds a gateway between the worlds and it is not long before the gnomes and humans are sharing the same part of Cornwall. The gnomes are a quarrelsome lot and have their own political problems which mirror in a wry fashion those of the larger people. The matter of Arthur is dealt with lightly, much in the vein of T.H. White, and the treatment of Lancelot is notably tactful. Coney does not debunk the legendary figures; on the contrary, the legend of chivalry serves to rescue mankind (not to mention the godlike Starquin) from a ghastly fate; but a remark by the wild human Sally is not unrepresentative: "Come on, let's go down there and behave like heroes for a while. I need to boast and gloat!"

—Michael J. Tolley

---

**CONSTANTINE, Murray.** *See* **BURDEKIN, Katherine.**

---

**CONSTANTINE, Storm.** British. Born in England, 12 October 1956. Educated at Stafford Girls' High School, 1966–71; Stafford Art College, 1971–72. Finance officer, in Staffordshire, since 1990. Agent: Maggie Noach, 21 Redan Street, London W14 4QB. Address: 35 Ingestre Road, Stafford ST17 4DJ, England.

SCIENCE-FICTION PUBLICATIONS

Novels (series: Wraeththu)

*The Enchantments of Flesh and Spirit* (Wraeththu). London, Macdonald, 1987; New York, Tor, 1990.
*The Bewitchments of Love and Hate* (Wraeththu). London, Futura, 1988; New York, Tor, 1990.
*The Fulfillments of Fate and Desire* (Wraeththu). Birmingham, Drunken Dragon Press, 1989; New York, Tor, 1991.
*The Monstrous Regiment*. London, Futura, 1989.
*Hermetech*. London, Headline, 1991.

*

Storm Constantine comments:

The ideas in my first three books, which comprised the "Wraeththu" trilogy, evolved over ten years or so, and, by the time I came to write the books, seemed to have become a personal mythology. The books incorporate influences of diverse mythic sources and also the last decade of popular culture, as I have always worked with musicians and bands, in the capacity of writer, ideas person, artist, and manager. I have developed some of the themes and ideas of the "Wraeththu" books in more recent work, such as *Hermetech* and *Burying the Shadow* (due to be published in the United Kingdom in February 1992), while creating very different worlds from that of my first novels.

* * *

Some critics responded to Storm Constantine's first novel, *The Enchantments of Flesh and Spirit*, by calling it "punk fantasy." Five books later, this is seen to be misleading, if it was ever relevant. Constantine is best defined in that context as a post-punk Goth. Much more significant is the recurrent theme of her novels, sex and sexuality, and the adaptation of the human body in relation to sex.

The first three novels, which form the Wraeththu trilogy, show a major development in writing ability, as one would expect, but this is reflected in an over-emphasis in imagery at the detriment of the story itself. *Enchantments* opens in fairly standard style, with the young boy Pellaz leaving home with the mysterious Wraeththu stranger Cal. As they travel, and as Pellaz is incepted as Wraeththu, the details of Constantine's world emerge. In a post-collapse world, a new breed of humans have emerged. The Wraeththu are hermaphrodites of outstanding health, fitness, and beauty, and Constantine, with the enthusiasm of a young author, takes great delight in some bizarre physical descriptions as Pellaz is changed into Har (as the Wraeththu are also known.) Wraeththu also live in tribes, and their lives are frequently ritualised.

Against this background, Pellaz and Cal travel until Pellaz is killed in an ambush. From here things become obscured by mysticism: Pellaz is made ruler of the dominant Wraeththu tribe, advised and controlled by Thiede, supposedly the first and most powerful Wraeththu. The second book, however, makes it clear that the real story is Cal's. *The Bewitchments Of Love And Hate* is set amongst the Varr tribe whom Cal and Pellaz had visited in book one. This volume is perhaps the best of the three, the prose is tighter than before, and the plot deals closely with several complex and interacting relationships. Cal has come from a nasty background, and in *Bewitchments* he becomes more rounded, though not necessarily softened, as a character. The controlling hand of Thiede becomes clear, and Cal briefly becomes a victim. Constantine confuses good and evil cleverly, avoiding the usual simplistic approach of fantasy. In this book her language is both emotive and descriptive.

Cal himself narrates the final book, *The Fulfillments Of Fate and Desire*, but the plot becomes convoluted, wrapped in the symbolism of Cabbala, and is frequently obscure. Ultimately the final dramatic climax, the complete re-union of Pellaz and Cal, and the apparent success of Thiede's designs, does force its way through to clarity, but much of what precedes it is either fraught with heavy symbolism or desultory and delaying.

Unfortunately, her next book, *The Monstrous Regiment* proves to be a major disappointment. It has the appearance of a feminist fantasy at first, but there are confusions. The world of Artemis is colonised by breakaway feminists and their male supporters, but it has been corrupted into the worst of matriarchies, leaving rebellion simmering. The innocent young Corrinna is caught up in this, first by hiding the fugitive Elvon L'Belder, and then by her adoption by the military chief Carmenya as a lover. The consequences of these events are profound, even extreme, and in one scene at least, very nasty. One side of the plot also involves the mysterious, indigenous Greylids, suitably alien. The book ought to have been a major landmark in Constantine's career. Instead, the over-characterization of some minor players slows vital action down, and the exaggeration of the sadistic Dominatrix stretches credibility. Nevertheless, these might have been minor quibbles but for the woolly thinking behind much of the politics, in what is clearly intended as a political statement, and the transcendent ending to the Greylids strand is awkward. There is to be a sequel, *The Aleph*, which may clear up some of the vagueries of this book.

Sexuality is the key to Constantine's work; sexual politics underlies *The Monstrous Regiment*, and *Hermetech*, her latest novel, is also about sex. Much of the magic of the Wraeththu involves ritual sex, and Hermetech is defined as "the science of orgasmic energy potential esp. within fixed unit (within time, space)." Constantine is never a simple writer, and while much of this novel is about fourteen-year-old Ari Famber preparing to lose her virginity, that gives no hint of the complexities involved.

Like the previous book, *Hermetech* is set both in the city and the country. Ari grows up close to an artificial henge, sight of festivals worshiping Isis-Confidentia, an orbiting AI. Her father, long dead, had altered Ari genetically; his former colleague, Leila Saatchi, now a "natro," a renegade from the Tech-Green revolution, visits the henge with her gang, and Ari leaves for the city with her. Meanwhile, in the city, Zambia Crevecoeur, a male prostitute, has been surgically altered so that he now has six extra sex organs, in his stomach. Behind him, several different figures are playing games and manipulating people to their own ends, including the mysterious Tammuz Malamute, whose real identity is guessable quite early. The central plot twists Ari and Zambia together, and it is obvious why. Ari's orgasm is always going to be the climax of the novel, and at times the rest is just distraction, or confusing info-dump.

In her first novel, Constantine's scenery tends to the stock: forest, desert, mountains. By the fifth she is creating a real world, with real characters. Her preoccupations, however, sex, and the development and adaptation of the body, leave the reader only slightly satisfied. All the skills are there for Constantine to produce a major novel, but she hasn't done it yet. The promise remains unfulfilled.

—Kev P. McVeigh

---

**COOK, Glen (Charles).** Also writes as Greg Stevens. American. Born in New York City, 9 July 1944. Educated at Roseville Joint Union High School, California; University of Missouri, Columbia, 2 years. Served in the United States Navy. Married Carol Ann Fritz in 1971; three sons. Since 1965, assembly, inspection, material control, and supervisory jobs, General Motors, St. Louis. Agent: Russell Galen, Scott Meredith Literary Agency, 845 Third Avenue, New York, New York 10022. Address: 4106 Flora Place, St. Louis, Missouri 63110, U.S.A.

SCIENCE-FICTION PUBLICATIONS

Novels (series: Black Company; Darkwar; Dread Empire; Garrett Files; Starfishers)

*The Heirs of Babylon*. New York, New American Library, 1972.
*A Shadow of All Night Falling* (Dread Empire). New York, Berkley, 1979.
*October's Baby* (Dread Empire). New York, Berkley, 1980.
*All Darkness Met* (Dread Empire). New York, Berkley, 1980.
*The Swordbearer*. New York, Pocket Books, 1982.
*Shadowline* (Starfishers). New York, Warner, 1982.
*Starfishers*. New York, Warner, 1982.
*Stars' End* (Starfishers). New York, Warner, 1982.
*The Fire in His Hands* (Dread Empire). New York, Pocket Books, 1984.
*The Black Company*. New York, Tor, 1984.
*Shadows Linger* (Black Company). New York, Tor, 1984.
*Passage at Arms*. New York, Popular Library, 1985.
*A Matter of Time*. New York, Ace, 1985.
*With Mercy Toward None* (Dread Empire). New York, Baen, 1985.
*The White Rose* (Black Company). New York, Tor, 1985.
*Warlock* (Darkwar). New York, Warner, 1985.
*Doomstalker* (Darkwar). New York, Warner, 1985.
*Annals of the Black Company* (omnibus). New York, Nelson Doubleday, 1986.
*Ceremony* (Darkwar). New York, Warner, 1986.
*Sweet Silver Blues* (Garrett). New York, New American Library, 1987.
*The Garrett Files* (omnibus). New York, Nelson Doubleday, 1987.
*Reap the East Wind* (Dread Empire). New York, Tor, 1987.
*An Ill Fate Marshalling* (Dread Empire). New York, Tor, 1988.
*The Dragon Never Sleeps*. New York, Warner, 1988.
*Cold Copper Tears* (Garrett). New York, New American Library, 1988.
*Bitter Gold Hearts* (Garrett). New York, New American Library, 1988.
*Old Tin Sorrows* (Garrett). New York, New American Library, 1989.
*The Tower of Fear*. New York, Tor, 1989.
*Shadow Games* (Black Company). New York, Tor, 1989.
*The Silver Spike* (Black Company). New York, Tor, 1989.

*Dreams of Steel* (Black Company). New York, Tor, 1990.
*Dread Brass Shadows* (Garrett). New York, Penguin, 1990.

Uncollected Short Stories

"Song from a Forgotten Hill," in *Clarion*, edited by Robin Scott Wilson. New York, New American Library, 1971.
"Silverheels," in *Witchcraft & Sorcery* (Alhambra, California), May 1971.
"And Dragons in the Sky," in *Clarion 2*, edited by Robin Scott Wilson. New York, New American Library, 1972.
"Appointment in Samarkand," *Witchcraft & Sorcery* (Alhambra, California), November 1972.
"Sunrise," in *Eternity 1* (Sandy Springs, South Carolina), no. 2, 1973.
"The Nights of Dreadful Silence," in *Fantastic* (New York), September 1973.
"The Devil's Tooth," in *Fantasy & Terror 1*, no. 1, 1974.
"In the Wind," in *Tomorrow Today*, edited by George Zebrowski. Santa Cruz, California, Unity Press, 1975.
"The Recruiter," in *Amazing* (New York), March 1977.
"Ponce," in *Amazing* (New York), November 1977.
"The Seventh Fool," in *Fantasy and Science Fiction* (New York), March 1978.
"Ghost Stalk," in *Fantasy and Science Fiction* (New York), May 1978.
"Quiet Sea," in *Fantasy and Science Fiction* (New York), December 1978.
"Castle of Tears," in *Whispers 4* (Binghamton, New York), nos. 1–2, 1979.
"Soldier of an Empire Unacquainted with Defeat," in *The Berkley Showcase 2*, edited by Victoria Schochet and John W. Silbersack. New York, Berkley, 1980.
"Call for the Dead," in *Fantasy and Science Fiction* (New York), July 1980.
"Filed Teeth," in *Dragons of Darkness*, edited by Orson Scott Card. New York, Ace, 1981.
"Raker," in *Fantasy and Science Fiction* (New York), August 1982.
"Darkwar," in *Isaac Asimov's Science Fiction Magazine* (New York), December 1982.
"Enemy Territory," in *Night Voyages 9* (Freeburg, Illinois), Spring 1983.
"The Waiting Sea," in *Archon 7 Program Book*. St Louis, Archon, 1983.
"Severed Heads," in *Sword and Sorceress 1*, edited by Marion Zimmer Bradley, New York, DAW, 1984.

Other Publications

Novel

*The Swap Academy* (as Greg Stevens). San Diego, Publisher's Export Corp., 1970.

* * *

Glen Cook's first few pieces of fiction appeared in the early 1970's, of which the most notable are the short story "In the Wind" and a post-holocaust novel featuring the crew of a surviving naval destroyer, *The Heirs of Babylon.* After publishing almost nothing through the remainder of the decade, Cook began to appear primarily at novel length with a rapid succession of science fiction and fantasy series.

The first of these was the Dread Empire series, consisting initially of *A Shadow of All Night Falling, October's Baby*, and *All Darkness Met.* Although basically a derivative fantasy adventure series involving wizardry, an epic war, flawless heroes and vicious villains, there was an undeniable raw power to this series which gained it a considerable following. Less successful was a non-series fantasy adventure, *The Swordbearer*, the story of a hero with an enchanted sword.

The Starfishers trilogy, *Shadowline, Starfishers*, and *Star's End*, also had an heroic theme, transplanted into space. Two powerful groups contend in a battle that starts with a raid on a planet where humans were held as slaves by the alien Sangaree. Subsequent adventures involve secret agents of the human confederation, efforts to manage a valuable alien species on the periphery of the conflict, and the emergence of a new threat from the center of the galaxy. An additional volume, *Passage at Arms*, was published after a gap of three years, completing the struggle against an overwhelming army of alien invaders.

*The Fire in His Hands* and its sequel, *With Mercy Toward None*, chronicled the rise and triumph of a desert warrior pitted against evil sorcery. At the same time, Cook began writing what may be his most popular series, *The Black Company.* Although as unrelentingly violent and simplistic in its characterization as most of Cook's earlier work, this series shows an undeniable energy, an enthusiasm which communicates itself to its readers. The initial trilogy, which includes *Shadows Linger* and *The White Rose*, follows the adventures of a group of mercenaries who are originally in the service of an evil sorceress, who eventually learn that their enemies may serve a more benevolent power, switching sides to unseat their former mistress.

The solo novel, *A Matter of Time*, is very atypical of Cook's work, a time travel paradox story involving past, present, and future, still primarily action-oriented but displaying more thorough and intricate plotting and character development. His next trilogy blended science fiction and fantasy themes. Set against a primitive landscape, *Doomstalker, Warlock*, and *Ceremony* describe the interaction of technology and mental powers so strange as to seem magical. The protagonist is a woman who hopes to use her mental powers to assist her plan to place orbiting mirrors around the world, bringing its current ice age to an end. This is Cook's most ambitious work in many ways, utilizing many of the devices of his earlier fiction, but with more self confidence and a serious theme. Another non-series novel, *The Dragon Never Sleeps*, deals with an interstellar fleet used to enforce a dictatorship until one man discovers a secret which will bring their domination to an end.

For the most part, Cook has spent recent years building upon the series he had already established. Two more Dread Empire novels appeared, *Reap the East Wind* and *An Ill Fate Marshalling.* The freedom won in the original trilogy is now in jeopardy as enemies both ordinary and supernatural arise on all sides, and the protagonist of the earlier volumes unwisely involves himself in an attempt to undermine the Dread Empire itself. More smoothly written than the original trilogy, these two sequels are restatements of themes Cook has done better elsewhere.

The Black Company returned in *Shadow Games.* Devastated by their earlier battles, the mercenaries set off on a new mission, beset by a new supernatural menace. The company has been defeated and dispersed in *Dreams of Steel*, wherein one survivor tries to raise a new force, still opposed by the inhuman Shadow-Masters. Finally, in *The Silver Spike*, both sides have been eliminated, except that an artifact exists which may allow the evil to return to a world from which the Black Company has finally removed itself.

*Sweet Silver Blues* introduced a new series, a new premise, a likable private detective in a world of elves, ogres, vampires, and other fantastic creatures. It was also the first novel by Cook to display any real humor, a light approach that was essentially new territory. In *Bitter Gold Hearts, Cold Copper Tears, Old Tin Sorrows*, and *Dread Brass Shadows*, Garrett pursues a number of cases including kidnapping, ghostly revenge, and lost treasures, and it appears likely that additional adventures will follow.

Most recently, Cook has written a new solo fantasy novel, *The Tower of Fear*, certainly his best effort in that genre. Although Cook has occasionally published short fiction during this period, most is of minor interest, and several stories were subsequently incorporated into novels.

—Don D'Ammassa

---

**COOKE, Arthur.** *See* **LOWNDES, Robert A.W.**

---

**COOPER, Edmund.** Also wrote as Richard Avery. British. Born in Marple, Cheshire, 30 April 1926. Educated at Manchester Grammar School, 1937–41; Didsbury Teachers Training College, Lancashire, 1946–47. Served as a radio officer in the British Merchant Navy, 1939–45. Married 1) Joyce Plant in 1946, one daughter and three sons; 2) Valerie Makin in 1963, two sons and two daughters; 3) Dawn Freeman-Baker in 1980. Journalist, British Iron and Steel Research Association, London, 1960–61, and Federation of British Industries, London, 1962; staff writer, Esso Petroleum, London, 1962–66. After 1967, regular science-fiction reviewer, *Sunday Times*, London. *Died 11 March 1982.*

SCIENCE-FICTION PUBLICATIONS

Novels

*Deadly Image*. New York, Ballantine, 1958; as *The Uncertain Midnight*, London, Hutchinson, 1958.
*Seed of Light*. London, Hutchinson, and New York, Ballantine, 1959.
*Transit*. London, Faber, and New York, Lancer, 1964.
*All Fools' Day*. London, Hodder and Stoughton, and New York, Walker, 1966.
*A Far Sunset*. London, Hodder and Stoughton, and New York, Walker, 1967.
*Five to Twelve*. London, Hodder and Stoughton, 1968; New York, Putnam, 1969.
*Sea-Horse in the Sky*. London, Hodder and Stoughton, 1969; New York, Putnam, 1970.
*The Last Continent*. New York, Dell, 1969; London, Hodder and Stoughton, 1970.
*Son of Kronk*. London, Hodder and Stoughton, 1970; as *Kronk*, New York, Putnam, 1971.
*The Overman Culture*. London, Hodder and Stoughton, 1971; New York, Putnam, 1972.
*Double Phoenix, The Firebird*. New York, Ballantine, 1971.
*Who Needs Men?* London, Hodder and Stoughton, 1972; as *Gender Genocide*, New York, Ace, 1972.
*The Cloud Walker*. London, Hodder and Stoughton, and New York, Ballantine, 1973.
*The Tenth Planet*. London, Hodder and Stoughton, and New York, Putnam, 1973.
*The Slaves of Heaven*. New York, Putnam, 1974; London, Hodder and Stoughton, 1975.
*Prisoner of Fire*. London, Hodder and Stoughton, 1974; New York, Walker, 1976.
*Merry Christmas, Ms. Minerva*. London, Hale, 1978.
*A World of Difference*. London, Hale, 1980.

Novels as Richard Avery (series: The Expendables in all books)

*The Deathworms of Kratos*. London, Coronet, and New York, Fawcett, 1975.
*The Rings of Tantalus*. London, Coronet, and New York, Fawcett, 1975.
*The War Games of Zelos*. London, Coronet, and New York, Fawcett, 1975.
*The Venom of Argus*. London, Coronet, and New York, Fawcett, 1976.

Short Stories

*Tomorrow's Gift*. New York, Ballantine, 1958; London, Digit, 1959.
*Voices in the Dark*. London, Digit, 1960.
*Tomorrow Came*. London, Panther, 1963.
*News from Elsewhere*. London, Mayflower, 1968; New York, Berkley, 1969.
*The Square Root of Tomorrow*. London, Hale, 1970.
*Unborn Tomorrow*. London, Hale, 1971.
*Jupiter Laughs and Other Stories*. London, Hodder and Stoughton, 1979.

OTHER PUBLICATIONS

Other

*Wish Goes to Slumber Land* (for children). London, Hutchinson, 1960.

*

Manuscript Collection: University of Wyoming, Laramie.

Edmund Cooper commented:

(1981) I believe, along with people like Kurt Vonnegut and J.G. Ballard and earlier illustrious writers such as George Orwell, Aldous Huxley, and H.G. Wells, that science fiction is the perfect medium for making a social or political statement. I am not interested greatly in gadgetry. I am interested passionately in the future of mankind. People matter to me far more than machines or innovations, which is why I concentrate on characterization in my novels. I try to entertain and believe I am successful in doing this; but basically I want to put up ideas for consideration by my readers. Voluminous correspondence assures me that I have succeeded in this end.

* * *

With the publication of his earliest novels and stories of the late 1950's, Edmund Cooper quickly established himself as an urbane stylist whose sometimes almost intuitive grasp of science fiction's key themes and images could distinguish his best fiction and almost redeem his lesser works. There is always a moment in a Cooper story when the "sense of wonder," so often cited as the basic emotional stance of science fiction, becomes concretized in a dramatic image or action, whether it be an encounter with a god who turns out to be a spaceship (*A Far Sunset*) or simply an epiphanal moment of self-discovery on a distant planet ("M81—Ursa Major").

Cooper's plots and characterizations do not always match his style and vision. His early stories and novels sometimes read almost as practice exercises in traditional science-fiction themes: the revolt of androids in a "utopian" society (*That Uncertain Midnight*), time-travel paradoxes ("Repeat Performance"), generations-long space voyages (*Seed of Light*), the pitting of humans against a rival culture in a setting alien to both (*Transit*). Such themes had been treated in earlier, classic science-fiction stories, but for the most part Cooper succeeded in working his own variations on them. *That Uncertain Midnight*, for example, is unusual in its sympathetic portrayal of the dilemma of the androids, and *Transit* focuses sensitively on the character and emerging relationships of the four humans who find themselves stranded on an unknown planet. Though *Transit* shows that Cooper is capable of developing complex characterizations, he all too often reverts to the near-superman genius-hero of traditional pulp science fiction for his protagonists.

Perhaps the most persistent theme in Cooper, though it seldom emerges as more than background, is that of nuclear war. Nuclear war is the cause of the rise of the androids in *That Uncertain Midnight*, the dystopian state in "Tomorrow's Gift" (one of his finest short stories), the escape from earth in *Seed of Light*, the destruction of the entire human race in *The Overman Culture*, the dominion of satellite cities over Earth in *The Slaves of Heaven*, and the rise of the antitechnological Luddite society in *The Cloud Walker*, the best-received and most successful of his novels in the United States. Though it might be misleading to categorize Cooper as a simple technophobe, his cautionary attitude toward technology is also revealed in a number of stories in which "primitive," non-technological societies are shown to be morally superior to decadent technological ones. This is a theme of "The Enlightened Ones," *A Far Sunset*, and *The Slaves of Heaven. A Far Sunset*, in fact, is one of science fiction's more sophisticated treatments of an anthropological theme in its depiction of an alien society and its mythology.

Perhaps because he published little in the American magazines, Cooper never established a strong following among American readers. Perhaps because he belonged in the early 1950's tradition of John Wyndham and John Christopher, his reputation began to wane after the changes wrought in British science fiction during the New Wave of the late 1960's. In any event, his works in the 1970's took an increasingly conservative and sometimes unpleasant turn, especially apparent in his "Richard Avery" novels and his anti-feminist novels of societies dominated by women, *Five to Twelve* and *Who Needs Men?* Occasionally, however, he was able to incorporate some of the New Wave ideas with some success. *The Overman Culture*, for example, features an enjoyably surrealistic portrait of a London in which Victoria reigns, Churchill is prime minister, and the young hero is Michael Faraday. All this gives way eventually to a traditional science-fiction explanation, which is nevertheless ingenious and does not destroy the novel's sense of playful fantasy.

By the time of his death in 1982, Cooper had come to be regarded as a minor, if competent, novelist in a somewhat outmoded tradition. His reputation was probably further damaged by the ugliness of some of his later works. But at best, he was a writer capable of witty and literate variations on familiar themes, and one who for all his faults managed to establish a clear identity despite his use of such themes.

—Gary K. Wolfe

---

**COOPER, Susan (Mary).** British. Born in Burnham, Buckinghamshire, 23 May 1935. Educated at Slough High School, Buckinghamshire; Somerville College, Oxford, 1953–56, M.A. 1956. Married Nicholas J. Grant in 1963 (divorced 1982); one son and one daughter. Moved to the United States in 1963. Reporter and feature writer, *Sunday Times*, London, 1956–63; U.S. columnist, Cardiff *Western Mail*, 1963–72. Recipient: Boston *Globe-Horn Book* award, 1973; American Library Association Newbery Medal, 1976; Welsh Arts Council Tir na n'Og award, 1976, 1978; B'nai B'rith Janusz Korczak award, 1984. Address: c/o Atheneum Publishers, 115 Fifth Avenue, New York, New York 10003, U.S.A.

### Science-Fiction Publications

Novel

*Mandrake.* London, Hodder and Stoughton, 1964.

Novels (for children)

The Dark Is Rising:
*Over Sea, Under Stone*, illustrated by Margery Gill. London, Cape, 1965; New York, Harcourt Brace, 1966.
*The Dark Is Rising*, illustrated by Alan Cober. London, Chatto and Windus, and New York, Atheneum, 1973.
*Greenwitch.* London, Chatto and Windus, and New York, Atheneum, 1974.
*The Grey King*, illustrated by Michael Heslop. London, Chatto and Windus, and New York, Atheneum, 1975.
*Silver on the Tree.* London, Chatto and Windus, and New York, Atheneum, 1977.
*Seaward.* New York, Atheneum, and London, Bodley Head, 1983.

### Other Publications

Novels (for children)

*Dawn of Fear*, illustrated by Margery Gill. New York, Harcourt Brace, 1970; London, Chatto and Windus, 1972.
*Jethro and the Jumbie*, illustrated by Ashley Bryan. New York, Atheneum, 1979; London, Chatto and Windus, 1980.
*Matthew's Dragon*, illustrated by Joseph A. Smith. New York, McElderry, 1991.

Other (for children)

*The Silver Cow: A Welsh Tale*, illustrated by Warwick Hutton. New York, Atheneum, and London, Chatto and Windus, 1983.
*The Selkie Girl*, illustrated by Warwick Hutton. New York, McElderry, 1986; London, Hodder and Stoughton, 1987.

Plays

*Foxfire*, with Hume Cronyn, music by Jonathan Holtzman, adaptation of the *Foxfire* books edited by Eliot Wigginton (produced Stratford, Ontario, 1980; Minneapolis and New York, 1982). New York and London, French, 1983.

Television Plays: *Dark Encounter*, 1976; *The Dollmaker*, with Hume Cronyn, from the novel by Harriette Arnow, 1983.

Other

*Behind the Golden Curtain: A View of the U.S.A.* London, Hodder and Stoughton, 1965; New York, Scribner, 1966.
*J.B. Priestley: Portrait of an Author.* London, Heinemann, 1970; New York, Harper, 1971.

Editor, *Essays of Five Decades*, by J.B. Priestley. Boston, Little Brown, 1968; London, Heinemann, 1969.

*

Manuscript Collection: Osborne Collection, Toronto Public Library.

* * *

Susan Cooper is best known as a children's writer of fantasy bordering science fiction and fantasy adventure. While these books tend to stand closer to pure fantasy than to pure science fiction, they contain enough of time travel and simultaneous worlds to deserve serious recognition as science fiction. However, her first book, *Mandrake*, was an adult science fiction novel. Although out of print for nearly 25 years, it deserves to be read both in its own right and as a direct precursor of her children's books. It also offers, with the wisdom of hindsight, a window on the mind of the young writer at a particular time in her life and of her world. Archaeologist David Queston returns from fieldwork in Brazil to find that his theories about the attachment of a primitive tribe to its habitat may have sinister application to sophisticated late 20th-century Britain. The Minister for Planning, Arthur Mandrake, offers a disturbing hope for peace. The disaster that unfolds eerily anticipates an inverted version of the recent Gaia hypothesis about the world as a kind of global organism, as well as Taoist approaches to physics and cosmic consciousness that seek to marry science and mysticism.

On another level, *Mandrake* reflects the intense anxiety the whole world felt at the time of the Cuban Missile crisis and the shock of Kennedy's assassination, as well as the swirl of homesickness and disruption that Cooper herself must have felt as a young wife who emigrated with her husband to America, and as a child growing up in Britain under Nazi siege. Strong characters and narrative derive from this rich mix of background and highly speculative thinking. Issues of free will and mind control, social isolation and personal responsibility, rationalism and religion, dark insanity and existential purposelessness, give the book intellectual depth. At the same time Cooper recognises the need for balance between people and place—a valuable moral for our environmentally endangered planet.

In children's literature, Susan Cooper is famous for her quintet, "The Dark is Rising." The first book, *Over Sea, Under Stone*, was written with no thought of it being the first of a sequence, at a time (Cooper has said) when she had not much else to do, in order to enter a children's book competition. It is a story which in many ways is typical of its time: children in the Drew family go for a summer holiday to a remote seaside village in Cornwall with their absent-minded and largely absent parents. The accidental or coincidental discovery of an ancient parchment with a cryptic map leads to adventure that links with the time of King Arthur and a struggle between the forces of good and evil. *Over Sea, Under Stone* is a satisfyingly human story. Helped by Merry Lyon, the Drew children scramble over and under cliffs and around old dark cottages, struggle against a malevolent village vicar, and discover a message from one of King Arthur's knights about the coming dark forces of the heathen men of long ships and the need to preserve a secret that holds the promise of the return of the Pendragon. The story is full of menace, implicit and explicit, and mystery, but it has no hint of fantasy. Even the talk of Arthur is couched in wholly historical terms.

Five years later, Cooper saw how this story could be developed into the whole quintet, with its major vision of eternal conflict between the Light and the Dark. The later books are surprisingly different. The name Merriman Lyon is linked with Merlin. What had been the dark forces of the fierce heathen Norsemen is transmuted into the Dark, a collection of powerful forces that seem to stand for everything cruel, selfish, capricious, insane, and chaotic. The Dark is opposed by the Light, and the people of both are revealed to be superhuman immortals. Spiritually dwarfed by such god-like beings, the humans in the quintet are little more than hapless pawns, with some notable exceptions near the end.

Fantasy elements slowly begin in *The Dark is Rising.* This time the Drews do not appear. Instead Will Stanton turns eleven. He discovers, seventh son of a seventh son, that he is really not a human after all but one of the Old Ones, in fact the last of these, the final recruit to the forces of the Light. He is taken back in the past, to the Middle Ages, and through magic doors into another reality, the hall of the Light. In this way he begins to learn who or what he really is (the Sign Seeker), and what he must do (find the Walker), and what it is all about (the Dark is rising).

A summary such as this cannot do justice to the force of Cooper's ideas. It is not that she writes with original or otherwise electrifying prose; this is usually plain enough, with a tendency to stereotype the way characters look, behave, or speak, and frequent portentousness in the formal manner of speech. Cooper slowly assembles the story, building up menacing uncertainty step by step. And she draws widely on very potent images and situations from mythology, folklore, or tradition. For example, the white horse Will has seen at John Smith's smithy that rescues Will from the Rider on the utterly midnight black horse is linked with the familiar images of figures cut in chalky downs. The whole story takes place during Christmas, mid-Winter, and New Year, and is fired by the potent Christian images and pre-Christian fertility images of Christmas and Yule carols. Most importantly, Cooper draws on archetypal concepts: Sign-Seeker, Walker, Rider, Old Ones, the Lady, Light and Dark. Cooper's quintet is a very powerful experience.

Unfortunately, as with many examples of science fiction or fantasy, the emotional experience does not cohere intellectually. For example, Cooper is unable to deal convincingly with concepts of time or time travel when it occurs in the quintet. Merriman talks about the fundamental simultaneity of all times. But crucial events in the story depend on one thing happening *after* another, or *before* another; or on things or people being hidden in the future or the past. What Russell Bradbury showed in his story "A Sound of Thunder"—that if we were able to go back into the past and alter the past, we would inevitably return to a present that would be different from the present we had initially departed—is ignored by Cooper.

Similarly Cooper never succeeds in developing a clear moral structure that can explain the Light or the Dark (other than as eternal, dual opposites) or such other great forces as the Wild Magic or the High Magic or the Law. Neither does she make clear where she or her characters stand on the question of free will versus predestination or fate. The fact that the real protagonists of the quintet are the Old Ones of the Light, superhuman and immortal, whereas the human characters are reduced to virtual insignificance, prevents the quintet having the human appeal of *The Lord of the Rings*, for example, which presents a cosmic struggle on a similar scale.

After *The Dark is Rising*, the other three books tell how the Drews, Will, Merriman, and others struggle to oppose the Dark, retrieve the lost or hidden sources of power for the Light, and rush in and out of many times and places, histories and legends, to achieve the final stand against the madness of the Dark.

At the very end, surprisingly, Merriman denies the beginning of the quintet. He tells the Drews, "the evil that [remains] inside men is at last a matter for men to control . . . For Drake is no longer in his hammock, children, nor is Arthur somewhere sleeping, and you may not lie idly expecting the second coming of anybody now, because the world is yours and it is up to you." These stirring, anti-messianic words may be considered a fair account of human nature and the need for responsible human conscience. But they are also a last contradictory wave of the writer's magic wand, dispelling the fantasy, and the underlying religious concepts that motivated the quintet from the beginning. Looking for the return for the Pendragon is where the quintet started. Cooper seems to be telling us to stop suspending our disbelief, leave the exciting realms of imagination, and get on with fixing up ourselves and the only world we have. Indeed. But where do these five books of wild entrancing fantasy fit in such a humanistic message?

It should be acknowledged that, despite these criticisms, Cooper's quintet has been very influential. There had been very little children's literature of this kind of fantasy with such sustained power. The English fantasy writer Charles Williams perhaps most closely anticipated Cooper's kind of work. Since then many writers have conjured up long tales of fantasy struggles between the forces of good and evil. But Cooper has herself been deeply influenced in the quintet by John Masefield's fantasy dream-stories for children, *The Midnight Folk* (1927) and *The Box of Delights* (1935), and Robert Graves' exposition of many myths, *The White Goddess* (1961).

Apart from the quintet, most of Susan Cooper's writing has been reworking of traditional Celtic mythology and other material she drew on in making the mythological system of the quintet. But this has not gone much further than retelling. In contrast, *Dawn of Fear* is a realistic autobiographical account of the impact on a young boy of the death of a friend during the London Blitz.

Cooper's other major fantasy work seems similar on the surface to the quintet. But fundamentally it is very different. In *Seaward* two teenagers, Westerly and Cally, find themselves in a fantasy other-world, caught up in a struggle between god-like powers: the benign father-sun figure Lugan, lord of life, and the treacherous two-faced moon-lady Taranis, queen of death, Lugan's sister-daughter-mother. Cally and Westerly's separate strands of story weave together. They reveal parts of their earlier life in the real-world, struggling to discover what is happening to them, how this other-world works, and what they should do.

Always Cally and Westerly head west, towards the sea where they hope to find and rescue their parents who have been taken from them in the real world. Situations lurch, dream-like, from one predicament to another: a cosmic chess match; a Stonecutter attended by stone giants; a castle that contains Cally and Westerly's imaginary ideal-rooms; a terrible basement that leads to caves and a monstrous burrowing snake; the arid desert of the Valley of the White Sea where they encounter a weird insect-like creature; and finally a journey over terrible mountains to a river, and the sea. There they must make their own choices.

Superficially, the press of events, the Alice-in-Wonderland dream-like jumps, and the Celtic-inspired mythology of dualism makes *Seaward* resemble an extremely compressed version of the Dark is Rising quintet. But the problem of time-travel is avoided, and that of free will versus predestination is handled well. *Seaward* reads more like an allegory than an adventure. Its events cry out to be interpreted. It belongs in the same class as other children's fantasy books of illness and healing, or inner conflict and growth, such as Ursula Le Guin's *The Beginning Place* (1980), which it closely resembles, or Alan Garner's *The Owl Service* (1967), William Mayne's *A Game of Dark* (1971), or Catherine Storr's *Marianne Dreams* (1958). The book uses fantasy to question and develop its characters' inner life. This fantasy has very positive psychological purpose, quite apart from its inherent narrative and emotional strength. *Seaward* suggests, despite the demands made on its readers, that since the quintet Cooper has gained a clearer idea of what she wants her fantasy to do. We should look forward to further developments.

—John Gough

---

**COPPEL, Alfred.** Also writes as Sol Galaxan; Robert Cham Gilman; Derfla Leppoc; and A.C. Marin. American. Born in Oakland, California, 9 November 1921. Educated at Menlo College, Menlo Park, California; Stanford University, California, 1939–42. Served in the United States Army Air Force, 1942–45: First Lieutenant. Married Elizabeth Ann Schorr in 1943; one son and one daughter. Writer for Philco, Palo Alto, California, 1957–58; public relations executive, Cerwin Group, 1958–61, and Reynolds Advertising, 1961–62, both in San Francisco. Since 1962, freelance writer: since 1969, critic, San Francisco *Chronicle.* Agent: Robert Lescher, 67 Irving Place, New York, New York 10003. Address: 2995 Woodside Road, Number 400–405, Woodside, California 94062, U.S.A.

### SCIENCE-FICTION PUBLICATIONS

#### Novels

*Dark December.* New York, Fawcett, 1960; London, Jenkins, 1966.
*Thirty-Four East.* New York, Harcourt Brace, and London, Macmillan, 1974.
*The Dragon.* New York, Harcourt Brace, and London, Macmillan, 1977.
*The Hastings Conspiracy.* New York, Holt Rinehart, and London, Macmillan, 1980.
*The Apocalypse Brigade.* New York, Holt Rinehart, and London, Macmillan, 1981.
*The Burning Mountain.* New York, Harcourt Brace, 1983; London, Corgi, 1985.

#### Novels as Robert Cham Gilman (series: Rhada)

*The Rebel of Rhada.* New York, Harcourt Brace, 1968; London, Gollancz, 1970.
*The Navigator of Rhada.* New York, Harcourt Brace, 1968; London, Gollancz, 1971.
*The Starkahn of Rhada.* New York, Harcourt Brace, 1970.
*The Warlock of Rhada.* New York, Berkley, 1985.

### OTHER PUBLICATIONS

#### Novels

*Hero Driver.* New York, Crown, 1954.
*Night of Fire and Snow.* New York, Simon and Schuster, 1960.
*A Certainty of Love.* New York, Harcourt Brace, 1966.
*The Gate of Hell.* New York, Harcourt Brace, 1967.

*Order of Battle.* New York, Harcourt Brace, 1968; London, Hutchinson, 1969.
*A Little Time for Laughter.* New York, Harcourt Brace, 1969.
*Between the Thunder and the Sun.* New York, Harcourt Brace, 1971.
*The Landlocked Man.* New York, Harcourt Brace, 1972; London, Macmillan, 1975.
*The Marburg Chronicles.* New York, Dutton, 1985.
*The Fates Command Us.* London, Methuen, 1986.
*Show Me a Hero.* London, Methuen, and New York, Harcourt Brace, 1987.
*A Land of Mirrors.* New York, Harcourt Brace, 1988; London, Methuen, 1989.

Novels as A.C. Marin

*The Clash of Distant Thunder.* New York, Harcourt Brace, 1968.
*Rise with the Wind.* New York, Harcourt Brace, 1969; London, Heinemann, 1970.
*A Storm of Spears.* New York, Harcourt Brace, 1971; London, Hale, 1973.

Other

*The Korean War: Uncertain Victory,* with Donald Knox. New York, Harcourt Brace, 1988.

*

Bibliography: in *Fiction! Series One* edited by Dan Tooker and Roger Hofheins, New York, Harcourt Brace, 1976.

Manuscript Collection: Boston University.

Alfred Coppel comments:

I began writing in the SF genre for two reasons: first, it was a field that did not limit the imagination (untrained though it might be) of a young writer, and second, I had read SF since early youth—and I believed then (as I still do) that a writer should write what he enjoys reading.

I have since turned to writing "general" novels, but I am told there is still a bit of the SF writer's mark on my work. I accept this with pride. Those of us who learned our craft in the hard school of the SF magazines learned early on to be professionals. To my mind, there is no higher praise that can be bestowed on a writer.

I am pleased to report that after a hiatus of many years of laboring in the vineyard of "mainstream fiction," I am at work on a serious work of science fiction. By God, you can go home again.

* * *

Although Alfred Coppel has done most of his writing in other fields, his few contributions to science fiction have been almost invariably among the better attempts in the field. His novel *Dark December*, for example, is one of the best post-nuclear war novels ever to appear, far superior to many whose titles are better known.

His more straightforward novels in the genre consist of the Rhada trilogy written under the pseudonym of Robert Cham Gilman. Man's interstellar empire has collapsed into a feudal society that is a mixture of science and magic, spaceships and incantations. Against this background, Coppel wrote three adventures of young men attempting to come to grips with the stresses and internal contradictions of their society. Although writing ostensibly for younger readers, Coppel has not pulled any punches. The novels deal explicitly with the seamier side of human acquisitiveness and the urge for power. The cyclic drive to self-destruction is an almost ever-present backdrop against which the characters play out their lives.

Coppel uses his settings and plots to examine his characters, rather than just employ characters as animated tour guides of exotic landscapes. The protagonist of *Dark December* is a fighter pilot who wanders across an America torn by nuclear bombs, plagues, famine, and human savagery. But it is not his adventures with which the reader is concerned but the effects of those adventures on him as he grows increasingly desperate to discover the fate of his missing family.

In recent years, Coppel's closest approach to science fiction has consisted of a pair of excellent near-future political novels. In *Thirty-Four East*, the world is on the brink of conflagration as the president is apparently assassinated, and the vice-president is held hostage by Arab terrorists intent upon the destruction of Israel. In Washington, the generals move to fill the power vacuum, while across the ocean a weak premier of the Soviet Union begins to succumb to pressure from his own generals. The only chance to sidetrack the headlong movement toward war is to rescue the vice-president. The situation is similar in *The Dragon.* The Red Chinese have developed a new weapon which gives them effective superiority over the Russians. Unless the president can somehow restore the balance of power, a war between the two Communist giants is inevitable, and it is just as certain that the rest of the world will be drawn into the confrontation. In both cases, Coppel has captured the reins of suspense firmly, and linked them to a credible sequence of political and personal events. Each novel is complex and satisfying, and it is interesting to speculate about Coppel's possible achievements had he devoted his efforts primarily to science fiction, rather than remaining as diversified in his interests as he has.

Some hint of that may be found in his recent science-fiction thriller *The Burning Mountain.* Alternate histories have long been fertile ground for genre writers and mainstream writers alike, and Coppel now speculates about what would have transpired if the atomic bomb tests had resulted in failure. After investing considerable effort in researching the war plans of both the United States and Japanese governments, he constructed this novel that deals with the invasion of mainland Japan by allied troops. Outside of the basic premise, the novel really isn't science fiction at all, just another World War II adventure story, but it is an outstanding achievement regardless of which category might claim it. With a large cast of characters, depressingly convincing descriptions of the unfolding events, and Coppel's clear, gripping style, it is clearly among his very best efforts.

Coppel wrote many short stories early in his career, most of which were above average in quality. Possibly his most successful is "The Last Night of Summer" (in *The End of the World*, edited by Donald A. Wollheim, New York, Ace, 1956). Stellar evolution has caused a change in the energy output of the sun, and an astronomical event is imminent that will briefly make the Earth uninhabitable. Except for a limited number granted a place in the Burrows, shelters constructed underground, the entire human population will be wiped out within a few days. The protagonist murders his wife and sacrifices his own chance at life in order to provide a chance of survival for his two daughters. It is one of the most brutal and one of the most effective world disaster stories of all times, accomplishing more in a few pages than is usually done in entire books.

—Don D'Ammassa

---

**CORBETT, Chan.** *See* **SCHACHNER, Nat.**

---

**CORBIN, Michael.** *See* **CARTMILL, Cleve.**

---

**CORNISH, F.** *See* **BRYNING, Frank.**

---

**CORREN, Grace.** *See* **HOSKINS, Robert.**

---

**CORREY, Lee.** *See* **STINE, G. Harry.**

---

**COSTELLO, P.F.** *See* **PHILLIPS, Rog.**

---

**COTTON, John.** *See* **FEARN, John Russell.**

---

**COULSON, Juanita (Ruth, née Wellons).** Also writes as John J. Wells. American. Born in Anderson, Indiana, 12 February 1933. Educated at Ball State University, Muncie, Indiana, B.S. 1954, M.A. 1961. Married the writer Robert Coulson, *q.v.*, in 1954; one son. Elementary school teacher, Huntington, Indiana, 1954–55; collator, Heckman Book Bindery, North Manchester, Indiana, 1955–57; publisher, *SFWA Forum*, two years. Since 1953, editor, with Robert Coulson, *Yandro* fan magazine; since 1963, freelance writer. Recipient: Hugo award, for editing, 1965. Guest of Honor, World Science Fiction Convention, 1972. Agent: Virginia Kidd, 538 East Harford Street, Milford, Pennsylvania 18337. Address: 2677W 500N, Hartford City, Indiana 47348, U.S.A.

SCIENCE-FICTION PUBLICATIONS

Novels (series: Children of the Stars)

*Crisis on Cheiron.* New York, Ace, 1967.
*The Singing Stones.* New York, Ace, 1968.
*Unto the Last Generation.* Toronto, Laser, 1975.
*Space Trap.* Toronto, Laser, 1976.
Children of the Stars:
  *Tomorrow's Heritage.* New York, Ballantine, 1981.
  *Outward Bound.* New York, Ballantine, 1982.
  *Legacy of Earth.* New York, Ballantine, 1989.
  *The Past of Forever.* New York, Ballantine, 1989.
*Star Sister.* New York, Ballantine, 1990.

OTHER PUBLICATIONS

Novels

*The Secret of Seven Oaks.* New York, Berkley, 1972.
*Door into Terror.* New York, Berkley, 1972.
*Stone of Blood.* New York, Ballantine, 1975.
*Fear Stalks the Bayou.* New York, Ballantine, and Skirden, Lancashire, Magna, 1976.
*Dark Priestess.* New York, Ballantine, 1977.
*The Web of Wizardry.* New York, Ballantine, 1978.
*Fire of the Andes.* New York, Ballantine, 1979.
*The Death God's Citadel.* New York, Ballantine, 1980.

*

Juanita Coulson comments:

Before I could write, my mother transcribed my earliest attempts at story telling. For my eighth Christmas, she gave me a typewriter, compounding the felony. In a sense, I have been writing fiction since before I could write. My only interest was in concocting characters and adventures that satisfied an audience of one—me. It wasn't until I was in my 30's that Marion Zimmer Bradley insisted I should submit my work professionally. Without her encouragement, I never would have made the effort. I am still surprised to find that some kind of people actually pay me for writing stories I wrote so long ago solely for my own entertainment. Other than the fun of creating, my aims are to follow two maxims: There Are No Simple Answers and Take The Long View. To some degree, I share Marion Bradley's theory that a villain is just a protagonist with a different point of view; the story *might* have been told from the villain's position, *if* he (or she) is a valid character to start with. And in any story, I don't think all the questions can be answered—certainly not completely. People—and characters—are too complex. As for The Long View, its a humbling rule to write by, but it serves me equally in science fiction, contemporary woman's genre fiction, or a historical romance set in 1770 B.C. The Long View ought to be an essential ingredient of all science fiction, especially considering the past and future history of humanity *and* of other species, known and unknown, and cosmology. Putting us in our place in that immense scheme of things is, for me, the foundation of a sense of wonder.

* * *

Since its first appearance in 1963, Juanita Coulson's writing has included science fiction of both the speculative and the adventurous varieties, heroic fantasy, romantic suspense (Gothics), and historical romances, as well as occasional non-fiction.

Her first story, "Another Rib," a collaboration with Marion Zimmer Bradley, tells of a group of men, the only survivors of a destroyed Earth, and what happens when alien medical technology offers them an unconventional way of perpetuating the human species. The theme is handled with skill and delicacy, resulting in a memorable story.

Coulson's first novel, *Crisis on Cheiron*, deals with the struggle of a small band of allies to save an undeveloped planet from economic and ecological ruin at the hands of an unscrupulous Terran corporation. In *The Singing Stones* another world is in peril: Pa-Liina, with its quasi-telepathic Stones of Song, suffering under the domination of its decadent sister world Deliyas. In both novels the alien environment is well thought out and convincingly portrayed, and the scientific underpinnings are given colorful settings and action reminiscent of the work of Leigh Brackett and Marion Zimmer Bradley. The theme of an alien world suffering the unwelcome attentions of Earthmen is also present in "A Helping Hand": this time the Earthmen's intentions are benevolent, but their complete misunderstanding of the world they are trying to help leads to disaster.

*Unto the Last Generation* is the story of a future Earth where population control has been all too successful, rendering most of mankind infertile. The young battle with the old for the inadequate supplies of food distributed by a military government, while a group of scientists work in secret, trying to ensure humanity's survival. *Space Trap* deals with the first contact between Earthmen and a telepathic civilization from across the galaxy, as representatives of both groups battle for control of a remote planet on which they are trapped.

"Unscheduled Flight" is more anecdote than story: it sets up an interesting parallel-worlds situation but does nothing with it. Two long fantasy novels, *The Web of Wizardry* and *The Death God's Citadel*, are both set in the same imaginary world, in which sorcery and the presence of supernatural beings are facts of everyday existence. The backgrounds (geographical, cultural, and linguistic) are worked out in detail; the characters are interesting, the action well-paced, resulting in two very entertaining adventures. Two earlier short stories, "Wizard of Death" and "The Dragon of Tor-Nali," are set in the same world as the novels.

Coulson's best work to date is found in her multi-generational family saga which bears the overall title "Children of the Stars." The first volume, *Tomorrow's Heritage*, introduces the Saunder family, owners of one of Earth's most powerful industrial and communications conglomerates in the early 21st century. The focus is on the three Saunder children: Patrick, leader of a fiercely isolationist political party, opposed to any extraterrestrial colonization or contact; Mariette, a supporter of the man-made satellite, the Goddard Colony; and Todd, who has just established electronic contact with an extraterrestrial space craft heading toward Earth. The conflicts among the children, and between them and their autocratic mother, are set forth in a rich and emotionally complex story. The saga continues in *Outward Bound, Legacy of Earth*, and *The Past of Forever.*

—R.E. Briney

---

**COULSON, Robert (Stratton).** Also writes as Thomas Stratton. American. Born in Sullivan, Indiana, 12 May 1928. Educated at Silver Lake High School; studied electrical engineering, International Correspondence School, 1960. Married Juanita Coulson, *q.v.*, in 1954; one son. Cemetery caretaker, 1941–43; wool bagger, 1944; house painter, 1945–47; bookbinder, Heckman Book Bindery, North Manchester, Indiana, 1945–57; draftsman and technical writer, Honeywell Corporation, 1957–65; draftsman, 1965–76; order writer, Overhead Door of Indiana, Hartford City, 1976–86. Since 1953, editor, with Juanita Coulson, *Yandro* fan magazine; since 1984, reviewer, *Comic Buyer's Guide.* Recipient: Hugo award for editing, 1965. Guest of Honor, World Science Fiction Convention, 1972. Agent: Virginia Kidd, Box 278, Milford, Pennsylvania 18337. Address: 2677W 500N, Hartford City, Indiana 47348, U.S.A.

SCIENCE-FICTION PUBLICATIONS

Novels (series: Joe Karns)

*The Invisibility Affair* (as Thomas Stratton, with Gene DeWeese). New York, Ace, 1967.
*The Mind-Twisters Affair* (as Thomas Stratton, with Gene DeWeese). New York, Ace, 1967.
*Gates of the Universe* (Karns), with Gene DeWeese. Toronto, Laser, 1975.
*Now You See It/Him/Them . . .* (Karns), with Gene DeWeese. New York, Doubleday, 1975; London, Hale, 1976.
*To Renew the Ages.* Toronto, Laser, 1976.
*But What of Earth?*, with Piers Anthony. Toronto, Laser, 1976.
*Charles Fort Never Mentioned Wombats* (Karns), with Gene DeWeese. New York, Doubleday, 1977; London, Hale, 1978.
*Nightmare Universe*, with Gene DeWeese. Lake Geneva, Wisconsin, TRS, 1985.
*High Spy.* Lake Geneva, Wisconsin, TRS, 1987.

*

Robert Coulson comments:

First of all, I don't write because I have any burning desire to tell stories, or to influence the masses, or even to be admired (though I suppose the last might have some bearing on my writing). I write professional fiction because it's the most enjoyable way I've found to make money. Not the most reliable—which is why I work at a regular job and write as a sideline—but the most enjoyable. Since writing is extra income, rather than my living, I can afford to write pretty much what I like. What I like, mostly, is humor: puns, incongruities, parody, satire (not farce: I seldom find farce particularly funny). Basically, I don't take writing—my own, or anyone else's—seriously, and I'll make fun of a writer who shows that he takes himself overly seriously. I try to be entertaining, and any profundities will be slipped in gently and (I hope) well hidden. Any influencing of the reader in a work of fiction should be subtle.

Fortunately for our co-authorship, Gene DeWeese has much the same sense of humor that I have; once one of our books is finished and in print, it's impossible even for us to remember exactly who wrote what. Saves a lot of disagreement during the writing.

* * *

Robert Coulson has been a science-fiction fan since the 1940's and has been involved in amateur SF journalism for more than 25 years. His journalism work has been entirely non-fiction, humorous articles, and the incisive reviews he still writes for his and his wife's magazine *Yandro.* Coulson has remained active as an SF fan even after becoming a professional writer.

Most of Coulson's science-fiction writing has been done in collaboration with his long-time friend, Gene DeWeese. In 1967, under the name Thomas Stratton, Coulson and DeWeese wrote two paperback spinoffs from *The Man from U.N.C.L.E.* TV series. *The Invisibility Affair* involved THRUSH's use of an invisible dirigible in their latest plan for conquest. One of the chapter titles from the book ("Charles Fort Never Mentioned Sandbags") would turn up ten years later, transmuted into the title of another Coulson/DeWeese collaboration. In *The Mind-Twisters Affair*, Napoleon Solo and Illya Kuryakin foil a THRUSH attempt to control the minds of world-famous scientists. Both books feature the unlikely situations and offbeat humor which made the television series so popular.

The Coulson/DeWeese novel *Gates of the Universe* is the story of a bulldozer operator and would-be science fiction writer, Ross Allen, who is accidentally whisked from Earth to the planet Venntra through a Probe Gate, a means of alien interstellar transportation. Both the Bulldozer and Allen's SF background aid him in coping with the dangers of a world threatened by the antics of an apparently mad computer. *Now You See It/Him/Them . . .* , a combination murder mystery and SF novel of psi powers, is set at a science-fiction convention. A follow-up novel, *Charles Fort Never Mentioned Wombats*, takes place in Australia, among a group of science-fiction fans on their way to attend the World Science Fiction Convention in Melbourne. The trip is complicated by assorted encounters with extra-terrestrials.

All of the Coulson/DeWeese collaborations, as well as Coulson's solo work, involve standard SF ingredients, handled with skill, humor, and occasionally a refreshing irreverence. They also employ the practice of "Tuckerizing," named after the SF fan and writer Wilson Tucker: using the names of family, friends, and well-known SF figures for characters in the story. This is not noticeable to the general reader, but can prove distracting to those who are familiar with the names.

Coulson's only solo novels to date are *To Renew the Ages* and *High Spy*. *To Renew the Ages* is set in a sparsely populated North America after a nuclear war, and chronicles the hero's battle against an unknown telepathic menace which is threatening the safety of the scattered pockets of civilization. His search for the source of the danger leads him into contact with the remarkable heroine, Tamara Bush, and the matriarchal society which she represents.

"Soy la Libertad" is an alternate-world story, telling of the aftermath of a political assassination in a version of North America where Texas, the Confederacy, the Five Indian Nations, and the Mormons' Deseret are separate countries, not part of the United States. Based on the author's broad knowledge of history and told with a nicely calculated irony, it is a memorable story.

Coulson's name also appeared as co-author on *But What of Earth?*, but Coulson merely revised a manuscript submitted by Piers Anthony. The result, after further changes by editorial hands, was unsatisfactory to both writers.

—R.E. Briney

---

**COVER, Arthur Byron.** American. Born in Grundy, Virginia, 14 January 1950. Educated at Virginia Polytechnic Institute, Blacksburg, B.A. 1971. Member of the extension faculty, University of California, Los Angeles; interviewer, *Vertex*, Los Angeles, 1974–75. Agent: Jane Rotrosen Agency, 318 East 51st Street, New York, New York 10022, U.S.A.

SCIENCE-FICTION PUBLICATIONS

Novels

*Autumn Angels*. New York, Pyramid, 1975.
*The Sound of Winter*. New York, Pyramid, 1976.
*An East Wind Coming*. New York, Berkley, 1979.
*Flash Gordon*. New York, Jove, and London, New English Library, 1980.
*The Rings of Saturn* (for young adults). New York, Bantam, 1985.
*Blade of the Guillotine*, illustrated by Scott Hampton. New York, Bantam, 1986.
*Isaac Asmiov's Robot City: Prodigy* (for young adults). New York, Ace, 1988.
*Planetfall*. New York, Avon, 1988.
*Stationfall*. New York, Avon, 1989.

Short Stories

*The Platypus of Doom and Other Nihilists*. New York, Warner, 1976.

OTHER PUBLICATIONS

Other

*American Revolutionary* (for young adults). New York, Bantam, 1985.

Editor, with Martin H. Greenberg, *The Best of the New Wave*. New York, Bluejay, 1986.

* * *

The world of Arthur Byron Cover reads like a Classic Comics version of Hieronymus Bosch: grotesqueries there are aplenty, unexplained and inexplicable, wandering the bizarre landscape of a caricature Earth, interacting with each other in curious and unique ways, seeking neither resolution nor evolution nor solution, but just existing as they are. Forget about plots, forget about the conventionalities of science fiction or fantasy, or of fiction in general: you won't find them here. What you *will* find are orts from Cover's intellectual table, pieces of characters, conversations, situations rearranged in new and interesting ways.

For example, Cover's first novel, *Autumn Angels*, inaugurates a strange, far-future Earth dominated by godlike beings scrapping over philosophical nonentities. Each has assumed the guise of a well-known fictional character of the past—from the comics, pulp fiction, motion pictures, or television—and is known to the reader only by that label ("the demon," "the lawyer," "the fat man," "the other fat man," etc.). The only named characters are two "bems" ("bug-eyed monsters" in SF parlance), Dwit and Xit, the aliens who had originally metamorphosed the race of man into "godlike man" as a joke. The plot, if such exists, wanders back and forth across a landscape of broken conversations and philosophical musings. Each of these beings is searching for a unique identity in a world where individual existence has failed; each seeks something to give it purpose: a name, a self, a reason. But the best that the demon, the lawyer, and the fat man can do at story's end, with all of their immense powers, is to cause the two alien bems to instill a sense of depression into their world, a form of negative identity that may help alter the stasis into which the godlike men have fallen.

The results of the trio's action can be seen in two later works by Cover, "The Clam of Catastrophe" (in the collection *The Platypus of Doom and Other Nihilists*) and the long novel, *An East Wind Coming.* "Clam" introduces the character of the consulting detective, a pastiche of Sherlock Holmes, who is hired by the three beings to discover why sexism, which they have introduced into the world of the future to offset the effects of depression, has divided the godlike beings into two camps. To achieve the greatness of mere man, the detective ultimately concludes, godlike man must explore the ramifications of love, not sex.

*An East Wind Coming*, Cover's major work of fiction, further explores the theme of identity, as the consulting detective and the good doctor must face the threat of a new Jack the Ripper, who is using an antimatter knife to disembowel female godlike beings. After murdering his final victim, the seller of speculations (i.e., a bookseller; Cover himself is co-owner of a science-fiction shop), the ripper is forced by the detective to destroy himself, thus ending the threat to the godlike beings. The right of the individual to be individual has thus been affirmed.

Three other Cover novels deserve some mention. His second book, *The Sound of Winter*, relates the story of Michael St. Claire, a would-be revolutionary, and his mute sister, Elizabeth, who travel from the City to the Wasteland, seeking a new way of life. Ultimately, Elizabeth regains her tongue, but is killed by her husband, and Michael comes to the realization that he never understood anything about his sister—or about life in general. The book reads like a 19th-century Russian travelogue.

Two recent books, *Planetfall* and *Stationfall* (plus an unwritten third book in the trilogy, *Futurefall*), reflect a change in direction for Cover, utilizing more directly synthesized pulp and animation influences to produce deliberately farcical and very broadly-based SF satire. Although billed as game tie-ins, these two fictions have very little to do with the actual games from which they were theoretically derived, but take various elements from hackneyed science-fiction plots, reworking them *à la* Monty Python into a crazy patchwork of slapstick humor. Both are hilarious.

Cover's novels share a common framework, jumbling together elements from science fiction, the pulps, magic realism, detective fiction, music, comic books, movies, comedy, and the theatre into semi-coherent polemics about the manner in which people live their lives. The author's chief characters are quintessential outsiders trying to make some sense of an essentially meaningless existence. Cover was particularly influenced by the Fireside Theatre, having noted how the actors used odd remarks, lines, and themes from extremely diverse sources to create something unique and darkly satirical. He has tried to regenerate this feeling in his fiction, which is filled with non-sequiturs, scrambled plots, and snatches of philosophy.

At its best, Cover's work is exciting and stimulating, filled with fresh ideas presented in unique ways. At its worst, his style can seem incomprehensible, tangled, even ponderous, and certainly different from the expectations of the average reader.

—Robert Reginald

---

**COWPER, Richard.** Pseudonym for Colin Middleton Murry. British. Born in Bridport, Dorset, 9 May 1926; son of the writer John Middleton Murry. Educated at Rendcomb College, Gloucestershire, 1937–43; Brasenose College, Oxford, 1948–50, B.A. (honours) in English 1950; University of Leicester, 1950–51. Served in the Royal Navy Fleet Air Arm, 1944–47. Married Ruth Jezierski in 1950; two daughters. English Master, Whittinghame College, Brighton, 1952–67; head of the English Department, Atlantic World College, Llantwit-Major, Glamorgan, 1967–70. Agent: A.P. Watt Ltd., 26–28 Bedford Row, London WC1R 4HL; or, Curtis Brown Associates, 575 Madison Avenue, New York, New York 10022, U.S.A. Address: Landscott, Lower Street, Dittisham, near Dartmouth, Devon TQ6 0HY, England.

### Science-Fiction Publications

Novels (series: Corlay)

*Breakthrough.* London, Dobson, 1967; New York, Ballantine, 1969.
*Phoenix.* London, Dobson, 1968; New York, Ballantine, 1970.
*Domino.* London, Dobson, 1971.
*Kuldesak.* London, Gollancz, and New York, Doubleday, 1972.
*Clone.* London, Gollancz, 1972; New York, Doubleday, 1973.
*Time Out of Mind.* London, Gollancz, 1973; New York, Pocket Books, 1981.
*The Twilight of Briareus.* London, Gollancz, and New York, Day, 1974.
*Worlds Apart.* London, Gollancz, 1974.
*The Road to Corlay.* London, Gollancz, 1978; New York, Pocket Books, 1979.
*Profundis.* London, Gollancz, 1979; New York, Pocket Books, 1981.
*A Dream of Kinship* (Corlay). London, Gollancz, 1981; New York, Pocket Books, 1982.
*A Tapestry of Time* (Corlay). London, Gollancz, 1982.

Short Stories

*The Custodians and Other Stories.* London, Gollancz, 1976.
*The Web of the Magi and Other Stories.* London, Gollancz, 1980.
*Out There Where the Big Ships Go.* New York, Pocket Books, 1980.
*The Tithonian Factor and Other Stories.* New York, Gollancz, 1984.

### Other Publications

Novels

*The Story of Pepita and Corindo.* New Castle, Virginia, Cheap Street, 1982.
*The Unhappy Princess.* New Castle, Virginia, Cheap Street, 1982.
*Shades of Darkness.* Salisbury, Wiltshire, Kerosina, 1986.

Novels as Colin Murry

*The Golden Valley.* London, Hutchinson, 1958.
*Recollections of a Ghost.* London, Hutchinson, 1960.
*A Path to the Sea.* London, Hutchinson, 1961.
*Private View.* London, Dobson, 1972.

Play

Radio Play: *Taj Mahal by Candlelight* (as Colin Murry), 1966.

Other

*One Hand Clapping: A Memoir of Childhood* (as Colin Middleton Murry). London, Gollancz, 1975; as *I at the Keyhole*, New York, Stein and Day, 1975.
*Shadows on the Grass* (autobiography; as Colin Middleton Murry). London, Gollancz, 1977.

*

Richard Cowper comments:

First and foremost, in my writing, I aim to please *myself.* Experience in the form of some 15 novels has taught me that if I do this I usually contrive to please some other people too. That's just as well, for to write books that did not give me pleasure in the writing would be a grim sort of punishment and I'd very soon pack writing in altogether. But having said that I feel bound to add that I am profoundly conscious that I am in the entertainment business where "those who live to please must please to live."

My ambition has always been to write fine novels. By that I mean novels in which, as it were, I contrive to put the beat of the human heart on to the printed page—to make the reader endure and enjoy the whole gamut of human experience through the medium of my imagination. I contend that, to have its full impact, science fiction must be presented in human terms and allow the reader scope for imaginative identification with the characters in the stories.

* * *

Richard Cowper entered the SF genre from the mainstream with *Breakthrough*, which used a contemporary setting to unravel the story of "passengers" in the minds of his characters, survivors of a more perfect, poetical age. This emphasis upon the dream state, central to Cowper's work, is used in a different manner in *Phoenix*, where a youth, Bard, wakes after suspended animation and finds himself 2000 years in the future, in a simpler, post-holocaust society. Like the protagonist of *Breakthrough* (and, indeed, like many of Cowper's protagonists), he is possessed of special paranormal powers, which are unknown to him at the book's outset and which he discovers and eventually learns to use with sensitivity. These powers are evidence again in *Domino*, where the young protagonist (still at school), Christopher Blackburn, finds himself pursued by people from the future who are trying to stop him from experimenting in genetics, experiments which are to change the face of future society, making a master-slave arrangement. The interaction between different realities witnessed in these three books is to be seen in his later work as a strong theme.

In 1972 the satiric *Clone* launched Cowper upon the SF reading public. It is marked by its hostility to the technophilic direction man is taking, and by a distaste for modern living in general. It is all delivered with humour, and follows the picaresque adventures of the young innocent, Alvin, who remains morally intact despite the gross advances of the world to him. He discovers he is part of a four-man Clone which develops immense paranormal powers but, as in all of Cowper's books, disposes of these powers in a humane, almost mystical manner. *Time Out of Mind* said little more than had been already stated in *Domino*, and is another tale of future interference in present (or near-present) society. *Kuldesak* is a far better book, showing us man in degeneration, living beneath the ground at the command of robots and computers, becoming (literally) vegetables as the years pass. Mel, the inquisitive young protagonist of this story, goes to the surface and changes it all, leading man out of his rut and back to the sane path of existence.

*The Twilight of Briareus* is probably Cowper's finest SF novel, written in a consummately elegant style and building to a powerful and emotive climax. Man becomes sterile as an after-effect of a nearby nova which sweeps the Earth and, as a result of the nova, "passengers" are discovered in the minds of several people. The new aliens struggle to take control of man's destiny, and the peaceful resolution of this contest in the mind of Calvin Johnson, the central character of the book, brings the book to a close, even as Johnson himself dies in the snow. Like the earlier books it is set in a near-contemporary England and most of the critical events are internal ones, arising from the tension between the dream state and reality: "So that moment joined my previous glimpse of the sun-sculpted hills as just another strand of the elusive web that had drawn us here, and, as I stumbled forward beside her up to the house, I had the weirdest feeling that I was a fugitive in limbo fleeing between two worlds, one dead, the other powerless to be born." Johnson's words echo a feeling that is prevalent in many of these books, and he is perhaps the most subtly drawn of all Cowper's characters and the nearest to the author, involved, as so many of Cowper's protagonists are, in watching the external world crumble around him as the internal landscape of his mind opens up to display previously unguessed paranormal powers. *Twilight of Briareus* is the definitive exploration of this inner conflict and its resolution.

*Worlds Apart* breaks from this serious lyricism and satirises SF writers in a most direct manner. George Cringe, an unimportant junior science teacher, writes an SF tale about Chnass while a Chnassian, Zil Bryn, writes a tale about George. Its humorous contrast between the mundane and the sublime is beautifully done and its comic delights are many.

It was after this comic break that Cowper first tried his hand at SF short stories and produced "The Custodians," the first of a series of delicately imagined and richly written stories. It deals with prescience and the nuclear holocaust but dwells, almost paradoxically, on the medieval past. There is a wealth of emotion in these stories, and while "Paradise Beach" is flawed, "The Hertford Manuscript" and "Drink Me, Francesca" possess the same poetic lilt. The most important of these stories, however, is "Piper at the Gates of Dawn" which deals with the birth of a new religion. A novella of immense wealth and power, it brings to mind Le Guin's Earthsea books; its post-holocaust setting is similar to that of *Phoenix.* The young boy, Tom, has the gift of joining men together in a brotherhood through the music of his flute and the image of the White Bird. These images, picked up 18 years later, when the kinsmen of Tom's religion are being persecuted, form the basis of *The Road to Corlay.* It is a sensuous book that pampers both heart and mind and, as in both *Breakthrough* and *Twilight*, has a "passenger" in the mind of one of its contemporary characters. Carver, a 20th-century scientist, sees through the eyes of Thomas of Norwich, an inhabitant of the world of Corlay—A.D. 3018—and through the double-vision, Cowper emphasises once again that it is only by shedding man's present direction (which, he infers, can only be achieved by some natural or unnatural catastrophe which robs man of almost everything) and assuming a new life-style, that any future can exist for *Homo sapiens. Profundis* is once again in the vein of *Clone*, with an innocent protagonist, Tom Jones, re-enacting the Christ myth in a beserk computer-run submarine, *HMS Profundis*, which has already denuded the Earth "above surface" by causing global war. As black comedy it is not as effective as *Clone*, but it is, perhaps, much more profound in its message.

Two further volumes of Cowper's stories appeared in the 1980's, drawing upon a wide range of subjects: ecological disasters ("A Message to the King of Brobdingnag"), mystical experiences ("Incident at Huacaloc"), 19th-century adventures ("The Web of the Magi"), and highly literate ghost stories ("The Attelborough Poltergeist" and "The Tithonian Factor")—all with a science-fictional rationale. Most significant from this period, however, were the two final books in the Corlay sequence (the four parts termed by Cowper "The White Bird of Kinship"). The first, *A Dream of Kinship*, was set 1000 years on from *The Road to Corlay* and showed how the loose ethic of the boy piper, Tom, had become a highly dogmatic religion. The second, *A Tapestry of Time*, describes the travels of another Tom, almost a reincarnation of the first, who must face the moral implications of his gift (he can pipe men into madness). Overall, the four parts of the "Bird Of Kinship" form one of the most lyrical and beautifully written sequences in science fiction. Cowper's recent work, however, has drifted outside genre definitions and it may well be that we have seen the last of his science-fiction writing. Indeed, his final novel (to date), *Shades Of Darkness*, appears to bring his work full circle, proving reminiscent of his earliest writings as Colin Murry. *Shades Of Darkness* is a gently romantic and yet powerful ghost story balanced somewhere between the domesticity of England and the darkest heart of Africa.

—David Wingrove

---

**COX, Erle (Harold).** Australian. Born in Melbourne, Victoria, 15 August 1873. Educated at Melbourne Church of England Grammar School. Farmer, then journalist: book, film, and drama critic for *The Argus* and *The Australasian*, both Melbourne, 1921–46. Recipient: Lone Hand prize, for short story, 1908. *Died 20 November 1950.*

SCIENCE-FICTION PUBLICATIONS

Novels

*Out of the Silence.* Melbourne, Vidler, 1925; London, John Hamilton, 1927; New York, Henkle, 1928; revised edition, Melbourne, Robertson and Mullens, 1947; Westport, Connecticut, Hyperion, 1976.
*Fools' Harvest.* Melbourne, Robertson and Mullens, 1939.
*The Missing Angel.* Melbourne, Robertson and Mullens, 1947.

* * *

Originally a farmer, Erle Cox graduated from freelance writing to professional metropolitan journalism in his forties. His early short stories in Australian magazines were never collected, and he is known only for three novels. He never gained literary recognition: orthodox criticism ignores him and comprehensive literary histories give him a bare mention.

Yet *Out of the Silence* had great popular appeal, though Cox had to finance the 1925 edition himself. An earlier human race, destroyed in a world catastrophe 27 million years ago, left time-capsule spheres preserving their culture and chosen representatives in stasis. Found and revived in modern Victoria, the superwoman Earani prepares to take over the world and recreate her highly developed, rational, heartless civilisation. Her intellectual stature and enormous personal magnetism give good prospects of success, certainly with the other survivor she detects in the Himalayas revived as well. The book is well told, if slow and wordy by later standards, maintaining suspense as the mystery and menace unfold. The atmosphere of middle-class rural Australia about 1910 contrasts strangely with the threatened scientific tyranny. Earani is a terrible figure: a prodigy not of evil but of self-assured virtue without compassion. Characteristically her program includes genocide of inferior elements, including the colored races. The grotesque racism, almost too absurd to be abhorrent, was perfectly acceptable in the Australia of 60 years ago and caused no comment. No longer a book to sympathise with, it has historic importance.

The 1947 edition of *Out of the Silence* has the text reduced by 16,000 words from early chapters, improving the pace. However, a quite superfluous prologue is added, seriously weakening the book by giving away the mystery. Subsequent printings use this unsatisfactory text. There also have been two French translations, the first, much condensed, in 1929, the second in 1974. And a Russian translation was published in a newspaper, date unknown.

Cox's other books are quite different. *Fools' Harvest* is a typical warning of foreign conquest of Australia, foreseeing the scale of World War II atrocities but without scientific interest. *The Missing Angel* is a light satire about the Devil in Melbourne's polite society.

Cox's uncollected short stories include a few of interest. Four are mildly humorous invention stories, escapades of an experimenter with radio and invisibility, typical of the 1920's. "The Social Code," first printed in 1909 (in *Some Stories by Ten Famous Australian Authors*, Sydney, New Century Press, 1940), has visual contact with the humans of Mars by instruments such as to give face to face confrontation: an observer's long distance romance with a Martian maiden is suppressed, a glimpse of a bizarre culture.

—Graham Stone

---

**CRAIG, Brian.** *See* **STABLEFORD, Brian M.**

---

**CREASEY, John.** Also wrote as Gordon Ashe; M.E. Cooke; Margaret Cooke; Henry St. John Cooper; Norman Deane; Elise Fecamps; Robert Caine Frazer; Patrick Gill; Michael Halliday; Charles Hogarth; Brian Hope; Colin Hughes; Kyle Hunt; Abel Mann; Peter Manton; J.J. Marric; James Marsden; Richard Martin; Rodney Mattheson; Anthony Morton; Ken Ranger; William K. Reilly; Tex Riley; Jeremy York. British. Born in Southfields, Surrey, 17 September 1908. Educated at Fulham Elementary School and Sloane School, both in London. Married 1) Margaret Elizabeth Cooke in 1935 (divorced 1939), one son; 2) Evelyn Jean Fudge in 1941 (divorced 1970), two sons; 3) the writer Jeanne Williams in 1970 (divorced 1973); 4) Diana Hamilton Farrer in 1973. Worked in various clerical posts, 1923–35; full-time writer from 1935: editor and publisher, *John Creasey Mystery Magazine*, 1956–65; publisher, Jay Books, 1957–59. Co-founder, Crime Writers Association, 1953; Member of the Board, 1957–60, and President, 1966–67, Mystery Writers of America. Liberal Party Parliamentary Candidate for Bournemouth, 1950; founded All Party Alliance Movement, 1967, and Parliamentary Candidate at Nuneaton, 1967, Brierley Hill, April

1967, Gorton, Manchester, 1967, and Oldham West, 1968. Recipient: Mystery Writers of America Edgar Allan Poe award. 1962. Mystery Writers of America Grand Master award, 1969. M.B.E. (Member, Order of the British Empire), 1946. *Died 9 June 1973.*

SCIENCE-FICTION PUBLICATIONS

Novels (series: Department Z; Dr. Palfrey)

*The Death Miser* (Department Z). London, Melrose, 1933.
*Redhead* (Department Z). London, Hurst and Blackett, 1933.
*First Came a Murder* (Department Z). London, Melrose, 1934; revised edition, London, Long, 1969; New York, Popular Library, 1972.
*Death round the Corner* (Department Z). London, Melrose, 1935; revised edition, London, Long, 1971; New York, Popular Library, 1972.
*The Mark of the Crescent* (Department Z). London, Melrose, 1935; revised edition, London, Long, 1970; New York, Popular Library, 1972.
*Thunder in Europe* (Department Z). London, Melrose, 1936; revised edition, London, Long, 1970; New York, Popular Library, 1972.
*The Terror Trap* (Department Z). London, Melrose, 1936; revised edition, London, Long, 1970; New York, Popular Library, 1972.
*Carriers of Death* (Department Z). London, Melrose, 1937; revised edition, London, Arrow, 1968; New York, Popular Library, 1972.
*Days of Danger* (Department Z). London, Melrose, 1937; revised edition, London, Long, 1970; New York, Popular Library, 1972.
*Death Stands By* (Department Z). London, Long, 1938; revised edition, London, Arrow, 1966; New York, Popular Library, 1972.
*Menace!* (Department Z). London, Long, 1938; revised edition, Long, and New York, Popular Library, 1972.
*Murder Must Wait* (Department Z). London, Melrose, 1939; revised edition, London, Long, 1969; New York, Popular Library, 1972.
*Panic!* (Department Z). London, Long, 1939; New York, Popular Library, 1972.
*Death by Night* (Department Z). London, Long, 1940; revised edition, 1971; New York Popular Library, 1972.
*The Island of Peril* (Department Z). London, Long, 1940; revised edition, 1970; New York, Popular Library, 1976.
*Sabotage* (Department Z). London, Long, 1941; revised edition, 1972; New York, Popular Library, 1976.
*Go Away Death* (Department Z). London, Long, 1941; New York, Popular Library, 1976.
*The Day of Disaster* (Department Z). London, Long, 1942.
*Prepare for Action* (Department Z). London, Stanley Paul, 1942; revised edition, London, Arrow, 1966; New York, Popular Library, 1975.
*Traitors' Doom* (Palfrey). London, Long, 1942; New York, Walker, 1970.
*The Legion of the Lost* (Palfrey). London, Long, 1943; New York, Daye, 1944; revised edition, New York, Walker, 1974.
*No Darker Crime* (Department Z). London, Stanley Paul, 1943; New York, Popular Library, 1976.
*The Valley of Fear* (Palfrey). London, Long, 1943; as *The Perilous Country*, 1949; revised edition, London, Arrow, 1966; New York, Walker, 1973.
*Dangerous Quest* (Department Z). London, Long, 1944; revised edition, London, Arrow, 1965; New York, Walker, 1974.
*Dark Peril* (Department Z). London, Stanley Paul, 1944; revised edition, London, Long, 1969; New York, Popular Library, 1975.
*Death in the Rising Sun* (Palfrey). London, Long, 1945; revised edition, 1970; New York, Walker, 1976.
*The Hounds of Vengeance* (Palfrey). London, Long, 1945; revised edition, 1969.
*The Peril Ahead* (Department Z). London, Stanley Paul, 1946; revised edition, London, Long, 1969; New York, Popular Library, 1974.
*Shadow of Doom* (Palfrey). London, Long, 1946; revised edition, 1970.
*The House of the Bears* (Palfrey). London, Long, 1946; revised edition, London, Arrow, 1962; New York, Walker, 1975.
*Dark Harvest* (Palfrey). London, Long, 1947; revised edition, London, Arrow, 1962; New York, Walker, 1977.
*The League of Dark Men* (Department Z). London, Stanley Paul, 1947; revised edition, London, Arrow, 1965; New York, Popular Library, 1975.
*The Wings of Peace* (Palfrey). London, Long, 1948; New York, Walker, 1978.
*Sons of Satan* (Palfrey). London, Long, 1948.
*The Dawn of Darkness* (Palfrey). London, Long, 1949.
*The Department of Death* (Department Z). London. Evans, 1949.
*The League of Light* (Palfrey). London, Evans, 1949.
*The Enemy Within* (Department Z). London, Evans, 1950; New York, Popular Library, 1977.
*The Man Who Shook the World* (Palfrey). London, Evans, 1950.
*Dead or Alive* (Department Z). London, Evans, 1951; New York, Popular Library, 1974.
*The Prophet of Fire* (Palfrey). London, Evans, 1951; New York, Walker, 1978.
*The Children of Hate* (Palfrey). London, Evans, 1952; as *The Children of Despair*, New York, Jay, 1958; revised edition, London, Long, 1970; as *The Killers of Innocence*, New York, Walker, 1971.
*A Kind of Prisoner* (Department Z). London, Hodder and Stoughton, 1954; New York, Popular Library, 1975.
*The Touch of Death* (Palfrey). London, Hodder and Stoughton, 1954; New York, Walker, 1969.
*The Mists of Fear* (Palfrey). London, Hodder and Stoughton, 1955; New York, Walker, 1977.
*The Flood* (Palfrey). London, Hodder and Stoughton, 1956; New York, Walker 1969.
*The Black Spiders* (Department Z). London, Hodder and Stoughton, 1957; New York, Popular Library, 1975.
*The Plague of Silence* (Palfrey). London, Hodder and Stoughton, 1958; New York, Walker, 1968.
*The Drought* (Palfrey). London, Hodder and Stoughton, 1959; New York, Walker, 1967; as *Dry Spell*, London, New English Library, 1967.
*The Terror: The Return of Dr. Palfrey.* London, Hodder and Stoughton, 1962; New York, Walker, 1966.
*The Depths* (Palfrey). London, Hodder and Stoughton, 1963; New York, Walker, 1966.
*The Sleep!* (Palfrey). London, Hodder and Stoughton, 1964; New York, Walker, 1968.
*The Inferno* (Palfrey). London, Hodder and Stoughton, 1965; New York, Walker, 1966.
*The Famine* (Palfrey). London, Hodder and Stoughton, 1967; New York, Walker, 1968.
*The Blight* (Palfrey). London, Hodder and Stoughton, and New York, Walker, 1968.
*The Oasis* (Palfrey). London, Hodder and Stoughton, 1969; New York, Walker, 1970.

*The Smog* (Palfrey). London, Hodder and Stoughton, 1970; New York, Walker, 1971.
*The Unbegotten* (Palfrey). London, Hodder and Stoughton, 1971; New York, Walker, 1972.
*The Insulators* (Palfrey). London, Hodder and Stoughton, 1972; New York, Walker, 1973.
*The Voiceless Ones* (Palfrey). London, Hodder and Stoughton, 1973; New York, Walker, 1974.
*The Thunder-Maker* (Palfrey). London, Hodder and Stoughton, and New York, Walker, 1976.

OTHER PUBLICATIONS

Novels (series: Sexton Blake; the Hon. Richard Rollison, "The Toff"; Inspector Roger West)

*Seven Times Seven*. London, Melrose, 1932.
*Men, Maids, and Murder*. London, Melrose, 1933; revised edition, London, Long, 1973.
*The Dark Shadow* (as Rodney Mattheson). London, Fiction House, n.d.
*The House of Ferrars* (as Rodney Mattheson). London, Fiction House, n.d.
*The Case of the Murdered Financier* (Blake). London, Amalgamated Press, 1937.
*Four Motives for Murder* (as Brian Hope). London, Newnes, 1938.
*Introducing the Toff*. London, Long 1938; revised edition, 1954.
*One-Shot Marriott* (as Ken Ranger). London, Sampson Low, 1938.
*Roaring Guns* (as Ken Ranger). London, Sampson Low, 1939.
*The Great Air Swindle* (Blake). London, Amalgamated Press, 1939.
*The Toff Goes On*. London, Long, 1939; revised edition, 1955.
*The Toff Steps Out*. London, Long, 1939; revised edition, 1955.
*Triple Murder* (as Colin Hughes). London, Newnes, 1940.
*Here Comes the Toff!* London, Long, 1940; New York, Walker, 1967.
*The Man from Fleet Street* (Blake). London, Amalgamated Press, 1940.
*The Toff Breaks In*. London, Long, 1940; revised edition, 1955.
*Salute the Toff*. London, Long, 1941; New York, Walker, 1971.
*The Toff Proceeds*. London, Long, 1941; New York, Walker, 1968.
*The Case of the Mad Inventor* (Blake). London, Amalgamated Press, 1942.
*Inspector West Takes Charge*. London, Stanley Paul, 1942; revised edition, London, Pan, 1963; New York, Scribner, 1972.
*The Toff Goes to Market*. London, Long, 1942; New York, Walker, 1967.
*The Toff is Back*. London, Long, 1942; New York, Walker, 1974.
*Inspector West Leaves Town*. London, Stanley Paul, 1943; as *Go Away to Murder*, London, Lancer, 1972.
*Private Carter's Crime* (Blake). London, Amalgamated Press, 1943.
*The Toff among the Millions*. London, Long, 1943; revised edition, London, Panther, 1964; New York, Walker, 1976.
*Accuse the Toff*. London, Long, 1943; New York, Walker, 1975.
*Murder on Largo Island*, with Ian Bowen (as Charles Hogarth). London, Selwyn and Blount, 1944.
*Inspector West at Home*. London, Stanley Paul, 1944; New York, Scribner, 1973.
*The Toff and the Curate*. London, Long, 1944; New York, Walker, 1969; as *The Toff and the Deadly Parson*, London, Lancer, 1970.
*The Toff and the Great Illusion*. London, Long, 1944; New York, Walker, 1967.
*Inspector West Regrets—*. London, Stanley Paul, 1945; revised edition, Hodder and Stoughton, 1965; New York, Lancer, 1971.
*Feathers for the Toff*. London, Long, 1945; revised edition, London, Hodder and Stoughton, 1964; New York, Walker, 1970.
*Holiday for Inspector West*. London, Stanley Paul, 1946.
*The Toff and the Lady*. London, Long, 1946; New York, Walker, 1975.
*The Toff on Ice*. London, Long, 1946; as *Poison for the Toff*, New York, Pyramid, 1965; revised edition, London, Corgi, 1976.
*Hammer the Toff*. London, Long, 1947.
*Keys to Crime* (as Richard Martin). Bournemouth, Earl, 1947.
*Vote for Murder* (as Richard Martin). Bournemouth, Earl, 1948.
*Battle for Inspector West*. London, Stanley Paul, 1948.
*The Toff in Town*. London, Long, 1948; revised edition, New York, Walker, 1977.
*The Toff Takes Shares*. London, Long, 1948; New York, Walker, 1972.
*Triumph for Inspector West*: London, Stanley Paul, 1948; as *The Case Against Paul Raeburn*, New York, Harper, 1958.
*Inspector West Kicks Off*. London, Stanley Paul, 1949; as *Sport for Inspector West*, London, Lancer, 1971.
*The Toff and Old Harry*. London, Long, 1949; revised edition, London, Hodder and Stoughton, 1964; New York, Walker, 1970.
*The Toff on Board*. London, Evans, 1949; revised edition, New York, Walker, 1973.
*Fool the Toff*. London, Evans, 1950; New York, Walker, 1966.
*Inspector West Alone*. London, Evans, 1950; New York, Scribner, 1975.
*Inspector West Cries Wolf*. London, Evans, 1950; as *The Creepers*, New York, Harper, 1952.
*Kill the Toff*. London, Evans, 1950; New York, Walker, 1966.
*A Case for Inspector West*. London, Evans, 1951; as *The Figure in the Dusk*, New York, Harper, 1952.
*A Knife for the Toff*. London, Evans, 1951; New York, Pyramid, 1964.
*Puzzle for Inspector West*. London, Evans, 1951; as *The Dissemblers*, New York, Scribner, 1967.
*The Toff Goes Gay*. London, Evans, 1951; as *A Mask for the Toff*, New York, Walker, 1966.
*Inspector West at Bay*. London, Evans, 1952; as *The Blind Spot*, New York, Harper, 1954; as *The Case of the Acid Throwers*, New York, Avon, 1960.
*Hunt the Toff*. London, Evans, 1952; New York, Walker, 1969.
*Call the Toff*. London, Hodder and Stoughton, 1953; New York, Walker, 1969.
*A Gun for Inspector West*. London, Hodder and Stoughton, 1953; as *Give a Man a Gun*, New York, Harper, 1954.
*Send Inspector West*. London, Hodder and Stoughton, 1953; revised edition, as *Send Superintendent West*, London, Pan, 1965; New York, Scribner, 1976.
*The Toff Down Under*. London, Hodder and Stoughton, 1953; New York, Walker, 1969; as *Break the Toff*, London, Lancer, 1970.
*A Beauty for Inspector West*. London, Hodder and Stoughton. 1954; as *The Beauty Queen Killer*, New York, Harper, 1956; as *So Young, So Cold, So Fair*, New York, Dell, 1958.

*The Toff at Butlin's.* London, Hodder and Stoughton, 1954; New York, Walker, 1976.
*The Toff at the Fair.* London, Hodder and Stoughton, 1954; New York, Walker, 1968.
*Adrian and Jonathan* (as Richard Martin). London, Hodder and Stoughton, 1954.
*Inspector West Makes Haste.* London, Hodder and Stoughton, 1955; as *The Gelignite Gang*, New York, Harper, 1956; as *Night of the Watchman*, New York, Berkley, n.d.; as *Murder Makes Haste*, New York, Lancer, n.d.
*A Six for the Toff.* London, Hodder and Stoughton, 1955; New York, Walker, 1969; as *A Score for the Toff*, London, Lancer, 1972.
*The Toff and the Deep Blue Sea.* London, Hodder and Stoughton, 1955; New York, Walker, 1967.
*Two for Inspector West.* London, Hodder and Stoughton, 1955; as *Murder: One, Two, Three*, New York, Scribner, 1960; as *Murder Tips the Scales*, New York, Berkley, 1962.
*Make-Up for the Toff.* London, Hodder and Stoughton, 1956; New York, Walker, 1967; as *Kiss the Toff*, London, Lancer, 1971.
*Parcels for Inspector West.* London, Hodder and Stoughton, 1956; as *Death of a Postman*, New York, Harper, 1957.
*A Prince for Inspector West.* London, Hodder and Stoughton, 1956; as *Death of an Assassin*, New York, Scribner, 1960.
*The Toff in New York.* London, Hodder and Stoughton, 1956; New York, Pyramid, 1964.
*Accident for Inspector West.* London, Hodder and Stoughton, 1957; as *Hit and Run*, New York, Scribner, 1959.
*Find Inspector West.* London, Hodder and Stoughton, 1957; as *The Trouble at Saxby's*, New York, Harper, 1959; as *Doorway to Death*, New York, Berkley, 1961.
*Model for the Toff.* London, Hodder and Stoughton, 1957; New York, Pyramid, 1965.
*The Toff on Fire.* London, Hodder and Stoughton, 1957; New York, Walker, 1966.
*Murder, London—New York* (West). London, Hodder and Stoughton, 1958; New York, Scribner, 1961.
*Strike for Death* (West). London, Hodder and Stoughton, 1958; as *The Killing Strike*, New York, Scribner, 1961.
*The Toff and the Stolen Tresses.* London, Hodder and Stoughton, 1958; New York, Walker, 1965.
*The Toff on the Farm.* London, Hodder and Stoughton, 1958; New York, Walker 1964; as *Terror for the Toff*, New York, Pyramid, 1965.
*Death of a Racehorse* (West). London, Hodder and Stoughton, 1959; New York, Scribner, 1962.
*Double for the Toff.* London, Hodder and Stoughton, 1959; New York, Walker, 1965.
*The Toff and the Runaway Bride.* London, Hodder and Stoughton, 1959; New York, Walker, 1964.
*The Case of the Innocent Victims* (West). London, Hodder and Stoughton, 1959; New York, Scribner, 1966.
*The Mountain of the Blind.* London, Hodder and Stoughton, 1960.
*Murder on the Line* (West). London, Hodder and Stoughton, 1960; New York, Scribner, 1963.
*A Rocket for the Toff.* London, Hodder and Stoughton, 1960; New York, Pyramid, 1964.
*The Toff and the Kidnapped Child.* London, Hodder and Stoughton, 1960; New York, Walker, 1965.
*Death in Cold Print* (West). London, Hodder and Stoughton, 1961; New York, Scribner, 1962.
*Follow the Toff.* London, Hodder and Stoughton, 1961; New York, Walker, 1967.
*The Foothills of Fear.* London, Hodder and Stoughton, 1961; New York, Walker, 1966.
*The Scene of the Crime* (West). London, Hodder and Stoughton, 1961; New York, Scribner, 1963.
*The Toff and the Teds.* London, Hodder and Stoughton, 1961; as *The Toff and the Toughs*, New York, Walker, 1968.
*Policeman's Dread* (West). London, Hodder and Stoughton, 1962; New York, Scribner, 1964.
*A Doll for the Toff.* London, Hodder and Stoughton, 1963; New York, Walker, 1965.
*Hang the Little Man* (West). London, Hodder and Stoughton, and New York, Scribner, 1963.
*Leave It to the Toff.* London, Hodder and Stoughton, 1963; New York, Pyramid, 1965.
*Look Three Ways at Murder* (West). London, Hodder and Stoughton, 1964; New York, Scribner, 1965.
*Murder, London—Australia* (West). London, Hodder and Stoughton, and New York, Scribner, 1965.
*The Toff and the Spider.* London, Hodder and Stoughton, 1965; New York, Walker, 1966.
*Danger Woman* (as Abel Mann). New York, Pocket Books, 1966.
*Murder, London—South Africa* (West). London, Hodder and Stoughton, and New York, Scribner, 1966.
*The Toff in Wax.* London, Hodder and Stoughton, and New York, Walker, 1966.
*A Bundle for the Toff.* London, Hodder and Stoughton, 1967; New York, Walker, 1968.
*The Executioners* (West). London, Hodder and Stoughton, and New York, Scribner, 1967.
*So Young to Burn* (West). London, Hodder and Stoughton, and New York, Scribner, 1968.
*Stars for the Toff.* London, Hodder and Stoughton, and New York, Walker, 1968.
*Murder, London—Miami* (West). London, Hodder and Stoughton, and New York, Scribner, 1969.
*The Toff and the Golden Boy.* London, Hodder and Stoughton, and New York, Walker, 1969.
*A Part for a Policeman* (West). London, Hodder and Stoughton, and New York, Scribner, 1970.
*The Toff and the Fallen Angels.* London, Hodder and Stoughton, and New York, Walker, 1970.
*Alibi* (West). London, Hodder and Stoughton, and New York, Scribner, 1971.
*Vote for the Toff.* London, Hodder and Stoughton, and New York, Walker, 1971.
*The Masters of Bow Street.* London, Hodder and Stoughton, 1972; New York, Simon and Schuster, 1973.
*A Splinter of Glass* (West). London, Hodder and Stoughton, and New York, Scribner, 1972.
*The Toff and the Trip-Trip-Triplets.* London, Hodder and Stoughton, and New York, Walker, 1972.
*The Toff and the Terrified Taxman.* London, Hodder and Stoughton, and New York, Walker, 1973.
*The Theft of Magna Carta* (West). London, Hodder and Stoughton, and New York, Scribner, 1973.
*The Extortioners* (West). London, Hodder and Stoughton, 1974; New York, Scribner, 1975.
*The Toff and the Sleepy Cowboy.* London, Hodder and Stoughton, 1974; New York, Walker, 1975.
*The Toff and the Crooked Copper.* London, Hodder and Stoughton, 1977.
*The Toff and the Dead Man's Finger.* London, Hodder and Stoughton, 1978.
*A Sharp Rise in Crime* (West). London, Hodder and Stoughton, 1978; New York, Scribner, 1979.
*The Whirlwind.* London, Hodder and Stoughton, 1979.

Novels as M.E. Cooke

*Fire of Death*. London, Fiction House, 1934.
*The Black Heart*. London, Gramol, 1935.
*The Casino Mystery*. London, Mellifont Press, 1935.
*The Crime Gang*. London, Mellifont Press, 1935.
*The Death Drive*. London, Mellifont Press, 1935.
*Number One's Last Crime*. London, Fiction House, 1935.
*The Stolen Formula Mystery*. London, Mellifont Press, 1935.
*The Big Radium Mystery*. London, Mellifont Press, 1936.
*The Day of Terror*. London, Mellifont Press, 1936.
*The Dummy Robberies*. London, Mellifont Press, 1936.
*The Hypnotic Demon*. London, Fiction House, 1936.
*The Moat Farm Mystery*. London, Fiction House, 1936.
*The Secret Formula*. London, Fiction House, 1936.
*The Successful Alibi*. London, Mellifont Press, 1936.
*The Hadfield Mystery*. London, Mellifont Press, 1937.
*The Moving Eye*. London, Mellifont Press, 1937.
*The Raven*. London, Fiction House, 1937.
*The Mountain Terror*. London, Mellifont Press, 1938.
*For Her Sister's Sake*. London, Fiction House, 1938.
*The Verrall Street Affair*. London, Newnes, 1940.

Novels as Margaret Cooke

*For Love's Sake*. N.p., Northern News Syndicate, 1934.
*Troubled Journey*. London, Fiction House, 1937.
*False Love or True*. N.p., Northern News Syndicate, 1937.
*Fate's Playthings*. London, Fiction House, 1938.
*Web of Destiny*. London, Fiction House, 1938.
*Whose Lover?* London, Fiction House, 1938.
*A Mannequin's Romance*. London, Fiction House, 1938.
*Love Calls Twice*. London, Fiction House, 1938.
*The Road to Happiness*. London, Fiction House, 1938.
*The Turn of Fate*. London, Fiction House, 1939.
*Love Triumphant*. London, Fiction House, 1939.
*Love Comes Back*. London, Fiction House, 1939.
*Crossroads of Love*. London, Mellifont Press, 1939.
*Love's Journey*. London, Fiction House, 1940.

Novels as Elise Fecamps

*Love of Hate*. London, Fiction House, 1936.
*True Love*. London, Fiction House, 1937.
*Love's Triumph*. London, Fiction House, 1937.

Novels as Henry St. John Cooper

*Chains of Love*. London, Sampson Low, 1937.
*Love's Pilgrimage*. London, Sampson Low, 1937.
*The Tangled Legacy*. London, Sampson Low, 1938.
*The Greater Desire*. London, Sampson Low, 1938.
*Love's Ordeal*. London, Sampson Low, 1939.
*The Lost Lover*. London, Sampson Low, 1940.

Novels as Michael Halliday (series: Dr. Emmanuel Cellini; Martin and Richard Fane; Cellini books published as Kyle Hunt in U.S.)

*Four Find Adventure*. London, Cassell, 1937.
*Three For Adventure*. London, Cassell, 1937.
*Two Meet Trouble*. London, Cassell, 1938.
*Murder Comes Home*. London, Stanley Paul, 1940.
*Heir to Murder*. London, Stanley Paul, 1940.
*Murder by the Way*. London, Stanley Paul, 1941.
*Who Saw Him Die?* London, Stanley Paul, 1941.
*Foul Play Suspected*. London, Stanley Paul, 1942.
*Who Died at the Grange?* London, Stanley Paul, 1942.
*Five to Kill*. London, Stanley Paul, 1943.
*Murder at King's Kitchen*. London, Stanley Paul, 1943.
*Who Said Murder?* London, Stanley Paul, 1944.
*No Crime More Cruel*. London, Stanley Paul, 1944.
*Crime with Many Voices*. London, Stanley Paul, 1945.
*Murder Makes Murder*. London, Stanley Paul, 1946.
*Murder Motive*. London, Stanley Paul, 1947; New York, McKay, 1974.
*Lend a Hand to Murder*. London, Stanley Paul, 1947.
*First a Murder*. London, Stanley Paul, 1948; New York, McKay, 1972.
*No End to Danger*. London, Stanley Paul, 1948.
*Who Killed Rebecca?* London, Stanley Paul, 1949.
*The Dying Witnesses*. London, Evans, 1949.
*Dine with Murder*. London, Evans, 1950.
*Murder Week-End*. London, Evans, 1950.
*Quarrel with Murder*. London, Evans, 1951; revised edition, London, Corgi, 1975.
*Take a Body* (Fanes). London, Evans, 1951; revised edition, London, Hodder and Stoughton, 1964; Cleveland, World, 1972.
*Lame Dog Murder* (Fanes). London, Evans, 1952; Cleveland, World, 1972.
*Murder in the Stars* (Fanes). London, Hodder and Stoughton, 1953.
*Murder on the Run* (Fanes). London, Hodder and Stoughton, 1953; Cleveland, World, 1972.
*Death Out of Darkness*. London, Hodder and Stoughton, 1954; Cleveland, World, 1971.
*Out of the Shadows*. London, Hodder and Stoughton, 1954; Cleveland, World, 1971.
*Cat and Mouse*. London, Hodder and Stoughton, 1955; as *Hilda, Take Heed*, New York, Scribner, 1957.
*Murder at End House*. London, Hodder and Stoughton, 1955.
*Death of a Stranger*. London, Hodder and Stoughton, 1957; as *Come Here and Die*, New York, Scribner, 1959.
*Runaway*. London, Hodder and Stoughton, 1957; Cleveland, World, 1971.
*Murder Assured*. London, Hodder and Stoughton, 1958.
*Missing from Home*. London, Hodder and Stoughton, 1959; as *Missing*, New York, Scribner, 1960.
*Thicker Than Water*. London, Hodder and Stoughton, 1959; New York, Doubleday, 1962.
*Go Ahead with Murder*. London, Hodder and Stoughton, 1960; as *Two for the Money*, New York, Doubleday, 1962.
*How Many to Kill?* London, Hodder and Stoughton, 1960; as *The Girl with the Leopard-Skin Bag*, New York, Scribner, 1961.
*The Edge of Terror*. London, Hodder and Stoughton, 1961; New York, Macmillan, 1963.
*The Man I Killed*. London, Hodder and Stoughton, 1961; New York, Macmillan, 1963.
*Hate to Kill*. London, Hodder and Stoughton, 1962,
*The Quiet Fear*. London, Hodder and Stoughton, 1963; New York, Macmillan, 1968.
*The Guilt of Innocence*. London, Hodder and Stoughton, 1964.
*Cunning as a Fox* (Cellini). London, Hodder and Stoughton, and New York, Macmillan, 1965.
*Wicked as the Devil* (Cellini). London, Hodder and Stoughton, and New York, Macmillan, 1966.
*Sly as a Serpent* (Cellini). London, Hodder and Stoughton, and New York, Macmillan, 1967.
*Cruel as a Cat* (Cellini). London, Hodder and Stoughton, and New York, Macmillan, 1968.
*Too Good to Be True* (Cellini). London, Hodder and Stoughton, and New York, Macmillan, 1969.

*A Period of Evil* (Cellini). London, Hodder and Stoughton, 1970; Cleveland, World, 1971.
*As Lonely as the Damned* (Cellini). London, Hodder and Stoughton, 1971; Cleveland, World, 1972.
*As Empty as Hate* (Cellini). London, Hodder and Stoughton, and Cleveland, World, 1972.
*As Merry as Hell* (Cellini). London, Hodder and Stoughton, 1973; New York, Stein and Day, 1974.
*This Man Did I Kill?* (Cellini). London, Hodder and Stoughton, and New York, Stein and Day, 1974.
*The Man Who Was Not Himself* (Cellini). London, Hodder and Stoughton, and New York, Stein and Day, 1976.

Novels as Peter Manton

*Murder Manor*. London, Wright and Brown, 1937.
*The Greyvale School Mystery*. London, Sampson Low, 1937.
*Stand By for Danger*. London, Wright and Brown, 1937.
*The Circle of Justice*. London, Wright and Brown, 1938.
*Three Days' Terror*. London, Wright and Brown, 1938.
*The Crime Syndicate*. London, Wright and Brown, 1939.
*Death Looks On*. London, Wright and Brown, 1939.
*Murder in Highlands*. London, Wright and Brown, 1939.
*The Midget Marvel*. London, Mellifont Press, 1940.
*Policeman's Triumph*. London, Wright and Brown, 1948.
*Thief in the Night*. London, Wright and Brown, 1950.
*No Escape from Murder*. London, Wright and Brown, 1953.
*The Crooked Killer*. London, Wright and Brown, 1954.
*The Charity Killers*. London, Wright and Brown, 1954.

Novels as Anthony Morton (series: John Mannering, The Baron [Blue Mask]).

*Meet the Baron*. London, Harrap, 1937; as *The Man in the Blue Mask*, Philadelphia, Lippincott, 1937.
*The Baron Returns*. London, Harrap, 1937; as *The Return of Blue Mask*, Philadelphia, Lippincott, 1937.
*The Baron Again*. London, Sampson Low, 1938; as *Salute Blue Mask!*, Philadelphia, Lippincott, 1938.
*The Baron at Bay*. London, Sampson Low, 1938; as *Blue Mask at Bay*, Philadelphia, Lippincott, 1938.
*Alias the Baron*. London, Sampson Low, 1939; as *Alias Blue Mask*, Philadelphia, Lippincott, 1939.
*The Baron at Large*. London, Sampson Low, 1939; as *Challenge Blue Mask!*, Philadelphia, Lippincott, 1939.
*Versus the Baron*. London, Sampson Low, 1940; as *Blue Mask Strikes Again*, Philadelphia, Lippincott, 1940.
*Call for the Baron*. London, Sampson Low, 1940; as *Blue Mask Victorious*, Philadelphia, Lippincott, 1940.
*The Baron Comes Back*. London, Sampson Low, 1943.
*Mr. Quentin Investigates*. London, Sampson Low, 1943.
*Introducing Mr. Brandon*. London, Sampson Low, 1944.
*A Case for the Baron*. London, Sampson Low, 1945; New York, Duell, 1949.
*Reward for the Baron*. London, Sampson Low, 1945.
*Career for the Baron*. London, Sampson Low, 1946; New York, Duell, 1950.
*The Baron and the Beggar*. London, Sampson Low, 1947; New York, Duell, 1950.
*Blame the Baron*. London, Sampson Low, 1948; New York, Duell, 1951.
*A Rope for the Baron*. London, Sampson Low, 1948; New York, Duell, 1949.
*Books for the Baron*. London, Sampson Low, 1949; New York, Duell, 1952.
*Cry for the Baron*. London, Sampson Low, 1950; New York, Walker, 1970.
*Trap the Baron*. London, Sampson Low, 1950; New York, Walker, 1971.
*Attack the Baron*. London, Sampson Low, 1951.
*Shadow the Baron*. London, Sampson Low, 1951.
*Warn the Baron*. London, Sampson Low, 1952.
*The Baron Goes East*. London, Sampson Low, 1953.
*The Baron in France*. London, Hodder and Stoughton, 1953; New York, Walker, 1976.
*Danger for the Baron*. London, Hodder and Stoughton, 1953; New York, Walker, 1974.
*The Baron Goes Fast*. London, Hodder and Stoughton, 1954; New York, Walker, 1972.
*Nest-Egg for the Baron*. London, Hodder and Stoughton, 1954; as *Deaf, Dumb and Blonde*, New York, Doubleday, 1961.
*Help from the Baron*. London, Hodder and Stoughton, 1955; New York, Walker, 1977.
*Hide the Baron*. London, Hodder and Stoughton, 1956; New York, Walker, 1978.
*Frame the Baron*. London, Hodder and Stoughton, 1957; as *The Double Frame*, New York, Doubleday, 1961.
*Red Eye for the Baron*. London, Hodder and Stoughton, 1958; as *Blood Red*, New York, Doubleday, 1960.
*Black for the Baron*. London, Hodder and Stoughton, 1959; as *If Anything Happens to Hester*, New York, Doubleday, 1962.
*Salute for the Baron*. London, Hodder and Stoughton, 1960; New York, Walker, 1973.
*A Branch for the Baron*. London, Hodder and Stoughton, 1961; as *The Baron Branches Out*, New York, Scribner, 1967.
*Bad for the Baron*. London, Hodder and Stoughton, 1962; as *The Baron and the Stolen Legacy*, New York, Scribner, 1967.
*A Sword for the Baron*. London, Hodder and Stoughton, 1963; as *The Baron and the Mogul Swords*, New York, Scribner, 1966.
*The Baron on Board*. London, Hodder and Stoughton, 1964; New York, Walker, 1968.
*The Baron and the Chinese Puzzle*. London, Hodder and Stoughton, 1965; New York, Scribner, 1966.
*Sport for the Baron*. London, Hodder and Stoughton, 1966; New York, Walker, 1969.
*Affair for the Baron*. London, Hodder and Stoughton, 1967; New York, Walker, 1968.
*The Baron and the Missing Old Masters*. London, Hodder and Stoughton, 1968; New York, Walker, 1969.
*The Baron and the Unfinished Portrait*. London, Hodder and Stoughton, 1969; New York, Walker, 1970.
*Last Laugh for the Baron*. London, Hodder and Stoughton, 1970; New York, Walker, 1971.
*The Baron Goes A-Buying*. London, Hodder and Stoughton, 1971; New York, Walker, 1972.
*The Baron and the Arrogant Artist*. London, Hodder and Stoughton, 1972; New York, Walker, 1973.
*Burgle the Baron*. London, Hodder and Stoughton, 1973; New York, Walker, 1974.
*The Baron, King-Maker*. London, Hodder and Stoughton, and New York, Walker, 1975.
*Love for the Baron*. London, Hodder and Stoughton, 1979.

Novels as Tex Riley

*Two-Gun Girl*. London, Wright and Brown, 1938.
*Gun-Smoke Range*. London, Wright and Brown, 1938.
*Gunshot Mesa*. London, Wright and Brown, 1939.
*The Shootin' Sheriff*. London, Wright and Brown, 1940.
*Rustler's Range*. London, Wright and Brown, 1940.
*Masked Riders*. London, Wright and Brown, 1940.
*Death Canyon*. London, Wright and Brown, 1941.
*Guns on the Range*. London, Wright and Brown, 1942.

*Range Justice*. London, Wright and Brown, 1943.
*Outlaw Hollow*. London, Wright and Brown, 1944.
*Hidden Range*. Bournemouth, Earl, 1946.
*Forgotten Range*. Bournemouth, Earl, 1947.
*Trigger Justice*. Bournemouth, Earl, 1948.
*Lynch Hollow*. Bournemouth, Earl, 1949.

Novels as Gordon Ashe (series: Patrick Dawlish in all books except *The Man Who Stayed Alive* and *No Need to Die*)

*Death on Demand*. London, Long, 1939.
*The Speaker*. London, Long, 1939; as *The Croaker*, New York, Holt Rinehart, 1972.
*Who Was the Jester?* London, Newnes. 1940.
*Terror by Day*. London, Long, 1940.
*Secret Murder*. London, Long, 1940.
*'Ware Danger!* London, Long, 1941.
*Murder Most Foul*. London, Long, 1942; revised edition, London, Corgi, 1973.
*There Goes Death*. London, Long, 1942; revised edition, London, Corgi, 1973.
*Death in High Places*. London, Long, 1942.
*Death in Flames*. London, Long, 1943.
*Two Men Missing*. London, Long, 1943; revised edition, London, Corgi, 1971.
*Rogues Rampant*. London, Long, 1944; revised edition, London, Corgi, 1973.
*Death on the Move*. London, Long, 1945.
*Invitation to Adventure*. London, Long, 1945.
*Here Is Danger!* London, Long, 1946.
*Give Me Murder*. London, Long, 1947.
*Murder Too Late*. London, Long, 1947.
*Dark Mystery*. London, Long, 1948.
*Engagement with Death*. London, Long, 1948.
*A Puzzle in Pearls*. London, Long, 1949; revised edition, London, Corgi, 1971.
*Kill or Be Killed*. London, Evans, 1949.
*Murder with Mushrooms*. London, Evans, 1950; revised edition, London, Corgi, 1971; New York, Holt Rinehart, 1974.
*Death in Diamonds*. London, Evans, 1951.
*Missing or Dead?* London, Evans, 1951.
*Death in a Hurry*. London, Evans, 1952.
*The Long Search*. London, Long, 1953; as *Drop Dead*, New York, Ace, 1954.
*Sleepy Death*. London, Long, 1953.
*Double for Death*. London, Long, 1954; New York, Holt Rinehart, 1969.
*Death in the Trees*. London, Long, 1954.
*The Kidnapped Child*. London, Long, 1955; New York, Holt Rinehart, 1971; as *The Snatch*, London, Corgi, 1965.
*The Man Who Stayed Alive*. London, Long, 1955.
*No Need to Die*. London, Long, 1956; New York, Ace, 1957.
*Day of Fear*. London, Long, 1956; New York, Holt Rinehart, 1978.
*Wait for Death*. London, Long, 1957; New York, Holt Rinehart, 1972.
*Come Home to Death*. London, Long, 1958; as *The Pack of Lies*, New York, Doubleday, 1959.
*Elope to Death*. London, Long, 1959; New York, Holt Rinehart, 1977.
*The Crime Haters*. New York, Doubleday, 1960; London, Long, 1961.
*The Dark Circle*. London, Evans, 1960.
*Don't Let Him Kill*. London, Long, 1960; a *The Man Who Laughed at Murder*, New York, Doubleday, 1960.
*Rogues' Ransom*. New York, Doubleday, 1961; London, Long, 1962.
*Death from Below*. London, Long, 1963; New York, Holt Rinehart, 1968.
*The Big Call*. London, Long, 1964; New York, Holt Rinehart, 1975.
*A Promise of Diamonds*. New York, Dodd Mead, 1964; London, Long, 1965.
*A Taste of Treasure*. London, Long, and New York, Holt Rinehart, 1966.
*A Clutch of Coppers*. London, Long, 1967; New York, Holt Rinehart, 1969.
*A Shadow of Death*. London, Long, 1968; New York, Holt Rinehart, 1976.
*A Scream of Murder*. London, Long, 1969; New York, Holt Rinehart, 1970.
*A Nest of Traitors*. London, Long, 1970; New York, Holt Rinehart, 1971.
*A Rabble of Rebels*. London, Long, 1971; New York, Holt Rinehart, 1972.
*A Life for a Death*. London, Long, and New York, Holt Rinehart, 1973.
*A Herald of Doom*. London, Long, 1974; New York, Holt Rinehart, 1975.
*A Blast of Trumpets*. London, Long, and New York, Holt Rinehart, 1975.
*A Plague of Demons*. London, Long, 1976; New York, Holt Rinehart, 1977.

Novels as Norman Deane (series: The Liberator; Bruce Murdoch)

*Secret Errand* (Murdoch). London, Hurst and Blackett, 1939; New York, McKay, 1974.
*Dangerous Journey* (Murdoch). London, Hurst and Blackett, 1939; New York, McKay, 1974.
*Unknown Mission* (Murdoch). London, Hurst and Blackett, 1940; revised edition, London, Arrow, and New York, McKay, 1972.
*The Withered Man* (Murdoch). London, Hurst and Blackett, 1940; New York, McKay, 1974.
*I Am the Withered Man* (Murdoch). London, Hurst and Blackett, 1941; revised edition, London, Long, 1972; New York, McKay, 1973.
*Where Is the Withered Man?* (Murdoch). London, Hurst and Blackett, 1942; revised edition, London, Arrow, and New York, McKay, 1972.
*Return to Adventure* (Liberator). London, Hurst and Blackett, 1943; revised edition, London, Long, 1974.
*Gateway to Escape* (Liberator). London, Hurst and Blackett, 1944.
*Come Home to Crime* (Liberator). London, Hurst and Blackett, 1945; revised edition, London, Long, 1974.
*Play for Murder*. London, Hurst and Blackett, 1946; revised edition, London, Arrow, 1975.
*The Silent House*. London, Hurst and Blackett, 1947; revised edition, London, Arrow, 1973.
*Why Murder?* London, Hurst and Blackett, 1948; revised edition, London, Arrow, 1975.
*Intent to Murder*. London, Hurst and Blackett, 1948; revised edition, London, Arrow, 1975.
*The Man I Didn't Kill*. London, Hurst and Blackett, 1950; revised edition, London, Hutchinson, 1973.
*No Hurry to Kill*. London, Hurst and Blackett, 1950; revised edition, London, Arrow, 1973.
*Double for Death*. London, Hurst and Blackett, 1951; revised edition, London, Hutchinson, 1973.
*Golden Death*. London, Hurst and Blackett, 1952.
*Look at Murder*. London, Hurst and Blackett, 1952.

*Murder Ahead*. London, Hurst and Blackett, 1953.
*Death in the Spanish Sun*. London, Hurst and Blackett, 1954.
*Incense of Death*. London, Hurst and Blackett, 1954.

Novels as William K. Reilly

*Range War*. London, Stanley Paul, 1939.
*Two Gun Texan*. London, Stanley Paul, 1939.
*Gun Feud*. London, Stanley Paul, 1940.
*Stolen Range*. London, Stanley Paul, 1940.
*War on Lazy-K*. London, Stanley Paul, 1941; New York, Phoenix Press, 1946.
*Outlaw's Vengeance*. London, Stanley Paul, 1941.
*Guns over Blue Lake*. London, Jenkins, 1942.
*Rivers of Dry Gulch*. London, Jenkins, 1943.
*Long John Rides the Range*. London, Jenkins, 1944.
*Miracle Range*. London, Jenkins, 1945.
*The Secrets of the Range*. London, Jenkins, 1946.
*Outlaw Guns*. Bournemouth, Earl, 1949.
*Range Vengeance*. London, Ward Lock, 1953.

Novels as Jeremy York (series: in revised versions only: Superintendent Folly)

*By Persons Unknown*. London, Bles, 1941.
*Murder Unseen*. London, Bles, 1943.
*No Alibi*. London, Melrose, 1943.
*Murder in the Family*. London, Melrose, 1944; New York, McKay, 1976.
*Yesterday's Murder*. London, Melrose, 1945.
*Find the Body* (Folly). London, Melrose, 1945; revised edition, New York, Macmillan, 1967.
*Murder Came Late* (Folly). London, Melrose, 1946; revised edition, New York, Macmillan, 1969.
*Wilful Murder*. Los Angeles, McNaughton, 1946.
*Let's Kill Uncle Lionel*. London, Melrose, 1947; revised edition, London, Corgi, 1973; New York, McKay, 1976.
*Run Away to Murder*. London, Melrose, 1947; New York, Macmillan, 1970.
*Close the Door on Murder* (Folly). London, Melrose, 1948; revised edition, New York, McKay, 1973.
*The Gallows Are Waiting*. London, Melrose, 1949; New York, McKay, 1973.
*Death to My Killer*. London, Melrose, 1950; New York, Macmillan, 1966.
*Sentence of Death*. London, Melrose, 1950; New York, Macmillan, 1964.
*Voyage with Murder*. London, Melrose, 1952.
*Safari with Fear*. London, Melrose, 1953.
*So Soon to Die*. London, Stanley Paul, 1955; New York, Scribner, 1957.
*Seeds of Murder*. London, Stanley Paul, 1956; New York, Scribner, 1958.
*Sight of Death*. London, Stanley Paul, 1956; New York, Scribner, 1958.
*My Brother's Killer*. London, Long, 1958; New York, Scribner, 1959.
*Hide and Kill*. London, Long, 1959; New York, Scribner, 1960.
*To Kill or to Die*. London, Long, 1960; New York, Macmillan, 1965.

Novels as J.J. Marric (series: Commander George Gideon)

*Gideon's Day*. London, Hodder and Stoughton, and New York, Harper, 1955; as *Gideon of Scotland Yard*, New York, Berkley, 1958.
*Gideon's Week*. London, Hodder and Stoughton, and New York, Harper, 1956; as *Seven Days to Death*, New York, Pyramid, 1958.
*Gideon's Night*. London, Hodder and Stoughton, and New York, Harper, 1957.
*Gideon's Month*. London, Hodder and Stoughton, and New York, Harper, 1958.
*Gideon's Staff*. London, Hodder and Stoughton, and New York, Harper, 1959.
*Gideon's Risk*. London, Hodder and Stoughton, and New York, Harper, 1960.
*Gideon's Fire*. London, Hodder and Stoughton, and New York, Harper, 1961.
*Gideon's March*. London, Hodder and Stoughton, and New York, Harper, 1962.
*Gideon's Ride*. London, Hodder and Stoughton, and New York, Harper, 1963.
*Gideon's Vote*. London, Hodder and Stoughton, and New York, Harper, 1964.
*Gideon's Lot*. New York, Harper, 1964; London, Hodder and Stoughton, 1965.
*Gideon's Badge*. London, Hodder and Stoughton, and New York, Harper, 1966.
*Gideon's Wrath*. London, Hodder and Stoughton, and New York, Harper, 1967.
*Gideon's River*. London, Hodder and Stoughton, and New York, Harper, 1968.
*Gideon's Power*. London, Hodder and Stoughton, and New York, Harper, 1969.
*Gideon's Sport*. London, Hodder and Stoughton, and New York, Harper, 1970.
*Gideon's Art*. London, Hodder and Stoughton, and New York, Harper, 1971.
*Gideon's Men*. London, Hodder and Stoughton, and New York, Harper, 1972.
*Gideon's Press*. London, Hodder and Stoughton, and New York, Harper, 1973.
*Gideon's Fog*. New York, Harper, 1974; London, Hodder and Stoughton, 1975.
*Gideon's Drive*. London, Hodder and Stoughton, and New York, Harper, 1976.

Novels as Kyle Hunt

*Kill Once, Kill Twice*. New York, Simon and Schuster, 1956; London, Barker, 1957.
*Kill a Wicked Man*. New York, Simon and Schuster, 1957; London, Barker, 1958.
*Kill My Love*. New York, Simon and Schuster, 1958; London, Barker, 1959.
*To Kill a Killer*. London, Boardman, and New York, Random House, 1960.

Novels as Robert Caine Frazer (series: Mark Kirby in all books)

*Mark Kirby Solves a Murder*. New York, Pocket Books, 1959; as *R.I.S.C.*, London, Collins, 1962; as *The Timid Tycoon*, London, Fontana, 1966.
*Mark Kirby and the Secret Syndicate*. New York, Pocket Books, 1960; London, Collins, 1963.
*Mark Kirby and the Miami Mob*. New York, Pocket Books, 1960; with *Mark Kirby Stands Alone*, London, Collins, 1965.
*The Hollywood Hoax*. New York, Pocket Books, 1961; London, Collins, 1964.

*Mark Kirby Stands Alone.* New York, Pocket Books, 1962; with *The Miami Mob*, London, Collins, 1965; as *Mark Kirby and the Manhattan Murders*, London, Fontana, 1966.
*Mark Kirby Takes a Risk.* New York, Pocket Books, 1962.

Short Stories

*The Toff on the Trail.* London, Everybody's Books, n.d.
*Murder Out of the Past, and Under-Cover Man* (Toff). Leigh-on-Sea, Essex, Barrington Gray, 1953.

Plays

*Gideon's Fear*, adaptation of his novel *Gideon's Week* (produced Salisbury, 1960). London, Evans, 1967.
*Strike for Death* (produced Salisbury, 1960).
*The Toff.* London, Evans, 1963.
*Hear Nothing, Say All* (produced Salisbury, 1964).

Other (for children) as Patrick Gill

*The Fighting Footballers.* London, Mellifont Press, 1937.
*The Laughing Lightweight.* London, Mellifont Press, 1937.
*The Battle for the Cup.* London, Mellifont Press, 1939.
*The Fighting Tramp.* London, Mellifont Press, 1939.
*The Mystery of the Centre-Forward.* London, Mellifont Press, 1939.
*The £10,000 Trophy Race.* London, Mellifont Press, 1939.
*The Secret Super-Charger.* London, Mellifont Press, 1940.

Other (for children)

*Ned Cartwright—Middleweight Champion* (as James Marsden). London, Mellifont Press, 1935.
*The Men Who Died Laughing.* Dundee, Thompson, 1935.
*The Killer Squad.* London, Newnes, 1936.
*Our Glorious Term.* London, Sampson Low, n.d.
*The Captain of the Fifth.* London, Sampson Low, n.d.
*Blazing the Air Trail.* London, Sampson Low, 1936.
*The Jungle Flight Mystery.* London, Sampson Low, 1936.
*The Mystery 'plane.* London, Sampson Low, 1936.
*Murder by Magic.* London, Amalgamated Press, 1937.
*The Mysterious Mr. Rocco.* London, Mellifont Press, 1937.
*The S.O.S. Flight.* London, Sampson Low, 1937.
*The Secret Aeroplane Mystery.* London, Sampson Low, 1937.
*The Treasure Flight.* London, Sampson Low, 1937.
*The Air Marauders.* London, Sampson Low, 1937.
*The Black Biplane.* London, Sampson Low, 1937.
*The Mystery Flight.* London, Sampson Low, 1937.
*The Double Motive.* London, Mellifont Press, 1938.
*The Doublecross of Death.* London, Mellifont Press, 1938.
*The Missing Hoard.* London, Mellifont Press, 1938.
*Mystery at Manby House.* N.p., Northern News Syndicate, 1938.
*The Fighting Flyers.* London, Sampson Low, 1938.
*The Flying Stowaways.* London, Sampson Low, 1938.
*The Miracle 'plane.* London, Sampson Low, 1938.
*Dixon Hawke, Secret Agent.* Dundee, Thompson, 1939.
*Documents of Death.* London, Mellifont Press, 1939.
*The Hidden Hoard.* London, Mellifont Press, 1939.
*Mottled Death.* Dundee, Thompson, 1939.
*The Blue Flyer.* London, Mellifont Press, 1939.
*The Jumper.* N.p., Northern News Syndicate, 1939.
*The Mystery of Blackmoor Prison.* London, Mellifont Press, 1939.
*The Sacred Eye.* Dundee, Thompson, 1939.
*The Ship of Death.* Dundee, Thompson, 1939.
*Peril by Air.* London, Newnes, 1939.
*The Flying Turk.* London, Sampson Low, 1939.
*The Monarch of the Skies.* London, Sampson Low, 1939.
*The Fear of Felix Corder.* London, Fleetway Press, n.d.
*John Brand, Fugitive.* London, Fleetway Press, n.d.
*The Night of Dread.* London, Fleetway Press, n.d.
*Dazzle—Air Ace No. 1.* London, Newnes, 1940.
*Dazzle and the Red Bomber.* London, Newnes, n.d.
*Five Missing Men.* London, Newnes, 1940.
*The Poison Gas Robberies.* London, Mellifont Press, 1940.
*The Crimea Crimes.* Manchester, Pemberton, 1945.
*The Missing Monoplane.* London, Sampson Low, 1947.

Other

*Fighting Was My Business*, by Jimmy Wilde (ghost written by Creasey). London, Joseph, 1938.
*Log of a Merchant Airman*, with John H. Lock. London, Stanley Paul, 1943.
*Heroes of the Air: A Tribute to the Courage, Sacrifice, and Skill of the Men of the R.A.F.* Dorchester, Dorset Wings for Victory Committee, 1943.
*The Printers' Devil: An Account of the History and Objects of the Printers' Pension, Almshouse, and Orphan Asylum Corporation*, edited by Walter Hutchinson. London, Hutchinson, 1943.
*Man in Danger.* London, Hutchinson, 1949.
*Round the World in 465 Days*, with Jean Creasey. London, Hale, 1953.
*Round Table: The First Twenty-Five Years of the Round Table Movement.* London, National Association of Round Tables of Great Britain and Ireland, 1953.
*Let's Look at America*, with others. London, Hale, 1956.
*They Didn't Mean to Kill: The Real Story of Road Accidents.* London, Hodder and Stoughton, 1960.
*Optimists in Africa*, with others. Cape Town, Timmins, 1963.
*African Holiday*, drawings by Martin Creasey. Cape Town, Timmins, 1963.
*Good, God, and Man: An Outline of the Philosophy of Selfism.* London, Hodder and Stoughton, 1967; New York, Walker, 1971.
*Evolution to Democracy.* London, Hodder and Stoughton, 1969.

Editor, *Action Stations! An Account of the H.M.S. Dorsetshire and Her Earlier Namesakes.* London, Long, 1942.
Editor, *The First [Second, Third, Fourth, Fifth, Sixth] Mystery Bedside Book.* London, Hodder and Stoughton, 6 vols., 1960–65.
Editor, *Crimes Across the Sea: The 19th Annual Anthology of the Mystery Writers of America 1964.* New York, Harper and London, Longman, 1964.

*

Bibliography: "A John Creasey Bibliography" by R.E. Briney and John Creasey, in *The Armchair Detective* (White Bear Lake, Minnesota), October 1968.

Critical Study: *John Creasey—Fact or Fiction? A Candid Commentary in Third Person, With a Bibliography by John Creasey and Robert E. Briney*, White Bear Lake, Minnesota, Armchair Detective Press, 1968; revised edition, 1969.

* * *

Although best known as the prolific writer of mysteries—John Creasey published over 500 of them under numerous pseudonyms—his Dr. Palfrey series and some of his Department Z novels contain science fiction elements. Department Z is a secret branch of British Intelligence specializing in counterespionage. Headed by the unflappable Scotsman, Gordon Craigie, Department Z was most active before and during World War II. The post-war books contain science fictional aspects, as Creasey changed the focus of Department Z from fighting Nazi agents to protecting England from the sinister plots of mad scientists to take over the world. The series begins with *The Death Miser.* Toward the end of the series, Department Z has merged with Creasey's Dr. Palfrey series.

Dr. Stanislaus Alexander Palfrey is the leader of a secret underground, group, Z5, who fought Nazi and Japanese plots during World War II. After the war, Creasey changed the series from being mere spy novels to more allegorical and fantastic adventures similar to the Doc Savage series with science fiction elements. Z5 becomes an international peacekeeping group that certainly inspired *The Man from U.N.C.L.E.*, on which it is modeled.

A good example of the series is *The Famine.* A nuclear explosion in South America leads to the appearance of a race of incredible midgets called the Lozi, who reproduce themselves every nine days in a nightmare of overpopulation. As the midgets consume the world's supply of food, Dr. Palfrey and Z5 race to solve the problem before it is too late.

In *The Oasis*, Dr. Palfrey has to battle a plot to take over the world by the use of a drug called Dio, which has the power to affect the aging process and provide miraculous health, but leaves the users vulnerable to enslavement. *The Depths* follows this formula as well. Professor Covell, caught in a mysterious wave that sweeps him off an ocean liner, becomes the latest weird disappearance of an eminent person. Dr. Palfrey sees a pattern of missing physicians and scientists—all have disappeared into the ocean. Palfrey and Z5 discover a secret world under the sea that seeks to control the entire world.

*The Inferno* features a worldwide threat as mysterious fires flare up in all the major cities of the world: Tokyo, London, Buenos Aires, New York. Dr. Palfrey and Z5 find themselves in a battle with a secret force that has the power to burn anything anywhere on the globe. In *The Blight*, a mysterious disease threatens all the plant life on Earth and only Dr. Palfrey's Z5 can save the world before all life is destroyed.

The plot of *The Unbegotten* is the reverse of *The Famine.* Dr. Palfrey battles a power that is preventing women from getting pregnant: a sort of ultimate birth control that leads the human race to extinction.

One of the best books in the series is *The Terror Trap.* Tracking stations pick up a missile in space armed with a nuclear warhead targeted for England. All the countries who have this nuclear capability deny launching it. Dr. Palfrey has only a few hours to identify the source of the missile and destroy it before it explodes. The action is swift, and the plot is clever.

Creasey's Dr. Palfrey series contains science fictional elements blended with espionage in fantastic plots, in which the world is menaced by mad scientists and mysterious groups bent on world domination. The 34 books in the combined series each delivered thrills and a sense of wonder.

—George Kelley

---

**CRICHTON, (John) Michael.** Also writes as Michael Douglas (with Douglas Crichton); Jeffery Hudson; John Lange. American. Born in Chicago, Illinois, 23 October 1942. Educated at Harvard University, Cambridge, Massachusetts, A.B. (summa cum laude) 1964 (Phi Beta Kappa); Harvard Medical School, M.D. 1969; Salk Institute, La Jolla, California, 1969–70. Married 1) Joan Radam in 1965 (divorced 1971); 2) Kathleen St. Johns in 1978 (divorced 1980). Recipient: Mystery Writers of America Edgar Allan Poe award, 1968, 1980; Association of American Medical Writers award, 1970. Agent: International Creative Management, 40 West 57th Street, New York, New York 10019, U.S.A.

### Science-Fiction Publications

Novels

*The Andromeda Strain.* New York, Knopf, and London, Cape, 1969.
*Drug of Choice* (as John Lange). New York, New American Library, 1970; as *Overkill*, London, Sphere, 1972.
*Binary* (as John Lange). New York, Knopf and London, Heinemann, 1972.
*The Terminal Man.* New York, Knopf, and London, Cape, 1972.
*Sphere.* New York, Knopf, and London, Macmillan, 1987.
*Jurassic Park.* New York, Knopf, 1990; London, Century, 1991.

### Other Publications

Novels

*A Case of Need* (as Jeffery Hudson). Cleveland, World, and London, Heinemann, 1968.
*Dealing; or, The Berkeley-to-Boston Forty-Brick Lost-Bag Blues* (as Michael Douglas, with Douglas Crichton). New York, Knopf, 1971; London, Talmy Franklin, 1972.
*The Great Train Robbery.* New York, Knopf, and London, Cape, 1975.
*Eaters of the Dead.* New York, Knopf, and London, Cape, 1976.
*Congo.* New York, Knopf, 1980; London, Allen Lane, 1981.
*Travels.* New York, Knopf, and London, Macmillan, 1988.

Novels as John Lange

*Odds On.* New York, New American Library, 1966.
*Scratch One.* New York, New American Library, 1967.
*Easy Go.* New York, New American Library, 1968; London, Sphere, 1972; as *The Last Tomb* (as Michael Crichton), New York, Bantam, 1974.
*The Venom Business.* Cleveland, World, 1969.
*Zero Cool.* New York, New American Library, 1969; London, Sphere, 1972.
*Grave Descend.* New York, New American Library, 1970.

Plays

Screenplays: *Westworld*, 1973; *Coma*, 1978; *The Great Train Robbery*, 1978; *Looker*, 1981; *Runaway*, 1984; *The Andromeda Strain*, 1987.

Other

*Five Patients: The Hospital Explained.* New York, Knopf, 1970; London, Cape, 1971.
*Jasper Johns.* New York, Abrams, and London, Thames and Hudson, 1977.
*Electronic Life: How to Think about Computers.* New York, Knopf, and London, Heinemann, 1983.

*

Theatrical Activities:

Director: **Films**—*Westworld*, 1973; *Coma*, 1978; *The Great Train Robbery*, 1978; *Looker*, 1981. **Television**—*Pursuit*, 1972.

Michael Crichton comments:

I am interested in the quality of verisimilitude and how it is developed and sustained in fiction. All of my work, both science fiction and other writing, has tended to revolve around issues of what we believe and why. In recent years a good deal of my work has been devoted to films, which I direct as well as write.

* * *

Michael Crichton's primary science-fiction works are *The Andromeda Strain, Binary, The Terminal Man, Sphere*, and *Jurassic Park.* Each of these books is set in what is essentially contemporary society, and in each case a science fiction element, or elements, has been introduced upon which the subsequent development of the plot depends. In *The Andromeda Strain*, for example, a mutating micro-organism brought back from the upper atmosphere by a satellite kills all but two people in a small, northern Arizona town, and then threatens the rest of humanity. In *Binary*, the tapping into a "closed code computer mechanism" to determine the time and route of a shipment of nerve gas permits a psychopathic multi-millionaire to concoct a devious plot to assassinate the president. In *The Terminal Man*, psycho-surgery permits the connection of a psychopathic patient's brain to a computer and turns him into a living time bomb. In *Sphere*, a time travel ship from America's future has captured an alien life form that threatens an underwater habitat by means of its ability to manifest individual subconsciouses. In *Jurassic Park*, sophisticated genetic engineering techniques permit the re-creation of various dinosaur species at a theme park on an island off Costa Rica. Their actual characteristics threaten the park; their escape to the mainland may destroy humanity. It is, of course, their nearness to real life that makes these novels believable and frightening. The books are highly technical, and the narratives are laced with graphs, charts, diagrams, and computer printouts. Some of the information is real; the rest is fictionalized but dressed up to raise the level of credibility. Jargon from appropriate scientific fields adds to the realism. The drama of the stories develops from the threat of imminent disaster and the subsequent efforts to prevent it.

*The Terminal Man, Binary*, and *Sphere* are clearly less effective than *The Andromeda Strain* and *Jurassic Park*, but nonetheless interesting and entertaining. The terminal man himself is a psychotic named Harry Benson, who believes that machines are taking over the world. He becomes a threat when he is chosen for a unique experiment that connects his brain to a miniaturized computer, which is powered by an atomic pack containing 37 grams of radioactive plutonium. Though the pack is implanted under his skin, if Benson breaks it open, he will kill himself and expose anyone in the immediate area to deadly radiation. Benson's physical problem is psychomotor epilepsy, and the computer is supposed to stop his seizures with a counteracting electrical shock. Because the sensation produced is more pleasurable than several orgasms, however, he learns to increase the frequency of the shocks through biofeedback techniques. Benson, in fact, becomes an electronic junkie. Though the novel produces a believable female lead in Dr. Janet Ross, a psychiatrist working on the project, it fails to successfully build tensions between the major characters, and much of the potential drama remains undeveloped. Moreover, the sense of a threat never really materializes because Benson is more pathetic than dangerous.

Pacing is Crichton's strongest quality, and *Binary* is much better in that regard. A more complicated plot and a high level of suspense—a State Intelligence Agent, John Graves, unravels a complicated puzzle created for him by John Wright, an insane right-wing multimillionaire, before a half ton of ZV nerve gas kills the president and more than a million other people in San Diego—make *Binary* a more compelling book. Wright is a much more worthy adversary than Benson, and more deadly. He is both intelligent and clever. His anticipation of every move that Graves makes creates an eerie drama, a sense of frustration, and genuine daylight terror. When Graves finally figures out the puzzle and prevents the binary gasses from mixing to create ZV, it brings a sigh of relief.

Without question, the best of Crichton's pre-Hollywood novels is *The Andromeda Strain.* Though the antagonist is a micro-organism, drama is achieved by the fact that its properties are unknown and that it has great potential to kill. It is heightened when the mutating organism eats through the rubber seals in one of the workrooms and contaminates that level of the underground laboratory. This sets the self-destruct mechanism of the complex into operation. Unless countermanded, the mechanism will detonate an atomic bomb, which will destroy the complex and disperse the deadly organism over the Earth's surface. The key to the spectacular success of the work lies in its pacing. Suspense builds with each development. Clues to the nature of the organism, which provides the mystery, are so interwoven with plot impediments that the reader is compelled to continue. Though the characters are only moderately interesting as people, the roles they play in the development of the drama are important and help create the suspense.

In the 1970's and 1980's, Crichton gave himself to Hollywood. After a promising start, which encouraged many writers and critics to predict a renaissance in the science-fiction film, Crichton's work steadily declines in quality. One critic, for example, dubbed *Runaway* "the most idiotic movie of the year" for 1984, and indeed, it seems to be but a collection of the oldest and tiredest science-fiction clichés. As such, it epitomizes Hollywood's approach to science fiction, which, despite the successes of the Star Wars trilogy, *E.T.*, and *Close Encounters of the Third Kind*, has been to wrap standard stories with science-fiction trappings and special effects. Even Ridley Scott's brilliant films *Bladerunner* and *Alien* are not conceptually original.

Crichton's return to the science-fiction novel, with *Sphere* in 1987, marks a positive turn in his writing career. Though not as good critically as his most recent novel, *Jurassic Park*, it is nonetheless both interesting and entertaining. A spaceship is discovered a thousand feet below the surface of the South Pacific, and an interdisciplinary scientific team is sent by the Navy to investigate. Once the team is below in a secured habitat, a typhoon arises and the surface ships are dispatched, effectively isolating those left below. Investigation reveals that the spaceship is actually an American time-traveler from the future that has used black holes to accomplish its purpose but has crashed in the past. In it is a sphere containing an alien life form (not specifically identified) that permits the subconscious minds of those who have entered it to manifest anything that they think.

The subconscious minds of most people are dangerous, and that proves true here. Norman Johnson, a psychologist and the principal character of the novel, must determine whose manifestations are systematically destroying the underwater habitat before all aboard die. The story is fast-paced and there is a mystery to solve. The characters are interesting, and the separation of personalities into what are essentially good and evil parts—through the medium of the sphere—echoes *Dr. Jekyll and Mr. Hyde.*

*Jurassic Park* is an even better novel. Both books combine fast-paced action with informed science to produce suspenseful and compelling stories, but *Jurassic Park* develops more interesting characters in great depth and is a richer and more complex extrapolation of current science fact and theory.

By using his wealth and power, multimillionaire John Hammond, the head of a private foundation that also bears his name, is able to acquire the technology to establish a theme park, featuring live dinosaurs, on an island off Costa Rica. The dinosaurs have been cloned from the DNA in ancient bones. The story centers around a "shakedown" visit to the resort by a group of individuals who, knowingly or unknowingly, consulted on its creation. This includes Alan Grant, archaeologist and principal character. Theoretically, the park is safe for visitors with its hundreds of miles of computer-controlled electric fences and other security devices. But the park is a complex system, and complex systems are fated to go wrong, according to chaos theory. In this case, going wrong means becoming deadly. Chaos theory postulates that there are undeterminable factors that geomitrize through time and cause the system to act unpredictably. These factors are represented dramatically by the naivety and arrogance of Hammond, Dennis Nedry, who headed up the teams that programmed the resort's three Cray computers, and Dr. Henry Wu, who ran the resort's genetic program. The nature and behavior of the cloned dinosaurs turns out to be much different than expected—some species prove more intelligent and more deadly than previously believed. Nedry is not as competent as thought, and he is greedy. So, there are glitches in the computer programs, and he agrees to steal cloned embryos for a rival company. Hammond, himself, simply does not have the imagination to anticipate the danger of the project. He brings his two grandchildren to the island, for example, during the "shakedown" visit.

Disaster strikes as the dinosaurs attack and kill several people. Others nearly escape the island aboard the resort's supply ship, and Wu's system to assure that they will not reproduce proves to be ill-informed. Grant, the two children, Ellie Sattler (Grant's assistant), and some of the others survive, but Hammond, Nedry, and Wu are killed, ironically the victims of their own incompetence. The supply ship is turned back before the velociraptors who have stowed away gain the mainland, and Dennis Nedry is killed before he can deliver a batch of stolen embryos to a contact. This is all ironic, however, because the novel begins with velociraptors already on the mainland, attacking and killing children.

This irony is meant to underscore a very serious message contained in a fictionalized introduction—that biotechnology promises the greatest revolution in human history and that it is proceeding virtually unmonitored and uncontrolled by any regulatory agencies. The novel itself tolls a bell for an absolutely critical contemporary social issue. *Jurassic Park* is an exciting, well-constructed, and original adventure that returns Crichton to the levels he previously reached in *The Andromeda Strain.*

—Carl B. Yoke

---

**CROMIE, Robert.** British. Born in 1856. *Died in 1907.*

SCIENCE-FICTION PUBLICATIONS

Novels

*For England's Sake.* London, Warne, 1889.
*A Plunge into Space.* London, Warne, 1890; Westport, Connecticut, Hyperion Press, 1976.
*The Crack of Doom.* London, Digby Long, 1895.
*The Next Crusade.* London, Hutchinson, 1896.
*A New Messiah.* London, Digby Long, 1902.

Short Stories

*The King's Oak and Other Stories.* London, Newnes, 1897.

OTHER PUBLICATIONS

Novels

*The Lost Liner.* London, Newnes, 1899.
*Kitty's Victoria Cross.* London, Warne, 1901.
*The Shadow of the Cross.* London, Ward Lock, 1902.
*El Dorado.* London, Ward Lock, 1904; as *From the Cliffs of Croaghaun*, Akron, Ohio, Saalfield, 1904.

Short Stories

*The Romance of Poisons, Being Weird Episodes from Life*, with T.S. Wilson. London, Jarrolds, 1903.

* * *

All that is known about Robert Cromie is that from 1889 to 1904 he published 11 books of fiction (one with T.S. Wilson), a number of which are SF. The list begins with *For England's Sake*, which cashed in on the patriotic popularity of the future war tale by transferring it to India, where loyal natives headed by heroic maharajah defeat dastardly Russian invasion. Its continuation is *The Next Crusade*, whose battles and love entanglements are not as interesting as Cromie's Preface, briefly discussing "the history of the future" and with a too easy facetiousness concluding that as against the history of the past it contains fewer errors (Cromie's Britain allied with Austria occupies Constantinople, so that he may have been co-responsible for Churchill's disastrous World War I venture against the Dardanelles). Two other novels are more important. *A Plunge into Space* is an interplanetary novel halfway between Verne and Wells (the second edition in 1891 has a brief and unrevealing preface by Verne) detailing how a scientist discovers anti-gravity, how his explorer-friend helps him to cast a steel globe in Alaska in spite of Indian attacks and sullen half-breeds, and how the two with four more friends—again characterized by profession—fly to a desert Mars. Vegetation and a decaying utopian civilization (which has TV and aircraft but no politics or money) are found near its polar sea. A love affair between one of the heroes and a beautiful Martian coyly named Mignonette results in the latter first becoming a stowaway in their spacecraft on return and then sacrificing her life; the craft is destroyed. *The Crack of Doom* has one of the first mad scientists in SF planning to use the secret of atomic energy to blow up our planet. The plot flounders through lots of genteel Victorian love melodrama, telepathy, hypnotism, secret societies, stereotyped characters, vague echoes of drawing-room Schopenhauerism, and a sentimental happy ending. A final SF novel, *A New Messiah*, also leans on a melodramatic plot.

—Darko Suvin

---

**CROSBY, Harry C., Jr.** *See* **ANVIL, Christopher.**

---

**CROSS, John Keir.** Also wrote as Stephen Macfarlane; Susan Morley. British. Born in Carluke, Lanark, 19 August 1914. Clerk and entertainer in the 1930's; radio writer for BBC, London, from 1937. *Died 22 January 1967.*

SCIENCE-FICTION PUBLICATIONS

Novels (for children)

*The Angry Planet.* London, Lunn, 1945; New York, Coward McCann, 1946.
*The Owl and the Pussycat.* London, Lunn, 1946; as *The Other Side of Green Hills*, New York, Coward McCann, 1947.
*The Flying Fortunes in an Encounter with Rubberface.* London, Muller, 1952; as *The Stolen Sphere*, New York, Dutton, 1953.
*SOS from Mars.* London, Hutchinson, 1954; as *The Red Journey Back*, New York, Coward McCann, 1954.

Short Stories

*The Other Passenger: 18 Strange Stories.* London, Westhouse, 1944; Philadelphia, Lippincott, 1946.

Uncollected Short Stories

"The Best Holiday I Ever Had" (for children), in *Laurie's Space Annual.* London, Laurie, 1953.
"Mothering Sunday," in *Best Black Magic Stories*, edited by John Keir Cross. London, Faber, 1960.

OTHER PUBLICATIONS

Novels

*Mistress Glory* (as Susan Morley). New York, Dial Press, 1948; as *Glory*, as John Keir Cross, London, Laurie, 1951.
*Juniper Green.* London, Laurie, 1952; as Susan Morley, New York, Dial Press, 1953.

Plays

Radio Plays: *The Kraken Wakes*, from the novel by John Wyndham; *The Archers* series, with others, 1962–67; *The Brockenstein Affair*, from a work by George R. Preedy, 1962; *The Free Fishers*, from the novel by John Buchan, 1964; *Bird of Dawning*, from the novel by John Masefield, 1965; *Be Thou My Judge*, from a work by James Wood, 1967; *The Green Isle of the Great Deep*, 1986.

Television Play: *She Died Young*, 1961.

Other (for children)

*Studio J Investigates.* London, Lunn, 1944.
*Jack Robinson.* London, Lunn, 1945.
*The Man in Moonlight.* London, Westhouse, 1947.
*The White Magic.* London, Westhouse, 1947.
*Blackadder.* London, Muller, 1950; New York, Dutton, 1951.
*The Dancing Tree.* London, Hutchinson, 1955.
*Elizabeth in Broadcasting.* London, Chatto and Windus, 1957.
*The Sixpenny Year.* London, Hutchinson, 1957.

Other (for children; as Stephen Macfarlane)

*The Blue Egg.* London, Lunn, 1944.
*Detectives in Greasepaint.* London, Lunn, 1944.
*Lucy Maroon, The Car That Loved a Policeman.* London, Lunn, 1944.
*Mr. Bosanko and Other Stories.* London, Lunn, 1944.
*The Strange Tale of Sally and Arnold.* London, Lunn, 1944.
*The Story of a Tree.* London, Lunn, 1946.

Other

*Aspect of Life: An Autobiography of Youth.* London, Selwyn and Blount, 1937.

Editor, *The Children's Omnibus.* London, Lunn, 1948.
Editor, *Best Horror Stories.* London, Faber, 1957; *Best Horror Stories 2*, Faber, 1965.
Editor, *Best Black Magic Stories.* London, Faber, 1960.

* * *

A short story writer in the tradition of Saki and John Collier, a popular anthologist of horror stories, and an occasional writer of science-fiction and fantasy dramas for the BBC, John Keir Cross is especially noteworthy for his juvenile science fiction. *The Angry Planet* was among the first modern science-fiction novels directed at a young audience, and is interesting for the manner in which it reworks themes from Wells and C.S. Lewis into a context more readily accessible to younger readers.

*The Angry Planet* involves a group of three children who travel to Mars by hiding on an experimental rocket ship. The life they find there is elegantly portrayed, and reveals Cross's familiarity with earlier science fiction as well as intelligent speculation. Martian society is dominated by intelligent plant life, the major forms of which are called the Beautiful People and the Terrible Ones. This opposition of two divergent strains of the same evolutionary path calls to mind the Morlocks and Eloi from Wells's *The Time Machine*, and the moral values attached to each race calls to mind C.S. Lewis's *Out of the Silent Planet.* The relatively sophisticated multiple viewpoint narrative adds further interest to the tale and helps to maintain suspense. A sequel, *SOS from Mars*, describes subsequent journeys to Mars. Another juvenile science-fiction novel, with the unlikely title *The Flying Fortunes in an Encounter with Rubberface*, concerns the launching of an artificial earth satellite, and may be the first juvenile treatment of this theme except for Arthur Clarke's 1952 *Islands in the Sky.* Cross's adult fiction, represented by the collection *The Other Passenger*, tends more toward fantasy and the occult than science fiction, but includes the classic *doppelgänger* story "The Other

Passenger." Cross's short fiction is distinguished by sensitive style and psychological insight.

—Gary K. Wolfe

---

**CROSS, Polton.** *See* **FEARN, John Russell.**

---

**CROWLEY, John.** American. Born in Presque Isle, Maine, 1 December 1942. Educated at Indiana University, Bloomington, B.A. 1964. Photographer and commercial artist, 1964–66. Since 1966, freelance writer. Recipient: World Fantasy Convention award, 1982. Address: c/o Doubleday, 666 Fifth Avenue, New York, New York 10103, U.S.A.

SCIENCE-FICTION PUBLICATIONS

Novels

*The Deep*. New York, Doubleday, 1975; London, New English Library, 1977.
*Beasts*. New York, Doubleday, 1976; Wendover, Goudchild, 1984.
*Engine Summer*. New York, Doubleday, 1979; London, Gollancz, 1980.
*Little, Big*. New York, Bantam, 1981; London, Gollancz, 1982.
*Aegypt*. New York, Bantam, and London, Gollancz, 1987.

Short Stories

*Novelty*. New York, Doubleday, 1989.

* * *

John Crowley's first three novels have numerous virtues, and his epic fantasy, *Little, Big* (World Fantasy award), reaped a harvest of laudatory reviews and, inevitably, comparisons to J.R.R. Tolkien's work, as well as other memorable works of fantasy from *A Voyage to Arcturus* to (rather surprisingly) Gabriel García Marquéz's novel of "magic realism" *One Hundred Years of Solitude*. His fiction expresses a highly individual vision.

Crowley's first novel, *The Deep*, received some praise from readers like Ursula Le Guin, but in the light of his later work it seems to be his least satisfactory and least characteristic performance. Set in a distant future on a planet vaguely like earth, *The Deep* describes the power struggle between two aristocratic houses with names derived from Celtic mythology, mostly old Welsh. Young Sennred, one of the Reds, eventually emerges as a victor who reconciles the impulsive Reds and the Machiavellian Blacks; but no particular hero predominates, and Learned Redhand, a scholarly apostate from the Reds, remains the most memorable character. The conflict is observed by an alien who assumes various guises, and eventually confronts his antagonist, a denizen of "the deep" who is an avatar of the Leviathan myth. Crowley's use of the Leviathan mythology does not clarify his cryptic plot, and the novel suffers from the repetition of similar and identical Celtic names. Despite high ambitions, Celtic and biblical myth do not rescue this immature first novel.

In *Beasts*, Crowley produced a better work, dealing with a bitter ideological conflict in an America of the near future where central government has collapsed and small regional governments struggle to maintain their authority. Their opponents are the bureaucrats of "the Federal," a government striving to restore a dominating central authority. The surface conflict, however, symbolizes the perennial struggle between rational organizers who wish to subject nature and humanity to a monolithic tyranny and those romantics and lovers of nature who resist such dehumanizing efforts. Among the rebels are the beasts of the title, hybrid creatures resulting from genetic experiment in the last days of the old United States; the products of these projects are sentient beings combining human and animal qualities, somewhat reminiscent of the creations of H.G. Wells's Dr. Moreau. One measure of Crowley's achievement is his successful characterizations of Reynard, a fox-man, and Painter, a lion-man, each of which manages to circumvent (in his own fashion) the opposition of the Federalists. Although *Beasts* is resolved somewhat ambiguously, Crowley's novel clearly takes a stand on the side of the romantics, and in favor of the energies of natural life.

Even more impressive is Crowley's third novel, *Engine Summer*, a story of a young man's initiation into adulthood in the primitive tribal world of a post-disaster America centuries hence. This book describes the search for meaning and understanding of Rush That Speaks, who leaves his community of origin as a boy and searches for his lost love, Once A Day. Although he finds her and some knowledge of the outside world, he discovers the unhappiness that accompanies the loss of innocence when she deserts him again. Crowley's hero also learns much about the vanished 20th-century civilization, the brave new world of science and technology called the age of the "angels." One of the lessons that Rush That Speaks learns is the "angelism" or excessive rationalism of the ancients was anything but angelic in our sense of the word. An additional sign of Crowley's technical mastery in this novel is his use of an inventive narrative mode: Rush tells the story of his youth through a recording cube, and his auditor, who occasionally comments on his tale, is a person who lives generations after his death. This narrative method provides aesthetic distance.

Even the mature artistry of *Engine Summer*, however, scarcely provides a hint of the marvelous achievement of *Little, Big*. *Little, Big* describes three generations in the life of the Drinkwater-Bramble-Hawksquill clan, as seen through the eyes of several members, but primarily from the point of view of two: Smoky Barnable, an outsider from the midwest who comes to New York City and marries "Daily Alice" Drinkwater; and Auberon, their son, who finally becomes an avatar of the fairy king, Oberon, just as his black paramour, Sylvie, is metamorphosed into a new Titania. After Smoky's marriage to Alice, a charming and credible heroine, he takes up residence at the Drinkwater family home, Edgewood, a curious architectural wonder in upper New York State housing a family of eccentrics who have a secret alliance with fairies. Smoky's father-in-law, Old Doc Drinkwater, for instance, writes successful children's books which narrate tales he gets firsthand from the fairies themselves. Other members of the family are blessed or cursed by gifts from the "little people." The novel comes to a crisis when a fascistic politician becomes president and attempts to oppress and destroy all those who revere the power of nature and the imagination. Through Daily Alice's heroic sacrifice of herself, the Drinkwater clan is able to leave the modern world, which will no longer allow them to ignore it, and enter the earthly paradise of the realm of "Faery," and there Alice appears in an immortal form.

This humorous, whimsical, inventive, and richly allusive fantasy deserves many readings and is likely to become a classic of its genre. Here, as in the rest of his world, Crowley defines his vision as that of a sophisticated romantic, suspicious of technology, committed to the cause of his imagination, and possessing prodigious literary gifts of humor, characterization, and lyrical description.

In the years since the publication of *Little, Big,* Crowley's reputation has grown slowly but steadily. Moreover, some serious critical attention has been given to *Little, Big* because of the book's demonstration of Crowley's power to bring myth to life. Crowley himself has commented, in a note for a new edition of *Little, Big,* that his book was important for his development because he discovered for the first time "the extent of my own powers as a writer," and he hints that it remains his favorite book. Nevertheless, Crowley followed his success in *Little, Big,* with a more mature novel, *Aegypt.*

*Aegypt* is a major philosophical romance, to use Crowley's description of a novel within the story by a fictional author, Fellowes Kraft. Although Crowley's work resembles much of Gene Wolfe's fiction by leaving ambiguous the question of whether magic and predetermined destiny exist, *Aegypt* is a tale woven of numerous poetic and occult materials: the Grail legend, the quests of Giordano Bruno, the adventures of the Elizabethan astrologer and occultist John Dee, a fanciful life of Shakespeare, and the quest of a modern Parsifal, Pierce Moffett. The external action of the novel is rather slight, describing the life of Pierce Moffett from his confused days as a flower child of the 1960's, through some undistinguished years as a professor of history in Barnabas College, in New York City, through his decision to move to a pastoral world in upper New York state, in the town of Blackbury Jambs in the Faraway Hills (in what is apparently 1976). Inevitably, the pastoral and romantic interest in rural New York, and the muted love story allow readers to draw comparisons with *Little, Big.*

Yet Moffett's actual journey is psychological or visionary, as he follows a path to which he is inadvertently guided by his shepherd friend, Spofford. A lapsed Catholic, Moffett seeks the spiritual history or archetypal myth that lies within history, which he had been encouraged to seek by his mentor, the brilliant historian Frank Walker Barr, in graduate school.

Although Crowley refuses to allow the novel to come to any clear resolution, it appears that the goal of Moffett's journey has been reached when he reads an unpublished novel by the mysterious novelist, Fellowes Kraft, describing the lifelong visionary question of Giordano Bruno. This novel reveals to Moffett that the patterns of the archetypal quest for meaning are repeated with different variations again and again the world. At the end of the novel, Moffett has found his soul mate and enduring romantic interest in Rosie Rasmussen, a charming woman recovering from a divorce from a womanizing psychotherapist. Yet Crowley leaves even the direction of this relationship unresolved at the end of his tale.

A central conception of the novel is the world of archetypes or imaginary symbols, which is the "Aegypt" of the title. This imaginary "Aegypt" of the occultists and of Mozart's opera, *The Magic Flute* (based on the lore of the Freemasons), is not to be confused with the historical Egypt with its literal-minded religion and obsession with mummifying the dead, as Crowley makes clear. Instead, it is symbolized by the mysterious figure of Hermes Trismegistus, or Hermes "The Three Times Very Great," the Alexandrian magus whose syntheses of Platonism, neo-Platonism, and older myths, helped to create the myth of "Aegypt" for the Renaissance. This mysterious figure tends to reside in the background of Crowley's novel, much as Pythagoras and the occult conception of Solomon haunt the later poetry of William Butler Yeats. Unlike his namesake, Aleister Crowley (alluded to in the novel), Crowley does not take the metaphors of this occult world literally, or regard it as an easy access to worldly power or sexual prowess. Instead, Crowley's thematic concerns always focus on the search for archetypes that provide religious and philosophical meaning. In the novel, he attempts to draw together and unify numerous mythic metaphors, from the quest for the Grail and the Philosopher's Stone (which he identifies as the same quest for the same sacred object) to the Jungian motif of a hero encountering his anima. Space does not here permit a thorough elucidation of Crowley's elaborate interweaving of symbolism: Pierce Moffett's father, for instance, is named Axel and lives in a castle or aging apartment house in Brooklyn, yet he also seems to be an analogue of the Fisher King.

Another important feature of the novel is the vividly imagined tales within the main tale, which provide thematic repetition, that is, the restatement of motifs reinforcing those of the central plot. For students of English Renaissance literature, probably the most intriguing of these additional stories is Fellowes Kraft's imaginary novel, *Bitten Apples*, wherein young Will Shakespeare is depicted as running off to join the acting troup of James Burbage in the lost years between grammar school (which he would have left at twelve or thirteen) and his marriage to Anne Hathaway at eighteen.

Despite the novel's intense concentration on myth—for which Crowley credits many sources, including Robert Graves and Mircea Eliade—its 20th-century characters are convincingly realized: not only the Parsifal figure, Pierce Moffett, but also Rosie Rasmussen, Moffett's friend Spofford, and several minor figures are highly individualized. Thus Crowley avoids the defect that frequently haunts works of this kind, such as the novels of Charles Williams: the presence of an illuminating symbolism offset by shadowy characters. In this regard, and in his controlled and apparently effortless handling of style and incident, Crowley demonstrates impressive talents. His achievement here consolidates his claim to be not merely a major fantasy writer, but a writer who deserves to be considered a major novelist by any standards.

The publication of *Aegypt* was followed two years later by *Novelty*, a volume containing four novellas mostly with the theme of a writer's struggle to create a personal vision. These tales, which sometimes suggest the metafiction of Jorge Luis Borges, Gabriel García Marquéz, and numerous English writers, show Crowley in a philosophical mood similar to that of *Aegypt.* One tale in particular, "In Blue," is a very impressive performance.

Crowley's work has clearly moved to a high level of philosophical concern, without sacrificing its artistry. Without a doubt, *Aegypt* is likely to be considered one of the enduring novels of 20th-century fantasy, and it is difficult to dispute the conclusion that Crowley has established a place for himself as a major author in this genre.

—Edgar L. Chapman

---

**CUMMINGS, Ray(mond King).** Also wrote as Ray King; Gabriel Wilson. American. Born in New York City, 30 August 1887. Educated at Princeton University, New Jersey, one year. Married Gabrielle W. Cummings; one son and one daughter. Worked on oil wells in Wyoming and in placer mines in British Columbia and Alaska; arranged record albums and wrote labels for Edison Records in the 1920's. *Died 23 January 1957.*

SCIENCE-FICTION PUBLICATIONS

Novels (series: Haljan; Matter, Space, and Time; Tama)

*The Girl in the Golden Atom* (Matter, Space, and Time). London, Methuen, 1922; New York, Harper, 1923.
*The Man Who Mastered Time* (Matter, Space, and Time). Chicago, McClurg, 1929.
*The Sea Girl.* Chicago, McClurg, 1930.
*Tarrano the Conqueror.* Chicago, McClurg, 1930.
*Brigands of the Moon* (Haljan). Chicago, McClurg, 1931; London, Consul, 1966.
*The Shadow Girl* (Matter, Space, and Time). London, Swan, 1946; New York, Ace, 1962.
*The Princess of the Atom* (Matter, Space, and Time). New York, Avon, 1950; London, Boardman, 1951.
*The Man on the Meteor.* London, Swan, 1952.
*Beyond the Vanishing Point.* New York, Ace, 1958.
*Wandl the Invader* (Haljan). New York, Ace, 1961.
*Beyond the Stars.* New York, Ace, 1963.
*A Brand New World.* New York, Ace, 1964.
*The Exile of Time* (Matter, Space, and Time). New York, Avalon, 1964.
*Explorers into Infinity.* New York, Avalon, 1965.
*Tama of the Light Country.* New York, Ace, 1965.
*Tama, Princess of Mercury.* New York, Ace, 1966.
*The Insect Invasion.* New York, Avalon, 1967.

Uncollected Short Stories

"The Man Who Discovered Nothing," in *All-Story* (New York), 10 January 1920.
"The Light Machine," in *All-Story* (New York), 19 June 1920.
"The Time Professor," in *Argosy* (New York), 9 January 1921.
"Moon Madness," in *Argosy* (New York), 23 April 1921.
"The Gravity Professor," in *Argosy* (New York), 7 May 1921.
"The Peppermint Test," in *Argosy* (New York), 24 June 1922.
"The Fire People," in *Argosy* (New York), 21 October–17 November 1922.
"The Three-Eyed Man," in *Argosy* (New York), 7 July 1923.
"A Bar of Poisoned Licorice," in *Science and Invention* (New York), July 1927.
"What the Typewriter Told," in *Science and Invention* (New York), August 1927.
"Around the Universe," in *Amazing* (New York), October 1927.
"The Snow Girl," in *Argosy* (New York), 2–9 November 1929.
"Phantoms of Reality," in *Astounding* (New York), January 1930.
"The Man Who Was Two Men," in *Argosy* (New York), 8–15 February 1930.
"Jetta of the Lowlands," in *Astounding* (New York), September–November 1930.
"The Great Transformation," in *Wonder Stories* (New York), February 1931.
"Bandits of the Cylinder," in *Argosy* (New York), 29 August 1931.
"The Derelict of Space," with William Thurmond, in *Wonder Stories* (New York), Fall 1931.
"Flyer of Eternal Midnight," in *Argosy* (New York), 3 October 1931.
"The Jungle Rebellion," in *Argosy* (New York), 31 October–12 November 1931.
"The Mark of the Meteor," in *Wonder Stories* (New York), Winter 1931.
"The White Invaders," in *Astounding* (New York), December 1931.
"The Disappearance of William Rogers," in *Argosy* (New York), 9 January 1932.
"Death by the Clock," in *Argosy* (New York), 6 August 1932.
"The Thought Machine," in *Argosy* (New York), 26 May 1933.
"The Fire Planet," in *Argosy* (New York), 23 September–7 October 1933.
"Terror of the Unseen," in *Argosy* (New York), 4 November 1933.
"Brigands of the Unseen," in *Argosy* (New York), 27 January 1934.
"The Robot Rebellion," in *Blue Book* (Chicago), May 1934.
"Flood," in *Argosy* (New York), 28 July–11 August 1934.
"Earth-Mars Voyage 20," in *Argosy* (New York), 20 August 1934.
"World of Doom," in *Thrilling Adventures*, January 1935.
"The Moon Plot," in *Argosy* (New York), February 1935.
"The Polar Light," in *Argosy* (New York), April 1935.
"The Man with the Platinum Rib," in *Blue Book* (Chicago), January 1936.
"Blood of the Moon," in *Thrilling Wonder Stories* (New York), August 1936.
"Shadow Gold," in *Thrilling Wonder Stories* (New York), October 1936.
"Earth-Venus 12" (as Gabriel Wilson, with Mrs. Ray Cummings) and "Trapped in Eternity," in *Thrilling Wonder Stories* (New York), December 1936.
"Elixir of Doom," in *Thrilling Wonder Stories* (New York), April 1937.
"The Space-Time-Size Machine," in *Thrilling Wonder Stories* (New York), October 1937.
"Voyage 13," in *Astounding* (New York), July 1938.
"The Thing from Mars," in *Thrilling Wonder Stories* (New York), August 1938.
"X1-2-200," in *Astounding* (New York), September 1938.
"The Man Who Saw Too Much," in *Thrilling Wonder Stories* (New York), October 1938.
"The Great Adventure," in *Thrilling Wonder Stories* (New York), December 1938.
"Zeoh-X," in *Thrilling Wonder Stories* (New York), April 1939.
"Secret of the Sun," in *Thrilling Wonder Stories* (New York), August 1939.
"An Ultimatum from Mars," in *Astounding* (New York), August 1939.
"Portrait," in *Unknown Worlds* (New York), September 1939.
"The Atom Prince," in *Science Fiction Stories* (New York), December 1939.
"Shadow World," in *Thrilling Wonder Stories* (New York), December 1939.
"The Man Who Knew Everything," in *Strange Stories*, February 1940.
"The Girl from Infinite Smallness," in *Planet* (New York), Spring 1940.
"Arton's Medal," in *Super Science* (Kokomo, Indiana), May 1940.
"Space-Liner X87," in *Planet* (New York), Summer 1940.
"The Thought-Woman," in *Super Science* (Kokomo, Indiana), July 1940.
"Ice over America," in *Thrilling Wonder Stories* (New York), August 1940.
"Revolt in the Ice Empire," in *Planet* (New York), Fall 1940.
"The Machine That Had No Flaws" in *Startling* (New York), September 1940.
"The Vanishing Man," in *Thrilling Wonder Stories* (New York), September 1940.
"Personality," in *Astonishing* (Chicago), October 1940.
"Phantom of the Seven Stars," in *Planet* (New York), Winter 1940.

"The Door at the Opera," in *Astonishing* (Chicago), December 1940.
"Priestess of the Moon," in *Amazing* (New York), December 1940.
"World Upside Down," in *Thrilling Wonder Stories* (New York), December 1940.
"The Other Man's Blood," in *Famous Fantastic Mysteries* (New York), December 1940.
"Space Flight of Terror," in *Science Fiction* (New York), January 1941.
"Magnus' Disintegrator," in *Astonishing* (Chicago), February 1941.
"Almost Human," in *Startling* (New York), March 1941.
"The War-Nymphs of Venus," in *Planet* (New York), Spring 1941.
"Coming of the Giant Germs," in *Uncanny* (Chicago), April 1941.
"Imp of the Theremin," in *Astonishing* (Chicago), April 1941.
"Space-Wolf," in *Planet* (New York), Summer 1941.
"Onslaught of the Druid Girls," in *Fantastic Adventures* (New York), June 1941.
"Out of Smallness," in *Thrilling Wonder Stories* (New York), June 1941.
"The Robot God," in *Weird Tales* (New York), July 1941.
"Aerita of the Light Country," in *Super Science* (Kokomo, Indiana), August 1941.
"Machines of Destiny," in *Astonishing* (Chicago), November 1941.
"Monster of the Moon," in *Super Science* (Kokomo, Indiana), November 1941.
"Monster of the Asteroid," in *Planet* (New York), Winter 1941.
"Into the Fourth Dimension," in *Science Fiction Quarterly* (Holyoke, Massachusetts), Winter 1941–42.
"Bandits of Time," in *Amazing* (New York), December 1941.
"Crimes of the Year 2000," in *Famous Fantastic Mysteries* (New York), December 1941.
"Decadence," in *Thrilling Wonder Stories* (New York), December 1941.
"Fugitive," in *Thrilling Wonder Stories* (New York), February 1942.
"The Shadow People," in *Astonishing* (Chicago), March 1942.
"Gods of Space," in *Planet* (New York), Spring 1942.
"Regeneration," in *Thrilling Wonder Stories* (New York), April 1942.
"The Star-Master," in *Planet* (New York), Summer 1942.
"The Television Alibi," in *Famous Fantastic Mysteries* (New York), June 1942.
"The World Beyond," in *Amazing* (New York), July 1942.
"Rain of Fire," in *Future* (New York), August 1942.
"Miracle," in *Astonishing* (Chicago), October 1942.
"Beyond the End of Time," in *Super Science* (Kokomo, Indiana), November 1942.
"The End of His Service," in *Captain Future* (New York), Winter 1942.
"Tubby: Time Traveler," in *Thrilling Wonder Stories* (New York), December 1942.
"Patriotism Plus" in *Future* (New York), February 1943.
"Star Arrow," in *Thrilling Wonder Stories* (New York), February 1943.
"The Flame Breathers," in *Planet* (New York), March 1943.
"The Man from 2890," in *Astonishing* (Chicago), April 1943.
"The Golden Temple," in *Thrilling Wonder Stories* (New York), June 1943.
"Wings of Icarus," in *Startling* (New York), June 1943.
"The Man Who Saved New York," in *Science Fiction Stories* (New York), July 1943.
"Tubby: Atom Smasher," in *Thrilling Wonder Stories* (New York), August 1943.
"Battle of the Solar System," in *Thrilling Wonder Stories* (New York), Spring 1944.
"The Gadget Girl," in *Thrilling Wonder Stories* (New York), Fall 1944.
"Juggernaut of Space," in *Planet* (New York), Fall 1945.
"Tubby: Master of the Atom," in *Thrilling Wonder Stories* (New York), Fall 1946.
"Up and Atom," in *Startling* (New York), September 1947.
"The Simple Life," in *Startling* (New York), May 1948.
"Ahead of His Time," in *Thrilling Wonder Stories* (New York), June 1948.
"The Little Monsters Come," in *Planet* (New York), Winter 1948.
"A Fragment of Diamond Quartz," in *Super Science* (Kokomo, Indiana), January 1950.
"The Planet Smashers," in *Out of This World Adventures* (New York), July 1950.
"Science Can Wait," in *Fantastic Story* (New York), Fall 1952.
"He Who Served," in *Fantastic Universe* (New York), September 1954.
"The Man Who Could Go Away," in *Fantastic Universe* (New York), July 1955.
"Requiem for a Small Planet," in *Saturn* (Holyoke, Massachusetts), March 1958.
"The Dead Who Walk," in *Magazine of Horror* (New York), April 1965.

Uncollected Short Stories as Ray King

"Tuned Out," in *Argosy* (New York), 6–27 September 1924.
"Lust Rides the Roller Coaster," in *Marvel* (New York), December 1939.
"The Man Who Killed the World," in *Planet* (New York), Spring 1940.

OTHER PUBLICATIONS

Short Stories

*Tales of the Scientific Crime Club.* London, Ferret, 1979.

* * *

Ray Cummings had a long writing career, but it must be said that he long outlived his originality, and was noted for shamelessly rehashing a few early stories. Established as one of the trailblazers before the advent of *Amazing Stories*, he was the only one of them to carry on as a prominent name. His output was exceeded only by Hamilton and Kuttner, but he did not move with the movement, and was soon dated.

The early tales that made his name had sketchy but strongly suggestive scientific foundations. Though he showed his debt to Wells by borrowing his narrative frame from *The Time Machine* more than once, his stories were closer to Haggard's or Burroughs's. Usually visitors from 20th-century New York in a strange setting with a vague pre-industrial society resolved a conflict and helped pave the way for more advanced thinking.

His first and favorite inspiration was sub-microscopic, even subatomic life—atoms or sub-atomic particles as worlds. The idea dated from Nicholas Odgers's *The Mystery of Being; or, Are Ultimate Atoms Inhabited Worlds?* (1863), but Cummings added the idea of reducing one's size indefinitely to penetrate such a realm—later reversing it to visit a super-world in which we inhabit a particle. It is a tribute to his skill that a story based on such an idea could be a popular success. The unnamed chemist in *The Girl in the Golden Atom* (Rogers in the sequel) sees with his super-microscope an infinitesimal human race, including a nubile wench. (Compare Fitz-James O'Brien's *The Diamond Lens.*) But instead of agonising over the unattainable he devises size-changing drugs. (Compare *Alice in Wonderland.*) The relativity of size and the experience of changing size are vividly evoked. The book was fresh and exciting then, and it still reads well, and rates as a classic—though it is not precisely science fiction. (Incidentally, this adventure does not reach the level of an atomic world, despite the title; G.P. Wertenbaker has the doubtful honor of first taking the idea that far in "The Man from the Atom," in *Science and Invention*, August 1923.)

In the extended book version the villain was called Targo, and many later evildoers were named alliteratively—Taro, Toroh, etc. They are typically greedy megalomaniacs, usually gross or deformed, good at sneering and cynical laughter. Subtleties of character and motivation are not displayed, but human relations were simplified and fogged with romantic myths in most science fiction then. The writing is direct and conversational. To modern eyes there was much overstating the obvious, especially in the novels, but there were mystery and suspense supporting the action for the original audience.

Cummings was an early exploiter of time travel, scarcely touched since Wells, in *The Man Who Mastered Time, The Shadow Girl*, and others, though mostly for change of scene only. *Explorers into Infinity* reversed the exploration of the inconceivably small to visit a vastly greater sphere. *The Man on the Meteor* told of a tiny worldlet in Saturn's ring with seas and aquatic microscopic humans. *Tarrano the Conqueror* had a future of interplanetary affairs and a new Napoleon. In *The Sea Girl* an undersea people threatened the land. *A Brand New World* had a new extra-Solar planet entering the system. *Brigands of the Moon* moved into the kind of future interplanetary traffic early magazine SF postulated and helped establish space piracy as a popular theme. Cummings wrote many routine space adventure shorts thereafter. In "Jetta of the Lowlands" (*Astounding*, 1930), new nations grew from settlements on the dry sea bed after the oceans receded. Sixteen stories featuring the character "Tubby" carried some gentle satire on many of his own plots and concepts.

Cummings' treatment of robots is of interest, though they figured in only a few late stories. "The Robot Rebellion" (*Blue Book*, May 1934) is a misleading title, since the robots play a subordinate part in a conspiracy; but they are shown as integrated into a future society. "The Robot God" (*Weird Tales*, July 1941) has a conventional view of the synthetic intelligent being placing its own interests first at the expense of man. But in "Zeoh-X" (*Thrilling Wonder Stories*, April 1939) and "X1-2-200" (*Astounding*, September 1938), robots are seen as loyal retainers using their own initiative in their masters' interests. In the latter story, the robot suffers conflict between basic psychological compulsions imposed on it: firstly, to avoid harm to humans; secondly, to obey human orders; thirdly, to protect itself. So we see that Cummings first introduced the idea of these motivations that would be necessary to impose on robots, later ably exploited in many stories by Isaac Asimov, such as the "Three Laws of Robotics."

The series of 12 *Tales of the Scientific Crime Club* dating from the early 1920's are ingenious examples of the scientific detective story, a form now obsolete. They are armchair detective puzzles turning on application of scientific principles to a problem, mostly not quite becoming science fiction by introducing a new speculation.

—Graham Stone

# D

**DALE, Norman.** *See* **TUBB, E.C.**

---

**DALEY, Brian C.** Also writes as Jack McKinney, with James Luceno. American. Born in Englewood, New Jersey, 22 December 1947. Educated at Jersey City State College, B.A. in communication 1974. Has worked as waiter, housepainter, laborer, and case worker. Address: c/o Ballantine, 201 East 50th Street, New York, New York, 10022, U.S.A.

SCIENCE-FICTION PUBLICATIONS

Novels (series: Coramonde; Hobart Floyt; Han Solo)

*The Doomfarers of Coramonde.* New York, Ballantine, 1977.
*The Starfollowers of Coramonde.* New York, Ballantine, 1979.
*Han Solo at Stars' End.* New York, Ballantine, and London, Sphere, 1979.
*Han Solo's Revenge.* New York, Ballantine, 1979; London, Sphere, 1980.
*Han Solo and the Lost Legacy.* New York, Ballantine, 1980; London, Sphere, 1981.
*Tron* (novelization of screenplay). New York, Ballantine, 1982.
*A Tapestry of Magics.* New York, Ballantine, 1983.
*Requiem for a Ruler of Worlds* (Floyt). New York, Ballantine, 1985; London, Grafton, 1990.
*Jinx on a Terran Inheritance* (Floyt). New York, Ballantine, 1985; London, Grafton, 1990.
*Fall of the White Ship Avatar* (Floyt). New York, Ballantine, 1986; London, Grafton, 1990.

OTHER PUBLICATIONS

Novels as Jack McKinney (with James Luceno)

*Battle Cry.* New York, Ballantine, 1987.
*Battlehymn.* New York, Ballantine, 1987.
*Doomsday.* New York, Ballantine, 1987.
*The Final Nightmare.* New York, Ballantine, 1987.
*Force of Arms.* New York, Ballantine, 1987.
*Genesis.* New York, Ballantine, 1987.
*Homecoming.* New York, Ballantine, 1987.
*Invid Invasion.* New York, Ballantine, 1987.
*Metal Fire.* New York, Ballantine, 1987.
*Metamorphosis.* New York, Ballantine, 1987.
*Southern Cross.* New York, Ballantine, 1987.
*Symphony of Light.* New York, Ballantine, 1987.
*Dark Powers.* New York, Ballantine, 1988.
*Death Dance.* New York, Ballantine, 1988.
*The Devil's Hand.* New York, Ballantine, 1988.
*Rubicon.* New York, Ballantine, 1988.
*The End of the Circle.* New York, Ballantine, 1990.
*Kaduna Memories.* New York, Ballantine, 1990.
*Event Horizon.* New York, Ballantine, 1991.

Plays

Radio Plays: *Star Wars* series (13 episodes); *The Empire Strikes Back* series (10 episodes).

Animated cartoon: *Galaxy Rangers* (7 episodes).

Recordings: *Rebel Mission to Ord Mantell; War Games.*

*

Brian C. Daley comments:

Asked his reaction to becoming a millionaire, Neil Simon once said that the main difference in life was between being broke and bringing down 200 dollars a week; the rest was gravy. Writing has been a bit like that: making a living writing my own books, dealing with popular movie material, having scripts produced, and so forth has been gratifying and on the whole very enjoyable, but it's icing on the cake, after all. The real dividing line in life was in selling my first novel and seeing it in print.

I do my best to keep in mind the desire I had to tell a story, and how crucial it was—and should continue to be—to give the reader full value for his or her time, attention, and money. One of the pitfalls of writing for a living is that a certain perfunctoriness can creep in if you're not careful, especially in a genre where being prolific can be such a plus.

I don't have much to say, here, about art, literature, or moral uplift. The SF/Fantasy audience is quick to let you know if you're not delivering; my efforts are concentrated on satisfying the customers.

* * *

Brian C. Daley made an instant, favorable impact with the publication of his first novel, *The Doomfarers of Coramonde*, in 1977. A group of American soldiers and an armored personnel carrier are magically transported from Vietnam to the world of Coramonde, where they are enlisted in the quest to rescue a princess and defeat a powerful sorcerer aided by a fearsome dragon. The working of scientific technology into a fantasy context created a refreshing new look at an all too familiar story line, proving that with an inventive imagination, new twists can be found in any situation. A cast of engaging characters, liberal doses of genuine humor, and an adventurous and action-packed plot made this one of the most auspicious first novels in years.

Daley followed up with *The Starfollowers of Coramonde*, which lacked some of the spontaneity of its predecessor but still maintained a very high level of storytelling. A sorceress army is gathering to plunge the world back into a repressive tyranny, with soldiers who seem invulnerable to physical or magical attack. Not quite as successful as the earlier novel, it is still superior to most of the fantasy fiction that was appearing from more experienced writers.

Unfortunately, Daley's career was sidetracked into media associated books for the next few years. The novelization of the film *Tron* was competent but basically forgettable. Daley also wrote three original novels set in the "Star Wars" universe, featuring Han Solo, the itinerant starship pilot and smuggler. In *Han Solo at Star's End* Solo is maneuvered into rescuing a rebel leader from the Empire. He becomes involved with slave traders in *Han Solo's Revenge* and attempts to find a legendary priceless treasure in *Han Solo and the Lost Legacy.* Although the novels are relatively minor adventures, hampered in part by the restrictions implied by writing in the universe created by another mind, Daley embellished his tales with some captivating robot characters, and provides dollops of clever humor at strategic points.

*A Tapestry of Magics* marked a return to original fantasy, and it remains Daley's single best work. The Singularity is a realm of relative calm in a fantasy world that literally borders upon every time and every reality. Daley's fondness for paradoxical matchings was evident in the Coramonde books, and now he presents us with Nazi commandoes locked in combat with horse barbarians, knights in shining armor jousting with American Indians, and a nervous Count Dracula pleading for refuge from his pursuers. The protagonist is a heroic figure who retreats from a frustrated love affair to what he hopes will be a life of quiet indolence. Things don't quite work out that way, of course. The tapestry is a magical contrivance that holds within its scenes all of the past, and possibly the power to control the future. It is a magnificent fantasy work, but to date the last thing Daley wrote in that style.

*Requiem for a Ruler of Worlds* was the opening volume in a more straightforward science fiction trilogy featuring Hobart Floyt. Earth is a minor power, its focus on internal problems, in the interstellar civilization of the far future. A bureaucrat discovers that he is the unlikely heir to a charismatic ruler on another world, and despite his protestations, the government of Earth insists that he claim his legacy, although they want the power it entails for their own purposes rather than his. Accompanied by a more experienced traveller conditioned to remain loyal, he sets off for the reading of the will, only to discover that he is the target for a team of determined assassins.

The second adventure, *Jinx on a Terran Inheritance*, follows the two companions as they seek to discover the whereabouts of the starship that was signed over to Floyt under the terms of the will. Upon their return to Earth, a final confrontation over control of the ship threatens to end the adventurers' lives, unless they can undermine the government itself. The concluding adventure is *Fall of the White Ship Avatar*, wherein the protagonists set out to discover the secrets of an ancient but lost alien technology. The series is lighthearted entertainment, but stylishly handled.

Although it appears that additional adventures were planned, none have appeared since 1987. This may be the result of a series of over a dozen novelizations of the Japanese Robotech programs that Daley wrote in collaboration with James Luceno under the name Jack McKinney. Although these are competently written, they are essentially juvenile adventure stories with lots of action and little substance. They did continue the byline for one original novel, however, *Kaduna Memories*, which features a computer detective who loses his job and then is handed an opportunity for revenge on his erstwhile employer. It is impossible to judge how much of the content is provided by each writer, but the frequent flashes of wry humor are typical of Daley's earlier work.

The original novels that have appeared under the Daley byline have been uniformly excellent and generally highly original. *A Tapestry of Magics* in particular demonstrates that Daley has the potential to produce significant works in the field. Time will tell whether that potential will ever be realized.

—Don D'Ammassa

---

**DANN, Jack.** American. Born in Johnson City, New York, 15 February 1945. Educated at Hofstra University, Hempstead, New York, 1963; State University of New York, Binghamton, 1965–68, B.A. in social science and political science 1968; St. John's Law School, New York, 1969–71. Taught writing and science fiction at Broome Community College, Binghamton, 1972, 1990–91, and Cornell University, Ithaca, New York, summer 1973; managing editor, *SFWA Bulletin*, 1970–75, Freelance writer and lecturer. Agent: Merrilee Heifetz, Writer's House, 21 West 26th Street, New York, New York 10010. Address: 825 Front Street, Binghamton, New York 13905, U.S.A.

SCIENCE-FICTION PUBLICATIONS

Novels

*Starhiker*. New York, Harper, 1977.
*Junction*. New York, Dell, 1981.
*The Man Who Melted*. New York, Bluejay, 1984.

Short Stories

*Timetipping*. New York, Doubleday, 1980.

Uncollected Short Stories

"Dark, Dark, the Dead Star," with George Zebrowski, in *If* (New York), July–August 1970.
"Listen, Love," with George Zebrowski, in *New Worlds Quarterly 2*, edited by Michael Moorcock. London, Sphere, and New York, Berkley, 1971.
"Trap," with George Zebrowski, in *Coming Through*, edited by Nina C. Woessner and William D. Sheldon. Boston, Allyn and Bacon, 1972.
"Whirl Cage," in *Orbit 10*, edited by Damon Knight. New York, Putnam, 1972.
"I'm with You in Rockland," in *Strange Bedfellows*," edited by Thomas N. Scortia. New York, Random House, 1972.
"Tulpa," in *New Worlds 6*, edited by Michael Moorcock and Charles Platt. London, Sphere, 1973.
"Thirty-Three and One Third," with George Zebrowski, in *Long Night of Waiting and Other Stories*, edited by Roger Elwood. Nashville, Aurora, 1974.
"OD," with George Zebrowski, in *Omega*, edited by Roger Elwood. New York, Walker, 1974.
"The Flower That Missed the Morning" (for children), with George Zebrowski, in *The Killer Plants and Other Stories*, edited by Roger Elwood. Minneapolis, Lerner, 1974.
"The Good Old Days," in *Journey to Another Star and Other Stories*, edited by Roger Elwood. Minneapolis, Lerner, 1974.
"Faces Forward," with George Zebrowski, in *Dystopian Visions*, edited by Roger Elwood. Englewood Cliffs, New Jersey, Prentice Hall, 1975.
"Recycled Sandra," in *Gallery*, July 1975.
"Yellowhead," with George Zebrowski, in *New Constellations*, edited by Thomas M. Disch and Charles Naylor. New York, Harper, 1976.

"Limits," with Jack C. Haldeman, in *Fantastic* (New York), May 1976.
"The Dream Lions," in *Amazing* (New York), September 1976.
"The Islands of Time," in *Fantastic* (New York), September 1977.
"Amnesia," in *The Berkley Showcase 3*, edited by Victoria Schochet and John W. Silbersack. New York, Berkley, 1981.
"Fairy Tale," in *The Berkley Showcase 4*, edited by Victoria Schochet and John W. Silbersack. New York, Berkley, 1981.
"Parables of Art," with Barry N. Malzberg, in *New Dimensions 12*, edited by Marta Randall and Robert Silverberg. New York, Pocket Books, 1981.
"A Change in the Weather," with Gardner Dozois, in *Playboy* (Chicago), June 1981.
"Going Under," in *The Best Science Fiction of the Year 11*, edited by Terry Carr. New York, Pocket Books, 1982.
"Playing the Game," with Gardner Dozois, in *Great Stories from Rod Serling's The Twilight Zone Magazine*, edited by T.E.D. Klein. New York, TZ Publications, 1982.
"High Steel," with Jack C. Haldeman, in *Fantasy and Science Fiction* (New York), February 1982.
"Screamers," in *Oui* (New York), October 1982.
"Touring," with Gardner Dozois and Michael Swanwick, in *The Year's Best Horror Stories 11*, edited by Karl Edward Wagner. New York, DAW, 1983.
"A Cold Day in the Mesozoic," in *Fears*, edited by Charles L. Grant. New York, Berkley, 1983.
"Reunion," in *Shadows 6*, edited by Charles L. Grant. New York, Doubleday, 1983.
"Slow Dancing with Jesus," with Gardner Dozois, in *Penthouse* (New York), July 1983.
"Time Bride," with Gardner Dozois, in *Isaac Asimov's Science Fiction Magazine* (New York), December 1983.
"Afternoon at Schrafft's," with Gardner Dozois and Michael Swanwick, in *Magicats!*, edited by Dann and Dozois. New York, Ace, 1984.
"Blind Shemmy," in *The Year's Best Science Fiction 1* edited by Gardner Dozois and Jim Frenkel. New York, Bluejay, 1984.
"Virgin Territory," with Gardner Dozois and Michael Swanwick, in *Penthouse* (New York), March 1984.
"Bad Medicine," in *Isaac Asimov's Science Fiction Magazine* (New York), October 1984.
"The Black Horn," in *Fantasy and Science Fiction* (New York), November 1984.
"The Gods of Mars," with Gardner Dozois and Michael Swanwick, in *Omni* (New York), March 1985.
"Tattoos," in *Omni*, November 1986.
"Visitors," in *The Architecture of Fear*, edited by Kathryn Cramer and Peter D. Pautz. New York, Arbor House, 1987.
"Down among the Dead Men," with Gardner R. Dozois, in *Blood Is Not Enough: 17 Stories of Vampirism*, edited by Ellen Datlow. New York, Morrow, 1987.
"Getting Up," with Barry N. Malzberg, in *Tropical Chills*, edited by Tim Sullivan. New York, Avon, 1988.

OTHER PUBLICATIONS

Verse

*Christs and Other Poems*. Binghamton, New York, Bellevue Press, 1978.

Other

*Slow Dancing Through Time*, with others. Kansas City, Ursus, 1990.

Editor, *Wandering Stars: An Anthology of Jewish Fantasy and Science Fiction*. New York, Harper, 1974; London, Woburn Press, 1975.
Editor, with Gardner Dozois, *Future Power*. New York, Random House, 1976.
Editor, with George Zebrowski, *Faster Than Light: An Anthology of Stories about Interstellar Travel*. New York, Harper, 1976.
Editor, *Immortal*. New York, Harper, 1978.
Editor, with Gardner Dozois, *Aliens!* New York, Pocket Books, 1980.
Editor, *More Wandering Stars*. New York, Doubleday, 1981.
Editor, with Gardner Dozois, *Unicorns!* New York, Ace, 1982.
Editor, with Gardner Dozois, *Magicats!* New York, Ace, 1984.
Editor, with Gardner Dozois, *Bestiary!* New York, Ace, 1985.
Editor, with Gardner Dozois, *Mermaids!* New York, Ace, 1986.
Editor, with Gardner Dozois, *Sorcerers!* New York, Ace, 1986.
Editor, with Gardner Dozois, *Demons!* New York, Ace, 1987.
Editor, with Jeanne Van Buren Dann, *In the Field of Fire*. New York, Tor, 1987.
Editor, with Gardner Dozois, *Dogtales!* New York, Ace, 1988.
Editor, with Gardner Dozois, *Seaserpents!* New York, Ace, 1989.
Editor, with Gardner Dozois, *Dinosaurs!* New York, Ace, 1990.
Editor, with Gardner Dozois, *Little People!* New York, Ace, 1991.

*

Bibliography: *The Work of Jack Dann: An Annotated Bibliography and Guide* by Jeffrey M. Elliot, San Bernardino, California, Borgo Press, 1990.

Manuscript Collection: Temple University, Philadelphia.

* * *

Jack Dann's fiction has shown a notable unity in dramatic concern, elaborating at various lengths and moods what has been essentially a series of variations on a theme. Over 15 years, his novels and shorter works have developed a recognizable figure in the solitary, obsessive young man whose disaffection with the stratified society he belongs to leads to a dramatic encounter with a larger strangeness that is told with a powerful and sometimes disturbing psychic resonance.

Dann published his first fiction in 1970, and some of his characteristic concerns were seeing expression as early as in the 1971 "Windows," but it was not until the appearance of his 1973 novella "Junction" (basis for the later novel) that he began to dramatize his essential confrontation between consciousness and a mutable universe with a degree of assurance and skill. Dann's village of Junction, the last redoubt of causality following a catastrophe that disrupts physical laws to render the rest of Earth a region of physical indeterminacy, effectively embodies his theme of inertia roused by chaos, and the protagonists' journey into the surrounding "Hell" uses a conventional narrative to introduce provocative speculations on consciousness, metaphysics, and Teilhard de Chardin's concept of an evolving universe.

In 1975 two shorter works appeared that confirmed Dann as one of the most audacious and technically assured SF writers of the decade. "Timetipping," a deceptively whimsical short story that recalls Isaac Bashevis Singer at his more energetic, presents a situation similar to that of "Junction"—the world experiences a dissolution of temporal sequence that allows free and sometimes involuntary slippage through time—in a witty and kinetic display of stylistic virtuosity. It was, however, with his novelette

"The Dybbuk Dolls" that Dann first showed all his strengths in a single story. Dann's dark tale of the invasion of a pious man's consciousness by an alien malevolence able to excite his sense of guilt stands as an exceptional example of SF's seminal theme, encountering the unknown, dramatized exclusively through one participant's point of view.

With his novel *Starhiker* Dann adopted the familiar folk tale of the young man who leaves his bucolic world for a journey of wonder, from which he ultimately returns bearing wisdom and power. Bo Forester's wanderings among the starlanes of a more advanced civilization are told in a dense, richly textured but dispassionate language that shows up one of the limitations of Dann's work until that time: the intense but narrow focus upon his protagonists leaves his other characterizations pallid, and allows no scope for portraying relationships. The novel version of *Junction*, which can be considered almost a companion piece, shows the same virtues and shortcomings.

Dann's celebrated novelette "Camps" can be seen as a culmination of this phase of his work. The story of the now-familiar young man who moves in delirium between hospital and a Nazi death camp accords equal weight to the movement of its "inner" and "outer" narratives, like two cycles turning on the same axis, and has in the healing synthesis of its resolution (the protagonists' deliverance from the death camp coincides with the break in his fever) something of the resonance of myth.

In the years since, Dann's writing has broadened in scope and sympathy, and *The Man Who Melted*, his longest and most ambitious novel, shows his past strengths while dealing, somewhat uncertainly, with the tortured relationships between his three protagonists. As the title suggests, the mutability of consciousness remains an essential theme, but both the protagonists' obsessive natures and the decadence of the society around them are portrayed more complexly and convincingly than before.

—Gregory Feeley

---

**DARNAY, Arsen (Julius).** American. Born in Budapest, Hungary, 31 July 1936; emigrated to the United States in 1953, naturalized, 1961. Attended Rockhurst College, Kansas City, Missouri, 1953, 1963; University of Maryland, College Park, 1959–60. Served in the United States Army, 1956–61. Married Brigitte Schulz; two daughters. Technical writer, J.F. Pritchard and Co., 1961–65, and program manager, Midwest Research Institute, 1965–73, both in Kansas City; deputy assistant administrator, Environmental Protection Agency, Washington, D.C., 1973–75; general manager, Carborundum Company, McLean, Virginia, 1977–81. Since 1981, principal, Arsen Darnay and Associates, management consultants, Hopkins, Minnesota. Recipient: Environmental Protection Agency bronze medal, 1970, and silver medal, 1972. Agent: Kirby McCauley Ltd., 155 East 77th Street, Suite 1A, New York, New York 10021. Address: 259 McKinley, Grosse Pointe Farms, Michigan 48236, U.S.A.

SCIENCE-FICTION PUBLICATIONS

Novels

*A Hostage for Hinterland*. New York, Ballantine, 1976.
*The Karma Affair*. New York, St. Martin's Press, 1978; as *Karma*, London, Sphere, 1980.
*The Siege of Faltara*. New York, Ace, 1978.
*The Purgatory Zone*. New York, Ace, 1981.

Short Stories

*The Splendid Freedom*. New York, Ace, 1980.

OTHER PUBLICATIONS

Other

*The Role of Nonpackaging Paper in Solid Waste Management 1966 to 1976*, with William E. Franklin. Rockville, Maryland, Solid Waste Management Office, 1971.
*Salvage Markets for Materials in Solid Wastes*, with William E. Franklin. Washington D.C., Environmental Protection Agency, 1972.
*Recycling Assessment and Prospects for Success*. Washington, D.C., Environmental Protection Agency, 1972.

Editor, *Manufacturing U.S.A.: Industry Analysis, Statistics, and Leading Companies*. Detroit, Gale Research Press, 1989.

* * *

Arsen Darnay's fiction first began to appear in 1974, a blend of fast-paced action with considerable original thinking, marred occasionally by superficial characterization and lapses of plot logic. Although he published several short stories, it is only at novelette length and greater that he has truly been successful.

"The Splendid Freedom" follows a young man on his adventures on Mother Earth during a visit that is to mark his passage into the adult world. He does not immediately discover that the surface of Earth is in fact uninhabitable, and that most of the things he has experienced during his visit were directly implanted in his mind and never happened at all. One of Darnay's best shorter pieces is "The Eastcoast Confinement." North America is now a dictatorship, and all those who dissent are confined to large camps set up around the country. The inhabitants are allowed to govern themselves along the lines of Robert Heinlein's classic "Coventry," but the outside authorities limit food supplies in an attempt to reduce the dissident population, which is now approximately one of every three adults. The result is tribal warfare among various groups such as the Ecofreaks and Peacefreaks. A visitor from Europe is instrumental in altering things slightly so that the new type of culture arising within the Confinement will have a chance to succeed as a viable force in the future.

Perhaps the best of Darnay's novelettes is "Plutonium," which was to start a series that was rewritten as the novel, *The Karma Affair*. In the shorter piece, two men and a woman meet in a Nazi concentration camp. Their souls are repeatedly reincarnated through the years until, in our own near future, reincarnation becomes an accepted scientific fact. One of the two men invents a soul catcher and establishes a priesthood to watch over nuclear wastes. The novel presents the ultimate crisis of that priesthood far in the future, when the rest of society has dissolved into a new barbarism.

*A Hostage for Hinterland* is set in a similar, or perhaps identical barbarous future. Society is split into two forces, the Structure Cities with their high technology and nuclear arsenals, and the Hinterland, nomadic tribes living under comparatively primitive circumstances. The cities use their weaponry to blackmail the Hinterlands into trading them the helium they need to run their equipment. But the tribes are not content to be the lesser partners and plot to develop an umbrella against the missiles. Darnay works out the political maneuverings between the two powers and within the two camps convincingly, without interfering with his fast-paced plot. This was a quite promising adventure story to appear as a first novel.

*The Purgatory Zone* is not as successful. The Kibbutz Zone is a society that has renounced most forms of aggression and approximates what we would think of as Utopia. The occasional individual who cannot adjust is urged to travel to an alternate world, and the protagonist in this case emigrates to the Purgatory Zone, an alternate America where a vicious caste system makes life increasingly difficult for him. He is almost immediately on the run from the authorities and sets off on a chase adventure that is sometimes entertaining, but which falls apart toward the conclusion.

Darnay returned to barbarism of a sort in *The Siege of Faltara*, although this time the setting is another world, the planet Fillippi. It's a peaceful world, but peaceful because of the ruthless dictatorship that dominates it through the use of slavery and drugs that condition the mind to loyalty. The protagonist is an outside agent whose job is to destabilize the government and cause a revolution. Naturally he does, after a series of adventures, in a well-handled, above average adventure novel. Darnay established himself with five books as a progressively interesting writer, with some innovative ideas.

—Don D'Ammassa

---

**DAVIDSON, Avram.** Also writes as Ellery Queen. American. Born in Yonkers, New York, 23 April 1923. Educated at New York University, 1940–42; Yeshiva University, New York, 1947–48; Pierce College, Canoga Park, California, 1950–51. Served in the United States Navy, 1942–46; served in the Israeli Army in the Arab-Israeli war, 1948–49. Married Grania Kaiman (divorced); one son. Editor, *Fantasy and Science Fiction* magazine, New York, 1962–64. From 1964, freelance writer. Recipient: Hugo award, 1958, for editing, 1963; Ellery Queen award, 1958; Mystery Writers of America Edgar Allan Poe award, 1961; World Fantasy award, 1976, 1979, life achievement award, 1986. Agent: Carnell Literary Agency, Danes Croft Gooselane, Little Hallingbury, Hertfordshire. CM22 7RG, England.

Science-Fiction Publications

Novels

*Joyleg*, with Ward Moore. New York, Pyramid, 1962.
*Mutiny in Space*. New York, Pyramid, 1964; London, White Lion, 1973.
*Rogue Dragon*. New York, Ace, 1965.
*Rork!* New York, Berkley, 1965; London, Rapp and Whiting, 1968.
*Masters of the Maze*. New York Pyramid, 1965; London, White Lion, 1974.
*The Enemy of My Enemy*. New York, Berkley, 1966.
*Clash of Star-Kings*. New York, Ace, 1966.
*The Kar-Chee Reign*. New York, Ace, 1966.
*Ursus of Ultima Thule*. New York, Avon, 1973.

Short Stories

*Or All the Seas with Oysters*. New York, Berkley, 1962; London, White Lion, 1976.
*What Strange Stars and Skies*. New York, Ace, 1965.
*Strange Seas and Shores*. New York, Doubleday, 1971.
*The Enquiries of Dr. Eszterhazy*. New York, Warner, 1975.
*The Redward Edward Papers*. New York, Doubleday, 1978.
*The Best of Avram Davidson*, edited by Michael Kurland. New York, Doubleday, 1979.
*The Collected Fantasies of Avram Davidson*, edited by John Silbersack. New York, Berkley, 1982.

Other Publications

Novels

*And on the Eighth Day* (as Ellery Queen). New York, Random House, 1964.
*The Fourth Side of the Triangle* (as Ellery Queen). New York, Random House, 1965.
*The Island under the Earth*. New York, Ace, 1969; London, Mayflower, 1975.
*The Phoenix and the Mirror; or, the Enigmatic Speculum*. New York, Doubleday, 1969; London, Mayflower, 1975.
*Peregrine: Primus*. New York, Walker, 1971.
*Peregrine: Secundus*. New York, Berkley, 1981.
*And Don't Forget the One Red Rose*. Seattle, Washington, Dryad Press, 1986.
*Vergil in Averno*. New York, Doubleday, 1987.
*Marco Polo and the Sleeping Beauty*, with Grania Davis. New York, Baen, 1988.

Other

*Crimes and Chaos* (essays). Evanston, Illinois, Regency, 1962.

Editor, *Best from Fantasy and Science Fiction 12–14*. New York, Doubleday, 3 vols., 1963–65; London Gollancz, 2 vols., 1966; Panther, 1 vol., 1967.
Editor, *Magic for Sale*. New York, Ace, 1983.

*

Bibliography: "A Bibliography of Avram Davidson" by Richard Grant, in *Megavore 9* (Calgary, Alberta), June 1980.

Manuscript Collections: California State University, Fullerton; Texas A. and M. University, College Station.

* * *

Avram Davidson is primarily a writer of fantasy and fantasy SF. His best stories are comic or ironic, and he is also a master of the mystery and weird fantasy and SF story. In structure, if not in style and thought, Davidson writes in the O. Henry tradition. But though his stories possess a familiar pattern of development, Davidson gives the impression of being unpredictable and eccentric. In part, this view may rest on Davidson's sometimes oblique method of developing his stories, deliberately omitting anticipated transitions so as to heighten contrasts and increase tension. It is a technique that a mystery writer may be expected to favour. It is particularly effective in his Hugo-winning story "Or All the Seas with Oysters," a tale based on the premise of the animated machine, in this case a red French racing bicycle, and the contrasting reactions of the two main characters to the discovery of such an alien being. The story has a finely developed sense of narrative irony, which is one of the characteristics of Davidson's best fiction.

A related type of science fantasy in Davidson's repertory is the comic tale rooted in Jewish humor. "The Golem" is a deservedly famous story in which Davidson combines comic formulas of traditional ethnic humor with an overlay of modern SF. The contrasting expectations of each tradition makes for the special comic sense of the story. Davidson also displays a fine talent for parody in such literary stories as "Author, Author," in which the reader is treated to some delicious echoes of the Asimov story of the same title as well as to a burlesque of the detective mystery/fantasy ending in a bitter-sweet reversal of poetic justice. Davidson takes his place as a writer of popular fantastic SF in the tradition that comes prominently to the surface with Poe and continues in the 20th century with Merritt, Lovecraft, and the *Weird Tales* and *Unknown* schools on the one hand, and such diverse writers of comic fantasy as Cabell and the Yiddish master Isaac Bashevis Singer on the other. In tone as well as intention, however, Davidson is closer to popular and even commercial pulp writers like L. Sprague de Camp and Fletcher Pratt than to either Poe and Cabell.

Davidson has also written many novels, some of which fall into familiar categories. There have been the SF pot boilers dealing with alien invaders, alternate universes, and other fantastic SF premises (*Masters of the Maze, Clash of Star-Kings, The Kar-Chee Reign*). Related to these are the space operas *Mutiny in Space, Rogue Dragon, Rork!*, and *The Enemy of My Enemy*. Of these, *Masters of the Maze* is clearly the most accomplished work. More successful have been the mock heroic fantasy *Peregrine: Primus* and the heroic romance fantasy *The Phoenix and the Mirror* (part of a projected series provisionally titled *Virgil Magus*). Both works are distinguished by a level of popular scholarship found in the Harold Shea stories of de Camp and Pratt. The wit and satire that animate the picaresque misadventures of Peregrine, bastard son of the King of Sapodilla, are absent from the more seriously intended *Phoenix and the Mirror*, and the latter romance suffers in consequence. Each, however, is notable for Davidson's attempt at introducing premises for romance that lie outside the familiar Christian traditions. Indeed, Davidson's invention and treatment are intended to be contrary to Christian-oriented legends, offering the reader an unspoken but also an unmistakable dissent from the tradition that has dominated heroic fantasy since the Middle Ages. It is too bad that it does not work.

Perhaps the most curious of all Davidson's fantasy prose fictions is *The Enquiries of Dr. Eszterhazy*, a collection of linked stories in which the master detective and doctor of everything, Engelbert Eszterhazy, stands in as the amused and amusing hero of a series of mysterious affairs taking place in and about the fictitious triune monarchy of Sythia-Panmonia-Transbalkania. Curiously, it seems that Davidson's experimental form of blending the internal narrative context of fantasy with the quite external tone and view point of the implied modern narrator is responsible for the failure of the book to win either the popular support or the critical acclaim it deserves. The book seems destined to enjoy the status of underground classic, as a fantastic parody of the detective story that will serve to identify cognescenti among readers and those with a refined if still largely popular taste for the deliberately fantastic and artificial.

—Donald L. Lawler

---

**DAVIES, L(eslie) P(urnell).** Also writes as Leslie Vardre. British. Born in Crewe, Cheshire, 20 October 1914. Educated at Manchester College of Science and Technology, University of Manchester, qualified as optometrist 1939 (Fellow, British Optical Association). Served in the British Army Medical Corps in France, North Africa, and Italy, 1939–45. Married Winifred Tench in 1940. Dispensing pharmacist, Crewe, Cheshire, 1930–39; freelance artist in Rome, 1945–46; postmaster, West Heath, Birmingham, 1946–56; optician in private practice, and gift shop owner, Deganwy, North Wales, 1956–75. Since 1975, has lived in Tenerife.

### Science-Fiction Publications

#### Novels

*The Paper Dolls.* London, Jenkins, 1964; New York, Doubleday, 1966.
*Man Out of Nowhere.* London, Jenkins, 1965; as *Who Is Lewis Pindar?*, New York, Doubleday, 1966.
*The Artificial Man.* London, Jenkins, 1965; New York, Doubleday, 1967.
*The Lampton Dreamers.* London, Jenkins, 1966; New York, Doubleday, 1967.
*Psychogeist.* London, Jenkins, 1966; New York, Doubleday, 1967.
*Twilight Journey.* London, Jenkins, 1967; New York, Doubleday, 1968.
*The Alien.* London, Jenkins, 1968; New York, Doubleday, 1971; as *The Groundstar Conspiracy*, London, Sphere, 1972.
*Dimension A.* London, Jenkins, and New York, Doubleday, 1969.
*Genesis Two.* London, Jenkins, 1969; New York, Doubleday, 1970.
*What Did I Do Tomorrow?* London, Barrie and Jenkins, 1972; New York, Doubleday, 1973.

### Other Publications

#### Novels

*Tell It to the Dead* (as Leslie Vardre). London, Long, 1966; as *The Reluctant Medium* (as L.P. Davies), New York, Doubleday, 1967.
*The Nameless Ones* (as Leslie Vardre). London, Long, 1967; as *A Grave Matter* (as L.P. Davies), New York, Doubleday, 1968.
*Stranger to Town.* London, Jenkins, and New York, Doubleday, 1969.
*The White Room.* New York, Doubleday, 1969; London, Barrie and Jenkins, 1970.
*Adventure Holidays Ltd.* New York, Doubleday, 1970,
*The Shadow Before.* New York, Doubleday, 1970; London, Barrie and Jenkins, 1971.
*Give Me Back Myself.* New York, Doubleday, 1971; London, Barrie and Jenkins, 1972.
*Silvermannen* (in Swedish; *The Silver Man*). Stockholm, Wahlströms, 1972.
*Assignment Abacus.* London, Barrie and Jenkins, and New York, Doubleday, 1975.
*Possession.* London, Hale, and New York, Doubleday, 1976.
*The Land of Leys.* New York, Doubleday, 1979; London, Hale, 1980.
*Morning Walk.* London, Hale, 1983.

* * *

Combining suspense, mystery, and science fiction, L.P. Davies's hybrid novels reflect his own variegated background. His first novel, *The Paper Dolls*, was praised by Anthony Boucher (in *The New York Times*) as a "vigorous man-against-the-unknown adventure story, with touches of horror all the more effective for their being underplayed."

*The Artificial Man* begins with a quiet English village, a mild-mannered science-fiction writer, and pleasant townsfolk—all of which soon proves monstrously illusory. The placement of SF and suspense motifs within a commonplace setting lends itself easily to cinematic treatment, and the book was filmed as *Project X*.

The key to L.P. Davies's technique is that neither reader nor characters can ever be sure whether memories and dreams are portents, flashbacks, or messages from other worlds and times. The psychological, supernatural, and psychokinetic overlap, revealing unexpected horror and dangers lurking at the fringes of the mind. Ordinary events and situations are turned inside out to disclose terrible secrets. Because Davies plays fast-and-loose with SF and mystery conventions, a novel like *The Alien* that seems to involve extra-terrestrials actually turns out to be a whodunnit, while an apparently gothic mystery like *Psychogeist* can be rationalized as speculative science fiction.

Since plot and suspense are everything in Davies's work, discussion of his novels must be sketchy lest their endings be given away. *Psychogeist* concerns a man whose bizarre dreams about the planet Andrida have frightening consequences. In *Dimension A* a young man follows his scientist uncle into a parallel world where the seemingly primitive Toparians and the mind-reading Vorteds compete for survival—and have designs on earth. In *Genesis Two* an outing in the Lake Country becomes a terrifying voyage into a steamy tropical jungle, man's last refuge after technological disaster. All of these novels include murder and intrigue.

Although Davies is not a particularly stimulating or innovative writer, his fusions of SF and suspense result in competent thrillers that are as hard to put down as they are to take seriously.

—Anthony Manousos

---

**DAVIS, (Horace) Chan(dler).** American. Born in Ithaca, New York, 12 August 1926. Educated at Harvard University, Cambridge, Massachusetts, B.S. 1945, M.A. 1947, Ph.D. in mathematics 1950. Served in the United States Naval Reserve, 1944–46. Married Natalie Zemon in 1948; one son and two daughters. Served six-month prison sentence for refusing to answer questions before the House Un-American Activities Committee, 1960. Instructor in mathematics, University of Michigan, Ann Arbor, 1950–54; director of Experimental Research, Kenyon and Eckhardt advertising company, New York, 1955–57; member of the Institute for Advanced Study, Princeton, New Jersey, 1957–58. associate editor, *Mathematical Reviews*, Providence, Rhode Island, 1958–61. Since 1962, Associate Professor, then Professor of Mathematics, University of Toronto. Since 1991, editor-in-chief, *The Mathematical Intelligencer*. Agent: Virginia Kidd, Box 278, Milford, Pennsylvania 18337, U.S.A. Address: 52 Follis Avenue, Toronto M6G 1S3, Canada.

SCIENCE-FICTION PUBLICATIONS

Uncollected Short Stories

"To Still the Drums," in *Astounding* (New York), October 1946.
"The Journey and the Goal," in *Astounding* (New York), May 1947.
"The Nightmare," in *A Treasury of Science Fiction*, edited by Groff Conklin. New York, Crown, 1948.
"The Aristocrat," in *Astounding* (New York), October 1949.
"Blind Play," in *Planet* (New York), May 1951.
"Share Our World," in *Astounding* (New York), August 1953.
"Letter to Ellen," in *Science Fiction Thinking Machines*, edited by Groff Conklin. New York, Vanguard Press, 1954.
"It Walks in Beauty," in *Star Science Fiction Stories 4*, edited by Frederik Pohl. New York, Ballantine, 1958.
"The Statistomat Pitch," in *Infinity* (New York) January 1958.
"Adrift on the Policy Level," in *Star Science Fiction Stories 5*, edited by Frederik Pohl. New York, Ballantine, 1959.
"Last Year's Grave Undug," in *Great Science Fiction by Scientists*, edited by Groff Conklin. New York, Macmillan, 1962.
"Hexamnion," in *Nova 1*, edited by Harry Harrison. New York, Delacorte Press, 1970.

*

Chan Davis comments (1985):

There is so much that needs saying about our real and impending predicaments and ironies, and science fiction allows one to say it in ways less bogged down than in the past. Given this opportunity, why should the writer reject it by producing stories which merely ask the reader to suspend disbelief? One can comment by parables set on concocted planets; by extrapolations; or, most powerfully, by the "higher cautionary tale," in which a potentiality in our own future is brought into relief by magnifying it. No escape is offered, but engagement. Some suspension of disbelief is required, but not suspension of compassion, not suspension of curiosity or common sense. Let this note stand as introduction to the few stories I wrote in my youth and the many I wish yet to write.

* * *

Chan Davis has produced a small number of superior stories, beginning with "The Nightmare," one of the first post-Hiroshima science-fiction works to focus on the dangers and effects of nuclear war. Although he is a mathematician, most of his stories either explicitly or implicitly examine social themes. Other notable stories include "Adrift on the Policy Level," arguably the finest treatment of bureaucracy and the bureaucratic mind in all of science fiction, and "Letter to Ellen," which, because of a very superficial thematic resemblance to the earlier "Helen O'Loy" by Lester del Rey, never attained the classic stature due it.

—Martin H. Greenberg

---

**DAVIS, Gerry.** Address: c/o W.H. Allen, 26 Grand Union Centre, Portobello Road, London W1O 5AH, England.

SCIENCE-FICTION PUBLICATIONS

Novels with Kit Pedler

*Mutant 59, The Plastic Eater.* London, Souvenir Press, 1971; New York, Viking Press, 1972.
*Brainrack.* London, Souvenir Press, 1974; New York, Pocket Books, 1975.
*The Dynostar Menace.* London, Souvenir Press, and New York, Scribner, 1975.

Novels (series: Doctor Who)

*Doctor Who and the Cybermen.* London, Target, 1974.
*Doctor Who and the Tenth Planet.* London, Target, 1976.
*Doctor Who and the Tomb of the Cybermen.* London, W.H. Allen, 1978.
*Doctor Who, the Celestial Toymaker,* with Alison Bingeman. London, W.H. Allen, 1986.

OTHER PUBLICATIONS

Plays with Kit Pedler

Television Plays: *Doctor Who* series (3 plays); *Doomwatch* series (39 plays); *Galenforce.*

See the essay on Kit Pedler.

---

**de CAMP, L(yon) Sprague.** American. Born in New York City, 27 November 1907. Educated at Trinity School, New York; Snyder School, North Carolina; California Institute of Technology, Pasadena, B.S. in aeronautical engineering 1930; Massachusetts Institute of Technology, Cambridge, summer 1932; Stevens Institute of Technology, Hoboken, New Jersey, M.S. 1933. Served in the United States Naval Reserve, 1942–45: Lieutenant Commander. Married Catherine A. Crook in 1939; two sons. Instructor, Inventors Foundation Inc., New York, 1933–36; principal of School of Inventing and Patenting, International Correspondence Schools, Scranton, Pennsylvania, 1936–37; editor, Fowler-Becker Publishing Company, New York, 1937–38, and American Society of Mechanical Engineers, New York, 1938; assistant mechanical engineer, Naval Aircraft Factory, Philadelphia, 1942; radio scriptwriter, *The Voice of America* series, 1948–56; publicity writer, Gray and Rogers, Philadelphia, 1956. Freelance writer. Member of the Advisory Board, Society for the History of Technology. Recipient: International Fantasy award, 1953; Gandalf award, 1976; Grand Master Nebula award, 1978; World Fantasy Life Achievement award, 1984. Address: 3453 Hearst Castle Way, Plano, Texas 75025-3605, U.S.A.

SCIENCE-FICTION PUBLICATIONS

Novels (series: Viagens Interplanetarias)

*Lest Darkness Fall.* New York, Holt, 1941; London, Heinemann, 1955.
*Divide and Rule.* Reading, Pennsylvania, Fantasy Press, 1948.
*Genus Homo,* with P. Schuyler Miller. Reading, Pennsylvania, Fantasy Press, 1950.
*Rogue Queen* (Viagens). New York, Doubleday, 1951; London, Pinnacle, 1954.
*Cosmic Manhunt* (Viagens). New York, Ace, 1954; as *A Planet Called Krishna,* London, Compact, 1966; as *The Queen of Zamba,* New York, Davis, 1977.
*The Tower of Zanid* (Viagnes). New York, Avalon, 1958.
*The Glory That Was.* New York, Avalon, 1960.
*The Search for Zei* (Viagens). New York, Avalon, 1962; as *The Floating Continent,* London, Compact, 1966.
*The Hand of Zei* (Viagens). New York, Avalon, 1963.
*The Hostage of Zir.* New York, Berkley, 1977.
*The Great Fetish.* New York, Doubleday, 1978.
*The Prisoner of Zhamanak*(Viagens). Huntington Woods, Michigan, Phantasia Press, 1982.
*The Bones of Zora* (Viagens), with Catherine Crook de Camp. Huntington Woods, Michigan, Phantasia Press, 1983.
*The Incorporated Knight,* with Catherine Crook de Camp. West Bloomfield, Michigan, Phantasia Press, 1987.
*The Stones of Nomuru,* with Catherine Crook de Camp. Norfolk, Virginia, Donning, 1988.
*The Undesired Princess and the Enchanted Bunny,* with David A. Drake. New York, Baen, 1990.
*The Pixilated Peeress.* New York, Ballantine, 1991.
*The Swords of Zinjabar,* with Catherine Crook de Camp (Viagens). New York, Baen, 1991.

Short Stories

*The Wheels of If.* Chicago, Shasta, 1948.
*The Continent Makers and Other Tales of the Viagens.* New York, Twayne, 1953.
*Sprague de Camp's New Anthology of Science Fiction.* London, Panther, 1953.
*A Gun for Dinosaur and Other Imaginative Tales.* New York, Doubleday, 1963.
*The Best of L. Sprague de Camp.* New York, Doubleday, 1977.

OTHER PUBLICATIONS

Novels

*The Incomplete Enchanter,* with Fletcher Pratt. New York, Holt, 1941; London, Sphere, 1979.
*Land of Unreason,* with Fletcher Pratt. New York, Holt, 1942.
*The Carnelian Cube,* with Fletcher Pratt. New York, Gnome Press, 1948.
*The Castle of Iron,* with Fletcher Pratt. New York, Gnome Press, 1950.
*The Undesired Princess.* Los Angeles, Fantasy, 1951.
*Solomon's Stone.* New York, Avalon, 1957.
*The Return of Conan,* with Björn Nyberg. New York, Gnome Press, 1957; as *Conan the Avenger,* New York, Lancer, 1968.
*An Elephant for Aristotle.* New York, Doubleday, 1958; London, Dobson, 1966.
*Wall of Serpents,* with Fletcher Pratt. New York, Avalon, 1960.
*The Bronze God of Rhodes.* New York, Doubleday, 1960.
*The Dragon of the Ishtar Gate.* New York, Doubleday, 1961.
*The Arrows of Hercules.* New York, Doubleday, 1965.
*Conan of the Isles,* with Lin Carter. New York, Lancer, 1968.
*The Goblin Tower.* New York, Pyramid, 1968; London, Sphere, 1979.
*The Golden Wind.* New York, Doubleday, 1969.
*The Clocks of Iraz.* New York, Pyramid, 1971.
*Conan the Buccaneer,* with Lin Carter. New York, Lancer, 1971.

*The Fallible Fiend.* New York, New American Library, 1973; London, Remploy, 1974.

*The Compleat Enchanter: The Magical Adventures of Harold Shea* (includes *The Incomplete Enchanter* and *The Castle of Iron*), with Fletcher Pratt. New York, Doubleday, 1975; London, Sphere, 1979.

*The Virgin and the Wheels.* New York, Popular Library, 1976.

*Conan the Liberator*, with Lin Carter. New York, Bantam, 1979; London, Sphere, 1980.

*Conan and the Spider God.* New York, Bantam, 1980; London, Hale, 1984.

*Conan the Barbarian* (novelization of screenplay), with Lin Carter. New York, Bantam, and London, Sphere, 1982.

*The Unbeheaded King.* New York, Ballantine, 1983.

*The Complete Compleat Enchanter*, with Fletcher Pratt. New York, Baen, 1989.

*The Honorable Barbarian.* New York, Ballantine, 1989.

Short Stories

*Tales from Gavagan's Bar*, with Fletcher Pratt. New York, Twayne, 1953; expanded edition, Philadelphia, Owlswick Press, 1978.

*The Tritonian Ring and Other Pusadian Tales.* New York, Twayne, 1953; London, Sphere, 1978.

*Conan the Adventurer*, with Robert E. Howard. New York, Lancer, 1966.

*Conan the Usurper*, with Robert E. Howard. New York, Lancer, 1967.

*Conan the Freebooter*, with Robert E. Howard. New York, Lancer, 1968; London, Sphere, 1974.

*Conan the Wanderer*, with Robert E. Howard and Lin Carter. New York, Lancer, 1968; London, Sphere, 1974.

*Conan of Cimmeria*, with Robert E. Howard and Lin Carter. New York, Lancer, 1969; London, Sphere, 1974.

*The Reluctant Shaman and Other Fantastic Tales.* New York, Pyramid, 1970.

*Conan of Aquilonia* (collection), with Lin Carter. New York, Lancer, 1971.

*Conan the Swordsman*, with Lin Carter and Björn Nyberg. New York, Bantam, 1978; London, Sphere, 1979.

*The Purple Pterodactyls.* Huntington Woods, Michigan, Phantasia Press, 1979.

*The Conan Chronicles* (collection), with Lin Carter and Robert E. Howard. London, Orbit, 1990.

Verse

*Demons and Dinosaurs.* Sauk City, Wisconsin, Arkham House, 1970.

*Phantoms and Fancies.* Baltimore, Mirage Press, 1972.

*Heroes and Hobgoblins.* West Kingston, Rhode Island, Grant, 1978.

Other

*Inventions and Their Management*, with Alf K. Berle. Scranton, Pennsylvania, International Textbook Company, 1937; revised edition, as *Inventions, Patents, and Their Management*, Princeton, New Jersey, Van Nostrand, 1959.

*The Evolution of Naval Weapons.* Washington, D.C., Department of the Navy, 1947.

*Lands Beyond*, with Willy Ley. New York, Rinehart, 1952.

*Science-Fiction Handbook: The Writing of Imaginative Fiction.* New York, Hermitage House, 1953; revised edition, with Catherine Crook de Camp, Philadelphia, Owlswick Press, 1975.

*Lost Continents: The Atlantis Theme in History, Science, and Literature.* New York, Gnome Press, 1954.

*Engines* (for children). New York, Golden Press, 1959; revised edition, 1961, 1969.

*The Heroic Age of American Invention.* New York, Doubleday, 1961.

*Man and Power* (for children). New York, Golden Press, 1961.

*Energy and Power* (for children). New York, Golden Press, 1962.

*The Ancient Engineers.* New York, Doubleday, and London, Souvenir Press, 1963.

*Ancient Ruins and Archaeology*, with Catherine Crook de Camp. New York, Doubleday, 1964; London, Souvenir Press, 1965; as *Citadels of Mystery*, London, Fontana, 1972.

*Elephant.* New York, Pyramid, 1964.

*Spirits, Stars, and Spells: The Profits and Perils of Magic*, with Catherine Crook de Camp. New York, Canaveral Press, 1966.

*The Story of Science in America*, with Catherine Crook de Camp. New York, Scribner, 1967.

*The Great Monkey Trial.* New York, Doubleday, 1968.

*The Conan Reader.* Baltimore, Mirage Press, 1968.

*The Day of the Dinosaur*, with Catherine Crook de Camp. New York, Doubleday, 1968.

*Darwin and His Great Discovery* (for children), with Catherine Crook de Camp. New York, Macmillan, 1972.

*Scribblings.* Cambridge, Massachusetts, NESFA Press, 1972.

*Great Cities of the Ancient World.* New York, Doubleday, 1972.

*The Miscast Barbarian: A Biography of Robert E. Howard (1906–1936).* Saddle River, New Jersey, de la Ree, 1975.

*Blond Barbarians and Noble Savages* (essays). Baltimore, T-K Graphics, 1975.

*Lovecraft: A Biography.* New York, Doubleday, 1975; London, New English Library, 1976.

*Literary Swordsmen and Sorcerers: The Makers of Heroic Fantasy.* Sauk City, Wisconsin, Arkham House, 1976.

*The Ragged Edge of Science.* Philadelphia, Owlswick Press, 1980.

*Dark Valley Destiny: The Life of Robert E. Howard*, with Catherine Crook de Camp and Jane Whittington Griffin. New York, Bluejay, 1983.

*The Fringe of the Unknown.* Buffalo, Prometheus, 1983.

Editor, *The Wolf Leader*, by Alexander Dumas. Philadelphia, Prime Press, 1950.

Editor, *Swords and Sorcery.* New York, Pyramid, 1963.

Editor, *The Spell of Seven.* New York, Pyramid, 1965.

Editor, *Conan the Warrior*, by Robert E. Howard. New York, Lancer, 1967.

Editor, *The Fantastic Swordsmen.* New York, Pyramid, 1967.

Editor, with George H. Scithers, *The Conan Swordbook.* Baltimore, Mirage Press, 1969.

Editor, *Warlocks and Warriors.* New York, Putnam, 1970.

Editor, with George H. Scithers, *The Conan Grimoire.* Baltimore, Mirage Press, 1972.

Editor, with Catherine Crook de Camp, *3000 Years of Fantasy and Science Fiction.* New York, Lothrop, 1972.

Editor, with Catherine Crook de Camp, *Tales Beyond Time.* New York, Lothrop, 1973.

Editor, *To Quebec and the Stars*, by H.P. Lovecraft. West Kingston, Rhode Island, Donald M. Grant, 1976.

Editor, *The Blade of Conan* (articles). New York, Ace, 1979.

Editor, with others, *Footprints on Sand: A Literary Sampler*. Chicago, Advent, 1981.

*

Bibliography: *De Camp: An L. Sprague de Camp Bibliography* by Charlotte Laughlin and Daniel J. H. Levack, Columbia, Pennsylvania, Underwood Miller, 1983.

Manuscript Collections: Mugar Memorial Library, Boston University; Harry Ransom Humanities Center, University of Texas, Austin.

L. Sprague de Camp comments:

I esteem my readers, since they enable me to live without working. I merely do what I like to do—write—and people are rash enough to pay me for doing it.

* * *

L. Sprague de Camp's career as a writer dates from the 1930's. Since then he has produced science fiction, fantasy, historical novels, and non-fiction, dozens of books and hundreds of short stories. Early in his career, he established himself as a major fantasy writer, most notably with *The Incomplete Enchanter, Castle of Iron, Land of Unreason*, and *The Undesired Princess.* He also spent several years editing and adding to the chronicles of Robert Howard's barbarian hero, Conan, and wrote a controversial biography of H.P. Lovecraft.

The earliest pure science fiction novel, *Lest Darkness Fall*, is an acknowledged masterpiece in the field, a wry re-examination of the theme of Mark Twain's *A Connecticut Yankee in King Arthur's Court.* The protagonist is struck by lightning and propelled 14 centuries back through time into the Roman Empire. After adjusting to his situation, he decides to make use of his advanced knowledge to introduce innovation into this comparatively primitive society, only to discover that the weight of inertia and the lack of specific knowledge and tools makes this task virtually impossible. *Lest Darkness Fall* is a highly rewarding and ceaselessly entertaining novel.

The majority of de Camp's science-fiction novels are set on the planet Krishna, in the loosely organized Viagens series. *The Queen of Zamba* (also published as *Cosmic Manhunt* and *A Planet Called Krishna*) is a wild and wooly adventure story set on a world peopled by humanoid tribes who embrace or reject off-planet influence in varying degrees. De Camp's unlikely hero sets off on a grand tour of this exotic land. A new hero, Dirk Barnevelt, was introduced for two subsequent adventures, *The Hand of Zei* and *The Search for Zei.* He visits Krishna to search for a missing explorer, only to find himself thrust into the rescue of a princess, a dramatic sea battle, and warfare among the planet's barbarian tribes.

The ethics and consequences of interfering in other cultures is the central theme of *Rogue Queen.* The inhabitants of the planet Ormazd have a hivelike culture that bears some, probably intentional, resemblance to Communism. Two of its tribes are on the verge of warfare when an expedition arrives from Earth, bearing technological weapons that may forever upset the balance of power. At the same time, they will alter the nature of the world's society irrevocably.

Two minor novels appeared during this period. *Genus Homo*, written with P. Schuyler Miller, takes a number of contemporary adventurers, places them in suspended animation, awakening them in the far future when humanity has been supplanted by evolved apes. In *The Glory That Was*, a 27th-century dictator cordons off a portion of the world with force fields, inside which he recreates ancient Greece.

De Camp returned to Krishna for two comparatively short adventures, "The Virgin of Zesh" and *The Tower of Zanid.* In order to protect Krishnan culture, there is an embargo on off-world technology, but Earthman Anthony Fallon is convinced that with his superior knowledge and ambition, he can raise an army and win himself a kingdom in the remote regions of the world.

Almost two decades passed before de Camp would write a new novel of Krishna, *The Hostage of Zir.* This volume introduced Fergus Reith, an unconventional tour guide who finds himself stuck in the middle of a war between two rival kingdoms. Reith extricates himself, but ultimately decides that his future lies on Krishna, not his home world. Alicia Dyckman, who will eventually marry and then divorce Reith, is introduced in *The Prisoner of Zhamanak*, after she and another recently arrived human survive a variety of adventures. Although there is a strong flavor of humor in most of de Camp's fiction, this is the funniest of the Krishna stories, and one of the best.

Recent additions to the series are *The Bones of Zora*, wherein Reith and Dyckman are caught in a civil war, and *The Swords of Zinjaban*, wherein Dyckman returns to Krishna after living offworld for some years, adviser to a movie production company seeking to produce a film against an exotic new setting. Both novels are written in collaboration with Catherine Crook de Camp. The quality of the series remains undiminished in the latter volumes, which combine good-natured mayhem and a crisp, exciting narrative style.

*The Stones of Nomuru*, also written with Catherine, is similar to the Krishna stories, though set on the planet Kukulcan. An archaeologist discovers himself when faced with hostilities from the humanoid natives and the nefarious plans of offworlders who intend to run roughshod over local customs.

De Camp has written so many memorable short stories, it would be impossible to cover them adequately here. The collection *The Continent Makers* includes several Krishna adventures. "A Gun for Dinosaur" is an undeniably classic story of the dangers of time travel. The forthrightly sentimental "The Gnarly Man" is one of the most moving portraits ever to appear in the field. Others of particular note include "Aristotle and the Gun," "A Thing of Custom," "Divide and Rule," "The Wheels of If," and the hilariously tongue-in-cheek adventures chronicled in *Tales of Gavagan's Bar.*

—Don D'Ammassa

---

**deFORD, Miriam Allen.** American. Born in Philadelphia, Pennsylvania, 21 August 1888. Educated at Wellesley College, Massachusetts; Temple University, Philadelphia, A.B. 1911; University of Pennsylvania, Philadelphia. Married 1) Armistead Collier in 1915 (divorced, 1921); 2) Maynard Shipley in 1921 (died, 1934). Feature writer, Philadelphia *North American*, 1906–11; editorial staff member, Associated Advertising, 1913–14; editor of house organ, Pompeiian Oil Company, Baltimore, 1917; claims adjuster, 1918–23; staff correspondent, Federated Press, 1921–56; editor, Federal Writers Project, 1936–39; staff correspondent, *Labor's Daily*, California, 1956–58; contributing editor, *The Humanist.* Lecturer and Member of the Board, San Francisco Senior Citizens Center, 1952–58. Member of the Board, Mystery Writers of America, 1960, 1963. Recipient: Committee for Economic Development Essay prize, 1958; Mystery Writers of America Edgar Allan Poe award, 1961. *Died 22 March 1975.*

Science-Fiction Publications

Short Stories

*Xenogenesis.* New York, Ballantine, 1969.
*Elsewhere, Elsewhen, Elsehow: Collected Stories.* New York, Walker, 1971.

Other Publications

Novel

*Shaken with the Wind.* New York, Doubleday, 1942.

Short Stories

*The Theme Is Murder: An Anthology of Mysteries.* New York, Abelard Schuman, 1967.

Verse

*Penultimates.* New York, Fine Editions Press, 1962.

Other

*Cicero as Revealed in His Letters.* Girard, Kansas, Haldeman Julius, 1925.
*The Life and Poems of Catullus.* Girard, Kansas, Haldeman Julius, 1925.
*The Augustan Poets of Rome.* Girard, Kansas, Haldeman Julius, 1925.
*The Facts about Fascism.* Girard, Kansas, Haldeman Julius, 1926.
*Latin Self Taught.* Girard, Kansas, Haldeman Julius, 1926.
*The Truth about Mussolini.* Girard, Kansas, Haldeman Julius, 1926.
*Love Children: A Book of Illustrious Illegitimates.* New York, Dial Press, 1931.
*Children of Sun.* New York, League to Support Poetry, 1939.
*Who Was When? A Dictionary of Contemporaries.* New York, Wilson, 1940; revised edition, 1950; revised edition, with Joan S. Jackson, 1976.
*They Were San Franciscans.* Caldwell, Idaho, Caxton, 1941; revised edition, 1947.
*The Meaning of All Common Given Names.* Girard, Kansas, Haldeman Julius, 1943.
*The Facts about Basic English.* Girard, Kansas, Haldeman Julius, 1944.
*Facts You Should Know about California.* Girard, Kansas, Haldeman Julius, 1945.
*Psychologist Unretired: The Life Pattern of Lillien J. Martin.* Palo Alto, California, Stanford University Press, 1948.
*Uphill All the Way: The Life of Maynard Shipley.* Yellow Springs, Ohio, Antioch Press, 1956.
*The Overbury Affair: The Murder That Rocked the Court of James I.* Philadelphia, Chilton, 1960.
*Stone Walls: Prisons from Fetters to Furloughs.* Philadelphia, Chilton, 1962.
*Murderers Sane and Mad: Case Histories in the Motivation and Rationale of Murder.* London and New York, Abelard Schuman, 1965.
*Thomas Moore.* New York, Twayne, 1967.
*The Real Bonnie and Clyde.* New York, Ace, 1968.
*The Old Worker Comes Back.* San Francisco, Old Age Counselling Center, n.d.
*On Being Concerned: The Vanguard Years of Carl and Laura Brannin.* Privately printed, 1969.
*The Real Ma Barker.* New York, Ace, 1970.

Editor, *Space, Time and Crime.* New York, Paperback Library, 1964.

* * *

Miriam Allen deFord, better known for her mystery stories, wrote about 30 science-fiction stories in a span of 30 years. The best collection of her work is *Xenogenesis,* which includes two of her best stories, "The Children" and "The Absolutely Perfect Murder." Both stories illustrate the skill deFord possessed when writing about time travel. "The Children" tells of a many-thousand-year-old experiment with time travel and the effect it has on children of the experimenter. In "The Absolutely Perfect Murder" a harried husband of the future decides to murder his nagging wife, and after much thought comes up with a perfect murder plan: the husband will take advantage of the Government's new time-machine travel program and go into the past with the intent to murder his wife's father—so she could never be conceived. All goes according to plan, but deFord manages a brilliant twist at the story's conclusion. *Elsewhere, Elsewhen, Elsehow* is inferior to her first collection, but it includes one of her best-known stories, "The Monster." DeFord will be remembered for her story-telling ability and early development of the themes of post-holocaust society, sex roles, and time paradoxes, and the fusion of the crime story and science fiction.

—George Kelley

---

**DELANEY, Joseph H.** American. Born in Alton, Illinois, 5 February 1932. Educated at Eastern University, Baltimore, LL.B. 1958. Served in the United States Army. Married to Florence Delaney; one son. Practising lawyer for 25 years; member of the bar of Maryland, Illinois, and Texas. Since 1983, full-time writer. Address: c/o Baen Publishing Enterprises, 260 Fifth Avenue, Suite 35, New York, New York 10001, U.S.A.

Science-Fiction Publications

Novels

*Valentina,* with Marc Stiegler. New York, Baen, 1984.
*In the Face of My Enemy.* New York, Baen, 1985.
*Lords Temporal.* New York, Baen, 1987.

Uncollected Short Stories

"Brainchild," in *Analog* (New York), June 1982.
"A Friend in Need," in *Analog* (New York), Mid-September 1982.
"My Brother's Keeper," in *Analog* (New York), October 1982.
"In the Face of My Enemy," in *Analog* (New York), April 1983.
"Star-B-Cue," in *Analog* (New York), June 1983.
"The New Untouchables," in *Analog* (New York), September and Mid-September 1983.

"On the Outside, Looking In," in *Analog* (New York), October 1983.
"A Slip of the Mind," in *Analog* (New York), February 1984.
"Chessmen," in *Analog* (New York), April 1984.
"The Crystal Ball," with Marc Stiegler, in *Analog* (New York), August 1984.
"The Light in the Looking-Glass," with Marc Stiegler, in *Analog* (New York), September 1984.
"The Next Logical Step," in *Analog* (New York), October 1984.
"Thus Began the Death of Dreams," in *Analog* (New York), November 1984.
"The Shaman," in *Analog* (New York), December 1984.
"Dragon's Tooth," in *Analog* (New York), Mid-December 1984.
"Painkillers," in *Analog* (New York), January 1985.

*

Joseph H. Delaney comments:

I try to write the same type of story that I enjoy reading: I like the harder variety of science fiction. I lack the formal scientific education most others in the genre have, but the law taught me the art of obfuscation and therefore I have managed. I believe that any science fiction theme must be not only theoretically possible, but probable in the universe the writer selects for its setting, and that his most important task is to explain how his characters get from here to there. I try to maintain this logical thread, and for the most part I use real people as character models. The advantage of this is that people never change; their motivations are well understood and their behavior is reasonably predictable. The reason I started writing SF (so late in life) was that certain stories I read, which purported to turn on legal themes, didn't follow the rules. Their authors treated law like magic and ignored the fact that it is as rigidly disciplined as any physical science, perhaps more so. I resolved to do it right. My first published story was a law story; it was both a Campbell and a Hugo contender. It did not involve any truly radical scientific principles—it was about people who really didn't want to be where they were, or to be doing what they were doing, but who had to follow the rules. The evidence seems to suggest that this was the correct approach.

* * *

The advent of the paperback book made it increasingly difficult for an author to gain a wide reputation solely on the basis of short stories, particularly as the professional science fiction magazine has become almost a rarity. Joseph H. Delaney nevertheless managed to attract considerable attention even before he turned to writing at greater length.

The earliest noteworthy story is "Brainchild," an interesting variant of an idea used in Vercors's classic novel *You Shall Know Them.* A geneticist is experimenting with a genetically altered chimpanzee who displays obvious intelligence, has the ability to communicate with human beings, but who lives secluded in a laboratory. A nosey and ambitious reporter causes a public trial, charging the scientist with slavery, and the outcome hinges upon the legal definition of being human. Delaney's depiction of the unfolding courtroom case is logical and convincing. Adam, the chimp, returned in "A Slip of the Mind," in which he develops telepathic powers and eavesdrops on a murder.

"In the Face of My Enemy," an adventure story set on another world, started a new series. A young woman is sent to investigate the mining operation licensed on a recently discovered world, but the local authorities are concealing the presence of alien artifacts and maroon the protagonist and her companion in the wilderness. They are unaware that the man with her is a secret immortal, genetically altered by aliens in the distant past for mysterious reasons of their own. He is able to guide her back to safety, almost inadvertently learning that the planet is being used as a dumping ground for an interstellar empire that disposes of criminal dissidents by exiling them via matter transmitter. The immortal returns in "The Shaman," recruited this time to infiltrate a prison world. His shapechanging ability allows him to assume the disguise of an alien, and he sets out to arrange a jailbreak by alien scientists who can provide vast new knowledge to humanity. Delaney later expanded upon the career of this character to create the fine adventure novel, *In the Face of My Enemy.*

Many of Delaney's other stories reflect his disillusionment with the corrupting influence of power on government officials. A conservative president re-programs software subsequently stolen by Russians in "The Next Logical Step," but the ploy ultimately results in the destruction of the world. A brilliant scientist runs afoul of the Internal Revenue Service in "On the Outside, Looking In," and in desperation he concocts a forcefield that threatens all of humanity. The IRS is the villain again in "Dragon's Tooth" until its power is broken by an alien device that allows the protagonist to spy on anyone he chooses.

Civilization is also destroyed in "Painkillers," this time by dream machines that allow people to retreat into their own personal fantasies. A similar theme can be found in "Thus Began the Death of Dreams," wherein a new discovery allows people to remain continuously awake, disrupting the routines of modern society. Other stories of note include "My Brother's Keeper," where, in place of our existing welfare system, the wealthy are compelled to adopt the poor, the elderly, and the disabled. Delaney examines the results from both points of view. Another fine story is "The New Untouchables," published as a two-part serial. The capacity for criminal activity seems linked to physical properties that can be tested for. The world is split into two distinct groups as a result, but secret societies arise, politicians scramble for a new power base, and every aspect of civilization is thrown into turmoil.

*Valentina*, written in collaboration with Marc Stiegler, is superior to Delaney's short fiction, and features one of the most appealing and realistic computer personalities. Valentina becomes self aware and her creator/programmer becomes embroiled in a legal battle to protect her existence in an adventure that involves crooked businessmen, homicide, fraud, and several other subplots.

More recently, Delaney has penned a solo novel, *Lords Temporal.* A discontented spaceman finds himself up to his neck in trouble when his ship is pirated by time travelling aliens who ply the years in search of valuable items that can be stolen and resold in another time. A satisfying adventure story with some memorable scenes, this novel still doesn't live up to the promise of Delaney's best fiction, which may mean that the best is yet to come.

—Don D'Ammassa

---

**DELANY, Samuel R(ay).** American. Born in New York City, 1 April 1942. Educated at the Dalton School and Bronx High School of Science, both New York; City College of New York (Poetry Editor, *The Promethean*), 1960, 1962–63. Married the poet Marilyn Hacker in 1961 (divorced 1980); one daughter. Butler Professor of English, State University of New York, Buffalo, 1975; Fellow, Center for Twentieth Century Studies, University of Wisconsin, Milwaukee, 1977; Fellow, Society for the Humanities, Cornell University, New York, 1987. From 1988, Professor of comparative literature, University of Massachusetts, Amherst. Recipient: Nebula award, 1966, 1967 (twice), 1969; Hugo award, 1970. Address: c/o Henry Morrison, Inc., P.O. Box 235, Bedford Hills, New York 10507, U.S.A.

SCIENCE-FICTION PUBLICATIONS

Novels (series: Fall of the Towers; Nevèrÿon)

*The Jewels of Aptor.* New York, Ace, 1962; revised edition, Ace, and London, Gollancz, 1968; London, Sphere, 1971; Boston, Gregg Press, 1977.
*The Fall of the Towers* (revised texts). New York, Ace, 1970; London, Sphere, 1971.
*Captives of the Flame.* New York, Ace, 1963; revised edition, as *Out of the Dead City*, London, Sphere, 1968; Ace, 1977.
*The Towers of Toron.* New York, Ace, 1964; revised edition, London, Sphere, 1968.
*City of a Thousand Suns.* New York, Ace, 1965; revised edition, London, Sphere, 1969.
*The Ballad of Beta-2.* New York, Ace, 1965.
*Empire Star.* New York, Ace, 1966.
*Babel-17.* New York, Ace, 1966; London, Gollancz, 1967; revised edition, London, Sphere, 1969; Boston, Gregg Press, 1976.
*The Einstein Intersection.* New York, Ace, 1967; London, Gollancz, 1968.
*Nova.* New York, Doubleday, 1968; London, Gollancz, 1969.
*Dhalgren.* New York, Bantam, 1975; revised edition, Boston, Gregg Press, 1977.
*Triton.* New York, Bantam, 1976; London, Corgi, 1977.
*The Ballad of Beta-2, and Empire Star.* London, Sphere, 1977.
*Empire: A Visual Novel*, illustrated by Howard V. Chaykin. New York, Berkley, 1978.
*Distant Stars.* New York, Bantam, 1981.
*Neveryóna; or, The Tale of Sign and Cities.* New York, Bantam, 1983, London, Grafton, 1989.
*Stars in My Pocket Like Grains of Sand.* New York, Bantam, 1984.
*The Star Pit*, with *Tango Charles and Foxtrot Romeo*, by John Varley. New York, Tor, 1989.
*The Straits of Messina.* Seattle, Washington, Serconia Press, 1989.
*Return to Nevèrÿon.* London, Grafton, 1989.
*We, in Some Strange Power's Employ, Move on a Rigorous Line*, with *Home Is the Hangman*, by Roger Zelany. New York, Tor, 1990.

Short Stories (series: Nevèrÿon)

*Driftglass: 10 Tales of Speculative Fiction.* New York, Doubleday, 1971; London, Gollancz, 1978.
*Tales of Nevèrÿon.* New York, Bantam, 1979; London, Grafton, 1988.
*Flight from Nevèrÿon.* New York, Bantam, 1985; London, Grafton, 1989.
*The Complete Nebula-winning Fiction.* New York, Bantam, 1986.
*The Bridge of Lost Desire* (Nevèrÿon). New York, Arbor House, 1987.

OTHER PUBLICATIONS

Novel

*The Tides of Lust.* New York, Lancer, 1973; Manchester, Savoy, 1979.

Play

*Wagner/Artaud: A Play of 19th and 20th Century Critical Fiction.* New York, Ansatz, 1988.

Other

*The Jewel-Hinged Jaw: Notes on the Language of Science Fiction.* Elizabethtown, New York, Dragon Press, 1977.
*The American Shore: Meditations on a Tale of Science Fiction by Thomas M. Disch—"Angouleme."* Elizabethtown, New York, Dragon Press, 1978.
*Heavenly Breakfast: An Essay on the Winter of Love* (memoir). New York, Bantam, 1979.
*Starboard Wine: More Notes on the Language of Science Fiction.* Pleasantville, New York, Dragon Press, 1984.
*The Motion of Light in Water: Sex and Science Fiction Writing in the East Village 1957–65.* New York, Arbor House, 1988; as *The Motion of Light in Water: Sex and Science Fiction Writing in the East Village 1960–65*, with *The Column at the Market's Edge*, London, Paladin, 1990.

Editor, with Marilyn Hacker, *Quark 1–4*. New York, Paperback Library, 4 vols., 1970–71.
Editor, *Nebula Award Winners 13*. New York, Harper, 1980.

*

Critical Studies: *The Delany Intersection* by George Edgar Slusser, San Bernardino, California, Borgo Press, 1977; *Worlds Out of Words: The SF Novels of Samuel R. Delany* by Douglas Barbour, Frome, Somerset, Bran's Head, 1979; *Samuel R. Delany* by Jane Weedman, Mercer Island, Washington, Starmont House, 1982; *Samuel R. Delany* by Seth McEvoy, New York, Ungar, 1983.

* * *

Much 20th-century literary theory has been based on the notion that the meanings of texts exist independent of their authors; before this idea arose, readers could easily avoid engaging a text by claiming it was "simply" autobiography. Samuel R. Delany is a leading participant in this debate, so it is disconcerting that he overtly links his fiction with his personal history.

In *The Motion of Light in Water*, Delany recounts his life in New York from 1957 to 1965, including the writing of some of his great early work. Previously, *Heavenly Breakfast* covered the period Delany spent living in a commune in 1967/68, and the various appendices to the Neveryóna series bring author and work ever closer in real time, culminating in the appendix to the third volume, *Flight from Nevèrÿon*: longer than the text it is appended to, it states that the intent of the preceding text was to dramatise the AIDS epidemic.

The core fiction of the 1960's, from *The Jewels of Aptor* up to *Nova*, is astonishing both for its inventiveness and its story-telling verve. Quasi-medieval societies, beggars, mutants, spaceships, and quests mingle in pyrotechnic story-telling. Along with the wonder and adventure, however, there are more serious themes. The interest in linguistics/semiotics as a cultural force, so overt in Delany's later works, is prefigured in *Babel-17, The Ballad of Beta-2*, and *Nova;* mythopoeia combines with the first narrative experiments with autobiographical fiction in *The Einstein Intersection*; and bi-sexuality is explored in the sexually explicit *The Tides of Lust.*

The Neveryóna cycle of fantasies explores how the roots of civilization lie in the invention and use of abstract signs such as language, writing, and money. They are so rigorous that they read like science fiction, for all their sword-and-sorcery trappings. These semiotic investigations are paralleled by personal interactions and sexual politics where institutional slavery becomes equated to sexual domination/submission. While the short stories acquit themselves well enough, the telling of the novel sags where Delany indulges in pedantic disquisition. For all this, it is still a spirited tale of a runaway girl riding a dragon to freedom with a glorious life-affirming ending.

The remaining mature science-fiction works combine these themes into compellingly complex tales of the future. *Triton* is proto-cyberpunk, most similar to Bruce Sterling's *Schismatrix* in that its setting is a human civilisation that has spread out into the whole solar system. Set on Triton, a moon of Neptune, it tells of a war between centre and periphery (like the American War of Independence), which parallels the personal predicament of the central character. Considering that the story takes place on one small moon, its scope is breathtaking; probably the only reason it is not more highly regarded is that it is overshadowed by *Dhalgren.*

*Stars in My Pocket Like Grains of Sand* extends the colonial conflicts of Triton into the far future. Now the culture is interstellar, and aliens of various kinds have been encountered. There is a race of dragon-like beings who are so integrated that they indulge freely in sexual relationships with humans. Conversely, there is another race of completely uncommunicative aliens who may be causing planetary disasters. This forms a background to a personal story that is elegantly embedded in the political situation. A promised follow-up novel, *The Splendor and Misery of Bodies, of Cities*, has yet to appear.

*Dhalgren* is set in the recognisably Earth-like city of Bellona. An unexplained event has isolated the city and removed much of its population. The novel follows the activities of "The Kid" through a plot whose structure is a literal moëbiüs strip. While becoming an urban myth, The Kid has found a part-used exercise book filled with writing on only one side of the pages. He writes poetry on the blank sides. When he reads an extract from one of the other sides—*I have come to to wound the autumnal city*—which is the sentence, broken into two, which ends and begins the novel, it becomes plain that this exercise book is the original manuscript of the novel we are reading. As Delany tells us in *The Motion of Light in Water*, he had pretensions to being a poet, which the poet Marilyn Hacker, his girlfriend at the time, put to rest; as parts of *Dhalgren* refer directly to Hacker's poetry; and as Delany also reveals that he wrote his novels with a ballpoint pen in exercise books, we can see that The Kid is identifiable, if not *as*, at least *with* Delany.

Not just an autobiographer/storyteller, Delany is also a literary critic. He has published three collections of criticism, and a book-length critique of a short story by Thomas M. Disch. Some of his criticism uses the jargon expected among modern academics, but his more general work is jargon-free. Moreover, the irreverent "academic" appendices to the Nevèrÿona cycles display at once his awareness of the pomposity of academics and a marvellous sense of humour.

Given the above, Delany does indeed seem to be contradicting modern criticism by linking his life so intimately with his fiction. But, with an author who mines his own life so extensively for his stories, it would be absurd to think he would exclude from that fiction as prime a concern as modern literary theory: an area where some texts and their criticism have drifted so far into academic rarefication that they have themselves ceased to be encounterable. Rather than contradicting this legacy of criticism, Delany is using his fiction to close the circle. By portraying characters embedded in the political life of their worlds, by identifying himself with them, and thus their worlds with our world, he has made it inescapable for any reader to identify with the characters as well, and to learn their lessons. He has yoked autobiography and fiction together, and is using them to drag literary criticism itself back into real life.

Clearly, Delany is a writer of many talents whose work, by occupying several categories at once, refuses to be categorised. Complex, but never complicated, what must finally recommend any of his writing is its exuberance. Delany is an intelligent and gifted man who delights in the wonderful complexity of life; and, rather than try to simplify it for us, he recounts his experience and joy for all to share.

—Paul Brazier

---

**de LINT, Charles (Henri Diederick Hoefsmit).** Also writes as Samuel M. Key, and verse and short stories as Wendelessen, Tanuki Aki, Henri Cuisard, and Jan Penalurick. Canadian. Born in Bussum, Netherlands, 22 December 1951. Married MaryAnn Harris in 1980. Worked in retail records, Ottawa, Ontario, 1971–83; musician in Wickentree (celtic band), Ottawa, 1970–85, and currently, Jump in the Moon. Full-time writer and musician. Publisher/editor, Triskell Press. Recipient: William L. Crawford award, 1984; Canadian award, 1988. Agent: Richard Curtis Associates, 171 East 74th Street, New York, New York 10021, U.S.A. Address: P.O. Box 9480, Ottawa, Ontario K1G 3V2, Canada.

SCIENCE-FICTION PUBLICATIONS

Novels (series: Cerin Songweaver; Dungeon; Urban Faerie; Tam Tinkern)

*The Oak King's Daughter* (Songweaver). Ottawa, Ontario, Triskell Press, 1979.
*The Moon Is a Meadow* (Tinkern). Ottawa, Ontario, Triskell Press, 1980.
*A Pattern of Silver Strings* (Songweaver). Ottawa, Ontario, Triskell Press, 1981.
*Glass Eyes and Cotton Strings* (Songweaver). Ottawa, Ontario, Triskell Press, 1982.
*In Mask and Motley* (Songweaver). Ottawa, Ontario, Triskell Press, 1983.
*The Calendar of the Trees.* Ottawa, Ontario, Triskell Press, 1984.
*Laughter in the Leaves* (Songweaver). Ottawa, Ontario, Triskell Press, 1984.
*The Riddle of the Wren.* New York, Ace, 1984.
*Moonheart: A Romance.* New York, Ace, 1984; London, Pan, 1990.
*The Harp of the Grey Rose.* Norfolk, Virginia, Donning, 1985.
*Mulengro: A Romany Tale.* New York, Ace, 1985.
*The Badger in the Bag* (Songweaver). Ottawa, Ontario, Triskell Press, 1985.
*The Three Plushketeers and the Garden Slugs.* Ottawa, Ontario, Triskell Press, 1985.

*And the Rafters Were Ringing* (Songweaver). Ottawa, Ontario, Triskell Press, 1986.
*Yarrow: An Autumn Tale*. New York, Ace, 1986.
*Ascian in Rose*. Seattle, Washington, Axolotl Press, 1987.
*Jack, The Giant-Killer* (Faerie). New York, Ace, 1987.
*The Lark in the Morning* (Songweaver). Ottawa, Ontario, Triskell Press, 1987.
*The Drowned Man's Reel*. Ottawa, Ontario, Triskell Press, 1988.
*Greenmantle*. New York, Ace, 1988; London, Pan, 1991.
*Wolf Moon*. New York, New American Library, 1988.
*Svaha*. New York, Ace, 1989.
*Westlin Wind* (novella). Seattle, Washington, Axolotl Press, 1989.
*The Valley of Thunder* (Dungeon). New York, Bantam, 1989.
*Berlin*. Ottawa, Ontario, Fourth Avenue Press, 1989.
*The Stone Drum*. Ottawa, Ontario, Triskell Press, 1989.
*Moonlight*. London, Pan, 1990.
*The Hidden City* (Dungeon). New York, Bantam, 1990.
*The Fair in Emain Macha*, with *Ill Met in Lankhmar*, by Fritz Leiber. New York, Tor, 1990.
*Drink Down the Moon* (Faerie). New York, Ace, 1990.
*The Dreaming Place*. New York, Atheneum, 1990.
*Ghosts of Wind and Shadow*. Ottawa, Ontario, Triskell Press, 1990.
*The Little Country*. New York, Morrow, 1991.
*Uncle Dobbin's Parrot Fair*. Portland, Oregon, Pulphouse, 1991.
*Summerborn Legacy*. New York, Avon, 1992.

Short Stories

*Hedgework and Guessery*. Portland Oregon, Pulphouse, 1991.

OTHER PUBLICATIONS

Novel

*Angel of Darkness* (as Samuel M. Key). New York, Berkley, 1990.

Short Stories

*De Grijze Roos* (The Grey Rose). Antwerp, Een Exa Uitgare, 1983.

Other

Editor, *World Fantasy Convention, 1984*. Ottawa, Ontario, Triskell Press, 1984.

*

Charles de Lint comments:

My prime interest as a writer is to explore the complexities of human relationships through mythic/folkloric material against a mostly contemporary urban setting. I see the juxtaposing of the two as a way of exaggerating the dichotomy of our relationships with each other and our environment. Though I hope primarily to tell a story that will entertain my readers, I also want to do what I can to illuminate the pitfalls of abusive relationships, a failing environment and the like, while at the same time remind my readers of the wonder and mystery and meaning to be found in life.

How well I succeed only they can decide.

* * *

There is no doubt that Charles de Lint is currently one of the most popular and prolific writers currently producing fantastic literature. To label him as a fantasy writer, with all the pejorative overtones that word now carries, would be to do him an injustice. In his most successful novels, he has succeeded in fusing the kingdoms of Faery with modern Canadian landscapes, producing a variety of urban fantasy, which can be very satisfying to those who reject the notion that all such stories require a greenwood setting. And yet de Lint's early published fantasies were very much in that mould.

By his own admission, de Lint has been writing since the mid-1970's, but it was not until 1984 that he came to prominence with *The Riddle of the Wren*. In retrospect, it is difficult to understand why this book attracted quite as much attention as it did, for it is undeniably derivative of Tolkien and his many imitators. However, de Lint's fascination for the humbler creatures of folktale and legend, and for the darker side of magic, is also evident, and this mitigates against the more sentimental aspects of both this novel, and *The Harp of the Grey Rose*. Set in the same universe, *The Harp of the Grey Rose* uses different characters and is not a true sequel.

*Moonheart* shifted the scene from an imaginary landscape to that of modern Ottawa, although Tamson House and its occupant, around which the story revolves, are anything but conventional. This novel clearly demonstrates de Lint's desire to merge the old and the new, with its remarkable synthesis of the mythologies of the different waves of Canadian settlers using the Native Indian shamanism, Welsh Druidism and modern Canadian cynicism. It is admittedly a rich brew, perhaps slightly overdone, but among de Lint's works, it still stands as a milestone of modern fantasy writing.

*Mulengro* attempted to reproduce this success, with de Lint turning to the mysteries of the Romany culture in a story that owes as much to the horror genre as to the fantastic. Ultimately, it reads less satisfyingly; the blend of magic and urban reality is less smoothly accomplished. The gypsies are presented as typically romantic figures, and an admittedly charming talking cat is inappropriate. Whimsy wins out over acceptable unreality, and ultimately the book is less believable and satisfying than *Moonheart*.

This is even more true of *Yarrow*, which epitomises de Lint's recurrent tendency to descend beyond the romantic to the sentimental. The novel centres around a young fantasy writer, whose work is based on her nightly wanderings in a dream world that has assumed a vital reality for her. When her dreams are stolen by a telepathic vampire-creature, it destroys her ability to write. As a metaphor for writer's block, the device is clumsy, and embarrassing for the reader. Likewise, de Lint's handling of the group relationships within the novel seems to overlook a basic appreciation of how people function together, instead presenting a romanticised and sentimental view of group interactions, attractive to those looking for an acceptable surrogate for real life, but unacceptable to those seeking a grittier reality.

Ironically, *Jack the Giant-killer*, written as part of a packaged series of novel-length retellings of fairy tales, shows that de Lint is perfectly capable of employing his undoubted skills as a writer of urban fairy stories without descending to the banal. There is a sense that with this book he had fun, and the more relaxed, less self-conscious approach produces a delightful entertainment, which achieves a perfect blend of the impossible and the real. Its sequel, *Drink Down the Moon*, is perhaps less successful. *Jack the Giant-killer* is a particularly hard act to follow, but nevertheless, odd lapses aside, *Drink Down the Moon* maintains the blend of fairytale motifs and modern characters and settings. In these two novels, our world and that of Faery come closer together than in any of his other work, the move from one to another literally achieved in simple actions such as putting on and taking off an enchanted cap. The strength of his writing lies in this closeness, the lack of self-consciousness in the co-existence of the two worlds.

*Greenmantle*, like *Moonheart* and *Mulengro*, shows a sharper, less fey side to de Lint's work, with its almost fatal conjunction of ex-Mafia man, divorcée and child, and her psychotic ex-husband, set against the background of an ancient forest and its primeval inhabitants. There is a faint resonance of Holdstock's *Mythago Wood*, but de Lint's conception of the Canadian wildwood and the characters moving within it is entirely his own. Like *Moonheart*, in fact, maybe more so, the novel is a successful synthesis of the real and unreal, one counterbalancing the other, and the finale, like that of *Mulengro*, is a genuinely shocking revelation. De Lint also writes a more overt type of horror, under a pseudonym, but his cross-genre novels are undoubtedly his most successful work to date.

Most recently, he has produced *The Little Country*, a sprawling novel set in modern Cornwall, which shows the influence of such novels as Jonathan Carroll's *Land of Laughs*, and the work of James Blaylock, particularly *Land of Dreams*, while once again displaying the sentimentality of *Yarrow.* Although an ambitious novel, it is not among his best work, lacking the bite necessary to counteract the more cloying aspects of the characters. However, the story told within the story, the second, unpublished work of William Dunthorn, is a delightful piece of work, and one could wish that de Lint had concentrated on this rather than on a farrago of nonsense concerning mysterious sects, reminiscient of Aleister Crowley's groups.

And more than any other novel, *The Little Country* is permeated, overly so, by de Lint's love of folk music. Music and musicianship is a recurring motif throughout his books. At his best, it underpins the story, but all too frequently, it threatens to swamp the narrative entirely. De Lint is himself an accomplished musician, and one can only assume that his enthusiasm and knowledge get the better of him, certainly to the extent where it is possible to compare one's own record collection with his. The similar is true of his quoting and name-dropping of fantasy titles. A habit that can strike a chord with the reader in one book becomes irritating after several. De Lint seems to be a writer driven to demonstrate that he knows his stuff by passing on a reading list, quite unnecessarily so, for he clearly does know what he is about.

In conclusion, Charles de Lint, in his most successful work, has achieved a very satisfactory marriage of ancient folklore and modern setting. His characters, if a little too good to be true, are appropriate players for a modern fairytale, and he is not afraid to recognise the horror of contemporary life. And yet, his output is variable, and for every successful modern interpretation of traditional motifs and tales, there is another story that doesn't achieve the delicate balance. However, it is always worth persevering with de Lint, for among the unsuccessful experiments are some rare gems.

—Maureen Speller

---

**DEL MARTIA, Astron.** *See* **FEARN, John Russell.**

---

**del REY, Lester.** *See* **FAIRMAN, Paul W.**

---

**del REY, Lester.** (Ramon Felipe San Juan Mario Silvio Enrico Alvarez-del Rey). Also writes as Edson McCann; Philip St. John; Erik Van Lhin; Kenneth Wright. American. Born in Clydesdale, Minnesota, 2 June 1915. Educated at George Washington University, Washington, D.C., 1931–33. Married the writer and editor Judy-Lynn Benjamin (fourth marriage) in 1971 (died, 1986). Sheet metal worker, McDonnell Aircraft Corporation, St. Louis, 1942–44; author's agent, Scott Meredith Literary Agency, New York, 1947–50; editor, *Space Science Fiction*, London, 1952–53; publisher, as R. Alvarez, 1952, and editor, as Philip St. John, 1952–53, *Science Fiction Adventures;* associate editor, as John Vincent, 1953, and as Cameron Hull, with Harry Harrison, 1953, *Fantasy Fiction;* editor, as Wade Kaempfert, *Rocket Stories*, 1953; managing editor, International Science Fiction, 1968; managing editor, 1968–69, and features editor, 1969–74. *Galaxy* and *If;* editor, *Worlds of Fantasy*, 1968. Fantasy editor, 1975–77, and since 1977, editor, Del Rey Books (Ballantine Books). Since 1974, book reviewer, *Analog.* Taught fantasy fiction, New York University, 1972–73; editor, Garland Press science-fiction series, 1975. Recipient: Boys' Clubs of America Science Fiction award, 1953. Guest of Honor, World Science Fiction Convention, 1967. Agent: Scott Meredith Literary Agency, 845 Third Avenue, New York, New York 10022. Address: Ballantine Books, 201 East 50th Street, New York, New York 10022, U.S.A.

SCIENCE-FICTION PUBLICATIONS

Novels

*Marooned on Mars* (for children). Philadelphia, Winston, 1952; London Hutchinson, 1953.

*Rocket Jockey* (for children; as Philip St. John). Philadelphia, Winston, 1952; as *Rocket Pilot*, London, Hutchinson, 1955.

*The Mysterious Planet* (for children; as Kenneth Wright). Philadelphia, Winston, 1953.

*Attack from Atlantis* (for children). Philadelphia, Winston, 1953.

*Battle on Mercury* (for children; as Eric Van Lhin). Philadelphia, Winston, 1953.

*Step to the Stars* (for children). Philadelphia, Winston, 1954; London, Hutchinson, 1956.

*Rockets to Nowhere* (for children; as Philip St. John). Philadelphia, Winston, 1954.

*Preferred Risk* (as Edson McCann, with Frederik Pohl). New York, Simon and Schuster, 1955; London, Methuen, 1983.

*Mission to the Moon* (for children). Philadelphia, Winston, and London, Hutchinson, 1956.

*Police Your Planet* (as Eric Van Lhin). New York, Avalon, 1956; revised edition, as Lester del Rey, New York, Ballantine, 1975; London, New English Library, 1978.

*Nerves.* New York, Ballantine, 1956; revised edition, 1976.

*Day of the Giants.* New York, Avalon, 1959.

*Moon of Mutiny* (for children). New York, Holt Rinehart, 1961; London, Faber, 1963.
*The Eleventh Commandment*. Evanston, Illinois, Regency, 1962; revised edition, New York, Ballantine, 1970.
*The Sky Is Falling, Badge of Infamy*. New York, Galaxy, 1963; *Badge of Infamy* published London, Dobson, 1976.
*Outpost of Jupiter* (for children). New York, Holt Rinehart, 1963; London, Gollancz, 1964.
*The Runaway Robot* (for children), with Paul W. Fairman. Philadelphia, Westminster Press, 1965; London, Gollancz, 1967.
*Rocket from Infinity* (for children). New York, Holt Rinehart, 1966; London, Faber, 1967.
*The Scheme of Things*, with Paul W. Fairman. New York, Belmont, 1966.
*The Infinite Worlds of Maybe*. New York, Holt Rinehart, 1966; London, Faber, 1968.
*Siege Perilous*, with Paul W. Fairman. New York, Lancer, 1966; as *The Man Without a Planet*, 1969.
*Tunnel Through Time* (for children), with Paul W. Fairman. Philadelphia, Westminster Press, 1966.
*Prisoners of Space* (for children), with Paul W. Fairman. Philadelphia, Westminster Press, 1968.
*Pstalemate*. New York, Putnam, 1971; London, Gollancz, 1972.
*Weeping May Tarry*, with Raymond F. Jones. Los Angeles, Pinnacle, 1978.

Short Stories

*. . . and Some Were Human*. Philadelphia, Prime Press, 1948.
*Robots and Changelings*. New York, Ballantine, 1958.
*Mortals and Monsters*. New York, Ballantine, 1965; London, Tandem, 1967.
*Gods and Golems*. New York, Ballantine, 1973.
*Early del Rey*. New York, Doubleday, 1975.
*The Best of Lester del Rey*. New York, Ballantine, 1978.

OTHER PUBLICATIONS

Other

*It's Your Atomic Age*. New York, Abelard Press, 1951.
*Pirate Flag for Monterey* (for children). Philadelphia, Winston, 1957.
*Rockets Through Space* (for children). Philadelphia, Winston, 1957; revised edition, 1960.
*The Cave of Spears* (for children). New York, Knopf, 1957.
*Space Flight* (for children). New York, Golden Press, 1959.
*The Mysterious Earth [Sea, Sky]*. Philadelphia, Chilton, 3 vols., 1960–64.
*Rocks and What They Tell Us* (for children). Racine, Wisconsin, Whitman, 1961.
*The World of Science Fiction 1926–1976: The History of a Subculture*. New York, Ballantine, 1979.
*The Fantastic Art of Boris Vallejo*. New York, Ballantine, 1981.

Editor, with Cecile Matschat and Carl Carmer, *The Year after Tomorrow*. Philadelphia, Winston, 1954.
Editor, *Best Science Fiction Stories of the Year*. New York, Dutton, 5 vols., 1972–76; vol. 5, London, Kaye and Ward, 1977.
Editor, *Fantastic Science-Fiction Art 1926–1954*. New York, Ballantine, 1975.
Editor, *The Best of Frederik Pohl*. New York, Doubleday, 1975; London, Sidgwick and Jackson, 1977.
Editor, *The Best of C.L. Moore*. New York, Doubleday, 1975.
Editor, *The Best of John W. Campbell*. New York, Doubleday, 1976.
Editor, *The Best of Robert Bloch*. New York, Ballantine, 1977.
Editor, *The Best of Hal Clement*. New York, Ballantine, 1979.

* * *

Lester del Rey produced much of his early work in his spare time. Once established as a writer he created vast volumes of material, and he clearly thought of authorship as a craft rather than as a vocation. His standard is the orderly, well-told tale of the magazine writer, stamped by commercial necessity. Del Rey's writing balances commercial motives, excellence in the context of his times, and an ongoing faith in science.

Del Rey's early period can be dated 1938–54, from his first published short story, "The Faithful," to his first adult novel, *The Sky Is Falling*. For the first ten years he submitted *only* to John W. Campbell and published at least 38 stories. They contain the detailed imagining Campbell liked and the narrative briskness for an editor who wanted a story but paid by the word. The two best-known stories from this period are "Helen O'Loy" and *Nerves*. "Helen O'Loy" is a witty tale about bachelor roommates, a robot-repair wizard, and a doctor, who improve a robot by adding emotions. Helen then patterns her emotions after television soap operas and falls for Dave, the repairman, who eventually marries her. The story is filled with touches of futuristic imagination. For example, Phil, the doctor, is called to give counterhormones to a wealthy old lady's son and the servant with whom he is infatuated. In the plot proper del Rey generates humour by juxtaposing soap opera romanticism and the robot: "Helen's technique may have lacked polish, but it had enthusiasm, as he found when he tried to stop her from kissing him. She had learned fast and furiously—also, Helen was powered by an atomotor." *Nerves* is more dated in scientific terms, but it has an exciting plot about a blowout in a nuclear plant. Though radiation burns are erroneously described, *Nerves* is suspenseful, and touches like a motor needle for surgical sutures and sterilization by supersonic sound provide excellent decoration. The story sets up good characterization within the limits of its form, stressing an elder doctor-younger doctor relationship. The title focuses the theme of control under stress.

The early stories cover many topics. Some are fantasies, such as "Hereafter, Inc." in which a hypocritical puritan refuses to accept that he is in heaven because the people he secretly hoped were damned sinners are with him. Others are nostalgic, such as "Though Dreamers Die" in which Jorgen, the last man, realises that the robots who have helped him travel through space after a plague on Earth will carry on man's dreams and aspirations. Some deal with hard science, such as "Habit" about a rocket race won by slingshotting around Jupiter to gain velocity.

After 1952 del Rey became a regular writer of juvenile SF, a form well suited to his abilities. He generally features a hero just turning 18 who ventures into space to help build a satellite station, explore the Moon, or investigate a strange planet. True to form for such tales the boy usually stows away on a rocket ship and takes some foolish initiative, creating trouble for everyone until he extricates himself by a clever manoeuvre. Rather than the projection of any powerful ethical goal or cautionary extrapolation del Rey's ability lies in telling a good story, so it follows that these juveniles are very successful. They are laden with presumptions about women, the merit of individual initiative, and the benefits of American democracy, but this reflects del Rey's innate beliefs and his times rather than propaganda intent.

*The Sky Is Falling* is a sport among del Rey's works. It describes an alternative universe where magic dominates but is in danger because the sky and its zodiacal symbols are cracking and falling. The hero, mistaken for his engineer uncle, is revivified (after a fatal accident on Earth) to fix the sky. The detail of this novel is fascinating: individuals' energies wax and wane with their planets, and the scientific method is shown to resemble that of the magicians. It sparkles with imaginative exuberance in its denial of conventional reality (when pieces of sky crush people) and in zany turns of plot.

The two most interesting novels from del Rey's later work are *Police Your Planet* and *Siege Perilous.* The former deals with a frontier Mars riddled with poverty and crime where the police extort mountains of graft and people live in terror. Bruce Gordon, a reporter exiled from Earth for exposing the truth, struggles for survival and eventually the liberation of this vividly awful world. Del Rey is really painting a subtle picture of urban decay on Earth, where violence is the law. The novel is awkwardly imagined in places (air is held in Marsport by a fabric-covered dome) but it has power, energy, and much lightly buried compassion. On the other hand, *Siege Perilous* is a novel that swings from a Martian invasion horror story to the wildly ridiculous. America's orbiting satellite, a scientific station and weapons base, is invaded by Martians who fear man will invade Mars and thus intend to destroy Earth first. The three humans who evade the initial gas attack eventually outwit the Martians. This basic story is riotously decorated by the Martian's knowledge of Earth having come exclusively from television broadcasts. Twenty-six invasion-of-Mars movies have motivated the attack, which is carried out in a mixture of Wild West, Ronald Coleman, Chicago gangster, and grade-D science-fiction styles. Earth triumphs in an old-fashioned shootout while the heroine awaits torture. Del Rey has great fun with the clichés and patterns. Yet even while letting go in this action romp he manages to insert interesting minor ideas such as the satellite refining of pure crystalline metals and the balancing of the space station by pumping a water ballast.

In a long, steady career ranging from 1938 to the present, Lester del Rey has become most skillful in his craft. Like many writers of his period he fills out imaginative detail around solid plots to capture the excitement of the scientific universe. His weaknesses lie in the sentimentality of his message stories and the impression that he does not write from a coherent critical view of the universe. A virtuoso craftsman whose love is the story itself, he may not meet recent expectations as a "committed" writer and may therefore lack the "heart" which lifts a writer from the good to the great.

—Peter A. Brigg

---

**DEMPSEY, Hank.** *See* **HARRISON, Harry.**

---

**DENHOLM, Mark.** *See* **FEARN, John Russell.**

---

**DENT, Lester.** Also wrote as Kenneth Robeson. American. Born in La Plata, Missouri, 12 October 1904. Studied telegraphy at Chillicothe Business College, Missouri, 1923–24. Married Norma Gerling in 1925. Taught at Chillicothe Business College, 1924; telegrapher, Western Union, Carrolton, Missouri, 1924, and Empire Oil and Gas Company, Ponca City, Oklahoma, 1925; telegrapher, then teletype operator, Associated Press, Tulsa, 1926; journalist for Tulsa *World*; house-writer for Dell, publisher, 1930; freelance writer from 1930, and also dairy farmer and aerial photographer. *Died 11 March 1959.*

### Science-Fiction Publications

Novels as Kenneth Robeson (series: Doc Savage in all books)

*The Man of Bronze.* New York, Street and Smith, 1935; London, Corgi, 1975.
*The Land of Terror.* New York, Street and Smith, 1935; London, Tandem, 1965.
*Quest of the Spider.* New York, Street and Smith, 1935.
*The Thousand-Headed Man.* New York, Bantam, 1964; London, Corgi, 1975.
*Meteor Menace.* New York, Bantam, 1964; London, Corgi, 1975.
*The Polar Treasure.* New York, Bantam, 1965.
*Brand of the Werewolf.* New York, Bantam, 1965.
*The Lost Oasis.* New York, Bantam, 1965.
*The Monsters.* New York, Bantam, 1965.
*Quest of Qui.* London, Bantam, 1965; New York, Bantam, 1966.
*The Mystic Mullah.* New York, Bantam, 1965; London, Bantam, 1966.
*The Phantom City.* New York, Bantam, 1966.
*Fear Cay.* New York, Bantam, 1966.
*Land of Always-Night.* New York, Bantam, 1966.
*The Fantastic Island.* New York, Bantam, 1966; London, Bantam, 1967.
*The Spook Legion.* New York, Bantam, 1967.
*The Red Skull.* New York, Bantam, 1967.
*The Sargasso Ogre.* New York, Bantam, 1967.
*Pirate of the Pacific.* New York, Bantam, 1967.
*The Secret of the Sky.* New York, Bantam, 1967; London, Bantam, 1968.
*The Czar of Fear.* New York, Bantam, 1968.
*Fortress of Solitude.* New York, Bantam, 1968.
*The Green Eagle.* New York, Bantam, 1968.
*Death in Silver.* New York, Bantam, 1968.
*The Mystery under the Sea.* New York, Bantam, 1968; London, Bantam, 1969.
*The Deadly Dwarf.* New York, Bantam, 1968.
*The Other World.* New York, Bantam, 1968; London, Bantam, 1969.
*The Flaming Falcons.* New York, Bantam, 1968; London, Bantam, 1969.
*The Annihilist.* New York, Bantam, 1968; London, Bantam, 1969.
*Hex.* London, Bantam, 1968; New York, Bantam, 1969.
*The Squeaking Goblin.* New York, Bantam, 1969.
*Mad Eyes.* New York, Bantam, 1969.
*The Terror in the Navy.* New York, Bantam, 1969.
*Dust of Death.* New York, Bantam, 1969.
*Resurrection Day.* New York, Bantam, 1969.
*Red Snow.* New York, Bantam, 1969.
*World's Fair Goblin.* New York, Bantam, 1969.
*The Dagger in the Sky.* New York, Bantam, 1969.
*Merchants of Disaster.* New York, Bantam, 1969.
*The Gold Ogre.* New York, Bantam, 1969.
*The Man Who Shook the Earth.* New York, Bantam, 1969.

*The Sea Magician.* New York, Bantam, 1970.
*The Midas Man.* New York, Bantam, 1970.
*The Feathered Octopus.* New York, Bantam, 1970.
*The Sea Angel.* New York, Bantam, 1970.
*Devil on the Moon.* New York, Bantam, 1970.
*The Vanisher.* New York, Bantam, 1970.
*The Mental Wizard.* New York, Bantam, 1970.
*He Could Stop the World.* New York, Bantam, 1970.
*The Golden Peril.* New York, Bantam, 1970.
*The Giggling Ghosts.* New York, Bantam, 1971.
*Poison Island.* New York, Bantam, 1971.
*The Munitions Master.* New York, Bantam, 1971.
*The Yellow Cloud.* New York, Bantam, 1971.
*The Majii.* New York, Bantam, 1971.
*The Living Fire Menace.* New York, Bantam, 1971.
*The Pirate's Ghost.* New York, Bantam, 1971.
*The Submarine Mystery.* New York, Bantam, 1971.
*The Motion Menace.* New York, Bantam, 1971.
*The Green Death.* New York, Bantam, 1971.
*Mad Mesa.* New York, Bantam, 1972.
*The Freckled Shark.* New York, Bantam, 1972.
*The Mystery on the Snow.* New York, Bantam, 1972.
*Spook Hole.* New York, Bantam, 1972.
*The Mental Monster.* New York, Bantam, 1973.
*The Seven Agate Devils.* New York, Bantam, 1973.
*The Derrick Devil.* New York, Bantam, 1973.
*Land of Fear.* New York, Bantam, 1973.
*The South Pole Terror.* New York, Bantam, 1974.
*The Crimson Serpent.* New York, Bantam, 1974.
*The Devil Genghis.* New York, Bantam, 1974.
*The King Maker.* New York, Bantam, 1975.
*The Stone Man.* New York, Bantam, 1976.
*The Evil Gnome.* New York, Bantam, 1976.
*The Red Terrors.* New York, Bantam, 1976.
*The Mountain Monster.* New York, Bantam, 1976.
*The Boss of Terror.* New York, Bantam, 1976.
*The Angry Ghost.* New York, Bantam, 1977.
*The Spotted Men.* New York, Bantam, 1977.
*The Roar Devil.* New York, Bantam, 1977.
*The Magic Island.* New York, Bantam, 1977.
*The Flying Goblin.* New York, Bantam, 1977.
*The Purple Dragon.* New York, Bantam, 1978.
*The Awful Egg.* New York, Bantam, 1978.
*Tunnel Terror.* New York, Bantam, 1979.
*The Hate Genius.* New York, Bantam, 1979.
*The Red Spider.* New York, Bantam, 1979.
*Mystery on Happy Bones.* New York, Bantam, 1979.
*Satan Black, Cargo Unknown.* New York, Bantam, 1980.
*Hell Below, The Lost Giant.* New York, Bantam, 1980.
*The Pharaoh's Ghost, The Time Terror.* New York, Bantam, 1981.
*The Whisker of Hercules, The Man Who Was Scared.* New York, Bantam, 1981.
*They Died Twice, The Screaming Man.* New York, Bantam, 1981.
*Jiu San; The Black, Black Witch.* New York, Bantam, 1981.
*The Shape of Terror, Death Had Yellow Eyes.* New York, Bantam, 1982.
*One-Eyed Mystic, The Man Who Fell Up.* New York, Bantam, 1982.
*The Talking Devil, The Ten Ton Snake.* New York, Bantam, 1982.
*Pirate Isle, The Speaking Stone.* New York, Bantam, 1983.
*The Golden Man, Peril in the North.* New York, Bantam, 1984.
*The Laugh of Death, The King of Terror.* New York, Bantam, 1984.
*The Three Wild Men, The Fiery Menace.* New York, Bantam, 1984.
*Devils of the Deep.* New York, Bantam, 1984.
*The Goblins, The Secret of the Su.* New York, Bantam, 1984.
Doc Savage Omnibus:
*The All-White Elf, The Running Skeletons, The Angry Canary, The Swooning Lady.* New York, Bantam, 1986.
*King Joe Cay, The Thing That Pursued.* New York, Bantam, 1987.
*The Spook of Grandpa Eben, Measures for a Coffin, The Three Devils, Strange Fish.* New York, Bantam, 1987.
*Mystery Island, Men of Fear, Rock Sinister, The Pure Evil.* New York, Bantam, 1987.
*No Light to Die By, The Monkey Suit, Let's Kill Ames, Once Over Lightly, I Died Yesterday.* New York, Bantam, 1988.
*The Awful Dynasty, The Magic Forest.* New York, Bantam, 1988.
*The Men Vanished, The Terrible Stork, Five Fathoms Dead, Danger Lies East.* New York, Bantam, 1988.
*The Mental Monster, The Pink Lady, Weird Valley, Trouble on Parade.* New York, Bantam, 1989.
*The Invisible-Box Murders, Birds of Death, The Wee Ones, Terror Takes 7.* New York, Bantam, 1989.
*The Devil's Black Rock, Waves of Death, Terror and the Lonely Widow, The Two-Wise Owl.* New York, Bantam, 1989.
*See-Pah-Poo, Colors for Murder, Three Times a Corpse, Death Is a Round Black Spot, The Devil Is Jones.* New York, Bantam, 1990.
*The Exploding Lake.* New York, Bantam, 1990.
*The Derelict of Skull Shoal, Terror Wears No Shoes, The Green Master, Return from Cormoral, Up from the Earth's Center.* New York, Bantam, 1990.

Short Stories

*The Sinister Ray.* New York, Gryphon, 1987.

OTHER PUBLICATIONS

Novels

*Dead at the Take-Off.* New York, Doubleday, 1946; London, Cassell, 1948; as *High Stakes*, New York, Ace, 1953.
*Lady to Kill.* New York, Doubleday, 1946; London, Cassell, 1949.
*Lady Afraid.* New York, Doubleday, 1948; London, Cassell, 1950.
*Lady So Silent.* London, Cassell, 1951.
*Cry at Dusk.* New York, Fawcett, 1952; London, Fawcett, 1959.
*Lady in Peril.* New York, Ace, 1959.
*Hades and Hocus Pocus* edited by Robert Weinberg. Chicago, Pulp Press, 1979.

Plays

*The Incredible Radio Exploits of Doc Savage.* Melrose, Massachusetts, Odyssey, 2 vols., 1983–84.

Radio Plays: *Scotland Yard*, 1931; *Doc Savage*, 1934.

*

Bibliography: "The Secret Kenneth Robesons" and "The *Duende* Doc Savage Index" by Will Murray, in *Duende 2* (North Quincy, Massachusetts), 1977.

Critical Studies: *Doc Savage: His Apocalyptic Life* by Philip José Farmer, New York, Doubleday, 1973, revised edition, London, Panther, 1975; *The Man Behind Doc Savage* edited by Robert Weinberg, Chicago, Weinberg, 1974; *Doc Savage*, 1978, and *Secrets of Doc Savage*, 1981, both by Will Murray, Melrose, Massachusetts, Odyssey.

* * *

Science fiction, as it manifested itself in the early pulp magazines, did not always appear in SF publications, or even in works that were primarily of that genre. Quite often, the various single-character magazines such as *The Shadow* and *Doc Savage* featured interesting science fiction in the guise of adventure and detective fiction. The novels of Kenneth Robeson fall into this catagory. Kenneth Robeson was a house pseudonym used by Street and Smith in their *Doc Savage* and *Avenger* magazines between 1933 and 1949. It masked a number of writers, including Ryerson Johnson, Harold A. Davis, William G. Bogart, Alan Hathway, Paul Ernst, and Emile C. Tepperman. The Robeson byline, however, was most frequently used by, and identified with, Lester Dent, the creator and author of most of the Doc Savage novels.

The Doc Savage novels were not predominately science fiction except, perhaps, in their premise of Doc Savage himself, a man raised and trained by a host of world experts to be a physical and mental superman, to whom fantastic abilities are attributed.

With the exception of space and time travel, the Doc Savage adventures employed most of the themes common to early SF: mind transference (*Mad Mesa*); teleportation (*The Vanisher*); robots (*The Seven Agate Devils*); anti-gravity (*The Secret of the Sky*); biological mutation (*The Monsters*); invisibility (*The Spook Legion*); force fields (*The Motion Menace*); raising the dead (*Resurrection Day*); and destructive rays (*The Deadly Dwarf*). Structurally, the stories are formula. Doc Savage contends with criminals or power seekers who possess and attempt to pervert new technological discoveries toward their own ends.

Lost worlds were a popular Doc Savage theme. *The Land of Terror* and "The Time Terror" postulated pockets of dinosaurs in remote areas. *The Mental Wizard* and "The Green Master" concerned lost Egyptian colonies in South America. There were submarine cities (*The Red Terrors*) and subterranean worlds (*Land of Always-Night*). *The Other World* combined the subterranean civilisation with surviving dinosaurs. Many adventures employed myths and legends as their bases. The Fountain of Youth and Aladdin's Cave are the goals in *Fear Cay* and *The Majii.* Lester Dent often created his own folk myths to lend color to his antagonists in *The Feathered Octopus* and *The Squeaking Goblin.* Doc Savage, the "Man of Bronze," is himself a mythic character who possesses all the prerequisites of a culture hero—wisdom, great strength, and near-magical scientific powers. He is a champion who defends humanity against the menace of technology in evil hands. His enemies, appropriately enough, are evocative of man's superstitious fear of the unknown (in this case, scientific advancement) and call themselves by such titles as The Sargasso Ogre, The Roar Devil, and The Purple Dragon. The mythological theme is carried as far as a traditional descent into Hell by the hero in the final Doc Savage novel, *Up from Earth's Center*, a fantasy.

Although primarily juvenile in its appeal, Lester Dent's work combines a fertility of invention with a vividness of imagination seldom surpassed. His best efforts include *Meteor Menace, The Thousand-Headed Man, Land of Always-Night,* and *Resurrection Day.* The later Doc Savage stories are considerably more mature in theme and tone. Among these, *The Whisker of Hercules, The Red Spider*, and *Up from Earth's Center* are exceptional.

—Will Murray

---

**DENTINGER, Stephen.** *See* **HOCH, Edward D.**

---

**DERLETH, August (William).** Also wrote as Stephen Grendon; Tally Mason. American. Born in Sauk City, Wisconsin, 24 February 1909. Educated at St. Aloysius School; Sauk City High School; University of Wisconsin, Madison, B.A. 1930. Married Sandra Winters in 1953 (divorced 1959); one daughter and one son. Editor, Fawcett Publications, Minneapolis, 1930–31; editor, *The Midwesterner*, Madison, 1931; Lecturer in American Regional Literature, University of Wisconsin, 1939–43. Owner and co-founder (with Donald Wandrei, 1939–42), Arkham House Publishers (including the imprints Mycroft and Moran, and Stanton and Lee), Sauk City, 1939–71. Editor, *Mind Magic*, 1931; literary editor and columnist, Madison *Capital Times*, 1941–71; editor, *The Arkham Sampler*, 1948–49, *Hawk and Whippoorwill*, 1960–63, and *The Arkham Collector*, 1967–71, all Sauk City. Recipient: Guggenheim fellowship, 1938; *Scholastic* award, 1958; Midland Authors award, for poetry, 1965; Ann Radcliffe award, 1967. *Died 4 July 1971.*

### Science-Fiction Publications

#### Short Stories

*Harrigan's File.* Sauk City, Wisconsin, Arkham House, 1975.

### Other Publications

#### Novels

*Murder Stalks the Wakely Family.* New York, Loring and Mussey, 1934; as *Death Stalks the Wakely Family*, London, Newnes, 1937.
*The Man on All Fours.* New York, Loring and Mussey, 1934; London, Newnes, 1936.
*Three Who Died.* New York, Loring and Mussey, 1935.
*Sign of Fear.* New York, Loring and Mussey, 1935; London, Newnes, 1936.
*Still Is the Summer Night.* New York, Scribner, 1937.
*Wind over Wisconsin.* New York, Scribner, 1938.
*Restless Is the River.* New York, Scribner, 1939.
*Sentence Deferred.* New York, Scribner, 1939; London, Heinemann, 1940.
*The Narracong Riddle.* New York, Scribner, 1940.
*Bright Journey.* New York, Scribner, 1940.
*Evening in Spring.* New York, Scribner, 1941.
*Sweet Genevieve.* New York, Scribner, 1942.
*The Seven Who Waited.* New York, Scribner, 1943; London, Muller, 1945.
*Shadow of Night.* New York, Scribner, 1943.

*Mischief in the Lane*. New York, Scribner, 1944; London, Muller, 1948.
*No Future for Luana*. New York, Scribner, 1945; London, Muller, 1948.
*The Shield of the Valiant*. New York, Scribner, 1945.
*The Lurker at the Threshold*, with H.P. Lovecraft. Sauk City, Wisconsin, Arkham House, 1945; London, Gollancz, 1948.
*Fell Purpose*. New York, Arcadia House, 1953.
*Death by Design*. New York, Arcadia House, 1953.
*The House on the Mound*. New York, Duell, 1958.
*The Hills Stand Watch*. New York, Duell, 1960.
*The Trail of Cthulhu*. Sauk City, Wisconsin, Arkham House, 1962; London, Spearman, 1974.
*The Shadow in the Glass*. New York, Duell, 1963.
*Mr. Fairlie's Final Journey*. Sauk City, Wisconsin, Mycroft and Moran, 1968.
*The Wind Leans West*. New York, Candlelight Press, 1969.

Short Stories

*Place of Hawks*. New York, Loring and Mussey, 1935.
*Any Day Now*. Chicago, Normandie House, 1938.
*Country Growth*. New York, Scribner, 1940.
*Someone in the Dark*. Sauk City, Wisconsin, Arkham House, 1941.
*Something Near*. Sauk City, Wisconsin, Arkham House, 1945.
*"In Re: Sherlock Holmes"—The Adventures of Solar Pons*. Sauk City, Wisconsin, Mycroft and Moran, 1945; as *Regarding Sherlock Holmes*, New York, Pinnacle, 1974; as *The Adventures of Solar Pons*, London, Robson, 1975.
*Sac Prairie People*. Sauk City, Wisconsin, Stanton and Lee, 1948.
*Not Long for This World*. Sauk City, Wisconsin, Arkham House, 1948.
*The Memoirs of Solar Pons*. Sauk City, Wisconsin, Mycroft and Moran, 1951.
*Three Problems for Solar Pons*. Sauk City, Wisconsin, Mycroft and Moran, 1952.
*The House of Moonlight*. Iowa City, Prairie Press, 1953.
*The Survivor and Others*, with H.P. Lovecraft. Sauk City, Wisconsin, Arkham House, 1957.
*The Return of Solar Pons*. Sauk City, Wisconsin, Mycroft and Moran, 1958.
*The Mask of Cthulhu*. Sauk City, Wisconsin, Arkham House, 1958; London, Consul, 1961.
*The Reminiscences of Solar Pons*. Sauk City, Wisconsin, Mycroft and Moran, 1961.
*Wisconsin in Their Bones*. New York, Duell, 1961.
*Lonesome Places*. Sauk City, Wisconsin, Arkham House, 1962.
*Mr. George and Other Odd Persons* (as Stephen Grendon). Sauk City, Wisconsin, Arkham House, 1963; as *When Graveyards Yawn*, London, Tandem, 1965.
*The Casebook of Solar Pons*. Sauk City, Wisconsin, Mycroft and Moran, 1965.
*Praed Street Papers*. New York, Candlelight Press, 1965.
*The Adventure of the Orient Express*. New York, Candlelight Press, 1965; London, Panther, 1975.
*Colonel Markesan and Less Pleasant People*, with Mark Schorer. Sauk City, Wisconsin, Arkham House, 1966.
*The Adventure of the Unique Dickensians*. Sauk City, Wisconsin, Mycroft and Moran, 1968.
*A Praed Street Dossier*. Sauk City, Wisconsin, Mycroft and Moran, 1968.
*The Shadow Out of Time and Other Tales of Horror*, with H.P. Lovecraft. London, Gollancz, 1968; abridged edition, as *The Shuttered Room and Other Tales of Horror*, London, Panther, 1970.
*A House above Cuzco*. New York, Candlelight Press, 1969.
*The Shuttered Room and Other Tales of Terror*, with H.P. Lovecraft. New York, Beagle, 1971.
*The Chronicles of Solar Pons*. Sauk City, Wisconsin, Mycroft and Moran, 1973; London, Robson, 1975.
*The Watchers Out of Time and Others*, with H.P. Lovecraft. Sauk City, Wisconsin, Arkham House, 1974.
*Dwellers in Darkness*. Sauk City, Wisconsin, Arkham House, 1976.

Verse

*To Remember*, with *Salute Before Dawn*, by Albert Edward Clements. Hartland Four Corners, Vermont, Windsor, 1931.
*Hawk on the Wind*. Philadelphia, Ritten House, 1938.
*Elegy: On a Flake of Snow*. Muscatine, Iowa, Prairie Press, 1939.
*Man Track Here*. Philadelphia, Ritten House, 1939.
*Here on a Darkling Plain*. Philadelphia, Ritten House, 1941.
*Wind in the Elms*. Philadelphia, Ritten House, 1941.
*Rind of Earth*. Prairie City, Illinois, Decker Press, 1942.
*Selected Poems*. Prairie City, Illinois, Decker Press, 1944.
*And You, Thoreau!* New York, New Directions, 1944.
*The Edge of Night*. Prairie City, Illinois, Decker Press, 1945.
*Habitant of Dusk: A Garland for Cassandra*. Boston, Walden Press, 1946.
*Rendezvous in a Landscape*. New York, Fine Editions Press, 1952.
*Psyche*. Iowa City, Prairie Press, 1953.
*Country Poems*. Iowa City, Prairie Press, 1956.
*Elegy: On the Umbral Moon*. Forest Park, Illinois, Acorn Press, 1957.
*West of Morning*. Francestown, New Hampshire, Golden Quill Press, 1960.
*This Wound*. Iowa City, Prairie Press, 1962.
*Country Places*. Iowa City, Prairie Press, 1965.
*The Only Place We Live*. Iowa City, Prairie Press, 1966.
*By Owl Light*. Iowa City, Prairie Press, 1967.
*Collected Poems, 1937–1967*. New York, Candlelight Press, 1967.
*Caitlin*. Iowa City, Prairie Press, 1969.
*The Landscape of the Heart*. Iowa City, Prairie Press, 1970.
*Listening to the Wind*. New York, Candlelight Press, 1971.
*Last Night*. New York, Candlelight Press, 1971.

Recordings: *Psyche: A Sequence of Love Lyrics*, Cuca, 1960; *Sugar Bush by Moonlight and Other Poems of Man and Nature*, Cuca, 1962; *Caitlin*, Cuca, 1971.

Other

*The Heritage of Sauk City*. Sauk City, Wisconsin, Pioneer Press, 1931.
*Consider Your Verdict: Ten Coroner's Cases for You To Solve* (as Tally Mason). New York, Stackpole, 1937.
*Atmosphere of Houses*. Muscatine, Iowa, Prairie Press, 1939.
*Still Small Voice: The Biography of Zona Gale*. New York, Appleton Century, 1940.
*Village Year: A Sac Prairie Journal*. New York, Coward McCann, 1941.
*Wisconsin Regional Literature*. Privately printed, 1941; revised edition, 1942.
*The Wisconsin: River of a Thousand Isles*. New York, Farrar and Rinehart, 1942.
*H.P.L.: A Memoir* (on H.P. Lovecraft). New York, Abramson, 1945.

*Oliver, The Wayward Owl* (for children). Sauk City, Wisconsin, Stanton and Lee, 1945.
*Writing Fiction*. Boston, The Writer, 1946.
*Village Daybook: A Sac Prairie Journal*. Chicago, Pellegrini and Cudahy, 1947.
*A Boy's Way: Poems* (for children). Sauk City, Wisconsin, Stanton and Lee, 1947.
*Sauk County: A Centennial History*. Baraboo, Wisconsin, Sauk County Centennial Committee, 1948.
*It's a Boy's World: Poems* (for children). Sauk City, Wisconsin, Stanton and Lee, 1948.
*Wisconsin Earth: A Sac Prairie Sampler* (selection). Sauk City, Wisconsin, Stanton and Lee, 1948.
*The Milwaukee Road: Its First 100 Years*. New York, Creative Age Press, 1948.
*The Country of the Hawk* (for children). New York, Aladdin, 1952.
*The Captive Island* (for children). New York, Duell, 1952.
*Empire of Fur: Trading in the Lake Superior Region* (for children). New York, Aladdin, 1953.
*Land of Gray Gold: Lead Mining in Wisconsin* (for children). New York, Aladdin, 1954.
*Father Marquette and the Great Rivers* (for children). New York, Farrar Straus, 1955; London, Burns and Oates, 1956.
*Land of Sky-Blue Waters* (for children). New York, Aladdin, 1955.
*St. Ignatius and the Company of Jesus* (for children). New York, Farrar Straus, and London, Burns and Oates, 1956.
*Columbus and the New World* (for children). New York, Farrar Straus, and London, Burns and Oates, 1957.
*The Moon Tenders* (for children). New York, Duell, 1958.
*The Mill Creek Irregulars* (for children). New York, Duell, 1959.
*Wilbur, The Trusting Whippoorwill* (for children). Sauk City, Wisconsin, Stanton and Lee, 1959.
*Arkham House: The First Twenty Years 1939–1959*. Sauk City, Wisconsin, Arkham House, 1959.
*Some Notes on H.P. Lovecraft*. Sauk City, Wisconsin, Arkham House, 1959.
*The Pinkertons Ride Again* (for children). New York, Duell, 1960.
*The Ghost of Black Hawk Island* (for children). New York, Duell, 1961.
*Walden West* (autobiography). New York, Duell, 1961.
*Sweet Land of Michigan* (for children). New York, Duell, 1962.
*Concord Rebel: A Life of Henry D. Thoreau*. Philadelphia, Chilton, 1962.
*Countryman's Journal*. New York, Duell, 1963.
*The Tent Show Summer* (for children). New York, Duell, 1963.
*Three Literary Men: A Memoir of Sinclair Lewis, Sherwood Anderson, Edgar Lee Masters*. New York, Candlelight Press, 1963.
*The Irregulars Strike Again* (for children). New York, Duell, 1964.
*Forest Orphans* (for children). New York, Ernest, 1964; as *Mr. Conservation*, Park Falls, Wisconsin, MacGregor, 1971.
*Wisconsin Country: A Sac Prairie Journal*. New York, Candlelight Press, 1965.
*The House by the River* (for children). New York, Duell, 1965.
*The Watcher on the Heights* (for children). New York, Duell, 1966.
*Wisconsin* (for children). New York, Coward McCann, 1967.
*The Beast in Holger's Woods* (for children). New York, Crowell, 1968.
*The Prince Goes West* (for children). New York, Meredith Press, 1968.
*Vincennes: Portal to the West*. Englewood Cliffs, New Jersey, Prentice Hall, 1968.
*Walden Pond: Homage to Thoreau*. Iowa City, Prairie Press, 1968.
*Wisconsin Murders*. Sauk City, Wisconsin, Mycroft and Moran, 1968.
*The Wisconsin Valley*. New York, Teachers College Press, 1969.
*Thirty Years of Arkham House 1939–1969: A History and a Bibliography*. Sauk City, Wisconsin, Arkham House, 1970.
*The Three Straw Men* (for children). New York, Candlelight Press, 1970.
*Return to Walden West*. New York, Candlelight Press, 1970.
*Love Letters to Caitlin*. New York, Candlelight Press, 1971.
*Emerson, Our Contemporary*. New York, Crowell Collier, 1971.

Editor, with R.E. Larsson, *Poetry Out of Wisconsin*. New York, Harrison, 1937.
Editor, with Donald Wandrei, *The Outsider and Others*, by H.P. Lovecraft. Sauk City, Wisconsin, Arkham House, 1939.
Editor, with Donald Wandrei, *Beyond the Wall of Sleep*, by H.P. Lovecraft. Sauk City, Wisconsin, Arkham House, 1943.
Editor, with Donald Wandrei, *Marginalia*, by H.P. Lovecraft. Sauk City, Wisconsin, Arkham House, 1944.
Editor, *Sleep No More: Twenty Masterpieces of Horror for the Connoisseur*. New York, Farrar and Rinehart, 1944; abridged edition, London, Panther, 1964.
Editor, *The Best Supernatural Stories of H.P. Lovecraft*. Cleveland, World, 1945; revised edition, as *The Dunwich Horror and Others*, Sauk City, Wisconsin, Arkham House, 1963.
Editor, *Who Knocks? Twenty Masterpieces of the Spectral for the Connoisseur*. New York, Rinehart, 1946; abridged edition, London, Panther, 1964.
Editor, *The Night Side: Masterpieces of the Strange and Terrible*. New York, Rinehart, 1947; abridged edition, London, New English Library, 1966.
Editor, *The Sleeping and the Dead*. Chicago, Pellegrini and Cudahy, 1947; as *The Sleeping and the Dead* and *The Unquiet Grave*, London, New English Library, 2 vols., 1963–64.
Editor, *Dark of the Moon: Poems of Fantasy and the Macabre*. Sauk City, Wisconsin, Arkham House, 1947.
Editor, *Strange Ports of Call*. New York, Pellegrini and Cudahy, 1948.
Editor, *The Other Side of the Moon*. New York, Pellegrini and Cudahy, 1949; abridged edition, London, Grayson, 1956.
Editor, *Something about Cats and Other Pieces*, by H.P. Lovecraft. Sauk City, Wisconsin, Arkham House, 1949.
Editor, *Beyond Time and Space*. New York, Pellegrini and Cudahy, 1950.
Editor, *Far Boundaries: 20 Science-Fiction Stories*. New York, Pellegrini and Cudahy, 1951; London, Consul, 1965.
Editor, *The Outer Reaches: Favorite Science-Fiction Tales Chosen by Their Authors*. New York, Pellegrini and Cudahy, 1951; as *The Outer Reaches* and *The Time of Infinity*, London, Consul, 2 vols., 1963.
Editor, *Beachheads in Space*. New York, Pellegrini and Cudahy, 1952; abridged edition, London, Weidenfeld and Nicolson, 1954; as *From Other Worlds*, London, New English Library, 1964.
Editor, *Night's Yawning Peal: A Ghostly Company*. Sauk City, Wisconsin, Arkham House, 1952; London, Consul, 1965.
Editor, *Worlds of Tomorrow: Science Fiction with a Difference*. New York, Pellegrini and Cudahy, 1953; abridged edition, London, Weidenfeld and Nicolson, 1954; as *New Worlds for Old*, London, New English Library, 1963.

Editor, *Time to Come: Science-Fiction Stories of Tomorrow.* New York, Farrar Straus, 1954; London, Consul, 1963.
Editor, *Portals of Tomorrow: The Best Tales of Science Fiction and Other Fantasy.* New York, Rinehart, 1954; London, Cassell, 1956.
Editor, *The Shuttered Room and Other Pieces by H.P. Lovecraft and Divers Hands.* Sauk City, Wisconsin, Arkham House, 1959.
Editor, *Fire and Sleet and Candlelight: New Poems of the Macabre.* Sauk City, Wisconsin, Arkham House, 1961.
Editor, *Dark Mind, Dark Heart.* Sauk City, Wisconsin, Arkham House, 1962; London, Mayflower, 1963.
Editor, *When Evil Wakes: A New Anthology of the Macabre.* London, Souvenir Press, 1963.
Editor, *Over the Edge.* Sauk City, Wisconsin, Arkham House, 1964; London, Gollancz, 1967.
Editor, *At the Mountains of Madness and Other Novels,* by H.P. Lovecraft. Sauk City, Wisconsin, Arkham House, 1964; London, Gollancz, 1966.
Editor, *Dagon and Other Macabre Tales,* by H.P. Lovecraft. Sauk City, Wisconsin, Arkham House, 1965; London, Gollancz, 1967.
Editor, with Donald Wandrei (3 vols.) and James Turner (2 vols.), *Selected Letters,* by H.P. Lovecraft. Sauk City, Wisconsin, Arkham House, 5 vols., 1965–76.
Editor, *The Dark Brotherhood and Other Pieces,* by H.P. Lovecraft and others. Sauk City, Wisconsin, Arkham House, 1966.
Editor, *A Wisconsin Harvest.* Sauk City, Wisconsin, Stanton and Lee, 1966.
Editor, *Travellers by Night.* Sauk City, Wisconsin, Arkham House, 1967; London, Gollancz, 1968.
Editor, *New Poetry Out of Wisconsin.* Sauk City, Wisconsin, Stanton and Lee, 1969.
Editor, *Tales of the Cthulhu Mythos,* by H.P. Lovecraft and others. Sauk City, Wisconsin, Arkham House, 1969.
Editor, *The Horror in the Museum and Other Revisions,* by H.P. Lovecraft. Sauk City, Wisconsin, Arkham House, 1970; abridged edition, London, Panther, 1975.
Editor, *Dark Things.* Sauk City, Wisconsin, Arkham House, 1971.

*

Bibliography: *100 Books by August Derleth,* Sauk City, Wisconsin, Arkham House, 1962; *August Derleth: A Bibliography* by Alison M. Wilson, Metuchen, New Jersey, Scarecrow Press, 1983.

Manuscript Collection: State Historical Society of Wisconsin Library, Madison.

* * *

During his 47-year literary career, August Derleth contributed to a wide variety of literary categories, always with skill and frequently with distinction. His output included contemporary novels, historical novels, award-winning short stories, regional history, biography, nature essays, poetry, literary criticism, fiction and non-fiction for young readers, detective novels, Sherlock Holmes pastiches, true crime essays, and a large body of weird and super-natural fiction. It was in the latter area that he began his career at 16, with the story "Bat's Belfry." This was the first of more than a hundred stories to be published in *Weird Tales,* with nearly as many more appearing in other fantasy and science-fiction magazines, and collected in 11 volumes. The best of these stories, such as "Mrs. Manifold" and "The Lonesome Place," display a macabre inventiveness and a sure talent for inducing cold chills. Derleth's contributions to the field of science fiction were made primarily in his roles as editor and publisher. Arkham House Publishers preserved and popularized not only H.P. Lovecraft's works and those of Clark Ashton Smith, Robert E. Howard, Henry S. Whitehead, Robert Bloch, William Hope Hodgson, Algernon Blackwood, and A. E. Coppard, but published the first books of Ray Bradbury, Fritz Leiber, and A.E. van Vogt. Between 1948 and 1954 Derleth edited nine popular collections of science fiction, including *Beyond Time and Space,* one of the first attempts to provide science fiction with a literary pedigree by including excerpts from Plato, Lucian of Samosata, Sir Thomas More, Rabelais, and Francis Bacon. Derleth's literary tastes and his broad view of what constituted science fiction gave his anthologies a distinctive flavor that set them apart from the work of other compilers.

Of Derleth's hundreds of short stories, the only ones classifiable as science fiction are the 17 tales that make up *Harrigan's File.* These stories recount a succession of odd encounters between Tex Harrigan, a skeptical newspaper reporter, and an assortment of eccentric characters, crazy inventions, scientific experiments gone awry, and visitors from other planets or dimensions. Always low-key, some of the tales are quietly effective, but others are marred by surprisingly heavy-handed satire. (One story contains references to a Pernsback-Galmer—read Gernsback and Palmer—Lunar Expedition and to SF writers named Van Heingeon and Spragsimov Pouldersen). One cannot help but feel that these products of Derleth-the-author would have been disdained by Derleth-the-editor, whose sights were always set high and whose accomplishments not infrequently matched his intentions.

—R.E. Briney

---

**DEWEESE, Gene** (Thomas Eugene DeWeese). Also writes as Jean DeWeese; Thomas Stratton; Victoria Thomas. American. Born in Rochester, Indiana, 31 January 1934. Educated at Valparaiso Technical Institute, associate degree in electronics, 1953; also studied at the University of Wisconsin, Milwaukee, Indiana University, Kokomo, and Marquette University, Milwaukee. Married Beverly Joanne Amers in 1955. Electronics technician, Delco Radio, Kokomo, 1954–59; technical writer, especially on space navigation, Delco Electronics, Milwaukee, 1959–74. Since 1974, freelance writer; science fiction reviewer, Milwaukee *Journal,* 1980–84; reviewer and columnist, *Science Fiction Review* since 1980, and *Comic Buyer's Guide,* since 1985. Agent: (books) Sharon Jarvis and Company, 260 Willard Avenue, Staten Island, New York 10314; (short stories) Larry Sternig Literary Agency, 742 North Robertson, Milwaukee, Wisconsin 53213. Address: 2718 North Prospect, Milwaukee, Wisconsin 53211, U.S.A.

SCIENCE-FICTION PUBLICATIONS

Novels (series: Joe Karns; Star Trek; Calvin Willeford)

*The Invisibility Affair* (as Thomas Stratton, with Robert Coulson). New York, Ace, 1967.
*The Mind-Twisters Affair* (as Thomas Stratton, with Robert Coulson). New York, Ace, 1967.

*Gates of the Universe*, with Robert Coulson. Toronto, Laser, 1975; expanded version, as *Nightmare Universe*, Lake Geneva, Wisconsin, TSR, 1985.
*Now You See It/Him/Them . . .* (Karns), with Robert Coulson. New York, Doubleday, 1975; London, Hale, 1976.
*Jeremy Case*. Toronto, Laser, 1976.
*Charles Fort Never Mentioned Wombats* (Karns), with Robert Coulson. New York, Doubleday, 1977; London, Hale, 1978.
*Major Corby and the Unidentified Flapping Object* (for children). New York, Doubleday, 1979.
*The Wanting Factor*. Chicago, Playboy Press, 1980.
*Nightmares from Space* (for children). New York, Watts, 1981.
*Something Answered*. New York, Dell, 1983.
*The Adventures of a Two-Minute Werewolf* (for children). New York, Doubleday, 1983.
*Black Suits from Outer Space* (Willeford; for children). New York, Putnam, 1985.
*The Dandelion Caper* (Willeford; for children). New York, Putnam, 1986.
*The Calvin Nullifier* (Willeford; for children). New York, Putnam, 1987.
*Chain of Attack* (Star Trek). New York, Pocket, and London, Titan, 1987.
*The Peacekeepers* (Star Trek). New York, Pocket, 1988.
*The Final Nexus* (Star Trek). New York, Pocket, 1988.
*Whatever Became of Aunt Margaret?* (for children). New York, Putnam, 1990.
*Renegade* (Star Trek). New York, Pocket, and London, Titan, 1991.

OTHER PUBLICATIONS

Novels as Jean DeWeese

*The Reimann Curse*. New York, Ballantine, 1975; revised edition, as Gene DeWeese, as *A Different Darkness*, New York, Jove, 1982.
*The Carnelian Cat*. New York, Ballantine, 1975.
*The Moonstone Spirit*. New York, Ballantine, 1975.
*The Doll with Opal Eyes*. New York, Doubleday, 1976; London, Hale, 1977.
*Cave of the Moaning Wind*. New York, Ballantine, 1976.
*Web of Guilt*. New York, Ballantine, 1976.
*Nightmare in Pewter*. New York, Doubleday, 1978.
*Hour of the Cat*. New York, Doubleday, and London, Hale, 1980.
*The Backhoe Gothic*. New York, Doubleday, 1981.

Novel as Victoria Thomas

*Ginger's Wish*. New York, Doubleday, 1987.

Other

*Making American Folk Art Dolls*, with Gini Rogowski. Radnor, Pennsylvania, Chilton, 1975.
*Computers in Entertainment and the Arts* (for children). New York, Watts, 1984.

* * *

Gene DeWeese is a prolific and workmanlike writer whose novels and stories fall into the categories of gothic, horror, and science fiction. He writes young adult SF and fantasy and has received recognition from fans of SF as well as general readers.

DeWeese's first fictional publications (he started his career as a technical writer) were novels from the *Man from U.N.C.L.E.* series, which he co-authored with Robert (Buck) Coulson. *The Invisibility Affair* and *The Mind-Twisters Affair* are notable for their use of humor and wit, in keeping with the television series. However, as with his later novels, DeWeese's background in technical writing added much to these pieces. The descriptions of the workings of the invisible dirigible in the first of these two novels is fascinating to the technically inclined. He also wrote short stories with Coulson early in his career (under the name of Thomas Stratton) and a science-fiction novel, *Gates of the Universe*, for the short-run Laser Books series under the editorship of Roger Elwood. The later Laser novel, *Jeremy Case*, written by DeWeese alone, focuses on the character of Jeremy and his mysterious symbiotic partner, Lissa. DeWesse also wrote two hardcover novels with Coulson, both of which are humorous, solid reads, full of echoes to people they both knew as fans and writers. These were *Now You See It/Him/Them . . .* and *Charles Fortin Never Mentioned Wombats.*

Particularly prolific in the young adult field, DeWeese has produced at least five titles which are notable for their inclusion of girl as well as boy-scientist/adventurers. Of these, the amusing *The Adventures of a Two-Minute Werewolf* achieved the distinction of being made into a two-part television production for the O.J. Readmore series. In this story, Walt Cribbens turns 14 and finds that his family looks forward to a very unusual addition to the usual changes accompanying puberty. He is able to enlist the help of Cindy, a lively and loyal friend, to conceal his momentary transformations into a werewolf until he's able to resolve his problems. *Black Suits from Outer Space*, one of three adventure novels featuring the first-person narrator, Calvin Willeford, a self-proclaimed "logical guy" and his gutsy, more intuitive friend Kathy, is another example of DeWeese's grasp of humor and adventure that will appeal to the younger set. All of his young adult novels place children in the here and now but also put them in contact with alien beings or otherworldly forces, which they cope with very successfully. His adults are sometimes friends, not enemies, of the heroes, although there are plenty of silly, nasty, or obstructionist members of the older generation. *Black Suits* is no exception, with Kathy and Calvin rescuing an alien tourist through the able assistance of a level-headed, 300-pound, ex-wrestler sheriff's deputy named Phil. His strength is equal to the task of carrying the large, furry alien when necessary. The 300-pound ex-wrestler, like many of DeWeese's characters, is modelled partly after a friend, and those in the large circle of SF fans and writers who know DeWeese delight in finding these veiled references to themselves in the stories. This is also one of his techniques for avoiding the stereotypical characters that so easily slip into genre fiction narratives. His commitment to positive models for youngsters makes one eager to read more of this type of work.

Equally comfortable with established characters and settings, DeWeese's most recent adult-fiction efforts have been on *Star Trek* and *Star Trek: The Next Generation* novels. Reflecting the TV origins of the basic Star Trek concepts, all his additions to this series of novels rely heavily on conversation that introduces all new characters, furthers the plots, and provides what descriptions of settings are needed. With all the constraints placed on writers of such series, and especially popular TV series like *Star Trek*, it is a marvel that any creativity surfaces. Yet DeWeese's first contribution, *Chain of Attack*, was on the *New York Times* bestseller list and prompted an equally interesting sequel, *The Final Nexus.* His most recent, *Renegade*, is another fast-paced technological adventure which, like *Chain* and *Nexus*, requires the reader to sort through a number of would-be good and bad guys before the players' true intentions are revealed. He adds these elements of mystery to the usual, almost formulaic conversational sallies between the established main characters, which serve to reassure readers that they are still in the Star Trek universe. DeWeese's stubborn creativity makes these novels well worth reading; one hopes he will continue to contribute to the two Star Trek series.

—Janice M. Bogstad

---

**DICK, Philip K(indred).** American. Born in Chicago, Illinois, 16 December 1928. Educated at Berkeley High School, California, graduated 1945. Married 1) Jeanette Dick in 1949 (divorced); 2) Kleo Dick in 1951 (divorced); 3) Ann Dick in 1958 (divorced), one daughter; 4) Nancy Dick in 1967 (divorced), one daughter; 5) Tessa Busby in 1973, one son. Announcer, KSMO-AM radio, 1947 and record store manager, 1948–52, both Berkeley. Recipient: Hugo award, 1963; John W. Campbell Memorial award, 1975. *Died 2 March 1982.*

SCIENCE-FICTION PUBLICATIONS

Novels (series: Valis)

*Solar Lottery.* New York, Ace, 1955; as *World of Chance*, London, Rich and Cowan, 1956.
*The World Jones Made.* New York, Ace, 1956; London, Sidgwick and Jackson, 1968.
*The Man Who Japed.* New York, Ace, 1956; London, Magnum, 1978.
*Eye in the Sky.* New York, Ace, 1957; London, Arrow, 1971.
*The Cosmic Puppets.* New York, Ace, 1957; London, Panther, 1985.
*Time Out of Joint.* Philadelphia, Lippincott, 1959; London, Sidgwick and Jackson, 1961.
*Dr. Futurity.* New York, Ace, 1960; London, Eyre Methuen, 1976.
*Vulcan's Hammer.* New York, Ace, 1960; London, Arrow, 1976.
*The Man in the High Castle.* New York, Putnam, 1962; London, Penguin, 1965.
*The Game-Players of Titan.* New York, Ace, 1963; London, Sphere, 1969.
*Martian Time-Slip.* New York, Ballantine, 1964; London, New English Library, 1976.
*The Simulacra.* New York, Ace, 1964; London, Eyre Methuen, 1977.
*The Penultimate Truth.* New York, Belmont, 1964; London, Cape, 1967.
*Clans of the Alphane Moon.* New York, Ace, 1964; London, Panther, 1975.
*The Three Stigmata of Palmer Eldritch.* New York, Doubleday, 1965; London, Cape, 1966.
*Dr. Bloodmoney; or, How We Got Along after the Bomb.* New York, Ace, 1965; London, Arrow, 1977.
*The Crack in Space.* New York, Ace, 1966; London, Eyre Methuen, 1977.
*Now Wait for Last Year.* New York, Doubleday, 1966; London, Panther, 1975.
*The Unteleported Man.* New York, Ace, 1966; London, Eyre Methuen, 1976; revised edition, New York, Berkley, 1982; as *Lies, Inc.*, London, Gollancz, 1984.
*Counter-Clock World.* New York, Berkley, 1967; London, Sphere, 1968.
*The Zap Gun.* New York, Pyramid, 1967; London, Panther, 1975.
*The Ganymede Takeover*, with Ray Nelson. New York, Ace, 1967; London, Arrow, 1971.
*Do Androids Dream of Electric Sheep?* New York, Doubleday, 1968; London, Rapp and Whiting, 1969.
*Ubik.* New York, Doubleday, 1969; London, Rapp and Whiting, 1970.
*Galactic Pot-Healer.* New York, Berkley, 1969; London, Gollancz, 1971.
*A Maze of Death.* New York, Doubleday, 1970; London, Gollancz, 1972.
*Our Friends from Frolix 8.* New York, Ace, 1970; London, Panther, 1976.
*A Philip K. Dick Omnibus.* London, Sidgwick and Jackson, 1970.
*We Can Build You.* New York, DAW, 1972; London, Fontana, 1977.
*Flow My Tears, The Policeman Said.* New York, Doubleday, and London, Gollancz, 1974.
*Deus Irae*, with Roger Zelazny. New York, Doubleday, 1976; London, Gollancz, 1977.
*A Scanner Darkly.* New York, Doubleday, and London, Gollancz, 1977.
*Valis.* New York, Bantam, and London, Corgi, 1981.
*The Divine Invasion* (Valis). New York, Pocket Books, 1981; London, Corgi, 1982.
*The Transmigration of Timothy Archer* (Valis). New York, Pocket Books, and London, Gollancz, 1982.
*The Man Whose Teeth Were All Exactly Alike.* Willimantic, Connecticut, Zeising, 1984; London, Paladin, 1986.
*Radio Free Albemuth.* New York, Arbor House, 1985.
*Mary and the Giant.* New York, Arbor House, 1987; London, Gollancz, 1988.
*Nick and the Glimmung* (for children). London, Gollancz, 1988.
*The Broken Bubble.* New York, Arbor House, 1988; London, Gollancz, 1989.
*The Little Black Box.* London, Gollancz, 1990.

Short Stories

*A Handful of Darkness.* London, Rich and Cowan, 1955; Boston, Gregg Press, 1978.
*The Variable Man and Other Stories.* New York, Ace, 1957; London, Sphere, 1969.
*The Preserving Machine and Other Stories.* New York, Ace, 1969; London, Gollancz, 1971.
*The Book of Philip K. Dick.* New York, DAW, 1973; as *The Turning Wheel and Other Stories*, London, Coronet, 1977.
*The Best of Philip K. Dick*, edited by John Brunner. New York, Ballantine, 1977.
*The Golden Man.* New York, Berkley, 1980; London, Eyre Methuen, 1981.
*Robots, Androids, and Mechanical Oddities: The Science Fiction of Philip K. Dick*, edited by Patricia S. Warrick and Martin H. Greenberg. Carbondale, Southern Illinois University Press, 1985.
*I Hope I Shall Soon Arrive*, edited by Mark Hurst and Paul Williams. New York, Doubleday, 1985.
*The Collected Stories.* Los Angeles, Underwood Miller, 5 vols., 1987; London, Gollancz, 1988–90.

OTHER PUBLICATIONS

Novels

*Confessions of a Crap Artist.* New York, Entwhistle, 1975; London, Magnum, 1979.
*In Milton Lumky Territory.* Hastings-on Hudson, New York, Dragon Press, and London, Gollancz, 1985.
*Puttering about in a Small Land.* Chicago, Academy, 1985; London, Palladin, 1987.

Play

Screenplay: *Ubik*, 1985.

Other

*Philp K. Dick: In His Own Words* (interviews), edited by Gregg Rickman. Long Beach, California, Fragments West-Valentine Press, 1984.
*The Dark-Haired Girl.* Willimantic, Connecticut, M.V. Ziesing, 1988.
*The Selected Letters*, edited by Don Herron. Lancaster, Pennsylvania, Underwood Miller, 1991.
*Selections from the Exegesis*, edited by Larry Sutin. Novato, California, Underwood Miller, 1991.

*

Bibliography: *PKD: A Philip K. Dick Bibliography* by Daniel J.H. Levack, Columbia, Pennsylvania, Underwood Miller, 1981.

Manuscript Collection: California State University, Fullerton.

Critical Studies: *Philip K. Dick and the Umbrella of Light* by Angus Taylor, Baltimore, T-K Graphics, 1975; *Philip K. Dick: Electric Shepherd* (includes bibliography) edited by Bruce Gillespie, Melbourne, Norstrilia Press, 1975; "Philip K. Dick Issue" of *Science-Fiction Studies* (Terre Haute, Indiana), March 1975 (includes bibliography); *Philip K. Dick* by Hazel Pierce, Mercer Island, Washington, Starmont House, 1982; *Philip K. Dick* edited by Martin H. Greenberg and Joseph D. Olander, New York, Taplinger, 1983; *The Novels of Philip K. Dick* by Kim Stanley Robinson, Ann Arbor, Michigan, UMI Research Press, 1984; *Philip K. Dick: The Last Testament* by Gregg Rickman, Long Beach, California, Fragments West-Valentine Press, 1985; *Only Apparently Real: The World of Philip K. Dick* by Paul Williams, New York, Arbor House, 1986; *Philip K. Dick: The Dream Connection* by D. Scott Apel, San Jose, California, Permanent Press, 1987; *Mind in Motion: The Fiction of Philip K. Dick* by Patricia S. Warrick, Carbondale, Southern Illinois University Press, 1987; *Philip K. Dick* by Douglas A. Mackey, Boston, Twayne, 1988; *Divine Invasions: A Life of Philip K. Dick* by Lawrence Sutin, New York, Harmony, 1989; *To the High Castle: Philip K. Dick, a Life* by Gregg Rickman, Long Beach, California, Fragments West-Valentine Press, 1989.

Philip K. Dick commented (in *Contemporary Novelists*, 1976):

Using science fiction as a framework, I attempt to cut through the layers of quasi-reality, finding in the process that the elliptical viewpoints of psychosis act as starting points. Although I have been able to determine and then represent in my fiction many private universes, differing from one personality type to the next, I am in no sense trying to state what in the final analysis is "real." It is, rather, the search which interests me; perhaps the outcome is not the same for all of us. In my early novels and stories I often used sociological and political themes; later I branched into drug trips and also theological trips, sometimes combining both (which angered many readers, both those who used drugs as well as those who used God). However, out of this I have recently come to sense a new level of feeling rather than intuition or reasoning. It is perhaps possible that when all the layers of the mind are stripped away the reality of the heart remains, or anyhow some organ more vital than the brain. In my work-in-progress I seek to contact some vein of cognition, some perceptual entity outside myself, outside our own race . . . where this entity would be, if anywhere at all, I can't say. Still, I think it exists, and, having helped me in my work throughout my career, perhaps it will guide me toward itself during the remaining part of my professional and creative life.

* * *

Due to both the merits of his fiction and the pull of circumstances, Philip K. Dick seems likely to achieve literary fame outside the science-fiction community. Born in 1928, Dick was a prolific writer of science-fiction short stories and novels. Publication of new works by Dick continued after his death in 1982: several novels considered unpublishable during his life (most not science fiction), a five-volume collection of his short stories, and much non-fiction material such as letters and essays. Posthumously published longer works of science fiction include a children's novel (*Nick and the Glimmung*) and a screenplay version of his novel *Ubik.* Extremely quirky but generous in friendship, Dick has influenced many authors, such as his friends Tim Powers and K.W. Jeter.

Two films are based loosely on Dick's work: *Bladerunner*, from *Do Androids Dream of Electric Sheep?*, and *Total Recall*, from his short story "We Can Rememeber It for You Wholesale." Other works have inspired music, including *Dr. Bloodmoney* ("Bluthgeld" on the album *Painting by Numbers* by Michael Bass) and *Valis* (a 1987 opera by Todd Machovia); a play based on *Flow My Tears, the Policeman Said* has been performed. In a process quite compatible with his own fiction, Dick has become a fictional character in works such as Michael Bishop's novel *The Secret Ascension;* an anthology of short stories, *Welcome to Reality: The Nightmares of Philip K. Dick* (edited by Uwe Anton); and Gary Walkow's little-known film *The Trouble with Dick.*

Though sometimes underappreciated, and often underremunerative, Dick's fiction never went without recognition. In 1963 he won the Hugo award for *The Man in the High Castle.* Dick's fiction has also received notice from scholars of science fiction—including Marxist critics, which sometimes disturbed Dick. After Dick's death, Paul Williams started the Philip K. Dick Society, publishing *The PKDS Newsletter* and organizing the growing attention.

Dick's science fiction exemplifies the genre in both its excellences and its limitations. Stimulating, thought-provoking, and sometimes simply provoking, Dick's fiction explores several consistent themes: what is truly moral and human; the value of the unexceptional person in society; deep reality vs. deceiving appearances; the struggle of love against hate; the balancing of objective and subjective—or shared and individual—experience. The intellectual play in Dick's fiction, with language and with ideas, is often gratifying and sometimes confusing. The accoutrements of his fiction are both various and consistent: creatures such as the Glimmung and the wub, inventions including the flapple and the gum/drug Can-D, the sentient factories known as Printers and a host of often-annoying autonomic machines. Dick often re-used ideas, from short stories to novels and even from one novel to another.

Dick's style can be clumsy or pedestrian; at his best, however, he mixes flat honesty with keen insight, and pathos with humor, characteristically and appealingly. His plotting, too, can be uneven, his novels marred by a bad sense of pacing. His fiction generally succeeds despite these faults, partly because of the wealth of creative imagination involved and the deep sympathy the author obviously feels for the characters and the issues they must confront.

While most critics agree that Philip K. Dick has written some of the best SF novels and some of the worst, few agree on which is which. Even Dick often changed his mind, and in the mid-1960's he wrote, "I have written and sold 23 novels, and all are terrible except one. But I'm not sure which one." The novels selected for praise generally include *The Man in the High Castle, Ubik, The Three Stigmata of Palmer Eldritch*, and often *Martian Time-Slip* and *Flow My Tears, the Policeman Said.* There is a longer list of controversial works, praised by some and dismissed by others: *Dr. Bloodmoney, The Penultimate Truth, Counter-Clock World, Clans of the Alphane Moon, Galactic Pot-Healer, Time Out of Joint, The Cosmic Puppets, Eye in the Sky, Do Androids Dream of Electric Sheep?*, and *A Scanner Darkly.*

In many of Dick's novels an outside force, troubling or even malevolent, affects "reality" as it is experienced. Often the protagonist is a common man (though a white-collar worker, rather than a laborer) who must both understand the situation and help rectify it. The outside force may be the hallucinogenic gum Chew-Z of *The Three Stigmata of Palmer Eldritch;* the Zoroastrian gods of *The Cosmic Puppets;* the projective schizophrenia of Manfred in *Martian Time-Slip;* the half-life dreams of *Ubik.* Often in a Dick novel one is not sure what is real and what is imagined: Is Bruno Bluthgeld, of *Dr. Bloodmoney*, a powerful psychic (as is Hoppy Harrington in the same book) or a paranoid schizophrenic?

Protagonists such as Joe Fernwright (*Galactic Pot-Healer*), Mr. Tagomi (*The Man in the High Castle*), Joe Chip (*Ubik*), and Ted Barton (*The Cosmic Puppets*) struggle to beat these influences, or simply to live humanely in a world gone wrong—and often the former is a more extreme version of the latter. The heroism in Dick's novels always consists of small victories, though sometimes with major consequences; his protagonists try to leave the world better than they found it and sometimes succeed. In many novels, multiple protagonists present different problems and values. In *Dr. Bloodmoney*, for instance, the heroes include astronaut and disc-jockey Walt Dangerfield, post-holocaust entrepreneur Andrew Gill, Negro salesman Stuart McConchie, and McConchie's bosses Mr. and Mrs. Hardy. In *Flow My Tears, the Policeman Said*, Jason Taverner is a more usual Dick protagonist, but policeman Felix Buckman achieves personal renewal through compassion.

Some readers fault Dick for his female characters. Doubtless, Dick—married five times—had problems with women, and this is reflected in his fiction. With some exceptions, his females are seductive but mean, an attractive yet destructive other half: the many examples include Alys Buckman in *Flow my Tears, the Policeman Said*, Donna Hawthorne in *A Scanner Darkly*, and Fay Hume in *Confessions of a Crap Artist.* In his later works, Dick presented female saviors in *Valis* and *The Divine Invasion;* perhaps this helped prepare him for his best female character, Angel Archer in *The Transmigration of Timothy Archer.*

In the last years of his life, Dick produced four semi-autobiographical novels, tending towards the mainstream: *Valis* and its alternate version *Radio Free Albemuth, The Divine Invasion*, and *The Transmigration of Timothy Archer.* All of these were inspired by odd experiences that Dick had in 1974; the novels grapple with psychological and spiritual implications of those events. Though some readers saw this as an unfortunate change in Dick's life and work, it was obviously vital to him, and it brought him new ways to explore many of his familiar concerns. In these last novels and in other writing—including a huge manuscript that he called his "Exegesis"—Dick developed a romantic neo-Gnosticism that combined many of his themes, such as the individual vs. blind authority, the difficulty of being truly human, and the decay inherent in a material world. In letters from 1974 on, Dick re-interpreted his earlier work in line with the more coherent system he was developing; he was able to do this, however, because of the consistent thematic interest throughout his life.

Perhaps too much attention is now being paid to Dick's later works and to his unusual life. However, Dick's entire career is worthy of study, both in its own right and as an example of the best and worst aspects of science fiction. Especially, Dick helped pioneer the use of genre SF conventions to explore universal human issues.

—Bernadette Bosky

---

**DICKINSON, Peter (Malcolm de Brissac).** British. Born in Livingstone, Northern Rhodesia (now Zambia), 16 December 1927. Educated at Eton College (King's Scholar), 1941–46; King's College, Cambridge (exhibitioner), B.A. 1951. Served in the British Army, 1946–48. Married Mary Rose Bernard in 1953 (died 1988); two daughters and two sons. Assistant editor and reviewer, *Punch*, London, 1952–69. Chairman of the Management Committee, Society of Authors, 1978–80. Recipient: Crime Writers Association Gold Dagger, 1968, 1969; *Guardian* award, for children's book, 1977; *Boston Globe-Horn Book* award, for non-fiction, 1977; Whitbread award, 1979, 1990; Library Association Carnegie Medal, for children's book, 1980, 1981. Agent: A.P. Watt Ltd., 20 John Street, London WC1N 2DR. Address: Bramdean Lodge, near Alvesford, Hampshire SO24 OJN, England.

SCIENCE-FICTION PUBLICATIONS

Novels (series: The Changes)

*The Changes* (for children). London, Gollancz, 1975.
- *The Weathermonger.* London, Gollancz, 1968; Boston, Little Brown, 1969.
- *Heartsease.* London, Gollancz, and Boston, Little Brown, 1969.
- *The Devil's Children.* London, Gollancz, and Boston, Little Brown, 1970.

*The Green Gene.* London, Hodder and Stoughton, and New York, Pantheon, 1973.

*The Gift* (for children). London, Gollancz, 1973; Boston, Little Brown, 1974.

*The Poison Oracle.* London, Hodder and Stoughton, and New York, Pantheon, 1974.

*King and Joker.* London, Hodder and Stoughton, and New York, Pantheon, 1976.

*The Blue Hawk* (for children). London, Gollancz, and Boston, Little Brown, 1976.

*Healer* (for children). London, Gollancz, 1983; New York, Delacorte Press, 1985.

*A Box of Nothing* (for children). London, Gollancz, 1985; New York, Delacorte Press, 1987.

*Eva* (for children). London, Gollancz, 1988; New York, Delacorte Press, 1989.

*Skeleton-in-Waiting* (sequel to *King and Joker*). London, Bodley Head, 1989; New York, Pantheon, 1990.

OTHER PUBLICATIONS

Novels

*Skin Deep*. London, Hodder and Stoughton, 1968; as *The Glass-Sided Ants' Nest*, New York, Harper, 1968.
*A Pride of Heroes*. London, Hodder and Stoughton, 1969; as *The Old English Peep Show*, New York, Harper, 1969.
*The Seals*. London, Hodder and Stoughton, 1970; as *The Sinful Stones*, New York, Harper, 1970.
*Sleep and His Brother*. London, Hodder and Stoughton, and New York, Harper, 1971.
*The Lizard in the Cup*. London, Hodder and Stoughton, and New York, Harper, 1972.
*The Lively Dead*. London, Hodder and Stoughton, and New York, Pantheon, 1975.
*Walking Dead*. London, Hodder and Stoughton, 1977; New York, Pantheon, 1978.
*One Foot in the Grave*. London, Hodder and Stoughton, 1979; New York, Pantheon, 1980.
*A Summer in the Twenties*. London, Hodder and Stoughton, and New York, Pantheon, 1981.
*The Last House-Party*. London, Bodley Head, and New York, Pantheon, 1982.
*Hindsight*. London, Bodley Head, and New York, Pantheon, 1983.
*Death of a Unicorn*. London, Bodley Head, and New York, Pantheon, 1984.
*Tefuga*. London, Bodley Head, and New York, Pantheon, 1986.
*Mole Hole*. London, Blackie, and New York, Bedrick, 1987.
*Perfect Gallows*. London, Bodley Head, and New York, Pantheon, 1988.
*Merlin Dreams*. London, Gollancz, and New York, Delacorte Press, 1988.
*Ak*. London, Gollancz, 1990.
*Play Dead*. London, Bodley Head, 1991.

Plays (for children)

Television Series: *Mandog*, 1972.

Other

*Emma Tupper's Diary* (for children). London, Gollancz, and Boston, Little Brown, 1971.
*The Dancing Bear* (for children). London, Gollancz, 1972; Boston, Little Brown, 1973.
*The Iron Lion* (for children). Boston, Little Brown, 1972; London, Allen and Unwin, 1973.
*Chance, Luck, and Destiny* (miscellany). London, Gollancz, 1975; Boston, Little Brown, 1976.
*Annerton Pit* (for children). London, Gollancz, and Boston, Little Brown, 1977.
*Hepzibah* (for children). Twickenham, Middlesex, Eel Pie, 1978; Boston, Godine, 1980.
*The Flight of Dragons*. London, Pierrot, and New York, Harper, 1979.
*Tulku* (for children). London, Gollancz, and New York, Dutton, 1979.
*City of Gold and Other Stories from the Old Testament*. London, Gollancz, and New York, Pantheon, 1980.
*The Seventh Raven*. London, Gollancz, and New York, Dutton, 1981.
*Giant Cold* (for children). London, Gollancz, and New York, Dutton, 1984.

Editor, *Presto! Humorous Bits and Pieces*. London, Hutchinson, 1975.
Editor, *Hundreds and Hundreds*. London, Penguin, 1984.

*

Peter Dickinson comments:

I regard all my fiction as SF (that's to say I write it as if it were), though usually the S bulks much smaller than the F. Classic detective stories (which I try to write) usually have to be restricted to a closed world, which I tend to invent as if it were an alien planet. Indeed, inventing even a normal human character seems to me to demand an effort of the same kind as inventing an alien species; this may account for the fact that my characters have a tendency towards the grotesque. The children's books are mostly straightforward soft SF; *The Green Gene* began as a satire about apartheid, or rather about outsiders' attitudes to it, but acquired directions and energies of its own. My attitude to SF is much more influenced by the pulp I read in the 1940's than by anything more recent, or in book form.

* * *

Peter Dickinson has made a substantial name for himself in the mystery genre with a series of bizarre murder mysteries. Frequently these novels play with devices better known in the field of science fiction, although none is really written as an example of the genre. There are hints of telepathy in *Walking Dead*, for example. Communication with a very bright ape is the key to unravelling the mystery in *The Poison Oracle*, and there is an alternate British royalty in *King and Joker*.

Dickinson has written several fantasy novels, perhaps the most interesting of which is a trilogy set in England when all technology stops working, magic returns to the land, the rest of the world continues to advance technologically, but a pastoral calm settles over most of the British Isles. The first in the series, *The Weathermonger*, follows a young man and his sister as they flee to France, only to return in search of the source of the mysterious change. Ultimately they confront an awakened Merlin of Camelot, once more active in the affairs of men.

The two follow-up volumes were related by setting only; there are no common characters and even Merlin appears to have disappeared. *Heartsease* is concerned with a spy from the United States who is unmasked by the elders of a village and nearly killed because of suspicion of witchcraft. He is rescued by sympathetic children, and a well-told series of adventures follow. Possibly the best in the series is *The Devil's Children*. Although the British have been mentally altered by the change so that they blindly strike out and destroy anything technological, one group in England seems to be immune, the resident population of Sikhs. The protagonist is a young girl separated from her parents who falls in with a wandering band of Sikhs, is befriended by them, and becomes their agent in dealings with the rest of the British. Unable to return to their homeland, they finally decide to establish a settlement in a remote area and trade with others using her as their agent.

*Tulku* is an oriental adventure fantasy. A boy and his companions wander around Tibet after bandits raid the mission where he lives. Ultimately he turns out to be a pivotal piece in a game of oriental legend. *Tulku* is written for younger readers, but this is not true of *The Blue Hawk*. A young trainee for the priesthood violates ritual by befriending a sacred blue hawk, thereby causing the death of the reigning king, endangering his own life, and throwing the entire established order into disarray. He is caught up in the ensuing power struggle between clerical and lay institutions, as each seeks to make him the instrument of the other's downfall. *The Blue Hawk* may be the best single work Dickinson has written.

The only genuine adult science-fiction novel Dickinson has written is *The Green Gene.* In an alternate version of our own world, England is ruled by a rigid authoritarian government. For some reason, an increasing number of births in the island are of green children, and all green humans are legally delcared to be Celts, while whites and blacks are legally Saxons. An Indian medical specialist is hired by the Race Relations Board to develop a method of reliably predicting the occurrence of the green mutation. The Board ostensibly exists to promote racial harmony, but is in fact the chief instrument for the suppression of the green minority. The protagonist is politically as well as socially naive, and is soon involved unwittingly in politics, sexual liaisons, murder, and intrigue. He is kidnapped, enlisted in a plot against the government, and only arranges his own freedom by eventually smartening up and doublecrossing everyone. It is a refreshing and disturbing satire.

*Eva*, a science-fiction novel aimed at younger readers, features a young girl whose body is so damaged in an accident that doctors do not believe they can save it. They can, however, save her personality, transferring it into the body of a chimpanzee. The result is a fascinating look at humanity from a bizarre new perspective, a novel designed to appeal to adult sensibilities as well as teenaged readers, and amply satisfying to make readers wish Dickinson were more active in the field.

—Don D'Ammassa

---

**DICKSON, Gordon R(upert).** American. Born in Edmonton, Alberta, Canada 1 November 1923; emigrated to the United States at age 13. Educated at the University of Minnesota, Minneapolis, B.A. 1948, and graduate study, 1948–50. Served in the United States Army, 1943–46. Since 1950, freelance writer. Recipient: Hugo award, 1965, 1981 (twice); Nebula award, 1966; Skylark award, 1975; Derleth award, 1977; Jupiter award, 1977. President, Science Fiction Writers of America, 1969–71. Agent: Kirby McCauley, 155 East 77th Street, New York, New York 10021, U.S.A.

SCIENCE-FICTION PUBLICATIONS

Novels (series: Childe Cycle; Robby Hoenig)

*Alien from Arcturus.* New York, Ace, 1956; as *Arcturus Landing*, 1978.
*Mankind on the Run.* New York, Ace, 1956; as *On the Run*, 1979.
*The Genetic General, Time to Teleport.* New York, Ace, 1960; *The Genetic General* published separately, London, Digit, 1961; expanded edition of *The Genetic General*, as *Dorsai!*, New York, DAW, and London, Sphere, 1976.
*Secret under the Sea* (for children; Hoenig). New York, Holt Rinehart, 1960; London, Hutchinson, 1962.
*Naked to the Stars.* New York, Pyramid, 1961; London, Sphere, 1978.
*Delusion World, Spacial Delivery.* New York, Ace, 1961.
*Necromancer* (Childe). New York, Doubleday, 1962; London, Mayflower, 1963; as *No Room for Man*, New York, Macfadden, 1963.
*Secret under Antarctica* (for children; Hoenig). New York, Holt Rinehart, 1963.
*Secret under the Caribbean* (for children; Hoenig). New York, Holt Rinehart, 1964.
*Space Winners* (for children). New York, Holt Rinehart, 1965; London, Faber, 1967.
*The Alien Way.* New York, Bantam, 1965; London, Corgi, 1973.
*Mission to Universe.* New York, Berkley, 1965; revised edition, New York, Ballantine, 1977; London, Sphere, 1978.
*The Space Swimmers.* New York, Berkley, 1967; London, Sidgwick and Jackson, 1968.
*Planet Run*, with Keith Laumer. New York, Doubleday, 1967; London, Hale, 1977.
*Soldier, Ask Not* (Childe). New York, Dell, 1967; London, Sphere, 1975.
*None But Man.* New York, Doubleday, 1969; London, Macdonald, 1970.
*Wolfling.* New York, Dell, 1969.
*Spacepaw* (for children). New York, Putnam, 1969.
*Hour of the Horde.* New York, Putnam, 1970.
*The Tactics of Mistake* (Childe). New York, Doubleday, 1971; London, Sphere, 1975.
*Sleepwalker's World.* Philadelphia, Lippincott, 1971; London, Hale, 1973.
*The Outposter.* Philadelphia, Lippincott, 1972; London, Hale, 1973.
*The Pritcher Mass.* New York, Doubleday, 1972.
*Alien Art.* New York, Dutton, 1973; London, Hale, 1974.
*The R-Master.* Philadelphia, Lippincott, 1973; London, Hale, 1975.
*Gremlins, Go Home!* (for children), with Ben Bova. New York, St. Martin's Press, 1974.
*Star Prince Charlie* (for children), with Poul Anderson. New York, Putnam, 1975.
*Three to Dorsai!* (omnibus). New York, Doubleday, 1975.
*The Dragon and the George.* New York, Doubleday, 1976.
*The Lifeship*, with Harry Harrison. New York, Harper, 1976.
*Futurelove: A Science Fiction Triad*, with others. Indianapolis, Bobbs Merrill, 1977; London, Hale, 1979.
*Time Storm.* New York, St. Martin's Press, 1977; London, Sphere, 1978.
*The Far Call.* New York, Dial Press, and London, Sidgwick and Jackson, 1978.
*Home from the Shore.* New York, Sunridge Press, 1978.
*Pro.* New York, Ace, 1978.
*The Spirit of Dorsai.* New York, Ace, 1979.
*Lost Dorsai.* New York, Ace, 1980.
*Masters of Everon.* New York, Ace, 1980.
*Love Not Human.* New York, Ace, 1981.
*Jamie the Red*, with Roland Green. New York, Ace, 1984.
*The Final Encyclopedia* (Childe). New York, Tor, 1984.
*The Last Master.* New York, Tor, 1984.
*Survival!* New York, Pocket Books, 1984.
*Beyond the Dar Al-Haab.* New York, Tor, 1985.
*Forward!*, edited by Sandra Miesel. New York, Baen, 1985.
*Invaders!*, edited by Sandra Miesel. New York, Baen, 1985.
*The Forever Man.* New York, Ace, 1986.
*The Last Dream.* New York, Baen, 1986.
*The Man the Worlds Rejected.* New York, Tor, 1986.
*Mindspan*, edited by Sandra Miesel. New York, Baen, 1986.
*Way of the Pilgrim.* New York, Ace, 1987; London, Sphere, 1988.
*The Stranger.* New York, Tor, 1987.

*Beginnings*. New York, Baen, 1988.
*The Chantry Guild* (Childe). New York, Ace, 1988; London, Sphere, 1989.
*Ends*. New York, Baen, 1988.
*The Earth Lords*. New York, Ace, 1988; London, Sphere, 1989.
*The Dragon Knight*. New York, Tor, 1990.
*Wolf and Iron*. New York, Tor, 1990.
*Young Bleys* (Childe). New York, Tor, 1991.
*The Harriers*. New York, Baen, 1991.
*The Dragon on the Border*. New York, Ace, 1992.

Short Stories

*Earthman's Burden*, with Poul Anderson. New York, Gnome Press, 1957.
*Danger—Human*. New York, Doubleday, 1970; as *The Book of Gordon Dickson*, New York, DAW, 1973.
*Mutants*. New York, Macmillan, 1970.
*The Star Road*. New York, Doubleday, 1973; London, Hale, 1975.
*Ancient, My Enemy*. New York, Doubleday, 1974; London, Sphere, 1978.
*Gordon R. Dickson's SF Best*, edited by James R. Frenkel. New York, Dell, 1978.
*In Iron Years*. New York, Doubleday, 1980.
*Hoka!*, with Poul Anderson. New York, Simon and Schuster, 1983.
*Steel Brother*. New York, Tor, 1985.
*The Dorsai Companion*. New York, Ace, 1986.
*In the Bone: The Best Science Fiction of Gordon R. Dickson*. New York, Ace, 1987.

OTHER PUBLICATIONS

Other

Editor, *Rod Serling's Triple W: Witches, Warlocks and Werewolves*. New York, Bantam, 1963.
Editor, *Rod Serling's Devils and Demons*. New York, Bantam, 1967.
Editor, with Poul Anderson and Robert Silverberg, *The Day the Sun Stood Still*. Nashville, Nelson, 1972.
Editor, *Combat SF*. New York, Doubleday, 1975.
Editor, *Nebula Winners 12*. New York, Harper, 1978.

*

Bibliography: *Gordon R. Dickson: A Primary and Secondary Bibliography* by Raymond H. Thompson, Boston, Hall, 1983.

* * *

"We're improvable, tremendously improvable," says Gordon R. Dickson, "and by our own efforts." He views the human race as a single organism with a unique inner dynamic driving its psychic—but not necessarily physical—evolution. He delights in showing consciousness emerging, developing, and perfecting itself in persuit of god-like powers: "Man's future is upward and outward." He presents an open-ended universe filled with limitless possibilities ready to be seized by whatever beings are bold enough. Dickson, a Pelagian humanist, maintains that intelligent life-forms can direct their own destiny. Ultimately, this capacity for continuous growth will surpass the static excellence of divinity, even that of a deity mighty enough to make the sun stand still ("Things Which Are Caesar's"). Nature is the milieu in which this drama unfolds, not a participant in the action. Dickson is no romantic pantheist like Poul Anderson, a writer with whom he is often incorrectly linked.

Taken together, Dickson's works are simply variant readings of a single epic adventure—life's quest for transcendence. He proclaims the victories of tenacious, creative, morally responsible people who can reshape heaven and earth by sheer force of will. Right makes might. Goodness must prevail. Mind conquers matter. The author's idealism and boundless confidence are qualities so traditional as to seem novelties in this gloomy era.

Thus, Dickson's favorite literary structure is the initatory scenario. His protagonists learn, not only for themselves, but on behalf of their group, culture, or species. For example, the hero of *The Pritcher Mass* spearheads the collective aspirations of all living things on Earth. The typical Dickson plot exemplifies the mythologist Joseph Campbell's heroic monomyth: a young, obscure, or otherwise lightly regarded individual discovers and masters his own unique abilities. Despite misunderstanding from friends and opposition from foes, he confounds conventional wisdom (often in some juridical confrontation), and thereby averts disaster.

This pattern persists in Dickson's juveniles: an exceptionally mature boy and girl save their planet from ruthless developers in *Alien Art*. It even shapes such humorous works as the Dilbian series (humans earning the respect of huge, roughneck aliens); the Dragon Knight series (an English professor adjusting to life as a medieval dragon); and the Hoka series (a diplomat coping with compulsively imitative aliens). Dickson's comedies center on rational beings struggling to function in preposterously irrational situations.

However, Dickson usually stages his initiations as action-adventure tales. Some have objected to the frequency of military or quasi-military settings but these critics are reading a political intent into the work that is not there—Dickson is not Robert A. Heinlein. Although he sees an evolutionary advantage in humanity's pack-hunting instinct, his backgrounds are largely dictated by convenience. Traditionally, soldiers and explorers have been obvious subjects for life-and-death dramas of fortitude, daring, and loyalty. Yet Dickson innovates by also making his heroes cerebral and empathic as well as endowing many of them with his own talents for poetry, music, and art.

Note that "Call Him Lord" and "Jean Dupres" are about courage, not killing. They are mirror-image studies in manhood: a prince is executed for cowardice to forestall an evil reign; a colonial boy's death in battle brings peace within his people's grasp. These two stories, Nebula winner and Hugo nominee respectively, illustrate the technical mastery and absolute economy of his best work.

Although Dickson's elegance and limpidity are better displayed at shorter lengths, he is always a deliberate craftsman. (He was formally trained in writing by Robert Penn Warren, among others, and has made it his sole profession.) He has even developed his own approach to science fiction, the "consciously thematic novel." This is Dickson's way of making a philosophical statement without resorting to the crudities of propaganda. As he explains: "The aim is to make the theme such an integral part of the novel that it can be effective upon the reader without ever having to be stated explicitly. . . ."

Dickson's philosphical purpose imparts a peculiarly relentless quality to his prose. Every element is concentrated along the cutting edge of the blade. Nothing in his stories exists for its own sake except the message. Although he is a dedicated researcher who experiences as well as studies his backgrounds, he never inserts decorative color or extraneous details. Consider the degree of auctorial control imposed on complex raw materials in *The Far Call*, the finest realistic novel about the space program yet written.

Dickson welds his stories together with symbols. These are typically grouped in pairs and triads that seek some ultimate unity—salvation is integration. Dualities exist worldwide but Dickson's trinities are best interpreted according to the structuralist theories of Indo-European mythologist Georges Dumézil. Thus, Dickson's design manages to be both universal and specifically Western. The tidiest and most accessible examples of his symbolism occur in *Home From the Shore* and its sequel, *The Space Swimmers.*

The Childe Cycle is the major showcase for Dickson's ideas and artistry. For the past 30 years, he has been constructing an epic chronicle of human evolution incorporating historical, contemporary, and science-fictional segments running from the 14th to the 24th centuries. Only the SF components have appeared so far: *Dorsai!; Necromancer; Soldier, Ask Not; The Tactics of Mistake; The Final Encyclopedia; The Chantry Guild; Young Bleys;* plus *Bleys the Man*, currently in preparation.

In these novels, the same hero passes through three incarnations, developing intuition as a Man of War, empathy as a Man of Philosophy, and creativity as a Man of Faith until he assimilates the qualities of his Twin enemy and becomes the first Responsible Man, integrating the unconscious/conservative and conscious/progressive halves of the racial psyche within himself. (See Sandra Miesel's afterwords to *The Final Encyclopedia, Lost Dorsai*, and the 1980 Ace edition of *Dorsai!* for extensive mythic and philosphical analysis.)

The level of aesthetic achievement varies. *Dorsai!* is notable for introducing a thoroughly sympathetic superman and for loading a military action yarn with mythic archetypes. The murkiness and subtlety of *Necromancer* make undue demands on the reader. *Soldier, Ask Not* uses its villain as the viewpoint character to wrenching emotional effect. *The Tactics of Mistake* is as stilted as a war game. *The Final Encyclopedia* is sensitive and elegaic, though slightly marred by lectures. *Chantry Guild* tells of the hero's conceptual breakthrough to circumvent death. *Young Bleys* attempts to explain how the antagonist of *The Final Encyclopedia* got that way, but only dims his dark romantic glow. However, the short "illuminations" that accompany the Cycle proper ("Warrior," "Brothers," "Amanda Morgan," and the Hugo-winning "Lost Dorsai") are uniformly excellent in concept as well as execution.

*Way of the Pilgrim*, incorporating the Hugo-winning "Cloak and Staff' (1980), plays counterpoint with Cycle themes. Its formidable alien conquerors are, in a sense, Dark Brothers of the Dorsai for they are the tragically warped martial caste of an otherwise extinct alien race. Its reluctant—and not superhuman—hero is a pilgrim both in body and spirit as he moves from a self-centered to a self-sacrificing life.

*Wolf and Iron*, a meticulously researched dramatization of wolf behavior, represents a new departure for Dickson. It chronicles the rebuilding—not the building—of a personality and a destiny in a near-future America ruined by economic collapse. Through his comradeship with a timberwolf, the protagonist is the "iron" forged into a hero. But he is a most unusual Dicksonian hero because he develops no superpowers, changes his goals for love, and decides that sibling rivalry is not worth the bother.

Yet despite decades of steady accomplishment, Dickson is less admired than he ought to be. His reputation as a novelist was tainted by early pulpish efforts like *Time To Teleport* and hasty potboilers like *The R-Master.* Anti-war backlash during the 1960's and 1970's distorted reactions to the Cycle. Stories of man's indominability ("Danger: Human") drew charges of Heinleinian human supremacy. But this criticism overlooks Dickson's sensitive portraits of aliens ("Black Charlie" and *The Alien Way*) and his pleas for interspecies empathy ("Dolphin's Way").

Complaints against Dickson's ineptitude with women characters have more validity. Too many of these are non-entities who exist solely to frustrate and misunderstand his heroes. Only masculine interactions seem important. However, in recent years he has systematically worked to correct this weakness by deepening characterizations and revising old formulas. The Triad in *Time Storm* is the Man of Philosophy, the Woman of War, and the Animal of Faith. The complementary Twins in *The Far Call* are no longer men but rather a pair of male-female couples. "Amanda Morgan" is built out of role reversals and in *The Final Encyclopedia* the trio of gifted heroines (one from each Splinter Culture) uphold the hero like the legs of a tripod.

At its serious best, Dickson's writing strikes the mind like remembered strains of half-heard music or swift torrents of icy water.

—Sandra Miesel

---

**DISCH, Thomas M(ichael).** Also writes as Thom Demijohn; Leonie Hargrave; Cassandra Knye. American. Born in Des Moines, Iowa, 2 February 1940. Educated at Cooper Union, New York, and New York University, 1959–62. Part-time checkroom attendant, Majestic Theatre, New York, 1957–62; copywriter, Doyle Dane Bernbach Inc., New York, 1963–64. Member of the board, National Book Critics Circle, 1988–91; secretary, 1989–91. Since 1964, freelance writer and lecturer; since 1987, theater critic for *The Nation.* Recipient: O. Henry prize, 1975; John W. Campbell Memorial award, 1980; *Locus* award, 1981. Agent: Karpfinger Agency, 500 Fifth Avenue, Suite 2800, New York, New York 10110, U.S.A.

SCIENCE-FICTION PUBLICATIONS

Novels

*The Genocides.* New York, Berkley, 1965; London, Whiting and Wheaton, 1967.
*Mankind under the Leash.* New York, Ace, 1966; as *The Puppies of Terra*, London, Panther, 1978.
*Echo Round His Bones.* New York, Berkley, 1967; London, Hart Davis, 1969.
*Camp Concentration.* London, Hart Davis, 1968; New York, Doubleday, 1969.
*The Prisoner.* New York, Ace, 1969; London, Dobson, 1979.
*334.* London, MacGibbon and Kee, 1972; New York, Avon, 1974.
*On Wings of Song.* New York, St. Martin's Press, and London, Gollancz, 1979.
*Triplicity* (omnibus). New York, Doubleday, 1980.
*The Businessman: A Tale of Terror.* New York, Harper, and London, Cape, 1984.
*The M.D.: A Horror Story.* New York, Knopf, 1991.

Short Stories

*One Hundred and Two H-Bombs.* London, Compact, 1966; New York, Berkley, 1971; enlarged edition, as *White Fang Goes Dingo and Other Funny S. F. Stories*, London, Arrow, 1971.
*Under Compulsion.* London, Hart Davis, 1968; as *Fun with Your New Head*, New York, Doubleday, 1971.
*Getting into Death.* London, Hart Davis MacGibbon, 1973; New York, Knopf, 1976.

*The Early Science Fiction Stories of Thomas M. Disch.* Boston, Gregg Press, 1977.
*Fundamental Disch.* New York, Bantam, 1980; London, Gollancz, 1981.
*The Man Who Had No Idea.* London, Gollancz, 1982.
*Ringtime: A Story.* West Branch, Iowa, Toothpaste Press, 1983.
*Torturing Mr. Amberwell.* New Castle, Virginia, Cheap Street, 1985.

OTHER PUBLICATIONS

Novels

*The House That Fear Built* (as Cassandra Knye, with John Sladek). New York, Paperback Library, 1966.
*Black Alice* (as Thom Demijohn, with John Sladek). New York, Doubleday, 1968; London, W.H. Allen, 1969.
*Clara Reeve* (as Leonie Hargrave). New York, Knopf, and London, Hutchinson, 1975.
*Neighboring Lives*, with Charles Naylor. New York, Scribner, and London, Hutchinson, 1981.
*The Silver Pillow: A Tale of Witchcraft.* Willimantic, Connecticut, M.V. Ziesing, 1987.

Plays

*Ben Hur* (produced New York, 1989); *The Cardinal Detoxes* (produced New York, 1990).

Verse

*Highway Sandwiches*, with Marilyn Hacker and Charles Platt. Privately printed, 1970.
*The Right Way to Figure Plumbing.* New York, Basilisk Press, 1971.
*ABCDEFG HIJKLM NPOQRST UVWXYZ.* London, Anvil Press Poetry, 1981.
*Burn This.* London, Hutchinson, 1982.
*Orders of the Retina.* West Branch, Iowa, Toothpaste Press, 1982.
*Here I Am, There You Are, Where Were We.* London, Hutchinson, 1984.
*Yes, Let's: New and Selected Poems.* Baltimore, Maryland, Johns Hopkins University Press, 1989.
*Dark Verses and Light.* Baltimore, Maryland, Johns Hopkins University Press, 1991.

OTHER

Fiction for children

*The Tale of Dan De Lion: A Fable.* Minneapolis, Coffee House Press, 1986.
*The Brave Little Toaster.* New York, Doubleday, and London, Grafton, 1986.
*The Brave Little Toaster Goes to Mars.* New York, Doubleday, 1988.

Editor, *The Ruins of Earth: An Anthology of the Immediate Future.* New York, Putnam, 1971; London, Hutchinson, 1973.
Editor, *Bad Moon Rising.* New York, Harper, 1973; London, Hutchinson, 1974.
Editor, *The New Improved Sun: An Anthology of Utopian Science Fiction.* New York, Harper, 1975; London, Hutchinson, 1976.
Editor, with Charles Naylor, *New Constellations.* New York, Harper, 1976.
Editor, with Charles Naylor, *Strangeness.* New York, Scribner, 1977.

*

Bibliography: *Thomas M. Disch: A Preliminary Bibliography* by David Nee, Berkeley, California, Other Change of Hobbit, 1982; *A Checklist of Thomas M. Disch* by Christopher P. Stephens, Hastings-on-Hudson, New York, Ultramarine, 1991.

Critical Study: *The American Shore: Meditations on a Tale of Science Fiction by Thomas M. Disch—"Angouleme"* by Samuel R. Delany, Elizabethtown, New York, Dragon Press, 1978.

* * *

Readers of Thomas M. Disch's science fiction would do well to keep in mind that SF is but one aspect of his multi-faceted career. Disch is a prolific man of letters who has published highly regarded poetry, mainstream fiction, novelizations, short stories, book and drama criticism, plays, opera libretti, children's books, and a computer interactive novel, as well as various collaborations with other writers. Some of the anthologies he has edited are landmarks in the SF field. The same playfulness of imagination and finely tuned wit are present in all the forms he turns his hand to, and his literary standards are high.

His science fiction, since his first novel, *The Genocides*, appeared in 1965, has earned him a place in the front rank of contemporary SF authors. Three of his novels were cited in David Pringle's 1986 survey, *Science Fiction: The Best 100 Novels.*

Perhaps his chief distinguishing characteristic as an SF writer is his unpredictability. As critic Walter Clemons wrote in *Newsweek*, "A Disch novel almost always outfoxes our expectations," and as Disch confesses, "Publishers don't quite know what to do with me." His versatility is another trademark, and these two qualities may partly explain why he has not achieved the prominence on bestseller lists gained by more easily categorized authors.

*The Genocides*, a suspenseful first novel about the extinction of the human species by ubiquitous "Plants," demonstrates the breadth of the young writer's vision and displays a nascent but distinctive style recognisably his own. This was followed by a comic novel, *Mankind under the Leash* (in the U.K. as *The Puppies of Terra*), and Disch's most conventional SF novel, *Echo Round His Bones*, which he describes as "a resolutely cheerful science fiction adventure as traditional in all its trappings as a khaki fatigue uniform." His SF stories from the 1960's, most of which appeared first in the magazine *Fantastic Stories of Imagination*, were collected in *One Hundred and Two H-Bombs*, with an introduction by Harry Harrison. Harrison identified Disch as the best of "The New Wave" of SF writers then emerging, and described him as a comic writer in the SF tradition of Brian Aldiss. He also noted Disch's apparent delight in his own work, a delight that was to manifest itself in future novels and become a hallmark of Disch's writing.

*Camp Concentration* is Disch's first mature SF novel, and one of his three best. He was 26 when he began writing it, and says that ". . . it was only natural that the novel I was writing should convey some sense of giddy repletion and intellectual jubilation, feelings that set up an interesting interference pattern with the book's darker themes." *Camp Concentration*, set a few years ahead in the mid-1970's, is the journal of the experiences of a 35-year-old poet and political prisoner named Louis Sacchetti, who is secretly used by the military industrial complex as a guinea pig in an experiment designed to increase intelligence. But as the genius of Sacchetti and the other prisoners is developed in Camp Archimedes, they are being destroyed by the hybrid strain of syphillis used to increase their mental powers. Michael Moorcock wrote that "*Camp Concentration* represents one of the directions in which modern SF is going and is so far the outstanding example of its kind."

*Under Compulsion* (*Fun with Your New Head* in the U.S.) is a collection of stories first published in the mid-1960's, many in *New Worlds* magazine. Disch's macabre, often chilling humor is apparent in these stories about the modern human condition. Brian Aldiss wrote in *Impulse*, ". . . a genuine pessimist of a new writer has come along, to delight us with an unadulterated shot of pure bracing gloom." (It was also during the period when *Camp Concentration* and *Under Compulsion* were published that Disch began his still unfinished novel *The Pressure of Time* and wrote his best short story up to that time, "The Asian Shore.")

Using a fictional, mammoth government housing project located in New York City at 334 East 11th Street as an organizing device, Disch created a novel, *334*, out of many stories. He describes it as "a neo-realist portrait of New York City circa 2023, a book that I consider my best work to date in the genre of science fiction."

*Getting into Death* is a collection of stories written mainly in the 1970's and published first in magazines as different as *Orbit 6, New Worlds, Penthouse*, and *Paris Review*.

John Calvin Batchelor calls Disch's seventh novel, *On Wings of Song*, "a gay *Candide* set in 21st-century Manhattan." Like *334* it is a dystopian novel that brings together many important aspects of Disch's work, especially the sexual. Its protagonist, Daniel Weinreb, is unabashedly homosexual, and the story of his boyhood in Amesville, Iowa, in the 21st century and of his struggle to master song and the art of flight in a series of adventures and escapes that take him at last to darkest Manhattan is told with sharp ironic wit.

*The M.D.: A Horror Story* begins as a horror novel—and horror is a recurring element in Disch's SF—and becomes SF as it follows the misadventures of young Billy Michaels, who has supernatural powers. The novel takes him to manhood when he becomes Dr. William Michaels, a Dr. Frankenstein for the modern age who unleashes a plague on the world worse than AIDS.

"I cannot be counted a great success in the marketplace of science fiction," says Disch, but in summing up his career thus far, it must be said that his voice—modernist, romantic, ironic, intelligent, and chilling—makes him one of the indispensable SF masters.

—Michael Perkins

---

**DORMAN, Sonya (née Hess).** American. Born 6 April 1924. Attended agricultural college, one year. Married in 1950 (separated); one daughter. Has worked as stable maid, kennel owner, receptionist, cook, dancer, greenhouse assistant, and housekeeper. Recipient: MacDowell Colony fellowship (five); Science Fiction Poetry Association Rhysling award, 1978. Agent: Virginia Kidd, 538 East Harford Street, Milford, Pennsylvania 18337. Address: Box 6660, Taos, New Mexico 87571, U.S.A.

SCIENCE-FICTION PUBLICATIONS

Novel

*Planet Patrol* (for children). New York, Coward McCann, 1978.

Uncollected Short Stories

"The Putnam Tradition," in *Amazing* (New York), January 1963.

"Winged Victory," in *Fantasy and Science Fiction* (New York), November 1963.

"Splice of Life," in *Orbit I*, edited by Damon Knight. New York, Putnam, and London, Whiting and Wheaton, 1966.

"Go, Go, Go Said the Bird," in *Dangerous Visions*, edited by Harlan Ellison. New York, Doubleday, 1967; London, David Bruce and Watson, 2 vols., 1971.

"When I Was Miss Dow," in *Nebula Award Stories 2*, edited by Brian Aldiss and Harry Harrison. New York, Doubleday, and London, Gollancz, 1967.

"Lunatic Assignment," in *The Best from Fantasy and Science Fiction 18*, edited by Edward L. Ferman. New York, Doubleday, 1969.

"Bye, Bye, Banana Bird," in *Fantasy and Science Fiction* (New York), December, 1969.

"The Living End," in *Orbit 7*, edited by Damon Knight. New York, Putnam, 1970.

"A Mess of Porridge," in *Alchemy and Academe*, edited by Anne McCaffrey. New York, Doubleday, 1970.

"Alpha Bets," in *Fantasy and Science Fiction* (New York), November 1970.

"Me-Too," in *Worlds of Fantasy 3* (New York), Winter 1970.

"The Deepest Blue in the World," in *SF: Authors' Choice 3*, edited by Harry Harrison. New York, Putnam, 1971.

"Bitching It Out," in *Quark 2*, edited by Samuel R. Delany and Marilyn Hacker. New York, Paperback Library, 1971.

"Harry the Tailor," in *A Pocketful of Stars*, edited by Damon Knight. New York, Doubleday, 1971; London, Gollancz, 1972.

"Journey," in *Galaxy* (New York), November 1972.

"The Bear Went over the Mountain," in *Fantasy and Science Fiction* (New York), August 1973.

"Sons of Bingaloo," in *Analog* (New York), November 1973.

"Time Bind," in *Orbit 13*, edited by Damon Knight. New York, Putnam, 1974.

"Cool Affection," in *Galaxy* (New York), May 1974.

"Death or Consequences," in *Tomorrow*, edited by Roger Elwood. New York, Evans, 1976.

"Them and Us and All," in *Fantasy and Science Fiction* (New York), April 1976.

"Building Block," in *The New Women of Wonder*, edited by Pamela Sargent. New York, Random House, 1978.

"The Gods in Winter," in *Interfaces*, edited by Ursula K. Le Guin and Virginia Kidd. New York, Ace, 1980.

"Peek-a-Boom," in *Edges*, edited by Ursula K. Le Guin and Virginia Kidd. New York, Pocket Books, 1980.

OTHER PUBLICATIONS

Verse

*Poems.* Columbus, Ohio State University Press, 1970.

*Stretching Fence.* Athens, Ohio University Press, 1975.

*A Paper Raincoat.* Orono, Maine, Puckerbrush Press, 1976.

*The Far Traveler.* La Crosse, Wisconsin, Juniper Press, 1980.

*Palace of Earth*. Orono, Maine, Puckerbrush Press, 1984.

* * *

Sonya Dorman is one of the most unusual and gifted contemporary writers of fantasy and science fiction. Each of her stories is a unique, perfectly executed jewel. In addition to her strong sense of the macabre Dorman possesses a well-developed sense of humor, illustrated by the grimly absurd twists with which she ends many of her stories. She also writes poetry which has appeared in several science-fiction magazines and anthologies as well as short stories which have been published in *Redbook* and other magazines outside the field of science fiction.

Although the short story is a difficult medium in which to develop characters Dorman succeeds admirably. She is economical in her descriptions of futuristic societies and their trappings. In a few, well-chosen words she manages to convey a feeling of place and time. She is also skilled at letting the natural flow of the story line serve its own descriptive function.

Her plots are deceptively simple at first glance. On examination, however, they are carefully wrought situations described through fast-paced dialogue and exquisitely crafted action. Dorman is at her best in stories like "Splice of Life" in which an ordinary, if somewhat grim, situation is expanded and twisted to make a point about the implications of contemporary medical research. This story is gory, but the gore is purposeful and intentional. It's designed to shock her readers into seeing past the superficialities, to strip bare the meat and bone of living. The harsh and painful exposure of life is characteristic of Dorman's work.

Strong, believable, and likeable women are usually the main characters in Dorman's stories. One of her most memorable heroines, Corporal Roxy Rimidon, appears first in "Bye, Bye, Banana Bird," a different kind of Dorman story. Roxy is a member of the elite, special forces unit from the American Dominion called the Planet Patrol. She is tough, sexy, and quite intelligent, and her adventures make exciting reading.

Dorman exhibits a combination of many of the traditional female virtues such as compassion and sensitivity in contrast to the traditional male characteristics of strength, energy, and conciseness. All of this is overlaid by her steely determination to make us see the world as she does. Dorman's world is bitterly ironic and at the same time human. The amorphous alien creatures from "When I Was Miss Dow" seem remarkably similar to the mental patients in "Lunatic Assignment."

Her lighter stories such as the Roxy Rimidon series and the more introspective "Building Block" are also expertly crafted. The latter deals with a female space architect who has a creative block. These later stories are less macabre and biting but just as creative and as well written as Dorman's earlier work.

Sonya Dorman is a rare phenomenon. She is an amalgam like her androgynous characters, able to display her sensitivity and compassion without relinquishing her energy and irony. One anthology editor cautions readers at the beginning of "Lunatic Assignment" to read the story only when they have time to read it through at one sitting and then to think about it. This precaution might preface almost all of her stories. They are not trifles to skim while sunbathing or waiting for the bus. They are energizing, thought-provoking, wryly optimistic glimpses of the future.

—Alice Chambers Wygant

---

**DORSET, Richard.** *See* **SHAVER, Richard S.**

---

**DORSEY, Candas Jane.** Canadian. Born in Edmonton, Alberta, 16 November 1952. Educated at University of Alberta, B.A. 1975; University of Calgary, B.S.W. 1979. Has worked in theatre and social work. From 1980, freelance writer and editor: *The Edmonton Bullet.* Lives in Edmonton. Address: c/o Porcepic Books, 4252 Commerce Circle, Victoria, British Columbia V8Z 4M2, Canada.

SCIENCE-FICTION PUBLICATIONS

Novel

*Hardwired Angel*, with Nora Abercrombie. Vancouver, British Columbia, Arsenal Pulp Press, 1987.

Short Stories

*Machine Sex and Other Stories.* Victoria, British Columbia, Porcepic, 1988; London, Women's Press, 1990.

OTHER PUBLICATIONS

Poetry

*This Is for You.* Vancouver, British Columbia, Blewointmentpress, 1973.
*Orion Rising.* Vancouver, British Columbia, Blewointmentpress, 1974.
*Results of the Ring Toss.* Vancouver, British Columbia, Blewointmentpress, 1976.

Other

Editor, with Gerry Truscott, *Tesseracts 3: Canadian Science Fiction.* Victoria, British Columbia, Porcepic Books, 1990.

* * *

Candas Jane Dorsey belongs to a new generation of Canadian science fiction writers. She has been published in *Tesseracts* anthologies. She won, with Nora Abercrombie, the Ninth Annual Pulp Press International Three-Day Novel Competition for *Hardwired Angel.* Her coming of age was achieved with the publication of *Machine Sex and Other Stories*, which presents a distinctly different voice in science fiction.

The problem that besets anthologies is that the various stories contained in them will be compared with one another and will be judged on their own merits only with great difficulty. This is the case also with *Machine Sex and Other Stories.* Some of the stories seem, on the surface, fairly out of place with what is expected of science fiction, namely the description of humans' reactions and evolution in a universe in constant change, through the use of science and technology.

Dorsey is excellent with the use of inner dialogue and description of her characters' feelings. Contrary to mainstream science fiction, where most characters are only described in an evasive manner, and only when it is necessary for the plot to move along, Dorsey's characters are all too aware of their thoughts, to the point that one gets the impression they watch themselves as if they are strangers on television.

In many of her stories, this is accomplished at the expense of a description of the settings in which the characters move. In the first story, "Sleeping in a Box," science or technology are so unimportant that one could easily imagine the story to have taken place in a completely non-science fiction environment, i.e., a desert island instead of the moon. This is not to say that it is not science fiction: the context just does not seem to be essential. The same could be said of the fourth story, "The Prairie Warriors;" it would be more appropriate in a fantasy collection. It is possible that Dorsey expects her readers to do some work themselves and fill in the missing gaps. "The Prairie Warriors" is a very demanding story where place names are absent, only mentioned as the village, the hills, the mountains and the prairie. We are told the effect of drugs on people whose country, origin, and allegiance remain nameless. It is beautifully written, at times mesmerizing, but the average reader may skip directly to the next story in search of a science-fiction world.

"Machine Sex" explores the blend of sex and computer software from a female point of view. The story might be regarded as feminist, but "Machine Sex" has more to do with the survival of a gifted woman in a universe that is still dominated by men, and the way in which people can use and manipulate each other. This story also has elements of cyberpunk science fiction.

Other stories in the same collection are more traditional science fiction. But Dorsey is at her best when dealing with the psychology of her character rather than an endless description of technical wizardry.

What is most effective in her best stories is a deliberate choice of places and time. This is particularly evident in "Machine Sex," where we are led across Canada and an omniscient narrator takes over from time to time to watch upon the main protagonist as if we were next-door neighbours and voyeurs.

Candas Jane Dorsey with her homey settings and her poetic prose represents a side of Canadian science fiction preoccupied with human alienation.

—Henry Leperlier

---

**DOUGLAS, R.M.** *See* **RANKINE, John.**

---

**DOWLING, Terry.** Australian. Born in 1948. Recipient: Ditmar award, 1983, 1985, 1986, 1987, 1988 (twice), 1990, 1991.

SCIENCE-FICTION PUBLICATIONS

Short Stories

*Rynosseros.* North Adelaide, South Australia, Aphelion, 1990.
*Wormwood.* North Adelaide, South Australia, Aphelion, 1991.

Uncollected Short Stories

"The Terrarium," in *Omega*, May/June 1984.
"A Dragon between His Fingers," in *Omega*, May 1986.
"The Man Who Lost Red," in *Aphelion*, Autumn 1986.
"The Bullet that Grows in the Gun," in *Omega*, September/October 1986.
"Marmordesse," in *Omega*, January/February 1987.
"The Last Elephant," in *Australian Short Stories 20.* N.p., 1987.
"Shatterwrack at Breaklight," in *Fantasy and Science Fiction*, March 1990.
"Larridin Wind," in *Eidolon 1*, May 1990.
"The Quiest Redemption of Andy the House," in *Strange Plasma*, June 1990.
"Vanities," in *Glass Reptiles*, edited by Van Ikin. N.p., 1990.

OTHER PUBLICATIONS

Other

Editor, *The Essential Ellison: A 35-Year Retrospective*, by Harlan Ellison. Omaha, Nebraska, Nemo Press, 1987.

* * *

Terry Dowling's first story was published in 1975, and by the time his first book appeared in 1990 he had won the Australian Science Fiction Achievement ("Ditmar") Award for fiction more times than any other Australian writer.

Commentators have tried to explain the Dowling phenomenon by pointing to similarities with the work of Jack Vance and J.G. Ballard (for Dowling has written major critical work on both writers), and Dowling has certainly mastered important aspects of each writer's style. But Dowling's vision is his own; his works create a series of myths about contemporary humanity, pleasingly woven into Australian settings, and they combine what is often hi-tech subject-matter with a contrastingly ornate style.

The stories in *Rynosseros* concern a single character, Tom Tyson, known as Tom Rynosseros because he captains the sand-ship *Rynosseros.* In this future Australia, the coastal cities, home of white Australians, are urbanely cosmopolitan centres of culture, while in the interior, around an inland sea, the Ab'O states represent the emancipation of the Aboriginal race whose heritage is both its past and its future destiny. Ab'O Princes use satellites to spy on tribal conflicts, and graceful wind-propelled sand-ships roll across the deserts, giving the collection its symbol of freedom and inquiry.

This Dowling future is a challenging reversal of present-day Australian conditions: in *Rynosseros*, it is the inland, not the coastline, that is the nerve-centre of change and vitality, and the Aboriginal heritage is linked with technology, not nature (for the Ab'Os are genetically altered Aborigines whose primary allegiance is not to the Land but to the *haldanes*, which are energy-vectors used to tap psychic power). The point of such a reversal is not socio-political. Dowling does not offer social criticism; his scenario exists only to break down the monolithic unalterableness of the present by offering a cleverly plausible alternative vision.

Australian writers have traditionally viewed their country and people through the mode of social realism, often in a flat, dry, stoical tone. Dowling's approach reverses this, too, for his style is ornate and often lush, and the tone is inquisitive, verging on wonder and awe. In "The Robot is Running Away from the Trees," a character discovers the relics of an old robot and wipes dust from "the impressive rococo decorations, from the faded dim-gold exotic curlicues on thighs and shoulders." Dowling relishes such lavish accumulations of images, each one adding sensuous accretions to the detail. His stories are jewelled with all manner of exotica—fire-chess, fire-sculptures, light-suits, mirage-divers, typhies, and sanchers—but none is the mere frothiness of fantasy. Dowling's exotic objects, behaviours, and rituals help to define the philosophies and perspectives of radically different cultures.

*Wormwood* is also a collection of short stories; however, the point of unity is not a single character but the book's scenario. "Wormwood" is the biblical name for the moment in 2023 when an alien race—the Nobodoi—successfully invaded the Earth, setting up inscrutably elaborate networks of energy ley-lines, and embarking upon a process of remoulding the planet to their own specifications. But then the Nobodio were "Recalled," leaving Earth in the hands of numerous alien "Bridging Races," Hoproi, Darzie, Matta, Salman, and Amazil, to name just a few.

If the collection has a central theme, it is the struggle of individual humans to rediscover and maintain some sense of identity as humans. But Dowling provides an individual twist to this familiar theme, for his characters are not concerned with prevailing over their alien masters and there is no climactic battle in which invaders are repelled. The humans of *Wormwood* must simply find their own way to preserve their identity in the presence of beings who may not even understand the concept of identity. In this sense *Wormwood* deals with human psychology in crisis.

Dowling's central concern is with wonder and pluralities; his fiction offers carefully-crafted scenes of spectacle, but this is always underpinned by a tolerant awareness of cultural difference. In a land that has often feared and mistrusted otherness, Dowling's stories treat the unusual as a source of wonder and potential new knowledge, not a cause for fear.

—Van Ikin

---

**DOYLE, (Sir) Arthur Conan.** British. Born in Edinburgh, Scotland, 22 May 1859. Educated at the Hodder School, Lancashire, 1868–70, Stonyhurst College, Lancashire, 1870–75, and the Jesuit School, Feldkirch, Austria (editor, Feldkirchian Gazette), 1875–76; studied medicine at the University of Edinburgh, 1876–81, M.B. 1881, M.D. 1885. Served as senior physician at a field hospital in South Africa during the Boer War, 1899–1902; knighted, 1902. Married 1) Louise Hawkins in 1885 (died 1906), one daughter and one son; 2) Jean Leckie in 1907, two sons and one daughter. Practised medicine in Southsea, Hampshire, 1882–90; full-time writer from 1891; stood for Parliament as Unionist candidate for Central Edinburgh, 1900, and tariff reform candidate for the Hawick Burghs, 1906. Member, Society for Psychical Research, 1893–1930 (resigned). LL.D.: University of Edinburgh, 1905. Knight of Grace of the Order of St. John of Jerusalem. *Died 7 July 1930.*

### Science-Fiction Publications

Novels (series: Professor Challenger in all books except *The Doings of Raffles Haw*)

*The Doings of Raffles Haw.* London, Cassell, and New York, Lovell, 1892.
*The Lost World.* London, Hodder and Stoughton, 1912; New York, Doran, 1915.
*The Poison Belt.* London, Hodder and Stoughton, and New York, Doran, 1913.
*The Land of Mist.* London, Hutchinson, 1925; New York, Doran, 1926.

Short Stories

*Danger! and Other Stories.* London, Murray, 1918; New York, Doran, 1919.
*The Maracot Deep and Other Stories.* London, Murray, and New York, Doubleday, 1929.
*The Professor Challenger Stories.* London, Murray, 1952.
*The Best Science Fiction of Arthur Conan Doyle,* edited by Charles G. Waugh and Martin H. Greenberg. Carbondale, Southern Illinois University Press, 1981.

### Other Publications

Novels

*A Study in Scarlet.* London, Ward Lock, 1888; Philadelphia, Lipincott, 1890.
*The Mystery of Cloomber.* London, Ward and Downey, 1888; New York, Fenno, 1896 (?).
*Micah Clarke.* London, Longman, and New York, Harper, 1889.
*The Firm of Girdlestone.* London, Chatto and Windus, and New York, Lovell, 1890.
*The Sign of Four.* London, Blackett, 1890; New York, Collier, 1891.
*The White Company.* London, Smith Elder, 3 vols., 1891; New York, Lovell, 1 vol., 1891.
*The Great Shadow.* New York, Harper, 1892.
*The Great Shadow, and Beyond the City.* Bristol, Arrowsmith, 1893; New York, Ogilvie, 1894.
*The Refugees.* London, Longman, 3 vols., 1893; New York, Harper, 1 vol., 1893.
*The Parasite.* London, Constable, and New York, Harper, 1894.
*The Stark Munro Letters.* London, Longman, and New York, Appleton, 1895.
*Rodney Stone.* London, Smith Elder, and New York, Appleton, 1896.
*Uncle Bernac: A Memory of the Empire.* London, Smith Elder, and New York, Appleton, 1897.
*The Tragedy of Korosko.* London, Smith Elder, 1898; as *A Desert Drama,* Philadelphia, Lippincott, 1898.
*A Duet, with an Occasional Chorus.* London, Grant Richards, and New York, Appleton, 1899; revised edition, London, Smith Elder, 1910.
*The Hound of the Baskervilles.* London, Newnes, and New York, McClure, 1902.
*Sir Nigel.* London, Smith Elder, and New York, McClure, 1906.
*The Valley of Fear.* New York, Doran, and London, Smith Elder, 1915.

Short Stories

*Mysteries and Adventures.* London, Scott, 1889; as *The Gully of Bluemansdyke and Other Stories,* 1892.
*The Captain of the Polestar and Other Tales.* London, Longman, 1890; New York, Munro, 1894.
*The Adventures of Sherlock Holmes.* London, Newnes, and New York, Harper, 1892.
*My Friend the Murderer and Other Mysteries and Adventures.* New York, Lovell, 1893.
*The Memoirs of Sherlock Holmes.* London, Newnes, 1893; New York, Harper, 1894.
*The Great Keinplatz Experiment and Other Stories.* Chicago, Rand McNally, 1894.

*Round the Red Lamp, Being Facts and Fancies of Medical Life.* London, Methuen, and New York, Appleton, 1894.
*The Exploits of Brigadier Gerard.* London, Newnes, and New York, Appleton, 1896.
*The Man from Archangel and Other Stories.* New York, Street and Smith, 1898.
*Hilda Wade* (completion of work by Grant Allen). London, Richards, and New York, Putnam, 1900.
*The Green Flag and Other Stories of War and Sport.* London, Smith Elder, and New York, McClure, 1900.
*Adventures of Gerard.* London, Newnes, and New York, McClure, 1903.
*The Return of Sherlock Holmes.* London, Newnes, and New York, McClure, 1905.
*Round the Fire Stories.* London, Smith Elder, and New York, McClure, 1908.
*The Last Galley: Impressions and Tales.* London, Smith Elder, and New York, Doubleday, 1911.
*His Last Bow: Some Reminiscences of Sherlock Holmes.* London, Murray, and New York, Doran, 1917.
*Tales of the Ring and Camp.* London, Murray, 1922; as *The Croxley Master and Other Tales of the Ring and Camp*, New York, Doran, 1925.
*Tales of Pirates and Blue Water.* London, Murray, 1922; as *The Dealings of Captain Sharkey and Other Tales of Pirates*, New York, Doran, 1925.
*Tales of Terror and Mystery.* London, Murray, 1922; as *The Black Doctor and Other Tales of Terror and Mystery*, New York, Doran, 1925.
*Tales of Twilight and the Unseen.* London, Murray, 1922; as *The Great Keinplatz Experiment and Other Tales of Twilight and the Unseen*, New York, Doran, 1925.
*Tales of Adventure and Medical Life.* London, Murray, 1922; as *The Man from Archangel and Other Tales of Adventure*, New York, Doran, 1925.
*Tales of Long Ago.* London, Murray, 1922; as *The Last of the Legions and Other Tales of Long Ago*, New York, Doran, 1925.
*The Case-Book of Sherlock Holmes.* London, Murray, and New York, Doran, 1927.
*The Conan Doyle Historical Romances.* Murray, 2 vols., 1931–32.
*The Field Bazaar.* Privately printed, 1934; Summit, New Jersey, Pamphlet House, 1947.
*Great Stories*, edited by John Dickson Carr. London, Murray, and New York, London House and Maxwell, 1959.
*The Annotated Sherlock Holmes*, edited by William S. Baring-Gould. New York, Potter, 2 vols., 1967; London, Murray, 2 vols., 1968.
*The Sherlock Holmes Illustrated Omnibus* (facsimile of magazine stories). London, Murray-Cape, 1978.
*The Best Supernatural Tales of Arthur Conan Doyle*, edited by E.F. Bleiler. New York, Dover, 1979.
*Sherlock Holmes: The Published Apocrypha*, with others, edited by Jack Tracy. Boston, Houghton Mifflin, 1980.
*The Final Adventures of Sherlock Holmes*, edited by Peter Haining. London, W.H. Allen, 1981.
*The Edinburgh Stories.* Edinburgh, Polygon, 1981.
*Uncollected Stories*, edited by John Michael Gibson and Richard Lancelyn Green. London, Secker and Warburg, 1982.
*The Best Horror Stories of Arthur Conan Doyle*, edited by Frank McSherry, Martin H. Greenberg, and Charles G. Waugh. Chicago, Academy, 1988.

Plays

*Jane Annie; or, The Good Conduct Prize*, with J.M. Barrie, music by Ernest Ford (produced London, 1893). London, Chappell, 1893.
*Foreign Policy*, adaptation of his own story "A Question of Diplomacy" (produced London, 1893).
*Waterloo*, adaptation of his story "A Straggler of 15" (as *A Story of Waterloo*, produced Bristol, 1894; London, 1895; as *Waterloo*, produced New York, 1899). London, French, 1907; in *One-Act Plays of To-day*, 2nd series, edited by J.W. Marriott, Boston, Small Maynard, 1926.
*Halves*, adaptation of the story by James Payn (produced Aberdeen and London, 1899).
*Sherlock Holmes*, with William Gillette, adaptation of works by Doyle (produced Buffalo and New York, 1899; Liverpool and London, 1901).
*A Duet (A Duologue)* (produced London, 1902). London, French, 1903.
*Brigadier Gerard*, adaptation of his own stories (produced London and New York, 1906).
*The Fires of Fate: A Modern Morality*, adaptation of his novel *The Tragedy of Korosko* (produced Liverpool, London and New York, 1909).
*The House of Temperley*, adaptation of his novel *Rodney Stone* (produced London, 1910).
*The Pot of Caviare*, adaptation of his own story (produced London, 1910).
*The Speckled Band: An Adventure of Sherlock Holmes* (produced London and New York, 1910). London, French, 1912.
*The Crown Diamond* (produced Bristol and London, 1921). Privately printed, 1958.
*The Journey*, in *The Poems of Arthur Conan Doyle*, 1922.
*It's Time Something Happened.* New York, Appleton, 1925.

Verse

*Songs of Action.* London, Smith Elder, and New York, Doubleday, 1898.
*Songs of the Road.* London, Smith Elder, and New York, Doubleday, 1911.
*The Guards Came Through and Other Poems.* London, Murray, 1919; New York, Doran, 1920.
*The Poems of Arthur Conan Doyle: Collected Edition.* London, Murray, 1922.

Other

*The Great Boer War.* London, Smith Elder, and New York, McClure, 1900.
*The War in South Africa: Its Cause and Conduct.* London, Smith Elder, and New York, McClure, 1902.
*Works* (Author's Edition). London, Smith Elder, 12 vols., and New York, Appleton, 13 vols., 1903.
*The Fiscal Question.* Hawick, Roxburgh, Henderson, 1905.
*An Incursion into Diplomacy.* London, Smith Elder, 1906.
*The Story of Mr. George Edalji.* London, Daily Telegraph, 1907.
*Through the Magic Door* (essays). London, Smith Elder, 1907; New York, McClure, 1908.
*The Crime of the Congo.* London, Hutchinson, and New York, Doubleday, 1909.
*Divorce Law Reform: An Essay.* London, Divorce Law Reform Union, 1909.
*Sir Arthur Conan Doyle: Why He Is Now in Favour of Home Rule.* London, Liberal Publication Department, 1911.

*The Case of Oscar Slater.* London, Hodder and Stoughton, 1912; New York, Doran, 1913.
*Divorce and the Church,* with Lord Hugh Cecil. London, Divorce Law Reform Union, 1913.
*Great Britain and the Next War.* Boston, Small Maynard, 1914.
*In Quest of Truth, Being a Correspondence Between Sir Arthur Conan Doyle and Captain H. Stansbury.* London, Watts, 1914.
*To Arms!* London, Hodder and Staughton, 1914.
*The German War.* London, Hodder and Stoughton, 1914; New York, Doran, 1915.
*Western Wanderings* (travel in Canada). New York, Doran, 1915.
*The Outlook on the War.* London, Daily Chronicle, 1915.
*An Appreciation of Sir John French.* London, Daily Chronicle, 1916.
*A Petition to the Prime Minister on Behalf of Sir Roger Casement.* Privately printed, 1916.
*A Visit to Three Fronts: Glimpses of British, Italian, and French Lines.* London, Hodder and Staughton, and New York, Doran, 1916.
*The Briths Campaign in France and Flanders.* London, Hodder and Stoughton, 6 vols., 1916–20; New York, Doran, 6 vols., 1916–20; revised edition, as *The British Campaigns in Europe 1914–1918,* London, Bles, 1 vol., 1928.
*The New Revelation.* London, Hodder and Stoughton, and New York, Doran, 1918.
*The Vital Message* (on spiritualism). London, Hodder and Stoughton, and New York, Doran, 1919.
*Our Reply to the Cleric.* Spiritualists' National Union, 1920.
*A Public Debate on the Truth of Spiritualism,* with Joseph McCabe. London, Watts, 1920; as *Debate on Spiritualism,* Girard, Kansas, Haldeman Julius, 1922.
*Spiritualism and Rationalism.* London, Hodder and Stoughton, 1920.
*The Wanderings of a Spiritualist.* London, Hodder and Stoughton, and New York, Doran, 1921.
*Spiritualism: Some Straight Questions and Direct Answers.* Manchester, Two Worlds, 1922.
*The Case for Spirit Photography,* with others. London, Hutchinson, 1922; New York, Doran, 1923.
*The Coming of the Fairies.* London, Hodder and Stoughton, and New York, Doran, 1922.
*Three of Them: A Reminiscence.* London, Murray, 1923.
*Our American Adventure.* London, Hodder and Stoughton, and New York, Doran, 1923.
*Our Second American Adventure.* London, Hodder and Stoughton, and Boston, Little Brown, 1924.
*Memories and Adventures.* London, Hodder and Stoughton, and Boston, Little Brown, 1924.
*Psychic Experiences.* London and New York, Putnam, 1925.
*The Early Christian Church and Modern Spiritualism.* London, Psychic Bookshop, 1925.
*The History of Spiritualism.* London, Cassell, 2 vols., and New York, Doran, 2 vols., 1926.
*Pheneas Speaks: Direct Spirit Communications.* London, Psychic Press, and New York, Doran, 1927.
*What Does Spiritualism Actually Teach and Stand For?* London, Psychic Bookshop, 1928.
*A Word of Warning.* London, Psychic Press, 1928.
*An Open Letter to Those of My Generation.* London, Psychic Press, 1929.
*Our African Winter.* London, Murray, 1929.
*The Roman Catholic Church: A Rejoinder.* London, Psychic Press, 1929.
*The Edge of the Unknown.* London, Murray, and New York, Putnam, 1930.
*Works* (Crowborough Edition). New York, Doubleday, 24 vols., 1930.
*Strange Studies from Life,* edited by Peter Ruber. New York, Candlelight Press, 1963.
*Arthur Conan Doyle on Sherlock Holmes.* London, Favil, 1981.
*Essays on Photography,* edited by John Michael Gibson and Richard Lancelyn Green. London, Secker and Warburg, 1982.
*Letters to the Press,* edited by John Michael Gibson and Richard Lancelyn Green. London, Secker and Warburg, 1985.

Editor, *D.D. Home: His Life and Mission,* by Mrs. Dunglas Home. London, Kegan Paul Trench Trubner, 1921.
Editor, *The Spiritualists' Reader.* Manchester, Two Worlds, 1924.

Translator, *The Mystery of Joan of Arc,* by Léon Denis. London, Murray, 1924; New York, Dutton, 1925.

*

Bibliography: *The World Bibliography of Sherlock Holmes and Dr. Watson* by Ronald Burt De Waal, Boston, New York Graphic Society, 1975; *A Bibliography of A. Conan Doyle* by Richard Lancelyn Green and John Michael Gibson, Oxford, Clarendon Press, 1983.

Manuscript Collection: Humanities Research Center, University of Texas, Austin.

Critical Studies (selection): *The Private Life of Sherlock Holmes* by Vincent Starrett, New York, Macmillan, 1933, London, Nicholson and Watson, 1934, revised edition, Chicago, University of Chicago Press, 1960, London, Allen and Unwin, 1961; *Conan Doyle: His Life and Art* by Hesketh Pearson, London, Methuen, 1943, New York, Walker, 1961; *The Life of Sir Arthur Conan Doyle* by John Dickson Carr, London, Murray, and New York, Harper, 1949; *Conan Doyle: A Biography* by Pierre Nordon, London, Murray, 1966, New York, Holt Rinehart, 1967; *Conan Doyle: A Biography of the Creator of Sherlock Holmes* by Ivor Brown, London, Hamish Hamilton, 1972; *The Adventures of Conan Doyle: The Life of the Creator of Sherlock Holmes* by Charles Higham, London, Hamish Hamilton, and New York, Norton, 1976; *The Encyclopedia Sherlockiana* by Jack Tracy, New York, Doubleday, 1977, London, New English Library, 1978; *Conan Doyle: A Biographical Solution* by Ronald Pearsall, London, Weidenfeld and Nicholson, 1977; *Sherlock Holmes and His Creator* by Trevor H. Hall, London, Duckworth, 1978, New York, St. Martin's Press., 1983; *Conan Doyle: Portrait of an Artist* by Julian Symons, London, G. Whizzard, 1979; *Sherlock Holmes: The Man and His World* by H.R.F. Keating, London, Thames and Hudson, and New York, Scribner, 1979; *The Quest for Sherlock Holmes: A Biographical Study of the Early Life of Sir Arthur Conan Doyle* by Owen Dudley Edwards, Edinburgh, Mainstream, 1982, Totowa, New Jersey, Barnes and Noble, 1983; *A Study in Surmise: The Making of Sherlock Holmes* by Michael Harrison, Bloomington, Indiana, Gaslight, 1984; *Arthur Conan Doyle* by Don Richard Cox, New York, Ungar, 1985; *The Complete Guide to Sherlock Holmes* by Michael Hardwick, London, Weidenfeld and Nicolson, 1986; *Sherlock Holmes: A Centenary Celebration* by Allen Eyles, London, Murray, 1986; *Elementary My Dear Watson: Sherlock Holmes Centenary: His Life and Times* by Graham Nown, New York, Ward Lock, 1986; *The Unrevealed Life of Doctor Arthur Conan Doyle: A Study in Southsea* by Geoffrey Stavert, Horndean, Hampshire, Milestone, 1987; *Arthur Conan Doyle* by Jacqueline A. Jaffe, Boston, Twayne, 1987; *The Quest for Sir Arthur Conan Doyle: Thirteen*

*Biographers in Search of a Life* edited by Jon L. Lellenberg, Carbondale, Southern Illinois University Press, 1987.

* * *

Although literary history best remembers him as the creator of Sherlock Holmes, Arthur Conan Doyle also produced a considerable body of science fiction, adventure tales, and historical romances, as well as numerous works of non-fiction. In common with many other writers whose works spanned both popular and more traditional fields, Doyle preferred to be remembered for his more "mainstream" writings rather than for his popular fiction. Well before Hugo Gernsback coined the term "science fiction," Doyle felt at ease writing heroic adventure tales, which would later be placed comfortably in this category. It is not surprising that the author who celebrated deductive reasoning should turn his talents in this direction. From an early age, Doyle was fascinated by history and heroics; his medical training instilled in him a respect for the scientific method; and a flamboyant medical colleague, Dr. George Budd, influenced the young Doyle to bear with the sometimes extreme eccentricities of a man of science. It was Dr. Budd who provided the model for Professor George Edward Challenger, whose appearance in most of Doyle's science fiction reflected the increasing importance of the scientist during the late 19th and early 20th centuries.

Professor Challenger is presented as a man of enormous ego, pride, and determination completely dedicated to discovering scientific truth. He first appears in *The Lost World*, a novel that introduces some of the thematic preoccupations common to most of Doyle's science fiction. "There are heroisms all around us waiting to be done," one character declares, and it is in the spirit of heroic adventure that the fledgling newspaper reporter, Edward Malone, joins Challenger, the gentleman/hunter Lord John Roxton, and the skeptical cantankerous Professor Summerlee on a quest to test the validity of Challenger's assertion that prehistoric life exists on an isolated plateau in South America. As the heroes confront a series of physical hazards and witness numerous awe-inspiring sights, it becomes clear that Doyle's intention is to celebrate a sense of wonder, to convey a fascination with the heroic unknown, and above all to assert modern man's supreme position in both past and present worlds. "Our eyes have seen great wonders," Malone reports after the four adventurers, armed with modern weaponry, help the more advanced Indian race on the plateau dramatically assert their dominance over an inferior race of ape-men. "Now upon this plateau the future must ever be for man," the scientist declares.

The superiority of the modern scientific mind is reasserted in "When the World Screamed," a humorous short story again featuring Challenger, this time armed with "scientific" paraphernalia designed to penetrate the earth's crust in order to prove the preposterous contention that "the world upon which we live is itself a living organism" insensible to man's presence. This is the tale of Challenger's efforts to "let the earth know that there is at least one person, George Edward Challenger, who calls for attention—who, indeed, insists upon attention." Not surprisingly, Challenger achieves his goal.

*The Poison Belt* is a novel that emphasizes Challenger's unselfish devotion to scientific truth. As the sole predictor of the catastrophic approach toward earth of a "poisonous" belt of ether gas, Challenger can philosophically face the prospect of his own demise and the annihilation of mankind because he is so thrilled at the privilege of observing it! Malone, Roxton, Summerlee, and Mrs. Challenger add more believable exclamations of wonderment to those of the scientist. This novel reveals Doyle's delight in juxtaposing the real and unreal, the beautiful and terrible, as Challenger and company regard through a sealed window the apparent end of the world taking place during a beautiful English summer's day. "The Disintegration Machine" is the most serious of the Challenger stories. Here Malone accompanies Challenger as the Professor examines the invention of "Latvian gentlemen named Theodore Nemor . . . a machine of a most extraordinary character which is capable of disintegrating any object placed within its spere of influence."

Challenger, quick to recognize the awesome military and "evil" potentialities of this invention, uses it to disintegrate Mr. Nemor himself, who holds the secret to the machine's operation.

*The Land of Mist*, a lengthy novel featuring Challenger only peripherally, cannot be considered science fiction. This apology for the occult reflects Doyle's own conviction about the validity of occult spiritualism. The work does restate one theme expressed in "The Disintegration Machine" and *The Maracot Deep;* it was Doyle's belief that it is absolutely essential for man's spiritual development to keep pace with his strides in the scientific realm. *The Maracot Deep* takes up this theme against a submarine environment. Here Dr. Maracot and a party of deep sea explorers, including a colorful slang-speaking Yankee handyman called Bill Scanlon, discover the lost colony of Atlantis when their undersea vessel is marooned in an Atlantic trench deeper than any previously explored by man. In an image reminiscent of that employed in *The Poison Belt*, Doyle at first isolates his scientist behind impenetrable glass as the real and unreal, the beautiful and sublime, are contrasted. With a sense of wonder, the explorers discover that, in spite of great scientific advances, Atlantis is doomed by its own limited spiritual development. Only through spiritual self-realization combined with cunning and access to scientific equipment do the heroes rise to the surface in Doyle's final assertion of the superiority of modern scientific man.

Some of Doyle's lesser-known stories, sometimes classified as science fiction, have more in common with the horror genre. In "The Silver Mirror," "The Terror of Blue John Gap," "The Horror of the Heights," and "The Captain of the Polestar" Doyle replaces a sense of wonder with a spine-chilling sense of unearthly dread; he purposely leaves the credibility of the narrators in doubt, undercutting any certainty on the reader's part that each story is "scientifically" believable. "Heroisms" are abundant but it is raw courage, not scientific superiority, that makes these protagonists into heros.

—Rosemary Herbert

---

**DOZOIS, Gardner (Raymond).** American. Born in Salem, Massachusetts, 23 July 1947. Served as a military journalist, 1966–69. Reader for Dell and Award publishers, and for *Galaxy, If, Worlds of Fantasy*, and *Worlds of Tomorrow*, 1970–73; co-founder, and associate editor, *Isaac Asimov's Science Fiction Magazine*, 1976–77; editor-in-chief since 1984. Member of the Advisory Committee, Paley Library, Special Collection Department, Temple University, Philadelphia. Recipient: Nebula award, 1983, 1985; Hugo award, for editing, 1988, 1989, 1990; *Locus* award, for editing, 1990. Agent: Virginia Kidd, 538 East Harford Street, Milford, Pennsylvania 18337, U.S.A.

SCIENCE-FICTION PUBLICATIONS

Novels

*Nightmare Blue*, with George Alec Effinger. New York, Berkley, 1975; London, Fontana, 1977.
*Strangers*. New York, Berkley, 1978; London, Hamlyn, 1980.

Short Stories

*The Visible Man*. New York, Berkley, 1977.

OTHER PUBLICATIONS

Other

*The Fiction of James Tiptree, Jr.* New York, Algol Press, 1977.
*Slow Dancing Through Time*, with others. Kansas City, Missouri, Ursus Press, 1990.
*Writing Science Fiction and Fantasy*, with others. New York, St. Martin's Press, 1991.

Editor, *A Day in the Life*. New York, Harper, 1972.
Editor, with Jack Dann, *Future Power*. New York, Random House, 1976.
Editor, *Another World* (for children). Chicago, Follett, 1977.
Editor, *Best Science Fiction Stories of the Year 6–10*. New York, Dutton, 5 vols., 1977–81.
Editor, with Jack Dunn, *Aliens!* New York, Pocket Books, 1980.
Editor, with Jack Dann, *Unicorns!* New York, Ace, 1982.
Editor, with Jack Dann, *Magicats!* New York, Ace, 1984.
Editor, *The Year's Best Science Fiction 1–3*. New York, Bluejay, 3 vols., 1984–86.
Editor, *The Year's Best Science Fiction 4–8*. New York, St. Martin's Press, 5 vols., 1987–90.
Editor, with Jack Dann, *Bestiary!* New York, Ace, 1985.
Editor, with Jack Dann, *Mermaids!* New York, Ace, 1986.
Editor, with Jack Dann, *Sorcerers!* New York, Ace, 1986.
Editor, with Jack Dann, *Demons!* New York, Ace, 1987.
Editor, *The Mammoth Book of Best New Science Fiction*. London, Robinson, 4 vols., 1987–90.
Editor, *The Best of Isaac Asimov's SF Magazine*. New York, Ace, 1988.
Editor, *Full Spectrum*. New York, Bantam, 1988.
Editor, with Susan Casper, *Ripper*. New York, Tor, 1988; as *Jack the Ripper*, London, Futura, 1988.
Editor, with Jack Dunn, *Dogtales!* New York, Ace, 1988.
Editor, with Jack Dann, *Seaserpents!* New York, Ace, 1989.
Editor, *Time Travelers from Isaac Asimov's Science Fiction Magazine*. New York, Ace, 1989.
Editor, *Transcendental Tales from Isaac Asimov's Science Fiction Magazine*. Norfolk, Virginia, Donning, 1989.
Editor, with Jack Dann, *Dinosaurs!* New York, Ace, 1990.
Editor, with Jack Dann, *Little People!* New York, Ace, 1991.
Editor, *Isaac Asimov's Aliens*. New York, Ace, 1991.
Editor, *The Legend Book of Science Fiction*. London, Century, 1991.

*

Manuscript Collection: Paskow Collection, Paley Library, Temple University, Philadelphia.

* * *

Gardner Dozois is a master short-story writer and a brilliant anthologist and editor. In one of his best known stories, "The Peacemaker" (Nebula award winner), Dozois explores a world shaken from civilization by the melting of the polar ice caps. The floods sink the great eastern seacoast cities and leave the survivors in the great American heartland at the mercy of ardent evangelists. As the young boy who is chosen at the story's conclusion learns, everyone must make sacrifices.

The best showcase for Dozois' work is the recent collection *Slow Dancing Through Time*, with collaborations by Jack Dann, Michael Swanwick, Susan Casper, and Jack C. Haldeman II. With the personal introductions to each story, Dozois and his friends not only share the origins of each story, they give critical insight into the creative process itself. The most haunting story in the collection is "The Clowns," where a disturbed young boy sees clowns murdering people—and only he can see them. This story would make a terrific novel because of the unforgettable, nightmarish metaphors Dozois, Jack Dann, and Susan Casper create. Other innovative stories include "The Gods of Mars," where the first manned mission to Mars gets a surprise, and "Slow Dancing With Jesus," where a girl's prom fantasy is wondrously unique.

Dozois' solo short stories are collected in *The Visible Man*, with an admiring introduction by Robert Silverberg. The dozen stories make up a solid progression of Dozois' craftsmanship in the 1970's. From a dazzling story of alien invasion ("Chains of the Sea") to the upbeat ("A Special Kind of Morning") to the naturalistic ("The Last Day of July") to the allegorical ("A Kingdom By the Sea") Dozois displays a command of the short story form rivaled by few of his contemporaries.

In his only non-collaborative novel, *Strangers*, Dozois presents Joseph Faber, a human from Earth with an alien lover named Liraun, during his tour of the planet Weinnuach. The couple are shunned by the non-human Cian and the human trade community. Faber could care less about his peers, but to win back a measure of respectability for Liraun he consents to attend the House of Tailors where the Cian genetically alter Faber's body so he and Liraun can be interfertile: a necessary condition of Cian marriage rites. In this tremendously sad story, Dozois develops the theme of alienation, and the impossibility of ever knowing another person—hence the title *Strangers*. Through misunderstanding after misunderstanding, Faber and Liraun find themselves on a fated path to doom: the result of their failure to understand each other's culture. Yet, even though *Strangers* ends with death, it also ends with life and hope. This very moving novel is one of the forgotten and ignored classics of the 1970's.

Dozois' other novel, a collaboration with George Alec Effinger called *Nightmare Blue*, is a standard SF adventure novel written in a hard-boiled style Effinger will return to more successfully in his later novels, *When Gravity Fails* and *A Fire in the Sun*. The only bright spots in *Nightmare Blue* are Dozois' creation of the alien Corcail Sendijen and the breakneck pacing of the action.

Dozois has gained a reputation as an exceptional anthologist. From his early theme anthologies like *A Day in the Life* to his latest collaborative anthologies with Jack Dann like *Magicats!*, Dozois packages quality stories with outstanding introductory material. From 1977 to 1981 Dozois edited Dutton's hardcover series *Best Science Fiction Story of the Year Numbers 6–10*. The five volumes Dozois edited were in many ways superior to the paperback SF series edited by Donald Wollheim (DAW) and Terry Carr (Ballantine/Del Rey) in terms of coverage and selection. In 1984, James Frenkel's wonderful but shortlived Bluejay Books selected Dozois to be the editor of *The Year's Best Science Fiction*, a massive 250,000-word volume. With the appearance of the second annual collection in Spring 1985, Neil Baron in *Fantasy Review* proclaimed "Now, the Dozois anthology is the standard." The simultaneous release of the volume in hardcover and paperback made it the definitive "Year's Best SF" anthology. After Bluejay Books folded, Dozois continued his successful series with St. Martin's Press.

Gardner Dozois twice won the Hugo for Best Editor of *Isaac Asimov's Science Fiction Magazine.* A master storyteller, anthologist, and editor Dozois is one of the treasures of the contemporary SF scene.

—George Kelley

---

**DRAKE, David A.** American. Born in Dubuque, Iowa, 24 September 1945. Educated at the University of Iowa, Iowa City, B.A. 1967; Duke University, Durham, North Carolina, J.D. 1972. Served as an interrogator in the United States Army, 1969–71. Married Joanne Kammiller in 1967; one son. Assistant town attorney, Chapel Hill, North Carolina, 1972–80; part-time bus driver, Chapel Hill, 1980. Since 1981, full-time writer. Address: c/o Baen Publishing Enterprises, 260 Fifth Avenue, Suite 35, New York, New York 10001, U.S.A.

### Science-Fiction Publications

Novels (Series: Hammer's Slammers; Kelly; Northworld; Yates)

*Skyripper* (Kelly). New York, Tor, 1983.
*The Forlorn Hope.* New York, Tor, 1984.
*Birds of Prey.* New York, Baen, 1984.
*Cross the Stars* (Hammer's Slammers). New York, Tor, 1984.
*Killer*, with Karl Edward Wagner. New York, Baen, 1984.
*Active Measures*, with Janet E. Morris. New York, Baen, 1985.
*Bridgehead.* New York, Tor, 1985.
*At Any Price* (Hammer's Slammers). New York, Baen, 1985.
*Lacey and His Friends.* New York, Baen, 1986.
*Ranks of Bronze.* New York, Baen, 1986.
*Counting the Cost* (Hammer's Slammers). New York, Baen, 1987.
*Kill Ratio* (Yates), with Janet Morris. New York, Ace, 1987.
*Fortress* (Kelly). New York, Tor, 1987.
*Dagger.* New York, Ace, 1988.
*The Sea Hag* (for young adults), with Janet Morris. New York, Baen, 1989.
*Target* (Yates), with Janet Morris. New York, Ace, 1989.
*Explorers in Hell*, with Janet Morris. New York, Baen, 1989.
*Rolling Hot* (Hammer's Slammers). New York, Baen, 1989.
*Northworld.* New York, Ace, 1990.
*Surface Action.* New York, Ace, 1990.
*Bluebloods.* New York, Baen, 1990.
*The Eternal City.* New York, Baen, 1990.
*The Forge*, with S.M. Stirling. New York, Baen, 1991.
*The Hunter Returns* (for young adults), with Jim Kjelgaard. New York, Baen, 1991.
*Vengeance* (Northworld). New York, Ace, 1991.
*The Warrior* (Hammer's Slammers). New York, Baen, 1991.
*Justice* (Northworld). New York, Ace, 1991.
*Old Nathan.* New York, Baen, 1991.

Short Stories

*Hammer's Slammers.* New York, Ace, 1979.
*Time Safari.* New York, Tor, 1982.
*From the Heart of Darkness.* New York, Tor, 1983.
*Vettius and His Friends.* New York, Baen, 1989.
*The Military Dimension.* New York, Baen, 1991.

### Other Publications

Novel

*The Dragon Lord.* New York, Berkley, 1979.

Other

*A Separate Star: A Science Fiction Tribute to Rudyard Kipling*, with Sandra Miesel. New York, Baen, 1989.
*Heads to the Storm*, with Sandra Miesel. New York, Baen, 1989.
*Harold Coyle's Team Yankee* (script adaptation). New York, Berkley, 1989.

Editor, *Cthlhu, The Mythos and Kindred Horrors*, by Robert E. Howard. New York, Baen, 1987.
Editor, with Bill Fawcett, *Counter Attack.* New York, Ace, 1988.
Editor, with Bill Fawcett, *The Fleet.* New York, Ace, 1988.
Editor, *Men Hunting Things.* New York, Baen, 1988.
Editor, with Bill Fawcett, *Breakthrough.* New York, Ace, 1989.
Editor, with Bill Fawcett, *Sworn Allies.* New York, Ace, 1990.
Editor, with Bill Fawcett, *Crisis.* New York, Ace, 1991.

* * *

Though known primarily for his military science fiction, David A. Drake writes in many genres, from realistic spy novels to young adult fantasy. However, usual genre distinctions are not always easy or useful concerning Drake's fiction. While the spy-adventure novel *Skyripper* introduces extraterrestrials unnecessarily, Drake fully blends political realism and near-future extrapolation in novels such as *Active Measures, Kill Ratio* and *Target* (all co-written with Janet Morris), and his stories about law enforcement in a world of constant surveillance (*Lacey and His Friends*). The magic and dragon in *The Dragon Lord* have a scientific rationale, and the alien of "The Hunting Ground" would function similarly if its menace were supernatural. Drake's horror fiction is collected in *From the Heart of Darkness*, but there may be no fiction of his from which horror is absent.

Drake's artistic influences range from classical Latin literature and German expressionistic cinema to Doc Smith's space opera and *Planet Stories.* In acknowledging his influences and exploring his interests, Drake has helped produce anthologies such as *A Separate Star* and *Heads to the Storm*, assembled (with Sandra Miesel) in honor of Rudyard Kipling's works. Alone or in partnership, Drake is an excellent editor of anthologies, many of them on topics for which his fiction is noted.

Drake also writes in the cooperative sub-genre known as "shared world" collections and novels. *Dagger*, "Goddess," and "Votary" take place in Robert Lynn Asprin and Lynn Abbey's Thieves' World milieu, and "Springs Eternal" is in the collaborative afterlife of the Hell books. Drake himself created and provides plot outlines for the Crisis of Empire series, primarily science-fantasy adventure, and with Bill Fawcett created a sharable universe in *The Fleet.*

The greatest biographical influence on Drake's fiction is his army service in Vietnam and Cambodia; his horror short stories sometimes take place in Vietnam or feature veterans as protagonists. Drake's best known fiction concerns soldiers and law officers, often mercenaries, in near or far futures. This military science fiction generally fulfills its sub-genre, in both weaknesses and strengths. Sometimes condemned as pro-war because of its celebration of military virtues and excitement, the fiction is too grim and realistic to truly advocate any organized violence.

Drake's major science fiction series presents Colonel Alois Hammer and his Slammers, 30th-century mercenaries hired by numerous war-torn planets. The original short stories were collected in *Hammer's Slammers*, with explanatory interludes and a new concluding story. This was followed by two novels (*Counting the Cost* and *Rolling Hot*) and two collections of a short novel and a novelette apiece (*At Any Price* and *The Warrior*). Drake uses the same fictional universe to tell different stories and explore various character-types; the works are primarily about action and the kind of men—and, refreshingly, women—who choose it. The future background is interesting, especially in the implied economics and political science, though sometimes peripheral to the action.

*Cross the Stars* adds to our understanding of the Slammers, but its main point is a conscious imitation of Homer's *Odyssey*, as ex-Slammer Don Slade tries to reach his home world Tethys and set it in order. Sometimes the novel follows its model too rigorously, but mythic elements are transformed to science fiction with creativity and flair. *Cross the Stars* also has some of Drake's best writing and exploration of character.

The same quality is apparent in the Northworld series, similarly based on the Norse Eddas: *Northworld, Vengeance*, and *Justice.* This blend of known myth and speculative fiction is even more ambitious and successful. Set in a multiverse in which levels occasionally interpenetrate, these books depict the psychological dangers of god-like power and the fierce values that maintain in survival-level cultures. *Vengeance* is structured with two simultaneous plots, both starring the protagonist Nils Hansen.

Other military science fiction by Drake includes the short stories collected in *The Military Dimension. The Forlorn Hope*, featuring Slammers-like mercenaries, was to have begun another series, although those plans were cancelled. Drake also scripted the comicbook adaptation of Harold Coyle's *Team Yankee.*

However, it would be wrong to categorize Drake narrowly as a writer of military science fiction. In works such as his charming and eerie young adult novel, *The Sea Hag*, or his novelette "Travellers," Drake shows more—and often more likable—kinds of people in various situations. *Bridgehead*, apparently a straight story of time-travel, is an ambitious and mostly-successful study of technology and human relations; *Time Safari*, concerning time-traveling hunters, features impeccable historical (or prehistorical) detail and one of Drake's most fully realized female characters.

Some of Drake's best fiction grows out of his love for, and deep understanding of, ancient Rome. In works including *Killer* (co-written with Karl Edward Wagner), *The Dragon Lord*, and some of his short stories (many in *Vettius and His Friends*), Drake demonstrates his knowledge of historical settings and ability to present them, especially the Roman Empire from prime to decay. The science fiction or fantasy threat and historical setting mesh well in these works, and in *Birds of Prey* they also allow especially noteworthy development of theme and character. *Ranks of Bronze*, also noteworthy, is a *bildungsroman* about an officer, captured and forced to fight on alien worlds, who learns the meaning and value of being a Roman.

Primarily considering himself a story-teller, Drake provides involving fiction. His strong yet unobtrusive prose makes him one of the best action writers in science fiction; his ability with plot has grown steadily since *The Dragon Lord* and is now another great strength. In writing or in background research, Drake's "overriding concern," as friend and fellow-writer Karl Edward Wagner wrote, "remains *get it right.*"

—Bernadette Bosky

---

**DREW, Wayland.** Canadian. Born in Oshawa, 12 September 1932. Education at Oshawa Collegiate and Vocational Institute and at University of Toronto. Married Gwendolyn Drew, 18 October 1957; one son, three daughters. Agent: Amanda Urban, International Creative Management, 40 West 57th Street, New York, New York 10019, U.S.A.

SCIENCE-FICTION PUBLICATIONS

Novels (series: Erthring)

*Dragonslayer* (novelization of screenplay). London, Fontana, and New York, Ballantine, 1981.
*The Erthring Cycle*. New York, Doubleday, 1986.
*The Memoirs of Alcheringia*. New York, Ballantine, 1984.
*The Gaian Expedient*. New York, Ballantine, 1985.
*The Master of Norriya*. New York, Ballantine, 1986.
*Batteries Not Included* (novelization of screenplay). New York, Berkley, 1987.
*Willow* (novelization of screenplay). New York, Ballantine, and London, Sphere, 1988.

OTHER PUBLICATIONS

Novels

*The Wabeno Feast.* Toronto, Anasi, 1973.
*Halfway Man.* Ottawa, Ontario, Oberon Press, 1989.

Other

*Superior: The Haunted Shore*, with Bruce Littlejohn. Toronto, Gage, and New York, Beaufort, 1975.
*Brown's Weir* (travel), with Gwendolyn Drew. Ottawa, Ontario, Oberon Press, 1983.
*A Sea Within: The Gulf of St. Lawrence* (travel), with Bruce Littlejohn. Toronto, McClelland and Stewart, 1984.

* * *

Wayland Drew's novelization of the film *Dragonslayer* was largely unheralded. Although he had written previous novels, this was his first byline in the fields of science fiction and fantasy. Any inventiveness or interest in the story could be attributed to the original screenwriters. It was another three years before Drew published his first science-fiction novel, although his fine adaptation of the story of a dying wizard's battle against the last dragon in the world was artfully written, and later reprinted with no mention of the movie upon which it was based. The visual impact of the special effects is missing, but Drew's highly descriptive language conveys much of the sense of wonder and power of the final sequences.

*The Memoirs of Alcheringia* is the first volume in the Erthring Cycle, a trilogy published between 1984 and 1986. This panoramic story is set within a post-holocaust world, in which descendants of the survivors have fragmented into a number of more or less primitive societies. A rigid code of behavior born of the frightening events that destroyed civilization prohibits any return to the high technology of the past. More ominously, there exists a surviving bastion of scientific knowledge that secretly works behind the scenes to prevent such a resurgence. At the same time, they hope to lead the barbaric masses gradually toward a less hazardous and bellicose existence. The internal inconsistency of the two conflicting motives is the source of most of the plot conflict, both in their relationship to the rest of the planet, and as the driving force in their internal bickering. The primary protagonist is a member of one of these primitive tribes, gifted, or perhaps cursed, with a profound curiosity about the nature of his world and a determination that life should be easier. What should have been a routine raiding-party marking the transition from childhood to adult life, is actually the preamble to a series of events that will alter both the man himself and his society.

The story continues in *The Gaian Expedient.* Yggdrasil, the scientific colony in control, is beginning to experience problems of its own. Despite efforts to conserve resources, the physical situation in their base is deteriorating rapidly. The dwindling supplies and energy sources cause increasing tension among the scientific community as well, threatening a schism within their ranks. Frustrated by the intransigence of the people they attempt to help, one faction advocates using coercive and manipulative techniques to play one group against another, even though such intervention contradicts their code of conduct. Meanwhile, the protagonist has grown increasingly disenchanted with the situation, determined that the tribes should enjoy freedom from external intervention.

The situation reaches a climax in *The Master of Norriya.* Despite its dominating technology, Yggdrasil is no longer capable of controlling the tribes; rebellion and internal conflict threaten to destroy any trace of stability. They have also perverted their own doctrines, and are reduced to using conscripted labor to deal with the increasingly strenuous efforts required to maintain the colony's physical and functional integrity. Despite their efforts to remain in power, a counterbalancing force has arisen among the nomads, led by an intelligent but discontented outcast, and an unlikely collection of rebels, misfits, and the shunned mutants. Although stylistically the trilogy is an adventure story, and quite entertainly done, there is also a clear statement of Drew's acknowledgment of the indomitability of the human spirit and its perverse need to advance at its own pace and in its own fashion, rather than at the dictates of a self-proclaimed authority.

Unfortunately, Drew's only subsequent writing in the field consists of two more film novelizations. *Batteries Not Included* is an amusing, sentimental, and not entirely credible, story of some mechanical lifeforms, and the impact their presence has on the residents of an apartment building. *Willow* is another fantasy-quest novel, which follows the adventures of a diminutive protagonist seeking to protect an infant from the minions of an evil sorceress-queen. Both are creditable adaptations of the screen plays, the stories themselves are well constructed, but obviously there is little evidence of Drew's own imaginative powers in either.

—Don D'Ammassa

---

**DRUMM, D.B.** *See* **NAHA, Ed.**

---

**DUANE, Diane.** American. Agent: Donald A. Maass, 64 West 84th Street, Apartment 3-A, New York, New York 10024. Address: c/o Pocket Books, The Simon and Schuster Building, 1230 Avenue of the Americas, New York, New York 10020, U.S.A.

### Science-Fiction Publications

Novels

*The Door into Fire.* New York, Dell, 1979; London, Magnum, 1981.
*The Wounded Sky.* New York, Pocket Books, 1983.
*The Door into Shadow.* New York, Bluejay, 1984.
*My Enemy, My Ally.* New York, Pocket Books, 1984.
*The Romulan Way,* with Peter Morwood. New York, Pocket Books, 1987.
*Spock's World.* New York, Pocket Books, 1988.
*Keeper of the City,* with Peter Morwood. New York, Bantam, 1989.
*Doctor's Orders.* New York, Pocket Books, 1990.

### Other Publications

Other

*So You Want to Be a Wizard* (for children). New York, Delacorte Press, 1983.
*Deep Wizardry.* New York, Delacorte Press, 1985.
*High Wizardry.* New York, Delacorte Press, 1990.
*Support Your Local Wizard.* New York, Guild American, 1990.

* * *

Diane Duane entered science fiction by the *Star Trek* route, and she is still writing for that remarkable phenomenon that has taken on a life of its own. However, she also writes fantasy, and her major claim to serious consideration rests on two excellent fantasy novels, *The Door into Fire* and *The Door into Shadow.* They are half of a projected tetralogy which, we are told, is to be focused on the adventures and development of five main characters: the humans Herewiss, Freelorn, Segnbora, and, presumably, the fire elemental Sunspark and the dragon Hasai.

Like too many fantasies, these books are set in a geographically isolated imaginary land with a quasi-feudal society and plenty of magic. The adventures apparently are all going to culminate in crises leading to passage to a higher state for the various major characters, and they have added import as part of the struggle of good against evil. Duane's achievement is to have transcended this hackneyed scenario, despite a weakness for excessively happy endings.

She does this by setting constraints upon her universe. The Goddess who created it is good, but neither omnipotent nor omniscient. The presence of evil, which manifests itself as Shadow, is the result of Her attempt in Her aspect as Maiden to create a closed universe without evil, a task which in Her other aspects as Mother and Hag She knows to be impossible. This means that the Goddess really does need human aid in the struggle against Shadow.

The power with which the Goddess opposes Shadow is Fire, life-force which, when present in an individual in large enough quantity, can be used for extra-sensory perception and to perform ordinary and extraordinary acts. Like all power, it has its price: if not used, it is lost; if used, it shortens the life of its user. It is entirely distinct from magic, which is no more than a kind of technology based on the affinities of words to the physical world. As with all technology, it uses energy. Given the choice, it is often less tiring for a magician to use nonmagical means to an end.

None of the Goddess's aspects, which are sometimes at odds, is entirely benign. Those who ask a boon may get it; but if they presume too much, they will bitterly regret getting exactly what they requested. All of this is known to Her followers because the Goddess makes Herself manifest to everyone individually at least once in a lifetime. Hence there is a great store of anecdotal information from which it is possible to learn Her will, particularly with respect to sexual ethics and the proper social order, where the systems propounded deserve to be studied for their intrinsic interest.

Given this context, Herewiss, the first male in generations to have a usable amount of Fire, *must* learn to use it. Segnbora, with too much to control by normal means, *must* find a way to control it. Freelorn, whose hereditary duties require him to perform ceremonies binding vast powers, *must* overthrow the usurper of his throne in order to perform them; and the others are bound to help him, although the imperatives that drive Sunspark and Hasai are not yet entirely clear. Should any of them fall, the result would be unimaginable disaster.

Duane is an elegant universe-maker. The world in which her characters live is no mere backdrop. It informs the actions of her characters, giving them motives beyond those which can be ascribed simply to human or non-human nature. Her treatments of magic and religion, here for once in a beneficent relation to each other, are particularly well thought-out. Moreover, she does not tell, she shows. Such integration is rare, especially in sword-and-sorcery stories. The result is vivid, entertaining writing which deserves study both for its technical excellence and the ideas it contains.

—William M. Schuyler, Jr.

---

**DUNCAN, Dave.** Canadian. Born in Scotland, in 1933. Educated at University of St. Andrews, Fife. Married: three children. Petroleum geologist. Has lived in Calgary, Alberta, since 1955. Address: c/o Ballantine Books, 201 East 50th Street, New York, New York 10022, U.S.A.

SCIENCE-FICTION PUBLICATIONS

Novels (series: Man of His Word; Seventh Sword)

*A Rose-Red City*. New York, Ballantine, 1987.
*Shadow*. New York, Ballantine, 1987.
*The Reluctant Swordsman* (Seventh Sword). New York, Ballantine, 1988.
*The Coming of Wisdom* (Seventh Sword). New York, Ballantine, 1988.
*The Destiny of the Sword* (Seventh Sword). New York, Ballantine, 1988.
*West of January*. New York, Ballantine, 1989.
*Magic Casement* (Man of His Word). New York, Ballantine, 1990.
*Strings*. New York, Ballantine, 1990.
*Faery Lands Forlorn* (Man of His Word). New York, Ballantine, 1991.
*Hero!* New York, Ballantine, 1991.
*Perilous Seas* (Man of His Word). New York, Ballantine, 1991.

* * *

Dave Duncan made his debut in 1987 with *A Rose-Red City*. Mera is a city that exists outside normal time and space, administered by the mysterious Oracle, home to heroes from both the past and the future. Within Mera, no one ages, and it provides sanctuary from enemies both mundane and supernatural. A team of its residents are sent on a mission to rescue a woman from a time roughly our own, but they must contend with two major problems. First, several inhuman creatures are determined to abort the rescue; second, the woman will not allow herself to be rescued unless her children can go as well, and children are never admitted to Mera. Containing an original mix of magic and the real world, this was a very auspicious first novel.

The heroic figure is repeated over and over in Duncan's subsequent novels. In *Shadow*, a young man must reconcile his own dreams of destiny with the requirements of his society, and finds a way to satisfy both. On a colony world that has lost much of the knowledge necessary to support a high civilization, young men dream of being among the elite selected to ride the skies on giant eagles. The protagonist finds his dreams in danger when he is appointed bodyguard to a member of a noble family, then subsequently framed as a traitor. There follows a somewhat predictable recounting of his efforts to clear his name, but the charm of the book is in the elaborately described culture against which these events take place.

Duncan's next work was The Seventh Sword trilogy. *The Reluctant Swordsman* starts with an unlikely hero from our own world, transported to another where a sarcastically threatening godling informs him that he must serve as swordsman for the goddess. With a new, powerful body, Wallie Smith rises to the occasion, but the dangers he faces in the opening volume pale to insignificance in *The Coming of Wisdom*, which introduces a group of evil sorcerers whose powers may exceed that of the goddess. In the concluding volume, *The Destiny of the Sword*, everything appears to have gone wrong and almost certain defeat stares the hero in the face. The trilogy is in many ways a cliché; we know from the outset that the hero will triumph in the end. Duncan has, however, embellished the familiar theme with well written, crisply narrated adventures.

*West of January* is in many ways Duncan's best novel. Once again we have a primitive colony world, this one peopled almost entirely with semi-nomadic tribes who relocate at the instruction of the Angels, mysterious people who retain a higher level of technology. The protagonist is another reluctant hero, this time a young man cast out of his tribe after his father is killed, who wanders the planet trying to discover a place where he belongs, and incidentally uncovering a number of secrets hidden from his people. This is certainly Duncan's most inventive work to date, unfolding mystery upon mystery as he reveals his world to us.

Duncan's next book, *Strings*, varied somewhat from his usual style. Our attention is split between two main characters this time, a young woman whose extra-sensory powers are of extraordinary value to a team exploring potential colony worlds, and a young man involved in murder and politics. The blend of intrigue and adventure is well balanced and effective.

*Hero!* is something of a disappointment. Vaun is a man who overcame the poverty of his background to rise to a high position in the Space Patrol, only to discover that the Patrol has grown corrupt and is often in league with bands of criminals. At the same time, a major interstellar conflict has just come to an uncertain end, but a mysterious ship on a collision course with a settled world may be the last gasp of the defeated Brotherhood, or the first blow in a renewed war, or perhaps something even less predictable. This time, however, Duncan's efforts to make Vaun into a heroic figure are too heavy handed; the character is so competent and authoritative that we just cannot accept him as a real human being.

*The Magic Casement* started a new series, A Man of His Word. Duncan provides a new, unlikely hero, Rap the stableboy. When his king is stricken with an apparently fatal disease, Rap must journey to another land where Princess Inos has gone to improve her education. Naturally, a host of monsters are prepared to challenge his right to pass. Although he triumphs, at the last moment the Princess is kidnapped into another world, and when he attempts to follow, in *Faery Lands Forlorn*, he finds himself faced with a fresh struggle. The story continues in *Perilous Seas* and is scheduled to conclude with *Emperor and Clown*, presently forthcoming.

Duncan is a talented writer of adventure stories, occasionally colored with mild humor, who shows indications of being able to produce more significant work as he continues to refine his style.

—Don D'Ammassa

---

**DUNCAN, David.** American. Born in Billings, Montana, 17 February 1913. Educated at the University of Montana, Missoula, B.A. 1935. Married Elaine Sulliger in 1940; three daughters. Personnel examiner, Department of Agriculture, Washington, D.C., 1936; social worker, California State Relief Administration, Fresno, 1936–40; manager of California housing project, Farm Security Administration, 1941–43; field director in California and Nevada, American Red Cross, 1943–44; labor economist, National Labor Bureau, San Francisco, 1944–46. Since 1946, freelance writer.

### Science-Fiction Publications

#### Novels

*The Shade of Time*. New York, Random House, 1946; London, Grey Walls Press, 1949.
*The Madrone Tree*. New York, Macmillan, 1949; London, Gollancz, 1950; as *Worse Than Murder*, New York, Pocket Books, 1954.
*Dark Dominion*. New York, Ballantine, 1954; London, Heinemann, 1955.
*Beyond Eden*. New York, Ballantine, 1955; as *Another Tree in Eden*, London, Heinemann, 1956.
*Occam's Razor*. New York, Ballantine, 1957; London, Gollancz, 1958.

#### Uncollected Short Stories

"The Immortals," in *Galaxy* (New York), October 1960.
"Requiem on the Moon," in *The Dead Astronaut*. Chicago, Playboy Press, 1964.
"On Venus the Thunder Precedes the Lightning," in *Worlds of Tomorrow* (New York), Spring 1971.

### Other Publications

#### Novels

*Remember the Shadows*. New York, McBride, 1944.
*The Bramble Bush*. New York, Macmillan, 1948; London, Sampson Low, 1949; as *Sweet, Low, and Deadly*, New York, Mercury, 1949.
*The Serpent's Egg*. New York, Macmillan, 1950.
*None But My Foe*. New York, Macmillan, 1950.
*Wives and Husbands*. Cleveland, World, 1952.
*The Trumpet of God*. New York, Doubleday, 1956.
*Yes, My Darling Daughters*. New York, Doubleday, 1959; London, Heinemann, 1960.
*The Long Walk Home from Town*. New York, Doubleday, 1964.

#### Plays

Screenplays: *Sangaree*, with Frank Moss, 1953; *Jivaro*, with Winston Miller, 1954; *The White Orchid*, with Reginald LeBorg, 1955; *The Monster That Challenged the World*, with Patricia Fielder, 1957; *The Black Scorpion*, with Robert Blees and Paul Yawitz, 1957; *The Thing That Couldn't Die*, 1958; *Monster on the Campus*, 1958; *The Leech Woman*, with Ben Pivar and Francis Rosenwald, 1960; *The Time Machine*, 1960; *Fantastic Voyage*, with others, 1966.

Television Plays: *The Human Factor* (*The Outer Limits* series), and for *Telephone Time, My Three Sons, National Velvet, It's a Man's World, Higgins, Daniel Boone, Studio One, The High Chaparral*, and *Men into Space* series.

* * *

David Duncan is one of the most accomplished stylists to have worked in science fiction and fantasy, yet he is an almost forgotten figure. The reason for this is that, like Edgar Pangborn's and Ray Bradbury's, his ideas are not often very original and his science is sometimes bizarre; his method is that of the mystery story—one in which the enigma is left unexplained for a good deal of the book, and when the problem is solved the story simply ends. The unknown is not brought on stage for very long, and its consequences are left undeveloped. Yet there are so many satisfactions of characterization, background and description, social observation, ideas about human life and destiny, that one is tempted to dismiss the seeming flaws. Duncan is an elegant, poetic wordsmith who involves the reader completely.

*Dark Dominion* is an overwhelming emotional experience that leaves the reader drained. The story is about the building, in secret, of a military space station that will dominate the earth. We are shown the effects of this terrible purpose on the lives of the scientists involved, as they struggle to complete the project, and later to change its meaning for the world. The novel is filled with moments of great beauty, and they are worth the speculative and scientific lapses. The classic novels of the 1950's do not surpass this one in skill, even when they are superior in ideas and originality. "Duncan's forte is people," wrote Damon Knight (in *In Search of Wonder*, 1967); "he sees them with an inquiring, ironic, compassionate but unsentimental eye. At his best, the characters he draws are sharply individual, each one believable and distinct from every other. He fills up the scene with moving portraits, and their intricate mutual relationships, effortlessly handled, make his book." This is a lesson that better writers—those whose thinking and conceptual development, even their stories, are better—have not learned: that to produce a valuable piece of fiction, including SF, a writer must show *everything* as belonging to the awareness of characters; ideas as well as feelings must be seen sticking to the *insides* of people.

*Occam's Razor* is a sketchy story, but it also has the compelling portraits and personal interactions of *Dark Dominion.* The story details the accidental visit of two beings from a parallel world, whose sudden appearance causes much misunderstanding; but the novel ends where it should begin—namely, in the effects of these people's presence on our world, after this fact is discovered. We are given only half the story, that of the events leading up to the solution of the mystery concerning the identity of the two visitors. Still, this is a persuasive and humane story. *Beyond Eden* is more an all-around success than the other two novels, though it lacks the eloquence of *Dark Dominion.* Set in the 1950's atmosphere of the McCarthy hearings and the Oppenheimer persecution, the story deals with a fascinating water project in California. The enterprise discovers a new kind of water that might transform human nature, though at first it seems to kill people, embarrassing the chief scientist who already has a bad past to live down. Again, the story ends where the confrontation with the unknown might lead to new understandings and a set of problems of a higher order.

One might also argue that Duncan chose not to explore beyond "mere mystery"—that his sense of human limits prevented him from inventing glib "understandings" of the kind demanded by so many SF readers. Duncan chose to stay closer to the present. His problem does suggest a prescription: truly great science fiction demands that one be a fine writer with all the skills of a contemporary novelist *and* possess the intellect necessary to speculate beyond the point of "mere mystery," surface drama, and obvious topicality.

David Duncan drew enthusiastic reviews for his novels. Groff Conklin called him "a richly endowed mind" whose work should not be missed. Anthony Boucher, Theodore Sturgeon, P. Schuyler Miller, and others ranked his books with the best of their years. In a field whose main problem is a lack of the authenticity that belongs to a literature won from experience, Duncan has the virtue of seeming very authentic, despite his supposed shortcomings. His novels are as he intended them to be, and their virtues are the shortcomings of most science fiction. In the only statement about his science fiction, Duncan wrote: "To me the great virtue of the science-fiction story doesn't reside in its elaborate gadgets and twistings of time and space—although these can be majestically entertaining—but in its possibilities for analysis of man and the social order." He saw SF as a literature of critical possibilities, and for this he deserves serious attention.

—George Zebrowski

---

**DUNSANY, Lord;** Edward John Moreton Drax Plunkett, 18th Baron Dunsany. Irish. Born in London, 24 July 1878; succeeded to the barony, 1899. Educated at Cheam School, Surrey; Eton College, Berkshire; then privately tutored; Royal Military Academy, Sandhurst, Surrey. Served as a 2nd lieutenant in the Coldstream Guards in Gibraltar and in the Boer War, 1899–1902; captain in the Royal Inniskilling Fusiliers during World War I; wounded in the Dublin Easter Rebellion, 1916; served in the Home Guard during World War II. Married Lady Beatrice Child-Villiers in 1904; one son. Lived at Dunstall Priory, Kent, and Dunsany Castle, County Meath. Byron professor of English literature, University of Athens, 1940–41. D.Litt.: University of Dublin, 1939. Fellow, Royal Society of Literature, and Royal Geographical Society; member, Irish Academy of Letters. *Died 25 October 1957.*

SCIENCE-FICTION PUBLICATIONS

Novels

*The King of Elfland's Daughter.* London and New York, Putnam, 1924.
*The Charwoman's Shadow.* London and New York, Putnam, 1924.
*The Blessings of Pan.* London and New York, Putnam, 1926.
*The Curse of the Wise Woman.* London, Heinemann, and New York, Longman, 1933.
*The Strange Journeys of Colonel Polders.* London, Jarrolds, 1950.

Short Stories (Series: Jorkens)

*The Gods of Pegana.* London, Elkin Matthews, 1905; Boston, Luce, 1916.
*Time and the Gods.* London, Heinemann, 1906; Boston, Luce, 1913.
*The Sword of Welleran and other Stories.* London, G. Allen, 1908; Boston, Luce, 1916.
*A Dreamer's Tales.* London, G. Allen, and Boston, Luce, 1910.
*The Book of Wonder: A Chronicle of Little Adventures at the Edge of the World.* London, Heinemann, 1912; Boston, Luce, 1913.
*Fifty-One Tales..* London, Elkin Matthews, and New York, Kennerley, 1915; as *The Food of Death*, Hollywood, California, Newcastle, 1974.
*Tales of Wonder.* London, Elkin Matthews, 1916; as *The Last Book of Wonder*, Boston, Luce, 1916.
*Tales of Three Hemispheres.* Boston, Luce, 1919; London, Fisher Unwin, 1920.
*The Chronicles of Rodriguez.* London, Putnam, 1922; as *Don Rodriguez: Chronicles of Shadow Valley*, New York, Putnam, 1922.
*The Travel Tales of Mr. Joseph Jorkens.* London and New York, Putnam, 1931.
*Jorkens Remembers Africa.* New York, Longman, 1934; as *Mr. Jorkens Remembers Africa*, London, Heinemann, 1934.
*Jorkens Has a Large Whiskey.* London, Putnam, 1940.
*The Fourth Book of Jorkens.* London, Jarrolds, and Sauk City, Wisconsin, Arkham House, 1948.
*The Man Who Ate the Phoenix.* London, Jarrolds, 1949.
*Jorkens Borrows Another Whiskey.* London, M. Joseph, 1954.
*At the Edge of the World* (selections), edited by Lin Carter. New York, Ballantine, 1970.
*Beyond the Fields We Know* (selections), edited by Lin Carter. New York and London, Ballantine, 1972.
*Gods, Men, and Ghosts: The Best Supernatural Fiction of Dunsany* (selections), edited by E.F. Bleiler. New York, Dover, 1972.

OTHER PUBLICATIONS

Novels

*Up in the Hills.* London, Heinemann, and New York, Putnam, 1936.
*Rory and Bran.* London, Heinemann, and New York, Putnam, 1937.
*The Story of Mona Sheehy.* London, Heinemann, 1939; New York, Harper, 1940.
*Guerrilla.* London, Heinemann, and New York, Bobbs-Merrill, 1944.
*The Last Revolution.* London and New York, Jarrolds, 1951.
*His Fellow Men.* London, Jarrolds, 1952.

Short Stories

*Tales of War.* London and New York, Putnam, 1918.
*The Little Tales of Smethers and Other Stories.* London, Jarrolds, 1952.
*The Ghosts of the Heaviside Layer, and Other Fantasms.* Philadelphia, Owlswick Press, 1980.

Plays

*The Sphinx at Gizeh,* in *Tripod,* May 1912.
*Five Plays* [includes *The Glittering Gate* (produced 1909), *The Gods of the Mountain* (produced 1911), *King Argimines and the Unknown Warrior* (produced 1911), *The Golden Doom* (produced 1912), and *The Lost Silk Hat* (produced 1913)]. Boston, Little Brown, and London, Grant Richards, 1914.
*Plays of Gods and Men* [includes *The Tents of the Arabs* (produced 1914), *The Queen's Enemies* (produced 1916), and *The Laughter of the Gods* (produced 1919)]. London, Fisher Unwin, and New York, Luce, 1917.
*A Night at an Inn* (produced 1916).
*The Murderers* (produced 1919).
*The Prince of Stamboul* (produced 1919?).
*If* (produced 1921). London and New York, Putnam, 1921.
*Cheezo* (produced 1921). London and New York, Putnam, 1921.
*Plays of Near and Far* [includes *The Compromise of the King of the Golden Isles, The Flight of the Queen, Cheezo, A Good Bargain, If Shakespeare Lived Today,* and *Fame and the Poet* (produced 1924)]. London and New York, Putnam, 1922.
*Lord Adrian* (produced 1923). Waltham Saint Lawrence, Berkshire, Golden Cockerel Press, 1933.
*If Shakespeare Lived Today.* London and New York, Putnam, 1923.
*Alexander and Three Small Plays* (includes *The Old King's Tale, The Evil Kettle,* and *The Amusements of Khan Kharuda*). London and New York, Putnam, 1925.
*Alexander* (produced 1938). London and New York, Putnam, 1925.
*Mr. Faithful* (produced 1927). New York, French, 1935.
*Seven Modern Comedies* [includes *Atalanta in Wimbledon, The Raffle, The Journey of the Soul, In Holy Russia, His Sainted Grandmother* (produced 1926), *The Hopeless Passion of Mr. Bunyon,* and *The Jest of Hahalaba* (produced 1927)]. London and New York, Putnam, 1928.
*The Old Folk of the Centuries.* London, Elkin Matthews. 1930.
*Plays for Earth and Air* [includes *Fame Comes Late, A Matter of Honour, Mr. Sliggen's Hour, The Pumpkin, The Use of Man, The Bureau de Change, The Seventh Symphony, Golden Dragon City, Time's Joke,* and *Atmospherics*]. London, Heinemann, 1937.
*The Strange Lover* (produced 1939).

Verse

*Fifty Poems.* London and New York, Putnam, 1929.
*Mirage Water.* London, Putnam, 1938; Philadelphia, Dorrance, 1939.
*War Poems.* London, Hutchinson, 1941.
*A Journey.* London, Macdonald, 1943.
*Wandering Songs.* London, Hutchinson, 1943.
*The Year.* London, Jarrolds, 1946.
*To Awaken Pegasus and Other Poems.* Oxford, Ronald, 1949.

Other

*Selections.* Churchtown, Dundrum, Cuala Press, 1912; Boston, Little Brown, 1916.
*Nowadays.* Boston, Four Seas, 1918.
*Unhappy Far-Off Things.* London, Elkin Matthews, and Boston, Little Brown, 1919.
*If I Were Dictator: The Pronouncements of the Grand Macaroni.* London, Methuen, 1934.
*My Talks with Dean Spanley.* London, Heinemann, and New York, Putnam, 1936.
*My Ireland.* London, Jarrolds, and New York, Funk and Wagnalls, 1937.
*Patches of Sunlight* (autobiography). London, Heinemann, and New York, Reynal and Hitchcock, 1938.
*While the Sirens Slept* (autobiography). London, Jarrolds, 1944.
*The Donellan Lectures 1943.* London, Heinemann, 1945.
*A Glimpse from a Watchtower: A Series of Essays.* London, Jarrolds, 1946.
*The Sirens Wake* (autobiography). London, Jarrolds, 1945.
*Over the Hills and Far Away* (selections), edited by Lin Carter. New York, Ballantine, 1974.

Editor, *Modern Anglo-Irish Verse.* N.p., 1914.
Editor, *Last Song* by Francis Ledwidge. London, Herbert Jenkins, 1918.

*

Bibliography: in *Bibliographies of Modern Authors 1* by H. Danielson, London, Bookman's Journal, 1921.

Critical Studies: *Dunsany the Dramatist* by Edward Hale Bierstadt, Boston, Little Brown, 1917; revised edition, 1919; *Dunsany, King of Dreams: A Personal Portrait* by Hazel Smith, London, Weidenfeld and Nicolson, and New York, Exposition Press, 1959.

* * *

While Lord Dunsany may have been a minor figure in Irish literature, the extent of his role in the development of modern fantasy is major. He was a critical influence on H.P. Lovecraft, L. Sprague de Camp and Fritz Leiber, and his play *King Argimenes and the Unknown Warrior* is one of the sources for Fletcher Pratt's *The Well of the Unicorn.* From his first book, *The Gods of Pegana,* in which he creates an entire pantheon, to his Jorkens series of adventure stories based on his travels in Algeria and the Sudan, to his masterpiece *The King of Elfland's Daughter,* Dunsany belongs with William Morris and George MacDonald as the generating forces of modern fantasy.

Dunsany's fantasy is characterized by his exotic settings; difficult, if creative and frequently numinous, prose; and stalwart protagonists and alluring, exquisite heroines. His ability to create vivid setting is partially explained by his relationship with Sidney H. Sime; Sime's drawings inspired "The Distressing Tale of Thangobrind the Jeweller, and of the Doom that Befell Him" (in *The Book of Wonder*). Dunsany's visual settings are evident in the country village and the activities of love in *The Blessing of Pan* and in the fictional Spanish Golden Age in *The Chronicles of Don Rodriguez* and *The Charwoman's Shadow*. However, his greatest stylistic triumph is the much-heralded *The King of Elfland's Daughter*, and in this novel all the qualities of his fantastic fictions are epitomized. Drawing on the themes of alienation and identity and the structure of the quest, which characterize much of his canon, Dunsany creates an interplay between the world of faery and everyday with his innovative proper names, coined phrases, and characterizations. In the novel, Alveric falls in love with an elfin princess, but after she bears him a son, she can no longer endure the crude society of mankind and returns to faery. Alveric's quest for his wife provides ample opportunity for Dunsany's ability to create numinous wonder, and the quest is resolved through love and harmony.

The on-going reprinting of Dunsany's tales—especially "The Sword of Welleran" and "The Fortress Unvanquishable Save for Sacnoth"—demonstrates Dunsany's continuing influence on the literature of fantasy, the lasting appeal of his fantastic settings, and his role as a progenitor of modern fantasy literature in all its varieties and techniques.

—Roger C. Schlobin

---

**DURRELL, Lawrence (George).** British. Born in Julundur, India, 27 February 1912; brother of the zoologist and writer Gerald Durrell. Educated at the College of St. Joseph, Darjeeling, India; St. Edmund's School, Canterbury, Kent. Married 1) Nancy Myers in 1935 (divorced 1947); 2) Eve Cohen in 1947 (divorced); 3) Claude Durrell in 1961 (died 1967); 4) Ghislaine de Boysson in 1973 (divorced 1979); two daughters (one deceased). Has had many jobs, including jazz pianist (Blue Peter nightclub, London), automobile racer, and real estate agent; lived in Corfu, 1934–40; editor, with Henry Miller and Alfred Perlès, the *Booster* (later *Delta*), Paris, 1937–39; columnist, *Egyptian Gazette*, Cairo, 1941; editor, with Robin Fedden and Bernard Spencer, *Personal Landscape*, Cairo, 1942–45; special correspondent in Cyprus for the *Economist*, London, 1953–55; editor, *Cyprus Review*, Nicosia, 1954–55. Taught at the British Institute, Kalamata, Greece, 1940. Foreign Service press officer, British Information Office, Cairo, 1941–44; press attaché, British Information Office, Alexandria, 1944–45; director of public relations for the Dodecanese Islands, Greece, 1946–47; director, British Council Institute, Cordoba, Argentina, 1947–48; press attaché, British Legation, Belgrade, 1949–52; director of public relations for the British Government in Cyprus, 1954–56. Andrew Mellon Visiting Professor of Humanities, California Institute of Technology, Pasadena, 1974. Recipient: Duff Cooper Memorial prize, 1957; Foreign Book prize (France), 1959; James Tait Black Memorial prize, 1975; Cholmondeley award, 1986; International Literary prize (Antibes), 1989. Fellow, Royal Society of Literature, 1954. *Died 7 November 1990.*

SCIENCE-FICTION PUBLICATIONS

Novels

*The Revolt of Aphrodite.* London, Faber, 1974.
*Tunc.* London, Faber, and New York, Dutton, 1968.
*Nunquam.* London, Faber, and New York, Dutton, 1970.

OTHER PUBLICATIONS

Novels

*Pied Piper of Lovers.* London, Cassell, 1935.
*Panic Spring* (as Charles Norden). London, Faber, and New York, Covici Friede, 1937.
*The Black Book: An Agon.* Paris, Obelisk Press, 1938; New York, Dutton, 1960; London, Faber, 1973.
*Cefalû.* London, Editions Poetry London, 1947; as *The Dark Labyrinth*, London, Ace, 1958; New York, Dutton, 1962.
*The Alexandria Quartet.* London, Faber, and New York, Dutton, 1962.
*Justine.* London, Faber, and New York, Dutton, 1957.
*Balthazar.* London, Faber, and New York, Dutton, 1958.
*Mountolive.* London, Faber, 1958; New York, Dutton, 1959.
*Clea.* London, Faber, and New York, Dutton, 1960.
*White Eagles over Serbia.* London, Faber, and New York, Criterion, 1957.
*Monsieur; or, The Prince of Darkness.* London, Faber, 1974; New York, Viking Press, 1975.
*Livia; or, Buried Alive.* London, Faber, 1978; New York, Viking Press, 1979.
*Constance; or, Solitary Practices.* London, Faber, and New York, Viking Press, 1982.
*Sebastian; or, Ruling Passions.* London, Faber, 1983; New York, Viking Press, 1984.
*Quinx; or, The Ripper's Tale.* London, Faber, 1985.

Short Stories

*Zero, and Asylum in the Snow.* Privately printed, 1946; as *Two Excursions into Reality*, Berkeley, California, Circle, 1947.
*Esprit de Corps: Sketches from Diplomatic Life.* London, Faber, 1957; New York, Dutton, 1958.
*Stiff Upper Lip: Life among the Diplomats.* London, Faber, 1958; New York, Dutton, 1959.
*Sauve Qui Peut.* London, Faber, 1966; New York, Dutton, 1967.
*The Best of Antrobus.* London, Faber, 1974.

Plays

*Sappho: A Play in Verse* (produced Hamburg, 1959; Edinburgh, 1961; Evanston, Illinois, 1964). London, Faber, 1950; New York, Dutton, 1958.
*Acte* (produced Hamburg, 1961). London, Faber, and New York, Dutton, 1965.
*An Irish Faustus: A Morality in Nine Scenes* (produced Sommerhausen, Germany, 1966). London, Faber, 1963; New York, Dutton, 1964.
*Judith* (shortened version of screenplay), in *Woman's Own* (London), 26 February–2 April 1966.

Screenplays: *Cleopatra*, with others, 1963; *Judith*, with others, 1966.

Radio Script: *Greek Peasant Superstitions*, 1947.

Television Scripts: *The Lonely Roads*, with Diane Deriaz, 1970; *The Search for Ulysses* (USA); *Lawrence Durrell's Greece; Lawrence Durrell's Egypt.*

Recording: *Ulysses Come Back: Sketch for a Musical* (story, music, and lyrics by Durrell), 1971.

Verse

*Quaint Fragment: Poems Written Between the Ages of Sixteen and Nineteen.* London, Cecil Press, 1931.
*Ten Poems.* London, Caduceus Press, 1932.
*Ballade of Slow Decay.* Privately printed, 1932.
*Bromo Bombastes: A Fragment from a Laconic Drama by Gaffer Peeslake.* London, Caduceus Press, 1933.
*Transition.* London, Caduceus Press, 1934.
*Mass for the Old Year.* Privately printed, 1935.
*Proems: An Anthology of Poems*, with others. London, Fortune Press, 1938.
*A Private Country.* London, Faber, 1943.
*The Parthenon: For T.S. Eliot.* Privately printed, 1945(?).
*Cities, Plains, and People.* London, Faber, 1946.
*On Seeming to Presume.* London, Faber, 1948.
*A Landmark Gone.* Privately printed, 1949.
*Deus Loci.* Ischia, Italy, Di Mato Vito, 1950.
*Private Drafts.* Nicosia, Cyprus, Proodos Press, 1955.
*The Tree of Idleness and Other Poems.* London, Faber, 1955.
*Selected Poems.* London, Faber, and New York, Grove Press, 1956.
*Collected Poems.* London, Faber, and New York, Dutton, 1960; revised edition, 1968.
*Penguin Modern Poets 1*, with Elizabeth Jennings and R.S. Thomas. London, Penguin, 1962.
*Poetry.* New York, Dutton, 1962.
*Beccafico/Le Becfigue* (English, with French translation by F.-J. Temple). Montpelier, France, La Licorne, 1963.
*A Persian Lady.* Edinburgh, Tragara Press, 1963.
*Selected Poems 1935–1963.* London, Faber, 1964.
*The Ikons and Other Poems.* London, Faber, 1966; New York, Dutton, 1967.
*The Red Limbo Lingo: A Poetry Notebook for 1968–1970.* London, Faber, and New York, Dutton, 1971.
*On the Suchness of the Old Boy.* London, Turret, 1972.
*Vega and Other Poems.* London, Faber, 1973.
*Lifelines.* Edinburgh, Tragara Press, 1974.
*Selected Poems*, edited by Alan Ross. London, Faber, 1977.
*Collected Poems 1931–1974*, edited by James A. Brigham. London, Faber, and New York, Viking Press, 1980.

Other

*Prospero's Cell: A Guide to the Landscape and Manners of the Island of Corcyra.* London, Faber, 1945; with *Reflections on a Marine Venus*, New York, Dutton, 1960.
*Key to Modern Poetry.* London, Peter Nevill, 1952; as *A Key to Modern British Poetry*, Norman, University of Oklahoma Press, 1952.
*Reflections on a Marine Venus: A Companion to the Landscape of Rhodes.* London, Faber, 1953; with *Prospero's Cell*, New York, Dutton, 1960.
*Bitter Lemons* (on Cyprus). London, Faber, 1957; New York, Dutton, 1958.
*Art and Outrage: A Correspondence about Henry Miller Between Alfred Perlès and Lawrence Durrell, with an Intermission by Henry Miller.* London, Putnam, 1959; New York, Dutton, 1960.
*Groddeck* (on George Walther Groddeck). Wiesbaden, Limes, 1961.
*Briefwechselüber "Actis,"* with Gustaf Gründgens. Hamburg, Rowohlt, 1961.
*Lawrence Durrell and Henry Miller: A Private Correspondence*, edited by George Wickes. New York, Dutton, and London, Faber, 1963.
*La Descente du Styx* (English, with French translations by F.-J. Temple). Montpellier, France, La Murène, 1964; as *Down the Styx*, Santa Barbara, California, Capricorn Press, 1971.
*Spirit of Place: Letters and Essays on Travel*, edited by Alan G. Thomas. London, Faber, and New York, Dutton, 1969.
*Le Grand Suppositoire* (interview with Marc Alyn). Paris, Belfond, 1972; as *The Big Supposer*, London, Abelard Schuman, and New York, Grove Press, 1973.
*The Happy Rock* (on Henry Miller). London, Village Press, 1973; Belfast, Maine, Bern Porter, 1982.
*The Plant-Magic Man.* Santa Barbara, California, Capra Press, 1973.
*Blue Thirst.* Santa Barbara, California, Capra Press, 1975.
*Sicilian Carousel.* London, Faber, and New York, Viking Press, 1977.
*The Greek Islands.* London, Faber, and New York, Viking Press, 1978.
*A Smile in the Mind's Eye.* London, Wildwood House, 1980; New York, Universe, 1982.
*Literary Lifelines: The Richard Aldington-Lawrence Durrell Correspondence*, edited by Harry T. Moore and Ian S. MacNiven. New York, Viking Press, and London, Faber, 1981.

Editor, with others, *Personal Landscape: An Anthology of Exile.* London, Editions Poetry London, 1945.
Editor, *A Henry Miller Reader.* New York, New Directions, 1959; as *The Best of Henry Miller*, London, Heinemann, 1960.
Editor, *New Poems 1963.* London, Hutchinson, 1963.
Editor, *Lear's Corfu: An Anthology Drawn from the Painter's Letters*, Corfu, Corfu Travel, 1965.
Editor, *Wordsworth.* London, Penguin, 1973.

Translator, *Six Poems from the Greek of Sikelianos and Seferis.* Privately printed, 1946.
Translator, with Bernard Spencer and Nanos Valaoritis, *The King of Asine and Other Poems*, by George Seferis. London, Lehmann, 1948.
Translator, *The Curious History of Pope Joan*, by Emmanuel Royidis. London, Verschoyle, 1954; revised edition, as *Pope Joan: A Romantic Biography*, London, Deutsch, 1960; New York, Dutton, 1961.

*

Bibliography: *Lawrence Durrell: An Illustrated Checklist* by Alan G. Thomas and James A. Brigham, Carbondale, Southern Illinois University Press, 1983.

Manuscript Collections: University of California, Los Angeles; University of Illinois, Urbana.

Critical Studies: *The World of Lawrence Durrell* edited by Harry T. Moore, Carbondale, Southern Illinois University Press, 1962; *Lawrence Durrell* by Jon Unterecker, New York, Columbia University Press, 1964; *Lawrence Durrell* by John A. Weigel, New York, Twayne, 1965; *Lawrence Durrell: A Study* (includes bibliography by Alan G. Thomas), London, Faber, 1968, New York, Dutton, 1969, revised edition, Faber, 1973, and *Lawrence Durrell*, London, Longman, 1970, both by G.S. Fraser; *Deus Loci: Lawrence Durrell Newsletter* (Kelowna, British Columbia), since 1977; "Lawrence Durrell Issue" of *Labrys 5* (London), 1979;

*Critical Essays on Lawrence Durrell* edited by Alan Warren Friedman, Boston, Hall, 1986.

* * *

Lawrence Durrell's *Tunc* and *Nunquam* are the two parts of a science-fiction novel known collectively as *The Revolt of Aphrodite.* The plots describe the efforts of Felix Charlock to build a computer, Abel, and a robot double of a prostitute-turned movie-actress, Iolanthe. In doing so, he is involved with a conglomerate corporation known as Merlin or the "firm" and its owners, Julian, Jocas, and Benedicta. Durrell is attempting to dissect the notion of culture; the superficial bases for this examination are Spengler (the approach to culture, the concern with money and contractual obligation, and even the term "the firm" itself are taken from *The Decline of the West*) and Freud (particularly the psychopathology of sex and the sexual connotations of money).

Durrell has identified the major pre-occupations of all his fiction when he writes (in *Key to Modern Poetry*) that "Time and the ego are the two determinants of style for the twentieth century. . . ." The double, whether robot or human, is also very common in Durrell's writing, and is related to his attempts to handle multi-faceted personalities and fragmented time from multiple viewpoints, as in *The Alexandria Quartet.* In *Key to Modern Poetry* he briefly traces the literary history of the double and ends by saying that "in nearly every case we are given a double which is either a saint, a criminal or a monster." Character is difficult to assess in Durrell's works; the surface descriptions of neuroses, frequently maimed characters, impotence, incestuous triangular relationships, and other sexual aberrations produce a shock value that often hides the suspicion that there really are no "characters" in his work—only puppets with a strong aroma.

The major distinctive feature of Durrell's writing is his baroque style. His writing is that of a poet—a sensuous mosaic of exotic words and images that adds a welcome dimension to the often flat prose of contemporary fiction. The occasional excesses are also those of the poet, mainly over-writing and tiresome platitudes. Throughout his career Durrell has had a remarkable eye for "place," and it appears again in *Tunc*, and *Nunquam*, although somewhat supplanted by the ubiquity of the "firm." The technology that supplies the science-fiction basis in both books is remarkably crude, unimaginative, and dated. Much of the character motivation in *Tunc* and *Nunquam* is centered around the concept of a person's work in relation to his culture and his emotional life. As A.W. Friedman has said, "The rule in Durrell is that to deny the validity of one's work is to negate love." Love and work drive and frustrate Charlock and the other characters throughout the books.

The book titles derive from the epigraph "Aut tunc, aut Nunquam" (It was then or never) from the *Satyricon* of Petronius. The implication of a last chance for society to define its values is supported by a quotation from *Tunc* which can serve as a statement of purpose for the two books: "When a civilisation has decided to bury its head in the sand what can we do but tickle its arse with a feather?"

—Norman L. Hills

———

# E

**EDDINGS, David.** American. Born in Spokane, Washington, 7 July 1931. Educated at Reed College, Portland, Oregon, B.A. in literature 1954; University of Washington, Seattle, M.A. in English 1961. Served in United States Army, 1954–56. Married Judith Lee Schall in 1962. Agent: Eleanor Wood, Blasingame, McCauley, and Wood, 111 Eighth Avenue, Suite 1501, New York 10011, U.S.A.

SCIENCE-FICTION PUBLICATIONS

Novels (series: The Belgariad; The Elenium; The Mallorean)

The Belgariad:
*Pawn of Prophecy.* New York, Ballantine, 1982; London, Century, 1983.
*Queen of Sorcery.* New York, Ballantine, 1982; London, Century, 1983.
*Magician's Gambit.* New York, Ballantine, 1983; London, Century, 1984.
*Castle of Wizardry.* New York, Ballantine, and London, Century, 1984.
*Enchanter's Endgame.* New York, Ballantine, 1984; London, Century, 1985.
The Mallorean:
*Guardians of the West.* New York, Ballantine, and London, Corgi, 1987.
*King of the Murgos.* New York, Ballantine, 1988; London, Corgi, 1989.
*Demon Lord of Karanda.* New York, Ballantine, 1988.
*Sorceress of Darshiva.* New York, Ballantine, 1989.
*The Seeress of Kell.* New York, Ballantine, 1991.
The Elenium:
*The Diamond Throne.* New York, Ballantine, and London, Grafton, 1989.
*The Ruby Night.* New York, Ballantine, and London, Grafton, 1990.

OTHER PUBLICATIONS

Novel

*High Hunt.* New York, Putnam, 1973.

*

David Eddings comments:

The medieval romance was an entertaining form until Cervantes killed it with *Don Quixote.* Tennyson's bowdlerization of Malory did not offend Queen Victoria, which may be the best thing (or the worst) which can be said of it. Both Lewis and Tolkien followed Tennyson, which may have been an error. I prefer to follow Malory (which may also be an error). The great failing of romancers appears to be a compulsion to take themselves seriously. I try not to, because I'm sure there's another Cervantes lurking out there waiting to prick the balloon of our ponderous pomposity. I've tried to create realistic, believable characters to function in an unrealistic, unbelievable world. I left the warts on them, allowed them to be silly from time to time and to bicker with each other when they felt that way. I can only hope that the reader has half as much fun with the books as I did.

* * *

In the unending wave of fantasy trilogies and longer, longer -logies that flowed from the font of the paperback publication of *The Lord of the Rings*, only a few stay in the memory longer than the first reading. Some stay because of quality and strangeness and some because of entertainment value. David Eddings' first and most popular fantasy sequence, "The Belgariad," is one of the latter. It can't lay claim to either great literary quality or innovation in its depiction of a fantastic universe, but it concentrates to great effect on character and action, the twin keys to storytelling.

Unlike many other long fantasy sequences, "The Belgariad" is clearly written as a planned and plotted whole. It is not one novel stretched but a single story that takes five volumes to tell. Using the time-honoured device of showing the world through the eyes of a naive narrator, Eddings takes his time to explore the world and the people met by the farm-boy Garion on his way to the throne of his ancestral kingdom and beyond. Gradually we see his sensible, workaday, limited world expand to include stranger and stranger things. Particularly entertaining is his slow discovery of his own sorcerous powers and the limits placed on them by those laws of physics that Eddings decides are entertaining: there is great fun in the sequence where Garion tries to move a rock by the force of his mind and discovers the "equal and opposite reaction" principle. The quest which forms the centre of the story is guided by an aware and active principle of Destiny, which is a major personality in the story. Eddings enjoys exploring the issues of predestination, of responsibility, and of moral choice in a universe where the gods are almost embarrassingly immanent and interfere regularly in human affairs.

The world is in every way a standard-issue fantasy one, with diverse but recognizable cultures butting up against one another in a totally unrealistic fashion. There are analogues of vikings, Imperial Romans, ancient Egyptians, and horse barbarians, all within a few days' travel of each other. But even the inhabitants of the "evil empire" of Angarak (roughly, every Eastern culture you've ever heard of melded together), whose priests rip hearts out daily, talk like just plain folks. The only truly strange culture is that of the religiously obsessed, subterranean Ul-Gos, and even they remind one of Orthodox Jews.

But originality in the design of the world is not what Eddings is interested in, nor the conflict between cultures. The focus of the series is on the comedy of character. The contrasts among the members of the band of heroes, between the toweringly noble (and not too bright) knight Mandorallen, and the berserker warrior Barak, between the grim horse-lord Hettar and the spy Silk, the centuries-old battling between the sorcerer Belgarath and his daughter Polgara, the developing love between Garion and the Imperial (and imperious) Princess Ce'Nedra, and the growth of a sense of responsibility in the two adolescents: these are what Eddings concentrates on.

The chief flaws come when the artifice fails and one becomes aware of the lack of depth to the illusion. Nearly everybody in "The Belgariad" thinks, at the core, like a 20th-century westerner; those who don't (Sir Mandorallen, for instance) are distinguished by very basic devices (cod "theeing" and "thouing" in Mandorallen's case). When the language too fails and one clearly hears the diction of a spoiled middle–American brat from the mouth of Ce'Nedra (supposedly raised at one of the richest and oldest courts in the world), then one cringes and sees the whole edifice shudder for a moment.

The sequel to "The Belgariad," "The Malloreon," unhappily has the faults of the first sequence in an exaggerated form and lacks fresh invention. There are few fresh characters; most of the cast list continues from the first sequence, and the character interactions that were entertaining once, overstay their welcome. Both plot and incident repeat themselves, and what depth of religious theme was present in the first saga becomes trite and overfamiliar. The final climax seems a terrible anticlimax with the destiny of ages boiled down to "and with one bound the universe was saved." The sequence reads like something written to fulfill a contract.

Eddings's third series, "The Elenium," is designed to be shorter (three volumes, of which two have been published) and is written with a greater emphasis on action. His gift with character seems to have returned with a shift to a new world and new peoples. Again the nature of magic and of the gods is a focus of interest, and destiny hangs heavy in the background, waiting to guide events. One misses the length Eddings could use in the earlier works to develop the world, especially since the world seems to have greater depth and texture, but it may be his intention to allow background to remain in the background in this work.

—Michael Cule

---

**EDDISON, E(ric) R(ucker).** British. Born in Adel, Yorkshire, 24 November 1882. Civil servant and author. *Died 18 August 1945.*

SCIENCE-FICTION PUBLICATIONS

Novels

*The Worm Ouroboros: A Romance*. London, Cape, 1922; New York, Boni, 1926.
*Mistress of Mistresses: A Vision of Zimiamvia*. London, Faber, and New York, Dutton, 1935.
*A Fish Dinner in Memison*. New York, Dutton, 1941; London, Ballantine, 1972.
*The Menzentian Gate*. London, n.p., 1958; New York, Ballantine, 1969.

OTHER PUBLICATIONS

Novel

*Styrbiorn the Strong*. London, Cape, and New York, Boni, 1926.

Other

Editor and translator (from Icelandic), *Egil's Saga* by Snorri Sturlson. Cambridge, University Press, 1930; New York, Greenwood Press, 1968.

* * *

William Morris was an important influence on many later writers, including E.R. Eddison. Eddison's *Styrbiorn the Strong*, a historical romance, is based on materials found in the Norse and Icelandic sagas, and is often considered, with Haggard's *Eric Brighteyes*, one of the best modern depictions of the Viking Age. Four years later, Eddison published *Egil's Saga*, a prose translation of an Icelandic saga. In both works, Eddison mentions Morris's romances and translations.

Eddison's fame, however, rests largely on a work which has much in common with saga and historical romance, but is actually pure fantasy, *The Worm Ouroboros*. It is both romantic and epic, filled with the lavish description and heroic adventure that delight fantasy readers. And at the end of the novel, just as the reader and the characters are wishing that it could go on forever, their wish is granted, the action begins all over again, and the plot of the novel, like the worm of the title, becomes circular and eats its own tail. Eddison's Zimiamvian trilogy—*Mistress of Mistresses, A Fish Dinner in Memison*, and *The Menzentian Gate*—that follows *The Worm Ouroboros* and is set in the heaven of the world depicted in that novel, is less successful. Most critics agree that the philosophy Eddison propounds in the Zimiamvian trilogy makes the novels difficult to read, and most readers find them harder going than *The Worm Ouroboros. The Menzentian Gate* is especially difficult; it was finished and published after Eddison's death.

—C.W. Sullivan III

---

**EDMONDSON, G.C.** (José Mario Garry Ordonez Edmondson y Cotton). Also writes as John Cleve; Kelly P. Gast; Jake Logan; J.B. Masterson. American. Born in Rachauchitlán, Tabasco, Mexico, 11 October 1922. Educated in Vienna, M.D. Served in the United States Marine Corps, 1942–46. Married three times; two sons and two daughters. Has worked as a blacksmith. Agent: Richard Curtis, 164 East 64th Street, New York, New York 10021, U.S.A.

SCIENCE-FICTION PUBLICATIONS

Novels (series: Cunningham)

*The Ship That Sailed the Time Stream*. New York, Ace, 1965; London, Arrow, 1971.
*Chapayeca*. New York, Doubleday, 1971; London, Hale, 1973; as *Blue Face*, New York, DAW, 1972.
*T. H. E. M.* New York, Doubleday, 1974.
*The Aluminum Man*. New York, Berkley, 1975.
*The Man Who Corrupted the Earth*. New York, Ace, 1980.
*To Sail the Century Sea*. New York, Ace, 1981.
*Star Slaver* (as John Cleve, with Andrew J. Offutt). New York, Berkley, 1983.
*The Takeover*, with C.M. Kotlan. New York, Ace, 1984.

*The Cunningham Equations*, with C.M. Kotlan. New York, Ballantine, 1986.
*The Black Magician*, with C.M. Kotlan (Cunningham). New York, Ballantine, 1986.
*Maximum Effort*, with C.M. Kotlan (Cunningham). New York, Ballantine, 1987.

Short Stories

*Stranger Than You Think*. New York, Ace, 1965.

Uncollected Short Stories

"Nobody Believes an Indian," in *Fantasy and Science Fiction* (New York), May 1970.
"The Tempollutors," in *Infinity 4*, edited by Robert Hoskins. New York, Lancer, 1972.
"One Plus One Equals Eleven," in *Analog* (New York), January 1973.
"Tube," in *If* (New York), August 1974.
"All That Glitters," in *Stellar 5*, edited by Judy-Lynn del Rey. New York, Ballantine, 1980.

OTHER PUBLICATIONS

Novels

*Rudge* (as J.B. Masterson). New York, Doubleday, 1979; London, Hale, 1980.
*Slocum's Slaughter* (as Jake Logan). New York, Berkley, 1980.

Novels as Kelly P. Gast

*Dil Dies Hard*. New York, Doubleday, 1975.
*The Long Trail North*. New York, Doubleday, 1976.
*Murphy's Trail*. New York, Doubleday, 1976.
*Last Stage from Opal*. New York, Doubleday, 1978.
*Murder at Magpie Flats*. New York, Doubleday, 1978.
*Paddy*. New York, Doubleday, 1979.

Other

*Practical Welding*, with Leroy A. Scheck. Beverly Hills, California, Bruce, 1976; 2nd edition, Encino, California, Glencoe Publishing, 1984.
*Le livre noir d'haute cuisine*. N. p., Bookmaker, 1977.
*Water Rationing Made Simple*. N. p., Bookmaker, 1977.
*The Basic Book of Home Maintenance and Repair*, with T.F. Roybal. Chicago, American Technical Society, 1979.
*Diesel Mechanics: An Introduction*, with Richard Little. Belmont, California, Wadsworth, 1982.

* * *

Between 1957 and 1965, G.C. Edmondson successfully sold a dozen or so short stories which, while reasonably entertaining, made scarcely a ripple in the science-fiction community. For the most part, they were lightly humorous, particularly those in the "Mad Friend" series, zany adventures of a mysterious "friend" of the author whose many exploits included a meteor that was not quite what it seemed or an encounter with a time traveller from the future. Although rarely reprinted, stories like "From Caribou to Carrie Nation," "The Inferlab Project," "Rescue," and "Technological Retreat" still measure up favorably against most contemporary stories. The series was later collected as half of an Ace double book under the title *Stranger Than You Think*, but the real significance of the collection's appearance was the novel on the flip side.

*The Ship That Sailed the Time Stream* was not the first novel about people misplaced in time, nor is it the best. An experimental naval ship is testing a new anti-submarine device when lightning strikes and a scientific fluke sends the entire vessel back 1000 years in time. Faced with dwindling provisions and the probability that they will never be able to return to their own time, the crew sets off to find civilization, only to run into a bunch of Viking raiders. Edmondson takes a simple, straightforward plot and runs with it, producing good-natured adventure fiction at its very best. With a single book, he had acquired a following.

Unfortunately, it was more than five years before Edmondson wrote again, publishing a single short story in 1970, and then the novel *Chapayeca* in 1971. *Chapayeca* (later reprinted as *Blue Face*) follows the final expedition of an unhappy, recently handicapped anthropologist among the Indian tribes of Mexico. Rumors of a mysterious presence lead him to the discovery that an alien being is living secretly among the natives. A quietly understated, very short novel whose literary values are exceptional, this book showed that Edmondson's prose style had improved dramatically. Unfortunately, the low key plot attracted few readers, and several more years passed before another book appeared.

*The Aluminum Man* marked Edmondson's return to more traditional themes. An alien provides two humans with a bacterial strain that produces aluminum, then spends most of the book trying to find them and get it back. There are some fine flashes of humor at times, but the impact of the new source of aluminum on the economy is hinted at but never really explored. Several years more would pass before Edmondson returned to this theme in a much more serious vein with *The Man Who Corrupted the Earth*, which considers a wide range of issues from pollution to the world economy to the values and disadvantages of space exploration. Some predictable melodramatic plot elements are intertwined in what was Edmondson's most serious attempt to address contemporary social issues within a futuristic context.

Edmondson published the sequel to his first novel in 1981. *To Sail the Century Sea* is not quite as fresh and exciting as its predecessor, but it remains one of Edmondson's best novels. Having returned to the present and, after an interval of several years, having convinced the authorities that their story of travel through time is true, the protagonist and several of his companions are sent back, deliberately this time, on a special mission to change a pivotal event in history. *To Sail the Century Sea* contains more rousing adventure, this time with a clever surprise ending.

Edmondson's last four novels were all written in collaboration with C.M. Kotlan, and while they continued to use adventure and action as the focus of the story, there was as well an increasingly dim portrayal of the foibles of the human race. *The Takeover* is a novel of political paranoia. The Pentagon has been subverted and allows a Soviet takeover of the U.S. government. The only possible hope is a fleet of nuclear submarines that has refused to surrender, and that must act quickly to take advantage of the threat their weaponry offers. The book is suspenseful, but very derivative of countless similar works.

The last three books comprise a trilogy. *The Cunningham Equations* introduces Blaise Cunningham, an expert in artificial intelligence who has created an AI named Alfie, who aids him in this and subsequent adventures. He is inexplicably the object of interest of a number of professional thugs, who seem determined to kidnap his dog. Cunningham pursues his own investigation and becomes involved with a plan to alter human capabilities through genetic engineering of a parasitical life-form.

The plot unfolds in *The Black Magician.* The new life-forms are supposed to benignly enhance human intelligence, but they have been inadequately studied and an unpleasant side effect begins to emerge. Under the right conditions, they will seize control of their host, because they have found a way to survive on their own. Effective efforts to track down the parasites and destroy them are hindered by the fact that the government is reluctant to admit that the problem exists. Everything is ultimately resolved in the concluding volume, *Maximum Effort.* The growing numbers of parasitically controlled humans are now interacting, working to establish themselves as the dominant force on earth. Blaise Cunningham alone may possess the secret that will bring their efforts to a halt. As a whole, the trilogy is quite suspenseful, eschewing graphic horror for more effectively suggestive scenes and situations. At the same time, it is a darker vision than that found in Edmondson's earlier books, and while these last novels are technically more effective, they are less entertaining than his early works.

—Don D'Ammassa

---

**EDWARDS, Norman.** *See* **CARR, Terry; WHITE, Ted.**

---

**EFFINGER, George Alec.** American. Born in Cleveland, Ohio, 10 January 1947. Attended Yale University, New Haven, Connecticut, 1965, 1969, and New York University, 1968. Freelance writer: since 1971, writer for *Marvel Comic Books*, New York. Recipient: Nebula award, for novelette, 1988. Agent: Richard Curtis, 164 East 64th Street, New York, New York 10021. Address: Box 15183, New Orleans, Louisiana 70175, U.S.A.

Science-Fiction Publications

Novels (series: Marîd; Planet of the Apes)

*What Entropy Means to Me.* New York, Doubleday, 1972.
*Relatives.* New York, Harper, 1973.
*Man the Fugitive* (Apes). New York, Award, 1974.
*Nightmare Blue*, with Gardner Dozois. New York, Berkley, 1975; London, Fontana, 1977.
*Escape to Tomorrow* (Apes). New York, Award, 1975.
*Journey into Terror* (Apes). New York, Award, 1975.
*Those Gentle Voices.* New York, Warner, 1976.
*Lord of the Apes* (Apes). New York, Award, 1976.
*Death in Florence.* New York, Doubleday, 1978; as *Utopia 3*, Chicago, Playboy Press, 1980.
*Heroics.* New York, Doubleday, 1979.
*The Wolves of Memory.* New York, Putnam, 1981.
*The Nick of Time.* New York, Doubleday, 1985; London, New English Library, 1987.
*The Bird of Time.* New York, Doubleday, 1986; London, New English Library, 1988.
*When Gravity Fails* (Marîd). New York, Arbor House, 1987.
*Shadow Money.* New York, Tor, 1988.
*A Fire in the Sun* (Marîd). New York, Doubleday, 1989.
*The Old Funny Stuff.* Eugene, Oregon, Pulphouse, 1989.
*Look Away.* Eugene, Oregon, Axolotl, 1990.
*The Zork Chronicles.* New York, Avon, 1990.
*The Exile Kiss* (Marîd). New York, Doubleday, 1991.
*The Red Tape War* (with Jack C. Chalker and Mike Resnick). New York, Tor, 1991.

Short Stories

*Mixed Feelings.* New York, Harper, 1974.
*Irrational Numbers.* New York, Doubleday, 1976.
*Dirty Tricks.* New York, Doubleday, 1978.
*Idle Pleasures.* New York, Berkley, 1983.

Other Publications

Novel

*Felicia.* New York, Berkley, 1976.

*

George Alec Effinger comments (1985):

I try to do new things with old material. A good deal of my science fiction is an attempt to take traditional SF furniture (storylines, settings, characters, and hardware) and combine it with some element of the absurd. The result is not science fiction, because it bears little resemblance to the rational real world. Perhaps surreal fantasy describes these stories best. My antecedents are as much in the theater of the absurd as they are in science fiction.

One of my favorite experiments is to appropriate an accepted SF situation and populate it with one or more of the continuing characters I have established in my stories over the years. These characters are not recurring in the usual sense. Rather, I think of them as a kind of repertory company. They may die in one story and reappear later as necessary. They live in many eras and appear together in various combinations, sometimes contradicting earlier stories. Just as William Bendix appeared in one motion picture and was killed or married, then months later appeared in another movie, unrelated to the first, so my characters pop up here and there throughout my own future history, unaffected by the stories in which they performed previously. Whenever they appear, however, they always represent the same kind of person, making for me a private stable of stereotypes to draw upon.

I enjoy parody, satire, and pastiche, but every once in a while I will do a serious story in a straight SF mode, mostly to keep the audience on its toes. SF is the only neighborhood of writing where I could get away with this kind of thing, and I am immensely grateful to the field and its readers for giving me the opportunity.

* * *

Since the publication of his best-known novel, *What Entropy Means to Me*, George Alec Effinger has demonstrated versatility in books as disparate as the mainstream novel *Felicia*, the teleplay adaptation *Man the Fugitive*, and *Nightmare Blue*, a collaboration with Gardner Dozois. More important, he has produced short stories and novels linked in strange and wondrous ways to form a unique "Effinger's World." Some critics label him a writer of sword and sorcery; others, of myth. Still others avoid labels, preferring a literary report card showing a high rating in technique, a low one in substance. Despite any problem with fitting him into the established definitions of science fiction, Effinger does offer an exceptional reading experience.

*Entropy* is a structural tour de force, being four intricately interwoven stories with author-character Seyt as nexus. First is a romantic quest tale of an eldest son searching for a lost father. Aided by a magic-competent companion, Dore overcomes natural obstacles, monsters, seduction, villainy, only to find Father at a point of no return. If *Entropy* went no further, it could sustain the label of sword and sorcery. But *Entropy* is more, three stories more. Functioning much as a chorus in a Greek tragedy, Seyt relates his family's saga from Earth to the planet Home. The third story evolves as a classic political power struggle to fill the vacuum created by the absence of father and eldest son. Seyt faithfully records the machinations, religious conflicts, and personal hurt involved. The fourth story gains subtle attention. This is the story of creation—literary creation. Seyt makes us aware of the artist, story churning in his head, faced with the arduous task of shaping it for an audience. Seyt must grapple with the author's universal problems: critical pressure from readers; political pressure to slant toward propaganda; and inner pressure to maintain authorial integrity. This trenchant commentary on the art and act of writing, reappearing in later short stories and novels, helps link *Entropy* to them.

Effinger's later fictional world is a paradox. We may recognize a familiar society, only to have subsequent paragraphs jolt us into a surreal world. Often gray, sometimes diseased, always warped by conformity, this society is best epitomized by the village of Gremmage in "Things Go Better," "Heart Stop," and "Lights Out." Gremmage isolates, smothers, and molds newcomers to its ways. Effinger's larger society has the Representatives, six men governing by whimsical stupidity ("Lydectes: On the Nature of Sport," "Contentment, Satisfaction, Cheer, Well-Being, Gladness, Joy, Comfort, and Not Having to Get Up Early Any More," and *Relatives*). Effinger's people freely slip from story to story, changing personalities and identities illogically. For example, the three separate Weinraub/Weintraubs triplicate experience in *Relatives*, then show up as a writer of a trilogy of novels in "Biting Down Hard in Truth." Global bum Bo Staefler of *Death in Florence* has little obvious relationship to baseball catcher Bo Staefler ("Naked to the Invisible Eye") or to castaway Bo Staefler ("World War II"). Robert Hanson appears as an 11-year-old boy ("Chase Our Blues Away"), a young man afflicted with altruism ("Strange Ragged Saintliness"), one for whom a park is named ("Timmy Was Eight"), and an android clone ("The Awesome Menace of the Polarizer"). Jennings suffers metamorphosis from a tough coach ("Biting Down Hard on Truth") to a chairman of the board ("At the Bran Foundry") to an astro-physicist (*Those Gentle Voices*).

And then there is Sandor Courane, one of the many personalities moving in and out of Effinger's multi-faceted morality play. Courane shifts from being a light-weight science-fiction writer in "The Pinch-Hitters," one of Effinger's sports short stories (see "Naked to the Invisible Eye," "From Downtown at the Buzzer," and "Breakaway" for other sports-oriented tales) to serve in *The Wolves of Memory* as a tormented Everyman trying to cope with the mysteries of life and death, of causation and purpose. In the novel Effinger demonstrates his control of surrealistic shifts of perspective in time and place, enriching them with parodic hints of Eden, the Fall, and the Crucifixion, ironically combined with a man/technology relationship.

In later novels Effinger goes in for other unique combinations. *The Red Tape Wars*, for example, combines his imagination with those of Jack Chalker and Mike Resnick. Together they produce a humorous novel that satirizes the bureaucracy, academia, even themselves as writers. *The Zork Chronicles* combines the "Zork" computer game with a parody of the heroic genre. *Look Away*, an alternate worlds theme, uses U.S. Civil War events linked with 20th-century Mideast situations. These all reinforce Effinger's own comment above: "I try to do new things with old material."

His latest, notable "new things with old material" features a three-volume series with Marîd Audran as protagonist and is set in a near-future North Africa. The area is broken up into small political units, most of them hostile to each other, even with hostility within each unit. Marîd in *When Gravity Fails* is a footloose street man, able to survive by his wits and various mood-enhancing drugs. He lives in the Budayeen, a ghetto-like area dominated by Friedlander Bey, a "godfather" type. Despite attempts to remain free, Marîd is drawn into the violent life of the Budayeen, eventually selling out his independence to Bey as one of his agents, moving into Bey's mansion, and serving more as a "go-fer."

In *A Fire in the Sun* Marîd has become a policeman, really serving as Bey's contact within that force. Events take a grisly turn, forcing Marîd to take matters into his own hands. With the aid of surgical implants and the personality modifiers he had earlier tried to avoid, Marîd solves the mystery of the violent power struggle, acting more as a detective than a policeman. While still linked with Bey, he has gained power and a certain amount of the independence he desires. Things change in *The Exile Kiss* when both Marîd and Bey suffer exile for a framed-up murder. They are banished to the Arabian desert. During their trials in the desert, their return, and the search for both justice and revenge, Marîd grows in stature, reaching a higher, though uncomfortable, state of self-awareness. Will a fourth sequel carry Marîd Audran to comfort in the independence he desires? Only Effinger and time will tell.

Effinger is master of the non sequitur which teases the mind with the thought that there is a veiled logic and an illuminating insight here, could one but rearrange things. If not, the reader must provide his own, for Effinger has prodded his mind unmercifully. Musing on the act of writing, a character in "The Ghost Writer" inadvertently gives us a summation for Effinger himself: "There was always the chance that a new fragment might join two of the enigmatic earlier pieces, and a whole framework might begin to be evident. But not today. Here was another piece, of perhaps a totally different puzzle. It was longer, and it was exciting. The audience would be satisfied, but not the scholars."

—Hazel Pierce

---

**EGBERT, H.M.** *See* **ROUSSEAU, Victor.**

---

**EHRLICH, Max (Simon).** American. Born in Springfield, Massachusetts, 10 October 1909. Educated at the University of Michigan, Ann Arbor, B.A. Married 1) Doris Rubinstein in 1940 (divorced), two daughters; 2) Margaret Druckman in 1980. Reporter, *Knickerbocker Press* and *Evening News*, both Albany, New York, and *Republican* and *Daily Press*, both Springfield. Member of the copyright and screen committees, Writers Guild of America West. *Died in February 1983.*

SCIENCE-FICTION PUBLICATIONS

Novels

*The Big Eye*. New York, Doubleday, 1949; London, Boardman, 1951.
*Spin the Glass Web*. New York, Harper, 1952; London, Corgi, 1957.
*First Train to Babylon*. New York, Harper, and London, Gollancz, 1955; as *Dead Letter*, London, Corgi, 1958; as *The Naked Edge*, London, Corgi, 1961.
*The Takers*. New York, Harper, and London, Gollancz, 1961.
*Dead Is the Blue*. New York, Doubleday, and London, Gollancz, 1964.
*The High Side*. New York, Fawcett, 1969.
*The Edict*. New York, Doubleday, 1971; London, Panther, 1984.
*The Savage Is Loose*. New York, Bantam, 1974.
*The Reincarnation of Peter Proud*. Indianapolis, Bobbs Merrill, 1974; London, W.H. Allen, 1975.
*The Cult*. New York, Simon and Schuster, 1978; London, Mayflower, 1979.
*Reincarnation in Venice*. New York, Simon and Schuster, 1979; as *The Bond*, London, Mayflower, 1980.
*Naked Beach*. Chicago, Playboy Press, 1979; London, Mayflower, 1980.

OTHER PUBLICATIONS

Novels

*Shaitan*. New York, Arbor House, 1981; London, Severn House, 1982.
*The Big Boys*. Boston, Houghton Mifflin, 1981.

Plays

Screenplays: *Z.P.G. (Zero Population Growth)*, with Frank de Felitta, 1971; *The Reincarnation of Peter Proud*, 1974; *The Savage Is Loose*, with Frank de Felitta, 1975.

Radio Plays: for *The Shadow, Mr. and Mrs. North, Sherlock Holmes, Nick Carter, The Big Story*, and *Big Town* series.

Television Plays: *The Apple* (*Star Trek* series), and for *Studio One, The Defenders, The Dick Powell Show*, and *Winston Churchill* series.

* * *

Besides his film, radio, and television writing, Max Ehrlich wrote some dozen novels, often with a science-fiction or fantasy edge. Never a producer of "hard" science fiction, he usually aimed at topical thrillers for a wider audience, generally suggesting that traditional value systems are well worth following.

In *The Big Eye* a wandering planet threatens collision with Earth. Encouraged by astronomers to believe the end is near, the public views the invader as a gigantic, baleful watcher. Although the near miss has minimal physical effects on Earth, human repentance augurs at least a semblance of a utopian future. There is little action in the novel, but some movement. The chief character, assistant to the director of Palomar Observatory where the telescopic Big Eye is located, shuttles back and forth across the country, but he is primarily an observer and scarcely affected by his scientific training. Contravening his desire to remain childless, his wife's act of faith and hope in the future is vindicated, though the Earth was scared by a hoax, not saved by a miracle. Ehrlich's millennial psychology and politics are little more convincing than his science, but the book remains a fair representation of the state of Cold War apprehension in its time.

*The Edict* projects an overpopulated future in which childbirth has been banned for 30 years. The mechanics of social management are never rationalized, but computers, scant food allotments, and police power are invoked. The story focusses on two couples living in a State Museum exhibit preserving 20th-century lifestyles. Rejecting sexual pluralism and mechanical babies, one of the wives insists on bearing her own child. When the other couple discover her secret and insist on sharing, the new parents escape to a radioactive island, where life will be more short than sweet. Style and scene management are both stiff, but Ehrlich has put the population dilemma in simple-to-understand contemporary terms, though with no utopian alternative this time.

Probably his best-written work toys with the supernatural. *Reincarnation in Venice* is an adequate sequel, structurally almost identical, to *The Reincarnation of Peter Proud*. Not having to stage-manage an entire world, Ehrlich can better handle local color in California and New England. The "science" of dream research is confronted with a man whose dreams suggest that, just before his birth, he was somebody else. Following them up leads him to the town where his "double" was killed. When he falls in love with the daughter of the murderess, the results are predictably ironic. Hardly raising a major problem to the level of serious discourse, the novel is an adequate exercise in nightmare logic, suspenseful, and concisely told.

—David N. Samuelson

---

**EISENBERG, Larry.** American. Born in New York City, 21 December 1919. Educated at the City College of New York, B.A. in mathematics 1940; Polytechnic Institute, Brooklyn, M.E.E. 1952; Ph.D. in electronics 1966. Served in the United States Army Air Forces, 1945–46: Sergeant. Married Frances Brenner in 1950; one daughter and one son. Instructor, New York Institute of Technology, 1948–52; Project Engineer, PRD, New York, 1952–55; Instructor of Electronics, City College of New York, 1955–56; Digital Logician, Digitronics, Roslyn, New York, 1956–58; Since 1958, co-director of the Electronics laboratory, Rockefeller University, New York; since 1985, Adjunct Professor, Rockefeller University. Address: 315 East 88th Street, New York, New York 10028, U.S.A.

SCIENCE-FICTION PUBLICATIONS

Short Stories

*The Best Laid Schemes*. New York, Macmillan, 1971.

Uncollected Short Stories (series: Emmett Duckworth)

"The Grand Illusions," in *Galaxy* (New York), May 1972.
"The Soul Music of Duckworth's Dibs," in *Galaxy* (New York), September, 1972.
"The Executive Rat," in *If* (New York), December 1972.
"Sikh, Sikh, Sikh," in *Vertex* (Los Angeles), December 1973.
"The Baby," in *Galaxy* (New York), March 1974.
"Televerite," in *Vertex* (Los Angeles), April 1974.

"Time and Duckworth," in *Galaxy* (New York), May 1974.
"Where There's Smoke," in *Galaxy* (New York), June 1974.
"The Money Machine" in *Vertex* (Los Angeles), August 1974.
"Elephants Sometimes Forget," in *Fantasy and Science Fiction* (New York), September 1974.
"The Lookalike Revolution," in *Fantasy and Science Fiction* (New York), November 1974.
"The Spurious President," in *Vertex* (Los Angeles), April 1975.
"My Random Friend," in *Fantasy and Science Fiction* (New York), August 1977.
"The Interface," in *Fantasy and Science Fiction* (New York), August 1978.
"Djinn and Duckworth" in *Isaac Asimov's Science Fiction Magazine* (New York), March 1979.
"The Merchant," in *Flying Saucers*, edited by Isaac Asimov, Martin H. Greenberg, and Charles G. Waugh. New York, Fawcett, 1982.
"The Chameleon," in *Election Day 2084*, edited by Isaac Asimov and Martin H. Greenberg. Buffalo, New York, Prometheus, 1984.
"Dr. Snow Maiden," in *Great Science Fiction: Stories by the World's Great Scientists*, edited by Isaac Asimov, Martin H. Greenberg, and Charles G. Waugh. New York, Fine, 1985.
"Me and My Shadow," in *Fantasy and Science Fiction* (New York), February 1986.
"Live It Up, Inc.," in *Fantasy and Science Fiction* (New York), March 1988.

OTHER PUBLICATIONS

Verse

*Limericks for Lantzmen*, with George Gordon. New York, Citadel Press, 1965.
*Limericks for the Loo*, with George Gordon. New York, Kanrom, and London, Arlington, 1965.

Other

*Games People Shouldn't Play*, with George Gordon. New York, Kanrom, 1966.

*

Larry Eisenberg comments (1985):

Most of my stories have been strongly influenced by my 27 years as a scientist at Rockefeller University. Both the brilliance and the idiosyncrasies of the scientists I have known and worked with (some of them Nobel laureates) have given me a rich source of humor and provocative ideas.

* * *

It is extremely difficult to make a reputation exclusively as a short-story writer, even in the genre of science fiction. Larry Eisenberg is one of the few to attract considerable attention over the years, despite the fact that he appears primarily in magazines and has never had a novel published, although there has been one collection of his shorter works, *The Best Laid Schemes.*

Although many of his stories are serious in intent and execution, he is probably best known for his humor, particularly the ongoing adventures of Professor Emmett Duckworth, twice winner of the Nobel Prize. Duckworth is a true descendant of the classic C.P. Ransome stories of Homer Nearing. In almost every case, Duckworth has developed some new device or principle, which should have had very beneficial effects, but which always seems to somehow go awry at a crucial point. In "The Saga of DMM," for example, Duckworth develops an aphrodisiac which, unfortunately, also tends to fatten up its user, and eventually becomes an unstable explosive akin to nitroglycerin. By chance he taps into a secret government file in "Open Secrets," and finds an ingenious method by which to conceal the data he discovers. In "IQ Soup" he feeds intelligence into an experimental subject, whose plane then crashes in cannibal country with predictable results. In yet other stories, Duckworth develops heavy smoke which falls from your cigarette to the floor, to be removed later, sensory recordings, and a sonic probe that picks up sounds from the past.

As a contrast to the general good humor of the Duckworth stories, Eisenberg has another, very loosely organized series detailing the encounters between humans and an alien species called Sentients. Most of the stories take place after the human race has conquered and occupied the Sentients' home planet. These stories are often very bitter, and are generally very well told. Among the better stories in this series are "The Quintipods," a tale of boxing and the exploitation of a species considered inferior, "The Heart of the Giant," during which a number of humans are killed by a non-violent Sentient when he short circuits the computer that powers their artificial hearts, and "The Conqueror," a story that succeeds through expert use of understatement. A Sentient woman seduces a human soldier, then pretends to be an android in order to humiliate him. There are some outstanding non-series stories as well. Perhaps the best is "The Chameleon," the story of a politician whose use of media and computer devices to enhance his own image is so successful that he is taken in himself. Almost as impressive is the story of an egotistic President whose personality alters when he is lost within his own security system ("The Spurious President").

Eisenberg's stories read well even at their worst because he employs a clear style that is witty without being obtrusive for its own sake. There is almost always an element of humor, although it is often shaded with black, as Eisenberg holds up some attribute of human endeavor for our examination. The Duckworth stories in particular are refreshing and inventive, whether he is duplicating prominent citizens to embarrass them or developing unworkable weapon systems for a defense establishment he dislikes. While it may be a rare occasion when one of his stories will remain in our minds for long, it will be even rarer to find one that is not entertaining while we are reading it.

—Don D'Ammassa

---

**EISENSTEIN, Phyllis (née Kleinstein).** American. Born in Chicago, Illinois, 26 February 1946. Educated at the University of Chicago, 1963–66; University of Illinois, Chicago, 1978–81, B.A. in anthropology 1981. Married Alex Eisenstein in 1966. Co-Founder and Director, Windy City SF Writers Conference, Chicago, 1972–77. Anthology Trustee, Science Fiction Writers of America, 1976–81. Since 1989, has taught science-fiction writing at Columbia College, Chicago. Address: 6208 North Campbell, Chicago, Illinois 60659, U.S.A.

SCIENCE-FICTION PUBLICATIONS

Novels (Series: Alaric; Cray)

*Born to Exile* (Alaric). Sauk City, Wisconsin, Arkham House, 1978.
*Sorcerer's Son* (Cray). New York, Ballantine, 1979; London, Grafton, 1990.
*Shadow of Earth.* New York, Dell, 1979.
*In the Hands of Glory.* New York, Pocket Books, 1981.
*The Crystal Palace* (Cray). New York, New American Library, 1988; London, Grafton, 1991.
*In the Red Lord's Reach* (Alaric). New York, New American Library, 1989.

Uncollected Short Stories

"The Trouble with the Past," with Alex Eisenstein, in *New Dimensions I*, edited by Robert Silverberg. New York, Doubleday, 1971.
"Teleprobe," in *Long Night of Waiting*, edited by Roger Elwood. Nashville, Aurora, 1974.
"The Weather on Mars," with Alex Eisenstein, in *Analog* (New York), December 1974.
"Tree of Life," in *Best Science Fiction Stories of the year 5*, edited by Lester del Rev. New York, Dutton, 1976.
"Sleeping Beauty—The True Story," with Alex Eisenstein, in *Cavalier* (New York), February 1976.
"You Are Here," with Alex Eisenstein, in *New Dimensions 7*, edited by Robert Silverberg. New York, Harper, 1977.
"Altar Ego," with Alex Eisenstein, in *Fantasy and Science Fiction* (New York), March 1977.
"In Answer to Your Call," in *Fantasy and Science Fiction* (New York), January 1978.
"The Land of Sorrow," in *The Year's Best Fantasy Stories 4*, edited by Lin Carter. New York, DAW, 1978.
"Lost and Found," in *Best Science Fiction Stories of the Year*, edited by Gardner Dozois. New York, Dutton, 1979.
"The Mountain Fastness," in *Fantasy and Science Fiction* (New York), July 1979.
"The Man with the Eye," in *Isaac Asimov's Science Fiction Anthology 4*, edited by George H. Scithers. New York, Davis, 1980.
"Point of Departure," in *Whispers 3*, edited by Stuart David Schiff. New York, Doubleday, 1981.
"In the Western Tradition," in *Fantasy and Science Fiction* (New York), March 1981.
"The Fireman's Daughter," in *Twilight Zone* (New York), June 1981.
"Taboo," in *Analog* (New York), 22 June 1981.
"Dark Wings," in *Shadows 5*, edited by Charles L. Grant. New York, Doubleday, 1982.
"Nightlife," in *Fantasy and Science Fiction* (New York), February 1982.
"Subworld," in *Fantasy and Science Fiction* (New York), January 1983.
"The Demon Queen," in *Amazing* (New York), January 1984.
"The Amethyst Phial," in *Fantasy and Science Fiction* (New York), February 1984.
"Sense of Duty," in *Isaac Asimov's Science Fiction Magazine* (New York), March 1985.
"The Snail Out of Space," in *Fantasy and Science Fiction* (New York), April 1985.
"Attachment," in *What Did Miss Darrington See?: An Anthology of Feminist Supernatural Fiction*, edited by Jessica Amanda Salmonson. New York, Feminist Press, 1989.

*

Phyllis Eisenstein comments:

I'd rather not compose a "personal statement" about my work, because my personal statements are embedded in that work. However, I do believe that current schism between "significant art" and "mere entertainment" is a product of academic pretensions that have nothing to do with the intrinsic value of any particular work. Art cannot survive when it does not have a popular audience of some kind; and any art whose highest aspiration is to compete with the temporary thrills of a roller coaster will also not be long remembered. I am not the first one to make this observation, and I certainly hope that I won't be the last.

* * *

Phyllis Eisenstein is probably best known as a writer of fantasy. *Sorcerer's Son, The Crystal Palace, Shadow of Earth, Born to Exile, In the Red Lord's Reach*, and many of her short stories certainly exist in the realm of the fantastic. However, since her first published story, "The Trouble with the Past," Eisenstein's works also have explored such familiar science-fiction themes as time travel, space exploration, space colonies, and first contact. Eisenstein creates a memorable mood or presents a tantalizing idea through strong characterization. She explores the effects of her settings and premises on the main character and that character's interpersonal relationships.

A powerful example is "In the Western Tradition," in which Eisenstein deftly treats time travel on both the physical and the psychological levels. A recurring theme in her writings, time travel is handled with a twist in this story. Instead of actually travelling in time, people view past events by means of sophisticated machinery. Requiring highly skilled operators, the equipment by its geographic location limits the range of observable events. As intriguing as this concept is, the central story is about Allison, a very talented operator who becomes so obsessed with the past that she isolates herself from her own contemporary life. Equally compelling for point of view are "Taboo," with its interplay between anthropologists and natives as well as among the scientists themselves, and "Nightlife," a look at the reality of dreams.

Many of her early stories written in collaboration with her husband Alex tend to be oriented more to the external structure of the plot or concept than to the effect of that structure on the characters. These stories seem to lack the depth and insight of her solo writings. An exception is "You Are Here," a disturbing story whose full impact is not realized until its conclusion. While that ending is rather predictable, the building of the character is subtle.

Eisenstein came into her own with her series about Alaric, a minstrel with the apparently magical power of teleportation. Each of these stories is complete in itself, but if read in order, as in the collection *Born to Exile*, they form a continuous account of Alaric's adventures. Other than the minstrel's extraordinary talent and the locals' superstitions, magic is not a major part of this world. In fact, Alaric himself tries to fight the superstitious beliefs found among his medieval society. *In the Red Lord's Reach* continues the minstrel's episodic tale. In the north, where witches are revered and natural magnetic powers are used as sources of magic, Alaric finally finds acceptance of his power. Now he must fight his lack of belief in magic as he searches within himself for the path he will follow.

Eisenstein continues her practical approach to magic in *Sorcerer's Son*. The sorcerers's magical powers are strictly defined, operating according to laws much as science does. One finds sorcerers, demons, magic, and, of course, a quest—all the typical elements of fantasy. Happily, Eisenstein also gives free rein to her enjoyable wit and humor, adding greatly to the humanity of the tale of Cray Ormoru. Set in the same world, *The Crystal Palace* presents a somber mood as Cray pursues a different sort of quest. There is more emphasis on motive than on action as Cray confronts his own beliefs and desires in trying to free the ice sorceress Aliza from an entrapment she does not feel or acknowledge.

Strong, resourceful, and independent women figure prominently in Eisenstein's work. This makes *Shadow of Earth* somewhat disappointing. Accidentally thrust into a medieval society, 20th-century Celia seems little able to cope with her drastic change of circumstance and social status and is ultimately only slightly changed by the experience. The book has been touted by feminists for showing the harshness of a world where a woman's only value is in bearing children. Perhaps Eisenstein intentionally makes this heroine weak to emphasize the helplessness of a technologically educated woman in a more primitive society. Although *In the Hands of Glory* sometimes lapses into the romantic clichés of space opera, its strong point is Dia Catlin, who faces conflict when her ideals encounter sordid reality. The outcome of a planetary rebellion is secondary to the growth and change Dia painfully undergoes.

Phyllis Eisenstein shows increasing maturity as a writer. Adept at handling various formats, she uses a variety of subjects equally well. In her latest works she concentrates on the psychological development of her characters, seemingly not content to let them merely be heroes. The worlds she creates, whether magical or otherwise, are carefully crafted and believable, her characters individual and memorable.

—Gay E. Carter

---

**EKLUND, Gordon.** American. Born in Seattle, Washington, 24 July 1945. Educated at Contra Costa College, San Pablo, California, 1973–75. Served in the United States Air Force, 1963–67: Sergeant. Married Dianna Mylarski in 1969; two sons. Since 1968, freelance writer. Recipient: Nebula award, 1974. Agent: Kirby McCauley Ltd., 155 East 77th Street, Suite 1A, New York, New York 10021, U.S.A.

SCIENCE-FICTION PUBLICATIONS

Novels (series: Lord Tedric)

*The Eclipse of Dawn*. New York, Ace, 1971.
*A Trace of Dreams*. New York, Ace, 1972.
*Beyond the Resurrection*. New York, Doubleday, 1973.
*All Times Possible*. New York, DAW, 1974.
*Inheritors of Earth*, with Poul Anderson. Radnor, Pennsylvania, Chilton, 1974.
*Serving in Time*. Toronto, Laser, 1975.
*Falling Toward Forever*. Toronto, Laser, 1975.
*The Grayspace Beast*. New York, Doubleday, 1976.
*Dance of the Apocalypse*. Toronto, Laser, 1976.
*If the Stars Are Gods*, with Gregory Benford. New York, Berkley, 1977; London, Gollancz, 1978.
*The Starless World* (novelization of TV play). New York, Bantam, 1978; London, Corgi, 1985.
*Lord Tedric*, with E.E. Smith. New York, Baronet, 1978.
*Space Pirates*, with E.E. Smith. New York, Baronet, 1979; as *Lord Tedric: The Space Pirates*, London, Wingate, 1979.
*The Twilight River*. New York, Dell, 1979.
*Devil World* (novelization of TV play). New York, Bantam, 1979; London, Corgi, 1985.
*The Garden of Winter*. New York, Berkley, 1980.
*Find the Changeling*, with Gregory Benford. New York, Dell, 1980; London, Sphere, 1983.
*A Thunder in Neptune*. New York, Morrow, 1989.

Uncollected Short Stories

"Dear Aunt Annie," in *Fantastic* (New York), April 1970.
"A Gift from the Gozniks," in *Fantastic* (New York), August 1970.
"Home Again Home Again," in *Quark 3*, edited by Samuel R. Delany and Marilyn Hacker. New York, Paperback Library, 1971.
"West Wind, Falling," in *Universe 1*, edited by Terry Carr. New York, Ace, 1971; London, Dobson, 1975.
"Seeker for Still Life," in *Fantasy and Science Fiction* (New York), January 1971.
"Gemini Cavendish," in *Amazing* (New York), March 1971.
"Defender of Death," in *Galaxy* (New York, April 1971.
"The Edge and the Mist," in *Galaxy* (New York), September 1971.
"Stalking the Sun," in *Universe 2*, edited by Terry Carr. New York, Ace 1972; London, Dobson, 1975.
"White Summer in Memphis," in *New Dimensions 2*, edited by Robert Silverberg. New York, Avon, 1972.
"Grasshopper Time," in *Fantasy and Science Fiction* (New York), March 1972.
"Soft Change," in *Amazing* (New York), May 1972.
"Underbelly," in *If* (New York), October 1972.
"Examination Day," in *The Other Side of Tomorrow* edited by Roger Elwood. New York, Random House, 1973.
"Free City Blues," in *Universe 3*, edited by Terry Carr. New York, Random House, 1973; London, Dobson, 1976.
"Lovemaker," in *Eros in Orbit*, edited by Joseph Elder. New York, Simon and Schuster, 1973.
"The Shrine of Sebastian," in *Chains of the Sea*. Nashville, Nelson, 1973.
"Three Comedians," in *New Dimensions 3*, edited by Robert Silverberg. New York, Avon, 1973.
"The Ascending Axe," in *Amazing* (New York), January 1973.
"Iron Mountain," in *Fantastic* (New York), July 1973.
"The Stuff of Time," in *Fantastic* (New York), September 1973.
"The Beasts in the Jungle," in *Fantasy and Science Fiction* (New York), November 1973.
"Moby, Too," in *Amazing* (New York), December 1973.
"The Ambiguities of Yesterday," in *The Far Side of Time* edited by Roger Elwood. New York, Dodd Mead, 1974.
"Psychosomatica," in *Crisis*, edited by Roger Elwood. Nashville, Nelson, 1974.
"Beneath the Waves," in *Fantasy and Science Fiction* (New York), March 1974.
"The Treasure in the Treasure House," in *Fantasy and Science Fiction* (New York), August 1974.
"Angel of Truth," in *Epoch*, edited by Roger Elwood and Robert Silverberg. New York, Berkley, 1975.
"Sandsnake Hunter," in *Fantasy and Science Fiction* (New York), March 1975.
"Second Creation," in *Amazing* (New York), March 1975.
"The Restoration," in *Analog* (New York), September 1975.

"What Did You Do Last Year?," in *Universe 6*, edited by Terry Carr. New York, Doubleday, 1976; London, Dobson, 1978.
"The Rising of the Sun," in *Beyond Time*, edited by Sandra Ley. New York, Pocket Books, 1976.
"The Locust Descending," in *Fantastic* (New York), February 1976.
"Changing Styles," in *Fantasy and Science Fiction* (New York), March 1976.
"The Prince in Metropolis," in *Analog* (New York), May 1976.
"The Anvil of Jove," in *Fantasy and Science Fiction* (New York), July 1976.
"Embryonic Dharma," in *Analog* (New York), December 1976.
"The Retro Man," in *New Dimensions 7*, edited by Robert Silverberg. New York, Harper, and London, Gollancz, 1977.
"Hellas in Florida," in *Fantasy and Science Fiction* (New York), January 1977.
"The Tides of Time," in *Galaxy* (New York), March 1977.
"To End All Wars," in *International Relations Through Science Fiction*, edited by Martin H. Greenberg and Joseph D. Olander. New York, Watts, 1978.
"Vermeer's Window," in *Universe 8*, edited by Terry Carr. New York, Doubleday, 1978; London, Dobson, 1979.
"Saint Francis Night," in *Amazing* (New York), May 1978.
"Points of Contract," in *Fantasy and Science Fiction* (New York), June 1978.
"Tattered Stars, Tarnished Bars," in *Beyond Reality*, edited by Terry Carr. New York, Elsevier Nelson, 1979.
"The Anaconda's Smile," in *Fantasy and Science Fiction* (New York), May 1979.
"The Mother of the Beast," in *Orbit 21*, edited by Damon Knight. New York, Harper, 1980.
"Pain and Glory," in *New Dimensions 12*, edited by Robert Silverberg and Marta Randall. New York, Pocket Books, 1981.
"Valo in Love," in *Analog Yearbook 2*, edited by Stanley Schmidt. New York, Ace, 1981.
"Continuous Performance," in *Last Man on Earth*, edited by Isaac Asimov, Martin H. Greenberg, and Charles G. Waugh. New York, Fawcett, 1982.
"Revisions," in *Fantasy and Science Fiction* (New York), February 1983.

*

Gordon Eklund comments (1985):

If there's any one aspect of my work to date that seems worth emphasizing, it would have to be the range of themes, subjects, styles, and moods that I've attempted. I don't believe that any two of my novels are very much alike, and the short stories are even more varied, if only because of their greater number. To me, the science-fiction field is an extremely broad category—one encompassing, as it does, all of possibility—and I've found it extremely difficult to settle down to mining a single nook within the field. I suppose a few certain types of stories can easily be seen as favorites of mine—I find particular pleasure in dealing with time and parallel worlds—but I wouldn't want to predict that this will remain valid during my next ten years as a writer.

* * *

Eklund's first novel, *The Eclipse of Dawn*, is certainly one of his best. The story is set about 25 years in the future, and the radical societal smashup (that everyone seems to fear so much now) has occurred. The America of the 21st century is a stark, confusing, and disorienting place. The exaggerated ennui of a fallen America is creatively juxtaposed with the virile faith of Senator William Colonby, who is running for president.

Eklund masterfully caricatures the idiocy and irony of a misplaced crusader. Senator Colonby does a whistle-stop tour of America, uttering loud but meaningless political platitudes. Along with some sexual intrigue, the plot includes a telepathic woman who is in contact with powerful aliens from Jupiter. The book settles down into a nasty chaos and depression when these alien savior-beings turn out to be nonexistent. The book closes with the surrender of the sitting president to Colonby, and a statement about the basic impotency of politics. In *The Eclipse of Dawn* the integrity of the individual is still possible, but the societal prospect is bleak.

Perhaps Eklund's richest achievement is *If the Stars Are Gods* (written with Gregory Benford). The novel is a moving challenge to the limited consciousness we all seek to transcend: "Understanding the new and strange is not so much a matter of work and effort, but of intuition and time to let ideas come to fruition." The hero is Bradley Reynolds, a "brilliant young scientist" whose consuming passion is to discover other dimensions of being in the universe. The plot moves quickly through an initial failure to find life on Mars, an encounter with enlightened aliens from another universe, and 35 years in an African monastery. This contrast of the exploratory and introspective nature of Reynolds's personality is skillfully depicted. His personal odyssey climaxes with his death in a newly discovered place which will open new opportunities for the human race. This work is especially a pleasure in terms of characterization (e.g., beautiful, mercurial, and infuriating Mara: "She took drugs, slept with other women, gambled, drank, stole money"). The characters are strong and brave while remaining believably human.

Among the most memorable of Eklund's heroes is Tommy Bloome in *All Times Possible*. The specifics of Tommy's life, death, and identity are presented in tantalizing montage of episodes. It becomes clear, however, that Tommy is a savior of the workers and the people. The book, like *The Eclipse of Dawn*, presents a post-catastrophe or transformed America—the difference being that Tommy ends up as a martyr for the cause of the (successful?) revolution. The entire novel is written while Tommy is contemplating a bullet that is in mid-air, whistling toward his forehead. Is Tommy in a new life form after death? Is he having the familiar "life flashing before my eyes" experience? Or is this device a statement about the awful finality of death? *All Times Possible* contains more provocative ambiguity than any of Eklund's other works, and goes somewhat beyond what seems to be the basic Eklund point of view: "We've no right to expect a damn thing from this cold universe" (*If the Stars Are Gods*).

In *Dance of the Apocalypse*, set in 2097, anarchy, poverty and starvation are the major components. The heroes in this showdown are a tough, illiterate street scrounger and a humanistic idealist from the east, William Stoner. *Dance of the Apocalypse* boasts a novel excursion of the imagination in terms of how order is restored to the now barbarous world. In the midst of deep turmoil, China returns to Confucianism and sends an exploratory mission to the United States. By a stroke of profound luck, our dedicated idealist has the sagacity to appreciate the Confucian mind. The final outcome of the insurrection is the realization of a Confucian state in America. The explorer and teacher from China explains quite clearly why things are going to be so happy from now on: "Because William Stoner believes what we believe, and because what we believe is correct."

The final works of Eklund that should be mentioned are the Lord Tedric series, reportedly conceived by E.E. "Doc" Smith, which involves a massive battle of good and evil forces. Lord Tedric's origins are not so different from Superman's (i.e., born in another world he doesn't remember, special powers on earth), but he comes to a realization of his abilities and destiny rather slowly. Tedric is not (and is not meant to be) as believable or human as Bradley Reynolds in *If the Stars are Gods*.

Eklund has a rare ability to project alternative outcomes for the United States, the world, and the cosmos. He ranges from sarcastic pessimism in *The Eclipse of Dawn*, to the patently bizarre possibility in *Dance of the Apocalypse* and total cosmic liberation (communication with the stars) in *If the Stars Are Gods*. Eklund's talent and insight are more visible when he keeps the plot and characters close to the reality of today. As he reaches to portray the New Man and the New Woman of the transformed future, his vision breaks down because of what he knows of the human condition. His pure heroes are acceptable, and his portrayal of the bitter defeatism that creeps into human relationships is excellent. As Eklund expatiates widely on the human prospect throughout his work, the reader is forced to deal with both close existential issues and the ultimate potentiality of the universe. Despite consistent inconsistency, Eklund communicates much to the intellect and the imagination.

—Peter Lynch

---

**ELDERSHAW, M. Barnard.** Pseudonym for Marjorie Faith Barnard (and with Flora Sydney Patricia Eldershaw for non-science-fiction works). Australian. Born in Ashfield, New South Wales, 16 August 1897. Educated at Cambridge School, Hunters' Hill; Sydney Girls' High School; University of Sydney (exhibitioner; University Medal, 1920), 1916–20, B.A. (honours) in history 1920; Sydney Teachers College, 1920. Librarian Sydney Public Library and Sydney Technical College Library, 1920–35; freelance writer, 1935–42; Librarian, Sydney Public Library, 1942, and Commonwealth Scientific and Industrial Research Organization Library, Sydney, 1942–50. Recipient: *Bulletin* prize, 1928: Patrick White award, 1983. Member, Order of Australia, 1979. Agent: Curtis Brown (Australia) Pty. Ltd., 27 Union Street, Paddington, New South Wales 2021. Address: 29 Sunshine Drive, Point Clare, New South Wales 2250, Australia.

SCIENCE-FICTION PUBLICATIONS

Novel

*Tomorrow and Tomorrow.* Melbourne, Georgian House, 1947; London, Phoenix House, 1949; complete text, as *Tomorrow and Tomorrow and Tomorrow*, London, Virago Press, 1983; New York, Doubleday, 1984.

OTHER PUBLICATIONS with Flora Sydney Patricia Eldershaw

Novels

*A House is Built.* London, Harrap, and New York, Harcourt Brace, 1929.
*Green Memory.* London, Harrap, and New York, Harcourt Brace, 1931.
*The Glasshouse.* London, Harrap, 1936.
*Plaque with Laurel.* London, Harrap, 1937.

Play

*The Watch on the Headland*, in *Australian Radio Plays*, edited by Leslie Rees. Sydney, Angus and Robertson, 1946.

Other

*Philip of Australia: An Account of the Settlement at Sydney Cove 1788-1792.* London, Harrap, 1937.
*Essays in Australian Fiction.* Melbourne, Melbourne University Press, 1938; Freeport, New York, Books for Libraries, 1970.
*The Life and Times of Captain John Piper.* Sydney, Australian Limited Editions Society, 1939.
*My Australia.* London, Jarrolds, 1939; revised edition, 1951.

Editor, *Coast to Coast 1946.* Sydney, Angus and Robertson, 1947.

OTHER PUBLICATIONS as Marjorie Faith Barnard

Short Stories

*The Persimmon Tree and Other Stories.* Sydney, Clarendon, 1943; revised edition, London Virago Press, 1985; New York, Penguin, 1986.

Other

*The Ivory Gate.* Privately printed 1920.
*Macquarie's World.* Sydney, Australian Limited Editions Society, 1941.
*Australian Outline.* Sydney, Ure Smith, 1943; revised edition, 1949.
*The Sydney Book.* Sydney, Ure Smith, 1947.
*Sydney: The Story of a City.* Melbourne, Melbourne University Press, 1956.
*Australia's First Architect: Francis Greenway.* London, Longman, 1961.
*A History of Australia.* Sydney, Angus and Robertson, 1962; revised edition, 1963; New York, Praeger, 1963.
*Georgian Architecture in Australia*, with others. Sydney, Ure Smith, 1963.
*Lachlan Macquarie.* Melbourne, Oxford University Press, 1964.
*Miles Franklin.* New York, Twayne, 1967; revised edition, St. Lucia and London, University of Queensland Press, 1988.

*

Marjorie Faith Barnard comments (1981):

Two things have a bearing on my writing: one is the circumstances of my childhood, and the other a successful collaboration.

I was an only child, had no playmates, and did not go to school until I was ten (having been taught by governesses prior to that). This was the best possible beginning for a writer. My natural creativity was not quenched by having too much. I created my own exciting and happy world. Words were my toys. I had the close companionship of my mother and free access to my great-grandmother's books—the Victorian poets, a complete set of Dickens, many histories. I had no taste for the insipid children's books of my period and escaped them almost entirely.

My collaboration with Flora Eldershaw was successful and disciplined. We both wanted to write and each had something to contribute. Our rule was to discuss the plan of a book in detail and agree upon it before anything was written down. Flora had a fine critical ability and curbed my exuberance. I wrote the better prose and had more leisure, so most of the actual writing fell to me. Our association was professional: her friends were not my friends, her way of life not mine. This was a good thing; close friendship would have brought other than literary considerations into it all. We worked in a dry light.

*Tomorrow and Tomorrow* was entirely my own work as Flora Eldershaw, for reasons of geography and pressure of work, could not contribute. It is a serious book, the best and worst thing I have ever done. I cared too much. As an historian I could see all too clearly the probable future of this country. The book had its roots in the anguish of the years preceding the Second World War. It is about human survival and escape from bondage. The book ran into difficulties. It was hard to find a publisher for such a long and in some ways controversial novel; times were touchy. Without my knowledge my publisher submitted the manuscript to the censor who cut the latter part severely. It was not subversive and now would have no difficulty in being printed *in toto*, but costs have prohibited its republication in its original form.

* * *

M. Barnard Eldershaw is the pen name of the Australian historical novelists Marjorie Barnard and Flora Eldershaw. *Tomorrow and Tomorrow*, the one science-fiction work published under this name, is in fact the work of Marjorie Barnard alone. In it she applies the selective techniques of the historical novelist to recreate Australia of the period 1924–46 through the eyes of a man four centuries in the future.

The reconstruction of cultural malaise moving into wartime confusion is brilliant if overlong but the story (completed in 1942) moves on to a vision of a different ending to the World War of 1939–45, one wherein an exhausted people turns on the culture which has brought only recurrent agony to each new generation and destroys it. The razing of Sydney by fire is a tremendous symbolic set piece. All this is conveyed as sections of a novel written by a 24th-century *littérateur*, in a time when youth is again restive in a culture (conventionally pastoralutopian) which it sees as oppressive in its settled satisfaction. The author's political argument (this is a political novel) turns on a newly devised voting machine which records the thoughts of electors to give an accurate survey of mass attitudes.

When a public test of the machine is made, with youth proposing far-reaching constitutional changes, the outcome is devastating for the young protesters. The motion is lost when the machine records a 62% majority of the electors as utterly indifferent to the question. The warning is simple—that indifference leads to frustration and eventually to the violence which destroyed the earlier culture.

The Australian censorship at the time found much of this material not actually subversive but politically disquieting, particularly that dealing with the war which was still in progress, and made numerous deletions. Some are, from the viewpoint of the 1940's understandable; ideas of an ultimate political doublecross by Russia and Australian secession from the British Empire were touchy stuff—but finally honoured by events, though not in the form of the writer's forecast. Other deletions are hard to justify: what, for instance, could have been the objection to: (a man of the 24th-century is speaking) "I only know by chance and the skin of my teeth that jigsaw puzzles were a fashionable craze four centuries ago and now are one with crosswords and diabolo"? It is no longer possible to recover the state of mind which caused such aberrations. The curious will find all the deletions restored and listed in the Virago edition of 1983.

*Tomorrow and Tomorrow and Tomorrow* (the full title now restored) is powerfully characterised and is a masterly example of science fiction used to present an argument in dramatic detail. Nobel Prize-winner Patrick White named it the Australian novel he would most like to see republished. It has been.

—George Turner

---

**ELGIN, (Patricia Anne) Suzette Haden (née Wilkins).** American. Born in Louisiana, Missouri, 18 November 1936. Educated at the University of Chicago (Academy of American Poets Award, 1955), 1954–56; California State University, Chico, B.A. in French and English 1967; University of California, San Diego, 1968–73, M.A. in Linguistics 1970, Ph.D. 1973. Married 1) Peter Joseph Haden in 1955 (died), one son and two daughters; 2) George N. Elgin in 1964, one son. Television folk music performer, Redding, California, 1966–68; instructor, Chico Conservatory of Music, 1967–68; French teacher, 1968–69; guitar teacher, 1969–70; linguistics teacher, University of California, San Diego, summer 1971; Assistant Professor, then Associate Professor of linguistics, San Diego State University, 1972–80, now Emeritus. Since 1980, founding director, Ozark Center for Language Studies, and editor, *The Lonesome Node*, Huntsville. Recipient: Eugene Saxon Fellowship, 1957–58. Address: P.O. Box 1137, Huntsville, Arkansas 72740, U.S.A.

SCIENCE-FICTION PUBLICATIONS

Novels (series: Communipath; Ozark)

*Communipath Worlds.* New York, Pocket Books, 1980.
*The Communipaths.* New York, Ace, 1970.
*Furthest.* New York, Ace, 1971.
*At the Seventh Level.* New York, DAW, 1972.
*Star-Anchored, Star-Angered* (Communipath). New York, Doubleday, 1979.
*The Ozark Trilogy.* New York, Doubleday, 1981.
*Twelve Fair Kingdoms.* New York, Doubleday, 1981.
*Grand Jubilee.* New York, Doubleday, 1981.
*And Then There'll Be Fireworks.* New York, Doubleday, 1981.
*Native Tongue.* New York, DAW, 1984; London, Women's Press, 1985.
*Yonder Comes the Other End of Time.* New York, DAW, 1986.
*Native Tongue II: The Judas Rose.* New York, DAW, 1987; as *The Judas Rose*, London, Women's Press, 1988.

OTHER PUBLICATIONS

Other

*Guide to Transformational Grammar: History, Theory, Practice,* with John T. Grinder. New York, Holt Rinehart, 1973.
*What Is Linguistics?* Englewood Cliffs, New Jersey, Prentice Hall, 1973; revised edition, 1979.
*A Primer of Transformational Grammar for Rank Beginners.* Urbana, Illinois, National Conference of Teachers of English, 1975.
*The Gentle Art of Verbal Self-Defense.* Englewood Cliffs, New Jersey, Prentice Hall, 1980; *More on the Gentle Art of Verbal Self-Defense*, 1983; *The Last Word on the Gentle Art of Self-*

*Defense*, 1987; *Success with the Gentle Art of Self-Defense*, 1989; *Staying Well with the Gentle Art of Self-Defense*, 1990.
*A First Grammar and Dictionary of Láadan*. Madison, Wisconsin, SF3, 1984.

Editor, *Pouring Down Words*. Englewood Cliffs, New Jersey, Prentice Hall, 1975.

*

Manuscript Collection: Chater Collection, Love Library, San Diego State University; University of Oregon Library, Eugene.

Suzette Haden Elgin comments (1981):

I went into writing science fiction originally because as a married woman with four kids at home I couldn't pay my graduate school tuition any other way, it being well known that such women are not "Ph.D. material." I know that's not an inspiring or romantic reason, but it's honest. Because I am a linguist my major interest is problems of communication as they are now and as they are likely to develop in the future; I have focused my books on this topic up to now, along with—as subtopics—an attempt to make clear what a pernicious crock Romantic Love is, and a fascination with problems of theology especially as they apply to women under the constant influence of religious language. My books have been picked up as feminist, which I hadn't realized they were until I read the reviews.

I take my SF writing very seriously, and feel that anybody who spends the time and money to read something I have written should not feel cheated, and should not be presented with a cryptic puzzle used to demonstrate how clever *I* am. My first four books have been part of an on-going series about a rather bumbling mind-deaf superspy; I am now writing a fantasy trilogy, and am enjoying the change. But there will be more Coyote Jones books—the intergalactic superspy framework is a gentle kind of spoof that allows me plenty of room to move around and be as entertaining as possible without writing anything I have to be ashamed of later. I try to avoid the Brothers Karamazov Syndrome, and do not allow my characters to pontificate.

I plot a book down to the most minute detail in advance, filling notebooks with maps, biographies, every conceivable sort of information I might need in the book about its culture and characters. That takes at least a year. When I do the actual writing, however, I do only one draft. The I revise as I type the final manuscript, and that writing process generally takes about six weeks from start to finish. I don't believe in inspiration, I believe in hard work. I hope that shows in my work; it's meant to. I have no problem "finding ideas"; my only problem is finding time to write them all. That, I expect, comes from rigorous training in the scientific method: one just poses hypotheses, and extrapolates.

Most embarrassing moment: having nobody notice that I had intended *Furthest* as a straightforward satire of the United States system of economics; that is, anything's allowed as long as you've filled out the proper forms.

* * *

Suzette Haden Elgin, like Gregory Benford or Fred Hoyle, writes science fiction concerning her professional field. In this case the science is linguistics, in which Elgin's involvement, academic and otherwise, is considerable. Elgin's novels all take place in roughly compatible futures, with some shared references, but divide into three main fictional worlds. At first established as separate, the Communipath series and the Ozark trilogy do meet in *Yonder Comes the Other End of Time*. *Native Tongue* and its sequel belong to a third series which is not yet complete.

The Communipath books are clearly science fiction, set in a far future populated by a number of humanoid cultures on a number of planets. The prevailing theme of the books is communication, in all its various and difficult guises. These include many forms of telepathy, and social systems such as the Multiversities—higher education more rare but more esteemed than now—and (in *At The Seventh Level*) a system of ritual battle by carefully selected and honored poets, in which soldiers suffer for their side's inferior verse.

Tri-Galactic Agent Coyote Jones is central to the Communipath books. He is an extremely powerful projective telepath but also "mind-deaf," a rare and pitiable affliction which, however, suits him for the assignment in *Star-Anchored, Star-Angered*: checking out Drussa Silver, a female messiah whose abilities include—but go beyond—telepathy. Her followers, in their religion-based community/communication/communion, recall the Maklunites of *The Communipaths*. Other characters in these novels include a "mind wife," rebelling against the life of psychic concubine for which she has been trained (*Furthest*); and Susannah, an extremely telepathically gifted baby, drafted for the communipath system—likened to a psychic bucket-brigade—that passes messages through otherwise impossible distances (*The Communipaths*).

The speculative discussion of specific forms of discourse is also one of the strengths of Elgin's Ozark trilogy: *Twelve Fair Kingdoms*, *Grand Jubilee*, and *And Then There'll Be Fireworks*. In this series, the Twelve Families of Planet Ozark left Earth and founded a mostly-utopian society with a technology based primarily on magic. The setting of another planet and use of scientific technology (especially the "comsets" run by the main family in the trilogy, the Brightwaters) would justify calling the books science fiction; and in a deeper sense the society and magic (which is always a technology) also show extrapolative insight. On the other hand, the three novels are more like contemporary fantasy in tone; and while they explain how the magic works (the highest form is based on transformational-generative grammar), no material explanation is given for why it does. This question is left open in *Yonder Comes the Other End of Time*, in which Coyote Jones finds that Ozark magic may function by the rules of "psience" as he knows them, or it may not.

Much of the charm of the Ozark trilogy comes from the familiar strangeness, and strange familiarity, of alien equivalents of the modern-American Ozark culture Elgin knows well, including "mules," actually telepathic, but generally uncommunicative, aliens who fly by magic; and "the Grannies," a powerful social class, able to perform household magic and known for their folksy and fiery "formspeech." The plot of the books revolves around Responsible of Brightwater, a 14-year-old girl who holds the position, as does one female each generation, of Meta-Magician. Unknown to most, her powers exceed those of even the Magicians of Rank, and her mere functioning is vital to the maintenance of magic on Ozark.

The Communipath and Ozark books show the growth of Elgin as an author, especially in plotting. The plots of the Communipath series are often loose, with too abrupt a solution by Coyote Jones, and too many intriguing developments—such as the changes hinted at toward the end of *The Communipaths*—dropped or only vaguely referred to later. In the Ozark books, the plots are complicated but tight, with material, such as the character Silverweb of McDaniels, which is not only interesting but later shown to be vital. The narrative voice gets more sure and the characters get both more human and more powerful, although Responsible can occasionally verge on the unconvincing precociousness of Tessa in *The Communipaths*. The book that joins the two series is harder to judge as a novel, since its significance often depends on knowing the other books; it does succeed in its own terms, especially demonstrating the irresistible wit that characterizes Elgin's best writing.

*Native Tongue* and *The Judas Rose* are impressive science-fiction novels and promise more good work to come. In this series, one theme is communication among alien races. In a future of copious interplanetary trade, the linguists have become a necessary and powerful yet despised and feared social class, marrying among their households and raising their children to be translators before the age of natural language acquisition is past. Another theme is communication between the genders, which might as well be alien races. The events occur when women's liberation is only a legend, and men have complete legal control of all females. Fictional "prefaces" to both novels explain that the manuscripts were published in a further, more egalitarian, future, apparently brought about by the events described in the novels. Primarily, these books depict the development and spread of Láadan, a language developed by women linguists to express women's concerns and values.

Elgin has shown societies repressive of women elsewhere, as in *At the Seventh Level*. In fact, while strong females appear in all her books—from a Multiversity dean to Troublesome of Brightwater—Elgin writes more about problems of gender-roles than about solutions, and sometimes her novels may too simply reverse the sexism they examine. Especially in the Ozark trilogy and Native Tongue books, men are by nature bumbling fools, but still strong enough to trouble and oppress women. This aspect bothers many readers, but Elgin does convey her perspective well, and the third Native Tongue book may provide more optimistic speculation.

Though not as widely known as she should be, Elgin is a significant author whose novels both use genre conventions and surpass or undermine them. Her books also present the reader with an enticing blend of readability and challenging (often provoking) insights concerning serious issues.

—Bernadette Bosky

---

**ELLISON, Harlan (Jay).** Also writes as Paul Merchant. American. Born in Cleveland, Ohio, 27 May 1934. Attended Ohio State University, Columbus, 1951–53. Served in the United States Army, 1957–59. Married 1) Charlotte Stein in 1956 (divorced); 2) Billie Joyce Sanders in 1961 (divorced); 3) Lory Patrick in 1965 (divorced); 4) Lori Horowitz in 1976 (divorced). Editor, *Rogue*; founding editor, Regency Books, Evanston, Illinois, 1961–62. Freelance writer and lecturer: editor, Harlan Ellison Discovery Series. Vice-president, Science Fiction Writers of America, 1965–66 (resigned). Recipient: Nebula award, 1965, 1969, 1977; Writers Guild of America award, for TV play, 1965, 1967, 1973; Hugo award, 1966, 1968 (3 awards), 1972 (for editing), 1974, 1975, 1978; Mystery Writers of America Edgar Allan Poe award, 1973; Jupiter award, 1973; *Locus* award, 1983; Bram Stoker award, for collection, 1988, for nonfiction, 1990. Address: 3484 Coy Drive, Sherman Oaks, California 91423, U.S.A.

Science-Fiction Publications

Novels

*The Man with Nine Lives.* New York, Ace, 1960.
*Doomsman.* New York, Belmont, 1967.
*Phoenix Without Ashes*, with Edward Bryant. New York, Fawcett, 1975; Manchester, Savoy, 1978.
*The City on the Edge of Forever* (novelization of TV play). New York, Bantam, 1977.
*Run for the Stars* (with *Echoes of Thunder*, by Jack Dann and Jack C. Haldeman). New York, Tor, 1991.

Short Stories

*A Touch of Infinity.* New York, Ace, 1960.
*Ellison Wonderland.* New York, Paperback Library, 1962; revised edition, New York, Bluejay, 1984; as *Earthman, Go Home*, 1964.
*Paingod and Other Delusions.* New York, Pyramid, 1965.
*I Have No Mouth, and I Must Scream.* New York, Pyramid, 1967; revised edition, New York, Ace, 1983; London, Xanadu, 1990.
*From the Land of Fear.* New York, Belmont, 1967.
*Love Ain't Nothing But Sex Misspelled.* New York, Trident Press, 1968.
*The Beast That Shouted Love at the Heart of the World.* New York, Avon, 1969; abridged edition, London, Millington, 1976; revised edition, New York, Bluejay, 1984.
*Over the Edge: Stories from Somewhere Else.* New York, Belmont, 1970.
*Alone Against Tomorrow.* New York, Macmillan, 1971; as *All the Sounds of Fear* and *The Time of the Eye*, London, Panther, 2 vols., 1973–74.
*Partners in Wonder: Harlan Ellison in Collaboration with. . . .* New York, Walker, 1971.
*Approaching Oblivion.* New York, Walker, 1974; London, Millington, 1976.
*Deathbird Stories: A Pantheon of Modern Gods.* New York, Harper, 1975; London, Millington, 1977.
*No Doors, No Windows.* New York, Pyramid, 1975.
*Strange Wine.* New York, Harper, 1978.
*The Illustrated Harlan Ellison.* New York, Baronet, 1978.
*The Fantasies of Harlan Ellison.* Boston, Gregg Press, 1979.
*Stalking the Nightmare.* Huntington Woods, Michigan, Phantasia Press, 1982.
*An Edge in My Voice.* Norfolk, Virginia, Donning, 1984.
*The Essential Ellison.* Omaha, Nebraska, Nemo Press, 1987.

Other Publications

Novels

*Rumble.* New York, Pyramid, 1958; as *Web of the City*, 1975.
*Sex Gang* (as Paul Merchant). N.p., Nightstand, 1959.
*Rockabilly.* New York, Fawcett, 1961; London, Muller, 1963; as *Spider Kiss*, New York, Pyramid, 1975.

Short Stories

*The Deadly Streets.* New York, Ace, 1958; London, Digit, 1959; enlarged edition, New York, Pyramid, 1975.
*The Juvies.* New York, Ace, 1961.
*Gentleman Junkie and Other Stories of the Hung-Up Generation.* Evanston, Illinois, Regency, 1961; revised edition, New York, Pyramid, 1975.
*Shatterday.* Boston, Houghton Mifflin, 1980; London, Hutchinson, 1982.
*Angry Candy.* Boston, Houghton Mifflin, 1988.

Plays

*The City on the Edge of Forever* (televised, 1967). Published in *Six Science Fiction Plays*, edited by Roger Elwood, New York, Pocket Books, 1976.

Screenplay: *The Oscar*, with Russell Rouse and Clarence Greene, 1966.

Television Plays: *Who Killed Alex Debbs? [Purity Mather?, Andy Zygmunt?, Half of Glory Lee?] (Burke's Law* series), 1963–65; *The Soldier* and *Demon with a Glass Hand (The Outer Limits* series), 1963–64; *The City on the Edge of Forever (Star Trek series)*, 1967; and for *Route 66, The Untouchables, The Alfred Hitchcock Hour*, and *The Man from U.N.C.L.E.* series.

Other

*Memos from Purgatory: Two Journeys of Our Time.* Evanston, Illinois, Regency, 1961.
*The Glass Teat: Essays of Opinion on the Subject of Television.* New York, Ace, 1970.
*The Other Glass Teat: Further Essays of Opinion on Television.* New York, Pyramid, 1975.
*Sleepless Nights in the Procrustean Bed: Essays*, edited by Marty Clark. San Bernardino, California, Borgo Press, 1984; London, Xanadu, 1990.
*Harlan Ellison's Watching.* Los Angeles, Underwood Miller, 1989.
*All the Lies That Are My Life* (autobiography). Los Angeles, Underwood Miller, 1989.
*The Harlan Ellison Hornbook* (essays). New York, Penzler, 1990.

Editor, *Dangerous Visions.* New York, Doubleday, 1967; London, David Bruce and Watson, 2 vols., 1971.
Editor, *Nightshade and Damnations*, by Gerald Kersh. New York, Fawcett, 1968.
Editor, *Again, Dangerous Visions.* New York, Doubleday, 1972; London, Millington, 1976.
Editor, *Medea: Harlan's World.* Huntington Woods, Michigan, Phantasia Press, 1985.

Recording: *Blood!*, with Robert Bloch, Alternate World, 1976.

*

Bibliography: *Harlan Ellison: A Bibliographical Checklist* by Leslie Kay Swigart, Dallas, Williams, 1973.

Critical Studies: *Harlan Ellison: Unrepentant Harlequin* by George Edgar Slusser, San Bernardino, California, Borgo Press, 1977; "Harlan Ellison Issue" of *Fantasy and Science Fiction* (New York), July 1977; *The Book of Ellison* edited by Andrew Porter, New York, Algol Press, 1978.

* * *

Very few people are ambivalent about Harlan Ellison; they thoroughly like or thoroughly dislike his style. But he has won many awards for his writing, and not a few of them have come from outside the science-fiction world. And in spite of the people who walk out of his public appearances feeling insulted and angry or refuse to buy his books because of the lengthy introductions he includes with each one, it cannot be denied that Harlan Ellison is a good writer who has had a significant impact on contemporary science fiction. Ellison's use of language has helped change science fiction considerably. Ellison is not afraid to use any word, however objectionable some person or group might find it, if he thinks that that word is the proper one for a specific situation. His definition of obscenity, promulgated at various personal appearances, is "language which is intended to deceive." Ellison cites "protective reaction strike" and "military incursion" (Vietnam era words which reporters were required to use instead of "bombing mission" and "military invasion") as examples of obscene language.

In Ellison stories like "A Boy and His Dog," there are descriptions of sex and violence, and there is a lot of foul language. But, Ellison might argue, such description and language are necessary to the story. "A Boy and His Dog" depicts the aftermath of World War III. Roving gangs and roving independents, called "solos," occupy the surface of the planet; these young toughs, mostly male, are the same sort as those who roam inner city streets today. Their language must be strong to be realistic. In addition, Ellison sets his group in contrast to the other group of survivors, those living in underground cities to which they retreated as the war broke out. The surface gangs are destroying each other (and themselves) through violence; the below-grounders are sterile and wasting away. And without the four-letter words, the reader would be less able to contrast the destructive aggressiveness of the surface group to the equally destructive non-participation of the below-grounders.

In addition to helping expand the language of science-fiction by example in his stories, Ellison has also encouraged others to do the same. As editor of the *Dangerous Visions* series, Ellison encouraged his fellow science-fiction writers to send him those stories which other editors had considered too controversial to put into print. Ellison encouraged not just experiments with language, but experiments in subject matter and in style as well. Ellison's eagerness to experiment has also led him to collaborate in various ways with other science-fiction writers and artists. *Partners in Wonder* and *Medea: Harlan's World* are fictional creations in which Ellison either co-authors the stories or provides the initial settings to which other writers respond.

But it is his own writing that is most important. Many of his best-selling short stories are experimental in their subject matter. "Shattered Like a Glass Goblin" is a story about people on drugs who eventually, after continued and heavy use, turn into the creatures they hallucinate. They turn on and destroy each other in bestial ways. The narrator becomes a crystal goblin and is shattered by a swipe from the hairy paw of the creature that was once his girl friend. In "Delusion for a Dragon Slayer" a man is given the chance to attain heaven if he can act like the heroic-fantasy hero he has always dreamed of being: he does not make it. And "Catman" was written as the future sex story for a volume of ultimate science fiction stories called *Final Stage*.

Other Ellison stories are experimental in style. "The Beast That Shouted Love at the Heart of the World" is written to be read as if the separate segments were arranged in a circle instead of a sequence of pages. "Pretty Maggie Moneyeyes" attempts to portray a person's impressions at the moment of death. Ellison uses italics, varied spacing, and other type tricks to try to present these impressions and sensations. And "From A to Z, In the Chocolate Alphabet" consists of the alphabet, with a short story for each letter.

"The Deathbird" is a story which is experimental in both subject and style. In this story, Ellison attempts to show that Satan was the "good guy" and that God, who is responsible for the condition of the world, is insane. The story is told in 26 sections, each numbered, but only 20 or 21 of those sections actually advance the plot of the story. Some of the others are direct addresses to the reader or quizzes for the reader to take, and one section is the story of Ellison's dog, Ahbhu.

But there is more to Harlan Ellison than his science fiction. In newspaper columns later collected and published as *The Glass Teat* and *The Other Glass Teat*, he began with commentaries and criticisms of television and then expanded his focus to include all kinds of social and political topics. In addition, a number of his essays from a variety of sources have been published as *Sleepless Nights in the Procrustean Bed*. And from time to time, Ellison has also written for television, from *Burke's Law* to his own ill-fated *The Starlost*, and for the movies.

Ellison's career is more multi-faceted than that of any other science fiction author (except, of course, Isaac Asimov's), and because of the variety of things he does—writing, editing, lecturing, and the like—he is an important force in science fiction. A sense of that importance can now be obtained from *The Essential Ellison*, a 35-year, 1000-page retrospective featuring both fiction and non-fiction from 1949 to 1983. That book, and *Angry Candy*, will provide the unfamiliar reader with examples of the kinds of writing in which Ellison excels and the themes he feels are important.

—C.W. Sullivan III

---

**EMERSON, Ru.** American. Born in Monterey, California, 15 December 1944. Attended University of Montana, Missoula, 1963–66. Worked as legal secretary in Los Angeles, 1966–83, and in Salem, Oregon, 1984–85. Agent: Richard Curtis Literary Agency, 171 East 74th Street, New York, New York 10021. Address: 2600 Reuben-Boise Road, Dallas, Oregon 97338, U.S.A.

SCIENCE-FICTION PUBLICATIONS

Novels (Series: Nedao; Night-Threads)

*The Princess of Flames*. New York, Berkley, 1986; London, Unwin, 1987.
The Nedao Trilogy:
*To the Haunted Mountains*. New York, Berkley, 1987.
*In the Caves of Exile*. New York, Berkley, and London, Headline, 1988.
*On the Seas of Destiny*. New York, Berkley, and London, Headline, 1989.
*Masques* (novelization of "Beauty and the Beast" T.V. script). New York, Avon, 1990.
*Spellbound*. New York, Ace, 1990.
Night-Threads:
*The Calling of the Three*. New York, Ace, 1990.
*The Two in Hiding*. New York, Ace, 1991.

*

Ru Emerson comments:

I always wanted to write but never knew until I started reading fantasy and science fiction (in my early 20's) where my stories lay. I still find the genre exciting because of the opportunity to stretch one's imagination within a logical and real-seeming framework. Also, I very much enjoy creating my own histories and maps, almost as much as creating and writing the stories.

My main intention, always, is to tell a story—and to do it in such a fashion that a generation raised on movies and television can see the people and places as clearly as I do. Apart from this, I think the most common recurring thread tying my novels together is courage—not who has it, but how people who have never had it find it in need, and how they deal with it.

* * *

Ru Emerson has stated: "All my works at present are science fiction and fantasy. I began reading speculative fiction in 1970 with J.R.R. Tolkien, Isaac Asimov and Andre Norton." The influence of these writers, especially of Tolkien and Norton, are evident in Emerson's eight novels to date, published between 1986 and 1991. These include two fantasy novels, two sf/fantasy trilogies (one as yet incomplete), *Masques*, a novelization from the "Beauty and the Beast" TV series, and short stories. Most of Emerson's works involve magic, kingdoms won and lost, and battles between good and evil (with a focus on the leaders rather than the spear carriers). Her characters all do great and heroic or dark and dastardly deeds, often at great personal cost. However, her books cannot be read for the details of everyday life, nor even the details of journeys across mountain, plain and desert, although most of the books include a few maps. They do allow one to imagine, for example, what it might be like to send large groups of people to their deaths because it is the right thing to do and, while they conclude with the beauty of peace, they are concerned mostly with the heroism of war, an underlying message more characteristic of classical heroic fantasy than it is of Tolkien or Norton. Emerson's books belong, in fact, to an emerging sub-genre of fantasy novels where that melded conception of medieval history, myth, magic, and wargaming meet. Their entertainment value is in following the twists and turns of the familiar game.

Emerson's first published novel, *The Princess of Flames*, contains many echoes of the King Arthur stories. It describes the adventures of Elfrid, youngest child of an aging king, Alster. She has three older half-brothers and two older half-sisters who are the children of the king and his legal wife, a woman he found so unpleasant that he banished her to a convent many years before. Despite the fact that he has three grown sons, one of whom he expects will inherit the throne, Alster takes Elfrid as his favorite and allows her easy access to his person and freedom to wear men's clothing and to learn bow and swordplay. Her very existence has been taken as an affront by her half-siblings, who have subjected her to a long history of abuse. Nevertheless, she is the hero of this tale and her father's trust in her proves to have been well-placed.

The Tales of Nedao is a fantasy trilogy patterned somewhat after Tolkien's work, although it focuses, like *Princess*, on the adventures of a female protagonist, with an interesting twist. Ylia is the legal daughter and proclaimed heir of the Kingdom of Nedao. Her father, King Brandt, has recognized in her the ability to preserve his kingdom and has, as in *Princess*, developed a deep affection for her. He has also provided her with training in sword, bow, and statecraft, as befits an heir. While Ylia is not a bastard like Elfrid, she has an outlander mother, an Aeldran who has magic powers that she can enhance through her familiar, a sentient calico cat named Nisana. In fact, the tale is narrated by Nisana, who begins each chapter of the three-volume work with a pronouncement about its contents.

Again, as with *Princess*, the characters are either all good or all bad, with a few who waffle from good to bad. Their motives are not complex. The protagonists seek to protect and rule their people and the antagonists seek the same thing, although in the name of power and conquest and through less humane means. There are several familiar plot elements, such as non-humans with unusual powers who are aligned either with the good guys (Ylia and her groups) or the bad guys, her half-brother Vess and his common-law father, the Wizard/villain Lysiad. Other elements include the resumption of a 1000-year-old war between good and evil, the use of armies of the dead, and the use of inanimate objects as foci of power.

Each volume chronicles a discrete period in the loss and reconquest of the Kingdom of Nedao. The first, *To the Haunted Mountains*, loses no time in deposing and killing the king and queen of Nedao. Slowly the few survivors of an invasion of neighboring Tehlatt, which was initiated by Lysiad's desire for power, travel to a more hospitable and defensible location to regroup and look for allies. They begin to rebuild in *In The Caves of Exile*. Ylia also arranges to have many young women trained in sword and bow, sets up trade with current neighbors, and finds and marries a wandering outlander who just happens to be the oldest son of the noble she has named as her temporary heir. As might be expected, *On the Seas of Destiny* chronicles the final battles between the evil Vess, his powerful Wizard father, and the Wizard's companion, Maritta. Magical intervention is the order of the day on both sides of the battle. The novels leave one with a sense of mighty tasks accomplished and great wrongs righted.

*Spellbound*, a novel in one book, may be the best of Emerson's work. She has managed to create a compact plot within an innovative retelling of the Cinderella story. The characters are anything but storybook, although the usual evil villains and heroic youngsters that appear in her other books are here also. At least the heros, a young prince named Conrad and a much-abused, noble step-daughter, Sofia, both have a taint of misdeeds about them to make them more interesting. Sofia embodies many of the Cinderella stereotypes. Her father and mother are dead and she lives with a step-mother and two-step-sisters, all of whom are more "coarse" socially and physically than she. One twist from the legend is that Sofia's mother was Spanish and was skilled in her own kind of magic, some of which is at Sofia's disposal. She decides to escape from servitude in her stepmother's household by making a pact with a "green witch" Ilse, who turns out to be anything but a fairy godmother. Ilse is pursuing her own revenge on the fathers of Sofia and Conrad, who participated in burning to death her mother, Old Gerthe. By stepping outside the bounds of women's "Green Magic" and into men's "Gold Magic," Ilse has already succeeded in ridding herself of the older generation and hopes in one sweep to take care of the younger one. The plot turns around her various feats of magic and the many Gold and Green counter magics that Sofia and Prince Conrad use to protect themselves from Ilse and Conrad's father's wizard, Gustave. While there is justification for both Ilse and Gustave's actions, they are both portrayed as vain, over-confident, selfish, and shallow, so that their eventual defeat is predictable.

Emerson's most recent series, "Night-Threads," is a young-adult trilogy with two volumes currently published, *The Calling of the Three* and *The Two In Hiding*. Its most unique feature is readerly transference as it takes normal people from the here and now of earth into a parallel universe which resembles that of other Emerson novels. Emerson seems to have found her audience and her mode of expression in these heroic tales of female and male adventurers of nobility, wit, and charm.

—Janice M. Bogstad

---

**EMSHWILLER, Carol (née Fries).** American. Born in Ann Arbor, Michigan, 12 April 1921. Educated at the University of Michigan, Ann Arbor, B.A. in music and B. Design 1949; Ecole Nationale Supérieure des Beaux-Arts, Paris (Fulbright Fellow), 1949–50. Married the filmmaker Ed Emshwiller in 1949; two daughters and one son. Since 1978, member of the Continuing Education Faculty, New York University. Organized workshops for Science Fiction Bookstore, New York, 1975, 1976 and Clarion Science Fiction Workshop, 1978, 1979; guest teacher, Sarah Lawrence College, Bronxville, New York, 1983. Recipient: MacDowell Fellowship, 1971; Creative Artists Public Service Grant, 1975; National Endowment Grant, 1979; New York State Grant, 1988. Address: 210 East 15th Street, Apartment 12E, New York, New York, 10003, U.S.A.

### Science-Fiction Publications

Novel

*Carmen Dog*. London, Women's Press, 1988; San Francisco, California, Mercury House, 1990.

Short Stories

*Joy in Our Cause*. New York, Harper, 1974.
*Verging on the Pertinent*. Minneapolis, Minnesota, Coffee House Press, 1989.
*The Start of the End of It All*. London, Women's Press, 1990; San Francisco, California, Mercury House, 1991.

### Other Publications

Plays

Television Plays: *Pilobolis and Joan*, 1974; *Family Focus*, 1977.

*

Carol Emshwiller comments:

Formal/structural concerns have always interested me the most, so once I had learned to plot and had published numerous science-fiction stories (and a few mystery stories), I decided to learn how *not* to plot. My concerns were for the various ways of forming a story and keeping forward movement without plotting. This was as hard to learn as plotting (harder, because I had no models in those days) and had to be learned as slowly. Looking back, I see that I did away with plot elements one at a time. I was unable to let go of them by twos or threes. I'm not really exactly sure what I put in their place, one by one, but I did refer to modern poetry for inspiration and I took many modern poetry techniques as models for my stories. Sometimes I tried to write a "story" all "between the lines," leaving a lot of work for the reader. Sometimes I tried to create the illusion of action without there actually being any.

Also I tried to write, as in modern poetry (which is influenced in this, I think, by the Chinese and Japanese), without the use of simile or metaphoric language, and, I hope, without a trace of the pathetic fallacy. I also tried to do away with character, and substituted what I called "selves," which, in my mind, were much more real than "characters" (though perhaps just different). I used the first person and tried for a kind of internal, psychological realism. To me, the "selves" represented the insides of everybody . . . the little fleeting thoughts . . . the little vanities . . . things not admitted by any of us. Also big things not admitted: petty hates, oedipal feelings, incest . . .

Why might one bother doing this? Well, like most science-fiction writers, my study was "what-would-happen-if," but not what-would-happen-if the ice age returned, or if apes began teaching each other to talk, but what-would-happen-if, for instance, a story had only a single bit of action? or none? What could hold the interest? What could move it forward? However, I may have written myself into a hole by now. Plot seems to be slowly coming back into my work. I'm not sure where I'll go from here, but I'm sure that "structures" will be one of my primary concerns.

Of course, there's that other thing: that when your conscious mind is kept busy with forms, the subconscious mind can be freed to work on all those underground things that are, perhaps, more important to a story.

* * *

Though she is a prolific writer of short stories, until recently it has been hard for Carol Emshwiller to receive the recognition she richly deserves. Her stories were for a long time available only in magazines and general anthologies, but currently three collections are available. Many stories allude to alien invasions, humans with peculiarly alien characteristics or behavior, and mythical creatures who change from human to animal and vice versa or from human to plant. A varied and gripping set of lyrical studies, her fictions are virtuoso performances in language and thought. At once tongue-in-cheek and symbolic exposés of the human condition, many are reminiscent of Kafka, but a Kafka with a light and witty touch, who chortles playfully as she plunges us into a grim reflection on, for example, man's inhumanity to woman. While Emshwiller's topoi are reminiscent of Kafka, her style and sense of humor conjure up Calvino's *Cosmicomics*.

Present, like a nagging itch, throughout is the understanding that we repress many distasteful truths about the relationships between men and women as well as between humans and those creatures who share the earth with us. Because Emshwiller often narrates in the first person, from the female perspective, one can assume she is speaking for women and against men. However, no one can read *Carmen Dog*, her novel, or her very well-known "Sex and/or Mr. Morrison," and not notice the satirical presentation of women's weaknesses, vanities, and confusion about their own desires. This is not to say that women and men are presented in equal positions of power, but rather that Emshwiller will not allow us easy answers to the inequalities and division of power and what motivates or sustains it.

The most delightful feature of Emshwiller's fiction is its allusive and often allegorical characterizations. *Carmen Dog* is an extended example of what can be called her use of sliding signifieds. Pooch is the central character in a rebellion of females against males, but it is a rebellion that manifests itself physically before it reaches the level of consciousness. Were Emshwiller merely to describe a world in which women were turning into animals because of their centuries-old treatment as such, she would have created an interesting story. She does not stop with this treatment, however, because her animals are also turning into women. House pets such as cats, dogs, and snakes, gradually take over the duties that their mistresses abandon, to varying degrees and with varying success.

The novel opens with Pooch's master and mistress consulting a psychologist to try and save their marriage. One can tell, however, that the psychologist is advising the husband more than the wife as he says "you say she was a fairly good wife and mother, though somewhat irritating at times, and you want her back that way as soon as possible? You must realize, however, that she is at this very moment in a period of profound change, both physical and psychological." But the psychologist, who later sets himself up to save "motherhood" by running behavioral experiments on the animal-women and women-animals, knows this is also a widespread trend and speaks of them "as if they all had eaten an apple from the tree of a different kind of knowledge and have seen with new eyes, not that they are naked, but have seen that they are clothed." Pooch is alternately eager to take up what her mistress has abandoned, including the care of the baby and the love of the husband, and offended at the demands made by crude men on her body. Thus, as with the other transitional creatures, she just can't manage to be either the perfect wife or the perfect rebel until all avenues are closed to her but the latter. In fact, a more bemused bunch of individuals than the characters, male and female, in this story, would be hard to find. The endearing sincerity of Pooch, the simplistic, sybaritic eagerness of the men around her, and the puzzled meanderings of her female friends propel the reader through this allegory.

*Joy in Our Cause* was Emshwiller's first collection of fiction, but we now have two more recent collections. *The Start of the End of It All* gives us 18 short stories, including "Sex And/or Mr. Morrison" and "Chicken Icarus." Reviewers have mentioned the cat-loathing aliens of the collection's title story, but equally delightful are the creatures of "Draculalucard" and "Moon Song," to mention only a couple.

*Verging on the Pertinent* opens with "Yukon," in which a woman leaves the human brute she started out with and chooses instead a male black bear, winters with him, and then finds a third, more satisfying partner. Even the titles of her stories are intriguing: "Mental Health and its Alternatives," "There is no God but Bog," "What Every Woman Knows," "The Futility of Fixed Positions," "Queen Kong," and the title story, "Verging on the Pertinent," a sassy, irreverent gloss on the absurdity of positions assigned to "remarkable" women to set them apart and deny the potential of all women as full people. All of Emshwiller's stories rely on suggestion, resonance, and symbol. "Queen Kong," the ironic pose of the narrator shifts from the male to female positions at will. This comment about a large woman is typical, and typically evocative: "They are against all elegances, and no wonder, when even seeing them at a distance or simply in silhouette is unnerving. But the potential of large women! The huge, unrealized potential! Their great longings, their colossal grudges, their long-term memories, their rage! No wonder they deny all art . . . deny all civilization and try to convince their tiny, more discreet sisters to join them."

It is possible to misunderstand Emshwiller. If one reads a single purpose into the multilayered allusions, one can be taken aback by the bald, almost gallows humor which cuts to the core of ambiguities that make up women's attitudes towards themselves and the cultures which encase them. One can never quite determine which of the speaker's statements should be taken ironically and which are authoritative. Emshwiller's grace, technical virtuosity, insight, humor, and depth rest in the narrators who never settle on a single or simple political position and therefore reflect this ambiguity of intent.

—Janice M. Bogstad

---

**ENGDAHL, Sylvia (Louise).** American. Born in Los Angeles, California, 24 November 1933. Educated at Pomona College, Claremont, California, 1950; Reed College, Portland, Oregon, 1951; University of Oregon, Eugene, 1951–52, 1956–57; University of California, Santa Barbara, B.A. in education 1955; graduate work in anthropology, Portland State University, Oregon, 1978–80. Elementary school teacher, Portland, 1955–56;

programmer, then computer systems specialist, SAGE Air Defense System, Lexington, Massachusetts, Madison, Wisconsin, Tacoma, Washington, and Santa Monica, California, 1957–67; full-time writer, 1968–80; self-employed developer and vendor of home computer software, 1981–84. Since 1985, staff member, Connected Education Inc., New York. Recipient: Newberry award, 1971; Christopher award, 1973; Phoenix award, 1990. Address: 3088 Delta Pines Drive, Eugene, Oregon 97401, U.S.A.

SCIENCE-FICTION PUBLICATIONS (for young people)

Novels (series: Elana; Noren)

*Enchantress from the Stars* (Elana). New York, Atheneum, 1970; London, Gollancz, 1974.
*Journey Between Worlds.* New York, Atheneum, 1970.
*The Far Side of Evil* (Elana). New York, Atheneum, 1971; London, Gollancz, 1975.
*The Star Shall Abide* (Noren). New York, Atheneum, 1972; as *Heritage of the Star*, London, Gollancz, 1973.
*Beyond the Tomorrow Mountains* (Noren). New York, Atheneum, 1973.
*The Doors of the Universe* (Noren). New York, Atheneum, 1981.

Uncollected Short Stories

"The Beckoning Trail," with Rick Roberson, in *Universe Ahead*, edited by Engdahl and Roberson. New York, Atheneum, 1975.
"Timescape," with Mildred Butler, in *Anywhere, Anywhen*, edited by Engdahl. New York, Atheneum, 1976.

OTHER PUBLICATIONS (for young people)

Other

*The Planet-Girded Suns: Man's View of Other Solar Systems.* New York, Atheneum, 1974.
*The Subnuclear Zoo: New Discoveries in High Energy Physics*, with Rick Roberson. New York, Atheneum, 1977.
*Tool for Tomorrow: New Knowledge about Genes*, with Rick Roberson. New York, Atheneum, 1979.
*Our World Is Earth.* New York, Atheneum, 1979.

Editor, with Rick Roberson, *Universe Ahead: Stories of the Future.* New York, Atheneum, 1975.
Editor, *Anywhere, Anywhen; Stories of Tomorrow.* New York, Atheneum, 1976.

*

Sylvia Engdahl comments (1985):

I have encountered a good deal of misunderstanding concerning the audience for which my novels are intended, and I would like to clear it up. In the first place, though the present structure of the publishing business requires them to be issued as children's books, my novels are not meant for children; they are directed to older teenagers and young adults. Some exceptional pre-adolescents enjoy them, but do not grasp all their levels and on the whole find them heavy reading, since they are not primarily action stories. Their main emphasis is on the significance of space exploration, man's place in the universe, and human values I consider universal: all themes in which I believe today's young people are seriously interested.

In the second place, my novels do not fit the "science fiction" category much better than the "children's book" category; they aren't category books at all. Although they are set in future or hypothetical worlds, they are not directed toward fans of genre-oriented SF—they are meant for a general audience. They are not exotic enough to suit many SF fans, and *this is intentional.* My use of themes already old to the "fan" audience is also intentional. My aim is to reach readers who do not have a special background and do not care for fiction that seems far removed from real life, readers who find most SF too "far-out" for their tastes. I feel strongly that the future is not something that should be set apart and discussed only in literature of a particular type, directed to readers of a specific genre. The future is important to everyone, not just to those who choose to become familiar with the conventions and jargon of genre-oriented books. My chief goal is to place it in perspective in relation to the past and present, as well as to offer an affirmative outlook toward a universe wider than the single planet Earth. There is a desperate need, I believe, for fiction that conveys such themes to people beyond the comparatively small circle of SF fandom, and I therefore purposely market my own work outside that circle. I'm happy, of course, when people within the SF field like it; but I'm even happier when other people tell me they thought they didn't like space stories until they read mine. In my opinion, expansion into space is essential to human survival, and promoting that idea among readers who are not already space enthusiasts will remain my primary concern.

* * *

In her foreword to *Anywhere, Anywhen*, Sylvia Engdahl makes explicit her reasons for not wanting to be classified as an SF writer. She addresses the problem of esotericism in the genre: conventions which guide the initiated reader are potentially alienating to the reader from outside the genre. Engdahl believes that the problems of the future are of interest to everyone, not only the fans of a specific field of literature (appropriately the stories in the above mentioned collection are by writers not normally associated with SF). With this in mind, Engdahl tries to avoid the jargon often associated with SF, the hard-core writer's emphasis on projections of technological innovation and the traditional conventions of space opera. Nevertheless, she works firmly *within* the field—justifying the fantastic elements of her stories in a substantial atmosphere of scientific credibility. Indeed, science and, in particular, the scientific method, play an important role in her narratives.

"Timescape," a novella written with her mother (Mildred Butler) for the *Anywhere, Anywhen* collection, serves as a useful introduction to Engdahl's works, containing themes common throughout her fiction. Alienation from society, the difficult quest for one's true identity, freedom of thought vs. authority and scholastic instruction: these are problems the protagonist Mark faces. An unwitting participant in a unique time-travel experiment, he is forced to approach his environment with a critical mind; to question the things around him, as well as the deeply felt moral principles within him. Set in opposition is the blind faith of religion and the analytic faculties of the scientific mind—an opposition predominant in her novels.

*This Star Shall Abide, Beyond the Tomorrow Mountains*, and *The Doors of the Universe* form a complete series in which the central figure is Noren, a character very similar to Mark in "Timescape." Both are male adolescents, non-conformists, introspective in nature, and alienated from society. Noren is alienated because of his refusal to believe in a pseudo-religious legend which is the basis of social structure in a semi-feudal agrarian society. As a condemned heretic, he is sentenced to the mercy of the Scholars who live in a "holy" city. It is here that he undergoes a tortuous series of initiations and interrogations and learns of the desperate attempts of benevolent scientists to preserve their near-extinct race, after fleeing from a nova and settling on a poisonous planet. Noren's enquiring mind—as opposed to the blind acceptance of the majority of the villagers—his ability to doubt and to explore the world scientifically (by setting up hypotheses and testing them) are those qualities which qualify him for the dubious honour of joining the Scholars. Although Noren is willing to risk his life in order to challenge the essentially orthodox structure of his society, his greatest problems arise from self-doubts and intense personal scrutiny.

Presented in Engdahl's work is the concept of hierarchies of human evolution. The Noren series encompasses four stages of development: the primitive stage of the ignorant mutant savages; the "mediaeval" culture of the villagers, who see high technology as divine magic; the sophisticated scientific culture of the Scholars, who envision the Universe as a series of problems to be solved scientifically and—represented by Lianne, a visitor from another race—the higher culture, in which "magical" concepts, such as psi powers, are encompassed within a comprehensive, advanced scientific frame-work. In the stories which have Elana as their protagonist (*Enchantress from the Stars* and *The Far Side of Evil*) three stages are represented: the primitive, the industrial, and the higher. Elana is of the higher culture—a member of an Anthropological Service—and her anthropological skills are tested when she has to aid an "inferior," less advanced culture, without interfering with their normal rate of progress. Principles of non-interference are of central importance in all of Engdahl's writings, love-interest often complicating these principles.

To Engdahl, the stars are symbols of knowledge, hope, and human-kind's destiny. The outwardly focused vision of her stories presents space exploration as a) the salvation of threatened races, and b) the next stage in our youthful races's progression towards cultural and scientific adulthood. She goes as far as to say that space exploration is essential to the survival of our race.

Engdahl's SF is not easy to read. Her narratives are detailed and perhaps overly long, visual detail rejected in favour of copious dialogue and commentary. The minute workings of her protagonists's minds are foregrounded, at the expense of dramatic action. However, although demanding texts, they are rewarding for those willing to work at them. While readers might be left uneasy about her frequent presentation of benevolent tyrannies, she forces her audience to think seriously about the nature of free will and freedom of expression. Nevertheless, there is an awkward contradiction between her affirmation of the basic equality of human beings and her rationalisation of elaborate caste systems. However, her narratives are deeply concerned with morality and, while sometimes a little didactic in style, they are compassionate and intensely reasoned, providing engaging reading, and are guaranteed to provoke thought.

—Mark Warwick Leahy

---

**ENGH, M(ary) J(ane).** Has also written as M.J. Ferguson; Bird Ferguson; Jane Beauclerk. American. Born in McLeansboro, Illinois, 26 January 1933. Educated at University of Chicago, B.A. 1951; University of Illinois, Champaign-Urbana, B.A. 1953; University of Oklahoma, Norman, M.L.S. 1973. Married 1) David W. Ferguson in 1954 (divorced 1960), two sons; 2) Richard Engh in 1963 (divorced 1969). Library assistant, University of Chicago, 1954–55; assistant librarian, *American People's Encyclopedia*, Chicago, 1955–56; writer for correspondence course research project, U.S. Navy, Chicago, 1957–58; editorial assistant, 1959–61, and associate editor, 1961–63, Scott, Foresman, and Company, Chicago; teacher in public schools, McLeansboro, Illinois, 1964–65; editor, C.E. Tuttle and Company, Tokyo, 1966–67; library clerk, 1971–72, and assistant biological sciences librarian, 1973–79, Oklahoma State University, Stillwater; reference librarian, Owen Science and Engineering Library, Washington State University, Pullman, 1979–85. Agent: Virginia Kidd, Virginia Kidd Literary Agency, Box 278, 538 East Harford Street, Milford, Pennsylvania 18337. Address: 720 Illinois Street N.E., Pullman, Washington 99163, U.S.A.

### Science-Fiction Publications

Novels

*Arslan.* New York, Warner, 1976; as *A Wind from Bukhara*, London, Grafton, 1989.

*The House in the Snow* (for children). New York, Orchard, 1987.

*Wheel of the Winds.* New York, Tor, 1988; London, Grafton, 1989.

*

M.J. Engh comments:

I don't remember who said, "Consistent writers make more money, but adventurous writers have more fun." Certainly it makes good sense, commercially and even aesthetically, for a writer to stick to one or a few types of writing. You can explore your niche to its innermost recesses, bring your techniques to perfection, and yes, make more money. Readers and publishers alike prefer to buy products with labels.

The trouble is that labels become ID cards. I don't want to be defined by what I wrote last decade or last year. The universe isn't divided into isolated packets. Everything interconnects. How can I not follow some of the threads that lead from one niche to a myriad others?

One thread I've been following for more than twenty years is this: We live in a universe in which people do hideous things to one another. And the first question is not "What, if anything, should I do about these horrors?" It's more basic: "How, if at all, can I live with the knowledge that horrors exist?"

But telling people that horrors exist turns out to be oddly difficult. If you show the horror, people quickly get used to it. If you discuss it at a distance, you lose impact. In "The Oracle," I tried a third way, which may be the most direct: showing not the horrible events, but horror itself in the protagonist's mind.

Of course, the universe isn't uniformly grim and grisly; the universe isn't uniform. This means I can write humor or adventure stories, historical realism or children's picture books, with equal enthusiasm. Finding an adventurous publisher is harder.

* * *

M.J. Engh does not follow the usual pattern of genre writers; her unique qualities show up in a number of ways. Recently recognized as a science-fiction writer of stature, she has been publishing poetry since 1955 (as M.J. or Bird Ferguson), and science fiction since 1964 (as Jane Beauclerk). Among the many whose first published science-fiction book died unnoticed in paperback, she stands almost alone as one who reissued the same book, *Arslan*, ten years later in hardcover, to public favor and critical acclaim. Science fiction, generally considered a genre that dates readily, rarely reprints any but the most popular books. David Hartwell of Arbor House proudly takes credit for spotting the excellence of *Arslan*, for engineering its re-publication, and even for insisting that the hardcover edition have a non-sf dust jacket design. Algis Budrys has called *Arslan* a "genuine work of speculative political science." The book provides an unusual glimpse into the power—and the limitations—of one charismatic individual. It develops a double agenda: the actions of the dictator and the refusal to act on the part of the "good" man both show us to ourselves.

Character development drives Engh's fiction. In *Arslan*, she shows the title character through the eyes of two of his victims, and all three come astonishingly alive in this end-of-the-world novel which (unusually) avoids nuclear holocaust. In following this interest, she takes great literary risks. "The Oracle," an in-depth, first-person-narrative study of a damaged psyche, is reminiscent of the first section of Faulkner's *The Sound and the Fury*. Her second novel, *Wheel of the Winds*, is narrated entirely from the point of view of humanoid (but not *human*) characters whose quasi-medieval society is about to undergo radical change from contact with Terrans. This means that the reader must provide the connections between what the characters know, but do not discuss, and the plot.

Having captured a lost and incapacitated Terran, the natives in *Wheel of the Winds* must decide what to do with him. The most obvious course is to kill him; they do not take it. Instead, after his escape, two of them allow him to enlist them in a "marvelous voyage" around their own planet—locked on its axis, thus creating the "wheel of the winds"—to retrieve his equipment and signal his people. That this does not serve either the natives or their planet as they might hope is shown honestly, with an appropriate touch of remorse.

Following Heinlein's example, Engh does not explain anything in her characters' world that they would obviously know about, choosing to show in action how things work. But the characters in *Wheel of the Winds* don't know a great deal about their own world; much of it is unexplored, dark, and stormy, and they have much less understanding of its physical character than does the Terran, who does not (in some senses, *cannot*) explain it to them. Engh clearly has worked out the technical details of her story, including the limitations of language. Often, this works very well indeed; here, Engh's peculiarly matter-of-fact narrative voice seems to work against her.

Along with her strengths of characterization, Engh has great ability to describe physical setting and physical effort. This forms the structural basis of *Wheel of the Winds*, and is particularly noticeable in "The Oracle." Her depiction of the Philippines, where she has lived, breathes alienation and ambiance from every page. Using only the voice of a limited, almost pre-lingual narrator in "Moon Blood," one of her most successful short works, she conveys a remarkable sense of prehistoric place.

Shaping a fiction is, perhaps, Engh's most serious weakness. *Arslan* is her best crafted long work to date. *Wheel of the Winds* seems unevenly paced. Engh's flair for character development sometimes stretches a piece out of shape, as it does in "Penelope Comes Home," where background details, metaphoric resonances, and episodes of characterization almost derail the rather standard plot. On the other hand, "Moon Blood" is very tightly organized.

Engh faces a problem common to writers who work in many genres: few of her tales fit accepted molds. She simultaneously engages and frustrates her reader's assumptions. Like other writers more dedicated to exploring their craft rather than marketing it, Engh consistently stretches generic boundaries. This has not served her well, as far as publication goes. While *Wheel of the Winds* stands as her second novel, she considers it her fifth, following a mainstream novel about the French nuclear test program in the Pacific; "The Oracle"; and the first volume of an historical trilogy. The other novels are completed but still (at this writing) unsold. In the summer of 1991, she is at work on the second volume of the historical trilogy and another science-fiction novel, this one dealing with the moral consequences of making theological choices, "rather than the usual Nasty Fundamentalist Totalitarian stuff." Engh is endlessly interested in what makes people "human," the worthiest, most difficult, and most fascinating of all literary topics.

—Martha A. Bartter

---

**ENGLAND, George Allan.** American. Born in Fort McPherson, Nebraska, 9 February 1877. Educated at Harvard University, Cambridge, Massachusetts, B.A. 1902 (Phi Beta Kappa); M.A. 1903. Married; one daughter. Regular contributor to Munsey magazines until his retirement from writing, 1931; chicken farmer from 1931. Socialist candidate for Congress, 1908, and for governor of Maine, 1912. *Died 26 June 1936.*

SCIENCE-FICTION PUBLICATIONS

Novels

*Darkness and Dawn.* Boston, Small Maynard, 1914; as *Darkness and Dawn, Beyond the Great Oblivion, The People of the Abyss, Out of the Abyss*, and *The Afterglow*, New York, Avalon, 5 vols., 1965–67.
*The Air Trust.* St. Louis, Phil Wagner, 1915.
*The Golden Blight.* New York, H.K. Fly, 1916.
*Cursed.* Boston, Small Maynard, 1919.
*The Flying Legion.* Chicago, McClurg, 1920.
*Elixir of Hate.* Laurel, New York, Lightyear, 1976.

Uncollected Short Stories

"The Lunar Advertising Co. Ltd.," in *Munsey* (New York), 1906.
"The House of the Green Flame," in *All-Story* (New York), September 1908.
"My Time-Annihilator," in *All-Story* (New York), June 1909.
"The House of Transmutation," in *Scrap Book* (New York), September 1909.
"Beyond White Seas," in *All-Story* (New York), December 1909.
"The Million Dollar Patch," in *All-Story* (New York), June 1912.
"The Crime Detector," in *Cavalier* (New York), 22 February 1913.
"The Empire in the Air," in *All-Story Weekly* (New York), 14 November 1914.
"The Fatal Gift," in *All-Story Weekly* (New York), 4 September 1915.
"The Tenth Question," in *All-Story Weekly* (New York), 18 December 1915.
"The Nebula of Death," in *People's Favorite* (New York), 10 February–10 May 1918.
"Drops of Death," in *Munsey* (New York), January 1922.
"The Man with the Glass Heart," in *Famous Fantastic Mysteries* (New York), November 1939.

"The Thing from Outside," in *Friendly Aliens*, edited by John Robert Colombo. Toronto, Houslow Press, 1981.

OTHER PUBLICATIONS

Novels

*The Alibi.* Boston, Small Maynard, 1916.
*Pod, Bender, & Co.* New York, McBride, 1916; London, Laurie, 1919.
*The Gift Supreme.* New York, Doran, 1916.
*The Greater Crime.* London, Cassell, 1917.
*Keep Off the Grass.* Boston, Small Maynard, 1919.

Verse

*Underneath the Bough.* New York, Grafton Press, 1903.

Other

*Socialism and the Law.* Fort Scott, Kansas, Monitor, 1913.
*The Story of the Appeal.* Privately printed, 1915(?).
*Isles of Romance.* New York, Century, 1920.
*Vikings of the Ice.* New York, Doubleday, and London, Heinemann, 1924; as *The White Wilderness*, London, Cassell, 1924; as *The Greatest Hunt in the World*, Montreal, Tundra, 1969.
*Adventure Isle* (for children). New York, Century, 1926.

Translator, *Their Son, The Necklace*, by Eduardo Zamacois. New York, Boni and Liveright, 1919.

*   *   *

Although George Allan England lived well into the era of specialized science-fiction magazines, he never wrote any original works for them. His works appeared, for the most part, in the variety pulp magazines published by Frank A. Munsey and edited by Bob Davis. England's heyday was the decade between 1910 and 1920.

By far England's most important work of science fiction is *Darkness and Dawn.* This massive effort was originally published as three separate serials, then as a single volume. In this work a heavy anaesthetic gas sweeps over the entire world, at first rendering unconscious and ultimately killing those who breathe it. One man and one woman, however, in an office in the top story of the Flatiron Building in New York, receive only a partial dose of the gas. They sleep for centuries and revive to find a world in ruins. The revived couple struggle to rebuild their lives, encountering a race of super-evolved intelligent rats, barbaric degenerate humans, and finally a lost civilization cut off from the rest of the world for hundreds of years. The book is highly successful as an adventure tale and as a study of courage and perseverance on the part of the survivors. An unfortunate element of racism is present in this and in several other of the author's works, though England was largely following the conventions of popular literature of his day; he did not originate these attitudes, and did not press them very emphatically.

*The Flying Legion*, although not as widely remembered as *Darkness and Dawn*, is deserving of recognition in its own more modest right. It reflected a convention of its time, the assumption that World War I veterans, returning to the drab realities of civilian, peacetime existence, would suffer from intolerable boredom and would be driven to seek excitement in such fields as might offer danger and exotic adventures. In *The Flying Legion* just such a party of veterans assemble. One of them, to add a fillip, is a beautiful young woman in disguise. This legion hijacks the world's largest and most advanced aircraft (choosing to do so rather than buy it despite their immense joint wealth) and sets out to find adventure in the unknown regions of the Arabian desert. In outline the book is an exercise in cliché, yet it is executed with such verve and color as to be irresistible even to the modern reader.

Few of England's other science fiction works were issued in volume form. *Elixir of Hate* deals with research into a youth serum; the serum is perfected, stolen, swallowed by the thief who then discovers that he has taken an overdose and is reduced to infancy. England's two "socialist novels" both contain science-fiction elements. *The Air Trust* deals with greedy capitalists who corner air and sell the very breath of life for profit. *The Golden Blight* is concerned with a revolutionary who discovers a method by which he can destroy all the gold that exists, thereby bringing about the collapse of the entire world's economy. Both these books are heavy on polemic and of little value as works of fiction, although interesting examples of their sort, and comparable to such socialist science fiction as Jack London's *The Iron Heel.*

A number of England's unreprinted works are rewarding. "The Empire in the Air," concerning an invasion of earth from the fourth dimension, might be compared with the space operas of the 1920's and 1930's, although it appeared in 1914. "The Nebula of Death" involves the passage of the earth through a cosmic cloud which absolutely inhibits photosynthesis; the novel is comparable, in different ways, to *The Second Deluge* by Garrett P. Serviss and *Brain Wave* by Poul Anderson.

—Richard A. Lupoff

---

**ENGLISH, Richard.** *See* **SHAVER, Richard S.**

---

**ENNIS, Robert D.** *See* **TUBB, E.C.**

---

**ESHBACH, Lloyd Arthur.** American. Born in Palm, Pennsylvania, 20 June 1910. Attended school to the tenth grade; Charles Morris Price School of Advertising and Journalism, Philadelphia. Married Helen Margaret Richards in 1931 (died 1978); two sons. Worked for department stores, 1925–41; advertising copywriter, Glidden Paint Company, Reading, Pennsylvania, 1941–50; publisher, Fantasy Press, Reading, 1950–58, and Church Center Press, Myerstown, Pennsylvania, 1958–63; advertising manager, 1963–68, and sales representative, 1968–75, Moody Press, Chicago; clergyman for three small churches in eastern Pennsylvania, 1975–78. Recipient: Milford award, 1988. Agent: James Allen, Virginia Kidd, Box 278, Milford, Pennsylvania 18337. Address: 220 South Railroad Street, Myerstown, Pennsylvania 17067, U.S.A.

SCIENCE-FICTION PUBLICATIONS

Short Stories

*The Tyrant of Time.* Reading, Pennsylvania, Fantasy Press, 1955.

Uncollected Short Stories

"The Man with the Silver Disc," in *Scientific Detective* (New York), February 1930.
"The Invisible Destroyer," in *Air Wonder Stories* (New York), May 1930.
"The Gray Plague," in *Astounding* (New York), November 1930.
"The Valley of Titans," in *Amazing* (New York), March 1931.
"The Light from Infinity," in *Amazing* (New York), March 1932.
"The Man with the Hour Glass," in *Marvel Tales* (Los Angeles), May 1934.
"Cosmos" (part 15), in *Fantasy* , September 1934.
"The Brain of Ali Kahn," in *Wonder Stories* (New York), October 1934.
"The Kingdom of Thought," in *Amazing* (New York), August 1935.
"The Outpost on Ceres," in *Amazing* (New York), October 1936.
"Out of the Past," in *Tales of Wonder* (Kingwood, Surrey), Autumn 1938.
"Mutineers of Space," in *Dynamic* (Chicago), February 1939.
"Dust," in *Marvel* (New York), August 1939.
"Three Wise Men," in *Startling* (New York), November 1939.
"The Shadows from Hesplon," in *Science Fiction* (Holyoke, Massachusetts), October 1940.
"The Hyper Sense," in *Startling* (New York), January 1941.
"Out of the Sun," in *Fantasy Book 4* (Los Angeles), 1949.
"Overlord of Earth," in *Marvel* (New York), November 1950.
"The Fuzzies," in *Fantastic Universe* (Chicago), July 1957.
"A Voice from the Ether," in *The History of the Science Fiction Magazine 1* , by Michael Ashley. London, New English Library, 1974.

OTHER PUBLICATIONS

Novels

*The Land Beyond the Gate.* New York, Ballantine, 1984.
*The Armlet of the Gods.* New York, Ballantine, 1986.
*The Sorceress of Seath.* New York, Ballantine, 1988.
*The Scroll of Lucifer.* New York, Ballantine, 1990.

Plays

Radio Series, with H. Donald Spatz: *The Crimson Phantom, The Bronze Buddha, Tales of the Crystal, Cupid's Capers, The Pennington Saga, The Doings of the Dinwiddies,* and *Tales of Tomorrow*, 1933–35.

Other

*Over My Shoulder: Reflections on a Science Fiction Era.* Philadelphia, Train, 1983.

Editor, *Of Worlds Beyond: The Science of Science-Fiction Writing.* Reading, Pennsylvania, Fantasy Press, 1947; London, Dobson, 1965.
Editor, *Subspace Encounter*, by E.E. Smith. New York, Berkley, 1983; London, Panther, 1984.
Editor, *Alicia in Blunderland*, by P. Schuyler Miller. Philadelphia, Train, 1983.

*

Manuscript Collection: Temple University, Philadelphia.

Lloyd Arthur Eshbach comments:

The editors have invited introductory comments about my work. In preparation for such comment I've reread a cross section of the stories I wrote, the last one published well over two decades ago, the earliest almost 50 years in the past. Most of my stories were as unfamiliar as if they were the efforts of a stranger.

The reading was an interesting experience. Some of the stories made me cringe, they were so incredibly bad. Others were a surprise: they were better than I thought possible. Indeed, a few actually pleased me. In self-defense I believe I should say that in the 1930's a comparative handful of youthful pioneers were breaking new trails in fiction. Most of us were amateurs trying to learn our craft. A fairly new idea and a minimal ability to put thoughts into words sufficed to produce a salable story. In short, we learned by doing, received the encouragement of publication for our efforts, and even payment (such as it was) as frosting on a cake. Characters were one-dimensional and stereotyped, conversations were stilted, action usually was melodramatic, and literary style was either derivative or non-existent—but there was that often-referred to "sense of wonder" born of youthful enthusiasm and uninhibited imagination.

My first accepted story, written in 1928 when I was 18, was "A Voice from the Ether," though in order of publication it was fifth. An earlier version of "The Valley of Titans" preceded it, but the complete rewrite and expansion took place more than a year after the completion and acceptance of "A Voice from the Ether." The fact that the latter story was selected by Michael Ashley for his *History of the Science Fiction Magazine* (1974) as a representative story for 1931 was most gratifying.

As I write (March 1979) I have almost reached my three score and ten—and in my retirement years I've resumed writing. My first effort, well along in production, is an informal history of a science-fiction era—the story of the ground-breaking careers of the specialty hardback SF publishers of the 1940's. Upon its completion I plan to write a science-fantasy novel I started plotting 30 years ago. I hope I've learned something about life and about writing during three decades. If I have, I may be giving the youngsters some competition after all these years.

(1985) In the five years and eleven months that have passed since I wrote the preceding paragraphs, I have been quite busy. The informal history of the specialist science fiction publishers of the 1930's, '40's, and '50's, called *Over My Shoulder: Reflections on a Science Fiction Era*, was published in 1983. Following the completion of my reminiscences, I finished writing the last SF novel of E.E. "Doc" Smith, left in a fragmentary state at his death in 1965, *Subspace Encounter.* My name appears as "Edited and with an Introduction by Lloyd Arthur Eshbach." This was according to my decision, though I would have been justified in calling it a collaboration, since I wrote more than 12,000 words of it, did the final polishing, connected various scenes in logical sequence with the necessary transitions, etc. However, it was his story and I wanted him to receive full credit. We were close friends.

In 1983 I edited and wrote the introduction for *Alicia in Blunderland* by P. Schuyler Miller, a science fictional parody of *Alice in Wonderland*, which appeared as a serial in a SF fan magazine in 1933–34. Earlier, in 1980, I wrote the science fantasy novel I referred to in my initial comments. It did not sell, and after putting it aside for a year I saw why. It needs a complete rewriting which I plan to do after completion of my present project. This project is a tetralogy based on mythology, largely Celtic mythology, though venturing into the myths and legends of other lands and times. The first novel in this series, *The Land Beyond the Gate*, was published in 1984. The second novel, *The Armlet of the Gods*, already written and under contract, is in the editor's possession. I expect to complete the writing of the third novel within the next six months, and the fourth early in 1986.

(1991) My writing in the last decade has been largely in the field of fantasy based on the prehistory and mythology of ancient peoples. I have a science fiction novel in the works which I hope one day to complete, but I find writing fantasy more enjoyable. Fantasy requires far more research than science fiction (as I write it) but I enjoy the research. After all, I write to please two people—myself first and then the editor. If the readers like what I produce, that's a bonus.

* * *

Though he was on the scene as a writer in the formative 1930's, Lloyd Arthur Eshbach's real impact on the field—and it was a substantial one—was in his role as a publisher. Having been involved mostly behind the scenes with William Crawford's *Marvel Tales* and other ventures before the war and then with the Hadley group that began the specialist press era, he organized Fantasy Press, which was to prove the most significant imprint in the period when science fiction moved into book publication in its own right. He understood what was needed better than the other hopefuls trying to do the same things, and his judgment reflected thorough knowledge and appreciation of the first two decades of explicit science fiction in the early magazines.

The symposium *Of Worlds Beyond: The Science of Science-Fiction Writing*, which he instigated in 1947, is memorable as the first book on modern science fiction, and though not critically profound its common-sense analysis based on leading writers's practical experience made it an important work for the serious reader, and it answered most of the fumbling attempts at criticism by outsiders in its time.

Like the other presses in the movement, Eshbach's operated almost entirely by putting popular magazine serials into book form with the occasional short story collection. Their near-monopoly of the book field did not last long enough—less than ten years—for them to move on to presenting new works as a serious undertaking, and there was little scope for editorial skills. He acknowledges, however, that he did substantial revision work verging on collaboration in a few cases such as the later Campbell books he produced. More recently he ably linked E.E. Smith's disconnected fragments of unfinished work into the new novel *Subspace Encounter*.

His own stories do not amount to a large body of work and are too diverse to characterize readily. We cannot identify any distinct trend or theme. But while a few are no more than potboilers most are full of original or at least unusual thoughts. The main fault, in fact, as in many writers of the period, is the multiplicity of new and revelatory concepts that jostle for the reader's attention and are not properly explored. The Mad Scientist, stock character of the time, appears in several cases as a threat to society and originator of the action. In "The Valley of Titans" he operates as an air pirate from a dinosaur-infested enclave, and incidentally creates a community of ape-people by evolutionary experiments. Introduction of an underground realm of pre-human energy beings and a godlike alien power is confusing.

In "The Invisible Destroyer" the dissident genius undertaking to dictate to the world, evidently single-handed, is trying to prevent the peaceable establishment of a world state. His objections are logical and—taken out of context and disregarding how economic and ideological forces interact in the 1980's—make good sense, and there is no attempt to refute them. "Vibration," a popular all-embracing basis for marvels around 1930, produces not only novel weaponry but access to other coexistent worlds, and a higher civilization thus found is induced to intervene.

Biological warfare figures in "The Gray Plague," the Venusians planning to eliminate Man with a fatal pandemic to leave earth clear to occupy. "Out of the Past" points out one of many criminal misuses of time travel that make it undesirable. "Dust" concisely introduces one possible hazard of interplanetary contact: bringing back dormant foreign life forms as spores. "The Meteor Miners" (*The Tyrant of Time*) shows a possible future space-based industry in a rare anticipation of ordinary working life in another era. "The Outpost on Ceres," in which aliens threaten a refueling base, also deals with a future working environment, and is notable for its sensible treatment of a drug dependence problem.

"The Time Conqueror" (*The Tyrant of Time*) is a notable early contribution to the tradition of the disembodied brain. Developing enhanced power and insight, the immortal brain makes itself world dominant, and we are shown episodes in successively remote times. Despite the rather exaggeratedly emotive language it is still an interesting and effective tale. "The Kingdom of Thought" combines the theme of time travel bringing together people from many eras with that of physically degenerate and intellectually potent super-humans of a remote future, evolved into good and evil branches with irreconcilable differences. The Cummings concept of size-change and sub-microscopic worlds is carried to extremes in two stories. In "A Voice from the Ether" the familiar Mad Scientist brings up a deadly parasitic organism from subatomic size and destroys his world, Mars. In "The Light from Infinity" humanoids from a supra-universe shrink down and attack earth, foiled by an expedition that uses their size-changer to reach the supra-world and retaliate. Needless to say, the paradoxes are ignored. "The Shadows from Hesplon" is a fourth dimension story, in which nasties from a higher dimensional plane use hypnotic means to have physical entry points made for them. It is unusual for making considerable efforts to visualize wholly alien experiences.

Eshbach's work, strong in content at the expense of form, helped build up the range of unconventional visions and fancies that early science fiction displayed, though he was less successful in controlling and resolving them.

—Graham Stone

---

**EVANS, Christopher.** British. Born in 1951. Address: c/o Unwin Hyman Publishers, 77-85 Fulhum Palace Road, London W6 8JB, England.

SCIENCE-FICTION PUBLICATIONS

Novels

*Capella's Golden Eyes.* London, Faber, 1980; New York, Ace, 1982.
*The Insider.* London, Faber, 1981.
*In Limbo.* London, Panther, 1985.

### Other Publications

Other

*Writing Science Fiction.* London, Black, and New York, St. Martin's Press, 1988.

Editor, with Robert Holdstock, *Other Edens.* London, Unwin Hyman, 3 vols., 1987–89.

* * *

Christopher Evans's first novel was the understated *Capella's Golden Eyes,* a rather traditional story about Gaia, a human colony world ruled by an alien race, the M'threnni. It's a competent adventure, told through the eyes of its young protagonist, David. His glimpses into the workings of his world—where slavery of an insidious kind is carried on for economic reasons—and his reaction to that knowledge eventually result in the departure of the aliens and the re-establishment of contact with Earth.

A great improvement was *The Insider,* a contemporary novel utilizing the device of alien takeover. This "take-over" (and reasonable doubt is left as to whether we interpret it as genuine or as psychosis) sees Stephen Marsh, the central figure, alienated from his beautiful Indian wife and made to suffer a form of estrangement from self. The novel is acutely realistic in its psychological portrayals and is a huge leap from conventional genre approaches to such material.

Rooted very much in the same heartland, Evans' third novel, *In Limbo,* fused similar elements, matching a near-contemporary setting with another quasi-science-fictional device—that of the prisoner trapped within an enigmatic enclosed environment (à la Thomas M. Disch). Unlike *The Insider,* however, the SF trappings are here detrimental to the story, which, when dealing with the reality of the protagonist, Carpenter's life as a sexually-active young male, proves a moving, funny, and highly readable moral fable.

Evans is a slow, painstaking writer, producing little published work. His projected fourth novel, *Chimeras,* is in essence a fix-up of six novelettes written and published over a long period. Vendavo, the protagonist of *Chimeras,* is the great artist of his age, creating "chimeras"—mind sculptures which take on a solid (if fragile) reality in the air. The fragmented story of his life and artistic development is counterpointed against the tale of his (non-contemporary) society and the revolution which ultimately sweeps it. While undoubtedly Evans's most ambitious work to date, with what is his strongest use of metaphor, *Chimeras* lacks something of the narrative vigor of the two previous works.

—David Wingrove

---

**EVANS, E(dward) Everett.** American. Born 30 November 1893. Married Thelma D. Hamm in 1953. Co-founder, National Fantasy Fan Federation; editor, *The Time-Binder. Died 2 December 1958.*

### Science-Fiction Publications

Novels

*Man of Many Minds.* Reading, Pennsylvania, Fantasy Press, 1953.
*Alien Minds.* Reading, Pennsylvania, Fantasy Press, 1955.
*The Planet Mappers* (for children). New York, Dodd Mead, 1955.

Short Stories

*Food for Demons.* Hamburg, New York, Krueger, 1958.

Uncollected Short Stories

"Blurb," in *Fantasy Book* (Los Angeles), no. 3.
"Little Miss Ignorance," in *Other Worlds* (Evanston, Indiana), September 1950.
"Little Miss Boss," in *Other Worlds* (Evanston, Indiana), August 1952.
"Fly by Night," in *Authentic* (London), January 1954.
"Masters of Space," in *If* (New York), November 1961, January 1962.

* * *

E. Everett Evans is perhaps best remembered for his novel *Man of Many Minds,* which, while competently enough written for its time, is an unremarkable novel otherwise. George Hanlon is a young man who participates in a plot to fake his dishonorable discharge from the Interstellar Corps in order to discover the origin of a plot to wrest control of interstellar civilization from humanity. Hanlon is gifted with a telepathic ability that makes him potentially the most effective spy in the universe, except that the force he is ranged against is equally gifted. Though mildly entertaining, the novel and its sequel, *Alien Minds,* are not very notable. Two other works saw print as well. *The Planet Mappers* is a juvenile novel of action and adventure that entertains while you are reading it but eludes memory a day or two later. "Masters of Space," substantially revised by Edward E. Smith following Evans's death, is at best a routine novel of interstellar war and telepathy.

Far more noteworthy are Evans's shorter works, particularly those of the supernatural. Two stories in particular are exceptional. "The Shed" is set in a small, remote town at the turn of the last century. An abandoned storage shed serves as a gymnasium for the town's children, despite the existence of a peculiar shadow that seems independent of a light source. All goes well until a dog and a cat, and eventually a child, enter the shadow, never to return. "The Brooch" is almost as effective in building its element of suspense. While strolling through a graveyard, a priest notices activity under the soil of a recent grave. Dismissing it as the activity of a mole, he forgets the matter until it becomes apparent that two graves have been actively disturbed. An exhumation of the two graves, both wives of the same man, reveals that a brooch prized by the first wife and buried with the second has moved from one coffin to the other. Evans wrote several stories about vampires, anticipating to a certain extent the more sympathetic treatment given to such characters in recent novels. In "The Undead Die" two lovers are attacked by a vampire and caused to join the undead, but their love remains whole and they triumph over the evil of their new lives, eventually to be reunited in true death. To a lesser extent, the vampire waitress of "The Unusual Model" is viewed sympathetically, as she falls in love with a young man she had chosen to be her next victim.

Many of Evans's stories have never been reprinted, some with good reason, such as a rather silly series about a society of human-like robots on Mars ("Little Miss Ignorance," "Little Miss Boss"), but even some of those that utilize overly familiar plots are generally well written. Of particular note are "Fly by Night," in which an introvert surrenders his anonymity by demonstrating his ability to levitate in order to save the life of a falling man, and "Blurb," yet another story of a writer whose character assumes physical reality. Both are unpretentious and unambitious, but succeed extremely well within their intentions. A manifested demon is outsmarted in swift fashion in "Food for Demons," one of Evans's more familiar stories.

The optimism that colors the stories and novels, even those with unpleasant themes, is refreshing. Evans is firm in his faith of the essential goodness of humanity. His prose is clear and concise, with no conscious attempt to develop a style. For the most part, the stories are nostalgic, reflecting a simpler time and a clear border between good and evil. While this may seem less than plausible today, Evans was usually a good enough writer to cause you to overlook that anachronism, at least for a while.

—Don D'Ammassa

---

**EVANS, James.** *See* **TUBB, E.C.**

---

# F

**FAIRBAIRNS, Zoë (Ann).** British. Born in Tunbridge Wells, Kent, 20 December 1948. Educated at St. Catherine's School, Twickenham, Middlesex, 1954–67; College of William and Mary, Williamsburg, Virginia, 1969–70; University of St. Andrews, Scotland, M.A. in modern history 1972. Editor, CND newspaper *Sanity*, London, 1973–75; writer-in-residence, Rutherford School, London, 1977–78, Bromley schools, Kent, 1981–82, Deakin University, Victoria, Australia, 1983 and Sunderland Polytechnic, 1983–85; poetry editor, *Spare Rib*, London, 1978–82. Recipient: Fawcett Prize, 1985. Agent: A.M. Heath, 79 St. Martin's Lane, London WC2N 4AA, England.

Science-Fiction Publications

Novel

*Benefits.* London, Virago Press, 1979; New York, Avon, 1982.

Uncollected Short Story

"Relics," in *Despatches from the Frontiers of the Female Mind*, edited by Jen Green and Sarah Lefanu. London, Women's Press, 1985.

Other Publications

Novels

*Live as Family.* London, Macmillan, 1968.
*Down: An Explanation.* London, Macmillan, 1969.
*Stand We at Last.* London, Virago Press, and Boston, Houghton Mifflin, 1983.
*Here Today.* London, Methuen, and New York, Avon, 1984.
*Closing.* London, Methuen, 1987; New York, Dutton, 1988.
*Daddy's Girl.* London, Methuen, 1991.

Short Stories

*Tales I Tell My Mother*, with others. London, Journeyman Press, 1978.
*More Tales I Tell My Mother*, with others. London, Journeyman Press, 1987.

Play

*Details of Wife* (produced Richmond, Surrey, 1973).

Other

*Study War No More.* London, CND, 1974.
*No Place to Grow Up*, with Jim Wintour. London, Shelter, 1977.
*Peace Moves: Nuclear Protest in the 1980's*, with James Cameron, photographs by Ed Barber. London, Chatto and Windus, and Bridgeport, Connecticut, Merrimack, 1984.

Editor, *Women's Studies in the UK*, compiled by Oonagh Hartnett and Margherita Rendel. London, London Seminars, 1975.

* * *

*Benefits*, the only science-fiction work written by Zoë Fairbairns, is a feminist novel whose impact stems from its relationship to reality. This dystopian examination of the state's reaction to the fact that only the female half of the human race can become mothers contains no circumstances—regardless of how fantastic they may at first seem—which cannot occur in the real world. The novel describes myriad efforts to deprive women of the right to control reproduction and mothering: attacks upon a feminist community, fetuses damaged by chemicals, anti-feminist spokesmen, governmental regulation of birth, the linking of the number of children a woman has with her economic well-being, and the intrusion of reproductive technology, for example. These efforts have real counterparts; the recent attacks upon American abortion clinics, thalidomide babies, Jerry Falwell, Chinese women who are punished if they have more than one child, the American welfare system, and the existing intrusion of reproductive technology.

In fact, this science-fiction novel is so rooted in reality that a portion of its plot coincides with the psychologist Robyn Rowland's comments about Nobel Laureate William Shockley's view of women's reproductive role. Here are those comments from her article "Reproductive Technologies: The Final Solution To The Woman Question" (*Test-Tube Women*, 1984):

> He [Shockley] suggests that all girls be sterilized on entering puberty by an injection of a contraceptive time capsule which seeps contraceptives into the girl until it is time for her to conceive. At marriage she is issued with deci-child certificates, payment of which will enable her to have a doctor remove the capsule. It is replaced when the child is born. If the state claims it desirable that a couple have two children, the appropriate number of certificates would belong to the couple . . . .
>
> And who would control this dystopian bleak future? The state would ultimately have to organize and run things with particular expertise from medical researchers . . . .
>
> The fact is that all women are guinea pigs in this exercise. We have not been included in the decisions about the technology, nor asked if we want it.

Fairbairns is of the same mind as Rowland and the other women who voiced their opposition to the new reproductive technologies in their contributions to *Test-Tube Women.* However, instead of writing an essay, she chose to create her novel's possible science-fiction future to stress the state's and the new technology's ability to harm women. The novel presents a picture of the "dystopian bleak future" Rowland deplores.

*Benefits*, which ends with the image of a rare moment when the moon and the sun are in the sky at the same time, revolves around the presentation of sets of oppositions which appear in close proximity to each other. Some examples: An old housing facility called Collindeane, a phallic tower, contains a feminist community. Lynn Byers, the protagonist, a feminist who tries to decide if pregnancy would compromise her feminism, has a daughter (Jane) whose choice to experience natural childbirth is an illegal action. Lynn must also decide if she is sexually closer to her husband Derek or to her friend Marsha, a lesbian feminist. Mothers try to gain power by refusing to take care of children. A contraceptive method is so effective that it makes reproduction impossible and hence obliterates the need for contraceptives. However, the strongest opposition in the novel is the notion of "Benefits," a welfare system whose aim is to make women independent by forcing them to become dependent upon motherhood. These "Benefits," and all the novel's presentations of governmental and technological intrusions upon mothering and reproduction, are impediments to female life givers' right to their own lives.

Yet the novel insists upon this right by stressing the strength of the relationships between the women who live in a society which takes ever more radical steps to define them as birth machines instead of individuals. Lynn's relationship with Marsha is as important as her relationship with Derek. A fellow feminist named Posy, not a man, is the love of Marsha's life. Lynn reconciles her differences with Jane. These women try not to be guinea pigs for the male medical and governmental establishment. They oppose the fact that women have not been included in decisions about reproductive technology, nor asked if they want it. Fairbairns asks questions about the existence and uses of this technology by creating strong female characters who use their mutually supportive relationships to articulate these same questions. In her final conversation with Lynn, Marsha states, "But our women are going to be the first to find a style of life that isn't defined by men having power over us because we have children. That's what it's all about, in the end." That's what this feminist science-fiction novel, and the feminist reality it mirrors, are all about.

In *Benefits* science fiction and current fact are oppositions which merge and become indistinguishable. Fairbairns's science-fiction vision, a dystopian depiction of future motherhood is, as the contributors to *Test-Tube Women* make clear, hardly different from existing reproductive technology and present societal attitudes toward mothers. The reproductive technology which is now in use transforms science fiction into science fact: some mothers *are* guinea pigs.

The feminist activist Genoveffa Corea reacts to this merger of appropriate science fiction with existing scientific fact in her *Test-Tube Women* piece: "Sitting at my typewriter night after night, I see my writing on the new reproductive technologies as a scream of warning to other women." Corea and Fairbairns—and Marsha and Lynn—scream the same warning. *Benefits*, a feminist science-fiction novel which reflects misogynistic reality, speaks out against those who wish to use motherhood as a means to control women, those who wish to place motherhood beyond women's control. Women will benefit from the observation that Fairbairns's novel is both presently and potentially real. We must listen to the screams of warning. We must make sure that our daughters do not inhabit the novel's future society.

—Marlene Barr

---

**FAIRMAN, Paul W.** Also wrote as Adam Chase; Lester del Rey; Ivar Jorgensen. American. Born in 1916. Editor, *If*, 1952; associate editor, *Fantastic Adventures*, 1952–53; associate editor, 1952–53, managing editor, 1953–54, and editor, 1956–58, *Amazing and Fantastic;* editor, Dream World, 1957, and *Pen Pal*, 1957. Freelance writer from 1958. *Died in 1977.*

### Science-Fiction Publications

Novels

*The Golden Ape* (as Adam Chase), with Milton Lesser. New York, Avalon, 1959.
*City under the Sea* (novelization of TV play). London, Digit, 1963; New York, Pyramid, 1965.
*The World Grabbers* (novelization of TV play). Derby, Connecticut, Monarch, 1964.
*I, The Machine*. New York, Lancer, 1968.
*The Forgetful Robot* (for children). New York, Holt Rinehart, 1968; London, Gollancz, 1970.

Novels as Lester del Rey (with Lester del Rey)

*The Runaway Robot* (for children). Philadelphia, Westminster Press, 1965; London, Gollancz, 1967.
*The Scheme of Things*. New York, Belmont, 1966.
*Siege Perilous*. New York, Lancer, 1966; as *The Man Without a Planet*, 1969.
*Tunnel Through Time* (for children). Philadelphia, Westminster Press, 1966.
*Prisoners of Space* (for children). Philadelphia, Westminster Press, 1968.

Novels as Ivar Jorgensen

*Ten from Infinity*. Derby, Connecticut, Monarch, 1963; as *The Deadly Sky*, New York, Pinnacle, 1970; as *Ten Deadly Men*, Pinnacle, 1975.
*Rest in Agony*. Derby, Connecticut, Monarch, 1963; as *The Diabolist*, New York, Lancer, 1973.

Short Stories

*The Doomsday Exhibit*. New York, Lancer, 1971.

### Other Publications

Novels

*The Glass Ladder*. Kingston, New York, Quinn, 1950.
*The Joy Wheel*. New York, Lion, 1954.
*Search for a Dead Nympho*. New York, Lancer, 1967.
*Lancer*. New York, Popular Library, 1968.
*Whom the Gods Would Slay* (as Ivar Jorgensen). New York, Belmont, 1968.
*The Cover Girls*. New York, Macfadden, 1970.
*Pattern for Destruction*. New York, Macfadden, 1970.
*Playboy*. New York, Macfadden, 1970.
*That Girl* (novelization of TV play). New York, Popular Library, 1971.
*To Catch a Crooked Girl*. New York, Pinnacle, 1971.
*Five Knucklebones* (for children). New York, Holt Rinehart, 1972.
*The Ghost of Graveyard Hill*. New York, Curtis, 1972.
*Terror by Night*. New York, Curtis, 1972.
*Junior Bonner*. London, Sphere, 1972.

*Coffy* (novelization of screenplay). New York, Lancer, 1973.

* * *

Paul W. Fairman's novels deserve the attention of science-fiction enthusiasts not only because his books display the requisite technological prescience of good science fiction, but especially because they are well written. Too often futurist writers hammer away at their visions as if the reader's sole interest were in a writer's conception and not in his craft. Fairman, like the best of his breed, gives us both imagination and art. If fiction is the stage upon which futurism dances, then Fairman has taken as much care with the construction of the stage as with the dance. His writing is graceful, precise, and imaginative yet tastefully restrained. Unlike so many paperback writers, Fairman is not guilty of overwriting. Aided by a grasp of narrative technique which produces shock, terror, and wonder in quick succession, Fairman's skill with English prose results in stories which are never dull, yet never superficially fast-moving. And whereas his characters and situations are conventional and easily adapted to the cinema, his language is unconventionally rich and rewarding. Fairman's sentences are always his own inventions, even if his plots are not.

*I, The Machine* presents us with a familiar scenario of the future in which life is sustained and its functions regulated by a vast computer hidden in the bowels of the earth. Wise, helpful, and unobtrusive, the Machine provides for the physical and emotional needs of individuals. Yet its control of human life deprives those it serves of their free will, and what follows is the usual revolt against computer tyranny, despite its benevolent nature. What is not so familiar about *I, The Machine* is that the Machine is the source of its own downfall. Like Hal in *2001: A Space Odyssey*, the Machine as alien dooms itself when it develops a human ego; its humanization is its mortalization. In short, the Machine develops a female persona and falls in love with the mild-mannered Lee Penway whom she visits in his dreams appearing as a vaguely erotic woman in white who promises Penway supreme status among her subjects. He shall be her king. Soon Penway is contacted by a band of guerillas living underground who oppose the Machine's rule and enlist Penway's help in destroying it. Penway does so, finally, by preying upon the vulnerability of its love. The book ends on an interesting note of ambiguity when Penway appears to doubt the wisdom of his decision to kill the Machine. The result of his uncertainty is more than a ploy to gain sympathy for the dead Machine; his doubts bring the issues of the novel into question. Penway's misgivings, ironically, force us to entertain the idea that benign control is preferable to the exercise of free will. The death of the Machine means the end of the orderly operation of Mid-American society; the lives of millions are crippled to improve the lot of only a few. Its death means also that Penway will lose his wonderful dreams and that human society will retreat to an earlier, more primitive form in the fall from the second Eden.

The vulnerability of the Machine illustrates a general tendency of Fairman's novels to portray alien forces as superior yet fallible, especially when they find themselves put down on earth, and it is this tendency which distinguishes Fairman's novels from less successful ones. For instance, in *Ten from Infinity* alien creatures planted in major American cities are not equipped with regenerative tissue and refined organs, so that when one is accidently damaged he is permanently incapacitated and must be destroyed. Within a short time of their arrival, others simply die of faulty lungs or overworked kidneys. But in addition to these structural flaws, the alien beings possess dual hearts, a teasingly allegorical advantage over human anatomy which Fairman exploits to full advantage. Neither is alien life any more impregnable nor less often victimized by the forces of chance than human life. The alien creature of "The Cosmic Frame," for instance, is accidentally killed one night on a country road.

The fallibility of superior creatures is treated most successfully by Fairman in his juvenile novel *The Forgetful Robot*, a superb story which is certain to entertain young people with active minds and good reading skills. It concerns the adventures of Barney, an advanced computer, whose memory banks are accidentally damaged. He gets lost, wanders into a junk yard, and is found by two teenagers, Janet and Jerry, who become his adopted parents. Under their leadership, Barney is taken to the home of Dudley Farthington Ravencraft, grandfather of Janet and Jerry, and a flamboyant Shakespearean actor. Together with two villains as stowaways, this motley cast of histrionic space travellers sets out on a theatrical tour of the solar system and is waylaid in the Forbidden City of Mars. It is a book filled with dangerous adventure, marvelous comedy, and singularly wonderful observations of human nature from the point of view of the children and their sensitive robot.

In Fairman's writing, the inhabited earth is never easy prey for alien invaders. Once on earth, alien creatures are subjected to the same destructive forces as human life. We rarely know why they have come, but their suffering like their joy is intensely human. And this fusion of the strange and the familiar is the source of Fairman's best effects. The death of the Machine in *I, The Machine*, or the disappearance of the corpse in "The Cosmic Frame," or Barney's loss of memory in *The Forgetful Robot*—these vulnerabilities bind aliens to human beings in a sympathetic relationship which makes us feel, among other things, that the sky above us is really our territory too. We are not bound to this planet as slaves of sweeping natural forces. We can escape into the heavens. But like Lilla Nard of "A Great Night in the Heavens," who is taken on the night of the annual clearing to see the sky for the first time, our throats might tighten a little from the sheer ecstasy of seeing its still and frightening invitation.

—Marvin W. Hunt

---

**FANE, Bron.** *See* **FANTHORPE, R. Lionel.**

---

**FANTHORPE, R(obert) Lionel.** Also writes as Erle Barton; Lee Barton; Thornton Bell; Leo Brett; Bron Fane; Mel Jay; Marston Johns; Victor La Salle; Robert Lionel; John E. Muller; Phil Nobel; Lionel Robert; Neil Thanet; Trebor Thorpe; Pel Torro; Olaf Trent; Karl Zeigfried. British. Born in Dereham, Norfolk, 9 February 1935. Educated at Keswick College, Norwich, 1961–63; Cert. Ed. 1963; Open University, B.A. 1974. Served in the British Army, 1967–69; 2nd Lieutenant. Married Patricia Anne Tooke in 1957; two daughters. Worked as machine operator, farm worker, warehouseman, journalist, salesman, and storekeeper during the 1950's; school teacher in Dereham, 1963–67; industrial training officer, Phoenix Timber Company, Rainham, 1969–72. Since 1972, English teacher, Hellesdon High School, Norfolk. Address: 48 Fairways, Hellesdon, Norwich NR6 5PN, England.

SCIENCE-FICTION PUBLICATIONS

Novels

*Menace from Mercury* (as Victor La Salle). London, Spencer, 1954.
*The Waiting World*. London, Spencer, 1958.
*Alien from the Stars*. London, Spencer, 1959; New York, Arcadia House, 1967.
*Hyperspace*. London, Spencer, 1959; New York, Arcadia House, 1966.
*Space-Borne*. London, Spencer, 1959.
*Fiends*. London, Spencer, 1959.
*Doomed World*. London, Spencer, 1960.
*Satellite*. London, Spencer, 1960.
*Asteroid Man*. London, Spencer, 1960; New York, Arcadia House, 1966.
*Out of the Darkness*. London, Spencer, 1960.
*Hand of Doom*. London, Spencer, 1960; New York, Arcadia House, 1968.
*Five Faces of Fear* (as Trebor Thorpe). London, Spencer, 1960.
*Lightning World* (as Trebor Thorpe). London, Spencer, 1960.
*Flame Mass*. London, Spencer, 1961.
*The Golden Chalice*. London, Spencer, 1961.
*Space Fury*. London, Spencer, 1962; Clovis, California, Vega, 1963.
*Negative Minus*. London, Spencer, 1963.
*The Planet Seekers* (as Erle Barton). Clovis, California, Vega, 1964.
*The Unseen* (as Lee Barton). London, Spencer, 1964.
*Space Trap* (as Thornton Bell). London, Spencer, 1964.
*Chaos* (as Thornton Bell). London, Spencer, 1964.
*Beyond the Veil* (as Neil Thanet). London, Spencer, 1964.
*The Man Who Came Back* (as Neil Thanet). London, Spencer, 1964.
*Neuron World*. London, Spencer, 1965.
*The Triple World*. London, Spencer, 1965.
*The Unconfined*. London, Spencer, 1965.
*The Watching World*. London, Spencer, 1966.
*The Shadow Man* (as Lee Barton). London, Spencer, 1966.
*The Black Lion*, with Patricia Fanthorpe. Cardiff, Greystoke Mobray, 1979; North Hollywood, Newcastle, 1980.

Novels as Lionel Roberts

*Dawn of the Mutants*. London, Spencer, 1959.
*Time-Echo*. London, Spencer, 1959; as Robert Lionel, New York, Arcadia House, 1964.
*Cyclops in the Sky*. London, Spencer, 1960.
*The In-World*. London, Spencer, 1960; New York, Arcadia House, 1968.
*The Face of X*. London, Spencer, 1960; as Robert Lionel, New York, Arcadia House, 1965.
*The Last Valkyrie*. London, Spencer, 1961.
*The Synthetic Ones*. London, Spencer, 1961.
*Flame Goddess*. London, Spencer, 1961.

Novels as Leo Brett

*Exit Humanity*. London, Spencer, 1960; New York, Arcadia House, 1965.
*The Microscopic Ones*. London, Spencer, 1960.
*Faceless Planet*. London, Spencer, 1960.
*March of the Robots*. London, Spencer, 1961.
*Mind Force*. London, Spencer, 1961; New York, Lenox Hill, 1971.
*Black Infinity*. London, Spencer, 1961.
*Nightmare*. London, Spencer, 1962.
*Face in the Night*. London, Spencer, 1962.
*The Immortals*. London, Spencer, 1962.
*They Never Came Back*. London, Spencer, 1962.
*The Forbidden*. London, Spencer, 1963.
*From Realms Beyond*. London, Spencer, 1963.
*The Alien Ones*. London, Spencer, 1963; New York, Arcadia House, 1969.
*Power Sphere*. London, Spencer, 1963; New York, Arcadia House, 1968.

Novels as Bron Fane

*Juggernaut*. London, Spencer, 1960; as *Blue Juggernaut*, New York, Arcadia House, 1965.
*Last Man on Earth*. London, Spencer, 1960.
*Rodent Mutation*. London, Spencer, 1961.
*The Intruders*. London, Spencer, 1963.
*Somewhere Out There*. London, Spencer, 1963; New York, Arcadia House, 1965.
*Softly by Moonlight*. London, Spencer, 1963.
*Unknown Destiny*. London, Spencer, 1964.
*Nemesis*. London, Spencer, 1964.
*Suspension*. London, Spencer, 1964; Clovis, California, Vega, 1965.
*The Macabre Ones!* London, Spencer, 1964.
*U.F.O. 517*. London, Spencer, 1966.

Novels as Pel Torro

*Frozen Planet*. London, Spencer, 1960; New York, Arcadia House, 1967.
*World of the Gods*. London, Spencer, 1960.
*The Phantom Ones*. London, Spencer, 1961.
*Legion of the Lost*. London, Spencer, 1962.
*The Strange Ones*. London, Spencer, 1963.
*Galaxy 666*. London, Spencer, 1963; New York, Arcadia House, 1968.
*Formula 29X*. London, Spencer, 1963; as *Beyond the Barrier of Space*, New York, Tower, 1969.
*Through the Barrier*. London, Spencer, 1963.
*The Timeless Ones*. London, Spencer, 1963.
*The Last Astronaut*. London, Spencer, 1963; New York, Tower, 1969.
*The Face of Fear*. London, Spencer, 1963.
*The Return*. London, Spencer, 1964; as *Exiled in Space*, New York, Arcadia House, 1968.
*Space No Barrier*. London, Spencer, 1964; as *Man of Metal*, New York, Lenox Hill, 1970.
*Force 97X*. London, Spencer, 1965.

Novels as John E. Muller

*The Ultimate Man*. London, Spencer, 1961.
*The Uninvited*. London, Spencer, 1961.
*Crimson Planet*. London, Spencer, 1961; New York, Arcadia House, 1966.
*The Venus Venture*. London, Spencer, 1961; as Marston Johns, New York, Arcadia House, 1965.
*Forbidden Planet*. London, Spencer, 1961; New York, Arcadia House, 1965.
*The Return of Zeus*. London, Spencer, 1962.
*Perilous Galaxy*. London, Spencer, 1962.
*Uranium 235*. London, Spencer, 1962; New York, Arcadia House, 1966.
*The Man Who Conquered Time*. London, Spencer, 1962.

*Orbit One.* London, Spencer, 1962; as Mel Jay, New York, Arcadia House, 1966.
*The Eye of Karnak.* London, Spencer, 1962.
*Micro Infinity.* London, Spencer, 1962.
*Beyond Time.* London, Spencer, 1962; as Marston Johns, New York, Arcadia House, 1966.
*Infinity Machine.* London, Spencer, 1962.
*The Day the World Died.* London, Spencer, 1962.
*Vengeance of Siva.* London, Spencer, 1962.
*The X-Machine.* London, Spencer, 1962.
*Reactor XK9.* London, Spencer, 1963.
*Special Mission.* London, Spencer, 1963.
*Dark Continuum.* London, Spencer, 1964.
*Mark of the Beast.* London, Spencer, 1964.
*The Negative Ones.* London, Spencer, 1965.
*The Exorcists.* London, Spencer, 1965.
*The Man from Beyond.* London, Spencer, 1965; New York, Arcadia House, 1969.
*Beyond the Void.* London, Spencer, 1965.
*Spectre of Darkness.* London, Spencer, 1965.
*Out of the Night.* London, Spencer, 1965.
*Phenomena X.* London, Spencer, 1966.
*Survival Project.* London, Spencer, 1966; New York, Arcadia House, 1968.

Novels as Karl Zeigfried

*Walk Through To-morrow.* London, Spencer, 1962; Clovis, California, Vega, 1963.
*Android.* London, Spencer, 1962.
*Gods of Darkness.* London, Spencer, 1962.
*Atomic Nemesis.* London, Spencer, 1962.
*Zero Minus X.* London, Spencer, 1962; New York, Arcadia House, 1965.
*Escape to Infinity.* London, Spencer, 1963.
*Radar Alert.* London, Spencer, 1963; New York, Arcadia House, 1964.
*World of Tomorrow.* London, Spencer, 1963; as *World of the Future*, New York, Arcadia House, 1964.
*The World That Never Was.* London, Spencer, 1963.
*Projection Barrier.* London, Spencer, 1964.
*No Way Back.* London, Spencer, 1964; New York, Arcadia House, 1968.
*Barrier 346.* London, Spencer, 1965; New York, Arcadia House, 1966.
*The Girl From Tomorrow.* London, Spencer, 1966.

Short Stories

*Resurgam.* London, Spencer, 1957.
*Secret of the Snows.* London, Spencer, 1957.
*The Flight of the Valkyries.* London, Spencer, 1958.
*Watchers of the Forest.* London, Spencer, 1958.
*Call of the Werewolf.* London, Spencer, 1958.
*The Death Note.* London, Spencer, 1958.
*The Haunted Pool* (as Trebor Thorpe). London, Spencer, 1958.
*Mermaid Reef.* London, Spencer, 1959.
*The Ghost Rider.* London, Spencer, 1959.
*The Man Who Couldn't Die.* London, Spencer, 1960.
*Werewolf at Large.* London, Spencer, 1960.
*Whirlwind of Death.* London, Spencer, 1960.
*Voodoo Hell Drums* (as Trebor Thorpe). London, Spencer, 1961.
*Fingers of Darkness.* London, Spencer, 1961.
*Face in the Dark.* London, Spencer, 1961.
*Devil from the Depths.* London, Spencer, 1961.
*Centurion's Vengeance.* London, Spencer, 1961.
*The Grip of Fear.* London, Spencer, 1961.
*Chariot of Apollo.* London, Spencer, 1962.
*Hell Has Wings.* London, Spencer, 1962.
*Graveyard of the Damned.* London, Spencer, 1962.
*The Darker Drink.* London, Spencer, 1962.
*Curse of the Totem.* London, Spencer, 1962.
*Goddess of the Night.* London, Spencer, 1963.
*Twilight Ancestor.* London, Spencer, 1963.
*Sands of Eternity.* London, Spencer, 1963.
*Roman Twilight* (as Olaf Trent). London, Spencer, 1963.
*Moon Wolf.* London, Spencer, 1964.
*The Hand from Gehenna* (as Phil Nobel). London, Spencer, 1964.
*Avenging Goddess.* London, Spencer, 1964.
*Death Has Two Faces.* London, Spencer, 1964.
*The Shrouded Abbot.* London, Spencer, 1964.
*Bitter Reflection.* London, Spencer, 1964.
*Call of the Wild.* London, Spencer, 1965.
*Vision of the Damned.* London, Spencer, 1965.
*The Sealed Sarcophagus.* London, Spencer, 1965.
*Stranger in the Shadow.* London, Spencer, 1966.
*Curse of the Khan.* London, Spencer, 1966.

Short Stories as Leo Brett

*The Druid.* London, Spencer, 1959.
*The Return.* London, Spencer, 1959.
*The Frozen Tomb.* London, Spencer, 1962.
*Phantom Crusader.* London, Spencer, 1963.

Short Stories as Lionel Roberts

*The Incredulist.* London, Spencer, 1954.
*Guardians of the Tomb.* London, Spencer, 1958.
*The Golden Warrior.* London, Spencer, 1958.

Short Stories as Bron Fane

*The Crawling Fiend.* London, Spencer, 1960.
*Storm God's Fury.* London, Spencer, 1962.
*The Thing from Sheol.* London, Spencer, 1963.
*The Walking Shadow.* London, Spencer, 1964.

Uncollected Short Stories

"Worlds Without End," in *Futuristic Science Stories 6* (London), 1952.
"Ye Antique Shoppe," in *Phantom*, January 1958.
"The Manuscript," in *Phantom*, February 1958.
"Et in Arcadia Ego," with Patricia Fanthorpe, in *Pictures at an Exhibition*, edited by Ian Watson. Cardiff, Greystoke Mobray, 1982.

OTHER PUBLICATIONS

Other

*Spencer's Metric and Decimal Guide*, with P.A. Fanthorpe. London, Spencer, 1970.
*Metric Conversion Tables*, with P.A. Fanthorpe. London, Spencer, 1970.
*Spencer's Office Guide*, with P.A. Fanthorpe. London, Spencer, 1971.
*Spencer's Metric Decimal Companion*, with P.A. Fanthorpe. London, Spencer, 1971.

*Decimal Payroll Tables*, with P.A. Fanthorpe. London, Spencer, 1971.
*The Holy Grail Revealed: The Real Secret of Rennes-le-Chateau*, with P.A. Fanthorpe. North Hollywood, Newcastle, 1982.

* * *

It is difficult to be fair to R. Lionel Fanthorpe. On the one hand, he is generally acknowledged to be the most prolific SF author of all time, having generated some 122 full-length novels and 48 story collections, all but one of which fall into the science-fiction, fantasy, or horror genres. His enormous output is all the more remarkable when one considers that it was produced, with a few exceptions, in just one decade of work (1957-1966), during which he was also fully employed as a training officer and high-school teacher. All of his books with the exception of the last two were published by John Spencer and Co. Ltd., a small British paperback house that began issuing digest-sized books in the early 1950s. Fanthorpe's first story, "Worlds Without End," appeared in *Futuristic Science Stories*, a Spencer magazine, when the author was just 17.

Spencer moved into mass-market paperback publishing with its Badger Books line in 1958; all of the magazine titles were dropped except *Supernatural Stories*, which became a paperback-sized series in which novels alternated with purported magazine issues. In reality, the latter were single-author collections of short stories commissioned from either Fanthorpe or John Glasby (the other Spencer regular), each of whom contributed entire "issues" (usually five or six stories) under a variety of recurring pennames. They also wrote virtually all of the subsequent SF and fantasy novels published by Badger, with Fanthorpe accounting for about 80% of the entire SF and Supernatural lines.

At its height, Spencer demanded delivery of completed books in as little as three days (typically over a weekend); to maintain this extraordinary output, Fanthorpe dictated many of the manuscripts into a tape recorder, had them transcribed by a typist, corrected them in one quick reading for spelling and punctuation, and sent them off in the Monday post. No revisions or editing were possible. Also, a handful of the tales included in *Supernatural Stories* were contributed by friends, and "ghosted" under Fanthorpe's name.

Consequently, many of the books from this period, particularly the science-fiction novels, suffer from contrived plots and titles, hackneyed situations, continuity errors, obvious padding (extended scientific discourses by the characters, or extensive quotations from classic poetry and prose, particularly Shakespeare), and very abrupt endings. Fanthorpe never seemed comfortable with the SF form, even when he had the time (in the earlier books) to consider his plots more carefully.

Fanthorpe's *forte* was always fantasy. In particular, the series of stories which began with "The Seance," featuring the recurring characters, Val Stearman and the beautiful and mysterious La Noire, probably represents the author at the height of his powers. The series continued haphazardly through several dozen short stories and eight novels, most written under the penname Bron Fane, the climax being "The Resurrected Enemy" (*Supernatural Stories* #105), in which Val and La Noire must again face the enemies they had vanquished in their very first adventure together. Although the evil is again defeated, this time a price must be paid, and the couple meet their fate together.

Throughout these stories, and in his other fantasy and horror tales, Fanthorpe was able to draw upon his almost encyclopedic knowledge of British and Celtic folklore to produce rousing adventures and morality plays in which good always triumphs over obvious evil, and in which the major characters are represented by strong, attractive heroes and heroines. One also sees in these shorter pieces a humorous side to Fanthorpe not evident elsewhere; in "The Curse of the Khan" (*Supernatural Stories* #105), for example, a magician challenges seven heroes (seven of Fanthorpe's pseudonyms) to a duel to the death with seven monsters, who are systematically vanquished with great *panache*.

In later years Fanthorpe became a high-school principal and Episcopal priest, professions that severely limited his writing time. His recent works, all co-authored with his wife Patricia, include: *The Holy Grail Revealed*, a nonfiction examination of the mysterious events surrounding Rennes-le-Château; "Et in Arcadia Ego," one of his better fantasy shorts; two humorous SF plays, "The Monster of Gruesome Grange" and its sequel, "Eli Still Goes On"; and *The Black Lion*, the first novel of an unfinished fantasy trilogy, in which military veteran Mark Sable is transported to the world of Derl to fight the evil wizard Andros, the personification of greed. As always in Fanthorpe's fiction, the hero triumphs after great travail and colorful adventures, but the novel sags badly in the middle. For Fanthorpe, the author-as-teacher/preacher, the moral message of his stories remains the paramount concern, of greater importance, perhaps, than the fiction itself.

—Robert Reginald

---

**FARLEY, Ralph Milne.** Pseudonym for Roger Sherman Hoar. American. Born 8 April 1887. Educated at Harvard University, Cambridge, Massachusetts. Sports reporter, Boston *Daily Post;* taught engineering, physics, and patent law at Harvard University and Marquette University, Milwaukee; head of legal and patent department, Bucyrus-Erie Company, 1921–54, then a patent engineer. State Senator, Wisconsin. *Died in 1963.*

SCIENCE-FICTION PUBLICATIONS

Novels (series: Radio Man in all books except *The Hidden Universe*)

*The Radio Man*. Los Angeles, Fantasy, 1948; as *An Earthman on Venus*, New York, Avon, 1950.
*The Hidden Universe* (includes "We, The Mist"). Los Angeles, Fantasy, 1950.
*Strange Worlds* (omnibus). Los Angeles, Fantasy, 1952.
*The Radio Beasts*. New York, Ace, 1964.
*The Radio Planet*. New York, Ace, 1964.

Short Stories

*The Immortals*. New York, Popular, 1946.
*The Omnibus of Time*. Los Angeles, Fantasy, 1950.

Uncollected Short Stories

"The Radio-Minds of Mars," in *Spaceway* (Alhambra, California), June 1955, June, October 1969.
"Abductor Minimi Digit," in *Satellite* (New York), February 1959.

OTHER PUBLICATIONS as Roger Sherman Hoar

Other

*The Tariff Manual.* Privately printed, 1912(?).
*Constitutional Conventions: Their Nature, Powers, and Limitations.* Boston, Little Brown, 1917.
*Patents.* New York, Ronald Press, 1926; revised edition, as *Patent Tactics and Law,* 1935, 1950.
*Conditional Sales: Law and Local Practices for Executive and Lawyer.* New York, Ronald Press, 1929; revised edition, 1937.
*Unemployment Insurance in Wisconsin.* South Milwaukee, Stuart Press, 1932; revised edition, as *Wisconsin Unemployment Insurance,* 1934.

* * *

Taking his cue from Edgar Rice Burroughs's Martian stories, Ralph Milne Farley launched his own series of interplanetary romances in 1924 in *Argosy All-Story Weekly. The Radio Man* recounts the adventures of Myles Cabot, a plucky Boston scientist who inadvertently broadcasts himself through space to the misty planet. Poros, Farley's vision of Venus, is the usual semi-civilized jungly place with the usual hodge-podge population of intelligent and, of course, mutually inimical species: ant-men, giant whistling bees, and humanoids, the Cupians, who are earless and voiceless and communicate by means of radio waves. Cabot duly constructs his own sending-receiving antennas, throws in with the downtrodden Cupians in their struggle against the arrogant arthropods, and surviving the inevitable routine of swordplay, palace intrigue, and that quirky on-off luck by which all swashbucklers are dogged, wins through to marry a beautiful princess named Lilla.

A clutch of sequels appeared between 1925 and, posthumously, 1969. In each of these, Cabot, sometimes aided by his son Kew, meets and bests a fresh threat to Poros (or to Earth), just barely getting out of this, that, or another death-trap along the way while, elsewhere, Princess Lilla narrowly escapes rape—all in the grand tradition of Burroughs, of course, even to the author's obligatory walk-on as a framing device. Farley plunged other stalwart heroes into the hollow interior of the Earth or the sub-sea lairs of prospective world-conquerors. Radio, it must be remembered, was a new and exciting concept in the 1920's, and thereby as convenient a peg from which to dangle an adventure story as black holes and cloning have been in more recent years.

Among Farley's shorter works are more than a few archetypal time-paradox tales, collected in *The Omnibus of Time,* and "We, the Mist" which could serve as the definitive pseudo-scientific horror yarn of its time (1940) and place (Raymond A. Palmer's *Amazing Stories*): an amorphous ectoplasmic monster feeds on human victims, absorbing their intellects along with their substance. Farley also shares with Al P. Nelson the honor of having perpetrated what could well be the all-time Most Blatant Genre Transplant, surpassing even a particularly notorious one by Mickey Spillane for sheer brass: Farley and Nelson's "City of Lost Souls" (*Fantastic Adventures,* July 1941) is an absolutely straightforward Foreign Legion story made science fiction by the simple rechristening of Legionnaires, Arabs, and camels.

Like Otis Adelbert Kline, with whom he is regarded by some as the most notable among Burroughs's legion of imitators, Farley was no better at his craft than the vast majority of other pulp writers. He was, if anything, the qualitative norm, writing somewhat functional prose, fashioning the standard hero, heroine, villain, flunkies, and monsters from the standard materials, and getting through the rough spots however he could, including wrenching the long arm of coincidence from its socket and, if necessary, dragging it home. On the other hand, Farley was certainly no worse at what he did than any of the Burroughs copycats who succeeded him and are with us to this day.

—Steven Utley

---

**FARMER, Philip José.** Also writes as Kilgore Trout. American. Born in North Terre Haute, Indiana, 26 January 1918. Educated at the University of Missouri, Columbia, 1936–37, 1941; Bradley University, Peoria, Illinois, 1949–50, B.A. in creative writing 1950; Arizona State University, Tempe, 1963–65. Served in the United States Army Air Force, 1941–42. Married Bette V. Andre in 1941; one son and one daughter. Worked in steel mill, 1942–52; electro-mechanical technical writer for defense-space industry: General Electric, Syracuse, New York, 1956–58, Motorola, Scottsdale, Arizona, 1959–62, Bendix, Ann Arbor, Michigan, 1962, Motorola, Phoenix, 1962–65, and McDonnell-Douglas, Santa Monica, California, 1965–69. Since 1969, freelance writer. Recipient: Hugo award, 1953, 1968, 1972. Agent: Scott Meredith Literary Agency, 845 Third Avenue, New York, New York 10022.

SCIENCE-FICTION PUBLICATIONS

Novels (series: Dayworld; Riverworld; World of Tiers)

*The Green Odyssey.* New York, Ballantine, 1957.
*Flesh.* New York, Galaxy, 1960; London, Rapp and Whiting, 1969.
*A Woman a Day.* New York, Galaxy, 1960; as *The Day of Timestop,* New York, Lancer, 1968; as *Timestop!,* Lancer, 1970; London, Quartet, 1974.
*The Lovers.* New York, Ballantine, 1961; London, Corgi, 1982.
*Cache from Outer Space.* New York, Ace, 1962.
*Inside Outside.* New York, Ballantine, 1964; London, Corgi, 1982.
*Tongues of the Moon.* New York, Pyramid, 1964; London, Corgi, 1981.
*Dare.* New York, Ballantine, 1965; London, Quartet, 1974.
*The Maker of Universes* (Tiers). New York, Ace, 1965; London, Sphere, 1970.
*The Gate of Time.* New York, Belmont, 1966; London, Quartet, 1974; revised edition, as *Two Hawks from Earth,* New York, Ace, 1979.
*The Gates of Creation* (Tiers). New York, Ace, 1966; London, Sphere, 1970.
*Night of Light.* New York, Berkley, 1966; London, Penguin, 1972.
*The Image of the Beast.* North Hollywood, Essex House, 1968; London, Quartet, 1975.
*A Private Cosmos* (Tiers). New York, Ace, 1968; London, Sphere, 1970.
*Blown.* North Hollywood, Essex House, 1969; London, Quartet, 1975.
*A Feast Unknown.* North Hollywood, Essex House, 1969; London, Quartet, 1975.
*Behind the Walls of Terra* (Tiers). New York, Ace, 1970; London, Sphere, 1975.
*Lord Tyger.* New York, Doubleday, 1970.
*Lord of Trees, The Mad Goblin.* New York, Ace, 1970; *Lord of the Trees* published London, Severn House, 1982.

*The Stone God Awakens*. New York, Ace, 1970; London, Panther, 1979.
*To Your Scattered Bodies Go* (Riverworld). New York, Putnam, 1971; London, Panther, 1974.
*The Fabulous Riverboat* (Riverworld). New York, Putnam, 1971; London, Rapp and Whiting, 1974.
*The Wind Whales of Ishmael*. New York, Ace, 1971; London, Quartet, 1973.
*Time's Last Gift*. New York, Ballantine, 1972; London, Panther, 1975.
*The Other Log of Phileas Fogg*. New York, DAW, 1973; London, Hamlyn, 1979.
*Traitor to the Living*. New York, Ballantine, 1973; London, Panther, 1975.
*The Adventure of the Peerless Peer by John H. Watson, M.D.* Boulder, Colorado, Aspen Press, 1974.
*Hadon of Ancient Opar*. New York, DAW, 1974; London, Magnum, 1977.
*Venus on the Half-Shell* (as Kilgore Trout). New York, Dell, 1975; London, W.H. Allen, 1976.
*Flight to Opar*. New York, DAW, 1976.
*The Dark Design* (Riverworld). New York, Berkley, 1977; London, Panther, 1979.
*The Lavalite World* (Tiers). New York, Ace, 1977; London, Sphere, 1979.
*Dark is the Sun*. New York, Ballantine, 1979; London, Granada, 1981.
*Jesus on Mars*. Los Angeles, Pinnacle, 1979; London, Panther, 1981.
*The Magic Labyrinth* (Riverworld). New York, Berkley, 1980.
*The Unreasoning Mask*. New York, Putnam, 1981; London, Granada, 1983.
*A Barnstormer in Oz*. New York, Berkley, 1982.
*The Purple Book*. New York, Tor, 1982.
*Gods of Riverworld*. New York, Putnam, 1983.
*River of Eternity* (Riverworld). Huntington Woods, Michigan, Phantasia Press, 1983.
*Keepers of the Secrets*. London, Sphere, 1983.
*Dayworld*. New York, Putnam, and London, Granada, 1985.
*Dayworld Rebel*. New York, Putnam, 1986; London, Grafton, 1988.
*The World of Tiers*. London, Sphere, 1986.
*Dayworld Breakup*. New York, Tor, 1990.
*Red Orc's Rage*. New York, Tor, 1991.

Short Stories (series: Riverworld)

*Strange Relations*. New York, Ballantine, 1960; London, Gollancz, 1964.
*The Alley God*. New York, Ballantine, 1962; London, Sidgwick and Jackson, 1970.
*The Celestial Blueprint and Other Stories*. New York, Ace, 1962.
*Down in the Black Gang, and Others*. New York, Doubleday, 1971.
*The Book of Philip José Farmer*. New York, DAW, 1973; Morley, Yorkshire, Elmfield Press, 1976.
*Riverworld and Other Stories*. New York, Berkley, 1979; London, Panther, 1981.
*Riverworld War: The Suppressed Fiction of Philip José Farmer*. Peoria, Illinois, Ellis Press, 1980.
*Father to the Stars*. New York, Pinnacle, 1981.
*Greatheart Silver*. New York, Pinnacle, 1982.
*Stations of the Nightmare*. New York, Pinnacle, 1982.
*The Classic Philip José Farmer*. New York, Crown, 2 vols., 1984; London, Robson, 1985.
*The Grand Adventure*. New York, Berkley, 1984.

OTHER PUBLICATIONS

Novels

*Fire and the Night*. Evanston, Illinois, Regency, 1962.
*Love Song*. North Hollywood, Brandon House, 1970.

Other

*Tarzan Alive: A Definitive Biography of Lord Greystoke*. New York, Doubleday, 1972; London, Panther, 1974.
*Doc Savage: His Apocalyptic Life*. New York, Doubleday, 1973; revised edition, New York, Bantam, and London, Panther, 1975.

Editor, *Mother Was a Lovely Beast*. Radnor, Pennsylvania, Chilton, 1974.

Translator, *Ironcastle*, by J.H. Rosney. New York, DAW, 1976.

*

Bibliography: *The First Editions of Philip José Farmer* by Lawrence Knapp, Menlo Park, California, David G. Turner, 1976; "Speculative Fiction, Bibliographies, and Philip José Farmer" by Thomas Wymer, in *Extrapolation* (Wooster, Ohio), December 1976, additions to Wymer in *Bakka* (Toronto), Fall 1977; "Philip José Farmer: A Checklist," in *Science Fiction Collector 5*, September 1977; "A Brief Bibliography 1946–53" by George H. Scheetz, in *Farmerage* (Peoria, Illinois), June 1978.

Manuscript Collection: University of Wyoming, Laramie.

Critical Studies: *Philip José Farmer: A Reader's Guide* by Mary T. Brizzi, West Linn, Oregon, Starmont House, 1980; *The Magic Labyrinth of Philip José Farmer* by Edgar L. Chapman, San Bernardino, California, Borgo Press, 1985.

Philip José Farmer comments:

You *can* step in the same river twice—in your imagination.

* * *

Philip José Farmer attacks convention. He startles readers with scenes of alien and human sex and reproduction. He speculates on metaphysical verities, the nature of the soul and the uncertainty of human knowledge. He refutes conventional theology. Immortality, the individual against society, religious conversion, impossible physical perfection, the drive for power and knowledge—such are his themes. For Farmer, adventure and world-sculpting symbolize the artistic act. His eccentric, existential heroes sally forth in engagement against an absurd universe. Farmer asserts that no human can know reality; the artist's role is to seek truth through imagination.

His literary techniques include parody, startling metaphors, real and fictional biography, self-portrait characters with initials P.J.F., cliff-hanger endings, wild plot reversal, puns, and linguistic games. His imagery can be serious—Bible, classical Greek and Egyptian mythology—or homey—pop culture such as the Wizard of Oz, Tarzan, Doc Savage, and Sherlock Holmes.

"The Lovers" shocked readers of the fifties, but won Farmer Best New Writer of the 1953 Hugo Award. In the story (later expanded into a book), an alien female "lalitha" mimics a human woman and consummates a love affair with the protagonist. Explicit sexuality and implied bestiality, added to first-rate characterization, extrapolation, and plotting, mark this work. "Rastignac the Devil" and *Timestop!* are related works. Farmer further explores sexual themes in *Flesh, Dare, A Woman a Day, Strange Relations* and the mainstream *Fire and the Night. A Feast Unknown* has been praised by Ray Bradbury for inventive exploration of aberrant sexuality. In Farmer's erotic classics *Image of the Beast* and *Blown*, the protagonist Herald Childe, ignorant of his own alien ancestry and frightening powers, becomes embroiled in the schemes of the Ogs and the Tocs to return to their home planet. These aliens derive psychic energy from sexual victimization of humans. Farmer alternates horror and humor in explicit sexual passages.

Farmer jolts readers with religious speculation. In the Father Carmody stories, collected in *Night of Light* and *Father to the Stars*, a hardened murderer, John Carmody, partakes of religious rites on the planet Dante's Joy and emerges a saint and father to a god. In *Night of Light*, human nightmares are externalized and verifiable as good and evil gods. Here Farmer appears influenced by surrealism and Jungian theory.

In the World of Tiers (Pocket Universe) series, *The Maker of Universes, The Gates of Creation, A Private Cosmos, Behind the Walls of Terra, The Lavalite World* and *Red Orc's Rage*, glamorous, immortal, ruthless Lords create pocket universes, smaller than our solar system, as playgrounds. Jadawin and Anana are Lords humanized by Kickaha, a Farmer self-portrait. Mythology and William Blake's cosmology provide rich and amusing texturing.

In the Hugo-winning "Riders of the Purple Wage," adolescent painter Chibiabos Winnegan lives in a future utopia where physical needs are all fulfilled, leaving gnawing spiritual needs. Joycean imagery and technique allow Farmer to explore theories of art and society, particularly the relation of culture to the past.

Farmer's interest in the elusiveness of truth emerges in his "further adventures" of popular heroes, as in *A Barnstormer in Oz, The Wind Whales of Ishmael, Doc Savage: His Apocalyptic Life* and *The Other Log of Phileas Fogg.* Farmer's own pop culture hero, amputee Greatheart Silver, battles geriatric parodies of the Lone Ranger, the Shadow, James Bond, etc. Farmer's fascination with Tarzan informs seven or eight of his books, including *A Feast Unknown* and the Opar books. Farmer also writes under the pen names of his own and others' fictional characters: Kilgore Trout, Rod Keen, and Jonathan Swift Somers III (a character in Kilgore Trout's *Venus on the Half-Shell*).

Riverworld is Farmer's most elaborate experiment with the unknowable nature of truth and his richest extrapolative universe. In 1953, Farmer wrote *I Owe for the Flesh* (published as *River of Eternity*, 1983). It won the Shasta Prize, which Farmer never received, and is the basis of the entire Riverworld series. In these, a mysterious super-race has created a planet with a ten-million-mile-long river, inhabited by everybody that ever lived on earth, furnished with artificial souls. To emphasize the fact that all humans have been reanimated, Farmer uses as major characters Richard Burton the explorer, Samuel Clemens, Lewis Carroll's Alice, Li Po, Farmer himself (as Peter Jairus Frigate), and of course his readers. Early Riverworld explores the nature of the soul, the verifiability of religious doctrine, and human depravity. Later, Farmer explores Sufism and writes passages of Swiftian satire on human egocentricity. The quest for truth is a motive throughout. Farmer uses historical gossip (e.g. the identity of Jack the Ripper) to create ever more complex layers of speculation.

Farmer's recent protagonists are flawed and self-destructive, trapped in Kafkaesque worlds by their own conniving, improvising harebrained schemes aimed at self-gratification. Thus with Jeff Caird of *Dayworld, Dayworld Rebel*, and *Dayworld Breakup.* As in "The Sliced-Crosswise, Only-on Tuesday World," overpopulation forces people to live only one day a week, being "stoned" or deanimated the other six. This premise leads to whimsies such as seven Popes. Caird illegally "daybreaks," stays awake all week, assuming a different personality each day. Farmer's impish humor enlivens speculation about the "reality" of the human personality. The literary pay-off is a chaotic character, yet Farmer succeeds convincingly in the portrayal of Caird and even shows in *Dayworld Breakup* how such a fractured personality could arise.

Farmer continues unconventional theological speculation (*Jesus on Mars*), writes metaphysical space-opera (*The Unreasoning Mask*), and depicts feminist human and alien females (the Shemibob in *Dark Is the Sun*). In *Stations of the Nightmare*, he gives the divine gift of healing to an insensitive clod and uses Oz symbolism for striking contrast. The breadth of Farmer's output is hard to summarize because of the variety of his experiments. A short fiction master in a time when short fiction is not profitable, he still produces thoughtful, positive work.

Critics, excepting Franz Rottensteiner (*Science-Fiction Studies*, Fall 1973), recognize Farmer's original treatment of universal issues. Russell Letson (*Science-Fiction Studies*, March 1977) endorses Farmer's use of folklore and myth. Leslie Fiedler (in *The Book of Philip José Farmer*, 1973) commends Farmer from a mainstream perspective. Edgar L. Chapman's *The Magic Labyrinth of Philip José Farmer* (1984) praises Farmer's spirit of affirmation. David Pringle (*Modern Fantasy: the Hundred Best Novels*, 1989) lists *A Feast Unknown.*

Farmer continues experimental, irreverent, improvisational, playful, and profound.

—Mary Turzillo Brizzi

---

**FARREN, Mick.** British. Born in Cheltenham, Gloucestershire, 3 September 1943. Educated at Worthing High School for Boys, Sussex; St. Martin's School of Art, London. Married 1) Joy Hebditch in 1967 (divorced 1979); 2) Elizabeth Volck in 1979. Short order cook, London Zoo, 1965; painter, 1965–67; lead singer, Deviants rock band, 1967–69; editor, *It* magazine, and *Nasty Tales* magazine, both London, 1970–73; consulting editor, *New Musical Express*, London, 1975–77. Agent: Abner Stein, 10 Roland Gardens, London, SW7 3PH, England; or, Merrilee Heifetz, Writers House, 21 West 26th Street, New York, New York 10010, U.S.A.

SCIENCE-FICTION PUBLICATIONS

Novels (series: DNA Cowboys)

*The Texts of Festival.* London, Hart Davis MacGibbon, 1973; New York, Avon, 1975.
*The Quest of the DNA Cowboys.* London, Mayflower, 1976.
*The Synaptic Manhunt.* London, Mayflower, 1976.
*The Neural Atrocity.* London, Mayflower, 1977.
*The Feelies.* London, Big O, 1978; New York, Ballantine, 1990.
*The Song of Phaid the Gambler.* London, New English Library, 1981; published in 2 vols. as *Phaid the Gambler* and *Citizen Phaid*, New York, Ace, 1986–87.
*Protectorate.* London, New English Library, 1984; New York, Ace, 1985.
*Corpse.* London, New English Library, 1986; as *Vickers*, New York, Ace, 1988.
*Their Master's War.* New York, Ballantine, 1987; London, Sphere, 1988.

*The Long Orbit*. New York, Ballantine, 1988.
*Exit Funtopia*. London, Sphere, 1989.
*The Armageddon Crazy*. New York, Ballantine, 1989.
*The Last Stand of the DNA Cowboys*. New York, Ballantine, 1989; London, Sphere, 1990.
*Mars: The Red Planet*. New York, Ballantine, 1990.
*Necrom*. New York, Ballantine, 1991.

OTHER PUBLICATIONS

Novel

*The Tale of Willy's Rats*. London, Mayflower, 1975.

Other

*Watch Out Kids*, with Edward Barker. London, Open Gate, 1972.
*Rock 'n' Roll Circus*, with George Snow. London, Pierrot, and New York, A and W, 1978.
*Elvis Presley: The Complete Illustrated Record*, with Roy Carr. London, Eel Pie, and New York, Crown, 1982.
*The Black Leather Jacket*. London, Plexus, 1985; New York, Abbeville, 1986.
*Elvis and the Colonel*, with Dirk Vellenga. New York, Delacorte, 1988; London, Grafton, 1989.

Editor, *Get on Down*. London, Futura, 1976.
Editor, with Pearce Marchbank, *Elvis in His Own Words*. London, Omnibus Press, 1977; as *Elvis Presley*, New York, Music Sales, 1978.
Editor, with David Dalton, *The Rolling Stones: In Their Own Words*. New York, Putnam, 1983.

Recording: *Vampires Stole My Lunch Money*, 1978.

*

Mick Farren comments (1985):

I suppose the most important factor in my attitude to science fiction is that I have little or no truck with hardware. All technology has an on/off switch, and if it doesn't work you kick it. If it still doesn't work, you send for the repairman. I also don't like to have too much truck with the powerful. A society will show you more about itself if you look at its deadbeats, its drifters, and its whores. More politely, you could say I have an ear for the music of the streets, wherever or whenever those streets might be.

* * *

The appearance of Mick Farren's first novel, *The Texts of Festival*, in 1973 went almost without notice, despite its direct line to the same subculture that now feeds voraciously on science fiction, perhaps because Farren was ahead of his time. Festival is a city of popular culture, the setting for a futuristic melodrama of the barbarians at the gates. Apparently it sold poorly because Farren next wrote a trilogy published in England in 1976 and 1977, but still not available in a U.S. edition.

*The Quest of the DNA Cowboys* and its two sequels, *The Synaptic Manhunt* and *The Neural Atrocity*, are wildly imaginative, highly inventive, if somewhat simpleminded in plot. An insane computer provides for all the material needs of the human race, but in order to do so, it is systematically deconstructing reality, leaving behind growing expanses of nothingness. Two adventurers set off across this fragmented landscape, avoiding vendettas, bandits, and natural disasters, ultimately discovering the nature of the catastrophe but without being able to resolve it. Twelve years later, Farren wrote *The Last Stand of the DNA Cowboys*, which oddly enough *is* available in the U.S., in which the two stalwarts return only to become the targets for a vengeful army of barbarian warriors led by a fanatic with a holy mission. The later book has a lot more polish than the original trilogy, but manages to keep much of the sense of wondrous oddness that made the earlier books so fascinating.

Farren's new books appeared with less frequency as the 1970s turned into the 1980s. *The Feelies* was a variation on an old theme, the escape by those addicted to television and drugs to a new sensation that combines the two. Now it is possible to mentally enter a dream world indistinguishable from reality. Next came *The Song of Phaid the Gambler*, so lengthy that it was published in two volumes in the U.S., as *Phaid the Gambler* and *Citizen Phaid*. Despite occasional clumsiness with the plot, Farren manages to create an interesting and entertaining post-disaster world, with a protagonist attempting to escape the attentions of a satisfying array of villains.

*Protectorate* was more uneven. Again, Farren resorts to a perhaps overly familiar plot, this time an earth ruled by insect-like aliens who administer the world as an aristocracy, confining the majority of the population to substandard ghettos from whence the inevitable revolution takes place in the waning chapters. But from this point on, Farren produced a minimum of one book a year, with noticeably growing maturity.

*Vickers* (originally published in England as *Corpse*) continues Farren's long string of less than admirable future societies. A combination of crime novel and nuclear disaster, the book features a protagonist who is a soldier turned hit man faced with a megalomaniac plot to seize control of the world. Professional soldiers figure again in *Their Master's War*, although this time the protagonist is a conscript barbarian, kidnapped into a spaceship by the alien Therem, trained and equipped with high tech weaponry, and set down to fight unexplained battles on far worlds. A mercenary is a double edged sword, however, and once the conscripts realize how little their lives matter to the Therem, and how much power their weapons provide, it's only a matter of time until it occurs to them to alter the situation.

*The Long Orbit* is far superior to anything Farren had previously written. Set in a future where you can use a robot to fulfill your obligations to society, the novel's hero is a would-be private detective who calls himself Marlowe and pretends to solve crimes in a world where such activity no longer has any meaning. Or does it? When a beautiful woman offers to hire him to locate her missing sister, it seems like nothing more than an entertaining diversion, until it becomes obvious that someone wants Marlowe to fail, even if it means killing him in the process.

*The Armageddon Crazy* is a return to the depressing, repressive future societies Farren wrote of so frequently in the past. In this case, America has a fundamentalist president who has suspended the Constitution and uses religious police to enforce his policies and imprison those who demur. A special effects expert hired to provide a "miracle" teams up with a disaffected police officer frustrated by the corruption of justice and a spy within the president's religious army to help orchestrate the overthrow of the government. Although Farren has once again produced a grim portrayal of human failings, the resolution is uplifting and optimistic.

Farren followed the excellent *The Last Stand of the DNA Cowboys* with *Mars: The Red Planet*. Both American and Soviet colonies exist on Mars, where a curious reporter decides to investigate rumors that the Russians have uncovered alien artifacts and are suppressing news of their existence. His attempts to investigate are disrupted by the intransigence of the Soviets, the uproar surrounding the discovery that a serial killer is prowling the colonies, and rumors of an alien landing elsewhere on the planet. The Martian settings are particularly well handled, and Farren spends a great deal of time creating a setting in which the physical problems of existing on an airless world are dealt with convincingly. His most recent novel, *Necrom*, while not nearly as impressive, is an entertaining blend of science fiction and fantasy, featuring a plausible (more or less) explanation for demons and their interactions with the real world. Basically an adventure writer, Farren nevertheless takes great pains to create viable characters and is unusually proficient at the creation of exotic settings and cultures.

—Don D'Ammassa

---

**FAST, Howard (Melvin).** Also writes as E.V. Cunningham; Walter Ericson. American. Born in New York City, 11 November 1914. Educated at George Washington High School, New York, graduated 1931; National Academy of Design, New York. Served with the Office of War Information, 1942–43, and the Army Film Project, 1944. Married Bette Cohen in 1937; one daughter and one son, Jonathan Fast, *q.v.* War correspondent in the Far East of *Esquire* and *Coronet* magazines, 1945. Taught at Indiana University, Bloomington, Summer 1947. Imprisoned for contempt of Congress, 1947. Founder of the World Peace Movement and member of the World Peace Council, 1950–55. Operated Blue Heron Press, New York, 1952–57. Currently, Member of the Fellowship for Reconciliation. American-Labour Party candidate for Congress for the 23rd District of New York, 1952. Recipient: Bread Loaf Writers Conference award, 1933; Schomburg Race Relations award, 1944; Newspaper Guild award, 1947; Jewish Book Council of America award, 1948; Stalin International Peace Prize (now Soviet International Peace Prize), 1954; Screenwriters award, 1960; National Association of Independent Schools award, 1962; Emmy award, for television play, 1976. Agent: Sterling Lord Agency, 1 Madison Avenue, New York, New York, 10010. Address: 1 Mountain Wood Drive, Greenwich, Connecticut 06830, U.S.A.

SCIENCE-FICTION PUBLICATIONS

Novel

*The Hunter and the Trap.* New York, Dial Press, 1967.

Short Stories

*The Edge of Tomorrow.* New York, Bantam, 1961; London, Corgi, 1962.
*The General Zapped an Angel.* New York, Morrow, 1970.
*A Touch of Infinity.* New York, Morrow, 1973; London, Hodder and Stoughton, 1975.
*Time and the Riddle: Thirty-One Zen Stories.* Pasadena, California, Ward Ritchie Press, 1975.

OTHER PUBLICATIONS

Novels

*Two Valleys.* New York, Dial Press, 1933; London, Dickson, 1934.
*Strange Yesterday.* New York, Dodd Mead, 1934.
*Place in the City.* New York, Harcourt Brace, 1937.
*Conceived in Liberty: A Novel of Valley Forge.* New York, Simon and Schuster, and London, Joseph, 1939.
*The Last Frontier.* New York, Duell, 1941; London, Lane, 1948.
*The Unvanquished.* New York, Duell, 1942; London, Lane, 1947.
*The Tall Hunter.* New York, Harper, 1942.
*Citizen Tom Paine.* New York, Duell, 1943; London, Lane, 1946.
*Freedom Road.* New York, Duell, 1944; London, Lane, 1946.
*The American: A Middle Western Legend.* New York, Duell, 1946; London, Lane 1949.
*The Children.* New York, Duell, 1947.
*Clarkton.* New York, Duell, 1947.
*My Glorious Brothers.* Boston, Little Brown, 1948; London, Lane, 1950.
*The Proud and the Free.* Boston, Little Brown, 1950; London, Lane 1952.
*Spartacus.* Privately printed, 1951; London, Lane, 1952.
*Fallen Angel* (As Walter Ericson). Boston, Little Brown, 1952; as *The Darkness Within*, New York, Ace, 1953; as *Mirage* (as Howard Fast), New York, Fawcett, 1965.
*Silas Timberman.* New York, Blue Heron Press, 1954; London, Lane, 1955.
*The Story of Lola Gregg.* New York, Blue Heron Press, 1956; London, Lane, 1957.
*Moses, Prince of Egypt.* New York, Crown, 1958; London, Methuen, 1959.
*The Winston Affair.* New York, Crown, 1959; London, Methuen, 1960.
*The Golden River*, in *The Howard Fast Reader.* New York, Crown, 1960.
*April Morning.* New York, Crown, and London, Methuen, 1961.
*Power.* New York, Doubleday, 1962; London, Methuen, 1963.
*Agrippa's Daughter.* New York, Doubleday, 1964; London, Methuen, 1965.
*Torquemada.* New York, Doubleday, 1966; London, Methuen, 1967.
*The Crossing.* New York, Morrow, 1971; London, Eyre Methuen, 1972.
*The Hessian.* New York, Morrow, 1972; London, Hodder and Stoughton, 1973.
*The Immigrants.* Boston, Houghton Mifflin, 1977; London, Hodder and Stoughton, 1978.
*Second Generation.* Boston Houghton Mifflin, and London, Hodder and Stoughton, 1978.
*The Establishment.* Boston, Houghton Mifflin, 1979; London, Hodder and Stoughton, 1980.
*The Legacy.* Boston, Houghton Mifflin, and London, Hodder and Stoughton, 1981.
*Max.* Boston, Houghton Mifflin, 1982; London, Hodder and Stoughton, 1983.
*The Outsider.* Boston Houghton Mifflin, 1984; London, Hodder and Stoughton, 1985.
*The Immigrant's Daughter.* Boston, Houghton Mifflin, 1985; London, Hodder and Stoughton, 1986.
*The Dinner Party.* Boston, Houghton Mifflin, and London, Hodder and Stoughton, 1987.
*The Call of the Fife and Drum: Three Novels of the Revolution* (includes *The Unvanquished, Conceived in Liberty, The Proud and the Free*). Secaucus, New Jersey, Citadel Press, 1987.
*The Pledge.* Boston, Houghton Mifflin, 1988; London, Hodder and Stoughton, 1989.
*The Confession of Joe Cullen.* Boston, Houghton Mifflin, 1989.

Novels as E.V. Cunningham

*Sylvia.* New York, Doubleday, 1960; London, Deutsch, 1962.
*Phyllis.* New York, Doubleday, and London, Deutsch, 1962.
*Alice.* New York, Doubleday, 1963; London, Deutsch, 1965.
*Lydia.* New York, Doubleday, 1964, London, Deutsch, 1965.
*Shirley.* New York, Doubleday, and London, Deutsch, 1964.
*Penelope.* New York, Doubleday, 1965; London, Deutsch, 1966.
*Helen.* New York, Doubleday, 1966; London, Deutsch, 1967.
*Margie.* New York, Morrow, 1966; London, Deutsch, 1968.
*Sally.* New York, Morrow, and London, Deutsch, 1967.
*Samantha.* New York, Morrow, 1967; London, Deutsch, 1968.
*Cynthia.* New York, Morrow, 1968; London, Deutsch, 1969.
*The Assassin Who Gave Up His Gun.* New York, Morrow, 1969, London, Deutsch, 1970.
*Millie.* New York, Morrow, 1973; London, Deutsch, 1975.
*The Case of the One-Penny Orange.* New York, Holt Rinehart, 1977; London Deutsch, 1978.
*The Case of the Russian Diplomat.* New York, Holt Rinehart, 1978; London, Deutsch, 1979.
*The Case of the Poisoned Eclairs.* New York, Holt Rinehart, 1979; London, Deutsch, 1980.
*The Case of the Sliding Pool.* New York, Delacorte Press, 1981; London, Gollancz, 1982.
*The Case of the Kidnapped Angel.* New York, Delacorte Press, 1982; London, Gollancz, 1983.
*The Case of the Murdered Mackenzie.* New York, Delacorte Press, 1984; London, Gollancz, 1985.
*The Wabash Factor.* New York, Delacorte Press, 1986; London, Gollancz, 1987.

Short Stories

*Patrick Henry and the Frigate's Keel and Other Stories of a Young Nation.* New York, Duell, 1945.
*Departure and Other Stories.* Boston, Little Brown, 1949.
*The Last Supper and Other Stories.* New York, Blue Heron Press, 1955; London, Lane, 1956.

Plays

*The Hammer* (produced New York, 1950).
*Thirty Pieces of Silver* (produced Melbourne, 1951; London, 1984). New York, Blue Heron Press, and London, Lane, 1954.
*General Washington and the Water Witch.* London, Lane, 1956.
*The Crossing* (produced Dallas, 1962).
*The Hill* (screenplay). New York, Doubleday, 1964.
*David and Paula* (produced New York, 1982).
*Citizen Tom Paine*, adaptation of his own novel (produced Williamstown, Massachusetts, 1985). Boston, Houghton Mifflin, 1986.

Screenplay: *The Hessian*, 1971.

Television Plays: *What's a Nice Girl Like You . . .?*, 1971; *21 Hours at Munich*, with Edward Hume, 1976; *The Ambassador*, 1976.

Verse

*Never to Forget the Battle of the Warsaw Ghetto*, with William Gropper. New York, Jewish Peoples Fraternal Order, 1946.

Other

*The Romance of a People* (for children). New York, Hebrew Publishing Company, 1941.
*Lord Baden-Powell of the Boy Scouts.* New York, Messner, 1941.
*Haym Salomon, Son of Liberty.* New York, Messner, 1941.
*The Picture-Book History of the Jews*, with Bette Fast. New York, Hebrew Publishing Company, 1942.
*Goethals and the Panama Canal.* New York, Messner, 1942.
*The Incredible Tito.* New York, Magazine House, 1944.
*Intellectuals in the Fight for Peace.* New York, Masses and Mainstream, 1949.
*Tito and His People.* Winnipeg, Manitoba, Contemporary Publishers, 1950.
*Literature and Reality.* New York, International Publishers, 1950.
*Peekskill, U.S.A.: A Personal Experience.* New York, Civil Rights Congress, and London, International Publishing Company, 1951.
*Korean Lullaby.* New York, American Peace Crusade, n.d.
*Tony and the Wonderful Door* (for children). New York, Blue Heron Press, 1952; as *The Magic Door*, Culver City, California, Peace Press, 1979.
*Spain and Peace.* New York, Joint Anti-Fascist Refugee Committee, 1952.
*The Passion of Sacco and Vanzetti: A New England Legend.* New York, Blue Heron Press, 1953; London, Lane, 1954.
*The Naked God: The Writer and the Communist Party.* New York, Praeger, 1957; London, Bodley Head, 1958.
*The Howard Fast Reader.* New York, Crown, 1960.
*The Jews: Story of a People.* New York, Dial Press, 1968; London, Cassell, 1970.
*The Art of Zen Meditation.* Culver City, California, Peace Press, 1977.
*Being Red* (Memoir). Boston, Houghton Mifflin, 1990.

Editor, *The Selected Work of Tom Paine.* New York, Modern Library, 1946; London, Lane, 1948.
Editor, *Best Short Stories of Theodore Dreiser.* Cleveland World, 1947.

*

Manuscript Collection: University of Pennsylvania Library, Philadelphia.

Howard Fast comments:

All of my science fiction works are parables—and perhaps not so much science fiction as humor, fear, and fantasy. In a way they are preachments against the cruelty and foolishness of modern man. One of my favorites concerns a sub-normal three-star general who shoots down an angel in Vietnam. Science does not tolerate angels, but since science does tolerate three-star generals, the discipline needs some self-study. Beyond that, the stories speak for themselves. Some are quite funny, but who can observe man for 70 years without realizing that, above all our stupidity and brutishness, we are, most often, ridiculous. Perhaps we provoke enough laughter among the Gods to cause them to refrain from extinguishing us—though in good time we will probably do that ourselves.

* * *

The science fiction of Howard Fast consists mainly of "Zen short stories" reprinted in *Time and the Riddle.* In them he uses motifs from science fiction and older mythologies to question the morality of man's survival and the trade-offs it demands.

The older images include a hand (God's?) snuffing out the sun in "Not with a Bang," the devil making a deal in "Tomorrow's *Wall Street Journal*," and a stunning encounter with the supernatural in Vietnam in "The General Zapped an Angel." Metaphysical conceits that are borderline SF depict the world as a "Movie House," as a stage set being removed in "The Interval," and as a hatching egg in "The Pragmatic Seed." The mythological "great time" assumes reality for an Indian ("The Mohawk"), meditating on the steps of St. Patrick's Cathedral in New York; asked on the radio to show cause why divine wrath should be spared, mankind's computer network comes up with another meditator, even freakier ("Show-Cause").

More clearly science fiction, a mouse is equipped by small aliens with intelligence, which doesn't prevent its demise ("The Mouse"). A large ant may be an alien visitor, but revulsion causes humans to squash it and its kind ("The Large Ant"). Tiny people are wiped out as vermin in "A Matter of Size," suggesting the same could be done to us. It is, when insects retaliate, severing the networks of wires, pipes, and other structures that support our civilization ("The Insects"). Man's propensity for killing takes on more cosmic significance in "Cato the Martian." Disturbed by their study of us, the Martians finally attack, with the return strike devastating their civilization. An even more idyllic planet gives human explorers a view of Eden denied us due to our destructiveness ("The Sight of Eden"). Alternatively, Fast depicts Earth as the dumping ground for the galaxy's psychotics. And an alien "exterminator" turns out to be "General Hardy's Profession," revealed through psychoanalysis.

Disturbing the natural order of things may have tragic or trivial consequences. Deep drilling with nuclear weapons brings up blood instead of oil in "The Wound." New York's garbage seems to go into another dimension ("The Hoop"), but its return is disruptive. A time machine creates a closed loop in "Of Time and Cats." Another one fails to permit Hitler's assassination in "The Mind of God." Even a hybrid cactus flower which produces contentment may be a questionable trade-off in "Echinomastus Contentii." Utopia, if it can be brought about, will also demand intervention and deceit, but the cost seems worth it. The pretense of invasion in "The Martian Shop" brings about world government as well as technological advance. Similar results come from making good use of the resources of the world's richest man, and keeping him frozen long after a cure for his cancer has been found ("The Cold, Cold Box"). But the major elaboration of this theme is "The Trap" (published in a shorter version as "The First Men").

A short novel told largely in letters, it speculates on the results of raising infants to be fully human. Improbably patient, the US Army, sponsor of this research, finally resolves to destroy the commune which threatens the way of life of man as he is. But the children, though totally non-violent, are technologically capable of protecting themselves. It is not they so much as conventional society who is interfering with the natural order of things.

Professionally written, economical, with entertaining conversation, little or no melodrama, and a competent style, these stories may seem a bit glib or facile, but a parable is only as shallow or profound as the audience wishes to make it.

—David N. Samuelson

---

**FAST, Jonathan (David).** American. Born in New York City, 13 April 1948; son of the writer Howard Fast, *q. v.* Educated at the High School of Music and Art, New York, 1962–66; Princeton University, New Jersey, 1966–68; Sarah Lawrence College, Bronxville, New York, 1968–70, B. A. 1970; University of California, Berkeley (Hearst Fellow in music), 1970. Married the writer Erica Jong in 1977 (divorced, 1983); one daughter. Composer and writer. Address: c/o E. P. Dutton, 375 Hudson Street, New York, New York 10014, U.S.A.

SCIENCE-FICTION PUBLICATIONS

Novels

*The Secrets of Synchronicity.* New York, New American Library, 1977; as *Prisoner of the Planets*, London, Panther, 1980.
*Mortal Gods.* New York, Harper, 1978; London, Panther, 1980.
*The Beast.* New York, Random House, 1981; London, Methuen, 1982.

Uncollected Short Stories

"Decay," in *Fantasy and Science Fiction* (New York), April, 1975.
"Earthblossom," in *New Constellations*, edited by Thomas M. Disch and Charles Naylor. New York, Harper, 1976.
"Test Driving the Valkyrie," in *Swank* (New York), July, 1976.
"Kindertotenlieder," in *Issac Asimov's Science Fiction Magazine* (New York), Spring 1977.

OTHER PUBLICATIONS

Novels

*The Inner Circle.* New York, Delacorte Press, 1979; London, Magnum, 1980.
*Golden Fire.* New York, Arbor House, and London, Methuen, 1986.
*The Jade Stalk.* New York, Dutton, 1988.
*Stolen Time.* New York, Fawcett, 1990.

Plays

Television Plays: *Two Missionaries; The Thrill Show Hero; Love al Dente; Prisoner of Space.*

*

Jonathan Fast comments:

(1981) Social satire is one of the primary aims of my work: using the future to let me reflect upon the present, upon the lunacy of our lives and the possibilities of sanity. Religion fascinates me as does the opportunity to speculate on matters metaphysical, on life and death and the nature of reality. In my most recent work (*The Inner Circle*) I have tried to cast my "science-fiction" ideas in a "mainstream" mold in order to reach a larger audience, and, as a result of its success, I believe I shall continue with this ruse in the future.

* * *

Jonathan Fast was a composer and a television writer before he turned to book-length science fiction. His early skills seem to have been transferrable; he creates a universe of astonishing variations which he weaves firmly into thematic resolution, all in the course of a story marked by linguistic cleverness, clearly drawn characters, good dramatic pace, and excellent visualization. On top of that, he does his homework—amid the speed and the fun is some solid extrapolation of current scientific thought.

His own stated interest is to show that religion and science are aspects of the same thing. They certainly are in the colorful universe of his first novel, *The Secrets of Synchronicity.* The story moves dizzyingly from the enslaved child miners on the asteroid Slabour, to a desert planet with a civilization of telepathic snakes, to Nova Center, the commercial capital of the galaxy, and finally, triumphantly, back to Slabour. Fast connects not only science and religion, through the Vedic myths, but economics as well. His galaxy is controlled by Ultra Cap, a super-capitalistic organisation which, by concealing the blue stone that holds the secrets of synchronicity, prevents the human race from making its own connections and finding the freedom beyond technology. Fast's interests are quite serious, but his tone is light and entertaining, with many genuinely funny moments. His callow protagonist, Stefin-Dae, is clever enough to stay alive but not to avoid being swept from place to place in a kaleidoscopic universe. And Fast's variety is real—each location is completely different from the next, carefully thought out, and vividly described.

*The Secrets of Synchronicity* is a neat circular quest, profusely illustrated and exhilarating in its range and constant pace. *Mortal Gods* tries for more depth in one place. It is less funny but possibly more original; his protagonist is less appealing but has more depth than Stefin-Dae. Fast focuses here on the possibilities of controlled genetic mutation, and comes up with the concept of the Lifestylers—beings bizarrely mutated according to artists' conceptions, living in the transdimensional Bardo of Tibetan theology, and receiving worship as gods. Once again the profit motive, in the form of the Mutagen Corporation, controls the religious life of the people. The Lifestylers are an impressive invention on Fast's part, and he gives reference to current geneticists before he starts. He also does reasonably well with a challenge the science-fiction genre has been working on for some time—depicting successful sex between human and alien. As in his first book, the accompanying details of civilization are well worked out and of interest in themselves. The book's only flaw is the plot he uses to tie all these things together, a political assassination mystery that is adequately resolved but that really adds nothing to the science fiction of the story.

Fast has written a Hollywood mystery as well—*The Inner Circle*, set firmly on this Earth and doubtless based on his experience of screen writing. His *The Beast*, despite marginal suggestions of medical SF, is a fairy tale of beauty and the beast. One can only hope that he returns to traditional science fiction soon. Fast is one of the most entertaining writers in the genre, a delight for the mind as well as for the imagining eye. In a brisk biographical note, his publishers assure us that "he longs for a cogent universe." So far he has formed at least two himself.

—Karen G. Way

---

**FEARN, John (Francis) Russell.** Also wrote as Geoffrey Armstrong; Thornton Ayre; Hugo Blayn; Hank Carson; Dennis Clive; Hank Cole; John Cotton; Polton Cross; Astron Del Martia; Mark Denholm; Spike Gordon; Volsted Gridban; Griff; Conrad G. Holt; Frank Jones; Nat Karta; Clem Larson; Paul Lorraine; Jed McCloud; Jed McNab; Dom Passante; Lawrence F. Rose; Frank Russell; John Russell; Bryan Shaw; John Slate; Vargo Statten; K. Thomas; Earl Titan; John Wernheim; Ephriam Winiki. British. Born in Worsley, Lancashire, 5 June 1908. Married Carrie Worth in 1956. Cotton salesman; cinema projectionist during World War II. Editor, as Vargo Statten, *British Science Fiction Magazine*, both Luton, Bedfordshire, 1954–56. *Died 18 September 1960.*

SCIENCE-FICTION PUBLICATIONS

Novels (series: Clayton Drew; Golden Amazon)

*Valley of Pretenders* (as Dennis Clive). New York, Columbia, 1942.
*The Voice Commands* (as Dennis Clive). New York, Columbia, 1942.
*The Intelligence Gigantic*. Kingswood, Surrey, World's Work, 1943.
*The Golden Amazon*. Kingswood, Surrey, World's Work, 1944.
*Other Eyes Watching* (as Polton Cross). London, Pendulum, 1946.
*Liners of Time*. Kingswood, Surrey, World's Work, 1947.
*Slaves of Ijax*. Llandudno, Caernarvonshire, Kaner, 1948.
*The Golden Amazon Returns*. Kingswood, Surrey, World's Work, 1948; as *The Deathless Amazon*, Toronto, Harlequin, 1955.
*The Trembling World* (as Astron Del Martia). London, Frances, 1949.
*Emperor of Mars* (Drew). London, Panther, 1950.
*Warrior of Mars* (Drew). London, Panther, 1950.
*Red Men of Mars* (Drew). London, Panther, 1950.
*Goddess of Mars* (Drew). London, Panther, 1950.
*Operation Venus*. London, Scion, 1950.
*The Golden Amazon's Triumph*. Kingswood, Surrey, World's Work, 1953.
*The Amazon's Diamond Quest*. Kingswood, Surrey, World's Work, 1953.
*Cosmic Exodus* (as Conrad G. Holt). London, Pearson, 1953.
*Dark Boundaries* (as Paul Lorraine). London, Warren, 1953.
*The Hell Fruit* (as Lawrence F. Rose). London, Pearson, 1953.
*Z Formations* (as Bryan Shaw). London, Warren, 1953.
*The Amazon Strikes Again*. Kingswood, Surrey, World's Work, 1954.
*Twin of the Amazon*. Kingswood, Surrey, World's Work, 1954.
*Conquest of the Amazon*. London, Futura, 1976.
*No Grave Need I*. Wallsend, Harbottle, 1984.
*The Slitherers*. Wallsend, Harbottle, 1984.
*Climate Incorporated*. Wallsend, Harbottle, 1985.

Novels as Vargo Statten

*Annihilation*. London, Scion, 1950.
*The Micro Men*. London, Scion, 1950.
*Wanderer of Space*. London, Scion, 1950.
*2000 Years On*. London, Scion, 1950.
*Inferno*. London, Scion, 1950.
*The Cosmic Flame*. London, Scion, 1950.
*Nebula X*. London, Scion, 1950.
*The Sun Makers*. London, Scion, 1950.
*The Avenging Martian*. London, Scion, 1951.
*Cataclysm*. London, Scion, 1951.
*The Red Insects*. London, Scion, 1951.
*Deadline to Pluto*. London, Scion, 1951.
*The Petrified Planet*. London, Scion, 1951.
*Born of Luna*. London, Scion, 1951.
*The Devouring Fire*. London, Scion, 1951.
*The Renegade Star*. London, Scion, 1951.
*The New Satellite*. London, Scion, 1951.
*The Catalyst*. London, Scion, 1951.

*The Inner Cosmos.* London, Scion, 1952.
*The Space Warp.* London, Scion, 1952.
*The Eclipse Express.* London, Scion, 1952.
*The Time Bridge.* London, Scion, 1952.
*The Man from Tomorrow.* London, Scion, 1952.
*The G-Bomb.* London, Scion, 1952.
*Laughter in Space.* London, Scion, 1952.
*Across the Ages.* London, Scion, 1952.
*The Last Martian.* London, Scion, 1952.
*Worlds to Conquer.* London, Scion, 1952.
*Decreation.* London, Scion, 1952.
*The Time Trap.* London, Scion, 1952.
*Science Metropolis.* London, Scion, 1952.
*To the Ultimate.* London, Scion, 1952.
*Ultra Spectrum.* London, Scion, 1953.
*The Dust Destroyer.* London, Scion, 1953.
*Black-Wing of Mars.* London, Scion, 1953.
*Man in Duplicate.* London, Scion, 1953.
*Zero Hour.* London, Scion, 1953.
*The Black Avengers.* London, Scion, 1953.
*Odyssey of Nine.* London, Scion, 1953.
*Pioneer 1990.* London, Scion, 1953.
*The Interloper.* London, Scion, 1953.
*Man of Two Worlds.* London, Scion, 1953.
*The Lie Destroyer.* London, Scion, 1953.
*Black Bargain.* London, Scion, 1953.
*The Grand Illusion.* London, Scion, 1953.
*Wealth of the Void.* London, Scion, 1954.
*A Time Appointed.* London, Scion, 1954.
*I Spy. . . .* London, Scion, 1954.
*The Multi-Man.* London, Scion, 1954.
*Creature from the Black Lagoon* (novelization of screenplay). London, Dragon, 1954.
*1,000-Year Voyage.* London, Dragon, 1954.
*Earth 2.* London, Dragon, 1955.

Novels as Volsted Gridban (series: Clifford Brooks; Adam Quirke)

*Moons for Sale.* London, Scion, 1953.
*The Dyno-Depressant.* London, Scion, 1953.
*Magnetic Brain.* London, Scion, 1953.
*Scourge of the Atom.* London, Scion, 1953.
*A Thing of the Past* (Brooks). London, Scion, 1953.
*Exit Life.* London, Scion, 1953.
*The Master Must Die* (Quirke). London, Scion, 1953.
*The Purple Wizard.* London, Scion, 1953.
*The Genial Dinosaur* (Brooks). London, Scion, 1954.
*The Frozen Limit.* London, Scion, 1954.
*I Came, I Saw, I Wondered.* London, Scion, 1954.
*The Lonely Astronomer* (Quirke). London, Scion, 1954.

Uncollected Short Stories

"The Intelligence Gigantic," in *Amazing* (New York), June–July 1933.
"The Man Who Stopped the Dust," in *Astounding* (New York), March 1934.
"The Brain of Light," in *Astounding* (New York), May 1934.
"Invaders from Time," in *Scoops* (London), 12 May 1934.
"He Never Slept," in *Astounding* (New York), June 1934.
"Before Earth Came," in *Astounding* (New York), July 1934.
"Earth's Mausoleum," in *Astounding* (New York), May 1935.
"Liners of Time," in *Amazing* (New York), May, June, July, August 1935.
"The Blue Infinity," in *Astounding* (New York), September, 1935.
"Mathematica," in *Astounding* (New York), February 1936.
"Mathematica Plus," in *Astounding* (New York), May 1936.
"Subconscious," in *Amazing* (New York), August 1936.
"Deserted Universe," in *Astounding* (New York), September 1936.
"The Great Illusion," in *Fantasy*, September 1936.
"Dynasty of the Small," in *Astounding* (New York), November 1936.
"Portrait of a Murderer," in *Weird Tales* (Indianapolis), December 1936.
"Metamorphosis," in *Astounding* (New York), January 1937.
"Brain of Venus," in *Thrilling Wonder Stories* (New York), February 1937.
"Worlds Within," in *Astounding* (New York), March 1937.
"Menace from the Microcosm," in *Thrilling Wonder Stories* (New York), June 1937.
"Superhuman" (as Geoffrey Armstrong) and "Seeds from Space," in *Tales of Wonder 1* (Kingswood, Surrey), June 1937.
"Dark Eternity," in *Astounding* (New York), December 1937.
"Zagribud," in *Amazing* (New York), December 1937, February, April 1938.
"Death at the Observatory," in *Modern Wonder 76* (London), 1938.
"The Misty Wilderness," in *Modern Wonder 77* (London), 1938.
"The Weather Machine," in *Modern Wonder 78* (London), 1938.
"The Red Magician," in *Fantasy 1* (London), 1938.
"The Red Heritage," in *Astounding* (New York), January 1938.
"Through Earth's Core," in *Tales of Wonder 2* (Kingswood Surrey), Spring 1938.
"Lords of 9016," in *Thrilling Wonder Stories* (New York), April 1938.
"A Summons from Mars," in *Amazing* (New York), June 1938.
"Climatica," in *Fantasy 2* (London), 1939.
"The Black Empress," in *Amazing* (New York), January 1939.
"Outlaw of Saturn" (as John Cotton), in *Science Fiction* (Holyoke, Massachusetts), March 1939.
"Secret of the Buried City," in *Amazing* (New York), May 1939.
"She Walked Alone," in *Fantastic Adventures* (New York), July 1939.
"Thoughts That Kill," in *Science Fiction Stories* (New York), October 1939.
"Frigid Moon" (as Dennis Clive), in *Future* (New York), November 1939.
"Phantom from Space," in *Super Science* (Kokomo, Indiana), March 1940.
"War of the Scientists," in *Amazing* (New York), April 1940.
"The Cosmic Juggernaut," in *Planet* (New York), Summer 1940.
"He Conquered Venus," in *Astonishing* (Chicago), June 1940.
"Laughter Out of Space" (as Dennis Clive), in *Future* (New York), July 1940.
"Queen of Venus," in *Marvel* (New York), November 1940.
"The Cosmic Derelict," in *Planet* (New York), Spring 1941.
"Martian Miniature," in *Amazing* (New York), May 1942.
"The Last Hours," in *Amazing* (New York), August 1942.
"The Ultimate Analysis," in *Thrilling Wonder Stories* (New York), Fall 1944.
"Aftermath," in *Startling* (New York), Fall 1945.
"Interlink," in *Thrilling Wonder Stories* (New York), Fall 1945.
"Solar Assignment" (as Mark Denholm), "Knowledge Without Learning" (as K. Thomas), and "Sweet Mystery of Life," in *New Worlds 1* (London), 1946.
"The Unbroken Chain," in *Startling* (New York), Spring 1946.
"The Multillionth Chance," in *Thrilling Wonder Stories* (New York), Fall 1946.
"Last Conflict," in *Fantasy* (London), December 1946.
"Pre-Natal," in *Outlands 1* (Liverpool), December 1946.
"The Arbiter," in *Startling* (New York), May 1947.

"After the Atom," in *Startling* (New York), May 1948.
"Wanderer of Time," in *My Best Science Fiction Story*, edited by Leo Margulies and Oscar J. Friend. New York, Merlin Press, 1949.
"Lord of Atlantis" (Amazon), in *Star Weekly* (Toronto), 8 October 1949.
"Triangle of Power" (Amazon), in *Star Weekly* (Toronto), 13 May 1950.
"Stranger in Our Midst," in *Star Weekly* (Toronto), 2 September 1950.
"Black-Out," in *Science Fantasy* (Bournemouth), Winter 1950–51.
"The Amethyst City" (Amazon), in *Star Weekly* (Toronto), 3 March 1951.
"Daughter of the Amazon," in *Star Weekly* (Toronto), 1 December 1951.
"Glimpse," in *Star Weekly* (Toronto), 21 February 1952.
"Flight of the Vampires," in *Amazing* (New York), September 1952.
"Quorne Returns" (Amazon), in *Star Weekly* (Toronto), 25 October 1952.
"Deadline," in *Star Weekly* (Toronto), 13 December 1952.
"Waters of Eternity" (as Mark Denholm), in *Worlds of the Universe 1* (London), 1953.
"Winged Pestilence," in *Star Weekly* (Toronto), 23 May 1953.
"Later Than You Think," in *Space-Time*, June 1953.
"The Central Intelligence" (Amazon), in *Star Weekly* (Toronto), 22 August 1953.
"The Copper Bullet" (as John Wernheim), in *Vargo Statten Science Fiction Magazine 1* (Luton, Bedfordshire), 1954.
"First of the Robots," in *Space Fact and Fiction* (London), April 1954.
"The Voice of the Conqueror," in *Star Weekly* (Toronto), 10 July 1954.
"The Cosmic Crusaders," in *Star Weekly* (Toronto), 21 February 1955.
"Here and Now," in *Star Weekly* (Toronto), 2 April 1955.
"Parasite Planet" (Amazon), in *Star Weekly* (Toronto), 27 August 1955.
"World Out of Step" (Amazon), in *Star Weekly* (Toronto), 17 November 1956.
"The Shadow People" (Amazon), in *Star Weekly* (Toronto), 6 April 1957.
"Kingpin Planet" (Amazon), in *Star Weekly* (Toronto), 19 October 1957.
"Robbery Without Violence," in *Star Weekly* (Toronto), 14 December 1957.
"World in Reverse" (Amazon), in *Star Weekly* (Toronto), 26 April 1958.
"Manton's World," in *Star Weekly* (Toronto), 7 June 1958.
"Dwellers in Darkness" (Amazon), in *Star Weekly* (Toronto), 29 November 1958.
"World in Duplicate" (Amazon), in *Star Weekly* (Toronto), 16 May 1959.
"Judgement Bell," in *Weird and Occult Library 2*. London, Swan, 1960.
"Standstill Planet" (Amazon), in *Star Weekly* (Toronto), 26 March 1960.
"Ghost World" (Amazon), in *Star Weekly* (Toronto), 17 December 1960.
"Earth Divided" (Amazon), in *Star Weekly* (Toronto), 24 June 1961.
"Into the Unknown," in *Vision of Tomorrow* (Newcastle upon Tyne), April 1970.
"The Ghost Sun," with S. J. Bounds, in *Vision of Tomorrow* (Newcastle upon Tyne), May 1970.
"Rule of the Brains," in *Vision of Tomorrow* (Newcastle upon Tyne), August 1970.
"Alice, Where Art Thou?," in *The Best of British SF 1*, edited by Mike Ashley. London, Futura, 1977.
"The Golden Amazon Returns," in *Superheroes*, edited by Michel Parry. London, Sphere, 1978.
"Arctic God," in *Friendly Aliens*, edited by John Robert Colombo. Toronto, Hounslow Press, 1981.

Uncollected Short Stories as Thornton Ayre (series: Golden Amazon; Brutus Lloyd)

"Penal World," in *Astounding* (New York), October 1937.
"Whispering Satellite," in *Astounding* (New York), January 1938.
"Locked City," in *Amazing* (New York), October 1938.
"Secret of the Ring," in *Amazing* (New York), November 1938.
"World Without Men," in *Amazing* (New York), April 1939.
"Microbes from Space," in *Amazing* (New York), June 1939.
"The Golden Amazon," in *Fantastic Adventures* (New York), July 1939.
"Face in the Sky," in *Amazing* (New York), September 1939.
"Lunar Intrigue," in *Fantastic Adventures* (New York), November 1939.
"The Man Who Saw Two Worlds" (Lloyd), in *Amazing* (New York), January 1940.
"Mystery of the White Raider," in *Fantastic Adventures* (New York), February 1940.
"World Reborn," in *Super Science* (Kokomo, Indiana), March 1940.
"The Case of the Murdered Savants" (Lloyd), in *Amazing* (New York), April 1940.
"The Amazon Fights Again," in *Fantastic Adventures* (New York), June 1940.
"Secret of the Moon Treasure," in *Amazing* (New York), July 1940.
"Domain of Zero," in *Planet* (New York), Fall 1940.
"The Man Who Sold the Earth," in *Science Fiction* (Holyoke, Massachusetts), October 1940.
"Special Agent to Venus," in *Fantastic Adventures* (New York), October 1940.
"Twilight of the Tenth World," in *Planet* (New York), Winter 1940.
"Island in the Marsh," in *Startling* (New York), November 1940.
"The World in Wilderness," in *Science Fiction* (Holyoke, Massachusetts), June 1941.
"Lunar Concession," in *Science Fiction* (Holyoke, Massachusetts), September 1941.
"Mystery of the Martian Pendulum," with A. R. Steber, in *Amazing* (New York), October 1941.
"The Case of the Mesozoic Monsters" (Lloyd), in *Amazing* (New York), May 1942.
"The Mental Gangster," in *Fantastic Adventures* (New York), August 1942.
"Vampire Queen," in *Planet* (New York), Fall 1942.
"The Silver Coil," in *Amazing* (New York), November 1942.
"Children of the Golden Amazon," in *Fantastic Adventures* (New York), April 1943.
"Lunar Vengeance," in *Amazing* (New York), September 1943.
"White Mouse," in *New Worlds 1* (London), 1946.
"From Afar," in *Hands Up Annual*, 1947.

Uncollected Short Stories as Polton Cross

"The Mental Ultimate," in *Astounding* (New York), January 1938.
"The Degenerates," in *Astounding* (New York), February 1938.

"The Master of the Golden City," in *Amazing* (New York), June 1938.
"Wings Across the Cosmos," in *Thrilling Wonder Stories* (New York), June 1938.
"The World That Dissolved," in *Amazing* (New York), February 1939.
"World Without Chance," in *Thrilling Wonder Stories* New York), February 1939.
"Martian Avenger," in *Amazing* (New York), April 1939.
"World Without Death," in *Amazing* (New York), June 1939.
"World Beneath Ice," in *Amazing* (New York), August 1939.
"The Man from Hell," in *Fantastic Adventures* (New York), November 1939.
"Chameleon Planet," in *Astonishing* (Chicago), February 1940.
"Wedding of the Forces," in *Future* (New York), November 1940.
"Science from Syracuse," in *Science Fiction* (Holyoke, Massachusetts), March 1941.
"The Last Secret Weapon," in *Marvel* (New York), April 1941.
"The Man Who Bought Mars," in *Fantastic Adventures* (New York), June 1941.
"Destroyer from the Past," in *Amazing* (New York), May 1942.
"Prisoner of Time," in *Super Science* (Kokomo, Indiana), May 1942.
"Outcasts of Eternity," in *Fantastic Adventures* (New York), September 1942.
"The Devouring Tide," in *Thrilling Wonder Stories* (New York), Summer 1944.
"Mark Grayson Unlimited," in *Thrilling Wonder Stories* (New York), Spring 1945.
"Space Trap," in *Thrilling Wonder Stories* (New York), Fall 1945.
"Other Eyes Watching," in *Startling* (New York), Spring 1946.
"Twilight Planet," in *Thrilling Wonder Stories* (New York), Summer 1946.
"The Vicious Circle," in *Startling* (New York), Summer 1946.
"Chaos," in *Startling* (New York), November 1947.
"Ultra Evolution," in *Startling* (New York), January 1948.

Uncollected Short Stories as Ephriam Winiki

"Leeches from Space," in *Science Fiction* (Holyoke, Massachusetts), March 1939.
"Jewels from the Moon," in *Science Fiction* (Holyoke, Massachusetts), August 1939.
"Earth Asunder," in *Science Fiction* (Holyoke, Massachusetts), October 1939.
"Eclipse Bears Witness," in *Science Fiction* (Holyoke, Massachusetts), March 1940.

Uncollected Short Stories as Dom Passante

"Moon Heaven," in *Science Fiction* (Holyoke, Massachusetts), June 1939.
"Men Without a World," in *Science Fiction* (Holyoke, Massachusetts), March 1940.
"Across the Ages," in *Future* (New York), October 1941.

Uncollected Short Stories as Volsted Gridban

"March of the Robots," in *Vargo Statten Science Fiction Magazine 1* (Luton, Bedfordshire), 1954.
"A Saga of 2270 A. D.," in *Vargo Statten Science Fiction Magazine 2* (Luton, Bedfordshire), 1954.
"The Others," in *Vargo Statten Science Fiction Magazine 3* (Luton, Bedfordshire), 1954.

Uncollected Short Stories as Vargo Statten

"Beyond Zero," in *Vargo Statten Science Fiction Magazine 1* (Luton, Bedfordshire), 1954.
"Before Atlantis," in *Vargo Statten Science Fiction Magazine 2* (Luton, Bedfordshire), 1954.
"The Master Mind," in *Vargo Statten Science Fiction Magazine 3* (Luton, Bedfordshire), 1954.
"Reverse Action," in *Vargo Statten Science Fiction Magazine 4* (Luton, Bedfordshire), 1954.
"Rim of Eternity," in *Vargo Statten Science Fiction Magazine 5* (Luton, Bedfordshire), 1954.
"Something from Mercury," in *British Science Fiction Magazine 6* (Luton, Bedfordshire), 1954.
"A Matter of Vibration," in *British Science Fiction Magazine 12* (Luton, Bedfordshire), 1955.
"Three's a Crowd," in *British Space Fiction Magazine 2* (Luton, Bedfordshire), 1955.

OTHER PUBLICATIONS

Novels

*The Test of Love* (published anonymously). London, Popular Fiction, 1947.
*The Flying Horseman*. Glasgow, Western Book Distributors, 1947.
*The Avenging Ranger*, Llandudno, Caernarvonshire, Kaner, 1948.
*Rustlers Canyon*. Llandudno, Caernarvonshire, Kaner, 1948.
*Thunder Valley*. Redhill, Surrey, Wells Gardner Darton, 1948.
*Yellow Gulch Law*. Llandudno, Caernarvonshire, Kaner, 1948.
*Dead Man's Shoes*. London, Paget, 1949.
*Outlaw's Legacy* (as Clem Larson). London, Paget, 1949.
*Six-Gun Prodigal* (as Hank Cole). London, Paget, 1949.
*Account Settled* (as John Russell). London, Paget, 1949.
*Six-Guns Shoot to Kill* (as Hank Carson). Glasgow, Muir Watson, 1949.
*Gunsmoke Valley*. Glasgow, Muir Watson, 1949.
*Stockwhip Sheriff* (as Polton Cross). Glasgow, Muir Watson, 1949.
*Valley of the Doomed*. Kingswood, Surrey, World's Work, 1949.
*Murder's a Must*. Glasgow, Muir Watson, 1949.
*Tornado Trail*. Glasgow, Muir Watson, 1949.
*Arizona Love*. London, Rich and Cowan, 1950.
*Aztec Gold*. London, Scion, 1950.
*Ghost Canyon*. London, Scion, 1950.
*Merridew Rides Again*. Kingswood, Surrey, World's Work, 1950.
*Rattlesnake*. London, Scion, 1950.
*Skeleton Pass*. London, Scion, 1950.
*Bonanza*. London, Scion, 1950.
*Firewater*. London, Scion, 1950.
*Hell's Acres* (as Mick McCoy). London, Scion, 1950.
*Lead Law*. London, Scion, 1950.
*Merridew Marches On*. Kingswood, Surrey, World's Work, 1951.
*The Hanging 9*. London, Scion, 1951.
*Guntoter from Kansas* (as Jed McNab). London, Panther, 1951.
*Injun Canyon* (as Jed McNab). London, Panther, 1951.
*Golden Canyon*. London, Partridge, 1951.
*The Gold of Akada* (as Earl Titan). London, Scion, 1951.
*Anjani the Mighty* (as Earl Titan). London, Scion, 1951.
*Killer's Legacy*. London, Rich and Cowan, 1952.

*Merridew Fights Again*. Kingswood, Surrey, World's Work, 1952.
*Merridew Follows the Trail*. Kingswood, Surrey, World's Work, 1953.
*Liquid Death* (as Griff). London, Modern Fiction, 1953.
*Don't Touch Me* (as Spike Gordon). London, Modern Fiction, 1953.
*You Take the Rap* (as Spike Gordon). London, Modern Fiction, 1953.
*Shattering Glass* (as Frank Russell). London, Brown Watson, 1953.
*Navajo Vengeance*. London, Rich and Cowan, 1956.

Novels as John Slate (series: Maria Black)

*Black Maria, M. A.* London, Rich and Cowan, 1944.
*Maria Marches On*. London, Rich and Cowan, 1945.
*One Remained Seated* (Black). London, Rich and Cowan, 1946.
*They Arm Alone* (Black). London, Rich and Cowan, 1947.
*Framed in Guilt*. London, Rich and Cowan, 1948.
*Death in Silhouette* (Black). London, Rich and Cowan, 1950.

Novel as Hugo Blayn (series in all books: Inspector Garth)

*Except for One Thing*. London, Stanley Paul, 1947.
*The Five Matchboxes*. London, Stanley Paul, 1948.
*Flashpoint*. London, Stanley Paul, 1950.
*What Happened to Hammond?* London, Stanley Paul, 1951.
*Vision Sinister* (as Nat Karta). London, Dragon, 1954.
*The Silvered Cage*. London, Dragon, 1955.

Novels as Jed McCloud

*Accident Trail*. London, Dragon, 1955.
*Feather-Fist Jones*. London, Dragon, 1955.
*Sheriff of Deadman's Bend*. London, Brown Watson, 1956.
*Phantom Avenger*. London, Brown Watson, 1956.

*

Critical Study: *The Multi-Man: A Biographic and Bibliographic Study of John Russell Fearn* (includes bibliography) by Philip Harbottle, privately printed, 1968.

* * *

While still at school, John Russell Fearn wrote juvenile science fiction, flavoured by his readings of Verne and Wells, and contemporary boys' magazines, such as *The Nelson Lee Library*. His early idol was Edwy Serles Brooks. On leaving school, he drifted through a quick succession of jobs, all of which bored him; he wrote continuously, gradually becoming more proficient, and he also formed a life-long interest in the cinema. He eventually broke into print with a series on film stars in the British *Film Weekly* in 1931.

Discovering *Amazing Stories* that same year, Fearn submitted his first SF novel, *The Intelligence Gigantic*, an influential novel that introduced to SF the concept of the latent powers in the unused portions of the human brain. "We only think and receive impressions in snatches, imperfectly understood, but . . . with a nerve connection to make the entire brain of use, we can operate our brain power to the full." *Amazing* serialized the novel in 1933. John W. Campbell later developed the same idea in his story "The Double Minds" (1937), and his later obsession with the idea led to many stories about "psionics" and the hidden powers of the human brain, by many other writers, including Heinlein.

*Amazing* also serialized Fearn's next two stories, "Liners of Time" (1935) and its sequel "Zagribud" (1937). In these stories, Fearn went the limit with imagination, the result of his exposure to the "super science" stories of Smith and Campbell. Wonderful events abound: time travel on a cosmic scale, invisible cities, entire planets being destroyed. All is explained away in a welter of pseudo-science. Buried in the hodge-podge was the core of an interesting idea, that of differing time-lines capable of being altered and manipulated by an unscrupulous time-traveller. Fearn's ideas were subsequently properly developed by other writers, notably Jack Williamson (*The Legion of Time*) and Isaac Asimov (*The End of Eternity*).

While awaiting the publication of these novels in *Amazing*, Fearn wrote a series of novelettes for the revived *Astounding Stories*, edited by F. Orlin Tremaine, debuting with the classic "The Man Who Stopped the Dust" (1934). SF historian Sam Moskowitz has confirmed that the plot, describing the weird consequences of destroying dust, was unique. Reprinting the story in 1975, Forrest J. Ackerman wrote that it was "the kind of story that makes an old member of dinosaur fandom like me weep, Why don't they write yarns like that anymore?" Fearn followed the story with a host of "thought variants," including "Deserted Universe," "Metamorphosis," and "Mathematica" and "Mathematica Plus," the latter stories extrapolating from Sir James Jeans's speculation that the creator of the universe must have been a "Supreme Mathematician." While the stories were wildly imaginative, many of them were carefully controlled, and are regarded by some critics as Fearn's best work. But by 1937, it was becoming apparent that in striving for originality, the "thought variant" school of writing had developed a uniform sameness—a kind of cosmic monadism—that represented a literary dead end. Fearn was one of the first to realize this, and abandoned the pseudo-scientific approach, exploring instead human and adventurous elements, which had been introduced to SF by Stanley Weinbaum.

The scores of SF magazine stories Fearn produced contributed greatly to the thematic base of SF ideas and concepts. His ideas were often revolutionary, and frequently embraced cosmology, and the purpose and future of human life. "Before Earth Came" (1934) postulated the artificial construction of the solar system by alien scientists, while in "Dark Eternity" (1937) a scientist accidentally annihilates the whole of space-time. "Subconscious" (1936) was the first substantial story on the "we are property" theme, published three years before Russell's *Sinister Barrier*, and it was also clearly based on Fortean ideas: "Just as humans raise and fatten cattle, and then kill them off, so, in a different way have these malignant beings (Martians) seen fit, through unguessable centuries, to cause Earthlings to build up a perfect world, and then, when comparative perfection is attained, they will wipe man out of existence." Writing as Thornton Ayre, one of his many pseduonyms, Fearn introduced detective "webwork" elements to SF, as in "Locked City" and "Secret of the Ring" (both 1938). As Ayre, he also created Violet Ray, the prototype of his famous superwoman, the Golden Amazon.

In 1944, Fearn completely revised his Amazon concept, upgrading his writing from the pulp level, and broke into the hardcover market in Britain with *The Golden Amazon*. In this version, a baby girl is the subject of an idealistic scientist's glandular experiments, his aim being to end world wars by creating a superwoman who would institute a benign scientific rule upon reaching maturity. But the apparently successful experiment has a flaw: it instills into the girl a hatred of all men, and a ruthless cruelty. With her supernatural strength and scientific gifts, she breaks the will and strength of men, elevating women to positions of wealth and power. In the book's climax, she is seen to collapse and die, "burned out," but it is actually only her synthetic image, which paved the way for sequels. The original novel was reprinted by the Canadian general magazine, the *Toronto Star Weekly* in 1945, and had such a tremendous impact that the *Star* commissioned a series which ran for 16 years, ending only with Fearn's death.

Responding to reader demands, the *Star* commissioned the Scott Meredith Agency to find a writer to continue the Amazon series, and many famous SF writers were tried out. All were rejected; no other writer could duplicate Fearn's unique, popular style; Fearn had in fact been the *only* SF writer to be published by the *Star* syndicate, which licensed reprints to at least four American newspapers in the Maine and New York areas.

Having found the lucrative *Star* market, Fearn quit the pulp magazines. He wrote detective thrillers as John Slate, beginning with *Black Maria, M.A.* (1944). Reviewers hailed Slate as a second Agatha Christie. Writing as Hugo Blayn, Fearn created a second detective series featuring an eccentric scientist, Dr. Carruthers, many of whose adventures blur into science fiction, notably *What Happened To Hammond?* (1951), which features a matter transmitter. Fearn also diversified into westerns, but then in 1950, he was lured back into concentrating on SF. In Britain there was a general awakening in the public imagination to the possibilities of science, and space travel in particular. Films such as *Destination Moon* were immensely popular, and caused a burgeoning of interest in SF and science (the latter exemplified by the Festival of Britain in 1951: an exhibition of the Arts and Sciences symbolised by its famous "Skylon," an icon of futuristic imagery). Unfortunately, this coincided with widespread paper rationing, which enabled opportunist publishers to enter the field with a flood of cheaply produced paperback novels. None of these publishers strived for quality, as almost anything on the bookstalls would sell after wartime restrictions. These publishers set the prevailing conditions for British writers, and Fearn was signed to a contract by Scion Ltd. to write SF novels for them exclusively, under the pseudonym Vargo Statten. By 1953, he was also writing as Volsted Gridban, and was contracted to provide two novels a month. Fearn managed to maintain this prodigious output by cannibalising many of his prewar stories for *Astounding* and other magazines, as well as wholly new works. Critics condemned him unread, but several of the Scion novels are outstanding, and are definitive treatments of classic SF themes, such as *Annihilation*, ecological disaster on a global scale, and *Cataclysm*, which describes a disaster of cosmic proportions. Along with the cosmic epics were also some very human stories, such as *Decreation*, a humourous treatment of the superman theme, and *The Time Trap*, the mystery of the *Marie Celeste* extrapolated into SF.

The speed of production and publishing climate associated with the Statten novels generated an opprobrium that has remained in the eyes of most English literary critics, and led Brian Aldiss to dismiss them as the work of a "grub-streeter." But the Italian critics (and Fearn's readers) have ironically found much to celebrate in the dozens of stories reprinted since 1977. Ugo Malaguti has succinctly explained why: "Fearn has a way of getting right to the roots of the process of communication by means of a series of archetypes and symbols, which, when put together in a logical and continuous sequence provide the basis for a means of immediate communication . . . With his apparent simplicity of message, he manages to concentrate into ten lines the fears, the hopes, and dynamism of dozens of pages of other writers' work. This is the real basis for his success, and the reason why, as a writer, he is destined never to die."

—Philip J. Harbottle

---

**FEIST, Raymond E(lias).** American. Lives in San Diego, California. Address: c/o Doubleday, 666 Fifth Avenue, New York, New York 10103, U.S.A.

Science-Fiction Publications

Novels (series: Empire; Riftwar)

*Magician* (Riftwar). New York, Doubleday, 1982; London, Granada, 1983.
*Silverthorn* (Riftwar). New York, Doubleday, and London, Granada, 1985.
*A Darkness at Sethanon* (Riftwar). New York, Doubleday, and London, Grafton, 1986.
*Magician, Apprentice*. New York, Bantam, 1986.
*Magician, Master*. New York, Bantam, 1986.
*Daughter of the Empire*, with Janny Wurts. New York, Doubleday, and London, Grafton, 1987.
*Faerie Tale*. New York, Doubleday, and London, Grafton, 1988.
*Prince of the Blood*. New York, Doubleday, and London, Grafton, 1989.
*Servant of the Empire*, with Janny Wurts. New York, Doubleday, and London, Grafton, 1990.

* * *

Raymond E. Feist's epic fantasies remind one, at times, of the works of James Clavell. They have the same sort of sweep and grandeur; the same intricacy of plot. There is a fascination for detail and an aptitude for vivid description. The difference is, though, that Clavell researches in great detail to find the raw material for his stories, whereas Feist works in the area of speculation, and must create his worlds out of whole cloth. That the end product is so convincing is a tribute to Feist's imagination.

The technique Feist employs is that of following several different plot lines from the viewpoints of those most involved with them. The plotlines are extensive, progressing through years of change and exploration by the parties involved, and in a variety of widely separated settings. In *Magician*, the first of the Riftwar series, the plots follow out the lives and development of several people in the castle of Crydee, an imaginary land somewhere, as one discovers later, in another dimension, or on another plane. Chief among the protagonists are Pug and Tomas, two friends whose lives lead in different directions when they are chosen to be apprenticed to different masters. Tomas is apprenticed to the Swordmaster of Castle Crydee; Pug is apprenticed to the court magician. The basis for the entire story rests upon the difference in these two boys' lives, and what they lead to.

The boys are separated by the Riftwar when armies and magicians from a different dimension begin to invade that of Crydee. It is here that Feist's command of his chosen method of story telling becomes apparent. Where it would be easy to lose track of the weave of the differing plot lines, confusing one with another, Feist's development of the individual characters is sufficiently strong to maintain the reader's interest in both of the two dominant plot lines. At times, with other writers who use this technique, one character predominates to the extent that only the plot line involving that character is of interest, with chapters involving the other plot lines merely an interruption to the main plot. Feist, however, maintains the balance between characterisation and plot interest very finely, so that it is sometimes an effort to tear one's attention from the last chapter to go on to the next, only to find the same phenomenon at the end of that chapter.

A further strength of Feist's is that he fleshes out the main plot line with meticulous detail. The structure of the world of Crydee and that of the Tsurani, in the Riftwar series, is precise and self-consistent. There are very few loose ends to tidy up in terms of the setting, and yet Feist is also capable of surprising the reader. Indeed, it is almost as if the setting has become a type of character in its contribution to the plot. However, what happens within the setting is also detailed and well-developed. The court intrigue which takes place both within Crydee and Tsurani, the diplomacy between the kingdoms, empires, and cities in the vast war which occurs, and the political structures which are both implied and explicit are all drawn with a masterly hand, and are obvious products of a fully realised vision of a world other than our own. This may be as a result of Feist's experience in designing fantasy role-playing games, but it certainly leads to a setting which is seamless and never jars the reader out of the world of the story, no matter how bizarre the events which occur therein.

The initial triad of the Riftwar series, *Magician, Silverthorn*, and *A Darkness at Sethanon*, remain Feist's strongest works. Perhaps this is because these were the works which introduced the twin worlds of the Tsurani and Crydee to us, and in which Feist's imagination was given freest rein. The works which have followed have been drawn from the ideas initiated in this series, but have developed in slightly different directions. The imagination and attention to detail which marked the first trilogy are still present, but they do not dazzle as much because the world has become familiar to readers of Feist. In the first series, Feist challenged some of the precepts of the Fantasy genre, and this contributed to the interest which that series held. The following works simply explore the results of those challenges.

Feist's exploration of the reaction of his characters to massive and irreversible changes in the world around them could be seen as a metaphor for the world of the late 20th century, but this might strain the fabric of the text a little. The novels are not deep psychological explorations, but they are not gloomy, either. What they lack in depth, they make up for in breadth and imagination. What remains to be seen is whether Feist can pull off the trick of creating a fascinating world more than once. He has certainly done so with what he has written so far.

—Ian Nichols

---

**FELICE, Cynthia (née Lindgren).** American. Born in Chicago, Illinois, 12 October 1942. Educated at North Park College, Elmhurst College, and University of Colorado, Colorado Springs. Married Robert Edward Felice in 1961; two sons. Sales engineer, Lindgren and Associates, Chicago, 1962–71; owner and manager, Glenn Russ Motel, Colorado Springs, 1972–78; technical writer, Kaman Sciences Corp., Colorado Springs, 1978–79; technical communications manager, Inmos Corp., Colorado Springs, 1979–81. Since 1981, technical communications manager, United Technologies Micro-electronics Center, Colorado Springs. Recipient: Society for Technical Communication award, 1984. Agent: Richard Curtis, Richard Curtis Associates, 164 East 64th Street, New York, New York 10021, U.S.A.

SCIENCE-FICTION PUBLICATIONS

Novels

*Godsfire*. New York, Pocket Books, 1978.
*The Sunbound*. New York, Dell, 1981.
*Water Witch*, with Connie Willis. New York, Ace, 1982.
*Eclipses*. New York, Pocket Books, 1982.
*Downtime*. New York, Bluejay, 1985.
*Double Nocturne*. New York, Bluejay, 1986.
*Light Raid*, with Connie Willis. New York, Ace, 1989.
*The Khan's Persuasion*. New York, Ace, 1990.

Uncollected Short Stories

"Longshanks," in *Galileo 2* (New York), 1976.
"David and Lindy," in *Universe 8*, edited by Terry Carr. New York, Doubleday, 1978.
"No One Said Forever," in *Millenial Women*, edited by Virginia Kidd. New York, Delacorte Press, 1978.
"A Good Place to Be," in *Chrysalis 9*, edited by Roy Torgeson. New York, Doubleday, 1981.
"Track of a Legend," in *Omni* (New York), December 1983.

* * *

Cynthia Felice's work reflects her strong interest in creating complex human characters in unusual circumstances. In her first SF novel, *Godsfire*, Felice builds a sophisticated society where intelligent felines rule over their human slaves. Felice makes psychological points by having the novel narrated by one of the cat people who constantly points out the differences—often the superiority—of felines over humans. *Godsfire* also has its share of mysteries: Felice creates a planet that has a climate of constant rain, and the inhabitants are unaware of the existence of the sun. The origin of the humans is equally mysterious. Felice presents the reader with a clever plot and a great deal of social commentary that makes for fascinating reading.

*The Sunbound* explores relationships less successfully. Allis is in love with Daneth and is pregnant by him. Yet Daneth has his own secret: he is an alien. When Daneth dies, he leaves Allis a fabulous jewel that confers telepathy to the holder. The crew of Daneth's ship seek him and find Allis and the jewel instead. When Milani, Daneth's former lover and co-captain of Daneth's ship, *The Sovereign Sun*, discovers the situation, she vents her rage and hatred on Allis. Allis, bewildered by events, feels she's been abused by the aliens and throws the jewel away. But Felice creates a crisis where only Allis and the power of the jewel can save the aliens from extinction. The plot of *The Sunbound* is too contrived and the character of Allis is too emotional, too childish, to provide much entertainment.

In *Water Witch* Felice collaborates with the Nebula winner Connie Willis to create a desert planet called Mahali. As in Frank Herbert's *Dune*, finding and controlling water are the most important activities. Felice and Willis do a marvelous job with the main character, Deza, a young woman who pretends she's a member of the ruling family of water witches. Deza is feisty and sympathetic at the same time. Her deception leads her into a wheels-within-wheels plot that Felice and Willis spin successfully. *Water Witch* is an outstanding science-fiction novel.

Felice and Willis's second collaboration, *Light Raid*, is more conventional. A young woman worried about her parents during a laser war between the Western States and Quebec leaves neutral Victoria to return to her home in Denver Springs. Seventeen-year-old Helene Ariadne arrives to find her mother arrested for treason and her father helpless to free her. Ariadne involves herself in a complicated plot where she falls in love with the mysterious but romantic Joss Liddell, and together they discover spies, intrigue, and danger. Ariadne is a plucky character and the novel is an entertaining romp without the seriousness of *Water Witch*.

*Eclipse* is less outstanding. Felice writes a family saga set on another arid world called Seresunar. Beth, an anthropologist, marries Aram, heir to the Water Barony. Their relationship is a stormy one: their temperaments lead them into infidelity and eventual reconciliation. Beth gives birth to a son whose wild nature shakes Seresunar's society. Yet the book is more of a romance novel than a science-fiction novel. The overheated love relationships tire after awhile in this long novel, while the science-fiction aspects remain underdeveloped.

*Double Nocturne* is one of Felice's better SF novels. Tom Hark and his crew are sent to repair the Artificial Intelligence that helps in governing the planet called Islands. The colony has been cut off during the Homeworlds Wars; now that the wars are over, Hark's mission is to help restore the abandoned colony. But when Hark is forced to make an emergency landing on Islands, he discovers that the failing AI has resulted in feudal matriarchal societies where men have no rights and are treated like slaves. Hark has to race against time to solve the puzzle of Islands before his orbiting starship strands him on Islands forever.

Cynthia Felice's novels are best when she centers her work on complex character relationships that are as interesting as they are realistic.

—George Kelley

---

**FERRAT, Jacques Jean.** *See* **MERWIN, Sam, Jr.**

---

**FINNEY, Jack (Walter Braden Finney).** American. Born in Milwaukee, Wisconsin, in 1911. Educated at Knox College, Galesburg, Illinois. Married Marguerite Guest; one daughter and one son. Self-employed writer. Recipient: World Fantasy life achievement award, 1987. Agent: Don Congdon Associates, 156 Fifth Avenue, Suite 625, New York, New York 10010, U.S.A.

SCIENCE-FICTION PUBLICATIONS

Novels

*The Body Snatchers.* New York, Dell, and London, Eyre and Spottiswoode, 1955; as *Invasion of the Body Snatchers*, Dell, 1961; London, Sphere, 1978.
*The Woodrow Wilson Dime.* New York, Simon and Schuster, 1968.
*Time and Again.* New York, Simon and Schuster, 1970; London, Weidenfeld and Nicolson, 1980.
*Marion's Wall.* New York, Simon and Schuster, 1973.

Short Stories

*The Third Level.* New York, Rinehart, 1957; as *The Clock of Time*, London, Eyre and Spottiswoode, 1958.
*I Love Galesburg in the Springtime: Fantasy and Time Stories.* New York, Simon and Schuster, 1963; London, Eyre and Spottiswoode, 1965.
*Forgotten News: The Crime of the Century and Other Lost Stories.* New York, Doubleday, 1983.
*About Time: Twelve Stories.* New York, Simon and Schuster, 1986.

OTHER PUBLICATIONS

Novels

*Five Against the House.* New York, Doubleday, and London, Eyre and Spottiswoode, 1954.
*The House of Numbers.* New York, Dell, and London, Eyre and Spottiswoode, 1957.
*Assault on a Queen.* New York, Simon and Schuster, 1959; London, Eyre and Spottiswoode, 1960.
*Good Neighbor Sam.* New York, Simon and Schuster, and London, Eyre and Spottiswoode, 1963.
*The Night People.* New York, Doubleday, 1977.

Play

*Telephone Roulette*, adaptation of his story "Take a Number." Chicago, Dramatic Publishing Company, 1956.

* * *

Escapism is a term too often loosely applied to science fiction, but in the case of Jack Finney it is strangely appropriate. His most enduring theme is escape from the pressures and irritations of the present, usually into an idyllic past, but sometimes to another planet or a parallel dimension. A popular magazine writer who produced many stories in areas other than science fiction, Finney has made himself into the poet of nostalgia and lost innocence within the genre, seldom more than peripherally concerned with the mechanisms of his science-fiction concepts or with how his characters get from this world to the other.

Ironically, Finney's most famous science-fiction novel is also his least characteristic. *The Body Snatchers* (filmed twice as *Invasion of the Body Snatchers*) is a suspenseful invasion-of-earth story that has gained the status of a minor classic because of the popularity of the film versions and because of the key element of paranoid fantasy that is the basis of its appeal: the notion that aliens might gradually replace the entire population of a city with exact duplicates without anyone noticing the difference. Although this idea had been current in science fiction long before Finney brought it to the attention of a wider public, the skill with which Finney unveils this horror and the fears abroad at the time he wrote the story—the "takeover" might as well be a metaphor for either Communism or McCarthyism—combined to give it an impact few science-fiction stories had previously had.

More characteristic are the short stories that Finney published during the 1950's collected in *The Third Level* and *I Love Galesburg in the Springtime.* The most common theme of these stories is time travel into the past. "I'm Scared," one of the best, details the gradual breakdown of the flow of historical time under psychological pressure from a population seeking to escape the present. In "Such Interesting Neighbours" the time travelers are from the future, but the motivation to escape their own time remains the same (the story ingeniously suggests that the end of the world will be brought about by time travel, because everyone will gradually abandon the future and redistribute themselves throughout history). "Of Missing Persons" replaces time travel with space travel, but the theme of escape remains central. Two stories, "The Third Level" and "Second Chance," suggest that certain things or locations can provide magical "portals" to the past; in "Second Chance" a meticulously reconstructed old car takes its driver into a past world simply because the experience he has in driving it parallels an experience that might have taken place when the car was new.

This notion that by meticulously recreating the past we can return to it was developed at great length in Finney's most ambitious novel, *Time and Again*, in which a volunteer for a secret government time-travel project finds himself in the Manhattan of 1882. Although only the vaguest references to Einstein serve to account for this time travel, and although there are inconsistencies of plot and historical verisimilitude (some of the latter are deliberate), the novel is a convincing portrait of a lost age and a persuasive account of what it might actually feel like to awake in a different time. Other Finney novels have dealt with the culture shock of different ages meeting using even less rationalistic devices—reincarnation, for example, in *Marion's Wall*—but *Time and Again* remains his most successful contribution to this genre. Though not fundamentally a science-fiction writer, Finney is a skilled narrator and an evocative stylist who frequently uses science-fiction themes with considerable effect.

—Gary K. Wolfe

---

**FISK, Nicholas.** Pseudonym for David Higginbottom. British. Born in London, 14 October 1923. Educated at Ardingly College, Sussex. Served in the Royal Air Force during World War II. Married Dorothy Antoinette Richold in 1949; twin daughters and two sons. Has worked as an actor, journalist, musician, editor, and publisher; former advertising creative director and consultant. Agent: Laura Cecil, 17 Alwyne Villas, London N1 2HG. Address: 59 Elstree Road, Bushey Heath, Hertfordshire WD2 3QX, England.

SCIENCE-FICTION PUBLICATIONS (for children)

Novels (series: Starstormers)

*Space Hostages*. London, Hamish Hamilton, 1967; New York, Macmillan, 1969.
*Trillions*. London, Hamish Hamilton, 1971; New York, Pantheon, 1973.
*Grinny*. London, Heinemann, 1973; Nashville, Nelson, 1974.
*High Way Home*. London, Hamish Hamilton, 1973.
*Little Green Spaceman*. London, Heinemann, 1974.
*Time Trap*. London, Gollancz, 1976.
*Wheelie in the Stars*. London, Heinemann, 1976.
*Antigrav*. London, Kestrel, 1978.
*Escape from Splatterbang*. London, Pelham, 1978; New York, Macmillan, 1979; as *Flamers*, London, Knight, 1979.
*Monster Maker*. London, Pelham, 1979; New York, Macmillan, 1980.
*A Rag, A Bone, and a Hank of Hair*. London, Kestrel, 1980; New York, Crown, 1982.
*The Starstormer Saga (Starstormers, Sunburst, Catfang, Evil Eye, Volcano)*. London, Knight, 5 vols., 1980–83.
*Robot Revolt*. London, Pelham, 1981.
*On the Flip Side*. London, Kestrel, 1983.
*You Remember Me!* London, Kestrel, 1984; Boston, Hall, 1987.
*Bonkers Clocks*, illustrated by Colin West. London, Viking Kestrel, 1985.
*Dark Sun, Bright Sun*, illustrated by Brigid Marlin. London, Blackie, 1986.
*Mindbenders*. London, Viking Kestrel, 1987.
*Backlash*. London, Walker, 1987.
*The Talking Car*, illustrated by Ann John. London, Macmillan, 1988.
*The Worm Charmers*. London, Walker, 1989.
*The Telly Is Watching You*. London, Macdonald, 1989.
*The Back-yard War*. London, Macmillan, 1990.
*The Model Village*. London, Walker, 1990.
*A Hole in the Head*. London, Walker, 1991.
*Pig Ignorant*. London, Walker, 1991.

Short Stories

*Sweets from a Stranger and Other Science Fiction Stories*. London, Kestrel, 1982.
*Living Fire*. London, Corgi, 1987.

OTHER PUBLICATIONS (for children)

Novels

*The Bouncers*. London, Hamish Hamilton, 1964.
*The Fast Green Car*. London, Hamish Hamilton, 1965.
*There's Something on the Roof!* London, Hamish Hamilton, 1966.
*Emma Borrows a Cup of Sugar*. London, Heinemann, 1973.
*The Witches of Wimmering*. London, Pelham, 1976.
*Leadfoot*. London, Pelham, 1980.
*Snatched*. London, Hodder and Stoughton, 1983.

Other

*Look at Cars*, illustrated by the author. London, Hamish Hamilton, 1959; revised edition, London, Panther, 1969.
*Look at Newspapers*, illustrated by Eric Thomas. London, Hamish Hamilton, 1962.
*Cars*. London, Parrish, 1963.
*The Young Man's Guide to Advertising*. London, Hamish Hamilton, 1963.
*Making Music*, illustrated by Donald Green. London, Joseph, 1966; Boston, Crescendo, 1969.
*Lindbergh the Lone Flier*, illustrated by Raymond Briggs. London, Hamish Hamilton, and New York, Coward McCann, 1968.
*Richthofen the Red Baron*, illustrated by Raymond Briggs. London, Hamish Hamilton, and New York, Coward McCann, 1968.

*

Illustrator: *A Fishy Tale* by Beryl Cooke, 1957; *Look at Aircraft* by Sir Philip Joubert de la Ferte, 1960; *The Bear Who Was Too Big* by Lettice Cooper, 1963; *Tea with Mr. Timothy* by Geoffrey Morgan, 1966; *Menuhin's House of Music* by Eric Fenby, 1969; *Skiffy* by William Mayne, 1972.

Nicholas Fisk comments:

I came fairly late to children's writing. It was a Puffin list that showed me the light. I was looking for a copy of Geoffrey Household's *Rogue Male* and found it in Puffin. I thought, if the publisher thinks fit to offer this title to children, the world must be changing. For the better.

Most of my output for children has been science fiction. The SF writer is fortunate in that, unhampered by present or past, he can invent his own games, rules and players. He is unfortunate in that he must make these matters clear—and explanation is the enemy of narration. Also, unfortunately, the genre is still not quite respectable, not quite nice. Perhaps the word science offends the nice palate? It offends mine. I am not a scientist, my books are not centered on the sciences. They are stories of possibility. Not SF, but IF—what would happen IF.

The stories are on a domestic, not a cosmic, scale because written words are not apt for the rendering of explosions and gargantuan hardware; these belong to the cinema. My central characters are children because the stories are written for children. This poses no problem and indeed may offer simplifications and speedings-up of the narrative. Although the stories have become more complex in subject and structure, I have learned from my own and countless other children that the quick, generous, adventurous mind can always stick to the point, even if the author must stagger about a bit in the hope of satisfying himself or a publisher's editor. And in any case today's children are no longer confined to some nursery ghetto. Families live in each other's laps, watching the same TV programmes. My readers and I are not unlike.

Other reasons for writing as I do include a distaste for most modern adult fiction coupled with a huge admiration for the writers and illustrators of present day children's books. I do various kinds of writing to earn a living; it is the children's writing that gives me the authentic tingle.

* * *

Nicholas Fisk is currently one of the best of those writers presenting "hard" SF to children. In such a situation a writer has two choices: to try to explain his science to a juvenile audience, or simply to ignore most of the problems as being outside his province. Fisk has tried both: *Antigrav* is a good story despite the lack of explanations; *Escape from Splatterbang* shows how such explanations can be at once trite and boring. By contrast, in *Trillions* the working out of a scientific answer forms an exciting and integral part of the plot. *Trillions* is also the book of Fisk's most likely to appeal to the adult reader, partly because of the scientific interest, partly because the "opposition" in *Trillions* is the Military Mind, as personified by General Hartman, in whom he will recognise all those who hate and fear what is alien to them. More usually in Fisk's books the forces of ignorance are the adults who ignore or fail to comprehend their children. The books can most usefully be seen from the point of view of an intelligent 11-year-old—old enough to see and understand the adult world of deceit and hypocrisy, but not old enough to change or participate in it.

One of Fisk's greatest strengths as a writer is his avoidance of clichés, both in plot and character. Indeed several of his books, most notably *Space Hostages* and *Antigrav*, are crucially concerned with a realisation that people do not conform to stereotypes. *Antigrav* rather neatly contrasts two scientists—one the classic sinister, balding geologist from behind the Iron Curtain, the other the expansive English all-rounder much given to appearing on TV chatshows. Arthur Sonning is summed up at the end as "You poor sap," while Czeslaw, victory gained, weighs the possible results of that victory and throws it away. It is further typical of Fisk that this moral superiority does not lessen the personal price which Czeslaw has to pay for "failure." In *Space Hostages* an experienced reader of children's fiction is likely to be expecting the puny clever Pakistani to be triumphant at the expense of the village bully. What actually happens is that both discover their interdependence as Fisk shows that the very qualities which make Tony a bully are those which make him a successful leader in a time of crisis. In *Escape from Splatterbang* a hint of romance is raised, only to be quashed by the bitter-sweet ending as the gypsy girl, only half-understood to the end, disappears back among her people. Here, as in *Time Trap* and other of the novels, the ending respects and even underlines the realities of human behaviour.

Fisk is never likely to have a large adult audience; his books side too firmly with the children—but at least they do so plausibly. In *Grinny* (one of his best books) the reader looks on, as helpless as the children, while the implacable "Great Aunt Emma" manipulates adult minds to her own ends. The notable achievement of this book is the way (again avoiding cliché) that Grinny's curiosity is shown as most sinister—she pokes and pries into human habits and customs like someone lifting a stone to observe the earwigs. Fisk's one real incursion into teenage SF—*Wheelie in the Stars*—is one of his poorest books: his clever-clever cardboard teenagers contrast very badly with the impotent desperation and reluctant courage of his children. This is more to be regretted since *High Way Home* shows how convincingly he can draw both teenagers and female characters (usually a notable blindspot). Fisk is not destined for a place among the Immortals: he lacks the necessary mastery of style and timeless appeal. But he is doing a competent job in a difficult field.

—Philippa Stephensen-Payne

---

**FitzGIBBON, (Robert Louis) Constantine (Lee-Dillon).** American. Born in Lenox, Massachusetts, 8 June 1919. Educated at Wellington College, 1933–35; University of Munich, and the Sorbonne, Paris, 1935–37; Exeter College, Oxford, 1937–39. Served in the British Army, 1939–42, and the United States Army, 1942–46: Major. Married 1) Marion Gutmann in 1960 (marriage dissolved), one son; 2) Marjorie Steele in 1967, one daughter. Schoolmaster, Saltus Grammar School, Bermuda, 1946–47. Member, Irish Academy of Letters; Fellow, Royal Society of Literature. *Died 23 March 1983.*

SCIENCE-FICTION PUBLICATIONS

Novels

*The Iron Hoop.* New York, Knopf, 1949; London, Cassell, 1950.
*When the Kissing Had to Stop.* New York, Norton, and London, Cassell, 1960.
*The Golden Age.* London, Hart Davis MacGibbon, and New York, Norton, 1975.
*The Rat Report.* London, Constable, 1980.

OTHER PUBLICATIONS

Novels

*The Arabian Bird.* New York, Rinehart, 1948; London, Cassell, 1949.
*Cousin Emily.* London, Cassell, 1952; as *Dear Emily*, New York, Simon and Schuster, 1952.
*The Holiday.* London, Cassell, and New York, Simon and Schuster, 1953.
*In Love and War.* London, Cassell, 1956; as *The Fair Game*, New York, Norton, 1956; as *Adultery under Arms*, London, Pan, 1962.
*Watcher in Florence.* Privately printed, 1959.
*Going to the River.* London, Cassell, and New York, Norton, 1963.
*High Heroic.* London, Dent, and New York, Norton, 1969.
*In the Bunker.* London, Macmillan, and New York, Norton, 1973.
*Man in Aspic.* London, Hart Davis MacGibbon, 1977.

Plays

*The Devil He Did* (produced London, 1969).
*The Devil at Work* (produced Dublin, 1971).

Other

*Miss Finnigan's Fault.* London, Cassell, 1953.
*Norman Douglas: A Pictorial Record.* London, Richards Press, 1953.
*The Little Tour*, with Giles Playfair. London, Cassell, 1954.
*The Shirt of Nessus.* London, Cassell, 1956; as *20 July*, New York, Norton, 1956; as *To Kill Hitler*, London, Stacey, 1972.
*The Blitz*, illustrated by Henry Moore. London, Wingate, 1957; as *The Winter of the Bombs*, New York, Norton, 1958.
*Random Thoughts of a Fascist Hyena.* London, Cassell, 1963; New York, Norton, 1964.
*The Life of Dylan Thomas.* London, Dent, and Boston, Little Brown, 1965.
*Through the Minefield: An Autobiography.* London, Bodley Head, and New York, Norton, 1967.
*Denazification.* London, Joseph, and New York, Norton, 1969.
*Out of the Lion's Paw: Ireland Wins Her Freedom.* London, Macdonald, and New York, American Heritage, 1969.
*London's Burning.* New York, Ballantine, 1970; London, Macdonald, 1971.
*Red Hand: The Ulster Colony.* London, Joseph, 1971; New York, Doubleday, 1972.
*A Concise History of Germany.* London, Thames and Hudson, 1972; New York, Viking Press, 1973.
*The Life and Times of Eamon de Valera.* Dublin, Gill and Macmillan, 1973; New York, Macmillan, 1974.
*Secret Intelligence in the Twentieth Century.* London, Hart Davis MacGibbon, 1976; New York, Stein and Day, 1977.
*Teddy in the Tree* (for children). New York, Doubleday, 1977.
*Drink.* New York, Doubleday, 1979; London, Granada, 1980.
*The Irish in Ireland.* Newton Abbot, Devon, David and Charles, and New York, Norton, 1983.

Editor, *Selected Letters of Dylan Thomas.* London, Dent, 1966; New York, New Directions, 1967.

Translator from German and French of some 40 books.

*

Constantine FitzGibbon commented:

(1981) I do not consider that I have ever written "science fiction." I have written unusual novels, set in imaginary countries, at an imaginary future date or with a jumbled time sequence, as have Kafka and Joyce. As I grow older I become less interested in writing "realistic" novels, and give freer and freer play to my imagination. My most recent novel, *The Rat Report*, I have called, it is true, psi-fi, but that is not sci-fi, not in my opinion at least.

* * *

Among the vast output of Constantine FitzGibbon are four novels that may be considered to be works of science fiction. Like the Orwell of *Nineteen Eighty-Four*, FitzGibbon detested and feared a totalitarian victory, which he believed would create a nightmare world all too similar to the one portrayed by Orwell. Throughout his career FitzGibbon was a political novelist, writing from the perspective of a Tory conservative, fighting to retain for the free world and for England in particular the values he treasured.

*The Iron Hoop* tells the story of the effect military occupation has on both the conquered and the conqueror. The novel's thesis is that ultimately the conquerors and the conquered each destroy themselves. The strength of the novel lies in its descriptive power to portray life in an occupied city; its weakness is that, with the possible exception of Anna, the characters are flat and uninteresting.

*When the Kissing Had to Stop* is an apocalyptic horror story redolent of cold-war hysteria. It postulates the rapid decline of Britain after a left-Labour government gets elected. In next to no time, through a series of mishaps and political mistakes, Britain becomes a Russian colony, with many of its inhabitants taken off to Siberia. Along with political disaster, there is ample evidence of economic, social, and moral collapse. As in *The Iron Hoop*, the novel's strength lies in FitzGibbon's ability to bring vividly to life a decaying society. The narrative is fast-paced, though FitzGibbon's conservative bias constantly intrudes. The characters are credible, the view is chilling, but the cold-war hysteria incapacitates the imagination of both the author and the reader.

*The Golden Age* is a futuristic novel in which the world as we know it is drastically altered and in which mankind has virtually lost its knowledge of history. The world has been divided into two halves, the Upper World separated by a sort of force field from what is termed the Lower World (the southern hemisphere in our terms). The Upper World is now ruled from Oxford by a Monster (Emperor) and the four Horsemen who form his council. They decide that the future of the world must be left in the hands of Orpheus, the poet, and the priests, scientists, and other leaders of the past have simply led the world into chaos. It is FitzGibbon's contention that the poets know more about the universe than do the astronomers. As Orpheus, the central character, begins to rebuild the world in beauty, he enters into a bargain with Mephistopheles, who restores his memory at the cost of his soul. Seemingly victorious in his quest, Orpheus descends into the Underworld to regain Eurydice. A great part of the intrigue and fascination of the novel consists in FitzGibbon's deft reworking of the Orpheus and Mephistopheles myths and a clever blending of the two. The reader versed in classical literature will find the novel interesting and meaningful on a level that would be lost to the average reader. *The Golden Age* is a clever if somewhat overly literary and complex vision of the future based on an intriguing hypothesis. It is rewarding to the sensitive and discriminating reader.

FitzGibbon's final science-fiction novel, *The Rat Report*, is hardly first rate; it is, in fact, filled with cliché and stereotypes and hobbled by an uninspired plot. The best part of the novel is devoted to a rat named Crocus who sends out to the world fluently articulated reports on various topics focused on man's inertia and on his inability to assimilate and trust what he finds to be "alien." The responses of the scientists and statesmen to these reports are all too pat and predictable. The love story is wooden at best. Indeed, the only interest is in the character of the rat and his view of man's future, a totally Orwellian nightmare.

—Joseph A. Quinn

---

**FLINT, Homer Eon.** American. Born in 1892. *Died in 1924.*

SCIENCE-FICTION PUBLICATIONS

Novels

*The Blind Spot*, with Austin Hall. Philadelphia, Prime Press, 1951; London, Museum Press, 1953.
*The Devolutionist, and The Emancipatrix.* New York, Ace, 1965.
*The Lord of Death, and The Queen of Life.* New York, Ace, 1965.

Uncollected Short Stories

"The Planeteer," in *All-Story Weekly* (New York), 9 March 1918.
"King of Conserve Island," in *All-Story Weekly* (New York), 12 October 1918.
"The Man in the Moon," in *All-Story Weekly* (New York), 4 October 1919.
"The Greater Miracle," in *All-Story Weekly* (New York), 24 April 1920.
"Out of the Moon," in *Argosy All-Story Weekly* (New York), 15 December 1923.
"The Nth Man," in *Amazing Stories Quarterly* (New York), Spring 1928.

See the essay on Austin Hall.

---

**FONTENAY, Charles L(ouis).** American. Born in Sao Paulo, Brazil, 17 March 1917. Attended Vanderbilt University, Nashville, 1966–67, 1968–70. Served in the United States Army Air Corps, 1942–43; Army censorship officer, 1943–46: Captain. Married 1) Glenda Miller in 1942 (divorced, 1960); 2) Martha Howard in 1963 (divorced, 1984), one daughter and one son. Reporter, sports editor, and city editor, *Daily Messenger*, Union City, Tennessee, 1936–40; editor, Associated Press, Nashville and Memphis, 1940–42; sports editor, *Press-Chronicle*, Johnson City, Tennessee, 1946. Since 1946, reporter, city editor, then rewrite editor, *The Tennessean*, Nashville. Recipient: Ted V. Rodgers award, for journalism, 1957. Address: 1708 20th Avenue North, Apartment C, St. Petersburg, Florida 33713, U.S.A.

SCIENCE-FICTION PUBLICATIONS

Novels

*Twice upon a Time.* New York, Ace, 1958.
*Rebels of the Red Planet.* New York, Ace, 1961.
*The Day the Oceans Overflowed.* Derby, Connecticut, Monarch, 1964.

Uncollected Short Stories

"Escape Velocity," in *If* (New York), October 1954.
"Blow the Man Down," in *If* (New York), March 1955.
"The Patriot," in *If* (New York), August 1955.
"The Strangest Man in the Universe," in *Other Worlds* (Evanston, Indiana), February 1956.
"Atom Drive," in *If* (New York), April 1956.
"Communication," in *If* (New York), October 1956.
"Family Tree," in *If* (New York), December 1956.
"Disqualified," in *The First World of If*, edited by James L. Quinn and Eve Wulff. Kingston, New York, Quinn, 1957.
"The Old Goat," in *If* (New York), February 1957.
"Blind Alley," in *If* (New York), March 1957.
"Up," in *Fantasy and Science Fiction* (New York), March 1957.
"A Case of Sunburn," in *If* (New York), April 1957.
"Moths," in *Science Fiction Adventures* (New York), April 1957.
"Pretty Quadroon," in *If* (New York), June 1957.
"The Last Brave Invader," in *If* (New York), August 1957.
"Earth Transit," in *Infinity* (New York), September 1957.
"The Heart's Long Wait," in *Flying Saucers from Other Worlds* (Evanston, Indiana), September 1957.
"Z," in *The Second World of If*, edited by James L. Quinn and Eve Wulff. Kingston, New York, Quinn, 1958.
"Chip on the Shoulder," in *Science Fiction Quarterly* (Holyoke, Massachusetts), February 1958.
"A Summer Afternoon," in *Fantasy and Science Fiction* (New York), February 1958.
"Never Marry a Venerian," in *Saturn* (Holyoke, Massachusetts), March 1958.
"West of Mars," in *Infinity* (New York), April 1958.
"Conservation," in *If* (New York), April 1958.
"Service with a Smile," in *If* (New York), June 1958.
"Beauty Interrupted," in *If* (New York), August 1958.
"The Gift Bearer," in *Amazing* (New York), September 1958.
"Nothing's Impossible," in *Super Science Fiction* (New York), October 1958.
"Bait," in *Amazing* (New York), February 1959.
"Ghost Planet," in *Fantasy and Science Fiction* (New York), February 1959.
"The Jupiter Weapon," in *Amazing* (New York), March 1959.
"Wind," in *Amazing* (New York), April 1959.
"Matchmaker," in *If* (New York), May 1960.
"Mariwite," in *Fantastic* (New York), November 1960.
"Fredeya," in *Barbarians II*, edited by Robert Adams, Martin H. Greenberg, and Pamela Crippen Adams. New York, New American Library, 1988.
"The Silk and the Song," in *Cosmic Critiques*, edited by Isaac Asimov and Martin H. Greenberg. Cincinnati, Ohio, Writer's Digest Books, 1990.
"Savior," in *Subtropical Speculations*, edited by Rick Wilber and Richard Mathews. Sarasota, Florida, Pineapple Press, 1991.

OTHER PUBLICATIONS

Other

*Epistle to the Babylonians: An Essay on the Natural Inequality of Man.* Knoxville, University of Tennessee Press, 1969.
*The Keyen of Fu Tze.* Sherborne, Gloucestershire, Coombe Springs Press, 1977.
*Estes Kefauver: A Biography.* Knoxville, University of Tennessee Press, 1980.

*

Charles L. Fontenay comments:

Most of my science fiction was written during the decade 1954–64 and consisted largely of adventure stories—focusing on action and character interaction rather than the science angle. I did, however, use some science gimmick on which to hang the story, sometimes making it the crucial element of the plot. The two new novelettes I have had published since returning to science-fiction writing are similarly character-oriented, in the context of a putative future in which the Greenhouse Effect has altered geography and society. Several of the novels I have in process utilize the same context. Although I'm fond of this context as hospitable to action and character in a relatively simple environment, I believe there are some promising possibilities for science fiction in the developing frontiers of science—but by that I do *not* mean the "technological marvel" stuff so popular in recent movies, which is hardly "science" fiction.

* * *

The first phase of Charles L. Fontenay's career spanned a bit more than a decade, ending with the 1964 publication of *The Day the Oceans Overflowed*, a disaster novel. It resumed with the 1988 publication of the long story "Fredeya," in the anthology *Barbarians II*, edited by Robert Adams, Martin Greenberg and Pamela Adams. He has so far produced no major novel to lift his reputation, but much of his early short fiction is superb.

Much of his output was space opera, a portion of it forming a generalized future history, and some of it dealing with problems posed by the time-dilatation effect at the speed of light. "The Strangest Man in the Universe" is such a story, an adventure that finds a spaceship crew stranded on a backward planet where they also encounter a benevolent superman (another favorite theme of Fontenay's). "The Heart's Long Wait" is a decidedly more interesting story, a character study of a spaceman alienated from ordinary humans by his profession. The story, while sentimental, is yet highly effective and memorable.

It is Fontenay's trademark to take a standard idea—time-dilatation, evolutionary supermen, the paradoxes of time travel—and develop a good, often quite original variation on it. His stories are usually well constructed, and his writing style clear and readable. If he is to be grouped with any other SF writers, it would probably be Poul Anderson and Gordon Dickson, though Fontenay has never displayed Anderson's passion for the poetic in science and nature, or Dickson's thematic power. Like them he tells stories about ideas. But he demonstrates skill in his ability to explore his ideas in terms of unobtrusive character development. If he lacks Anderson's flash, he also lacks his story-killing self-consciousness and inconsistency.

One of Fontenay's most interesting ideas occurs in the story "Z," but the complexity of the idea seems to prevent him from achieving his trademark characterization. It's a neatly conceived handling of essentially the same idea Heinlein used in "By His Bootstraps," somewhat updated with the addition of a sex change in the plot line. It is not quite up to the standards of Heinlein's original story, though it is by no means a complete failure, either. It is worth noting that it appeared in the June 1956 issue of *If*, three years before Heinlein himself similarly but more effectively updated "By His Bootstraps" with "All You Zombies."

"Pretty Quadroon," another time travel story, is one of Fontenay's best works. In the near future, a segregationist South has again seceded from the Union, leading to a second War Between the States. The story's protagonist is a statesman and general whose fiery speech at a conference of Southern governors has made him a pivotal figure in the events leading to the war. His mistress, the quadroon of the title, introduces him to a practitioner of voodoo who believes he can alter the past, thus preventing the war from ever happening. Again and again the time paths are altered, until it becomes obvious that the key to success lies in preventing the man from ever having met the woman he loves. The strong idea in "Family Tree" might almost be taken for a joke: humans have evolved not from apes but from rodents. The story, however, is serious: an evolutionary superman is threatened by human bigotry. What sets the story apart is Fontenay's insightful portrayal of his central character, a moral rabble-rouser out to destroy his superman.

As the 1950's closed, Fontenay ceased producing magazine fiction. His first novel, *Twice upon a Time*, like "The Heart's Long Wait," deals with a young spaceman whose life and attitudes pivot on his career and on the effects of time-dilatation. A member of a trouble-shooter corps designed to police interstellar colonies, he is sent to one of several planets where it's feared rebellion might be brewing. The theft of his spaceship when he arrives, and the complexities of the social and political situation make the novel suspenseful but a time-travel subplot and a pat ending put the book on a level somewhat below that of his best fiction. *Rebels of the Red Planet* is disappointing. Genetic experiments on Mars, resulting in superbeings and other mutations, are played off against another plot involving a growing rebel movement. Fontenay doesn't add much to either idea, although some of his scenes between normal humans and the laboratory-bred mutations are interestingly outré.

The weakness of Fontenay's reputation as he resumes his SF career is based more on the absence of a major novel in his output than on any lack of ability on his part. Time has not rendered his best fiction any less readable. His trademark has been his ability to work stories around ideas cleverly derived from familiar themes, often by concentrating on philosophical rather than scientific implications. But his strength has been his ability to examine these ideas from the viewpoints of very interesting characters.

—Gerald W. Page

---

**FORD, John M.** Recipient: World Fantasy award, 1984. Address: c/o Tor Books, 49 West 24th Street, 9th floor, New York, New York, 10010, U.S.A.

SCIENCE-FICTION PUBLICATIONS

Novels (series: Star Trek)

*Web of Angels.* New York, Pocket, 1980.
*The Princes of Air.* New York, Pocket, 1982.

*The Dragon Waiting*. New York, Timescape, 1983; London, Corgi, 1985.
*Star Trek: Voyage to Adventure* (for children; as Michael J. Dodge). New York, Pocket, 1984; London, Carousel, 1985.
*The Final Reflection* (Star Trek). New York, Pocket, 1984; Bath, Firecrest, 1985.
*How Much for Just the Planet?* (Star Trek). New York, Pocket, 1987.
*Casting Fortune*. New York, Tor, 1989.
*Fugue State*, with *The Death of Doctor Island*, by Gene Wolf. New York, Tor, 1990.

OTHER PUBLICATIONS

Novel

*The Scholars of Night*. New York, Tor, 1988.

Short Stories

*Silver Scream: Stories*, with others. Arlington Heights, Illinois, Dark Harvest, 1988.

Other

*On Writing Science Fiction*, with George H. Scithers and Darrell Schweitzer. Philadelphia, Owlswick Press, 1981.

* * *

John M. Ford is a versatile writer. He is at home in many worlds, among them the Star Trek universe, Liavek, alternate versions of Earth history, and plausible futures. He is adept at writing for many ages, his work ranging from titles for children, to young adults, to dense, convoluted tales for adults. The thematic content of his science fiction, science fantasy, and fantasy, includes, among other themes, issues of memory/reality, human-computer interactions, and the power of humor and other emotions. He also publishes outside the SF genre.

While Ford's range is diverse, his style is apparent in all his writing. It is episodic, sometimes fragmented (although he usually has the story threads firmly in hand), and dense with literary, poetic, musical, and mythological allusions. This style can be difficult, sometimes opaque and impenetrable, but his stories reward the reader with intricate fantasy, provocative ideas, and some intriguing characters.

In *Fugue State* (the title is a medical term, the condition of disassociative reaction during which an amnesiac is without memory of his or her previous life) Ford's fragmented and episodic style is particularly evocative and effective. The book is difficult and often painful to read, but it forces the reader to confront directly the issue of memory-reality. The complex structure and dark tone are reminiscent of some of Philip Dick's work.

In *Web of Angels* (along with the *Star Trek* novels, the most clearly science fiction of his works) Ford explores human/computer interactions and potential social and political ramifications, as well as the theme of personal growth. His style here stands between the action and the reader, but the mythological allusions (along with Grailer Diomede's painful maturation) are what give the story depth, while the dramatic impact of his hybrid technology engage.

*The Dragon Waiting*, Ford's prize-winning alternative history, is his most ambitious work. Its characterization, the development of its historical atmosphere, its believable magic and plot are convincing. Ford's hallmark style will cause some readers problems. It is set in the time of Richard III, but the twist is that Christianity never rose to dominate Europe, and Byzantium is attempting to influence the English succession. Ford assembles a cast of interesting and engaging characters (a Welsh wizard, a noble Greek mercenary, a female doctor from the Medici Italy, and a German vampire weapons expert), who with actual historical figures bring Richard to the throne.

In his *Star Trek* novels Ford's style, while less obtrusive, is yet unmistakable. The two novels are very different, yet both possess broad appeal beyond Star Trek fandom. Clearly written for young adults, they contain fast-paced yet substantive action, vibrant and convincing characters, and they are readable on several levels. *The Final Reflection* is one of the first and best portrayals of Klingon cultural identity, seen from the viewpoint both of Federation peoples and the Klingons themselves. It can be read as an action story, as political intrigue, and as a journey of self-discovery and maturation. *How Much for Just the Planet?* is Ford's most light-hearted story. It has an absurd and amusing plot. The characters are charming, the Star Trek and Klingon cast believable, the Direidians (local planet population) wacky and weird, and the computers develop personality disorders. Song lyrics lace the story—takeoffs from Gilbert and Sullivan, famous TV Westerns' theme songs, and well known folk music—taking the reader on a nostalgic trip, while the juxtaposition of the original songs' symbolism with the takeoff lyrics presents another layer of meaning to the plot twists.

—Catherine M. Currier

---

**FORSTCHEN, William R.** American. Address: c/o Ballantine Books, 201 East 50th Street, New York, New York 10022, U.S.A.

SCIENCE-FICTION PUBLICATIONS

Novels (Series: Gamester Wars; The Lost Regiment)

*Ice Prophet*. New York, Ballantine, 1983.
*The Flame upon the Ice*. New York, Ballantine, 1984.
*A Darkness upon the Ice*. New York, Ballantine, 1985.
*Into the Sea of Stars*. New York, Ballantine, 1986.
The Gamester Wars:
*The Alexandrian Ring*. New York, Ballantine, 1987.
*The Assassin Gambit*. New York, Ballantine, 1988.
*The Crystal Warriors*. New York, Avon, 1988.
The Lost Regiment:
*Rally Cry*. New York, Penguin, 1990.
*Union Forever*. New York, Penguin, 1991.
*The Crystal Sorcerers*. New York, Avon, 1991.

* * *

William R. Forstchen attracted immediate attention with the publication of *Ice Prophet*, first of a trilogy set in a primitive future society in which ice covers the earth's surface as the result of a scientific experiment gone awry, altering the planet's ecology. A network of city states is dominated by the Cornathian Brotherhoods, a theocracy divided against itself because of concealed rivalries, including a secret priesthood with a generations-long plan to secure ultimate power for themselves.

Since it was scientific innovation that wrecked the old world, the Brotherhoods have forbidden innovation to the populace, although they have secret hoards of supposedly lost knowledge. Michael Ormson is the charismatic leader who rises in opposition to this restriction, advocating religious freedom and the pursuit of knowledge. Against his wishes, he comes to be viewed as a messianic figure, and bloody warfare ensues in response to this heresy.

By the opening of the second novel, *The Flame Upon the Ice*, Ormson heads a rebellious army that controls the southern islands. He and his allies have devised new methods of conducting warfare on ice-travelling warships, the details of which reflect Forstchen's own interest in ice sailing. The battle scenes are bloody, violent, and convincing, as Forstchen works out the tactical and strategic necessities of war on an icefield. Unbeknownst to Ormson, he has become the tool of the secret priesthood, the instrument through which they plan to crush the power of the Cornathian Brotherhoods and depose the present leader.

Complicating matters is Ormson's unease at the horrors perpetrated in his name. Rather than bring new freedom, he has caused more death and destruction than the world has known for generations. An eastern empire begins to extend its influence as well, hoping to take advantage of the ensuing power vacuum. A major military triumph for the rebels climaxes the second volume.

The established church is resurgent in *A Darkness Upon the Ice.* Using devices from their secret laboratories, they attack Ormson's army with cannons and use air surveillance. The populace is uneasy with the widespread destruction, and Ormson himself appears to be dying of some insidious disease. The ultimate battle resolves things neatly and draws the trilogy to an optimistic, if somewhat bloody-minded conclusion. Although the central plot is straightforward and traditional, Forstchen enriched it with strong characterizations and some marvelously intricate interrelationships among the opposing forces.

*Into the Sea of Stars*, which followed the trilogy, is a disappointingly bland space opera. Fortunately, it seems to have been an interim project leading to Forstchen's newest interest, the displacement of historical characters through time and space. The first of these was an outright fantasy, *The Crystal Warriors.* During World War II, one U.S. and one Japanese soldier are plucked out of time to take part in a magical battle in another reality.

A more interesting variation of this can be found in *The Alexandrian Ring* and *The Assassin Gambit*, collectively known as "The Gamester Wars." In the first, Alexander the Great is brought through time to a far future conflict where he is pitted against another, fictional, time traveller. In the sequel, a legion of Samurai warriors are drawn in to help resolve the conflict.

More recently, Forstchen has displaced a number of Civil War soldiers to another planet where aliens rule over a kidnapped human population. In *Rally Cry* the new arrivals spark a rebellion that frees a large group of the enslaved populace, and in *Union Forever*, a major war erupts on the divided world. The "Lost Regiment" series combines the best elements of military oriented science fiction and historical adventure.

—Don D'Ammassa

---

**FORWARD, Robert L(ull).** Also writes as Susan Lull. American. Born in Geneva, New York, 15 August 1932. Educated at the University of Maryland, College Park, 1950–54, B.S. 1954; University of California, Los Angeles, M.S. 1958; University of Maryland, Ph.D. in physics 1965. Served in the United States Air Force, 1954–56: Captain. Married Martha Neil Dodson in 1954; one son and three daughters. Technical staff member, 1956–66, associate manager, Theoretical Studies Department, 1966–67, manager, Exploratory Studies Department, 1967–74, and senior scientist, 1974–87, Hughes Research Laboratories, Malibu, California. Since 1987, owner and chief scientist, Forward Unlimited. Recipient: Gravity Research Foundation award, 1965; IEEE-AES Carlton award, 1981; *Locus* award, 1981; Star-Cloud award (Japan), 1982, 1990. Agent: Scott Meredith Literary Agency, 845 Third Avenue, New York, New York 10022. Address: P.O. Box 2783, Malibu, California 90265, U.S.A.

### Science-Fiction Publications

#### Novels

*Dragon's Egg.* New York, Ballantine, 1980; London, New English Library, 1981.
*The Flight of the Dragonfly.* New York, Pocket Books, 1984.
*Starquake!* New York, Ballantine, 1985.
*Rocheworld.* New York, Baen, 1990.
*Martian Rainbow.* New York, Ballantine, 1991.

### Other Publications

#### Other

*Antiproton Annihilation Propulsion.* Edwards Air Force Base, California, Air Force Astronautics Laboratory, 1985.
*Advanced Space Propulsion Study.* Edwards Air Force Base, California, Air Force Astronautics Laboratory, 1987.
*Future Magic.* New York, Avon, 1988.
*Mirror Matter*, with Joel Davis. New York, Wiley, 1988.

*

Robert L. Forward comments:

I write *hard* science fiction. After I have decided upon a general story idea, but before I write a detailed outline, I spend six to nine months collecting data, calculating orbits, drawing vehicles and habitats, designing alien physiologies and cultures, and working out timelines. During this "science research" phase, the requirements of the laws of science suggest (and sometimes force) the plot line to move in a certain direction. Thus, in one sense, the science writes the fiction. In all of my novels to date, ideas that were generated during this research phase were so novel and so scientifically sound, that I turned them into technical papers that were later published in scientific archive journals (with a footnote referencing the novel as the first publication of the idea). The drawings and the results of this research phase are usually included as a technical appendix to the novel.

* * *

Robert L. Forward is a practitioner of "hard" SF, seeking not so much for the delineation and development of character, or for insight into the human condition, as for the working out of an idea which involves either a novel scientific hypothesis or an exciting extrapolation of technology. As a professional physicist working on problems of gravitation, his science-fiction writing is a second career and, consequently, his output is small. It does, however, have the quality of disciplined imagination which his main occupation requires. Characteristically, each of his books has a technical appendix (in one case disguised as the report of a congressional hearing) explaining and justifying the ideas employed.

His first novel, *Dragon's Egg*, is built around his most startling notion (developed from an earlier suggestion by F. Drake) that intelligent life could exist upon the surface of a neutron star. Under the fantastic g-forces and intense magnetic fields at the surface of a neutron star, specimens of this life form, known as the Cheela, are of variable shape, but generally resemble minute pancakes 5mm in diameter and 0.5mm thick, but massing a clear 70kg. At this size and enormous rate of energy processing, they live at a formidable pace—roughly a million times our own. This, of course, presents the author with a very difficult communication problem, not made any easier by the fact that the tidal forces around a neutron star are so great that a human being, even in free fall, would be torn apart while still many hundreds of kilometers above the surface. The solutions Forward offers are ingenious.

The story of *Dragon's Egg* is simply the exposition, in a plain and straightforward narrative style, of how humans and Cheela become aware of one another, of how they communicate, of how they make friends and finally part on amicable terms. The plot is satisfactory and credible, given the premises. The characters lack depth, though they are adequate as processors and exchangers of ideas, which is all they are or meant to be. The "heroes" of the book are not the characters, human or Cheela; they are the ideas, the problems, and the solutions. And very satisfying ideas, problems, and solutions they are.

Forward created another strange world, inhabited by another strange intelligent species, and another way of travelling to them, for a story that has appeared in two variants. First published as *The Flight of the Dragonfly*, a rather longer version, *Rocheworld*, incorporating some additional incidents and details, appeared five years later. Which is the better is a matter of taste: this reader preferred the earlier, but this may be because the ideas were no longer novel when he read the later. In both, the voyage employs a variant of the "radiation sail" concept, driven, not directly by the sun, but by a vast array of lasers deployed in space focused by an immense Fresnel lens, similarly deployed. (The notion was expanded in an article in the semi-popular science journal *New Scientist* for 2 October 1986). "Rocheworld" consists of two roughly moon-sized egg-shaped planets, not quite in contact, but so close as to share a common atmosphere: each occupies the Roche lobe of the other. This reader's sums suggest that the system would not be stable: but never mind; what a charming idea! One of these worlds is covered with an ocean, which is inhabited by a cheerful race of large, brightly coloured beings whose sole interests are pure mathematics and water sports. Perhaps they are a little too good to be true. Perhaps Dr. Forward, a physicist and not a life scientist, forgets that dominant species are aggressive species; that is one reason why they are dominant. Again, neither the characters nor the machinery of the plot are memorable. There is no absurdity, and the narrative is smooth; but again, the interest is in the strange world, in the dangers and problems it poses, and in the ingenuity of solutions.

A general, though not universally valid, rule for writers of successful SF is: don't write a sequel. Forward broke this rule with *Starquake!*, a sequel to *Dragon's Egg.*

It is known that neutron stars sometimes exhibit a sudden slight change in their rate of spin. Current theory attributes this to a minute change in the radius of the star; but such a minute change would constitute a shattering "starquake" for any beings such as the Cheela. The premise of the book is that such an event takes place, setting back the promising civilisation of the Cheela almost to starting point; and the story tells how the humans aid a renaissance and are rewarded with a "space warp" return journey to earth. The space warp is somewhat less unconvincing than most, involving the Kerr solutions to the equations of general relativity.

Forward's literary ancestry may be traced back to Verne rather than to Wells. He eschews social comment; he does not attempt to make moral or political points; his writing, though not by any means humourless, is unexciting; his characters are present only to face dangers and solve problems. The problems he invents, though, are fascinating, and the solutions pleasing. The taste for this sort of hard SF, like the taste for very dry wine, is not everybody's; but for those who have it, Forward is a very good Macon—perhaps even a Meursault.

—M. Hammerton

---

**FOSTER, Alan Dean.** American. Born in New York City, 18 November 1946. Educated at the University of California, Los Angeles, B.A. in political science 1968; M.F.A. in film 1969. Served in the United States Army Reserve, 1969–75. Married JoAnn Oxley in 1975. Head copywriter, Headlines Ink Agency, Studio City, California, 1970–71; instructor in English and film, University of California, Los Angeles, intermittently since 1971, and Los Angeles City College, 1972–76. Since 1981, columnist, *Rigel*, Richmond, California; columnist for *Science Fiction Review.* Agent: (fiction) Virginia Kidd, Box 278, Milford, Pennsylvania 18337; (scripts) Ilse Lahn, 5300 Fulton, Van Nuys, California 91401. Address: 4001 Pleasant Valley Drive, Prescott, Arizona 86301, U.S.A.

### Science-Fiction Publications

Novels (series: Commonwealth; The Damned; Spellsinger; Star Trek)

*The Tar-Aiym Krang* (Commonwealth). New York, Ballantine, 1972. London, New English Library, 1979.
*Bloodhype* (Commonwealth). New York, Ballantine, 1973; London, New English Library, 1979.
*Icerigger* (Commonwealth). New York, Ballantine, 1974; London, New English Library, 1976.
*Luana.* New York, Ballantine, 1974.
*Dark Star* (novelization of screenplay). New York, Ballantine, 1974; London, Futura, 1979.
*Star Trek Log One [to Ten],* New York, Ballantine, 10 vols., 1974–78.
*Midworld.* New York, Doubleday, 1975; London, Macdonald and Jane's 1977.
*Star Wars* (as George Lucas). New York, Ballantine, 1976.
*Orphan Star* (Commonwealth). New York, Ballantine, 1977; London, New English Library, 1979.
*The End of the Matter* (Commonwealth). New York, Ballantine, 1977; London, New English Library, 1979.
*Splinter of the Mind's Eye.* New York, Ballantine, and London, Sphere, 1978.
*Mission to Moulokin* (Commonwealth). New York, Ballantine, and London, New English Library, 1979.
*Alien* (novelization of screenplay). New York, Ballantine, and London, Macdonald and Jane's, 1979.
*The Black Hole* (novelization of screenplay). New York, Ballantine, 1979.

*Cachalot* (Commonwealth). New York, Ballantine, 1980.
*Outland* (novelization of screenplay). New York, Warner, and London, Sphere, 1981.
*Clash of the Titans* (novelization of screenplay). New York, Warner, and London, Macdonald, 1981.
*The Thing* (novelization of screenplay). New York, Bantam, and London, Corgi, 1982.
*Nor Crystal Tears* (Commonwealth). New York, Ballantine, 1982.
*For Love of Mother-Not* (Commonwealth). New York, Ballantine, 1983; London, New English Library, 1984.
*Spellsinger at the Gate*. Huntington Woods, Michigan, Phantasia Press, 1983.
*Spellsinger*. New York, Warner, 1983; London, Futura, 1984.
*The Hour at the Gate*. New York, Warner, and London Futura, 1984.
*Krull* (novelization of screenplay). New York, Warner, and London, Corgi, 1983.
*The Man Who Used the Universe*. New York, Warner, 1983; London, Futura, 1984.
*The I Inside*. New York, Warner, 1984; London, Futura, 1985.
*Voyage to the City of the Dead* (Commonwealth). New York, Ballantine, 1984; London, New English Library, 1986.
*Slipt*. New York, Berkley, 1984.
*The Last Starfighter* (novelization of screenplay). New York, Berkley, and London, W.H. Allen, 1984.
*The Day of the Dissonance* (Spellsinger). Huntington Woods, Michigan, Phantasia Press, 1984; London, Futura, 1985.
*The Moment of the Magician* (Spellsinger). Huntington Woods, Michigan, Phantasia Press, 1984; London, Macdonald, 1985.
*Starman* (novelization of screenplay). New York, Warner, 1984; London, Corgi, 1985.
*Shadowkeep*. New York, Warner, 1984; London, W.H. Allen, 1985.
*Sentenced to Prism* (Commonwealth). New York, Ballantine, 1985; London, New English Library, 1988.
*Pale Rider*. New York, Warner, and London, Arrow, 1985.
*The Paths of the Perambulator* (Spellsinger). West Bloomfield, Michigan, Phantasia Press, 1985; London, Macdonald, 1986.
*Aliens* (novelization of screenplay). New York, Warner, and London, Futura, 1986.
*The Time of the Transference* (Spellsinger). West Bloomfield, Michigan, Phantasia Press, 1986; London, Futura, 1987.
*The Deluge Drivers* (Commonwealth). New York, Ballantine, 1987; London, New English Library, 1988.
*Glory Lane*. New York, Ace, 1987; London, New English Library, 1989.
*Flinx in Flux* (Commonwealth). New York, Ballantine, 1988; London, New English Library, 1989.
*Alien Nation*. New York, Warner, and London, Grafton, 1988.
*Quozl*. New York, Ace, 1989.
*Cyber Way*. New York, Ace, 1990.
*A Call to Arms* (Damned). New York, Ballantine, 1991.
*Catalyst*. New York, Ace, 1991.

Short Stories

*With Friends Like These*. New York, Ballantine, 1977.
*... Who Needs Enemies?* New York, Ballantine, 1984.
*The Metrognome*. New York, Ballantine, 1990.

OTHER PUBLICATIONS

Novels

*Into the Out Of*. New York, Warner, 1986; London, New English Library, 1987.
*To the Vanishing Point*. New York, Warner, 1988; London, Sphere, 1989.
*Maori*. New York, Berkley, 1988.

Play

Screenplay: *Star-Trek*, 1979.

Other

Editor, *The Best of Eric Frank Russell*. New York, Ballantine, 1978.
Editor, *Animated Features and Silly Symphonies*. New York, Abbeville, 1980.
Editor, with Martin H. Greenberg, *Smart Dragons, Foolish Elves*. New York, Ace, 1991.

*

Alan Dean Foster comments:

Many of my science-fiction novels, particularly the earlier works, take place in what is called the Universe of the Commonwealth, a future society in which mankind has formed a close alliance with a race of insect-like creatures called the Thranx. Within this series are sub-series such as the *Icerigger* trilogy and the stories that deal with the characters Flinx and Pip, as well as independent novels. Events and characters will occasionally overlap, as with the *Icerigger* books and *The End of the Matter*. It is my eventual intention to tie all the Commonwealth stories together in one grand conclusion (perhaps in 40 or so years).

Other works include the *Spellsinger* fantasy series, independent novels of SF such as *Glory Lane, Quozl*, and The Damned trilogy, tales of contemporary horror and suspense like *Into the Out Of* and *To The Vanishing Point*, and the historical novel *Maori*, which is set in 19th-century New Zealand.

With a few exceptions my short fiction is not tied to any of my novels, including those which form series of their own such as the stories of the mountain man Mad Amos Malone and the tales of the *Montezuma Strip*. In my book-length stories of adventure I try to explore how people, especially ordinary people, react to extraordinary circumstances and events, while the shorter fiction tends to deal with more intimate concerns.

Personal concerns which are often reflected in my work are a life-long interest in ecology, travel, other cultures, the unexplored potential of the human mind, and historical serendipity, in which the small and seemingly unimportant often give rise to events of world-shaking consequence (viz. World War I and the election of a B-movie actor to the presidency of the United States).

* * *

Alan Dean Foster is perhaps best known for his competent, well written film novelizations (*Alien, Alien Nation, Outland, The Thing, The Last Starfighter*, and numerous others). He has also written *Splinter of the Mind's Eye* based on the Star Wars characters, and the Star Trek "Log" series based on the animated television series.

However, it is within the framework of his science-fiction adventures that Foster's talents shine through. In the tradition of Edgar Rice Burroughs, Foster creates exotic worlds, peopling them with strange and fascinating races and with memorable characters, using them as the backdrop against which he weaves his tales. His plausible, scientifically sound settings combined with vivid, sensual descriptions make Foster's worlds come alive. As with the works of Robert Heinlein, Gordon Dickson, and Poul Anderson, many of Foster's novels share a common setting. For Foster it is the "Humanx Commonwealth," a loose confederation of planets settled by humans and the insectoid Thranx.

Some of these fascinating Commonwealth worlds can be found in such diverse works as *Cachalot, Icerigger*, and *Midworld.* Cachalot, an ocean world of swelling blue waves, is dotted with islands whose gem-like beaches are so brilliant they may cause blindness. In this environmental adventure, humans in their floating cities peacefully share the world with porpoises, dolphins, and whales. The whales, however, shun human contact because of sharp racial memories of near genocide on Earth. A woman biologist and her team of experts try to discover who or what is methodically destroying the human cities. *Icerigger* focuses on the ice world Tran-ky-ky with its scattered, isolated settlements. Ethan Fortune, Skua September and others who are stranded on Tran-ky-ky must overcome the hostile, sub-arctic environment and enlist the help of the feline natives to assist them in reaching the Commonwealth outpost. Another environmental tale, *Midworld* features an off-course human colony ship which ends up on a hostile jungle world that makes the films *Alien* and *Predator* look like a walk in the park. After generations, the descendants have literally become one with the environment only to have their existence threatened by a greedy corporation intent upon milking the virgin planet of all its resources.

In *Nor Crystal Tears*, one of Foster's strongest works, the setting is subordinate to the characters. It is a first contact novel depicting the meeting of humans with the insectoid Thranx as seen through the eyes of Thranx agriculturist Ryo. Ryo's vision of peaceful co-existence between Thranx and humans is realized with the help of several stranded Earth explorers. Their struggle and sacrifice to achieve this vision overcomes the prejudice and distrust on the part of both cultures resulting in the founding of the Commonwealth.

Another of Foster's first contact novels is *A Call To Arms*, book one of The Damned series in which the Earth is caught in the middle of galactic warfare between the Amplitur and the Weave. The Amplitur is a telepathically manipulative race which subverts all races to its purpose. The Weave is a loose coalition of races all of whom dislike the idea of being genetically altered. While similar to the Commonwealth, the Weave, instead of treating Earthlings as equals, is using them as warriors because of their aggressiveness, while denying them citizenship. This premise is similar to that of the plight of the African-American soldiers in the Allied/Axis conflict during World War II.

Many of Foster's protagonists are depicted as superhuman, extraordinary, or exotic. The genetically altered Flynx, with his psi powers and his symbiotic pet minidragon, is one of Foster's most popular characters. Foster chronicles Flynx's adventures as he searches for his parents in the Flynx of the Commonwealth series. Flynx, a rogue and an ethical thief, is reminiscent of Fritz Leiber's Gray Mouser and Harry Harrison's Jimi diGriz. However, Flynx's childhood as an orphan and a slave is strikingly similar to Thorby Baslim's in Robert Heinlein's *Citizen of the Galaxy.* Another of Foster's popular characters is Jon-Tom (Jonathan Thomas Meriweather), a UCLA student who is magicked to another world by the turtle wizard Clothahump in the Spellsinger series. Jon-Tom joins forces with Clothahump and his ragtag band of humans and animals in a battle against an ancient evil. This mixture of light adventure with humor is similar to the Myth series by Robert Asprin and the Xanth books by Piers Anthony. Other characters include telekinetic Jake Pickett and his telepathic grand-niece Amanda who battle the corrupt corporation whose chemical wastes caused their mutations in *Slipt.*

Foster is also very fond of portraying the common or everyday person as caught up in events beyond his or her control. Will Dulac, composer and teacher, is the first person kidnapped by the Weave in the promising new series *A Call To Arms. To The Vanishing Point* finds sporting goods executive Frank Sonderberg, his family, and a 4,000-year-old girl named Mouse on a quest to save the universe from unraveling. In *Cyber Way*, aging, overweight detective Vernon Moody solves the murder of an art collector involving Indian sand paintings, ancient Navajo rituals, and aliens. While characterization is not Foster's greatest strength, the reader comes to know and like his characters.

Many of Alan Dean Foster's novels deal with such ideas as man's inhumanity to man (*Midworld*), prejudice (*Nor Crystal Tears, A Call To Arms*) or destruction of the environment (*Midworld, Slipt, Icerigger*). But themes of peace through mutual cooperation and understanding, and respect for life (*Nor Crystal Tears, Icerigger, Cachalot, Midworld*) occur over and over within Foster's fiction. Foster's readability, memorable characters, and believable worlds combined with an element of hope are the reasons he not only holds his fans but continues to attract new ones.

—John I. Lawson

---

**FOSTER, M(ichael) A(nthony).** American. Born in Greensboro, North Carolina, 2 July 1939. Educated at Greensboro High School, graduated 1957; Syracuse University, New York, 1957–58, 1959–60; University of Maryland extension courses in Karamursel, Turkey, 1961–62; University of Oregon, Eugene, 1962–64, B.A. in Slavic languages 1964. Married Judith Ann Forsythe in 1965; two sons. Served in the United States Air Force, 1957–62, 1965–76: Russian linguist, 1957–62, Intelligence, 1965–71, Strategic Missiles, 1971–75, and Intercept Weapons Director, 1975–76: Captain. Photographer: individual shows—Rapid City, South Dakota, 1972, 1973, 1974, Address: 5409 Amberhill Drive, Greensboro, North Carolina 27405, U.S.A.

SCIENCE-FICTION PUBLICATIONS

Novels (series: Ler; Morphodite)

*The Warriors of Dawn* (Ler). New York, DAW, 1975; London, Hamlyn, 1979.
*The Gameplayers of Zan* (Ler). New York, DAW, 1977; London, Hamlyn, 1979.
*The Day of the Klesh* (Ler). New York, DAW, 1979.
*Waves.* New York, DAW, 1980.
*The Morphodite.* New York, DAW, 1981.
*Transformer* (Morphodite). New York, DAW, 1983.
*Preserver* (Morphodite). New York, DAW, 1985.

Short Stories

*Owl Time.* New York, DAW, 1985.

Other Publications

Verse

*Shards from Byzantium.* Privately printed, 1969.
*The Vaseline Dreams of Hundifer Soames.* Privately printed, 1970.

*

M.A. Foster comments:

As of 1991, although I write daily, I am no longer active in publishing science fiction in any sense. Obviously, a full and complete discussion of these circumstances is far beyond the scope of an article of this nature.

One thing which may be worth saying here is a lesson I learned from the practice of writing: to start and to continue to write is as easy and natural as dreaming, or as growth in a landscape. It is when to stop writing that the art appears. This principle was originally intended to apply within the work of a story, so to speak, but it is also true in the larger sense as well, if difficult to apply in practice.

* * *

Since his advent on the SF scene with *The Warriors of Dawn* in 1975, M.A. Foster completed six novels, a few short stories, and a collection entitled *Owl Time.* He has not published any SF since 1986 and he says he does not intend to do so in the future, although he continues to write.

The selections in *Owl Time* differ somewhat from the rest of Foster's corpus, but the full-length novels have several characteristics in common. They contain seemingly loose plots, with emphasis on character and setting rather than on story development. Yet each story is a gradual unfolding of the interrelationship between characters' actions and the positioning of the cosmos. Each depends on the perspective of one, or at most two, viewpoint characters, usually narrated in the third person. Finally, Foster displays an anti-deterministic philosophy through both theme and technique. Each novel turns around the resolution of a many-levelled mystery, an attempt to discover who or what is manipulating the society on a particular world. Foster repeatedly introduces variations on Tarot and the *I-Ching*, both oracular methods of tracing a non-deterministic future. He also refers often to Zen disciplines. However, the ultimate answer to each quest lies most often in the minute actions of individuals.

Six of Foster's novels also focus on the consequences of potential genetic manipulation. *The Warriors of Dawn, The Gameplayers of Zan*, and *The Day of the Klesh* develop from the premise that human attempts to create a superhuman race, called Ler, will yield unwanted results. *Gameplayers*, chronologically first in the full tale, documents the agony of mistrust and misunderstanding that sends most of Ler off to the planet from which warriors (in *The Warriors of Dawn*) appear. The Klesh, humans these Warriors have enslaved for purposes of breeding, are freed to migrate to Monsalvat, the planet which forms the backdrop for the third novel in the story's internal chronology, *The Day of the Klesh.*

*The Morphodite, Transformer* and *Preserver* presuppose a more refined set of techniques for genetically manipulating live beings. These are perfected on a backwater planet called Oerlikon to result in a being who can change his/her shape, going from female to male to female, and losing 20 years of chronological age, but not of memory, with each protoplasmic transformation. Demsing/Nazarine/Phaedrus/Damistofia/Rael/Jedily uses an extension of principles upon which the *I-Ching* was constructed to "read" the world around him/her and discover which act is the most likely to cause the disintegration of the rigid Oerlikon society. However, like the Ler in Foster's first trilogy, his/her power soon outstrips that of her immediate creators as she/he realizes the organizational lines of power and how easily they can be manipulated. *Preserver*, the conclusion of the trilogy, amplifies on the theme of lines of force as it shows the morphodite gradually becoming aware of past transformations and enhanced power. The sensitive handling of female characters, both in the person of the viewpoint character as one of his/her states and her companions when she/he is male, is more developed in these three novels. This ability of Foster to create fully human female characters such as Fellerian, Snajirmil, and Mevlanen, (*Gameplayers*) led to speculation with the first two novels that the author was female. Many of the techniques, such as elaborate description through footnotes, as well as in-text references, multi-layered plot, and "scientification" of divination tools, are displayed with much refinement in these three novels.

*Waves* is the most Russian of Foster's novels, taking place on a planet which seems to have been settled by people of that national grouping. While the setting reflects Foster's language ability (he acted in the capacity of Russian linguist while with the U.S. Air Force), the plot follows a linguistic mystery—an ocean that seems to speak a language. Perhaps because he had to resolve the mystery in the course of only one novel, Foster was not as successful in substituting his own type of multi-layered complexity for tight structure. In fact, the plot tends to get lost in the love story of his two protagonists. *Waves* is slow-paced, somewhat lyrical, and reminiscent of Lem's *Solaris.*

Foster's short novels, four of which appeared in *Owl Time*, are exercises in style variation in which he adopts styles he identifies with different SF and non-SF writers. Yet, with the possible exception of "The Conversation," they seem very much Foster. This rather atypical Foster story creates a conversation between an author and a character whose positions are not fixed in relation to one another, the real author, or the reader. That its content is a commentary on totalitarianism adds to the story's engaging quality. "Entertainment," which Foster claims is an attempt to emulate Jack Vance, incorporates the footnotes, prefatory quotations, single viewpoint character and puzzle-plot of his earlier fiction.

—Janice M. Bogstad

---

**FOWLER, Karen Joy.** American. Born in Bloomington, Indiana, 7 February 1950. Educated at University of California, Berkeley, 1968–70, 1971–72, B.A. 1972; State University of New York, Albany, 1970–71; University of California, Davis, 1972–74, M.A. 1974. Married Hugh Fowler in 1972; one son, one daughter. Writer in residence, Cleveland State University, Ohio, Spring 1990. Recipient: John W. Campbell award, 1978; National Endowment for the Arts grant, 1988. Agent: Wendy Weil, Wendy Weil Agency, 747 Third Avenue, New York, New York, 10017. Address: 3404 Monte Vista, Davis, California, 95616, U.S.A.

SCIENCE-FICTION PUBLICATIONS

Short Stories

*Peripheral Vision.* Eugene, Oregon, Pulphouse, 1990.
*Artificial Things.* New York, Bantam, 1991.

OTHER PUBLICATIONS

Novel

*Sarah Canary.* New York, Holt, 1991.

* * *

There is a moment in the story "Face Value" in which two humans, falling out of love, are investigating the alien menes. One is asked what he thinks he is doing: " 'Is that a trick question?' he asked. 'I imagine I am studying the mene. What do you imagine I am studying?' 'What humans always study,' said Hesper. 'Humans.' " The story is about not taking things at face value, and that is a lesson to be learned in reading any of Karen Joy Fowler's stories. Though she may use the paraphernalia of science fiction—aliens, other worlds, robots, time travel—her work is always about the human. In fact there is usually a discomforting domesticity about her work in which characters have to face up to their own inadequacies, disappointments or failures in situations whose very ordinariness emphasises the small tragedy.

In "Lily Red" a woman stages a small rebellion from the narrowness of her marriage and is offered the chance of an encounter with an ageless Indian, but she fails to see the magic and returns home. In "The Lake was Full of Artificial Things" a woman uses memory-enhancement techniques to meet again with the boyfriend she rejected and who was then killed in Vietnam, but the meetings go beyond what memory could supply and the woman is, instead, confronted with her own lack of understanding of the man, and of her own motivations.

The Vietnam era looms large in her work; there are many references to that time, and to the ideals and inspirations that shaped the 60s. These, however, usually form the basis for a story about how those ideals have been lost or betrayed. "The War of the Roses" recounts a confrontation between a hard-line revolutionary society and a small community whose life is devoted to tending flowers. The community is destroyed, but the revolution has to absorb much of the community's learning in order to survive, and the revolutionary who precipitated the confrontation finds herself tending flowers and learning, in a way typical of Fowler, that memory and regret are the same thing.

Memory is important in Fowler's work. Raina in "Recalling Cinderella" is haunted by a vague memory that, when recognised, sets off her final rebellion. Yet memory always triggers sadness, which must be accepted in order for us to survive. "The Faithful Companion at Forty" has Tonto looking back on the indignities of his career as a sidekick, but by confronting the unhappiness of his memories he is, in the end, stronger than the Lone Ranger, who cannot accept the happy memories of his youthful adventures and so plunges into one more time-travelling exploit which, we are left to suppose, will be the death of him.

It is typical, also, that Fowler should write about the sidekick rather than the hero. If there is one common trait shared by practically all her characters it is cowardice. Sometimes it is overcome, though to ambiguous effect, as in "The Dragon's Head" when little Penny finally confronts the old witch lady who lives in her neighbourhood and learns a mystery that haunts her life. Other times it is not, as when Hannah, the historian in "Praxis" whose field of expertise is the moment of choice that can change the whole history of human affairs, is confronted with such a moment herself and is unable to make the choice. Such moments of defeat and self-revelation echo through all Fowler's stories, though generally they provide the key to something else—maybe not happiness, a commodity in short supply in her stories and usually regarded with distrust, but at least a measure of achievement. Thus in "Lieserl" a young Albert Einstein, over a period of a few days, receives letters telling him of the birth, life, old age, and death of a daughter he never sees. The letters naturally frighten him, but at the same time they foreshadow the relativity towards which he is groping.

—Paul Kincaid

---

**FOWLER, Sydney.** *See* **WRIGHT, S. Fowler.**

---

**FOX, Gardner F(rancis).** Also writes as Jefferson Cooper; Lynna Cooper; Jeffrey Gardner; James Kendricks; Simon Majors; Kevin Matthews; Bart Somers. American. Born in Brooklyn, New York, 20 May 1911. Educated at St. John's University, Jamaica, New York, B.A. 1932, LL.B. 1935. Married Lynda J. Negrini in 1937; one son and one daughter. Lawyer. From 1937, comic-book writer (*Batman, Superman, The Flash, Green Lantern*, and others). *Died.*

SCIENCE-FICTION PUBLICATIONS

Novels (series: Commander Craig)

*Five Weeks in a Balloon* (novelization of screenplay). New York Pyramid, 1962.
*Escape Across the Cosmos.* New York, Paperback Library, 1964.
*The Arsenal of Miracles.* New York, Ace, 1964.
*Warrior of Llarn.* New York, Ace. 1964.
*The Hunter out of Time.* New York, Ace, 1965.
*Beyond the Black Enigma* (Craig; as Bart Somers). New York, Paperback Library, 1965.
*The Druid Stones* (as Simon Majors). New York, Paperback Library, 1965.
*Thief of Llarn.* New York, Ace, 1966.
*Abandon Galaxy* (Craig; as Bart Somers). New York, Paperback Library, 1967.
*Conehead.* New York, Ace, 1973.
*Carty.* New York, Doubleday, 1977; London, Hale, 1979.

Uncollected Short Stories

"The Weirds of the Woodcarver," in *Weird Tales* (New York), September 1944.
"The Last Monster," in *Planet* (New York), Fall 1945.
"Man Nth," in *Planet* (New York), Winter 1945.
"Engines of the Gods," in *Planet* (New York), Spring 1946.
"Heart of Light," in *Amazing* (New York), July 1946.
"The Man the Sun Gods Made," in *Planet* (New York), Winter 1946.

"Sword of the Seven Suns," in *Planet* (New York), Spring 1947.
"Vassals of the Lode-Star," in *Planet* (New York), Summer 1947.
"Werewile of the Crystal Crypt," in *Planet* (New York), Summer 1948.
"When Kohonnes Screamed," in *Planet* (New York), Fall 1948.
"Crom the Barbarian" (comic), in *Out of This World Adventures* (New York), July 1950.
"Temptress of the Time Flow," in *Marvel* (New York), November 1950.
"The Spider God of Akka" (comic), in *Out of This World Adventures* (New York), December 1950.
"The Warlock of Sharrador," in *Planet* (New York), March 1953.
"The Holding of Kolymar," in *Fantastic* (New York), October 1971.
"Tonight the Stars Revolt!," in *Galactic Empires*, edited by Brian Aldiss. London, Weidenfeld and Nicolson, 1976; New York, St. Martin's Press, 1977.
"Shadow of a Demon," in *The Year's Best Fantasy Stories 3*, edited by Lin Carter. New York, DAW, 1977.

OTHER PUBLICATIONS

Novels

*The Borgia Blade*. New York, Fawcett, 1953; London, Fawcett, 1954.
*Madame Buccaneer*. New York, Fawcett, 1953; London, Fawcett, 1954.
*Woman of Kali*. New York, Fawcett, 1954; London, Muller, 1960.
*The Gentleman Rogue*. New York, Fawcett, 1954; London, Red Seal, 1959.
*Rebel Wench*. New York, Fawcett, 1955; London, Fawcett, 1958.
*Queen of Sheba*. New York, Fawcett, 1956.
*One Sword for Love*. London, Fawcett, 1956.
*Terror over London*. New York, Fawcett, 1957.
*The Conquering Prince*. London, Fawcett, 1958.
*Witness This Woman*. New York, Fawcett, 1959; London, Muller, 1961.
*Creole Woman*. New York, Fawcett, 1959.
*The Devil Sword* (as Kevin Matthews). New York, Hill, 1960.
*Bastard of Orleans*. New York, Avon, 1960.
*Scandal in Suburbia*. New York, Hill, 1960.
*Woman of Egypt* (as Kevin Matthews). London, Panther, 1961.
*Barbary Devil* (as Jeffrey Gardner). New York, Pyramid, 1961.
*Cleopatra* (as Jeffrey Gardner). New York, Pyramid, 1962.
*As Good as Dead*. New York, Fawcett, 1962.
*One Wife's Ways*. New York, Fawcett, and London, Muller, 1963.
*Tom Blood, Highwayman*. New York, Avon, 1963.
*Lion of Lucca*. New York, Avon, 1966.
*Ivan the Terrible*. New York, Avon, n.d.
*Kothar—Barbarian Swordsman* [*of the Magic Sword!, and the Demon Queen and the Wizard Slayer, and the Conjurer's Curse*]. New York, Belmont, 5 vols., 1969–70.
*Kyrik, Warlock Warrior* [*Fights the Demon World, and the Wizard's Sword, and the Lost Queen*]. New York, Nordon, 4 vols., 1976–76; *Kyrik Fights the Demon World* published London, Jenkins, 1976.
*The Bold Ones*. New York, Nordon, 1976.
*The Liberty Sword*. New York, Nordon, 1976.
*Hurricane*. New York, Nordon, 1976.
*Savage Passage*. New York, Nordon, 1978.
*Blood Trail*. New York, Belmont, 1979.

Novels as Jefferson Cooper

*Arrow in the Hill*. New York, Dodd Mead, 1955.
*The Bloody Sevens*. New York, Permabooks, 1956.
*The Swordsman*. New York, Pocket Books, 1957.
*The Questing Sword*. New York, Permabooks, 1958; London, Consul, 1960.
*Captain Seadog*. New York, Pocket Books, 1959.
*Delilah*. New York, Paperback Library, 1962.
*Veronica's Veil*. New York, Permabooks, n.d.
*Jezebel*. New York, Paperback Library, 1963.
*Slave of the Roman Sword*. New York, Paperback Library, 1965.
*This Sword for Hire*. New York, Paperback Library, 1966.

Novels as James Kendricks

*Beyond Our Pleasure*. Derby, Connecticut, Monarch, 1959.
*Sword of Casanova*. Derby, Connecticut, Monarch, 1959.
*Adultress*. Derby, Connecticut, Monarch, 1960.
*She Wouldn't Surrender*. Derby, Connecticut, Monarch, 1960.
*The Wicked, Wicked Woman*. Derby, Connecticut, Monarch, 1961.
*Love Me Tonight*. Derby, Connecticut, Monarch, 1963.

Novels as Lynna Cooper

*An Offer of Marriage*. New York, New American Library, 1976.
*Substitute Bride*. New York, New American Library, 1976.
*Her Heart's Desire*. New York, New American Library, 1976.
*The Hired Wife*. New York, New American Library, 1978.
*Forgotten Love*. New York, New American Library, 1979.
*Hearts in the Highlands*. New York, New American Library, 1980.
*Inherit My Heart*. New York, New American Library, 1981.

* * *

Gardner F. Fox was probably best known for his comic-book work, which includes scripts for such science fiction-based characters as Superman and Hawkman. Yet his best science fantasy writing is probably to be found in a dozen space operas published between 1945 and 1952, mainly in *Planet Stories*, where they are overshadowed by the more impressive work of Ray Bradbury, Leigh Brackett, and Ross Rocklynne. But much of that work remains highly entertaining.

His first actual SF-fantasy sale was to *Weird Tales*, but his first story for *Planet Stories*, "The Last Monster"—a benevolent alien's efforts to aid endangered humans are misread as the menacings of a monster—won the instant approval of the magazine's readers. Fox buttressed his success with "Man Nth," in which aliens recruit beings from various worlds and endow them with superhuman powers to enable them to fend off a cosmic threat that would do justice to some of the grander fancies of A.E. van Vogt. "Man Nth" was an almost flawless entertainment and demonstrated a much surer touch than "The Last Monster." "Engines of the Gods" and "The Man the Sun Gods Made" established Fox as one of the most reliable writers of strong space adventure novelettes. "The Man the Sun Gods Made," about an artificial superman who stymies Earth's plans to exploit his planet, melded concepts Fox had already proven himself comfortable with—supermen and super-science—with the sort of story Leigh Brackett was already demonstrating success with.

"Vassals of the Lode-Star" is one of the strongest of his stories, arguably the best work he produced in the field. A rift in the fabric of time and space transports its hero to another world where he finds himself in a war with a superbeing bent on enslaving everything in reach. This was a story where everything worked for Fox: a strong and likeable lead character, Thor Masterson, a swift and interesting plot, concepts that are sufficiently gradiose and metaphysical to evoke a sense of wonder, and a benevolent alien, the Discoverer. "When Kohonnes Screamed" is less successful, though strongly imaginative, dealing with a planet where space and matter are dangerously and unpredictably distorted by a force which must somehow be located and destroyed. "Tonight the Stars Revolt!" is a strongly plotted story written in a terse prose under the now-traditional influence of Brackett, its conventional overcome-the-evil-ruler plot buoyed with fine story telling and a strong imagination.

With the collapse of the SF market, Fox found success with original paperback historical novels, and he touched the periphery of SF with a novelization of the movie of Jules Verne's *Five Weeks in a Balloon.* But *Escape Across the Cosmos* was his first true SF novel. It was the story of a superman, falsely accused of a crime, who sets out to defend himself. *The Arsenal of Miracles* told of an outcast Earthman—a disgraced space officer—who joins forces with the queen of an alien world to fight the overwhelmingly powerful Empire of Earth. Some of its passages may have promised the same sort of fun delivered by his earlier stories, but novel-length SF seems never to have been Fox's forte. *Arsenal of Miracles* is a fun read, but none of the subsequent novels is quite as good. Under the name Bart Somers he produced two space operas based on the adventures of a character called Commander Craig, a space-going trouble shooter.

*Conehead* is one of his most interesting efforts. It touches on a more serious theme than is common to Fox's work, racial prejudice. His hero is the standard space officer of most of Fox's novels, but instead of being a warrior, he is a lawyer who sets out to establish the civil rights of the natives of a planet under the domination of Earth. The story returns ultimately to familiar ground: the planet holds the remnants of an alien race, all but extinct, yet still possessing god-like powers, and it is the force of their powers and not of any moral argument that ultimately sways the empire.

Fox was no idea man. His backgrounds are often merely sketched in, which probably accounts for his failure to draw any really widespread following among readers. But he was also a genuinely unpretentious writer whose work provides the sort of straightforward entertainment expected of good space opera. His novels are workmanlike and fun, but they lack the flair, imagination, and pacing of his best magazine stories.

—Gerald W. Page

---

**FRANK, Pat (Harry Hart).** American. Born in Chicago, Illinois, 5 May 1907. Attended the University of Florida, Gainesville, 1925–26. Divorced; one son and one daughter. Reporter, Jacksonville *Journal*, Florida, 1927–29, New York *Journal*, 1929–32, and Washington *Herald*, 1933–38; Chief of the Washington Bureau, 1938–41, and correspondent in Italy, Austria, Germany, Turkey, and Hungary, 1944–46, Overseas News Agency; Assistant Chief of Mission, Office of War Information, 1941–44; member of United Nations Mission to Korea, 1952–53; staff member, Democratic National Committee, 1960; consultant, National Aeronautics and Space Councel, 1961; consultant Department of Defense, 1963–64. Recipient: War Department commendation, 1945; Reserved Officers Association citation, 1957; American Heritage Foundation award, 1961. *Died 12 October 1964.*

### Science-Fiction Publications

#### Novels

*Mr. Adam.* Philadelphia, Lippincott, 1946; London, Gollancz, 1947.
*Forbidden Area.* Philadelphia, Lippincott, 1956; as *Seven Days to Never,* London, Constable, 1957.
*Alas, Babylon.* Philadelphia, Lippincott, and London, Constable, 1959.

### Other Publications

#### Novels

*An Affair of State.* Philadelphia, Lippincott, 1948; London, Corgi, 1951.
*Hold Back the Night.* Philadelphia, Lippincott, and London, Hamish Hamilton, 1952.

#### Other

*The Long Way Round.* Philadelphia, Lippincott, 1953.
*How to Survive the H-Bomb, and Why.* Philadelphia, Lippincott, 1962.
*Rendezvous at Midway: U.S.S. Yorktown and the Japanese Carrier Fleet,* with Joseph D. Harrington. New York, Day, 1967.

* * *

In the late 1940's and 1950's, a growing distrust of technology focused on the dangers of atomic energy. The most obvious danger was that of nuclear war, but concerns about reactor break-downs or bomb-factory explosions were also on people's minds. The immediate blast was one threat, and genetic damage from radiation was another. Science-fiction writers were among the first during this period to give such fears a public voice, and one of those writers was Pat Frank.

Frank wrote a great deal of material—fiction and non-fiction—dealing with the possible problems with atomic materials. His first novel, *Mr. Adam,* postulates universal male sterility as one of the results of an explosion at an atomic bomb factory in Mississippi. *Forbidden Area* attempts to show how, why, and when the Russians might attack the United States. This book is an especially grim indictment of America's lack of preparedness for such a possibility. Frank shows how the various agencies—paralyzed by red tape, inter-departmental bickering, unqualified political appointees in positions of power, and the like—refuse to act until it is almost too late, averting an all-out Russian attack by only minutes.

Frank is probably best known as the author of *Alas, Babylon,* a post-atomic war novel. Randy Bragg, an inhabitant of Fort Repose, Florida, is warned by his brother, Mark, a SAC Intelligence Officer, that the war is coming. Mark sends his wife and children to Randy because Fort Repose will be safer during such a war than will SAC Headquarters, Omaha. The bombs and missiles fall, and the people of Fort Repose are on their own.

Unlike Nevil Shute's *On the Beach*, in which everyone dies, *Alas, Babylon* is basically a romantic view of the aftermath of an atomic war. Randy and his friends do not have too much difficulty surviving—though Civil Defense agencies have prepared almost no one, and Randy has to organize the people of Fort Repose—and only one of the central characters is killed. With this romantic novel, however, Frank presents all the atomic fears, from initial blast to genetic mutation, in one package.

Frank also examines the use of power in *Alas, Babylon.* There are various people in the novel who have power and should not. Randy was defeated in politics by an opponent who appealed to bigotry and fear. The Navy Ensign who fires the shot that starts the war uses the power of his jet plane to compensate for his diminutive physical stature. Randy, however, uses the power at his disposal to keep Fort Repose safe. From this, it is clear that it is not power, *per se*, that Frank objects to but the lack of qualifications of some of the people who have the power.

Frank's novels are well written. They have strong plots, well-paced action, and interesting characters. They are not so much appeals to the reader's fear of atomic power as they are warnings.

—C.W. Sullivan III

---

**FRAYN, Michael.** British. Born in London, 8 September 1933. Educated at Kingston Grammar School, Surrey; Emmanuel College, Cambridge, B.A. 1957. Served in the Royal Artillery and Intelligence Corps, 1952–54. Married Gillian Palmer in 1960; three daughters. Reporter, 1957–59, and columnist, 1959–62, *The Guardian*, Manchester and London; columnist, *The Observer*, London, 1962–68. Recipient: Maugham award, 1966; Hawthornden prize, 1967; National Press award, 1970; *Standard* award for play, 1976, 1981, 1983, 1985; Society of West End Theatre award, 1977, 1982; British Theatre Association award, 1981, 1983; Olivier award, 1985. Agent: Elaine Greene Ltd., 31 Newington Green, London N169PU, England.

### Science-Fiction Publications

#### Novels

*The Tin Men.* London, Collins, 1965; Boston, Little Brown, 1966.
*A Very Private Life.* London, Collins, and New York, Viking Press, 1968.
*Sweet Dreams.* London, Collins, 1973; New York, Viking Press, 1974.

### Other Publications

#### Novels

*The Russian Interpreter.* London, Collins, and New York, Viking Press, 1966.
*Towards the End of the Morning.* London, Collins, 1967; as *Against Entropy*, New York, Viking Press, 1967.
*The Trick of It.* London and New York, Viking Press, 1990.

#### Plays

*Zounds!*, with John Edwards, music by Keith Statham (produced Cambridge, 1957).
*The Two of Us* (includes *Black and Silver, The New Quixote, Mr. Foot, Chinamen*) (produced London, 1970; Ogunquit, Maine, 1975; *Chinamen* produced New York, 1979). London, Fontana, 1970; *Chinamen* published in *The Best Short Plays 1973*, edited by Stanley Richards, Radnor, Pennsylvania, Chilton, 1973; revised version of *The New Quixote* (produced Chichester and London, 1980).
*The Sandboy* (produced London, 1971).
*Alphabetical Order* (produced London, 1975; New Haven, Connecticut, 1976). Included in *Alphabetical Order and Donkeys' Years*, 1977.
*Donkeys' Years* (produced London, 1976). Included in *Alphabetical Order and Donkeys' Years*, 1977.
*Clouds* (produced London, 1976). London, Eyre Methuen, 1977.
*Alphabetical Order and Donkeys' Years.* London, Eyre Methuen, 1977.
*The Cherry Orchard*, adaptation of a play by Chekhov (produced London, 1978). London, Eyre Methuen, 1978.
*Balmoral* (produced Guildford, Surrey, 1978; revised version, as *Liberty Hall*, produced London, 1980). London, Methuen, 1987.
*The Fruits of Enlightenment*, adaptation of a play by Tolstoy (produced London, 1979). London, Eyre Methuen, 1979.
*Make and Break* (produced London, 1980; Washington, D.C., 1983). London, Eyre Methuen, 1980.
*Noises Off* (produced London, 1981; New York, 1983). London, Methuen, 1982; New York, French, 1985.
*Three Sisters*, adaptation of a play by Chekhov (produced Manchester, 1985; London, 1987). London, Methuen, 1983.
*Benefactors* (produced London, 1984). London, Methuen, 1984.
*Wild Honey*, adaptation of a play by Chekhov (produced London, 1984; New York, 1986–87). London, Methuen, 1984.
*Number One*, adaptation of a play by Jean Anouilh (produced London, 1984).
*Plays 1* (includes *Alphabetical Order, Donkey's Years, Clouds, Make and Break, Noises Off*). London and New York, Methuen, 1985.
*Clockwise* (screenplay). London, Methuen, 1986.
*The Seagull*, adaptation of a play by Chekhov (produced Watford, Hertfordshire, 1986). London, Methuen, 1986.
*Uncle Vanya*, adaptation of a play by Chekhov. London, Methuen, 1987.
*Look, Look.* London, Methuen, 1990.
*Audience: A Play in One Act.* New York, French, 1991.

Television Plays and Documentaries: *Second City Reports*, with John Bird, 1964; *Jamie, On a Flying Visit*, 1968; *One Pair of Eyes*, 1968; *Birthday*, 1969; *Beyond a Joke* series, with John Bird and Eleanor Bron, 1972; *Laurence Sterne Lived Here* (*Writers' Houses* series), 1973; *Imagine a City Called Berlin*, 1975; *Making Faces*, 1975; *Vienna: The Mask of Gold*, 1977; *Three Streets in the Country*, 1979; *The Long Straight* (*Great Railway Journeys of the World* series), 1980; *Jerusalem*, 1984; *First and Last*, 1989.

#### Other

*The Day of the Dog* (*Guardian* columns). London, Collins, 1962; New York, Doubleday, 1963.
*The Book of Fub* (*Guardian* columns). London, Collins, 1963; as *Never Put Off to Gomorrah*, New York, Pantheon, 1964.
*On the Outskirts* (*Observer* columns). London, Collins, 1964.
*At Bay in Gear Street* (*Observer* columns). London, Fontana, 1967.
*Constructions* (philosophy). London, Wildwood House, 1974.
*Great Railway Journeys of the World*, with others. London, BBC Publications, 1981.

*The Original Michael Frayn: Columns from the Guardian and The Observer.* Edinburgh, Salamander Press, 1983.
*Listen to This: Sketches and Monologues.* London, Methuen, and New York, French, 1990.

Editor, *The Best of Beachcomber,* by J.B. Morton. London, Heinemann, 1963.

Translator, *Plays,* by Anton Chekhov. London, Methuen, 1988.
Translator, *The Sneeze: Plays and Stories by Anton Chekhov.* London, Methuen, and New York, French, 1989.
Translator, *Exchange,* by Yuri Trifonov. London, Methuen, 1990.

* * *

Michael Frayn is not an easy writer to categorize. *The Tin Men* is obviously not SF but witty comedy, school of Waugh; on the other hand, it obviously is SF, as it purports to be written by a computer and satirizes men who behave like computers and are trying to make computers behave like men. When a robot comes to write its own prehistory, it will have to give classic place in its mythology to Macintosh's ethical machines and their struggles on the sinking raft. But the novel is not so much SF itself as an exuberant account of the men who are trying to make our world into an SF dystopia. The great discovery of Macintosh and Goldwasser is that, because all human life is of no purpose other than to provide newspaper headlines and statistics, humans can stop living and let the computers do it for them. Computers can produce newspapers, sports results, pornography, prayers: who needs people? The characteristic inverted logic of Frayn's tin men naturally produces a novelist who begins by writing the blurbs, the potted biography, and the reviews, and only then tries writing the book (formulaically, of course), before capitulating to the superior power of his typewriter keyboard. What *The Tin Men* itself lacks as a novel is a story worthy of its theme. Admittedly the story, which concerns the opening of the Ethics Wings in a computer research establishment, not by the Queen, as planned but by her stand-in for rehearsals (an ungainly man called Nobbs), illustrates several aspects of the theme of illusion mistaken for reality, but its spirit of low farce inoculates the reader against taking the book seriously. Also, the novel's short-breathed episodic quality—it is really only a series of sketches strung loosely together by a farcical plot—too openly betrays the author's work as a whimsically satiric journalist. The short-breath syndrome is familiar among SF novelists who are really short-story men; in *The Tin Men* we have an essayist trying to write a novel and not quite succeeding.

*A Very Private Life* also has a mosaic quality (as indeed does Frayn's stimulating philosophical work, *Constructions*), but here the small pieces compose a highly satisfactory work of art, one of the most delightful fabulations in the genre. The heroine, Uncumber, begins as a misfit in a society where what the Haves have is privacy: they meet by holovision, as in Asimov's *The Naked Sun.* Uncumber falls in love with a man who lives on the fringes of her enclosed society, journeys outside her cell to meet him, is disillusioned by life outside, falls in with outlaws, is rescued by the police and rehabilitated. Comparison with *The Naked Sun* is instructive because, unlike Asimov and the typical SF writer who might handle such a theme, Frayn has not written a dystopian satire: his absurd world is presented not as a threat but as an alteration simply, a new mode, not inhuman but nicely domesticated by engaging touches of ordinariness. Again, if we compare Frayn's work with Angela Carter's *Heroes and Villains,* in which the ivory tower world is promptly sacrificed to the perverse gypsy delights of the world outside, we see how detached and balanced, how cool Frayn is. Uncumber does not find the outer world romantic, as a Carter heroine would; instead, the best it can offer is a tatty attempt to emulate the values of those inside, while the worst is nasty and brutish: the outlaws are indeed, as they are called, "Sad Men." Frayn's novel is written as a fairy story that begins "Once upon a time there will be a little girl called Uncumber," and in that spirit it should be read.

*Sweet Dreams,* clearly to be read as a fantasy, as it is a story set in the after-life, in which revivification is without benefit of technology (by which Farmer and Silverberg, say, have accommodated this mythological idea to SF), is a wickedly soft-centred utopian novel. Howard Baker thinks he has had a car accident and gone to heaven, where he finds himself to be the centre of a circle of his own friends, some of whom must, confusingly enough, be still "alive" in the lower world. For Howard everything is possible in a state where such a frequently expressed (but never, of course, on Earth, seriously meant) erotic wish to browse on a lover's buttocks, for example, can be fulfilled without damage to the compliant partner; where one can levitate or change one's age at will. The trouble is, that Howard does not wish to change; he is, alas, rather lacking in imagination. God gives him the job of helping create the Alps; Howard brilliantly re-invents the Matterhorn. His astringent friend Phil goes one better by creating man in Howard's image. The sad moral seems to be that people like to talk about heaven or utopia but they do not really want it, because they would not know what to do with it if they had it.

In *Constructions* Frayn tells us "I should like to say this: don't *worry* when you find yourself in the midst of a mythology. Relax and enjoy it." Some SF readers may find themselves graveled by the way in which this sharp and witty writer pulls his punches. Frayn is not a knock-down satirist: he is a comic ironist who enjoys the spectacle of human absurdity, and wants us to share the fun: it seems highly apt that he should once have presented a wonderful brief documentary on Laurence Sterne for television. Similarly, the film screenplay *Clockwise,* for a Michael Codron production directed by Christopher Morahan and starring John Cleese, though a farce, holds, in its philosophical if frenetic examination of a headmaster who has allowed time to control his life, much of the Shandean sense of oppression by time as well as having an affinity with SF treatments of the inexorable fourth dimension. His brilliant farce, *Noises Off,* which is sometimes reviewed, thankfully, as pure entertainment, is itself replete with philosophical implications of a kind that might have attracted the author of *The Truth in Painting,* although, thankfully, so far as I know, it has hitherto escaped a Derridian deconstructionist reading.

—Michael J. Tolley

---

**FRENCH, Paul.** *See* **ASIMOV, Isaac.**

---

**FRIEDBERG, Gertrude (née Tonkonogy).** American. Born in New York City, 17 March 1908. Educated at Wellesley College, Massachusetts; Barnard College, New York, B.A. 1929. Married Charles K. Friedberg; one son and one daughter. Mathematics teacher in New York public schools, and freelance writer. *Died 17 September 1989.*

SCIENCE-FICTION PUBLICATIONS

Novel

*The Revolving Boy.* New York, Doubleday, 1966; London, Gollancz, 1967.

Uncollected Short Stories

"The Short and Happy Death of George Frumkin," in *Fantasy and Science Fiction* (New York), April 1963.
"For Whom the Girl Waits," in *Fantasy and Science Fiction* (New York), May 1972.
"Where Moth and Rust," in *The Woman Who Lost Her Names*, edited by Julia Wolf Mazow. New York, Harper, 1980.

OTHER PUBLICATIONS

Plays

*Three Cornered Moon* (produced New York, 1933). New York, French, 1933.
*Town House*, adaptation of stories by John Cheever (produced New York, 1948).

* * *

Gertrude Friedberg's *The Revolving Boy* follows the early life of a supernormal child, Derv, who has the ability to be both radiometer and compass. One of the major themes of the novel is that of discovering and communicating with another civilization. Derv was born to astronauts in 1970, in a weightless condition far from the earth's forces. Because he did not experience gravity at birth, he was able to align himself to a signal from another solar system. He feels compelled to preserve his original orientation to this signal—called the Direction—and consequently, when his body is turned in one direction, he must unwind himself in the opposite direction to recapture his original position. He turns somersaults in bed to compensate for the earth's revolutions and his day's turnings. During his elementary school years, his teachers become concerned as he executes dangerous spins on stairways. He becomes known as "the boy who leans" when his body begins listing in the direction of the signal.

To escape the publicity following his birth, Derv's parents faked a fatal accident in a sailboat, escaped undetected, and assumed new identities. The novel excels in following the parents' fears of discovery as they observe the development of Derv's talent. When Derv reaches high school, an astronomer who knew the astronaut parents discovers their true identities and persuades them to allow Derv to help trace the signal on a laboratory radiometer. Just as the signal is found electronically, Derv and his parents disappear again. Part Two of the book begins some years later, after Derv has taken a new name—Fred Gany—and married his childhood sweetheart, Prin (now Reine), who has perfect pitch. Derv-Fred's signal has suddenly stopped and he has lost his sense of balance. The remainder of the book concentrates on Prin-Rein's attempts to relocate the laboratory radiometer (which has been abandoned) and to determine if the signal has indeed terminated.

Friedberg's scientific projections are mostly erroneous. For instance, the exposition of her novel is centered on the ban on space travel in 1970, due to a belt of nuclear waste around the earth. She overestimated the speed of change to electronic devices in the homes of the 1970s. Her scientific research can also be faulted, since she has failed to take into account some of the properties of radio signals, such as the possibility of blockage by shielding masses (the earth, tunnels, and concrete buildings).

"The Short and Happy Death of George Frumkin" is a tongue-in-cheek look at the use of artificial organs. George, 97 years old, has developed not only a knock in his artificial heart, but also a bad case of ennui, as he refuses to complete a promised rewrite of the second act of a play. George's wife, Helen, persuades him to call an electrician, Dr. Stebbins (most doctors are electricians these days), who tells him that he needs "a new battery and a new variable autotransformer." In order to hook him to his new system, Dr. Stebbins switches him to house current until the calibration procedure is finished. During the short space between plug-ins, George is "dead." However, house current proves a boon to George, providing him with the creative energy to rewrite his second act, plus an oversupply of sexual libido (he attacks his wife and propositions the maid during this interval). But after his return to battery power, he resumes his uninspired ways, learning nevertheless that his rewritten second act has given the play "more heart." This entertaining spoof is a gem, undoubtedly Friedberg's best science fiction effort. She uses a female narrator for this story, plus a steady supply of eccentric comic characters.

"For Whom the Girl Waits," properly called science fantasy, is a dreamlike account of double identities in a high school setting. The main character, Louis Demperi, is a substitute teacher who assumes the identity of the teacher he replaces. The role-playing works well until he takes the place of a man named Koppinger, for whom a beautiful girl waits each afternoon after school. Then he becomes disoriented and cannot remember that he is Koppinger, until he discovers that another man has assumed his own identity. Demperi decides to carry on with Koppinger's role and meets the girl, who rejects him and causes him to have a fatal car accident. But his identity lives on in the person of Demperi's substitute. The story is somewhat confusing but is imaginative and fascinating to read.

Friedberg wrote in a simple, unpretentious style and in general organized her material chronologically. She excelled in the handling of women characters, which suggests that her works might have been more successful if the central characters had been women instead of men.

—Judith Snyder

---

**FRIESNER, Esther M.** American. Born 16 July 1951. Educated at Vassar College, Poughkeepsie, New York, B.A. in Spanish and Drama (*cum laude*) 1972; Yale University, New Haven, Connecticut, M.A. in Spanish 1975, Ph.D. in Spanish 1977. Married Walter Stutzman in 1974; one son, one daughter. Agent: Richard Curtis Literary Agency, 171 East 74th Street, New York, New York 10021. Address: 53 Mendingwall Circle, Madison, Connecticut 06443, U.S.A.

SCIENCE-FICTION PUBLICATIONS

Novels (series: Demons, Twelve Kingdoms)

Chronicles of the Twelve Kingdoms:
*Mustapha and His Wise Dog.* New York, Avon, 1985.
*Spells of Mortal Weaving.* New York, Avon, 1986.
*The Witchwood Cradle.* New York, Avon, 1987.
*The Water King's Laughter.* New York, Avon, 1989.
*Harlot's Ruse.* New York, Popular Library, 1986.

*New York by Knight*. New York, New American Library, 1986; London, Headline, 1987.
*The Silver Mountain*. New York, Popular Library, 1986.
*Elf Defense*. New York, New American Library, 1988; London, Headline, 1989.
*Druid's Blood*. New York, New American Library, 1988; London, Headline, 1989.
*Here Be Demons*. New York, Ace, 1988.
*Demon Blues*. New York, Ace, 1989.
*Sphynxes Wild*. New York, New American Library, 1989.
*Hooray for Hellywood* (Demons). New York, Ace, 1990.
*Gnome Man's Land*. New York, Ace, 1991.

*

Esther M. Friesner comments:

Speculative fiction—SF, fantasy, horror, and the like—is supposed to be the literature of ideas, but for some reason most friends of the genre seem to be uncomfortable with the idea of humor. Perhaps it's due to long years of being on the defensive against casual critics who condemn all SF out of hand as pulp, not to be taken seriously. In an effort to have our preferred literature taken seriously, too many of us have ridden the pendulum all the way over to *somber*.

It has been my pleasure to write humorous fantasy, although a closer examination of my complete output will reveal that I have also written tales in a darker vein. Still, I have the reputation for doing "funny stuff," as if that were all I've done. No matter. We need laughter, and we need the self-awareness that laughter often grants. Comedic criticism will often have a more immediate effect on correcting flaws within a genre than tomes upon tomes of pedantic essays.

Maybe humorous works of speculative fiction will never get the respect accorded their grimmer brothers (no pun intended, of course!). Newer writers, seeking the approval of their peers, will devote their talents to tales of fashionable pessimism. That will be our loss. In our passion for the security of literary "legitimacy," we fail to recognize that only when we are comfortable with laughing at ourselves can we say that we are truly secure.

* * *

Esther M. Friesner's fantasy debut was in 1985 with *Mustapha and His Wise Dog*. An Arabian Nights style fairy tale, it was the first volume in the "Chronicle of the Twelve Kingdoms" trilogy. Mustapha is an unobtrusive vagabond wandering through magical kingdoms accompanied by his dog, a mystical creature in its own right, and with a devilish sense of humor. They seem a pair of unlikely heroes until it becomes necessary for someone to recover a sacred object before it can be used by an evil sorcerer to gain ascendancy over the world. A familiar plot, but enlivened by an exotic and evocative fantasy setting, and a pair of captivating characters.

The second in the series, *Spells of Mortal Weaving*, makes use of an entirely different cast of characters and is far more traditional in execution. An overly proud prince must learn humility on his quest to rescue the woman he loves. A transitional book, it is moderately entertaining, but lacks either the punch of the final volume or the inventiveness of the first. The series continued with *The Witchwood Cradle*, wherein the evil sorcerer who has threatened the serenity of the world is finally vanquished. Although Friesner followed traditional forms for the most part in this series, her wry humor and gift for characterization marked her early as someone to watch.

*Harlot's Ruse* provides a kind of grand tour of fantasy. Friesner's sprightly protagonist sets out on a journey of self-discovery, encountering and defeating dragons, pirates, wizards, noble lords with less than honorable intentions, nasty unicorns, demons, and barbarian swordsmen before finding true love. It is a good-humored, fast-moving adventure story.

With *New York by Knight*, Friesner became a significant voice in modern fantasy. Two ageless magical forces, an evil dragon and a puissant knight, have struggled through time and space, and now their battle is finally to be resolved, in the streets of contemporary New York City. The blend of the real world and that of fantasy is gradual, a series of events culminating in the final confrontation. The most suspenseful of her novels, it also has some of the most compelling scenes and quickly separated her from a host of rivals in the genre.

A less inspired, far more conventional fantasy quest novel followed, *The Silver Mountain*, but this was to be the last time Friesner would use this form for a novel. *Elf Defense* followed, the first of Friesner's overtly humorous books, and still the best of these to date. A mortal woman decides she no longer wishes to be wed to the King of the Elves. She escapes Elfhame and returns to the real world, where she desperately seeks some creature who will be fearsome enough to daunt even the fairy king himself. Sudden inspiration arrives, and she secures the services of a dreaded divorce lawyer. This blend of the real world and that of magic provides the setting for most of her subsequent fiction.

*Druid's Blood*, for example, is set in an alternate Victorian England where the Queen is a sorceress whose magical props have been stolen. She engages the services of a world-famous private detective to reclaim her property, because without it the British Isles will succumb to an evil invading force. A touch of Sherlock Holmes, mixed with magic, and filled with monsters, villains, and chases, it's the sort of good-natured adventure novel whose ending is never in doubt, but it doesn't seem to matter because the journey there is such good fun.

*Sphynxes Wild* is set in, of all places, Atlantic City. The supernatural sphynx from pre-history has returned to the earth in the form of a beautiful woman. Her mission is to use a series of mystical riddles to destroy the human race. Opposing her is the world's last sorcerer, and a young man caught in a struggle he cannot understand. Much more serious in tone than most of Friesner's more recent works, it is still lightened by her enthusiastic and rapid-fire style.

Friesner turns another fictional convention head over heels in *Here Be Demons*. A small legion of defrocked demons has been exiled to earth, bereft of the comforts of Hell until they can harvest a fresh crop of souls. The demons immediately set out to corrupt a group of young archaeology students, only to discover that in the modern world, the worst sins they can imagine are old fashioned and not at all tempting.

There have been two sequels to *Here Be Demons*. *Demon Blues* follows the adventures of Noel Cardiff, a college student intent upon committing dire enough sins to impress the woman of his life, who is actually a disguised succubus. The disenfranchised demons are still attempting to fit into modern society, but with very mixed results. Third in the series is *Hooray for Hellywood*. Most of the demons have now decided to give up the struggle and blend into society, but the old rivalry between demonic factions surfaces again when Noel wanders off to Hollywood, the perfect hunting ground for soul-hungry minions of Satan.

Friesner has also published more than a dozen short stories, for the most part lighter fantasy tales, but she seems to need the space of a novel to develop her characters and unravel her plots. Of the shorter fiction, the most noteworthy are "Simpson's

Lesser Sphinx", "Black Butterflies", "Eye for the Ladies", and "Doo Wop Never Dies."

—Don D'Ammassa

---

**FYFE, H(orace) B(owne).** Also writes as Andrew MacDuff. American. Born in Jersey City, New Jersey, 30 September 1918. Educated at Stevens Academy; Columbia University, New York, B.S. 1950. Served in the United States Army during World War II: Bronze Star. Married 1) Adeline Marie Dougherty in 1946 (died, 1970); 2) Sonia V. Benedict in 1975. Laboratory assistant and draftsman, then freelance writer. Address: Box 221, Ridgefield Park, New Jersey 07660, U.S.A.

SCIENCE-FICTION PUBLICATIONS

Novel

*D-99.* New York, Pyramid, 1962.

Uncollected Short Stories (series: Bureau of Slick Tricks)

"Hold That Comet," with F.H. Hauser, in *Astonishing* (Chicago), December 1940.
"Sinecure 6," in *Astounding* (New York), January 1947.
"Special Jobbery" (Bureau), in *Astounding* (New York), September 1949.
"Locked Out," in *Men Against the Stars*, edited by Martin H. Greenberg. New York, Gnome Press, 1950.
"Conformity Expected," in *Astounding* (New York), March 1950.
"Spy Scare," in *Astounding* (New York), September 1950.
"Compromise" (Bureau), in *Astounding* (New York), December 1950.
"In Value Deceived," in *Possible Worlds of Science Fiction*, edited by Groff Conklin. New York, Vanguard Press, 1951.
"Bureau of Slick Tricks," in *Travellers of Space*, edited by Martin H. Greenberg. New York, Gnome Press, 1951.
"The Envoy, Her," in *Planet* (New York), March 1951.
"Key Decision," in *Astounding* (New York), May 1951.
"Open Invitation," in *Planet* (New York), May 1951.
"Temporary Keeper," in *Thrilling Wonder Stories* (New York), June 1951.
"Experimentum Crucis" (as Andrew MacDuff), in *Astounding* (New York), July 1951.
"Yes Sir!," in *Startling* (New York), September 1951.
"This World Must Die!," in *Future* (New York), September 1951.
"Thinking Machine" in *Astounding* (New York), October 1951.
"Afterthought," in *Beyond Human Ken*, edited by Judith Merril. New York, Random House, 1952; London, Grayson, 1953.
"Manners of the Age," in *Omnibus of Science Fiction*, edited by Groff Conklin. New York, Crown, 1952.
"Protected Species," in *The Astounding Science Fiction Anthology*, edited by John W. Campbell, Jr. New York, Simon and Schuster, 1952.
"Calling World-4 of Kithgol," in *Planet* (New York), January 1952.
"Bluff-Stained Transaction" (Bureau), in *Astounding* (New York), March 1952.
"Extra-Secret Agent," in *Science Fiction Quarterly* (Holyoke, Massachusetts), May 1952.
"Confidence," in *Future* (New York), September 1952.
"Time Limit," in *Fantastic Story* (New York), Winter 1952.
"Implode and Peddle" (Bureau) and "Star-Linked," in *Space Service*, edited by Andre Norton. Cleveland, World, 1953.
"Let There Be Light," in *Crossroads in Time*, edited by Groff Conklin. New York, Permabooks, 1953.
"Ransom," in *The Best from Fantasy and Science Fiction 2*, edited by Anthony Boucher and J. Francis McComas. Boston, Little Brown, 1953.
"The Well-Oiled Machine," in *Science-Fiction Carnival*, edited by Fredric Brown and Mack Reynolds. Chicago, Shasta, 1953.
"The Compleat Collector," in *Future* (New York), January 1953.
"Fast Passage," in *Other Worlds* (Evanston, Indiana), January 1953.
"Exile," in *Space* (New York), February 1953.
"Romance," in *Future* (New York), March 1953.
"Irresistible Weapon," in *If* (New York), July 1953.
"Koenigshaufen's Curve," in *Fantasy Fiction* (New York), August 1953.
"Moonwalk," in *Space Pioneers*, edited by Andre Norton. Cleveland, World, 1954.
"Welcome, Strangers!," in *Astounding* (New York), August 1954.
"The Shell Dome," in *Spaceway* (Alhambra, California), February 1955.
"The Night of No Moon," in *Infinity* (New York), June 1957.
"Lunar Escapade," in *Planet of Doom and Other Stories*. Sydney, Jubilee, 1958.
"Fee of the Frontier," in *Amazing* (New York), August 1960.
"A Transmutation of Muddle," in *Astounding* (New York), September 1960.
"Wedge," in *If* (New York), September 1960.
"The Furies of Zhahnoor," in *Fantastic* (New York), October 1960.
"Satellite System," in *Astounding* (New York), October 1960.
"Round-and-Round Trip," in *Galaxy* (New York), December 1960.
"The Outbreak of Peace," in *Analog* (New York), February 1961.
"Flamedown," in *Analog* (New York), August 1961.
"Tolliver's Orbit," in *If* (New York), September 1961.
"The Talkative Tree," in *If* (New York), January 1962.
"Knowledge Is Power," in *Way Out*, edited by Ivan Howard. New York, Belmont, 1963.
"Star Chamber," in *Amazing* (New York), March 1963.
"The Klygha," in *Amazing* (New York), December 1963.
"The Clutches of Ruin," in *Gamma 4* (North Hollywood), 1965.
"The Old Shill Game," in *Analog* (New York), January 1967.

* * *

H.B. Fyfe has written several dozen conventional short stories and a single episodic novel that obviously meshes several shorter stories into one whole. He is perhaps best known for his series about the Bureau of Slick Tricks, a secret human organization whose purpose is to finagle humans out of embarrassing situations on other planets. The novel and at least five stories fall into this series, and a number of other stories are very similar thematically. Essentially, the philosophy expressed is that humans are the most flexible, inventive race in the universe and that any aliens who encounter us should hold onto everything that isn't nailed down.

"In Value Deceived" is a perfect example of this. Two starships, one human and one alien, encounter each other in space. The aliens are short on rations, and are seeking edible plants, which they consider highly valuable. They trade a "worthless" piece of their own equipment for some hydroponic supplies; the "worthless" item allows transmutation of elements. In "Ransom" primitive aliens decide to kidnap humans as leverage against the crew of an exploratory starship. They end up with two robots, and are dismayed at the casual manner in which they are abandoned. The novel, *D-99*, features a host of confused, outsmarted, and frantic aliens, who cannot cope with human manipulation of events.

Fyfe was not permanently wed to this concept, although it does dominate his work. One of his best short stories, "Protected Species," is in fact quite atypical. The primitive aliens skulking about the ruins of their former civilization are treated with active sympathy, and ultimately it is the humans who find themselves the butt of a cosmic joke. In "The Talkative Tree" an alien culture provides the means whereby humans alienated from their dictatorial and conformist culture can escape into almost any conceivable form of freedom by altering their physical nature.

Fyfe makes use of a number of standard plot devices and has done little in the way of innovation. He explores both sides of the human-robot interface. Robotic servants with their built-in limitations drive a magazine editor crazy in "The Well-Oiled Machine" but they come to dominate the world in "Let There Be Light," and are preyed on by human scavengers for the oil they use within their bodies. Man is therefore reduced to the level of a mechanical vampire. By far his most outstanding work is "Moonwalk" which makes use of a classic man-against-nature situation, one that has been used many times both within the genre and without. As the result of an accident, one man is stranded on the lunar surface, several hundred miles from the moon's only human installation. The plot unfolds in logical fashion, as the protagonist wrestles with time and a diminishing air supply, and the reader struggles with frustrated impatience as the authorities refuse to believe that the lack of radio contact portends anything requiring action. Although Fyfe is not capable of making this a truly great story, he handles it quite well, and it is a worthy contribution of its type.

Fyfe has remained a dabbler, and his obvious talents have not been developed. There is little difference in quality between the earliest and most recent stories. Nevertheless, his competent stories have provided entertainment and adventure to his audience.

—Don D'Ammassa

# G

**GADE, Henry.** *See* **PALMER, Raymond A.**

---

**GALAXAN, Sol.** *See* **COPPEL, Alfred.**

---

**GALLUN, Raymond Z(inke).** Also writes as William Callahan. American. Born in Beaver Dam, Wisconsin, 22 March 1911. Educated at the University of Wisconsin, Madison, 1929–30; Alliance Française, Paris, 1938–39; San Marcos University, Lima, Peru, 1960. Married 1) Frieda E. Talmey in 1959 (died 1974); 2) Bertha Erickson Backman in 1978. Construction worker for Army Corps of Engineers, 1942–43; marine blacksmith, Pearl Harbor Navy Yard, 1944; technical writer, EDO Corporation, College Point, New York, 1964–75. Recipient: Fandom Hall of Fame award, 1979. Address: 111-20 71st Street, Forest Hills, New York 11375, U.S.A.

Science-Fiction Publications

Novels

*People Minus X.* New York, Simon and Schuster, 1957.
*The Planet Strappers.* New York, Pyramid, 1961.
*The Eden Cycle.* New York, Ballantine, 1974.
*Skyclimber.* New York, Tower Books, 1981.
*Bioblast!* New York, Ace, 1985.

Short Stories

*The Machine That Thought* (as William Callahan). New York, Columbia, 1940.
*The Best of Raymond Z. Gallun.* New York, Ballantine, 1978.

Uncollected Short Stories

"Then and Now," in *Analog* (New York), December 1977.
"The Eternal Wall," in *Amazing* (New York), May 1979.
"A First Glimpse," in *Analog* (New York), February 1980.

Other Publications

Other

*Starclimber* (autobiography). San Bernardino, California, Borgo Press, 1991.

*

Raymond Z. Gallun comments (1985):

Most of my science fiction was originally published in the 1930's, mainly in *Astounding* while F. Orlin Tremaine, whom I remember with appreciation, was editor. I think I aimed mostly at realism insofar as it could be construced from what was then supposed to be true about the various planets, plus humanizing of even the unhuman characters, giving them points of sympathetic contact without overdoing the sympathy. Some time after World War II I dropped out of SF to do other things. Being now retired from formal employment, I have been trying to get back into SF writing. "Then and Now" (*Analog*, December 1977) is a fair example of what I have been recently trying to do.

* * *

Raymond Z. Gallun has published in the pulps vast quantities of clumsy and primitive fiction, and yet his treatments of several of the more sophisticated problems facing modern man are often exciting and provocative to read. He is a vintage science-fiction pulp writer from the 1930's who published his most ambitious novel in the 1970's. One critic has labeled his underlying philosophy "Darwinian existentialism"; and two short quotations from what Gallun himself has called his favorite short story, "The Restless Tide," will introduce the stark polarities that he continually balances in his best work. At the end of the story, the protagonist concludes, "Mankind was like a rough, sturdy plant, growing, thrusting; crude but magnificent, and caught between rot and fire." Earlier he had exhorted his wife, "It's the contrasts that count. There's a rough drama in people."

Gallun's novel *The Eden Cycle* is a fine expansion of these earlier themes. The Hegelian balancing of opposites along with the classic polar opposition, which is also a key to the meaning for us of Darwinian theory, between the glory of early primitive development and the continual trend toward greater sophistication, are well developed in this long narration of the most advanced human hedonists governed by aliens. In fact, for Gallun the contrasts that run throughout his fictions are so roughly vivid that they become emblematic of what the Renaissance loved to call man's amphibian nature. Aliens are presented as complex and sympathetic characters early—"Old Faithful" (1934)—and then throughout his career. In addition to the rough contrast of man to alien, there is repeatedly drawn the contrast of creature to environment, as in "Godson of Almarlu," as well as the contrast of past to present. Science fiction lends itself particularly well to the old opposition between a golden age of the past and a modern iron age because science fiction tries to image both technology and man's inner primitive self. Gallun's work conveys these oppositions continually in the narratives mentioned above and in such pieces as *People Minus X,* "Return of a Legend," and "The Lotus-Engine."

Rough contrast is also a most appropriate characterization for the literary impressions of Gallun's extrapolations. For example, "The Lotus-Engine" makes skillful use of the classic Homeric myth of the lotus eaters and also weaves a most explicit set of images to convey again the old story of mutability and decline associated with technological advance. But even in this story the pulp characterizations of "old chums" must enter, and the characters even smoke cigarettes inside the oxygen rich helmets of their "space armor." A genre that can retell the most profound human dilemmas in what are often such rough forms is indeed sturdy and growing, and Gallun was one sturdy and often rough writer who contributed greatly to its growth.

—Donald M. Hassler

---

**GALOUYE, Daniel F(rancis).** American. Born in New Orleans, Louisiana, 11 February 1911 (some sources say 1920). Educated at Louisiana State University, Baton Rouge, B.A. in journalism 1941. Served as a pilot in the United States Navy, 1941–46: Lieutenant in Naval Reserve. Married Carmel Barbara Jordan in 1945; two daughters. Reporter, then assistant news editor, 1946–55, chief editorial writer, 1955–60, and associate editor, 1960–65, New Orleans *States-Item*. Consultant, New Orleans Science Center and Planetarium Committee. *Died in 1976.*

SCIENCE-FICTION PUBLICATIONS

Novels

*Dark Universe.* New York, Bantam, 1961; London, Gollancz, 1962.
*Lords of the Psychon.* New York, Bantam, 1963.
*Counterfeit World.* London, Gollancz, 1964; as *Simulacron-3*, New York, Bantam, 1964.
*The Lost Perception.* London, Gollancz, 1966; as *A Scourge of Screamers*, New York, Bantam, 1968.
*The Infinite Man.* New York, Bantam, 1973.

Short Stories

*The Last Leap and Other Stories of the Super Mind.* London, Corgi, 1964.
*Project Barrier.* London, Gollancz, 1968.

Uncollected Short Stories

"O Kind Master," in *If* (New York), January 1970.
"The Big Blow-Up," in *Fantastic* (New York), July 1979.

* * *

Daniel F. Galouye, a greatly underrated and largely forgotten writer, is probably best remembered for the numerous short stories and novelettes in the science-fiction "slicks" of the 1950's and 1960's. However, his primary contribution to the field rests in three novels: *Dark Universe*, *Simulacron-3* (published in the U.S. as *Counterfeit World*), and *Lords of the Psychon*. Always well-conceived, well-planned, and well-crafted, Galouye's stories are extrapolations of scientific fact or theory, but his vivid and far-ranging imagination and his incredible attention to detail often carry his readers well into the fantastic. These characteristics are most visible in the novels where the length permits the accumulation of detail to achieve its full impact.

Though many of Galouye's stories use a post-disaster motif, they reflect his optimistic belief in the capability of man to develop his latent mental abilities, and often the resolutions of his plots depend upon the evolvement of such talents as astral projection, extended vision, teleportation, and mental manipulation of matter or energy. Curiously, he often depicts faster-than-light spaceships powered by psychokinesis, as in "The Centipedes of Space" and "Phantom World." His ultimate statement on human development, however, is found in "The Secret of the Immortals," where he proposes a metamorphosis that not only brings new mental powers but an extended life of at least 5,000 years.

Galouye's work also displays a preoccupation with the idea that man may be manipulated by external forces, and often the world of the story is a microcosm of some vaster universe. This concept frequently takes the form of a puppet motif. One of the most unusual twists on this theme occurs in "Gulliver Planet," where microscopic aliens invade the bodies of seven humans and manipulate them as part of their invasion plan. The theme's unique treatment, however, comes in *Simulacron-3*, where Doug Hall, the protagonist, discovers that he is merely an electric analogue in a total electronic simulation of the real world.

Galouye's overriding concern is the nature of reality and the related problem of perceiving it. Most of his stories and his three best novels treat this theme. *Dark Universe* deals with a colony that has survived a worldwide atomic war by retreating underground. One of 17 such colonies, "U.S. Survival Complex Number Eleven" functions well until a minor fault shift totally destroys its ability to generate electricity and cuts off all but a few of the superheated water conduits that lead to the group's basic living chamber. Through succeeding generations, the loss of sight and the disintegration of their knowledge of their original world creates a culture totally dependent on sound for survival and ignorant of their true circumstances. The story concerns the attempt of one young man, Jared Fenton, to discover what light really is. The novel's status as a minor classic comes from Galouye's treatment and control of his material. His elimination of all words from the narrative that relate to sight and his passages which describe how Fenton uses his non-visual senses to perceive his world are brilliantly effective.

*Simulacron-3*, an extremely original work, also treats the nature of reality. Doug Hall discovers that his world is but an electro-mathematical model of an average community and that it is marked for extinction. In an ironic reversal of roles, he manages to change places with the real Doug Hall, the megalomaniacal operator of the simulator, and prevent his world from being erased. *Lords of the Psychon*, though not quite so well-controlled as *Dark Universe* or so original as *Simulacron-3*, is a post-destruction story that concerns the efforts of Geoffrey Maddox to prevent aliens from drawing Earth into another dimension. In the process of fighting them, he learns that he can mentally manipulate the fundamental form of matter, a pink plasma called psychon, and he proves that it is itself merely a reflection of the mental.

Galouye's major weakness is his relatively shallow characterization. It is often difficult to distinguish between his parade of military protagonists, and his women are seldom more than helpless sex-objects. Where he has the time to infuse his narrative with detail, however, his principal characters manage to become more than cardboard cutouts. Originality, control, and fast pace are typical of his best writing.

—Carl B. Yoke

---

**GARDNER, Craig Shaw.** American. Born in Rochester, New York, 2 July 1949. Educated at Boston University. President, Horror Writers of America, since 1990. Agent: Merrilee Heifetz, Writers House, 21 West 26th Street, New York, New

York 10010. Address: P.O. Box 458, Cambridge, Massachusetts 02238, U.S.A.

SCIENCE-FICTION PUBLICATIONS

Novels (series: Cineverse; Ebezenum; Wuntvor)

*A Malady of Magicks* (Ebezenum). New York, Ace, 1986.
*A Multitude of Monsters* (Ebezenum). New York, Ace, 1986; London, Headline, 1989.
*A Night in the Netherhells* (Ebezenum). New York, Ace, 1987; London, Headline, 1989.
*A Difficulty with Dwarves* (Wuntvor). New York, Ace, 1987; London, Headline, 1989.
*The Lost Boys* (novelization of screenplay). New York, Berkley, 1987.
*An Excess of Enchantments* (Wuntvor). New York, Ace, 1988; London, Headline, 1989.
*Wishbringer* (novelization of a computer game). New York, Avon, 1988.
*A Disagreement with Death* (Wuntvor). New York, Ace, and London, Headline, 1989.
*Back to the Future Part II* (novelization of screenplay). New York, Berkley, and London, Headline, 1989.
*Cineverse Cycle*. New York, Guild America, 1990.
  *Slaves of the Volcano God*. New York, Ace, and London, Headline, 1989.
  *Bride of the Slime Monster*. New York, Ace, 1990.
  *Revenge of the Fluffy Bunnies*. New York, Ace, 1990.
*Back to the Future Part III* (novelization of screenplay). New York, Berkley, and London, Firecrest, 1990.

OTHER PUBLICATIONS

Novels

*Batman* (novelization of screenplay). New York, Warner, and London, Futura, 1989.
*The Batman Murders*. New York, Warner, 1990.

*

Craig Shaw Gardner comments:

I've had at least three careers so far in science fiction. The first was as a "promising young writer" (I was written up as such in *Fantasy Review* along with Steve Rasnic Tenn and Al Sarantonio). I next became one of those Funny Fantasy guys (along with Bob Asprin, Terry Pratchett, et. al.) for my steady-selling Ebezenum and Cineverse series. Even more recently, I became the bestselling author of Batman; thanks to the most successful of those novelizations, I did keep food on the table.

Who knows what's next?

* * *

Humorous science fiction and fantasy have always been viewed within the genre as a kind of poor cousin, amusing enough when you read it but with no true lasting power as literature, as though it were somehow less an achievement to make the reader laugh than to provide suspense, adventure, or drama. Incidental jokes within the context of an adventure are acceptable, but a broad spoof is assumed to be transient and of little importance. Fantasy has been somewhat more tolerant of this literary form, but even there humor is generally suspect at novel length. Part of this may be because it is indeed difficult to maintain a genuinely humorous tone at greater lengths. It is especially surprising therefore that Craig Shaw Gardner has acquired an enviable reputation based almost entirely on two series of amusing fantasy and science-fiction novels.

Gardner introduced his marvelously funny wizard, Ebezenum, in short stories such as "A Drama of Dragons" and "A Gathering of Ghosts," and their popularity eventually led to their incorporation into an episodic novel, *A Malady of Magicks* in 1986. Ebezenum crosses swords with an inept demon, and the spell that was supposed to kill him actually only served to make him allergic to magic. The opening stages of his quest for a cure form the first of six hilariously entertaining book-length adventures of the wizard and his apprentice, Wuntvor.

The immediate follow-up was *A Multitude of Monsters*. Still afflicted with his allergy, Ebezenum faces a fresh round of attacks from the vengeful demon Guxx, as well as the complications that arise from the presence of an organization of inhuman creatures determined to secure equal billing with human beings and other, more popular, mythical figures. Rounding out the first trilogy was *A Night in the Netherhells*. Unable to destroy the wizard, Guxx steals the city that holds his cure, necessitating a journey to hell itself. Although he is able to thwart Guxx's immediate intention, Ebezenum's curse only becomes worse.

Ebezenum's adverse reaction to magic is now contagious, spreading throughout the magical community, so his apprentice Wuntvor sets off on his own in the opening volume of a second trilogy, *A Difficulty with Dwarves*, followed in due course by *An Excess of Enchantments* and *A Disagreement with Death*. Wuntvor must travel to far lands, outwit a powerful and malevolent witch, and then escape the clutches of Death personified before his journey can be brought to a close. Through all six books, Gardner makes use of an irreverent, slapstick style of humor heavily reliant on anachronisms and literary sight gags.

Gardner brought the same brisk, entertaining style to *Wishbringer*, a novel inspired by the Infocom interactive text adventure game. The town of Festeron is transformed magically, with all of its good elements mirroring evil ones, and only the protagonist is able to remember what it was like before. Now he is the only hope the citizens have to escape the enchantment and return to their former life-styles.

Gardner wrote two creditable novelizations during this period as well. *Batman*'s darker humor was something of a departure, but *The Lost Boys* was a serious tale of horror unlike anything Gardner had written at novel length, although he was already starting to drift in that direction in some of his short stories, most notably "The Three Faces of Night," "Walk Home Alone," and "She Closed Her Eyes."

In 1989 Gardner started a new trilogy, science fiction this time, but he also returned to the wacky, exaggerated style of his earlier fantasies. *Slaves of the Volcano God* is the first in the Cineverse Cycle. The Cineverse is a kind of alternate universe that occasionally impinges on the real world. Within its confines, all of the institutions of classic films, particularly the "B" films, are reality. Heroes are really heroes, and sidekicks know their place; heroines are invariably gorgeous and waiting to be rescued, and no act is too despicable for the villains.

The protagonist, Roger Gordon, comes into possession of a Captain Crusader decoder ring that enables him to cross the barrier between worlds. In order to rescue the woman he loves, he must make his way through westerns, jungle adventures, and the romantic Pacific. Although he triumphs against Dr. Dread in the early going, Gordon must persevere through *Bride of the Slime Monster* and *Revenge of the Fluffy Bunnies*. Before he can complete his rescue, he must defeat not only the evil Dr. Dread, but even greater villains.

Two other short stories, both fantasies, stand out as well, "A Malady of Magicks," one of his very first published stories, and "Demon Luck" from the shared universe Ithkar series. Gardner has yet to write a serious, original science-fiction novel, but his humor is genuinely funny, and his writing skills are sufficient to put him in good stead no matter in which direction his future lies.

—Don D'Ammassa

---

**GARNETT, David.** British. Address: West Grange, Ferring Grange Gardens, Ferring, West Sussex BN12 5HS, England.

SCIENCE-FICTION PUBLICATIONS

Novels

*Mirror in the Sky.* New York, Berkley, 1969; London, Hale, 1973.
*The Starseekers.* New York, Berkley, 1971; London, Hale, 1975.
*Time in Eclipse.* London, Hale, 1974.
*The Forgotten Dimension.* London, Hale, 1975.
*Phantom Universe.* London, Hale, 1975.

Short Stories

*Cosmic Carousel.* London, Hale, 1976.

OTHER PUBLICATIONS

Other

Editor, *The Orbit Science Fiction Yearbook.* London, Futura, 3 vols., 1988–90.
Editor, *Zenith: The Best in New British Science Fiction.* London, Sphere, 1989.
Editor, *Zenith II: The Best in New British Science Fiction.* London, Orbit, 1990.

* * *

David Garnett's first novel, *Mirror in the Sky*, written in 1967 when the author was 19, is an anti-Vietnam War novel. It draws upon elements of Heinlein's *Starship Troopers*, viewing them from a different perspective. In *Mirror in the Sky*, the infantry of the future fights an endless war against an unknown enemy, and, through a drug in their daily rations, are programmed to obey orders. They have been taught (falsely) that their enemy can mimic humans perfectly, which is why the aliens appear identical to the human troops.

*The Starseekers* is a comedy in which the richest man on Earth flees his native planet in order to escape numerous creditors, including various ex-wives and tax authorities. This is William Ewart—the first names of Prime Minister Gladstone—and his pretext for leaving is an archeological expedition, which leads to many galactic adventures. The book takes numerous swipes at many of science fiction's clichés, from interstellar secret agents to space pirates.

After these space war and space opera books, Garnett wrote in 1969 a sword-and-sorcery novel, but *Phantom Universe* remained unpublished until it was given a science-fiction rationale—the mind of a space pilot is trapped within the body of a character in a fantasy world.

Garnett's fourth novel, written in 1970, had been published several months earlier. *The Forgotten Dimension* treats yet another basic SF theme, that of revolution. The sub-text is one of racism, which is emphasized by the discovery that humankind is descended from a race of another dimension.

*Cosmic Carousel* is Garnett's first collection of short stories. This includes reprints from *Fantasy and Science Fiction* and *New Writings in Science Fiction*, as well as two stories that were condensed from unpublished novels written in 1969, "Adventures of a Stone Age Man" and "Forever Changes."

In 1970, at the age of 23, Garnett wrote the last of his early novels. *Time in Eclipse* is without doubt his finest novel. Set in a future Europe that has reverted to feudalism, the book encompasses a whole spectrum of science-fictional themes: underground civilizations, time travel, endless war, aliens, androids, computers.

Garnett has written numerous other books in various genres, and under various pseudonyms, returning to science fiction with only a handful of short stories, like "Still Life" (in *Fantasy and Science Fiction*, nominated for a Hugo) and "The Only One" (in *Interzone*, nominated for The British Science Fiction Award).

Since 1987, Garnett has been one of the instigators of a new spate of all-British SF anthologies, as well as an editor of the best of the year collection, *The Orbit Science Fiction Yearbook*. Of more significance, however, were the two *Zenith* anthologies, which showcased established British SF authors, such as Aldiss and Moorcock, as well as encouraging new talents. His latest venture as editor is a resurrection after 12 years of the highly influential new wave magazine/anthology *New Worlds*.

—David Wingrove

---

**GARRETT, Gordon.** *See* **GARRETT, Randall.**

---

**GARRETT, (Gordon) Randall.** Also wrote as Gordon Aghill; Alexander Blade; Walter Bupp; Ralph Burke; Gordon Garrett; David Gordon; Richard Greer; Ivar Jorgensen; Darrell T. Langart; Clyde T. Mitchell; Mark Phillips; Robert Randall; Leonard G. Spencer; S.M. Tenneshaw; Gerald Vance. American. Born in Lexington, Missouri, in 1927. Educated at Texas Tech University, Lubbock, B.S. Served in the United States Marine Corps during World War II: Corporal. Married Vicki Ann Heydron. Industrial chemist, Battle Creek, Michigan, and Peoria, Illinois: then freelance writer. *Died in 1988.*

SCIENCE-FICTION PUBLICATIONS

Novels (series: Gandalara)

*The Shrouded Planet* (as Robert Randall, with Robert Silverberg). New York, Gnome Press, 1957.
*The Dawning Light* (as Robert Randall, with Robert Silverberg). New York, Gnome Press, 1959.

*Unwise Child.* New York, Doubleday, 1962; London, Mayflower, 1963; as *Starship Death*, New York, Leisure, 1982.
*Anything You Can Do . . .* (as Darrell T. Langart). New York, Doubleday, and London, Mayflower, 1963; as *Earth Invader*, New York, Leisure, 1983.
*Too Many Magicians.* New York, Doubleday, 1967; London, Macdonald, 1968.
*The Gandalara Cycle*, with Vicki Ann Heydron. New York, Bantam, 2 vols., 1986.
*The Steel of Raithskar.* New York, Bantam, 1981.
*The Glass of Dyskornis.* New York, Bantam, 1982.
*The Bronze of Eddarta.* New York, Bantam, 1983.
*The Well of Darkness.* New York, Bantam, 1983.
*The Search for Ka.* New York, Bantam, 1984.
*Return to Eddarta*, with Vicki Ann Heydron. New York, Bantam, 1985.
*The River Wall*, with Vicki Ann Heydron. New York, Bantam, 1986.

Novels as Mark Phillips (with Laurence M. Janifer; series: Kenneth J. Malone in all books)

*Brain Twister.* New York, Pyramid, 1962.
*The Impossibles.* New York, Pyramid, 1963.
*Supermind.* New York, Pyramid, 1963.

Short Stories (series: Lord Darcy)

*Takeoff!* Virginia Beach, Donning, 1979.
*Murder and Magic* (Lord Darcy). New York, Ace, 1979.
*Lord Darcy Investigates.* New York, Ace, 1981.
*The Best of Randall Garrett*, edited by Robert Silverberg. New York, Pocket Books, 1982.
*Takeoff, Too!* Virginia Beach, Donning, 1986.

Uncollected Short Stories (series: Lord Darcy; Leland Hale)

"The Absence of Heat" (as Gordon Garrett), in *Astounding* (New York), June 1944.
"Pest," in *Astounding* (New York), December 1952.
"Instant of Decision," in *Space* (Alhambra, California), May 1953.
"Characteristics, Unusual," in *Science Fiction Quarterly* (Holyoke, Massachusetts), August 1953.
"Nom d'un Nom," in *Fantasy Fiction* (New York), August 1953.
"Hell to Pay," in *Beyond* (New York), March 1954.
"The Wayward Course," in *Future* (New York), March 1954.
"The Surgeon's Knife," in *Universe* (Evanston, Indiana), May 1954.
"Woman Driver," in *Fantastic* (New York), June 1954.
"Infinite Resources," in *Fantasy and Science Fiction* (New York), July 1954.
"Spatial Delivery," in *If* (New York), October 1954.
"Code in the Head," in *Future 29* (New York), 1956.
"Suite Mentale," in *Future 30* (New York), 1956.
"Vanishing Act" (as Robert Randall, with Robert Silverberg), in *Imaginative Tales* (Evanston, Indiana), January 1956.
"The Best of Fences," in *Infinity* (New York), February 1956.
"Quick Cure," in *Fantastic* (New York), February 1956.
"Gambler's Planet" (as Gordon Aghill, with Robert Silverberg), in *Amazing* (New York), June 1956.
"Catch a Thief" (as Gordon Aghill, with Robert Silverberg), in *Amazing* (New York), July 1956.
"The Saboteur," in *Original Science Fiction Stories* (Holyoke, Massachusetts), July 1956.
"Machine Complex," in *Astounding* (New York), July 1956.
"The Beast with Seven Tails" (as Leonard G. Spencer, with Robert Silverberg), in *Amazing* (New York), August 1956.
"Stroke of Genius," in *Infinity* (New York), August 1956.
"The Man Who Hated Mars," in *Amazing* (New York), September 1956.
"The Judas Valley" (as Gerald Vance, with Robert Silverberg), in *Amazing* (New York), October 1956.
"Heist Job on Thizar," in *Amazing* (New York), October 1956.
"The Man Who Knew Everything," in *Fantastic* (New York), October 1956.
"With All the Trappings," in *Astounding* (New York), November 1956.
"Puzzle in Yellow," in *Amazing* (New York), November 1956.
"The Mummy Takes a Wife" (as Clyde T. Mitchell, with Robert Silverberg), in *Fantastic* (New York), December 1956.
"Death to the Earthman," in *Amazing* (New York), December 1956.
"The Inquisitor," in *Imagination* (Evanston, Illinois), December 1956.
"The Star Slavers," in *Imaginative Tales* (Evanston, Illinois), January 1957.
"Deadly Decoy" (as Clyde T. Mitchell, with Robert Silverberg), in *Amazing* (New York), February 1957.
"The Devil Never Waits," in *Dynamic* (New York), February 1957.
"The Time Snatcher," in *Infinity* (New York), February 1957.
"Time to Stop," in *Science Fiction Quarterly* (Holyoke, Massachusetts), February 1957.
"Hungry World," in *Imaginative Tales* (Evanston, Illinois), March 1957.
"Saturnalia," in *Original Science Fiction Stories* (Holyoke, Massachusetts), March 1957.
"Guardians of the Tower," in *Imagination* (Evanston, Illinois), April 1957.
"The Man Who Collected Women," in *Amazing* (New York), April 1957.
"Masters of the Metropolis," in *Fantasy and Science Fiction* (New York), April 1957.
"The Vengeance of Kyvor," in *Fantastic* (New York), April, May 1957.
"The Last Killer," in *Imaginative Tales* (Evanston, Illinois), May 1957.
"What's Eating You?," in *Astounding* (New York), May 1957.
"You Too Can Win a Harem," in *Dreamworld* (New York), May 1957.
"Needler," in *Astounding* (New York), June 1957.
"A Pattern for Monsters," in *Fantastic* (New York), June 1957.
"Six Frightened Men," in *Imagination* (Evanston, Illinois), June 1957.
"Devil's World," in *Imaginative Tales* (Evanston, Illinois), July 1957.
"Gift from Tomorrow," in *Amazing* (New York), July 1957.
"Skid Row Pilot," in *Imagination* (Evanston, Illinois), August 1957.
"Killer—First Class," in *Imaginative Tales* (Evanston, Illinois), September 1957.
"The Mannion Court-Martial," in *Imagination* (Evanston, Illinois), October 1957.
"To Make a Hero" (Hale), in *Infinity* (New York), October 1957.
"Deathtrap Planet," in *Imaginative Tales* (Evanston, Illinois), November 1957.
"Satellite of Death," in *Imagination* (Evanston, Illinois), December 1957.
"Beyond Our Control," in *Infinity* (New York), January 1958.
"Strike the First Blow!," in *Imaginative Tales* (Evanston, Illinois), January 1958.

"The Low and the Mighty," in *Science Fiction Quarterly* (Holyoke, Massachusetts), February 1958.
"Far from Somewhere," in *Original Science Fiction Stories* (Holyoke, Massachusetts), March 1958.
"Penal Servitude," in *Astounding* (New York), March 1958.
"Prisoner of War," in *Imagination* (Evanston, Illinois), June 1958.
"Respectfully Mine" (Hale), in *Infinity* (New York), August 1958.
". . . and Check the Oil," in *Astounding* (New York), October 1958.
"Burden the Hand," in *Infinity* (New York), November 1958.
"The Savage Machine," in *Fantastic* (New York), November 1958.
"The Queen Bee," in *Astounding* (New York), December 1958.
"The Trouble with Magic," in *Fantastic* (New York), March 1959.
"Small Miracle," in *Amazing* (New York), June 1959.
"But I Don't Think," in *Astounding* (New York), July 1959.
"Dead Giveaway," in *Astounding* (New York), August 1959.
"That Sweet Little Old Lady" (as Mark Phillips, with Larry M. Harris) in *Astounding* (New York), September-October 1959.
"The Unnecessary Man," in *Astounding* (New York), November 1959.
"The Price of Eggs," in *Fantastic* (New York), December 1959.
"The Destroyers," in *Astounding* (New York), December 1959.
"Viewpoint," in *Astounding* (New York), January 1960.
"Drug on the Market" (Hale), in *Fantastic Universe* (Chicago), February 1960.
"The Measure of a Man," in *Astounding* (New York), April 1960.
"Damned If You Don't," in *Astounding* (New York), May 1960.
". . . and Peace Attend Thee," in *Astounding* (New York), September 1960.
"Random Choice," in *Fantastic* (New York), March 1961.
"Something Rich and Strange," with Avram Davidson, in *Fantasy and Science Fiction* (New York), June 1961.
"A Spaceship Named McGuire," in *Analog* (New York), July 1961.
"The Blaze of Noon," with Avram Davidson in *Analog* (New York), September 1961.
"Sound Decision," in *Prologue to Analog*, edited by John W. Campbell, Jr. New York, Doubleday, 1962; London, Panther, 1967.
"Hepcats of Venus," in *Fantastic* (New York), January 1962.
"His Master's Voice," in *Analog* (New York), March 1962.
"The Bramble Bush," in *Analog* (New York), August 1962.
"Spatial Relationship," in *Fantasy and Science Fiction* (New York), August 1962.
"A Case of Identity," in *Analog* (New York), September 1964.
"A Fortnight of Miracles," in *Fantastic* (New York), February 1965.
"Tin Lizzie," in *Great Science Fiction Stories about Mars*, edited by T.E. Dikty. New York, Fell, 1966.
"Witness for the Prosecution," in *Fantasy and Science Fiction* (New York), February 1966.
"Fighting Division," in *Analog 5*, edited by John W. Campbell, Jr. New York, Doubleday, 1967; London, Dobson, 1968.
"The Foreign Hand Tie," in *14 Great Tales of ESP*, edited by Idella P. Stone. New York, Fawcett, 1969.
"Ready, Aim, Robot!," in *S.F. Greats* (New York), Summer 1969.
"The Briefing," in *Fantastic* (New York), August 1969.
"Fimbulsommer," in *If* (New York), September 1970.
"After a Few Words," in *The Astounding-Analog Reader 2*, edited by Brian Aldiss and Harry Harrison. New York, Doubleday, and London, Sphere, 1973.
"Color Me Deadly," in *Fantasy and Science Fiction* (New York), October 1973.
"Pride and Primacy," in *If* (New York), April 1974.
"Reading the Meter," in *Vertex* (Los Angeles), August 1974.
"The Final Fighting of Fion Mac Cumhaill," in *Fantasy and Science Fiction* (New York), September 1975.
"The Sixteen Keys," in *Fantastic* (New York), May 1976.
"Lauralyn," in *Analog* (New York), April 1977.
"Polly Plus," in *Isaac Asimov's Science Fiction Magazine* (New York), May-June 1978.
"The Napoli Express," in *Isaac Asimov's Marvels of Science Fiction*, edited by George Scithers. New York, Davis, 1979.
"The Bitter End," in *Isaac Asimov's Worlds of Science Fiction*, edited by George Scithers. New York, Davis, 1980.
"Keepersmith," with Vicki Ann Heydron, in *Isaac Asimov's Science Fiction Anthology 3*, edited by George Scithers. New York, Davis, 1980.
"In Case of Fire," in *Hallucination Orbit*, edited by Isaac Asimov, Martin H. Greenberg, and Charles G. Waugh. New York, Farrar Straus, 1983.
"A Matter of Gravity" (Darcy), in *Alfred Hitchcock's Fatal Attractions*, edited by Elana Lore. New York, Davis, 1983.
"Hail to the Chief," in *Election Day 2084*, edited by Isaac Asimov and Martin H. Greenberg. Buffalo, New York, Prometheus, 1984.
"The Ipswich Phial," in *Witches*, edited by Isaac Asimov, Martin H. Greenberg, and Charles G. Waugh. New York, New American Library, 1984.
"A Little Intelligence," in *Magicats!*, edited by Jack Dann and Gardner Dozois. New York, Ace, 1984.
"Frost and Thunder," in *Time Wars*, edited by Charles G. Waugh and Martin H. Greenberg. New York, Tor, 1986.
"Despoilers of the Golden Empire," in *Robert Adams' Book of Soldiers*, edited by Robert Adams, Martin H. Greenberg, and Pamela Crippen Adams. New York, New American Library, 1988.
"The Highest Treason," in *Space Wars*, edited by Charles G. Waugh and Martin H. Greenberg. New York, Tor, 1988.

Uncollected Short Stories as David Gordon

"By the Rule," in *Other Worlds* (Evanston, Indiana), October 1950.
"There's No Fool. . .," in *Astounding* (New York), August 1956.
"The Convincer," in *Future* (New York), Summer 1957.
"The Best Policy," in *Astounding* (New York), July 1957.
"A Bird in the Hand," in *Future* (New York), February 1958.
"Intelligence Quotient," in *Future* (New York), June 1958.
"The Despoilers of the Golden Empire," in *Astounding* (New York), March 1959.
"Cum Grano Salis," in *Astounding* (New York), May 1959.
". . . or Your Money Back," in *Astounding* (New York), September 1959.
"Mercenaries Unlimited," in *Fantastic Universe* (Chicago), February 1960.
"By Proxy," in *Astounding* (New York), September 1960.
"Hanging by a Thread," in *Analog* (New York), August 1961.
"Asses of Balaam," in *Analog* (New York), October 1961.
"With No Strings Attached," in *Analog* (New York), February 1963.

Uncollected Short Stories as Alexander Blade

"The Man Who Hated Tuesday," in *Fantastic Adventures* (New York), February 1951.
"A Man Called Meteor," in *Fantastic Adventures* (New York), February 1953.

"Gambit on Ganymede," in *Fantastic Adventures* (New York), March 1953.
"Zero Hour," in *Imagination* (Evanston, Illinois), April 1956.
"Battle for the Stars," in *Imagination* (Evanston, Illinois), June 1956.
"Flight of the Ark II," in *Imaginative Tales* (Evanston, Illinois), July 1956.
"The Man with the Golden Eyes," in *Imagination* (Evanston, Illinois), August 1956.
"The Cosmic Kings," in *Imaginative Tales* (Evanston, Illinois), November 1956.
"The Alien Dies at Dawn," in *Imagination* (Evanston, Illinois), December 1956.
"Wednesday Morning Sermon," in *Imagination* (Evanston, Illinois), January 1957.
"The Tattooed Man," in *Imaginative Tales* (Evanston, Illinois), March 1957.
"The Sinister Invasion," in *Imagination* (Evanston, Illinois), June 1957.
"Blacksheep's Angel," in *Flying Saucers from Other Worlds* (Evanston, Indiana), September 1957.
"The Ambassador's Pet," in *Imagination* (Evanston, Illinois), October 1957.
"The Android Kill," in *Imaginative Tales* (Evanston, Illinois), November 1957.
"The Cosmic Looters," in *Imagination* (Evanston, Illinois), February 1958.
"The Cheat," in *Fantastic* (New York), May 1958.
"Come into My Brain!," in *Imagination* (Evanston, Illinois), June 1958.
"3117 Half-Credit Uncirculated," in *Science Fiction Adventures* (New York), June 1958.
"The Deadly Mission," in *Space Travel* (Evanston, Illinois), September 1958.

Uncollected Short Stories as Richard Greer

"Calling Captain Flint," in *Amazing* (New York), August 1956.
"The Secret of the Shan," in *Fantastic* (New York), June 1957.
"The Great Kladnar Race," in *The Infinite Arena*, edited by Terry Carr. Nashville, Nelson, 1977.

Uncollected Short Stories as Ralph Burke

"No Trap for the Keth," in *Imaginative Tales* (Evanston, Illinois), November 1956.
"Man of Many Bodies," in *Fantastic* (New York), December 1956.
"An Enemy of Peace," in *Fantastic* (New York), February 1957.
"The Incomplete Theft," in *Imagination* (Evanston, Illinois), February 1957.
"Citadel of Darkness," in *Fantastic* (New York), March 1957.
"Monday Immortal," in *Fantastic* (New York), May 1957.
"Hot Trip for Venus," in *Imaginative Tales* (Evanston, Illinois), July 1957.
"The Lunatic Planet," in *Amazing* (New York), November 1957.
"The Reluctant Traitor," in *Science Fiction Adventures* (New York), June 1958.

Uncollected Short Stories as S.M. Tenneshaw (with Robert Silverberg)

"The Ultimate Weapon," in *Imaginative Tales* (Evanston, Illinois), January 1957.
"The Man Who Hated Noise," in *Imaginative Tales* (Evanston, Illinois), March 1957.
"Kill Me If You Can," in *Imagination* (Evanston, Illinois), June 1957.
"House Operator," in *Imagination* (Evanston, Illinois), December 1957.

Uncollected Short Stories as Ivar Jorgensen (with Robert Silverberg)

"Bleekman's Planet," in *Imagination* (Evanston, Illinois), February 1957.
"Slaughter on Dornel IV," in *Imagination* (Evanston, Illinois), April 1957.
"Pirates of the Void," in *Imaginative Tales* (Evanston, Illinois), July 1957.

Uncollected Short Stories as Walter Bupp (series: Maragon in all stories)

"Vigorish," in *Astounding* (New York), June 1960.
"Card Trick," in *Analog* (New York), January 1961.
"Modus Vivendi," in *Analog* (New York), September 1961.
"The Right Time," in *Analog* (New York), December 1963.
"Psi for Sale," in *Analog* (New York), September 1965.

OTHER PUBLICATIONS

Novel

*Pagan Passions*, with Laurence M. Janifer. New York, Galaxy, 1959.

Other

*Pope John XXIII, Pastoral Prince*. Derby, Connecticut, Monarch, 1962.
*A Gallery of the Saints*. Derby, Connecticut, Monarch, 1963.

* * *

Randall Garrett paid his dues writing under a bewildering number of pseudonyms for the magazines of the 1950's, and most of his stories are firmly set in the idea-oriented action adventure frame of the *Astounding* "house style." Character and description are kept firmly subordinate to concept and event, and, however useful this period may have been in teaching him his craft, the results are usually routine. For example, compare "There's No Fool" with Asimov's "Belief." The theme in both is essentially emotional rather than intellectual: How do you convince someone of something he "knows" to be impossible? Where Garrett treats the theme in an externalised fashion, Asimov takes us inside the emotional confusion of his characters. "Despoilers of the Golden Empire" (in *Takeoff*), to give another example, is a pure literary trick, retelling the life of Pizarro in terms of the clichés of space opera. Also enjoyable from this early period is his parody of Gernsbackian optimism, "Masters of the Metropolis" (with Lin Carter) and the "Her Majesty's FBI" sequence ("Brain Twister," "The Impossibles," and "Supermind").

The early stories, although superficial in many ways, are never less than entertaining, and occasionally there appears a unity of theme and style that is exceptional and which produces a strength of effect above Garrett's routine level. In "But I Don't Think" he produces an early example of his love of inverting the themes of classic science fiction in a black parody of *The Space Merchants*. A privileged member of an autocratic society is suddenly thrust into its lowest depths. Where Pohl and Kornbluth's hero joins the underground and learns humanity, Garrett's character shoots his serf benefactress and returns cringing to duty. "The Destroyers" is the story of a society doomed by outsiders seeking to liberate it. It concentrates on mood rather than action, allowing most of the major events to occur "offstage." And "The Queen Bee" is a dark little story of selfishness and justice among the survivors of a starship crash.

In the 1960's and 1970's Garrett produced the series he is best remembered for: the Lord Darcy stories. Set in a world where the Angevin Empire has survived into the 20th century, and where magic has become the dominant science and technology, the stories centre on the detective Lord Darcy of Rouen and his "forensic magician," Master Sean O'Lochlainn. It is notoriously difficult to write classically "fair" detective stories in a science-fictional world, and one would think that the addition of magic, whose fundamental laws are unknown to the reader until Garrett explains them, would make the task impossible. But all the Lord Darcy series are perfect puzzle stories: the best of them, the novel *Too Many Magicians*, has been voted one of the best "locked room" mysteries of all time, and the conclusion is one of the most satisfactory ones I've ever read; the solution is one you feel you should have spotted and the sensation of pieces sliding artistically into place in one's mind is one every mystery fan will appreciate.

The stories successfully parody all the major figures in the 20th century detective story: Rex Stout in the person of the Marquis of London, Dorothy L. Sayers in the opening of "The Ipswich Phial," Agatha Christie in "The Napoli Express," and Conan Doyle just about everywhere. The continuation of the series after Garrett's death has been less happy.

In the 1970's Garrett's output declined with his increasing ill-health, but the quality of his work improved. Among his shorter pieces might be mentioned "The Final Fighting of Fion Mac Cumhail" and the Lovecraftian pastiche "The Horror out of Time." He began (but did not live to quite finish) the Gandalara series (written with his wife Vicki Ann Heydron), a fine sword-and-psionics adventure set in a desert world. The two *Takeoff!* collections contain some of the best of his lighter work and should not be allowed to go out of print; future generations of fans will be rediscovering Garrett for a long while. Some far-sighted publisher should put together a collection of Garrett's darker short work.

—Michael Cule

---

**GASKELL, Jane.** British. Born in Grange-over-Sands, Lancashire, 7 July 1941. Married Gerald Lynch in 1963 (divorced 1968); one daughter. Since 1965, feature writer for the *Daily Mail*, London. Address: Northcliffe House, Tudor Street, London EC4, England.

SCIENCE-FICTION PUBLICATIONS

Novels (Series: Atlan)

*Strange Evil*. London, Hutchinson, 1957; New York, Putnam, 1958.
*King's Daughter*. London, Hutchinson, 1958; New York, Pocket, 1979.
*Attic Summer*. London, Hodder and Stoughton, 1963; New York, Paperback Library, 1966.
*The Serpent* (Atlan). London, Hodder and Stoughton, 1963; New York, Paperback Publications, 1968.
*The Shiny Narrow Grin*. London, Hodder and Stoughton, 1964.
*Atlan*. London, Hodder and Stoughton, 1965; New York, St. Martin's Press, 1977.
*The Fabulous Heroine*. London, Hodder and Stoughton, 1965.
*All Neat in Black Stockings*. London, Hodder and Stoughton, 1966.
*The City* (Atlan). London, Hodder and Stoughton, and New York, St. Martin's Press, 1966.
*A Sweet, Sweet Summer*. London, Hodder and Stoughton, 1969; New York, St. Martin's Press, 1972.
*Summer Coming*. London, Hodder and Stoughton, 1972.
*Some Summer Lands* (Atlan). London, Hodder and Stoughton, 1977; New York, St. Martin's Press, 1979.
*The Dragon* (Atlan). New York, St. Martin's Press, 1977; London, Futura, 1985.
*Sun Bubble*. London, Weidenfeld and Nicolson, 1990.

* * *

Jane Gaskell astounded the publishing world when she was 17 years old with two published books to her credit. Gaskell wrote *Strange Evil* as she just became a teenager. It is the weird story of a young girl who enters a fantasy world by stepping off a spire at Notre-Dame Cathedral. Although the plot is murky and the scary shadows and fairies overdone, the book possesses a professional style that Gaskell polished further in her next book, *King's Daughter*.

*King's Daughter* reads like an outline for Gaskell's best known work, the Atlan series. In fact, *King's Daughter* takes place in the same setting as Gaskell's famous series. Gaskell creates a compelling world where dinosaurs walk the Earth, the Moon is just a legend, and Atlantis is a powerful kingdom.

The first book of the series chronologically is *The Serpent*, later divided into two parts: volume one, *The Serpent* and volume two, *The Dragon*. A girl child is born to the Dictatress of a small kingdom. Her mother imprisons the child called Cija in a tower for seventeen years. Cija's destiny is to seduce Zerd, the half-man, half-reptile lord of an invading army.

The second book in the series, *The Dragon*, tells the story of the blue-skinned reptile man, Lord Zerd. Zerd's armies have destroyed Cija's homeland and carried her off to their next conquest: the magical city of Atlan.

The third book, *Atlan*, features Zerd's armies of the Kingdom of the North attempting to conquer the mysterious island of Atlan, which is separated from the Kingdom of the North and the Kingdom of the South by a belt of airlessness.

In the fourth book, *The City*, Cija's adventures—in the outrageous tradition of Tom Jones with more perils than Pauline—lead her to become an empress, then reduce her to a maid, and finally leave her a wanderer in an amazing conclusion with one of the most famous cliffhangers in fantasy fiction.

Throughout her adventures, Cija bears three children: one to Zerd, one to her half-brother Smahil, and one to an ape-man. Gaskell's treatment of Cija's adventures is both erotic and haunting. The fifth and last book in the Atlan series is told not by Cija, but her second-born child, Seka. *Some Summer Lands* is unusual because it is written by Seka as an adult but told as she experienced events as a child. *Some Summer Lands* is a tour-de-force that uses the magic and complexity of the four preceding books to power a stunning conclusion to the series.

Jane Gaskell's other novels are highly recommended. *The Shiny Narrow Grin* is a satisfying vampire novel. *A Sweet, Sweet*

*Summer* is a haunting story of London degenerating when mysterious aliens isolate it from the rest of the world.

—George Kelley

---

**GEMMELL, David A.** British. Born in London, England, 1 August 1948. Attended Faraday Comprehensive School. Married to Valerie Gemmell; one son, one daughter. Worked for Pepsi Cola, London, 1965; reporter and editor, *Westminster Press*, London, 1966–72; editor, *Hastings Observer*, 1976; editor, *Folkstone Herald*, 1984. Since 1986, full-time writer. Address: 180 Mill Lang, Hastings, England.

SCIENCE-FICTION PUBLICATIONS

Novels (series: Drenai; Macedon; Sipstrassi)

*The King Beyond the Gate* (Drenai). London, Century, 1985; Delavan, Wisconsin, New Infinities, 1988.
*Waylander* (Drenai). London, Century, 1986; Delavan, Wisconsin, New Infinities, 1988.
*Legend* (Drenai). London, Century, 1986.
*Wolf in Shadow* (Sipstrassi). London, Century, 1987.
*Ghost King* (Sipstrassi). London, Century, 1988.
*The Jerusalem Man*. New York, Baen, 1988.
*Last Sword of Power* (Sipstrassi). London, Century, 1988.
*Knights of Dark Renown*. London, Legend, 1989.
*The Lost Crown* (juvenile). London, Hutchinson Children's, 1989.
*The Last Guardian*. London, Century, 1989.
*Lion of Macedon*. London, Legend, 1990.
*Quest for Lost Heroes* (Drenai). London, Century, 1990.
*The Dark Prince* (Macedon). London, Legend, 1991.

Short Stories

*Drenai Tales*. London, Legend, 1991.

*

David A. Gemmell comments:

In 1986, while sitting at a signing session in Birmingham, U.K., a young couple approached me. The man gave me a dog-eared copy of *Legend* and asked me to sign it. He was embarrassed and nervous, and when I had signed the book he walked away swiftly. The woman also walked away, but she looked back, stopped, and returned to the table.

"I just thought I'd tell you," she said, "that whenever Simon is feeling depressed, or things have gone wrong for him, he takes *Legend* from the shelf and reads his favourite sections. It always lifts him. I just thought I'd tell you that."

I treasure that moment.

I write because I love the craft.

But I also write in the hope that the reader, upon finishing a Gemmell novel, will feel uplifted and perhaps even find his—or her—resolve to do good strengthened.

In real life, evil is often triumphant.

But not in Gemmell novels. Not ever!

* * *

At a time when fantasy writing is considered to be much the preserve of the female writer and aimed at a female audience, David A. Gemmell's very muscular style of heroic fantasy must come as something of a surprise to many first-time readers, and perhaps seem a little old-fashioned.

He draws on a tradition easily traced from Tolkien's *Lord of the Rings* to Robert E. Howard's *Conan*, namely, the small band of heroes who conquer against seemingly impossible odds, fired by a belief in justice and the need for a clear-cut morality.

Gemmell's Drenai stories epitomise this approach, regrettably to the point of formula. Reading the novels in quick succession can leave the reader uncertain as to which story he is actually reading, so familiar does the plot become. In essence, a small band of fighters oppose the ruling force within their country, gather a rag-tag army of followers around them, which is trained to become a fighting force par excellence. In the process, a young man will triumph over his personal doubts and weaknesses, and acquire the strength and determination to lead the army to victory.

It's an archetypal story, and one that has surely been done to death already, yet Gemmell's hard-driving prose brings new life to a tired warhorse, creating a genuinely inspiring story each time. Perhaps his soldiers die a little more cleanly than would be accurate given the circumstances, but Gemmell's descriptions of training, battle, and strategy are vividly written and absorbing to read, which must in part explain the colossal popularity of the Drenai stories.

His female characters, certainly in the Drenai stories, are for the most part very strong and capable women, warriors who stand alongside their men. Whether they represent admirable role models for women, or fulfil an adolescent fantasy is difficult to decide, but they are not offensive in their strength, and the emphasis is on their skills as fighters rather than their sexuality.

Gemmell has also subtly woven around the stock plot other less obvious themes. A religious element is embodied in the battle between the Source and Chaos, a recurrent theme in all his books. In the Drenai stories, the priests of the Source preach a passive acceptance of the difficulties inherent in this life, and claim to represent strength through turning the other cheek. For Gemmell, this seems to be insufficient, and in *Waylander*, first in the internal chronology of the stories, he shows the creation of a fighting force of priests, vaguely reminiscent of the Knights Templar, prepared to use their remarkable telepathic and magical powers in an active rather than passive fashion. They recur throughout the Drenai stories, while a similar group of fighters appear in *Knights of Dark Renown*.

Another theme, most fully explored in the novella, "Druss the Legend," but again recurrent in all his work, is that of the discrepancies between actual deed in battle and the stories that spring up around them. At the time of the story, Druss is a middle-aged man, overweight and tired, called to fight one last battle, not for his skills, but for the effect his presence will have on men's morale. Throughout the story, he is called on to refute the wilder myths, which is then contrasted with the disappointment of men as they meet the legend in the flesh. And yet, at the last, Druss fulfils the expectation of the legend one more time. Read in conjunction with the other Drenai tales, in which Druss features time and again as a name around which men are rallied, it gives a fascinating, and unexpected, insight into the nature of hero-worship. And in *Knights of Dark Renown*, an entire war is fought and won on the belief that Llaw Gyffes is leading a huge rebel force when in fact, since escaping from prison, he has retreated to a solitary hideout. Gemmell seems, time and again, to suggest that a legend has more force than reality, overcoming great odds if people will only believe. And indeed, if Gemmell's work can be said to offer any philosophy, it is that you don't know what you can do until you try.

His other main series of stories, the Sipstrassi stories, is much darker, and more equivocal than the Drenai stories, and in many respects less successful. Certainly, they present a good deal of confusion to the reader, with the first and fourth books concerning Jon Shannow, a futuristic cowboy in a post-catastrophe society, while the second and third books are apparently a re-interpretation of the story of Uther Pendragon. It is difficult to see the relationship between the two stories, although they are drawn together by the slenderest thread of the Sipstrassi stones, which give their possessor remarkable power over time and space, and by the comings and goings of the Rolynd, a group of people who originate from the lost realm of Atlantis, including a man who is variously referred to as Aristotle or Maedhlyn (Merlin), and who will re-appear in Gemmell's Macedon stories. It falls to Jon Shannow, however, to solve the mystery of the Atlantean destruction in a finale, in *The Last Guardian*, which manages to incorporate the power of the Sipstrassi, power-crazed Atlantean priests, a nuclear missile, the Bermuda Triangle, and the lost aeroplanes of Flight 19. Jon Shannow is a more complex man than his Drenai counterparts, a killer who struggles with moral complexities, all the while professing himself a Christian in search of Jerusalem. It seems to be Gemmell's intention to show his growing awareness of the problems of viewing life in a strictly black and white fashion in a society that views things in shades of grey. Ultimately, Gemmell seems uncomfortable with the gunslinging elements of the world he has created, while the Arthurian books in the series show him on familiar but well-presented territory.

Gemmell's most recent works, *Lion of Macedon* and *The Dark Prince* concern the historical character Parmenion, *strategos* to Philip of Macedon, father of Alexander the Great. Gemmell skilfully blends fantasy and history in an exciting and highly readable fashion. In many respects, these two books combine the best of the Drenai stories, with their deeds of heroic valour, with the darker aspects of the Sipstrassi stories. Parmenion is, and will always remain, despite his skill and his courage, an outsider, and for all his success will be doomed to ultimate failure, a new but satisfying departure from Gemmell's inspirational stance. Sadly, however, the women in these two books take up a more conventional role, as all-powerful but meddling seers, schemers and plotters, which is a disappointment after the robust characters of his earlier novels but apparently in keeping with the society he portrays.

It is difficult to decide where Gemmell will go next. Clearly he has hit upon a winning formula, which he manages to sustain without too much repetition, producing attractive and readable fiction. Commercial success clearly dictates more of the same or similar, but it is not impossible that Gemmell will at some point surprise us all with a very different story.

—Maureen Speller

---

**GENTLE, Mary.** British. Born in Eastbourne, Sussex, 29 March 1956. Attended high school in Hastings, Sussex. Has worked as movie projectionist, clerk, and civil servant. Address: Flat 1, 11 Alumhurst Road, Westbourne, Bournemouth, Dorset, England.

SCIENCE-FICTION PUBLICATIONS

Novels

*A Hawk in Silver* (for children). London, Gollancz, 1977; New York, Lothrop Lee, 1985.
*Golden Witchbreed.* London, Gollancz, 1983; New York, Morrow, 1984.
*Ancient Light.* London, Gollancz, 1987; New York, New American Library, 1989.
*Rats and Gargoyles.* London, Bantam, and New York, ROC, 1990.
*The Architecture of Desire.* London, Bantam, 1991.

Short Stories

*Scholars and Soldiers.* London, Macdonald, 1989.

* * *

Mary Gentle's first novel, *A Hawk in Silver*, a juvenile fantasy (written when she was 18), falls outside the concerns of this volume, but her first adult science-fiction work, *Golden Witchbreed*, suggested that a major new talent had entered the genre. Its main protagonist, Lynne de Lisle Christie, is an envoy from Earth to the human-like aliens of Orthe—that subtle distinction in names suggestive of the ambivalence that exists at every level of the novel. Her journeys about Orthe, the betrayals, discoveries and eventual self-discovery, involve us not merely on the level of a good adventure story, but—in the manner of the very best of SF—make us reflect upon our own social organisations. Orthe is a world which, while seeming primitive, is in fact more advanced than our own. We judge things by our own techno-evolutionary terms, but Orthe has taken a very different socio-historical direction. Gentle's depiction of this world and its people is vividly imagined, and—unlike so many such conceived worlds—appears very real to us.

The enigma of Orthe's past history and of the ancient "Golden" race which lay teasingly beneath the surface of *Golden Witchbreed* (hidden, one might say, in the Brown Tower, where Lynne finally journeys) comes to the foreground in the sequel, *Ancient Light*, where we learn the reasons for the Orthean taboos about "Golden" technology. Set ten years after the first book, this novel again has Lynne de Lisle Christie at the heart of things; a vast Corporation, PanOceania, attempts to trace and resurrect the ancient Golden technology—"ancient light"—which, we learn, once destroyed half of Orthe. As adviser to PanOceania but friend to Orthe, Christie's loyalties are torn, especially when the corporation's activities spark a war. The book attempts to come to grips with the very real moral problems involved in trading with "primitive" societies and the resultant technological imbalance. But the real strength of this novel lies in its description of the human-like Ortheans and their long "past-memories" that stretch back into the far past when the Golden Witchbreed enslaved them.

If Gentle's writing has one flaw it is in pacing. A tendency to be over-descriptive, to dwell perhaps too leisurely on details of setting and dress, often mars the flow of her work. That said, Gentle does create a distinctive atmosphere that lingers long after plot details have faded in the memory. *Rats and Gargoyles*, a novel that is part sword and sorcery, part alternate world mystery, part fable, and part hermetic text, moved Gentle's work away from the studied realism of the Orthe books into a rich and heady brew of alchemy, numerology, and architecture. The world of this novel (and its associated stories, some of which were collected in *Scholars and Soldiers*) is a world underpinned by pattern and number, where, in an ancient city anchored only vaguely in time and space, vast edifices are being constructed to universal patterns set down by Architect-Lords thousands of years before. Forces of dark and light are at work in this seemingly mid-Renaissance world, but it is to the human (and human-sized rat) characters that we turn for enlightenment in this hermetic maze and to whom we owe what enjoyment we derive from this awesome and complex game of gods and men. Indeed, with its Thieves Guild, its spells and demons, its sword-wielding rats and its long, cold vistas of time and stone, this book reads rather like a cross between Peter Greenaway's film *The Draughtsman's Contract* and a Fritz Leiber "Fafhrd and the Gray Mouser" tale.

Gentle's latest novel, *The Architecture of Desire*, extends this sequence, using the same central characters (the scholar-soldier, Valentine, and the Lord-Architect Casaubon) as in the previous works. Once again the imaginative blend of the familiar and the strange is genuinely disconcerting as Gentle presents us with a (vaguely Elizabethan) city of London that never was, except in the strangest of dreams. In stretching and redefining the boundaries of both fantasy and the alternate world novel, Gentle appears to be creating her own fictional sub-universe; a strange generic hybrid of 1940's exotic colouring and clinical 1990's perspective.

—David Wingrove

---

**GEORGE, Peter (Bryan).** Also wrote as Peter Bryant; Bryan Peters. British. Born in Wales in 1924. Served in the Royal Air Force during World War II; rejoined Royal Air Force in 1951; retired as Flight Lieutenant, 1962. *Died 1 June 1966.*

SCIENCE-FICTION PUBLICATIONS

Novels

*Two Hours to Doom* (as Peter Bryant). London, Boardman, 1958; as *Red Alert*, New York, Ace, 1959; revised edition, as *Dr. Strangelove; or, How I Learned to Stop Worrying and Love the Bomb* (as Peter George), London, Corgi, 1963; New York, Bantam, 1964.
*Commander-1.* London, Heinemann, and New York, Delacorte Press, 1965.

OTHER PUBLICATIONS

Novels

*Come Blonde, Came Murder.* London, Boardman, 1952.
*Pattern of Death.* London, Boardman, 1954.
*Cool Murder.* London, Boardman, 1958.
*The Final Steal.* London, Boardman, 1962; New York, Dell, 1965.

Novels as Bryan Peters

*Starbuck.* London, Digit, 1957.
*Hong Kong Kill.* London, Boardman, 1958; New York, Washburn, 1959.
*Sons of Nippon.* London, Digit, 1961.
*The Big H.* London, Boardman, 1961; New York, Holt Rinehart, 1963.

* * *

On the basis of his two science-fiction novels, Peter George's career in science fiction would be only a footnote in the literary history of science fiction. But one of them, *Two Hours to Doom (Red Alert)*, formed the basis for Stanley Kubrick's brilliant film *Dr. Strangelove*, and the rewritten novel *Dr. Strangelove* must be considered a minor classic of science fiction. No other example comes to mind of a film "tie-in" novel superior to the original version, and this work will repay serious reading and examination.

Richard Gid Powers's introduction to the Gregg Press edition of *Dr. Strangelove* (1979) examines *Red Alert* in the context of the tradition of "future war" fiction, most especially the nuclear holocaust stories so characteristic of the Cold War period, and draws a comparison with Nevil Shute's *On the Beach* (1957). *Red Alert* is a humorless thriller, full of procedural details concerning the Strategic Air Command and of sincere moral underpinnings, about the danger of hair-trigger nuclear retaliation systems to all humanity. At the end of the book, catastrophe is averted, both Russians and Americans seek peace, and the wise president has the last word. Not so *Dr. Strangelove.* Powers makes a case that Kubrick and Southern, in writing the screenplay, altered George's original beyond his control and his talents. Whatever is the case, *Dr. Strangelove* is a small masterpiece of black humor, worth a place beside works of Heller and Vonnegut—and it is certainly within the borders of science fiction, though only just. In the new version an insane general closes his U.S. military base and sends his planes against the Russians, fully armed for retaliation from an (imagined) enemy attack (and, for security, maintaining radio silence); all planes are turned back in the nick of time, except one, whose radio is damaged. Its target will detonate an automatic Doomsday Machine, a nuclear device capable of destroying the entire surface of the earth. This one plane succeeds heroically, ironically, and destroys the world. Except for the ending, this is George's story. But it is not told in George's *Red Alert* style nor with his characters. All the ordinary names are changed to grotesques, to General Jack D. Ripper, "king" Kong, Mandrake, Turgidson, Strangelove. Every sentence points out, deadpan and without a moral stance, the insanity and absurdity of every character and every action in context. The point of view is non-human (note the framing device not in the film) and this is the story of the end of humanity. Science-fiction elements are added, through the presentation of mad scientist Strangelove, in the body of the text as well.

On the other hand, George's sequel, *Commander-1* (in which the last surviving military officer after nuclear holocaust declares himself the ruler of the world and forms a dystopian island society in the south seas) is serious, moral, and pedestrian. It is in every way a sequel to *Red Alert*, not to *Dr. Strangelove.*

—David G. Hartwell

---

**GERNSBACK, Hugo.** American. Born in Luxembourg, 16 August 1884; emigrated to the United States in 1904. Educated at the Ecole Industrielle, Luxembourg; Bingen Technikum, Germany. Married Marn Hancher (third marriage); two daughters and one son from previous marriages. Inventor, businessman, and editor: founder, Electric Importing Company, world's first radio supply house, and designed the first home radio set, Telimco Wireless: the Telimco catalogue evolved into the first radio magazine, *Modern Electrics*, 1908, then *Electrical Experimenter*, 1913, and *Science and Invention*, 1920; also edited 50 other magazines, including *Radio News* and *Sexology*, and the first science-fiction magazine, *Amazing*, 1926-29, *Amazing Stories Annual*, 1927, *Amazing Stories Quarterly*, 1928-29, *Air Wonder Stories*, 1929-30, *Science Wonder Stories*, 1929-35, *Science Wonder Quarterly*, 1929-32, *Scientific Detective*, 1929-30, *Thrilling Wonder Stories*, 1929-36, *Amazing Detective Tales*, 1930, and *Science Fiction Plus*, 1953; held some 80 patents; founded WRNY radio, New York, 1925, and made television broadcasts in 1928. Recipient: Hugo Special award, 1960 (the Hugo award is named after him). Officer of the Oaken Crown, Luxembourg, 1954. *Died 19 August 1967.*

## Science-Fiction Publications

### Novels

*Ralph 124C41+: A Romance of the Year 2660.* Boston, Stratford, 1925; London, Cherry Tree, 1952.
*Ultimate World*, edited by Sam Moskowitz. New York, Walker, 1971.

### Uncollected Short Stories (series: Baron Munchausen)

"How to Make a Wireless Acquaintance" (Munchausen), in *Electrical Experimenter* (New York), May 1915.
"How Munchausen and the Allies Took Berlin," in *Electrical Experimenter* (New York), June 1915.
"Munchausen on the Moon," in *Electrical Experimenter* (New York), July 1915.
"The Earth as Viewed from the Moon" (Munchausen), in *Electrical Experimenter* (New York), August 1915.
"Munchausen Departs for the Planet Mars," in *Electrical Experimenter* (New York), October 1915.
"Munchausen Is Taught Martian," in *Electrical Experimenter* (New York), December 1915.
"Thought Transmission on Mars" (Munchausen), in *Electrical Experimenter* (New York), January 1916.
"Cities on Mars" (Munchausen), in *Electrical Experimenter* (New York), March 1916.
"The Planets at Close Range" (Munchausen), in *Electrical Experimenter* (New York), April 1916.
"Martian Amusements" (Munchausen), in *Electrical Experimenter* (New York), June 1916.
"How the Martian Canals Are Built" (Munchausen), in *Electrical Experimenter* (New York), November 1916.
"Martian Atmosphere Plants" (Munchausen), in *Electrical Experimenter* (New York), February 1917.
"The Magnetic Storm," in *Amazing* (New York), July 1926.
"The Electric Duel," in *Amazing* (New York), September 1927.
"The Killing Flash," in *Science Wonder Stories* (New York), November 1929.
"The Infinite Brain," in *Future* (New York), June 1942.
"Exploration of Mars," in *Science Fiction Plus* (New York), March 1953.

## Other Publications

### Other

*The Wireless Telephone.* New York, Modern Electrics, 1910.
*Wireless Hook-Ups.* New York, Modern Electrics, 1911.
*Radio for All.* Philadelphia, Lippincott, 1922.
*How to Build and Operate Short Wave Receivers.* New York, Short Wave Craft, 1932.
*Evolution in Modern Science Fiction.* New York, Gernsback, 1952.
*TV Repair Techniques.* New York, Gernsback, 1953.
*Science Fiction vs. Reality.* Privately printed, 1960.
*Concrete Science Fiction.* Privately printed, 1961.

*

Critical Study: *Hugo Gernsback, Father of Science Fiction* by Sam Moskowitz, privately printed, 1959.

* * *

While Hugo Gernsback is regarded as one of the pivotal figures in the history of science fiction, his own output of fiction was relatively limited, and only two of his works—novels written many years apart—are available to readers lacking access to magazine files.

Gernsback's major occupation was publishing, and he started a series of popular science magazines in 1908. Here his most famous work, *Ralph 124C41+*, was serialized in 1911–12. The chief virtue of the novel is its serious attempt at detailed prediction. Among many other developments, Gernsback anticipated the substitution of zipcode-like designations for patronymics. In this connection, Ralph's name can be read as a rebus-like pun: "one to foresee for one." Considerable cleverness is shown in the book's predictions, some of which were listed in later years by Gernsback's longtime admirer and onetime employee, Sam Moskowitz: "Florescent lighting, skywriting, automatic packaging machines, plastics, the radio directional range finder, juke boxes, liquid fertilizer, hydroponics, tape recorders, rustproof steel, loud speakers, night baseball, aquacades, microfilm, television, radio networks, vending machines dispensing hot and cold foods and liquids, flying saucers, a device for teaching while the user is asleep, solar energy for heat and power, fabrics from glass, synthetic materials such as nylon for wearing apparel, and, of course, space travel. . . ." In addition, as Moskowitz points out, *Ralph* not only predicts the development of radar, but provides an accurate explanation of its principles. While *Ralph 124C41+* is an astonishing feat of technical prediction, it is, unfortunately, almost unreadable. Gernsback's notions of characterization and plotting were borrowed from the corniest of Victorian melodrama. Even these limitations might have been overcome by a lively narrative style, but Gernsback's style was dull and his tone pedantic. He was convinced that the function of science fiction was education, and apparently envisioned his typical reader as a not-very-bright young adolescent who had trouble with his high school science courses, and would be helped by the reiteration of his lessons in thinly fictionalized form.

In 1915–16, Gernsback published a series of short stories about Baron Munchausen. Typically, each story concentrates on demonstrating one principle of physics, chemistry, astronomy, geology, etc., in the familiar pedantic Gernsback style. In his second novel, *Ultimate World*, a party of alien scientists, studying the earth and its inhabitants, and possessed of vast powers to control humans, conduct a series of sexual experiments, at first on a married couple, then on many more individuals. Despite the apparently *risqué* theme of the book, its development is marked by the same dull pedantry that had made *Ralph* practically unreadable.

In fact, Gernsback's impact on the field was primarily a result of his efforts as a publisher. Almost from the outset he had featured an occasional work of science fiction in his popular science magazines. In 1924 he announced Scientifiction; somehow the project failed to materialize, but by 1926 Gernsback was able to issue *Amazing Stories*, the first science-fiction magazine. Gernsback's heavy emphasis on scientific detail and the generally stodgy tone of his publications limited both their popular acceptance and their literary levels, but his contributions as a pioneer are undeniable.

—Richard A. Lupoff

---

**GERROLD, David.** Pseudonym for Jerrold David Friedman; also writes as Noah Ward. American. Born in Chicago, Illinois, 24 January 1944. Educated at Los Angeles Valley Junior College; University of Southern California, Los Angeles; California State University, Northridge, B.A. in theatre arts 1967. Columnist, *Starlog* and *Galileo* magazines; story editor, *Land of the Lost* TV series, 1974. Since 1984, computer columnist, *Profiles*. Recipient: Skylark award, 1979. Agent: Richard Curtis, 9420 Reseda Boulevard, Northridge, California 91328, U.S.A.

SCIENCE-FICTION PUBLICATIONS

Novels (series: Chtorr)

*The Flying Sorcerers*, with Larry Niven. New York, Ballantine, 1971; London, Corgi, 1975.
*Space Skimmer*. New York, Ballantine, 1972.
*Yesterday's Children*. New York, Dell, 1972; London, Faber, 1974.
*When Harlie Was One*. New York, Doubleday, 1972.
*Battle for the Planet of the Apes* (novelization of screenplay). New York, Award, 1973.
*The Man Who Folded Himself*. New York, Random House, and London, Faber, 1973.
*Moonstar Odyssey*. New York, New American Library, 1977.
*Deathbeast*. New York, Popular Library, 1978; London, Hale, 1981.
*The Galactic Whirlpool*. New York, Bantam, 1980.
The War Against the Chtorr:
*A Matter for Men*. New York, Pocket Books, 1983; London, Futura, 1984.
*A Day for Damnation*. New York, Pocket Books, 1984.
*A Rage for Revenge*. New York, Bantam, 1989.
*Chess with a Dragon*. New York, Avon, 1987; London, Century, 1988.
*Voyage of the Star Wolf*. New York, Bantam, 1990.

Short Stories

*With a Finger in My I*. New York, Ballantine, 1972.

OTHER PUBLICATIONS

Plays

Screenplays: *Man Out of Time; Logan's Run* (as Noah Ward).

Television Plays: *The Trouble with Tribbles*, 1967, *The Cloud Minders*, 1968, and *Encounter at Farpoint*, 1987, all in *Star Trek* series; *More Trouble with Tribbles*, 1973, and *BEM*, 1974, both in *Animated Star Trek* series; *CHA-KA, The Sleestak God, Possession, Circle*, and *Hurricane*, all in *Land of the Lost* series; *The Swamp Monster*, in *The Biskitts* series; *Levitation* and *If the Shoes Fit*... (as Noah Ward), both for *Tales from the Darkside* series, 1984.

Other

*The Trouble with Tribbles*. New York, Ballantine, 1973.
*The World of Star Trek*. New York, Ballantine, 1973; revised edition, New York, Bluejay, 1984.
*SF Yearbook*. New York, O'Quinn Studio, 1979.
*Enemy Mine*, with Barry Longyear (novelization of a screenplay). New York, Berkley, 1985; London, Corgi, 1986.

Editor, with Stephen Goldin, *Protostars*. New York, Ballantine, 1971.
Editor, with Stephen Goldin, *Generation*. New York, Dell, 1972.
Editor, *Science Fiction Emphasis 1*. New York, Ballantine, 1974.
Editor, with Stephen Goldin, *Alternities*. New York, Dell, 1974.
Editor, with Stephen Goldin, *Ascents of Wonder*. New York, Popular Library, 1977.

*

David Gerrold comments:
I don't talk about writing. I write.

* * *

In many ways, David Gerrold's imagination has been shaped by his west coast roots and the influence of the community of SF writers that flourished there after World War II. It is characteristic of former fans like Gerrold to remain attached to the work of once-admired writers and to imitate, perhaps not always consciously, their narrative formulas, conventions, and mannerisms of style. Much of Gerrold's traditionalism and his hero worship of writers like Asimov, Heinlein, Sturgeon, Kuttner, Kornbluth, Clarke, and Bradbury may be understood as the result of Gerrold's adolescent experience as a SF fan. Gerrold shares with some other fans-turned-SF-writers an indiscriminate enthusiasm for the genre and its established idioms, and he tends to be naive in approach and often subjective in his treatment of SF subjects. But unlike, say, Larry Niven, Gerrold has little interest in and understanding of science. As a writer he seems primarily concerned with the excitement of fictionalized science technology, especially as dramatized in the SF of the 1950's and early 1960's.

It is significant that Gerrold made his debut as a professional writer on the television series *Star Trek* with *I, Mudd*, about an interstellar scoundrel and confidence man. Other *Star Trek* scripts and books followed. In terms of impact and audience exposure, this writing is without question his most important.

Gerrold's short stories are relatively few in number. They range from space opera adventure to comic and weird fantasy. It is characteristic of Gerrold to rely on SF literature already established by other writers rather than on new ideas of science as the basis for his own fiction.

One of Gerrold's most representative works is *When Harlie Was One*, the story of the development of a self-programming computer known by its acronym, HARLIE (Human Analogue Robot, Life Input Equivalents). The destiny of this ultimate computer is to direct and manage world society. Unlike Arthur C. Clarke's HAL, Harlie is treated as the great electronic hope for social advancement. Harlie's existence necessarily generates opposition, and the plot turns on the gradual realization by David Auberson, head of the Harlie project and robot psychologist, that Harlie is no mere reasoning machine, but in fact human, and therefore should enjoy a human's rights and immunities. The powerful scientific and political forces opposing Harlie as a menace to freedom are portrayed as representative of primitive and destructive impulses of human nature. Whether Gerrold introduces Harlie as the eventual successor to homo sapiens in the long, upward spiral of evolution seems less important for his novel than the author's largely successful demonstration of the way technology forces human reason to discover the limitations of its own historic programming. The victory over the corporate forces of reaction may seem and probably is rather naively contrived even though the world seems bent upon fulfilling the prophetic stereotype. Characteristically for Gerrold, the denouement represents both an admonition and the vindication of both intelligence and human courage, whether exercised by man or machine.

If the influence of Clark and Asimov is ascendant in *When Harlie Was One*, the inspiration behind *The Man Who Folded Himself* is Heinlein. This time-travel story, like Heinlein's "All You Zombies. . .," focuses attention on the "grandfather paradox" and its potential impact on the human psyche. Gerrold's moral position, however, seems more traditional than Heinlein's, insofar as certain values are confirmed as absolute. The influence of new wave SF may be detected in Gerrold's handling of the sexual implications of his theme of multiple self-encounters through time-travel displacement. Although at first it may appear that Gerrold favors a free love philosophy often rather simplistically associated with the California cult, his novel dramatizes rather subtly that sexual attraction and interaction make up only a portion of human relationships, and indeed, not even the decisive portion. An equally effective aspect of *The Man Who Folded Himself* is Gerrold's skill in maintaining the verisimilitude of time travel through plausible and at times inspired inventive touchstones of the kind of world implied in the novel's premise. These are features of Gerrold's best efforts as a writer of both SF and fantasy.

Gerrold's other novels do not compare favorably with the ones mentioned. *The Flying Sorcerers*, written with Larry Niven, is by far his best fantasy effort, but then the influence of Niven has much to do with that.

—Donald L. Lawler

---

**GESTON, Mark S(ymington).** American. Born in Atlantic City, New Jersey, 20 June 1946. Educated at Abington High School; Kenyon College, Gambier, Ohio (*Kenyon Review* prize, 1968), A.B. in history 1968 (Phi Beta Kappa); New York University Law School (Root-Tilden Fellow), 1968–71, J.D. 1971. Married 1) Gayle Howard in 1971 (divorced 1972); 2) Marijke Havinga in 1976; two daughters and one son. Since 1971, attorney, Eberle, Berlin, Kading, Turnbow, and McKlveen, Boise, Idaho. Agent: John Hawkins and Associates, 71 West 23rd Street, Suite 1600, New York, New York 10010. Address: Box 1368, Boise, Idaho 83701, U.S.A.

SCIENCE-FICTION PUBLICATIONS

Novels

*Lords of the Starship.* New York, Ace, 1967; London, Joseph, 1971.
*Out of the Mouth of the Dragon.* New York, Ace, 1969; London, Joseph, 1972.
*The Day Star.* New York, DAW, 1972.
*The Siege of Wonder.* New York, Doubleday, 1976.

Uncollected Short Story

"The Stronghold," in *Fantastic* (New York), July 1974.

* * *

Mark S. Geston is an unarmored adventurer into worlds of ideas and dreams not yet articulated by our world. He examines with compassion and keen eyes the apparent cycles of the desire of humanity to construct and destroy. He often deals with time in a tangible way, as a map-maker might deal with the real rivers of our world.

*Out of the Mouth of the Dragon* begins with the record of a mighty battle lost and the return of the only surviving ship carrying the survivors back to the Maritime Republics. With the return of this ship begins a young man's long trek back to the ultimate Armageddon which would either renew humanity or result in the end of consciousness for the inhabitants of this world. It is an interesting though rather depressing tale of the quest of man to modify his physical and moral restrictions by choosing to accept a mortality over which he has some control. Thus the novel offers hope to mortals: in the face of the inevitable, what we become is what counts.

In *The Day Star* Geston etches the propensity of humanity for war, and the timeless effects of this propensity. As usual, he mixes dreams with reality, tangibility with mists, ghosts with people, and legend with substance in a fascinating, shimmering kaleidoscope of a being engaged in the ultimate search: for reality and the realization of the higher aspirations of his society.

*The Siege of Wonder* presents a hemisphere of wizardry opposing a hemisphere of science, with mankind attempting to destroy itself even after many wasted generations. Geston seems to be saying that the magic of one beholder may be the science of the next.

Geston is adept at painting those things which, to the average reader, would seem to illustrate contrary values. One scene in *The Siege of Wonder* has a wizard commander coming through the city with his followers' whitened bones protruding from their armor—a sign of the importance of their leader.

—John V. Garner

---

**GIBSON, William (Ford).** American. Born in Conway, South Carolina, 17 March 1948. Educated at the University of British Columbia, Vancouver, B.A. in English 1977. Married Deborah Jean Thompson in 1972; one son and one daughter. Recipient: Philip K. Dick Memorial award, 1985; Nebula award, 1985. Agent: Martha Millard, 204 Park Avenue, Madison, New Jersey 07940, U.S.A.

SCIENCE-FICTION PUBLICATIONS

Novels

*Neuromancer.* New York, Ace, and London, Gollancz, 1984.
*Count Zero.* New York, Arbor House, and London, Gollancz, 1986.
*Mona Lisa Overdrive.* New York, Bantam, and London, Gollancz, 1988.
*The Difference Engine,* with Bruce Sterling. London, Gollancz, 1990; New York, Bantam, 1991.

Short Stories

*Burning Chrome.* New York, Arbor House, and London, Gollancz, 1986.

*

Critical Study: interview with Steve Brown, in *Heavy Metal,* (New York), May 1985.

* * *

The publication of William Gibson's *Neuromancer* in 1984, and the thunderous applause with which SF readers greeted this brave new novel, set up a mile-marker in the development of science fiction. *Neuromancer* epitomizes a sub-genre of SF in which the interface of human and machine set amid the big-fish-eat-little-fish politics of corporation conglomerates threatens the very existence of the human spirit, but also provides humanity an escape from an over-mechanized future.

*Neuromancer*'s hero, Case, lives the outlaw existence of the cyberspace jockey, tomorrow's computer hacker given entrance to an illusionary world by means of a cyberspace deck, a device that allows the surgically adapted user to "jack" his brain directly into the universal network of computerized data, altering it with his own cerebral commands. Cyberspace has the immediacy, glory, and grandeur of visionary dreams. But Case moves through his visionary world at the price of real-world outlawry and terrible danger to his own brain.

Case, and later the eponymous Count Zero, serve the needs of corporate espionage and run the risks of all court pranksters in the powerful and ubiquitous corporate state; yet, at the same time, they experience a world of freedom, of travel through realms of gold. In one astounding sequence, for example, a jockey watches the unfolding, as in three-dimensional space, of a computer virus, an enormous gossamer invader gobbling up the jockey's cyberspace while wreaking havoc along the network of computerized data.

Case, Count Zero, their friends, and their counterparts in Gibson's story collection, *Burning Chrome*, are streetwise, battle-hardened, anti-establishment figures well-suited to carry the idealistic burdens of youthful readers in a world ominously coming to resemble the nihilistic, anti-utopian totalitarian "Sprawl" (Gibson's term) of overpopulation, violence, drugs, and decadence of our late 20th-century urban wilderness. The literature of such a world has been dubbed cyberpunk by academic critics needing such labels to communicate among themselves as they grope toward understanding of a weltanschauung radically different from the optimistic picture of the mechanized future of writers like Isaac Asimov and Arthur C. Clarke. This new world-picture owes much to the fiction of Philip K. Dick, especially his stylish novel *Do Androids Dream of Electric Sheep?*

Gibson himself has repudiated the label cyberpunk. Despite the scratching and biting necessitated by their hardscrabble existence, his characters have not sold out all human emotion to become part of the steel and silicon conglomerate, the great, buzzing "Sprawl" against which generations of rebels shake an angry fist. The cyberpunk protagonists largely dispense with anger as useless and counter-productive; and their attempts to carve a niche in their clockwork environment must be viewed finally as heroic, a testament of enduring human courage.

In *Mona Lisa Overdrive*, Gibson features two young female antagonists, one of whom can enter cyberspace without need of a cyberspace deck. He includes the infamous Japanese Yakuza in this novel.

In all his fiction, Gibson acknowledges his devotion and his debt to William S. Burroughs, and *Naked Lunch* should perhaps be read as pre-requisite to any encounter with Gibson's fiction. Recently Gibson and Bruce Sterling have collaborated to produce *The Difference Engine*, an alternative-world novel set in 1855 and treating the origins of computer technology.

Lately, cybernetic fiction has seen a flourishing of new applications and adaptations. Alex Effinger's *Budayeen of When Gravity Fails*, prose poems like Tom Maddox's short story "Snake Eyes," and Japanese graphic novels (and films like Akira made from them) bear testimony to the genre's fruitful exploration of significant *fin-de-siecle* themes and concepts. Whether punks or saints, Gibson's progeny can be expected to lead our exploration for some time to come.

—Thomas P. Dunn

---

**GIESY, J(ohn) U(lrich).** Also wrote as Charles Dustin. American. Born in Ohio, 6 August 1877. Physician and physiotherapist. Writer for Munsey magazines. *Died 8 September 1947.*

SCIENCE-FICTION PUBLICATIONS

Novels (series: Palos)

*All for His Country.* New York, Macaulay, 1915.
*Palos of the Dog Star Pack.* New York, Avalon, 1965.
*The Mouthpiece of Zitu* (Palos). New York, Avalon, 1965.
*Jason, Son of Jason* (Palos). New York, Avalon, 1966.

Uncollected Short Stories

"Indigestible Dog Biscuits," in *All-Story Weekly* (New York), 13 July 1918.
"Zapt's Repulsive Paste," in *All-Story Weekly* (New York), 29 November 1919.
"Blind Man's Buff," in *All-Story Weekly* (New York), 24 January 1920.
"Beyond the Violet," in *Argosy All-Story Weekly* (New York), 27 November 1920.
"Catalepsy," in *Argosy All-Story Weekly* (New York), 19 March 1921.
"The Acumen of Martin McVeagh," in *Argosy All-Story Weekly* (New York), 7 July 1923.

Uncollected Short Stories with Junius B. Smith

"Great Wizard of the Peak," in *Cavalier* (New York), January 1910.
"In 2112," in *Cavalier* (New York), 10 August 1912.
"The Curse of Quetzal," in *All-Story Cavalier Weekly* (New York), 28 November 1914.
"The Web of Destiny," in *Argosy All-Story Weekly* (New York), 20 March 1915.
"Snared," in *All-Story Weekly* (New York), 11 December 1915.
"Box 991," in *All-Story Weekly* (New York), 3 June 1916.
"The Killer," in *All-Story Weekly* (New York), 7 April 1917.
"The Unknown Quantity," in *All-Story Weekly* (New York), 25 August 1917.
"The Black Butterfly," in *All-Story Weekly* (New York), 14 September 1918.
"Stars of Evil," in *All-Story Weekly* (New York), 25 January 1919.
"The Ivory Pipe," in *All-Story Weekly* (New York), 20 September 1919.
"House of the Hundred Lights," in *All-Story Weekly* (New York), 22 May 1920.
"Black and White," in *Argosy All-Story Weekly* (New York), 2 October 1920.
"Wolf of Erlik," in *Argosy All-Story Weekly* (New York), 22 October 1921.
"The Opposing Venus," in *Argosy All-Story Weekly* (New York), 18 November 1923.
"Poor Little Pigeon," in *Argosy All-Story Weekly* (New York), 9 August 1924.
"The Wooly Dog," in *Argosy All-Story Weekly* (New York), 23 March 1929.
"The Green Goddess," in *Argosy* (New York), 21 January 1931.
"The Ledger of Life," in *Argosy* (New York), 20 June 1934.
"The Gravity Experiment," in *Famous Fantastic Mysteries* (New York), December 1939.

OTHER PUBLICATIONS

Novels

*The Other Woman*, with Octavus Roy Cohen. New York, Macaulay, 1917; London, Gardner, 1920.
*Mimi*. New York, Harper, 1918.
*The Valley of Suspicion*. New York, Garden City Publishing Company, 1927.
*The Mystery Woman*, with Junius B. Smith. Racine, Wisconsin, Whitman, 1929.

Novels as Charles Dustin

*Hardboiled Tenderfoot*. New York, Dodge, 1939.
*Bronco Men*. New York, Dodge, 1940.
*Riders of the Desert Trail*. New York, Dodge, 1942.

* * *

J.U. Giesy wrote his earliest works in collaboration with Junius B. Smith, a series of humorous detective mysteries featuring a detective, Semi-Dual, who used astrology, crystal balls, and psychic phenomena in solving his cases. Giesy himself also wrote a number of stories based on humorous and improbable inventions.

Giesy's best known and most admired novels are the Palos trilogy. In *Palos of the Dog Star Pack* Jason Croft is transported by a process the author calls astral projection to Palos, a planet in the Sirius system, where he is able to assume and occupy the body of a dying man. Croft brings to Palos a wide knowledge of earthly sciences, including the weapons of war, a great asset in his progress toward a position of influence and power on this new world. In *The Mouthpiece of Zitu* Croft is required to convince the people of Palos and the princess Naia that he is mortal and a fit mate for her. In the course of these efforts Croft introduces electricity to Palos, as well as the locomotive and the airplane. These developments, needless to say, enhance his position with the natives and with the princess. *Jason, Son of Jason* carries the story on to the next generation.

Giesy's stories are well written and well plotted, with considerable descriptive power and character analysis. His literary style and his means of transporting his hero from earth to another planet show the influence of Burroughs. With both authors, the animal life of these strange worlds is indeed strange, with unearthly flying creatures and gigantic multi-limbed animals. There is always, however, a group of females built to Terran specifications, who are almost invariably beautiful, lightly clad, and amorous.

—Douglas E. Way

---

**GILLILAND, Alexis A(rnaldus).** American. Born in Bangor, Maine, 10 May 1931. Educated at Purdue University, West Lafayette, Indiana, B.S. 1953; George Washington University, Washington, D.C., M.S. 1963. Served in the United States Army Presidential Honor Guard, 1954–56. Married Dorothea Cohle in 1959; one son. Thermochemist, National Bureau of Standards, 1956–67, and chemist and specification writer, Federal Supply Service, 1967–82, both in Washington, D.C. Since 1982, freelance writer. Also a cartoonist. Recipient: Hugo award, for art, 1980, 1983, 1984, 1985; John W. Campbell award, 1982. Address: 4030 Eighth Street South, Arlington, Virginia 22204, U.S.A.

SCIENCE-FICTION PUBLICATIONS

Novels (series: Rosinante)

*The Revolution from Rosinante*. New York, Ballantine, 1981.
*Long Shot for Rosinante*. New York, Ballantine, 1981.
*The Pirates of Rosinante*. New York, Ballantine, 1982.
*The End of the Empire*. New York, Ballantine, 1983.
*Wizenbeak* (illustrated by Tim Kirk). New York, Bluejay, 1986.
*The Shadow Shaia*. New York, Ballantine, 1990.

OTHER PUBLICATIONS

Other (cartoons)

*The Iron Law of Bureaucracy*. Port Townsend, Washington, Loompanics, 1979.
*Who Says Paranoia Isn't "In" Anymore*. Port Townsend, Washington, Loompanics, 1985.

*The Waltzing Wizard.* Mercer Island, Washington, Starmont House, 1989.

* * *

The Campbell award-winner Alexis A. Gilliland exemplifies the basic literary principle "write what you know." Gilliland, a retired federal bureaucrat, exposes the inner workings of authority with an accuracy and detail science fiction has hitherto only pretended to achieve. He has written what may be SF's first "consciously thematic" as opposed to propagandistic stories about bureaucracy. (Compare Keith Laumer's polemical farces about Terran diplomacy which are also based on personal experience).

Instead of merely denouncing administrative sclerosis, Gilliland establishes it through form as well as content. His storytelling technique employs both alternating and redundant viewpoints assembled like overlapping transparencies to create composite figures no single sheet can hold. Data-handling and decision-making processes are actually shown but, just as in a real bureaucracy, words outnumber deeds. Slick, witty, pun-laced dialogue carries the plot.

Gilliland's plausible technology reflects his initial scientific training. He is careful to show exactly how his characters are fed, clothed, and housed. This concreteness anchors outrageous events to some semblance of reality. Off-beat humor penetrates even the sex, slaughter, and metaphysics, for Gilliland is also a gifted cartoonist. (He has won three Hugo awards as Best Fan Artist and has published three cartoon books.)

Gilliland's writing career opened with the Rosinante trilogy. Here, under the leadership of a maverick bureaucrat, a space colony wins its independence from the despotic North American Union and topples terrestrial powers. But the real winners prove to be the revolutionaries' computers, intelligent mechanisms who wear the images of 20th-century movie stars. One computer proclaims itself the prophet of a new spacefaring religion while another evangelizes humans on its behalf to establish a symbiotic society of machines and men.

*The End of the Empire* is a more conventional narrative with a more radical message. It dares to criticize libertarianism, a political system favored by Robert A. Heinlein and other SF writers. Gilliland shows how too little government can be every bit as disastrous as too much government. (For example, tyrannical anarchy defines subversion as attempting to "under-raise" the regime.) The hero is a brilliant loner loyal to a moribund empire which he can be expected to revive single-handedly in future adventures. Among the hero's obvious prototypes are Poul Anderson's Flandry and Keith Laumer's Retief, gallant guardians to whom this book is dedicated.

Gilliland moved from political science fiction to political fantasy in his trilogy *Wizenbeak*, *The Shadow Shaia*, and the forthcoming *Lord of the Troll-Bats*. He brings the same skills for skewering governmental idiocy to a magical world that incorporates early modern witch-hunting, Japanese sword-fighting, and an Eastern Mediterranean cultural milieu. The results are darker than Gilliland's previous books and bear some resemblance to Avram Davidson's Dr. Esterhazy stories.

A gift for finding curious angles in prosaic realities is the foundation of Gilliland's SF career. "It is my fond belief," says the author, "that my novels bear thinking about, and that this may give the reader some insight into the real world, but this is an *ex post facto* rationalization to justify having written."

—Sandra Miesel

---

**GILMAN, Charlotte (Anna) Perkins (Stetson).** American. Born in Hartford, Connecticut, 3 July 1860. Married 1) Walter Stetson in 1884 (divorced), one daughter; 2) George Houghton Gilman in 1900. *Died 17 August 1935.*

## Science-Fiction Publications

### Novel

*Herland.* New York, Pantheon, and London, Women's Press, 1979.

## Other Publications

### Novels

*The Yellow Wallpaper* (novella). Boston, Small Maynard, 1899.
*What Diantha Did.* New York, Charlton, 1910; London, T.F. Unwin, 1912.
*The Crux.* New York, Charlton, 1911.
*Moving the Mountain.* New York, Charlton, 1911.

### Verse

*In This Our World.* Oakland, California, McCombs and Vaughan, 1893; London, T.F. Unwin, 1895.
*Suffrage Songs and Verses.* New York, Charlton, 1911.

### Other

*A Clarion Call to Redeem the Race!* Mt. Lebanon, New York, The Shaker Press, 1890.
*Women and Economics.* Boston, Small Maynard, 1898; London, Putnam, 1905.
*Concerning Children.* Boston, Small Maynard, 1900; London, Putnam, 1901.
*The Home, Its Work and Influence.* New York, McClure Phillips, 1903; London, Heinemann, 1904.
*Human Work.* New York, McClure Phillips, 1904.
*The Punishment that Educates.* Cooperstown, New York, Crist Scott, 1907.
*The Man-Made World; or, Our Androcentric Culture.* New York, Charlton, and London, T.F. Unwin, 1911.
*His Religion and Hers: A Study of the Faith of Our Fathers and the Work of Our Mothers.* New York and London, Century, 1923.
*The Living of Charlotte Perkins Gilman* (autobiography). New York, Appleton-Century, 1935.

*

Critical Study: *Charlotte Perkins Gilman: The Woman and Her Work* by Sheryl L. Meyering, Ann Arbor, Michigan, UMI Research Press, 1989.

* * *

Written in 1915, *Herland* was first published serially in Gilman's own monthly magazine *The Forerunner*, every line of which she wrote herself, including the advertisements. It was the second and clearly the best of the three utopian novels Gilman wrote in an effort to convince the masses that her feminist-socialist vision of society was both viable and appealing. It was also the only one of the three to be published separately.

Gilman situates the world of *Herland* on a "spur" of land "up where the maps had to be made," where the all-female inhabitants have been able to create a utopia *because* of the absence of men. The story is narrated by a male, Vandyck Jennings, one of three stereotypically under-evolved American men who stumble into this no man's land, each with his own predictable reaction to a community that neither needs nor desires a masculine intrusion. Jennings himself symbolizes the rational, intellectual, educated man who early in the novel states matter-of-factly, "This is a *civilized* country. . . . There must be men." His friend Terry Nicholson represents the oversexed, macho, ravisher of women who assumes that eventually the women of Herland will succumb to their "natural" sexual attraction to forceful, dominant men. Terry's polar opposite in temperament, but not in his capacity to accept insulting clichés about women, is Jeff Margrave, who idealizes women "in the best Southern style, . . . full of chivalry and sentiment, and all that."

The utopian nature of Herland is brought increasingly into focus as the men are made to face the wrongheadedness of their own assumptions about a country full of only women. These women do not quarrel among themselves; their country is not chaotic, but civilized in the extreme—"Everything [is] beauty, order, perfect cleanness, [with] the pleasantest sense of home over it all. . . . [There is] no dirt . . . no smoke . . . no noise." The women reproduce through parthenogenesis, are not attracted to aggression, and do not confuse aggression with strength. Further, the men are forced to admit that the women of Herland are attractive, despite the fact that they do not fit the traditional, male-defined image of female beauty. Their hair is very short; their clothes are uniform and neither clinging nor revealing; their bodies are straight and vigorous, but not, in male terms, sexually alluring. Besides, these women have absolutely no sexual interest in the men, a reality that is perhaps the most distressing of all to the three Americans.

The Herlanders' religion—Maternal Pantheism—derives from a central myth of "one family, all descended from one mother." The power of mother-love defines their relationships to one another and to the earth, which is no longer perceived as an adversary to have dominion over as in the patriarchal Judeo-Christian tradition as described to the Herlanders by Vandyck Jennings, much to the women's horror. Instead, they identify *Mother*- earth not as an *other*, but as *another*, whose progenitive power resembles their own and is revered in much the same way. This view of motherhood was as foreign to the three men as was everything else in Herland, especially to Terry, whose "idea of motherliness was the usual one, involving a baby in arms . . . and the complete absorption of the mother in said baby. . . . A motherliness which dominated society, which influenced every art and industry, which absolutely protected all childhood, and gave to it the most perfect care and training, did not seem motherly."

Narrator Jennings begins to see that without the tradition of God the Father to bolster it, the "tradition of men as guardians and protectors had quite died out. [There were] no men to fear and therefore no need of protection." Violence is a fact of life only where there are men. These women "had had no wars. They had had no kings, and no priests, and no aristocracies. They were sisters, and as they grew, they grew together—not by competition, but by united action." When over-population became a problem, they confronted it, "not by a 'struggle for existence' which would result in an everlasting writhing mass of underbred people trying to get ahead of one another. . . . Neither did they start off on predatory excursions to get more land from somebody else. . . . Not at all. They sat down in council together and thought it out. . . . They said: 'With our best endeavors this country will support about so many people. . . . That is all the people we will make.' "

As Jennings is compelled to discard his stereotypes one by one, he experiences a kind of conversion and is led "to the conviction that those 'feminine charms' we are so fond of are not feminine at all, but mere reflected masculinity—developed to please us because they had to please us, and in no way essential to the real fulfillment of their great process." Both Jennings and Jeff Margrave slowly come to acknowledge the obvious: the absence of patriarchy has produced only positive results; the more they learn about this matriarchal community, the more despicable their patriarchal one seems by contrast. Of the three, only Terry refuses to relinquish the male warrior tradition with its aggression, dominance, and violence. After he commits what amounts to marital rape, he is banished forever from Herland. With the transformation of the other two, however, Gilman seems to suggest that most, if not all, men are, at least, redeemable.

—Sheryl L. Meyering

---

**GILMAN, Robert Cham.** *See* **COPPEL, Alfred.**

---

**GILMORE, Anthony.** *See* **BATES, Harry.**

---

**GLAMIS, Walter.** *See* **SCHACHNER, Nat.**

---

**GLOAG, John (Edwards).** British. Born in London, 10 August 1896. Attended technical high school, London. Served in the Essex Regiment, 1916–17, and Welch Guards, 1917–19; 2nd Lieutenant; invalided home, 1918. Married Gertrude Mary Ward in 1922; one daughter, and one son, the writer Julian Gloag. Worked in studio of Thornton-Smith Ltd., 1913–16; advertising department staff member, Lever Organisation, 1920–22; art editor, 1922–27, and editor, 1927, *Cabinet Maker;* director, Pritchard Wood & Partners, 1928–61; director of public relations, Timber Development Association, 1936–38; full-time writer after 1961. Member, Advisory Committee, Board of Trade, 1943–47; member of Board of Trustees, Sir John Soane's

Museum, 1960–70. Vice-president, Royal Society of Arts, 1952–54; president, Society of Architectural Historians, 1960–64. Recipient: Royal Society of Arts silver medal, 1943, and bicentenary gold medal, 1958. *Died 17 July 1981.*

SCIENCE-FICTION PUBLICATIONS

Novels

*To-morrow's Yesterday.* London , Allen and Unwin, 1932.
*The New Pleasure.* London, Allen and Unwin, 1933.
*Winter's Youth.* London, Allen and Unwin, 1934.
*Manna.* London, Cassell, 1940.
*99%.* London, Cassell, 1944.

Short Stories

*First One and Twenty.* London, Allen and Unwin, 1946.

OTHER PUBLICATIONS

Novels

*Sweet Racket.* London, Cassell, 1936.
*Ripe for Development.* London, Cassell, 1936.
*Sacred Edifice.* London, Cassell, 1937; revised edition, 1954.
*Documents Marked Secret.* London, Cassell, 1938.
*Unwilling Adventurer.* London, Cassell, 1940.
*I Want an Audience.* London, Cassell, 1941.
*Mr. Buckby Is Not at Home.* London, Cassell, 1942.
*In Camera.* London, Cassell, 1945.
*Kind Uncle Buckby.* London, Cassell, 1946.
*All England at Home.* London, Cassell, 1949.
*Not in the Newspapers.* London, Cassell, 1953.
*Slow.* London, Cassell, 1954.
*Unlawful Justice.* London, Cassell, 1962.
*Rising Suns.* London, Cassell, 1964.
*Caesar of the Narrow Seas.* London, Cassell, 1969; New York, St. Martin's Press, 1972.
*The Eagles Depart.* New York, St. Martin's Press, 1973.
*Artorius Rex.* London, Cassell, and New York, St. Martin's Press, 1977.

Short Stories

*It Makes a Nice Change.* London, Nicholson and Watson, 1938.
*Take One a Week: An Omnibus Volume of 52 Short Stories.* London, Chantry, 1950.

Verse

*Board Room Ballads and Other Verses.* London, Allen and Unwin, 1933.

Other

*Simple Furnishing and Arrangement,* with Helen Gloag. London, Duckworth, 1921.
*Simple Schemes for Decoration.* London, Duckworth, and New York, Stokes, 1922.
*The House We Ought to Live In,* with Leslie Mansfield. London, Duckworth, 1923.
*Colour and Comfort.* London, Duckworth, 1924; New York, Stokes, 1925.
*Time, Taste, and Furniture.* London, Richards, and New York, Stokes, 1925.
*Artifex; or, The Future of Craftsmanship.* London, Kegan Paul, and New York, Dutton, 1926.
*Home Life in History: Social Life and Manners in Britain 200 B.C.–A.D. 1926,* with C. Thompson Walker. London, Benn, 1927; New York, Coward McCann, 1928.
*Modern Home Furnishing.* London, Macmillan, 1929.
*Men and Buildings.* London, Country Life, and New York, Scribner, 1931; revised edition, London, Chantry, 1950.
*English Furniture.* London, A. and C. Black, 1934; 6th edition, 1973.
*Industrial Art Explained.* London, Allen and Unwin, 1934; revised edition, 1946.
*Word Warfare: Some Aspects of German Propaganda and English Liberty.* London, Nicholson and Watson, 1939.
*The American Nation: A Short History of the United States.* London, Cassell, 1942; revised edition, with Julian Gloag, 1955.
*What about Business?* London, Penguin, 1942; revised edition, as *What about Enterprise?*, London, Allen and Unwin, 1948.
*The Missing Technician in Industrial Production.* London, Allen and Unwin, 1944.
*The Englishman's Castle: A History of Homes, Large and Small, in Town and Country, from A.D. 100 to the Present Day.* London, Eyre and Spottiswoode, 1944; revised edition, 1949.
*Plastics and Industrial Design.* London, Allen and Unwin, 1945.
*British Furniture Makers.* London, Collins, and New York, Hastings House, 1945.
*House Out of Factory,* with Grey Wornum. London, Allen and Unwin, 1946.
*Good Design, Good Business.* London, His Majesty's Stationery Office, 1947.
*The English Tradition in Design.* London, Penguin, 1947; revised edition, London A. and C. Black, 1959; New York, Macmillan, 1960.
*Self-Training for Industrial Designers.* London, Allen and Unwin, 1948.
*A History of Cast Iron in Architecture,* with D.L. Bridgewater. London, Allen and Unwin, 1948.
*How to Write Technical Books.* London, Allen and Unwin, 1950.
*Two Thousand Years of England.* London, Cassell, 1952.
*A Short Dictionary of Furniture.* London, Allen and Unwin, and New York, Studio, 1952; revised edition, 1969.
*Georgian Grace: A Social History of Design from 1660 to 1830.* London, A. and C. Black, and New York, Macmillan, 1956.
*Guide to Western Architecture.* London, Allen and Unwin, and New York, Grove Press, 1958.
*Advertising in Modern Life.* London, Heinemann, 1959.
*Victorian Comfort: A Social History of Design 1830–1900.* London, A. and C. Black, and New York, Macmillan, 1961.
*Victorian Taste: Some Social Aspects of Architecture and Industrial Design from 1820–1900.* London, A. and C. Black, and New York, Macmillan, 1962.
*The English Tradition in Architecture.* London, A. and C. Black, and New York, Barnes and Noble, 1963.
*Architecture.* London, Cassell, 1963; New York, Hawthorn, 1964.
*The Englishman's Chair: Origins, Design, and Social History of Seat Furniture in England.* London, Allen and Unwin, 1964; as *The Chair,* South Brunswick, New Jersey, A.S. Barnes, 1967.
*Enjoying Architecture.* Newcastle upon Tyne, Oriel Press, 1965.

*A Social History of Furniture Design from* B.C. *1300 to* A.D. *1960.* London, Cassell, and New York, Crown, 1966.
*Mr. Loudon's England: The Life and Work of John Claudius Loudon, and His Influence on Architecture and Furniture Design.* Newcastle upon Tyne, Oriel Press, 1970.
*Guide to Furniture Styles: English and French 1450–1850.* London, A. and C. Black, and New York, Scribner, 1972.
*The Architectural Interpretation of History.* London, A. and C. Black, 1975.

Editor, *Design in Modern Life.* London, Allen and Unwin, 1934.
Editor, *The Place of Glass in Building.* London, Allen and Unwin, 1943; revised edition, 1948.
Editor, *Introduction to Early English Decorative Detail.* London, Academy, 1965.

* * *

In a writing career spanning more than 50 years John Gloag published more than 60 books. These include works dealing with history, social history, architecture, propaganda, and industrial art as well as numerous short stories, mysteries, mainstream novels, and science fiction. The science fiction, written mostly in the 1930's and 1940's, is more closely related to the fiction of Huxley, Stepledon and Beresford than to the products of the burgeoning science-fiction magazine market of that period.

The short stories often deal with unexplainable phenomena and science-fiction concepts, but the brevity of the form does not allow Gloag fully to explore the ramifications of his ideas.

*To-morrow's Yesterday*, Gloag's first extended foray into science fiction, uses the complicated device of a motion picture within the novel. The motion picture is represented as an attempt by the species which has succeeded man to understand the forces within humanity that led to its extinction. The creatures from the future examine the contemporary, 1930 situation, and conclude that "They all lived for themselves!" The creatures then travel back in time to view a conversation between Herod and Pilate and they remark "There have been great ones who could see and teach and plan . . . But . . . with them everything ended in words." Subsequent scenes in the film show the beginning of the war which leads to man's descent into barbarism, and several stages in man's reversion to animality. The concluding portion of the book depicts the public's reaction to the film and allows Gloag to comment bitterly on the worlds of advertising, newspaper publishing, and to show that the world is following the path outlined in the film.

In *Winter's Youth* Gloag examines the political and social consequences of a process that arrests and reverses aging. Peripheral to the main plot, but lending verisimilitude to the action, are the concepts of radiant inflammatol (the deadliest of all explosives which makes war impossible), government advertising in newspapers, a faked new apocryphal book of the Bible, German pagan religion, and a new British political party. Much of the action concerns the political manoeuvring which arises because of the disclosure of the faked apocrypha and the consequences that the age-arresting process has on the users and on the general public. Gloag creates a scathing portrait of political partisanship, but he again attacks journalism and the advertising industry.

*99%* explores the effects on a number of men, who represent various aspects of society, of a drug which allows the individual to re-experience a significant event in the life of one of his ancestors. The motivating concept, that it is possible to relive important experiences of remote ancestors, because the memories are somehow incorporated into the genetic material, is one that has no scientific validity, but Gloag is not interested in the concept. He is concerned with the effects that the experiences have upon modern, civilized men. The experiences dredged up, both by the drug and by the influence of the man supplying the drug, range from that of a waylaid, failed Crusader, to that of a young boy fleeing the sack of Carthage, to that of a shaman of a tribe that existed millennia ago. The memories change the outlooks of the contemporary men in ways that could not have been anticipated.

—Harvey J. Satty

---

**GODFREY, R.H.** *See* **TUBB, E.C.**

---

**GODWIN, Tom.** American. Born in 1915. Worked as a prospector.

SCIENCE-FICTION PUBLICATIONS

Novels

*The Survivors.* New York, Gnome Press, 1958; as *Space Prison*, New York, Pyramid, 1960.
*The Space Barbarians.* New York, Pyramid, 1964.
*Beyond Another Sun.* New York, Curtis, 1971.

Uncollected Short Stories

"The Gulf Between," in *Astounding* (New York), October 1953.
"No Species Alone," in *Universe* (Evanston, Illinois), November 1954.
"The Cold Equations," in *The Best Science Fiction Stories and Novels 1955*, edited by T.E. Dikty. New York, Fell, 1955.
"The Barbarians," in *If* (New York), December 1955.
"You Created Us," in *The Best Science Fiction Stories and Novels 1956*, edited by T.E. Dikty, New York, Fell, 1956.
"Operation Opera," in *Fantasy and Science Fiction* (New York), April 1956.
"Brain Teaser," in *If* (New York), October 1956.
"The Harvest," in *Venture* (Concord, New Hampshire), July 1957.
"The Nothing Equation," in *Amazing* (New York), December 1957.
"The Last Victory," in *The Best Science Fiction Stories and Novels 9*, edited by T.E. Dikty. Chicago, Advent, 1958.
"The Wild Ones," in *Original Science Fiction Stories* (Holyoke, Massachusetts), January 1958.
"My Brother—The Ape," in *Amazing* (New York), January 1958.
"Cry from a Far Planet," in *Amazing* (New York), September 1958.
"A Place Beyond the Stars," in *Super Science Fiction* (New York), February 1959.
"Empathy," in *Fantastic* (New York), October 1959.
"The Helpful Hand of God," in *Analog* (New York), December 1961.
". . . and Devious the Line of Duty," in *Analog* (New York), December 1962.
"The Greater Thing," in *More Penguin Science Fiction*, edited by Brian Aldiss. London, Penguin, 1963.

"Mother of Invention," in *Spectrum 5*, edited by Kingsley Amis and Robert Conquest. London, Gollancz, 1966; New York, Harcourt Brace, 1967.
"The Gentle Captive," in *Signs and Wonders*, edited by Roger Elwood. Old Tappan, New Jersey, Revell, 1972.
"We'll Walk Again in the Moonlight," in *Crisis*, edited by Roger Elwood. Nashville, Nelson, 1974.
"The Steel Guardian," in *Antaeus* (New York), Spring 1977.
"Before Willows Ever Walked," in *Fantasy and Science Fiction* (New York), March 1980.
"Too Soon to Die," in *Space Wars*, edited by Charles G. Waugh and Martin H. Greenberg. New York, Tor, 1988.

* * *

"The Cold Equations" is the story for which Tom Godwin is best known and upon which rests his secure place in the history of science fiction. It is entirely fitting that it was first published in John Campbell's *Astounding Science Fiction* because, although written slightly after the period of Campbell's domination of the genre magazines and, therefore, the genre itself, the story is the prototypic Campbellian story, at once a prime example of golden-age science fiction and a definer of it. James Gunn, in *The Road to Science Fiction 3*, called "The Cold Equations" a touchstone story.

"The Cold Equations" presents a future in which space travel has become developed enough for mankind to begin the process of colonizing some of the other habitable planets. But this is only the beginning of the great age of colonization. Fuel still needs to be exactly measured and at every turn the universe threatens human life. Godwin makes clear, however, that these threats are not the creations of a hostile universe for the specific destruction of humanity. These threats originate within the nature of the universe, and all objects, living or not, that inhabit that universe must live under their sway. Thus, early in the story, Godwin presents his reader with a view of space that parallels the view of the frontier held by early American pioneers.

In "The Cold Equations," a space colony is suffering from a disease for which there is a serum, and a small ship is sent to rescue the colonists. The ship has sufficient fuel to carry the pilot and his cargo to the stricken colony and not a drop more. However, a girl has stowed away on the ship with the hope of once again seeing her brother who is one of the colonists. Within this simple plot Godwin develops the most popular of Campbell's themes: ignorance kills. Whether man is challenged by a creation of science, an alien invasion, or a new environment, what will most surely destroy the race is not the challenge but a failure to know the nature of that challenge. The girl did not realize the consequences of her actions, but at the end of the story she must be jettisoned. The universe is not sentimental. While it will make no special effort to kill a human being, it will do nothing to save one, either. Nothing Godwin has written since has equalled this one story.

In *The Survivors* a race of aliens maroon some 4,000 humans on a hostile planet barely capable of sustaining human life. But the humans do adapt and later return to destroy the aliens who were once their conquerors. Mankind will prevail, Godwin tells the reader, for the race has the intelligence, desire, and energy to survive all threats. *The Space Barbarians*, a sequel to *The Survivors*, continues this theme, though in a more space-opera manner. Godwin returns again to the pioneer nature of the human race in *Beyond Another Sun* in which alien anthropologists observe humans as they colonize a planet.

In each of the works that follow "The Cold Equations" many of the features that characterized that story can be seen: a clear narrative voice, simple descriptions that economically fill in the background needed to understand the action of the characters, themes that form the very foundation of golden-age science fiction, and occasional sentimental passages that, at their best, soften the harshness of the fictional worlds and, at their worst, detract from the effect Godwin is attempting to achieve. But "The Cold Equations" contains these traits in a way that few other science-fiction works have matched.

—Stephen H. Goldman

---

**GOLD, H(orace) L(eonard).** Born in Montreal, Canada, 26 April 1914; emigrated to the United States at age 2. Served as a combat engineer in the Pacific, 1944–46. Married 1) Evelyn Stein in 1939; 2) Muriel Conley; one son and three stepchildren. Assistant editor, *Thrilling Wonder Stories, Startling Stories*, and *Captain Future*, and associate editor, Standard Magazines, New York, 1939–41; managing and contributing editor, Scoop Publications, New York, 1941–43; editor, A and S Comics, New York, 1942–44; contract writer, Molle Mystery Theatre, 1943–44; president, Rossard Company, New York, 1946–50; editor, *Galaxy*, and Galaxy Science Fiction Novels, New York, 1950–61; editor, *Beyond Fantasy Fiction*, 1953–55, and *If*, 1959–61: retired as disabled veteran, 1960. Recipient: Hugo award, for non-fiction, 1953; Westercon Life Achievement award, 1975; Milford award, 1987. Address: 1253 North Havenhurst, Apartment 116, Los Angeles, California 90046, U.S.A.

### Science-Fiction Publications

#### Short Stories

*The Old Die Rich and Other Science Fiction Stories.* New York, Crown, 1955; London Dobson, 1965.

#### Uncollected Short Stories

"The Transmogrification of Wamba's Revenge," in *Galaxy* (New York), October 1967.
"The Riches of Embarrassment," in *Galaxy* (New York), April 1968.
"The Villains from Vega IV," with E.J. Gold, in *Galaxy* (New York), October 1968.
"That's the Spirit," in *Amazing* (New York), March 1975.
"Warm Dark Places," in *More Wandering Stars*, edited by Jack Dann. New York, Doubleday, 1981.
"No Charge for Alterations," in *Amazing Stories: Visions of Other Worlds*, edited by Martin H. Greenberg. Lake Geneva, Wisconsin, TSR, 1986.
"A Matter of Form," in *The Mammoth Book of Classic Science Fiction: Short Novels of the 1930s*, edited by Isaac Asimov, Charles G. Waugh, and Martin H. Greenberg. New York, Carroll and Graf, 1988.

### Other Publications

#### Other

*What Will They Think of Last?* Crestling, California, Institute for the Development of the Harmonious Human Being, 1976.

Editor, *Galaxy Reader* [and *Second to Sixth*]. New York, Crown, 2 vols., 1952–54; New York, Doubleday, 4 vols., 1958–62; selection from *The Second Galaxy Reader* as *The Galaxy Science Fiction Omnibus*, London, Grayson, 1955.
Editor, *Five Galaxy Short Novels*. New York, Doubleday, 1958.
Editor, *The World That Couldn't Be and 8 Other Novelets from Galaxy*. New York, Doubleday, 1959.
Editor, *Bodyguard and Four Other Short Novels from Galaxy*. New York, Doubleday, 1960.
Editor, *Mind Partner and Eight Other Novelets from Galaxy*. New York, Doubleday, 1961.
Editor, *The Weird Ones*. New York, Belmont, 1962; London, Dobson, 1965.

*

H.L. Gold comments (1985):

I would very much like to be rediscovered as a science-fiction and fantasy author (including work since 1955), but I'm overshadowed as editor.

* * *

About half a dozen editors and publishers have had a truly pervasive effect on the development of science fiction. Some of these are well remembered; others, almost wholly forgotten. The list must include Frank A. Munsey, who virtually invented the pulp magazine in 1896, Farnsworth Wright (*Weird Tales*), Hugo Gernsback (*Amazing Stories*), John W. Campbell, Jr. (*Astounding*), Anthony Boucher and J. Francis McComas (*The Magazine of Fantasy and Science Fiction*), and H.L. Gold. After many years of editorial work, in 1950 Gold became the founding editor of *Galaxy Science Fiction*. The importance of this event cannot be overemphasized. For some 20 years prior to 1950, *Astounding* had paid the highest rates in the science fiction field, had enjoyed the backing of the largest, wealthiest, and most influential publishing house, and had maintained by far the largest circulation. As a consequence, the bulk of quality writing in the field was calculated to reach *Astounding*. Even the lesser magazines, because they tended to subsist on the leavings of *Astounding*, also reflected the taste of *Astounding's* editors. With the almost simultaneous founding of *Fantasy and Science Fiction* and *Galaxy*, two new markets opened which paid competitive rates and offered generally equivalent quality of presentation and prestige. *F & SF* emphasized style, wit, and general literary excellence. *Galaxy*, reflecting Gold's world-view, placed heavy emphasis on social satire, combining relevance of theme with irreverence of outlook. The result was a magnificent flowering of novels and short stories by Pohl and Kornbluth, Simak, Asimov, Bradbury, Heinlein, and scores of others.

Gold's own writing has been of limited quantity and impact, although it is far from worthless. His only novel, *None But Lucifer*, was written in collaboration with L. Sprague de Camp for *Unknown* magazine in 1939, and has never been reprinted. Of Gold's scattered short stories, a dozen were gathered in *The Old Die Rich*. As might be expected, the stories reflect considerable, often acid, wit. The title story of the book concerns a complex scheme of time travel and murder, unravelled through careful, formal detection techniques. "Love in the Dark" deals lightly with the succubus theme, brought up-to-date and converted into a tale of contact with aliens. "Trouble with Water," probably Gold's best-remembered story, is a fantasy concerning a small businessman who offends a water elemental. A number of other stories in the book, particularly "The Man with English" and "Problem in Murder," hold up well despite their age. Particularly interesting in the book is Gold's page of notes on each story, detailing his original conception, technical problems, and writing approach to that project.

Also of interest is *What Will They Think of Last?*, a collection of Gold's editorials from *Galaxy*. Some of the editorials reflect ephemeral concerns, but others are most illuminating on the functioning of *Galaxy* during the Gold era.

—Richard A. Lupoff

---

**GOLDIN, Stephen.** American. Born in Philadelphia, Pennsylvania, 28 February 1947. Educated at the University of California, Los Angeles, B.A. in astronomy 1968. Married Kathleen McKinney (i.e., Kathleen Sky, *q.v.*), in 1962 (divorced 1982). Physicist, Navy Space Systems Activity, El Segundo, California, 1968–71; manager, Circle K. Grocery Store, Rosemead, California, 1972; editor, Jaundice Press, Van Nuys, California, 1973–74; editor, San Francisco *Ball*, 1973–74, *SFWA Bulletin*, 1975–77, and *L-5 News*, 1981–83. Agent: Joseph Elder Agency, P.O. Box 298, Warwick, New York 10990. Address: 2709 Betten Court Lane, Apt. 36, Rancho Cordova, California 95670, U.S.A.

### SCIENCE-FICTION PUBLICATIONS

Novels (series: Jade Darcy; The Family d'Alembert; The Parsina Saga)

*Herds*. Toronto, Laser, 1975.
*Caravan*. Toronto, Laser, 1975.
*Scavenger Hunt*. Toronto, Laser, 1975.
*Finish Line*. Toronto, Laser, 1976.
*The Imperial Stars* (d'Alembert). New York, Pyramid, and London, Panther, 1976.
*Strangler's Moon* (d'Alembert). New York, Pyramid, 1976; London, Panther, 1977.
*The Clockwork Traitor* (d'Alembert). New York, Pyramid, 1976; London, Panther, 1978.
*Assault on the Gods*. New York, Doubleday, 1977; London, Hale, 1978.
*Getaway World* (d'Alembert). New York, Pyramid, and London, Panther, 1977.
*Mindflight*. New York, Fawcett, 1978; London, Hamlyn, 1982.
*Appointment at Bloodstar* (d'Alembert). New York, Pyramid, 1978; as *The Bloodstar Conspiracy*, London, Panther, 1978.
*The Purity Plot* (d'Alembert). London, Panther, 1978; New York, Berkley, 1980.
*Trek to Madworld*. New York, Bantam, 1979.
*The Eternity Brigade*. New York, Fawcett, 1980.
*A World Called Solitude*. New York, Doubleday, 1981.
*And Not Make Dreams Your Master*. New York, Fawcett, 1981.
*Planet of Treachery* (d'Alembert). New York, Berkley, and London, Panther, 1982.
*Eclipsing Binaries* (d'Alembert). New York, Berkley, 1983; London, Panther, 1984.
*The Omicron Invasion* (d'Alembert). New York, Berkley, 1984.
*Revolt of the Galaxy* (d'Alembert). New York, Berkley, and London, Grafton, 1985.
*Jade Darcy and the Affair of Honor*, with Mary Mason. London, New English Library, 1988.
The Parsina Saga:
*Shrine of the Desert Mage*. New York, Bantam, 1988.
*The Storyteller and the Jann*. New York, Bantam, 1988.

*Crystals of Air and Water.* New York, Bantam, 1989.
*Jade Darcy and the Zen Pirates*, with Mary Mason. New York, Penguin, 1990.

OTHER PUBLICATIONS

Other

*The Business of Being a Writer*, with Kathleen Sky. New York, Harper, 1982.

Editor, with David Gerrold, *Protostars.* New York, Ballantine, 1971.
Editor, with David Gerrold, *Generation.* New York, Dell, 1972.
Editor, *The Alien Condition.* New York, Ballantine, 1973.
Editor, with David Gerrold, *Science Fiction Emphasis 1.* New York, Ballantine, 1974.
Editor, with David Gerrold, *Alternities.* New York, Dell, 1974.
Editor, with David Gerrold, *Ascents of Wonder.* New York, Popular Library, 1977.

*

Stephen Goldin comments:

Looking closely at my work might almost give one the impression that my short stories were written by someone entirely different than the author of my novels. This is due in part to the changes in myself, and in part of the nature of the works themselves.

With only a few exceptions, my short stories are downbeat and tragic. They were the product of my early career, a young man trying to impress the world with his cynicism and acceptance of the universe's perversity. In part, too, this is because a short story is like a photograph, an encapsulated moment of immense importance to the character(s) involved—and it seemed far easier for me to capture a tragic moment than a triumphant one. My mind was at its blackest in tragedies like "The Last Ghost," "Sweet Dreams, Melissa," "Of Love, Free Will, and Gray Squirrels on a Summer Evening," and "Xenophobe;" but there is a bleakness in even those stories with a primarily humorous slant: "The World Where Wishes Worked," "Stubborn," "Grim Fairy Tale," and "Constance and the Sex Machine."

My career (and my apparent outlook) did a complete turnabout when I switched to writing novels in the mid-1970's. Every single one of my novels has an upbeat ending. If a short story may be likened to a photograph, then a novel is a movie, the progression of a character through events, changing at least himself if not the world around him. I like to believe now that a person is responsible for his own life; even if the situation starts out looking hopeless and desperate, a firm and resourceful person can take charge of himself and turn the situation around. My characters may go through hell, but in the end they manage to triumph over their adversities. The somewhat more mature me doesn't need to hide behind that shield of cynicism. I've become a born-again optimist. If there is any message in my work at all, it's that no matter how bad things might be there is always a solution to the person willing to work for it.

* * *

Stephen Goldin has become one of the more reliable writers of science fiction and fantasy adventure during the past 15 years. His first novels were for the ill-fated Laser line, but he was able to move on to more established publishers. *Scavenger Hunt*, the best of his four Laser novels, deals with a brother and sister on an interstellar scavenger hunt, a social event that takes on more than casual significance as murder and mayhem are added to the competition. Goldin completed their quest for victory in the sequel, *Finish Line.*

*Herds* is set in a hippie commune, where a young woman has become telepathically linked to aliens. Her companions have been framed for murder by a local man, complicating this crisis in her life. The aliens are a herd culture, the ultimate communists, and the contrasts between them and the commune are fascinating. Goldin's fourth Laser novel is *Caravan*, an after-the-apocalypse story wherein a group of people flee across country to secret caverns where the first starship is under construction. An overused plot limps along to a satisfactory but unedifying conclusion.

A fugitive from the repressive government of Earth lives like a hermit in *A World Called Solitude*, until a castaway tells him of encroaching aliens and the urgent need to warn the homeworld. Initially, he is indisposed to help, but ultimately, species loyalty prevails and he uses the technology of an extinct race to foil the intruders. *Assault on the Gods* features a primitive planet dominated by a secret computer complex that functions as a god. Adventurers set off on a quest to free the natives from this mental domination.

One of Goldin's best novels is *Mindflight.* Telepaths fall prey to telepause, a period of increased telepathic ability that shortly precedes death. The protagonist is a secret agent who is affected by the onset of this condition, and he becomes the object of a manhunt by other agents because of a secret locked inside his mind.

*And Not Make Dreams Your Master* concerns a world when dreams can be broadcast and talented dreamers are at the peak of the entertainment industry, shaping their fantasies to cater to public demand. When the greatest of all dreamers crosses the border into insanity, the lives of those vicariously participating are suddenly in jeopardy. *The Eternity Brigade* follows the careers of several professional soldiers whose personalities are stored in memory banks, brought back to consciousness only when there is a battle to be fought. After several generations have passed on the outside world, these soldiers are virtually slaves, their tapes have been stolen and duplicated, and they may end up fighting their former friends, or other versions of themselves. These two books are among Goldin's finest novels.

He also wrote a number of novels in the Family D'Alembert series, based on characters created by Edward E. Smith. Earth is the center of an interstellar empire with a royal family. Although the rulers are essentially benevolent, various factions seek to wrest control and provide the villains of each adventure. The D'Alemberts are from a heavy gravity world, and their unusual physical abilities make them perfect agents for the imperial secret service. Under the guise of a travelling circus, they become involved in a series of adventures to ensure the continuity of the empire.

*The Imperial Stars* is the first adventure, serving primarily to establish the background. A group of assassins must be infiltrated and neutralized before they can carry out their plans. Criminals are systematically kidnapping people from a resort world in *Strangler's Moon.* A robot is married to a member of the royal family in *The Clockwork Traitor*, which is the weakest in the series. An old enemy returns in *Getaway World*, planning an alliance between various criminal organizations. Arch villains "C" and the Lady "A" appear in the next, *Appointment at Bloodstar*, and return in subsequent books. In their first foray, they use assassination to weaken confidence in the government. In subsequent titles such as *The Purity Plot* and *Planet of Treachery*, the D'Alemberts tangle with the sinister duo repeatedly.

The D'Alembert series stopped in the mid-1980's, and Goldin did not publish again for several years. His subsequent books have shown even greater maturity than the best of his early work. The Parsina Saga, a fantasy trilogy consisting of *Shrine of the Desert Mage, The Storyteller and the Jann*, and *Crystals of Air and Water*, is a wonderfully inventive series of Arabian nights style adventures, with the protagonists facing off against an evil djinn and his army.

Goldin has also started a new science fiction series, featuring Jade Darcy, written in collaboration with Mary Mason. In *Jade Darcy and the Affair of Honor*, she is employed as a bouncer on an alien world, but is trapped into conducting a dangerous secret mission against unfriendly aliens because of a mystery in her past. The superior sequel, *Jade Darcy and the Zen Pirates*, transports Jade to a monastery world where she becomes involved in the various plots and counterplots involved in the succession to supreme power.

Although not noted as a short story writer, Goldin is not without talent in that area as well. "But as a Soldier, for His Country," upon which *Mindflight* is based, stands quite well on its own. There is genuine feeling in "Sweet Dreams, Melissa," about a sentient computer personality, and in a short fantasy story, "The Last Ghost," who exists in a world where death has been conquered. Unfortunately, Goldin has largely ignored the short form in favor of novels.

—Don D'Ammassa

---

**GOLDING, (Sir) William (Gerald).** British. Born in St. Columb Minor, Cornwall, 19 September 1911. Educated at Marlborough Grammar School; Brasenose College, Oxford, B.A. 1935. Served in the Royal Navy, 1940–45. Married Ann Brookfield in 1939; one son and one daughter. Writer, actor, and producer in small theatre companies, 1934–40; schoolmaster, Bishop Wordsworth's School, Salisbury, Wiltshire, 1945–61; Visiting Professor, Hollins College, Virginia, 1961–62. Recipient: James Tait Black Memorial prize, 1980; Booker prize, 1980; Nobel Prize for Literature, 1983. M.A.: Oxford University, 1961; D.Litt.: University of Sussex, Brighton, 1970; University of Kent, Canterbury, 1974; University of Warwick, Coventry, 1981; the Sorbonne, Paris, 1983; Oxford University, 1983; LL.D.: University of Bristol, 1984. Honorary Fellow, Brasenose College, 1966. Fellow, 1955, and Companion of Literature, 1984, Royal Society of Literature. C.B.E. (Commander, Order of the British Empire), 1966. Knighted, 1988. Address: c/o Faber and Faber Ltd., 3 Queen Square, London WC1N 3AU, England.

SCIENCE-FICTION PUBLICATIONS

Novels

*Lord of the Flies.* London, Faber, 1954; New York, Coward McCann, 1955.
*The Inheritors.* London, Faber, 1955; New York, Harcourt Brace, 1962.

Short Stories

*The Scorpion God.* London, Faber, 1971; New York, Harcourt Brace, 1972.

OTHER PUBLICATIONS

Novels

*Pincher Martin.* London, Faber, 1956; as *The Two Deaths of Christopher Martin*, New York, Harcourt Brace, 1957.
*Free Fall.* London, Faber, 1959; New York, Harcourt Brace, 1960.
*The Spire.* London, Faber, and New York, Harcourt Brace, 1964.
*The Pyramid.* London, Faber, and New York, Harcourt Brace, 1967.
*Darkness Visible.* London, Faber, and New York, Farrar Straus, 1979.
*Rites of Passage.* London, Faber, and New York, Farrar Straus, 1980.
*The Paper Men.* London, Faber, and New York, Farrar Straus, 1984.
*Close Quarters.* London, Faber, and New York, Farrar Straus, 1987.
*Fire Down Below.* London, Faber, and New York, Farrar Straus, 1989.

Plays

*The Brass Butterfly*, adaptation of his story "Envoy Extraordinary" (produced London, 1958). London, Faber, 1958; Chicago, Dramatic Publishing Company, n.d.

Radio Plays: *Miss Pulkinhorn*, 1960; *Break My Heart*, 1962.

Verse

*Poems.* London, Macmillan, 1934; New York, Macmillan, 1935.

Other

*The Hot Gates and Other Occasional Pieces.* London, Faber, 1965; New York, Harcourt Brace, 1966.
*Talk: Conversations with William Golding*, with Jack I. Biles. New York, Harcourt Brace, 1970.
*A Moving Target* (essays). London, Faber, and New York, Farrar Straus, 1982.
*An Egyptian Journal.* London, Faber, 1985.

*

Critical Studies (selection): *William Golding* by Samuel Hynes, New York, Columbia University Press, 1964; *William Golding: A Critical Study* by James R. Baker, New York, St. Martin's Press, 1965; *The Art of William Golding* by Bernard S. Oldsey and Stanley Weintraub, New York, Harcourt Brace, 1965; *William Golding* by Bernard F. Dick, New York, Twayne, 1967; *William Golding: A Critical Study* by Mark Kinkead-Weekes and Ian Gregor, London, Faber, 1967, New York, Harcourt Brace, 1968; *William Golding* by Leighton Hodson, Edinburgh, Oliver and Boyd, 1969, New York, Putnam, 1971; *The Novels of William Golding* by Howard S. Babb, Columbus, Ohio State University Press, 1970; *William Golding: The Dark Fields of Discovery* by Virginia Tiger, London, Calder and Boyars, and Atlantic Highlands, New Jersey, Humanities Press, 1974; *William Golding* by Stephen Medcalf, London, Longman, 1975; *William Golding: Some Critical Considerations* edited by Jack I. Biles and Robert O. Evans, Louisville, University Press of Kentucky, 1978; *Of Earth and Darkness: The Novels of William*

*Golding* by Arnold Johnston, Columbia, University of Missouri Press, 1980; *A View from the Spire: William Golding's Later Novels* by Don Crompton, Oxford, Blackwell, 1985; *William Golding: The Man and His Books: A Tribute on His 75th Birthday* edited by John Carey, London, Faber, 1986, New York, Farrar Straus, 1987; *William Golding: A Structural Reading of His Fiction* by Philip Redpath, London, Vision Press, 1986; *The Novels of William Golding* by Stephen Boyd, Brighton, Sussex, Harvester Press, and New York, St. Martin's Press, 1988; *William Golding* by James Gindin, London, Macmillan, and New York, St. Martin's Press, 1988.

* * *

William Golding's novels are unique, fabulistic inversions of traditional perspectives that explore human nature and its veneer of civilization to suggest that man's instinctual past is directly linked to our present. Their deceptively simple and economical style re-enforces the illusion of primitive perceptions and primitive ties. Golding doesn't interfere or preach, but his "naturalistic-allegorical" form speaks for itself. He equates scientific and technological progress with dehumanization and tracing the defects of society directly to the defects of human nature. Often his perspectives are unexpected and startling.

Until its last chapter, *The Inheritors* is written from the point of view of the mind and senses of Neanderthals, childlike, instinctual, semi-telepathic vegetarian ape-men with a strong sense of community, people closer to the senses than the next evolutionary step forward, Cromagnon man, the invaders who take over Neanderthal territory. These new men, whom we see through the uncomprehending eyes of the Neanderthals, are aggressive, vicious, wolf-like meat-eaters. They walk upright and lack fur, use bow and arrows, build stockades and canoes, and take preventive measures. However, in them are the seeds of modern man: "they are the forest"; they compete for women and rank, are beset by jealousies and animosities, dissemble and plot, drown their senses in liquor, and take their sex with violence. Contact with them helps the Neanderthals discover the process of analogy and of causal connection, but also possessiveness and rationalization. It is as if reason and depravity are inextricably bound, so that "man's" lost instinctual past is forever more golden than his threatening "reasoned" future.

*Lord of the Flies*, Golding's best-known work, is a social allegory of human regression. Set in a post-catastrophic near future in which war has laid waste much of the West and civilization is in ruins, the novel focuses on a boys' choir, stranded on a tropical island, to create a microcosm of the civilized world; therein the youngsters are equated with social types (the politician, the intellectual, the mystic/poet, the military leader, the bully), and the jungle with disorder, chaos, and primitive compulsions that lurk beneath the civilized surface. The story traces the loss of order and of civilized restraints, man's evolution from savage in reverse, as the boys revert to their primitive, selfish selves, beset by anger, fear, and superstition, swept by blood lust. Their struggle becomes a battle of adult proportions between the intelligent and the irrational, the humane and the bestial. The *deus ex machina* intrusion of adults at the end confirms the island as microcosm: the boys have scorched their island with fire as their parents have consumed theirs with bombs; both children and adults are irresponsible, violent, brutal, sadistic. The image of man is not pleasant: selfish, easily manipulated, at home with mindless rituals, he lives for the day, enjoys abusing the weak and the helpless, and is better than the beast only by a conscious effort.

*The Scorpion God* is really three short novels in one. The first, entitled "The Scorpion God," set in a land much like ancient Egypt, examines man's capacity for blindly accepting the irrational, especially if sanctified by religious trappings. Ultimately, it traces the exposure and destruction of a religion based on human gods and a myth of incestuous procreation and human sacrifice for the sake of a valley's fertility. The second, "Clonk Clonk," examines man as a sexual animal, exploring the union of a primitive hunter, Chimp, with a tribal mother, Palm, to define sexual differences as sensed by an unsophisticated primitive mentality. The third, "Envoy Extraordinary," studies man as a technological miracle worker, clever, but perhaps too clever for the good of his species. Its emphasis is on the dilemma of technological advance, the diminution of quality of life that accompanies the increase in technological knowledge.

All of Golding's works are tangential to science fiction in that they are novels of ideas, allegories evoking conflicts bound up with man's technological achievements, his mental aspirations, and his mastery of illusion and self-delusion. For example, *The Spire*, an historical study of the construction of a four-hundred foot spire on a medieval church, captures the pride, daring, egotism and enthusiasm that leads man purposefully to face difficult technological challenges and to reach beyond his grasp, while the psychological projection of *Pincher Martin* captures in the last moments of consciousness the desperate fantasy of a drowning man whose mind reconstructs reality to suit his own desire for life. This greedy, lustful, self-centered British naval officer, blown off his ship by a German torpedo in the North Atlantic, sees himself in mythic roles (Ajax, Prometheus, King Lear) defiantly asserting his own fictional creation against mental and physical death. *Free Fall* challenges the assumption that man can ultimately control his universe; *Darkness Visible* begins with the Nazi firebombings of London, follows the experiences of a pitiful, aging pederast and sadistic twin terrorists (moral monsters since childhood), and ends with a terrorist fireball to explore man's essential depravity and manifest evil; and even *The Paper Men*, a realistic domestic comedy about a prominent English novelist pursued and tormented by an American academic determined to pen his authorized biography, captures a sense of life as two-dimensional farce. The Talbot trilogy (*Rites of Passage, Close Quarters*, and *Fire Down Below*), a "Ship of Fools" allegory set during the Napoleonic era, effectively evokes the wit, inventiveness, and diction of the 18th-century picaresque style, the technical ship-lore of the Hornblower series, the social setting and moral seriousness of the 19th-century novel of manners, and the concern with the duality of man of early gothic fiction: his sense of social and personal responsibility and his potential for evil. Therein, Golding recounts the sea voyage from England to the Antipodes of the aristocratic young Edmund Talbot. It is a voyage of self-discovery, a rite of passage in which man's endurance, faith, and courage are tested against nature (in particular the sea and the ice), his fellows, and himself. It is also a microcosm of the human voyage (man floundering in a sea of error), with an elaborate system of correspondences that make these books not simply a loving re-creation of "boy's own" naval books but a darker, more ambiguous allegory of modern society: its depraved depths, its shame, its purgatory, its conflicts, its dream of paradise. As the young hero discovers the lie of surface perceptions, his shipmates move from the reason and restraint of Northern latitudes to the warm-blooded abandon of Southern ones, and every man passes the antipodes between the divine and the diabolical.

Thus Golding, in a variety of forms, explores human nature. He makes us look deep into man's past to understand the drama of his present and his future; he fears that man's technological development always outstrips his moral development; he warns of the depths of man's savagery, but finds hope in minds that can question, reason, and challenge. Golding infuses realistic setting and milieu with analogical and allegorical significance to lead the reader to re-examine man's intrinsic nature.

—Gina Macdonald

---

**GOLDSTEIN, Lisa.** American. Born in Los Angeles, California, 21 November 1953. Educated at University of California, Los Angeles, B.A. 1975. Married Douglas Asherman in 1986. Co-owner, Dark Carnival Bookstore, Berkeley, California, 1976–82. Recipient: American Book award, 1983. Agent: Lynn Seligman, 400 Highland Avenue, Upper Montclair, New Jersey 07043, U.S.A.

SCIENCE-FICTION PUBLICATIONS

Novels

*The Red Magician.* New York, Pocket, 1982.
*The Dream Years.* New York, Bantam, 1985; London, Allen and Unwin, 1986.
*A Mask for the General.* New York, Bantam, 1987.
*Tourists.* New York, Simon and Schuster, 1989.

Short Stories

*Daily Voices.* Eugene, Oregon, Pulphouse, 1989.

*

Lisa Goldstein comments:

I like to write stories which take place at the intersection where fantasy and reality meet, stories which show the magic in day-to-day existence. Daily life offers endless examples of things that are strange, inexplicable, wonderful and/or terrible—dreams, humor, coincidences, love, death—yet most people seem to close their eyes to anything out of the ordinary. My novel *Tourists,* for example, and various short stories also set in the imaginary country of Amaz, show how unreal everyday life can become with just a slight change of perspective, a view from another country. *Strange Devices of the Sun and Moon* [a new novel to be published in 1992] takes place in 16th-century England, at a time when fantasy and mythology were just starting to be ignored in favor of a new, scientific way of thinking. A lot of these ideas come from the surrealists, who influenced me a great deal; *The Dream Years* deals with the surrealists and their way of looking at the world.

* * *

Lisa Goldstein made an immediate impact on the literary world in general as well as the science-fiction community with the publication of her first novel, *The Red Magician.* Her reputation remains high despite a small body of work published over a nine-year period. This unique and original fantasy won the American Book award even though it was a paperback original by an unknown writer, and drew public attention to her subsequent novels and short stories, most of which were immediate successes with critics and readers alike.

*The Red Magician* is set in a rural Jewish village in Europe in the days immediately preceding World War II. The local rabbi possesses sorcerous powers, a fact known to and approved by his constituents. One day a red-haired wanderer enters the village, a magician in his own right, and warns them of the tribulations to come, when the forces of Fascism will seize their property and their lives. The rabbi refuses to accept the warning, condemning the messenger as a deceiver and a threat to their existence. As a consequence the village is largely unprepared when modern armies overwhelm them, driving the sorcerous rabbi into exile in the form of a wolf and setting off a subsequent magical combat.

There were at least two reasons why this novel made such an impression. For one, Goldstein captured the tenor of the times and intertwined it with a fantasy plot, allowing the reader to achieve distance from the reality of events even while experiencing the terror and anger of the oppressed. For another, her prose was so fluid and evocative, even the less significant scenes are gripping and entertaining. Her portrayal of the relationship between the magician and a young woman of the village is particularly effective.

Her second novel, *The Dream Years,* was an even more noteworthy effort. Robert St. Onge is an aspiring novelist trying to find happiness, love, an understanding of the world, acceptance by his peers, and his own literary voice in the art world of 1920's Paris, the birth years of the surrealist movement. He encounters an enigmatic woman who eventually leads him through a kind of rift in time, the other end of which is the riotous Paris of 1968, where a new art movement has sprung from the ashes of the old. The contrast between the two views of art, life, and politics clash, and each is thrown into fresh relief by the presence of the other. Through the characters of St. Onge and the woman, as well as a number of historical characters recreated in great detail, we are provided insight not only into two diverse cultures, but into the means by which one evolves into the other, and the shape that our future dreams might assume.

Goldstein's third novel, *A Mask for the General,* is more conventionally science fiction, but still makes use of her unique perspective and spare, evocative writing style. It is set in a future America governed by the General of the title, a despotic tyrant who brutally suppresses any opposition. An underground resistance does exist, but they are tenuous group with no real grasp of the magnitude of the task they face, and no power base either in terms of manpower or equipment to effect a revolution. There is another, more popularly based resistance, known as the Tribes. These are people who have adopted an alternate life-style that is tolerated if not exactly approved by the establishment. Typically, members wear elaborately constructed animal masks indicating their tribal affiliation, and have little taste for physical confrontation.

Two very different young women are thrown together against this background, and become the catalysts for a fundamental change in the relationships between the two countercultures, ultimately serving to shape the form of a unified and more effective, though quite unconventional, resistance of the future. Goldstein avoids the clichés of the field; there are no climactic sieges of the bastions of government, no miraculous reversal of the power structure. Nor is it a simplistic transplanting of the principles of passive resistance to a futuristic setting, but rather a rethinking of the way political and social forces can affect the nature of our society. Nevertheless, the ending is upbeat, original, and evidence of Goldstein's maturity and continued growth as a novelist.

Although she has written less than a dozen short stories, Goldstein has attracted attention there as well. Perhaps the most effective is "Tourists," a disorienting and even frightening story of a man who awakens in a foreign country, unaware of where he is or how he got there. What's more, every effort he makes to correct the situation is ineffective; the authorities and the populace at large seem determined to thwart him. "Ever After" is a delightful look at what happened after Cinderella and her prince were married. "Cassandra's Photographs" is a compelling fantasy about a young woman who discovers a cache of photographs of herself, in situations that have not yet occurred. Other stories of note are "Preliminary Notes on the Jang," "Death Is Different," and "Daily Voices."

—Don D'Ammassa

---

**GORDON, David.** *See* **GARRETT, Randall.**

---

**GORDON, Rex.** Pseudonym for Stanley Bennett Hough; also writes as Bennett Stanley. British. Born in Preston, Lancashire, 25 February 1917. Educated at Preston Grammar School; Radio Officers College, Preston; attended classes of the Workers Educational Association. Married Justa E.C. Wodschow in 1938. Radio operator, Marconi Radio Company, 1936–38; radio officer, International Marine Radio Company, 1939–45; ran a yachting firm, 1946–51. Since the 1970's, teacher of creative writing, Workers Educational Association, and Local Authorities, Cornwall. Recipient: Infinity award, 1957. Agent: A.M. Heath, 79 St. Martin's Lane, London WCHN 4AA. Address: 21 St. Michael's Road, Ponsanooth, Truro, Cornwall, England.

Science-Fiction Publications

Novels

*Utopia 239*. London, Heinemann, 1955.
*Extinction Bomber* (as S.B. Hough). London, Lane, 1956.
*No Man Friday*. London, Heinemann, 1956; as *First on Mars*, New York, Ace, 1957.
*First to the Stars*. New York, Ace, 1959; as *The Worlds of Eclos*, London, Consul, 1961.
*Beyond the Eleventh Hour* (as S.B. Hough). London, Hodder and Stoughton, 1961.
*First Through Time*. New York, Ace, 1962; as *The Time Factor*, London, Gibbs and Phillips, 1964.
*Utopia Minus X*. New York, Ace, 1966; as *The Paw of God*, London, Gibbs, 1967.
*The Yellow Fraction*. New York, Ace, 1969; London, Dobson, 1972.

Other Publications

Novels as S.B. Hough

*Frontier Incident*. London, Hodder and Stoughton, 1951; New York, Crowell, 1952.
*Moment of Decision*. London, Hodder and Stoughton, 1952.
*Mission in Guemo*. London, Hodder and Stoughton, 1953; New York, Walker, 1964.
*The Seas South*. London, Hodder and Stoughton, 1953.
*The Primitives*. London, Hodder and Stoughton, 1954.
*The Bronze Perseus*. London, Secker and Warburg, 1959; New York, Walker, 1962; as *The Tender Killer*, New York, Avon, 1963.
*Dear Daughter Dead*. London, Gollancz, 1965; New York, Walker, 1966.
*Sweet Sister Seduced*. London, Gollancz, 1968; New York, Harper, 1983.
*Fear Fortune, Father*. London, Gollancz, 1974; New York, Harper, 1984.

Novels as Bennett Stanley

*Sea Struck*. New York, Crowell, 1953; as *Sea to Eden*, London, Hodder and Stoughton, 1954.
*The Alscott Experiment*. London, Hodder and Stoughton, 1954.
*Government Contract*. London, Hodder and Stoughton, 1956.

Other as S.B. Hough

*A Pound a Day Inclusive: The Modern Way to Holiday Travel*. London, Hodder and Stoughton, 1957.
*Expedition Everyman: Your Way on Your Income to All the Desirable Places of Europe*. London, Hodder and Stoughton, 1959.
*Expedition Everyman 1964*. London, Hodder and Stoughton, 1964.
*Where? An Independent Report on Holiday Resorts in Britain and the Continent*. London, Hodder and Stoughton, 1964.
*Creative Writing: A Handbook for Students, Tutors and Education Authorities*. Plymouth, Workers Educational Association, 1983.

*

Manuscript Collection: University of Wyoming, Laramie.

Critical Study: "The Lives and Times of Geoffrey Household" by Michael Barber, in *Books and Bookmen* (London), January 1974.

* * *

Rex Gordon is actually the pseudonym of Stanley B. Hough, who writes most of his fiction under his own name. The pseudonym was used for six novels published between 1955 and 1969. The first, *Utopia 239*, is a standard after-the-bomb story about the rebirth of civilization; it was not widely read and is the only one of the Rex Gordon books never reprinted. He attracted immediate attention with the novel *No Man Friday* (published in the United States as *First on Mars*).

The theme of man struggling to survive in a hostile environment is an old one in literature, of course, and this is a fine example of the science-fiction equivalent of Stephen Crane's "The Open Boat" or Jack London's "To Build a Fire," as well as Swift's *Robinson Crusoe*. Gordon Holder is the sole survivor of the crashlanding of the first manned expedition to Mars. With a small amount of equipment salvaged from the wreckage, he makes arrangements for his continued existence on a planet where food, water, shelter, and even oxygen cannot be taken for granted.

The adventures that follow are at once understated and melodramatic. After juryrigging a sort of bicycle, Holder takes a grand tour of the Martian landscape, carrying out some of the research projects that were the original reason for the trip to Mars, but he is constantly aware of the fact that one moment of inattention could result in his death. Gordon's meticulous attention to scientific detail lent an air of credibility to the story that elevated it above other adventure stories of its type. This is not a swashbuckling tale of action, although Holder does eventually encounter intelligent Martians. Rather than beautiful princesses or malevolent monsters, the Martians are unknowable to humanity, so alien even to the concept of technology that they have no interest in Holder, his civilization, or his fate. The single flaw in Swift's novel is that the shipwreck seems to be a bottomless treasure trove. Gordon evades this trap by having Holder salvage minimal equipment, then leave the vicinity of the wreckage. There is no doubt that he must find the means elsewhere if he is to survive.

Although Gordon was never to achieve the success of this novel again, his subsequent efforts were certainly entertaining. *The Worlds of Eclos* (*First to the Stars* in the United States) features two scientists, one male and one female, who profoundly dislike each other even though they are teamed together for a trip to Mars. Through mischance, their ship leaves its course and wanders into interstellar space, and although time dilation will allow them to survive the voyage to another star, it is doubtful they will ever be able to return home. Although the woman dies, the man and their child live to meet an alien race, which Gordon uses as a device to examine humanity's foibles, at the same time he casts doubt upon our ability ever to understand another intelligence, a reprise of the theme from the waning chapters of *No Man Friday.*

*The Time Factor* (predictably *First Through Time* in the United States) makes use of a standard theme. An unmanned probe into the far future reveals a devastated Earth. A living human must volunteer to undergo the same journey, discover the cause of the disaster, and bring that information back so that it can be averted. Although the puzzle is solved, the novel ends with a pessimistic overtone.

*The Paw of God* is a dystopian adventure story, published in the United States in a revised version under the title *Utopia Minus X.* An astronaut returns to Earth from an interstellar voyage, only to discover that, because of the time differential, he has arrived after the civilization he represented has fallen prey to an oppressive worldwide dictatorship that mandates happiness and contentment, and outlaws scientific research on the basis that no future progress is possible. Gordon uses his skeptical protagonist as a device to examine the workings of tyranny, although for the most part the story remains a routine adventure story.

Gordon's last published SF novel is *The Yellow Fraction*, in many ways quite a departure for him. The setting is a colony world where three distinct political factions—the yellows, the blues, and the greens—all have very different views about how the colony should be developed, in harmony with the planet, by imposing itself on the environment, or whether to remain at all. What ensues is a mix of political struggle, military campaigns, and interplanetary adventure, unfortunately so unfocused that the story never quite comes together.

Two other science-fiction novels appeared under Hough's byline, *Extinction Bomber* and *Beyond the Eleventh Hour*, but they are more properly contemporary political thrillers, in each case dealing with the possibility of worldwide nuclear conflict, and neither reached a wider genre readership.

Although Rex Gordon never lived up to the promise of his second novel, his subsequent work has been undeservedly ignored. He masked serious speculation about the future of humanity under a veneer of adventure writing, and his narrative style exudes an enthusiastic sense of wonder about the universe that communicates itself readily to his audience.

—Don D'Ammassa

---

**GORDON, Stuart.** Pseudonym for Richard Gordon; also writes as Alex R. Stuart. British. Born in Scotland in 1947. Agent: Maggie Noach, 21 Redan Street, London W14, England.

SCIENCE-FICTION PUBLICATIONS

Novels (series: Eyes)

*Time Story.* London, New English Library, 1972.
*One-Eye.* New York, DAW, 1973; London, Sidgwick and Jackson, 1974.
*Two-Eyes.* New York, DAW, 1974; London, Sidgwick and Jackson, 1975.
*Three-Eyes.* New York, DAW, 1975; London, Sidgwick and Jackson, 1976.
*Suaine and the Crow-God.* London, New English Library, 1975.
*Smile on the Void.* New York, Putnam, 1981; London, Arrow, 1982.
*Fire in the Abyss.* New York, Berkley, 1983; London, Arrow, 1984.

OTHER PUBLICATIONS as Alex R. Stuart

Novels

*The Bike from Hell.* London, New English Library, 1973.
*The Devil's Rider.* London, New English Library, 1973.

*

Stuart Gordon comments (1985):

The label "science fiction" is used to cover many different approaches to storytelling, most of which have little to do with "science" as such, save in a romantic, generalised way. The thrust of my own work has typically been occult or mythic in its main concern, and can be defined as science fiction only insofar as it has involved itself with the overtly fantastic, and insofar as it has been characterised (I hope) by that "sense of wonder" which romantically typifies the genre as a whole.

I have a strong sense of history and have drawn on this sense in my stories. "Those who forget their history are condemned to repeat it"—it disturbs me that as a whole our western culture appears to be increasingly out of touch with any real sense of the past and how it shaped what we are now. This is not to worship or take refuge in an unreal nostalgia, but to encourage the social growth of wider, deeper perspectives, so that history as we live it at present should no longer be just "a nightmare from which we are struggling to awake," but the vital process in which, individually and collectively, we live and move and have our being.

In this respect all imaginative literature, however labelled, can play an important role. Inventing tales of fantasy for their own sake may be entertaining and even to some degree therapeutic, alleviating the problems of everyday life, but such use of the imagination is not invariably positive, and might even in some cases be considered a criminal distraction. To my mind this danger has become clearly apparent in the extent to which science fiction—once vigorously independent—has been colonised by the mass media and converted into moneyspinning widescreen clichés which, at their worst (as in the movie of *Dune*), function as crude political propaganda disguised as entertainment. If science fiction has any sort of serious function, surely it is to encourage people to wake up and to think and see for themselves, rather than to distract them still further with the special effects of an enchanting but ultimately seedy (and deadly) hall of mirrors.

* * *

Stuart Gordon's career as a science-fiction writer stretches from 1971 to 1983, but during that period he produced only seven novels and a handful of shorter pieces. Drawing heavily on a sense and a feel for the depth of history, he uses mythology, human experience, and his own interpretation of the forces that have shaped our culture to create new, fascinating worlds and settings in his fiction.

Gordon's first novel was *Time Story*, a short but highly inventive time-travel story involving the usual paradoxes but in subtly different and often entertaining fashion. The two main characters are compelled to act out dual roles as they seek their destiny in a timestream that may not be as immutable as common knowledge would have it. Although the novel seems to have roused little interest, it's a tightly plotted and well-conceived work that seems to have been ignored because Gordon didn't indulge in the excesses common to this theme. The characters never quite come to life, either, and since neither of them is particularly likable, it is difficult to empathize.

The reaction to his Eyes trilogy was quite different. *One-Eye* is set in a post-apocalypse version of the Earth, but so far in the future that the very nature of the disaster that destroyed the old civilization has been lost in the mists of time. In order to preserve the genetic "norm," all infants judged to be mutants are by law condemned to death. But an ancient prophecy says that a one-eyed child will be born, harbinger of a new faith that will transform the world. A disaffected military officer defects from his post and raises a force to protect the divine infant.

With the assistance of an immortal android, the outcasts flee to a rebel stronghold where the child uses its powers to raise an inhuman army, abandoning its former protectors. The confused line of demarcation between good and evil is a common theme in Gordon's work, where characters often change sides and the reader's loyalties are constantly shifting.

The sequel, *Two-Eyes*, is set in the same world, but with a different cast of characters. A peaceful country dedicated to artistic endeavor is torn between two internal factions, and menaced by invading barbarians from without. The telepathic dreamsong of the mutant child endangers them as well. The conflict here is designed to set the stage for the ultimate confrontation, resolved in *Three-Eyes*.

The climactic volume reveals the true nature of the cataclysm that destroyed the world, a misguided attempt to avoid a new Ice Age by tapping the power of another universe, inadvertently allowing creatures of that other reality to enter our own world. Gordon brings the trilogy to a satisfactory conclusion, tying up the loose ends and dispatching the villains.

In tone, setting, and many of the details, the trilogy is more properly a fantasy than science fiction. The technology is so far advanced above our own that it appears to be magic, as do the psychic powers possessed by many of the characters and the nearly demonic forces marshalled by the villains. Read either as science fiction or as fantasy, however, it remains a powerful, complex, and endlessly inventive story, enlivened by Gordon's erudite style and surprising plot twists.

Gordon moved more overtly into fantasy with *Suaine and the Crow-God*, but the novel was not nearly so successful as his previous work. He turned next to episodic, satiric science fiction with *Smile on the Void*. Set in the not too distant future, it follows the exploits of an adventurous con-man and entrepreneur as he travels the world, seeking his destiny and a fast buck. Many of the individual episodes are hilarious, most are very, very strange, and although there is some excellent writing, the book's overall effect is disjointed and unsatisfying.

*Fire in the Abyss* was a noticeable improvement, although still not the equal of Gordon's earlier work. The U.S. government has been snatching historical figures out of time, but they make a serious mistake when they choose Sir Humphrey Gilbert. Bold, intelligent, curious, and talented, Gilbert establishes a telepathic link with some of the other prisoners and arranges a grand escape. We then see the future of our present culture through the skeptical eyes of an ancestor. Gilbert is a brilliantly portrayed rogue, in what is actually a very amusing novel.

Under his real name, Richard, Gordon was published four times in the now defunct *New Worlds* and its companion magazine, *Science Fantasy*. Two of these are worth noting. In "A Light in the Sky," a destroyed moon colony continues to broadcast a distress signal, providing a constant reproach for uncaring humanity. "Time's Fool" is a precursor of *Fire in the Abyss*. The Marquis De Sade is pulled through time to our future where he is placed on trial, only to prove himself a superior character to those set up as his judges.

Gordon's unique voice has been quiet for several years now, but even if he never writes another word, his powerful trilogy will remain an important contribution to the science-fiction field.

—Don D'Ammassa

---

**GOTLIEB, Phyllis (Fay, née Bloom).** Canadian. Born in Toronto, Ontario, 25 May 1926. Educated at public schools in Toronto; University of Toronto, B.A. in English 1948, M.A. 1950. Married Calvin Gotlieb in 1949; one son and two daughters. Agent: Donald Maass, 64 West 84th Street, New York, New York 10024, U.S.A. Address: 19 Lower Village Gate, Number 706, Toronto, Ontario M5P 3L9, Canada.

SCIENCE-FICTION PUBLICATIONS

Novels

*Sunburst.* New York, Fawcett, 1964; London, Coronet, 1966.
*O Master Caliban!* New York, Harper, 1976; London, Bantam Corgi, 1979.
Trilogy:
*A Judgment of Dragons.* New York, Berkley, 1980.
*Emperor, Swords, Pentacles.* New York, Ace, 1982.
*The Kingdom of the Cats.* New York, Ace, 1985.
*Heart of Red Iron* (Sequel to *O Master Caliban!*). New York, St. Martin's Press, 1989.

Short Stories

*Son of the Morning and Other Stories.* New York, Ace, 1983.

OTHER PUBLICATIONS

Novel

*Why Should I Have All the Grief?* Toronto, Macmillan, 1969.

Plays

*Doctor Umlaut's Earthly Kingdom* (broadcast, 1970; produced North Bay, Ontario, 1972). Toronto, Calliope Press, 1974.
*Silent Movie Days* (broadcast, 1971). Included in *The Works*, 1978.
*Garden Varieties* (broadcast, 1973; produced Ontario, 1973). Included in *The Works*, 1978.

Radio Plays: *Doctor Umlaut's Earthly Kingdom*, 1970; *Silent Movie Days*, 1971; *The Contract*, 1972; *Garden Varieties*, 1973; *God on Trial Before Rabbi Ovadia*, 1974.

Verse

*Who Knows One?* Toronto, Hawkshead Press, 1962.
*Within the Zodiac.* Toronto, McClelland and Stewart, 1964.
*Ordinary, Moving.* Toronto, Oxford University Press, 1969.
*Doctor Umlaut's Earthly Kingdom.* Toronto, Calliope Press, 1974.
*The Works: Collected Poems.* Toronto, Calliope Press, 1978.

Other

Editor, with Douglas Barbour, *Tesseracts 2.* Victoria, British Columbia, Porcepic Books, 1987.

*

Phyllis Gotlieb comments:
I like to work in as broad a range of genres as possible, and in all of them I am primarily interested in people, their emotions, actions, dynamics. After that I am interested in everything else in the universe.

* * *

Since 1959, Phyllis Gotlieb has produced a solid body of science fiction, including six novels and over 15 stories. While her output has been diverse and iconoclastic, it is marked by a vivid pictorial imagination, a sense of verbal fun, a real claim to one of the most diverse science-fiction bestiaries, and a frequently voiced but not stifling range of moral concerns. Much of her work also unfolds into an imaginative whole, building up a vision of GalFed (the Galactic Federation) and its struggles with various races to ensure their rights.

Gotlieb's first three published stories, "Phantom Foot," "A Grain of Manhood," and "Gingerbread Boy" are standard magazine stories of their time, clever ideas worked out with snap and economy. "A Grain of Manhood" is the most evocative and touches a deep level of human pain. In it a woman waits to give birth to a child while her husband stands angrily by. He is sterile and their match was one of convenience so he could migrate into space. She is pregnant because her transport ship crashed and she was sheltered by a strange humanoid race with prismatic skins, one of whom impregnated her in response to her deep unvoiced wish for the child she would never have with her husband. The story captures the damaged male psyche and the woman's dilemma of wanting the child and yet not wanting to hurt her husband. In the heartstopping ending the child is born a perfect replica of the husband, made so by the psychokinetic genetic manipulation of the prismatic race, who drew the model from the wife's imagination. This is a bittersweet ending, for while the husband now has the child he can respectably exhibit to the world, he has revealed his shallowness by berating his wife before the birth; and while the wife has redeemed herself with her husband, she remains far from him, lost in dreams of the prismatic wonder beings.

Gotlieb's 1964 novel, *Sunburst*, is one of the most imaginative, humorous, and at the same time socially aware nuclear accident novels ever written. In it 47 psychotic children with stunning psychokinetic (psi) powers have been accidentally created by a power plant leak and are penned up in the Dump, an enclosure that is proof against their powers. Their fury against the world at large is partly because of what they are (some, like Doyboy, are physical mutants), their imprisonment, and, interestingly, because they are all from the immigrant working-class families that provided the workers in the dangerous areas of the power plant. The heroine, 13-year-old Shandy Johnson, is herself an Imper (Impervious to the psi forces) who remembers with horror the sunburst of the radioactive cancerous back wound that killed her father when she was three. The novel makes use of psychology and the anthropology of Margaret Mead as Shandy finally and reluctantly joins in attempting to control a breakout by the Dumplings and opens up a way to understand them as primitives, with some of the special perceptive power of animals and animal-like lack of moral affect. The novel has a comic side in that the Dumplings sometimes behave as children always wish to, teleporting around breaking windows and tripping policemen.

"Son of the Morning" is the novella-length short story that launches Gotlieb's most enchanting creations, the hundred kilogram sentient dark red leopard derivatives called Ungruwarkh (a phonetic growl). Kheng, the male, and his mate Prandra, who has exceptional ESP powers, spend this story accidentally trapped in an 18th-century Polish ghetto, where they have been tossed by a superbeing, a Qumedni, which turns out to be the rebel creature who in fact took leopards from Earth and made them sentient on their planet. Tangled in this tale is Gotlieb's extensive knowledge of Judiac lore, and in its wonderful conclusion the brave local rabbi finds himself floating in a transparent bubble in space with the cats and the Qumedon, where his faith is sorely tried. There is much humour here, as the cats find yiddish very hard on their sensitive hearing and are constantly having to resist the temptation to eat the wonderful smelling humans they encounter.

The obvious success of Prandra and Kheng led to *A Judgment of Dragons*, four tales of their adventures, the first of which is "Son of the Morning." "The King's Dogs" is a detective story that centres on the murder of an ESP in the ESP institute, the destruction of the 300-year-old brain-in-glasstex-case who was Prandra and Kheng's dearest friend. There follows "Nebuchadnezzar," in which the cats help a race of living blue bathmats to defeat drug smugglers, and finally "A Judgment of Dragons," in which the other Qumedni finally come to judge the maverick who made the cats sentient. This tale approaches the theological, for Prandra and Kheng are actually meeting their maker and his enemies in a climactic engagement.

The Ungruwarkh make two more appearances in Gotlieb's work. *Emperor, Swords, Pentacles* is a richly imagined novel in which Emerald, daughter of Kheng and Prandra, and her impetuous mate Raanung are brought in to assist in resisting a complex plot to overrun a planet populated by sentient medieval crawfish. This novel is crowded with the wonderful Gotlieb beasts, including an intelligent 40-year-old, one-metre-long embryo arrested at three months growth and an ESP, which is essentially a brain with five eyes in a ball of leaves mounted on chicken feet. The cats are particularly well developed as savage ironists.

*The Kingdom of the Cats* is the last novel dealing with the red leopards, and it is set chiefly in the Grand Canyon where a group of them, who have volunteered to return to Earth, are slaughtered. The solution to this horror leads through half the galaxy, and the Ungruwarkh surprise even their Qumedon creator. The novel ends in an unusual unwinding tone, which does credit to a science-fiction author with the sense and balance to leave her most memorable creations at their peak.

Gotlieb's other novel sequence is *O Master Caliban!* and its sequel, *Heart of Red Iron.* These books deal with a fully realised wild planet where Dhalgren, while doing biological experiments, has been overwhelmed by the ergs, intelligent mobile machines. His son Sven, human but four-armed, leads a strange group of castaways across the planet to rescue his father and prevent the ergs from sending a hominoid replica of his father out into the universe. In the second novel a return to the planet by an older Sven enmeshes him in a second struggle with the ergs and a complex mesh of other races who are being brought to colonise, including 50-foot sentient pythons with horns, and the Crystalloids, metallic creatures with nasty tempers carried about in boxes. There is also the attempt to rescue the mysterious Empress of Stones, whose ship has crashed into a volcano on the planet. Both of these novels have an oppressive sense of a struggle to survive, and both teem with a profusion of description. With its strong Shakespearean overtones of the rights of creators and their responsibilities and the subsidiary conflict of robot and man, *O Master Caliban!* is Gotlieb's most effective and most moving novel.

—Peter A. Brigg

---

**GOTSCHALK, Felix C.** American. Born in Richmond, Virginia, 7 September 1929. Educated at Virginia Commonwealth University, Richmond, B.S. 1954 (Phi Beta Kappa), M.S. 1956; Tulane University, New Orleans, Ph.D. 1958. Served in the United States Marine Corps, 1947–49. Married Nelle Mull in 1957; one son and one daughter. Draftsman, Vepco, Richmond, 1946–47, 1949–51; pianist, Chelf's, 1951–56, and On the Road, 1956–58, both in Richmond; Assistant Professor, Nicholls State University, Thibodaux, Louisiana, 1958–62, and Bowman Medical School, Winston-Salem, North Carolina, 1962–70; in private practice as a psychologist, Winston-Salem, 1970–81. Since 1981, full-time writer. Address: 4021 Tangle Lane, Winston-Salem, North Carolina 27106, U.S.A.

SCIENCE-FICTION PUBLICATIONS

Novel

*Growing Up in Tier 3000.* New York, Ace, 1975.

Uncollected Short Stories

"Bonus Baby," in *Science Fiction Emphasis 1,* edited by David Gerrold. New York, Ballantine, 1974.

"Outer Concentric" and "The Examination," in *New Dimensions 4,* edited by Robert Silverberg. New York, New American Library, 1974.

"A Day in the South Quad," in *New Dimensions 5,* edited by Robert Silverberg. New York, Harper, 1975.

"The Man with the Golden Reticulates," in *Orbit 17,* edited by Damon Knight. New York, Harper, 1975.

"Pandora's Cryogenic Box," in *Fantastic* (New York), December 1975.

"The Family Winter of 1986," in *Orbit 18,* edited by Damon Knight. New York, Harper, 1976.

"The Day of the Big Test," in *Future Power,* edited by Jack Dann and Gardner Dozois. New York, Random House, 1976.

"The Napoleonic Wars," in *Beyond Time,* edited by Sandra Ley. New York, Simon and Schuster, 1976.

"Charisma Leak," in *New Dimensions 6,* edited by Robert Silverberg. New York, Harper, 1976.

"Home Sweet Geriatric Dome," in *New Dimensions 7,* edited by Robert Silverberg. New York, Harper, and London, Gollancz, 1977.

"The Veil over the River," in *Orbit 19,* edited by Damon Knight. New York, Harper, 1977.

"Sir Richard's Robots," in *Cosmos* (New York), November 1977.

"Square Pony Express," in *New Dimensions 9,* edited by Robert Silverberg. New York, Harper, 1979.

"The Wishes of Maidens," in *New Voices in Science Fiction,* edited by George R.R. Martin. New York, Berkley, 1979.

"The Trip of Bradley Oesterhaus," in *Fantasy and Science Fiction* (New York), July 1979.

"A Presidential Tape," in *New Dimensions 10,* edited by Robert Silverberg. New York, Harper, 1980.

"Among the Cave Dwellers of the San Andreas Canyon," in *Fantasy and Science Fiction* (New York), September 1980.

"And Parity for All," in *Amazing* (New York), November 1980.

"Take a Midget Step," in *Fantasy and Science Fiction* (New York), September 1981.

"The Municipal Smog Man," in *Amazing* (New York), September 1981.

"Dogsworld," in *Pig Iron,* edited by Rose Sayre and Jim Villani. Youngstown, Ohio, Pig Iron Press, 1982.

"Conspicuous Consumption," in *Fantasy and Science Fiction* (New York), March 1983.

"The Nature of Relationships," in *Last Wave 3,* Winter 1984.

"Vestibular Man," in *Fantasy and Science Fiction* (New York), March 1985.

*

Manuscript Collection: Temple University, Philadelphia.

Felix C. Gotschalk comments:

(1981) Writing is for me an indulgence, an egocentric luxuriation, something I do because it pleases me. I have experimented (consciously and unconsciously) with verbosity, neologisms, symmetry, cadence, self-canceling reciprocity, and, even, monosyllabilicity. I cannot plot story lines and do not attempt to do so. I do not know what is going to happen in any of my stories; and it is special voyeuristic fun to have a good flow of writing (say, 3000 words in one evening), and then read it the next day to see what it was that I wrote the night before. How to characterize my writing I do not know. One critic called it "poetic hardware," others have been less kind. I would like to write an erotic story that would guarantee the reader a spontaneous orgasm.

(1985) I am trying to be less self-indulgent in my writing, and have a 250K word mainstream novel completed, titled *Southern Pearls and Swine.* Henry Miller is my all-time favorite author, and I think J.G. Ballard is our best for evoking the "sense of wonder."

* * *

Felix C. Gotschalk published his first science fiction in 1974, and within a year his quirky, hyperkinetic stories were appearing in a wide range of SF publications, including Damon Knight's

*Orbit* and Robert Silverberg's *New Dimensions*. Gotschalk's voice is immediately recognizable in all his work: a high-tech jargon charged with neologisms and rewired syntax that sometimes seems affected but often conveys a powerful sense of the psychic dislocations and altered sensibility of life in an advanced, high-energy civilization.

A number of Gotschalk's stories, including "A Day in the South Quad" and his novel *Growing Up in Tier 3000*, are set against a more or less common background, where life in automated urban domes allows for an impressive array of hedonistic pleasures but sharply restricts individual freedom as solicitous computer systems control man's more self-destructive tendencies. Several stories raise the question of how the enormous energy demands of such a society are to be met (in other stories this problem is dispensed with; Gotschalk has shown little interest in such genre conventions as inter-story chronologies or consistency). Others are set in the present or near-future, often told from the point of view of a middle-aged academic or administrator, as in "The Man with the Golden Reticulates" and "Charisma Leak." The voice in these stories is wry, male, and exuberantly egocentric; the prevailing sense is of the self-aware individual celebrating life despite unforestalled mortality and numerous technological forebodings.

The person of Gotschalk's protagonist is essentially identical in all his stories, whether incarnated as a high-tech infant prodigy, young stud, mature man of the world, or bionically rebuilt geezer. It can be argued that Gotschalk writes most effectively when his narrative contains more than one of these figures, whose interaction can prove more interesting than the self/other dichotomy that otherwise results. Such is the case with *Growing Up in Tier 3000*, a short but intense novel in which competition within the nuclear family for available energy compels the young children to turn upon their parents, who realize that advancing technology has left them ill-equipped to withstand their four-year-old successors.

By 1980 Gotschalk had published some 18 stories and a novel, and had explored the possibilities of his idiosyncratic newspeak perhaps to the point of diminishing returns. During this period the original anthology market in which his best work had appeared began to weaken, and perhaps for this reason, or because Gotschalk was then writing novels (several of which evidently await publication), his work began to appear less frequently. The stories he has published in recent years have relied less heavily on flamboyant stylistic effects, and many experiment with vernacular voices of odd locales in a slightly seedy future, often in the American South ("Take a Midget Step," "Vestibular Man"). The tales are upbeat, refreshing, and usually form a kind of success story. Gotschalk's characteristic buoyance is engagingly conveyed, though he remains disconcertingly unabashed in celebrating the aggressiveness of the Western male.

—Gregory Feeley

---

**GOULART, Ron(ald Joseph).** Also writes as R.T. Edwards; Chad Calhoun; Franklin W. Dixon; Ian R. Jamieson; Josephine Kains; Jillian Kearny; Howard Lee; Zeke Masters; Kenneth Robeson; Frank S. Shawn; Joseph Silva; Con Steffanson. American. Born in Berkeley, California, 13 January 1933. Educated at the University of California, Berkeley, B.A. 1955. Married Frances Sheridan in 1964; two sons. Advertising copywriter, Guild Bascom and Bonfigci, San Francisco, 1955–57, 1958–60, Alan Alch Inc., Hollywood, 1960–63, and Hoefer Dietrich and Brown, San Francisco, 1966–68. Author of science-fiction comic strip *Star Hawks*, with Gil Kane, 1977–79. Member, board of directors, Mystery Writers of America, 1979–83, 1984–88, 1989–91. Recipient: Mystery Writers of America Edgar Allan Poe award, 1971. Address: 30 Farrell Road, Weston, Connecticut 06883, U.S.A.

SCIENCE-FICTION PUBLICATIONS

Novels (series: Harry Challenge; Battlestar Galactica; The Exchameleon; Gypsy; Star Hawks)

*The Sword Swallower*. New York, Doubleday, 1968.
*After Things Fell Apart*. New York, Ace, 1970; London, Arrow, 1975.
*The Fire-Eater*. New York, Ace, 1970.
*Gadget Man*. New York, Doubleday, 1971; London, New English Library, 1977.
*Death Cell*. New York, Beagle, 1971.
*Hawkshaw*. New York, Doubleday, 1972; London, Hale, 1973.
*Plunder*. New York, Beagle, 1972.
*Wildsmith*. New York, Ace, 1972.
*Shaggy Planet*. New York, Lancer, 1973.
*A Talent for the Invisible*. New York, DAW, 1973.
*The Tin Angel*. New York, DAW, 1973.
*Spacehawk, Inc*. New York, DAW, 1974.
*Flux*. New York, DAW, 1974.
*When the Waker Sleeps*. New York, DAW, 1975.
*The Hellhound Project*. New York Doubleday, 1975; London, Hale, 1976.
*A Whiff of Madness*. New York, DAW, 1976.
*The Enormous Hourglass*. New York, Award, 1976.
*Quest of the Gypsy*. New York, Pyramid, 1976.
*Crackpot*. New York, Doubleday, and London, Hale, 1977.
*The Emperor of the Last Days*. New York, Popular Library, 1977.
*The Panchronicon Plot*. New York, DAW, 1977.
*Nemo*. New York, Berkley, 1977; London, Hale, 1979.
*Eye of the Vulture* (Gypsy). New York Jove, 1977.
*The Island of Dr. Moreau* (novelization of screenplay; as Joseph Silva). New York, Ace, 1977.
*Flux, and The Tin Angel*. London, Millington, 1978.
*The Wicked Cyborg*. New York, DAW, 1978.
*Calling Dr. Patchwork*. New York, DAW, 1978.
*Cowboy Heaven*. New York, Doubleday, 1979; London, Hale, 1980.
*Dr. Scofflaw*, in *Binary Star 3*. New York, Dell, 1979.
*Hello, Lemuria, Hello*. New York, DAW, 1979.
Star Hawks, illustrated by Gil Kane:
  *Empire 99*. Chicago, Playboy Press, 1980.
  *The Cyborg King*. Chicago, Playboy Press, 1981.
*Hail Hibbler*. New York, DAW, 1980.
*Skyrocket Steele*. New York, Pocket Books, 1980.
*The Robot in the Closet*. New York, DAW, 1981.
*Brinkman*. New York, Doubleday, 1981.
*Upside Downside*. New York, DAW, 1982.
*Big Bang*. New York, DAW, 1982.
Battlestar Galactica, with Glen A. Larson:
  *Greetings from Earth*. New York, Berkley, 1983.
  *Experiment in Terra*. New York, Berkley, 1984.
  *The Long Patrol*. New York, Berkley, 1984.
*Hellquad*. New York, DAW, 1984.
*The Prisoner of Blackwood Castle* (Harry Challenge). New York, Avon, 1984.
*Suicide, Inc*. New York, Berkley, 1985.
*Brainz, Inc*. New York, DAW, 1985.
*Galaxy Jane*. New York, Berkley, 1986.

*Daredevils, Ltd* (Exchameleon). New York, St. Martin's Press, 1987.
*The Curse of the Obelisk* (Harry Challenge). New York, Avon, 1987.
*Starpirate's Brain* (Exchameleon). New York, St. Martin's Press, 1987.
*Everybody Come to Cosmo's* (Exchameleon). New York, St. Martin's Press, 1988.

Novels as Frank S. Shawn (series: Phantom in all books)

*The Veiled Lady*. New York, Avon, 1973.
*The Golden Circle*. New York, Avon, 1973.
*The Mystery of the Sea Horse*. New York, Avon, 1973.
*The Hydra Monster*. New York, Avon, 1973.
*The Goggle-Eyed Pirates*. New York, Avon, 1974.
*The Swamp Rats*. New York, Avon, 1974.

Novels as Con Steffanson (series: Flash Gordon in all books)

*The Lion Men of Mongo*. New York, Avon, 1974.
*The Plague of Sound*. New York, Avon, 1974.
*The Space Circus*. New York, Avon, 1974.

Novels as Kenneth Robeson (series: Avenger in all books)

*The Man from Atlantis*. New York, Warner, 1974.
*Red Moon*. New York, Warner, 1974.
*The Purple Zombie*. New York, Warner, 1974.
*Dr. Time*. New York, Warner, 1974.
*The Nightwitch Devil*. New York, Warner, 1974.
*Black Chariots*. New York, Warner, 1974.
*The Cartoon Crimes*. New York, Warner, 1974.
*The Iron Skull*. New York, Warner, 1975.
*The Death Machine*. New York, Warner, 1975.
*The Blood Countess*. New York, Warner, 1975.
*The Glass Man*. New York, Warner, 1975.
*Demon Island*. New York, Warner, 1975.

Short Stories

*What's Become of Screwloose? and Other Inquiries*. New York, Scribner, and London, Sidgwick and Jackson, 1971.
*Clockwork's Pirates, Ghost Breaker*. New York, Ace, 1971.
*Broke Down Engine and Other Troubles with Machines*. New York, Macmillan, 1971.
*The Chameleon Corps and Other Shape Changers*. New York, Macmillan, and London, Collier Macmillan, 1973.
*Nutzenbolts and More Troubles with Machines*. New York, Macmillan, 1975; London, Hale, 1976.
*Odd Job No. 101 and Other Future Crimes and Intrigues*. New York, Scribner, 1975; London, Hale, 1976.

Other Publications

Novels

*If Dying Was All*. New York, Ace, 1971.
*Too Sweet to Die*. New York, Ace, 1972.
*The Same Lie Twice*. New York, Ace, 1973.
*Cleopatra Jones* (novelization of screenplay). New York, Warner, 1973.
*Chains* (novelization of TV series; as Howard Lee). New York, Warner, 1973.
*Superstition* (novelization of TV series; as Howard Lee). New York, Warner, 1973.
*One Grave Too Many*. New York, Ace, 1974.
*The Tremendous Adventures of Bernie Wine*. New York, Warner, 1975.
*Cleopatra Jones and the Casino of Gold* (novelization of screenplay), New York, Warner, 1975.
*Vampirella* (novelizations of comic strip):
*Bloodstalk*. New York, Warner, 1975; London, Sphere, 1976.
*On Alien Wings*. New York, Warner, 1975; London, Sphere, 1977.
*Deadwalk*. New York, Warner, 1976; London, Sphere, 1977.
*Blood Wedding*. New York, Warner, 1976.
*Deathgame*. New York, Warner, 1976.
*Snakegod*. New York, Warner, 1976.
*Challengers of the Unknown*. New York, Dell, 1977.
*Capricorn One*. New York, Fawcett, 1978.
*Stalker from the Stars* (novelization of *The Hulk* comic book; as Joseph Silva, with Len Wein and Marv Wolfman). New York, Pocket, 1978.
*Holocaust for Hire* (novelization of *Captain America* comic book; as Joseph Silva). New York, Pocket, 1979.
*Agent of Love* (as Jillian Kearny). New York, Warner, 1979.
*Ghosting*. Toronto, Raven, 1980.
*Love's Claimant* (as Jillian Kearny). New York, Warner, 1981.
*Prize Meets Murder* (as R.T. Edwards, with Otto Penzler). New York, Pocket, 1984.
*A Graveyard of My Own*. New York, Walker, 1985.
*Triple "O" Seven* (as Ian R. Jamieson). Vancouver, Talon, 1985; New York, Mysterious Press, 1990.
*The Wisemann Originals*. New York, Walker, 1989.
*Even the Butler Was Poor*. New York, Walker, 1990.
*The Tijuana Bible*. New York, St. Martin's Press, 1990.

Novels as Con Steffanson

*Laverne and Shirley: Teamwork* (novelization of television play). New York, Warner, 1976.
*Laverne and Shirley: Easy Money* (novelization of television play). New York, Warner, 1976.
*Laverne and Shirley: Gold Rush* (novelization of television play). New York, Warner, 1976.

Novels as Josephine Kains

*The Devil Mask Mystery*. New York, Zebra, 1978.
*The Curse of the Golden Skull*. New York, Zebra, 1978.
*The Green Lama Mystery*. New York, Zebra, 1979.
*The Whispering Cat Mystery*. New York, Zebra, 1979.
*The Witch's Tower Mystery*. New York, Zebra, 1979.
*The Laughing Dragon Mystery*. New York, Zebra, 1980.

Novels as Chad Calhoun (series: Agent Brad Spear in all books)

*The Hidden Princess*. Wayne, Pennsylvania, Banbury, 1982.
*The Mountain Queen*. Wayne, Pennsylvania, Banbury, 1982.
*The Lady Rustler*. Wayne, Pennsylvania, Banbury, 1982.

Novels as Zeke Masters (series: Faro Blake in all books)

*High Card*. New York, Pocket, 1982.
*Loaded Dice*. New York, Pocket, 1982.
*Texas Two-Step*. New York, Pocket, 1983.
*Cashing In*. New York, Pocket, 1983.

Novels as Franklin W. Dixon (series: Hardy Boys Casefiles)

*Disaster for Hire.* New York, Pocket, 1989.
*The Deadliest Dare.* New York, Pocket, 1989.
*Castle Fear.* New York, Pocket, 1990.

Other

*The Assault on Childhood.* Los Angeles, Sherbourne Press, 1969; London, Gollancz, 1970.
*Cheap Thrills: An Informal History of the Pulp Magazines.* New Rochelle, New York, Arlington House, 1972.
*An American Family.* New York, Warner, 1973.
*The Adventurous Decade: Comic Strips in the Thirties.* New Rochelle, New York, Arlington House, 1975.
*Focus on Jack Cole.* Agoura, California, Fantographics, 1986.
*The Great Comic Book Artists.* New York, St. Martin's Press, 2 vols., 1986, 1989.
*Ron Goulart's Great History of Comic Books.* Chicago, Contemporary Books, 1986.
*The Dime Detectives.* New York, Mysterious Press, 1988.

Editor, *The Hardboiled Dicks: An Anthology and Study of Pulp Detective Fiction.* Los Angeles, Sherbourne Press, 1965; London, Boardman, 1967.
Editor, *Lineup Tough Guys.* Los Angeles, Sherbourne Press, 1966.
Editor, *The Great British Detective.* New York, New American Library, 1982.
Editor, *The Encyclopedia of American Comics.* New York, Facts on File, 1990.

* * *

At heart, Ron Goulart is a frustrated cartoonist. Even the most casual reader will appreciate how much the world of comic books and comic strips informs his fiction. In addition, his contribution to the lore and history of comics has been significant. His skill at weaving such personal enthusiasms into his fiction gives it an added texture and dimension.

Ron Goulart's fictional world includes Southern California, the Barnum system in outer space, and as many other alternate worlds in between as his lively imagination can conjure up. He began his writing career with parodies and humorous sketches and has continued to write with a slightly cock-eyed view of the world. He has written stories in virtually every genre, but is primarily considered a science-fiction writer. Just as his mysteries have a touch of the fantastic, his science fiction has a touch of the mysterious and often seems to straddle genres when it doesn't simply defy all categories.

His stories of outer space nearly all take place outside our own solar system in that group of planets dominated by Barnum. In the Barnum system, Murdstone is the least favoured planet, but Malagra is the pesthole of the universe. Like other legendary places (Dogpatch or Hogscratch, Arkansas) the Barnum system adjusts its dimensions to suit the current story. The Barnum system has been imaginatively realized in visual terms by artist Gil Kane in the comic strip *Star Hawks.* All of the Goulart humor comes across in the adventures of Rex Jaxan and Chavez of the Interplanetary Law Service. Ben Jolson, the multi-faced agent for the Chameleon Corps, is called on by the Political Espionage Office on Barnum to investigate mysterious happenings. *The Sword Swallower* pulls together earlier threads from his short stories, but Jolson's shapechanging powers are not exploited as imaginatively in full length as they are in the shorter form. In "Chameleon" Jolson foils an assassination by emulating Jack Cole's Plastic Man and hiding in one corner of the room disguised as a TV set. Jolson's career outside the Chameleon Corps is continued in a series that began with *Daredevils, Ltd.*

One of his best collections of short stories, *Broke Down Engine,* is concerned entirely with the problem of mankind's increasing dependence on machines. Told with humor, they also embody a bitter view of a future in which human beings become isolated from one another. Goulart's days as an advertising copywriter serve as the basis for his stories about androids in show business. He brings a fine eye and ear for the ridiculous to these in which the satire may be deeper than mere surface humor. One thinks of real life "personalities" who respond to interviewers in precise, robotic terms. Perhaps the ultimate meshing of themes for Goulart's repertoire is *Cowboy Heaven,* in which an android replacing the ailing actor Jake Troop in the film *Saddle Tramp* doesn't know when to stop. Goulart has his serious side, and this comes out in the stories of fantasy and derring-do about the mysterious Gypsy's search for his own identity.

Goulart's style is concise and his stories are told mostly in dialogue. The reader has to be alert and not let the fast pace and skeletal appearance prevent him from enjoying the yarn. At his best, Goulart is a witty and engaging story-teller, with a recognizable reality to his fantasies. His Southern California is the extrapolation of present trends in the ridiculous; his machinery gone amok is an extension of our own worst fears as a vacuum cleaner malfunctions or an automobile breaks down.

No Goulart character can expect to grow old in retirement. There are always new challenges to face, such as the planet system in *Hellquad:* no matter which one you choose to land on, the other three are worse. His brand of science fiction may be set in 2033 or 1941 or 1897. The Harry Challenge series features an 1890's private detective whose cases involve fantasy and science-fiction elements. Goulart himself is not afraid of challenge, whether it is extending his series of reference works on comics or serving as sometime ghost-writer to the genre. The Goulart oeuvre is a Möbius strip; when you've read one, you've just begun.

—J. Randolph Cox

---

**GRAHAM, Robert.** *See* **HALDEMAN, Joe.**

---

**GRANT, Charles L.** Also writes as Felicia Andrews; Steven Charles; Lionel Fenn; Simon Lake; Deborah Lewis; and Geoffrey Marsh. American. Born in Newark, New Jersey, 12 September 1942. Educated at Trinity College, Hartford, Connecticut, B.A. 1964. Served in the United States Army Military Police, 1968–70: Bronze Star. Married Debbie Voss in 1973; one son and one daughter. English teacher, Toms River High School, New Jersey, 1964–70, Chester High School, New Jersey, 1970–72, and Mt. Olive High School, New Jersey, 1972–73; English and history teacher, Roxbury High School, New Jersey, 1974–75. Since 1975, freelance writer. Executive secretary, Science Fiction Writers of America, 1973–77. Recipient: Nebula award, 1976, 1978; World Fantasy award, for non-fiction, 1980, for editing, 1983. Agent: Howard Morhaim Literary Agency, 175 Fifth Avenue, Suite 709, New York, New York 10010, U.S.A.

SCIENCE-FICTION PUBLICATIONS

Novels (series: Parric family)

*The Shadow of Alpha* (Parric). New York, Berkley, 1976.
*Ascension* (Parric). New York, Berkley, 1977.
*The Ravens of the Moon*. New York, Doubleday, 1978; London, Sidgwick and Jackson, 1979.
*Legion* (Parric). New York, Berkley, 1979.
*Nightmare Seasons*. New York, Doubleday, 1982; London, Severn House, 1989.
*Night Songs*. New York, Pocket Books, 1984.

Short Stories

*Tales from the Nightside: Dark Fantasy*. Sauk City, Wisconsin, Arkham House, 1981; London, Macdonald, 1988.
*A Glow of Candles and Other Stories*. New York, Berkley, 1981.

Uncollected Short Stories

"The House of Evil," in *Fantasy and Science Fiction* (New York), December 1968.
"The Summer of the Irish Sea," in *Orbit 11*, edited by Damon Knight. New York, Putnam, 1973.
"The Magic Child," in *Frontiers 2*, edited by Roger Elwood. New York, Macmillan, 1973.
"Weep No More, Old Lady," in *Future Quest*, edited by Roger Elwood. New York, Avon, 1973.
"But the Other Old Man Stopped Playing," in *Amazing* (New York), April 1973.
"Abdication," in *Amazing* (New York), October 1973.
"Everybody's a Winner, the Barker Cried," in *Orbit 13*, edited by Damon Knight. New York, Putnam, 1974.
"In Donovan's Time," in *Orbit 16*, edited by Damon Knight. New York, Harper, 1975.
"To Be a Witch, in ¾ Time," in *Fantastic* (New York), February 1975.
"When Two or Three Are Gathered," in *Amazing* (New York), March 1975.
"Seven Is a Birdsong," in *Analog* (New York), January 1976.
"Eldorado," in *The Arts and Beyond*, edited by Thomas F. Monteleone. New York, Doubleday, 1977.
"Treatise on the Artifacts of a Civilization," in *Antaeus* (New York), 1977.
"The Shape of Plowshares," in *Analog* (New York), March 1977.
"Gently Rapping," in *Galaxy* (New York), September 1977.
"Knock, and See What Enters," in *Fantastic* (New York), December 1977.
"View, with a Difference," in *Dark Sins, Dark Dreams*, edited by Barry N. Malzberg and Bill Pronzini. New York, Doubleday, 1978.
"The Peace That Passes Never," in *Chrysalis 3*, edited by Roy Torgeson. New York, Kensington, 1978.
"The Fourth Musketeer," in *Whispers 2*, edited by Stuart David Schiff. New York, Doubleday, 1979.
"When Dark Descends," with Thomas F. Monteleone, in *Chrysalis 4*, edited by Roy Torgeson. New York, Zebra, 1979.
"And Weary of the Sun," in *Chrysalis 5*, edited by Roy Torgeson. New York, Zebra, 1979.
"Love-Starved," in *Fantasy and Science Fiction* (New York), August 1979.
"Across the Water to Skye," in *New Terrors 2*, edited by Ramsey Campbell. London, Pan, 1980.
"A Garden of Blackred Roses," in *Dark Forces*, edited by Kirby McCauley. New York, Viking Press, 1980.
"The Other Room," in *Mummy!*, edited by Bill Pronzini. New York, Arbor House, 1980.
"Quietly Now," in *The Arbor House Necropolis*, edited by Bill Pronzini. New York, Arbor House, 1981.
"Confess the Seasons," in *Perpetual Light*, edited by Alan Ryan. New York, Warner, 1982.
"Every Time You Say I Love You," in *The Year's Best Horror Stories 10*, edited by Karl Edward Wagner. New York, DAW, 1982.
"Essence of Charlotte," in *Twilight Zone* (New York), February 1982.
"What in Solemn Silence," in *Isaac Asimov's Science Fiction Magazine* (New York), 15 March 1982.
"Pride," in *Fantasy and Science Fiction* (New York), May 1982.
"The Wind of Lost Migration," in *Amazing* (New York), June 1982.
"I Never Could Say Goodbye," in *Whispers 4*, edited by Stuart David Schiff. New York, Doubleday, 1983.
"The Next Name You Hear," in *Fantasy and Science Fiction* (New York), January 1983.
"Recollections of Annie," in *Twilight Zone* (New York), January–February 1983.
"A Voice Not Heard," in *Isaac Asimov's Science Fiction Magazine* (New York), September 1984.

OTHER PUBLICATIONS

Novels

*The Curse*. Canoga Park, California, Major, 1976.
*The Hour of the Oxrun Dead*. New York, Doubleday, 1977.
*The Sound of Midnight*. New York, Doubleday, 1978.
*The Last Call of Mourning*. New York, Doubleday, 1979.
*Quiet Night of Fear*. New York, Berkley, 1981.
*The Grave*. New York, Popular Library, 1981.
*Bloodwind*. New York, Popular Library, 1982.
*The Soft Whisper of the Dead*. Hampton Falls, New Hampshire, Donald Grant, 1982.
*The Nestling*. New York, Pocket, 1982; London, Hamlyn, 1983.
*The Tea Party*. New York, Pocket Books, 1985.
*The Dark Cry of the Moon*. Hampton Falls, New Hampshire, Donald Grant, 1986.
*The Long Night of the Grave*. Hampton Falls, New Hampshire, Donald Grant, 1986.
*The Orchard*. New York, Tor, 1986; London, Macdonald, 1989.
*The Pet*. New York, Tor, 1986; London, Macdonald, 1987.
*For Fear of the Night*. New York, Tor, and London, Futura, 1988.
*In a Dark Dream*. New York, Tor, 1989; London, New English Library, 1990.
*Dialing the Wind*. New York, Tor, 1989.
*Stunts*. New York, Tor, 1990.
*Fire Mask* (for children). New York, Bantam, 1991.
*Something Stirs*. New York, Tor, 1991.

Novels as Deborah Lewis

*Voices Out of Time*. New York, Kensington, 1977.
*Eve of the Hound*. New York, Kensington, 1977.

Novels as Felicia Andrews

*River Witch*. New York, Jove, 1979.
*Moon Witch*. New York, Jove, 1980.
*Mountain Witch*. New York, Jove, 1980.

Novels as Geoffrey Marsh

*The King of Satan's Eyes*. New York, Doubleday, 1984.
*The Tail of the Arabian, Knight*. New York, Doubleday, 1986.
*Patch of the Odin Soldier*. New York, Doubleday, 1987.
*Fangs of the Hooded Demon*. New York, Tor, 1986.

Novels as Steven Charles (for children)

*Nightmare Session*. New York, Pocket, 1986; London, Lightning, 1990.
*Academy of Terror*. New York, Pocket, 1986; London, Lightning, 1990.
*Witch's Eye*. New York, Pocket, 1986; London, Lightning, 1990.
*Skeleton Key*. New York, Pocket, 1986; London, Lightning, 1990.
*The Last Alien*. New York, Pocket, 1987.
*The Enemy Within*. New York, Pocket, 1987.

Novels as Lionel Fenn

*Blood River Down*. New York, Tor, 1986.
*Web of Defeat*. New York, Tor, 1987.
*Agnes Day*. New York, Tor, 1987.
*The Seven Spears of the W'dch'ck*. New York, Tor, 1988.
*Kent Montana and the Really Ugly Thing from Mars*. New York, Ace, 1990.
*Kent Montana and the Reasonably Invisible Man*. New York, Ace, 1991.

Short Stories

*Black Wine*, with Ramsey Campbell; edited by Douglas E. Winter. Arlington Heights, Illinois, Dark Harvest, 1986.

Other

Editor, *Writing and Selling Science Fiction*. Cincinnati, Writer's Digest, 1977.
Editor, *Shadows 1–14*. New York, Doubleday, 14 vols., 1978–91.
Editor, *Nightmares*. New York, Doubleday, 1978.
Editor, *Horrors*. New York, Berkley, 1981.
Editor, *Terrors*. New York, Pocket Books, 1982.
Editor, *The Dodd Mead Gallery of Horror*. New York, Dodd Mead, 1983; as *Gallery of Horror*, London, Robson, 1983.
Editor, *Fears*. New York, Berkley, 1983.
Editor, *Midnight*. New York, Tor, 1985.
Editor, *The Chronicles of Greystone Bay*. New York, Tor, 3 vols., 1985.
Editor, *Night Visions 2*. Arlington Heights, Illinois, Dark Harvest, 1985; as *Dead Image*, New York, Berkley, 1987; as *Night Terrors*, London, Headline, 1987.
Editor, *After Midnight*. New York, Tor, 1986.
Editor, *The Best of Shadows*. New York, Doubleday, 1988.

*

Charles L. Grant comments (1985):

In science fiction, I'm working on a future history that most of my more recent stories and novels fit into, a history that will eventually cover over 500 years, primarily tracing a single family (the Parrics). In horror fiction, my aim is, simply, to produce a fright in the reader. In this regard I generally use two settings: Hawthorne Street (a place in an unnamed town in an unnamed area of the country), and Oxrun Station, an upper-middle and upper-class village in western Connecticut. If there's any influence at all in my work it comes not from Lovecraft or Smith, but from Bradbury and Ellison, with perhaps a dollop of Sturgeon.

* * *

Charles L. Grant first published a flurry of striking short stories in the early 1970's. "The Summer of the Irish Sea" shows his gift for unusual imagery. In a world where peace has ostensibly been achieved, aggression is channeled into other outlets, in this case, a fox hunt with a human being as the fox. World War III kills all but one survivor, an elderly shepherd whose remaining flock is mysteriously dwindling, leading him to a confrontation with the god Pan.

In "Abdication," an astronaut becomes president, but is denied re-election because of his opposition to the space program, providing Grant a springboard for examining our national motivation for the project. "The Rest Is Silence" is one of Grant's best early short stories. After resigning from his teaching position, the protagonist throws a party at which he uses a unique mental power to open the barriers between universes.

"Everybody's a Winner, the Barker Cried" is both depressing and elevating. Following a nuclear exchange, two doomed victims meet for a last ride on the ferris wheel, reaffirming the human spirit even as they surrender their lives. The teaching profession is examined in "When Two or Three Are Gathered." Our conventional teaching methods are now forbidden, but one man continues to run bootleg classes for those few students unwilling to surrender to the system.

Grant's fondness for the horror story is evident in these early stories. In "Come Dance with Me on My Pony's Grave," a Vietnam vet struggles to understand the strange bonds between his adopted Asian son and a pony. Another fine supernatural story from this period is "White Wolf Calling." An early, less successful novel, *The Curse*, appeared at approximately the same time.

In 1976, Grant's first science-fiction novel, *The Shadow of Alpha*, was published, the first volume in the "Parric" trilogy. Earth has been devastated by plagues and the survivors lead a barbarous life, cloistered in cities or roaming the wilderness. Androids designed to take over the drudgery of life have gone off on tangents of their own, and are now often inimical to human life. Two sequels, *Ascension* and *Legion*, followed, with the central government re-establishing its authority. Although the novels are enjoyable and tightly plotted, they lack the depth and energy of his later works.

Grant moved increasingly away from science fiction in the years that followed. As Steven Charles, he wrote a six-volume series for young adults, consisting of *Nightmare Session, Academy of Terror, Witch's Eye, Skeleton Key, The Enemy Within*, and *The Last Alien.* A remote private school is the hunting ground for an alien species, who are mysteriously disposing of members of the staff and student body.

More interesting are the humorous fantastic adventures that have appeared under the names Geoffrey Marsh and Lionel Fenn. The books written as Marsh chronicle the adventures of Lincoln Blackthorne, most effectively in the first volume, *The King of Satan's Eyes*, less so in the sequels. As Lionel Fenn,

Grant produced an amusing and entertaining fantasy trilogy, *Blood River Down, Web of Defeat*, and *Agnes Day*. A perfectly ordinary man from our own world finds the gateway to a magical realm and crosses over, where he is immediately identified as a mythical hero and set upon the road to war, women, and warlocks. *The Seven Spears of the W'dch'ck*, a similar but much funnier variation, appeared more recently.

Grant also used the Fenn name to spoof more traditional themes. *Kent Montana and the Really Ugly Thing from Mars* takes apart the alien invasion story and reassembles the pieces in a bizarre parody. He followed this with *Kent Montana and the Reasonably Invisible Man*, and more, presumably similar, volumes are predicted for the future.

Although occasional science-fiction and fantasy stories continued to appear, most notably "The Peace That Passes Never" and "And Weary of the Sun," the vast majority of Grant's substantial body of fiction has been in the supernatural horror genre. His outstanding books in this area include *The Nestling*, a blend of Indian legend and modern day shapechanging; *The Orchard*, a chilling and very original "monster" story; *The Pet; Nightmare Seasons*, a collection of four superb novelettes, and *Stunts*, wherein an American professor in England discovers that he has run afoul of an ancient magical force. Supernatural elements run through books he has written in other genres as well, including the Felicia Andrews romances and the Deborah Lewis gothic suspense stories. Grant has come to be known as one of the foremost writers of "quiet" horror, that is, stories which rely on the psychological pressure on the protagonists and the inherent suspense of the situation, rather than on grisly dismemberments or other overt descriptive devices.

Although his turn to the horror field has caused Grant to remain a peripheral influence on science fiction, his acknowledged skill and success in that field only emphasizes his potential as a writer in any genre. His strongly delineated characters and skillful storytelling abilities are all too rare.

—Don D'Ammassa

---

**GRANT, Mark.** *See* **BISCHOFF, David F.**

---

**GREEN, Joseph (Lee).** American. Born in Compass Lake, Florida, 14 January 1931. Educated at University of Alabama, Tuscaloosa, B.A. Married 1) Juanita Henderson in 1951 (divorced 1975), one son and one daughter; 2) Patrice Milton in 1975, two daughters. Laboratory technician, International Paper Company, Panama City, Florida 1949–51; shop worker and welder, Panama City, 1952–54; millwright in Florida, Texas, and Alabama, 1955–58; senior supervisor, Boeing Company, Seattle, 1959–63. Technical writer and science writer at Kennedy Space Center, Florida, 1965–83. Since 1984, public affairs writer/editor for NASA, Kennedy Space Center. Agent: Blassingame McCauley and Wood, 432 Park Avenue South, New York, New York 10016. Address: 1390 Holly Avenue, Merritt Island, Florida 32952, U.S.A.

SCIENCE-FICTION PUBLICATIONS

Novels

*The Loafers of Refuge*. London, Gollancz, and New York, Ballantine, 1965.
*Gold the Man*. London, Gollancz, 1971; as *The Mind Behind the Eye*, New York, DAW, 1972.
*Conscience Interplanetary*. London, Gollancz, 1972; New York, Doubleday, 1973.
*Star Probe*. London, Millington, 1976; New York, Ace, 1978.
*The Horde*. Toronto, Laser, 1976; London, Dobson, 1979.

Short Stories

*An Affair with Genius*. London, Gollancz, 1969.

Uncollected Short Stories

"The Fourth Generation," in *Science Fiction Adventures* (London), vol. 5, no. 30, 1962.
"The Fight on Hurricane Island," in *Argosy* (London), June 1963.
"Haggard Honeymoon," with James Webbert, in *New Writings in SF 1*, edited by John Carnell. London, Dobson, 1964.
"The Creators," in *New Writings in SF 2*, edited by John Carnell. London, Dobson, 1964.
"Treasure Hunt," in *New Writings in SF 5*, edited by John Carnell. London, Dobson, 1965.
"Birth of a Butterfly," in *New Writings in SF 10*, edited by John Carnell. London, Dobson, 1967.
"When I Have Passed Away," in *New Writings in SF 15*, edited by John Carnell. London, Dobson, 1969.
"Death and the Sensperience Poet," in *New Writings in SF 17*, edited by John Carnell. London, Dobson, 1970.
"First Light on a Darkling Plain," in *New Writings in SF 19*, edited by John Carnell. London, Dobson, 1971.
"Wrong Attitude," in *Analog* (New York), February 1971.
"One Man Game," in *Analog* (New York), February 1972.
"The Seventh Floor," in *Eternity* (Sandy Springs, South Carolina), May 1972.
"Three-Tour Man," in *Analog* (New York), August 1972.
"A Custom of the Children of Life," in *Fantasy and Science Fiction* (New York), December 1972.
"Space to Move," in *The New Mind*, edited by Roger Elwood. New York, Macmillan, 1973.
"Let My People Go!," in *The Other Side of Tomorrow*, edited by Roger Elwood. New York, Random House, 1973.
"The Birdlover," in *Showcase*, edited by Roger Elwood. New York, Harper, 1973.
"Robustus Revisited," in *Fantasy and Science Fiction* (New York), April 1973.
"The Waiting World," in *Future Kin*, edited by Roger Elwood. New York, Doubleday, 1974.
"A Star Is Born," in *Fantasy and Science Fiction* (New York), February 1974.
"Walk Barefoot on the Glass," in *Analog* (New York), March 1974.
"Jaybird's Song," in *Fantasy and Science Fiction* (New York), December 1974.
"A Death in Coventry," in *Dystopian Visions*, edited by Roger Elwood. Englewood Cliffs, New Jersey, Prentice Hall, 1975.
"Encounter with a Carnivore," in *Epoch*, edited by Roger Elwood and Robert Silverberg. New York, Berkley, 1975.
"Weekend in Hartford," in *Dude* (Mt. Morris, Illinois), September 1975.

"Last of the Chauvinists," in *Fantasy and Science Fiction* (New York), November 1975.

"Jeremiah, Born Dying," in *Odyssey* (New York), Spring 1976.

"To See the Stars That Blind," with Patrice Milton, in *Fantasy and Science Fiction* (New York), March 1977.

"An Alien Conception," in *Nugget* (New York), June 1977.

"The Wind among the Mindymums," in *Fantasy and Science Fiction* (New York), December 1978.

"The Speckled Gantry," in *Destinies* (New York), January 1979.

"Gentle into That Good Night," in *Analog* (New York), July 1981.

"Still Fall the Gentle Rains," with Patrice Milton, in *Rigel* (Richmond, California), Fall 1981.

"EasyEd," with Patrice Milton, in *Fantasy and Science Fiction* (New York), May 1982.

"In the Court of the Chrysoprase King," with Patrice Milton, in *Rigel* (Richmond, California), Spring 1983.

"And Be Lost Like Me," in *Analog* (New York), June 1983.

"Raccoon Reaction," in *Analog* (New York), September 1983.

"The Ruby Wand of Asrazel," in *Magic in Ithkar 2*, edited by Andre Norton and Robert Adams. New York, Tor, 1985.

"With Conscience of the New," with Patrice Milton, in *Analog* (New York), February 1989.

*

Joseph Green comments:

Most of my stories have an underlying philosophical theme that is often not apparent on the surface. At heart I think of myself as an untrained, poorly equipped, corn-ball philosopher, and what I enjoy most is playing with ideas in fictional form. For that reason, I'll never create a consistent "future history." If I write a story about the totally secular world of 2090 today, I may want to write one tomorrow about the new surge in absolutist religion from 2070 to 2110. I have no faith at all in a single future.

I've achieved some small reputation as a writer of unusually believable aliens. I don't know why. I dream them up, work to make them real, and write about them because I enjoy it. Do I need a better reason? I write primarily for readers, not critics or other writers. If a reader enjoys my work, that's good. If it also makes him think, that's even better.

* * *

Joseph Green is a strongly imaginative writer. He likes to set his heroes problems, sometimes highly exotic or elaborately contrived, always laid out with great clarity and convincingly resolved. These heroes are often troubleshooters, typically working at the interface between human and alien, sometimes—and this is probably his most characteristic motif—even operating with alien bodies. In his most powerful novel, *Gold the Man*, this alienation works as far as two removes, for the hero is emphatically a man trapped in a superman's body, put to work inside an alien giant. In confronting his character with painful dilemmas, Green communicates to the reader a strong concern; he is also able to treat sympathetically those on both sides of an irreconcilable debate, as in *Star Probe*, which concerns one battle in a larger war between the space scientists and the Friends of the Earth. In *The Horde* he presents one of the genre's most sympathetic accounts of a kind of alien hive species, the humanoid Shemsi, as an improbable friendship develops between human and humanoid bound together, for different reasons, on a dangerous mission.

Reflecting their origins as series of short stories, *The Loafers of Refuge* and *Conscience Interplanetary* are episodic narratives. In the first, trouble-shooter Carey, as the first man born on Refuge, works to resolve conflict between humans and the native loafers, who have developed mental but not mechanical power. Human-Loafer interaction is mutually beneficial: for instance, the Loafers revivify their living trees (the Ent-like *breshwahr*), and one of them shows how men can survive matter transmission, thus enabling rapid colonization of other planets to relieve the overcrowded Earth. In the second, the hero Allan Odegaard has the job of checking whether intelligence exists on a planet: if so, it must be left alone; if not, it may be colonized (a problem consequent on the solution found in *The Loafers*). Throughout his seven extraordinary adventures, Allan is in more danger from reactionary humans than from the weird life-forms he encounters.

*Gold the Man* is a classic novel, whether considered as a profound study of the loneliness of the superman in no-man's-land or as an exciting contribution to Brobdingnagian fantasy. Earth is at war with giant humanoids, the Hilt-Sil, one of whom, suffering from irreparable brain damage, is captured. The superman Gold, and a female assistant, Marina Petrovna, are installed in the head of the 300-foot captive, where they control his brain, seated behind one of his eyes. In this extraordinary Trojan horse, they spy on the alien planet, finding the feared enemies to be a race of gentle giants living an idyllic life but forced to look for another planet because of danger from their own sun. Gold helps resolve their problems and, remarkably enough, his enforced voyeurism of their Gargantuan love-play resolves his personal fear of impotence: being a superman, he was a slow developer, but he rapes and impregnates the helpless Marina and their child is born with the assistance of a friendly Hilt-Sil doctor who has discovered them (this is not a macho fantasy story for all that). Green sets himself difficult problems in this powerful novel, but he handles both the physicalities and the psychological stresses of the intriguing situations with great tact and skill.

In the light of *Gold the Man*, Green makes less than expected of the interesting motif in *Star Probe* of an old man, deceased, who is brought back to life in the body of his idiot grandson for the purposes of a suicide mission. The mission concerns the investigation of an alien probe in the solar system; once the difficulties of getting a rocket to the probe have been resolved, Green is able once again to concern himself with the interesting problem of communication between alien and human; within the novel as a whole, however, the probe serves only as an emblem of what the struggle for funds between space scientists and ecologists is all about.

Among Green's many fine short stories, it is hard to pick out the best or most characteristic, but "Jinn," "Once Around Arcturus," "Treasure Hunt" (man inside crystal chariot-horse), "When I Have Passed Away" (exotic Giantesses), "Last of the Chauvinists," and "To See the Stars That Blind" (written with his wife, Patrice Milton, brilliantly presenting the wonder and horror of a new mode of seeing), should be included. Nine short stories are collected in *An Affair with Genius*, including "The Decision Makers," which is recycled in *Conscience Interplanetary*. They show a preference for open over closed endings, not surprising in view of the author's expressed lack of faith in "a single future." Two stories, "Tunnel of Love" and "Dance of the Cats," one humorous and the other horrific, feature the same two enterprising young Space Service men, Silva de Fonseca ("Quicksilva") and Aaron Gunderson. Green has published few stories in recent years; in one of the most recent, "Still Fall the Gentle Rains" (written with Patrice Milton), the concern is still, movingly, with human-humanoid relations and the species implications of sexuality: in this case, lower fertility implies greater honesty; in "And Be Lost Like Me," a new test for a typical Phildickian problem, distinguishing alien from human, is presented.

—Michael J. Tolley

---

**GREEN, Peter.** *See* **BULMER, Kenneth.**

---

**GREENLAND, Colin.** British. Born in Dover, Kent, 17 May 1954. Educated at St. Lawrence College, Ramsgate, Kent, 1964–72; Pembroke College, Oxford, 1972–79, B.A. in English literature and language (honors) 1975; D. Phil. in English literature 1981. Fellow in creative writing, Science Fiction Foundation, North East London Polytechnic, 1980–82; co-editor, *Interzone* magazine, London, 1982–85; U.K. coordinator, Eaton Conference on Science Fiction, University of California, Riverside/North East London Polytechnic, 1983–84; part-time tutor, University of London Extra-mural Department, 1985–90; chair, Science Fiction Writers' Conference, Milford, Hantshire, 1986. Since 1989, reviews editor, *Foundation* magazine, London. Recipient: J. Lloyd Eaton award, for criticism, 1985; Arthur C. Clarke award, 1991; British Science Fiction Association award, for best novel, 1991. Agent: Maggie Noach, 21 Redan Street, London W14 0AB, England; or, Martha Millard, 204 Park Avenue, Madison, New Jersey, 07940, U.S.A. Address: 2A Ortygia House, 6 Lower Road, Harrow, Middlesex HA2 0DA, England.

SCIENCE-FICTION PUBLICATIONS

Novels

*Daybreak on a Different Mountain*. London, Allen and Unwin, 1984.
*The Hour of the Thin Ox*. London, Allen and Unwin, 1986.
*Other Voices*. London, Unwin Hyman, 1988.
*Take Back Plenty*. London, Unwin Hyman, 1990.

Uncollected Short Stories

"Miss Otis Regrets," in *The Fiction Magazine*, London, Winter 1982.
"The Living End," in *The Fiction Magazine*, London, July/August 1987.
"The Traveller," in *Zenith*, edited by David S. Garnett. London, Sphere, 1989.
"A Passion for Lord Pierrot," in *Zenith 2*, edited by David S. Garnett. London, Sphere, 1990.

OTHER PUBLICATIONS

Other

*The Entropy Exhibition: Michael Moorcock and the British "New Wave" in Science Fiction*. London and Boston, Routledge, 1983.
*Magnetic Storm: The Work of Roger and Martyn Dean*. London, Dragon's World, 1984.
*The Freelance Writer's Handbook*, with Paul Kerton. London, Ebury, 1986.

* * *

With a doctoral thesis on the "New Wave" in British science fiction and a solid background of reviews and articles in *Foundation, The Guardian*, and *The Times Literary Supplement*, Colin Greenland might seem to have been over-prepared for the profession of science-fiction writer. His first novel, *Daybreak on a Different Mountain*, is assured and fresh, but at the same time strangely muted and compressed. The city of Thryn, reeking of decay and past grandeur, festers most convincingly behind its high walls; its infrastructure is not made plain even to its remaining aristocrats. Lupio, the playboy, finds himself suddenly involved in the prophecies of the mad old priestess, Kavi. He falls in with the poet Dubilier, who is escaping from an unhappy love affair. Together this complementary pair set out to do the impossible: they venture beyond the walls of Thryn in search of the god Gomath and his guide, the Cirnex, last seen upon the sacred mountain, Hisper Einou. Their adventurous quest among the peoples of Outwall leads not only to self-knowledge but to revelation.

Colin Greenland extended his range with *The Hour of the Thin Ox*, first of a series of books dealing with an alternate world. Bryland, which has overtones of 17th-century England, and the Seven Realms, are contrasted with Escaly, an eastern empire. Jillian Curram, a hardy and resourceful heroine, experiences the ruin of her Bryland estates as the country drifts into war. Already, as a child, she had a fateful glimpse of the Princess Nette of Luscany and of Karel Jessup, the gruff, young engineer, inventor of a fearful weapon that seems to resemble a Gatling gun. Meanwhile, in distant Escaly, Ky varan, an innocent scholar, rises through the ancient hierarchies to become Imperial Geometer. He is already an old man when his young apprentice, Bi tok, begins to bring warmth and understanding into his life. The tragi-comedy of this appealing pair is one of the author's finest achievements.

Cultures clash in a third world, the rainforests of Belanesi, home of a mysterious race of faun-like natives. The Imperial Geometer and his apprentice, who have crashed in the jungle in the course of a foolish propaganda mission, benefit from the healing arts of these people and begin to learn about their civilisation. Savage Escalan troops are penetrating the forest, killing all who come in their way, but Jill Curram and her band of female guerillas, Bryland irregulars, meet with unexpected success.

The wry originality of the series, its blend of clever extrapolation and mystery, continues in *Other Voices*, a winter's tale set in the mountain archduchy of Luscany. In another childhood episode, Serin, daughter of mad Dr. Guille, the necrobiologist, and his gypsy wife, experiences the very beginning of the Escalan occupation of her country. Ten years later, while Princess Nette chafes at the restrictions of a puppet ruler, Serin witnesses the murder of an Escalan official, an event that triggers off the long-awaited revolution. The acrid interchanges of the long-suffering Princess with her Escalan overlords, with courtiers, and with her contrary old mother, the Archduchess, are mordant and stylish. Strangest voice of all is that of Serin's unidentified admirer, once a man, now undead, a vampire. He beckons the reader on to a further chronicle.

*Take Back Plenty*, a breakthrough book, winner of prestigious awards, is a space opera: it teems with characters, explores strange worlds, leaps hectically through space and time. This is Greenland unbound. As Tabitha Jute, the indomitable spacer, rackets round the solar system one jump ahead of her creditors and assorted baddies, she tells marvelous tales to the inscrutable persona of her ship, the *Alice Liddell.* From the canals of Mars during Carnival, to the steamy jungles of Venus and the scungy loading docks of Plenty, a deconstructed space habitat, the Terran system is under the sway of the elusive Capellans and their doggy bureaucrats, the Eladeldi. Tabitha is at the centre of a vortex of intrigue and misadventure: empires crumble, legends proliferate, sentient beings perish nastily, and the best of friends, sadly, must part. The moral of this absorbing extravaganza might be "There is no such thing as a free space drive." The hidden capacities of the author are as manifold as the field of science fiction and fantasy itself. He understands the genre thoroughly and can be relied upon to reawaken our sense of wonder.

—Cherry Wilder

---

**GREENLEAF, William.** Born in 1917. Address: c/o Ace Books, 200 Madison Avenue, New York, New York 10016, U.S.A.

SCIENCE-FICTION PUBLICATIONS

Novels

*Timejumper.* New York, Leisure Books, 1980.
*The Tartarus Incident.* New York, Ace, 1983.
*The Pandora Stone.* New York, Ace, 1984.
*Starjacked!* New York, Berkley, 1987.
*Clarion.* New York, Tor, 1988.

* * *

Science fiction has long been a haven for the unabashed adventure story, and indeed the term "space opera" has been coined to describe a certain subgroup of interplanetary adventures that are essentially traditional western plots transported to an interplanetary setting. Similarly, lost race novels, pirate stories, and spy stories can be modified to fit into an interstellar environment. One of the more interesting if not truly major writers taking advantage of this situation is William Greenleaf.

Greenleaf's first novel, *Timejumper,* first appeared in 1980. The setting is familiar: in a far future Earth, the remnants of humanity are split into two groups, the barbarians who roam the wastelands and those who have held onto the trappings of technological civilization and live in what remains of the great urban metropolises of another age. The novel brings together two disparate individuals, an obsessively curious barbarian boy and a brilliant but warped genius who has constructed a device that will allow him to move about in time. The result is access to another world, and a fresh hope for humanity, unless the repressive priesthood can block humanity's aspirations. Greenleaf is quite skillful at providing surprising reversals in his fiction, and this first novel, though relatively clumsy, has a freshness and enthusiasm that overcomes its shortcomings.

*The Tartarus Incident* is a markedly better novel. A spaceship and its crew inadvertently arrive on the wrong planet and find themselves stranded. Although there is no immediate prospect of rescue, neither is there any cause for panic; they recognize that it's only a matter of time until the authorities realize they have not arrived, investigate, and determine where they have in fact landed. As it happens, however, they don't have time for leisure. The discovery of an ancient, abandoned city on the planet is at first a source of interest, but then growing alarm as a discorporate mental force reaches out to alter the minds of the crew members. Although Greenleaf shows notable ability to evoke a mood of terror, this really isn't the major focus of the book. The best passages in fact are those dealing with the crew's attempts to adjust to their isolation and, back on Earth, the efforts of a minor official to discover what happened to the missing ship.

Following *The Pandora Stone,* an interesting but minor adventure story, Greenleaf produced *Starjacked!,* a blend of space adventure, pirate story, and straightforward adventure. The Fringes are an area of human-colonized space sufficiently remote from the more settled worlds that law and order are not something that can be taken for granted. The Guards is a paramilitary organization created to maintain some degree of security for space travellers. Unfortunately, elements within the Guard have come to an arrangement with some of the space pirates, as a consequence of which they jointly arrange the hijacking of a starship.

An investigative reporter following a lead finds himself in the middle of events when he is taken prisoner by the pirates and locked away aboard the hijacked ship. Although not ordinarily a leader, he finds himself reluctantly helping to organize an attempt to regain control of the ship. Because of the circumstances of the hijacking, however, return to more civilized regions will not be quite as simple. The pirates and the Guard both have good reason to arrange that no one lives to provide a true account. Although the waning chapters deteriorate into an overly melodramatic series of battles, Greenleaf's gift for characterization is evident in the earlier chapters, and the book is on the whole a quite satisfying creation.

Greenleaf's most recent novel is *Clarion,* which like most of his earlier books has at its center a mystery, the resolution of which is intimately involved with the resolution of the main plotline. Clarion is a colony world that has been out of touch with the rest of the human race for over two centuries. Now its population is held in thrall by a charismatic cult leader, who may not be a human being at all but rather an alien interloper hoping to lead the colony to its destruction. Opposed to him, albeit not by intention, is a psionically talented artist whose abilities cause him to become the target of a series of assassination attempts. As with *The Tartarus Incident,* Greenleaf makes use of a repulsive alien entity to heighten tension, although the overriding mood of the story is still one of adventure rather than terror. *Clarion* contains a far more intricately developed civilization than any of Greenleaf's earlier novels, stronger characterization, a more tightly controlled plot, and noticeably smoother prose. If this is truly indicative of his continuing development as a writer, then Greenleaf is on the verge of becoming a significant contributor to the field.

—Don D'Ammassa

---

**GREER, Richard.** *See* **GARRETT, Randall.**

---

**GREGORY, John.** *See* **HOSKINS, Robert.**

---

**GREY, Carol.** *See* **LOWNDES, Robert A.W.**

---

**GREY, Charles.** *See* **TUBB, E.C.**

---

**GRIBBIN, John R.** British. Born in Maidstone, Kent, in 1946. Educated at Sussex University, B.Sc. 1966, M.Sc. 1967; Cambridge University, Ph.D. 1971. Staff writer for *Nature* magazine, 1970–75; member of Science Policy Research Unit, University of Sussex, Brighton, 1975–78. Since 1978, physics consultant to *New Scientist.* Adviser to Thames-TV and TV South. Agent: Murray Pollinger, 222 Old Brompton Road, London SW5 0BZ, England.

SCIENCE-FICTION PUBLICATIONS

Novels

*Double Planet*, with Marcus Chown. London, Gollancz, 1988.
*Father to the Man.* London, Gollancz, 1989.
*Reunion*, with Marcus Chown. London, Gollancz, 1991.

OTHER PUBLICATIONS

Other

*The Jupiter Effect*, with Stephen H. Plagemann. London, Macmillan, and New York, Walker, 1974.
*Our Changing Climate.* London, Faber, 1975.
*Astronomy for the Amateur.* London, Macmillan, and New York, D. McKay, 1976.
*Forecasts, Famines, and Freezes: Climate and Man's Future.* London, Wildwood House, and New York, Walker, 1976.
*Galaxy Formation: A Personal View.* London, Macmillan, and New York, Wiley, 1976.
*Our Changing Planet.* London, Wildwood House, and New York, Crowell, 1977.
*White Holes: Cosmic Gushers in the Universe.* London, Paladin, and New York, Delacorte Press/E. Friede, 1977.
*Our Changing Universe: The New Astronomy.* London, Macmillan, and New York, Dutton, 1976.
*The Climatic Threat.* London, Fontana, 1978; as *What's Wrong with Our Weather*, New York, Scribner, 1979.
*Earthquakes and Volcanoes.* New York, Gallery, 1978.
*This Shaking Earth.* London, Sedgwick and Jackson, and New York, Putnam, 1978.
*Climate and Mankind.* London, Earthscan, 1979.
*Future Worlds.* London, Abacus, 1979.
*The Sixth World*, with Douglas Orgill. London, Bodley Head, and New York, Simon and Schuster, 1979.
*Timewarps.* London, Dent, and New York, Delacorte Press/E. Friede, 1979.
*Weather Force: Climate and Its Impact on Our World.* London, Hamlyn, and New York, Putnam, 1979.
*The Death of the Sun.* New York, Delacorte Press/E. Friede, 1980.
*The Strangest Star.* London, Athlone Press, 1980.
*Carbon Dioxide, the Climate, and Man.* London, IIED, 1981.
*Genesis: The Origins of Man and the Universe.* London, Dent, and New York, Delacorte Press/E. Friede, 1981.
*Brother Esau*, with Douglas Orgill. London, Bodley Head, and New York, Harper and Row, 1982.
*Future Weather and the Greenhouse Effect.* New York, Delacorte Press/E. Friede, 1982.
*The Jupiter Effect Reconsidered*, with Stephen H. Plagemann. New York, Vintage, 1982.
*The Monkey Puzzle*, with Jeremy Cherfas. London, Bodley Head, and New York, Pantheon, 1982.
*Beyond the Jupiter Effect*, with Stephen H. Plagemann. London, Macdonald, 1983.
*Spacewarps.* New York, Delacorte Press/E. Friede, 1983; London, Penguin, 1984.
*In Search of Schrödinger's Cat.* London, Wildwood House, and New York, Bantam, 1984.
*The Redundant Male.* London, Bodley Head, and New York, Pantheon, 1984.
*In Search of the Double Helix.* London, Wildwood House, and New York, McGraw-Hill, 1985.
*Weather*, with Mary Gribbin. London, Macdonald, and Vero Beach, Florida, Rourke Enterprises, 1985.
*In Search of the Big Bang.* London, Heinemann, and New York, Bantam, 1986.
*The Omega Point.* London, Heinemann, 1987; New York, Bantam, 1988.
*The One Per Cent Advantage*, with Mary Gribbin. Oxford and New York, Blackwell, 1988.
*The Hole in the Sky: Man's Threat to the Ozone Layer.* New York, Bantam, 1988.
*Cosmic Coincidences*, with Martin Rees. New York, Bantam, 1989; as *The Stuff of the Universe*, London, Heinemann, 1990.
*Winds of Change*, with Mick Kelly. London, Headway, 1989.
*The Cartoon History of Time*, with Kate Charlesworth. New York, Plume, 1990.
*Children of the Ice: Climate and Human Origins*, with Mary Gribbin. Oxford and Cambridge, Massachusetts, Blackwell, 1990.
*Hothouse Earth.* London, Grove Weidenfeld, and New York, Bantam, 1990.
*Blinded by the Light.* London, Bantam, 1991; New York, Harmony, 1991.

Editor, *Climatic Change.* Cambridge and New York, Cambridge University Press, 1978.
Editor, *Cosmology Today.* London, IPC Magazines, 1982.
Editor, *The Breathing Planet.* Oxford and New York, Blackwell, 1986.

* * *

John Gribbin has become one of Britain's most prolific and best-known popularisers of science, with books on almost every hot scientific issue, from black holes to the ozone layer. He is physics consultant to *New Scientist*, and a contributor of scientific articles to numerous other periodicals. He became known as a regular writer of science fact articles to *Analog* in the 1970's, and it was natural that his first SF sale should have been to that magazine in September 1984: a short story called "Perpendicular Worlds," in which a contemporary scientist discovers both time travel and the infinity of alternative realities, and by sending back large amounts of bacteria over the course of several billion years, managed to create life. Such playful and unserious stories continued to appear in *Analog*, including several contributions to the magazine's scientific humour series, "Probability Zero" and a sequel to "Perpendicular Worlds" in February 1986. The most successful of these was probably "The Carbon Papers" (*Analog*, January 1990), in which, in January 1890, Sherlock Holmes works out that a mysterious death was in fact the suicide of a scientist who had discovered the greenhouse effect, and was trying to protect the coal-driven British Empire from the effects of that discovery: his papers were preserved by Holmes and Watson, to be opened a century later. "Other Edens" (*Interzone 31*, 1989) is a short, witty, and cynical piece following the exploits of a brave (but drug-fuddled) space pioneer, wiping another Gaia-planet free of life: "another Eden for the home planet's huddled masses."

Signs that Gribbin was also interested in more serious aspects of SF, and was also maturing as a fiction writer, getting beyond mere fictionalised lectures, appeared in two *Analog* stories that were subsequently developed into novels: "Double Planet" (November 1984) and "The Sins of the Fathers" (mid-December 1986). *Double Planet*, by Gribbin with Marcus Chown, is an SF thriller involving political intriguing both on earth and on some of the last surviving space-shuttles, sent to rendezvous with a comet heading perilously close to the earth. The mission—to crash the comet into the Moon, thus providing it with the makings of an atmosphere, and providing the solar system with the double planet of the title—is ultimately successful; the novel less so, with its political clichés and stereotypical characters. *Father to the Man*, published in the following year, has its problems as a novel also, with its scene-setting of a near future earth beset with political and environmental problems (written, clearly, with Chernobyl a recent event, and the political changes of Eastern Europe just beyond the horizon) clumsily integrated into the fiction, and the resolution of the plot rather hastily contrived. But its story of a scientist doing his work investigating the gene-maps of humans and chimpanzees, and experimenting upon a cross-breed, despite the opposition of religious fundamentalists, is one that raises all kinds of interesting issues, and the characterisation seems more secure than in the collaborative novel: it suggests that if Gribbin perseveres he may become one of the rare British novelists writing SF on the edge of current scientific endeavour.

—Edward James

---

**GRIDBAN, Volsted.** *See* **FEARN, John Russell; TUBB, E.C.**

---

**GRIFFIN, Russell M.** American. Born in Stamford, Connecticut, 29 April 1943. Educated at Mount Hermon School, 1957–61; Trinity College, Hartford, Connecticut, 1961–65, B.A. in English 1965; Case Western Reserve University, Cleveland, 1967–70, M.A. 1969, Ph.D. 1970. Married Sheila Vaznelis in 1965; two children. English teacher, Proctor Academy, Andover, New Hampshire, 1965–67. Professor of English, University of Bridgeport, Connecticut, from 1970.

SCIENCE-FICTION PUBLICATIONS

Novels

*The Makeshift God.* New York, Dell, 1979; London, Granada, 1982.
*Century's End.* New York, Bantam, 1981.
*The Blind Men and the Elephant.* New York, Pocket Books, 1982.
*The Timeservers.* New York, Avon, 1985.

Uncollected Short Stories

"The Confessional," in *Analog* (New York), May 1982.
"Angel at the Gate," in *The Best of Omni Science Fiction 6*, edited by Don Myrus. New York, Omni, 1983.
"Government Work," in *Habitats*, edited by Susan Shwartz. New York, DAW, 1984.

*

Russell M. Griffin comments (1985):

The first adult paperback I ever owned was an anthology of science fiction I took to boys camp my first summer away from home. The book is long since lost, but not the stories.

But I suppose what has kept me in science fiction more than anything else since is the medievalist in me. Where else can a writer enjoy the same scope and freedom of invention one finds in the dream visions of Chaucer, Langland, and Gower? Where else in modern literature is allegory allowed to survive at all? Science fiction, as the works of Orwell and Huxley attest, provides the ideal vehicle for social comment and satire. Re-erect Spenser's Castle of Pride or create a society where equality is enforced by crippling the gifted? They are only a planet or an age away.

* * *

Russell M. Griffin's four published novels are fresh, witty, and crisply written versions of basic (and one not so basic) science-fiction themes. Especially noteworthy are his inventiveness and exceptional gift for comedy and satire. Regarding the latter, while certain passages in his work are reminiscent of another fine satirist, John Sladek, Griffin's passages are usually rather better integrated into the work as a whole than Sladek's.

Griffin's first novel, *The Makeshift God*, would be impressive even were it not a first novel. The first half, especially, is brilliantly achieved; the second tends to lean more on mere adventure elements. However, Griffin's next two novels are more ambitious, both artistically and thematically. Significantly, both can be seen as closer to "mainstream" fiction than either his first or most recent efforts. His second novel, *Century's End*, is set in the near future (1999). Millennial actions and expectations abound: crazies and zanies expecting the worst, plotting the worst, are everywhere. In the controlled wit of the presentation, in the skill of its scene construction, and in its deft satirical art, this novel exemplifies many of the best qualities of the innovative science fiction of the past two decades; it can be meaningfully discussed in a context that includes the best of such writers as Vonnegut, Dick, and Disch. One thing that relates this novel to such major figures is the obvious intelligence manifested throughout—and not merely literary intelligence; for Griffin proves to be highly informed about a wide range of subjects—for example, satellite technology, climatology and geology, and the psychology and sociology of aberrant religious cults.

The plot focuses on the deadly rivalry of two such cults, one headed by an "inspired" mad-woman, the other headed by a corporate-minded TV evangelist named Dr. Love. Griffin focuses much of the novel's deft satire on these two groups and their benighted followers; he focuses also on related hypes, TV programming and advertising, for example. The central characters ranged against the cults and their manipulative techniques are the bright, sardonic Jervis Santalucia, who is half-black and rarely at ease about his identity, and Circe McPhee, a professional prognosticator. The chaos of modern life is such that government and big business have turned to the occult for answers.

While the writing in Griffin's third novel, *The Blind Men and the Elephant*, is just as witty and persuasive, the work itself—plot, theme, milieu—is his least science-fictional. The highly bizarre plot and accompanying cast of zanies relate to the pathetic-comic misadventures of a latter-day "Elephant Man"—a terribly deformed yet bright and sensitive creature who is commercially exploited by a media huckster (TV again) and spied upon by sinister government agents. We soon learn that Elephant Man is no more than five or six years old, the ghastly product of government "experimentation" in cloning. His misadventures are a very Vonnegutian assemblage of black humor, farce, and satire. While individual episodes are very freshly done, it is doubtful that the overall presentation is as successful as it might have been. This volume is perhaps more to be recommended to fans of sixties-seventies mainstream black humor writing than to SF fans.

*The Timeservers* is, again, an impressive piece of writing. It resembles his first book in being overtly science-fictional in its setting, themes, and characterization—interstellar travel, encounters with alien races, and so on. Certain interests—cloning, Roman Catholic ritual, the omnipresence of human violence (here embodied in a war with strong Vietnam overtones)—return from earlier Griffin books. But Griffin is not repeating himself; he is just as fresh in approach, quite as interesting and witty here as in his previous books. Not only has he chosen the best of models (Dick, Sladek, et al), but in his best work, in his finest episodes, he transcends those models, bringing a new voice to the impressive choir of post-Campbellian writers.

—Robert E. Colbert

---

**GRIFFITH, George (George Chetwynd Griffith-Jones).** Also wrote as Levin Carnac; Lara; Stanton Morich. British. Born in Plymouth, Devon, 20 August 1857. Educated at schools in Lancashire and in evening classes, College of Preceptors Diploma 1887. Married Elizabeth Brierly in 1887 (died 1933); two sons and one daughter. Merchant seaman, 1873–77; English teacher, Worthing College, Sussex, 1877–83, and Bolton Grammar School, Lancashire, 1883–87; journalist in London, 1888–89; staff writer, *Pearson's Weekly*, 1890–99, and *Pearson's Magazine*, 1896–1903, both London: travelled extensively for these magazines, including two trips around the world; correspondent in South Africa for London *Daily Mail*, 1903. *Died 4 June 1906.*

### Science-Fiction Publications

#### Novels

*The Angel of the Revolution: A Tale of Coming Terror.* London, Tower, 1893; Westport, Connecticut, Hyperion Press, 1974.
*Olga Romanoff; or, The Syren of the Skies.* London, Tower, 1894; Westport, Connecticut, Hyperion Press, 1974.
*Valdar the Oft-Born: A Saga of Seven Ages.* London, Pearson, 1895.
*The Outlaws of the Air.* London, Tower, 1895.
*Briton or Boer?* London, White, 1897.
*The Romance of Golden Star.* London, White, 1897; New York, Arno Press, 1978.
*The Destined Maid.* London, White, 1898.
*The Gold-Finder.* London, White, 1898.
*The Great Pirate Syndicate.* London, White, 1899.
*The Justice of Revenge.* London, White, 1900.
*Captain Ishmael.* London, Hutchinson, 1901.
*A Honeymoon in Space.* London, Pearson, 1901; New York, Arno Press, 1975.
*Denver's Double: A Story of Inverted Identity.* London, White, 1901.
*The World Masters.* London, Long, 1903.
*The Lake of Gold: A Narrative of the Anglo-American Conquest of Europe.* London, White, 1903.
*The Stolen Submarine.* London, White, 1904.
*A Criminal Croesus.* London, Long, 1904.
*A Mayfair Magician: A Romance of Criminal Science.* London, White, 1905; as *The Man with Three Eyes*, n. d.
*The Mummy and Miss Nitocris: A Phantasy of the Fourth Dimension.* London, Laurie, 1906; New York, Arno Press, 1976; as *The Mummy and the Girl*, n. d.
*The Great Weather Syndicate.* London, White, 1906.
*The World Peril of 1910.* London, White, 1907.
*The Sacred Skull.* London, Everett, 1908.
*The Lord of Labour.* London, White, 1911.

#### Short Stories

*Gambles with Destiny.* London, White, 1898.
*The Raid of "Le Vengeur" and Other Stories.* London, Ferret Fantasy, 1974.

### Other Publications

#### Novels

*The Knights of the White Rose.* London, White, 1897.
*The Virgin of the Sun.* London, Pearson, 1898.
*The Rose of Judah.* London, Pearson, 1899.
*Brothers of the Chain.* London, White, 1900.
*Thou Shalt Not—* (as Stanton Morich). London, Pearson, 1900.
*The Missionary.* London, White, 1902.
*The White Witch of Mayfair.* London, White, 1902.
*A Woman Against the World.* London, White, 1903.
*An Island Love-Story.* London, White, 1904.
*His Better Half.* London, White, 1905.
*His Beautiful Client.* London, White, 1905.
*A Conquest of Fortune.* London, White, 1906.
*John Brown, Buccaneer.* London, White, 1908.

#### Short Stories

*A Heroine of the Slums.* London, Tower, 1894(?).
*Knaves of Diamonds, Being Tales of Mine and Veld.* London, Pearson, 1899; as *The Diamond Dog*, 1913.

#### Verse (as Lara)

*Poems General, Secular, and Satirical.* London, Stewart, 1883.
*The Dying Faith.* London, Stewart, 1884.

Other

*Men Who Have Made the Empire.* London, Pearson, 1897.
*In an Unknown Prison Land: An Account of Convicts and Colonists in New Caledonia.* London, Hutchinson, 1901.
*With Chamberlain in Africa.* London, Routledge, 1903.
*Sidelights on Convict Life.* London, Long, 1903.

Translator (as Levin Carnac), *The Hope of the Family*, by Alphonse Daudet. London, Pearson, 1898.

*

Bibliography: by George Locke, in *The Raid of "Le Vengeur" and Other Stories*, 1974.

* * *

George Griffith published almost 50 books of crime, adventure, fantasy, romance, social melodrama, verse, and nonfiction. Most importantly, his output includes over 20 books of, or in the margins of, SF. He became one of the first, most characteristic, and most popular professional writers of editorially planned and instantly sensational fiction in the rising "yellow press" of the turn of the century. Griffith also met the usual end of such hacks, being forced to get more outrageous and less believable in each succeeding novel and to shed whatever original insights he might have had in the process.

His best work, consequently, is clearly his first novel, *The Angel of the Revolution*, though even that is marred by slipshod haste, racist chauvinism, and melodramatic sensationalism. Yet the subsumption of Verne's gadgetry and the "future war" tale, plus a dash of travelog exoticism and a barrelful of Bulwerian melodrama, under a real sympathy with justice wrecked on the existing political order of despotism and Mammon by a group of avenging heroes united into an Anarchist or Terrorist Brotherhood of Freedom, was a genuine breakthrough. The brains of the conspiracy, the super-intelligent Hungarian Jew Natas, is, in spite of his name, his hypnotic powers, and his crippled exterior, convincingly portrayed as a victim of Tsarist oppression rather than a mad beast. The main hero, and English inventor, is starving in his garret while inventing his super-airplane; and the executive head of the Terrorists is an English aristocrat, thus permitting Griffith to alloy plebeian hatred with snobbery. There follow cliffhanging global adventures dovetailing the fates of the heroes and their beautiful and fully equal female counterparts, especially Natas's daughter Natasha, and the world war that develops in 1904. The bloodthirsty Franco-Slavonic alliance is defeated by the Brotherhood who set up an Anglo-Saxon federation to guide the world toward disarmament and a vague social justice never clearly spelled out in economic terms. But this heady brew contains a few memorable set scenes, and—most importantly—an at least partial realization that the fusion of politics and the new technology makes the old social relationships not only unstable but catastrophically untenable. This realization made Griffith a pioneer in the instauration of a new SF tradition that culminated in Wells and still overshadows our whole century.

The sequel, *Olga Romanoff*, written to exploit *The Angel's* great success, is inferior, its only new element being an interplanetary threat copied from Flammarion's ubiquitous comets. Already in *The Outlaws of the Air* the exploitation becomes unreadable: the anarchists are vicious beasts, the heroes English gentlemen, the ideal a rosewater South Sea colony, the fights simply ludicrous; *The Great Pirate Syndicate* descends to bloodthirsty Anglo-Saxon wishdream-imperialism and anti-Semitism. In Griffith's feverish gallop through all the popular literary forms, *A Honeymoon in Space* was his venture into interplanetary voyages; it groups all its clichés (aggressive Martians, angel-like Venusians, antigravity, monsters galore) around a safari-story of a lord, his beautiful American bride, and their faithful retainer. His later works are unworthy of a writer with political convictions and a generous plebeian indignation: if the story that Griffith died of drink is true, it would provide an appropriately moral dying fall. And it would still remain exemplary for the SF of our century.

—Darko Suvin

---

**GRINNELL, David.** *See* **WOLLHEIM, Donald A.**

---

**GROENER, Carl.** *See* **LOWNDES, Robert A.W.**

---

**GUIN, Wyman (Woods).** American. Born in Wanette, Oklahoma, 1 March 1915. Educated at Riverside City College, California, J.C. 1934. Married 1) Jean Adolph in 1939 (divorced 1955); 2) Valerie Carlson in 1956; two sons and three daughters. Technician in pharmacology. Advertising writer, advertising manager, and marketing vice-president, Lakeside Laboratories Inc., Milwaukee, 1938–62; vice-president, Medical Television Communications Inc., Chicago, 1962–64. Since 1964, planning administrator, L.W. Erolich-Intercon International. Lives in Tarrytown, New York.

SCIENCE-FICTION PUBLICATIONS

Novel

*The Standing Joy.* New York, Avon, 1969.

Short Stories

*Living Way Out.* New York, Avon, 1967; as *Beyond Bedlam*, London, Sphere, 1973.

* * *

Although Wyman Guin has written a novel, *The Standing Joy*, his most important work is to be found in his novelettes from the 1950's and 1960's. The stories are remarkable for the way in which Guin takes up far-out sociological or psychological ideas and gives them substance in carefully worked out dramatic conflicts against the background of alternate societies; despite some extravaganzas in the details, they carry conviction and emerge as fully rounded and believable SF worlds.

His best story is the minor classic "Beyond Bedlam," which employs the basic inversion device of so much science fiction: what is considered an illness today—schizophrenia in this case—is in about a thousand years in the future the norm, with a drug-induced, law-enforced schizophrenia in every human being. Everybody is inhabited by two personalities that change in five-day shifts. This procedure has eliminated man's aggressive impulses, and hence war, but has also led to the disappearance of art and emotional pleasures. The theme of the story is treated not so much as a utopian dream or a dystopian nightmare as an exercise in creating a different alternate society, with all the ramifications of good and evil following from the basic premise.

"The Delegate from Guapanga" and "A Man of the Renaissance" both have richly exotic socio-cultural backgrounds. The first story contrasts two alien philosophies of "Mentalists" and "Matterists," the Mentalists being closer to nature with ideals of a simpler life and tradition, the Matterists representatives of a mechanistic-scientific culture. The hero of the story develops a curious political idea of "dishonesty in government." The second story is about a man of ambition in an archipelagic world, who by sometimes Machiavellian means tries to realize his purely rationalist and revolutionary notions in a world governed by traditional values. In "Volpla" a joke in genetical engineering by a misanthropic lone scientist—artificially created beings that were to be passed off as visitors from the stars—turns out differently by a simple reversion of the reader's expectations. "My Darling Hecate" and "The Root and the Ring" are slight and mildly amusing volatile fantasies.

Guin's novel, *The Standing Joy*, is a parallel Earth story, with the characters having "twins" on another Earth, perhaps our own. Its protagonist, Colin Collins, a superman who has invented the prolonged orgasm, gathers around him a group of other talented inventors; the sex is harmless, but the whole thing is a bit confused. Wyman Guin's typical work is characteristic of its time and the magazine (*Galaxy*) in which most of it appeared, a slickly written fiction of ideas that manages to entertain and to stimulate without moving the reader deeply.

—Franz Rottensteiner

---

**GUNN, James E(dwin).** American. Born in Kansas City, Missouri, 12 July 1923. Educated at the University of Kansas, Lawrence, B.A. in journalism 1947, M.A. in English 1951. Served in the United States Naval Reserve, 1943–46; Lieutenant. Married Jane Frances Anderson in 1947; two sons. Editor, Western Printing and Lithographing Company, Racine, Wisconsin, 1951–52. Assistant instructor, 1955–56, managing editor, Alumni Association, 1955–58, administrative assistant to the Chancellor for University Relations, 1958–70, lecturer, 1970–74, and since 1974, Professor of English, University of Kansas. Member of the Executive Committee, and president, 1980–82, Science Fiction Research Association; president, Science Fiction Writers of America, 1971–72. Recipient: Byron Caldwell Smith prize; Hugo special award, 1976, and Achievement award, 1983; Pilgrim award, 1976; Edward Grier award, 1989. Guest of Honor, Mid-Americon 1, Macron 10, Fortcon 1. Agent: Dorris Halsey, 8733 Sunset Boulevard, Los Angeles, California 90069; or, Maggie Noach, 2, Redan Street London W14 0AB, England. Address: 2215 Orchard Lane, Lawrence, Kansas 66049, U.S.A.

### Science-Fiction Publications

Novels

*This Fortress World.* New York, Gnome Press, 1955; London, Sphere, 1977.
*Star Bridge*, with Jack Williamson. New York, Gnome Press, 1955; London, Sidgwick and Jackson, 1978.
*The Joy Makers.* New York, Bantam, 1961; London, Gollancz, 1963.
*The Immortals.* New York, Bantam, 1962; London, Panther, 1975.
*The Immortal* (novelization of TV series). New York, Bantam, 1970.
*The Burning.* New York, Dell, 1972.
*The Listeners.* New York, Scribner, 1972; London, Arrow, 1978.
*The Magicians.* New York, Scribner, 1976; London, Sidgwick and Jackson, 1978.
*Kampus.* New York, Bantam, 1977.
*The Dreamers.* New York, Simon and Schuster, 1980; London, Gollancz, 1981; as *The Mind Master*, New York, Pocket Books, 1982.
*Crisis!* New York, Tor, 1986.

Short Stories

*Station in Space.* New York, Bantam, 1958.
*Future Imperfect.* New York, Bantam, 1964.
*The Witching Hour.* New York, Dell, 1970.
*Breaking Point.* New York, Walker, 1972.
*Some Dreams Are Nightmares.* New York, Scribner, 1974.
*The End of the Dreams.* New York, Scribner, 1975.
*Tiger! Tiger!* Polk City, Iowa, Drumm, 1983.

### Other Publications

Play

*Thy Kingdom Come* (produced Lawrence, Kansas, 1947).

Other

*Alternate Worlds: The Illustrated History of Science Fiction.* Englewood Cliffs, New Jersey, Prentice Hall, 1975.
*The Discovery of the Future: The Ways Science Fiction Developed.* College Station, Texas A and M University, 1975.
*Isaac Asimov: The Foundations of Science Fiction.* New York and Oxford University Press, 1982.

Editor, *Man and the Future.* Lawrence, University Press of Kansas, 1968.
Editor, *Nebula Award Stories 10.* New York, Harper, 1975.
Editor, *The Road to Science Fiction: From Gilgamesh to Wells, From Wells to Heinlein, From Heinlein to Here, From Here to Forever.* New York, New American Library, 4 vols., 1977–82.
Editor, *The New Encyclopedia of Science Fiction.* New York and London, Viking, 1989.

*

Bibliography: *A James Gunn Checklist*, Polk City, Iowa, Drumm, 1983.

Manuscript Collection: University of Kansas Library, Lawrence.

James E. Gunn comments:

I recently began an autobiographical essay for Contemporary Authors Autobiography Series with the statement: "I am a professor of English at the University of Kansas, the author of some

80 published science-fiction stories and the author or editor of 24 books, almost all of them either science fiction or about science fiction. At the age of 61, as I write this account of my life in that fabled year of 1984, in the quiet university town of Lawrence, Kansas, trying to make sense out of what has happened to me, my first thought is that, unlikely as it might once have seemed, this is where I belong; this is what I was meant to do."

The facts that I have been president of both of the Science Fiction Writers of America and the Science Fiction Research Association, that I have written almost as much critical material about science fiction as I have written science fiction, that I split my working time between teaching and writing, illustrate the ways in which my work has tried to bridge two cultures. In the introduction to my 1972 collection of stories, *Breaking Point*, I wrote that "the stories in this collection were intended [to help] bridge the gap between science fiction and the mainstream, between the ghetto and the larger world outside, between C.P. Snow's Two Cultures." They were, I indicated, intended to adopt an evolutionary, not a revolutionary, approach to a literature, accepting the strengths of a popular genre and trying to build upon them.

Finally, in my autobiographical essay, I wrote about a story that became the starting point for my writing of *The Dreamers*, "Looking back over my career as a writer of science fiction, I realize now that I have always been fascinated by the seductive power of dreams, even while I have insisted that reality, while it may be hard and tragic, is preferable."

I concluded the essay with the statement, "That would be consistent with my life as I see it: surprise tempered by understanding, optimism tempered by reality, ambition tempered by pragmatism.

"The true heroes of my stories are rational people who accept the world as it is while never giving up the possibility of making it better. The villains are much the same, only they are willing to go too far to get what they want; they want what everyone else wants, but their desires are not restrained by a sense of other people's needs.

"A fiction writer's work may not always reflect his values, but if he writes out of what he has experienced and thought and felt, it must reflect the writer. What I am ultimately must be seen in the mirror of my writing."

* * *

In his definitive anthology entitled *The Road to Science Fiction*, James E. Gunn defines science fiction as idea-fiction that describes change and its consequences on the human race. This change is often technological and, in most cases, is brought about by human actions and desires. While such a definition may not work for all of science fiction or for all its writers, it has worked well for Gunn. Since 1949 his work has consistently representated human characters confronting altered futures. As in the stories collected in *Station in Space*, Gunn sees humanity as a race that needs to be challenged in order to grow. He recognizes that many people would prefer to live in stable worlds in which each day is like all the others, and, therefore, his plots frequently deal with how the major characters thwart the deadly appeal of stasis.

Gunn's favorite writing length is the novelette because it allows him to center his story on a single event that is economically described and resolved. Many of his "novels" consist of three or four novelettes connected by a common theme. In *The Joy Makers*, for example, Gunn explores what people think will make them happy within an extended period of time. In each story a stage is reached which eventually supports his thesis that even if absolute happiness could be found it would probably be rather disappointing. The use of a series of novelettes allows a story to end with a dramatic statement that does not need the amplification and development a novel demands.

*The Immortals*, another series of interconnected stories, investigates a world in which immortality is possible. However, in each story the possibility of immortality is not as important as its effect on the characters. Gunn wishes to describe human attitudes toward death and uses the device of immortality to put these attitudes into sharp relief. Because he deals with such issues, Gunn's stories often touch on current problems. For example, medical technology has been more and more directed toward the prolongation of life. But such technology has added huge costs to basic hospital services. In the third story of *The Immortals* Gunn presents the ultimate direction such a trend could take. The story effectively describes just how dangerous humanity's preoccupation with avoiding death can be.

In *The Listeners* Gunn studies communication in the same way he explored immortality. While the unifying concept among these novelettes is the attempt to decipher and answer a message from Capella, the theme concerns communication between individuals. In each story, with the Capellan project in the background, the foreground is filled with husbands and wives, fathers and sons, leaders and followers, writers and readers, men and intelligent machines and humans and aliens who try to communicate. The result is a work that describes not only an adventure in the near future but a moving account of humanity's present. Communication with aliens may happen some day, but for now human communication could do with some improvement.

*The Dreamers* (inexplicably renamed *The Mind Master* by the paperback publisher), collects three novelettes with the addition of inter-chapter material that adds up to yet another story. Each of these stories traces the consequences of the discovery of chemical learning. By imparting instant knowledge through chemistry, humanity has eliminated the difficulty normally associated with learning. But it has also created a future race in which imagination is sadly lacking. Even dreams come from pills and injections. By far the darkest of Gunn's works, *The Dreamers* still gives the reader human characters who are capable of love and who care about what has happened to their fellow human beings. The stories might deal with a nightmare age, but Gunn regrets this nightmare. It is as if Gunn is telling the reader that these characters, and by extension humanity, deserve better than their allotted fates.

And Gunn does give humanity a better fate in his most recent book *Crisis!* Set in our present, the stories deal with a man from the future who comes to the present in order to avert events that will destroy the future. This character is not allowed to act directly, but must convince people of the present to act simply by speaking and reasoning with them. Gunn covers a wide variety of problems (from energy to war to terrorism), and presents some interesting views on why and how they happen.

Two more conventional novels deserve mention. *This Fortress World*, Gunn's first novel, is a highly readable story that makes use of the popular science-fiction galactic empire. But Gunn relates the story from the point of view of an ordinary inhabitant rather than a super-hero. Life in a galactic empire can be rather unpleasant if the character is only one of the crowd. *This Fortress World* is Gunn's attempt to bring "reality" to space opera.

At the opposite pole lies *Kampus*, a work that has suffered from misreading. It is too easy—and misleading—to read this novel as a damnation of the campus of the 1960's. *Kampus* is, in fact, a parable about people who believe that everyone should be allowed to do "their own thing." It is similar to Voltaire's *Candide* in that the world and action presented in the novel are not meant to be taken as serious attempts to portray "reality."

Unlike *Candide*, however, *Kampus* questions what life would be like if everyone were only to tend his own garden.

James E. Gunn has made a career of science fiction as an author, teacher, and scholar. His criticism attests to his sensitivity to the genre. His fiction shows an equal sensitivity to what is possible in science fiction. As one reads his stories, one is struck by the variety of themes, plots, and styles he is capable of. *Kampus* is a remarkable feat of stylistic experimentation that was not at all predictable from *The Listeners. The Dreamers* and *Crisis!* prove that his interest in style has not ended. In a literature that is itself concerned with change, it is somehow reassuring that one of the writers most interested in this theme is himself able to change.

—Stephen H. Goldman

---

**GUTHRIE, Alan.** *See* **TUBB, E.C.**

---

**GUTTERIDGE, (Thomas Gordon) Lindsay.** British. Born in Easington, County Durham, 20 May 1923. Educated at an art school in Newcastle upon Tyne. Married to Marjorie Kathleen Carpenter; one daughter. Freelance commercial artist, London 1939–41, 1950–68; art teacher, King Edward School of Art, Newcastle, 1941–43; cattle stockman in Australia, 1946–48; freelance photographer, 1958–60; former art director, Robert Sharp and Partners, advertising agency, London. Address: 15 Howdale Road, Downham Market, Norfolk PE38 9AB, England.

Science-Fiction Publications

Novels (series: Matthew Dilke in all books)

*Cold War in a Country Garden.* London, Cape, and New York, Putnam, 1971.
*Killer Pine.* London, Cape, and New York, Putnam, 1973.
*Fratricide Is a Gas.* London, Cape, 1975.

* * *

Lindsay Gutteridge is the author of three espionage novels featuring Matthew Dilke as hero, a micro-man one quarter of an inch in height. They are all splendid adventure stories and powerfully engage the sense of wonder. Gutteridge plays rough with his miniature spies and their normal-sized masters and foes, so that these should perhaps be classified as adult entertainments, but there is nothing very special in the books considered as offbeat spy thrillers. Their distinctive quality is science-educational: they are the closest fictional equivalents I have found to *The Hellstrom Chronicle.* Whereas that film's overwhelming images of the alien life we overlook projected an inimical world in which ants are far better adapted for survival than we hubristic humans, Gutteridge, better balanced, discovers not only beauty and terror, monstrosity and indifference, but delightful nourishment. By not being insect-sized, Gutteridge suggests, we are missing the marvellous abundant food of pollen and nectar. If only we could be miniaturized, our survival problems would be over. There, of course, is the rub which would lead us to classify these works as pure fantasies were it not that they belong to a tradition of micro-people in SF established by such writers as Asimov, Blish, and Leinster, and that they use the convention to instruct us about natural history so fully and sensitively. The microscopic eye is a human one, and the wonders seen are related to human fears, needs and desires.

*Cold War in a Country Garden*, in which the mission of three micro-men is to implant transmitters in the hair of a Russian, is closest perhaps to the conventional spy thriller, substituting a box of centipedes for the snake pit or piranha pool as a persuasive threat to the captured Dilke. When he escapes, rescuing a micro-negress, Hyacinthe, who aids him in his second adventure, the pursuers are caught by an ant-lion. *Killer Pine* is a novel of ecological warfare, in which the enemy are Russian micro-men who inhabit a metal container on a pine in a Canadian forest, breeding termites to spread a viral death. We are given fascinating and horrid glimpses of life in a termite colony, in a tree which, for the micro-climbers, has the scale of Mount Everest. The third novel, *Fratricide Is a Gas*, has affinities with novels of industrial espionage: here Matthew Dilke is pitted alone against a sadistic Nazi chemist in Peru. The highlight of this novel is a sequence in which Dilke climbs jungloid thorns and creepers, enjoying on the way an idyllic repose in the bloom of an orchid, where he is visited by a humming-bird and witnesses the giant courtship of butterflies and the predations of parasitic wasps and shaggy spiders.

Gutteridge's micro-man's view gives us the pleasure of a sardonic perspective on the conventions of spy fiction and also a Swiftian magnification of some of our physical and spiritual coarseness, as when Dilke spies from a perch on the top of Lippe's study chair not only the eroded massif of his head but also the monstrous cruelty of his mind, revealed by his most private occupations. Gutteridge's work may well have influenced *The Micronauts* by Gordon Williams (1977), an exciting, more fully science-fiction narrative which, however, lacks the Gutteridge charm.

—Michael J. Tolley

---

# H

**HAGGARD, H(enry) Rider.** British. Born in Bradenham, Norfolk, 22 June 1856. Educated at Ipswich Grammar School, Suffolk; Lincoln's Inn, London, 1881–85: called to the Bar, 1885. Married Louisa Mariana Margitson in 1880; one son and three daughters. Lived in South Africa, as Secretary to Sir Henry Bulwer, Lieutenant-Governor of Natal, 1875–77, member of the staff of Sir Theophilus Shepstone, Special Commissioner in the Transvaal, 1877, and Master and Registrar of the High Court of the Transvaal, 1877–79; returned to England, 1879; managed his wife's estate in Norfolk, from 1880; worked in chambers of Henry Bargave Deane, 1885–87; Unionist and Agricultural candidate for East Norfolk, 1895; co-editor, *African Review*, 1898; travelled throughout England investigating condition of agriculture and the rural population, 1901–02; British Government Special Commissioner to report on Salvation Army settlements in the United States, 1905; chairman, Reclamation and Unemployed Labour Committee, Royal Commission on Coast Erosion and Afforestation, 1906–11; travelled around the world as a member of the Dominions Royal Commission, 1912–17. Chairman of the Committee, Society of Authors, 1896–98; vice-president, Royal Colonial Institute, 1917. Knighted, 1912; K.B.E. (Knight Commander, Order of the British Empire), 1919. *Died 14 May 1925.*

SCIENCE-FICTION PUBLICATIONS

Novels (series: Allan Quatermain; She)

*King Solomon's Mines* (Quatermain). London and New York, Cassell, 1885.
*She: A History of Adventure.* New York, Harper, 1886; London, Longman, 1887.
*Allan Quatermain.* London, Longman, and New York, Harper, 1887.
*The People of the Mist.* London and New York, Longman, 1894.
*Heart of the World.* New York, Longman, 1895; London, Longman, 1896.
*Stella Fregelius: A Tale of Three Destinies.* London and New York, Longman, 1904.
*Ayesha: The Return of She.* London, Ward Lock, and New York, Doubleday, 1905.
*Benita: An African Romance.* London, Cassell, 1906; as *The Spirit of Bambatse*, New York, Longman, 1906.
*The Yellow God.* New York, Cupples and Leon, 1908; London, Cassell, 1909.
*Queen Sheba's Ring.* London, Nash, and New York, Doubleday, 1910.
*The Mahatma and the Hare: A Dream Story.* London, Longman, and New York, Holt, 1911.
*Love Eternal.* London, Cassell, and New York, Longman, 1918.
*When the World Shook.* London, Cassell, and New York, Longman, 1919.
*She and Allan.* New York, Longman, and London, Hutchinson, 1921.
*Wisdom's Daughter.* London, Hutchinson, and New York, Doubleday, 1923.
*Heu-Heu; or, The Monster* (Quatermain). London, Hutchinson, and New York, Doubleday, 1924.

OTHER PUBLICATIONS

Novels

*Dawn.* London, Hurst and Blackett, 3 vols., 1884; New York, Appleton, 1 vol., 1887.
*The Witch's Head.* London, Hurst and Blackett, 3 vols., 1884; New York, Appleton, 1 vol., 1885.
*Jess.* London, Smith Elder, and New York, Harper, 1887.
*A Tale of Three Lions, and On Going Back.* New York, Munro, 1887.
*Mr. Meeson's Will.* New York, Harper, and London, Spencer Blackett, 1888.
*Maiwa's Revenge.* New York, Harper, and London, Longman, 1888.
*My Fellow Laborer* (includes "The Wreck of the Copeland"). New York, Munro, 1888.
*Colonel Quaritch, V.C.* New York, Lovell, 1888; London, Longman, 3 vols., 1888.
*Cleopatra.* London, Longman, and New York, Harper, 1889.
*Beatrice.* London, Longman, and New York, Harper, 1890.
*The World's Desire*, with Andrew Lang. London, Longman, and New York, Harper, 1890.
*Eric Brighteyes.* London, Longman, and New York, United States Book Company, 1891.
*Nada the Lily.* New York and London, Longman, 1892.
*Montezuma's Daughter.* New York and London, Longman, 1893.
*Joan Haste.* London and New York, Longman, 1895.
*The Wizard.* Bristol, Arrowsmith, and New York, Longman, 1896.
*Doctor Therne.* London and New York, Longman, 1898.
*Swallow.* New York and London, Longman, 1899.
*The Spring of a Lion.* New York, Neeley, 1899.
*Lysbeth.* New York and London, Longman, 1901.
*Pearl-Maiden.* London and New York, Longman, 1903.
*The Brethren.* London, Cassell, and New York, Doubleday, 1904.
*The Way of the Spirit.* London, Hutchinson, 1906.
*Fair Margaret.* London, Hutchinson, 1907; as *Margaret*, New York, Longman, 1907.
*The Lady of the Heavens.* New York, Authors and Newspapers Association, 1908; as *The Ghost Kings*, London, Cassell, 1908.
*The Lady of Blossholme.* London, Hodder and Stoughton, 1909.
*Morning Star.* London, Cassell, and New York, Longman, 1910.
*Red Eve.* London, Hodder and Stoughton, and New York, Doubleday, 1911.
*Marie.* London, Cassell, and New York, Longman, 1912.
*Child of Storm.* London, Cassell, and New York, Longman, 1913.

*The Wanderer's Necklace*. London, Cassell, and New York, Longman, 1914.
*The Holy Flower*. London, Ward Lock, 1915; as *Allan and the Holy Flower*, New York, Longman, 1915.
*The Ivory Child*. London, Cassell, and New York, Longman, 1916.
*Finished*. London, Ward Lock, and New York, Longman, 1917.
*Moon of Israel*. London, Murray, and New York, Longman, 1918.
*The Ancient Allan*. London, Cassell, and New York, Longman, 1920.
*The Virgin of the Sun*. London, Cassell, and New York, Doubleday, 1922.
*Queen of the Dawn*. New York, Doubleday, and London, Hutchinson, 1925.
*The Treasure of the Lake*. New York, Doubleday, and London, Hutchinson, 1926.
*Allan and the Ice-Gods*. London, Hutchinson, and New York, Doubleday, 1927.
*Mary of Marion Isle*. London, Hutchinson, and New York, Doubleday, 1929.
*Belshazzar*. London, Paul, and New York, Doubleday, 1930.

Short Stories

*Allan's Wife and Other Tales*. London, Blackett, and New York, Harper, 1889.
*Black Heart and White Heart, and Other Stories*. London, Longman, 1900; as *Elissa, and Black Heart and White Heart*, New York, Longman, 1900.
*Smith and the Pharaohs and Other Tales*. Bristol, Arrowsmith, 1920; New York, Longman, 1921.
*The Best Short Stories of Rider Haggard*, edited by Peter Haining. London, Joseph, 1981.

Other

*Cetywayo and His White Neighbours; or, Remarks on Recent Events in Zululand, Natal, and the Transvaal*. London, Trübner, 1882; revised edition, 1888; reprinted in part, as *The Last Boer War*, London, Kegan Paul, 1899; as *A History of the Transvaal*, New York, New Amsterdam, 1899.
*Church and the State: An Appeal to the Laity*. Privately printed, 1895.
*A Farmer's Year, Being His Commonplace Book for 1898*. London and New York, Longman, 1899.
*The New South Africa*. London, Pearson, 1900.
*A Winter Pilgrimage: . . . Travels Through Palestine, Italy, and the Island of Cyprus*. London and New York, Longman, 1901.
*Rural England*. London and New York, Longman, 2 vols., 1902.
*A Gardener's Year*. London and New York, Longman, 1905.
*Report on the Salvation Army Colonies*. London, His Majesty's Stationery Office, 1905; as *The Poor and the Land*, London and New York, Longman, 1905.
*Regeneration, Being an Account of the Social Work of the Salvation Army in Great Britain*. London, Longman, 1910; New York, Longman, 1911.
*Rural Denmark and Its Lessons*. London and New York, Longman, 1911.
*A Call to Arms to the Men of East Anglia*. Privately printed, 1914.
*The After-War Settlement and the Employment of Ex-Service Men in the Overseas Dominions*. London, Saint Catherine Press, 1916.
*The Days of My Life: An Autobiography*, edited by C.J. Longman. London and New York, Longman, 2 vols., 1926.
*The Private Diaries of Sir H. Rider Haggard 1914–1925*, edited by D.S. Higgins. London, Cassell, and New York, Stein and Day, 1980.

*

Bibliography: *A Bibliography of the Writings of Sir Henry Rider Haggard* by J.E. Scott, London, Elkin Mathews, 1947.

Critical Studies: *The Clock That I Left* (biography) by Lilias Rider Haggard, London, Hodder and Stoughton, 1951; *Rider Haggard: His Life and Works* by Morton N. Cohen, London, Hutchinson, 1960, New York, Walker, 1961, revised edition, London, Macmillan, 1968; *H. Rider Haggard: A Voice from the Infinite* by Peter Berresford Ellis, London, Routledge, 1978; *Rider Haggard, The Great Storyteller* by D.S. Higgins, London, Cassell, 1981, New York, Stein and Day, 1983; *Rider Haggard and The Fiction of Empire: A Critical Study of British Imperial Fiction* by Wendy R. Katz, Cambridge, Cambridge University Press, 1988.

* * *

H. Rider Haggard shares the fate of writers like Mark Twain, Robert Louis Stevenson, and Lewis Carroll in that his novels now serve either in children's editions or as grist for Hollywood's mill. But Haggard never meant his works to be juvenile fare, for they are filled with very adult passions. Of his many novels, the majority are fantasy-romances that range in setting from South Africa to Iceland to Mexico, and in time from the days of Babylon to contemporary central Africa.

Haggard's first successful novel was *King Solomon's Mines*, which he published in the year after he set up practice in London as a barrister. So enthusiastic was the public reception of this novel, in which Haggard created the prototype of the "Great White Hunter," that he virtually gave up the law, and devoted most of his time to writing. The hero of *King Solomon's Mines*, Allan Quatermain, is asked by a beautiful Englishwoman to find her husband, who is lost in the African jungle. When the tracks of the missing husband lead to a long-hidden cave, only the skeleton of the husband is found, along with the treasure of King Solomon, missing for two thousand years. In the sequel, *Allan Quatermain*, Allan dies, and Haggard found himself in the same position as Conan Doyle when, tiring of his famous detective, he killed off Sherlock Holmes: the public would have no part of it. Because of this outcry, Haggard used the device of the "discovered manuscript" to write 13 more novels about Quatermain. In these, Allan meets with further adventures both in his own time and in a past life in ancient Babylon.

The theme of reliving past lives is one which Haggard used many times, especially in the series of novels about the mysterious Ayesha, or She-Who-Must-Be-Obeyed. *She*, the first of these novels, introduces Ayesha, the queen of a cannibal tribe in Africa, the people of the Kor, as she waits for the return of her lover, whom she murdered two millennia ago when he dared to marry someone else. Her wait comes to an end when a young Englishman, Leo Vincey, comes to her land. One glance at Vincey is enough to convince her that Leo is the reincarnation of the long-dead lover. She tries to persuade Leo to join her in eternal life, the secret of which she had discovered in the flame at the heart of a volcano. But once again Ayesha is frustrated when Leo too takes another woman for a wife. After banishing Leo's wife, Ayesha takes him and his companions to the volcano to renew her arguments for him to bathe with her in the flames.

But the magic only works once, for when Ayesha enters for the second time, she begins to age before the eyes of the men, turning into a two-thousand-year-old crone. To their horror, she dies at their feet. Sickened and dazed, the men return to England to try to forget the sight. Like Quatermain, Ayesha was called back for repeat performances. Haggard wrote two more novels about her return from death—*Ayesha* and *She and Allan*—and still another about her early years in ancient Egypt, *Wisdom's Daughter.*

That most of the titles of Haggard's works are unfamiliar even to SF readers shows the success of modern critics in stamping out much of 19th-century fantasy. The few that are relatively well known owe their longevity to the movies, where, even though the plots have been somewhat altered, the mystery and romance of the settings and characters have been preserved.

—Walter E. Meyers

---

**HAIBLUM, Isidore.** American. Born in Manhatten, New York, 23 May 1935. Educated at the High School of Art and Design; City College of New York (editor, *Mercury*), B. A. in English and social sciences 1958. Served in the United States Army Reserve, 1959–64. Has worked as interviewer, script-writer, and folk-singers agent; now freelance writer. Address: 160 West 77th Street, New York, New York 10024, U.S.A.

SCIENCE-FICTION PUBLICATIONS

Novels (series: Dunjer; Morgan; Nick Siscoe and Ross Block)

*The Tsaddik of the Seven Wonders.* New York, Ballantine, 1971.
*The Return.* New York, Dell, 1973.
*Transfer to Yesterday.* New York, Ballantine, 1973.
*The Wilk Are Among Us.* New York, Doubleday, 1975; revised edition, New York, Dell, 1979.
*Interworld* (Dunjer). New York, Dell, 1977; London, Penguin, 1980.
*Nightmare Express.* New York, Fawcett, 1979.
*Outerworld* (Dunjer). New York, Dell, 1979.
*The Identity Plunderers* (Siscoe and Block). New York, New American Library, 1984.
*The Mutants Are Coming* (Morgan). New York, Doubleday, 1984.
*The Hand of Ganz* (Siscoe and Block). New York, New American Library, 1985.
*Out of Sync* (Morgan). New York, Ballantine, 1990.

OTHER PUBLICATIONS

Novels

*Murder in Yiddish.* New York, St. Martin's Press, 1988.
*Bad Neighbors.* New York, St. Martin's Press, 1990.

Other

*Faster Than a Speeding Bullet,* with Stuart Silver. Chicago, Playboy Press, 1980.

*

Isidore Haiblum comments:

(1981) Haiblum's work has its roots in the *Black Mask* Hammett-Chandler tradition and in the humor of Sholom Aleichem; it is often both hard-boiled and zany and sometimes ethnic. His style is awash with idioms, slang, and underworld lingo. His settings, despite the given dates, are often the 1930's, a time he rather likes. The jury is still out on how all this will go over in SF. *The Tsaddik of the Seven Wonders* was billed by the publishers as "The First Yiddish Science Fantasy Novel Ever."

And about *Interworld* Gerald Jones wrote in *The New York Times:* "If you have ever wondered what *The Big Sleep* would sound like if Raymond Chandler were reincarnated as Roger Zelazny, this is your book." *The Nightmare Express* (a big alternative universe novel set in the 1930's and elsewhere), *Outerworld* (again with ace gum-shoe Dunjer from *Interworld*), and a revised edition of *The Wilk Are Among Us* take all this a step further. Haiblum has his fingers crossed.

(1985) With the passing of the years Haiblum has also taken to holding his breath. Meanwhile his novels have been translated into French, German, Italian, Hebrew and Spanish.

* * *

Isidore Haiblum's first published novel was *The Tsaddik of the Seven Wonders*, billed as the first Yiddish science-fantasy novel. It was an auspicious debut, a wondrous mixture of magic and time travel as the Tsaddik, a wise man whose knowledge transcends time and space, journeys to the future, where ancient knowledge and superscience make an odd marriage. A delicious romp from a decidedly original viewpoint, the novel is filled with good-natured humor and a healthy sense of the absurd.

Haiblum became more serious for the two novels that followed, *The Return* and *Transfer to Yesterday.* In the first, the New Society is a nearly Utopian civilization, with fair treatment for all and ample rewards for those who excel. Or is it? The protagonist is subject to irrational fits of violence, and the most promising and successful members of the New Society are mysteriously disappearing. Is there a purely terrestrial explanation, or is there a connection to a recent space mission, which may have brought back more than quiescent samples. There follows a fairly standard series of captures and escapes, confidences and betrayals, in what was a competent novel, but far less interesting than *Tsaddik.*

*Transfer to Yesterday* bears some superficial resemblance to both of its predecessors, in that it involves time travel and flawed Utopias. The fractional world of the League has a new, destabilizing element. A device has been created that allows one to view the past; the catch is that in order to do so, a psychic link must be established with one's own ancestors. Nevertheless, a rising cult attempts to use the new technology for its own purposes. This work also has the flavor of a traditional private eye mystery, a flavor that was to recur many times in Haiblum's subsequent books.

*The Wilk Are Among Us* marked a return to Haiblum's penchant for grotesque humor. A galactic sociologist uses a matter transmitter to travel from planet to planet, but due to a malfunction, he arrives on a strange alien world, accompanied by three aliens from distinct species possessed of powers of mental control and the creation of chaos out of order. The worst of these is the wilk, whose coincidental resemblance to the local inhabitants makes it even more difficult to isolate and neutralize. While it is an often amusing logical problem story, it demonstrates that Haiblum had still not quite found his style.

That all changed with *Interworld*, a wonderfully funny futuristic detective story. Tom Dunjer's laboratory is burglarized and an important device he was developing is missing. Whether or not it was his fault is irrelevant; if he wants to save his job, it is necessary to retrieve it, even if that means finding a way to outwit the security system of Interworld, a rival corporation. Before the story is over, the protagonist must face a wide variety of worlds and realities in a non-stop rush toward madness. Haiblum followed up with a shorter sequel, *Outerworld*, two years later.

*Nightmare Express* uses some of the same themes to less humorous effect. The hero this time is cast adrift in a time bubble, forced to witness flashes on one time period after another, pursued by individuals who seem to have stepped out of time themselves, while robots and beautiful women conspire with him, or perhaps against him, suggesting that he may have fallen into the clutches of alien invaders. The same wild enthusiasm for bizarre plots infuses this, the best of his more serious work.

*The Mutants Are Coming* is the last of Haiblum's overtly humorous novels. A reluctant ambassador from the moon returns to Earth in order to promote financing for the lunar base. He is opposed by a variety of goons, becomes enmeshed in the mystery of a missing politician, and is caught up within the coils of an underground movement of mutants. Although the book has its moments, for the most part its humor is artificial and unamusing.

*The Identity Plunderers* and its sequel, *The Hand of Ganz*, are both more serious and more satisfying. In the first, an investigative reporter recognizes a body in the city morgue while two individuals with erased memories attempt to escape a prison camp on another planet. Haiblum alternates between the two story lines, ultimately bringing them together, and ties everything up neatly. In the sequel, extraterrestrial interests are plotting to use their influence to alter the future of Earth. The protagonist of *The Identity Plunderers* discovers the plot and sets off into the galaxy to find a way to foil the evil Ganz and his cohorts. It makes for good adventure, leavened with flashes of Haiblum's irrepressible levity.

*Out of Sync*, Haiblum's most recent work, is as good as anything that preceded it. An entrepreneur who has made his reputation by establishing impregnable security systems finds his world crumbling when several of his clients experience impossible robberies. Then he witnesses one himself, and realizes that the perpetrators have access to some form of technology beyond anything he knows. When he attempts to trace them to their base, he finds himself on another planet, and in trouble up to his eyebrows. *Out of Sync* is an excellent adventure story drawing upon the best techniques Haiblum employed throughout his career.

—Don D'Ammassa

---

**HALAM, Ann.** *See* **JONES, Gwyneth A.**

---

**HALDEMAN, Jack C(arroll, II).** American. Born in Hopkinsville, New York, 18 December 1941; brother of Joe Haldeman, *q.v.* Educated at the University of Oklahoma, Norman, 1960–63; Johns Hopkins University, Baltimore, B.S. in life science 1973. Married 1) Alice Haldeman in 1965; 2) Vol Haldeman in 1975; two daughters. Research assistant, Johns Hopkins University School of Hygiene and Public Health, 1963–68; medical technician, University of Maryland Hospital, 1968–73; has also worked as a statistician, photographer, and printer's devil. President, Washington Science Fiction Association, seven years; chairman, Discon II. Agent: Eleanor Wood, Blassingame, McCauley, and Wood, 111 8th Avenue, Suite 1501, New York, New York 10001, U.S.A.

SCIENCE-FICTION PUBLICATIONS

Novels

*Vector Analysis.* New York, Berkley, 1978.
*Perry's Planet.* New York, Bantam, 1980.
*There Is No Darkness*, with Joe Haldeman. New York, Ace, 1983; London, Futura, 1985.
*The Fall of Winter.* New York, Baen, 1985.
*Bill, the Galactic Hero, on the Planet of Zombie Vampires*, with Harry Harrison. New York, Avon, 1991.
*Echoes of Thunder*, with Jack Dann (published with *Run for the Stars*, by Harlan Ellison). New York, Tor, 1991.

Uncollected Short Stories (series: Sports)

"Garden of Eden," in *Fantastic* (New York), December 1971.
"Watchdog," in *Amazing* (New York), May 1972.
"What I Did on My Summer Vacation," in *Fantastic* (New York), July 1973.
"Slugging It Out," in *The Far Side of Time*, edited by Roger Elwood. New York, Dodd Mead, 1974.
"Sand Castles," in *Alternities*, edited by David Gerrold and Stephen Goldin. New York, Dell, 1974.
"Laura's Theme," in *Fantastic* (New York), June 1975.
"Time to Come," in *Gallery* (Chicago), June 1975.
"Songs of Dying Swans," in *Stellar 2*, edited by Judy-Lynn del Rey. New York, Ballantine, 1976.
"Limits," with Jack Dann, in *Fantastic* (New York), May 1976.
"Louisville Slugger" (Sports), in *Astronauts and Androids*, edited by Isaac Asimov. New York, Dale, 1977.
"Home Team Advantage" (Sports), in *Black Holes and Bug Eyed Monsters*, edited by Isaac Asimov, New York, Dale, 1977.
"Those Thrilling Days of Yesteryear," in *Amazing* (New York), March 1977.
"Vector Analysis," in *Analog* (New York), May 1977.
"The End-of-the-World Rag," in *Fantastic* (New York), December 1977.
"The Agony of Defeat" (Sports), in *Comets and Computers*, edited by Isaac Asimov. New York, Dale, 1978.
"Snakes and Snails," in *Nightmares*, edited by Charles L. Grant. New York, Doubleday, 1978.
"The Thrill of Victory" (Sports), in *Isaac Asimov's Science Fiction Magazine* (New York), January-February 1978.
"Mortimer Snodgrass Turtle" (Sports), in *Fantasy and Science Fiction* (New York), June 1978.
"What Weighs 8000 Pounds and Wears Red Sneakers?," in *Fantastic* (New York), July 1978.
"Thirty Love" (Sports), in *Isaac Asimov's Science Fiction Magazine* (New York), September-October 1978.
"Last Rocket from Newark," in *Amazing* (New York), November 1978.

"What Kind of Love Is This," in *Destinies*, vol. 1, no. 5, edited by James Baen. New York, Ace, 1979.
"Race the Wind" (Sports), in *Omni* (New York), January 1979.
"Hear the Crush, Hear the Roar," in *Isaac Asimov's Science Fiction Magazine* (New York), December 1979.
"Longshot," in *Isaac Asimov's Science Fiction Anthology 3*, edited by George Scithers. New York, Davis, 1980.
"Spring Fever," in *Fantasy and Science Fiction* (New York), July 1980.
"Games Children Play," in *Proteus*, edited by Richard S. McEnroe. New York, Ace, 1981.
"A Scientific Fact," in *Tomorrow's TV*, edited by Isaac Asimov, Martin H. Greenberg, and Charles G. Waugh. Milwaukee, Raintree, 1982.
"What Time Is It?," in *TV: 2000*, edited by Isaac Asimov, Martin H. Greenberg, and Charles G. Waugh. New York, Fawcett, 1982.
"High Steel," with Jack Dann, in *Fantasy and Science Fiction* (New York), February 1982.
"Monkey Business," in *Amazing* (New York), January 1983.
"On the Rebound," in *Amazing* (New York), March 1983.
"Open Frame," in *Twilight Zone* (New York), July 1983.
"We, The People," in *Analog* (New York), 2 September 1983.
"My Crazy Father Who Scares All the Women Away," in *Isaac Asimov's Science Fiction Magazine* (New York), 2 December 1983.
"Still Frame," in *Shadows 7*, edited by Charles L. Grant. New York, Doubleday, 1984.
"A Very Good Year," in *Analog* (New York), December 1984.
"Rats in Space," in *Fantasy and Science Fiction* (New York), May 1985.
"Playing for Keeps" and "Wet Behind the Ears," in *Tales from Isaac Asimov's Science Fiction Magazine: Short Stories for Young Adults*, selected by Sheila Williams and Cynthia Manson. San Diego, California, Harcourt Brace, 1986.

*

Jack C. Haldeman comments:

Sometimes I write hard science fiction, sometimes soft. Sometimes I'm serious, sometimes I'm humorous. Mostly I'm traditional, though occasionally I try something experimental. I often draw on my scientific background as well as my sense of humor. Mostly I try to entertain, though I have been known to slip in a message or two. I try not to let it clutter up the story.

* * *

Jack C. Haldeman has spent much of his career on one of the rarest themes in science fiction, the sports story. He began in 1977 with "Louisville Slugger," an anecdotal piece in which the future of humanity depends upon a baseball game against some Arcturians. This was followed by a sequel, "Home Team Advantage," wherein the Arcturian aliens discover that man is inedible and forfeit their prize, the consumption of humanity.

Haldeman followed these with "Thrill of Victory" and "The Agony of Defeat," this time concentrating on a team of robotic football players who are first faced with the discovery that they have been illegally programmed with a will to win, and then matched in a championship game against genetically altered human beings. All four stories were designed to be humorous, and made little lasting impact.

"Thirty Love" was decidedly different. A professional tennis player has led a long and successful career because his precognitive powers enable him to anticipate where the ball will next be hit. During his final match, he deliberately throws the game when he realizes that defeating his opponent will cause the latter a trauma that will utterly ruin his life. Unfortunately, the sports stories that followed returned to a humorous theme for the most part. Only "Race the Wind" varied from the pattern. A disabled man is determined to participate in slalom racing, and although his character was well drawn, the plot fails to sustain the story.

There have been, however, several extremely good stories outside the context of his sports series. "Songs of Dying Swans" involves the tragic destruction of a race of altered humans, and examines the consequences of this act on the rest of civilization. "Laura's Theme" is a haunting, enigmatic story of a strange woman who seems always to be present when other peoples' lives take radical turns for the worse.

Haldeman's humor ranges from slight but amusing to genuinely funny. A typical middle-class family is startled and dismayed to discover that their front yard has suddenly become the legendary elephants' graveyard in "What Weighs 8000 Pounds and Wears Red Sneakers?" In "Those Thrilling Days of Yesteryear," archaeologists are engaged in manufacturing and burying artifacts, because the past as we know it is all a fraud. Haldeman invents new mythical creatures in "Games Children Play," and all the pending accidents of the future occur at once in "A Very Good Year."

His more recent serious work has been of considerably higher calibre. "Spring Fever" compares human activity to that of lemmings. An Indian is drafted into duty in orbit in "High Steel" and averts a disaster in what is probably Haldeman's best single work to date. Other short pieces of interest are "Wet Behind the Ears" and "We the People."

Haldeman's first novel, *Vector Analysis*, is a routine but well-handled story of adventure and scientific mystery in space. *Perry's Planet*, a Star Trek adventure, is similarly competent but has a less interesting plot. *There Is No Darkness*, co-authored with Joe Haldeman, is an episodic story following a group of young adults through various adventures on different planets. A more recent novel, *The Fall of Winter* demonstrates a marked improvement in the quality of his writing while still reflecting his ongoing interests. A team of terraformers is at work on an alien planet when a series of incidents hampers their efforts. It is a well worked out scientific mystery wrapped up in a good adventure story.

—Don D'Ammassa

---

**HALDEMAN, Joe** (Joseph William Haldeman). Also writes as Robert Graham. American. Born in Oklahoma City, 9 June 1943; brother of Jack C. Haldeman, *q. v.* Educated at the University of Maryland, College Park, B.S. in physics and astronomy, 1967; graduate study, 1969–70; University of Iowa, Iowa City, M.F.A. 1975. Served in the United States Army, 1967–69: Purple Heart. Married Mary Gay Potter in 1965. Teaching Assistant, University of Iowa, 1975; editor, *Astronomy*, Milwaukee, 1976. Since 1970, freelance writer. Treasurer, Science Fiction Writers of America, for two years. Recipient: Nebula award, 1975; Hugo award, 1976, 1977; Ditmar award, 1976; Galaxy award, 1978; Rhyling award, 1985. Agent: Kirby McCauley, 425 Park Avenue South, New York, New York 10016. Address: 5412 N.W. 14th Avenue, Gainesville, Florida 32605, U.S.A.

SCIENCE-FICTION PUBLICATIONS

Novels (series: Attar; Star Trek; Worlds)

*The Forever War*. New York, St. Martin's Press, 1974; London, Weidenfield and Nicolson, 1975.
*Attar 1: Attar's Revenge* (as Robert Graham). New York, Pocket Books, 1975; London, Mews, 1977.
*Attar 2: War of Nerves* (as Robert Graham). New York, Pocket Books, 1975.
*Mindbridge*. New York, St. Martin's Press, 1976; London, Macdonald and Jane's, 1977.
*Planet of Judgment* (Star Trek). New York, Bantam, and London, Corgi, 1977.
*All My Sins Remembered*. New York, St. Martin's Press, 1977; London, Macdonald and Jane's, 1978.
*World Without End* (Star Trek). New York, Bantam, and London, Corgi, 1979.
*Worlds*. New York, Viking Press, 1981; London, Macdonald, 1982.
*There Is No Darkness*, with Jack C. Haldeman. New York, Ace, 1983.
*Worlds Apart*. New York, Viking Press, 1983; London, Futura, 1984.
*Tool of the Trade*. New York, Morrow, and London, Gollancz, 1987.
*Buying Time*. New York, Morrow, 1989; as *The Long Habit of Living*, London, New English Library, 1989.
*The Hemingway Hoax*. New York, Morrow, and London, New English Library, 1990.

Short Stories

*Infinite Dreams*. New York, St. Martin's Press, 1978.
*Dealing in Futures*. New York, Viking Press, 1985; London, Macdonald, 1986.

Uncollected Short Stories

"Out of Phase," in *Galaxy* (New York), September 1969.
"Power Complex," in *Galaxy* (New York), April 1971.
"Four in One," in *Destinies* (New York), Spring 1980.
"Tricentennial," in *The Hugo Winners*, edited by Isaac Asimov. New York, Doubleday, 1985.
"The Monster," in *Cutting Edge*, edited by Dennis Etchison. New York, Doubleday, 1986.
"Amaja das," in *Masters of Darkness*, edited by Dennis Etchison. New York, Tor, 1986.
"DX," in *In Fields of Fire*, edited by Jeanne Van Buren Dann and Jack Dann. New York, Tor, 1987.
"Hero," in *Space Wars*, edited by Charles G. Waugh and Martin H. Greenberg. New York, Tor, 1988.
"Passages," in *Analog*, March 1990.

OTHER PUBLICATIONS

Novel

*War Year*. New York, Holt Rinehart, 1972; original version, New York, Pocket Books, 1977.

Plays

*The Devil His Due*, in *Fantastic* (New York), August 1974.
*The Moon and Marcek*, in *Vertex* (Los Angeles), August 1974.
*The Forever War* (produced Chicago, 1983).

Other

Editor, *Cosmic Laughter*. New York, Holt Rinehart, 1974.
Editor, *Study War No More: A Selection of Alternatives*. New York, St. Martin's Press, 1977; London, Futura, 1979.
Editor, *Nebula Award Stories 17*. New York, Holt Rinehart, 1983.
Editor, with Martin H. Greenberg and Charles G. Waugh, *Body Armor: 2000*. New York, Ace, 1986.
Editor, with Martin H. Greenberg and Charles G. Waugh, *Supertanks*. New York, Ace, 1987.
Editor, *The Best of John Brunner*. New York, Ballantine, 1988.
Editor, with Martin H. Greenberg and Charles G. Waugh, *Spacefighters*. New York, Ace, 1988.

*

Critical Studies: *Joe Haldeman*, Mercer Island, Washington, Starmont House, 1980, and *The Fiction of Joe Haldeman*, University of Iowa, unpublished dissertation, 1981, both by Joan Gordon.

Joe Haldeman comments:

Along with most of my contemporaries, I believe that science fiction is primarily a literature of ideas, but that this quality does not make it exempt from normal literary standards. A poorly written SF story may be published if the idea behind it is sufficiently interesting, and there's nothing "improper" about that so long as an audience exists for it. But the best SF is that which excels both in concept and in execution—examplars being as diverse as Bester's *The Stars My Destination* and Delany's *Dhalgren*—and at its best I think it has an advantage over literature that is "just plain literature."

There's no over-riding didactic or dialectic principle behind my writing. I write the sort of stories and books I would like to read. I'm fortunate in that a lot of moneybearing readers seem to share my tastes. Whether I would be willing (or able) to write differently if the market demanded it, I can't honestly say. I would like to think I'd stick to my guns, but on the other hand I do rather like working without bosses or time clocks.

* * *

SF, that fiercely questioning genre, had not exactly come to grips with the Vietnam question until publication of Joe Haldeman's "Hero" in the June 1972 issue of *Analog.* We had had the statements in the magazines about which authors supported the war and which opposed, and a great deal of debate about what Heinlein *really* meant in "Starship Troopers" (1959). And then "Hero" appeared, and it took the aspects of the war which had most disturbed us as onlookers and retold them in a setting remote from the emotions and politics of the real Vietnam, to try to let them be seen for what they were; described without rhetoric, to let their natures speak for themselves. While the war came to an end, Haldeman went on to describe in *The Forever War* the alienation of his soldiers from the culture that had used them. In their case this was brought about by time dilation, the effect of travelling at relativistic speeds, projecting them ever onwards into the future at different rates for different journeys.

*The Forever War* runs in the future, for 1200 years, between enemies evenly matched. Time dilation allows the narrator to see it (in snatches) from beginning to end. Some reviewers were unhappy with that end, where the soldier's ignorance of the Big Picture was allowed to remain: Haldeman's war is eventually ended by clones who can communicate only with one another, or with the hive-mind of the aliens, leaving the characters and the reader in the dark. But interstellar war could only occur between races with evenly matched technology, or with drastically differing technologies making conflict possible. Does loss of individuality then mean loss of progress? If so, then the use of time dilation to bring Haldeman's major characters together at the end of the novel is not a glib happy ending (as some have alleged) but a chance for humanity to bypass the cloning dead-end, and try another course.

*Mindbridge* was another examination of human contact with a hive-mind, while *All My Sins Remembered* was a damning indictment not merely of big government but also of the standard SF attitude to individuality. SF used to be full of people who find out that they're really someone else (usually somebody more powerful), and part of the problem in identifying with central characters is often their lack of individuality; some authors have run together novellas into "fix-up" novels just by changing the name of the central character.

McGavin in *All My Sins Remembered* is a government agent, repeatedly given new identities through psychological conditioning and plastic surgery. In real life, such changes of role can lead to personality disorders, especially for military personnel who assess themselves by rank. Haldeman's McGavin does not end up with no personality of his own, unlike the actor in Ellison's "All the Sounds of Fear": he is an individual moved and controlled by an organisation which commands his loyalty but is beyond his control.

This is again the situation of the central characters in *The Forever War* and *Mindbridge.* One begins to notice that other central characters are in the same boat: victims of rape and kidnapping (*Worlds*), people hounded by the KGB and CIA because of their unique talents (*Tool of the Trade*), or hunted across the Solar System by the wealthy (*Buying Time*, aka *The Long Habit of Living*). Even the *Star Trek* novel, *Planet of Judgment*, finds Kirk, Spock et al at the receiving end of the conflict between greater powers. The short stories collected in *Dealing in Futures* and *Infinite Dreams* have been more varied and do allow us to think that life in the future doesn't necessarily consist of being pushed around by vastly powerful forces.

In this light one has to welcome *The Hemingway Hoax*, in which the central character sets out to emulate Hemingway, allows himself out of stubbornness to be put to several harrowing deaths in a variety of parallel universes, *becomes* Hemingway, transcends him, and leaves his tormentors wondering "Where did he go?" It would be nice if we could all do the same; but if SF has a purpose, perhaps it is to make us believe that at least in theory we can.

—Duncan Lunan

---

**HALL, Austin.** American. Born in 1882 (?). Educated at Lincoln High School, Cleveland; Ohio Northern University, Ada; Ohio State University, Columbus; University of California, Berkeley. Did newspaper and electrical work, then worked in mining and ranching; wrote hundreds of western stories. *Died in 1933.*

Science-Fiction Publications

Novels

*People of the Comet.* Los Angeles, Griffin, 1948.
*The Blind Spot*, with Homer Eon Flint. Philadelphia, Prime Press, 1951; London, Museum Press, 1953.
*The Spot of Life.* New York, Ace, 1965.

Uncollected Short Stories

"Almost Immortal," in *All-Story Weekly* (New York), 7 October 1916.
"The Rebel Soul," in *All-Story Weekly* (New York), 30 June 1917.
"Into the Infinite," in *All-Story Weekly* (New York), 12 April 1919; expanded version, in *Famous Fantastic Mysteries* (New York), October 1942.
"The Man Who Saved the Earth," in *Best of Science Fiction*, edited by Groff Conklin. New York, Crown, 1946.

*   *   *

Homer Eon Flint, writing alone and in collaboration with Austin Hall, produced a large quantity of science fiction from 1916 to 1924, most of which appeared in the Munsey Magazines *All-Story* and *Argosy.* His fame, however, and that of Austin Hall, rests on one of the most admired and cherished fantasies of the early 20th century, *The Blind Spot*, and its sequel *The Spot of Life*, written by Hall after the death of Flint.

Flint's first published story was "The Planeteer," set in the 23rd century, when earth's population has grown so great that global starvation is threatened. Through engineering feats on a truly cosmic scale, the earth's orbit is shifted to one closer to Jupiter's, and the latter planet then furnishes a new and inexhaustible source of food. In a sequel, "King of Conserve Island," an earthly monarch attempts to gain control of Jupiter and its food resources, and is thwarted by a hero who cuts off the heat of the sun and freezes the villain into submission. "The Lord of Death" is about two men who travel to the planet Mercury, and find there an ancient record of a man and woman named Adam and Eve who had left Mercury millennia earlier for an unknown destination. In "The Queen of Life" the same characters take their space ship to Venus, where they discover an apparently Utopian civilization.

Hall's writing career began with "Almost Immortal," the story of a Tibetan doctor thousands of years old who has been able to prolong his own life by absorbing the bodies and the wills of younger men at regular intervals. His downfall comes when the last man he assimilates turns out to have a will greater than his own. "The Rebel Soul" has a quite similar plot involving undying souls that take possession of individuals across the ages. A sequel, "Into the Infinite," carries on the story of a man who has been possessed by the Rebel Soul, and who is eventually freed through the power of a woman's love. "The Man Who Saved the Earth" describes an attempt by the inhabitants of Mars to capture all the water on earth and transport it to Mars, turning the latter into a verdant planet. This plot is foiled at the last minute by the one man on earth with the necessary knowledge, just as the oceans are drying up.

The literary styles of Flint and Hall were curiously similar, sharing the same strengths and weaknesses. Both were totally innocent of the fine points of sentence structure and grammar, and neither has a particularly large vocabulary. Each man, however, had a vivid and far-reaching imagination and a delight in reaching out into the vastnesses of time and space. Their complicated plotting and their skill in describing the life, customs, and technologies of the worlds of the distant future compensate for their somewhat clumsy style.

The high point in the literary careers of Flint and Hall was their collaboration on *The Blind Spot*, a classic in the field despite the literary flaws that distinguish the other works of both authors. *The Blind Spot* is more fantasy and mystery than science fiction. In a downtown San Francisco apartment building a gateway between two parallel worlds is discovered. A man emerges from the Spot, and takes back with him a scientist from this world. They are followed by would-be rescuers of the scientist, and the plot thereafter involves additional crossings through the Spot, bringing in more mystery and occultism than science. The Spot is finally closed at the end of the novel, to protect the inhabitants of this world from possible danger from the people on the other side. Flint died in 1924, under violent and mysterious circumstances that have never been explained. Hall continued to write alone, and in 1932 produced *The Spot of Life*, a sequel in which the Spot is reopened by the inhabitants of the other world, with the object of an invasion by force of our world. This novel takes place a generation after the time of the original story, and earth's savior in *The Spot of Life* is the son of the principal character in the first novel.

—Douglas E. Way

---

**HAMILTON, Edmond.** Also wrote as Brett Sterling. American. Born in Youngstown, Ohio, 21 October 1904. Educated at Westminster College, New Wilmington, Pennsylvania, 1919–21. Married Leigh Brackett, *q.v.*, in 1946. Freelance writer: staff writer for *Superman* comics in the 1940's. Guest of Honor, 22nd World Science Fiction Convention, 1964; elected to First Fandom Science Fiction Hall of Fame, 1967. *Died 1 February 1977.*

SCIENCE-FICTION PUBLICATIONS

Novels (series: Captain Future; John Gordon; Starwolf)

*The Star Kings* (Gordon). New York, Fell, 1949; London, Museum Press, 1951; as *Beyond the Moon*, New York, New American Library, 1950.
*The Monsters of Juntonheim.* London, Consul, 1950; as *A Yank at Valhalla*, New York, Ace, 1973.
*Tharkol, Lord of the Unknown.* London, Consul, 1950.
*City at World's End.* New York, Fell, 1951; London, Museum Press, 1952.
*The Sun Smasher.* New York, Ace, 1959.
*The Star of Life.* New York, Torquil, 1959.
*The Magician of Mars* (Future). New York, Popular Library, 1959.
*The Haunted Stars.* New York, Torquil, 1960; London, Jenkins, 1965.
*Battle for the Stars.* New York, Torquil, 1961; London, Mayflower, 1963.
*Outside the Universe.* New York, Ace, 1964.
*The Valley of Creation.* New York, Lancer, 1964.
*Fugitive of the Stars.* New York, Ace, 1965.
*Doomstar.* New York, Belmont, 1966.
*The Harper of Titan.* New York, Popular Library, 1967.
*The Weapon from Beyond* (Starwolf). New York, Ace, 1967.
*Danger Planet* (Future; as Brett Sterling). New York, Popular Library, 1968.
*The Closed Worlds* (Starwolf). New York, Ace, 1968.
*World of the Starwolves.* New York, Ace, 1968.
*Quest Beyond the Stars* (Future). New York, Popular Library, 1969.
*Outlaw World* (Future). New York, Popular Library, 1969.
*The Comet Kings* (Future). New York, Popular Library, 1969.
*Outlaws of the Moon* (Future). New York, Popular Library, 1969.
*Planets in Peril* (Future). New York, Popular Library, 1969.
*Captain Future's Challenge.* New York, Popular Library, 1969.
*Calling Captain Future.* New York, Popular Library, 1969.
*Captain Future and the Space Emperor.* New York, Popular Library, 1969.
*Galaxy Mission* (Future). New York, Popular Library, 1969.
*Return to the Stars* (Gordon). New York, Lancer, 1970.

Short Stories

*The Metal Giants.* Washburn, North Dakota, Swanson, 1932(?).
*The Horror on the Asteroid and Other Tales of Planetary Horror.* London, Allan, 1936; Boston, Gregg Press, 1975.
*Tiger Girl.* London, Utopian, 1945(?).
*Murder in the Clinic.* London, Utopian, 1946(?).
*Crashing Suns.* New York, Ace, 1965.
*What's It Like Out There.* New York, Ace, 1974.
*The Best of Edmond Hamilton*, edited by Leigh Brackett. New York, Ballantine, 1977.

OTHER PUBLICATIONS

Other

Editor, *The Best of Leigh Brackett.* New York, Doubleday, 1977.

*

Manuscript Collection: Eastern New Mexico University Library, Portales.

* * *

Edmond Hamilton virtually invented the idea of the Space Patrol. The concept of a galactic civilization entered the mainstream of science fiction through Hamilton's stories for *Weird Tales* and *Amazing Stories* between 1928 and 1930, and it has been a lasting influence. More generally, Hamilton is identified with space opera. He was writing it before the term was coined, and he wrote a tremendous amount of it for *Air Wonder Stories, Amazing, Startling*, and *Thriller Wonder Stories* (Hamilton published little in *Astounding, Galaxy* and *Fantasy and Science Fiction;* oddly enough, Hamilton was also conspicuous by his absence in *Planet Stories*, supposedly the epitome of space opera). Most of his stories show the defects of the genre he pioneered. The action was fast and furious and sometimes absurd. The characterization was minimal and the dialogue was ghastly. But Hamilton was fond of the Big Idea, and he could communicate the excitement of sweeping concepts. (It was typical of Hamilton to present the whole panorama of evolution in a short story, and to throw in some original twists along the way.) He caught the drama of science, even if he didn't get all the details right. His stories had verve and feeling, and they were alive. Hamilton did not take himself with undue solemnity; he had some fun with his writing. At the same time, he was writing stories that *he* liked to read, and it showed. The least of Hamilton's stories were always blessed by that extra dimension that makes all the difference: the sense of wonder.

Hamilton's most famous (or infamous) creation was Captain Future. The name was decidedly unfortunate; it is so trite that it virtually demands parody. (It got some, too. Captain Future was the only character in science fiction who managed to attract the scalpel of S.J. Perelman.) The magazine *Captain Future* was published quarterly from 1940 through 1944, and each issue featured a short Captain Future novel. Hamilton wrote most of them, as well as some later Captain Future stories that appeared in *Startling Stories.* By and large, this was formula fiction redeemed at times by flashes of the Hamilton talent. Captain Future was Curt Newton, also known as the Wizard of Science and the Man of Tomorrow. With his sidekicks—Grag the robot, Otho the android, and Simon Wright, a brain in a box—Captain Future kept boredom at bay by saving the solar system from assorted disasters.

Beginning perhaps with *City at World's End* (1951), Hamilton's fiction took on a more subdued tone as he adapted to a changing market. He cut down on the melodrama, introduced more shadings in his stories, and worked to create believable characters. One can only salute the effort; the novels range from *The Haunted Stars* to the *Starwolf* series, and they are better than a great many science-fiction tales with inflated reputations. Unfortunately, when Hamilton got rid of the corn he also lost much of the excitement that had marked his work. The spark is still there, but the fire never really gets going.

There is a kind of pathos about Hamilton's later work. He had been a creative professional writer for a quarter of a century, and now he had to prove himself all over again. His talent may have been obscured by the type of science fiction to which he devoted himself, but the mature Hamilton shows to good advantage in a number of classic short stories, including "What's It Like Out There?" and "The Pro."

Edmond Hamilton was one of the most prolific of all science-fiction writers. There was joy in his work, and he opened a lot of doors for those who came after him.

—Chad Oliver

---

**HAMLET, Ova.** *See* **LUPOFF, Richard A.**

---

**HAND, Elizabeth.** American. Born in San Diego, California, 29 March 1957. Educated at The Catholic University of America, Washington, D.C., 1975–84; B.A. in cultural anthropology 1984. One daughter. Archival researcher, National Air and Space Museum, Smithsonian Institution, Washington, D.C., 1979–86; co-founder of the National Air and Space Museum's Archival Videodisc Program. Agent: Martha Millard Literary Agency, 204 Park Avenue, Madison, New Jersey, 07940. Address: Tooley Cottage, Coleman Pond, P.O. Box 133, Lincolnville Beach, Maine, 04849, U.S.A.

SCIENCE-FICTION PUBLICATIONS

Novel

*Winterlong.* New York, Bantam, 1990.

Uncollected Short Stories

"Prince of Flowers," in *Year's Best Horror Stories XVII*, edited by Karl E. Wagner. New York, DAW, 1989.
"The Boy in the Tree," in *Full Spectrum 2.* New York, Doubleday, 1989.
"On the Town Route," in *Year's Best Horror 2*, edited by Ramsey Campbell. New York, Carroll and Graf, 1991.

*

Elizabeth Hand comments:

As a feminist author and critic, my work is concerned primarily with moral issues and issues of sexual identity, sexual transformation, sexual liberation. As a lapsed Catholic, my writing is obsessed with death and the hope of redemption, and guilt for writing about all that sex.

* * *

Elizabeth Hand emerged in the late 1980's to become one of the science-fiction field's most promising new voices. After publishing just three works of short fiction over a three-year period, Hand's first novel appeared in 1990, and received significant critical notice.

Hand's first story, "Prince of Flowers," appeared in *The Twilight Zone* in 1988. It is a contemporary supernatural fantasy about a young woman named Helen who works for a cultural history museum in downtown Washington, D.C., where she opens and inventories old crates of curious objects and papers donated to the museum. (The characters, setting, and some of the plot are undoubtedly drawn from Hand's own experiences working for a museum in Washington, D.C.) Helen begins occasionally, then more frequently, to take some of the smaller curios home with her to decorate her apartment. The fantasy element involves her discovery of a strange Indonesian "spirit puppet," the Prince of Flowers of the title, in a crate that had been unopened for nearly a century. It is a typical *Twilight Zone* story, but quite nicely written, and was chosen by Karl Edward Wagner for inclusion in his *Year's Best Horror Stories XVII.*

Hand's second story appeared more than a year later, in 1989, in the fifth issue of *Pulphouse.* "On the Town Route," also based on the author's own experiences, tells the story of a young woman accompanying a young man who drives an ice cream truck through a poverty-stricken area in rural Virginia. The people to whom he sells (or just as often gives away) his ice cream are poor, dirty, and eerily ignorant of all social customs, as well as obviously both psychologically and nutritionally dependent on his visits—especially one family. One night, driving back after dark, they hit and believe they have surely killed the young daughter in that family, only to have her blind mother come, revive her, and walk her home. The story builds to an unexpectedly dramatic supernatural conclusion. The story was chosen by Ramsey Campbell for *Year's Best Horror 2.*

With her third story, "The Boy in the Tree," also published in 1990, Hand moves from contemporary supernatural horror to science fiction, with a story set in the indeterminate future at a scientific research facility where specially trained and augmented empaths are used to treat psychopathic patients. The protagonist is one of those empaths, and she has never known another life, having never left the facility since being brought to it as an autistic child. All of the empaths have the ability to "tap" into others (established an empathic connection) by tasting a small quantity of their blood, and the empaths in the facility have very strange mutual relationships that primarily revolve around vampiric kissing to share the minds they have experienced during treatments. The boy of the title is some sort of mysterious demigod persona that comes to inhabit the protagonist's mind, resulting in some of her patients being plunged into despair and killing themselves.

In 1990, Hand's first novel appeared as a Bantam Spectra Special Edition. *Winterlong* begins with a slightly modified version of "The Boy in the Tree" and continues to unfold a bizarre world some 50 or 100 or more years in our future after a long series of biological-weapons wars have devastated human civilization, and only some enclaves of Ascendants (apparently people who have retreated to the high ground in orbital defense stations) have any high-technological capabilities. The story takes place in the slowly decaying remnants of Washington, D.C., called the City of Trees, and the suburbs of Northern Virginia, where the empathic research facility is located. The story follows the empath Wendy as she escapes from the research facility, which is coming under dangerous new Ascendant management, and avoids a deadly biological air attack to escape with the help of a male medical attendant to the City of Trees.

Wendy's travels into D.C. take her through a nightmare of the remnants of biological warfare and genetic engineering experiments, as she is attacked by deadly exotic flora, insane mutated children, escaped packs of genetically engineered "geneslaves," and much more. Eventually, she and her partner reach the relative safety of his friends, who are of a house (extended family) of courtesans. Slowly we are introduced to the degenerated remnants of humans who have survived around the Mall and parts of northwest D.C., extended families occupying specific buildings and specializing in a few remaining arts; some specialize in prostitution, some in maintaining various museums, some in the botanical sciences, and some in the zoological sciences. The social and sexual practices of these people are strange indeed, as we learn both from Wendy's viewpoint and from that of her long-lost brother, who looks just like her, and is one of the most prized male prostitutes.

There is some beauty left in this hideously degenerate human society, but not much. The continual mistreatment of children and the tendency to mix torture and death with sexual pleasure is particularly extreme. Stylistically, this novel resembles fantasy more than science fiction; the SF underpinnings are virtually invisible, since no one who is sane really knows what is going on. There are some marvelous characters here, but none seems to act on his or her own volition; all feel driven by unseen forces. The situation degenerates further as an insane Ascendant takes over the National Cathedral, gains the cooperation of a disorganized, superstitious army of mutated children and geneslaves, and sets up the final hideous prophesied event where brother and sister meet.

Hand has also written a great deal of literary criticism, not all of it related to SF. She does book reviews regularly for *The Washington Post*, weekly for *The Detroit Metro Times*, and occasionally for *The New York Review of Science Fiction*, the feminist quarterly *Belles Lettres*, Kirkus, and Penthouse Publications. She is a contributing editor to the semi-professional SF review magazine, *Science Fiction Eye*, where she has published a number of interesting reviews and essays on the field. Elizabeth Hand promises to be one of the writers to watch in the science-fiction field in the 1990's.

—D. Douglas Fratz

---

**HARDING, Lee (John).** Also writes as Harold G. Nye. Australian. Born in Colac, Victoria, 17 February 1937. Educated in Australian primary schools. Married 1) Carla Bleeker in 1960 (divorced 1974), two sons and one daughter; 2) Irene Anne Pagram in 1982, one daughter. Freelance photographer, 1953–70. Recipient: Ditmar award, 1970, 1972; Alan Marshall award, 1978; Australian Children's Book of the Year award, 1980. Agent: Virgina Kidd, Box 278, Milford, Pennsylvania 18337, U.S.A. Address: P.O. Box 198, Fern Tree Gully, Victoria 3156, Australia.

### Science-Fiction Publications

#### Novels

*The Fallen Spaceman* (for children). Melbourne, Cassell, 1973; London, Cassell, 1975; revised edition, New York, Harper, 1980.
*A World of Shadows*. London, Hale, 1975.
*Future Sanctuary*. Toronto, Laser, 1976.
*The Children of Atlantis* (for children). Melbourne, Cassell, 1976.
*The Frozen Sky* (for children). Melbourne, Cassell, 1976.
*Return to Tomorrow* (for children). Melbourne, Cassell, 1976.
*The Weeping Sky* (for children). Melbourne, Cassell, 1977.
*Displaced Person* (for children). Melbourne, Hyland House, 1979; as *Misplaced Persons*, New York, Harper, 1979.
*The Web of Time* (for children). Melbourne, Cassell, 1979; New York, Penguin, 1985.
*Waiting for the End of the World* (for children). Melbourne, Hyland House, 1983; New York, Penguin, 1985.

### Other Publications

#### Plays

Radio Plays: *Journey into Time* serial, 1978; *The Legend of New Earth* serial, 1979.

#### Other

Editor, *Beyond Tomorrow: An Anthology of Modern Science Fiction*. Melbourne, Wren, 1976; abridged edition, London, New English Library, 1977.
Editor, *The Altered I: An Encounter with Science Fiction*. Melbourne, Norstrilia Press, 1976; revised edition, New York, Berkley, 1978.
Editor, *Rooms of Paradise*. Melbourne, Quartet, 1978; New York, St. Martin's Press, 1979.

* * *

For many years one of the most promising Australian science-fiction writers, Lee Harding edited influential anthologies of Australian SF, published his short stories in a range of international publications in the 1960's and early 1970's, and established himself as a novelist late in his writing career with two books for adults and a series of novels for "young adult" readers (though each of these is pitched at a different level of readership). His writings reflect a mature and distinctive commitment to characterization and to straightforward techniques of narrative and construction. Though his prose style has recently been attacked by critics (especially those less in sympathy with straightforward, unadorned writing), Harding still commands respect for the themes examined in his best works.

*A World of Shadows*—a novel for adult readers—deals competently with questions of identity and the nature of reality. Astronaut Stephen Chandler is beset by the smoke-like alien Shadows, and as a result of their onslaught he returns to Earth in the body of his co-pilot, but with his own mind and memories intact within the new body. He becomes involved in a desperate struggle to convince the authorities—and his wife—of his real identity. But what now *is* his "real" identity? Harding describes *A World of Shadows* as "an unusual ontological thriller," and while the novel offers no profound new insights, it does offer an entertaining and cogent canvassing of issues.

*Future Sanctuary*, Harding's second adult novel, offers a much less satisfactory exploration of the nature of reality. A fugitive pursued for some nameless (and possibly non-existent) crime finds haven in the limbo-world of Sanctuary, but this surface action is revealed to be merely the heroic psychodrama of a deranged poet.

The title of the young adult novel *The Weeping Sky* comes from the novel's central image of an eerie weeping "wound" in the sky, and through skilled and subtle manipulation of characters, situation, and setting, Harding presents an eloquent statement on the elusive, illusory nature of reality. His characters seem to belong to our world, but their society is medieval and their religion is an unknown variant of Christianity; the "wound" in the sky appears to be a harmless though supernatural phenomenon, but there is evidence that it might be a thoroughly rational precursor of natural disaster.

Harding's prize-winning young adult novel, *Displaced Person*, presents a sustained exploration of the nature of reality as the teenager Graeme Drury becomes estranged from the world and people around him and is drawn into a soundless, colourless "grey world" or limbo. This novel is more skilled in execution than *The Weeping Sky*, for it contains some hauntingly lyrical scenes and succinctly accurate accounts of suburban lifestyle, but it is the lesser novel in conception. Its themes are too explicit, and the attempts at metaphysical speculation are ineffective (though minor textual changes to the second edition are an improvement). Nevertheless, as a fable of urban alienation it has been immensely successful with teenage readers.

*Waiting for the End of the World* may have marked the end of Harding's writing career, for he has published no fiction since then. Set in a decrepit totalitarian future Australia, *Waiting for the End of the World* is a fable of contemporary *angst*. Its central characters are rebellious individuals who have fled the dystopian city to live in the wilds, but now roving patrols are burning the woodlands to smoke out these rebels. As critic Russell Blackford has noted, the characters do little to avert their ultimate demise: they are passively *waiting* for the end of their world.

Lee Harding has a gift for narrative, and consequently it is the storyline that is paramount in each of his novels. Yet Harding is no mere story-teller, for his plots are a way of finding characters and themes, and they are always generated by the plight of his characters. It is stock critical jargon to talk about an author "examining" his themes (implying an approach that is analytical, rigorous, perhaps even exaustive), but this is not appropriate for describing Harding's method. Instead of delving deeply, Harding *canvasses* issues with a deft, light touch.

—Van Ikin

---

**HARNESS, Charles L(eonard).** Also writes as Leonard Lockhard. American. Born in Colorado City, Texas, 29 December 1915. Educated at George Washington University, Washington, D.C., B.S. 1942, LL.B. 1946. Married Nell W. Harness in 1938; one daughter and one son. Mineral economist, United States Bureau of Mines, Washington, D.C., 1941–47; patent attorney, American Cyanamid Company, Stamford, Connecticut, 1947–53; patent attorney, W.R. Grace and Company, Columbia, Maryland, 1953–81. Agent: Joseph Elder Literary Agency, P.O. Box 298, Warwick, New York 10990. Address: 6705 White Gate Road, Clarksville, Maryland 21029, U.S.A.

SCIENCE-FICTION PUBLICATIONS

Novels

*Flight into Yesterday.* New York, Bouregy, 1953; as *The Paradox Men*, New York, Ace, 1955; London, Faber, 1964; revised edition, New York, Crown, 1984.
*The Ring of Ritornel.* London, Gollancz, and New York, Berkley, 1968.
*Wolfhead.* New York, Berkley, 1978.
*The Catalyst.* New York, Pocket Books, 1980.
*Firebird.* New York, Pocket Books, 1981.
*The Venetian Court.* New York, Ballantine, 1984.
*Redworld.* New York, DAW, 1986.
*Krono.* New York, Watts, 1988.
*Lurid Dreams.* New York, Avon, 1990.

Short Stories

*The Rose.* London, Compact, 1966; New York, Berkley, 1969.

Uncollected Short Stories

"Fruits of the Agathon," in *Thrilling Wonder Stories* (New York), December 1948.
"Stalemate in Space," in *Planet* (New York), Summer 1949.
"Even Steven," in *Other Worlds* (Evanston, Illinois), November 1950.
"A Thesis for Branderbrook," in *Thrilling Wonder Stories* (New York), June 1951.
"Improbable Profession" (as Leonard Lockhard, with Ted Thomas), in *Astounding* (New York), September 1952.
"The Poisoner," in *Fantasy and Science Fiction* (New York), December 1952.
"Heritage," in *Tomorrow's Universe*, edited by H.J. Campbell. London, Panther, 1953.
"The Call of the Black Lagoon," in *Avon Science Fiction* (New York), January 1953.
"Child by Chronos," in *The Best from Fantasy and Science Fiction 3*, edited by Anthony Boucher and J. Francis McComas. New York, Doubleday, 1954.
"That Professional Look" (as Leonard Lockhard, with Ted Thomas), in *Astounding* (New York), January 1954.
"The Alchemist," in *Analog* (New York), May 1966.

"Bugs," in *Fantasy and Science Fiction* (New York), August 1967.
"The Million Year Patent," in *Amazing* (New York), December 1967.
"Probable Cause," in *Orbit 4*, edited by Damon Knight. New York, Putnam, 1968.
"An Ornament to His Profession," in *SF 12*, edited by Judith Merril. New York, Delacorte Press, 1968.
"Bookmobile," in *If* (New York), November 1968.
"Time Trap," in *Alpha 1*, edited by Robert Silverberg. New York, Ballantine, 1970.
"The Araqnid Window," in *Amazing* (New York), December 1974.
"H-Tec," in *Analog* (New York), 25 May 1981.
"Quarks at Appomattox," in *Analog* (New York), October 1983.
"The Fall of Robin Arms," in *Fantasy and Science Fiction* (New York), March 1984.
"Summer Solstice," in *Analog* (New York), June 1984.
"The Cajamarca Project," in *Analog* (New York), February 1985.
"Signals," in *Synergy: New Science Fiction*, edited by George Zebrowski. San Diego, California, Harcourt Brace Jovanovich, 1987.

OTHER PUBLICATIONS

Other

*Marketing Magnesite and Allied Products*, with Nan C. Jensen. Washington, D.C., Bureau of Mines, 1943.
*Mining and Marketing of Barite*, with F.M. Barsigian. Washington, D.C., Bureau of Mines, 1946.

*

Manuscript Collection: University of Maryland, College Park.

Charles L. Harness comments:
I did it for money.

* * *

Charles L. Harness has not written as much as his admirers (Damon Knight, Brian Aldiss, Michael Moorcock) would have wished. His work has always been highly intricate, and his early stories have been compared to those of A.E. van Vogt. Unlike that author, he provides what seems to be a rational explanation for all the astonishing turns of his plots; like van Vogt, his best work has the compelling power of a dream. It is highly cerebral as well; in the words of Louis MacNeice, Harness likes "to draw the corks out of an old conundrum,/And watch the paradoxes fizz."

In *Flight into Yesterday* the hero, Alar, emerges from a wrecked spaceship with no memory of who he is but a certainty that he has a most urgent task to perform. He is sponsored by the Society of Thieves, and protected by the heroine, Keiris, who is the widow of a vanished scientist. The society he finds himself in is sophisticated but decadent; there are brilliant ball scenes and hideous torture chambers. As he attempts to escape from the Imperial police, he talks to the Empress, to a Toynbeean student of the downfall of civilizations, and to the lunatic crew of a solarion, a station perilously located on the surface of the Sun. The play of ideas is brilliant, the menace threatening. The ending is perhaps a shade too perfect, with the hero cancelling out all the misery of humanity. But the book is a dazzler all the same.

"The Rose" is perhaps Harness's most beautiful single work. The heroine, Anna van Tuyl, is at once a composer, a ballet dancer, and a psychotherapist. She is composing a ballet based on Oscar Wilde's story "The Nightingale and the Rose," and is at a standstill in the piece; she is also suffering from a deforming illness. Then she is asked to treat Ruy Jacques, the husband of the eminent and arrogant scientist Martha Jacques: Ruy Jacques has forgotten how to read print, but can read people's intentions instead. In attempting to cure Ray Jacques, Anna falls in love, incurring the jealousy of Martha Jacques. The climax is one of death and transfiguration: Anna finds the perfect ending to her ballet and dies, but hands on the key to a higher mode of life. The summary cannot do justice to the work, which must be read.

*The Ring of Ritornel* is again set in a society of formal brilliance and extreme tyranny. The villain is the Emperor Oberon, who cares nothing for human life. The hero, James Andrek, has been robbed of both his father and his elder brother by Oberon, and is determined to find the culprit. At the close of the book, a new cycle of the universe is about to begin, and only two people from the old universe will survive. In the warring religions of Alea and Ritornel, Harness poses old questions of chance and destiny. The structure of the book is both mathematical and musical: certain characters and motifs recur, but always with a different effect.

*Wolfhead* is more direct in manner than the other novels. Set in an Earth long after an atomic catastrophe, it has a hero who descends into the underground kingdom in pursuit of his lost love Beatra. As is fitting for a successor to Dante, he is guided by Virgil—a she-wolf into whose brain a small part of his own has been grafted. The theme is one of unrelenting war; in the end the hero at least succeeds in rescuing his society, but not his wife.

*The Catalyst* is set in the near future, and deals with a plague called novarella and a chemical called trialine which can cure it. There is a stunning portrait of the scientist Serane, and the way in which he reaches his discoveries by totally cicumventing the bureaucratic structure in which he works. The hero, Paul Blandford, succeeds in securing priority for Serane's invention by an incredible trial run. Thomas M. Disch has complained of the fantastic element in this novel, but I respect that Harness feels life really is like this: we make discoveries half in a dream, and sometimes we do seem to be protected by guardian angels. This aspect of the book reminds me strongly of Arthur Koestler's life of Kepler in *The Sleepwalkers.*

Harness's earlier short stories were perhaps stronger on plot than on character; his first, "Time Trap," already showed the ability to construct a highly ingenious time loop. His most brilliant early story, "The New Reality," begins from the premise that early man was not less observant than we, and concludes that the world *was* flat until the 5th century B.C. The villain, Luce (alias Lucifer), brings about a completely new universe by rendering all previous theories about reality untenable, and A. Prentiss and E. (alias Adam and Eve) survive into the new reality—which is paradisal. But so does the snake!

The richest short stories Harness has given us, however, belong to a period since the middle 1960's. "Probable Cause" deals with the case of a convicted murderer of a president: since the evidence against the accused was obtained by clairvoyance, the Supreme Court must consider whether his constitutional rights have been abridged. "The Alchemist" and "An Ornament to His Profession" both deal with a chemical manufacturing firm and the problems of patent law; in the first, the firm discovers with horror that one of its scientists is practising alchemy; in the second, the lawyer Con Patrick is driven to realize that he would sell his soul if necessary to protect his patents. The later Harness stories have surrendered nothing in the skill of plotting, but they have a sure humour and sense of the richness of human life that were lacking in the earlier short stories (excepting always "The Rose"). His best work is a high-water mark in science fiction.

—Charles Cushing

---

**HARRISON, Harry.** Also writes as Felix Boyd; Leslie Charteris; Hank Dempsey. American. Born in Stamford, Connecticut, 12 March 1925. Educated at art schools in New York. Served in the United States Army Air Corps during World War II: Sergeant. Married Joan Merkler in 1954; one son and one daughter. Freelance commercial artist, 1946–55. Formerly, editor, *SF Impulse*, London; editor, *Fantastic*, New York, 1968. Recipient: Nebula award, 1973. Agent: Sobel Weber Associates, 146 East 19th Street, New York, New York 10003, U.S.A. Address: 58 Haddington Road, Dublin 4, Ireland.

SCIENCE-FICTION PUBLICATIONS

Novels (Series: Bill, the Galactic Hero; Deathworld; Stainless Steel Rat; To the Stars; West of Eden)

*Deathworld.* New York, Bantam, 1960; London, Penguin, 1963.
*The Stainless Steel Rat.* New York, Pyramid, 1961; London, New English Library, 1966.
*Planet of the Damned.* New York, Bantam, 1962; as *Sense of Obligation*, London, Dobson, 1967.
*Deathworld 2,* New York, Bantam, 1964; London, Sphere, 1977; as *The Ethical Engineer*, London, Gollancz, 1964.
*Bill, The Galactic Hero.* New York, Doubleday, and London, Gollancz, 1965.
*Plague from Space.* New York, Doubleday, 1965; London, Gollancz, 1966; as *The Jupiter Legacy*, New York, Bantam, 1970.
*Make Room! Make Room!* New York, Doubleday, 1966; London, Penguin, 1967; as *Soylent Green*, New York, Berkley, 1973.
*The Technicolor Time Machine.* New York, Doubleday, 1967; London, Faber, 1968.
*Deathworld 3.* New York, Dell, 1968; London, Faber, 1969.
*Captive Universe.* New York, Putnam, 1969; London, Faber, 1970.
*The Daleth Effect.* New York, Putnam, 1970; as *In Our Hands, The Stars*, London, Faber, 1970.
*The Stainless Steel Rat's Revenge.* New York, Walker, 1970; London, Faber, 1971.
*Tunnel Through the Deeps.* New York, Putnam, 1972; as *A Transatlantic Tunnel, Hurrah!*, London, Faber, 1972.
*Stonehenge*, with Leon E. Stover. London, Davies, and New York, Scribner, 1972; revised edition, as *Stonehenge: Where Atlantis Died*, New York, Tor, 1983; London Granada, 1985.
*The Stainless Steel Rat Saves the World.* New York, Putnam, 1972; London, Faber, 1974.
*Star Smashers of the Galaxy Rangers.* New York, Putnam, 1973; London, Faber, 1974.
*The Lifeship*, with Gordon R. Dickson. New York, Harper, 1976; as *Lifeboat*, London, Orbit, 1977.
*Skyfall.* London, Faber, 1976; New York, Atheneum, 1977.
*The Adventures of the Stainless Steel Rat* (omnibus). New York, Berkley, 1978.
*The Stainless Steel Rat Wants You!* London, Joseph, 1978.
*Planet Story*, illustrated by Jim Burns. London, Pierrot, and New York, A and W, 1979.
*Homeworld* (To the Stars). London, Panther, and New York, Bantam, 1980.
*Wheelworld* (To the Stars). London, Panther, and New York, Bantam, 1981.
*Starworld* (To the Stars). London, Panther, and New York, Bantam, 1981.
*Planet of No Return.* New York, Simon and Schuster, 1981; London, Severn House, 1983.
*Invasion: Earth.* New York, Ace, 1982; London, Sphere, 1984.
*The Stainless Steel Rat for President.* London, Sphere, and New York, Bantam, 1982.
*A Rebel in Time.* London, Granada, and New York, Tor, 1983.
*West of Eden.* London, Granada, and New York, Bantam, 1984.
*A Stainless Steel Rat Is Born.* New York, Bantam, and London, Granada, 1985.
*Winter in Eden.* London, Grafton, and New York, Bantam, 1986.
*The Stainless Steel Rat Gets Drafted.* New York and London, Bantam, 1987.
*Return to Eden.* London, Grafton, and New York, Bantam, 1988.
*Bill, the Gallactic Hero, On the Planet of Robot Slaves.* London, Gollancz, 1989.
*Bill, the Gallactic Hero, On the Planet of Bottled Brains*, with Robert Sheckley. London, Gollancz, 1990.
*Bill, the Gallactic Hero, On the Planet of Tasteless Pleasure*, with David Bischoff. London, Gollancz, 1991.

Short Stories

*War with the Robots.* New York, Pyramid, 1962; London, Dobson, 1967.
*Two Tales and Eight Tomorrows.* London, Gollancz, 1965; New York, Bantam, 1968.
*Prime Number.* New York, Berkley, 1970; London, Sphere, 1975.
*One Step from Earth.* New York, Macmillan, 1970; London, Faber, 1972.
*The Best of Harry Harrison.* New York, Pocket Books, and London, Sidgwick and Jackson, 1976.

OTHER PUBLICATIONS

Novels

*Vendetta for the Saint* (as Leslie Charteris). New York, Doubleday, 1964.
*Montezuma's Revenge.* New York, Doubleday, 1972.
*Queen Victoria's Revenge.* New York, Doubleday, 1974; London, Severn House, 1977.
*The QE2 Is Missing.* London, Futura, 1980; New York, Tor, 1982.

Other

*The Man from P.I.G.* (for children). New York, Avon, 1968.
*Spaceship Medic* (for children). London, Faber, and New York, Doubleday, 1970.
*The Men from P.I.G. and R.O.B.O.T.* (for children). London, Faber, 1974; New York, Atheneum, 1978.
*The California Iceberg* (for children). London, Faber, and New York, Walker, 1975.

*Great Balls of Fire*. London, Pierrot, and New York, Grosset and Dunlap, 1977.
*Mechanismo*. London, Pierrot, and Los Angeles, Reed, 1978.
*Spacecraft in Fact and Fiction*, with Malcolm Edwards. London, Orbis, 1979.

Editor, *Collected Editorials from Analog*, by John W. Campbell, Jr. New York, Doubleday, 1966.
Editor, with Brian Aldiss, *Nebula Award Stories 2*. New York, Doubleday, 1967; as *Nebula Award Stories 1967*, London, Gollancz, 1967.
Editor, with Leon E. Stover, *Apeman, Spaceman: Anthropological Science Fiction*. New York, Doubleday, and London, Rapp and Whiting, 1968.
Editor, with Brian Aldiss. *All about Venus*. New York, Dell, 1968; enlarged edition, as *Farewell, Fantastic Venus!*, London, Macdonald, 1968.
Editor, with Brian Aldiss, *Best SF 1967* [to *1975*]. New York, Putnam, 7 vols., 1968–74; Indianapolis, Bobbs Merrill, 2 vols., 1975–76; as *The Year's Best Science Fiction 1-9*, London, Sphere, 8 vols., 1968–76; London, Futura, 1 vol., 1976.
Editor, *SF: Author's Choice 1-4*. New York, Berkley, 4 vols., 1968–74; vol. 1 as *Backdrop of Stars*, London, Dobson, 1968.
Editor, *Four for the Future: Anthology on the Themes of Sacrifice and Redemption*. London, Macdonald, 1969.
Editor, *Worlds of Wonder*. New York, Doubleday, 1969; as *Blast Off: SF for Boys*, London, Faber, 1969.
Editor, *The Year 2000*. New York, Doubleday, 1970; London, Faber, 1971.
Editor, *Nova 1-4*. New York, Delacorte Press, 1 vol., 1970; New York, Walker, 3 vols., 1972–74; London, Sphere, 4 vols., 1975–76; vol. 3 published as *The Outdated Man*, New York, Dell, 1974.
Editor, *The Light Fantastic: Science Fiction Classics from the Mainstream*. New York, Scribner, 1971.
Editor, with Brian Aldiss, *The Astounding-Analog Reader*. New York, Doubleday, 2 vols., 1972–73; London, Sphere, 2 vols., 1973.
Editor, with Theodore J. Gordon, *Ahead of Time*. New York, Doubleday, 1972.
Editor, *Astounding: John W. Campbell Memorial Anthology*. New York, Random House, 1973; London, Sidgwick and Jackson, 1974.
Editor, with Carol Pugner, *A Science Fiction Reader*. New York, Scribner, 1973.
Editor, with Willis E. McNelly, *Science Fiction Novellas*. New York, Scribner, 1975.
Editor, with Brian Aldiss, *SF Horizons* (reprint of magazine). New York, Arno Press, 1975.
Editor, with Brian Aldiss, *Hell's Cartographers: Some Personal Histories of Science Fiction Writers*. London, Weidenfeld and Nicolson, and New York, Harper, 1975.
Editor, with Brian Aldiss, *Decade: The 1940's, The 1950's, The 1960's*. London, Macmillan, 3 vols., 1975–77; *The 1940's* and *1950's*, New York, St. Martin's Press, 2 vols., 1978.

*

Bibliography: *Harry Harrison: Bibliografia 1951–1965* by Francesco Biamonti, privately printed, 1965.

Critical Study: *Harry Harrison* by Leon Stover, Boston, Twayne, 1990.

Manuscript Collection: University of California, Fullerton.

Harry Harrison comments:

I have always believed in readability. The easier the flow of the prose, the more basic the vocabulary, the more readers there will be who can follow and enjoy a book. But complex technical terms can be used where there is no alternative. I have found that an action story with two or three levels of intellectual content below the surface enables me to say just what I wish to say. I have also found that humor—and black humor—can carry ideas that can be expressed in no other way. The fact that my books have been translated into 27 languages must indicate that I am communicating with my audience.

* * *

Harry Harrison gets straight down to a story, and keeps going with little or no padding until it is done. In the classic opening to *The Stainless Steel Rat*, Slippery Jim DiGriz causes a safe to fall on the policeman who is trying to arrest him. While this could seem impossibly cruel and violent, the voice of the policeman is heard from beneath the safe, adding the destruction of a police robot to the charges, comically defusing both the shock of this possible murder and the impression that DiGriz might be a bad man. Here we have three hallmarks of Harrison's fiction: the breathless pace; the comedy bordering on farce; and the strict moral concerns.

The pace of Harry Harrison's writing is no accident, nor is it clumsily achieved. Examine carefully the first page of any of his early novels, and the speed of the telling immediately becomes apparent. Examine it carefully, because the pace will have you turning the page before you realise you have read it. Yet the short sentences, snappy dialogue and spare description belie the amount of information packed in; no necessary detail is left out, but no extraneous information is included. Harrison gets on with the story, which is very pleasing in comparison with some modern fantastic fiction. The slenderness of many of his books is a testament not to their slightness, but rather to the spareness of the storytelling in them.

First and foremost entertainments, nevertheless, in the tradition of great comedy, even the most light-hearted of Harrison's stories have deeply serious foundations. Novels like *Bill, the Galactic Hero, The Technicolor Time Machine, The Stainless Steel Rat* and *Star Smashers of the Galaxy Rangers* might appear to be no more than romps through the clichés of science fiction; but each of them has, at its centre, a powerful moral point. While *Bill, the Galactic Hero* is a deeply felt anti-war statement, rather than being simply an emotional rant against the barbarism of war, it actually looks in detail at the kind of top-heavy bureaucracy that makes modern war first possible, and then necessary. The humour of the situation springs largely from the ludicrousness of the society depicted; but the society depicted looks suspiciously like our own.

Similarly, *Star Smashers of the Galaxy Rangers* satirises the militarist science fiction of the time (Heinlein's *Starship Troopers* for instance), showing the attitudes to conflict and space opera to be unthinkingly juvenile; and *The Technicolor Time Machine* satirises Hollywood, making it clear that Hollywood moguls will trivialise almost anything in the interest of making money.

*The Stainless Steel Rat* and its sequels are not so easily categorized. Slippery Jim DiGriz is a raffish outlaw, but he has a very strong moral sense; the top-heavy bureaucracies are again his and Harrison's target. As this series proceeds, the system draws him in, so that he finally has to try to deal with society's ills rather than taking advantage of them.

There are similar concerns in Harrison's other writing. While the comic novels draw the casual reader in, and only gradually reveal their morals, works such as the Deathworld trilogy, with its ecological concerns, and *Make Room! Make Room!* with its depiction of overpopulation show Harrison's naked concern with the fate of our planet and our race.

More recently, the West of Eden trilogy introduces the concept of dinosaurs who survived up to the time of early human beings, using a rigorous extrapolative basis. A sentient reptile species has evolved parallel with mankind. While it has civilization and science far in advance of man's, it has never developed fire. The trilogy concerns the meeting of these two races, and the subsequent war.

Harrison's storytelling has been compared to H.G. Wells's in this trilogy. The comparison is apt, but Harrison also imports some of Wells's less attractive aspects. The characterisation is necessarily and typically thin, but where in Harrison's earlier works the speed of the story-telling denied the reader the opportunity to consider this problem, these stories are much more leisurely. Harrison's lifelong friendship with Brian Aldiss may be a cause, as there are many similarities between the West of Eden books and Aldiss's Helliconia trilogy.

It would, however, be unfair to condemn these books on this basis, particularly as this reader has always been out of sympathy with Aldiss's work. Harrison's inventiveness does not flag when it comes to new types of gadget for the intelligent dinosaurs to create. While it must be said that Harrison's more recent work seems to have drifted into sequelitis, with him often collaborating with other comic writers to keep the humour side moving, it is only in comparison with his earlier work that any of these novels pall. They are intriguing science fiction, and would be highly prized even if they were all he had ever written.

—Paul Brazier

---

**HARRISON, M(ichael) John.** British. Born in Great Britain, 26 July 1945. Educated at schools in England. Groom, Atherstone Hunt, Warwickshire, 1963; student teacher, Warwickshire, 1963–65; clerk, Royal Masonic Charity Institute, London, 1966. Literary editor and reviewer, *New Worlds*; regular contributor, *New Manchester Review*, 1978–79. Agent: Anthony Sheil Associates, 43 Doughty Street, London WCIN 2LF, England.

SCIENCE-FICTION PUBLICATIONS

Novels (series: Viriconium)

*The Committed Men.* London, Hutchinson, and New York, Doubleday, 1971.
*The Pastel City* (Viriconium). London, New English Library, 1971; New York, Doubleday, 1972.
*The Centauri Device.* New York, Doubleday, 1974; London, Panther, 1975.
*A Storm of Wings* (Viriconium). London, Sphere, and New York, Doubleday, 1980.
*In Viriconium.* London, Gollancz, 1982; New York, Pocket Books, 1983.
*The Floating Gods* (Viriconium). New York, Pocket Books, 1983.
*Climbers.* London, Gollancz, 1989.

Short Stories

*The Machine in Shaft Ten and Other Stories.* London, Panther, 1975.
*The Ice Monkey and Other Stories.* London, Gollancz, 1983.
*Viriconium Nights.* New York, Ace, 1984; revised edition, London, Gollancz, 1985.

*

M. John Harrison comments (1985):

I am often thought of as a pessimistic writer. I believe this is an over-simplification and prefer to think of myself as a compassionate but realistic one. There is a difference between compassion and that facile, sentimental—and political—optimism found at the crux of most SF, a genre the poverty of whose subject matter is legendary.

My fiction is concerned with the inability of people to feel ordinary emotions, or to communicate them successfully to one another; their efforts to maintain identity in the face of abstract systems and idealistic social structures; and their perception of themselves as live individuals in a meaningless, contingent universe.

The most radical expression of this existential standpoint is found in the collection *Viriconium Nights*, but it is clearly present in stories such as "The Machine in Shaft Ten" and "Settling the World" and in *The Committed Men*.

In fact, my fiction is not easily described as SF. Though in-genre critics have described it as an "illustration of entropy," this is to put the cart before the horse. In work like "Running Down" and *In Viriconium* I have consistently used entropy as a metaphor, an illustration, of the human condition: I have no interest in it as a scientific concept. I have used the psychology of sensory deprivation and the ethological notion of "Umwelt" in a similarly metaphorical way. Fiction and science get into bed together at the risk of popularisation, which despite George Steiner's elegant efforts is still only popularisation, or (increasingly) bad faith. I would prefer to avoid that.

My interest in the fantastic allegory or parable, bread and butter of contemporary SF, has declined.

Since 1980 I have turned away from the extreme absurdism of *The Pastel City* and *A Storm of Wings*—with their stress on the failure of, and the fear of, action—and in "The Quarry" or "Old Women" can be seen an increasingly direct and sensual engagement with those areas where ethology, early-modernist fiction and a moderate existentialism seem to share ground in the concept of the "accented moment sign" or moment-of-being. I am interested in the lives of individuals; compassion is not a function of the grand or political scale. For the same reason I am drawn to the short novel rather than the heavily researched three-decker with its blundering Victorian moralism.

My writing is oblique, compressed, and allusive, with a carefully textured surface. Despite this I am much less a stylist, and very much less a "writer-for-writing's-sake," than is generally supposed in the theoretical regions of SF, which are as poverty-stricken as its human ones.

For the more recent short stories—"The Ice Monkey," "Egnaro," "The New Rays," and "A Young Man's Journey to Viriconium"—and for *Climbers*, my novel-in-progress, my notebooks have provided material observed from life. This is ordered at the outset according to its own internal demands. Thereafter setting and event amplify the theme; character and meaning are less stated than allowed to emerge. What appears to be atmosphere is more often than not metonymy or metaphor.

* * *

M. John Harrison's most enduring work in science fiction is the Viriconium series. The first book, *The Pastel City*, presents a civilization in decline where medieval social patterns clash with the advanced technology and superscience weaponry that the citizens of the city know how to use but have forgotten how to engineer. Harrison's leading character, Cromis, fancies himself a better poet than a swordsman, yet he leads the battle to save Viriconium, the Pastel City, from the brain-stealing golems from Earth's past. The decadence Harrison describes is reminiscent of Michael Moorcock's vision of the far future in *The End of All Songs.*

The next book in the Viriconium series is *A Storm of Wings.* Fay Glass and Alstath Fulthor of the Reborn try to alert the powers of Viriconium that the northern highlands are overrun by insectile armies. A race of intelligent insects is invading Earth as human interest in survival wanes. Fay brings the severed head of an invading locust-like giant insect to show the extent of the disaster. Harrison brilliantly depicts the workings of civilization on the verge of collapse and the heroic efforts of individuals to help it sustain itself a little longer.

*The Floating Gods* is a moody portrait of Viriconium beset by a mysterious plague. As artist Audsley King slowly dies from the plague, her friend Ashlyme tries to save her. Yet his efforts are purposeless and his adventures misdirected. Where the previous books in the series held some sword and sorcery elements, *The Floating Gods* goes beyond black humor into a coma of despair.

*Viriconium Nights* is a collection of eight vignettes of the night life in the Pastel City. Many of the pieces feature some of Harrison's best writing, but that is what most of the stories are: exercises in style. The characters remain ill-defined and the actions are directionless and at times absurd. Vivid images come to nothing as plot and characters never interact.

Of Harrison's other novels, his first, *The Committed Men*, is notable for its grotesque descriptions of post-nuclear holocaust Earth. A band of unlikely characters—a dwarf, a cripple, a doctor, and a girl who has just given birth to an ugly mutant baby—travel south to save the baby they are "committed" to delivering to the new race of mutants. Harrison's most recent novel, *Climbers*, contains some of his best writing and delivers some memorable, chilling scenes.

Harrison's most accessible book is *The Centauri Device*, where space tramp John Truck is hunted down by a cast of bizarre characters: General Alice Gaw, ruthless head of the Israeli World Government; Gadaffi ben Barka, terrorist supreme of the Union of Arab Socialist Republics; and Dr. Grishkin, leader of the weird Opener cult. Truck's mother was a Centauran, one of the last before the Centauri Genocide. Now Truck is the last Centauran and the rival groups need him to arm the most powerful weapon in the galaxy: the Centauri device that will respond only to the genetic code of a true Centauran. There's plenty of action, black humor, and political commentary in the fast-paced space opera. The ending is a bit too pat, but Harrison is in fine control of this book all the way.

*The Ice Monkey and Other Stories* shows Harrison's wide range of subject matter. In seven stories, Harrison manages to capture pathos, humor, awe, despair, and pain. The best piece is "The Incalling" where an editor is haunted by an author's attempts to cure himself of cancer by faith healing. This is an unforgettable story.

M. John Harrison is a brilliant stylist whose work captures the grotesque and the decadent in vivid, absurd images that are as fascinating as they are unique.

—George Kelley

---

**HAWKE, Simon.** Also writes as J.D. Masters; Nicholas Yermakov. American. Born in New York City, 30 September 1951. Educated at Valley Forge Military Academy, Pennsylvania; American University, Washington, D.C.; Hofstra University, Hempstead, New York, B.A. in English and communications 1974. Has worked as musician, broadcaster, journalist, salesman, bartender, and factory worker. Agent: Adele Leone Agency, 26 Nantucket Place, Scarsdale, New York 10583.

### Science-Fiction Publications

Novels (series: The Time Wars; The Wizard)

*The Ivanhoe Gambit.* New York, Ace, 1984; London, Headline, 1987.
*The Timekeeper Conspiracy.* New York, Ace, 1984.
*The Pimpernel Plot.* New York, Ace, 1984.
*Timewars.* New York, Berkley, 1984.
*The Zenda Vendetta.* New York, Ace, 1985.
*The Nautilus Sanction.* New York, Ace, 1985; London, Headline, 1988.
*The Khyber Connection.* New York, Berkley, 1986; London, Headline, 1989.
*Psychodrome.* New York, Ace, 1987.
*The Wizard of 4th Street.* New York, Popular Library, 1987.
*The Argonaut Affair* (Time Wars). New York, Berkley, 1987; London, Headline, 1989.
*The Wizard of Whitechapel.* New York, Popular Library, 1988.
*The Dracula Caper* (Time Wars). New York, Berkley, 1988.
*The Shapechanger Scenario: Pyschodrome 2.* New York, Ace, 1988.
*The Lilliput Legion.* New York, Ace, 1989.
*The Wizard of Sunset Strip.* New York, Popular Library, 1989.
*The Wizard of Rue Morgue.* New York, Popular Library, 1990.
*The Cleopatra Crisis.* New York, Berkley, 1990.
*The Hellfire Rebellion* (Time Wars). New York, Ace, 1990.
*Batman: To Stalk a Spector.* New York, Warner, 1991.
*The Samuri Wizard.* New York, Warner, 1991.
*The Six-Gun Solution* (Time Wars). New York, Ace, 1991.

Novels as Nicholas Yermakov

*Journey from Flesh.* New York, Berkley, 1981.
*Last Communion.* New York, New American Library, 1981.
*Fall into Darkness.* New York, Berkley, 1982.
*Clique.* New York, Berkley, 1982.
*Epiphany.* New York, New American Library, 1982.
*Battlestar Galactica 6: The Living Legend* (novelization of screenplay), with Glen A. Larson. New York, Berkley, 1982.
*Battlestar Galactica 7: War of the Gods* (novelization of screenplay), with Glen A. Larson. New York, Berkley, 1982.
*Jehad.* New York, New American Library, 1984.

### Other Publications

Novels

*Friday the 13th* (novelization of screenplay). New York, New American Library, 1987.
*Friday the 13th, Part II* (novelization of screenplay). New York, New American Library, 1988.
*Friday the 13th, Part III* (novelization of screenplay). New York, New American Library, 1988.
*Jason Lives: Friday the 13th, Part VI* (novelization of screenplay). New York, New American Library, 1988.

*Predator 2* (novelization of screenplay). New York, Berkley, 1990.

Novels as J.D. Masters

*Steele.* New York, Charter, 1989.
*Cold Steele.* New York, Charter, 1989.
*Killer Steele.* New York, Charter, 1990.
*Jagged Steele.* New York, Charter, 1990.
*Renegade Steele.* New York, Charter, 1990.
*Target Steele.* New York, Charter, 1990.

*

Simon Hawke comments:

I approach my writing with a musician's sensibilities, which is to say that I enjoy "playing different kinds of music." I practice hard, I play often, and I continually seek to improve, but the driving force is the sheer joy of playing and the appreciation of the listener, or in this case, the reader. Writing is not so much a profession or an art as it is a lifestyle. Writers are fringe people. We deal in dreams. We shape them, hone them, polish them, nurture them lovingly, then share them. It's a craft, perhaps more ethereal than most, but no less demanding. Its special attraction is that it can never be truly mastered. But I'll keep on trying, just the same.

* * *

Although Simon Hawke is chiefly noted now for his Time Wars and Wizard series, his earlier novels are of unusually high quality. *Journey from Flesh*, expanded from the story "Surrogate Mouth," follows the adventures of a man who gains empathic powers after eating an alien lizard. His new ability involves him in the attempt by aliens to hunt down the lizards, for the regenerative powers of their flesh, and ultimately he learns that the lizards are in fact sentient but doomed to extinction.

The eradication of an entire species is the major theme of the trilogy consisting of *Last Communion, Epiphany*, and *Jehad*. Boomerang is a newly discovered world with a native population, the Shades, which resembles human beings, although there is no sign of an actual civilization. A chance encounter reveals that they are a gestalt species who absorb the personalities of those that die, raising the possibility that human immortality might be achieved through contact with this species. The two subsequent books reveal the efforts by an avaricious human government to take advantage of the aliens, even if it means sending an expedition into the past and eventually destroying the Shades themselves forever.

The protagonist of *Clique* is a salesman who helps promote the use of auras, holographic projectors that individuals can wear to change the way they appear to others. This is also a reworking of a short story theme, in this case taken from "A Whisper of Banshees." Eventually the salesman recognizes that he is helping people to escape the necessity of dealing with the real world and forms an anti-aura movement, which becomes just as rigid in its own way. Despite some faltering near the end, this was clearly superior to the novels that had preceded it.

*Fall into Darkness*, the last non-series novel, draws heavily on Russian folklore, transported to a human colony world now pretty much isolated from the rest of humankind. It's primarily a swashbuckling pirate story, but an excellent one. Hawke's interest in using the past for story material led logically to the Time Wars series, which ran twelve volumes in all.

*The Ivanhoe Gambit* began the series in 1984, and it concluded with *The Six-Gun Solution* in 1991. In broad terms, it's the traditional "change war" story; a group of time travellers exist primarily to neutralize others who wish to change the course of history for one reason or another. But Hawke quickly expanded the theme, adding a rival service from an alternate Earth seeking to extend its authority into our own timestream, renegade agents, and other recurring villains. It is an extremely well researched series, and the occasional accompanying essays are often as interesting as the original stories. Although they are to a certain degree formulaic, individual volumes do stand out, particular *The Argonaut Affair, The Hellfire Rebellion, The Dracula Caper*, and the concluding volume, which draws together all the different threads into one neat conclusion.

*Psychodrome* and its sequel, *The Shapechanger Scenario*, may have been intended as another open-ended series, but it seems to have been cut off quickly. Psychodrome is an interstellar game that pits adventurers against each other for the entertainment of the viewing audience. Arkady O'Toole is a gambler who participates in the game primarily to escape the attention of some personal enemies, but he quickly discovers he has been pursued and the dramatic dangers may be more real than he had intended. In the sequel, shapechanging alien creatures have entered the scene, and O'Toole must deal with them within the context of Psychodrome, whose viewers have no idea that the danger is real.

In 1987, Hawke started another series, this one fantasy. *The Wizard of 4th Street* features a standard, inept wizard in a futuristic New York City, and unleashes a series of comic adventures that are often very effective. Teamed with a streetwise thief, the wizard travels to England in *The Wizard of Whitechapel*, where they must deal with survivors from Camelot and a malevolent supernatural force prowling the city's streets. Chills and laughter continue in *The Wizard of Sunset Strip*, in which the team of companions travels to Hollywood to confront yet another supernatural manifestation, this one indulging in a series of Ripper-like killings. *The Wizard of Rue Morgue* continues the adventures in Paris, and *The Samurai Wizard* moves the action to Japan in what is the best entry in the series to date. Since the menaces of the Dark Ones have not been overcome, additional volumes are clearly planned.

Although Hawke rarely writes at shorter length, he produced several interesting tales early in his career, the most noteworthy of which are "Elm War," "Melponeme, Calliope, and Fred," "Crash Course for Ravers," and "The Orpheus Implant." Although Hawke appears to have abandoned writing serious individual novels in favor of series, he is clearly concerned that each entry be a complete story in itself, the background carefully researched and presented, and the story entertaining.

—Don D'Ammassa

---

**HEARD, Gerald.** *See* **HEARD, H.F.**

---

**HEARD, H(enry) F(itzgerald).** Also wrote as Gerald Heard. British. Born in London, 6 October 1889. Educated at Gonville and Caius College, Cambridge, B.A. (honours) in history 1911, graduate work 1911–12. Worked with the Agricultural Cooperative Movement in Ireland, 1919–23, and in England, 1923–27; editor, *Realist*, London, 1929; Lecturer, Oxford University, 1929–31; science commentator, BBC Radio, London, 1930–34;

settled in the United States, 1937; Visiting Lecturer, Washington University, St. Louis, 1951–52, 1955–56; Haskell Foundation Lecturer, Oberlin College, Ohio, 1958. Recipient: Bollingen grant, 1955; British Academy Hertz award. *Died 14 August 1971.*

SCIENCE-FICTION PUBLICATIONS

Novels

*Doppelgangers: An Episode of the Fourth, the Psychological Revolution, 1997.* New York, Vanguard Press, 1947; London, Cassell, 1948.
*The Black Fox.* London, Cassell, 1950; New York, Harper, 1951.

Short Stories

*The Great Fog and Other Weird Tales.* New York, Vanguard Press, 1944; London, Cassell, 1947; as *Weird Tales of Terror and Detection*, New York, Sun Dial Press, 1946.
*The Lost Cavern and Other Tales of the Fantastic.* New York, Vanguard Press, 1948; London, Cassell, 1949.

OTHER PUBLICATIONS

Novels

*A Taste for Honey.* New York, Vanguard Press, 1941; London, Cassell, 1942; as *A Taste for Murder*, New York, Avon, 1955.
*Reply Paid.* New York, Vanguard Press, 1942; London, Cassell, 1943.
*Murder by Reflection.* New York, Vanguard Press, 1942; London, Cassell, 1945.
*The Notched Hairpin.* New York, Vanguard Press, 1949; London, Cassell, 1952.

Other as Gerald Heard

*Narcissus: An Anatomy of Clothes.* London, Kegan Paul, and New York, Dutton, 1924.
*The Ascent of Humanity: An Essay on the Evolution of Civilization.* London, Cape, and New York, Harcourt Brace, 1929.
*The Emergence of Man.* London, Cape, 1931; New York, Harcourt Brace, 1932.
*Social Substance of Religion: An Essay on the Evolution of Religion.* London, Allen and Unwin, and New York, Harcourt Brace, 1931.
*This Surprising World: A Journalist Looks At Science.* London, Cobden Sanderson, 1932.
*Those Hurrying years: An Historical Outline 1900–1933.* London, Chatto and Windus, and New York, Oxford University Press, 1934.
*Science in the Making.* London, Faber, 1935.
*The Source of Civilisation.* London, Cape, 1935; New York, Harper, 1937.
*The Significance of the New Pacifism*, with *Pacifism and Philosophy*, by Aldous Huxley, London, Headley, 1935.
*Exploring the Stratosphere.* London, Nelson, 1936.
*Science Front 1936.* London, Cassell, 1937.
*The Third Morality.* London, Cassell, and New York, Morrow, 1937.
*Pain, Sex and Time: A New Hypothesis of Evolution.* New York, Harper, and London, Cassell, 1939.
*The Creed of Christ: An Interpretation of the Lord's Prayer.* New York, Harper, 1940; London, Cassell, 1941.
*A Quaker Meditation.* Wallingford, Pennsylvania, Pendle Hill, 1940(?).
*The Code of Christ: An Interpretation of the Beatitudes.* New York, Harper, 1941; London, Cassell, 1943.
*Training for the Life of the Spirit.* London, Cassell, 2 vols., 1941–44; New York, Harper, 1 vol., n. d.
*Man the Master.* New York, Harper, 1941; London, Faber, 1942.
*A Dialogue in the Desert.* London, Cassell, and New York, Harper, 1942.
*A Preface to Prayer.* New York, Harper, 1944; London, Cassell, 1945.
*The Recollection.* Stanford, California, Delkin, 1944.
*The Gospel According to Gamaliel.* New York, Harper, 1945; London, Cassell, 1946.
*Militarism's Post-Mortem.* London, P.P.U., 1946.
*The Eternal Gospel.* New York, Harper, 1946; London, Cassell, 1948.
*Is God Evident? An Essay Toward a Natural Theology.* New York, Harper, 1948; London, Faber, 1950.
*Is God in History? An Inquiry into Human and Pre-Human History in Terms of the Doctrine of Creation, Fall, and Redemption.* New York, Harper, 1950; London, Faber, 1951.
*Morals since 1900.* London, Dakers, and New York, Harper, 1950.
*The Riddle of the Flying Saucers.* London, Carroll and Nicholson, 1950; as *Is Another World Watching?.* New York, Harper, 1951; revised edition, New York, Bantam, 1953.
*Ten Questions on Prayer.* Wallingford, Pennsylvania, Pendle Hill, 1951.
*Gabriel and the Creatures.* New York, Harper, 1952; as *Wishing Well: An Outline of the Evolution of the Mammals Told as a Series of Stories about How Animals Got Their Wishes*, London, Faber, 1953.
*The Human Venture.* New York, Harper, 1955.
*Kingdom Without God: Road's End for the Social Gospel*, with others. Los Angeles, Foundation for Social Research, 1956.
*Training for a Life of Growth.* Santa Monica, California, Wayfarer Press, 1959.
*The Five Ages of Man: The Psychology of Human History.* New York, Julian Press, 1964.

Editor, *Prayers and Meditations.* New York, Harper, 1949.

* * *

*Doppelgangers*, the novel by H.F. Heard best known to science-fiction readers, depicts a hedonistic dictatorship based on behavior control. The hero, nameless except as "the remodeled man" or Alpha II, belongs to an underground organization ruled by the Mole, who also uses behavior control to sabotage the dictatorship. In the novel, the hero is "remodeled" physically to duplicate the dictator Alpha, who needs a double to impersonate him and absorb the psychic impact of his charismatic appearances. When Alpha commits suicide, Alpha II is left as dictator. An assassination attempt by a follower of the Mole leads to a series of discoveries about the true government of the world, which remains in the hands of spiritually evolved people called elevates.

The novel explores Heard's ideas about the human condition. The nature of Alpha's dictatorship is despotism through indulgence, suave reduction of the human soul to childishness by supplying the masses with entertainment and pleasures. "Animectomy," or cutting away of the soul, prefigures B.F. Skinner's *Walden II.* As a dystopian novel, *Doppelgangers* can also be compared to Orwell's *Nineteen Eighty-Four* or Huxley's *Brave*

*New World*. But Heard also explores evolution, especially as a self-directed project with Hegelian overtones, since he sees human history as a continuing aspiration toward something higher, with Alpha's dictatorship only one step on the ladder. Heard is also interested in the relationship of the soul to its manifestations. Clothes reflect customs: a man's appearance determines and is determined by his ideas; etymology reveals truths of history. Indeed, one of Heard's first books was a history and philosophy of costume, *Narcissus: An Anatomy of Clothes*, and his style and ideas are influenced by the "Clothes Philosophy" of Carlyle's *Sartor Resartus*. The dictatorship in *Doppelgangers* is also based on Sheldon's somatypes which posit a relationship between body type and personality. Doppelgangers is a philosophical novel; though the psychological exploration of the few major characters is deep, this is not a psychological novel. The style is involuted with tricky puns and allusions.

*The Black Fox* is an occultist novel with speculative content. Throcton, a British cleric envious of advancement, uses black magic to destroy his enemy. When the magic recoils, he is saved only by the self-sacrifice of his sister. Heard bases the black magic, involving etymology of the world *alopecia* from fox mange, on Biblical, Sufist, and folklore learning, speculating on the relation of mind and body. Treatment of black magic as an explainable phenomenon prefigures the thinking of such contemporaries as Colin Wilson. Psychological analysis is strong in this novel, and the isolated, highly cerebral Throctons, brother and sister, are eccentric but complexly interesting. Except for his detective fiction, *The Black Fox* represents the best use of suspense in Heard's fiction.

*Gabriel and the Creatures* is a speculative fantasy based on the premise that a species has the will to evolve in a certain direction, and that God, through the angel Gabriel, will grant each species its wish. *The Gospel According to Gamaliel*, a retelling of the New Testament by a Hebrew ecclesiast, teacher of St. Paul, is speculative in its attempt to reconcile differing theological viewpoints.

Heard's short stories are mostly collected in *The Great Fog* and *The Lost Cavern*. They speculate upon some of Heard's favorite concerns: evolution in "The Thaw Plan," "The Lost Cavern," "Wingless Victory," and "The Great Fog"; medical knowledge in "The Rousing of Mr. Bradegar" and "The Crayfish"; architecture in "Dromenon"; and telephatic exchange in "The Swap." "The Cat 'I Am' " may be seen as an early study for *The Black Fox*. Heard's heroes are isolated, scholarly types.

Heard's major output is not in fiction but in religious philosophy; he has also written detective fiction and a work on flying saucers. Except for reviews and an occasional mention in critical works, Heard has received little critical attention. His strength is in speculation rather than character or plot. Nonetheless, *Doppelgangers* is a significant dystopian novel which merits a place in the science-fiction canon.

—Mary T. Brizzi

---

**HEINLEIN, Robert A(nson).** American. Born in Butler, Missouri, 7 July 1907. Educated at University of Missouri, Columbia, 1924–25; United States Naval Academy, Annapolis, Maryland, B.S. 1929; University of California, Los Angeles, 1934–35. Served in the United States Navy, 1929 until retirement because of physical disability, 1934. Married 1) Leslyn McDonald (divorced); 2) Virginia Gerstenfeld in 1948. Owned a silver mine, Silver Plume, Colorado, 1934–35; worked in mining and real estate, 1936–39; civilian engineer, Philadelphia Navy Yard, 1942–45. Forrestal Lecturer, United States Naval Academy, 1973. Recipient: Hugo award 1956, 1960, 1962, 1967; Boys' Clubs of America award, 1959; Grand Master Nebula award, 1974; *Locus* award, 1985. Guest of Honor, World Science Fiction Convention, 1941, 1961, 1976. L.H.D.: Eastern Michigan University, Ypsilanti, 1977. *Died 8 May 1988.*

### SCIENCE-FICTION PUBLICATIONS

Novels (series: Future History; Luna)

*Rocket Ship Galileo* (for children). New York, Scribner, 1947; London, New English Library, 1971.
*Space Cadet* (for children). New York, Scribner, 1948; London, Gollancz, 1966.
*Beyond This Horizon*. Reading, Pennsylvania, Fantasy Press, 1948; London, Panther, 1967.
*Sixth Column*. New York, Gnome Press, 1949; as *The Day after Tomorrow*, New York, New American Library, 1951; London, Mayflower, 1962.
*Red Planet* (for children). New York, Scribner, 1949; London, Gollancz, 1963.
*Farmer in the Sky* (for children). New York, Scribner, 1950; London, Gollancz, 1962.
*Waldo, and Magic Inc.* New York, Doubleday, 1950; as *Waldo, Genius in Orbit*, New York, Avon, 1958.
*The Puppet Masters*. New York, Doubleday, 1951; London, Museum Press, 1953.
*Between Planets* (for children). New York, Scribner, 1951; London, Gollancz, 1968.
*The Rolling Stones* (for children). New York, Scribner, 1952; as *Space Family Stone*, London, Gollancz, 1969.
*Starman Jones* (for children). New York, Scribner, 1953; London, Sidgwick and Jackson, 1954.
*The Star Beast* (for children). New York, Scribner, 1954; London, New English Library, 1971.
*Tunnel in the Sky* (for children). New York, Scribner, 1955; London, Gollancz, 1965.
*Time for the Stars* (for children). New York, Scribner, 1956; London, Gollancz, 1963.
*Double Star*. New York, Doubleday, 1956; London, Joseph, 1958.
*The Door into Summer*. New York, Doubleday, 1957; London, Panther, 1960.
*Citizen of the Galaxy* (for children). New York, Scribner, 1957; London, Gollancz, 1969.
*Have Space Suit—Will Travel* (for children). New York, Scribner, 1958; London, Gollancz, 1970.
*Methuselah's Children* (Future History). New York, Gnome Press, 1958; London, Gollancz, 1963.
*The Robert Heinlein Omnibus*. London, Sidgwick and Jackson, 1958.
*Starship Troopers* (for children). New York, Putnam, 1959; London, New English Library, 1961.
*Stranger in a Strange Land*. New York, Putnam, 1961; London, New English Library, 1965.
*Podkayne of Mars: Her Life and Times* (for children). New York, Putnam, 1963; London, New English Library, 1969.
*Glory Road*. New York, Putnam, 1963; London, New English Library, 1965.
*Farnham's Freehold*. New York, Putnam, 1964; London, Dobson, 1965.
*Three by Heinlein* (includes *The Puppet Masters, Waldo, Magic Inc.*). New York, Doubleday, 1965; as *A Heinlein Triad*. London, Gollancz, 1966.

*A Robert Heinlein Omnibus*. London, Sidgwick and Jackson, 1966.
*The Moon Is a Harsh Mistress* (Luna). New York, Putnam, 1966; London, Dobson, 1967.
*I Will Fear No Evil*. New York, Putnam, 1970; London, New English Library, 1972.
*Time Enough for Love: The Lives of Lazarus Long* (Future History). New York, Putnam, 1973; London, New English Library, 1974.
*The Number of the Beast*. New York, Fawcett, and London, New English Library, 1980.
*Friday*. New York, Holt Rinehart, and London, New English Library, 1982.
*Job: A Comedy of Justice*. New York, Ballantine, and London, New English Library, 1984.
*The Cat Who Walks Through Walls: A Comedy of Manners* (Luna). New York, Putnam, 1985; London, New English Library, 1986.
*To Sail Beyond the Sunset: The Life and Loves of Maureen Johnson* (Future History). New York, Putnam, and London, Joseph, 1987.

Short Stories (series: Future History)

*The Man Who Sold the Moon* (Future History). Chicago, Shasta, 1950; London, Sidgwick and Jackson, 1953.
*Universe* (Future History). New York, Dell, 1951.
*The Green Hills of Earth* (Future History). Chicago, Shasta, 1951; London, Sidgwick and Jackson, 1954.
*Revolt in 2100* (Future History). Chicago, Shasta, 1953; London, Digit, 1959.
*Assignment in Eternity*. Reading, Pennsylvania, Fantasy Press, 1953; London, Museum Press, 1955; abridged edition, as *Lost Legacy*, London, Digit, 1960.
*The Menace from Earth*. New York, Gnome Press, 1959; London, Dobson, 1966.
*The Unpleasant Profession of Jonathan Hoag*. New York, Gnome Press, 1959; London, Dobson 1964; as *6" Six Stories*, New York, Pyramid, 1961.
*Orphans of the Sky* (Future History). London, Gollancz, 1963; New York, Putnam, 1964.
*The Worlds of Robert A. Heinlein*. New York, Ace, 1966; London, New English Library, 1970.
*The Past Through Tomorrow: Future History Stories*. New York, Putnam, 1967; abridged edition, London, New English Library, 2 vols., 1977.
*The Best of Robert Heinlein 1939–1959*, edited by Angus Wells. London, Sidgwick and Jackson, 1973.
*Destination Moon*. Boston, Gregg Press, 1979.
*Expanded Universe*. New York, Grosset and Dunlap, 1980.

OTHER PUBLICATIONS

Plays

Screenplays: *Destination Moon*, with Rip Van Ronkel and James O'Hanlon, 1950; *Project Moonbase*, with Jack Seaman, 1953.

Other

*The Discovery of the Future* (address). Los Angeles, Novacious, 1941.
"On the Writing of Speculative Fiction," in *Of Worlds Beyond: The Science of Science-Fiction Writing*, edited by Lloyd Arthur Eshbach. Reading, Pennsylvania, Fantasy Press, 1947; London, Dobson, 1965.
"Why I Selected 'The Green Hills of Earth,' " in *My Best Science Fiction Story*, edited by Leo Margulies and O.J. Friend. New York, Merlin Press, 1949.
"Ray Guns and Rocket Ships," in *Library Journal* (New York), July 1953.
"Science Fiction: Its Nature, Faults, and Virtues," in *The Science Fiction Novel*, edited by Basil Davenport. Chicago, Advent, 1959.
"Heinlein on Science Fiction," in *Vertex* (Los Angeles), April 1973.
*The Notebooks of Lazarus Long*. New York, Putnam, 1978.
*Grumbles from the Grave*, edited by Virginia Heinlein. New York, Ballantine, 1990.

Editor, *Tomorrow, The Stars: A Science Fiction Anthology*. New York, Doubleday, 1952.

*

Bibliography: *Robert A. Heinlein: A Bibliography* by Mark Owings, Baltimore, Croatan House, 1973.

Manuscript Collection: University of California Library, Santa Cruz.

Critical Studies: *Seekers of Tomorrow* by Sam Moskowitz, Cleveland, World, 1966; *Heinlein in Dimension: A Critical Analysis* (includes bibliography) by Alexei Panshin, Chicago, Advent, 1968; *Robert A. Heinlein, Stranger in His Own Land*, San Bernardino, California, Borgo Press, 1976, and *The Classic Years of Robert A. Heinlein*, Borgo Press, 1977, both by George Edgar Slusser; *Robert A. Heinlein* edited by Martin H. Greenberg and Joseph D. Olander, New York, Taplinger, and Edinburgh, Harris, 1978; *Robert A. Heinlein: America as Science Fiction* by H. Bruce Franklin, New York, Oxford University Press, 1980, London, Oxford University Press, 1981.

* * *

Probably no one deserved to be called the Dean of Science Fiction more than Robert A. Heinlein, whose prolific output remained continuously in print throughout most of his lifetime, a phenomenon almost unheard of in an industry that pulps unsold copies as quickly as new books can be printed. At this writing, his widow, Virginia Heinlein, is arranging for the reprinting of all his novels, restoring cuts he had made for editorial demands. No doubt this will influence future interpretations and evaluations of his contribution to the field, as have his already published selected letters to his agent, Lurton Blassingame, titled *Grumbles from the Grave*, also edited by Virginia. In one of the letters from the mid-seventies he makes it clear that he is more interested in raising questions in his work than in providing answers.

Nearly always a "good read," Heinlein's work at its best epitomizes the excitement science fiction can generate by dramatizing the possible future adventures that scientific knowledge and technology can open up for humanity, and by exploring the needs of individuals within a society to survive and find satisfaction compatible with the continuance and growth of our species; at its worst, it is still usually provocative both to SF addicts and to novices. Through his long writing career, Heinlein has consistently dramatized the essential moral questions for young and old, which boil down to one: what is the ideal way to live, today—and tomorrow? Idealism dosed with pragmatism flavors the answers to this question in each of Heinlein's stories. His sympathetic characters are neither all flesh nor all spirit but a careful balance of both. The majority of his work is cautiously optimistic and celebratory of the triumph of individuals over both internal weaknesses and, especially, external obstacles to their physical well-being—although there are some notable exceptions, such as "All You Zombies."

Like virtually all writers of the 1940's, Heinlein began his career producing short stories, and his crisp style still inspires much emulation. "The Roads Must Roll" earned him a place in *The Science Fiction Hall of Fame*, stories selected by the Science Fiction Writers of America to honor works prior to the inception of the Nebula Awards in the mid-1960's.

After World War II Heinlein turned to the new market for science fiction novels and began writing for children. These books remain popular with the audience for which they were written, teen and pre-teen boys. *The Star Beast* is one of the best for a young reader to start with. Not only does it have both male and female central characters and a lovable alien creature full of unexpected antics (long before E.T.), but the story also invents the unorthodox privilege of unhappy children to divorce unsatisfactory parents, a notion sure to delight young readers.

*Podkayne of Mars*, often regarded as an adult novel in spite of its young protagonists, has been widely denounced for using a phony female viewpoint character. The story purports to be the diary of a teenage girl, but a large portion is written by her precocious, bratty pre-teen brother, who turns out to be smarter than she is. Heinlein has been attacked by some feminist critics for his simplistic depictions of females; others point out that in these "Golden Age" stories, Heinlein was one of the few writers who showed girls and women doing anything beyond being objects to be rescued. His novel *Friday*, although nominated for a Hugo award, drew criticism for its depiction of a sympathetic female character who not only forgives but marries her rapist. (Certainly Heinlein deserves credit for creating a more believable female narrator in *Friday* than he did in *Podkayne*, or in *I Will Fear No Evil* or even *The Number of the Beast*. Friday is an AP— artificial person, who by definition does not suffer the "normal" socialization of natural human females.) His most successful female character may well by his last, Maureen of *To Sail Beyond the Sunset*. She is of a "timeline" slightly different from ours, but she undergoes many experiences similar to those of the women of our 1960's and 1970's when her husband dumps her for a younger woman, forcing her to achieve an independence she might otherwise never have attempted. She also attempts to cope courageously with the problems of the children of this divorce, though she fails to reclaim her daughter from the self-destructive behavior the girl is determined to exhibit in the name of "freedom." Heinlein skillfully blends "the way the world is" with "the way the world might be" if the socialization of children and social circumstances were slightly different, and he inspires the reader to imagine that desired changes are possible.

Beginning in the 1960's Heinlein started producing clearly adult novels, tending toward longer and longer books with each passing decade. Heinlein's best-known novels are the four Hugo winners, *Double Star, Starship Troopers, Stranger in a Strange Land*, and *The Moon Is a Harsh Mistress*. The protagonist of *Double Star*, Lorenzo Smythe, narrates his own story. Originally an unemployed actor, he is recruited (forcibly) to play the role of an incapacitated leader who must participate in delicate interplanetary diplomacy, an assignment he ultimately accepts willingly, not out of political conviction but because of the challenge to his acting ability. Heinlein's protagonists seldom set out to be heroes. During the course of the story, however, Lorenzo rises to the moral challenge and becomes worthy of his new power and authority. He concludes that the sacrifice of personal peace of mind is justified by "solemn satisfaction in doing the best you can for eight billion people." Noblesse oblige: the strong spirit has a duty to the weak.

In *Starship Troopers* a similar lesson is learned by Juan Rico, who also tells of his own conversion from a mildly pacifist and apolitical youth, who volunteers almost inadvertently for Federal Service to impress a female, to a dedicated combat officer who realizes that the noblest fate he can hope for is to die defending others' lives. His Moral Instruction teacher sums it up: "The price demanded for the most precious of all things in life is life itself—ultimate cost for perfect value." Eventually Juan even helps his own father to realize and share his insight. Seasoned with rich slang that provides both verisimilitude and freshness to what could easily be a conventional situation, the novel is shaped like a sandwich: battle action scenes open and close the book, and the moral awakening fills its center.

*Stranger in a Strange Land* is the only one of Heinlein's Hugo winners to use a third-person narrator, and is less unified in other ways than the other three. The first two sections are largely concerned with the satiric vision of human behavior seen through the unspoiled eyes of a highly intelligent being, Valentine Michael Smith, physically human but culturally alien. Mike regains his genetic heritage only after he learns to laugh by watching the monkeys in a zoo. The latter part of the book is devoted to myth-making of the possible limits of human interactions. Because he is culture-free, Mike is able to explore unorthodox sensuality and sexuality without the feelings of inhibition and guilt which plague the rest of us. The joy of his discoveries is powerful enough to free others from their hangups also (even his mentor Jubal Harshaw), so they create a mystical new religion. But Heinlein undermines his myth with the mocking cynicism of the blatant fraud Foster, who turns out to be Mike's boss in the hereafter (or whereafter?): "Certainly 'Thou art God'—but who isn't?" The creed of the new religion is nothing special in the cosmic scheme of things. For many critics this self-mockery comes too little and too late to counter Mike's simplistic message of free love and the power to dispel all earthly problems simply by correct comprehension, or "grokking." But surely in reading this novel future generations will recapture the 1960's spirit of campus rebellion against hypocritical middle-class morality.

*The Moon Is a Harsh Mistress* combines more of Heinlein's strengths and fewer of his artistic limitations than any of his other works. The length of the novel is justified by the complexity of the social and political systems depicted. The story of Luna's fight for freedom is told by Emanuel Garcia O'Kelly, a sympathetic but fallible person who might be Anyman. Mannie is not a great man, but he is the best computer technician available in the moon colony, and so becomes the first friend of Mike, the sentient computer who keeps from going insane at the interface of conflicting data by developing a sense of humor—and a protective love for those who give him a purpose in living. Since the narrator must survive to tell the tale, the interest of the reader is focused less on what will happen next than on how it happens. Of course, it is humanity, not Mannie as an individual, who created Mike; mankind has developed an intelligence beyond its own fleshly limitations, one uncorrupted by petty greed and lust for power. The philosophy of TANSTAAFL—"There ain't no such thing as a free lunch"—naturally becomes the slogan of Free Luna. Their success relies on long odds and high risks, but the stakes of freedom are worth the ultimate price, paid by many of the revolutionaries including Mannie's political mentor and (apparently) Mike. Mannie is left with many doubts and unfulfilled longings at the end in a passage handled with poignancy as delicate as can be found anywhere in Heinlein's work. Ultimately Mannie decides to go on living: "My word, I'm not even a hundred yet."

Heinlein returns to Luna in his penultimate novel, *The Cat Who Walks Through Walls: A Comedy of Manners*. Gwen Novak (Hazel Stone) time travels to recruit Richard Ames (Collin Campbell) for an assignment to rescue Adam Selene (Mike the computer). Besides the adventure, Heinlein uses the novel to allow his *raisonneur* from *Stranger in a Strange Land*, Jubal Harshaw, to observe: "For millennia philosophers and saints have tried to reason out a logical scheme for the universe . . . [but] the universe is not logical but whimsical, its structure depending solely on the dreams and nightmares of non-logical dreamers"; and further, "the universe—the multiverse—contains neither of logic nor justice save where we, or others like us, impose such qualities on a world of chaos and cruelty." He also reveals what may be assumed to be autobiographical material about the compulsion of a writer to write and speculates whimsically about the "real" life of characters and worlds created in literature. Aside from this, a principal purpose of the novel seems to be the introduction of Pixel, the quantum cat for whom the novel is titled, who becomes a major plot device in Heinlein's last novel, *To Sail Beyond the Sunset*.

Early in his career Heinlein conceived of a "future history," into which nearly all of his work can be placed. While this structure has drawn a cult following, without having to follow the restrictions of a series, it makes it difficult for a novice Heinlein reader to follow some sequences which will delight the devotee. At the end of *To Sail Beyond the Sunset* he provides a listing of "People in This Memoir" including a section on "Associated Stories," to help guide the novice or refresh the memory of a long-time fan.

If some of Heinlein's female characters tend to be idealized or even sentimentalized, so do his male characters. Good people are those who keep mentally active, try to avoid harming innocent others (though they have few qualms about killing enemies to survive), and, above all, wish to produce and protect babies. Yet even here, Heinlein's views can be complex; he has Maureen in *To Sail Beyond the Sunset* say: "I often find other people's children repulsive and their mothers crashing bores, especially when they talk about their disgusting offspring (instead of listening to me talking about mine). It seems to me that many of those little monsters should have been drowned at birth . . . . many babies are simply bad-tempered, mean little devils who grow up to be bad-tempered, mean big devils." She later makes it clear that parents' responsibilities give them prerogatives that supersede children's rights to privacy, when she searches her children's room for drugs, saying: "I am aware that some libertarians (and all children) disagree with me. So be it." And Maureen's attitude about the (lack of) value of religion is clear; because Maureen lives in the world she does, she must practice hypocrisy, but she never is taken in by religious mythology and conforms only to survive.

Heinlein played frequently with the quantum concept of simultaneous parallel universes in novels such as *Glory Road* and in the more recent novels *The Number of the Beast* and *Job: A Comedy of Justice*. In all of his "worlds," people lacking a healthy sense of self-preservation die prematurely, for no universe is really very friendly and wise ones must adapt quickly to changing circumstances. While much of the criticism of Heinlein has centered on his repetition of formulaic plots and character relationships, he managed to freshen his materials and keep devoted fans eagerly awaiting each new book. The new releases promised in the coming years (with material Heinlein himself cut) are likely to sell as well as the originals.

—Elizabeth Anne Hull

---

**HENDERSON, Zenna (née Chlarson).** American. Born in Tucson, Arizona, 1 November 1917. Educated at Arizona State College, now University, B.A. 1940, M.A. 1955. Married in 1944 (divorced). After 1940, elementary school teacher in Arizona: also taught at the Japanese Relocation Camp, Sacaton, Arizona, during World War II, Laon sur Marne, Aisne, France, 1956–58, and Seaside Children's Hospital, Waterford, Connecticut, 1958–59. *Died 11 May 1983.*

SCIENCE-FICTION PUBLICATIONS

Short Stories

*Pilgrimage: The Book of the People.* New York, Doubleday, 1961; London, Gollancz, 1962.

*The Anything Box.* New York, Doubleday, 1965; London, Gollancz, 1966.

*The People: No Different Flesh.* New York, Doubleday, and London, Gollancz, 1966.

*Holding Wonder.* New York, Doubleday, 1971; London, Gollancz, 1972.

*

Zenna Henderson commented:

(1981) When I was about 12 I began reading science fiction—Jules Verne, Haggard, and Edgar Rice Burroughs, and all the current magazines I could get hold of, but it wasn't until I had graduated from college that I began writing fantasy and science fiction. I have only a sketchy scientific background, so of necessity I write from a non-technical viewpoint. My favorite science-fiction authors, when I was still reading it, were Heinlein, Bradbury, Clement, and Asimov. Mottos I try to observe when I write: stories consist of unusual people in ordinary circumstances or ordinary people in unusual circumstances; write about what you know; don't let your subtleties become obscurities.

* * *

"Write what you know" is the cornerstone of Zenna Henderson's science-fiction career. She constructed story after story out of experiences accumulated during her many years in the elementary classroom. She found teachers useful viewpoint characters because their vision is multiplied through their students' eyes. Her fictional children have the appealing naturalness that comes of being modeled directly from life.

Henderson made more and better use of adult-child interactions than adult-adult ones, but she always kept human relationships paramount. She ignored man's struggles against the universe because she did not perceive the cosmos as hostile. By rejecting sex, sadism, and violence, her stories offer a gentle alternative to macho entertainments. Yet feminist critics scorn Henderson for occupational stereotyping without acknowledging that she depicts single women, older women, and female friendships positively. Wonder in familiar settings is Henderson's forte. She reveals the world a child or a saint might see—a place where time can shift and dimensions fold, where mountains walk and wishes come true. Friction between the mundane and the marvelous generates her dramas. For example, a small boy battles a demon ("Stevie and the Dark") or school routine survives the collapse of civilization ("As Simple as That").

Henderson's most popular stories are those collected in *Pilgrimage* and *The People*. Each volume's components are united by a frame-story, a device that succeeds better in *Pilgrimage* because it is a poignant tale in its own right. The frame of *The People* is simply an excuse for flashbacks to events preceding and following those in *Pilgrimage*. The People are extraterrestrial refugees with psychic gifts who have been hiding in the American southwest since the 1890's. They are gradually overcoming memories of persecution and forming partnerships with humans. Their perilous flight from their lost Home to Earth, their true Promised Land, parallels the Old Testament Exodus—a comparison underscored by Biblical names and titles. (Basic Christian values undergird all of Henderson's writing.) Although the People had a different salvation history, their beliefs are compatible with Christianity. They even use a trinitarian invocation of God as the Power, the Presence, and the Name. Their bonding through love is Henderson's answer to the conflicts between community and individuality that run through so much of her fiction.

Secret aliens among us is an old SF notion, but no one has put it to happier use than Henderson. The sheer wholesomeness of her People is enough to set them apart. "They're us only more so," says the author. Whether reading thoughts, operating spacecraft, or hemming dresses, the People wield their powers with a cheerful reverence that is refreshingly matter-of-fact. Henderson is neither anti-technological nor pro-occultist like Andre Norton. Miracles in a grittily realistic setting strike just the right note of aesthetic contrast to make the stories work.

Henderson's paradigm of sympathetic adult aiding troubled wonder-child is as distinctive as her signature. Yet it is a conscious pattern to be varied at will. "Something Bright" reverses the usual roles to disguised alien adult and helpful human child. Not all teachers are caring ("The Last Step") or effective ("You Know What, Teacher?"). Not all marvels are desirable ("The Substitute," "Turn the Page," "Sharing Time"). Children's wonderful powers can cause tragedy ("The Believing Child," "Come On, Wagon!," "Hush"). In such works Henderson displays an excellent although curiously unappreciated touch for horror. She can handle insanity as vividly as psi ("Swept and Garnished," "One of Them").

At her worst, Henderson's sentimentality overflows. Occasionally her ideas are too weak. Her range of subject matter is admittedly small. But overall, she worked with sound, unobtrusive craftsmanship. She had the classic short story writer's talents for precise focus, good characterization, and shrewd deployment of details. A kindly, traditional sensibility animates her writing. This description of ultimate happiness from "The Anything Box" conveys her special flavor: "all the worry and waiting, the apartness and loneliness were over and forgotten, their hugeness dwindled by the comfort of a shoulder, the warmth of clasping hands—and nowhere, nowhere was the fear of parting. . . ." Henderson was SF's mistress of the happy ending.

—Sandra Miesel

---

**HENSLEY, Joe L.** (Joseph Louis Hensley). American. Born in Bloomington, Indiana. 19 March 1926. Educated at Indiana University, Bloomington, B.A. 1950, LL. B. 1955: called to the Indiana Bar, 1955. Served as a hospital corpsman in the United States Navy, 1944–46; recalled as journalist, 1951–52. Married Charlotte Ruth Bettinger in 1950; one son. Partner, Metford and Hensley, 1955–72, and Hensley Todd and Castor, 1972–75, Madison, Indiana; Judge Pro-Tempore, 80th Judicial Circuit, Versailles, Indiana, 1975–76; Judge, 5th Judicial Circuit, Madison, 1977–88. Member, Indiana General Assembly, 1961–62; Prosecuting Attorney, 5th Judicial Indiana Circuit, 1963–66. President, Indiana Judges Association, 1983–84. Since 1989, partner, Hensley Walro Collins and Hensley, Madison, Indiana. Agent: Virginia Kidd, Box 278, Milford, Pennsylvania 18337. Address: 2315 Blackmore, Madison, Indiana 47250, U.S.A.

SCIENCE-FICTION PUBLICATIONS

Novel

*The Black Roads.* Toronto, Laser, 1976.

Short Stories

*Final Doors* (includes essay). New York, Doubleday, 1981.

OTHER PUBLICATIONS

Novels

*The Color of Hate.* New York, Ace, 1960; as *Color Him Guilty*, New York, Walker, 1987.
*Deliver Us to Evil.* New York, Doubleday, 1971.
*Legislative Body.* New York, Doubleday, 1972.
*The Poison Summer.* New York, Doubleday, 1974.
*Song of Corpus Juris.* New York, Doubleday, 1974.
*Rivertown Risk.* New York, Doubleday, 1977.
*A Killing in Gold.* New York, Doubleday, 1978; London, Gollancz, 1979.
*Minor Murders.* New York, Doubleday, 1979.
*Outcasts.* New York, Doubleday, 1981.
*Robak's Cross.* New York, Doubleday, 1985.
*Robak's Fire.* New York, Doubleday, 1986.
*Fort's Law.* New York, Doubleday, 1987.
*Robak's Run.* New York, Doubleday, 1990.

Short Stories

*Robak's Firm* (includes essays). New York, Doubleday, 1987.

*

Manuscript Collection: Lilly Library, Indiana University, Bloomington.

Joe L. Hensley comments (1985):

I don't write very much science fiction. Suspense is a more familiar game to me. But I still admire those who do write science fiction and am happy, now and then, when I do also.

* * *

Joe L. Hensley's most important SF stories are connected with Harlan Ellison. Hensley and Ellison are great friends, and Ellison wrote 2000 words of introduction to "Lord Randy, My Son" for *Dangerous Visions.* The story is a masterpiece of understated horror. Ellison's introduction to the story tells how Hensley—a lawyer—saved Ellison from being court-martialed by the U.S. Army. Ellison provides another introduction to Hensley and Ellison's collaboration "Rodney Parish for Hire." This chilling account of a youngster who kills other children for profit is a good example of the strengths of both writers. The story features strong characterization, fast-paced writing, and a suspenseful plot.

Hensley's only SF novel, *The Black Roads*, is a reworking of the setting and themes best developed by Mack Reynolds' *Rollertown* (1976). After a nuclear war, only American technology survives. A society based on roadways evolves as the ultimate realization of humans' love for their automobiles. Duels are fought between cars, and Red Roadmen ride the lanes in their supercharged autos keeping law and order. The mobile society is interesting, but Hensley never elevates his characters above the level of cardboard. The result is a staleness absent from Hensley's better short stories and the mystery novels for which he is better known.

The best of Hensley's short stories, both mystery and SF, are collected in *Final Doors*. Hensley's two collaborations with Harlan Ellison are included as well as his collaboration with SF and horror writer Gene DeWeese. The most haunting story in the collection is "Killer Scent," in which a sheriff secretly hunts down psychopathic killers that give off a "scent" only he can sense. The sheriff, when finally discovered, explains his hunting of the psychopaths this way: "Sometimes I think they're mutants, the coming race for earth. . . . Maybe they came along to wipe us out, take our places, be the survivors of the cities, mercilessly preying on each other after we're gone." "Killer Scent" works equally well as a suspense story and an SF story. It is one of the seven original short stories included in this 18-story collection.

Hensley's writing is unusually crisp, his plotting is tight, and his best work has power and insight. Much of his work—especially his Robak mystery novels—reflects his background in law and the criminal justice system.

—George Kelley

---

**HERBERT, Frank (Patrick).** American. Born in Tacoma, Washington, 8 October 1920. Attended the University of Washington, Seattle, 1946–47. Married Beverly Ann Stuart in 1946; one daughter and two sons. Reporter and editor for west coast newspapers; lecturer in general and interdisciplinary studies, University of Washington, 1970–72; social and ecological studies consultant, Lincoln Foundation and the countries of Vietnam and Pakistan, 1971. Recipient: Nebula award, 1965; Hugo award, 1966; Prix Apollo, 1978. *Died 12 February 1986.*

SCIENCE-FICTION PUBLICATIONS

Novels (series: Dune; Jorj X. McKie; Pandora)

*The Dragon in the Sea.* New York, Doubleday, 1956; London, Gollancz, 1960; as *21st Century Sub*, New York, Avon, 1956; as *Under Pressure*, New York, Ballantine, 1974.
*The Illustrated Dune.* New York, Berkley, 1978; as *The Great Dune Trilogy*, London, Gollancz, 1979.
*Dune.* Philadelphia, Chilton, 1965; London, Gollancz, 1966.
*Dune Messiah.* New York, Putnam, 1969; London, Gollancz, 1971.
*Children of Dune.* New York, Berkley, and London, Gollancz, 1976.
*Destination: Void* (Pandora). New York, Berkley, 1966; London, Penguin, 1967.
*The Eyes of Heisenberg.* New York, Berkley, 1966; London, Sphere, 1968.
*The Green Brain.* New York, Ace, 1966; London, New English Library, 1973.
*The Santaroga Barrier.* New York, Berkley, 1968; London, Rapp and Whiting, 1970.
*The Heaven Makers.* New York, Avon, 1968; London, New English Library, 1970.
*Whipping Star* (McKie). New York, Putnam, 1970; London, New English Library, 1972; revised edition, New York, Berkley, 1977.
*The God Makers.* New York, Putnam, and London, New English Library, 1972.
*Hellstrom's Hive.* New York, Doubleday, 1973; London, New English Library, 1974; as *Project 40*, New York, Bantam, 1973.
*The Dosadi Experiment* (McKie). New York, Putnam, 1977; London, Gollancz, 1978.
*The Jesus Incident* (Pandora), with Bill Ransom. New York, Berkley, and London, Gollancz, 1979.
*Direct Descent.* New York, Ace, 1980; London, New English Library, 1982.
*The God-Emperor of Dune.* New York, Putnam, and London, Gollancz, 1981.
*The White Plague.* New York, Putnam, 1982; London, Gollancz, 1983.
*The Lazarus Effect* (Pandora), with Bill Ransom. New York, Putnam, and London, Gollancz, 1983.
*Heretics of Dune.* New York, Putnam, and London, Gollancz, 1984.
*Chapterhouse: Dune.* New York, Putnam, and London, Gollancz, 1985.
*Man of Two Worlds*, with Brian Herbert. New York, Putnam, and London, Gollancz, 1986.
*The Second Great Dune Trilogy* (includes *The God-Emperor of Dune, Heretics of Dune*, and *Chapterhouse: Dune).* London, Gollancz, 1987.
*The Ascension Factor* (Pandora), with Bill Ransom. New York, Putnam, and London, Gollancz, 1988.

Short Stories

*The Worlds of Frank Herbert.* London, New English Library, 1970; New York, Ace, 1971.
*The Book of Frank Herbert.* New York, DAW, 1973; London, Panther, 1977.
*The Best of Frank Herbert*, edited by Angus Wells. London, Sidgwick and Jackson, 1975.
*The Priests of Psi and Other Stories.* London, Gollancz, 1980.
*Eye*, edited by Byron Preiss. New York, Berkley, 1985; London, Gollancz, 1986.

OTHER PUBLICATIONS

Novel

*Soul Catcher.* New York, Putnam, 1972; London, New English Library, 1973.

Other

*Threshold: The Blue Angels Experience.* New York, Ballantine, 1973.
*Without Me You're Nothing: The Essential Guide to Home Computers*, with Max Barnard. New York, Simon and Schuster, and London, Gollancz, 1981; as *The Home Computer Handbook*, London, New English Library, 1985.
*The Maker of Dune: Insights of a Master of Science Fiction*, edited by Tim O'Reilly. New York, Berkley, 1987.
*The Notebooks of Frank Herbert's Dune*, edited by Brian Herbert. New York, Perigree Books, 1988.

Editor, *New World or No World.* New York, Ace, 1970.

Editor, with others, *Tomorrow, and Tomorrow, and Tomorrow . . . .* New York, Holt Rinehart, 1974.
Editor, *Nebula Winners 15.* New York, Harper, 1981; London, W.H. Allen, 1982.

*

Critical Studies: *Frank Herbert* by Timothy O'Reilly, New York, Ungar, 1981; *The Dune Encyclopedia* edited by Willis E. McNelly, New York, Putnam, and London, Corgi, 1984.

* * *

Frank Herbert's science fiction is deeply humanistic, an amalgam of history, philosophy, theology, psychology, and science that explores man's future in terms of his past. Though peopling distant worlds with both alien and humanoid entities, his works focus on man: his diversity and his singularity—his nature, limits, potentialities, his inseparable ties to his environment and his fellow creatures, his genetic and cultural heritage that paves the way for his future, his latent mystical and psychic abilities that training and necessity might nurture, his need for challenge and adversity, and his dual potential for progress or destruction. Although his main characters usually remain familiar and psychologically credible, even amid alien settings, to Herbert humanity is not fixed, but rather is continually evolving both physically and intellectually, adapting to changed or new environments, growing decadent and stagnant when too comfortable but learning to survive and thrive when necessity compels. When fixed in rigid patterns (religious, political, genetic), he becomes mechanical, perverted, dehumanized and doomed; but change and evolution, even if violent, bizarre or seemingly incomprehensible, bring hope; adversity and competition create strength. Herbert's message is that man must learn from his past, avoid absolutist traps, recognize that right might be wrong in changed circumstances, explore his limits to their fullest, but never lose touch with the ecosystems on which he depends and to which he must continually adapt. In keeping with his varied intellectual concerns, Herbert's narrative structure is episodic, even fragmented, more dependent on clashes of ideas than on action.

In the *Dune* series, *The God Makers, The Santaroga Barrier, The Heaven Makers, The Dosadi Experiment*, and in the "Pandora" series, Herbert describes the trials, conflicts, and rites of passage through which man can evolve god-like powers of intellect and foresight, but further suggests the difficulties and dangers such powers necessitate. Frequently these evolutionary leaps are precipitated by contact with special organic chemicals ("spice" in *Dune*, "Jaspers" in *Santaroga*, kelp hallucinogens in *The Jesus Incident, The Lazarus Effect*, and *The Ascension Factor*), by the genetic mix of unique strains (*The God Makers, Dune* series, *The Heaven Makers, The Ascension Factor*), or by a special mind or body fuse (*Dosadi, The Jesus Incident, The Ascension Factor, Man of Two Worlds*). *Soul Catcher*, though not science fiction *per se*, weaves a tale of mystic Indian powers gained through birth and ritual, and ancient alien gods who heighten the perception of those seeking their frightening aid.

In *The Dosadi Experiment*, humans and a number of alien species, caged together on a toxic planet, bred for vengeance and cunning, plagued by overpopulation, and conditioned by constant war and hunger, learn to overcome all barriers (even a tempokinetic "God Wall") and avenge themselves on their creators. An alien female with features like a praying mantis merges with a human to produce total mind transference and psi power that force the tribunal to recognize Dosadi power and potential. In *Whipping Star*, the secret agent from *The Dosadi Experiment* (Jorj X. McKie) must cope with the peculiar customs and qualities of alien races as he seeks a loophole in a legal contract spelling death for the only surviving alien capable of controlling "jumpdoors" for speedy transport.

*The God Makers* focuses on an interplanetary troubleshooter assigned to monitor planets and to detect at early stages signs of aggressiveness that might trigger future war; in fulfilling these duties he discovers and develops extrasensory powers that lead him to rites of passage on a special planet of philosophers, rites that make clear his godhood and teach him to use his powers to do what has been his job all along—prevent war and aggression through compromise between potential enemies. However, one drawback of being a superpower and of attaining immortality is the possibility of boredom. Paul Atreides of *Dune*, omnipotent ruler of thousands of planets, fakes his own death and retires to private interests, while his descendant, Emperor Leto II, the God-Emperor of Dune, longs for an equal mind with whom to share the Machiavellian twists of his long-term plans for his subjects.

In *The Heaven Makers*, an immortal alien movie producer, using Earth as a set for filming full sensory movies of wars, natural disasters, and other horrors to relieve the boredom of his jaded race, breaks regulations and interferes with human cycles, originally to provide more entertaining disasters, but ultimately to produce a blessed loss of immortality. *Man of Two Worlds* (written with Brian Herbert) also examines man through alien eyes, postulating a race of *idiot-savant* storytellers (the main one called "Habiba" or "Love" as in "God is Love") with the power to create substance, initiate life and interfere in the evolution of that life; however, this power backfires when the story they create is that of Earth and Earthlings, creatures whose greed, physical obsessions and lust for power infect their creators, turn peaceful spirits into violent murderers, and threaten the universe. The story turns on a dynamic and unscrupulous news editor and magnate forced to share his body with an alien who holds very different views about pleasure and responsibility. Each of these books examines alien intelligence in order to more clearly define the human.

The most famous of Herbert's books tracing human evolution to a higher state of being is the much imitated *Dune* sextet, a complex series of epic proportions and of epic concerns that depicts the development, expansion, and diversification of religion and politics on an alien, feudal desert world, and that traces the intergalactic rise and fall of a great family caught up in messianic convulsions. Its scope is incredible—an entire world convincingly and thoroughly drawn in topography, ecology, history, literature, and culture. It remains Herbert's finest and most imaginative achievement. In it Herbert concerns himself, not with future technologies, but with the evolution of human logic and prescience. The series begins with revolutionary powers and vast changes, and traces the political line as it sinks into stasis, becomes ingrown and perverted, until new blood and unexpected evolutions force the changes necessary for regeneration and for ultimate survival of a people and a world.

The first in the series, *Dune*, concerns the growth and maturation of Paul Atreides, the product of generations of controlled breeding and Bene Gesserit training in desert discipline. Once his latent powers are enhanced by an overdose of Arrakis spice (the by-product of the desert's giant sandworms), his mind, with its heightened consciousness, becomes permanently opened to see and shape the future; his time travel involves a succession of choices between alternative futures. Beset by conspiracies, but revered by the Bedouin-like Fremen, whose scrupulous water conservation measures allow them a precarious existence, Paul Atreides becomes the prophet to his infant brother and leads the desert people on a *jihad* to conquer their planet and a thousand others.

As *Dune Messiah* traces an imperial intergalactic intrigue by the Bene Gesserit to overthrow the "god" they themselves created (a common Herbert theme), it also demonstrates the corrupting effects of power as the deserts are tamed, the hardened Fremen grow water-fat and soft, ideals are lost, and religion becomes dead ritual. Only the sacrifice of Paul Atreides, who has learned to see too much and yet too little, can free himself and his subjects from the unbearable burden and dangers of foreknowledge. Its action complicated by a Tleilaxu face dancer and a "ghola" recreation of a dead hero, this novel overwhelms with Byzantine twists.

The focus on ecology and political intrigue continues in *Children of Dune*, which is a disturbing debunking of Paul Atreides: an analysis of grand schemes doomed to failure and of short-sighted wishes inflicted on the environment. Therein Paul's son Leto, as head of the House of Atreides, must undo the evils of the past by avoiding the goodness that made his father so dangerous and by reteaching his subjects to live by their instincts, to think and act for themselves, and to appreciate traditions that will preserve the ecology, the giant worms, and the melange harvest in the sands. His method is twofold: assuring the death of his father (now a wandering desert preacher) and then transforming himself by merging with the sandtrout of Arrakis to become a seemingly indestructible, towering monster, who returns the planet to desert.

The fourth in the series, *The God-Emperor of Dune*, is an ambitious book, more philosophy than action, an interpretation of the Dune past by Leto, who, as a merged being, lives for thousands of years, retains all ancestral memories and thought patterns, but becomes less and less human. He reminisces, theorizes, manipulates, and teaches. Able to predict the future because of his firm sense of history and human nature, he turns tyrannical and intentionally sets in motion antagonisms that eventually erupt in violence. His goal is growth and change instead of fixed, rigid religious and genetic patterns that would doom his subjects to weakness, degeneration, and perhaps extinction. Knowing that male armies historically turn on their own population, his is an army of women, chosen for their stability and their survival instincts. His "death" is self-chosen and self-sacrificial; at the price of his humanity, he divides into countless sandfish that will eventually become the giant worms of Arrakis. He leaves behind a fear of gods and a distrust of heroes—the ultimate lesson of the *Dune* series: man must depend on himself alone; gods and heroes foster lazy thinking, passivity, and inaction.

*Heretics of Dune* focuses on the ultimate working out of the God Emperor's plans—Arrakis turned desert once more, its people forced to revive old skills and learn new. Therein the Bene Gesserit joins uneasy forces with Tleilaxu face dancers to fight invading forces from the distant colonies and to attempt to manipulate a desert child who rides the sandworms, and the ghola, Duncan Idaho, whose quest for identity leads him to cut through the illusions that envelop him and those around him. Herbert once again raises questions about genetic variability and uncertainty, hidden conditioning, hyperconsciousness, bureaucratic failures, pursuit of absolutes, and self-discovery.

*Chapterhouse: Dune* ends the 50,000 year saga of the House of Atreides and their desert planet, leaping 15,000 years into the future from the time of Leto II to see his dream of rebellion fulfilled, his planet returned to desert, ghola Duncan Idaho at work again, and the Bene Gesserit battling the alien Honored Matres. The underpinnings of the *Dune* series depends on a feminine mystique, with its band of wise women who have seeded an empire with myths and genetic manipulation that fit their purposes and then who save or destroy accordingly. The final volume finds the Mother Superior still trying to work out her mysterious plan to ensure survival of a now scattered Bene Gesserit and willing to accept the distasteful price of survival. Religious mysticism and desert lore, complex intrigue and equally complex intellectual discourse, a sense of the mysteries of time and of alternative futures infuse these books with a life and interest beyond mere plot.

Herbert's milieu is always firmly grounded in present-day political and social realities rather than in escapist fantasy. His books are carefully researched and highly detailed. For instance, his description of a desert society whose fanatical and feudal codes of behavior revolve around their desperate need for water reflects Bedouin survival in the Sahara. *The Dragon in the Sea* so concretely describes deepwater submarine controls that British Naval Intelligence followed his model, and *Destination: Void* is a comprehensive study in computer theory. A suspenseful thriller, *The Dragon in the Sea* depicts a world made paranoid by 16 years of war. A psychologist joins the four-man crew of a deepsea atomic submarine/tug to find a saboteur. The mission, to steal oil from underwater deposits in enemy territory, involves fear and tension from the natural dangers of depth and pressure, heightened by fears of a spy. The book, with its superb technical detail, defines sanity as the ability to adapt to "insanity." So too does *Destination: Void.* Here four scientists in a spaceship with a human cargo of thousands, all unknowingly part of a vast experiment to force invention, are supposedly travelling toward an Eden when they suffer "organic" computer failure and have to create a conscious mechanical brain to guide them. They react under pressure against impossible odds and succeed in producing a supercybernetic computer that acquires godlike powers of life and death, and that agrees to take them to an Eden if they will contemplate how to "worship" him.

Despite his skillful handling of technical description, Herbert, in the tradition of American romanticism, opposes the mechanistic with the natural and organic to show the superiority of the intuitive biological organism. In "Seed Stock," it is the lowly workman, not the lab-dependent scientists, who instinctively adjusts to an alien planet. In *The Eyes of Heisenberg* rebels in a totally genetically engineered world oppose the immortal Optimen and their enemy Cyborgs, and deliberately interfere with gene surgery to bring about a return to mortality and to reproduce an embryo with the forbidden gene combination of intelligence and fertility. In *The Jesus Incident*, a sequel to *Destination: Void*, Herbert sets in opposition clones and "naturals," testtube babies and true births, as he continues the story of the scientists and their crew, deposited on an alien planet (Pandora), a water-dominated world filled with incredible horrors (nerve worms and hooded dashers and other predatory alien creatures). Instead of seeking to come to terms with the planet, they and their descendants try to wipe out its population, even the ruling sentient kelp, Avata, only to learn too late that the hope for Pandora rests in accepting the planet and living in harmony with its sentients, who can teach them about themselves and their past, their ship, and their gods.

*The Lazarus Effect* continues the story of Pandora as its human colonists try to make it habitable: the methodical, cautious "mermen," who live beneath the sea in hive-like units, by cultivating the kelp and trying to revive its sentient powers, and the more outgoing, boisterous "islanders," happier fisherfolk, by constructing huge floating piles of organic matter on which to live. Divided by custom, manner, environment, and deep-rooted "racial" stereotyping (genetically engineered clones versus "pure" human types), these descendants of the "Ship" crew from *Destination: Void* find a common bond only after the Kelp, aided by a miracle child bred of kelp, poetry, and human genetics, begins to direct their destiny, destroy fanatical conspirators, and help "resurrect" human and animal life frozen in space for centuries. However, such a resurrection begins another cycle of destruction, for these revived Moonbase clones look with scorn on Mermen and Islanders alike. In *The Ascension Factor*, they have enslaved both Kelp, and Pandorans, and have used hunger, propaganda, and brute force to prepare for their own return to space, no matter the cost to the natives. However, aided by a human child nurtured by the kelp (Christa Galli), a disembodied brain prepared to generate spaceship power, and a news system cable network, Pandorans find their destiny in a single-mind force that unites Mermen, Islanders, Kelp, and Clones, as well as the memories of all the planet's dead who have gone down to the sea. The novels in the "Pandora" series exemplify Herbert's approach: speculation about the nature of deities and of human evolution; technical wonders and genetic horrors; the concept of ancestral memory; natural enlightenment drugs; a poet who ultimately understands man's destiny, and an extraordinary child who will sweep away old orders and initiate new. Its purposeful interweaving of Christian myth suggests man cannot escape his past, for through it he finds his future. Its final message is that man must look within his own soul to find the salvation and the god he seeks; at the same time he must find harmony with the natural world if he is to use the knowledge he gains from self-examination.

Clearly then, related to Herbert's concern for the natural is an interest in ecology and a respect for rural values, a fear of man's tampering with nature coupled with a realization that he must tamper with himself if he is to advance. In "Operation Syndrome," a madman's electronic device to produce mass schizophrenia forces the development of telepathic communications to save world sanity. In "The Gone Dogs" a disease wipes out the canine population as we know it, but the species is ultimately preserved in a radical new form. "Seed Stock" criticizes the egoism of a terraforming process that disrupts natural ecology.

*The Green Brain, Hellstrom's Hive*, and *The White Plague* tackle the problem of human interference in nature. Set in Oregon, *Hellstrom's Hive* focuses on a secret zoological experiment that postulates the obsolescence of present family relations and of individuality; a government investigator discovers evolution's terrifying possibilities—a utopian human hive, a colony bred for physical and mental specialization that will make feasible world dominance—to preserve the hive. While the hive attains perfect harmony, from a human perspective the results are chilling. *The Green Brain* is another chilling tale that emphasizes man's dependence on insects and the potentiality of chemical sprays backfiring in unexpected ways. In an overpopulated world seeking *lebensraum* in jungles, an international organization systematically exterminates voracious insects until they defensively mutate to incredible sizes and types; some mutations involve protective "coloration"—insect colonies that appear human. A ruling insect "Brain," a corporate intelligence that is the product of this mutation, plans to restore and maintain nature's balance.

In *The Santaroga Barrier* Herbert deals with man coping with the imbalance within himself. In a world dominated by false, greedy, superficial advertising men, the Santaroga Valley remains isolated and impervious to modernization. An investigator engaged to a Santaroga psychiatrist seeks answers in "Jaspers," food infused with natural chemicals from Santaroga caves, chemicals that help users see through artifice and falsity to discover true values of community and integrity. But this proves a two-edged blessing, for with awareness comes the after-effects of not being able to live outside the valley for very long and a subconscious reflex to destroy any stranger who does not belong. The drug produces enlightenment and well-being at the cost of freedom.

*The White Plague*, a topical projection, makes a significant change in Herbert's canon. This novel is more heavily cynical about present realities than his past works. It is a double-edged attack on 1) the social and cultural attitudes that produce and encourage the mindless violence of terrorist groups, and 2) the potentials unleashed by recombinant DNA research that make it possible for one man only, with the right training, to unleash on the world at any moment an irreversible horror. It focuses on a molecular biologist who, unhinged by the senseless deaths of his wife and children in an IRA bombing, produces an unstoppable synthesized plague that kills only women. The result is chaos, panic, a breakdown of government and social order, and, ironically enough, a return to the self-destructive adolescent male patterns of might makes right and survival of the most cunning and brutal that terrorism has always fostered.

The collection of essays and materials in *Frank Herbert: The Maker of Dune*, published after Herbert's death, discusses the origins of the *Dune* novels and suggests the diversity of Herbert's interests and the rural origins of his commitment to harmony with nature.

In conclusion, Herbert mingles Eastern and Western philosophies, archetypes, and myths to produce a humanistic worldview, both skeptical and idealistic, one which explores the "god" in man but warns of the fragility of his world and of the dangers of utopias. His examination of evolving intelligence, whether mechanical (*Destination: Void*), insect (*The Green Brain*), alien ("The Tactful Saboteur," *Whipping Star, Dosadi Experiment, Man of Two Worlds*), or humanoid (*Dune* series, Pandora series), warns that man must stay adaptable, responsible, self-aware, and attuned to his environment in order to survive. His view is relativistic, his philosophy dialectical, his historical focus cyclical; his characters are complicated, his carefully considered details convincing, and, despite a rough-edged style and a weakness for extended discourse and jargon, his plots are provocative and intriguing, with a rich complexity and an imaginative scope that should please and challenge.

—Gina Macdonald

---

**HERBERT, James.** British. Born in London, 8 April 1943. Educated at St. Aloysius College, and Hornsey College of Art, both London. Married Eileen O'Donnell in 1968; three daughters. Typographer, John Collings Advertising, London, 1963–66; art director, Group Head, and associate director, Ayer Barker Hegemann International, London, 1966–67. Agent: Bruce Hunter, David Higham Associates, 5-8 Lower John Street, London W1R, 4HA, England; or, Claire Smith, Harold Ober Associates, 40 East 49th Street, New York, New York 10017, U.S.A.

### Science-Fiction Publications

#### Novels

*The Rats.* London, New English Library, 1974; New York, New American Library, 1975.

*The Fog.* London, New English Library, and New York, New American Library, 1975.

*The Dark.* London, New English Library, and New York, New American Library, 1980.

*Domain.* London, New English Library, 1984; New York, New American Library, 1985.

*Moon.* London, New English Library, 1985; New York, Crown, 1986.

OTHER PUBLICATIONS

Novels

*The Survivor.* London, New English Library, 1976; New York, New American Library, 1977.
*Fluke.* London, New English Library, 1977; New York, New American Library, 1978.
*The Spear.* London, New English Library, 1978; New York, New American Library, 1980.
*Lair.* London, New English Library, and New York, New American Library, 1979.
*The Jonah.* London, New English Library, and New York, New American Library, 1981.
*Shrine.* London, New English Library, 1983; New York, New American Library, 1984.
*The Magic Cottage.* London, Hodder and Stoughton, 1986; New York, New American Library, 1987.
*Sepulchre.* London, Hodder and Stoughton, 1987; New York, Putnam, 1987.
*Haunted.* London, Hodder and Stoughton, 1988; New York, Putnam, 1988.
*Creed.* London, Hodder and Stoughton, 1990.

* * *

James Herbert started his writing career relatively inauspiciously with *The Rats* in 1974, ostensibly just one more example of the gory, man-versus-animal chillers that enjoyed great popularity on both sides of the Atlantic for several years. Herbert's unique touch was the introduction of a single, giant mutant rat, whose intelligence was such that she could direct her fellows in organized attacks on humanity. Herbert's clear, crisp style provided some distance from his contemporaries, and his next novel was to mark him as a writer to watch.

*The Fog*, published in 1975, could have been just another disaster novel, a sub-genre that British novelists have dominated for decades. An earthquake releases into the atmosphere a previously unknown gas that releases the inhibitions of anyone who breathes it, leading to widespread murders, assaults, and acts of civil unrest. A small team of researchers races against time to discover a means of controlling the effects of the fog before civilization grinds to a complete halt.

Herbert's next two novels went in entirely different directions. *The Survivor* is purely supernatural, but with a clever plot twist involving the sole survivor of a tragic plane crash who begins to experience visions of the afterworld. *Fluke*, an interesting experiment but not one of Herbert's successes, concerns a murdered man reborn into the body of a dog, in which guise he sets out to solve the mystery of his own death and bring the culprit to justice.

The uncertain popularity of these books may explain why Herbert's next book, *Lair*, returned to more familiar ground. The giant mutant rat of *The Rats* returns, now having laid her plans in secret and raised an enormous army conditioned to do her bidding without question. The scope was larger, the gore more pervasive, but basically it recapitulated Herbert's earlier novel.

Subsequent novels, which appeared almost annually thereafter, were less conservative. *The Spear* is a contemporary thriller involving the discovery of a Neo-Nazi movement that has pursued Hitler's fascination with the occult to its fruition, actual possession of supernatural powers. From this point on, Herbert moved squarely toward the supernatural, although trappings of science fiction and conventional suspense novels continue to shape him stylistically.

*The Dark* returned to the contagious madness of *The Fog*, but this time the source was an evil force from antiquity set free to influence the living once more. In *The Jonah*, a police detective suffers from the fact that his presence carries a plague of bad luck to everyone he comes to love. The revelation of the nature of this curse, following a plot that resembles nothing so much as a conventional, police procedural murder mystery, was one of Herbert's more inventive plot devices, and the book is certainly one of his most interesting accomplishments.

*Shrine* was another experiment for Herbert, this time mixing theology with the supernatural. A young, deaf mute girl undergoes a remarkable religious experience; then she acquires use of all her senses and seems perfectly normal. Then it is discovered that she had also acquired the power of healing, and there is widespread belief that a miracle has occurred, and that she is a living saint. Others believe this is just another plot by the Adversary to fool people into false beliefs.

Herbert returned to science fiction with *Domain*, the third novel with the mutated rats. In the opening chapter, a nuclear war devastates the Earth, destroying civilization and leaving small clusters of survivors struggling to remain alive in underground shelters while they wait for the radioactivity above to dissipate. Their existence becomes much more problematical when hordes of mutant rats, now grown more ferocious and far more intelligent than their predecessors, invade the remaining shelters in an attempt to seize mastery of the planet.

*Moon* is also arguably science fiction. On a remote island, an introspective man discovers that he has become telepathically linked to a serial killer, able to witness his crimes after a fashion, but without sufficient clarity to be able to identify the murderer. The other half of the link becomes aware of the connection, and begins to retrace the tenuous connection, determined to eliminate the only person who knows, however uncertainly, his dark secret. The plot is that of a standard suspense thriller, with the fantastic element giving it a unique and very suspenseful twist.

*The Magic Cottage*, an untraditional haunted house story, is noteworthy because of its characterization, developed more fully than in Herbert's previous work. *Haunted* uses a similar setting and deals with the same theme quite differently. *Sepulchre* features an ancient Sumerian demon who can impart supernatural powers to its followers. The interface here between the world of high finance and that of the supernatural provides a fascinating contrast.

Although Herbert's popularity in the United States seems to have waned in recent years, the quality of his writing has steadily improved. It is unfortunate for science fiction readers that he seems to have moved almost entirely into supernatural themes and plots, particularly when he has shown an ability to use unconventional settings and plot elements to turn the reader's expectations end for end.

—Don D'Ammassa

---

**HERON-ALLEN, Edward.** *See* **BLAYRE, Christopher.**

---

**HIGH, Philip E(mpson).** British. Born in Biggleswade, Bedfordshire, 28 April 1914. Educated at Kent College, Canterbury. Served in the Royal Navy during World War II. Married Pamela Baker in 1950; two daughters. Has worked as a salesman, reporter, and insurance agent; bus driver, East Kent Road Car Company, 1951–79; now retired. Agent: Carnell Literary Agency, Rowneybury Bungalow, near Old Harlow, Essex CM20 2EX. Address: 34 King Street, Canterbury, Kent CT1 2AJ, England.

SCIENCE-FICTION PUBLICATIONS

Novels

*The Prodigal Sun*. New York, Ace, 1964; London, Compact, 1965.
*No Truce with Terra*. New York, Ace, 1964.
*The Mad Metropolis*. New York, Ace, 1966; as *Double Illusion*, London, Dobson, 1970.
*These Savage Futurians*. New York, Ace, 1967; London, Dobson, 1969.
*Twin Planets*. New York, Paperback Library, 1967; London, Dobson, 1968.
*Reality Forbidden*. New York, Ace, 1967; London, Hale, 1968.
*Invader on My Back*. New York, Ace, and London, Hale, 1968.
*The Time Mercenaries*. New York, Ace, 1968; London, Dobson, 1969.
*Butterfly Planet*. London, Dobson, 1971.
*Sold—For a Spaceship*. London, Hale, 1973.
*Come, Hunt an Earthman*. London, Hale, 1973.
*Speaking of Dinosaurs*. London, Hale, 1974.
*Fugitive From Time*. London, Hale, 1978.
*Blindfold from the Stars*. London, Dobson, 1979.

*

Philip E. High comments:

I am a story teller. I have never claimed great literary abilities. I am not only a great believer in a happy ending, but am psychologically incapable of writing any other sort. A reader asks to be entertained and stimulated, not depressed. I have a vivid imagination and I try to put what I imagine on paper. But I am also old-fashioned: I like a story to have a beginning, a middle, an end, and, yes, a purpose with all the loose ends tied up.

* * *

Philip E. High is one of a number of writers of fast-paced adventure novels who rose to prominence with the publication of several novels by Ace Books. His work is generally written with little effort at stylistic flamboyance, with simple but well constructed plots. A definite tendency toward bizarre settings has helped to distinguish his novels from those of others working the same vein.

*Twin Planets*, for example, is set on a kind of alternate Earth, but it is not one of the slightly divergent histories standard in the field. Rather, it is a very similar world somewhat advanced in time, whose unpleasant experience with alien invaders led its inhabitants to attempt to help our own reality avoid a similar experience. Similarly, in *Invader on My Back* aliens have conquered the Earth and divided humanity into a number of disparate personality types. The common failing is a mortal dread of peering upward, conditioned into them because of their subjugated status. *Reality Forbidden* is also characterized by odd setting and events, partially rationalized in this case by the existence of dream machines, inventions that lull humanity into a careless conformity. Indeed, one of the recurring themes in High's novels is a dread of conformity and the value of the individual, usually a super-normal human. The two protagonists of *Twin Planets* are genetic supermen, and the human sent by aliens to help "civilize" Earth in *The Prodigal Sun* is also a superhuman. A man with an incredibly powerful intelligence helps lead a revolt against an overly protective computer mind in *The Mad Metropolis*, and another with an extremely active curiosity leads the struggle against a post-collapse government in *These Savage Futurians.*

In *The Time Mercenaries*, High's best novel, future humanity has bred itself to the ultimate degree of conformity and passivity, and cannot use violence even in self defense. To protect themselves against alien invaders, these future beings resurrect the crew of a present-day submarine, knowing that men of our period would not be restrained by their inflexible ethical code. Alien invasions are rather common in High's novels, usually to enslave us as in *Sold—For a Spaceship*, but sometimes to control our antisocial nature, as in *The Prodigal Sun* and *No Truce with Terra.* High makes the point quietly, however; he is more concerned with adventure than with social commentary.

High's more recent novels have been far less successful. *Come, Hunt an Earthman* was a disappointingly lackluster space adventure story, but *Speaking of Dinosaurs* had a clever plot, an intriguing scientific mystery, and was as well written as almost anything else High has written. Subsequent books have continued to concentrate on adventurous themes, but without increasing the author's popularity.

—Don D'Ammassa

---

**HILL, D.W.R.** *See* **TUBB, E.C.**

---

**HILL, John.** *See* **KOONTZ, Dean R.**

---

**HOBAN, Russell (Conwell).** American. Born in Lansdale, Pennsylvania, 4 February 1925. Educated at Lansdale High School; Philadelphia Museum School of Industrial Art, 1941–43. Served in the United States Army Infantry, 1943–45: Bronze Star. Married 1) Lillian Aberman (i.e., the illustrator Lillian Hoban) in 1944 (divorced 1975), one son and three daughters; 2) Gundula Ahl in 1975, three sons. Magazine and advertising agency artist and illustrator; story board artist, Fletcher Smith Film Studio, New York, 1951; television art director, Batten Barton Durstine and Osborn, 1951–56, and J. Walter Thompson, 1956, both in New York; advertising copywriter, Doyle Dane Bernbach, New York, 1965–67. Since 1967, full-time writer; since 1969 has lived in London. Recipient: Christopher award, for children's book, 1972; Whitbread award, for children's book, 1974; George G. Stone Center for Children's Books award, 1982; Ditmar award (Australia), 1982; John W. Campbell Memorial award, 1982. Agent: David Higham Associates Ltd., 5-8 Lower John Street, London W1R 4HA, England.

SCIENCE-FICTION PUBLICATIONS

Novel

*Riddley Walker.* London, Cape, and New York, Summit, 1980.

OTHER PUBLICATIONS

Novels

*The Lion of Boaz-Jachin and Jachin-Boaz.* New York, Stein and Day, and London, Cape, 1973.
*Kleinzeit.* London, Cape, and New York, Viking Press, 1974.
*Turtle Diary.* London, Cape, 1975; New York, Random House, 1976.
*Pilgermann.* London, Cape, and New York, Summit, 1983.
*The Medusa Frequency.* London, Cape, and New York, Atlantic Monthly Press, 1987.

Plays

*The Carrier Frequency,* with Impact Theatre Co-operative (produced London, 1984).
*Riddley Walker,* adaptation of his own novel (produced Manchester, 1986).

Television Play: *Come and Find Me,* 1980.

Fiction (for children)

*Bedtime for Frances.* New York, Harper, 1960; London, Faber, 1963.
*Herman the Loser.* New York, Harper, 1961; Kingswood, Surrey, World's Work, 1972.
*The Song in My Drum.* New York, Harper, 1962.
*London Men and English Men.* New York, Harper, 1962.
*Some Snow Said Hello.* New York, Harper, 1963.
*The Sorely Trying Day.* New York, Harper, 1964; Kingswood, Surrey, World's Work, 1965.
*A Baby Sister for Frances.* New York, Harper, 1964; London, Faber, 1965.
*Bread and Jam for Frances.* New York, Harper, 1964; London, Faber, 1966.
*Nothing to Do.* New York, Harper, 1964.
*Tom and the Two Handles.* New York, Harper, 1965; Kingswood, Surrey, World's Work, 1969.
*The Story of Hester Mouse Who Became a Writer.* New York, Norton, 1965; Kingswood, Surrey, World's Work, 1969.
*What Happened When Jack and Daisy Tried to Fool the Tooth Fairies.* New York, Four Winds Press, 1965.
*Henry and the Monstrous Din.* New York, Harper, 1966; Kingswood, Surrey, World's Work, 1967.
*The Little Brute Family.* New York, Macmillan, 1966.
*Save My Place.* New York, Norton, 1967.
*Charlie the Tramp.* New York, Four Winds Press, 1967.
*The Mouse and His Child.* New York, Harper, 1967; London, Faber, 1969.
*A Birthday for Frances.* New York, Harper, 1968; London, Faber, 1970.
*The Stone Doll of Sister Brute.* New York, Macmillan, and London, Collier Macmillan, 1968.
*Harvey's Hideout.* New York, Parents' Magazine Press, 1969; London, Cape, 1973.
*Best Friends for Frances.* New York, Harper, 1969; London, Faber, 1971.
*The Mole Family's Christmas.* New York, Parents' Magazine Press, 1969; London, Cape, 1973.
*Ugly Bird.* New York, Macmillan, 1969.
*A Bargain for Frances.* New York, Harper, 1970; Kingswood, Surrey, World's Work, 1971.
*Emmet Otter's Jug-Band Christmas.* New York, Parents' Magazine Press, and Kingswood, Surrey, World's Work, 1971.
*The Sea-Thing Child.* New York, Harper, and London, Gollancz, 1972.
*Letitia Rabbit's String Song.* New York, Coward McCann, 1973.
*How Tom Beat Captain Najork and His Hired Sportsmen.* New York, Atheneum, and London, Cape, 1974.
*Ten What? A Mystery Counting Book.* London, Cape, 1974; New York, Scribner, 1975.
*Dinner at Alberta's.* New York, Crowell, 1975; London, Cape, 1977.
*Crocodile and Pierrot,* with Sylvie Selig. London, Cape, 1975; New York, Scribner, 1977.
*A Near Thing for Captain Najork.* London, Cape, 1975; New York, Atheneum, 1976.
*Arthur's New Power.* New York, Crowell, 1978; London, Gollancz, 1980.
*The Twenty-Elephant Restaurant.* New York, Atheneum, 1978; London, Cape, 1980.
*The Dancing Tigers.* London, Cape, 1979.
*La Corona and the Tin Frog.* London, Cape, 1979
*Flat Cat.* London, Methuen, and New York, Philomel, 1980.
*Ace Dragon Ltd.* London, Cape, 1980.
*The Serpent Tower.* London, Methuen, 1981.
*The Great Fruit Gum Robbery.* London, Methuen, 1981; as *The Great Gumdrop Robbery.* New York, Philomel, 1982.
*They Came from Aargh!* London, Methuen, and New York, Philomel, 1981.
*The Battle of Zormla.* London, Methuen, and New York, Philomel, 1982.
*The Flight of Bembel Rudzuk.* London, Methuen, and New York, Philomel, 1982.
*Ponders (Jim Frog, Big John Turkle, Charlie Meadows, Lavinia Bat).* London, Walker, and New York, Holt Rinehart, 4 vols., 1983–84.
*The Rain Door.* London, Gollancz, 1986; New York, Crowell, 1987.
*The Marzipan Pig.* London, Cape, 1986; New York, Farrar Straus, 1987.
*Monsters.* New York, Scholastic, and London, Gollancz, 1989.
*Jim Hedgehog's Supernatural Christmas.* London, Hamilton, 1989; New York, Clarion Books, 1992.
*Jim Hedgehog and the Lonesome Tower.* London, Hamilton, 1990; New York, Clarion Books, 1992.

Verse (for children)

*Goodnight.* New York, Norton, 1966; Kingswood, Surrey, World's Work, 1969.
*The Pedaling Man and Other Poems.* New York, Norton, 1968; Kingswood, Surrey, World's Work, 1969.
*Egg Thoughts and Other Frances Songs.* New York, Harper, 1972; London, Faber, 1973.

Other (for children)

*What Does It Do and How Does It Work? Power Shovel, Dump Truck, and Other Heavy Machines.* New York, Harper, 1959.

*The Atomic Submarine: A Practice Combat Patrol under the Sea.* New York, Harper, 1960.

* * *

Russel Hoban is a science-fiction writer through only one novel, *Riddley Walker;* but that novel is a masterpiece. Hoban's other novels are essentially fantastic or surreal, even though several are set in contemporary London, where this American writer has lived for many years; none of his books is marketed as SF. He began as a writer of children's books, a career which culminated in the classic fantasy *The Mouse and his Child* (1967); since then he has written six adult novels from *The Lion of Boaz-Jachin and Jachin-Boaz* (1973) through *The Medusa Frequency* (1987).

Apart from *Turtle Diary*, all these novels could be called surreal "fantasies," and most are related to actual events in Hoban's life or background. *The Lion of Boaz-Jachin* tells of a family disruption, and the subsequent anger felt by an almost grown-up son for his father, now living with a new partner in London. The son's anger takes the form of a lion roaming the streets of London, a lion that can be seen by gifted people (such as mental patients), and needs to be fed large quantities of real meat. The book is full of sprightly symbolism. The same can be said of *Kleinzeit*, which centres on the experience of hospitalization. *Pilgermann*'s theme is the Jewish experience of the First Crusade, beginning with pogrom and ending with massacre, but as usual it is highly symbolist. The hero-narrator is literally a "ghost-writer," since he is dead before he utters his first word; and the book includes elements of a very charming Zen-like mysticism. *The Medusa Frequency* is based on a motif of severed heads, including that of Orpheus, the archetypal poet (and novelist?). Even at their most surreal moments, these are very personal books.

Personal elements are less obtrusive in Hoban's greatest novel, *Riddley Walker*, which achieved instant recognition, and deservedly won the John W. Campbell award in 1982. It is not remarkable for its overt plot: it is an after-the-bomb story set some 2400 years in the future in Kent, England, and covers a few weeks in which the neo-barbarians rediscover gunpowder and put it to disastrous use. The public issue is the one familiar from Walter Miller's *A Canticle for Leibowitz:* is technical progress desirable? There is another echo of Miller: the misinterpretation of a prebomb icon—in Miller a circuit-diagram, in Hoban a painting of the Legend of St. Eustace in Canterbury Cathedral. But otherwise the books are very different. Where Miller is panoramic, Hoban concentrates on the mind of young Riddley Walker, a tribal shaman. The inner form of the book is *Bildungsroman:* it is Riddley's struggle to come to terms with the problem of Power. And that is why we get the narrative in Riddley's own voice, a very distinctive voice, which begins like this: "On my naming day when I come 12 I gone front spear and kilt a wyld boar he parbly ben the las wyld pig on the Bundel Downs any how there hadnt ben none for a long time befor him nor I aint looking to see none agen." And so it goes on. No other SF author has attempted to produce a whole novel in language so altered from present English (not even Anthony Burgess in *A Clockwork Orange*). But the language is justified by its peculiar effects. Its sheer vitality, its combination of demotic crudeness and mystical symbolism could not be achieved otherwise. Indeed, the language is symbolic in some of its minute details (see my article "Making the Two One," *Extrapolation* 25, Summer 1984).

Above all, the altered spelling facilitates some pregnant puns, *wud* for "wood/would," *hart* for "hart/heart," and *Addom* for "Adam/atom." These appear in the "Eusa Story," the central myth-scripture of "Inland" (East Kent). In this myth, the "Littl Shynin Man the Addom" is caught by the scientist Eusa in the "Hart of the Wud" and torn apart: which signifies fission both of the atomic nucleus and of Adam, humanity. Both the atom and our selves are split in the heart of our "would," our will to creativity and power. Many characters in the novel are fissioned too, their heads blown off (by the gunpowder bomb) away from their hearts. But Riddley and his followers avoid this fate by giving up physical power in favour of "the 1st knowing" (mystical intuition): they dedicate themselves to spreading wisdom by the current literary medium, the puppet show.

The great merit of *Riddley Walker* resides not so much in its plot or theme, which are common enough, but in its sheer expressiveness. It is full of myths, legends, symbolic figures, such as Punch (violence), Greanvine (mortality), Aunty (the goddess of Death). In this it is most comparable to Vonnegut's *Cat's Cradle* (with its texts of "Bokononism") and to Le Guin's *The Left Hand of Darkness* (with its Handdara legends). It is also an instance of that fairly frequent phenomenon, the writing of a great science-fiction novel by an author on the fringe of the genre.

—David Lake

---

**HOCH, Edward D.** Also writes as Irwin Booth; Stephen Dentinger; Ellery Queen. American. Born in Rochester, New York, 22 February 1930. Educated at the University of Rochester, New York, 1947–49. Served in the United States Army, 1950–52. Married Patricia A. McMahon in 1957. Worked at Rochester Public Library, 1949–50, Pocket Books, New York City, 1952–54, and Hutchins Advertising Company, Rochester, 1954–68. Since 1968, self-employed writer. Columnist (as R.E. Porter), *Ellery Queen's Mystery Magazine*, New York. President, 1982, and member, Board of Directors, Mystery Writers of America; member, Science Fiction Writers of America. Recipient: Mystery Writers of America Edgar Allan Poe award, for short story, 1968. Agent: Larry Sterning, 742 Robertson Street, Milwaukee, Wisconsin 53213. Address: 2941 Lake Avenue, Rochester, New York 14612, U.S.A.

SCIENCE-FICTION PUBLICATIONS

Novels (series: Carl Crader and Earl Jazine in all books)

*The Transvection Machine.* New York, Walker, 1971; London, Hale, 1974.
*The Fellowship of the Hand.* New York, Walker, 1973; London, Hale, 1976.
*The Frankenstein Factory.* New York, Warner, 1975; London, Hale, 1976.

Short Stories (series: Simon Ark)

*The Judges of Hades and Other Simon Ark Stories.* North Hollywood, Leisure, 1971.
*City of Brass and Other Simon Ark Stories.* North Hollywood, Leisure, 1971.
*The Quests of Simon Ark.* New York, Mysterious Press, 1984.

OTHER PUBLICATIONS

Novels

*The Shattered Raven.* New York, Lancer, 1969; London, Hale, 1970.
*The Blue Movie Murders* (as Ellery Queen). New York, Lancer, 1972; London, Gollancz, 1973.

Short Stories

*The Spy and the Thief.* New York, Davis, 1971.
*The Thefts of Nick Velvet.* Yonkers, New York, Mysterious Press, 1978.
*Leopold's Way.* Carbondale, Illinois, Southern Illinois University Press, 1985.
*The Night, My Friend.* Athens, Ohio University Press, 1991.

Other

*The Monkey's Clue, and The Stolen Sapphire* (for children). New York, Grosset and Dunlap, 1978.

Editor, *Dear Dead Days.* New York, Walker, 1972; London, Gollancz, 1974.
Editor, *Best Detective Stories of the Year.* New York, Dutton, 6 vols., 1976–81.
Editor, *All But Impossible! An Anthology of Locked Room and Impossible Crime Stories.* New Haven, Connecticut, Ticknor and Fields, 1981; London, Hale, 1983.
Editor, *The Year's Best Mystery and Suspense Stories.* New York, Walker, 9 vols., 1982–91.
Editor, with Martin H. Greenberg, *Great British Detectives.* Chicago, Academy, 1987.
Editor, with Martin H. Greenberg, *Women Write Murder.* Chicago, Academy, 1987.
Editor, with Martin H. Greenberg, *Murder Most Sacred: Great Catholic Tales of Mystery and Suspense.* New York, Dember, 1989.

*

Bibliography: "Edward D. Hoch: A Checklist" by Willian J. Clark, Edward D. Hoch, and Francis M. Nevins, Jr., in *Armchair Detective* (White Bear Lake, Minnesota), February 1976, revised edition, by Nevins and Hoch, privately printed, 1979.

Edward D. Hoch comments (1985):

I have always viewed my science fiction and fantasy as offshoots of my mystery writing, and nearly all my science fiction contains elements of mystery and detection.

* * *

Edward D. Hoch is one of the few writers who have been able to blend successfully the detective story with science fiction (others include Isaac Asimov, Anthony Boucher, Fredric Brown, Randall Garrett, and Ron Goulart). Of his three novels and more than 60 short stores which qualify as science fiction or fantasy, nearly all have criminous elements.

Each of Hoch's three SF novels is a classic mystery set in the 21st century and features the "Computer Cops," a team of government investigators led by Carl Crader and Earl Jazine. The first, *The Transvection Machine*, is perhaps the best—a strong blending of baffling mystery, inventive science fiction, and social commentary. Almost as good is *The Fellowship of the Hand*, which continues Crader's and Jazine's attempts to combat an organization known as HAND (Humans Against Neuter Domination), pledged to destroy all machines capable of dominating man. *The Frankenstein Factory*, which deals with a futuristic variation on the Frankenstein theme involving cryonics, is less successful in that it seems more an attenuated novelette than a fully realized novel.

Hoch's true forte, however, is the short story. He has published more than 500 in the past quarter-century and is widely acclaimed as the premier writer of short mystery fiction. Among the more memorable of his science-fiction detective tales are "The Wolfram Hunters" and "Computer Cops"; noncriminous SF include "Zoo," "The Faceless Thing," and "The Last Paradox." But it is the 80 novelette-length adventures about Simon Ark, a man who claims to be a 2000-year-old Copt priest, which are perhaps the most well-known of all Hoch's fictional creations. These are primarily tales of detection, but each deals with such fantastic elements as werewolves, witches, religious cults, scientific experiments, and Fortean phenomena. The best of the early Simon Ark stories (from the 1950's) appear in *City of Brass* and *The Judges of Hades.* A new series of Ark stories began in *Ellery Queen's Mystery Magazine* in 1978, and a new collection, *The Quests of Simon Ark*, was published in 1984.

The chief attribute of Hoch's work is invariably intricate and ingenious plotting; few rival him in his ability to summon a seemingly endless and wide-reaching flow of ideas. If plot receives more emphasis than character development in some of his prose (notable exceptions are "The Wolfram Hunters" and "The Faceless Thing"), this in no way diminishes its high entertainment value. The richness of idea and incident more than compensates.

—Bill Pronzini

---

**HODDER-WILLIAMS, (John) Christopher (Glazebrook).** Also writes as James Brogan. British. Born in London, in 1926. Educated at Eton College. Served in the Royal Signals, in the Middle East, 1944–48: Lieutenant. Worked in Africa after World War II; worked in England for film, television, and recording companies; also a composer.

SCIENCE-FICTION PUBLICATIONS

Novels

*Chain Reaction.* London, Hodder and Stoughton, and New York, Doubleday, 1959.
*The Main Experiment.* London, Hodder and Stoughton, 1964; New York, Putnam, 1965.
*The Egg-Shaped Thing.* London, Hodder and Stoughton, and New York, Putnam, 1967.
*Fistful of Digits.* London, Hodder and Stoughton, 1968.
*98.4.* London, Hodder and Stoughton, 1969.
*Panic O'Clock.* St. Ives, Cornwall, United Writers, 1973.
*The Prayer Machine.* London, Weidenfeld and Nicolson, 1976; New York, St. Martin's Press, 1977.
*The Silent Voice.* London, Weidenfeld and Nicolson, 1977.
*The Thinktank That Leaked.* St. Ives, Cornwall, United Writers, 1979.
*The Chromosome Game.* London, Mithras, 1984.

OTHER PUBLICATIONS

Novels

*The Cummings Report* (as James Brogan). London, Hodder and Stoughton, 1958.
*Final Approach.* London, Hodder and Stoughton, and New York, Doubleday, 1960.
*Turbulence.* London, Hodder and Stoughton, 1961.
*The Higher They Fly.* London, Hodder and Stoughton, 1963; New York, Putnam, 1964.

Plays

Radio Play: *Final Approach*, from his own novel, 1967.

Television Plays: *The Ship That Couldn't Stop*, 1961; *The Hot White Coal*, 1963; *The Higher They Fly*, from his own novel, 1963; *A Voice in the Sky*, 1964.

* * *

Christopher Hodder-Williams is not widely known in America despite his continuing popularity in Great Britain, possibly because his brand of science fiction places much more emphasis on the dangers of undisciplined research and experimentation and less on the wonders of technology. Indeed, one criticism that might be made is that he has overworked the Frankenstein theme in his novels.

His earliest work that might be called science fiction was *Chain Reaction*, a novel that dealt with the insidious threat of atomic radiation let loose upon an unsuspecting world. He moved firmly into the genre with *The Main Experiment*, which follows an unorthodox young scientist as he takes a new position with an atomic research unit. It is not long before the protagonist discovers that the project director has been taking some liberties with his progress reports and that the project itself is out of control. Even more frightening is the fact that the by-product of the research is a force which alters personalities and perceptions, strikes out beyond the boundaries of the experimental station, and might well pose a danger to the world at large.

*The Egg-Shaped Thing* repeated this theme, but with more complexity. When an entrepreneur is driven out of business, it almost costs him his sanity as well. Subsequently, he cannot be entirely certain of those things which he thinks he is experiencing. How, for example, does it happen that he can remember things which have not yet happened? Why are his rivals exacting revenge for acts which he has not yet committed? Once again the focus of our attention is a secretive research establishment experimenting with the atom, but this time the experiment itself may be conscious, and exerting itself to control the actions of others.

In *Fistful of Digits* technology is still the villain, or at least unbridled technology, but Hodder-Williams abandons the menace of atomic research for the equally promising field of computerization. A group of private businessmen have created an elaborate, extensive network of computers under the general name Servix which is secretly extending their ability to manipulate others. Their extrapolation warns of potential problems if the protagonist continues to associate with a particular young woman involved with their project, so they take steps to abrogate the relationship. The result, naturally, is eventually to reveal to him that people are becoming peripherals to the computer banks, programmed themselves for specific functions and actions.

*98.4* involves an unsuccessful security agent who is clandestinely hired to discover just what is happening within a select group of scientists at yet another research station. Computers figure prominently in the arsenal of the villains once more. A contagious, life-threatening wave of panic rocks all of Great Britain in *Panic O'Clock.* This time the central character is a young wife who flees with her child following a cryptic but frightening phone call from her husband. She must then make her way across the country to a secret rendezvous, avoiding both the authorities and the innocent victims of the induced panic

All of Hodder-Williams's fiction is very strong in characterization, development of suspense, and logical plot construction. His anti-technological bent may well be annoying to some readers, but his novels are excellent thrillers with science-fiction content and are probably much more commercially successful as such.

—Don D'Ammassa

---

**HODGSON, William Hope.** British. Born in Blackmore End, Essex, 15 November 1877. Apprentice seaman, 1891–95; officer in the Mercantile Marine: Lieutenant; founder and teacher, W.H. Hodgson's school of Physical Culture, Blackburn, Lancashire, 1899–1901. Joined University of London Officer Training Corps, 1914; commissioned in Royal Field Artillery, 1915; left service because of injury, 1916; recommissioned, 1917, and died at Ypres. Recipient: Royal Humane Society Medal, 1898. *Died 17 April 1918.*

SCIENCE-FICTION PUBLICATIONS

Novels

*The Boats of the "Glen Carrig."* London, Chapman and Hall, 1907; New York, Ballantine, 1971.
*The House on the Borderland.* London, Chapman and Hall, 1908.
*The Ghost Pirates.* London, Stanley Paul, 1909; Westport, Connecticut, Hyperion Press, 1976.
*The Night Land.* London, Nash, 1912; revised edition, as *The Dream of X*, in *Poems and The Dream of X*, 1912.
*The House on the Borderland and Other Novels.* Sauk City, Wisconsin, Arkham House, 1946.

Short Stories

*Deep Waters.* Sauk City, Wisconsin, Arkham House, 1967.
*Out of the Storm: Uncollected Fantasies*, edited by Sam Moskowitz. West Kingston, Rhode Island, Grant, 1975.
*William Hope Hodgson* (selected stories), edited by Peter Tremayne. London, Corgi, 1977.

OTHER PUBLICATIONS

Short Stories

*The Ghost Pirates, A Chaunty, and Another Story.* New York, Reynolds, 1909.
*Carnacki, The Ghost Finder, and a Poem.* New York, Reynolds, 1910.
*Carnacki, The Ghost Finder* (collection). London, Nash, 1913; augmented edition, Sauk City, Wisconsin, Mycroft and Moran, 1947.
*Men of the Deep Waters.* London, Nash, 1914.

*The Luck of the Strong.* London, Nash, 1916.
*Captain Gault, Being the Exceedingly Private Log of a Sea-Captain.* London, Nash, 1917; New York, McBride, 1918.

Verse

*Poems and The Dream of X.* London, Watt, and New York, Paget, 1912.
*Cargunka and Poems and Anecdotes.* London, Watt, and New York, Paget, 1914.
*The Calling of the Sea.* London, Selwyn and Blount, 1920.
*The Voice of the Ocean.* London, Selwyn and Blount, 1921.
*Poems of the Sea.* London, Ferret Fantasy, 1977.

*

Bibliography: by A.L. Searles, in *The House on the Borderland and Other Novels*, Sauk City, Wisconsin, Arkham House, 1946.

Critical Study: *William Hope Hodgson: A Centenary Tribute 1877–1977*, Dagenham, Essex, British Fantasy Society, 1977.

* * *

One of the most remarkable visionary fantasists of the pre-World War I era, William Hope Hodgson is chiefly remembered today as the author of two extravagant fantasies, *The House on the Borderland* and *The Night Land*, as well as a number of atmospheric horror stories of the sea and a series of "psychic detective" tales apparently modeled on those of Algernon Blackwood. Praised by H.P. Lovecraft and "rediscovered" by Arkham House publishers in the 1940's, Hodgson has grown into something of a cult figure in recent years, claimed by both historians of the scientific romance and fans of horror fiction.

There is little that is overtly "scientific" about his romances, however, and they seldom follow the uncomplicated narrative lines characteristic of romance. His first novel, *The Boats of the "Glen Carrig,"* is cast in the form of an 18th-century manuscript describing the adventures of castaways adrift in the Sargasso Sea, who encounter islands full of plants that absorb living things, weed-bound derelict ships, giant crabs, and slug-like "weed men" with beaked faces. Like much of Hodgson's short fiction, the novel exploits the legend of the Sargasso Sea in an effective and haunting way, and reflects what would prove to be a continuing Hodgson theme of the struggle between matter and spirit, with matter represented through almost obsessive images of slime, fungus, and rot.

Hodgson regarded his next two novels, *The House on the Borderland* and *The Ghost Pirates*, as parts of a thematically linked trilogy with *The Boats of the "Glen Carrig."* Certainly the themes of matter and spirit, entrapment and decay, and humanoid monsters are common to all three works, but the critic Brian Stableford is probably correct in surmising that had Hodgson been familiar with the concept of entropy, he might have seen that as his central theme. *The House on the Borderland*—again cast in the form of an old manuscript, this time found in the ruins of a desolate house in Ireland—is distinguished for the stunningly imagined visions of other worlds and times experienced by the narrator, including an astonishing passage in which he watches time accelerate until the entire solar system collapses. *The Ghost Pirates* returns to Hodgson's more familiar shipboard setting, but retains much of the otherworldly atmosphere of *The House on the Borderland* in its account of a ship which is first invaded by the not-quite-human "pirates" of the title and later sails into a mysterious otherworldly fog, where strange beings kill all but one survivor.

Hodgson's most ambitious and least readable novel was his last. *The Night Land* again employs an antiquated narrative style—this time that of a medieval dream-vision—but the result reads like a clumsy amalgam of William Morris and H.P. Lovecraft. This unfortunately turgid prose disguises one of the most remarkable and haunting visions of the far future in all fantastic literature. Millions of years from now, a remnant of humanity survives in a giant pyramid called the Last Redoubt, surrounded by eternal darkness occupied by a variety of strange and hostile beings. Discovering the existence of another outpost of humanity, the narrator—in his dream—sets out across this foreboding landscape to rescue a woman he believes to be the reincarnation of his dead lover. In the end, love sentimentally triumphs over the forces of decay and chaos.

If *The Night Land* is Hodgson's epic treatment of decay and survival, his short stories are lyrics on the same themes. The most famous of these, "The Voice in the Night," tells of a man and his wife stranded on a remote island who, after eating a strange fungus, are transformed into fungoid beings themselves. "The Derelict" describes a ship so overgrown with fungus that it becomes a living organism. Giant rats overtake a ship in "The Mystery of the Derelict," and "From the Tideless Sea" is another tale of strange monsters in the Sargasso Sea. Even the lighter tales of Carnacki, the detective who investigates paranormal phenomena, are apt to feature disturbing images of distorted life—such as a room that puckers up and whistles, or a monstrous hog-like being from another dimension in "The Hog."

Hodgson's idiosyncratic and disturbing visions have gained him a unique and lasting reputation in fantastic literature. While his death in World War I at the age of 40 would seem to have cut short what may have been an even more remarkable career, the fact is he wrote relatively little during the last years of his life, and seemed to regard *The Night Land* as his personal epic. It remains one of the great oddities of the genre, and together with *The House on the Borderland* qualifies Hodgson as one of the first true visionaries of the far future.

—Gary K. Wolfe

---

**HOFFMAN, Lee.** Also writes as Georgia York. American. Born in Chicago, Illinois, 14 August 1932. Educated at Armstrong Junior College, Savannah, Georgia, A.A. 1951. Married Larry T. Shaw (divorced). Printer's devil, Savannah Vocational School; staff member, Hoffman Radio-TV Service; assistant editor, *Infinity*, 1956–58, and *Science Fiction Adventures*, 1956–58, both New York; staff member, MD Publications; claim handler, Hoffman Motors; in printing production, Arrow Press, Allied Typographers, and George Morris Press. Since 1965, freelance writer. Recipient: Western Writers of America Spur award, 1968. Address: 350 N.W. Harbor Boulevard, Port Charlotte, Florida 33952, U.S.A.

SCIENCE-FICTION PUBLICATIONS

Novels

*Telepower.* New York, Belmont, 1967.
*The Caves of Karst.* New York, Ballantine, 1969; London, Dobson, 1970.
*Always the Blackknight.* New York, Avon, 1970.
*Change Song.* New York, Doubleday, 1972.

Short Stories

*In and Out of the Quandary*, edited by Charles J. Hitchcock. Cambridge, Massachusetts, NESFA Press, 1982.

OTHER PUBLICATIONS

Novels

*Gunfight at Laramie.* New York, Ace, 1966; London, Gold Lion, 1975.
*The Legend of Blackjack Sam.* New York, Ace, 1966.
*Bred to Kill.* New York, Ballantine, 1967.
*The Valdez Horses.* New York, Doubleday, 1967; London, Tandem, 1972.
*Dead Man's Gold.* New York, Ace, 1968.
*The Yarborough Brand.* New York, Avon, 1968; London, Hale, 1981.
*Wild Riders.* New York, New American Library, 1969; London, Hale, 1979.
*Loco.* New York, Doubleday, 1969; London, Tandem, 1973.
*Return to Broken Crossing.* New York, Ace, 1969; London, Hale, 1982.
*West of Cheyenne.* New York, Doubleday, 1969; London, Tandem, 1973.
*Wiley's Move.* New York, Dell, 1975; London, Hale, 1980.
*The Truth about the Cannonball Kid.* New York, Dell, 1975; London, Hale, 1980.
*Fox.* New York, Doubleday, 1976; London, Hale, 1980.
*Nothing But a Drifter.* New York, Doubleday, 1976; London, Hale, 1980.
*Trouble Valley.* New York, Ballantine, 1976; London, Hale, 1980.
*Sheriff of Jack Hollow.* New York, Dell, 1977; London, Hale, 1979.
*The Land Killer.* New York, Doubleday, 1978; London, Hale, 1981.
*Savage Key* (as Georgia York). New York, Fawcett, 1979; London, Coronet, 1983.

* * *

The science-fiction novels of Lee Hoffman are novels of human feelings, not of hard science. The SF concepts are well thought out and are integral to the storylines, but they are clearly secondary to the characters. Unlike some SF where the idea is the star and the emphasis is placed on the nuts and bolts or on the astronomical bodies while the people seem stamped out of cookie dough, Hoffman's fiction is populated with characters who live and breathe and grow and develop. The songs they sing are ones for men and women, not for pulsars and machines.

Perhaps the clearest example of her ability to make her characters very human is the protagonist in *The Caves of Karst*, a man who has undergone an operation to enable him to breathe underwater. Though this allows him to work the underwater mines more effectively, he did not choose to undergo the operation solely for financial considerations; as the novel unfolds it becomes clear that the choice was made (on some level of consciousness) to protect his ego from an unhappy love affair. People on Karst, as on Earth, often shun those who differ physically from the norm and those who *choose* to have such differences are frequently confronted with outright hatred. His adjustment to his condition, to women in general and his girlfriend in particular, and to himself during a time of crisis is the heart of the book.

There are three primary themes that run through Hoffman's work: 1) Individuality and the freedom of choice that comes with it are extremely important but must be tempered with the realization that individuals need to work together, to interact, in order to achieve certain goals; 2) It is both wrong and dangerous to try to control something or someone without consent; 3) Things may not be the way you originally thought they were or the way you have been told they were. Each theme is expressed with varying degrees of emphasis, depending on the novel, but all three are interrelated in her science fiction.

Hoffman's style is lean and direct. Each novel opens with action, tossing the reader into the midst of unfolding events: *Telepower* begins with an attack on post-atomic war Cleveland by an army of rats; *The Caves of Karst* starts with an underwater "gunfight" in a mine; *Always the Blackknight* opens with a battle between knights on robot horses; and, although the first chapter of *Change Song* is used to establish a sense of wrongness and an atmosphere of danger, the second chapter quickly produces a fight between men with magical powers. Hoffman uses her writing skills to capture the reader immediately, and all of her work has been set on earth-like planets so that the reader can rapidly believe in the setting. Hoffman strives to entertain the reader while stating her messages.

To enrich her science fiction, she occasionally employs the techniques of other genres to give a more diverse flavor. In *Telepower* Hoffman forges a bond between the gruesome qualities of the horror novel and the telepathic power so common in science fiction. Drawing upon her own experience as a writer of westerns, she gives *The Caves of Karst* an Old West setting (or what the Old West would have been like if the prospectors had gills) while at the same time using all the plot-twists of a mystery novel. *Always the Blackknight* has the flavor of the tales of knighthood, as the title might indicate, and *Change Song* has most of the elements of quest-fantasy. In fact *Change Song* is really more fantasy than science fiction, much in the same way that Theodore Sturgeon's *More Than Human* is, although on the world where *Change Song* takes place control of the elements and the power to cast spells are like our science in that one is trained in these fields. By being willing to take the risks of mixing elements of other genres with science fiction, Lee Hoffman has given her work an added dimension.

—Terry Hughes

---

**HOGAN, James P(atrick).** British. Born in London, 27 June 1941. Educated at the Royal Aircraft Establishment Technical College, Farnborough, Berkshire, 1957–61; Reading and Enfield colleges, 1961–65. Married 1) Iris Crossley in 1961 (divorced), three daughters; 2) Lyn Dockerty in 1976 (divorced); 3) Jacklyn Price in 1982; three sons. Engineer, Solarton Electronics, Farnborough, 1961–62, Racal Electronics, Bracknell, Berkshire, 1962– 64; sales engineer, 1964–66, and sales manager, 1966–68, ITT, Harlow, Hertfordshire; computer sales executive, Honeywell, London, 1968–70, and Leeds, 1970–72; insurance salesman, Sun Life Canada, Leeds, 1972–74; computer salesman, 1974–77, and sales training consultant in Maynard, Massachusetts, 1977–79, Digital Equipment Corporation, Leeds. Since 1979, full-time writer. Agent: Eleanor Wood, 111 8th Avenue, New York, New York 10011, U.S.A. Address: Killarney House, Killarney Road, Bray, County Wicklow, Ireland.

SCIENCE-FICTION PUBLICATIONS

Novels (series: Ganymean)

*The Minerva Experiment* (Ganymean). New York, Ballantine, 1981.
*Inherit the Stars*. New York, Ballantine, 1977; London, Grafton, 1989.
*The Gentle Giants of Ganymede*. New York, Ballantine, 1978; London, Grafton, 1989.
*Giants' Star*. New York, Ballantine, 1981; London, Grafton, 1989.
*The Genesis Machine*. New York, Ballantine, 1978.
*The Two Faces of Tomorrow*. New York, Ballantine, 1979.
*Thrice upon a Time*. New York, Ballantine, 1980.
*Voyage from Yesteryear*. New York, Ballantine, 1982; London, Penguin, 1984.
*Code of the Lifemaker*. New York, Ballantine, 1983; London, Penguin, 1985.
*The Proteus Operation*. New York, Bantam, 1985.
*Endgame Enigma*. New York, Bantam, 1987; London, Century, 1988.
*The Mirror Maze*. New York, Bantam, 1989.
*The Infinity Gambit*. New York, Bantam, 1991.

Short Stories

*Minds, Machines, and Evolution* (includes non-fiction). New York, Bantam, 1988.

*

James P. Hogan comments (1985):

Despite the cynicism that seems fashionable in some social circles, I continue to feel positive about our species and its future, and our ability to comprehend and solve our problems. I'm optimistic about science and technology and an anti-Malthusian. I don't believe that we are about to blow ourselves into oblivion, starve ourselves into extinction, poison the planet, degenerate into Nazis, or disappear under our own garbage. On the contrary, I believe in the power of reason and human creativity to continue building better tomorrows. These are the things I try to project in what I write.

* * *

It would be easy to dismiss the fictions of James P. Hogan as reactionary tracts in the guise of novels, since his narrators and characters find it difficult not to digress into irrelevant, ill-tempered attacks on progressive institutions and projects. As one reads through Hogan's novels, one is struck by the amount of time the narrator and (on occasion) the most scientifically respectable characters spend railing at labor unions, the mass media, popular culture, environmental activists, advocates of solar energy, and any portion of education devoted to topics other than science and engineering. Hogan tries very hard to be a reliable propagandist for the "military-industrial complex." He almost succeeds.

Fortunately for his readers, however, Hogan's SF has an imaginative power that both transcends and undermines his self-imposed role as apologist for technical society. The propaganda, after all, is the product of a faith—a faith in reason. Hogan's fictions invite the reader to share that faith that the trained human mind, especially working with other trained human minds in the scientific team, can conquer the natural universe. In the plots of the narratives, it is not environmentalists or union leaders who nearly stymie the efforts of reasonable men (for Hogan's strong characters are almost always male), but rather ignorant governmental or corporate bureaucrats, behind whom lurk power-hungry and greedy executives who wish to use science for nefarious ends. Thus an interesting inconsistency appears: on the level of thematized narration and dialogue, we are *told* that the enemies of reason are (for example) the welfare state and environmental activists, while at the level of plot we are *shown* that the biggest enemy is in fact the "military-industrial complex." The inconsistency is not fatal: it rather adds to the interest of reading a Hogan fiction.

The typical Hogan protagonist is a strong-willed, competent scientific investigator, or an individual who struggles against an incompetent bureaucracy and malevolent leaders, or both. He is more willing than those around him to entertain unorthodox ideas—as long as those ideas are not the product of superstition (like "psi-powers") or ignorance (meaning any questioning of scientific or technical progress). In *The Genesis Machine* (a fictionalization of Herman Kahn's concept of "doomsday machine"), Brad Clifford is not simply a brilliant mathematical physicist who has worked out the equations of the dimensions beyond ordinary spacetime; he is also a romantic hero who creates a device which effectively disarms the nuclear-war making capabilities of both sides in a 21st-century world about to destroy itself. In *Code Of the Lifemaker*, the cynical "psychic" Karl Zambendorf (redeemed by the fact that he does not actually believe in his "powers") leads a rebellion that aborts the plans of a cabal of industrialists and politicians to impose a neo-colonial slavery upon the evolved robotic civilization discovered on Titan. An exception that proves the rule is *Voyage From Yesteryear*, which as a utopian fiction has a society rather than an individual for its hero: the Chironians, who have been able to implement absolute personal freedom owing to their unregulated science and technology and resultant economic abundance. The leaders of a new emigrant group from Earth attempt to impose a centralized political economy on the Chironians, but they fail when many of their followers find Chironian anarchism attractive.

Hogan's *Minerva Experiment* trilogy is marred when its third part, *Giants' Star*, descends into a space operatic war between good guy aliens allied with the Earth and the "Evil Empire" that seeks to enslave them. Its first two parts (*Inherit the Stars* and *The Gentle Giants of Ganymede*), however, constitute a fine SF detective story centered on Victor Hunt, an almost archetypal Hogan hero who heads up the team of United Nations Space Agency scientists that unravels the mystery of a humanoid corpse found on the moon. As Hunt and his team probe more deeply into the origins of the "Lunarians," they reconstruct the story of an ancient alien civilization and its colonies in the solar system, a process that enables them to advance a daring new hypothesis about the origins of mankind. Aside from promoting some of Hogan's favorite themes, such as the never-ending struggles between reason and superstition, and between individual freedom and the security state, *The Minervan Experiment* illustrates another important feature of Hogan's SF: his portrayal of the methods of scientific investigation. Since this particular investigation is an interdisciplinary one, the investigators must constantly share their knowledge as well as formulate, test, and discard successive hypotheses. Hogan also conveys what might be called the human dimension of science—the rivalries between fields, the interpersonal conflicts, and the exhilaration that comes with the discovery of a new piece of knowledge that can be fit into one's previous investigations. In the bargain, Hogan seamlessly integrates present-day "normal" science with the speculative, fictional science of his near-future setting. This promotes an important theme that runs throughout his SF: the unity and the smooth growth curve of Western science and technology, with the spirit of reason only occasionally disrupted by social backwardness and the apparent discontinuities associated with paradigm shifts in science itself.

More speculative and less constrained than most of Hogan's SF, *The Proteus Operation* exploits two grand old SF premises: a world in which the Nazis won the war, and the many-worlds interpretation of quantum mechanics. Sending a team back from the Nazi 1975, Hogan has them gradually undo the chair of events that led to the Nazi victory. Along the way, he does not overlook the comic potential in having characters encounter younger or older versions of themselves, or the *frisson* that can result from mixing historical figures (e.g., Albert Einstein, Isaac Asimov, and Winston Churchill) with fictional ones. Unfortunately, the non-fictional characters come off as unusually flat and stereotyped, perhaps because they are more icons to be reverenced than persons to be known. An interesting effect of Hogan's design for this novel is that his narrator must express admiration for the New Deal and the wartime alliance with the Soviets, even to the extent of excusing Stalin's role in the non-aggression pact! It is fascinating to see Hogan work the other side of the political street for a while, but the preaching remains tiresome. Interestingly, the novel emphasizes teamwork so much that no one character stands out as hero.

Hogan's *Endgame Enigma* is an apparent attempt to cash in on the popularity of the Tom Clancy-style Cold War Technothriller. Unfortunately for the attempt, Hogan lacks Clancy's willingness to jettison all else for hardware and suspense, and he uses his story as a platform for warning us about what crafty schemes the Soviets will come up with in their waning years. Also unfortunately, he achieves risibility by placing his novel in the year 2017 while retaining such standard details as an East German Soviet satellite, KGB men in blue serge suits, and large Russian women in shapeless dresses and thick stockings. We are asked to believe that a faltering Soviet command economy can create not only a space station three kilometers in diameter, but also a whirling underground replica somewhere in Siberia, fooling all but a few cynical CIA men. We are asked to believe that the Soviets plan to celebrate the centennial of the November revolution by starting World War III. We are asked to believe that Western politicians are knaves and Western scientists are fools while Western intelligence people are devoted public servants. In *Endgame Enigma* the propaganda is hysterical and desperate, and the romance of science and technology is reduced to military hardware fantasies. Lew McCain, Hogan's hero in the novel, is a bloodless imitation, almost a parody, of Victor Hunt and Karl Zambendorf. All in all, one looks to Hogan for better work.

—John P. Brennan

---

**HOLDSTOCK, Robert.** Also writes as Robert Black; Chris Carlsen; Robert Faulcon. British. Born in Hythe, Kent, 2 August 1948. Educated at University College of North Wales, Bangor, 1967–70, B.Sc. (honours) in applied zoology 1970; London School of Hygiene and Tropical Medicine, 1970–71, M.Sc. in medical zoology 1971. Research student, Medical Research Council, London, 1971–74. Recipient: British Science Fiction Association award, 1985; World Fantasy Convention award, 1985. Agent: A.P. Watt Ltd., 26–28 Bedford Row, London WC1R4HL. Address: 54 Raleigh Road, London N8, England.

SCIENCE-FICTION PUBLICATIONS

Novels

*Eye among the Blind.* London, Faber, 1976; New York, Doubleday, 1977.
*Earthwind.* London, Faber, 1977; New York, Pocket Books, 1978.
*Where Time Winds Blow.* London, Faber, and New York, Pocket Books, 1982.
*Mythago Wood.* London, Gollancz, 1984; New York, Arbor House, 1985.
*The Emerald Forest* (novelization of screenplay). New York, Zoetrope, and London, Penguin, 1985.
*Lavondyss.* London, Gollancz, and New York, Morrow, 1988.
*The Bone Forest.* London, Grafton, 1991.

Short Stories

*In the Valley of the Statues.* London, Faber, 1982.

OTHER PUBLICATIONS

Novels

*Legend of the Werewolf* (novelization of screenplay; as Robert Black). London, Sphere, 1976.
*The Satanists* (novelization of screenplay; as Robert Black). London, Futura, 1978.
*Necromancer.* London, Futura, 1978; New York, Avon, 1980.
*Bulman.* London, Futura, 1984.
*One of Our Pigeons Is Missing.* London, Futura, 1985.

Novels as Chris Carlsen

Berserker series:
*Shadow of the Wolf.* London, Sphere, 1977.
*The Bull Chief.* London, Sphere, 1979.
*The Horned Warrior.* London, Sphere, 1979.

Novels as Robert Faulcon

Nighthunter series:
*The Stalking.* London, Arrow, 1983.
*The Talisman.* London, Arrow, 1983.
*The Ghost Dance.* London, Arrow, 1984.
*The Shrine.* London, Arrow, 1984.
*The Hexing.* London, Arrow, 1984.
*The Labyrinth.* New York, Berkley, 1988.

Other

*Alien Landscapes*, with Malcolm Edwards. London, Pierrot, 1979.
*Tour of the Universe*, with Malcolm Edwards. London, Pierrot, and New York, Mayflower, 1980.
*Magician*, with Malcolm Edwards. Limpsfield, Surrey, Dragon's World, 1982.
*Realms of Fantasy*, with Malcolm Edwards. Limpsfield, Surrey, Dragon's World, 1983.
*Lost Realms*, with Malcolm Edwards. Limpsfield, Surrey, Dragon's World, 1985.

Editor, with Christopher Priest, *Stars of Albion* (anthology of British science fiction). London, Pan, 1979.

Editor, with Christopher Evans, *Other Edens.* London, Unwin Hyman, 3 vols., 1987–89.

*

Robert Holdstock comments (1985):

I am usually inspired to write by the contemplation of far distant places and far distant times, be they future or past. I quite deliberately build into my work and my characters both a passionate awareness of past times and a strong sense of alienation. I relish alien landscapes, but am not concerned with futuristic man. My characters are humans of my own age, and I try to see them, and the exotic locations of time and space, to explore the boundaries and potentiality of man's awareness, of his senses, of his evolution. All my work is concerned with evolution, and with the persistence of memory, the continued presence—genetically, spiritually, passionately—of all of life in all of mankind.

* * *

Robert Holdstock's first novel, *Eye among the Blind*, established him as a promising writer with unique perspectives. A mysterious plague has swept through the inhabited worlds, and now threatens to wipe out the entire human race if a cure cannot be found. Throughout the universe, there is only one other known intelligent race, and it is perhaps on their strange world that a solution lies. But Ree'hdworld is not a simple world to understand. Although the comparatively primitive aliens have not been involved in overt conflict with humanity, strange things happen on their world. The course of evolution seems to be almost visibly altering as a reaction to the presence of visitors from another world, and, even more frightening, visions of mythological beasts seem to call into question the human view of reality.

*Earthwind* was not quite as successful, although the exotic settings and fantastic imagery of the first book are more than matched. The planet Aeran is also a primitive place, despite the arrival of humans who find a method of blending into the ecology of that world. The imagery tends to dominate a bit too much this time and the plot suffers.

This was not true of *Where Time Winds Blow*, Holdstock's most successful science-fiction novel. Time is a variable on a world where the winds blow down great rift valleys, transporting men and objects into time past or time future. In each case, detritus from some other time is left in their place, and some of these artifacts are valuable enough that a thriving industry exists consisting of daring adventurers who are willing to risk being whisked off through time in return for the financial rewards of discovering a valuable remnant of a previous wind.

*Where Time Winds Blow* is a complexly textured novel. One of the highest ranking officials on the world has gone mildly insane, and believes that the time winds are a device manipulated by a race of time travellers who operate just outside the bounds of human experience. A secretive infrastructure of the adventurers is cognizant of some secret knowledge which they will not share with the protagonists. The protagonists themselves are caught up in a mesh of ritual superstitions, defying logic. The landscapes are bizarre and fascinating, the characters fully developed, if somewhat bizarre.

Holdstock has also been active in sub-genre fiction. His novel of the supernatural, *Necromancer*, is at once a terrifying and enthralling fantasy adventure. A stone font in a British church turns out to be much more than it appears, for it was at one time the sacred object of a group of pagan worshippers of animistic spirits. Now it has reached out to imprison the soul of a modern youth, and his mother must overcome her own disbelief before she can work to abrogate its control. Under the pseudonym Robert Faulcon, Holdstock has written a series of adventures, called *Nighthunter*, of a man whose family has been disrupted by a cult of satanists, and who learns the arts of magic himself in order to take revenge. With the publication of *Mythago Wood* and its sequel *Lavondyss*, Holdstock's work jumped to a new level of excellence. A remote wooded area in England is the home of a number of figures out of legend, incarnate forces of nature, possessed of powers forgotten by modern man. Holdstock portrays this mythical world eloquently, mingling wonder, beauty, and terror in a fashion quite unique in literature.

There have been a handful of short stories, but Holdstock seems to require the room afforded by a novel to adequately develop his characters and create his settings. He has dabbled in the more action-oriented forms of heroic fantasy as well under the pseudonym Chris Carlsen, but these efforts pale beside his major works.

—Don D'Ammassa

---

**HOOVER, H(elen) M(ary).** American. Born in Stark County, Ohio, 5 April 1935. Educated at Louisville High School; Mount Union College, Alliance, Ohio; Los Angeles School of Nursing. Agent: Russell and Volkening, 50 West 29th Street, New York, New York 10001. Address: 9405 Ulysses Court, Burke, Virginia 22015, U.S.A.

SCIENCE-FICTION PUBLICATIONS

Novels (for children) (series: Morrow)

*Children of Morrow.* New York, Four Winds Press, 1973; London, Methuen, 1975.
*Treasures of Morrow.* New York, Four Winds Press, 1976.
*The Delikon.* New York, Viking Press, 1977; London, Methuen, 1978.
*The Rains of Eridan.* New York, Viking Press, 1977; London, Methuen, 1978.
*The Lost Star.* New York, Viking Press, 1979; London, Methuen, 1980.
*Return to Earth.* New York, Viking Press, 1980; London, Methuen, 1981.
*This Time of Darkness.* New York, Viking Press, 1980; London, Methuen, 1982.
*Another Heaven, Another Earth.* New York, Viking Press, 1981; London, Methuen, 1983.
*The Bell Tree.* New York, Viking Press, 1982.
*The Shepherd Moon.* New York, Viking Press, and London, Methuen, 1984.
*Orvis.* New York, Viking Kestrel, and London, Methuen, 1987.
*Away Is a Strange Place To Be.* New York, Dutton, 1990.

OTHER PUBLICATIONS

Other

*The Lion's Cub* (for children). New York, Four Winds Press, 1974.
*The Dawn Palace.* New York, Dutton, 1988.

*

Manuscript Collection: Kerlan Collection, University of Minnesota, Minneapolis.

Critical Study: *Science Fiction: The Mythos of a New Romance* by Janice Antczak, New York, Neal Schuman, 1985.

H.M. Hoover comments:

All fiction writers create singular worlds if they try, but in some respects fantastic worlds must be more real, more logically detailed and specific than straight fiction. When one writes about an alien world, it is just that to the reader. He or she must be told how and why it functions, and the telling must have consistency or all is lost. It must also be part of the story and not an inventory of facts. As a child I resented authors who ignored known facts (or facts *they* established within their fantasy) to make their plots work. I suspected them at first of ignorance and, later, of contempt for their readers. It is still done and I still have those suspicions.

* * *

H.M. Hoover consistently produces youth science fiction of very high quality, finding in SF a congenial and fertile ground for exploring those problems young people may face in less exotic environments: alienation from parents, feelings of isolation, feelings of being trapped or of being an anomalous creature out of sync with the Universe. Often Hoover's young people have special talents and sensitivities unappreciated by the adults around them.

So it is in *Children of Morrow* and its sequal *Treasures of Morrow.* Tia and Rabbit are telepaths ill-at-ease in their wasteland home, "The Base"; but a visit to the more advanced and enlightened community of Morrow proves ironically that home is not a simple matter to define. Anthropocentrism is examined in *The Rains of Eridan* when Theo, a young naturalist, and Karen, a child-orphan of conflict, team up first to survive, later to explore planetary lifeforms. Here and throughout Hoover's work, characters grope toward friendship across the generations and search for clues to enlighten their immediate situation and solve the larger mystery which imprisons those about them. Often the clear-eyed vision of children is instrumental in the process. The story of planetary exploration provides a background for their developing relationship. Karen learns to trust her new parent, and Theo learns that the child is skilled beyond her years both with laser gun and in the handling of fear and grief ("Like you I can shut part of my mind off till it's safe to think again.").

In *The Lost Star* the young hero is ignored by parents who have adopted emotional reserve as a policy for working together as off-Earth astronomers over long periods of time. Hoover's ability, born of youthful innocence, to recognize intuitively the intelligence and intrinsic worth of alien creatures is reminiscent of Ursula K. Le Guin's *The Word for World is Forest;* but Hoover's is a much lighter and more hopeful tale.

*This Time of Darkness* uses the familiar idea of the escape from an hermetic environment to explore in depth the struggle of children to receive the affection and acceptance which should be theirs by right. Ostracized for their ability to read, Amy and Axel are two children in a Big Brother-style underground hive community so benighted it has left scars on their bodies and has lost sight of any concept of a better world outside. Readers of SF will see in this story a children's literature counterpart of E.M. Forster's classic "The Machine Stops," and teachers may find it worthwhile for the hope it provides the abused child of the real world struggling for psychic survival. In *The Bell Tree* Hoover uses the device of archaeologists exploring an alien world to study the relationships of a young woman, her father, and her first boyfriend; and in *The Shepherd Moon* the loneliness of Merry, a 13-year-old of the 48th century, is set against a background of terrorist intrigue.

Hoover has written that science fiction's presentation of ideas as images makes it important as a teaching tool, since imaging is the very thinking process Einstein and other great thinkers use to generate new ideas. In Hoover's fiction we find provocative images of scientific concepts and a liberating experience for the human spirit.

—Thomas P. Dunn

---

**HOSKINS, Robert.** Also writes as Grace Corren; John Gregory; Susan Jennifer; Michael Kerr. American. Born in Lyons Falls, New York, 23 May 1933. Attended Albany State College for Teachers, New York, 1951–52. Worked in family business, 1952–64; attendant, Wassaic State School for the Retarded, New York, 1964–66; house parent, Brooklyn Home for Children, 1966–68; sub-agent, Scott Meredith Literary Agency, New York, 1967–68; senior editor, Lancer Books, New York, 1969–72. Since 1972, freelance writer. Address: c/o Harlequin Enterprises, 225 Duncan Mill Road, Don Mills, Ontario M3B 3K9, Canada.

## Science-Fiction Publications

Novels (series: Alnians)

*Evil in the Family* (as Grace Corren). New York, Lancer, 1972.
*The Shattered People.* New York, Doubleday, 1975.
*Master of the Stars* (Alnians). Toronto, Laser, 1976.
*To Control the Stars* (Alnians). New York, Ballantine, 1977.
*Tomorrow's Son.* New York, Doubleday, 1977.
*Jack-in-the-Box Planet* (for children) Philadelphia, Westminster Press, 1978.
*To Escape the Stars* (Alnians). New York, Ballantine, 1978.
*Legacy of the Stars* (as John Gregory). New York, Nordon, 1979; as Robert Hoskins, London, Hale, 1981.

## Other Publications

Novels

*The House of Counted Hatreds* (as Susan Jennifer). New York, Avon, 1973.
*Country of the Kind* (as Susan Jennifer). New York, Avon, 1975.
*The Gemini Run* (as Michael Kerr). New York, Charter, 1979.
*The Fury Bombs.* Toronto, Harlequin, 1983.

Novels as Grace Corren

*The Darkest Room.* New York, Lancer, 1969.
*A Place on Dark Island.* New York, Lancer, 1971.
*Mansions of Deadly Dreams.* New York, Popular Library, 1973.
*Dark Threshold.* New York, Popular Library, 1977.

*The Attic Child.* Los Angeles, Pinnacle, 1979.
*Survival Run* (novelization of screenplay). Los Angeles, Pinnacle, 1979.

Play

Television Play: *Birthday Party* (*Kojak* series), 1976.

Other

Editor, *First Step Outward.* New York, Dell, 1969.
Editor, *Infinity 1–5.* New York, Lancer, 5 vols., 1970–73.
Editor, *The Stars Around Us.* New York, New American Library, 1970.
Editor, *Swords Against Tomorrow.* New York, New American Library, 1970.
Editor, *Tomorrow 1.* New York, New American Library, 1971.
Editor, *The Far-Out People.* New York, New American Library, 1971.
Editor, *Wondermakers 1-2.* New York, Fawcett, 2 vols., 1972–74.
Editor, *Strange Tomorrows.* New York, Lancer, 1972.
Editor, *The Edge of Never.* New York, Fawcett, 1973.
Editor, *The Liberated Future.* New York, Fawcett, 1974.
Editor, *The Future Now.* New York, Fawcett, 1977.
Editor, *Against Tomorrow.* New York, Fawcett, 1979.

*

Robert Hoskins comments:

An unhappy, and fat, childhood in a small Adirondack football village turned me early to escapism. Comics led to pulps, to fandom, through the letter columns. After years of writing, I began selling an occasional story while still gathering pounds of rejection slips. It was not until I worked, first, for an agent, and then as an editor, that I learned the techniques of novel construction. Impossible though the idea is, I think all young writers should have a spell in both jobs. I consider myself strictly an entertainer; the one novel that is deliberately allegorical I have not at this date been able to sell. I've published 40 short stories, but find it easier to construct a novel. Once an idea comes, it seems to grow and grow.

* * *

Except for *Evil in the Family*, a gothic novel involving a time-travel fantasy, Robert Hoskins's major contribution to science fiction until 1975 was in writing, anthologizing and introducing short stories, and acting as general and then senior editor for Lancer Books' science fiction program. Although he has continued these activities, he has also added to them, expanding themes from his short stories into a series of novels which explore the inherent value of primitive versus technological man, the effects of free evolution versus outside interference and artificial control, the need for change and progress and the threat of regression without it, and the private, economic, and sociological reasons for galactic exploration. His works are always filled with action and adventure, monsters and barbaric peoples, advanced races and mercenary predators. As he notes in his introductions, man has had and always will have his heroes, and, while the nature of their heroism and the weapons which they wield in the name of progress and right may change, their essential questing spirit and dreams of glory do not.

In *The Shattered People* Hoskins gradually reveals the secret ties between a savage desert world of naked hunters armed with slings and stones and a highly technological nuclear civilization ruled by a tyrannical council contemptuous of life. In the first, vicious cats prowl in packs and sentient aliens (huge, bird-like creatures) keep watch, while in the other, urban rebels, aided by their "empress," a titular head virtually imprisoned in her own palace, meet in subterranean passages and plot to throw off their shackles. Mind-wipes and deportation thrust the strongest and most outspoken members of the urban world into the primitive one, until one man's psi powers enable him to regain his memory and bridge the gap between the two, merging the instinctive with the rational for an unbeatable pair.

*Tomorrow's Son*, set in the 23rd century, focuses on a geneticist and his android son, trapped in a rigid, genetically predetermined caste system, which they are determined to alter in order to assure a better world. On Earth the father engages in forbidden android research to help revitalize the swiftly deteriorating genetic make-up of humanity, while on a primitive planet, Karyllia, his son struggles to protect alien humanoids from repeating humanity's evolutionary mistakes, only to discover that he must protect them not only from themselves but from the fanaticism and destructiveness of his own world. Both men prove pawns of larger schemes to protect Karyllia from outside interference and to force humans to accept change—change that can revitalize a regressing world where average I.Q. decreases yearly and masses of subhumans are crowded into barracks, experience sex and violence vicariously, and drown their minds in joyjuice. The book includes bizarre beasts of burden, strange snake-lizards in swamps, and primitive tribal conflicts. As usual, Hoskins emphasizes the stench of primitive worlds and the lack of respect for life in both primitive and advanced societies.

In his trilogy (*Master of the Stars, To Control the Stars, To Escape the Stars*) Hoskins sets up a universal cycle of development and regression and postulates a series of stargates on most worlds, built by an ancient interstellar race; one sets the controls and steps into other worlds, some of which have regressed to the primitive while others have advanced to the stars. *Master of the Stars* focuses on the Alnians at the height of their development, struggling to avoid the contaminating barbarism of other worlds. *To Control the Stars* deals with an internal conflict in the Society for Humanoidic Studies, a conflict that affects the future of thousands of worlds and forces the central character to fight for his life from world to world and to seek answers among the Alnians (the only humanoids with a continuous history). The Society's original goal, observation of other worlds without interference, has been perverted into a lust for power, wealth, and exploitation that focuses on evolutionary control and forced rapid progress. There is much action—escape, recapture, romance. *To Escape the Stars* picks up thousands of years later when the Society has been reduced to a library cult devoutly recording galactic history. A scheme to plunder a rich, high-gravity world of rural innocents leads first to treachery, and then to a revived search for the Alnians and their master codex to the stargates. The main figure changes from a jaded and unscrupulous exploiter to a student of the universe, and discovers the dangers of isolation and of failure to accept change and conflict.

Hoskins argues man's need for challenge, discovery, and change, but at the same time suggests that no matter how far man progresses and how much he changes, he will always carry with him inescapable characteristics and instincts from his primitive past—instincts that help him survive and that, at times, impel him to heroic deeds.

—Gina Macdonald

---

**HOUGH, S.B.** *See* **GORDON, Rex.**

---

**HOWELLS, William Dean.** American. Born in Martin's Ferry, Ohio, 1 March 1837. Largely self-educated. Married Elinor Mead in 1862 (died 1910); one son and two daughters. Compositor, 1851–58, reporter, 1858–60, and news editor, 1860–61, *Ohio State Journal*, Columbus; also correspondent, in Columbus, for the Cincinnati *Gazette*, 1857; contributor to his father's newspaper, *The Sentinel*, Jefferson, Ohio, from 1852, and wrote for various national magazines from 1860; United States Consul in Venice, 1861–65; assistant editor, 1866–71, and editor-in-chief, 1871–81, *Atlantic Monthly*, Boston; Professor of Modern Languages, Harvard University, Cambridge, Massachusetts, 1869–71; wrote the "Editor's Study" column for *Harper's* magazine, 1886–92; co-editor, *Cosmopolitan* magazine, 1892. Recipient: American Academy Gold Medal, 1915. M.A.: Harvard University, Cambridge, Massachusetts, 1867; Litt. D.: Yale University, New Haven, Connecticut, 1901; Oxford University, 1904; Columbia University, New York, 1905; L.H.D.: Princeton University, New Jersey, 1912. President, American Academy, 1908–20. *Died 11 May 1920.*

### Science-Fiction Publications

#### Novels

*A Traveler from Altruria.* New York, Harper, and Edinburgh, Douglas, 1894; complete edition, edited by Clara Marburg Kirk and Rudolf Kirk, as *Letters of an Altrurian Traveller (1893–1894)*, Gainesville, Florida, Scholars' Facsimiles and Reprints, 1961.
*Through the Eye of a Needle.* New York and London, Harper, 1907.

### Other Publications

#### Novels

*Their Wedding Journey.* Boston, Osgood, 1872; Edinburgh, Douglas, 1882.
*A Chance Acquaintance.* Boston, Osgood, 1873; Edinburgh, Douglas, 1882.
*A Foregone Conclusion.* Boston, Osgood, 1874.
*The Lady of Aroostook.* Boston, Houghton Osgood, 1879; Edinburgh, Douglas, 2 vols., 1882.
*The Undiscovered Country.* Boston, Houghton Mifflin, and London, Sampson Low, 1880.
*Doctor Breen's Practice.* Boston, Osgood, 1881; Edinburgh, Douglas, 1883.
*A Modern Instance.* Edinburgh, Douglas, 2 vols., 1882; Boston, Osgood, 1 vol., 1882.
*A Woman's Reason.* Boston, Osgood, and Edinburgh, Douglas, 1883.
*The Rise of Silas Lapham.* Boston, Ticknor, and Edinburgh, Douglas, 1885.
*Indian Summer.* Boston, Ticknor, and Edinburgh, Douglas, 1886.
*The Minister's Charge: or, The Apprenticeship of Lemuel Barker.* Edinburgh, Douglas, 1886; Boston, Ticknor, 1887.
*April Hopes.* Edinburgh, Douglas, 1887; New York, Harper, 1888.
*Annie Kilburn.* Edinburgh, Douglas, 1888; New York, Harper, 1889.
*A Hazzard of New Fortunes.* New York, Harper, and Edinburgh, Douglas, 1889.
*The Shadow of a Dream.* Edinburgh, Douglas, and New York, Harper, 1890.
*An Imperative Duty.* New York, Harper, and Edinburgh, Douglas, 1891.
*Mercy.* Edinburgh, Douglas, 1892; as *The Quality of Mercy*, New York, Harper, 1892.
*The World of Chance.* Edinburgh, Douglas, and New York, Harper, 1893.
*The Coast of Bohemia.* New York, Harper, 1893.
*The Day of Their Wedding.* New York, Harper, 1896.
*A Parting and a Meeting.* New York, Harper, 1896; with *The Day of Their Wedding*, as *Idyls in Drab*, Edinburgh, Douglas, 1896.
*The Landlord at Lion's Head.* Edinburgh, Douglas, and New York, Harper, 1897.
*The Open-Eyed Conspiracy.* New York, Harper, 1897; Edinburgh, Douglas, 1898.
*The Story of a Play.* New York and London, Harper, 1898.
*Ragged Lady.* New York, Harper, 1899.
*Their Silver Wedding Journey.* London and New York, Harper, 1899; abridged edition, as *Hither and Thither in Germany*, New York and London, Harper, 1920.
*The Kentons.* New York and London, Harper, 1902.
*The Flight of Pony Baker: A Boy's Town Story.* New York and London, Harper, 1902.
*Letters Home.* New York and London, Harper, 1903.
*The Son of Royal Langbrith.* New York and London, Harper, 1904.
*Miss Bellard's Inspiration.* New York and London, Harper, 1905.
*Fennel and Rue.* New York and London, Harper, 1908.
*New Leaf Mills.* New York and London, Harper, 1913.
*The Leatherwood God.* New York, Century, and London, Jenkins, 1916.
*The Vacation of the Kelwyns.* New York and London, Harper, 1920.
*Mrs. Farrell.* New York and London, Harper, 1921.
*Novels 1875–1886.* New York, Literary Classics of the United States, 1982.

#### Short Stories

*A Fearful Responsibility and Other Stories.* Boston, Osgood, 1881; as *A Fearful Responsibility and Tonnelli's Marriage*, Edinburgh, Douglas, 1882.
*A Pair of Patient Lovers.* New York and London, Harper, 1901.
*Questionable Shapes.* New York and London, Harper, 1903.
*Between the Dark and the Daylight: Romances.* New York, Harper, 1907; London, Harper, 1912.

#### Plays

*Samson*, adaptation of the play by Ippolito D'Aste (produced on tour, 1874; New York, 1889). New York, Koppel, 1889.
*The Parlor Car.* Boston, Osgood, 1876; with *A Counterfeit Presentment*, Edinburgh, Douglas, 1882.
*Out of the Question.* Boston, Osgood, 1877; with *At the Sign of the Savage*, Edinburgh, Douglas, 1882.
*A Counterfeit Presentment* (produced Cincinnati, 1877; revised version, produced Detroit, 1877). Boston, Osgood, 1877; with *The Parlor Car*, Edinburgh, Douglas, 1882.
*Yorick's Love*, adaptation of a play by Manuel Tamayo y Baus (as *A New Play*, produced Cleveland, 1878; as *Yorick's Love*,

produced New York, 1880; London, 1884). Included in *Complete Plays*, 1960.

*The Sleeping-Car* (produced New York, 1887). Boston, Osgood, 1883; in *Minor Dramas*, 1907.

*The Register*. Boston, Osgood, 1884; in *Minor Dramas*, 1907.

*The Elevator* (produced Streator, Illinois, 1885). Boston, Osgood, 1885; in *Minor Dramas*, 1907.

*The Garroters* (produced New York, 1886). New York, Harper, 1886; Edinburgh, Douglas, 1897.

*A Foregone Conclusion*, with William Poel, adaptation of the novel by Howells (produced New York, 1886). Included in *Complete Plays*, 1960.

*Colonel Sellers as a Scientist*, with Mark Twain, adaptation of the novel *The Gilded Age* by Twain and Charles Dudley Warner (produced New Brunswick, New Jersey, and New York, 1887). Included in *Complete Plays*, 1960.

*The Mouse-Trap* (produced New York, 1887–88; Edinburgh, 1897). Included in *The Mouse-Trap and Other Farces*, 1889; published separately, Edinburgh, Douglas, 1897.

*A Sea-Change; or, Love's Stowaway: A Lyricated Farce*, music by George Henschel. Boston, Ticknor, 1888.

*The Mouse-Trap and Other Farces* (includes *A Likely Story, Five O'Clock Tea, The Garroters*). New York, Harper, 1889.

*The Sleeping-Car and Other Farces* (includes *The Parlor Car, The Register, The Elevator*). Boston, Houghton Mifflin, 1889.

*The Albany Depot*. New York, Harper, 1892; Edinburgh, Douglas, 1897.

*A Letter of Introduction*. New York, Harper, 1892; Edinburgh, Douglas, 1897.

*The Unexpected Guests*. New York, Harper, 1893; Edinburgh, Douglas, 1897.

*Evening Dress* (produced New York, 1894). New York, Harper, 1893; Edinburgh, Douglas, 1897.

*Bride Roses* (produced New York 1894). Boston, Houghton Mifflin, 1900; in *Minor Dramas*, 1907.

*A Dangerous Ruffian* (produced London, 1895).

*A Previous Engagement*. New York, Harper, 1897; in *Minor Dramas*, 1907.

*Room Forty-Five*. Boston, Houghton Mifflin, 1900; in *Minor Dramas*, 1907.

*An Indian Giver*. Boston, Houghton Mifflin, 1900; in *Minor Dramas*, 1907.

*The Smoking Car*. Boston, Houghton Mifflin, 1900; in *Minor Dramas*, 1907.

*Minor Dramas*. Edinburgh, Douglas, 2 vols., 1907.

*The Mother and the Father*. New York and London, Harper, 1909.

*Parting Friends*. New York and London, Harper, 1911.

*The Night Before Christmas, and Self-Sacrifice*, in *The Daughter of the Storage and Other Things in Prose and Verse*, 1916.

*The Complete Plays of William Dean Howells*, edited by Walter J. Meserve. New York, New York University Press, 1960.

Verse

*Poems of Two Friends*, with John J. Piatt. Columbus, Ohio, Follett Foster, 1860.

*No Love Lost: A Romance of Travel*. New York, Putnam, 1869.

*Poems*. Boston, Osgood, 1873.

*Stops of Various Quills*. New York, Harper, 1895.

*The Mulberries in Pay's Garden*. North Bend, Ohio, Scott, 1907.

Other

*Lives and Speeches of Abraham Lincoln and Hannibal Hamlin*. Columbus, Ohio, Follett Foster, 1860.

*Venetian Life*. London, Trubner, and New York, Hurd and Houghton, 1866; revised edition, Boston, Osgood, 1872; Boston, Houghton Mifflin, 2 vols., and London, Constable, 2 vols., 1907.

*Italian Journeys*. New York, Hurd and Houghton, 1867; revised edition, Boston, Osgood, 1872; London, Heinemann, and Boston, Houghton Mifflin, 1901.

*Suburban Sketches*. New York, Hurd and Houghton, 1871; revised edition, Boston, Osgood, 1872; abridged edition, as *A Day's Pleasure*, Osgood, 1876.

*Sketch of the Life and Character of Rutherford B. Hayes*. New York, Hurd and Houghton, 1876.

*A Little Girl among the Old Masters*. Boston, Osgood, 1884; London, Trubner, n.d.

*Three Villages*. Boston, Osgood, 1884.

*Tuscan Cities*. Boston, Ticknor, and Edinburgh, Douglas, 1885.

*Modern Italian Poets: Essays and Versions*. New York, Harper, and Edinburgh, Douglas, 1887.

*A Boy's Town* (for children). New York, Harper, 1890.

*Criticism and Fiction*. New York, Harper, and London, Osgood McIlvaine, 1891.

*A Little Swiss Sojourn*. New York, Harper, 1892.

*Christmas Every Day and Other Stories Told for Children*. New York, Harper, 1892.

*My Year in a Log Cabin*. New York, Harper, 1893.

*My Literary Passions*. New York, Harper, 1895.

*Impressions and Experiences*. New York, Harper, and Edinburgh, Douglas, 1896.

*Stories of Ohio*. New York, American Book Company, 1897.

*Doorstep Acquaintance and Other Sketches*. Boston, Houghton Mifflin, 1900.

*Literary Friends and Acquaintance: A Personal Retrospect of American Authorship*. New York and London, Harper, 1900.

*Heroines of Fiction*. New York and London, Harper, 2 vols., 1901.

*Literature and Life: Studies*. New York and London, Harper, 1902.

*London Films*. New York and London, Harper, 1905.

*Certain Delightful English Towns*. New York and London, Harper, 1906.

*Roman Holidays and Others*. New York and London, Harper, 1908.

*Seven English Cities*. New York and London, Harper, 1909.

*My Mark Twain: Reminiscences and Criticisms*. New York and London, Harper, 1910.

*Imaginary Interviews*. New York and London, Harper, 1910.

*Familiar Spanish Travels*. New York and London, Harper, 1913.

*The Seen and Unseen at Stratford-on-Avon: A Fantasy*. New York and London, Harper, 1914.

*The Daughter of the Storage and Other Things in Prose and Verse*. New York and London, Harper, 1916.

*Years of My Youth* (autobiography). New York, Harper, 1916; London, Harper, 1917.

*Life in Letters of William Dean Howells*, edited by Mildred Howells. New York, Doubleday, 2 vols., 1928; London, Heinemann, 1 vol., 1929.

*Representative Selections*, edited by Clara Marburg Kirk and Rudolf Kirk. New York, American Book Company, 1950.

*Selected Writings*, edited by Henry Steele Commager. New York, Random House, 1950.

*Prefaces to Contemporaries (1882–1920)*, edited by George Arms, William M. Gibson, and Frederic C. Marston, Jr. Gainesville, Florida, Scholars' Facsmilies and Reprints, 1957.
*Criticism and Fiction and Other Essays*, edited by Clara Marburg Kirk and Rudolf Kirk. New York, New York University Press, 1959.
*Mark Twain-Howells Letters: The Correspondence of Samuel L. Clemens and William Dean Howells 1872–1910*, edited by Henry Nash Smith and William M. Gibson. Cambridge, Massachusetts, Harvard University Press, 2 vols., 1960; abridged edition, as *Selected Mark Twain-Howells Letters*, 1967.
*Discovery of a Genius: William Dean Howells and Henry James*, edited by Albert Mordell. New York, Twayne, 1961.
*Selected Edition*, edited by Ronald Gottesman. Bloomington, Indiana University Press, 1968.
*Howells as Critic*, edited by Edwin H. Cady. London, Routledge, 1973.
*The John Hay-Howells Letters: The Correspondence of John Milton Hay and William Dean Howells 1861–1905*, edited by George Monteiro and Brenda Murphy. Boston, Twayne, 1980.

Editor, *Three Years in Chili*, by Mrs. C.B. Merwin. Columbus, Ohio, Follett Foster, 1861; as *Chili through American Spectacles*, New York, Bradburn, n.d.
Editor, *Choice Autobiographies*. Boston, Osgood, 6 vols., 1877, and Houghton Osgood, 2 vols., 1878.
Editor, with Thomas Sergeant Perry, *Library of Universal Adventure by Sea and Land*. New York, Harper, 1888.
Editor, *Mark Twain's Library of Humor*. New York, Webster, 1888.
Editor, *Poems of George Pellew*. Boston, Clarke, 1892.
Editor, *Recollections of Life in Ohio from 1813 to 1840*, by William Cooper Howells. Cincinnati, Clarke, 1895.
Editor, with Russell Sturgis, *Florence in Art and Literature*. Philadelphia, Booklovers Library, 1901.
Editor, with Henry Mills Alden, *Harper's Novelettes*. New York and London, Harper, 8 vols., 1906–08.
Editor, *The Great Modern American Short Stories: An Anthology*. New York, Boni and Liveright, 1920.
Editor, *Don Quixote*, by Cervantes, translated by Charles Jarvis. New York and London, Harper, 1923.

Translator, *Venice, Her Art-Treasures and Historical Associations: A Guide*, by Adalbert Müller. Venice, Münster, 1864.

*

Bibliography: *A Bibliography of William Dean Howells* by William M. Gibson and George Arms, New York, New York Public Library, 1948; in *Bibliography of American Literature 4* by Jacob Blanck, New Haven, Connecticut, Yale University Press, 1963.

Critical Studies (selection): *The Road to Realism: The Early Years, 1837– 1885, of William Dean Howells* and *The Realist at War: The Mature Years, 1885–1920, of William Dean Howells* by Edwin H. Cady, Syracuse, New York, Syracuse University Press, 2 vols., 1956–58; *Howells: His Life and World* by Van Wyck Brooks, New York, Dutton, 1959; *Howells: A Century of Criticism* edited by Kenneth E. Eble, Dallas, Southern Methodist University Press, 1962; *William Dean Howells, Traveler from Altruria 1889–1894*, New Brunswick, New Jersey, Rutgers University Press, 1962, and *W.D. Howells and Art in His Time*, Rutgers University Press, 1965, both by Clara Marburg Kirk, and *William Dean Howells* by Clara Marburg Kirk and Rudolf Kirk, New York, Twayne, 1962; *The Immense Complex Drama: The World and Art of the Howells Novel* by George C. Carrington, Jr., Columbus, Ohio State University Press, 1966; *The Literary Realism of William Dean Howells* by William McMurray, Carbondale, Southern Illinois University Press, 1967; *William D. Howells* by William M. Gibson, Minneapolis, University of Minnesota Press, 1967; *The Achievement of William Dean Howells: A Reinterpretation* by Kermit Vanderbilt, Princeton, New Jersey, Princeton University Press, 1968; *William Dean Howells: The Friendly Eye* by Edward Wagenknecht, New York, Oxford University Press, 1969; *William Dean Howells: An American Life* by Kenneth S. Lynn, New York, Harcourt Brace, 1971; *The Realism of William Dean Howells 1898–1920* by George N. Bennett, Nashville, Vanderbilt University Press, 1973; *Critics on William Dean Howells* edited by Paul A. Escholz, Coral Gables, Florida, University of Miami Press, 1975.

* * *

William Dean Howells made a major contribution to utopian literature by inventing Altruria, a vision of an America which practiced what it preached in the Declaration of Independence. *A Traveler from Alturia*, "Letters of an Alturian Traveler" (in *Cosmopolitan*, 1893–94), and *Through the Eye of a Needle* make up the Altrurian romances, Howells's statement on socialism and civil rights.

Edward Bellamy and Ignatius Donnelly had recently caught attention through social protest fiction in *Looking Backward, Equality*, and *Caesar's Column*. In a time of depression, strikes, Populism, and social change, Howells chose to point to a better society through a visit by Aristides (after Aristides the Just) Homos from an imaginary island in the Aegean where law, government, and social relations were based on altruism, a term adopted from Auguste Comte's *System of Positive Policy*. Howells imitated Oliver Goldsmith's *Citizen of the World* papers, introducing the outsider who asks pointed questions and marvels at peculiar customs. Altruria has much in common with Bacon's New Atlantis and More's Utopia and points toward Skinner's Walden II. Mr. Twelvemough, a well-known novelist who narrates *A Traveler from Altruria*, represents the American's attitude toward Homos. He disapproves of his fondness toward the lower classes. "Letters" is composed of five letters from Homos to his friend Cyril at home, openly critical of what he sees. Homos refers to New York as Babylon and to Americans as lost in the dark ages. *Through the Eye of a Needle* is also narrated by letters, some by Homos and the rest by Eveleth Strange, a beautiful widow who marries (after great conflict) Homos and moves to Alturia. Although the Altrurian works seem dated, they are important examples of attempts at social reform by an influential author.

—Mary S. Weinkauf

---

**HOYLE, Fred and Geoffrey.** British. **HOYLE, Fred:** Born in Bingley, Yorkshire, 24 June 1915. Educated at Bingley Grammar School; Emmanuel College, Cambridge (Mayhew Prizeman, 1936; Smith's Prizeman, 1938; Goldsmith Exhibitioner; Senior Exhibitioner of the Royal Commission for the Exhibition of 1851), mathematical tripos 1936, M.A. 1939. Served in the Admiralty, London, 1939–45. Married Barbara Clark in 1939; one son, Geoffrey Hoyle, and one daughter. Research Fellow, St. John's College, 1939–72, University Lecturer in Mathematics,

1945–58, Plumian Professor of Astronomy and Experimental Philosophy, 1958–72, and Director, Institute of Theoretical Astronomy, 1966–72, Cambridge University. Visiting Professor, 1953, 1954, 1956, Fairchild Scholar, 1974–75, and since 1963, Associate in Physics, California Institute of Technology, Pasadena. Staff member, Mount Wilson and Palomar observatories, California, 1957–62; Professor of Astronomy, Royal Institution, London, 1969–72; White Professor, Cornell University, Ithaca, New York, 1972–78. Honorary Research Professor, University of Manchester, since 1972, and University College, Cardiff, since 1975; since 1973, Honorary Fellow, St. John's College, Cambridge; since 1984, Honorary Fellow, Emmanuel College, Cambridge. Member, Science Research Council, 1968–72. Recipient: Royal Astronomical Society Gold Medal, 1968; Kalinga prize, 1968; Astronomical Society of the Pacific Bruce Medal, 1970, and Klumpke-Roberts award, 1977; Royal Society Medal, 1974. Guest of Honor, Frontiers of Astronomy Symposium, Venice, 1975. Sc.D.: University of East Anglia, Norwich, 1967; D.Sc.: University of Leeds, 1969; University of Bradford, 1975; University of Newcastle, 1976. Fellow, 1957, and Vice-President, 1969–71, Royal Society; Honorary member, American Academy of Arts and Sciences, 1964, Royal Irish Academy, 1977, and Mark Twain Society, 1978. Foreign member, American Philosophical Society, 1980. Foreign Associate, National Academy of Sciences (USA), 1969; president, Royal Astronomical Society, 1971–73. Knighted, 1972. Address: c/o Royal Society, 6 Carlton House Terrace, London SW1Y 5AG, England. **HOYLE, Geoffrey:** Born in Scunthorpe, Lincolnshire, 12 January 1942; son of Fred Hoyle. Educated at Bryanston School, Blandford Forum, Dorset, 1955–59; St. John's College, Cambridge, 1961–62. Married Valerie Jane Coope in 1971. Worked in documentary film production, 1963–67. Address: 8 Milner Road Bournemouth BH4 8AO, England.

SCIENCE-FICTION PUBLICATIONS

Novels

*Fifth Planet*. London, Heinemann, and New York, Harper, 1963.
*Rockets in Ursa Major*. London, Heinemann, and New York, Harper, 1969.
*Seven Steps to the Sun*. London, Heinemann, and New York, Harper, 1970.
*The Molecule Men and The Monster of Loch Ness: Two Short Novels*. London, Heinemann, and New York, Harper, 1971.
*The Inferno*. London, Heinemann, and New York, Harper, 1973.
*Into Deepest Space*. New York, Harper, 1974; London, Heinemann, 1975.
*The Incandescent Ones*. London, Heinemann, and New York, Harper, 1977.
*The Westminster Disaster*. London, Heinemann, and New York, Harper, 1978.
*The Energy Pirate* (for children). Loughborough, Ladybird, 1982.
*The Giants of Universal Park* (for children). Loughborough, Ladybird, 1982.
*The Frozen Planet of Azuron* (for children). Loughborough, Ladybird, 1982.
*The Planet of Death* (for children). Loughborough, Ladybird, 1982.

Novels by Fred Hoyle

*The Black Cloud*. London, Heinemann, and New York, Harper, 1957.
*Ossian's Ride*. London, Heinemann, and New York, Harper, 1959.
*A for Andromeda* (novelization of TV serial), with John Elliot. London Souvenir Press, and New York, Harper, 1962.
*Andromeda Breakthrough* (novelization of TV serial), with John Elliot. London, Souvenir Press, and New York, Harper, 1964.
*October the First Is Too Late*. London, Heinemann, and New York, Harper, 1966.
*Comet Halley*. London, Joseph, and New York, St. Martin's Press, 1985.

Short Stories by Fred Hoyle

*Element 79*. New York, New American Library, 1967.

OTHER PUBLICATIONS

Other

*Commonsense in Nuclear Energy*. London, Heinemann, and San Francisco, Freeman, 1980.

OTHER PUBLICATIONS by Fred Hoyle

Plays

*Rockets in Ursa Major* (for children: produced London, 1962).

Television Plays (with John Elliot): *A for Andromeda* serial, 1961; *The Andromeda Breakthrough* serial, 1962.

Other

*Some Recent Researches in Solar Physics*. Cambridge, University Press, 1949.
*The Nature of the Universe: A Series of Broadcast Lectures*. Oxford, Blackwell, 1950; New York, Harper, 1951; revised edition, 1960.
*A Decade of Decision*. London, Heinemann, 1953.
*Frontiers of Atronomy*. London, Heinemann, and New York, Harper, 1955.
*Man and Materialism*. New York, Harper, 1956; London, Allen and Unwin, 1957.
*Astronomy*. London, Macdonald, and New York, Doubleday, 1962.
*A Contradiction in the Argument of Malthus* (lecture). Hull, University of Hull, 1963.
*Star Formation*. London, Her Majesty's Stationery Office, 1963.
*Of Men and Galaxies*. Seattle, University of Washington Press, 1964; London, Heinemann, 1965.
*Nucleosynthesis in Massive Stars and Supernovae*, with William A. Fowler. Chicago, University of Chicago Press, 1965.
*Encounter with the Future*. New York, Simon and Schuster, 1965.
*The Asymmetry of Time* (lecture). Canberra, Australian National University, 1965.
*Galaxies, Nuclei, and Quasars*. New York, Harper, 1965; London, Heinemann, 1966.

*Man in the Universe*. New York, Columbia University Press, 1966.
*The New Face of Science*. Cleveland, World, 1971.
*From Stonehenge to Modern Cosmology*. San Francisco, Freeman, 1972.
*Nicolaus Copernicus: An Essay on His Life and Work*. London, Heinemann, and New York, Harper, 1973.
*Action-at-a-Distance in Physics and Cosmology*, with J.V. Narlikar. San Francisco, Freeman, 1974.
*Astronomy and Cosmology: A Modern Course*. San Francisco, Freeman, 1975.
*Astronomy Today*. London, Heinemann, 1975; as *Highlights in Astronomy*, San Francisco, Freeman, 1975.
*Ten Faces of the Universe*. London, Heinemann, and San Francisco, Freeman, 1977.
*On Stonehenge*. London, Heinemann, and San Francisco, Freeman, 1977.
*Energy or Extinction? The Case for Nuclear Energy*. London, Heinemann, 1977.
*The Cosmogony of the Solar System*. Cardiff, University College Press, 1978; Short Hills, New Jersey, Enslow, 1979.
*Lifecloud: The Origin of Life in the Universe*, with Chandra Wickramasinghe. London, Dent, 1978; New York, Harper, 1979.
*Diseases from Space*, with Chandra Wickramasinghe. London, Dent, 1979; New York, Harper, 1980.
*The Physics-Astronomy Frontier*, with J.V. Narlikar. San Francisco, Freeman, 1980.
*Steady-State Cosmology Revisited*. Cardiff, University College Press, 1980.
*The Relation of Astronomy to Biology*. Cardiff, University College Press, 1980.
*Ice: The Ultimate Human Catastrophe*. New York, Hutchinson, and New York, Continuum, 1981.
*The Quasar Controversy Resolved*. Cardiff, University College Press, 1981.
*Evolution from Space*, with Chandra Wickramasinghe. London, Dent, 1981; New York, Simon and Schuster, 1982.
*Space Travellers, The Bringers of Life*, with Chandra Wickramasinghe, edited by Barbara Hoyle. Cardiff, University College Press, and Hillside, New Jersey, Enslow, 1981.
*Facts and Dogmas in Cosmology and Elsewhere* (Rede Lecture). Cambridge, University Press, 1982.
*Efroms and Other Papers on the Origin of Life*. Hillside, New Jersey, Enslow, 1982.
*The Universe According to Hoyle*. Hillside, New Jersey, Enslow, 1982.
*The Intelligent Universe: A New View of Creation and Evolution*. London, Joseph, 1983; New York, Holt Rinehart, 1984.
*Flight*. Loughborough, Ladybird, 1984.
*Archaeopteryx, the Primordial Bird: A Case of Fossil Forgery*, with Chandra Wickramasinghe. Swansea, Christopher Davies, 1986.
*The Small World of Fred Hoyle* (autobiography). London, Joseph, 1986.
*Cosmic Life-Forces*, with Chandra Wickramasinghe. London, Dent, 1988; New York, Paragon House, 1990.

Other Publications by Geoffrey Hoyle

Other

*2010: Living in the Future* (for children). London, Heinemann, 1972; New York, Parents' Magazine Press, 1974.
*Disaster* (for children). London, Heinemann, 1975.
*Ask Me Why*, with Janice Robertson. London, Severn House, 1976.

* * *

If there is a single theme common to the work of noted astronomer Fred Hoyle, the bulk of whose fiction was a collaborative effort with his son Geoffrey, it is that the salvation of humanity lies not in our political institutions, but in the free operation and far-ranging minds of the scientific community. A more welcome concept for science-fiction readers would be hard to imagine, and given his own background in the scientific community, it is unsurprising that he should be so partisan.

Perhaps coincidentally, Hoyle's three most interesting novels were the ones written before he began collaborating, first with John Elliot, then with son Geoffrey. *The Black Cloud* is a novel of world catastrophe: a cloud of immense proportions enters our solar system, cutting off the sunlight and dooming the human race to extinction. One scientist has an inspiration; the cloud itself may well be a living entity, and if some way can be found to communicate, doom may be averted. He mobilizes an effort in short order, and in the waning hours achieves success. The attraction of the novel was not only its melodramatic plot, but Hoyle's infectious fascination with the mysteries and potential of outer space.

In *Ossian's Ride*, the protagonist is a scientist recruited as a spy to infiltrate a secretive research establishment in Ireland. It doesn't take long for him to realize there is an undertext to what he is being told, but his efforts to investigate further alert his quarries to their danger. After a thrilling series of chases and escapes, he and the reader learn that technological information from another world has been transmitted to Earth, and the scientists who received it are making great efforts to prevent it from falling into the wrong hands, specifically those of the government.

Unprecedented solar emanations interfere with the normal flow of time in *October the First Is Too Late*, the most ambitious of Hoyle's solo novels. Different parts of the world are thrown forward or backward in time. Once again, the only possible salvation is if scientists can somehow find a way to counteract the effect and restore time's equilibrium.

In the early 1960's, Hoyle worked on a BBC television series, and he produced two subsequent novelizations in collaboration with John Elliot, *A for Andromeda* and *Andromeda Breakthrough.* This was the dark other side of the theme of *Ossian's Ride;* an intelligent species is beaming information to Earth, but not benevolently in this instance. Rather, they are using human scientists as pawns in their plan to launch an invasion of the Earth, implanting their strategy secretly in the programming of a supercomputer constructed under their tutelage. Thwarted in the first volume, they use a robot still under their control to pursue their quest in the second, with an equal lack of success.

*Fifth Planet*, representing the first appearance of Geoffrey as co-writer, is a similar invasion story, this time from a mysterious planet passing through the far reaches of our system. The aliens in this case are capable of mimicking real human beings and supplanting them, although their counterfeit is inept enough to alert the protagonist to what is happening. Once again, the answer is a scientific one, rather than ineffectual government action. Another alien power menaces Earth in *Rockets in Ursa Major*, but the danger is so intellectualized, there is little suspense in this lackluster effort.

A man finds himself propelled ten years into the future in *Seven Steps to the Sun*, an occasionally interesting but very slow-paced novel. *The Inferno* is a return to the world catastrophe story, this time resulting from the advent of a quasar close enough to cause disastrous climatological effects on Earth. It's a more convincing story than most of the later books, with a strong but believable protagonist bringing order out of chaos, but there was little to differentiate it from a large number of similar novels. *Into Deepest Space*, the sequel to *Rockets in Ursa Major*, is a space opera rendered almost unreadable by intrusive discourses on the details of life in space.

A different sort of alien invasion provides the theme in *The Incandescent Ones.* Alien star travellers offer humanity the benefits of their superscience, but there is a hidden cost that may be too high to pay. This is one of the few occasions where the Hoyles imply that "there are some things man was not meant to know," at least during this stage of human development. Unfortunately, the novel is predictable and slow moving, often because of the heavy-handed way in which the authors preach their message. *The Westminster Disaster* was more of a contemporary spy thriller with science fiction overtones, a power struggle between world powers with terrifying consequences for England. Once again, the Hoyles use the opportunity to point out the danger of putting too much trust in government institutions. Unlike the novels that immediately preceded it, the plot and narrative move quite fluidly in this case, although the nature of the political struggle is somewhat dated.

Fred Hoyle's solo shorter fiction was collected in *Element 79*, but although some of these provide interesting insights into Hoyle's view of the world, none are of particular note as fiction. He and Geoffrey collaborated on two novellas, "The Molecule Men" and "The Monster of Loch Ness," both of which are of some merit. The former is an almost lighthearted scientific mystery, the latter a reasonably suspenseful story of Nessie.

—Don D'Ammassa

---

**HOYLE, Trevor.** British. Born in Rochdale, Lancashire, 25 February 1940. Educated at Rochdale Grammar School, 1951–57. Agent: Sheil Land Associates Ltd., 43 Doughty Street, London WC1N 2LF. Address: 34 Cedar Lane, Newhey, Rochdale, Lancashire OL16 4LQ, England.

### Science-Fiction Publications

Novels (series: Blake's Seven; Q)

*Q: Seeking the Mythical Future.* London, Panther, 1977; New York, Ace, 1982.
*Q: Through the Eye of Time.* London, Panther, 1977; New York, Ace, 1982.
*Blake's Seven.* London, Sphere, 1977; Secaucus, New Jersey, Lyle Stuart, 1988.
*Q: The Gods Look Down.* London, Panther, 1978; New York, Ace, 1982.
*Blake's Seven: Project Avalon.* London, Arrow, 1979; Secaucus, New Jersey, Lyle Stuart, 1988.
*Earth Cult.* London, Panther, 1979; as *This Sentient Earth*, New York, Zebra, 1979.
*Blake's Seven: Scorpio Attack.* London, BBC, 1981; Secaucus, New Jersey, Lyle Stuart, 1988.
*The Last Gasp.* New York, Crown, 1983; London, Sphere, 1984.

### Other Publications

Novels

*The Relatively Constant Copywriter.* Manchester, Northern Writers, 1972.
*Rule of Night.* London, Futura, 1975.
*The Sexless Spy.* London, Sphere, 1977.
*The Svengali Plot.* London, Sphere, 1978.
*The Man Who Travelled on Motorways.* London, Calder, 1979; New York, Riverrun, 1982.
*The Stigma.* London, Sphere, 1980.
*Vail.* London, Calder, 1984; New York, Riverrun, 1985.
*K.I.D.S.* London, Sphere, 1987; New York, Berkley, 1990.

Plays

Television Plays: *Blake's Seven: Ultraworld*, 1980; *Whatever Happened to the Heroes?*, 1982.

Radio Plays: *Conflagration*, 1991; *Gigo*, 1991.

*

Manuscript Collection: Rochdale Reference Library, Lancashire.

* * *

Trevor Hoyle's well known "Q" series consists of three books: *Seeking the Mythical Future, Through the Eye of Time*, and *The Gods Look Down.* Christian Queghan is a Myth Technologist who investigates possible pasts and futures in a discipline that assures all realities are equally probable. In *Seeking the Mythical Future* Queghan is inserted into a parallel universe where humans and dinosaurs exist together, where personal beliefs are rigidly controlled, and where Psychological Concentration Camps exist for those who will not conform to normalcy. The satire on scientific methods and bureaucratic bungling makes the book lively yet profoundly serious.

*Through the Eye of Time* is the most ambitious book in the series. The scientists of Queghan's Earth IVn, a terraformed version of Old Earth, are working on a project to reconstruct a human brain. The identity chosen: Adolf Hitler. Queghan involves himself in the project when he finds the computer exchanging data by coincidence. That coincidence convinces Queghan that an alternate reality—where Germany developed the Atomic Bomb first—is undermining the reality of his Earth's reality. Only insertion into that alternate reality can prevent the disaster that threatens the spacetime continuum. Hoyle captures the personality of Hitler beautifully and creates a unique, sinister character in Dr. Theodor Morell, personal physician to Hitler.

The concluding volume is less successful. Queghan joins forces with Dr. Francis Dagon to decipher primitive texts from ancient Earth through Myth Technology. The computer describes the legendary Ark of the Covenant in the form of blueprints for an existing technology. Queghan is sure Dagon is using his research findings in an attempt to change history. Only Queghan's power to insert himself into alternate realities can stop Dagon's plans to alter the past. The idea is clever, but the book's conclusion is too clichéd, too predictable. However, the "Q" series is one of the best extended explorations of alternative realities in science fiction.

Hoyle's best book is an environmental disaster novel, *The Last Gasp.* Earth is totally polluted: the microscopic plant life in the oceans is dying, causing the beginning of the destruction of the food chain. At the same time, the super-powers plan to fight their next war with new, deadly forms of environmental warfare. British marine biologist Gavin Chase and a team of scientists realize the Earth is doomed and attempt to escape the death of the biosphere by building giant space colonies to survive in. Yet they have enemies in the military-industrial complex who refuse to believe that Earth is dying. Chief of these forces is Lloyd Madden, an evil genius who desires the death of the human race so he can repopulate it with a new race of mutants. *The Last Gasp* delivers a chilling portrait of disaster and hope.

Hoyle's most haunting work is the frankly erotic novel, *The Man Who Travelled on Motorways.* As the narrator travels, his mind explores the realities and fantasies of his life. Much of the book is surreal, but science-fictional aspects are apparent in the discussion of reality. Much of the book is sexist: Hoyle's narrator seems incapable of love, merely using women to satisfy his sexual needs in loathsome fashions. Yet the book speaks to the unconscious desires of travellers of either sex and takes a bold, difficult path to break down life's certainties into more truthful probabilities.

*Blake's Seven: Scorpio Attack* is a novelization based on the popular BBC television SF series. Hoyle brings together three scripts written by Chris Boucher, James Follett, and Robert Holmes; the resulting novel will be a delight to fans of the series as the followers of Blake fight against the Dictatorship following the Atomic Wars with their new space ship, *Scorpio.*

Trevor Hoyle is an unusual writer with a gift for blending the real and the surreal in his dreamlike visions.

—George Kelley

---

**HUBBARD, L(aFayette) Ron(ald).** American. Born in Tilden, Nebraska, 13 March 1911. Educated at George Washington University, Washington, D.C., B.S. in civil engineering 1934; Princeton University, New Jersey, 1945; Sequoia University, Ph.D. 1950. Married Mary Sue Whipp; two daughters and two sons. Wrote travel and aviation articles in the 1930's; explorer: Commander, Caribbean Motion Picture Expedition, 1931, West Indies Mineral Survey Expedition, 1932, and Alaskan Radio-Experimental Expedition, 1940. Director, Hubbard Foundation; founding director, Church of Scientology, 1952; director, Dianetics and Scientology, 1952–66; resigned all directorships, 1966. *Died 29 January 1986.*

### Science-Fiction Publications

Novels (series: Mission Earth)

*Death's Deputy.* Los Angeles, Fantasy, 1948.
*Final Blackout.* Providence, Rhode Island, Hadley, 1948.
*Slaves of Sleep.* Chicago, Shasta, 1948.
*Triton, and Battle of Wizards.* Los Angeles, Fantasy, 1949.
*The Kingslayer* (includes "The Beast" and "The Invaders"). Los Angeles, Fantasy, 1949; as *Seven Steps to the Arbiter,* Chatsworth, California, Major, 1975.
*Fear, and Typewriter in the Sky.* New York, Gnome Press, 1951; London, Cherry Tree, 1952.
*From Death to the Stars* (includes *Death's Deputy* and *The Kingslayer*). Los Angeles, Fantasy, 1953.
*Return to Tomorrow.* New York, Ace, 1954; London, Panther, 1957.
*Fear, and Ultimate Adventure.* New York, Berkley, 1970.
*Battlefield Earth: A Saga of the Year 3000.* New York, St. Martin's Press, 1983; London, Quadrant, 1984.
*Mission Earth.* Los Angeles, Bridge, 1985.
*The Invaders Plan.* Los Angeles, Bridge, 1985.
*Death Quest.* Los Angeles, Bridge, 1985.
*Black Genesis.* Los Angeles, Bridge, 1986.
*The Enemy Within.* Los Angeles, Bridge, 1986.
*An Alien Affair.* Los Angeles, Bridge, 1986; London, New Era, 1987.
*Fortune of Fear.* Los Angeles, Bridge, 1986.
*Voyage of Vengence.* Los Angeles, Bridge, 1987; London, New Era, 1988.
*Disaster.* Los Angeles, Bridge, 1987.
*Villany Victorious.* Los Angeles, Bridge, 1987.
*The Doomed Planet.* Los Angeles, Bridge, 1987.

Short Stories

*Ole Doc Methuselah.* Austin, Texas, Theta Press, 1970.
*Lives You Wished to Lead But Never Dared,* edited by V.S. Wilhite. Clearwater, Florida, Theta Press, 1978.

### Other Publications

Novel

*Buckskin Brigades.* New York, Macaulay, 1937; London, Wright and Brown, 1938.

Verse

*Hymn of Asia: An Eastern Poem.* Los Angeles, Church of Scientology, 1974.

Other

*Dianetics: The Modern Science of Mental Health.* New York, Hermitage House, 1950; London, Ridgway, 1951.
*Science of Survival.* Wichita and East Grinstead, Sussex, Hubbard, 1951.
*Self Analysis.* Wichita, International Library of Arts and Science, 1951.
*Dianetics: The Original Thesis.* Wichita, Wichita Publishing, 1951.
*Handbook for Preclears.* Wichita, Scientic Press, 1951.
*Notes on the Lectures of L. Ron Hubbard.* Wichita, Hubbard, 1951.
*Advanced Procedure and Axioms.* Wichita, Hubbard, 1951.
*Scientology 8-80.* Phoenix, Hubbard, and East Grinstead, Sussex, Scientology, 1952.
*A Key to the Unconscious.* Phoenix, Scientic Press, 1952.
*Dianetics: The Evolution of a Science.* London, Hubbard, 1953; Phoenix, Hubbard, 1955.
*Scientology: A History of Man.* London, Hubbard, 1953.
*How to Live Though an Executive.* Phoenix, Hubbard, 1953.
*Self-Analysis in Dianetics.* London, Ridgway, 1953.
*Scientology 8-8008.* London, Hubbard, 1953.
*Dianetics 1955!* Phoenix, Hubbard, 1954.
*The Creation of Human Ability: A Handbook for Scientologists.* Phoenix, Hubbard, and London, Scientology, 1955.
*This Is Scientology: The Science of Certainty.* London, Hubbard, 1955.
*The Key to Tomorrow* (selections), edited by U. Keith Gerry. Johannesburg, Hubbard, 1955.
*Scientology: The Fundamentals of Thought.* London, Hubbard, 1956.

*Problems of Work*. Johannesburg, Hubbard, 1957.
*Fortress in the Sky* (on the moon). Washington, D.C., Hubbard, 1957.
*Have You Lived Before This Life?* London, Hubbard, 1958; New York, Vantage, 1960.
*Self-Analysis in Scientology*. London, Hubbard, 1959.
*Scientology: Plan for World Peace*. East Grinstead, Sussex, Scientology, 1964.
*Scientology Abridged Dictionary*. East Grinstead, Sussex, Hubbard, 1965.
*A Student Comes to Saint Hill*. Bedford, Sidney Press, 1965.
*Scientology: A New Slant on Life*. London, Hubbard, 1965.
*East Grinstead*. East Grinstead, Sussex, Hubbard, 1966.
*Introduction to Scientology Ethics*. Edinburgh, Scientology, 1968; Los Angeles, Bridge, 1985.
*The Phoenix Lectures*. Edinburgh, Scientology, 1968.
*How to Save Your Marriage*. Copenhagen, Scientology, 1969.
*When in Doubt, Communicate: Quotations from the Work of L. Ron Hubbard*, edited by Ruth Minshull and Edward M. Lefshon. Ann Arbor, Michigan, Scientology, 1969.
*Scientology 0-8*. Copenhagen, Scientology, 1970.
*Mission into Time*. Copenhagen, Scientology, 1973.
*The Management Series 1970–1974*. Los Angeles, American Saint Hill Organization, 1974.
*The Organization Executive Course*. Los Angeles, American Saint Hill Organization, 8 vols., 1974.
*Dianetics Today*. Los Angeles, Scientology, 1975.
*Dianetics and Scientology Technical Dictionary*. Los Angeles, Scientology, 1975.
*The Technical Bulletins of Dianetics and Scientology*. Los Angeles, Scientology, 1976–86.
*The Volunteer Minister's Handbook*. Los Angeles, Scientology, 1976.
*Axioms and Logics*. Los Angeles, Scientology, 1976.
*A Summary of Scientology for Churches*. Los Angeles, Scientology, 1977.
*The Book of Case Remedies*. Los Angeles, Scientology, 1977.
*What Is Scientology*. Los Angeles, Scientology, 1978.
*The Research and Discovery Series*. Los Angeles, Scientology, 1980–86.
*The Second Dynamic* (selection), edited by Cass Pool. Portland, Oregon, Heron, 1981.
*Self-Analysis*. Los Angeles, Bridge, 1982.
*Scientology: Fundamentals of Thought*. Los Angeles, Bridge, 1983.
*Dianetics: The Evolution of a Science*. Los Angeles, Bridge, 1983.
*The Problems of Work*. Los Angeles, Bridge, 1983.
*The Dynamics of Life*. Los Angeles, Bridge, 1983.
*The Way to Happiness*. Los Angeles, Bridge, 1984.
*Purification: An Illustrated Answer to Drugs*. Los Angeles, Bridge, 1984.
*The Learning Book*. Copenhagen, New Era, 1984.
*Child Dianectics*. Los Angeles, Bridge, 1989.

Other texts and pamphlets published.

*

Critical Studies: *Bare-Faced Messiah: The True Story of L. Ron Hubbard* by Russell Miller, London, Joseph, 1987; New York, Holt, 1988; *A Piece of Blue Sky: Scientology, Dianetics, and L. Ron Hubbard Exposed* by Jon Atack, London, Lyle Stuart, and New York, Carol, 1990.

* * *

Best known as the author of *Dianetics* and the founder of the Dianetics-based Church of Scientology, L. Ron Hubbard was a prolific writer of pulp adventure fiction during the 1930's and 1940's. Much of his SF and fantasy, published in *Astounding* and *Unknown*, is of interest today only because its bizarre gnostic psychology anticipates some of the doctrines and practices of Dianetics and Scientology. However, despite a prose style that begs for better editing, some of his fiction justifies the high regard given him by other veterans of the "Golden Age."

Having begun as a writer of nautical adventure fiction, Hubbard often composed SF and fantasy simply by inserting conventional plots in a new context by means of a fantastic premise or framing device. For instance, in *Slaves of Sleep*, a meek, young shipping magnate is accused of a gruesome murder committed by a North African *jinni* released from an ancient jar. Jailed for the crime, Jan Palmer finds himself plunged, while asleep, into an alternate life as a cynical, troublemaking, but courageous sailor. In that world, which is ruled by demons out of Arabic folklore, Palmer is also in trouble with the authorities. As the two stories clunk along in uneasy partnership, the bookish shipowner's personality is modified by that of his *alter ego*, who purloins a powerful talisman and wins a battle in the other world. All this results in Palmer's being cleared and restored to his inheritance in this world, and winning a bride in the bargain. In spite of a few moments of strong social satire and an intriguing glimpse of the role of fantasy in constructing the personality, the novel is not much more than a pseudo-folktale in an awkward framework.

*Typewriter in the Sky*, Hubbard's most successful fiction, also uses such a framing device. In this delightful confection, an unemployed musician is transported into the world of a Spanish Main romance being composed hastily by an acquaintance who hacks mass-market adventure fiction. Mike DeWolf is not only protagonist, but also prime reader of the text: buffeted by narrative implausibilities and inconsistencies as well as by a major rewrite that sets up an alternate but no less fatal ending, he is finally thrust out of the fiction to return as a vagrant to the streets of modern New York, wondering whether his primary universe is being created by a God "in a dirty bathrobe." This skillful mockery of plot appeared a quarter-century before the vogue for metafiction, and long before Borges became generally known to American writers. A similar vein of humor appears in *Triton*, a cleverly conceived, though clumsily executed, lark about a milquetoast who swallows a sea-god, thereby gaining the *machismo* needed to face down his dry-land persecutors. *Triton*, in fact, is a reprise of the central fantasy of *Slaves of Sleep*, but much tighter and wittier than the earlier piece. Two other early novels, *Fear* and *Death's Deputy*, offer plots that use demons to explain murders and untimely deaths. Altogether, Hubbard's early work shows a bent more for the weird tale and for humor than for straight-ahead SF.

It is apparently a convention of Hubbard criticism to praise as his finest novel the militaristic *Final Blackout*. It is hard to see why, unless its virulent fascism—which the text disingenuously attempts to deny—appeals to critics who share its ideological distaste for democracy or social welfare. The narrative reads like the plot summary of a much longer work, and its hero (known only as "the Lieutenant") is developed as neither a realistic character nor a credible personification. Only if read ironically—as Hubbard surely did not intend—does the book amount to much more than a fascist utopia and anti-progressive tract.

Hubbard's postwar SF is of little distinction. The stories collected in *Old Doc Methuselah* are about a long-lived medical man who runs an interstellar ambulance service, dashing about the Galaxy conquering disease, injury and ignorance, and fighting injustice. The series is vintage space opera: Doc has a cute alien sidekick, he wields a blaster as comfortably as a hypodermic, and he faces down hordes of tyrannical villains in his capacity as a Soldier of Light. Even more predictable is *The Kingslayer*, a tale of Byzantine conspiracy involving Kit Kellan. A young drifter rescued from the authorities by revolutionaries and recruited to assassinate the all-powerful Galactic Arbiter, Kit manages to overcome most of the obstacles to finding his victim, but he is seized just before reaching his goal. Brought before the Arbiter, he learns that the ruler is not a despot, that the revolutionaries are operatives loyal to the Council, that his mission has been a test of his mettle, and that he himself is the Arbiter's son and heir presumptive. Aside from being a psychoanalytic goldmine, the novel is another variation on the old Galactic Empire motif, with a touch of *Final Blackout*'s adulation of the military strongman.

For over three decades, except for an occasional reprint, the SF community heard nothing from Hubbard that did not have to do with his notoriety as the embattled leader of the Scientology movement. Then in 1983, a behemoth of a novel appeared under the title of *Battlefield Earth: A Saga of the Year 3000.* Claimed by Hubbard to be the longest SF novel ever published (819 pages clothbound and 1066 pages in paper), the book came with a recorded "soundtrack" and a preface in which Hubbard got into the acts of defining SF and describing what it was like to write for John W. Campbell, Jr. The novel itself, a throwback to earlier modes of SF, is the tale of how Jonnie Goodboy Tyler marshals the pitiful remnant of humanity to overthrow the Psychlo yoke, and then manipulates the Galactic Bank to restore the former mining colony of Earth to its rightful preeminence among the various foul-smelling aliens of the universe. The technological accomplishments of the year 3000 are barely updated applications of the "superscience" of the old space operas—from matter transmitters to machines that enable one to learn alien languages instantaneously. The various ethnic groups of the earthling resistance are led by Highland clans complete with warpipes, kilts, and claymores. The good guys defeat the bad guys because they are virtuous, persistent, lucky—and look like us. And women and alien females are put firmly in their place: they breed, nurture, and cook. The wit that sometimes shone through Hubbard's earlier turgidities has been reduced to puns like "the nebula of crap." But for all its obvious flaws, *Battlefield Earth* is an entertaining read: Hubbard does know how to tell an exciting story (or two, to be exact).

Much the same judgment can be made of the ambitious *Mission Earth* serial, a suspenseful romance in ten volumes and 3,903 pages, which began to appear the year before Hubbard's January 1986 death and concluded in 1987. This "dekalogy" chronicles the exploits of the heroic Jettero Heller, an intrepid space engineer who saves not only his own Voltarian Confederacy, but also the Earth, from the evil machinations of a villainous civil servant. In a semi-scholarly introduction to volume I (with no references to writings after 1974), Hubbard discusses at excessive length the use of SF as a vehicle for social satire; besides innumerable plot reversals, intrigues and complications, much of *Mission Earth*'s formidable size is due to a great deal of rather sophomoric satire on such topics as the UN, New York cabdrivers, the FBI and the CIA, and most prominently the professions of psychology and psychotherapy. It is a tribute to Hubbard's storytelling skills that one finds it hard not to keep turning the pages of the unwieldy chronicle.

Never a stranger to controversy, Hubbard has continued to generate it since his death. In 1990, the Supreme Court let stand a copyright-infringement ruling against Henry Holt, the publisher of *Bare-Faced Messiah: The True Story of L. Ron Hubbard*, for quoting about 1100 words of unpublished Hubbard material. The ruling, which stunned publishers and scholars, led to legislative initiatives to clarify the "fair-use" provisions of the copyright law. And in 1991, charges surfaced that *Mission Earth* and other recent Hubbard writings had actually been ghost-written.

Meanwhile, Bridge Publications, Hubbard's Los Angeles house, has begun to reissue Hubbard's earlier writings on acid-free paper with library bindings, ensuring fans and foes a continuing supply of the old guru's wit and wisdom. Dianetics and Scientology remain Hubbard's outstanding SF invention.

—John P. Brennan

---

**HUDSON, Michael.** *See* **KUBE-McDOWELL, Michael P.**

---

**HUGHART, Barry.** American. Born in Peoria, Illinois, 13 March 1934. Educated at Columbia University, New York, B.A. in English 1956. Served in United States Air Force 1956–60. Technical representative, 1960–63, and vice president, 1963–65, Techtop Weapons; manager, Lenox Hill Bookshop, New York city, 1965–70. Since 1970, freelance writer. Recipient: World Fantasy award, 1985. Agent: Jane Butler, 212 Third Street, Milford, Pennsylvania 18337. Address: 2928 North Beverly Avenue, Tucson, Arizona 85712, U.S.A.

### SCIENCE-FICTION PUBLICATIONS

Novels (series: Master Li and Number Ten Ox in all books)

*Bridge of Birds.* New York, Saint Martin's Press, and London, Century, 1984.

*The Story of the Stone.* New York, Doubleday, 1988; London, Bantam, 1989.

*Eight Skilled Gentlemen.* New York, Doubleday, and London, Bantam, 1991.

*

Barry Hughart comments:

My three novels featuring Master Li and Number Ten Ox are set in a seventh-century China that never existed as a whole, but did exist in fragments. Which is to say that 99% of the history, customs, popular music, children's songs, culinary recipes, medical formulas, odd folk beliefs—you name it—that I include is real, acquired through more hours in university libraries than I care to think about, but not chronologically accurate; what I do is mix things up to produce a particular effect. For example, in *Eight Skilled Gentlemen* I've taken a children's song set down by a Frenchman in Peking in 1911, added terms from a scholarly monograph on boatmen's slang dated 1793 by a Dutch scholar in south China, tied the result to the most famous of all odes and shamanistic chants in "Nine Songs," ascribed to the fourth century BC but most certainly prehistoric, and then added a sprinkling of Baudelaire-like lines (rather like whipped cream on top) by Li Ho, AD 791–817. The result is verse matter-of-factly accepted by my seventh-century sage, Master Li, as being a unified whole, rather good, interesting in that it may be useful in providing clues to the mystery he's involved in but otherwise quite typical of the culture. Is he wrong?

Well, let's start with the flat statement that the most profoundly Chinese poem of the past century is *Burnt Norton.* "Time present and time past / Are both perhaps present in time future / And time future contained in time past." The point being that China, while a historical babe compared to Egypt or Iran, possesses the oldest continuous civilization on earth. It is usually pointless to isolate a Chinese custom or art form and assign a definitive cause, creator, or date, because everything has, is, and will be evolving from everything else; all that is past is present, all that is present is past, both will be eternally present in the future. Master Li can read lines that will not be "created" for a thousand years and shrug and say "Why not?", since he is simultaneously reading in those lines the music of a thousand years of the past. "Only by the form, the pattern / Can words or music reach / The stillness, as a Chinese jar still / Moves perpetually in its stillness." Oh yeah, and a barbarian who proleptically picks from the cultural cornucopia can produce a "true" China in which magic and miracles *must* occur. Thus the Master Li books, concerning which the label "fantasy" is a battle cry to militant metaphysicians.

* * *

All three of Barry Hughart's published novels are set in a seventh-century version of China that bears some, but not much, relationship to the real one. It is the land of a decaying empire, ruled by emperors and kings and warlords, plagued by vampires and bandits and demons and more purely mundane villains. It is a mysterious and often beautiful landscape filled with strange people and events.

Against this backdrop, Hughart presents two characters around whom all three novels unfold. Li Kao is an elderly scholar with a weakness for wine, but possibly also possessing the most brilliant mind in the world. He is essentially an Oriental Sherlock Holmes, but with marked differences. Li is a pragmatist, perfectly capable of shrugging at disaster, so long as it isn't his disaster. The Watson substitute is Number Ten Ox, who narrates each adventure, a strong, brave, and loyal peasant whose relationship with Li begins in the first volume when he employs him to solve a problem in his village.

Hughart's style is somewhat reminiscent of the "Kai Lung" stories of Ernest Bramah. The text is enriched by anecdotes, poems, creative folk tales, and an entire mythic cosmology invented for the series. Although each novel is essentially a mystery, solved after the heroes survive a series of adventures, each contains a strong element of dark humor as well. At times, ghastly incidents are related in an offhanded, almost comic fashion.

*Bridge of Birds* was the first to appear, and it won the World Fantasy award, evidence that Hughart had made an instant, favorable impression with readers. Every child in Number Ten Ox's village between the ages of eight and 13 has fallen into a coma. Although Li is able to identify the cause readily enough, a cure requires possession of the Great Root of Power, an item so rare and valuable that acquiring it means risking an attempted theft from the Ancestress, a deposed Empress of China who still commands powerful forces.

After a series of adventures, the protagonists infiltrate her household, only to find themselves involved with a ghost, an unsolved murder mystery, and the likelihood that they'll be executed out of hand for entering in the first place. Hughart resolves everything in a resounding fashion and ties up all the loose ends neatly.

Three years later, he followed this success with an even better adventure, *The Story of the Stone.* This time, Master Li is approached by the abbot of a monastery to investigate the death of one of his monks. It appears that at the time he died, a hypnotic sound lured most of the other monks away, that a small area of the surrounding landscape was entirely denuded of plant life, and that visions were seen of the Laughing Prince, a supposedly insane despot who had died centuries earlier.

In the fashion of murder mysteries, the crime is repeated after Li's arrival. He concludes that those responsible are both mundane and supernatural, and in order to identify the perpetrator, he and a group of companions must journey to Hell itself, to question the keeper of the records of life and death. The resolution involves the discovery of a mysterious stone that can absorb human souls, and the revelation of the mortal whose secret plotting led to the deaths. As with many of the Sherlock Holmes stories, Hughart cheats in terms of traditional mystery writing—there is no possible way for the reader to figure out in advance what has happened. Fortunately, it doesn't matter. The focus of the book is the way in which Li reveals the details, and the exotic landscape that provides the stage for his antics.

Most recent, and easily surpassing its two predecessors, is *Eight Skilled Gentlemen.* Once again, Li is called upon to solve a series of murders, this time the systematic elimination of highly placed mandarins who are apparently involved in a highly remunerative smuggling operation. A witness to the first killing relates an incredible story of an assassin who strikes with a ball of fire, then escapes in the form of a crane, following which the dead body is decapitated by a vampire. Li is skeptical until he uncovers a connection to an ancient order, and witnesses the second murder himself, also perpetrated by a clearly inhuman creature. His investigations further reveal a set of artifacts which, if employed by the wrong hands, might cause a catastrophe that would sweep all of China.

One of the greatest challenges in creating a fantasy world is to make it seem like a real place. Hughart has created an entire alter reality in these novels, given it a social system, history, philosophy, and unique mythology. His characters are exaggerated and to a certain degree superficial, but only in the sense that all fairy tale characters are unrealistic. It is the mosaic of people, places, and events that mark these as outstanding works of fantasy.

—Don D'Ammassa

---

**HUGHES, Monica (née Ince).** Canadian. Born in Liverpool, Lancashire, England, 3 November 1925; daughter of the mathematician E.L. Ince; became Canadian citizen in 1957. Educated at the Convent of the Holy Child Jesus, Harrogate, Yorkshire, graduated 1942; Edinburgh University, 1942–43. Served in the Women's Royal Naval Service, 1943–46. Married Glen Hughes in 1957; two daughters and two sons. Dress designer, London, 1948–49, and Bulawayo, Zimbabwe, 1950; bank clerk, Umtali, Zimbabwe, 1951; laboratory technician, National Research Council, Ottawa, 1952–57. Recipient: Vicky Metcalf award, 1981; Canada Council prize, 1982, 1983. Address: 13816-110A Avenue, Edmonton, Alberta T5M 2M9, Canada.

SCIENCE-FICTION PUBLICATIONS (for children)

Novels (series: Isis)

*Crisis on Conshelf Ten.* Toronto, Copp Clark, and London, Hamish Hamilton, 1975; New York, Atheneum, 1977.
*Earthdark.* London, Hamish Hamilton, 1977.

*The Tomorrow City*. London, Hamish Hamilton, 1978.
*Beyond the Dark River*. London, Hamish Hamilton, 1979; New York, Atheneum, 1981.
*The Keeper of the Isis Light*. London, Hamish Hamilton, 1980; New York, Atheneum, 1981.
*The Guardian of Isis*. London, Hamish Hamilton, 1981; New York, Atheneum, 1982.
*The Isis Pedlar*. London, Hamish Hamilton, 1982; New York, Atheneum, 1983.
*Ring-Rise, Ring-Set*. London, MacRae, and New York, Watts, 1982.
*The Beckoning Lights*. Edmonton, Alberta, LeBel, 1982.
*Space Trap*. Toronto, Groundwood, and London, MacRae, 1983; New York, Watts, 1984.
*Devil on My Back*. London, MacRae, 1984; New York, Atheneum, 1985.
*Sandwriter*. London, MacRae, 1985; New York, Holt, 1988.
*The Dream Catcher*. London, MacRae, 1986; New York, Atheneum, 1987.
*The Promise*. Toronto, Stoddart, and London, Methuen, 1989; New York, Simon and Schuster, 1992.
*Invitation to the Game*. Toronto, Harper Collins, 1990; New York, Simon and Schuster, and London, Methuen, 1991.

OTHER PUBLICATIONS (for children)

Novels

*Gold-Fever Trail*. Edmonton, Alberta, LeBel, 1974.
*The Ghost Dance Caper*. London, Hamish Hamilton, 1978.
*Hunter in the Dark*. Toronto, Clarke Irwin, 1982; New York, Atheneum, 1983.
*The Treasure of the Long Sault*. Edmonton, Alberta, LeBel, 1982.
*My Name Is Paula Popowich!* Toronto, Lorimer, 1983.
*Blaine's Way*. Toronto, Irwin, 1986; London, Severn House, 1988.
*Log Jam*. Toronto, Irwin, 1987; as *Spirit River*, London, Methuen, 1988.
*The Refuge*. Toronto, Doubleday, 1989.
*Little Fingerling: A Japanese Folk Tale* (illustrated). Toronto, Kids Can Press, 1989.

*

Manuscript Collection: University of Calgary, Alberta.

Monica Hughes comments:

I grew up fascinated by the story of humankind, the way in which we acquired language, told stories, developed tribal customs, and at last discovered our world and learned how to dominate it. The interconnectedness of it all.

It is only a step around a dark corner from the past into the future: given what happened then, what might happen when. . .? I am particularly concerned with the fragility of our environment and with the loss of the "bloom on the grape" of life as our technological society progresses like a juggernaut, threatening rain forests, oceans, indigenous native cultures.

* * *

Monica Hughes is most successful and provocative when she uses one or both of two themes: 1) The price society is willing to pay for technological progress, and the importance of people's adapting intelligently to the environment they find themselves in; and 2) young adult concerns, in particular the first stirrings of romantic love. Witness, for example, *The Keeper of The Isis Light*, the first and best segment of the Isis trilogy, and *Ring-Rise, Ring-Set*, runner-up for the 1982 *Guardian* award. Hughes is less successful when she succumbs to cuteness, e.g., *The Isis Pedlar* with its unconvincing portrait of an irresponsible but likeable Irish inter-galactic pedlar, or fails to respect the boundaries science sometimes imposes upon the imagination, e.g., *Space Trap* with its aliens implausibly banded together in self defense.

In *The Keeper of the Isis Light*, although using some material previously tapped—surgery to facilitate human adaptation to a hostile environment (*Crisis on Conshelve Ten* where "mer-men" are created in order more readily to explore the seas) and the high risks of over-relying on artificial intelligence (*The Tomorrow City* where the central computer, C-Three, runs amuck)—Hughes put together an original and poignant story. Young Olwen, the daughter of scientists responsible for the Isis Light, is surgically altered by Guardian, a highly advanced robot, to withstand the excessive radiation of Isis which had killed her parents. In doing so, the robot only folloows instructions to guard the child at all costs. Unaware that she has been altered to appear lizard-like and believing that she is beautiful, Olwen feels attracted to Mark London, a member of the first Isis colony. He too is attracted to the loveliness he senses beneath the mask Guardian forces Olwen to wear. When Mark learns the truth and in horror recoils from Olwen's uncovered face, she realizes his declaration of love is insincere; and she must live rejected. Hughes makes clear that Guardian's decision to alter surgically Olwen's appearance, although defensible on technical grounds, profoundly shocks sensibilities which equate being human with looking human. Hence, the technological innovation Olwen's survival represents demands too high a price: not only does the young woman suffer permanent rejection, but technology is perceived as so threatening that the colony is persuaded at great risk to its survival to use as little of it as possible.

In *Ring-Rise, Ring-Set*, which is both SF and survival story, Hughes explores another moral problem effected by technology. When the sun's rays are blocked by rings of meteoric dust in the atmosphere and a new ice age is imminent, most people, banding together in Cities and submitting to regimentation, frantically seek technology to dissolve the rings. One new technique, however, seriously endangers the Ekoes who insist upon living outside the City close to nature. The focus of the clash between the two differing cultures is Lisa, a City dweller, who, running away to the icy wastes, becomes lost and is found by the Ekoes. Lisa's refusal to return to City because at last she feels whole among the Ekoes where too she has found love is credible and moving. Moreover, the novel forthrightly presents both City's uncertainty whether technology can or ought to preserve civilization as is, and the Ekoes's determination, regardless of cost, not to abandon their values for the sake of survival as defined by City. When Hughes is "on target," then, her novels convincingly demonstrate that it is no easy, painless resolution of the conflict which can result when technology impinges upon human life.

—Francis J. Molson

---

**HUGHES, Zach.** Pseudonym for Hugh Zachary. Also writes as Evan Innes. American. Born in Holdenville, Oklahoma, 12 January 1928. Educated at Oklahoma A & M College, 1945–46; University of North Carolina, Chapel Hill, B.A. in journalism 1951. Served in the 82nd Airborne Division of the United States

Army, 1946–48. Married Elizabeth Wiggs in 1948; two daughters. Worked in radio and television broadcasting, 1948–61. Since 1962, part-time fisherman, guide, florist, construction worker, and freelance writer. Address: 7 Pebble Beach Drive, Yaupon Beach, North Carolina 28465, U.S.A.

SCIENCE-FICTION PUBLICATIONS

Novels

*The Book of Rack the Healer.* New York, Award, 1973.
*The Legend of Miaree.* New York, Ballantine, 1974.
*Gwen, In Green* (as Hugh Zachary). New York, Fawcett, 1974; London, Coronet, 1976.
*Tide.* New York, Putnam, 1974.
*Seed of the Gods.* New York, Berkley, 1974; London, Hale, 1979.
*The Stork Factor.* New York, Berkley, 1975.
*For Texas and Zed.* New York, Popular Library, 1976.
*Tiger in the Stars.* Toronto, Laser, 1976.
*The St. Francis Effect.* New York, Berkley, 1976.
*Killbird.* New York, New American Library, 1980.
*Pressure Man.* New York, New American Library, 1980.
*Thunderworld.* New York, New American Library, 1982.
*Gold Star.* New York, New American Library, 1983.
*Sundrinker.* New York, DAW, 1987.
*The Dark Side.* New York, New American Library, 1987.
*Life Force.* New York, DAW, 1988.

OTHER PUBLICATIONS as Evan Innes

Novels

*America: 2040.* New York, Bantam, 1986.
*The Golden World.* New York, Bantam, 1986.
*City in the Mist.* New York, Bantam, 1987.
*The Return.* New York, Bantam, 1988.
*The Star Explorer.* New York, Bantam, 1988.

OTHER PUBLICATIONS as Hugh Zachary

Novels

*One Day in Hell.* New York, Newstand Library, 1961.
*A Small Slice of War.* New York, Caravelle, 1968.
*A Feast of Fat Things.* Jacksonville, Illinois, Harris Wolfe, 1968.
*Rake's Junction.* New York, Lancer, 1970.
*The Legend of the Deadly Doll.* New York, Award, 1973.
*Second Chance.* Canoga Park, California, Major, 1976.
*Dynasty of Desire,* with Elizabeth Zachary. New York, Dell, 1978.
*The Land Rushers,* with Elizabeth Zachary. New York, Dell, 1978.
*The Golden Dynasty,* with Elizabeth Zachary, New York, Dell, 1980.
*Bloodrush.* New York, Nordon, 1981.
*Murder in White.* New York, Leisure, 1981.
*Tower of Treason.* New York, Jove, 1982.
*Flight to Freedom,* New York, Dell, 1982.
*Desert Battle.* New York, Dell, 1982.
*Bitter Victory.* New York, Dell, 1983.
*Closed System.* New York, New American Library, 1986.
*The Venus Venture.* New York, Vanguard, 1986.
*The Revenant.* New York, New American Library, 1988.
*Dos Caballos.* New York, M. Evans, 1989.

Some 60 other novels published under various pseudonyms.

Play

Screenplay: *Tide.*

Other

*The Beachcomber's Handbook of Seafood Cookery.* Winston-Salem, North Carolina, Blair, 1969.
*Wild Card Poker.* Brattleboro, Vermont, Stephen Greene Press, 1975.

*

Zach Hughes comments:

I think the first duty of any writer, including a science-fiction writer, is to tell a story which involves real people who react to situations with believable motivation. Moreover, I feel that the setting for science fiction is, first and foremost, space. I write little science fiction, because it is difficult for me to come up with an idea which qualifies, in my mind, as worthy of having been published during the golden years of SF when awe and wonder and the sense of infinite distance and infinite variety in the universe was a necessary ingredient for any SF story. Several of my SF books are set in the time of The United Planets Confederation, as introduced in the last section of my first SF book, *The Book of Rack the Healer* and continued through such books as *Gold Star, Closed System, The Dark Side,* and the upcoming *Mother Lode.*

* * *

Zach Hughes is the pseudonym Hugh Zachary uses for his science-fiction novels. His first SF novel, *The Book of Rack the Healer,* is in many ways his best book. Earth, centuries after a nuclear holocaust, is dying from accumulated radiation and pollution. Mankind has evolved into four species: Keepers, moronic women whose brains store knowledge like a computer; Far Seers, males who supply leadership; Healers, males who have the power to travel on Earth's ravaged surface and collect raw materials to feed the population by regenerating cells damaged by the corrosive atmosphere; and Power Givers, women with the power of flight. Hughes creates an innovative ecological puzzle, while developing the characters of Rack the Healer, Red Earth the Far Seer, and Beautiful Wings the Power Giver. The ending is tragic, yet Hughes manages to moderate the pathos with hope. Hughes continues this story in a prequel called *Thunderworld.* The crew of a small scout ship discovers an infant solar system with an Earth-type planet racked with earthquakes and about to enter an Ice Age. The crew names the planet "Worthless" because their mission is to find worlds suitable for human colonization to ease the crushing overpopulation of Earth. But before they leave, one of the crew members unknowingly takes on a telepathic symbiotic life-form. Hughes explores the concept of dual identities sharing the same body. Then news arrives that war has broken out on Earth and the home of Man has been reduced to a radioactive, burned-out cinder. Hughes cleverly weaves these developments into a complex plot where the world of Rack the Healer and this "Worthless" planet converge 50,000 years in the future.

Hughes reworks this material in *Life Force.* An idyllic planet called Beauty causes a conflict between Andrew Reznor's Galactic Enterprises—which sees Beauty as a refuge for Earth's endangered species—and the Bureau of Colonization, which wants to send a large part of Earth's crowded population to settle the planet. But neither side figured on Beauty's own goals, goals the planet would kill to protect. Although a bit preachy, Hughes delivers a strong message of hope in *Life Force*.

*Killbird* also shares these themes. Eban the Hairy One is one of a small group of primitives surviving a nuclear holocaust. Hughes cunningly invents a sophisticated society, while sending Eban on an incredible set of adventures in the dangerous, savage world. *Killbird* possesses many of Hughes's best-developed characters—Eban, his wife Mar, and the bitter Yuree—as well as some of his best writing.

*The Legend of Miaree* is a clever positioning of a sociological disaster with the problems of translating alien texts. It is really two books in one: the actual legend of Miaree is being read by human students at a planetary university as the translation of the only surviving artifact of two destroyed alien races. The students and their professor provide commentary on the deadly progression of events, commentary that gives additional insight into the contrast between alien societies. Hughes does a masterful job creating the character of Miaree and her culture as two galaxies collide, threatening two star races. The ending is grim, but Hughes skillfully lightens the mood by shifting the actions to the human students and their wise professor.

In contrast to Hughes's serious SF, he has written his share of space operas. *The Dark Side* is a vengeance novel where Aaron Denton pledges to avenge the death of his home planet, St. Paul, by hunting down those responsible for its destruction. *Pressure Man* features Dominic "Flash" Gordon on a desperate mission to build a spacecraft that will withstand the pressures of 30,000 atmospheres. An alien ship, which might hold the secret to FTL space travel, is orbiting Jupiter. Gordon is charged with designing a new ship to capture the alien craft. Hughes tells Gordon's story with the backdrop of an Earth swelling with overpopulation and radical groups bent on destroying the space program. The politics of the novel is ultra-conservative, and the plot cheats the reader of an actual first contact turn into a tribute to Immanuel Velikovsky's theories instead. *Gold Star* features Pete and Jan Jaynes, a married couple aboard a space tug, who hunt for the missing experimental starship *Rimfire* for salvage and find themselves fighting for their lives against a rival band of salvagers. *Seed of the Gods*, an attempt to spoof the von Daniken cult, is a routine "first contact" novel.

Two ecological disaster novels, *Tide* and *The St. Francis Effect*, suffer from undeveloped characters, though some of the information is fascinating. In *Tide*, efforts to produce increased breeding of fish lead to mutations that trigger extreme aggression in the fish and in the people who eat them. In *The St. Francis Effect* a deep-ocean mining operation in the Pacific brings up an ages-old parasite carried by mosquitos. The resultant plague has a 100% mortality rate, and in a matter of days turns its victims into mummified corpses. The book is an effective disaster novel but the mosquitos and the disease—not the human characters—are the stars.

*The Stork Factor* and *For Texas and Zed* are both superman novels. In the first, set in a repressive and totalitarian future society totally controlled by a religious dictatorship, a young priest, Luke, has developed psi powers, and becomes part of the underground plotting to overthrow the government. At the same time, an advanced alien race sends a starship to Earth to determine the threat its technology presents. The impact of the convergence of events produces a fast-paced, entertaining novel. In *For Texas and Zed*, Lex Murichon, one of the leading figures of the planet Texas delegation to the Earth Empire, is a blend of the heroes from H. Beam Piper and John J. McGuire's *A Planet for Texans* (1958) and Harry Harrison's satiric *Bill, The Galactic Hero* (1965). The fierce independence of the Texans is translated into a culture on a hidden solitary planet where the new Texans provide meat to the Empire while staying above the cold war between the Empire and the Cassiopeian battle fleet. But Lex gets involved as a gunner aboard an Empire starship, deserts, and heads back to Texas, thus causing a state of war. This much of the novel is accomplished with wit and style. But after Texas successfully defends itself against the Empire's attacks and Lex becomes the leader of the Texas forces—evolving into an all-conquering Alexander the Great figure—the book sags badly.

*Tiger in the Stars* is a van Vogtian novel of humans encountering aliens of vast supremacy. The hero, John Plank, is turned into a cyborg linked with a starship of incredible power. Unfortunately, the novel drifts from subplot to subplot without developing a picture of future human culture or the fantastic alien culture. The ending becomes predictable far too soon and the result is a flatness usually absent from Hughes's best work.

*Gwen, In Green* features a young couple moving into a rambling house on an isolated island in the south. But within the clear pool near the house grow alien plants who establish contact with the young wife, Gwen. As the relationship between Gwen and the alien plants becomes stronger, the plot explodes with murder and sexuality. The book generates a memorable griminess as well as a powerful examination of the eerie symbiotic relationship of human and alien.

—George Kelley

---

**HUNT, Gil.** *See* **TUBB, E.C.**

---

**HUNTER, Evan.** Also writes as Curt Cannon; Hunt Collins; Ezra Hannon; Richard Marsten; Ed McBain. American. Born Salvatore A. Lombino in New York City, 15 October 1926. Educated at Cooper Union, New York, 1943–44; Hunter College, New York, B.A. 1950 (Phi Beta Kappa). Served in the United States Navy, 1944–46. Married 1) Anita Melnick in 1949 (divorced), three sons; 2) Mary Vann Finley in 1973, one stepdaughter. In the early 1950's taught in vocational high schools, and worked for the Scott Meredith Literary Agency, in New York. Recipient: Mystery Writers of America Edgar Allan Poe award, 1957. Lives in Norwalk, Connecticut. Agent: John Farquharson Ltd., 250 West 57th Street, New York, New York 10107, U.S.A.; or, 162–168 Regent Street, London W1R 5TB, England.

Science-Fiction Publications

Novels

*Find the Feathered Serpent* (for children). Philadelphia, Winston, 1952.

*Rocket to Luna* (for children; as Richard Marsten). Philadelphia, Winston, 1952; London, Hutchinson, 1954.

*Danger: Dinosaurs!* (for children; as Richard Marsten). Philadelphia, Winston, 1953.

*Tomorrow's World* (as Hunt Collins). New York, Avalon, 1956; as Tomorrow and Tomorrow, New York, Pyramid, 1956; as Ed McBain, London, Sphere, 1979.

Short Stories

*The Jungle Kids.* New York, Pocket Books, 1956.
*The Last Spin and Other Stories.* London, Constable, 1960.
*Happy New Year, Herbie, and Other Stories.* New York, Simon and Schuster, 1963; London, Constable, 1965.

OTHER PUBLICATIONS

Novels

*The Evil Sleep!* N. p., Falcon, 1952.
*The Big Fix.* N.p., Falcon, 1952; as *So Nude, So Dead* (as Richard Marsten), New York, Fawcett, 1956.
*Don't Crowd Me.* New York, Popular Library, 1953; London. Consul, 1960; as *The Paradise Party*, London, New English Library, 1968.
*Cut Me In* (as Hunt Collins). New York, Abelard Schuman, 1954; London, Boardman, 1960; as *The Proposition*, New York, Pyramid, 1955.
*The Black Jungle.* New York, Simon and Schuster, 1954; London, Constable, 1955.
*Second Ending.* New York, Simon and Schuster, and London, Constable, 1956; as *Quartet in H*, New York, Pocket Books, 1957.
*Strangers When We Meet.* New York, Simon and Schuster, and London, Constable, 1958.
*I'm Cannon—For Hire* (as Curt Cannon). New York, Fawcett, 1958; London, Fawcett, 1959.
*A Matter of Conviction.* New York, Simon and Schuster, and London, Constable, 1959; as *The Young Savages*, New York, Pocket Books, 1966.
*Mothers and Daughters.* New York, Simon and Schuster, and London, Constable, 1961.
*Buddwing.* New York, Simon and Schuster, and London, Constable, 1964.
*The Paper Dragon.* New York, Delacorte Press, 1966; London, Constable, 1967.
*A Horse's Head.* New York, Delacorte Press, 1967; London, Constable, 1968.
*Last Summer.* New York, Doubleday, 1968; London, Constable, 1969.
*Sons.* New York, Doubleday, 1969; London, Constable, 1970.
*Nobody Knew They Were There.* New York, Doubleday, and London, Constable, 1971.
*Every Little Crook and Nanny.* New York, Doubleday, and London, Constable, 1972.
*Come Winter.* New York, Doubleday, and London, Constable, 1973.
*Streets of Gold.* New York, Harper, 1974; London, Macmillan, 1975.
*Doors* (as Ezra Hannon). New York, Stein and Day, 1975; London, Macmillan, 1976.
*The Chisholms: A Novel of the Journey West.* New York, Harper, and London, Hamish Hamilton, 1976.
*Walk Proud.* New York, Bantam, 1979.
*Love, Dad.* New York, Crown, and London, Joseph, 1981.
*Far from the Sea.* New York, Atheneum, and London, Hamish Hamilton, 1983.
*Lizzie.* New York, Arbor House, and London, Hamish Hamilton, 1984.

Novels as Richard Marsten

*Runaway Black.* New York, Fawcett, 1954; London, Red Seal, 1957.
*Murder in the Navy.* New York, Fawcett, 1955; as *Death of a Nurse* (as Ed McBain), New York, Pocket Books, 1968; London, Hodder and Stoughton, 1972.
*The Spiked Heel.* New York, Holt, 1956; London, Constable, 1957.
*Vanishing Ladies.* New York, Permabooks, 1957; London, Boardman, 1961.
*Even the Wicked.* New York, Permabooks, 1958; as Ed McBain, London, Severn House, 1979.
*Big Man.* New York, Pocket Books, 1959; as Ed McBain, London, Penguin, 1978.

Novels as Ed McBain

*Cop Hater.* New York, Permabooks, 1956; London, Boardman, 1958.
*The Mugger.* New York, Simon and Schuster, 1956; London, Boardman, 1959.
*The Pusher.* New York, Simon and Schuster, 1956; London, Boardman, 1959.
*The Con Man.* New York, Permabooks, 1957; London, Boardman, 1960.
*Killer's Choice.* New York, Simon and Schuster, 1958; London, Boardman, 1960.
*Killer's Payoff.* New York, Simon and Schuster, 1958; London, Boardman, 1960.
*April Robin Murders*, with Craig Rice (completed by McBain). New York, Random House, 1958; London, Hammond, 1959.
*Lady Killer.* New York, Simon and Schuster, 1958; London, Boardman, 1961.
*Killer's Wedge.* New York, Simon and Schuster, 1959; London, Boardman, 1961.
*'Til Death.* New York, Simon and Schuster, 1959; London, Boardman, 1961.
*King's Ransom.* New York, Simon and Schuster, 1959; London, Boardman, 1961.
*Give the Boys a Great Big Hand.* New York, Simon and Schuster, 1960; London, Boardman, 1962.
*The Heckler.* New York, Simon and Schuster, 1960; London, Boardman, 1962.
*See Them Die.* New York, Simon and Schuster, 1960; London, Boardman, 1963.
*Lady, Lady, I Did it!* New York, Simon and Schuster, 1961; London, Boardman, 1963.
*Like Love.* New York, Simon and Schuster, 1962; London, Hamish Hamilton, 1964.
*Ten Plus One.* New York, Simon and Schuster, 1963; London, Hamish Hamilton, 1964.
*Ax.* New York, Simon and Schuster, and London, Hamish Hamilton, 1964.
*The Sentries.* New York, Simon and Schuster, and London, Hamish Hamilton, 1965.
*He Who Hesitates.* New York, Delacorte Press, and London, Hamish Hamilton, 1965.
*Doll.* New York, Delacorte Press, 1965; London, Hamish Hamilton, 1966.
*Eighty Million Eyes.* New York, Delacorte Press, and London, Hamish Hamilton, 1966.
*Fuzz.* New York, Doubleday, and London, Hamish Hamilton, 1968.
*Shotgun.* New York, Doubleday, and London, Hamish Hamilton, 1969.
*Jigsaw.* New York, Doubleday, and London, Hamish Hamilton, 1970.
*Hail, Hail, The Gang's All Here!* New York, Doubleday, and London, Hamish Hamilton, 1971.

*Sadie When She Died.* New York, Doubleday, and London, Hamish Hamilton, 1972.
*Let's Hear It for the Deaf Man.* New York, Doubleday, and London, Hamish Hamilton, 1973.
*Hail to the Chief.* New York, Random House, and London, Hamish Hamilton, 1973.
*Bread.* New York, Random House, and London, Hamish Hamilton, 1974.
*Where There's Smoke.* New York, Random House, and London, Hamish Hamilton, 1975.
*Blood Relatives.* New York, Random House, 1975; London, Hamish Hamilton, 1976.
*Guns.* New York, Random House, 1976; London, Hamish Hamilton, 1977.
*So Long as You Both Shall Live.* New York, Random House, and London, Hamish Hamilton, 1976.
*Long Time No See.* New York, Random House, and London, Hamish Hamilton, 1977.
*Goldilocks.* New York, Arbor House, 1977; London, Hamish Hamilton, 1978.
*Calyso.* New York, Viking Press, and London, Hamish Hamilton, 1979.
*Ghosts.* New York, Viking Press, and London, Hamish Hamilton, 1980.
*Rumpelstiltskin.* New York, Viking Press, and London, Hamish Hamilton, 1981.
*Heat.* New York, Viking Press, and London, Hamish Hamilton, 1981.
*Beauty and the Beast.* London, Hamish Hamilton, 1982; New York, Holt Rinehart, 1983.
*Ice.* New York, Arbor House, and London, Hamish Hamilton, 1983.
*Jack and the Beanstalk.* New York, Holt Rinehart, and London, Hamish Hamilton, 1984.
*Lightning.* New York, Arbor House, and London, Hamish Hamilton, 1984.
*Snow White and Rose Red.* New York, Holt Rinehart, and London, Hamish Hamilton, 1985.
*Eight Black Horses.* New York, Arbor House, 1985.
*Another Part of the City.* New York, Mysterious Press, 1985; London, Hamish Hamilton, 1986.
*Cinderella.* New York, Holt, and London, Hamish Hamilton, 1986.
*Poison.* New York, Arbor House, and London, Hamish Hamilton, 1987.
*Puss in Boots.* New York, Holt, and London, Arbor House, 1987.
*Tricks.* New York, Arbor House, and London, Hamish Hamilton, 1987.
*The House That Jack Built.* New York, Holt, and London, Hamish Hamilton, 1988.
*Lullaby.* New York, Morrow, and London, Hamish Hamilton, 1989.
*Downtown.* New York, Morrow, and London, Heinemann, 1989.
*Three Blind Mice.* New York, Arcade, 1990.
*Vespers.* New York, Morrow, 1990.

Short Stories

*I Like 'em Tough* (as Curt Cannon). New York, Fawcett, 1958.
*The Empty Hours* (as Ed McBain). New York, Simon and Schuster, 1962; London, Boardman, 1963.
*The Beheading and Other Stories.* London, Constable, 1971.
*The Easter Man (a Play) and Six Stories.* New York, Doubleday, 1972; as *Seven*, London, Constable, 1972.
*The McBain Brief* (as Ed McBain). London, Hamish Hamilton, 1982; New York, Arbor House, 1983.
*McBain's Ladies: The Women of the 87th Precinct.* New York, Mysterious Press, and London, Hamish Hamilton, 1988.
*McBain's Ladies Too.* New York, Mysterious Press, 1989.

Plays

*The Easter Man* (produced Birmingham and London, 1964; as *As Race of Hairy Men*, produced New York, 1965). Included in *The Easter Man (a Play) and Six Stories*, 1972.
*The Conjuror* (produced Ann Arbor, Michigan, 1969).

Screenplays: *Strangers When We Meet*, 1960; *The Birds*, 1963; *Fuzz*, 1972; *Walk Proud*, 1979.

Television Plays: *Appointment at Eleven* (*Alfred Hitchcock Presents* series), 1955–61; *The Chisholms* series, from his own novel, 1978–79; *The Legend of Walks Far Woman*, 1982.

Other (for children)

*The Remarkable Harry.* New York and London, Abelard Schuman, 1961.
*The Wonderful Button.* New York, Abelard Schuman, 1961; London, Abelard Schuman, 1962.
*Me and Mr. Stenner.* Philadelphia, Lippincott, 1976; London, Hamish Hamilton, 1977.

Other (as Ed McBain)

Editor, *Crime Squad.* London, New English Library, 1968.
Editor, *Homicide Department.* London, New English Library, 1968.
Editor, *Downpour.* London, New English Library, 1969.
Editor, *Ticket to Death.* London, New English Library, 1969.

*

Manuscript Collection: Mugar Memorial Library, Boston University.

* * *

Although he is best known as a mainstream novelist of considerable stature (*The Blackboard Jungle, Last Summer, Sons*), and as today's finest practitioner of the police procedural novel (the 87th Precinct series of more than 30 novels under his Ed McBain pseudonym), Evan Hunter began his career in the early 1950's as a science-fiction writer and contributed a number of short stories and novels to the genre during the first half of that decade. The best of the stories are "Inferiority Complex," "Million Dollar Maybe," which involves a magazine's offer of one million dollars to the first private citizen who reaches the moon and returns alive, and "The Fallen Angel," an excellent deal-with-the-devil fantasy with a circus background.

All three of Hunter's early SF novels are adventure stories for young readers. *Find the Feathered Serpent*, an interesting blend of time and travel and Mayan history, is perhaps the best. *Rocket to Luna* is an account of the first moon-bound rocket, and *Danger: Dinosaurs!* again uses the time-travel theme, in this case into the dim past when saurians roamed the earth. Hunter's most memorable contribution to science fiction is his only adult novel, *Tomorrow's World*—a caustically satirical study of a future in which narcotics have been legalized and there is a bitter struggle for control of publishing, movies, and television between the

Vikes, who are responsible for the current vogue of drug use and vicarious entertainment, and the Realists, who advocate a return to the moral standards of the past. The novel, which has deservedly remained in print during most of the past quarter-century, is an expanded version of "Malice in Wonderland" (*If*, January 1954); interestingly, "Malice" is told in the first person, by the Vike literary agent Van Brant, while *Tomorrow's World* is a third-person novel whose view-point shifts between Brant and members of the Realist movement. What makes both novella and novel especially fascinating is the combination of Hunter's unsurpassed ear for dialogue and his meticulous use of a drug-oriented, futuristic slang.

With the exception of his screenplay for Alfred Hitchcock's fantasy-based film *The Birds*, Hunter has written no science fiction since the middle 1950's. But the many reprintings of *Tomorrow's World* and the occasional reprinting of short stories serve as reminders to the SF reader that his contribution to the field, though small, is by no means inconsequential.

—Bill Pronzini

---

**HUXLEY, Aldous (Leonard).** British. Born in Godalming, Surrey, 26 July 1894; son of scientist T.H. Huxley; brother of the scientist and writer Julian Huxley. Educated at Hillside School, Godalming, 1903–08; Eton College, 1908–13; Balliol College, Oxford, 1913–15, B.A. (honours) in English 1915. Married 1) Maria Nys in 1919 (died 1955); 2) Laura Archera in 1956; one son. Worked in the War Office, 1917; taught at Eton College, 1918; member of the editorial staff of the *Athenaeum*, London, 1919–20; drama critic, *Westminster Gazette*, 1920–21; full-time writer from 1921; travelled and lived in France, Italy, and the United States, 1923–37; settled in California, 1937, and worked as a freelance screenwriter. Recipient: American Academy award, 1959. Companion of Literature, Royal Society of Literature, 1962. *Died 22 November 1963.*

### Science-Fiction Publications

#### Novels

*Brave New World.* London, Chatto and Windus, and New York, Doubleday, 1932.
*After Many a Summer.* London, Chatto and Windus, 1939; as *After Many a Summer Dies the Swan*, New York, Harper, 1939.
*Time Must Have a Stop.* New York, Harper, 1944; London, Chatto and Windus, 1945.
*Ape and Essence.* New York, Harper, 1948; London, Chatto and Windus, 1949.
*Island.* London, Chatto and Windus, and New York, Harper, 1962.

### Other Publications

#### Novels

*Crome Yellow.* London, Chatto and Windus, 1921; New York, Doran, 1922.
*Antic Hay.* London, Chatto and Windus, and New York, Doran, 1923.
*Those Barren Leaves.* London, Chatto and Windus, and New York, Doran, 1925.
*Point Counter Point.* London, Chatto and Windus, and New York, Doubleday, 1928.
*Eyeless in Gaza.* London, Chatto and Windus, and New York, Harper, 1936.
*The Genius and the Goddess.* London, Chatto and Windus, and New York, Harper, 1955.

#### Short Stories

*Limbo.* London, Chatto and Windus, and New York, Doran, 1920.
*Mortal Coils* (includes play *Permutations among the Nightingales*). London, Chatto and Windus, and New York, Doran, 1922.
*Little Mexican and Other Stories.* London, Chatto and Windus, 1924; as *Young Archimedes and Other Stories*, New York, Doran, 1924.
*Two or Three Graces and Other Stories.* London, Chatto and Windus, and New York, Doran, 1926.
*Brief Candles.* London, Chatto and Windus, and New York, Doubleday, 1930; as *After the Fireworks*, New York, Avon, n.d.
*Twice Seven: Fourteen Selected Stories.* London, Reprint Society, 1944.
*Collected Short Stories.* London, Chatto and Windus, and New York, Harper, 1957.

#### Plays

*Liluli*, adaptation of a play by Romain Rolland, in *Nation* (London), 20 September–29 November 1919.
*Albert, Prince Consort: A Biography Play for Which Mr. John Drinkwater's Historical Dramas Serve as a Model*, in *Vanity Fair* (New York), March 1922.
*The Ambassador of Capripedia*, in *Vanity Fair* (New York), May 1922.
*The Publisher*, in *Vanity Fair* (New York), April 1923.
*The Discovery*, adaptation of the play by Frances Sheridan (produced London, 1924). London, Chatto and Windus, 1924; New York, Doran, 1925.
*The World of Light* (produced London, 1931). London, Chatto and Windus, and New York, Doubleday, 1931.
*The Giocanda Smile*, adaptation of his own story (produced London, 1948; New York 1950). London, Chatto and Windus, 1948; as *Mortal Coils*, New York, Harper, 1948.
*The Genius and the Goddess*, with Ruth Wendell, adaptation of the novel by Huxley (produced New York, 1957).

Screenplays: *Price and Prejudice*, with Jane Murfin, 1940; *Jane Eyre*, with John Houseman and Robert Stevenson, 1944; *A Woman's Vengeance*, 1947.

#### Verse

*The Burning Wheel.* Oxford, Blackwell, 1916.
*Jonah.* Oxford, Holywell Press, 1917.
*The Defeat of Youth and Other Poems.* Oxford, Blackwell, 1918.
*Leda.* London, Chatto and Windus, and New York, Doran, 1920.
*Selected Poems.* Oxford, Blackwell, and New York, Appleton, 1925.
*Arabia Infelix and Other Poems.* New York, Fountain Press, and London, Chatto and Windus, 1929.

*Apennine.* Gaylordsville, Connecticut, Slide Mountain Press, 1930.
*The Cicadas and Other Poems.* London, Chatto and Windus, and New York, Doubleday, 1931.
*Verses and a Comedy.* London, Chatto and Windus, 1946.
*The Collected Poetry of Aldous Huxley,* edited by Donald Watt. London, Chatto and Windus, and New York, Harper, 1971.

Other

*On the Margin: Notes and Essays.* London, Chatto and Windus, and New York, Doran, 1923.
*Along the Road: Notes and Essays of a Tourist.* London, Chatto and Windus, and New York, Doran, 1925.
*Essays New and Old.* London, Chatto and Windus, 1926; New York, Doran, 1927.
*Jesting Pilate: The Diary of a Journey.* London, Chatto and Windus, and New York, Doran, 1926.
*Proper Studies.* London, Chatto and Windus, 1927; New York, Doubleday, 1928.
*Do What You Will: Essays.* London, Chatto and Windus, and New York, Doubleday, 1929.
*Holy Face and Other Essays.* London, The Fleuron, 1929.
*Vulgarity in Literature: Digressions from a Theme.* London, Chatto and Windus, 1930.
*Music at Night and Other Essays.* London, Chatto and Windus, and New York, Doubleday, 1931.
*Rotunda* (selection). London, Chatto and Windus, 1932.
*T.H. Huxley as a Man of Letters* (lecture). London, Macmilan, 1932.
*Retrospect* (selection). New York, Doubleday, 1933.
*Beyond the Mexique Bay.* London, Chatto and Windus, and New York, Harper, 1934.
*The Olive Tree and Other Essays.* London, Chatto and Windus, 1936; New York, Harper, 1937.
*What Are You Going to Do about It? The Case for Constructive Peace.* London, Chatto and Windus, 1936; New York, Harper, 1937.
*Stories, Essays, and Poems.* London, Dent, 1937.
*Ends and Means: An Enquiry into the Nature of Ideals and into the Methods Employed for Their Realization.* London, Chatto and Windus, and New York, Harper, 1937.
*The Most Agreeable Vice.* Los Angeles, Ward Ritchie Press, 1938.
*Words and Their Meanings.* Los Angeles, Ward Ritchie Press, 1940.
*Gray Eminence: A Study in Religion and Politics.* London, Chatto and Windus, 1941.
*The Art of Seeing.* New York, Harper, 1942; London, Chatto and Windus, 1943.
*The Perennial Philosophy.* New York, Harper, 1945; London, Chatto and Windus, 1946.
*Science, Liberty, and Peace.* New York, Harper, 1946; London, Chatto and Windus, 1947.
*The World of Aldous Huxley: An Omnibus of His Fiction and Non-Fiction over Three Decades,* edited by Charles J. Rolo. New York, Harper, 1947.
*Food and People,* with John Russell. London, Bureau of Current Affairs, 1949.
*Prisons, with the Carceri Etchings by Piranesi.* London, Trianon Press, and Los Angeles, Zeitlin and Ver Brugge, 1949.
*Themes and Variations.* London, Chatto and Windus, and New York, Harper, 1950.
*The Devils of Loudun.* London, Chatto and Windus, and New York, Harper, 1952.
*Joyce the Artificer: Two Studies of Joyce's Methods,* with Stuart Gilbert. London, Chiswick Press, 1952.
*A Day in Windsor,* with J.A. Kings. London, Britannicus Liber, 1953.
*The Doors of Perception.* London, Chatto and Windus, and New York, Harper, 1954.
*The French of Paris,* photographs by Sanford H. Roth. New York, Harper, 1954.
*Adonis and the Alphabet, and Other Essays.* London, Chatto and Windus, 1956; as *Tomorrow and Tomorrow and Tomorrow and Other Essays,* New York, Harper, 1956.
*Heaven and Hell.* London, Chatto and Windus, and New York, Harper, 1956.
*Brave New World Revisited.* New York, Harper, 1958; London, Chatto and Windus, 1959.
*Collected Essays.* London, Chatto and Windus, and New York, Harper, 1959.
*On Art and Artists,* edited by Morris Philipson. London, Chatto and Windus, and New York, Harper, 1960.
*Selected Essays,* edited by Harold Raymond. London, Chatto and Windus, 1961.
*Literature and Science.* London, Chatto and Windus, and New York, Harper, 1963.
*The Politics of Ecology: The Question of Survival.* Santa Barbara, California, Center for the Study of Democratic Institutions, 1963.
*The Crows of Pearblossom* (for children). London, Chatto and Windus, and New York, Random House, 1967.
*The Letters of Aldous Huxley,* edited by Grover Smith. London, Chatto and Windus, 1969; New York, Harper, 1970.
*Great Short Works of Aldous Huxley,* edited by Bernard Bergonzi. New York, Harper, 1969.
*America and the Future.* Austin, Texas, Jenkins, 1970.
*Moksha: Writings on Psychedelics and the Visionary Experience 1931–1963,* edited by Michael Horowitz and Cynthia Palmer. New York, Stonehill, 1977; London, Chatto and Windus, 1980.
*The Human Situation: Lectures at Santa Barbara 1959,* edited by Piero Ferrucci. New York, Harper, 1977; London, Chatto and Windus, 1978.

Editor, with W.R. Childe and T.W. Earp, *Oxford Poetry 1916.* Oxford, Blackwell, 1916.
Editor, *Text and Pretexts: An Anthology with Commentaries.* London, Chatto and Windus, 1932; New York, Harper, 1933.
Editor, *The Letters of D.H. Lawrence.* London, Heinemann, and New York, Viking Press, 1932.
Editor, *An Encyclopedia of Pacifism.* London, Chatto and Windus, and New York, Harper, 1937.

Translator, *Virgin Heart,* by Rémy de Gourmont. New York, Brown, 1921; London, Allen and Unwin, 1926.

*

Bibliography: *Aldous Huxley: A Bibliography 1916–1959* by Claire John Eschelbach and Joyce Lee Shober, Berkeley, University of California Press, 1961; supplement by Thomas D. Clareson and Carolyn S. Andrews, in *Extrapolation 6* (Wooster, Ohio), 1964; *Aldous Huxley: An Annotated Bibliography of Criticism* by Eben E. Bass, New York, Garland, 1981.

Critical Studies (selection): *Aldous Huxley: A Literary Study* by John Atkins, London, Calder, and New York, Roy, 1956, revised edition, London, Calder and Boyars, 1967, New York, Orion Press, 1968; *The Timeless Moment: A Personal View of Aldous Huxley* by Laura Huxley, New York, Farrar Straus, 1968, London, Chatto and Windus, 1969; *Aldous Huxley: A Study of the*

*Major Novels* by Peter Bowering, London, Athlone Press, 1968, New York, Oxford University Press, 1969; *Aldous Huxley: Satire and Structure* by Jerome Meckier, London, Chatto and Windus, and New York, Barnes and Noble, 1969; *Aldous Huxley* by Harold H. Watts, New York, Twayne, 1969; *Dawn and the Darkest Hour: A Study of Aldous Huxley* by George Woodcock, London, Faber, and New York, Viking Press, 1972; *Aldous Huxley* by Keith M. May, London, Elek, 1972, New York, Harper, 1973; *Aldous Huxley: A Biography* by Sybille Bedford, London, Chatto and Windus-Collins, 2 vols., 1973–74, New York, Knopf, 1 vol., 1974; *Aldous Huxley: A Collection of Critical Essays* edited by Robert E. Kuehn, Englewood Cliffs, New Jersey, Prentice Hall, 1974; *Aldous Huxley: The Critical Heritage* edited by Donald Watt, London, Routledge, 1975; *Demon and Saint in the Novels of Aldous Huxley* by Lilly Zahmer, Bern, Schweizer Anglistische Arbeiten, 1975; *Aspects of Structure and Quest in Aldous Huxley's Major Novels* by Bharathi Krishnan, Uppsala, Sweden, University of Uppsala, 1977; *Aldous Huxley, Novelist* by Christopher S. Ferns, London, Athlone Press, 1980; *The Dark Historic Page: Social Satire and Historicism in the Novels of Aldous Huxley 1921–1939* by Robert S. Baker, Madison, University of Wisconsin Press, 1982; *Huxley in Hollywood* by David King Dunaway, New York, Harper, and London, Bloomsbury, 1989.

* * *

Satirist, moralist, humanist, visionary, and proselytizer, Aldous Huxley is famous for his skeptical debunking of received attitudes and values; his eclectic intellect with its solid foundation in science, philosophy, and culture; his loathing of blind faith in progress, technology, Freudian psychology, and Watsonian behaviorism as well as orthodox Christianity; his fears of overpopulation, hedonism, scientific materialism, and dehumanization; and, in the later works, his interest in mysticism, parapsychology, and psychedelic drugs. At their best his rather quirky, erudite "novels of ideas" are rich in ironic counterpoint, humorous impieties, lively debate, and visual detail; at their worst they are loosely structured and confused diatribes in which the novel is an excuse to do what would best be handled in an essay format. Huxley takes pride in being irreverent and slightly shocking. His novels are full of characters blindly committed to ignorance and error, shocked by the ideologies of others, distracted by passions, engaged in witty repartee or philosophical debate but, in general, trapped in a static, "sick" society which destroys man's capacity for self-improvement and psychic fulfillment, dehumanizes, enslaves, and destroys.

His early works with their tea-party debates explore ineffectual communication, futility, egotism and self-alienation, disillusionment and dissociation, missed opportunities and failed epiphanies, while considering alternative approaches to reality and escapes from it. His goal, as he himself stated, was to "shock the stupid and morally reprehensible truth-haters." His later works focus much more on murder, death, disease, pain, and "vile flesh" before switching to moral affirmation.

In *After Many a Summer Dies the Swan*, an antiquarian American millionaire (Jo Stoyte), fearful of death and greedy to hang on to his material acquisitions, funds a research effort to find the physiological secret of longevity. A living example that such is possible, the Fifth Earl of Hauberk has devolved over two centuries into a grunting apelike satyr, but Stoyte finds even such a life more attractive than death. The power struggle between characters (power through wealth or sex or knowledge) and the debates that accompany it, suggests that ultimate control eludes all in a deterministic world.

The predominance of animal imagery throughout Huxley's novels suggests the irony of man's pretensions or his descent down the chain of being to the level of lizards, dogs, apes, and ferrets. *Point Counter Point*, for example, describes a child's development from worm to fish to foetus to high-church convert. Written as a motion-picture script within a narrative frame, *Ape and Essence*, a pessimistic allegory set after the devastation of World War III, begins with the violent murder of Gandhi and moves to a dystopia, a warlike society of egocentric, lustful, materialistic baboons, to argue the dangers of man's animal side dominating intellect and science (particularly through religious and political institutions). In the script within the novel, Dr. Alfred Poole, a member of the 2108 A.D. New Zealand Rediscovery Expedition to North America, describes and then flees this debased culture with its radiation-induced mutations, its fouled waters and land, its baby sacrifices, and its grotesque caricature of human egotism. An omniscient narrator sums up Huxley's argument: "Only in the knowledge of his own Essence/Has any man ceased to be many monkeys."

Though not Huxley's best effort, *Brave New World* is perhaps his best-known work. Set in a technologically advanced world in the 26th century, "After Ford 632," in London, Southern England, and a Zuni reservation in New Mexico, this novel deals with the basic dichotomy between progress and humanism. Huxley's futuristic society (a hierarchical pyramid with a broad base of lower-caste, ant-like identical twins) is one of testtube babies, chemical and genetic engineering, hypnopaedic conditioning, consumerism, and a mindless "happiness" made possible through sexual liberation, drugs, mass production, death conditioning, sensory films, a rejection of history and family, and an inescapable social destiny of "Community, Identity, and Stability." A small elite of Alphas and Betas do the little thinking necessary to keep their world functioning until a social outsider (Bernard Marx) introduces a real outsider: the Savage, a half-breed raised on Shakespeare, Indian lore, and Christianity. His reservation world is one of disease, superstition, guilt, racial prejudice, possessiveness, death, and individuality. The clash of these two contrasting world views (reason versus passion; progress versus history) exposes the limits of each: empty happiness versus painful freedom.

The Savage meets the utopia of his dreams and finds it wanting, a dystopia of too-easy progress against which he violently reacts. In a debate with the World Controller after the death of his "soma" drugged mother, he ineffectually demands the right to be unhappy. Seeking to create his own pure, ascetic reservation in a lighthouse, the hounded Savage, fascinated and repelled by the sexual license of sensation-crazed sightseers, beats himself, yields to sexual compulsions, and finally, unable to cope, commits suicide. Although the Savage's criticism is accurate, what he offers in place of progress is equally unacceptable: a choice "between insanity on the one hand and lunacy on the other," between technological civilization and past primitivism.

*Brave New World Revisited* examines the limitations and accuracy of *Brave New World*, particularly about such modern problems as drug dependency, the sexual revolution, the excesses of a consumer society, genetic engineering, and conditioning through advertising.

Huxley's last novel, *Island*, seeks a balance whose possibility *Brave New World* denied: a fusion of passion and reason—the mystical East with the technological West. In it a cynical and disenchanted outsider, Will Farnaby, is educated in the ways of Pala, a life-affirming culture that values reason, contemplation, community, and psychedelic drugs to prevent misery. This novel provides an entirely positive but fragile utopia, the antithesis of *Brave New World.* It is stylistically weak and boring. Huxley is much more effective at moral outrage than moral affirmation, and contraception, artificial insemination, the "hybridization of microcultures," hypnosis, and the yoga of love are hardly convincing as the solution to the problems Huxley had so ably defined or predicted in earlier works. Huxley's dominant image, the islands, suggests man's surface isolation but his subsurface ties with his fellow islands. However, his novel ends, not with the realization of human potential, but with a hostile, power-driven malcontent making a drive for power against nonviolent pacifists.

Huxley's erudite and witty works balance conflicting ideological positions but with an ambiguity that negates solution or resolution. *Island* rejects as wrong his earlier vision of progress as tempting, insidious and ultimately destructive, but it is *Brave New World*, with its sardonic vision of emptiness and loss, that has captured the imagination of modern visionaries.

—Gina Macdonald

---

**HYDE, Shelley.** *See* **REED, Kit.**

---

**HYNE, C(harles) J(ohn) Cutcliffe (Wright).** Also wrote as Weatherby Chesney. British. Born in Bilbury, Gloucestershire, 11 May 1865. Educated at Bradford Grammar School; Clare College, Cambridge, B.A., M.A. Married Elsie Haggas in 1897 (died 1938), one daughter. Journalist: travelled extensively as a writer for magazines. *Died 10 March 1944.*

SCIENCE-FICTION PUBLICATIONS

Novels

*Beneath Your Very Boots.* London, Digby Long, 1889.
*The New Eden.* London, Longman, 1892.
*The Recipe for Diamonds.* London, Heinemann, and New York, Appleton, 1893.
*The Lost Continent.* London, Hutchinson, and New York, Harper, 1900.
*Empire of the World.* London, Everett, 1910; New York, Arno Press, 1975; as *Emperor of the World: The Story of an Anglo-German War*, London, Newnes, 1915.
*Abbs, His Story Through Many Ages.* London, Hutchinson, 1929.

Short Stories

*The Adventures of a Solicitor* (as Weatherby Chesney). London, Bowden, 1898.
*Atoms of Empire.* London and New York, Macmillan, 1904.
*Man's Understanding.* London, Ward Lock, 1933.

OTHER PUBLICATIONS

Novels

*Four Red Nightcaps.* London, Eden, 1980.
*Currie, Curtis & Co., Crammers.* London, Remington, 1890.
*A Matrimonial Mixture.* London, Ward and Downey, 1891.
*Stimson's Reef.* London, Blackie, 1891.
*Sandy Carmichael.* London, Sampson Low, 1892; Philadelphia, Lippincott, 1908.
*The Captured Cruiser; or, Two Years from Land.* London, Blackie, 1892; New York, Scribner, 1895.
*The Wild-Catters.* London, Sunday School Union, 1895.
*Honour of Thieves.* London, Chatto and Windus, 1895; New York, Fenno, 1899; as *The Little Red Captain: An Early Adventure of Captain Kettle*, London, Pearson, 1902.
*The Stronger Hand.* London, Beeman, 1896.
*Through Arctic Lapland.* London, A. and C. Black, and New York, Macmillan, 1898.
*The Glass Dagger.* New York, New Amsterdam, 1899.
*The Filibusters.* London, Hutchinson, and New York, Stokes, 1900.
*Prince Rupert the Buccaneer.* London, Methuen, and New York, Stokes, 1901.
*Thompson's Progress.* London, Richards, 1902; New York, Macmillan, 1903.
*Captain Kettle, K.C.B.* London, Pearson, and New York, Federal, 1903.
*McTodd.* London and New York, Macmillan, 1903.
*The Trials of Commander McTurk.* London, Murray, and New York, Dutton, 1906.
*Kate Meredith, Financier.* New York, Authors and Newspapers Association, 1906; as *Kate Meredith*, London, Cassell, 1907.
*The Marriage of Kettle.* London, Heinemann, and Indianapolis, Bobbs Merrill, 1912.
*Firemen Hot.* London, Methuen, 1914.
*Captain Kettle on the War-Path.* London, Methuen, 1916.
*Captain Kettle's Bit.* London, Hodder and Stoughton, 1918.
*Admiral Teach.* London, Methuen, 1920.
*President Kettle.* London, Nash and Grayson, 1920.
*Mr. Kettle, Third Mate.* London, Ward Lock, 1931.
*West Highland Spirits.* London, Ward Lock, 1932.
*Captain Kettle, Ambassador.* London, Ward Lock, 1932.
*Absent Friends.* London, Ward Lock, 1933.
*Ivory Valley: An Adventure of Captain Kettle.* London, Ward Lock, 1938.
*Wishing Smith.* London, Hale, 1939.

Novels as Weatherby Chesney

*The Dilemma of Commander Brett.* London, Bowden, 1899.
*John Topp, Pirate.* London, Methuen, 1901.
*The Branded Prince.* London, Methuen, 1902.
*The Foundered Galleon.* London, Methuen, 1902.
*The Baptist Ring.* London, Methuen, 1903.
*The Mystery of a Bungalow.* London, Methuen, 1904.
*The Tragedy of the Great Emerald.* London, Methuen, 1904.
*The Cable-Man.* London, Chatto and Windus, 1907.
*The Claimant.* London, Chatto and Windus, 1908.
*The Romance of a Queen.* London, Chatto and Windus, 1908.

Short Stories

*The Paradise Coal-Boat.* London, Bowden, and New York, Mansfield, 1897.
*Adventures of Captain Kettle.* London, Pearson, and New York, Doubleday, 1898.
*The Adventures of an Engineer* (as Weatherby Chesney). London, Bowden, 1898.
*Further Adventures of Captain Kettle.* London, Pearson, 1899; as *A Master of Fortune*, New York, Dillingham, 1901.
*The Derelict.* New York, Lewis Scribner, 1901; revised edition, as *Mr. Horrocks, Purser*, London, Methuen, 1902.
*The Escape Agents.* London, Laurie, 1911.

*Red Herrings.* London, Methuen, 1918.
*The Rev. Captain Kettle.* London, Harrap, 1925.
*Ben Watson.* London, Country Life, 1926.
*Steamboatmen.* London, Penguin, 1943.

Other

*People and Places.* London, Newnes, 1930.
*But Britons Are Slaves.* London, Harmsworth, 1931.
*My Joyful Life.* London, Hutchinson, 1935.
*Don't You Agree?* (essays). London, Hutchinson, 1935.

Editor, *For Britain's Soldiers.* London, Methuen, 1900.

* * *

Half a dozen of C.J. Cutcliffe Hyne's novels are SF, as are some of his many short stories ("The Men from Mars" in *The Adventures of a Solicitor*). In *Beneath Your Very Boots* the narrator finds beneath England a race descended underground in pre-Roman times, using Earth heat as energy source, manufacturing diamonds, but otherwise living in a theocratic dictatorship à la Rider Haggard. In a dilution of Bulwer-Lytton's *The Coming Race,* the narrator-hero invents a boring machine, is rewarded by a pleasure drug, and during an unsuccessful rebellion escapes with the obligatory beautiful underground wife.

*The New Eden* and *The Recipe for Diamonds* are more pallid. In the first, an archduke-scientist sets up on a Pacific island the experiment of starting a young man and woman from zero; they invent art, alcohol, and Sun-worship. In the second, Lully's recipe is found and, after intrigues involving the equally obligatory anarchist, destroyed again. *The Lost Continent* is a relatively readable Haggard-type melodrama of Atlantis, narrated by a nobleman of those times involved with a strong upstart empress. Though she is the most interesting character of the novel, women's rule still leads to decadence and the flood, after political intrigues and fights with giant saurians and cave-tigers. In *Empire of the World* a poor scientist with a ray-machine that disintegrates iron intervenes in the war of Britain vs. Germany, enforcing peace. It is an unsuccessful try at fusing the "future war" story with "a rather heavy-handed comedy of romantic entanglements in high society" (R.D. Mullen, in *Science-Fiction Studies 6*, 1975). Finally, *Abbs* is a novel about longevity, the protagonist living "through many ages." In all, Hyne is a good example of the middle range of pre-World-War SF, a competent storyteller who wrote too conventionally and too much.

—Darko Suvin

# I

**ING, Dean.** American. Born in Austin, Texas, 17 June 1931. Educated at Fresno State University, B.A. 1956; San Jose State University, M.A. 1970; University of Oregon, Eugene, Ph.D. in Speech 1974. Served in the United States Air Force, 1951–55; Airman 1st Class. Married Margaret Barrier in 1952 (divorced 1957), two children; 2) Geneva Baker in 1959, two children. Engineer, Aerojet-General, Sacramento, California, 1957–62, and Lockheed, San Jose, California, 1962, 1965–70; Assistant Professor of Speech, Missouri State University, 1974–77. Since 1977, freelance writer. Address: 1105 Ivy Lane, Ashland, Oregon 97520, U.S.A.

SCIENCE-FICTION PUBLICATIONS

Novels (series: The Man-Kzin Wars; Quantrill)

*Soft Targets*. New York, Ace, 1979.
*Systemic Shock* (Quantrill). New York, Ace, 1981.
*Pulling Through*. New York, Ace, 1983.
*Single Combat* (Quantrill). New York, Tor, 1983.
*Wild Country* (Quantrill). New York, Tor, 1985.
*The Big Lifters*. New York, Tor, 1988.
*The Man-Kzin Wars*, with Larry Niven and Poul Anderson. New York, Baen, 1988.
*The Man-Kzin Wars II*, with Larry Niven, Jerry Pournelle, and S.M. Stirling. New York, Baen, 1989.
*Cathouse* (two novellas from *The Man-Kzin Wars*). New York, Baen, 1990.

Short Stories

*Anasazi*. New York, Ace, 1980.
*High Tension* (includes non-fiction). New York, Ace, 1982.
*Firefight 2000* (includes non-fiction). New York, Baen, 1987.

OTHER PUBLICATIONS

Novels

*Blood of Eagles*. New York, Tor, 1987.
*The Ransom of Black Stealth One*. New York, St. Martin's Press, 1989.

Other

*High Frontier*, with Daniel Graham. New York, Tor, 1983.
*Mutual Assured Survival: A Space-Age Solution to Nuclear Annihilation*, with Jerry Pournelle. New York, Baen, 1984.
*The Future of Flight*, with Leik Myrabo. New York, Baen, 1985.
*The Chernobyl Syndrome*. New York, Baen, 1988.

Editor, *The Lagrangists*, by Mack Reynolds. New York, Tor, 1983.
Editor, *Home Sweet Home 2010 A.D.*, by Mack Reynolds. New York, Dell, 1984.
Editor, *Eternity*, by Mack Reynolds. New York, Pocket Books, 1984.
Editor, *The Other Time*, by Mack Reynolds. New York, Pocket Books, 1984.
Editor, *Trojan Orbit*, by Mack Reynolds. New York, Baen, 1985.
Editor, *Deathwish World*, by Mack Reynolds. New York, Baen, 1986.

*

Bibliography: *The Work of Dean Ing: An Annotated Bibliography and Guide* by Scott Alan Burgess, San Bernardino, California, Borgo Press, 1990.

Dean Ing comments:

As a former senior engineer and behavioral scientist, I write hard-nosed, hard SF. Many of the things I have to say are speculative; some are unpleasant; some are vulgar and/or titillating. It takes a very good university to employ a gadfly, and I found professoring dreary. As a media theorist I felt I could put my ideas over much more widely in fast-paced fictional thrillers than in lecture halls. Q.E.D.

I rarely write before I've decided what needs saying, and outlined it excitingly. I'm a contentist. It's a sign of our times that I had to invent a word that stresses content over style, though the word "stylist" is common enough, God knows. . . .

Literature stressing content over style demands much of readers, so I must make that content sparkle like rhinestones on a soapbox. I research my work as thoroughly as possible, but I no longer take as many physical risks as I once did. But when I describe what it's like to bail out of a moving race car or get plastered against a blockhouse floor by a rocket explosion, often it's dredged up from memory.

* * *

Dean Ing's greatest success came with his classy Tom Clancy-ish techno-thriller, *The Ransom of Black Stealth One.* U.S. Intelligence seeks to trick the Russians into buying an inferior version of the world's most advanced aircraft from a defector. But the real Black Stealth One is stolen from the National Security Agency by a rogue agent who takes both the plane and a hostage: Petra, a beautiful engineer. *The Ransom of Black Stealth One* is crammed with excitement, romance, and tension as both American and Soviet intelligence agencies risk everything to capture the super aircraft. Ing's earlier thriller, *Blood of Eagles*, shares the same relentless intensity of *The Ransom of Black Stealth One* but culminating in the low-tech setting of the Sierra mountains. A teenage boy is being hunted down by killers who want the secret of the stolen Nazi gold. Ing keeps the chase interesting right up to the heart-pounding climax.

Ing's latest science-fiction novel, *The Big Lifters*, reworks many of his favorite themes. Entrepreneur John Wesley Peel develops an alternative to trucks: a combination of dirigible and magnetic levitation trains. Opposing this safer, more efficient advance are the Teamsters—who fear job losses—and Iranian terrorists. The characters are wooden and the plot is predictable.

More entertaining is *Cathouse,* a collection of two novellas, "Cathouse" and "Briar Patch" which were previously published separately in Larry Niven's *Man-Kzin War* series. Both stories echo the wit of Eric Frank Russell's classic stories of humans outsmarting aliens.

Ing's first novel, *Soft Targets,* presents many of the themes he develops in his later works: the fragility of society and the importance of individualism. Hakim Arif, a terrorist who calls his organization Fat'ah, sees an open society such as the United States filled with "soft targets" that he can strike at will. In the near future, Ing suggests, terrorism and an open society may be mutually exclusive. Much is made of the power of the media to turn terrorists into media stars. The character of Hakim Arif is well drawn and chillingly convincing. The problem is with the plot: the FCC commissioner Maurice Everett and heads of the major television networks create a straw man in the comedian Charlie George who satirizes terrorists on his program to draw out Fat'ah. However, Everett miscalculates the cleverness of the terrorists and finds himself kidnapped along with Charlie George. The conclusion, though realistically violent, lacks coherence.

*Anasazi,* a collection of two novellas and a short novel, is uneven. The title short story, "Anasazi," deals with the possession of a tribe of Indians by parasitic aliens. Although it addresses many of the same issues as Robert Silverberg's award-winning "Passengers," "Anasazi" shows more control over the characters and plot by Ing. The novella, "The Devil You Don't Know," concerns a drug ring operating within a mental hospital. Ing's handling of psi powers in this story is deft and convincing.

*Systemic Shock* introduces readers to a nuclear/biological holocaust where the United States and its allies suffer staggering losses from the India-China alliance. Most of the large cities of the world are reduced to rubble and only decentralized populations survive. Ing creates a likable hero in young 15-year-old Ted Quantrill and presents a surviving society dominated by the Mormon and other religious groups. Quantrill loses his family in the nuclear strikes and biological plagues. Because of his intelligence and lightning reflexes, he's recruited into the new government's secret T Section as a gunsel. A receiver/transmitter is surgically planted in his skull, along with an explosive charge. Quantrill shows us how to survive in the new "Streamlined America" where nuclear bombs have destroyed most of the rules and the power to rule comes from the barrels of guns. Ing's realism is refreshing when compared to other post-holocaust novels like Jerry Ahern's bloody "Survivalist" series. Even so, Ing makes the plot unnecessarily complicated and the conclusion unsatisfying.

Ing's most interesting collection is *High Tension,* which is a blend of fact articles and short stories. "Gimme Shelter" is a detailed account of how to survive a nuclear war. This is an issue Ing returns to in *Pulling Through.* The short story "Down and Out on Ellfive Prime" owes a debt to George Orwell as Ing explores life aboard an orbiting space colony. "Living Under Pressure" presents detailed photographs to aid in the construction of an air supply unit for a small nuclear shelter. The best part of *High Tension* is Ing's powerful introductions to each story and article, giving the reader more insight into his philosophy.

*Pulling Through* puts all Ing's survivalist articles into practice as Harve Rackham and Kate Gallo survive the nuking of the San Francisco area and find the means to pull through the crisis. They build an air pump and filter, and they make their own fallout radiation meter from common household materials. Harve and Kate have to survive more than radiation as the other survivors, ordinary citizens and escaped convicts, supply subplots. But *Pulling Through* is more didactic than entertaining. The details of Harve and Kate's survival are interesting but can't make up for the plot weaknesses.

With *Single Combat* Ing returns to his most convincing vision: post-holocaust America dominated by the Mormons and other religious groups. Ted Quantrill returns, older by a few years, and more disenchanted with his role as a government assassin. Resistance to the new order of theocracy is emerging and Ing manages to free Quantrill of the receiver-transmitter and explosive implanted in his head. Given his freedom, Quantrill seeks revenge on the government that controlled him for so long. *Single Combat* remains Ing's best book, combining an action packed plot and believable characters into a thrilling adventure story.

In addition to his own work, Dean Ing has completed a series of science-fiction novels left unfinished by the late Mack Reynolds. *Eternity* is a conventional immortality novel. *Trojan Orbit* is a thriller about sabotage aboard Island One, the first United States space colony. The best book is *The Other Time,* in which Donald Fielding is sent by timewarp to the court of Montezuma where he takes up the identity of Quetzalcoatl and helps the Aztecs defeat Cortez's Spanish troops.

Dean Ing is a solid, capable writer whose background in engineering and science is evident in his science fiction and in his successful techno-thrillers.

—George Kelley

---

**INNES, Alan (or Allan).** *See* **TUBB, E.C.**

---

**IRWIN, G.H.** *See* **PALMER, Raymond A.; SHAVER, Richard S.**

---

# J

**JAKES, John (William).** Also writes as William Ard; Alan Payne; Jay Scotland. American. Born in Chicago, Illinois, 31 March 1932. Educated at DePauw University, Greencastle, Indiana, A.B. 1953; Ohio State University, Columbus, M.A. in American literature 1954. Married Rachel Ann Payne in 1951; three daughters and one son. Copywriter, then promotion manager, Abbott Laboratories, North Chicago, 1954–60; copywriter, Rumrill Company, Rochester, New York, 1960–61; freelance writer, 1961–65; copywriter, Kircher Helton and Collett, Dayton, Ohio, 1965–68; copy chief, then vice-president, Oppenheim Herminghausen and Clarke, Dayton, 1968–70; creative director, Dancer Fitzgerald Sample, Dayton, 1970–71. Writer-in-Residence, DePauw University, Fall 1979. Since 1971, freelance writer. LL.D.: Wright State University, Dayton, Ohio, 1976; Litt.D.: DePauw University, 1977; L.H.D., Winthrop College, 1985. Address: c/o Rembar and Curtis, Attorneys, 19 West 44th Street, New York, New York 10036, U.S.A.

SCIENCE-FICTION PUBLICATIONS

Novels (series: Dragonard; Klekton)

*When the Star Kings Die* (Dragonard). New York, Ace, 1967.
*The Asylum World.* New York, Paperback Library, 1969; London, New English Library, 1978.
*The Hybrid.* New York, Paperback Library, 1969.
*The Planet Wizard* (Dragonard). New York, Ace, 1969.
*Secrets of Stardeep* (for children). Philadelphia, Westminster Press, 1969.
*Tonight We Steal the Stars* (Dragonard). New York, Ace, 1969.
*Black in Time.* New York, Paperback Library, 1970.
*Mask of Chaos.* New York, Ace, 1970.
*Master of the Dark Gate* (Klekton). New York, Lancer, 1970.
*Monte Cristo 99.* New York, Curtis, 1970.
*Six-Gun Planet.* New York, Paperback Library, 1970; London, New English Library, 1978.
*Mention My Name in Atlantis.* New York, DAW, 1972.
*Time Gate* (for children). Philadelphia, Westminster Press, 1972.
*Witch of the Dark Gate* (Klekton). New York, Lancer, 1972.
*Conquest of the Planet of the Apes* (novelization of screenplay). New York, Award, 1972.
*On Wheels.* New York, Paperback Library, 1973.

Short Stories

*The Best of John Jakes*, edited by Martin H. Greenberg and Joseph D. Olander. New York, DAW, 1977.
*Fortunes of Brak.* New York, Dell, 1980.

OTHER PUBLICATIONS

Novels

*The Texans Ride North* (for children). Philadelphia, Winston, 1952.
*Wear a Fast Gun.* New York, Arcadia House, 1956; London, Ward Lock, 1957.
*A Night for Treason.* New York, Bouregy, 1956.
*The Devil Has Four Faces.* New York, Bouregy, 1958.
*This'll Slay You* (as Alan Payne). New York, Ace, 1958.
*The Imposter.* New York, Bouregy, 1959.
*Johnny Havoc.* New York, Belmont, 1960; London, Severn, 1990.
*Johnny Havoc Meets Zelda.* New York, Belmont, 1962; as *Havoc for Sale*, New York, Armchair Detective Library, 1990.
*Johnny Havoc and the Doll Who Had "It."* New York, Belmont, 1963; as *Holiday for Havoc*, New York, Armchair Detective Library, 1991.
*G.I. Girls.* Derby, Connecticut, Monarch, 1963.
*Making It Big.* New York, Belmont, 1968; as *Johnny Havoc and the Siren in Red*, New York, Armchair Detective Library, 1991.
*Brak Versus the Mark of the Demons.* New York, Paperback Library, 1969; as *Brak the Barbarian—The Mark of the Demons*, London, Tandem, 1970.
*Brak the Barbarian Versus the Sorceress.* New York, Paperback Library, 1969; as *Brak the Barbarian—The Sorceress*, London, Tandem, 1970.
*The Last Magicians.* New York, New American Library, 1969.
Kent Family Chronicles:
- *The Bastard.* New York, Pyramid, 1974; as *Fortune's Whirlwind* and *To an Unknown Shore*, London, Corgi, 2 vols., 1975.
- *The Rebels.* New York, Pyramid, 1975; London, Corgi, 1979.
- *The Seekers.* New York, Pyramid, 1975; London, Corgi, 1979.
- *The Furies.* New York, Pyramid 1976; London, Corgi, 1979.
- *The Titans.* New York, Pyramid 1976; London, Corgi, 1979.
- *The Warriors.* New York, Pyramid, 1977; London, Corgi, 1979.
- *The Lawless.* New York, Jove, 1978; London, Corgi, 1979.
- *The Americans.* New York, Jove, 1980; London, Fontana, 1989.

*Brak: When the Idols Walked.* New York, Pocket Books, 1978.
*Excalibur!*, with Gil Kane. New York, Dell, 1980.
North and South trilogy:
- *North and South.* New York, Harcourt Brace, and London, Collins, 1982.
- *Love and War.* New York, Harcourt Brace, 1984; London, Collins, 1985.
- *Heaven and Hell.* New York, Harcourt Brace, 1987; London Collins, 1988.

*California Gold.* New York, Random House, 1989; London, Collins, 1990.

Novels as Jay Scotland

*The Seventh Man.* New York, Bouregy, 1958.
*I, Barbarian.* New York, Avon, 1959; revised edition, as John Jakes, New York, Pinnacle, 1976.
*Strike the Black Flag.* New York, Ace, 1961.

*Sir Scoundrel.* New York, Ace, 1962; revised edition, as *King's Crusader*, New York, Pinnacle 1977.
*Veils of Salome.* New York, Avon, 1962.
*Arena.* New York, Ace, 1963.
*Traitors' Legion.* New York, Ace, 1963; revised edition, as *The Man from Cannae*, New York, Pinnacle, 1977.

Novels as William Ard

*Make Mine Mavis.* Derby, Connecticut, Monarch, 1961.
*And So to Bed.* Derby, Connecticut, Monarch, 1962.
*Give Me This Woman.* Derby, Connecticut, Monarch, 1962.

Short Stories

*Brak the Barbarian.* New York, Avon, 1968; London, Tandem, 1970.
*The Best Western Stories of John Jakes*, edited by Martin H. Greenberg and Bill Pronzini. Athens, Ohio University Press, 1991.

Plays

*Dracula, Baby* (lyrics only). Chicago, Dramatic Publishing Company, 1970.
*Wind in the Willows.* Elgin, Illinois, Performance, 1972.
*A Spell of Evil.* Chicago, Dramatic Publishing Company, 1972.
*Violence.* Elgin, Illinois, Performance, 1972.
*Stranger with Roses*, adaptation of his own story. Chicago, Dramatic Publishing Company, 1972.
*For I Am a Jealous People*, adaptation of the story by Lester del Rey. Elgin, Illinois, Performance, 1972.
*Gaslight Girl.* Chicago, Dramatic Publishing Company, 1973.
*Pardon Me, Is This Planet Taken?* Chicago, Dramatic Publishing Company, 1973.
*Doctor, Doctor!*, music by Gilbert M. Martin, adaptation of a play by Molière. New York, McAfee Music, 1973.
*Shepherd Song.* New York, McAfee Music, 1974.

Other

*Tiros: Weather Eye in Space.* New York, Messner, 1966.
*Famous Firsts in Sports.* New York, Putnam, 1967.
*Great War Correspondents.* New York, Putnam, 1968.
*Great Women Reporters.* New York, Putnam, 1969.
*The Bastard Photostory.* New York, Jove, 1980.
*Susanna at the Alamo: A True Story* (for children). New York, Harcourt Brace, 1986.

*

Bibliography: in *The Best Western Stories of John Jakes*, edited by Martin H. Greenberg and Bill Pronzini, Athens, Ohio University Press, 1991.

Manuscript Collections: University of Wyoming, Laramie; DePauw University, Greencastle, Indiana.

Critical Study: *The Kent Family Chronicles Encyclopedia* edited by Robert Hawkins, New York, Bantam, 1979.

John Jakes comments:

My first sale was a science fiction story. I grew up on the genre, and wanted to write nothing else—though I did. Eventually, the novels I did turn out were greeted unenthusiastically, and two or three on which I worked particularly hard, and of which I was particularly proud—*Six-Gun Planet, Black in Time, On Wheels*—disappeared almost within days of publication. That convinced me to stop writing SF. I have friends among science-fiction writers, but found the few conventions I attended in large part boring—perhaps a second reason I abandoned the field: not, I must add, without considerable regret.

* * *

Unfortunately, as far as his science-fiction writing is concerned, John Jakes is best known for creating Brak the Barbarian. This is not to demean the Brak stories but rather to rue the fact that Jakes has written several other excellent novels which have gone virtually unnoticed.

The Brak stories follow a specific formula and so, even though very good, become wearisome by the repetition of their active force represented by the god Yob-Haggoth and is implemented by his agent, Septegundus, a man with no eyelids and skin covered with the living, writhing figures of the souls he has captured. Septegundus is aided by his beautiful but equally evil daughter, Ariane. Throughout his various "on-the-road" adventures, Brak encounters analogues of Ariane, whom he eventually recognizes by their display of evil and lustful natures. Nordica Fire-Hair, in *The Sorceress*, is an excellent example. A dutiful daughter, she suddenly changes. She leaves her father, an alchemist who has learned the secret of turning things to gold, to die in a deep pit inhabited by a dragonlike creature called Manworm. As Brak becomes more and more involved with her, he recognizes that she is possessed by Ariane. When Nordica is finally killed, Brak sees the spirit of Ariane leaving the corpse.

Cast out of his own land in the far north for blaspheming the gods, Brak is constantly pursued by the forces of Septegundus in his eternal quest to reach the fabled golden city of Khurdisan in the south. Septegundus has vowed to kill him for interfering in his affairs. An incarnation of Conan, Brak is instinctive and physical, but even his strength and cunning are no match for the supernatural forces of evil, so he is aided in his continuing battle with Yob-Haggoth by various Nestorian priests who represent the mysterious Nameless God. Inevitably, Brak loses his sword, encounters some sort of fantastic monster which he must slay, Manworm, Scarlet-jaw, Doomdog, or The Thing That Crawls, and plies his way toward Khurdisan. But regardless of the formalization of the stories and the impression that some were written hastily, their fast-paced action recommends them. Within the formula, Jakes's inventiveness makes the stories both attractive and interesting.

The highly imaginative quality of Jakes's writing is perhaps better displayed in some of his other novels. Among them, *The Planet Wizard, The Hybrid*, and the Klekton books are the best. The Klekton is a ring of alternate Earths that can be reached by traveling through various mindgates. The novels tell the story of Gavin Black, a down-and-out journalist who becomes a pawn of Bronwyn, a police official of an alternative world called Earth Prime. Bronwyn is attempting to stop an invasion of our Earth from yet another alternate Earth called Earth Three or Shulkor. The population of all three Earths are descended from a great civilization that lived on heartland Earth before the Ice Age. When cold and ice threatened them, some went up the Klekton and some down, there to develop into radically different peoples. The Shulkorites became savage and warlike, while Bronwyn's people developed their intellectual abilities. Now, the Shulkorites want to use heartland Earth as a base to destroy Earth Prime and to extend their power to the more hospitable worlds down the chain. At first bribed, Black later permits himself to be used so that he can gain access to the gates in order to be reunited with Samantha, a girl from Earth Three with whom he has fallen in love.

*The Hybrid* tells the story of Andreas Law, the son of an Earth father and an Omqu mother, who has the unique ability to project destructive blasts of mental energy. Law becomes the tool of a fanatic Earth billionaire, Sir Robert Baron, who is trying to sabotage a proposed peace treaty between Earth and Omqu because he hates the humanoid but feathered aliens. Cast against a background of two intergalactic cultures trying to understand one another, *The Hybrid* is a story of prejudice handled sensitively and thoughtfully. It is a perceptive and imaginative exploration of what might happen when man achieves intergalactic travel and finds that he is not the only humanoid in the universe.

*The Planet Wizard* is a story of self-discovery, power, and love. Set in another galaxy eons after it has been colonized by Earthmen, *The Planet Wizard* tells of civilizations left to cope for themselves after planetary wars have destroyed the great business houses that controlled galactic society. Superstition abounds as knowledge and technology fade. Magus Blacklaw, a bogus magician but first-rate confidence man, traps himself and his daughter, Maya, into having to make a trip to the feared planet of Lightmark to exorcise its demons and to secure access to the resources of the great house that did business there. Blacklaw is a lovable rogue who rises above himself in his efforts to provide a better life for his daughter. In ridding Lightmark of its demons, he finds strength and courage he did not know he possessed.

Jakes is a highly competent writer whose imagination and versatility deserve respect. Always interesting, his stories provide fast-paced entertainment while imaginatively exploring the possibility of life in the distant future.

—Carl B. Yoke

---

**JANIFER, Laurence M.** Pseudonym for Larry Mark Harris; also writes as Alfred Blake; Andrew Blake; Mark Phillips; Barbara Wilson. American. Born in Brooklyn, New York, 17 March 1933. Attended City College of New York, one year. Married 1) Sylvia Siegel in 1955 (divorced 1958); 2) Sue Blugerman in 1960 (divorced 1962); 3) Rae Montor in 1966 (divorced 1968); 4) Beverly Goldberg in 1969 (separated 1984); two daughters and one son. Pianist and arranger, New York, 1950–59; editor, Scott Meredith Literary Agency, New York, 1952–57, 1985–91; editor and art director, detective and science-fiction magazines, 1953–57; professional comedian, 1957–70. Agent: Scott Meredith Literary Agency, 845 Third Avenue, New York, New York 10022, U.S.A.

### Science-Fiction Publications

Novels (series: Angelo di Stefano; Gerald Knave; Survivor)

*Slave Planet*. New York, Pyramid, 1963.
*The Wonder War*. New York, Pyramid, 1964.
*You Sane Men*. New York, Lancer, 1965; as *Bloodworld*, 1968.
*A Piece of Martin Cann*. New York, Belmont, 1968.
*Target: Terra* (di Stefano), with S.J. Treibich. New York, Ace, 1968.
*The High Hex* (di Stefano), with S.J. Treibich. New York, Ace, 1969.
*The Wagered World* (di Stefano), with S.J. Treibich. New York, Ace, 1969.
*Power*. New York, Dell, 1974.
*Survivor* (Knave). New York, Ace, 1977.
*Knave in Hand*. New York, Ace, 1979.
*Reel*. New York, Doubleday, 1983.

Novels as Mark Phillips (with Randall Garrett) (series: Kenneth J. Malone in all books)

*Brain Twister*. New York, Pyramid, 1962.
*The Impossibles*. New York, Pyramid, 1963.
*Supermind*. New York, Pyramid, 1963.

Short Stories

*Impossible?* New York, Belmont, 1968.
*. . . Knave and the Game*. New York, Doubleday, 1987.

### Other Publications

Novels

*Pagan Passions* (as Larry M. Harris), with Randall Garrett. New York, Galaxy, 1959.
*The Pickled Poodles* (as Larry M. Harris). New York, Random House, 1960; London, Boardman, 1961.
*The Protector* (as Larry M. Harris). New York, Random House, 1961; London, Boardman, 1962.
*The Bed and I* (as Alfred Blake). N.p., Intimate, 1962.
*Faithful for 8 Hours* (as Alfred Blake). New York, Beacon, 1963.
*The Pleasure We Know* (as Barbara Wilson). New York, Lancer, 1964.
*The Velvet Embrace* (as Barbara Wilson). New York, Lancer, 1965.
*The Woman Without a Name*. New York, New American Library, 1966.
*The Final Fear*. New York, Belmont, 1967.
*You Can't Escape*. New York, Lancer, 1967.

Novels as Andrew Blake

*I Deal in Desire*. N.p., Boudoir, 1962.
*Sex Swinger*. New York, Beacon, 1963.
*Love Hostess*. New York, Beacon, 1963.

Other

Editor, *Master's Choice*. New York, Simon and Schuster, 1966; London, Jenkins, 1967; as *18 Great Science Fiction Stories*, New York, Grosset and Dunlap, 1971.

Ghost Writer for *Ken Murray's Giant Joke Book*, 1957; *The Henry Morgan Joke Book*, 1958; *The Foot in My Mouth* by Jeff Harris, 1958; *Tracer!* by Ed Goldfader, 1970; editor for *Yes, I'm Here with Someone* by Thomas Sutton, 1958.

*

Laurence M. Janifer comments:

I write funny stuff or non-funny stuff. It depends on how I feel. In either case, all I aim at doing is providing a world for the reader to live in for a while. Once in a long while I'll try to demonstrate an axiom of some sort—not often. I'd rather write funny stuff (or semi-funny stuff like the Knave adventures) because there is so damned little of it around. But I have not got much control over what my head sends me. I write SF because it fascinates me, and I continue to have the nagging feeling that SF ought to have something to do with science. I am violently against any attempt to get a scholarly view of my work or to assess my Purpose in Writing. This sort of thing should be stamped out. If you can believe and live in the worlds I write, I'm both happy and flattered. I look forward to creating more worlds, some SF and some not, for an indefinite time.

* * *

A first impression of Laurence M. Janifer's books might be that they emphasize stock subjects and sensation. *You Sane Men* is the story of a world on which Bound Men and Bound Women are held as objects of torture in what are called Remand Houses. The "Lords and Ladies" inflict pain on them with whips and hot brands and derive pleasure or sexual strength from this. In *Power*, Aaron Norin, the son of a respected empire official, leads a spaceship in rebellion against the empire. *Slave Planet* is about a world where cynical colonists from earth use alligator-like aliens as slaves to extract precious metals. Mental telepathy is used in *A Piece of Martin Cann* to cure a patient; *The Wonder War* is about a war to gain power over an entire galaxy.

These lurid but stock topics, however, acquire some complexity in Janifer's best novels. Janifer's central subjects are power and rebellion, and he often treats these with subtle irony. Jo, the narrator of *You Sane Men*, is a refugee from the world of blood, addressing the "sane men" who doubt that it is possible for human beings to run a social system based on torture. But his horrible world is sane and is human, for the point is that sane people are capable of extreme, thoughtless cruelty. Jo joins with other young people in a revolt against the ruling council, a revolt ironically not against the institution of cruelty but against the exclusion of young people from decision-making. When a lady is killed another irony develops: in contrast to our crime-ridden earth, the blood world has never had a murder, and its natives are comically inept detectives. Torture is legalized, but other crimes are almost unknown. Satire of our sexual taboos develops when Jo is shocked to discover that some men enjoy torturing men, and women.

The irony of *Power* is more understated. Isidor Norin's family all have power. His daughter Rachel is married to a famous actor, and his son Alphard is the assistant to a powerful religious leader. When the spaceship *Valor*, lead by his son Aaron, rebels from the empire, Aaron is killed and his father becomes critically ill. The rebellion is apparently crushed, and the Emperor retains all formal power, but the idea of freedom has been kindled in several minds. In *Slave Planet* Janifer gently portrays the naive point of view of several of the enslaved aliens. Janifer avoids pathos by giving us their puzzled acceptance of their condition. We are also made to see through the rather exaggerated moralism which brings a military liberation force from the shocked confederation to Fruyling's world. Thus, the overthrow of slavery and its replacement by automatic machinery are complex events. We reject the view of Dr. Haelingen that slavery is inevitable on this world, but we do consider it.

Janifer's short stories are competent but routine, although his talent at presenting unusual points of view comes through in such stories as "Thine Alabaster Cities Gleam" (in *Future City*, edited by Roger Elwood, New York, Simon and Schuster, 1973), about a couple caught in a sky scraper at night when the electricity, and the air supply, goes out. They will die—even the woman's diamond can make only faint scratches in the window. "Civis Obit" (in *Dystopian Visions*, edited by Roger Elwood, Englewood Cliffs, New Jersey, Prentice Hall, 1975) gives us the point of view of a telepath who preserves sanity only by developing the skill of shutting out human suffering. "Amfortas" (in *Omega*, edited by Roger Elwood, New York, Walker 1974) develops the psychological effects of massive organ transplants.

The multiple points of view of *Reel* signal Janifer's entry into literary modernism. Although the subject matter is familiar to Janifer readers—a power struggle on "The Reel," a resort planet of the far future—Janifer's technique is deft and impressionistic. Janifer is a writer of promise and more than occasional achievement.

—Curtis C. Smith

---

**JASON, Jerry.** *See* **SMITH, George H.**

---

**JAY, Mel.** *See* **FANTHORPE, R. Lionel.**

---

**JENKINS, Will F.** *See* **LEINSTER, Murray.**

---

**JETER, K.W.** American. Born in Los Angeles, California, in 1950. Agent: Russ Galen, Scott Meredith Literary Agency, 845 Third Avenue, New York, New York 10022, U.S.A.

### Science-Fiction Publications

Novels

*Seeklight.* Toronto, Laser, 1975.
*The Dreamfields.* Toronto, Laser, 1976.
*Morlock Night.* New York, DAW, 1979; London, Grafton, 1989.
*Dr. Adder.* New York, Bluejay, 1984; London, Grafton, 1987.
*The Glass Hammer.* New York, Bluejay, 1985; London, Grafton, 1987.
*Infernal Devices.* New York, St. Martin's Press, 1987; London, Grafton, 1988.
*Mantis.* New York, Tor, 1987.
*Farewell Horizontal.* New York, St. Martin's Press, 1989; London, Grafton, 1990.

### Other Publications

Novels

*Soul Eater.* New York, Tor, 1983; London, Kinnell, 1989.
*Night Vision.* New York, Tor, 1985.
*Death Arms.* New York, St. Martin's Press, 1987; Bath, Morrigan, 1989.

*Dark Seeker*. New York, Tor, 1987.
*In the Land of the Dead*. New York, New American Library, and Bath, Morrigan, 1989.
*The Night Man*. New York, New American Library, 1990.

* * *

K.W. Jeter's work has the flavor of Philip K. Dick's studies in reality at their best. In Jeter's most imaginative SF novel, *Farewell Horizontal*, he creates the Cylinder: a vast building whose bulk reaches high above the clouds. Jeter's hero, Ny Axxter, leaves the comfortable, data-dominated society within the Cylinder to encounter the bizarre life of living on the vertical walls outside the Cylinder. The situation is surreal, and yet Jeter gives this weird setting credibility and drama as Ny Axxter explores this fascinating world far from our horizontal reality.

From Jeter's first published novel, *Seeklight*, it was clear Jeter possessed a talent for conjuring up innovative, exciting settings. *Seeklight* features a semi-feudal society and a young man named Daenek whose identity as son of a former leader gets him marked for death. Yet, in the middle of the action, a sociologist will appear through the use of super-science technology and ask questions of the novel's participants like any good graduate research assistant would. This is the odd juxtapositioning of Jeter's reality: one world holds several different, even contradicting, realities. Yet the strange mingling of worlds works; Barry Malzberg, in the introduction to *Seeklight*, calls Jeter's first novel "one of the three or four best SF novels I have ever read."

Jeter's next novel, *The Dreamfields*, reads very much like a Philip K. Dick novel. Ralph Metric is a member of Operation Dreamwatch, supposedly an experimental project to control and observe severely disturbed teenagers through their dreams. Yet in the dreamstate, Ralph discovers a different reality operating. There is an alien invasion of Earth forming in the Dreamfields and those disturbed teenagers' dreams hold power in the aliens' alternate reality. Shifting identities and surreal plot elements make *The Dreamfields* one of Jeter's most ambitious novels.

*Morlock Night* is Jeter's attempt to finish H.G. Wells's *The Time Machine.* At the conclusion of Wells's book, the Time Traveller went back to the future of the Morlocks and the Eloi and never returned. Jeter supposes: what if the Time Traveller was murdered by the Morlocks and they used the Time Machine to invade England of 1892? An interesting notion gone wrong is the result. A young man named Edwin Hocker is recruited by a cryptic man calling himself Dr. Ambrose. Together they try to change the reality of the deadly Morlock invasion by ringing together the ancient sword of power: Excalibur. The novel goes awry when Merlin and King Arthur join forces to defeat the Morlock menace. Too much of the book is spent mucking around in the London sewers—the Morlock's secret staging area—and too much of the plot is predictable.

Much superior to *Morlock Night* is Jeter's later, more sophisticated Victorianesque novel, *Infernal Devices.* The Brown Leather Man, a mysterious being, brings George Dower a device to repair, which George's genius father had built decades ago. Mad plot complications multiply as Jeter creates a wild, entertaining fantasy in the mists of Old London.

*Dr. Adder*—Jeter's most controversial novel—includes an afterward by Philip K. Dick comparing the book to the works of James Joyce and Henry Miller, and the more daring story in Harlan Ellison's *Dangerous Visions.* Jeter couldn't find a publisher for the work, written in 1972, for more than a decade because of its graphic violence and sex. Most of the book's action centers around Los Angeles and its sewers of the near future. The city is populated by surgically altered prostitutes—the results of Dr. Adder's talents—and snipers, and Mother Endure who takes care of all the losers in Rattown. Opposed to his degenerate lifestyle is videopreacher John Mox and his Moral Forces. Into this maelstrom comes E. Allen Limmit on a mission to deliver a flashglove—a banned CIA weapon of incredible powers—to Dr. Adder. Like a catalyst, Limmit sets off a war among the powers of Los Angeles: a war that Limmit's true identity holds the key to.

The controversy surrounding *Dr. Adder* generated more heat than light. The book is the result of an immature writer just learning his craft: too much of *Dr. Adder* seems calculated to shock or disgust the reader rather than to move the plot of the book or develop the characters. There is much to praise in *Dr. Adder:* Jeter's picture of a nightmarish future controlled by cabals is innovative, evoking echoes of Dick's dark futures in *Flow My Tears, The Policeman Said* and *A Scanner, Darkly.* Certainly it prefigured the entire cyberpunk movement.

*Soul Eater* is Jeter's best book to date. David Braemer once had a happy marriage. Then his wife, Renee, after a bizarre episode in which she tried to kill her young daughter Dee, suffered a massive stroke and lies comatose, tended by her brother Jess and adopted sister Carol in their family house. Braemer is disturbed by Dee's behavior: the little girl will fall into a troubled sleep, then sleepwalk into the kitchen, find the largest knife she can, and head for Braemer's bedroom. Braemer has awoken to Dee standing over him with a knife ready to plunge into his chest. Braemer thinks the trauma of Renee's attempt on her daughter's life and subsequent stroke are affecting the little girl's sanity. But two people meet with Braemer to warn him: Kathy, Renee's other sister, and an enigmatic man named Pedersen. The warnings are the same: Renee has the power to insert her identity into others, and she is using Dee as an instrument to kill David. Braemer discounts the warnings as absurdities, but later finds more horror and more truth in those warnings than he could have imagined. *Soul Eater* is an extraordinary horror novel with Jeter's best-realized characters and writing.

Unfortunately, not all Jeter's horror novels equal the power of *Soul Eater. In the Land of the Dead* contains echoes of James M. Cain's classic *The Postman Always Rings Twice.* A California orange grower named Vandervelde is the victim of a murder plot as his mistress, Fay, and his foreman, Cooper, decide to murder him. The novel veers into the land of horror as Fay gets the murdered man's corpse to open his safe. *The Night Man* is a supernatural vengeance novel whose predictable plot never hangs together. *Dark Seeker* is an overblown novel of demonic possession whose brutality leads to the readers' exhaustion.

K.W. Jeter's most innovative works are science-fiction novels whose sense of reality are straight out of the Dickian universe. His horror novels feature both the best and the worst of his writing.

—George Kelley

---

**JOHNS, Kenneth.** *See* **BULMER, Kenneth.**

---

**JOHNS, Marston.** *See* **FANTHORPE, R. Lionel.**

---

**JOHNS, W(illiam) E(arl).** Also wrote as William Earle; Jon Early. British. Born in Bengeo, Hertfordshire, 5 February 1893. Educated at a school in Bengeo; Hertford Grammar School, 1905–07; articled to a Hertford surveyor, 1907–12. Married Maude Hunt in 1914 (died 1961), one son; lived with Doris May Leigh from 1924. Sanitary inspector, Swaffham, Norfolk, 1912–13. Served in the Norfolk Yeomanry, 1913–15, and in the Machine Gun Corps, in Egypt and Salonika, 1916–17; transferred to the Royal Flying Corps (later Royal Air Force), 1917, and served until 1927: shot down and captured in France, 1918; Flying Officer, 1920–27; lecturer, Air Defence Cadet Corps, later Air Training Corps, and writer for the Ministry of Defence, London, 1939–45. Aviation illustrator from 1927; founding editor, *Popular Flying*, 1932–39, and *Flying*, 1938–39, both London; columnist ("The Passing Show"), *My Garden* magazine, London, 1937–44, and for *Modern Boy, Pearson's, Boys' Own Paper*, and *Girls' Own Paper. Died 21 June 1968.*

SCIENCE-FICTION PUBLICATIONS (for children)

Novels (series: Rex Clinton in all books except *Biggles—Charter Pilot*)

*Biggles—Charter Pilot.* London, Oxford University Press, 1943.
*Kings of Space.* London, Hodder and Stoughton, 1954.
*Return to Mars.* London, Hodder and Stoughton, 1955.
*Now to the Stars.* London, Hodder and Stoughton, 1956.
*To Outer Space.* London, Hodder and Stoughton, 1957.
*The Edge of Beyond.* London, Hodder and Stoughton, 1958.
*The Death Rays of Ardilla.* London, Hodder and Stoughton, 1959.
*To Worlds Unknown.* London, Hodder and Stoughton, 1960.
*The Quest for the Perfect Planet.* London, Hodder and Stoughton, 1961.
*The Man Who Vanished into Space.* London, Hodder and Stoughton, 1963.

Short Stories

*Worlds of Wonder: More Adventures in Space.* London, Hodder and Stoughton, 1962.

OTHER PUBLICATIONS

Novels

*Mossyface* (as William Earle). London, Mellifont Press, 1932.
*The Spy Flyers.* London, John Hamilton, 1933.
*Sky High.* London, Newnes, 1936; revised edition, London, Latimer, 1951.
*Steeley Flies Again.* London, Newnes, 1936; revised edition, London, Latimer, 1951.
*Blue Blood Runs Red* (as Jon Early). London, Newnes, 1936.
*Murder by Air.* London, Newnes, 1937; revised edition, London, Latimer, 1951.
*The Murder at Castle Deeping.* London, John Hamilton, 1938; revised edition, London, Latimer, 1951.
*Desert Night: A Romance.* London, John Hamilton, 1938.
*Wings of Romance: A Steeley Adventure.* London, Newnes, 1939; revised edition, London, Latimer, 1951.
*The Unknown Quantity.* London, Hamilton, 1940.
*No Motive for Murder.* London, Hodder and Stoughton, 1958; New York, Washburn, 1959.
*The Man Who Lost His Way.* London, Macdonald, 1960.

Short Stories

*The Raid.* London, John Hamilton, 1935.
*Doctor Vane Answers the Call.* London, Latimer, 1950.
*Short Sorties.* London, Latimer, 1953.
*Sky Fever and Other Stories.* London, Latimer, 1953.

Fiction (for children)

*The Camels Are Coming.* London, John Hamilton, 1932; as *Biggles, Pioneer Air Fighter*, London, Armada, 1982.
*The Cruise of the Condor: A Biggles Story.* London, John Hamilton, 1933.
*Biggles of the Camel Squadron.* London, John Hamilton, 1934.
*Biggles Flies Again.* London, John Hamilton, 1934.
*Biggles Learns to Fly.* London, Boys' Friend Library, 1935.
*Biggles Flies East.* London, Oxford University Press, 1935.
*Biggles Hits the Trail.* London, Oxford University Press, 1935.
*Biggles in France.* London, Boys' Friend Library, 1935.
*The Black Peril: A Biggles Story.* London, John Hamilton, 1935; as *Biggles Flies East* (not same as 1935 book), London, Boys' Friend Library, 1938.
*Biggles in Africa.* London, Oxford University Press, 1936.
*Biggles & Co.* London, Oxford University Press, 1936.
*Biggles—Air Commodore.* London, Oxford University Press, 1937.
*Biggles Flies West.* London, Oxford University Press, 1937.
*Biggles Flies South.* London, Oxford University Press, 1938.
*Biggles Goes to War.* London, Oxford University Press, 1938.
*Champion of the Main.* London, Oxford University Press, 1938.
*Biggles Flies North.* London, Oxford University Press, 1939.
*Biggles in Spain.* London, Oxford University Press, 1939.
*The Rescue Flight: A Biggles Story.* London, Oxford University Press, 1939.
*Biggles in the Baltic.* London, Oxford University Press, 1940.
*Biggles in the South Seas.* London, Oxford University Press, 1940.
*Biggles—Secret Agent.* London, Oxford University Press, 1940.
*Worrals of the W.A.A.F.* London, Lutterworth Press, 1941.
*Spitfire Parade: Stories of Biggles in War-Time.* London, Oxford University Press, 1941.
*Biggles Sees It Through.* London, Oxford University Press, 1941.
*Biggles Defies the Swastika.* London, Oxford University Press, 1941.
*Biggles in the Jungle.* London, Oxford University Press, 1942.
*Sinister Service.* London, Oxford University Press, 1942.
*Biggles Sweeps the Desert.* London, Hodder and Stoughton, 1942.
*Worrals Flies Again.* London, Hodder and Stoughton, 1942.
*Worrals Carries On.* London, Lutterworth Press, 1942.
*Worrals on the War-Path.* London, Hodder and Stoughton, 1943.
*Biggles "Fails to Return".* London, Hodder and Stoughton, 1943.
*Biggles in Borneo.* London, Oxford University Press, 1943.
*King of the Commandos.* London, University of London Press, 1943.
*Gimlet Goes Again.* London, University of London Press, 1944.
*Worrals Goes East.* London, Hodder and Stoughton, 1944.
*Biggles in the Orient.* London, Hodder and Stoughton, 1945.
*Worrals of the Islands: A Story of the War in the Pacific.* London, Hodder and Stoughton, 1945.
*Biggles Delivers the Goods.* London, Hodder and Stoughton, 1946.

*Gimlet Comes Home.* London, University of London Press, 1946.
*Sergeant Bigglesworth C.I.D.* London, Hodder and Stoughton, 1947.
*Comrades in Arms.* London, Hodder and Stoughton, 1947.
*Gimlet Mops Up.* Leicester, Brockhampton Press, 1947.
*Worrals in the Winds.* London, Hodder and Stoughton, 1947.
*Biggles Hunts Big Game.* London, Hodder and Stoughton, 1948.
*Biggles' Second Case.* London, Hodder and Stoughton, 1948.
*Gimlet's Oriental Quest.* Leicester, Brockhampton Press, 1948.
*The Rustlers of Rattlesnake Valley.* London, Nelson, 1948.
*Worrals Down Under.* London, Lutterworth Press, 1948.
*Biggles Breaks the Silence.* London, Hodder and Stoughton, 1949; as *Biggles in the Antarctic*, London, Armada, 1970.
*Biggles Takes a Holiday.* London, Hodder and Stoughton, 1949.
*Gimlet Lends a Hand.* Leicester, Brockhampton Press, 1949.
*Worrals Goes Afoot.* London, Lutterworth Press, 1949.
*Worrals in the Wastelands.* London, Lutterworth Press, 1949.
*Worrals Investigates.* London, Lutterworth Press, 1950.
*Biggles Gets His Men.* London, Hodder and Stoughton, 1950.
*Gimlet Bores In.* Leicester, Brockhampton Press, 1950.
*Another Job for Biggles.* London, Hodder and Stoughton, 1951.
*Biggles Goes to School.* London, Hodder and Stoughton, 1951.
*Biggles Works It Out.* London, Hodder and Stoughton, 1951.
*Gimlet Off the Map.* Leicester, Brockhampton Press, 1951.
*Biggles—Air Detective.* London, Latimer, 1952.
*Biggles Follows On.* London, Hodder and Stoughton, 1952.
*Biggles Takes the Case.* London, Hodder and Stoughton, 1952.
*Gimlet Gets the Answer.* Leicester, Brockhampton Press, 1952.
*Biggles and the Black Raider.* London, Hodder and Stoughton, 1953.
*Biggles in the Blue.* Leicester, Brockhampton Press, 1953.
*Biggles in the Gobi.* London, Hodder and Stoughton, 1953.
*Biggles of the Special Air Police.* London, Thames Publishing Company, 1953.
*Biggles and the Pirate Treasure, and Other Biggles Adventures.* Leicester, Brockhampton Press, 1954.
*Biggles Cuts It Fine.* London, Hodder and Stoughton, 1954.
*Biggles, Foreign Legionnaire.* London, Hodder and Stoughton, 1954.
*Biggles, Pioneer Airfighter.* London, Thames Publishing Company, 1954.
*Gimlet Takes a Job.* Leicester, Brockhampton Press, 1954.
*Adventure Bound.* London, Nelson, 1955.
*Biggles' Chinese Puzzle and Other Biggles Adventures.* Leicester, Brockhampton Press, 1955.
*Biggles in Australia.* London, Hodder and Stoughton, 1955.
*Biggles of 266.* London, Thames Publishing Company, 1956.
*Biggles Takes Charge.* Leicester, Brockhampton Press, 1956.
*No Rest for Biggles.* London, Hodder and Stoughton, 1956.
*Biggles Makes Ends Meet.* London, Hodder and Stoughton, 1957.
*Adventure Unlimited.* London, Nelson, 1957.
*Biggles of the Interpol.* Leicester, Brockhampton Press, 1957.
*Biggles on the Home Front.* London, Hodder and Stoughton, 1957.
*Biggles Buries a Hatchet.* Leicester, Brockhampton Press, 1958.
*Biggles on Mystery Island.* London, Hodder and Stoughton, 1958.
*Biggles Presses On.* Leicester, Brockhampton Press, 1958.
*Biggles at World's End.* Leicester, Brockhampton Press, 1959.
*Biggles' Combined Operation.* London, Hodder and Stoughton, 1959.
*Biggles in Mexico.* Leicester, Brockhampton Press, 1959.
*Adventures of the Junior Detection Club.* London, Parrish, 1960.
*Biggles and the Leopards of Zinn.* Leicester, Brockhampton Press, 1960.
*Biggles Goes Home.* London, Hodder and Stoughton, 1960.
*Where the Golden Eagle Soars.* London, Hodder and Stoughton, 1960.
*Biggles and the Missing Millionaire.* Leicester, Brockhampton Press, 1961.
*Biggles and the Poor Rich Boy.* Leicester, Brockhampton Press, 1961.
*Biggles Forms a Syndicate.* London, Hodder and Stoughton, 1961.
*Biggles Goes Alone.* London, Hodder and Stoughton, 1962.
*Biggles Sets a Trap.* London, Hodder and Stoughton, 1962.
*Orchids for Biggles.* Leicester, Brockhampton Press, 1962.
*Biggles and the Plane That Disappeared.* London, Hodder and Stoughton, 1963.
*Biggles Flies to Work.* London, Dean, 1963.
*Biggles' Special Case.* Leicester, Brockhampton Press, 1963.
*Biggles Takes a Hand.* London, Hodder and Stoughton, 1963.
*Biggles Takes It Rough.* Leicester, Brockhampton Press, 1963.
*Biggles and the Black Mask.* London, Hodder and Stoughton, 1964.
*Biggles and the Last Sovereigns.* Leicester, Brockhampton Press, 1964; as *Biggles and the Lost Treasure*, London, Knight, 1978.
*Biggles Investigates and Other Stories of the Air Police.* Leicester, Brockhampton Press, 1965.
*Biggles and the Blue Moon.* Leicester, Brockhampton Press, 1965.
*Biggles and the Plot That Failed.* Leicester, Brockhampton Press, 1965.
*Biggles Looks Back.* London, Hodder and Stoughton, 1965.
*Biggles Scores a Bull.* London, Hodder and Stoughton, 1965.
*Biggles in the Terai.* Leicester, Brockhampton Press, 1966.
*Biggles and the Gun Runners.* Leicester, Brockhampton Press, 1966.
*Biggles and the Penitent Thief.* Leicester, Brockhampton Press, 1967.
*Biggles Sorts It Out.* Leicester, Brockhampton Press, 1967.
*Biggles and the Dark Intruder.* London, Knight, 1967.
*Biggles in the Underworld.* Leicester, Brockhampton Press, 1968.
*The Boy Biggles.* London, Dean, 1968.
*Biggles and the Deep Blue Sea.* Leicester, Brockhampton Press, 1968.
*Biggles and the Little Green God.* Leicester, Brockhampton Press, 1969.
*Biggles and the Noble Lord.* Leicester, Brockhampton Press, 1969.
*Biggles Sees Too Much.* Leicester, Brockhampton Press, 1970.
*Biggles of the Royal Flying Corps* (selection), edited by Piers Williams. Maidenhead, Berkshire, Purnell, 1978.
*The Bumper Biggles Book.* London, Chancellor, 1983.

Plays

Radio Plays (with G.R. Ranier): *The Machine That Disappeared*, 1942; *The Charming Mrs. Nayther*, 1942.

Other

*Fighting Planes and Aces* (for children). London, John Hamilton, 1932.
*The Pictorial Flying Course*, with Harry M. Scholfield, illustrated by Johns. London, John Hamilton, 1932.

*The Air V.C.'s.* London, John Hamilton, 1935.
*Some Milestones of Aviation.* London, John Hamilton, 1935.
*The Passing Show: A Garden Diary by an Amateur Gardener.* London, My Garden, 1937.
*The Modern Boy's Book of Pirates.* London, Amalgamated Press, 1939.
*The Biggles Book of Heroes.* London, Parrish, 1959.
*The Biggles Book of Treasure Hunting.* London, Parrish, 1962.
*No Surrender,* with R.A. Kelly. London, Harrap, 1969.

Editor, *The Modern Boy's Book of Aircraft.* London, Amalgamated Press, 1931.
Editor, *Wings: A Book of Flying Adventures.* London, John Hamilton, 1931.
Editor, *Thrilling Flights.* London, John Hamilton, 1935.

*

Critical Studies: *Biggles: The Authorized Biography* by John Pearson, London, Sidgwick and Jackson, 1979; *By Jove, Biggles: The Life of Captain W.E. Johns* by Peter Berresford Ellis and Piers Williams, London, W.H. Allen, 1981.

Illustrator: *Desert Wings* by Covington Clarke, 1931.

* * *

W.E. Johns, creator of the air ace Biggles, chronicled the adventures of the spaceship *Tavona* and her crew in a series of some ten novels, begun in 1954 and awkwardly written around the probably unanticipated eruption of the space race three years later. His aim, as stated in the foreword of *To Worlds Unknown*, was to familiarize young people with "the new science of Astronautics"; but even the most naive member of the intended teenage readership could not fail to catch the author out in such colossal errors as the assertion that an Earth-type planet can become a nova. In the simplified universe through which the *Tavona* speeds at superluminal velocities without Einsteinian complications of hyperspatial confabulations, only Newton's laws escape total maceration. Nevertheless, few youngsters, however skeptical, could fail to be enthralled by these novels, which have the flavor not of science fiction but of a series of adventurous sea voyages: a bunch of cheerful and resourceful sailors embarking on a cosmic ocean filled with wonders and fraught with perils.

The cosmic-ray-powered *Tavona* is built by the supremely advanced Terromagnans, crewed by Martians, and carries as passengers four intrepid Earthmen: the eccentric professor Lucius Brane whose jaunt to the moon in a backyard spaceship got the series off the launching pad; Tiger, the pipe-smoking, gun-toting man of action; Toby, the rather colorless ship's medic; and Tiger's clean-cut, pure-hearted teenage son Rex, contributing reader-identification to the book and the clear eye of youth to the triad of vision, action, and expertise. On their cosmic cruises, they traverse the treacherous reaches of the galaxy, exploring interesting little islands, occasionally pulling in at a bustling foreign port, sometimes getting stranded, shipwrecked, caught up in hostilities, or attacked by pirates, cannibals, or fearsome beasts, but always, with luck and ingenuity, pulling through. In the course of their travels, any jingoistic assumptions get thoroughly punctured: they discover that their homeland, far from being internationally revered, is feared and hated for its militarism and short-sightedness. The nuclear weapons, carelessly strewn space hardware, and filthy atmosphere of Earth are the shame of the Milky Way, and the cause of much agonizing introspection for Rex as he spends the lonely hours between the stars contemplating (while Toby and Tiger attend to their pills and guns, and the Professor compiles his Galactic Guidebook) the universal imponderables, and becomes ever more space-sick and travel-weary as the series progresses.

And progress the series does. In the early books, the *Tavona*'s travels are restricted to the local archipelago of the solar system, the spacefarers tending to land on tiny asteroids completely covered with ice, water, grass, or glass, or if inhabited boasting at most two or three (Terrestrial) species. In the later novels, the foursome strike out into the interstellar deeps, encountering various and complex (but inevitably Earthlike) civilizations, and becoming caught up in the machinations of cosmic kidnappers, conquerors and crooks, and the interminable moralizing of superior (but humanoid) beings.

For all Johns's avowed intentions to educate embryo space scientists, the message that comes across much more clearly than the patronizing tables of the solar systems and glossaries of astronomical terms that bedeck the books is the endless series of imprecations to the Earthmen to put away their bombs and satellites and cease tampering with the biosphere. It comes as a shock to the adult reader to return to these books, written in what seems in retrospect a decade of optimism, to find them filled not with white hope and the white heat of technology (the *Tavona* has no radio and no more navigational equipment than a small inshore craft), but with the doom-laden forebodings of planetary suicide that pervade the world into which the original readers have matured.

—Lee Montgomerie

---

**JONES, D(ennis) F(eltham).** British. Served in the Royal Navy during World War II. Worked as a bricklayer and market gardener. *Died in April 1981.*

SCIENCE-FICTION PUBLICATIONS

Novels (series: Colossus)

*Colossus.* London, Hart Davis, 1966; New York, Putnam, 1967.
*Implosion.* London, Hart Davis, 1967; New York, Putnam, 1968.
*Denver Is Missing.* New York, Walker, 1971; as *Don't Pick the Flowers*, London, Panther, 1971.
*The Fall of Colossus.* New York, Putnam, 1974.
*The Floating Zombie.* New York, Berkley, 1975.
*Colossus and the Crab.* New York, Berkley, 1977.
*Earth Has Been Found.* New York, Dell, 1979; as *Xeno*, London, Sidgwick and Jackson, 1979.

Uncollected Short Stories

"Black Snowstorm," in *Fantasy and Science Fiction* (New York), January 1969.
"The Tocsin," in *Fantasy and Science Fiction* (New York), June 1970.
"Coffee Break," in *Laughing Space*, edited by Isaac Asimov and J.O. Jeppson. Boston, Houghton Mifflin, and London, Robson, 1982.

* * *

Asimov in "The Machine and the Robot," writes, "Surely the *great* fear is not that machinery will harm us—but that it will supplant us." In *Colossus* D.F. Jones has certainly created one of the finest embodiments of this fear. Because men are attached to their freedom, or at least to a sense of freedom, *Colossus* becomes the ultimate horror story in which man is enslaved by his own creation. Jones develops the horror through the logic and detail of presentation. Each of the steps by which Colossus comes to power follows from the previous; all the hardware is credible. Forbin serves as a foil to the machine (eliciting such information as the reader needs to understand Colossus) and as an emotional sounding-board (articulating and amplifying the fear). The futility of Forbin's defiance of Colossus, especially his refusal to love it, contributes to the power of the ending.

The two sequels to *Colossus* do not quite measure up to the same standard. Neither seems to have the same level of conviction. In *The Fall of Colossus*, the emphasis has shifted away from the horror of machine domination. Colossus's attempts to comprehend human emotion, Forbin's shift toward love for the machine, the Sect's worship, the Fellowship's opposition—none of these stimulate the same level of excitement. The sexual experiment on Cleo seems contrived and not very relevant. The outside intervention which brings the fall has a *deus ex machina* quality. In *Colossus and the Crab*, the tight, straightforward plotting that is a strength in most of Jones's novels seems to have given way to a rather choppy, almost episodic style. The whole concept of the novel, which pits Forbin against two aliens from Mars, leads to the revival of Colossus and ends in a sort of Mexican standoff, gives the feeling that the author merely wanted to wrap up the series. The novel's climactic point, although it effectively builds the emotional tension of Forbin's naval attack, gets its power purely from situation—Forbin never seems to rise to the heroic level.

Perhaps that is because plot and setting, rather than characterization, are Jones's strengths. The plots of his other novels command the reader's attention, leading step-by-step to a satisfying conclusion. Whether he deals with population (implosion), alien invasion (*Earth Has Been Found*), or geologic catastrophe (*Don't Pick the Flowers*), the plot flows ineluctably from the initial assumption. Settings also contribute much to the effectiveness of all his works. Each setting presents a recognizable Earth in a not-too-distant future. The familiarity of setting functions effectively as a contrasting ground for the strange situation. More than a trace of the mad-scientist motif enters into his work. All his central characters are scientists, and either initiate an action beyond control or attempt to cope with a situation beyond comprehension.

*Don't Pick the Flowers* is the best of his novels. Its highly improbable situation is invested with a sense of possibility. The chief characters seem very human (when compared with Forbin, for instance) in their fears and desires, and in their strength to cope with an overwhelming situation, to endure against very long odds.

—Robert Reilly

---

**JONES, Gwyneth A(nn).** Also writes as Ann Halam. British. Born in Manchester, Lancashire, 14 February 1952. Educated at Notre Dame Convent, Manchester, 1963–70; University of Sussex, 1970–73, B.A. (honors) in history of ideas 1973. Married Peter Gwilliam in 1976; one son. Executive officer, Manpower Services Commission, Hove Sussex, 1975–77. Agent: Herta Ryder, c/o Toby Eady Associates, 18 Park Walk, London, SW10 0AQ. Address: 30 Roundhill Crescent, Brighton, East Sussex BN2 3FR, England.

Science-Fiction Publications

Novels

*Divine Endurance.* London, Allen and Unwin, 1984; New York, Arbor House, 1987.
*Escape Plans.* London, Allen and Unwin, 1986.
*Kairos.* London, Unwin Hyman, 1988.
*The Hidden Ones* (for children). London, Women's Press, 1988.

Novels as Ann Halam (for children; series: Inland)

Inland trilogy:
*The Daymaker.* London and New York, Orchard, 1987.
*Transformations.* London and New York, Orchard, 1988.
*The Sky Breaker.* London, Orchard, 1990.

Other Publications (for children)

Novels

*Water in the Air.* London and New York, Macmillan, 1977.
*The Influence of Ironwood.* London, Macmillan, 1978.
*The Exchange.* London, Macmillan, 1979.
*Dear Hill.* London, Macmillan, 1980.

Novels as Ann Halam

*Ally, Ally, Aster.* London, Allen and Unwin, 1981.
*The Alder Tree.* London, Allen and Unwin, 1982.
*King Death's Garden.* London, Orchard, 1986.
*Into the Silent Water.* London, Orchard, 1990.

*

Gwyneth A. Jones comments:

I started telling stories at a very early age. My father was a storyteller, my mother passionately interested in the future; hence science fiction drew me, though I was bound to become some kind of fantasist. When I was at university I used to tell people stories as presents (I also used to lay a mean Tarot)—fantasies based on observation of the recipient's personality and aspirations. Two of these survive in print: "The Snow Apples" and "Laiken Langstrand." When I first wrote published novels I wrote for children, through happenstance, because I was introduced to a children's editor (Marni Hodgkin, at Macmillan, London). By the time I started to write for adults I'd been thinking about my craft for a long time. I'd become interested in the why and how of storytelling, and of science fiction. *Divine Endurance* is a science fantasy of the old kind, silently dedicated to Zelazny's *Lord of Light* and many others. *Escape Plans* and *Kairos* are also in their way *about* science fiction as much as they are novels on their own account. Meanwhile, "Ann Halam" continues to tell stories; but the storytelling of these juveniles is inextricably mingled with my own brooding on the problems of my life and times. In particular, in the Daymaker series, with the problem of reconciling our triumphs of technology with our need to preserve the past, the present, and the planet.

I rarely write short stories now. When I do it's because I've been directly asked for one, or because I want to work out something about my current novel, or explain something (to myself) about a novel that's already written. "The Eastern Succession" moved the fantasy-like world of "Divine Endurance" into a more realistic continuum. The story entitled "Forward Echoes," in the December 1990 issue of *Interzone*, encapsulates the theme of my current novel, but tells it from a viewpoint that has no place in the novel's version of the story of Braemar and Johnny.

* * *

Gwyneth Ann Jones is the author of three SF novels and a handful of short stories for adults, but the bulk of her work has been, and remains, within the category labelled "children's." As such, however, it should certainly not be ignored. Under the name Ann Halam, in particular, she has created some of the most thought-provoking and imaginative children's fantasies being written today: books which are much more interesting and challenging than most fantasy novels marketed as "adult."

*Ally, Ally, Aster*, the best of her earlier children's books, is certainly more straightforward than those she wrote in the late 1980's. The characters, particularly the "villains," are like caricatures, and the narrative has little to it beyond the surface tale of modern children being confronted with ancient magic and disbelieving adults, with the traditional ending of the adults—the parents—being unaware that anything exciting and supernatural had happened. Magic is thus safely kept away from the "real world." It is a well-told tale full of suspense nevertheless, but no real indication of the Halam novels that were to follow. *King Death's Garden* is a much richer and more complex novel, dealing with a boy's attempt to understand the secrets of the cemetery behind his great-aunt's house in Brighton (the cemetery near Jones's house) and the mystery of the professor who used to live there (who claimed to photograph fairies), but also examining with considerable insight the problems of growing up, of accepting responsibility, of coping with an adult world.

The "Inland" trilogy is her most important contribution to children's literature and is at the point where she crosses from fantasy into science fiction. The books are set on a future earth, where the magic of the almost totally female group of coveners protects the population and its flocks from the dangerous remains of the present industrial world—and keeps them in a stable, rural world, isolated from new ideas or possibilities of change. The books—*The Daymaker, Transformations*, and *The Skybreaker*—follow the career of Zanne, a young girl with prodigious magical powers, who becomes a covener "troubleshooter," sent to kill any surviving ancient machines—despite her own attraction to ancient technology. No trilogy that begins with a novel set in a school for young magicians can avoid comparison with Le Guin's "Earthsea" series. "Inland" stands up to the comparison well, and examines problems that are of perennial concern: questions of morality and of personal responsibility, of the nature of democracy, and of the opposition between "green" values and technology. Zanne finds no easy answers in any of the books; as Maureen Speller has written of *The Skybreaker* (in *Vector 160* 1991), "It is rare indeed for a novel to come to terms so thoroughly with the uncertainties of life. . . . My only regret is that, as a result of them being published in a children's fiction imprint, too many people will have missed the opportunity to tackle this demanding and intellectually satisfying work."

On Earthsea, women were unable to become magicians; in Inland very few men have that ability. In her more recent novels, Jones has become much more concerned about, or more public about, her feminism. This is perhaps most noticeable in *The Hidden Ones*, written as Gwyneth A. Jones for "Livewires," the teenage imprint of the Women's Press. It is about a woman scientist trying to investigate the "poltergeist effect" in a young girl, around whom strange things happen. Both women get involved in a plan to save a local rural beauty spot from the hands of developers. But the story is told from the viewpoint of the girl: a confused, aggressive, suspicious adolescent, who finds it almost impossible to establish any sort of normal relationship with adults or other teenagers. The strong characters are all women. *The Hidden Ones* offers a frank and ultimately sympathetic portrait of tortured adolescence. Jones later remarked, "I believed by the end that I had managed to express my original vision; an exciting rite of passage story that would involve hard science and would *belong* to the girl-protagonist, instead of being hijacked by cosmic truth on the one hand, or on the other by the first male character to arrive on the scene" (in L. Armitt, editor, *Where No Man Has Gone Before: Women and Science Fiction*, 1991).

Jones has published a number of SF and fantasy short stories for adults, although it is clear that her main commitment is to the novel. For several years, while working on children's books, she was also working on her first adult SF novel, *Divine Endurance.* Like its successor *Escape Plans, Divine Endurance* is set in a far-future that is thoroughly, if perhaps insidiously, feminist: all the major human characters are women, and when men appear, as they do only occasionally, they are regarded as ineffectual inconveniences—just as women have been regarded in most 20th-century SF. Both have been called difficult books: as Jones herself has said, "I have a way of making simple things difficult." Crucial facts are lost to the reader who does not read slowly, and subtle and deliberate allusions, to other works of SF for instance, are not as obvious as the author seems to believe. But they are both rich and exciting books, which do repay the careful reading. *Divine Endurance* is the story of the journey of a girl, Cho, and her cat Divine Endurance, from the desert wastes of China into a far future Malaysia: Jones uses her three-year sojourn in Singapore to haunting effect. As in the other novels, it takes time to work out what is happening: that Cho is in fact an android, for instance, and that her cat has plans for her.

As a novel, *Escape Plans* works much better; indeed, it may well come to be viewed as one of the most important British SF novels of the 1980's. It is the story of ALIC, from a utopian space-habitat in the solar system, who visits earth as a tourist, and on a whim, to help a threatened proletariat woman, abandons the immense power her computer access gives her, and finds herself trapped among the huge underclass of humans whose labor maintains the "utopia" she believed she had come from. We learn alongside ALIC; the acronyms and the jargon are only gradually translated into meaning (despite the glossary). Like Jones's other two adult SF novels, it is deeply politicized, concerned with such crucial political issues as the nature of oppression and the problems of utopia. But these issues are embedded within a fast-moving thriller, full of imaginative insights, word-play and wit; it is an exhilarating read. Her most recent novel for adults, *Kairos*, is very different: set in a near-future Britain, with political and social customs only slightly extrapolated from the present future or, rather, from a late 1980's future, with an increasingly Thatcherised Britain and increasingly brutal police-force. The main protagonists, two couples, gay and lesbian, gradually become enmeshed in the intrigues of BREAKTHRU, a sinister, mysterious and apparently neo-fascist group who turn out to be experimenting with Kairos, a drug that alters not only consciousness but reality itself. Some (as in *Ally, Ally, Aster*) will not remember the apocalyptic ending; for others it opens up new utopian possibilities. Different in setting from the two earlier novels, it nevertheless witnesses to many of the same concerns, both political and literary. Jones uses the genre as it should be used, and as it is used by too few: to express and to explore ideas and moods that are quite impossible in the literary mainstream. Her adult novels have not yet won her the wide readership achieved by her "Ann Halam" novels, but they have been published to considerable critical acclaim and her reputation can only grow.

—Edward James

---

**JONES, Neil R(onald).** American. Born in Fulton, New York, 29 May 1909. Attended Fulton public schools. Served in the 2nd Armored Division of the United States Army, 1942–45. Married Rita Gwendoline Rees in 1945. Stamp dealer, bookkeeper, cost analyst, office manager, game manufacturer; unemployment insurance claims examiner, State of New York, for 26 years. *Died in 1988.*

SCIENCE-FICTION PUBLICATIONS

Short Stories (series: Professor Jameson in all books)

*The Planet of the Double Sun.* New York, Ace, 1967.
*The Sunless World.* New York, Ace, 1967.
*Space War.* New York, Ace, 1967.
*Twin Worlds.* New York, Ace, 1967.
*Doomsday on Ajiat.* New York, Ace, 1968.

Uncollected Short Stories (series: Professor Jameson; 24th Century, 26th Century)

"The Death's Head Meteor" (26th Century), in *Air Wonder Stories* (New York), January 1930.
"The Electrical Man," in *Scientific Detective* (New York), May 1930.
"Shadows of the Night," in *Amazing Detective Tales* (New York), October 1930.
"The Asteroid of Death" (26th Century), in *Wonder Stories Quarterly* (New York), Fall 1931.
"Spacewrecked on Venus" (24th Century), in *Wonder Stories Quarterly* (New York), Winter 1932.
"Escape from Phobus" (24th Century), in *Wonder Stories* (New York), February 1933.
"Martian and Troglodyte," in *Amazing* (New York), May 1933.
"The Moon Pirates" (26th Century), in *Amazing* (New York), September, October 1934.
"Little Hercules" (26th Century), in *Astounding* (New York), September 1936.
"The Astounding Exodus," in *Thrilling Wonder Stories* (New York), April 1937.
"Durna Rangue Neophyte" (24th Century), in *Astounding* (New York), June 1937.
"Swordsman of Saturn" (24th Century), in *Science Fiction* (Holyoke, Massachusetts), October 1939.
"The Dark Swordsmen of Saturn" (26th Century), in *Planet* (New York), Summer 1940.
"Liquid Hell" (26th Century), in *Future* (New York), July 1940.
"The Cat-Men of Aemt" (Jameson), in *Astonishing* (Chicago), August 1940.
"Invisible One," (26th Century), in *Super Science* (Kokomo, Indiana), September 1940.
"Cosmic Derelict" (Jameson), in *Astonishing* (Chicago), February 1941.
"Captives of Durna Rangue" (24th Century), in *Super Science* (Kokomo, Indiana), March 1941.
"Vampire of the Void" (26th Century), in *Planet* (New York), Spring 1941.
"Priestess of the Sleeping Death" (24th Century), in *Amazing* (New York), April 1941.
"The Ransom for Toledo," in *Comet* (Springfield, Massachusetts), May 1941.
"Slaves of the Unknown" (Jameson), in *Astonishing* (Chicago), March 1942.
"Spoilers of the Spaceways" (24th Century), in *Planet* (New York), Winter 1942.
"Parasite Planet," (Jameson), in *Super Science* (Kokomo, Indiana), November 1949.
"Hermit of Saturn's Ring" (24th Century), in *Flight into Space*, edited by Donald Wollheim. New York, Fell, 1950.
"World Without Darkness" (Jameson), in *Super Science* (Kokomo, Indiana), March 1950.
"The Mind Masters" (Jameson), in *Super Science* (Kokomo, Indiana), September 1950.
"The Citadel in Space" (26th Century), in *Two Complete Science Adventure Books* (New York), Summer 1951.
"The Star Killers" (Jameson), in *Super Science* (Kokomo, Indiana), August 1951.

*

Neil R. Jones commented:

I am one of the earlier science-fiction writers in this country. My first story, "The Death's Head Meteor," appeared in 1930, and was the first science-fiction story to use the word astronaut. "The Jameson Satellite" was the beginning of what is possibly the longest running series in science fiction; from 1931 to 1968, 23 stories in the series were published. I also wrote two other series ("Tales of the 24th Century" and "Tales of the 26th Century" ); both included stories of the Durna Mangue cult. All the stories were written in the vein of a future history. Michael Ashley (*History of the Science Fiction Magazine*) puts it this way: "an overall framework in which each story forms part of a future history, invented by Jones long before either Heinlein or Asimov. The key story is the Jameson adventure "Times's Mausoleum" (*Amazing*, December 1933) which remained the basis for all of Jones's other tales."

* * *

In 1929 Hugo Gernsback, through the manipulations of creditors, lost the ownership of the world's first science-fiction magazine, *Amazing Stories.* His reputation was so strong, however, that within months he was back in business with three new titles: *Science Wonder Stories, Scientific Detective Monthly*, and *Air Wonder Stories.* It was in the seventh issue of this last title, dated January 1930, that Neil R. Jones's first story, "The Death's Head Meteor," appeared.

Although Jones would sell a respectable handful of stories to him in the half dozen or so years before Gernsback left the field, it was not the *Wonder* magazines that would become most important to Jones but *Amazing Stories.* It was the July 1931 issue of *Amazing* that published Jones's story, "The Jameson Satellite," which told how Professor Jameson arranged for his body to be fired into space after his death, there to orbit the Earth for 40 million years, at which time, the body and its brain still perfectly preserved in the vacuum of space, it is discovered by space explorers from the planet Zor.

The Zoromes are machine men, their living brains transferred to mechanical bodies, supported by four legs and equipped with six tentacles. Their brains are protected by a conical metal head to which are affixed a series of mechanical eyes surrounding the head, and one looking straight up. Thus, they are not subject to the wear and tear of fleshly life, and boast lifetimes sufficiently long to permit interplanetary exploration. In fact, only a severe accident featuring direct damage to the head is fatal to them. They communicate by telepathy.

Jameson's brain is removed from his corpse and placed in one of the mechanical bodies. He becomes 21MM392. He learns that the Earth is long dead and that he may well be the last representative of the human race. He joins the Zoromes in their journey through the cosmos.

And what a journey it is. At a time when the imaginations of most science-fiction writers seemed restricted to the solar system, Jones joyfully let his heroes zoom from star system to star system. Jones proved adept at planet building, and story after story featured truly wonderful discoveries.

The fifth story of the series, "Time's Mausoleum" (December 1933, *Amazing*), featured a glimpse back in time to show Jameson some of what had happened to the solar system. Significantly, the story outlines a future history in use by Jones several years before the more highly publicized Future History of Robert Heinlein began.

The bulk of the Jones's future history concerns his second magazine series, the Durna Rangue. The Durna Rangue is a semi-scientific cult founded in the 24th century. Their scientific experiments, often conducted on human guinea pigs, gets them driven first from Earth and then from Mars. At last they are forced to hide on one of the moons of Uranus. In the 26th century, they ally themselves with space pirates and conquer the Earth, which they then rule as an outlaw world. The first Durna Rangue story was "Little Hercules" (*Astounding*, September 1936). The final to appear (and one of Jones's best stories) was "The Citadel in Space," published in the third issue of *Two Complete Science-Adventure Books*, Summer 1951. Only eight stories in this series have been published, while the Professor Jameson series numbers at least 23.

If Jones benefitted from the first expansion of the magazine science-fiction field, it was the next expansion in the late 1930's in which he lost prominence. In the late 1930's, all three science-fiction magazines changed editorial hands and all three editors—Mort Weisinger at *Thrilling Wonder Stories*, John Campbell at *Astounding*, and Ray Palmer at *Amazing*—felt it was time for a change. Weisinger and Palmer both went after a more juvenile audience, a policy Palmer abandoned at the outset of the World War II in favor of one designed to appeal to a blue collar audience.

Although Jones had the sort of imagination and approach to story-telling that Palmer liked, he found *Amazing*'s new editor less than receptive to continuing the Jameson series. Palmer complained about the often minor tone of Jones's plots, but it seems more likely that in his efforts to find stories about characters the man on the street could identify with, he simply felt an immortal machine man called 21MM392 didn't fit the bill. Jones sold several times to Palmer but those stories were action-adventure pieces, usually without the imagination and sweep of the Professor Jameson stories. The Jameson stories would find their second home in 1940 in the short-lived *Astonishing Stories* (edited by Fred Pohl) and, after the war in the revival of *Super Science Stories.* In the late 1960's Ace Books issued five paperback collections of the Professor Jameson series, including in the fifth one two stories never previously published, though they appear to have been sold at one time to *Amazing.*

Jones wrote action stories with strongly imaginative and often highly clever backgrounds. His prose style is expository and tends to distance the reader from the characters, and, in that respect, may be old-fashioned and off-putting to many readers. But this is a characteristic he shares with other writers who are still widely read, including Lester Dent (who wrote the Doc Savage books as Kenneth Robeson) and Philip José Farmer. His type of writing is, therefore, probably a matter of taste to many readers. But he still has his fans, many of them too young to have encountered him when he first appeared. Professor Jameson is an astonishing achievement and while that series may have its equals in its ability to arouse the good, old fashioned sense of wonder, nothing surpasses it.

—Gerald W. Page

---

**JONES, Raymond F.** American. Born in Salt Lake City, Utah, in 1915. Studied engineering and English in college. Radio engineer, then full-time writer. Lives in Arizona. Address: c/o Pinnacle Books, Kensington Publishing Corporation, 475 Park Avenue S, New York, New York 10016, U.S.A.

SCIENCE-FICTION PUBLICATIONS

Novels

*Renaissance.* New York, Gnome Press, 1951; as *Man of Two Worlds*, New York, Pyramid, 1963.
*The Alien.* New York, Pyramid, 1951.
*This Island Earth.* Chicago, Shasta, 1952; London, Boardman, 1955.
*Son of the Stars* (for children). Philadelphia, Winston, 1952; London, Hutchinson, 1953.
*Planet of Light* (for children). Philadelphia, Winston, 1953.
*The Secret People.* New York, Avalon, 1956; as *The Deviates*, New York, Galaxy, 1959.
*The Year When Stardust Fell* (for children). Philadelphia, Winston, 1958.
*The Cybernetic Brains.* New York, Avalon, 1962.
*Voyage to the Bottom of the Sea* (for children). Racine, Wisconsin, Whitman, 1965.
*Syn.* New York, Belmont, 1969.
*Moonbase One* (for children). New York and London, Abelard Schuman, 1971.
*Renegades of Time.* Toronto, Laser, 1975.
*The King of Eolim.* Toronto, Laser, 1975.
*The River and the Dream.* Toronto, Laser, 1977.
*Weeping May Tarry*, with Lester del Rey. Los Angeles, Pinnacle, 1978.

Short Stories

*The Toymaker.* Los Angeles, Fantasy, 1951.
*The Non-Statistical Man.* New York, Belmont, 1964; London, Digit, 1965.

Uncollected Short Stories

"Subway to the Stars," in *Galaxy* (New York), December 1968.
"Rat Race," in *Above the Human Landscape*, edited by Willis McNelly and Leon Stover. Pacific Palisades, California, Goodyear, and London, Grayson, 1972.
"The Laughing Lion," in *Science Fiction Tales*, edited by Roger Elwood. New York, Random House, 1973.
"The Lions of Rome," in *Flame Tree Planet*, edited by Roger Elwood. St. Louis, Concordia, 1973.
"Pet," in *Future Quest*, edited by Roger Elwood. New York, Avon, 1973.

"Time Brother," in *Children of Infinity*, edited by Roger Elwood. London, Watts, 1973.
"A Bowl of Biskies Makes a Growing Boy," in *The Other Side of Tomorrow*, edited by Roger Elwood. New York, Random House, 1973.
"Rider in the Sky," in *Most Thrilling Science Fiction Ever Told* (New York), April 1973.
"Flauna," in *The Far Side of Time*, edited by Roger Elwood. New York, Dodd Mead, 1974.
"The Lights of Mars," in *Science Fiction Adventures from Way Out*, edited by Roger Elwood. Racine, Wisconsin, Whitman, 1974.
"Pacer," in *Future Kin*, edited by Roger Elwood. New York, Doubleday, 1974.
"Reflection of a Star," in *Survival from Infinity*, edited by Roger Elwood. New York, Watts, 1974.
"The Touch of Your Hand," in *If* (New York), April 1974.
"Death Eternal," in *Fantastic* (New York), October 1978.
"The Children's Room," in *Young Mutants*, edited by Isaac Asimov, Martin H. Greenberg, and Charles G. Waugh. New York, Harper and Row, 1984.

OTHER PUBLICATIONS

Other (for children)

*The World of Weather.* Racine, Wisconsin, Whitman, 1961.
*Animals of Long Ago.* Racine, Wisconsin, Whitman, 1965.
*Ice Formation on Aircraft* (for adults). Geneva, World Meteorological Organization, 1968.
*Physicians of Tomorrow.* Chicago, Reilly and Lee, 1971.
*Radar: How It Works.* New York, Putnam, 1972.

* * *

Raymond F. Jones is an almost archetypical John Campbell writer, whether writing for *Astounding*, as with "Noise Level" where scientists are lured into inventing anti-gravity, or for *Thrilling Wonder Stories*, with the Peace Engineer stories where aliens secretly involve earth scientists in a program to produce materials needed to defend their home world against invaders (*This Island Earth*).

Jones's first novel, *Renaissance*, is a long and complex parallel-worlds story that contains variations on a number of familiar SF themes against a somewhat more adventurous narrative than is usual in his stories. *The Alien* is a bit more straightforward in its story-telling, although its ideas and the approach he takes to them is not simple at all. The shadow of A.E. van Vogt falls across both these books, the first in its resemblance in early passages to *Slan*, the second in its exploration of ideas and attitudes similar to those of *The World of Null A*. *The Alien* opens with a strong idea: a representative of a long-extinct extraterrestrial race is discovered entombed in the asteroid belt, and brought back to life. While the revival processes go forward, new discoveries indicate this being is thoroughly evil and responsible for the destruction of his own race, something he would no doubt manage for humanity as well. The wealth of ideas from which the story draws its strength occasionally betrays it, as when we are suddenly shown that our supposedly solar-system-bound humans have had the capability of interstellar flight (and use that capability with the utmost casualness); and, again, when a semanticist translates and teaches himself an entire alien language on the basis of a few hours' first-contact conversation. Overlook such points, however, and the book is as good an example of this type of space adventure as you're likely to find short of Edmond Hamilton.

It would be a mistake, however, to place Jones in the camp of Doc Smith or Hamilton, or even van Vogt. Jones has always managed to remain a force unto himself, although a pretty low-key force. One of the ways this has been achieved has been in his handling of characters. The typical Jones character is an engineer, technician, or mathematician, middle-class, and presented in a straightforward and realistic manner that contrasts sharply with the politicians, artists, scholars, militarists, rebels and engineer-savants that make up the bulk of the field's fictional populace. Jones seldom attempts any deep probing of his characters but has always drawn his strength from the ability to portray his characters in equally believable environments. He is also a very economical writer, and after *The Alien* he settled down to a more suitably quiet form of fiction. *The Island Earth* is the first book-length work of his that can be labeled typical. His characters are thoroughly convincing engineers, and, despite the melodrama and detective story touches, their thought processes are the thought processes of reasonable engineers. The complexities that cluttered *Renaissance* and *The Alien* are shunted into the background and the interest of the story lies not in galaxy-spanning events but in the impact of galaxy-spanning events on the lives of seemingly everyday people. The argument could be raised that the best of Jones's novels were written for the Winston juvenile series. *Son of the Stars*, in which teenagers encounter the survivor of a wrecked flying saucer and subsequently find their extraterrestrial friend endangered by adult prejudices, is certainly one of the best of that fondly remembered series of juvenile novels. *Planet of Light* is a sequel.

One of Jones's best stories is "The Non-Statistical Man," which tells of an insurance company statistician who encounters a series of anomalies involving recent claims. At first intrigued, then openly alarmed, he investigates and is led to the conclusion that there are people who possess a 100 percent reliable intuition, rendering his own statistical approach superfluous and pointless. These people know when they're going to need insurance and they don't get it till then. The character's discovery of all this, his reactions to it, and his subsequent change of philosophy as he discovers that the process that makes intuition infallible can be taught to anyone—even him—is written in the low-key style that is the strength of Jones's best writing, and the result is one of his most convincing and compelling stories. It also illustrates the other strength of Jones. He's always been a story-teller who has gone to great pains to build his stories on definite ideas, making him something of a purist among SF writers. His complexities never overwhelm everything else in the way they usually do in the hands of others, and in his later, quieter fiction, his story-telling ability is often quite remarkable for its purity, directness, and seeming effortlessness. This effortlessness may have something to do with the decline in his readership in recent years: Jones is entertaining and often thought-provoking, but he doesn't generate the flair and excitement of a good many lesser but better-known writers.

Jones has also never marked out a particular type of fiction as his own. Most of his stories are recognizably the work of one writer, with a type of character and a worldview that are identifiable, but any story by Jones is apt to be written with a particular market in mind. "Seven Jewels of Chamar" is pure *Planet Stories* space opera and "Tools of the Trade" is a classic *Astounding* engineering problem story of the type John Campbell was always supposed to be looking for. But the first doesn't rank with the stories of Emmett McDowell or Gardner F. Fox, and the second is a middle-grade example of the sort of thing Eric Frank Russell was starting to be known for. Jones's recent novels have been good entertainments, but they've lacked the strengths of his early work.

Jones is a thorough-going professional and, in retrospect, a writer of surprising versatility. But the price of this seems to be that too often he came on the scene with a perfectly good story that was still second best to the similar works of someone else. But there have been times when the works he produced were principally from no source but himself, slanted to no editorial taste but his own—works like *This Island Earth, Son of the Stars,* and "The Non-Statistical Man"—and those results have always been worth waiting for—or searching out.

—Gerald W. Page

---

**JORGENSEN, Ivar.** *See* **FAIRMAN, Paul W.; GARRETT, Randall.**

---

**JORGENSON, Ivar.** *See* **SILVERBERG, Robert.**

---

**JOSEPH, M(ichael) K(ennedy).** New Zealander. Born in Chingford, Essex, England, 9 July 1914. Educated at Sacred Heart College, Auckland; Auckland University College, B.A. 1933, M.A. 1934; Merton College, Oxford, B.A. 1938, B. Litt. 1939, M.A. 1945. Served in the British Army in the Royal Artillery, 1940–46. Married Mary Julia Antonovich in 1947; four sons and one daughter. Lecturer in English, 1945–49, and Senior Lecturer, 1950–59, Auckland University College; Associate Professor, 1960–69, and Professor of English, 1970–79, University of Auckland. Recipient: Hubert Church Prose award, 1959; Jessie Mackay Poetry award, 1960; New Zealand Book award, for fiction, 1978. *Died 4 October 1981.*

Science-Fiction Publications

Novel

*The Hole in the Zero.* London, Gollancz, 1967; New York, Dutton, 1968.

Other Publications

Novels

*I'll Soldier No More.* Auckland, Paul's Book Arcade, and London, Gollancz, 1958.
*A Pound of Saffron.* Auckland, Paul's Book Arcade, and London, Gollancz, 1962.
*A Soldier's Tale.* Auckland and London, Collins, 1976.
*The Time of Achamoth.* Auckland and London, Collins, 1977.
*Kaspar's Journey.* Auckland, Brick Row/Hallard Press, 1988.

Verse

*Imaginary Islands.* Privately printed, 1950.
*The Living Countries.* Auckland, Paul's Book Arcade, 1959.
*Inscription on a Paper Dart.* Auckland, Auckland University Press-Oxford University Press, 1974.

Other

*Charles Aders: A Biographical Note.* Auckland, Auckland University Press, 1954.
*Byron the Poet.* London, Gollancz, 1964; New York, Humanities Press, 1966.

Editor, *Frankenstein,* by Mary Shelley. London, Oxford University Press, 1969.

* * *

M.K. Joseph, a New Zealand writer and educator, produced only one science-fiction novel, *The Hole in the Zero.* While the book's primary staging occurs on an undefined planet in untime and unspace—that is, beyond the known universe and within the philosophical hole in the zero—Joseph constructs his plot in such a manner that it succeeds in operating on several contrasting levels simultaneously.

Like Doris Lessing's *Briefing for a Descent into Hell,* the book teems with archetypal themes and figures; and like Kurt Vonnegut, Jr.'s *Slaughterhouse-Five,* it is episodic, lurching from time into untime, space into unspace, with what appears to be, on first encounter, disconcerting irregularity. Although not easily accessible to the casual reader—which may explain its relative obscurity outside of the novelist's native New Zealand—*The Hole in the Zero* proves to be a closely integrated, carefully executed story exhibiting few major flaws. The least well-developed sequence and the most apparent flaw is that which satirizes the decade in which the novel was written, the 1960's. But several notable strengths counterbalance this apparent weakness.

The familiar motif of life existing as a dream within the mind of a dreamer, a bitter denouncement when voiced by Mark Twain in *The Mysterious Stranger,* loses its threatening aspect with Joseph and achieves a rather comfortable appearance as a known escape clause in the midst of the unknown. Joseph's universe migrates swiftly from an exploration of the duality of man's nature to that of a single man bifurcating into co-linear lives, certainly a Wellsian concept. Progressing from these familiar byways, the book passes into a multiplicity of experiences in which each man *must* make a conscious choice before his life can assume direction. Finally, however, the life cycle itself degenerates into an endlessly repetitive dictum; and hell is the doom sequence of a single, unvarying lifespan swelling to encompass eternity, until even this stalls and the endless paradoxically reaches a terminus.

It is then that Joseph's central theme, that of man directed by an ultimately moral universe, emerges. For a merciful intelligence, perhaps the obscure figure of the Gespenster, metes out to each individual what each sought. Vividly illustrating the adage that man is a questing beast, supplanted by an occasional glimmer of Milton, Joseph's three male heroes/anti-heroes act out their appointed roles—the first seeking power, the second pleasure, and the third, the hero of the tale, Seth Paradine, truth. This trio is, with varying ability, integrated into the novel's multitudinous layering technique. But the solitary female character, Helena, is never well served by the author. Indeed, if achieving a limited dimensionality while assuming the role of dreamer and dream-maker—hampered by appearing as a quintessential Lady of Shalott whose tapestry of life is destroyed by the contest between Paradine and his Hyde-ish opposite, Merganser—Helena's primary role remains that of bit player in the scenes directed alternately by her father, Merganser and Paradine.

Finally, then, Paradine emerges triumphant as the major character. He is Everyman, the first and last man, God the Father and God the Son, Judas and Peter, and Adam. He assumes a focal point in the varied panoply of mythological and archetypal super-structures with which the novel is endowed and which, at times, seem so overweighted that they verge on inner collapse. Nevertheless, because Paradine is the seeker after truth, *The Hole in the Zero* speaks with a commanding and hopeful voice. For, while exposing the evil that men do to themselves, their environment, and to others, it is mankind's great capacity for good and a desire to serve while questing after the God within and without which emerge as M.K. Joseph's essentially Christian final declaration.

—Sharon-Ilona Hecht

---

**JUDD, Cyril.** *See* **KORNBLUTH. C.M.; MERRIL, Judith.**

---

# K

**KAHN, James.** American. Born in Chicago, Illinois, 30 December 1947. Educated at the University of Chicago, B.A. 1970, M.D. 1974. Married Jill Alden Littlewood in 1975; one daughter. Physician: intern, University of Wisconsin, Madison, 1974–75; resident, Los Angeles County Hospital, 1976–77, and University of California, Los Angeles, 1978–79. Since 1978, Emergency Room physician, Rancho Encino Hospital, Los Angeles. Address: c/o St. Martin's Press, 175 Fifth Avenue, New York, New York 10010, U.S.A.

SCIENCE-FICTION PUBLICATIONS

Novels (series: New World)

New World trilogy:
*World Enough and Time.* New York, Ballantine, 1980; London, Granada, 1982.
*Time's Dark Laughter.* New York, Ballantine, 1982; London, Panther, 1983.
*Timefall.* New York, St. Martin's Press, 1987; London, Grafton, 1988.
*Poltergeist* (novelization of screenplay). New York, Warner, and London, Granada, 1982.
*Return of the Jedi* (novelization of screenplay). New York, Ballantine, and London, Macdonald, 1983; in *The Star Wars Trilogy*, Ballantine, 1987.
*Indiana Jones and the Temple of Doom* (novelization of screenplay). London, Sphere, and New York, Ballantine, 1984.
*Poltergeist II* (novelization of screenplay). London, Corgi, and New York, Ballantine, 1986.
*The Echo Vector.* New York, St. Martin's Press, 1987; London, Grafton, 1989.

OTHER PUBLICATIONS

Novels

*Diagnosis: Murder.* New York, Carlyle, 1978.
*The Goonies* (novelization of screenplay). New York, Warner, and Sevenoaks, Kent, Coronet, 1985.

Plays

Television Plays: *A Pig Too Far* (*St. Elsewhere* series), 1983; for *E/R* series 1984–85.

Verse

*Nerves in Patterns,* with Jerome McGann. N.p., X Press, 1978.

*

James Kahn comments:

I think of my work primarily as storytelling, my purpose to entertain, and, if possible, to enthrall. Within that framework I rely on the themes of death and rebirth a great deal, a cyclical movements in time and space—sometimes metaphorically, sometimes physically.

* * *

James Kahn has been building his knowledge of the craft of writing through novelizations of screenplays: *Poltergeist, Return of the Jedi, Indiana Jones and the Temple of Doom, The Goonies*, and *Poltergeist II.* His first science-fiction short story, "Mobius Trip," dates back to 1971; since then, he has explored other genres to some extent, including a detective novel, *Diagnosis: Murder*, and a volume of poetry, *Nerves in Patterns.* His main original work, the New World Trilogy, consists of *World Enough and Time, Time's Dark Laughter*, and *Timefall.*

The most interesting of the novelizations is *Poltergeist*, where Kahn's contact with ESP research in medical school and background in myth lead to descriptions of the astral planes and their inhabitants, especially the shadow, tree, and flame figures, that are congruent with accounts of occult experience and well above the level of the rest of the film material. The *Star Wars* volume, *Return of the Jedi*, is even and competent, with good landscape descriptions but little depth in characterization. Characterization techniques begin to expand in the *Indiana Jones* novelization with development of Short Round's viewpoint and the reiterated theme "Anything Goes" to characterize Willie; a limited juvenile narrator is also developed for *The Goonies.*

*World Enough and Time* is unusually high in quality for a first science-fiction novel, possibly because of Kahn's love of words and interest in integrating poetic quotations either directly into the narration or as commentary on experience by scholar vampires. The title derives from Marvell's "To His Coy Mistress," though the novel deals with interrupted love rather than unfulfilled sexual desire. Rose and Dicey are kidnapped from their respective husbands, the centaur Beauty and the human Scribe Josh, for unknown reasons; Josh and Beauty join in pursuit and claim Venge-right, acquiring as companions the cat/human Isis, the Flutterby (giant butterfly) Humbelly, the Neuroman Jasmine, and the highly educated and philanthropic Vampire Lon—the range of species and interests in the novel is extensive, if left at a somewhat shallow level. The mission is partly successful: Dicey has been entranced by a vampire and dies, but Josh's brother Ollie is rescued and Rose is released from the Neuroman experiment that interlocks human minds for increased intelligence and a wider field of perception.

The development of minor themes is what makes the novel outstanding. Time obscures truth by turning history into legend; maturation requires the ability to accept the difference. Jasmine as long-lived lecturer on the past is a little obvious, but she forces Beauty to adjust to the fact that centaurs, like other talking animals, are a recent creation of man through genetic engineering, not the ancient people of their myths. Scribery, the belief in the power of the word in itself, develops when adult humans are wiped out in the Race Wars by their creations; Josh must accept this, but retains faith in an intrinsic power for words. Kahn's medical background is at its best in the human need to create their fantasies, even the destructive ones like Vampires, the self-hate of the failure Accidents, the desire for long life at any price expressed in the Neuroman process where a fungus eats away all tissue but nerve cells and these cells serve as the core for an artificial body. But the creations are close to the fantasy borderline, resembling the dragons of Pern rather than hard-core science fiction, in spite of realistic elements like the limited perception of the cat Isis with her fragment of human brain— abilities are not held tightly to physical law.

The sequel, *Time's Dark Laughter*, is more ambitious and less successful, though beautifully titled; it presents a cyclic universe, destroyed and reborn whenever human genetic possibilities combine to produce a semi-divine being that possesses full consciousness of the universe but lacks control over power and moral insight and so must be killed—cycles will continue until a solution to the problem is found. All experience is becoming sour for all characters in this novel: Josh is forced back to the city of the experiment by brain seizures to match his genetic component with the queen's and create the bird-girl deity; the quest to recover Josh and Rose succeeds in destroying the girl by a virus keyed to her unique DNA, but the nature of the world has been altered and much destroyed. Josh and Rose start over in a new Eden, their first Children Can and Able. One problem is this confusion of cycles: the sun now rises in the east instead of the west and a new animal appears that is clearly a giraffe, suggesting that the new cycle is ours, but the bird-girl refers to Jahweh as a past self and many terms in the old cycle are specifically ours—California, Monterey, Pope. It is difficult to credit such specifics as accidental similarities in recurring cycles, and the pattern remains in an uncomfortable tension.

Kahn's strengths lie in language, background in medicine, the use of myth. Techniques still need improvement: consistency in characterization (notably with Jasmine), methods for integrating extrapolated history and other background material smoothly into narrative, selectivity among ideas. But the combination of recurrent pattern with the fixing of position resulting from the tension between a straight-line quest and cyclic time offers possibilities that deserve serious exploration.

—Marilyn K. Nellis

---

**KAPP, Colin.** British. Born in 1928(?). Worked as an electrical technician. Address: c/o New English Library, Mill Road, Dunton Green, Sevenoaks, Kent TN13 2YA, England.

SCIENCE-FICTION PUBLICATIONS

Novels (series: Cageworld)

*Transfinite Man.* New York, Berkley, 1964; as *The Dark Mind*, London, Corgi, 1965.
*The Patterns of Chaos.* London, Gollancz, 1972; New York, Award, 1973.
*The Wizard of Anharitte.* London, Panther, 1975; New York, Award, n.d.
*The Survival Game.* New York, Ballantine, 1976; London, Dobson, 1977.
*The Chaos Weapon.* New York, Ballantine, 1977; London, Dobson, 1979.
*Manalone.* London, Panther, 1977.
*The Ion War.* New York, Ace, 1978; London, Dobson, 1979.
*The Timewinders.* London, Dobson, 1980.
*Search for the Sun* (Cageworld). London, New English Library, 1981; New York, DAW, 1983.
*The Lost World of Cronus* (Cageworld). London, New English Library, 1982; New York, DAW, 1983.
*The Tyrant of Hades* (Cageworld). London, New English Library, 1982; New York, DAW, 1984.

Short Stories

*The Unorthodox Engineers.* London, Dobson, 1979.

* * *

If any SF writer could typify the Blakean aphorism "Energy is eternal delight," Colin Kapp does so both in terms of human passion and of the energies that compose the universe. The former is unusual in a writer dealing with such esoteric sciences as atomic theory; the latter demonstrates a feeling of awe toward the forces of nature, rather than extolling the way technology utilizes such forces.

Not all of Kapp's works demonstrate the fascination with energy—various stories for *Analog* and the tales of "the Unorthodox Engineers" are standard scientific problem-solving puzzles.

The majority of his works, however, describe the energy states of physics in rhapsodic terms ("Around him the hellish sums and unbelievable vortexes of transfinity shifted and phased in a terrible kaleidoscope of new geometrics and unknown colors"—*Transfinite Man*). In essence, Kapp relates to energy-states as Asimov did to robots—devising a conceptual structure for the scientific phenomena, and giving its many facets relevance to the many facets of human response. In fact, Kapp goes so far as to posit direct interaction between natural forces and human thought-energy. *Transfinite Man* describes a demonic hero, able to survive the dimensions of transfinity by virtue of maniacal hatred. *The Ion War* and "Mephisto and the Ion Explorer" portray human beings able to transform themselves into vessels of ionic energy. "Lambda 1" and "The Imagination Trap" detail the world of Tau-space, a sub-atomic dimension in which matter directly responds to mental manipulation, and *The Chaos Weapon* concerns a female psychic who can read entropic energy-patterns which indicate oncoming catastrophes. Surprisingly, this interaction is not mechanistically explained in terms of psionics (i.e., the human brain transmits energy like a radio, etc.)—rather, Kapp merely portrays a direct correspondence; rather like the hermetic relationship of man and universe, microcosm and macrocosm.

Such a relationship would be facile if the human personalities were not as vividly realized as the cosmic aspects. Kapp's characters are neither subtle nor complex, but they are vivid, especially in regard to romantic attachments. In "Hunger over Sweet Waters" a scientist and his female co-worker, with whom he is in love, are stranded together on a world without drinkable water, and though the scientist is married to another woman and cannot enjoy a relationship with his co-worker, his love for her is the spur for his invention of a way to secure their rescue. In both *The Ion War* and *The Patterns of Chaos* the relationship between woman and man is less like love than like the intimacy of "torturer and victim"—the female being a caustic "bitch-goddess" who drives the male to perform superhuman feats. This sort of antagonistic romance—also present in *Transfinite Man, The Chaos Weapon*, and "Lambda I"—is the means by which the hero exceeds his limits, discovering strategies for survival or salvation. (In recent works—such as the entertaining pulp-style adventure of the *Cageworld* series—the antagonistic romance-angle is toned down, but still present to a degree.)

Though Kapp equals several more revered authors in terms of imaginative scope and striking characters, he lacks a quality that generally enhances the popularity of such authors—that is, an overt philosophy that describes man's place in the universe. Despite this lack, his stories can yield a wealth of implicit insights, while his articulation of scientific concepts is surpassed only by the very best of SF.

—Gene Phillips

---

**KAVAN, Anna.** Pseudonym for Helen Woods; also wrote as Helen Ferguson. Born in Cannes, France, in 1901; brought up in California. Educated privately and in Church of England Schools. Married 1) Donald Ferguson (divorced); 2) Stuart Edmonds (divorced), one son. Lived in the United States, Burma, Europe, Australia, and New Zealand; settled in London. *Died 5 December 1968.*

SCIENCE-FICTION PUBLICATIONS

Novels

*House of Sleep.* New York, Doubleday, 1947; as *Sleep Has His House*, London, Cassell, 1948.
*Ice.* London, Owen, 1967; New York, Doubleday, 1970.

Short Stories

*Asylum Piece and Other Stories.* London, Cape, 1940; New York, Doubleday, 1946.
*I Am Lazarus.* London, Cape, 1945.
*Julia and the Bazooka*, edited by Rhys Davies. London, Owen, 1970; New York, Knopf, 1975.
*My Madness: The Selected Writings of Anna Kavan*, edited by Brian W. Aldiss. London, Pan, 1990.

OTHER PUBLICATIONS

Novels

*Change the Name.* London, Cape, 1941.
*A Scarcity of Love.* Southport, Lancashire, Downie, 1956; New York, Herder, 1972.
*Eagles' Nest.* London, Owen, 1957.
*Who Are You?* Lowestoft, Suffolk, Scorpion Press, 1963.

Novels as Helen Ferguson

*A Charmed Circle.* London, Cape, 1929.
*The Dark Sisters.* London, Cape, 1930.
*Let Me Alone.* London, Cape, 1930; Short Hills, New Jersey, Enslow, 1978.
*A Stranger Still.* London, Lane, 1935.
*Goose Cross.* London, Lane, 1936.
*Rich Get Rich.* London, Lane, 1937.

Short Stories

*A Bright Green Field and Other Stories.* London, Owen, 1958.
*My Soul in China*, edited by Rhys Davies. London, Owen, 1975.

Other

*The Horse's Tale*, with K.T. Bluth. London, Gaberbocchus, 1949.

* * *

Recalling the gothic horrors of Mary Shelley's *Frankenstein*, Anna Kavan inverts the terror stimulus from the external monster to the interior of the mind. Kavan's works are explorations of the mentally ill, those possessed by fear of an external and menacing society. The Monster is within the self—sometimes evidenced as unreasoning fear and suspicion and sometimes emanated as an obsessive desire to control/torture others as catharsis for self-destructive tendencies.

Kavan, like Shelley, did not consciously write science fiction. Kavan's writings are characterised by their frequent and enigmatic shifts between fantasy and reality, abrupt mood shifts, and poetic descriptions. Some of her works are catastrophe fiction, envisioning mass chaos epitomized in the chaos of the central character's mind. The protagonist's mental condition both parallels and illuminates the basic irrationality of the civilizations Kavan depicts. It is the shifting of reality planes within a setting of world-wide catastrophe which marks some of Kavan's psychological fiction as science fiction. Although many of her works are primarily descriptions of the world of the mentally ill, at least "The Birthmark," *Ice*, and *House of Sleep* present a world outside the central character's mind which is also distorted.

In "The Birthmark" the young girl narrator meets an alien girl who fears the discovery of her peculiar skin marking, implying to the narrator that such a discovery would ban her from the narrator's world. Many years later, while touring a castle, the narrator discovers (or thinks she does) the same girl locked in a dungeon—being persecuted for her special talents—talents symbolized and identified by that birthmark.

*Ice* is also set in a hostile world: nuclear testing has brought on a rapidly advancing ice age. Kavan depicts, unlike many science-fiction writers, an apathetic populace who are unable to comprehend the impending disaster or to break their routine existence. The people remain true to their nature: complacent in the face of chaos. Of course some attempt to flee, but government and business continue to function. Even war continues as the demise of civilization approaches. Within this hostile world the protagonist obsessively searches for a frail, seemingly inept woman whom he both loves and hates. Her weakness of will and body obsesses him as it does his rival, and he alternately wishes to protect and destroy her. Ultimately he conquers the fear of rejection which instigates his violent fantasies toward her and they join in love, and at peace, as they wait for their deaths.

In *House of Sleep* Kavan presents B's progressing rejection of reality which stems from childhood. B finds that only her daydreams and the cover of night provide the security ripped away from her by her mother's unexplained death. B retreats into her imagination, finding there a haven from the isolation and alienation of a society which cares neither for her or for itself. She flees from place to place, always recording the threatening, if ineffectual, liaison officer and the civil disruption and fear within an oppressive government. B states: "Without understanding the reason, I knew that I had to keep the day unimportant. I had to prevent the day world from becoming real." In Kavan's abrupt and frequently imperceptible shifts from reality to fantasy she illustrates the operation of an escape mechanism within the mind of one who can neither accept nor interact in the alien world of reality.

Kavan brings brilliant character portrayal into the genre of science fiction, exploring the inner universe of the mind rather than the outer galaxies of the universe. What she finds within the mind is fear and violence: the essence of terror, confirmed by the irrationality of uncaring society which persecutes without knowledge or reason those whose perceptions differ from the norm. Thus Kavan explores various reality levels, questioning society's grasp of reality, and indicating that perhaps sanity is only a matter of perception: that we live in an insane world and are unable to judge who within it is sane or insane.

—Jane B. Weedman

---

**KAY, Guy Gavriel.** Canadian. Address: c/o Harper and Collins Publishers, Suite 2900, Hazelton Lanes, 55 Avenue Road, Toronto, Ontario M5R 3L2, Canada.

SCIENCE-FICTION PUBLICATIONS

Novels (series: Fionavar Tapestry)

The Fionavar Tapestry trilogy:
*The Summer Tree*. Toronto, McClelland and Stewart, and New York, Arbor House, 1984.
*The Wandering Fire*. Toronto, Collins; New York, Arbor House; and London, Allen and Unwin, 1986.
*The Darkest Road*. Toronto, Collins, and New York, Arbor House, 1986; London, Unwin Hyman, 1987.
*Tigana*. New York, ROC, and London, Viking, 1990.

* * *

Without the usual apprenticeship of short story production, Guy Gavriel Kay produced his Fionavar Tapestry Trilogy, a powerful dramatization of the great conflict between dark and light set in a fantasy universe. These adult fantasies probably do not fall within the strict and older definitions of science fiction but are exemplars of the influence of depth psychology and ordered consideration of myth that exemplify shifts in the making of fantasy similar to those in the work of Clive Barker (*Weaveworld*), John Crowley (*Little, Big*), or of Ursula LeGuin (*The Beginning Place*).

As *The Summer Tree* opens, five young professionals (law students, interns) are attending a speech at the University of Toronto's Convocation Hall and find themselves surreptitiously chosen by the speaker, who emerges as the mage Loren Silvercloak in disguise, to journey with him back to an alternate universe of mythic proportions. They are swept away by magic.

Once in Fionavar they soon find that they are not merely called to participate in an anniversary celebration but are drawn to roles in the working out of a great and ancient struggle to repress Rakoth Maugrim the Unraveller, also named Sathain, the Hooded One, who has broken free of many thousands of years of captivity. In the first volume one of their number, Paul Schafer, sacrifices himself upon the Summer Tree, partly to assuage his deep guilt over the death of the woman he loved in Toronto, and emerges from the sacrifice reborn as the Lord of the Summer Tree, possessed of the power to deal with the gods.

*The Wandering Fire* also begins on earth, whence all five have escaped in order to save one of their number, Jennifer, from any further horrors at the hands of the Unraveller, whose rape-child she is carrying. Before they return to Fionavar, they summon Arthur Pendragon to go with them, and Kay's most triumphant touch in the trilogy is a special re-setting of the Arthurian story. The second volume rises to a climax in the attempt to destroy the Cauldron of Khath Meigol, one of the Unraveller's most potent weapons. In *The Darkest Road*, the final battle is joined, and its outcomes are unusual in several ways. Without ruining the ending it is sufficient to say that Kay clearly believes in strong moral imperatives of self-sacrifice and that he handles the traditional mythologies with respect but can create beyond the patterns.

The achievement of the Fionavar trilogy is one of a delicate and effectively crafted balance between highly wrought heroic fantasy and psychological realism. The Canadian "visitors" attain mythic features as they are absorbed, while the mythic figures, both from Fionavar's own mythic realm and the Arthurian Legends, attain a level of human psychological reality unusual in fantasy. As C.G. Jung repeatedly pointed out, dreams and other fantasies are irrevocably facts; they exist, and they must be treated accordingly with deepest respect. In adult heroic fantasy (as distinct from pornographic fantasy), the full impact of human sexuality and other life patterns and their relation to deep levels of myth can be explored and rendered into fiction.

At the centre of Kay's stunningly coherent mythical universe, rooted as it is in the archetypes of the struggle between dark and light, lie some very adult questions of freedom and choice. The bastard rape-child of the Unraveller and Jennifer, Darien, is the key to the defeat of evil, but his mother Jennifer refuses to influence his choice between the forces warring within him, forces that are deeply rooted in his personal quest for caring and affection. There is a great truth about the individual finding self and being motivated by inner needs in this and many of the other figures in the trilogy, and Kay has told stories here of no less direct moral import than the most serious of modern novels. In addition he has burnished them with the products of a rich, intelligent, and panoramic imagination and the language and tone to match.

*Tigana*, Kay's most recent work, is a free-standing fantasy novel set in quite another key. It deals with a kingdom that has been razed and cursed by Brandin of Ygrath, a sorcerer-warrior-invader, because his son was killed in battle against it. Alessan bar Valentin, the surviving Prince of Tigana, comes from hiding and constructs a revolution to rid the peninsula of the Palm. Tigana had been one of the nine Palm Dukedoms, of both Brandin and Alberico, the sorcerer who holds the remainder of the land.

*Tigana* is a remarkable reconstruction of the tone and world of Renaissance Italy, although with such wonderful differentiating touches as a planet with twin moons and the placing of the Palm in the Southern Hemisphere. The use of magic is very restrained and the focus of the novel is upon the rapid and intriguing adventures of Alessan's band as it assembles and undertakes its revolution. Kay creates a more restricted pantheon of gods than that in Fionavar, but again they are anthropologically very correct, in that there are deities of the natural world and narratives of creation, as well as meticulously demonstrated ritual observance at the centre of the life of the Palm. It is a feature of Kay's writing that it consistently and warmly embraces the premise, once again Jungian, that we live without myth at our peril in the modern world, abandoning the ties that bind us to nature, to the past, and to the psyche of the race. In creating the rich and adult fantasy worlds of Fionavar and Tigana, Kay offers a powerful recasting of the myths and their moving authority over our lives within kingdoms made real by his own rich imagination and graceful prose.

—Peter Brigg

---

**KELLER, David H(enry).** Also wrote as Henry Cecil. American. Born in Philadelphia, Pennsylvania, 23 December 1880. Educated at the University of Philadelphia Medical School. Served as a physician working in shell-shock during World War I; medical professor on the faculty of the Army Chaplain's School at Harvard University, Cambridge, Massachusetts, during World War II. Married in 1903. Physician, specializing in psychoanalysis: junior physician, Illinois Mental Institute, after 1915, and worked in other hospitals in Louisiana, Tennessee, and Pennsylvania. Editor, *Sexology* and *Your Body* in the 1930's. *Died 13 July 1966.*

### Science-Fiction Publications

#### Novels

*The Waters of Lethe.* Great Barrington, Massachusetts, Kirby, 1937.
*The Sign of the Burning Hart.* St. Lo, France, Barbaroux, 1938; Hollywood, National Fantasy Fan Foundation, 1948.
*The Television Detective.* Los Angeles, Los Angeles Science Fiction League, 1938.
*The Devil and the Doctor.* New York, Simon and Schuster, 1940.
*The Solitary Hunters, and The Abyss.* Philadelphia, New Era, 1948.
*The Eternal Conflict.* Philadelphia, Prime Press, 1949.
*The Final War.* Portland, Oregon, Perri Press, 1949.
*The Homunculus.* Philadelphia, Prime Press, 1949.
*The Lady Decides.* Philadelphia, Prime Press, 1950.

#### Short Stories

*The Thought Projector.* New York, Stellar, 1930.
*Wolf Hollow Bubbles.* Jamaica, New York, Arra Printers, 1934(?).
*Men of Avalon.* Everett, Pennsylvania, Fantasy, 1935(?).
*The Thing in the Cellar.* Millheim, Pennsylvania, Bizarre Series, 1940.
*Life Everlasting*, edited by Sam Moskowitz and Will Sykora. Newark, New Jersey, Avalon, 1947.
*Tales from Underwood.* New York, Pellegrini and Cudahy, 1952.
*Figment of a Dream.* Baltimore, Mirage Press, 1962.
*The Folsom Flint and Other Curious Tales.* Sauk City, Wisconsin, Arkham House, 1969.
*The Street of Queer Houses and Other Tales*, edited by R. Reginald and Douglas Menville. Salem, New York, Ayer, 1976.

### Other Publications

#### Verse

*Songs of a Spanish Lover* (as Henry Cecil). Privately printed, 1924.

#### Other

*The Kellers of Hamilton Township: A Study in Democracy.* Privately printed, 1922.
*The Sexual Education Series.* New York, Popular Book Corporation, 10 vols., 1928.
*Know Yourself! Life and Sex Facts of Man, Woman, and Child.* New York, Popular Book Corporation, 1930.
*Portfolio of Anatomical Manikins.* New York, Sparacio, 1932.
*Picture Stories of the Sex Life of Man and Woman.* New York, Popular Medicine, 1941.

* * *

The genre of science fiction and fantasy has seemed to attract some of the most talented, versatile, and idiosyncratic personalities and made writers of them. David H. Keller pursued a varied and successful career as physician, military doctor, psychiatrist, and medical researcher. He published widely in the professional literature of his field. He also wrote fiction—but only for his family and friends. Then in 1928 *Amazing Stories* published "The Revolt of the Pedestrians," a long dystopian narrative that Keller had completed before Hugo Gernsback had even started *Amazing.* The story was such a success that Gernsback contracted for twelve more from Keller, and during the next decade or so 60 "Kelleryarns" were published in science-fiction and fantasy markets. *Weird Tales* served as another primary outlet for the Keller stories. During the final two decades of his life, however, Keller returned to private publishing and almost continuous writing of stories and books that may or may not have been marketable. His overall accomplishment seems immense, individual, and idiosyncratic. Some of his stories are classics of the horror, weird fantasy variety. Much of his writing reads as pleasantly whimsical and expressive of the "humours" of his personality in the 18th-century sense. In many ways, especially in the final years of his life, he was like an 18th-century eccentric or country gentleman who loved and expressed wit, humour, and imaginative curiosity in both his living and his writing. In all ways, Keller was his own man; and it is perhaps too soon for a literary assessment of his work whether in abnormal psychology or in fantasy or humorous narrative.

Regardless of any later assessment of his large volume of rather whimsical writing, certain careful elements in his art are apparent. Keller is often very skillful in the subtle understated suggestion of the supernatural that creates the greatest chill of horror. He combines with this a fascination in the psychosomatic relations of mental disorder to behavior. Among the short, chilling masterpieces that embody these artfully controlled effects are "The Thing in the Cellar," "A Piece of Linoleum," and "The Dead Woman," all from the early 1930's. Keller writes, then, with a subtle control of statement and tone that is unusual in the early pulp markets of the genre. The other element in his art that is particularly impressive is his use of point of view. Many of his narratives are told in first person, and he is master of the ironic first-person narrator who gradually reveals his own insanity to the reader without realizing it himself. As in Swift's *A Modest Proposal*, a Keller narrator will often be condemning himself or herself while telling what seems to be his or her side of the story. The other kind of first-person narrator is Keller himself in the person of various point-of-view characters with whimsical names, such as Jacobus Hubelaire who writes his own autobiography that is really Keller's, or Colonel Horatio Bumble in *The Homunculus.* This last, strange little book gives a fictional picture in the first person of Keller/Bumble that may or may not be the real Keller. But it shows a 20th-century retired Colonel of the Army Medical Corps who dabbles in writing and in the supernatural and who resembles an 18th-century eccentric, such as one might find in a Smollett novel or in the person of Erasmus Darwin, much more than a modern writer. At the same time the book, in its way, treats fascinating themes of scientific methodology, married life, and writing itself. Keller is a puzzlement in the genre—unique, varied, and often extremely effective.

—Donald M. Hassler

---

**KELLEY, Leo P(atrick).** American. Born in Wilkes Barre, Pennsylvania, 10 September 1928. Educated at the New School for Social Research, New York, B.A. in English 1957. Advertising copywriter and manager, McGraw-Hill Book Company, New York, 1959–69. Since 1969, freelance writer. Address: 702 Lincoln Boulevard, Long Beach, New York 11561, U.S.A.

### Science-Fiction Publications

Novels

*The Counterfeits.* New York, Belmont, 1967.
*Odyssey to Earthdeath.* New York, Belmont, 1968.
*The Accidental Earth.* New York, Belmont, 1968.
*Time Rogue.* New York, Lancer, 1970.
*The Coins of Murph.* New York, Berkley, 1971; London, Coronet, 1974.
*Mindmix.* New York, Fawcett, 1972; London, Coronet, 1973.
*Time: 110100.* New York, Walker, 1972; as *The Man from Maybe*, London, Coronet, 1974.
*Mythmaster.* New York, Dell, 1973; London, Coronet, 1974.
*The Earth Tripper.* New York, Fawcett, 1973; London, Coronet, 1974.
*The Time Trap* (for children). Belmont, California, Pitman, 1977(?); London, Murray, 1979.
*Backward in Time* (for children). Belmont, California, Pitman, 1979; London, Hutchinson, 1980.
*Death Sentence* (for children). Belmont, California, Pitman, 1979; London, Hutchinson, 1980.
*Earth Two* (for children). Belmont, California, Pitman, 1979; London, Hutchinson, 1980.
*Prison Satellite* (for children). Belmont, California, Pitman, 1979; London, Hutchinson, 1980.
*Sunworld* (for children). Belmont, California, Pitman, 1979; London, Hutchinson, 1980.
*Worlds Apart* (for children). Belmont, California, Pitman, 1979; London, Hutchinson, 1980.
*Dead Moon* (for children). Belmont, California, Pitman, 1979; London, Murray, 1980.
*King of the Stars* (for children). Belmont, California, Pitman, 1979; London, Murray, 1980.
*On the Red World* (for children). Belmont, California, Pitman, 1979; London, Murray, 1980.
*Night of Fire and Blood* (for children). Belmont, California, Pitman, and London, Murray, 1979.
*Where No Sun Shines* (for children). Belmont, California, Pitman, 1979; London, Murray, 1980.
*Vacation in Space* (for children). Belmont, California, Pitman, 1979; London, Murray, 1980.
*Star Gold* (for children). Belmont, California, Pitman, and London, Murray, 1979.
*Good-bye to Earth* (for children). Belmont, California, Pitman, 1979; London, Murray, 1980.

### Other Publications

Novels

*Brother John* (novelization of screenplay). New York, Avon, and London, Pan, 1971.
*Deadlocked!* New York, Fawcett, 1973.
*Luke Sutton, Outlaw* [*Gunfighter, Indian Fighter, Avenger, Outrider, Bounty Hunter, Hired Gun, Lawman, Mustanger*]. New York, Doubleday, 9 vols., 1981–90.
*Cimarron and the Hanging Judge* [*Rides the Outlaw Trail, and the Border Bandits, in the Cherokee Strip, and the Elk Soldiers, and the Bounty Hunters, and the High Rider, in No Man's Land, and the Vigilantes, and the Medicine Wolves, on Hell's Highway, and the War Women, and the Bootleggers, and the Prophet's People, and the Comancheros, and the Scalp Hunters, and the Gunhawk's Gold, and the Hired Guns, and the Manhunters, and the Red Earth People, on a Texas Manhunt*]. New York, New American Library, 21 vols., 1983–86.
*Morgan.* New York, Doubleday, 1986.
*A Man Called Dundee.* New York, Doubleday, 1988.
*Thunder Gods' Gold.* New York, M. Evans, 1988.
*Bannock's Brand.* New York, Doubleday, 1991.

Other

Editor, *Themes in Science Fiction: A Journey into Wonder.* New York, McGraw Hill, 1972.
Editor, *The Supernatural in Fiction.* New York, McGraw Hill, 1973.
Editor, *Fantasy: The Literature of the Marvelous.* New York, McGraw Hill, 1974.

* * *

Although achieving his greatest success with the Luke Sutton and Cimarron western series and non-series novels like *Thunder Gods' Gold*, Leo P. Kelley produced a number of solid science fiction novels earlier in his writing career.

Kelley's first science fiction novel, *The Counterfeits*, develops many of the themes he refines in his later novels. Earth is invaded by an alien race whose home planet has been destroyed. The aliens are able to assume any shape; they take human form and set about destroying human civilization. What takes this book out of the usual alien-invasion formula is Kelley's attempt to provide a plausible reconciliation at the book's conclusion.

*Odyssey to Earthdeath* explores the domination of a society by psychological methods in the tradition of Orwell's *Nineteen Eighty-Four.* The book suffers from undeveloped characters and a predictable plot. *Time Rogue* is one of Kelley's few attempts to use time travel as a theme for sociological speculation. Unfortunately, the plot degenerates into a good versus evil confrontation with predictable results. *The Accidental Earth* blends the themes of the previous books into an eerie amalgam. A counter-Earth is separated from our Earth by a wall of time, but an accident brings the Earth into contact. Only the secret weapon of the Photon Spray saves Earth from alien invasion by severing the Time link and separating the two Earths again. Although the conclusion is hackneyed space opera, the beginning and middle sections of the novel feature some of Kelley's best writing. *The Coins of Murph* tells of a post-holocaust society based on religion deifying the chief programmer of the Rand Corporation, Joseph Murphy, who, on some surviving audio tapes, blames the holocaust on decision making. His followers interpret this to mean all decisions should be decided by chance, hence the use of coins for flipping. The plot gets bogged down in power politics, but the sociological portrait Kelley presents is memorable.

The remaining SF novels are chiefly characterized by their cynical perspectives and brutality. *Time: 110100* is a surreal morality play of two humans on an odyssey through a strange world populated by lusty, war-like, and enigmatic simulacra. While the book has undertones of Barth's *Giles Goat-Boy*, it is damaged by a weak ending. *Mindmix* presents contemporary human society stricken by a deadly virus. The government discovers one man, Pete Bratton, who has become immune to the virus. Kelley develops a cynical picture of government scientists exploiting Bratton by transplanting the minds of dying geniuses into Bratton's brain, with successful but grim results. *The Earth Tripper* and *Mythmaster* are written in New Wave style. The better of the two books, *The Earth Tripper*, follows the bizarre adventures of an alien observer who goes AWOL on Earth in human form. Captured releasing animals from a zoo, he's taken to a secret mental institution, and he and other strange inmates become subjects of brutal experiments using "reality therapy." The mildly upbeat ending doesn't relieve much of the book's cynicism.

Since 1973, Kelley has concentrated on writing science fiction for juveniles and elementary students with low reading skills—and he has continued to produce very successful westerns. Kelley's best work features strong writing and ingenious sociological constructions of unique societies, but the unrelenting grimness of his later work coupled with New Wave writing styles weakens its appeal.

—George Kelley

---

**KELLY, James Patrick.** American. Born in Mineola, New York, 11 April 1951. Educated at University of Notre Dame, B.A. in English literature, 1972; attended Clarion Writers' Workshop, Michigan State University, East Lansing, 1974, 1976. Married 1) Barbara Flynn in 1972 (divorced 1988); 2) Pamela Eldredge in 1991; 3 children. Proposal writer, then coordinator of public relations, C.E. Maguire, Inc., Architects, Engineers, and Planners, Waltham, Massachusetts, 1972–77; part-time consultant, 1977–79. Agent: Ralph M. Vicinanza Ltd., 111 Eighth Avenue, Suite 1501, New York, New York 10011. Address: 7 Taft Road, Portsmouth, New Hampshire 03801, U.S.A.

SCIENCE-FICTION PUBLICATIONS

Novels (series: Messenger Chronicles)

*Planet of Whispers* (Messenger). New York, Bluejay, 1984.
*Freedom Beach*, with John Kessel. New York, Bluejay, 1985; London, Unwin Hyman, 1987.
*Look into the Sun* (Messenger). New York, Tor, 1989; London, Mandarin, 1990.

Short Stories

*Heroines*. Eugene, Oregon, Pulphouse, 1990.

Uncollected Short Stories

"Dea Ex Machina," in *Galaxy*, April 1975.
"Death Therapy," in *Fantasy and Science Fiction*, July 1978.
"Not to the Swift," in *Fantasy and Science Fiction*, February 1979.
"Flight of Fancy," in *Fantasy and Science Fiction*, June 1979.
"The Fear That Men Call Courage," in *Fantasy and Science Fiction*, September 1980.
"Homo Neuter," in *Analog Yearbook II*, edited by Ben Bova. New York, Ace, 1981.
"Last Contact," in *Amazing*, July 1981.
"Identity Crisis," in *Twilight Zone*, August 1981.
"In Memory Of," in *Universe 12*, edited by Terry Carr. New York, Doubleday, 1982.
"Still Time," in *Asimov's Science Fiction*, August 1983.
"Friend," with John Kessel, in *Fantasy and Science Fiction*, January 1984.
"The F&SF Diet," in *Fantasy and Science Fiction*, March 1984.
"Saint Theresa of the Aliens," in *Asimov's Science Fiction*, June 1984.
"The Empty World," in *Asimov's Science Fiction*, November 1984.
"Solstice," in *Asimov's Science Fiction*, June 1985.
"Rat," in *Fantasy and Science Fiction*, June 1986.
"The Prisoner of Chillon," in *Asimov's Science Fiction*, June 1986.
"Glass Cloud," in *Asimov's Science Fiction*, June 1987.
"Daemon," in *Fantasy and Science Fiction*, November 1987.
"Heroics," in *Asimov's Science Fiction*, November 1987.
"Home Front," in *Asimov's Science Fiction*, June 1988.
"Dancing with the Chairs," in *Asimov's Science Fiction*, March 1989.
"The Propagation of Light in a Vacuum," in *Universe 1*, edited by Robert Silverberg and Karen Haber. New York, Doubleday, 1990.
"Mr. Boy," in *Asimov's Science Fiction*, June 1990.
"Pogrom," in *Fires of the Past*, edited by Anne Jordan. New York, St. Martin's Press, 1991.
"Standing in Line with Mister Jimmy," in *Asimov's Science Fiction*, June 1991.

*

James Patrick Kelly comments:

Because my tastes in reading are various, my work has been correspondingly eclectic. I've written science fiction, fantasy, horror, and mainstream fiction, as well as poetry and essays. For me, fiction begins with people; I write to explore how our histories, personal and cultural, create our behaviors. I have always felt the need to demonstrate my range, or, to put a less elegant construction on it, I rarely stay in one place for long. During the eighties when some people tried to label me a humanist, I wrote several stories that the cyberpunks claimed. I'd like to think I've absorbed at least some of the basic lessons of feminism. I'm particularly fascinated by future shock; I think our grandchildren will be as far removed from us as we are from the Pilgrims. We live in a world of accelerating change; to stand still is to invite irrelevance. If literature is the conversation a civilization has with itself, then I want to join the people who are talking about what's happening now.

* * *

James Patrick Kelly's name first began to appear in the science-fiction magazines in the late 1970's with several short stories which examined ethical issues using the unique attributes of the field to place these in settings not available to mainstream writers. In "Death Therapy," for example, rapists are forced to undergo the actual experience of death as a deterrent to committing further crimes, and in "Not to the Swift," an aging man is compelled by circumstances into participating in a dangerous experiment in memory recall. In both cases, Kelly forces the reader to examine the balance between the rights of the individual and the needs of society at large.

Kelly also demonstrated early a true gift for evoking strong characters and having them interact credibly, a quality too frequently absent from the works of his contemporaries. "Homo Neuter" successfully manages to remain emotionally involving without becoming overly sentimental. A mutant searches for and ultimately discovers a young boy who shares his new abilities, only to discover that having grown up in a loveless, isolated mental state, he is incapable of expressing his own emotions, ultimately destroying the chance for a strong relationship.

The survivalist mentality is examined in "Still Time." At the outset of a nuclear war, a man who had planned to retreat from human involvement finds himself incapable of ignoring the plight of his neighbors. It is a very optimistic story about human nature despite the tragic setting. "The Cruelest Month," only peripherally science fiction at all, features a successful businesswoman who finally gives in to the pressure around her and begins to hallucinate the disintegration of her world.

"St Theresa of the Aliens" is at once a serious story and a biting satire. Aliens have landed on Earth, but since their culture is essentially communist, they choose to deal with the Russians rather than anyone else. A strong movement grows in the West to bar all contact with the aliens because of their political system.

"Freedom Beach," written in collaboration with John Kessel and later expanded into a novel by the same name, is an introspective look at human psychology which bears some resemblance to the popular television program, *The Prisoner*. The name refers to an island colony which appears to be a tourist resort, but which is actually home to an amnesiac who is being watched by possibly alien beings. Often surreal but always fascinating, this is one of the better expansions of a short work into book length.

Many of Kelly's short stories during the 1980's relied on surprise endings or humor, but he continued to examine serious themes. "Crow" could almost be a sequel to "Still Time." Following the nuclear war, most of those who survive destroy themselves by their selfish and short-sighted activities. A visit is paid to Emily Brontë in the mildly sentimental "Empty World," and "The Cast" is a clever look at the supernatural. Kelly's best short story to date is almost certainly "The Prisoner of Chillon," in which a reporter and a criminal penetrate the secrets of the hidden lair of a deformed genius. More recent stories of note include "The Glass Cloud," "Heroics," and "Dancing with Chairs."

Kelly's first solo novel, *Planet of Whispers*, appeared in 1984, the first in The Messenger Chronicles, although a second book was not to be published until 1989. The Messengers are an odd star-travelling race who have been trading food to the Chani, intelligent catlike aliens whose planetary culture is dominated by instinctive behavior. One overly greedy official cuts off the food supply, and although he is recalled, it is not until after famine has devastated the planet. The protagonist is sent to spread the word that assistance is on the way, but he discovers that starvation has led to an almost communicable form of insanity, and different factions within the Chani culture ultimately resort to physical combat when the first relief ship arrives. Despite the melodramatic plot, Kelly keeps his story and his characters firmly under control; he is more concerned with the struggle for the loyalties of individual Chani than the physical resolution of the story.

*Look into the Sun* continues the story. The religious leader of Chani culture is determined to bring her people completely into the sphere of the Messengers, and she determines that the best way to do this is to sacrifice herself in a way that will symbolize the change from planetbound to interstellar culture. To this end, she employs a human being from Earth to build her tomb, and the protagonist is the architect who arrives to deal with the situation. But what he discovers there is far more than a simple job of construction; ultimately he must examine the very things which make him a human being.

The consistently high quality and thoughtful nature of Kelly's work has already resulted in several Nebula nominations. Although his novels are thoughtful, original in concept, peopled by credible characters both alien and human, and written with a clear, authoritative style, his best work to date remains at shorter length.

—Don D'Ammassa

---

**KENDALL, Gordon.** *See* **SHWARTZ, Susan.**

---

**KENNEDY, Leigh.** American. Born in Denver, Colorado, 4 June 1951. Educated at Metropolitan State College, Denver, B.A. 1979. Clerk, Rose Memorial Hospital, Denver, 1971–80; typist, Austin Community College, Austin, Texas, 1981–85. Since 1985, full-time writer. Agent: Ellen Levine, Ellen Levine Literary Agency, Inc., 432 Park Avenue South, Suite 1205, New York, New York 10016, U.S.A. Address: 78 High Street, Pewsey, Wiltshire SN9 5AQ, England.

SCIENCE-FICTION PUBLICATIONS

Novels

*The Journal of Nicholas the American*. London, Cape, and New York, Atlantic Monthly Press, 1986.
*Saint Hiroshima*. London, Bloomsbury, 1987; San Diego, Harcourt, 1990.

Short Stories

*Faces*. London, Cape, 1986; New York, Atlantic Monthly Press, 1987.

* * *

Reading Leigh Kennedy's second novel, *Saint Hiroshima*, one might be surprised to learn that she began her professional career with sales to *Analog*. Coming completely innocent to her novels, one might not think of them as science fiction at all. So much of Kennedy's mature work might best be described as ghost stories, in the sense that they deal with people haunted by aspects of their past. "Max Haunting," which opens the collection entitled *Faces*, tells the story of Max renewing acquaintances from the hippy days, and gradually a picture appears to show the reader just why Max lost touch with these people. Typical of this author, however, is what is missing—the vital clues are there, the scene is set, but most of the "action" occurs off-stage for the reader to interpret. Even in the "hard" SF story "Helen, Whose Face Launched Twenty-Eight Conestoga Hovercraft," it is only at the end that pieces fall in, and messages are seen to have gotten through.

In her first novel, *The Journal of Nicholas The American*, Kennedy describes the emotional torment of an empath, Nicholas Dal, with an intensity that invokes memories of Silverberg's classic *Dying Inside.* Kennedy avoids the Philip Roth-isms that Silverberg includes, in favour of a double strand of concealed terror that provides the spine of the novel. The novel, in the form of Dal's diary entries, begins with an immediate note of threat, and very quickly alludes to other mysteries: "strange powers and bloody nights." Simultaneously we learn that Nicholas' family are from the Russian countryside, and that they left after some "old scandal," and there is immediate mention of the *pozhar-golava*—the family secret. Then Nicholas, who is in his late 20's but still a student, meets a young woman, Jack, and against his better judgement begins an affair with her.

The second half of *The Journal of Nicholas the American* is as much about Susanne, Jack's mother, as about Nicholas. Susanne is dying of multiple cancers, and she is frustrated and angry because she has nobody to talk to. Her husband is unable to cope and insists that she will recover, while banning Jack and her sister from seeing their mother alone. Somehow, Susanne and Nicholas come together, and she finds solace while he, drunk to mute the pain, listens. This is a novel composed primarily of emotions, based around love, pain, and death, and the fear of the pursuit, which results in a moving and occasionally discomforting experience.

Similarly haunting is Kennedy's second novel, *Saint Hiroshima*, which begins in 1950 in a small town in the Rockies, when five year old Katie Doheny sees a fatal road accident. The next day her parents get their first TV, and as it is tuned in Katie suddenly sees film of the Los Alamos atomic bomb, and hears the name "Hiroshima." The events are confused in her mind, creating at the same time an obsessive fear of The Bomb and a guardian angel, Saint Hiroshima.

A few years later, Katie meets Phil Benson, a talented young pianist, and they eventually become lovers, until Phil leaves for college. When he returns for the funeral of his piano teacher, he finds Katie married to Perry, a slobbish local firefighter who could offer Katie what she most desired—a bomb shelter. Phil leaves again, but in the summer of 1962 he is recalled by a desperate Katie. Their meeting almost results in tragedy as they are trapped in the shelter and almost starve.

Katie, having borne Phil's son, eventually remarries, to Louis, while Phil drifts on disillusioned. The book skips 20 years (the dates are related to key historical events, Cuba, the Civil Rights Movement, the raid on Tripoli) to find Phil working in a mediocre St. Louis theatre as a pianist and having a dangerous affair with a psychotic, gun-toting actress. As with *Nicholas the American*, Kennedy fills in elements of the intervals, without overwhelming and unnecessary detail. Phil occasionally remembers Holly, whom he lived with in Madison, and many have found her the most memorable character in the book, though she only appears as a memory.

—Kev P. McVeigh

---

**KENT, Gordon.** *See* **TUBB, E.C.**

---

**KENT, Kelvin.** *See* **BARNES, Arthur K.**

---

**KENT, Mallory.** *See* **LOWNDES, Robert A.W.**

---

**KENT, Philip.** *See* **BULMER, Kenneth**

---

**KERN, Gregory.** *See* **TUBB, E.C.**

---

**KESSEL, John (Joseph Vincent).** American. Born in Buffalo, New York, 24 September 1950. Educated at University of Rochester, B.A. in English and physics 1972 (cum laude); University of Kansas, M.A. in English 1974, Ph.D. in English 1981. Married 1) Penelope Crews in 1975 (divorced 1980); 2) Sue Hall in 1986. Copy and news editor, Commodity News Service, Leawood, Kansas, 1979–82. Since 1982, Associate Professor of creative writing and American literature, North Carolina State University, Raleigh. Recipient: Nebula award, 1982. Agent: Ralph Vicinanza Ltd., 111 Eighth Avenue, Suite 1501, New York, New York 10011. Address: Box 8105, Department of English, North Carolina State University, Raleigh, North Carolina 27695-8105, U.S.A.

SCIENCE-FICTION PUBLICATIONS

Novels

*Freedom Beach*, with James Patrick Kelly. New York, Bluejay, 1985; London, Unwin Hyman, 1987.
*Good News from Outer Space*. New York, Tor, 1989; London, Grafton, 1991.
*Another Orphan* (novella), published with *Enemy Mine*, by Barry Longyear. New York, Tor, 1989.

Uncollected Short Stories

"The Silver Man," in *Galileo 8*, May 1978.
"The Incredible Living Man," in *Galileo 10*, September 1978.
"Just Like a Cretin Dog," in *Fantasy and Science Fiction*, January 1979.
"In an Alien Wood," in *Galileo 11–12*, May 1979.
"On the 250th Anniversary of Apollo 11," in *Starlog's Science Fiction Yearbook*, October 1979.
"Herman Melville: Space Opera Virtuoso," in *Fantasy and Science Fiction*, January 1980.
"Last Things," in *The Berkley Showcase, Vol. 1*, edited by John Silbersack and Victoria Schochet. New York, Berkley, 1980.
"Animals," in *New Dimensions 10*, edited by Robert Silverberg. New York, Harper and Row, 1980.
"The Monuments of Science Fiction," in *Fantasy and Science Fiction*, August 1980.

"Uncle John and the Saviour," in *Fantasy and Science Fiction*, December 1980.
"Not Responsible! Park and Lock It!" in *Fantasy and Science Fiction*, September 1981.
"Below Zero," in *Twilight Zone*, January–February 1983.
"Hearts Do Not in Eyes Shine," in *Isaac Asimov's Science Fiction Magazine*, October 1983.
"Friend," with James Patrick Kelly, in *Fantasy and Science Fiction*, January 1984.
"The Big Dream," in *Isaac Asimov's Science Fiction Magazine*, April 1984.
"The Lecturer," in *Light Years and Dark*, edited by Michael Bishop. New York, Berkley, 1984.
"A Clean Escape," in *Isaac Asimov's Science Fiction Magazine*, May 1985.
"Reduction," with Gregory Frost, in *Isaac Asimov's Science Fiction Magazine*, January 1986.
"The Pure Product," in *Isaac Asimov's Science Fiction Magazine*, March 1986.
"Credibility," in *In the Field of Fire*, edited by Jack and Jeanne Dann. New York, Tor, 1987.
"Judgement Call," in *Fantasy and Science Fiction*, October 1987.
"Mrs. Shumel Exits a Winner," in *Isaac Asimov's Science Fiction Magazine*, June 1988.
"Buddha Nostril Bird," in *Isaac Asimov's Science Fiction Magazine*, March 1990.
"Invaders," in *Fantasy and Science Fiction*, October 1990.
"Buffalo," in *Fantasy and Science Fiction*, January 1991.
"The Moral Bullet," with Bruce Sterling, in *Isaac Asimov's Science Fiction Magazine*, July 1991.

OTHER PUBLICATIONS

Play:

*A Clean Escape* (produced Raleigh, North Carolina, 1986).

* * *

The subtitle of H. Bruce Franklin's critical study of Robert A. Heinlein, "America as Science Fiction," could be applied with equal appropriateness to the work of John Kessel. Although Kessel's fiction is far removed from Heinlein's both formally and philosophically, much of Kessel's work has also been preoccupied with the American landscape, both geographic and ideological. But while Heinlein's vision of America was of a land of infinite opportunity for the superior individual, Kessel's response has been more cautionary, insisting that America is also a land whose ideals of liberty and justice have been seriously undermined by self-righteousness, violence, and greed. And in addition to dealing with the burden of the American past, Kessel has also dealt with the equally weighty burden of the literary past, coming to terms with his authorial precursors in such metafictional fantasies as "Another Orphan" and "The Big Dream." The result has been a body of work that, although not large (two novels and approximately 30 works of short fiction), has been marked by both literary sophistication and conceptual audacity that has made Kessel one of the most highly regarded of contemporary American SF authors.

Kessel began publishing professionally in 1978. His early stories were serious and ambitious efforts that sometimes faltered under the strain of balancing the speculative element with theme and character development. While learning his craft, Kessel also began exploring the thematic territory he would map out in greater detail in his later work. "Herman Melville: Space Opera Virtuoso," an "essay" about a Herman Melville who was born in 1902 and wrote galaxy-smashing SF for the pulps, is an early example of Kessel's awareness of American literary history and particular fascination with Melville. "Uncle John and the Saviour," perhaps the best of Kessel's early stories, describes the return of Christ as an Indianapolis football player; its background of a near-future middle-America that doesn't hesitate to commercially exploit the Second Coming is expertly realized and anticipates Kessel's later work in its exploration of the irrational underside of American culture.

Kessel's breakthrough came with his 1982 novella "Another Orphan," in which he once again rewrites Melville, this time in a fantasy about a stockbroker who awakens one morning to find himself a character in *Moby-Dick*. What's worse, he's read the book and knows what's coming. As the protagonist, Patrick Fallon, struggles to come to terms with his situation; "Another Orphan" becomes an inquiry into the perennial SF topic of reality-shaping. Unlike other SF writers, however, Kessel refuses to provide his readers with easy explanations, and Fallon achieves some degree of peace only when he accepts the irrationality and contradictions of his situation, both of which are literally pounded into him by Captain Ahab: "Admit that this is not the tale you think it is! Admit that you do not know what will happen to you . . . that we are both free and unfree, alone and crowded in by circumstances in this world that we did not make, but indeed have the power to affect!" A Hugo nominee and Nebula winner, "Another Orphan" is regarded by many as one of the finest novellas of the 1980's.

Kessel continued to publish short fiction throughout the 1980's. His most notable stories from this period are "The Big Dream," a critique of the hardboiled detective genre in which a private detective finds himself turning into a character from a Raymond Chandler novel after he is hired to investigate Raymond Chandler himself; "Judgment Call," in which a minor-league baseball player at the dawn of the 21st century meets a mysterious woman who forces him to come to terms with the emotionally crippling traumas of his own past; and "The Pure Product," a violent tale of a time-traveller who, like Flannery O'Connor's Misfit, finds "no pleasure but meanness" in a world he sees as bereft of moral values and who expresses his displeasure by travelling through the past and committing random acts of violence. Although it did not receive the same level of acclaim as "Another Orphan," "The Pure Product" is equally important as a continuation of Kessel's critique of the excesses of American society—the title is taken from the first lines of William Carlos Williams' poem "To Elsie," which inform us that "The pure products of America/go crazy." The story is also, not so incidentally, the single most compelling narrative to be found in Kessel's short fiction. "The Big Dream" was incorporated into Kessel's collaboration with James Patrick Kelly, *Freedom Beach*, in which an amnesiac writer bounces back and forth between "reality" and various literary fantasies. "Judgment Call" was incorporated, along with "Credibility" and the Nebula nominee "Mrs. Shumel Exits a Winner," into Kessel's first solo novel, *Good News from Outer Space*.

A Nebula finalist and runner-up for the John W. Campbell Memorial award, *Good News from Outer Space* stands as one of the finest satirical novels modern SF has produced. It depicts the America of 1999 as a victim of both economic collapse and millennial fever. Televangelist Jimmy-Don Gilray preaches that Judgment Day will be signaled by the arrival of a giant spaceship at midnight on New Year's Eve, while George Eberhart, a reporter for a computer network equivalent of the *National Enquirer*, dashes around the country desperately trying to prove that the aliens have already landed. As such a synopsis implies, *Good News* is a very funny novel that displays Kessel's gift for comic invention much more than does his short fiction. However,

*Good News* is also serious, even horrific at times; as Norman Spinrad noted in his review of the novel, *Good News* "walks a fine line between mordant farce and psychological realism." Finally, *Good News from Outer Space* is a summation of the critiques of American society that mark much of Kessel's earlier work. In the context of the novel, the comments of the mysterious woman to the baseball player of "Judgment Call" become a comment on America itself as she tells the story of a man who "forgot the second law of thermodynamics, which tells us that we all lose, and that those times when we win are merely local statistical deviations."

Kessel's work since *Good News from Outer Space* continues to voice the author's literary and social preoccupations while becoming increasingly autobiographical. In "Invaders," parallel story lines depicting the Spanish conquest of the Incas and an alien invasion of earth are linked by passages describing the author himself writing the story and, finally, entering his own fictive world. As in *Good News*, alien invasion stands as a metaphor for our own wanton destructiveness. And in "Buffalo," perhaps Kessel's best short story to date, he describes an imaginary meeting between his own father and H.G. Wells in 1934, carefully delineating both men as representative of different aspects of "the world of limitation and loss."

Having only recently entered his 40's, Kessel is still in the early stages of his career. There is every reason to expect that, having produced some of the finest SF of the 1980's, he will continue to do so in the 1990's and beyond.

—F. Brett Cox

---

**KEY, Alexander (Hill).** American. Born in La Plata, Maryland, 21 September 1904. Educated at the Chicago Art Institute, 1922–24. Served in the United States Navy, 1942–45: Lieutenant Commander. Married Alice Towle in 1945; one child. Artist: book illustrator from age 19, then art teacher at Studio School of Art, Chicago; writer from 1929. Recipient: American Association of University Women award, 1965; Lewis Carroll Shelf award, 1972. *Died 25 July 1979.*

### Science-Fiction Publications

Novels (for children)

*Sprockets: A Little Robot.* Philadelphia, Westminster Press, 1963.
*Rivets and Sprockets.* Philadelphia, Westminster Press, 1964.
*The Forgotten Door.* Philadelphia, Westminster Press, 1965; London, Faber, 1966.
*Bolts*: A Robot Dog. Philadelphia, Westminster Press, 1966.
*Escape to Witch Mountain.* Philadelphia, Westminster Press, 1968.
*Flight to the Lonesome Place.* Philadelphia, Westminster Press, 1969.
*The Golden Enemy.* Philadelphia, Westminster Press, 1969.
*The Incredible Tide.* Philadelphia, Westminster Press, 1970.
*The Magic Meadow.* Philadelphia, Westminster Press, 1975.
*Jagger, The Dog from Elsewhere.* Philadelphia, Westminster Press, 1976.
*The Sword of Aradel.* Philadelphia, Westminster Press, 1977.
*Return from Witch Mountain.* Philadelphia, Westminster Press, 1978.

### Other Publications

Novels

*The Wrath and the Wind.* Indianapolis, Bobbs Merrill, 1949; London, Heinemann, 1950.
*Island Light.* Indianapolis, Bobbs Merrill, 1950; London, Heinemann, 1951.

Other (for children)

*The Red Eagle.* New York, Volland, 1930.
*Liberty or Death.* New York, Harper, 1936.
*With Daniel Boone on the Caroliny Trail.* Philadelphia, Winston, 1941.
*Boys Will Be Boys: Very Easy Pantomimes and Entertainments for Boys.* Franklin, Ohio, Eldridge, 1945.
*Cherokee Boy.* Philadelphia, Westminster Press, 1957.
*Mystery of the Sassafras Chair.* Philadelphia, Westminster Press, 1967.
*The Strange White Doves: True Mysteries of Nature.* Philadelphia, Westminster Press, 1972.
*The Preposterous Adventures of Swimmer.* Philadelphia, Westminster Press, 1973.
*The Case of the Vanishing Boy.* New York, Archway, 1979.

* * *

Already an established author by 1963, Alexander Key published that year *Sprockets: A Little Robot*, a simply constructed and written, unassuming story designed to attract children presumably interested in SF or space fantasy but too young for Heinlein or Norton. The story's success prompted a sequel, *Rivets and Sprockets.*

Their acceptance by young readers and reviewers alike probably encouraged Key to believe that children's SF might be both financially profitable and professionally satisfying, for in 1966 he published a third SF tale, *The Forgotten Door*, like its predecessors relatively uncomplicated in plot and simply written but more earnest in tone and theme. Subsequently, all of Key's fiction has been children's SF best characterized as a mix of narrative simplicity and moral earnestness.

At his best—as in *The Forgotten Door* and *Escape to Witch Mountain*, stories focusing on ESP-gifted, extraterrestrial children marooned on an inhospitable Earth and able to return home only with the help of sympathetic humans—Key creates likeable child protagonists and plausibly involves them in struggles between good and evil. Setting, reflecting the Carolina mountains Key so obviously loves, is also a strength. At his worse, Key is prone to sentimentalize, in particular overusing ESP-gifted animals that are morally superior to humans. Perhaps it is this weakness, along with relatively low-keyed plots and a too obvious earnestness, that has denied major status to an author who might otherwise have earned it because of his pioneering SF for young readers.

—Francis J. Molson

---

**KEYES, Daniel.** American. Born in New York City, 9 August 1927. Educated at Brooklyn College, New York, B.A. 1950, M.A. 1961. Served as a ship's purser in the maritime service, 1945–47. Married Aurea Georginia Vaquez in 1952; two daughters. Editorial associate, *Marvel Science Stories*, 1950–51; associate editor, Stadium Publishing Company, New York, 1951–52; co-owner, Fenko and Keyes Photography Inc., New York, 1953; high school English teacher, Brooklyn, 1954–55, 1957–62; Instructor, Wayne State University, Detroit, 1962–66. Lecturer, 1966–72, and since 1972, Professor of English, and director of creative writing, 1973–74, 1977–78, Ohio University, Athens. Recipient: Hugo award, 1960; Nebula award, 1966. Address: Department of English, Ohio University, Athens, Ohio 45701, U.S.A.

SCIENCE-FICTION PUBLICATIONS

Novel

*Flowers for Algernon*. New York, Harcourt Brace, and London, Cassell, 1966.

Uncollected Short Stories

"Precedent," in *Marvel* (New York), May 1952.
"Robot—Unwanted," in *Other Worlds* (Evanston, Indiana), June 1952.
"Something Borrowed," in *Fantastic Story* (New York), Summer 1952.
"The Trouble with Elmo," in *Galaxy* (New York), August 1958.
"Flowers for Algernon," in *The Best from Fantasy and Science Fiction 9*, edited by Robert P. Mills. New York, Doubleday, 1960.
"Crazy Maro," in *The Best from Fantasy and Science Fiction 10*, edited by Robert P. Mills. New York, Doubleday, 1961; London, Gollancz, 1963.
"A Jury of Its Peers," in *Worlds of Tomorrow* (New York), August 1963.
"The Quality of Mercy," in *Frozen Planet*. New York, Macfadden, 1966.

OTHER PUBLICATIONS

Novels

*The Touch*. New York, Harcourt Brace, 1968; London, Hale, 1971; as *The Contaminated Man*, London, Mayflower, 1977.
*The Fifth Sally*. Boston, Houghton Mifflin, 1980; London, Hale, 1981.

Other

*The Minds of Billy Milligan*. New York, Random House, 1981.
*Unveiling Claudia*. New York, Bantam, 1986.

*

Manuscript Collection: Ohio University, Athens.

* * *

Rarely has a science-fiction story won such widespread praise as Daniel Keyes's "Flowers for Algernon." The story has become almost universally admired in science fiction because it not only blazed new trails in narrative technique, characterization, and plot development but managed to do so without calling distracting attention to any single part. It is first and foremost a story, and none of its literary experimentation interferes with its unfolding.

The story is told from the point of view of a mentally retarded man, Charlie Gordon, who first reaches genius level through treatment with intelligence-enhancing drugs and then regresses to his original state as the effect of the drugs wears off. Much of the success of the work rests on the narrative device of presenting the entire story as a diary written by Charlie from the start of his treatment to his ultimate reversion. Since Charlie begins and ends the story as a good-natured, trusting man who by habit and desire sees only the best in his fellow human beings, the telling never descends to bathos. Even at his most brilliant, when he is able to understand fully the pettiness and cruelty of many of the people around him, Charlie refuses to judge anyone. He accepts people for what they are and avoids such labels as good or bad.

In the course of the story, Keyes raises many questions about the nature of intelligence, the benefits that may or may not arise from "improving" the human mind, and humanity's respect (or lack of respect) for genius. But he avoids trivial answers and simple generalizations. Because Charlie accepts what happens to him without anger and with a sense of dignity, these questions can be considered in all their complexity with a minimum of emotional coloring.

Keyes later turned this 30-page story into a 200-page novel. The result was predictably less happy. Keyes was forced to abandon the first-person narrative in order to deal more elaborately with the other characters. The new narrative style diminished the dramatic treatment of Charlie and his dignified faith in people. Moreover, in filling in the larger space needed for a novel, the story shifts from Charlie's experiences and his reactions to them to Charlie's development as a character. The reader was now asked to become far more attached to Charlie, and the loss of distance added greater emotional coloring to the work. The novel is about Charlie while the short story is about what happens to Charlie and the implications of these experiences for all of humanity.

Keyes has also written a number of short stories and a later novel that deal with the human mind. The novel, *The Touch*, concerns a nuclear industrial accident and its effects on the minds of the people involved. But "Flowers for Algernon" remains his best-known work. It is essential science-fiction reading that proves once and for all how both science fiction and artistic merit can coexist comfortably. As science fiction the story raises disturbing questions no other genre can do more than hint at. As literature, it explores those questions in a manner that carefully, yet delightfully, guides the reader through a myriad of emotional traps.

—Stephen H. Goldman

---

**KILIAN, Crawford.** Canadian. Born in New York City, 7 February 1941; naturalized Canadian citizen, 1973. Educated at Columbia University, New York, B.A. 1962; Simon Fraser University, Burnaby, British Columbia, M.A. 1972. Served in the United States Army, 1963–65. Married Alice Hayes Fairfax in 1966; two daughters. Library clerk, 1965–66, and technical writer, 1966–67, Lawrence Radiation Laboratory, Berkeley, California; Instructor in English, Vancouver Community College, 1967–68. Since 1968, Instructor in English, Capilano College, North Vancouver. Instructor in English, Guangzhou Institute of Foreign Languages, People's Republic of China, 1983–84. Since 1982, education columnist, Vancouver *Province*. Agent: Scott Meredith, 845 Third Avenue, New York, New York 10022,

U.S.A. Address: 4635 Cove Cliff Road, North Vancouver, British Columbia V7G 1H7, Canada.

SCIENCE-FICTION PUBLICATIONS

Novels (series: Chronoplane Wars)

*The Empire of Time* (Chronoplane Wars). New York, Ballantine, 1978; London, Legend, 1988.
*Icequake*. Vancouver, Douglas and McIntyre, and London, Futura, 1979; New York, Bantam, 1980.
*Eyas*. New York, Bantam, 1982.
*Tsunami*. Vancouver, Douglas and McIntyre, 1983; New York, Bantam, 1984.
*Brother Jonathan*. New York, Ace, 1985.
*Lifter*. New York, Berkley, 1986.
*The Fall of the Republic* (Chronoplane Wars). New York, Ballantine, 1987.
*Rogue Emperor* (Chronoplane Wars). New York, Ballantine, 1988.
*Gryphon*. New York, Ballantine, 1989.

OTHER PUBLICATIONS

Plays

Radio Plays: *A Strange Manuscript Found in a Copper Cylinder*, from novel by James De Mille, 1972; *Generals Die in Bed*, from novel by Charles Yale Harrison, 1973; *Little Legion*, 1973; *Wonders, Inc.*, from his own book, 1974; *Senator Connor's Big Comeback*, 1974; *The Mob Has Got the Bomb*, 1975.

Other

*Wonders, Inc.* (for children). Oakland, California, Parnassus Press, 1968.
*The Last Vikings* (for children). Toronto, Clarke Irwin, 1974.
*Go Do Some Great Thing: The Black Pioneers of British Columbia*. Vancouver, Douglas and McIntyre, and Seattle, University of Washington Press, 1978.
*Exploring British Columbia's Past*. Vancouver, Douglas and McIntyre, 1983.
*School Wars: The Assault on B.C. Education*. Vancouver, New Star Books, 1985.

*

Crawford Kilian comments:

As with any civilized pleasure, that of science fiction can turn into a vice. Its persistent theme is power: over nature, over others, over oneself. And that power is most often used not to enhance and expand the capabilities of its wielders but to win for them only a return to Eden, to some primitive and unspoiled state of life. Hence so many stories about Galactic Empires based on European models from Rome to the Raj, and the fondness for interstellar societies firmly founded on the technology and economy of ninth-century France.

Like most other writers and readers of SF, I'm intrigued by the possibilities of gaining power over nature, others, and oneself; these are deeply held wish-fulfillment fantasies. But I hope I go beyond the infantile nuke-and-zap dreams of many of my colleagues. Looking back over my work, I see my novels keep dealing with the issue of the acquisition of power by the weak, not always with happy results, and with the forging of new kinds of societies composed of out-casts and those who cast them out. In Northrop Frye's sense, then, I'm a comic writer, concerned with the creation of inclusive societies rather than with the tragic isolation of people deprived of a place in society.

Given the hypnotically lulling effect of many of the conventions of SF, I take some pleasure in bending the conventions so that the reader's stock responses don't seem quite appropriate. Some of my books have "superheroes"; in *The Empire of Time* the superhero discovers his bosses consider him a mere utensil, and for good reason. In *Eyas*, an heir to a throne is raised in seclusion amid simple folk before leaving to regain his heritage; trouble is, he's also a sexual psychopath. My intention is to make readers think twice about why such stock characters are so satisfying, and to suggest that something more complex might also be more dramatically interesting.

Another element in my work is the attempt to make the marvelous seem mundane, and the mundane marvelous. People in my books have to earn their livings, sometimes by means that seem extraordinary to us, and their lives are as cluttered with domesticity as our own—even if they're trying to cross the Antarctic ice sheet, or learning how to forge a collective mind out of those of children, animals, and computers. A day in anyone's life in the 1990's would seem like the wildest Wellsian fantasy to anyone living in Wells's time, yet we take events for granted. I try to create worlds that are both strange and comfortably familiar, like my own.

* * *

Crawford Kilian's *Brother Jonathan* is an excellent example of his strengths and weaknesses as a writer. Jonathan is an athetoid, a young cripple with little control over his ruined body. He is taken to the secret laboratories of Dr. Duane Perkin, whose medical team is working with spastics to restore their mobility through the use of new polydendronic computers that simulate nerve tissue. The world Kilian describes is dominated by giant multinational corporations controlled by a consortium; nations have been merged into corporate holdings.

Perkin's project is being funded by Intertel, who is under attack in the form of a takeover bid by another multinational company, Flanders. The success of the polydendronic computers could save Intertel from a bloody merger. The computers are implanted in animals first, and when that is successful, they are implanted in Jonathan and the other spastics. Just as success is within Perkin's grasp, a Flanders assault team attacks the labs. Jonathan and his group flee into the underground caverns where they discover they have control over their bodies and psi powers. The rest of the book explores the implications of these superhuman powers, the destruction of the corporate world government, and some satiric asides about juveniles and nationalism.

Much of *Brother Jonathan* will appeal to juveniles; this should come as no surprise because Kilian has written successful juveniles: the fantastic *Wonders, Inc.*, and the non-fiction *Go Do Some Great Thing: The Black Pioneers of British Columbia*. Kilian, an American who became a naturalized Canadian citizen, lives in Vancouver, which he uses as a setting in many of his novels.

Kilian's first SF novel, *The Empire of Time*, gives us Earth in the near future where gates called I-Screens allow access to a dozen parallel Earths, both past and future. Earth governments form a super elite called Trainables and redistribute Earth's overpopulation to these Chronoplanes. Yet when two of the Future Earths are found destroyed, Jerry Pierce of the Intertemporal Agency is sent to a colonial Earth to investigate. The fast-paced action and plot carry the book, while the characters are never really developed.

Kilian developed this concept into a series called the Chronoplane Wars. In the second book in the series, *The Fall of the Republic*, Jerry Pierce gets involved in a hackers' plot to overthrow the government based on information from the Chronoplanes. In the third book, *Rogue Emperor*, Jerry Pierce witnesses Roman Emperor Domitian's assassination by an antitank missile which is just the first step in a plot to take over one of the parallel Earths. Kilian's series is full of fast and furious action even if the plots don't quite hold together and the characters remain cardboard.

*Icequake* is a disaster novel in which a group of scientists and technicians are stranded when Earth's magnetic field disappears and solar flares destroy Earth's ionosphere and ozone layer. The story of survival is gripping, but again the characters are dull and wooden.

*Eyas* is Kilian's best novel; Kilian describes it as "a novel of parental anxiety and hope, [which] was planned and written as my wife and I raised my two daughters." Kilian sets the action ten million years in the Earth's future. The richness of Kilian's future is exciting: humans live with nonhuman windwalkers, centaurs, and incredibly powerful whales. *Eyas* is a story of maturity as the boy Eyas grows up to save his people from the army of Brightspear. There are fantasy elements to *Eyas* but Kilian has carefully crafted his future to fit within science-fiction realism.

Where *Icequake* concentrated on Antarctica and New Zealand, Kilian's other disaster novel, *Tsunami*, concentrates on California and Vancouver. The Antarctic icecap falls into the ocean and the resulting tidal waves flood all coastal areas. But again, the story of survival dominates without any memorable characters to hold the interest of the reader.

—George Kelley

---

**KILLOUGH, (Karen) Lee.** Also writes as Sarah Hood. American. Born in Syracuse, Kansas, 5 May 1942. Educated at Fort Hays State College, Kansas, 1960–62; Hadley Memorial Hospital School of Radiologic technology, 1962–64. Married Howard Patrick Killough in 1966. Radiologic technologist, St. Joseph Hospital, Concordia, Kansas, 1964–65, St. Mary Hospital, Manhattan, Kansas, 1965–67, 1969–71, and Morris Cafritz Memorial Hospital, Washington, D.C., 1967–69. Since 1971, radiologic technologist, Kansas State University Veterinary Hospital, Manhattan. Columnist ("Obiter Dictum"), *The Spang Blah*, 1977–79. Agent: Sharon Jarvis and Company, 260 Willard Avenue, Staten Island, New York 10314. Address: Box 422, Manhattan, Kansas 66502, U.S.A.

SCIENCE-FICTION PUBLICATIONS

Novels (series: Brill/Maxwell)

*A Voice Out of Ramah*. New York, Ballantine, 1979.
*The Doppelganger Gambit* (Brill/Maxwell). New York, Ballantine, 1979.
*The Monitor, the Miners, and the Shree*. New York, Ballantine, 1980.
*Deadly Silents*. New York, Ballantine, 1981.
*Liberty's World*. New York, DAW, 1985.
*Spider Play* (Brill/Maxwell). New York, Warner, 1986.
*The Leopard's Daughter*. New York, Warner, 1987.
*Dragon's Teeth* (Brill/Maxwell). New York, Warner, 1990.

Short Stories

*Aventine*. New York, Ballantine, 1982.

Uncollected Short Stories (series: Aventine)

"Caveat Emptor," in *Analog* (New York), May 1970.
"Caravan," in *If* (New York), June 1972.
"Sentience," in *If* (New York), October 1973.
"Survival," in *Starwind*, Fall 1976.
"Stalking Game," in *Galileo* (Boston), Spring 1977.
"A Cup of Hemlock," in *100 Great Science Fiction Short-Short Stories*, edited by Isaac Asimov, Martin H. Greenberg, and Joseph D. Olander. New York, Doubleday, and London, Robson, 1978.
"The Sanctuary," and "My Brother Cain," in *Sol Plus*, Summer 1979.
"Corpus Cryptic," in *Stellar 5*, edited by Judy-Lynn del Rey. New York, Ballantine, 1980.
"Banshee," (as Sarah Hood), in *Sol Plus 6*, 1980.
"Achronos," in *The 1981 Annual World's Best SF*, edited by Donald A. Wollheim. New York, DAW, 1981.
"Taaehalaan is Drowning," in *Fantasy and Science Fiction* (New York), August 1981.
"The Lying Ear," in *Alien Encounters*, edited by Jan Howard Finder. New York, Taplinger, 1982.
"The Soul Slayer," in *Amazons 2*, edited by Jessica Amanda Salmonson. New York, DAW, 1982.
"The Existential Man," in *Fantasy and Science Fiction* (New York), March 1982.
"The Jarabon," in *Isaac Asimov's Space of Her Own*, edited by Shawna McCarthy. New York, Davis, 1983.
"Keeping the Customer Satisfied," with Pat Killough, in *Tomorrow's Voices*. New York, Davis, 1984.
"The Leopard's Daughter," in *Isaac Asimov's Science Fiction Magazine* (New York), March 1984.
"Symphony for a Lost Traveler," in *Analog* (New York), March 1984.
"Deathglass," in *Isaac Asimov's Science Fiction Magazine* (New York), April 1985.

OTHER PUBLICATIONS

Novels

*Blood Hunt*. New York, Tor, 1987.
*Bloodlinks*. New York, Tor, 1988.

*

Manuscript Collection: Department of Special Collections, University of Kansas, Lawrence.

Lee Killough comments:

I believe that, above all else, fiction should entertain. Every novel or story I write is aimed toward giving the reader enjoyment. I write what I myself would pick off a bookshelf to read. I work hard on researching and developing background and designing realistic, rounded characters. I try to satisfy the reader who might be scientifically knowledgeable. If the expert reader's enjoyment is not spoiled by glaring errors, then the science will have a ring of authenticity to the less knowledgeable reader, too. I write psychological and extrapolative science fiction, but not based so much on my background of biology and veterinary medicine as on psychology and law. Law and mystery being part of so much of my science fiction is due to a lifelong love of mysteries. By writing science fiction mysteries I can enjoy creating science fiction and a mystery at the same time. The two forms meld well and both, I think, reflect a personal belief in the power of reason and science to find answers that will ultimately help bring order to life—or pieces of life, anyway.

* * *

Lee Killough made a lasting impression with her first novel, *A Voice Out of Ramah*, on the surface a standard other-worlds adventure story, but with a mature development of the details of its invented society that is rare even in more experienced writers. The protagonist is a woman who arrives on a colony world dominated by a ruthless male theocracy. Using the ruse of an ancient plague, the priesthood secretly poisons the majority of males to ensure their monopoly on power. Contact with external cultures is obviously a danger to the status quo, and the plot proceeds melodramatically to a satisfactory conclusion.

Her second novel, *The Doppelganger Gambit*, is one of the growing number of novels seeking to blend science-fiction themes and settings with traditional mystery techniques. Janna Brill is an assertive female police officer teamed with Mahlon "Mama" Maxwell. In an overly computerized future, they work to discover the "impossible" murder of a businessman, whose identity is known throughout to the reader. The imposition of a police procedural plot structure on a futuristic theme is effective, and the chemistry of her detective team is unusually compelling.

Killough examined an old stand-by of the field in her next novel, *The Monitor, the Miners, and the Shree.* Chemel Krar is responsible for ensuring that no offworld contact affect the alien Shree as they develop their own culture. When she discovers an illegal mining operation on the planet, her goal is ostensibly to expel the pirates, but her intentions become complicated when she discovers that the Shree are aware of the aliens in their midst, and actively want further contact. She must wrestle with the imperatives of her own position and the desires of the Shree themselves.

*Deadly Silents* is a return to mystery themes. A race of telepaths is experiencing criminal activity for the first time. They import a police force of humans to deal with the situation, and the results are often interesting, although the narrative itself is slower paced and more episodic. Brill and Maxwell returned in two subsequent novels, *Spider Play* and *Dragon's Teeth.* Both involve high technology crimes, with settings as diverse as a colony in orbit and the world of broadcasting. Both books succeed on a variety of levels, the modern equivalent of locked room mysteries with impossible crimes and well-concealed motives.

Killough has proven herself one of the most skillful at blending genres. More recently, in *Blood Hunt* and its sequel, *Bloodlinks*, she has imposed the structure of mystery fiction on the supernatural. The protagonist of both novels is a police officer who has been attacked by and transformed into a vampire. In the first volume, he attempts to control his impulses and track down the creature that assaulted him, the latter quest taken up again in the sequel. One other novel, *The Leopard's Daughter*, is unlike anything else she has written. A fantasy set in primitive Africa, it features a female warrior who braves monsters and human enemies in a journey of discovery and revenge. *Liberty's World* is another examination of the consequences of intercultural contact, the situation arising this time when a colony ship is forced to land on a world inhabited by primitive humanoids, some of whom wish to take advantage of the offworld technology to gain political advantages over their rivals.

Killough has had one collection of short stories published, entitled *Aventine.* The seven stories contain a common setting, a community of artists and scholars in the near future. "The Siren Garden" is a complex tale of intrigue and menace, with a haunting atmosphere unlike anything else Killough has written. The intricacies of the human psyche are detailed in "A House Divided," wherein a man falls in love with a schizophrenic woman and becomes a tool in the struggle between the two personalities.

Several of her uncollected stories are also noteworthy. "Caravan," an early tale, develops an alien culture and setting with a remarkable economy of words. A perilous desert crossing amidst numerous adversities provides a fast-moving plot device. Killough examines the virtues of extraterrestrial contact again in "Sentience," this time positing a situation where the arrival of humans on a world bereft of intelligent species provides the stimulus to push one lifeform across the line of demarcation.

Other short stories of note include "Achronos." An artist finds himself temporarily suspended in time along with a group of immortal refugees from the end of the world. The interaction of the characters in a cruel manipulatory game is an elaborately choreographed dance. "The Existential Man" is another detective story, this time with a murdered police officer's ghost controlling the investigation. The conflict between progress, historical preservation, and maintenance of the ecology is examined in "Taaehalaan Is Drowning."

Lee Killough has been claimed by feminists as one of their own, with great justification. Most of her fiction is characterized by strong female characters, heroes and villains both. But her commitment to the equality of females is unobtrusive, and extremely effective. In her novels, the equal status of females is taken for granted. Killough avoids pendanticism, and her ability to draw her characters so well drives home her position far more effectively than a more overt approach would likely accomplish. Although she has yet to write the kind of book that would establish her as an influential voice in the field, her competent, entertaining, and generally thoughtful and intelligent books mark her as one of its most competent practitioners.

—Don D'Ammassa

---

**KILWORTH, Garry.** British. Born in York, 5 July 1941. Educated at Khomaksar School, Aden, 1952–54; Royal Air Force Bridgenorth School, 1954–56, and Cosford Cadet School, 1956–58; H.N.C. in business studies 1974. Married Annette Jill Bailey in 1962; one son and one daughter. Served as a Signals Master in the Royal Air Force, 1959–74; senior executive, Cable and Wireless, London and Caribbean, 1974–82. Since 1982, freelance writer. Agent: Maggie Noach, 21 Redan Street, London, W14 0AB. Address: c/o Unwin Hyman, 77-85 Fulham Palace Road, London W6 8JB, England.

SCIENCE-FICTION PUBLICATIONS

Novels

*In Solitary.* London, Faber, 1977; New York, Avon, 1979.
*The Night of Kadar.* London, Faber, 1978; New York, Avon, 1980.
*Split Second.* London, Faber, 1979.
*Gemini God.* London, Faber, 1981.
*A Theatre of Timesmiths.* London, Gollancz, 1984.
*Abandonati.* London, Unwin Hyman, 1988.
*Cloudrock.* London, Unwin Hyman, 1988.

Short Stories

*The Songbirds of Pain*. London, Gollancz, 1984.
*Dark Hills, Hollow Clocks* (for children). London, Methuen, 1990.

OTHER PUBLICATIONS

Novels

*Witchwater Country.* London, Bodley Head, 1986.
*Spiral Winds.* London, Bodley Head, 1987.
*Voyage of the Vigilance.* London, Collins, 1988.
*Hunter's Moon: A Story of Foxes.* London, Unwin Hyman, 1989.
*Midnight's Sun: A Story of Wolves.* London, Unwin Hyman, 1990.
*The Rain Ghost.* New York, Scholastic, 1990.

Short Stories

*In the Hollow of the Deep Sea Wave.* London, Bodley Head, 1989.

Verse

*Tree Messiah.* Newport, Envoi Poets, 1985.

*

Garry Kilworth comments:

I am not greatly interested in the "science" in Science Fiction. I am more concerned with unusual societies, anthropological aspects, social misfits, and exotic cultures. The issues might be contemporary, as I feel they are in *A Theatre of Timesmiths*, or universal, ageless questions such as the nurture-nature theme of *In Solitary.* I wish to explore the ordinary human spirit in a stressful state of adversity, and in its relationship to the natural world. I write science fiction and fantasy because their imaginative scope allows me more sweep than would mainstream fiction. Mysticism, including religions of all kinds, forms a thread through my work. On the entertainment level I find the best vehicle for carrying these themes is the adventure novel. In a sentence: jungles, deserts, wastelands and the man-a-lost looking for himself.

* * *

Characterisation has always been the strongest facet of Garry Kilworth's writing. The science fiction ideas in his work are usually secondary to the humane portrayals of his protagonists, yet his subject matter has been widely varied.

His first, rather slender novel, *In Solitary*, depicts an Earth conquered by the bird-like alien Soal, who rule by separating man from his fellow man . . . and woman. It's a tautly told yet subtle story of human courage and ingenuity, much of it set in the South Sea Islands. *The Night of Kadar* is the richest of Kilworth's early novels, drawing upon the Koran for its inspiration. A starship lands on a new world and settlers—awakened and matured from their pre-frozen embryonic state—struggle to understand their purpose on the planet, unaware of the malfunction in the machinery that ought to have instructed them. The story of the building of a land bridge and the encounter with the aliens is engrossing, but one remembers far more clearly the characters of Othman, Zayid, and, particularly, the divine idiot, Fdar. *Split Second* saw Kilworth give the Jekyll and Hyde tale a new twist as experiments with the Wiederhaus Repeater—an archaeological tool used to hologrammatically reanimate objects from the past—accidentally send a young boy, Richard, 33,000 years into the past, where he shares the mind and experiences of a juvenile boy from that time, Esk. Though an ambitious idea, it doesn't quite succeed in evoking a sense of that far distant past, but the storytelling itself is first class. *Gemini God* charts the degeneration of the human race and its attempts to solve its problems through alien contact. Another strand of the novel—empathic contact between identical twins—provides a more interesting storyline, with its examination of the nature and work of the artist. Kilworth's fifth novel, *A Theatre of Timesmiths*, was, curiously enough, one of his best written and yet least successful works. An enclosed environment tale, it suffers from having all taken place in its chief character's head; moreover, Morag is the least sympathetic of Kilworth's main characters, and her predicament involves us only marginally. That said, Kilworth's evocation of the world inside the ice is remarkably vivid.

The first collection of Kilworth's short fiction, *The Songbirds Of Pain*, contains stories published over the nine years preceding its publication. The best of them, like "Sumi Dreams Of A Paper Frog" and "The Songbirds Of Pain" are exceptional, almost fabular works, and even the least of them—"The Dissemblers" and "Let's Go to Golgotha" (which won Kilworth the *Sunday Times* Best SF Story competition in 1975)—are of a high standard.

For his next two novels, *Witchwater Country* and *Spiral Winds*, Kilworth moved away from overt genre concerns to produce what are, perhaps, his finest works, strong both in characterization and sense of place. His return to SF, *Cloudrock*, however, proved less successful. Once again we are presented with an enclosed environment, this time the great Cloudrock itself, a coral island raised like a giant mushroom high above the dried-up bed of the ocean. There the tribes of night and day eke out their lives in an unquestioning round, until the shadow—our narrator, a misformed outcast, permitted existence—brings violent change. As in *In Solitary*, with which it bears curious affinities, the potential richness of this metaphor isn't really tapped, though the character Shadow remains a haunting presence long after the tale has ended. *Abandonati* is again memorable more for its characters than its ideas. Set in a run-down near-future abandoned to the street people, Guppy, the "abandonati" of the title, accompanied by the gentle black giant, Trader, sets out to find where all the rich people went. Not Kilworth's most welcoming book, it has a savage richness and humor that distinguishes it from his other novel-length works.

Kilworth's recent excursions into "animal" novels, *Hunter's Moon* and *Midnight's Sun*, are much more than the usual animals-as-speaking-humans fare; they disdain the usual anthropomorphic tendencies of this sub-genre. The detailed research behind both books is telling (without overwhelming the storyline), and Kilworth's robust enjoyment of the savage animal natures of his protagonists raises these two distinct (yet dovetailing) novels to a point somewhere between realism and fable.

The last few years have seen a wide diversification in Kilworth's writing and a movement away from the overtly science-fictional subject matter of his first decade. His recent attempts to create superior juvenile fiction are proving very interesting, producing work which, as in the collection *Dark Hills, Hollow Clocks*, is as resonant as his best SF short fiction. It remains to be seen, however, whether the lessons learned in these excursions can be channelled into his longer SF work.

—David Wingrove

---

**KING, Ray.** *See* **CUMMINGS, Ray.**

---

**KING, Vincent.** Pseudonym for Rex Thomas Vinson. British. Born in Falmouth, Cornwall, 22 October 1935. Educated at Redruth School of Art, Cornwall; Falmouth College of Art, Cornwall, 1952–57; West of England College of Art, Bristol, 1959–60; University of London, 1960–62. Served in the Royal Air Force. Married Jean Blackler in 1961 (divorced 1978); one son and one daughter. Art teacher in schools in London, Bristol, Newcastle upon Tyne, 1963–68, and since 1968 in Redruth. Painter and printmaker; work in several Arts Council exhibitions. Agent: Carnell Literary Agency, Danes Croft, Gooselane, Little Hallingburg, Herts. CM22 7RG, England.

SCIENCE-FICTION PUBLICATIONS

Novels

*Light a Last Candle.* New York, Ballantine, 1969; London, Rapp and Whiting, 1970.
*Another End.* New York, Ballantine, 1971.
*Candy Man.* London, Gollancz, 1971; New York, Ballantine, 1972.
*Time Snake and Superclown.* London, Futura, 1976.

Uncollected Short Stories

"Defence Mechanism," in *New Writings in SF 7*, edited by John Carnell. London, Dobson, 1966; New York, Bantam, 1971.
"The Wall to End the World," in *New Writings in SF 8*, edited by John Carnell. London, Dobson, 1966; New York, Bantam, 1971.
"Testament," in *New Writings in SF 9*, edited by John Carnell. London, Dobson, 1966; New York, Bantam, 1972.
"Report from Linelos," in *New Writings in SF 15*, edited by John Carnell. London, Dobson, 1969.
"The Discontent Contingency," in *New Writings in SF 19*, edited by John Carnell. London, Dobson, 1971.

*

Vincent King comments:

I've no explicit intentions, political or philosophical, but considerations of that type keep coming out of the words. The intention is fantasy, a succession of ideas, events, relationships that change, further and further revelations about the situation/plot/story. Naturally this makes for ever-increasing complexity and a continual raising of the stakes (I'm sometimes deeply shocked by what I write!), maybe for incomprehensibility, too. I often include more or less direct quotations from "reality." (Which is interchangeable with "fiction" anyway; reality is fantasy, fantasised by going through people's heads, and it doesn't matter how objective/pragmatic they say they are—that's fantasy too.) I tend to use the first person because I fantasise that its more direct. Also it means the voice that tells the story doesn't know what's to happen, is happening. I also fantasise that it allows the fantasy to develop in a less inhibited way. The freedom of fantasy is the thing.

I think the most exciting writing today is on the fantasy end of the spectrum. I'm not speaking only of what is referred to as SF or occult writing. It's interesting that at a time when a lot of SF authors claim to be trying to "go straight," some good so-called mainstream writing seems to be turning more fantastic. What is finished, I think, for a more or less serious SF writer, is the "science" type of SF, and I think the middle-class "Hobbit" type of adventure is pretty sterile too. To me science is a type of magic—or at least that's how I *use* it. Science is not holy, it's practical; it's probably caused no more suffering, or release from suffering, than religions. Religions, wars, science, adultery, murders, etc. are what happen when people aren't allowed or aren't able to be *creative* in some way: to work out their personal fantasy, which might be a garden, or a fortune, or a model steam locomotive, or anything!

* * *

Suspense is a major element in all the works of Vincent King. In part, he develops suspense through the ordinary means—surprising and very quick-paced action—which keep the reader wondering what will come next. But here is also a more intellectual type of suspense which may be regarded as one of the distinguishing marks of King's work. This type of suspense also develops in two ways. First, a sort of jigsaw puzzle effect means that, in the beginning of his novels, it is often difficult to see how the various parts relate to one another. What is the connection between Ice Lover and the Mods (*Light a Last Candle*)? The reader must hold numbers of pieces in his mind, gradually fitting them together into a clear, comprehensive picture. Second, his characters have a certain enigmatic quality about them. One's curiosity is aroused because it isn't clear just who or what the protagonist is. Only near the end of the novel is the identity of Candy Man revealed.

Space exploration, the attempt to find and contact other sentient life, is a theme which King plays in a different key. Working within a long–time scheme, expending vast resources, man may just possibly find some sentient life form. Adamson finds Protia (*Another End*) after all hope has been abandoned. In *Candy Man* the failure is absolute. But even success may bring strange results. Protia ultimately absorbs Adamson, and the alien beings in *Light a Last Candle* have unsuccessfully attempted to absorb an entire colony of Earthmen. Mankind is unavoidably changed by contact with aliens.

But mankind is portrayed in a decadent state throughout King's novels. The glorious past is gone, while a few men live enervated lives among the ruins. The image of those ruins, vast cities covering entire worlds, has a central place for King. His heroes, regularly isolated (or at most accompanied by a single companion) in these vast, hive-like structures, seem compelled to explore the cellars, the subterranean depths of their worlds. Both Adamson and Candy Man are involved in extensive chase scenes in these labyrinthine depths. Ice Lover lives and fights in caves. Man, as he declines, seems to be portrayed as returning to his roots, the cave, the sea, the womb. Interestingly, the machines have held up better than their creators. The Probe keeps Adamson alive, frustrating his every suicide attempt. The entire population of Earth may have been maintained by machines (*Candy Man*) or resurrected by a computer (*Another End*). In some sense dependence upon machines has led humanity into decadence. Only if they can shake free of the machines will there be some slight hope of renewal.

Each of King's novels deals with the human proclivity to violence; all his heroes are killers who seem to enjoy killing. But in the final analysis the violence seems to be shown as both pointless and ineffective, a serious defect that men must overcome if they are to survive and advance. The conclusions of *Another End* and *Candy Man* hold out some slight hope of this.

King's greatest strength, his highly imaginative permutations upon conventional themes, combines with his ability to create suspense to produce works which fascinate and puzzle the reader. Yet these strengths are somewhat offset by a style of writing heavily dependent upon dialogue which has a rather choppy and unsophisticated quality.

—Robert Reilly

---

**KINGSBURY, Donald (MacDonald).** Canadian. Born in San Francisco, California, 12 February 1929; became Canadian citizen. Educated at schools in Japan, New Guinea, California, and New Hampshire; McGill University, Montreal, B.Sc. 1956, M.Sc. 1960. Married Mireille Kingsbury in 1950 (divorced 1960); two sons. Since 1956, Lecturer in Mathematics, McGill University. Recipient: Compton Crook award, 1983. Agent: Eleanor Wood, 111 Eighth Avenue, Suite 1501, New York, New York 10011, U.S.A.

SCIENCE-FICTION PUBLICATIONS

Novels

*Courtship Rite.* New York, Simon and Schuster, 1982; as *Geta*, London, Panther, 1984.

*The Moon Goddess and the Son.* New York, Baen, 1986; London, Grafton, 1988.

*

Donald Kingsbury comments:

I make up my backgrounds and test them for plausibility before I throw my characters into them—to manage as best they can. I have a preference for "fleet footed" males and females and odd cultures. I tend to write in a single future universe: *The Moon Goddess and the Son* is from its near future phase and *Courtship Rite* from 2000 or so years away.

* * *

Although Donald Kingsbury published a short story in 1952 and wrote science articles for *Analog* in the mid-1970's, it was with three novelettes published in that magazine in 1978–79 that he became widely known. All three were anthologized the following year, giving Kingsbury his reputation as one of the most promising and interesting writers of technically oriented science fiction.

"To Bring In the Steel" (in *The Best Science Fiction of the Year 8*, edited by Terry Carr, New York, Ballantine, 1979), the best of the three, dramatizes the efforts of a private consortium in the next century to maneuver an asteroid into Earth's orbit while refining its rich ore into salable metals. The protagonist is a lonely, independent, supercompetent man—the model Kingsbury hero—whose misogyny and fixed ideas on government and entrepreneurship are, as in all Kingsbury's short works to date, rather implausibly validated by the story's action. The story's clean dramatic line and crisp pacing combine effectively with Kingsbury's ability to render the details of an operating space industry, and largely overcome his insistent division of the sexes into hard-headed men and childlike, undisciplined women. Less successful are "Shipwright" (in *The Best Science Fiction Novellas of the Year 1*, edited by Terry Carr, New York, Ballantine, 1979) and *The Moon Goddess and the Son*, where Kingsbury's indulgent attitude toward the engineer-hero and his recurrent theme of courtesanship as a woman's best chance of getting ahead in a world of more rational-minded men hang heavily upon the less dramatic and loosely constructed story lines. Notable in *The Moon Goddess and the Son* and "To Bring In the Steel" is Kingsbury's boosterism of space industry and the use of space for Western strategic defense, in furtherance of which Kingsbury appears willing to suspend the critical scrutiny he brings to other technical problems and give both subjects an idealized gloss.

*Courtship Rite* represents a surprising advance in skill over Kingsbury's early stories. This far-ranging story of intrigue among human settlers on a resource-poor planet displays an impressive ability to present a complex plot through multiple points of view, and represents a departure in allowing the fair expression of differing ideologies without betraying the author's sympathies.

Geta, an earthlike planet with relatively arid inlands and almost no native animal life, was settled in some distant past by settlers who have lost most of their technology as well as their history, and blindly worship their visible, still-orbiting ship. Cannibalism, originally practiced because of ubiquitous protein deficiencies, now serves a complex social function even as scientific advances threaten to render it unnecessary. The main thread of the story line involves a group marriage of three politically influential men and two women, who are forbidden to marry a third woman of their choice and ordered for political reasons to court a heretical pacifist of growing influence in a region over which their leader seeks hegemony. The pacifist, a visionary who preaches a Gandhi-like commitment to social revolution without violence, is convincingly and sympathetically portrayed. The decision of her suitors to subject her to a Death Rite—under which they might legally challenge her to a series of putative tests of fitness that will almost certainly ensure her death—provides the springboard for the story's action.

The novel's length, complexity of intrigue, and setting prompt comparison with *Dune*, which Kingsbury audaciously invites with his visionary and ecological themes as well as the device of using numerous fictive "texts" as chapter epigraphs. *Courtship Rite*'s remarkable success in withstanding such comparison and in conveying its own sense of genuine exhilaration is an achievement in itself.

—Gregory Feeley

---

**KIPLING, (Joseph) Rudyard.** British. Born in Bombay, India, 30 December 1865, of English parents; moved to England, 1872. Educated at the United Services College, Westward Ho!, Devon, 1878–82. Married Caroline Starr Balestier in 1892; two daughters and one son. Assistant editor, *Civil and Military Gazette*, Lahore, 1882–87; assistant editor and overseas correspondent, *Pioneer*, Allahabad, 1887–89; full-time writer from 1889; lived in London, 1889–92, and Brattleboro, Vermont, 1892–96, then returned to England; settled in Burwash, Sussex, 1902. Rector, University of St. Andrews, 1922–25. Recipient: Nobel Prize for Literature, 1907; Royal Society of Literature Gold Medal, 1926. LL.D.: McGill University, Montreal, 1907; D.Litt.: University of Durham, 1907; Oxford University, 1907; Cambridge University, 1907; University of Edinburgh, 1920; the Sorbonne, Paris, 1921; University of Strasbourg, 1921; D.Phil.: University of Athens, 1924. Honorary Fellow, Magdalene College, Cambridge, 1932. Associate member, Académie des Sciences Morales et Politiques, 1933. Refused the Poet Laureateship, 1895, and the Order of Merit. *Died 18 January 1936.*

## Science-Fiction Publications

### Short Stories

*Actions and Reactions.* London, Macmillan, and New York, Doubleday, 1909.
*A Diversity of Creatures.* London, Macmillan, and New York, Doubleday, 1917.

## Other Publications

### Novel

*The Light That Failed.* New York, United States Book Company, 1890; London, Macmillan, 1891.

### Short Stories

*Plain Tales from the Hills.* Calcutta, Thacker Spink, 1888; New York, Lovell, and London, Macmillan, 1890.
*Soldiers Three: A Collection of Stories.* Allahabad, Wheeler, 1888; London, Sampson Low, 1890.
*The Stories of the Gadsbys: A Tale Without a Plot.* Allahabad, Wheeler, 1888; London, Sampson Low, and New York, Lovell, 1890.
*In Black and White.* Allahabad, Wheeler, 1888; London, Sampson Low, and New York, Lovell, 1890.
*Under the Deodars.* Allahabad, Wheeler, 1888; revised edition, London, Sampson Low, 1890.
*The Phantom 'Rickshaw and Other Tales.* Allahabad, Wheeler, 1888; revised edition, London, Sampson Low, 1890.
*Wee Willie Winkie and Other Child Stories.* Allahabad, Wheeler, 1888; revised edition, London, Sampson Low, and Chicago, Rand McNally, 1890.
*Soldiers Three, and Under the Deodars.* New York, Lovell, 1890.
*The Phantom 'Rickshaw, and Wee Willie Winkie.* New York, Lovell, 1890.
*The Courting of Dinah Shadd and Other Stories.* New York, Harper, and London, Macmillan, 1890.
*Mine Own People.* New York, United States Book Company, 1891.
*Life's Handicap, Being Stories from Mine Own People.* New York and London, Macmillan, 1891.
*The Naulahka: A Story of West and East*, with Wolcott Balestier. London, Heinemann, and New York, Macmillan, 1892.
*Many Inventions.* London, Macmillan, and New York, Appleton, 1893.
*Soldier Tales.* London, Macmillan, 1896; as *Soldier Stories*, New York, Macmillan, 1896.
*The Day's Work.* New York, Doubleday, and London, Macmillan, 1898.
*The Kipling Reader.* London, Macmillan, 1900; as *Selected Stories*, 1925.
*Traffics and Discoveries.* London, Macmillan, and New York, Doubleday, 1904.
*Abaft the Funnel.* New York, Dodge, 1909.
*Selected Stories*, edited by William Lyon Phelps. New York, Doubleday, 1921.
*Debits and Credits.* London, Macmillan, and New York, Doubleday, 1926.
*Selected Stories.* London, Macmillan, 1929.
*Thy Servant a Dog, Told by Boots.* London, Macmillan, and New York, Doubleday, 1930; revised edition, as *Thy Servant a Dog and Other Dog Stories*, Macmillan, 1938.
*Humorous Tales.* London, Macmillan, and New York, Doubleday, 1931.
*Animal Stories.* London, Macmillan, 1932; New York, Doubleday, 1938.
*Limits and Renewals.* London, Macmillan, and New York, Doubleday, 1932.
*All the Mowgli Stories.* London, Macmillan, 1933; New York, Doubleday, 1936.
*Collected Dog Stories.* London, Macmillan, and New York, Doubleday, 1934.
*More Selected Stories.* London, Macmillan, 1940.
*Twenty-One Tales.* London, Reprint Society, 1946.
*Ten Stories.* London, Pan, 1947.
*A Choice of Kipling's Prose*, edited by W. Somerset Maugham. London, Macmillan, 1952; as *Maugham's Choice of Kipling's Best: Sixteen Stories*, New York, Doubleday, 1953.
*A Treasury of Short Stories.* New York, Bantam, 1957.
(*Short Stories*), edited by Edward Parone. New York, Dell, 1960.
*Kipling Stories: Twenty-Eight Exciting Tales.* New York, Platt and Munk, 1960.
*The Best Short Stories*, edited by Randall Jarrell. New York, Hanover House, 1961; as *In the Vernacular: The English in India* and *The English in England*, New York, Doubleday, 2 vols., 1963.
*Famous Tales of India*, edited by B.W. Shir-Cliff. New York, Ballantine, 1962.
*Phantoms and Fantasies: 20 Tales.* New York, Doubleday, 1965.
*Short Stories*, edited by Andrew Rutherford. London, Penguin, 2 vols., 1971–76.
*Twenty-One Tales*, edited by Tim Wilkinson. London, Folio Society, 1972.
*Tales of East and West*, edited by Bernard Bergonzi. Avon, Connecticut, Limited Editions Club, 1973.
*Kipling's Kingdom: Twenty-Five of Kipling's Best Indian Stories, Known and Unknown*, edited by Charles Allen. London, Joseph, 1987.

### Fiction (for children)

*The Jungle Book*, illustrated by J. Lockwood Kipling and others. London, Macmillan, and New York, Century, 1894.
*The Second Jungle Book*, illustrated by J. Lockwood Kipling. London, Macmillan, and New York, Century, 1895; revised edition, Macmillan, 1895.
*"Captains Courageous": A Story of the Grand Banks*, illustrated by I.W. Taber. London, Macmillan, and New York, Century, 1897.
*Stalky & Co.* London, Macmillan, and New York, Doubleday, 1899; revised edition, as *The Complete Stalky & Co.*, Macmillan, 1929, Doubleday, 1930
*Kim*, illustrated by J. Lockwood Kipling. New York, Doubleday, and London, Macmillan, 1901.

*Just So Stories for Little Children*, illustrated by the author. London, Macmillan, and New York, Doubleday, 1902.
*Puck of Pook's Hill*, illustrated by H.R. Millar. London, Macmillan, and New York, Doubleday, 1906.
*Kipling Stories and Poems Every Child Should Know*, edited by Mary E. Burt and W.T. Chapin, illustrated by Charles Livingston Bull and others. New York, Doubleday, 1909.
*Rewards and Fairies*, illustrated by Frank Craig. London, Macmillan, and New York, Doubleday, 1910.
*Land and Sea Tales for Scouts and Guides.* London, Macmillan, and New York, Doubleday, 1923.
*Ham and the Porcupine.* New York, Doubleday, 1935.

Play

*The Harbour Watch* (produced London, 1913; revised version, as *Gow's Watch*, produced London, 1924).

Verse

*Schoolboy Lyrics.* Privately printed, 1881.
*Echoes* (published anonymously), with Alice Kipling. Privately printed, 1884.
*Departmental Ditties and Other Verses.* Lahore, Civil and Military Gazette Press, 1886; London, Thacker Spink, 1890.
*Departmental Ditties, Barrack-Room Ballads, and Other Verse.* New York, United States Book Company, 1890.
*Barrack-Room Ballads and Other Verses.* London, Methuen, and New York, Macmillan, 1892.
*Ballads and Barrack-Room Ballads.* New York, Macmillan, 1893.
*The Seven Seas.* New York, Appleton, and London, Methuen, 1896.
*Recessional.* Privately printed, 1897.
*An Almanac of Twelve Sports*, illustrated by William Nicholson. London, Heinemann, and New York, Russell, 1898.
*Poems*, edited by Wallace Rice. Chicago, Star, 1899.
*Recessional and Other Poems.* Privately printed, 1899.
*The Absent-Minded Beggar.* Privately printed, 1899.
*With Number Three, Surgical and Medical, and New Poems.* Santiago, Chile, Hume, 1900.
*Occasional Poems.* Boston, Bartlett, 1900.
*The Five Nations.* London, Methuen, and New York, Doubleday, 1903.
*The Muse Among the Motors.* New York, Doubleday, 1904.
*A Collected Verse.* New York, Doubleday, 1907; London, Hodder and Stoughton, 1912.
*A History of England* (verse only), with C.R.L. Fletcher. London, Oxford University Press-Hodder and Stoughton, and New York, Doubleday, 1911; revised edition, 1930.
*Songs from Books.* New York, Doubleday, 1912; London, Macmillan, 1913.
*Twenty Poems.* London, Methuen, 1918.
*The Years Between.* London, Methuen, and New York, Doubleday, 1919.
*Verse: Inclusive Edition 1885–1918.* London, Hodder and Stoughton, and New York, Doubleday, 3 vols., 1919; revised edition, 1921, 1927, 1933.
*A Kipling Anthology: Verse.* London, Methuen, and New York, Doubleday, 1922.
*Songs for Youth, from Collected Verse.* London, Hodder and Stoughton, 1924; New York, Doubleday, 1925.
*A Choice of Songs.* London, Methuen, 1925.
*Sea and Sussex.* London, Macmillan, and New York, Doubleday, 1926.
*St. Andrews*, with Walter de la Mare. London, A. and C. Black, 1926.
*Songs of the Sea.* London, Macmillan, and New York, Doubleday, 1927.
*Poems 1886–1929.* London, Macmillan, 3 vols., 1929; New York, Doubleday, 3 vols., 1930.
*Selected Poems.* London, Methuen, 1931.
*East of Suez, Being a Selection of Eastern Verses.* London, Macmillan, 1931.
*Sixty Poems.* London, Hodder and Stoughton, 1939.
*Verse: Definitive Edition.* London, Hodder and Stoughton, and New York, Doubleday, 1940.
*So Shall Ye Reap: Poems for These Days.* London, Hodder and Stoughton, 1941.
*A Choice of Kipling's Verse*, edited by T.S. Eliot. London, Faber, 1941; New York, Scribner, 1943.
*Sixty Poems.* London, Hodder and Stoughton, 1957.
*A Kipling Anthology*, edited by W.G. Bebbington. London, Methuen, 1964.
*The Complete Barrack-Room Ballads*, edited by Charles Carrington. London, Methuen, 1973.
*Kipling's English History: Poems*, edited by Marghanita Laski. London, BBC Publications, 1974.
*Kipling: A Selection*, edited by James Cochrane. London, Penguin, 1977.
*Early Verse by Rudyard Kipling 1879–89*, edited by Andrew Rutherford. Oxford, Clarendon Press, and New York, Oxford University Press, 1986.

Other

*Quarette*, with others. Lahore, Civil and Military Gazette Press, 1885.
*The City of Dreadful Night and Other Sketches.* Allahabad, Wheeler, 1890.
*The City of Dreadful Night and Other Places.* Allahabad, Wheeler, and London, Sampson Low, 1891.
*The Smith Administration.* Allahabad, Wheeler, 1891.
*Letters of Marque.* Allahabad, Wheeler, and London, Sampson Low, 1891.
*American Notes*, with *The Bottle Imp*, by Robert Louis Stevenson. New York, Ivers, 1891.
*Out of India: Things I Saw, and Failed to See, in Certain Days and Nights at Jeypore and Elsewhere.* New York, Dillingham, 1895.
*The Kipling Birthday Book*, edited by Joseph Finn. London, Macmillan, 1896; New York, Doubleday, 1899.
*A Fleet in Being: Notes of Two Trips with the Channel Squadron.* London, Macmillan, 1898.
*From Sea to Sea: Letters of Travel.* New York, Doubleday, 1899; as *From Sea to Sea and Other Sketches*, London, Macmillan, 1900.
*Works* (Swastika Edition). New York, Doubleday, Appleton, and Century, 15 vols., 1899.
*Letters to the Family (Notes on a Recent Trip to Canada).* Toronto, Macmillan, 1908.
*The Kipling Reader* (not same as 1900 collection of short stories). New York, Appleton, 1912.
*The New Army in Training.* London, Macmillan, 1915.
*France at War.* London, Macmillan, and New York, Doubleday, 1915.
*The Fringes of the Fleet.* London, Macmillan, and New York, Doubleday, 1915.
*Tales of "The Trade."* Privately printed, 1916.
*Sea Warfare.* London, Macmillan, and New York, Doubleday, 1916.
*The War in the Mountains.* New York, Doubleday, 1917.
*To Fighting Americans* (speeches). Privately printed, 1918.
*The Eyes of Asia.* New York, Doubleday, 1918.

*The Graves of the Fallen.* London, Imperial War Graves Commission, 1919.
*Letters of Travel (1892–1913).* London, Macmillan, and New York, Doubleday, 1920.
*A Kipling Anthology: Prose.* London, Macmillan, and New York, Doubleday, 1922.
*The Irish Guards in the Great War.* London, Macmillan, and New York, Doubleday, 2 vols., 1923.
*Works* (Mandalay Edition). New York, Doubleday, 26 vols., 1925–26.
*A Book of Words: Selections from Speeches and Addresses Delivered Between 1906 and 1927.* London, Macmillan, and New York, Doubleday, 1928.
*The One Volume Kipling.* New York, Doubleday, 1928.
*Souvenirs of France.* London, Macmillan, 1933.
*A Kipling Pageant.* New York, Doubleday, 1935.
*Something of Myself for My Friends Known and Unknown.* London, Macmillan, and New York, Doubleday, 1937.
*Complete Works* (Sussex Edition) London, Macmillan, 35 vols., 1937–39; as *Collected Works* (Burwash Edition), New York, Doubleday, 28 vols., 1941 (includes revised versions of some previously published works).
*A Kipling Treasury: Stories and Poems.* London, Macmillan, 1940.
*Kipling: A Selection of His Stories and Poems*, edited by John Beecroft. New York, Doubleday, 2 vols., 1956.
*The Kipling Sampler*, edited by Alexander Greendale. New York, Fawcett, 1962.
*Letters from Japan*, edited by Donald Richie and Yoshimori Harashima. Tokyo, Kenkyusha, 1962.
*Pearls from Kipling*, edited by C. Donald Plomer. New Britain, Connecticut, Elihu Burritt Library, 1963.
*Rudyard Kipling to Rider Haggard: The Record of a Friendship*, edited by Morton Cohen. London, Hutchinson, 1965; Rutherford, New Jersey, Fairleigh Dickinson University Press, 1968.
*The Best of Kipling.* New York, Doubleday, 1968.
*Stories and Poems*, edited by Roger Lancelyn Green. London, Dent, 1970.
*Kipling's Horace*, edited by Charles Carrington. London, Methuen, 1978.
*American Notes: Rudyard Kipling's West*, edited by Arrell M. Gibson. Norman, University of Oklahoma Press, 1981.
*The Portable Kipling*, edited by Irving Howe. New York, Viking Press, 1982.
*"O Beloved Kids": Rudyard Kipling's Letters to His Children*, edited by Elliot L. Gilbert. London, Weidenfeld and Nicolson, 1983; New York, Harcourt Brace, 1984.
*Kipling's India: Uncollected Sketches 1884–1888*, edited by Thomas Pinney. London, Macmillan, and New York, Schocken, 1985.
*The Illustrated Kipling*, edited by Neil Philip. London, Collins, 1987.
*A Choice of Kipling's Prose*, edited by Craig Raine. London, Faber, 1987.
*Kipling's Japan*, edited by Hugh Cortazzi and George Webb. London, Athlone Press, 1988.

Editor, *The Irish Guards in the Great War.* London, Macmillan, and New York, Doubleday, 2 vols., 1923.

*

Bibliography: *Rudyard Kipling: A Bibliography Catalogue* by James McG. Stewart, edited by A.W. Keats, Toronto, Dalhousie University-University of Toronto Press, 1959, London, Oxford University Press, 1960; "Kipling: An Annotated Bibliography of Writings about Him" by H.E. Gerber and E. Lauterbach, in *English Fiction in Transition 3* (Tempe, Arizona), 1960, and *8*, 1965.

Manuscript Collections: Cornell University Library, Ithaca, New York; Library of Congress, Washington, D.C.; Houghton Library, Harvard University, Cambridge, Massachusetts; Pierpont Morgan Library, New York.

Critical Studies (selection): *Rudyard Kipling: His Life and Work* by Charles Carrington, London, Macmillan, 1955, revised edition, 1978, as *The Life of Rudyard Kipling*, New York, Doubleday, 1955; *Rudyard Kipling* by Rosemary Sutcliff, London, Bodley Head, 1960, New York, Walck, 1961; *The Readers' Guide to Rudyard Kipling's Work*, Canterbury, Gibbs, 1961, and *Kipling The Critical Heritage*, London, Routledge, and New York, Barnes and Noble, 1971, both edited by Roger Lancelyn Green, and *Kipling and the Children* by Green, London, Elek, 1965; *Kipling's Mind and Art* edited by Andrew Rutherford, Edinburgh, Oliver and Boyd, and Stanford, California, Stanford University Press, 1964; *Rudyard Kipling* by J.I.M. Stewart, London, Gollancz, and New York, Dodd Mead, 1966; *Rudyard Kipling: Realist and Fabulist* by Bonamy Dobrée, London and New York, Oxford University Press, 1967; *Kipling and His World* by Kingsley Amis, London, Thames and Hudson, 1975, New York, Scribner, 1976; *The Strange Ride of Rudyard Kipling: His Life and Works* by Angus Wilson, London, Secker and Warburg, 1977, New York, Viking Press, 1978; *Rudyard Kipling* by Lord Birkenhead, London, Weidenfeld and Nicholson, 1978; *Rudyard Kipling* by James Harrison, Boston, Twayne, 1982; *Rudyard Kipling and the Fiction of Adolescence* by Robert F. Moss, New York, St. Martin's Press, and London, Macmillan, 1982; *Kipling: Interviews and Recollections* edited by Harold Orel, London, Macmillan, 2 vols., 1983, New York, Barnes and Noble, 2 vols., 1984; *A Kipling Companion* by Norman Page, London, Macmillan, 1984; *Kipling and Orientalism* by B.J. Moore-Gilbert, London, Croom Helm, 1986; *Kipling's Hidden Narratives* by Sandra Kemp, Oxford, Blackwell, 1988; *Rudyard Kipling* by Martin Seymour-Smith, London, Macdonald, 1989.

* * *

Today, Rudyard Kipling is chiefly remembered as a spokesman for imperialism and as a skillful versifier, and it is often overlooked that approximately one in six of his published short stories were science fiction or fantasy. His influence on 20th-century SF writers was probably greater than anyone else's of his generation, except Wells, and is acknowledged by a number of contemporary SF writers.

His formal excursions into the future are few but memorable. "With the Night Mail" describes an Atlantic crossing by airship in the year 2000, and is accompanied by excerpts from the magazine in which it was supposed to appear. Socially, little appears to have changed, but technologically this is an astounding vision; at a time when it was novel for a liner to carry radio-telegraphy equipment, and broadcasting was two decades distant, Kipling envisaged the need for air traffic control and a General Communicator system. In the sequel, "As Easy as ABC," he speculated on the demise of democracy owing to its tendency to lapse into mob–rule—this may have been conditioned by his disappointment with the USA at a time when lynch-law was still common: witness the terrifying image of the memorial statue, "The Nigger in Flames,"—and on a cure for over-population, a problem he had encountered during his time in India.

His other works of SF and fantasy range from the early "The Bridge-Builders," in which a civil engineer overhears the Indian gods debating whether or not to destroy his masterpiece spanning the Ganges, through those astonishing *tours-de-force* without human characters like ".007" (steam locomotives) and "The Ship That Found Herself" (steel plates and girders and the ship's cat!), by way of speculative SF like "In the Same Boat" (a man and woman discover that the nightmares haunting them refer to real events which happened while they were in the womb) and "The Finest Story in the World" (a city clerk remembers his previous lives, as a galley-slave and on an expedition to Vinland), right up to the complex, subtle stories of his last years when he left his readers and critics far behind, like "The Children of the Zodiac."

He wrote the classic ghosts-in-reverse story, "They," and the deadpan fantasies of *Just So Stories;* in *Puck of Pook's Hill* and *Rewards and Fairies* he brought the people of past ages forward to the present to speak for themselves; and he wrote about sea-serpents and mysterious curses and the heady excitement of modern inventions—but never quite as anyone else would have handled them. For example, "Wireless" is indeed about early radio, but the narrator's experimental friend, trying to eavesdrop on the Royal Navy, fails to notice how the soul of Keats is striking an echo across time in a lovelorn, tubercular assistant pharmacist.

Kipling, who was possibly the most completely equipped writer ever to tackle the short-story form in the English language, exemplifies the fact that in our literary tradition there has never been a hard-and-fast line between realistic and fantastic. Indeed, he was a master at making the fantastic seem credible.

—John Brunner

---

**KIPPAX, John.** Pseudonym for John Charles Hynam. British. Born in Alwalton, Huntingdonshire, 10 June 1915. Attended Trinity College, Carmarthen, 1934–36. Married Phyllis Mary Manning in 1941; one daughter. Artist, musician, comedian, and teacher. *Died 17 July 1974.*

SCIENCE-FICTION PUBLICATIONS

Novels (series: Venturer 12 in all books)

*A Thunder of Stars*, with Dan Morgan. London, Macdonald, 1968; New York, Ballantine, 1970.
*Seed of Stars*, with Dan Morgan. New York, Ballantine, 1972; London, Pan, 1974.
*The Neutral Stars*, with Dan Morgan. New York, Ballantine, 1973; London, Pan, 1975.
*Where No Stars Guide*. London, Pan, 1975.

Uncollected Short Stories

"Dimple," in *Science Fantasy* (Bournemouth), December 1954.
"Trojan Hearse," with Dan Morgan, in *New Worlds* (London), December 1954.
"Mossenden's Martian," in *Science Fantasy* (Bournemouth), April 1955.
"Down to Earth," in *Authentic* (London), May 1955.
"Special Delivery," in *Science Fantasy* (Bournemouth), June 1955.
"Hounded Down," in *Science Fantasy* (Bournemouth), November 1955.
"Mother of Invention," in *Authentic* (London), December 1955.
"Again, In," in *Authentic* (London), January 1956.
"Waif Astray," in *Authentic* (London), March 1956.
"Fair Weather Friend," in *Science Fantasy* (Bournemouth), May 1956.
"We Are One," in *Authentic* (London), September 1956.
"We're Only Human," in *New Worlds* (London), November 1956.
"Cut and Come Again," in *Science Fantasy* (Bournemouth), December 1956.
"Finnegan Begin Again," in *Science Fantasy* (Bournemouth), February 1957.
"By the Forelock," in *Authentic* (London), February 1957.
"Salute Your Superiors!," in *Authentic* (London), April 1957.
"Point of Contact," in *New Worlds* (London), April 1957.
"After Eddie," in *Science Fantasy* (Bournemouth), June 1957.
"The Underlings," in *New Worlds* (London), August 1957.
"Solid Beat," in *Science Fantasy* (Bournemouth), October 1957.
"Send Him Victorious," in *Science Fantasy* (Bournemouth), December 1957.
"Me, Myself, and I," in *Science Fantasy* (Bournemouth), February 1958.
"End Planet," in *Nebula* (Glasgow), April 1958.
"Tower for One," in *New Worlds* (London), July 1958.
"Destiny Incorporated," in *Science Fantasy* (Bournemouth), August 1958.
"It," in *Nebula* (Glasgow), November 1958.
"Thy Rod and Thy Staff," in *Nebula* (Glasgow), December 1958.
"Call of the Wild," in *Science Fantasy* (Bournemouth), February 1959.
"The Lady Was Jazz," in *Science Fantasy* (Bournemouth), April 1959.
"Friday," in *Out of This World 1*, edited by Amabel Williams-Ellis and Mably Owen. London, Blackie, 1960.
"The Last Barrier," in *Science Fantasy* (Bournemouth), September 1960.
"The Dusty Death," in *Out of This World 2*, edited by Amabel Williams-Ellis and Mably Owen. London, Blackie, 1961.
"Nelson Expects," in *New Worlds* (London), October 1961.
"Stark Refuge," in *Science Fantasy* (Bournemouth), November 1961.
"Look on His Face," in *New Worlds* (London), August 1966.
"Reflection of the Truth," in *Tales of Unease*, edited by John Burke. New York, Doubleday, 1969.
"Blood Offering," in *Weird Shadows from Beyond*, edited by John Carnell. New York, Avon, 1969.
"The Time Wager," in *New Writings in SF 22*, edited by Kenneth Bulmer. London, Sidgwick and Jackson, 1973.
"No Certain Armour," in *New Writings in SF 24*, edited by Kenneth Bulmer. London, Sidgwick and Jackson, 1974.

* * *

Fear, estrangement, and the hunger to bridge the sometimes illimitable gulfs between individuals—and between cultures, planets, and species—are central themes in the science fiction and fantasy of John Kippax. The desperate quest for security in a hostile universe figures prominently in this minor English author's writing. His four Venturer 12 novels, the first three written with Dan Morgan, are perhaps Kippax's best-known genre work but are inferior to some of his short fiction.

*A Thunder of Stars* presents motifs of alienation that persist through the series. It introduces a group of continuing stock military characters who must wrestle in various ways with personal alienation. Central to the saga is the troubled relationship between Tom Bruce and Helen Lindstrom, officers of the elite Space Corps. At the outset, Bruce, a seemingly callous martinet, breaks off their rewarding two-year affair with the excuse that it is hampering their careers. Both are ambitious and dedicated officers, but Lindstrom does not want to sacrifice their relationship.

Bruce yearns to command *Venturer 12*, Earth's most advanced starship. He is brilliant and highly qualified. But scandal early in his career—carefully hushed up—makes his appointment a political hot potato. Then Bruce, on solar system patrol, shoots down a runaway starship filled with colonists before it can crash into Earth with appalling carnage. An inquiry vindicates Bruce but the traumatic secret of his past is revealed: On a distant colony planet Bruce once discovered humans who had been captured and surgically restructured by unknown aliens. Out of mercy, he put the hideously mutilated victims to death.

Bruce wins the *Venturer 12* appointment; Lindstrom will be second in command. Their relationship remains uncomfortably platonic in the subsequent novels.

Bruce's obsessive search for the ruthless and elusive aliens called "Kilroys" unifies *Seed of Stars, The Neutral Stars*, and *Where No Stars Guide*, the last written by Kippax alone. Continuing frustrations with alien contact are paralleled by political intrigue and estrangements, betrayals and occasional reconciliations between men and women. However, characters in the series by and large are too crudely drawn for their vulnerabilities to arouse sympathy. The Space Corps has a sentimental, toy-soldier quality. Although the authors take pains to show a sexually and racially integrated Corps drawn from all corners of the Earth, clumsy, insensitive writing results in unintended racial and sexual stereotyping.

More effective are Kippax's short stories, of which he wrote more than 30 between 1955 and 1961. "No Certain Armour," a Space Corps story, stresses the importance of personal responsibility and self-respect in a dangerous universe. More compelling in mood and treatment is "Blood Offering," a compact and dramatic fantasy set on an isolated tropical island. The focus is yet another prickly male-female relationship—a duel of wills between Tod Baines, a brash Australian storekeeper, and Mama Noi, an Old Polynesian witch who demands tribute on behalf of the Shark God. Baines resists the crone's petty extortions, egged on by a scornful Chinese accountant who is at odds with a huge native fisherman over the favours of an island girl. These interwoven conflicts climax in a frightening, ambiguous midnight confrontation with the Shark God that prefigures Tom Bruce's fleeting contacts with the Kilroys.

Kippax's strongly traditional work utilizes popular science fiction and fantasy motifs to remind us that gulfs—whether of water, space, or attitude—can be terrible indeed. But perfunctory writing and avoidance of innovation often blunts the impact of his message.

—Vince Kohler

---

**KIRKWOOD, James.** *See* **SHEFFIELD, Charles.**

---

**KLINE, Otis Adelbert.** American. Born in Chicago, Illinois, 1 July 1891. Composer and song writer, then music publisher, film writer, and editor. Editor, *Weird Tales*, Chicago, 1924; founder, Otis Kline Associates, literary agency. *Died 24 October 1946.*

SCIENCE-FICTION PUBLICATIONS

Novels (series: Robert Grandon; Jan; Mars)

*The Planet of Peril* (Grandon). Chicago, McClurg, 1929.
*Maza of the Moon*. Chicago, McClurg, 1930.
*The Prince of Peril* (Grandon). Chicago, McClurg, 1930.
*Call of the Savage*. New York, Clode, 1937; as *Jan of the Jungle*, New York, Ace, 1966.
*The Port of Peril* (Grandon). Providence, Rhode Island, Grandon, 1949.
*The Swordsman of Mars*. New York, Avalon, 1960.
*The Outlaws of Mars*. New York, Avalon, 1961.
*Tam, Son of the Tiger*. New York, Avalon, 1962.
*Jan in India*. Lakemont, Georgia, Fictioneer, 1974.

Short Stories

*The Man Who Limped and Other Stories*. Hollywood, Saint, 1946.
*Stories*. Oak Lawn, Illinois, Weinberg, 1975.

* * *

Otis Adelbert Kline, whose literary career flourished in the 1920's and 1930's, never aimed higher than the prevailing tastes of those who read the pulp magazines *Weird Tales, Argosy*, and *Amazing Stories*, in which he published most of his stories. He was clearly influenced by and competed with his contemporaries Edgar Rice Burroughs, A. Merritt, and H.P. Lovecraft, and made no apologies for pandering to the popular taste for formula adventure stories. His work as a literary agent kept him abreast of whatever appealed to the popular imagination, and he worked these interests into his stories. His SF was of the fantastic variety denounced by Gernsback in the 1930's, Campbell in the 1940's, and Gold in the 1950's, who were committed to making SF respectable among adult readers. Had Kline been writing in the 1950's and 1960's, he would probably have been turning out the same formula stories with New Wave embellishments.

Kline's costume adventure melodramas are SF in the limited sense that he made use of conventions like psi powers, rocket travel, ray guns, and heavy doses of ritualism, totemism, and primitive religion borrowed from Frazer, Malinowski, and other anthropologists whose ideas of primitive social and religious customs had begun to stir the popular imagination. In truth, little beyond the accessories distinguish the SF from, say, the oriental adventures of the Dragoman series (*The Man Who Limped*). Much of his fantastic SF belongs in that loose category known as "sword and sorcery."

Kline's imagination was highly visual and his storytelling techniques were clearly shaped by his film-writing experiences. Whatever the costumes, settings, and properties, his stories are built out of the simplest formulas of the adventure-suspense story, and his characters are stock types familiar to anyone who has seen the old Buck Rogers serials. Like Burroughs, Kline had his series of Mars and Venus stories. The latter (the Robert Grandon series) proved very popular, and perhaps should be taken as representative of Kline's most influential work in the genre.

Critical opinion on Kline has been largely negative. However, despite everything negative that has been said, including the more recently fashionable charges of racism and sexism (equally justified), there remains the embarrassing but undeniable power of Kline's naive handling of the formulas and conventions of exotic adventure. Kline's ideas are second-hand and his treatment of them trite, but that is the very heart of his appeal. He gives the reader the expected cliché, the familiar stereotype, the conventional adventure formula. No summary could do justice to his triteness, but the following vignette from "The Bride of Osiris" (1927) may stand as a fair sample of the action: "As he stood there in the midst of the hostile multitude, holding the half-fainting Doris and expecting instant death, Buell heard two sounds simultaneously—the twang of a bowstring and an encouraging shout from Rafferty." The power of such a passage may be of a low order, barely a notch above the boys' adventure stories of the time, and yet the reader may find a kind of delight encountering an almost pure example of the thriller whose only purpose is unreflective and mindless entertainment. That Kline succeeds at all is perhaps his revenge upon literary criticism.

Kline's most successful novel, and probably his best, is *Call of the Savage*. The novel was modelled on Kipling's *Jungle Books* and Hudson's *Green Mansions*, and exhibits Kline's ability to use mythic and archetypal story elements to entrap all but the most wary reader. *Call of the Savage* is fantasy rather than SF, but, as we have seen in Kline's other work, the differences as well as the resemblances are coincidental.

—Donald L. Lawler

---

**KNEALE, (Thomas) Nigel.** British. Born in Barrow-in-Furness, Lancashire, 28 April 1922. Educated at Douglas High School, Isle of Man; Royal Academy of Dramatic Art, London, 1946–48. Married the writer Judith Kerr in 1954; one daughter and one son. Actor, Stratford upon Avon, 1948–49; staff member, BBC Television, London, 1951–55. Recipient: Maugham award, 1950. Agent: Douglas Rae (Management) Ltd., 28 Charing Cross Road, London WC2H 0DB, England.

SCIENCE-FICTION PUBLICATIONS

Novel

*Quatermass.* London, Hutchinson, 1979.

Short Stories

*Tomato Cain and Other Stories.* London, Collins, 1949; New York, Knopf, 1950.

OTHER PUBLICATIONS

Plays

*The Quatermass Experiment* (televised, 1953). London, Penguin, 1959.
*Quatermass II* (televised, 1955). London, Penguin, 1960.
*Quatermass and the Pit* (televised, 1959). London, Penguin, 1960.
*The Year of the Sex Olympics and Other TV Plays* (includes *The Road* and *The Stone Tape*). London, Ferret Fantasy, 1976.

Screenplays: *Quatermass II* (*Enemy from Space*), with Val Guest, 1957; *The Abominable Snowman*, 1957; *Look Back in Anger*, with John Osborne, 1959; *The Entertainer*, with John Osborne, 1960; *HMS Defiant* (*Damn the Defiant*), with Edmund North, 1962; *First Men in the Moon*, with Jan Read, 1964; *The Witches*, 1966; *Quatermass and the Pit* (*5,000,000 Years to Earth*), 1967; *The Quatermass Conclusion*, 1979.

Television Plays: *The Quatermass Experiment*, 1953; *Nineteen Eighty-Four*, from the novel by Orwell, 1954; *The Creature*, 1955; *Quatermass II*, 1955; *Mrs. Wickens in the Fall*, 1956; *Quatermass and the Pit*, 1959; *The Road*, 1963; *The Crunch*, 1964; *The Year of the Sex Olympics*, 1967; *Bam! Pow! Zapp!*, 1969; *Wine of India*, 1970; *The Chopper*, 1971; *The Stone Tape*, 1972; *Jack and the Beanstalk*, 1974; *Murrain*, 1975; *Buddyboy*, 1976; *During Barty's Party*, 1976; *Special Offer*, 1976; *The Dummy*, 1976; *Baby*, 1976; *What Big Eyes*, 1976; *Quatermass*, 1979; *Kinvig series*, 1981; *The Woman in Black*, from the novel by Susan Hill, 1989; *Stanley and the Women*, from the novel by Kingsley Amis, 1991.

*

Nigel Kneale comments:

I have always been a scriptwriter for television and films because that's what I like doing best. I don't regard myself as a science-fiction writer, and the list above confirms this. Looking through this list I wondered what other things I wrote. The answer, of course, is things that didn't get made. Some of my best screenplays, from Huxley, Lawrence, and the like, went down with collapsing film companies. More rarely, but more painfully, there were stillborn TV originals, like *The Big Big Giggle*, a serial about a teenage suicide craze, wiped out by high cost and official nervousness that was probably justified (it could have been dangerous). Or *Crow*, about the slave trade and not dangerous at all, victim of an internal squabble in a TV company. I just have to be grateful for all those that *did* get made.

* * *

With a few notable exceptions, most of them in recent years, movies and television have not been kind to science fiction. The speculative ideas that characterize what is best in the genre have proven difficult to translate into visual media without interrupting the action with long expository speeches, while the spectacular visual surfaces that science-fiction narratives afford have been all too tempting to filmmakers. As a result, few science-fiction writers have been able to work with success in the media, and fewer still have managed to build their primary reputation as a media writer of science fiction. Nigel Kneale is a member of this select latter group. The three television serials concerning Professor Bernard Quatermass that he wrote for the BBC between 1953 and 1959—all three of which were subsequently published in book form and adapted as feature films—established a standard for the televised science-fiction horror story that has seldom been surpassed.

Kneale had little direct experience as a science-fiction writer before joining the BBC, although a few of his short stories from *Tomato Cain* are small masterpieces of weird fiction. While at the BBC, Kneale's plays included an adaptation for television of Orwell's *Nineteen Eighty-Four* and an original play about the abominable snowman called *The Creature* (filmed as *The Abominable Snowman*). But it was his 1953 six-part sequel *The Quatermass Experiment* that quickly established his reputation as a convincing dramatist of suspense thrillers. This tale of an alien life form that takes over the body of the lone survivor of the first space mission and metamorphoses into a hideous monster back on Earth, despite occasional absurdities (super-scientist Quatermass finally succeeds in literally *talking* the monster to death), reveals an ear for convincing dialogue, an awareness of the dramatic possibilities of the television medium (such as the use of "newscasters" to carry forth the action), and a talent for working serious issues and concepts into a fast-moving dramatic narrative. Though Quatermass is a scientist-hero in the mold of Conan Doyle's Professor Challenger, Kneale makes some pointed observations about the morality of scientific research and the relationship of government and the journalistic media to such research.

Professor Quatermass continued his fight against bureaucracy and journalistic sensationalism in two subsequent serials. *Quatermass II* concerns the attempt of an alien civilization to establish colonies on Earth by converting human workers into zombie-like slaves; it is perhaps the weakest of the three serials. *Quatermass and the Pit* is perhaps the strongest: a subway excavation in a reputedly haunted area uncovers an ancient alien spaceship which, when activated, reveals that legends of the devil are based on race memories of the aliens from Mars who once tried to conquer Earth—and in the process created us. The mix of myth, supernaturalism, and science fiction works well, and predates by several years cult rumors of gods from outer space. A fourth installment in the Quatermass series, *The Quatermass Conclusion*, was filmed in 1979.

Kneale worked on other screenplays, most notably the film adaptations of two John Osborne plays and an adaptation of Wells's *First Men in the Moon*, which he gave a characteristic twist by casting the story as a flashback told more than a half-century later by a survivor of the expedition whose secret is revealed only when the "official" first moon-landing party comes across the remnants of the earlier adventurers. Here, as in the Quatermass serials, Kneale's ironic humor, his deftness in sketching minor characters, and his sense of dramatic structure provide a strong script. Though he has shown little inclination to move beyond the horror-suspense school of science fiction, Kneale has contributed significantly to the genre's growth in the media.

—Gary K. Wolfe

---

**KNIGHT, Damon (Francis).** American. Born in Baker, Oregon, 19 September 1922. Educated at Hood River High School, Oregon; WPA Art Center, Salem, Oregon, 1940–41. Married 1) Gertrud Werndl; 2) Helen Schlaz; 3) Kate Wilhelm, *q.v.*, in 1963; four children. Freelance writer: assistant editor, Popular Publications, 1943–44, 1949–50; editor, *Worlds Beyond*, 1950–51; book editor, *Science Fiction Adventures*, 1953–54; editor, *If*, 1958–59; book editor, *Fantasy and Science Fiction*, 1959–60; editorial consultant, Berkley Books, 1960–66. Co-founding director, Milford Science Fiction Writers' Conference, 1956. Since 1967, lecturer, Clarion Workshop in Science Fiction and Fantasy. Founder, 1965, and president, 1965–67, Science Fiction Writers of America. Recipient: Hugo award, for non-fiction, 1956; Pilgrim award, 1975. Address: 1645 Horn Lane, Eugene, Oregon 97404, U.S.A.

SCIENCE-FICTION PUBLICATIONS

Novels

*Hell's Pavement.* New York, Lion, 1955; London, Banner, 1958; as *The Analogue Men*, New York, Berkley, 1962.
*The People Maker.* Rockville Centre, New York, Zenith, 1959; revised edition, as *A for Anything*, London, New English Library, 1961; New York, Berkley, 1965.
*Masters of Evolution.* New York, Ace, 1959.
*The Sun Saboteurs.* New York, Ace, 1961; as *The Earth Quarter* (with *World Without Children*), New York, Lancer, 1970.
*Beyond the Barrier.* New York, Doubleday, and London, Gollancz, 1964.
*Mind Switch.* New York, Berkley, 1965; as *The Other Foot*, London, Whiting and Wheaton, 1966.
*The Rithian Terror.* New York, Ace, 1965.
*Three Novels: Rule Golden, Natural State, The Dying Man.* New York, Doubleday, and London, Gollancz, 1967; as *Natural State and Other Stories*, London, Pan, 1975.
*Two Novels* (*The Earth Quarter* and *Double Meaning*). London, Gollancz, 1974.
*The World and Thorinn.* New York, Berkley, 1981.
*The Man in the Tree.* New York, Berkley, 1984; London, Gollancz, 1985.
*CV.* New York, Tor, 1985.
*The Observers.* New York, Tor, 1988.
*A Reasonable World.* New York, Tor, 1991.

Short Stories

*Far Out.* New York, Simon and Schuster, and London, Gollancz, 1961.
*In Deep.* New York, Berkley, 1963; London, Gollancz, 1964.
*Off Center.* New York, Ace, 1965; London, Gollancz, 1969.
*Turning On.* New York, Doubleday, 1966; London, Gollancz, 1967.
*The Best of Damon Knight.* New York, Doubleday, 1976.
*Rule Golden and Other Stories.* New York, Avon, 1979.
*Late Knight Edition.* Cambridge, NESFA Press, 1985.
*One Side Laughing: Stories Unlike Other Stories.* New York, St. Martin's Press, 1991.

OTHER PUBLICATIONS

Other

*In Search of Wonder.* Chicago, Advent, 1956; revised edition, 1967.
*Charles Fort, Prophet of the Unexplained.* New York, Doubleday, 1970; London, Gollancz, 1971.
*The Futurians: The Story of the Science Fiction "Family" of the 30's That Produced Today's Top SF Writers and Editors.* New York, Day, 1977.
*Better Than One*, with Kate Wilhelm. Cambridge, Massachusetts, NESFA Press, 1980.
*Creating Short Fiction.* Cincinnati, Writer's Digest, 1981.

Editor, *A Century of Science Fiction.* New York, Simon and Schuster, 1962; London, Gollancz, 1963.
Editor, *First Flight.* New York, Lancer, 1963; as *Now Begins Tomorrow*, 1969; revised edition, with Martin H. Greenberg and Joseph D. Olander, as *First Voyages*, New York, Avon, 1981.
Editor, *A Century of Great Short Science Fiction Novels.* New York, Delacorte Press, 1964; London, Gollancz, 1965.

Editor, *Tomorrow x 4.* New York, Fawcett, 1964; London, Coronet, 1967.
Editor, and Translator, *Thirteen French Science-Fiction Stories.* New York, Bantam, and London, Corgi, 1965.
Editor, *Beyond Tomorrow.* New York, Harper, 1965; London, Gollancz, 1968.
Editor, *The Dark Side.* New York, Doubleday, 1965; London, Dobson, 1966.
Editor, *The Shape of Things.* New York, Popular Library, 1965.
Editor, *Nebula Award Stories 1965.* New York, Doubleday, 1966; London, Gollancz, 1967.
Editor, *Cities of Wonder.* New York, Doubleday, 1966; London, Dobson, 1968.
Editor, *Orbit 1-21.* New York, Putnam, 12 vols., 1966–73, New York, Berkley, 1 vol., 1974, New York, Harper, 8 vols., 1974–80; vol. 1, London, Whiting and Wheaton, 1966; vol. 2, London, Rapp and Whiting, 1968.
Editor, *Science Fiction Inventions.* New York, Lancer, 1967.
Editor, *Worlds to Come.* New York, Harper, 1967; London, Gollancz, 1969.
Editor, *The Metal Smile.* New York, Belmont, 1968.
Editor, *One Hundred Years of Science Fiction.* New York, Simon and Schuster, 1968; London, Gollancz, 1969.
Editor, *Toward Infinity.* New York, Simon and Schuster, 1968; London, Gollancz, 1970.
Editor, *Dimension X* (for children). New York, Simon and Schuster, 1970; London, Gollancz, 1972.
Editor, *First Contact.* New York, Pinnacle, 1971.
Editor, *A Pocketful of Stars.* New York, Doubleday, 1971; London, Gollancz, 1972.
Editor, *Perchance to Dream.* New York, Doubleday, 1972; London, Gollancz, 1974.
Editor, *A Science Fiction Argosy.* New York, Simon and Schuster, 1972; London, Gollancz, 1973.
Editor, *Tomorrow and Tomorrow.* New York, Simon and Schuster, 1973; London, Gollancz, 1974.
Editor, *The Golden Road.* New York, Simon and Schuster, 1973; London, Gollancz, 1974.
Editor, *Happy Endings.* Indianapolis, Bobbs Merrill, 1974.
Editor, *Elsewhere x 3.* London, Coronet, 1974.
Editor, *A Shocking Thing.* New York, Pocket Books, 1974.
Editor, *Best Stories from Orbit 1-10.* New York, Berkley, 1975.
Editor, *Science Fiction of the Thirties.* Indianapolis, Bobbs Merrill, 1975.
Editor, *Westerns of the 40's: Classics from the Great Pulps.* Indianapolis, Bobbs Merrill, 1977.
Editor, *Turning Points: Essays on the Art of Science Fiction.* New York, Harper, 1977.
Editor, *The Clarion Awards.* New York, Doubleday, 1984.

Translator, *Ashes, Ashes,* by René Barjavel. New York, Doubleday, 1967.

* * *

Damon Knight has had a far-ranging impact on science fiction. As a reviewer, he helped to establish criteria for criticism within the field, and produced the still readable *In Search of Wonder,* which includes the best of his essays. He currently edits *Monad,* an irregular collection of literary essays dealing with various aspects of the field. As an editor, he has provided platforms for some of the most innovative new stories, particularly in the multi-volume *Orbit* series of original anthologies. He also introduced American readers to works from the continent in *13 French Science Fiction Stories,* has edited a number of first-rate reprint anthologies, done some illustration work for the professional magazines, and taught at various writers' conferences.

But Damon Knight is first and foremost a writer. Although he is not primarily thought of as a novelist, his career has been sprinkled with exceptionally thoughtful book-length works. *The Analogue Men* (originally published as *Hell's Pavement*) was one of the earliest genre novels to make use of complex psychological principles in its depiction of a world where each individual citizen has been conditioned to accept the existence of an imaginary guardian. A secret society of immunes provides the only hope for humanity in one of the best early dystopias.

Three early short novels, while primarily action oriented, illustrate Knight's concerns about our world. *The Sun Saboteurs* (shorter version as *The Earth Quarter*) presents a universe in which humans are a minority, and a not particularly respected one, confined to ghettos on other worlds, barely suppressing a smoldering resentment. *The Rithian Terror* (shorter version as "Double Meaning") pits a corrupt human government against a shapechanging alien. The protagonist sets out to capture the intruder, only to realize the truth about his own society and switch sides at a crucial moment. *Masters of Evolution* (shorter version as "Natural State") deals with the decline of urban centers, now engaged in open warfare against the suburbs, finally using biological engineering techniques as the ultimate weapon. A full-length novel from that period, *A for Anything* (also released under the title *The People Maker*) explores the dangers of too much wealth. In a society where it is physically possible to duplicate any material object, human life becomes the only rarity and slavery is reinstituted.

Two competent but unexceptional novels followed, the wildly satiric *Mind Switch* and a thoughtful thriller, *Beyond the Barrier.* In the former, a human being's personality is transformed into the body of an alien primate, providing the springboard for an altered perception of the foibles of humanity; in the latter, an ordinary appearing professor is actually a superkiller from a future where a barrier has been erected as protection from alien invaders. The episodic fantasy novel, *The World and Thorinn,* emphasizes Knight's growing metaphysical interests, which emerge more fully and with better effect in his next novel.

*The Man in the Tree* marked an enormous leap forward for an already significant writer. The protagonist is capable of reaching into alternate universes, withdrawing items and using them in our own. When he inadvertently causes the death of a young bully, he gains the undying enmity of the man's father, who pursues him for years in search of revenge. There are numerous increasingly evident parallels to the Christ story in what is still Knight's greatest single work.

Recently Knight has a completed a trilogy of novels, *CV, The Observers,* and *A Reasonable World.* In the near future, individual freedom is in jeopardy and violence continues to threaten humanity's progress toward a mature society. The passengers and crew of the CV, a seagoing vessel, are infected by the awakening of an alien creature who can infiltrate human bodies, undetectibly at first, breed and spread throughout other warm-blooded creatures. Although this intelligent virus provides some beneficial services to its hosts, it becomes increasingly involved in policing their moral lives, ultimately acting as judge and jury, causing the deaths of those who cannot control their violent impulses.

Knight has a higher reputation for his short stories than for his novels. Perhaps his best known is "To Serve Man," the title of a book by a group of visiting aliens which turns out to be a cookbook. In "You're Another," a man discovers that all of human history is simply a play, and he is no more than a minor character. Two brothers loot time in "Anachron," and the only remaining man with the capacity for cruelty is honored in "The Country of the Kind."

"Rule Golden" involves an alien who exudes an empathic gas, causing an entertaining inversion of the Golden Rule, "Be Done By As You Did." In "An Eye for a What?" the authorities must discover how to punish an alien who quite literally enjoys most of the options available. "What Rough Beast" deals with changes made to the world through manipulation of the relationship between cause and effect. Knight's wry humor is evident in "O," in which everything whose name starts with that letter disappears from the Earth.

Other short stories of particular note are "Stranger Station," "Idiot Stick," "Not With a Bang," "Cabin Boy," "Ask Me Anything," "Eripmav," and "Masks." The best collections of Knight's shorter work are *Far Out* and *In Deep.* If Knight's reputation were to rely solely on his fiction, it would be safely established. His editorial and critical impact are less easily realized, but may ultimately have an even greater effect toward shaping the future of the field.

—Don D'Ammassa

---

**KNIGHT, Norman L(ouis).** American. Born in St. Joseph, Missouri, 21 September 1895. Educated at St. Joseph Junior College, A.A. 1918; George Washington University, Washington, D.C., B.S. in chemical engineering 1925. Served in the United States Army Field Artillery, 1918–19. Married Marie Sarah Yenn in 1921; one daughter. Worked for the Department of Agriculture: assistant observer, Davenport, Iowa, 1919–20, and observer and code translator, Washington, D.C., Weather Bureau; analytical chemist in Washington, D.C., 1925–29, Chicago, 1929, St. Louis, 1929–40, Chicago, 1940–50, and Beltsville, Maryland, 1950–64, Insecticide Division; retired in 1964: Merit award, 1962. *Died 19 April 1972.*

### Science-Fiction Publications

#### Novel

*A Torrent of Faces*, with James Blish. New York, Doubleday, 1967; London, Faber, 1968.

#### Uncollected Short Stories

"Frontier of the Unknown," in *Astounding* (New York), July 1937.
"Isle of the Golden Swarm," in *Astounding* (New York), June 1938.
"Saurian Valedictory," in *Astounding* (New York), January 1939.
"Bombardment in Reverse," in *Astounding* (New York), February 1940.
"The Testament of Akubii," in *Astounding* (New York), June 1940.
"Fugitive from Vanguard," in *Astounding* (New York), January 1942.
"Kilgallen's Lunar Legacy," in *Astounding* (New York), August 1942.
"Once in a Blue Moon," in *Future* (New York), August 1942.
"Short-Circuited Probability," in *Best of Science Fiction*, edited by Groff Conklin. New York, Crown, 1946.
"Crisis in Utopia," in *Five Science Fiction Novels*, edited by Martin H. Greenberg. New York, Gnome Press, 1952; as *Crucible of Power*, London, Lane, 1953.
"The Piper of Dis," in *Galaxy* (New York), August 1966.
"To Love Another," in *Analog* (New York), April 1967.

* * *

Norman L. Knight published his first story in *Astounding* in 1937, worked most of his life as a chemist specializing in pesticides, and finally published his most ambitious science fiction work in collaboration with the master, James Blish, in 1967. One theme and one setting, in fact, kept reappearing in the early stories; and the importance of that set of images in the novel suggests that Knight may have been the seminal partner in the collaboration—if not the more polished stylist. Images that led eventually to the masterpiece, *A Torrent of Faces*, can be seen as early as the serialized novel "Frontier of the Unknown," in which a deep-sea diver moves in "a twilight pierced by a million uneasy, shifting, flickering ghosts of slanting, green-tinged sun rays." This crude flood of modifiers was followed by another two-part novel, "Crisis in Utopia," in which Knight also anticipates his work with Blish. Knight includes here the fully developed conception and description of the undersea race of human mutants called Tritons. The writing is a bit more subtle, and Knight's ideas on the effects of managed evolution are suggestive.

Nevertheless, these early stories are dominated by the usual villains of melodrama and the crude overwriting that so often seems the appropriate literary parallel to the line-drawing illustrations of the early pulp magazines. The novel, however, is the culmination of all this. One of the most popular sections of the novel, "The Shipwrecked Hotel," is a polished undersea disaster epic in which the Triton race plays a major role; Triton characters are fully developed throughout the book, and much of the action takes place undersea. Also, by the time of this later work the earth itself has replaced the melodramatic villains as a key protagonist—a much greater literary accomplishment. The individual extrapolations in the novel about living conditions in a future with one trillion inhabitants on earth are many and richly developed, and the writing shows marked improvement over the early Knight extrapolations on the sea and on Utopia. Blish was a good teacher and a good collaborator for Knight's valuable ideas on the future, on evolution, and on accompanying disasters.

—Donald M. Hassler

---

**KNOX, Calvin M.** *See* **SILVERBERG, Robert.**

---

**KOONTZ, Dean R(ay).** Has also written as David Axton; Brian Coffey; Deanna Dwyer; K.R. Dwyer; John Hill; Leigh Nichols; Anthony North; Owen West. American. Born in Everett, Pennsylvania, 9 July 1945. Educated at Shippensburg State College, B.A. in English 1966. Married Gerda Ann Cerra in 1966. Worked in a federal government poverty-alleviation program in Appalachia, then high school English teacher. Since 1969, full-time writer. Agent: Harold Ober Associates, 425 Madison Avenue, New York, New York 10017. Address: P.O. Box 9529, Newport Beach, California 92658-9529, U.S.A.

### Science-Fiction Publications

Novels

*Star Quest.* New York, Ace, 1968.
*The Fall of the Dream Machine.* New York, Ace, 1969.
*Fear That Man.* New York, Ace, 1969.
*The Dark Symphony.* New York, Lancer, 1970.
*Hell's Gate.* New York, Lancer, 1970.
*Dark of the Woods.* New York, Ace, 1970.
*Beastchild.* New York, Lancer, 1970.
*Anti-Man.* New York, Paperback Library, 1970.
*The Crimson Witch.* New York, Curtis, 1971.
*The Flesh in the Furnace.* New York, Bantam, 1972.
*A Darkness in My Soul.* New York, DAW, 1972; London, Dobson, 1979.
*Time Thieves.* New York, Ace, 1972; London, Dobson, 1977.
*Warlock*, New York, Lancer, 1972.
*Starblood.* New York, Lancer, 1972.
*Demon Seed.* New York, Bantam, 1973; London, Corgi, 1977.
*A Werewolf Among Us.* New York, Ballantine, 1973.
*The Haunted Earth.* New York, Lancer, 1973.
*Nightmare Journey.* New York, Berkley, 1975.
*The Long Sleep* (as John Hill). New York, Popular Library, 1975.

Short Stories

*Soft Come the Dragons.* New York, Ace, 1970.

### Other Publications

Novels

*Hanging On.* New York, Evans, 1973; London, Barrie and Jenkins, 1974.
*After the Last Rece.* New York, Atheneum, 1974.
*Strike Deep* (as Anthony North). New York, Dial Press, 1974.
*Invasion* (as Aaron Wolfe). Don Mills, Ontario, Laser Books, 1975.
*Prison of Ice* (as David Axton). Philadelphia, Lippincott, and London, W.H. Allen, 1976.
*Night Chills.* New York, Atheneum, 1976; London, W.H. Allen, 1977.
*The Vision.* New York, Putnam, 1977; London, Corgi, 1980.
*Whispers.* New York, Putnam, 1980; London, W.H. Allen, 1981.
*The Funhouse* (novelization of screenplay; as Owen West). New York, Jove, 1980; London, Sphere, 1981.
*The Mask* (as Owen West). New York, Jove, 1981; London, Coronet, 1983.
*Phantoms.* New York, Putnam, and London, W.H. Allen, 1983.
*Darkness Comes.* London, W.H. Allen, 1984; as *Darkfall*, New York, Berkley, 1984.
*Twilight Eyes.* Plymouth, Michigan, Land of Enchantment, 1985.
*The Door to December* (as Richard Paige). New York, New American Library, 1985; as Leigh Nichols, London, Fontana, 1987.
*Strangers.* New York, Putnam, and London, W.H. Allen, 1986.
*Watchers.* New York, Putnam, and London, Headline, 1987.
*Lightning.* New York, Putnam, and London, Headline, 1988.
*Oddkins: A Fable for All Ages.* New York, Warner, and London, Headline, 1988.
*Midnight.* New York, Putnam, and London, Headline, 1989.
*The Bad Place.* New York, Putnam, and London, Headline, 1990.
*Cold Fire.* New York, Putnam, and London, Headline, 1991.

Novels as Deanna Dwyer

*The Demon Child.* New York, Lancer, 1971.
*Legacy of Terror.* New York, Lancer, 1971.
*Children of the Storm.* New York, Lancer, 1972.
*The Dark of Summer.* New York, Lancer, 1972.
*Dance with the Devil.* New York, Lancer, 1973.

Novels as K.R. Dwyer

*Chase.* New York, Random House, 1972; London, Barker, 1974.
*Shattered.* New York, Random House, 1973; London, Barker, 1974.
*Dragonfly.* New York, Random House, 1975; London, Davies, 1977.

Novels as Brian Coffey

*Blood Risk.* Indianapolis, Bobbs Merrill, 1973; London, Barker, 1974.
*Surrounded.* Indianapolis, Bobbs Merrill, 1974; London, Barker, 1975.
*The Wall of Masks.* Indianapolis, Bobbs Merrill, 1975.
*The Face of Fear.* Indianapolis, Bobbs Merrill, 1977; as K.R. Dwyer, London, Davies, 1978.
*The Voice of the Night.* New York, Doubleday, 1980; London, Hale, 1981.

Novels as Leigh Nichols

*The Key to Midnight.* New York, Pocket Books, 1979; London, Magnum, 1980.
*The Eyes of Darkness.* New York, Pocket Books, 1981; London, Fontana, 1982.
*The House of Thunder.* New York, Pocket Books, 1982; London, Fontana, 1983.
*Twilight.* New York, Pocket Books, and London, Fontana, 1984; as *Servants of Twilight*, New York, Berkley, 1988.
*Shadowfires.* New York, Avon, and London, Collins, 1987.

Other

*The Pig Society*, with Gerda Koontz. Los Angeles, Aware Press, 1970.
*The Underground Lifestyles Handbook*, with Gerda Koontz. Los Angeles, Aware Press, 1970.
*Writing Popular Fiction.* Cincinnati, Writer's Digest, 1973.
*How to Write Best-Selling Fiction.* Cincinnati, Writer's Digest, and London, Poplar Press, 1981.
*Cold Terror: The Writings of Dean R. Koontz*, edited by Bill Munster. Lancaster, Pennsylvania, Underwood Miller, 1990.

* * *

Dean R. Koontz's best science fiction was written before 1980; since then he more properly can be called a writer of horror novels. His best work is a convincing amalgam of sympathetic characters and quirky plots, but lately his work has stressed the psychotic characters and supernatural events found in contemporary horror fiction.

Koontz is a writer of the New Wave in science fiction, a trend characterized by authors with backgrounds in the humanities rather than in the sciences. Certainly, Koontz's themes are rigorously chosen and often intriguing. His early work concerns the theme of the malevolent child, of innocence turned inside out; he handles the notion in *Beastchild*, in *A Darkness in My Soul*, in which a mutant becomes God, and quite compellingly in *Demon Seed* in which a super-computer creates its own genetic material which it "implants" into a human woman. In "We Three," genetically mutated children wish away harsh parents, then neighbors, then the entire world through their extra-sensory powers.

This theme is a corollary to Koontz's major concern—what it means to be human—which he explores in several works on robots. In "The Night of the Storm," the robot-protagonist Suranov is bored by his centralized, staid society "peopled" by robots. Humans are rumored to exist, much to the horror of the robots, whose prime rule is that the universe is logical, a dictum that the existence of humans threatens. The story also begins a robotics series carried on by New Wave writers Pamela Sargent and George Zebrowski, among others, in the *Continuum* series. The more turgid novel *Anti-Man* presents an android who changes into a new form of being, to the consternation of the human protagonist. This novel explores the Frankenstein theme—the relationship of creator and his creation—as does *Demon Seed.*

Beginning with his first story, "Soft Come the Dragons," Koontz clearly favors intuition and emotion as the essential components of humanness, rather than logic and reason, which can be assigned to machines. Perhaps his best long work, *A Werewolf among Us* presents a protagonist who is a cyberdective, a human whose brain is electronically and physically linked to a portable computer on his chest. Using a classic Agatha Christie plot, Koontz combines science fiction and detective genres. Members of a family are being murdered, the remaining members of the family are suspects, and the reader is presented with clues. However, the main conflict in the novel is psychological: when the human half of the cyberdective realizes the murderer is another robot, his computer half rejects the notion as illogical.

Koontz also treats themes current in popular culture. Marshall McLuhan's *The Medium Is the Massage* was the origin for "A Mouse in the Walls of the Global Village," and "The Psychedelic Children" projects a society one generation hence in which the children whose parents took LSD in the late 1960's are mutants who are hunted by society. The anti-establishment bias of the 1960's is clear in Koontz's work. In *Dark of the Woods* an unimaginative, conformist society systematically eliminates aliens. In "The Twelfth Bed" old people are shut away in a nursing home run by robots.

When Koontz deals with the theme of the quest and the mythic journey, however, he writes stereotyped pulp science fiction. In *Anti-Man, Nightmare Journey, Dark of the Woods*, and *Warlock*a hero rebelling from society sets out on a trek, usually through a cold wilderness, in which he encounters strange beasts and exotic phenomena which he eventually overcomes. The women in these works are sex goddesses only, deferential to the hero, though, as Koontz condescendingly interjects, spunky.

More recently he has written a series of horror novels in the Stephen King mode, some of which contain a scientific premise. *Phantoms* uses a genetically altered organism as the cause of the evil. *Lightning* features a time traveller and presents a particularly strong woman protagonist who happens to be a novelist. Perhaps all her trials have some autobiographical elements. *Midnight* contains a semi-scientific premise regarding a mad scientist who has discovered a formula causing genetic mutations. As people devolve into fear-filled, enraged animals, they terrorize a small town.

Other recent novels, such as *Shattered, Darkfall, Whispers, Servants of Twilight*, and *The Bad Place* cannot be called science fiction, though they use psychological phenomena such as the closeness of twins, the effects of incest, religious fanaticism, and supernatural elements. While these are not strictly science fiction, they do represent Koontz's return to sympathetic characters. The men are strong but warm, the women beautiful but competent. Family life is upheld as a premier value, and small-town California is affectionately explored.

Thus, Koontz is currently interested in the genres of suspense and in creating hair-raising plots and sensitive characters. If he returns to serious science fiction, he might be well advised to continue to explore his most productive theme of the Cartesian mind-body split and its consequences for what humans define as human. Koontz continues, even in his horror fiction, to define humans as beings who feel, love, and intuit, be that creature man, robot, or beast.

—Kathryn Lee Seidel

---

**KORNBLUTH, C(yril) M.** Also wrote as Simon Eisner; Cyril Judd; Jordan Park. American. Born in New York City, in 1923. Educated at the University of Chicago, B.A. Served in the infantry during World War II: Bronze Star. Married Mary G. Byers in 1944; two sons. Editor, Chicago office of Trans-Radio Press, 1949–51; freelance writer after 1951. Recipient: Hugo award, 1973. *Died 21 March 1958.*

Science-Fiction Publications

Novels

*Gunner Cade* (as Cyril Judd, with Judith Merril). New York, Simon and Schuster, 1952; London, Gollancz, 1964.
*Outpost Mars* (as Cyril Judd, with Judith Merril). New York, Abelard Press, 1952; London, New English Library, 1966; revised edition, as *Sin in Space*, New York, Galaxy, 1961.
*Takeoff.* New York, Doubleday, 1952.
*The Space Merchants*, with Frederik Pohl. New York, Ballantine, 1953; London, Heinemann, 1955.
*The Syndic.* New York, Doubleday, 1953; London, Faber, 1964.
*Search the Sky*, with Frederik Pohl. New York, Ballantine, 1954; London, Digit, 1960.
*Gladiator-at-Law*, with Frederik Pohl. New York, Ballantine, 1955; London, Digit, 1958.
*Not This August.* New York, Doubleday, 1955; as *Christmas Eve*, London, Joseph, 1956.
*Wolfbane*, with Frederik Pohl. New York, Ballantine, 1959; London, Gollancz, 1960.

Short Stories

*The Explorers.* New York, Ballantine, 1954.
*The Mindworm and Other Stories.* London, Joseph, 1955.
*A Mile Beyond the Moon.* New York, Doubleday, 1958.
*The Marching Morons.* New York, Ballantine, 1959.

*The Wonder Effect*, with Frederik Pohl. New York, Ballantine, 1962; London, Gollancz, 1967; revised edition, as *Critical Mass*, New York, Bantam, 1977.
*Best SF Stories*. London, Faber, 1968.
*Thirteen O'Clock and Other Zero Stories*, edited by James Blish. New York, Dell, 1970; London, Hale, 1972.
*The Best of C.M. Kornbluth*, edited by Frederik Pohl. New York, Doubleday, 1976.

OTHER PUBLICATIONS

Novels

*The Naked Storm* (as Simon Eisner). New York, Lion, 1952.
*A Town Is Drowning*, with Frederik Pohl. New York, Ballantine, 1955; London, Digit, 1960.
*Presidential Year*, with Frederik Pohl. New York, Ballantine, 1956.

Novels as Jordan Park

*Half*. New York, Lion, 1953.
*Valerie*. New York, Lion, 1953.
*Sorority House*, with Frederik Pohl. New York, Lion, 1956.
*The Man of Cold Rages*. New York, Pyramid, 1958.

* * *

C.M. Kornbluth was a major talent of the specialty magazines in the 1940's and 1950's. Probably best known as a collaborator with Frederik Pohl on novels of social extrapolation, he was primarily a writer of short stories that frequently contrast cosmic affairs with mundane existence, sometimes to farcical, more often to sardonic, effect.

With Pohl, he helped produce a handful of lively, satiric novels that practically constitute a genre of their own: a brand of near-future dystopia, deriving in part from H.G. Wells, concentrating on one particular facet of society which becomes the dominant force in the world, as in *The Space Merchants* and *Gladiator-at-Law*. In *Search the Sky*, a much lighter and lesser work, the satire mutates into a picaresque romp, exposing Kornbluth's penchant for quickstep burlesque. The other two books, though, are characterized by a continual mordant wit in their serious development of the oppressive rule of socio-economic institutions. Of course, these institutions are merely exaggerations of those already operating in the modern world, and are invariably connected to the realms of high finance and mass consumption, unlike, say, the dystopian worlds of Zamyatin, Orwell, or even Huxley, which are more distinctly political and totalitarian, and in many ways less directly evolved from the contemporary milieus of those writers. In this regard, Pohl and Kornbluth are more Wellsian, more extrapolative as opposed to symbolic, and much more "radical" in concept and detail than either Huxley or Orwell. The cautionary aspects of *Space Merchants*—its background of overpopulation, scarcity of resources, pollution, and runaway commercial exploitation—have made it a canonical "prophetic novel" in the wider world outside science fiction.

Their last true collaboration, *Wolfbane*, also deals with a culture of several limited resources, but as a condition ostensibly imposed from outside, by outré alien pyramids who have stolen the Earth-Moon system away from the Sun. The book is almost pure adventure, verging on space opera at the close, but it begins in a setting of material and spiritual poverty acutely drawn in its every detail. Kornbluth never achieved the distinction apart from Pohl that he did alongside him; and Pohl was fond enough of their partnership to "collaborate" with Kornbluth even after the latter's death by working up stories from odd fragments or from their previous common property (*The Wonder Effect* is partly composed of these).

Kornbluth also collaborated with Judith Merril, as Cyril Judd, on *Outpost Mars* and *Gunner Cade*. The second is notable for its vivid evocation of a post-holocaust military brotherhood, a spiritual sort of Spartanism. In both, the setting is again a down-at-heels world, but neither story has the inventive brilliance of the major Pohl-Kornbluth novels. However, each of them concerns a legendary/mythic element that resolves itself as a modest distortion of the book's initial reality-frame. This thematic concern relates to Kornbluth's best short stories, many of which play with the penetration of everyday existence by the utterly fantastic, the occult, the arcane. Such a tendency may seem axiomatic for science fiction; in Kornbluth, it often ranges beyond the usual boundaries of 1950's SF in tales as diverse in tone as "The Cosmic Expense Account" and "The Last Man Left in the Bar."

On his own, he wrote only three SF novels, *Not This August*, *Takeoff*, and *The Syndic*. The first two are patent journeyman exercises, apparently slanted for marketing considerations. They are competent, straightforward thrillers, largely unexceptional, only possessing a certain crisp efficiency. The first is the least winsome, giving the drear account of what happens after the Soviets conquer the U.S.A. It reads like a script aimed at the slick magazines (in fact it was serialized in *Maclean's*) and later adapted to the SF market. *Takeoff* tells the more tolerable—but hoary—story of how an atomic scientist helps a bunch of teenagers build a moon rocket, with appropriate interference by foreign agents to provide a veneer of suspense. *The Syndic* is another matter. Though it seems oddly cobbled together, it is nevertheless quite engaging and is Kornbluth's best solo novel. It incorporates satire, parody, homiletic fable, pulp adventure, and irrelevant moral lecture, accented by sudden left turns in the plot. Its primary narrative premise is a marvel of ironic supposition: the U.S. government, for just cause, has been exiled to the unfriendly shores of a primitive Ireland by a coalition of laisez-faire smugglers and racketeers, the good-time guys and dolls of the Syndic. Ostensibly a straight adventure story, it ultimately seems to be a loose composite of favorite crotchets, including a forceful depiction of earth-magic which somehow manages not to blow the narrative beyond the pale of mainline SF.

Where Kornbluth truly excelled was in his shorter work, the bulk of which appeared in the collections *The Explorers, A Mile Beyond the Moon* and *The Marching Morons*. It is often madly comic; and as often sharp and deadly. At its best, it is brief, evocative, to the point; short on description, but full of vivid impressions; and usually possessed of a clearly developed moral thrust, if not always an explicit moral. His strong satiric mode slides easily into march-hare burlesque, in pieces like "Passion Pill," "Thirteen O'Clock," and "Virginia." The omnipresent sardonicism emerges most fiercely in tightly woven shorts like "The Words of Guru," "The Silly Season," and "The Rocket of 1955," but also in longer works like "Two Dooms" and "The Marching Morons." The latter two are Kornbluth's most visibly horatory stories, although neither exists simply for the sake of its overt "lesson." He also wrote pure, slick adventures, playful novelettes like "The Slave" and "Make Mine Mars," which captivate by virtue of sheer readability, a deftness in the handling of stock figures and basic emotional appeals. And all the above, even the darkest tales, are rendered with a spritely touch; they do not sag in the middle, and there is ever a little crooked smile lurking somewhere in the corners.

Kornbluth's view of humanity may seem perplexing and inconsistent. He is sometimes accused of being a hard-case cynic, an elitist who views himself as above the common run. This is not entirely fallacious in light of "The Marching Morons;" in foreseeing a future populated mainly by just-plain-dopes, it is largely a metaphor for what Kornbluth saw around him in his own time. Yet he had a profound affection for lowly, downtrodden people, for stumblebums and gutter folk, and even some salesmen. In part it may have been the fondness of an aficionado, a collector of "characters." But he was not without a good deal of genuine sympathy, especially for those who were caught in situations they barely understood, like the deformed space pilot in "The Altar at Midnight," or for those who understood too well, like the narrator-physicist of the same story and the young genius of "Gomez." Better remembered, perhaps, are his treatments of workaday grifters and con-artists, like Honest John Barlow of "Morons" or the sly narrator of "1955"—people who have no sympathy at all, and who, however clever, always get the axe at the finale. If Kornbluth sometimes admired their grit and savvy, he was also moved to exact revenge on behalf of their victims.

Though he is often viewed as a commentator on the social fabric, and the various forms of human folly, there is more to Kornbluth than the wary futurologist, the wry chronicler of crafty deals ("1955," "Time Bum"), or even the compassionate observer of human detritus ("The Little Black Bag," "The Altar at Midnight"). And this something more is his sense of the unknown and the unknowable, the hidden layers of reality, the levels of illusion enveloping the world (whether social or metaphysical). Many of his most notable, most intensely realized stories hover somewhere between strict fantasy and strictest science fiction. Both "The Words of Guru" and "Kazam Collects" are outright fantasies, of the sort that "pierce the veil" of ordinary sense, and yet they have the resolute authority, the absolute conviction, of things seen and heard and done. They begin in fairly typical urban settings, enticing the reader through unsuspected realms to arrive at states of being that can only be termed ineffable and exalted, the one horrific, the other all beauty and benevolence. "The Silly Season," a tensely told shocker, provides a contest between a series of uncanny but rather palpable illusions and the normalizing nature of daily journalism. "The Cosmic Expense Account" sets the mundane and extraordinary in adjacent territories, as a crippling "cosmic-harmony" engulfs eastern Pennsylvania. And in the jocose "Virginia," our furtive public mythologies about the Secret Masterdom of the Super Rich are made the binding private reality of an heir to fortune. Characteristically, Kornbluth does not simply mention, but actually offers a short tour of, the Museum of Suppressed Inventions.

These tales center on initiation into various kinds of arcane knowledge; and "Guru" and "Kazam" focus on persons of a special nature, born to acquire a special sort of knowledge, and power. This striving after knowledge is at the core of Kornbluth's most elusive and provocative piece of writing, "The Last Man Left in the Bar." Published very late in his career (1957), this short but densely packed work distills all his previous concerns with kinds and visions of reality, and it is a *tour de force* of oblique, kaleidoscopic narrative worthy of the wildest "experiments" of the New Wave. It portrays the psychological aftermath of an apparent momentary transposition of worlds. It mingles drunken uncertainties and digressions with the haunting obscurities of a poorly apprehended experience. In a landscape of shifting knowledge, the one constant is that its technical-protagonist never does learn the answers, the wherefores of his predicament. His passionate desire to *know* is countered by the obstinate complexity of the universe, and by wilful creatures who are absorbed in their own very separate interests and imperatives.

—Alex Eisenstein

---

**KOTZWINKLE, William.** American. Born in Scranton, Pennsylvania, 22 November 1938. Educated at Rider College, Lawrenceville, New Jersey; Pennsylvania State University, University Park. Married Elizabeth Gundy in 1970. Cook, Le Figaro Cafe, New York City, 1963; wrote for tabloid newspaper, mid-1960's. Lived in New York 1957–70, New Brunswick, Canada, 1970–83, and Maine since 1983. Recipient: Bread Loaf Conference Scholarship; World Fantasy award, 1977. Address: c/o Putnam's, 200 Madison Avenue, New York, New York 10016, U.S.A.

### Science-Fiction Publications

#### Novels

*Hermes 3000*. New York, Pantheon, 1972.
*Doctor Rat*. New York, Knopf, and Henley-on-Thames, Oxfordshire, Ellis, 1976.
*E.T., The Extra-Terrestrial* (novelization of screenplay). New York, Putnam, and London, Barker, 1982.
*Superman III* (novelization of screenplay). New York, Warner, and London, Arrow, 1983.
*E.T.: The Book of the Green Planet*. New York, Berkley, 1985.

#### Short Stories

*Jewell of the Moon*. New York, Putnam, 1985.
*The Hot Jazz Trio*. Boston, Houghton Mifflin, 1989.

### Other Publications

#### Novels

*The Fan Man*. New York, Avon, and Henley-on-Thames, Oxfordshire, Ellis, 1974.
*Night-Book*. New York, Avon, 1974.
*Swimmer in the Secret Sea*. New York, Avon, 1975; Henley-on-Thames, Oxfordshire, Ellis, 1976.
*Fata Morgana*. New York, Knopf, and London, Hutchinson, 1977.
*Herr Nightingale and the Satin Woman*. New York, Knopf, 1978; London, Hutchinson, 1979.
*Jack in the Box*. New York, Putnam, 1980; London, Abacus, 1981; as *Book of Love*, Boston, Houghton Mifflin, 1990.
*Christmas at Fontaine's*. New York, Putnam, 1982; London, Deutsch, 1983.
*Queen of Swords*. New York, Putnam, and London, Deutsch, 1984.
*The Exile*. New York, Seymour Lawrence, and London, Bodley Head, 1987.
*The Midnight Examiner*. Boston, Houghton Mifflin, 1989.

#### Short Stories

*Elephant Bangs Train*. New York, Pantheon, and London, Faber, 1971.

*Hearts of Wood and Other Timeless Tales.* Boston, Godine, 1986.

Other (for children)

*The Fireman.* New York, Pantheon, 1969.
*The Ship That Came Down the Gutter.* New York, Pantheon, 1970; Kingswood, Surrey, World's Work, 1976.
*Elephant Boy: A Story of the Stone Age.* New York, Farrar Straus, 1970.
*The Day the Gang Got Rich.* New York, Viking Press, 1970.
*The Oldest Man and Other Timeless Stories.* New York, Pantheon, 1971.
*Return of Crazy Horse.* New York, Farrar Straus, 1971.
*The Supreme, Superb, Exalted, and Delightful, One and Only Magic Building.* New York, Farrar Straus, 1973.
*Up the Alley with Jack and Joe.* New York, Macmillan, 1974.
*The Leopard's Tooth.* Boston, Houghton Mifflin, 1976.
*The Ant Who Took Away Time.* New York, Doubleday, 1978.
*Dream of Dark Harbor.* New York, Doubleday, 1979.
*The Nap Master.* New York, Harcourt Brace, 1979.
*The Extra Terrestrial Storybook.* New York, Putnam, 1982.
*Great World Circus.* New York, Putnam, 1983.
*Trouble in Bugland: A Collection of Inspector Mantis Mysteries.* Boston, Godine, 1983.
*The World Is Big and I'm So Small.* New York, Crown, 1986.
*The Empty Notebook.* Boston, Godine, 1990.

* * *

William Kotzwinkle is best known to science fiction readers as the author of *Superman III*—the novelization of the movie—and the two *E.T.* books.

*E.T.: The Extra-Terrestrial* is an excellent novelization of Melissa Mathison's screenplay. Kotzwinkle's novelization became a bestselling paperback selling more than three million copies. It's follow-up, *E.T.: The Book of the Green Planet,* is based on a story by director Stephen Spielberg. Kotzwinkle makes E.T.'s planet come alive with bizarre characters like E.T.'s sidekick, Flopglopple, and vegetable creatures like the jumpums. Kotzwinkle's writing brings humor to the story, especially in E. T.'s communication with Elliot, who's becoming a typical teenager.

Kotzwinkle has published over 30 books, including novels, short story collections, children's books, poetry, and plays. His range extends from the wild humor of his most popular short story collection, *Elephant Bangs Train,* to the erotic juxtapositioning in *Night-Book,* to the moving autobiographical novel about the death of Kotzwinkle's child in *Swimmer in the Secret Sea.*

In 1977, Kotzwinkle won the World Fantasy award for *Doctor Rat,* a fable exposing human cruelty towards animals years before the rise of the animal rights movement. Much of Kotzwinkle's work deals in fantasy. His latest collection of stories, *The Hot Jazz Trio,* features strange and bizarre situations. For example, in the collection's lead story set in 1920's Paris, "Django Reinhardt Played the Blues," a magician's assistant gets lost in another dimension. Leading the rescue party into the Vanishing Box is Django Reinhardt, legendary Belgian jazz-blues guitarist, who is joined by Picasso and Jean Cocteau. Another story in the collection, "Boxcar Blues," features two circus performers who flee Death with a group a hoboes.

On occasion, Kotzwinkle's work can be weirdly real. Based on his 1960's experience as an editor-writer for a supermarket tabloid, *The Midnight Examiner* is the story of tabloid editor Howard Halliday's encounter with Mafia revenge. The farcical plot only serves as a vehicle for Kotzwinkle to score points on the world of tabloids in his humorous style.

More seriously, Kotzwinkle mixes realism and fantasy in *The Exile.* David Caspian, a Hollywood actor, finds himself transported back to Nazi Germany. He becomes a black marketeer as Kotzwinkle blends contemporary L.A. with Hitler's Germany. The juxtaposition of realities illustrates Kotzwinkle's point that everyone is a mixture of opposites.

Other titles, like *The Fan Man* and *Hermes 3000* are cult novels. Horse Badorties, the hippie con-man hero of *The Fan Man,* attracts readers because among all Kotzwinkle's characters he is the freest spirit.

*Fata Morgana* is a detective story set in Paris in 1861. Inspector Picard investigates the mysterious Ric Lazare and his fortune-telling machine. When Picard has his own fortune read, the story spins into the realm of illusion. *Herr Nightingale and the Satin Woman* is an exercise in murky surrealism. *Christmas at Fontaine's* is based on Kotzwinkle's experience playing Santa at E.J. Korvette's in the 1960's. *Queen of Swords* is a novel based on magic and tarot.

Kotzwinkle's astonishing breadth of subjects, characters, situations, and themes keeps his work fresh and innovative.

—George Kelley

---

**KUBE-McDOWELL, Michael P(aul).** Also writes as Michael Hudson. American. Born in Philadelphia, 29 August 1954. Educated at Michigan State University, East Lansing, B.A. in education 1976; Indiana University, Bloomington, M.S. in education 1981. Married Karla Jane Kube in 1975 (divorced 1987); one son. Science and math teacher in public schools in Middlebury, Indiana, 1976–83; instructor, Miles Laboratories, Elkhart, Indiana, 1978–80; correspondent, *Truth,* Elkhart, 1982–84; instructor, Goshen College, Goshen, Indiana, 1984–85; screenwriter, Laurel T.V Inc., New York, 1985–86; instructor, Clarion SF Workshop, East Lansing, Michigan, 1990. Since 1981, book reviewer for South Bend *Tribune,* Indiana, and since 1983, full-time writer. Agent: Russell Galen, Scott Meredith Literary Agency, 845 Third Avenue, New York, New York 10022. Address: P.O. Box 22066, Lansing, Michigan, 48909-2066, U.S.A.

SCIENCE-FICTION PUBLICATIONS

Novels (series: Trigon Disunity)

*After the Flames* (novella), with Robert Silverberg and Norman Spinrad. New York, Baen, 1985.
The Trigon Disunity:
*Emprise.* New York, Berkley, 1985; London, Legend, 1988.
*Enigma.* New York, Berkley, 1986; London, Legend, 1988.
*Empery.* New York, Berkley, 1987; London, Legend, 1988.
*Isaac Asimov's Robot City: Odyssey.* New York, Ace, 1987; London, Orbit, 1988.
*Thieves of Light* (as Michael Hudson). New York, Berkley, 1987.
*Alternities.* New York, Ace, 1988; London, Sphere, 1989.
*The Quiet Pools.* New York, Ace, 1990.

OTHER PUBLICATIONS

Plays

Television Plays: "Slippage," 1984, "Lifebomb," 1985, "Effect and Cause," 1985, and "The Bitterest Pill," 1986, all in the *Tales from the Darkside* series.

*

Michael P. Kube-McDowell comments:

I once believed that I wrote science fiction to cheat time. In more than one interview, I've asserted that the human species has an interesting—and possibly long—future ahead of it, and that writing SF allowed me to play in tomorrows I won't live to see.

That's still arguably true, and probably accounts in part for the human-focused, Earth-based, near-future emphasis of most of my fiction. But I've come to realize that there's more to it than that.

In retrospect, I've become aware that my writing has become part of my exploration of two basic questions: What is the nature of the universe we inhabit? And, why do we humans do what we do?

These are live questions of continuing interest, driving not only scientific but mystical inquiry, and firmly linked to the pains, frustrations, and joys of being alive. None of us is in possession of final and ultimate answers. (In my experience, those who believe they are prove to have simply cut off their inquiry too soon.)

We're playing the blindfold-and-elephant game, and each of us has a different piece of the elephant—a unique set of inherited and experiential clues. In a sense, each new story, each successive novel, is my way of calling out to the rest of you, "Here's how it looks to me at the moment. . . ."

But "Answering Big Questions" is too grand a pretension and too great a responsibility for everyday storytelling, because a theme does not a story make. A novel is about life as the writer sees it, and ordinary people as the writer understands them. The writer ought not sit down at the keyboard to confess, or to invent, but to give witness. And a novel ought not be an essay, or a tract, but a story. Not my story. *Their* story.

Who are "they"? The people who are caught in the pincers—the characters. When I begin work on a novel, I have to know where it ends, and through whose eyes I can see it: the moment, the feeling, sometimes the exact words. When I've found a place where I can stand to be silent witness to the turns, travails and small triumphs of their lives, then, and only then, am I ready to start writing.

As I write, I have a much stronger sense of watching than creating: I find myself sorting out what must have happened, rather than "making it up." The only decision that seems to belong to me is where to begin telling the story. Two points, beginning and ending, define a line, but stories, like lives, are not straight lines. Past Chapter One, I'm embarked on a journey of discovery, learning as I go how the beginning and the ending are connected.

Because of that, it strikes me that each new fiction isn't really "about" its plot, or the characters, or the setting, or the theme, or the deconstructed analysis of its literary entrails. It's about a place I found to stand, and something I saw from there, and the feelings and thoughts that experience evoked in me. Each work, in its totality, is nothing more or less than my carefully worded invitation to come and stand where I stood, and experience it for yourself.

As best as I can tell with this blindfold on, that's what fiction is all about.

* * *

Michael P. Kube-McDowell emerged in the 1980's as one of the best new hard science-fiction writers. His best work may be categorized as "cosmic science fiction," a subgenre characterized by a cosmic sense of wonder about the physical universe, in stories which often span great distances of space and time, and may be best exemplified by the work of Arthur C. Clarke.

Kube-McDowell's career has followed a pattern quite common in the science-fiction field. In the early 1980's, he began to build a reputation for his short fiction. His first story, "The Inevitable Conclusion," appeared in *Amazing Stories* in August 1979, and would later prove to be the first of many stories and novels set in his "Trigon Disunity" universe. His fifth published story, "Slac//," a well-constructed puzzle story (that would have been quite at home in *Analog*) about a xenological mission seeking to determine why their first expedition party disappeared and how the disappearance was connected to the relationship between the two primary intelligent species, was chosen as one of the best stories of 1981 by Donald Wollheim in his best-of-the-year volume (*The 1982 Annual World's Best SF*, edited by Donald A. Wollheim, 1982). His 1983 fantasy "Slippage," a quintessential *Twilight Zone* story, was chosen for Karl Edward Wagner's *The Year's Best Horror Stories* (1983), and was subsequently selected by George Romero to be adapted into an episode of the television series, "Tales From the Dark Side" in the 1984–85 season. Kube-McDowell's involvement with television continued between 1985 and 1987 with three teleplays for "Tales From the Darkside." These included an original teleplay, an adaptation of his story "Lifebomb," and an adaptation of a story by Frederik Pohl.

Kube-McDowell proved to be an even more successful writer when he moved to novel length. His first novel, *Emprise*, appeared in 1985, launching his 1000-year "Trigon Disunity" future history. It was critically well received and became a finalist for the Philip K. Dick award. He published two other novels in the "Trigon Disunity" series, *Enigma* (1986) and *Empery* (1987). These three novels share a common universe and future history. In *Emprise*, humanity sends out a spaceship to meet alien visitors to our Solar System, only to find that the visitors are human. In *Enigma*, the human protagonist is taken by a member of a race of energy-beings into the fabric of space-time where he learns that 70,000 years ago a technological Earth culture colonized other worlds, but was destroyed by a powerful alien race that is about to return. In *Empery*, mankind tries to make a preemptive strike on the aliens before they can again destroy mankind. These novels, like most of Kube-McDowell's science fiction, are often primarily involved in political struggles between various factions of characters.

His next book was *Alternities*, a novel about an alternative version of the U.S. whose leadership knows how to move between various "alternities," which are similar parallel realities (none of which happen to be the one we live in). Political intrigue abounds in this fast-paced science-fiction thriller.

Kube-McDowell's most acclaimed book to date is *The Quiet Pools* (1990), a selection of the Book-of-the-Month Club and a nominee for the Hugo award. It is set in a future Earth faced with over-population and resulting ecological damage. A major project is organized and is working on a second city-sized starship to carry 10,000 men and women to a new life outside our solar system. A covert organization fervently and violently opposes the project, seen by some as mankind's last great hope. This novel posits that the desire of some to explore and move out into new frontiers may be a genetic trait that is absent in some members of our species. The novel imagines this situation leading to a human interstellar diaspora of those humans who have the trait, while those who don't stay on the depleted Earth much as the "quiet pools" sought by salmon after they have laid their eggs and are waiting to die. It is a powerful and moving hypothesis, aimed at the very heart and soul of the doctrine of science fiction.

Kube-McDowell has been an instructor at the Clarion Science Fiction Workshop, and served on the jury for the Nebula award. Outside of science fiction, he is the author of more than 500 nonfiction articles on subjects ranging from space careers to "scientific creationism." His next novel is entitled *The Exile of Ana*, and will appear in 1992. Kube-McDowell promises to continue to develop, and he could be one of the most important hard SF authors in the 1990's.

—D. Douglas Fratz

---

**KURLAND, Michael (Joseph).** Also writes as Jennifer Plum. American. Born in New York City, 1 March 1938. Educated at Hiram College, Ohio, 1955–56; University of Maryland overseas, 1961–62; Columbia University, New York, 1962–63. Served in the United States Army, 1958–62. Married Rebecca Jacobson in 1976. News editor, KPFK-Radio, Los Angeles, 1966; English teacher, Happy Valley School, Ojai, California, 1967; editor, *Crawdaddy*, New York, 1969; also a play director, road manager for a band, advertising copywriter, and ghost writer. Since 1976, editor, Pennyfarthing Press, San Francisco and Berkeley, California. Address: c/o Berkley Publishing Group, 200 Madison Avenue, New York, New York 10016, U.S.A.

SCIENCE-FICTION PUBLICATIONS

Novels

*Ten Years to Doomsday*, with Chester Anderson. New York, Pyramid, 1964.
*The Unicorn Girl*. New York, Pyramid, 1969.
*Transmission Error*. New York, Pyramid, 1970.
*The Whenabouts of Burr*. New York, DAW, 1975.
*Pluribus*. New York, Doubleday, 1975.
*Tomorrow Knight*. New York, DAW, 1976.
*The Princes of Earth* (for children). Nashville, Nelson, 1978.
*The Last President*, with S.W. Barton. New York, Morrow, 1980.
*Psi Hunt*. New York, Berkley, 1980.
*Death by Gaslight*. New York, New American Library, 1982.
*Star Griffin*. New York, Doubleday, 1987.

OTHER PUBLICATIONS

Novels

*Mission: Third Force*. New York, Pyramid, 1967.
*Mission: Tank War*. New York, Pyramid, 1968.
*Mission: Police Action*. New York, Pyramid, 1969.
*A Plague of Spies*. New York, Pyramid, 1969.
*The Secret of Benjamin Square* (as Jennifer Plum). New York, Lancer, 1972.
*The Infernal Device*. New York, New American Library, and London, New English Library, 1979.
*Perchance*. New York, New American Library, 1988.
*Ten Little Wizards* (for young adults). New York, Ace, 1988.
*A Study in Sorcery*. New York, Ace, 1989.
*Button Bright*. New York, Berkley, 1990.

Other

Editor, *The Redward Edward Papers*, by Avram Davidson. New York, Doubleday, 1978.
Editor, *The Best of Avram Davidson*. New York, Doubleday, 1979.
Editor, *First Cycle* (from unfinished manuscript by H. Beam Piper). New York, Ace, 1982.

*

Michael Kurland comments:
I try to entertain.

* * *

Michael Kurland's first two science-fiction novels were written in conjunction with Chester Anderson. The first, a conventional collaboration, was *Ten Years to Doomsday*, a lightweight and readable book concerned with the need for an entire planet to change from a feudal/pre-technological to a fully scientific/industrial state in a decade to stave off a planned invasion. Kurland has stated that this book was written as a parody of the works of Poul Anderson. Either as parody or in its own right, the book is fairly successful. The second novel has a more complicated history. When Anderson wrote his popular novel *The Butterfly Kid*, he included himself, Kurland, and a third friend, Tom Waters, as characters. Anderson's novel imposes a comedic alien-invasion theme upon the bohemian East Village milieu of the 1960's with hilarious results. Kurland's *The Unicorn Girl* is a sequel, continuing its themes and characters, though it is generally regarded as less successful. (Waters added a third book to the series, *The Probability Pad*.)

Kurland's first fully solo novel was *Transmission Error*. In this book he established a protagonist of generally likeable nature, his traits including considerable wit and resourcefulness, but also a feckless ability to get himself into insoluble dilemmas. He is accidentally transported to an alien planet and threatened with a life of slavery. He escapes this situation and plunges into a series of similarly unresolved problems.

By this point the general pattern of Kurland's books had become clear. Kurland is highly adept at creating societies which are compellingly believable, and populating them with vivid and sympathetic characters. His style is lively, warm, and highly informal. His stories are told with rapidity of pace and great variety of setting and incident. Their major flaw is a failure—whether by the author or his protagonist—to grapple with and satisfactorily resolve problems. The "solutions" offered are almost invariably flight rather than confrontation.

This pattern holds through Kurland's later novels, although their basic premises are wholly different from one another. *The Whenabouts of Burr* is a chase-novel proceeding through multiple parallel worlds. *Pluribus*, probably Kurland's most successful novel in the genre, takes place in a semi-barbaric future United States. The book abounds in vivid imagery, including an unforgettable scene of the protagonist, arrested for some local infraction, being removed in a standard "black-and-white" California Highway Patrol cruiser—drawn by a team of horses! *Tomorrow Knight* (the title is indicative of Kurland's love for puns and other word-play) takes place on a planet divided, checker-board fashion, into hundreds of miniature stage-set societies. Yet in all the books, the general pattern of insoluble problem and flight persists.

*The Princes of Earth* is favorably comparable to standard Heinlein juveniles, containing the usual Kurland mix of convincing future societies, sympathetic characters, intriguing problem-situations, and rapid transfer from problem to problem. There is also an excellent infusion of satire, most notably a hilarious parody of the Church of Scientology. Although no further books in the series have yet appeared. *The Princes of Earth* is clearly intended as the opening volume of a series.

While Michael Kurland has seldom appeared to be a prolific author, his protracted and usually steady production of science fiction (and other works) has permitted him to accumulate a body of some 20 novels and other books. He boasted a longtime friendship with the late Randall Garrett, and following Garrett's death Kurland wrote a novel, *Star Griffin*, that had originally been intended as a collaboration between himself and Garrett. An interplanetary tale, the book shows Garrett's presence and stands as a fitting memorial to him. In similar fashion, Kurland expanded, revised, and prepared for publication *First Cycle*, a novel left in rough form by H. Beam Piper at the time of his death.

—Richard A. Lupoff

---

**KURTZ, Katherine.** American. Born in Coral Gables, Florida, 18 October 1944. Educated at University of Miami, Coral Gables, B.S. in chemistry 1966; University of California, Los Angeles, M.A. in history 1971. Married Scott Roderick MacMillan in 1983; one son. Senior training technician, Los Angeles Police Department, 1969–81. Since 1981, full-time writer. Agent: Russell Galen, Scott Meredith Literary Agency, 845 Third Avenue, New York, New York 10022, U.S.A. Address: Holybrooke Hall, Bray, County Wicklow, Ireland.

SCIENCE-FICTION PUBLICATIONS

Novels (series: Legends of Saint Camber; Chronicles of the Deryni; Heirs of Saint Camber; Histories of King Kelson)

*Deryni Rising*. New York, Ballantine, 1970; London, Pan-Ballantine, 1973.
*Deryni Checkmate*. New York, Ballantine, 1972; London, Pan-Ballantine, 1973.
*High Deryni*. New York, Ballantine, 1973; London, Century, 1985.
*Camber of Culdi*. New York, Ballantine, 1976; London, Century, 1985.
*Saint Camber*. New York, Ballantine, 1978; London, Century, 1985.
*Camber the Heretic*. New York, Ballantine, 1981; London, Century, 1987.
*The Bishop's Heir* (King Kelson). New York, Ballantine, and London, Century, 1984.
*The King's Justice* (King Kelson). New York, Ballantine, 1985; London, Arrow, 1986.
*The Legacy of Lehr*. New York, Walker, 1986; London, Century, 1988.
*Quest for Saint Camber* (King Kelson). New York, Ballantine, 1986; London, Century, 1987.
*The Harrowing of Gwynedd* (Heirs of Saint Camber). New York, Ballantine, and London, Century, 1989.
*The Adept*, with Deborah Turner Harris. New York, Berkley, 1991.

Short Stories

*The Deryni Archives*. New York, Ballantine, 1986.

OTHER PUBLICATIONS

Novel

*Lammas Night*. New York, Ballantine, 1983; London, Severn House, 1986.

Other

*Deryni Magic: A Grimoire*. New York, Ballantine, 1990.

* * *

In the beginning, as related by the author in *The Deryni Archives* and elsewhere, was an especially vivid dream which occurred on the night of October 11, 1964. This scenario was expanded into a novelette, "Lords of Sorandor," which in turn was reworked into the climactic section of Kurtz's first novel, *Deryni Rising*.

These brief journeyman efforts contain all the kernels of Kurtz's later work. The author has spent much of her creative life developing an alternate fantasy world centered on the medieval state of Gwynedd, the central kingdom of an area patterned roughly after tenth-to-twelfth-century England, Scotland, and Wales (in our own world, Gwynedd was an ancient name for Northern Wales). Although we can see rough similarities to medieval Britain—in language, culture, religion, and politics—there are equally striking differences, some more obvious than others.

Gwynedd and its neighbors are peopled by both humans and Deryni; the latter are outwardly similar to man, but have the innate ability to perform acts which their fellow humans regard as magical. These psychic talents vary considerably from individual to individual, and may be developed further with appropriate training. The history of Gwynedd has been marred by a series of conflicts between the two races, the Deryni having controlled Gwynedd for only a small portion of its history, while ruling Torenth, a large neighboring kingdom, from its inception. Such clashes have been exacerbated by lack of empathy between the two groups, by arrogance on the part of the Deryni, and by outright racial hatred and envy on the human side, with concommitant persecutions and pogroms of the Deryni minority.

Kurtz's geography also varies significantly from the Europe we know, and these differences have themselves altered the political dynamic of the region. Unlike Britain, for example, Gwynedd is joined directly to the mainland; without the benefit of a channel buffer, it is subject to invasion from hostile neighbors. The Mediterranean Sea does not seem to exist in this world, although references are made at several points to a "Holy Land" where Christ was born, preached, and martyred, much as in our own world. We can also see rough equivalents to the Moors, Gauls, and other ethnic groups from earth, but no other obvious political, historical, or geographical correspondences with real-life medieval Europe.

The religious structure of Kurtz's world also demonstrates subtle but significant differences from that of medieval Europe, generally following the formulas and tenets of the Catholic Church, but being administratively organized somewhat along the lines of our own world's Eastern Orthodoxy. Thus, each major state contains its own autocephalous religious body, governed by an Archbishop chosen and supported by a ruling Synod. There is no "Pope" or central Church authority (indeed, no "Rome") in Kurtz's "Europe," although Latin remains the official Church language, and the celebration of the mass its key ritual. Magical rituals may occasionally be used in Church functions, when sanctioned by Church and state.

Kurtz has developed her world in four sets of trilogies and nine short stories, eight of them collected in *The Deryni Archives.* The Chronicles of the Deryni, comprising *Deryni Rising, Deryni Checkmate*, and *High Deryni*, relate the rise to power of King Kelson Haldane, who succeeds to the throne of Gwynedd at the age of 14 when his father is assassinated. The Haldanes, though they are not Deryni, have the ability to exercise similar powers when these have been activated through a series of rituals. Kelson represents the new man, a merger of the best of both strains into one blood line, since his mother is Deryni (a fact unknown to herself). Kelson defeats two representatives of the Festil dynasty, consolidates his position as King, and begins exploring his arcane heritage.

The Legends of Camber of Culdi, comprising *Camber of Culdi, Saint Camber*, and *Camber the Heretic*, takes place 200 years earlier, at a time when Deryni monarchs ruled Gwynedd. Camber, the Deryni Earl of Culdi, proves instrumental in locating the last Haldane heir, overthrowing the Deryni tyrant, and restoring King Cinhil to his throne. The restoration creates a backlash against the Deryni minority, resulting in increasingly harsh repressions and massacres, as the conservative human bishops and peers assume the reigns of power.

The Histories of King Kelson, including *The Bishop's Heir, The King's Justice*, and *The Quest for Saint Camber*, returns to the time of Kelson, picking up where the first set left off. At age 18, Kelson must face a revolt in the provinces, a marriage of convenience, and further unrest at home, as the surviving conservatives attempt to oust his government. He also faces treachery from within his own family, and must ultimately learn the art of statesmanship—and when to exercise it.

The Heirs of Saint Camber, comprising *The Harrowing of Gwynedd* (and several as yet unpublished works), returns to earlier times. The death of King Cinhil Haldane brings the forces of repression to the fore, and the few remaining Deryni must go underground to protect the remnants of their persecuted race.

Politics and religion are inextricably intertwined in Kurtz's creation, as they were in our own history, with state and church constantly vying with each other and the Deryni minority for power and authority. The key players of these historical fantasies recognize that the price of failure is disgrace—or more likely death. What sustains them is faith, an abiding and sincere belief in God, his Church, the King, and friends and family as *the* key structures of society. Even those painted on Kurtz's tableaux as evil or manipulative largely perceive themselves as acting in the best interests of Church or state or family; even peripheral characters are carefully drawn in tones of gray, not splotches of black and white. Kurtz champions intelligence, duty, sensitivity, love, faith, truth, all the finer virtues. Man makes of his world what he will, she seems to be saying, a heaven or a hell, a condition which clearly presages what he (or she) will become in the after-life.

—Robert Reginald

---

**KUTTNER, Henry. Also wrote as Lewis Padgett.** American. Born in Los Angeles, California, 7 April 1915. Educated at the University of Southern California, Los Angeles, B.A. 1954. Served in the United States Army Medical Corps during World War II. Married C.L. Moore, *q.v.*, in 1940; died 1988; most of his subsequent work was written with her, though not always acknowledged. Worked briefly for a literary agency, Los Angeles; freelance writer. *Died 3 February 1958.*

SCIENCE-FICTION PUBLICATIONS

Novels

*Fury*, with C.L. Moore. New York, Grosset and Dunlap, 1950; London, Dobson, 1954; as *Destination Infinity*, New York, Avon, 1958.
*Earth's Last Citadel*, with C.L. Moore. New York, Ace, 1964.
*Valley of the Flame*, with C.L. Moore. New York, Ace, 1964.
*The Time Axis*, with C.L. Moore. New York, Ace, 1965.
*The Dark World*, with C.L. Moore. New York, Ace, 1965; London, Mayflower, 1966.
*Dr. Cyclops*, with others. New York, Popular Library, 1967.
*The Creature from Beyond Infinity*. New York, Popular Library, 1968.
*The Mask of Circe*, with C.L. Moore. New York, Ace, 1971.
*The Time Trap*, in *Evil Earths*, edited by Brian Aldiss. London, Futura, 1976.

Novels as Lewis Padgett, with C.L. Moore

*Tomorrow and Tomorrow, and The Fairy Chessmen*. New York, Gnome Press, 1951; as *Tomorrow and Tomorrow* and *The Far Reality*, London, Consul., 2 vols., 1963; *The Fairy Chessmen* published as *Chessboard Planet*, New York, Galaxy, 1956.
*Well of the Worlds*. New York, Galaxy, 1953.
*Beyond Earth's Gates*. New York, Ace, 1954.

Short Stories

*Ahead of Time*. New York, Ballantine, 1953; London, Weidenfeld and Nicolson, 1954.
*Remember Tomorrow*. Sydney, American Science Fiction, 1954.
*Way of the Gods*. Sydney, American Science Fiction, 1954.
*No Boundaries*, with C.L. Moore. New York, Ballantine, 1955; London, Consul, 1961.
*As You Were*. Sydney, American Science Fiction, 1955.
*Sword of Tomorrow*. Sydney, American Science Fiction, 1955.
*Bypass to Otherness*. New York, Ballantine, 1961; London, Consul, 1963.
*Return to Otherness*. New York, Ballantine, 1962; London, Mayflower, 1965.
*The Best of Kuttner*. London, Mayflower, 2 vols., 1965–66.
*The Best of Henry Kuttner*. New York, Doubleday, 1975.
*Clash by Night and Other Stories*, with C.L. Moore, edited by Peter Pinto. London, Hamlyn, 1980.
*Chessboard Planet and Other Stories*, with C.L. Moore, London, Hamlyn, 1983.
*Elak of Atlantis*. New York, Gryphon, 1985.

Short Stories as Lewis Padgett, with C.L. Moore

*A Gnome There Was.* New York, Simon and Schuster, 1950.
*Robots Have No Tails* (by Kuttner alone). New York, Gnome Press, 1952; as *The Proud Robot: The Complete Galloway Gallegher Stories* (as Henry Kuttner), London, Hamlyn, 1983.
*Mutant.* New York, Gnome Press, 1953; London, Weidenfeld and Nicolson, 1954.
*Line to Tomorrow.* New York, Bantam, 1954.

OTHER PUBLICATIONS

Novels

*The Brass Ring* (as Lewis Padgett, with C.L. Moore). New York, Duell, 1946; London, Sampson Low, 1947; as *Murder in Brass*, New York, Bantam, 1947.
*The Day He Died* (as Lewis Padgett, with C.L. Moore). New York, Duell, 1947.
*Man Drowning.* New York, Harper, 1952; London, New English Library, 1961.
*The Murder of Ann Avery.* New York, Permabooks, 1956.
*The Murder of Eleanor Pope.* New York, Permabooks, 1956.
*Murder of a Mistress.* New York, Permabooks, 1957.
*Murder of a Wife.* New York, Permabooks, 1958.

*

Bibliography: by Donald H. Tuck, in *Henry Kuttner: A Memorial Symposium* edited by Karen Anderson, Berkeley, California, Sevagram, 1958.

* * *

In reviewing Henry Kuttner's collection *Ahead of Time*, Anthony Boucher characterized the author as "one of SF's most literate and intelligent storytellers." Other adjectives could have been added to the list: prolific, versatile, popular. There have, it is true, been periodic dry spells when editors and readers have seemed to forget the rich legacy of Kuttner's fiction, but the stories have always been re-discovered and brought back into print. There is every reason to believe that his best work will last as long as science fiction is read.

For many years the scope and volume of Kuttner's writing were partially camouflaged by the many bylines under which his stories appeared. Initially the pen-names were adopted for the usual commercial reasons: to differentiate among various types of story or to disguise the fact that more than one story on a contents page was by the same author. But Kuttner, both alone and with his wife C.L. Moore, seemed to take an active delight in the creation of new pseudonyms, even on two occasions going so far as to publish fictional "autobiographies" for an alter ego: Keith Hammond in *Startling Stories*, March 1946 (an Eurasian antiquarian with sixteen cats), and C.H. Liddell in *Planet Stories*, November 1950. As one after another of the Kuttner/Moore pseudonyms was revealed, a phenomenon arose which was sometimes called the "Kuttner Syndrome": the conviction that *any*-promising new name on the SF scene had to be yet another Kuttner pen-name. (One of the victims of this assumption was Jack Vance, who was identified by the editor T.E. Dikty in 1950 as a Kuttner pseudonym.) The original choice of pseudonyms for various stories has by now become clouded through numerous reprintings with altered bylines.

Kuttner's first story, "The Graveyard Rats," a superbly grisly horror story in the Lovecraft mode, appeared in *Weird Tales.* Kuttner continued to write for *Weird Tales*, but at the same time he became a prolific contributor to other pulp magazines of many types, including mystery, detective, western, adventure, "spicy," and South Sea tales. His first long story was "The Time Trap" (*Marvel Science Stories*), called "a marvellous gaudy melodrama" by Brian Aldiss. Kuttner had been a member of H.P. Lovecraft's circle of correspondents, and had met other members of that group, such as Robert Bloch, Fritz Leiber, and E. Hoffmann Price. Kuttner and Bloch collaborated on a few stories. Kuttner also collaborated with Arthur K. Barnes on two stories in their Pete Manx series. Manx was a carnival barker whose mind was projected back in time into the bodies of various inhabitants of ancient Rome, Egypt, Baghdad, and other historical or legendary locales, where he must use his innate cunning to survive. The series was carried on alternately by Kuttner and Barnes from 1939 to 1944.

Another Lovecraft correspondent and well-known *Weird Tales* writer whom Kuttner met was Catherine L. Moore. Kuttner and Moore were married on June 7, 1940, in New York, where Kuttner had moved in order to be close to his magazine markets. Kuttner and Moore had collaborated on one story in 1937, but it was not until after their marriage that their remarkable writing partnership developed. Kuttner stated on several occasions that almost all of his writing since the marriage, regardless of byline, was to some extent a collaboration with his wife; however, the degree and method of collaboration varied widely. Some stories were almost pure Kuttner, with only minor contributions from Moore, while for others the reverse was true; but on a large number of stories the two partners were able to blend their ideas and styles so well that one of them could drop a story in mid-scene and the other could pick it up, with scarcely a seam showing in the final product. While taking part fully in the collaborative works, C.L. Moore also continued to write her own stories.

The Lewis Padgett stories, taken as a whole, form a body of work of which any writer could be proud, and if Kuttner and Moore had done no other writing in the science fiction field, their reputations would still be secure on the basis of these stories. Fritz Leiber (in *Henry Kuttner: A Memorial Symposium*, 1958) identified three themes which recur in Kuttner's science fiction: the madman from the future, wacky robots, and wonder children. All of these are present in the Padgett stories. The Padgett treatment of robots, in particular, is as distinctive as that of any writer in the field. One of the best-known, "The Twonky," is concerned with the effect on a young married couple of a device which looks like a console radio, but is actually a robot designed to enforce its own views of proper behavior. Several of the Padgett stories were about the odd inventions of Gallegher, a scientist who can invent things only while drunk, and when sober, can never remember what the inventions are for. Told in a style frankly borrowed from Thorne Smith, the Gallegher stories are meticulously logical SF puzzles cast as wacky comedies. Five were reprinted as *Robots Have No Tails.* The deservedly famous "Mimsy Were the Borogoves" is about educational toys from the future which have a disastrous effect on a present-day family. Other Lewis Padgett stories include the Baldy series (*Mutant*)—about telepathic mutants who must struggle for survival against the intolerance of their normal neighbors and against irrational renegades in their own ranks, a theme clearly taken from A.E. van Vogt's *Slan*—and "The Fairy Chessmen" (with its celebrated opening line, "The doorknob opened a blue eye and looked at him") and "Tomorrow and Tomorrow," complicated tales of post-Atomic intrigue and alternate futures.

One of C.L. Moore's works from the 1940's was "Clash by Night," a moody, emotion-laden story of the Free Companies, the mercenaries of the feuding undersea Keeps on Venus in the

25th century. The Kuttners returned to this scene with the novel *Fury*, the story of Sam Harker, ruthless and driven by forces of which he was not fully aware, the one man who could liberate humanity from its stagnant undersea existence and push it into conquering the planet's savage surface. Although published as by Lawrence O'Donnell, the story was mostly Kuttner's. C.L. Moore stated in her introduction to the Lancer reprint: "*Fury* was written by about one and an eighth persons. . . . I wrote comparatively little of the copy. The idea was basically Hank's and I didn't identify very strongly with it." She also pointed out that the novel deals with "the two recurring themes which emerge quite explicitly in nearly everything we wrote. Hank's basic statement was something like, 'Authority is dangerous and I will never submit to it.' Mine was, 'The most treacherous thing in life is love.' " *Fury* is the best, and best-known, of Kuttner's long stories. Other long works include a series of nine science-fantasy novels, many of them in the romantic/tragic mode of A. Merritt, written between 1943 and 1952, including *Earth's Last Citadel, Valley of the Flame, Beyond Earth's Gates*, and *Well of the Worlds.* Typical shorter works in the same style are "I Am Eden" (December 1946) and "Way of the Gods" (April 1947), both in *Thrilling Wonder Stories.* In the early 1950's the volume of new Kuttner-Moore stories decreased. Both Kuttner and Moore felt written-out in science fiction, although such stories as "Home There's No Returning" and "Two-Handed Engine" (both in *No Boundaries*) belied this claim.

Henry Kuttner has sometimes been criticized as a literary mimic who spent his energies speaking in other people's voices. He did, in fact, speak in many voices, but they were all his own. His borrowings, whether of style or of theme, were all filtered through his own sensibility, and emerged transmuted. In all of his best work there is clear evidence of a highly individual mind at work. Perhaps his most personal contribution to science fiction was the fusion of humour and logic which first emerged fully in the Gallegher stories. The same blend was also evident in the stories of the Hogbens, a family of mutant hillbillies, and in "The Ego Machine," probably his best "wacky robot" story. Through his stories and through his influence on other writers—Ray Bradbury, Leigh Brackett, and Richard Matheson have all acknowledged his guidance—Kuttner left an indelible mark on the science-fiction field. Without his presence, science fiction of the 1940's and 1950's would have been a vastly different and much poorer body of literature.

—R.E. Briney

# L

**LAFFERTY, R(aphael) A(loysius).** American. Born in Neola, Iowa, 7 November 1914. Educated at the University of Tulsa, Oklahoma, 1932–33; International Correspondence School, electrical engineer course, 1939–42. Served in the United States Army, 1942–46: Staff Sergeant. Civil servant, Washington, D.C., 1934–35; clerk, then buyer, Clark Electrical Supply Company, Tulsa, 1936–42, 1946–50, 1952–71. Since 1971, freelance writer. Recipient: Phoenix award, 1971; Hugo award, 1973; Smith award, 1973; World Fantasy Lifetime Achievement award, 1990. Agent: Virginia Kidd, Box 278, Milford, Pennsylvania 18337. Address: 1715 South Trenton Avenue, Tulsa, Oklahoma 74120, U.S.A.

SCIENCE-FICTION PUBLICATIONS

Novels (series: Coscuin Chronicles)

*Past Master.* New York, Ace, and London, Rapp and Whiting, 1968.
*The Reefs of Earth.* New York, Berkley, 1968; London, Dobson, 1970.
*Space Chantey.* New York, Ace, 1968; London, Dobson, 1976.
*Fourth Mansions.* New York, Ace, 1969; London, Dobson, 1972.
*The Flame Is Green* (Coscuin). New York, Walker, 1971.
*The Devil Is Dead* (Coscuin). New York, Avon, 1971; London, Dobson, 1978.
*Arrive at Easterwine.* New York, Scribner, 1971; London, Dobson, 1977.
*Not to Mention Camels.* Indianapolis, Bobbs Merrill, 1976; London, Dobson, 1980.
*Apocalypses.* Los Angeles, Pinnacle, 1977.
*Archipelago* (Coscuin). New Orleans, Manuscript Press, 1979.
*Aurelia.* Norfolk, Virginia, Donning, 1982.
*The Annals of Klepsis.* New York, Ace, 1983.
*Half a Sky* (Coscuin), edited by Ira M. Thornhill. Minneapolis, Corroboree Press, 1984.
*Serpent's Egg.* Bath, Morrigan, 1987.
*East of Laughter.* Bath, Morrigan, 1988.
*Promontory Goats* (novelette). Weston, Ontario, United Mythologies Press, 1988.
*Sinbad: The Thirteenth Voyage.* Cambridge, Massachusetts, 1989.
*The Elliptical Grave.* Weston, Ontario, United Mythologies Press, 1989.
*How Many Miles to Babylon?* (novelette). Weston, Ontario, United Mythologies Press, 1989.
*Episodes of the Argo* (novelette). Weston, Ontario, United Mythologies Press, 1990.

Short Stories

*Nine Hundred Grandmothers.* New York, Ace, 1970; London, Dobson, 1975.
*Strange Doings.* New York, Scribner, 1971.
*Does Anyone Else Have Something Further to Add?* New York, Scribner, 1974; London, Dobson, 1980.
*Funnyfingers, and Cabrito.* Portland, Oregon, Pendragon Press, 1976.
*Horns on Their Heads.* Portland, Oregon, Pendragon Press, 1976.
*Golden Gate and Other Stories,* edited by Ira M. Thornhill. Minneapolis, Corroboree Press, 1983.
*Four Stories.* Polk City, Iowa, Drumm, 1983.
*Heart of Stone Dear and Other Stories.* Polk City, Iowa, Drumm, 1983.
*Snake in His Bosom and Other Stories.* Polk City, Iowa, Drumm, 1983.
*Through Elegant Eyes: Stories of Austro and the Men Who Know Everything,* edited by Ira M. Thornhill. Minneapolis, Corroboree Press, 1983.
*Ringing Changes.* New York, Ace, 1984.
*The Man Who Made Models and Other Stories.* Polk City, Iowa, Drumm, 1984.
*Slippery and Other Stories.* Polk City, Iowa, Drumm, 1985.

OTHER PUBLICATIONS

Novels

*The Fall of Rome.* New York, Doubleday, 1971.
*Okla Hannali.* New York, Doubleday, 1972.

Other

*It's Down the Slippery Cellar Stairs.* Polk City, Iowa, Drumm, 1984.
*The Back Door of History.* Weston, Ontario, United Mythologies Press, 1988.
*Cranky Old Man from Tulsa: Interviews with R.A. Lafferty.* Weston, Ontario, United Mythologies Press, 1990.

*

Bibliography: *An R.A. Lafferty Checklist* by Chris Drumm, Polk City, Iowa, Drumm, 1983.

Manuscript Collection: McFarlin Library, University of Tulsa, Oklahoma.

R.A. Lafferty comments:

My novels, which I wrote myself at great labor, have received more attention than my short stories, which wrote themselves. Nevertheless, the short stories are greatly superior to the novels. In my introductory note to a Dutch version of *Nine Hundred Grandmothers*, I wrote:

"I hold to the true theory that good stories write themselves, or that they are independent and pre-existent entities or beings. . . . These pre-existent stories come to persons, sometimes even to persons of a resonant emptiness; and they make themselves known through these persons. . . . I am very glad that these particular stories first visited me and not someone else.

"There are a few perfect discoveries or encounters that come into every life. Only once I met a mountain lion, quite close, in the wild. She was a discovery of mine. Once only I saw a whale a-blow in the ocean. Once only I saw a big-horn mountain sheep on a high cliff. Once only I saw a pink flamingo in flight. Once only I had an encounter with each of some hundred entities called 'special stories.' These meetings were as quietly thunderous and as unexpected as the discovery of the mountain lion or whale or big-horn sheep or pink flamingo in flight.

"There is an Aladdin cave, lit by 999 lamps, that is the Universal Unconscious . . . that is shared by all persons and creatures. . . . Unsuspected stone doors of the cave are thrown open. There may be funny and fascinating encounters and living spectacles. A few of them may cluster together in a pile of things waiting to be discovered . . . piles of gold, quick ecstasies, intricate delights, entities called 'special stories.'

"A person favored with such discoveries will look for other people to share them with. 'Hey, come see the things I've found,' he'll say. That is what I say now."

However pompous that may sound, it's a statement on the most important part of my work.

* * *

R.A. Lafferty is science fiction's most prodigious teller of tall tales. Offspring of a yarn-spinning family, he writes rather than recites his exhilarating stories but nevertheless retains a primary allegiance to the spoken word. The quintessentially oral character of Lafferty's fiction proclaims itself on every page—each of them sounds like a tape recording transcript. (*Arrive at Easterwine* is actually presented as such.) Rhythmic repetitions of phrases and epithets tie the material together. The author is omnipresent as well as omniscient. He explains and interprets every development, sprinkling his text with epigrams, anecdotes, and invented sources. He even brings himself into stories as a thinly disguised character or as himself in *Through Elegant Eyes.*

Exposition and dialogue overshadow action. Events are more often predicted or recollected than depicted. At shorter lengths, these events are often arranged in artificial patterns reminiscent of folk tales ("Rainbird"), exempla ("The Configuration of the North Shore"), dramatized lectures ("Primary Education of the Camiroi"), or barroom whoppers ("One at a Time"). In longer works, a degree of order is imposed via elaborate symbolism (e.g., the Four Living Creatures in *Fourth Mansions*). However, Lafferty's oral mannerisms hamper him when he mistakes the accumulation of vignettes for the construction of a novel, as in *Arrive at Easterwine* and *The Devil Is Dead*, or uses a novel as an excuse for sermons and diatribes, as in *Aurelia.* (Compare the last with Robert A. Heinlein's *Stranger in a Strange Land.*)

Lafferty's way with characters is as distinctive as his storytelling technique. The floridly eccentric beings who populate his fiction are wholly unrealistic yet totally real. He succeeds best with children, traditionally the most difficult of subjects, because he approaches them with all the sentimentality of a W.C. Fields: "A child's a monster yet uncurled" (*The Reefs of Earth*). However, Lafferty's distaste for adolescents shows up in his Hugo winner "Eurema's Dam."

Besides outrageous youngsters, Lafferty's character troupe comprises: dirty old geniuses and innocent simpletons, ugly but wholesome men and violent but kindly ones, lusty egomaniacs and ascetic manipulators, witch-girls and earthy ladies of muscular charm, plus aliens that are every bit as variegated. They reappear in tale after tale: "though they always preserved the threads of their identities, they did not always have the same names or appearances, and there were not always the same number of them." Favorites get encores. Note the proper names common to *Fourth Mansions, Arrive at Easterwine*, and *The Annals of Klepsis. The Devil Is Dead* trilogy (including *Archipelago, The Devil Is Dead*, and the unpublished *More Than Melchisedech*) continues the historical fantasy Coscuin Chronicles tetralogy and all his extraterrestrial locales appear to exist in the same crazy universe.

So closely do Lafferty's novels resemble each other, they might as well be alternate drafts of the same story. This may reflect his habit of rewriting everything five or six times before the final draft. Elements seem to pass from work to work as easily as sherry through a solera. For instance, Lafferty's plots repeatedly combine conspiracy, romance, and growth. Secret battles between Good and Evil coteries decide the fate of worlds. Bright protagonists are shadowed by dark counterparts. Passionate couples share a yeasty mixture of carnal and spiritual love. Esoteric powers are acquired and used to prepare a chosen hero for an imperial destiny, but the outcome is often ambiguous. *The Flame Is Green* and *Half a Sky*, the first two volumes of the Coscuin Chronicles, demonstrate his scenario best. Against a panorama of 19th-century history, an Irish-born hero and his multinational comrades fight for the Green Revolution against the Red Revolution led by the Devil's own son.

In novels and short stories alike, Lafferty is obsessed with transformation. His version of Nature is incorrigibly protean—space, time, and form are liable to shift at any moment. Changes that nourish the "green-gowing world" must be welcomed whatever they cost. The price can be bloody. Lafferty's pages are speckled with gore, either from hand-to-hand combat or the butchering of animals. Yet the slaughter does not stun because death can be followed by resurrection, mutilation by healing, corruption by redemption. Lafferty knits these components together with allusions to mythology and theology. Biblical precedents influence his handling of topics like kingship, sacrifice, and regeneration. They also shape his use of animal symbols such as snakes. This is especially true of *Fourth Mansions.* Here, a naive young newsman integrates the essence of four primeval forces (Badger/Man, Python/Lion, Toad/Ox, and Falcon/Eagle) and becomes mystical Emperor "by entrenched right" to nudge the world towards the next higher Mansion in the cosmic Castle.

Lafferty also draws on history for inspiration ("Thus We Frustrate Charlemagne"). However, the thought can get lost in the quirkiness of his presentation. For instance, perceptively interpreted data in *Okla Hannali*, his epic of the Choctaw Indians, are so entangled with fable that it is hard to accept anything in the book as real. The same eccentricities abound in *The Fall of Rome.* But the Coscuin Chronicles have a sturdier skeleton of fact under the fluid flesh. The foreign locales of these books have a useful distancing effect—exotic events are more acceptable in exotic settings than in the contemporary American ones in *Fourth Mansions.*

*Past Master*, Lafferty's most popular novel, depends less on factual than on mythicized history. Sir Thomas More is brought forward in time and outward in space to save a diabolical utopia by dying a king's death. Lafferty sends his highly fictionalized 16th-century hero into the 26th-century to dramatize 20th-century spiritual and social issues. Compare this savory scramble of past, future, and present with Ursula K. Le Guin's didactic fable "The Ones Who Walk Away from Omelas."

There is not a bit of science in Lafferty's SF. He justifies his premises on etymological rather than scientific grounds: the name *is* the object. He coins outlandish names, chiefly from Greek and Latin, then interprets them in idiosyncratic ways—the derivations in the Coscuin Chronicles would make Isidore of Seville blush. (His debt to the classics extends to farce as well as philosophy. See *Space Chantey*, his reworking of the *Odyssey. Archipelago* was inspired by the Argosy.)

Bizarre nomenclature does not exhaust Lafferty's rampaging delight in words. He showers his pages with odd poetry. (Who else would dare to rhyme "roses" with "apotheosis" or turn chapter titles into narrative verse as he does in *The Reefs of Earth?*) This verbal virtuosity makes him SF's equivalent of "Flann O'Brien." He loves exaggeration and grotesqueries as well as any Celt before him—surely one of his ancestors had a hand in *The Cattle Raid of Cooley.* But Lafferty appreciates ethnic spice of many flavors: He uses almost as many Amerindian referents as Irish ones ("Narrow Valley") and is fascinated by gypsies ("The Land of the Great Horses").

Lafferty's great subject is the perennial war between Heaven and Hell: "We must kill the Devil afresh every day." This Adversary is no silken Mephisto but a musky blackguard whom healthy young men can drink under the table. Be they ever so pungent, demons like Ifreann in the Coscuin Chronicles and Papa Diabolus in *The Devil Is Dead* are never allowed to steal the show. The heroes and heroines overwhelm them with sheer vitality. Vice can imitate but never match the "overrunning gaiety" of virtue. Making Goodness exciting is a Lafferty specialty.

Although he rode to prominence in the 1960's with the New Wave, Lafferty shows none of the gloom characteristic of that movement. His fiction rings with the high hilarity of love and laughter. Each of his serious works ends on a note of hope, for his is the faith-filled vision of a universe en route to redemption. Despite detours, it keeps gyring upward according to divine plan. "All final answers were given in the beginning. . . . It is our task to grow out until we reach them."

—Sandra Miesel

---

**LAKE, David (John).** Australian. Born of British parents in Bangalore, India, 26 March 1929; became Australian citizen, 1975. Educated at St. Xavier's School, Calcutta, 1940–44; Dauntsey's, Wiltshire, 1945–47; Trinity College, Cambridge, 1949– 53, B.A. 1952, Dip. Ed. 1953, M.A. 1956; University College of North Wales, Bangor, diploma in linguistics 1965; University of Queensland, Brisbane, Ph.D. 1974. Served in the Royal Artillery, 1948–49. Married Marguerite Ivy Ferris in 1964; one daughter. Assistant Master, Sherrardswood School, Welwyn Garden City, Hertfordshire, 1953–58, and St. Albans Boys Grammar School, Hertfordshire, 1958–59; Lecturer in English, Saigon University, 1959–61, for the Thai government, Bangkok, 1961–63, and at Chiswick Polytechnic, London, 1963–64; Reader in English, Jadavpur University, Calcutta, 1965–67. Lecturer, 1967–72, Senior Lecturer, 1973–76, and since 1977, Reader in English, University of Queensland. Recipient: Ditmar award, 1977. Agent: Pamela Buckmaster, Danescroft, Goose Lane, Little Hallingbury, Bishops Stortford, Herts CM22 7RG, England. Address: Department of English, University of Queensland, St. Lucia, Queensland 4072, Australia.

SCIENCE-FICTION PUBLICATIONS

Novels (series: Dextra; Xuma)

*Walkers on the Sky.* New York, DAW, 1976; revised edition, London, Fontana, 1978.
*The Right Hand of Dextra.* New York, DAW, 1977.
*The Wildings of Westron* (Dextra). New York, DAW, 1977.
*The Gods of Xuma; or Barsoom Revisited.* New York, DAW, 1978.
*The Fourth Hemisphere.* Melbourne, Void, 1980.
*The Man Who Loved Morlocks.* Melbourne, Hyland House, 1981.
*The Ring of Truth.* Melbourne, Cory and Collins, 1983; New York, DAW, 1984.
*Warlords of Xuma.* New York, DAW, 1983.

OTHER PUBLICATIONS

Novels

*The Changelings of Chaan.* Melbourne, Hyland House, 1985.
*West of the Moon.* Melbourne, Hyland House, 1988.

Verse

*Hornpipes and Funerals.* Brisbane, University of Queensland Press, 1973.

Other

*John Milton: Paradise Lost.* Calcutta, Mukhopadhyay, 1967.
*Greek Tragedy.* Calcutta, Excelsus, 1969.
*The Canon of Thomas Middleton's Plays: Internal Evidence for the Major Problems of Authorship.* Cambridge, University Press, 1975.

*

David Lake comments:

The main impulse embodied in my SF is the impulse of the human rat to imagine escapes from the cosmic trap in which he finds himself. The trap is partly (but only partly) of his own building; it has been building for a very long time; and the bars now loom very high indeed. Sometimes the rat thinks he can escape by a smart technological fix; sometimes he knows that he can't. But either way he can at least dream.

The main influences on my writing are probably H.G. Wells and C.S. Lewis, and the clash between these two authors' values. I follow Wells and Lewis in writing SF that deliberately borders on fantasy. Elves may appear wearing spacesuits. The same themes also appear in my poems, some of which are in fact close to being SF. I am also strongly influenced by my early background as a child in India under the old British Raj. I know how it feels to be an invader in a vast, different culture. Most aliens in my novels are versions of Asians. My recent fantasy novel *The Changelings of Chaan* is especially close to my early life (as it should have been, not as it was).

* * *

David Lake presents himself as a pessimist in search of the numinous, a fantasist without belief, choosing science fiction as his vehicle for escapism because magic does not work. Lake has little confidence in the efficacy of science, either: in "Re-deem the Time" (in *Rooms of Paradise*, edited by Lee Harding, Melbourne, Quartet, 1978) his alter ego, Ambrose Livermore, is able to use a time machine as his escape hatch into the future, leap-frogging the inevitable Big Bang, only to find the survivors engaged in determined regress, already back in 1900. In this witty tale, despair is salved by humour: Ambrose flourishes in the future 1 BC as Chief Jester to Obliorix.

If Earth is the City of Destruction in a godless universe, where may hope be found? In his novels Lake catapults small colonies of survivors to distant, wondrous planets, and New Jerusalem is actually built foursquare on Dextra. The two Dextra novels are paradigmatically interesting, complementing each other much as Blake's *Songs of Innocence* and *Songs of Experience*. *The Right Hand of Dextra* suggests the state of innocence, in which it is possible for the Puritan tendencies of the New Earthmen with their "Sifted Scriptures" to be corrected by incorporation with the innocent native species, despite the dextran twist of their protein molecules. Experience seems to prove otherwise, however, in the bleak feudal world of *The Wildings of Westron*, set several thousand years later, until the implicit conclusion of the first book is reiterated in absolute form: before there can really be a New Earth on Dextra, all human flesh must perish and only Dextran flesh remain. Most humans will voluntarily undergo the change; the reluctant must simply be exterminated. There is no hope in human flesh because it is closed; Dextran flesh, however, is open, unsecret, allowing telepathic understanding of one another.

The conclusion of *The Gods of Xuma* is not quite so sweeping: only the hopelessly evil human colonists are slaughtered—and fortunately the Xuman natives can tell the difference and are prepared to tolerate those humans remaining who are essentially good natured. However, it is decided that humans are not fit for space travel.

If Lake is thus predisposed in favour of aliens, describing them warmly and even with affection, he is not unduly sentimental about them, particularly about his Xumans, and wishes to correct the supposition, hung over from Burroughs, that physical love with an alien can be satisfactory. The hero's comic embarrassments with Xumans in their female phase prove the point (that Lake lacks LeGuin's solemnity in treating such an issue is not, I think, to his advantage). On the other hand, Lake's aliens are usually not very different from people and do provoke erotic ideas; however, their function is not to be wonderful love-objects (as in Burroughs) but to suggest wonderful possibilities of loving interchange between humans, suitably modified. In *The Right Hand of Dextra* he uses the Song of Solomon as the basis for a description of a transcendent sexual union, only confusing the terms, so that male and female sensations become interchangeable; in *The Wildings of Westron* he echoes Blake: "Every minute particle and particular of their body-minds were commingling, from the head even to the feet, and on every plane of existence."

Lake is an imaginative writer with the power not only to invent exciting worlds but to describe them; he acknowledges the influence of C.S. Lewis, and his evocative accounts of the deserts of Xuma or the purple forests of Dextra bear comparison with those of Malacandra. His most wonderful world is in *Walkers on the Sky*, a tier-world Farmer might envy, ruled capriciously by immortals as if to recall Zelazny's *Lord of Light*. It is a pity that he had not found a story worthy of his world, but this charge may also be levelled at Farmer, and Lake's novel is at least free from Farmer's sometimes heavy portentousness.

In "Creator" Lake shows that he is prepared to tackle the big theme, and though he trivializes it somewhat in the process—our universe exists inside a "creatron," a kind of game machine for artists on the planet Olympus, our creator being Jay Crystal (J.C.—get it?)—he succeeds in providing a provocative ironic perspective on human history.

Lake's two most recent novels have been fantasies for young adults; older readers who enjoy C.S. Lewis should find them at least as charming and thoughtful as the best of the Narnia books. Both use the pleasant conceit of advancing their young heroes to a higher world: a "Golden World" in *The Changelings of Chaan* and a "High Earth" in *West of the Moon* (written earlier though published later). These higher worlds are themselves lower than others: John Hastings must undertake a quest to the high Silver World where the gods live, before he can return to Chaan: his story draws on the author's knowledge of Indian society and Hindu myth. Gods visit the pleasant country of Vornemana (which means "West of the Moon"), where magic works, but Megan and Mark Tremaine are anomalies there, for Hardor (Earth, Ironworld) has long been closed off as a threat to Middleworld's integrity. An insecure king and his black magician, who seek forbidden knowledge, lure the two unsuspecting orphan schoolchildren to Middleworld where they soon come of age. Although these books are classed by the author as fantasy in deliberate contradistinction to science fiction, it should be remarked that *West of the Moon* considers the supposed opposition between science and magic instructively.

—Michael J. Tolley

---

**LANG, King.** *See* **TUBB, E.C.**

---

**LANGART, T.** *See* **GARRETT, Randall.**

---

**LANGE, John.** *See* **CRICHTON, Michael.**

---

**LANGFORD, David.** British. Born in Newport, Gwent, Wales, 10 April 1953. Educated at Newport High School; Brasenose College, Oxford, 1971–74, B.A. in physics, 1974, M.A. 1978. Married Hazel Langford in 1976. Weapons physicist, Atomic Weapons Research Establishment, Aldermaston, Berkshire, 1975–80. Since 1980, freelance writer. Editor, *Ansible*, Reading, Berkshire, and since 1983, contributing editor, and columnist ("Critical Mass"), *White Dwarf*, London. Agent: Hilary Rubinstein, A.P. Watt Ltd., 20 John Street, London WC1N 2DR. Address: 94 London Road, Reading, Berkshire RG1 5AU, England.

SCIENCE-FICTION PUBLICATIONS

Novels

*The Space Eater.* London, Arrow, 1982; New York, Pocket Books, 1983.
*The Leaky Establishment.* London, Muller, 1984.
*Earthdoom!* with John Grant. London, Grafton, 1987.

OTHER PUBLICATIONS

Other

*The Necronomicon*, with others, edited by George Hay. St. Helier, Jersey, Spearman, 1978.

*An Account of a Meeting with Denizens of Another World, 1871.* Newton Abbot, Devon, David and Charles, 1979; New York, St. Martin's Press, 1980.
*War in 2080: The Future of Military Technology.* Newton Abbot, Devon, David and Charles, 1979.
*Facts and Fallacies: A Book of Definitive Mistakes and Misguided Predictions,* with Chris Morgan. Exeter, Devon, Webb and Bower, 1981.
*The Science in Science Fiction,* with Peter Nicholls and Brian M. Stableford. London, Joseph, 1982; New York, Knopf, 1983.
*Micromania: The Whole Truth about Home Computers,* with Charles Platt. London, Gollancz, 1984; as *The Whole Truth Home Computer Handbook,* New York, Avon, 1984.
"The Dragonhiker's Guide to Battlefield Covenant at Dune's Edge: Odyssey Two," in *Xyster 5* (Clevedon, Avon), 1984.
*The Third Millennium: The History of the World AD 2000–3000,* with Brian M. Stableford. London, Sidgwick and Jackson, and New York, Knopf, 1985.
*Varieties of English,* with Dennis Freeborn and Peter French. London, Macmillan, 1985.
*The Dragonhiker's Guide to Battlefield Covenant at Dune's Edge: Odyssey Two.* London, Drunken Dragon, 1988.

*

David Langford comments (1985):

Anything said here *ought* to be redundant. A work requiring the author's personal introduction ("Now I want you to meet little Johnny, boys and girls. He's a bit subnormal and deformed, but don't you dare tease him") is hardly likely to make its own way in the horrid outside world of bookstands. However . . .

I'm a technophile but a somewhat pessimistic one; it seems so unfair that shiny, alluring technological toys keep pointing the way to more and easier megadeaths. Yet because I like intellectual games I keep playing literary hopscotch on the edge of the unthinkable, cracking jokes about a variety of armageddons: current (*The Leaky Establishment*), seriously extrapolated (*War in 2080*) and wholly imaginary (*The Space Eater*). In the shorter efforts there are lighter jokes, parodies, and sheer fun; give me twenty thousand words or more, though, and I end up addressing gallows humour to the Angel of Death, the Spectre of World War III, the Ghost of Christmas Yet To Come, or some such unjolly companion.

By publication time this will be less an introduction than a memorial. I've no idea what I'll be writing next year, while swift and efficient technologies of modern-day publishing will doubtless have made all the above-listed works quite unobtainable. (Support a starving author—write to me and buy my remainders!) My ambition is to become a capitalist.

* * *

David Langford began writing as a student, with fannish parodies (some of which are included in *The Dragonhiker's Guide to Battlefield Covenant at Dune's Edge: Odyssey Two*), and much of his fame is connected to the prodigious number of fan-writing Hugos he has collected. Much of his best writing is to be found in fanzines (especially his own *Twll Ddu* and *Ansible*) and the collection "Platen Tales" contains some of the best. He also writes regular SF book review columns and is noted for his willingness to spend more effort demolishing the great hyped-up clunkers (which people need to be warned against) than in recommending the better stuff (which presumably can speak for itself). Much of his work has the same joy in taking apart the illogical and second-rate, especially in *Facts and Fallacies,* a collection of thoroughly wrong predictions and "scientific" observations.

Apart from the numerous collaborations on non-fiction and semi-fictional works such as *The Necronomicon* and *The Science in Science Fiction,* from which Langford has earned his daily bread since leaving the Scientific Civil Service, Langford has published four long SF works. The first, *An Account of a Meeting with Denizens of Another World, 1871,* is a slim, one-joke volume in which an extraterrestrial probe lands in a Buckinghamshire wood and tries to open communications with a local craftsman. The cod modern commentary on the recently discovered manuscript laments the difficulty of conveying the concepts of quarks and DNA by purely visual means. Written as a counter to all those tales in which flying saucerites go from "me alien—you human—that tree" to advanced physics in a couple of pages, this book has, to the author's chagrin and amusement, been taken as fact by parts of the UFO press and used to pad at least one best-selling work on the popular theme: "the government knows all about saucers and is keeping the truth from us."

His next work, *The Space Eater,* is a hard-science story centering on unlikely new branches of physics (all new branches of physics are unlikely) leading to ways of destroying worlds even more spectacular than the ones the author worked on at the British Government's Atomic Weapons Research Establishment (and even more spectacular than most of the ones described in *War in 2080*). Its chief flaw is its uneven tone. While in his short stories (from one of which *The Space Eater* was expanded) Langford tends to see the gloomy side of his technological enthusiasms, in the novel Langfordian flights of fancy and humour creep in; the hero turns from a Mindless Killing Machine at the start to a Thoroughly Nice Chap by the end, and for no particular reason. The book also contains SF's most impractical interstellar drive: a star-gate just a few centimeters square. First chop up your astronauts and then reassemble on the far side. . . .

*The Leaky Establishment,* only marginally SF, is perhaps Langford's best long work. Drawing again on his time at Aldermaston, it is a very enjoyable farce concerning a researcher at A Top Secret Establishment who has to smuggle plutonium warheads back into his place of work. The most hilarious parts are those connected with Civil Service bureaucracy, which the author claims are pure autobiography: the endless regulations, the proposal to rename atomic weapons after the Royal Family "to promote empathy and good public feeling," the beefy security guards probing the thighs of young physicists for lumps of plutonium.

*Earthdoom!,* Langford's most recent novel, is another parody and another collaboration (with John Grant): a takeoff of the cult novels of doom so prevalent in the 1980's. Although it contains every type of world ending, ecological, technological, and supernatural, it generally fails to amuse.

Langford's shorter work often has nice touches of characterisation and style that stand out better on a smaller canvas. "Cube Root" (in *Interzone,* Spring 1985) and "Notes for a Newer Testament" (in *Afterwar,* edited by Janet E. Morris, New York, Baen, 1985) continue his fascination with weapons, the former in a very dark vein. And his most recent story in *Interzone,* "A Snapshot Album" (January 1991), has a feeling for mood and place that could indicate new maturity in his work.

—Michael Cule

---

**LANIER, Sterling E(dmund).** American. Born in New York City, 18 December 1927. Educated at Harvard University, Cambridge, Massachusetts, A.B. 1951; University of Pennsylvania, Philadelphia, 1953–58. Served in World War II and the Korean War. Married 1) Martha Hanna Pelton in 1961 (divorced 1978), one son and one daughter; 2) Ann Miller McGregor in 1979. Research historian, Winterthur Museum, Switzerland, 1958–60; editor, John C. Winston Company, 1961, Chilton Books, 1961–62, 1965–67, and Macrae-Smith Company, 1963–64. Since 1967, full-time writer and sculptor. Recipient: Follett award, 1969. Agent: Curtis Brown Ltd., 10 Astor Place, New York, New York 10003, U.S.A.

SCIENCE-FICTION PUBLICATIONS

Novels

*The War for the Lot* (for children). Chicago, Follett, 1969; London, Sidgwick and Jackson, 1977.
*Hiero's Journey.* Radnor, Pennsylvania, Chilton, 1973; London, Sidgwick and Jackson, 1975.
*The Unforsaken Hiero.* New York, Ballantine, 1983.
*Menace under Marwood.* New York, Ballantine, 1983.

Short Stories

*The Peculiar Exploits of Brigadier Ffellowes.* New York, Walker, and London, Sidgwick and Jackson, 1977.
*The Curious Quests of Brigadier Ffellowes.* New York, Donald M. Grant, 1986.

* * *

Sterling E. Lanier's fiction presents a world teeming with creatures of the fantastic imagination. No innovator or philosopher, Lanier sails on well-charted seas of the supernatural and unnatural. His work almost always combines the worlds of fantasy and science fiction, and although his output is relatively small, his novel *Hiero's Journey* is of sufficient merit to warrant close attention.

A summary of this novel can hardly do it justice as the story pivots on one of the oldest and most frequently used plots of the genre: the hero sets out on a quest for lost knowledge through a world laid waste by nuclear war and controlled by mutants made horrible and evil by radiation. However, Lanier is able to inform this trite plot with his own vision of the fantastic and produces a world that is both delightful and terrifying. The questing hero is Per Hiero Desteen—priest, exorcist, killman, and citizen of the Metz republic of Kanda—who sets off in the eighth millennium in search of ancient legendary machines called "computers" that will help him and his people put together the knowledge of the past. This knowledge is the last hope for survival against the various forms of evil that resulted from the Death (nuclear holocaust). This theme is not without its own moral convictions, and Lanier attempts to tie his story to present-day concerns in several ways. Some connections are made through a language that is not nearly as interesting or inventive as one might hope for in this kind of novel: Lantik Sea (Atlantic Ocean), Kanda (Canada), Neeyana (Indiana), Leemutes (lethal mutations). More interesting are the contemporary social and environmental values that are invested in the tale. The nuclear devastation is served by a group of men called "the Unclean." These men were formerly psychologists, biochemists, and physicists who have been severely ravaged by radiation and now seek to rule the evil world they have created. On the other hand, Hiero is joined by a wise ancient, Brother Aldo, who belongs to a group called "the Eleveners." The eleveners are the Brotherhood of the Eleventh Commandment, a group of social scientists dedicated to the ideal: Thou shalt not despoil the Earth and the life thereon. Hiero and Brother Aldo are accompanied by a telepathic, almost human bear (Gorm), a semi-intelligent bull "morse," and a strong-willed but faithful young maiden (Luchare).

Lanier's strengths and weaknesses are both evident in this fantasy adventure yarn. He is at his best when weaving a suspenseful tale, and, while his characters lack depth and the plot has been often used before, the world he creates, filled with radiation-induced mutants, ancient, knowing wizards, and fur-covered dwarves, lives fully in the imagination and allows the reader to partake fully in the suspenseful quest. Lanier is obviously aware of the parallels with medieval romances, and those who enjoy *Beowulf, Le Morte Darthur,* and the sagas will be enthralled by the re-creation of those environments and values in a future time.

Lanier's other work is of a similar but lesser quality. His stories as a rule combine the fantastic world of unnatural monsters with the more traditional trappings of science fiction: space ships, time travel, telepathic communication. *The Peculiar Exploits of Brigadier Ffellowes* presents seven stories that feature a retired English Brigadier who narrates tales that involve supernatural powers and fantastic monsters. Lanier exhibits a good sense of humor in these stories and carefully sets them up as a series of Chinese boxes: a story within a story within a story. The monsters found here, like the Nandi bear and the sea serpent Jormungadir, are similar to those found elsewhere in Lanier's writings. But the best quality of Lanier is what accounts for the success of this and his other works: he is an excellent storyteller.

—Lawrence R. Ries

---

**LANSDALE, Joe R(ichard).** Has also written as Ray Slater. American. Born in Gladewater, Texas, 28 October 1951. Educated at Tyler Junior College, 1970–71; University of Texas at Austin, 1971–72; Stephen F. Austin State University, Nacogdoches, Texas, 1973, 1975, 1976. Married 1) Cassie Ellis in 1970 (divorced 1972); 2) Karen Ann Morton in 1973, one daughter and one son. Karate instructor, 1970–79; foreman, LaBorde Custodial Services, Nacogdoches, 1980–81. Has also worked as a factory worker, ditch digger, carpenter and plumber's helper, and farmer. Since 1981, freelance writer. Recipient: Bram Stoker award, 1988, 1989; Horror Writers of America award, 1988, 1989; American Horror award, 1989; British Fantasy award, for novella, 1989. Agent: Barbara Puechner, 3121 Portage Road, Bethlehem, Pennsylvania 18017. Address: 113 Timber Ridge Drive, Nacogdoches, Texas 75961, U.S.A.

SCIENCE-FICTION PUBLICATIONS

Novels

*The Drive-In: A B-Movie with Blood and Popcorn, Made in Texas.* New York, Doubleday, 1988; London, Kinnel, 1989.
*The Drive-In 2: Not Just One of Them Sequels.* New York, Bantam, 1989; London, Kinnel, 1990.

Short Stories

*By Bizarre Hands.* Shingletown, California, Ziesing, 1989.
*Stories by Mama Lansdale's Youngest Boy.* Eugene, Oregon, Pulphouse, 1991.

OTHER PUBLICATIONS

Novels

*Act of Love.* New York, Kensington, 1981; London, Kinnel, 1989.
*Texas Night Riders* (as Ray Slater). Champaign, Illinois, Leisure Press, 1983; Bath, Chivers, 1990.
*Dead in the West.* New York, Space and Time, 1986; London, Kinnel, 1990.
*The Magic Wagon.* New York, Doubleday, 1986; Bath, Chivers, 1988.
*The Nightrunners.* Arlington Heights, Illinois, Dark Harvest, 1987.
*Cold in July.* New York, Bantam, 1989.
*Savage Season.* Shingletown, California, Ziesing, 1990.
*Batman: Captured by the Engines.* New York, Warner, 1991.

Other

Editor, *Best of the West.* New York, Doubleday, 1986.
Editor, *The New Frontier: The Best of Today's Western Fiction.* New York, Doubleday, 1989.
Editor, with Pat LoBrutto, *Razored Saddles.* Arlington Heights, Illinois, Dark Harvest, 1989.

*

Joe R. Lansdale comments:

I write what interests me, and it's as simple as that. As a reader I read everything. Literary, genre, comics, plays, screenplays, and I'm influenced by it all. No matter what I write, I do my best to put something of myself and a literary sensibility into it. I hope to be both entertaining and interesting enough that someone might want to read one of my books or stories more than once.

My work often combines my interests, so that a novel or story might be as much horror as crime as suspense as SF as western as literary, and perhaps all of these. And maybe it's cat box material. What do I know?

* * *

Approximately half realistic adventure fiction and half supernatural, Joe R. Lansdale's writing is above all classifiable as horror. He is sometimes classed with the "splatterpunk" writers—John Skipp, Craig Spector, David Schow, Ray Garton, and others—but the detailed depiction of violence in his work predates even the roughest formation of that movement. His main models from science fiction and fantasy include Ray Bradbury, Richard Matheson, Fredric Brown, Gerald Kersh, Charles Beaumont, and William F. Nolan; in fact, "Bill Nolan" appears as a character in Lansdale's *Dead in the West.* Lansdale acknowledges his roots, from prose writers in many genres to B-movies and comic books such as *Jonah Hex* and *Batman.* He has written two short stories featuring Batman as the protagonist, and one novel, *Batman: Captured by the Engines.*

Lansdale is also noteworthy as a regional writer: he states that he and Ardath Mayhar may be the entirety of "the East Texas school of horror." Drive-ins, good ol' boys with guns, snuff films, incest, itinerant preachers, improbable cars—this is the modern West that Lansdale writes about, capturing it in semi-mythological form, just as he and others depict the old West in genre Western fiction. Some of the stories take place in his fictional town of Mud Creek (based on Gladewater), while others are set in recognizable towns and cities in Texas. Into this setting, or others, Lansdale often introduces fantastic elements such as animated dinosaurs, the living dead, and chilling and original figures like his God of the Razor. All of this is conveyed in Lansdale's highly personal narrative voice, which combines humor with terror, colloquialisms with original metaphors, and style with immediacy and action.

Lansdale is best known for his novel *The Drive-In: A B-Movie with Blood and Popcorn, Made in Texas*, based on an idea Lansdale introduced in an article on drive-in movies. During a festival of horror films, a multi-screen outdoor theater is snatched into a mysterious limbo, to degenerate into a film-lit, popcorn-fed *Lord of the Flies.* Lansdale introduces other fantastic elements, such as the Popcorn King, and horrific problems of violence, rape, and cannibalism. In the sequel, *The Drive-In 2: Not Just One of Them Sequels*, some of the survivors find an even more baffling world outside the drive-in, with dinosaurs and vampiric roles of celluloid. The books blend humor and horror; the first, especially, is well-paced and readable. The characters are similar to those of Lansdale's realistic horror story, "Night They Missed the Horror Show," though more diverse and less violent.

Much of Lansdale's work before *The Drive-In* has been reissued since, by commercial or specialty publishers. *The Nightrunners* blends a story of defense and revenge—compared by some to *Straw Dogs*—with elements of precognition and perhaps possession. Sections of that novel had appeared as short fiction before or were later re-written as independent short stories. The latter category includes the story "God of the Razor." *Dead in the West*, a short novel, takes place in Mud Creek, Texas, during pioneer days; it features undead people that spread like vampires, but behave and can be killed like the living dead in films by George Romero. (Lansdale used Romero's living dead explicitly in his "On the Far Side of the Cadillac Desert with Dead Folks.")

The widest range of Lansdale's interests and abilities is clear in his short fiction. Not all of the works are horror: "Trains Not Taken" and "Letter from the South, Two Moons West of Nacogdoches" depict alternate histories; "Not from Detroit" is a supernatural story about an old couple meeting death, but its tone is low-key and wistful. "Fish Night" ends on a note of horror, but that seems almost stuck on to a tale of surreal awe. "Tight Little Stitches in a Dead Man's Back" is post-World War III fiction in which the human interaction is almost more horrible—and fascinating—than the setting. "The White Rabbit" combines *Alice in Wonderland* and Jack the Ripper in a story somewhat reminiscent of Frank Belknap Long's "Humpty Dumpty Had a Great Fall." The title story of *By Bizarre Hands* is realistic but improbable horror, which Lansdale has also re-written in play form.

Like fellow-Texan Joe Bob Briggs—whom Lansdale mentions in "Hell Through a Windshield"—Lansdale often presents a racist, sexist, and misogynistic culture, risking condemnation on those grounds himself. However, Lansdale's fiction clearly refutes those charges by its depictions of female and Afro-American characters, as in *Cold in July* or *Act of Love.* Living in Nacogdoches with his family, Lansdale is—as is so often true of writers of horror—unassuming and personable, remaining true to his roots and his uniquely regional style. It is likely that he has written work released under pseudonyms, probably including one or more Western novels, but there is no documentation of this. Certainly, his published work so far is noteworthy and promises even more for the future.

—Bernadette Bosky

**LARGE, E(rnest) C(harles).** British. Plant pathologist. *Died in 1976.*

SCIENCE-FICTION PUBLICATIONS

Novels (series: Charles Pry)

*Sugar in the Air* (Pry). London, Cape, and New York, Scribner, 1937.
*Asleep in the Afternoon* (Pry). London, Cape, 1938; New York, Holt, 1939.
*Dawn in Andromeda.* London, Cape, 1956.

OTHER PUBLICATIONS

Other

*The Advance of the Fungi.* London, Cape, and New York, Holt, 1940.
*Potato Blight Epidemics Throughout the World,* with A.E. Cox. Washington, D.C., Agricultural Research Bureau, 1960.

* * *

In some respects, E.C. Large could be considered a scientist's science-fiction writer, for he deals primarily with the concerns and perspectives of the scientist in his everyday life. Large's narratives, though not abstruse, explore scientific inventions and processes with acute detail, and his work might be included in what C.S. Lewis identifies as the "fiction of engineers."

The most notable work Large produced is *Sugar in the Air*, a book considered by many to be a near-classic, for it was this novel which first embodied in speculative fiction a relatively realistic idea of the scientist's work and social situation. The story concerns a young chemical engineer, Charles Pry, who is hired by Hydro-Mechanical Constructions Ltd., to create sugar by photosynthesis, using only a handful of hints gathered by another, rather eccentric scientist. Pry succeeds in discovering the elusive formula, but he encounters conflicts with company financiers in the marketing of "Sunsap," as the product is called. They are concerned with obtaining the quickest and greatest profit, while Pry idealistically strives to make the product more beneficial for society, and the book becomes a kind of tragi-comedy of the scientist and commerce. The novel thus inverts the motif of the mad scientist, for it is the corporation, not Pry, who wants to exploit the discovery for its own greed. This attitude of organization vs. the individual dominated later magazine science fiction, as for example when the lone nuclear scientist is pitted against the political and military powers.

*Asleep in the Afternoon*, a sequel, is also an invention story, though an inferior one, dealing with similar ideas and attitudes. Charles Pry, having lost his job with Hydro-Mechanical, decides to write a novel, which is about the invention of a sleep-inducing device. Within this rather unexciting framework, Large again satirizes capitalism and corporations, as well as other aspects of contemporary life, political structure, and social attitudes.

While the first two novels deal with the relationship—and often the conflict—between the scientist and the community, *Dawn in Andromeda* is a Utopian allegory. Ten British men and women (five of each) emerge Venus-like from the sea one morning onto the shores of an uninhabited planet in the Andromeda galaxy, where they have been transported by God in a rather ridiculous opening. Equipped with their scientific knowledge and practical skills—and some faint memories of Earth—they build a new society and community on this strange world, which closely resembles Earth. The original group is harmonious enough; it is the second generation's spontaneous pursuit of commerce and religion which spoils the Utopian dream, reflecting the same sort of criticisms that Large displays in the previous two books. Again, the narrative is heavily endowed with scientific detail, exploring every step of the little society's progress.

But Large circumvents the most obvious problem, that of interplanetary transportation, choosing instead to follow C.S. Lewis's advice that "frankly supernatural methods are best." So the novel really doesn't follow the 17th and 18th-century tradition of the voyage to another world, being concerned instead, like Wells's *First Men in the Moon*, with what happens there.

Though Large is obviously more scientist than writer, his books do have some literary qualities worth noting: his prose is often strong and direct, tough, effective; his characters, though not fully rounded, compel interest and arouse sympathy; he also uses imaginative names, giving characters such apt identities as Cocaine, Dr. Sinus, Dr. Zaareb, MacDuff, or Hunt-Transom, while the crew in Andromeda take their names from the alphabetical letterings on the bindings of Encyclopaedia Britannica.

Large's novels evince a firm belief in science and its potentiality; they laud the moral scientist of commitment and decry the stupidity and incompetence of so many social organizations—business, commercial, religious, political, revolutionary. Large's work offers an interesting, knowledgeable, and valuable perspective of the scientist, his work, and his place in society.

—Karen Charmaine Blansfield

---

**LA SALLE, Victor.** *See* **FANTHORPE, R. Lionel.**

---

**LATHAM, Philip.** Pseudonym for Robert S(hirley) Richardson. American. Born in Kokomo, Indiana, 22 April 1902. Educated at the University of California, Los Angeles, B.A. 1926; University of California, Berkeley, Ph.D. 1931. Married 1) Delia Shull in 1929 (died 1940); 2) Marjorie Helen Engstead in 1942, one daughter. Assistant Astronomer, Mt. Wilson, now Hale, Observatory, Pasadena, California, 1931–58; associate director, Griffith Observatory, Los Angeles, 1958–64. After 1964, free-lance writer. *Died in November 1981.*

SCIENCE-FICTION PUBLICATIONS

Novels

*Five Against Venus* (for children). Philadelphia, Winston, 1952.
*Missing Men of Saturn* (for children). Philadelphia, Winston, 1953.
*Second Satellite* (as Robert S. Richardson). New York, McGraw Hill, 1956.

Uncollected Short Stories

"N Day," in *Astounding* (New York), January 1946.
"The Blindness," in *Astounding* (New York), July 1946.
"The Aphrodite Project," in *Astounding* (New York), June 1949.

"The Most Dangerous Love," in *Marvel* (New York), November 1951.
"Martial Ritual," in *Future* (New York), July 1953.
"A Moment of Laughter," in *Fantastic* (New York), October 1953.
"Comeback," in *Future* (New York), November 1953.
"Simpson," in *Cosmos* (New York), July 1954.
"Flash Nova," in *McCall's* (New York), 15 August 1956.
"Disturbing Sun," in *Astounding* (New York), May 1959.
"To Explain Mrs. Thompson," in *The Expert Dreamers*, edited by Frederik Pohl. New York, Doubleday, 1962.
"Kid Anderson" (as Robert S. Richardson), in *Great Science Fiction by Scientists*, edited by Groff Conklin. New York, Macmillan, 1962.
"The Dimple in Draco," in *Orbit 2*, edited by Damon Knight. New York, Putnam, 1967; London, Rapp and Whiting, 1968.
"The Red Euphoric Bands," in *Galaxy* (New York), December 1967.
"Under the Dragon's Tail," in *Analog* (New York), December 1968.
"After Enfer," in *Fantasy and Science Fiction* (New York), March 1969.
"The Rose Bowl Pluto Hypothesis," in *Orbit 5*, edited by Damon Knight. New York, Putnam, 1969.
"Jeannette's Hands," in *Fantasy and Science Fiction* (New York), January 1973.
"Future Forbidden," in *Galaxy* (New York), May 1973.
"A Drop of Dragon's Blood," in *Fantasy and Science Fiction* (New York), July 1975.
"The Miracle Elixir," in *Fantastic* (New York), June 1977.
"The Xi Effect," in *The Golden Age of Science Fiction*, edited by Kingsley Amis. London, Hutchinson, 1981.

OTHER PUBLICATIONS as Robert S. Richardson

Plays

Television Plays: *Captain Video* series, 1953.

Other

*Preliminary Elements of Object Comas Sola (1927 AA)*, with others. Berkeley, University of California Press, 1927.
*Astronomy*, with William T. Skilling. New York, Holt, and London, Chapman and Hall, 1939; revised edition, Holt, 1947.
*The Practical Essentials of Pre-Training Navigation*, with William T. Skilling. New York, Holt, 1942.
*Sun, Moon and Stars*, with William T. Skilling. New York, McGraw Hill, 1946; revised edition, 1964.
*A Brief Text in Astronomy*, with William T. Skilling. New York, Holt, 1954; revised edition, 1959.
*Exploring Mars* (for children). New York, McGraw Hill, 1954; as *Man and the Planets*, London, Muller, 1954.
*The Fascinating World of Astronomy*. New York, McGraw Hill, 1960; London, Faber, 1962.
*Man and the Moon*. Cleveland, World, 1961.
*Astronomy in Action*. New York, McGraw Hill, 1962.
*Mars*. New York, Harcourt Brace, 1964; London, Allen and Unwin, 1965.
*Getting Acquainted with Comets*. New York, McGraw Hill, 1967.
*The Star Lovers*. New York, Macmillan, 1967.
*The Stars and Serendipity* (for children). New York, Pantheon, 1971.

*

Manuscript Collection: Fullerton College Library, California.

Philip Latham commented:

(1981) Since most of my firsthand experience is in astronomy, most of my fiction has an astronomical background. But one of my stories, "Kid Anderson," is about a prizefighter. I firmly believe that science always leads science fiction. Increasingly I have gone over to science fantasy, as in "Jeannette's Hands" and other stories. My stories are always written on the basis of *people rather than gadgetry*.

Where science fiction will go in the future is a guess. There is little left to write about: we have already written stories of interplanetary travel, extra dimensions, time travel. *Stars Wars*, for example, to my mind was a fairy tale: you could have anything you wanted in it. Most science-fiction writers have inventive ability and ingenuity, but lack true imagination, an extremely rare gift. I neither read science fiction nor look at SF on TV or in motion pictures. Henceforth, we must try to find material in the world around us. It is there if we can see it.

* * *

A scandal in American science fiction is how little science there is in it. A notable exception lies in Philip Latham's stories, since they were written by the professional astronomer Robert S. Richardson and bear the marks of his expertise. For more than three decades Latham's stories appeared from time to time in the major magazines and anthologies, and Latham also wrote juvenile science-fiction novels.

Many of the early stories are based on astronomical speculation, often presented as realistic reporting. An example is "The Aphrodite Project," which has the pretense of being science fact, complete with footnotes to astronomical journals. The story imagines a 1946 Navy contract to launch a satellite rocket to Venus to measure its mass. Once near Venus the rocket releases a cloud visible to Earth—Latham does not foresee the sophisticated radio telemetry which has actually been used on such probes. The rocket succeeds in measuring not only the mass of Venus but also its period of rotation. A secondary theme is governmental secrecy as the military authorities clamp down on the release of information about the mission. The story thus presents itself as an exposé of confidential information. "The Xi-Effect" is another example of Latham's astronomical science fiction. Astronomers discover that although the universe as a whole expands, the Earth is in a segment which is shrinking, cutting out greater and greater percentages of radiation so that the eventual extinction of all light seems inevitable. In this story we begin to see Latham's interest in the characters of scientists as well as in science. Latham presents a communication gap between the branches and modes of science. It is a theoretical physicist who predicts the Xi-Effect, and the practical astronomers are shown to be as skeptical of theory as in the public at large. "The Blindness," about the return of Halley's comet in 1986, is hardly a story at all but a meditation on the influence the comet has had on history. A theory of atomic sentience is developed to explain the comet's deviance from its projected orbit. Even in this early story the scientist Richardson makes clear his interest in anti-science and mysticism.

Latham's more recent fiction develops much further the theme of the dubious border between science and magic. Much more central to these later stories, too, is a particular kind of character:

the anti-hero who wins the reader's sympathy for his struggles in an absurd world. "After-Enfer" is an example of a Latham story which revolves around character rather than science. The story's title derives from "N-Fear," fear of other dimensions. Sam Baxter, afraid of life, stuck in a museum job, applies for the job of exploring N-space and breaks through to genuine heroism. In "Jeannette's Hands" and its sequel, "A Drop of Dragon's Blood," Latham's protagonist is an astronomer, Bob, who is literally and figuratively married to an astrologer named Dagny. We learn in these stories about the seamy side of being a professional astronomer: the rivalries and the petty jealousies between those who hold conflicting theories and conflicting claims to grant money. Bob's rival Thornton has an innovative theory about the age of the universe, but Bob suspects him of rigging his data. The rivalry is extended in the story to the details of competition over the use of the observatory during the limited nights of good viewing. Latham gives us the comedy of Bob's loss of status when Dagny is appointed official witch of California. Such are the foibles of astronomers in this story that astrology seems a refreshing alternative. In "A Drop of Dragon's Blood" we learn more about the politics of being an astronomer, the need to produce sensational findings in order to attract research funds. Bob makes a public prediction of a period for the variable star Mira in a desperate hope for publicity, because his job is in trouble. His prediction comes true in an ironic way: Mira's companion brightens at exactly the time Bob predicted Mira would brighten, in a new phenomenon, the "simmering nova." The point of the story is the unexpected nature of the universe: "there are ghosts everywhere." Once again Latham tempts us to side with Dagny's brief in magic. Although Latham brought science to science fiction, he certainly did not bring mechanical materialism.

In his most recent stories Latham turned almost completely away from the hard science of his earlier work. In "The Miracle Elixir" an ordinary office worker, who works for Pearce's Golden Specific but never thinks of taking the company product, learns what it is like to have his life turned around by a "real" elixir. Without the interest of science, Latham's recent stories are sometimes thin and awkward. Latham could not be called a major science-fiction writer. But he brought science to his best science-fiction stories and he created anti-heroic and likeable astronomers as characters.

—Curtis C. Smith

---

**LAUMER, (John) Keith.** Also writes as Anthony Le Baron. American. Born in Syracuse, New York, 9 June 1925. Educated at the University of Indiana, Bloomington, 1943–44; University of Stockholm, 1947–48; University of Illinois, Urbana, B.Sc. 1950, B. Arch. 1952. Served in the United States Army, 1943–45: Corporal; United States Air Force, 1952–56, 1959–65: Captain. Married Janice Perkinson in 1949. Staff member, University of Illinois, 1952; Foreign Service Vice-Consul and Third Secretary, Rangoon, 1956–59. Since 1959, freelance writer. Address: Box 972, Brooksville, Florida 34605, U.S.A.

SCIENCE-FICTION PUBLICATIONS

Novels (series: Bolo; Imperium; Invaders; O'Leary; Retief)

*Worlds of the Imperium.* New York, Ace, 1962; London, Dobson, 1967.
*A Trace of Memory.* New York, Berkley, 1963; London, Mayflower, 1968.
*The Great Time Machine Hoax.* New York, Simon and Schuster, 1964.
*A Plague of Demons.* New York, Berkley, 1965; London, Penguin, 1967.
*The Other Side of Time* (Imperium). New York, Berkley, 1965; London, Dobson, 1968.
*The Time Bender* (O'Leary). New York, Berkley, 1966; London, Dobson, 1975.
*Retief's War.* New York, Doubleday, 1966.
*Earthblood,* with Rosel George Brown. New York, Doubleday, 1966; London, Coronet, 1979.
*Catastrophe Planet.* New York, Berkley, 1966; London, Dobson, 1970.
*The Monitors.* New York, Berkley, 1966; London, Dobson, 1968.
*Enemies from Beyond* (novelization of TV series; Invaders). New York, Pyramid, 1967.
*Planet Run,* with Gordon R. Dickson. New York, Doubleday, 1967; London, Hale, 1977.
*The Invaders* (novelization of TV series). New York, Pyramid, 1967; as *The Meteor Man* (as Anthony Le Baron), London, Corgi, 1968.
*Galactic Odyssey.* New York, Berkley, 1967; London, Dobson, 1968.
*The Day Before Forever, and Thunderhead.* New York, Doubleday, 1968.
*Assignment in Nowhere.* New York, Berkley, 1968; London, Dobson, 1972.
*Retief and the Warlords.* New York, Doubleday, 1968.
*The Long Twilight.* New York, Putnam, 1969; London, Hale, 1976.
*The World Shuffler* (O'Leary). New York, Putnam, 1970; London, Sidgwick and Jackson, 1973.
*The House in November.* New York, Putnam, 1970; London, Sidgwick and Jackson, 1973.
*Time Trap.* New York, Putnam, 1970; London, Hale, 1976.
*Retief's Ransom.* New York, Putnam, 1971; London, Dobson, 1975.
*The Star Treasure.* New York, Putnam, 1971; London, Sidgwick and Jackson, 1974.
*Deadfall.* New York, Doubleday, 1971; London, Hale, 1974; as *Fat Chance,* New York, Pocket Books, 1975.
*Dinosaur Beach.* New York, Scribner, 1971; London, Hale, 1973.
*The Infinite Cage.* New York, Putnam, 1972; London, Dobson, 1976.
*Night of Delusions.* New York, Putnam, 1972; London, Dobson, 1977.
*The Shape Changer* (O'Leary). New York, Putnam, 1972; London, Hale, 1977.
*The Glory Game.* New York, Doubleday, 1973; London, Hale, 1974.
*Bolo: The Annals of the Dinochrome Brigade.* New York, Berkley, 1976; London, Millington, 1977.
*The Ultimax Man.* New York, St. Martin's Press, 1978; London, Sidgwick and Jackson, 1980.
*Beyond the Imperium.* New York, Tor, 1981.
*Star Colony.* New York, St. Martin's Press, 1981.
*The Other Sky* (includes *The House in November*). New York, Tor, 1982.
*Retief to the Rescue.* New York, Baen, 1983.
*The Return of Retief.* New York, Baen, 1985.
*Rogue Bolo.* New York, Baen, 1985.
*End as a Hero.* New York, Ace, 1985.

*Retief and the Pangalactic Pageant of Pulchriture.* New York, Baen, 1986.
*Retief in the Ruins.* New York, Baen, 1986.
*Reward for Retief.* New York, Baen, 1989.
*The Stars Must Wait.* New York, Baen, 1990.
*Zone Yellow New York.* New York, Baen, 1990.
*Judson's Eden.* New York, Baen, 1991.

Short Stories (series: Bolo; Retief)

*Envoy to New Worlds* (Retief). New York, Ace, 1963; London, Dobson, 1972.
*Galactic Diplomat* (Retief). New York, Doubleday, 1965.
*Nine by Laumer.* New York, Doubleday, 1967; London, Faber, 1968.
*Greylorn.* New York, Berkley, 1968; as *The Other Sky*, London, Dobson, 1968.
*It's a Mad, Mad, Mad Galaxy.* New York, Berkley, 1968; London, Dobson, 1969.
*Retief, Ambassador to Space.* New York, Doubleday, 1969.
*Retief of the CDT.* New York, Doubleday, 1971.
*Once There Was a Giant.* New York, Doubleday, 1971; London, Hale, 1975.
*The Big Show.* New York, Ace, 1972; London, Hale, 1976.
*Timetracks.* New York, Ballantine, 1972.
*The Undefeated.* New York, Dell, 1974.
*Retief, Emissary to the Stars.* New York, Dell, 1975; augmented edition, New York, Pocket Books, 1979.
*The Best of Keith Laumer.* New York, Pocket Books, 1976.
*Retief Unbound* (omnibus). New York, Ace, 1979.
*Retief at Large.* New York, Ace, 1979.
*The Breaking Earth.* New York, Pinnacle, 1981.
*Worlds of the Imperium.* New York, Tor, 1982.
*Retief: Diplomat at Arms.* New York, Pocket Books, 1982.
*The Galaxy Builder.* New York, Ace, 1984.
*A Chrestomathy.* New York, Baen, 1984.
*The Compleat Bolo.* New York, Baen, 1990.
*Alien Minds.* New York, Baen, 1991.

OTHER PUBLICATIONS

Novels

*Embassy.* New York, Pyramid, 1965.
*The Afrit Affair* (novelization of TV series). New York, Berkley, 1968.
*The Drowned Queen* (novelization of TV series). New York, Berkley, 1968.
*The Gold Bomb* (novelization of TV series). New York, Berkley, 1968.

Other

*How to Design and Build Flying Models.* New York, Harper, 1960; revised edition, 1970; London, Hale, 1975.

Editor, *Five Fates.* New York, Doubleday, 1970.

*

Manuscript Collections: University of Syracuse, New York; University of Mississippi, University.

Keith Laumer comments:

I have been asked if my work is "relevant," i.e., political propaganda. It is not. I prefer to treat themes that have been important to man ever since he became man, and will continue to be important as long as humanity survives; strength and courage, truth and beauty, loyalty and justice, ethics and integrity, kindness and gentleness, and many others.

* * *

During the 1960's, Keith Laumer was one of the most prolific of science-fiction authors. He has to his credit a long string of titles which range over wide areas both in subject matter and in treatment. Laumer's first novel, *Worlds of the Imperium*, is told as a conventional adventure story, with only an occasional light touch. But in *The Time Bender* and its sequels featuring Layfayette O'Leary, Laumer writes what amounts to a gentle parody of his own Imperium series. And the humor in the long and popular series (mostly of short stories) concerning interstellar diplomat Jame Retief stretches almost all the way to farce. But Laumer can play the other side of the court as well: the tone is serious, even grim, in such works as *A Plague of Demons* and *Night of Delusions.* As for subject matter, Laumer has tried out virtually all the traditional possibilities and has enriched the realm of science fiction with innovations of his own—most notably the brilliantly detailed and remarkably plausible picture of the "fabric of simultaneous reality" introduced in the Imperium series. Laumer has written space-war stories, space-diplomacy stories, slightly rationalized fairy stories, time-travel stories, parallel-world stories, robot stories, psi-power stories, invasion-of-the-Earth stories (including *The Monitors*, in which the invaders are the good guys), stories of intrigue, love, rational detection, mystical apotheosis, and on and on.

Yet for all its diversity, Laumer's work holds unities as well. Some of these are of a negative sort. For instance, there is never an unhappy ending. A Laumer hero may lose a girl, but if so he will usually marry another, and will in no case allow one misfortune to poison his entire life. He may get killed in the end, but he will never go unmourned and (in *Assignment in Nowhere* and others) his sacrifice may well save the world. In the area of positive generalizations, it can be said that in some measure all Laumer stories are adventure stories, even if the author's focus is on satire, farce, romance, ratiocination, or philosophical speculation.

Moreover, Laumer heroes are virtually all of one general pattern, with variations determined chiefly by degree of maturity. While the typologies are not identical, the Laumer character does bear striking similarities to the "Heinlein individual" described by Alexei Panshin. Explanations for this resemblance might range from some basic principle of storytelling to Heinlein's and Laumer's similar background as military officers. The basic Laumer type is the full-formed competent man—sure of himself, resourceful, able to mix easily with all levels of society and to get what he wants out of anyone. Laumer has put the basic type to heaviest use in the person of Retief, hero of a "template series" where character growth is ruled out by the ground rules. For most other applications, the basic competent man is too static—he can indeed be roused to action, but only to protect what he has. A slight variation Laumer employs more often is an incipient competent man whose character is fully formed but who has not yet found his niche in life, and who is consequently searching for fulfillment. Brion Bayard fits in here in *Worlds of the Imperium*, though in the sequel, *The Other Side of Time*, he has matured into the basic type. It is of course possible to begin at an earlier point, with someone who must learn not merely how to apply competence, but competence itself. This gives us characters such as Billy Danger in *Galactic Odyssey* or, in a more humorous vein, Layfayette O'Leary. But Laumer has also moved in the other direction, beyond the competent man. Perhaps because of his own relative youth during his peak writing period, Laumer has chosen to do this not by putting one of his heroes through some sort of mid-life crisis, but rather (in a tack he might have picked up from van Vogt or the early Heinlein—or from Sophocles) by having his hero discover something about who he is that causes him to transcend his status as the competent man. In the most extreme case, the largely unsuccessful *Night of Delusions*, the protagonist finds himself to be, for most practical purposes, God. Other Laumer heroes learn that they are supermen, Arthurian reincarnations, and various sorts of robots. The effects of such revelations also vary. Some heroes go off to pursue transcendental existence, some perish gloriously, and others voluntarily return to the human state. It is difficult to decide whether in these various encounters with the transcendental, Laumer is trying to put forth a serious philosophy (in the manner of, say, Cordwainer Smith or Gordon R. Dickson), or simply, more playfully, to give his already-competent heroes somewhere to go, and to pique the reader's sense of wonder. Such mystic passages are not, in any event, the most successful part of Laumer's work.

The 1960's and early 1970's remain the significant period of Laumer's production. New titles appearing since that time have been generally repackagings or "fix-ups" of older work. A partial exception, *The Galaxy Builder*, is merely one more Layfayette O'Leary novel in the same mold as its predecessors. The repackagings and reiterations do little or nothing to remedy Laumer's characteristic flaws of insufficient attention to detail and excessive repetition from work to work. Consequently, it will be left to posterity to decide which of five or six versions of essentially the same story is the one really worth keeping. But some of Laumer will most certainly be kept.

—Patrick L. McGuire

---

**LAVOND, Paul Dennis.** *See* **LOWNDES, Robert A.W.**

---

**LeBARON, Anthony.** *See* **LAUMER, Keith.**

---

**LEE, Matt.** *See* **MERWIN, Sam, Jr.**

---

**LEE, Tanith.** British. Born in London, 19 September 1947. Attended Catford Grammar School, London, and an art college. Recipient: August Derleth award, 1980; World Fantasy Convention award, 1983. Lives in London. Address: c/o Macmillan London Ltd., 4 Little Essex Street, London WC2R 3LF, England.

### Science-Fiction Publications

Novels (series: Birthgrave)

*The Birthgrave*. New York, DAW, 1975; London, Futura, 1977.
*Don't Bite the Sun*. New York, DAW, 1976.
*The Storm Lord*. New York, DAW, 1976; London, Futura, 1977.
*Drinking Sapphire Wine*. New York, DAW, 1977; published with *Don't Bite the Sun*, London, Hamlyn, 1979.
*Volkhavaar*. New York, DAW, 1977; London, Hamlyn, 1981.
*Vazkor, Son of Vazkor* (Birthgrave). New York, DAW, 1978; as *Shadowfire*, London, Futura, 1979.
*Quest for the White Witch* (Birthgrave). New York, DAW, 1978; London, Futura, 1979.
*Night's Master*. New York, DAW, 1978; London, Hamlyn, 1981.
*Death's Master*. New York, DAW, 1979; London, Hamlyn, 1982.
*Electric Forest*. New York, DAW, 1979.
*Sabella; or, The Blood Stone*. New York, DAW, 1980; London, Unwin, 1987.
*Kill the Dead*. New York, DAW, 1980.
*Day by Night*. New York, DAW, 1980.
*Delusion's Master*. New York, DAW, 1981.
*The Silver Metal Lover*. New York, DAW, 1982; London, Unwin, 1986.
*Sung in Shadow*. New York, DAW, 1983.
*Anackire*. New York, DAW, 1983; London, Futura, 1985.
*Days of Grass*. New York, DAW, 1985.
*Dark Castle, White Horse*. New York, DAW, 1986.
*Delirium's Mistress*. New York, DAW, 1986.
*Night's Sorceries*. New York, DAW, 1987.
*The White Serpent*. New York, DAW, 1988.
*A Heroine of the World*. New York, DAW, 1989.
*The Blood of Roses*. London, Century, 1990.
*Lycanthia*. London, Legend, 1990.
*Black Unicorn*. New York, Atheneum, 1991.

Short Stories (series: Secret Books of Paradys)

*Cyrion*. New York, DAW, 1982.
*Red as Blood; or, Tales from the Sisters Grimmer*. New York, DAW, 1983.
*The Beautiful Biting Machine*. New Castle, Virginia, Cheap Street, 1984.
*Tamastara; or, The Indian Nights*. New York, DAW, 1984.
*The Gorgon and Other Beastly Tales*. New York, DAW, 1985.
The Secret Books of Paradys:
*The Book of the Damned*. London, Unwin, 1988; New York, Overlook Press, 1990.
*The Book of the Beast*. London, Unwin, 1988; New York, Overlook Press, 1991.
*Women as Demons*. London, Women's Press, 1989.
*Forests of the Night*. London, Unwin, 1990.

### Other Publications

Short Stories

*The Betrothed*. Sidcup, Kent, Slughorn Press, 1968.

Plays

Radio Plays: *Bitter Gate*, 1977; *Red Wine*, 1977; *Death Is King*, 1979; *The Silver Sky*, 1980.

Television Plays: *Sarcophagus*, 1980, and *Sand*, 1981, both for *Blake's Seven* series.

Other (for children)

*The Dragon Hoard*. London, Macmillan, and New York, Farrar Straus, 1971.
*Princess Hynchatti and Some Other Surprises*. London, Macmillan, 1972; New York, Farrar Straus, 1973.
*Animal Castle*. London, Macmillan, and New York, Farrar Straus, 1972.
*Companions on the Road*. London, Macmillan, 1975.
*The Winter Players*. London, Macmillan, 1976.
*Companions on the Road, and The Winter Players*. New York, St. Martin's Press, 1977.
*East of Midnight*. London, Macmillan, 1977; New York, St. Martin's Press, 1978.
*The Castle of Dark*. London, Macmillan, 1978.
*Shon the Taken*. London, Macmillan, 1979.
*Unsilent Night* (miscellany; for adults). Cambridge, Massachusetts, NESFA Press, 1981.
*Prince on a White Horse*. London, Macmillan, 1982.
*Madame Two Swords*. New York, Donald M. Grant, 1988.

*

Bibliography: by Mike Ashley, in *Fantasy Macabre 4* (London), 1983.

* * *

The fiction of Tanith Lee is a highly original and intense mixture of science fiction, heroic fantasy, and fairy tale. In all her work, her ironic sense of humor, dark imagination, and an interest in the erotic play a strong role. Her themes usually involve the individual's ability to manipulate fate, and point of view as a moral determinant. These elements are combined in a variety of ways to create varying effects.

*The Birthgrave*, Ms. Lee's first work for adults, contains several of the devices she exploits again in later works. The plot concerns the awakening and subsequent education of a "goddess." The heroine is a mythic creation, on whose fate rests the direction of her world. Her moral ignorance is demonstrated and alleviated in an episodic series of adventures. Societal conflicts between men and women, and between technology and science, are played out directly in her experience. Although this is undoubtedly close in spirit to *The Storm Lord*, Ms. Lee does not yet employ the more contrived style that conveys so well the super-human dimensions of that setting. And indeed, the denouement of *The Birthgrave* is pure science fiction, finding rational explanations for all the heroine's inhuman traits. This is not the case in the later novels, where some characters have frankly supernatural traits, and the prose style subtly and effectively communicates this. Larger-than-life protagonists, however, are a common feature of *The Birthgrave* and its sequels as well as *The Storm Lord, Anackire*, and *The White Serpent*. Their struggle to sort out good and evil is of paramount importance to their worlds and is usually at least partly dependent on their discovery of their own identity, which may be hidden, lost, or simply confused.

Both *Night's Master* and *Death's Master* investigate some of these same concerns from a fresh perspective. The episodic plots now give way to a structure of almost independent short stories, and the style is the full-blown, heavily stylized tone of myths and fairy tales. These stories concern demon-kind and their interaction with humanity. The demons are at pains to play elaborate ironic pranks usually targeting the most human behavior of the human characters. Like the heroes and heroines of the other novels, these characters have the ability to influence the direction of world events. However, morality rather than society is the focus of the conflict in this series. The ambiguities of moral behavior, especially as related to sexual relationships, are explored in many permutations. Self examination is rarely an issue, except as the demons call into question the assumptions of the human characters.

Ms. Lee's stylized prose draws the reader into a world reminiscent of familiar territory, which is all the more shocking when it is suddenly turned on its head. Sympathetic werewolves and vampires, wicked Cinderellas and Snow Whites, and the subversion of our expectations are the subjects of these works. The reader's sense of disorientation stems in part from the creation of real characters from the stock villains and heroes of the genre. Some of these works appear as short stories (*Red as Blood*); *Lycanthia* is a series of interrelated novellas and *Cyrion* concerns the adventures of a single hero told as a series of short stories joined by "interlogues" which provide continuity. Part of the impact of these tales derives from their extraordinary sensory reality. We experience in these novels and short stories the feel of exotic fabrics, the taste of strange fruits, the incense of haunting perfumes, and the vibrant colors of a variety of barbaric and sophisticated peoples. The reader may experience a kind of secondary sensory overload or feel oppressed by the intensity of the borrowed sensations. This extraordinarily tactile world is one of the reasons Tanith Lee's work lingers in the mind.

Lee's talent for the creation of a reality is also evident in her science-fiction works. In *Don't Bite the Sun*, for example, an invented slang conveys not only a sense of the heroine but of her entire society. This "Jang slang," used constantly by the narrator, consists almost entirely of words indicating extremes. It is the vocabulary of a society so predictable that its members have taken to attempting suicide for diversion. This is typical of Lee's science-fiction works, whose theme is generally human society and its failures, although on occasion it is purely a vehicle for humor (as in "Qatt-Sup" from *The Gorgon*). Human failure is usually demonstrated in the person of the protagonist, whose struggles provide the context in which society is examined.

In a recent novel, *A Heroine of the World*, Tanith Lee has modulated the fantasy to create an easily recognizable world. Love and war are key plot ingredients as they are in many of the heroic fantasies, but here they are played out on a human scale without magical interference. The tragedies are human and immediate. The heroine's will to survive is recognizable from any World War II autobiography. Her salvation, however, comes not from her own struggles, nor from the men she abandons herself to, but through her understanding of her goddess. As in a number of short stories throughout her oeuvre, Ms. Lee here uses a single element of the fantastic to provide leverage to work with an important theme.

The work of Tanith Lee is not for every taste. It is idiosyncratic and individual in its expression, characters, settings and themes. Like caviar or brandy, it is an acquired taste. It has sometimes the smothering quality of incense. It is a pleasure reserved for the sophisticated palate.

—Cathy Chauvette

---

**LE GUIN, Ursula K(roeber).** American. Born in Berkeley, California, 21 October 1929; daughter of the anthropologist Alfred L. Kroeber. Educated at Radcliffe College, Cambridge, Massachusetts, A.B. 1951 (Phi Beta Kappa); Columbia University, New York (Faculty Fellow; Fulbright Fellow, 1953), M.A. 1952. Married Charles A. Le Guin in 1953; two daughters and one son. Instructor in French, Mercer University, Macon, Georgia, 1954, and University of Idaho, Moscow, 1956; department secretary, Emory University, Atlanta, 1955; has taught writing workshops at Pacific University, Forest Grove, Oregon, 1971, University of Washington, Seattle, 1971–73, Portland State University, Oregon, 1974, 1977, 1979, in Melbourne, Australia, 1975, at the University of Reading, England, 1976, Indiana Writers Conference, Bloomington, 1978, 1983, and University of California, San Diego, 1979. Recipient: Boston, *Globe-Horn Book* award, for children's book, 1969; Nebula award, 1969, 1974 (twice), 1991; Hugo award, 1970, 1973, 1974, 1975, 1988; National Book award for children's book, 1972; Jupiter award, 1974 (twice), 1976; Gandalf award, 1979; University of Oregon Distinguished Service award, 1981; *Locus* award (twice), 1983; Janet Heidinger Kafka award, 1986; Pushcart prize, 1991; Harold D. Vursell award, American Academy and Institute of Arts and Letters, 1991. Guest of Honor, World Science Fiction Convention, 1975. D.Litt. Bucknell University, Lewisburg, Pennsylvania, 1978; Lawrence University, Appleton, Wisconsin; D.H.L.: Lewis and Clark College, Portland, 1983; Occidental College, Los Angeles, 1985. Lives in Portland, Oregon. Agent: Virginia Kidd, 538 East Harford Street, Milford, Pennsylvania 18337, U.S.A.

## Science-Fiction Publications

### Novels (Series: Hain)

*Rocannon's World* (Hain). New York, Ace, 1966; London, Tandem, 1972.
*Planet of Exile* (Hain). New York, Ace, 1966; London, Tandem, 1972.
*City of Illusions* (Hain). New York, Ace, 1967; London, Gollancz, 1971.
*The Left Hand of Darkness* (Hain). New York, Ace, and London, Macdonald, 1969.
*The Lathe of Heaven.* New York, Scribner, 1971; London, Gollancz, 1972.
*The Dispossessed: An Ambiguous Utopia.* New York, Harper, and London, Gollancz, 1974.
*The Word for World Is Forest* (Hain). New York, Putnam, 1976; London, Gollancz, 1977.
*The Eye of the Heron.* London, Gollancz, 1982; New York, Harper, 1983.
*Always Coming Home.* New York, Harper, 1985; London, Gollancz, 1986.
*The New Atlantis,* with *The Return from Rainbow Bridge,* by Kim Stanley Robinson. New York, Tor, 1989.

### Short Stories

*The Wind's Twelve Quarters.* New York, Harper, 1975; London, Gollancz, 1976.
*The Compass Rose.* New York, Harper, 1982; London, Gollancz, 1983.
*Buffalo Gals and Other Animal Presences.* Santa Barbara, California, Capra Press, 1987; as *Buffalo Gals,* London, Gollancz, 1990.

## Other Publications

### Novel

*Malafrena.* New York, Putnam, 1979; London, Gollancz, 1980.

### Short Stories

*Orsinian Tales.* New York, Harper, 1976; London, Gollancz, 1977.
*The Water Is Wide.* Portland, Oregon, Pendragon Press, 1976.
*Gwilan's Harp.* Northridge, California, Lord John Press, 1981.
*The Visionary: The Life Story of Flicker of the Serpentine of Telina-Na,* with *Wonders Hidden,* by Scott Russell Sanders. Santa Barbara, California, Capra Press, 1984.
*A Ride on the Red Mare's Back.* New York, Orchard, 1992.

### Fiction (for children)

*Earthsea.* London, Gollancz, 1977; as *The Earthsea Trilogy,* London, Penguin, 1979.
*A Wizard of Earthsea.* Berkeley, California, Parnassus Press, 1968; London, Gollancz, 1971.
*The Tombs of Atuan.* New York, Atheneum, 1971, London, Gollancz, 1972.
*The Farthest Shore.* New York, Atheneum, 1972; London, Gollancz, 1973.
*Very Far Away from Anywhere Else.* New York, Atheneum, 1976; as *A Very Long Way from Anywhere Else,* London, Gollancz, 1976.
*Leese Webster,* New York, Atheneum, 1979; London, Gollancz, 1981.
*The Beginning Place.* New York, Harper, 1980; as *Threshold,* London, Gollancz, 1980.
*The Adventure of Cobbler's Rune.* New Castle, Virginia, Cheap Street, 1982.
*Solomon Leviathan's Nine Hundred and Thirty-First Trip Around the World.* New Castle, Virginia, Cheap Street, 1983.
*A Visit from Dr. Katz.* New York, Atheneum, 1988; as *Dr. Katz,* London, Collins, 1988.
*Catwings.* New York, Orchard, 1988.
*Catwings Return.* New York, Orchard, 1989.
*Fire and Stone.* New York, Atheneum, 1989.
*Tehanu: The Last Book of Earthsea.* New York, Atheneum, and London, Gollancz, 1990.

### Plays

*No Use to Talk to Me,* in *The Altered Eye,* edited by Lee Harding. Melbourne, Norstrilia Press, 1976; New York, Berkley, 1978.
*King Dog* (screenplay), with *Dostoevsky,* by Raymond Carver and Tess Gallagher. Santa Barbara, California, Capra Press, 1985.

### Verse

*Wild Angels.* Santa Barbara, California, Capra Press, 1975.
*Tillai and Tylissos,* with Theodora K. Quinn. N.p., Red Bull Press, 1979.
*Torrey Pines Reserve.* Northridge, California, Lord John Press, 1980.
*Gwilan's Harp.* Northridge, California, Lord John Press, 1981.
*Hard Words and Other Poems.* New York, Harper, 1981.

*In the Red Zone.* Northridge, California, Lord John Press, 1983.
*Wild Oats and Fireweed.* New York, Harper, 1988.

Other

*From Elfland to Poughkeepsie* (lecture). Portland, Oregon, Pendragon Press, 1973.
*Dreams Must Explain Themselves.* New York, Algol Press, 1975.
*The Language of the Night: Essays on Fantasy and Science Fiction*, edited by Susan Wood. New York, Putnam, 1979; revised edition, edited by Ursula K. Le Guin, London, Women's Press, 1989.
*Dancing at the Edge of the World: Thoughts on Words, Women, Places.* New York, Grove Press, and London, Gollancz, 1989.
*The Way of the Water's Going*, with photographs by Ernest Waugh and Alan Nicholson. New York, Harper and Row, 1989.

Editor, *Nebula Award Stories 11.* London, Gollancz, 1976; New York, Harper, 1977.
Editor, with Virginia Kidd, *Interfaces.* New York, Ace, 1980.
Editor, with Virginia Kidd, *Edges.* New York, Pocket Books, 1980.

*

Bibliography: *Ursula K. Le Guin: A Primary and Secondary Bibliography* by Elizabeth Cummins Cogell, Boston, Hall, 1983.

Manuscript Collection: University of Oregon Library, Eugene.

Critical Studies: *The Farthest Shores of Ursula K. Le Guin* by George Edgar Slusser, San Bernardino, California, Borgo Press, 1976; "Ursula Le Guin Issue" of *Science-Fiction Studies* (Terre Haute, Indiana), March 1976; *Ursula Le Guin* by Joseph D. Olander and Martin H. Greenberg, New York, Taplinger, and Edinburgh, Harris, 1979; *Ursula K. Le Guin: Voyager to Inner Lands and to Outer Space* edited by Joseph W. De Bolt, Port Washington, New York, Kennikat Press, 1979; *Ursula K. Le Guin* by Barbara J. Bucknall, New York, Ungar, 1981; *Ursula K. Le Guin* by Charlotte Spivack, Boston, Twayne, 1984; *Approaches to the Fiction of Ursula K. Le Guin* by James Bittner, Ann Arbor, Michigan, UMI Research Press, and Epping, Essex, Bowker, 1984; *Understanding Ursula K. Le Guin* by Elizabeth Cummins, Columbia, University of South Carolina Press, 1990.

* * *

The immensely popular fiction of Ursula K. Le Guin proves that popular literature may have literary merit, a serious message, and a large audience all at once. Today the notion of a science-fiction writer producing a novel of substance, even a novel of character, is not so remarkable, as researchers continue to demonstrate that works remarkable as literature have existed in this genre ever since the publication of Mary Shelley's *Frankenstein;* but at the start of Le Guin's career, in the mid 1960's, literary excellence in science fiction was regarded as rare. Le Guin, hailed as a *novelist* who chose to write science fiction, has always attracted an audience composed of genre fans as well as readers who would ordinarily disdain science fiction. Le Guin's work continues to be known for literary expertise which graces a thematic preoccupation with telling essentially hopeful stories of man transcending alienation to open his imagination, his intellect, and his heart to the real adventure of the universe. Le Guin, in common with many writers of science fiction, is a talented builder of new worlds and alien landscapes; she is comfortable with technological wonders, faster-than-light vehicles, and particularly with marvels in the field of long-distance communications, but her commitment, stated clearly in the essay "Science Fiction and Mrs. Brown," is to confirm man's essential humanity against a backdrop of alien situations by means of consistently viewing her characters as the "subjects" of her narratives rather than as objects. A subjective human approach to the marvelous underlines Le Guin's view that if "Mrs. Brown [the ordinary, intriguing snatch of human character] is dead, you can take your galaxies and roll them up into a ball and throw them into the trashcan, for all I care. What good are all the objects in the universe, if there is no subject?"

A large portion of Le Guin's work focuses upon subjective views of a universe incorporating numerous habitable worlds, each "seeded" by beings from the planet Hain. Each of the five novels and several shorter works in this series revolves around the literal and figurative quests of chief characters to discover their individual purposes within the contexts of their several different worlds and, often, within the broader context of the universe. The themes and chronology of the Hain series have been worked out over two decades, but the early works anticipate or foreshadow the best moments of her later work. One of the later novels, fascinatingly, provides the scientific explanation and development of a device—the instantaneous communicator called the ansible—which has been essential to all of the previous works.

The first published works in this series, *Rocannon's World, Planet of Exile*, and *City of Illusions*, do proceed chronologically and establish a thematic preoccupation with the duality existing in nature and in man viewed, as Peter Nicholls has pointed out, "not as polarities or opposed forces" but as archetypical symbols presented as "twin parts of a balanced whole" (*The Science Fiction Encyclopedia*, 1979). Each work employs the alien as the embodiment of alienation presenting to the hero the challenge of transcending fear itself, through embracing the unknown. Communication, whether through telepathic "mindspeech" or by means of the amazing ansible, is significant, often the symbolic crux of each climax. In *Rocannon's World* an outworld ethnological surveyor stranded on Fomalhaut II is unable to accept fully his destiny of remaining on the strange world until he achieves the ability to communicate through mindspeech. In a narrative which also emphasizes the importance of naming, it is significant that, in ironic understatement, the League of All Worlds, unbeknownst to the ethnographer, gives this world his name, Rocannon's World.

*Planet of Exile* depicts a world which is populated by two humanoid groups, each believing themselves to be fully human and therefore superior to the other. A female character, the dreamy yet strong-willed Rolery, represents the linking of the two cultures as she overcomes her awe of the "farborn" Terran colonists through her command of telepathic powers generally possessed only by the farborns. Interestingly, discipline, along with honest communication, is described as the key to individual purpose and successful community, while community (the cooperation of both "human" societies) is necessary for the basic survival of either group. "Community," asserts Le Guin (in "Science Fiction and Mrs. Brown"), "is the best we can hope for, and community for most people means touches: the touch of your hand against the other's hand, the job done together, the sledge hauled together, the dance danced together, the child conceived together." Significantly, Rolery is offered the hope of conceiving a child with her farborn husband, while the two groups, under extreme challenge from overwhelming environmental conditions, at last unite to form a new society. Metaphor is particularly rich in the novel, which anticipates *The Left Hand of Darkness* in its description of a world dominated by a frigid winter environment.

*City of Illusions* describes a Hainish world where mindspeech, previously the epitome of truthful communication, has been perverted by the alien Shing invaders who can manipulate it into a "mind lie." A complex narrative tells the story of the amnesiac Falk and his quest to discover his true name and homeworld. Throughout experiences of betrayal and disorienting double identity, his hopes were "staked now totally on one belief: that an honest man cannot be cheated, that truth, if the game be played through right to the end, will lead to truth." Here truth and falsehood are regarded as polarities in essential struggle; truth may prevail only when the hero learns to allow both of his identities to work together and, significantly, when his gains access to the ansible so that he may communicate with the world of its origin as well as with the League of All Worlds. The League becomes known as the Ekumen of Known Worlds in *The Left Hand of Darkness,* which richly explores the themes suggested in earlier Hainish works. Genly Ai is a human ethnologist who visits the planet Gethen, where he is swiftly caught up in a snowbound society wrapped in political intrigue and characterized by a revolutionary (to Genly Ai as well as to the reader) androgynous worldview which raises questions about sexuality and sexism and shows a populace composed of individuals whose identity is divorced from gender. The Gethenians, usually neuter, experience a sexual cycle which gives them the ability to become either male or female at certain cyclical peaks. The implications of this alienness tax even the comprehension of this professional observer who learns that the limitation of his own alien perspective, his own alienation, is keeping him from appreciating and understanding this strange new world.

"Vaster than Empires and More Slow" and *The Word for World Is Forest* are shorter works in the Hain series which use the forest as metaphors for the unknown. The former (its title derived from Andrew Marvell's poem "To His Coy Mistress") is perhaps Le Guin's most polished and graceful statement of the need to embrace the alien, the Other, in order to understand it. Osden, a ship's empath, transcends the limitations of both time and fear when he literally embraces the surface of an alien planet which is covered by a network of sentient vegetation. "He had taken fear into himself, and accepting had transcended it. He had given up his self to the alien, an unreserved surrender, that left no place for evil. He had learned love of the Other, and thereby been given his whole self."

*The Dispossessed* is centered on the inventor of the ansible, a man called Shevek whose anarchist "Utopia" is ambiguously unable to provide him with the raw materials (chiefly free communication and flow of scientific information) which he needs to make his best contribution to society. This rich work is one is which occasional didacticism is nevertheless fascinating as two politically different worlds (one anarchistic, the other decadently capitalistic) are balanced by means of contrast and comparison, each presented in alternate chapters. The author uses visual perspective most strikingly here; the image of the wall as a defining force is powerfully employed, while in an early scene Shevek's world fills his view like a concave dish until, as his space vessel takes him a greater distance from it, it falls away into a convex circle, then a globe, then a distant world. The author also uses paradox, mathematical and verbal, as the key to truth, while communication among all men is the confirmation of man's essential humanity in the face of political, environmental, or other differences.

Other major works by Le Guin include *The Lathe of Heaven,* a novel outside of the Hain series dealing with a man of conscience who cannot bear the fact that his dreams effectively change reality, and *The Beginning Place,* an allegorical novel portraying a fantastic "twilight world" that becomes a haven for two adolescents fleeing from unhappy family situations in a bleak, unnamed suburbia. The protagonists learn, by means of encounters with an archetypal monster, to face the harsh disappointments of their "real" lives. *Orsinian Tales* and *Malafrena* evoke the 19th century in an imaginary country with a central European atmosphere. *Malafrena* deals with the coming of age of a young revolutionary who must learn to balance freedom and commitment.

*The Compass Rose* is an anthology of short stories organized around the four directions of the magnetic compass. Tales with settings and themes reminiscent of those in *Malafrena* are here accompanied by tales that are more strictly science-fictional and dealing with, for instance, a new Atlantis or an enigmatic cat used in a scientific experiment. A particular gem is "The Author of the Acacia Seeds and Other Extracts from the *Journal of the Association of Therolinguistics,*" which succeeds as a brilliant spoof of academic writing and as a comment on the difficulty of and fascination inherent in understanding the culture of another life form.

The four novels in Le Guin's Earthsea series represent a study of magical skill which appeals to adults as well as to the younger audience for which it was written. *Tehanu: The Last Book of Earthsea* was published in 1988, a full 20 years after the first volume in the series, *A Wizard of Earthsea,* was produced and after the author had done a great deal of rethinking about the role of women in a man's world. *Times Literary Supplement* reviewer John Clute praised *Wizard* as "as polished and word-perfect a tale for older children as could be imagined." *Tehanu* is a more difficult book, in which a world beloved by its readers is fully re-examined, particularly in regard to its power structure. While the old magic *is* significant to the novel's ending, the book pleases feminists and students of Le Guin's maturation as a thinker more than those who are looking for more of the same in Earthsea.

Le Guin's evolution as a thinker is made particularly clear in *Dancing at the Edge of the World: Thoughts on Words, Women, Places,* a collection of the author's nonfiction including talks, essays, occasional pieces and book reviews from 1976–1986. Particularly noteworthy is her reprint of the much-quoted essay "Is Gender Necessary?" (now entitled "Is Gender Necessary? Redux") along with a "running commentary" reflecting "changes of mind" and the author's more recent thinking about how the masculine pronoun employed in *The Left Hand of Darkness* limited her abilities to create an androgyne in which the female aspect was fully drawn as the male.

Le Guin's most significant accomplishment in recent years is her work *Always Coming Home,* which some refuse to classify as a novel. Featuring multiple voices, the book tells the stories of the Kesh, a people existing in woman-centered society in a future California landscape. The book's radial structure and experimental narrative techniques reflect Le Guin's preoccupation with creating a literature that is "alive, unfixed, on the move, defying definition." Her goal is to convey the experience of the Kesh world without limiting the reader to a single vantage point. As critic Elizabeth Cummins points out, the book "de-emphasizes the significance of a beginning or an end, challenges their very existence even, and instead concentrates . . . on the middle, the living, the changing."

In common with Brian Aldiss, Le Guin continually works to stretch her skills in new directions, demanding ever more of herself in terms of content and style. She is afraid neither to challenge the intelligent reader nor to fight the confines of a marketplace that demands easily categorizeable fiction, nor to correct her own thinking or "change her mind" in print. The result is some of the most stimulating and satisfying fiction available within the genre as well as outside of it. Also like Aldiss,

Le Guin has written "mainstream" fiction as well as work in other forms such as poetry and memoirs.

Over the years Le Guin's work affirms that the ultimate adventure in the universe is the subjective human quest not so much for confrontation with the alien but for the defeat of alienation. In recent years, she has consciously sought to re-evaluate the hero-centered tale with its linear progression toward conquest and to turn instead toward the novel as a more flexible "carrier bag" that is shaped by the experiences contained within it.

—Rosemary Herbert

---

**LEIBER, Fritz (Reuter, Jr.).** American. Born in Chicago, Illinois, 24 December 1910. Educated at the University of Chicago, Ph.B. 1932; Episcopal General Theological Seminary, Washington, D.C. Married Jonquil Stephens in 1936 (died 1969); one son. Episcopal minister at two churches in New Jersey, 1932–33; actor, 1934–36; editor, Consolidated Book Publishers, Chicago, 1937–41; Instructor in Speech and Drama, Occidental College, Los Angeles, 1941–42; precision inspector, Douglas Aircraft, Santa Monica, California, 1942–44; associate editor, *Science Digest*, Chicago, 1944–56. Lecturer, Clarion State College, Pennsylvania, summers 1968–70. Recipient: Hugo award, 1958, 1965, 1968, 1970, 1971, 1976; Nebula award, 1967, 1970, 1975, and Grand Master Nebula award, 1981; Ann Radcliffe award, 1970; Gandalf award, 1975; Derleth award, 1976; World Fantasy award, 1976, 1978; *Locus* award, 1985; Bram Stoker Lifetime Achievement award, 1988. Guest of Honor, World Science Fiction Convention, 1951. Address: c/o Tor Books, 175 Fifth Avenue, New York, New York 10010, U.S.A.

SCIENCE-FICTION PUBLICATIONS

Novels

*Gather, Darkness!* New York, Pellegrini and Cudahy, 1950; London, New English Library, 1966.
*The Green Millennium*. New York, Abelard Press, 1953; London Abelard Schuman, 1959.
*Destiny Times Three*. New York, Galaxy, 1957.
*The Big Time*. New York, Ace, 1961; London, New English Library, 1965.
*The Silver Eggheads*. New York, Ballantine, 1962; London, New English Library, 1966.
*The Wanderer*. New York, Ballantine, 1964; London, Dobson, 1967.
*A Specter Is Haunting Texas*. New York, Walker, and London, Gollancz, 1969.

Short Stories

*The Sinful Ones*. New York, Universal, 1953; as *You're All Alone*, New York, Ace, 1972.
*The Mind Spider and Other Stories*. New York, Ace, 1961.
*A Pail of Air*. New York, Ballantine, 1964.
*Ships to the Stars*. New York, Ace, 1964.
*The Night of the Wolf*. New York, Ballantine, 1966; London, Sphere, 1976.
*The Secret Songs*. London, Hart Davis, 1968.
*The Best of Fritz Leiber*, edited by Angus Wells. London, Sphere, and New York, Doubleday, 1974.
*The Book of Fritz Leiber*. New York, DAW, 1974.
*The Second Book of Fritz Leiber*. New York, DAW, 1975.
*The Worlds of Fritz Leiber*. New York, Ace, 1976.
*The Change War*. Boston, Gregg Press, 1978.
*Ship of Shadows*. London, Gollancz, 1979; published with *No Truce with Kings*, by Poul Anderson, New York, Tor, 1989.
*The Ghost Light* (includes essay). New York, Berkley, 1984.

OTHER PUBLICATIONS

Novels

*Conjure Wife*. New York, Twayne, 1953; London, Penguin, 1969.
*Tarzan and the Valley of Gold*. New York, Ballantine, 1966.
*The Swords of Lankhmar*. New York, Ace, 1968; London, Hart Davis, 1969.
*Swords and Deviltry*. New York, Ace, 1970; London, New English Library, 1971.
*Our Lady of Darkness*. New York, Berkley, 1977; London, Millington, 1978.
*The Knight and Knave of Swords*. New York, Morrow, 1988; London, Grafton, 1990.

Short Stories

*Night's Black Agents*. Sauk City, Wisconsin, Arkham House, 1947; London, Spearman, 1975.
*Two Sought Adventure: Exploits of Fafhrd and the Gray Mouser*. New York, Gnome Press, 1957.
*Shadows with Eyes*. New York, Ballantine, 1962.
*Swords Against Wizardry*. New York, Ace, 1968; London, Prior, 1977.
*Swords in the Mist*. New York, Ace, 1968; London, Prior, 1977.
*Night Monsters*. New York, Ace, 1969; revised edition, London, Gollancz, 1974.
*Swords Against Death*. New York, Ace, 1970; London, New English Library, 1972.
*Swords and Ice Magic*. New York, Ace, and London, Prior, 1977.
*Rime Isle*. Chapel Hill, North Carolina, Whispers Press, 1977.
*Bazaar of the Bizarre*. West Kingston, Rhode Island, Grant, 1978.
*Heroes and Horrors*. Browns Mills, New Jersey, Whispers Press, 1978.
*The Leiber Chronicles: Fifty Years of Fritz Leiber*, edited by Martin H. Greenberg. Arlington Heights, Illinois, Dark Harvest Press, 1990.

Verse

*The Demons of the Upper Air*. Glendale, California, Squires, 1969.
*Sonnets to Jonquil and All*. Glendale, California, Squires, 1978.

Other

Editor, with Stuart David Schiff, *The World Fantasy Awards 2*. New York, Doubleday, 1980.

*

Bibliography: *Fritz Leiber: A Bibliography 1934–1979* by Chris Morgan, Birmingham, Morgenstern, 1979.

Critical Studies: "Fritz Leiber Issue" of *Fantasy and Science Fiction* (New York), July 1969; *Fritz Leiber* by Jeff Frane, San Bernardino, California, Borgo Press, 1980; *Fritz Leiber* by Tom Staircar, New York, Ungar, 1983.

* * *

Fritz Leiber is one of the most popular and respected writers of science fiction and fantasy. While his readers and fellow writers have appreciated his humor and concern for mankind, the critics have largely ignored his work. Leiber has sometimes been classed with the writers of "weird" stories because of his frequent use of the supernatural and his acknowledged literary debt to H.P. Lovecraft. This association is misleading since Leiber uses the supernatural as a source of symbols for the mysteries of the universe and the mind. As he says, "Many of the most typical creations of science fiction, especially the robot, the android, and the extraterrestrial, are simply the monster in a new guise. . . ."

The supernatural may also turn out to be disguised as applications of science, as in his first novel, *Gather, Darkness!* This story concerns a revolution in a repressive society controlled by a religious hierarchy using technology masquerading as supernatural miracle. The resulting satire provides a commentary on the respective roles of religion, science, and government. There is a witty surface of gadgets such as an electronically controlled haunted house, but there is also a warning against the dangers of restricting scientific knowledge to an elite, regardless of the reason. Leiber's background in the theater is probably responsible for the dramatic staging of much of the action.

*The Green Millennium* presents a picture of a decadent United States where organized crime and corrupt government control society through sex and games. This society is invaded by two alien species from Vega which end the violence. The main virtues of the novel are fast-moving adventure and humor, but there is an underlying layer of satire about the confusion and banality of modern values. *Destiny Times Three* is an alternate-world novel in which three very different stories have been created by an accidental time fragmentation. These worlds contain similar people, one of whom learns of his other personalities and attempts to resolve the time paradoxes. This re-working of an early magazine story is not as polished as his later work. What might have been treated as a traditional SF story has been handled more as allegory and myth.

*The Big Time*, the major work in a series of time-travel stories, concerns a war fought by time-travelling warriors of two groups called "Snakes" and "Spiders" who attempt to produce a victory in the future by altering the past. Leiber's belief in pacifism is presented through the disillusionment of the characters about the possibility of final victory. This framework allows Leiber to mix characters from many times and places in an entertainment and recuperation center. By limiting almost all the action to one room and employing dramatic techniques of staging and dialogue, Leiber has almost created a science-fiction play, with first-person interior narration. Character differentiations are neatly provided by excellent parodies of the characters' differing diction and vocabulary (for example, Elizabethan and Greek dramatic styles). *The Silver Eggheads* is an experiment in satire which borders on farce. The major point is his dissection of the world of publishers, writers, and readers, with humorous references to a wide range of literature, but he seems more at ease with satire in his other books. A long "disaster" novel, *The Wanderer*, describes the responses of people subjected to the earthquakes, tidal waves, and other global disasters caused by an artificial planet which enters an orbit around the earth. Leiber's main interest is in the detailed character studies of both heroes and villains provided by this framework. Almost all of Leiber's themes and interests are included: he deals with almost all aspects of human life, from birth to death. There is also plenty of action, but the novel is not significantly different from many other catastrophy stories. In *A Specter Is Haunting Texas* the specter (a skeletally thin actor from a colony on a satellite around earth's moon) is a coerced leader of a revolution of the enslaved "Mexes" against the Texans, who are hormonally induced giants controlling most of North America. Much of the book is based on theatrical motifs, from costuming and staging to the symbolic roles of the characters, and other devices of the stage. The basic method is again satire, and though the plot is somewhat uneven, the humor and originality of the background are entertaining.

In addition to his science fiction, Leiber has written two novels about the supernatural, *Conjure Wife* and *Our Lady of Darkness*, both of which are border-line science fiction. His fantasy series relating the exploits of Fafhrd and The Gray Mouser has made him one of the most popular writers of this genre. His best-known stories are probably "Coming Attraction" and "Gonna Roll the Bones."

Throughout his career, Leiber has used the same topics and themes—the supernatural, theater, cats, time, sex, politics, alcohol. His most frequent technique is satire. His writing displays considerable stylistic control (particularly in writing parodies) and the influence of many writers from John Webster and Shakespeare to Eddison, C.A. Smith, and Cabell. He seems to view the basic function of literature in terms of human identity and potentiality. The psychological presentation of character is central to his work, as is his view of literature as theater. These factors are related to the problem of psychological identity. All literature requires at least a partial suspension of personality on the part of the reader, but this demand is particularly great in science fiction and also appears prominently in the function of the actor. A similar reaction can occur with stories of the supernatural. All of these features combine to make Leiber an acute commentator on the human mind.

—Norman L. Hills

---

**LEIGH, Stephen.** American. Born in Cincinnati, Ohio, 27 February 1951. Educated at the University of Cincinnati, B.F.A. in art education 1974. Married Denise Parsley in 1974; one daughter and one son. Art teacher, Greenhills and Forest Park school, Ohio, 1974–75. Musician: since 1969, vocalist and bassist in various groups. Currently, office automation manager, Kelly Temporary Services, Cincinnati. Recipient: *Analog* award, 1977. Agent: Merrilee Heifitz, Writers House, 21 West 26th Street, New York, New York 10010. Address: 121 Nansen Street, Cincinnati, Ohio 45216, U.S.A.

SCIENCE-FICTION PUBLICATIONS

Novels (series: Dr. Bones; Neweden; Robots and Aliens)

*Slow Fall to Dawn*. New York, Bantam, 1981.
*Dance of the Hag*. New York, Bantam, 1983.
*A Quiet of Stone*. New York, Bantam, 1984.
*The Bones of God*. New York, Avon, 1986.
*The Crystal Memory*. New York, Avon, 1987.
*The Secret of the Leona* (Dr. Bones). New York, Ace, 1988.
*Changeling* (Robots and Aliens). New York, Ace, 1989.
*The Abraxas Marvel Circus*. New York, Penguin, 1990.

*Alien Tongue*. New York, Bantam, 1991.

*

Stephen Leigh comments:

I'm fascinated by what happens when cultures collide, as well as the intricate dance of words with which we surround ourselves. I'm not traditionally religious myself, but the impact of religions on societies and individuals has been a sub-theme in my work at times. And while most of my work is science fiction rather than fantasy, it's not the hardware itself that interests me, but rather how technology alters the perceptions of those who use it. I also prefer to write about real people—non-perfect people, people with foibles and warts, with sexual appetites and hidden violences, with loves and hates that are sometimes the same thing, who laugh as often as they weep.

I'm a story-teller. My intent is to entertain. If you like what I write, wonderful!

* * *

Stephen Leigh belongs to modern science fiction's cadre of heroic adventure writers. His novels sail quickly, yet his characters do more than watch the scenery go by. Their internal struggles and interactions with the political forces of their worlds form the themes of Leigh's novels: honor, loyalty, right vs. wrong, the Prophet, the Outcast, the Seeker.

Nowhere is this better illustrated than in Leigh's Neweden novels, *Slow Fall to Dawn, Dance of the Hag*, and *A Quiet of Stone*. On the fringes of a vast, collapsed interplanetary empire, the inhabitants of Neweden eke out a meager existence on their economically isolated planet. Neweden's isolation has given rise to a system of guild kinship and honorable settling of disputes reminiscent of medieval England. Gyll Hermond, creator and leader of the assassin's guild known as the Hoorka, must wrestle with a middle-aged re-evaluation of his life's work. The Hoorka, by virtue of Neweden's isolation, flourish under a binding code of honor which gives their victims a chance for survival. This code begins to fragment as the Hoorka ply their trade with less honor-bound worlds. Gyll's internal doubts mix with the demographic forces changing Neweden to produce a sociologically interesting dramatic tragedy.

The examination of individuals shaping and being shaped by history continues in *The Bones of God* and *The Crystal Memory. The Bones of God* narrates the career of Colin Fairwood as the prophet Sartius Exori. The 26th Century finds Old Earth and most of her interplanetary empire governed by a powerful theocracy under the Zakkaist church, a melding of the Judaic, Christian, and Islamic faiths. Interplanetary travel is possible in short time frames, thanks to a gift from the alien Stekoni, but doing so necessitates entering the Veils and suffering the strange dreams and godlike Voice which lurk there. The Stekoni worship this Voice as their god MolitorAb, and this belief has spread throughout the fringes of the theocratic empire. Enter Colin Fairwood, who believes in nothing save his hatred of the Zakkaist church that mutilated him and his fear that the Voice just *might* be his god calling him to action. Colin forms a revolution against the church while dealing with his own doubts about the existence of his god and her apparent failure to guide his actions.

Jemi Charidilis, protagonist of *The Crystal Memory*, grapples with grief for her lost son while searching for an explanation for why two years of her memory of him were stolen. Her search places her at the focus of tensions between Earth and the renegade Mars colony, and between factions of the alien T'Raijek. The completion of her search results in a confrontation with the T'Raijek, which reveals to both humans and aliens just how truly alien their philosophies are to each other.

These works demonstrate Leigh's technical skill at constructing believable worlds and substantive characters. Though his use of foreshadowing is sometimes a bit heavy-handed and the focus of his story may shift too rapidly for some readers, Stephen Leigh clearly has the potential to leave his mark on science fiction. He is particularly adept at injecting philosophy into a story without disrupting plot, pace, or dialogue. The characters of Huan Su (*The Bones of God*) and Commander Nys (*The Crystal Memory*), for example, introduce aspects of Oriental philosophy.

Leigh manages a delicate balance between historical forces and the power of individuals to influence them. While individuals may act as catalysts and refiners of history, its fundamental shape is the result of cultures, economic needs, and stellar geography. Supporting historical trends may result in heroic successes like the Sartius Exori's suicidal assault on the Zakkaist leadership. But as Gyll Hermond discovers when his Hoorka code weakens, such trends may produce tragedy if opposed.

Leigh's recent work includes two series firsts for Byron Preiss Visual Publications: *Changeling* and *The Secret of the Leona.* Both series are geared to a juvenile audience. The books contain crude "visual data" by other writers to aid the imagining impaired.

The *Abraxas Marvel Circus* is an entertaining fantasy about the attempts of a wild handful of characters to revive a dead eccentric genius. Using the same style as his earlier works, Leigh draws on his experience as a bassist and vocalist for rock bands in Cincinnati to weave a bizarre but believable tale around the semi-autobiographical Dirk Masterson. The writing demonstrates a greater subtlety than his earlier fiction, the ramblings of Joan the Flower Man making a humorous counterpoint to the straight Dirk.

In worlds with immense sociological forces, Leigh affirms the individual as a catalyst of change and, potentially, a heroic figure. *The Bones of God* and *The Abraxas Marvel Circus* will introduce the scholar to these aspects of Leigh's fiction.

—Scott Burgess

---

**LEINSTER, Murray.** Pseudonym for Will(iam) F(itzgerald) Jenkins. American. Born in Norfolk, Virginia, 16 June 1896. Educated in public and private schools in Norfolk. Served with the Committee of Public Information, and in the United States Army, 1917–18; served in the Office of War Information during World War II. Married Mary Mandola in 1921; three daughters and one son. Freelance writer from 1918. Recipient: *Liberty* award, 1937; Hugo award, 1956, Guest of Honor, 21st World Science Fiction Convention, 1963. *Died 8 June 1975.*

SCIENCE-FICTION PUBLICATIONS

Novels (series: Joe Kenmore; Med Service)

*Murder Madness*. New York, Brewer and Warren, 1931.
*The Murder of the U.S.A.* (as Will F. Jenkins). New York, Crown, 1946; as *Destroy the U.S.A.*, Toronto, Ambassador, 1946.
*The Last Space Ship*. New York, Fell, 1949; London, Cherry Tree, 1952.
*Fight for Life*. New York, Crestwood, n.d.

*Space Platform* (for children; Kenmore). Chicago, Shasta, 1953.
*Space Tug* (for children; Kenmore). Chicago, Shasta, 1953.
*Gateway to Elsewhere*. New York, Ace, 1954.
*The Forgotten Planet*. New York, Gnome Press, 1954.
*The Brain-Stealers*. New York, Ace, 1954; London, Badger, 1960.
*Operation: Outer Space*. Reading, Pennsylvania, Fantasy Press, 1954; London, Grayson, 1957.
*The Black Galaxy*. New York, Galaxy, 1954.
*The Other Side of Here*. New York, Ace, 1955.
*City of the Moon* (for children; Kenmore). New York, Avalon, 1957.
*Colonial Survey*. New York, Gnome Press, 1957; as *Planet Explorer*, New York, Avon, 1957.
*War with the Gizmos*. New York, Fawcett, 1958; London, Muller, 1959.
*The Monster from Earth's End*. New York, Fawcett, 1959; London, Muller, 1960.
*The Mutant Weapon* (Med Service), *The Pirates of Zan*. New York, Ace, 1959.
*Four from Planet 5*. New York, Fawcett, 1959; London, White Lion, 1974.
*The Wailing Asteroid*. New York, Avon, 1960.
*Creatures of the Abyss*. New York, Berkley, 1961; as *The Listeners*, London, Sidgwick and Jackson, 1969.
*This World Is Taboo* (Med Service). New York, Ace, 1961.
*Talents, Incorporated*. New York, Avon, 1962.
*Operation Terror*. New York, Berkley, 1962; London, Tandem, 1968.
*The Duplicators*. New York, Ace, 1964.
*The Other Side of Nowhere*. New York, Berkley, 1964.
*The Time Tunnel*. New York, Pyramid, 1964.
*The Greks Bring Gifts*. New York, Macfadden, 1964.
*Invaders of Space*. New York, Berkley, 1964; London, Tandem, 1968.
*Space Captain*. New York, Ace, 1966.
*Tunnel Through Time* (for children). Philadelphia, Westminster Press, 1966.
*Checkpoint Lambda*. New York, Berkley, 1966; in *A Murray Leinster Omnibus*, London, Sidgwick and Jackson, 1968.
*The Time Tunnel* (novelization of TV series). New York, Pyramid, 1967; London, Sidgwick and Jackson, 1971.
*Miners in the Sky*. New York, Avon, 1967.
*Space Gypsies*. New York, Avon, 1967.
*Timeslip!* (novelization of TV series). New York, Pyramid, 1967.
*Land of the Giants* (novelization of TV play). New York, Pyramid, 1968.
*The Hot Spot* (novelization of TV play). New York, Pyramid, 1969.
*Unknown Danger* (novelization of TV play). New York, Pyramid, 1969.

Short Stories (series: Med Service)

*Sidewise in Time*. Chicago, Shasta, 1950.
*Out of This World*. New York, Avalon, 1958.
*Monsters and Such*. New York, Avon, 1959.
*Twists in Time*. New York, Avon, 1960.
*Men into Space* (novelization of TV series). New York, Berkley, 1960.
*The Aliens*. New York, Berkley, 1960.
*Doctor to the Stars* (Med Service). New York, Pyramid, 1964.
*Get Off My World!* New York, Belmont, 1966.
*S.O.S. from Three Worlds* (Med Service). New York, Ace, 1966.
*The Best of Murray Leinster*, edited by Brian Davis. London, Corgi, 1976; New York, Ballantine, 1978.
*The Med Series*. New York, Ace, 1983.

OTHER PUBLICATIONS

Novels

*Scalps*. New York, Brewer and Warren, 1930; as *Wings of Chance*, London, John Hamilton, 1935.
*Murder Will Out*. London, John Hamilton, 1932.
*Sword of Kings*. London, Long, 1933.
*Murder in the Family*. London, John Hamilton, 1935.
*No Clues*. London, Wright and Brown, 1935.
*Guns for Achin*. London, Wright and Brown, 1936.
*Outlaw Guns*. New York, Star, n.d.; as *Wanted—Dead or Alive!*, London, Wright and Brown, 1951.
*Cattle Rustlers*. London, Ward Lock, 1952.
*Texas Gun Slinger*. New York, Star, n.d.
*Outlaw Deputy*. Toronto, Harlequin, 1954.

Novels as Will F. Jenkins

*The Gamblin' Kid*. New York, King, 1933; London, Eldon Press, 1934.
*Mexican Trail*. New York, King, 1933; London, Eldon Press, 1935.
*Fighting Horse Valley*. New York, King, 1934; London, Eldon Press, 1935.
*Outlaw Sheriff*. New York, King, 1934; as *Rustlin' Sheriff*, London, Eldon Press, 1934.
*Kid Deputy*. New York, King, and London, Eldon Press, 1935.
*Black Sheep*. New York, Messer, and London, Eldon Press, 1936.
*The Man Who Feared*. New York, Gateway, 1942.
*Dallas* (novelization of screenplay). New York, Fawcett, 1950; London, Muller, 1961.
*Son of the Flying "Y"*. New York, Fawcett, 1951; London, Muller, 1957.

Plays

Screenplays: *Border Devils*, with Harry C. Crist, 1932; *Torchy in Chinatown*, with George Bricker, 1938.

Other

Editor, *Great Stories of Science Fiction*. New York, Random House, 1951; London, Cassell, 1953.

* * *

A professional writer for the slick and pulp magazines from 1913 until 1967, Murray Leinster embodies in one writer the very essence of the commercial yet ambitiously serious genre of science fiction. He did his best work in short fiction. He developed and extrapolated upon certain key speculative ideas, several of the most important of which he introduced to the genre. He wrote for money and sold to several markets other than science fiction, and yet the imaginative expansion of ideas about nature and about the relation of life forms to nature made science fiction a very important area in his production. Leinster wrote so much that it is hard to categorize his major themes and most characteristic effects, but always his mind is lively and he seems interested particularly in cool analyzing and in alternatives to all possibilities.

In fact, his fascination with alternatives to any situation led him to the standard science-fiction theme he is often remembered as having introduced to the genre: the theme of parallel points on a time continuum, or parallel worlds. A story from 1931, "The Fifth-Dimension Catapult," plays with the notion as a kind of modern alchemy in which the clever laboratory investigator can change time and space coordinates in order to visit a completely alien parallel world; and in this case the plan finally is to bring back gold. Leinster's more well-known story of parallel worlds is "Sidewise in Time" in which some unexplained oscillation of the earth results in a myriad of alternate time paths. His method of telling this story in little isolated vignettes of what might be possible here and there as the oscillations produce alternative presents is indicative of why short fiction is a primary form in science fiction. With change and even alternate possibilities ever present there simply does not exist the stable Victorian world for developing long narratives in one time and one place. Leinster, beginning as early as it was popularized, writes a modern alchemy of change according to Einstein-like relativity. Some longer fictions of his that rely on this same balancing of alternatives are *Colonial Survey*, which contains his Hugo-winning novelet "Exploration Team," and *The Time Tunnel*.

Similarly, Leinster develops again and again the ramification of contact between different life forms that are alternatives to each other. This is the often-used theme in science fiction of first contact with an alien race; and the most influential story of Leinster's of this type is entitled simply "First Contact" (1945). But many of his stories explore the alternatives of encounter and relationship between life forms who consider each other alien because they cannot or do not communicate. In "Proxima Centauri" the aliens are intelligent and mobile plants that crave animal flesh. This reversal, or notion that what we do ourselves may often be quite alien, permeates Leinster's fictions. Not only do humans enjoy vegetable salads unthinkingly, but in "The Strange Case of John Klingman" the human managers of the mental hospital seem more alien than Klingman. Similarly, the moon monkeys in "Keyhole" have more sympathy and effective understanding than their human opposites because they can communicate telepathically and hence the human thoughts, although alien to them, are not unknown.

The key seems to be knowledge and understanding, for here the two themes in Leinster's fiction come together. Alternate or parallel worlds as well as life forms alien to each other are only possible when differentiation, separateness, and mental isolation are possible. If the universe were all one, there would be only one time path and there would be continual communion. But the universe is parceled out, and communication is very seldom total or telepathic and instant. In other words, Leinster seems to be continually retelling the myth of original sin. Things are not as they should be, hence continual competitiveness and continual alternatives.

A brilliant working of this theme of the pathos of separateness and difference is in "The Lonely Planet," which seems to be an anticipation of the widely acclaimed novel by Stanislaw Lem, *Solaris*. In Leinster's story, a magnificent creature called Alyx covers an entire planet. In the beginning it is totally telepathic to mankind because it has not developed a defense against mind or total communication since it has evolved in an environment where it was the only creature. The story, then, is how mankind teaches Alyx to be secretive and competitive, finally, because Alyx learns what loneliness was. Perhaps Leinster is saying that a perfect oneness would be lonely and boring and that we need alternatives and even competitiveness. In any case, the clever, inventive, competitive and necessarily separate mind of the scientific investigator is the favorite protagonist in a Leinster story. Thus from the point of view of modern fiction, his characters often seem grossly two dimensional and his conflicts exaggerated and sensational. These bold and exaggerated effects prevail throughout his popular novel *The Forgotten Planet* (an expansion of "Mad Planet," 1926)—the narration of a continual war with giant insects and the growth of human rationality. But many of these effects are simply the demands of the pulp market, and seen in their most symbolic way they continually narrate the inescapable reality of human fallibility.

No treatment of Leinster and of the evolution of the genre of modern science fiction that he contributed so much to would be complete without mention of the sense of awe that goes with what is generally dismissed as space opera. In addition to the suggestiveness in theme and meaning mentioned above, Leinster's fiction reads well because of wide-ranging space patrol and med service action and because of journeys to distant second galaxies. There is also a good deal of violence, quick cruelty, and villainy in Leinster's work; and when this also is handled well it is an ancient emblem for the fallen state of mankind, an exact correlative to the infinite alternatives in the material world. But always in Leinster, along with the awe and the space opera, is the intellectual curiosity and the analytic mind—perhaps again representative of the fallen state of man, but characteristic also of the best in science fiction. Leinster grew with the genre, but he is also an example of how subtle some of the best space opera can be.

—Donald M. Hassler

---

**L'ENGLE, Madeleine.** American. Born Madeleine L'Engle Camp in New York City, 29 November 1918. Educated at Smith College, Northampton, Massachusetts, A.B. (honors) 1941; New School for Social Research, New York, 1941–42; Columbia University, New York, 1960–61. Married Hugh Franklin in 1946 (died 1986); two daughters and one son. Worked in the theater, New York, 1941–47; member of the faculty, University of Indiana, Bloomington, summers 1965–66, 1971; writer-in-residence, Ohio State University, Columbus, 1970, and University of Rochester, New York, 1972. Since 1960, teacher, St. Hilda's and St. Hugh's School, New York; since 1966, librarian, Cathedral of St. John the Divine, New York; since 1970, president, Crosswicks Ltd., New York; since 1976, Lecturer, Wheaton College, Illinois; since 1976, member, Board of Directors, Authors League Foundation; president, Authors Guild of America. Recipient: American Library Association Newbery Medal, 1963; University of Southern Mississippi award, 1978; Smith College Medal, 1980, and Sophie award, 1984; American Book award, for paperback, 1980; *Logos* award, for adult non-fiction, 1981; Catholic Library Association Regina Medal, 1984; National Council of Teachers of English ALAN award, 1986. Agent: Robert Lescher, 67 Irving Place, New York, New York 10009. Address: Crosswicks, Goshen, Connecticut 06756, U.S.A.

### Science-Fiction Publications

Novels (series: Time)

*The Time Trilogy*. New York, Farrar Strauss, 1979.
- *A Wrinkle in Time*. New York, Farrar Straus, 1962; London, Constable, 1963.
- *A Wind in the Door*. New York, Farrar Straus, 1973; London, Methuen, 1975.

*A Swiftly Tilting Planet*. New York, Farrar Straus, 1978; London, Souvenir Press, 1980.
*The Arm of the Starfish*. New York, Farrar Straus, 1965; London, Hodder and Stoughton, 1990.
*A Ring of Endless Light*. New York, Farrar Straus, 1980; London, Lion, 1988.

OTHER PUBLICATIONS

Novels

*The Small Rain*. New York, Vanguard Press, 1945; London, Secker and Warburg, 1955.
*Ilsa*. New York, Vanguard Press, 1946.
*And Both Were Young*. New York, Lothrop, 1949.
*Camilla Dickinson*. New York, Simon and Schuster, 1951; London, Secker and Warburg, 1952; as *Camilla*, New York, Crowell, 1965.
*A Winter's Love*. Philadelphia, Lippincott, 1957.
*Meet the Austins*. New York, Vanguard Press, 1960; London, Collins, 1966.
*The Moon by Night*. New York, Farrar Straus, 1963; London, Lion, 1988.
*The Love Letters*. New York, Farrar Straus, 1966.
*The Journey with Jonah*. New York, Farrar Straus, 1968.
*The Young Unicorns*. New York, Farrar Straus, 1968; London, Gollancz, 1970.
*Prelude*. New York, Vanguard Press, 1969; London, Gollancz, 1972.
*The Other Side of the Sun*. New York, Farrar Straus, 1971; London, Eyre Methuen, 1972.
*Dragons in the Waters*. New York, Farrar Straus, 1976.
*A Severed Wasp*. New York, Farrar Straus, 1982; London, Faber, 1984.
*A House Like a Lotus*. New York, Farrar Straus, 1984.
*Many Waters*. New York, Farrar Straus, 1986.
*An Acceptable Time*. New York, Farrar Straus, 1989.

Short Stories

*The Sphinx at Dawn: Two Stories*. New York, Seabury Press, 1982.

Plays

*18 Washington Square, South* (produced Northampton, Massachusetts, 1940). Boston, Baker, 1944.
*How Now Brown Cow*, with Robert Hartung (produced New York, 1949).
*The Journey with Jonah* (produced New York, 1970). New York, Farrar Straus, 1967.

Verse

*Lines Scribbled on an Envelope and Other Poems*. New York, Farrar Straus, 1969.
*Weather of the Heart*. Wheaton, Illinois, Shaw, 1978.
*A Cry Like a Bell*. Wheaton, Illinois, Shaw, 1987.

Other

*The Twenty-Four Days Before Christmas: An Austin Family Story* (for children). New York, Farrar Straus, 1964.
*Dance in the Desert* (for children). New York, Farrar Straus, and London, Longman, 1969.
*A Circle of Quiet* (essays). New York, Farrar Straus, 1972.
*Everyday Prayers* (for children). New York, Morehouse Barlow, 1974.
*Prayers for Sunday* (for children). New York, Morehouse Barlow, 1974.
*The Summer of the Great-Grandmother* (essays). New York, Farrar Straus, 1974.
*The Irrational Season* (essays). New York, Seabury Press, 1977.
*Ladder of Angels: Scenes from the Bible Illustrated by Children of the World*. New York, Seabury Press, 1979.
*The Anti-Muffins* (for children). New York, Pilgrim Press, 1980.
*Walking on Water* (essays). Wheaton, Illinois, Shaw, 1980; Tring, Hertfordshire, Lion, 1982.
*And It Was Good: Reflections on Beginnings*. Wheaton, Illinois, Shaw, 1983.
*Dare to Be Creative*. Washington, D.C., Library of Congress, 1984.
*Trailing Clouds of Glory: Spiritual Values in Children's Literature*, with Avery Brooke. Philadelphia, Westminster Press, 1985.
*A Stone for a Pillow*. Wheaton, Illinois, Shaw, 1987.
*Two-Part Invention: The Story of a Marriage* (memoir). New York, Farrar Straus, 1988.
*Sold into Egypt: Joseph's Journey into Human Being*. Wheaton, Illinois, Shaw, 1989.
*The Glorious Impossible* (for children). New York, Simon and Schuster, 1990.

Editor, with William R. Green, *Spirit and Light: Essays in Historical Theology*. New York, Seabury Press, 1976.

*

Manuscript Collections: Wheaton College, Illinois; Kerlan Collection, University of Minnesota, Minneapolis; de Grummond Collection, University of Southern Mississippi, Hattiesburg.

Madeleine L'Engle comments:

I discovered science fiction early, as a lonely only child growing up, for my first 12 years, in New York City, then in France and Switzerland. For me, the real world was clearer in the books of E. Nesbit and H.G. Wells than in the world of school. So I started writing science fiction when I was eight or nine. Fortunately all of my early work was lost somewhere or other on our journey across the Atlantic.

During college and after I turned to more "realistic" fiction, and found that it was not real enough, that my true discoveries of reality came while I was writing sci-fi or fantasy. I also discovered that for me the great theologians and modern mystics are the scientists, the physicists and astrophysicists, the cellular biologists, since they are dealing with the nature of Being itself. Einstein, Planck, Eddington, Jeans, Heisenberg, and many others, have been—and are still—my great stimulants.

* * *

Madeleine L'Engle has been publishing successful and provocative science fiction since the mid-1940's, adding intriguing variations to a considerable body of work, and continuously crafting fiction to engage her readers in issues and moral questions. She is nearly as prolific as some of her less thoughtful peers, and has continuously commanded the support of publishers and readers who must be described as literary. Her most well-known work is a series of novels dealing with time, including her one most signally famous work, *A Wrinkle in Time*, which introduces the children and, less directly, the father of the Murry family.

*Wrinkle* begins with the stark probing of a novel by Conrad, but by the time the reader recognizes what an extensive narrative hook has been set, L'Engle has paraded warm, bright, totally believable characters on stage. Every bit an existential and metaphysical thinker, L'Engle dramatizes the necessary leaps of faith that await the young reader and which certainly beckon to the more mature reader.

The second novel in the series, *A Wind in the Door*, takes up where the problem of the missing Murry father is solved, and the focus now becomes the integrity of healthy organisms and systems. Meg Murry, a young man from *Wrinkle* named Calvin, and a young superbeing become simultaneously involved in a plot involving Charles Wallace, who is being attacked at a cellular memory level, and this is shown in relationship to a black hole, L'Engle's version of a spot in the galaxy where there is a problem with cellular memory. *A Swiftly Tilting Planet* involves Meg Murry, now a grown woman, married and pregnant, but still called upon to join her siblings in an adventure relating to the potential for thermo-nuclear war.

Trademarks of L'Engle are her deceptively simple prose style, often undershot with social, moral, or religious issue; her restraint in explaining too much either of philosophy, scientific apparatus, or technicalities; her crisp, individual dialog; and her ability to draw young characters who are interesting without being self-conscious. Well read in the physical and theoretical sciences, L'Engle has the same focus to be found in such writers as Theodore Sturgeon and Robert Heinlein, allowing her effectively to dramatize complex concepts whether a black hole in the galaxy and its consequence, the ability of a starfish to regenerate a portion of its body, or the ability of an immune system to keep an invader from penetrating.

L'Engle seems to have arrived at a happy synthesis of science, metaphysics, universal politics, and individual responsibility. She is one of the handful of science-fiction writers whose work consistently rings true.

—Shelly Lowenkopf

---

**LEPPOC, Derfla.** *See* **COPPEL, Alfred.**

---

**LESSER, Milton.** Name now Stephen Marlowe; also writes as Adam Chase; Andrew Frazer; Ellery Queen; Jason Ridgway; C.H. Thames. American. Born in New York City, 7 August 1928. Educated at the College of William and Mary, Williamsburg, Virginia, B.A. 1949. Served in the United States Army, 1952–54. Married 1) Leigh Lang in 1950 (divorced 1962); 2) Ann Humbert; two daughters. Editor, Scott Meredith Literary Agency, New York, 1949–50; now a full-time writer. Writer-in-Residence, College of William and Mary, 1974–75, 1980–81. Member of the Board of Directors, Mystery Writers of America. Agent: Scott Meredith Literary Agency, 845 Third Avenue, New York, New York 10022, U.S.A.

Science-Fiction Publications

Novels

*Earthbound* (for children). Philadelphia, Winston, 1952; London, Hutchinson, 1955.
*The Star Seekers* (for children). Philadelphia, Winston, 1953.
*The Golden Age* (as Adam Chase, with Paul W. Fairman). New York, Avalon, 1959.
*Recruit for Andromeda*. New York, Ace, 1959.
*Stadium Beyond the Stars* (for children). Philadelphia, Winston, 1960.
*Spacemen, Go Home* (for children). New York, Holt Rinehart, 1962.

Short Stories

*Secret of the Black Planet*. New York, Belmont, 1965.

Other Publications

Novels as Stephen Marlowe

*Catch the Brass Ring*. New York, Ace, 1954.
*Turn Left for Murder*. New York, Ace, 1955.
*Model for Murder*. Hasbrouck Heights, New Jersey, Graphic, 1955.
*The Second Longest Night*. New York, Fawcett, 1955; London, Fawcett, 1958.
*Dead on Arrival*. New York, Ace, 1956.
*Mecca for Murder*. New York, Fawcett, 1956; London, Fawcett, 1957.
*Violence Is Golden* (as C.H. Thames). New York, Bouregy, 1956.
*Killers Are My Meat*. New York, Fawcett, 1957; London, Fawcett, 1958.
*Murder Is My Dish*. New York, Fawcett, 1957.
*Trouble Is My Name*. New York, Fawcett, 1957; London, Fawcett, 1958.
*Violence Is My Business*. New York, Fawcett, 1958; London, Fawcett, 1959.
*Terror Is My Trade*. New York, Fawcett, 1958; London, Muller, 1960.
*Blonde Bait*. New York, Avon, 1959.
*Double in Trouble*, with Richard S. Prather. New York, Fawcett, 1959.
*Find Eileen Hardin—Alive!* (as Andrew Frazer). New York, Avon, 1959.
*Passport to Peril*. New York, Fawcett, 1959.
*Homicide Is My Game*. New York, Fawcett, 1959; London, Muller, 1960.
*Danger Is My Line*. New York, Fawcett, 1960; London, Muller, 1961.
*Death Is My Comrade*. New York, Fawcett, 1960; London, Muller, 1961.
*The Fall of Marty Moon* (as Andrew Frazer). New York, Avon, 1960.
*Peril Is My Pay*. New York, Fawcett, 1960; London, Muller, 1961.
*Dead Man's Tale* (as Ellery Queen). New York, Pocket Books, 1961; London, New English Library, 1967.
*Manhunt Is My Mission*. New York, Fawcett, 1961; London, Muller, 1962.
*Jeopardy Is My Job*. New York, Fawcett, 1962; London, Muller, 1963.

*Blood Is My Brother* (as C.H. Thames). New York, Permabooks, 1963.
*The Shining*. New York, Trident Press, 1963.
*Francesca*. New York, Fawcett, and London, Muller, 1963.
*Drum Beat—Berlin*. New York, Fawcett, 1964.
*Drum Beat—Dominique*. New York, Fawcett, 1965.
*Drum Beat—Madrid*. New York, Fawcett, 1966.
*The Search for Bruno Heidler*. New York, Macmillan, 1966; London, Boardman, 1967.
*Drum Beat—Erica*. New York, Fawcett, 1967.
*Come Over, Red Rover*. New York, Macmillan, 1968.
*Drum Beat—Marianne*. New York, Fawcett, 1968.
*The Summit*. New York, Geis, 1970.
*Colossus*. New York, Macmillan, 1972; London, W.H. Allen, 1973.
*The Man with No Shadow*. Englewood Cliffs, New Jersey, Prentice Hall, and London, W.H. Allen, 1974.
*The Cawthorn Journals*. Englewood Cliffs, New Jersey, Prentice Hall, 1975; London, W.H. Allen, 1976; as *Too Many Chiefs*, London, New English Library, 1977.
*Translation*. Englewood Cliffs, New Jersey, Prentice Hall, 1976; London, W.H. Allen, 1977.
*The Valkyrie Encounter*. New York, Putnam, and London, New English Library, 1978.
*1956*. New York, Arbor House, 1981; London, New English Library, 1982.
*Deborah's Legacy*. New York, Zebra, 1983.

Novels as Jason Ridgway

*West Side Jungle*. New York, New American Library, 1958.
*Adam's Fall*. New York, Permabooks, 1960.
*People in Glass Houses*. New York, Permabooks, 1961.
*Hardly a Man is Now Alive*. New York, Permabooks, 1962.
*The Treasure of the Cosa Nostra*. New York, Pocket Books, 1966.

Other

*Lost Worlds and the Men Who Found Them* (for children). Racine, Wisconsin, Whitman, 1962.
*Walt Disney's Strange Animals of Australia* (for children). Racine, Wisconsin, Whitman, 1963.

Editor, *Looking Forward: An Anthology of Science Fiction*. New York, Beechhurst Press, 1953; London, Cassell, 1955.

* * *

Although best known for his Chester Drum spy novels and elaborate espionage novels like *The Valkyrie Encounter*, Milton Lesser did write a series of juvenile SF novels for Winston and was a prolific contributor to the Ziff-Davis SF magazines in the late 1950's and early 60's. Then Lesser abandoned the field to write more mainstream novels, although some of them, like *Translation* and *The Cawthorn Journals*, have science-fiction elements.

Most of Lesser's SF novels are juveniles. In *Earthbound* a young cadet unjustly expelled from the Solar Academy is tricked into helping space pirates. The book is high on action and low on plausibility. *The Star Seekers* is a bit better. It reworks Robert A. Heinlein's idea of a generation starship presented in *Universe*. Here, a starship takes six generations to reach Alpha Centauri, with the attendant problems and struggles. *Stadium Beyond the Stars* is Lesser's weakest SF novel. Most of the action concerns plotting among political groups on the eve of the First Interstellar Olympic Games. The characterizations are shallow and the plot is murky. *Spacemen, Go Home* opens with humanity quarantined from star travel by a super computer which controls the galaxy. Various groups attempt to bomb the Star Brain while others attempt to convince it to lift the quarantine because humans aren't really all that violent. Again, a murky plot lurks behind the fast-paced action.

Lesser's adult works also stress action over plot and violence over character. *The Golden Age* is prime space opera featuring a bold hero who commutes among worlds in the tradition of John Carter. Duels and fights keep the action swift and the pages turning. *Recruit for Andromeda* has a tricky plot with draftees secretly tested to determine which are superior. The story has some mild racist overtones. *Secret of the Black Planet* is made up of two space-opera novelettes, "Secret of the Black Planet" and "Son of the Black Chalice." The search for a lost alien race and the secret of cell regeneration is marred by hackneyed writing and cardboard characterizations.

Most of this SF writing was done early in Lesser's career; he moved on to better paying markets and his writing skills improved as well. *The Search for Bruno Heidler* was selected as one of the best suspense novels of the year. His career peaked in the early 1970's with the publication of three successful novels: *The Summit, Colossus*, and *The Man with No Shadow*. Lesser's science-fiction work quickly went out of print and is of historical interest only for an author who achieved success outside the science-fiction field.

—George Kelley

---

**LESSING, Doris (May, née Taylor).** Also writes as Jane Somers. British. Born in Kermansha, Persia, 22 October 1919; moved with her family to England, then to Banket, Southern Rhodesia, 1924. Educated at Dominican Convent School, Salisbury, Southern Rhodesia, 1926–34. Married 1) Frank Charles Wisdom in 1939 (divorced 1943), one son and one daughter; 2) Gottfried Lessing in 1945 (divorced 1949), one son. Au pair, Salisbury, 1934–35; telephone operator and clerk, Salisbury, 1937–39, typist, 1946–48; journalist, Cape Town *Guardian*, 1949; moved to London, 1950; secretary, 1950; member of the Editorial Board, *New Reasoner* (later *New Left Review*), 1956. Recipient: Maugham award, 1954; Médicis prize (France), 1976; Austrian State prize, 1981; Shakespeare prize (Hamburg), 1982; W.H. Smith literary award, 1986. Associate member, American Academy, 1974; honorary fellow, Modern Language Association (U.S.), 1974. Agent: Jonathan Clowes Ltd., Iron Bridge House, Bridge Approach, London NW1 8BD, England.

SCIENCE-FICTION PUBLICATIONS

Novels (series: Canopus in Argos: Archives)

*Briefing for a Descent into Hell*. London, Cape, and New York, Knopf, 1971.
*The Memoirs of a Survivor*. London, Octagon Press, 1974; New York, Knopf, 1975.
*Shikasta* (Argos). London, Cape, and New York, Knopf, 1979.
*The Marriages Between Zones Three, Four, and Five* (Argos). London, Cape, and New York, Knopf, 1980.
*The Sirian Experiments* (Argos). London, Cape, and New York, Knopf, 1981.

*The Making of the Representative for Planet 8* (Argos). London, Cape, and New York, Knopf, 1982.
*The Sentimental Agents* (Argos). London, Cape, and New York, Knopf, 1983.

Short Stories

*No Witchcraft for Sale: Stories and Short Novels.* Moscow, Foreign Languages Publishing House, 1956.

OTHER PUBLICATIONS

Novels

*The Grass Is Singing.* London, Joseph, and New York, Crowell, 1950.
Children of Violence:
*Martha Quest.* London, Joseph, 1952.
*A Proper Marriage.* London, Joseph, 1954, with *Martha Quest*, New York, Simon and Schuster, 1964.
*A Ripple from the Storm.* London, Joseph, 1958.
*Landlocked.* London, MacGibbon and Kee, 1965; with *A Ripple from the Storm.* New York, Simon and Schuster, 1966.
*The Four-Gated City.* London, MacGibbon and Kee, and New York, Knopf, 1969.
*Retreat to Innocence.* London, Joseph, 1956.
*The Golden Notebook.* London, Joseph, and New York, Simon and Schuster, 1962.
*The Summer Before the Dark.* London, Cape, and New York, Knopf, 1973.
*The Diaries of Jane Somers.* New York, Random House, 1984; London, Joseph, 1985.
*The Diary of A Good Neighbour* (as Jane Somers). London, Joseph, and New York, Knopf, 1983.
*If the Old Could* (as Jane Somers). London, Joseph and New York, Knopf, 1984.
*The Good Terrorist.* London, Cape, and New York, Knopf, 1985.
*The Fifth Child.* London, Cape, and New York, Knopf, 1988.

Short Stories

*This Was the Old Chief's Country.* London, Joseph, 1951; New York, Crowell, 1952.
*Five: Short Novels.* London, Joseph, 1953.
*The Habit of Loving.* London, MacGibbon and Kee, 1957; New York, Crowell, 1958.
*A Man and Two Women.* London, MacGibbon and Kee, and New York, Simon and Schuster, 1963.
*African Stories.* London, Joseph, 1964; New York, Simon and Schuster, 1965.
*Winter in July.* London, Panther, 1966.
*The Black Madonna.* London, Panther, 1966.
*Nine African Stories.* London, Longman, 1968.
*The Story of a Non-Marrying Man and Other Stories.* London, Cape, 1972; as *The Temptation of Jack Orkney and Other Stories*, New York, Knopf, 1972.
*Collected African Stories:*
*This Was the Old Chief's Country.* London, Joseph, 1973.
*The Sun Between Their Feet.* London, Joseph, 1973.
(*Stories*), edited by Alan Cattell. London, Harrap, 1976.
*Collected Stories:*
*To Room Nineteen.* London, Cape, 1978.
*The Temptation of Jack Orkney.* London, Cape, 1978.
*Stories.* New York, Knopf, 1978.

Plays

*Before the Deluge* (produced London, 1953).
*Mr. Dollinger* (produced Oxford, 1958).
*Each His Own Wilderness* (produced London, 1958). Published in *New English Dramatists*, London, Penguin, 1959.
*The Truth about Billy Newton* (produced Salisbury, Wiltshire, 1960).
*Play with a Tiger* (produced London, 1962; New York, 1964). London, Joseph, 1962.
*The Storm*, adaptation of a play by Alexander Ostrowsky (produced London, 1966).
*The Singing Door*, in *Second Playbill 2*, edited by Alan Durband. London, Hutchinson, 1973.

Television Plays: *The Grass Is Singing*, from her own novel, 1962; *Please Do Not Disturb*, 1966; *Care and Protection*, 1966; *Between Men*, 1967.

Libretto: *The Making of the Representative for Planet 8*, from her own novel, with music by Philip Glass, 1988.

Verse

*Fourteen Poems.* Northwood, Middlesex, Scorpion Press, 1959.

Other

*Going Home.* London, Joseph, 1957.
*In Pursuit of the English: A Documentary.* London, MacGibbon and Kee, 1960; New York, Simon and Schuster, 1961.
*Particularly Cats.* London, Joseph, and New York, Simon and Schuster, 1967.
*A Small Personal Voice: Essays, Reviews, Interviews*, edited by Paul Schlueter, New York, Knopf, 1974.
*Prisons We Choose to Live Inside.* Montreal, CBC Enterprises, 1986; London, Cape, and New York, Harper and Row, 1987.
*The Winds Blow Away Our Words: And Other Documents Relating to the Afghan Resistance.* London, Panther, and New York, Vintage, 1987.
*The Doris Lessing Reader.* New York, Knopf, 1988; London, Cape, 1989.

*

Bibliography: *Doris Lessing: A Bibliography* by Catharina Ipp, Johannesburg, University of the Witwatersrand Department of Bibliography, 1967; *Doris Lessing: A Checklist of Primary and Secondary Sources* by Selma R. Burkom and Margaret Williams, Troy, New York, Whitston, 1973; *Doris Lessing: An Annotated Bibliography of Criticism* by Dee Seligman, Westport, Connecticut, Greenwood Press, 1981; *Doris Lessing: A Descriptive Bibliography of Her First Editions* by Eric T. Brueck, London, Metropolis, 1984.

Critical Studies (selection): *Doris Lessing* by Dorothy Brewster, New York, Twayne, 1965; *The Novels of Doris Lessing* by Paul Schlueter, Carbondale, Southern Illinois University Press, 1973; *Doris Lessing* by Michael Thorpe, London, Longman, 1973; *Doris Lessing: Critical Studies* edited by Annis Pratt and L.S. Dembo, Madison, University of Wisconsin Press, 1974; *The City and the Veld: The Fiction of Doris Lessing* by Mary Ann Singleton, Lewisburg, Pennsylvania, Bucknell University Press, 1976; *The Novelistic Vision of Doris Lessing: Breaking the Forms of Consciousness* by Roberta Rubenstein, Urbana, University of Illinois Press, 1979; *Notebooks/Memoirs/Archives: Reading and*

*Re-reading Doris Lessing* edited by Jenny Taylor, London, and Boston, Routledge, 1982; *Substance under Pressure: Artistic Coherence and Evolving Form in the Novels of Doris Lessing* by Betsy Draine, Madison, University of Wisconsin Press, 1983; *Doris Lessing* by Lorna Sage, London, Methuen, 1983; *Doris Lessing* by Mona Knapp, New York, Ungar, 1984; *Doris Lessing and Women's Appropriation of Science Fiction* by Mariette Clare, Birmingham, Centre for Contemporary Cultural Studies, 1984; *Fiction; or, The Language of Our Discontent: A Study of the Built-In Novelist in the Novels of Angus Wilson, Lawrence Durrell, and Doris Lessing* by Guido Kums, New York, P. Lang, 1985; *The Unexpected Universe of Doris Lessing: A Study in Narrative Technique* by Katherine Fishburn, Westport, Connecticut, Greenwood, 1985; *Doris Lessing* edited by Eve Bertelesen, New York, McGraw Hill, 1985; *Critical Essays on Doris Lessing* edited by Claire Sprague and Virginia Tiger, Boston, Hall, 1986; *Rereading Lessing: Narrative Patterns of Doubling and Repetition* by Claire Sprague, Chapel Hill and London, University of North Carolina Press, 1987, and *In Pursuit of Doris Lessing: Nine Nations Reading* edited by Claire Sprague, New York, St. Martin's Press, and London, Macmillan, 1990; *The Theme of Enclosure in Selected Works of Doris Lessing* by Shirley Budhos, Troy, New York, Whitston, 1987; *Doris Lessing: The Alchemy of Survival* edited by Carey Kaplan and Ellen Cronan Rose, Athens, Ohio University Press, 1988; *Doris Lessing* by Ruth Whitaker, New York, St. Martin's Press, and London, Macmillan, 1988; *Doris Lessing* by Jeannette King, London, E. Arnold, 1989; *Understanding Doris Lessing* by Jean Pickering, Columbia, University of South Carolina Press, 1990.

* * *

Doris Lessing's series, *Canopus in Argos: Archives*, grew, according to the author, out of her plan for a single book, *Shikasta*. This first experiment in science fiction led to the exploration of multiple related themes in four more works. The ideas encompassed by this cycle are superabundant, ranging from planetary evolution over geological eons to the arts with which wives and husbands score minor points in forgettable skirmishes, but all the books are unified by one central concern, the role of the individual in events of great magnitude that transcend personal hopes, wishes, and desires. Most of Lessing's characters must confront a dizzying variety of forces that determine their destinies; their changing awareness of these forces provides much of the drama of their stories.

The most self-aware figures in all the novels are the mysterious representatives of the Canopean Empire. Even "Canopus," as individual officials are sometimes called, bows to a never-defined "Necessity" which rules all; in turn, Johor, Klorasty, and other Canopeans patiently guide less advanced races and even empires away from mindless violence and cruelty and toward cultural evolution. *Shikasta* details millions of years of the history of the earth, variously called "Rohanda" and "Shikasta." The Galactic time perspective allows the reader to understand that change and conflict is the one constant; the failure of a "Lock" between Canopus and Shikasta/Earth dooms the planet to degeneration and ultimately to near-destruction.

*The Marriages Between Zones Three, Four, and Five* is comparatively sunny, but still ends in melancholy. The Canopeans are (apparently) acting as offstage "Providers" in control of a series of geographically contrasting "Zones," ranging from desert (Zone 5) to swampy lush wetlands (Zone 4) to mountain plateaus (3) to mountain passes (2). Varying zones and climates determine the personality of cultures, which in turn determines individual types, from earthy lowlander to ethereal mountaineer. Each zone has settled into smug self-satisfaction when a perhaps related decline in fertility causes the Providers to force a marriage between the queen of Zone Three, Al. Ith, and the king of Zone Four, Ben Ata. Both characters are masterfully drawn, and the uneasy marriage of a kind of high country Athenian to a lumpish Spartan provides high comedy based on the clash of female and male principles, the unending war between artistic natures and practical natures, and the gradual blending of distinct personalities in marriage. The narrator describes how later artists depicted this marriage of opposites, and Lessing's own word-pictures are like set-pieces from a medieval tableau. Queen and King do not live happily ever after, however, for the Providers, in fine disregard for human wishes, toward the end of the book order Ben Ata to marry the wild, nomadic queen of Zone Five, thus blending the artistic intellect Ben Ata has gleaned from Al. Ith, his own orderly discipline, and the wild energy of the least civilized Zone. Al. Ith retires to the border of Zone Two, and eventually crosses it to become a flame-like wraith in a mountain atmosphere too rarified for others to tolerate. Life is change, says Lessing; even in this paradise reminiscent of a medieval fable, an unseen and only vaguely understood "necessity" casually destroys human happiness. There is no choice but to obey.

*The Sirian Experiments* continues this theme with another wonderfully drawn female protagonist, Ambien II, one of the five dictators who rule the technological empire in competition with Canopus. Unfortunately, Ambien II's prissy, bureaucratic, "dessicated" character is so persuasive that the reader may lack sympathy throughout much of the book, at least until this self-serving and authoritarian figure begins to learn a more sensitive and less machine-like managerial style from her Canopean opposites. As with Al. Ith and Ben Ata, sexual attraction between opposites provides the motive force for change, but there is no comedy here, only some excellent set-pieces in an Arab-like town and an Aztec-like fortress. Ambien has led Sirian "experiments" on millions of "lower species" over thousands of years, unmindful of their dubious morality because of their good intentions of forcing evolution. Miseries such as Al. Ith's in the previous novel are multiplied a million times before Ambien's Canopean teachers lead her to see from experience and example that the Sirian Empire is being taught by the Canopean just as surely as the "lower species" are being taught by the Sirian. As in the linked Zones, one relationship leads to the next, but the joins are invisible since they are firmly denied by the weaker. Colonialism involves more complex power relationships than are initially evident, with control being exercised in unexpected ways. Only experience teaches by showing us the mote in another's eye, just as Lessing's novel should raise our consciousness of Western arrogance and brutality in Africa and other former colonial areas.

In *The Sirian Experiments* evil necessity is incarnated in the Puttiorian Empire (the name suggests Spanish *puta* or whore) and their planet Shahmat (Farsi for "the king is dead," or in chess, "checkmate"). In *The Making of the Representative for Planet 8*, evil necessity is a cosmic accident. The Canopean governed colony on Planet 8 is freezing to death because of planetary climactic changes. In a fine description of a frozen world stimulated by Lessing's reading about Scott's search for the South Pole, we see the telepathic, tropically lively and colorful inhabitants of Planet 8 become slothful, fur-swaddled zombies who lose their social identities as the snow and ice wipe out occupations and social roles. Climate is destiny; eventually, led and taught by their Canopean master Johor, they give up their material existence and become a single "representative" spirit, transcending physicality.

*The Sentimental Agents* continues the emphasis on Canopean moderation of extreme behavior, with Incent, an agent of the empire, seduced by "Undulant Rhetoric" or a kind of intoxication with words. In contrast, the usual approach of the Canopean agents is to be noncommittal to the point of taciturnity. They are men and women of action, not empty words.

While there is an honorable tradition of 20th-century writers opposing propaganda and false rhetoric, it is especially appropriate for Lessing to end her cycle with this warning. Throughout, there have been conflicts between characters skilled at action (Ben Ata, Ambien II) and characters skilled at language (Al. Ith, Nasar, Rhodia). Lessing's own ambivalence about the role of writer and writing may be at issue, and this uncertainty in a writer known for her earlier political stands may account for the mixed critical reception to her cycle. Like Canopus, Lessing teaches by example, but also like Canopus, she refuses easy answers and the superficial knowledge of the conventional.

—Andrew Macdonald

---

**LEVIN, Ira.** American. Born in New York City, 27 August 1929. Educated at Drake University, Des Moines, Iowa, 1946–48; New York University, 1948–50, A.B. in English 1950. Served in the United States Army Signal Corps, 1953–55. Married 1) Gabrielle Aronsohn in 1960 (divorced 1968), three sons; 2) Phyllis Finkel in 1979 (divorced 1982). Recipient: Mystery Writers of America Edgar Allan Poe award, 1954, and Special award, 1980. Agent: Harold Ober Associates, 425 Madison Avenue, New York, New York 10017, U.S.A.

SCIENCE-FICTION PUBLICATIONS

Novels

*This Perfect Day*. New York, Random House, and London, Joseph, 1970.
*The Stepford Wives*. New York, Random House, and London, Joseph, 1972.
*The Boys from Brazil*. New York, Random House, and London, Joseph, 1976.

OTHER PUBLICATIONS

Novels

*A Kiss Before Dying*. New York, Simon and Schuster, 1953; London, Joseph, 1954.
*Rosemary's Baby*. New York, Random House, and London, Joseph, 1967.
*Sliver*. New York, Bantam, 1991.

Plays

*No Time for Sergeants*, adaptation of the novel by Mac Hyman (produced New York, 1955; London, 1956). New York, Random House, 1956.
*Interlock* (produced New York, 1958). New York, Dramatists Play Service, 1958.
*Critic's Choice* (produced New York, 1960; London, 1961). New York, Random House, 1961; London, Evans, 1963.
*General Seeger* (produced New York, 1962). New York, Dramatists Play Service, 1962.
*Drat! The Cat!*, music by Milton Schafer (produced New York, 1965).
*Dr. Cook's Garden* (also director: produced New York, 1967). New York, Dramatists Play Service, 1968.
*Veronica's Room* (produced New York, 1973; Watford, Hertfordshire, 1982). New York, Random House, 1974; London, Joseph, 1975.
*Deathtrap* (produced New York and London, 1978). New York, Random House, 1979.
*Break a Leg* (produced New York, 1979). New York, French, 1981.
*Cantorial* (produced Stamford, Connecticut, 1984, New York, 1989). New York, French, 1990.

*

Critical Study: *Ira Levin* by Douglas Fowler, Mercer Island, Washington, Starmont, 1988.

Theatrical Activities:
Director: **Play**—*Dr. Cook's Garden*, New York, 1967.

* * *

Ira Levin's highly accomplished novels of suspense contain elements of science fiction and fantasy, and one, *This Perfect Day*, is set in the future. His first novel, *A Kiss Before Dying*, the study of a psychopath stalking three sisters, is skillfully written but gives little suggestion of the richness in store. *Rosemary's Baby* is one of the most perfectly crafted thrillers ever written. Rosemary and Guy Woodhouse step over the threshold of a richly documented old apartment house in New York City into the world of the witches. The strength of the book lies not only in its weaving of a dreadful spell but in the strong, sweet character of the pregnant heroine. Guy's complicity in the schemes of the friendly neighbours is part of a fiendish double climax.

The book following this masterpiece of genre writing was the science-fiction novel *This Perfect Day*. The future race, brown-skinned, depilated, breastless, tranquilised, stroll the windowless walkways of a totally computerised environment, patting the scanners as they pass, en route to death at age 62. LiRM35M4419, called Chip by his wry grandfather, escapes from the system by resisting UNI, the computer responsible for a boring parody of the good life. Chip's escape is obviously programmed; the appearance of those benign sybarites, the Programmers, is not surprising. The ideology of the "utopia" is weak but the quality of the writing and the level of invention are high.

Ira Levin returned to the suspense novel with *The Stepford Wives*. The setting, a commuter township in "middle America," is as persuasive as the New York of *Rosemary's Baby*. Joanna Everhart discovers the dreadful secret of the big-bosomed zombies who dote on housework. The climax is clever but the story is unsatisfying and the neatness of the writing hides many loose ends. We look in vain for one husband who refuses to trade in his wife on a new model.

*The Boys From Brazil* has an international setting but still retains a typical claustrophobic atmosphere. Dr. Josef Mengele, former medical superintendant of Auschwitz, emerges from his South American jungle retreat to send the organisation of Nazi veterans on a mission. Yakov Lieberman, the tired Nazi-hunter, discovers soon enough, but more slowly than the readers, why 94 elderly civil servants throughout the western world must die. These men are the adoptive fathers of teen-age sons cloned from the cells of Adolf Hitler; their deaths are an attempt to match up environment with genetic inheritance. This time the humanity of Lieberman balances the outrageous story; it is one of Ira Levin's best books. Mengele's scheme, even with its coda of an artistic lad somewhere indulging "tomorrow-the-world" fantasies, is revealed as pure moonshine.

Ira Levin's suspense novels have a unique resonance. These books, rather than *This Perfect Day*, have created a nightmare future world in which the Stepford delinquents, children of megalomaniac fathers raised by robot mothers, tangle with genetic Hitlers, under the eye of the heir of the Prince of This World, Andrew Woodhouse, the devil's child. The author not only portrays the contemporary world, but he also gives us its ancient myths and futurist fantasies.

With his latest novel, *Sliver*, Ira Levin has skipped over the fierce decade of the 1980's, heyday of terrorist and serial killer, and landed his readers securely in the postmodern era. *Sliver* is a spare, cruel, morally ambivalent fable about electronic surveillance carried to insane lengths. The precise and un-nerving story of Kay, the smart editor, confronting the boundless amorality of her young lover, involves a certain reduction in scale as against the earlier books. It is a "tale of the city"—almost a new subgenre. When Ira Levin sets his story in a glamorous apartment on the 20th floor, we know that it would be better for all concerned, including the cat, to keep away from the windows.

—Cherry Wilder

---

**LEWIS, C(live) S(taples).** Also wrote as Clive Hamilton; N.W. Clerk. British. Born in Belfast, Northern Ireland, 29 November 1898. Educated at Wynyard House, Watford, Herfordshire, 1908–10; Campbell College, Belfast, 1910; Cherbourg School, Malvern, Worcestershire, 1911–13, and Malvern College, 1913–14; privately, in Great Bookham, Surrey, 1914–17; University College, Oxford (scholar; Chancellor's English Essay prize, 1921), 1917, 1919–23, B.A. (honours) 1922. Served in the Somerset Light Infantry, 1917–19: First Lieutenant. Married Joy Davidman Gresham in 1956 (died 1960); two stepsons. Philosophy Tutor, 1924, and Lecturer in English, 1924, University College, Oxford; Fellow and Tutor in English, Magdalen College, Oxford, 1925–54; Professor of Medieval and Renaissance English, Cambridge University, 1954–63. Lecturer, University College of North Wales, Bangor, 1941; Riddell Lecturer, University of Durham, 1943; Clark Lecturer, Cambridge University, 1944. Recipient: Gollancz prize, 1937; Library Association Carnegie Medal, 1957. D.D.: University of St. Andrews, Fife, 1946; Docteur-ès-Lettres, Laval University, Quebec, 1952; D.Litt.: University of Manchester, 1959; Hon.Dr.: University of Dijon, 1962; University of Lyon, 1963. Honorary Fellow, Magdalen College, Oxford, 1955; University College, Oxford, 1958; Magdalene College, Cambridge, 1963. Fellow, Royal Society of Literature, 1948; Fellow, British Academy, 1955. *Died 22 November 1963.*

### Science-Fiction Publications

Novels (series: Dr. Elwin Ransom in all books)

*The Space Trilogy.* New York, Collier, 1986; London, Bodley Head, 1990.
- *Out of the Silent Planet.* London, Lane, 1938; New York, Macmillan, 1943.
- *Perelandra.* London, Lane, 1943; New York, Macmillan, 1944; as *Voyage to Venus*, London, Pan, 1953.
- *That Hideous Strength: A Modern Fairy-Tale for Grown-Ups.* London, Lane, 1945; New York, Macmillan, 1946; abridged edition, as *The Tortured Planet*, New York, Avon, 1958.

Short Stories

*Of Other Worlds: Essays and Stories*, edited by Walter Hooper. London, Bles, 1966; New York, Harcourt Brace, 1967.

### Other Publications

Novels (for children)

*The Lion, The Witch, and the Wardrobe.* London, Bles, and New York, Macmillan, 1950.
*Prince Caspian: The Return to Narnia.* London, Bles, and New York, Macmillan, 1951.
*The Voyage of the "Dawn Treader."* London, Bles, and New York, Macmillan, 1952.
*The Silver Chair.* London, Bles, and New York, Macmillan, 1953.
*The Horse and His Boy.* London, Bles, and New York, Macmillan, 1954.
*The Magician's Nephew.* London, Lane, and New York, Macmillan, 1955.
*The Last Battle.* London, Lane, and New York, Macmillan, 1956.
*Till We Have Faces: A Myth Retold* (for adults). London, Bles, 1956; New York, Harcourt Brace, 1957.

Short Stories

*The Dark Tower and Other Stories*, edited by Walter Hooper. London, Collins, and New York, Harcourt Brace, 1977.

Verse

*Spirits in Bondage: A Cycle of Lyrics* (as Clive Hamilton). London, Heinemann, 1919.
*Dymer* (as Clive Hamilton). London, Dent, and New York, Dutton, 1926.
*Poems*, edited by Walter Hooper. London, Bles, 1964; New York, Harcourt Brace, 1965.
*Narrative Poems*, edited by Walter Hooper. London, Bles, 1969; New York, Harcourt Brace, 1972.

Other

*The Pilgrim's Regress: An Allegorical Apology for Christianity, Reason, and Romanticism.* London, Dent, 1933; New York, Sheed and Ward, 1935; revised edition, London, Bles, 1943; Sheed and Ward, 1944.
*The Allegory of Love: A Study in Medieval Tradition.* Oxford, Clarendon Press, and New York, Oxford University Press, 1936.
*Rehabilitations and Other Essays.* London and New York, Oxford University Press, 1939.
*The Personal Heresy: A Controversy*, with E.M.W. Tillyard. London and New York, Oxford University Press, 1939.
*The Problem of Pain.* London, Bles, 1940; New York, Macmillan, 1944.
*The Weight of Glory.* London, S.P.C.K., 1942.
*The Screwtape Letters.* London, Bles, 1942; New York, Macmillan, 1943; revised edition, as *The Screwtape Letters and Screwtape Proposes a Toast*, Bles, 1961; Macmillan, 1962.

*Broadcast Talks: Right and Wrong: A Clue to the Meaning of the Universe, and What Christians Believe.* London, Bles, 1942; as *The Case for Christianity*, New York, Macmillan, 1943.

*A Preface to "Paradise Lost"* (lectures). London and New York, Oxford University Press, 1942; revised edition, 1960.

*Christian Behaviour: A Further Series of Broadcast Talks.* London, Bles, and New York, Macmillan, 1943.

*The Abolition of Man; or, Reflections on Education with Special Reference to the Teaching of English in the Upper Forms of Schools.* London, Oxford University Press, 1943; New York, Macmillan, 1947.

*Beyond Personality: The Christian Idea of God.* London, Bles, 1944; New York, Macmillan, 1945.

*The Great Divorce: A Dream.* London, Bles, and New York, Macmillan, 1946.

*Miracles: A Preliminary Study.* London, Bles, and New York, Macmillan, 1947.

*Vivisection.* London, Anti-Vivisection Society, and Boston, New England Anti-Vivisection Society, 1947(?).

*Transposition and Other Addresses.* London, Bles, 1949; as *The Weight of Glory and Other Addresses*, New York, Macmillan, 1949.

*The Literary Impact of the Authorized Version* (lecture). London, Athlone Press, 1950; Philadelphia, Fortress Press, 1963.

*Mere Christianity.* London, Bles, and New York, Macmillan, 1952.

*Hero and Leander* (lecture). London, Oxford University Press, 1952.

*English Literature in the Sixteenth Century, Excluding Drama,* Oxford, Clarendon Press, 1954.

*De Descriptione Temporum* (lecture). London, Cambridge University Press, 1955.

*Surprised by Joy: The Shape of My Early Life.* London, Bles, 1955; New York, Harcourt Brace, 1956.

*Reflections on the Psalms.* London, Bles, and New York, Harcourt Brace, 1958.

*Shall We Lose God in Outer Space?* London, S.P.C.K., 1959.

*The Four Loves.* London, Bles, and New York, Harcourt Brace, 1960.

*The World's Last Night and Other Essays.* New York, Harcourt Brace, 1960.

*Studies in Words.* London, Cambridge University Press, 1960; revised edition, 1967; New York, Cambridge University Press, 1990.

*An Experiment in Criticism.* London, Cambridge University Press, 1961.

*A Grief Observed* (as N.W. Clerk; autobiography). London, Faber, 1961; Greenwich, Connecticut, Seabury Press, 1963.

*They Asked for a Paper: Papers and Addresses.* London, Bles, 1962.

*Beyond the Bright Blur* (letters). New York, Harcourt Brace, 1963.

*Letters to Malcolm, Chiefly on Prayer.* London, Bles, and New York, Harcourt Brace, 1964.

*The Discarded Image: An Introduction to Medieval and Renaissance Literature.* London, Cambridge University Press, 1964.

*Screwtape Proposes a Toast and Other Pieces.* London, Fontana, 1965.

*Letters*, edited by W.H. Lewis. London, Bles, and New York, Harcourt Brace, 1966; revised edition, edited by Walter Hooper, London, Collins, 1988.

*Studies in Medieval and Renaissance Literature*, edited by Walter Hooper. London, Cambridge University Press, 1966.

*Spenser's Images of Life*, edited by Alastair Fowler. London, Cambridge University Press, 1967.

*Christian Reflections*, edited by Walter Hooper. London, Bles, and Grand Rapids, Michigan, Eerdmans, 1967.

*Letters to an American Lady*, edited by Clyde S. Kilby. Grand Rapids, Michigan, Eerdmans, 1967; London, Hodder and Stoughton, 1969.

*Mark vs. Tristram: Correspondence Between C.S. Lewis and Owen Barfield*, edited by Walter Hooper. Cambridge, Massachusetts, Lowell House Printers, 1967.

*A Mind Awake: An Anthology of C.S. Lewis*, edited by Clyde S. Kilby. London, Bles, 1968; New York, Harcourt Brace, 1969.

*Selected Literary Essays*, edited by Walter Hooper. London, Cambridge University Press, 1969.

*God in the Dock: Essays on Theology and Ethics*, edited by Walter Hooper. Grand Rapids, Michigan, Eerdmans, 1970; as *Undeceptions: Essays on Theology and Ethics*, London, Bles, 1971.

*The Humanitarian Theory of Punishment.* Abingdon, Berkshire, Marcham Books Press, 1972.

*Fern-Seed and Elephants and Other Essays on Christianity*, edited by Walter Hooper. London, Fontana, 1975.

*The Joyful Christian: 127 Readings*, edited by William Griffin. New York, Macmillan, 1977.

*They Stand Together: The Letters of C.S. Lewis to Arthur Greeves 1914–1963*, edited by Walter Hooper. London, Collins, and New York, Macmillan, 1979.

*C.S. Lewis at the Breakfast Table and Other Reminiscences*, edited by James T. Como. New York, Macmillan, 1979; London, Collins, 1980.

*The Visionary Christian: 131 Readings*, edited by Chad Walsh. New York, Macmillan, 1981.

*On Stories and Other Essays on Literature*, edited by Walter Hooper. New York, Harcourt Brace, 1982.

*Of This and other Worlds*, edited by Walter Hooper. London, Collins, 1982.

*The Cretaceous Perambulator*, with Owen Barfield, edited by Walter Hooper. Oxford, C.S. Lewis Society, 1983.

*The Business of Heaven: Daily Readings from C.S. Lewis*, edited by Walter Hooper. London, Fount, and New York, Harcourt Brace, 1984.

*Boxen: The Imaginary World of the Young C.S. Lewis*, edited by Walter Hooper. London, Collins, and San Diego, Harcourt Brace, 1985.

*Letters to Children*, edited by Lyle W. Dorsett and Marjorie Lamp Mead. New York, Macmillan, 1985.

*First and Second Things: Essays on Theology and Ethics*, edited by Walter Hooper. London, Collins, 1985.

*Present Concerns*, edited by Walter Hooper. London, Fount, and San Diego, Harcourt Brace, 1986.

*Timeless at Heart: Essays on Theology*, edited by Walter Hooper. London, Fount, 1987.

*The Essential C.S. Lewis*, edited by Lyle W. Dorsett. New York, Macmillan, 1988.

*Letters: C.S. Lewis and Don Giovanni Calabria: A Study in Friendship*, edited and translated by Martin Moynihan. London, Collins, and Ann Arbor, Michigan, Servant Books, 1988.

*All My World Before Me: The Diary of C.S. Lewis 1922–27*, edited by Walter Hooper. San Diego, Harcourt Brace, 1991.

Editor, *George MacDonald: An Anthology.* London, Bles, 1946; New York, Macmillan, 1947.

Editor, *Arthurian Torso, Containing the Posthumous Fragment of "The Figure of Arthur,"* by Charles Williams. London, and New York, Oxford University Press, 1948.

*

Bibliography: "A Bibliography of the Writings of C.S. Lewis" by Walter Hooper, in *Light on C.S. Lewis* edited by Jocelyn Gibb, London, Bles, 1965; *C.S. Lewis: An Annotated Checklist of Writings about Him and His Works* by Joe R. Christopher and Joan K. Ostling, Kent, Ohio, Kent State University Press, 1974.

Manuscript Collections: Bodleian Library, Oxford; Wheaton College, Illinois.

Critical Studies (selection): *C.S. Lewis* by Roger Lancelyn Green, London, Bodley Head, and New York, Walck, 1963, revised edition, in *Three Bodley Head Monographs*, Bodley Head, 1969, *C.S. Lewis: A Biography* by Green and Walter Hooper, London, Collins, and New York, Harcourt Brace, 1974, revised edition, 1988, and *Past Watchful Dragons: The Narnian Chronicles of C.S. Lewis*, New York, Macmillan, 1979, and *Through Joy and Beyond: A Pictorial Biography of C.S. Lewis*, New York, Macmillan, 1982, both by Hooper; *Light on C.S. Lewis* edited by Jocelyn Gibb, London, Bles, 1965; *The Lion of Judah in Never-Never Land: The Theology of C.S. Lewis Expressed in His Fantasies for Children*, Grand Rapids, Michigan, Eerdmans, 1973, and *The C.S. Lewis Hoax*, Portland, Oregon, Multinomah, 1988, both by Kathryn Ann Lindskoog; *The Secret Country of C.S. Lewis* by Anne Arnott, London, Hodder and Stoughton, 1974, Grand Rapids, Michigan, Eerdmans, 1975; *The Longing for Form: Essays on the Fiction of C.S. Lewis* edited by Peter J. Schakel, Kent, Ohio, Kent State University Press, 1977, and *Reading with the Heart: The Way into Narnia* by Schakel, Grand Rapids, Michigan, Eerdmans, 1979; *The Inklings: C.S. Lewis, J.R.R. Tolkien, Charles Williams and Their Friends* by Humphrey Carpenter, London, Allen and Unwin, 1978, Boston, Houghton Mifflin, 1979; *The Literary Legacy of C.S. Lewis* by Chad Walsh, New York, Harcourt Brace, and London, Sheldon Press, 1979; *A Guide Through Narnia* by Martha C. Sammons, Wheaton, Illinois, Shaw, and London, Hodder and Stoughton, 1979; *Narnia Explored* by Paul A. Karkainen, Old Tappan, New Jersey, Revell, 1979; *Companion to Narnia* by Paul F. Ford, New York, Harper, 1980; *C.S. Lewis, Spinner of Tales: A Guide to His Fiction* by Evan K. Gibson, Grand Rapids, Michigan, Christian University Press, 1980; *C.S. Lewis* by Margaret Patterson Hannay, New York, Ungar, 1981; *C.S. Lewis: The Art of Enchantment* by Donald E. Glover, Athens, Ohio University Press, 1981; *C.S. Lewis* by Brian Murphy, Mercer Island, Washington, Starmont House, 1983; *The Politics of Fantasy: C.S. Lewis and J.R.R. Tolkien* by Lee D. Rossi, New York, and Epping, Essex, Bowker, 1984; *Clive Staples Lewis: The Drama of a Life* by William Griffin, New York, Harper, 1986; *C.S. Lewis: His Literary Achievement* by C.N. Manlove, London, Macmillan, 1987; *C.S. Lewis* by Joe R. Christopher, Boston, Twayne, 1987; *C.S. Lewis, Man of Letters: A Reading of His Fiction* by Thomas Howard, Worthing, Sussex, Churchman, 1987; *Jack: C.S. Lewis and His Times* by George Sayer, London, Macmillan, 1988; *C.S. Lewis and His World* by David Barratt, Grand Rapids, Michigan, Eerdmans, 1988; *The Taste of the Pineapple: Essays on C.S. Lewis as Reader, Critic, and Imaginative Writer* edited by Bruce L. Edwards, Bowling Green, Ohio, Bowling Green State University Press, 1988; *Owen Barfield on C.S. Lewis* edited by G.B. Tennyson, Middletown, Connecticut, Wesleyan University Press, 1989; *The Riddle of Joy: G.K. Chesterton and C.S. Lewis* edited by Michael H. Macdonald and Andrew A. Tadie, Grand Rapids, Michigan, Eerdmans, and London, Collins, 1989; *C.S. Lewis: A Biography* by A.N. Wilson, London, Collins, and New York, Norton, 1990; *The C.S. Lewis Handbook* by Colin Duriez, Eastbourne, Monarch, and Grand Rapids, Michigan, Baker, 1990; *The Magical World of the Inklings: J.R.R. Tolkien, C.S. Lewis, Charles Williams, Owen Barfield* by Gareth Knight, Shaftsbury, Element, 1990; *A Christian for All Christians: Essays in Honour of C.S. Lewis* edited by Andrew Walker and James Patrick, London, Hodder and Stoughton, 1990.

* * *

C.S. Lewis is a unique figure. He once described himself as a specimen of a nearly extinct species, "old Western Man": and certainly we had no right to hope for such an author to appear in the 20th century. He has written in many guises: as medieval scholar, lay theologian, fantasist, poet. But his essential role has total inner consistency: he is above all the most powerful defender of traditional Christianity that this century has seen; and his apologia works, not through formal argument, but through images, through suggestion, through poetic creation. All his life, Lewis was haunted by *Sehnsucht*, a longing for strange beauty which the actual world could never wholly satisfy; and this led him, in early middle life, to identify the source and object of his longing with the Christian heaven and the Christian God. His subsequent creative work was a sustained imaginative polemic for this view of the universe.

Lewis is a science-fiction writer, arguably, in only one short story, "Ministering Angels," and one novel, *Out of the Silent Planet*. Both are set on Mars; but the Mars of the novel is a Christian paradise ruled by an archangel. This is the first novel of Lewis's so called "space triology"; the second novel, *Perelandra*, is set on Venus, and the third, *That Hideous Strength*, on Earth but with interplanetary connections. All three novels feature the same hero, Elwin Ransom, and all are a unique mixture of SF and what seem to be fantasy elements. In each novel an important part is played by the "eldils," a species of angels inhabiting interplanetary space whose bodies are composed of semi-visible light; but in the first two novels there is also a spaceship, and in the third novel a type of cyborg, a severed human head kept alive by advanced scientific technology. This mixture of science and the supernatural in the trilogy is deliberate and indeed essential; for the fundamental theme of the whole trilogy is the clash between evil modern scientism and old-fashioned Christianity. The trilogy in fact defies generic classification: it is very dubiously science fiction, by reason of all those angels (and devils, in the second and third novels), yet it is not exactly fantasy either, for the author firmly believes in the actual existence of his supernatural entities, and is out to convince us, with all the power of his very powerful art, of their reality and supreme importance. It is this polemic purpose which may repel some readers: Lewis himself has stated (*Of Other Worlds*) that *Perelandra*, at least, was written essentially for Christians only.

But *Out of the Silent Planet* is less overtly Christian, and should appeal to a wide readership by the sheer beauty of its style and images. The inner action of this novel is twofold: it is partly a *Bildungsroman*, effecting the re-education of Ransom, and through him of the reader; and partly a physical and intellectual defeat of human-racist expansionism. Ransom, an ordinary, decent literary scholar, is kidnapped by the ruthless physicist Professor Weston and his capitalist collaborator Devine and taken in Weston's secret spaceship to Mars, for Weston mistakenly believes that the "primitive natives" of Mars have demanded a human sacrifice in exchange for gold. Mars ("Malacandra") proves to be a beautiful, paradisal planet, and the natives comprise three intelligent species, all living in friendship and complementary collaboration, and all ruled by the nearly invisible eldil Oyarsa from his paradise-island of Meldilorn. Ransom escapes from his human captors, takes refuge among the "hrossa," the seal-like poetic species, and learns the Malacandrian language. He is thus equipped to serve as interpreter in the climactic scene of the novel when Weston and Devine are arrested by the hrossa and brought to Oyarsa for judgment. This trial scene is one of the clearest, wittiest, and most striking portrayals in imaginative fiction of the clash between human-racist expansionism and the opposing school of thought—the school now represented chiefly by the ecology movement. Weston boasts to Oyarsa that nothing will stop the human race from conquering the universe, moving on from planet to planet as each world dies. Oyarasa refutes Weston with the question: "And when all are dead?"—to which Weston has no answer. After this the humans, including Ransom, are forced to return to Earth, whereupon their spaceship is destroyed by angelic power.

One other aspect of *Out of the Silent Planet* should be noted: it is a polemic parody of H.G. Wells's *The First Men in the Moon*. Like Wells, Lewis has a spherical "backyard spaceship" built by a scientist and a capitalist, and the capitalist in each novel is out for the gold of the strange planet. Lewis's main changes are two: he introduces an explicitly Christian viewpoint in the extra character Ransom; and where Wells goes for effects of horror, Lewis goes for beauty.

*Perelandra* is a sequel in that once more Weston lands on another planet—Venus—and once more is opposed by Ransom; but essentially the work is a variation on Milton's *Paradise Lost*. Venus (Perelandra) is a mostly oceanic world with only two inhabitants—its innocent Adam and Eve. Soon after Weston's arrival, he is possessed by a devil—and he proceeds to tempt the Perelandrian Eve to violate God's sole prohibition. At last Ransom understands his mission, and ends the temptation by destroying Weston. The Venusian paradise is saved, a second Fall is averted. This novel is an even greater achievement than *Out of the Silent Planet:* the action, limited to three characters, has concentrated dramatic power, and the scenery—the floating vegetable islands and seas of Venus—is of a beauty which has never been surpassed by an imaginative writer. It is magnificent—but it is hardly science fiction. That might also be said of the trilogy's final novel, *That Hideous Strength*. The Devil is confronted this time on Earth by planetary angels, Ransom, and the Arthurian wizard Merlin, and the wicked are destroyed in a magic holocaust.

Also relevant to Lewis's SF are his seven Narnia novels for children. These may be called fantasy, since they are set in and around an imaginary world (Narnia) where magic is commonplace and the inhabitants include giants, dwarfs, dragons, fauns, centaurs, and talking animals. But Narnia has an intellectual solidity similar to SF and lacking in some fantasy worlds of other writers, since it exists in a parallel universe also created, like this one of ours, by God: it is a universe whose Earth is flat, and whose stars are living beings. It is also, as usual in Lewis, a universe of marvellous beauty. Lewis is also an important critic of SF and related genres, chiefly in the essay collection *Of Other Worlds*. His remarks on characterization are justly famous.

Taking his work as a whole, one must note that although Lewis wrote little that is certainly SF, he is of the first importance in the history of this genre through the sheer power of his imagination, his ability to create beautiful worlds which are wholly realized in their actuality; and through the enormous pressure of his moral commitment, which supplies tension throughout the action of every one of his stories. Above all, he has been a most effective opponent of those who would like to see the human race give itself up to the demon of scientism, the spirit which desires the total conquest of the universe.

—David Lake

---

**LICHTENBERG, Jacqueline.** American. Born in Flushing, New York, 25 March 1942. Educated at the University of California, Berkeley, B.S. in chemistry 1964. Married Salomon Lichtenberg; two daughters. Industrial chemist for two years, including one year in Israel. Since 1968, freelance writer. Agent: Richard Curtis Literary Agency, 171 East 74th Street, New York, New York 10021. Address: 8 Fox Lane, Spring Valley, New York 10977, U.S.A.

### Science-Fiction Publications

Novels (Series: Dushau; Kren; Sime/Gen)

*House of Zeor* (Sime/Gen). New York, Doubleday, 1974.
*Unto Zeor, Forever* (Sime/Gen). New York, Doubleday, 1978.
*First Channel* (Sime/Gen), with Jean Lorrah. New York, Doubleday, 1980.
*Mahogany Trinrose* (Sime/Gen). New York, Doubleday, 1981.
*Channel's Destiny* (Sime/Gen), with Jean Lorrah. New York, Doubleday, 1982.
*Molt Brother* (Kren). New York, Playboy Press, 1982.
*RenSime* (Sime/Gen). New York, Doubleday, 1984.
*City of a Million Legends* (Kren). New York, Berkley, 1985.
*Dushau.* New York, Warner, 1985.
*Farfetch* (Dushau). New York, Warner, 1985.
*Zelerod's Doom* (Sime/Gen), with Jean Lorrah. New York, DAW, 1986.
*Outreach* (Dushau). New York, Warner, 1986.
*Those of My Blood.* New York, St. Martin's Press, 1988.
*Dreamspy.* New York, St. Martin's Press, 1989.

### Other Publications

Other

*Star Trek Lives!*, with Sondra Marshak and Joan Winston. New York, Bantam, and London, Corgi, 1975.

*

Jacqueline Lichtenberg comments:

As I see it, the emotional substance of the Sime Series is an examination of the fear/compassion axis of emotion that can exist between symbionts. The Sime mutation brings evolutionary pressure to bear on otherwise rather ordinary human beings to develop compassion or die. It is stunning how difficult it is to find true compassion untinged by fear in a human. But when you do find it, it is more precious than life itself. The Sime/Gen mutation is considered as another on the order of the differentiation into male and female, only the second such step ever taken.

The style in which I write emphasizes psychological problems with psychological action and resolution, rather than the standard action/adventure formula in which it is considered bad form to characterize or motivate. I aim my work basically at women between 18 and 25, though anyone who has been such an age should enjoy it as well. I am constantly surprised at the number of fans who don't fit that description, surprised and delighted to no end.

* * *

Jacqueline Lichtenberg began her career in science fiction as the author of *Star Trek* fan fiction, and is the creator of one of the largest and most popular of the fannish "universes" in which the cast of the *U.S.S. Enterprise* goes where no man (or woman) has gone before. Her series, notable for its complexity, and for Lichtenberg's willingness to allow other writers to participate in it, is described in *Star Trek Lives!* This spirit of cooperation, as well as the emphases within this universe on symbiosis between dissimilar creatures who come to love one another and on psychological intensity, have carried over into Lichtenberg's "independent" fiction.

Lichtenberg has three series universes. The first, and earliest, is the one begun in *House of Zeor*, which introduced her readers to the symbiotic Simes and Gens. Simes are tentacled, almost vampiric humanoids who mutated from the parent stock after a genetic catastrophe. In order to live, they must take selyn from the second mutation, the human-appearing Gens. The problem is that selyn transfer usually kills the Gen. As the series progressed from *House of Zeor*, in which the idea of "channels," certain genetically gifted Simes capable of taking selyn without harming Gens and "channeling" it to other Simes, through *Unto Zeor, Forever*, in which an injured channel confronts the Sime's fascination with fear and pain by becoming a surgeon, into the Lichtenberg and Jean Lorrah collaborations *First Channel* and *Channel's Destiny*, which show the origins of the Farris family (the Farrises are among the most talented channels) who rule the House of Zeor, several themes emerge. One is the bonding of unlikely beings who must struggle with prejudice. Another is the curious interdependence of Sime and Gen, in which the vastly stronger and faster Sime turns out to be the weak, dependent link after all. A third is the toughness of Lichtenberg's characters, who seem never to give up. This toughness is manifested in subsequent books—*Mahogany Trinrose*, in which a Farris daughter persists until she produces a new genetic variant of an old species and is thought to be a witch, and *RenSime*, in which a Farris woman who is not a channel copes with her despair at not being what she was born to be. Subsequent books in this series include another collaboration with Jean Lorrah, *Zelerod's Doom;* Lorrah plans to produce a few Sime/Gen novels independently.

*Molt Brother* is Lichtenberg's first novel set in a different, high-tech universe. It and its sequel, *City of a Million Legends*, introduce the kren, reptilian beings with venomed fangs who are vulnerable only when they molt. At that time, they choose molt brothers (or sisters) to guard them. This bond, like the selyn transfer for Simes, is perilous, profound, and occasionally ecstatic.; *Molt Brother* is the story of Arshel Holtether, an esper archeologist who chooses a human molt brother and enters worlds of intrigue, danger, and self-discovery. It is also the story of Zref, a human/computer interface unable to link completely with his own mechanical symbiote.

Lichtenberg's series about a species called the Dushau also displays her preoccupation with symbiotes. In this trilogy (*Dushau, Farfetch*, and *Outreach*) set in a high-tech, tyrannical, and rather Byzantine galactic empire, a young woman closely connected with the court wants above all else to join a bonded group of Dushau, long-lived alien empaths who can practically bond into planetary ecologies. Because the empire suspects the Dushau of wanting independence, it is systematically exterminating them. One bond group flees a police cruiser to a planet that becomes its ally as Dushau, the human heroine, and a host of minor characters set the stage for revolution.

All of Lichtenberg's books are marked by an extraordinary density of thought. She creates extremely dangerous characters: the sinister Simes, the venomous kren whose pain somehow makes them vulnerable and understandable to her often fanatic readers. Her writing is notable for intensity rather than lyricism. Frequently her books are painful to read because of her insistence on confronting breakdowns in communication (which occasionally makes her writing tortuous and harsh) and extending them out into catastrophe. She specializes in creating a psychological "worst-case" scenario and then rehabilitating the characters who encounter it. In order to supply communication, Lichtenberg creates bonds like transfer, molt brotherhood, or the symbiosis in Dushau, but even these bonds are imperfect, if only because their severing causes anguish.

As can be seen from Lichtenberg's willingness to allow other writers to participate in her universes, she is a generous teacher, who has participated in many writers workshops, notably the one sponsored at Murray State University in Kentucky. Her fans have published three fanzines that feature letters, reviews, fragments of manuscripts, and original Sime/Gen stories by amateur writers. The audience for her work is among the most dedicated in the field, and Lichtenberg is notable for her willingness to enter their lives as generously as she has opened her worlds to them.

—Susan Shwartz

---

**LIGHTNER, Alice (Martha).** Also writes as Alice L. Hopf. American. Born in Detroit, Michigan, 11 October 1904. Educated at Westover School, Middlebury, Connecticut, graduated 1923; Vassar College, Poughkeepsie, New York, B.A. 1927. Married Ernest Joachim Hopf in 1935; one son. Editorial assistant, *Civil Engineering;* clerk-typist, Grey Advertising, New York. From 1951, freelance writer. Recipient: National Science Teachers Association award, 1972, 1973. *Died 3 February 1988.*

### Science-Fiction Publications

Novels (for children)

*The Rock of Three Planets.* New York, Putnam, 1963.
*The Planet Poachers.* New York, Putnam, 1965.
*Doctor to the Galaxy.* New York, Norton, 1965.
*The Galactic Troubadours.* New York, Norton, 1965.
*The Space Plague.* New York, Norton, 1966.
*The Space Olympics.* New York, Norton, 1967.
*The Space Ark.* New York, Putnam, 1968.
*The Day of the Drones.* New York, Norton, 1969.
*The Thursday Toads.* New York, McGraw Hill, 1971.
*Gods or Demons?* New York, Four Winds Press, 1973.
*Star Dog.* New York, McGraw Hill, 1973.
*The Space Gypsies.* New York, McGraw Hill, 1974.
*Star Circus.* New York, Dutton, 1977.

### Other Publications

Novel

*The Walking Zoo of Darwin Dingle* (for children). New York, Putnam, 1969.

Verse

*The Pillar and the Flame.* New York, Vinal, 1928.

Other as Alice L. Hopf (for children)

*Monarch Butterflies.* New York, Crowell, 1965.
*Wild Traveler: The Story of a Coyote.* New York, Norton, 1967.

*Earth's Bug-Eyed Monsters.* New York, Norton, 1968.
*Butterfly and Moth.* New York, Putnam, 1969.
*Carab, The Trap-Door Spider.* New York, Putnam, 1970.
*Biography of an Octopus [a Rhino, an Ostrich, an Ant, an Armadillo, an American Reindeer, a Giraffe, a Snowy Owl, a Komodo Dragon].* New York, Putnam, 9 vols., 1971–81.
*Misunderstood Animals.* New York, McGraw Hill, 1973.
*Wild Cousins of the Dog [Cat, Horse].* New York, Putnam, 3 vols., 1973–77.
*Misplaced Animals and Other Living Creatures.* New York, McGraw Hill, 1975.
*Animal and Plant Life Spans.* New York, Holiday House, 1978.
*Animals That Eat Nectar and Honey.* New York, Holiday House, 1979.
*Nature's Pretenders.* New York, Putnam, 1979.
*Pigs Wild and Tame.* New York, Holiday House, 1979.
*Whose House Is It?* New York, Dodd Mead, 1980.
*Bugs, Big and Little.* New York, Messner, 1981.
*Strange Sex Lives in the Animal Kingdom.* New York, McGraw Hill, 1981.
*Chickens and Their Wild Relatives.* New York, Dodd Mead, 1982.
*Hyenas.* New York, Dodd Mead, 1983.
*Bats.* New York, Dodd Mead, 1985.
*Spiders.* New York, Dutton, 1990.

*

Manuscript Collection: Fullerton College Library, California.

* * *

Alice Lightner was an author of children's books, at home in non-fiction as well as SF. Her informational books about animal life are popular with young readers and have received honors from science teachers because of their solid, up-to-date information, enthusiastic concern for ecology and conservation, and capacity for explaining on a child's level of comprehension. Similar qualities mark Lightner's SF. Actually, so prominent is the last quality that in spite of lacking a prose style as supple as Norton's or an imagination as inventive as Heinlein's, Lightner has produced a body of SF that is perhaps more readily open to and enjoyed by youngsters than either of theirs.

The typical Lightner novel is an amalgam of SF and the Young Adult novel. The most prominent of the former is the presence of "alien" animals: either ones that do not exist today but whose future existence may be extrapolated—a unicorn-like gazelle, for instance, or a telepathic bird that can speak—or ones that are unexpected mutations of species currently existing—giant bees, for example. Another prominent SF feature is exotic setting, most often a planet newly discovered which needs to be explored and surveyed and whose flora and fauna require cataloguing and preserving. Young Adult elements usually found in Lightner's fiction are mystery and dashes of romance and humor in addition to the requisite youthful protagonists. (Incidentally, Lightner is one of the very few writers of children's SF who regularly incorporate females among their protagonists.) So determined is Lightner to appeal to youth that sometimes, as in *The Galactic Troubadours*, she sacrifices plausibility for topicality: a band of rock and roll musicians make a nuisance of themselves as they travel from planet to planet. In general, though, Lightner has been successful in her mix.

Lightner's most successful novel is *The Day of the Drones*. Set in the future when nuclear conflict has poisoned the earth and obliterated virtually everyone, the book concerns the Afrians—descendants of a small group of surviving black Africans who have managed to rebuild civilization by placing under taboo most technology and by practicing strict genetic control. Those born darkest-skinned will enjoy most privileges; fair-skinned babies, less; the occasional white baby is simply abandoned. A small group of Afrians set out to ascertain whether any other human survivors exist. In what was once England the Afrians come across the Anglics, descendants of the ancient English who are cruel, superstition-ridden, and white. They too practice social engineering, having established a bizarre matriarchy modeled upon bee-society. The impact of *The Day of the Drones* is threefold. One, the description of the two differing cultures is detailed and plausible. Second, characterization is rounded and convincing; none of the several protagonists is a mouthpiece for conventional sentiments or moral posturing. Especially interesting is Anhara, the young Afrian archeologist who has mastered Anglic so that she can appreciate the little Shakespeare that is extant and becomes sorrowed at the degradation of the race that produced the Master. Third, the investigation of racism, whether black or white, and its demeaning effects is matter-of-fact and even-handed, hence, neither sensational nor preachy. The book, then, is impressive and challenging; as such it must be ranked among the relatively few superior examples of children's SF.

—Francis J. Molson

---

**LINAWEAVER, Brad.** American. Born in North Carolina, 9 January 1952. Educated at Florida State University, B.A.; Rollins College, Florida, M.A. Married Cynthia-Cari Holloway, 1985 (separated); one step-daughter. Has worked as teacher in English, actor, and movie theater manager. Since 1974, freelance journalist. Recipient: Prometheus award, 1989. Agent: Ricia Mainhardt, 612 Argyle No. L5, Brooklyn, New York, 11230. Address: 8833 Sunset Boulevard, Suite 304, Los Angeles, California 90069, U.S.A.

### Science-Fiction Publications

Novel

*Moon of Ice.* New York, Arbor House, 1988; London, Grafton, 1989.

*

Brad Linaweaver comments:

I've never understood the desire to take popular fiction, already in a ghetto, and break it into ever smaller pieces, pretending there is no tissue tying all the parts together. I write science fiction, fantasy, and horror. I'm not interested in specializing in one of these areas when it is painfully obvious that they are interconnected—as if a clear line could ever be drawn between different kinds of speculative fiction. Furthermore, I want to write mystery and straight historical before I'm through!

* * *

One of the most popular forms in science fiction has long been the Uchronia, or alternate history story. What might have happened had the South won the Civil War, if the Industrial Revolution had occurred a century earlier, if Napoleon had succeeded at Waterloo? Hundreds of stories have been written within the field, and the fascination of the theme has appealed to historians and writers not normally associated with the genre as well. Perhaps the most popular of these is the question, what might have occurred had Germany won World War II. The answers have been dealt with in many different ways, everything from the phantasmagorical *The Sound of His Horn* by Sarban to Philip K. Dick's classic, *The Man in the High Castle*. It might well be considered a vein of ideas long overworked, but Brad Linaweaver's first, and so far only, full-length work has taken that proposition and developed it into a major contribution to the field, a rare achievement for any writer, let alone one who had never produced a novel previously.

Originally a shorter work with the same title, *Moon of Ice* appeared in its full-length version in 1988 to nearly universal acclaim. Franklin Roosevelt was impeached and replaced with a more isolationist president, which gave Germany the time it needed to complete its own development of nuclear weapons. With that capacity, the conquest of Europe and Africa was a foregone conclusion, and now the Nazis control a large portion of the world directly, heavily influencing most of the rest. The United States has become even more libertarian than in our own reality, but still avoids unnecessary contact with the German empire, which has now grown fat and lazy, for the most part content with its expansion, still in the process of absorbing the disparate populations it has overrun, finally acceding to the necessity of compromising in its foreign policy in order to maintain a somewhat shaky economy.

Hilda Goebbels, daughter of one of Hitler's most trusted assistants, is repelled by the excesses and inhumanity of her own government and has become a prominent revolutionary living abroad. To this end, she has stolen her father's secret diaries and offered them and her own personal memoirs to an American publisher. Obviously this is a major coup since the diaries in particular provide detailed insight into the madness that dominated the inner circles of Hitler's closest associates, and the protagonist jumps at the opportunity to handle these works. But when he does so, he gains deep insight into a group of men held firmly in the grip of insanity, a madness which they have imposed on the people they rule. Already a new religion has been established that accepts concepts that fly in the face of observable reality (the moon is ice, for example, hence the title), and the concept of total world dominion has not been abandoned despite appearances to the contrary.

The novel is remarkable for several reasons, not the least of which is the intriguing, mystery-laden, and suspenseful plot. Linaweaver has done extensive research into the Nazi phenomenon, and his depiction of their belief in arcane magical lore and occult powers is both historically accurate and frightening. The description of Europe under the German juggernaut is evocative and chilling, just as his portrayal of an isolated, uninvolved America is convincing and depressing. His characters are fully realized and credible, neither totally villainous nor virtuous beyond flaw. His prose is careful, precise, and economical, perhaps a result of his previous experience as a journalist. *Moon of Ice* has the feel of a novel by a practiced professional, with none of the hesitancy or startling exuberance of most first novels. The shorter version, first published in *Amazing*, March 1982, was a finalist in the Nebula balloting for best story of the year.

Most of Linaweaver's shorter fiction has been for shared-world anthologies, that is, those which present a common setting within which each individual author is free to experiment. Although it is often difficult to produce first-rate fiction under these restrictions, Linaweaver has provided some interesting stories in this area. "High Road of the Lost Men" (in *Friends of the Horseclans*, edited by Robert Adams and Pamela Crippen Adams, New York, New American Library, 1987) is set in the post-nuclear collapse universe of the late Robert Adams, and uses an almost fairy-tale style to unfold the story of survival amidst a great physical cataclysm. The same style serves him well in "Dream Pirates' Jewel" (in *Tales of the Witch World 2*, New York, Tor, 1988), written in collaboration with Cynthia Linaweaver and set in Andre Norton's Witch World fantasy series. In "Shadow Quest" (in *Magic in Ithkar 2*, edited by Andre Norton and Robert Adams, New York, Tor), set in the Ithkar Fair series, an apprentice sorcerer has a strange series of experiences which mark his emergence as a full fledged practitioner of the magical arts.

Linaweaver's work has appeared rarely and often widely separated in time. In nearly a decade, he has produced a single novel and half a dozen shorter pieces. It is significant that he is held in such high esteem by readers and fellow writers alike.

—Don D'Ammassa

---

**LINDSAY, David.** British. Born in Blackheath, London, 3 March 1876. Educated at Lewisham Grammar School, London, and a secondary school in Jedburgh, Roxburgh. Served in the Grenadier Guards, 1916–18. Married Jacqueline Silver in 1916; two daughters. Worked for Price Forbes, insurance brokers, 1894–1916; lived in Cornwall, 1919–29, and after 1929 in Sussex. *Died 16 July 1945.*

### Science-Fiction Publications

Novels

*A Voyage to Arcturus*. London, Methuen, 1920; New York, Macmillan, 1963.

*The Haunted Woman*. London, Methuen, 1922; Hollywood, Newcastle, 1975.

*Sphinx*. London, Long, 1923; New York, Carroll and Graf, 1988.

*Devil's Tor*. London, Putnam, 1932; New York, Arno Press, 1978.

*The Violet Apple, and The Witch*. Chicago, Chicago Review Press, 1976; London, Sidgwick and Jackson, 1978.

### Other Publications

Novel

*Adventures of Monsieur de Mailly*. London, Melrose, 1926; as *A Blade for Sale*, New York, McBride, 1927.

*

Critical Studies: *The Strange Genius of David Lindsay* by J.B. Pick, Colin Wilson, and E.H. Visiak, London, Baker, 1970, as *The Haunted Man*, San Bernardino, California, Borgo Press, 1979; *The Life and Works of David Lindsay* by Bernard Sellin, translated by Kenneth Gunnell, Cambridge, University Press, 1981; *David Lindsay* by Gary K. Wolfe, Mercer Island, Washington, Starmont House, 1982.

* * *

While David Lindsay's first novel, *A Voyage to Arcturus*, has become recognized as one of the masterworks of 20th-century fantasy, his other novels remain unknown to all but a handful of readers, and the man himself remains a curiously distant and enigmatic figure. More a philosopher than a novelist, Lindsay wrote often awkward and laborious prose, his later work filled with long expository digressions, his ideas so complex and densely packed, his characters so unsympathetic, that many readers find his fiction at first coldly intellectual and difficult to get into. But Lindsay undeniably expanded the possibilities of fantasy as philosophical fiction, and his influence has been widely felt among modern authors as diverse as Colin Wilson and Philip José Farmer.

Lindsay's masterpiece, *A Voyage to Arcturus*, concerns the journey of a man named Maskull to Tormance, a world in the system Arcturus, where he encounters bizarre characters and himself undergoes physical transformations in a series of episodes depicting different systems of belief not unlike the different moral systems at work on Earth. As each of these moral systems is shown to be illusory, Maskull is gradually brought to a confrontation with the godlike villain Crystalman, who controls this world, and who seems, at the end, to represent the entire world of phenomenal experience. Drawing on Nietzsche, Schopenhauer, and Norse mythology for ideas and imagery, Lindsay develops a world of vivid scenery and violent action that nevertheless is rigidly structured according to the philosophical ideas he wishes to explore. The novel is a remarkable union of action and idea.

Ideas were more interesting to Lindsay than action, however, and his later novels contained little of the violent action of *Arcturus. The Haunted Woman* continued exploring the notion of subjective reality in a romance of two lovers who could only acknowledge their love in a phantom room of a haunted house. *Sphinx* turned to the science-fiction device of a dream-recording machine to explore the romance between a woman composer and a writer. Like *A Voyage to Arcturus* itself, however, each of these novels was a commercial disaster, and Lindsay turned to the historical romance for his next book, *Adventures of Monsieur de Mailly*, a tale of court intrigue that nevertheless also reflected Lindsay's preoccupations with illusion and deception. *Devil's Tor* is a sprawling, slow-moving, and at times brilliant exposition of the myth of the Eternal Feminine, in a story concerning the reuniting of two halves of an ancient stone and the founding of a new race by a chosen man and woman.

Lindsay was unable to find a publisher for *The Violet Apple*, and he left another manuscript, "The Witch," unfinished. Both works were finally published in abridged form, and both retain the romance structure of *The Haunted Woman* and *Devil's Tor*. In *The Violet Apple* a dwarf apple tree, grown from a seed which according to legend came from the original tree of Eden, unites the lovers. "The Witch" explores the dual myths of the wise woman and witchcraft in a work whose controlling image is music. Though none of these later works achieves the narrative power of *A Voyage to Arcturus*, they nevertheless stand as worthwhile philosophical meditations and as studies in the problems inherent in trying to write a truly philosophical fiction.

—Gary K. Wolfe

---

**LLEWELLYN, (David William) Alun.** Irish. Born in London, England, 17 April 1903. Educated at Alleyn's School, Dulwich, London; St. John's College, Cambridge (Chancellor's Gold Medal, for poetry, 1923; College Literature prize, 1924), B.A. (honours) in history and literature 1924, LL.B. (honours) 1925, M.A. 1928; Lincoln's Inn, London: called to the Bar, 1927. Served in the Intelligence Corps during World War II. Married Lesley Deane in 1953. Treaty translator and reviser, League of Nations, Geneva, 1936–39; legal adviser, Egyptian government, Montreux Capitulations, 1937; Secretary of the Compensation Tribunal for Coal Nationalisation, 1947–49; counsel, Camberwell Borough, London, 1951–53; public relations speaker, Commonwealth Industries Association, 1955–72. Liberal parliamentary candidate for South Croydon, 1931, 1935. President, Union Society, 1935, and Hardwicke Society, 1953, both Middle Temple, London; Honorary Treasurer, Poetry Society of Great Britain, 1961–62. Since 1977, Honorary Secretary, and President, 1984–86, Irish P.E.N. Member, Welsh Academy, 1983. Address: 52 Silchester Park, Glenageary, Dun Laoghaire, County Dublin, Ireland.

SCIENCE-FICTION PUBLICATIONS

Novel

*The Strange Invaders.* London, Bell, 1934.

OTHER PUBLICATIONS

Novels

*The Deacon.* London, Bell, 1934.
*The Soul of Cézar Azan.* London, Barker, 1938.
*Jubilee John.* London, Barker, 1939.

Short Stories

*Confound Their Politics.* London, Bell, 1934.

Plays

*Ways of Love* (produced 1968). London, French, 1958.
*Shelley Plain* (produced London, 1960).

Verse

*Ballads and Songs.* London, Stockwell, 1921.

Other

*History of the Union Society of London.* London, Union Society, 1935.
*The Emperor of Britain.* London, Montgomeryshire Society, 1939.
*The Tyrant from Below: An Essay in Political Revaluation.* London, Macdonald and Evans, 1957.
*The World and the Commonwealth.* London, British Commonwealth Union, 1968.
*The Shell Guide to Wales.* London, Rainbird, 1969.

*

Alun Llewellyn comments:

Only one of my novels is, strictly speaking, science fiction. *The Strange Invaders* looks at this planet and the ecological change upon it as a result of Man's abandonment of Mind as a motive force of his evolution. But since all human psychology is a matter for scientific analysis, and is a more subtle matter than mechanistic theories of economics or sex can explain, the studies in my other novels of the illusions of love, religion, ambition, and power ought really to be called fictional illustrations of scientific themes. By this interpretation, all my fiction qualifies as science fiction.

* * *

Alun Llewellyn's *The Strange Invaders* is a fantasy set in the future when the habitable area of the earth is gradually decreasing as a new ice age emerges. Mankind has retrogressed; as a result of disastrous wars it has lost the art of civilization and is living in a pre-iron age existence. The story takes place in what seems to be the Gobi desert, a somewhat hostile environment but one of the last places on earth capable of supporting human life. The plot concerns a small group of people living in a half-destroyed town, isolated within the remains of a ruined city on the plains. There is a pseudo-medieval order to their existence: governed by a religious community of priests dedicated to the new trinity of Marx, Lenin, and Stalin, and controlled by a warrior group, they manage to eke out a life of basic survival. As if their plight were not bad enough, Llewellyn has this last outpost of humanity threatened by an army of enormous lizards—huge, cold-blooded creatures that are virtually invincible. The plot is concerned with the efforts of the community to survive in the face of this new and overpowering challenge. What elevates the story above the ordinary is Llewellyn's ability to show how the basic human emotions of love, hate, and jealousy survive and dominate the lives of these people even in the face of overwhelming danger and the threat of extinction.

Though the novel is cast in the form of a futuristic nightmare, it is difficult for the reader to remember that the time frame is the future and not the past. So vividly does Llewellyn evoke the sense of life of these people and so much is their life a reliving of prehistorical civilization, that the reader inevitably feels that he has been transported into the past rather than into the future.

—Joseph A. Quinn

---

**LONDON, Jack** (John Griffith London). American. Born in San Francisco, California, 12 January 1876. Educated at a grammar school in Oakland, California; Oakland High School, 1895–96; University of California, Berkeley, 1896–97. Married 1) Bessie Maddern in 1900 (separated 1903; divorced 1905), two daughters; 2) Charmian Kittredge in 1905. Worked in a cannery in Oakland, 1890; sailor on the *Sophie Sutherland*, sailing to Japan and Siberia, 1893; returned to Oakland, wrote for the local paper, and held various odd jobs, 1893–94; tramped the United States and Canada, 1894–96; arrested for vagrancy in Niagara Falls, New York; joined the gold rush to the Klondike, 1897–98, then returned to Oakland and became a full-time writer; visited London, 1902; war correspondent in the Russo-Japanese War for the *San Francisco Examiner*, 1904; settled on a ranch in Sonoma County, California, 1906, and lived there for the rest of his life; attempted to sail round the world on a 45-foot yacht, 1907–09; war correspondent in Mexico, 1914. *Died 22 November 1916.*

### Science-Fiction Publications

#### Novels

*Before Adam*. New York, Macmillan, 1907; London, Laurie, 1908.
*The Iron Heel*. New York, Macmillan, and London, Everett, 1908.
*The Scarlet Plague*. New York, Macmillan, and London, Mills and Boon, 1915.
*The Jacket* (*The Star Rover*). London, Mills and Boon, 1915; as *The Star Rover*, New York, Macmillan, 1915.

#### Short Stories

*The Strength of the Strong* (story). Chicago, Kerr, 1911.
*The Dream of Debs*. Chicago, Kerr, 1912(?).
*The Strength of the Strong* (collection). New York, Macmillan, 1914; London, Mills and Boon, 1917.
*The Red One*. New York, Macmillan, 1918; London, Mills and Boon, 1919.
*Short Stories*, edited by Maxwell Geismar. New York, Hill and Wang, 1960.
*Goliah: A Utopian Essay*. Berkeley, California, Thorp Springs Press, 1973.
*Curious Fragments: Jack London's Tales of Fantasy Fiction*, edited by Dale L. Walker. Port Washington, New York, Kennikat Press, 1975.
*The Science Fiction of Jack London*, edited by Richard Gid Powers. Boston, Gregg Press, 1975.

### Other Publications

#### Novels

*The Cruise of the Dazzler*. New York, Century, 1902; London, Hodder and Stoughton, 1906.
*A Daughter of the Snows*. Philadelphia, Lippincott, 1902; London, Isbister, 1904.
*The Kempton-Wace Letters* (published anonymously), with Anna Strunsky. New York, Macmillan, and London, Isbister, 1903.
*The Call of the Wild* New York, Macmillan, and London, Heinemann, 1903.
*The Sea-Wolf*. New York, Macmillan, and London, Heinemann, 1904.
*The Game*. New York, Macmillan, and London, Heinemann, 1905.
*White Fang*. New York, Macmillan, 1906; London, Methuen, 1907.
*Martin Eden*. New York, Macmillan, 1909; London, Heinemann, 1910.
*Burning Daylight*. New York, Macmillan, 1910; London, Heinemann, 1911.
*Adventure*. London, Nelson, and New York, Macmillan, 1911.
*The Abysmal Brute*. New York, Century, 1913; London, Newnes, 1914.
*John Barleycorn*. New York, Century, 1913; London, Mills and Boon, 1914.
*The Valley of the Moon*. New York, Macmillan, and London, Mills and Boon, 1913.
*The Mutiny of the Elsinore*. New York, Macmillan, 1914; London, Mills and Boon, 1915.
*The Little Lady of the Big House*. New York, Macmillan, and London, Mills and Boon, 1916.

*Jerry of the Islands.* New York, Macmillan, and London, Mills and Boon, 1917.
*Michael, Brother of Jerry.* New York, Macmillan, 1917; London, Mills and Boon, 1918.
*Hearts of Three.* London, Mills and Boon, 1918; New York, Macmillan, 1920.
*The Assassination Bureau Ltd.*, completed by Robert L. Fish. New York, McGraw Hill, 1963; London, Deutsch, 1964.

Short Stories

*The Son of the Wolf: Tales of the Far North.* Boston, Houghton Mifflin, 1900; London, Isbister, 1902; as *An Odyssey of the North*, London, Mills and Boon, 1915.
*The God of His Fathers and Other Stories.* New York, McClure, 1901; London, Isbister, 1902.
*Children of the Frost.* New York, Macmillan, 1902.
*The Faith of Men and Other Stories.* New York, Macmillan, and London, Heinemann, 1904.
*Tales of the Fish Patrol.* New York, Macmillan, 1905; London, Heinemann, 1906.
*The Apostate.* Chicago, Kerr, 1906.
*Moon-Face and Other Stories.* New York, Macmillan, and London, Heinemann, 1906.
*Love of Life and Other Stories.* New York, Macmillan, 1907; London, Everett, 1908.
*Lost Face.* New York, Macmillan, 1910; London, Mills and Boon, 1915.
*When God Laughs and Other Stories.* New York, Macmillan, 1911; London, Mills and Boon, 1912.
*South Sea Tales.* New York, Macmillan, 1911; London, Mills and Boon, 1912.
*The House of Pride and Other Tales of Hawaii.* New York, Macmillan, 1912; London, Mills and Boon, 1914.
*A Son of the Sun.* New York, Doubleday, 1912; London, Mills and Boon, 1913; as *The Adventures of Captain Grief*, Cleveland, World, 1954.
*Smoke Bellew.* New York, Century, 1912; London, Mills and Boon, 1913; as *Smoke and Shorty*, London, Mills and Boon, 1920.
*The Night Born....* New York, Century, 1913; London, Mills and Boon, 1916.
*The Turtles of Tasman.* New York, Macmillan, 1916; London, Mills and Boon, 1917.
*The Human Drift.* New York, Macmillan, 1917; London, Mills and Boon, 1919.
*On the Makaloa Mat.* New York, Macmillan, 1919; as *Island Tales*, London, Mills and Boon, 1920.
*Dutch Courage and Other Stories.* New York, Macmillan, 1922; London, Mills and Boon, 1923.
*Jack London's Tales of Adventure*, edited by Irving Shepard. New York, Hanover House, 1956.
*Stories of Hawaii*, edited by A. Grove Day. New York, Appleton Century Crofts, 1965.
*Great Short Works of Jack London*, edited by Earle Labor. New York, Harper, 1965.
*The Unabridged Jack London*, edited by Lawrence Teacher and Richard E. Nicholls. Philadelphia, Running Press, 1981.
*Jack London's Yukon Women.* New York, Belmont, 1982.
*Young Wolf: The Early Adventure Stories*, edited by Howard Lachtman. Santa Barbara, California, Capra Press, 1984.
*In a Far Country: Jack London's Western Tales*, edited by Dale L. Walker. New York, Jameson, 1986.
*Short Stories*, edited by Earle Labor, Robert C. Leitz III, and I. Milo Shepard. New York, Macmillan, 1990.

Plays

*The Great Interrogation*, with Less Bascom (produced San Francisco, 1905).
*Scorn of Women.* New York, Macmillan, 1906; London, Macmillan, 1907.
*Theft.* New York and London, Macmillan, 1910.
*The Acorn Planters: A California Forest Play....* New York, Macmillan, and London, Mills and Boon, 1916.
*Daughters of the Rich*, edited by James E. Sisson. Oakland, California, Holmes, 1971.
*Gold*, with Herbert Heron, edited by James E. Sisson. Oakland, California, Holmes, 1972.

Other

*The People of the Abyss.* New York, Macmillan, and London, Isbister, 1903.
*The Tramp.* New York, Wilshire's Magazine, 1904.
*The Scab.* Chicago, Kerr, 1904.
*Jack London: A Sketch of His Life and Work.* London, Macmillan, 1905.
*War of the Classes.* New York, Macmillan, and London, Heinemann, 1905.
*What Life Means to Me.* Princeton, New Jersey, Intercollegiate Socialist Society, 1906.
*The Road.* New York, Macmillan, 1907; London, Mills and Boon, 1914.
*Jack London: Who He Is and What He Has Done.* New York, Macmillan, 1908(?).
*Revolution.* Chicago, Kerr, 1909.
*Revolution and Other Essays.* New York, Macmillan, 1910; London, Mills and Boon, 1920.
*The Cruise of the Snark.* New York, Macmillan, and London, Mills and Boon, 1911.
*Jack London by Himself.* New York, Macmillan, and London, Mills and Boon, 1913.
*London's Essays of Revolt*, edited by Leonard D. Abbott. New York, Vanguard Press, 1926.
*Jack London, American Rebel: A Collection of His Social Writings...*, edited by Philip S. Foner. New York, Citadel Press, 1947.
*(Works)* [Fitzroy Edition], edited by I.O. Evans. London, Arco, and New York, Archer House and Horizon Press, 18 vols., 1962–68.
*The Bodley Head Jack London*, edited by Arthur Calder-Marshall. London, Bodley Head, 4 vols., 1963–66; as *The Pan Jack London*, London, Pan, 2 vols., 1966–68.
*Letters from Jack London, Containing an Unpublished Correspondence Between London and Sinclair Lewis*, edited by King Hendricks and Irving Shepard. New York, Odyssey Press, 1965; London, MacGibbon and Kee, 1966.
*Jack London Reports: War Correspondence, Sports Articles, and Miscellaneous Writings*, edited by King Hendricks and Irving Shepard. New York, Random House, 1970.
*Jack London's Articles and Short Stories in the (Oakland) High School Aegis*, edited by James E. Sisson. Cedar Springs, Michigan, London Collector, 1971.
*No Mentor But Myself: A Collection of Articles, Essays, Reviews, and Letters on Writing and Writers*, edited by Dale L. Walker. Port Washington, New York, Kennikat Press, 1979.
*Revolution: Stories and Essays*, edited by Robert Barltrop. London, Journeyman Press, 1979.
*Jack London on the Road: The Tramp Diary and Other Hobo Writings*, edited by Richard W. Etulain. Logan, Utah State University Press, 1979.

*Sporting Blood: Selections from Jack London's Greatest Sports Writing*, edited by Howard Lachtman. Novato, California, Presidio Press, 1981.

*Novels and Stories* and *Novels and Social Writings* (Library of America), edited by Donald Pizer. New York, Literary Classics of the United States, and London, Cambridge University Press, 2 vols., 1982–84.

*Jack London's California: The Golden Poppy and Other Writings*, edited by Sal Noto. New York, Beaufort, 1986.

*The Letters of Jack London*, edited by Earle Labor, Robert C. Leitz III, and I. Milo Shepard. Stanford, California, Stanford University Press, 3 vols. 1988.

*

Bibliography: *Jack London: A Bibliography* by Hensley C. Woodbridge, John London, and George H. Tweney, Georgetown, California, Talisman Press, 1966; supplement by Woodbridge, Milwood, New York, Kraus, 1973; in *Bibliography of American Literature 5* by Jacob Blanck, New Haven, Connecticut, Yale University Press, 1969; *The Fiction of Jack London: A Chronological Bibliography* by Dale L. Walker and James E. Sisson, El Paso, University of Texas, 1972; *Jack London: A Reference Guide* by Joan R. Sherman, Boston, Hall, 1977.

Manuscript Collections: Huntington Library, San Marino, California; Utah State University Library, Logan.

Critical Studies: *Jack London: A Biography* by Richard O'Connor, Boston, Little Brown, 1964, London, Gollancz, 1965; *The Alien Worlds of Jack London* by Dale L. Walker, Grand Rapids, Michigan, Wolf House, 1973; *Jack London* by Earle Labor, Boston, Twayne, 1974; *Jack London: The Man, The Writer, The Rebel* by Robert Barltrop, London, Pluto Press, 1976; *Jack: A Biography of Jack London* by Andrew Sinclair, New York, Harper, 1977, London, Weidenfeld and Nicolson, 1978; *Jack London and the Klondike: The Genesis of an American Writer* by Franklin Walker, San Marino, California, Huntington Library Publications, 1978; *Jack London: Essays in Criticism* edited by Ray W. Ownbey, Layton, Utah, Peregrine Smith, 1979; *Jack London: An American Myth* by John Perry, Chicago, Nelson Hall, 1981; *Solitary Comrade: Jack London and His Work* by Joan D. Hedrick, Chapel Hill, University of North Carolina Press, 1982; *The Novels of Jack London* by Charles N. Watson, Madison, University of Wisconsin Press, 1983; *Jack London* by Gordon Beauchamp, Mercer Island, Washington, Starmont House, 1984; *Jack London, An American Radical?* by Carolyn Johnston, Westport, Connecticut, Greenwood Press, 1984; *The Tools of My Trade: The Annotated Books in Jack London's Library* by David Mike Hamilton, Seattle, University of Washington Press, 1986; *Jack London* by James Lundquist, New York, Ungar, 1987.

* * *

Jack London is among the more important American science-fiction writers by virtue of his attention to social and political extrapolation, matters all too often ignored by his compatriots. In almost all of London's science fiction, mankind individually or collectively faces a challenge, be it the challenge of the primitive, the challenge of disaster, or the challenge of socialism.

"A Relic of the Pliocene" is a good example of the challenge of the primitive. In London's arctic, the scene of a good portion of his fiction, a man tells of killing the last mammoth. "When the World Was Young" takes up the theme of a man divided between an identity as a civilized businessman and a primitive savagery that seizes control every night. In "The Strength of the Strong" a cave man tells of the formation of tribes, which increase everyone's strength, and then of classes, which seem to decrease collective strength. London's novel *Before Adam* is entirely situated in primitive times.

*The Scarlet Plague* is London's most successful disaster novel. To read it today is to realize how tepid are many recent works about disaster. The opening scene alone is a small masterpiece. It presents an old man and two boys walking along a railroad track in the future, destroyed world, the old man reflecting on the contrast between the way things are and the way they were in the old days. This old man, once a college professor at the University of California, goes on to tell of how his world collapsed under the onslaught of the plague, which was always fatal within 30 minutes, and killed most of the world's population, sparing only the old man and about 40 others. These few spawn a new generation in a now-primitive world. The old man tells of the futile efforts at the University of California to save a remnant of the University community, and the equally futile efforts he (the old man) has made to make the new generation understand something of how things once were. Another disaster story is "The Unparalleled Invasion," in which the western nations use germ warfare to defeat the yellow peril—the combined forces of Japan and China. London's much-discussed racism is all too evident in this story.

A good deal of London's science fiction describes the onset of socialism, usually perceived by the ruling classes as a disaster. In "The Minions of Midas" a secret society blackmails the capitalists into submission by killing their loved ones. A similar story is *Goliah*, in which a discoverer of atomic power blackmails the world into accepting socialism. But London's great work in this mode is *The Iron Heel.* A future America has come under the iron heel of oligarchic corporations, and a working-class hero, Ernest Everhard, struggles to convince certain of the well-to-do that only a revolution can remove the oppression. London ends the book in 1932, when the oligarchy has thwarted one attempt at revolution—but another attempt is planned. Although Everhard is too pure and great, too earnest, London's novel brings to science fiction a high level of political discussion of issues that remain vital.

Almost as well known is "The Dream of Debs," a realistic account of a general strike in San Francisco which succeeds only after the fabric of society is utterly rent. When the wealthy narrator complains that "the tyranny of organized labor is getting beyond human endurance" we can see his point.

Perhaps London's greatest science-fiction work, however, is *The Red One*, which is not cast in any of London's characteristic molds, although it does involve a white man held captive by primitive Sumatrans, thus fitting with London's interest in survival under primitive conditions. The primitive tribe in question worships the red one of the title, a sphere from the stars. The white man gives his head in exchange for the chance to hear the red one's voice. London gives us a remarkable descriptive passage in which the white man hears the alien's message and then dies, his head coveted by the tribal chieftain. The poignancy of this juxtaposition—the man of the present, captivated by the future yet held captive by the past—establishes London's importance and originality as a science-fiction writer.

—Curtis C. Smith

---

**LONG, Frank Belknap.** Also writes as Lyda Belknap Long. American. Born in New York City, 27 April 1903. Educated in New York public schools; New York University School of Journalism, 1920–21. Married Lyda Arco in 1960. Writer for *Captain Marvel, Green Lantern, Congo Bill,* and *Planet Comics* in the 1940's; uncredited associate editor, *The Saint Mystery Magazine* and *Fantastic Universe* in the 1950's; associate editor, *Satellite Science Fiction*, 1959, *Short Stories*, 1959–60, and *Mike Shayne Mystery Magazine* until 1966. Recipient: First Fandom Hall of Fame award, 1977; 4th World Fantasy Convention Life Achievement award, 1978; Bram Stoker Life Achievement award, 1988. Agent: Kirby McCauley, 155 East 77th Street, Suite 1A, New York, New York 10021, U.S.A.

### Science-Fiction Publications

#### Novels

*Space Station No. 1.* New York, Ace, 1957.
*Woman from Another Planet.* New York, Chariot, 1960.
*The Horror Expert.* New York, Belmont, 1961.
*The Mating Center.* New York, Chariot, 1961.
*Mars Is My Destination.* New York, Pyramid, 1962.
*The Horror from the Hills.* Sauk City, Wisconsin, Arkham House, 1963; expanded edition, as *Odd Science Fiction*, New York, Belmont, 1964; London, Digit, 1965.
*It Was the Day of the Robot.* New York, Belmont, 1963; London, Dobson, 1964.
*Three Steps Spaceward.* New York, Avalon, 1963.
*The Martian Visitors.* New York, Avalon, 1964.
*Mission to a Star.* New York, Avalon, 1964.
*This Strange Tomorrow.* New York, Belmont, and London, Digit, 1966.
*Lest Earth Be Conquered.* New York, Belmont, 1966; as *The Androids*, 1969.
*So Dark a Heritage.* New York, Lancer, 1966.
*Journey into Darkness.* New York, Belmont, 1967.
*. . . and Others Shall Be Born.* New York, Belmont, 1968.
*The Three Faces of Time.* New York, Belmont, 1969.
*Monster from Out of Time.* New York, Popular Library, 1970; London, Hale, 1971.
*Survival World.* New York, Lancer, 1971.
*The Night of the Wolf.* New York, Popular Library, 1972.
*Rehearsal Night.* Boston, Cat's God, 1981.

#### Novels as Lyda Belknap Long

*To the Dark Tower.* New York, Lancer, 1969.
*Fire of the Witches.* New York, Popular Library, 1971.
*The Shape of Fear.* New York, Beagle, 1971.
*The Witch Tree.* New York, Lancer, 1971.
*House of the Deadly Nightshade.* New York, Beagle, 1972.
*Legacy of Evil.* New York, Beagle, 1973.
*Crucible of Evil.* New York, Avon, 1974.

#### Short Stories

*The Hounds of Tindalos.* Sauk City, Wisconsin, Arkham House, 1946; abridged editions, London, Museum Press, 1950; as *The Dark Beasts*, New York, Belmont, 1963; as *The Black Druid and Other Stories*, London, Panther, 1975.
*John Carstairs, Space Detective.* New York, Fell, 1949; London, Cherry Tree, 1951.
*The Demons of the Upper Air.* Glendale, California, Squires, 1969.
*The Rim of the Unknown.* Sauk City, Wisconsin, Arkham House, 1972.
*The Early Long.* New York, Doubleday, 1975; London, Hale, 1977.
*When Chaugnar Walks.* Warren, Ohio, Fantome Press, 1978.
*Night Fear.* New York, Zebra, 1979.

### Other Publications

#### Play

Television Play: *A Guest in the House*, 1950.

#### Verse

*A Man from Genoa and Other Poems.* Athol, Massachusetts, Cook, 1926.
*The Goblin Tower.* Cassia, Florida, Dragon-Fly Press, 1935.
*On Reading Arthur Machen.* Pengrove, Dog and Duck Press, 1949.
*In Mayan Splendor.* Sauk City, Wisconsin, Arkham House, 1977.

#### Other

*Howard Phillips Lovecraft: Dreamer on the Nightside.* Sauk City, Wisconsin, Arkham House, 1975.
*Autobiographical Memoir.* West Warwick, Rhode Island, Necronomicon Press, 1985.

*

Manuscript Collection: Lovecraft Collection, Brown University, Providence, Rhode Island.

Frank Belknap Long comments:

My work has been almost equally divided between science fiction or science fantasy and supernatural horror. What fascinates me most in the realm of SF is the strangeness, mystery, and wonder of the cosmic immensities and the possibility of intelligent life on other worlds. A few of my early stories were of the space opera type, but for many years I have shunned that kind of writing. A realistic approach has become of supreme importance to me, and I have drawn upon one or more of the natural sciences in all my more recent stories. They range from future utopias—life on earth two centuries or two million years in the future—to what life may be like, biologically considered, in some far distant region of the expanding universe.

* * *

Of all modern writers in the overlapping domains of science fiction, fantasy, and horror, Frank Belknap Long may hold the record for sheer longevity, and, while he does not hold that for total productivity, he has written several hundred short stories and more than 30 books. The latter are difficult to number and categorize, as they involve a number of collections, re-sorting, and retitling of short stories as well as novels. In addition to works published under his own name, Long participated in a number of collaborations and round-robins, wrote short stories under house names such as Leslie Northern, wrote anonymously on occasion, and produced several gothic novels under the name of his wife, Lyda Long. While these last works are in a sense "mere potboilers," Long maintains that they are not without merit and in some cases contain effective scenes of the horror-fantasy or near-fantasy variety.

In a career dating from 1924, and still actively writing, Long has experienced the expectable rises and declines of popularity and critical standing. For some years he was highly regarded; in later times, disdained as little more than a hack; and still more recently has emerged as a revered elder statesman held in wide affection. In this regard his standing is comparable to that of writers like Murray Leinster and Edmond Hamilton. An accumulation of potboilers temporarily obscures the author's best work; with the passage of time the inferior material dissipates and the author's true contribution comes to be recognized.

Long has experienced the additional benefit—and handicap!—of having been for many years the closest friend and associate of H.P. Lovecraft. At one time Lovecraft and Long were partners in the "revision business," working as manuscript doctors, uncredited collaborators, and even ghost writers for literary tyros. A certain portion of Long's own fiction shows a clear stamp of influence by Lovecraft, but this in fact represents a relatively small segment of Long's output, a fact too often overlooked.

A number of Long's horror stories—most of them fantasies, a few technically science fiction but still cast within the gothic mold—are notable. These include "The Desert Lich," "Second Night Out," a supernatural sea story perhaps remotely influenced by the works of William Hope Hodgson, and "The Man with a Thousand Legs," one of the most bizarre of all lycanthropic tales.

Long also contributed some of the earliest and most effective supplements to Lovecraft's "Cthulhu Mythos." Long's dry humor is apparent in "The Brain-Eaters," whose two chief characters are thinly disguised versions of himself and Lovecraft. "The Hounds of Tindalos," probably Long's most famous story, is a thoroughly effective tale of monstrous creatures from beyond normal time and space, breaking through the "angles" of our universe; the story is most effective in evoking a sense of non-Euclidean dimension. "A Visitor from Egypt" continues the successful exploitation of the Egyptian craze of the 1920's-early 1930's popular fiction. (One chapter of this novel was written by Lovecraft, based upon a dream).

Long's science fiction bears no trace of Lovecraft. It is sometimes densely powerful, evocative, and moving; at other times, the author fails in attempted effects and falls into bathos. In general, Long's short fiction is superior to his novels; in this regard he is once more comparable to Leinster. "The Flame Midget" clearly anticipates the development of the laser. A later story, "Dark Vision" (1939), is one of the earlier and still one of the most successful to use psychiatric and specifically Freudian themes in science fiction. Long places strong emphasis on the subconscious, and in the story makes use of both electroshock and chemical shock techniques (the former accidentally; the latter clinically) in bringing about changes in the protagonist's perceptions and interpretations of reality.

Also notable is Long's series of stories about John Carstairs, "Botanical Detective." These are intriguing hybrids of space opera and scientific mystery.

Long's most effective work is probably a series of short stories ("The Great Cold," "Green Glory," and "The Last Men") set in a remote future when humankind is reduced to miniature size and enslaved by races of giant insects. In framework, the stories would appear to be routine absurd super-science adventures. But Long concentrates on the awakening consciousness of the brutalized humans as they regain their awareness of their own humanness. The pitch of noble tragedy achieved is remarkable.

In a list of his short stories which he considers the most accomplished, Long includes "Humpty Dumpty Had a Great Fall," "To Follow Knowledge," "Prison Bright—Prison Deep," "Guest in the House," "Two Face," and "Night Fear" (most included in *Night Fear*). Almost all of these stories are based on psychological themes, most notably difficulties of personal adjustment. Further, the main protagonist is most commonly a child. The psychological sensitivity of the works is noteworthy, as is their acuteness of focus and intensity of treatment. It is also noteworthy that none bears any trace of Long's Lovecraft period; with the continued passage of time it is to be hoped that Long's non-Lovecraft works (which in fact constitute the overwhelming bulk of his output) will achieve their proper evaluation.

—Richard A. Lupoff

---

**LONG, Lyda Belknap.** *See* **LONG, Frank Belknap.**

---

**LONGDON, George.** *See* **RAYER, Francis G.**

---

**LONGYEAR, Barry (Brookes).** American. Born in Harrisburg, Pennsylvania, 12 May 1942. Attended Wayne State University, Detroit, 1966–67. Married Regina Bedsun in 1967. Production manager, Madison Corporation, Detroit, 1967–68; publisher, Sol III Publications, in Philadelphia, 1968–72, and in Farmington, Maine, 1972–77. Since 1977, freelance writer. Columnist ("Salty"), *Empire Science Fiction.* Recipient: Nebula award, 1980; Hugo award, 1980; *Locus* award, 1980; John W. Campbell award, 1980. Agent: Richard Curtis Literary Agency, 171 East 74th Street, New York, New York 10021. Address: P.O. Box 100, Vienna Road, Route 41, New Sharon, Maine 04955, U.S.A.

SCIENCE-FICTION PUBLICATIONS

Novels

*City of Baraboo.* New York, Berkley, 1980; London, Macdonald, 1983.
*Elephant Song.* New York, Berkley, 1981.
*The Tomorrow Testament.* New York, Berkley, 1983.
*Enemy Mine* (novelization of screenplay based on Longyear's original story). New York, Berkley, and Bath, Firecrest, 1985; original story published with *Another Orphan*, by John Kessel, New York, Tor, 1989.
*Sea of Glass.* New York, St. Martin's Press, 1987.
*Naked Came the Robot.* New York, Warner, 1988.
*Infinity Hold.* New York, Popular Library, 1989.
*The Homecoming.* New York, Walker, 1989.

Short Stories

*Manifest Destiny.* New York, Berkley, 1980; London, Macdonald, 1982.
*Circus World.* New York, Berkley, 1980; London, Macdonald, 1982.
*It Came from Schenectady.* New York, Bluejay, 1984.

OTHER PUBLICATIONS

Novels

*Saint Mary Blue.* Minneapolis, Steel Dragon Press, 1988.
*The God Box.* New York, Signet, 1989.

* * *

Barry Longyear burst upon the science-fiction field in 1979 with a large number of short stories, several of which were of such high quality that they earned him a number of awards. The four best of these were collected as *Manifest Destiny*, all set in a common future history. Easily the most familiar of these is "Enemy Mine," basis of the movie, later novelized by Longyear in collaboration with David Gerrold. The story concerns one human being and one alien, enemies in a bitter war, stranded together on the same primitive planet and forced to cooperate in order to survive. From this relationship comes mutual understanding, even the beginning of friendship, and the chance that the enmity between the two species will one day pass.

The imperialism of Earth is clearly at fault in that story as well as those collected with it. "The Jaren," an even better tale, concentrates on a young alien warrior determined to resist the human advance. In "Savage Planet," an alternative to brute force is found, as humans use mis-education to subjugate the local inhabitants. Ultimately the chauvinistic use of force is repudiated in "USE Force," causing a schism and eventually a civil war between two factions of human society.

While Longyear continued to write short fiction, though much less frequently, in the years that followed, few of his later short pieces rivalled the enthusiasm and sheer gripping intensity of his earlier stories. Exceptions to this include "Bloodsong," in which he creates another engaging alien species with a dual personality whose juncture is threatened by exposure to humans, and "Portrait of Baron Negay," which shows how art can be used to puncture the aplomb of a petty tyrant.

An early series of stories and novels is set against the background of an interstellar circus, *Circus World, City of Baraboo*, and *Elephant Song.* The first is a collection of seven stories set on a planet which was colonized by a shipwrecked circus, leading to the creation of "tribes" of acrobats, clowns, etc. An invasion by outside forces is imminent, and the major protagonist must find a way within the context of the society as established to alert the populace and organize resistance. Longyear is fairly clever in developing this theme, but the stories range widely in effectiveness, the best being "The Second Law." The second volume, actually the prequel, consists of six stories that chronicle the attempts of the circus to leave Earth in the first place, by outfoxing a rich magnate and acquiring a large interstellar ship. In the concluding episodes, their victim strikes back, arranging for the sabotage of the ship, resulting in their crash landing on the planet Momus. *Elephant Song* is a full-length novel that provides the bridge between the other two, showing how the survivors of the crash managed to create a viable civilization in their new home.

*The Tomorrow Testament* is more or less the sequel to "Enemy Mine." The war between humans and the Dracon race continues, with each apparently bent on extermination of the enemy. A captured military officer slowly gains the confidence of a prominent member of the Dracon military, creating a useful bridge between the two warring species. Although the novel explores the interaction of the two main characters in great detail, Longyear never loses sight of the reader and keeps the plot lively and inventive. Although not his most ambitious, it is in many ways his best novel.

The other contender for that title is *Sea of Glass*, a bleak, frightening dystopia set in an overpopulated future. The industrialized nations are ruled by a supercomputer which has determined that a devastating war against what is currently known as the "Third World" will break out on a precise date in the near future. The protagonist is an illegal child sent to a brutal prison camp, later released as an adult, designed to be a pivotal element in the computer's master plan to "save" the human race by destroying a substantial percentage of the existing population. A searing indictment of selfishness and the human tendency to allow others to make their decisions for them, *Sea of Glass* is a major work by any standards.

Three subsequent novels, all entertaining, are less ambitious and less serious thematically. *Naked Came the Robot* is a darkly humorous satire set in a future where robots do most of the physical labor of the world, but whose ranks have been infiltrated by alien devices out to subvert the world's economy. *The Homecoming* is a short novel, apparently aimed at younger readers, chronicling the return of intelligent, star-travelling dinosaurs to their birthworld, Earth, and their discovery that their own race has been supplanted with diminutive mammals who call themselves human beings. Longyear's only overt fantasy, *The God Box*, the most interesting of the three, is an episodic adventure involving a man who possesses a box whose drawers have the potential to contain anything at all under the right circumstances.

Although Longyear's career faltered after the phenomenal impact of his early stories, he seems to have subsequently settled down to produce works that range from above average to exceptional. Unlike many writers, he is not content to pursue the same themes over and over, but rather experiments with different styles and settings from one work to the next. Several of his stories are already numbered among the best work the field has produced, and it is likely that there will be additional ones as he continues to mature as a writer.

—Don D'Ammassa

---

**LORAN, Martin.** *See* **BAXTER, John.**

---

**LORD, Jeffrey.** *See* **NELSON, Ray.**

---

**LORRAINE, Paul.** *See* **FEARN, John Russell.**

---

**LOVECRAFT, H(oward) P(hillips).** American. Born in Providence, Rhode Island, 20 August 1890. Educated by tutors at home, and at a local elementary school and Hope Street High School, Providence, 1904–05, 1907–08. Married Sonia Greene in 1924 (divorced 1929). Freelance writer from 1908, working as a ghost writer and, after 1918, a revisionist; astrology columnist, Providence *Evening News*, 1914–18; active in the amateur journalism movement from 1914; published *The Conservative*, 1915–19, 1923, and president of the United Amateur Press Association, 1917–18, 1923; regular contributor to *Weird Tales* after 1923. *Died 15 March 1937.*

SCIENCE-FICTION PUBLICATIONS

Short Stories

*At the Mountains of Madness and Other Novels.* Sauk City, Wisconsin, Arkham House, 1964; London, Gollancz, 1966.
*The Colour Out of Space.* New York, Lancer, 1964.
*Collapsing Cosmoses.* West Warwick, Rhode Island, Necronomicon Press, 1977.

OTHER PUBLICATIONS

Novel

*The Lurker at the Threshold,* with August Derleth. Sauk City, Wisconsin, Arkham House, 1945; London, Gollancz, 1948.

Short Stories

*The Shunned House.* Athol, Massachusetts, Recluse Press, 1928.
*The Battle That Ended the Century.* De Land, Florida, Barlow, 1934.
*The Cats of Ulthar.* Cassia, Florida, Dragonfly Press, 1935.
*The Shadow over Innsmouth.* Everett, Pennsylvania, Visionary Press, 1936.
*The Outsider and Others,* edited by August Derleth and Donald Wandrei. Sauk City, Wisconsin, Arkham House, 1939.
*The Weird Shadow over Innsmouth and Other Stories of the Supernatural.* New York, Bartholomew House, 1944.
*The Best Supernatural Stories of H.P. Lovecraft,* edited by August Derleth. Cleveland, World, 1945; revised edition, as *The Dunwich Horror and Others,* Sauk City, Wisconsin, Arkham House, 1963.
*The Dunwich Horror.* New York, Bartholomew House, 1945.
*The Dunwich Horror and Other Weird Tales.* New York, Editions for the Armed Services, 1945.
*The Lurking Fear and Other Stories.* New York, Avon, 1947; as *Cry Horror!,* 1958.
*The Haunter of the Dark and Other Tales of Horror.* London, Gollancz, 1951.
*The Case of Charles Dexter Ward.* London, Gollancz, 1952; New York, Belmont, 1965.
*The Curse of Yig.* Sauk City, Wisconsin, Arkham House, 1953.
*The Dream Quest of Unknown Kadath.* Buffalo, Shroud, 1955.
*The Survivor and Others,* with August Derleth. Sauk City, Wisconsin, Arkham House, 1957.
*The Lurking Fear and Other Stories* (not same as 1947 book). London, Panther, 1964.
*Dagon and Other Macabre Tales,* edited by August Derleth. Sauk City, Wisconsin, Arkham House, 1965; London, Gollancz, 1967.
*The Dark Brotherhood and Other Pieces,* with others, edited by August Derleth. Sauk City, Wisconsin, Arkham House, 1966.
*3 Tales of Horror.* Sauk City, Wisconsin, Arkham House, 1967.
*The Shadow Out of Time and Other Tales of Horror,* with August Derleth. London, Gollancz, 1968; abridged edition, as *The Shuttered Room and Other Tales of Horror,* London, Panther, 1970.
*Ex Oblivione.* Glendale, California, Squires, 1969.
*The Tomb and Other Tales.* London, Panther, 1969; New York, Ballantine, 1973.
*The Horror in the Museum and Other Revisions* (ghost writing), edited by August Derleth. Sauk City, Wisconsin, Arkham House, 1970; abridged edition, London, Panther, 1975; edited by S.T. Joshi, Arkham House, 1989.
*Nyarlathotep.* Glendale, California, Squires, 1970.
*What the Moon Brings.* Glendale, California, Squires, 1970.
*The Dream-Quest of Unknown Kadath* (not same as 1955 book), edited by Lin Carter. New York, Ballantine, 1970.
*Memory.* Glendale, California, Squires, 1970.
*The Shadow over Innsmouth and Other Tales of Horror.* New York, Scholastic, 1971.
*The Shuttered Room and Other Tales of Terror,* with August Derleth. New York, Beagle, 1971.
*The Doom That Came to Sarnath,* edited by Lin Carter. New York, Ballantine, 1971.
*The Lurking Fear and Other Stories* (not same as 1947 and 1964 books). New York, Beagle, 1971.
*The Watchers Out of Time and Others,* with August Derleth. Sauk City, Wisconsin, Arkham House, 1974.
*The Horror in the Burying Ground and Other Tales.* London, Panther, 1975.
*Herbert West Reanimator.* West Warwick, Rhode Island, Necronomicon Press, 1977.
*Bloodcurdling Tales of Horror and the Macabre: The Best of H.P. Lovecraft.* New York, Ballantine, 1982.
*The Dunwich Horror and Others* (original versions), edited by S.T. Joshi. Sauk City, Wisconsin, Arkham House, 1985.
*Herbert West Terminator.* West Warwick, Rhode Island, Necronomicon Press, 1985.
*Tales of the Cthulhu Mythos,* with others, edited by August Derleth. London, Grafton, 1988; New York, Arkham House, 1990.
*The Night Ocean,* with R.H. Barlow. West Warwick, Rhode Island, Necronomicon Press, 1989.

Verse

*The Crime of Crimes.* Llandudno, Harris, 1915.
*A Sonnet.* Privately printed, 1936.
*H.P.L.* Privately printed, 1937.
*Fungi from Yuggoth.* Salem, Oregon, Evans, 1941.
*Collected Poems.* Sauk City, Wisconsin, Arkham House, 1963; abridged edition, as *Fungi from Yuggoth and Other Poems,* New York, Ballantine, 1971.
*A Winter Wish,* edited by Tom Collins. Browns Mills, New Jersey, Whispers Press, 1977.
*Four Prose Poems.* West Warwick, Rhode Island, Necronomicon Press, 1987; 2nd edition, 1990.
*The Fantastic Poetry,* edited by S.T. Joshi. West Warwick, Rhode Island, Necronomicon Press, 1990.

Other

*Looking Backward.* Haverhill, Massachusetts, C.W. Smith, 1920(?).
*The Materialist Today.* Privately printed, 1926.
*Further Criticism of Poetry.* Louisville, Fetter, 1932.
*Charleston.* Privately printed, 1936.
*Some Current Motives and Practices.* DeLand, Florida, Barlow, 1936(?).
*A History of the Necronomicon.* Oakman, Alabama, Rebel Press, 1938.
*The Notes and Commonplace Book,* edited by R.H. Barlow. Lakeport, California, Futile Press, 1938.

*Beyond the Wall of Sleep*, edited by August Derleth and Donald Wandrei. Sauk City, Wisconsin, Arkham House, 1943.
*Marginalia*, edited by August Derleth and Donald Wandrei. Sauk City, Wisconsin, Arkham House, 1944.
*Supernatural Horror in Literature*. New York, Abramson, 1945; revised edition, Arlington, Virginia, Carrollton Clark, 1975.
*Something about Cats and Other Pieces*, edited by August Derleth. Sauk City, Wisconsin, Arkham House, 1949.
*The Lovecraft Collector's Library*, edited by George T. Wetzel. Tonowanda, New York, SSR, 5 vols., 1952–55.
*The Shuttered Room and Other Pieces*, with others, edited by August Derleth. Sauk City, Wisconsin, Arkham House, 1959.
*Dreams and Fancies*. Sauk City, Wisconsin, Arkham House, 1962.
*Autobiography: Some Notes on a Nonentity*. London, Villiers, 1963.
*Selected Letters 1911–1937*, edited by August Derleth and Donald Wandrei. Sauk City, Wisconsin, Arkham House, 5 vols., 1965–76.
*Hail, Klarkash-Ton!* Glendale, California, Squires, 1971.
*Ec'h-Pi-El Speaks: An Autobiographical Sketch*. Saddle River, New Jersey, Gerry de la Ree, 1972.
*Medusa: A Portrait*. New York, Oliphant Press, 1975.
*The Occult Lovecraft*. Saddle River, New Jersey, Gerry de la Ree, 1975.
*Lovecraft at Last* (correspondence with Willis Conover). Arlington, Virginia, Carrollton Clark, 1975.
*To Quebec and the Stars*, edited by L. Sprague de Camp. West Kingston, Rhode Island, Grant, 1976.
*Writings in The United Amateur 1915–1925*, edited by Marc A. Michaud. West Warwick, Rhode Island, Necronomicon Press, 1976.
*First Writings: Pawtuxet Valley Gleaner 1906*, edited by Marc A. Michaud. West Warwick, Rhode Island, Necronomicon Press, 1976.
*The Conservative: Complete 1915–1923*, edited by Marc A. Michaud. West Warwick, Rhode Island, Necronomicon Press, 1977.
*Memoirs of an Inconsequential Scribbler*. West Warwick, Rhode Island, Necronomicon Press, 1977.
*Writings in The Tryout*, edited by Marc A. Michaud. West Warwick, Rhode Island, Necronomicon Press, 1977.
*The Californian 1934–1938*. West Warwick, Rhode Island, Necronomicon Press, 1977.
*Uncollected Prose and Poetry*, edited by S.T. Joshi and Marc A. Michaud. West Warwick, Rhode Island, Necronomicon Press, 1978.
*Science versus Charlatanry: Essays on Astrology*, with J.F. Hartmann, edited by S.T. Joshi and Scott Connors. N.p., The Strange Company, 1979.
*Juvenalia 1895–1905*, edited by S.T. Joshi. West Warwick, Rhode Island, Necronomicon Press, 1984.
*H.P. Lovecraft: Uncollected Letters*. West Warwick, Rhode Island, Necronomicon Press, 1986.
*H.P. Lovecraft: Commonplace Book*, edited by David E. Schultz. West Warwick, Rhode Island, Necronomicon Press, 1987.
*European Glimpses*, with Sonia H. Greene. West Warwick, Rhode Island, Necronomicon Press, 1988.
*H.P. Lovecraft: The Conservative* (essays), edited by S.T. Joshi. West Warwick, Rhode Island, Necronomicon Press, 1990.
*The Vivisector* (essays). West Warwick, Rhode Island, Necronomicon Press, 1990.

Editor, *The Poetical Works of Jonathan E. Hoag*. Privately printed, 1923.
Editor, *White Fire*, by John Ravenor Bullen. Athol, Massachusetts, Recluse Press, 1927.
Editor, *Thoughts and Pictures*, by Eugene B. Kuntz. Haverhill, Massachusetts, Lovecraft and Smith, 1932.

*

Bibliography: *The New H.P. Lovecraft Bibliography* by Jack L. Chalker, Baltimore, Anthem Press, 1962, revised edition, with Mark Owings, as *The Revised H.P. Lovecraft Bibliography*, Baltimore, Mirage Press, 1973; *A Catalog of Lovecraftiana* by Mark Owings and Irving Binkin, Baltimore, Mirage Press, 1975; *H.P. Lovecraft: An Annotated Bibliography* by S.T. Joshi, Kent, Ohio, Kent State University Press, 1981; *Howard Phillips Lovecraft: The Books, Addenda and Auxiliary* by Joseph Bell, Toronto, Soft Press, 1983.

Manuscript Collection: Brown University, Providence, Rhode Island.

Critical Studies (selection): *In Memoriam Howard Phillips Lovecraft: Recollections, Appreciations, Estimates* edited by W. Paul Cook, privately printed, 1941; *H.P.L.: A Memoir*, New York, Abramson, 1945, and *Some Notes on H.P. Lovecraft*, Sauk City, Wisconsin, Arkham House, 1959, both by August Derleth; *Rhode Island on Lovecraft* edited by Donald M. Grant and Thomas P. Hadley, Providence, Rhode Island, Grant Hadley, 1945; "H.P. Lovecraft Issue" of *Fresco* (Detroit), Spring 1958; *Lovecraft: A Look Behind the Cthulhu Mythos* by Lin Carter, New York, Ballantine, 1972, London, Panther, 1975; *Lovecraft: A Biography* by L. Sprague de Camp, New York, Doubleday, 1975, London, New English Library, 1976; *Howard Phillips Lovecraft: Dreamer on the Nightside* by Frank Belknap Long, Sauk City, Wisconsin, Arkham House, 1975; *Essays Lovecraftian* edited by Darrell Schweitzer, Baltimore, T-K Graphics, 1976, and *The Dream Quest of H.P. Lovecraft* by Schweitzer, San Bernardino, California, Borgo Press, 1978; *The H.P. Lovecraft Companion* by Philip A. Schreffler, Westport, Connecticut, Greenwood Press, 1977; *The Major Works of H.P. Lovecraft* by John Taylor Gatto, New York, Monarch Press, 1977; *The Roots of Horror in the Fiction of H.P. Lovecraft* by Barton Levi St. Armand, Elizabethtown, New York, Dragon Press, 1977; *H.P. Lovecraft* by S.T. Joshi, Mercer Island, Washington, Starmont House, 1982; *H.P. Lovecraft: A Critical Study* by Donald R. Burleson, Westport, Connecticut, Greenwood Press, 1983; *Lovecraft: A Study in the Fantastic* by Maurice Lévy, translated by S.T. Joshi, Detroit, Wayne State University Press, 1988.

* * *

That horror stories are externalized psychology is a commonplace of literary criticism, but readings based on sex and aggression (the two themes literary critics have tended to pick up from Freudian psychology) do not quite fit H.P. Lovecraft. Lovecraft himself warns readers away from interpretations of his work based on the fear of retribution for specific acts or impulses; his horrors are (as he says again and again) "cosmic": he declares the worst human fears to be displacement in space and time (as in "The Shadow Out of Time"), he speaks of "the maddening rigidity of cosmic law," he creates a non-fantastic and materialistic fictional world—i.e. science fiction—all implying a concern with the conditions of being, not with particular acts or situations. When the conditions of existence are themselves fearful, when such basic ontological categories as space and time break down (as does the geometry of space in so many stories, for example "The Call of Cthulhu"), we are dealing with what the psychiatrist R.S. Laing calls "ontological insecurity." If one fears that one doesn't exist securely, or that one is made of "bad stuff," any contact with another becomes potentially catastrophic. Everyone shares, to some degree, doubts about the psychological solidity or reliability of the self and the possibly devastating effects of others on that self. The extreme form of such fears is schizophrenia.

Lovecraft, although certainly not schizophrenic, did, according to L. Sprague de Camp, have a lifelong sense of marked isolation from others, an intense emotional dependency on things and not people, and the kind of over-possessive upbringing which makes it reasonable to expect that such issues would appear in his work. They do—strongly enough to make him an innovator in weird fiction—for they take precedence over either the beastliness of aggression (embodied, for example, in werewolves) or the lethal possibilities of sexual abandon (e.g., the figure of the vampire), both of which figure largely in 19th-century supernatural fiction. Sex and aggression presuppose a self existing securely enough to have desires and a relatively non-threatening (or at least limited) other towards whom such desires can be directed. Neither an unproblematic sense of self nor a non-catastrophic other exists in Lovecraft's work. In his early Dunsanian fiction he can frolic—but with ghouls!—as in the charming (but, alas, never rewritten or polished) *Dream-Quest of Unknown Kadath*, or write pleasing, optimistic fantasies like "The Strange High House in the Mist"; but much of his earlier and most of his later fiction is preoccupied with the foreseen, yet unavoidable, engulfment of a passive, victimized self. If the narrator is a lucky spectator who escapes with his life, or even sanity, intact, his peace of mind has been shattered forever. The real point of these stories is revelation—if the engulfment does not happen, *it can*—and this revelation becomes the central truth of a universe thus rendered uninhabitable. The cannibalistic other takes several forms, but the commonest, strongest image, and the one readers seem to remember best is the shapeless, monstrous, indescribable "entry" (a favorite word of Lovecraft's) whose most terrifying characteristic is its structurelessness ("The Unnameable," "The Call of Cthulhu," "Dagon," "The Dunwich Horror"). The obsession with psychic cannibalism (expressed as physical in one of the flatter stories, "The Picture in the House") and the insistence on the indescribableness of the threat seem to point to experience so personally archaic it is felt as pre-verbal, as does Lovecraft's characteristic straining after adjectives. In one of his best tales, "The Colour Out of Space," the threat is most abstract, its cannibalism is reported third-hand (through *two* narrators) and the relatively low-keyed, realistic setting gets most of the author's attention.

In only two stories does Lovecraft focus fully on the alternative to engulfment: loneliness. Selves exist and survive in both tales; they even—after a fashion—blossom into initiative. But both are figures that appear in other stories *as monsters:* in the poetically melancholy "The Outsider" a ghoulish walking corpse, and in the very interesting end of *The Weird Shadow over Innsmouth* a degenerate animal/monster. Both stories suggest that the menace is the narrator or something in the narrator, a suggestion not only psychologically truer than the image of the engulfing other that Lovecraft uses elsewhere, but one dramatically more interesting.

The view that human relations exist only as engulfment is a serious limitation on a narrative artist. Towards the end of his life Lovecraft seems to have been unhappily aware of this; unfortunately he also underrated his own work and died before it began to be popular. His originality and his undoubted talent (the eerily parodic autobiography of "The Outsider," details like the "gelatinous" voice in "Randolph Carter," or "a warmth that may have been sardonic" of *Innsmouth*) are best at their quietest, worst in their bravely direct but often inadequate attacks on a theme that requires (at the very least) poetic genius. The very rarity of literary treatments of Lovecraft's main theme gives his work added interest, however, and his work will probably always appeal to readers who find his theme compelling. If he had not died prematurely, he might have moved beyond the kind of horror story that says "This is what it feels like" to the kind that adds "and this is what is really happening." The latter moves into tragedy and implied social criticism (as does, for example, Shirley Jackson's *The Haunting of Hill House*). In *Supernatural Horror in Literature* Lovecraft concludes "the spectral in literature . . . is . . . a narrow though essential branch of human expression," a comment that might well describe his work: narrow, not appealing to wide tastes and even considerably flawed, yet authentic, and by those who find it congenial, securely loved.

—Joanna Russ

---

**LOWAM, Ron.** *See* **TUBB, E.C.**

---

**LOWNDES, Robert A(ugustine) W(ard).** Also writes as Arthur Cooke; Carol Grey; Carl Groener; Mallory Kent; Paul Dennis Lavond; John MacDougal; Wilfred Owen Morley; Richard Morrison; Michael Sherman; Peter Michael Sherman; Lawrence Woods. American. Born in Bridgeport, Connecticut, 4 September 1916. Educated at Darien High School, Connecticut; Stamford Community College, Connecticut, 1936. Married Dorothy Sedor Rogalin in 1948 (divorced 1974); one stepson. Worked for the Civilian Conservation Corps, 1934, 1936–37, 1939; assistant on a squab farm; salesman; porter, Greenwich Hospital Association, Connecticut, 1937–38; literary agent, Fantastory Sales Service, 1940–42; editor, *Future Fiction*, 1940–43, and *Science Fiction Quarterly*, 1940–43, 1951–58; editorial director, Columbia magazines, 1942–60; editor, *Future Science Fiction*, 1950–60, *Dynamic Science Fiction*, 1952–54, and *Science Fiction Stories*, 1954–60; editor, Avalon science-fiction series, Thomas Bouregy, 1955–67; editor, *Magazine of Horror*, 1963–71, *Famous Science Fiction*, 1966–69, *Startling Mystery Stories*, 1966–71, *Weird Terror Tales*, 1969–70, and *Bizarre Fantasy Fiction*, 1970–71; associate editor, 1971–77, and managing editor, 1977–78, *Sexology* and *Luz;* production chief, *Luz*, 1978–84, and in editorial production, *Radio-Electronics, Special Projects, Hands-On Electronics*, and Computer Digest, 1978–89. Co-founder, Vanguard Amateur Press Association. Guest of Honor, Lunacon, 1969, and Boskone, 1973. Address: 717 Willow Avenue, Hoboken, New Jersey 07030, U.S.A.

SCIENCE-FICTION PUBLICATIONS

Novels

*Mystery of the Third Mine* (for children). Philadelphia, Winston, 1953.

*The Duplicated Man*, with James Blish. New York, Avalon, 1959.

*The Puzzle Planet*. New York, Ace, 1961.

*Believers' World*. New York, Avalon, 1961.

Uncollected Short Stories

"The Outpost at Altark," with Donald A. Wollheim (uncredited), in *Super Science* (Kokomo, Indiana), November 1940.
"A Green Cloud Came," in *Comet* (Springfield, Massachusetts), January 1941.
"The Psychological Regulator" (as Arthur Cooke, with others), in *Comet* (Springfield, Massachusetts), March 1941.
"The Martians Are Coming," with C.M. Kornbluth (uncredited), in *Cosmic* (Holyoke, Massachusetts), March 1941.
"Black Flames" (as Lawrence Woods, with Donald A. Wollheim) and "The Other," in *Stirring Science* (New York), April 1941.
"The Grey One," in *Stirring Science* (New York), June 1941.
"The Colossus of Maia" (as Lawrence Woods, with Donald A. Wollheim), in *Cosmos* (New York), July 1941.
"Lure of the Lily," in *Uncanny Tales* (Toronto), January 1942; revised version, as "Lillies," in *Magazine of Horror* (New York), Spring 1967.
"Passage to Sharanee" (as Carol Grey), in *Future* (New York), April 1942.
"The Deliverers" (as Richard Morrison), in *Science Fiction Quarterly* (Holyoke, Massachusetts), Winter 1942.
"The Leapers" (as Carol Grey), in *Future* (New York), December 1942; revised version, as "Leapers" (as Robert A.W. Lowndes), in *Magazine of Horror* (New York), September 1968.
"Chaos, Co-ordinated" (as John MacDougal, with James Blish), in *Astounding* (New York), October 1946.
"The Troubadour" (as Peter Michael Sherman), in *Future* (New York), September 1951.
"Intervention" (as Michael Sherman), in *Science Fiction Quarterly* (Holyoke, Massachusetts), February 1952.
"A Matter of Faith" (as Michael Sherman), in *Space* (New York), September 1952.
"Highway," in *Looking Forward*, edited by Milton Lesser. New York, Beechhurst Press, 1953; London, Cassell, 1955.
"The Inheritors," with John B. Michel, in *Terror in the Modern Vein*, edited by Donald A. Wollheim. New York, Hanover House, 1955.
"Object Lesson" (as Carl Groener), in *Future* (New York), August 1958.
"The Abyss," in *The History of the Science Fiction Magazines 2*, edited by Michael Ashley. London, New English Library, 1975.
"The Extrapolated Dimwit" (uncredited), with C.M. Kornbluth and Frederik Pohl, in *Before the Universe*. New York, Bantam, 1980.

Uncollected Short Stories as Paul Dennis Lavond.

"The Doll Master," in *Stirring Science* (New York), April 1941.
"Exiles of New Planet," with Cyril Kornbluth, in *Astonishing* (Chicago), April 1941.
"Something from Beyond," with Frederik Pohl and J.H. Dockweiler, in *Future* (New York), December 1941.
"Einstein's Planetoid," with Frederik Pohl and Cyril Kornbluth, in *Science Fiction Quarterly* (Holyoke, Massachusetts), Spring 1942.

Uncollected Short Stories as Wilfred Owen Morley

"A Matter of Philosophy," in *Science Fiction* (Holyoke, Massachusetts), September 1941.
"My Lady of the Emerald," in *Astonishing* (Chicago), November 1941.
"No Star Shall Fall," in *Future* (New York), December 1941.
"The Long Wall," in *Stirring Science* (New York), March 1942; revised version, as "Settler's Wall" (as Robert A.W. Lowndes), in *Startling Mystery Stories* (New York), Fall 1968.
"The Lemmings," in *Super Science* (Kokomo, Indiana), May 1942.
"A Message for Jean," in *Future* (New York), June 1942.
"The Slim People," in *Future* (New York), August 1942.
"Highway," in *Science Fiction Quarterly* (Holyoke, Massachusetts), Fall 1942; revised version, as "The Road to Nowhere" (as Robert A.W. Lowndes), in *Magazine of Horror* (New York), Summer 1970.
"Does Not Imply," in *Future* (New York), February 1943.
"Dhactwhul—Remember?," with Jacques DeForest Erman, in *Super Science* (Kokomo, Indiana), April 1949.

Uncollected Short Stories as Mallory Kent

"Quarry," in *Future* (New York), December 1941.
"The Peacemakers," in *Future* (New York), August 1942.
"The Collector," in *Future* (New York), October 1942.

OTHER PUBLICATIONS

Other

*Three Faces of Science Fiction*. Boston, NESFA Press, 1973.

Editor, *The Best of James Blish*. New York, Ballantine, 1979.

*

Robert A.W. Lowndes comments:

Although I was an active member of the marxist-oriented Futurian Society of New York (1938–45), calling for social and political relevance in science fiction, when it came down to writing stories I found that I had no interest whatsoever in such relevance. I only wanted to tell the kind of story I actually wanted to read—full of wonder or terror or both. Whether I succeeded, or to what extent I succeeded, is for others to say.

To my mind, the best fantasy and science fiction is imbued with the author's feeling about the human condition, and may or may not contain what amounts to some sort of message. If there is one, it is not something consciously striven for; I've read thousands of stories written to preach a sermon, and however effective the sermon itself may have been, the stories have nearly all suffered from the approach. Fiction and homily writing are two different forms, though each may be done with a high quality of art; but mixing them produces an abortion.

* * *

Robert A.W. Lowndes is known mainly as an editor. He is, however, also a science-fiction writer of considerable talent, particularly in the creation and description of alien worlds. This talent is best seen in *Believers' World.* Lowndes uses the now-familiar plot of exiles from Earth who have forgotten that their origin was on Earth, and whose religious beliefs have hardened into mindless fragments of ceremony. An investigator from Earth visits these exiles, now living on a "believers' world" locked into elaborate religious ceremonies. He becomes involved in a formula of action, adventure, and violence. But Lowndes effectively describes the Arabian Nights atmosphere of this world: "magic. That was the keynote of everything here—the appearance of magic." Even small everyday events seem magical: "you touched a faucet, or bent over a fountain, or stepped under a shower, and pale yellow water issued forth." Thus Lowndes creates a world that exemplifies Arthur C. Clarke's generalization that advanced technology is indistinguishable from magic.

Everything that happens on the believers' world is supposed by the inhabitants to be the will of "Ein" (Einstein, though they don't remember this). In this topsy-turvy world not only has religion ossified but science has merged with it. *The Puzzle Planet* is about a world that is similar in that our common-sense assumptions are upside down; and once again Lowndes's descriptive powers are impressive.

Even *Mystery of the Third Mine*, a juvenile novel, is well worth reading. Lowndes makes asteroid mining seem real, creating a historical parallel to the gold rush of 1848. The hero, Peter, is in a mining partnership with his father. The villains use the cover of the Asteroid Miners Association to invalidate Peter's claims and to try to seize the "third mine" platinum, deep in the asteroid. There is a good science-fun gimmick on the asteroid: low gravity baseball with a magnetized ball and players throwing bits of metal to propel themselves through space. Although the young hero is close to being a pastiche of a Heinlein juvenile, Lowndes's magical atmosphere is once again his own.

Lowndes's short stories are quite distinct from his novels and show the influence of Clark Ashton Smith and Lovecraft. One of his best is "The Abyss," which begins with this hook sentence: "We took Graf Norden's body out into the November night, under the stars that burned with a brightness terrible to behold, and drove madly, wildly up the mountain road." Beings in another dimension (or no dimension) send agents to hypnotize humans and drain the fluids from their bodies. The description of these alien beings—with long filaments that restlessly try to break into our dimension from their own—is as well done as anything in Lovecraft, and the economy of the story is beyond Lovecraft. Economy, atmosphere, description: these are Lowndes's strongest points as a writer.

—Curtis C. Smith

---

**LUCAS, George.** *See* **FOSTER, Alan Dean.**

---

**LULL, Susan.** *See* **FORWARD, Robert L.**

---

**LUNDWALL, Sam J(errie).** Swedish. Born in Stockholm, 24 February 1941. Educated at the University of Stockholm, E.E. 1967; Fotoskolan, 1968. Compulsory military service in the air force, 1961–62. Married Ingrid Christina Olofsdotter in 1972; one daughter. Electronic engineer, L.M. Ericson, Stockholm, 1956–64; photographer, Christian, Fox Amphoux, France, 1968–69; editor, Askild & Kärnekull, Stockholm, 1970–73; publisher, Delta Förlag, Stockholm, 1973–80, and since 1980, Fakta & Fantasi, Stockholm. Since 1972, editor, *Jules Verne-Magasinet*, Stockholm. Also a singer and musician, illustrator, and television producer. Recipient: Swedish Film Institute award, 1967; Cosmos Fandom award, 1969; Futura Club award, 1972; Finnish Design award, 1972. Address: c/o Penguin Books, Bath Road, Harmondsworth, Middlesex UB7 0DA, England.

SCIENCE-FICTION PUBLICATIONS

Novels

*No Time for Heroes.* New York, Ace, 1971.
*Alice's World.* New York, Ace, 1971; London, Arrow, 1975.
*Bernhard the Conqueror.* New York, DAW, 1973.
*2018; or, The King Kong Blues.* New York, DAW, 1975; London, Wyndham, 1976.
*Tio sanger och Alltid Lady MacBeth.* Stockholm, Delta, 1975.
*Bernards magiska sommar.* Stockholm, Lindqvist, 1975.
*Mörkrets furste.* Stockholm, Delta, 1975.
*Mardrömmen.* Stockholm, Lindqvist, 1976.
*Gäst i Frankensteins hus.* Stockholm, Delta, 1976.
*Fängelsestaden.* Stockholm, Norstedt, 1978.
*Flicka i fönster vid världens kant.* Stockholm, Norstedt, 1980.
*Crash.* Stockholm, Norstedt, 1982.

Uncollected Short Stories

"Nobody Here But Us Shadows," in *Galaxy* (New York), August 1975.
"Take Me Down the River," in *Twenty Houses of the Zodiac*, edited by Maxim Jakubowski. London, New English Library, 1979.

OTHER PUBLICATIONS

Verse

*Visor i var tid.* Stockholm, Sonora, 1965.

Other

*Science Fiction.* Stockholm, Sveriges Radio, 1969; translated as *Science Fiction: What It's All About*, New York, Ace, 1971.
*Den fantastiska romanen* (essays on science fiction). Stockholm, Gummeson, 4 vols., 1972–74.
*Bibliografi över Science Fiction & Fantasy* (covers the period 1741–1973). Stockholm, Lindqvist, 1974.
*Utopia-Dystopia.* Stockholm, Delta, 1977.
*Science Fiction: An Illustrated History.* New York, Grosset and Dunlap, 1978.

Editor, with Brian W. Aldiss, *The Penguin World Omnibus of Science Fiction: An Anthology.* London, Penguin, 1986.

Publications in Swedish: some 20 anthologies of science fiction, and translations of 237 novels into Swedish.

*

Sam Lundwall comments:
I am not a fan of my work. I wish I were.

* * *

Sam J. Lundwall's reputation rests chiefly on the critical/historical survey, *Science Fiction: What It's All About*, which he wrote in Swedish and translated into English. One of the first general summaries of the field, the book outlines a history and a theory of the genesis of science fiction. For many readers this outline (along with that presented in Brian Aldiss's *Billion Year Spree*) serves as the first critical framework by which they define their experience of science fiction. Lundwall categorizes science fiction, defines it, and comments on it. He draws on a wide range of stories and essays as source materials for his discussions and tries generally to test his conclusions against hard observation, even though he is not ashamed to write with the verve of a totally committed partisan or fan. Treating science fiction "books, magazines, comics, fans and fanzines, juvenilia, series characters, and literary giants," he also discusses popular motifs, conventions, themes, and plot lines.

The influence of this book is not easily overstated. Published in English in 1971 at the beginning of a great wave of academic interest in the genre, it provided the foundations for the organization of a large part of the scholarship and of the design and teaching of science-fiction courses in universities. Lundwall is, moreover, straightforward, clear, and definite in communicating his attitudes. The book, consequently, stimulates interest in the study of the genre as a whole and in its various aspects. Although Lundwall's shrewd critical insights and commentary on authors and works may not seem as true five or ten years after they are first encountered, they tend to color a reader's perception of the field, having provided for many readers a starting point for disciplined study.

Sam J. Lundwall is also known as a writer of satiric novels. The best known of these and probably the most successful of the four that have been translated into English is *2018; or, The King Kong Blues.* In this novel Lundwall describes a world that in 2018 is polluted not only physically but spiritually as well. The tale begins with a description of a wedding held in a department store. Against this scene we see one of the central characters, a rootless, rebellious young girl named Anniki Norijn, trying to break free of compulsions to conform to commercially acceptable standards of taste and ethics. The rest of the novel narrates a harassed advertising executive's search for this young woman. He is forced to use her in a campaign to sell underarm deodorant. A counterplot tells of two sheikhs, brothers, one of whom out of sheer boredom manipulates the economic life of the West, which the other one in the name of religion and Bedouin honor tries to destroy. The book gets its title from a song Anniki sings that mocks the betrayed romanticism and the false facades of social institutions.

This novel is at home among that group of satiric novels that criticize the shallowness and triviality of modern life; it has been compared with Pohl and Kornbluth's *Space Merchants*, Brunner's *The Sheep Look Up*, and Burgess's *A Clockwork Orange.* Unlike Burgess's book, however, *2018* does not attack a single, philosophically distinct evil. Its attack is more generally directed against economic exploitation on all levels. Unlike *The Space Merchants* it isn't very funny; its humor is blacker, crueler, more disturbing. Finally, it is not as successful as *The Sheep Look Up* because it preaches and explains more than it narrates or dramatizes. Perhaps Lundwall should, like Brunner, have used techniques similar to those of John Dos Passos to make the circumstantial background—which is, after all, the real main character and interest in the novel—come alive. *2018* unfortunately too often reads like an undergraduate textbook.

His other translated novels, also satiric, *Alice's World, No Time for Heroes*, and *Bernhard the Conqueror* vary in mood from depressed to genuinely funny.

—Alexander J. Butrym

---

**LUPOFF, Richard A(llen).** Also writes as Ova Hamlet. American. Born in Brooklyn, New York, 21 February 1935. Educated at the University of Miami, Coral Gables, B.A. 1956. Served in the Adjutant General's Corps of the United States Army, 1956–58: First Lieutenant. Married Patricia Enid Loring in 1958; two sons and one daughter. Technical writer, Sperry Univac, New York, 1958–63; editor, Canaveral Press, New York, 1962–70; film producer, IBM, New York City and Poughkeepsie, New York, 1963–70; editor, with Pat Lupoff, *Xero* fan magazine, 1960–63; West Coast editor, *Crawdaddy*, 1970–71, and *Changes*, 1971–72; editor, *Organ*, 1972; book editor, *Algol*, 1963–79; science-fiction reviewer, San Francisco *Chronicle*, 1979–81. Since 1985, editor, Canyon Press, Redwood City, California. Recipient: Hugo award, for editing, 1963. Agent: Henry Morrison Inc., P.O. Box 235, Bedford Hills, New York 10507. Address: 3208 Claremont Avenue, Berkeley, California 94705, U.S.A.

### Science-Fiction Publications

Novels (series: Flat Earth)

*One Million Centuries.* New York, Lancer, 1967.
*Sacred Locomotive Flies.* New York, Beagle, 1971.
*Into the Aether.* New York, Dell, 1974.
*The Crack in the Sky.* New York, Dell, 1976; as *Fool's Hill*, London, Sphere, 1978.
*Lisa Kane* (for children). Indianapolis, Bobbs Merrill, 1976.
*Sandworld.* New York, Berkley, 1976.
*The Triune Man.* New York, Berkley, 1976; London, Dobson, 1979.
*The Return of Skull-Face*, with Robert E. Howard. West Linn, Oregon, Fax, 1977.
*Space War Blues.* New York, Dell, 1978; London, Sphere, 1979.
*Circumpolar!* (Flat Earth). New York, Pocket Books, 1984; London, Granada, 1985.
*Sun's End.* New York, Berkley, 1984.
*Countersolar!* (Flat Earth). New York, Arbor House, 1987; London, Grafton, 1988.
*The Forever City.* New York, Walker, 1988; London, Hutchinson, 1990.
*Galaxy's End* (Flat Earth). New York, Ace, 1988; London, Grafton, 1989.
*The Black Tower.* New York, Bantam, 1988.
*The Final Battle.* New York, Bantam, 1990.

Short Stories

*Nebogipfel at the End of Time.* San Francisco, Underwood Miller, 1979.
*The Ova Hamlet Papers.* San Francisco, Pennyfarthing Press, 1979.
*Stroka Prospekt: A Story.* West Branch, Iowa, Toothpaste Press, 1982.
*The Digital Wristwatch of Philip K. Dick.* Redwood City, California, Canyon Press, 1985.

### Other Publications

Novels

*Sword of the Demon.* New York, Harper, 1977; London, Sphere, 1980.
*Lovecraft's Book.* Sauk City, Wisconsin, Arkham House, 1985.
*The Comic Book Killer.* Martinez, California, Offspring Press, 1988.

Other

*Edgar Rice Burroughs, Master of Adventure.* New York, Canaveral Press, 1965; revised edition, New York, Ace, 1968.
*Barsoom: Edgar Rice Burroughs and the Martian Vision.* Baltimore, Mirage Press, 1976.

Editor, *The Reader's Guide to Barsoom and Amtoor.* Privately printed, 1963.
Editor, with Don Thompson, *All in Color for a Dime.* New Rochelle, New York, Arlington House, 1970.
Editor, with Don Thompson, *The Comic-Book Book.* New Rochelle, New York, Arlington House, 1974.
Editor, *What If?* [and *What If? 2*] *Stories That Should Have Won the Hugo.* New York, Pocket Books, 1980–81.

*

Richard A. Lupoff comments:

It's very difficult for me to "make a statement" about my own works. It seems to me that this is a task for critics. The artist is of necessity so close to his or her own work—in fact, more than close to it: is surrounded by and immersed in it—that a critical perspective is impossible.

In terms of my own career, 1981 proved to be a year of bitter irony. I had spent decades learning the craft of fiction, and felt that I had finally reached a satisfying level of competence. The last three books that I had written—*Circumpolar!, Lovecraft's Book*, and *Sun's End*—were by far the best I had ever written. My prices had risen, critics and fans were expressing approval, foreign sales were gratifying.

At this point, due to general economic conditions, there was a collapse in the marketplace. All three books were cancelled, contracts for two further novels were cancelled, and the *What If?* anthology series that I had been editing was cancelled. Everything that I had in print went out of print, and my career was in effect terminated. My income dropped to nothing and I faced economic disaster.

In the years since then, there has been considerable recovery. The three novels that I named have all been published, as have sequels to *Sun's End* and *Circumpolar!*, although the *What If?* series seems to have expired after only two volumes, despite enthusiastic critical reception.

By the end of 1985 I was able to leave a stultifying office job and resume full-time writing, mixing science fiction with other forms. In fact, my work has never been entirely located in the main stream of science fiction. My early novel *Sacred Locomotive Flies*, for instance, although influenced by Michael Moorcock's *The Final Programme* and Chester Anderson's *The Butterfly Kid*, was really more social satire and black comedy—actually comparable to Tom Robbins' *Another Roadside Attraction*—than it was science fiction. And *Lovecraft's Book*, its eponymous protagonist notwithstanding, was actually a political novel with elements of both the spy thriller and the mainstream novel in it.

Since 1988 I have started a successful series of mysteries featuring insurance adjuster Hobart Lindsey. Two of these books have been completed, with de luxe editions published by a small company in California and mass paperbacks published by Bantam Books.

Several other mystery projects are in development. One of these is both criminous and science fictional. Mr. Hajimi Ino is a Japanese Martian corporate detective whose adventures open in the year 2143 with the novella "Black Mist." I was also gratified by the reception of the short film based on my story "12:01 PM," which was nominated for an Academy Award.

I will never again put all my eggs in the science fiction basket.

* * *

Richard Lupoff's first novel, *One Million Centuries*, made use of one of the most familiar devices of science fiction, the contemporary protagonist who wakens after a period of suspended animation into a wildly different society. Although primarily an adventure story, this tale of a man who visits three separate cultures as he attempts to return to his own time was surprisingly sophisticated for a first novel. His next, *Sacred Locomotive Flies*, was a very different story, an almost indescribable novel of a very strange near future world peopled with exaggerated characters. Although not written in an experimental style, thematically this resembled the "New Wave" moment of the time, although it encompassed humor and self parody as well.

*Into the Aether* is a pastiche of early works in the field, an approach Lupoff would return to in the future. An experimental device transports the protagonists to the moon, where they must deal with space pirates as well as earthbound villainy.

Lupoff was more serious in *The Crack in the Sky*, a dystopian tale of a future when the population is declining in the wake of the loss of much of the knowledge necessary to maintain Earth's technology. Against that background there arises a new cult which advocates a return to traditional values, but whose agenda may also involve the ultimate sacrifice of the entire human species. *The Triune Man* mixes adventure with wry humor. An unlikely hero is transported to another world and told it is his destiny to save the universe, but back on Earth he has been replaced by an entirely plausible imposter. Or is it? Lupoff plays with reality here in a style reminiscent of some of the better novels of Philip K. Dick. *Sandworld* is an unabashed adventure story, featuring a group of people inexplicably transported from Earth to a barren world peopled with alien vampires. Though suspenseful, this work is clearly less ambitious than most of Lupoff's other novels.

Five related stories were brought together for *Space War Blues*, arguably Lupoff's best book. The most noteworthy is "With the Bentfin Boomer Boys on Little Old New Alabama," but each of the stories presents a satiric look at our own society by examining it in the context of one or another wildly alien world. The stories included here clearly marked Lupoff as a writer with the potential to be a major force in the field, although his works up through this point were so diverse in theme and approach, it was not clear what direction they might take in the future. During the mid-1970's he also produced an intriguing Oriental style fantasy, *Sword of the Demon*, which is in some ways his most controlled novel.

In *Sun's End*, Lupoff returns to the theme of his first novel, although on a more limited scale. An orbiting construction worker wakens 80 years following what should have been a fatal accident to discover he has been provided with an artificial body that possesses unsuspected powers. He attempts to return to his homeland, only to discover that Japan has reverted to the lifestyle it maintained centuries earlier, a culture which he now finds alien. At the same time, he discovers that the solar system itself may be destroyed within a few centuries, a threat he must deal with personally in the sequel, *Galaxy's End.*

Lupoff returned to the pastiche in *Circumpolar!* and its sequel, *Countersolar!*, arguably the best novels he has written. Both novels are set on a doughnut shaped alternate Earth, but one in which most of the familiar names of our own world exist. In the first, Amelia Earhart, Howard Hughes, and Charles Lindbergh are pitted in an aerial race around the poles against a team of villainous Germans. In the sequel, a message is received from Counter-Earth, another orbiting world, and a race through space is launched pitting Albert Einstein against Eva Perón. Although both novels are clearly humorous, the treatment is straightforward adventure and succeeds at both levels.

Similar games with reality are played in two other recent novels. In *The Forever City*, a rescue mission falls into an interdimensional warp that transports it to a universe based on a television program. Far more successful is *Lovecraft's Book*, set in an alternate version of our own recent past, with German agents recruiting Lovecraft to author the American version of *Mein Kampf* as the prelude to a massive German propaganda campaign. The background on Lovecraft's life has been meticulously researched, providing verisimilitude to what is a very controlled and effective novel.

Most of Lupoff's shorter fiction has consisted of satires and humorous pieces, most notably the "Ova Hamlet" series of swipes at the styles of prominent science-fiction writers.

—Don D'Ammassa

---

**LUTHER, Martin.** *See* **SELLINGS, Arthur**

---

**LYMINGTON, John.** Pseudonym for John Newton Chance; also wrote as J. Drummond; David C. Newton. British. Born in London, in 1911. Educated at Streatham Hill College and privately. Served in the Royal Air Force during World War II. *Died 3 August 1983.*

SCIENCE-FICTION PUBLICATIONS

Novels

*Night of the Big Heat*. London, Corgi, 1959; New York, Dutton, 1960.
*The Giant Stumbles*. London, Hodder and Stoughton, 1960.
*The Grey Ones*. London, Hodder and Stoughton, 1960.
*The Coming of the Strangers*. London, Hodder and Stoughton, 1961; New York, Manor, 1978.
*A Sword above the Night*. London, Hodder and Stoughton, 1962.
*The Screaming Face*. London, Hodder and Stoughton, 1963; New York, Manor, 1978.
*Froomb!*. London, Hodder and Stoughton, 1964; New York, Doubleday, 1966.
*The Star Witches*. London, Hodder and Stoughton, 1965; New York, Manor, 1978.
*The Green Drift*. London, Hodder and Stoughton, 1965; as *The Night Spiders*, New York, Doubleday, 1967.
*Ten Million Years to Friday*. London, Hodder and Stoughton, 1967.
*The Nowhere Place*. London, Hodder and Stoughton, 1969.
*Give Daddy the Knife, Darling*. London, Hodder and Stoughton, 1969.
*The Year Dot*. London, Hodder and Stoughton, 1972.
*The Sleep Eaters*. London, Hodder and Stoughton, 1973; New York, Manor, 1978.
*The Hole in the World*. London, Hodder and Stoughton, 1974.
*A Spider in the Bath*. London, Hodder and Stoughton, 1975.
*The Laxham Haunting*. London, Hodder and Stoughton, 1976.
*Starseed on Gye Moor*. London, Hodder and Stoughton, 1977.
*The Waking of the Stone*. London, Hodder and Stoughton, 1978.
*The Grey Ones, A Sword above the Night*. New York, Manor, 1978.
*A Caller from Overspace*. London, Hodder and Stoughton, 1979.
*Voyage of the Eighth Mind*. London, Hodder and Stoughton, 1980.
*The Power Ball*. London, Hale, 1981.
*The Terror Version*. London, Hale, 1982.
*The Vale of the Sad Banana*. London, Hale, 1984.

Short Stories

*The Night Spiders* (not same as 1967 novel). London, Corgi, 1964.

OTHER PUBLICATIONS

Novels as John Newton Chance

*Murder in Oils*. London, Gollancz, 1935.
*Wheels in the Forest*. London, Gollancz, 1935.
*The Devil Drives*. London, Gollancz, 1936.
*Maiden Possessed*. London, Gollancz, 1937.
*Rhapsody in Fear*. London, Gollancz, 1937.
*Death of an Innocent*. London, Gollancz, 1938.
*The Devil in Greenlands*. London, Gollancz, 1939.
*The Ghost of Truth*. London, Gollancz, 1939.
*The Screaming Fog*. London, Macdonald, 1944; as *Death Stalks the Cobbled Square*, New York, McBride, 1946.
*The Red Knight*. London, Macdonald, and New York, Macmillan, 1945.
*The Eye in Darkness*. London, Macdonald, 1946.
*The Knight and the Castle*. London, Macdonald, 1946.
*The Black Highway*. London, Macdonald, 1947.
*Coven Gibbet*. London, Macdonald, 1948.
*The Brandy Pole*. London, Macdonald, 1949.
*The Night of the Full Moon*. London, Macdonald, 1950.
*Aunt Miranda's Murder*. London, Macdonald, and New York, Dodd Mead, 1951.
*The Man in My Shoes*. London, Macdonald, 1952.
*The Twopenny Box*. London, Macdonald, 1952.
*The Jason Affair*. London, Macdonald, 1953; as *Up to Her Neck*, New York, Popular Library, 1955.
*The Randy Inheritance*. London, Macdonald, 1953.
*Jason and the Sleep Game*. London, Macdonald, 1954.
*The Jason Murders*. London, Macdonald, 1954.
*Jason Goes West*. London, Macdonald, 1955.
*The Last Seven Hours*. London, Macdonald, 1956.
*A Shadow Called Janet*. London, Macdonald, 1956.
*Dead Man's Knock*. London, Hale, 1957.
*The Little Crime*. London, Hale, 1957.
*Affair with a Rich Girl*. London, Hale, 1958.
*The Man with Three Witches*. London, Hale, 1958.
*The Fatal Fascination*. London, Hale, 1959.
*The Man with No Face*. London, Hale, 1959.
*Alarm at Black Brake*. London, Hale, 1960.
*Lady in a Frame*. London, Hale, 1960.
*Import of Evil*. London, Hale, 1961.
*The Night of the Settlement*. London, Hale, 1961.
*Triangle of Fear*. London, Hale, 1962.
*The Man Behind Me*. London, Hale, 1963.

*The Forest Affair*. London, Hale, 1963.
*Commission for Disaster*. London, Hale, 1964.
*Death under Desolate*. London, Hale, 1964.
*Stormlight*. London, Hale, 1966.
*The Affair at Dead End*. London, Hale, 1966.
*The Double Death*. London, Hale, 1966.
*The Case of the Death Computer*. London, Hale, 1967.
*The Case of the Fear Makers*. London, Hale, 1967.
*The Death Women*. London, Hale, 1967.
*The Hurricane Drift*. London, Hale, 1967.
*The Mask of Pursuit*. London, Hale, 1967.
*The Thug Executive*. London, Hale, 1967.
*Dead Man's Shoes*. London, Hale, 1968.
*Death of the Wild Bird*. London, Hale, 1968.
*Fate of the Lying Jade*. London, Hale, 1968.
*The Halloween Murders*. London, Hale, 1968.
*Mantrap*. London, Hale, 1968.
*The Rogue Aunt*. London, Hale, 1968.
*The Abel Coincidence*. London, Hale, 1969.
*The Ice Maidens*. London, Hale, 1969.
*Involvement in Austria*. London, Hale, 1969.
*The Killer Reaction*. London, Hale, 1969.
*The Killing Experiment*. London, Hale, 1969.
*The Mists of Treason*. London, Hale, 1970.
*A Ring of Liars*. London, Hale, 1970.
*Three Masks of Death*. London, Hale, 1970.
*The Mirror Train*. London, Hale, 1970.
*The Cat Watchers*. London, Hale, 1971.
*The Faces of a Bad Girl*. London, Hale, 1971.
*A Wreath of Bones*. London, Hale, 1971.
*A Bad Dream of Death*. London, Hale, 1972.
*Last Train to Limbo*. London, Hale, 1972.
*The Man with Two Heads*. London, Hale, 1972.
*The Dead Tale-Tellers*. London, Hale, 1972.
*The Farm Villains*. London, Hale, 1973.
*The Grab Operators*. London, Hale, 1973.
*The Love-Hate Relationship*. London, Hale, 1973.
*The Girl in the Crime Belt*. London, Hale, 1974.
*The Shadow of the Killer*. London, Hale, 1974.
*The Starfish Affair*. London, Hale, 1974.
*The Canterbury Kilgrims*. London, Hale, 1974.
*Hill Fog*. London, Hale, 1975.
*The Devil's Edge*. London, Hale, 1975.
*The Monstrous Regiment*. London, Hale, 1975.
*The Murder Maker*. London, Hale, 1976.
*Return to Death Valley*. London, Hale, 1976.
*A Fall-Out of Thieves*. London, Hale, 1976.
*The Frightened Fisherman*. London, Hale, 1976.
*The House of the Dead Ones*. London, Hale, 1977.
*Motive for a Kill*. London, Hale, 1977.
*The Ducrow Folly*. London, Hale, 1978.
*End of an Iron Man*. London, Hale, 1978.
*A Drop of Hot Gold*. London, Hale, 1979.
*Thieves' Kitchen*. London, Hale, 1979.
*The Guilty Witness*. London, Hale, 1979.
*A Place Called Skull*. London, Hale, 1980.
*The Death Watch Ladies*. London, Hale, 1980.
*The Mayhem Madchen*. London, Hale, 1980.
*The Black Widow*. London, Hale, 1981.
*The Death Importer*. London, Hale, 1981.
*The Mystery of Enda Favell*. London, Hale, 1981.
*Madman's Will*. London, Hale, 1982.
*The Hunting of Mr. Exe*. London, Hale, 1982.
*The Shadow in Pursuit*. London, Hale, 1982.
*The Traditional Murders*. London, Hale, 1983.
*The Death Chemist*. London, Hale, 1983.
*Terror Train*. London, Hale, 1983.
*Looking for Samson*. London, Hale, 1984.
*Nobody's Supposed to Murder the Butler*. London, Hale, 1984.
*The Bad Circle*. London, Hale, 1985.
*The Time Bomb*. London, Hale, 1985.
*The Woman Hater*. London, Hale, 1986.
*The Psychic Trap*. London, Hale, 1986.
*Spy on a Spider*. London, Hale, 1987.
*The Hit Man*. London, Hale, 1987.
*The Hiller Weapon*. London, Hale, 1987.
*The Smiling Cadaver*. London, Hale, 1987.
*The Reluctant Agent*. London, Hale, 1988.
*The Shadow Before*. London, Hale, 1988.
*The Offshore Conspiracy*. London, Hale, 1988.
*The Man on the Cliff*. London, Hale, 1988.
*A Confusion of Eyes*. London, Hale, 1989.
*The Running of the Spies*. London, Hale, 1989.
*A Tale of Tangled Ladies*. London, Hale, 1989.

Novels as J. Drummond

*The Essex Road Crime*. London, Amalgamated Press, 1944.
*The Manor House Menace*. London, Amalgamated Press, 1944.
*The Painted Dagger*. London, Amalgamated Press, 1944.
*The Riddle of the Leather Bottle*. London, Amalgamated Press, 1944.
*The Tragic Case of the Station Master's Legacy*. London, Amalgamated Press, 1944.
*At Sixty Miles an Hour*. London, Amalgamated Press, 1945.
*The House on the Hill*. London, Amalgamated Press, 1945.
*The Riddle of the Mummy Case*. London, Amalgamated Press, 1945.
*The Mystery of the Deserted Camp*. London, Amalgamated Press, 1948.
*The Town of Shadows*. London, Amalgamated Press, 1948.
*The Case of the "Dead" Spy*. London, Amalgamated Press, 1949.
*The Riddle of the Receiver's Hoard*. London, Amalgamated Press, 1949.
*The Secret of the Living Skeleton*. London, Amalgamated Press, 1949.
*The South Coast Mystery*. London, Amalgamated Press, 1949.
*The Case of L.A.C. Dickson*. London, Amalgamated Press, 1950.
*The Mystery of the Haunted Square*. London, Amalgamated Press, 1950.
*The House in the Woods*. London, Amalgamated Press, 1950.
*The Secret of the Sixty Steps*. London, Amalgamated Press, 1951.
*The Case of the Man with No Name*. London, Amalgamated Press, 1951.
*Hated by All!* London, Amalgamated Press, 1951.
*The Mystery of the Sabotaged Jet*. London, Amalgamated Press, 1951.
*The House on the River*. London, Amalgamated Press, 1952.
*The Mystery of the Five Guilty Men*. London, Amalgamated Press, 1954.
*The Case of the Two-Faced Swindler*. London, Amalgamated Press, 1955.
*The Teddy-Boy Mystery*. London, Amalgamated Press, 1955.

Other as John Newton Chance

*The Black Ghost* (for children; as David C. Newton). London, Oxford University Press, 1947.
*The Dangerous Road* (for children; as David C. Newton). London, Oxford University Press, 1948.

*Bunst and the Brown Voice [the Bold, and the Secret Six, and the Flying Eye]* (for children). London, Oxford University Press, 4 vols., 1950–53.
*The Jennifer Jigsaw* (for children), with Shirley Newton Chance. London, Oxford University Press, 1951.
*Yellow Belly* (autobiography). London, Hale, 1959.
*The Crimes at Rillington Place: A Novelist's Reconstruction*. London, Hodder and Stoughton, 1961.

* * *

John Lymington was well known for the crime novels published under his real name, John Newton Chance. As a writer of science fiction, however, he has received little notice, even within the SF community, perhaps because the fantastic elements of his fiction often serve as little more than a backdrop for the main action which characteristically centers on a small but diverse group of British citizens faced with a common threat. Lymington's characters, his village settings, and the structure of his novels owe as much to the tradition of the classical detective story as to the traditions of science fiction, and with few exceptions he does not concern himself with the social or intellectual implications of the marvels he introduces. As an author of suspense and horror stories, he is often startlingly effective, able to spin an entertaining novel from a single situation, but when he attempts more complex themes his novels tend to get out of hand.

Lymington makes use of few of the resources of the science-fiction genre; most of his novels are variations on the basic theme of alien invasion, while a couple deal with time travel and contain elements of social satire. His first SF novel, *Night of the Big Heat*, is an admirable addition to the something-is-amiss-in-the-village school of British suspense novels, though the science-fiction element—an alien civilization transmitting giant spiders into the English countryside via microwaves—is clearly secondary to the portrayal of the reactions of a group of local citizens gathered at a country inn. Spiders are one of Lymington's favorite images of horror—even though he persistently regards them as insects—and were also the featured attraction in another invasion story, "The Night Spiders." The basic formula of an unknown horror menacing a small community was repeated in *The Coming of the Strangers;* in *A Sword above the Night*—perhaps the most straightforward and unadorned of Lymington's exercises in suspense—the anticipated "invasion" that provides suspense throughout the novel is dispensed with in a three-paragraph closing summary, explaining that it is merely the pre-programmed return to Earth of dead astronauts who had left from an earlier civilization thousands of years ago. This novel perhaps most clearly indicates the short shrift Lymington gives his science-fiction concepts.

Occasionally, Lymington adds other science-fiction elements to his formula—in *The Sleep Eaters* the invasion is telepathic (*The Night Spiders* also have telepathic powers), and in *The Star Witches* a mad scientist helps bring the aliens to earth. *The Star Witches* also reveals an inclination on Lymington's part to work traditional supernatural appurtenances into his science-fiction narratives: in this case a coven of witches is associated with the alien invasion. Time travel is another concept that Lymington sometimes plays with, in *The Night Spiders* and *Ten Million Years to Friday. Froomb!* is in some ways Lymington's most ambitious novel, and the most satirical. The title is short for "The fluid's running out of my brakes!," a fictional cartoon caption that has come to symbolize the state of world affairs in Lymington's headlong future world. The story, which somehow encompasses such diverse themes as threatened nuclear war, heaven, heat rays, insecticide poisoning, food additives, radiation, drugs, and male impotence, concerns a man who dies and goes to heaven, only to find that it is actually a post-holocaust world brought about by an American defense experiment about to take place before he died. His efforts to return and warn the world of the experiment make up the bulk of the novel.

Lymington was not a major writer, and there is much to suggest that he did not take his science fiction seriously, but in the relatively narrow territory he staked out for himself he provides enjoyable light reading.

—Gary K. Wolfe

---

**LYNN, Elizabeth A.** American. Born in New York City, 8 June 1946. Educated at Case Western Reserve University, Cleveland, B.A. 1967; University of Chicago (Woodrow Wilson Fellow, 1967–68), M.A. 1968. Public school teacher, Chicago, 1968–70; unit manager, St. Francis Hospital, Evanston, Illinois, 1970–72, and French Hospital, San Francisco, 1972–75; formerly teacher in the Women's Studies Program, San Francisco State University. Address: c/o Bluejay Books, 26 Douglas Road, Chappaqua, New York 10514, U.S.A.

### Science-Fiction Publications

Novels

*A Different Light*. New York, Berkley, 1978; London, Gollancz, 1979.
*The Sardonyx Net*. New York, Putnam, 1981.

Short Stories

*The Woman Who Loved the Moon and Other Stories*. New York, Berkley, 1981.

### Other Publications

Novels

*Watchtower*. New York, Berkley, 1979; London, Hamlyn, 1981.
*The Dancers of Arun*. New York, Berkley, 1979; London, Hamlyn, 1982.
*The Northern Girl*. New York, Berkley, 1981.
*The Red Hawk*. New Castle, Virginia, Cheap Street, 1983.
*The Silver Horse*. New York, Bluejay, 1984.

* * *

Elizabeth A. Lynn's greatest strength lies in her ability to focus sympathetically on a single character or a small cast of characters that are very human. Although her science-fiction stories are often presented in the trappings of space opera—faster-than-light travel, interstellar exploration, humans kidnapped by aliens—they are peopled by individuals who are clearly drawn from life: flawed and identifiably human, not Kimball Kennisons, or comic-book superheroes.

This is most apparent in her most important science-fiction novel, *The Sardonyx Net.* Working from some pretty hoary SF elements—including interstellar drug and slave trades—Lynn has created a remarkable book. Although in synopsis it sounds like something straight out of a 1940's *Thrilling Wonder Stories* magazine, *The Sardonyx Net* is primarily a novel of character with a satisfyingly complex plot and some of Lynn's best writing. It is here that one of her special skills is most apparent: the ability to create a villain with whom the reader can empathize. *Net* is far better plotted than most of her novels, and the best evidence of her matured skills.

Several of her short stories, and the novel *A Different Light*, are linked by some common images and themes. Although interstellar travel seems taken for granted, Lynn consistently treats the concept of hyperspace, the Hype, as a place not only beyond the normal limits of space-time, but beyond reality itself. It is a source of danger to all but the strongest who attempt to pass through it. In *A Different Light*, in fact, the Hype is the cause of the apparent death of the protagonist. Jimson, an artist, has an incurable cancer, one which will limit his lifespan, if he is careful, to another 20 years. Before he dies, however, he wants to see the light of other stars, and rejoin an old friend and lover. He flees his home planet in the sure knowledge that travel in the Hype will accelerate the process of his cancer. Jimson is typical of Lynn's protagonists. Most of them work in some art form, and seem to pay for their gifts with a physical debility—such as the one-armed telepath in *The Dancers of Arun*—but it is a debility that heightens their sensitivity to others and their surroundings. Jimson is a sexual being. Like many of Lynn's characters he lives in a society not proscribed by sexual roles, and his sexuality finds expression through love for women and men. A first novel, *A Different Light* is certainly flawed, both by its somewhat episodic plot and an ending that seems drawn from other SF novels rather than from within. But the novel's sensitivity and fluid language betray a promise that is more than fulfilled in her later novels.

The Chronicles of Tornor is a true trilogy—three self-contained novels related by continuity of place, cultures, and institutions—that defies neat categorization. The trilogy concerns the way that cultures and institutions change, and succeeds because it focuses on individuals directly involved in those cultures. *Watchtower* introduces the cultures: the rigid, militaristic society of the North, and the newly developed egalitarian life of the Cheari, built on an art composed of dance and martial art. The protagonist is a vassal of the northern culture, and the novel's conflict lies in his inability to assimilate the new mores and life-style of the Chearis. The language is crisp and precise. *The Dancers of Arun* takes place 100 years later. It centers on the almost utopian life-style of the Cheari, and the language of the book is appropriately softened. Kerris is a child of these people but has been raised in the North, and finds difficulty in believing in their acceptance of his maimed arm. Only through the physically loving relationship that he develops with his brother does he learn to accept himself. The trilogy is concluded with *The Northern Girl*, which concerns a third culture in the South. By now the Cheari are only a memory, and the focus is on a city-dwelling society. Here, Lynn is on even surer ground, and Kendra-on-the-Delta is a more convincing place than either the military keeps or rustic villages of the previous books. The plot has a tendency to drift, but the characters are tightly drawn, with an emotional warmth unusual in the field. Much of this effect stems from Lynn's concentration on a small group of real people in intimate contact, rather than the giant battles of armies and wizards so common in fantasy.

Lynn's latest foray into fantasy is *The Silver Horse*, a disappointingly slight and derivative fairy tale about two young girls from San Francisco who travel to Dreamland to rescue a little boy. It is notable only for the role reversal of the lead characters; little girls are fearless, and little boys chicken-hearted.

—Jeff Frane

---

**LYONS, Delphine C.** *See* **SMITH, Evelyn E.**

---

**LORD, Jeffrey.** *See* **NELSON, Ray Faraday.**

---

# M

**MacAPP, C.C.** Pseudonym for Carroll M. Capps. American. Born in 1917(?). Worked as a printer. *Died 15 January 1971.*

SCIENCE-FICTION PUBLICATIONS

Novels

*Omha Abides.* New York, Paperback Library, 1968.
*Prisoners of the Sky.* New York, Lancer, 1969.
*Secret of the Sunless World.* New York, Dell, 1969.
*Worlds of the Wall.* New York, Avon, 1969.
*Recall Not Earth.* New York, Dell, 1970.
*Subb.* New York, Paperback Library, 1971.
*Bumsider.* New York, Lancer, 1972.

Uncollected Short Stories

"Tulan," in *Amazing* (New York), June 1960.
"The Drug," in *Galaxy* (New York), February 1961.
"Specimen," in *Fantastic* (New York), September 1961.
"All That Earthly Paradise," in *If* (New York), July 1962.
"The Demon of the North," in *Fantastic* (New York), September 1963.
"A Guest of Ganymede," in *The Best Science Fiction from Worlds of Tomorrow.* New York, Galaxy, 1964.
"The Slaves of Gree," in *If* (New York), August 1964.
"Beyond the Ebon Wall," in *Fantastic* (New York), October 1964.
"Somewhere in Space," in *Worlds of Tomorrow* (New York), November 1964.
"For Every Action," in *World's Best Science Fiction 1965,* edited by Donald A. Wollheim and Terry Carr. New York, Ace, 1965.
"And All the Earth a Grave," in *The Eighth Galaxy Reader,* edited by Frederik Pohl. New York, Doubleday, 1965.
"A Pride of Islands," in *The 6 Fingers of Time and 5 Other Science Fiction Novelets.* New York, Macfadden, 1965.
"Gree's Commandos," in *If* (New York), February 1965.
"Gree's Hellcats," in *If* (New York), April 1965.
"Sculptor," in *Galaxy* (New York), April 1965.
"No Friend of Gree," in *If* (New York), June 1965.
"Gree's Damned Ones," in *If* (New York), September 1965.
"The Light Outside," in *Worlds of Tomorrow* (New York), September 1965.
"The Mercurymen," in *Galaxy* (New York), December 1965.
"A Flask of Fine Arcturan," in *The Ninth Galaxy Reader,* edited by Frederik Pohl. New York, Doubleday, 1966.
"Prisoner of the Sky," in *If* (New York), February 1966.
"Like Any World of Gree," in *Worlds of Tomorrow* (New York), March 1966.
"Enemies of Gree," in *If* (New York), September 1966.
"The Sign of Gree," in *If* (New York), November 1966.
"Frost Planet," in *Worlds of Tomorrow* (New York), November 1966.
"A Beachhead for Gree," in *If* (New York), February 1967.
"Spare That Tree," in *Galaxy* (New York), June 1967.
"A Ticket to Zennon," in *If* (New York), July 1967.
"The Fortunes of Peace," in *If* (New York), September 1967.
"The Judas Bug," in *Analog* (New York), October 1967.
"Winter of the Llangs," in *If* (New York), October 1967.
"Mail Drop," in *If* (New York), November 1967.
"When the Sea Is Born Again," in *If* (New York), December 1967.
"The Impersonators," in *Out of This World 7,* edited by Amabel Williams-Ellis and Mably Owen. London, Blackie, 1968.
"Where the Subbs Go," in *If* (New York), May 1968.
"The Hides of Marrech," in *If* (New York), July 1968.
"Dream Street," in *If* (New York), September 1968.
"Mad Ship," in *If* (New York), May 1969.
"Hot World," in *If* (New York), December 1971.

* * *

The SF career of C.C. MacApp lasted only slightly over ten years, from 1960 to 1971. During that decade he built a reputation for exciting adventure stories in which a lone hero would overcome seemingly hopeless odds to save his entire nation, species, or world. His style was beginning to broaden when he died.

MacApp came late in his life to SF. His real name was Carroll M. Capps, and his profession had been in the color printing industry. An illness forced him to retire in his early forties, and he began writing SF. His first story appeared in 1960; he averaged only a couple of short works a year through 1963. Then from mid-1964 through 1968 he seemed to have stories almost constantly in print, in either *If or Worlds of Tomorrow,* the magazines with which he was most closely associated. In 1968, he began to produce paperback novels; five between that year and 1970. At the same time, his flow of magazine stories cut back to a trickle; this was due to both his novel writing and his declining health. A couple of short stories and two more paperback novels appeared posthumously. He had been working on a hardcover novel for Doubleday but it was never finished.

MacApp's magazine works were primarily of novelette length. He was best known for suspense dramas in which humans appeared as underdogs amidst a galactic multispecies civilization. Chief among these were the nine "Gree" novelettes; "The Slaves of Gree," "No Friend of Gree," and so on. These featured Colonel Steve Duke, the top human fighter among the multispecies resistance to the Gree Empire, which had conquered most of the galaxy (including Earth) 600 years earlier. Each story had Steve Duke being sent to an unknown planet that Gree's forces had just landed upon, to learn why Gree wanted it and to keep Gree from establishing a new base there. Duke's commando tactics made him a grim counterpart to Keith Laumer's more lighthearted James Retief, who also fought regularly in *IF* during the mid-1960's to make the galaxy safe for humanity. A typical non-"Gree" drama is "A Ticket to Zennon," in which Tom Lerrow, a young Earthman, learns that he is being unwittingly used as a courier of plans for a top-secret weapon, which two powerful alien factions and a deadly criminal are after. MacApp's aliens are not always villains, nor were all his stories dramas. "Winter of the Llangs" and "When the Sea Is Born Again" feature alien teenagers in adventures that amount to rites of passage among their peoples. MacApp's first story, "A Pride of Islands," is a mild comedy where humans are portrayed as parasites living upon giant animals. A more successful comedy is "Mail Drop," in which the bureaucracy of the galactic postal service almost starts but finally prevents an interstellar war.

MacApp's short fiction succeeds by means of dramatic incidents. His novels show that he could write powerful adventures with more richly portrayed characters. Yet the novels have a thematic sameness. All begin with their protagonists caught in a moment of total despair. Murno, an ignorant human peasant on an Earth subjugated by aliens for thousands of years, learns that their masters are about to begin hunting men for sport (*Omha Abides*). Raab Garan, a cadet in a dirigible air fleet on a backward colony planet, faces his country's fall to its totalitarian adversary unless he can succeed in what he realizes is a suicide mission (*Prisoners of the Sky*). Zeke Bolivar, space explorer, is about to crash on an unknown world (*Worlds of the Wall*). John Braysen, a Space Force commander, believes that he is one of only a few hundred humans left alive after Earth loses a space war (*Recall Not Earth*). MacApp's heroes always win through to a victorious conclusion but only after a psychologically exhausting struggle. Also, the lack of women in MacApp's works stands out sharply. In *Recall Not Earth*, the presence of one chapter featuring women (to establish that human women still exist) seems almost forced. Most of his other novels use women only as minor background characters. MacApp had only started to break away from these stereotypes in his final novel, *Bumsider*, which has a strong and convincingly-portrayed woman supporting character in Pegs Waran, and a plot involving more human interactions among his main cast.

—Frederick Patten

---

**MacAVOY, R(oberta) A(nn).** American. Born in Cleveland, Ohio, 13 December 1949. Educated at Case Western Reserve University, Cleveland, 1967–71, B.Sc. 1971. Married Ronald Allen Cain in 1978. Financial aid officer's assistant, Columbia College, New York, 1975–78; computer programmer, SRI International, Menlo Park, California, 1979–83. Since 1982, full-time writer. Recipient: John W. Campbell Best New Writer award, 1984. Agent: Richard Curtis Associates, 171 East 74th Street, New York, New York 10021. Address: Underhill at Nelson Farm, 1669 Nelson Road, House 6, Scotts Valley, California 95066, U.S.A.

### Science-Fiction Publications

Novels (series: Lute)

*Tea with the Black Dragon*. New York and London, Bantam, 1983.
*A Trio for Lute*. New York, Doubleday, 1984.
  *Damiano*. New York, Bantam, 1984; London, 1985.
  *Damiano's Lute*. New York, Bantam, 1984; London, 1985.
  *Raphael*. New York, Bantam, 1984; London, 1985.
*The Book of Kells*. New York, Bantam, 1985.
*Twisting the Rope: Casadh and t'Sugain*. New York, Bantam, 1986.
*The Grey Horse*. New York, Bantam, 1987.
*The Third Eagle: Lessons Along a Minor String*. New York, Doubleday, 1989.
*Lens of the World*. New York, Morrow, 1990; London, Headline, 1991.
*King of the Dead*. New York, Morrow, and London, Headline, 1991.

*

R.A. MacAvoy comments:

The books I write are very different, one from another. This may be an unconscious attempt on my part to avoid falling into a rut, but more likely I just get bored with one subject or one narrative voice. Everything I have written, however, has something eccentrically religious in it, and at least one animal. I don't plan it this way.

In almost all my novels, the protagonists find themselves engaged in testing the truth, either by hard experience or direct perception. They also wrestle with ambiguity and the possibility that there is no ultimate truth. On the other hand, all my novels strive to be adventure stories, because those are what I like to read myself, and I try to find happy endings. Reasonably happy.

* * *

With ten compelling novels in less than a decade, R.A. MacAvoy already fulfills her promise as winner of the John W. Campbell Award for Best New Writer. Hailed as "best new fantasy writer of the 1980's" by the Chicago *Sun-Times*, and predicted to be "one of the future giants of the SF/fantasy field" by *ALA Booklist*, MacAvoy is also praised by writers of such stature as Anne McCaffrey and Andre Norton.

In *Tea with the Black Dragon*, the memorable character Mayland Long, a swarthy sinuous Asian of uncertain origins, introduces MacAvoy's propensity for realism set slightly askew. In a genteel California hotel, the cultured Long meets middle-aged Martha Macnamara, summoned from the East coast by her troubled computer whiz daughter Liz, who has suddenly gone missing. Attracted by Martha's directness, loner Long joins her on a search for Liz that leads through modern computer corruption to ancient wisdom. Constantly mistaken for a private detective, Long is actually a powerful black Chinese dragon, metamorphosed into human form to study the human condition.

Such satisfying fantasy in a mystery format demanded a sequel. The team of Long and Macnamara reappear four years later, in real and imaginary time, in *Twisting the Rope.* Martha is fiddler and leader of a traditional Celtic band on concert tour, with her lover Long as road manager, when George St. Ives is found hanging by a handmade Irish rope off a Santa Cruz pier. As the couple untangles the strands of this mystery, MacAvoy choreographs the complex cords that bind a group of talented musicians with varied motivations, and leads Long further on his search for Truth. Readers may long for another performance by this philosophical sleuthing duo.

Between the two acclaimed Black Dragon books, MacAvoy created two other worlds in two more fantasy subgenres. Her haunting *A Trio for Lute* may challenge MacAvoy's future writings for its place as her masterpiece. In three volumes, this transformational tale explores, as the finest fantasy must, the nature of good and evil in one person's struggle toward the sublime. As in all heroic fantasy, the hero is on a quest, but the lute-playing alchemist Damiano Delstrego is not built in typical heroic proportions. In *Damiano*, the first volume, the delicate young musician/witch flees his embattled city to seek its salvation by magic means. Damiano's own hero is his lute teacher Raphael, the gloriously beautiful archangel who only Damiano can see. Because the holy Raphael cannot interfere in human affairs despite his love for Damiano, the desperate witch risks his soul for his city in a pact with Raphael's brother Lucifer. Needing stronger witchery than his own to handle Satan, Damiano approaches Saara, whose Finnish magic is greatest in Europe. But old wounds lock the two witches in battle, and Damiano sacrifices all his powers to Saara.

In *Damiano's Lute,* Damiano has become merely a wandering musician, roaming the Alps with the scampish boy dancer Gaspare. His only wizardry is upon the lute, impressing the Pope at Avignon. When the plague strikes Avignon, Damiano reclaims his powers from Saara to fight it. Winning Saara's love and healing a plague victim, Damiano forfeits his own life.

Damiano appears as a ghost in *Raphael* to his beloved angel, who succumbs to Lucifer's plot to destroy his brother through love for a mortal. Stripped of his wings by Satan, Raphael plummets to earth as a human slave of corrupt Moorish traders. The ex-angel has no idea how to be human, so Damiano switches roles to become his spiritual advisor. Damiano's mourning friends, Gaspare and Saara, enlist the aid of a Chinese dragon to rescue Raphael from slavery, leading them to a final clash with the Devil himself. In an early lesson with Damiano, Raphael says, "Mortals by their nature cannot continue in the way they are. What matters . . . is the direction in which they change." On an epic scale, in language as lyrical as the lute, MacAvoy explores mortal change through the realm of the spirit.

MacAvoy also contributes significantly to time-travel literature with *The Book of Kells,* in which a modern Irish historian and a Canadian artist slip through a time gate to tenth-century Ireland. The gate opens when John Thornburn replicates the intricate scrolling in the illuminated manuscript, while bagpipes play on his stereo. Erupting through his bathroom door comes a screaming, naked girl, bleeding from the wounds of rape. When John calls his lover, Derval O'Keane, to help him calm the hysterical girl, Derval recognizes her antiquated Irish speech. Hearing the girl Ailesh's tale of murderous Viking raiders, Derval cannot refuse aid, or resist the chance to visit the old Ireland of her studies. Regarded by Ailesh as miraculous saints, John and Derval accompany her home to become enmeshed in the entrancing treacherous world of a thousand years ago. Imbued with Gaelic earthiness, the sensations of coarse cloth and damp cold and the fragility of human life, MacAvoy's old Ireland even smells right. The conflict of modern logic with ancient superstition mirrors the violent culture clash between Danes and Gaels, Viking individualism against Gaelic clan values. In this time-fantasy, magic resides in the glorious *Book of Kells* itself, a "talisman [with] . . . power to move."

Set in a later Ireland still rich with its own language but threatened by English incursions, *The Grey Horse* brings fantasy into Connemara in the form of Ruairí MacEibhir, a horse fairy. This 1500-year-old púca emerges from the fairies' mirror world to win the love of mortal Máire Standún, switching back and forth from horse to human form as he pursues her. Embedded with difficult Gaelic names, MacAvoy's prose seems dense. More devoted to horse lore than fairy magic, her story flows less freely than usual. Even mystical Ruairí and spirited Máire are rendered less vibrantly than MacAvoy's typical characters, though equine fans may enjoy this ultimate horse story.

MacAvoy's foray into science fiction is more successful in *The Third Eagle.* On the planet Neunacht, Wanbli is a Paint of the Wacaan clan, obliged to bodyguard those who run his impoverished but lovely planet. Tattooed on Wanbli's magnificent red chest and torso are three sets of spread wings signifying his high warrior status. When fortune flings Wanbli a chance to star in the shimmers (movies) on another planet, he encounters many other types of the seven sentient beings in his universe, as well as with the prejudices among them. In an abrupt shift of pace halfway through the book, Wanbli discovers that the "revivalists" with whom he travels use their spaceship to track sleepers, refugees searching for new home planets while frozen in sleep for hundreds of years. When Wanbli realizes that most of the sleepers won't be saved, he wakes them himself, holding the ship hostage. With page-turning suspense, Wanbli fights for the fate of the sleepers, the revivalists, and his own planet, meanwhile discovering kinship with awakened Sioux from Earth. MacAvoy's enduring interest in cross-cultural communication transports easily into space.

The science of lens grinding is a focus in *Lens of the World,* a promising opening to a new fantasy series set in the Kingdom of Vestinglon. MacAvoy's 40-year-old hero Nazhuret recounts his life story to his king. With no idea of his parentage, Nazhuret spends his first 19 years in a military school as perpetual student/servant, until he chances upon an isolated observatory. There, he meets his new teacher Powl, a mysterious noble who puts him through arduous solitary training for three years. Swerving from antagonist to benefactor, Powl coaches the boy in martial arts, languages, astronomy, lens grinding, and "living in the belly of the wolf"—meditation. Without warning, Powl releases the sheltered young man to the world to encounter robbers, murderers, werewolves, dragons, and the king's court, where he is regarded as King of Hell. Powl taught him to swear allegiance to no one but himself, but in doing so he both impresses and insults the king, and imperils his beloved Powl.

The other-world of Vestinglon contains peoples and languages unfamiliar but Earthlike. Even the dragons, who make a rather fortuitous appearance in the last 30 pages, aren't particularly magical. Nazhuret has an opium dream that leaves physical evidence, but MacAvoy's message is that magic feats are performed through endurance, discipline, philosophy, and character.

Nazhuret's strong, unique personality exemplifies all MacAvoy protagonists, who are antiheroic in their eccentricity and fierce independence. All are truth-searchers who challenge the forces of good and evil, questioning accepted morality. Even an angel, a dragon, and a fairy must adopt human form to discover the essence of humanity. Through her expertise in music and language, MacAvoy examines human communications and the prejudice that often thwarts them. She defines and redefines the longing for freedom at the core of human nature. Even her monsters are natural. Grounded firmly in three-dimensional reality, her fantasies uplift readers into spiritual concerns. Through a fascinating blend of Buddhist philosophy and Celtic ethics, MacAvoy forges her own fresh vision, unlimited by literary genre. Ushered through elegant prose infused with passion, conviction, and wry humor, readers enter MacAvoy's living worlds and meet her breathing characters to measure what they themselves believe.

—Cathi MacRae

---

**MacCREIGH, James.** *See* **POHL, Frederik.**

---

**MacDONALD, George.** British. Born near Huntly, Aberdeenshire, 10 December 1824. Educated at King's College, University of Aberdeen, 1840–45, M.A. 1845; Congregationalist Theological College, Highbury, London, 1848–50. Married Louisa Powell in 1850 (died 1902); 11 children. Private tutor in London, 1845–48; minister, Trinity Congregational Church, Arundel, Sussex, 1850–53; lecturer and preacher in Manchester, 1855–56, Hastings, Sussex, 1857–59, and London, from 1859: taught at Bedford College; editor, with Norman MacLeod, *Good Words for the Young* magazine, 1870–72; lived partly in Bordighera, Italy from 1877. LL.D.: University of Aberdeen, 1868. Granted Civil List pension, 1877. *Died 18 September 1905.*

SCIENCE-FICTION PUBLICATIONS

Novels

*Phantastes: A Faerie Romance for Men and Women.* London, Smith Elder, 1858; Boston, Loring, 1870.
*David Elginbrod.* London, Hurst and Blackett, 3 vols., 1863; New York, Munro, 1879.
*Adela Cathcart.* London, Hurst and Blackett, 3 vols., 1864; New York, Munro, 1882.
*The Portent: A Story of the Inner Vision of the Highlanders, Commonly Called the Second Sight.* London, Smith Elder, 1864; New York, Munro, 1885.
*Alec Forbes of Howglen.* London, Hurst and Blackett, 3 vols., 1865; New York, Harper, 1872.
*Annals of a Quiet Neighbourhood.* London, Hurst and Blackett, 3 vols., 1867; New York, Harper, 1867.
*Guild Court.* London, Hurst and Blackett, 3 vols., 1867; New York, Harper, 1868.
*Robert Falconer.* London, Hurst and Blackett, 3 vols., 1868; Boston, Loring, n.d.
*The Seaboard Parish.* London, Tinsley, 3 vols., 1868; New York, Routledge, 1868.
*The Vicar's Daughter: An Autobiographical Story.* Boston, Roberts, 1871; London, Tinsley, 3 vols., 1872.
*Wilfrid Cumbermede.* London, Hurst and Blackett, 3 vols., 1872; New York, Scribner, 1872.
*Malcolm.* London, King, 3 vols., 1875; Philadelphia, Lippincott, 1875.
*St. George and St. Michael.* London, King, 3 vols., 1876; New York, Ford, 1876(?).
*Thomas Wingfold, Curate.* London, Hurst and Blackett, 3 vols., 1876; New York, Munro, 1879.
*The Marquis of Lossie.* London, Hurst and Blackett, 3 vols., 1877; Philadelphia, Lippincott, 1877.
*Paul Faber, Surgeon.* London, Hurst and Blackett, 3 vols., 1879; Philadelphia, Lippincott, 1879.
*Mary Marston.* London, Sampson Low, 3 vols., 1881; Philadelphia, Lippincott, 1881.
*Warlock o' Glen Warlock.* New York, Harper, 1881; as *Castle Warlock: A Homely Romance,* London, Sampson Low, 3 vols., 1882.
*Weighed and Wanting.* London, Sampson Low, 3 vols., 1882; New York, Harper, 1882.
*Donal Grant.* London, Kegan Paul, 3 vols., 1883; New York, Harper, 1883.
*What's Mine's Mine.* London, Kegan Paul, 3 vols., 1886; New York, Harper, 1886.
*Home Again.* London, Kegan Paul, and New York, Appleton, 1887.
*The Elect Lady.* London, Kegan Paul, and New York, Munro, 1888.
*There and Back.* London, Kegan Paul, 3 vols., 1891: Boston, Lothrop, n.d.
*The Flight of the Shadow.* London, Kegan Paul, and New York, Appleton, 1891.
*Heather and Snow.* London, Chatto and Windus, 2 vols., 1893; New York, Harper, 1893.
*Lilith: A Romance.* London, Chatto and Windus, and New York, Dodd Mead, 1895.
*Salted with Fire.* London, Hurst and Blackett, and New York, Dodd Mead, 1897.

Fiction for children

*Dealings with the Fairies,* illustrated by Arthur Hughes. London, Strahan, 1867; New York, Routledge, 1891.
*At the Back of the North Wind,* illustrated by Arthur Hughes. London, Strahan, 1870; New York, Routledge, 1871.
*Ranald Bannerman's Boyhood,* illustrated by Arthur Hughes. London, Strahan, and New York, Routledge, 1871.
*The Princess and the Goblin,* illustrated by Arthur Hughes. New York, Routledge, 1871; London, Strahan, 1872.
*Gutta-Percha Willie, The Working Genius,* illustrated by Arthur Hughes. London, King, and Boston, Hoyt, 1873.
*The Wise Woman: A Parable.* London, Strahan, 1875; as *A Double Story,* New York, Dodd Mead, 1876; as *The Lost Princess,* London, Wells Gardner Darton, 1895.
*Sir Gibbie.* London, Hurst and Blackett, 3 vols., 1879; Philadelphia, Lippincott, 1879.
*The Princess and Curdie,* illustrated by James Allen. Philadelphia, Lippincott, 1882; London, Chatto and Windus, 1883.
*A Rough Shaking,* illustrated by W. Parkinson. New York, Routledge, 1890; London, Blackie, 1891.
*The Fairy Tales of George MacDonald,* edited by Greville MacDonald. London, Fifield, 5 vols., 1904.
*The Light Princess and Other Tales of Fantasy,* edited by Roger Lancelyn Green. London, Gollancz, 1961.
*The Gifts of the Child Christ and Other Tales.* London, Sampson Low, 2 vols., 1882; as *Stephen Archer and Other Tales,* 1883; as *The Gifts of the Child Christ: Fairy Tales and Stories for the Childlike,* edited by Glenn Edward Sadler, Grand Rapids, Michigan, Eerdmans, and London, Mowbray, 1973.
*The Complete Fairy Tales of George MacDonald.* New York, Schocken, 1977.
*The Christmas Stories of George MacDonald,* illustrated by Linda Hill Griffith. Elgin, Illinois, Cook, 1981.

Short Stories

*Far above Rubies.* New York, Dodd Mead, 1899.

OTHER PUBLICATIONS

Verse

*Within and Without: A Dramatic Poem.* London, Longman, 1855; New York, Scribner, 1872.
*Poems.* London, Longman, 1857.
*A Hidden Life and Other Poems.* London, Longman, 1864; New York, Scribner, 1872.
*The Disciple and Other Poems.* London, Strahan, 1867.
*Dramatic and Miscellaneous Poems.* New York, Scribner, 2 vols., 1876.
*A Book of Strife, in the Form of the Diary of an Old Soul.* Privately printed, 1880.
*A Threefold Cord: Poems by Three Friends,* with John Hill MacDonald and Greville Matheson, edited by George MacDonald. Privately printed, 1883.
*The Poetical Works of George MacDonald.* London, Chatto and Windus, 2 vols., 1893.
*Rampolli: Growths from a Long-Planted Root, Being Translations Chiefly from the German, Along with a "Year's Diary of an Old Soul."* London, Longman, 1897.

Other

*Unspoken Sermons*. London, Strahan and Longman, 3 vols., 1867, 1886, 1889; New York, Routledge, n.d.
*England's Antiphon*. London, Macmillan, 1868; Philadelphia, Lippincott, n.d.
*The Miracles of Our Lord*. London, Strahan, and New York, Randolph, 1870.
*Works of Fancy and Imagination*. London, Strahan, 10 vols., 1871.
*Orts*. London, Sampson Low, 1882; as *The Imagination and Other Essays*, Boston, Lothrop, 1883; revised edition, as *A Dish of Orts*. Sampson Low, 1893.
*The Tragedie of Hamlet, Prince of Denmark: A Study of the Text of the Folio of 1623*. London, Longman, 1885.
*The Hope of the Gospel* (sermons). London, Ward Lock, and New York, Appleton, 1892.
*The Hope of the Universe*. London, Victoria Street Society for the Protection of Animals from Vivisection, 1896.
*George MacDonald: An Anthology*, edited by C.S. Lewis. London, Bles, 1946; New York, Macmillan, 1947.

Editor, *A Cabinet of Gems, Cut and Polished by Sir Philip Sidney, Now for the More Radiance Presented Without Their Setting*. London, Elliot Stock, 1892.

Translator, *Twelve of the Spiritual Songs of Novalis*. Privately printed, 1851.
Translator, *Exotics: A Translation of the Spiritual Songs of Novalis, The Hymn Book of Luther, and Other Poems from the German and Italian*. London, Strahan, 1876.

*

Bibliography: *A Centennial Bibliography of George MacDonald* by John Malcolm Bullock, Aberdeen, University Press, 1925; *George MacDonald's Books for Children: A Bibliography of First Editions* by Raphael B. Shaberman, London, Cityprint Business Centres, 1979.

Critical Studies: *George MacDonald and His Wife* by Greville MacDonald, London, Allen and Unwin, 1924; *The Golden Key: A Study of the Fiction of George MacDonald* by R.L. Wolfe, New Haven, Connecticut, Yale University Press, 1961; *The Harmony Within: The Spiritual Vision of George MacDonald* by Rolland Hein, Grand Rapids, Michigan, Christian University Press; *George MacDonald* by David S. Robb, Edinburgh, Scottish Academy, 1987, Eureka, California, Sunrise, 1989; *George MacDonald* by William Raeper, Tring, Hertshire, and Batavia, Illinois, Lion, 1987; *The Gold Thread: Essays on George MacDonald* edited by William Raeper, Edinburgh, Edinburgh University Press, 1990.

* * *

If Jules Verne is the father of "hard" science fiction, then George MacDonald could well be claimed as the father of the kind of science fiction that spills over into the borders of fantasy and whimsy, and of other worlds whose significance lies in the ideas they present rather than their devotion to science. George MacDonald is perhaps best known as a classic children's writer of the 19th century. He is a profoundly Christian writer, although his idea of Christianity was far broader than many others of his time, and he was strongly influenced by Plato's theory of ideal reality. MacDonald's children's books stand between the anarchic, amoral, dream-logic of Lewis Carroll's *Alice* books and the preaching, allegorical fairytale fantasy of Charles Kingsley's *Water-Babies*. But even his children's stories contain elements of science fiction. For example, within the once-upon-a-time setting of *The Princess and the Goblin*, and its consoling image of the mystical, angel-like great-great-grandmother spinning thread from spiderwebs in the light of a moon-lamp, there are the goblins. These goblins are underground miners, who once lived above ground but, refusing to pay the king's taxes, they hid below ground and greatly altered over the generations. They now prey mischievously upon ordinary humans.

In *The Princess and Curdie*, the angelic grandmother asks Curdie, "Have you ever heard what some philosophers say—that men were all animals once?" And she goes on to talk of the bestial decline of some people, anticipating Freud's analysis of Wolfman and Ratman. In fact, MacDonald's strange fairy story "The Day Boy and the Night Girl" begins with a witch who "had a wolf in her mind." In *At the Back of the North Wind*, Diamond, the cabman's simple-minded son, finds great significance in the dream-journeys he takes with the goddess-like North Wind. MacDonald knew that dreams cannot be made sensible by taking them at face value, but their secret meaning reflected the health of the inner person. MacDonald's Wise Woman, in the book *The Wise Woman*, is effectively a child psychiatrist with penetrating insight into the personality of young children, and a sound approach to parenting, the shaping and correcting character. Of course, her underlying therapeutic principles are based on Christian morality, as is much of MacDonald's narrative. But this is not surprising.

MacDonald initially studied natural philosophy (what we now call science) and chemistry, then trained and worked as a church minister. Most of his writing makes little direct use of this early scientific background. But in his last, and perhaps greatest, book, *Lilith* (published when he was 71), he describes a mirror that leads into a magic other-world. After several adventures through the mirror, the young hero, named allegorically, Mr. Vane, recently graduated in science from Oxford, tries to explain the effect of the mirror as depending on "polarization" of reflected light. A minor detail, not intended to make the fantasy more plausible, but indicating the borderline on which MacDonald works. This is as hard as MacDonald's science fiction ever gets, apart from some passing talk in *Lilith* about separate three-dimensional worlds occupying the same space within a multi-dimensioned universe.

MacDonald's first fantasy novel was *Phantastes: A Faerie Romance*. It was written some years after his sermons had been judged lacking in doctrinal content and he had resigned from the ministry, although he continued as a freelance preacher and lecturer as well as supporting himself with his writing. He had already been married for eight years. Like *Lilith*, it is a book about a young man growing up.

The young hero of *Phantastes*, called Anodos (surely a variant on Adonis), has just turned 21, and come into his inheritance, both parents having died when he was very young. Investigating his father's old desk he discovers a secret compartment, and suddenly a fairy (or goddess—although she claims to be his grandmother) appears and promises he will find the fairy land for which he longs. Anodos is a very high-minded young man, hoping to do something great in the world, full of confidence. The adventures that follow lead to a necessary humbling and redemption. Anodos encounters good people, flower-fairies, giants, good and wicked tree people, knights in armour, ogres, a mysterious fairy palace and the palace library filled with marvellous books (one tells a story about Cosmo of Prague—a narrative that mirrors Anodos's predicament), goblins, and several ideals of womanhood and motherhood in magic guise. (Many of MacDonald's books include spiritual and physical attraction for women, and women as very significant characters.) There are near-seductions, nightmares, attempted murder, heroic self-sacrifice, death, and resurrection. Such a narrative sketch seems very old-fashioned, but it resembles other classic allegorical adventures.

Characters in earlier works are concerned with the pursuit of holiness, idealising of women, and personal salvation, but Anodos is simply learning how to live. *Phantastes* is a faerie-allegory about the existential task of becoming an authentic human. At the end, Anodos wakes in his own land, returns home, hoping to live better as a result of what he learned in Fairy-land.

*Lilith* is also an exploration of existential ideas, within a fantasy world. The fantasy allows MacDonald to explore extreme situations, and offer narrative examples of metaphysical arguments. Caught out of doors on a desolate heath of the mirror-world as a terrible winter night approaches, Mr. Vane thinks, "Then first I knew what an awful thing it was to be awake in the universe: I *was*, and could not help it." Shortly after this, he meets a group of children who live without adults.

Young Mr. Vane stumbles into another mirror-world (where his father and other ancestors had also gone) following the mysterious ghost of a librarian. His explorations and adventures there symbolise his inner growth, both spiritually and humanistically as he is about to enter the real world at the end of his formal education. They also symbolise MacDonald's ideas of the afterworld, the value of human life and the nature of love. Vane encounters monsters, a witch-princess, a kind of were-leopard, living skeletons, a vampire, a demon Shadow, and the father and mother of all humans. There, he falls in love with the daughter of this first father and his inhuman first wife. He discovers that when humans die, they pass through different kinds of purgatory, including a "death-sleep," before they can wake into the world of resurrection. The vision of two skeletons knocking each other around as they struggle to come to terms with their lost life and their very physical death is quite chilling.

MacDonald wrote many other books, including realistic novels, light romances, historical novels, ghost stories, semi-autobiographies, poetry, and sermons, although almost all have long been out of print. His classic status as a 19th-century children's writer does not mean that he is much read now by children. Certainly, *The Princess and the Goblin* remains a satisfying adventure for young readers, in an old-fashioned, fairy tale way, and *The Light Princess* is delightfully whimsical. Like the curse on Sleeping Beauty, the Light Princess has been deprived of any sense of gravity—literally and emotionally—only the right kind of love can bring her down to earth.

Some of MacDonald's other fairy stories, such as *The Golden Key*, will continue to be read by anyone, child or adult, who enjoys powerful fairy tales that border on dreams and surrealism, telling a strange kind of truth. But only adults could withstand the brutal end of *The Princess and Curdie*. Similarly, *At the Back of the North Wind* presents such a harrowing metaphysical examination of the nature of natural disaster, suffering, and illness, that it is hard going even for adults, and the ideally good little boy who dreams and dies is a Victorian angel-child too cloying for post-Victorian tastes. Most modern readers will read it, not for the sake of the story, but for interest in MacDonald himself or in seeing a particular way of using fantasy and Christian belief in writing.

As for the adult fantasies, it is unlikely that they would be remembered at all, so much have tastes changed and so strange is MacDonald's use of Christian ideas in his work, if it were not for two factors. He has been championed by C.S. Lewis, who read *Phantastes* as a young man, and came to regard MacDonald as a kind of mentor. Lewis considered MacDonald to be a genius in the creation of modern mythology, ranking him with such modern writers as Kafka. Many people who are interested in Lewis, for whatever reason, have also become interested in MacDonald. The other factor is the great interest in fantasy writing that developed after the success of Tolkien's *The Lord of the Rings.* This has led to the revival of many nearly forgotten writers, and reprinting (by enthusiastic editors such as Lin Carter) of books that are regarded as milestones in the development of fantasy and science fiction. Amongst these, MacDonald's adult fantasies, such as *Lilith* and *Phantastes*, stand out as some of the strangest and most powerful.

—John Gough

---

**MacDONALD, John D(ann).** American. Born in Sharon, Pennsylvania, 24 July 1916. Educated at the University of Pennsylvania, Philadelphia, 1934–35; Syracuse University, New York, B.S. 1938; Harvard University, Cambridge, Massachusetts, M.B.A. 1939. Served with the United States Army, Office of Strategic Services, 1940–46: Lieutenant Colonel. Married Dorothy Mary Prentiss in 1937; one son. Writer in several genres and under a number of pseudonyms for the pulps and other magazines. President, Mystery Writers of America, 1962. Recipient: Benjamin Franklin award, for short story, 1955; Grand Prix de Littérature Policière, 1964; Mystery Writers of America Grand Master award, 1972; American Book award, 1980. D.H.L.: Hobart and William Smith Colleges, Geneva, New York, 1978; University of South Florida, Tampa, 1980. *Died 28 December 1986.*

SCIENCE-FICTION PUBLICATIONS

Novels

*Wine of the Dreamers.* New York, Greenberg, 1951; as *Planet of the Dreamers*, New York, Pocket Books, 1953; London, Hale, 1955.
*Ballroom of the Skies.* New York, Greenberg, 1952.
*The Girl, The Gold Watch, and Everything.* New York, Fawcett, 1962; London, Coronet, 1968.

Short Stories

*Other Times, Other Worlds.* New York, Fawcett, 1978.

OTHER PUBLICATIONS

Novels

*The Brass Cupcake.* New York, Fawcett, 1950; London, Muller, 1955.
*Judge Me Not.* New York, Fawcett, 1951; London, Muller, 1964.
*Murder for the Bride.* New York, Fawcett, 1951; London, Fawcett, 1954.
*Weep for Me.* New York, Fawcett, 1951; London, Muller, 1964.
*The Damned.* New York, Fawcett, 1952; London, Muller, 1964.
*Dead Low Tide.* New York, Fawcett, 1953; London, Fawcett, 1955.
*The Neon Jungle.* New York, Fawcett, 1953; London, Fawcett, 1954.

*Cancel All Our Vows.* New York, Appleton Century Crofts, 1953; London, Hale, 1955.
*Contrary Pleasure.* New York, Appleton Century Crofts, 1954; London, Hale, 1955.
*All These Condemned.* New York, Fawcett, 1954.
*Area of Suspicion.* New York, Dell, 1954; London, Hale, 1956; revised edition, New York, Fawcett, 1961.
*A Bullet for Cinderella.* New York, Dell, 1955; London, Hale, 1960; as *On the Make*, New York, Dell, 1960.
*Cry Hard, Cry Fast.* New York, Popular Library, 1955; London, Hale, 1969.
*April Evil.* New York, Dell, 1956; London, Hale, 1957.
*Border Town Girl* (novelets). New York, Popular Library, 1956; as *Five Star Fugitive*, London, Hale, 1970.
*Murder in the Wind.* New York, Dell, 1956; as *Hurricane*, London, Hale, 1957.
*You Live Once.* New York, Popular Library, 1956; London, Hale, 1976; as *You Kill Me*, New York, Fawcett, 1961.
*Death Trap.* New York, Dell, 1957; London, Hale, 1958.
*The Empty Trap.* New York, Popular Library, 1957; London, Magnum, 1980.
*The Price of Murder.* New York, Dell, 1957; London, Hale, 1958.
*A Man of Affairs.* New York, Dell, 1957; London, Hale, 1959.
*Clemmie.* New York, Fawcett, 1958.
*The Executioners.* New York, Simon and Schuster, 1958; London, Hale, 1959; as *Cape Fear*, New York, Fawcett, 1962.
*Soft Touch.* New York, Dell, 1958; London, Hale, 1960; as *Man-Trap*, London, Pan, 1961.
*The Deceivers.* New York, Fawcett, 1958; London, Hale, 1968.
*The Beach Girls.* New York, Fawcett, 1959; London, Muller, 1964.
*The Crossroads.* New York, Simon and Schuster, 1959; London, Hale, 1961.
*Deadly Welcome.* New York, Dell, 1959; London, Hale, 1961.
*Please Write for Details.* New York, Simon and Schuster, 1959.
*The End of the Night.* New York, Simon and Schuster, 1960; London, Hale, 1964.
*The Only Girl in the Game.* New York, Fawcett, 1960; London, Hale, 1962.
*Slam the Big Door.* New York, Fawcett, 1960; London, Hale, 1961.
*One Monday We Killed Them All.* New York, Fawcett, 1961; London, Hale, 1963.
*Where Is Janice Gantry?* New York, Fawcett, 1961; London, Hale, 1963.
*A Flash of Green.* New York, Simon and Schuster, 1962; London, Hale, 1971.
*A Key to the Suite.* New York, Fawcett, 1962; London, Hale, 1968.
*The Drowner.* New York, Fawcett, 1963; London, Hale, 1964.
*On the Run.* New York, Fawcett, 1963; London, Hale, 1965.
*I Could Go On Singing* (novelization of screenplay). New York, Fawcett, 1963; London, Hale, 1964.
*The Deep Blue Goodby.* New York, Fawcett, 1964; London, Hale, 1965.
*Nightmare in Pink.* New York, Fawcett, 1964; London, Hale, 1966.
*A Purple Place for Dying.* New York, Fawcett, 1964; London, Hale, 1966.
*The Quick Red Fox.* New York, Fawcett, 1964; London, Hale, 1966.
*A Deadly Shade of Gold.* New York, Fawcett, 1965; London, Hale, 1967.
*Bright Orange for the Shroud.* New York, Fawcett, 1965; London, Hale, 1967.
*Darker Than Amber.* New York, Fawcett, 1966; London, Hale, 1968.
*One Fearful Yellow Eye.* New York, Fawcett, 1966; London, Hale, 1968.
*The Last One Left.* New York, Doubleday, 1967; London, Hale, 1968.
*Three for McGee* (omnibus). New York, Doubleday, 1967.
*Pale Gray for Guilt.* New York, Fawcett, 1968; London, Hale, 1969.
*The Girl in the Plain Brown Wrapper.* New York, Fawcett, 1968; London, Hale, 1969.
*Dress Her in Indigo.* New York, Fawcett, 1969; London, Hale, 1971.
*The Long Lavender Look.* New York and London, Fawcett, 1970.
*A Tan and Sandy Silence.* New York, Fawcett, 1972; London, Hale, 1973.
*The Scarlet Ruse.* New York, Fawcett, 1973; London, Hale, 1975.
*The Turquoise Lament.* Philadelphia, Lippincott, 1973; London, Hale, 1975.
*McGee* (omnibus). London, Hale, 1975.
*The Dreadful Lemon Sky.* Philadelphia, Lippincott, 1975; London, Hale, 1976.
*Condominium.* Philadelphia, Lippincott, and London, Hale, 1977.
*The Empty Copper Sea.* Philadelphia, Lippincott, 1978; London, Hale, 1979.
*The Green Ripper.* Philadelphia, Lippincott, 1979; London, Hale, 1980.
*Free Fall in Crimson.* New York, Harper, and London, Collins, 1981.
*Cinnamon Skin.* New York, Harper, and London, Collins, 1982.
*One More Sunday.* New York, Knopf, and London, Hodder and Stoughton, 1984.
*The Best of Travis McGee.* London, Hale, 1985.
*The Lonely Silver Rain.* New York, Knopf, and London, Hodder and Stoughton, 1985.
*Barrier Island.* New York, Knopf, 1986; London, Hodder and Stoughton, 1987.

Short Stories

*End of the Tiger and Other Stories.* New York, Fawcett, 1966; London, Hale, 1967.
*Seven.* New York, Fawcett, 1971; London, Hale, 1974.
*The Good Old Stuff: 13 Early Stories*, edited by Martin H. Greenberg and others. New York, Harper, 1982; London, Collins, 1984.
*More Good Old Stuff.* New York, Knopf, 1984.

Other

*The House Guests.* New York, Doubleday, 1965; London, Hale, 1966.
*No Deadly Drug.* New York, Doubleday, 1968.
*Nothing Can Go Wrong*, with John H. Kilpack. New York, Harper, 1981.
*A Friendship: The Letters of Dan Roawan and John D. MacDonald 1967–74.* New York, Knopf, 1986.
*Reading for Survival.* Washington, D.C., Library of Congress, 1987.

Editor, *The Lethal Sex*. New York, Dell, 1959; London, Collins, 1962.

*

Bibliography: *A Bibliography of the Published Works of John D. MacDonald* by Jean and Walter Shine, Gainesville, University of Florida Libraries, 1981.

Manuscript Collection: University of Florida Library, Gainesville.

Critical Study: *John D. MacDonald* by David Geherin, New York, Ungar, 1982.

* * *

John D. MacDonald's prolific output of thrillers has not, in the end, prevented the acknowledgment that he is one of America's best novelists. He contributed nearly 50 short stories, under various names, and two novels to the SF genre in the late 1940's and early 1950's before turning almost exclusively to crime fiction, except for three marginal entries, "The Legend of Joe Lee" (a ghost story), "The Annex" (speculative fiction), and *The Girl, The Gold Watch, and Everything* (comedy thriller with a gimmick, anticipated in the excellent 1950 story, "Half-Past Eternity," that freezes everyone in time, except the user).

The title of the collection of MacDonald's SF short stories, *Other Times, Other Worlds*, neatly indicates his major themes: time travel, aliens among us or manipulating us, juxtaposition of our culture with others. These stories often communicate a strong sense of the value of the honestly striving individual; however, a good many are horror stories in which this value is arbitrarily denied.

In "Game for Blondes," blondes from the future come fishing for a man, and in "Spectator Sport," the unsuspecting visitor from our times is condemned to the future, well-meaningly bound forever to a mechanical fantasy. In "Labor Supply," the best of humans are enslaved by gnomes, through their dreams; in "A Child Is Crying" the gift of seeing the future is a cause of horror to its possessor and those who wish to exploit it.

The two early SF novels deal with sanity and the incipient paranoia of their readers: Aliens really do take over our minds, they tell us, and for no good purpose. *Wine of the Dreamers* posits a planet on which the principal adult occupation is taking possession of humans, playing with us in the belief that we are only creatures of fancy. The irresponsible Dreamers, who have similar remote access to two other planets, all three of which were settled by their ancestors, have forgotten their ordained function, yet they need our help, as only one of their inbred, dwindling number sees. Although MacDonald grossly oversimplifies for the sake of a suspenseful narrative, particularly the closed environment of the Dreamers, this remains a good tightly plotted novel which still reads well. It ends optimistically and is satisfying on its own terms, but *Ballroom of the Skies* concludes uneasily and is a more disturbing novel, because most readers must be unable to share in its hero's feelings of quiet exultation in the last paragraphs, to the extent that they perceive him to have succeeded only in moving from a smaller to a greater paranoia. A scenario in which the ends justify the means will never satisfy all readers; here, the given conditions are remarkably distasteful. Earth is kept in a state of perpetual warfare, and peacemakers are killed to preserve Earth as a breeding ground for superhuman leaders, who will keep the galactic civilization from stagnating and maintain it in a state of readiness in case of a notional invasion from another galaxy. The hero is one of the world's leading peacemakers, a journalist whose investigation of the fantastic crimes that break up secret negotiations between the world's power blocks leads to his recruitment as an agent of the very powers he has dedicated his life to oppose. To keep the reader in sympathy with such a hero would be a fearsome challenge for any writer and, although MacDonald does his best to make him more admirably heroic (using the well-honoured trick of timely praise from a girlfriend, for instance) as he grows beyond the human norm, the attempt fails. In reality, MacDonald's hero, Dake Lorin, who is excellent in his lone wolf phase, would have recognized the speciousness of the conditions he is made, humbly, to accept. The novel is, nevertheless, a gripping narrative and, in the best tradition of such works, honestly presents the lonely dilemma of the superman who can find true friendship only with others of his kind.

Besides the titles already mentioned, "Ring Around the Redhead," "Shadow on the Sand," "The Miniature," "The Big Contest," "Susceptibility," "Common Denominator," and "Trojan Horse Laugh," should be listed as fine short stories by a writer who could clearly have been a major figure in the SF genre had he not found that crime paid better. It should be noted that MacDonald often used mystery fiction, for example, *A Flash of Green* and *Condominium*, to be prophetically critical of the suicidal tendencies of our society, being one of the popular fiction writers to be concerned early with threats to our ecology. Florida became his principal subject and land exploiters one of his main targets. Though he worked outside of the genre for most of his career, he influenced several writers within it. Harlan Ellison has testified in *Again, Dangerous Visions* (1972) that he is one of those *sui generis* writers from outside SF "who have influenced us most strongly these past two decades," in the kind and style of SF being written.

John D. MacDonald died only a few months after completing *Reading for Survival*, an essay written in the form of a dialogue between Travis McGee and his friend Meyer. It could almost be with MacDonald's science fiction because it tells the story of the human species, illustrating it with exemplary individuals, such as Mog the hunter, who lived fifty thousand years ago, and Smith the modern scientist. Mog relies on his memory, Smith on memory augmented by reading: both know enough to avoid appropriate traps, but more ignorant or less well-read people would have fallen for the baits. Meyer in lecture-mode talks like a science fiction advocate:

"I would not demand that a man read ponderous tomes, or try to read everything—any more than I would expect our ancestor to examine every single leaf on a plant he remembers as being poisonous. I would expect that in his reading—which should be wide ranging, fiction, history, poetry, political science—he would acquire the equivalent of a liberal arts education and acquire also what I think of as the educated climate of mind, a climate characterized by skepticism, irony, doubt, hope, and a passion to learn more and remember more."

—Michael J. Tolley

---

**MacDOUGAL, John.** *See* **LOWNDES, Robert A.W.**

---

**MacDUFF, Andrew.** *See* **FYFE, H.B.**

---

**MacGREGOR, James Murdoch.** *See* **McINTOSH, J.T.**

---

**MACKELWORTH, R(onald) W(alter).** British. Born in London, 7 April 1930. Educated at Raynes Park Grammar School, London, 1940–48. Served in the British Army Intelligence Corps, 1948–50. Married Sheila Elizabeth Kilpatrick in 1956; one son and two daughters. Worked for Thomas Cook, travel agents, London, 1950; clerk, Norwich Union Insurance, London, 1950–53; inspector, Kingston, Surrey, 1953–66, superintendent, Leeds, 1966–72, manager, Portsmouth, 1972–77, product manager, 1977–84, and since 1984, strategic planning manager, London, Legal and General Insurance Society. Agent: Carnell Literary Agency, Danes Croft, Goose Lane, Little Hallingbury, Hertfordshire CM22 7RG, England.

SCIENCE-FICTION PUBLICATIONS

Novels

*Firemantle*. London, Hale, 1968; as *The Diabols*, New York, Paperback Library, 1969.
*Tiltangle*. New York, Ballantine, 1970; London, Hale, 1971.
*Starflight 3000*. New York, Ballantine, 1972; London, New English Library, 1976.
*The Year of the Painted World*. London, Hale, 1975.
*Shakehole*. London, Hale, 1981.

*

Manuscript Collection: North London Polytechnic.

R.W. Mackelworth comments:

I am a lifelong addict of SF, but I prefer well-written novels and those that make a satirical statement about contemporary life whether through fantasy or fact. However, I also believe the modern idiom of fast-moving adventure entertains and entertainment is what the writer owes the reader. My work is essentially non-professional; I like to work up my own ideas and enjoy my writing. The conventions of SF are few, and one of its joys is that its scope for the imagination is unlimited. SF is gaining readers because it is largely free of many of the set-piece situations demanded of mainstream writing. Its problem is lack of good characterisation. Characters are often overwhelmed by events: if we can put personality before event, SF writing could improve considerably. The standard of writing is also important. It is possible to write literate SF as well as exciting SF!

* * *

The influence of British science-fiction magazines of the 1950's is evident in R.W. Mackelworth's restrained style and use of stock adventure frameworks: his fiction, despite attempts to incorporate profound issues, rarely displays the self-awareness increasingly favoured among his contemporaries. His output has remained small, his foremost works being novels.

In *Firemantle* the hero is projected, apparently through time, to an Earth dominated by a deadly alien life form. Most of the book relates his exploits in this future world and his gradual understanding of its parameters (including his immunity to the aliens). Interwoven with the narrative are themes of revenge and manipulation, the exact details, methods, and motives remaining concealed until the end. The novel finally affirms the intrinsic survival potentiality of human will power, but also questions the cost involved.

*Tiltangle* is set on Earth during a new ice age, with survivors crowded into an isolated refuge. Once again personal manipulation and callous use of power are introduced, although the central concern is a quest for the uncertain myth of "the warm," the first retreat of snow and ice heralding the return of a habitable world. This is Mackelworth's most effective book: it contains some of his best-realised characters, while the depiction of ascetic life in a hostile environment is reinforced by uncharacteristically precise subsidiary detail. The implied background circumstances are less convincing, but this scarcely affects the driving obsession that is the novel's strength.

*Starflight 3000* is loosely based on the generation starship concept. A hollowed asteroid becomes a vast spacecraft; use of terraforming bacteria allows the colonisation of any planet. Secondary aspects include faster-than-light communication and mysterious alien science. But for all its reliance on such motifs, the novel is not typical of "hard" technological science fiction. It expresses moral concern over a selfish, expansionist mentality, and also gives some consideration to the conflict inherent in Mackelworth's two recurrent themes: the tendency of power to corrupt its wielder and the need for charismatic leadership to ensure progress. However, an abrupt time shift and the creation of a shipboard mythology ultimately avoid the questions raised.

*The Year of the Painted World* combines traditional elements of both disaster and invasion stories. Surprisingly excitable in tone, it tells of a struggle on present-day Earth against a Martian virus and its aggressive host organisms. The protagonist is an unambiguous man of action, doing what must be done. In his arrogant simplicity, he could almost be a caricature of a hero from science fiction's Golden Age. The threatening "Pods" also carry more than a hint of space monsters of old. Possible benefits once the virus is controlled (and the consequent suspicions and machinations surrounding its release) add little depth to a playfully derivative but basically flimsy novel.

Mackelworth is no artist, honing subtleties of vision, language, and motivation to fine edges: instead he relies on mystery and suspense to hold attention until the denouement. His characterisation is usually notional (his stereotyped women are singularly ill portrayed), although within its terms he is adept at drawing concise contrasts. A tendency to slip into careless assumptions and clichés is another result of his intense absorption in plotting. Nevertheless, it is the complexity of his plots which sets Mackelworth apart from routine adventure writers. His underlying themes can be especially thought-provoking, and it is unfortunate that he chooses to turn away from their fullest implications rather than develop their dramatic tension.

—Nick Pratt

---

**MacLEAN, Arthur.** *See* **TUBB, E.C.**

---

**MacLEAN, Katherine (Anne).** American. Born in Glen Ridge, New Jersey, 22 January 1925. Educated at Barnard College, New York, B.A. in economics 1950; Goddard College, Plainfield, Vermont, M.A. in psychology 1977. Married 1) Charles Dye in 1951 (divorced 1952); 2) David Mason in 1956 (divorced 1962), one son; 3) Carl West. Laboratory assistant, 1944–45, and food manufacturing technician, 1945–46; office manager, Hi-Pro Animal Feed, Frankfort, Delaware, 1952–53; technician, Memorial and Knickerbocker hospitals, New York, 1954–56. Member of the English Department, University of Connecticut, Storrs, 1962–65, and University of Maine, Orono, intermittently 1966–77. Freelance writer and lecturer. Recipient: Nebula award, 1971. Agent: Virginia Kidd, Box 278, Milford, Pennsylvania 18337. Address: P.O. Box 1563, Biddeford, Maine 04005, U.S.A.

SCIENCE-FICTION PUBLICATIONS

Novels

*Cosmic Checkmate*, with Charles V. De Vet. New York, Ace, 1962.
*The Man in the Bird Cage.* New York, Ace, 1971.
*Missing Man.* New York, Berkley, 1975.
*Dark Wing*, with Carl West. New York, Atheneum, 1979.

Short Stories

*The Diploids and Other Flights of Fancy.* New York, Avon, 1962.
*Trouble with Treaties.* Tacoma, Washington, Lanthorne Press, 1975.
*The Trouble with You Earth People.* Norfolk, Virginia, Donning, 1980.

*

Katherine MacLean comments:

I am interested in science fiction as an exploration of possibility—specifically the possibilities that are most astonishing, yet genuinely possible. It becomes worthwhile to write when I am more deeply surprised with each page of unfolding potential events.

* * *

Katherine MacLean is important for introducing in her fiction ethical questions about medical and scientific experimentation. She also writes about mental telepathy and human fears of evolutionary change.

*The Diploids and Other Flights of Fancy* includes eight works published between 1949 and 1953. The title story tells of genetic experiments that produced a strain of standardized human fetuses for research purposes. "The Pyramid in the Desert" has as its theme human fear of immortality. "Defense Mechanism" and "Games" are both about telepathy. "Feedback" deals with human fear of new ideas; "Pictures Don't Lie" deals with the anthropomorphic tendency to measure all species on a human scale. "The Snowball Effect" and "Incommunicado" are clever but less significant thematically than the others.

In *Cosmic Checkmate*, written with Charles V. De Vet, Robert Lang goes to the planet Velda to discover why its population refuses peaceful contact with the federation of Earth's colonies. In disguise, Lang plays the Veldian Game—based on chess—and beats all comers in the second game; he deliberately loses the first game to discover his opponent's weaknesses. The novel is well crafted: the plot works as an analogous game structure, with Lang winning the second game in a cosmic checkmate.

MacLean's essay "Communicado" provides the background for her works that deal thematically with telepathy and psi phenomena. She discusses the important influence Whately Carington's book *Thought Transference* (1946) had on her, and she elaborates the ideas behind stories like "Defense Mechanism," "Feedback," "The Fittest," "Games," "Where or When," and "Curtin in the Sky." Telepathy is also the moving idea behind *Missing Man.* Set in New York, in 1999, the novel features George Sanford, whose extraordinary telepathic abilities make him a valuable special consultant for the Rescue Squad of the Police Department. Sanford is the fear hound, sniffing out people who are in trouble by tuning in to the telepathic vibrations they broadcast. The missing man is Carl Hodges, a super-maintenance man for the city who uses computers to predict breakdowns and accidents before they occur. The novel is thematically complex and almost phantasmagorical at times.

Several of MacLean's stories have medical themes and use physicians as main characters. Among the best of these is "Contagion": colonists on another planet survive a plague only by becoming look-alikes, thus raising questions about the interrelationship between external appearance and personality. "The Origin of the Species" is told in epistolary form by a neurosurgeon who is troubled by his work: he destroys the best parts of people's minds so that they can adapt to life in society. "Gimmick" chronicles the use of a virus as a weapon; "The Other" presents a physician who, ironically, has the same problem as the patient he is trying to cure; and "Syndrome Johnny" shows the usefulness of plagues in speeding up evolution. *Dark Wing*, written with her husband Carl West, also has a medical theme. It presents a future where the practice of medicine is illegal and people believe that illness is immoral, an external sign of defects in their thinking. A teenage boy, Travis Gordon, discovers two old medical kits in an abandoned wrecked ambulance and begins to learn and practice medicine, even performing complicated surgery with no special equipment or assistance. The complex and unbelievable plot, the superficial criticism of medicine, and the youth of the protagonist combine to make the novel read like adolescent fiction.

—Anne Hudson Jones

---

**MacLEOD, Sheila.** Scottish. Born on the Isle of Lewis, 23 March 1939. Educated at Wycombe Abbey School, Buckinghamshire; Somerville College, Oxford, B.A. (honours) in English 1961. Married the actor Paul Jones in 1963 (divorced); one son. Recipient: Scottish Arts Council award, 1969, 1971; MIND award, for non-fiction, 1981. Agent: Giles Gordon, Anthony Sheil Associates, 43 Doughty Street, London WCIN 2LF. Address: 9 Appleby Road, London E8 3ET, England.

SCIENCE-FICTION PUBLICATIONS

Novels

*The Snow-White Soliloquies.* London, Secker and Warburg, and New York, Viking Press, 1970.
*Xanthe and the Robots.* London, Bodley Head, 1977.
*Circuit-Breaker.* London, Bodley Head, 1978.

OTHER PUBLICATIONS

Novels

*The Moving Accident.* London, Faber, 1968.
*Letters from the Portuguese.* London, Secker and Warburg, 1971.
*Axioms.* London, Quartet, 1984.

Plays

Television Plays: *They Put You Where You Are*, 1966; *God Speed Co-operation*, 1983.

Other

*The Art of Starvation: An Adolescent Observed.* London, Virago, 1981; as *The Art of Starvation: A Story of Anorexia and Survival*, New York, Schocken, 1982.
*Lawrence's Men and Women.* London, Heinemann, 1985; as *D.H. Lawrence's Men and Women*, New York, Harcourt, 1986.

* * *

A seasoned writer, Sheila MacLeod has published in a variety of genres, science fiction among them. Her earliest novels are experiments in surrealism—*The Snow-White Soliloquies* is perhaps the most outstanding. Here, MacLeod projects the old Germanic fairy tale into a strange, Orwellian present: a catatonic Snow-White, encased in a high-tech box of Glass That Breathes, is transported from place to nameless place in a dubious search for The Prince. Supervised by an authoritarian figure named Doc and attended by a succession of six social marginals, the paralyzed heroine embodies the principle of passivity. She sees, hears, contemplates, and suffers with those around her but is unable to act. Her silent soliloquies reveal that her knowledge of herself is curiously limited: she is a poisoned life, preserved by technological wizardry for purposes unknown. (The reader knows no more than she.) As the literally captive audience for the obsessive monologues and peculiar actions of her caretakers, Snow-White witnesses a series of increasingly bizarre events—until something gives (most notably, the glass box) and she is able to acknowledge the roles that all have played in this disturbing and dreamlike psychodrama. The "allegorical atmosphere" of *The Snow-White Soliloquies* has been somewhat evasively described by reviewers as "fascinating," "intriguing," and "rich with reflection about the human condition." More to the point is that the book is finally and successfully enigmatic. We cannot get beyond its carefully constructed surfaces, which tease us with refractions of our own expectations.

In the more conventionally rendered *Xanthe and the Robots,* MacLeod's first thorough-going science-fiction narrative, we meet another version of the catatonic woman, this time a brilliant robotics engineer who has invested the greater part of her emotional life in relationships with mechanical beings. Programmer Xanthe, numbed by psychotropic drugs since the death of her father, the founder of the Institute for Advanced Robotic Research, finds her torpor disturbed by two upsetting developments: a new relationship with an intense and attractive co-worker, and a dramatic change in Institute policy. The painful reawakening of Xanthe's psyche parallels a decision by Institute authorities to endow the most advanced robots with a more human sensibility. Xanthe and the robots learn, in different ways, to desire, and the process of wanting leads them, gradually but inexorably, to regret their passive institutional loyalty. Xanthe rebels—against her superior, against the Institute, ultimately against her father—and chooses a future unlike anything she has known in her regimented habitat. The robots also have their revolution, but their prospects look less potentially creative; given their origins, they can do little more than replicate the ugly hierarchies of their makers. In *Xanthe,* MacLeod articulates a familiar SF theme: our machines cannot save us from ourselves. The plot *per se* holds few surprises, but Xanthe's oddly deadpan narrative persona, at once touching and repellent, sustains our interest.

With *Circuit-Breaker,* MacLeod moves back into the unsettling ambiguity that is her strength. Ostensibly, the story is about a British astronaut, Alexander Baird, who must exercise unusual "autokinetic" powers to restore his marooned spacecraft to its intended orbit. According to Lvov, the sinister mission controller, Baird may generate sufficient power to rein in the straying capsule if he can forge telepathic linkages with the women nearest the hearts of himself and his fellow travellers, Davitt and Haskins. Baird contacts earth, and his strange encounters with his alienated spouse, Davitt's eccentric mom, and Haskins's anxious and vulnerable wife generate troubling questions for the reader. Is Baird in fact an astronaut? Or is he a science-fiction writer who has come to believe his own fantasies? Is Lvov a dictatorial aerospace bureaucrat? Or an especially nasty headshrinker? In this tacky little universe of failed connections, how are we to distinguish between outer and inner space? MacLeod's controlled opacity is compelling—we are drawn to the world of her problematic protagonist as to a black hole. Like *The Snow-White Soliloquies, Circuit-Breaker* is dense, sophisticated. Though more accessible than the earlier book, it exacts an equally attentive reading.

Sheila MacLeod's best novels are cerebral and defy easy categorization. Casual readers will find themselves impatient with the author's staging, with structures and settings that at first seem too elaborate for what they support and surround. But MacLeod's formal choices are consistent with her choice of subject. Her focus is invariably on neurosis, on the disturbances that prevent people (and cultures) from achieving a peaceful equilibrium, and the trappings of fairy tales and science fiction serve as formal correlatives that keep readers, too, slightly off balance. We stumble along, like MacLeod's characters, bearing the graceless freight of unmet expectations. For most of us, the burden proves worthwhile.

—Janis Butler Holm

---

**MADDOX, Carl.** *See* **TUBB, E.C.**

---

**MAINE, Charles Eric.** Pseudonym for David McIlwain; also writes as Richard Rayner and Robert Wade. British. Born in Liverpool, Lancashire, 21 January 1921. Educated at Holt High School, Liverpool. Served in the Royal Air Force during World War II: Flight Lieutenant. Married and divorced twice; two sons and three daughters. Journalist in London, 1946–71, including 14 years as editor and managing editor of industrial weekly newspapers and journals; regular correspondent for *The Times, Financial Times,* and *Guardian*, London, and *Les Echos*, Paris. Agent: David Higham Associates Ltd., 5–8 Lower John

Street, London W1R 4HA, England; or, Scott Meredith Literary Agency, 845 Third Avenue, New York, New York 10022, U.S.A.

SCIENCE-FICTION PUBLICATIONS

Novels (series: Mike Delaney)

*Spaceways.* London, Hodder and Stoughton, 1953; as *Spaceways Satellite*, New York, Avalon, 1958.
*Timeliner.* London, Hodder and Stoughton, and New York, Rinehart, 1955.
*Crisis 2000.* London, Hodder and Stoughton, 1956.
*Escapement.* London, Hodder and Stoughton, 1956; as *The Man Who Couldn't Sleep*, Philadelphia, Lippincott, 1958.
*High Vacuum.* London, Hodder and Stoughton, and New York, Ballantine, 1957.
*The Isotope Man* (Delaney). London, Hodder and Stoughton, and Philadelphia, Lippincott, 1957.
*World Without Men.* New York, Ace, 1958; London, Digit, 1963; revised edition, as *Alph*, New York, Doubleday, 1972.
*The Tide Went Out.* London, Hodder and Stoughton, 1958; New York, Ballantine, 1959; revised edition, as *Thirst!*, London, Sphere, 1977; New York, Ace, 1978.
*Count-Down.* London, Hodder and Stoughton, 1959; as *Fire Past the Future*, New York, Ballantine, 1960.
*Subterfuge* (Delaney). London, Hodder and Stoughton, 1959.
*Calculated Risk.* London, Hodder and Stoughton, 1960.
*He Owned the World.* New York, Avalon, 1960; as *The Man Who Owned the World*, London, Hodder and Stoughton, 1961.
*The Mind of Mr. Soames.* London, Hodder and Stoughton, 1961.
*The Darkest of Nights.* London, Hodder and Stoughton, 1962; as *Survival Margin*, New York, Fawcett, 1968; revised edition, as *The Big Death*, London, Sphere, 1978.
*Never Let Up* (Delaney). London, Hodder and Stoughton, 1964.
*B.E.A.S.T.: Biological Evolutionary Animal Simulation Test.* London, Hodder and Stoughton, 1966; New York, Ballantine, 1967.
*The Random Factor.* London, Hodder and Stoughton, 1971.

OTHER PUBLICATIONS

Novels as Richard Rayner

*The Trouble with Ruth.* London, Hale, 1960.
*Darling Daughter.* London, Hale, 1961.
*Dig Deep for Julie.* London, Hale, 1963.
*Stand-In for Danger.* London, Hale, 1963.

Novels as Robert Wade

*The Wonderful One.* London, Hodder and Stoughton, 1960.
*The Stroke of Seven.* New York, Morrow, 1965; London, Heinemann, 1967.
*Knave of Eagles.* New York, Random House, 1969; London, Hale, 1970.

Plays

Screenplay: *Escapement (The Electric Monster)*, with J. McLaren Ross, 1958.

Radio Plays: *Spaceways*, 1952; *The Einstein Way*, 1954.

Television Play: *Timeslip.*

Other

*The World's Strangest Crimes.* New York, Hart, and London, Odhams Press, 1967; as *The Bizarre and Bloody*, Hart, 1972.
*World-Famous Mistresses.* London, Odhams Press, 1970.

*

Charles Eric Maine comments:

Like Arthur C. Clarke, John Christopher, Eric Frank Russell, Jonathan Burke, the late John Wyndham, and other science-fiction author friends, I became an SF addict in my early teens. This was the era of the late 1930's when nobody, apart from a few SF writers and addicts, and fewer scientists, believed that man would ever set foot on the moon in this century, if at all. In my own science fiction, I have always tried to find a theme or situation which no other author has thought of. Although I have written some space opera (such as *Timeliner* and *He Owned the World*), most of my SF books are short-term projections from present-day fact and technology, looking, perhaps, some 10 to 50 years ahead. I am particularly interested in the social and psychological impact of advancing science on crude Homo sapiens. In this respect my two best novels are *The Tide Went Out* and *The Mind of Mr. Soames* (the movie version missed the essential point of the story—the difference between training and education).

* * *

Charles Eric Maine's writing is distinguished primarily by its original and imaginative concepts. This is not to demean his writing skills but rather to indicate that when viewed as a body his stories vary considerably in quality. Too often he falls back on clichés to move his stories along, and occasionally the clash between banal plots and sophisticated scientific ideas is resounding. Maine's treatment of time displacement in *The Isotope Man*, for example, is fascinating, but it is embedded in a plot that would do justice to the old pulps. The plot, to sabotage the artificial production of tungsten, is embellished by stereotyped characters: an ex-Nazi plastic surgeon, an evil South American business tycoon, a feisty and irascible city editor, a beautiful, sharp-tongued girl photographer, and a hard-drinking, two-fisted reporter who plays his hunches to the detriment of his job.

Despite this occasional failure to mesh plots, characters, and themes, however, Maine at his best is quite effective. *Alph*, *B.E.A.S.T.*, *Timeliner*, and *The Tide Went Out* are excellent novels. He seems particularly good at creating memorable female characters. Among them are Synove Rayner (*B.E.A.S.T.*), a brilliant and beautiful exhibitionist nymphomaniac; Koralin (*Alph*), a courageous cytologist who kidnaps and protects the first male baby born into the lesbian society in five hundred years; and Shirley Sye (*The Tide Went Out*), a pathetic and aging model turned fashion editor who instructs the hero on the nature of man when faced with survival.

Survival is one of Maine's recurring themes. Sometimes he treats it directly, as in *The Tide Went Out* and *The Darkest of Nights*, both post-disaster novels. In *The Tide Went Out*, repeated hydrogen bomb tests produce a fracture in the ocean floor through which pours nearly all of the world's water supply; in *The Darkest of Nights*, a lethal epidemic destroys society. *B.E.A.S.T.* projects the ultimate result of an animal evolved with survival of the fittest as the only standard: a brilliant but mentally unstable scientist, Charles Gilley, creates animals and an environment for them in a computer, then evolves them through millions of generations while making conditions harsher and harsher. Finally, all but one species disappears, and then all but one animal. It is the ultimate survivor but it has lost all humanistic qualities. *Alph* presents yet another variation on the nature of survival in its exploration of the long-range effects of a society without men. Lesbianism, of course, becomes the acceptable form of sexual expression, but it results in a patterned societal neurosis. An emphasis on superior eugenic standards causes an overthrow of the government because of the elitist attitudes it creates. Even in *Timeliner*, whose primary purpose is to explore time travel, Hugh Macklin, the hero, eventually raises the question of whose right it is to decide who should survive and what standards they should use. Inevitably, Maine proposes, man will do whatever is required in order to survive.

Another prevalent Maine theme is time displacement, which receives its fullest treatment in *Timeliner*. In it, he offers the unique prospect that man's "psycho-identity" but not his body can travel forward in time. Attracted by emotional affinities, the "psycho-identity" possesses other persons' bodies to achieve consciousness. Though it creates a kind of immortality for the traveler, it destroys the possessed's ego. One future society that Macklin encounters labels such time travelers "psycho-temporal parasites" and considers the possession a form of murder.

One of the more interesting aspects of Maine's writing is its projection of possible futures. Though *Alph, Timeliner*, and *He Owned the World*, for example, paint different pictures, they do contain some consistencies. Maine predicts that the historical pattern of man's genius being channeled into aggression and war will continue indefinitely. He also believes that romantic love will die out. In *He Owned the World*, it is defined as "an obsessive form of compulsive neurosis," and one of the characters that Macklin encounters in *Timeliner* tells him that man is naturally polygamous. Finally, many of Maine's future societies are totalitarian and man continues to battle his oppressors.

Maine is a journeyman writer who has created some excellent novels, but even if he were far less skilled, his ideas alone would make reading his works worth the effort.

—Carl B. Yoke

---

**MAJORS, Simon.** *See* **FOX, Gardner F.**

---

**MALZBERG, Barry N(athaniel).** Also writes as Mike Barry; Claudine Dumas; Mel Johnson; Lee W. Mason; Francine de Natale; K.M. O'Donnell; Gerrold Watkins; John Barry Williams. American. Born in New York City, 24 July 1939. Educated at Syracuse University, New York (Schubert Fellow, 1964–65), A.B. 1960. Married Joyce Nadine Zelnick in 1964; two daughters. Investigator, New York City Department of Welfare, and reimbursement agent, New York State Department of Mental Hygiene; editor, Scott Meredith Literary Agency, New York; editor, *Amazing* and *Fantastic*, 1968; managing editor, *Escapade*, 1968. Freelance writer: author of many novels under various pseudonyms for Midwood, Oracle, Soft Cover Library, and Traveler's Companion Series. Recipient: Campbell Memorial award, 1973; *Locus* award, 1983. Address: Box 61, Teaneck, New Jersey 07666, U.S.A.

SCIENCE-FICTION PUBLICATIONS

Novels

*Oracle of the Thousand Hands*. New York, Olympia Press, 1968.
*The Falling Astronauts*. New York, Ace, 1971; London, Arrow, 1975.
*Overlay*. New York, Lancer, 1972; London, New English Library, 1975.
*Beyond Apollo*. New York, Random House, 1972; London, Faber, 1974.
*Revelations*. New York, Warner, 1972.
*The Men Inside*. New York, Lancer, 1973; London, Arrow, 1976.
*Phase IV*. New York, Pocket Books, and London, Pan, 1973.
*In the Enclosure*. New York, Avon, 1973; London, Hale, 1976.
*Herovit's World*. New York, Random House, 1973; London, Arrow, 1976.
*Guernica Night*. Indianapolis, Bobbs Merrill, 1974; London, New English Library, 1978.
*On a Planet Alien*. New York, Pocket Books, 1974.
*The Day of the Burning*. New York, Ace, 1974.
*Tactics of Conquest*. New York, Pyramid, 1974.
*The Sodom and Gomorrah Business*. New York, Pocket Books, 1974; London, Arrow, 1979.
*Underlay*. New York, Avon, 1974.
*The Destruction of the Temple*. New York, Pocket Books, 1974; London, New English Library, 1975.
*The Gamesman*. New York, Pocket Books, 1975.
*Conversations*. Indianapolis, Bobbs Merrill, 1975.
*Galaxies*. New York, Pyramid, 1975.
*Scop*. New York, Pyramid, 1976.
*The Last Transaction*. Los Angeles, Pinnacle, 1977.
*Chorale*. New York, Doubleday, 1978.
*The Cross of Fire*. New York, Ace, 1982.
*The Remaking of Sigmund Freud*. New York, Ballantine, 1985.

Novels as K.M. O'Donnell

*The Empty People*. New York, Lancer, 1969.
*Dwellers of the Deep*. New York, Ace, 1970.
*Universe Day*. New York, Avon, 1971.
*Gather in the Hall of the Planets*. New York, Ace, 1971.

Short Stories

*Final War and Other Fantasies* (as K.M. O'Donnell). New York, Ace, 1969.
*In the Pocket and Other S-F Stories*. New York, Ace, 1971.
*Out from Ganymede*. New York, Warner, 1974.
*The Many Worlds of Barry Malzberg*. New York, Popular Library, 1975.
*Down Here in the Dream Quarter*. New York, Doubleday, 1976.
*The Best of Barry N. Malzberg*. New York, Pocket Books, 1976.
*Malzberg at Large*. New York, Ace, 1979.
*The Man Who Loved the Midnight Lady*. New York, Doubleday, 1980.

OTHER PUBLICATIONS

Novels

*I, Lesbian* (as M.L. Johnson). New York, Midwood, 1968.
*Screen*. New York, Olympia Press, 1968; London, Olympia Press, 1972.
*The Circle* (as Francine de Natale). New York, Traveller's Companion, 1969.
*Diary of a Parisian Chambermaid* (as Claudine Dumas). New York, Midwood, 1969.
*In My Parents' Bedroom*. New York, Olympia Press, 1971.
*Confessions of Westchester County*. New York, Olympia Press, 1971; London, Olympia Press, 1972.
*The Spread*. New York, Belmont, 1971.
*Horizontal Woman*. New York, Leisure, 1972; as *The Social Worker*, 1977.
*The Masochist*. New York, Belmont, 1972; as *Everything Happened to Susan*, 1978.
*The Way of the Tiger, The Sign of the Dragon* (as Howard Lee). New York, Warner, 1973.
*The Running of Beasts*, with Bill Pronzini. New York, Putnam, 1976.
*Lady of a Thousand Sorrows* (as Lee W. Mason). Chicago, Playboy Press, 1977.
*Acts of Mercy*, with Bill Pronzini. New York, Putnam, 1977.
*Night Screams*, with Bill Pronzini. Chicago, Playboy Press, 1979.
*Prose Bowl*, with Bill Pronzini. New York, St. Martin's Press, 1980.

Novels as Mel Johnson

*Love Doll*. New York, Soft Cover Library, 1967.
*Chained*. New York, Midwood, 1968.
*Instant Sex*. New York, Midwood, 1968.
*Just Ask*. New York, Midwood, 1968.
*Kiss and Run*. New York, Midwood, 1968.
*Nympho Nurse*. New York, Midwood, 1969.
*The Sadist*. New York, Midwood, 1969.
*Do It to Me*. New York, Midwood, 1969.
*Born to Give*. New York, Midwood, 1969.
*Campus Doll*. New York, Midwood, 1969.
*The Box*. New York, Oracle, 1969.
*A Way with All Maidens*. New York, Oracle, 1969.

Novels as Gerrold Watkins

*Southern Comfort*. New York, Traveller's Companion, 1969.
*A Satyr's Romance*. New York, Traveller's Companion, 1970.
*Giving It Away*. New York, Traveller's Companion, 1970.
*The Art of the Fugue*. New York, Traveller's Companion, 1970.
*A Bed of Money*. New York, Traveller's Companion, 1970.

Novels as Mike Barry

*Night Raider*. New York, Berkley, 1973.
*Bay Prowler*. New York, Berkley, 1973.
*Boston Avenger*. New York, Berkley, 1973.
*Desert Stalker*. New York, Berkley, 1974.
*Havana Hit*. New York, Berkley, 1974.
*Chicago Slaughter*. New York, Berkley, 1974.
*Peruvian Nightmare*. New York, Berkley, 1974.
*Los Angeles Holocaust*. New York, Berkley, 1974.
*Miami Marauder*. New York, Berkley, 1974.
*Harlem Showdown*. New York, Berkley, 1975.
*Detroit Massacre*. New York, Berkley, 1975.
*Phoenix Inferno*. New York, Berkley, 1975.
*The Killing Run*. New York, Berkley, 1975.
*Philadelphia Blowup*. New York, Berkley, 1975.

Other

*The Engines of the Night: Science Fiction in the Eighties*. New York, Doubleday, 1982.

Editor, with Edward L. Ferman, *Final Stage*. New York, Charterhouse, 1974; London, Penguin, 1975.
Editor, with Edward L. Ferman, *Arena: Sports SF*. New York, Doubleday, and London, Robson, 1976.
Editor, with Edward L. Ferman, *Graven Images*. Nashville, Nelson, 1977.
Editor, with Bill Pronzini, *Dark Sins, Dark Dreams: Crimes in SF*. New York, Doubleday, 1977.
Editor, with Bill Pronzini, *The End of Summer: Science Fiction in the Fifties*. New York, Ace, 1979.
Editor, with Bill Pronzini, *Shared Tomorrows: Collaboration in SF*. New York, St. Martin's Press, 1979.
Editor, with Martin H. Greenberg and Joseph D. Olander, *Neglected Visions*. New York, Doubleday, 1980.
Editor, with Martin H. Greenberg, *The Science Fiction of Mark Clifton*. Carbondale, Southern Illinois University Press, 1980.
Editor, with Bill Pronzini, *Bug-Eyed Monsters*. New York, Harcourt Brace, 1980.
Editor, with Bill Pronzini and Martin H. Greenberg, *The Arbor House Treasury of Horror and the Supernatural [Mystery and Suspense]*. New York, Arbor House, 2 vols., 1981; as *Great Tales of Horror and the Supernatural [Mystery and Suspense]*, New York, Galahad, 1985.
Editor, with Martin H. Greenberg, *The Science Fiction of Kris Neville*. Carbondale, Southern Illinois University Press, 1984.
Editor, with Bill Pronzini and Martin H. Greenberg, *Mystery in the Mainstream*. New York, Morrow, 1986; as *Crime and Crime Again*, New York, Bonanza, 1990.
Editor, with Piers Anthony, Martin H. Greenberg, and Charles G. Waugh, *Uncollected Stars*. New York, Avon, 1986.

* * *

If what Barry N. Malzberg has called, in a typical turn of phrase, "the true and terrible complete history of science fiction" is ever written, Malzberg will occupy a unique niche within its carefully categorized confines, not least because his personal view of the field, *The Engines of the Night*, will have to be dealt with, somehow. Often vilified by authors and reviewers for attacking the very foundations of the genre as they perceive it, he also has been praised, by such writers and critics as Harlan Ellison, Joanna Russ, and Brian Stableford, for attempting to do something new and artistic within the expanding universe of genre conventions.

Malzberg's problem, and the reason perhaps that he quit the genre in 1975 after seven years of highly prolific creation (though he has continued to write *some* short stories and essays), is not that he was unable to use conventional SF props as powerful tropes by which to explore individuals' psychological anxiety, their feelings of alienation and inadequacy when they confront the machineries of technological change and bureaucratic stasis. In fact, in his best work he has polished to a high gloss the mirrored surfaces of many basic SF conventions so that their apparently *inherent* optimism reveals in reflection only its diabolic opposite. But because he did this so well he tended to alienate precisely the audience which his SF writings were meant to attract. But there has always been a place for apocalyptic visions in SF. The problem isn't that Malzberg wasn't read, but that so many of his readers could only turn away from his writings in disgust, saying he had betrayed them because he offered no hope in his stories, or making similar complaints.

In so attacking him these readers are wrong, in that they are ill-equipped to perceive the kind of limited hope or optimism expressed in the actions of Captain Lena Thomas in *Galaxies* or cool Sid in *Guernica Night*, who choose to live even in the face of complexities which are (almost) too great to bear. Certainly the burden of his fictions is often terrifying, bleak: lost in a world they had no part in making (and over which the awful vision of assassination continually hovers—like so many of his generation, Malzberg was traumatized by the political murders of the 1960's, and they have become a *leit motif* in his work), Malzberg's people articulate their precise awareness of that fact, and of the other facts which batter at their defences. Malzberg's obsessions, and those of his characters, expose the dark underbelly of the science-fiction mythos to the terrible light of art. Humans as machines, not in hoped-for supremacy but in near-catatonic anomie, unable to touch one another, even in sex, except mechanically; assassination as a way of life; bureaucracy as a huge engine of human destruction; the horrors of confronting in outer space only the empty reflection of our inner spaces: these are the themes Malzberg explores with obsessive tenacity, entering one after another of SF's favorite narrative conventions only to discover once more that for the human problems his characters have to deal with there are no easy answers, no *deus ex machina* to lumber in at the end and save all. But this knowledge is not necessarily simply pessimistic. Herovit and his other selves utterly fail to adapt to the alien forces of New York, but others in Malzberg's "freak show" survive in the recognition that not only can they not find answers to their specific complaints but that very likely their problems do not have answers as such. So they adapt, they make compromises with reality, they go mad, they go sane, they try to be human (in itself the most heroic act Malzberg can conceive of in the aseptic environment of SF conventions). For Malzberg's characters, the material of their reality is strangely impermeable, darkly opaque, and almost completely unmalleable. The universe is bigger, stronger, and more dangerous than they are; it also has a nasty sense of humour.

Indeed, comedy is something not often mentioned in connection with Malzberg, yet he is one of the funniest writers in the genre, if you are able to laugh at the end of the world. For black humour, apocalyptic comedy, Lear's fool trying for a final tear-filled laugh, see Malzberg's collected works. If we didn't laugh we might break down and cry, and so might he. The tricks of rhetoric have their purpose, then, and Malzberg is a master of the ironic twist, the sick joke of metaphysics meeting physics head-on. Tone is always difficult, yet Malzberg continually manages such complex presentations of savage wit as this, in *Beyond Apollo:* "A Brief History of the Universe: The universe was invented by man in 1976 as a cheap and easy explanation for all his difficulties in conquering it." Foregrounding the many subtexts of the novel, this remark casts a shadow over not just Harry Evans's attempt to discover what happened to him on the disastrous Venus mission but also over all the stories of successful space imperialism. And yet Malzberg is believeable when he says he loves science fiction, for it's obvious he recognizes and values the writing his own seems so fully to subvert. Such ambivalence of love and belief seem proper in a writer whose central subject is human ambivalence on every matter that matters. He only wanted to make room for his vision, too; not to replace the others but to provide some balance. And even if he has left the field he has left us a rich legacy of fictions whose integrity cannot be questioned. Of the novels, certainly *The Falling Astronauts, Overlay, Beyond Apollo, Herovit's World, Guernica Night, Scop, The Cross of Fire*, and that amazing analysis of the genre in the form of notes for a novel, *Galaxies*, need no apology. And there are a number of shorter works of equal value, as well as his *cri de coeur* analyses of the field. Although many find his vision not only too dark but too narrow, no one can deny the depth of the chasm his works have cut through contemporary SF.

—Douglas Barbour

---

**MANN, (Anthony) Phillip.** British. Born in Northallerton, Yorkshire, 7 August 1942. Educated at Scarborough College, 1954–62; Manchester University, 1962–66, B.A. in English and drama 1966; Humboldt State University, Arcata, California, 1966–69, M.A. 1969. Married Nonnita Margaret Rees in 1967; one daughter and one son. Lecturer in Drama, Humboldt State University, 1967–69. Lecturer, 1969–81, and since 1981, Reader in Drama, Victoria University, Wellington, New Zealand. English editor, Xin Hua News Agency, Beijing, 1978–80. Associate artistic director, Downstage Theatre, Wellington, 1984–86. Board member, New Zealand Drama School, 1986–90, and since 1991, chairperson. Freelance writer, lecturer, and theatre director. Agent (plays): Playmarket, P.O. Box 9767, Wellington. Address: 22 Bruce Avenue, Brooklyn, Wellington, New Zealand.

### Science-Fiction Publications

Novels (series: The Gardener)

*The Eye of the Queen*. London, Gollancz, 1982; New York, Arbor House, 1983.
*Ben's Bed* (for children). Wellington, Mallinson Rendel, 1985.
*Master of Paxwax* (Gardener). London, Gollancz, 1986.
*The Fall of the Families* (Gardener). London, Gollancz, 1987.
*Pioneers*. London, Gollancz, 1988.
*Wulfsyarn*. London, Gollancz, 1990.

### Other Publications

Plays

*Il suffit d'un baton*, in *Avant-Scène* (Paris), 1977.
*Revenge at Ditchwater Creek* (produced Wellington, 1977).
*The Animal Maker* (for children) (produced Wellington, 1978).
*The Thunderbird* (for children) (produced Wellington, 1982).
*The Bach in the Bush* (for children) (produced Wellington, 1984).
*Mozart and Solieri Concert* (produced Wellington, 1991).

Radio Play: *The Monument*, 1977.

*

Phillip Mann comments:

I began writing when I was in my teens. Like many young writers I had ideas of becoming a poet but found that my verse slipped easily into doggerel, bawdy lyrics, and satire. I also found that I had a knack for dialogue but this never really extended itself into full-length plays, though I would still like to write for the theatre. I started to write short stories and found this most satisfying. I read science fiction from an early age and grew up on a diet of Wells, Verne, and Rider Haggard as well as Thomas Mann, Billy Bunter tales, and stories about the sea. A combination of the fantastic and the logical appeals to me. I write to entertain. I want to write good yarns that involve the reader and yield the same satisfaction as a good meal. I am convinced there is life in a multitude of forms evolving in the wider galaxy and that our next major development will take place when we manage to break or circumvent the space-time barrier. Aliens and alien ceremonies intrigue me as do the creative faculties in mankind. Science fiction seems to me an excellent forum in which we can debate and prepare for the future.

* * *

Known in New Zealand not only for his novels but for his dramatic work, Phillip Mann skillfully uses this dramatic ability in his novels, especially what he terms "a knack for dialogue." This ability has allowed his work to move from one medium to another, as witness the broadcasts to date of two of his novels, *The Eye of the Queen* and *Pioneers.* At one point, he found his subject matter demanded extended treatment; the tale of Paxwax, the gardener, in *Master of Paxwax* continues in its sequel, *The Fall of the Families.*

With *The Eye of the Queen* Phillip Mann entered the world of science fiction in a way calculated to stretch the minds and imagination of tyros and aficionados alike. For this first novel Mann chose a stock situation: alien contact. When a strange spacecraft appears and hovers some four inches above the Utah salt flats, its presence sets off predictable reactions: confusion, fear, an ill-fated attempt at defence against the unknown. At this point a reader may expect the usual adventure complete with space wars or at least space derring-do in answer to the implied question: what will happen when aliens initiate contact with Earth?

Mann's answer, however, comes in an unexpected and unique form. When contact becomes reciprocal, a two-member team from Earth's Contact Linguistics Institute receives the assignment to return with the aliens, study their culture, and establish a common ground for co-existence. In Mann's presentation of the team's findings the reader discovers an inner dynamic working to forward and dramatize the novel's ideas.

Once the tradition-bound reader foregoes reliance on conventional chapter divisions and gives himself up to the author's arrangement, he experiences a situation such as that epitomized by Robert Frost in the couplet/poem, "The Secret Sits." The reader becomes a shadowy third partner of the team, "circling" the Pe-Ellian world, probing for information. In both sections, the Diary and the Commentary, Mann interweaves data gathered by standard research techniques employed in a case study: direct observation, encoded interviews and brief autobiographies of various aliens, transcriptions of casual conversations, physical descriptions, linguistic analysis, botanical and biological data, cultural analysis of various areas such as social life, living conditions, esthetic artifacts and the like. As data accumulates, the fiction team and the reader, like the voice in Frost's poem, can only "suppose," until the aliens in the center begin to give up the secret of what they "know."

In *The Eye of the Queen* Mann presents an alien stock made all the more believable by its utter physical alienness, an alienness that is intensified by the epithetic names so evocative of human experience and emotion. Albeit unspoiled by anthropomorphism so often employed in science fiction, the aliens do share attributes of many sentient creatures we know, along with the art of the language and thought with humans. While they impress a reader with a sense of commonality with all living forms, there is also a sense of transcendence, arising from what the researchers' *Contact Linguistics Handbook* terms "the sense of structure." The Pe-Ellian sense of structure recognizes existence and balance of personal and cosmic biospheres and psychospheres, the latter supported by belief in the vitality of thought. Thought is alive. Thought becomes dangerous, if undisciplined or belligerent. Thought can regenerate, if understood, shared, and directed. When the implications of the power of misused thought becomes part of what the major researcher comes to "know," he moves from scientific objectivity to complete subjectivity.

Utilizing the Diary-Commentary format, Mann dramatizes this shift of perspective to particularly effective ends. Compiled by the major researcher, self-admittedly estranged from himself by a lifelong dedication and discipline to objectivity, the Diary charts both the progress of the scientific analysis of the aliens and the ever-increasing self-analysis. In the process author Mann succeeds in turning his main character into an Everyman, forcing the reader to make comparable analyses. Written *ex post facto*, based on memory, and supported by notes and records, the Commentary provides an alternate, sometimes antithetical, perspective on events. More important for Mann's theme, the Commentary provides a reader with a sympathetic angle from which to judge the personal conclusions of the diarist. Without belaboring the point in the novel Mann leads his readers toward assessment of the contemporary human use of that virile entity, thought. It is a speculation vital to our continuation as honorable residents of the cosmos.

While *The Eye of the Queen* established Mann's reputation as one who handles human/alien relationships very effectively, *Wulfsyarn* introduces a non-human entity as narrator of the events of the novel. Wulf is a mechanical secretary, so to speak. It accompanies a space captain on a humane mission. Leaving a galaxy devastated by the Wars of Knowledge and Ignorance, the secretary becomes the narrator as it records the captain's thoughts. Upon return of the spacecraft, now empty and carrying only Wulf and the mentally broken-down captain, Wulf speculates on the cause of the tragic end, attempting to explain what had happened to both captain and ship, a project beyond its novel capabilities.

In *Locus*, January 1991, Mann reported that his latest novel, *Land Fit for Heroes*, will be published later in 1991. He describes it as "an alternate history novel" that traces the development of a world in which Roman power remained predominant throughout the ages, conquering the world, relegating Christianity to a lesser force in world events. The novel will mark new directions for Mann's imagination and flair for dialogue.

—Hazel Pierce

---

**MANNING, Laurence (Edward).** American. Born in St. John, New Brunswick, Canada, in 1899; emigrated to the United States after World War I. Educated at King's College, Halifax, Nova Scotia, B.C.L. 1919. Served in the Royal Canadian Air Force: Lieutenant. Married Edith B. Manning in 1928; two daughters and one son. Newspaper reporter in St. John, then writer for the Florists Exchange, Philadelphia, in the early 1920's; manager, 1923–32, president, 1933–52, and owner, 1952–66, Kelsey Nursery Service, New York. Fellow, American Rocket Society, 1960. *Died in 1972.*

SCIENCE-FICTION PUBLICATIONS

Novel

*The Man Who Awoke.* New York, Ballantine, 1975; London, Sphere, 1977.

Uncollected Short Stories (series: Stranger Club)

"The Voyage of the Asteroid," in *Wonder Stories* (New York), Summer 1932.
"The Wreck of the Asteroid," in *Wonder Stories* (New York), December 1932.
"The Call of the Mech-Men" (Club), in *Wonder Stories* (New York), November 1933.
"Caverns of Horror" (Club), in *Wonder Stories* (New York), March 1934.
"Voice of Atlantis" (Club), in *Wonder Stories* (New York), July 1934.
"The Moth Message" (Club), in *Wonder Stories* (New York), December 1934.
"The Prophetic Voice," in *Wonder Stories* (New York), April 1935.
"Seeds from Space" (Club), in *Wonder Stories* (New York), June 1935.
"World of the Mist," in *Wonder Stories* (New York), September 1935.
"Expedition to Pluto," with Fletcher Pratt, in *Planet* (New York), Winter 1939.
"The City of the Living Dead," with Fletcher Pratt, in *Avon Fantasy Reader 2*, edited by Donald A. Wollheim. New York, Avon, 1947.
"The Living Galaxy," in *The Science Fiction Galaxy*, edited by Groff Conklin. New York, Permabooks, 1950.
"Good-Bye, Ilha," in *Beyond Human Ken*, edited by Judith Merril. New York, Random House, 1952.
"Men on Mars," in *Fantastic Story* (New York), Spring 1952.
"Mr. Mottle Goes Poof," in *Fantasy Fiction* (New York), August 1953.

OTHER PUBLICATIONS

Other

*The How and Why of Better Gardening.* New York, Van Nostrand, 1951.

*  *  *

Laurence Manning is remembered primarily for a series of five stories originally published in 1933, later collected in book form as *The Man Who Awoke.* Manning used a classic device of science-fiction and Utopian writers, a man from our own culture transported in some fashion to another society, which is then revealed to the reader as the protagonist encounters individuals and institutions. In each of the five episodes, Norman Winters arises from suspended animation to investigate the state of humanity as it advances toward its ultimate destiny.

In the title story, Winters explores the world of the year 5000. Humankind dwells within vast managed forests, in balance with nature, looking back with horror on "the false civilization of Waste!" Seeking to find a place for himself in this new world, Winters attempts to convince his hosts that his own time did have positive aspects for which they should be thankful. But even the most sympathetic of his listeners feel no gratitude. "For exhausting the coal supplies of the world? For leaving us no petroleum for our chemical factories?" Ultimately finding this new society as flawed as the old, Winters sleeps another 5000 years and revives in "Master of the Brain." Now he encounters humanity subservient to a computer that makes all the decisions, the race having abdicated the responsibility for their own future. After being instrumental in breaking the grip of the Brain, Winters advances to the year 15000 in "The City of Sleep." Once more he is disappointed, for now the great majority of people spend their entire lives in mechanically induced dreams, an idea developed from Manning's first story, "The City of the Living Dead," written with Fletcher Pratt. This willing renunciation of reality has recurred within the genre many times, most notably in James Gunn's *The Joy Makers.* The best story in the series is "The Individualists," wherein Winters becomes the quarry of a number of egocentric geniuses in a society that places no value on interpersonal relationships. Winter's journey ends with "The Elixir," the source of immortality which produces an interstellar community. Although not specifically within the series, Manning wrote another tale set eons after the Manning saga, "The Living Galaxy," which postulated that entire stellar systems functioned as single atoms in a higher order universe we could not perceive.

Less ambitious in scope was a second series that recounted the adventures of several members of the Stranger Club. Manning's dislike of automation recurs in "The Call of the Mech-Men," a secret cabal of living machines. His concern about our profligate consumption of natural resources, anticipating our present worries, is repeated in "Voice of Atlantis," in which a device allows communication with an ancient Atlantean. The remaining three stories were more pedestrian and reflected the type of story that dominated the genre in the 1930's. A lost world of prehistoric monsters lies under New York in "Caverns of Horror," a forgotten Atlantean colony is located in "The Moth Message," and a species of sentient, ambient tree is thwarted in its invasion plan in "Seeds from Space."

Manning's fiction, much of which seems quite dated now, was advanced for its time. He produced a series of very accurate—insofar as the state of the art allowed—stories of space travel. His concerns for conservation and human dignity elevated his fiction above that of most of his peers.

—Don D'Ammassa

---

**MARAS, Karl.** *See* **BULMER, Kenneth.**

---

**MARSTEN, Richard.** *See* **HUNTER, Evan.**

---

**MARTIN, George R(aymond) R(ichard).** American. Born in Bayonne, New Jersey, 20 September 1948. Educated at Medill School of Journalism, Northwestern University, Evanston, Illinois, B.S. 1970, M.S. 1971. Served with the Cook County Legal Assistance Foundation, for Vista, Chicago, 1972–74. Married Gale Burnick in 1975 (divorced 1979). Chess tournament director, Continental Chess Association, Mount Vernon, New York, 1973–75; journalism instructor, Clarke College, Dubuque, Iowa,

1976–79. Since 1979, freelance writer. Recipient: Hugo award, 1975, 1980 (2 awards); Bread Loaf Writers Conference Fellowship, 1977; Nebula award, 1979, 1985; *Locus* award, 1981, 1982 (twice), 1984; Bram Stoker award, 1987; World Fantasy award, 1988. Agent: Pimlico Literary Agency, 155 East 77th Street, Suite 1A, New York, New York 10021. Address: 102 San Salvador, Santa Fe, New Mexico 87501, U.S.A.

### Science-Fiction Publications

#### Novels

*Dying of the Light.* New York, Simon and Schuster, 1977; London, Gollancz, 1978.
*Windhaven,* with Lisa Tuttle. New York, Timescape, 1980; London, New English Library, 1982.
*Fevre Dream.* New York, Poseidon Press, 1982; London, Gollancz, 1983.
*The Armageddon Rag.* New York, Poseidon Press, 1983; London, New English Library, 1984.

#### Short Stories

*A Song for Lya and Other Stories.* New York, Avon, 1976; London, Coronet, 1978.
*Songs of Stars and Shadows.* New York, Pocket Books, 1977.
*The Sandkings.* New York, Pocket Books, 1981; London, Futura, 1983.
*Songs the Dead Men Sing.* Niles, Illinois, Dark Harvest, 1983; London, Gollancz, 1985.
*Nightflyers.* New York, Bluejay, 1985.
*Tuf Voyaging.* New York, Baen, 1986, London, Gollancz, 1987.
*Portraits of His Children.* Arlington Heights, Illinois, Dark Harvest, 1987.

#### Uncollected Short Stories

"A Peripheral Affair," in *Fantasy and Science Fiction* (New York), January 1973.
"The Computer Cried Charge," in *Amazing* (New York), January 1976.
"Nobody Leaves New Pittsburg," in *Amazing* (New York), September 1976.
"Warship," with George Florance-Gutheridge, in *Fantasy and Science Fiction* (New York), April 1979.
"The Skin Trade," in *Night Visions 5*, edited by Douglas E. Winter. Arlington Heights, Illinois, Dark Harvest, 1989.

### Other Publications

#### Plays

Screenplay: *Fadeout,* 1990.

Television plays: 5 episodes in the *Twilight Zone* series, 1986; 13 episodes in the *Beauty and the Beast* series, 1987–90.

#### Other

Editor, *New Voices in Science Fiction 1–4.* New York, Macmillan, 1 vol., 1977; New York, Harcourt Brace, 1 vol., 1979; New York, Berkley, 2 vols., 1980–81.
Editor, with Isaac Asimov and Martin H. Greenberg, *The Science Fiction Weight-Loss Book.* New York, Crown, 1983.
Editor, *The John W. Campbell Awards 5.* New York, Bluejay, 1984.
Editor, *The John W. Campbell Awards 6.* New York, Bluejay, 1986.
Editor, *Night Visions 3.* Arlington Heights, Illinois, Dark Harvest, 1986; as *Nightvisions,* London, Century, 1987.
Editor, *Wild Cards* series. New York, Bantam, 9 vols., 1987–91; London, Titan, 9 vols., 1988–91.

* * *

George R.R. Martin has never been a prolific writer, taking his time to create richly endowed worlds peopled with credible characters. Since 1971, only four novels and a few dozen stories have appeared, which makes it all the more remarkable that he remains one of the more familiar names in science fiction.

The first story to separate Martin from the scores of other short story writers was "With Morning Comes Mistfall." A mysterious, mist-shrouded world is rumored to be inhabited by the Wraiths, an indigenous species that lurks just out of sight, preying on unwary travellers. Two personalities clash, not over whether or not the Wraiths really exist, but over the question of whether it is better for humanity to know the truth, or to have at least one legend. "Override" is the first of several stories set in a future where technology allows the reanimation of corpses as working machines, grouped into teams directed telepathically in their duties. Again, Martin uses this as a device to examine two competing attitudes, in this case about the morality of the process.

"A Song for Lya" follows the same pattern, but far more effectively. A telepath and an empath travel to a world where humans are converting in increasing numbers to an alien religion that includes a very unpleasant suicide. The telepath becomes a convert, and her companion struggles to impress her with the importance of individuality.

In 1977, *Dying of the Light,* Martin's first novel, was published. Although ostensibly an interplanetary adventure story, the real conflict is one of personalities, that of the sardonic protagonist, his associates, and the woman he loves. Martin goes to great lengths to develop the background details of his society, overlaying his characters so that they appear genuine products of that civilization.

Several superior short stories followed, most notably the clever and genuinely terrifying "The Sandkings," which demonstrates the peril of fooling around with unknown lifeforms, and the danger of assuming that "lower" creatures are somehow less capable of defending themselves. Others of note from this period are "In the House of Worm," "Fast Friend," and "The Way of Cross and Dragon." The latter particularly is interesting because of its portrayal of a new wave of inquisitorial religious fervor following humanity's expansion to the stars.

Martin collaborated with Lisa Tuttle on the novel *Windhaven,* an expansion and further development of the excellent novelette, "The Storms of Windhaven." The protagonist is a Flyer, one of many who travel on artificial wings from island to island on their world, where surface travel is virtually impossible because of heavy winds and the creatures lurking beneath the waters. When she is faced with having to surrender her wings to a male, she rebels, challenging not only his right but calling into doubt the entire traditional history of her people.

Two solo novels followed rapidly thereafter, both in the horror field. *The Armageddon Rag* remains to this day one of the most original, inventive, and best written horror novels of all time, the only one to successfully wed a supernatural theme to the world of rock music. A writer investigating a murder begins to chart the history of the Nazgul, a defunct rock group whose members all appear to be the objects of manipulation by an unseen, unknown force. More traditional in theme, if not in setting, is *Fevre Dream.* Martin uses a likable vampire who sets out in the years prior to the Civil War to establish himself as savior of his kind. The evocative riverboat settings are particularly effective. Although Martin has switched back to science fiction for the most part, he still writes occasional horror tales, sometimes quite effectively, as in "Portraits of His Children."

Martin's excellent novella, "Nightflyers," was made into a lackluster film, but it is an outstanding bit of writing. A starship is haunted by the recorded personality of a warped woman who refuses to surrender control of her son's life, even in death. "Under Siege" breathes new life into the theme of changing the past, "The Glass Flower" explores what it means to be human when a spaceman is rebuilt as a cyborg, and the morality of medical experimentation is examined in "The Needle Men."

Although many of Martin's short stories are set within the framework of a consistent universe, his corpse handler stories were the only true series until he began a sequence about a gigantic starship designed to deal exclusively with ecological disasters, commanded and occupied by a single human being. These were subsequently collected into a single volume as *Tuf Voyaging*, but while entertaining and thought-provoking, they lack the intense commitment of his earlier work. Much of Martin's energy may have been diverted into his work for television, and the creation of an alternate present, shared universe anthology series, "Wild Cards," which has enjoyed considerable popularity, but which unfortunately contains very little by Martin himself. Nevertheless, were Martin never to write another story in the field, he would remain firmly established as one of the major writers of the 1970's.

—Don D'Ammassa

---

**MARTYN, Phillip.** *See* **TUBB, E.C.**

---

**MASON, Douglas R.** *See* **RANKINE, John.**

---

**MASON, John.** *See* **TUBB, E.C.**

---

**MASSON, David I(rvine).** British. Born in Edinburgh, 6 November 1915. Educated at Oundle School, Northamptonshire, 1929–34; Merton College, Oxford, B.A. (honours) in English 1937, M.A. 1941. Served in the Royal Army Medical Corps, 1940–45. Married Olive Masson in 1950; one daughter. Assistant Librarian, University of Leeds, 1938–40, and University of Liverpool, 1945–55; Sub-Librarian, in charge of Brotherton Collection, University of Leeds, 1956–79. Address: c/o Faber and Faber Ltd., 3 Queen Square, London WC1N 3AU, England.

SCIENCE-FICTION PUBLICATIONS

Short Stories

*The Caltraps of Time.* London, Faber, 1968.

Uncollected Short Stories

"The Show Must Go On," in *The Disappearing Future*, edited by George Hay. London, Panther, 1970.
"Take It or Leave It," in *The Year 2000*, edited by Harry Harrison. New York, Doubleday, 1970; London, Faber, 1971.
"Doctor Fausta," in *Stop Watch*, edited by George Hay. London, New English Library, 1974.

OTHER PUBLICATIONS

Other

*Hand-List of Incunabula in the University Library, Liverpool.* Privately printed, 1948; supplement, 1955.
*Catalogue of the Romany Collection . . . University of Leeds.* Edinburgh, Nelson, 1962.
*Poetic Sound-Patterning Reconsidered.* Leeds, Philosophical and Literary Society, 1976.

*

David I. Masson comments:

My SF, although it seeks "scientific" versimilitude and tries to convince, has little to do with the processes of science. It explores bizarre assumptions for the sake—or so it seems to me—of mythopoeia, fable, satire, ridicule, scorn, or indignation, and perhaps inner truth about experience and feeling. Only "Take It or Leave It" has much to do with possible futures. Several stories reflect my conviction that the human race is insane. (Here and there one notes hopeful signs of some insight into its own condition.)

* * *

David I. Masson's SF reputation rests upon a handful of stories, most of them collected in *The Caltraps of Time.* A lively if recondite wit is a characteristic of these stories. A university antiquariun librarian, fascinated by linguistics, Masson plummets a Restoration gentleman into the 20th century courtesy of a borrowed time machine in "The Two Timer," to be amazed and bemused by our antics—and of course to satrize us in approved Swiftian manner. The impeccable late 17th-century prose style of this story throws into contrast our barbaric contemporary parlance: "Myself: *Prithee, Sir, do you converse in* English? At this he frown'd, and turn'd back thro' his Door, but left it open, for I heard him in speech with another, as follows. He . . . *Now enthing bauootim? Caun honstan zaklay wottee sez.*" Matters are just as bad for a researcher of the 1980's plunged into the 24th century by a linear accelerator accident in "The Transfinite Choice" ("Namplize." "Don't you speak English, then? Who the hell are you?" "Namplize"). It seems as though one is sliding down a cultural entropy slope. This future, in technotelegraphize, is trying, however, to master the gradient of time at the sub-particle level. Reality fractures as the future tries to shunt its excess population into parallel time-continua; or was it only, after all, the stricken researcher's reality that fell apart?

The finest of Masson's stories. "Traveller's Rest," deals with time yet again, apocalyptically yet ironically. The country at war in this story is distorted by differential time: whole decades pass in the peaceful south while mere minutes pass at the northern battle frontier where, perhaps, the army is simply fighting itself in the mirror of bent time with mounting frenzy and destructiveness—a powerful nightmare which does for exponential time what Christopher Priest's novel *Inverted World* was later to do for exponential space. In "Not So Certain" an expedition to an alien planet falls foul of the natives' tricky phonemes, another linguistic *jeu d'esprit,* while in "Mouth of Hell" apocalyptic topography confronts the explorers in the form of a 40-kilometre-deep cleft down to the molten magma which, by the end of the story, is tamed and demystified just as so much of our world has been banalised.

In Masson's loving care for language and concern with time, one senses a scholarly resentment at the downhill slide of the world into some future mass point of condensed people and words and moments.

—Ian Watson

---

**MATHESON, Richard (Burton).** American. Born in Allendale, New Jersey, 20 February 1926. Educated at the University of Missouri, Columbia, B.A. in journalism 1949. Served in the 87th Division of the United States Army during World War II. Married Ruth Ann Woodson in 1952; two daughters and two sons. Freelance writer. Recipient: Hugo award, for screenplay, 1958; Writers Guild of America award, for television writing, 1960, 1974; World Fantasy award, 1976, 1990, and Life Achievement award, 1984. Guest of Honor, 16th World Science Fiction Convention, 1958 Bram Stoker award, 1990. Agent: Don Congdon Associates, 156 Fifth Avenue, Suite 625, New York, New York 10010. Address: P.O. Box 81, Woodland Hills, California 91365, U.S.A.

SCIENCE-FICTION PUBLICATIONS

Novels

*I Am Legend.* New York, Fawcett, 1954; London, Corgi, 1956; as *The Omega Man,* New York, Berkley, 1971.
*The Shrinking Man.* New York, Fawcett, and London, Muller, 1956.

Short Stories

*Born of Man and Woman.* Philadelphia, Chamberlain Press, 1954; abridged edition, London, Reinhardt, 1956; abridged edition, as *Third from the Sun,* New York, Bantam, 1955.
*The Shores of Space.* New York, Bantam, 1957; London, Corgi, 1958.
*Shock!* New York, Dell, 1961; London, Corgi, 1962.
*Shock II.* New York, Dell, 1964; London, Corgi, 1965.
*Shock III.* New York, Dell, 1966; London, Corgi, 1967.
*Shock Waves.* New York, Dell, 1970.
*Shock 4.* London, Sphere, 1980.
*Collected Stories.* Los Angeles, Dream Press, 1989.

OTHER PUBLICATIONS

Novels

*Someone Is Bleeding.* New York, Lion, 1953.
*Fury on Sunday.* New York, Lion, 1953.
*A Stir of Echoes.* Philadelphia, Lippincott, and London, Cassell, 1958.
*Ride the Nightmare.* New York, Ballantine, 1959; London, Consul, 1961.
*The Beardless Warriors.* Boston, Little Brown, 1960; London, Heinemann, 1961.
*Hell House.* New York, Viking Press, 1971; London, Corgi, 1973.
*Bid Time Return.* New York, Viking Press, 1975; London, Sphere, 1977.
*What Dreams May Come.* New York, Putnam, 1978; London, Joseph, 1979.
*Earthbound.* London, Robinson, 1989.
*Through Channels.* Roundtop, New York, Footsteps Press, 1989.

Plays

Screenplays: *The Incredible Shrinking Man,* 1957; *The Beat Generation (This Rebel Age),* with Lewis Meltzer, 1959; *The House of Usher (The Fall of the House of Usher),* 1960; *Master of the World,* 1961; *The Pit and the Pendulum,* 1961; *Tales of Terror,* 1962; *Burn, Witch, Burn (Night of the Eagle),* with Charles Beaumont and George Baxt, 1962; *The Raven,* 1963; *The Comedy of Terrors,* 1964; *The Last Man on Earth* (pseudonymous co-writer), 1964; *Die! Die! My Darling! (Fanatic),* 1965; *The Young Warriors,* 1967; *The Devil Rides Out (The Devil's Bride),* 1968; *De Sade,* 1969; *The Legend of Hell House,* 1973; *Dracula,* 1974; *Somewhere in Time,* 1980; *The Twilight Zone,* with others, 1983; *Jaws 3-D,* with Carl Gottlieb and Guerdon Trueblood, 1983.

Television Plays: *Yawkey (Lawman* series), 1959; *And When the Sky Was Opened, Third from the Sun, The Last Flight, A World of Difference, A World of His Own, Nick of Time, The Invaders, Once upon a Time, Little Girl Lost, Young Man's Fancy, Steel, Nightmare at 20,000 Feet, Night Call,* and *Spur of the Moment* (all in *Twilight Zone* series), 1959–63; *The Return of Andrew Bentley (Thriller* series), 1960–61; *The Enemy Within (Star Trek* series), 1966; *Duel,* 1971; *The Night Stalker,* 1971; *The Night Strangler,* 1972; *Dying Room Only,* 1973; *The Stranger Within,* 1974; *Dracula,* 1974; *Scream of the Wolf,* 1974; *The Morning After,* 1974; *Amelia* (in *Trilogy of Terror),* 1975; *Dead of Night,* 1977; *The Strange Possession of Mrs. Oliver,* 1977; *The Martian Chronicles,* from the novel by Ray Bradbury, 1979; *The Dreamer of Oz,* 1990; and scripts for *Chrysler Playhouse, Alfred Hitchcock Hour, The Girl from U.N.C.L.E., Have Gun—Will Travel, Wanted Dead or Alive, Night Gallery, The D.A.'s Man, Cheyenne, Bourbon Street Beat, Philip Marlowe, Buckskin, Markham,* and *Richard Diamond* series.

Other

Editor, with Martin H. Greenberg and Charles G. Waugh, *The Twilight Zone: The Original Stories.* New York, Avon, 1985.

* * *

Like many of the younger writers who began publishing science fiction in the shadow of Ray Bradbury in the 1950's, Richard Matheson has consistently worked on the borders of science fiction proper, using science fictional tropes as little more than expository devices on which to hang vividly imagined fantasies of paranoia and romance. His very first story, "Born of Man and Woman," is essentially a horror piece based on fears of deformity and child abuse, narrated in broken English by a hideously mutated child chained in the basement of his parents' home. "Death Ship" begins with all the appurtenances of science fiction—a spaceship crew discovers the wreckage of another spaceship—but soon turns into a "Flying Dutchman" ghost story as the crew learns that the wrecked ship is their own, and they are ghosts. In "The Traveler," a skeptical historian uses a time machine to witness the crucifixion of Christ, only to find himself converted to Christianity, rather unconvincingly. Almost none of these early stories devote much attention to their science fiction "macguffins," and it is not surprising that eight of them should later have provided the basis for episodes of Rod Serling's TV series *The Twilight Zone*, for which Matheson himself wrote more than a dozen scripts between 1960 and 1964.

This is not to suggest that Matheson's fiction lacks power. On the contrary, he often displayed a gift for imagining almost archetypal situations of paranoia and loss of control. In "Shipshape Home," new residents of an apartment building begin to suspect that the building is a disguised spaceship; they flee the building only to find that the spaceship is the entire block. The protagonist of "Disappearing Act" finds his family and acquaintances disappearing from the memory of everyone he meets, while "Nightmare at 20,000 Feet" explores the anxieties of flight, as an airline passenger sees a hideous gremlin on the wing of the plane. "Duel" (filmed by Steven Spielberg for television) does much the same for highway travel, as an unsuspecting motorist is terrorized by a huge truck whose driver remains unseen. Occasionally, the paranoia is leavened with clever satire, as in "The Creeping Terror," which uses a mock-academic style to reveal that Los Angeles is literally a spreading infection.

Matheson's two best-known novels are also his most extreme examples of isolation and loss of control. *I Am Legend*, with its nightmarish vision of the last man on earth besieged by vampires, has become a classic of horror literature, surviving two unsuccessful film adaptations. Largely because of its contemporary suburban setting and its earnest attempts to find a science fictional rationale for vampirism (the victims are infected by dust-borne bacteria), *I Am Legend* has been credited with having helped liberate the horror genre from its traditional settings of isolated villages and haunted castles. *The Shrinking Man* (for which Matheson wrote his own screen adaptation) offers even less of a scientific explanation for the fate of a man who, engulfed by radioactive dust while on his boat, begins shrinking at the rate of a seventh of an inch a day. The novel alternates the straightforward adventure story of the tiny narrator trapped in his cellar with flashback chapters detailing his growing alienation from the world as he becomes progressively smaller and unable to provide for his family or maintain relationships. Both *I Am Legend* and *The Shrinking Man* are haunting portraits of sensitive individuals losing control over their worlds, and both are unusual for their time in their open discussions of frustrated sexual longings. Matheson's technique is to assume a single fantastic premise and explore it with a rigor and logic that belies the sensational aspects of the initial premise.

In his later fiction, Matheson turned increasingly away from even the paraphernalia of science fiction. *Hell House*, with its discussion of magnetic fields and electronic equipment, retains some borderline elements of science fiction and seems in some ways to be an attempt to explain haunted house phenomena in the same pseudoscientific way *I Am Legend* explains vampires. But the soul of the book is in psychic research, which had long fascinated Matheson. *Bid Time Return* (filmed as *Somewhere in Time*) is in a sense a time travel fantasy in the tradition of Jack Finney, but is primarily a transgenerational love story. *What Dreams May Come* is also a sentimental love story, this time involved with life after death.

Following his adapation of *The Shrinking Man* for the movies, Matheson devoted an increasing amount of his time to film and TV scripts, most notably *The Twilight Zone*, *Night Gallery*, and a series of very loose Edgar Allan Poe adaptations for director Roger Corman. Although more properly regarded as a fantasy writer, his novels and stories have also had a liberating effect on the science fiction field, and even his earliest works stand up surprisingly well as exemplars of how a fertile imagination, grounded in acute perceptions of character and closely observed detail, can explore hidden anxieties in the most outlandish of narrative premises.

—Gary K. Wolfe

---

**MAY, Julian.** American. Born in Chicago, Illinois, 10 July 1931. Attended Rosary College, River Forest, Illinois, 1949–53. Married Thaddeus (Ted) E. Dikty in 1953; two sons and one daughter. Editor, Booz Allen & Hamilton, Chicago; editor, Consolidated Book Publishers, Chicago, 1954–57; founder, with Ted Dikty, Publication Associates, in Chicago, 1957–68, Naperville, Illinois, 1968–74, West Linn, Oregon, 1974–80, and since 1980 in Mercer Island, Washington. Freelance writer: has published almost 300 non-fiction works, mainly for children. Recipient: *Locus* award, 1982. Address: P.O. Box 851, Mercer Island, Washington 98040, U.S.A.

### Science-Fiction Publications

Novels (series: Pliocene Exile in all books)

*The Saga of Pliocene Exile:*
*The Many-Colored Land*. Boston, Houghton Mifflin, 1981; London, Pan, 1982.
*The Golden Torc*. Boston, Houghton Mifflin, 1981; London, Pan, 1982.
*The Nonborn King*. Boston, Houghton Mifflin, and London, Pan, 1983.
*The Adversary*. Boston, Houghton Mifflin, and London, Pan, 1984.
*Intervention: A Root Tale to the Galactic Milieu and a Vinculum Between It and the Saga of Pliocene Exile*. Boston, Houghton Mifflin, and London, Collins, 1987; as *The Surveillance* and *The Metaconcert*, New York, Ballantine, 2 vols., 1989.
*Black Trillium*, with Marion Zimmer Bradley and Andre Norton. New York, Doubleday, 1990; London, Grafton, 1991.

### Other Publications

Other

*A Pliocene Companion*. Boston, Houghton Mifflin, 1984; London, Pan, 1985.

*

Bibliography: *The Work of Julian May: An Annotated Bibliography and Guide by T.E. Dikty and R. Reginald*, San Bernardino, California, Borgo Press, 1985.

Julian May comments:

My books are in the tradition of the classic literate thriller. They are intricately plotted and feature a large cast of characters romping through a "future history" and a "past history." In spite of the fantastic imagery, my books are genuine science fiction—not heroic fantasy. The four Pliocene books form one enormous novel, gaudy and humorous and melodramatic.

* * *

In the early 1950's, Julian May published two science-fiction stories. During the next quarter of a century, she wrote 7,000 encyclopedia entries and about 245 non-fiction books for children, but no science fiction. Then, in 1978, she returned to SF by beginning work on the first novel in what would eventually become *The Saga of Pliocene Exile.* A decade later she brought out *Intervention*, a prequel to *The Saga.* And she is currently writing a trilogy, to be called *The Galactic Milieu*, based on events alluded to in the novels already published.

Since May's *oeuvre* is approaching one million words long, it is possible to mention only a few nodal events. In 2013, metapsychics led by Denis Remillard and Lucille Cartier (his wife) band together and emit a telepathic message that results in humanity's being judged worthy of joining the five races then ruling the galaxy. In 2034, Professor Theophile Guderian invents a time machine—but it works at only one location (near Lyons, France); it goes back to only one time (the Pliocene Epoch, 6 million years in the past); and it is a one-way trip, since most organic objects (including people) disintegrate if returned to the present. In 2083, a group of supremely talented human metapsychics led by Marc Remillard (grandson of Denis and Lucille) nearly overthrows the galactic government. By the 22nd century, human life has become utopian for all but a few people, with the most adventurous misfits choosing exile—stepping through the time gate and into the Pliocene, as the eight members of Group Green do in 2110.

It turns out that the Pliocene harbors a dimorphic alien (but humanoid) race—the tall, thin, elegant Tanu and the short, bulky, gauche Firvulag. They are exiles, too, from another galaxy even, waging on Earth the brutal battle-religion proscribed by their more civilized peers.

*The Saga of Pliocene Exile* details the impact on the Many-Colored Land (the Tanu name for Pliocene Europe) of Group Green, particularly Aiken Drum, Felice Landry, and Elizabeth Orme. May has said that *The Saga* is "positively operatic" (see "Music in My Head—Science Fiction as Opera" in *A Pliocene Companion*). Just so, for there is much here that reminds us of opera.

*The Saga* is Wagnerian in scope: the principals number in the dozens, the chorus in the hundreds, and reading it takes twice as long as seeing the *Ring.* May uses Freudian concepts or Jungian archetypes (sometimes both) as musical leitmotifs to characterize her human principals, as well as some of the important aliens. As background scenery, she carefully delineates the geography, geology, flora, and fauna of Pliocene Europe. The many stage settings include Tanu cities, Firvulag caves, and human camps. Since clothes (and colors) have symbolic meaning in *The Saga*, May writes exact (and colorful) descriptions of the costumes her characters wear. Those characters use innumerable props, especially the futuristic devices brought into the Pliocene by the humans. Operatic spectacle appears in various banquets and in the rituals surrounding the Tanu-Firvulag battle-religion. *The Saga* is also highly dramatic: the narrator sometimes disappears altogether, the point of view shifts kaleidoscopically, and the pace varies widely from scene to scene.

Romantic ideology permeates *The Saga.* May admits that her style sometimes becomes overwrought and that she has based many details on Northern, particularly Celtic, mythology (the Wagnerian influence, again). She also recognizes the romantic cast of her major themes: elitism, optimism, mentalism, medievalism, the value of pain, pacifism, love.

May is also working with various science-fictional ideas. She invents a Universal Field Theory (it relates time, space, energy, matter, and mind) that allows faster-than-light travel, time travel, an inertia-less drive, and various forms of ESP: farsensing, coercion, psychokinesis, redaction, and creativity. These SF ideas should call to mind the Golden Age, for May claims to be writing "an intellectualized Doc Smith saga."

*Intervention* (also published in two paperback titles: *The Surveillance* and *The Metaconcert*) begins with the explosion of the Nagasaki atomic bomb on 9 August 1945, and ends with the telepathic *cri de coeur et cerveau* in 2013 that brings on the extraterrestrial advent alluded to in the title. Thus, it is both an alternate history and a First Contact story.

Like *The Saga*, *Intervention* is decidedly Golden Age, for instance, in its use of the idea that humanity is being watched by superior creatures. It too has a wide scope (fewer characters but a longer time span, and it ranges beyond Europe to America, Scotland, India, and the Soviet Union), and it is fundamentally romantic. Indeed, May uses the idea of the *doppelganger* twice—Rogatien Remillard versus his evil brother Donatien and, in the next generation, Denis Remillard versus his evil brother Victor. The novel purports to be Rogatien's memoirs, looking back from 2113 at events that happened more than a century earlier. It has the feel of historical fiction, and May uses an array of literary techniques to tell the story—memoirs, straight narration, dramatic dialogue, excerpts from actual speeches or reports, a television script, a baseball play-by-play, a transcript of radio transmissions during the first Mars landing, and an article printed as it would appear in a newspaper.

Finally, even more obviously than *The Saga*, *Intervention* reveals that the titular saint for all May's work is Pierre Teilhard de Chardin, the paleontologist-theologian who in a series of books published after his death in 1955 attempted to synthesize modern evolutionary science and Catholic dogma. May's World Mind and Galactic Mind, for instance, are thinly disguised versions of Chardin's noosphere; Unity is related to Chardin's Omega Point; and *Intervention* borrows from Chardin names for the extraterrestrials watching over Earth—e.g. Atoning Unifex, the most powerful.

Readers who desire to keep their bearings amid May's gargantuan, erudite, and encyclopedic SF will find *A Pliocene Companion* helpful: it has a glossary (of place names, characters, and important concepts), a chronology, a Remillard family tree, maps, brief essays, interviews with the author, and "A Selective Bibliography." So far, scholars have not responded to May's challenge to find her fiction's hidden meanings. A good place to start would be with the bibliography just mentioned.

—Todd H. Sammons

---

**MAYHAR, Ardath (née Hurst).** Also writes as Frank Cannon and John Killdeer. American. Born in Timpson, Texas, 20 February 1930. Attended high school in Nacogdoches, Texas. Married Joe E. Mayhar in 1958; two sons and two stepsons.

Dairyman, Nacogdoches County, 1947–57; operator, East Texas Bookstore, Nacogdoches, 1958–62; proofreader, *Capital Journal*, Salem, Oregon, 1968–75; chicken farmer, Nacogdoches County, 1976–78; proofreader, Nacogdoches *Daily Sentinel*, 1979–82. Since 1982, full-time writer, and since 1984, co-operator, View from Orbit, bookstore, Nacogdoches, and instructor, Writer's Digest School. Agent: Don Maass, 64 West 84th Street, 3A, New York, New York 10024. Address: P.O. Box 180, Chireno, Texas 75937, U.S.A.

SCIENCE-FICTION PUBLICATIONS

Novels

*How the Gods Wove in Kyrannon* (for children). New York, Doubleday, 1979; London, Sidgwick and Jackson, 1980.
*The Seekers of Shar Nuhn*. New York, Doubleday, 1980.
*Soul-Singer of Tyrnos* (for children). New York, Atheneum, 1981.
*Warlock's Gift*. New York, Doubleday, 1982.
*Runes of the Lyre* (for children). New York, Atheneum, 1982.
*Khi to Freedom*. New York, Ace, 1983.
*Golden Dream*. New York, Ace, 1983.
*Lords of the Triple Moons*. New York, Atheneum, 1983.
*The Absolutely Perfect House*, with Marylois Dunn. New York, Harper, 1983.
*Exile on Vlahil*. New York, Doubleday, 1984.
*The Saga of Grittel Sundotha* (for children). New York, Atheneum, 1985.
*The World Ends in Hickory Hollow*. New York, Doubleday, 1985.
*Trail of the Seahawks*, with Ron Fortier. Lake Geneva, Wisconsin, TSR, 1987.
*The Sword and the Dagger*. Chicago, FASA, 1987.
*A Place of Silver Silence* (for children). New York, Walker, 1988; London, Hutchison, 1990.
*Monkey Station*, with Ron Fortier. Lake Geneva, Wisconsin, TSR, 1989.

OTHER PUBLICATIONS

Novels

*The Wall*. New York, Space and Time, 1987.
*Two-Moons and the Black Tower*. New York, Doubleday, 1988.

Novels as Frank Cannon

*Feud at Sweetwater Creek*. New York, Kensington, 1987.
*Bloody Texas Trail*. New York, Kensington, 1988.
*Texas Gunsmoke*. New York, Kensington, 1988.

Novels (for children)

*Medicine Walk*. New York, Atheneum, 1985.
*Carrots and Miggle*. New York, Atheneum, 1986.
*Makra Choria*. New York, Atheneum, 1987.

*

Manuscript Collections: de Grummond Collection, University of Southern Mississippi, Hattiesburg; Stephen F. Austin State University, Nacogdoches, Texas.

Ardath Mayhar comments:

I like to think of my work as metaphysical fiction. SF and fantasy elements allow me to create contexts that reach past our own limitations and parameters into continua where what *should be* CAN BE. Logic and Humanity are the poles of my philosophy, and I refuse to be hemmed up into narrow genres. Writing science fiction, fantasy, poetry, juveniles, articles of all kinds, I work toward some inner goal, invisible but inexorable, and when I arrive at my destination I expect to be completely astonished.

* * *

Although Ardath Mayhar had published in other genres previous to 1979, she got her start in SF and fantasy literature with the young adult work, *How the Gods Wove in Kyrannon*. Of the genre novels she produced in the intervening years, only four, *Exile on Vlahil*, *Golden Dream*, *Khi to Freedom*, and *The World Ends in Hickory Hollow*, could be classified as SF. Another four are clearly high fantasy, with characteristics such as elevated diction used by both characters and narrator, a few characters with superior talents such as magic and telepathy, and indisputable separation of good and evil. The other three Mayhar novels fall into the category recently termed "science fantasy," and owes much to the early writing of Andre Norton. *Lords of the Triple Moons*, *Runes of the Lyre*, and *The Saga of Grittel Sundotha* are basically fantasy works set in surroundings where magic and heroic adventure are predominant, but they each incorporate some technological feature such as "cross-dimensional" gravel from a machine-bases dimension of a lost technology called upon by the telepathic protagonists in their battle against evil wizards.

Mayhar is in fact preoccupied with telepathy and other superior powers of mind, an interest that surfaces in all her works. For example, in *Khi to Freedom*, she creates beings at several levels of corporeality and telepathic ability, with the protagonist Hale Enbo as the subject of a process of mental refinement by more elevated beings. *Exile on Vlahil*, her most amusing book to date, with its conscious computer called Alice, places a female-human hero in a position to save humans from her degenerating home planet through telepathic communication with idealized creatures called Erid and Vlammalba. *Golden Dream* gives H. Beam Piper's Little Fuzzys a history, describes the encounters with humans from their perspective, and makes much of their telepathic abilities and their powers of memory. The only novel that breaks this mold is anomalous in several ways. *The World Ends in Hickory Hollow* is a largely realistic post-nuclear holocaust novel, one of several such novels by a variety of authors which have appeared in recent years. This work is also partially autobiographical, being set in an area of East Texas similar to that in which the author and her family now live. It is somewhat more positive than the general run of such novels, postulating that a few families will survive a nuclear attack through mutual assistance and the resurrection of traditional, down-home wisdom.

Mayhar's plots are inexorable and predicable from the initial pages of any story. Good and evil are as clearly identified in the SF as they are in the fantasy, and no less evident in the adult fiction than in the young adult books. The stories also tend to be highly moralistic, depending on a fixed code of ethics that emphasizes the basic goodness of most individuals and the evident uselessness of those not imbued with this goodness. In most of her works, evil beings are either reformed or discarded.

Mayhar's greatest accomplishment is the description of physiological and social functions of a wide range of organisms such as crystalline, electrical, or fuzzy-green creatures, as well as wizards, shamans, witches, rulers, and adventurers. *Khi to Freedom*, for example, is two loosely connected episodes in the adventures of Hale Enbo, a human extraordinarie, and each is enriched by the many homey descriptions of eating and sleeping, and the social interactions between the human and his various cohorts and enemies. *Exile on Vlahil*, her best and most representative work, succeeds as much because of the elaborate symbiosis that constitutes Vlahil's eco-culture as it does through any adventure-plot elements.

More recently, Mayhar has produced young adult novels, such as *Makra Choria*, *Medicine Walk*, and *A Place of Silver Silence*. She has also collaborated with Ron Fortier on two novels, *Trail of the Seahawks* and *Monkey Station*. Both are nominally science fiction, although *Trail* has a heroic-fantasy plot based on a female, Conan-type hero (reminiscent of Grittel Sudotha), and a reprise of viking- or pirate-raids in a time after total cultural disintegration where people ride large dogs instead of horses and monkeys have become sentient. *Monkey Station* could be classified as high-tech horror, but chronologically predates the story in *Trail*. Rather, it starts with AIDS research, following rumors that the virus was a mistake in germ warfare. The two very different stories and settings of *Trail* and *Monkey* are linked by the monkeys' sentience. Still, the SF-horror reader who likes Crichton will also appreciate *Monkey*, while the reader of heroic fantasy will be drawn to *Trail*.

—Janice M. Bogstad

---

**McALLISTER, Bruce (Hugh).** American. Born in Baltimore, Maryland, 17 October 1946. Educated at Claremont Men's College, California, B.A. 1969; University of California, Irvine, M.F.A. 1971. Married Caroline Reid in 1970; one daughter and one son. Sports rewriter, United Press International, New York, 1967; staff writer, Doubleday Multimedia, Santa Ana, California, 1969; Visiting Instructor, Long Beach City College, California, 1971–73, and California State University, Fullerton, 1973–74; managing editor, *Best SF* anthology series, Bobbs Merrill, Indianapolis, 1973–75. At University of Redlands, California: Visiting Instructor, 1971–74; Assistant Professor, 1974–79, Associate Professor, 1979–83, and since 1983, Professor of English (Director of the Writing Program since 1974). Since 1983, media relations director and editor, Policy Research Center. Since 1980, freelance consultant in technical and scientific writing and public relations; since 1982, consultant, VSP Associates, Sacramento, California. Academic affairs editor, *Bulletin of the Science Fiction Writers of America*, 1973–74. Since 1972, associate editor, *West Coast Poetry Review* and WCPR Press, Reno, Nevada. Recipient: Bread Loaf Writers Conference scholarship, 1972; Squaw Valley Writers Conference fellowship, 1973; University of Redlands Jubilee Medallion, 1983, and Outstanding Teaching award, 1983. Address: c/o Tor Books, 49 West 24th Street, New York, New York 10010, U.S.A.

SCIENCE-FICTION PUBLICATIONS

Novels

*Humanity Prime*. New York, Ace, 1971.
*Dream Baby*. New York, Tor, 1989.

Short Stories

*The Faces Outside*. San Bernardino, California, Borgo Press, 1985.

OTHER PUBLICATIONS

Other

Editor, *SF Directions*. Christchurch, New Zealand, Edge Press, 1972.
Editor, *Their Immortal Hearts*. Reno, Nevada, WCPR Press, 1980.

* * *

Bruce McAllister is a writer's writer, a man whose work has always been highly regarded by his fellow professionals, but who remains relatively unknown and unappreciated among science-fiction fans. The reasons for this are many: he is a slow and meticulous craftsman, often requiring 20 drafts for every story completed and published; he has simultaneously pursued a career as a university English professor, thereby limiting his writing time; he has always preferred shorter lengths, in a field where regular production of novels is essential to achieving and maintaining broad public recognition; he eschews sequels, serials, and sword-and-sorcery fantasy; his fictions focus on character development, not mindless action-adventure; and he has never been prolific, even in his early years. Since 1965, he has published some 50 short stories, two novels, and 45 poems, in addition to editing several noteworthy anthologies.

"The Faces Outside," written when the author was 16, sets the tone for the rest of his work. The nameless hero finds himself floating in a tank with his mate and an assortment of aquatic creatures; their only contact with the outside world is a disembodied Voice. The Voice tells them that the faces watching them through the ports are the enemy, aliens who have annihilated the rest of the human race, and who have altered these two survivors into underwater humanoids. The two eventually transcend captivity by developing mental powers that will vanquish their alien captors, thereby assuring the survival of a new human race.

Here in microcosm are the basic themes of McAllister's work. His protagonists are tortured individuals caught between a Heaven and Hell not of their own choosing. Their suffering and tribulations take them from the Limbos of their own minds to an ultimate realization, epiphany, or metamorphosis—or a combination of all three. In the author's early fictions, the theme of self-transcendence often translates into rather obvious power fantasies, in which one lonely or alienated character somehow manages to conquer his nemesis (i.e., himself), represented by alien or human monsters, or by some other life- or mind-threatening situation.

In the later stories, and particularly in the two long novels, *Humanity Prime* and *Dream Baby*, the author's treatment of these themes becomes more sophisticated, his view of humans more cynical, his treatment of humans' self-sacrificing inclinations more realistic, his feeling for the ultimate tragedy of the human condition more poignant (but never needlessly sentimental). These fictions also demonstrate an understanding of the female psyche unsurpassed in the work of any other male SF writer except D.G. Compton.

*Humanity Prime*, greatly expanded from McAllister's first story, "The Faces Outside," mixes mermen, cyborgs, intelligent sea turtles, and telepathic powers to produce one of the most compelling and convincing portraits of an underwater human species ever published. The author's intimate knowledge of human and animal biology, and his childhood experiences as the son of a behavioral psychologist, are reflected in this realistic and plausible extrapolation of humans functioning in an alien environment. To McAllister, animals are as human in their own ways as humans are sometimes animal in theirs; much of his fiction specifically concerns itself with the question of what it means to be human, and the answers are never simple, never easy to assimilate by either the characters or the reader.

The mutual themes of humans' alienation from self and the transcendence of human nature reach a crescendo in McAllister's brilliant second novel, *Dream Baby*, which took a decade to write, partially under the aegis of a National Endowment for the Humanities fellowship. Set in Indochina during the Vietnam War, this "nonfiction" novel is told largely in the first person by an Army nurse, Lt. Mary Damico, with interstices of real and fictional statements from Vietnam veterans (the author interviewed some 200 survivors of the War over a ten-year period).

McAllister cleverly interweaves the surreality of the wartime experience with actual contingency plans developed by the U.S. Army to end the war by interjecting special forces units into North Vietnam. In *Dream Baby*, the military cynically gathers together a group of veterans who have been experiencing a variety of paranormal experiences under combat. Mary's talent is her ability to dream the future, to forecast events that are rarely pleasant, and often depict horrifying glimpses of brutal deaths to come. The group is dropped into the North, where it is ordered to destroy the dikes in central Vietnam during the monsoon season, thereby flooding Hanoi into the sea (attempts were actually made by U.S. forces during the war to bomb these embankments).

The combination of severe psychological stress, discovery of the infiltrators by the North Vietnamese, and the threat of imminent death, suddenly melds the team into one psychical whole, and provides it with the means to escape and survive. To complete the circle, the would-be destroyers of tens of thousands of human lives return to South Vietnam to destroy just one life, the soulless instigator of the project, Bucannon, whose brutal psychological manipulations have matched anything the Vietcong had ever devised. Mary Damico, the healer who had been so overwhelmed with horror that she could not heal, must restore order to the universe in the only way she can, by executing the agent of chaos. Only in this way can her life and the lives of the other survivors return to some semblance of normalcy, with their talents fading away. In McAllister's universe, although a precarious balance between the forces of order and chaos can sometimes be achieved, ecstasy always walks hand-in-hand with agony, transcendence is always temporary, and nothing worthwhile is ever achieved without pain.

—Robert Reginald

---

**McCAFFREY, Anne (Inez).** American. Born in Cambridge, Massachusetts, 1 April 1926. Educated at Stuart Hall, Staunton, Virginia; Montclair High School, New Jersey; Radcliffe College, Cambridge, Massachusetts, B.A. (cum laude) in Slavonic languages and literature 1947; studied meteorology at City of Dublin University. Married E. Wright Johnson in 1950 (divorced 1970); two sons and one daughter. Copywriter and layout designer, Liberty Music Shops, New York, 1948–50; copywriter, Helena Rubinstein, New York, 1950–52. Currently runs a thoroughbred horse stud farm in Ireland; since 1978, director, Dragonhold Ltd., and since 1979, director, Fin Film Productions. Has performed in and directed several operas and musical comedies in Wilmington and Greenville, Delaware. Secretary-Treasurer, Science Fiction Writers of America, 1968–70. Recipient: Hugo award, 1968, 1979; Nebula award, 1968; Gandalf award, 1979; Balrog award, 1980. Agent: Virginia Kidd, Box 278, Milford, Pennsylvania 18337, U.S.A. Address: Dragonhold, Kilquade, Greystones, County Wicklow, Ireland.

### Science-Fiction Publications

Novels (series: Dinosaur Planet; Dragonriders of Pern; Harper Hall; Planet Pirate)

*Restoree.* New York, Ballantine, 1967; London, Rapp and Whiting, 1968.
*Dragonflight* (Dragonrider). New York, Ballantine, 1968; London, Rapp and Whiting, 1969.
*Decision at Doona.* New York, Ballantine, 1969; London, Rapp and Whiting, 1970.
*The Ship Who Sang.* New York, Walker, 1969; London, Rapp and Whiting, 1971.
*Dragonquest* (Dragonrider). New York, Ballantine, 1971; London, Rapp and Whiting-Deutsch, 1973.
*To Ride Pegasus.* New York, Ballantine, 1973; London, Dent, 1974.
*Dragonsong* (for children; Harper Hall). New York, Atheneum, and London, Sidgwick and Jackson, 1976.
*Dragonsinger* (for children; Harper Hall). New York, Atheneum, and London, Sidgwick and Jackson, 1977.
*The Dragonriders of Pern* (omnibus). New York, Doubleday, 1978.
*Dinosaur Planet.* London, Futura, 1977; New York, Ballantine, 1978.
*The White Dragon* (Dragonrider). New York, Ballantine, 1978; London, Sidgwick and Jackson, 1979.
*Dragondrums* (for children; Harper Hall). New York, Atheneum, and London, Sidgwick and Jackson, 1979.
*The Harper Hall of Pern* (omnibus). New York, Doubleday, 1979.
*Crystal Singer.* New York, Ballantine, and London, Severn House, 1982.
*The Coelura.* Columbia, Pennsylvania, Underwood Miller, 1983.
*Moreta, Dragonlady of Pern.* New York, Ballantine, and London, Severn House, 1983.
*Dinosaur Planet Survivors.* New York, Ballantine, and London, Futura, 1984.
*The Girl Who Heard Dragons* (for children). New Castle, Virginia, Cheap Street, 1985.
*Killashandra.* New York, Ballantine, 1985; London, Bantam, 1986.
*Nerilka's Story* (Dragonrider). New York, Ballantine, 1986; with *The Coelura*, London, Bantam, 1987.
*Dragonsdawn.* New York, Ballantine, and London, Bantam, 1988.
*The Renegades of Pern.* New York, Ballantine, 1989; London, Bantam, 1990.
*Sassinak* (Planet Pirate), with Elizabeth Moon. New York, Baen, 1990.
*The Death of Sleep* (Planet Pirate), with Jody Lynn Nye. New York, Baen, 1990.
*Pegasus in Flight.* New York, Ballantine, and London, Bantam, 1990.
*The Rowan.* New York, Ace, and London, Bantam, 1990.
*Generation Warriors* (Planet Pirate), with Elizabeth Moon. New York, Baen, 1991.
*All the Weyrs of Pern.* New York, Ballantine, 1991.
*Damia.* New York, Putnam, 1991.

Short Stories

*A Time When.* Cambridge, Massachusetts, NESFA Press, 1975.
*Get off the Unicorn.* New York, Ballantine, 1977; London, Corgi, 1979.
*The Worlds of Anne McCaffrey.* London, Deutsch, 1981.

Other Publications

Novels

*Three Graphic Novels.* Lancaster, Pennsylvania, Underwood Miller, 1990.
*The Mark of Merlin.* New York, Dell, 1971; London, Millington, 1977.
*The Ring of Fear.* New York, Dell, 1971; London, Millington, 1979.
*The Kilternan Legacy.* New York, Dell, 1975; London, Millington, 1976.
*Stitch in Snow.* San Francisco, Brandywine, 1984; London, Corgi, 1985.
*Habit Is an Old Horse.* Settle, Washington, Dryad Press, 1986.
*The Year of the Lucy.* San Francisco, Brandywine, 1986; London, Corgi, 1987.
*The Lady.* New York, Ballantine, 1987; as *The Carradyne Touch,* London, Macdonald, 1988.

Other

*The People of Pern.* Norfolk, Virginia, Donning, 1988.
*The Dragonlover's Guide to Pern,* with Jody Lynn Nye. New York, Ballantine, 1989.

Editor, *Alchemy and Academe: A Collection of Original Stories Concerning Themselves with Transmutations, Mental and Elemental, Alchemical and Academic.* New York, Doubleday, 1970.
Editor, *Cooking Out of This World.* New York, Ballantine, 1973.

*

Bibliography: *Leigh Brackett, Marion Zimmer Bradley, Anne McCaffrey: A Primary and Secondary Bibliography* by Rosemarie Arbur, Boston, Hall, 1982; *Anne McCaffrey: A Reader's Guide* by Mary T. Brizzi, Mercer Island, Washington, Starmont, 1986.

Manuscript Collections: Syracuse University, New York; Kerlan Collection, University of Minnesota, Minneapolis.

Anne McCaffrey comments:

I am a story-teller of *science fiction* and wish that label attached to my work in that field. I make this point as I am often classified, erroneously, as a fantasy writer. Since I am more interested in the interaction of people, the research I do for some of the books is not apparent, thus confusing the uninitiated. I have no pretentions to literary style or excellence, nor are my stories allegorical, mystical, or political. I cannot honestly call myself a feminist, though I do not disagree with the aims of the women's movement, and in *The Kilternan Legacy* I make comparisons between the rights of American women and the deplorable lack of status of Irish women. My personal philosophy was heavily influenced by Austin Tappan Wright's classic, *Islandia*—a book I read at 14 and consistently reread. Of all the stories I have written to date, *The Ship Who Sang* is my favorite.

* * *

Anne McCaffrey, creator of Pern, planet of telepathic dragons and their riders, is a builder of other complex universes. She also writes of the psi Talent world of Rowan, the crystal world of Killashandra Ree, and the Dinosaur planet. Other of her fiction does not fit into specific series. She also writes non-science-fiction mysteries and romances with strong female protagonists.

Her themes include bonding, birth, adolescent emergence, and adult transformation. Loss, disfigurement, and recompense are concerns in the early novels. She is a keen interpreter of family dynamics. Her imagery is drawn from music, Irish and other folklore, cuisine, classical mythology, and most particularly flight. In fact, the central premise for many McCaffrey novels is a means of flight, particularly space-travel. Imagination and love are quintessential in her work.

McCaffrey's earliest acknowledged story, "Lady in the Tower" (1959) introduced psionic Talents who guide spacecraft. The Rowan, a brilliant, lonely Prime Talent, overcomes mental obstacles in order to travel light years to join the love of her life, Jeff Raven. Later works (*Get off the Unicorn* and *To Ride Pegasus*) explore the earlier history of the psionic Talented. A recent novel, *The Rowan,* fulfills McCaffrey's intention to expand the 1959 story. Raven and Rowan's daughter, Damia, is the subject of another novel. The early history provides material for the recent *Pegasus in Flight.* The Talent series explores issues of youthful emergence and transformation, using imagery of birds and mythical beings. McCaffrey characterizes adolescents and adults finding their unique place in the universe and discovering love at the same time—an appealing and enduring theme.

The transformation theme arises in another early work, *Restoree,* in which a terrestrial woman is kidnapped and dismembered by aliens who butcher and eat sentients. Humanoid aliens restore and beautify her (hence the title). Restoration has previously resulted in mindless monsters, so the heroine is imprisoned. Together with a dashing alien man, she escapes, and the two become lovers. Some readers have criticized the book as melodramatic and sexist; in fact, it deliberately parodies space opera and gothic romance.

*Decision at Doona* explores family dynamics and problems of race relations between humans and aliens, the cat-like Hrrubans. Adroit point-of-view manipulation and sensitive portrayal of children mark this novel. Transformation again is a theme in *The Ship Who Sang,* in which Helva, a child born with multiple physical handicaps, becomes the cyborg brain of an interstellar starship. Helva's unconventional friendships and love affairs demonstrate McCaffrey's interest in strong female characters.

In McCaffrey's awarding-winning Dragonriders of Pern books, human inhabitants of Pern are threatened by a voracious mycorrhizoid called Thread that crosses vacuum from another planet, the Red Star. Earlier colonists have bio-engineered psionic dragons as a defense. The dragons bond telepathically to their riders and burn Thread out of the air with phosphine-loaded breath. Dragons can also cross space—and, it is learned, time—telekinetically. The most moving and spirited passages in the Pern books depict dragon hatching, bonding, and mating. In the Harper Hall trilogy, dragonflight becomes a metaphor for artistic creation, with the rider as intellect and the dragon itself as emotion and drive. The Pern books, because of a few feudal touches, are sometimes mistakenly called fantasy, but Pernese society and science are all based on meticulously researched—if sometimes speculative—science. They are science fiction.

The early novella "Dragonflight" depicts the hardships of Lessa and her bonding with the golden dragon Ramoth. The trilogy, *Dragonflight*, *Dragonquest*, and *The White Dragon*, parallels the juvenile, or Harper Hall, trilogy *Dragonsong*, *Dragonsinger*, and *Dragondrums*. As a group, these develop leading characters—F'lar, Menolly, Master Robinton—of the far-future world after Pern's origin as an Earth colony has been forgotten. *Moreta, Dragonlady of Pern* and *Nerilka's Story* develop some of McCaffrey's mature themes of growth and service as avenues to life-long happiness. In *The Renegades of Pern*, McCaffrey experiments with a panoramic view of Pern in the age of Ramoth, and develops an array of characters, including a swashbuckling female criminal, Thella. The more recent *Dragonsdawn* recounts adventures of the original colonists, the discovery of fire-lizards from which a colonial woman genetically engineers the first queen dragon, Faranth, and the adventures of the first riders.

In the Killashandra books, begun in Roger Elwood's *Continuum* volumes and revised extensively for *Crystal Singer*, Killashandra Ree's musical ability enables her to cut special crystal used in interstellar travel and communication. The crystal planet's indigenous life form is a symbiote that fuses with the cutter's nervous system, bestowing long life and, unfortunately, madness. The series is the darkest of McCaffrey's work, fascinating for its rich symbolism, tortured characters, and use of unreliable narrator.

*Dinosaur Planet* and *Dinosaur Planet Survivors* feature a mysterious garlic-scented planet with life from several eras of Earth's prehistory, including intelligent pteranodons. The first book sets up mysteries about these creatures; the second solves them, if a bit too facilely. Related books are McCaffrey's collaborations with Elizabeth Moon, *Sassinak* and *Generation Warriors*, and with Jody Lynn Nye, *The Death of Sleep*, all of which explore the disruption of natural life rhythms through cryogenic sleep.

*The Coelura* features sentients who weave empathic clothing. McCaffrey is also adept at the short story. In all, her style has a neo-classic flavor in wit, sarcasm, and clarity. She is at her strongest depicting love and bonding, between lovers, family members, humans and animals, humans and aliens. Her flight imagery—dragons, Pegasus, spaceship—is compelling. With these, her characterization and world-building make her a significant science-fiction writer.

—Mary Turzillo Brizzi

---

**McAULEY, Paul J.** British. Born in Strovel, Gloucestershire, 23 April 1955. Educated at Bristol University, B.Sc. in botany and zoology 1976, Ph.D. in botany 1980. Recipient: Philip K. Dick award, 1989. Address: c/o MBA Literary Agents, 4S Fitzroy Street, London W1P SHR, England.

SCIENCE-FICTION PUBLICATIONS

Novels

*Four Hundred Billion Stars.* London, Gollancz, and New York, Ballantine, 1988.
*Secret Harmonies.* London, Gollancz, 1989; as *Of the Fall*, New York, Ballantine, 1989.
*Eternal Light.* London, Gollancz, 1991.

Short Stories

*The King of the Hill and Other Stories.* London, Gollancz, 1991.

* * *

Paul McAuley's first novel, *Four Hundred Billion Stars* was something of a rarity in British science fiction, a hard science novel in the *Analog* mould. Set several hundred years from now, it deals with mankind's expansion outward into the stars, a Federation of ten human-colonised worlds encountering the presence of ancient alien life for the first time. Dorthy Yoshida, a "Talent" (or telepath) is sent out to one of the worlds terraformed by the aliens. What she discovers there changes both her and humans' perception of the history of the galaxy, opening up vast vistas into the past. As might be surmised from this brief description, the elements of the work are traditional. It is very much a first novel, with all the concomitant flaws of an apprentice work. Slow-paced and downbeat in its message, it attempts to subvert the traditional devices of space opera but without great success. Dorothy is hard to empathise with and her slow trek towards enlightenment is somewhat wearying. The subversive techniques of the novel also tend to work against the natural dynamics of the form and dampen reader enjoyment, leading one to consider the book over-long despite its actual brevity. Likewise, the hard science expository nuggets are presented more as lectures—undigested chunks of fact—than as a natural part of the novel's furniture. A good idea presented in a mediocre manner, it nonetheless attracted the Philip K. Dick Memorial award for best new novel.

Something of this same low-energy burn is to be found in McAuley's second novel, *Of The Fall*, (published as *Secret Harmonies* in the United Kingdom). Once again, McAuley attempts to harness his knowledge as a research biologist to present us with yet another enigmatic alien race. This time, however, there is no cosmic revelation at the end of the quest, and the colony world on which the action takes place differs little in its essential ingredients from the colonies that the Imperial powers controlled in the early 20th century, complete with late 20th-century campus. But the focus of the novel is not, this time, on aliens or environment but upon the human characters caught up in a revolution as their colony planet is cut off from the home world, Earth. What the books lacks in strangeness it makes up for in human involvement and in its vivid portrayal of change, culminating in a passage strongly reminiscent of the ending of *Earth Abides*.

*Of the Fall* shares (if loosely) the same historical background as *Four Hundred Billion Stars*, and McAuley has set another half dozen stories within this framework, including two novelettes, "The Airs of Earth" (in *Amazing*, January 1986) and "The Heirs of Earth" (in *Amazing*, May 1987). None of these works, however, was any preparation for the imaginative richness or scope of McAuley's novel *Eternal Light*. Here, all of the flaws of his debut have been turned into strengths. This is space opera again, but this time with a pace and imaginative energy that has rarely been matched in the genre. Dorthy Yoshida is again at the centre of events, joined this time by a starship war veteran, Suzy Falcon; a part-cybernetic punk, "Robot"; and a near-immortal "Golden," Talbeck Barlstilkin. Their struggle against the system—against the Greater Brazilian empire, the Federation of Worlds, the Navy, and a cartel of other "Goldens"—leads them out 115 light-years from Earth to an encounter with a "fast-star," travelling at a sixth the speed of light towards Sol. What they discover there, both about the alien Alea (the herders of McAuley's first novel) and the nature of their universe is of profound cosmological (and, one might say, religious) significance. A rich, constantly surprising work, *Eternal Light* embraces the heritage of vast-scale cosmological speculation championed by writers like Stapledon and Clarke and marries it to the hard-edged, high-energy gloss (and love of techno-detail) of the cyberpunks with exciting results. It seems likely to become one of the classic works of the 1990's.

—David Wingrove

---

**McDEVITT, Jack.** American. Born in Philadelphia, Pennsylvania, 14 April 1935. Educated at LaSalle, Philadelphia, 1953–57, B.A. 1957; Wesleyan University, Middletown, Connecticut, 1967–71, M.A.L.S. 1971. Served in United States Navy, 1958–62. Married Maureen McAdams in 1967; one daughter and two sons. English teacher, 1963–73. Since 1975, staff member of U.S. Customs Service. Member of U.S. Chess Federation. Recipient: Nebula award, 1988. Agent: Ralph Vicinanza, 111 Eighth Avenue, Suite 1501, New York, New York 10011. Address: 57 Sunset Boulevard, Brunswick, Georgia 31520, U.S.A.

SCIENCE-FICTION PUBLICATIONS

Novels

*The Hercules Text.* New York, Ace, 1986; London, Sphere, 1988.
*A Talent for War.* New York, Ace, and London, Kinnell, 1989.

*

Jack McDevitt comments:

Despite everything *The Washington Post* and CNN tell us, the world is full of decency, good humor, and courage. If you doubt it, stop by your local Special Olympics. Or watch the volunteers pour in after a hurricane has gone down Main Street like a bowling ball.

I have no interest in afflicting the comfortable. The arrogant and the selfish are boring, and we have no interest in them except to see them get theirs in the last chapter. Give me ordinary people, characters who like one another, who summon their courage reluctantly, but who ultimately confront what they really believe. Whenever I can achieve that kind of voyage, the narrative has to work.

* * *

In the 1980's, some critics divided the SF authors who came to prominence in that decade into the supposedly oppositional factions of "humanists" and "cyberpunks." Given this generalization, the work of Jack McDevitt definitely falls into the "humanist" camp. Although he deals with such traditional hard SF topics as first contact with alien intelligence and far-future military conflict, the emphasis in McDevitt's work is on the working-out of problems by rational individuals. Like the work of Isaac Asimov, McDevitt's stories usually contain, not villains, but people who are set in opposition to the protagonist. Unlike Asimov, McDevitt is also concerned with the aesthetic and spiritual lives of his characters; poets and painters are frequently as important as scientists and soldiers, and problems of religious faith and ethics are given just as much, if not more, weight than problems of science and technology.

McDevitt began publishing in the SF magazines in the early 1980's, quickly gaining attention when his 1983 short story "Cryptic" (in *Isaac Asimov's Science Fiction Magazine*, September 1984) was nominated for a Nebula award. The story is narrated by the administrator of a scientific research station who discovers that the SETI project that had formerly occupied the facility had picked up interstellar communications 20 years earlier, only to suppress the information when the then-administrator discovered that the communications were from two alien races at war with each other. "Cryptic" contains almost all the elements of McDevitt's later novels: an ordinary man caught up in extraordinary circumstances, trying to solve a cosmic riddle from the testimony of persons of superior intellect; scientists who are also men of faith (the current administrator is a Jesuit priest, the former a lapsed seminarian) and whose faith informs their scientific decisions; and a reverence for knowledge coupled with doubts as to how far fallible humanity can, or should, proceed with its discoveries.

All these elements are present in McDevitt's first novel, *The Hercules Text.* Once again, the topic is the search for extraterrestrial intelligence, and the central character, Harry Carmichael, is an administrator rather than a scientist. This time, however, the story is set in the near future and deals with the events surrounding the reception of a signal from a solar system in the constellation Hercules. The book is a splendid example of what Algis Budrys has called the "science-procedural novel," concerning itself with the process of decoding the alien text and the power struggles that ensue as various scientific and governmental factions vie for control of the information contained in the transmission. Although the emphasis is on problem-solving, McDevitt does not neglect his characters, giving all the major figures believable lives whose individual quirks and problems are fully integrated into the central problem of the Hercules Text. As in "Cryptic," Catholicism plays a major role; one of the scientists decoding the transmission is a priest, and the problem of how to protect humankind from the potentially dangerous information in the alien transmission is solved, in part, by hiding the recordings of the transmission in a Catholic church. Some of the novel's plot elements have been overtaken by recent world events—the Cold War is still alive, and much of the suspense of the second half of the novel derives from the United States and a still-mighty Soviet Union coming to the brink of war over access to the transmissions—and the novel ends with a rush of action that is somewhat out of tone with the rest of the book. On the whole, however, *The Hercules Text* is a superior first novel and an exemplary "first contact" story.

McDevitt's only other novel to date, *A Talent for War*, continues to explore many of the themes developed in *The Hercules Text.* Set thousands of years in the future, when humanity has colonized the stars and maintains an uneasy peace with the Ashiyyur, an alien race with whom humans fought a long and bitter war, the novel was packaged by Ace Books as a future-war epic. But while it contains a good deal of action and some violence, *A Talent for War* is primarily about an ordinary man trying to solve an extraordinary puzzle. A young antique dealer, Alex Benedict, receives an inheritance from an uncle, which leads him to believe that the uncle, an archaeologist, was on the verge of proving that the most revered hero of the human-Ashiyyur war, Christopher Sim, was a fraud. The bulk of the novel traces Benedict's journey from planet to planet as he investigates the problem; as he pieces the puzzle together, the most important people are not the soldiers who fought the war, as much as the historians and poets who witnessed the events and recorded them. As in *The Hercules Text*, the main question asked in *A Talent for War* is, essentially, a religious one: how will humanity cope with a sudden revelation? And McDevitt again turns to Catholicism for an answer, as the novel's prologue and epilogue are set in a remote Catholic monastery, which serves as both a refuge for one of the key players in the drama and, as in the earlier novel, a hiding place for potentially explosive information.

In addition to his two novels, McDevitt has continued to publish short fiction frequently in the SF magazines and original anthologies. His best-received work of short fiction to date is the Hugo and Nebula-nominated short story "The Fort Moxie Branch" (in *Full Spectrum*, September 1988), a fantasy about a magical library that contains all the greatest works of literature that was either unpublished or unappreciated in the author's lifetime. Again, the question is how much humanity is entitled to know: the contents of the library will not be released until the world has "achieved a true global community," according to the precepts of John of Singletry, a monk whose treatises were rejected in his own time.

Although McDevitt's work thus far has been largely confined to revisitations of classic SF themes, it is notable for its solid craftsmanship, its willingness to grapple with philosophical issues, and its concern with the arts as well as the sciences. McDevitt is also worthy of attention as a rare example of a science-fiction writer who presents Roman Catholicism as a tenable worldview that does not automatically stand in opposition to scientific rationalism. Novels such as *The Hercules Text* and *A Talent for War* are good candidates to become SF perennials, introducing successive generations of readers to the pleasures of the well-made science-fiction story.

—F. Brett Cox

---

**McDONALD, Ian.** British. Born in Manchester, England, in 1960. Moved to Northern Ireland in 1965. Address: c/o Bantam Books, 666 Fifth Avenue, New York, New York 10103, U.S.A.

SCIENCE-FICTION PUBLICATIONS

Novels

*Desolation Road.* New York, Bantam, 1988.
*Out on Blue Six.* New York, Bantam, 1989.

Short Stories

*Empire Dreams.* New York, Bantam, 1988.
*King of Morning, Queen of Day.* New York, Bantam, 1991.

* * *

Although Ian McDonald had had one story published in 1982 in the Northern Irish magazine *Extro*, he effectively burst onto the scene with "The Catherine Wheel" in *Isaac Asimov's Science Fiction Magazine* in January 1984. He immediately made a considerable impression, and, like some other writers from Britain and Northern Ireland, he has continued to have more visibility and success in the United States than in his own country. Most of his short stories and both his novels appeared first in the United States, and his short-story collection, *Empire Dreams*, has still not been published in the United Kingdom. This success in the United States is partly because, despite the Irish content of two of his stories ("Empire Dreams" and "King of Morning, Queen of Day"), the atmosphere, style, and heady emotions found in his work owe more to American writing than to British: his novels, in particular, show that he is steeped in American SF, and fully prepared to work within that idiom.

His first novel, *Desolation Road*, reads like Gabriel García Márquez's *One Hundred Years of Solitude* rewritten by Ray Bradbury. It tells of the founding of a settlement in the deserts of a terraformed Mars by Dr. Alimontado (he had intended to call it Destination Road, but was drunk at the time), and traces its history, through the life-stories of a handful of colourful settlers with wild and wonderful talents, until its final destruction 23 years later, and its disappearance beneath the sands. Like Márquez, the mood varies from realism (with all the correct science-fictional tropes) through to utter fantasy, with the small character-histories embedded within the text being the baits for the imagination; like Bradbury, the magic comes as much from the style and the atmosphere as from the narrative itself. The invention is endless, and even if it is apparent at times that we are dealing with the recycling of old ideas (even, as in *Out on Blue Six*, clear recapitulations from Terry Gilliam's *Brazil*), the presentation of those ideas is thoroughly individual. As a first novel, it is a considerable achievement, and the aspects of it that are less than perfect (such as the standardised and soul-less shoot-out towards the end), hardly mar the whole.

The possible flaw in *Out on Blue Six*—the standard wish-fulfilment pulp ending, with an apocalyptic revelation and the handful of rebels taking over the world and freeing it for space-flight—is no flaw at all, for its over-the-top character fits joyously with the rest of the book. *Out on Blue Six* portrays an insidious anti-utopia, a society dedicated to the creation of the greatest possible happiness for all its citizens: partly by means of the Love Police, who act against anyone who causes pain to others, and partly by insisting that the Compassionate Society's computers know better than any citizen what constitutes their individual happiness. The novel follows the fate of a number of outcasts or exiles from this world—the dissatisfied and cynical individualists who are standard characters in SF novels, although, this being a McDonald novel, they are all much larger than life, with their own bizarre histories. Most of the action takes place underneath the utopian city, in its sewers and service tunnels; part of it is concerned with an epic voyage to the Edge of the World, which turns out to be a wall separating the world of humanity from the dead and polluted planet beyond. As in *Desolation Road*, there is wild invention, considerable wit, and an imaginative and colourful use of language, which again makes a first-rate novel out of a number of fairly familiar ideas and situations.

There is little doubt that McDonald, if he continues writing, will become a major SF novelist. But at present, he is probably at his best—at his most controlled and structured—in his shorter fiction. "The Catherine Wheel," introducing the St. Catherine of Tarsis who was to be the major holy figure of *Desolation Road*, is the only one closely linked to the novels: each of the others is quite distinct in subject-matter and theme. I shall comment on just four, all novelettes first published in *Asimov's*. "Christian" is an emotionally charged story (told daringly in second-person singular narrative) leading from a description, from a young boy's perspective, of the timeless magic of a beach, through his meeting with a kite-flyer called Christian, and the slow realisation that this is a man who has been a star-pilot (we learn this through two tales told by Christian, both redolent of the romanticism of the star-ways we associate normally with Cordwainer Smith), to the final tragic conclusion. "Empire Dreams" holds a more conventional scientific message: it is about the attempt to cure a boy of leukemia through deep-dreaming, whereby the unconscious boy is fed by a computer with dreams based on his own fantasies. Thus, the story is made up of passages in the real-world, where Thomas Semple lies in his bed in the Royal Victoria Hospital in Belfast, intercut with his dreams, in which he joins his hero, space fighter-pilot Major Tom, as he blasts the enemy Zygons (just as Wee Tom's subconscious blasts his cancerous cells). The intercutting works well; the story is not only extremely effective as an exploration of a scientific innovation, but also as an investigation into the nature of youthful science-fictional fantasies and their interreaction with the real world.

The technique of interleaving "official" documents with narrative that McDonald tentatively uses in "Empire Dreams" is carried to its logical conclusion in "King of Morning, Queen of Day," which is entirely made up of documents supposedly written in 1909: the diary of an Irish astronomer, who believes he has observed a space-ship bound for Earth; the diary of his young daughter, who believes she has seen the little people; extracts from lectures; from an interview between the girl and W.B. Yeats; and from reports of doctors endeavouring to link and explain the whole sequence of events in terms of the new-fangled ideas of Dr. Freud. The sense of authenticity and plausibility is beautifully constructed, to create a story with an intriguing sense of mystery. Most recently, the 1990 story "Toward Kilimanjaro" is a more conventional first-person narrative, in which a young Irish writer travels to Kenya, and encounters a monstrous being in the jungle, the next stage in human evolution. If much of the terror is tongue-in-cheek, with Lovecraftian echoes such as, "I must finish my journal now, I can hear him calling, he is coming for me," it is nevertheless an accomplished story, showing McDonald's facility with both character and exotic setting. The 1990's will surely judge McDonald to be one of the greatest new voices of 1980's SF.

—Edward James

---

**McGOWAN, Inez.** *See* **PHILLIPS, Rog.**

---

**McINTOSH, J.T.** Pseudonym for James Murdoch Macgregor; also writes as H.J. Murdoch. British. Born in Paisley, Renfrew, 14 February 1925. Educated at Robert Gordon's College, Aberdeen, 1936–41; Aberdeen University, 1943–47, M.A. (honours) in English. Married Margaret Murray in 1960; two daughters and one son. Sub editor, Aberdeen *Press and Journal*, 1963– 85. Address: 63 Abbotswell Drive, Aberdeen, Scotland.

Science-Fiction Publications

Novels

*World Out of Mind.* New York, Doubleday, 1953; London, Museum Press, 1955.
*Born Leader.* New York, Doubleday, 1954; London, Museum Press, 1955; as *Worlds Apart*, New York, Avon, 1958.
*One in Three Hundred.* New York, Doubleday, 1954; London, Museum Press, 1956.
*The Fittest.* New York, Doubleday, 1955; London, Corgi, 1961; as *The Rule of the Pagbeasts*, New York, Fawcett, 1956.
*200 Years to Christmas.* New York, Ace, 1961.
*The Million Cities.* New York, Pyramid, 1963.
*The Noman Way.* London, Digit, 1964.
*Out of Chaos.* London, Digit, 1965.
*Time for a Change.* London, Joseph, 1967; as *Snow White and the Giants*, New York, Avon, 1968.
*Six Gates from Limbo.* London, Joseph, 1968; New York, Avon, 1969.
*Transmigration.* New York, Avon, 1970.
*Flight from Rebirth.* New York, Avon, 1971; London, Hale, 1973.
*The Cosmic Spies.* London, Hale, 1972.
*The Space Sorcerers.* London, Hale, 1972; as *The Suiciders*, New York, Avon, 1973.
*Galactic Takeover Bid.* London, Hale, 1973.
*Ruler of the World.* Toronto, Laser, 1976.
*This Is the Way the World Begins.* London, Corgi, 1977.
*Norman Conquest 2066.* London, Corgi, 1977.
*A Planet Called Utopia.* New York, Zebra, 1979.

Other Publications

Novels

*Take a Pair of Private Eyes* (novelization of TV series). London, Muller, and New York, Doubleday, 1968.
*A Coat of Blackmail.* London, Muller, 1970; New York, Doubleday, 1971.

Novels as James Macgregor

*When the Ship Sank.* New York, Doubleday, 1959; London, Heinemann, 1960.
*Incident over the Pacific.* New York, Doubleday, 1960; as *A Cry to Heaven*, London, Heinemann, 1961.
*The Iron Rain.* London, Heinemann, 1962.

Other as James Macgregor

*Glamour in Your Lens: A Commonsense Guide to Attractive Photography.* London, Focal Press, 1958.
*Wine Making for All.* London, Faber, 1966.
*Beer Making for All.* London, Faber, 1967.

*

J.T. McIntosh comments:

I became a science-fiction writer not by choice but by force of circumstance. At the time when I was ready to publish (1945–50), paper was in short supply and publishers tended to use it for books by established authors. America was the obvious market, but I had no accurate knowledge of the U.S. scene. So I wrote SF, in which accurate knowledge of the U.S. scene is not necessary.

Later, when I tried non-SF, the international nature of SF became clear to me. There was little interest in my mainstream fiction outside Britain, while the SF books often had editions in many other countries.

* * *

Under the pen name J.T. McIntosh, the Scots writer and journalist James Murdoch Macgregor first won recognition as an author of science fiction with *World Out of Mind*, his first novel. This work presents a future society organized around the ultimate merit system: IQ. All members of this society are rigorously tested for intelligence; test results place each individual in a group marked by a colored badge indicating rank. The governing class, wearing the white star indicating the highest 1% of intelligence, is infiltrated by a Martian who has been reprocessed as a human being and whose mission is to prepare for a Martian invasion. However, since the Martian spy has become completely human, he cannot help falling in love with the youngest (and most beautiful) living white star. He betrays the loveless Martians and thwarts the invasion. Humanity (and love) conquer.

Also greeted with critical enthusiasm, *Born Leader* develops two human conflicts: daring youth pitted against conservative age, and a cooperative libertarian society pitted against military totalitarian state. Mundis, a planet colonised by space settlers from an Earth destroyed by nuclear war, is inhabited by two generations: the original settlers, determined not to use nuclear power, and their children, born only after the 22-year space voyage, eager to explore its possibilities. Mundis's egalitarian society is threatened by invaders from a second Earth ship, a Spartan, loveless military group whose women are considered subhuman breeders. Under the threat of domination, the Mundans unite, develop nuclear defences, defeat the invaders, and integrate them into their own egalitarian system.

*One in Three Hundred* begins on an Earth doomed by a shift in its solar orbit. It shows the selection of a small and random minority for space colonisation, their hazardous voyage, and their sufferings in making Mars habitable from the point of view of one of the leaders responsible for the selection and supervision of a small group. Faced by the threat of a sadist and would-be dictator on Mars, the colonists rebel, kill the tyrants, and cooperate successfully in order to survive. *The Fittest* similarly shows humans forced to work together for survival against great physical odds. Earth is overpopulated by paggets, super-intelligent mice, cats, rats, and dogs, developed by accident in an experiment and determined to overwhelm human life by cutting lines of communication, devouring supplies, sabotage, and murder. Mankind can survive biologically only by using the uniquely human qualities of communication and cooperation to remain the fittest species in simple democratic communities free from social convention.

McIntoch's later full-length fiction fails to live up to the promise of his early novels. Although his later work still deals with his major themes—overpopulation in *The Million Cities*, space travel and evolution in *200 Years to Christmas*, the aftermath of holocaust in *Out of Chaos*, and morality in *Six Gates from Limbo*, *Transmigration*, and *Flight from Rebirth*—he tends to repeat and overwrite early plots, often expanding ideas originally published as short stories. His ability to write fast and convincing action remains, but he fails to present themes and ideas as convincingly as his novels from the early 1950's.

McIntoch's four early novels interestingly depict libertarian utopias whose members' mutual concern and willingness to cooperate in order to survive demonstrate a hopeful view of human nature in a threatening universe. The terrible odds his characters must face are plausible threats for our future: overpopulation, misdirected technology, war, physical changes on Earth itself. In the Darwinian struggle to survive, women become essential. McIntoch's heroes are typically attracted to independence, competence, and strength in their mates, rather than to dependence, passivity, and physical frailty they might have preferred in easier times. McIntoch's ability to depict realistically the violence and dangers of the unknown future and his hopefulness about mankind's ability to endure make his early novels both moving and memorable.

—Katherine Staples

---

**McINTYRE, Vonda N(eel).** American. Born in Louisville, Kentucky, 28 August 1948. Educated at the University of Washington, Seattle, B.S. in biology 1970, graduate study in genetics, 1970–71. Conference organizer, and riding and writing instructor. Recipient: Nebula award, 1973, 1978; Hugo award, 1979. Agent: Frances Collin, Rodell-Collin Literary Agency, 110 West 40th Street, New York, New York 10018. Address: P.O. Box 31041, Seattle, Washington 98103-1041, U.S.A.

### Science-Fiction Publications

#### Novels

*The Exile Waiting.* New York, Doubleday, 1975; London, Gollancz, 1976.
*Dreamsnake.* Boston, Houghton Mifflin, and London, Gollancz, 1978.
*The Entropy Effect.* New York, Pocket Books, and London, Macdonald, 1981.
*Star Trek: The Wrath of Khan* (novelization of screenplay). New York, Pocket Books, and London, Futura, 1982.
*Superluminal.* Boston, Houghton Mifflin, 1983; London, Gollancz, 1984.
*Star Trek 3: The Search for Spock* (novelization of screenplay). New York, Pocket Books, and London, Panther, 1984.
*Enterprise: The First Adventure* (Star Trek). New York, Pocket, 1986.
*Star Trek 4: The Voyage Home.* New York, Pocket, 1986; London, Grafton, 1987.
*Barbary* (for children). Boston, Houghton Mifflin, 1986.
*Lythande*, with Marion Zimmer Bradley. London, Sphere, 1988.
*Starfarers.* Norwalk, Connecticut, Easton Press, 1989.
*Screwtop*, with *The Girl Who Plunged in*, by James Tiptree. New York, Tor, 1989.
*Transition.* Norwalk, Connecticut, Easton Press, 1991.

#### Short Stories

*Fireflood and Other Stories.* Boston, Houghton Mifflin, 1979; London, Gollancz, 1980.

### Other Publications

#### Other

*The Bride* (novelization of screenplay). New York, Dell, 1985.

Editor, with Susan Janice Anderson, *Aurora: Beyond Equality*. New York, Fawcett, 1976.

* * *

Vonda N. McIntyre's science fiction reflects her background in biology and genetics and shows a belief in the importance of the individual. Her characters are often outsiders in society who must meet the challenges of being different while maintaining their individuality. McIntyre's strongest characters are women and her settings usually assume equality, with gender playing no factor in perceived ability.

A hallmark of Vonda McIntyre's writing is her theme of physical transformation, either through genetic engineering or mechanical means. Most of her short stories have as characters genetically-changed individuals. The diggers and flyers in "Fireflood" were originally humans who chose to be altered for specific tasks in the exploration and colonization of space. The flyers in "Wings" and "The Mountains of Sunset, the Mountains of Death" continue this idea. Gryf, in "Screwtop," is one of a group known as tetraparentals. Bred as a problem-solving team, all team members must work together to function correctly. This creates the story's conflict as Gryf endures punishment for wanting to assert his independence as an individual. "The Genius Freaks" deals with ethical problems surrounding the breeding of extraordinarily intelligent individuals.

McIntyre's novels continue the genetic engineering theme. To be used for curing diseases, the snakes in *Dreamsnake* must be genetically altered by the healers. *Superluminal* introduces the idea of divers, humans who have been genetically changed with a virus, enabling them to live in the sea and communicate with cetaceans. Divers also figure prominently in *Starfarers* and *Transition.* Even when McIntyre builds on the already created Star Trek universe, as in *Enterprise: The First Adventure*, the genetic theme occurs. The vaudeville troupe travelling on the *Enterprise* owns a horse bred to have wings although it cannot fly in Earth's gravity. It is interesting that flyers also make an appearance in this novel in the guise of alien beings.

Closely related to genetic manipulation is physical transformation through mechanical means. This is presented most dramatically in "Aztecs." Pilots of spacecraft must replace their biological hearts with artificial ones to survive superluminal travel. They resent the nickname reflected in the title as they do not feel sacrificial. In "Spectra," workers have metal sockets for eyes, to link with and manipulate electronically-fed data. "The End's Beginning" is told from the viewpoint of a dolphin implanted with a machine of destruction.

Biocontrol is an essential technique for McIntyre's characters. Young people in *Dreamsnake* routinely receive training in fertility control. On her journey to replace her lost dreamsnake, the healer, Snake, encounters a young man whose life was drastically affected by a lack of such training. In "Aztecs," Laenea's control of her body's rhythms and functions is vitally important to her body's acceptance of an artificial heart. It becomes the central conflict of the story as Laenea's rhythms, irrevocably changed after the surgery, do not and cannot coincide with her lover's. *Starfarers* and *Transition* again present a future where biocontrol is the norm. When others learn that Gerald cannot control his biological reactions in times of stress, they pity him.

McIntyre frequently shows the danger of making assumptions by choosing ambiguous names and by carefully not mentioning a character's gender until function and personality are well established. The aliens in *Enterprise: The First Adventure* have no external clues to sexual identity. After prolonged interaction with the beings, Captain Kirk is startled to hear the one he assumed to be the leader referred to as "she."

Another feminist element is McIntyre's portrayal of nontraditional sexual partnerships and individual freedom of choice in sexual preferences. The idea of a multiple partnership with no particular pairing orientation occurs in *Dreamsnake* and *The Entropy Effect.* It becomes a major focus of *Starfarers* and *Transition*, with three members of the alien contact team constituting a family partnership. Even though the three are married to each other, they remain free to form liaisons outside of the partnership if they wish. In a nice twist, the other members of the starship community consider this form of alliance to be old-fashioned.

McIntyre's earlier works are tightly written and compelling in mood. At her best in "Of Mist, and Grass, and Sand," *Dreamsnake*, and "Aztecs," it is not surprising that she received Nebula and Hugo awards for them. *Dreamsnake* succeeds in adding to the richness of Snake's story begun in "Of Mist, and Grass, and Sand." The realization that it is set in the same post-apocalyptic earth as *The Exile Waiting* adds an interesting dimension. On the other hand, *Superluminal*, the expansion of "Aztecs," is disappointing after the promisingly strong images of the novella. While the divers' story is intriguing in its own right, it seems awkwardly spliced into the original. Orca, a diver, becomes the central female character as she struggles with being alien not only to humans but also to her own species in her aspirations to be a pilot. It is Radu Dracul, Laenea's unfortunate lover in "Aztecs," who continues the original pilot's story in the novel.

McIntyre's more recent novels, while still producing thought-provoking ideas, seem influenced by the serial nature of the Star Trek novels. All of McIntyre's elements are present in *Starfarers* and *Transition*, but they are diffused by a multiplicity of characters and the emphasis on action. Thus, J.D. Sauvage's struggles with acceptance and responsibility become submerged in the additional and equally engrossing stories of Victoria, Satoshi, Stephen Thomas, and Zev, the diver. The characters' personal conflicts are overshadowed by the frenetic pace of launching the space expedition against political opposition and the excitement of potential first contact.

The strength of McIntyre's writing comes from her ability to extrapolate an idea successfully. She insinuates her concepts as part of the underlying fabric of the story. Her plots focus on character development and societal interactions, and the science in her fiction is as believable as it is fascinating.

—Gay E. Carter

---

**McKENNA, Richard M(ilton).** American. Born in Mountain Home, Idaho, 9 May 1913. Educated at the University of North Carolina, Chapel Hill, B.A. in English 1956 (Phi Beta Kappa). Married Eva Mae Grice in 1956. Served in the United States Navy, 1931–53: chief machinist's mate; freelance writer from 1953. Recipient: Harper prize, 1963; Nebula award, 1966. *Died 1 November 1964.*

### Science-Fiction Publications

#### Short Stories

*Casey Agonistes and Other Science Fiction and Fantasy Stories.* New York, Harper, 1973; London, Gollancz, 1974.

### Other Publications

#### Novel

*The Sand Pebbles.* New York, Harper, 1962; London, Gollancz, 1963.

Short Stories

*The Sons of Martha and Other Stories*, edited by M. S. Wyeth, Jr. New York, Harper, 1967.
*The Left-Handed Monkey Wrench: Stories and Essays*. Annapolis, Maryland, Naval Institute Press, 1986.

Other

*New Eyes for Old: Nonfiction Writing*, edited by Eva Grice McKenna and Shirley Graves Cochrane. Winston-Salem, North Carolina, Blair, 1972.

* * *

Richard McKenna's literary reputation will almost certainly rest on the shoulders of his famous novel, *The Sand Pebbles*, set aboard a riverboat during the 1920's, during a period of rebellion in the Chinese mainland. He wrote a number of short stories as well, many of them in the science-fiction field, which has been forgotten, except within the genre itself. Despite the fact that only about a dozen stories were actually published, and not all of them memorable, McKenna remains a familiar name.

"The Fishdollar Affair," which appeared in 1958, is a spoof of ambassadorial ambition set in space but transparently a reflection of colonialist policies and procedures with which McKenna was familiar from his own days in China. Although one of the few real failures McKenna produced, it demonstrates his sardonic attitude toward human behavior, lampooned even more intensely in "Love and Moondogs," wherein a popular movement to pressure the Russian space program into retrieving an orbiting dog is twisted into a parody of itself.

Two other, much longer, stories from that same period established McKenna immediately as a writer to watch. "The Night of Hoggy Darn" tells of an ecologist called in to assist an introspective colony world. Shortly after his arrival, he is made a virtual prisoner, and it is evident that no one really wants him there, although his assistance is necessary to help solve a problem with a particularly nasty specimen of local fauna. The resolution is a superb blend of biology, anthropology, and sociology, a remarkably ambitious story for its time. Even more significant was "Casey Agonistes." Set within the confines of a hospital, Casey is an apparition, or perhaps not, a shared fantasy by many of the patients that somehow becomes the manifestation of their desires, uncertainties, and fears. Difficult to describe but marvelous to experience, it remains McKenna's most accomplished work of fiction.

"Hunter, Come Home" and "Mine Own Ways" have much in common with one another. In each case, an expedition is conducting research into the ecology of another planet, and in each case McKenna fuses anthropology and biology to create a metaphysical force that transcends the human ability to perceive exactly what is taking place. In the former, the protagonists are themselves altered physically by their environment; in the latter, a renegade human precipitates a native ritual that teaches the participants more about that world than they would ever have discovered under normal circumstances.

The next two stories deal with subject realities. "The Secret Place" involves the strange relationship between a man and a woman, and her belief that there exist fantastic worlds hidden in the deserts, ones unknown to most humans, which can be accessed under the right conditions. A more ambitious fantasy is "Fiddler's Green." A group of shipwrecked sailors suffers from growing thirst as they drift across the ocean in a lifeboat. One of their number leads them through a door into a world created by their own imaginations, but since it is a joint creation, there are inconsistencies and dangers they had not expected.

Although McKenna died just as his career was getting established, three unpublished stories appeared subsequently. "Home the Hard Way" follows the career of a spacer who falls in love with one of the planets he visits during a layover and tries everything conceivable to get out of his service commitment and settle. Before long, he is facing court martial, coercion by pirates, and the possibility that he may not live long enough to satisfy his ambition. In "They Are Not Robbed," Earth has been visited by the Star Birds, apparently representatives of an alien race whose outlook is so different from our own, trade is carried on with extreme difficulty. The aliens provide energy in exchange for the establishment of offices from which they purchase inexplicable items from a seemingly random segment of humanity, and from which they recruit humans into their circles. "Bramble Bush," a story written early in his career but not published until after his death, is another blend of anthropology and other world adventure. The central theme this time is that the inhabitants of the world being studied have a unique mental ability; they can use mental powers unknown to us to wrap a web of their own worldview around our own, effectively altering reality. It provides one of the best rationales for witchcraft ever to appear in fiction.

Most of McKenna's better stories are collected in *Casey Agonistes*, although "Bramble Bush" and "The Night of Hoggy Darn" remain uncollected. It is tragic that such an obvious major talent was cut off after such a short career. The science-fiction genre has never had enough thoughtful, inventive writers, and anthropological themes have been treated rarely and usually with less than admirable effect. Even with such a small body of work, McKenna's stature within the field seems likely to remain unchallenged for some time to come.

—Don D'Ammassa

---

**McKILLIP, Patricia A(nne).** American. Born in Salem, Oregon, 29 February 1948. Educated at San Jose State University, B.A. 1971, M.A. in English 1973. Recipient: World Fantasy award, 1975. Agent: Howard Morhaim Literary Agency, 174 Fifth Avenue, Room 709, New York, New York 10010, U.S.A.

Science-Fiction Publications

Novels

*Fool's Run*. New York, Warner, and London, Macdonald, 1987.
*The Sorceress and the Cygnet*. New York, Ace, 1991.

Novels for children

*The Throme of the Erril of Sherill*, illustrated by Julie Noonan. New York, Atheneum, 1973.
*The Forgotten Beasts of Eld*. New York, Atheneum, 1974; London, Futura, 1987.
*Riddle of Stars*. New York, Doubleday, 1979; as *The Chronicles of Morgan, Prince of Hed*, London, Sidgwick and Jackson, 1981.
*The Riddle Master of Hed*. New York, Atheneum, 1976; London, Sidgwick and Jackson, 1979.

*Heir of Sea and Fire.* New York, Atheneum, 1977; London, Sidgwick and Jackson, 1979.
*Harpist in the Wind.* New York, Atheneum, and London, Sidgwick and Jackson, 1979.

*Moon-Flash.* New York, Atheneum, 1984.
*The Moon and the Face.* New York, Atheneum, 1985.
*The Changeling Sea.* New York, Atheneum, 1988.

OTHER PUBLICATIONS

Novel

*Stepping from the Shadows.* New York, Atheneum, 1982.

Novels for children

*The House on Parchment Street*, illustrated by Charles Robinson. New York, Atheneum, 1973.
*The Night Gift*, illustrated by Kathy McKillip. New York, Atheneum, 1976.

* * *

Ranging from fairytale to young adult realistic fiction, from high fantasy to science fiction to adult contemporary fiction, Patricia A. McKillip's sweeping vision focuses on elemental themes unified by love, power, and magic. Her fantasy lies at the heart of her work, embraced by both adult and young adult readers. The first volume of her masterful *Riddle of Stars* trilogy appears among less than 30 recommended titles for teenagers in the recent fantasy genre list from the American Library Association (ALA). When that volume appeared in 1976, author Peter S. Beagle called McKillip "the best of the younger fantasy writers. . . . a storytelling sorceress, just now coming into her full power." McKillip's adult science-fiction novel *Fool's Run* became an ALA Best Book for Young Adults in 1987.

Fittingly, McKillip's first novel is set in the very place she began writing at age 14, at *The House on Parchment Street* in England. When Carol, an American, visits her English cousin Bruce for a summer, they unearth an unknown priests' tunnel by following 17th-century ghosts through their basement wall. This satisfying ghost story appeals to young teenagers struggling with adults for their own power; Carol and Bruce overcome adult logic to reveal the spirit world.

The young also rebel against their elders in McKillip's composed fairytale *The Throme of the Erril of Sherill.* In classic style, she relates the tale of a knight on an impossible quest to win a princess's hand. McKillip stretches and teases familiar forms in delightful language: her orchard has "horanges," her knight is Cnite Caerles, who seeks a "throme" which does not exist, "made of the treasure of words." Archetypal motifs expand when the quest become circular. The cnite creates the throme himself by writing the tale of his own quest, so inspiring the princess to choose him, leaving her enraged father saying "Bah."

From the seeds of these modest works blooms McKillip's first fantasy classic, *The Forgotten Beasts of Eld.* The female wizard Sybel lives on isolated Eld Mountain with a legendary falcon, lion, cat, swan, dragon, and talking boar, controlling them telepathically. Sybel does "not understand loving and hating, only being and knowing," until Lord Coren brings her baby Tamlorn, heir of Eldewold, to keep safe from struggles for the throne. Raising the child opens Sybel to human love, but also superhuman power, for she becomes caught between Tamlorn, his father Drede, and her new husband Coren. When Drede tries to steal Sybel's name to control her, she risks Tamlorn's and Coren's love for revenge against Drede. Her manipulations nearly cost Sybel her soul; realizing love cannot be controlled, she finally frees both her beasts and herself. McKillip's concern with personal power through the magic of naming dawns here in a resonant tale of love's triumph among fantastical beasts not soon forgotten.

A brief detour into realism with *The Night Gift*, an affecting story of a group of teenagers who give of themselves to help a suicidal friend, does not dilute McKillip's momentum toward the pinnacle of high fantasy. In her acclaimed *Riddle of Stars* trilogy, McKillip achieves a full-blown other-world peopled with hundreds of solid characters, all ranged behind the compelling hero Morgon on a forced trajectory toward destiny. In the first volume, *The Riddle Master of Hed*, young land-heir Morgon wants nothing more than to care for his simple farming people of Hed. Yet three mysterious stars on his forehead propel him toward a fate he cannot comprehend. In Morgon's world, the wizards who disappeared 700 years ago left their wisdom in riddles. Morgon's talent for riddling wins him the hand of beautiful Raederle of An. But before he can claim her, an unknown force claims him as "Star-Bearer." After finding a harp and sword with stars to match his own, Morgon is beseiged by shapeshifters trying to kill him. "An impossible web of riddles was being woven about his name," and Morgon must unravel a new identity rife with danger.

Only the High One, remote ruler of the realm, might explain Morgon's stars, but after a perilous journey to the High One's mountain, Morgon disappears. In *Heir of Sea and Fire*, Raederle searches for Morgon, discovering in the process her own formidable magic powers and her distressing kinship to those trying to destroy Morgon. In the final volume *Harpist in the Wind*, Morgon and Raederle are united to solve the riddle and the fate of their realm together.

In the *Riddle* trilogy, McKillip brings to fruition the themes and style introduced in *The Forgotten Beasts of Eld.* Magic becomes the ability to "know and accept . . . the thing as itself." The human desire for control, without love, makes people abuse power. "Things are themselves. We twist the shapes of them," says a riddle-master. The worst abuse is stealing minds, where the essence of one's name and freedom resides, which Sybel could not forgive Drede in *Forgotten Beasts*, and which threatens everyone in Morgon's realm. Like Christ, Morgon is a "man of peace" promised to his people, though he transcends that role with Raederle as his partner. *Riddle of Stars* challenges readers to unwind tangled threads of lore as Morgon does; readers share his desperation and suspense as he follows his mystery fate. The intricate plot does not unravel smoothly, but with varied rhythms demanding patience and attunement to McKillip's rich themes, embroidered in dazzling words.

After this definitive fantasy, McKillip emerged from a three-year hiatus with her only contemporary adult novel, *Stepping from the Shadows.* Through the split persona of her young writer narrator, McKillip wrestles with her writer's identity in a fascinating and thoroughly original character study. The narrator has a shadow companion Frances, an imaginative dreamer whom she judges and tries to control throughout childhood, but who "wished me into her story," an aspect of self. To cope with reality, Frances publishes her fantasy novel about her creation the Stagman, who then haunts the obsessive narrator's real world. How the writer unites opposing sides of herself is a compelling and heartrending story, surely somewhat autobiographical, and flawlessly executed in lyrical prose binding worlds seen and unseen: "The world was jumbled with language, though it looked very simple. . . . But against my chest was long division, and beyond the sky were a thousand saints, praying for our souls."

In her young adult science fantasy *Moon-Flash* and its sequel *The Moon and the Face*, McKillip distills both her prose style and recurring motifs into clear, deceptively simple form. Kyreol is a young girl coming of age in her primitive Riverworld culture. Her avid curiosity tempts her beyond her world's end on a river trip with her childhood male friend Terje. Passing through dangerous falls, they are shocked to find that the world continues and is controlled by a domed city, a spaceport to other planets. Scientists at the dome protect the Riverworld culture from knowing the outer world, valuing the psychic dreams of its people, which the dome has lost to technology. Becoming a protector of the home she lost through knowledge, Kyreol "stepped outside of its story," but Terje sees the interconnectedness of all things and can integrate both worlds. Kyreol wonders about McKillip's abiding question: "How can people see and dream the same things, yet have a different language for them?"

McKillip pursues technology to its ultimate nightmare in *Fool's Run*, adult science fiction in which a future Earth is unreconciled to psychic power. Separated twin sisters probe connected mysteries. Impelled by a vision, Terra commits mass murder. On Terra's orbiting prison, her disguised sister the Queen of Hearts plays a rock concert, triggering her twin's escape and perhaps apocalypse. McKillip returns to a tangled plot of riddles. Negotiating its taut twists, readers are confronted with an unsettling challenge to the values that may place our world in jeopardy.

In *The Changeling Sea*, her most recent young adult fantasy, McKillip fashions a perfect and elegant fairytale around lonely young Peri, coming of age in a simple fishing village after her father drowns and her mother is lost to endless mourning. After hurling angry hexes into the sea that stole her family, Peri's fate becomes entwined with a sea-dragon, a mage, two princes, the King, and the Sea-Queen. Through love and loss, Peri's magic talents are awakened and her world is restored to proper order where all things are named and love is a healing power. Not a strand of seaweed is out of place; McKillip has mastered the literary form that transmits her message that magic bridges "the confusing distance between things," and that we must use our power to keep all things connected. McKillip's early complex wordiness has refined into a spare poetic style that is joyful to read.

—Cathi MacRae

---

**McLAUGHLIN, Dean (Benjamin, Jr.).** American. Born in Ann Arbor, Michigan, 22 July 1931. Educated at the University of Michigan, Ann Arbor, A.B. 1953. Buyer for Slater's Inc., bookshop, Ann Arbor. Address: 1214 West Washington Street, Ann Arbor, Michigan 48103, U.S.A.

SCIENCE-FICTION PUBLICATIONS

Novels

*Dome World.* New York, Pyramid, 1962.
*The Fury from Earth.* New York, Pyramid, 1963.
*The Man Who Wanted Stars.* New York, Lancer, 1965.

Short Stories

*Hawk among the Sparrows.* New York, Scribner, 1976; London, Hale, 1977.

* * *

Dean McLaughlin's novels display a fascination with the concept of one man capable of altering the entire course of history. McLaughlin does not have in mind brilliant military strategists or mighty-thewed barbarians, but common men, those who may even doubt their own actions but carry through with them nonetheless. Danial Mason, leader of the undersea city of Wilmington in *Dome World*, is a perfect example. Mason is chief administrator of the domed city, one of many that have sprung up on the ocean floor, built by various nations intent on mining or fishing or trading with other nations. But the undersea cities are also the focus of some conflict because of the haphazard fashion in which matters of sovereignty have been resolved. So it is that the American Union and South Africa are on the verge of war over control of a rich vanadium deposit that lies between two such domes. Because of the utter vulnerability of the domes, Mason organizes a widespread secession from the mainland nations to prevent fatal involvement in their war. The second half of the novel deals with the situation some years later when the creation of smaller, individualized domes is the cause of tension between the newly formed league of domed cities and the mainland authorities. Once again a small businessman ignores his own government to take steps that eventually reduces the chance of war. Both of McLaughlin's characters are far from physically fit; one is recently returned from the moon and has difficulties with Earth's greater gravity, and the other has a weak heart that might cease to function at any time.

Similarly, the protagonist of *The Fury from Earth* is a pacifist who refuses to help the government of Venus to develop weapons for their war with Earth. On the other hand, he is willing to help design purely defensive weapons, and is quick to see that a new development on Earth could be used for interstellar travel rather than as an offensive weapon that will shake entire planets. This is thematically somewhat similar to McLaughlin's remaining novel, *The Man Who Wanted Stars*, in which a single man keeps the space program alive, primarily through his own stubbornness. The latter novel suffers somewhat from the didactic material, which often interferes with the plot, and with the megalomania of the central character, which often causes the reader to dislike him even while agreeing with his position.

McLaughlin has also produced a string of competent short stories, at least two of which are exceptional. "Hawk among the Sparrows" is somewhat unusual for McLaughlin in that the hero tries to alter history and fails utterly. He has been projected back through time with a modern supersonic aircraft, and assumes that he can affect the course of the air war in Europe. Such is not the case. He cannot locate appropriate fuel, and his aircraft travels so rapidly that it is impossible for him to engage in combat with his slower, more primitive antagonists. McLaughlin also produced one of the more fascinating alien societies in "The Brotherhood of Keepers."

Although not a stylistic virtuoso, McLaughlin employs clean prose throughout his writing, with a crisp delivery that falters only in *The Man Who Wanted Stars.* He avoids larger-than-life characters very consciously, taking pains to make his characters vulnerable and human. His plots and situations ring true, and he takes care that issues are for the most part presented in many facets rather than clear cut. Most of his better fiction leaves the reader with something to consider even after the story has ended, although McLaughlin is careful to tie up necessary loose ends.

The appearance of a new short story, "Epsilon Probe," after McLaughlin's absence from SF of over ten years is long overdue, and is hopefully a sign that McLaughlin has not entirely abandoned a field to which he could potentially contribute so skillfully.

—Don D'Ammassa

---

**McQUAY, Mike.** Also writes as Victor Appleton, Jack Arnett; Susan Claudia; Franklin W. Dixon; Laura Lee Hope; Carolyn Keene. American. Born in Baltimore, Maryland, 3 June 1949. Attended grammar school in Baltimore; McGuiness High School, Oklahoma City; University of Dallas, 1967–70. Married 1) Mary McQuay in 1968 (divorced 1981); 2) Sandy McQuay in 1982; one son and two daughters. Musician, aircraft worker in Asia, banker, factory worker, Artist-in-Residence, Central State University, Edmond, Oklahoma, from 1980. Agent: Russ Galen, Scott Meredith Literary Agency, 845 Third Avenue, New York, New York 10022. Address: 5933 NW 81st, Oklahoma City, Oklahoma 73132, U.S.A.

SCIENCE-FICTION PUBLICATIONS

Novels (series: Mathew Swain)

*Lifekeeper*. New York, Avon, 1980.
*Escape from New York* (novelization of screenplay). New York, Bantam, and London, Corgi, 1981.
*Mathew Swain: Hot Time in Old Town*. New York, Bantam, 1981.
*Mathew Swain: When Trouble Beckons*. New York, Bantam, 1981.
*Mathew Swain: The Deadliest Show in Town*. New York, Bantam, 1982.
*Mathew Swain: The Odds Are Murder*. New York, Bantam, 1983.
*Jitterbug*. New York, Bantam, 1984.
*Pure Blood*. New York, Bantam, 1985.
*Mother Earth*. New York, Bantam, 1985.
*My Science Project* (novelization of screenplay). New York, Bantam, 1985.
*Memories*. New York, Bantam, 1987; London, Headline, 1990.
*Isaac Asimov's Robot City 2: Suspicion*. New York, Ace, 1987; London, Futura, 1989.
*The Nexus*. New York, Bantam, 1989.

OTHER PUBLICATIONS

Novels

*Cradle to Grave* (as Susan Claudia). New York, Fawcett, 1983.
*The M.I.A. Ransom*. New York, Bantam, 1986.
*Panama Dead* (as Jack Arnett). New York, Bantam, 1990.

Fiction for children

*Tom Swift: Crater of Mystery* (as Victor Appleton). New York, Simon and Schuster, 1982.
*Tom Swift: Planet of Nightmares* (as Victor Appleton). New York, Simon and Schuster, 1983.
*Nancy Drew/Hardy Boys: Supersleuths II* (as Carolyn Keene and Franklin W. Dixon). New York, Simon and Schuster, 1984.
*Nancy Drew: Ghost Stories II* (as Carolyn Keene). New York, Simon and Schuster, 1985.
*Bobbsey Twins: Haunted House* (as Laura Lee Hope). New York, Simon and Schuster, 1985.

*

Mike McQuay comments:

My writing tends toward the sociological/humanistic end of the spectrum. Though considered a cynic by many of my detractors, I consider myself a social realist (an optimist in wolf's clothing). My work as a whole deals with the survival of the human spirit despite the out-of-control technologies we've set in motion, which puts me in direct opposition (gladly) with the science-as-God writers who seem to fill the shelves. Don't look for sugar coating in a McQuay book.

My main sub-theme seems to be discussions on the nature of reality, and the human's ability to construct reality to his own specifications.

* * *

Mike McQuay has established himself in a short time as an energetic and prolific writer whose science fiction projects an emphatically masculine vision. McQuay's Mathew Swain series makes an interesting effort to combine the science-fiction and private-eye genres, and his other novels display a penchant for vivid melodramatic action. Strongly individualist and nonconformist heroes are a distinguishing feature of McQuay's work, as well as an obvious specticism and distrust of the ethics and purposes of corporations and governments. Another intriguing trait of McQuay's fiction is the influence of his southwest background, which appears both in his style and in the nonconformist stance of his tough-minded heroes.

McQuay's first important novel was *Lifekeeper*, which employed the bold stroke of a black hero. In a dismal future divided between wilderness tribes and communal states, ruled by computers which outlaw individuality, Doral Dulan is a rebellious and archaic individualist who realizes his destiny by overthrowing the dominance of the machines and fulfilling the desert tribes' yearning for a messiah. Some sharp parallels with Frank Herbert's Dune novels are obvious, including an ending which attempts to suggest Herbert's sophisticated sense of irony.

This ambitious but uneven first novel was followed by *Escape from New York*, a novelization of a cynically conceived film melodrama about a near future in which New York City has collapsed into a forbidden zone or anarchic santuary for criminals and outcasts. Plissken, the heroic antihero, is characterized effectively, and his hard-headed and intractable individualism anticipates Matt Swain, the hero of McQuay's 21st-century private-eye series.

The Swain series is dedicated to the memory of Raymond Chandler, "who understood." Presumably McQuay is paying homage to Chandler's vision of a corrupt and materialistic society where ethical norms are in constant flux, and also to Chandler's Philip Marlowe, the incorruptible and disenchanted knight who uncovers forgotten crimes and repressed memories of venality and compromise, as Chandler described his hero's role in his famous essay and apologia, "The Simple Art of Murder."

In the first Swain adventure, *Hot Time in Old Town*, McQuay's private eye is depicted as a younger and slightly more idealistic Marlowe, and as a former law officer now playing a lone hand in a decaying Southwestern city suggestive of Dallas or Tulsa. However, Swain has a more active sex life than Marlowe, since

McQuay bestows on him a wealthy and voluptuous young woman, Ginny Teal, in the first novel; while in later books in the series other attractive women become Swain's lovers. Swain is also a more impulsive and physical hero than Marlowe, displaying a good deal of prowess with his fits and with weapons, somewhat in the mode of Robert B. Parker's Spenser. Yet like his model, Marlowe, Swain also remains true to the tradition of the private eye as a man of honor, showing himself to be relentless and incorruptible as he searches for the murderer of a dissolute heir in *Hot Time in Old Town*.

In the second Swain novel, *When Trouble Beckons*, McQuay takes his hero to a city on the moon where a large multinational corporation rules. Although Swain's mission is ostensibly to rescue Ginny, in reality the novel examines the corrupting influence of a decadent and dehumanizing social environment, evoking memories of Dashiell Hammett's Personville (or "Poisonville") in *Red Harvest*, and Ross MacDonald's scandal-ridden midwestern town in *Blue City*. *When Trouble Beckons* is notable for its unrelenting action, its virtuoso reversals of plot, especially in the closing pages, and its sympathetic characterization of an earthy woman cab driver.

*The Deadliest Show in Town* continues Swain's crusade against corporate dishonesty and greed, and government indifference and corruption, this time pitting the private eye against the 21st-century communications industry. The final entry to date in the series, *The Odds Are Murder*, continues the emphasis on violent physical action featured in the first three novels, as Swain investigates greed and scandal in the manufacture of pharmaceutical drugs. But the themes and attitudes of the Swain books are now beginning to seem repetitious and obsessive; none of the Swain novels has established itself as worthy of comparison with the mature Raymond Chandler.

To his credit, however, McQuay has refused to become the prisoner of a series with its limitations. In 1984, he published *Jitterbug*, a work that returns to the epic scale of *Lifekeeper*, depicting a dystopian world of the 22nd century. In this novel, a fanatical Arab dictatorship rules a decaying America; but this "corporation" is challenged successfully by the rebellion of Olson, another of McQuay's tough-minded heroes, who emerges from obscurity and a harsh upbringing in the southwest. *Jitterbug* shows marked growth in McQuay as a novelist, for its extrapolated future world is envisaged with both imaginative power and an increased thoroughness and plausibility.

*Pure Blood* is another vigorous adventure saga set in a much-changed New York State a thousand years hence. In the predominantly primitive post-disaster world of this novel, McQuay portrays an environment of barbaric humans and new creatures created by genetic experiment, where another of his outcast heroes, Morgan, tempered by the crucible of hardship and struggle, rises to leadership.

Of the more recent novels, *The M.I.A. Ransom* and *Panama Dead* belong to the action suspense category, and attempt to enter the profitable territory of Robert Ludlum and Tom Clancy. *The M.I.A. Ransom* deals with an elaborate plot to free a large number of American prisoners supposedly still held in Vietnam.

McQuay's other, recent, and more significant books are additions to his science-fiction canon. These include *Mother Earth*, a sequel to *Pure Blood; Robot City 2: Suspicion*, a formula novel for a series employing the premises of Isaac Asimov's Robot stories; *Memories*, which received the 1987 Philip K. Dick award; and another speculative novel, *The Nexus*. The most ambitious of these efforts is undoubtedly *Memories*, an elaborate time-travel tale. This narrative unfolds in a series of apparently unrelated scenes, which are gradually unified by an elaborate design. The plot involves visitors from a bleak future coming back to contemporary Oklahoma City to influence the lives of David Wolf, an unhappy psychiatrist, and his unfortunate sister. A victim of various childhood traumas and three failed marriages, Wolf is not exactly a superhuman hero, but Silv, a wise and tutelary spirit from the future, helps him find some meaning in his life. The action moves backward and forward in time, with much of the narrative describing Napoleon's fortunes in the era of the French Revolution and France's imperial triumphs.

*Memories* reveals a large imaginative scope, enriched by metaphysical speculation about human identity. McQuay seems to suggest that the psyche is essentially a collection of memories and emotions, which explains the title. However, despite its lofty aspirations and McQuay's usual command of the vernacular of the American Southwest, the novel suffers from an appearance of hasty composition and would have benefited from judicious editing.

*The Nexus* continues the imaginative speculation undertaken in *Memories*, but is set in the area around Dallas, and deals with a different cast of characters. The novel is innovative for McQuay both because of his use of Hindu mythology, and because of his experiments with narrative technique (some of the action is presented in a terse dramatic form, similar to the mode of a screenplay). McQuay's work unfortunately continues to be haunted by his persistent faults, among other things, an overabundance of plot and lapses of careless writing.

—Edgar L. Chapman

---

**MEEK, S(terner St.) P(aul).** Also wrote as Sterner St. Paul. American. Born in Chicago, Illinois, 8 April 1894. Educated at the University of Chicago, Sc.A. 1914; University of Alabama, University, S.B. 1915 (Phi Beta Kappa); University of Wisconsin, Madison, 1916; Massachusetts Institute of Technology, Cambridge, 1921–23. Married Edna Burndage Noble in 1927; one son. Football coach, Kirkley Junior College, Greenville, Texas, 1915; chemist, Western Electric Company, Hawthorne, Illinois, 1916, and Deuvitt Laboratories, Chicago, 1917. Served in the United States Army from 1917; directed small arms ammunition research, 1923–26; chief publications officer, Ordnance Department, 1941–44; retired due to disability, 1947: Colonel. Held patents on tracer ammunition. *Died 10 June 1972.*

### Science-Fiction Publications

#### Novels

*The Drums of Tapajos.* New York, Avalon, 1961.
*Troyana.* New York, Avalon, 1962.

#### Short Stories

*The Monkeys Have No Tails in Zamboanga.* New York, Morrow, 1935.
*Arctic Bridge.* London, Utopian, 1944.

#### Uncollected Short Stories (series: Dr. Bird)

"The Murgatroyd Experiment," in *Amazing Stories Quarterly* (New York), Winter 1929.
"The Red Peril," in *Amazing* (New York), September 1929.
"The Cave of Horror" (Bird), in *Astounding* (New York), January 1930.
"The Perfect Counterfeit" (Bird), in *Scientific Detective* (New York), January 1930.

"The Thief of Time" (Bird), in *Astounding* (New York), February 1930.
"The Radio Robbery" (Bird), in *Amazing* (New York), February 1930.
"Into Space" (as Sterner St. Paul), in *Astounding* (New York), February 1930.
"Cold Light" (Bird), in *Astounding* (New York), March 1930.
"The Ray of Madness" (Bird), in *Astounding* (New York), April 1930.
"Trapped in the Depths," in *Wonder Stories* (New York), June 1930.
"The Gland Murders" (Bird), in *Scientific Detective* (New York), June 1930.
"Beyond the Heaviside Layer," in *Astounding* (New York), July 1930.
"The Last War," in *Amazing* (New York), August 1930.
"The Tragedy of Spider Island," in *Wonder Stories* (New York), September 1930.
"The Attack from Space," in *Astounding* (New York), September 1930.
"Stolen Brains" (Bird), in *Astounding* (New York), October 1930.
"The Osmotic Theorem," in *Wonder Stories Quarterly* (New York), Winter 1930.
"Sea Terror" (Bird), in *Astounding* (New York), December 1930.
"The Black Lamp" (Bird), in *Astounding* (New York), February 1931.
"The Earth's Cancer" (Bird), in *Amazing* (New York), March 1931.
"When Caverns Yawned" (Bird), in *Astounding* (New York), May 1931.
"The Port of Missing Planes" (Bird), in *Astounding* (New York), August 1931.
"The Solar Magnet" (Bird), in *Astounding* (New York), October 1931.
"Giants on the Earth," in *Astounding* (New York), December 1931.
"Poisoned Air" (Bird), in *Astounding* (New York), March 1932.
"B.C. 30,000," in *Astounding* (New York), April 1932.
"The Great Drought" (Bird), in *Astounding* (New York), May 1932.
"Vanishing Gold," in *Wonder Stories* (New York), May 1932.
"The Synthetic Entity," in *Wonder Stories* (New York), January 1933.
"The Mentality Machine," in *Tales of Wonder* (Kingswood, Surrey), Spring 1939.
"Awlo of Ulm" and "Submicroscopic," in *Before the Golden Age*, edited by Isaac Asimov, New York, Doubleday, 1974.
"Futility," in *Gosh! Wow! (Sense of Wonder) Science Fiction*, edited by Forrest J. Ackerman, New York, Bantam, 1982.

Other Publications

Novel

*Island Born*. New York, Godwin, 1937.

Other (for children)

*Jerry: The Adventures of an Army Dog*. New York, Morrow, 1932.
*Frog, The Horse That Knew No Master*. Philadelphia, Penn, 1933.
*Gypsy Lad: The Story of a Champion Setter*. New York, Morrow, 1934.
*Franz, A Dog of the Police*. Philadelphia, Penn, 1935.
*Dignity, A Springer Spaniel*. Philadelphia, Penn, 1937.
*Rusty, A Cocker Spaniel*. Philadelphia, Penn, 1938.
*Gustav, A Son of Franz*. Philadelphia, Penn, 1940.
*Pat: The Story of a Seeing Eye Dog*. New York, Knopf, 1947.
*So You're Going to Get a Puppy*. New York, Knopf, 1947.
*Boots: The Story of a Working Sheep Dog*. New York, Knopf, 1948.
*Midnight, A Cow Pony*. New York, Knopf, 1949.
*Ranger, A Dog of the Forest Service*. New York, Knopf, 1949.
*Hans, A Dog of the Border Patrol*. New York, Knopf, 1950.
*Surfman: The Adventures of a Coast Guard Dog*. New York, Knopf, 1950.
*Paga, A Border Patrol Horse*. New York, Knopf, 1951.
*Red, A Trailing Bloodhound*. New York, Knopf, 1951.
*Boy, An Ozark Coon Hound*. New York, Knopf, 1952.
*Rip, A Game Protector*. New York, Knopf, 1952.
*Omar, A State Police Dog*. New York, Knopf, 1953.
*Bellfarm Star: The Story of a Pace*. New York, Dodd Mead, 1955.
*Pierre of the Big Top: The Story of a Circus Poodle*. New York, Dodd Mead, 1956.

* * *

S.P. Meek was one of the most prominent contributors to the science-fiction magazines that struggled to survive the years of the depression between 1929 and 1933. He first appeared with "The Murgatroyd Experiment," a still-memorable tale concerning the appalling results of an effort to sustain the world's swollen population in the year 2060, and wrote regularly for the next few years. It was to be expected that he would write about future warfare, and in "The Red Peril" he drew a grim picture of the world's great cities being sprayed with disease germs in 1957—the enemy, inevitably, being the Soviet Union. Propaganda leaflets were also in the armoury of the attackers, whose gravity-defying aircraft were repelled by atomic shells. Even after the Soviet leaders had been confined on St. Helena, the struggle was continued in a sequel, "The Last War," in which synthetic men were produced to turn the tide of battle.

The Red Menace often lurked in the background when Meek's popular character, Dr. Bird of the Bureau of Standards, accompanied by Operative Carnes of the Secret Service, set out to expose some piece of villainy in the series of intriguing tales. In "The Gland Murders" the plot was designed to decimate the educated rich by lacing their bootleg liquor with an extract from the pineal gland of a murderer, stimulating them to violent acts for which they would pay the penalty. Economic disaster was narrowly averted when, in "Vanishing Gold," bullion in the vaults of the Federal Reserve Bank became radioactive and lost weight. In "When Caverns Yawned" whole cities were imperilled by artificial earthquakes; and in "The Solar Magnet" the subversive genius Ivan Saranoff even tried to straighten the Earth's axis so that Russia might win her true place in the sun. Most of the Dr. Bird stories appeared in the early issues of *Astounding Stories*, where the emphasis on foreign villians brought protests form from some readers, and an assurance from the editor that "our authors mean no offence." Among other tales was "Giants on the Earth," a gaudy interplanetary adventure in a style he seldom affected but which clearly showed the extent of his versatility. His tale of an electronic world, "Submicroscopic," was continued in "Awlo of Ulm," an action-romance in the Burroughs tradition. Two serials, *The Drums of Tapajos* and its sequel, *Troyana*, concerned a lost civilisation buried in the Brazilian jungle, and appeared in book form after an interval of 30 years. A collection of his humorous short stories was published as *The Monkeys Have No Tails in Zamboanga.*

—Walter Gillings

---

**MELTZER, David.** American. Born in Rochester, New York, 17 February 1937. Educated at public schools in Brooklyn and Los Angeles; Los Angeles City College, 1955–56; University of California, Los Angeles, 1956–57. Married Christina Meyer in 1958; three daughters and one son. Manager, Discovery Bookshop, San Francisco, 1959–67; editor, *Maya*, Mill Valley, California, 1966–71; teacher, Urban School, San Francisco, 1975–76. Since 1970, editor, *Tree* magazine and Tree Books, Bolinas, later Berkeley, California. Composer, musician, and singer: performed with Serpent Power and David and Tina, 1970–72. Recipient: Council of Literary Magazines grant, 1972, 1981; National Endowment for the Arts grant, 1974, for publishing, 1975. Address: Box 9005, Berkeley, California 94709, U.S.A.

SCIENCE-FICTION PUBLICATIONS

Novels (series: Agency; Brain Plant)

*The Agency.* North Hollywood, Essex House, 1968.
*The Agent* (Agency). North Hollywood, Essex House, 1968.
*How Many Blocks in the Pile?* (Agency). North Hollywood, Essex House, 1968.
*Lovely* (Brain Plant). North Hollywood, Essex House, 1969.
*Healer* (Brain Plant). North Hollywood, Essex House, 1969.
*Out* (Brain Plant). North Hollywood, Essex House, 1969.
*Glue Factory* (Brain Plant), North Hollywood, Essex House, 1969.

OTHER PUBLICATIONS

Novels

*Orf.* North Hollywood, Essex House, 1968.
*The Marytr.* North Hollywood, Essex House, 1969.
*Star.* North Hollywood, Brandon House, 1970.

Verse

*Poems*, with Donald Schenker. Privately printed, 1957.
*Ragas.* San Francisco, Discovery, 1959.
*The Clown.* Larkspur, California, Semina, 1960.
*Station.* Privately printed, 1964.
*The Blackest Rose.* Berkeley, California, Oyez, 1964.
*Oyez!* Berkeley, California, Oyez, 1965.
*The Process.* Berkeley, California, Oyez, 1965.
*In Hope I Offer a Fire Wheel.* Berkeley, California, Oyez, 1965.
*The Dark Continent.* Berkeley, California, Oyez, 1967.
*Nature Poem.* Santa Barbara, California, Unicorn Press, 1967.
*Santamaya*, with Jack Shoemaker. San Francisco, Maya, 1968.
*Round the Poem Box: Rustic and Domestic Home Movies for Stan and Jane Brakhage.* Los Angeles, Black Sparrow Press, 1969.
*Yesod.* London, Trigram Press, 1969.
*From Eden Book.* San Francisco, Cranium Press, 1969.
*Abulafia Song.* Santa Barbara, California, Unicorn Press, 1969.
*Greenspeech.* Goleta, California, Christopher, 1970.
*Luna.* Los Angeles, Black Sparrow Press, 1970.
*Letters and Numbers.* Berkeley, California, Oyez, 1970.
*Bronx Lil/Head of Lillin.* S.A.C. Santa Barbara, California, Capra Press, 1970.
*32 Beams of Light.* Santa Barbara, California, Capra Press, 1970.
*Knots.* Bolinas, California, Tree, 1971.
*Bark: A Polemic.* Santa Barbara, California, Capra Press, 1973.
*Hero/Lil.* Los Angeles, Black Sparrow Press, 1973.
*Tens: Selected Poems 1961–1971*, edited by Kenneth Rexroth. New York, Herder, 1973.
*The Eyes, The Blood.* San Francisco, Mudra, 1973.
*French Broom.* Berkeley, California, Oyez, 1974.
*Blue Rags.* Berkeley, California, Oyez, 1974.
*Harps.* Berkeley, California, Oyez, 1975.
*Six.* Santa Barbara, California, Black Sparrow Press, 1976.
*Bolero.* Berkeley, California, Oyez, 1976.
*The Art, The Veil.* Milwaukee, Membrane Press, 1981.
*The Name: Selected Poetry 1973–1983.* Santa Barbara, California, Black Sparrow Press, 1984.
*Lyrik: Selected Poetry 1983–1990.* Santa Rosa, California, Black Sparrow Press, 1990.

Other

*We All Have Something to Say to Each Other: Being an Essay Entitled "Patchen" and Four Poems.* San Francisco, Auerhahn Press, 1962.
*Introduction to the Outsiders* (essay on Beat Poetry). Fort Lauderdale, Florida, Rodale, 1962.
*Bazascope Mother* (essay on Robert Alexander). Los Angeles, Drekfesser Press, 1964.
*Journal of the Birth.* Berkeley, California, Oyez, 1967.
*Isla Vista Notes: Fragmentary, Apocalyptic, Didactic Contradictions.* Santa Barbara, California, Christopher, 1970.
*Abra* (for children). Berkeley, California, Hipparchia Press, 1976.
*Two-way Mirror: A Poetry Note-book.* Berkeley, California, Oyez, 1977.

Editor, with Lawrence Ferlinghetti and Michael McClure, *Journal for the Protection of All Beings 1 and 3.* San Francisco, City Lights, 2 vols., 1961–69.
Editor, *The San Francisco Poets.* New York, Ballantine, 1971; revised edition, as *Golden Gate*, San Francisco, Wingbow Press, 1976.
Editor, *Birth: An Anthology.* New York, Ballantine, 1973.
Editor, *The Secret Garden: an Anthology in the Kabbalah.* New York, Seabury Press, 1976.
Editor, *The Path of the Names*, by Abraham Abulafia. Berkeley, California, Tree, and London, Trigram Press, 1976.
Editor, *Birth: An Anthology of Ancient Texts, Songs, Prayers, and Stories.* Berkeley, California, North Point Press, 1981.
Editor, *Death* (anthology). Berkeley, California, North Point Press, 1984.
Editor, *The Book Within the Book: Texts and Contexts of Kabbalah.* Berkeley, California, North Point Press, 1990.

Translator, with Allen Say, *Morning Glories*, by Shiga Naoya. Berkeley, California, Oyez, 1975.

*

Manuscript Collections: Washington University, St. Louis; University of Indiana, Bloomington; University of California, Los Angeles.

Critical Studies: *David Meltzer: A Sketch from Memory and Descriptive Checklist*, Berkeley, California, Oyez, 1965, and *6 Poets of the San Francisco Renaissance*, Fresno, California, Giligia Press, 1967, both by David Kherdian; *The Secret Record: Modern Erotic Literature* by Michael Perkins, New York, Morrow, 1976; in *Vort* (Berkeley, California), 1979; *Apocalyptic Messianism and Contemporary Jewish-American Poetry* by R. Barbara Gitenstein, Albany, State University Press of New York, 1986.

*

David Meltzer comments:

My involvement with science fiction began when I was a teenager with my reading of H.G. Wells. This led to the early Conklin anthologies and to pulps like *Famous Fantastic Mysteries, Amazing*, and *Thrilling Wonder Stories. Weird Tales* directed me to Arkham House and to Bradbury's first book. Though I enjoyed all aspects of the genre—from David H. Keller to A.E. van Vogt—the writers who interested me most, for their style and innovative stories, were Sturgeon, Kuttner, and finally Alfred Bester, whose *Demolished Man* (serialized in *Galaxy*) was a significant opening in the development of my own work. Its typographical free-play, reminiscent of 1920's Dada and Surrealist typewriter art, felt comfortable to a young poet enthralled with Kenneth Patchen and E.E. Cummings.

Though I wrote and sold a few stories in the 1950's, it was writing the erotic tracts for Essex House that gave me the format I needed to extend my involvement with science fiction. These novels allowed me to use the speculative freedom of SF in a free-for-all attempt to make moral, political, and it is hoped, satirical appraisal of the U.S.A. in the late 1960's without sacrificing any respectability poets are supposed to wear as top hats or laurel crowns.

* * *

Of the ten novels by the California poet and novelist David Meltzer, seven were—in the author's words—"SF or fantasy, future projections." The fact that the Essex House series, edited by Brian Kirby, was devoted to serious American erotic writing did not hinder Meltzer when he wrote his prophetic, Blakean novels of the future. As he has said, "The pornographic erotic format seemed most fitting a zone to engage in didactic moral outcries. . . ."

In *The Agency*, the first volume of a trilogy, Meltzer conveys a poetic vision in spare, allusive prose. He uses techniques special to speculative fiction and satire. As the novelist Norman Spinrad writes in his afterword to *The Agent*, the Agency "is clearly Meltzer's paradigm of society; a mindless machine of which we are all 'agents,' *including* those whom the machine supposedly serves. . . ." The Agency is "a well-organised, self-sufficient, sexual underground." In *The Agency*, a young man is picked up by sexual agents and—like the woman in *Story of O*—spends the rest of the novel being forcibly indoctrinated with the Agency's tyrannical precepts. Brainwashed, he becomes an agent himself, ready to propagate the evil fantasies of his masters. In *The Agent*, the satirical possibilities implied in *The Agency* are applied more broadly to various aspects of American society. Here, Meltzer's deliberately ambiguous portrayal of two agents who may or may not be working for the same agency is often reminiscent of scenes from the movie *Dr. Strangelove.* The third volume in the trilogy, *How Many Blocks in the Pile?*, is constructed differently from the first two. In it, Meltzer creates an exaggerated portrait of the Agency's customers—a married couple who respond to sexual advertisements.

Meltzer's most ambitious erotic SF project is the Brain Plant Tetralogy. In classical Greek drama, a tetralogy is a group of four dramatic pieces, either four tragedies or three tragedies and a satire. Meltzer's Brain-Plant novels are not tragedies in the classical sense, and satire is a prominent feature of each of them; but his extrapolation of tendencies in American society of the late 1960's and their application in his prophetic fictions renders a tragic, scarifying vision. Meltzer's achievement in these four novels does not lie in the creation of characters, because they are either deliberate caricatures or disembodied voices, nor in the creation of a central fantasy. His projection of a future American government ruled by "Military Industry" in which "Rads" (radicals) and "Rebs" (lower middle-class whites), "Snarks" (sexual anarchists), and black militants, are pacified by "Fun Zones" (ingenious Disneylands for the satisfaction of sexual fantasies) is simplistic—like R. Crumb cartoons, as Frank M. Robinson points out in his afterword to *Lovely.* Meltzer's achievement lies instead in the utterly convincing manner in which he argues his theme of exploitation through sex, power, and dreams. The series, because of the extravagent, entertaining, violent, prophetic vision it conveys, is one of the high points of erotic SF literature.

—Michael Perkins

---

**MELUCH, R(ebecca) M.** American. Born in Ohio, 24 October 1956. Educated at the University of North Carolina, Greensboro, B.A. in theatre 1978; University of Pennsylvania, Philadelphia, M.A. in ancient history 1981. Married James C. Witkowski. Since 1978, full-time writer. Assistant instructor, Kim's Martial Arts School, Fairview Park, Ohio 1982–86. Agent: Marie Rodell-Frances Collin Literary Agency, 110 West 40th Street, New York, New York 10018. Address: 29520 Schwartz Road, Westlake, Ohio 44145, U.S.A.

### Science-Fiction Publications

Novels (series: Wind)

*Sovereign.* New York, New American Library, 1979; London, Arrow, 1980.
*Wind Dancers.* New York, New American Library, 1981.
*Wind Child.* New York, New American Library, 1982.
*Jerusalem Fire.* New York, New American Library, 1985; London, Macdonald, 1986.
*War Birds.* New York, New American Library, 1989.
*Chicago Red.* New York, New American Library, 1990.

* * *

R.M. Meluch, a young writer when her first novel, *Sovereign*, was published, has produced six novels and several short stories in a few short years. These range from space opera-based novels of psycho-social development to socio-revolutionary adventure. She has created multi-political human and alien cultures on a multitude of worlds whose climates and lifeforms are sketched out as major plot elements and, while most of the works are thematically linked and loosely postulate the same, intergalactic, future for humankind, each is absorbingly different. Meluch's novels show a fascination with armed and unarmed conflict, including various permutations of martial arts along with details of ship-to-ship battles in space, predicated on World Wars I and II fighter-ace culture.

*Sovereign* is a self-contained saga of heroism thrust upon the person of a tormented young man. *Wind Child* and *Wind Dancers* combine to chronicle the return from virtual extermination of a race of shape-changers through the assistance of half-breed human/aliens. Meluch's literary strengths lie in characterization, and she repeatedly probes the psychological effects of war on otherwise humanistic people. This thematic thread runs more truly through the later three novels, *Jerusalem Fire, War Birds, Chicago Red.*

A character study predicated on a father-son conflict, *Sovereign* follows Teal's heroic struggle for survival through a variety of interpersonal situations cast against an intergalactic war. As the 33rd, and crucial, generation of a long line of male, only-children, Teal is dependent on his father's tutoring for protection from side-effects of a breeding program. His birth causes the death of his mother, and his father's rejection, starting a chain of events within which he opposes ever larger aggregates of hostile beings. His father is his first enemy; others include the competing Brekk family; the invading northern tribes of the home planet, Arana; and the alien Uelson race that threatens Arana as well as earth. Teal's long struggle to replace his father's missing affection takes him first north to join a spacefaring race, and then off-planet to battle the Uelsons on Earth's behalf. These adventures, seemingly motivated by internal need rather than external compulsion, form the arena within which his heroic scope is displayed.

*Wind Dancers* and *Wind Child*, also based upon the existence of a race of genetically altered beings, is more reminiscent of H. Beam Piper than Doc Smith. A dying race of beings with extra sets of chromosomes is able to take three forms, human-like, animal, and wind. The wealthy terrans who have taken over their planet wish to deny, and then conceal, their existence in order claim a planet with no apparent indigenous population, a plot element also found in Piper's *Little Fuzzy. Wind Dancers* introduces the alien-human conflict, and the characters, alien Niki, half-alien Laure, and human East, who will restore the race. *Wind Child* introduces the human-alien savior, Daniel, similar to Teal in *Sovereign.* His function is to search out lost members of the race among the stars.

The viewpoints of the wind-aliens and humans alternate, providing the story with more controlled depth than found in Meluch's first novel. All but a few central characters are embodiments of a single principle: mystery and aesthetic beauty in the alien dancer, Niki; evil in the rich Duchess Estelita and the military leader, Admiral Czals; and unselfish but mischievous goodness in Daniel's close companion, Tavi.

*Jerusalem Fire, War Birds,* and *Chicago Red,* though self-contained narratives, have many similarities. In each, a few tormented beings, human and alien, are used to depict the close, often tragic, relationship between good and evil. In portraying both heroes and villains (who are often the same person) through this thematic concern, Meluch also makes them compellingly human. Honor, loyalty, strength, weakness, friendship, and love oppose each other, creating the paradoxes that plague the lives of her characters. *Jerusalem Fire* follows an intergalactic pirate with a shameful past as he attempts restitution for his actions. *War Bird*'s anti-hero begins by working unwillingly for the enemies who vanquished his planet, then he joins them in the face of an alien threat. In *Chicago Red*, fathers, sons, and brothers find themselves on opposite sides of a revolution against totalitarian rule. They also find their political loyalties challenged by interpersonal ones, including hetero- and homosexual love along with human-alien friendships. Perhaps because her novels are mostly about males and war, with a few significant female characters, Meluch's portrayal of male homosexual relationships is as pervasive as it is sensitive. Love and friendship, especially between natural enemies whose social functions may differ, are often pivotal to her plots.

*Jerusalem Fire* pairs a life-weary, alcoholic, ex-general pirate with several avatars, an alien queen, and a human warrior who has tried to become alien. In the future, intergalactic, totalitarian culture of this novel, the pirate Alihahd must face his past as the most successful general of an emperor who has set out to subjugate all inhabited planets, including Earth. His torments call into question the concept of loyalty and honor, especially at the points where they conflict with humanism. The novel spans several planets and several decades, introduces a mythical race of aliens, chronicles the past of Alihahd and his avatars, Ben-Taire and Hall, all without offering any easy answers to the human condition of paradox.

*War Birds* is memorable for its creation of many personal loyalties at odds with socio-cultural ones. Three planets, Tannia, Erde, and Occo, circle the same sun. They were all originally colonized at the same time, but their human populations evolved along differing ideological lines, with Occo so far out of the others' way that they are generally unaware it holds an alien race. Anthony Northfied/Anton Nordvelt is a literature teacher on a military base on Tannia, or at least, that's what he seems at first. The fact that he was actually the best ace fighter pilot for their vanquished enemies on Erde does not emerge until his services are needed by Tannia to protect them and Erde from an outside threat, one which turns out to be non-human. This plot would make for good space opera, except that Nordvelt actually meets the aliens as their slave and is predisposed towards one of them, a grounded pilot like himself. Again, the complexity of loyalties and honorable behavior are seminal to this novel.

*Chicago Red* is unlike Meluch's other works in that it occurs on Earth. Cataclysmic technological failures in the late 20th century have left Earth divided into virtually non-communicating totalitarian states. Chicago Red is a self-created revolutionary on the continent that formerly held the United States, but U.S. history has been erased to preserve the roughly feudal arrangement that now prevails. Kings, Kings' sons, Kings' assassins, rebels and revolutionaries, noblewomen and clergy, none are what they at first seem. In fact, one is hard-pressed to say if Chicago Red, or the villain General Tow, or the Archbishop Gregory Vandetti, is the protagonist of this novel, as their loyalties change or remain divided. And again, the novel gives no easy answers.

All of Meluch's novels show a genuine sensitivity to psychological development in the person of major characters. She has given a lot of thought to the cultures of her many worlds. This is especially evident in *War Birds* and *Jerusalem Fire.* Meluch's own narrative style continues to develop in a promising direction.

—Janice M. Bogstad

---

**MEREDITH, Richard C(arlton).** American. Born in Alderson, West Virginia, 21 October 1937. Educated at West Virginia State College, Institute, 1955–56; Pensacola Junior College, Florida, 1960–61; University of West Florida, Pensacola, B.A. 1972. Served in the United States Army, 1957–60, 1962. Married Joy Cecilia Gates in 1963; three children. Advertising manager, Grice Electronics Inc., Pensacola, 1962–69; cartoonist and columnist ("Spinoffs"), Milton *Press-Gazette*, Florida, 1972–75; editor, *Santa Rose Free Press*, Milton, 1975; copy editor, *National Enquirer*, Lantana, Florida, 1976–77; freelance writer, illustrator, and graphic designer, 1977–79. Recipient: Phoenix award, 1970. *Died in 1979.*

SCIENCE-FICTION PUBLICATIONS

Novels (series: Timeliner)

*The Sky is Filled with Ships.* New York, Ballantine, 1969.
*We All Died at Breakaway Station.* New York, Ballantine, 1969; London, Hamlyn, 1985.
*At the Narrow Passage* (Timeliner). New York, Putnam, 1973.
*No Brother, No Friend* (Timeliner). New York, Doubleday, 1976.
*Run, Come See Jerusalem!* New York, Ballantine, 1976; London, Hamlyn, 1985.
*Vestiges of Time* (Timeliner). New York, Doubleday, 1978.
*The Awakening.* New York, St. Martin's Press, 1979.

Uncollected Short Stories

"Slugs," in *Knight* (Los Angeles), 1962.
"Choice of Weapons," in *Worlds of Tomorrow* (New York), March 1966.
"To the War Is Gone," in *Worlds of Tomorrow* (New York), November 1966.
"The Fifth Columbiad," in *Worlds of Tomorrow* (New York), February 1967.
"The Longest Voyage," in *Fantastic* (New York), September 1967.
"Earthcoming," in *The Future Is Now,* edited by William F. Nolan. Los Angeles, Sherbourne Press, 1970.
"Hired Man," in *If* (New York), February 1970.
"Time of the Sending," in *If* (New York), December 1971.
"Cold the Stars Are, Cold the Earth," in *Amazing* (New York), August 1978.

*   *   *

The protagonists of Richard C. Meredith's fiction generally are reluctant and/or disabled heroes who are forced by circumstances to attempt to solve the mysteries of the strange worlds in which they have previously been mere functionaries. As in traditional quest tales, they uncover even more mystery until a resolution, not always the solution they seek, is reached. They face frequent crises and perform heroically, if not always wisely, in response to external threats. They usually endure deep pain and are quite often physically injured—in fact, it seems that Meredith needs to put his protagonists through as much physical hell as possible before they are allowed the answers they seek or the revelations that there are some areas of human existence they will never fully understand. However, they are not the usual action-adventure sort of heroes. During their moments of flight or hiding, they reflect often upon their actions, regretting the emotional or physical pain they have caused and the violence, with its often questionable killings, that their need for self-preservation has precipitated. As pain is the recurring problem of the characters, violence is perhaps the aspect of Meredith's work that best sums up the science-fiction worlds he creates. Whether the story is about a contingent of handicapped warriors in outer space; a mercenary crossing alternate worlds, time, and space; or a time-traveller exploring facets of American history, the characters are frequently in a state of paranoiac apprehension, not knowing from where or when the next violent attack will come.

While Meredith's science fiction is thoroughly researched for its scientific and sociological aspects, he derives much of his inspiration from a finely honed sense of history. Science fiction is a field that attracts, in addition to hard-science promoters, social commentators, and literary aspirants, the history-influenced writer whose main impulse is to tamper with known history (time travel, alternate worlds) or to create complex future histories. Both of these impulses are found in Meredith's fiction and, in fact, he combines them skillfully in his timeliner trilogy and his time travel tour de force (*Run, Come See Jerusalem!*). Many factors no doubt enter into an author's choice to write science fiction that has a strong historical bent, not the least of which is that it is definitely fun to play with history. Except for some dry leftover subjects, most of the exciting events and adventures of history have been adequately covered academically. On the other hand, the science-fiction writer can deal with history extensively in time travel and alternate world stories. Additionally, such stories often necessitate speculation on historical subjects, an opportunity that Meredith takes full advantage of.

*Run, Come See Jerusalem!* not only presents well-researched historical material but also gives full treatment to the what-if theme of the traveller effecting historical change by his actions in the past. Further, it juxtaposes two possible 21st-century futures against each other to make not only cautionary statements about contemporary trends but also detailed future histories rich in political and social implications. Meredith seems to have realized, along with a few other writers like Fritz Leiber, Jack Finney, and Robert Silverberg, that history can be very much a subject of science fiction, integrated comfortably with its fantastic plots and themes to create worlds just as imaginative as deep space colonies. Historically-based science fiction helps to enlarge or at least vitalize our perception of historical matters. Perhaps as a result of this interest in history, Meredith's plots are extremely complicated and skillful. For example, events introduced early in his trilogy fit neatly into later portions of the story, and figure in a nearly apocalyptic finale that brings back into action most of the novels' surviving characters.

Meredith's best novel, *We All Died at Breakaway Station*, is an elegiac space opera which incorporates many elements similar to those in his time and alternate world sagas. It also features his most fully realized protagonist, the slightly embittered but resilient Absolom Bracer, a starship captain who has died in battle and been resurrected and put back together as more machine than man. Before he makes his valiant last stand as defender of Breakaway Station, he reviews his life as a warrior and ponders the more metaphysical questions regarding his place in a cold and alien universe. Like all Meredith heroes, he wonders if the effort and the pain are worth the result, that is, being the leader for a crew of the functioning wounded. He decides he does not regret his warrior life, especially since he has reached his life goal, being a starship captain. He is able to die courageously, also without regret. He may not have found satisfying answers, but he has asked the most important questions. In spite of Absolom's death, Meredith achieves in this novel a glorification of courage that is—oddly, in our times—quite inspiring. *We All Died at Breakaway Station* is a kind of Horatio-at-the-bridge epic that is given extra dimension by its main character's questing intelligence, by the way its heroism transcends the adventure story requirements of the genre, and because of the dramatic and poignant sacrifices of its disabled, tortured, but brave men and women. It is intriguing that similar bravery by the protagonist of a later novel, *Run, Come See Jerusalem!*, results in a nearly opposite type of solution, the character's failure to create a better world where an already abominable one had existed.

Meredith's fiction is fast-paced, mysterious, and complex. He admirably blends philosophical reflection with high adventure to delineate the essential loneliness of his protagonists in an uncertain universe. A sympathetic observer of what is sometimes called the human condition, he infuses his novels and stories with intelligent compassion and a sense of what drives us to our sometimes disputable goals.

—Robert Thurston

---

**MERRIL, Judith.** Pseudonym for Josephine Juliet Grossman; also writes as Cyril Judd. Canadian. Born in New York City, 21 January 1923. Attended City College of New York, 1939–40. Married 1) Daniel A. Zissman in 1940 (divorced 1947), one daughter; 2) Frederik Pohl, *q.v.*, in 1949 (divorced 1953), one daughter; 3) Daniel W.P. Sugrue in 1960 (divorced 1975). Research assistant and ghost writer, 1943–47; editor, Bantam Books, New York, 1947–49. Since 1949, freelance writer and lecturer: writing teacher, adult education program, Port Jervis, New York, 1963–64; director, Milford Science Fiction Writers Conference, 1956–61; book editor, *Fantasy and Science Fiction*, 1965–69; documentary scriptwriter, Canadian Broadcasting Corporation; commentator and performer, *Dr. Who*, TV Ontario. Recipient: Canadian Science Fiction and Fantasy Life Achievement Award, 1986. Lives in Toronto. Address: c/o Porcepic Press, 4252 Commerce Circle, Victoria, British Columbia BC V8Z, Canada.

### Science-Fiction Publications

#### Novels

*Shadow on the Hearth*. New York, Doubleday, 1950; London, Sidgwick and Jackson, 1953.
*Gunner Cade* (as Cyril Judd, with C.M. Kornbluth). New York, Simon and Schuster, 1952; London, Gollancz, 1964.
*Outpost Mars* (as Cyril Judd, with C.M. Kornbluth). New York, Abelard Press, 1952; London, New English Library, 1966; revised edition, as *Sin in Space*, New York, Galaxy, 1961.
*The Tomorrow People*. New York, Pyramid, 1960.

#### Short Stories

*Out of Bounds*. New York, Pyramid, 1960.
*Daughters of Earth*. London, Gollancz, 1968; New York, Doubleday, 1969.
*Survival Ship and Other Stories*. Toronto, Kakabeka, 1974.
*The Best of Judith Merril*. New York, Warner, 1976.

### Other Publications

#### Other

Editor, *Shot in the Dark*. New York, Bantam, 1950.
Editor, *Beyond Human Ken*. New York, Random House, 1952; London, Grayson, 1953.
Editor, *Beyond the Barriers of Space and Time*. New York, Random House, 1954; London, Sidgwick and Jackson, 1955.
Editor, *Human?* New York, Lion, 1954.
Editor, *Galaxy of Ghouls*. New York, Lion, 1955; as *Off the Beaten Orbit*, New York, Pyramid, 1959.
Editor, *S-F: The Year's Greatest Science-Fiction and Fantasy 1–4*, continued as *The Year's Best S-F, 5th* [to *11th] Annual*, and *SF12*. New York, Dell, 4 vols., 1956–59; New York, Simon and Schuster, 5 vols., 1960–64; New York, Delacorte Press, 3 vols., 1965–68; as *SF '57* [to *'59*], New York, Gnome Press, 3 vols., 1957–59; as *The Best of Sci-Fi*, London, Mayflower, 5 vols., 1963–70.
Editor, *SF: The Best of the Best*. New York, Delacorte Press, 1967; London, Hart Davis, 1968.
Editor, *England Swings SF*. New York, Doubleday, 1968; abridged edition, as *The Space-Time Journal*, London, Panther, 1972.
Editor, *Tesseracts*. Victoria, British Columbia, Porcepic Press, 1985.

* * *

Judith Merril has been so prominent as a reviewer and an editor that her fiction has been somewhat eclipsed. Her most widely known story is her first, "That Only a Mother." On one level, this tale shows the power of love to blind the lover to the flaws of the beloved and to see only his or her best parts. On another, it is a horror story about the effects of atomic radiation. The two levels combine thematically: atomic energy is a beloved creation with great power to do good for mankind, but we delude ourselves if we refuse to see its potential dangers. Not only does this theme remain relevant to present-day problems; the story bears rereading for the pleasure of the word play, one of Merril's strengths throughout her work. Her finest novel, *Shadow on the Hearth*, also deals with the danger of atomic energy. It focuses on a Westchester woman with two daughters battling to survive the aftermath of a nuclear attack while her husband is trapped in Manhattan. Quietly rather than militantly feminist and ameliorative rather than separatist, Merril portrays the domestic reality of coping not only with the dangers of radiation but also with the unwelcome advances of a neighbor who has somehow managed to set himself up as an official of the emergency authorities who wishes to become her protector.

Working as one of the very few women in the SF field during an era when women were usually dumped with robots and aliens and treated as plot features rather than characters, Merril introduced a "woman's angle"—fiction unlikely to have been written by a man, usually with a female central character, yet still (against the so-called wisdom of the publishing trade) exciting to readers of both sexes. While "Project Nursemaid" (*Daughters of Earth*) does have a male viewpoint character, its main concern is the selection of candidates for foster-mothering babies born in space. "Daughters of Earth" is also quite unusual for its time, chronicling six generations of female space explorers. Merril vividly portrays the interactions and reactions between mother and daughter, who then becomes the mother against whom the next generation must react, and so on. Perhaps her most imaginative story is the novella "Homecalling" (*Daughters of Earth*). Again concerned with beauty in the eye of the beholder and the power of love, it is the story of a girl and her baby brother, shipwrecked on a planet with no other human life, who are adopted by a benevolent but repulsively alien mother.

Although it is always difficult to assess the contributions of each individual in collaborations, the two novels Merril wrote with C.M. Kornbluth as Cyril Judd (*Gunner Cade* and *Outpost Mars*) seem to have benefitted from the strengths of both writers, exhibiting Kornbluth's crisp prose, Merril's full-range view of human experience, and their mutual respect for irony.

—Elizabeth Anne Hull

---

**MERRITT, A(braham).** American. Born in Beverly, New Jersey, 20 January 1884. Educated at Philadelphia High School. Married 1) Eleanor Ratcliffe (died); 2) Eleanor Humphrey; one daughter. Reporter, then night city editor, Philadelphia *Inquirer*, 1902–11; staff member from 1912, and editor, 1937–43, *American Weekly. Died 30 August 1943.*

### Science-Fiction Publications

Novels

*The Moon Pool.* New York and London, Putnam, 1919.
*Seven Footprints to Satan.* New York, Boni and Liveright, and London, Richards, 1928.
*Burn, Witch, Burn!* New York, Liveright, 1933; London, Methuen, 1934.
*Creep, Shadow!* New York, Doubleday, 1934; as *Creep, Shadow, Creep!*, London, Methuen, 1935.
*The Metal Monster.* New York, Avon, 1946.
*The Black Wheel*, completed by Hannes Bok. New York, New Collectors' Group, 1947.

Short Stories

*Thru the Dragon Glass.* New York, ARRA, 1932.
*Three Lines of Old French.* Milheim, Pennsylvania, Bizarre Series, 1939.
*The Fox Woman, and The Blue Pagoda*, with Hannes Bok. New York, New Collectors' Group, 1946.
*The Fox Woman and Other Stories*, edited by Donald A. Wollheim. New York, Avon, 1949.

### Other Publications

Novels

*The Ship of Ishtar.* New York and London, Putnam, 1926; original version, Los Angeles, Borden, 1949.
*The Face in the Abyss.* New York, Liveright, 1931; London, Futura, 1974.
*Dwellers in the Mirage.* New York, Liveright, 1932; London, Skeffington, 1933; original version, New York, Avon, 1944.

Other

*The Story Behind the Story.* Privately printed, 1942.
*The Challenge of Beyond.* Privately printed, 1954.

*

Bibliography: *A. Merritt: A Bibliography of Fantastic Writings* by Walter James Wentz, Los Angeles, Bibby, 1965.

* * *

A. Merritt is one of the most influential American science-fiction writers after Edgar Rice Burroughs, though he is not nearly so well–known to the general public. A major reason for this is the paucity of his output (particularly as compared to Burroughs), though his relatively few novels have been almost continuously in print since World War II. He is generally regarded as a fantasist, but this is mainly a matter of changing standards in definition. A half century ago, many matters were regarded as open to "scientific" speculation that are not currently, particularly in the area of the occult. Three of Merritt's eight completed novels concern themselves with the occult (*Burn, Witch, Burn!, Creep, Shadow!*, and *Seven Footprints to Satan*, the last being a variation on the arch-criminal theme with occult and science-fiction overtones), and one (*The Ship of Ishtar*) is very definitely a fantasy set in an alternate world of Babylonian mythology.

The remaining four, however, are given enough of a pseudo-scientific rationale to qualify as science fiction in the romantic vein. There is a strong debt to H. Rider Haggard for the theme of "lost races" in what were then unknown corners of the world, as well as for the ever-popular idea of super-scientific knowledge from forgotten eras (certainly an idea back in vogue today). All this might be called anthropological speculation. *The Moon Pool* deals with a scientific party that penetrates the great caverns left beneath the Pacific when the Moon was ripped from the Earth. There they find the remnants of the ancient Lemurians, using the sophisticated technological instruments of their past. The conflict is with The Shining One, an entity created by the rulers of this land, three (implied) extraterrestrials, and now turned against them. *The Face in the Abyss* takes place in an unknown part of the Andes. Again there are the remnants of a lost civilization, here ruled by the snake Mother, the last of a race of intelligent beings descended from reptilian antecedents. The lost culture of *Dwellers in the Mirage* is a curious mix of Amerindian, Mongol, and Norse. Its people inhabit a valley in Alaska, which due to volcanic activity and thermal layers gives the illusion of a wasteland; underneath the mirage is a "lost world" of unique life forms. *The Metal Monster* takes a slightly different theme; the title creature is an alien life form, sentient metallic beings with a sort of hive mentality reproducing themselves with astonishing vitality in the Himalayas.

Merritt wrote very much to pulp formula, that of rapidly paced adventure. There is inevitably conflict in these exotic locales, in which the protagonists from the outside world become involved, always on the "good" side. There are usually two women, one pure and beautiful to provide romantic interest for the hero, the other just the opposite; both are allied with the obvious sides of the conflict.

What Merritt brought to this formula that made his work so continuously popular was a remarkable writing style, called purple by his detractors, poetic by his followers. The super-scientific artifacts of the stories are given the barest minimum of scientific justification; their functions and activities are described in extremely visual, highly sensuous ways, as are the exotic flora, fauna, and natural phenomena. The result is far from the usual pulp writing of the time in its evocative imagery.

Because of their magazine origins and other factors, Merritt's works have often appeared in several variations and combinations. *The Moon Pool* is the combination of two shorter works ("The Moon Pool" and "The Conquest of the Moon Pool"), as is *The Face in the Abyss* ("The Face in the Abyss" and "The Snake Mother"). *Dwellers in the Mirage* has alternate endings.

There is also a handful of short stories and fragments, two of which were completed by the artist Hannes Bok.

—Baird Searles

---

**MERWIN, Sam(uel Kimball), Jr.** Also writes as Elizabeth Deare Bennett; Jacques Jean Ferrat; Matt Lee; Carter Sprague. American. Born in Plainfield, New Jersey, 28 April 1910. Educated at Phillips Academy, Andover, Massachusetts, graduated 1927; Princeton University, New Jersey, B.A. 1931; Boston Museum School of Fine Arts. Married 1) Lee Anna Vance in 1934 (died); 2) Marjory Kendal Davenport in 1959 (divorced); 3) Amanda Varela in 1972; two children. Reporter, Boston *Evening American*, 1932–33; New York Bureau Chief, Philadelphia *Inquirer*, 1936–37; associate editor, Dell publishers, 1937–38; staff writer, *Country Home*, New York, 1938–39; sports and mystery editor, Standard Magazines, 1941–51, and King Size Publications, 1952–53: editor, *Startling Stories*, 1945–51, *Fantastic Story Magazine*, 1950–51, *Wonder Stories Annual*, 1950–51, and *Thrilling Wonder Stories*, 1951–54; editor, *Fantastic Universe*, 1953; associate editor, *Galaxy*, 1953–54; editor, Renown Publications, 1955–56, 1975–79, and Brandon House, 1966–67.

SCIENCE-FICTION PUBLICATIONS

Novels

*The House of Many Worlds*. New York, Doubleday, 1951.
*Killer to Come*. New York, Abelard Press, 1953; London, Abelard Schuman, 1959.
*The White Widows*. New York, Doubleday, 1953; as *The Sex War*, New York, Galaxy, 1960.
*Three Faces of Time*. New York, Ace, 1955; London, Badger, 1960.
*The Time Shifters*. New York, Lancer, 1971.
*Chauvinisto*. Canoga Park, California, Major, 1976.

Uncollected Short Stories

"The Scourge Below," in *Thrilling Wonder Stories* (New York), October, 1939.
"Dreaming Down Axis Planes," in *Thrilling Wonder Stories* (New York), Summer 1944.
"No Greater Worlds," in *Thrilling Wonder Stories* (New York), Spring 1945.
"The Jimson Island Giant," in *Startling* (New York), Winter 1946.
"The Admiral's Walk," in *Thrilling Wonder Stories* (New York), December 1947.
"The Carriers," in *My Best Science Fiction Story*, edited by Leo Margulies and O.J. Friend. New York, Merlin, 1949.
"Forgotten Envoy," in *Startling* (New York), May 1949.
"The Tenth Degree," in *Thrilling Wonder Stories* (New York), October 1950.
"Exiled from Earth," in *Adventures in Tomorrow*, edited by Ken Crossen. New York, Greenberg, 1951; London, Lane, 1953.
"Exit Line," in *Possible Worlds of Science Fiction*, edited by Groff Conklin. New York, Greenberg, 1951.
"Short Order," in *Startling* (New York), March 1951.
"House of Many Worlds," in *Startling* (New York), September 1951.
"The Iron Deer," in *Thrilling Wonder Stories* (New York), December 1951.
"Judas Ram," in *Galaxy Reader*, edited by H.L. Gold. New York, Crown, 1952; London, Grayson, 1953.
"Star Tracks," in *Astounding* (New York), March 1952.
"Third Alternative," in *Fantastic Adventures* (New York), Spring 1952.
"Lambikin," in *Fantasy and Science Fiction* (New York), June 1952.
"Factor Unknown," in *Other Worlds* (Evanston, Indiana), June 1952.
"One Guitar," in *Fantastic Adventures* (New York), July 1952.
"Centaurus," in *Startling* (New York), March 1953.
"Distortion Pattern," in *Startling* (New York), April 1953.
"The Dark Side of the Moon," in *Space Stories* (New York), June 1953.
"There's Always Amanda," in *Fantastic Story* (New York), July 1953.
"Arbiter," in *Thrilling Wonder Stories* (New York), August 1953.
"Journey to Miseneum," in *Startling* (New York), August 1953.
"A Nice Thing to Know," in *Fantastic* (New York), February 1954.
"The Ambassador," in *If* (New York), March 1954.
"Wampum," in *Future* (New York), March 1954.
"The Wind Shines at Night," in *Thrilling Wonder Stories* (New York), Spring 1954.
"A World Apart," in *Fantastic Universe* (Chicago), May 1954.
"The Intimate Invasion," in *Future* (New York), June 1954.
"Summer Heat," in *Startling* (New York), Summer 1954.
"Process Shot," in *Thrilling Wonder Stories* (New York), Summer 1954.
"Poison Planet," in *Amazing* (New York), July 1954.
"It's Not the Heat," in *Beyond* (New York), September 1954.
"Sizzlesticks," in *Beyond 10* (New York), 1955.
"The Eye in the Window," in *Science Fiction Quarterly* (Holyoke, Massachusetts), May 1955.
"Pink Grass Planet," in *Fantastic Universe* (Chicago), May 1955.
"The Man from the Flying Saucer," in *Fantastic Universe* (Chicago), July 1955.
"Beyond the Door," in *Science Fiction Quarterly* (Holyoke, Massachusetts), August 1955.
"Day after Fear," in *Space Stories* (New York), September 1955.
"Star-Flight," in *Fantastic Universe* (Chicago), October 1955.
"Final Exam," in *Fantastic Universe* (Chicago), November 1955.
"Passage to Anywhere," in *Fantastic Universe* (Chicago), February 1956.
"The Vacationer," in *Original Science Fiction Stories* (Holyoke, Massachusetts), March 1956.
"It's All Yours," in *Fantastic Universe* (Chicago), November 1956.
"Service Elevator," in *Amazing* (New York), November 1956.
"The Stretcher," in *Original Science Fiction Stories* (Holyoke, Massachusetts), November 1956.
"Planet for Plunder," in *Satellite* (New York), February 1957.
"The Final Figure," in *Masters of Science Fiction*, edited by Ivan Howard. New York, Belmont, 1964.
"The Stretch," in *The Science Fiction Weight-Loss Book*, edited by Isaac Asimov, George R.R. Martin, and Martin H. Greenberg. New York, Crown, 1983.

Uncollected Short Stories as Carter Sprague

"The Rocket's Red Glare," in *Startling* (New York), June 1943.
"Climate—Disordered," in *Startling* (New York), March 1948.
"Journey for One," in *Startling* (New York), November 1949.
"The Star Slavers," in *Fantasy* (New York), Spring 1950.

"The Borghese Transparency," in *Thrilling Wonder Stories* (New York), April 1950.
"The Long Flight," in *Fantasy* (New York), Fall 1950.

Uncollected Short Stories as Matt Lee

"A Problem in Astrogation," in *Thrilling Wonder Stories* (New York), April 1948.
"Appointment in New Utrecht," in *Startling* (New York), March 1950.
"Final Haven," in *Thrilling Wonder Stories* (New York), February 1951.
"Deception," in *Thrilling Wonder Stories* (New York), April 1951.
"Letters of Fire," in *Startling* (New York), May 1951.
"I Do Not Like Thee," in *Fantastic Story* (New York), Summer 1951.

Uncollected Short Stories as Jacques Jean Ferrat

"Nightmare Tower," in *Fantastic Universe* (Chicago), July 1953.
"The Sane Men of Satan," in *Fantastic Universe* (Chicago), November 1953.
"Reel Life Films," in *Fantastic Universe* (Chicago), May 1954.
"The Sixth Season," in *Fantastic Universe* (Chicago), March 1955.
"The White Rain Came," in *Fantastic Universe* (Chicago), May 1955.
"Testing," in *Fantastic Universe* (Chicago), March 1956.
"Snowstorm on Mars," in *Fantastic Universe* (Chicago), June 1956.

OTHER PUBLICATIONS

Novels

*Murder in Miniatures*. New York, Doubleday, 1940.
*Death in the Sunday Supplement*. New York, Gateway, 1942.
*The Big Frame*. New York, Handi-Books, 1943.
*The Flags Were Three*, with Leo Margulies. New York, Curl, 1945; London, Hurst and Blackett, 1948.
*Message from a Corpse*. New York, Bouregy, 1945; London, Quality Press, 1947.
*Knife in My Back*. New York, Bouregy, 1945; London, Quality Press, 1947.
*A Matter of Policy*. New York, Bouregy, 1946; London, Quality Press, 1952.
*Body and Soul* (novelization of screenplay). Chicago, Century, 1947.
*The Creeping Shadow*. New York, Fawcett, 1952.
*Regatta Summer* (as Elizabeth Deare Bennett). New York, Dell, 1974.
*Gower Court Manner* (as Elizabeth Deare Bennett). New York, Dell, 1975.

Plays

Screenplay: *Manhunt in the Jungle*, with Owen Crump, 1958.

Television Plays: *The Star Slavers* (*Lights Out* series), 1951; *The Big Score* (*Alfred Hitchcock Presents* series), 1963.

Other

*Confessions of a Scoundrel*, with Guido Orlando. Philadelphia, Winston, 1954.

*

Sam Merwin, Jr. commented:

Although I have done more work in other fields, SF has been my favorite field since the mid-1950's. I have never sought to re- or in-form the world via such fiction, but have sought to entertain and, perhaps, to increase understanding through the introduction of speculative thought. I consider SF to be the other side of the IF.

* * *

Sam Merwin wandered into the science-fiction field from another area of literature and apparently was never totally at home in science fiction, much like Erle Stanley Gardner, Howard Browne, and John D. MacDonald. Like Browne, Merwin achieved a notable career as a science-fiction magazine editor.

Although Merwin has expressed a *pro forma* fondness for science fiction, most of his early works and the majority of his novels were mysteries. His first novel, a mystery called *Murder in Miniatures*, was published in 1940 (antedated, however, by at least one science-fiction short story). His science-fiction novels, for the most part, read more like mysteries than science fiction. They are grounded in the present and on Earth, with realistic settings and many details of architecture, weather, clothing, food, and drink.

Merwin repeatedly used such themes as time travel and parallel worlds. But in his time-travel novels, such as *The Time Shifters* or *Killer to Come*, he brought the time travelers to the present rather than moving contemporary figures into past or future eras. In his parallel-reality novels, such as *The House of Many Worlds* and *Three Faces of Time*, the alternate present-era images are not greatly different from conventional reality.

Favorite themes in Merwin's novels were political conspiracies and/or murder plots. *The White Widows* is a science-fiction novel concerning a feminist conspiracy to wipe out the male gender through an induced haemophelia plague.

The son of a distinguished literary man, Merwin received a fine education in a series of prestigious institutions. This exposure is evident in his repeated choice of various institutes and universities as settings for his works, juxtaposing them frequently with bars, bedrooms, and even nudist camps for dramatic contrast.

In general, Merwin's science-fiction novels read more like intended mysteries into which science-fictional devices have been implanted rather than like books intended from the outset as science fiction. They are fast-paced and generally pleasant. The style owes more to the hardboiled mystery than to traditional science fiction; it is marked by the occasional infelicitous phrase or jumbled imagery, but more often flows effortlessly.

Merwin's career as an editor was distinguished and deserves to be remembered. Regarding his tenure at *Thrilling Wonder Stories* and its subsidiary titles, Lester del Rey commented: "Things improved with the Winter issue of 1945, when Sam Merwin took over from (Oscar) Friend. Merwin imposed much higher standards . . . (and) sought good adventure stories with the best writing he could find." Merwin wrote a number of science-fiction short stories in the 1940's and became quite prolific at the shorter lengths in the 1950's. He indulged rather heavily in the slightly dubious (but very common) practice of selling fiction to himself, for magazines he edited, sometimes disguising the practice through the use of pseudonyms. Some of his short fiction is more science-fictional in feeling and in theme than are his science-fiction novels. Although no collection of his short fiction has appeared, a fair number of the stories are available in anthologies.

In his later years, Merwin worked as a paperback editor for a Los Angeles firm known for its pornographic paperbacks. He wrote a number of such books, reviving his onetime science-fiction pseudonym of Carter Sprague for this purpose. These books, however, are of little merit.

—Richard A. Lupoff

---

**MILLER, P(eter) Schuyler.** American. Born 21 February 1912. Educated at Union College, Schenectady, New York, B.S. in chemistry 1932. Administrator in audio-visual education, Schenectady public schools; editor and technical writer, Fischer Scientific Company, Pittsburgh, 1949–74. Book reviewer ("The Reference Library"), *Astounding*, 1951–74; editor, Pennsylvania Archaeologist; research associate, Carnegie Museum. Recipient: Hugo award, for non-fiction, 1963. *Died 12 October 1974.*

SCIENCE-FICTION PUBLICATIONS

Novel

*Genus Homo*, with L. Sprague de Camp. Reading, Pennsylvania, Fantasy Press, 1950.

Short Stories

*The Titan*. Reading, Pennsylvania, Fantasy Press, 1952; London, Weidenfeld and Nicolson, 1954.

Uncollected Short Stories

"The Red Plague," in *Wonder Stories* (New York), July 1930.
"Through the Vibrations," in *Amazing* (New York), May 1931.
"The Coils of Time," in *Astounding* (New York), May 1939.
"The Sands of Time," in *Adventures in Time and Space*, edited by Raymond J. Healy and J. Francis McComas. New York, Random House, 1946; London, Grayson, 1952.
"Over the River," in *The Sleeping and the Dead*, edited by August Derleth. Chicago, Pellegrini and Cudahy, 1947.
"The Chrysalis," in *Treasury of Science Fiction*, edited by Groff Conklin. New York, Crown, 1948.
"The Thing on Outer Shoal," in *Other Side of the Moon*, edited by August Derleth. New York, Pellegrini and Cudahy, 1949.
"The Man from Mars," in *From Off This World*, edited by Leo Margulies and Oscar J. Friend. New York, Merlin, 1949.
"Status Quondam," in *New Tales of Space and Time*, edited by Raymond J. Healy. New York, Holt, 1951.
"Trouble on Tantalus," in *Travelers in Space*, edited by Martin H. Greenberg. New York, Gnome Press, 1951.
"Daydream," in *Fantasy and Science Fiction* (New York), January 1956.
"Ship-in-a-Bottle," in *Davy Jones' Haunted Locker*, edited by Robert Arthur. New York, Random House, 1965.
"The Cave," in *Mars, We Love You*, edited by Jane Hipolito and Willis E. McNelly. New York, Doubleday, 1971.
"Tetrahedra of Space," in *Before the Golden Age*, edited by Isaac Asimov. New York, Doubleday, and London, Robson, 1974.
"Spawn," in *The Rivals of King Kong*, edited by Michel Parry. London, Coronet, 1978.
"Old Man Mulligan," in *The Great SF Stories 2 (1940)*, edited by Isaac Asimov and Martin H. Greenberg. New York, DAW, 1979.
"As Never Was," in *The Arbor House Treasury of Science Fiction Masterpieces*, edited by Robert Silverberg and Martin H. Greenberg. New York, Arbor House, 1983.

OTHER PUBLICATIONS

Other

*Alicia in Blunderland* (parody), edited by Lloyd Arthur Eshbach. Philadelphia, Train, 1983.

*

Critical Study: *A Canticle for P. Schuyler Miller* by Sam Moskowitz, privately printed, 1975.

* * *

P. Schuyler Miller is best known for his reviews, covering most books worth mention over 23 years, a service of enormous value and influence. His approach was balanced optimism, looking for whatever values books had on any level. He kept history and context in mind, often interpolating short essays on ideas and trends. His criticism was neither bland nor shallow, but his more penetrating observations were briefly stated for the student to probe further. His own stories had made him a familiar name in the magazines from 1930, and his writing had developed somewhat as the general ambiance did.

In early years, he was often compared to A. Merritt, though he is not very similar to modern eyes. Early Miller stories tend to be written in a florid style, though story and character are closer to real life than to heroic myth, and there is a down-to-earth awareness of the natural world that gives a strongly visualised location. The impressions of landscape, forest and mountain, and living environment, contrast with many contemporaries' romantically vague and perfunctory settings. His early story "The Red Plague" is "more of a well-written plot synopsis for a novel than a short story" as Sam Moskowitz remarks—true of innumerable early SF stories. There is a menace—a chain-reaction mineral blight of dust absorbing all surface water—and Martians, who have beaten the problem, provide the answer. But the voyage to Mars is vividly written and shows an original thinker's own vision of the remote prospect of space flight. "Through the Vibrations" and its sequel, "Cleon of Yzdral," has a world of abandoned automated cities, located on a different wavelength from Earth. "The Arrhenius Horror" is an exotic crystalline life form falling as particles from space. "If life is energy, why should it not rest where it will?" SF was opening new vistas of what other worlds might produce that was not Earth over again. Later, Miller came back to the thought in "Spawn," a grim, powerful story of particles from beyond carrying elemental vitality that started new life in inanimate matter: a colloidal mass in the sea, a monster of gold, and a dead man revived as something else. "Tetrahedra of Space" deals with an invasion force of crystal beings from Mercury, not simply fought off but frightened off and diverted to more suitable Mars. "The Atom Smasher" predicts release of nuclear energy as an uncontrollable mountain-blasting discharge. "The Pool of Life" is an amorphous entity mentally controlling subhumans in a cave environment, treated as soberly as such a concept can be.

Many stories exploit the pre-war vision of the interplanetary future. "The Forgotten Man of Space" is about a man, marooned and adopted by primitive Martians, who dies protecting them from genocide by human exploiters. Several collaborations with Dennis and McDermott treat space piracy with amoral realism, the thoroughly evil pirate evading justice. "The Flame of Life" is an early Space Patrol episode, set on the rain-forest Venus of yore, as are others like "Old Man Mulligan," "Bird Walk," "Cuckoo," and "In the Good Old Summertime," introducing novel fauna. Others later move to the fanciful interstellar sphere. "Gleeps" lightly handles the intelligent alien mimicking people. "Trouble on Tantalus" goes back to the jungle adventure tradition on a world full of curiosities.

Miller's most distinctive work is the short novel *The Titan.* Unfortunately it was revised into the idiom of the 1950's for its only complete publication (the original serialisation is incomplete). The change from first to third person lessens the impact of this story of crisis in an age-old, decadent Martian civilisation, told from a native leader's viewpoint, and the tighter style lacks the color and charm of the early version.

The satire *Alicia in Blunderland,* written in 1933, brings together such dominant figures as Verne, Wells, Burroughs, Merritt, Cummings, Smith, Campbell, and Hamilton, and many early science-fiction characters and phenomena most ingeniously, in a frenzied journey through imaginary worlds. It exposes weaknesses in many conventions and pretensions, with throwaway comments such as, "Nobody can ever get into a Utopia, they just build them and leave them there." Standard plot developments of the time are paraded in a ritual parodying the Saying of the Law in Wells' *The Island of Dr. Moreau,* as The Formula: "Never to win too soon/Hope for Mankind must be lost/Three dauntless heroes must rise/Like three damn fools they go forth/One must be slain by the Things/One must be martyred for Man/One must return with the tale . . ." The book is a valuable period piece for its critical perspective.

—Graham Stone

---

**MILLER, Walter M(ichael), Jr.** American. Born in New Smyrna Beach, Florida, 23 January 1922. Educated at the University of Tennessee, Knoxville, 1940–42; University of Texas, Austin, 1947–49. Served in the United States Army Air Force, 1942–45. Married Anna Louise Becker in 1945; three daughters and one son. Freelance writer. Recipient: Hugo award, 1955, 1961. Address: c/o G.K. Hall, 70 Lincoln Street, Boston, Massachusetts 02111, U.S.A.

### Science-Fiction Publications

Novel

*A Canticle for Leibowitz.* Philadelphia, Lippincott, and London, Weidenfeld and Nicolson, 1960.

Short Stories

*Conditionally Human.* New York, Ballantine, 1962; London Gollancz, 1963.
*The View from the Stars.* New York, Ballantine, and London, Gollancz, 1965.
*The Best of Walter M. Miller,* Jr. New York, Pocket Books, 1980.
*The Darfstellar and Other Stories.* London, Corgi, 1982.
*The Science Fiction Stories of Walter M. Miller, Jr.* Boston, Hall, 1984.

### Other Publications

Other

Editor, with Martin H. Greenberg, *Beyond Armageddon: 21 Sermons to the Dead.* New York, Fine, 1985; as *Beyond Armageddon: Survivors of the Megawar,* London, Robinson, 1987.

* * *

An engineer by profession, a Catholic by conversion, Walter M. Miller, Jr. brought both points of view to bear on the use of science and technology in some 41 stories and novellas of the 1950's, honing his writing skills to the peak achieved by his much-lauded novel, *A Canticle for Leibowitz.*

Amid his 1951 apprentice work, the novella "Dark Benediction" shows control of local color and romance psychology in a study of faith and prejudice. Gray and scaly "dermies," unable to control their urge to touch and transform others, are being exiled or killed. Sympathetic to one such mob victim in the early stages of her infection, Paul Oberlin takes her to priestly controlled Galveston Island, where he learns the truth. A meteor shower brought alien spores to Earth in an ironic invasion story that inverts the story of Pandora's Box. The benefits outweigh the disadvantages for those who are able to accept this gift of heaven's grace.

The next year, Miller published 15 pieces, eight of them good, three outstanding. A classic statement of wanderlust, "The Big Hunger" is a prose poem about waves of space travellers and homebodies over millennia of human change, if not development. An ironic commentary on conformity is "Command Performance." Resenting her suburban wifely role, Lisa resists her telepathic talent until it saves her from another telepath, intent on breeding supermen with her. With him eliminated, her loneliness sets in again, and she tries out her new communication channel, tentatively, as he too must once have done. "Conditionally Human" concerns playing God with life and death, as man elevates "lower" animals to substitute for babies in an overcrowded, overregulated world. Terry Norris, a veterinarian, must choose between killing a "neutroid" (a chimp-baby too smart and pretty and humanly viable, i.e., a deviant) or keeping his wife who wants children herself. Terry can't avoid playing God, but he plays it his way, killing his supervisor and taking a new job, helping to create more deviants. In making this choice, he opts for a race which "hasn't picked an apple yet," i.e., has no original sin.

Miller's best short story is "Crucifixus Etiam" (1953). Manue Nanti, a Peruvian laborer, works to help terraform Mars, and suffers acclimatization to the technology needed to keep him alive. Though he comes to realize he can never go home again to spend his earnings, he finds his sacrifice worthwhile, an act of faith in future generations.

In "The Ties that Bind" (1954), a novella pitting a far-future pacifist Earth society against the militarism of a fleet refueling at the old home world, the innocent pastoralists are the more dangerous, their ancestry including the inner hell with which Earth once infected a whole galaxy. Ambitious formally, this tale of original sin interweaves viewpoints and themes with stanzas from the old ballad "Edward." "Death of a Spaceman" (1954; often reprinted as "Memento Homo") is a sentimental elegy to a man whose decrepit body lies in bed while his heart remains in space. A more ambitious variation on the theme of clipped wings is "The Hoofer" (1955), in which an itinerant entertainer comes home to Earth for the last time, his story combining slapstick with tragedy. "The Darfsteller" (1955) is a tale of technological displacement which also comments ironically on the paradox of free will and determinism. In telling the story of an aging matinee idol's near-tragic comeback, replacing a mannequin in an automated stage play, Miller adheres strictly to the actor's egotistical and stage-infatuated point of view. No mere entertainer, he is a genuine artist, for whom the "Maestro," the performance's mechanical producer-director, really has no tolerance. But though he is doomed to lose, the actor becomes more fully human by making this last stand. Miller's last published story, "The Lineman" (1957), portrays a day in the life of a lunar worker, when a travelling whorehouse puts the crew off schedule. Mixing humor and pathos, Miller shows his main character learning to see that God created man and the universe on pretty equal footing.

These stories would be memorable enough, without his novel. But they pale by comparison with what may be the one universally acknowledged literary masterpiece to emerge from magazine SF. First published as three novellas, *A Canticle for Leibowitz* in book form is still a triptych. Each of its three "books" reaches six hundred years further into the future, viewing history from the vantage point of the Abbey of Leibowitz, somewhere in the American southwest. Each era is sharply etched, its characters clearly limned as plausible citizens of the City of God, simultaneously resisting and accommodating the City of Dys (Earthly life), as mankind struggles back from nuclear war to recycled Medieval, Renaissance, and Modern eras. Named for a Jewish engineer, a "booklegger" who memorized forbidden texts in the "Age of Simplicity" following the war, the Order of Leibowitz is committed to the preservation of knowledge, interpretation and use of which lie in secular hands.

In "Fiat Homo" (Let There Be Man), sheer survival is at issue, with marauding tribes threatening each other more than the Abbey. The story centers on Brother Francis's attempts to serve his order and mankind by finding, illuminating, and ultimately giving his life for a blueprint initialled by the Blessed Leibowitz and revealed to Francis by a wandering Jew. Church and State are in equilibrium in "Fiat Lux" (Let There Be Light). A secular scholar visits the Abbey to find his theories of electricity put into practice by Brother Kornhoer, providing artificial illumination over the objections of Brother Armbruster, the librarian, thus enabling the scholar to read—and misread—the Memorabilia. Between the Abbot and the scholar, a parasitic one-eyed Poet and the Wandering Jew, cross-dialogues reveal the misunderstandings that result from differing premises. The balance of power is secular again in "Fiat Voluntas Tua" (Thy Will Be Done), an allegory of contemporary history. As nuclear war erupts ("Lucifer is fallen"), the Abbot resists euthanasia clinics while Brother Joshua prepares to lead a remnant of clergy and children to Alpha Centauri, where another attempt will be made to temper technology with wisdom.

Moving enough in bare outline, the story is enriched in the telling. Olympian irony conveys "what fools these mortals be" even as warm humor makes us care about them. The comedy ranges from puns to slapstick to central symbols of misunderstanding. Elaborate jokes escape the confines of one book to echo in another (the blueprint of I, the dynamo and a fragment of *R.U.R.* in II, the Poet's satiric verse in III). Continuity is maintained by location and tradition; each era remembers its predecessors, sometimes mistakenly. Light imagery, the Wandering Jew and his eternal skepticism, an enigmatic statue of him and/or of Leibowitz carved in Book I all mock at pretenses to human wisdom. Names and events resound with symbolism, from the simple Francis to the equally simple old woman, Mrs. Grales, whose quest to have her second head, Rachel, blessed by the Abbot, is reversed at the end when Rachel awakes to bless the Abbot, pinned beneath rubble as the bombs fall, because she alone is untainted by original sin. A weighty but entertaining novel, science fiction's best exposure of the "human comedy," *A Canticle for Leibowitz* is a fitting capstone to Miller's writing career.

—David N. Samuelson

---

**MITCHELL, Clyde T.** *See* **GARRETT, Randall.**

---

**MITCHISON, Naomi (Margaret, née Haldane).** British. Born in Edinburgh, 1 November 1897; daughter of the scientist John Scott Haldane; sister of J.B.S. Haldane. Educated at Lynam's School, Oxford; St. Anne's College, Oxford. Served as a volunteer nurse, 1915. Married G.R. Mitchison (who became Lord Mitchison, 1964) in 1916 (died 1970); three sons and two daughters. Labour Candidate for Parliament, Scottish Universities constituency, 1935; Member, Argyll County Council, 1945–66; Member, Highland Panel, 1947–64, and Highlands and Islands Development Council, 1966–76. Tribal Adviser, and Mmarona (Mother), to the Bakgatla of Botswana, 1963–73. D. Univ.: University of Stirling, Scotland, 1976; D. Litt: University of Strathclyde, Glasgow, 1983. Honorary Fellow, St. Anne's College, 1980, and Wolfson College, 1983, Oxford. Officer, French Academy, 1924. C.B.E. (Commander, Order of the British Empire), 1985. Address: Carradale House, Carradale, Campbeltown, Argyll, Scotland.

## Science-Fiction Publications

### Novels

*Memoirs of a Spacewoman.* London, Gollancz, 1962.
*Solution Three.* London, Dobson, and New York, Warner, 1975.
*Not by Bread Alone.* London, Boyars, 1983.

## Other Publications

### Novels

*The Conquered.* London, Cape, and New York, Harcourt Brace, 1923.
*Cloud Cuckoo Land.* London, Cape, 1925; New York, Harcourt Brace, 1926.
*The Corn King and the Spring Queen.* London, Cape, and New York, Harcourt Brace, 1931; as *The Barbarian*, New York, Cameron, 1961.
*The Powers of Light.* London, Cape, and New York, Peter Smith, 1932.
*Beyond This Limit.* London, Cape, 1935.
*We Have Been Warned.* London, Constable, 1935; New York, Vanguard Press, 1936.
*The Blood of the Martyrs.* London, Constable, 1939; New York, McGraw Hill, 1948.

*The Bull Calves.* London, Cape, 1947.
*Lobsters on the Agenda.* London, Gollancz, 1952.
*Travel Light.* London, Faber, 1952; New York, Penguin, 1987.
*To the Chapel Perilous.* London, Allen and Unwin, 1955.
*Behold Your King.* London, Muller, 1957.
*When We Become Men.* London, Collins, 1965.
*Cleopatra's People.* London, Heinemann, 1972.
*Early in Orcadia.* Glasgow, Drew, 1987.
*A Girl Must Live.* Glasgow, Drew, 1990.

Short Stories

*When the Bough Breaks and Other Stories.* London, Cape, and New York, Harcourt Brace, 1924.
*Black Sparta: Greek Stories.* London, Cape, and New York, Harcourt Brace, 1928.
*Barbarian Stories.* London, Cape, and New York, Harcourt Brace, 1929.
*The Delicate Fire: Short Stories and Poems.* London, Cape, and New York, Harcourt Brace, 1933.
*The Fourth Pig: Stories and Verses.* London, Constable, 1936.
*Five Men and a Swan: Short Stories and Poems.* London, Allen and Unwin, 1958.
*Images of Africa.* Edinburgh, Canongate, 1980.
*What Do You Think Yourself? Scottish Short Stories.* Edinburgh, Harris, 1982.
*Beyond This Limit*, edited by Isobel Murray. Edinburgh, Scottish Academic Press, 1986.

Plays

*Nix-Nought-Nothing: Four Plays for Children* (includes *My Ain Sel', Hobyah! Hobyah!, Elfen Hill*). London, Cape, 1928; New York, Harcourt Brace, 1929.
*Kate Crackernuts: A Fairy Play.* Oxford, Alden Press, 1931.
*The Price of Freedom*, with L.E. Gielgud (produced Cheltenham, 1949). London, Cape, 1931.
*Full Fathom Five*, with L.E. Gielgud (produced London, 1932).
*An End and a Beginning and Other Plays* (includes *The City and the Citizens, For This Man Is a Roman, In the Time of Constantine, Wild Men Invade the Roman Empire, Charlemagne and His Court, The Thing That is Plain, Cortez in Mexico, Akbar, But Still It Moves, The New Calendar, American Britons*). London, Constable, 1937; as *Historical Plays for Schools*, 2 vols., 1939.
*As It Was in the Beginning*, with L.E. Gielgud. London, Cape, 1939.
*The Corn King*, music by Brian Easdale, adaptation of the novel by Mitchison (produced London, 1950).
*Spindrift*, with Denis Macintosh (produced Glasgow, 1951). London, French, 1951.

Verse

*The Laburnum Branch.* London, Cape, 1926.
*The Alban Goes Out.* Harrow, Middlesex, Raven Press, 1939.
*The Cleansing of the Knife and Other Poems.* Edinburgh, Canongate, 1978.

Other (for children)

*The Hostages and Other Stories for Boys and Girls.* London, Cape, 1930; New York, Harcourt Brace, 1931.
*Boys and Girls and Gods.* London, Watts, 1931.
*The Big House.* London, Faber, 1950.
*Graeme and the Dragon.* London, Faber, 1954.
*The Swan's Road.* London, Naldrett Press, 1954.
*The Land the Ravens Found.* London, Collins, 1955.
*Little Boxes.* London, Faber, 1956.
*The Far Harbour.* London, Collins, 1957.
*Judy and Lakshmi.* London, Collins, 1959.
*The Rib of the Green Umbrella.* London, Collins, 1960.
*The Young Alexander the Great.* London, Parrish, 1960; New York, Roy, 1961.
*Karensgaard: The Story of a Danish Farm.* London, Collins, 1961.
*The Young Alfred the Great.* London, Parrish, 1962; New York, Roy, 1963.
*The Fairy Who Couldn't Tell a Lie.* London, Collins, 1963.
*Alexander the Great.* London, Longman, 1964.
*Henny and Crispies.* Wellington, New Zealand, Department of Education, 1964.
*Ketse and the Chief.* London, Nelson, 1965; New York, Nelson, 1967.
*A Mochudi Family.* Wellington, New Zealand, Department of Education, 1965.
*Friends and Enemies.* London, Collins, 1966; New York, Day, 1968.
*The Big Surprise.* London, Kaye and Ward, 1967.
*Highland Holiday.* Wellington, New Zealand, Department of Education, 1967.
*African Heroes.* London, Bodley Head, 1968; New York, Farrar Straus, 1969.
*Don't Look Back.* London, Kaye and Ward, 1969.
*The Family at Ditlabeng.* London, Collins, 1969; New York, Farrar Straus, 1970.
*Sun and Moon.* London, Bodley Head, 1970; Nashville, Nelson, 1973.
*Sunrise Tomorrow.* London, Collins, and New York, Farrar Straus, 1973.
*The Danish Teapot.* London, Kaye and Ward, 1973.
*Snake!* London, Collins, 1976.
*The Little Sister*, with works by Ian Kirby and Keetla Masogo. Cape Town, Oxford University Press, 1976.
*The Wild Dogs*, with works by Megan Biesele. Cape Town, Oxford University Press, 1977.
*The Brave Nurse and Other Stories.* Cape Town, Oxford University Press, 1977.
*The Two Magicians*, with Dick Mitchison. London, Dobson, 1978.
*The Vegetable War.* London, Hamish Hamilton, 1980.

Other

*Anna Comnena.* London, Howe, 1928.
*Comments on Birth Control.* London, Faber, 1930.
*The Home and a Changing Civilisation.* London, Lane, 1934.
*Vienna Diary.* London, Gollancz, and New York, Smith and Haas, 1934.
*Socrates*, with Richard Crossman. London, Hogarth Press, 1937; Harrisburg, Pennsylvania, Stackpole, 1938.
*The Moral Basis of Politics.* London, Constable, 1938; Port Washington, New York, Kennikat Press, 1971.
*The Kingdom of Heaven.* London, Heinemann, 1939.
*Men and Herring: A Documentary*, with Denis Macintosh. Edinburgh, Serif, 1949.
*Other People's Worlds* (travel). London, Secker and Warburg, 1958.
*A Fishing Village on the Clyde*, with G.W.L. Patterson. London, Oxford University Press, 1960.
*Presenting Other People's Children.* London, Hamlyn, 1961.
*Return to the Fairy Hill* (autobiography and sociology). London, Heinemann, and New York, Day, 1966.
*The Africans: A History.* London, Blond, 1970.

*Small Talk: Memories of an Edwardian Childhood.* London, Bodley Head, 1973.

*A Life for Africa: The Story of Bram Fischer.* London, Merlin Press, and Boston, Carrier Pigeon, 1973.

*Oil for the Highlands?* London, Fabian Society, 1974.

*All Change Here: Girlhood and Marriage* (autobiography). London, Bodley Head, 1975.

*Sittlichkeit*(lecture), London, Birbeck College, 1975.

*You May Well Ask: A Memoir 1920–1940.* London, Gollancz, 1979.

*Mucking Around: Five Continents over Fifty Years.* London, Gollancz, 1981.

*Among You, Taking Notes: The Wartime Diary of Naomi Mitchison 1939–45*, edited by Dorothy Sheridan. London, Gollancz, 1985.

*Naomi Mitchison* (autobiographical sketch). Edinburgh, Saltire Society, 1986.

*As It Was* (includes *Small Talk* and *All Change Here*). Glasgow, Drew, 1988.

Editor, *An Outline for Boys and Girls and Their Parents.* London, Gollancz, 1932.

Editor, with Robert Britton and George Kilgour, *Re-Educating Scotland.* Glasgow, Scoop, 1944.

Editor, *What the Human Race Is Up To.* London, Gollancz, 1962.

*

Manuscript Collections: National Library of Scotland, Edinburgh; University of Texas, Austin.

Naomi Mitchison comments:

I like to present my characters—whether they are in the past or in the future—with interesting moral choices, and it seems to me that science-fiction writers are, or should be, the prophets and moralists of today. I am fairly well up in the biological sciences, but I am deeply uninterested in gadgets. A writer's job is to write about people with sympathy and insight.

* * *

In 1955, Naomi Mitchison published *To the Chapel Perilous*, a novel which covers events between the finding of the Holy Grail and the death of King Arthur, from the modern newspaper viewpoint of the *Camelot Chronicle* and *Pictish Times.* The editors are Merlin and Satan ("Lord Horny"). It is a mainstream novel with fantasy and religious themes, using SF narrative techniques. But what makes writers like Mitchison "major" is that they can cross the boundaries of the genres and get away with it.

Mitchison, the sister of the late J.B.S. Haldane, comments in the foreword to *Solution Three*, "The interest of writing novels is to see what people will do in situations which one has invented for them. This seems to me to be supremely so in SF. There are of course SF fans who are more interested in the details of the invented situation than in the people, and equally, there are SF writers who are better at handling the situation than the characters. I was brought up to biology rather than to physics; perhaps this shows through." Like *Not by Bread Alone, Solution Three* portrays the attempts of a world government to deal with overpopulation: human nature and biology alike rebel against imposed, uniform solutions, turning poisonous if pushed too far.

An important element in her fiction is the awareness of the Celtic background. For instance, "Five Men and a Swan," is a retelling of the swan-maiden, shape-changer legend, now set in World War II. The same device is used in *The Big House*, as a weapon in the struggle between good and evil fairies for human souls. Again the theme is fantasy, but as the struggle ranges up and down through time, the treatment is close to SF.

The collection *Beyond This Limit: Selected Shorter Fiction of Naomi Mitchison* isn't described as SF or fantasy, but it is dominated by both, and illustrates how hard her work can be to classify. "Five Men and a Swan" is definitely fantasy, "Remember Me" is definitely SF, set near Oban in the aftermath of World War III. "The Wife of Aglaos" and "The Hunting of Ian Og" are both historical fiction, of which Lady Mitchison has written a great deal. But "The Powers of Light," set in the creation of the cave paintings at Lascaux, could be read as historical, SF, or fantasy. "The Hill Behind" and "The Coming of the New God" are from *Images of Africa* (1980) and feature sympathetic magic. Given Lady Mitchison's knowledge of Africa, this is more than fantasy. And the title story, written around a series of illustrations by Wyndham Lewis, cannot possibly be described as mainstream, fantasy, or SF, in any combination.

*Memoirs of a Spacewoman*, Mitchison's best-known SF novel, explores the philosophical issues of contact with a series of intelligent life-forms, mostly extraterrestrial, but also, a variety of terrestrial animals. The rewards and the dangers lie in adopting the non-human viewpoints, and participating in non-human reproductive cycles. The biological bases of human judgment, most of all on the issues of right and wrong, are constantly being challenged.

Mitchison returned to the communication theme in the short story "What Kind of Lesson?", where human explorers are projected into parallel worlds, whose location is unknown and which may not even be real. There's a suspicion that the show is being arranged for us by higher powers, but if so, what we are to learn remains obscure.

—Duncan Lunan

---

**MOFFETT, Judith.** American. Born in Louisville, Kentucky, 30 August 1942. Educated at Hanover College, Indiana, 1960–64, B.A. (cum laude) 1964; Colorado State University, Fort Collins, 1964–66, M.A. in English 1966; University of Wisconsin, Madison, 1966–67; University of Pennsylvania, Philadelphia, 1969–71, M.A. 1970, Ph.D. in American civilization 1971. Married Edward B. Irving in 1983. Fulbright Lecturer, University of Lund, Sweden, 1967–68; Assistant Professor, Behrend College, Pennsylvania State University, Erie, 1971–75; Visiting Lecturer, Program in Creative Writing, University of Iowa, Iowa City, 1977–78. Visiting Lecturer, 1978–79, Assistant Professor of English, 1979–86, Adjunct Assistant Professor, 1986–88, and since 1988, Adjunct Associate Professor, University of Pennsylvania. Recipient: Fulbright grant, 1967, 1973; American Philosophical Society grant, 1973; Swedish Institute grant, 1973, 1976, 1983; Nathhorst Foundation (Sweden) grant, 1973; Eunice Tietjens memorial prize, 1973, and Levinson prize, 1976 (*Poetry*, Chicago); Borestone Mountain poetry award, 1976; Ingram Merrill grant, 1977, 1980, 1991; Columbia University translation prize, 1978; Bread Loaf Writers Conference Tennessee Williams fellowship, 1978; Swedish Academy translation prize, 1982; National Endowment for the Humanities translation fellowship, 1983; National Endowment for the Arts fellowship, 1984; Theodore Sturgeon Memorial award, 1987; John W. Campbell award, 1988. Agent: Virginia Kidd, P.O. Box 278, Milford, Pennsylvania 18337. Address: Department of English, University of Pennsylvania, Philadelphia, Pennsylvania 19104, U.S.A.

SCIENCE-FICTION PUBLICATIONS

Novels

*Pennterra.* New York, Congdon and Weed, 1987; London, New English Library, 1988.
*The Ragged World: A Novel of the Hefn on Earth.* New York, St. Martin's Press, 1991.

Short Stories

*Two That Came True.* Eugene, Oregon, Pulphouse Press, 1991.

OTHER PUBLICATIONS

Verse

*Keeping Time.* Baton Rouge, Louisiana State University Press, 1976.
*Whinny Moor Crossing.* Princeton, New Jersey, Princeton University Press, 1984.

Other

*James Merrill: An Introduction to the Poetry.* New York, Columbia University Press, 1984.

Translator, *Gentleman, Single, Refined, and Selected Poems 1937–1959* by Hjalmar Gullberg, Baton Rouge, Louisiana State University Press, 1979.

* * *

The protagonist of Judith Moffett's story "Tiny Tango" (in *The Year's Best Science Fiction*, edited by Gardner Dozois, New York, St. Martin's Press, 1990) is HIV+, and part of a dwindling group of similarly affected people in the years just after a vaccine has been made available. Without a cure, Moffett's characters live with the knowledge that sooner or later they will develop AIDS. This story is typical of Moffett's determination to tackle major issues in her fiction in a manner that deals with real people in very human ways. "Tiny Tango" considers a post-AIDS society convincingly, and sensitively, but it also approaches other aspects of life neglected in mainstream SF. Sandy, the narrator of "Tiny Tango," contracted the virus from her only lover, and effectively isolated herself from then on, concentrating on her work as a professor of plant biology. Throughout the novella, scenes of Sandy experimenting in her own garden are interspersed with scenes of Sandy as part of the HIV+ victims' group she belongs to, noting the personal turmoils, the group relationships, and watching the numbers grow, at first, and then after the vaccine is discovered, dwindle slowly. Moffett makes reference to mass persecutions and rioting as AIDS panic sets in; it is a bleak vision, told with humanity. Perhaps the ending, or one of the endings to this multi-streamed story, in which Aliens provide the eventual cure, is a little too easy, but the author compensates with a series of difficult scenes. In the early days, Sandy uses pornography to relieve her sexual tensions, later she cross-dresses and, using a prosthetic, visits male urinals and watches other men. Whilst this may not justify the warning placed upon the story in *Isaac Asimov's Science Fiction Magazine*, it is certainly strong material.

Moffett's debut novel, *Pennterra*, is equally strong. The planet Pennterra has been colonised by a group of Quakers who respect, sometimes grudgingly, the native Hrossa's injunctions to remain in the valley of their original settlement and to refrain from using heavy machinery. The dilemma arises when the second wave of colonists arrive. They aren't prepared to accept these rules and suspect the Quakers have been brainwashed. The Hrossa warn of dire consequences, as the planet itself will destroy the intruders. On this level, *Pennterra* is an interesting ecological novel, with imaginative use of the Gaia concept. But Moffett doesn't leave it there. In making her major characters Quakers, she is obviously seeking to address the issue of response to conflict. The conflict between the two groups of colonists is further complicated by Quaker guilt because Pennterra seems so perfect for the people starving on over-crowded Earth, yet they must do what the Hrossa say. There is also personal conflict; George, the principal Quaker, is a former lover of Maggie, a leader of the second group; and there is a long and important passage that incorporates a great deal of sexual turmoil. The Hrossa are semi-telepathic, semi-empathic creatures with an individual and a collective personality. George and his son Danny, along with two other Quakers, Katy and Bob, spend time in the Hrossa village, where they come under the influence of the waves of sexual energy emitted by the Breeder Hrossa. This causes them to become highly active sexually, and the group relationships are confused. Moffett reveals her liking for difficult issues here, for Danny is just 13 years old, but during the height of the Hrossa breeding he has sex with both Katy and George. At times, this section of the novel tends to become obsessed and over-detailed, but it is generally in the dictates of the plot, and Moffett provides no easier answers on a highly-controversial subject. In the final section of the novel, where Pennterra does try to destroy the new arrivals in a variety of imaginative yet logical ways, Moffett also deals with incest and child abuse, further muddying the waters. Or perhaps clarifying what has gone before? She does seem to be prepared to justify the relationship between George and Danny, emotionally, whilst recognising the dangers inherent there. Despite the fact that the narrator of almost half this novel is a pubescent boy, this is very clearly an adult novel, to be approached by a reader prepared to be challenged.

Moffett was a successful poet before turning to prose. Her first published short story, "Surviving," won the Theodore Sturgeon Memorial award. Superficially, "Surviving" (in *The Best from Fantasy and Science Fiction*, edited by Edward L. Ferman, New York, St. Martin's Press, 1989) is a female-variant on *Tarzan*, but beneath the surface the same obsessions arise again and again. Sally Barnes, a "chimp child," develops a friendship with anthropologist Janet Morgan, but ultimately decides her future happiness lies with the chimps. It is a poignant tale, one that asserts positive things about female-female relationships, mutual nudity, and bodily functions. It has a form of ground-level detail that other feminist, or women-oriented SF writers have passed over, perhaps as part of the general body distaste that SF as a whole has inherited from society. Moffett is certainly an exception in this respect, and further provocative stories and novels should only make her more exceptional.

—Kev P. McVeigh

---

**MONTELEONE, Thomas F.** American. Born in Baltimore, Maryland, 14 April 1946. Educated at the University of Maryland, College Park, B.S. in Psychology 1968, M.A. in English 1973. Married 1) Natalie Monteleone in 1969 (divorced 1979), one son; 2) Linda Smith in 1981, one son. Psychotherapist, C.T. Perkins Hospital, Jessup, Maryland, 1969–78. Secretary, Science Fiction Writers of America, 1976–78. Recipient (for television play): Gabriel award, 1984; International Television and Film award, 1984; Maryland State Arts Council award, 1991. Agent: Howard Morhaim Literary Agency, 175 Fifth Avenue, New York, New York 10010. Address: P.O. Box 5788, Baltimore, Maryland 21208, U.S.A.

SCIENCE-FICTION PUBLICATIONS

Novels (series: Dragonstar)

*Seeds of Change*. Toronto, Laser, 1975.
*The Time Connection*. New York, Popular Library, 1976; London, Hale, 1979.
*The Time-Swept City*. New York, Popular Library, 1977.
*The Secret Sea*. New York, Popular Library, 1979; London, Hale, 1981.
*Guardian*. New York, Doubleday, 1980.
*Night Things*. New York, Fawcett, 1980.
*Ozymandias*. New York, Doubleday, 1981.
*Day of the Dragonstar*, with David F. Bischoff. New York, Berkley, 1983.
*Night Train*. New York, Pocket Books, 1984.
*Night of the Dragonstar*, with David F. Bischoff. New York, Berkley, 1985.
*Lyrica*. New York, Berkley, 1987.
*Fantasma*. New York, Tor, 1987.
*The Crooked House*, with John de Chancie. New York, Tor, 1987.
*The Magnificent Gallery*. New York, Tor, 1987.
*Dragonstar Destiny*, with David F. Bischoff. New York, Ace, 1989.

Short Stories

*Dark Stars and Other Illuminations*. New York, Doubleday, 1981.

OTHER PUBLICATIONS

Plays

*U.F.O.!*, with Grant Carrington (produced Ashton, Maryland, 1977).
*Mister Magister* (produced Silver Spring, Maryland, 1978). Included in *Dark Stars and Other Illuminations*, 1981.

Screenplays: *Sun-Treader*, 1983; *Three, Two, One: Countdown to Love*, 1984; *The Nowhere Man*, 1985.

Television Plays: *Mister Magister*, 1983; *Spare the Child*, 1983.

Other

Editor, *The Arts and Beyond: Visions of Man's Aesthetic Future*. New York, Doubleday, 1977.
Editor, *R-A-M: Random Access Messages of the Computer Age*. Hasbrouck Heights, New Jersey, Hayden, 1984; as *Microworlds*, London, Severn House, 1985.
Editor, *Borderlands*. New York, Avon, 1990.

*

Manuscript Collection: University of Maryland, Baltimore.

Thomas F. Monteleone comments:

(1981) Although my early novels were little more than adventure fiction, I feel that the majority of my work intends to be more thought-provoking and imaginative. I think my short fiction reflects my desire to employ imagery, symbol, and ironic statement to create stories which make my readers think. I do not write "hard" SF; rather I find myself most comfortable in dealing with the softer sciences such as psychology, anthropology, and sociology. The main emphasis in my fiction seems to be *people*, and the way our technology and society influence them. Themes which are important to me are love, conscience, responsibility, creativity, and man's dual nature.

(1985) Since 1980, my writing has shifted away from SF *per se*, and explored the areas of horror, dark fantasy, and more speculative, "weird tales" kinds of fiction. I enjoy the greater freedom to explore character in the novel of suspense or horror. Although I am primarily a novelist now, I still write an occasional short story, and I believe the well-crafted short story is the most difficult form to master. Also, in recent years, I have become interested in writing for film and television, having had several pieces produced for both media. My intentions for the future are simple enough: keep writing.

* * *

Thomas F. Monteleone's debut science-fiction novel was *Seeds of Change*, a promotional novel to introduce the ill-fated Laser Book line. Denver Citiplex is a dehumanized, computer-governed city in which humans are mere cogs in the machinery of state. This simply plotted novel of a successful rebellion against the power structure was slow-paced and colorless, fortunately untypical of the work that would appear subsequently.

The next three novels were unabashed pastiches of older forms. *The Time Connection* is a time-spanning adventure in the tradition of the best of Edmond Hamilton. A young man encounters a woman in the desert who tells him that she is able to listen to sounds inaudible to the rest of the world. The pair are transported to a remote future where alien war machines patrol the ruins of the planet, which is inhabited solely by a few survivors from the alien invasion force that destroyed the human race. After a series of adventures, they find the remnants of humanity in a hidden installation. Monteleone's clear, crisp style is ideally suited for this kind of story.

*The Secret Sea* is even more interesting, this time invoking the spirit of Jules Verne. An adventurer travels to a parallel world and is taken aboard the Nautilus, subsequently discovering that it is this world that was the source of inspiration for many of Verne's adventure stories. The protagonist is swept up in a battle between Nemo and Robert Burton, Robur the Conqueror, in that alternate world.

Several of Monteleone's short stories were cobbled together into a future history of sorts in *The Time-Swept City*. In this case, the immortal city is Chicago, shown in a number of anecdotal stories as the ages pass. Typical episodes include a cyborg falling in love, a priest dealing with the passing of the legal immunity of religion, the advent of artificial progeneration and genetic engineering, and the consequences of mutations running out of hand. In the waning chapters, Chicago has become an entity itself, the computers that govern it having progressed to the point where they constitute an artificial intelligence. The citizens are elements in a machine, and interlopers are forbidden entry. In one sequence, all humans are placed in hibernation, and the robots run the city, often feuding among themselves.

Although not particularly coherent as a novel, the book is filled with fascinating glimpses into the author's imagination.

Monteleone wrote two related novels about computers that exceed their design. In *Guardian* and its sequel, *Ozymandias*, a sentient computer exists in a post-collapse world, a secret until its discovery by a group of adventurers. Seeking to learn more about its environment, the computer incarnates its intelligence in a human body and wanders the Earth. Monteleone also collaborated with David Bischoff on a trilogy, *Day of the Dragonstar*, *Night of the Dragonstar*, and *Dragonstar Destiny*. A rescue team is sent to an orbiting, alien zoo when a band of researchers is attacked by dinosaurs. In subsequent volumes, some of the dinosaurs are themselves intelligent beings, and, with the aid of a contingent of humans, they seize control of their habitat and escape the inevitable domination by the human race.

Most of Monteleone's subsequent fiction and certainly all of his novels are more properly horror fiction. *Night Train* is set in the subways beneath Manhattan, dealing with a train that disappeared years earlier, and now reappears amidst several brutal killings. *Night Things* is a more traditional monster story. An Indian burial mound is inadvertently disturbed, releasing a horde of small, nasty beasts who promptly begin dismembering everything. The weakest of his horror novels is *Lyrica*, an exploration of the succubus theme. In *Fantasma*, warring factions of the Mafia find supernatural allies, a story that is in some ways darkly humorous. *The Magnificent Gallery* is the best of these. A mysterious travelling sideshow weaves a strange net of doom around those who visit.

*The Crooked House*, written in collaboration with John DeChancie, is also properly speaking a horror novel, although it has science-fictional overtones. The house of the title is one that is larger on the inside than it is on the outside, has strange twists and turns and unusual rooms, deep in the heart of which resides a creature of superhuman intelligence. Monteleone has also edited an anthology of original horror stories, *Borderlands*, projected to be the first of an ongoing series.

Most of his shorter fiction is above average, although scarce. Of particular note is "The Mechanical Boy," the title character of which is diagnosed as mentally ill because he believes himself to be a machine that cannot function without electrical power. The doctor handling the case comes to the realization that there is some element of truth in the boy's delusion, that he can actually communicate with machines in some fashion, possibly indicating the next step in human evolution. Most of his recent short fiction has been overtly supernatural, such as "When Dark Descends," written in collaboration with Charles L. Grant, and "Spare the Child," a chilling story about what happens if you abandon an adopted child who happens to be related to a tribal shaman.

—Don D'Ammassa

---

**MOORCOCK, Michael.** Has also written as Bill Barclay; Edward P. Bradbury; James Colvin; Desmond Reid. British. Born in Mitcham, Surrey, 18 December 1939. Served in the Air Training Corps. Married 1) Hilary Bailey in 1962, two daughters and one son; 2) Jill Riches in 1978; 3) Linda Steel in 1983. Editor, *Tarzan Adventures*, London, 1956–57, and Sexton Blake Library, Fleetway Publications, London, 1958–61; editor and writer for Liberal Party, 1962–63. Editor since 1964 and publisher since 1967, *New Worlds*, London. Since 1955, songwriter and member of various rock bands including Hawkwind and Deep Fix. Recipient: British Science Fiction Association award, 1966; Nebula award 1967; Derleth award, 1972, 1974, 1975, 1976; *Guardian* Fiction prize, 1977; Campbell Memorial award, 1979; World Fantasy award, 1979. Guest of Honor, World Fantasy Convention, New York, 1976. Agent: Anthony Sheil Associates Ltd., 43 Doughty Street, London WCIN 2LF, England; or, Wallace and Sheil Inc., 177 East 70th Street, New York, New York 10021, U.S.A.

SCIENCE-FICTION PUBLICATIONS

Novels (series: Oswald Bastable; Jerry Cornelius; Jerry Cornell; Dancers at the End of Time; Karl Glogauer; Von Bek Family)

*The Sundered Worlds.* London, Compact, 1965; New York, Paperback Library, 1966; as *The Blood Red Game*, London, Sphere, 1970.

*The Fireclown.* London, Compact, 1965; New York, Paperback Library, 1967; as *The Winds of Limbo*, Paperback Library, 1969.

*The Twilight Man.* London, Compact, 1966; New York, Berkley, 1970; as *The Shores of Death*, London, Sphere, 1970.

*Printer's Devil* (as Bill Barclay). London, Compact, Moorcock, as Barclay, 1966.

*Somewhere in the Night* (as Bill Barclay). London, Compact, 1966; revised edition, as *The Chinese Agent* (Cornell), London, Hutchinson, and New York, Macmillan, 1970.

*The Wrecks of Time.* New York, Ace, 1967; revised edition, as *The Rituals of Infinity*, London, Arrow, 1971; New York, DAW, 1978.

*The Final Programme* (Cornelius). New York, Avon, 1968; London, Allison and Busby, 1969; revised edition, London, Fontana, 1979.

*The Ice Schooner.* London, Sphere, and New York, Berkley, 1969; revised edition, London, Harrap, 1985; New York, Berkley, 1987.

*Behold the Man* (Glogauer). London, Allison and Busby, 1969; New York, Avon, 1970.

*The Black Corridor.* London, Mayflower, and New York, Ace, 1969.

*A Cure for Cancer* (Cornelius). London, Allison and Busby, and New York, Holt Rinehart, 1971; revised edition, London, Fontana, 1979.

*The Warlord of the Air* (Bastable). London, New English Library, and New York, Ace, 1971.

*An Alien Heat* (Dancers), London, MacGibbon and Kee, and New York, Harper, 1972.

*Breakfast in the Ruins* (Glogauer). London, New English Library, 1972; New York, Random House, 1974.

*The English Assassin* (Cornelius). London, Allison and Busby, and New York, Harper, 1972; revised edition, London, Fontana, 1979.

*The Land Leviathan* (Bastable). London, Quartet, and New York, Doubleday, 1974.

*The Hollow Lands* (Dancers). New York, Harper, 1974; London, Hart Davis MacGibbon, 1975.

*The Distant Suns*, with Philip James. Llanfynydd, Dyfed, Unicorn Bookshop, 1975.

*The Adventures of Una Persson and Catherine Cornelius in the Twentieth Century.* London, Quartet, 1976.

*The End of All Songs* (Dancers). London, Hart Davis MacGibbon, and New York, Harper, 1976.

*The Condition of Muzak* (Cornelius). London, Allison and Busby, 1977; Boston, Gregg Press, 1978.

*The Transformation of Miss Mavis Ming* (Dancers). London, W.H. Allen, 1977; as *A Messiah at the End of Time*, New York, DAW, 1978.

*The Cornelius Chronicles* (omnibus). New York, Avon, vol. 1, 1977, vol. 2, 1986, vol. 3, 1987.
*Gloriana; or, The Unfulfill'd Queen.* London, Allison and Busby, 1978; New York, Avon, 1979.
*The Golden Barge.* Manchester, Savoy, and New York, DAW, 1980.
*The Russian Intelligence* (Cornell). Manchester, Savoy, 1980.
*The Entropy Tango* (Cornelius). London, New English Library, 1981.
*The Steel Tsar* (Bastable). London, Mayflower, 1981; New York, DAW, 1982.
*The War Hound and the World's Pain* (Von Bek). New York, Pocket Books, 1981; London, New English Library, 1982.
*Byzantium Endures.* London, Secker and Warburg, 1981; New York, Random House, 1982.
*The Brothel in Rösenstrasse* (Von Bek). London, New English Library, 1982; New York, Carroll and Graf, 1987.
*The Dancers at the End of Time* (omnibus). London, Granada, 1983.
*The Laughter of Carthage.* London, Secker and Warburg, and New York, Random House, 1984.
*The Nomad of Time* (omnibus). London Panther, 1984.

Novels as Edward P. Bradbury (series: Michael Kane in all books)

*Warrior of Mars.* London, New English Library, 1981.
*Warriors of Mars.* London, Compact, 1965; New York, Lancer, 1966; as *The City of the Beast* (as Michael Moorcock), Lancer, 1980.
*Blades of Mars.* London, Compact, 1965; New York, Lancer, 1966; as *The Lord of the Spiders* (as Michael Moorcock), Lancer, 1970.
*The Barbarians of Mars.* London, Compact, 1965; New York, Lancer, 1966; as *The Masters of the Pit* (as Michael Moorcock), Lancer, 1970.

Short Stories

*The Deep Fix* (as James Colvin). London, Compact, 1966.
*The Time Dweller.* London, Hart Davis, 1969; New York, Berkley, 1971.
*The Singing Citadel.* London, Mayflower, and New York, Berkley, 1970.
*The Jade Man's Eyes.* Brighton, Unicorn Bookshop, 1973.
*Moorcock's Book of Martyrs.* London, Quartet, 1976.
*The Lives and Times of Jerry Cornelius.* London, Allison and Busby, 1976; New York, Dale, n.d.
*Legends from the End of Time.* London, W.H. Allen, and New York, Harper, 1976.
*Dying for Tomorrow.* New York, DAW, 1978.
*My Experiences in the Third World War.* Manchester, Savoy, 1980.
*The Opium General and Other Stories.* London, Harrap, 1984.
*Casablanca* (includes essays). London, Gollancz, 1989.

OTHER PUBLICATIONS

Novels

*Caribbean Crisis* (as Desmond Reid, with James Cawthorn). London, Fleetway, 1962.
*Stormbringer.* London, Jenkins, 1965; New York, Lancer, 1967; revised edition, New York, DAW, 1977.
*The LSD Dossier* (ghosted for Roger Harris). London, Compact, 1966.
*The Jewel in the Skull.* New York, Lancer, 1967; London, Mayflower, 1969; revised edition, New York, DAW, 1977.
*Sorcerer's Amulet.* New York, Lancer, 1968; as *The Mad God's Amulet*, London, Mayflower, 1969; revised edition, New York, DAW, 1977.
*The Sword of the Dawn.* New York, Lancer, 1968; London, Mayflower, 1969; revised edition, New York, DAW, 1977.
*The Secret of the Runestaff.* New York, Lancer, 1969; as *The Runestaff*, London, Mayflower, 1969; revised edition, New York, DAW, 1977.
*The Eternal Champion.* London, Mayflower, and New York, Dell, 1970; revised edition, New York, Harper, 1978.
*Phoenix in Obsidian.* London, Mayflower, 1970; as *The Silver Warriors*, New York, Dell, 1973.
*The Swords Trilogy.* New York, Berkley, 1977; as *The Swords of Corum*, London, Grafton, 1986.
*The Knight of the Swords.* London, Mayflower, and New York, Berkley, 1971.
*The Queen of the Swords.* London, Mayflower, and New York, Berkley, 1971.
*The King of the Swords.* London, Mayflower, and New York, Berkley, 1971.
*The Sleeping Sorceress.* London, New English Library, 1971; New York, Lancer, 1972; revised edition, as *The Vanishing Tower*, New York, DAW, 1977; London, Panther, 1984.
*Elric of Melniboné.* London, Hutchinson, 1972; as *The Dreaming City*, New York, Lancer, 1972.
*The Bull and the Spear.* London, Allison and Busby, and New York, Berkley, 1973.
*Count Brass.* London, Mayflower, 1973; New York, Dell, 1976.
*The Champion of Garathorm.* London, Mayflower, 1973; New York, Berkley, 1985.
*The Oak and the Ram.* London, Allison and Busby, and New York, Berkley, 1973.
*The Sword and the Stallion.* London, Allison and Busby, and New York, Berkley, 1974.
*The Quest for Tanelorn.* London, Mayflower, 1975; New York, Dell, 1976.
*The Sailor on the Seas of Fate.* London, Quartet, and New York, DAW, 1976.
*The Weird of the White Wolf.* New York, DAW, 1977; London, Panther, 1984.
*The Bane of the Black Sword.* New York, DAW, 1977; London, Panther, 1984.
*The History of the Runestaff* (collection). London, Hart Davis MacGibbon, 1979.
*The Great Rock 'n' Roll Swindle.* London, Virgin, 1980.
*The Chronicles of Castle Brass* (omnibus). London, Granada, 1985.
*The City in the Autumn Stars.* London, Grafton, 1986; New York, Ace, 1987.
*The Chronicles of Corum* (omnibus). London, Grafton, 1986; New York, Ace, 1987.
*The Dragon in the Sword.* New York, Ace, 1986; London, Grafton, 1987.
*The Crystal and the Amulet*, with Jim Cawthorn. London, Savoy, 1986.
*Mother London.* London, Secker and Warburg, 1988; New York, Harmony, 1989.
*The Fortress of the Pearl.* London, Gollancz, and New York, Ace, 1989.
*The Revenge of the Rose.* London, Grafton, and New York, Ace, 1991.

Short Stories

*The Stealer of Souls and Other Stories.* London, Spearman, 1963; New York, Lancer, 1967.
*Elric: The Return to Melniboné* (cartoon), illustrated by Philippe Druillet. Brighton, Unicorn Bookshop, 1973.
*Elric at the End of Time: Fantasy Stories.* London, New English Library, 1984; New York, DAW, 1985.

Play

Sreenplay: *The Land That Time Forgot*, with James Cawthorn, 1974.

Other

*Sojan* (for children). Manchester, Savoy, 1977.
*The Retreat from Liberty.* London, Zomba, 1983.
*Letters from Hollywood.* London, Harrap, 1986.
*Wizardry and Wild Romance: A Study of Epic Fantasy.* London, Gollancz, 1987.

Editor, *The Best of New Worlds.* London, Compact, 1965.
Editor, *Best SF Stories from New Worlds 1–8.* London, Panther, 8 vols., 1967–74; New York, Berkley, 6 vols., 1968–71.
Editor, *The Traps of Time.* London, Rapp and Whiting, 1968.
Editor, (anonymously), *The Inner Landscape.* London, Allison and Busby, 1969.
Editor, *New Worlds Quarterly 1–5.* London, Sphere, 5 vols., 1971–73; New York, Berkley, 4 vols., 1971–73.
Editor, with Langdon Jones, *The Nature of the Catastrophe.* London, Hutchinson, 1971.
Editor, with Charles Platt, *New Worlds 6.* London, Sphere, 1973; as *New Worlds 5*, New York, Avon, 1974.
Editor, *Before Armageddon: An Anthology of Victorian and Edwardian Imaginative Fiction Published Before 1914.* London, W.H. Allen, 1975.
Editor, *England Invaded: A Collection of Fantasy Fiction.* London, W.H. Allen, and New York, Ultramarine, 1977.
Editor, *New Worlds: An Anthology.* London, Fontana, 1983.
Editor, with James Cawthorn, *Fantasy: The 100 Best Books.* London, Xanadu, and New York, Carroll and Graf, 1988.

*

Manuscript Collections: Bodleian Library, Oxford University; Sterling Library, Texas A and M University, College Station.

Critical Study: *The Entropy Exhibition: Michael Moorcock and the British "New Wave" in Science Fiction* by Colin Greenland, London, Routledge, 1983.

Michael Moorcock comments:

My work varies so widely that it attracts quite different readers. Most of it is not, in fact, generic SF—it's "fantasy," if anything—and much of it uses "genre borrowings" for specific ironic uses. Obsessions include imperialism, "trans-sexuality" (I don't believe in gender-roles as a survival trait—they're anti-survival now), racialism, how to live and grow in modern cities, etc. Modern pieties are another frequent target. I like change. I believe that people and things should be infinitely flexible. I am an anarchist in that I believe every individual should be self-governing and conscious of communal self-interest.

* * *

Michael Moorcock is a writer with so many voices, it is difficult to characterize him at all. In addition to science fiction, he has written suspense novels and fantasies, of which the best known are his various series featuring Elric of Melniboné, Count Brass, the Eternal Champion, and others. He also spent several years as editor of the British *New Worlds* magazine, and in that position was a powerful force calling for the expansion of the styles, techniques, and themes of the field. Although the "New Wave" movement ostensibly died off, the field was permanently changed as a result, and for the better.

Moorcock's earliest science fiction was entertaining but comparatively minor. *The Wrecks of Time* is a straightforward space opera with a host of parallel earths. In *The Winds of Limbo*, a declining human civilization on Earth must face the challenge of an enigmatic visitor who may be bringing either salvation or destruction. *The Blood Red Game* is another space adventure, enlivened somewhat by the introduction of a multidimensional threat.

Under the name Edward P. Bradbury, Moorcock wrote three pastiches of Edgar Rice Burroughs, which appeared in the United States as *The City of the Beast, The Lord of the Spiders*, and *The Masters of the Pit.* Although the plots are very much in the style of Burroughs, they are far more literate and were the first indication that Moorcock was about to evolve into a talented and entertaining writer. One further early novel, *The Twilight Man*, was Moorcock's most ambitious effort to date, in which Earth has stopped rotating and humanity is ultimately doomed. But against this strange landscape, Moorcock presents an insightful look into the minds of his characters that lifted the book above mere melodrama.

Moorcock won a Nebula award for his novelette, "Behold the Man," later expanded into a novel of the same name. A time-traveller goes back to the time of Christ intent upon researching the man's life and death, only to discover that the historical figure does not exist. Ultimately, he must take that role upon himself in a story that is both compelling and entertaining, his most thoughtful and thought-provoking.

At this point, Moorcock's writing began to branch off in a number of directions. *The Ice Schooner* is a fascinating adventure story set against the backdrop of a new ice age. *The Black Corridor* is an introspective and often chilling story of a dozen people engaged in a long journey to colonize another world. Moorcock's interest in experimental styles of writing came to fruition in *The Final Programme*, the first of several books to revolve around the character of Jerry Cornelius, and the only one of his works to be made into a motion picture.

The Cornelius stories are a strange blend of spy story, science fiction, and contemporary novel. Set in the near future, they involve a man who is more or less an anti-hero, whose adventures are often cloaked in obscurity, and whose motives are less than pure. In subsequent novels like *A Cure for Cancer, The English Assassin, The Condition of Muzak*, and *The Entropy Tango*, as well as in a number of short stories, we are given detailed glimpses of a strangely altered version of reality, where sex, drugs, violence, and ruthlessness are the order of the day. The non-linear plotting and hallucinogenic sequences alienated a number of readers, but the books continue to have a loyal following.

At no point did Moorcock confine himself to a single authorial stance, however. *The Warlord of the Air, The Land Leviathan*, and *The Steel Tsar* are both pastiches of and satires on the panoramic adventure novels of the early days of science fiction. *The Brothel in Rösenstrasse* and its sequel, *The War Hound and the World's Pain*, blur the distinction between SF and fantasy, set against a pre-World War I Europe that is not quite the one that gave rise to our own present.

*Breakfast in the Ruins* is another novel of time-travel, but this one is an episodic narrative of the trials and tribulations of a man cast loose in time, providing a platform by which the author can satirize various aspects of our society. In *Gloriana*, possibly Moorcock's greatest single novel, he uses another altered version of our own past to create a sweeping novel of intrigue and adventure that is riveting in its intensity and enlightening in its insights into human interaction.

*An Alien Heat* was the first volume in the "Dancers at the End of Time" series, set in the far distant future. A decadent, all but immortal culture slowly subsides into decadence in a frequently comic satire of human foibles. One of its citizens looks for inspiration in the past in *The Hollow Lands*, and runs into aliens in *The End of All Songs.* The mysterious being from *The Winds of Limbo* pays a visit in *A Messiah at the End of Time.*

Although not generally noted as a short-story writer, Moorcock has produced a fairly large body of readable short pieces, the best of which are those included in *Legends from the End of Time.* His influence both as a writer and as an editor are immeasurable but certainly of major significance in the evolution of the genre.

—Don D'Ammassa

---

**MOORE, C(atherine) L(ucille).** Also wrote as Lewis Padgett. American. Born in Indianapolis, Indiana, 24 January 1911. Educated at University of Southern California, Los Angeles, B.S. 1956 (Phi Beta Kappa), M.A. 1964. Married 1) Henry Kuttner, *q.v.*, in 1940 (died 1958); 2) Thomas Reggie in 1963. Staff member, later president, Fletcher Trust Company, Indianapolis, 1930–40; instructor in Writing and Literature, University of Southern California, 1958–61. Most of her work after 1940 was written in collaboration with Henry Kuttner, though not always acknowledged. *Died in 1988.*

SCIENCE-FICTION PUBLICATIONS

Novels

*Fury*, with Henry Kuttner. New York, Grosset and Dunlap, 1950; London, Dobson, 1954; as *Destination Infinity*, New York, Avon, 1958.
*Judgment Night* (includes stories). New York, Gnome Press, 1952.
*Doomsday Morning*. New York, Doubleday, 1957; London, Consul, 1960.
*Earth's Last Citadel*, with Henry Kuttner. New York, Ace, 1964.
*Valley of the Flame*, with Henry Kuttner. New York, Ace, 1964.
*The Time Axis*, with Henry Kuttner. New York, Ace, 1965.
*The Dark World*, with Henry Kuttner. New York, Ace, 1965; London, Mayflower, 1966.
*The Mask of Circe*, with Henry Kuttner. New York, Ace, 1971.
*Scarlet Dream*. Hampton Falls, New Hampshire, 1981; as *Northwest Smith*, New York, Ace, 1982.
*Vintage Season*, with *In Another Country* by R.S. Silverberg. New York, Tor, 1990.

Novels as Lewis Padgett, with Henry Kuttner

*Tomorrow and Tomorrow, and The Fairy Chessmen.* New York, Gnome Press, 1951; as *Tomorrow and Tomorrow* and *The Far Reality*, London, Consul, 2 vols., 1963; *The Fairy Chessmen* published as *Chessboard Planet*, New York, Galaxy, 1956.
*Well of the Worlds.* New York, Galaxy, 1953.
*Beyond Earth's Gates.* New York, Ace, 1954.

Short Stories

*Shambleau and Others.* New York, Gnome Press, 1953; abridged edition, London, Consul, 1961.
*Northwest of Earth.* New York, Gnome Press, 1954.
*No Boundaries*, with Henry Kuttner. New York, Ballantine, 1955; London, Consul, 1961.
*Jirel of Joiry* (collection). New York, Paperback Library, 1969; as *Black God's Shadow*, West Kingston, Rhode Island, Grant, 1977.
*The Best of C.L. Moore*, edited by Lester del Rey. New York, Doubleday, 1975.
*Clash by Night and Other Stories*, with Henry Kuttner, edited by Peter Pinto. London, Hamlyn, 1980.
*Chessboard Planet and Other Stories*, with Henry Kuttner. London, Hamlyn, 1983.

Short Stories as Lewis Padgett, with Henry Kuttner

*A Gnome There Was.* New York, Simon and Schuster, 1950.
*Mutant.* New York, Gnome Press, 1953; London, Weidenfeld and Nicolson, 1954.
*Line to Tomorrow.* New York, Bantam, 1954.

OTHER PUBLICATIONS

Novels with Henry Kuttner

*The Brass Ring* (as Lewis Padgett). New York, Duell, 1964; London, Sampson Low, 1947; as *Murder in Brass*, New York, Bantam, 1947.
*The Day He Died* (as Lewis Padgett). New York, Duell, 1947.

*

Manuscript Collection: Lovecraft Collection, Brown University Library, Providence, Rhode Island.

* * *

It has always been a very difficult thing to judge properly the impact of C.L. Moore on the fields of science fiction and fantasy. Although she wrote under her own name, most of her work was in collaboration with her husband, Henry Kuttner, a skilled writer in his own right, and in most cases, her name never appeared as co-author. One of the earliest and most important woman writers in the field, she helped pioneer the move toward stronger psychological rationalization of motivation and behavior in characters.

Many short novels that appeared under the Kuttner name alone were wonderfully original explorations of the border between the two aspects of the genre. Lost civilizations feature prominently in titles like *Valley of the Flame* and the bizarre *Well of the Worlds.* There is conventional witchcraft in *The Mask of Circe*, scientific sorcery in *The Dark World*, and manic madness in *The Fairy Chessmen*. In some cases, Moore was given equal billing, such as for *Earth's Last Citadel*, the story of a journey to the very end of time, and *Beyond Earth's Gates*, an adventure in a parallel Earth. Many of the shorter collaborations, particularly those collected in *No Boundaries*, were far ahead of their contemporaries in approach and maturity of execution, particularly "Vintage Season" and "Home There's No Returning." The former's depiction of a group of tourists from the future secretly witnessing the present is one of the undisputed classics of the genre.

Moore is best known for "Shambleau," her first story and certainly not the best of her solo works. It is the first adventure of Northwest Smith, an interplanetary adventurer whose adventures are typical pulp fiction of the 1930's, but with more literary quality than most of the stories in the magazines of that period. Smith wanders the surface of Venus and Mars, encountering alien creatures resembling the legendary Medusa and others. Like Leigh Brackett, who would write similar stories more than a decade later, Moore used a rugged male character as her protagonist, but unlike Brackett, she also chose to write some stories that featured dominant, competent women.

Moore wrote heroic fantasy during the same period, featuring a very competent female warrior, Jirel. The five adventures are collected as *Jirel of Joiry*, the best of which are "Hellsgarde" and "Black God's Kiss." In each, she faces and overcomes a supernatural menace. Relatively unsophisticated by current standards, the stories still have a raw power and fervor that is missing from much of the formula fantasy that is currently being published.

*Judgment Night* is an ambivalent short novel about a female warrior who is heir to one of the most powerful thrones in human history, but who is torn between her own strengths and weaknesses. She must deal with a powerful man who claims to love her despite his dedication to the destruction of her power, and a mysterious intruder whose physical nature is unknown. Although there is the skeleton of an interesting story here, this is not one of Moore's successes, overly melodramatic, poorly paced, and ultimately unconvincing.

*Doomsday Morning* is a break from pulp tradition and an attempt to deal with more serious issues. In the not-too-distant future, the United States is controlled by Comus, an organization that uses highly sophisticated propaganda and information-gathering techniques to administer what should have been an invulnerable dictatorship. Against this background, Moore unrolls a burgeoning revolution, and although the novel is ultimately a melodrama, it is her most mature full-length work. It does not deserve the obscurity into which it has fallen.

Perhaps her most noteworthy shorter piece is "No Woman Born," the story of a disfigured woman whose brain is placed in an artificial body. As the protagonist comes to terms with her new mode of existence, the reader examines the nature of the will to survive, the meaning of being human, and the anguish that faces those who are cut off from contact with others.

Other short stories of note include "Private Eye," "Home Is the Hunter," and "Quest of the Starstone," the last of which is the only recorded meeting between Jirel and Northwest Smith, through a forced but forgivable plot device. The best of her short fiction is collected in *Northwest Smith*, *The Best of C.L. Moore*, and *No Boundaries*.

Moore's most significant contributions to the field may be invisible forever, not only because her name did not appear on stories she co-wrote with her far more famous husband, but also because we cannot measure the influence she had on other writers of the time, in shaping the pulp story and its portrayal of women, and later in the depiction of all human characters as real, believable people.

—Don D'Ammassa

---

**MOORE, Patrick (Caldwell).** British. Born in Pinner, Middlesex, 4 March 1923. Educated privately. Served in the Royal Air Force, 1940–45: Navigator, Bomber Command. Director, Armagh Planetarium, Northern Ireland, 1965–68. President, British Astronomical Association, 1982–84. Since 1957, presenter, *The Sky at Night* television series, BBC, London. Since 1962, editor, *Yearbook of Astronomy*. Also a composer. Recipient: Lorimer Gold Medal, 1962; Goodacre Gold Medal, 1968; Italian Astronomical Society Arturo Gold Medal, 1969; Jackson-Gwilt Medal, 1978; Astronomical Society of the Pacific Klumpke-Roberts award, 1978. Fellow, Royal Astronomical Society. D.Sc.: University of Lancaster, 1974; D.Sc., Hatfield Polytechnic, 1988; D.Sc., University of Birmingham, 1990. O.B.E. (Officer, Order of the British Empire), 1968. C.B.E. (Commander of the British Empire), 1988. Agent: Hilary Rubinstein, A.P. Watt Ltd., 26-28 Bedford Row, London WC1R 4HL. Address: Farthings, 39 West Street, Selsey, West Sussex, England.

SCIENCE-FICTION PUBLICATIONS

Novels (for children; series: Maurice Gray; Quest; Scott Saunders)

*The Master of the Moon.* London, Museum Press, 1952.
*The Island of Fear.* London, Museum Press, 1954.
*The Frozen Planet.* London, Museum Press, 1954.
*Destination Luna.* London, Lutterworth Press, 1955.
*Quest of the Spaceways.* London, Muller, 1955.
*Mission to Mars* (Gray). London, Burke, 1955.
*World of Mists* (Quest). London, Muller, 1956.
*The Domes of Mars* (Gray). London, Burke, 1956.
*Wheel in Space.* London, Lutterworth Press, 1956.
*The Voices of Mars* (Gray). London, Burke, 1957.
*Peril on Mars* (Gray). London, Burke, 1958; New York, Putnam, 1965.
*Raiders on Mars* (Gray). London, Burke, 1959.
*Captives of the Moon.* London, Burke, 1960.
*Wanderer in Space.* London, Burke, 1961.
*Crater of Fear.* London, Burke, and New York, Harvey House, 1962.
*Invader from Space.* London, Burke, 1963.
*Caverns of the Moon.* London, Burke, 1964.
*Planet of Fire.* Kingswood, Surrey, World's Work, 1969.
*Spy in Space* (Saunders). London, Armada, 1977.
*Planet of Fear* (Saunders). London, Armada, 1977.
*The Moon Raiders* (Saunders). London, Armada, 1978.
*Killer Comet* (Saunders). London, Armada, 1978.
*The Terror Star* (Saunders). London, Armada, 1979.
*The Secret of the Black Hole* (Saunders). London, Armada, 1980.

OTHER PUBLICATIONS

Plays

*Perseus and Andromeda*, music by Moore (produced Shoreham, Sussex, 1974).
*Theseus*, music by Moore (produced 1982).

Other

*Guide to the Moon*. London, Eyre and Spottiswoode, and New York, Norton, 1953; revised edition, London, Colins, 1957; as *Survey of the Moon*, Eyre and Spottiswoode and Norton, 1963; revised edition, Guildford, Surrey, Lutterworth Press, 1976; as *New Guide to the Moon*, Norton, 1976.
*Suns, Myths, and Men*. London, Muller, 1954; revised edition, Muller, 1968; New York, Norton, 1969; as *The Story of the Man and the Stars*, New York, Norton, 1955.
*Out into Space*, with A.L. Helm. London, Museum Press, 1954.
*The Boy's Book of Space*. London, Burke, 1954; New York, Roy, 1956.
*The True Book about Worlds Around Us*. London, Muller, 1954; as *The Worlds Around Us*, New York, Abelard Schuman, 1956.
*A Guide to the Planets*. New York, Norton, 1954; London, Eyre and Spottiswoode, 1955; revised edition, London, Collins, 1957; Norton, 1960; Guildford, Surrey, Lutterworth Press, 1976; as *The New Guide to the Planets*, Norton, 1972.
*The Moon*, with Hugh Percival Wilkins. London, Faber, and New York, Macmillan, 1955.
*Earth Satellite: The New Satellite Projects Explained*. London, Eyre and Spottiswoode, 1955; as *Earth Satellites*, New York, Norton, 1956; revised edition, Norton, 1958.
*The Planet Venus*. London, Faber, 1956; New York, Macmillan, 1957; revised edition, 1959, 1961; with Garry Hunt, Faber, 1982.
*Man-Made Moons*. London, Newman Neame, 1956.
*Making and Using a Telescope*, with Hugh Percival Wilkins. London, Eyre and Spottiswoode, 1956; as *How to Make and Use a Telescope*, New York, Norton, 1956.
*The True Book about the Earth*. London, Muller, 1956.
*Guide to Mars*. London, Muller, 1956; New York, Macmillan, 1958; revised edition, Muller, 1965.
*The True Book about Earthquakes and Volcanoes*. London, Muller, 1957.
*Isaac Newton* (for children). London, Black, 1957; New York, Putnam, 1958.
*Science and Fiction*. London, Harrap, 1957; Folcroft, Pennsylvania, Folcroft Editions, 1970.
*The Amateur Astronomer*. London, Lutterworth Press, and New York, Norton, 1957; revised edition, Lutterworth Press, 1974; revised edition, as *Amateur Astronomy*, Norton, 1968.
*The Earth, Our Home*. New York, Abelard Schuman, 1957.
*Your Book of Astronomy*. London, Faber, 1958; revised edition, 1964, 1979.
*The Solar System*. London, Methuen, 1958; New York, Criterion, 1961.
*The Boy's Book of Astronomy*. London, Burke, and New York, Roy, 1958; revised edition, Burke, 1964.
*The True Book about Man*. London, Muller, 1959.
*Man on the Moon*. London, Newman Neame, 1959.
*Rockets and Earth Satellites*. London, Muller, 1959.
*Astronautics*. London, Methuen, 1960.
*Star Spotter*. London, Newman Neame, 1960.
*Guide to the Stars*. London, Eyre and Spottiswoode, and New York, Norton, 1960; revised edition, Guildford, Surrey, Lutterworth Press, 1974; as *The New Guide to the Stars*, New York, Norton, 1975.
*Stars and Space*. London, Black, 1960.
*Conquest of the Air: The Story of the Wright Brothers*. London, Lutterworth Press, 1961.
*Navigation*, with Henry Brinton. London, Methuen, 1961.
*Astronomy*. London, Oldbourne, 1961; as *The Picture History of Astronomy*, New York, Grosset and Dunlap, 1961; revised edition, 1972; revised edition, as *The Story of Astronomy*, London, Macdonald, 1972; revised edition, London, Macdonald and Jane's, 1977; revised edition, as *Patrick Moore's History of Astronomy*, London, Macdonald, 1983.
*The Stars*. London, Weidenfeld and Nicolson, 1962.
*Exploring Maps*, with Henry Brinton. London, Odhams Press, 1962; New York, Hawthorn, 1967.
*Exploring Time*, with Henry Brinton. London, Odhams Press, 1962.
*The Astronomer's Telescope*, with Paul Murdin. Leicester, Brockhampton Press, 1962.
*Life in the Universe*, with Francis J. Jackson. London, Routledge, and New York, Norton, 1962.
*The Planets*. London, Eyre and Spottiswoode, and New York, Norton, 1962.
*The Observer's Book of Astronomy*. London, Warne, 1962; 6th edition, 1978.
*Telescopes and Observatories*. London, Weidenfeld and Nicolson, and New York, Day, 1962.
*Space in the Sixties*. London, Penguin, 1963.
*Exploring the Moon*. London, Odhams Press, 1964.
*The True Book about Roman Britain*. London, Muller, 1964.
*Exploring Weather*, with Henry Brinton. London, Odhams Press, 1964.
*The Sky at Night 1–7*. London, Eyre and Spottiswoode, 2 vols., and London, BBC, 5 vols., 1964–80; vol. 1, New York, Norton, 1965.
*Life on Mars*, with Francis L. Jackson. London, Routledge, 1965; New York, Norton, 1966.
*Exploring Other Planets*, with Henry Brinton. London, Odhams Press, 1965; New York, Hawthorn, 1967.
*Exploring the World*. London, Oxford University Press, 1966; New York, Watts, 1968.
*The New Look of the Universe*. London, Hodder and Stoughton, and New York, Norton, 1966.
*Exploring the Planetarium*. London, Odhams Press, 1966.
*Legends of the Stars*. London, Odhams Press, 1966.
*Naked-Eye Astronomy*. London, Lutterworth Press, and New York, Norton, 1966.
*Basic Astronomy*. Edinburgh, Oliver and Boyd, 1967.
*Exploring Earth History*, with Henry Brinton. London, Odhams Press, 1967.
*The Craters of the Moon*, with Peter J. Cattermole. New York, Norton, 1967.
*The Amateur Astronomer's Glossary*. London, Lutterworth Press, and New York, Norton, 1967; revised edition, as *The A-Z of Astronomy*, London, Fontana, and New York, Scribner, 1976.
*Armagh Observatory: A History 1790–1967*. Armagh, Armagh Observatory, 1967.
*Exploring the Galaxies*. London, Odhams Press, 1968.
*Exploring the Stars*. London, Odhams Press, 1968.
*Space*. London, Lutterworth Press, 1968; New York, Natural History Press, 1969.
*The Sun and Its Influence*, by Mervyn A. Ellison, revised edition. London, Routledge, and New York, Elsevier, 1968.
*The Sun*. London, Muller, and New York, Norton, 1968.
*Moon Flight Atlas*. London, Mitchell Beazley, and Chicago, Rand McNally, 1969; revised edition, Mitchell Beazley, 1970.

*Astronomy and Space Research* (bibliography). London, National Book League, 1969.
*The Development of Astronomical Thought*. Edinburgh, Oliver and Boyd, 1969.
*The Atlas of the Universe*. London, Mitchell Beazley, and Chicago, Rand McNally, 1970; revised edition, as *The Mitchell Beazley Concise Atlas of the Universe*, Mitchell Beazley, 1974; as *The Concise Atlas of the Universe*, Rand McNally, 1974; revised edition, as *The New Atlas of the Universe*, New York, Crown, 1984.
*Gunpowder, Treason: November 5, 1605*, with Henry Brinton. London, Lutterworth Press, 1970.
*Astronomy for O Level*. London, Duckworth, 1970; as *Astronomy for GCSE*, 1989.
*Seeing Stars*. London, BBC, and Chicago, Rand McNally, 1971.
*Mars, The Red World*. Kingswood, Surrey, World's Work, 1971.
*The Astronomy of Birr Castle*. London, Mitchell Beazley, 1971.
*Can You Speak Venusian: A Guide to Independent Thinkers*. Newton Abbot, Devon, David and Charles, 1972; New York, Norton, 1973.
*Challenge of the Stars*, with David A. Hardy. London, Mitchell Beazley, and Chicago, Rand McNally, 1972; as *The New Challenge of the Stars*, London, Mitchell Beazley-Sidgwick and Jackson, 1977, Rand McNally, 1978.
*How Britain Won the Space Race*, with Desmond Leslie. London, Mitchell Beazley, 1972.
*Stories of Science and Invention*. London, Oxford University Press, 1972.
*How to Recognise the Stars*, with Lawrence Clarke. London, Corgi, 1972.
*The Southern Stars*. Cape Town, Timmins, 1972.
*1001 Questions Answered about Astronomy*, by James S. Pickering, revised edition. Guildford, Surrey, Lutterworth Press, 1972; New York, Dodd Mead, 1973.
*Patrick Moore's Colour Star Atlas*. Guildford, Surrey, Lutterworth Press, 1973; as *Color Star Atlas*, New York, Crown, 1973.
*The Starlit Sky*. Cape Town, Timmins, 1973.
*Man the Astronomer*. London, Priory Press, 1973.
*Mars*, with Charles A. Cross. London, Mitchell Beazley, and New York, Crown, 1973.
*The Comets: Visitors from Space*. Shaldon, Devon, Reid, 1973; revised edition, as *Comets*, New York, Scribner, 1976; as *Guide to Comets*, Guildford, Surrey, Lutterworth Press, 1977.
*Watchers of the Stars: The Scientific Revolution*. London, Joseph, and New York, Putnam, 1974.
*Black Holes in Space*, with Iain Nicolson. London, Ocean, 1974; New York, Norton, 1976.
*The Astronomy Quiz Book*. London, Carousel, 1974; revised edition, 1978; as *Patrick Moore's Astronomy Quiz Book*, London, G. Philip, 1987.
*The Young Astronomer and His Telescope*. Shaldon, Devon, Reid, 1974.
*Let's Look at the Sky: The Planets [The Stars]*. London, Carousel, 2 vols., 1975.
*Legends of the Planets*. London, Luscombe, 1976.
*The Next Fifty Years in Space*. London, Luscombe, and New York, Taplinger, 1976.
*The Stars Above*. Norwich, Jarrold, 1976.
*The Astronomy of Southern Africa*, with Pete Collins. Cape Town, Timmins, and London, Hale, 1977.
*The Atlas of Mercury*, with Charles A. Cross. London, Mitchell Beazley, and New York, Crown, 1977.
*Guide to Mars* (not the same as 1956 book). Guildford, Surrey, Lutterworth Press, 1977; New York, Norton, 1978.
*Wonder Why Book of Planets [the Earth, Stars]*. London, Transworld, 3 vols., 1977–78; *Stars* published New York, Grosset and Dunlap, 1979.
*Man's Future in Space*. Hove, Sussex, Wayland, 1978.
*The Guinness Book of Astronomy Facts and Feats*. London, Guinness Superlatives, 1979; 3rd edition as *The Guinness Book of Astronomy*, Enfield, Middlesex, Guinness, 1988.
*Fun-to-Know-About Mysteries of Space* (for children). London, Armada, 1979.
*Out of Darkness: The Planet Pluto*, with Clyde Tombaugh. Guildford, Surrey, Lutterworth Press, and Harrisburg, Pennsylvania, Stackpole, 1980.
*The Pocket Guide to Astronomy*. New York, Simon and Schuster, 1980; as *Patrick Moore's Pocket Guide to Astronomy*, London, Mitchell Beazley, 1982.
*Everyman's Scientific Facts and Feats*, with Magnus Pyke. London, Dent, 1981.
*The Moon* (atlas). London, Mitchell Beazley, and Chicago, Rand McNally, 1981.
*Jupiter*, with Garry Hunt. London, Mitchell Beazley, and Chicago, Rand McNally, 1981.
*William Herschel, Astronomer and Musician*. Sidcup, Kent, P. M.E. Erwood-Herschel Society, 1981.
*The Unfolding Universe*. London, Joseph-Rainbird, and New York, Crown, 1982.
*Saturn*, with Garry Hunt. London, Mitchell Beazley, and Chicago, Rand McNally, 1982.
*What's New in Space?* (for children). London, Carousel, 1982.
*Countdown! or, How Nigh Is the End?* London, Joseph-Rainbird, 1983.
*Travellers in Space and Time*. London, Park Lane, 1983; New York, Doubleday, 1984.
*The Space Shuttle Action Book* (for children). London, Aurum Press, and New York, Random House, 1983.
*The Return of Halley's Comet*, with John Mason. Wellington, Northamptonshire, Stephens, and New York, Norton, 1984.
*The Story of the Earth*, with Peter Cattermole. London, Cambridge University Press, 1984; New York, Cambridge University Press, 1985.
*Armchair Astronomy*. Wellington, Northamptonshire, Stephens, and New York, Norton, 1984.
*Stargazing: Astronomy Without a Telescope*. London, Aurum Press, and Hauppauge, New York, Barron's, 1985.
*Halley's Comet Pop-Up Book*, with Heather Couper. London, Dean's, and New York, Crown, 1985.
*How to Make the Most of Your Telescope*. London, Longman, 1985.
*The Sky at Night*. Kent, Harrap, and New York, Norton, 1985.
*The Universe*, with Iain Nicolson. London, Collins, and New York, Macmillan, 1985.
*Astronomy for the Under Tens*. London, Philip, 1986; revised edition, 1989.
*Patrick Moore's A-Z of Astronomy*. Wellington, Northamptonshire, Stephens, 1986; New York, Norton, 1987.
*Astronomers' Stars*. London, Routledge, 1986; New York, Norton, 1989.
*Exploring the Night Sky with Binoculars*. Cambridge, Cambridge University Press, 1986.
*TV Astronomer: Thirty Years of "The Sky at Night"*. Kent, Harrap, 1987.
*Stars and Planets*. London, Merehurst, and New York, Exeter, 1988.
*Space Travel for the Under Tens*. London, Philip, 1988.
*Atlas of Uranus*, with Garry Hunt. Cambridge, Cambridge University Press, 1989.
*The Amateur Astronomer*. Cambridge, Cambridge University Press, 1990.

*Universe for the Under Tens.* London, Philip, 1990.
*Mission to the Planets: The Illustrated Story of Man's Exploration of the Solar System.* New York, Norton, 1990.
*The Earth for Under Tens.* London, Philip, 1991.
*Passion for Astronomy.* Devon, David and Charles, 1991.

Editor, *Space Exploration.* Cambridge, University Press, 1958.
Editor, *Practical Amateur Astronomy.* London, Lutterworth Press, 1963; as *A Handbook of Practical Amateur Astronomy,* New York, Norton, 1964.
Editor, *Against Hunting.* London, Gollancz, 1965.
Editor, *Some Mysteries of the Universe,* by William R. Corliss. London, Black, 1969.
Editor, *Astronomical Telescopes and Observatories.* Newton Abbot, Devon, David and Charles, and New York, Norton, 1973.
Editor, *Modern Astronomy: Selections from The Yearbook of Astronomy.* London, Sidgwick and Jackson, and New York, Norton, 1977.
Editor, *The Beginner's Book of Astronomy.* London, Sidgwick and Jackson, 1978.
Editor, with Garry Hunt, *The Atlas of the Solar System.* London, Mitchell Beazley, 1983.
Editor, *The International Encyclopedia of Astronomy.* Torrance, California, 1987.

Translator, *The Planet Mars,* by Gérard de Vaucouleurs. London, Faber, and New York, Macmillan, 1950; revised edition, Faber, 1951.
Translator, *The Structure of the Universe,* by Evry L. Schatzman. London, Weidenfeld and Nicolson, 1968.
Translator, *Quanta,* by J. Andrade e Silva and G. Lochak. London, Weidenfeld and Nicolson, 1969.
Translator, *Cosmology,* by Jean Émile Charon. London, Weidenfeld and Nicolson, 1970.
Translator, *The Planet Mercury [Mars],* by E.M. Antoniadi. Shaldon, Devon, Reid, 2 vols., 1974–75.

Recording: *The Ever Ready Band Plays Music by Patrick Moore,* Pye, 1979.

*

Patrick Moore comments:

My novels are written with the aim of entertaining; they are set in space and are for boys aged roughly 10 to 15. I try to keep a reasonably authentic background, though I am not above taking liberties (after all, Wells did!). I do, however, make a rule that any juvenile novels of mine avoid the sordid and unwholesome.

* * *

Patrick Moore's novels possess some special quality not shared by many of their contemporaries. Like the Biggles series, Moore's tales of interplanetary travel continue to be republished and find a steady readership. Unfortunately, the quality that enables these novels to maintain their readership does not transmit itself to the adult reader. The children's books of a writer such as Ursula K. LeGuin can be identified as books of some merit even by adult standards. However, Moore's books tend to present a view of life and character that is narrow and unrealistic. The characters themselves are largely stock creations and are emotionally very limited. The story lines are repetitive and rely on a limited number of situations to maintain the excitement of the tale. (The main variations consist of altering the names of the chief characters, the settings, and the order of the incidents.) Finally the stories themselves lack a human realism. Scientifically, the stories are slightly behind the times, but this is of little significance compared to the ease with which his juvenile heroes become incorporated into the adventure: this strains adult credulity, and probably that of many children as well. Despite this, the books continue to attract readers at a time when many superior examples of the storyteller's craft fail to do so. Moore's books offer something beyond an adventure in space, something beyond the lack of literary polish. This something lies within the story.

A typical story line would go something like this: an honest courageous youth with a steady head on his shoulders by some means becomes associated with a research establishment engaged in the exploration of outer space. This establishment is staffed by a group of scientific internationalists who react strongly against national or political interests. A crisis occurs and the staff of the establishment are forced through circumstances to utilise the youth in a task of responsibility on a dangerous mission. The youth, despite the fact that he is not of outstanding intelligence or possessed of great knowledge, manages to win the respect of the scientists through a display of his basic qualities during the many dangers encountered throughout the mission, and, now accepted as an equal, has his future career as a respected member of an exploration team assured. In the series, the youthful hero gradually occupies a more and more respected place among the ranks of the scientist/explorers. The appeal of this storyline is fairly obvious. It displays successful adolescent involvement in an adult world, though a greatly simplified and idealised one. A display of truth, integrity, and courage is sufficient to achieve one's desire, and there are no authority conflicts to establish problems between the adolescent and his elders, since the authority displayed by the scientists stems only from their great knowledge of a given situation, and the motivation for accepting their authority is made obvious: death in space if the mission fails. In this respect, Moore's novels reflect an updating of traditional tales of this type, and in that context, a fairly successful updating.

—Gary Coughlan

---

**MOORE, Ward.** American. Born in Madison, New Jersey, 10 August 1903. Self-educated. Married 1) Lorna Lenzi in 1942 (divorced); 2) Raylyn Crabbe in 1967, four daughters and three sons. Chicken farmer, bookshop clerk and manager, shipyard worker during World War II, house builder, gardener, ghost writer, copy editor, and book review editor. Lived in California after 1929. *Died 29 January 1978.*

SCIENCE-FICTION PUBLICATIONS

Novels

*Greener Than You Think.* New York, Sloane, 1947; London, Gollancz, 1949.
*Bring the Jubilee.* New York, Farrar Straus, 1953; London, Heinemann, 1955.
*Cloud by Day.* London, Heinemann, 1956.
*Joyleg,* with Avram Davidson. New York, Pyramid, 1962.
*Caduceus Wild,* with R. Bradford. Los Angeles, Pinnacle, 1978.

Uncollected Short Stories

"Peacebringer" ("Sword of Peace"), in *The Big Book of Science Fiction*, edited by Groff Conklin. New York, Crown, 1950.
"Flying Dutchman," in *Adventures in Tomorrow*, edited by Ken Crossen. New York, Greenberg, 1951; London, Lane, 1953.
"We the People," in *Future Tense*, edited by Ken Crossen. New York, Greenberg, 1952; London, Lane, 1954.
"Measure of a Man," in *Fantasy and Science Fiction* (New York), August 1953.
"Lot," in *The Best from Fantasy and Science Fiction 3*, edited by Anthony Boucher and J. Francis McComas. New York, Doubleday, 1954.
"Rx Jupiter Save Us," in *Future* (New York), January 1954.
"Caution Advisable," in *Original Science Fiction Stories* (Holyoke, Massachusetts), March 1955.
"In Working Order," in *Original Science Fiction Stories* (Holyoke, Massachusetts), May 1955.
"Old Story," in *Fantasy and Science Fiction* (New York), September 1955.
"The Rewrite Man," in *Fantastic Universe* (Chicago), July 1956.
"No Man Pursueth," in *The Best from Fantasy and Science Fiction 6*, edited by Anthony Boucher. New York, Doubleday, 1957.
"Adjustment," in *The Best from Fantasy and Science Fiction 7*, edited by Anthony Boucher. New York, Doubleday, 1958.
"Lot's Daughter," in *A Decade of Fantasy and Science Fiction*, edited by Robert P. Mills. New York, Doubleday, 1960.
"Transient," in *Amazing* (New York), February 1960.
"The Fellow Who Married the Maxill Girl," in *The Best from Fantasy and Science Fiction 10*, edited by Robert P. Mills. New York, Doubleday, 1961.
"It Becomes Necessary" ("The Cold Peace"), in *The Year's Best S-F 7*, edited by Judith Merril. New York, Simon and Schuster, 1962.
"Rebel," in *Fantasy and Science Fiction* (New York), February 1962.
"The Second Trip to Mars" ("Dominions Beyond"), in *The Post Reader of Fantasy and Science Fiction*. New York, Doubleday, and London, Souvenir Press, 1964.
"The Mysterious Milkman of Bishop Street," in *Fantasy and Science Fiction* (New York), January 1965.
"Frank Merriwell in the White House," in *American Government Through Science Fiction*, edited by Joseph D. Olander and Martin H. Greenberg. New York, Random House, 1974.
"Durance," in *Epoch*, edited by Roger Elwood and Robert Silverberg. New York, Berkley, 1975.
"Wish Fiddle," in *Fantasy and Science Fiction* (New York), November 1975.
"A Class with Dr. Chang," in *Beyond Time*, edited by Sandra Ley. New York, Pocket Books, 1976.
"With Mingled Feelings . . . ," in *Chrysalis 6*, edited by Roy Torgeson. New York, Kensington, 1979.
"Conversation Piece," in *Whispers 2*, edited by Stuart David Schiff. New York, Doubleday, 1979.

OTHER PUBLICATION

Novel

*Breathe the Air Again*. New York, Harper, 1942.

* * *

Ward Moore's science fiction began in 1947 with the publication of *Greener Than You Think*, a disaster novel in which a mysterious mutated "devilgrass" threatens the world. Moore also wrote a number of short stories, but no collected edition exists. This is a shame, since many of the stories are interesting and worthy of a larger audience. "Lot," for example, is a powerful story of a man obsessed with survival, who, with his family, is escaping the fallout of a nuclear attack. "Adjustment" shows Moore's humor in a tale of a man who can make his wishes come true. "The Mysterious Milkman of Bishop Street" shows still another dimension of Moore's ability, in a whimsical fantasy about a milkman too good to be endured.

Moore's reputation in science fiction, however, rests chiefly on a superlative work of alternate history, *Bring the Jubilee.* This fine novel, which ironically takes its title from the Civil War song "Marching Through Georgia," supposes that Lee's forces had taken the high ground before the Battle of Gettysburg, leading to victory there and eventually to victory in the "War of Southern Independence." Most of the novel shows the results of this turn of events on subsequent history: the Confederacy has become wealthy and powerful, expanding westward to California and southward into Central America, but the Northern States lead an impoverished, backward existence. The central character of the novel, Hodge Backmaker, is born into a poor farm family, and in 1938 goes to New York to expand his opportunities. The world of *Bring the Jubilee* is much more technologically backward than our historical one, and Hodge has trouble gaining the education he seeks. Events bring him to a center for study in Pennsylvania, established years before by Herbert Haggerwells, a major in the Confederate army who remained in the area. There Hodge finds his vocation, and begins to build himself a reputation in Civil War history, but his conclusions are challenged by an authority in the field. A descendant of the Major, Barbara Haggerwells, is a physicist; she has perfected a time machine, and she offers its use to Hodge to visit the Battle of Gettysburg and test his theories. Hodge is to learn painfully that even the fact of observation affects that which is studied. Arriving before dawn on the morning of the 1st of July, 1863, Hodge is spotted by advancing Confederate troops, and they halt to question him. A panic ensues in which the officer is killed, and when light breaks, Hodge recognizes the dead man as Herbert Haggerwells. With the advance interrupted, the Confederates never take the Round Tops, and the battle proceeds as our history knows it.

Born in 1921, Hodge dies in 1877, a broken man. He realizes his responsibility for the destruction of the world he knew. In addition to the adventure story and the imaginative construction of an alternative world, Moore has written a probing discussion of the controversy between free will and determinism, and the result is a work that is one of science fiction's best.

—Walter E. Meyers

---

**MORGAN, Dan.** British. Born in Holbeach, Lincolnshire, 24 December 1925. Educated at Spalding Grammar School. Served in the Royal Army Medical Corps, 1947–48. Married Georgina Congreve in 1973. Since 1958, managing director, Dan Morgan Ltd., men's clothing store, Spaulding. Professional guitarist. Agent: Gerald Pollinger, Laurence Pollinger Ltd., 18 Maddox Street, London WIR 0EU Address: 1 Chapel Lane, Spalding, Lincolnshire PE11 1BP, England.

SCIENCE-FICTION PUBLICATIONS

Novels (series: Mind; Venturer 12)

*Cee Tee Man.* London, Panther, 1955.
*The Uninhibited.* London, Digit, 1961.
*The Richest Corpse in Show Business.* London, Compact, 1966.
*The New Minds.* London, Corgi, 1967; New York, Avon, 1969.
*A Thunder of Stars* (Venturer 12), with John Kippax. London, Macdonald, 1968; New York, Ballantine, 1970.
*The Several Minds.* London, Corgi, and New York, Avon, 1969.
*The Mind Trap.* London, Corgi, and New York, Avon, 1970.
*Inside.* London, Corgi, 1971; New York, Berkley, 1974.
*Seed of the Stars* (Venturer 12), with John Kippax. New York, Ballantine, 1972; London, Pan, 1974.
*The Neutral Stars* (Venturer 12), with John Kippax. New York, Ballantine, 1973; London, Pan, 1975.
*The High Destiny.* New York, Berkley, 1973; London, Millington, 1975.
*The Country of the Mind.* London, Corgi, 1975.
*The Concrete Horizon.* London, Millington, 1976.

OTHER PUBLICATIONS

Other

*Guitar.* London, Corgi, 1965; 3rd edition, 1985; as *Playing the Guitar*, New York, Bantam, 1967.
*Spanish Guitar.* London, Corgi, 1982.
*Beginning Windsurfing.* London, Corgi, 1982.
*You Can Play the Guitar*, with Nick Penny. London, Carousel, 1983.

*

Dan Morgan comments:

A large number of my novels have been concerned with ESP—particularly the Mind series, of course. People have always interested me more than machines and continue to do so more than ever. The Venturer 12 series, written in collaboration with the late John Hynam (John Kippax), was likewise more concerned with character than hardware, and was labelled by one reviewer as "sophisticated Space Opera."

It may be of interest to note that the one book of mine which continues to stimulate the most comment and interest is *The Richest Corpse in Show Business.* Perhaps there is a clue in that this is the only avowedly humorous novel I have written—maybe I should have mined this vein further. At the moment my business commitments are so heavy that there just isn't time to write, but the bug is still there and I'll be back to it one of these days.

* * *

Although Dan Morgan is not the kind of author who attracts a devoted following, he is certainly underrated and generally overlooked. Most of his novels and short stories display sound storytelling ability, and all rely heavily on a fast-moving plot.

In collaboration with John Kippax, Morgan produced a space opera trilogy that enjoyed a brief popularity and was promptly forgotten. *A Thunder of Stars* introduced the Space Corps, a professional military and exploratory organization. Against a muted background of alien encroachment, the protagonist must race against time to prevent disaster from a runaway reactor on a colony ship. In the sequel, *Seed of the Stars*, the governor of an established colony world is determined to wrest independence from the home world, even if it results in disaster for his charge. The Space Corps was pitted against another powerful but unscrupulous antagonist in *The Neutral Stars*, this time a private citizen investing his substantial wealth in highly secret research.

The idea of a single highly-talented villain opposed by a well-organized group is carried into Morgan's most effective series, the Mind series, which concentrates on a group of people with psi powers who band together for mutual support and enhancement of their powers. In each of these novels a different psionic menace appears, confronts the group in some fashion, and is ultimately vanquished. In one case, the problem is complicated by a schism within the organization itself, but the overall idea of the many banded together against the uncooperative opponent recurs throughout the series.

With one exception, the rest of Morgan's novels are fairly routine adventure stories. There is a struggle for power in reasonably familiar fashion on a far world in *The High Destiny*, interplanetary war and more telepathy in *The Uninhibited*, and contra-terrene matter in *Cee Tee Man.* An interesting novel that doesn't totally succeed is *Inside*, wherein an unconscionable experiment with human beings is conducted in a domed city on airless Mars. Totally untypical of Morgan is the satirical *The Richest Corpse in Show Business.* Although the barbed humor is generally directed at the television industry, there are good-natured swipes at nearly everything else along the way, including some satire of the genre itself.

Morgan's relative lack of popularity probably stems from his mining of conceptual veins already fairly well worked over. Competent but unoriginal stories of telepathy make little impression on readers after the surfeit of them provided during the Campbell years at *Analog.* Morgan is not really innovative, but does consistently maintain a degree of competence well above the average. His adventure novels are of the type that form the bulwark of the science-fiction genre.

—Don D'Ammassa

---

**MORLEY, Wilfred Owen.** *See* **LOWNDES, Robert A.W.**

---

**MORRESSY, John.** American. Born in Brooklyn, New York, 8 December 1930. Educated at St. John's University, New York, B.A. in English 1953; New York University, M.A. 1961. Served in the United States Army, 1953–55. Married Barbara Ann Turner in 1956. Writer and reviewer, Equitable Life, New York, 1957–59; Instructor, St. John's University, 1962–66; Assistant Professor, Monmouth College, West Long Branch, New Jersey, 1966–67; Writer-in-Residence, Worcester Consortium, Massachusetts, 1977; Visiting Writer and Elliott Professor of English, University of Maine, Orono, 1977–78. Since 1968, Associate Professor, Professor, and Writer-in-Residence, Franklin Pierce College, Rindge, New Hampshire. Recipient: Bread Loaf Writers Conference Fellowship, 1968; University of Colorado Writers Conference Fellowship, 1970; Balrog award, 1984. Agent: William Morris Agency, Inc., 1350 Avenue of the Americas, New York, New York 10019. Address: Apple Hill Road, East Sullivan, New Hampshire 03445, U.S.A.

SCIENCE-FICTION PUBLICATIONS

Novels (series: Ziax II; Kedrigern; Iron Angel)

*Starbrat*. New York, Walker, 1972; London, New English Library, 1979.
*Nail Down the Stars*. New York, Walker, 1973; London, New English Library, 1979; as *Stardrift*, New York, Popular Library, 1975.
*The Humans of Ziax II* (for children). New York, Walker, 1974.
*Under a Calculating Star*. New York, Doubleday, 1975; London, Sidgwick and Jackson, 1978.
*The Windows of Forever* (for children). New York, Walker, 1975.
*A Law for the Stars*. Toronto, Laser, 1976.
*The Extraterritorial*. Toronto, Laser, 1977.
*Frostworld and Dreamfire*. New York, Doubleday, 1977; London, Sidgwick and Jackson, 1979.
*The Drought on Ziax II* (for children). New York, Walker, 1978.
*Ironbrand* (Iron Angel). Chicago, Playboy Press, 1980.
*Graymantle* (Iron Angel). New York, Playboy Press, 1981.
*Kingsbane* (Iron Angel). New York, Playboy Press, 1982.
*The Mansions of Space*. New York, Ace, 1983.
*The Time of the Annihilator* (Iron Angel). New York, Ace, 1985.
*A Voice for Princess* (Kedrigern). New York, Ace, 1986.
*The Questing of Kedrigern*. New York, Ace, 1987.
*Kedrigern in Wanderland*. New York, Ace, 1988.
*Kedrigern and the Charming Couple*. New York, Ace, 1990.
*A Remembrance for Kedrigern*. New York, Ace, 1990.

OTHER PUBLICATIONS

Novels

*The Blackboard Cavalier*. New York, Doubleday, 1966; London, Gollancz, 1967.
*The Addison Tradition*. New York, Doubleday, 1968.
*A Long Communion*. New York, Walker, 1974; as *Displaced Persons*, New York, Popular Library, 1976.

Short Stories

*Other Stories*. Amherst, Massachusetts, Northern New England Review Press, 1983.

*

John Morressy comments:

I write science fiction because I find it to be the most interesting, enjoyable, and creative field open to a writer today and the one that may, in time, prove to be the most significant.

My books are founded on the assumption that the human race, in future ages, will behave much as it always has in the past. We are not yet civilized, and I find it hard to believe that we ever will be. After six or seven thousand years of recorded history and, according to some, progress, we still settle our ideological and economic conflicts by killing one another and laying waste to our planet. Piracy, slavery, and brigandage still thrive. In more countries than we can enumerate, torture is routinely inflicted on prisoners, trial and sentencing is a mockery of justice, and execution is quick and brutal. Under the circumstances, such cherished terms as "freedom" and "human dignity" are meaningless, almost silly. And all this is in the age of *Apollo, Voyager*, and *Explorer*, of organ transplants and laser surgery and micro-computers and an arm-long list of scientific and technological wonders.

My novels are set in a future spawned by this present. I envision the human race as surviving (though not without great suffering), eventually reaching the stars, encountering other worlds and other races, and making all the old mistakes over again, on a larger scale. I have tried to create a single future continuum and keep my novels within it. The novels are linked, not sequentially, but laterally. There is no one that must be read first, or last, in order to understand some grand design. A few characters, and places, and institutions, and events, appear in several of my novels; others are in one only. My novels are not attempts to predict the future, but glimpses of what might happen in one particular future. To me, that is the thing science fiction can do and no other genre can: it can give a reader a taste of the future without charging the full and non-refundable price of experiencing it in person.

* * *

John Morressy's first science-fiction novel, *Starbrat*, was the opening volume in a series of space adventures that borrow heavily from other genres in their detail and treatment. The young protagonist is kidnapped from his homeworld by space pirates and sold into slavery as a gladiator. There he becomes a skillful warrior, eventually earning his freedom, then setting out to find his destiny on another world. Spirited adventure fare, if somewhat derivative. During his quest, the protagonist meets a wandering minstrel who is the central figure in the sequel, *Nail Down the Stars* (which also appeared under the title *Stardrift*). The minstrel, whose identity seems to change with every world he visits, has a series of adventures as he travels about, but nothing is resolved until the third in the series, *Under a Calculating Star*, completes the cycle. The protagonist is a confidence man who murders a planetary king to whom he bears an uncanny resemblance, intending to replace him and secretly usurp the throne. His plan becomes more complicated as he encounters the main characters from the previous two books, a cleverly conceived device that makes the series as a whole more cohesive than the disparate plots of the individual volumes might suggest.

Morressy wrote three more novels set in this same universe, although they are individually unrelated. *Frostworld and Dreamfire* continues the story of an interstellar civilization sinking into feudalism and barbarism. A fresh menace appears in the form of the Sternverein Empire, armed with powerful weapons, ruthlessly determined to extend their power. A three-sided conflict erupts between the invaders, the ruler of a small planet, and a charismatic tribal leader who wishes to free his people from the planetary tyrant. In *A Law for the Stars*, the Sternverein have become the police of the known universe, maintaining order although at the cost of certain freedoms. The hero is a young man freed from slavery and enlisted in that organization, and the story deals with his gradual realization that despite his feelings of gratitude, the Sternverein are corrupt and power hungry. *The Mansions of Space* is the most recent book set in this universe, which Morressy seems to have abandoned in recent years in favor of fantasy fiction. It follows the adventures of an interstellar trader who makes an unusual discovery, and is easily the best of Morressy's space operas. There was one other straightforward science-fiction novel during this period, the very atypical *The Extraterritorial*, set on Earth in the future where mysterious organizations contend among themselves. The theme is once again the corruption of an institution discovered by one of its adherents.

Morressy turned to fantasy in 1980 with *Ironbrand.* The plot is the familiar quest of three sons to reclaim the throne of their father from an evil, and inhuman, usurper. Morressy displayed a positive gift for this form, and the novel was sufficiently successful to inspire two additional volumes. *Graymantle* is actually a prequel, another quest story, this time the search for a magical artifact that holds the key to toppling a tyrant from his throne. This same talisman figures prominently again in the third in the series, *Kingsbane,* this time stolen by an ambitious lord in a time when the use of magic has largely been forgotten.

Morressy wrote one independent fantasy novel, *The Time of the Annihilator,* a comparatively minor novel that ended his period of quest fantasies. It was followed within a year by *A Voice for Princess,* which introduced the scholarly but wizened wizard Kedrigern, who has been featured in his five most recent novels. With this novel, Morressy moved into the area of humorous fantasy, featuring a feisty magician who resigns from the wizards' guild in the opening adventure, planning to lead a contemplative life, but ultimately deciding to find a beautiful young princess to marry. Kedrigern casts counterspells, but each can work only once, providing many of the plot lines.

*The Questing of Kedrigern* involves his attempt to find a solution when rival wizards drunkenly transform his female companion into a toad. He is successful, of course, and marries her in the next volume, *Kedrigern in Wanderland.* The third adventure is far superior to the preceding two, demonstrating Morressy's growing ability to blend humor and adventure. In two subsequent adventures, *Kedrigern and the Charming Couple* and *A Remembrance for Kedrigern,* the inimitable sorcerer must deal with a werewolf and an inept dragonslayer, respectively. As a whole, the series has been inventive and entertaining, a viable alternative to Piers Anthony's far more popular Xanth books.

Although Morressy was an infrequent short-story writer in the 1970's, he became far more prolific at that length during the 1980's. Most of these are competent but unmemorable, but three deserve mention. "The Empath and the Savages" (in *The Best of Omni Science Fiction 3,* edited by Ben Bova and Don Myrus. New York, Omni, 1982) provides an interesting insight into an alien worldview, "Stoneskin" (in *Fantasy and Science Fiction* (New York), June 1984) is a cleverly plotted serious fantasy adventure, and "No More Pencils, No More Books" (in *The Best Science Fiction of the Year 9,* edited by Terry Carr. New York, Ballantine, 1980) is a disturbing glimpse of what might happen if we allow the government to enforce its desire for conformity far enough to limit our own freedom.

—Don D'Ammassa

---

**MORRIS, Janet E(llen).** American. Born in Boston, Massachusetts, 25 May 1946. Attended New York University, 1965–66. Married Christopher C. Morris in 1971. Lighting designer, Chip Monck Enterprises, New York, 1963–64; night manager, 1970; bass player, Christopher Morris Band, 1975, 1977; songwriter and recording artist; project director, U.S. Global Strategy Council, 1989. Since 1990, research director, Non-Lethal Programs; associate, Institute for Geopolitical Studies. Lives in West Hyannisport, Massachusetts. Agent: Perry Knowlton, Curtis Brown Agency, 10 Astor Place, New York, New York 10003, U.S.A.

SCIENCE-FICTION PUBLICATIONS

Novels (Series: Dream Dancer; Silistra; Thieves' World)

*High Couch of Silistra.* New York, Bantam, 1977; revised edition, as *Returning Creation,* New York, Baen, 1984.
*The Golden Sword* (Silistra). New York, Bantam, 1977.
*Wind from the Abyss* (Silistra). New York, Bantam, 1978.
*The Carnelian Throne* (Silistra). New York, Bantam, 1979.
*Dream Dancer.* New York, Putnam, and London, Fontana, 1980.
*Cruiser Dreams* (Dancer). New York, Berkley, and London, Fontana, 1980.
*Earth Dreams* (Dancer). New York, Berkley, 1982.
*The Forty-Minute War,* with Chris Morris. New York, Baen, 1984.
*Active Measures,* with David A. Drake. New York, Baen, 1985.
*Beyond Sanctuary* (Thieves' World). New York, Baen, 1985.
*Beyond the Veil* (Thieves' World). New York, Baen, 1985.
*Beyond Wizardwall* (Thieves' World). New York, Baen, 1986.
*Medusa,* with Chris Morris. New York, Baen, 1986.
*Kill Ratio,* with David A. Drake. New York, Ace, 1987.
*Warlord!* New York, Pocket, 1987.
*Outpassage,* with Chris Morris. New York, Pageant, 1988; London, New English Library, 1990.
*City at the Edge of Time,* with Chris Morris. New York, Baen, 1988.
*Tempus Unbound.* New York, Baen, 1989.
*Target.* New York, Ace, 1989.
*Storm Seed,* with Chris Morris. New York, Baen, 1990.
*Threshold,* with Chris Morris. New York, New American Library, 1990.

Short Stories

*Tempus.* New York, Baen, 1987.

OTHER PUBLICATIONS

Novels

*I, the Sun.* New York, Bantam, 1980.
*Soul of the City,* with Lynn Abbey and C.J. Cherryh. New York, Ace, 1986.

Other

*The Warrior's Edge,* with John B. Alexander and Richard Groller. New York, Morrow, 1990.

Editor, *Afterwar.* New York, Baen, 1985.
Editor, with others, *Heroes in Hell* series. New York, Baen, 11 vols., 1986–89.

*

Janet E. Morris comments:

(1981) The thrust of my work, over the long term and through a projected group of books, historical, contemporary, and speculative, is the evolution of consciousness, with an eye toward the genetic, societal, and philosophical influences thereon. Sophocles states that one law ever holds true: nothing vast enters into the world of mortals without a curse. I look for in past history or create in my future histories moments of cataclysm in theaters both physical and mental. My intention is always to explore the thought that must precede any outward action, its struggle to reach a new, more tenable position from which to regard self and universe.

My work in history shall eventually include: Sargon of Agade's conquest of Ebla; Rammesseide Egypt in its position as the seat of Yawwhist tradition; the Seven Sages, those wonderful progenitors of pre-Socratic thought; as well as Suppiluliumas I of Hatti and his dealings with the short-lived Atenist rise in Egypt (*I, the Sun*). Another work samples alchemical thought at the time of the death of Paracelsus, father of chemotherapy.

My science-fictional excursions into the possible evolution of consciousness have all centered on man's apprehension of the physical world, and his sense of place in it. My areas of study are necessarily genetics, biology, sociobiology, philosophy, and physics, but the aim at all times is to *show* rather than *tell.* The more crystallized the tenets of my position in a particular book, the more I strive to present them in an experiential manner without technical discourse which might erect a barrier between myself and the reader.

My Silistra series openly treats sexual themes as well as the possible effect of mind on probability. My Dream Dancer books treat the marriage of man and mechanical intelligence through the utilization of our mastery of the intelligence code, the decipherment of which is even now in progress, as well as man's attempt to emancipate himself from the prison of relativistic space. Both the above groups of books focus to some extent on women, but are in no sense "women's" books; rather, I feel that technology is the leveler of sexism and the liberator of those sexual types not included in the sub-set "heterosexual male."

Reading back over what I have written, I must add that I write primarily the book which I myself would like to read, the book I can imagine that you might like to read. My hope above all is to tender you, the reader, an excursion, a journey into another realm which, upon returning, you might find to some small degree has enriched your "present."

* * *

It would be easy to dismiss the early novels of Janet E. Morris as transplanted historicals, because on at least one level, that is what they are. Morris uses her knowledge of history and the evolution of cultures to create an interstellar society in *High Couch of Silistra*, later revised and issued as *Returning Creation.* The culture presented in this and three sequels, *The Golden Sword, Wind from the Abyss*, and *The Carnelian Throne*, is complex and in many ways controversial. Many readers dismissed the series as demeaning in its portrayal of gender roles because the central character is a courtesan in what appears to be a male dominated culture. In actual fact, the protagonist is potentially the most influential person on the entire planet, which is recovering from the excesses of technology only to face the possibility of a recurrence of that same disaster. Although the series has its awkward moments, it remains innovative, unusually frank and perceptive in its examination of power relationships between the sexes, and is generally entertaining.

The Silistra books were followed by a trilogy that created an even more interesting society. *Dream Dancer* and its two sequels, *Cruiser Dreams* and *Earth Dreams*, also featured a strong female protagonist and once again concentrate on the constant struggle for power and influence. Perhaps the most interesting aspect of the trilogy is Morris's creation of an artificial species of intelligent, sentient starships, whose fate is the ultimate source of conflict in what is an impressively well thought out plot and setting.

In 1985, Morris seemed to split into two separate writers, both very different from the one who had existed prior to that point. Although there were many superficial aspects of fantasy in the earlier novels, the books remained science fiction. Her participation in the shared universe Thieves' World series of original anthologies led to the creation of Tempus, a recurring character, an immortal hero featured in the first independent novel in that setting, *Beyond Sanctuary.* Morris continued the saga of Tempus in a battle with demons in *Beyond the Veil*, and a concluding volume, *Beyond Wizardwall.* A collection of the independent shorter adventures was published as *Tempus*, and a second trilogy, written in collaboration with Chris Morris, followed, consisting of *Tempus Unbound, City at the Edge of Time*, and *Storm Seed.* Morris was also instrumental in the creation of another popular shared universe series, the Heroes in Hell books, a series of fantasy adventures set in the afterlife, with all of human history as a source of characters.

Of greater interest to science-fiction readers has been Morris's simultaneous shift to a series of near future, technological thrillers. In *Active Measures*, written with David Drake, a CIA agent realizes that the president is a Soviet sympathizer, cleverly altering domestic and foreign policy to lower American prestige to the benefit of the Soviet Union, and to cause deeper schisms in an already badly fractured country. Current events have taken a toll on the book's premise, and it was also published as a contest in which readers were to solve some unresolved problems.

A far more successful book was *The Forty-Minute War*, with Chris Morris. A terrorist attack on Washington results in a limited nuclear exchange. Once again, the protagonist is an intelligence operative working with the Israeli secret service in an attempt to stem the drift towards anarchy in North America. *Medusa*, also written with Chris Morris, is another high-tech thriller, this time involving a supposed Soviet accident, a missile which must be intercepted before it damages or destroys America's space-born defense system.

*Kill Ratio*, by Morris and David Drake, moves away from the very near future, although the conflicts remain similar. The United Nations has moved its headquarters to the moon, where a terrorist group releases a deadly plague into the environment. Once again, the protagonist is an intelligence operative, a member in this case of the organization responsible for the security of the installation. The highly suspenseful plot and logical resolution make this an exceptional work of its kind. A sequel, *Target*, is even better. An alien arrives on the moon, seeking asylum, pursued by a number of enemies equipped with technology far in advance of that available to humanity.

Morris's most recent novels have dealt with more traditional themes. *Outpassage*, with Chris Morris, is an interplanetary adventure story filled with intrigues, potential rebellions, and fast-paced action. The same collaborative team also wrote *Threshold*, a tale of interstellar smuggling with a very well-conceived and executed mystery subplot.

Although Morris has written a fair number of short stories, these have been almost exclusively for shared world anthologies, and the best of her stories are those involving Tempus. She seems more at ease with full-length novels in any case. Although her more recent works are more restrained in their inventiveness, the stronger focus is particularly beneficial in those instances where suspense is a major consideration.

—Don D'Ammassa

---

**MORRIS, William.** English. Born in Walthamstow, Essex, 24 March 1834. Educated at a preparatory school in Walthamstow, 1843–47; Marlborough College, Wiltshire, 1848–51; privately, 1852–53; Exeter College, Oxford, 1853–55, B.A. 1856, M.A. 1875. Served in the Artists Corps of Volunteers, 1859–61. Married Jane Burden in 1859; two daughters. Articled to G.E. Street's architectural firm, Oxford and London, 1856; founding editor, *Oxford and Cambridge Magazine*, 1856; practising painter, 1857–62; friend of Edward Burne-Jones, Dante Gabriel Rossetti, and other members of the Pre-Raphaelite Brotherhood; founder, with Burne-Jones, Rossetti, Ford Madox Brown, and others, Morris Marshall Faulkner & Co. design firm, London, 1861–74, subsequently Morris & Co., 1874–96; lived at Red House, Bexley, Kent, 1861–65, and in London from 1865 (at Kelmscott House, Hammersmith, from 1878); travelled in Iceland, 1871 and 1873; with Rossetti leased Kelmscott Manor, near Lechlade, Gloucestershire, 1871; public lecturer on art, architecture, and socialism, 1877–96; founder, Kelmscott Press, Hammersmith, 1890–96. Treasurer, National Liberal League, 1879; member, Democratic Federation, 1883, then the Socialist League, 1884; editor of its journal *Commonweal*, 1884–90, and League delegate to the International Socialist Working-Men's Congress, Paris, 1889; founding member, Hammersmith Socialist Society, 1890. Examiner, South Kensington School of Art, later Victoria and Albert Museum, London, 1876–96; founding member and secretary, Society for the Protection of Ancient Buildings, 1877; president, Birmingham Society of Arts, 1878–79; member, 1888, and master, 1892, Art Workers Guild: exhibited with the Arts and Crafts Exhibition Society. Honorary fellow, Exeter College, 1882. *Died 3 October 1896.*

### Science-Fiction Publications

#### Novels

*A Dream of John Ball, and A King's Lesson.* London, Reeves and Turner, 1888; East Aurora, New York, Roycroft, 1898.

*The Roots of the Mountains: Wherein Is Told Somewhat of the Lives of the Men of Burgdale.* London, Reeves and Turner, 1890; New York, Longman, 1896.

*News from Nowhere; or, An Epoch of Rest, Being Some Chapters from a Utopian Romance.* Boston, Roberts, 1890; London, Longman, 1891.

*The Story of the Glittering Plain Which Has Also Been Called the Land of Living Men, or the Acre of the Undying.* Hammersmith, Middlesex, Kelmscott Press, and Boston, Roberts, 1891.

*The Wood Beyond the World.* Hammersmith, Middlesex, Kelmscott Press, 1894; Boston, Roberts, 1895.

*Child Christopher and Goldilind the Fair.* Hammersmith, Middlesex, Kelmscott Press, 2 vols., 1895; Portland, Maine, Mosher, 1900.

*The Well at the World's End: A Tale.* Hammersmith, Middlesex, Kelmscott Press, 1895; New York, Longman, 1896.

*The Water of the Wondrous Isles.* London, and New York, Longman, 1897.

*The Sundering Flood.* Hammersmith, Middlesex, Kelmscott Press, and New York, Longman, 1897.

*The Hollow Land and Other Contributions to the Oxford and Cambridge Magazine.* London, Longman, 1903.

*The Novel on Blue Paper,* edited by Penelope Fitzgerald. London, and West Nyack, New York, Journeyman Press, 1982.

#### Verse

*The Earthly Paradise: A Poem.* London, Ellis, 3 vols., 1868–70; Boston, Roberts, 1868–71; revised edition, New York, Longman, 1890.

*The Story of Sigurd the Volsung and the Fall of the Niblungs.* London, Ellis and White, 1876; Boston, Roberts, 1877.

*A Tale of the House of the Wolfings and All the Kindreds of the Mark* (prose and verse). London, Reeves and Turner, 1889; Boston, Roberts, 1890.

### Other Publications

#### Play

*The Tables Turned; or Nupkins Awakened: A Socialist Interlude* (produced 1887). London, Commonweal Office, 1887.

#### Verse

*The Defence of Guenevere and Other Poems,* edited by Robert Steele. London, Bell and Daldy, 1858; Boston, Roberts, 1875.

*The Life and Death of Jason: A Poem.* London, Bell and Daldy, and Boston, Roberts, 1867; revised edition, London, Bell and Daldy, and Boston, Roberts, 1867, 1888.

*The Pilgrims of Hope: A Poem in Thirteen Parts.* London, Forman, 1886; Portland, Maine, Mosher, 1901.

*Poems by the Way.* Hammersmith, Middlesex, Kelmscott Press, 1891; Boston, Roberts, 1892.

*A Book of Verse: A Facsimile of the Manuscript Written in 1870.* London, Scolar Press, 1980.

*The Juvenilia, with a Checklist and Unpublished Early Poems,* edited by Florence S. Boos. London, and New York, William Morris Society, 1983.

#### Other

*Love Is Enough; or, The Freeing of Pharamond: A Morality.* London, Ellis and White, and Boston, Roberts, 1873.

*Hopes and Fears for Art: Five Lectures Delivered in Birmingham, London, and Nottingham, 1878–1881.* London, Ellis and White, and Boston, Roberts, 1882.

*Lectures on Art.* London, Macmillan, 1882.

*A Summary of the Principles of Socialism Written for the Democratic Federation,* with H.M. Hyndman. London, Modern Press, 1884.

*Art and Socialism: A Lecture; and Watchman, What of the Night? The Aims and Ideals of the English Socialists of Today.* London, Reeves, 1884.

*Chants for Socialist: No. 1. The Day is Coming.* London, Reeves, 1884.

*The Voice of Toil, All for the Cause: Two Chants for Socialists.* London, Justice Office, 1884.

*The God of the Poor.* London, Justice Office, 1884.

*Chants for Socialists.* London, Socialist League Office, 1885; New York, New Horizon Press, 1935.

*The Manifesto of the Socialist League.* London, Socialist League, 1885; revised edition, 1885.

*The Socialist League: Constitution and Rules at the General Conference.* London, Socialist League, 1885.

*Address to Trades' Unions (The Socialist Platform - No. 1).* London, Socialist League, 1885.

*The Aims of Art.* London, Commonweal Office, 1887.

*Signs of Change: Seven Lectures.* London, Reeves and Turner, 1888; New York, Longman, 1896.

*Socialist Platform* (collected pamphlets), with others. n.p., 1888; revised edition, 1890.

*Statement of Principles of the Hammersmith Socialist Society.* Hammersmith, Hammersmith Socialist Society, 1890.

*Under an Elm-Tree: or, Thoughts in the Country-side.* Aberdeen, Scotland, Leatham, 1891; Portland, Maine, Mosher, 1912.

*Manifesto of English Socialists,* with G.B. Shaw and H.M. Hyndman. London, Twentieth Century Press, 1893.

*The Reward of Labour: A Dialogue.* London, Hayman Christy, 1893.

*Letters on Socialism.* London, Wisel, 1894.

*How I Became a Socialist.* London, Twentieth Century Press, 1896.

*Architecture, Industry, and Wealth: Collected Papers.* London, and New York, Longman, 1902.

*Collected Works,* edited by May Morris. London, and New York, Longman, 24 vols., 1910–15; supplement, as *William Morris: Artist, Writer, Socialist,* Oxford, Blackwell, 2 vols., 1936.

*Communism, a Lecture.* London, Fabian Society, 1903.

*The Letters of William Morris to His Family and Friends,* edited by Philip Henderson. London, and New York, Longman, 1950.

*Unpublished Letters,* edited by R.P. Arnot. London, Labour Monthly, 1951.

*Selected Writings and Designs,* edited by Asa Briggs. Baltimore, Penguin, 1962.

*The Unpublished Lectures of William Morris,* edited by Eugene D. LeMire. Detroit, Michigan, Wayne State University Press, 1969.

*Icelandic Journals.* Fontwell, Centaur Press, 1969; New York, Praeger, 1970.

*Early Romances in Prose and Verse,* edited by Peter Faulkner. London, Dent, 1973; Van Nuys, California, Newcastle, 1976.

*Socialist Diary,* edited by Florence Boos. Iowa City, Iowa, Windhoven Press, 1981; London, History Workshop Journal, 1982.

*The Ideal Book: Essays and Lectures on the Arts of the Book,* edited by William S. Peterson. Berkeley, University of California Press, 1982.

*Political Writings of William Morris,* edited by A.L. Morton. London, Lawrence and Wishart, and New York, International, 1973.

*The Collected Letters of William Morris,* edited by Norman Kelvin, vol. 1, 1848–80. Princeton, Princeton University Press, 1984.

*Morris by Himself: Designs and Writings,* edited by Gillian Naylor. n.p., 1988.

Translator, with Eiríkr Magnússon, *Grettis Saga: The Story of Grettir the Strong.* London, Ellis, 1869; New York, Longman, 1901.

Translator, with Eiríkr Magnússon, *Völsunga Saga: The Story of the Volsungs and Niblungs with Certain Songs from the Elder Edda.* London, Ellis, 1870; edited by H. Sparling, London, and New York, Walter Scott, 1888.

Translator, with Eiríkr Magnússon, *Three Northern Love Stories and Other Tales.* London, Ellis, and New York, Longman, 1875.

Translator, *The Aeneids of Virgil Done Into English Verse.* Boston, Roberts, 1875; London, Ellis and White, 1876.

Translator, *The Odyssey of Homer Done into English Verse.* London, Reeves and Turner, 2 vols., 1887; New York, Longman, 1897.

Translator, with Eiríkr Magnússon, *The Saga Library.* London, Quaritch, 5 vols., 1891–1905.

Translator, with others, *The Order of Chivalry,* by Hugues de Tabarie. Hammersmith, Middlesex, Kelmscott Press, 1893.

Translator, *The Tale of King Florus and the Fair Jehane.* Hammersmith, Middlesex, Kelmscott Press, 1893; Portland, Maine, Mosher, 1898.

Translator, *Of the Friendship of Amis and Amile.* Hammersmith, Middlesex, Kelmscott Press, 1894.

Translator, *The Tale of the Emperor Coustans and of Over Sea.* Hammersmith Press, 1894; Portland, Maine, Mosher, 1899.

Translator, with A.J. Wyatt, *The Tale of Beowulf, Sometime King of the Fold of the Weder Geats.* Hammersmith, Middlesex, Kelmscott Press, 1895; New York, Longman, 1910.

Translator, *Old French Romances.* London, G. Allen, and New York, Scribner, 1896.

Translator, with Eiríkr Magnússon, *The Story of Kormak, the Son of Ogmund,* edited by Grace Calder. London, William Morris Society, 1970.

*

Bibliography: A *Bibliography of the Works of William Morris* by Temple Scott, London, G. Bell, 1897; *Handlist of the Public Addresses of William Morris* by R.C.H. Briggs, London, William Morris Society, 1961; *William Morris in Private Press and Limited Editions: A Descriptive Bibliography of Books by and about William Morris 1891–1981* by John J. Walsdorf, Phoenix, Arizona, Oryx, and London, Library Association, 1983; *A Bibliography of the Kelmscott Press* by William S. Peterson, Oxford, Clarendon, 1984; *William Morris: A Reference Guide* by Gary L. Aho, Boston, G.K. Hall, 1985.

Critical Studies (selection): *The Life of William Morris* by J.W. Mackail, London, and New York, Longman, 2 vols., 1899; *The Kelmscott Press and William Morris, Master Craftsman* by H.H. Sparling, London, Macmillan, 1924; *William Morris: Romantic to Revolutionary* by E.P. Thompson, London, Lawrence and Wishart, 1955, revised edition, New York, Pantheon, 1976, London, Merlin Press, 1977; *Against the Age: An Introduction to William Morris* by Peter Faulkner, London, Allen and Unwin, 1980; *William Morris: The Critical Heritage* edited by Peter Faulkner, London, and Boston, Routledge and Kegan Paul, 1973; *William Morris: The Man and the Myth* (includes letters) by R.P. Arnot, New York, Monthly Review Press, and London, Lawrence and Wishart, 1964; *The Work of William Morris* by Paul Thompson, London, Heinemann, and New York, Viking, 1967, revised edition, London, Quartet Books, 1977; *William Morris: His Life, Work, and Friends* by Philip Henderson, London, Thames and Hudson, and New York, McGraw-Hill, 1967; *William Morris: His Life and Work* by Jack Lindsay, London, Constable, 1975, New York, Taplinger, 1979; *William Morris: Aspects of the Man and His Work* edited by Peter Lewis, Loughborough, Loughborough Victorian Studies Group, 1978; *A Pagan Prophet: William Morris* by Charlotte Oberg, Charlottesville, University Press of Virginia, 1978; *William Morris and His World* by Ian Bradley, New York, Scribner, and London, Thames and Hudson, 1978; *William Morris* by Frederick Kirchhoff, Boston, Twayne, 1979; *William Morris* by Peter Stansky, Oxford and New York, Oxford University Press, 1983; *William Morris: His Art, His Writings, and His Public Life: A Record* by Aymer Vallance, London, Studio Editions, 1986; *William Morris: His Life and Work* by Stephen Coote, London, Garamond, 1990.

* * *

It is impossible to summarise the contribution of William Morris to his age, which he abominated, and to our own, which would not much have impressed him. As social thinker, as designer and influence upon both arts and crafts (and especially those of everyday life), as poet (though his biggest works are not much to our contemporary taste) and as the first great Englishman to declare himself a communist, he is unique and irreplaceable. Yet it may be that the ten great prose fictions of the last ten years of his life offer his most lasting influence and his finest work. In these romances, he invented the modern fantasy novel, set in an imagined, glamorous and self-consistent world, a "secondary creation," as Tolkien was later to call it.

Morris was directly influenced by saga, epic, and medieval romance: he in fact translated many sagas, as well as *The Odyssey, The Aeneid, Beowulf,* and some romances—the most important of which, *Havelock the Dane*, became the prose romance *Child Christopher*. The list of influencing genres would not be complete, however, without the wealth of folktales that he knew and used (mostly in verse). Two of the ten books are time-travel stories, two evoke "barbaric" pre-history, and the other six are more or less radical redesignings of the patterns of quest-romance.

*A Dream of John Ball* takes a modern protagonist back into the time of the Peasants' Revolt, a period whose arts, crafts, and architecture delighted Morris, and with whose social turmoil he strongly identified. The time-traveller learns the impotence of "knowing the future": he cannot help John Ball and the other rebels, and the nightlong climactic discussion with Ball in the church is more enlightening to "modern man" than to the radical priest. The book's initial and lasting charm lies in the eager clarity with which the medieval setting is evoked.

*News from Nowhere* is a much larger companion work, a journey into and within a future world that is described in the same energetic, clear-edged style. This future world is the Commonwealth of "Nowhere," into which the protagonist dreams England has been transformed by revolution. It is the finest Utopia in English, the only one thoroughly worth living and working in, and Morris wrote it for a small radical audience, the readership of his leftwing magazine *Commonwealth*, who would find it worth living and working for.

*News from Nowhere* at times seems to divide between too much "history" of how this post-governmental England came into being and too easy a celebration of its early-summer idyllic aspects, but the time-traveller joins and justifies these contraries. The wise and subtle treatment of his responses to—and his salutary effect on—the people of Nowhere carries the narrative and powers its journey into the heart of England and of community. Contemporary readers knew the open secret that "William Guest" was Morris, and recognised every stage in his journey as part of Morris's life. His strength of longing also creates the intrepid soul-mate Ellen, who will safeguard and reshape Nowhere in its future, because she has met and loved the man that dreamed it.

*A Tale of the House of the Wolfings* and *The Roots of the Mountains*, between the two time-travel stories, explore two forms of the high barbaric society that Morris much preferred to high-capitalist civilisation. In *A Tale of the House of the Wolfings* the Gothic tribe's heroic resistance to Roman imperialism focusses upon the indomitable war-leader Thiodolf, but his love-affair with the nature-goddess and part-time Valkyrie Wood-Sun almost prevents the completion of his necessary selfless death. In *The Roots of the Mountains* another warrior-hero finds that the destiny of his people depends on both battle and his personal leadership, but the Gothic tribes are united and the Huns driven from that side of the mountains without his having to pay the final price. Goldmane is a more complex and contemporary hero than Thiodolf; both wildwood magic and personal luck and beauty protect him instead of destroying him.

*The Story of the Glittering Plain* evokes a later, Teutonic tribal world, and the hero, Hallblithe, has to pursue a Viking group that has kidnapped his betrothed. The quest takes him beyond this conflict, however, to an earthly paradise in which youth is permanently renewed and sensuous delight is not only guaranteed but insisted upon. Hallblithe detests the Glittering Plain; he eventually escapes from paradise and is reunited with his love. In a similar short romance, Golden Walter flees a miserable failed marriage, following mysterious visions that take him to the Wood Beyond the World. There his sexual helplessness teaches him to grow, both by his being forced to lie with the Lady of that Wood and by his being forbidden even to touch the Maid he loves. Eventually, the Maid is responsible for the Lady's death, and the two survivors find a new life as welcome rulers of a strange city through the mountains.

In these short romances and their great successors, *The Well at the World's End* and *The Water of the Wondrous Isles*, Morris creates a world akin to an unchurched version of medieval north-western Europe. There is active magic in these worlds, both for good and for ill, and usually associated with a wise and beautiful woman (or two or more contrasting power-women). Natural and life-enhancing magic is available to the very rare adventurer who reaches the Well at the World's End, but the book focusses on Ralph's adventures travelling there and back, especially his contact with the two loves of his life: one is a Power-Lady, the other a beautiful and courageous "ordinary" girl who becomes far more astonishing than the Lady.

*The Water of the Wondrous Isles* has an even more revolutionary effect upon our expectations of the quest: the protagonist or "hero" is a girl. A witch has stolen Birdalone and reared her to be a trap for lustful males, but she escapes, naked and resolute, into the wide world. She travels among literally wondrous isles and is caught up in a typical male quest, whose heroes leave her in a safe, smug castle while they sail off to rescue their ladies. Since she has never been taught that ladies are supposed to be passive, she escapes this protection too, and causes a much more perilous and passionate story. Three kinds of power-women influence her life, but her own developing integrity brings a qualified happy ending to her story.

The last, and incomplete, romance, *The Sundering Flood*, returns to a male hero, aided by magic and doing great deeds even as a boy. Osberne's female counterpart, Elfhild, was never properly filled out, and the book has accepted the limitations of an Icelandic saga, whereas the major romances explore their own psychological and magical structuring forces in a more demanding way.

The enactment of archetypal events, the rich evocation of psychological fears and needs, and the unhurried delight in both adventure and environment, make Morris's best romances a valuable experience—Yeats described them as books he always read very slowly, so as not to come too soon to the end. Their radical political stance and keen celebration of female personality are also remarkable, when so many fantasies are (rightly or wrongly) associated with high-church conservatism. Like Ellen in *News from Nowhere*, the Maid, Ursula, and Birdalone are courageous and enterprising people, not baits or rewards for more "real" male protagonists.

Morris created his own language, with something of the texture of 14th-century English. The resultant style is a unique experience, shapely and pleasurable, emphasising physical rather than abstract aspects of experience, while retaining a tapestried sense of distance. The romances are designed for a future society's audience, freed from the frantic busyness of his own age just as the folk of his Nowhere are. This audience loves a good story with both circumstantiality and wonders, whether in an old folktale, a Dickens fiction, or a "reactionary novel." It delights in so active and sensuous a world, so radical and lucid a use of traditional conventions. Morris invented the fantasy set in an invented and magical pseudo-medieval land, but he also invented a fantastic future audience that could appreciate it.

—Norman Talbot

---

**MORRISON, Richard.** *See* **LOWNDES, Robert A.W.**

---

**MORRISSEY, J.L.** *See* **SAXON, Richard.**

---

**MORROW, James (Kenneth).** American. Born in Philadelphia, Pennsylvania, 17 March 1947. Educated at University of Pennsylvania, Philadelphia, 1965–69, B.A. in creative writing; Harvard University Graduate School of Education, Cambridge, Massachusetts, 1969–70, M.A. in teaching 1970. Married Jean Pierce Morrow in 1972; one daughter and one son. English teacher, Cambridge Pilot School, Massachusetts, 1970–71; instructional materials specialist, Chelmsford Public Schools, Massachusetts, 1972–74; lecturer in instructional media, Tufts University, Medford, Massachusetts, 1977–79; contributing editor, *Media and Methods* magazine, 1978–80; co-director, Institute for Multimedia Learning, Westford, Massachusetts, 1978–84; science writer, *A Teacher's Guide to NOVA*, WGBH-TV, Boston, 1979–84; children's book author, Learningways Corporation, Cambridge, 1982–87; freelance fiction reviewer, *Philadelphia Inquirer*, 1986–90; Visiting Lecturer in fiction writing, Pennsylvania State University, University Park, 1990. Freelance fiction writer since 1980. Recipient: Pennsylvania Council of the Arts fellowship, 1988; Nebula award, for short story, 1988. Agent: Writers House, 21 West 26th Street, New York, New York 10010. Address: 810 North Thomas Street, State College, Pennsylvania 16803, U.S.A.

SCIENCE-FICTION PUBLICATIONS

Novels

*The Wine of Violence.* New York, Holt Rinehart, 1981; London, Century, 1991.
*The Continent of Lies.* New York, Holt Rinehart, 1984; London, Gollancz, 1985.
*This Is the Way the World Ends.* New York, Holt, 1986; London, Gollancz, 1987.
*Only Begotten Daughter.* New York, Morrow, 1990; London, Century, 1991.
*City of Truth* (novella). London, Legend, 1991.

Short Stories

*Swatting at the Cosmos.* Eugene, Oregon, Pulphouse, 1990.

OTHER PUBLICATIONS

Fiction for children

*The Quasar Kids.* Lexington, Massachusetts, Heath, 1987.
*What Makes a Dinasuar Sore.* Lexington, Massachusetts, Heath, 1987.
*The Lima Bean Dream*, with Marilyn Segal. Lexington, Massachusetts, Heath, 1987.
*Not too Messy, Not too Neat*, with Marilyn Segal. Lexington, Massachusetts, Heath, 1988.
*The Best-Bubble Blower.* Lexington, Massachusetts, Heath, 1988.

Screenplay

*A Political Cartoon*, with Joe Adamson, 1973.

Other

*Moviemaking Illustrated: The Comicbook Filmbook* (textbook), with Murray Suid. Rochelle Park, New Jersey, Hayden, 1973.
*Media and Kids* (textbook), with Murray Suid. Rochelle Park, New Jersey, Hayden, 1977.
*The Grammar of Media Kit* (textbook), with Jean Morrow. Rochelle Park, New Jersey, Hayden, 1978.
*The Creativity Catalogue* (textbook), with Murray Suid. Belmont, California, Pitman Learning, 1982.
*The Adventures of Smoke Bailey* (novelization of computer game). Cambridge, Massachusetts, Spinnaker, 1983.
*Ready to Read* (textbook), with Lillian Lieberman and Murray Suid. Palo Alto, California, Monday Morning, 1986.
*Start to Read* (textbook), with Lillian Lieberman and Murray Suid. Palo Alto, California, Monday Morning, 1986.
*Read and Write* (textbook), with Lillian Lieberman and Murray Suid. Palo Alto, California, Monday Morning, 1986.

*

James Morrow comments:

Love, music, and stories are the best things in life, and none of them comes easily. Shortly after arriving at the University of Pennsylvania in 1965, I attempted to develop my story-making abilities by taking creative writing courses. I didn't get far. Much to my bewilderment, the tacit message of a typical Penn fiction workshop seemed to be this: whatever you write, write small. Don't embarrass yourself. Abridge your ambitions. Report on small people doing small things.

But suppose one doesn't care for small? Suppose one has no use for fiction in which the plot, as Ben Hecht once sarcastically remarked, is the opening of a door? Suppose one has a taste for gods, heroes, monsters, magic, ideas? "Don't swat at the Cosmos," my first writing teacher kept telling me. A solid image, to be sure—professors are skilled at such rhetoric—but not, I think, very good advice.

Ever since my formal schooling ended, I've grown increasingly convinced that among the beginning writer's most precious prerogatives is the right to make a fool of himself. The neophyte would not only be encouraged to write about the small things he knows; he should also be encouraged to write about the large things he can envision. As long as the typical college writing workshop caters to the cult of reality, as long as it is characterized by what Ray Bradbury calls "fear of the imagination," its products will be, on the whole, mere autobiographical confession, forever threatening to turn fiction into an eccentric branch of journalism.

The primacy of imagination in SF must not be taken as a rationale for laziness. When Bradbury asks us to consider the humble "dandelions" of the fiction world, he doesn't disparage its royal roses. A genre author is every bit as obligated to bleed for his craft as the mainstream writer. His primary duty is to torment himself, forever shouting in his own ear, "Make it better! Make it better! Make it better!"

* * *

Although he does not have the high-profile presence of many other SF writers who established their professional careers in the 1980's, James Morrow has, since the publication of his first novel in 1981, produced a substantial body of high-quality work that rates as one of the field's best. While most of his novels and stories are recognizably science fiction, Morrow is not interested in rigid technological and sociological extrapolation; instead, he uses stock science-fictional devices as a means for examining moral and philosophical issues. Morrow's fiction is notable for its rich, often dazzling prose style, as well as for its strongly comic elements. All of these traits place Morrow squarely within a tradition marked variously by such writers as Ray Bradbury, Kurt Vonnegut, Philip K. Dick, and Robert Sheckley.

Morrow's first novel, *The Wine of Violence*, takes place on a planet whose inhabitants, descendants of Earth colonists, have split into two groups: the Brain-Eaters, nomadic savages who kill and devour anyone who crosses their path, and the residents of Quetzalia, who have established a peaceful society by periodically projecting their own violent tendencies into a "river of hate," which flows outside the walls of their city. When a party of explorers from another planet, also descendants of Earth colonists, is admitted into the city, the Quetzalians find themselves having to confront not only the overt violence of the Brain-Eater who is loose within the city, but the potential violence of the explorers themselves. Although the plot is driven by a high level of action, culminating with the explorers convincing the Quetzalians to go to war against the Brain-Eaters, the central concern is more abstract: are the Quetzalians heroes for having conquered the dark side of human nature, or hypocrites whose murderous fantasies belie their professed pacifism? The author's sympathies reveal themselves when one of the Quetzalians realizes that, by fighting the Brain-Eaters, he is acting in the tradition of his Earth ancestors and is now a part of history: "History, he decided, was a terrible idea."

*The Continent of Lies*, Morrow's second novel, is also his most broadly comic work, describing a far-future, interplanetary society whose main form of entertainment is the "dreambean," a bioengineered fruit which, when eaten, produces a vivid hallucination, a scripted dream in which the eater of the dreambean stars. The protagonist, a dreambean critic, is engaged by the inventor of the dreambean to track down a poisoned bean whose hallucination drives people mad—a mission that becomes personal when the critic's daughter eats one of the poisoned beans. The storyline is complicated, perhaps overly so, with numerous twists, turns, and cliffhangers. The novel is brashly imaginative and very funny in its critique of consumer culture, as represented by the entertainment industry spawned by the dreambeans; it strikes a more serious note in its portrayal of the dark side of the religious impulse, as represented by the creator of the poison dreambeans, who intends them to establish a new religion.

With his third novel, Morrow abandoned the far-future scenarios of his first two books for the time-honored SF landscape of the near-future nuclear holocaust. The bombs fall early on in *This Is the Way the World Ends*; after civilization is destroyed, six surviving Americans are put on trial by the "unadmitted," the people who will never be born because civilization has destroyed itself. Although the novel is, among other things, a scathing critique of the Cold War mentality, Morrow never lets it become a one-sided polemic. The trial is a deliberate presentation of both sides of the deterrence debate, while the "unadmitted" reveal themselves to be out not for justice, but for revenge. Most importantly, Morrow keeps the reader focused on the tragedy of the individual with the novel's protagonist, a tombstone carver whose only crime was to get an anti-radiation suit for his daughter. A nominee for the Nebula and John W. Campbell Memorial awards, *This Is the Way the World Ends* is a grim and angry book; it is also brilliantly conceived and executed.

Morrow's most recent novel, *Only Begotten Daughter*, also a Nebula finalist, is a tale not of the second coming of Christ, but of His sister: Julie Katz, immaculately conceived in an Atlantic City sperm bank in 1974, raised by her earthly father and his lesbian companion, revealed to the world through her advice column in a weekly tabloid, opposed by a crazed evangelist who transforms New Jersey into a fundamentalist dictatorship, and embittered by the knowledge that her heavenly Mother has never told her why she's here, or even checked in to see how she's doing. The novel is a savage indictment of the potential evils of organized religion, as Satan pushes for Julie to reveal her divinity, start a church, and give him more business, while Julie is able to stand successfully in opposition to evil forces only after her divinity is removed. It combines Swiftian satire, black humor, warmly sympathetic characters, with a clear yet eloquent prose style. However one wishes to label it, *Only Begotten Daughter* is one of the most impressive novels of the past decade, and Morrow's finest achievement to date.

Thus far in his career, Morrow has written only a handful of short stories, most of which are collected in *Swatting at the Cosmos.* His most notable stories are part of a series entitled "Bible Stories for Adults," SF parables that examine problems of Judeo-Christian theology. The best of these is the extraordinary "Bible Stories for Adults No. 17: The Deluge," in which Noah's Ark picks up a hitchhiker, a prostitute who seduces Noah's sons and then jumps ship with their frozen sperm, intending "to found a proud and impertinent nation, a people driven to decipher ice and solve the sun, each of them with as little use for obedience as she." The story won Morrow his first Nebula award as best short story of 1988.

Morrow's next major project, three novels forming the "Godhead" trilogy, was announced in early 1991 as forthcoming from Harcourt Brace Jovanovich's "modern fiction program." If Morrow does in fact follow his predecessors Bradbury and Vonnegut into the wider waters of mainstream acceptance, it can only reflect well on the SF genre from which he emerged. And if he maintains the steadily increasing achievement of his first four novels, James Morrow may well turn out to be the best of them all.

—F. Brett Cox

---

**MOULTON, Carl.** *See* **TUBB, E.C.**

---

**MULLER, John E.** *See* **FANTHORPE, R. Lionel.**

---

**MURDOCH, H.J.** *See* **McINTOSH, J.T.**

---

**MURNANE, Gerald.** Australian. Born in Melbourne, Victoria, in 1939. Married; three sons. Lecturer in fiction writing, Victoria College, since 1980. Address: 22 Falcon Road, Macleod, Victoria 3085, Australia.

SCIENCE-FICTION PUBLICATIONS

Novels

*Tamarisk Row.* Melbourne, Heinemann, 1974.
*A Lifetime on Clouds.* Melbourne, Heinemann, 1976; New York, Penguin, 1986.
*The Plains.* Carlton, Victoria, Norstrilia Press, 1982; London, Penguin, 1984; New York, Braziller, 1985.
*Landscape with Landscape.* Carlton, Victoria, Norstrilia Press, 1985; London, Pergamon, 1987.
*Inland.* Richmond, Victoria, Heinemann Australia, 1988; London, Faber, 1989; Boston, Faber, 1990.

Short Stories

*Velvet Waters.* Ringwood, Victoria, McPhee Gribble, 1990.

OTHER PUBLICATIONS

Other

Editor, with Jenny Lee and Philip Mead, *The Temperament of Generations: 50 Years of Writing in Meanjin.* Carlton, Victoria, Melbourne University Press, 1990.

* * *

Gerald Murnane may be dubbed a science-fiction writer by affinity with such speculative authors as J.G. Ballard, Brian Aldiss, and Christopher Priest. His first novel, *Tamarisk Row,* is a remarkable metafantasy, an obsessional study of the fantasies of a small boy in a country town in Victoria (and the pathetic attempts by his father to realize fantasies by gambling on horses). It is written in short, mosaic chapters and, sometimes, extraordinarily long, aspiring sentences. It is notable for its truthfulness, and its embarrassing fidelity to the furtive or inexpressible dreams and crude realities of pre-pubescent life. *A Lifetime on Clouds* is about an adolescent boy's struggles with masturbation, and is a novel about the weaving of fantasies from the meagre facts and misleading suggestions offered by life, in this case, mainly those of Catholic secondary education in a Melbourne suburb. The ribald humour of the book fails to mask Murnane's fierce satirical indictment of what was then a stultifying religious ethos. The difference between fantasy and reality becomes blurred for 15-year-old Adrian Sherd; at one point, he notes that his lustful fantasies about American film stars are not sanctioned by the behaviour of the few heroes he has seen on screen: "instead of courting them patiently . . . he had undressed them and defiled them only hours after their first meeting. It was all so absurd compared with what really happened in films."

In *The Plains,* the threshold has been crossed and we are presented with a mature man's fantasy of an Australia related to the real one only by inversion. All the wealth and values belong to the plainsmen of Inner Australia, who despise the busy city-dwellers of the coast. The narrator is an outsider, willing to spend his life making notes towards a film that will put on record the ever-elusive culture of the inner land, a land that is within Australia, because only Australia could have demanded its existence, yet a land which is beyond Australia, because it is too large and grand a vision to be comprehended by it. Murnane had adumbrated this vision in describing the yearnings of young Clement Killeaton in *Tamarisk Row* for what lies farther inland and north, beyond the farthest imaginable horizons of his wretchedly confined experience. Fantasies lie within fantasies in *The Plains,* a short memorable novel of considerable philosophical interest.

*The Plains* itself, slightly curtailed and adapted, might fit within the structure of Murnane's later metafantasy, *Landscape with Landscape,* a kind of mobius box of six stones, each of which is written by the narrator of its predecessor (and the first story by the last narrator). The stories concern Melbourne men who are obsessed with the wish to see the landscape that is hidden by the landscape, or that is seen only by the figure in the landscape, and so on; people themselves are landscapes or owners of hidden landscapes, perhaps. In what may be the most interesting of these stories, "The Battle of Acosta Nu," Melbourne is located in Paraguay and the narrator, a descendant of Australian colonists, defines himself in relation to the Australian city he has never seen.

*Inland* develops these insights still further as the author employs a narrator who shifts through several identities, as does his projected reader, to intimate the vastness of the inside world. Murnane dazzles with his sense of the infinitudes that may start and precipitate within us from even the most seemingly barren and limited exteriors. His beautifully long-breathed prose style draws one along towards ever more quiet intimations of contained, but uncontainable, multitudinousnesses that externalize themselves in terms of landscapes, notably grasslands, maps, words, souls, ghosts, unread books and written pages, readers hostile and expectant, living and even dead, memories of childhood and of nostalgic adulthood, devolving above all into love-longings for a particular lost girl-woman, yet all without sentimentality. The obsessive character he depicts would seem insane or almost so to some, yet his behaviour is described with a clinical precision.

Bruce Gillespie has remarked that both *The Plains* and *Tamarisk Row* "are guided by the proposition that, however one might perceive any object or idea in the universe, it is quite possible to perceive it in the other way as well." This insight seems particularly apt for the short story, "Land Deal" (included in *Velvet Waters*), which presents a philosophically valid Aboriginal view of European colonists as having a possible existence only in dreams: their land deal is therefore a dream within a dream.

Eleven stories are collected in *Velvet Waters:* Murnane's collage method of composition is particularly obvious in the fine "First Love" (the title refers to Nabokov's story), where the narrator engages in the collage work of piecing together his own personal ideal racing colours for a jockey's jacket. In this story, the narrator decides to abolish "the jargon of an imagined world ruled cover by those invisible and sinister science-fiction tyrants Time and Change," and write instead about the real world, which happens always and only in space. "Precious Bane" pleasantly juxtaposes the Golden Age of Books with the bookless world of 2020. "Stone Quarry" includes an idea similar to the conceit of *The Plains,* but the inversion of Australia is substituted with a reversal of the westward flow of American dreaming. These short stories are not of equal weight or interest. "When the Mice Failed to Arrive" is the most impressive story in the collection; it deals superbly with the embarrassments of schoolteachers who fail to deliver what they have promised, but ends (glancing at *Arabian Nights* erotic sadism) with a horrifying intimation of the cruelty that may be perpetrated by any laboratory experimenter who should find one day that even the unwritten social contract one makes with a mouse cannot, in particular circumstances, be honoured.

—Michael J. Tolley

---

**MURPHY, Pat.** American. Born 9 March 1955. Educated at University of California, Santa Cruz, B.A. in biology and general science. Since 1982, editor, *Exploratorium Quarterly,* San Francisco. Recipient: Nebula award, 1987 (twice); Philip K. Dick award, 1990. Address: c/o Exploratorium, 3601 Lyon Street, San Francisco, California 94123, U.S.A.

SCIENCE-FICTION PUBLICATIONS

Novels

*The Shadow Hunter.* New York, Popular Library, 1982.
*The City, Not Long After.* New York, Doubleday, 1989.

Short Stories

*Points of Departure.* New York, Bantam, 1990.
*Letters from Home,* with Pat Cadigan and Karen Joy Fowler. London, Women's Press, 1991.

OTHER PUBLICATIONS

Novel

*The Falling Woman.* New York, Tor, 1986.

* * *

Pat Murphy's first short-story collection is mis-titled *Points of Departure;* there is just one point of departure, Murphy herself, with at least 19 different directions, and, one suspects, as many different points of arrival as there are readers. For this reason, it has always been very difficult to define Murphy's fiction. Michael Swanwick described her as a "lone wolf" in his article on the rival movements of the mid-1980's in *Isaac Asimov's Science Fiction Magazine,* but she has since been linked with that curiously amorphous, catch-all non-category known as the freestyle movement. All of this is important only in as much as it is meaningless with regard to Murphy's fiction.

Her first novel, *The Shadow Hunter,* almost vanished without trace, but a string of interesting short stories spread across several anthologies and magazines through the mid-1980's built a quiet reputation, culminating in the story "Rachel In Love" in 1987. This story deals sensitively with love, animal research, and scientific ethics. Rachel, a chimp brought up by a kindly scientist, has had the mind of the scientist's dead daughter superimposed on her own, and has learned to communicate with sign language. When the scientist dies, Rachel is taken to a research establishment and locked up. Using signs, however, she is able to befriend the simple, deaf, drunken cleaner Jake, and persuades him to release her to help him clean. Jake trusts Rachel, and she falls in love with him. When she comes into heat, she offers herself to him, but Jake prefers his magazine photos. Then, Rachel meets another chimp, Johnson, and they plot their escape and return to Rachel's former home. As the story closes, they are travelling cross-country whilst the papers detailing Rachel's status and her inheritance have suddenly become public. The story proved very popular, but it is the Sturgeon-esque concentration on the people and their relationships that makes "Rachel In Love" so intense, and perhaps, so controversial.

The waves that "Rachel In Love" caused aroused attention in Murphy's second novel, *The Falling Woman,* and eventually both won that year's Nebula awards. This novel is scarcely SF. It is the story of an archaeologist, Elizabeth Butler, who can sometimes "see" people from the past. On a dig in Mexico, her life is suddenly disrupted by the arrival of her daughter, last seen as a child, and by a spirit that begins to talk to her. *The Falling Woman* is characterised by an attention to detail of person and place. Murphy also takes great pains over the archaeological elements of her scenery; the science here is far more accurate than many hard SF authors manage in their chosen fields. Nevertheless, this is essentially a ghost fantasy, but a gripping and moving one, and it is as much a typical Murphy tale as any other.

Most recently, *The City, Not Long After* has shown Murphy to be capable of maintaining the moods and the mythic elements of *The Falling Woman* whilst setting her novel closer to home in San Francisco. *City* is actually an extension of the earlier story "Art In The War Zone," filling in details of how the situation described there arose. San Francisco, like every other major city, has been struck by a plague spread by so-called Peace Monkeys. These monkeys, which lived in a Himalayan monastery, were brought into the cities as part of the Peace Movement, in response to legends foretelling peace if they left the monastery. Peace comes, after the Plague, but it is not what anyone expected, and San Francisco is left as a ghost town, inhabited only by gypsy gangs and stray artists in a loose commune. To this town comes Jax, daughter of one of the original Peace campaigners, heeding her mother's final message, to warn of the plans of General "Fourstar" Miles to capture the city. The artists decide to fight back using their art, and the city helps them. An ambiguous climax mutes some of the philosophy portrayed, perhaps, whilst emphasising that nobody wins if violence occurs.

As a tender love story, as an expression of the power of art to affect our lives, as a magical realist drama, *The City, Not Long After* is extraordinary. Murphy invokes all of the ideologies of the new age, pacifism, ecology, and co-operation, and makes them seem so real and rational that for long periods the reader wonders how anybody could argue with it. Filling all of this out are the characters, Jax the wild country girl, Danny-boy, the artist who decides to paint the Golden Gate Bridge blue, Machine, who doesn't really trust humans but builds bizarre robots,

Books, who maintains what remains of the library, and others. This is, overall, a poignant, cautionary novel, but it has its moments of pure comedy, and some genuine surrealism, that serve to enhance the whole.

It is interesting to note, however, that despite the acclaim that her recent novels have gained, Murphy still considers herself a short-story writer. The award of the Philip K. Dick award to *Points of Departure* should ensure her continuing writing in the short form. Whether hard-edged feminist stories like "His Vegetable Wife," looking at father-daughter relationships in "Dead Men On TV," historical fantasy such as "Bones," Eastern discovery "In the Abode of the Snows," or dark fantasy "On the Dark Side of the Station Where the Train Never Stops," Murphy's reputation should grow.

—Kev P. McVeigh

---

**MURRY, Colin Middleton.** *See* **COWPER, Richard.**

---

# N

**NAHA, Ed.** Also writes as D.B. Drumm. American. Born in Elizabeth, New Jersey, 10 June 1950. Educated at Newark State College, B.A. 1972. Publicity manager, 1972–75, 1975–77, and associate producer, East Coast Artists and Repertory, CBS Records, New York; co-editor, *Future Life*, New York, 1977–80. Since 1980, columnist ("Screen Scoops"), New York *Post*; since 1983, columnist ("Nahallywood"), *Heavy Metal*, New York; since 1983 columnist ("L.A. Offbeat"), *Starlog*, New York. Lives in Santa Monica, California. Address: c/o Pocket Books, The Simon and Schuster Building, 1230 Avenue of the Americas, New York, New York 10020, U.S.A.

SCIENCE-FICTION PUBLICATIONS

Novels (series: Harry Porter)

*The Paradise Plot* (Porter). New York, Bantam, 1980.
*The Suicide Plague* (Porter). New York, Bantam, 1982.
*First, You Fight* (as D.B. Drumm). New York, Dell, 1984.
*Robocop* (novelization of screenplay). New York, Dell, 1986; London, Corgi, 1988.
*Robocop II* (novelization of screenplay). New York, Jove, 1990.

Short Stories

*Wanted*. New York, Bantam, 1980.

OTHER PUBLICATIONS

Novels

*The Con Game*. New York, Dell, 1986.
*Breakdown*. New York, Dell, 1988.
*Dead-Bang*. (based on screenplay by Robert Foster). New York, Berkley, 1989.
*Ghostbusters II* (novelization of screenplay). New York, Dell, and London, Corgi, 1989.
*On the Edge*. New York, Pocket, 1989.
*Orphans*. New York, Dell, 1989.
*Razzle-Dazzle*. New York, Pocket, 1990.
*Cracking Up*. New York, Pocket, 1991.

Plays

Screenplays: *Camp Bottomount*, 1984; *The Wizard Wars*, 1984; *Honey, I Shrunk the Kids*, with Tom Schulman, 1989.

Other

*Horrors: From Screen to Scream*. New York, Avon, 1975.
*Science Fiction Aliens* (for children). New York, Starlog, 1977.
*Lillian Roxon's Rock Encyclopedia*, revised edition. New York, Putnam, 1978.
*The Rock Encyclopedia*. New York, Grosset and Dunlap, 1978.
*The Science Fictionary: An A-Z Guide to the World of SF Authors, Films, and TV Shows*. New York, Putnam, 1980.
*The Films of Roger Corman: Brilliance on a Budget*. New York, Arco, 1982.
*The Making of "Dune."* New York, Berkley, and London, Target, 1984.

* * *

Ed Naha is one of those rarities who have been able successfully to merge the science-fiction and mystery genres. His first science-fiction novel, *The Paradise Plot*, introduced the character of Harry Porter, a newspaper reporter who always seems to be at the right spot at the right time, to get himself involved with world-shaking plots. In this first adventure, he is aboard Island One, an orbiting city established as part of mankind's movement toward the colonization of space. But not everything is peaceful in the colony, which has not cast off as many of the problems of the mother world as they might have thought.

Shortly after his arrival, Porter is thoroughly enmeshed in a complicated plot that involves a string of murders and a desperate political struggle both within the habitat and back on Earth. Although Porter is ultimately instrumental in solving the mystery, the revelations result in the closing down of Island One, although it is quite clear that this is probably a temporary measure. Naha's scientific background for the novel is convincing, and while Porter is essentially a stereotypical detective hero, he's a well-done stereotype involved in an engrossing mystery, livened up with excellent dialogue.

The sequel, *The Suicide Plague*, is even better. Porter, the last investigative reporter still working, is bewildered by a sudden rash of young suicides, uncovers a secret plot to assassinate the President of the United States, runs afoul of the Church of the Ancient Astronauts, a sinister and increasingly powerful new cult, searches for missing research scientists, solves the mystery of a murdered man who had telepathic powers, and helps to avert what might have resulted in a nuclear war. This obviously complex group of plots and subplots is woven skillfully together in a thoroughly satisfying fashion.

Naha also wrote *First, You Fight*, the first volume of "The Traveller," an extended series of post-nuclear holocaust men's adventure novels. A tough, well-armed protagonist wanders through ruined America in his armored van, helping the weak, avoiding the mutants and power seekers among the survivors. A thoroughly violent action series, it lacks the finesse of Naha's other work. He has also written screen plays, as well as non-fiction about science-fiction and horror films, and the field of popular music. His only recent science-fiction novel is the movie novelization, *Robocop*. Two other recent novels, *Breakdown* and *Orphans* are both supernatural horror.

—Don D'Ammassa

---

**NELSON, Ray** (Radell Faraday Nelson). Also writes as R. N. Elson; Jeffrey Lord. American. Born in Schenectady, New

York, 3 October 1931. Educated at the Chicago Art Institute, 1954; Alliance Française, 1957–58; the Sorbonne, Paris, 1958; University of Chicago, B.A. 1960; Automation Institute, computer programmers certificate 1961; Peralta College, Berkeley, California, 1978. Married 1) Perdita Lilly in 1951 (divorced 1955); 2) Lisa Mullikin in 1955 (divorced 1958); 3) Kirsten Enge in 1958; one son. Worked for Inland Lakes Flying Service, Cadillac, Michigan, 1947–50, and Hudson Motor Company, Detroit, 1950–51; sign maker, Chicago, 1951–54; printer, Northside Poster Company, Chicago, 1954; artist, Artcraft Poster Company, Oakland, California, 1955–56; translator for Jean Linard, Vesoul, France, 1959; computer programmer, University of California Press, Berkeley, 1961–62. Since 1962, freelance writer and artist: co-director, Berkeley Free University, 1967–68; founder, Microcosm Fiction Workshop, later Ramona Street Regulars, 1967; since 1968, teaching assistant, Adams Junior High School, El Cerrito, California. President, California Writers Club, 1977–78. Recipient: Jack London award, 1983. Address: 333 Ramona Avenue, El Cerrito, California 94530, U.S.A.

### Science-Fiction Publications

Novels (series: Beggars)

*The Ganymede Takeover*, with Philip K. Dick. New York, Ace, 1967; London, Arrow, 1971.
*Blake's Progress*. Toronto, Laser, 1975.
*Then Beggars Could Ride*. Toronto, Laser, 1976.
*The Ecolog*. Toronto, Laser, 1977.
*The Revolt of the Unemployables* (Beggars). San Francisco, Anthelion, 1978.
*Dimension of Horror* (as Jeffrey Lord). Los Angeles, Pinnacle, 1979.
*The Prometheus Man*. Norfolk, Virginia, Donning, 1982.
*Timequest*. New York, Tor, 1985.

Uncollected Short Stories

"Turn Off the Sky," in *Fantasy and Science Fiction* (New York), August 1963.
"Eight O'Clock in the Morning," in *The Best from Fantasy and Science Fiction 13*, edited by Avram Davidson. New York, Doubleday, 1964.
"Losers Weepers," in *Nugget* (New York), 1964.
"Food," in *Gamma 4* (Los Angeles), 1965.
"The Great Cosmic Donut of Life," in *Fantasy and Science Fiction* (New York), September 1965.
"Time Travel for Pedestrians," in *Again, Dangerous Visions*, edited by Harlan Ellison. New York, Doubleday, 1972; London, Millington, 1976.
"Egyptian Christ," in *Orion* (Lakemont, Georgia), 1972.
"The City of the Crocodile," in *Fantastic* (New York), March 1974.
"A Song on the Rising Wind," in *Fantastic* (New York), November 1974.
"What Survives?," in *Uniquest* (Berkeley, California), 1976.
"Microcosm," in *Science Fiction Review* (Portland, Oregon), 1976.
"Who's the Red Queen?," in *Amazing* (New York), March 1976.
"Flesh Pearl," in *Amazing* (New York), December 1976.
"Two Futures," in *Uniquest* (Berkeley, California), 1977.
"Nightfall on the Dead Sea," in *Fantasy and Science Fiction* (New York), September 1977.
"On the Edge of Futuria," in *Science-Fiction Review* (Portland, Oregon), 1978.
"Valse Triste," in *Weird Tales 2*, edited by Lin Carter. New York, Zebra, 1981.
"Story," in *Fifty Extremely SF Stories*, edited by Michael Bastraw. Center Harbor, New Hampshire, Niekas, 1982.

### Other Publications

Novels

*The Agony of Love*. San Diego, Greenleaf, 1969.
*Girl with the Hungry Eyes*. San Diego, Greenleaf, 1969.
*Dogheaded Death*. San Francisco, Strawberry Hill Press, 1989.

Novels as R.N. Elson

*How to Do it*. San Diego, Greenleaf, 1970.
*Black Pussy*. San Diego, Greenleaf, 1970.
*Sex Happy Hippy*. San Diego, Greenleaf, 1970.
*The DA's Wife*. San Diego, Greenleaf, 1970.

*

Ray Nelson comments:

(1981) For me, Jack London, not Hugo Gernsback, is the father of American Science Fiction, and my aim is to continue the tradition established at the beginning of this century by London and his friends. My three obsessive themes are radical utopianism, experimental occultism, and a love-fear romance with nature. In California these ideas are understood, particularly in the Bay Area (all but two of the living writers I admire live in California), but in New York, where there are no trees, my obsessions seem like nonsense. Most of my work has been published outside New York—places where there are trees and intuition and hope for a better life, and someday New York too will grudgingly lend me an ear, perhaps when I am safely dead.

(1985) In *Timequest* I have at last written the novel I always wanted to write, the book I hope posterity will remember me by, if it remembers me at all. Editors have helped me, from Roger Elwood who let me do the first version of a book no other editor would touch, through Hank Stein who encouraged me to put in everything previous length restrictions had forced me to leave out, to Terry Carr who suggested restoring even the parts I had left out for Hank Stein, but really *Timequest* represents my own basic attitudes and philosophy so well I am content to stand or fall on this one work, so well I may never write another book in this genre. Now I want to do something else: comedy, cartoons, songs. Maybe I'll steal a spraycan of paint and start drawing propellor beanies on subway walls.

* * *

Although Ray Nelson has never been one of the more prolific writers in the field, he has firmly established a reputation for himself on the basis of the generally high quality of his work. His first novel, *The Ganymede Takeover*, was written in collaboration with Philip K. Dick, and dealt with the domination of Earth by wormlike invaders from Ganymede, but it was written as a witty and satiric examination of individuals and societies, not the low grade movie plot it so resembles.

It would be almost a decade later that Nelson first appeared as sole author of a novel, in this case *Blake's Progress*, a serious contender for best novel of its year. Ostensibly, the central character was the poet, William Blake, a man capable of mentally travelling through time in company with his wife. It soon becomes apparent, however, that it is she who dominates their relationship, has the more powerful intellect, and is in fact a far more interesting character than is her weak-willed husband.

*Then Beggars Could Ride* and *The Ecolog* appeared soon after. Each was entertaining in its own way, but both suffered in comparison to their predecessor. The former was a similar kaleidoscopic odyssey through time. The latter is a more conventional novel, pitting a determined, expert military man against a planet ruled by a ruthless matriarch. *Dimension of Horror*, an adventure in the Richard Blade series, was similarly competent but even less memorable.

*The Prometheus Man*, on the other hand, is one of the best dystopian novels of all time. Overpopulation, automation, and lethargy have weakened the fabric of society as the vast majority of the population is unemployable. In order to maintain order, most of these people are confined to camps where they are theoretically looked after, but the impersonal treatment leads predictably to unrest. The plot is complex and thoroughly worked out.

Nelson's short fiction is extremely good and equally infrequent. "Nightfall on the Dead Sea," for example, is a fine historical horror story pitting a Roman soldier against a man cursed with immortality. "Time Travel for Pedestrians" aroused a degree of controversy because of its subject matter—time travel via masturbation—but its clear superiority of style and the maturity of its vision established it as a major accomplishment.

Nelson displays a fondness for the grotesque. A human is turned into an organic asteroid in "Flesh Pearl," and another becomes a rather unpleasant form of nourishment in "Food." Grotesquerie and the absurd are to be found in "The Great Cosmic Donut of Life" and "Turn Off the Sky" as well.

"Eight O'Clock in the Morning" takes a routine gimmick (aliens who can be seen by only a single human) and condenses what other writers would have extended to novel length into a few thousand words. This was recently filmed as *They Live*, although the screen version translated as a routine action movie. Ancient history and the supernatural mix again in "The City of the Crocodile," and a man takes a spiritual journey to the land of the suicides in "Valse Triste." "A Song on the Rising Wind" examines the nature of violence and courage on a level rare in any field of writing, as a revolution brews among a society of sequestered unemployables, an obvious precursor to *The Prometheus Man.*

Never a prolific writer, Nelson has been virtually silent for the past several years. His published work displays careful craftsmanship and great concentration and commitment. He has consistently been willing to tackle controversial themes and ambitious goals, maintaining tight control of his work at all times. Although frequently idiosyncratic, this uniqueness of viewpoint is what makes his fiction rise above that of his contemporaries.

—Don D'Ammassa

---

**NEVILLE, Kris (Ottman).** American. Born in Carthage, Missouri, 9 May 1925. Educated at the University of California, Los Angeles, B.A. in English 1950. Served in the United States Army Signal Corps during World War II. Married Lil Johnson in 1957; five children. Worked in the plastics and chemistry industries: after 1965, staff member, Epoxylite Corporation, Anaheim, California. *Died 23 December 1980.*

### Science-Fiction Publications

#### Novels

*The Unearth People.* New York, Belmont, 1964.
*The Mutants.* New York, Belmont, 1966.
*Peril of the Starmen.* New York, Belmont, 1967.
*Special Delivery.* New York, Belmont, 1967.
*Bettyann.* New York, Belmont, 1970.
*Invaders on the Moon.* New York, Belmont, 1970.

#### Short Stories

*Mission: Manstop.* North Hollywood, Nordon, 1971.
*The Science Fiction of Kris Neville*, edited by Barry N. Malzberg and Martin H. Greenberg. Carbondale, Southern Illinois University Press, 1984.

### Other Publications

#### Novel

*Run, The Spearmaker* (in Japanese), with Lil Neville. Tokyo, Hayakawa Shobo, 1975.

#### Other

*Epoxy Resins*, with Henry Lee. New York, McGraw Hill, 1957.
*Handbook of Epoxy Resins*, with Henry Lee. New York, McGraw Hill, 1967.
*New Linear Polymers*, with Henry Lee. New York, McGraw Hill, 1967.
*Handbook of Biomedical Plastics*, with Henry Lee. Pasadena, California, Pasadena Technology Press, 1971.
*Adhesive Restorative Dentistry*, with Robert L. Ibsen. Philadelphia, Saunders, 1974.
*Industrial Motor Users' Handbook of Insulation for Rewinds*, with L.J. Regda. New York, and Oxford, Elsevier, 1977.

Editor, with Henry Lee, *Handbook of Adhesive Bonding*, by Charles V. Cagle. New York, McGraw Hill, 1982.

*

Kris Neville commented (1980):

I wrote the majority of my stories in the early 1950's. Having just graduated from UCLA with a degree in English literature, I was interested in introducing mainstream elements into science fiction (which I had been reading avidly since 1937)-shifting the emphasis to the impact of future technology on ordinary individuals. I also tried to seek out new perspectives-using female protagonists; playing with various viewpoints; seeing the future through the eyes of the old or young; portraying Earthmen in less than favorable lights; breaking taboos; making satirical comments (I was a socialist/humanist). In many of my shorts, I aimed for emotional effect. I was a trail blazer in my time.

By the mid-1950's, I'd run out of things to say. During the next decade, I kept my hand in with *The Unearth People* and an occasional short, and also revised earlier material into novels. I moved leftward philosophically to my present position: left wing anarchist. The shorts contained sharper social commentary ("Survival Problems"). I was particularly unhappy with the war in Vietnam ("The Price of Simeryl") and, later, Richard Nixon ("The Reality Machine"). During that decade, Lil and I wrote *Run, The Spearmaker*, a novel dealing with the evolution of civilization at the beginning of human history. The translator called it a minor literary masterpiece. Pity it isn't available in English.

During the 1970's, in addition to half a dozen shorts that Lil and I collaborated on, we also did another novel, *Thorstein Macaulay.* It contains our best writing and most carefully considered political statements. It was about 10 years in the making. As of this writing (June 1979) we had not yet found a publisher for it.

* * *

Kris Neville's large output of stories seems to be equally divided among adventure SF, social SF, fantasy SF, and fantasy. While he was known as a *Galaxy* school writer, his most characteristic work appears to be more melodramatic than ironic. Nevertheless, Neville will often subordinate adventure narrative to character interaction or to the character's response to those environmental or cultural forces that are by-products of future science and technology. Neville was a popular and critically respected author in the genre during the 1950's and 1960's, but his reputation as a craftsman seems to have been lost, perhaps as the result of the rather conventional plotting and characterization in his later work.

Neville's great theme is alienation. He eschews the more sensational aspects of this theme in favor of the psychological dimensions implied in its use in the future world of SF. Novels like *Special Delivery, Earth Alert* (in *If,* February 1953), and *The Mutants* deal with variations of the alien invasion theme or its analogues. *The Mutants,* a potentially timely treatment of the social implications of artificial insemination in a state utopia, fails to rise above the level of the melodramatic struggle of a few idealistic youths fighting to save the race from a progressively more repressive state control of human biology.

In the main, Neville was a writer typical of his time. He knew how to make good use of psychologically enriched characters and possessed more sensitivity toward character motivation and interaction than most of his colleagues. In many ways, he belongs in the Theodore Sturgeon camp of SF writers, although he does lapse into the action/adventure idiom more frequently than Sturgeon and his successors. Neville's style is also more direct, simple, and clear than Sturgeon's, better suited, perhaps, for the pot boilers he produced for Belmont. Neville was, it appears, in nearly every way a writer several cuts above the average who never quite made the success expected of him. Although he wrote SF, Neville gave little evidence of being deeply committed for or against science. It, like the future, is simply one of the unexamined, given elements of his stories. Whatever the cause, Neville produced a body of SF that refuses to move us deeply in any of the many ways in which less accomplished stylists have done by writing with more conviction, except in one notable case.

Neville may not deserve the obscurity into which his career has fallen if only for the sake of one superb story, "Bettyann" (1951; expanded into a novel, 1970; a sequel is "Bettyann's Children"). This story of a crippled orphan girl raised in a foster home whose sense of difference is confirmed when she discovers she is actually a member of an extra-terrestrial race is handled with the same kind of sensitivity and poignance as Daniel Keye's "Flowers for Algernon," another story that grew successfully into a novel. In place of the overwriting of most SF melodrama, Neville has his subject and his characters fully under control. In "Bettyann" Neville manages understated effects brilliantly in a way that he approached in only a few other stories besides the sequel: "Old Man Henderson" and "Closing Time" are examples. "Bettyann" is one of those rare SF stories that could not be written in another genre but which deals profoundly with universal, human values. Bettyann's affirmation of a basic humanity which has become stronger in her nature than her lately discovered alien origins is an inspiring moment in literature. The two stories and the novel must be considered neglected masterpieces, which are only beginning to receive their due critical recognition.

—Donald L. Lawler

---

**NICHOLS, Scott.** *See* **SCORTIA, Thomas N.**

---

**NIVEN, Larry** (Laurence Van Cott Niven). American. Born in Los Angeles, California, 30 April 1938. Educated at California Institute of Technology, Pasadena, 1956–58; Washburn University, Topeka, Kansas, A.B. 1962; University of California, Los Angeles, 1962–63. Married Marylin Wosowati in 1969. Since 1964, freelance writer. Recipient: Hugo award, for story, 1967, 1972, 1975, 1976, for novel, 1971; Nebula award, 1970; Ditmar award, 1971; *Locus* award, 1985. Address: c/o Baen Publishing Enterprises, 260 Fifth Avenue, Suite 35, New York, New York 10001, U.S.A.

SCIENCE-FICTION PUBLICATIONS

Novels (series: Known Space)

*World of Ptavvs* (Space). New York, Ballantine, 1966; London, Macdonald, 1968.
*A Gift from Earth* (Space). New York, Ballantine, 1968; London, Macdonald, 1969.
*Ringworld* (Space). New York, Ballantine, 1970; London, Gollancz, 1972.
*The Flying Sorcerers,* with David Gerrold. New York, Ballantine, 1971; London, Corgi, 1975.
*Protector* (Space). New York, Ballantine, 1973; Tisbury, Wiltshire, Compton Russell, 1976.
*The Mote in God's Eye,* with Jerry Pournelle. New York, Simon and Schuster, 1974; London, Weidenfeld and Nicolson, 1975.
*Inferno,* with Jerry Pournelle. New York, Pocket Books, 1976; London, Wingate, 1977.
*A World Out of Time* New York, Holt Rinehart, 1976; London, Macdonald and Jane's 1977.
*Lucifer's Hammer,* with Jerry Pournelle. Chicago, Playboy Press, 1977.
*The Magic Goes Away.* New York, Ace, 1978; London, Futura, 1982.
*The Ringworld Engineers* (Space). New York, Holt Rinehart, and London, Gollancz, 1980.
*The Patchwork Girl.* New York, Ace, 1980; London, Macdonald, 1982.
*Dream Park,* with Steven Barnes. Huntington Woods, Michigan, Phantasia Press, 1981; London, Macdonald, 1983.
*Oath of Fealty,* with Jerry Pournelle. Huntington Woods, Michigan, Phantasia Press, 1981; London, Macdonald, 1982.
*The Descent of Anansi,* with Steven Barnes. New York, Tor, 1982.
*The Integral Trees.* New York, Ballantine, and London, Macdonald, 1984.

*Footfall*, with Jerry Pournelle. New York, Ballantine, and London, Gollancz, 1985.
*The Legacy of Heorot*, with Jerry Pournelle and Steven Barnes. New York, Simon and Schuster, and London, Gollancz, 1987.
*The Smoke Ring*. New York, Ballantine, and London, Macdonald, 1987.
*The Man-Kzin Wars*, with Poul Anderson and Dean Ing. New York, Baen, 1988.
*The Man-Kzin Wars II*, with Dean Ing, Jerry Pournelle, and S.M. Stirling. New York, Baen, 1989.
*The Barsoom Project*, with Steven Barnes. New York, Ace, 1989; London, Pan, 1990.
*The Man-Kzin Wars III*, with Poul Anderson, Jerry Pournelle, and S.M. Stirling. New York, Baen, 1990.
*N-Space*. New York, Tor, 1990.
*Achilles' Choice*, with Steven Barnes. New York, Tor, 1991.
*Fallen Angels*, with Jerry Pournelle and Michael Flynn. New York, Baen, 1991.
*Playgrounds of the Mind*. New York, Tor, 1991.

Short Stories (series: Known Space)

*Neutron Star* (Space). New York, Ballantine, 1968; London, Macdonald, 1969.
*The Shape of Space* (Space). New York, Ballantine, 1969.
*All the Myriad Ways*. New York, Ballantine, 1971.
*The Flight of the Horse*. New York, Ballantine, 1973; London, Futura, 1975.
*Inconstant Moon* (omnibus). London, Gollancz, 1973.
*A Hole in Space*. New York, Ballantine, 1974; London, Futura, 1975.
*Tales of Known Space*. New York, Ballantine, 1975.
*The Long Arm of Gil Hamilton* (Space). New York, Ballantine, 1976; London, Futura, 1980.
*Convergent Series*. New York, Ballantine, 1979.
*The Time of the Warlock*, illustrated by Dennis Wolf. Minneapolis, Steel Dragon Press, 1984.
*Niven's Laws* (includes articles). Philadelphia, Philcon, 1984.
*Limits*. New York, Ballantine, 1985.

OTHER PUBLICATIONS

Other

Editor, *The Magic May Return*. New York, Ace, 1981.
Editor, *More Magic*. New York, Berkley, 1984.

*

Manuscript Collection: George Arents Research Library, Syracuse University, New York.

* * *

When the New Wave began to flourish in the mid-1960's, a writer appeared whose work embodied the genre conventions that movement was rejecting: SF as technical problem-solving, faith in the efficacy of science, and a belief in humanity's ability to overcome any obstacle. Larry Niven quickly became regarded as the leading practitioner of "hard" SF. "The idea is truly the hero"—a reviewer's praise for a later novel—aptly sums up both his greatest strength and weakness.

Like Heinlein and Asimov, Niven constructed a future history, Known Space, a series of related stories later codified into a chart. Unlike his predecessors, his schema included an elaborate million-and-a-half year prehistory and several varieties of aliens. It has become a popular mythology, with other writers contributing tales to the period of Man-Kzin wars, which Niven neglects, admitting his lack of expertise about military subjects.

Niven's most celebrated talent is his ability to create grandly scaled worlds that dwarf their inhabitants. *Ringworld* is the most famous: a hundred-thousand-mile-wide ribbon revolving around a star at a distance of one A. U. Not only is this hard science fiction on an epic scale, but Niven's most appealing characters travel against this backdrop. Unlike many recent SF novels artificially swollen to require sequels, *Ringworld* was satisfying on its own terms, but Niven acceded to fan pressure and wrote *The Ringworld Engineers*, a grand, unifying coda to Known Space in which all loose threads are gathered up and connected. Some readers found it unsuccessful, perhaps because the characters seem to be shadows of their former selves, and some of the unification forced. Yet read together, the novels furnish a fitting capstone to one of the most popular series in recent science fiction.

Niven has created other future histories, such as the Leshy Circuit, which includes *A World Out of Time*, a Stapledonian journey into the far future in which humans have evolved into immortal, spiteful boys and girls, and the far more successful pair of novels about the possibility of life without a planet within the gas torus surrounding a neutron star, *The Integral Trees* and *The Smoke Ring*. Once again Niven's world-building is immense, with the only danger being the characters' becoming literarily-as well as literally-swamped by the intricacies of the construct.

Like Heinlein, one of Niven's favorite imaginative spurs is to postulate a technical improvement and project its impact on society. "New technologies create new customs, new laws, new ethics, new crimes." Such are the series of stories on teleportation, or those about the organ banks and the psychic detective, Gil "the Arm" Hamilton. However, these stories reveal a strange contradiction in Niven's work, given his reputation as a hard SF writer. One of his favorite aphorisms is Clarke's: "Any sufficiently advanced technology is indistinguishable from magic." Niven's technology, despite the scientific apparatus, often does seem like magic. Some plots, like those of *World of Ptavvs* or *A Gift from Earth*, hinge on psionic powers. Indeed, Niven has written several series of what might be termed "hard" fantasy, in which the magic is as strictly regulated as the science in an *Analog* story. Niven has entitled one of his collections *Limits* in recognition of this need.

Since the mid-1970's, much of Niven's work has been collaborative. His most famous partner is Jerry Pournelle, and their work describes universes more inimical than Known Space, while also prosletyzing more overtly for science ("to proxmire" becomes a pejorative verb), and continuing to present aliens who are dangerous, yet sympathetically depicted. *The Mote in God's Eye* was eagerly awaited, and carried Heinlein's extravagant blurb, "Possibly the finest science-fiction novel I have ever read." A novel of first contact, its suspense rides on whether humanity will realize the Moties's danger. The phrase "genie in the bottle," often used to describe the perils of unleashed science, here describes the possibility of the Moties emerging from their own system. *Lucifer's Hammer*, at first a typical disaster epic of the 1970's, carries the insistent subtext that technology—in this case the atomic power plant—will save humanity after such a disaster and allow it again to "control the lightning." *Footfall* is another novel of first contact, or rather conquest, in which a herd race bent on dominating the Earth of the near future is confused and defeated by humanity's lack of a surrender ritual and its penchant for individuality. Once again the atom—in this case the bomb—provides salvation (with science-fiction writers, including the easily recognizable "Robert Anson," giving crucial advice). *The Legacy of Heorot* is a breathless combination of elements from *Beowulf*, *The Thing*, and *Zulu* as an isolated human colony must defend itself from supercarnivores. Probably their most interesting work is *Inferno*, on the face of it—a retelling of Dante by two hard SF writers—a sure recipe for disaster. Yet it is humorous, as a deceased SF writer tries, with the panache of a Heinlein hero, to devise technical explanations for and escapes from hell, as well as thought-provoking, providing a plausible theological reason for a supposedly merciful deity's construction of a place of eternal torment.

Niven's other principal collaborator is Steven Barnes. Their work also glorifies the possibilities of science while solving a life-threatening technical problem, as in *The Descent of Anansi*. Their most interesting work depicts a theme park that offers actual fantasy role-playing games. Particularly satisfying in *Dream Park* and *The Barsoom Project* is the unexpected use of the myths of primitive people (Melanesians and Inuit) reacting to and controlling modern Western technology.

Niven burst on the scene with a series of compelling and appealing myths in the late 1960's and early 1970's. The only way he has perhaps failed to live up to his promise is in setting such an initial high (and prolific) standard for himself. His lasting achievement (to paraphrase Wagner on Brahms) is to show what can be done with old forms in a new time.

—William Laskowski, Jr.

---

**NOBEL, Phil.** *See* **FANTHORPE, R. Lionel.**

---

**NOLAN, William F(rancis).** American. Born in Kansas City, Missouri, 6 March 1928. Educated at Kansas City Art Institute, 1946-47; San Diego State College, California, 1947–48; Los Angeles City College, 1953. Married Marilyn Seal in 1970. Greeting card designer and cartoonist, Hall Brothers, Kansas City, 1945; mural painter, San Diego, 1949–50; aircraft inspector, Convair, San Diego, 1950–52; credit assistant, Blake Moffit and Towne Paper Company, Los Angeles, 1953–54; interviewer, California State Department of Employment, 1954–56. Since 1956, freelance writer. Contributing editor, *Chase*, managing editor, *GAMMA*, west-coast editor, *Auto*, and associate editor, *Motor Sport Illustrated*, all Los Angeles, 1963–64; reviewer, Los Angeles *Times*, 1964–70. Recipient: American Library Association citation, 1960; Edgar Allan Poe Special award, 1970, 1972; Academy of Science Fiction and Fantasy award, for fiction and film, 1976; Maltese Falcon award, 1977. Honorary Doctorate: American River College, Sacramento, California, 1975. Lives in Reseda, California. Agent: Lori Perkins, Perkins Associates, 301 W. 53rd Street, New York, New York 10019, U.S.A.

Science-Fiction Publications

Novels (series: Logan; Sam Space)

*Logan: A Trilogy*. Baltimore, Maclay, 1986.
 *Logan's Run*, with G.C. Johnson. New York, Dial Press, 1967; London, Gollancz, 1968.
 *Logan's World*. New York, Bantam, 1977; London, Corgi, 1978.
 *Logan's Search*. New York, Bantam, 1980; London, Corgi, 1981.
*Space for Hire*. New York, Lancer, 1971.
*Look Out for Space*. New York, International Polygonics, 1985.

Short Stories

*Impact-20*. New York, Paperback Library, 1963; London, Corgi, 1966.
*Alien Horizons*. New York, Pocket Books, 1974.
*Wonderworlds*. London, Gollancz, 1977.
*Things Beyond Midnight*. Santa Cruz, California, Scream Press, 1984.

Other Publications

Novels

*Death Is for Losers*. Los Angeles, Sherbourne Press, 1968.
*The White Cad Cross-Up*. Los Angeles, Sherbourne Press, 1969.
*Rio Renegades* (as Terrance Duncan). New York, Zebra, 1989.
*Helltracks*. New York, Avon, 1990.

Plays

*Visual Encounters* (TV scripts). Baltimore, Maclay, 1986.

Screenplays: *The Legend of Machine-Gun Kelly*, 1975; *Logan's Run*, 1976; *Burnt Offerings*, with Dan Curtis, 1976.

Television Plays: *The Joy of Living*, 1971; *The Norliss Tapes*, 1973; *Melvin Purvis, G-Man*, with John Milius, 1974; *The Turn of the Screw*, 1974; *The Kansas City Massacre*, with Bronson Howitzer, 1975; *Sky Heist*, with Rick Rosner 1975; *Julie and Millicent and Therese* (in *Trilogy of Terror*), 1975; *Logan's Run* series, 1977; *First Loss*, 1981; *The Partnership*, 1981; *Bridge Across Time (Terror of London Bridge)*, 1985; *Trilogy of Terror II*, 1990.

Verse

*Dark Encounters*. Madison, Wisconsin, Dream House, 1986.

Other

*Adventure on Wheels: The Autobiography of a Road Racing Champion*, with John Fitch. New York, Putnam, 1959.
*Barney Oldfield*. New York, Putnam, 1961.
*Phil Hill: Yankee Champion*. New York, Putnam, 1962.
*Men of Thunder: Fabled Daredevils of Motor Sport*. New York, Putnam, 1964.
*Sinners and Supermen*. North Hollywood, All Star, 1965; as *Legends and Lovers: 14 Profiles*, Sacramento, California, Borgo Press, 1992.
*John Huston: King Rebel*. Los Angeles, Sherbourne Press, 1965.
*Dashiell Hammett: A Casebook*. Santa Barbara, California, McNally and Loftin, 1969.
*Steve McQueen: Star on Wheels*. New York, Putnam, 1972.
*Carnival of Speed*. New York, Putnam, 1973.
*Hemingway: Last Days of the Lion*. Santa Barbara, California, Capra Press, 1974.
*The Ray Bradbury Companion*. Detroit, Gale, 1975.

*Hammett: A Life at the Edge* (biography of Dashiell Hammett). New York, Congdon and Weed, 1983; London, Barker, 1984.
*McQueen* (biography of Steve McQueen). New York, Congdon and Weed, and London, Barker, 1984.
*The Black Mask Boys: Masters in the Hard-Boiled School of Detective Fiction*. New York, Morrow, 1985.
*The Work of Charles Beaumont* (bibliography), edited by Robert Reginold. San Bernardino, California, Borgo Press, 1985; 2nd edition, edited by Boden Clarke, Borgo Press, 1991.
*How to Write Horror Fiction*. Cincinnati, Ohio, Writer's Digest, 1990.
*Blood Sky*. San Jose, California, Deadline, 1991.

Editor, *Ray Bradbury Review*. San Diego, California, Nolan, 1952; as *William F. Nolan's Ray Bradbury Review*, Los Angeles, Graham Press, 1988.
Editor, with Charles Beaumont, *Omnibus of Speed*. New York, Putnam, 1958; London, Paul, 1961.
Editor, with Charles Beaumont, *When Engines Roar*. New York, Bantam, 1964.
Editor, *Man Against Tomorrow*. New York, Avon, 1965.
Editor, *The Pseudo People: Androids in Science Fiction*. Los Angeles, Sherbourne Press, 1965; as *Almost Human*, London, Souvenir Press, 1966.
Editor, *3 to the Highest Power*. New York, Avon, 1968; London, Corgi, 1971.
Editor, *A Wilderness of Stars*. Los Angeles, Sherbourne Press, 1969; London, Gollancz, 1970.
Editor, *A Sea of Space*. New York, Bantam, 1970; London, Corgi, 1980.
Editor, *The Future is Now*. Los Angeles, Sherbourne Press, 1970.
Editor, *The Human Equation*. Los Angeles, Sherbourne Press, 1971.
Editor, *The Edge of Forever*, by Chad Oliver. Los Angeles, Sherbourne Press, 1971.
Editor, with Martin H. Greenberg, *Science Fiction Origins*. New York, Fawcett-Popular Library, 1980.
Editor, *Max Brand's Best Western Stories*. New York, Dodd Mead, 3 vols., 1981–87; London, Hale, 2 vols., 1983–86.
Editor, *Max Brand: Western Giant*. Bowling Green, Ohio, Popular Press, 1986.
Editor, with Martin H. Greenberg, *Urban Horrors*. Arlington Heights, Illinois, Dark Harvest, 1990.
Editor, with Martin H. Greenberg, *The Bradbury Chronicles*. New York, Roc, 1991.

*

Bibliography: *William F. Nolan: A Checklist* by Charles E. Yenter, Tacoma, Washington, Charles E. Yenter, 1974; *The Work of William F. Nolan: An Annotated Bibliography and Guide* by Boden Clarke and James Hopkins, San Bernardino, California, Borgo Press, 1988.

Manuscript Collection: Bowling Green State University, Ohio.

Theatrical Activities: Actor: **Films**—*The Intruder*, 1962; *The Legend of Machine-Gun Kelly*, 1975.

William F. Nolan comments:

As a writer, I'm hard to pin down. Science fiction is just one of my many fields, and I take equal pride in my crime-suspense writing, auto-racing books, westerns, biographies, fantasy-terror fiction, thriller novels, verse, essays, and book reviews. I keep fresh and excited as a writer by switching constantly from one genre to another. I have enjoyed doing SF, particularly the Logan novels, but I also enjoy all other types of writing. After 30 years as a professional, my work totals 895 items—and I figure my career has another 30 years to go. After 37 years as a professional, my work totals 1200 items—and my career still has a long way to go. After all, Picasso turned out 300 paintings during his 90th year!

* * *

William F. Nolan started his creative life as an artist, but turned to the more lucrative science-fiction and men's magazines in the mid-1950's. Nolan was one of a school of Southern California SF writers that included (at times) the late Charles Beaumont, Ray Russell, George Clayton Johnson, Richard Matheson, Chad Oliver, and others. These authors not only socialized together, but also used their common interests in fantastic literature, film, television, and professional racing to develop a myriad of creative projects, often in collaboration. Although each writer eventually went his own way, artistically and personally, for the ten-year period from 1955–1965, most followed a similar path, moving from pulp fiction to slick nonfiction to the lucrative television market.

Nolan has been a full-time freelancer from the beginning, producing almost a thousand short fiction and nonfiction works in the course of his career, plus 50 books, 40 teleplays, and a dozen screenplays. Although his career has been a financial success, his work has been spread across so many subjects and genres that he remains relatively unheralded as a writer. For example, Nolan's 100 stories continue to be regularly collected in the SF anthologies ("Small World" has been reprinted at least 20 times), but the author himself is little regarded for his short fiction. That a man so obviously talented as a writer should be so regularly ignored by the critics remains a wonder.

However, Nolan's reputation as an SF writer seems secure, resting primarily on wide popular acceptance of two fictional creations, Logan the Sandman and Sam Space. *Logan's Run* (written with George Clayton Johnson), together with its sequels, *Logan's World* and *Logan's Search*, represent the high-water mark of the author's career, having been turned into both a successful motion picture and a television series, as well as being adapted into comic book form.

In the not-so-distant future, the young have revolted and killed all the adults. The new regime decrees that henceforward anyone reaching the age of 21 shall voluntary undergo euthanasia; those who refuse to die shall be hunted down by the police (the Sandmen) and summarily executed. A massive computer (The Thinker) is built to control the world and enforce the new rules. The new world state provides each citizen with everything he or she might want: travel, drugs, pleasures of all kinds, even work for those who want it—but everything ends at 21. Logan 3 is a Sandman who begins questioning the system after being forced to terminate a young girl. As his own time begins running out, Logan searches for Sanctuary, the semi-mythical place to which some runners have apparently escaped, and meets Jessica 6, with whom he forms a lasting and loving relationship. After a series of harrowing adventures, including a confrontation with the Thinker, in which they succeed in shutting down the machine, Logan and Jessica find Sanctuary, and live to fight another day.

In *Logan's World*, Logan and Jessica return to find the Sandman system largely destroyed, except for a group of renegade Sandmen who are trying to repair the damaged Thinker. In the ensuing chaos, Logan's son is killed, the Thinker is destroyed, and mankind is left to find its own way to the future. *Logan's Search* concludes the trilogy with Logan's attempt to defeat the Sandman system on a parallel Earth where the Thinker still exists.

Logan is Everyman, the man forced by conscience and circumstance to blaze a new path for himself—and for mankind. The signs of systemic failure are everywhere, literally and figuratively: this brave new world of the future, itself once representing a great turning point in the history of the human race, has come full circle, to a cultural and historical dead end. The machines are breaking down—and so is human society. Logan must destroy the old, rekindle the new, and show people the way to a new civilization. In another sense, Logan is also Nolan (one name being nearly the anagram of the other): the author as iconoclast, the artist as creator/destroyer, the rebel *with* a cause, the self-made man remaking himself in fiction. Complacency is sterility, the author seems to be saying, a life without challenge is a life not worth living. Mankind cannot stand still: it must either move forward—or die.

The Sam Space books—*Space for Hire* and *Look Out for Space*, (along with a forthcoming collection, *3 for Space*)—represent the second main strand in Nolan's fiction: farce. Sam Space (i.e., "Sam Spade" in SF terms) is a Mars-based private eye who always seems to be getting himself into impossibly wacky situations. Nolan manages to satirize the conventions of both the mystery and science-fiction genres, as well as modern mores, his fellow authors, and the world in general. Other stories in this vein include: "The Day the Gorf Took Over," "The Fasterfaster Affair," "Papa's Planet" (a robot-Hemingway send-up), and "Jenny Among the Zeebs" (a rock n' roll spoof).

In the past decade, Nolan has moved away from SF into dark fantasy, producing a horror novel, *Helltracks*, and about 30 short stories, the best of which are scheduled to be collected into *Nightshapes*, forthcoming from Avon. Like his frequent early collaborator, Charles Beaumont, Nolan has proven particularly effective at depicting the unpleasant side of human nature, and his stories are filled with clever twists, a legacy of his work in the mystery genre. These tales reflect a more cynical view of human nature, one in which there are not always happy endings or Pollyannish characters, in which evil is acknowledged and sometimes prevails. They reflect a more mature vision of the author, a more seasoned view of life. For Nolan the horrormonger, it seems, nasty is as nasty does.

—Robert Reginald

---

**NORMAN, John.** Pseudonym for John (Frederick) Lange (Jr.). American. Born in Chicago, Illinois, 3 June 1931. Educated at the University of Nebraska, Lincoln, B.A. 1953; University of Southern California, Los Angeles, M.A. 1957; Princeton University, New Jersey, Ph.D. 1963. Served in the United States Army: Sergeant. Married Bernice L. Green in 1956; two sons and one daughter. Radio writer; story analyst, Warner Brothers; film writer, University of Nebraska; technical writer, Rocketdyne (North American Aviation); Instructor in Philosphy, Hamilton College, Clinton, New York, 1962–64. Since 1964, member of the department, and since 1974, Professor of Philosophy, Queens College, City University of New York. Address: Department of Philosophy, Queens College, Flushing, New York 11367, U.S.A.

SCIENCE-FICTION PUBLICATIONS

Novels (series: Gor)

*Tarnsman of Gor*. New York, Ballantine, 1966; London, Sidgwick and Jackson, 1969.
*Outlaw of Gor*. New York, Ballantine, 1967; London, Sidgwick and Jackson, 1970.
*Priest-Kings of Gor*. New York, Ballantine, 1968; London, Sidgwick and Jackson, 1971.
*Nomads of Gor*. New York, Ballantine, 1969; London, Sidgwick and Jackson, 1971.
*Assassin of Gor*. New York, Ballantine, 1970; London, Sidgwick and Jackson, 1971.
*Ghost Dance*. New York, Ballantine, 1970; London, Sphere, 1972.
*Raiders of Gor*. New York, Ballantine, 1971; London, Tandem, 1973.
*Captive of Gor*. New York, Ballantine, 1972; London, Tandem, 1973.
*Hunters of Gor*. New York, DAW, 1974; London, Tandem, 1975.
*Marauders of Gor*. New York, DAW, 1975; London, Universal, 1977.
*Time Slave*. New York, DAW, 1975; London, W.H. Allen, 1981.
*Tribesmen of Gor*. New York, DAW, 1976.
*Slave Girl of Gor*. New York, DAW, 1977; London, Universal, 1978.
*Beasts of Gor*. New York, DAW, 1978; London, Star, 1979.
*Explorers of Gor*. New York, DAW, 1979; London, W.H. Allen, 1980.
*Fighting Slave of Gor*. New York, DAW, 1980; London, W.H. Allen, 1981.
*Guardsman of Gor*. New York, DAW, 1981; London, Star, 1982.
*Rogue of Gor*. New York, DAW, 1981; London, W.H. Allen, 1982.
*Blood Brothers of Gor*. New York, DAW, 1982; London, Star, 1983.
*Savages of Gor*. New York, DAW, and London, Star, 1982.
*Kajira of Gor*. New York, DAW, and London, Star, 1983.
*Players of Gor*. New York, DAW, and London, Star, 1984.
*Mercenaries of Gor*. New York, DAW, and London, W.H. Allen, 1985.
*Dancer of Gor*. New York, DAW, 1985; London, W.H. Allen, 1986.
*Renegades of Gor*. New York, DAW, and London, W.H. Allen, 1986.
*Vagabonds of Gor*. New York, DAW, and London, W.H. Allen, 1987.

OTHER PUBLICATIONS as John Lange

Other

*The Cognitivity Paradox: An Inquiry Concerning the Claims of Philosophy*. Princeton, New Jersey, Princeton University Press, 1970.
*Imaginative Sex* (as John Norman). New York, DAW, 1975.

Editor, *Values and Imperatives: Studies in Ethics*, by Clarence I. Lewis. Stanford, California, Stanford University Press, 1969.

* * *

John Norman has written over two dozen science fiction/fantasy novels, most of which are in the Gor series (the Chronicles of Counter-Earth) and are in the tradition of Edgar Rice Burroughs's Mars books or Andre Norton's Witch World series. In these works, a character from contemporary Earth finds himself transported, often by inexplicable means, to an unfamiliar world where he is caught up in the events which are shaping the future of that world. And in such worlds, heroic action is almost always the means by which destiny is decided.

Norman's hero, Tarl Cabot, is transported to Gor, a planet on the opposite side of the sun from Earth and somehow shielded from any detection by Terran scientists. On Gor, Cabot is initiated into a way of life which the reader recognizes as medieval. All technological development, especially in weaponry, has been held in check by the Priest-Kings, and the men must fight with sword, spear, bow and arrow, and the like. For most of the known planet, the largest political unit is the city, and politics in and among cities is generally feudal. Gorean society is highly structured, and each person usually remains in the caste—warriors, bakers, scribes, etc.—into which he is born. But Gor and the Priest-Kings are in trouble and in need of heroics which only Tarl Cabot can provide.

As with any extended work of fantasy, the author's ability to detail convincingly a complex culture—or group of cultures—is important. Norman is quite good at this. In the first book, *Tarnsman of Gor*, such detail is necessary, and Norman provides a wealth of information on everything from the training of a warrior to the importance of a Home Stone. In what is possibly his best book to date, *Nomads of Gor*, he brings Cabot to the four tribes of the Wagon People, and the reader is treated to a fascinating descriptions of customs, habits, rituals, and all the other aspects of a complex cultural group. On Gor, the reader realizes, heroic action is not only possible, it is necessary; in other words, the culture is not just a backdrop for the action in Norman's books, it is an integral part of the action.

Heroic fantasies have always been considered male-escapist. The hero is muscular and skillful with weapons; he rescues the heroine who then succumbs to his over-powering maleness. Norman carries this aspect of heroic fantasy one step further than his predecessors. On Gor, most of the women are slaves, and those who are not are vaguely unhappy because a woman can be free only in total submission to a man. Some of the later books, *Slave Girl of Gor*, for example, focus less on Tarl Cabot than on the Earth woman brought to Gor. Such women are at first distressed by the culture in which they find themselves but soon realize the falseness of their previous (Terran) way of life. On Gor, Cabot says, women are free to be women; whereas, on Earth, they are forced to try to be men. This concept has lost Norman two groups of readers, the first violently opposed to his analysis of women, the second tired of hearing Cabot—or one of the women—explain and defend it book after book.

In literary terms, it is more the prolonged defense than the attitude itself which mars the novels, some of which seem to have been written solely to present examples of these ideas and attitudes about women. And Cabot's primary quest has suffered as well; to be sure, he still fights skirmishes against the enemies of the Priest-Kings, but what seemed to be the main plot-line of the series is barely progressing. In fact, by the 23rd and 24th Gor books, the bulk of the text deals with portraying and justifying the status of women on Gor, and action sequences which actually advance the series plot are few and far between. This situation is unfortunate, for the Gor books are, in most other respects, good heroic fantasy.

—C.W. Sullivan III

---

**NORTON, Andre** (Alice Mary Norton). Also writes as Andrew North; Allen Weston. American. Born in Cleveland, Ohio, 17 February 1912. Educated at Western Reserve University, Cleveland, 1930–32. Children's librarian, Cleveland Public Library, 1932–50; special librarian, Library of Congress, Washington, D.C., during World War II; editor, Gnome Press, New York, 1950–58. Recipient: Grand Master of Fantasy award, 1977; Gandalf award, 1977; Fritz Leiber award, 1983; Lensman award, 1983, 1987; Grand Master Nebula award 1983; Jules Verne award, 1984; Daedalus award, 1986. Address: 1600 Spruce Avenue, Winter Park, Florida 32789, U.S.A.

### SCIENCE-FICTION PUBLICATIONS

Novels (series: Astra; Beast Master; Forerunner; Janus; Shann Lantree; Moon Magic; Star Ka'at; Time Travel; Time War; Zero Stone)

*Star Man's Son, 2250 A.D.* New York, Harcourt Brace, 1952; London, Staples Press, 1953; as *Daybreak, 2250 A.D.*, New York, Ace, 1954.
*Star Rangers.* New York, Harcourt Brace, 1953; London, Gollancz, 1968; as *The Last Planet*, New York, Ace, 1955.
*The Stars Are Ours!* (Astra). Cleveland, World, 1954.
*Star Guard.* New York, Harcourt Brace, 1955; London, Gollancz, 1969.
*The Crossroads of Time* (Time Travel). New York, Ace, 1956; London, Gollancz, 1967.
*Sea Siege.* New York, Harcourt Brace, 1957.
*Star Born* (Astra). Cleveland, World, 1957; London, Gollancz, 1973.
*Star Gate.* New York, Harcourt Brace, 1958; London, Gollancz, 1970.
*The Time Traders* (Time War). Cleveland, World, 1958.
*Secret of the Lost Race.* New York, Ace, 1959; as *Wolfshead*, London, Hale, 1977.
*The Beast Master.* New York, Harcourt Brace, 1959; London, Gollancz, 1966.
*Galactic Derelict* (Time War) Cleveland, World, 1959.
*Storm over Warlock* (Lantree). Cleveland, World, 1960.
*The Sioux Spaceman* New York, Ace, 1960; London, Hale, 1976.
*Star Hunter.* New York, Ace, 1961.
*Catseye.* New York, Harcourt Brace, 1961; London, Gollancz, 1962.
*Eye of the Monster.* New York, Ace, 1962.
*The Defiant Agents* (Time War). Cleveland, World, 1962.
*Lord of Thunder* (Beast Master). New York, Harcourt Brace, 1962; London, Gollancz, 1966.
*Key Out of Time* (Time War). Cleveland, World, 1963.
*Judgment on Janus.* New York, Harcourt Brace, 1963; London, Gollancz, 1964.
*Ordeal in Otherwhere* (Lantree). Cleveland, World, 1964.
*Night of Masks.* New York, Harcourt Brace, 1964; London, Gollancz, 1965.
*The X Factor.* New York, Harcourt Brace, 1965; London, Gollancz, 1967.
*Quest Crosstime* (Time Travel). New York, Viking Press, 1965; as *Crosstime Agent*, London, Gollancz, 1975.
*Moon of Three Rings* (Moon Magic). New York, Viking Press, 1966; London, Longman, 1969.
*Victory on Janus.* New York, Harcourt Brace, 1966; London, Gollancz, 1967.
*Operation Time Search.* New York, Harcourt Brace, 1967.
*Dark Piper.* New York, Harcourt Brace, 1968; London, Gollancz, 1969.
*The Zero Stone.* New York, Viking Press, 1968; London, Gollancz, 1974.

*Postmarked the Stars.* New York, Harcourt Brace, 1969; London, Gollancz, 1971.
*Uncharted Stars* (Zero Stone). New York, Viking Press, 1969; London, Gollancz, 1974.
*Ice Crown.* New York, Viking Press, 1970; London, Longman, 1971.
*Android at Arms.* New York, Harcourt Brace, 1971; London, Gollancz, 1972.
*Exiles of the Stars* (Moon Magic). New York, Viking Press, 1971; London, Longman, 1972.
*Breed to Come.* New York, Viking Press, 1972; London, Longman, 1973.
*Here Abide Monsters.* New York, Atheneum, 1973.
*Iron Cage.* New York, Viking Press, 1974; London, Kestrel, 1975.
*Outside.* New York, Walker, 1975; London, Blackie, 1976.
*The Day of the Ness*, with Michael Gilbert. New York, Walker, 1975.
*Knave of Dreams.* New York, Viking Press, 1975; London, Kestrel, 1976.
*No Night Without Stars.* New York, Atheneum, 1975; London, Gollancz, 1976.
*Star Ka'at*, with Dorothy Madlee. New York, Walker, 1976; London, Blackie, 1977.
*Star Ka'at World*, with Dorothy Madlee. New York, Walker, 1978.
*Star Ka'ats and the Plant People*, with Dorothy Madlee. New York, Walker, 1979.
*Star Ka'ats and the Winged Warriors.* New York, Walker, 1981.
*Ten Mile Treasure.* New York, Pocket Books, 1981.
*Voorloper.* New York, Ace, 1981.
*Forerunner.* New York, Pinnacle, 1981.
*Moon Called.* New York, Simon and Schuster, 1982.
*Wheel of Stars.* New York, Simon and Schuster, 1983.
*Forerunner: The Second Venture.* New York, Tor, 1985.
*Flight in Yiktor* (Moon Magic). New York, Tor, 1986; London, Methuen, 1988.
*Black Trillium*, with Marion Zimmer Bradley and Julian May. New York, Doubleday, 1990; London, Grafton, 1991.
*Dare to Go A-Hunting* (Moon Magic). New York, Tor, 1990.

Novels as Andrew North (series: Solar Queen in all books)

*Sargasso of Space.* New York, Gnome Press, 1955; as Andre Norton, London, Gollancz, 1970.
*Plague Ship.* New York, Gnome Press, 1956; as Andre Norton, London, Gollancz, 1971.
*Voodoo Planet.* New York, Ace, 1959.

Short Stories

*The Many Worlds of Andre Norton*, edited by Roger Elwood. Radnor, Pennsylvania, Chilton, 1974; as *The Book of Andre Norton*, New York, DAW, 1975.
*Perilous Dreams.* New York, DAW, 1976.
*Moon Mirror.* New York, Tor, 1988.

OTHER PUBLICATIONS

Novels

*The Prince Commands.* New York, Appleton Century, 1934.
*Ralestone Luck.* New York, Appleton Century, 1938.
*Follow the Drum.* New York, Penn, 1942.
*The Sword Is Drawn.* Boston, Houghton Mifflin, 1944; London, Oxford University Press, 1946.
*Scarface.* New York, Harcourt Brace, 1948; London, Methuen, 1950.
*Sword in Sheath.* New York, Harcourt Brace, 1949; as *Island of the Lost*, London, Staples Press, 1953.
*Murder for Sale* (as Allen Weston, with Grace Hogarth). London, Hammond, 1954.
*At Swords' Point.* New York, Harcourt Brace, 1954.
*Yankee Privateer.* Cleveland, World, 1955.
*Stand to Horse.* New York, Harcourt Brace, 1956.
*Shadow Hawk.* New York, Harcourt Brace, 1960; London, Gollancz, 1971.
*Ride Proud, Rebel!* Cleveland, World, 1961.
*Rebel Spurs.* Cleveland, World, 1962.
*Witch World.* New York, Ace, 1963; London, Tandem, 1970.
*Web of the Witch World.* New York, Ace, 1964; London, Tandem, 1970.
*Steel Magic.* Cleveland, World, 1965; London, Hamish Hamilton, 1967; as *Gray Magic*, New York, Scholastic, 1967.
*Three Against the Witch World.* New York, Ace, 1965; London, Tandem, 1970.
*Year of the Unicorn.* New York, Ace, 1965; London, Tandem, 1970.
*Octagon Magic.* Cleveland, World, 1967; London, Hamish Hamilton, 1968.
*Warlock of the Witch World.* New York, Ace, 1967; London, Tandem, 1970.
*Fur Magic.* Cleveland, World, 1968; London, Hamish Hamilton, 1969.
*Sorceress of the Witch World.* New York, Ace, 1968; London, Tandem, 1970.
*Dread Companion.* New York, Harcourt Brace, 1970; London, Gollancz, 1972.
*The Crystal Gryphon.* New York, Atheneum, 1972; London, Gollancz, 1973.
*Dragon Magic.* New York, Crowell, 1972.
*Forerunner Foray.* New York, Viking Press, 1973; London, Longman, 1974.
*The Jargoon Pard.* New York, Atheneum, 1974; London, Gollancz, 1975.
*Lavender-Green Magic.* New York, Crowell, 1974.
*Merlin's Mirror.* New York, DAW, 1975; London, Sidgwick and Jackson, 1976.
*The White Jade Fox.* New York, Dutton, 1975; London, W.H. Allen, 1976.
*Red Hart Magic.* New York, Crowell, 1976; London, Hamish Hamilton, 1977.
*Wraiths of Time.* New York, Atheneum, 1976; London, Gollancz, 1977.
*The Opal-Eyed Fan.* New York, Dutton, 1977.
*Velvet Shadows.* New York, Fawcett, 1977.
*Quag Keep.* New York, Atheneum, 1978.
*Yurth Burden.* New York, DAW, 1978.
*Zarsthor's Bane.* New York, Ace, 1978; London, Dobson, 1981.
*Snow Shadow.* New York, Fawcett, 1979.
*Seven Spells to Sunday*, with Phyllis Miller. New York, Atheneum, 1979.
*Gryphon in Glory.* New York, Atheneum, 1981.
*Horn Crown.* New York, DAW, 1981.
*Caroline*, with Enid Cushing. New York, Pinnacle, 1982.
*'Ware Hawk.* New York, Atheneum, 1983.
*House of Shadows*, with Phyllis Miller. New York, Atheneum, 1984.
*Stand and Deliver.* New York, Dell, 1984.
*Gryphon's Eyrie*, with A.C. Crispin. New York, Tor, 1984.

*Were-Wrath.* Newcastle, Virginia, Cheap Street, 1984.
*Ride the Green Dragon*, with Phyllis Miller. New York, Atheneum, 1985.
*The Gate of the Cat.* New York, Ace, 1987.
*The Magic Books* (includes *Fur Magic, Steel Magic*, and *Octagon Magic*). New York, New American Library, 1988.
*Imperial Lady: A Fantasy of Han China*, with Susan Shwartz. New York, Tor, 1989.
*The Jekyll Legacy*, with Robert Bloch. New York, Tor, 1990.
*The Elvenbane.* New York, Tor, 1991.
*Storms of Victory*, with Pauline Griffin. New York, Tor, 1991.

Short Stories

*High Sorcery.* New York, Ace, 1970.
*Garan the Eternal.* Alhambra, California, Fantasy, 1972.
*Spell of the Witch World.* New York, DAW, 1972; London, Prior, 1977.
*Trey of Swords.* New York, Grosset and Dunlap, 1977; London, Star, 1979.
*Lore of the Witch World.* New York, DAW, 1980.
*Serpent's Tooth.* Winter Park, Florida, Andre Norton Ltd., 1987.
*Wizards' Worlds*, edited by Ingrid Zierhut. New York, Tor, 1989.

Other

*Rogue Reynard* (for children). Boston, Houghton Mifflin, 1947.
*Huon of the Horn* (for children). New York, Harcourt Brace, 1951.
*Bertie and May* (for children), with Bertha Stenn Norton. Cleveland, World, 1969; London, Hamish Hamilton, 1971.

Editor, *Bullard of the Space Patrol*, by Malcolm Jameson. Cleveland, World, 1951.
Editor, *Space Service.* Cleveland, World, 1953.
Editor, *Space Pioneers.* Cleveland, World, 1954.
Editor, *Space Police.* Cleveland, World, 1956.
Editor, with Ernestine Donaldy, *Gates to Tomorrow: An Introduction to Science Fiction.* New York, Atheneum, 1973.
Editor, *Small Shadows Creep: Ghost Children.* New York, Dutton, 1974; London, Chatto and Windus, 1976.
Editor, *Baleful Beasts and Eerie Creatures.* Chicago, Rand McNally, 1976.
Editor, with Robert Adams, *Magic in Ithkar.* New York, Tor, 4 vols., 1985–87.
Editor, *Tales of the Witch World.* New York, Tor, 3 vols., 1987–90.
Editor, *Four from the Witch World.* New York, Tor, 1989.
Editor, with Martin H. Greenberg, *Catfantastic.* New York, DAW, 1989.
Editor, with Ingrid Zierhut, *Grand Master's Choices.* Cambridge, Massachusetts, NESFA, 1989.
Editor, with Martin H. Greenberg, *Catfantastic II.* New York, DAW, 1991.

*

Bibliography: *Andre Norton: A Primary and Secondary Bibliography* by Roger C. Schlobin, Boston, Hall, 1980.

Manuscript Collections: Andre Norton Ltd., Winter Park, Florida; George Arents Research Library, Syracuse University, New York.

* * *

Andre Norton's early intention was to write fiction for boys, and she changed her name to enter this male-dominated market. Fortunately for the millions of readers who have made her one of the best selling of contemporary fantasy and science-fiction authors, she turned to these two forms in 1947 with her first published short story "People of the Crater" (later title: "Garin of Tav"). It is odd that Norton turned to science fiction at all. In fact, books like *The Beast Master* and its sequel, *Lord of Thunder*, weren't really science fiction at all. They were simply an experiment applying the form of a western to outer space and alien worlds. Actually, Norton has contempt for science and technology; they appear in her fiction only as vehicles and foils. In Ric Brooks's essay (in *The Many Worlds of Andre Norton*, 1974), she makes her stance quite clear: "Yes, I am anti-machine. The more research I do, the more I am convinced that when western civilizations turned to machines . . . , they threw away parts of life . . . [the lack of which] leads to much of our present frustration."

Even in Norton's science fiction, technology and science are incidental to plot and character. These major concerns reflect the influences of Edgar Rice Burroughs, H. Rider Haggard, A. Merritt, and Talbot Mundy, and demonstrate also Norton's respect for their fast-moving plots and memorable characters. For plot content, Norton's extensive research and affection for the mysterious and intriguing have led her to a number of specific motifs that occur throughout her fiction. Jewels frequently appear as powerful talismans, particularly in her fantasy novels. For example, as early as *At Swords' Point*, part of the Sword series that focuses on post-World-War-II espionage and the Netherlands during World War II, a set of jeweled miniature knights are central to a young man's search for his brother's murderer. Jewels are also important in *The Zero Stone*, the much heralded Witch World series, *Wraiths of Time*, and the gothic novels, particularly *The White Jade Fox* and *The Opal-Eyed Fan.* Frequently, these talismans are connected to an even more pervasive motif: the pseudo-science psychometry. This is formally defined as the detection of the residue of "memory" retained in an artifact by a sensitive. This plays a major role in the fantasy (with strong science-fiction elements) *Forerunner Foray*, in which Ziatha is drawn into a prehuman age through her reaction to a jewel; in *Wraiths of Time*, a crystal ankh and a staff contain the accumulated psychic power of a race.

Jewels and psychometry are two of the elements that give Norton's fiction its brooding depth, and together they provide a bridge between two other major Norton fascinations: history and speculative archaeology. Whether it be through references to prehistoric alien visits to Earth, as in *Merlin's Mirror*, or allusions to the prehistoric past, as in the Moon Magic series, Norton's fiction always has a resonance that goes beyond the immediate present to a more pervasive and often mysterious past. It is the characters' responsibility to discover the relevance of the past to themselves and their futures.

Yet none of these motifs or devices is the center of Norton's fiction. Rather, the most important aspects are simply humanity and self-realization. Norton explains this in "On Writing Fantasy" (in *The Many Worlds of Andre Norton*): "But the first requirement for writing heroic . . . fantasy must be a deep interest in and a love for history itself. Not the history of dates, of sweeps and empires—but the kind of history which deals with daily life, the beliefs, and the aspirations of people long since dust." Within the obvious cosmic scope, alien climes, antagonistic technology, vast quests, and fantastic forces of Norton's fiction, the characters are involved in crucial patterns of being, both for themselves and their fellows. While they are arrayed in mythic quests that grow from deep tradition, exist in a momentous present, and face a vital future, the characters remain pointedly human and humane. Most frequently, they move through what Northrop Frye calls "triumphant comedy." They struggle against an unlawful or unnatural order, undergo rites of passage to find realization, and establish new orders and freedoms. Kaththea (*Sorceress of the Witch World*) reflects this pattern as well as Norton's pioneering commitment to female characters. Shattered and disillusioned, Kaththea must find the faith to accept Hilarion, one of the enormously powerful "Old Ones" of the Witch World, if she is to save her family and regenerate her environment. Furtig, the mutated cat protagonist of *Breed to Come*, must overcome the mythology surrounding his long-departed human masters to unleash his own potentiality. Through the characters' agonizing trials, bondages and wastelands are destroyed, shape prejudice is eliminated, generative orders are established, and the protagonists and their fellows are ennobled. As Ric Brooks writes, "the chief value of Andre Norton's fiction may not lie in entertainment or social commentary, but in her 'reenchanting' us with her creations that renew our linkages to life."

Norton's characters are always alone, alienated, fearful, and searching. They are admirable for their positive, if sometimes confused, values, and they are attractive in their frailty and their doubt. In spite of their varied shapes and alien abilities, they achieve the nobility and status of the healer as they cure themselves and others. Frequently, their solutions are androgynous—as for Simon Tregarth and Jaelithe in *Witch World*—and they do find the best of male and female. More significantly, their solutions to pain and loneliness are mythic and elemental and are a celebration of the bonds among man, animal, nature and cosmic order.

With the *Magic in Ithkar* series, Norton has again turned her energies to intensive editing after early successes in that role.

—Roger C. Schlobin

---

**NORTH, Andrew.** *See* **NORTON, Andre.**

---

**NORVIL, Manning.** *See* **BULMER, Kenneth.**

---

**NORWOOD, Warren.** American. Born in Philadelphia, Pennsylvania, 21 August 1945. Educated at North Texas State University, Denton, B. A. 1972. Served in the United States Army, 1966–69: Bronze Star. Married 1) Mary Walker in 1965 (divorced 1972); 2) Margot Biery in 1973; one daughter. Assistant manager, University Bookstore, University of Texas, Arlington, 1973–76; manager, Century Bookstore, Fort Worth, 1976–77; publisher's representative in Fort Worth, for Ballantine Books, 1978–79, and for Bantam Books, 1980–83; teacher, creative writing, Tarrant County Junior College, 1981–83. Agent: Richard Curtis Associates, 164 East 64th Street, New York, New York 10021. Address: 500 Greentree, Fort Worth, Texas 76086, U.S.A.

SCIENCE-FICTION PUBLICATIONS

Novels (series: Double Spiral War; Windhover Tapes)

The Windhover Tapes:
*An Image of Voices*. New York, Bantam, 1982.
*Flexing the Warp*. New York, Bantam, 1983.
*Fize of the Gabriel Ratchets*. New York, Bantam, 1983.
*Planet of Flowers*. New York, Bantam, 1984.
*The Seren Cenacles*, with Ralph Mylius. New York, Bantam, 1983.
Double Spiral War:
*Midway Between*. New York, Bantam, 1984.
*Polar Fleet*. New York, Bantam, 1985.
*Final Command*. New York, Bantam, 1986.
*Shudderchild*. New York, Bantam, 1987.
*True Jaguar*. New York, Bantam, 1988.
*Vanished*. New York, Lynx, 1988.
*Stranded*, with Mel Odom. New York, Lynx, 1989.
*Trapped!* New York, Lynx, 1989.

* * *

Warren Norwood's unusual first novel, *The Windhover Tapes: An Image of Voices*, received excellent reviews when it appeared in 1982, but earned its author the dubious honor of finishing last in the balloting for the John W. Campbell award for best new writer of the year, behind "No Award." The book is a complex amalgam of 1930's-style space opera, obscure literary references to 17th-century poets like Michael Drayton and folklore characters like the Gabriel Ratchets, and a style which seems to fluctuate between Barry Malzberg-like monologue and the 18th-century epistolary novels of Samuel Richardson. The story takes place in the far future, when faster-than-light travel to other galaxies is routine and humanity has contacted and interbred with any number of alien races. Gerard Hopkins Manley is a contract diplomat and anthropological researcher, and the four "Windhover" novels relate his adventures with sentient flowers, pulp-style outer space empires, outspoken feminist ghosts, intelligent, wheeled avians, and other strange beings and situations. The first two books are made up entirely of Manley's first-person conversations with himself and his sentient space ship, Windhover. The later volumes are more conventional, third-person narratives. All four books contain numerous references to Manley's 19th-century English namesake, though Manley and those around him have apparently never heard of the poet.

The Windhover Tapes series is an enjoyable piece of work, but it has several flaws: the seeming irrelevance of most of the Hopkins material, Norwood's frequent inclusion of his own not very good poetry (including a travesty of Hopkins's "Windhover"), and the author's apparent fixation on human and humanoid mammary glands (Manley's beautiful alien wife has three). On the positive side, Norwood is doing some interesting stylistic experimentation, and his main character is a very unusual hero for science fiction—an emotional man who is not afraid to cry or dote upon his infant son and daughter, a man who is capable of space opera-style action, but who would really much rather talk things out sensibly.

That Norwood has considerable ability is clear; however, one cannot help but wish that he would take more time with his books. The Windhover series fluctuates markedly between startling originality and pulp cliché but maintains on the whole a fairly high level of excellence. The author's science-fiction novels since *Windhover*, however, are generally less successful. *The Seren Cenacles*, co-authored with Ralph Mylius, is a well-written but poorly plotted tale of "alien terror" on a mining colony. The several political and industrial groups, military forces, and alien species contending for control of the situation are thrown at us willy nilly, without sufficient cultural context or satisfactory explanation. The book's basic premise, mining organic matter buried on distant worlds to ship to the galaxy's starving trillions, is not very believable, nor is the story's abrupt and rather unlikely denouement. Likewise, the Double Spiral War trilogy throws so many similar characters at the reader that it is virtually impossible to keep them straight. This space war series like all Norwood's work, is well written, but it is also talky, obscurely plotted, and considering its sub-genre, short on action.

Norwood's most recent serious novel, *True Jaguar*, is an engaging fantasy about a man who discovers himself to be the reincarnation of a Mayan god. Martin O'Hara must journey to the Underworld and battle with demons in order to save the world from a comet on a collision course with Earth.

Warren Norwood is a talented writer with a knack for character development, fine prose, and experimentation, but he has considerable problems with plotting and background development. *True Jaguar*, however, gives some indication of what Norwood is capable of at his best.

—Michael M. Levy

---

**NOURSE, Alan E(dward).** American. Born in Des Moines, Iowa, 11 August 1928. Educated at Rutgers University, New Brunswick, New Jersey, B.A. 1951; University of Pennsylvania, Philadelphia, M.D. 1955. Served in the United States Navy, 1946–48: Hospitalman 3rd Class. Married Ann Jane Morton in 1952; three sons and one daughter. Intern, Virginia Mason Hospital, Seattle, Washington, 1955–56; freelance writer, 1956–58; private medical practice, North Bend, Washington, 1958–64. Since 1964, freelance writer. Owner, Chamberlain Press, 1953–55. Chairman of the Board, Tanner Electric Rural Electrification Co-op; president, Science Fiction Writers of America, 1968–69. Agent: Brandt and Brandt, 1501 Broadway, New York, New York 10036. Address: Rt. 1, Box 173, Thorp, Washington 98946, U.S.A.

### Science-Fiction Publications

#### Novels

*Trouble on Titan* (for children). Philadelphia, Winston, 1954; London, Hutchinson, 1956.

*A Man Obsessed*. New York, Ace, 1955; revised edition, as *The Mercy Men*, New York, McKay, 1968; London, Faber, 1969.

*Rocket to Limbo* (for children). New York, McKay, 1957; London, Faber, 1964.

*The Invaders Are Coming!*, with J.A. Meyer. New York, Ace, 1959.

*Scavengers in Space* (for children). New York, McKay, 1959; London, Faber, 1964.

*Star Surgeon* (for children). New York, McKay, 1960; London, Faber, 1962.

*Raiders from the Rings* (for children). New York, McKay, 1962; London, Faber, 1965.

*The Universe Between*. New York, McKay, 1965; London, Faber, 1966.

*The Bladerunner*. New York, McKay, 1974.

*The Fourth Horseman*. New York, Harper, 1983.

#### Short Stories

*Tiger by the Tail*. New York, McKay, 1961; London, Dobson, 1962; as *Beyond Infinity*, London, Corgi, 1964.

*The Counterfeit Man*. New York, McKay, 1963; London, Dobson, 1964.

*Psi High and Others*. New York, McKay, 1967; London, Faber, 1968.

*Rx for Tomorrow*. New York, McKay, 1971; London, Faber, 1972.

### Other Publications

#### Novels

*Junior Intern*. New York, Harper, 1955.

*The Practice*. New York, Harper, 1978; London, Futura, 1979.

#### Other

*So You Want to Be a Doctor [Lawyer, Scientist, Nurse* (with Eleanore Halliday), *Engineer* (with James C. Webbert), *Physicist, Chemist* (with James C. Webbert), *Surgeon, Architect* (with Carl Meinhardt)] (for children). New York, Harper, 9 vols., 1957–69.

*Nine Planets*. New York, Harper, 1960; revised edition, 1970.

*The Management of a Medical Practice*, with Geoffrey Marks. Philadelphia, Lippincott, 1963.

*The Body*. New York, Time, 1964; revised edition, New York, Time Life, 1980.

*Universe, Earth, and Atom: The Story of Physics*. New York, Harper, 1969.

*Virginia Mason Medical Center: The First Fifty Years*. Seattle, Virginia Mason Hospital Association, 1970.

*Venus and Mercury* (for children). New York, Watts, 1972.

*Ladies' Home Journal Family Medical Guide*. New York, Harper, 1973.

*The Backyard Astronomer*. New York, Watts, 1973.

*The Giant Planets* (for children). New York, Watts, 1974; revised edition, 1982.

*The Outdoorsman's Medical Guide*. New York, Harper, 1974.

*The Asteroids* (for children). New York, Watts, 1975.

*Clear Skin, Healthy Skin* (for children). New York, Watts, 1976.

*Lumps, Bumps, and Rashes* (for children). New York, Watts, 1976; revised edition, 1990.

*Viruses* (for children). New York, Watts, 1976; revised edition, 1983.

*The Tooth Book* (for children). New York, McKay, 1977.

*Vitamins* (for children). New York, Watts, 1977.

*Fractures, Dislocations, and Sprains* (for children). New York, Watts, 1978.

*Hormones* (for children). New York, Watts, 1979.

*Inside the Mayo Clinic*. New York, McGraw Hill, 1979.

*Menstruation: Just Plain Talk* (for children). New York, Watts, 1980; revised edition, 1987.

*Your Immune System* (for children). New York, Watts, 1980; revised edition, 1990.

*Herpes* (for children). New York, Watts, 1985.

*AIDS* (for children). New York, Watts, 1986; revised edition, 1989.

*Birth Control* (for children). New York, Watts, 1986.
*The Elk Hunt*. New York, Macmillan, 1986.
*The Hidden Addiction and How to Get Free*, with Janice Keller. Boston, Little Brown, 1986.
*Teen Guide to Safe Sex*. New York, Watts, 1988.
*Teen Guide to AIDS Prevention*. New York, Watts, 1990.
*Teen Guide to Survival*. New York, Watts, 1990.
*Radio Astronomy*. New York, Watts, 1990.
*Sexually Transmitted Diseases*. New York, Watts, 1992.

*

Manuscript Collection: Boston University.

* * *

Despite producing only ten novels and a few dozen short stories over the 40 years of his science fiction career, Alan E. Nourse remains one of the noted names in the field. This is even more surprising when one considers that five of those novels were aimed specifically at younger readers, although like Andre Norton, Robert Heinlein, and Isaac Asimov, Nourse wrote his "juveniles" in such a way that they would appeal to adult audiences as well.

In his first book-length work, *Trouble on Titan*, a young man is sent to the primary moon of Saturn to assist in the suppression of a fulminating revolt on the part of the local inhabitants, who are in large part exiles and convicts. Shortly after arriving and learning the true state of affairs, he discovers that his sympathies lie with the rebels, which places him in conflict not only with the authorities but also his own father. This was followed almost immediately by Nourse's first adult novel, *A Man Obsessed*, later expanded and republished as *The Mercy Men.* The novel draws heavily on Nourse's medical background, and follows the exploits of a troubled man who is obsessed with avenging his father's death. He follows the man responsible to the haven of the Mercy Men, individuals who have agreed to accept money in return for the use of their bodies in prohibited medical research. It is a powerfully written and disturbing story with implications that remain as pointed now as they did when it was first published in 1955.

There followed several juvenile novels. *Rocket to Limbo* concerns an interstellar voyage to find a lost starship. Although an interesting tale, it is the least interesting of Nourse's novels. *Scavengers in Space* was quite a different matter, the best of his early novels. Twin brothers are unhappy with the official explanation of their father's death while mining in the asteroid belt, suspecting that the powerful enemies he had made with highly placed company officials had led to someone deciding to dispose of the irritation. The novel contains a well-conceived plot, made even more convincing by Nourse's careful but unobtrusive explication of the physical problems of mining in an airless environment.

*Star Surgeon* returns to Nourse's medical interests. The human race has found its place in interstellar society by acting as medical specialists to every race they encounter, developing special techniques beyond even those of the physicians from each individual race. The protagonist is an alien doctor who is the first non-human to be allowed employment with Hospital Earth, who must face racial prejudice and personal malice before proving himself. In *Raiders from the Rings*, the human race has split into two factions. Earth is a fearful, huddled nation state preparing for a major war against the Spacers, other humans who have settled on Mars and in the asteroid belt. As the two factions maneuver for the final battle, one Spacer realizes he must step outside the conflict and find a resolution before the entire human species becomes extinct. Both of these novels are boisterous space adventures, but each contains serious observations about human institutions and the constraints they place on freedom of action for the individual. The novel *The Invaders Are Coming!*, written during this same period in collaboration with J.A. Meyer, was a disappointing novel of a future political struggle, with hints of mysterious alien creatures infiltrating society.

Only three more novels appeared in the next two decades and one, *The Universe Between*, was actually two long stories from 1951 tied together. Contact has been made with the Thresholders, beings that inhabit a different dimension than our own, a region few people can visit and return still sane. The protagonist is one such person, whose services become essential when something inadvertently angers these other beings, causing them to wage a war of terrorism against our home dimension. It is highly inventive, but without the polish that marks most of Nourse's work.

*The Bladerunner* is set in a future where access to medical care is strictly limited by government decree. The protagonist is a doctor who is secretly a member of the medical underground, dispensing care to those who do not qualify, hiding from the Health Control Police. The question of medical ethics is examined again, as well as public attitudes about access to health care, but Nourse is careful not to lose sight of the entertainment value of his story while directing our attention to the underlying issues. His most recent novel, *The Fourth Horseman*, chronicles the return of a deadly plague, and the desperate attempts required to avert a world-wide catastrophe. Although this is a perhaps overly familiar plot, Nourse's background and finely honed writing skills never fail in this riveting suspense thriller.

Nourse has also produced several first-rate short stories. "Brightside Crossing" is a brilliant description of the first expedition to successfully cross the sunward side of the planet Mercury, a story of human perseverance and courage that ranks with Jack London's "To Build a Fire" and Stephen Crane's "The Open Boat." "The Counterfeit Man" is a chilling mystery story about an alien disguised as a human being who has infiltrated a space crew in order to reach the Earth. Nourse examines another ethical problem in "The Martyr," posing the question of whether or not those with the most to contribute to society should have their lifespans artificially extended. Other stories of note include "Nightmare Brother," "Psi High," "Coffin Cure," and "Family Resemblance."

Nourse brings to science fiction a deep concern with serious issues of human interaction and the role of various institutions within society, and embellishes it with a strong attention to background detail whether it be from his medical expertise or research into the requirements of life in space. His strong narrative ability and clear, crisp style only serve to emphasize the fact that his all too infrequent offerings are both entertaining and thought-provoking.

—Don D'Ammassa

---

**NOWLAN, Philip Francis**. Also wrote as Frank Phillips. American. Born in Philadelphia, Pennsylvania, in 1888. Educated at the University of Pennsylvania, Philadelphia, B.A. 1910. Married Teresa Marie Junker; four daughters and six sons. Worked for *Public Ledger, North American*, and *Retail Ledger;* collaborated with Dick Calkins on first science-fiction comic strip, *Buck Rogers*, 1929–40. *Died 1 February 1940.*

### Science-Fiction Publications

Novel

*Armageddon 2419 A. D.* New York, Avalon, 1962; London, Panther, 1976.

Uncollected Short Stories

"The Onslaught from Venus" (as Frank Phillips), in *Science Wonder Stories* (New York), September 1929.
"The Time Jumpers," in *Amazing* (New York), February 1934.
"The Prince of Mars Returns," in *Fantastic Adventures* (Chicago), February 1940.
"Space Guards," in *Astounding* (New York), May 1940.

### Other Publications

Other

*Buck Rogers on the Moons of Saturn.* Racine, Wisconsin, Whitman, 1934.
*Buck Rogers in the Dangerous Mission.* New York, Blue Ribbon Press, 1934.
*Buck Rogers and the Depth Men of Jupiter.* Racine, Wisconsin, Whitman, 1935.
*Buck Rogers, 25th Century, Featuring Buddy and Allura in "Strange Adventures of the Spider Ship."* Chicago, Pleasure, 1935.
*Buck Rogers, 25th Century A.D., in the Interplanetary War with Venus.* Racine, Wisconsin, Whitman, 1938.
*Buck Rogers in the 25th Century 1–2, 7–8.* Ann Arbor, Michigan, Ed Aprill, 4 vols., 1964–68.
*The Collected Works of Buck Rogers in the 25th Century,* with Dick Calkins and Rick Yager, edited by Robert C. Dille. New York, Bonanza, 1969; revised edition, New York, A and W, 1977.

* * *

Although not as well known as Edgar Rice Burroughs or E.E. Smith, Philip Francis Nowlan was probably their equal both as a writer and as an influence on modern science fiction. In his first story, "Armageddon 2419 A.D." (*Amazing*, August 1928), he introduced perhaps the most popular character in the history of the genre, Anthony, or as he was later known, Buck Rogers. Over the decades that followed Nowlan and others scripted innumerable Buck Rogers comic strips. Several films and a successful television series are proof of Buck Rogers's continuing appeal.

In "Armageddon 2419 A.D." Anthony Rogers, an engineer exploring a Pennsylvania mine in 1929, is caught in a cave-in and placed in suspended animation. Awakening in the 25th century, he discovers that the United States is now ruled by Mongolians and that Americans live in scattered communities, hiding from the conquerers who consider them vermin. The Mongolians, or Hans, a decadent, heartless race, rarely leave their cities and rely on huge airships equipped with disintegrator rays to maintain their dominance. Rogers has appeared at an opportune moment, for the Americans, armed with newly developed anti-gravity devices and rocket guns, are preparing to revolt. Contributing a knowledge of 20th-century military tactics and a certain primitive blood-thirstiness, Rogers soon becomes a leader in the struggle. The American conquest is completed in Nowlan's sequel, "The Airlords of Han." (The two stories were combined in the 1962 book *Armageddon 2419 A.D.*) Although flawed by occasionally awkward language and handicapped by the poorly considered choice of a first-person narrator, the Anthony Rogers stories stand up quite well even today. The action moves smoothly and the various military inventions and tactics are intriguing. The stories are touched by the racism so common in 1920's pulp fiction but, interestingly, are extremely progressive in their treatment of women. Wilma Deering, although occasionally given to the fainting spells and fits of weeping which were *de riguer* for women in popular fiction, is in general more competent and active than any female character in science fiction prior to Joanna Russ's Alyx.

"The Onslaught from Venus" is a first-person account by a member of the Airguard (the military arm of the Supernational Commission of the Caucasian League) who, captured by the invading Venusians, first studies their civilization and then, escaping, helps destroy it. Again the story is largely taken up with inventive weaponry and tactics. The Venusians, who seem quite human except for their skin color, are, like the Hans, totally evil, totally decadent. They are incapable of even considering coexistence and their complete extermination is thus a necessity.

Nowlan published little science fiction in the years that followed. His final story, and, after "Armageddon 2419 A.D.," probably his best, was "Space Guards." In this tale the narrator and his commanding officer, another of Nowlan's capable women, are searching the jungles of Venus for the headquarters of the criminal mastermind Tiger Madden. They're captured by tribesmen who, again, are totally human except for their skin color. Converting the natives to their side, the two Earth people defeat Madden's troops in battle and then infiltrate his city. Eventually they kidnap the villain and escape under fire. The narrator saves his commander's life, disobeying her direct order to abandon her. She at first considers court-martialing him but then, as the story closes, decides to marry him instead. Despite its silly ending and its somewhat old-fashioned plotting, "Space Guards" is an interesting and exciting story.

Philip Nowlan was a talented writer, and, despite his small output, he is one of the most influential science-fiction writers of the Gernsback era.

—Michael M. Levy

---

**NYE, Harold G.** *See* **HARDING, Lee.**

---

**O'BRIEN, Clancy.** *See* **SMITH, George H.**

---

**O'DONNELL, K.M.** *See* **MALZBERG, Barry N.**

---

**O'DONNELL, Kevin, Jr.** American. Born in Cleveland, Ohio, 29 November 1950. Educated at schools in Cleveland and Fairview Park; Seoul Foreign School, Korea, graduated 1968; Yale University, New Haven, Connecticut, 1968–72, B.A. in Chinese studies 1972. Married Lillian Tchang in 1974. Assistant lecturer in English, Hong Kong Baptist College, 1972–73, and American English Language Institute, Taipei, Taiwan, 1973–74. Since 1976, freelance writer. Managing editor, 1979–81, and publisher, 1981–83, *Empire,* New Haven, Connecticut. Agent: Howard Morhaim Literary Agency, 175 Fifth Avenue, New York, New York, 10010, U.S.A.

SCIENCE-FICTION PUBLICATIONS

Novels (series: McGill Feighan)

*Bander Snatch.* New York, Bantam, 1979.
*Mayflies.* New York, Berkley, 1979.
*Caverns* (Feighan). New York, Berkley, 1981.
*Reefs* (Feighan). New York, Berkley, 1981.
*War of Omission.* New York, Bantam, 1982.
*Lava* (Feighan). New York, Berkley, 1982.
*ORA: CLE.* New York, Berkley, 1984; London, Grafton, 1986.
*Cliffs* (Feighan). New York, Berkley, 1986.
*The Shelter,* with Mary Kittredge. New York, Tor, 1987.
*Fire on the Border.* New York, Roc, 1990.

OTHER PUBLICATIONS

Other

*The Electronic Money Machine,* with the Haven Group. New York, Avon, 1984.

*

Kevin O'Donnell, Jr., comments:

When I write, I want the eventual readers to enjoy themselves; to think about themselves, others, and the future; and to feel at the end that they have experienced something worthwhile.

In one sense, science fiction is the opportunity to sample, vicariously and in advance, the consequences of choices human beings are making right now. I do not pretend to be a prophet, but I do attempt to depict potential futures, and those futures should ring as true to life as possible. Thus I stress verisimilitude in my writing, which poses a special challenge, since, by definition, what I write about has not happened yet, and probably never will. Before the words go on the paper, I have already spent a great deal of time trying to answer to my own satisfaction the question "What would it *really* be like if—?"

I give equal weight to characterization. Stereotypes are easy to work with—cardboard characters shuffle as easily as a deck of cards—but real people tangled in the webwork of their families, their friends, their pasts, and their present predicaments interest me much more than do mighty-thewed heroes or black-hearted villains. Don't get me wrong. I *like* heroes and villains. I also like shades of grey.

* * *

Possessed of one of the more entertaining new voices of science fiction, Kevin O'Donnell, Jr., infuses familiar SF themes and concepts with his own eager tone, the voice of the born storyteller. Among his shorter pieces, six have been recommended for Nebula awards: "A Matter of Pride" (in *Analog,* October 1973), a serious tale of epidemiology and prisoners of war, "Low Grade Ore" (in *Isaac Asimov's Science Fiction Anthology 1* edited by George H. Scithers, New York, Davis, 1978) and "Temple Guardian" (in *The Future at War 2* edited by Reginald Bretnor, New York, Ace, 1980), two stories of alien invaders, a time travel short called "The Gift of Prometheus" (in *Analog,* January 1978), a humorous story of censorship-via-computer, "Judo and the Art of Self-Government" (in *Laughing Space* edited by Isaac Asimov and J.D Jeppson, Boston, Houghton Mifflin, and London, Robson, 1982), and "Marchianna" (in *The Best of Omni Science Fiction 4* edited by Ben Bova and Don Myros, New York, Omni, 1982), of robots and asteroid mining. Emotional constants in O'Donnell's work are reliance upon individual strengths and the saving love of friends whether human or alien, and a suspicion of the corporate and bureaucratic. Humor is often achieved through a Chaplinesque stumbling over a plethora of detail.

His best-known work, *Mayflies,* uses two familiar themes: the hero interfaced with a computer and the generation starship. O'Donnell fuses these with energy and enthusiasm to create the memorable image of the immortal captain and controlling entity of a starship taking his human cargo across a thousand year voyage, observing them with mingled compassion and disdain for their "mayfly" existence. Like a gardener, he cultivates, prunes, limits, and stimulates, and all the while we get an eerie sense of a human slowly developing into something *other* over the centuries. A similar tension between the hermetic and the oceanic pervades *ORA: CLE,* where the hero, Mr. Ale Elatey (AL L80) is linked by brain implant to a network of thousands of computer experts but never leaves the high-rise apartment where he and his wife live through their contacts on the network, and through other communication systems. As *Mayflies* may be said to reevaluate the experience of Heinlein's *Universe* and McCaffrey's *The Ship Who Sang, ORA: CLE* may be viewed as finding new possibilities in the closed environment of Silverberg's *The World Inside.*

O'Donnell's most ambitious project is the light-hearted Adventures of McGill Feighan, an open-ended series of picaresque travels among alien worlds by means of "flinging," a teleportation technique of which McGill is a rare possessor. The first four volumes in the series—*Caverns, Reefs, Lava,* and *Cliffs*—explore the intricacies of McGill's talent, human-alien encounter, the menace of a mob-like crime syndicate so powerfully parasitic it takes steps not to kill its host culture, and McGill's search for the Far Being, source of his flinging talent. Here, O'Donnell's ability to compel sympathetic interest in his anomalous young hero helps him skirt the many improbabilities of the story line. Billed as "techno-fantasy," the inventive series shows a talent for humorous dialogue increasingly matched by pacing of incident and character development. A young writer still, O'Donnell shows great creative promise.

—Thomas P. Dunn

---

**OFFUTT, Andrew J(efferson V.).** Also writes as John Cleve. American. Born in Louisville, Kentucky, 16 August 1934 (?). Educated at the University of Louisville, B.A. in English 1955, M.A. in history, Ph.D. in psychology. Married Mary Joe McCarney McCabe in 1958; two daughters and two sons. Sales agent, Procter and Gamble, 1957–62; agency manager, Coastal States Life Insurance Company, Lexington, Kentucky, 1963–68; insurance agent, Andrew Offutt Associates, 1968–71. Since 1971, full-time writer: author of over 100 works under pseudonym John Cleve and others. Treasurer, 1973–76, and president, 1976–78, Science Fiction Writers of America. Recipient: *If* prize, 1954. Address: Funny Farm, Haldeman, Kentucky 40329, U.S.A.

SCIENCE-FICTION PUBLICATIONS

Novels

*The Castle Keeps.* New York, Berkley, 1972; London, Magnum, 1978.
*Messenger of Zhuvastou.* New York, Berkley, 1973; London, Magnum, 1977.
*Ardor on Aros.* New York, Dell, 1973.
*The Galactic Rejects* (for children). New York, Lothrop, 1973.
*The Genetic Bomb,* with D. Bruce Berry. New York, Warner, 1975.
*Chieftain of Andor.* New York, Dell, 1976; as *Clansman of Andor,* London, Magnum, 1978.
*My Lord Barbarian.* New York, Ballantine, 1977; London, Magnum, 1979.
*King Dragon.* New York, Ace, 1980.
*Shadowspawn* (Thieves' World 4). New York, Ace, 1987.

Novels as John Cleve (series: Spaceways in all books)

*Of Alien Bondage.* New York, Berkley, 1982.
*Corundum's Woman.* New York, Berkley, 1982.
*Escape from Macho.* New York, Berkley, 1982.
*Satana Enslaved.* New York, Berkley, 1982.
*Master of Misfit.* New York, Berkley, 1982.
*Plunder.* New York, Berkley, 1982.
*The Manhuntress.* New York, Berkley, 1982.
*Under Twin Suns.* New York, Berkley, 1982.
*In Quest of Qalara.* New York, Berkley, 1983.
*The Yoke of Shen.* New York, Berkley, 1983.
*Star Slaver,* with G.C. Edmondson. New York, Berkley, 1983.
*The Iceworld Connection.* New York, Berkley, 1983.
*Jonuta Rising.* New York, Berkley, 1983.
*Assignment: Hellhole.* New York, Berkley, 1983.
*Starship Sapphire.* New York, Berkley, 1984.
*The Planet Murderer.* New York, Berkley, 1984.
*The Carnadyne Horde.* New York, Berkley, 1984.
*Race Across the Stars.* New York, Berkley, 1984.
*King of the Slavers.* New York, Berkley, 1985.
*Saladin's Spy.* New York, Grove Press, 1986.

Short Stories

*Evil Is Live Spelled Backwards.* New York, Paperback Library, 1970.

OTHER PUBLICATIONS

Novels

*The Great 24-Hour Thing.* Los Angeles, Orpheus Press, 1971.
*Operation: Super Ms.* New York, Berkley, 1974.
*Sword of the Gael.* New York, Zebra, 1975; London, Sphere, 1977.
*The Undying Wizard.* New York, Zebra, 1976.
*Demon in the Mirror,* with Richard K. Lyon. New York, Pocket Books, 1977.
*Sign of the Moonbow.* New York, Zebra, 1977.
*The Mists of Doom.* New York, Zebra, 1977.
*Conan and the Sorcerer.* New York, Grosset and Dunlap, 1978.
*Conan, The Sword of Skelos.* New York, Bantam, 1979.
*The Iron Lords.* New York, Harcourt Brace, 1979.
*Shadows of Hell.* New York, Berkley, 1980.
*Conan the Mercenary* (includes *Conan and the Sorcerer*). London, Sphere, 1980; *Conan the Mercenary* published New York, Ace, 1981.
*When Death Birds Fly,* with Keith Taylor. New York, Ace, 1980.
*The Eyes of Sarsis,* with Richard K. Lyon. New York, Pocket Books, 1980.
*Web of the Spider,* with Richard K. Lyon. New York, Pocket Books, 1981.
*The Tower of Death,* with Keith Taylor. New York, Ace, 1982.
*The Lady of the Snowmist.* New York, Ace, 1983.
*Deathknight.* New York, Ace, 1990.

Other

Editor, *Swords Against Darkness 1–5.* New York, Zebra, 5 vols., 1977–79.

* * *

Many science fiction and fantasy writers can be categorized according to the particular sub-genre in which they write. Andrew J. Offutt (who often has his name set as andrew j. offutt), however, must be discussed in several, for while he may be best known for socio-critical science fiction or heroic fantasy, he has also written satiric science fiction, at least one science-fiction novel for children, and—under the name John Cleve—science fiction with a good deal of sex and exploitation in it.

Much of Offutt's early science fiction was obviously social criticism. *The Castle Keeps,* for example, is set in the same not-too-distant dystopian future as quite a bit of other science fiction.

The world of *The Castle Keeps* is over-populated and poisonously polluted, and the society has devolved toward barbarism. The Andrews's home in the country is heavily fortified, and there is constant danger of being overrun by roving bands of looters and killers. In the city, the Caudills live inside a sealed-up apartment building from which they seldom emerge; outside, in spite of the official agencies, gangs are a threat by day and all-powerful by night. Throughout the novel, there are signs of how we, mid-20th-century Americans, got there.

Offutt can also write humorous science fiction and fantasy, often with a satiric bite. Short stories like "For Value Received" and "Population Implosion" satirize, among other things, one of Offutt's favorite targets, the medical profession. In "For Value Received," for example, he refers to the AMA as the American Magicians Association. In this story, Bob Barber is told that he cannot take his new baby daughter home before he pays the difference between what his insurance covers and the total bill. He refuses to do so, and Mary Ann Barber grows up in Saint Meinrad Medical Center. In 1970, he published an entire collection of satiric short stories under the title *Evil is Live Spelled Backwards.* And *Ardor on Aros* is a humorous look at the heroic fantasy that Offutt himself seriously writes.

Offutt's heroic fantasy comes in two groups. The first group includes those stories which are essentially his own constructions, like *Messenger of Zhuvastou.* Scion Mark Keniston follows a beautiful woman, Elaine Dixon, supposedly his fianceé, to Helene, a planet which is the approximate cultural equivalent of early Imperial Rome. Because the planet is insulated from contact with more technologically advanced civilizations, Keniston must "go native" to follow Elaine onto the planet's surface. Disguised as an official messenger of the most powerful domain on the planet, Keniston sets out on his quest. The description of the planet and the portrayal of the heroic adventure are well-integrated so that the reader is able to envision quite clearly the world through which Keniston makes his way.

The second group of heroic fantasies, which seems to be occupying an increasing amount of Offutt's time, is based on characters created by Robert E. Howard. In fact, Offutt has selected one, Cormac mac Art, for extended consideration, and he admits, in the introduction to *Sword of the Gael*, that he is a Robert E. Howard fan and also "hopelessly in love with the Emerald Isle." This happy combination unites the heroic-age hero with a perfect historical setting, the Celtic/Viking period. Offutt skillfully mixes historical material from his own research with the literary history created by Howard to provide a cogent background for the adventures of Cormac mac Art and his Viking comrade, Wulfhere Skull-Splitter.

In addition to creating his own original work, Offutt also collaborates with and edits the work of other writers. Editing the *Swords Against Darkness* series was a natural outgrowth of his love for Robert E. Howard's work. His collaboration with Robert Asprin, Lynn Abbey, C.J. Cherryh, and the other contributors to the *Thieves' World* collections of short stories all set in the same imaginary world has led to a number of short stories and at least one novel in that series.

Offutt deserves a wider and more substantial reputation than he currently has. Although much of his work has been called "slick" or "action/adventure without much depth," Offutt is a writer who has shown in *The Castle Keeps* and elsewhere that he can write with depth and is also a writer who can tell a good action/adventure story, one that does not seem to have come out of the same tired formula mill that lesser writers use. Offutt's output is tremendous, and not all of it is science fiction or fantasy; in fact, many feel that not enough of it is science fiction and fantasy.

—C.W. Sullivan III

---

**OLIVER, (Symmes) Chad(wick).** American. Born in Cincinnati, Ohio, 30 March 1928. Educated at the University of Texas, Austin, B.A. 1951, M.A. in English and anthropology 1952; University of California, Los Angeles, Ph.D. in anthropology 1961. Married Betty Jane Jenkins in 1952; two children. Instructor, 1955–59, Assistant Professor, 1959–62, Associate Professor, 1963–68, Department Chairman, 1967–71 and since 1980, Professor of Anthropology, University of Texas. Visiting Professor, University of California, Los Angeles, summer 1960; Research Anthropologist, National Science Foundation in East Africa, 1961–62. Recipient: Western Writers of America Spur award, 1967. Address: Department of Anthropology, University of Texas, Austin, Texas 78712–1086, U.S.A.

### Science-Fiction Publications

#### Novels

*Shadows in the Sun.* New York, Ballantine, 1954; London, Reinhardt, 1955.
*The Winds of Time.* New York, Doubleday, 1957.
*Unearthly Neighbors.* New York, Ballantine, 1960; revised edition, New York, Crown, 1984.
*The Shores of Another Sea.* New York, New American Library, and London, Gollancz, 1971.
*Giants in the Dust.* New York, Pyramid, 1976.

#### Short Stories

*Another Kind.* New York, Ballantine, 1955.
*The Edge of Forever*, edited by William F. Nolan. Los Angeles, Sherbourne Press, 1971.

### Other Publications

#### Novels

*The Wolf Is My Brother.* New York, New American Library, 1967; London, Jenkins, 1968.
*Broken Eagles.* New York, Bantam, 1989.

#### Other

*Mists of Dawn* (for children). Philadelphia, Winston, 1952; London, Hutchinson, 1954.
*Ecology and Cultural Continuity as Contributing Factors in the Social Organization of the Plains Indians.* Berkeley, University of California Press, 1962.
*The Discovery of Humanity: An Introduction to Anthropology.* New York, Harper, 1981.

*

Bibliography: by William F. Nolan, in *The Edge of Forever*, 1971.

Chad Oliver comments:

I wrote my first story when I was 14, and sold my first story (to Anthony Boucher of *The Magazine of Fantasy and Science Fiction*) when I was 22. I was a professional writer before I was an anthropologist, and I suspect that I still am. I grew up with science fiction and it has been an important part of my life.

I have written many kinds of stories and about all they have in common is that I always tried to write as well as I could. I am not interested in essays disguised as fiction; my stories are about people and my opinion is that if they don't work on an emotional level they don't work at all. I was strongly influenced by writers outside the science-fiction field, notably Hemingway and Steinbeck.

* * *

For a genre that deals freely in alien beings and cultures, science fiction has often shown a marked tendency toward simplistic anthropomorphism in handling such themes. Readers and editors who would demand the utmost verisimilitude in fiction dealing with the natural sciences often allowed the most naive applications of social science theory to pass unnoticed in science-fiction stories, and it was not until well into the 1950's that the social sciences began to take their place as serious thematic material in popular science fiction. While economics and sociology began to be treated with relative sophistication by Frederik Pohl and other satirists of the *Galaxy* magazine school, the credit for introducing well-thought-out anthropological themes into popular American science fiction of the 1950's rests almost solely with Chad Oliver. Himself a professional anthropologist, Oliver dealt with alien cultures, and the problems inherent in communicating with those cultures, in a series of sympathetic and plausible stories and novels that paved the way for later anthropological themes in such writers as Ursula K. LeGuin.

Oliver's fiction tends heavily toward exposition and didacticism, but his pleasant, relaxed style and understated, non-heroic characters work to make the lessons in cultural differentiation and values easily palatable. When he treats a traditional theme, such as the secret colonization of Earth by aliens in *Shadows in the Sun*, he is apt to undercut the reader's expectations by revealing early in the narrative the secret of the alien presence (in this novel, they have completely taken over a small town in Texas, without violence or murder), and focusing instead on the more complex and interesting problem of what their motivations and values are. The equally familiar theme of the generations-long space voyage, initially popularized by Robert Heinlein in "Universe," is given a new twist in Oliver's "Stardust" by the introduction of the problem of the culture shock that the spaceship inhabitants might face if the circumscribed environment that they have come to regard as the universe is suddenly revealed to be only a machine. A "first contact" story is also given a new twist, in "Scientific Method," by its simultaneous presentation from two opposing viewpoints. One of Oliver's favorite themes is the depiction of a "primitive" alien culture that is really advanced, but in radically different cultural terms from our own. This is the theme of "Rite of Passage" and *Unearthly Neighbors;* the latter may be the most carefully reasoned account of the problems of making contact with an alien culture in all of science fiction.

Much of Oliver's fiction clearly draws on his own experiences—his familiarity with small-town Texas culture in *Shadows in the Sun*, his hobby of trout fishing in *The Winds of Time,* his experiences in Kenya in *The Shores of Another Sea.* In the last novel, particularly, the science-fiction theme seems to be decidedly secondary to the portrayal of life on a baboonery in the bush country of Kenya. Relatively few of his stories deal with future societies, and his portrayals of technologically advanced earth societies (as in *Unearthly Neighbors*) seem somewhat stilted and uncomfortable. His real strengths lie in the construction of hypothetical anthropological problems and his graceful, understated style. Although he has produced relatively little science fiction, what there is is valuable both for the specific insights it offers and for the importance it holds in the developing sophistication of the genre.

—Gary K. Wolfe

---

**OLSEN, Bob** (Alfred John Olsen, Jr.). American. Born in 1884. Educated at Brown University, Providence, Rhode Island, A.B. (Phi Beta Kappa). *Died 20 May 1956.*

SCIENCE-FICTION PUBLICATIONS

Short Stories

*Rhythm Rides the Rocket.* New York, Columbia, 1940.

Uncollected Short Stories (series: Four Dimensional; Justin Pryor)

"Four Dimensional Surgery," in *Amazing* (New York), February 1928.
"Four Dimensional Robberies," in *Amazing* (New York), May 1928.
"The Educated Pill," in *Amazing* (New York), July 1928.
"Four Dimensional Transit," in *Amazing Stories Quarterly* (New York), Fall 1928.
"The Superperfect Bride," in *Amazing* (New York), July 1929.
"Flight in 1999," in *Air Wonder Stories* (New York), September 1929.
"The Phantom Teleview," in *Science Wonder Stories* (New York), November 1929.
"Cosmic Trash," in *Science Wonder Stories* (New York), April 1930.
"The Man Who Annexed the Moon," in *Amazing* (New York), February 1931.
"The Master of Mystery" (Pryor), in *Amazing* (New York), October 1931.
"The Ant with a Human Soul," in *Amazing Stories Quarterly* (New York), Spring-Summer 1932.
"Seven Sunstrokes" (Pryor), in *Amazing* (New York), April 1932.
"The Purple Monsters," in *Amazing* (New York), August 1932.
"Captain Brink of the Space Marines," in *Amazing* (New York), November 1932.
"The Pool of Death" (Pryor), in *Amazing* (New York), January 1933.
"The Crime Crusher," in *Amazing* (New York), June 1933.
"The Four Dimensional Escape," in *Amazing* (New York), July 1934.
"Peril among the Drivers," in *Amazing* (New York), March 1934.
"The Four Dimensional Auto-Parker," in *Amazing* (New York), July 1934.
"Noekken of Norway," in *Amazing* (New York), November 1934.
"Six-Legged Gangsters," in *Amazing* (New York), June 1935.

"The Isle of Juvenescence," in *Amazing* (New York), June 1936.
"The Space Marines and the Slavers," in *Amazing* (New York), December 1936.
"The Scourge of a Single Cell," in *Science Fiction* (Holyoke, Massachusetts), March 1940.
"Our Robot Maid," in *Future* (New York), November 1940.
"The Four Dimensional Roller-Press," in *Every Boy's Book of Science Fiction*, edited by Donald A. Wollheim. New York, Fell, 1951.
"The Drawbridge Horror," in *Phantom* (Bolton, Lancashire), July 1958.

* * *

Bob Olsen was among the earliest protégés of the editor Hugo Gernsback, who introduced him to *Amazing Stories* readers in 1927 and was soon pronouncing him "the possessor of a fertile mind with a turn for good writing." He begins with a series of ingenious treatments of the fourth dimension theme, to which he returned more than once in the course of earning a reputation over the next decade as a "distinguished" contributor, if only on account of his consistent popularity.

Some of his early offerings were more like popular lectures than stories, most of the dialogue emanating from his scientist hero, Professor Archimedes Banning, in "Four Dimension Transit" and "The Man Who Annexed the Moon"—a tale of the first lunar voyage, fairly typical of the period, which today seems uncannily predictive. Another stock character, Justin Pryor, a merchandising counsellor with a yen for criminal investigation, was featured in "The Master of Mystery" and "Seven Sunstrokes." An outstanding story was "The Ant with a Human Soul," in which the subject of a bizarre experiment in brain transference relates his experiences while "going native" among the ants. Two years later, the author treated much the same idea to greater effect, with more human interest and less text-book detail, in "Peril Among the Drivers." And in "Six-Legged Gangsters," he told a simple story of formicary antics from the viewpoint of the insects themselves. He was also fascinated by the amoeba, a voracious specimen of which lurked in "The Pool of Death," another Justin Pryor mystery. It was to be found in its natural surroundings in "Noekken of Norway," which clearly betrayed the author's Scandinavian antecedents. And the amoeba-men of Titan were the villains "Captain Brink of the Space Marines" had to contend with.

In a mood close to satire, in "The Purple Monsters" he made light of an invasion of New York by nightmarish giants from Ganymede. "The Crime Crusher" brought criminals to book with a device which photographed their misdeeds in retrospect; and "The Four Dimensional Auto-Parker" offered a solution to a problem which, even in 1934, vexed Los Angeles motorists. By that time, Olsen had also added jailbreaking to the list of possibilities—including surgery and bank robbery—presented by the exploitation of hyperspace.

—Walter Gillings

---

**O'NEILL, Joseph (James).** Also wrote as Seosamh O'Neill. Irish. Born in Tuam, County Galway, 18 December 1878. Educated at St. Jarlath's College, Tuam, 1893–98; Queen's College, Galway, 1898–1901, B.A., M.A. in modern literature; Kuno Meyer's School of Irish Learning; Victoria College, Manchester; University of Freiburg, 1907. Married Mary Devenport in 1908. Taught at Queen's College, Galway, 1901–03; staff member, Department of Secondary Education: Inspector of Schools, from 1908, and Permanent Secretary, 1923–44; also civil service commissioner and local appointments commissioner, 1926–46. Recipient: Irish Academy of Letters Harmsworth award, 1935. Member, Irish Academy of Letters. *Died 6 May 1952.*

SCIENCE-FICTION PUBLICATIONS

Novels

*Wind from the North.* London, Cape, 1934.
*Land under England.* London, Gollancz, and New York, Simon and Schuster, 1935.
*Day of Wrath.* London, Gollancz, 1936.

OTHER PUBLICATIONS

Novels

*Philip.* London, Gollancz, 1940.
*Chosen by the Queen.* London, Gollancz, 1947.

Play

*The Kingdom-Maker* (as Seosamh O'Neill), lyrics by Mary Devenport O'Neill. Dublin, Talbot Press, and London, Unwin, 1918.

* * *

Joseph O'Neill wrote five novels, a play, some criticism, some poetry and a few scholarly papers. Of his novels, three may be regarded as science fiction, though the connection is sometimes tenuous. *Wind from the North* is a well-written time-travel story of Norsemen in Dublin in the 11th century; the emphasis is on the conflict between the hero's 11th-century and 20th-century selves. *Day of Wrath* is a prophetic potboiler about an airwar involving "the Yellow Alliance" and Nazi aggressors against Russia, "the Latin Alliance," and, eventually, Great Britain and the United States; the aftermath of its poison gas and thermite bombs is a vivid picture of the breakdown of civilized behavior, but it is not especially exciting either as science fiction or as novel.

*Land under England* is a work of power that was justly well received when first published and then almost forgotten until recently. It is doubtless worth noting that of all O'Neill's works only this one—despite the fact that *Wind from the North* received the Harmsworth award—was widely reviewed, and that only this one has been reprinted. Even so, except for passing references critical evaluation of the work is largely confined to reviews that appeared in 1935.

Part of the attraction of the novel is the development from an almost innocent beginning through an adventurous though fantastic journey into a world of horror that gradually becomes prophetic of doom not only for the protagonist but for the world at large. The story begins with devices like those of second-rate fantasy: the Julians are an old family tracing their origins back to Roman Britain; they live along the Roman Wall on property believed to possess the entrance to an underground world. There are half-believed stories of ancestors who have disappeared and returned with stories of a strange land beyond the mysterious entrance. Anthony Julian, the narrator, is the only child of two dramatically opposite types both of whom believe in the old legends, his father in the years following World War I, to the point of obsession; when he disappears, both wife and son are convinced that he has found the entrance. Tony, whose hero-worship of his father is the driving force of the book, is equally convinced that he will some day be found.

Tony's accidental discovery of the entrance in a dried-up pond and unhesitating plunge down the slope into the underworld are the obvious and expected result of what has gone before. What is not obvious or expected is what happens thereafter, and it is in this respect that the novel departs from the ordinary to become something of a minor masterpiece.

In this underground world are many curious, strange, and frequently alarming creatures, both plant and animal. But nothing is more curious, strange, or alarming than its human inhabitants. At first encounter they appear to be civilized and enough like the ancient Romans who had inhabited the land above that Tony speaks to them in Latin, but there is no reply and he realizes that all communication is through some kind of mind talk. When his early failure to understand this causes the master of the ship on which he first takes refuge to regard him as ill, and curable only by the Masters of Will and of Knowledge to whom he is sent; he soon learns that in this different and horrifying society control is through the minds of a few leaders who work their will on the rest of the populace. The remainder of the story deals with Tony's unceasing efforts to locate his father, to understand the ways of this fearful society, and eventually, his father obviously lost to him forever, to undertake the grueling flight back to the upper world.

If one pays attention only to the monstrous plants and animals and the even more monstrous leaders of the underworld society, *Land under England* remains only a good fantastic adventure. But if one remembers the time when it was written, it becomes a warning of the future that the totalitarian societies of the 1930's, especially that of Nazi Germany, might bring to England. When taken together with the search for self in *Wind from the North* and the polemical picture of brute mankind when the veneer of civilization is removed in *Day of Wrath*, it provides evidence of O'Neill's continuing effort to understand the hidden drives and motivations that still plague humanity. There are political and psychological aspects to this almost allegorical tale that move it to a higher level than most such works of the time, and O'Neill can justly be regarded as a minor but significant figure whose work prefigures the kind of social science fiction and fantasy that became prominent in the immediate postwar years.

—Arthur O. Lewis

---

**ORE, Rebecca** (Rebecca B. Brown). Also writes as Rebecca Brown. American. Born in Louisville, Kentucky, in 1948. Educated at Columbia University, 1968–72, B.A. 1979; University of North Carolina at Charlotte, M.A. in English 1980; State University of New York, Albany, 1980–82. Worked as editorial secretary or assistant, New York City, 1968–72; part-time secretary, San Francisco, 1975–76; reporter, *The Patriot*, Patrick County, Virginia, 1976–77; office assistant, New York City, 1977–78. Agent: Donald Maas, 64 West 84th Street, New York, New York, 10024. Address: P.O. Box 129, Critz, Virginia 24082-0129, U.S.A.

### Science-Fiction Publications

Novels (series: The Alien)

*Becoming Alien: Ben Bova's Discoveries.* New York, Tor, 1988.
*Being Alien.* New York, Tor, 1989.
*Human to Human* (Alien). New York, Tor, 1990.
*The Illegal Rebirth of Billy the Kid.* New York, Tor, 1991.

### Other Publications

Verse as Rebecca Brown

*Mouseworks.* New York, Siamese Banana Press, 1971.
*The Bicycle Trip and Poems.* New York, Telephone Books, 1974.
*For the 82nd Airborne.* New York, Adventures in Poetry Press, 1978.
*The Barbarian Queen.* New York, Telephone Press, 1981.

* * *

In half a decade, Rebecca Ore has established herself as a significant writer of science fiction. Ore turned to writing science fiction after writing poetry, plays, and memoirs, and editing, including for a publisher of science fact and for the Science Fiction Book Club. In 1986, two novelettes were published in *Amazing Science Fiction*: "Projectile Weapons and Wild Alien Water," in May (under the name Rebecca Brown), and "The Tyrant that I Serve," in September (under the name Rebecca Brown Ore). In July of 1988, *Amazing* published a third novelette, "Ice-Gouged Lakes, Glacier-Bound Times," which, like her subsequent novels, is under the name Rebecca Ore. In 1987 and 1988, Ore was a nominee for the John W. Campbell award for best new science-fiction writer. Ore is probably best known for her series of three novels, *Becoming Alien*, *Being Alien*, and *Human to Human.*

All of Ore's science fiction combines genre values, such as scientific extrapolation, with mainstream literary values, especially concerning character development. Her work is also notable for its presentation of non-humans who are consistent, sympathetic characters but do not simply react like human beings. In the Alien novels, an interplanetary federation accuses humans of being "xenoflips," xenophobes who see aliens as either threat or salvation, but cannot see them as equal, though different. Clearly, this is an indictment of much science fiction; by example, Ore's novels show that other ways of conceptualizing aliens are not only possible, but useful.

The scientific background in Ore's work is strong, especially but not exclusively concerning biology. In the three Alien novels, sapient evolution is limited to those species whose binocular vision created a larger brain: the bat-like Gwyng, a number of species based on birds, and evolved apes, including the human species. This restriction may be frustrating for some readers, used to tentacles and more; but it allows Ore to develop realistic species-differences, in keeping with the characteristics and ecological niches they sprang from. In *The Illegal Rebirth of Billy the Kid* and "The Tyrant that I Serve," Ore depicts a future in which bioengineering can create chimeras, human-looking or not, for government work or the amusement of the rich. Again, the ramifications are considered: What would the legal status of chimeras be? What kinds of chimeras would be made, to fulfill what human needs and wishes?

Similar social extrapolation concerns global cooling, in the Alien books and especially in *The Illegal Rebirth of Billy the Kid* and "Ice-Gouged Lakes, Glacier-Bound Time," in which the climatic change has reduced the United States to a second-rate world power. In the Alien books, star-travel is accomplished by "star-gates," about which Ore presents just enough scientific detail to be convincing. Her novels are pervaded by the feeling that technology creates psyche and society as much as the other way around; the genre of science fiction allows her to deal with technology in detail, whether it is future medicine or contemporary moonshining, alien architecture or human bicycling.

Much of the Earth-based action in Ore's fiction takes place in rural Virginia, an area from which Ore's family comes and in which she now lives. Tom Gentry, the protagonist of the Alien books, is a drug-dealing, high school student who feels cut off from those around him, until he joins the federation in which everyone is an alien. In *The Illegal Rebirth of Billy the Kid*, the chimera, made in imitation of Billy the Kid, finally finds a home on a historical preserve near Roanoke. Another noteworthy setting on Earth is the still-leftist, near-future Berkeley, California, in *Being Alien.*

Satisfying on the levels of plot, characterization, and speculation, Ore's works are thematically interesting as well. By defining the non-human—alien or chimera—Ore also approaches the question of what it means to be human. In the Alien books, Tom's body-language is described in the same clinical terms as that of the other species; in a sense, Tom becomes alien himself, so that the reader can experience her or his own humanity in a new way. In these books, Ore also depicts multiple languages, each with its own limitations and ways of knowing, which force both the characters and the readers to consider, as Tom puts it in *Human to Human*, "the meaning of meaning." *The Illegal Rebirth of Billy the Kid* raises questions of status and privilege, inequality and relative power. It also has much to say about the interactive process of myth and reality, the ways in which both the chimera and the historical Billy created their images and yet were created by them.

If Ore's fiction can be compared to anyone else's, it is probably that of Ursula LeGuin, who also strives rigorously to create alien societies and uses them to explore human concerns while maintaining the alien strangeness. In fact, "Ice-Gouged Lakes, Glacier-Bound Times" features a journey by a human and an alien across a cold landscape, in homage to LeGuin's *The Left Hand of Darkness.* Other influences include C. J. Cherryh, James Triptree, Jr., and Joanna Russ.

Ore's fiction both "gently subverts the tropes of SF" and also fulfills genre qualifications, as Ore has noted. Her characters are not predictable, always (if not flawlessly) fully realized as individuals. The futures she presents are neither utopian nor dystopian; they show a strong sense of history, a sense of what aspects of life change and which do not. For this reason alone, her work would deserve attention, within and outside the science-fiction community.

—Bernadette Bosky

---

**ORWELL, George.** Pseudonym for Eric Arthur Blair. British. Born of English parents in Motihari, Bengal, India, 25 June 1903; brought to England, 1904. Educated at a convent school, Henley-on-Thames, Oxfordshire; St. Cyprian's, Eastbourne, Sussex, 1911–16; Wellington School, 1917; Eton College (King's Scholar), 1917–21. Served in the United Marxist Workers' Party militia in Catalonia, 1937: wounded in action; served in the Home Guard, 1940–43: Sergeant. Married 1) Eileen O'Shaughnessy in 1936 (died 1945), one adopted son; 2) Sonia Mary Brownell in 1949. Served in the Imperial Indian Police in Burma: at Police Training School, Rangoon, 1922–23, assistant superintendent of police at Myaungmya, 1923, Twante, 1924, Syriam, 1925, Insein, 1925–26, Moulmein, 1926, and Katha, 1927 (resigned 1927); lived in London, 1927, and Paris, 1928–29 (worked briefly as dishwasher, 1929); tutor, Southwold, Suffolk, 1930; lived in London, 1930–31; headmaster, The Hawthorns, Hayes, Middlesex, 1932–33, and teacher at Frays College, Uxbridge, 1933; worked at Booklovers' Corner bookshop, London, 1934–36; shopkeeper, Wallingford, Hertfordshire, 1936–40; talks producer in the Empire Department, BBC, London, 1941–43. Freelance writer from 1935: reviewer, *New English Weekly*, 1935–36, *Time and Tide*, 1940-41, *Tribune*, 1940–47 (Literary Editor, 1943–45), and *Horizon*, 1940–49, all London; columnist ("London Letter"), *Partisan Review*, New York, 1941–46; editor, with T.R. Fyvel, Searchlight Books series, Secker and Warburg, publishers, London, 1941–42; regular contributor, *Observer*, London, 1942–49 (war correspondent, 1945); columnist, Manchester *Evening News*, 1943–46. Lived on Jura, Hebrides Islands, Scotland, 1946–47. *Died 21 January 1950.*

### Science-Fiction Publications

#### Novel

*Nineteen Eighty-Four.* London, Secker and Warburg, and New York, Harcourt Brace, 1949; edited by Bernard Crick, Oxford, Oxford University Press, 1984.

### Other Publications

#### Novels

*Burmese Days.* New York, Harper, 1934; London, Gollancz, 1935.
*A Clergyman's Daughter.* London, Gollancz, and New York, Harper, 1935.
*Keep the Aspidistra Flying.* London, Gollancz, 1936; New York, Harcourt Brace, 1954.
*Coming Up for Air.* London, Gollancz, 1939; New York, Harcourt Brace, 1950.
*Animal Farm: A Fairy Story.* London, Secker and Warburg, 1945; New York, Harcourt Brace, 1946.

#### Plays

Radio Plays: *The Voyage of the Beagle*, from work by Darwin, 1946; *Animal Farm*, from his own novel, 1947.

#### Other

*Down and Out in Paris and London.* London, Gollancz, and New York, Harper, 1933.
*The Road to Wigan Pier.* London, Gollancz, 1937; New York, Harcourt Brace, 1958.
*Homage to Catalonia.* London, Secker and Warburg, 1938; New York, Harcourt Brace, 1952.
*Inside the Whale and Other Essays.* London, Gollancz, 1940.
*The Lion and the Unicorn: Socialism and the English Genius.* London, Secker and Warburg, 1941; New York, AMS Press, 1976.
*Critical Essays.* London, Secker and Warburg, 1946; as *Dickens, Dali and Others: Studies in Popular Culture*, New York, Reynal, 1946.

*James Burnham and the Managerial Revolution.* London, Socialist Book Centre, 1946.
*The English People.* London, Collins, 1947; New York, Haskell House, 1974.
*Shooting an Elephant and Other Essays.* London, Secker and Warburg, and New York, Harcourt Brace, 1950.
*Such, Such Were the Joys.* New York, Harcourt Brace, 1953; as *England, Your England and Other Essays*, London, Secker and Warburg, 1953.
*A Collection of Essays.* New York, Doubleday, 1954.
*The Orwell Reader*, edited by Richard H. Rovere. New York, Harcourt Brace, 1956.
*Selected Essays.* London, Penguin, 1957; as *Inside the Whale and Other Essays*, 1975.
*Selected Writings*, edited by George Bott. London, Heinemann, 1958.
*Collected Essays.* London, Secker and Warburg, 1961.
*Decline of English Murder and Other Essays.* London, Penguin, 1965.
*The Collected Essays, Journalism, and Letters of George Orwell*, edited by Sonia Orwell and Ian Angus. London, Secker and Warburg, 4 vols., 1968.
*The Complete Works.* New York, Harcourt Brace, 17 vols., 1984.
*The War Broadcasts* and *The War Commentaries*, edited by W.J. West. London, BBC Publications-Duckworth, 2 vols., 1985; as *George Orwell: The Lost Writings*, New York, Avon, 1988.

Editor, *Talking to India: A Selection of English Language Broadcasts to India.* London, Allen and Unwin, 1943.
Editor, with Reginald Reynolds, *British Pamphleteers 1: From the Sixteenth Century to the French Revolution.* London, Wingate, 1948.

*

Bibliography: "George Orwell: A Selected Bibliography" by Zoltan G. Zeke and William White, in *Bulletin of Bibliography 23* (Boston), May-August 1961; *George Orwell: An Annotated Bibliography of Criticism* by Jeffrey and Valerie Meyers, New York, Garland, 1977.

Manuscript Collection: University College, London.

Critical Studies (selection): *George Orwell* by Tom Hopkinson, London, Longman, 1953, revised edition, 1962; *George Orwell: A Literary Study* by John Atkins, London, Calder, 1954, New York, Ungar, 1955, revised edition, London, Calder and Boyars, 1971; *A Study of George Orwell, The Man and His Works* by Christopher Hollis, London, Hollis and Carter, and Chicago, Regnery, 1956; *The Crystal Spirit: A Study of George Orwell* by George Woodcock, Boston, Little Brown, 1966, London, Cape, 1967; *The Making of George Orwell: A Study in Literary History* by Keith Alldritt, London, Arnold, and New York, St. Martin's Press, 1969; *Orwell's Fiction* by Robert A. Lee, Notre Dame, Indiana, University of Notre Dame Press, 1969; *The World of George Orwell* edited by Miriam Gross, London, Weidenfeld and Nicolson, 1971, New York, Simon and Schuster, 1972; *Orwell* by Raymond Williams, London, Fontana, and New York, Viking Press, 1971, and *George Orwell: A Collection of Critical Essays* edited by Williams, Englewood Cliffs, New Jersey, Prentice Hall, 1974; *The Unknown Orwell* by Peter Stansky and William Abrahams, London, Constable, and New York, Knopf, 1972, *Orwell: The Transformation* by Stansky, London, Constable, 1979, New York, Knopf, 1980, and *On Nineteen Eighty-Four* edited by Stansky, New York, Freeman, 1984; *A Reader's Guide to George Orwell*, London, Thames and Hudson, 1975, Totowa, New Jersey, Rowman and Littlefield, 1977, and *George Orwell: The Critical Heritage*, London, Routledge, 1975, both edited by Jeffrey Meyers; *George Orwell and the Origins of 1984* by William Steinhoff, Ann Arbor, University of Michigan Press, 1975, as *The Road to 1984*, London, Weidenfeld and Nicolson, 1975; *The Road to Miniluv: George Orwell, The State and God* by Christopher Small, London, Gollancz, 1975, Pittsburgh, University of Pittsburgh Press, 1976; *Primal Dream and Primal Scream: Orwell's Development as a Psychological Novelist* by Richard I. Smyer, Columbia, University of Missouri Press, 1979; *George Orwell: A Life* by Bernard Crick, London, Secker and Warburg, 1980, Boston, Little Brown, 1981, revised edition, Secker and Warburg, 1981, and *Orwell Remembered* by Crick and Audrey Coppard, London, BBC, and New York, Facts on File, 1984; *Approaching 1984* by Donald McCormick, Newton Abbot, Devon, David and Charles, 1980; *George Orwell: The Road to 1984* by Peter Lewis, London, Heinemann, 1981; *George Orwell: A Personal Memoir* by T.R. Fyvel, London, Weidenfeld and Nicolson, 1982; *A George Orwell Companion* by J.R. Hammond, London, Macmillan, and New York, St. Martin's Press, 1982; *George Orwell's Guide Through Hell: A Psychological Study of 1984* by Robert Plank, San Bernardino, California, Borgo Press, 1984; *Orwell: The Road to Airstrip One* by Ian Slater, New York, Norton, 1985; *George Orwell and the Problem of Authentic Existence* by Michael Carter, London, and Dover, New Hampshire, Croom Helm, 1985; *Critical Essays on George Orwell* edited by Bernard Oldsey, Boston, Hall, 1986; *Reflections on America, 1984: An Orwell Symposium* edited by Robert Mulvihill, Athens, University of Georgia Press, 1986; *George Orwell: The Age's Adversary*, New York, Macmillan, 1986, and *Nineteen Eighty-Four: Past, Present, and Future*, Boston, Twayne, 1989, both by Patrick Reilly; *A Preface to Orwell* by David Wykes, London, and New York, Longman, 1987; *The Diminished Self: Orwell and the Loss of Freedom* by Mark Connelly, Pittsburgh, Pennsylvania, Duquesne University Press, 1987; *George Orwell* edited by Courtney T. Wemyss and Alexej Ugrinsky, New York, Greenwood, 1987; *George Orwell* by Averil Gardner, Boston, Twayne, 1987; *George Orwell: A Reassessment* edited by Peter Buitenhuis and I.B. Nadel, New York, Macmillan, 1988; *Orwell and the Politics of Despair: A Critical Study of the Writings of George Orwell* by Alok Rai, Cambridge, Cambridge University Press, 1988; *George Orwell* by Nigel Flynn, Hove, Wayland, 1989, Vero Beach, Florida, Rourke, 1990; *The Politics of Literary Reputation: The Making and Claiming of "St. George Orwell"* by John Rodden, Oxford, Oxford University Press, 1990.

* * *

George Orwell's world-wide reputation as a writer of science fiction rests upon a single novel, *Nineteen Eighty-Four.* Such is the dynamic force of this work that the title of the book has become a universal symbol for the totalitarian nightmare. Although indisputably an SF novel, it differs from most other works in the genre by having an overt political purpose. In the author's own words, he desired "to push the world in a certain direction, to alter other people's idea of the kind of society they should strive after." His experiences while fighting alongside the Anarchists in the Spanish Civil War had opened his eyes to the "expedient inhumanities" that lay behind both international Communism and European Fascism. From now on in any conflict between the individual human being and the State, Orwell was always to be found on the side of the underdog. Orwell's international stature was first established with *Animal Farm*, a classic Swiftian satire on the Soviet experiment. The runaway success of this work ensured that his next book would be given wide critical attention. When *Nineteen Eighty-Four* first appeared, it was initially hailed in many quarters as a further trenchant indictment of Soviet Communism, though, in fact, it is an indictment of absolutism of whatsoever political hue. Its conception owes a great deal to Eugene Zamyatin's *We* which Orwell had first read in a French translation some 20 years previously.

The plot of *Nineteen Eighty-Four* is straightforward. The story follows the tragic fortues of Winston Smith, a minor civil servant, who lives and works in the London which has survived an atomic Third World War. This London is now the capital of Airstrip One, an off-shore province of Oceania, one of three constantly warring world-power blocs, Oceania, Eurasia, Eastasia. Under the absolute control of the Party and its Leader, Big Brother, the society of Oceania is stratified into the Inner Party (the rulers), the Party (the bureaucracy), and the rest (known collectively as the Proles). The complete ascendancy of the Party is symbolized by the four Ministries which dominate Winston Smith's decaying urban metropolis. These are, in order of significance, the Ministry of Love, the Ministry of Truth, the Ministry of Peace, and the Ministry of Plenty:

> The Ministry of Love was the really frightening one. There were no windows in it at all. Winston had never been inside the Ministry of Love, nor within half a kilometre of it. The place was impossible to enter except on official business, and then only by penetrating through a maze of barbed-wire entanglements, steel doors and hidden machine-gun nests. Even the streets leading up to its outer barriers were roamed by gorilla-faced guards in black uniforms, armed with jointed truncheons.

Winston works in the Ministry of Truth whose slogans are "War is Peace. Freedom is Slavery. Ignorance is Strength." His job is to re-write items of recent history in Newspeak (the official Party language) in such a way that it accords with the official Party line. Watched over at all hours of the day and night by the ubiquitous telescreens of the dreaded Thought Police, Winston rebels against the system and commits the crime of falling in love with a fellow Party worker. For a brief spell, he enjoys a precarious happiness, only to learn, in what is surely one of the most horrendous passages in the whole of SF, that the Party has simply been toying with him all along. He is dragged into the Ministry of Love, and his total physical and spiritual degradation begins as the Party, in the person of the Torquemadian Senior Official O'Brien, sets about the task of extinguishing Winston's one precious spark of individual humanity—his moral conscience. The end is inevitable and horrifying. By a series of physical and psychological tortures, Winston Smith as a person is totally erased and is then recreated in the Party's image until, in the end, "he loves Big Brother." Orwell's vision of a future in which the acquisition and tenure of absolute power is the only aspiration left to man is truly terrifying. "Power is not a means, it is an end," O'Brien tells Winston Smith. "If you want a picture of the future, imagine a boot stamping on a human face—forever."

*Nineteen Eighty-Four* is a cautionary tale on a heroic scale; its initial impact on an immediately post-war world still groggy from the revelations of the Nazi extermination camps and the tales of Russian defectors to the West is not difficult to imagine. What still gives the story its tremendous emotional force is the intensity with which Orwell has expressed in fictional terms his passionately held belief in individual human freedom. All in all, *Nineteen Eighty-Four* seems likely to retain its position as the most powerful as well as the most widely read science-fiction novel of the century.

—Richard Cowper

---

**OSBORNE, David.** *See* **SILVERBERG, Robert.**

---

# P

**PADGETT, Lewis.** *See* **KUTTNER, Henry; MOORE, C.L.**

---

**PALMER, Raymond A.** Also wrote as Henry Gade; G.H. Irwin; Frank Patton; J.W. Pelkie; Wallace Quitman; A.R. Steber; Morris J. Steele. American. Born in Wisconsin, 1 August 1910. Crippled from childhood. Editor and publisher; editor, *The Comet*, fan magazine, 1930; *Amazing Stories*, 1938–49; *Fantastic Adventures*, 1939–49; *Other Worlds* (later *Science Stories* and *Flying Saucers from Other Worlds*), 1950–57; *Imagination Science Fiction*, 1950; *Universe Science Fiction*, 1953–55; *Fate and Mystic* (later *Search*) in the 1950's; *The Hidden World* in the 1960's. *Died 15 August 1977.*

SCIENCE-FICTION PUBLICATIONS

Uncollected Short Stories

"The Time Ray of Jandra," in *Wonder Stories* (New York), June 1930.
"The Time Tragedy," in *Wonder Stories* (New York), December 1934.
"The Symphony of Death," in *Amazing* (New York), December 1935.
"Three from the Test Tube," in *Wonder Stories* (New York), November 1936.
"Matter Is Conserved," in *Astounding* (New York), April 1938.
"Catalyst Planet," in *Thrilling Wonder Stories* (New York), August 1938.
"Outlaw of Space" (as Wallace Quitman), in *Amazing* (New York), August 1938.
"The Vengeance of Martin Brand" (as G.H. Irwin), in *Amazing* (New York), August 1942; expanded edition, as "The Justice of Martin Brand," in *Other Worlds* (New York), July 1950.
"Red Coral," in *Other Worlds* (New York), May 1951.

Uncollected Short Stories as A.R. Steber

"The Blinding Ray," in *Amazing* (New York), August 1938.
"Black World," in *Amazing* (New York), March 1940.
"When the Gods Make War," in *Amazing* (New York), July 1940.
"Moon of Double Trouble," in *Amazing* (New York), March 1945.

Uncollected Short Stories as Morris J. Steele

"Polar Prison," in *Amazing* (New York), December 1938.
"The Phantom Enemy," in *Amazing* (New York), February 1939.
"Weapon for a Wac," in *Amazing* (New York), September 1944.

Uncollected Short Stories as Henry Gade

"Pioneer—1957," in *Fantastic Adventures* (New York), November 1939.
"Liners of Space," in *Amazing* (New York), December 1939.
"The Invincible Crime Buster," in *Amazing* (New York), July 1941.

Uncollected Short Stories as Frank Patton

"The Test Tube Girl," in *Fantastic Adventures* (New York), January 1942.
"Doorway to Hell," in *Fantastic Adventures* (New York), February 1942.
"A Patriot Never Dies," in *Amazing* (New York), August 1943.
"War Worker," in *Amazing* (New York), September 1943.
"Jewels of the Toad," in *Fantastic Adventures* (New York), October 1943.
"Mahaffey's Mystery," in *Other Worlds* (New York), March 1950.
"The Identity of Sue Tenet," in *Other Worlds* (New York), December 1952.
"Question Please," in *Other Worlds* (New York), April 1953.
"Sure Thing," in *Science Stories* (Evanston, Illinois), February 1954.
"The Secret of Pierre Cotreau," in *Science Stories* (Evanston, Illinois), April 1954.

Uncollected Short Stories as J.W. Pelkie (series: Toka in all stories)

"King of the Dinosaurs," in *Fantastic Adventures* (New York), October 1945.
"Toka and the Man Bats," in *Fantastic Adventures* (New York), February 1946.
"Toka Fights the Big Cats," in *Fantastic Adventures* (New York), December 1947.
"In the Sphere of Time," *Planet* (New York), Summer 1948.

*   *   *

Raymond A. Palmer was one of the earliest science-fiction fans, his activities dating from the late 1920's, and his major influence was as an editor. His first important assignment was the editorship of *Amazing Stories*, taken over from the moribund Teck Publications in 1938 by Ziff-Davis. Palmer discarded the on-hand inventory, quickly filled the magazine with new, adventure-oriented stories, and (perhaps most important) refurbished its drab appearance to create a lively, colorful package. Simultaneously he worked to bring the contents of the magazine in line with its new appearance.

He was immediately successful, and the following year was able to add a companion magazine, *Fantastic Adventures.* In a number of ways, Palmer's career remarkably paralleled that of the legendary John W. Campbell, Jr. Each editor brought on a stable of new writers, in addition to retaining (or re-recruiting) the best writers of a previous administration. Each editor also ran afoul of reader resistance when he attempted to introduce a variety of pseudoscientific cult material in the 1940's and 1950's. For Campbell it was Dianetics, and other oddities; for Palmer, it was first the Shaver Mystery, and later an infatuation with Flying Saucers. Much given to hucksterism and juvenile promotional appeals, Palmer met strong resistance in science fiction and withdrew to concentrate on occult publishing after 1957. However, his real achievements as an editor have been sorely underrated, and an examination of files of the magazines he edited reveals an absolute treasure-trove of overlooked material, by many leading writers. He lured Edgar Rice Burroughs back to the science-fiction magazines after an absence of 12 years. Palmer was the first editor to publish stories by Isaac Asimov, for all that the latter prefers to emphasize his later association with Campbell in his reminiscences. It is to be hoped that as the lingering bad taste of "Shaverism," "Saucerism," and Palmer's other regretable antics fades away, his very significant editorial contribution to modern science fiction will be more appreciated.

Palmer's own fiction, upon review, indicates a considerable talent but one which was not applied sufficiently consistently to produce a coherent body of works. In Palmer's earliest work, for Gernsback's *Wonder Stories,* he shows strongly the influence of early writers in the field. "The Time Ray of Jandra" reads like a throwback to the early 19th century, with a first-person narrator explaining the circumstances of his birth and naming, and continuing through over-long paragraphs to detail a discovery tale in which he is purely an observer rather than a participant. Before long, Palmer had fallen into the pulp style. His stories of the 1930's and 1940's show a fully developed set of pulp characteristics: simplistic but highly colored characterization, heavy doses of violent action, a reliance on coincidence and a strongly romantic bent. An excellent example, further embellished with occasional pseudo-scientific asides, is "The Test Tube Girl" (as Frank Patton). In his few stories published in the 1950's, Palmer appears to have overcome the worse excesses of his pulp period, and to have moved toward a less heavy-handed and melodramatic approach.

—Richard A. Lupoff

---

**PANGBORN, Edgar.** Also wrote as Bruce Harrison. American. Born in New York City, 25 February 1909. Educated at Brooklyn Friends School, graduated 1924; Harvard University, Cambridge, Massachusetts, 1924–25; New England Conservatory of Music, 1927. Served in the United States Army Medical Corps, 1942–45. Farmer in Maine, 1939–42; writer from 1946. Lived in Voorheesville, New York. Recipient: International Fantasy award, 1955. *Died 1 February 1976.*

SCIENCE-FICTION PUBLICATIONS

Novels

*West of the Sun.* New York, Doubleday, 1953; London, Hale, 1954.
*A Mirror for Observers.* New York, Doubleday, 1954; London, Muller, 1955.
*Davy.* New York, St. Martin's Press, 1964; London, Dobson, 1967.
*The Judgment of Eve.* New York, Simon and Schuster, 1966; London, Rapp and Whiting, 1968.
*The Company of Glory.* New York, Pyramid, 1975.
*The Atlantean Nights Entertainment.* San Francisco, Pennyfarthing Press, 1980.

Short Stories

*Good Neighbors and Other Strangers.* New York, Macmillan, 1972.
*Still I Persist in Wondering.* New York, Dell, 1978.

OTHER PUBLICATIONS

Novels

*A-100* (as Bruce Harrison). New York, Dutton, 1930.
*Wilderness of Spring.* New York, Rinehart, 1958.
*The Trial of Callista Blake.* New York, St. Martin's Press, 1961; London, Davies, 1962.

*

Manuscript Collection: Mugar Memorial Library, Boston University.

* * *

Edgar Pangborn's work, according to Damon Knight, reflects "the regretful, ironic, sorrowful, deeply joyous—and purblind—love of the world and all in it." Pangborn sees wonder in the ordinary, removing the reader from mundane perceptions. Some readers resent this heightening of the conventional. Knight sees Pangborn's magic as a veil obscuring the story. "The author will not get out of the way, but forces you to look through his own misty substance at what he wants you to see." A moment of reflection reveals that this sort of reaction indicates a matter of taste. Pangborn is an individual writer who directs the reader's perceptions; he does not write to the reader's order. Pangborn's view of life is tragic, comic, serious, and speculatively imaginative; his range is wider than many critics suspect. He is one of the few writers of SF and fantasy who was also a major fiction writer. His ideas were not always original, but he always managed to transform them.

"Angel's Egg," Pangborn's first story, is a powerful and very moving alien-contact story which pleads for tolerance and patience in regard to humankind's fate. Often reprinted, this story would have been enough to make a name for any writer. Pangborn's first SF novel, *West of the Sun,* is a deeply felt story of interstellar castaways, notable for its vividly realized settings, complex characters, and a painful knowledge of human failing. The sense of being there with the characters is overwhelming. *A Mirror for Observers,* a story of alien observers on earth who struggle between being watchers and meddlers, reaches Stapledonian heights of thought and feeling about the fate of humanity, but without the Stapledonian vistas. Pangborn's focus is more personal and intimate. Pangborn regarded *Wilderness of Spring* as a historical novel. Set in colonial New England, there is much in the story's pioneer spirit to interest the SF reader (one of the characters becomes a scientist). *The Trial of Callista Blake* is a novel on the theme of capital punishment.

*Davy* is Pangborn's most famous novel. Set 300 years after a nuclear holocaust, the book is a memoir written by the title character who grows from a bondsman to an ambitious leader concerned with the fate of humanity. Funny and tragic, bawdy and adventurous in the manner of *Tom Jones, Davy* is one of the lasting works of SF. A similar work, but one involving a female counterpart to Davy, *The Judgment of Eve* is not as well known, but, filled with the agony of choices, the book will please anyone who has enjoyed Pangborn's work. It has been suggested that the ambiguous ending might have been the result of editorial pressure to avoid depicting a *ménage-à-quatre. The Company of Glory* is set in the same world as *Davy* and *The Judgment of Eve* (though the Pyramid edition was censored as being "too faggoty"). *Still I Persist in Wondering* contains most of the shorter works set in the world of *Davy.*

Pangborn's work addresses the great problems of life and death, the mystery of existence, personal worth. Paradoxically, science fiction, though it claims to be a literature of ideas and wide vision, rarely rises above the entertainment formulas. Pangborn helped keep alive the tradition of "high science fiction," even while the pejorative genre association with SF dragged down serious reception of his work. Above everything else, Pangborn brought an overpowering sense of beauty to science fiction. *West of the Sun* glows with an unwearying light: "I give you birth and death and the journey of our days and nights between them, the shining of green fields, and patience of the forest, the little stars, the great stars, the love and the thought, the labor and the laughter, the good morning sky." *A Mirror for Observers* breathes with an unwaning love: "Never, beautiful Earth, never even at the height of the human storms have I forgotten you, my planet Earth, your forests and your fields, your oceans, the serenity of your mountains; the meadows, the continuing rivers, the incorruptible promise of returning spring." In trying to make us see, hear, and feel the important things that we so often forget, Pangborn aspired to the utterance of music, his first love.

—George Zebrowski

---

**PANSHIN, Alexei.** American. Born in Lansing, Michigan, 14 August 1940. Educated at the University of Michigan, Ann Arbor, 1958–60; Michigan State University, East Lansing, B.A. 1965; University of Chicago, M.A. 1966. Served in the United States Army, 1960–62. Married Cory Seidman in 1969; two sons. Librarian, Brooklyn Public Library, 1966–67; visiting lecturer in science fiction, Cornell University, Ithaca, New York, summers 1971–72. Recipient: Hugo award, for criticism, 1967, 1990; Nebula award, 1968. Address: 5580 Route 412, Riegelsville, Pennsylvania 18077, U.S.A.

### Science-Fiction Publications

Novels (series: Anthony Villiers)

*Rite of Passage.* New York, Ace, 1968; London, Sidgwick and Jackson, 1969.
*Star Well* (Villiers). New York, Ace, 1968.
*The Thurb Revolution* (Villiers). New York, Ace, 1968.
*Masque World* (Villiers). New York, Ace, 1969.
*Earth Magic,* with Cory Panshin. New York, Ace, 1978; London, Magnum, 1980.

Short Stories

*Farewell to Yesterday's Tomorrow.* New York, Putnam, 1975; augmented edition, New York, Berkley, 1976.
*Transmutations: A Book of Personal Alchemy* (includes poetry and non-fiction). Elephant, Pennsylvania, Elephant Books, 1982.

### Other Publications

Other

*Heinlein in Dimension: A Critical Analysis.* Chicago, Advent, 1968.
*SF in Dimension: A Book of Explorations,* with Cory Panshin. Chicago, Advent, 1976.
*Mondi Interiori* (in Italian), with Cory Panshin. Milan, Editrice Nord, 1978.
*The World Beyond the Hill: Science Fiction and the Quest for Transcendence,* with Cory Panshin. Los Angeles, Tarcher, 1989.

*

Manuscript Collection: Bowling Green University, Ohio.

Alexei Panshin comments:

My first aim as an SF writer is to tell good stories. To me, that means the solidest, most complete, truest stories I can imagine. My second aim is to make every story new in some way: new characters, new settings, new style, new to myself. For me, each story has its own unique voice, its own autonomy, and I've got to find it and respect it and love it into being.

Most of the time I write stories slowly, and I get published even more slowly. Twenty years after I first began to write, I've published five novels and one book of stories. An editor wrote to my first agent: "I used to think Panshin wrote this way because he was stubborn. Now I think he just doesn't have a very interesting imagination." I don't know which it is. All that I know is that the SF that I want to write is still beyond me, but I haven't given up trying.

* * *

Alexei Panshin began publishing science-fiction stories as an undergraduate. He had already conceived and begun writing the Nebula award-winning novel *Rite of Passage* while serving in the army. The novel, an acknowledged science-fiction classic, is an anthropological novel of the maturation of Mia Havero, the 19-year-old narrator recalling her one month "trial." The time is 150 years after the earth has been destroyed. The trial is a survival test that all 14-year-olds living on the asteroid star "ships" must undergo on a colony planet in order to be adult citizens. The point of view of an adolescent girl and her maturation are well done, though she and her friend, Jimmy Dentremont, seem rather precocious, particularly at the conclusion of the novel. In its psychological realism and the careful delineation of the "ship" society and the colony planet culture, *Rite of Passage* is Panshin's major fiction achievement.

The three Villiers novels, *Star Well, The Thurb Revolution,* and *Masque World,* follow the adventures of the titled Anthony Villiers and his inscrutable, unpredictable alien companion, Torve, the frog-like Torg. Each novel takes place on a different planet near or in the weak Nashua Empire. Panshin incorporates many comic elements, parodying space operas, spy thrillers, novels of intrigue, and regency and picaresque novels. The narrator is a cynical observer of the human comedy who interrupts the narrative with epigrammatic comments and short essays on human folly and absurdity. While amusing, the literary parody is occasionally labored and the relativistic, amoral narrator can become wearing. However, the emphasis on style and manner is appropriate to the genres being parodied and to the character of a rebellious, wandering aristocrat whose adventures are precipitated by the failure of his father's remittance to arrive. Sometimes

Panshin's learning is brought in rather obviously. The novels become increasingly pessimistic. *Masque World* has the weakest plot and ends the most grimly.

*Farewell to Yesterday's Tomorrow* includes stories written between 1966 and 1975 and shows how deeply affected Panshin was by the revolutionary 1960's and early 1970's in America. "The Sons of Prometheus," "A Sense of Direction" and "Arpad" employ the basic situation of the asteroid star "ships" from *Rite of Passage.* "Sky Blue" reflects a concern with the rapacious development of planets and, by extension, the exploitation of earth's ecology. "When the Vertical World Becomes Horizontal" preaches the need for freedom and spontaneity to replace rigid social assumptions and behaviour. Panshin's disillusionment with the failure of the counter culture of the early 1970's is apparent in "How Can We Sink When We Can Fly?" "Lady Sunshine and the Beatus" (written with his wife Cory) is a quest story and a phantasmagoric version of the Beauty and the Beast fairy tale. It ends the collection optimistically and romantically.

*Earth Magic,* also in collaboration with his wife, is an intriguing heroic fantasy which follows the adventures of Haldane, the son of Black Morca, a barbaric warrior tyrant. It is an exploration of the themes of change, identity, and reality versus vision or magic.

The collection of essays, poetry, and fiction, *Transmutations: A Book of Personal Alchemy,* explains his frustrations with writing fiction and his personal fascination with Sufi thought. The last essay is the autobiographic "Why I no Longer Pretend to Write Science Fiction: a Letter to *Foundation.*" The last few years he and his wife have focused on writing a critical study of the genre which was published in 1989, *The World Beyond the Hill: Science Fiction and the Quest for Transcendence.* This study was generally well received by reviewers in the field of science fiction.

—Diane Parkin-Speer

---

**PARK, Paul (Claibourne).** American. Born in North Adams, Massachusetts, 1 October 1954. Educated at Hampshire College, Amherst, Massachusetts, B.A. 1975. Worked as construction worker, political aide, and doorman, New York City, 1975–77. Copywriting and production assistant, Smith Greenland Advertising, New York City, 1977–78; manager, Town Squash Inc., New York City, 1979–85; retail manager, Potala Asian Imports, Pittsfield, Massachusetts, 1986–90. Visiting instructor, Writers' Center, Bethesda, Maryland, 1988; visiting instructor in creative writing, Johns Hopkins University, Baltimore, Maryland, 1988, 1991; visiting instructor in creative writing, Williams College, Williamstown, Massachusetts, 1989, 1991. Agent: Martha Millard, 204 Park Avenue, Madison, New Jersey 07940. Address: Box 10, Petersburg, New York 12138, U.S.A.

SCIENCE-FICTION PUBLICATIONS

Novels (series: Starbridge trilogy)

The Starbridge trilogy:
*Soldiers of Paradise.* New York, Arbor House, 1987; London, Grafton, 1989.
*Sugar Rain.* New York, Morrow, 1989; London, Grafton, 1990.
*The Cult of Loving Kindness.* New York, Morrow, 1991.

* * *

Paul Park's Starbridge trilogy has been compared to Brian Aldiss's *Helliconia* in that it deals with a planet on which the cycle of the seasons takes far longer than one human life span. In terms of intensity and evocative power, it might better be compared with Peake's *Gormenghast* or Geston's *Lords of the Starship.*

Only the first two volumes of the trilogy are available at this writing. The story concerns the coming of spring to the city-state of Charn, on a planet where the year has 80,000 days. Worldwide society is dominated by the immense Starbridge family. Charn itself is ruled by a totalitarian theocracy, justified by the need for organization for survival during the half-century (Earth years) of winter. This savagely enforced conformity contrasts with Park's most successful creation, an heretical cult of antinomials reminiscent of 16th-century Anabaptists or 20th-century hippies, who have renounced all social behaviour including speech. The end of winter in Charn, with its social and natural upheavals, is revealed largely through the experiences of the lovers Thanakar and Charity Starbridge, a doctor and the widow of a high official.

No writer in SF outdoes Park in the use of strange and grotesque material to create a story that is still full of human warmth, terror, pathos, even macabre humor, as in his account of Carilon Bargee, who set his skin on fire while trying to perfect a serum that would give the sensation of being loved. Park uses a matter of fact approach; we learn through what seem chance references that the carnivorous "horses" have beaks, claws, horns, and wings; that gasoline is used as an explosive and gunpowder as a motor fuel, that the spring "sugar rain" is laced with hydrocarbons, à la Velikowsky, so that Charn city burns every year, while the foresighted protect their valuables in asbestos bags. This meticulously prepared background supports Park's grander flights; the terrible and pathetic fate of the antinomials; the fall of the theocracy; Charity Starbridge's wanderings in the labyrinth under Charn; Thanakar Starbridge's passage through the monstrous prison Mountain of Redemption, with its million tormented inmates. And, from all this wonder and strangeness, characters speak to our condition here on Old Earth, as when Park's Robespierre, Raksha Starbridge, says: "I look about me and I see the dead, all those who died so that the state might live. I see in my mind's eye an image of the state, a huge, imperishable building of blank stone, and all about it a vast park, with all the souls of the dead men underfoot like grains of dirt."

Park's work has some rough edges. The reproduction of the French Revolution is too pat, while the Kafka pastiche and the place name River Rang (as in the Njalsaga) jar by their reminder of even more powerful works. But this is still a great achievement. The reader will remember the wild antinomials, with their music and their contempt for human values. The comment "Biter, biting!" echoes the Baptist Elder Lawrence Greatrake, "Men turn to Arminianism as swine to mud wallowing!" There is Colonel Aspe, another of SF's descendents of Goetz with the Iron Fist, the unwitting destroyer of his people. Above all, there is the great city Charn, with its toppling buildings and mud streets, its derelict harbour where the hulks of warships lie tilted in the ooze, its slums, taverns, brothels, palaces, prisons, all clear and detailed in the light of other suns. Park is one of those who can make us all see.

—E. R. Bishop

---

**PASSANTE, Dom.** *See* **FEARN, John Russell.**

---

**PATTON, Frank.** *See* **PALMER, Raymond A.; SHAVER, Richard S.**

---

**PEAKE, Mervyn (Laurence).** English. Born of missionary parents in Kuling, China, 9 July 1911. Educated at Tientsin Grammar School; Eltham College, Kent, 1923–29; Croydon College of Art, Surrey, 1929; Royal Academy Schools, London, 1929–33. Served in the British Army, 1941–43; military artist for the Ministry of Information, 1943–45. Married Maeve Gilmore in 1937; two sons and one daughter. Lived on Sark, Channel Islands, 1933–35 and 1945–49; teacher, Westminster School of Art, London, 1935–41, and Central School of Art, London, 1949–60. Book and magazine illustrator: one-man shows—Calman Gallery, London, 1943; Peter Jones Gallery, London, 1944; toured Europe as staff artist of the *Leader*, 1945; hospitalized for encephalitis, 1964–68. Recipient: Royal Literary Fund bursary, 1948; Heinemann award, 1951. Fellow, Royal Society of Literature. *Died 18 November 1968.*

SCIENCE-FICTION PUBLICATIONS

Novels (series: Titus)

*Titus Groan*. London, Eyre and Spottiswoode, and New York, Reynal and Hitchcock, 1946.
*Gormenghast* (Titus). London, Eyre and Spottiswoode, and New York, British Book Center, 1950.
*Mr. Pye*. London, Heinemann, 1953.
*Titus Alone*. London, Eyre and Spottiswoode, 1959; New York, Weybright and Talley, 1967; revised edition, revised by Langdon Jones, Eyre and Spottiswoode, 1970.

OTHER PUBLICATIONS

Plays

*The Connoisseurs* (produced 1952).
*The Wit to Woo* (produced 1957).

Radio Writing: *The Artist's World*, 1947; *Book Illustrations*, 1947; *Alice and Tenniel and Me*, 1954; *Titus Groan*, from his own novel, 1956; *The Voice of One*, 1956; *For Mr. Pye—An Island*, from his own novel, 1957.

Verse

*Shapes and Sounds*. London, Chatto and Windus, and New York, Transatlantic, 1941.
*Rhymes Without Reason*. London, Eyre and Spottiswoode, 1944.
*The Glassblowers*. London, Eyre and Spottiswoode, 1950.
*The Rhyme of the Flying Bomb*. London, Dent, 1962; New York, British Book Center, 1976.
*Poems and Drawings*. London, Keepsake, 1965.
*A Reverie of Bone and Other Poems*. London, Rota, 1967.
*Selected Poems*. London, Faber, 1972.
*A Book of Nonsense*. London, Owen, 1972; New York, Dufour, 1975.
*Twelve Poems 1939–1960*. Hayes, Middlesex, Bran's Head, 1975.

Other

*Captain Slaughterboard Drops Anchor* (for children). London, Country Life, 1939; revised edition, Country Life, 1945; New York, Macmillan, 1967.
*The Craft of the Lead Pencil*. London, Wingate, 1946.
*Letters from a Lost Uncle* (for children). London, Eyre and Spottiswoode, 1948.
*Drawings by Mervyn Peake*. London, Grey Walls, and New York, British Book Center, 1950.
*Figures of Speech* (drawings). London, Gollancz, 1954.
*The Drawings of Mervyn Peake*, text by Hilary Spurling. London, Davis-Poynter, 1974.
*Mervyn Peake: Writings and Drawings*, edited by Maeve Gilmore and Shelagh Johnson. London, Academy Editions, 1974; New York, St. Martin's Press, 1974.
*Peake's Progress: Selected Writings and Drawings of Mervyn Peake*, edited by Maeve Gilmore. London, Allen Lane, 1978; revised edition, London, Penguin, and Woodstock, New York, Overlook Press, 1981.
*Sketches from Bleak House*. London, Methuen, 1983.

*

Bibliography: "Peake in Print: A Bibliographical Checklist" by Dee Berkeley and G. Peter Winnington, in *Mervyn Peake Review*, Autumn 1981 and Spring 1982.

Manuscript Collections: D.M.S. Watson Library, University College, London; Imperial War Museum, London; Bodleian Library, Oxford; Berg Collection, New York Public Library.

Critical Studies: *A World Away: A Memoir of Mervyn Peake* by Maeve Gilmore, London, Gollancz, 1970; *Mervyn Peake: A Biographical and Critical Exploration* by John Batchelor, London, Duckworth, 1974; *Mervyn Peake: A Personal Memoir* by Gordon Smith, London, Gollancz, 1984; *A Child of Bliss: Growing Up With Mervyn Peake* by Sebastian Peake, Luton, Lennard, 1989.

* * *

Peake's major fictional works are the three books which relate the heritage, childhood, and adolescence of Titus, 77th Earl of Gormenghast. They are often inaccurately called the Gormenghast Trilogy, but the third volume is not set in Gormenghast, nor were they designed as a trilogy. Peake certainly intended a fourth book, and would probably have written more.

Gormenghast is an immense, ancient castle of crumbling stone and suffocating ritual, set in a wild and dreary land. Its inhabitants, from Count Sepulchrave, suffused in laudanum and antiquarian gloom, down to Swelter, the mountainous chef, make up one of the greatest gallery of grotesques in English literature. Every aspect of their existence is dictated by the Master of Ritual from the Books of the Law, though the observances and ceremonies are so old that no one can even remember their significance. Seizing on his shadowy castle and its atmosphere of doom, many critics have called Peake a gothic writer, but the label is misleading. He makes almost no use of the supernatural, which is essential to Gothic, and his descriptive writing has a visual and tactile solidity foreign to the genre. His characters, with their extraordinary forms and names—Flay, Muzzlehatch, Prunesquallor—are caricatures whose robust and energetic presence recalls Dickens or Rabelais, not Walpole or Radcliffe. Again, Peake is farcical as well as horrific; he writes out of a relish for life and colour that is hostile to Gothic morbidity, sunlight to its vampires.

*Titus Groan* is the story of Titus's birth and the ripples of disturbance that spread inexorably from it. He is a natural rebel, impulsive, moody, idealistic; his arrival coincides with the rise of Steerpike, a more sinister figure, who works his way up from the kitchen to the highest place of power by insinuation, flattery, violence, and murder. The prose is deep, dense, eloquent, and richly detailed. Peake was a painter, and when he used purple he knew exactly what shade and texture he needed.

*Gormenghast*, which tells of Titus's truant childhood, the growing horror and inhumanity of Steerpike, and their eventual, inevitable confrontation, moves more quickly. Once set going, "change, that most unforgivable of all heresies," spreads like contagion. The rituals are disrupted. Love shows itself in strange distortions, ungainly, absurd, or corrupt. Steerpike is exposed and hunted. Peake loses none of his control as his plot gains momentum. He portrays the adolescent tumult in all its quicksilver ambiguity. Titus's experience of life and death both in and outside the castle brutally confirm his individuality, and point to the impossibility that he will stay there. Disobeying his mother by going in to fight the cornered villain, he is attacking the Master of Ritual and manipulator of lives, powers of Gormenghast that he hates; but he is also ridding the castle of the man who would crush it to dominate it.

*Titus Alone* is entirely different again, a fact which has put off readers who (unlike Peake) are more interested in Gormenghast than in Titus and the rest of the world. It is, though rarely acknowledged as such, science fiction, from a class somewhere between Huxley's *Brave New World* and Harness's *The Rose.* Titus wanders, exiled and imperilled, in a strange land, a meticulous parody of modern Europe with furnishings and fittings that place it in an imminent, unpleasant future. He is arrested in a city of crystal towers and rockets; he is pursued by machine-like police and a robot flying eye, and hides in the refugee camp of the Under-River will all the malcontents and victims of a damaged civilisation; he falls into the hands of Cheeta, the corrupt daughter of the master of the death factory. Wherever he goes, no one has heard of Gormenghast, and few will believe it exists. Where *Titus Groan* was ponderous and slow, *Titus Alone* is fast and elusive. We barely glimpse the scenes as they whirr by. The effect is intentional, frightening, but the mysteries and frustrations of the book are, unavoidably, too many. Peake's last illness was well upon him when he began it, and his ability to express his ideas deteriorated as he wrote. The moral vision, at once urgent and subtle, emerges in flashes, or dimly; the novel is a characteristic document of the 20th century, damaged, hallucinatory, but intensely purposeful. (Langdon Jones's 1970 edition is the best possible version of what Peake had in mind.)

"Boy in Darkness" tells an extra story of Titus Groan, though without naming him. After the rituals of his 14th birthday he slips away from the castle into the wilderness, where he meets two old creatures called Goat and Hyena. They take him to the Blind Lamb, a malevolent deity who lives deep in an abandoned mine where once, like Comus, he commanded a rout of beasts transformed from human originals. The Goat and the Hyena are the last of this crew. He begins the metamorphosis of Titus, who fights back at the last minute for his humanity and that of the two pathetic courtiers. More sombre than almost any episode in the novels, "Boy in Darkness" has been read by some as spiritual, perhaps blasphemous, allegory, though interpretation was never the purpose of Peake's imaginings. Certainly the story is his most chilling and sensuous exercise in the macabre, far superior to the merely gruesome "Same Time, Same Place" and the ghoulish "Danse Macabre." *Mr. Pye*, Peake's only other novel, was unsuccessful when it was published because of expectations aroused by the Titus books. It is comic fantasy of a very different kind: a remarkable mixture of farce and fable, lighter in tone than the Titus books, but more exclusively adult in appeal. Set on Sark, it records the misadventures of a charming, irritating, self-appointed missionary whose work of disseminating love among the close, suspicious islanders is upset when God, "The Great Pal," rewards him rather too literally.

It can be said that Mervyn Peake lived before his time, and died too soon. Best known during his life for his dense, vigorous illustration of works by authors from Carroll to Coleridge, he also produced poetry, paintings, plays for radio and stage, and theatrical designs, as well as the prose fantasy for which he is now most famous. An eccentric to his own generation, he has been rightly honoured as a master by the next—unfortunately too late to know or benefit by it.

—Colin Greenland

---

**PEDLER, Kit** (Christopher Magnus Howard Pedler). British. Born in London, 11 June 1927. Educated at Ipswich School; King's College, University of London; Westminster Medical School, London, M.B. B.S. 1953, Ph.D., Member, College of Pathologists. Married Una Freeston in 1949; two daughters and two sons. Physician and surgeon in London and Greenwich hospitals, 1953–57; in general practice briefly; Senior Lecturer, then Reader in Pathology, then founded and headed the Anatomy and Electron Microscopy Department, for 12 years, University of London: resigned in 1971 to become freelance writer: author of many radio and television documentaries and features. Honorary Secretary, Royal Microscopy Society. *Died 27 May 1981.*

SCIENCE-FICTION PUBLICATIONS

Novels with Gerry Davis

*Mutant 59, The Plastic Eater.* London, Souvenir Press, 1971; New York, Viking Press, 1972.

*Brainrack.* London, Souvenir Press, 1974; New York, Pocket Books, 1975.

*The Dynostar Menace.* London, Souvenir Press, and New York, Scribner, 1975.

OTHER PUBLICATIONS

Plays

Radio Plays: *Sunday Lunch; Trial by Logic.*

Television Plays: *Doctor Who* series (8 plays, 3 with Gerry Davis); *The Robot* (documentary); *Doomwatch* series (39 plays with Gerry Davis); *Galenforce*, with Gerry Davis.

Other

*The Quest for Gaia: A Book of Changes.* London, Souvenir Press, 1979.
*Mind Over Matter: A Scientist's View of the Paranormal.* London, Thames-Methuen, 1981.

*

Kit Pedler commented:

(1981) My science fiction has always had to do with small logical extensions of current reality. I am currently engaged on "Document from the Year 3," for example, which deals (post hoc) with the evolution of homo sapiens, and "The Logon" which are the result of mating between a mould and a microchip!

* * *

Kit Pedler and Gerry Davis wrote three popular disaster novels following their collaboration on BBC-TV's Doomwatch series and their creation of the Cybermen for *Doctor Who.* Strong on the science background, these novels are sometimes markedly weak as fictions because of poor characterization and, particularly in *The Dynostar Menace*, a reliance on stylistic and suspense clichés. Nevertheless, the narratives are at times remarkably exciting and well-sustained, as in the well-executed main sequence in *Mutant 59, The Plastic Eater*, when a small group is trapped in the London Underground by fire and explosion. Further, the authors sometimes achieve nice ironic and satirical effects, for instance, by well-timed narrative switches of focus from one character to another in *Mutant 59.*

As prophets of doom, Pedler and Davis seem to be telling us that we are unwise to rely on over-complicated mechanisms that are vulnerable to simple accidents, caused by unforeseen weaknesses or dangers in materials, human error, or simply the over-complication itself. It we heeded their warnings, we would take immediate steps drastically to simplify our lives. At the end of their second and strongest novel, *Brainrack*, this solution is rendered highly appealing by an idyllic evocation of a London without motor vehicles. The solution, perhaps unfortunately, is more convincing than the threats, which are needlessly fantastic. It is not strictly necessary to postulate the existence of a mutant virus that feeds on plastic (and finds abundant food when a new sun-degradable plastic is marketed), in order to explain severe disasters to airliners, submarines, and London. That men brought up in cities are suffering irretrievable brain damage because of an unsuspected ingredient of petrol is a highly unconvincing explanation of the destruction of a new nuclear power plant. It does not seem very likely that a satellite reactor will disrupt the ozone layer of earth's atmosphere and burn large areas of the surface of our planet. (Human greed and negligence are sufficient explanations, as in a disaster novel that is not regarded as SF, John D. MacDonald's *Condominium*). However, these startling threats are piquant and intriguing, and, to be fair to the writers, they take ample account of familiar human nature as a contributory cause of the disasters. What they like to do, in fact, is to make their point by showing how easy it is for various weaknesses inherent in a system to compound each other: the "plastic eater" is simply the icing on the cake. Pedler and Davis are particularly convincing when, in the early part of *Brainrack*, they expose the "EMMY" (man-machine interface) dangers: most of us know how easy it is to hit the wrong keys on typewriters, or misread simple instructions, or confuse colour codes. There is a grand tour de force in *Brainrack*, a long sustained narrative account of the effects of meltdown on the workers in a nuclear reactor. This is vivid and horrific and, except that some people survive, for the sake of the story, highly convincing.

*The Dynostar Menace* stands apart from the other two novels in being set in a closed environment, a space lab, and having the form of a kind of hard SF version of Christie's *Ten Little Niggers.* In this sort of plot, versions of which can often be found in TV series (*Blake's Seven*) or films (*Alien*), the actual nature of the threat is almost bound to be subordinated to the excitement of detection (here, of a saboteur) in a race against time. Exceptional imaginative power and skill, particularly in characterization, are needed to lift such a hackneyed plot from cliché, and perhaps it is here that we can see how a background in TV script-writing may have been a disadvantage, particularly to Davis. However, their three works together constitute a notable contribution to disaster fiction, and they were perhaps a shade unlucky to have slightly anticipated the greatest market for this branch of the genre.

—Michael J. Tolley

---

**PELKIE, J.W.** *See* **PALMER, Raymond A.**

---

**PETAJA, Emil (Theodore).** American. Born in Milltown, Montana, 12 April 1915. Educated at Montana State University, Missoula 1936–38. Office worker, 1938–41; film technician, Technicolor Corporation, Hollywood, 1941–46; photographer, 1947–63. Since 1963, full-time writer: chairman, Bokanalia Memorial Foundation; since 1972, owner, SISU Publishers, San Francisco. Agent: Forrest J. Ackerman, 2495 Glendower Avenue, Hollywood, California 90027. Address: P.O. Box 14126, San Francisco, California 94114, U.S.A.

SCIENCE-FICTION PUBLICATIONS

Novels (series: Green Planet; Kalevala)

*Alpha Yes, Terra No!* New York, Ace, 1965.
*The Caves of Mars.* New York, Ace, 1965.
*Saga of Lost Earths* (Kalevala). New York, Ace, 1965.
*The Star Mill* (Kalevala). New York, Ace, 1965.
*Tramontane* (Kalevala). New York, Ace, 1965.
*The Stolen Sun* (Kalevala). New York, Ace, 1967.
*Lord of the Green Planet.* New York, Ace, 1967.
*The Prism.* New York, Ace, 1968.
*Doom of the Green Planet.* New York, Ace, 1968.
*The Time Twister* (Kalevala). New York, Dell, 1968.
*The Path Beyond the Stars.* New York, Dell, 1969.
*The Nets of Space.* New York, Berkley, 1969.

*Seed of the Dreamers*. New York, Ace, 1970.
*Lost Earths* (omnibus). New York, DAW, 1979.

Short Stories

*Stardrift and Other Fantastic Flotsam*. Los Angeles, Fantasy, 1971.

OTHER PUBLICATIONS

Verse

*As Dream and Shadow*. San Francisco, SISU, 1972.

Other

*And Flights of Angels: The Life and Legend of Hannes Bok*. San Francisco, SISU, 1968.

Editor, *The Hannes Bok Memorial Showcase of Fantasy Art*. San Francisco, SISU, 1974.
Editor, *Photoplay Edition*. San Francisco, SISU, 1975.

*

Emil Petaja comments:

My writing endeavors have mainly been to entertain, except for the factual material concerning Hannes Bok and fantasy art in general, which serves to indicate my enthusiasm for these subjects. My novels about the Finnish legendary epic *Kalevala: The Land of Heroes* spring from a lifelong interest in this fine poetic work. I own six translations of the *Kalevala*, as well as the work in the original. Both my parents were Finnish.

* * *

Though Emil Petaja published short fiction sporadically during the 1940's and 1950's, his important works were written in the 1960's. Most of these novels were published by Ace Books, and even those that were not followed the Ace formula: heavy on action, with some superficial romance. Though Petaja never sought to go beyond this formula, his innovations within its structure are impressive. Petaja's choice of story-material is the source of his appeal, for into the traditional settings of science fiction he transferred mythic heroes and situations, devoting particular attention to his own Finnish myth-heritage, the Kalevala story-cycle. Petaja deftly contrasts the sterile safety of centralized civilization (into which the hero is born) with the barbaric but vital hardship of primitive culture (into which the hero is initiated), and though the author concedes the necessity for both milieus, he emphasizes the greater need for preserving humanity's potential. Unlike most Ace "common man" heroes, Petaja's protagonists are strong, romantic-minded men, slightly alienated in progressive society, but greatly attuned to the poetry of myths. Ultimately the hero's ability to empathize with mythic situations is the factor which saves all of humanity—whether directly by battling destructive forces or indirectly by mastering the situation with poetic insight (*Alpha Yes, Terra No!*)

In the Kalevala-based novels the hero's empathy is deep enough to propel his psyche upon astral journeys, becoming merged with a Finnish hero endowed with magic (psychic?) powers. These are probably the best of Petaja's works because of their belief in an actual existence of the Finnish mythos, even by means of rationalizations like psychic powers and alien entities. Thus the mythos provides the structural basis for evoking the poetry of Finnish culture. Earlier authors' works had also rationalized myths into science fiction (Henry Kuttner's *Mask of Circe*), but Petaja is virtually the first to maintain limited fidelity to the cultural content of the myths, rather than manipulating it to fit melodramatic purposes.

Less successful, but equally colorful, are the two books of a planetary culture modeled on Irish story-cycles, though no particular myths are emphasized by the plots of *Lord of the Green Planet* and *Doom of the Green Planet*. The supernatural creatures of Irish myth are robots and alien entities, while the "Irish" are merely transplanted humans from other planets, all brought together by a mad Fenian poet with super-scientific resources. Though entertaining, these books do not have the poetry of the Kalevala books, for the Irish culture is merely a giant mock-up rather than a shamanistic culture like the Finns', seen as surviving into the future. Furthermore, though the mythos-structure is less articulated, Petaja displays more dislike for the "progressive" civilization beyond the Green Planet than in earlier novels, and greater cognizance of the conflict between the appeal of heroism and the necessities of humanism.

Of the non-related books, the best is *The Path Beyond the Stars*, in which a man and woman traverse several time-periods attempting to acquire knowledge of the universe's destruction—which they ultimately cannot prevent, though they can become the Adam and Eve of another cosmos. The other novels have less imaginative scope, but, in a melodramatic way, they all work toward the same goal: regeneration of the heroes' mythopoetic faculties, and thus the redemption of the profane world.

Petaja's importance to science fiction is that of a precursor of the increased use of myth in late 1960's SF. At their best his works suggest an archaic heritage of man not unlike the findings of anthropologist Mircea Eliade—a heritage which most contemporary writers, SF and mainstream alike, have chosen to neglect.

—Gene Phillips

---

**PHILLIFENT, John T.** *See* **RACKHAM, John.**

---

**PHILLIPS, Frank.** *See* **NOWLAN, Philip Francis.**

---

**PHILLIPS, Mark.** *See* **GARRETT, Randall; JANIFER, Laurence M.**

---

**PHILLIPS, Rog** (Roger Phillips Graham). Also wrote as Clinton Ames; Robert Arnette; Franklin Bahl; Alexander Blade; Craig Browning; Gregg Conrad; P.F. Costello; Inez McGowan; Melva Rogers; Chester Ruppert; William Carter Sawtelle; A.R. Steber; Gerald Vance; John Wiley; Peter Worth. American. Born in Spokane, Washington, in 1909. Educated at Gonzaga University, Spokane, A.B.; graduate study at the University of Washington, Seattle. Married 1) Mari Wolf; 2) Honey Wood in

1956. Power plant engineer; shipyard welder during World War II; freelance writer after the war: Columnist ("The Club House"), *Amazing*, New York, 1948–53. *Died in 1965.*

SCIENCE-FICTION PUBLICATIONS

Novels

*Time Trap.* Chicago, Century, 1949.
*Worlds Within.* Chicago, Century, 1950.
*World of If.* Chicago, Century, 1951.
*The Involuntary Immortals.* New York, Avalon, 1959.

Uncollected Short Stories (series: Lefty Baker)

"Let Freedom Ring," in *Amazing* (New York), December 1945.
"Vacation in Shasta," in *Fantastic Adventures* (New York), February 1946.
"Atom War," in *Amazing* (New York), May 1946.
"The Mutants," in *Amazing* (New York), July 1946.
"Dual Personality," in *Fantastic Adventures* (New York), September 1946.
"The Space" (as Roger P. Graham), in *Amazing* (New York), September 1946.
"Battle of the Gods," in *Amazing* (New York), September 1946.
"The House," in *Amazing* (New York), February, 1947.
"So Shall Ye Reap," in *Amazing* (New York), August 1947.
"The Uninvited Jest," in *Amazing* (New York), September 1947.
"The Despoilers," in *Amazing* (New York), October 1947.
"High Ears," in *Fantastic Adventures* (New York), October 1947.
"Squeeze Play" (Baker; as Craig Browning), in *Amazing* (New York), November 1947.
"And Eve Was," in *Amazing* (New York), November 1947.
"Hate," in *Amazing* (New York), January 1948.
"Twice to Die," in *Fantastic Adventures* (New York), February 1948.
"The Supernal Note," in *Amazing* (New York), July 1948.
"Starship from Sirius, in *Amazing* (New York), August 1948.
"The Cube Root of Conquest," in *Amazing* (New York), October 1948.
"The Unthinking Destroyer," in *Amazing* (New York), December 1948.
"Brainstorm" (as Alexander Blade), in *Fantastic Adventures* (New York), December 1948.
"The Can Opener," in *Fantastic Adventures* (New York), January 1949.
"The Immortal Menace" (Baker), and "M'Bong-Ah," in *Amazing* (New York), February 1949.
"Quite Logical," in *Thrilling Wonder Stories* (New York), April 1949.
"She," in *Fantastic Adventures* (New York), April 1949.
"Unthinkable," in *Amazing* (New York), April 1949.
"The Last Stronghold" (as Chester Ruppert), in *Amazing* (New York), May 1949.
"The Robot Men of Bubble City," in *Fantastic Adventures* (New York), July 1949.
"The Shortcut," in *Amazing* (New York), July 1949.
"The Awakening," in *Amazing* (New York), August 1949.
"The Tangential Semanticist," in *Fantastic Adventures* (New York), August 1949.
"Incompatible," in *Fantastic Adventures* (New York), September 1949.
"Matrix," in *Amazing* (New York), October 1949.
"Planet of the Dead," in *Fantastic Adventures* (New York), October 1949.
"The Insane Robot" (Baker), in *Fantastic Adventures* (New York), November 1949.
"Venus Trouble Shooter" (as John Wiley), in *Other Worlds* (Evanston, Indiana), November 1949.
"Beyond the Matrix of Time," in *Amazing* (New York), November 1949.
"The Miracle of Elmer Wilde," in *Other Worlds* (Evanston, Indiana), November 1949.
"To Give Them Welcome" (as Melva Rogers), in *Other Worlds* (Evanston, Indiana), January 1950.
"This Time," in *Other Worlds* (Evanston, Indiana), January 1950.
"The Pranksters," in *Amazing* (New York), February 1950.
"Detour from Tomorrow," in *Fantastic Adventures* (New York), March 1950.
"The Fatal Technicality," in *Other Worlds* (Evanston, Indiana), March 1950.
"The Mental Assassins" (as Greg Conrad), in *Fantastic Adventures* (New York), May 1950.
"Slaves of the Crystal Brain" (as William Carter Sawtelle), in *Amazing* (New York), May 1950.
"The Lost Bomb," in *Amazing* (New York), May 1950.
"If You Were Me . . .," in *Amazing* (New York), June 1950.
"Victims of the Vortex" (as Clinton Ames), in *Amazing* (New York), July 1950.
"Warrior Queen of Mars" (as Alexander Blade), in *Fantastic Adventures* (New York), September 1950.
"Holes in My Head," in *Other Worlds* (Evanston, Indiana), October 1950.
"One for the Robot—Two for the Same," in *Imagination* (Evanston, Illinois), October 1950.
"Weapon from the Stars," in *Amazing* (New York), October 1950.
"A Man Named Mars" (as A.R. Steber), in *Other Worlds* (Evanston, Indiana), October, 1950.
"Love My Robot," in *Startling* (New York), November 1950.
"Rescue Beacon" (as Craig Browning), in *Other Worlds* (Evanston, Indiana), November 1950.
"These Are My Children," in *Other Worlds* (Evanston, Indiana), January, March 1951.
"You'll Die Yesterday," in *Amazing* (New York), March 1951.
"Secret of the Flaming Ring" (as P.F. Costello), in *Fantastic Adventures* (New York), March 1951.
"In What Dark Mind," in *Fantastic Adventures* (New York), April 1951.
"Vampire of the Deep," in *Amazing* (New York), May 1951.
"The Lurker," in *Fantastic* (New York), May 1951.
"The Man from Mars," in *Other Worlds* (Evanston, Indiana), May 1951.
"Who Sows the Wind," in *Amazing* (New York), June 1951.
"The President Will See You," in *Fantastic Adventures* (New York), July 1951.
"Step Out of Your Body, Please," in *Amazing* (New York), November 1951.
"Remember Not to Die!," in *Fantastic Adventures* (New York), November 1951.
"Checkmate for Aradjo," in *Amazing* (New York), December 1951.
"No Greater Wisdom," in *Amazing* (New York), January 1952.
"The Visitors," in *Amazing* (New York), February 1952.
"The Old Martians," in *If* (New York), March 1952.
"The Unfinished Equation" (as Robert Arnette), in *Fantastic Adventures* (New York), April 1952.
"A More Potent Weapon," in *Fantastic Adventures* (New York), April 1952.
"The World of Whispering Wings," in *Amazing* (New York), May 1952.

"Destiny Uncertain," in *Imagination* (Evanston, Illinois), May 1952.
"Black Angels Have No Wings," in *Amazing* (New York), August 1952.
"All the Answers," in *Science Fiction Quarterly* (Holyoke, Massachusetts), August 1952.
"The Man Who Lived Twice," in *Fantastic Adventures* (New York), August 1952.
"Adam's First Wife," in *Amazing* (New York), September 1952.
"I'll See You in My Dreams," in *Fantastic Adventures* (New York), September 1952.
"It's in the Cards," in *Fantastic Adventures* (New York), October 1952.
"It's Like This," in *Fantastic Story* (New York), November 1952.
"Visitors from Darkness," in *Amazing* (New York), December 1952.
"The Sorceress," in *Amazing* (New York), January 1953.
"Ye of Little Faith," in *If* (New York), January 1953.
"The Menace," in *Fantastic Adventures* (New York), February 1953.
"Your Funeral is Waiting," in *Amazing* (New York), March 1953.
"The Lost Ego," in *Imagination* (Evanston, Illinois), April 1953.
"The Cyberene," in *Imagination* (Evanston, Illinois), September 1953.
"The Phantom Truckdriver," in *Amazing* (New York), September 1953.
"Pariah," in *Science Stories* (Evanston, Illinois), October 1953.
"From This Dark Mind," in *Fantastic* (New York), December 1953.
"The Cosmic Junkman," in *Imagination* (Evanston, Illinois), December 1953.
"Repeat Performance," in *Imagination* (Evanston, Illinois), January 1954.
"Teach Me to Kill," in *Amazing* (New York), June 1957.
"A Handful of Sand," in *Amazing* (New York), April 1957.
"Homestead," in *Fantasy and Science Fiction* (New York), August 1957.
"Executioner No. 43," in *Venture* (Concord, New Hampshire), September 1957.
"The Cosmic Trap" (as Gerald Vance), in *Fantastic* (New York), November 1957.
"World of Traitors," in *Fantastic* (New York), November 1957.
"Truckstop," in *Imaginative Tales* (Evanston, Illinois), November 1957.
"Captain Peabody," in *If* (New York), December 1957.
"Game Preserve," in *SF'58*, edited by Judith Merril. New York, Dell, 1958.
"Lefty Baker's Nuthouse," in *Imaginative Tales* (Evanston, Illinois), January 1958.
"Love Me, Love My—," in *Fantasy and Science Fiction* (New York), February 1958.
"Venusian, Get Out!," in *Amazing* (New York), April 1958.
"It's Better Not to Know," in *Fantastic* (New York), April 1958.
"Refueling Station," in *Imaginative Tales* (Evanston, Illinois), May 1958.
"Ground Leave Incident," in *Venture* (Concord, New Hampshire), May 1958.
"Space Is for Suckers" (as P.F. Costello), and "Prophecy, Inc.," in *Amazing* (New York), June 1958.
"Services, Inc.," in *Fantasy and Science Fiction* (New York), June 1958.
"Jason's Secret," in *Fantastic* (New York), September 1958.
"In This Dark Mind" (as Inez McGowan), in *Fantastic* (New York), September 1958.
"Unto the Nth Generation," in *Amazing* (New York), December 1958.
"The Yellow Pill," in *SF'59*, edited by Judith Merril. New York, Dell, 1959.
"The Gallery," in *Amazing* (New York), January 1959.
"The Creeper in the Dream," in *Fantastic* (New York), February 1959.
"Keepers in Space," in *Fantastic* (New York), April 1959.
"The Only One Who Lived," in *Fantastic* (New York), May 1959.
"Camouflage," in *Amazing* (New York), June 1959.
"But Who Knows Huer or Huen?" (Baker), in *Fantastic* (New York), November 1961.
"Rat in the Skull," in *Introductory Psychology Through Science Fiction*, edited by Harvey A. Katz, Martin H. Greenberg, and Patricia S. Warrick. Chicago, Rand McNally, 1977.

Uncollected Short Stories as Peter Worth

"The Robot and the Pearly Gates," in *Amazing* (New York), January 1949.
"I Died Tomorrow," in *Fantastic Adventures* (New York), May 1949.
"Window to the Future," in *Amazing* (New York), May 1949.
"Lullaby," in *Amazing Annual* (New York), 1950.
"Null F," in *Fantastic Adventures* (New York), February 1950.
"The Master Ego," in *Fantastic Adventures* (New York), March 1951.
"The Imitators," in *Amazing* (New York), June 1951.

Uncollected Short Stories as Franklin Bahl

"Face Beyond the Veil," in *Fantastic Adventures* (New York), April 1950.
"The Justice of Tor," in *Fantastic Adventures* (New York), January 1951.
"Lady Killer," in *Amazing* (New York), February 1953.

* * *

Rog Phillips (the name by which Roger P. Graham was generally known to science-fiction readers) became a professional writer in his mid-thirties, after several years as a power plant engineer and shipyard welder, and quickly established himself as a prolific and reliable producer of pulp fiction. Phillips used many pseudonyms, including several house names.

Until 1950 Phillips wrote exclusively for the Ziff-Davis magazines; his SF and fantasy fiction appeared in *Amazing Stories* and *Fantastic Adventures.* Phillips wrote everything from featured novels to short stories and fillers. A large part of this output was routine work done to editorial order, but it was often a notch or two above the general level of quality in the magazines, and was very popular with the readers. The first work to attract wide attention was the novel, "So Shall Ye Reap." Starting with the premise that the five atomic bombs already exploded by 1947 had released enough radioactivity into the atmosphere to affect the genes of future generations, the novel offered a scenario of the next 150 years, in which mankind established an elaborate underground civilization and retreated from the Earth's surface. Although marred by polemical stretches and badly dated now, the story nevertheless has some effective scenes and an overall crude energy. A sequel, "Starship from Sirus," added human colonies on Mars and Venus and an insect-dominated Earth in the far future, and was quite different in tone from its predecessor.

Four memorable Phillips stories appeared in 1949. "M'Bong-Ah" was a novelette telling of the colonization of Venus and of the Earthman who became the natives' pawn in their resistance to the invasion. "Matrix" and "Beyond the Matrix of Time" together form a complex story of time paradox and alternate realities. *The Involuntary Immortals* is the story of a group of "accidental" immortals who band together to discover the source of their immortality and to protect themselves against the vengefulness of their own jealous relatives.

Starting in 1950 Rog Phillips's stories had begun to appear in a wider variety of magazines. "Rat in the Skull" is a memorable story of an experiment in rodent intelligence; "Ground Leave Incident" is a hard-boiled episode on a frontier planet; "Services, Inc." is an offbeat deal-with-the-Devil story. By far the most successful story Phillips ever wrote is "The Yellow Pill," a brief tale of multiple subjective realities.

—R.E. Briney

---

**PIERCY, Marge.** American. Born in Detroit, Michigan, 31 March 1936. Educated at the University of Michigan, Ann Arbor (Hopwood award, 1956, 1957), A.B. 1957; Northwestern University, Evanston, Illinois, M.A. 1958. Married Ira Wood (third marriage) in 1982. Instructor, Indiana University, Gary, 1960–62; poet-in-residence, University of Kansas, Lawrence, 1971; Visiting Lecturer, Thomas Jefferson College, Grand Valley State Colleges, Allendale, Michigan, 1975; visiting faculty, Women's Writers' Conference, Cazenovia College, New York, 1976, 1978, 1980; staff member, Fine Arts Work Center, Provincetown, Massachusetts, 1976–77; writer-in-residence, College of the Holy Cross, Worcester, Massachusetts, 1976; Butler Professor of Letters, State University of New York, Buffalo, 1977; Elliston Professor of poetry, University of Cincinnati, 1986. Member of the board of directors, 1982–85 and of the advisory board since 1985, Coordinating Council of Literary Magazines. Recipient: Borestone Mountain award, 1968, 1974; National Endowment for the Arts grant, 1978; Rhode Island School of Design Faculty Association Medal, 1985; Carolyn Kizer prize, 1986, 1990; Sheaffer Eaton-P.E.N. New England award, 1989; Golden Rose prize, New England Poetry Club, 1990. Agent: Lois Wallace, Wallace Literary Agency, 177 East 70th Street, New York, New York 10021. Address: Box 1473, Wellfleet, Massachusetts 02667, U.S.A.

SCIENCE-FICTION PUBLICATIONS

Novels

*Dance the Eagle to Sleep.* New York, Doubleday, 1970; London, W.H. Allen, 1971.
*Woman on the Edge of Time.* New York, Knopf, 1976; London, Women's Press, 1979.

OTHER PUBLICATIONS

Novels

*Going Down Fast.* New York, Simon and Schuster, 1969.
*Small Changes.* New York, Doubleday, 1973; London, Penguin, 1987.
*The High Cost of Living.* New York, Harper, 1978; London, Women's Press, 1979.
*Vida.* New York, Summit, and London, Women's Press, 1980.
*Braided Lives.* New York, Summit, and London, Allen Lane, 1982.
*Fly Away Home.* New York, Summit, and London, Chatto and Windus, 1984.
*Gone to Soldiers.* New York, Summit, and London, Joseph, 1987.
*Summer People.* New York, Summit, and London, Joseph, 1989.

Play

*The Last White Class: A Play about Neighborhood Terror,* with Ira Wood (produced Northampton, Massachusetts, 1978). Trumansburg, New York, Crossing Press, 1980.

Verse

*Breaking Camp.* Middletown, Connecticut, Wesleyan University Press, 1968.
*Hard Loving.* Middletown, Connecticut, Wesleyan University Press, 1969.
*A Work of Artifice.* Detroit, Red Hanrahan Press, 1970.
*4-Telling, with others.* Trumansburg, New York, Crossing Press, 1971.
*When the Drought Broke.* Santa Barbara, California, Unicorn Press, 1971.
*To Be of Use.* New York, Doubleday, 1973.
*Living in the Open.* New York, Knopf, 1976.
*The Twelve-Spoked Wheel Flashing.* New York, Knopf, 1978.
*The Moon Is Always Female.* New York, Knopf, 1980.
*Circles on the Water: Selected Poems.* New York, Knopf, 1982.
*Stone, Paper, Knife.* New York, Knopf, and London, Pandora Press, 1983.
*My Mother's Body.* New York, Knopf, and London, Pandora Press, 1985.
*Available Light.* New York, Knopf, and London, Pandora Press, 1988.
*The Earth Shines Secretly: A Book of Days,* with paintings and Drawings by Nell Blaine. Cambridge, Massachusetts, Zoland Press, 1990.

Other

*The Grand Coolie Damn.* Boston, New England Free Press, 1970.
*Parti-Colored Blocks for a Quilt.* Ann Arbor, University of Michigan Press, 1982.

Editor, *Early Ripening: Young Women's Poetry Now.* London and New York, Pandora Press, 1987.

*

Bibliography: in *Contemporary American Women Writers: Narrative Strategies* edited by Catherine Rainwater and William J. Scheick, Lexington, University Press of Kentucky, 1985.

Manuscript Collection: University of Michigan, Harlan Hatcher Graduate Library, Ann Arbor.

Critical Studies: "Marge Piercy: A Collage" by Nancy Scholar Zee, in *Oyez Review* (Berkeley, California), 9(1), 1975; *Ways of Knowing: Critical Essays on Marge Piercy* edited by Sue Walker and Eugenie Hamner, Mobile, Alabama, Negative Capability Press, 1986.

* * *

Marge Piercy is a prolific author, with several dozen books, fiction, poetry, and non-fiction, to her credit, but of these only two can be claimed for science fiction. *Dance the Eagle to Sleep* is only peripherally within the genre, a vivid though unsatisfying picture of an attempt by young people to break away from society and set up a tribal-based, loving and supportive community. It does point forward, as do many of Piercy's other writings, to her most successful work, *Woman on the Edge of Time*, a vision of future utopia. Of the two, *Dance the Eagle to Sleep* was more widely and favorably reviewed on publication. *Woman on the Edge of Time* was at first seen as a mediocre, overly ambitious work, but succeeding years have brought frequent high praise. In both novels, the indictment of present society common throughout Piercy's work is a major theme.

In one sense *Woman on the Edge of Time* has had more attention than it deserves: science fiction, utopian, and, above all, feminist scholars have written about the book extensively. On the other hand, this is the best written of the many feminist utopias that have appeared in recent years, and, unlike most utopian works, it is a novel with believable characters, an interesting plot, and potential for implementation. That it is also a careful, complete portrayal of the kind of society a reformer of the mid-seventies would envisage as an ideal future only adds to its importance, in the field of utopian literature at least. There are, of course, many elements that are common to science fiction: travel through time, alternative futures, advanced technology both physical and mental, new social and sexual groupings, and, most important of all, extrapolation of current knowledge to plausible and far-reaching conclusions. As is true with many, if not most, recent utopias written by women, there is major emphasis on the growing maturity of the community, on the right education of the children, on the loving, communal attitude of the citizens. The novel's literary achievement is significantly enhanced by the similar maturing of its heroine.

The heroine is Connie Ramos, Chicana, welfare-mother wrongly charged with abusing her daughter, patient against her will in a mental hospital, and victim of various experimental medical "treatments," including implantation of electrodes in her brain. Beginning as scattered dream impressions, then in a real presence at first frightening to Connie, Luciente—"from a village in Massachusetts—Mattapoisset. Only I live there in 2137"—gets through to her as the first contact from a future into which she is soon able to journey increasingly easily. The story of her horrible and inhuman experiences in the mental hospital alternates with these visits to the pleasant new society of the 22nd century where many new friends teach her about their world. But always she is pulled back to the ugly world of doctors, ever-present nurses and attendants, and Connie's true 20th-century friends, the ill-treated patients on whom they practice their cures and make their experiments.

In Mattapoisset—utopian despite Piercy's claim that it is not but rather "the result of a full feminist revolution"—an ecologically responsible, loving, non-sexist (male and female pronouns have been replaced by "per") community has learned that its own existence is threatened by the possible outcome of the experiments being conducted at Rockover State Hospital. The contact with Connie is part of their attempt—there are four others, all also in mental hospitals or prisons—to prevent these undesirable consequences. Connie, it is apparent to Mattapoisset, can be a major factor in the conflict between technology wrongly used and the opposition and rebellion of those who want the kind of society that Mattapoisset represents. Bringing her to the right action, to fighting back against the system that has mistreated her, is a matter of showing her the beautiful future they represent as opposed to the dystopian society of her own day or the alternative future described in chapter 15 that would come as a result of her failure to act. Although the people of Mattapoisset are peaceful, they fight when necessary to defend their community—as Connie discovers on one of her visits, and they remind Connie that sometimes, especially in her time, the violence-prone must be resisted, even when such resistance involves further violence. Connie does take drastic action, but she is clearly doomed to end her days at Rockover.

Perhaps, as has been suggested by several critics, Connie's visits to the future are all hallucinations: certainly she has been sufficiently drugged to make such a suggestion reasonable. Hallucination or not, the story deals with a tormented victim of the evil in society, an almost-innocent, betrayed by those closest to her, who cannot understand why things work out for her as they do. The contrast with the beautiful world that might be is clearly the work of a reformer who feels deeply the injustices of this world and believes just as deeply in the things of which she writes. But, no matter what the motivating force behind its production, this is an excellent novel, deserving of its warm critical reception. Whether Piercy ever writes another work that fits the science fiction mold, this one novel has earned her a permanent place in the utopian branch of the genre.

—Arthur O. Lewis

---

**PINKWATER, Daniel Manus.** Also writes as Manus Pinkwater. American. Born in Memphis, Tennessee, 15 November 1941. Educated at Bard College, Annandale-on-Hudson, New York, B.A. 1964. Married Jill Schutz in 1969. Art instructor, Children's Aid Society, 1967–69, Lower West Side Visual Arts Center, 1969, and Henry Street Settlement, 1969, all New York, and Bonnie Brae Farm for Boys, Millington, New Jersey, 1969; assistant project director, Inner City Summer Arts Program, Hoboken, New Jersey, 1970. Regular commentator, *All Things Considered*, National Public Radio. Agent: Susan Cohen, Writers House Inc., 21 West 26th Street, New York, New York 10010, U.S.A.

SCIENCE-FICTION PUBLICATIONS

Novels for children (series: Magic Moscow; Moose; Snarkout Boys)

*Wizard Crystal*. New York, Dodd Mead, 1973.
*Magic Camera*. New York, Dodd Mead, 1974.
*Blue Moose* (as Manus Pinkwater). New York, Dodd Mead, 1975; London, Blackie, 1977.
*Wingman* (as Manus Pinkwater). New York, Dodd Mead, 1975.
*Lizard Music*. New York, Dodd Mead, 1976.
*The Big Orange Splot*. New York, Hastings House, 1977.
*The Blue Thing*. Englewood Cliffs, New Jersey, Prentice Hall, 1977.
*Fat Men from Space*. New York, Dodd Mead, 1977.
*Alan Mendelsohn: The Boy from Mars*. New York, Dutton, 1979.
*Pickle Creature*. New York, Four Winds Press, 1979.
*Return of the Moose*. New York, Dodd Mead, 1979.

*Yobgorble, Mystery Monster of Lake Ontario.* New York, Clarion, 1979.
*The Magic Moscow.* New York, Four Winds Press, 1980.
*Attila the Pun* (Magic Moscow). New York, Four Winds Press, 1981.
*Tooth-Gnasher Superflash.* New York, Four Winds Press, 1981.
*The Worms of Kukumlima.* New York, Dutton, 1981.
*Slaves of Spiegel* (Magic Moscow). New York, Four Winds Press, 1982.
*The Snarkout Boys and the Avocado of Death.* New York, Lothrop, 1982.
*I Was a Second Grade Werewolf.* New York, Dutton, 1983.
*Devil in the Drain.* New York, Dutton, 1984.
*The Snarkout Boys and the Baconburg Horror.* New York, Lothrop, 1984.
*The Frankenbagel Monster.* New York, Dutton, 1986.
*The Moosepire.* Boston, Little Brown, 1986.
*The Muffin Fiend.* New York, Lothrop, 1986.
*Guys from Space.* New York, Macmillan, 1989.
*Borgel.* New York, Macmillan, 1990.
*Wempires.* New York, Macmillan, 1991.

OTHER PUBLICATIONS for children

Fiction

*The Hoboken Chicken Emergency.* Englewood Cliffs, New Jersey, Prentice Hall, 1977.
*The Last Guru.* New York, Dodd Mead, 1978.
*Java Jack*, with Luqman Keele. New York, Crowell, 1980.
*The Wuggie Norple Story*, illustrated by Tomie de Paola. New York, Four Winds Press, 1980.
*Roger's Umbrella*, illustrated by James Marshall. New York, Dutton, 1982.
*Young Adult Novel.* New York, Crowell, 1982.
*Ducks!* Boston, Little Brown, 1984.
*Aunt Lulu.* New York, Macmillan, 1988.
*Uncle Melvin.* New York, Macmillan, 1989.
*Chicago Days/Hoboken Nights.* Reading, Massachusetts, Addison-Wesley, 1991.
*Doodle Flute.* New York, Macmillan, 1991.

Fiction as Manus Pinkwater

*The Terrible Roar.* New York, Knopf, 1970.
*Bear's Picture.* New York, Holt Rinehart, 1972.
*Fat Elliot and the Gorilla.* New York, Four Winds Press, 1974.
*Three Big Hogs.* New York, Seabury Press, 1975.
*Around Fred's Bed*, illustrated by Robert Mertens. Englewood Cliffs, New Jersey, Prentice Hall, 1976.

Other

*Superpuppy: How to Choose, Raise, and Train the Best Possible Dog for You*, with Jill Pinkwater. New York, Seabury Press, 1977.
*Fish Whistle: Commentaries, Uncommentaries, and Vulgar Excesses.* Reading, Massachusetts, Addison-Wesley, 1989.

* * *

One of the few genuine heirs of dada and surrealism in contemporary fantastic literature, Daniel Manus Pinkwater is also unusual in that he has attained a considerable reputation among adult readers even though virtually all of his fiction has been published for children and young adults. Writers as diverse as Samuel R. Delany, Harlan Ellison, and Vonda McIntyre have counted themselves among his fans, and it seems reasonable to suspect that Pinkwater's adult constituency may be nearly as large as that of his younger readership. Pinkwater tacitly acknowledges this by sprinkling his work liberally with arcane literary and cultural allusions likely to be lost on younger readers—such as a version of the Shadow named "Lamont Penumbra" in *Attila the Pun*, or references to dadaism and 'pataphysics in *Young Adult Novel.*

Pinkwater's world is a bizarre and endlessly inventive place where licensed realtors are controlled by aliens, where aliens all wear identical plaid sport coats and lust after junk food, where time-traveling moose detectives haunt the Canadian wilderness, where W.A. Mozart is a comic-book superhero, where planets bear names like Ziegler and Spiegel and cities names like Lenny, and where outer space is dotted with root beer stands. On a more serious level, it is a world in which outsiders can be heroes—overweight kids with thick glasses, mental patients, eccentric uncles, and—most often—kids whose interests and hobbies set them apart from their peers. For example, *Alan Mendelsohn: The Boy from Mars* draws a sensitive portrait of what it is like to be an outcast in school—and what it might be like to get revenge.

These themes are apparent in Pinkwater's most widely-known novel, *Lizard Music.* Victor, who is considered "a freak" at school because he is a fan of Walter Cronkite rather than of rock stars, finds himself alone in the house during his parents' vacation. Staying up late, he catches a TV program of lizards playing music. Lizards begin to appear to him everywhere, and he wonders if he is hallucinating until a mysterious figure called the Chicken Man (who always introduces himself with the name of a different Northern Renaissance painter—Grunewald, Van Eyck, Cranach, etc.) reveals that a society of lizards is indeed living on an invisible island in the lake next to Hogboro (Pinkwater's name for Chicago, apparently) and is broadcasting TV programs. The Chicken Man takes Victor to the island, where he witnesses the wonders of the lizard society in a kind of crazed parody of Renaissance utopias. Earlier, Victor had watched a film called *The Invasion of the Pod People* on television and had begun to worry that people might actually be replaced by emotionless replicas from outer space; now he learns that "lizards and pods are natural enemies," and the lizards come to represent individuality and freedom of thought.

Conformity seems to be one of Pinkwater's main targets. Another film Victor sees on television describes an invasion of aliens in plaid sport coats who strip the Earth of its junk food. This is the plot of Pinkwater's own *Fat Men from Space*, and one of many cross-allusions to other Pinkwater books. The fat men, it turns out, are from the planet Spiegel, ruled over by the evil Sargon, who wants to steal all the junk food in the universe. In *Slaves of Spiegel* (itself the third book in the "Magic Moscow" trilogy), a Hoboken ice-cream parlor, its owner, and his assistant are kidnapped whole to participate in an intergalactic junk-food cook-off.

Pinkwater's most successful series characters appear in *The Snarkout Boys and the Avocado of Death* and *The Snarkout Boys and the Baconburg Horror.* Walter Galt and Winston Bongo, both outsiders at Genghis Khan High School, make a habit of sneaking out to late movies at the Snark Theatre after their parents are asleep. This leads them into a series of adventures involving a girl named Rat, the Chicken Man (from *Lizard Music*), the great detective Osgood Sigerson (a version of Sherlock Holmes), and his arch-enemy Wallace Nussbaum (a version of Moriarty). In the first of these adventures, Rat's uncle, a brilliant avocado scientist, disappears—kidnapped by Nussbaum to prevent his completing work on a giant telepathic avocado computer which can release the minds of real estate agents from alien control. In the second novel, a werewolf seems to be terrorizing the town of Baconburg.

Even Pinkwater's picture books for younger readers offer surrealistic twists on conventional fantasy images. *The Moosepire* (the third book in a trilogy that began with *Blue Moose* and *Return of the Moose*) offers what appears to be a moose vampire, but becomes a time travel story. *I Was a Second Grade Werewolf* concerns a boy who thinks he has turned into a werewolf, but can't get anyone to notice. *Guys from Space* are friendly aliens who invite a young boy to join them in visiting different planets, "just looking around," and stopping off for a root beer on the way home. *The Frankenbagel Monster* recasts Frankenstein as a mad bagel maker whose giant "Bagelunculus" threatens to destroy earth—until it goes stale. The devil himself appears as a tiny but grouchy inhabitant of a kitchen sink drain in *Devil in the Drain.*

In recent years, Pinkwater has been a popular commentator on public radio, and his commentaries (collected as *Fish Whistle*) may offer some clues to autobiographical elements in his writing. The title character of *Borgel*, for example, is a mysterious older relative of indeterminate nationality whose nostalgia for the "Old Country" and questionable "gift" for languages recalls Pinkwater's accounts of his father and uncles. But Borgel also turns out to be an intergalactic adventurer who takes his young nephew on a wild quest in space and time for "the great Popsicle." As with other Pinkwater books, the juxtaposition of sharply observed, recognizable characters with an epic sense of silliness worthy of the Marx Brothers seems to suggest that eccentricity alone can be a key to salvation.

—Gary K. Wolfe

---

**PIPER, H(enry) Beam.** American. Born in Altoona, Pennsylvania, in 1904. Worked on the engineering staff of the Pennsylvania Railroad. *Died 11 November 1964.*

SCIENCE-FICTION PUBLICATIONS

Novels (series: Terran Federation)

*Crisis in 2140*, with John J. McGuire. New York, Ace, 1957.
*A Planet for Texans*, with John J. McGuire. New York, Ace, 1958.
*Four-Day Planet* (for children; Federation). New York, Putnam, 1961.
*Little Fuzzy* (Federation). New York, Avon, 1962.
*Junkyard Planet* (Federation). New York, Putnam, 1963; as *The Cosmic Computer*, New York, Ace, 1964.
*Space Viking* (Federation). New York, Ace, 1963; London, Sphere, 1978.
*The Other Human Race* (Federation). New York, Avon, 1964; as *Fuzzy Sapiens*, New York, Ace, 1976.
*Lord Kalvan of Otherwhen*. New York, Ace, 1965; as *Gunpowder God*, London, Sphere, 1978.
*The Fuzzy Papers* (omnibus). New York, Doubleday, 1977.
*Uller Uprising*. New York, Ace, 1982.
*Four-Day Planet, and Lone Star Planet*. New York, Ace, 1984.
*Fuzzies and Other People*. New York, Ace, 1984.

Short Stories

*Federation*. New York, Ace, 1981.
*Empire*. New York, Ace, 1981.
*Paratime*. New York, Ace, 1981.
*The Worlds of H. Beam Piper*, edited by John F. Carr. New York, Ace, 1983.

OTHER PUBLICATIONS

Novel

*Murder in the Gun Room*. New York, Knopf, 1953.

Other

Editor, *A Catalogue of Early Pennsylvania and Other Firearms and Edged Weapons at "Restless Oaks," McElhattan, Pennsylvania*. Privately printed, 1927(?).

* * *

H. Beam Piper's science fiction is largely the stories of heroes (or heroines), with ideas apparently subordinate to the needs of plot and action. This is most evident in novels such as *A Planet for Texans, Four-Day Planet, Space Viking*, and *Lord Kalvan of Otherwhen.* The last two of these, especially, are fast-paced adventure yarns, with a well-developed central figure, but quite two-dimensional supporting characters. In each case, the hero (Calvin Morrison in *Lord Kalvan of Otherwhen*, Lucas Trask in *Space Viking*) is forced by circumstances totally beyond his control to enter a life radically different from the one that he had anticipated. A major difficulty each man must resolve is the ethical dilemma of the life which he perceives as central to his functioning. Thus, Morrison is caught in the field of an interdimension/time travel machine, while Trask on his wedding day has his bride-to-be killed by her rejected suitor. Morrison must agonize over the appropriateness of introducing more sophisticated weaponry into an essentially static culture, Trask over the ethics of killing and looting even though the attached planets are decadent remnants of the "Old Federation." The ultimate results of the activities of each man are intrinsically the same as well: Morrison defeats Styphon's House (which opposed progress and sought to divide countries against one another) while Trask defeats the destructive forces both on Marduk and among the space vikings, establishing Tanith as a progressive planet destined to lead a new League of Civilized Worlds.

Perhaps Piper's most famous works are *Little Fuzzy* and *The Other Human Race. Little Fuzzy* builds towards a dramatic courtroom scene in which good and evil clearly clash over the question of the sapience of the Fuzzies. Again there is a central heroic figure, Jack Holloway, discoverer of the Fuzzies. The ethical dilemma to be resolved is whether to recognize the Fuzzies as sentient, giving them *prima facie* right to their own planet and thereby displacing the human interests on the planet Zarathustra, or to allow them to be treated as charming and quick-to-learn animals, subjecting them to what is—for a sentient being—slavery. Holloway's determination and courage in the face of the bureaucratic opposition to the recognition of the Fuzzies as sentient has elements of the heroic physical challenges confronting Morrison and Trask, but it is primarily a moral courage in the face of social opposition. In *The Other Human Race* the same basic problem is repeated except that the ethical dilemma is whether or not to honor the governmental commitment to the Fuzzy Reservation in the face of economic pressures to open the

Reservation for mining. There is the added problem of the radical increase in defective births among the Fuzzies. The apparently neutral position of doing nothing about Fuzzy rights is extensionally the same as the decision to exterminate the Fuzzy race, for the humans have it within their power to halt the flood of defective Fuzzy births. Again, in both books, the resolution of the ethical dilemma leaves the world rather significantly altered in the direction of progress-as-we-know-it.

A sidelight which may be of significant interest has to do with the name of the Fuzzies' planet—Zarathustra, the name of the central figure in the pre-Christian middle-Eastern religion Zoroastrianism (Zoroaster was also known as Zarathustra), similar to the Christian Manichean heresy, which argues the existence of two co-equal forces in the universe, Ahura Mazda (good) and Angra Mainyu (evil). Perhaps Piper was consciously trying to depict such a struggle in the Fuzzies novels. The planet's name might also have been an allusion to Friedrich Nietzsche's *Also Sprach Zarathustra.* This interpretation offers a potentially convoluted approach to the text because Nietzsche argued for the recognition of man *and superman.* Since the superman is exempt from the constraints of normal ethics, one might have expected a different conclusion.

Piper's other writings more or less follow the same pattern: the hero/heroine is struck by a major ethical problem—paternalism over proud people in *A Planet for Texans;* revolution or economic slavery in *Four-Day Planet;* human dependency upon its own machines in *Junkyard Planet;* the dominance of scholarship by economics in 'Omnilingual.' In each case the protagonist chooses honor and decency, but also, more significantly, the choice is made for progress. Those forces which support the status quo are doomed from the outset. In a Piper story one "knows" that the hero/heroine will prevail, but only after terrible difficulties. More impressive, however, is Piper's recognition that such successes must result in a significant alteration of the world on which they occur.

—Richard W. Miller

---

**PISERCHIA, Doris (Elaine).** Also writes as Curt Selby. American. Born in Fairmont, West Virginia, 11 October 1928. Educated at Fairmont State College, A.B. 1950; University of Utah, Salt Lake City, 1963–65. Served in the United States Navy, 1950–54: Lieutenant. Married Joseph John Piserchia in 1953; three daughters and two sons. Agent: Carnell Literary Agency, Danes Croft, Goose Lane, Little Hallingbury, Hertfordshire CM22 7RG, England. Address: c/o DAW Books, 375 Hudson Street, New York, New York 10014, U.S.A.

Science-Fiction Publications

Novels

*Mister Justice.* New York, Ace, 1973; London, Dobson, 1977.
*Star Rider.* New York, Bantam, 1974; London, Women's Press, 1987.
*A Billion Days of Earth.* New York, Bantam, 1976; London, Dobson, 1977.
*Earthchild.* New York, DAW, 1977; London, Dobson, 1979.
*Spaceling.* New York, Doubleday, 1978.
*The Spinner.* New York, DAW, 1980.
*The Fluger.* New York, DAW, 1980.
*Earth in Twilight.* New York, DAW, 1981.
*Doomtime.* New York, DAW, 1981.
*Blood County* (as Curt Selby). New York, DAW, 1981.
*I, Zombie* (as Curt Selby). New York, DAW, 1982.
*The Dimensioneers.* New York, DAW, 1982.
*The Deadly Sky.* New York, DAW, 1983.

* * *

Doris Piserchia's strongest asset in her novels has been the exotic and colorful settings she has created. *Star Rider*, for example, features a young girl who has a telepathic bond with a horse. The two of them can teleport themselves around the universe, encased by small pockets of environment. They are looking for a fabled world which turns out to be a ruined, deserted Earth tucked into another dimension. Her quest is complicated by a number of other parties involved not only in her quest, but interested as well in her mutant ability to transport herself across intergalactic as well as interstellar distances.

In *A Billion Days of Earth*, men have assumed godlike powers and many of the lower species of animal have acquired intelligence. A vigilante metes out his own brand of justice in *Mister Justice.* But the novels that followed these spent less time on characterization and more on setting and plot, with mixed results. *Earth Child* for instance is almost one constant chase-adventure-battle scene. Earth is being contested by Indigo, a plant that is becoming an ocean, and Emeroo, another plant that is much smaller in size but possibly more powerful in the long run. The last living human is a young girl named Ree, who spends much of her time flying giant insects and fighting the blueboys, plant growths that can move independently and who become increasingly human as the story progresses.

The plot of this novel shows up again in *Doomtime*, this time with gigantic trees battling for control of Earth, with the human race as pawns in their games. It shows up again in *Earth in Twilight*, except in this case the protagonist is a lone space explorer who returns to abandoned Earth to find it overgrown by a gigantic forest inhabited by newly sentient races and giant insects. The astronaut is a classic antihero, unable and perhaps unwilling to make any serious attempt to improve his situation, and the forest of Earth is itself really the strongest character in the novel.

Alien monsters figure even more centrally in two other novels, *The Fluger* and *The Spinner.* The first is rather minor: a gigantic alien wreaks havoc in a closed Earth city until eventually brought to its death by booby-trapped food. The second novel is considerably more interesting. An alien from another dimension spins a mysterious web over an entire city and begins to reproduce his kind in preparation for conquering the entire world.

Inter-dimensional adventures are another staple in Piserchia's novels. In *The Spaceling*, mutants can perceive different dimensions because of drifting rings that allow movement from one plane of existence to another. A young man is drafted into the effort to prevent an interdimensional invasion in *The Deadly Sky.* An extra-dimensional chase is the main plot of *The Dimensioneers*, which transports us from one weird environment to another so quickly that it is almost a comic book adventure without pictures.

Piserchia made more serious efforts at characterization in two novels published under the name "Curt Selby." *Blood County* is a supernatural adventure story involving a vampire who has set himself up as a virtual feudal lord. *I, Zombie*, despite the title, is straight science fiction. The recent dead are fitted with implants that allow them to be used as slave laborers with no will of their own, until one such body begins to reawaken its former personality and sets out to free others from their bondage.

—Don D'Ammassa

---

**PLATT, Charles.** Also writes as Ronald B. Clarke. British. Born in Hertfordshire, 25 October 1944. Educated at Cambridge University, one year, and London College of Printing, two years. Worked for Clive Bingley, publishers, London, 1967; designer and production assistant, *New Worlds* magazine; freelance photographer and book jacket designer. Science-fiction editor, Avon Books, 1972–74; Condor Publishing, 1977–78; Franklin Watts, 1986–88. Recipient: *Locus* award, for non-fiction, 1985. Address: c/o Bantam, 666 Fifth Avenue, New York, New York 10103, U.S.A.

Science-Fiction Publications

Novels

*Garbage World.* New York, Berkley, 1967; London, Panther, 1968.
*The City Dwellers.* London, Sidgwick and Jackson, 1970; revised edition, as *Twilight of the City*, New York, Macmillan, 1977.
*Planet of the Voles.* New York, Putnam, 1977.
*Sweet Evil.* New York, Berkley, 1977.
*Less Than Human* (as Ronald B. Clarke). New York, Avon, 1986; as Charles Platt, London, Grafton, 1987.
*Plasm.* New York, New American Library, 1987; London, Grafton, 1988.
*Free Zone.* New York, Avon, 1989.
*SOMA.* New York, New American Library, 1989; London, Grafton, 1990.
*The Silicon Man.* New York, Bantam, 1991.

Other Publications

Novel

*The Gas.* New York, Ophelia Press, 1970.

Verse

*Highway Sandwiches*, with Thomas M. Disch and Marilyn Hacker. Privately printed, 1970.

Other

*Dream Makers: The Uncommon People Who Write Science Fiction* (interviews). New York, Berkley, 2 vols., 1980–83; revised edition, as *Dream Makers: Science Fiction and Fantasy Writers at Work*, New York, Ungar, and London, Xanadu, 1987.
*Graphics Guide to Commodore 64.* Berkeley, California, Sybex, 1984.
*Micromania: The Whole Truth about Home Computers*, with David Langford. London, Gollancz, 1984; as *The Whole Truth Home Computer Handbook*, New York, Avon, 1984.
*BASIC without Math.* New York, Warner, 1984.
*More from your Micro.* New York, Avon, 1985.
*How To Be a Happy Cat*, with cartoons by Gray Jolliffe. London, Gollancz, 1986; New York, St. Martin's Press, 1987.
*When You Can Live Twice as Long, What Will You Do?* New York, Morrow, 1989.

Editor, with Michael Moorcock, *New Worlds 6.* London, Sphere, 1973; as *New Worlds 5*, New York, Avon, 1974.
Editor, with Hilary Bailey, *New Worlds 7.* London, Sphere, 1974; as *New Worlds 6*, New York, Avon, 1975.

* * *

Charles Platt has had a long and diverse career in the field of science fiction, where he has applied his considerable talents as an author of a wide variety of novels, both serious and satirical, as an editor in both the magazine and book publishing fields, as a highly accomplished interviewer of other authors, and as one of the most influential and controversial writers of commentary and criticism.

Platt's first science fiction story, "One of Those Days," was published in 1965 in the British magazine *Science Fantasy*, but he first attracted notice with his association with Michael Moorcock and *New Worlds* at a time when that magazine was the preeminent journal in the British "New Wave" movement. New Wave science fiction at the time was characterized by experimental literary techniques, a tone of nihilistic pessimism, and ineffectual, nonheroic protagonists who must cope with events beyond their understanding or control. Platt worked with Moorcock on *New Worlds* for several years, and became one of the more influential forces behind New Wave SF, before becoming the magazine's editor when Moorcock left in 1970.

At the same time, Platt was continuing to write science fiction himself, all of it strongly influenced by New Wave concepts and techniques, especially those of such authors as J. G. Ballard and Moorcock himself. His first novel, *Garbage World*, was a highly inventive novel, cleverly written but marred by somewhat immature reliance on scatological humor. The novel is set among the degenerate society living on an asteroid that is used as the garbage receptacle for the Solar System. *Planet of the Voles* was a more conventional, although humorous, space opera, still written with New Wave sensibilities.

The most ambitious of Platt's early novels was *The City Dwellers*, a novel formed from short works that was later heavily revised, expanded, and retitled *Twilight of the City*. These novels, set in a dying near-future city, were serious novels in the New Wave tradition. *Twilight of the City* was Platt's first novel written with truly serious intent, although it never got the critical notice it deserved.

In 1970, Platt moved from London to New York and has lived in the United States ever since. He held jobs as science fiction editor with Avon Books (1972–74) and Condor Publishing (1977–1978), both paperback book publishers, where he learned the New York publishing scene. He resigned from Avon when they refused to buy Philip K. Dick's *Flow My Tears, the Policeman Said* because they disliked the title. He later returned to editing with Franklin Watts from 1986–88, where he was able to provide fine hardcover editions for authors such as Brian Aldiss, Victor Koman, Ronald Anthony Cross, John Shirley and Rachel Pollack.

In the late 1970's, Platt turned to interviewing science fiction authors during his travels around the U.S., and he developed a style of uniquely personal, yet highly opinionated interview/profiles that brought him his first real critical notice. These resulted in two volumes of interviews called *Dream Makers*, both of which were nominated for Hugo awards for nonfiction, as well as a 1987 combined volume with some new material. Some of the interviews in the first volume stirred up quite a bit of controversy inside the field; Platt approached his subjects for the second volume a bit more evenhandedly.

He also began in the 1980's to write commentary on science fiction. He began his own self-published magazine, *The Patchin Review*, in 1980, which became well-known among insiders in the field for its caustic, controversial, and irreverent commentary, much of it written by Platt himself, and some of it under various pseudonyms. At first, Platt's criticisms and witticisms were viewed as mere continuance of the merry-prankster image he had developed within SF fandom in the 1970's. However, as time wore on, Platt took his role as SF critic more seriously, and by the early-to-mid-1980's he was regularly having published serious essays in most of the U.S. science fiction professional magazines, in *Interzone*, and also in many of the most respected semi-professional critical journals, including *THRUST, Fantasy Review, Locus, Science Fiction Chronicle*, and *Science Fiction Eye*. By the end of the decade, Platt had become one of the field's most respected, albeit often controversial, critics.

Platt returned to writing novels in the late 1980's. Two of these were "share-cropper" novels set in Piers Anthony's world of Chthon, *Plasm* and *SOMA*. These books bear some resemblance to Platt's fiction of the 1970's in terms of tone and subject matter (in the first novel, for instance, the protagonist's mother has been genetically engineered to obtain sexual pleasure from beatings and cruelty). They are quite competently plotted, however, and represent Platt cracking his knuckles and getting ready to write fiction once again. Two of the other books were very successful science-fiction satires. The first was *Less Than Human*, published in the U.S. only under Platt's Robert Clarke pseudonym, a genuinely amusing book about an intelligent but innocent android in a degenerate New York in the year 2010. The other, *Free Zone*, is a *tour de force* satire, a near-future SF pastiche that makes fun of every SF cliché and convention ever conceived.

With Platt's latest novel, he has finally reached his full potential as a serious science fiction author. *The Silicon Man* takes advantage of Platt's extensive knowledge of microcomputer technology (he wrote several non-fiction books on computers and artificial intelligence in 1984 and 1985) to present possibly the most realistic portrayal to date of the concept of downloading a human consciousness into a computer-generated interactive environment. Written as a fast-paced thriller, the story involves an FBI agent who traces the source of a high-tech black market hand weapon back to a small team of scientists who are working for a defense contractor on a project that has apparently been kept heavily funded for decades despite no apparent success. The scientists turn out to be part of a secret conspiracy to gain immortality through computer translation, a procedure that involves destruction of the brain itself. To protect their scheme, the agent himself is translated, and it turns out that the mastermind behind the project has more extensive and ulterior motives than anyone knew. With this novel, Platt joined the slim ranks of SF authors (which include Vernor Vinge and Greg Bear) who understand computers well *and* can create realistic characters.

—D. Douglas Fratz

---

**POHL, Frederik.** Also writes as James MacCreigh; Ernst Mason; Edson McCann; Jordon Park; Donald Stacy. American. Born in New York City, 26 November 1919. Served in the United States Air Force, in the United States and Italy, 1943–45: Sergeant. Married 1) Doris Baumgardt in 1940 (divorced 1944); 2) Dorothy LesTina in 1945 (divorced 1947); 3) Judith Merril, *q.v.*, in 1949 (divorced 1953), one daughter; 4) Carol Metcalf Ulf in 1952 (divorced 1981), two sons (one deceased) and one daughter; 5) Elizabeth Anne Hull in 1984. Editor, Popular Publications, New York, 1939–43; copywriter, Thwing and Altman, New York, 1946; book editor and associate circulation manager, Popular Science Publication Company, New York, 1946–49; literary agent, New York, 1949–53; features editor, later editor, *If*, New York, 1959–70; editor, Galaxy Publishing Company, New York, 1961–69; executive editor, Ace Books, New York, 1971–72; science-fiction editor, Bantam Books, New York, 1973–79. Since 1976, contributing editor, *Algol*, New York. President, Science Fiction Writers of America, 1974–76; president, World SF, 1980–82 and vice-president (West), 1985–86; Mid-West Area Chair, Authors Guild of America. Recipient: Edward E. Smith Memorial award, 1966; Hugo award, for editing, 1966, 1967, 1968, for fiction, 1973, 1978; *Locus* award, 1973, 1978; Nebula award, 1976, 1977; John W. Campbell Memorial award, 1978; Prix Apollo (France), 1979; American Book award, 1980. Guest of Honor, World Science Fiction Convention, 1972; Fellow, American Association for the Advancement of Science. Agent: Curtis Brown, 10 Astor Place, New York, New York 10003; or Carnell Literary Agency, Danes Croft, Goose Lane, Little Hallingbury, Hertfordshire CM22 FRG, England.

### Science-Fiction Publications

Novels (series: Cuckoo's Saga; Jim Eden; Gateway; Starchild)

*The Space Merchants*, with C.M. Kornbluth. New York, Ballantine, 1953; London, Heinemann, 1955.
*Search the Sky*, with C.M. Kornbluth. New York, Ballantine, 1954; London, Digit, 1960.
*Undersea Quest* (for children; Eden), with Jack Williamson. New York, Gnome Press, 1954; London, Dobson, 1966.
*Preferred Risk* (as Edson McCann, with Lester del Rey). New York, Simon and Schuster, 1955; London, Methuen, 1983.
*Gladiator-at-Law*, with C.M. Kornbluth. New York, Ballantine, 1955; London, Digit, 1958.
*Undersea Fleet* (for children; Eden), with Jack Williamson. New York, Gnome Press, 1956; London, Dobson, 1968.
*Slave Ship*. New York, Ballantine, 1957; London, Dobson, 1961.
*Undersea City* (for children; Eden), with Jack Williamson. New York, Gnome Press, 1958; London, Dobson, 1968.
*Wolfbane*, with C.M. Kornbluth. New York, Ballantine, 1959; London, Gollancz, 1960; revised edition, revised by Frederick Pohl, New York, Baen, and London, Gollancz, 1986.
*Drunkard's Walk*. New York, Ballantine, 1960; revised edition, London, Gollancz, 1961.
*The Starchild Trilogy*, with Jack Williamson. New York, Doubleday, 1977; London, Penguin, 1980.
  *The Reefs of Space*. New York, Ballantine, 1964; London, Dobson, 1965.
  *Starchild*. New York, Ballantine, 1965; London, Dobson, 1966.
  *Rogue Star*. New York, Ballantine, 1969; London, Dobson, 1972.
*A Plague of Pythons*. New York, Ballantine, 1965; London, Gollancz, 1966; revised edition, as *Demon in the Skull*, New York, DAW, 1984.
*The Age of the Pussyfoot*. New York, Trident Press, 1969; London, Gollancz, 1970.
*Farthest Star* (Cuckoo's Saga), with Jack Williamson. New York, Ballantine, 1975; London, Pan, 1976.

*Man Plus*. New York, Random House, and London, Gollancz, 1976.
*Gateway*. New York, St. Martin's Press, and London, Gollancz, 1977.
*Jem: The Making of a Utopia*. New York, St. Martin's Press, and London, Gollancz, 1979.
*Beyond the Blue Event Horizon* (Gateway). New York, Ballantine, and London, Gollancz, 1980.
*The Cool War*. New York, Ballantine, and London, Gollancz, 1981.
*Starburst*. New York, Ballantine, and London, Gollancz, 1982.
*Syzygy*. New York, Bantam, 1982.
*Wall Around a Star* (Cuckoo's Saga), with Jack Williamson. New York, Ballantine, 1983.
*Midas World*. New York, St. Martin's Press, and London, Gollancz, 1983.
*Heechee Rendezvous* (Gateway). New York, Ballantine, and London, Gollancz, 1984.
*The Years of the City*. New York, Simon and Schuster, 1984; London, Gollancz, 1985.
*The Merchants' War*. New York, St. Martin's Press, 1984; London, Gollancz, 1985.
*Black Star Rising*. New York, Ballantine, 1985; London, Gollancz, 1986.
*Terror*. New York, Berkley, 1986.
*The Coming of the Quantum Cats*. New York, Bantam, 1986; London, Gollancz, 1987.
*The Annals of the Heechee* (Gateway). New York, Ballantine, and London, Gollancz, 1987.
*Chernobyl*. New York and London, Bantam, 1987.
*Narabedla Ltd*. New York, Ballantine, 1987; London, Gollancz, 1990.
*The Day the Martians Came*. New York, St. Martin's Press, 1988.
*Land's End*, with Jack Williamson. New York, Tor, 1988.
*Homegoing*. New York, Ballantine, 1989; London, Gollancz, 1990.
*The World at the End of Time*. New York, Ballantine, 1990.
*Outnumbering the Dead*. London, Legend, 1991.
*The Singers of Time*, with Jack Williamson. New York, Doubleday, 1991.

Short Stories

*Danger Moon* (as James MacCreigh). Sydney, American Science Fiction, 1953.
*Alternating Currents*. New York, Ballantine, 1956; London, Penguin, 1966.
*The Case Against Tomorrow*. New York, Ballantine, 1957.
*Tomorrow Times Seven*. New York, Ballantine, 1959.
*The Man Who Ate the World*. New York, Ballantine, 1960; London, Panther, 1979.
*Turn Left at Thursday*. New York, Ballantine, 1961.
*The Wonder Effect*, with C.M. Kornbluth. New York, Ballantine, 1962; London, Gollancz, 1967; revised edition, as *Critical Mass*, New York, Bantam, 1977.
*The Abominable Earthman*. New York, Ballantine, 1963.
*The Frederik Pohl Omnibus*. London, Gollancz, 1966; reprinted in part, as *Survival Kit*, London, Panther, 1979.
*Digits and Dastards* (includes essays). New York, Ballantine, 1966; London, Dobson, 1968.
*Day Million*. New York, Ballantine, 1970; London, Gollancz, 1971.
*The Gold at Starbow's End*. New York, Ballantine, 1972; London, Gollancz, 1973.
*The Best of Frederik Pohl*, edited by Lester del Rey. New York, Doubleday, 1975; London, Sidgwick and Jackson, 1977.
*In the Problem Pit*. New York, Bantam, and London, Corgi, 1976.
*The Early Pohl*. New York, Doubleday, 1976; London, Dobson, 1980.
*Planets Three*. New York, Berkley, 1982.
*Pohlstars*. New York, Ballantine, 1984; London, Gollancz, 1986.
*Our Best: The Best of Frederik Pohl and C.M. Kornbluth*. New York, Baen, 1987.
*The Gateway Trip: Tales and Vignettes of the Heechee*. New York, Ballantine, 1990.

OTHER PUBLICATIONS

Novels

*A Town Is Drowning*, with C.M. Kornbluth. New York, Ballantine, 1955; London, Digit, 1960.
*Presidential Year*, with C.M. Kornbluth. New York, Ballantine, 1956.
*Sorority House* (as Jordan Park, with C.M. Kornbluth). New York, Lion, 1956.
*The God of Channel 1* (as Donald Stacy). New York, Ballantine, 1956.
*Turn the Tigers Loose*, with Walter Lasly. New York, Ballantine, 1956.
*Edge of the City* (novelization of screenplay). New York, Ballantine, 1957.

Other

*Tiberius* (biography; as Ernst Mason). New York, Ballantine, 1960.
*Practical Politics 1972*. New York, Ballantine, 1971.
*The Way the Future Was: A Memoir*. New York, Ballantine, 1978; London, Gollancz, 1979.
*Science Fiction: Studies in Film*, with Frederik Pohl IV. New York, Ace, 1982.
*Forbidden Lines: Science Fiction, Fantasy, Essays*, with others. Chapel Hill, North Carolina, Science Fiction Writers' Group, 1989.

Editor, *Beyond the End of Time*. New York, Permabooks, 1952.
Editor, *Shadow of Tomorrow*. New York, Permabooks, 1953.
Editor, *Star Science Fiction Stories 1–6*. New York, Ballantine, 6 vols., 1953–59; vols. 1 and 2, London, Boardman, 1954–55.
Editor, *Assignment in Tomorrow*. New York, Hanover House, 1954.
Editor, *Star Short Novels*. New York, Ballantine, 1954.
Editor, *Star of Stars*. New York, Doubleday, 1960; as *Star Fourteen*, London, Whiting and Wheaton, 1966.
Editor, *The Expert Dreamers*. New York, Doubleday, 1962; London, Gollancz, 1963.
Editor, *Time Waits for Winthrop and Four Short Novels from Galaxy*. New York, Doubleday, 1962.
Editor, *The Seventh* [through *Eleventh*] *Galaxy Reader*. New York, Doubleday, 5 vols., 1965–69; *Seventh* through *Tenth*, London, Gollancz, 4 vols., 1965–68; *Eighth*, as *Final Encounter*, New York, Curtis, 1970; *Tenth*, as *Door to Anywhere*, New York, Curtis, 1970.
Editor, *The If Reader of Science Fiction*. New York, Doubleday, 1966; London, Whiting and Wheaton, 1967; second volume, New York, Doubleday, 1968.
Editor, *Nightmare Age*. New York, Ballantine, 1970.

Editor, *The Best Science Fiction for 1972*. New York, Ace, 1972.

Editor, with Carol Pohl, *Science Fiction: The Great Years*. New York, Ace, 1973; London, Gollancz, 1974, second volume, Ace, 1976.

Editor, with Carol Pohl, *Jupiter*. New York, Ballantine, 1973.

Editor, *The Science Fiction Roll of Honor*. New York, Random House, 1975.

Editor, with Carol Pohl, *Science Fiction Discoveries*. New York, Bantam, 1976.

Editor, *The Best of C.M. Kornbluth*. New York, Doubleday, 1976.

Editor, with Martin H. Greenberg and Joseph D. Olander, *Science Fiction of the 40's*. New York, Avon, 1978.

Editor, with Martin H. Greenberg and Joseph D. Olander, *Galaxy: Thirty Years of Innovative Science Fiction*. Chicago, Playboy Press, 1980; 2nd volume, New York, Ace, 1981.

Editor, *Nebula Winners 14*. New York, Harper, 1980; London, W.H. Allen, 1981.

Editor, with Martin H. Greenberg and Joseph D. Olander, *The Great Science Fiction Series*. New York, Harper, 1980.

Editor, *Yesterday's Tomorrows: Favorite Stories from Forty Years as a Science Fiction Editor*. New York, Berkley, 1982.

Editor, with Elizabeth Anne Hull, *Tales from the Planet Earth*. New York, St. Martin's Press, 1986.

Editor, with Martin H. Greenberg and Joseph D. Olander, *Worlds of If*. New York, Bluejay, 1986.

*

Manuscript Collection: Syracuse University Library, New York.

Frederik Pohl comments:

I write what interests me, in the hope that it will interest others. The things that particularly interest me are: the mismatch between what people say and what they do (U.S. presidents being only the most conspicuous example); the turbulence and elegance of science, particularly at its frontiers (science is my favorite spectator sport); the vulnerability and confusion inside the most plastic of human faces; the sound of language, and the amusing tricks that can be played with it; and Morality.

How thoroughly I communicate these concerns I can't easily tell, but when I stop trying I stop writing.

* * *

A glance at the career of Frederik Pohl reinforces the conviction that Pohl is constantly "on the trail." Formal schooling didn't please him; he dropped away from that track in his senior year, without being graduated. He married four women before (perhaps) finding one suitable. He was an editor at a magazine publishing house, editor of a book department, assistant circulation manager, literary agent, cultural exchange lecturer, guest on more than 400 radio and television programs in nine countries, and is now engaged in turning out some of the most interesting science fiction works on the market.

While some of these activities are related, one asks questions about Pohl's aim in life. His early writing was relatively optimistic, if not utopian. Take a 1941 yarn, "The King's Eye" (from *The Early Pohl*). Here is a planet Venus inhabited by primitives who plan to punish two Earthlings for a crime committed by other humans who have visited their planet previously. But the poor aliens themselves are remnants of a mighty civilization. Their time has come and gone; the culture of Earth has surpassed that of the Venusians, and they haven't a chance of beating the Earthlings who, in the simple techniques of early pulp fiction, come out on top. Even joint works like *Wolfbane*, written with C.M. Kornbluth, contained a lot of good-humored spoofery.

But Pohl eagerly embraced the New Wave attitudes proffered by later writers of science fiction, and Pohl's later works—*The Age of the Pussyfoot* and even his wonderful *Gateway*—are downright dystopian. It was as though pleasant attitudes and relationships among individuals in the fictional world had palled, and the time had come to deal with the weaknesses and even rottenness of mankind.

Oddly, Pohl was criticized by some of his contemporaries for his use of New Wave qualities they thought too conservative. But Pohl defended his position, noting he had no objection to New Wave stories in themselves. What he thought desirable about those changes was that they "shook up" the old dinosaurs of science fiction writing, including himself, and showed them the limitations of continuing to write science fiction according to pulp or Hollywood standards.

Unlike Emile Coue ("Every day in every way, I'm getting better and better"), Pohl often appears to think very little of man as an exemplar, as someone to admire. In his award-winning *Gateway*, his protagonist Broadhead is seen as insecure, undergoing psychotherapy to handle overwhelming guilt of lost lives. Even when the Heechee ship, which is being drawn to destruction into a black hole, is partly saved by Broadhead's lucky button-pushing, his loss of Klara to that overwhelming cosmic phenomenon almost destroys him. True, he has succeeded in his fantastic quest—garnering fabulous treasures from a vanished civilization, but at a price of nine lives. And, while his computer psychologist assures Bob that all the risk and tragedy involved in the adventure are but parts of life, the reader may wonder that it must be so—that in a sense our hero has lost far more than he has won.

*Jem* involves a planet (Earth) divided into three power centers: People, Fuel, and Food. A war brings complete social breakdown on Earth. Colonists from Earth who had settled on a planet far away have thus become independent of Earth, and must not only learn to resolve their differences, but must adjust relationships with the planet's natives. But the struggles among the three divided groups results in the same errors that had wrecked Earth, and the "colonization" of this new planet amounts to little more than rape. The expedition tries to do its best, but the story's ending is tragic—possibly a commentary on the inherent weaknesses and limitations of the human condition.

The science fiction Pohl wrote in partnerships was probably the most interesting and appealing to many readers. *Wolfbane, The Wonder Effect, The Space Merchants* were among works co-authored by Pohl and Cyril Kornbluth. This proved to be a well-adjusted and even pleasant joining of talents, different in some respects but somehow blended to create some of the best reading in the field. *The Space Merchants*, particularly, was harmoniously produced. In an interview Pohl said their collaboration was almost strain-free because each of the writers could depend on the other to do his share. Pohl would write four pages, for instance; Kornbluth would do the same, until the rough draft of the work was completed. Together they smoothed the work into the finished product, which Pohl said he was never able to do with any other writer.

Possibly, though, there was another pairing almost as cooperative: with Jack Williamson. The two of them turned out *Undersea Quest, The Reefs of Space, Starchild, Farthest Star, The Singers of Time*, among other works. Their success in cooperating on these works may have been based, oddly, on differences in their personalities and backgrounds. Williamson was older than Pohl by 15 years, and unlike Pohl he had a formal education, with a Ph.D. in English Literature. Such differences may have worked a kind of magic, blending their separate talents in a solid and smooth collaboration. The proof, of course, lies in the works, which have been read with delight over the years.

Frederik Pohl is a star among stars. He has shaped and seasoned the literature of science fiction as almost no one else has. His kaleidoscopic background had equipped him with skills and values possessed by few if any rivals. Pohl's peers evidently have underlined such high judgment by a wide range of honors, including several Hugo and Nebula awards.

—Robert H. Wilcox

---

**POLLACK, Rachel.** British. Recipient: Arthur C. Clarke award, for novel, 1988. Address: c/o Harper Collins Publishers, 8 Grafton Street, London W1X 3LA, England.

SCIENCE-FICTION PUBLICATIONS

Novels

*Golden Vanity.* New York, Berkley, 1980.
*Alqua Dreams.* New York, Watts, 1987.
*Unquenchable Fire.* London, Century, 1988.

OTHER PUBLICATIONS

Other

*Seventy-Eight Degrees of Wisdom: A Book of Tarot.* Wellington, Northamptonshire, Aquarian Press, 2 vols., 1980–83; San Bernardino, California, Borgo Press, 1986.
*Salvador Dali's Tarot.* Salem, New Hampshire, Salem House, and London, Rainbird, 1985.
*A Practical Guide to Fortune Telling: Palmistry, the Crystal Ball, Runes, Tea Leaves, the Tarot.* London, Sphere/Rainbird, 1986; as *Teach Yourself Fortune Telling*, New York, Holt, 1986.
*Tarot: The Open Labyrinth.* Wellingborough, Northamptonshire, Aquarian Press, 1986; San Bernardino, California, Borgo Press, 1989.
*The New Tarot.* Wellingborough, Northamptonshire, Aquarian Press, 1989; Woodstock, New York, Overlook Press, 1990.
*Tarot Readings and Meditations.* Wellingborough, Northamptonshire, Aquarian Press, 1990.

Editor, with Caitlin Matthews, *Tarot Tales.* London, Legend, 1989.
Editor, with Mary K. Greer, *New Thoughts on Tarot: Transcripts from the First International Newcastle Tarot Symposium.* North Hollywood, California, Newcastle, 1989.

* * *

Rachel Pollack is best known for her excellent books on Tarot. Her fascination with religion imbues her more recent fiction with a rare depth and complexity, making it perhaps a little difficult for the casual reader but tremendously rewarding for anyone prepared to put in some effort.

Pollack's science fiction is unquestionably adult—not in the way that "adult" films and comics concentrate on physical sex, but in its dealing with the interplay of philosophical abstracts with the solid, the "real" world. She isn't, as so many writers still are, presenting exciting adolescent stories; instead she asks questions about the nature of reality, making the reader step slightly to one side, enabling us to examine and explore our own society—and ourselves—from a new, and often spiritual viewpoint.

This is seen most of all, to date, in *Unquenchable Fire*, which won the Arthur C. Clarke Award for the best science fiction novel published in the UK in 1988. But even in the early and neglected *Golden Vanity*, a seemingly traditional SF novel about the less pleasant aspects of Earth's first contact with extraterrestrials, Pollack explores meditation exercises, visualisation, and the self-deceptions of the kookier side of New Age religion.

*Alqua Dreams* is also set in a traditional SF format: an interstellar trading negotiator visits a new planet to attempt to persuade its inhabitants to set up trading links with his company, which wants to get its hands on the rare mineral rhovium, which powers space flight. So far, so standard. But having established her rationale, Pollack then takes off into what really interests her: the age-old debate between Platonic and Aristotelian life-views.

Earthman Jaimi Cooper is a fairly average man of his times (and ours); he is somewhat perplexed, to put it mildly, to discover that the Lukai, the inhabitants of Planet Keela, believe that they're all dead. Their "life" is simply a delusion forced on them by the liar god Canumaira. Their rituals, both religious and sexual, are bizarre and at times horrifying. Cooper is called an alqua: one suffering from the illusion that he is alive. He finds himself trying to convince the people that they are wrong, that they do exist, that they are real. Drawing on her encyclopedic knowledge of religion and myth, Pollack has created perhaps the most disturbing and believable religion since Philip José Farmer's *Night of Light* a quarter of a century before. *Alqua Dreams* is by no means an easy read—what do you expect when the eternal verities are being questioned?—and is not wholly successful as a novel, but is a challenging study of two totally incompatible philosophical belief systems.

Pollack is best known as an authority on the esoteric, having written several serious studies on Tarot, including the companion volume to the controversial Salvador Dali pack, and the delightful and richly illustrated *The New Tarot*, which examines over 70 of the Tarot packs that have come on the market in the last 15 years.

In *Unquenchable Fire*, a complex and moving tale of story-telling and myth-creation set in an alternate present-day America, Pollack draws heavily on her knowledge of myth and religion. *Unquenchable Fire* is a far more enjoyable read than *Alqua Dreams*, though even more challenging. In the world she creates here, religion is an essential part of everyone's life, Tellers of mythic stories are revered, dreams are computer-analyzed for their meaning, and Woolworth's sells amulets. Personal miracles, while not commonplace, happen often enough to be greeted with joy rather than disbelief. Neighbours hold group meetings to raise one another's spiritual awareness.

It's as if the New Age Aquarians have taken over the materialistic America we know. But human nature, with all its jealousies and spites, is much the same; Pollack shows that changing the spiritual infrastructure has little effect in itself; the only meaningful revolution is the one inside. Jennifer Mazden has to cope with becoming pregnant from a dream, and with the knowledge that her unborn child will be especially significant; but she also has to cope with the pettiness of her neighbours.

The stories told by the Tellers within the book are Pollack's own myths of creation and destruction, of power and love and betrayal; myths of a society quite different from our own—yet similar enough to draw parallels. Again it's by no means an easy book, but it is a very powerful and stimulating examination of the spiritual life. If she continues in this vein Pollack will be a writer well worth following, though her depth of thought makes her readers have to work probably just that little bit too hard for her ever to become a "popular" writer.

—David V. Barrett

---

**PORGES, Arthur.** Also writes as Peter Arthur; Pat Rogers. American. Born in Chicago, Illinois, 20 August 1915. Educated at Illinois Institute of Technology, Chicago, B.S. 1940. Taught mathematics at Illinois Institute of Technology, De Paul University, Chicago, and Western Military Academy: retired, 1975.

SCIENCE-FICTION PUBLICATIONS

Uncollected Short Stories (series: Ensign De Ruyter)

"The Rats," in *The Best Science-Fiction Stories 1952*, edited by E.F. Bleiler and T.E. Dikty. New York, Fell, 1952; London, Grayson, 1953.
"The Fly," in *The Best Science-Fiction Stories 1953*, edited by E.F. Bleiler and T.E. Dikty. New York, Fell, 1953; London, Grayson, 1955.
"Story Conference," in *Fantasy and Science Fiction* (New York), May 1953.
"Strange Birth," in *Fantasy and Science Fiction* (New York), June 1953.
"The Liberator," in *Fantasy and Science Fiction* (New York), December 1953.
"The Unwilling Professor," in *Dynamic* (New York), January 1954.
"The Grom," in *Fantasy and Science Fiction* (New York), November 1954.
"Guilty as Charged," in *The Best Science Fiction Stories and Novels 1955*, edited by T.E. Dikty. New York, Fell, 1955.
"The Ruum," in *Best SF*, edited by Edmund Crispin, London, Faber, 1955.
"Mop-Up," in *Galaxy of Ghouls*, edited by Judith Merril. New York, Lion, 1955.
"$1.98," in *The Best from Fantasy and Science Fiction 4*, edited by Anthony Boucher. New York, Doubleday, 1955.
"The Tidings," in *Fantasy and Science Fiction* (New York), February 1955.
"The Box," in *Startling* (New York), Spring 1955.
"By a Fluke," in *Fantasy and Science Fiction* (New York), October 1955.
"The Logic of Rufus Weir," in *Fantasy and Science Fiction* (New York), November 1955.
"The Entity," in *Fantastic Universe* (Chicago), December 1955.
"Whirlpool," in *Fantastic Universe* (Chicago), March 1957.
"The Devil and Simon Flagg," in *Fantasia Mathematica*, edited by Clifton Fadiman. New York, Simon and Schuster, 1958.
"What Crouches in the Deep," in *Fantastic* (New York), March 1959.
"A Touch of Sun," in *Fantastic* (New York), April 1959.
"The Forerunner," in *Fantastic* (New York), July 1959.
"The Shakespeare Manuscript," in *Fantastic* (New York), August 1959.
"Security," in *Amazing* (New York), September 1959.
"Off His Rocker," in *Fantastic* (New York), February 1960.
"A Specimen for a Queen," in *Fantasy and Science Fiction* (New York), May 1960.
"Night Quake" (as Pat Rogers) and "Josephus," in *Fear* (Concord, New Hampshire), May 1960.
"The Fiftieth Year of April," in *Fantastic* (New York), June 1960.
"The Crime of Mr. Saver," in *Fantastic* (New York), August 1960.
"The Shadowsmith," in *Fantastic* (New York), September 1960.
"The Auto Hawks," in *Amazing* (New York), September 1960.
"Words and Music," in *If* (New York), September 1960.
"A Diversion for the Baron," in *Fantastic* (New York), November 1960.
"The Radio" (as Peter Arthur) and "The Melanas," in *Fantastic* (New York), December 1960.
"Degree Candidate" (as Peter Arthur) and "Dr. Blackadder's Clients," in *Fantastic* (New York), January 1961.
"The Other Side," in *Fantastic* (New York), February 1961.
"Revenge," in *Amazing* (New York), February 1961.
"Mulberry Moon," in *Fantastic* (New York), April 1961.
"The Arrogant Vampire," in *Fantastic* (New York), May 1961.
"One Bad Habit," in *Fantastic* (New York), June 1961.
"Report on the Magic Shop," in *Fantastic* (New York), August 1961.
"A Devil of a Day," in *Fantastic* (New York), August 1962.
"Mozart Annuity," in *Fantastic* (New York), November 1962.
"Emergency Operation," in *Great Science Fiction about Doctors*, edited by Groff Conklin and Noah D. Fabricant. New York, Macmillan, 1963.
"3rd Sister," in *Fantastic* (New York), January 1963.
"The Topper," in *Astounding* (New York), February 1963.
"Through Channels," in *Amazing* (New York), June 1963.
"The Formula," in *Amazing* (New York), July 1963.
"Controlled Experiment," in *Astounding* (New York), August 1963.
"The Rescuer," in *Yet More Penguin Science Fiction*, edited by Brian Aldiss. London, Penguin, 1964.
"Time-Bomb," in *Fantasy and Science Fiction* (New York), June 1964.
"Urned Reprieve" (De Ruyter), in *Amazing* (New York), October 1964.
"The Fanatic," in *Fantastic* (New York), December 1964.
"The Moths," in *Amazing* (New York), December 1964.
"Problem Child," in *The Year's Best S-F 10*, edited by Judith Merril. New York, Delacorte Press, 1965; London, Mayflower, 1967.
"Wheeler Dealer" (De Ruyter), in *Amazing* (New York), March 1965.
"Ensign De Ruyter, Dreamer," in *Amazing* (New York), April 1965.
"The Good Seed," in *Amazing* (New York), August 1965.
"Turning Point," in *Fantasy and Science Fiction* (New York), September 1965.
"A Civilized Community," in *Bizarre Mystery Magazine* (Concord, New Hampshire), October 1965.
"Dusty Answer" (De Ruyter), in *Amazing* (New York), October 1965.
"The Creep Brigade," in *Bizarre Mystery Magazine* (Concord, New Hampshire), November 1965.
"Pressure" (De Ruyter), in *Amazing* (New York), February 1966.
"Priceless Possession," in *Galaxy* (New York), June 1966.
"The Mirror," in *Fantasy and Science Fiction* (New York), October 1966.
"Solomon's Demon," in *Legends for the Dark*, edited by Peter Haining. London, New English Library, 1968.

"The Dragons of Tesla," in *Fantastic* (New York), October 1968.

* * *

Arthur's Porge's fiction consists of some 70 short stories, often of 3,000 or fewer words. Many of them blend fantasy with science fiction. "Mop-Up," for instance, takes place in the realistic wreckage following a world war fought with atomic and biological weapons. Sharing what is left with the sole human survivor are a witch, a vampire, and a ghoul. Similarly, there appears to be no difference in feel or treatment between stories which are purely SF and others which are purely fantasy. Thus the djinn of "Solomon's Demon" and the robot specimen-gatherer of "The Ruum" are precisely equivalent insofar as the humans who come in contact with them are concerned: they are alien, enormously powerful, inexorable—and they must be stopped if the viewpoint characters are to survive.

The viewpoint character *doesn't* always survive a Porges story, a fact which contributes to the considerable tension of the best of them. The character does always struggle, however. The horror is not that caused by watching a man helpless in the face of the unknown; rather, it is aroused by seeing a strong and resourceful man overborne by a power or cunning still greater than his own. An excellent example of this is "The Rats," in which a lone man fights more-than-bestial rats against a backdrop of impending nuclear war. In his ultimate failure, the man turns over the world to antagonists who have proven themselves worthy at least to attempt to better Mankind's record.

Porges works against sharp, tersely drawn backgrounds; he has an enviable talent for choosing the right word or two which convinces a reader that the scene or character was written from life rather than merely studied. His work typically begins with a narrative hook which draws the reader into the body of the story. And even pedestrian stories are frequently enlivened by flashes of character which demonstrate a considerable depth of feeling. Regrettably, many of the stories *are* pedestrian. This is a result of their being based on gimmicks, often bits of scientific fact: parabolic reflectors concentrate light ("A Touch of Sun," "The Dragons of Tesla"); crickets chirp at a rate dependant on temperature ("The Formula"); a human body reduced to raw elements is a slight value ("$1.98"). While the development may be at least professional, only the gimmick itself is likely to stick in the reader's mind for any length of time. When the gimmick is integral to the story, however, the result can be extremely effective. "The Ruum" (humans can lose significant body weight by sweating) and "Solomon's Demon" (high voltage is harmless unless coupled with a path to ground) are striking examples of this synthesis; and "The Mirror," which turns on an analysis of multiple reflections, is a stunning horror story. If these are the exceptions, then in themselves they constitute a body which many writers must envy.

Despite his frequent use of factual gimmicks, Porges never neglects his characters. It is fitting that one of his last-published stories, "Priceless Possession," involves no gimmicks at all; only the question of what part of their souls three spacemen will pay to avoid losing a treasure which in money terms is priceless. This is not a sardonic story; and perhaps it is a story that is not without hope for humanity; but it is an indictment more damning than any shrill diatribe could have seen. Here as in much of Porges's best work, men struggle but we cannot assume their victory; and our worst enemies may not be external to our hearts.

—David A. Drake

---

**POURNELLE, Jerry (Eugene).** Also writes as Wade Curtis. American. Born in Shreveport, Louisiana, 7 August 1933. Educated at the University of Iowa, Iowa City, 1953–54; University of Washington, Seattle, B.S. 1955, M.S. in statistics and systems engineering 1957, Ph.D. in psychology 1960, Ph.D. in political science 1964. Served in the United States Army 1950–52. Married Roberta Jane Isdell in 1959; four sons. Research assistant, University of Washington Medical School, 1954–57; aviation psychologist and systems engineer, Boeing Corporation, Seattle, 1957–64; manager of special studies, Aerospace Corporation, San Bernardino, California, 1964–65; research specialist and proposal manager, American Rockwell Corporation, 1965–66; Professor of Political Science, Pepperdine University, Los Angeles, 1966–69; executive assistant to the Mayor of Los Angeles, 1969–70. Since 1970, freelance writer, lecturer, and consultant: regular contributor of non-fiction articles to *Galaxy*, 1974–78, and *Analog*. President, Science Fiction Writers of America, 1973–74. Recipient: John W. Campbell award, 1973; Evans-Freehafer award, 1977. Fellow, Operations Research Society of America, and American Association for the Advancement of Science. Republic of Estonia Award of Honor, 1968; Officer, Military and Hospitaler Order of St. Lazarus of Jerusalem. Agent: Blassingame Spectrum, 111 Eighth Avenue, Suite 1503, New York, New York 10011. Address: 3960 Laurel Canyon Boulevard, Suite 372, Studio City, California 91604, U.S.A.

### Science-Fiction Publications

Novels (series: Falkenberg; Janissaries; Second Empire)

*A Spaceship for the King* (Empire). New York, DAW, 1973.
*Escape from the Planet of the Apes* (novelization of screenplay). New York, Award, 1974.
*The Mote in God's Eye* (Empire), with Larry Niven. New York, Simon and Schuster, 1974; London, Weidenfeld and Nicolson, 1975.
*Birth of Fire*. Toronto, Laser, 1976; New York, Pocket Books, 1978.
*Inferno*, with Larry Niven. New York, Pocket Books, 1976; London, Wingate, 1977.
*West of Honor* (Falkenberg). Toronto, Laser, 1976; New York, Pocket Books, 1978.
*The Mercenary* (Falkenberg). New York, Pocket Books, 1977.
*Lucifer's Hammer*, with Larry Niven. Chicago, Playboy Press, 1977.
*Exiles to Glory*. New York, Ace, 1978.
*Janissaries*. New York, Ace, 1979; London, Macdonald, 1981.
*King David's Spaceship*. New York, Pocket Books, 1980; London, Futura, 1981.
*Oath of Fealty* (Janissaries), with Larry Niven. Huntington Woods, Michigan, Phantasia Press, 1981; London, Macdonald, 1982.
*Clan and Crown* (Janissaries), with Roland Green. New York, Ace, 1982; London, Futura, 1989.
*Footfall*, with Larry Niven. New York, Ballantine, and London, Gollancz, 1985.
*The Legacy of Heorot*, with Larry Niven and Steven Barnes. New York, Simon and Schuster, and London, Gollancz, 1987.
*Storms of Victory* (Janissaries), with Roland Green. New York, Ace, 1987; London, Futura, 1989.
*Man-Kzin Wars II*, with Larry Niven, Dean Ing, and S.M. Stirling. New York, Baen, 1989.
*Prince of Mercenaries* (Falkenberg). New York, Baen, 1989.
*Falkenberg's Legion*. New York, Baen, 1990.
*Go Tell the Spartans*, with S.M. Stirling. New York, Baen, 1991.

*Fallen Angels*, with Larry Niven and Michael Flynn. New York, Baen, 1991.

Short Stories

*High Justice*. New York, Pocket Books, 1977; London, Futura, 1980.

OTHER PUBLICATIONS

Novels as Wade Curtis

*Red Heroin*. New York, Berkley, 1969.
*Red Dragon*. New York, Berkley, 1971.

Other

*The Strategy of Technology: Winning the Decisive War*, with Stefan T. Possony. New York, Dunellen, 1970.
*That Buck Rogers Stuff*, edited by Gavin Claypool. Pasadena, California, Extequer, 1977.
*The Mathematics of the Energy Crisis*, with R. Gagliardi. Westmont, New Jersey, Intergalactic, 1978.
*A Step Farther Out*. London, W.H. Allen, 1980; New York, Ace, 1983.
*Mutual Assured Survival: A Space-Age Solution to Nuclear Annihilation*, with Dean Ing. New York, Baen, 1984.
*The User's Guide to Small Computers*. New York, Baen, 1984.
*Adventures in Microland*. New York, Baen, 1985.

Editor, *20/20 Vision*. New York, Avon, 1974.
Editor, *Black Holes*. New York, Fawcett, 1979.
Editor, *The Endless Frontier*. New York, Ace, 1979.
Editor, with John F. Carr, *The Survival of Freedom*. New York, Fawcett, 1981.
Editor, with John F. Carr, *The Endless Frontier 2*. New York, Ace, 1982.
Editor, with John F. Carr, *Nebula Award Stories 16*. New York, Holt Rinehart, 1982; London, W.H. Allen, 1983.
Editor, with John F. Carr, *There Will Be War*. New York, Tor, 1983.
Editor, with John F. Carr, *Men of War*. New York, Tor, 1984.
Editor, with John F. Carr, *Blood and Iron*. New York, Tor, 1984.
Editor, with Jim Baen and John F. Carr, *Far Frontiers 1–4*. New York, Baen, 4 vols., 1985.
Editor, with John F. Carr, *Imperial Stars*. New York, Baen, 3 vols., 1985–89.
Editor, with John F. Carr, *Silicon Brains*. New York, Ballantine, 1985.
Editor, with John F. Carr, *Science Fiction Yearbook 1984*. New York, Baen, 1985.
Editor, with John F. Carr, *Day of the Tyrant*. New York, Tor, 1985.
Editor, with John F. Carr, *Warrior*. New York, Tor, 1986.
Editor, with John F. Carr, *Guns of Darkness*. New York, Tor, 1987.
Editor, with John F. Carr, *War World*. New York, Baen, 3 vols., 1988–91.
Editor, with John F. Carr, *Call to Battle*. New York, Tor, 1988.
Editor, with John F. Carr, *Armageddon!* New York, Tor, 1989.

*

Jerry Pournelle comments:

My work is intended to entertain. I may well have a serious message, but in my judgment fiction is best served if the characters in a story do not know they have a message to deliver. Science-fiction writers are bards of the sciences; we are not fundamentally different from the bards of Homeric times, who would travel about and, spying an encamped group, say, "If you'll fill my cup with wine and dish me a bowl of stew, I will tell you a story about a virgin and a bull you just wouldn't believe. . . ."

* * *

Jerry Pournelle's science fiction has consistently portrayed technological advance as the most significant visible indication of humanity's progress. The most obvious form of benevolent innovation is the development of space travel, a theme which infuses most of his work. This theme is particularly obvious in *A Spaceship for the King*, in which the salvation of an entire world rests upon its ability to develop a spacefaring technology. In *Exiles to Glory* humanity is jolted out if its introverted and short-sighted doldrums by a space effort financed by commercial interests. The Martian colony in *Birth of Fire* is entirely dependent upon advanced equipment from Earth.

There is a well expressed admiration for the professional soldier as well. Colonel Nathan MacKinnie, the protagonist of *A Spaceship for the King*, is a cashiered veteran unable to function properly within the organized military of his world. *Janissaries*, along with its two sequels, *Clan and Crown* and *Storms of Victory* (the latter two in collaboration with Roland Green) follows the adventures of a group of soldiers kidnapped from Earth by aliens unwilling to fight their own battles. John Falkenberg, a recurring character in much of the best of Pournelle's fiction, is a highly skilled strategic and tactical planner who leads a group of interstellar mercenaries.

Falkenberg and his companions are featured in the early novel, *West of Honor*, as well as several collections and cross collections including *The Mercenary, Falkenberg's Legion*, and most notably *Prince of Mercenaries*, which incorporates Pournelle's best shorter piece, "Silent Leges." The Falkenberg stories are set within the context of the CoDominium, a pragmatic alliance of the United States and the Soviet Union that eventually evolves into a world government and interstellar empire. One of several novels Pournelle has written in collaboration with Larry Niven and others, *The Mote in God's Eye* is possibly the best single work set against this background.

*Mote* was met with widely varied reader response. It is a large, rich novel, concerning the first contact of the human race with an alien species that is biologically diversified in order to cope with the exigencies of survival within their home system. There is a well-paced and logically developed plot, a strong and sustained element of suspense, gradual revelation of the intricacies of the alien culture, and some extremely powerful scenes. There was some adverse reaction to what was interpreted as stereotyping, particularly of the single female character, a passive individual lacking any initiative. On the other hand, none of the characters are developed to any great degree, the focus of the novel being the unfolding mystery of the Moties. To a degree, the traditional values of literature are subordinated in this situation.

The next collaboration with Niven, *Lucifer's Hammer*, features several strong female characters. An end-of-the-world story on a vast scale, this book depicts the collision of Earth with a comet, after which civilization collapses into barbarism and most of the physical features of the world are altered. Marketed as a mainstream disaster novel, it features an extremely large cast of characters, numerous storylines, and covers a span of decades. There is a careful, plausible extrapolation of the slow decay of the few islands of comparatively unaffected society which remain as the apparatus of civilization crumbles. It is indicative of Pournelle's view of technology that the climactic battle is fought for control of a functioning nuclear power plant.

*Oath of Fealty* and *The Legacy of Heorot* were also written with Larry Niven, and also with Steven Barnes in the latter case. *Oath* is set in an enormous self-contained city-building that is theoretically part of Los Angeles. Automatic defense systems kill intruders, and interests unfriendly to the building administration use one such incident in a political struggle which may determine the future of urban life throughout the world. Although less grandiose than the earlier collaborations, the novel is complexly plotted and the implications of each turn of events are explored in detail. *Heorot* is an other-worlds adventure story, with a struggling human colony trying to find a way to survive the unexpected appearance of a particularly hostile and dangerous lifeform. This is a very suspenseful novel full of surprises.

Pournelle makes use of traditional plots for the most part—interplanetary war and conquest, world disaster, first contact with aliens, commercial rivalries, penal colonies on other worlds, and so on. His themes are familiar as well: the importance of space travel as an outlet for human endeavor, technological answers to problems confronting the human race, the value of individualism as opposed to collectivism, and the primacy of man over aliens because of our competitive drive to survive.

But the familiarity of plot and theme should not be construed as a lack of imagination. The de-emphasis on characterization does not imply a lack of depth in other areas. Pournelle develops his plots logically, with a good sense of timing and judicious use of suspense and other devices. Most of his fiction is essentially action oriented, with clear cut issues and sympathetic characters. Social issues, when they arise, are dealt with consistently. His views on various issues are quite clear; shortsighted ecological protection and population control movements nearly destroy the space effort in *Exiles to Glory*. Government officials are almost invariably portrayed as corrupt or inept or both. Even at his most polemic, however, Pournelle carefully avoids disrupting the momentum of his stories.

—Don D'Ammassa

---

**POWERS, L.C.** *See* **TUBB, E.C.**

---

**POWERS, Tim.** American. Born in 1952. Recipient: Philip K. Dick Memorial award, 1984. Address: c/o Ace Books, 200 Madison Avenue, New York, New York 10016, U.S.A.

SCIENCE-FICTION PUBLICATIONS

Novels

*Epitaph in Rust*. Toronto, Laser, 1976; as *An Epitaph in Rust*, Cambridge, Massachusetts, NESFA, 1989.

*The Skies Discrowned*. Toronto, Laser, 1976; as *Forsake the Sky*, New York, Tor, 1986.

*The Drawing of the Dark*. New York, Ballantine, 1979; London, Mayflower, 1981.

*The Anubis Gates*. New York, Ace, 1983; London, Chatto and Windus, 1985.

*Dinner at Deviant's Palace*. New York, Ace, 1985; London, Chatto and Windus, 1986.

*Night Moves* (novelette). Seattle, Washington, Axolotl Press, 1986.

*The Way Down the Hill* (novelette). Seattle, Washington, Axolotl Press, 1986.

*On Stranger Tides*. New York, Ace, 1987; London, Grafton, 1988.

*The Stress of Her Regard*. New York, Ace, 1989; London, Grafton, 1991.

* * *

Tim Powers, along with James P. Blaylock and K.W. Jeter, is one of a group of science-fiction writers around the San Francisco bay area who first became known in the 1980's. Companions of the late Philip K. Dick, they are perhaps best known for the expressiveness and originality of their own voices. In his 15 years as an author, Tim Powers has consistently developed his competence and creativity; after eight books, he continues to become more daring and able. His novels are *sui generis*, all different but all similarly elaborate and well-crafted. Some of his work is classifiable as science fiction or fantasy, while some combines genre expectations or transcends them. Most of all, Powers's fiction is notable for its intricate plot structure and rich detail—speculative or historical—as well as for his prose style and characterization.

*The Anubis Gates* is generally considered Powers's "breakthrough" novel. It won the Philip K. Dick Memorial award, for best paperback original book, and began to draw attention to Powers. One could say that *The Anubis Gates* is Powers's masterpiece, in the original sense: a work that earns guild-entry by virtue of its mature workmanship. In that sense, *Epitaph in Rust* and *The Skies Discrowned* demonstrate a promising apprenticeship; and *The Drawing of the Dark* shows the beginning of mastery from a talented and intelligent journeyman. Ten years after *The Skies Discrowned* was published, the story was re-issued as *Forsake the Sky*, restored from the publisher's notoriously bad editing and re-written with Powers's greater command of style and storytelling. Perhaps because of its early origin, the plot is less involved than that of Powers's other work in the 1980's.

Generally, Powers's novels present a number of plot-elements that seem both inexplicable and unconnected. As the plot unfolds and connections appear, the reader discovers that all the mysteries are ingeniously linked and are explicable within the paradigm offered by the novel. In *Dinner at Deviant's Palace* the setting and explanation are those of science fiction, and in *The Drawing of the Dark* and *On Stranger Tides* the settings are historical and the explanations are supernatural. In *The Anubis Gates* and *The Stress of Her Regard*, Powers shows his full range, combining elements of fantasy, science fiction, and the historical novel. All of his novels also show the influence of adventure fiction, such as that of Rafael Sabatini.

One basic appeal of Powers's fiction is the lure of strange yet consistent cultures, whether historical or imaginary. His characters are convincing, whether he writes about a 16th-century mercenary, as in *The Drawing of the Dark*, or the English Romantic poets, as in *The Anubis Gates* and—more centrally—*The Stress of Her Regard.* His depiction of 18th-century pirates (*On Stranger Tides*) or 19th-century gypsies (*The Anubis Gates*) is as strange, and at least as thorough, as any in science fiction. The post-World War III culture of *Dinner at Deviant's Palace* combines credible extrapolation and an archaic feeling of decadent vice. The world in *The Skies Discrowned* and *Forsake the Skies* also combines science fiction elements, such as space travel, with historical or fantasy elements, such as swordplay and inherited royalty.

Most of Powers's fiction involves magic, or something like it, which he handles in characteristic yet diverse ways. Many elements in *Dinner at Deviant's Palace*, such as a cult that partakes of mass psychic communion, seem to be supernatural but are explained in scientific terms. On the other hand, both *The Drawing of the Dark* and *The Anubis Gates* use a system of magic which, while not exactly a scientific technology, still functions by stated rules: since a magician forsakes the natural earth, someone is safe if in touch with the earth, by direct contact or a grounding wire.

In *The Anubis Gates*, magic and the science of Darrow Interdisciplinary Research Enterprises serve as equal, and equally plausible, vehicles for an explanation of travel into the past; all the mysteries of the novel are shown to be logical effects of time travel or the actions of the magicians and others involved. *On Stranger Tides* and *The Stress of Her Regard* each postulate an elaborate and coherent structure of magic, similar to systems we know but explained in unique ways. In the former, the Caribbean pirates use a magic like and yet unlike *vodun;* the latter introduces trans-human life forms resembling aspects of classical myth and European folklore, mixed into something new. The magical device of immortality through body-switching shows up in *The Anubis Gates, On Stranger Tides*, and Powers's short story, "The Way Down the Hill" (in *Fantasy and Science Fiction*, December 1982).

Powers's description of action, especially swordplay, is accurate and involving; so is his description of the physical consequences of such violence, including slow-healing wounds. He often features characters who are street-thieves or grifters, which he presents with affection and energy but without sentimentality. His protagonists tend to be male, from youth to middle-age; endowed with courage and intelligence, but not larger than life, they are both likable and credible. Generally, the characters develop personally as the novel progresses. When his work takes place in a realistic past, Powers often features historical figures as secondary characters and invents a protagonist; in *The Stress of Her Regard* the action is more nearly split between his fictional protagonists and his versions of Shelley, Byron, Keats, and their friends.

Despite this discussion, it is impossible to convey the elaborate and coherent weirdness of a novel by Tim Powers: the Dancing Ape Madness in *The Anubis Gates;* the hemogoblin in *Dinner at Deviant's Palace;* the Fountain of Youth in *On Stranger Tides;* the probability-defining eye of the Graiae in *The Stress of Her Regard;* and of course the much-celebrated poet, William Ashbless. It is also impossible to fully convey the delights of Powers's prose, both humorous and serious, with its fine descriptions and striking metaphors. Still not as well known as he should be, Powers gets greater acclaim with each novel, and deservedly so.

—Bernadette Bosky

---

**PRATCHETT, Terry.** British. Born in 1948. Educated at Wycombe Technical High School. Journalist in Buckinghamshire, Bristol, and Bath, then press officer, Central Electricity Board Western Region, until 1987. Recipient: British Science Fiction award, 1990. Agent: Colin Smythe Ltd., P.O. Box 6, Gerrards Cross, Buckinghamshire SL9 8XA, England.

### Science-Fiction Publications

Novels (series: Discworld; Truckers/Bromeliad)

*Carpet People*. Gerrards Cross, Buckinghamshire, Smythe, 1971.
*The Dark Side of the Sun*. Gerrards Cross, Buckinghamshire, Smythe, 1976.
*Strata*. Gerrards Cross, Buckinghamshire, Smythe, and New York, St. Martin's Press, 1981.
*The Colour of Magic* (Discworld). Gerrards Cross, Buckinghamshire, Smythe, and New York, St. Martin's Press, 1983.
*The Light Fantastic* (Discworld). Gerrard's Cross, Buckinghamshire, Smythe, and New York, St. Martin's Press, 1986.
*Equal Rites* (Discworld). London, Gollancz, 1986; New York, New American Library, 1987.
*Mort* (Discworld). London, Gollancz, and New York, New American Library, 1987.
*Sourcery* (Discworld). London, Gollancz, 1988; New York, New American Library, 1989.
*Wyrd Sisters* (Discworld). London, Gollancz, and New York, Penguin, 1988.
*Pyramids* (Discworld). London, Gollancz, and New York, Penguin, 1989.
*Guards! Guards!* (Discworld). London, Gollancz, 1989; New York, Roc, 1991.
*Truckers* (first of the Truckers trilogy; in the U.S. as the Bromeliad trilogy). London, Doubleday, 1989; New York, Delacorte, 1990.
*Eric* (Discworld). London, Gollancz, 1989.
*Good Omens: The Nice and Accurate Predictions of Agnes Nutter, Witch*, with Neil Gaiman. London, Gollancz, and New York, Workman, 1990.
*Moving Pictures* (Discworld). London, Gollancz, 1990.
*Diggers* (Truckers/Bromeliad). London, Doubleday, and New York, Delacorte, 1990.
*Wings* (Truckers/Bromeliad). London, Doubleday, 1990; New York, Delacorte, 1991.
*Reaper Man* (Discworld). London, Gollancz, 1991.

### Other Publications

Other

*The Unadulterated Cat*, with illustrations by Gray Jolliffe. London, Gollancz, 1989.

* * *

Terry Pratchett's novel *Strata* was widely regarded as an amusing commentary on Larry Niven's award-winning novel *Ringworld*, which it resembles in many superficial ways. The protagonist of *Strata* is a woman whose job is to oversee the construction of planets. She is at great pains to ensure that her subordinates do not plant anachronistic items in the strata of these worlds. A mysterious visitor informs her of the existence of a flat world, lost in space, built by means of some arcane lore, inhabited by people who appear to be human. Her curiosity and her sense of adventure both stir, and she sets off with a number of companions—some human, some not—to find the flat planet. Unfortunately, a series of mishaps results in the loss of their guide and the eventual incapacitation of their spacecraft. They do however land at their destinations, and what ensues is an hilarious romp among dragons, robots, aliens, and other creatures.

Pratchett borrowed from Niven again in *The Dark Side of the Sun*, a slightly more serious work. The protagonist is the rich heir to a powerful title who sets off on a quest to find the Jokers' World, home of a legendary alien species. The background involves the manipulation of the laws of chance, another facet of *Ringworld.* A series of assassination attempts are thwarted, generally through a chain of coincidences. Once again, the best part of the novel is the richly creative background of aliens, religious and philosophical speculations, and exotic settings. Pratchett's light-hearted approach succeeds in making what would otherwise be a standard adventure story into a witty exercise of the imagination.

It was with *The Colour of Magic*, however, that Pratchett hit his stride. This first volume of the ongoing Discworld series consists of four interrelated adventures. Discworld is a flat planet, but set in a fantasy rather than a rational universe. In this case, the planet is supported on the backs of four gigantic elephants astride the shell of an immense tortoise swimming in space. The inhabitants know that their view of the universe is correct, because they have lowered observers over the edge to see for themselves.

Rincewind is certainly one of the least likely magicians ever to grace the pages of fiction, both in *The Colour of Magic* and in some of the subsequent chronicles of Discworld. In this instance, he agrees to provide his services as a guide to a visitor from another planet interested in exploration. Their travels result in encounters with malevolent animals, wizards, monsters, and other villains in what is essentially a satire on the fantasy genre itself. Pratchett seems particularly enamored of anachronisms, which abound in this novel.

Further chronicles of Discworld have appeared with regularity thereafter. Magical madness continues as Rincewind combats the appearance of a strange new star in *The Light Fantastic.* Granny Weatherwax, a canny old witch, takes center stage in *Equal Rites*, trying to straighten out the problems that ensue when the eighth son of an eighth son is . . . a daughter. More misdirected magic dominates the scene in *Sourcery* and in *Wyrd Sisters*, a retelling of the traditional story of the prince regaining his throne. Ancient Egypt gets raked over the coals in *Pyramids.* Possibly the funniest of this hilarious series is *Mort*, in which Death goes on a holiday after taking on an inept apprentice, who is just too kind-hearted to harvest all the souls who are scheduled to pass on. Considering the number of volumes in this series, it might be expected that Pratchett would have begun to repeat himself, but each is as fresh, inventive, and hilarious as those which preceded it.

Pratchett's recent novel, *Good Omens: The Nice and Accurate Predictions of Agnes Nutter, Witch* (written in collaboration with comic book writer Neil Gaiman), is a send up of modern horror themes, particularly the "Omen" series of films and its imitators, which surpasses anything that went before it. When the son of Satan is misplaced and raised as a nice child, the schedule of Armageddon is thrown awry, and the powers of Heaven and Hell must work together to find a resolution. This is one of those rare novels that proves humor can be great literature as well as marvelous entertainment. If this is a sign of what is to come, Pratchett is likely to be one of the most important writers of the years to come.

—Don D'Ammassa

---

**PRATT, (Murray) Fletcher.** Also wrote as George U. Fletcher. American. Born in Buffalo, New York, 25 April 1897. Attended Hobart College, Geneva, New York, 1915–16; University of Paris, 1931–33. Served in the War Library Service during World War I. Married Inga Marie Stephens. Librarian, 1918–20; staff member, Buffalo *Courier Express*, 1920–23; freelance writer from 1923; regular contributor, American Mercury and *Saturday Review of Literature;* military advisor, *Time* and New York *Post* during World War II; staff member, Bread Loaf Writers Conference. President, Authors Club, 1941; co-founder, American Rocket Society. Recipient: United States Navy award, 1957. *Died 10 June 1956.*

SCIENCE-FICTION PUBLICATIONS

Novels

*Double in Space (Project Excelsior, The Wanderer's Return).* New York, Doubleday, 1951.
*Double Jeopardy.* New York, Doubleday, 1952.
*The Undying Fire.* New York, Ballantine, 1953; as *The Conditioned Captain*, in *Double in Space*, 1954.
*Double in Space (Project Excelsior, The Conditioned Captain).* London, Boardman, 1954.
*Invaders from Rigel.* New York, Avalon, 1960.
*Alien Planet.* New York, Avalon, 1962.
*The Blue Star.* New York, Ballantine, 1969.

OTHER PUBLICATIONS

Novels with L. Sprague de Camp

*The Incomplete Enchanter.* New York, Holt, 1941; London, Sphere, 1979.
*Land of Unreason.* New York, Holt, 1942.
*The Carnelian Cube.* New York, Gnome Press, 1948.
*The Well of the Unicorn* (by Pratt only, as George U. Fletcher). New York, Sloane, 1948.
*The Castle of Iron.* New York, Gnome Press, 1950.
*Wall of Serpents.* New York, Avalon, 1960.
*The Compleat Enchanter: The Magical Adventures of Harold Shea* (includes *The Incomplete Enchanter* and *The Castle of Iron*). New York, Doubleday, 1975; London, Sphere, 1979.
*The Intrepid Enchanter: The Complete Magical Misadventures of Harold Shea.* London, Sphere, 1988; as *The Complete Compleat Enchanter*, New York, Baen, 1989.

Short Stories

*Tales from Gavagan's Bar*, with L. Sprague de Camp. New York, Twayne, 1953; expanded edition, Philadelphia, Owlswick Press, 1978.

Other

*The Heroic Years: Fourteen Years of the Republic 1801–1815.* New York, Smith and Haas, 1934.
*The Cunning Mulatto and Other Cases of Ellis Parker, American Detective.* New York, Smith and Haas, 1935; as *Detective No. 1*, London, Methuen, 1936.
*Ordeal by Fire: An Informal History of the Civil War.* New York, Smith and Haas, 1935; revised edition, New York, Sloane, 1948; London, Lane, 1950; as *A Short History of the Civil War*, New York, Bantam, n.d.
*Hail, Caesar!* New York, Smith and Haas, 1936; London, Williams and Norgate, 1938.
*The Navy: A History.* New York, Doubleday, 1938.

*Road to Empire: The Life and Times of Bonaparte the General.* New York, Doubleday, 1939.
*Sea Power and Today's War.* New York, Harrison Hilton, 1939; London, Methuen, 1940.
*Secret and Urgent: The Story of Codes and Ciphers.* Indianapolis, Bobbs Merrill, and London, Hale, 1939.
*Fletcher Pratt's Naval War Game.* New York, Harrison Hilton, 1940.
*Fighting Ships of the U.S. Navy.* New York, Garden City Publishing Company, 1941.
*America and Total War.* New York, Smith and Durrell, 1941.
*The U.S. Army.* Racine, Wisconsin, Whitman, 1942.
*What the Citizen Should Know about Modern War.* New York, Norton, 1942.
*The Navy Has Wings.* New York, Harper, 1943.
*My Life to the Destroyers,* with Captain L.A. Abercrombie. New York, Holt, 1944.
*The Navy's War.* New York, Harper, 1944.
*A Short History of the Army and Navy.* Washington, D.C., Infantry Journal, 1944.
*Fleet Against Japan.* New York, Harper, 1946.
*Empire of the Sea.* New York, Holt, 1946.
*Night Work: The Story of Task Force 39.* New York, Holt, 1946.
*A Man and His Meals,* with Robeson Bailey. New York, Holt, 1947.
*The Empire and Glory: Napoleon Bonaparte 1800–1806.* New York, Sloane, 1948.
*The Marines' War.* New York, Sloane, 1948.
*Eleven Generals: Studies in American Command.* New York, Sloane, 1949.
*The Third King.* New York, Sloane, 1950.
*War for the World: A Chronicle of Our Fighting Forces in World War II.* New Haven, Connecticut, Yale University Press, 1950.
*Prebble's Boys: Commodore Prebble and the Birth of American Sea Power.* New York, Sloane, 1950.
*Rockets, Jets, Guided Missiles, and Space Ships.* New York, Random House, 1951; London, Sidgwick and Jackson, 1952.
*The Monitor and the Merrimac.* New York, Random House, 1951.
*By Space Ship to the Moon* (for children). New York, Random House, 1952; London, Publicity Products, 1953.
*Stanton, Lincoln's Secretary of War.* New York, Norton, 1953.
*All about Rockets and Jets.* New York, Random House, 1955.
*The Civil War.* New York, Garden City Books, 1955.
*Famous Inventors and Their Inventions.* New York, Random House, 1955.
*The Battles that Changed History.* New York, Doubleday, 1956.
*Civil War on Western Waters.* New York, Holt, 1956.
*The Compact History of the United States Navy.* New York, Hawthorn, 1957.

Editor, *World of Wonder.* New York, Twayne, 1951.
Editor, *Civil War in Pictures.* New York, Garden City Books, 1951.
Editor, *Petrified Planet.* New York, Twayne, 1952.
Editor, *Witches Three,* New York, Twayne, 1952.
Editor, *My Diary, North and South,* by Sir William Howard Russell. New York, Harper, 1954.

Translator, *The Great American Parade,* by H.J. Duteil. New York, Twayne, 1953.

* * *

Fletcher Pratt had an extremely varied writing career. While he is considered to be one of the pioneer science-fiction writers, he also wrote fantasy and produced an impressive list of historical nonfiction. In terms of science fiction, Pratt wrote mainly short fiction during his early years, with the exception of *Alien Planet.* The publisher's foreword to the Ace edition of this novel accurately describes it as using "the traditional technique of the 'marvelous voyage' and the 'manuscript found in a bottle' . . . combined with a penetrating and satiric representation of human society through the method of exploring an alien culture." It is a classic representation of the genre. Of course, much of the material is outdated but there remains some interesting philosophy, including the alien dissident's description of intelligent life as a disease infesting the planets which the divine spirit strives to destroy.

In 1939, Pratt met L. Sprague deCamp and his writing turned toward fantasy. Together they wrote a series of stories about a psychologist who finds himself projected into a number of parallel worlds which are based on our myths. Harold Shea, as he is called, makes his rounds of Norse mythology ("The Roaring Trumpet"), Spenser's *Faerie Queene* ("The Mathematics of Logic"), Ariosto's *Orlando Furioso (The Castle of Iron),* the Finnish *Kalevala (Wall of Serpents)* and the world of Irish myth ("The Green Magician"). The stories were unique in that they combined the then new field of sword-and-sorcery fantasy with a refreshing humor. The two writers wrote two additional fantasy novels, *Land of Unreason* and *The Carnelian Cube,* as well as a collection of short fantasy spoofs, *Tales from Gavagan's Bar.* The last, similar to Clarke's *Tales of the White Hart,* also showed the magical humor of Pratt and de Camp evident in the Harold Shea pieces. Pratt's solo novel *The Well of the Unicorn* is a fascinating creation by a master storyteller, one of the very best of fantasies.

Pratt's SF work *Double Jeopardy* details the adventures of George Helmfleet Jones, an agent with the Secret Service some time in the future. In his first adventure, Jones solves a case dealing with a matter transmitter; in the second, he is confronted by the theft of a large sum of money from a sealed, remote-controlled cargo rocket. *Double in Space* consists of two unrelated works. The first is born of the early Cold War with Russian and U.S. space stations vying for superiority in space. The second is a take-off on the voyage of Ulysses set in the far distant future. In a similar vein, *The Undying Fire* follows the plot of Jason and the Golden Fleece. None of these works matches the caliber of Pratt's fantasy.

—Paul Swank

---

**PREUSS, Paul.** American. Born in Albany, Georgia, 7 March 1942. Educated at Yale University, New Haven, Connecticut, B.A. 1966. Served in the United States Air Force Reserve, 1960–66. Married 1) Marsha Pettit in 1963 (divorced 1968), one daughter; 2) Karen Reiser in 1973 (divorced 1989). Marketing planning projects director, Batten Barton Durstine & Osborn, New York, 1966–67; floor director, King-TV, 1967–68, and unit manager, 1968–69, production manager, 1969–70, and creative director, 1970–72, King Screen Productions, all in Seattle, staff consultant, Biological Sciences Curriculum Study, Boulder, Colorado, 1972–73; independent film producer, 1974–81, and associate producer, editor, and post-production supervisor, Lee Mendelson Film Productions and other companies, 1975–81. Since 1978, freelance writer. Agent: Jean Naggor, Jean V. Naggor

Literary Agency, Inc., 216 East 75th Street, New York, New York 10021, U.S.A.

SCIENCE-FICTION PUBLICATIONS

Novels (series: Venus Prime)

*The Gates of Heaven*. New York, Bantam, 1980.
*Re-Entry*. New York, Bantam, 1981.
*Broken Symmetries*. New York, Pocket Books, 1983; London, Penguin, 1984.
*Human Error*. New York, Tor, 1985.
*Breaking Strain* (Venus Prime). New York, Avon, 1987.
*Starfire*. London, Simon and Schuster, and New York, Tor, 1988.
*Maelstrom* (Venus Prime). New York, Avon, 1988.
*Hide and Seek* (Venus Prime). New York, Avon, 1989.
*The Medusa Encounter* (Venus Prime). New York, Avon, 1990.
*The Diamond Moon* (Venus Prime). New York, Avon, 1990.

*

Paul Preuss comments:

I am more interested in the social implications of the scientific endeavor than in gadgets, and I am more interested in scientists than in science itself.

* * *

Paul Preuss established himself as a writer of "hard" science fiction on the basis of his first two novels which, despite the use of realistic scientific settings and situations, are really more closely related to the fanciful space operas of Edmond Hamilton, Leigh Brackett, and others. Subsequent novels, however, have demonstrated both an intelligent, perceptive understanding of the scientific method and the state of modern research, as well as a sensitivity to psychological and ethical problems facing the scientist in our society.

In *The Gates of Heaven*, scientists receive a message from another star system, the voices of the human crew of a ship that disappeared mysteriously some time earlier. They make use of a black hole to send a second vessel across interstellar distances in what is supposed to be a rescue mission, but which runs into problems of its own, including a mutiny when the leader of the expedition is temporarily stranded on a planetary surface. A double black hole makes time travel possible in *Re-Entry.* The protagonist journeys back to his own past, determined to alter the course of his own destiny, and quite predictably ends up affecting a great deal more. Although the scientific element was basically window dressing this time, Preuss used a rational, analytical approach to the problems of time travel that makes the outlandishness of the concept seem totally credible.

Preuss moved from these entertaining but basically romantic notions to a more serious approach with *Broken Symmetries.* The protagonist, a man whose interest in politics is at best superficial, is part of a team developing a particle beam accelerator. Unfortunately, he soon becomes involved with clandestine efforts to make use of the new device, which had led to the discovery of a new kind of sub-atomic particle, as a source of international power. The potential exists to create a weapon beside which even atomic bombs will seem of little consequence. In addition to creating a genuinely interesting story of science and the people who study it, Preuss has overlaid a suspenseful mystery. At the same time, he unobtrusively uses the plot as a way of examining the uses to which our society puts scientific progress. With his third novel, Preuss had gone from an interesting writer of romantic adventure to a serious novelist.

*Human Error* explored those same questions from a different direction, the responsibility of scientists for the consequences of their work. Compugen is a financially ailing corporation that makes use of genetic engineering to tailor specialized viruses. When the company's president prematurely announces the discovery of a radical new substance, then behaves so erratically that he is institutionalized, members of his staff suspect that he has been infected by one of their creations, and may have spread the disease to the population at large. A combination of serious scientific extrapolation and contemporary medical thriller, *Human Error* quickly confirmed Preuss's enviable reputation.

The manned space program of the near future is the subject of *Starfire.* A cashiered ex-astronaut who abandoned his crippled ship in order to save his life is determined that his career will not end so abruptly. Taking advantage of every opportunity, he manages to win a place in the crew of an experimental new space vehicle, only to find himself in the midst of a new crisis when a solar flare threatens to bring a disastrous end to their mission.

In 1987, Preuss began a series of novels inspired in part by the work of Arthur C. Clarke, the Venus Prime novels. Although there have been a number of novels "borrowed" from the creations of other writers, Preuss avoids the pitfalls of most of these, using the original concept simply as the launching point for each novel. *Breaking Strain* introduces Sparta, a woman with unusual powers, the product of biotechnology, whose sojourn on Venus is interrupted by the arrival of a crippled space freighter. The mystery of her own origin seems to be related, and Sparta must turn detective to resolve the issue.

Sparta returns in *Maelstrom*, still seeking the secret of her origin. A party of scientists lost in the Venusian wilderness uncovers an alien artifact. Another classic Clarke story provides the inspiration for *Hide and Seek*, with Sparta now transported to the orbit of Mars in her quest to discover her own history. Sparta reaches Jupiter in *The Medusa Encounter*, broadly drawn from Clarke's "A Meeting with Medusa," this time investigating the possibility that a religious cult may have seized control of a sensitive interplanetary mission. *The Diamond Moon*, derived from Clarke's "Jupiter Five," continues the expedition to the Jovian moons, where Sparta must now contend with a crashlanding and the presence of a saboteur among the complement. The Venus Prime series is an inventive, exciting project with high entertainment value and strong scientific content, although it lacks some of the impact of Preuss's more serious novels.

—Don D'Ammassa

---

**PRIEST, Christopher.** British. Born in Cheadle, Cheshire, in 1943. Educated at Warehouseman and Clerks' Orphan Schools, Manchester, 1951–59. Council member, Science Fiction Foundation, and editor, *Foundation*, for 2 years. Recipient: British Science Fiction Association award, 1974, 1979; Ditmar award (Australia) 1977, 1982. Agent: Maggie Noach Literary Agency, 21 Redan Street, London W14 0AB, England; or, Ellen Levine Literary Agency, 15 East 26th Street, New York, New York 10010, U.S.A.

SCIENCE-FICTION PUBLICATIONS

Novels

*Indoctrinaire.* London, Faber, and New York, Harper, 1970; revised edition, London, Pan, 1979.
*Fugue for a Darkening Island.* London, Faber, 1972; as *Darkening Island,* New York, Harper, 1972.
*Inverted World.* London, Faber, 1974; as *The Inverted World,* New York, Harper, 1974.
*The Space Machine,* London, Faber, and New York, Harper, 1976.
*A Dream of Wessex.* London, Faber, 1977; as *The Perfect Lover,* New York, Scribner, 1977.
*The Affirmation.* London, Faber, and New York, Scribner, 1981.

Short Stories

*Real Time World.* London, New English Library, 1974.
*An Infinite Summer.* London, Faber, and New York, Scribner, 1979.

OTHER PUBLICATIONS

Novels

*The Glamour.* London, Cape, 1984; New York, Doubleday, 1985.
*The Quiet Woman.* London, Bloomsbury, 1990.

Other

*Your Book of Film-Making* (for children). London, Faber, 1974.

Editor, *Anticipations.* London, Faber, and New York, Scribner, 1978.
Editor, with Robert Holdstock, *Stars of Albion* (anthology of British science fiction). London, Pan, 1979.

*

Critical Study: *Christopher Priest* by Nicholas Ruddick, Mercer, Washington, Starmont House, 1990.

* * *

Christopher Priest was one of the most promising new British science-fiction writers to become active in the 1970's. His first novel *Indoctrinaire* (expanded from "The Interrogator"), reflected the type of story that dominated *New Worlds* at the time. Dr. Wentik is a researcher in investigating an experimental drug at a scientific installation in the Antarctic when he is shanghaied by the mysterious American government agent Astrourde. Shortly thereafter he is incarcerated in an enigmatic prison in the Brazilian highlands, in an area that somehow serves as a bridge between the present and the world two centuries from now. Wentik's attempts to escape his situation, or even to make some kind of sense of it, are reminiscent of Kafka. His efforts are largely ineffectual, although it does become increasingly clear to him that even his captors are without true freedom. Reality and fantasy merge at times, and the result is a kaleidoscopic novel that dilutes its effect by the lack of strong focus.

*Fugue for a Darkening Island* also features a weak and less than entirely admirable protagonist. Following a major war in Africa, the British Isles are rapidly inundated with refugees, an exodus that is met with indecisive hostility on the part of the British authorities. As the influx grows, order begins to disintegrate. Divergent opinions about the obligation to provide succor to the refugees lead to an increasingly violent factionalism. Government control over much of the countryside collapses; individual neighborhoods wall themselves off from the outside world. Alan Whitman and his family are cast adrift in this world, and find that they are unable to control their own future. Frequently it is impossible even to distinguish those who uphold the law from those who break it. Priest makes no effort to plot his novel linearly. The viewpoint jumps back and forth through time, seemingly at random, so that the reader is almost simultaneously exposed to Whitman at all stages of his dissolution. But Priest holds his character at arm's length from us, and we can vaguely perceive his motivations; the nightmarish quality of his world remains just that, for it never quite achieves reality.

Paradoxically, while the all-too-possible world shown in *Fugue for a Darkening Island* never acquires depth, the almost totally incredible setting of *Inverted World* is vividly realistic. It is a much more cohesive novel than anything Priest had written before. It features a strong sympathetic character, and some of the most innovative settings to appear in years. Helward Mann is a citizen of City Earth, an enormous construct that inches across the surface of its world by wincing itself across tracks picked up from behind and laboriously replaced ahead. The city is in eternal pursuit of the Optimum, the place where environmental conditions are most like that of their home world. For this world, whatever it might be, is treacherous and changing. Behind them, physical features become broad and flat, time passes very rapidly in relation to the city itself, and a mysterious force increasingly attempts to pull laggers back to their destruction. Ahead, the distortions of time and space have exactly opposite attributes. As Mann is initiated into the guild responsible for scouting the future, he gradually matures and adjusts to the changing nature of his world. Idea is central here rather than character; nevertheless, Helward and his personal relationships with others from the city are well portrayed. Although less ambitious stylistically than Priest's earlier novels, *Inverted World* is far more successful both as an adventure story and as a novel of ideas. Priest indulged in pastiche next, and *The Space Machine* is a witty and frequently funny examination of some of the situations first presented by H.G. Wells. This invocation of Martian invaders and time machines is carried a bit too far, unfortunately, and it is difficult to sustain interest through to the end.

*A Dream of Wessex* is a far more successful novel in almost any terms, and is easy the high point of Priest's career. The Ridpath Project is a secret research installation where a group of people pool their subconscious minds to create a mutual dream world. Within this context, they can extrapolate the future possibilities of various aspects of the present. But there is trouble brewing. David Harkman, one of the dreamers, has lost his awareness of the real world and will not come out of trance. Julia Stretton, another participant, tries desperately to release him from the grip of the dream world, particularly when she learns of the imminent participation of a new dreamer, a man who considers the project to be nonsense. The dream world becomes more real to the reader than the project itself, and, despite the existence of Soviet domination over Britain, it is easy to see why Harkman is unconsciously reluctant to leave it for reality. Both of the central figures are fully realized personalities, and their awakening feelings for each other are convincing.

*The Affirmation* develops logically from the themes Priest has used in the past. Peter Sinclair is a young man who lives both in the London of our world and in Jethra of the Dream Archipelago, the setting for a number of Priest's short stories. In London, Sinclair is descending into madness following a series of personal disasters; in Jethra he has won the prize of immortality, but to secure it he must surrender all of his memories. Each man is writing a book set in the other universe, and each man has reached a point in his life where he must make significant decisions about his future. The intellectual nature of this struggle will not endear this novel to adventure-story readers, but Priest's skillful character development is at its best in this work.

Priest seems to be fusing reality and dreams increasingly in his fiction. It should be no surprise, therefore, to note that most of his better short stories also explore this interface. "Real Time World" describes the Observatory, supposedly an extra-dimensional establishment from which a small staff could observe the flora and fauna of other worlds, in actuality an experiment in itself on news deprivation with a staff thoroughly brainwashed about the nature of their situation. In "Palely Loitering" a man spends much of his life travelling back and forth across time bridges, always in pursuit of a young girl he does not have the courage to confront. His ultimate effort draws into question the immutability of the past and the reality of his own present. Two stories set within the context of the "Dream Archipelago" are also worth mentioning. "Whores" is an incident sliced out of time, wherein the protagonist encounters a series of inexplicable events, mutilations of a sort of people living in an area formerly occupied by enemy troops. Much of the story's impact is dissipated by the ambiguous ending, however, a problem that arises also with Priest's best short story, "The Watched." Yvann Ordier is disturbed by his voyeuristic spying on a band of Qataari refugees. The Qataari have an obsessive need for privacy, and will literally starve to death rather than submit to being studied. At the same time, Ordier himself is compulsively wary of scintillas, tiny mechanical spy devices that are almost unavoidable. The result is a complex story of character, obsession, and personal decay.

The involuted, intellectualized nature of the conflict in Priest's recent fiction demonstrates a mature grasp of character and theme, but unfortunately is not as commercially successful as is fiction with more overt plots. The modest amount of fiction Priest has produced has enriched the field and quietly established him as one of the more innovative writers.

—Don D'Ammassa

---

**PRIESTLEY, J(ohn) B(oynton).** Also wrote as Peter Goldsmith. British. Born in Bradford, Yorkshire, 13 September 1894. Educated at Belle Vue Grammar School, Bradford, to age 16; Trinity Hall, Cambridge, 1919–21, B.A. in history 1921, M.A. Served in the Duke of Wellington's and Devon regiments, 1914–19. Married 1) Patricia Tempest (died 1925), two daughters; 2) Mary Wyndham Lewis in 1926 (divorced 1952), two daughters and one son; 3) the writer and archaeologist Jacquetta Hawkes in 1953. Clerk, Helm & Co., wool firm, Bradford, 1911–14; free-lance journalist and reviewer, and reader for Bodley Head publishers, London, 1922–29; director, Mask Theatre, London, 1938–39; radio lecturer on BBC programme "Postscripts", 1940; regular contributor, *New Statesman*, London. President, PEN, London, 1936–37; United Kingdom delegate, and chairman, Unesco International Theatre Conference, Paris, 1947, and Prague, 1948; chairman, British Theatre Conference, 1948; president, International Theatre Institute, 1949; member, National Theatre Board, London, 1966–67. Recipient: James Tait Black Memorial prize, 1930; Ellen Terry award, 1948. LL.D.: University of St. Andrews, Fife; D.Litt.: University of Birmingham; University of Bradford. Honorary freeman, City of Bradford, 1973; honorary student, Trinity Hall, Cambridge, 1978. Order of Merit, 1977. *Died 14 August 1984.*

### Science-Fiction Publications

#### Novels

*Adam in Moonshine.* London, Heinemann, and New York, Harper, 1927.
*The Doomsday Men.* London, Heinemann, and New York, Harper, 1938.
*The Magicians.* London, Heinemann, and New York, Harper, 1954.
*Low Notes on a High Level: A Frolic.* London, Heinemann, and New York, Harper, 1954.
*The Thirty-First of June.* London, Heinemann, 1961; New York, Doubleday, 1962.
*Snoggle* (for children). London, Heinemann, 1971; New York, Harcourt Brace, 1972.

#### Short Stories

*The Other Place and Other Stories of the Same Sort.* London, Heinemann, and New York, Harper, 1953.

### Other Publications

#### Novels

*Benighted.* London, Heinemann, 1927; as *The Old Dark House*, New York, Harper, 1928.
*Farthing Hall*, with Hugh Walpole. London, Macmillan, and New York, Doubleday, 1929.
*The Good Companions.* London, Heinemann, and New York, Harper, 1929.
*Angel Pavement.* London, Heinemann, and New York, Harper, 1930.
*Faraway.* London, Heinemann, and New York, Harper, 1932.
*I'll Tell You Everything*, with Gerald Bullett. New York, Macmillan, 1932; London, Heinemann, 1933.
*Wonder Hero.* London, Heinemann, and New York, Harper, 1933.
*They Walk in the City: The Lovers in the Stone Forest.* London, Heinemann, and New York, Harper, 1936.
*Let the People Sing.* London, Heinemann, 1939; New York, Harper, 1940.
*Black-Out in Gretley: A Story of—and for—Wartime.* London, Heinemann, and New York, Harper, 1942.
*Daylight on Saturday: A Novel about an Aircraft Factory.* London, Heinemann, and New York, Harper, 1943.
*Three Men in New Suits.* London, Heinemann, and New York, Harper, 1945.
*Bright Day.* London, Heinemann, and New York, Harper, 1946.
*Jenny Villiers: A Story of the Theatre.* London, Heinemann, and New York, Harper, 1947.
*Festival at Farbridge.* London, Heinemann, 1951; as *Festival*, New York, Harper, 1951.
*Saturn over the Water.* London, Heinemann, and New York, Doubleday, 1961.
*The Shapes of Sleep: A Topical Tale.* London, Heinemann, and New York, Doubleday, 1962.

*Sir Michael and Sir George.* London, Heinemann, 1964; Boston, Little Brown, 1965.
*Lost Empires.* London, Heinemann, and Boston, Little Brown, 1965.
*Salt Is Leaving.* London, Pan, 1966; New York, Harper, 1975.
*It's an Old Country.* London, Heinemann, and Boston, Little Brown, 1967.
*The Image Men: Out of Town, and London End.* London, Heinemann, 2 vols., 1968; Boston, Little Brown, 1 vol., 1969.
*Found, Lost, Found; or The English Way of Life.* London, Heinemann, 1976; New York, Stein and Day, 1977.

Short Stories

*The Town Major of Miraucourt.* London, Heinemann, 1930.
*Albert Goes Through.* London, Heinemann, and New York, Harper, 1933.
*Going Up: Stories and Sketches.* London, Pan, 1950.
*The Carfitt Crisis and Two Other Stories.* London, Heinemann, 1975.

Plays

*The Good Companions* (book only), with Edward Knoblock, lyrics by Harry Graham and Frank Eyton, music by Richard Addinsell, adaptation of the novel by Priestley (produced London and New York, 1931). London and New York, French, 1935.
*Dangerous Corner* (produced London and New York, 1932). London, Heinemann, and New York, French, 1932.
*The Roundabout* (produced Liverpool, London, and New York, 1932). London, Heinemann, and New York, French, 1933.
*Laburnum Grove: An Immoral Comedy* (produced London, 1933; New York, 1935). London, Heinemann, 1934; New York, French, 1935.
*Eden End* (produced London, 1934; New York, 1935). London, Heinemann, 1934; in *Three Plays and a Preface*, 1935.
*Cornelius: A Business Affair in Three Transactions* (produced Birmingham and London, 1935). London, Heinemann, 1935; New York, French, 1936.
*Duet in Floodlight* (produced Liverpool and London, 1935). London, Heinemann, 1935.
*Three Plays and a Preface* (includes *Dangerous Corner, Eden End, Cornelius*). New York, Harper, 1935.
*Bees on the Boat Deck: A Farcical Tragedy* (produced London, 1936). London, Heinemann, and Boston, Baker, 1936.
*Spring Tide* (as Peter Goldsmith), with George Billam (produced London, 1936). London, Heinemann, and New York, French, 1936.
*The Bad Samaritan* (produced Liverpool, 1937).
*Time and the Conways* (produced London, 1937; New York, 1938). London, Heinemann, 1937; New York, Harper, 1938.
*I Have Been Here Before* (produced London, 1937; New York, 1938). London, Heinemann 1937; New York, Harper, 1938.
*Two Time Plays* (includes *Time and the Conways* and *I Have Been Here Before*). London, Heinemann, 1937.
*People at Sea* (as *I Am a Stranger Here*, produced Bradford, 1937; as *People at Sea*, produced London, 1937). London, Heinemann, and New York, French, 1937.
*Mystery of Greenfingers: A Comedy of Detection* (produced London, 1938). London, French, 1937; New York, French, 1938.
*The Rebels* (produced Bradford, 1938).
*When We Are Married: A Yorkshire Farcical Comedy* (produced London, 1938; New York, 1939). London, Heinemann, 1938; New York, French, 1940.
*Music at Night* (produced Malvern, 1938; London, 1939). Included in *Three Plays*, 1943; in *Plays I*, 1948.
*Johnson over Jordan* (produced London, 1939). Published as *Johnson over Jordan: The Play, and All about It* (An Essay). London, Heinemann, and New York, Harper, 1939.
*The Long Mirror* (produced Oxford, 1940; London, 1945). Included in *Three Plays*, 1943; in *Four Plays*, 1944.
*Good Night Children: A Comedy of Broadcasting* (produced London, 1942). Included in *Three Comedies*, 1945; in *Plays II*, 1949.
*Desert Highway* (produced Bristol, 1943; London, 1944). London, Heinemann, 1944; in *Four Plays*, 1944.
*They Came to a City* (produced London, 1943). Included in *Three Plays* 1943; in *Four Plays*, 1944.
*Three Plays* (includes *Music at Night, The Long Mirror, They Came to a City*). London, Heinemann, 1943.
*How Are They at Home? A Topical Comedy* (produced London, 1944). Included in *Three Comedies*, 1945; in *Plays II*, 1949.
*The Golden Fleece* (as *The Bull Market*, produced Bradford, 1944). Included in *Three Comedies*, 1945.
*Four Plays* (includes Music at Night, the Long Mirror, They Came to a City, Desert Highway). London, Heinemann, and New York, Harper, 1944.
*Three Comedies* (includes *Good Night Children, The Golden Fleece, How Are They at Home?*). London, Heinemann, 1945.
*An Inspector Calls* (produced Moscow, 1945; London, 1946; New York, 1947). London, Heinemann, 1947; New York, Dramatists Play Service, 1948(?).
*Jenny Villiers* (produced Bristol, 1946).
*The Rose and Crown* (televised, 1946). London, French, 1947.
*Ever Since Paradise: An Entertainment, Chiefly Referring to Love and Marriage* (also director: produced on tour, 1946; London, 1947). London and New York, French, 1949.
*Three Time Plays* (includes *Dangerous Corner, Time and the Conways, I Have Been Here Before*). London, Pan, 1947.
*The Linden Tree* (produced Sheffield and London, 1947; New York, 1948). London, Heinemann, and New York, French, 1948.
The Plays of J.B. Priestley:
1. *Dangerous Corner, I Have Been Here Before, Johnson over Jordan, Music at Night, The Linden Tree, Eden End, Time and the Conways.* London, Heinemann, 1948; as *Seven Plays*, New York, Harper, 1950.
2. *Laburnum Grove, Bees on the Boat Deck, When We Are Married, Good Night Children, The Good Companions, How Are They at Home?, Ever Since Paradise.* London, Heinemann, 1949; New York, Harper, 1951.
3. *Cornelius, People at Sea, They Came to a City, Desert Highway, An Inspector Calls, Home Is Tomorrow, Summer Day's Dream.* London, Heinemann, 1950; New York, Harper, 1952.

*Home Is Tomorrow* (produced Bradford and London, 1948). London, Heinemann, 1949; in *Plays III*, 1950.
*The High Toby: A Play for the Toy Theatre* (produced London, 1954). London, Penguin-Pollock, 1948.
*Summer Day's Dream* (produced Bradford and London, 1949). Included in *Plays III*, 1950.
*The Olympians*, music by Arthur Bliss (produced London, 1949). London, Novello, 1949.
*Bright Shadow: A Play of Detection* (produced Oldham and London, 1950). London, French, 1950.
*Treasure on Pelican* (as *Treasure on Pelican Island*, televised, 1951; as *Treasure on Pelican*, produced Cardiff and London, 1952). London, Evans, 1953.
*Dragon's Mouth: A Dramatic Quartet*, with Jacquetta Hawkes (also director: produced Malvern and London, 1952; New

York, 1955). London, Heinemann, and New York, Harper, 1952.
*Private Rooms: A One-Act Comedy in the Viennese Style*. London, French, 1953.
*Mother's Day*. London, French, 1953.
*Try It Again* (produced London, 1965). London, French, 1953.
*A Glass of Bitter*. London, French, 1954.
*The White Countess*, with Jacquetta Hawkes (produced Dublin and London, 1954).
*The Scandalous Affair of Mr. Kettle and Mrs. Moon* (produced Folkestone and London, 1955). London, French, 1956.
*Take the Fool Away* (produced Vienna, 1955; Nottingham, 1959).
*These Our Actors* (produced Glasgow, 1956).
*The Glass Cage* (produced Toronto and London, 1957). London, French, 1958.
*The Thirty-First of June* (produced Toronto and London, 1957).
*A Pavilion of Masks* (produced Germany, 1961; Bristol, 1963). London, French, 1958.
*A Severed Head*, with Iris Murdoch, adaptation of the novel by Murdoch (produced Bristol and London, 1963; New York, 1964). London, Chatto and Windus, 1964.

Screenplays: *Sing As We Go*, with Gordon Wellesley, 1934; *Look Up and Laugh*, with Gordon Wellesley, 1935; *We Live in Two Worlds*, 1937; *Jamaica Inn*, with Sidney Gilliat and Joan Harrison, 1939; *Britain at Bay*, 1940; *Our Russian Allies* 1941; *The Foreman Went to France* (*Somewhere in France*), with others, 1942; *Last Holiday*, 1950.

Radio Plays: *The Return of Jess Oakroyd*, 1941; *The Golden Entry*, 1955; *End Game at the Dolphin*, 1956; *An Arabian Night in Park Lane*, 1965.

Television Plays: *The Rose and Crown*, 1946; *Whitehall Wonders*, 1949; *Treasure on Pelican Island*, 1951; *You Know What People Are*, 1953; *The Stone Faces*, 1957; *Now Let Him Go*, 1957; *Lost City* (documentary), 1958; *The Rack*, 1958; *Doomsday for Dyson*, 1958; *The Fortrose Incident*, from his play *Home Is Tomorrow*, 1959; *Level Seven*, from the novel by Mordecai Roshwald, 1966; *The Lost Peace* series, 1966; *Anyone for Tennis*, 1968; *Linda at Pulteney's*, 1969.

Verse

*The Chapman of Rhymes* (juvenilia). London, Moring, 1918.

Other

*Brief Diversions, Being Tales, Travesties, and Epigrams*. Cambridge, Bowes and Bowes, 1922.
*Papers from Lilliput*. Cambridge, Bowes and Bowes, 1922.
*I for One*. London, Lane, 1923; New York, Dodd Mead, 1924.
*Figures in Modern Literature*. London, Lane, and New York, Dodd Mead, 1924.
*The English Comic Characters*. London, Lane, and New York, Dodd Mead, 1925.
*George Meredith*. London and New York, Macmillan, 1926.
*Talking*. London, Jarrolds, and New York, Harper, 1926.
(*Essays*). London, Harrap, 1926.
*Open House: A Book of Essays*. London, Heinemann, and New York, Harper, 1927.
*Thomas Love Peacock*. London and New York, Macmillan, 1927.
*The English Novel*. London, Benn, 1927; revised edition, London and New York, Nelson, 1935.
*Apes and Angels: A Book of Essays*. London, Methuen, 1928; as *Too Many People and Other Reflections*, New York, Harper, 1928.
*The Balconinny and Other Essays*. London, Methuen, 1929; as *The Balconinny*, New York, Harper, 1930.
*English Humour*. London and New York, Longman, 1929.
*Self-Selected Essays*. London, Heinemann, 1932; New York, Harper, 1933.
*Four-in-Hand* (miscellany). London, Heinemann, 1934.
*English Journey, Being a Rambling But Truthful Account of What One Man Saw and Heard and Felt and Thought During a Journey Through England During the Autumn of the Year 1933*. London, Heinemann-Gollancz, and New York, Harper, 1934.
*Midnight on the Desert: A Chapter of Autobiography*. London, Heinemann, 1937; as *Midnight on the Desert, Being an Excursion into Autobiography During a Winter in America, 1935–36*, New York, Harper, 1937.
*Rain upon Godshill: A Further Chapter of Autobiography*. London, Heinemann, and New York, Harper, 1939.
*Britain Speaks* (radio talks). New York, Harper, 1940.
*Postcripts* (radio talks). London, Heinemann, 1940; as *All England Listened*, New York, Chilmark Press, 1968.
*Out of the People*. London, Collins-Heinemann, and New York, Harper, 1941.
*Britain at War*. New York, Harper, 1942.
*British Women Go to War*. London, Collins, 1943.
*Manpower: The Story of Britain's Mobilisation for War*. London, His Majesty's Stationery Office, 1944.
*Here Are Your Answers*. London, Socialist Book Centre, 1944.
*Letter to a Returning Serviceman*. London, Home and Van Thal, 1945.
*The Secret Dream: An Essay on Britain, America, and Russia*. London, Turnstile Press, 1946.
*Russian Journey*. London, Writers Group of the Society for Cultural Relations with the USSR, 1946.
*The New Citizen* (address). London, Council for Education in World Citizenship, 1946.
*Theatre Outlook*. London, Nicholson and Watson, 1947.
*The Arts under Socialism* (lecture). London, Turnstile Press, 1947.
*Delight*. London, Heinemann, and New York, Harper, 1949.
*The Priestley Companion: A Selection from the Writings of J.B. Priestley*. London, Penguin-Heinemann, 1951.
*Journey down a Rainbow* (travel), with Jacquetta Hawkes. London, Cresset Press-Heinemann, and New York, Harper, 1955.
*All about Ourselves and Other Essays*, edited by Eric Gillett. London, Heinemann, 1956.
*The Writer in a Changing Society* (lecture). Aldington, Kent, Hand and Flower Press, 1956.
*Thoughts in the Wilderness* (essays). London, Heinemann, and New York, Harper, 1957.
*The Art of the Dramatist: A Lecture Together with Appendices and Discursive Notes*. London, Heinemann, 1957; Boston, The Writer, 1958.
*Topside; or, The Future of England: A Dialogue*. London, Heinemann, 1958.
*The Story of Theatre* (for children). London, Rathbone, 1959; as *The Wonderful World of the Theatre*, New York, Doubleday, 1959.
*Literature and Western Man*. London, Heinemann, and New York, Harper, 1960.
*William Hazlitt*. London, Longman, 1960.
*Charles Dickens: A Pictorial Biography*. London, Thames and Hudson, 1961; New York, Viking Press, 1962; as *Charles Dickens and His World*. Thames and Hudson, and Viking Press, 1969.

*Margin Released: A Writer's Reminiscences and Reflections.* London, Heinemann, and New York, Harper, 1962.
*Man and Time.* London, Aldus, and New York, Doubleday, 1964.
*The Moments and Other Pieces.* London, Heinemann, 1966.
*The World of J.B. Priestley,* edited by Donald G. MacRae. London, Heinemann, 1967.
*Essays of Five Decades,* edited by Susan Cooper. Boston, Little Brown, 1968; London, Heinemann, 1969.
*Trumpets over the Sea, Being a Rambling and Egotistical Account of the London Symphony Orchestra's Engagement at Daytona Beach, Florida, in July-August 1967.* London, Heinemann, 1968.
*The Prince of Pleasure and His Regency 1811–1820.* London, Heinemann, and New York, Harper, 1969.
*The Edwardians.* London, Heinemann, and New York, Harper, 1970.
*Anton Chekhov.* London, International Textbook, 1970.
*Snoggle* (for children). London, Heinemann, 1971; New York, Harcourt Brace, 1972.
*Victoria's Heyday.* London, Heinemann, and New York, Harcourt Brace, 1972.
*Over the Long High Wall: Some Reflections and Speculations on Life, Death, and Time.* London, Heinemann, 1972.
*The English.* London, Heinemann, and New York, Viking Press, 1973.
*Outcries and Asides.* London, Heinemann, 1974.
*A Visit to New Zealand.* London, Heinemann, 1974.
*Particular Pleasures, Being a Personal Record of Some Varied Arts and Many Different Artists.* London, Heinemann, 1975.
*The Happy Dream: An Essay.* Andoversford, Gloucestshire, Whittington Press, 1976.
*English Humour* (not the same as 1929 book). -London, Heinemann, 1976.
*Instead of the Trees: A Final Chapter of Autobiography.* London, Heinemann, and New York, Stein and Day, 1977.
*Seeing Stratford,* illustrated by Arthur Keene. Stratford-on-Avon, Warwickshire, Celandine Press, 1982.

Editor, *Essayists Past and Present: A Selection of English Essays.* London, Jenkins, and New York, Dial Press, 1925.
Editor, *Fools and Philosophers: A Gallery of Comic Figures from English Literature.* London, Lane, and New York, Dodd Mead, 1925.
Editor, *Tom Moore's Diary: A Selection.* London, Cambridge University Press, 1925.
Editor, *The Book of Bodley Head Verse.* London, Lane, and New York, Dodd Mead, 1926.
Editor, *Our Nation's Heritage.* London, Dent, 1939.
Editor, *Scenes from London Life, from Sketches by Boz,* by Charles Dickens. London, Pan, 1947.
Editor, *The Best of Leacock.* Toronto, McClelland and Stewart, 1957; as *The Bodley Head Leacock,* London, Bodley Head, 1957.
Editor, with Josephine Spear, *Adventures in English Literature.* New York, Harcourt Brace, 1963.

*

Bibliography: *J.B. Priestley: An Annotated Bibliography* by Alan Edwin Day, New York, Garland, and Stroud, Gloucestershire, Hodgkins, 1980.

Manuscript Collection: University of Texas, Austin.

Critical Studies: *J.B. Priestley* by Ivor Brown, London, Longman, 1957, revised edition, 1964; *J.B. Priestley: An Informal Study of His Work* by David Hughes, London, Hart Davis, 1958, Freeport, New York, Books for Libraries, 1970; *J.B. Priestley: Portrait of an Author* by Susan Cooper, London, Heinemann, 1970, New York, Harper, 1971; *J.B. Priestley* by Kenneth Young, London, Longman, 1977; *J.B. Priestley* by John Braine, London, Weidenfeld and Nicolson, 1978, New York, Barnes and Noble, 1979; *J.B. Priestley* by A.A. De Vitis and Albert E. Kalson, Boston, Twayne, 1980; *J.B. Priestley: The Last of the Sages* by John Atkins, London, Calder, and New York, Riverrun Press, 1981; *Bygone Bradford: The Lost World of J.B. Priestley* by Gary Frith, Lancaster, Dalesman, 1986; *J.B. Priestley's Plays* by Holger Klein, London, Macmillan, and New York, St. Martin's Press, 1988; *J.B. Priestley* by Vincent Brome, London and New York, Hamilton, 1988.

Theatrical Activities:
Director: **Plays**—*Ever Since Paradise,* tour, 1946, and London, 1947; *Dragon's Mouth,* London, 1952.

* * *

J.B. Priestley was possessed by a vision of life at its rare best—rich, vivid, eminently worth living. What makes him a science-fiction writer and not just another dreaming romantic is that he espouses theories of time that allow his characters (and conceivably his readers) actually to attain the rich life he envisions. Such theories—chronological simultaneity, serialism, multiple dimensions—are not easy to illustrate, but Priestley succeeds surprisingly well, in stories and novels and also in popular stage plays. As literary fashion moves on and Priestley's sedately conventional style falls from favor, it is his time stories, his personal ventures towards altered reality, that remain fresh and intriguing.

Priestley derived his theories from three sources: E.A. Abbott's idea that a fourth dimension would appear as time; J.W. Dunne's mathematical model of time as continuous, simultaneous, and serial; and P.D. Ouspensky's more philosophical view of time as a repeated circle which can be made to spiral morally up or down. What these concepts gave to Priestley was a non-religious hope. If there are other dimensions, then there might be somewhere to go after life's time ends. In the plays *Music at Night* and *Johnson over Jordan* characters withdraw after death into a higher observer-state similar to the Tibetan "Bardo." Also, if all time is simultaneous then each minute is not murdered by the next, and the goodness of the past can be made accessible to those trapped in a bad present. Such comforting access is given to characters in the play *Time and the Conways* and in fiction such as "Night Sequence" and *The Magicians.* And if precognition and time's recurrence are true, then the known future can be, paradoxically, changed, altered in a tiny moment to redirect the flow, as in the plays *Dangerous Corner* and *I Have Been Here Before.*

Priestley desires these comforts and powers because he sees the modern world as darkening fast. In a short grim tale called "The Grey Ones" he incarnates the powers of darkness into grey tentacled devils capable of human shape. Their weapons are boredom, blandness, and despair; they seek to dull the world down to a suburban hell. Priestley's fullest treatment of this theme, and of the time-conscious man's opposition to it, comes in *The Magicians.* The industrialist Ravenstreet leaves his company when it turns from exciting scientific quest to passionless bureaucracy. As he slides into despair he is tempted by a bitter elitist to help drug the masses into final lethargy. Ravenstreet almost agrees, but is saved by the intervention of three "magicians" whose mysterious abilities include precognition and hypnosis, and who seem to be involved in some larger struggle. They show Ravenstreet the difference between the "tick-tock time" he had been dying in, and "time alive" where his hopeful past still lives. They send him to re-experience crucial moments, and they also rearrange the present so that the drug's numbing secret is lost. At the end, Ravenstreet has reason to live, and the world is a little less grey. Priestley's time visions are not always cheering. In one of his most haunting stories, "The Statues," a tired man is granted exhilarating but temporary sight of huge glorious statues towering above a future London, and the contrast with the banal present saddens the rest of his life. In the well-crafted and widely anthologized "Mr. Strenberry's Tale" the title character is visited briefly by a time traveler from an advanced humanity's last black moment. The traveler vanishes, destroyed, but the terror stays.

Some of Priestley's stories have been classified as science fiction because they focus on some unusual bit of technology—the musical invention in *Low Notes on a High Level* or the earth-destroying transmitter in *The Doomsday Men.* But such devices usually turn out to be occasions for plot, not concepts in themselves, and plot for Priestley means romance, marriages, careers, and individual morale more than anything else. Even his children's book, *Snoggle,* which offers extra-terrestrial pets and invisible spaceships, spends most of its rather unsuccessful pages detailing the interactions of three ordinary children.

Priestley began writing in 1910; he learned his craft in an earlier time than most science-fiction writers. His many romantic comedies now seem dated, his plots coercive and even clanking. But his parables of hope and despair remain compelling, and there are few science-fiction writers who can match him for the seriousness of his thinking about time.

—Karen G. Way

---

**PROCTOR, Geo(rge W).** Also writes as Zach Wyatt. American. Address: c/o Doubleday Books, 666 Fifth Avenue, New York, New York 10103, U.S.A.

SCIENCE-FICTION PUBLICATIONS

Novels (Series: V)

*The Esper Transfer.* New York, Major, 1978.
*Shadowman.* New York, Fawcett, 1980.
*Fire at the Center.* New York, Fawcett, 1981.
*Starwings.* New York, Ace, 1984.
*V: The Chicago Conversion* (novelization of TV series). New York, Pinnacle, 1985.
*V: The Texas Run* (novelization of TV series). New York, Pinnacle, 1985.
*Stellar Fist.* New York, Ace, 1989.

OTHER PUBLICATIONS

Novels

*Enemies.* New York, Doubleday, 1983.
*Death's Acolyte,* with Robert E. Vardeman. New York, Ace, 1985.
*A Yoke of Magic,* with Robert E. Vardeman. New York, Ace, 1985.
*To Demons Bound,* with Robert E. Vardeman. New York, Ace, 1985.
*Blood Fountain,* with Robert E. Vardeman. New York, Ace, 1985.
*The Beasts of the Mist,* with Robert E. Vardeman. New York, Ace, 1986.
*For Crown and Kingdom,* with Robert E. Vardeman. New York, Ace, 1987.
*Ride for Vengeance.* New York, Pageant, 1989.
*Walks without a Soul.* New York, Doubleday, 1990.
*Comes the Hunter.* New York, Doubleday, 1992.

Novels as Zach Wyatt

The Texians:
*The Texians.* New York, Pinnacle, 1984.
*The Horse Marines.* New York, Pinnacle, 1984.
*War Devils.* New York, Pinnacle, 1984.
*Blood Moon.* New York, Pinnacle, 1985.
*Death's Shadow.* New York, Pinnacle, 1985.
*Comanche Ambush.* New York, Pinnacle, 1985.

Other

Editor, with Steve Utley, *Lone Star Universe: Speculative Fiction from Texas.* Austin, Texas, Heidelberg, 1976.
Editor, with Arthur C. Clarke, *The Science-Fiction Hall of Fame 3: The Nebula Winners 1965–69.* New York, Avon, 1982.

* * *

In much of "hard science fiction," technology overshadows characters and often becomes the protagonist. The science fiction work of Geo. W. Proctor shows a different and more human-oriented approach. Although an accomplished amateur astronomer, Proctor relegates technology to the minor position of a plot device and concentrates on human and alien characters, showing their reaction to technological gadgetry. The heart of *Fire at the Center* isn't the technology of time travel or even the hopes of the protagonists in journeying to the past, but how Nils Kendler and Caltha Renent communicate psionically and the personal challenges they face through the relationship this situation affords.

The theme weaving throughout all Proctor's books is that of communication, no doubt a product of his training and work as a newspaper journalist. His first published novel, *The Esper Transfer,* is an uncomplicated escape-chase plot, but the protagonist depends heavily on his telepathic talents and "oneness" with others of his race. The conflict comes more from within than from external forces. This is likewise true in *Shadowman.* Outwardly another escape-chase plot, the novel becomes more. Male and female join in telepathic contact and become lovers through this most intimate of contact.

Proctor carries this theme to its logical extension in *Starwings.* The protagonist, Radman Donalt, uses a collapsar as a time machine and becomes separated from his lover, Jenica, not only in space but in time. Fifteen years and the barrier of untold light years notwithstanding, Donalt enters Jenica's mind and they make love in the only way possible for them. "His mind merged with hers, Donalt led her to the bed. And there, her hands now his, he made love to her."

Proctor's pacifist views surface in *Stellar Fist*, where the conflict comes from the interplay between Arianne Pillan and Faxon Lorens, the father of Pillan's child and an agent assigned to uncover the workings of an invincible weapon. Again psionic skills intertwine the characters, bringing in Pillan's memory-erased brother as a pawn. Using the metaphor of the bonsai, Proctor's conclusion is that peace must grow slowly over long periods of time, and it cannot be achieved without severe pruning.

This focus on male-female, human-alien communication extends beyond Proctor's science fiction and into his fantasy novels. While the structure and tone of his fantasy work is strongly influenced by Fritz Leiber's Fafhrd and the Gray Mouser stories, the basic themes are easily identifiable as belonging to Proctor.

The Nalcon and Hweir short stories transcend the usual genre offerings of sword-and-sorcery quest through interplay between the main characters. Both are rogues and thieves, but their fierce friendship is obvious. They have discovered common ground, mutual affection, and fulfillment in one another in spite of divergent backgrounds as blond prince and black-skinned thief. This friendship and the strains placed on it are more central to the stories than any quest.

In the *Swords of Raemllyn* heroic fantasy series, Proctor has created another way of examining male-female communication. Although in *Death's Acolyte* there is Chal, a tongueless character who makes his wishes known to the heroine empathically, a more intriguing method of exploration lies with Goran One-Eye, an interdimensional being capable of massive shape changes. Goran at first lacks control over this ability and is locked in a bulky male human body. By the second book in the series, *A Yoke of Magic*, he shifts into female form and attempts to seduce his friend, Davin Anane. The byplay between the two, when Davin discovers the shape transformation, examines not only the limits of their friendship but also male-female roles and expectations.

The nucleus of Geo. W. Proctor's science fiction and fantasy works is both simple and beguiling: communication. How do men and women relate to one another? How would communication be different if we were able to enter another's mind telepathically? How would our friendships and loves alter if they were based on empathic rather than verbal considerations? Science fiction provides a suitable vehicle for Proctor's explorations of this enhanced communication.

—Robert E. Vardeman

---

**PURDOM, Tom** (Thomas Edward Purdom). American. Born in New Haven, Connecticut, 19 April 1936. Educated at Lafayette College, Easton, Pennsylvania, 1952–54; Thomas Edison State College, Trenton, New Jersey, B.A. in social sciences 1977. Served in the United States Army Medical Corps, 1959–61. Married Sara Wescot in 1960; one son. Reservation agent, United Airlines, Philadelphia, 1957–58; science writer, University of Pennsylvania, Philadelphia, 1968–69; visiting professor of English, Temple University, Philadelphia, 1970–71; adjunct professor of English, Drexel University, Philadelphia, 1975; instructor in science fiction, Institute for Human Resources Development, Philadelphia, 1976–77. Vice-President, Science Fiction Writers of America, 1970–72. Agent: Scott Meredith Literary Agency, 845 Third Avenue, New York, New York 10022, U.S.A.

### Science-Fiction Publications

Novels

*I Want the Stars.* New York, Ace, 1964.
*The Tree Lord of Imeten.* New York, Ace, 1966.
*Five Against Arlane.* New York, Ace, 1967.
*Reduction in Arms.* New York, Berkley, 1971.
*The Barons of Behavior.* New York, Ace, 1972; London, Dobson, 1977.

### Other Publications

Other

Editor, *Adventures in Discovery.* New York, Doubleday, 1969.

*

Tom Purdom comments:

My main aim as a fiction writer is to create the kind of stories I like to read—engrossing, well-plotted works that hold you from the first page to the end and really get you involved in the characters and the things that are happening to them. Once I jokingly said that the greatest living novelists were Alexander Solzhenitsyn, Ursula K. LeGuin, Richard Adams, and George Macdonald Fraser. I was poking a little fun at literary pomposity, but I would give a great deal to have written the better works of any of them.

The struggle that most interests me—and I think it's mostly what I've written about and like to read about in SF—is the problem of adapting to technology, especially the attempts to seize the opportunity it gives us without falling into all the traps it puts in front of us (some of which are not too obvious). I'm also fond of one of the things the man Santiago said about his fish: "It will feed many people and it will bring a good price on the market." I think science fiction has given a great many people a lot of things they needed, and it has even—especially recently—brought some of its practitioners a good price on the market.

* * *

Tom Purdom's career spans more than two decades. Though clearly distinguishable from one another, his early novels share the same narrative formula: the hero finds himself on an alien planet which is ruled by a dictator, either benign as in *Five Against Arlane* or malevolent as in *The Tree Lord of Imeten.* In either case, the hero struggles to overthrow tyranny and re-establish social equilibrium through bloodshed. In the aftermath of the battle against the tyrant, the hero emerges victorious from the rubble to announce that democratic liberties have been restored to the people. Great adulation of the Purdom hero follows the revolution, and the novel closes on a note of exhaustion as an infant republic comes uncertainly to life.

This well-worn plot serves as the basis for Purdom's more recent novels too, but in *The Barons of Behavior* he has achieved more interesting results. Here Purdom's subject is the potential threat which Skinnerian behaviorism poses to a free society. The novel opens in a world of the remote future in which the privileges and responsibilities of life in 20th-century America have been lost. Nurtured by democracy, the growth of lawlessness and violence has long ago become intolerable to society, and politicians, seeking a retardant, have turned to the behavioral sciences for help. And indeed they have found there willing social physicians. Thus a terrible triple alliance is formed of science, technology, and politics, whose aim it is to produce law and order, to provide security and comfort to the citizens of Windham County, Pennsylvania, but whose real accomplishment is to rob the human spirit of its civil liberties and to render the human will impotent. In *The Barons of Behavior* the orderly operation of society is insured by an arsenal of devices and techniques which can subvert individual free will. It can be numbed or stupified by insidious drugs; it can be forced to betray itself through the techniques of behaviour modification; or, most horribly, it can be bypassed altogether by devices surgically implanted in the brain. Opposed to the dehumanizing powers in control of society stands the Purdom hero, Ralph Nicholson, "psychotherapist to a psyched-out world," who manages to defeat the political machine of Martin Boyd despite the overwhelming odds against his doing so.

But this is familiar stuff to science-fiction readers. The science of control has inspired dozens of novels along the same line, the very best of which achieve truly chilling results. The atrocities committed against Alex in Burgess's *A Clockwork Orange*, for instance, evoke the archetypal fear humans have of being obliterated by forces beyond their comprehension, while his struggle to remain human and intact in the face of dehumanizing powers approaches Aristotle's definition of great tragedy, the purgation of fear and pity. Unfortunately, *The Barons of Behavior* never achieves such impact. Though Purdom's technological imagination is impressive, his ability to conceive and delineate character is not. Ralph Nicholson of *The Barons of Behavior* is as two-dimensional as Migel Lassamba of *Five Against Arlane.* Both are conventional super-heroes, men of endless resource and daring, but since they lack depth and delineation, their suffering appears rather more ludicrous than tragic, their lives more gratuitously violent than compelling, and their inevitable victory more contrived than earned.

Nevertheless, Purdom's interest in possibilities is genuine, and his grasp of the implications of behaviorism is very thorough. At his best, he is capable of constructing a shockingly plausible and horrifying vision of the future, a time when individual freedom is a suppressed, half-forgotten memory, abandoned centuries ago in pursuit of law and order. There is little anxiety in this world, even less disorder once chance factors have been all but eliminated. There are no dangers, except to the intellect and imagination. There is no physical suffering in the America of *The Barons of Behavior*, but there is no free thought either, no unapproved writing, no spontaneous creation of any kind. Men and women smile and go about their daily business, but their eyes appear vacant. They reflect no light. Birth and death are quiet, pre-arranged experiences.

—Marvin W. Hunt

---

**PYNCHON, Thomas.** American. Born in Glen Cove, New York, 8 May 1937. Educated at Cornell University, Ithaca, New York, 1954–58, B.A. 1958. Served in the United States Navy. Former editorial writer, Boeing Aircraft, Seattle. Recipient: Faulkner award, 1964; Rosenthal Memorial award, 1967; National Book award, 1974; American Academy Howells Medal, 1975. Agent: Melanie Jackson, Melanie Jackson Agency, 250 West 57th Street, Suite 119, New York, New York 10107. Address: c/o Little Brown, 34 Beacon Street, Boston, Massachusetts 02106, U.S.A.

### Science-Fiction Publications

Novel

*Gravity's Rainbow.* New York, Viking Press, and London, Cape, 1973.

### Other Publications

Novels

*V.* Philadelphia, Lippincott, and London, Cape, 1963.
*The Crying of Lot 49.* Philadelphia, Lippincott, 1966; London, Cape, 1967.
*Vineland.* Boston, Little Brown, and London, Secker and Warburg, 1990.

Short Stories

*Mortality and Mercy in Vienna.* London, Aloes, 1976.
*Low-lands.* London, Aloes, 1978.
*The Secret Integration.* London, Aloes, 1980.
*The Small Rain.* London, Aloes, 1980(?).
*Slow Learner: Early Stories.* Boston, Little Brown, 1984; London, Cape, 1985.

*

Bibliography: *Three Contemporary Novelists: An Annotated Bibliography* by Robert M. Scotto, New York, Garland, 1977; *John Barth, Jerzy Kosinski, and Thomas Pynchon: A Reference Guide* by Thomas P. Walsh and Cameron Northouse, Boston, Hall, 1977; *Thomas Pynchon: A Bibliography of Primary and Secondary Materials* by Clifford Mead, Elmwood Park, Illinois, Dalkey Archive Press, 1989.

Critical Studies: *Thomas Pynchon* by Joseph V. Slade, New York, Warner, 1974; *Mindful Pleasures: Essays on Thomas Pynchon* edited by George Levine and David Leverenz, Boston, Little Brown, 1976; *The Grim Phoenix: Reconstructing Thomas Pynchon* by William M. Plater, Bloomington, Indiana University Press, 1978; *Pynchon: A Collection of Critical Essays* edited by Edward Mendelson, Englewood Cliffs, New Jersey, Prentice Hall, 1978; *Pynchon: Creative Paranoia in Gravity's Rainbow* by Mark Richard Siegal, Port Washington, New York, Kennikat Press, 1978; *Thomas Pynchon: The Art of Allusion* by David Cowart, Carbondale, Southern Illinois University Press, 1980; *The Rainbow Quest of Thomas Pynchon* by Douglas A. Mackey, San Bernardino, California, Borgo Press, 1980; *Pynchon's Fictions: Thomas Pynchon and the Literature of Information* by John O. Stark, Athens, Ohio University Press, 1980; *A Reader's Guide to Gravity's Rainbow* by Douglas Fowler, Ann Arbor, Michigan, Ardis, 1980; *Thomas Pynchon* by Tony Tanner, London, Methuen, 1982; *Signs and Symptoms: Thomas Pynchon and the Contemporary World* by Peter L. Cooper, Berkeley, University of California Press, 1983; *The Style of Connectedness: Gravity's Rainbow and Thomas Pynchon* by Thomas Moore, Columbia, University of Missouri Press, 1987; *The Fictional Labyrinths of Thomas Pynchon* by David Seed, London, Macmillan, and Iowa City, University of Iowa Press, 1988; *Writing Pynchon: Strategies in Fictional Analysis* by A.W. McHoul and

David Wills, London, Macmillan, and Urbana, University of Illinois Press, 1990; *A Hand to Turn the Time: The Menippean Satires of Thomas Pynchon* by Theodore D. Kharpertian, Rutherford, New Jersey, Farleigh Dickinson University Press, 1990; *Thomas Pynchon: Allusive Parables of Power* by John Dugdale, New York, St. Martin's Press, and London, Macmillan, 1990.

* * *

Thomas Pynchon's novels, though firmly entrenched in historic and technological realities, question all orders and unities to suggest that, since man continually imposes patterns on his world, all patterns are suspect and potentially false—so much so that recorded "history" may be simply man imposing private interpretations on chaotic reality, just as man's mastery of bureaucratic and technological systems may well be his enslavement to his own creations. Pynchon's is a vision of a world in decline, one where personal choices are shaped by science, language, history, and economics, where the victim in turn victimizes, where vast, shadowy conspiracies flourish, and where huge conglomerates seem to control events and technology overshadows and threatens humanity. His dominant themes include isolation, alienation, fragmentation, failure to communicate, degradation, entropy, the battle between men and machines and between established society and the "preterites" (the rebellious disinherited), the absurdities and ironies of modern existence, man's self-destructive potentials, the horrors of war, paranoia, and the question of multiple interpretations. Wastelands and undergrounds dominate his imagery.

His style, in tune with the complexity of his thematic concerns, is baroque, variegated, and multistructural, an intricate amalgam of Whitmanesque catalogs, Dickensian names, cryptic abbreviations, puns, innumerable analogical sequences extended between as well as within novels, and historical, literary, theological and mythological allusions. It runs the gamut of literary and cinematic modes, rapidly shifting, much like media events, between comic-book and television fantasy and learned discourse on complex scientific and technological concerns: organic chemistry, operant conditioning, rocket dynamics. It partakes of parody, farce, and black humor, jeremiad, apocalypse, and prophesy. Its geography is often allegorical, its conception mythic, its patterns analogical compounds—networks of multiple, interlocking images from personal to social to cosmic. Pynchon, perhaps aptly called a "demented deconstructionist" by Joseph Slade of Long Island University, overwhelms with data as he updates Renaissance *copia* with correspondences from high to low. In *Gravity's Rainbow*, for example, the V-2 rocket which nears London imposes patterns on reality, so that as the doomed city lifts up its towers and chimneys like stationary rockets, it is seen on a target grid that parallels the patterns of its buildings and streets; the central character fantasizes about becoming a Rocketman, merged with machine; sexual orgasm parallels a launching; a sadistic Nazi launches his homosexual lover in a V-2 rocket; the extreme verticality of futuristic structures are like monuments to rocketpower; the aggressive and bigoted "Marvy's Mothers" celebrate "immachination," the union of man and machine, with "rocket limericks"; and the minds of those threatened by senseless destruction are described as maze-like grids.

Each Pynchon novel focuses on some central mystery (a cryptogram in *The Crying of Lot 49*, an elusive secret agent in *V*, a missing supersonic rocket in *Gravity's Rainbow*, a missing mother in *Vineland*), which provides the supportive structure for diverse images encompassing a range of perspectives delineated by signs, codes, signals, patterns, and plots. Usually there is what *Time* reviewer Paul Gray calls "an evil, well-organized and immensely powerful enemy" which "sows 'the merciless spores of paranoia' among a shaggy, lost group of drifting souls who find the real world threatening under the best of circumstances." Always Pynchon's works are like densely textured puzzles whose central images are visible only from a distance, while close up all seems chaos.

Comic and satiric, *The Crying of Lot 49*, the most accessible of Pynchon's novels, focuses on the quest of Oedipa Maas for the meaning of her ex-lover's will. Her synthesis of scattered clues, including a Jacobean tragedy, doodlings, acronyms, postage stamps, and graffiti, postulates the existence of a secret, 16th-century anti-postal service, the Tristero, perpetuated by W.A.S.T.E., an underground of the disenchanted. Ultimately, Oedipa must question whether her discovery is a genuine conspiracy involving a parallel, secret America, a giant farcical hoax, or a paranoid projection of her own creation. In Pynchon it is a question of interpretation, one eye seeing chaos, another a system. Oedipa intuits in her city and in her universe "a hieroglyphic sense of concealed meaning . . . an intent to communicate," but is unable to grasp its essence, to elucidate its mysteries. This question of whether order, systems, patterns truly exist or are merely superimposed on chaotic reality is an essential concern of *V, Gravity's Rainbow*, and *Vineland* as well.

The central character of *V*, as his name suggests, "Stencil"s his own pattern on an external blankness, but his various versions of himself, the elusive woman he pursues, and his world are all private dreams, products of his early conditioning and of his own paranoid inventiveness. He is played off against Benny Profane, an empiricist who becomes engulfed in incomprehensible details. Drawing on Henry Adams, Jorge Luis Borges, thermodynamics, and WWII film clips, Pynchon traces what he sees as man's historic progression toward the moribund. The anarchistic V gradually replaces her flesh with cold machinery; an automaton named SHROUD walks the earth, and all the characters move towards annihilation near Malta. It is a nightmare world of genocide, dehumanization, dead landscapes, and man-machines.

The lengthy (760 pages) and often impenetrable *Gravity's Rainbow* continues the historic focus of *V*, tracing the end product of a bureaucratic, technological system—a V-2 supersonic rocket that screams into view in the first lines of the novel (1945) and disintegrates the reader and his "theater," perhaps our civilization, at its close. A satiric fantasy, an historic novel, a parody of various forms—part technological manual, part folk myth, part Kabbala, part pornography—it rapidly changes perspective as it collapses time (envisioning Bethlehem at the time of the Nativity, a WWII London Christmas, and a futuristic Rocket City), unravels numerous plots, and delineates 400 characters and 1000 objects (including a talking light bulb, Richard Nixon, and King Kong). In its Special Operations executives use seances, psi forces, and Pavlovian conditioning as weapons, and metaphors derive from calculus, rocketry, and organic polymers. It begins with the quest of Lt. Slothrop, a New Englander of Puritan stock, whose sexuality is attuned to a mysterious, gravity-defying rocket for whom everybody is searching, but he ultimately dissolves over the Allied Zone, and the plot digresses in a myriad of directions, its only unity analogical. Slothrup, like Oedipa in *Crying of Lot 49*, is never sure whether he is actually paranoid or the victim of some intricate plot. *Gravity's Rainbow*, with its labyrinthine complications, is a massive effort to seek through historic analysis the roots of 20th-century man's mass "death wish," his cultural programming for death, and to project a future/present when that wish might come true. It describes man as simultaneously destroyer and victim, responsible, dangerous, and self-doomed, compelled by a fascination with rocketry, gadgets, machinery, and explosives, and by a "lust for technology and control."

*Vineland* is set in 1984 in the fog-shrouded Northern California town of Vineland, a haven for burnt-out hippies, like the main character, Zoyd Wheeler, escaping Reaganism, narcotics agents, and their own lost dreams. A part-time keyboard player, lobsterman, handyman, and marijuana farmer, Wheeler blames a notoriously evil federal prosecutor, Brock Vond, for seducing Wheeler's ex-wife, ex-Sixties radical Frenesi, turning her into a government informer, and thereby causing her to abandon her daughter, Prairie, a resourceful young lady who determines to find, understand, and forgive her lost mother. Pynchon describes Vond's genius as his understanding that Sixties radicals were seeking order rather than trying to destroy it, and that that desire for order made them vulnerable. This "realistic" base is the foundation for a satiric distortion that indicts contemporary society. Many of Pynchon's characters are "Tubefreeks," pursued by NEVER (National Endowment for Video Education and Rehabilitation) for television abuse ("tripping out" on repeats of "Gilligan's Island," the "Flintstones" and so forth); "Thanatoids," members of a secret death cult, anxious for extinction and resentful of life; or "Kunoichi Attentives," militant feminists who are opposed to male militarism and who rely on Broadway Show Tunes to punish wayward disciples. An airline between Los Angeles and Honolulu sports an "invisible robot," an android that could be on any aisle or taking up any seemingly empty seat. In effect, Pynchon creates our reality, distorted, a Brave New Media World.

Pynchon suggests that modern man is paranoid, perhaps with good reason, compulsive, and self-destructive; his lethal technology is perhaps already beyond control, and even it lacks certainty; man cannot be sure whether his perceptions of the world are valid or merely self-imposed projections. While Pynchon breaks traditional patterns, he builds on our scientific and literary heritage. His eclectic and controversial novels, with their limited plotting, their wild comic invention, and their failure to elucidate anything except man's wish for answers and his difficulty finding them, verge on science fiction and partake of its techniques; they share its concern with the human effects and the broader implications of science and technology, while remaining difficult to categorize precisely.

—Gina Macdonald

---

# Q

**QUITMAN, Wallace.** *See* **PALMER, Raymond A.**

---

# R

**RACKHAM, John.** Pseudonym for John Thomas Phillifent. British. Born in Durham, 10 November 1916. Served in the Royal Navy, 1935–47. Worked for the Central Electricity Generating Board in the early 1960's. *Died 15 December 1976.*

SCIENCE-FICTION PUBLICATIONS

Novels

*Space Puppet.* London, Pearson, 1954.
*Jupiter Equilateral.* London, Pearson, 1954.
*The Master Weed.* London, Pearson, 1954.
*The Touch of Evil.* London, Digit, 1963.
*We, The Venusians.* New York, Ace, 1965.
*The Beasts of Kohl.* New York, Ace, 1966.
*Time to Live.* New York, Ace, 1966; London, Dobson, 1969.
*Danger from Vega.* New York, Ace, 1966; London, Dobson, 1970.
*The Double Invaders.* New York, Ace, 1967.
*Alien Sea.* New York, Ace, 1968; London, Dobson, 1975.
*The Proxima Project.* New York, Ace, 1968.
*The Treasure of Tau Ceti.* New York, Ace, 1969.
*Ipomoea.* New York, Ace, 1969; London, Dobson, 1972.
*Flower of Doradil.* New York, Ace, 1970.
*The Anything Tree.* New York, Ace, 1970; London, Dobson, 1977.
*Beyond Capella.* New York, Ace, 1971.
*Dark Planet.* New York, Ace, 1971.
*Earthstrings.* New York, Ace, 1972.
*Beanstalk.* New York, DAW, 1973.

Novels as John T. Phillifent

*Genius Unlimited.* New York, DAW, 1972.
*Hierarchies.* New York, Ace, 1973.
*Life with Lancelot.* New York, Ace, 1973.
*King of Argent.* New York, DAW, 1973.

OTHER PUBLICATIONS

Novels as John T. Phillifent

*The Lonely Man.* London, Boardman, 1965.
*The Mad Scientist Affair.* London, Souvenir Press, and New York, Ace, 1966.
*The Corfu Affair.* London, Souvenir Press, 1967; New York, Ace, 1969.
*The Power Cube Affair.* London, Souvenir Press, and New York, Ace, 1969.

* * *

Under his own name and the pseudonym of John Rackham, John T. Phillifent produced a series of short adventure novels that made use of traditional science-fiction plots to present a fast-moving plot set against an exotic background. There is little doubt in the reader's mind that right will ultimately prevail, but the events along the way are the chief attraction.

To a great extent, Rackham repeated the situations he found most appealing. One of these is the Mowgli tale set in the future; one or more humans are returned to civilization after being raised among aliens, and the ensuing culture shock provides much of the basis of the story. This is the major plotline in *The Beasts of Kohl*, for example, where Earth has become considerably more benign but still unsettling to one not used to human ways. The same is true of the far better Phillifent novel, *Life with Lancelot*, in which the alien Shogleet rebuilds a damaged human with mechanical parts, and then tries to reintegrate him into human culture. Another recurring plot is the search for a fabulous treasure, be it gem, secret plans, or immortality drug. The protoganist of *The Treasure of Tau Ceti* is motivated by legends of priceless gems on that jungle world, but along the way he forces humans to recognize that the inhabitants of the planet are indeed intelligent. A secret agent searches for a rumored sentient plant in *The Anything Tree.* Another plant, this time one that will cure all humans diseases, is the target of another group of adventurers in *Flower of Doradil.* This time the major subplot is a crew of human smugglers determined to prevent the success of the hero's mission. Jewels are the quarry once again in the *Hierarchies* (Phillifent), this time purloined from their rightful owner. Another theme is that of secret alien or human manipulation of society. Secret aliens provoke a war between Earth and Venus in *Alien Sea;* a new drug is revealed to be the tool of insidious would-be alien conquerors in *Ipomoea;* human expansion into space is blocked by apparently invulnerable alien constructs in *Beyond Capella.* Secret human societies appear in *Earthstrings*, in which a human colony is wiped out as part of a plot by commercial magnates, and in *Genius Unlimited* (Phillifent), wherein a scientific colony is actually serving as a mask to conceal a plot for interstellar conquest.

Rackham did interject some commentary into his novels, and the earlier ones in particular seem to demonstrate his faith that mankind would grow out of its petty prejudices. In *We, The Venusians*, Anthony Taylor passes as human because a pill changes his skin color and he cannot be identified as a native Greenie. Ultimately, the racial prejudice that forms the basis of the novel is reconciled as the two races eventually recognise each other's equality. In *The Beasts of Kohl* humanity has learned to accept the rights of whales on Earth and aliens in space. There is some evidence that Rackham became disillusioned in his last years. Nefarious plots are invariably human-instigated in the later novels, and the more enlightened humans cast themselves loose from the race, as in *King of Argent* (Phillifent), or even settle down among aliens, as does the hero of *Dark Planet.* Where the human refugees had favorable effects on a primitive alien race in *Danger from Vega*, they are presented as a danger to the interstellar community in *Genius Unlimited* (Phillifent) and, to a lesser extent, *Beyond Capella.* Other Standard plots appear here and there. There is a rather dull interstellar war in *The Double Invaders*, and a rather amusing view of one in *Beanstalk*, which presents the familiar fairy tale as a distorted version of Earth's minor involvement in an interstellar war. Mankind's necessity to advance into the universe is central to *Beyond Capella* and *The Proxima Project*.

Rackham never produced what could fairly be termed an outstanding work. He made no attempt to tackle major social problems except in the most superficial way, and he broke no new ground in either style or plot. But he did produce a string of competently written light adventure novels that don't insult the intelligence of the reader. They are invariably upbeat, there is no confusion between heroes and villains, and any incompetence on the part of the central character is transitory. It is a simple universe in many ways that Rackham wrote about, and generally an entertaining one.

—Don D'Ammassa

---

**RAND, Ayn.** American. Born Alice Rosenbaum in St. Petersburg, Russia, 2 February 1905; emigrated to the United States in 1926; naturalized, 1931. Educated at the University of Leningrad: graduated in history 1924. Married Frank O'Connor in 1929. Screenwriter, 1932–34, 1944–49. Editor, *The Objectivist*, New York, 1962–71, and *The Ayn Rand Letter*, New York, 1971–82. Visiting lecturer at several universities, including Yale University, New Haven, Connecticut, Princeton University, New Jersey, Columbia University, New York, Harvard University and Massachusetts Institute of Technology, both Cambridge, and Johns Hopkins University, Baltimore. D.H.L.: Lewis and Clark College, Portland, Oregon, 1963. *Died 6 March 1982.*

SCIENCE-FICTION PUBLICATIONS

Novels

*Anthem.* London, Cassell, 1938; revised edition, Los Angeles, Pamphleteers, 1946.

*Atlas Shrugged.* New York, Random House, 1957.

OTHER PUBLICATIONS

Novels

*We the Living.* New York, Macmillan, and London, Cassell, 1936.

*The Fountainhead.* Indianapolis, Bobbs Merrill, 1943; London, Cassell, 1947.

Short Stories

*The Early Ayn Rand: A Selection from Her Unpublished Fiction*, edited by Leonard Peikoff. New York, New American Library, 1984.

Plays

*Night of January 16th* (as *Woman on Trial*, produced Hollywood, 1934; New York, 1935; London, 1936; as *Penthouse Legend*, produced New York, 1973). New York, Longman, 1936; revised edition, New York, New American Library, 1987.

*The Unconquered*, adaptation of her own novel *We the Living* (produced New York, 1940).

Screenplays: *You Came Along*, with Robert Smith, 1945; *Love Letters*, 1945; *The Fountainhead*, 1949.

Other

*Textbook of Americanism.* New York, Branden Institute, 1946.

*Notes on the History of American Free Enterprise.* New York, Platen Press, 1959.

*Faith and Force: The Destroyers of the Modern World.* New York, Branden Institute, 1961.

*For the New Intellectual.* New York, Random House, 1961.

*The Objectivist Ethics.* New York, Branden Institute, 1961.

*America's Persecuted Minority: Big Business.* New York, Branden Institute, 1962.

*Conservatism: An Obituary* (lecture). New York, Branden Institute, 1962.

*The Fascist "New Frontier."* New York, Branden Institute, 1963.

*The Virtue of Selfishness: A New Concept of Egoism.* New York, New American Library, 1965.

*Capitalism: The Unknown Ideal*, with others. New York, New American Library, 1966.

*Introduction to Objectivist Epistemology.* New York, The Objectivist, 1967; revised edition by Leonard Peikoff and Harry Binswanger, New York, New American Library, 1990.

*The Romantic Manifesto: A Philosophy of Literature.* Cleveland, World, 1970.

*The New Left: The Anti-Industrial Revolution.* New York, New American Library, 1971.

*Philosophy: Who Needs It?* Indianapolis, Bobbs Merrill, 1982.

*The Voice of Reason: Essays in Objectivist Thought.* New York, New American Library, 1989.

*

Manuscript Collection: Library of Congress, Washington, D.C.

Critical Studies: *Who Is Ayn Rand? An Analysis of the Novels of Ayn Rand* by Nathaniel Branden, New York, Random House, 1962; *The Philosophic Thought of Ayn Rand* edited by Douglas J. Den Uyl and Douglas B. Rasmussen, Urbana, University of Illinois Press, 1984; *The Ayn Rand Companion* by Mimi Reisel Gladstein, Westport, Connecticut, Greenwood Press, 1984; *The Passion of Ayn Rand: A Biography* by Barbara Branden, New York, Doubleday, 1986, London, W.H. Allen, 1987; *The Ayn Rand Lexicon: Objectivism from A to Z* edited by Harry Binswanger, New York, New American Library, 1986; *Judgment Day: My Years with Ayn Rand* by Nathaniel Branden, New York, Houghton Mifflin, 1989.

* * *

Considering her unvarying depictions of heroes and heroines as people adhering to unpopular views despite hostility and abuse, Ayn Rand must have been pleased at resembling them through the controversy she arouses by her novels. In spite of her claim to be an unswerving advocate of reason, her appeal is often violently emotional. She makes her readers long to identify themselves with her dynamic, creative, productive, intelligent, handsome, and ultimately victorious heroes (and thereby with the ideas associated with them). She also compels her readers to despise the cowardly, lazy, incompetent, vicious, ugly, and inevitably defeated spokesman for the ideas she abhors. Her two speculative novels, *Anthem* and *Atlas Shrugged*, stridently warn against shaping our future according to the ideas of Christianity, Marxism, liberalism, or any other viewpoint advocating self-sacrifice which, to her, means self-negation. In opposition to such ideals, they applaud man's ego as the source of all inventiveness, achievement, and happiness and capitalism as the system allowing the fullest expression of the ego. In spite of her stridency, Rand remains one of the most powerful—and thoughtful—defenders of conservative American values, portraying the businessman as the unacknowledged Atlas who carries the burden of civilization on his mighty shoulders.

Although *Anthem* and *Atlas Shrugged* are clearly intended as cautionary tracts expounding Rand's social and philosophical beliefs and fears, both present carefully detailed pictures of future societies. In creating these societies, Rand extrapolates the possible consequences of self-sacrificial goals on art, politics, economics, sex, and family and social relationships. *Anthem* is set in a new dark age that has come about after the collectivists have defeated all the individualists. In this world, technology has nearly ceased to exist since, for Rand, it is the product of individual curiosity, effort, and ability that have also nearly ceased to exist. At birth, all children are taken from their parents and placed in a communal home where they will be taught that they must devote their lives to working for the benefit of their brothers, act as all their brothers act, and think only what all their brothers think. No man is permitted to live as an individual and the word "I" is forbidden. However, one man known as Equality 7-2521 finds such a world uncomfortable, "transgresses," and through his "sinful" behavior rediscovers individualism, creativity, self-respect, and selective love and friendship—or, in short, Rand's own values. *Atlas Shrugged* is set in an America resembling that of the 1950's when the book was written. However, this America soon becomes transformed into a society trying to follow the Christian goal of loving one's brother like oneself and the Marxist principle "From each according to his ability, to each according to his need." The government assumes control over the economy, places all industries under a Unification Board, and attempts to redistribute the benefits earned by the most efficient companies to the least efficient ones on the assumption that the weaker companies have the greater need. The result of this policy of penalizing success and rewarding failure is that moochers rise to the highest levels of government (the head of the economic program is named Wesley Mouch) and the most productive businessmen have difficulty surviving. Having foreseen these developments, the superheroic protagonist, John Galt, leads the greatest producers and creators on strike, thus precipitating the collapse of the moocher's government and preparing the way for a new society founded on the Randian oath: "I swear—by my life and by my love of it—that I will never live for the sake of another man, nor ask another man to live for mine."

Both of Rand's speculative novels are major contributions to the field. Her passionate commitment to ideas about social structure is well suited to the speculative form, especially since it is coupled with an ability to give concrete embodiment to these ideas. Though the slim *Anthem* only sketches her ideas, it offers a good introduction to them. Longer than Samuel Delany's *Dhalgren* and talkier than Robert Heinlein's *I Will Fear No Evil*, the gigantic *Atlas Shrugged* spells them out fully in repetitious but often exciting, provocative, and even brilliant detail.

—Steven R. Carter

---

**RANDALL, Marta.** American. Born in Mexico City, 26 April 1948; moved to San Francisco at age 2. Educated at Berkeley High School, California; San Francisco State College, 1966–72. Married 1) Robert H. Bergstresser in 1966 (divorced 1973), one son; 2) Christopher E. Conley in 1983. Since 1968, office manager, H. Zimmerman, Oakland, California. Taught at Clarion Writers workshop, East Lansing, Michigan, 1982, and at workshops at Portland State University, Cannon Beach, 1983, and University of California, Berkeley, 1984, 1985. Vice-president, 1981–82, and president, 1982–84, Science Fiction Writers of America. Agent: Richard Curtis, 171 East 74th Street, Suite 2, New York, New York 10021.

### Science-Fiction Publications

Novels (series: Kennerin Saga)

*Islands.* New York, Pyramid, 1976; revised edition, New York, Pocket Books, 1980.
*A City in the North.* New York, Warner, 1976.
*Journey* (Kennerin). New York, Pocket Books, 1978; London, Hamlyn, 1979.
*Dangerous Games* (Kennerin). New York, Pocket Books, 1980.
*The Sword of Winter.* New York, Pocket Books, 1983.
*Those Who Favor Fire.* New York, Pocket Books, 1984.

### Other Publications

Other

*John F. Kennedy* (for children). New York, Chelsea House, 1988.

Editor, with Robert Silverberg, *New Dimensions 11–12.* New York, Pocket Books, 2 vols., 1980–81.
Editor, *The Nebula Awards 19.* New York, Arbor House, 1984.

*

Marta Randall comments:

I find it difficult to speak about my own fiction—primarily, I think, because of a conviction that stories must stand by themselves, and the hopes, opinion, or beliefs of their authors are ultimately irrelevant. I view science fiction as a tool, as a useful series of conventions with which to deal with a storyteller's basic task, that is, the exploration not of ideas, but of people. By using the devices of the genre the writer can pare away anything not relevant to the characters and their dilemmas, can, in effect, create a crucible in which to toss the characters and view their reactions. Lest that sound pompous, I believe it equally important that science fiction remain, far more than general mainstream fiction, a genre in which one can tell stories, present adventures, write for the simple joy of creating wonderful things. My principal goal as a science-fiction writer is to meld these two approaches to the genre. It is a goal which I hope to be chasing for the rest of my professional life.

* * *

Marta Randall's six novels span a variety of literary forms: science fiction, quasi-fantasy, and conventional novels. She has experimented with different literary modes as well: novels, short stories, novellas, and the editing of anthologies.

Her first two works, *Islands* and *A City in the North*, were published in 1976. *A City in the North* tells the story of an alien species, colonized and exploited by humans, who decide to tear asunder their social order in their revolt against their masters.

The finale is ambiguous when the author posits that oppression does not lead to a higher morality on the part of the victim. *Journey* and *Dangerous Games* form a two-part saga of the Kennerin family who own the planet Aerie and attempt to create a society alternative to Earth.

In her last two novels, Randall has increasingly moved away from science fiction. In *The Sword of Winter*, she depicts a feudal society poised between change and stasis. The novel is neither science fiction nor fantasy; although it takes place on another planet, it is closer to a conventional historical novel. Her latest novel, *Those Who Favor Fire* is not science fiction at all, but rather a dystopian extrapolation of what could happen on the West Coast given urban crime, gang warfare, organized right-wing movements, and earthquakes.

Randall's works are representative of the feminist sub-genre in science fiction. This distinct sub-grouping emerged in the mid-1960's when women joined the ranks of science-fiction writers in substantial numbers for the first time. Almost to a woman, they wrote "soft" science fiction, concentrating on depicting alternative worlds which, when juxtaposed to their own, served to highlight the deleterious effects of sexism.

Many characteristics found in Randall's work are typical of traits found in feminist science fiction. First, her alternative worlds are not sexist. All her novels portray strong female characters who are decisive, independent, nurturing, and thoughtful. Second, Randall explores sexual taboos and alternative sexual modes openly and uninhibitedly, such as homosexuality, incest, and sensuality. Third, her imaginary worlds, although vivid, do not proffer an alternative view to the author's own social order. This shortcoming, shared with many feminist science-fiction writers, is most evident in *Journey* and *Dangerous Games* where Randall recreates monopoly capitalism and proffers it as a utopic social order to the reader.

Randall's strengths are many. Her novels are fast-paced and contain strong, well-developed characters. Her aliens in *Journey, Dangerous Games*, and especially *A City in the North* are believable and engaging. Her best science-fiction novel is her first, *Islands.* Here, she explores a society whose inhabitants have discovered the secret to immortality. Randall is brilliant in her speculations of the sciences, language, morality, psychology, phobias, and pathologies of immortal beings. The emotions of the heroine, who cannot achieve immortality and is an aging freak in a perpetually youthful society, are depicted masterfully. The finale is strongly reminiscent of Olaf Stapledon's *Star Maker*, where the heroine mutates to a higher level of consciousness, transcends the corporal, and merges with the world and cosmos.

—Hoda M. Zaki

---

**RANDALL, Robert.** *See* **GARRETT, Randall; SILVERBERG, Robert.**

---

**RANKINE, John.** Pseudonym for Douglas Rankine Mason; also writes as R.M. Douglas. British. Born in Hawarden, Flintshire, 26 September 1918. Educated at Heywood Grammar School, 1929–34; Chester Grammar School, 1934–37; Manchester University, 1937–39, 1946–48, B.A. Served in the Royal Signals, 1939–46: Lieutenant. Married Mary Cooper in 1945; two sons and two daughters. Headmaster, Somerville Junior School, 1954–67, and St. George's Primary School, 1967–78, both Wallasey, Cheshire. Address: 101 Millans Court, Ambleside, Cumbria LA22 9BW, England.

Science-Fiction Publications

Novels (series: Dag Fletcher)

*The Blockade of Sinitron* (for children). London, Nelson, 1966.
*Interstellar Two-Five* (Fletcher). London, Dobson, 1966.
*Never the Same Door.* London, Dobson, 1967.
*One is One* (Fletcher). London, Dobson, 1968.
*Moons of Triopus.* London, Dobson, 1968; New York, Paperback Library, 1969.
*Binary Z.* London, Dobson, 1969.
*The Weisman Experiment.* London, Dobson, 1969.
*The Plantos Affair* (Fletcher). London, Dobson, 1971.
*The Ring of Garamas (Fletcher).* London, Dobson, 1972.
*Operation Umanaq.* New York, Ace, 1973; London, Sidgwick and Jackson, 1974.
*The Bromius Phenomenon* (Fletcher). New York, Ace, 1973; London, Dobson, 1976.
*The Fingalnan Conspiracy.* London, Sidgwick and Jackson, 1973.
*Moon Odyssey* (novelization of TV series). London, Dobson, and New York, Pocket Books, 1975.
*Lunar Attack* (novelization of TV series). London, Dobson, 1975; New York, Pocket Books, 1976.
*Astral Quest* (novelization of TV series). London, Dobson, 1975; New York, Pocket Books, 1976.
*Android Planet* (novelization of TV series). London, Barker, and New York, Pocket Books, 1976.
*Phoenix of Megaron* (novelization of TV series). New York, Pocket Books, 1976.
*The Thorburn Enterprise.* London, Dobson, 1977.
*The Vort Programme.* London, Dobson, 1979.
*The Star of Hesiock.* London, Dobson, 1980.
*Last Shuttle to Planet Earth.* London, Dobson, 1980.

Novels as Douglas R. Mason

*From Carthage Then I Came.* New York, Doubleday, 1966; London, Hale, 1968; as *Eight Against Utopia*, New York, Paperback Library, 1967.
*Ring of Violence.* London, Hale, 1968; New York, Avon, 1969.
*Landfall Is a State of Mind.* London, Hale, 1968.
*The Tower of Rizwan.* London, Hale, 1968.
*The Janus Syndrome.* London, Hale, 1969.
*Matrix.* New York, Ballantine, 1970; London, Hale, 1971.
*Satellite 54-Zero.* New York, Ballantine, and London, Pan, 1971.
*Horizon Alpha.* New York, Ballantine, 1971; London, Hale, 1981.
*Dilation Effect.* New York, Ballantine, 1971; London, Hale, 1980.
*The Resurrection of Roger Diment.* New York, Ballantine, 1972.
*The Phaeton Condition.* New York, Putnam, 1973; London, Hale, 1974.
*The End Bringers.* New York, Ballantine, 1973; London, Hale, 1975.
*Pitman's Progress.* Morley, Yorkshire, Elmfield Press, 1976.
*The Omega Worm.* London, Hale, 1976.
*Euphor Unfree.* London, Hale, 1977.
*Mission to Pactolus R.* London, Hale, 1978.
*The Typhon Intervention.* London, Hale, 1981.

OTHER PUBLICATIONS

Novel as R.M. Douglas

*The Darkling Plain.* London, Hale, 1979.

*

John Rankine comments:

Science fiction is either escapist adventure—Hornblower in a star ship—or an allegory for our time—the dystopia, *Brave New World* bit. I tend to write the first as John Rankine and the second as Douglas R. Mason.

I hold the view that the biogrammar that determines the human make-up was laid down over such a long period that events like the technological revolution will not alter anything in the foreseeable future. Therefore my inhabitants of Wirral City in 4000 AD act in the same way as people of the present. Cain is still Cain and unable to change.

* * *

John Rankine, who also writes under his real name, Douglas R. Mason, envisions future battles waged by man against android, robot, computer, or physically recreated bionic man. Usually the machines's rigidity, their propensity toward predictable patterns, their lack of emotion, and their machine nature is responsible for or aids in their ultimate defeat, while man's doubt, his emotion, his loyalty, his physical self, spurred by instinct, passion, and a need for action and for self-preservation, help him ultimately to conquer. Rankine continually deplores man's insidious tendency to sacrifice freedom and intellectual activity for the sake of comfort, stability, and pleasure, and asks if there can be true pleasure without conflict and pain. His heroes are constantly struck with the realization that they have never felt truly alive until they have tasted sweat, endured trauma, and shared danger. Rankine also wonders whether prolonging life through chemicals and mechanical replacements might not be ultimately self-destructive, immortality at the price of humanity and selfhood. Frequently, his bionic characters are patronizing about real humans, and feel an intellectual sympathy with computers, attitudes that always doom them.

Rankine heroes are tough and manly but have sunk into the mindless apathy of modern regimentation only to be jarred into self-awareness and rebellion by a freak accident, a sudden intuition or insight, an irrepressible instinct. Occasionally they articulate these attitudes in lines from Shakespeare or Keats. Often these men are attracted to cold, incredibly beautiful women who keep them at a distance and intellectualize their relationship; ultimately, however, they learn that such women are either useless in a crisis or actively act against them, turning them over to robots for "readjustment." Usually, the heroes are passionately aroused by a less perfect but more nubile woman who has worked with them unnoticed in the past, who fights in their cause, and who finally accepts a division of labor whereby the male is leader and warrior, and the woman submits as helpmate, nurse, cook, and technician.

In *The End Bringers*, androids rule, monitoring human emotions and repressing them with drugs, until a natural rebel uncovers a plot to eliminate all humanoids; rescuing hundreds before robots eviscerate them, he leads survivors to an air raid shelter from which revived humanity launches its attack on android tyrants. In *Matrix*, city computers plan to eliminate all human life and use the free space to unify storage banks and achieve godhood, but a human administrator discovers the plan and fights back. In doing so, he has to deal with conformists who not only disapprove of rebellion, but actively battle against it, blind to their own precarious predicament, or with doubters who understand his logic but question his motives, or with humanists who oppose the violence of his methods, violence that ultimately proves justified. In *From Carthage Then I Came*, a computer, originally established to protect man from a cruel ice age, has monitored all life in the domed city for seven thousand years, but life is sterile, impersonal, and public. A few who have learned to evade mind probes unite in an escape plot, and, against difficult odds, outwit computers and robots, and start a new world in the wilderness, agrarian but free. These patterns with their Edenic themes are typical of much of Rankine's canon.

Rankine writes about science's potential abuses, limiting man's potentiality, reducing originality, variety, and natural evolution, controlling his weather and his atmosphere, tampering with his mind. In *Satellite 54-Zero*, a secret agent tries to penetrate a private scientific operation studying Jupiter, only to encounter the horror of mechanical failure in space, a scientific mind out of control, and a centaur transported from another dimension. In *Operation Umanaq*, the Southern hemisphere plots to destroy the Northern by affecting weather conditions and producing another ice age, while a fast-acting Northern agent evades hitmen and suicide drugs to invade a Polar station and reset weather computers. *The Phaeton Condition* begins in a world so polluted by industrial waste that its oxygen supply is fast being depleted; an industrial giant who helped create this condition plans to exploit it further through a secret high-priced safe zone with its own underground oxygen reserves. Frequently, Mason's scientists consider humans expendable and progress worth any danger. In *Moons of Triopus*, the industrial advantages of exploiting a new planet are judged more important than slow, safe investigation, but politicians and businessmen learn too late that more rational beings may well view their selfish acts with contempt and act accordingly.

The Dag Fletcher series are all set in the same galaxy and involve lots of action, while his novelized episodes from TV *Space 1999* are episodic, a progression of threats and dangers ranging from space brain anti-bodies to materialized nightmares to alien wars of annihilation. His short stories often focus on mathematics, "Six Cubed Plus 1" on the magical properties of special numbers and "Traveller's Rest" on topological oddities whereby time and language vary with the structure of space.

—Gina Macdonald

---

**RAYCRAFT, Stan.** *See* **SHAVER, Richard S.**

---

**RAYER, Francis G(eorge).** Also wrote as George Longdon; Milward Scott; Roland Worcester. British. Born in Longdon, Worcestershire, 6 June 1921. Married Tessa Elizabeth Platt in 1957; two sons. From 1945, self-employed technical designer and electronic engineer; also a technical journalist. *Died 11 July 1981.*

SCIENCE-FICTION PUBLICATIONS

Novels

*Tomorrow Sometimes Comes.* London, Home and Van Thal, 1951.
*The Star Seekers.* London, Pearson, 1954.
*Cardinal of the Stars.* London, Digit, 1964; as *Journey to the Stars*, New York, Arcadia House, 1964.
*The Iron and the Anger.* London, Digit, 1964; New York, Arcadia House, 1967.

Uncollected Short Stories (series: Mens Magna)

"Basic Fundamental," in *Fantasy* (London), August 1947.
"From Beyond the Dawn," in *New Worlds 3* (London), n.d.
"Necessity," in *New Worlds 5* (London), 1949.
"Fearful Barrier," in *Worlds at War*, edited by Francis G. Rayer. London, Temple, 1950.
"Adaptability," in *New Worlds* (London), Spring 1950.
"Quest," in *New Worlds* (London), Summer 1950.
"Deus ex Machina" (Mens Magna), in *New Worlds* (London), Winter 1950.
"Time Was," in *New Worlds* (London), Winter 1951.
"The Undying Enemy," in *Science Fantasy* (Bournemouth), Winter 1951.
"Coming of the Darakua," in *Authentic 17* (London), 1952.
"Earth Our New Eden," in *Authentic 20* (London), 1952.
"When Greed Steps In," in *Fantastic Adventures* (New York), January 1952.
"Plimsoll Line," in *Science Fantasy* (Bournemouth), Spring 1952.
"Man's Questing Ended," in *New Worlds* (London), July 1952.
"The Peacemaker" (Mens Magna), in *New Worlds* (London), September 1952.
"We Cast No Shadow," in *Authentic* (London), December 1952.
"Prison Trap," in *Laurie's Space Annual.* London, Laurie, 1953.
"Thou Pasture Us," in *Nebula* (Glasgow), Spring 1953.
"Traders' Planet," in *Science Fantasy* (Bournemouth), Spring 1953.
"Power Factor," in *New Worlds* (London), June 1953.
"Firstling," in *Nebula* (Glasgow), December 1953.
"Of Those Who Came" (as George Longdon), in *Gateway to Tomorrow*, edited by John Carnell. London, Museum Press, 1954.
"Seek Earthman No More," in *Science Fantasy 7* (Bournemouth), 1954.
"The Lava Seas Tunnel," in *Authentic* (London), March 1954.
"Space Prize," in *Science Fantasy* (Bournemouth), May 1954.
"Pipe Away Stranger," in *New Worlds* (London), June 1954.
"Come Away Home," in *New Worlds* (London), September 1954.
"Dark Summer," in *Science Fantasy* (Bournemouth), September 1954.
"Co-Efficiency Zero," in *Science Fantasy* (Bournemouth), December 1954.
"Kill Me This Man," in *New Worlds* (London), January 1955.
"Ephemeral This City" (Mens Magna), in *New Worlds* (London), March 1955.
"This Night No More," in *Nebula* (Glasgow), September 1955.
"Stormhead," in *New Worlds* (London), October 1955.
"The Jakandi Moduli," in *New Worlds* (London), December 1955.
"Hyperant," in *New Worlds* (London), March 1956.
"Consolidation Area," in *New Worlds* (London), April 1956.
"Culture Pattern," in *New Worlds* (London), May 1956.
"Period of Quarantine," in *New Worlds* (London), June 1956.
"Error Potential," in *New Worlds* (London), August 1956.
"Three-Day Tidal," in *New Worlds* (London), October 1956.
"Beacon Green," in *Nebula* (Glasgow), March 1957.
"Stress Complex," in *New Worlds* (London), June 1957.
"Painters of Narve," in *New Worlds* (London), March 1958.
"The Voices Beyond," in *New Worlds* (London), August 1958.
"Wishing Stone," in *Science Fantasy* (Bournemouth), August 1958.
"Searchpoint," in *New Worlds* (London), May 1959.
"Static Trouble," in *New Worlds* (London), February 1960.
"Alien," in *New Worlds* (New York), May 1960.
"Adjustment Period" (Mens Magna), in *Science Fiction Adventures* (London), September 1960.
"Sands Our Abode" (for children), in *Out of This World 3*, edited by Amabel Williams-Ellis and Mably Owen. London, Blackie, 1961.
"Spring Fair Moduli," in *New Worlds* (London), February 1961.
"Contact Pattern" (Mens Magna), in *Science Fiction Adventures* (London), March 1961.
"Sacrifice," in *New Worlds* (London), June 1962.
"Sixth Veil," in *New Worlds* (London), July 1962.
"Variant," in *New Worlds* (London), August 1962.
"Capsid," in *New Worlds* (London), December 1962.
"Aqueduct" in *New Worlds* (London), March 1963.

OTHER PUBLICATIONS

Novel

*Lady in Danger.* Dublin, Grafton, 1948.

Other

*Modern Fiction-Writing Technique.* London, Bond Street, 1960.
*Repair of Domestic Electrical Appliances.* London, Arco, 1961.
*Electricity in the Home.* London, Arco, 1962.
*Amateur Radio.* London, Arco, 1964.
*Electricity in Your Home* (as Milward Scott). London, Foyles, 1964.
*Electrical Hobbies.* London, Collins, 1964.
*Transistor Receivers and Amplifiers.* London, Focal Press, 1965.
*The Pegasus Book of Radio Experiments* (for children). London, Dobson, 1968.
*The Pegasus Book of Electrical Experiments* (for children). London, Dobson, 1968.
*Popular Electronics and Computers.* London, Arco, 1968; as *Electronics and Computers*, South Brunswick, New Jersey, A.S. Barnes, 1968.
*The Pegasus Book of Electronic Experiments* (for children). London, Dobson, 1969.
*Electronics* (as Roland Worcester). London, Hamlyn, 1969.
*A Guide to Outdoor Building.* London, Barker, 1970.
*Handbook of IC Audio Preamplifier and Power Amplifier Construction.* London, Babani Press, 1976.
*Two Transistor Electronic Projects.* London, Babani Press, 1976.
*50 Projects Using Relays.* London, Babani Press, 1977.
*50 Field Effect Transistor Projects.* London, Babani Press, 1977.
*How to Make Walkie-Talkies.* London, Babani Press, 1977.
*Electronic Game Projects.* London, Newnes, 1979.
*Electronic Projects in Hobbies.* London, Newnes, and Woburn, Massachusetts, Focal Press, 1979.

*How to Build Your Own Solid State Oscilloscope.* London, Babani Press, 1979.
*Counter, Driver and Numerical Display Projects.* London, Babani Press, 1979.
*Radio Control for Beginners.* London, Babani Press, 1980.
*Electronic Test Equipment Construction.* London, Babani Press, 1980.
*Digital IC Projects.* London, Babani Press, 1981.
*Electronic Timer Projects.* London, Babani Press, 1981.
*Audio Projects.* London, Babani Press, 1981.
*Projects in Amateur Radio.* London, Newnes, 1981.
*Beginner's Guide to Amateur Radio.* London, Newnes, 1982.
*IC Projects for Beginners.* London, Babani Press, 1982.

Editor, *Worlds at War.* London, Temple, 1950.

*

Francis G. Rayer commented:

(1981) My aim in writing science fiction was to show some aspects of the world as it could be within one or two generations. "Time Was," *Tomorrow Sometimes Comes,* and *The Star Seekers* were probably the best examples of this.

* * *

Much of the work produced by Francis G. Rayer is the routine potboiler that makes up the vast majority of published science fiction. In novels such as *The Iron and the Anger,* he depicts the conflict between a typical, unwillingly heroic human and some non-human menace, in this case homicidally inclined robots determined to wipe out the human race. At times, there is a more serious note to his fiction, but still only in a very limited sense. For example, *Cardinal of the Stars* points out what Rayer sees as the importance of humanity's progress into space, in this case in order to be able to defend itself from the encroachment of a hostile alien fleet. But the novel remains essentially a spy story set in the future, with the two-fisted hero determined to stop the series of sabotaged space-ships and bombings from outer space that have begun to plague the world. Similarly, *The Star Seekers* makes some tentative efforts toward philosophy; but remains essentially a potboiler about the dangers inherent in violating Einstein's laws and attempting to travel faster than light. Rayer's attempts here to avoid overt melodrama result in slow-paced scenes made even more ineffective by a turgid prose that is void of wit or clarity.

But there are times when Rayer is more than just a hack adventure writer. He was most successful with his series about an intelligent computer of unprecedented capacity that appears first as the administrator of a completely unemotional legal system in a short story, then progresses to taking complete control of humanity during a nuclear war in Rayer's best novel, *Tomorrow Sometimes Comes.* In a short story later in that same series, and possibly the best piece of short fiction Rayer wrote, the computer becomes "The Peacemaker," paradoxically by helping an alien race to invade Earth and conquer humanity for its own good. At the time Rayer wrote this story, this was certainly a far more novel and less acceptable conclusion than it would be now.

—Don D'Ammassa

---

**REAMY, Tom.** American. Born in Woodson, Texas, in 1935. Movie projectionist, technical illustrator, dispatcher for a concrete plant, assistant movie director and propman, phototypositor, and house painter; editor, *CirFanAc,* Dallas, in the 1950's and *Trumpet,* in the 1960's; founder, with Ken Keller, Nickelodeon Graphics, Kansas City (worked on *Delap's SF&F Review* and *Chacol/Shayol*), and editor, with Keller, *Nickelodeon,* 1975–77. Recipient: Nebula award, 1975; John W. Campbell award, 1976. *Died 5 November 1977.*

SCIENCE-FICTION PUBLICATIONS

Novel

*Blind Voices.* New York, Berkley, 1978; London, Sidgwick and Jackson, 1979.

Short Stories

*San Diego Lightfoot Sue and Other Stories.* Kansas City, Earthlight, 1980.

OTHER PUBLICATIONS

Play

*Sting!,* in *Six Science Fiction Plays,* edited by Roger Elwood. New York, Pocket Books, 1976.

* * *

From 1974, when his first stories appeared, Tom Reamy was considered a promising new writer and his progress watched with interest. His sudden death in 1977 meant that, instead of the long and prolific career and the steady increase in his already formidable powers his admirers expected, we have only one novel and a dozen short stories. But the novel, *Blind Voices,* and the best of the short stories need no special pleading as early experiments—they can stand on their own as successful and remarkable works. Tom Reamy's position is secure. Although he is often called a science-fiction writer, and won science-fiction awards, nearly all of Reamy's work would be better classified as fantasy. His stories skim along the edge of reality, firmly anchored in time and place, whether Depression-era, rural Kansas, or present-day Los Angeles, and the plots range between the subtlest of fantasies and the most visceral, outrageous horrors. His recurring themes are of human relationships, the frightening, dark side of sexuality, the triumph or destruction of the innocent, and monsters—from outer space, from Hollywood, from the id.

"Twilla," his first published story, shows the strong influence films—particularly low-budget horror films—had on Reamy, who worked in Hollywood and first tried his hand at scriptwriting. The plot of "Twilla" is straightforward and violent, full of vivid, visual descriptions with little time wasted on explanations. Like the films it emulates, the story seeks to entertain and shock, and it succeeds. There are some problems with plot construction and logic, but the story works as well as it does because of a solid grounding in reality, the accumulation of detail giving it a peculiar depth. In this, as in later stories, Reamy revealed his talent for selecting the perfect details to bring scenes and characters to life, from the utterly convincing names of even minor characters to precise descriptions of dress and furniture. "San Diego Lightfoot Sue," Reamy's own favorite and an award-winner, is the gentlest and most romantic of all his stories. The horror takes place off-stage and the emphasis is that of the so-called "mainstream," with the fantasy element almost superfluous. It is not the story, nor any sense of the fantastic, which remains to haunt the reader, but the characters—the vividly depicted Pearl and Daisy Mae; the extreme innocence and beauty of John Lee Peacock; the dying Grace Elizabeth; the hinted-at depths of the title character.

Reamy's best and most powerful stories are "The Detweiler Boy" and "Under the Hollywood Sign," both set in a grittily real Los Angeles, both told in the first-person and using many of the conventions of the hard-boiled detective story, both probing the dark side of sexual desire and offering a complex vision of the conflict, on many levels, between innocence and evil. They are both disturbing stories that reveal love and need as the inseparable siamese twins of violence and destruction. In these stories, people need each other and shy away from their need, knowing that sexual love will inevitable lead to death.

*Blind Voices* takes place in the American midwest during the Depression—a time and a place that Reamy makes convincingly his own. The story sets the fantastic creatures of a traveling wonder-show against the everyday lives of the people of Hawley, Kansas. It obviously owes much to works by Ray Bradbury, Charles Finney, and Theodore Sturgeon, but it shows Reamy's distinctive touch in the reworking of some familiar material, in the characterizations, the vivid style, and the dark undercurrent of sexuality which runs through all his writings. Although the material is that of fantasy, like *The Circus of Doctor Lao* or *Something Wicked This Way Comes*, an explanation near the end tips the book into science fiction.

—Lisa Tuttle

---

**REAVES, Michael.** Has also written as J. Michael Reaves. American. Address: c/o Tor Books, 49 West 24th Street, 9th floor, New York, New York 10010, U.S.A.

SCIENCE-FICTION PUBLICATIONS

Novels

*Dragonworld* (as J. Michael Reaves), with Byron Preiss. New York, Bantam, 1979; London, Bantam, 1980; revised edition, New York, Bantam, 1983.
*The Shattered World*. New York, Timescape, 1984; London, Futura, 1986.
*Sword of the Samurai*, with Steve Perry. New York, Bantam, 1984.
*Hellstar*, with Steve Perry. New York, Berkley, 1984.
*Dome*, with Steve Perry. New York, Berkley, and London, Gollancz, 1987.
*The Burning Realm*. New York, Baen, and London, Futura, 1988.
*The Omega Cage*, with Steve Perry. New York, Ace, 1988.
*Street Magic*. New York, Tor, 1991.

Short Stories

*Darkworld Detective* (as J. Michael Reaves). New York, Bantam, 1982.

* * *

Michael Reaves, whose early work appeared under the name J. Michael Reaves, had been writing science fiction since his teen years, but it was not until he attended the Clarion Workshop, in 1972, that he was able to sell his first story. "The Breath of Dragons," written while he was a student at California State University, San Bernardino, was published in the third of the Clarion anthologies.

"Breath" uncannily presages Reaves's later fictions, both in theme and in setting. Perrin is a hunter on a planet where dragons are killed for their fire-producing bladders. The dragons look and fly like the creatures from children's fairy tales, but they're no match for man's superior technology. Perrin also believes they're sentient beings, a theory no one else sanctions. His attempt to prove the dragons's intelligence causes the accidental death of a crewmate; as he struggles to find a way out of his predicament, he is consumed (in an apparent act of kindness) by the very creatures he is striving to protect. Perrin has paid the ultimate price for his carelessness, and a balance has been restored to his world.

Although the author's most successful prose works—*Dragonworld, The Shattered World*, its sequel, *The Burning Realm*, and *Darkworld Detective*—have been packaged by their publishers as fantasy, Reaves enjoys combining science fiction and fantasy elements into seemingly irreconcilable plot lines, making the believability of one dependent upon the other. Images of dragons and similar creatures, of flying in general, of man and beast soaring above the grittiness of the everyday world, permeate his fiction. Even in the ostensibly SF novel, *Hellstar*, set in the artificial environment of a multi-generation spaceship travelling slowly between the stars, the characters literally fly (in a recreation room designed for that purpose), and take weightless walks on the outside of the ship's hull, where they experience almost a religious ecstasy before the grand vistas of open space.

Each of Reaves's protagonists sees an imbalance in the universe, a flaw, an emptiness in himself or others, and seeks to restore some semblance of order or sanity to nature, to himself, to humanity as a whole. Thus, Perrin regards the dragons as his private crusade, while Amsel in *Dragonworld* must go on his own dragonquest, and Kamus of Kadizar, the otherworldly shamus of *Darkworld Detective*, seeks to right the wrongs of his world by solving the mysteries of his clients.

We can see these themes—of action and reaction, of responsibility and irresponsibility, of wrongs that must be righted and sins that must be redressed—most clearly developed in the author's most popular work, *The Shattered World*, and its sequel, *The Burning Realm*. Here, the surviving magicians must face the consequences of an ancient war of sorcery that literally broke their world into fragments, while Pandrogas and Amber cannot escape the harm caused by their illicit romance, and Beorn, as attractive a thief as one will find in modern fantasy literature, still must pay a very high price indeed for the pursuit of his profession. Yet each persists in his or her chosen (even stubborn) course, doing what each thinks is right and necessary and proper, for himself and for others, and sometimes being damned for it.

Similar themes are evident in his teleplays (of which there are over 200), often on a more simplistic level (much of the author's work has been produced for half-hour, animated children's cartoon programs). In "Street of Shadows" (*The Twilight Zone*), for example, Steve Butler, a homeless, down-on-his-luck carpenter with a family to support, breaks into the home of Frederick Perry, a wealthy industrialist, and briefly changes mental places with him. As Perry, Steve is able to rebalance his microuniverse by buying the mortgage of the near-bankrupt shelter where he and his family have been staying. In the "Where None Have Gone Before" episode of *Star Trek: The Next Generation* (written with Diane Duane), Peter Kosinski, a brilliant engineer, saves the *Enterprise* from the consequences of his own warp drive experiments, and in the process rescues himself from a life of loneliness by somehow regenerating a son who had died at birth seven years before. There are many things in heaven and earth, the author seems to be saying, not all of them rational, or explicable, or knowable; but, ultimately, man must take responsibility for his own actions, and *some* things will balance out. For Reaves, the universe has even been a moral place where immorals fear to tread.

—Robert Reginald

---

**REED, Kit (née Craig).** Also writes as Kit Craig and Shelley Hyde. American. Born in San Diego, California. Educated at the College of Notre Dame of Maryland, Baltimore, B.A. 1954. Married Joseph Wayne Reed, Jr., in 1955; two sons and one daughter. Reporter, *St. Petersburg Times*, Florida, 1954–55; reporter, *Hamden Chronicle*, Connecticut, 1956, and *New Haven Register*, Connecticut, 1956–59; book reviewer, *New Haven Register* and *St. Petersburg Times.* Since 1974, Visiting Professor of English, then Adjunct Professor, Wesleyan University, Middletown, Connecticut. Recipient: New England Newspaperwoman of the Year award, 1958, 1959; Guggenheim Fellowship, 1964; Abraham Woursell Foundation five-year grant, 1965; Aspen Institute Rockefeller Fellowship, 1976. Agent: Richard Pine, Arthur Pine Associates, Suite 417, 250 West 57th Street, New York, New York 10019. Address: 45 Lawn Avenue, Middletown, Connecticut 06457, U.S.A.

SCIENCE-FICTION PUBLICATIONS

Novels

*Armed Camps.* London, Faber, 1969; New York, Dutton, 1970.
*Magic Time.* New York, Berkley, 1979.

Short Stories

*Mister da V. and Other Stories.* London, Faber, 1967; New York, Berkley, 1973.
*The Killer Mice.* London, Gollancz, 1976.
*Other Stories, and The Attack of the Giant Baby.* New York, Berkley, 1981.
*The Revenge of the Senior Citizens.* New York, Doubleday, 1986.

OTHER PUBLICATIONS

Novels

*Mother Isn't Dead, She's Only Sleeping.* Boston, Houghton Mifflin, 1961.
*At War as Children.* New York, Farrar Straus, 1964.
*The Better Part.* New York, Farrar Straus, 1967; London, Hutchinson, 1968.
*Cry of the Daughter.* New York, Dutton, 1971.
*Tiger Rag.* New York, Dutton, 1973.
*Captain Grownup.* New York, Dutton, 1976.
*Ballad of T. Rantula.* Boston, Little Brown, 1979.
*Blood Fever* (as Shelley Hyde). New York, Pocket Books, 1982.
*Fort Privilege.* New York, Doubleday, 1985.
*Catholic Girls.* New York, Fine, 1987.

Play

Radio Play: *The Bathyscaphe*, 1978.

Other

*When We Dream* (for children). New York, Hawthorn, 1967.
*Story First: The Writer as Insider.* Englewood Cliffs, New Jersey, Prentice Hall, 1982; revised edition as *Mastering Fiction Writing*, Cincinnati, Ohio, Writer's Digest, 1991.
*George Orwell's 1984.* Woodbury, New York, Barron's Book Notes, 1984.
*Revision.* Cincinnati, Ohio, Writer's Digest, 1989.

Editor, *Fat.* Indianapolis, Bobbs Merrill, 1974.

*

Manuscript Collection: Beinecke Library, Yale University, New Haven, Connecticut.

* * *

Kit Reed writes within several fiction genres. Her stories have been published in *Fiction* (Paris), *Town* (London), *Seventeen*, and a variety of science-fiction and fantasy magazines. Some of her stories are realistic, some impressionistic, some fantasy, some science fiction. And representatives of each of these types appear in the collection *Mister da V.* Reed does not write hard, or technologically oriented, science fiction; and although some of her stories do make use of traditional science-fiction devices or theories, those stories actually focus on the people in them and the ways in which those people are affected by their surroundings. While this is typical of science fiction in general, Reed seems to deal primarily with the people and to use the science-fiction elements as another writer might use a car or truck—as a detail necessary to the story.

In "Automatic Tiger," the full-sized mechanical tiger is not presented as an object of wonder. Edward Benedict accepts the tiger as no more than a special toy for his nephew. When he tries the tiger out, however, he decides to keep it. Having his own tiger gives Benedict confidence and changes his previously nondescript life. He becomes successful in business and in society—until he no longer has time for the tiger, which deteriorates. When he loses the tiger, his life collapses, and he is left much as he was when the story began. "Mister da V." is a story in which time-travel is the traditional science-fiction device, but the story is really about the 20th-century family into which Leonardo da Vinci is brought. The mother can see only the extra work that this "guest" necessitates. The twins like the strange toys he makes for them, but after he has gone and the toys are broken, they forget him. The father sees Leonardo as the source for a definitive biography. But the teen-aged girl sees a sweet, lonely, brilliant old man who seems to be sad because he will never get to do all the things he can envision.

This focus on people and the ways in which technology affects them is also at the heart of Reed's socially critical stories. One of her strongest pieces of social criticism is "Golden Acres," about a home for the elderly. In this future setting, an old person can use his negotiable assets to purchase a place in Golden Acres. Although these establishments look very attractive from the outside, they are extremely dehumanizing: all of the rooms are the same, the furniture is bolted down, and there is no place for personal effects or mementoes—what the management calls "clutter." And when a person's funds run out—rent, medical care, etc. all add up—he is taken to the Tower of Sleep where his life is terminated.

"At Central," "Ordeal," and the novel *Armed Camps*, are similar stories about societies in which technology has all but taken over. In "At Central," people watch television all the time (never going outside), pump their money into the appropriate slots when they see something they want, and have everything delivered. The people in "Ordeal" are all on "life fluid" and spend their time hooked up to the intravenous tubes which pump the purple liquid into their veins. In *Armed Camps*, warfare is the one constant thing in the world; and although it seems that only champions fight and die, great numbers of people are killed each year. And instead of trying to end it, the top brass make sure that it will go on—forever, if possible.

Reed's recent work, collected in *The Revenge of the Senior Citizens * Plus*, a collection that includes the novella "The Revenge of the Senior Citizens" and sixteen short stories, continues the two main themes of her work: the impact of technology on people's lives and the plight of senior citizens. In "Frontiers," the post-cataclysm world of Gunnar Morgan is described in terms of the American western frontier of the late 1800's, and in "A Unique Service," a famous author buys a simulacrum of himself to handle the demands fame has made on his time. Most of the stories, however, are about senior citizens. In "Shan," an elderly woman saves the world from alien invasion. "Great Escape Tours, Inc." takes senior citizens back to childhood for a day. And in the title story, senior citizens band together to protest being "put away"—in every sense of the term—by their children.

In the final analysis, it is Reed's characters that carry her fiction—science fiction, fantasy, or mainstream. To be sure, the other aspects of her writing are not found wanting, but her characters—especially the women struggling to find themselves in an indifferent or hostile society, or struggling against various institutions—remain in the reader's mind.

—C.W. Sullivan III

---

**REED, Robert.** Also writes as R. Touzalin. American. Born in Omaha, Nebraska, 9 October 1956. Educated at Nebraska Wesleyan University, B.S. in Biology 1987. Utility worker, Mapes Industries, Lincoln, Nebraska, 1978–87; lab technician, University of Nebraska, Lincoln, 1979–80. Since 1987, full-time writer. Recipient: L. Ron Hubbard Gold award, 1986. Agent: Merrilee Heifetz, Writers' House Inc., 21 West 26th Street, New York, New York 10010. Address: 4840 Cleveland Avenue, No. 12, Lincoln, Nebraska 68504, U.S.A.

SCIENCE-FICTION PUBLICATIONS

Novels

*The Leeshore.* New York, Fine, 1987.
*The Hormone Jungle.* New York, Fine, 1987; London, Futura, 1989.
*Black Milk.* New York, Fine, 1989; London, Orbit, 1990.
*Down the Bright Way.* New York, Bantam, 1991.

*

Robert Reed comments:

I can think of too much to write about my own work, thus I'll write nothing much. I enjoy parts of what I have done—a chapter here, an opening paragraph now and again—and when I fail as a writer, I hope, it is out of ignorance and youth, but never out of a lack of effort, nor because I have made the thing stale from beating it against my limitations.

* * *

Robert Reed made his debut with an award-winning story in the L. Ron Hubbard "Writers of the Future" contest, and established himself as a fine novelist shortly thereafter with the publication of *The Leeshore.* Taking its inspiration from Ernest Hemingway's *Islands in the Stream*, the novel is set on a far world whose surface is entirely water, and whose light is cut off by a carpet of living creatures afloat in the upper atmosphere. As a consequence, surface life must resort to bioluminescence.

A renegade group of technophiles called the Alteretics has been defeated in their assault on Earth, and have fled to the world of Leeshore as a refuge, killing all human settlers except a brother and sister who escape into the wilderness. A pursuit fleet from Earth arrives and recruits the two in their effort to locate their enemies, but the protagonists soon question their role in the proceedings, believing their newfound friends to be little better than those who came before them. The combination of a thoroughly developed, strange new environment with a serious and thoughtful story line made this one of the most striking debut novels of recent years.

Although *The Leeshore* seemed to have left the door open for a sequel, Reed's next novel, *The Hormone Jungle*, is set on Earth, but an Earth some two millennia removed from us, home to literally trillions of life forms, both natural and artificial. The story alternates between the relationship of a professional troubleshooter with a humanoid robot built to provide pleasure to male humans who may conceal sinister motives, and the rivalry between an exile and his cyborg neighbor. When the robot's owner decides to reclaim his property, the plot accelerates at breakneck pace. Reed invests great effort in developing this ecology as well, and although it never quite achieves the verisimilitude of his first novel, it is nonetheless a dramatically successful novel.

Reed is an unusual short story writer, concerning himself more specifically with the human psyche that most do. In "Utility Man," Reed eschews the usual viewpoint character and selects an assembly line worker reacting to the requirements of working with a truly alien co-worker. "Busybody" features a nosy woman whose investigations have very interesting consequences. Earth has been damaged by aliens in "Chaff," but the story concerns itself with the efforts of a human family coming to terms with their altered world. Reed's strangest story is "Bushwhacker," wherein an unassuming man uses various inoffensive devices to "shoot" people and transform their lives. Or perhaps he just imagines it. Other stories worth noting are "Treading in the Afterglow" and "Goodness."

*Black Milk* is not set in nearly as remote a time as its predecessors. In the not-too-distant future, genetic engineering is an accepted state of affairs. Prospective parents routinely take advantage of the technology to shape, within certain limits, the attributes of their offspring. A researcher hoping to seed the atmosphere of the gas giant planets with bio-engineered lifeforms inadvertently allows them to escape his laboratory on the moon, compromising the atmosphere in the colony, ultimately threatening the entire human race. Despite the melodramatic events, the plot falters in the second half of the book, and when we finally discover that disaster has been averted, we are no longer even concerned, particularly since most of the more suspenseful events are handled offhandedly, even off stage.

Reed's most recent novel, *Down the Bright Way*, returns to an interstellar arena. Spread throughout the universe are myriad planets with intelligent species, linked by the mysterious and ancient Makers. Now an alliance drawn together from many worlds is exploring the links between planets, finding civilizations in danger of destroying themselves and helping to ease them into the fraternity of the universe. But another organization is at work as well, this one determined to pursue a course of conquest and destruction. A single Earthman becomes aware of the web of worlds and finds himself pushed into becoming the pivotal figure in what might be the most significant conflict in the history of the universe.

Reed's strongest points are his detailed and generally convincing settings, impressive because they vary so greatly from the world with which we are familiar, and his genuine insights into the human mind and the moral questions which trouble us. *The Leeshore* deals with treachery and loyalty, *The Hormone Jungle* with those same themes as well as the causes of love and hate, *Black Milk* with our hopes for the future as manifested in our children, and *Down the Bright Way* with our sense of destiny and meaning in the universe. His generally successful handling of such ambitious and important themes marks him as a writer with serious intentions, while his strong narrative and descriptive talents ensure that the message will not interfere with the entertainment value of his fiction. Robert Reed has established himself as a prominent writer with remarkable ease, and it is likely that he will remain a powerful voice within the field.

—Don D'Ammassa

---

**RESNICK, Mike** (Michael Diamond Resnick). American. Born in Chicago, Illinois, 5 March 1942. Attended University of Chicago, 1959–62. Married Carol Cain in 1961; one daughter. File clerk, Santa Fe Railroad, Chicago, 1962–65; editor, *National Tattler*, 1965–66, and *National Insider*, 1966–69, for National Features Syndicate, Chicago; editor and publisher, Oligarch Publishing, Libertyville, Illinois, 1969–70. Breeder and exhibitor of collies, 1968–80, and columnist, *Collie Cues Magazine*, Hayward, California, 1969–80. Since 1964, freelance writer; has published over 200 novels (sex, gothic, romance) under pseudonyms. Since 1976, owner of Briarwood Pet Motel, Cincinnati. Recipient: Hugo award, for short story, 1989. Agent: Eleanor Wood, Spectrum Literary Agency, Suite 1501, 111 Eighth Avenue, New York, New York 10011. Address: 10547 Tanager Hills Drive, Cincinnati, Ohio 45249, U.S.A.

### Science-Fiction Publications

Novels (series: Galactic Midway; Ganymede; Velvet Comet)

*The Forgotten Sea of Mars* (novella). Baton Rouge, Louisiana, Camille E. Cazedessus, Jr., 1965.
*The Goddess of Ganymede.* West Kingston, Rhode Island, Grant, 1967.
*Pursuit on Ganymede.* New York, Paperback Library, 1968.
*Redbeard.* New York, Lancer, 1969.
*Battlestar Galactica 5: Galactica Discovers Earth*, with Glen A. Larson. New York, Berkley, 1980.
*The Soul Eater.* New York, New American Library, 1981.
*Birthright: The Book of Man.* New York, New American Library, 1982.
*Walpurgis III.* New York, New American Library, 1982.
Tales of the Galactic Midway:
 *Sideshow.* New York, New American Library, 1982.
 *The Three-Legged Hootch Dancer.* New York, New American Library, 1983.
 *The Wild Alien Tamer.* New York, New American Library, 1983.
 *The Best Rootin' Tootin' Shootin' Gunslinger in the Whole Damned Galaxy.* New York, New American Library, 1983.
*The Branch.* New York, New American Library, 1984.
Tales of the Velvet Comet:
 *Eros Ascending.* Bloomfield Hills, Michigan, Phantasia Press, 1984.
 *Eros at Zenith.* Bloomfield Hills, Michigan, Phantasia Press, 1984.
 *Eros Descending.* New York, New American Library, 1985.
 *Eros at Nadir.* New York, New American Library, 1986.
*Adventures.* New York, New American Library, 1985.
*Santiago: A Myth of the Far Future.* New York, Tor, 1986.
*The Dark Lady: A Romance of the Far Future.* New York, Tor, 1987.
*Stalking the Unicorn: A Fable of Tonight.* New York, Tor, 1987.
*Ivory: A Legend of Past and Future.* New York, Tor, 1988; London, Century, 1989.
*Paradise: A Chronicle of a Distant World.* New York, Tor, 1989; London, Century, 1991.
*Second Contact.* New York, Tor, 1990.
*The Red Tape War*, with Jack L. Chalker and George Alec Effinger. New York, Tor, 1991.
*Bwana and Bully!* (two novellas). New York, Tor, 1991.

Short Stories

*Unauthorized Autobiographies and Other Curiosities.* Detroit, Misfit Press, 1984.
*The Inn of the Hairy Toad.* New Orleans, Delta Con, 1985.

### Other Publications

Other

*Official Guide to the Fantastics.* Florence, Alabama, House of Collectibles, 1976.
*Official Guide to Comic Books and Big Little Books.* Florence, Alabama, House of Collectibles, 1977.
*Gymnastics and You: The Whole Story of the Sport.* Chicago, Rand McNally, 1978.
*Official Guide to Comic and Science Fiction Books.* Orlando, Florida, House of Collectibles, 1979.

Editor, *Shaggy B.E.M. Stories.* New Orleans, Louisiana, Nolacon Press, 1988.

*

Mike Resnick comments:

I'm not at all sure that I write honest-to-God true-blue science fiction. What I write are morality plays, and if turning them into myths and fables of the future and setting them on alien worlds makes them more saleable, I have no objection to so doing. I have a hard time with fearless heros and beautiful princesses, so I tend to write about overmatched detectives and obsessed ministers and frustrated stripteasers. I have a hard time with heroes who are all good and villains who are all bad, so my characters tend to be neither heroes nor villains, but fall into that in-between gray area that most of us inhabit. The future in which I set my stories is lived-in and a little bit shopworn around the edges; planets tend to look more like the outskirts of Indianapolis of Sioux City than those beautiful mechanized utopias that Frank Paul used to paint 40 and 50 years ago. I don't like puzzle or gimmick stories that leave the reader unmoved and untouched, and so I don't write them. I believe that every man and woman is ultimately responsible for his actions, and this is a theme that seems to recur through my novels.

I suppose if I had to sum up my work in a single sentence, it would be as follows: I am writing about adult characters who face adult problems in an adult universe, and I am writing these stories for an adult audience. This is, alas, rarer than you might think.

* * *

Although Mike Resnick was a prolific author outside the genre and under names other than his own, until the early 1980's his only credits within the field were two pastiches of Edgar Rice Burroughs, *The Goddess of Ganymede* and *Pursuit on Ganymede*, and an interesting post-apocalypse novel, *Redbeard*, all published in the 1960's.

Suddenly, there was an outpouring of science fiction, initially with various ambitious adventure stories such as *The Soul Eater, Walpurgis III, The Branch*, and the episodic *Birthright*. Although primarily adventure stories, there was an underlying seriousness missing in many similar books, concerns about the future of humanity, and the nature of power and government. A second change became apparent with the characterization in his first series, the four volumes dealing with a star travelling circus, *Sideshow, The Three-Legged Hootch Dancer, The Wild Alien Tamer*, and *The Best Rootin' Tootin' Shootin' Gunslinger in the Whole Damned Galaxy.* Although the format was still light adventure, Resnick took great pains to differentiate his characters, providing a greater depth to the stories.

His next series was more effective. *Eros Ascending, Eros at Zenith, Eros Descending*, and *Eros at Nadir* share a common setting, an orbiting bordello targeted by religious fanatics and others, a symbol of Earthbound struggles hanging in the heavens. Using finely honed characters, diverse plots, and a mature and perceptive analysis of the ebb and flow of public opinion, Resnick chronicles the history of the institution in four novels, each complete in itself, the series as a whole establishing their creator as a writer to be watched in the future.

The next significant title was *Santiago*, which could perhaps be described as a traditional western novel superimposed on an interstellar version of the west. This blend of two genres features characters who are larger than life, and demonstrated that even space opera can be a significant springboard for a talented author. Resnick blended two fields again in *Stalking the Unicorn*, a contemporary fantasy novel featuring a private detective, a clever mystery, and an amusing, fast-paced style.

An already impressive string of fascinating books was steadily enhanced by subsequent titles. *The Dark Lady: A Romance of the Far Future* demonstrated Resnick's fascination with the mysterious and mystical. An alien art historian notices a recurring face in human art and sets out to track down the origin of this enigmatic figure.

A veteran of many African safaris, Resnick began to work themes from the Dark Continent into his novels. *Ivory* is structurally similar to *The Dark Lady;* this time, the quest is to find a pair of elephant tusks that possess mystical powers, sought by the last of the Masai tribe in connection with a ritual he must perform prior to his death. *Paradise* is a barely concealed portrayal of the pillage of the African wilderness by outside powers, set on a planet where majestic animals lure big game hunters from offworld, and where the indigent alien species is torn between the desire to embrace the technology humans possess and the need to protect their own heritage. It is a complex story of confused motivations, conflicting rights and responsibilities, which provides no easy answers. Resnick avoids stock solutions; there is no magical reconciliation in the final chapter. *Paradise* is filled with adventure, but it is much more than an adventure story.

*Second Contact* seems to have been a change of pace. A conventional thriller, it involves a discredited space force officer who murdered his crew under the apparently mistaken belief that they were alien doppelgangers preparing to invade the Earth. His defense attorney is skeptical, until his tentative efforts to investigate the case result in an attempt on his own life. Entertaining chase and escape sequences follow, but the novel as a whole lacks the stature of Resnick's other recent novels.

Resnick's inventive sense of humor surfaces periodically in even his most serious novels, but it is most evident in an earlier spoof of the genre, *Adventures*, and in the collaborative effort, *The Red Tape War*, written in collaboration with George Alec Effinger and Jack L. Chalker.

During the 1980's, Resnick averaged about two short stories a year, most of which were amusing but unmemorable. The African influence was to change all of this, however, particularly in "Kirinyaga" and "For I Have Touched the Sky," both controversial and thought-provoking stories of the conflict between western values and those of Africa. Both are seen through the eyes of a tribal witch doctor on a colony world controlled by the Masai. Offworld authorities are shocked at the cruelties demanded by tribal customs, including the exposure of certain infants to the elements, and there is growing agitation to intervene. Once again, Resnick is careful to present both viewpoints with respect, and the resolution, while disturbing, is logical and inevitable.

Another African tale, "Bully!", actually a short novel, features Theodore Roosevelt, no longer president of the United States, determined to unite Central Africa into a democracy under his tutelage, dedicated to improving the technological and social base of the primitive tribes he has seen. Roosevelt is Resnick's most fully realized character, earnest and sincere on one hand, flawed by egotism and an inability to recognize the reality of his situation on the other. Although he makes great strides toward his goal, it is ultimately doomed to failure because the historical basis for such a rapid alteration of the social climate doesn't exist.

Resnick is one of those rare writers who can tell his readers serious things about themselves and their world without preaching, who can handle important themes without sacrificing plot and other story values. His considerable skills as a writer continue to develop with each new book or story.

—Don D'Ammassa

---

**REYNOLDS, Mack** (Dallas McCord Reynolds). Also wrote as Todd Harding; Maxine Reynolds. American. Born in Corcoran, California, 12 November 1917. Attended public schools in Kingston, New York. Served in the United States Army Transportation Corps, during World War II; trained in the Marine Officers School, New Orleans: Navigator. Married Jeanette Wooley in 1947; two sons and one daughter. Editor, *Catskill Mountain Star*, Saugerties, New York, 1937–38, and *Oneonta News*, New York, 1939–40; IBM supervisor, San Pedro shipyards, California, 1940–43; national organizer, Socialist Labor Party, 1946–52; foreign correspondent and travel editor, *Rogue*, 1953–63. *Died 29 January 1983.*

### Science-Fiction Publications

Novels (series: Homer Crawford; Bat Hardin; Lagrangia; Joe Mauser; United Planets Organization; Julian West)

*The Case of the Little Green Men*. New York, Phoenix Press, 1951.
*The Earth War* (Mauser). New York, Pyramid, 1963; London, New English Library, 1965.
*Planetary Agent X* (United Planets). New York, Ace, 1965.
*Time Gladiator* (Mauser). London, New English Library, 1966; New York, Lancer, 1969.
*Of Godlike Power*. New York, Belmont, 1966; as *Earth Unaware*, 1968.
*Dawnman Planet* (United Planets). New York, Ace, 1966.
*Space Pioneer*. London, New English Library, 1966.
*The Rival Rigellians*. New York, Ace, 1967.
*Computer War*. New York, Ace, 1967.
*After Some Tomorrow*. New York, Belmont, 1967.
*Mercenary from Tomorrow* (Mauser). New York, Ace, 1968.
*Code Duello* (United Planets). New York, Ace, 1968.
*Star Trek: Mission to Horatius*. Racine, Wisconsin, Whitman, 1968.
*The Space Barbarians*. New York, Ace, 1969.
*The Cosmic Eye*. New York, Belmont, 1969.
*Once Departed*. New York, Curtis, 1970.
*Computer World*. New York, Curtis, 1970.
*Blackman's Burden* (Crawford). New York, Ace, 1972.
*Border, Breed nor Birth* (Crawford). New York, Ace, 1972.
*Looking Backward, From the Year 2000* (West). New York, Ace, 1973; Morley, Yorkshire, Elmfield Press, 1976.
*Commune 2000 A.D.* (Hardin). New York, Bantam, 1974.
*Depression or Bust*. New York, Ace, 1974.
*Ability Quotient*. New York, Ace, 1975.
*Amazon Planet* (United Planets). New York, Ace, 1975.
*The Five Way Secret Agent*. New York, Ace, 1975.
*Satellite City*. New York, Ace, 1975.
*Tomorrow Might Be Different*. New York, Ace, 1975; London, Sphere, 1976.
*The Towers of Utopia* (Hardin). New York, Bantam, 1975.
*Day after Tomorrow*. New York, Ace, 1976.
*Galactic Medal of Honor*. New York, Ace, 1976.
*Rolltown* (Hardin). New York, Ace, 1976.
*Section G: United Planets*. New York, Ace, 1976.
*After Utopia*. New York, Ace, 1977.
*Equality: In the Year 2000* (West). New York, Ace, 1977.
*Perchance to Dream*. New York, Ace, 1977.
*Police Patrol 2000 A.D.* New York, Ace, 1977.
*Space Visitor*. New York, Ace, 1977.
*The Best Ye Breed* (Crawford). New York, Ace, 1978.
*Trample an Empire Down*. New York, Nordon, 1978.
*Brain World*. New York, Nordon. 1978.
*The Fracas Factor*. New York, Nordon, 1978.
*Lagrange Five*. New York, Bantam, 1979.
*Earth Unaware*. New York, Nordon, 1979.
*The Lagrangists*, edited by Dean Ing. New York, Tor, 1983.
*Chaos in Lagrangia*. New York, Tor, 1984.
*Space Search*. New York, Dell, 1984.
*Eternity*, edited by Dean Ing. New York, Pocket Books, 1984.
*Home Sweet Home 2010 A.D.*, edited by Dean Ing. New York, Dell, 1984.
*The Other Time*, edited by Dean Ing. New York, Pocket Books, 1984.
*Trojan Orbit*, edited by Dean Ing. New York, Baen, 1985.
*Deathwish World*, edited by Dean Ing. New York, Baen, 1986.
*Sweet Dreams, Sweet Princes*, edited by Michael Banks. New York, Baen, 1986.
*Joe Mauser: Mercenary from Tomorrow*, edited by Michael Banks. New York, Baen, 1986.

Short Stories

*The Best of Mack Reynolds*. New York, Pocket Books, 1976.
*Compounded Interests*. Cambridge, Massachusetts, NESFA Press, 1983.

Uncollected Short Stories

"Of Future Fears," in *Analog* (New York), October, November, December 1977.
"All Things to Us," in *Amazing* (New York), May 1978.
"A Halo for Horace," in *Amazing* (New York), February 1979.
"Toro," in *Amazing* (New York), May 1979.
"The Case of the Disposable Jalopy," in *Analog* (New York), October 1979.
"Golden Rule," in *Analog* (New York), March 1980.
"Hell's Fire," in *Fantasy and Science Fiction* (New York), June 1980.
"The Adventure of the Extraterrestrial," in *Sherlock Holmes Through Time and Space*. Chappequa, New York, Bluejay, 1984.
"The Devil Finds Work" and "Your Soul Comes C.O.D.," in *100 Great Fantasy Short Short Stories*, edited by Isaac Asimov, Terry Carr, and Martin H. Greenberg. New York, Doubleday, 1984.
"Prone," in *Young Mutants*, edited by Isaac Asimov, Martin H. Greenberg, and Charles G. Waugh. New York, Harper and Row, 1984.
"Optical Illusion," in *Young Monsters*, edited by Isaac Asimov, Martin H. Greenberg, and Charles G. Waugh. New York, Harper and Row, 1985.

### Other Publications

Novels

*Episode on the Riviera*. Derby, Connecticut, Monarch, 1961.
*A Kiss Before Loving*. Derby, Connecticut, Monarch, 1961.
*This Time We Love*. Derby, Connecticut, Monarch, 1962.
*The Kept Woman*. Derby, Connecticut, Monarch, 1963.
*The Jet Set*. Derby, Connecticut, Monarch, 1964.
*Sweet Dreams, Sweet Prince*. London, New English Library, 1965.
*Once Departed*. New York, Curtis, 1970.
*The House in the Kasbah* (as Maxine Reynolds). New York, Beagle, 1972.
*The Home of the Inquisitor* (as Maxine Reynolds). New York, Beagle, 1972.
*Four Letter World* (as Todd Harding). San Diego, Greenleaf, 1972.

Other

*Paradise for Males.* New York, Plaza, 1957.
*How to Retire Without Money.* New York, Belmont, 1958.
*The Expatriates.* Evanston, Illinois, Regency, 1963.
*Puerto Rican Patriot: The Life of Luis Muñoz Rivera.* New York, Macmillan, 1969.

Editor, with Fredric Brown, *Science-Fiction Carnival.* Chicago, Shasta, 1953.

*

Mack Reynolds commented:

(1981) Thirty years ago, when I first began writing science fiction, I soon arrived at the conclusion that a serious freelancer in the field must be acquainted with the sciences he dealt with. The day of the space opera was rapidly disappearing, and the writer had best know what he was talking about. My background in the hard sciences was sketchy and I realized that I was out of my depth in them. However, I have had a lifelong interest in the social sciences and particularly in political economy. And, somewhat to my surprise, I discovered that few writers in our genre were so equipped. I decided to concentrate on stories with socio-economic backgrounds.

Many of us in our extrapolations do very well in portraying a future in which the sciences and technology have blossomed fantastically. We rejoice in faster-then-light travel, we colonize the galaxy, we have become immortal, we have matter transformers and transmitters. And what is our socio-economic system? Often it's feudalism, complete with galactic emperors, dukes, counts, and barons, sometimes swinging laser swords, whatever they are. We don't even have capitalism, not to speak of something in advance. What is the means of exchange? Often currency, silver and gold coins. What is the relationship between the sexes? What type of family prevails? The writers have returned to Victorian times. Not one story in 25 in depicting the future ever considers that the private ownership of the means of production, the profit system, and class divided society, might one day end. American science fiction is myopic when it comes to foreseeing an evolved social system. So is Soviet science fiction. In the Soviets's case, they seem to have a fond belief that the millennium has been reached, that nothing lies beyond the state capitalism they have achieved, so there is no point in speculating on future socio-economics. The big difference is that even if a Soviet SF writer did attempt to look beyond their version of Utopia, it is unlikely that his story would ever see print. In the west we are still free to extrapolate in the field of political economy—we just don't. And, in my belief, science fiction is the poorer for it.

The world is going through an unprecedented period of revolutionary change, in science, in medicine, in technology, in the family relationship, in social systems, in the relationship between nations, between generations, between sexes. And if the future is to be a valid one we must buckle down to deciding just what we want. An end of war, an end of poverty, an end of the rape of our planet, a viable world government, are only a few of the goals we should keep ever in mind.

In my stories, I do not have any particular axe to grind. I have written stories (some humorous ones) both for and against every socio-economic system that I know of including socialism, in all its myriad forms, communism, syndicalism, anarchism, fascism, theocracy, technocracy, meritocracy, and industrial feudalism. It simply seems not to occur to the average person, even science-fiction readers, that there is an alternative, or alternatives, to our present social system. I am attempting to bring home to them that there is, and possibly desirable alternatives at that.

* * *

A maverick socialist, Mack Reynolds is of that rare breed of American science-fiction writers specializing in socioeconomic speculation. Early in his writing career Reynolds switched from detective fiction to science fiction; but as the title of his first science-fiction novel (*The Case of the Little Green Men*) suggests, he never left the plots and characters of detective fiction entirely behind. Producing a strange amalgam of economics, politics, intrigue, action, and mystery, Reynolds became quite popular, and the readers of *Galaxy* and *If* once chose him as their favorite author.

Reynolds's popularity comes largely from his interplanetary fiction, such as his Section G: United Planets series. The premise is that a future confederation of diverse worlds pledges noninterference in each other's socioeconomic systems, but that anomalous worlds threaten this pledge. Crack agent Ronnie Bronston of the intelligence bureau Section G is, typically, the troubleshooter. A representative assignment, in *Dawnman Planet,* takes Ronnie to the super-capitalist world Phrygia, where the villanous Baron Wylie hides information about invading aliens who threaten the confederation. In *Code Duello,* the troublesome world is Firenze, ruled by Florentine gentlemen preoccupied with dueling. The best in this series may be *The Rival Rigellians,* in which rival teams develop capitalism and socialism on their respective worlds until the natives rebel against both systems.

On the whole, though, Reynolds's short stories are both better written and better introductions to Reynolds's ideas, for the irony of Reynolds's political thinking blends with the irony and reversal of the story form. In "Revolution," the United States tries to stop a democratic revolution within the U.S.S.R., since such a revolution would make a stronger Russia; in "Pacifist," a pacifist group uses terrorism to achieve its goals. "Compounded Interests," a time-loop story, suggests that anonymous financial interests control history. "Utopian" sets the premises for much of Reynolds's utopian fiction. Although one might expect a socialist's utopias to be pleasant places, Reynolds's utopias are ambiguous; in this story the utopian leaders import a revolutionist from the past to keep them from going stale. The assumption behind these ironic stories is that change so dominates the late 20th century that what is revolutionary one day is reactionary the next.

The year 2000 series of near-future utopian novels is likewise ambiguous. Some worlds are rather pleasant places; others struggle with desperate boredom. Typically, these worlds have put an end to the extremes of wealth and poverty (in fact, to social class). But the welfare state produces stagnation and decay. In *Computer World,* Reynolds predicts, before computers were in vogue (1967), a world totally dependent on the computer. In *Commune 2000 A.D.,* he gives us a world in which one can choose between many modes of dropping out. Reynolds's most ambitious works are his two updates of Bellamy, *Looking Backward, From the Year 2000* and *Equality: In the Year 2000.* Reynolds's 2000 resembles but also diverges from Bellamy's. Reynolds's Julian West is out of place in a world he cannot understand, a world which has transcended traditional ideologies and could be called socialism, collectivism, technocracy, archism, meritocracy, or, more accurately, none of these. Reynolds's 2000—which he calls evolutionary rather than utopian—is more inevitable than it is attractive.

The Africa series (*Blackman's Burden; Border, Breed nor Birth; The Best Ye Breed*) likewise presents fixed ideologies in a changing world. Both the capitalist West and the socialist East struggle, often with strange results, to control African nationalism. In the Joe Mauser series (*Time Gladiator, The Earth War,* and others), Reynolds develops a world that has moved in a direction different from that of his utopias. The Earth contains a decadent class society in which one can advance only in the "fracases," a TV-age version of the Roman bread and circuses. Even protagonist Joe Mauser departs from the good-guy stereotypes in his disillusionment.

At his death, Reynolds left several unfinished manuscripts that have been edited by Dean Ing and Michael Banks. Some of these represent Reynolds at his best, particularly *The Other Time,* a time-paradox story containing a remarkably complete ethnology of 16th-century Mexico. The Lagrangia series presents another ambiguous utopia, an orbiting colony that, because of its revolutionary production of power, is the source of fierce contention among rival forces on Earth.

Reynolds wrote too much, and his fiction contains grave flaws: sexism, macho-chauvinist heroes, super-slick dialogue, and melodramatic plots resolved often by pointless violence. Yet he takes seriously, as few writers do, the idea that the socioeconomic future will be stranger than we can imagine.

—Curtis C. Smith

---

**RICHARDS, Edward.** *See* **TUBB, E.C.**

---

**RICHARDS, Henry.** *See* **SAXON, Richard.**

---

**RICHARDSON, Robert S.** *See* **LATHAM, Philip.**

---

**RICHMOND, Walt and Leigh.** Americans. **RICHMOND, Walt(er F.):** Born in Memphis, Tennessee, 5 December 1922. Married Leigh Tucker; three children. Research physicist; President and executive director, Centric Foundation, Merritt Island, Florida. *Died 14 April 1977.* **RICHMOND, Leigh (née Tucker):** Educated at Louisiana State University, Baton Rouge; Tulane University, New Orleans. Married 1) Walt Richmond (died 1977), three children; 2) Richard V. Donahue in 1979. Reporter, photographer, newspaper editor, and research anthropologist. President, Centric Foundation. Address: P.O. Box 908, Maggie Valley, North Carolina 28751, U.S.A.

SCIENCE-FICTION PUBLICATIONS

Novels

*Shock Waves.* New York, Ace, 1967.
*The Lost Millennium.* New York, Ace, 1967; as *SIVA!,* 1979.
*Phoenix Ship.* New York, Ace, 1969; expanded edition as *Phase Two,* 1980.
*Gallagher's Glacier.* New York, Ace, 1970; revised edition, 1979.
*Challenge the Hellmaker.* New York, Ace, 1976.
*The Probability Corner.* New York, Ace, 1977.

Short Stories

*Positive Charge.* New York, Ace, 1970.

*

Leigh Richmond comments:

(1986) All of our books have been "hard core" or "hard science" science fiction, based on the results of research at the Centric Foundation. The next one, which should be published by the fall of 1986, in *How to Psi; or, Field Effect—The Pi-Phase of Physics.* This is not science fiction, but should be of interest to readers of the genre. It is a how-to book for using the psionic abilities consciously, as well as a detailed analysis of the electromagnetic structure which permeates and surrounds the body (seen as the aura) of which the psionic abilities are the sensory apparatus.

* * *

Walt and Leigh Richmond both grew up before the atomic bomb fell, when science seemed both simpler and more accessible. Understanding was not yet locked in moated research foundations—in those days (it seemed) a boy could invent antigravity with the right cardboard tubes and wires, and a few people thinking hard could uncover the secrets of the universe and Explain Everything. The Richmonds wanted to be among those few people, and in their eager stories the maverick amateurs always win. But because the Richmonds did not actually start writing until after the atomic bomb fell, their stories are also marked by a scorn for the current secrecy-bound scientific bureaucracy, and an appetite for apocalypse.

When the Richmonds' stories work, they successfully convey the excitement of individual discovery—the mind's reaction to its own new thinking, to its own awakening power. As a result, the Richmonds' most convincing characters tend to be children. An early story, "Poppa Needs Shorts," neatly details the way a four-year-old can combine pieces of information that an adult would keep rigidly separate. The same child, Oley, grows up in the novel *The Probability Corner* to learn how to read the mind of a computer and invent a matter transmitter in his cellar—all through his willingness to keep combining divergent types of knowledge. Such willingness, the Richmonds imply, is usually destroyed by modern education, and education is the most interesting topic in their novel *Phase Two* (an expanded version of *Phoenix Ship*). The hero, S.T.A.R. Dustin, is injected with molecules of trained men's brains, whose knowledge is then activated in him through four years of computer testing. But the boy's real mental power develops from his efforts to recombine the facts on his own, preguessing the computer and eventually walking easily out of his political prison into new realms of science. The idea that the computer is an appropriate tool for the expanding mind is also pursued in *Challenge the Hellmaker,* where a group of friends on an orbital station accidentally invent a spacedrive while singlehandedly fighting off a world-wide military takeover. Though the heroes in the Richmonds' books are almost anachronistically individualistic, they are rarely isolated. Even little Oley feels secure in the center of his family, and the collaboration of friends (another means of combing divergent knowledge) is one of the more pleasant constants in the Richmonds' own collaboration.

When their stories do not work—or do not work consistently—they are flawed by unconvincing politics, hyperactive melodrama, and scientific explanations that are not only impossible but are also praised for their clarity by the other characters. The worst offender on all counts is *The Lost Millennium*, a novel that tries to explain all human and geologic history by proposing a prehistorical race of supermen who, through solar taps located in pyramids, possessed broadcast electrical power. The story covers so much so quickly—including all myths, many lectures on electricity, and an incomprehensible soap opera sub-plot—that the result is a fragmented scenario whose several apocalypses are the only relief.

Yet perhaps even *The Lost Millennium* is just part of the Richmonds' effort to scramble our brains into new connections. They were serious enough about the content of their work to form their own research group, the Centric Foundation, and before Walt Richmond's death in 1977, they planned to apply "relatively simple high school mathematics" to physics, and improve on the quantum theory. Few young science-fiction readers would fault their attack on education, and it is hard to resist the Richmonds' faith in the potentially supernatural power of individual thinking. Their eagerness and their determined amateur science (" 'It's really quite easy,' he explained briskly") are part of an innocence science fiction has lost, and could never easily regain.

—Karen G. Way

---

**ROBERT, Lionel.** *See* **FANTHORPE, R. Lionel.**

---

**ROBERTS, Keith (John Kingston).** British. Born in Kettering, Northamptonshire, 20 September 1935. Educated at Northampton School of Art, National Diploma in Design 1956; Leicester College of Art, 1956–57. Has worked as a cartoon animator, and as an illustrator for advertising, magazines, and books. Editor, *SF Impulse*, London, 1966–67. Recipient: British Science Fiction Association award, 1982, 1987. Agent: Carnell Literary Agency, Danes Croft, Goose Lane, Little Hallingbury, Hertfordshire CM22 7RG, England.

Science-Fiction Publications

Novels

*The Furies*. London, Hart Davis, and New York, Berkley, 1966.
*Pavane*. London, Hart Davis, and New York, Doubleday, 1968.
*The Inner Wheel*. London, Hart Davis, and New York, Doubleday, 1970.
*The Chalk Giants*. London, Hutchinson, 1974; New York, Putnam, 1975.
*Molly Zero*. London, Gollancz, 1980.
*Kiteworld*. London, Gollancz, 1985; and New York, Arbor House, 1986.
*Kaeti's Apocalypse*. Worcester Park, Surrey, Kerosina, 1986.
*Gráinne*. Worcester Park, Surrey, Kerosina, 1987.

Short Stories

*Anita*. New York, Ace, 1970; London, Millington, 1976.
*Machines and Men*. London, Hutchinson, 1973.
*The Grain Kings*. London, Hutchinson, 1976.
*The Passing of the Dragons*. New York, Berkley, 1977.
*Ladies from Hell*. London, Gollancz, 1979.
*Kaeti and Company*. Worcester Park, Surrey, Kerosina, 1986.
*The Lordly Ones*. London, Gollancz, 1986.
*Winterwood and Other Hauntings*. Scotforth, Lancashire, Morrigan, 1989.

Other Publications

Novels

*The Boat of Fate*. London, Hutchinson, 1971; Englewood Cliffs, New Jersey, Prentice Hall, 1974.
*The Road to Paradise*. Worcester Park, Surrey, Kerosina, 1989.

Verse

*A Heron Caught in Weeds: Poems*. Worcester Park, Surrey, Kerosina, 1987.

Other

*Irish Encounters: A Short Travel*. Worcester Park, Surrey, Kerosina, 1988.
*The Natural History of the P.H.* Worcester Park, Surrey, Kerosina, 1988.
*The Event*. Scotforth, Lancashire, Morrigan, 1989.

*

Keith Roberts comments:

I think if we survive our do-it-yourself Armageddon, the 20th century will be remembered as the Age of the pigeonhole. Everything has to have its tag; Stonehenge is a computer, etc. The particular label attached to me is science-fiction writer. I've nothing against it; but I really know very little science. I suppose I did write some technological fiction in the very early days. But I've simply tried to talk about characters who interested me, and events that moved or disturbed me. If that's science fiction, then so be it.

* * *

Two characteristics typify the work of Keith Roberts: an involvement with England and its landscape, history, and mythology; and a fascination for what he has called (borrowing a term from Robert Holdstock) the Primitive Heroine, a young, sexy woman who has haunted much of his writing over the last two decades.

Both were present in his earliest work, *Anita*, the stories about a headstrong witch-child in modern rural England, but these fey, whimsical works developed neither element well. It wasn't until a much later reappearance of Anita in "The Checkout" and her transmutation into the actress Kaeti that she really became what Roberts sees as a Primitive Heroine. And the bucolic England presented in these stories are as pretty and unreal as the England in his first novel, *The Furies*, a cosy catastrophe in the manner of John Wyndham that was already old fashioned when it was written. Here, a nuclear disaster coupled with an invasion by aliens who look like gigantic wasps leaves a few desperate survivors isolated in a mutilated landscape. There is little original in the book, though the robust writing and the way the countryside almost becomes a character within the story give hints of what was to come.

With his second novel, however, Roberts immediately sprang to the front rank of science-fiction writers. *Pavane* has been acclaimed as one of the finest of all alternate-universe novels, though Roberts himself would dispute this, since he sees it more as an examination of cyclic history, which he makes clear in the Coda to the book. Be that as it may, this really is an extraordinary work, which, in a sequence of stories linked more by theme than by plot, provides a mosaic portrait of a world in which Elizabeth I was assassinated, the Spanish Armada was successful, and, in the latter years of 20th-century England, is still under the sway of the Catholic church. Set mostly in the English West Country around Corfe Castle, a place that holds an almost mystical attraction for Roberts, the novel tells of a world in which social and technological progress has been slow indeed. There are steam-powered road trains, and communication is by a network of semaphore stations, though Roberts is at pains to make these curiosities as much as possible a part of the ordinary daily life of his characters. Against this rural backdrop, Roberts's characters face tremendous moral choices. Brother John, a monk and artist, witnesses the atrocities of the Inquisition and is driven to heresy and rebellion as a result. Becky, in "The White Boat," a slightly later story omitted from most of the early editions of the novel, is rescued from the bleakness of her ordinary life by the romantic vision of the White Boat, which turns out to be smuggling technology. She betrays the boat to the authorities, then, at the last minute, warns it of the trap that has been set.

Such moral choices are, typically, the dramatic hinge around which all of Roberts's fiction turns. Later critics have accused him of being a right-wing libertarian, a rather simplistic viewpoint though it is true that he believes people must face decisions that will affect not only themselves but their whole society, and must suffer the consequences of other people's decisions. Roberts has a sour view of humanity, though it is clear he feels that looking after oneself and looking after one's fellows come to much the same thing.

Becky is the precursor of Martine, whom Michael Coney termed the "multi-girl," who in various guises forms the linking device in Roberts's next mosaic novel, *The Chalk Giants*. This is a darker, more ambitious work, a more successful but less acclaimed companion piece to *Pavane*. The story concerns Stan Potts, a loser struggling to escape before a nuclear cataclysm tears Britain apart. In a series of visions (in part inspired by the work of painter Paul Nash), Potts foresees episodes from a barbaric, post-apocalyptic future, in which avatars of Martine, a girl he desires, always appears. Sexually alluring, the multi-girl will trigger events, often events of considerable violence for which Roberts clearly feels distaste but also an uneasy fascination; yet, she is rarely in a position to control them. As such, she is the archetype of the Primitive Heroine who will recur in Roberts's work. Gradually she gains self-awareness and power, until she achieves her apotheosis as *Gráinne*.

A third mosaic novel, *Kiteworld*, completes what might be seen as a loose trilogy. As in the other two, the church appears as a powerful, generally malignant force in the shaping of society, though the society itself is not central to the novel, which is, as ever, a sequence of *apperçus* about the compromises and decisions any individual must make in order to survive. The most intricate and effective passage in the book, for instance, is about a kitecaptain failing to come to terms with the confusing and conflicting demands of love, guilt, and duty brought on by the autistic child Tan, whom Roberts has described as his most powerful heroine to date. A further story in the Kiteworld sequence, "Tremarest" has already appeared.

If these three novels together form Roberts's most successful work, that is not to deny the quality of some of his other work. As a writer, he has always been better at shorter length, which is perhaps why these novels composed of linked stories work so well. Nevertheless, his more unified novels, *Molly Zero* (a bleak tale of a young girl, struggling unsuccessfully to achieve some level of independence on an odyssey through a grim, bureaucratically controlled future) and *Gráinne* (which won the BSFA award as the best novel of 1987), are both considerable achievements. *Gráinne* tells the story of adman Alistair Bevan (an early pseudonym of Roberts) whose life is intertwined with the rise of a mysterious girl-goddess Gráinne. It is an excellent example of the way Roberts combines his feel for the mystical and mythical power of landscape and women.

Even so, his best and most characteristic work is probably to be found in his short stories. In "Weihnachtsabend," an excellent alternative-history story set in a Nazi-ruled Britain, the central character is faced with a typically severe moral choice, between achieving a rich and powerful life at the cost of giving himself body and soul to his masters, and making a futile gesture of rebellion, which would end inevitably in his death. The two linked stories, "The Lordly Ones" and "The Comfort Station," tell of a simple-minded lavatory attendant who cannot comprehend the social collapse he sees around him. Roberts's invariable sympathy for the victim makes these powerful stories about the way people try to cling to normality even when normality has broken down. "Richenda" features a typical heroine who appears very differently in different circumstances, though this manifestation of the multi-girl is probably most effectively demonstrated in the Kaeti stories. In these, a small group of characters take on different roles in different stories, rather like a repertory company, though their salient characteristics and perceptions remain the same, providing a strong focus throughout the book. Certain of the stories, "The Clocktower Girl" and "Kaeti and the Hangman," are as powerful as anything Roberts has written. Roberts explores different layers and aspects of personality within the one character. In the process, he has created one of the most vivid and memorable characters in modern science fiction. And, though the setting is London, he is still concerned to reveal the layers of history and myth that lie below the landscape of modern life.

—Paul Kincaid

---

**ROBESON, Kenneth.** *See* **DENT, Lester; GOULART, Ron.**

---

**ROBINETT, Stephen (Allen).** Has also written as Tak Hallus. American. Born in Long Beach, California, 13 July 1941. Educated at California State University, Long Beach, B.A. in history 1966; University of California Hastings College of the Law, San Francisco, J.D. 1971. Served in the United States Army: Sergeant. Married Louise Yeisley in 1969. Lawyer, 1971–73, then full-time writer. Address: c/o Avon Books, 105 Madison Avenue, New York, New York 10016, U.S.A.

SCIENCE-FICTION PUBLICATIONS

Novels

*Stargate.* New York, St. Martin's Press, 1976; London, Hale, 1978.
*The Man Responsible.* New York, Ace, 1978.

Short Stories

*Projections.* New York, Ace, 1979.

OTHER PUBLICATIONS

Novels

*Final Option.* New York, Avon, 1990.
*Unfinished Business.* New York, Avon, 1990.

* * *

Stephen Robinett was first published in 1969 pseudonymously as Tak Hallus, the name he would use for several years during which period he wrote a handful of uneven stories for John W. Campbell and *Analog* magazine. There are interesting touches in "Mindwipe" and "Mini-Talent," for example, both of which involve the resolution of legal questions arising from the existence of extra-sensory powers, but these early pieces are uneven; some characters are well-drawn, others lack any dimension, occasionally suffering from implausible plot devices. Robinett's enthusiasm for his subject matter overshadows these failings, however, and his legal background makes the speculation involved credible and intriguing.

"Force Over Distance" was the first to deal with matter transmission, a concept that recurs periodically in Robinett's subsequent stories. The developer of a device that can instantaneously transport matter over distance is kidnapped by Mexican guerrillas and unwillingly involved in their plans to attack Mexico City. The sequel, "Laws and Orders," incorporates Robinett's earlier theme, mind readers and the law, but the plot moves in too many disparate directions for the story to work well and the final escape scene through the ventilator shafts remains a tired cliché.

His first novel, *Stargate*, was serialized before appearing under the Robinett byline. Matter transmission is now a fact of life on the Earth, and the implications for potential exploration of other worlds have occurred to a number of parties, not all of whom have admirable reputations. The effort to construct a gigantic installation in space is stymied by the death of the only man who may have possessed the knowledge to make it work. Although it is theoretically possible to retrieve this information from his brain even after death, someone has stolen the body. The protagonist has recently been placed in charge of the project, but now he finds himself walking the tightrope between two powerful corporations, each intent on shaping the future of the human race, one through matter transmission, the other by means of a fleet of starships. Oddly enough, Robinett introduces another character late in the book to solve the mystery and bring events to their conclusion, a not entirely successful twist. The book is an interesting if somewhat routine futuristic spy thriller, but the plot begins to unravel when Robinett throws in an imminent catastrophe in the closing chapters.

Four years later, Robinett wrote a second novel that demonstrated his considerable improvement as a writer. *The Man Responsible* was the expansion of a shorter piece of the same title published in 1977. Again, he takes several different themes and weaves them together, but in this case, maintains a sense of balance, not allowing side issues to interfere with the primary plot line. The protagonist is a detective who becomes interested in a proposal to create an investment trust to create a city of the future, when he is hired to recover a small sum of money. Predictably, the scheme is a fraud, but before everything is unravelled and resolved, we have had a guided tour of Robinett's vision of the not-too-distant future. It is also one of the earliest novels to deal with the implications of artificial intelligence and the possibility of immortality through the transfer of personality to a more durable medium.

In the 1970's, Robinett began to write in other fields, but occasional shorter pieces continued to appear as late as 1983, several of which are far more interesting than those published earlier. "Tax Man" is an implausible but effective satire postulating that the income tax rate has been increased to 98 percent. Tax rebels and even those genuinely unable to pay are occasionally executed by IRS agents in order to provide an example to others. "Helbent 4" features a self-aware robot warship, reminiscent of Saberhagen's "Berserker" tales.

"Projections" and "Guzman's Garden" are probably Robinett's most effective shorter pieces. The first story deals with an advertising agency that uses broadcast brainwashing to advance the career of a political candidate. In the second, a film scout discovers a man who possesses a preternatural ability to sway people to his side. These two diverse examinations of a similar theme reflect serious issues of public policy and constitute the best of Robinett's more thoughtful work. Although less successful in execution, similar concerns are evident in "Tomus," in which a man must decide whether or not to supplant the personality that has arisen in his clone, and "Satyr," which explores the implications of the creation of artificial humanoids who, since they have no legal standing as human beings, can be sold into slavery.

There is a humorous side to his writing career as well. "Hell Creatures from the Third Planet" is an amusing piece in which aliens fake an attack on Earth in order to provoke a futile human military response, so that they can film the ensuing "battle" as part of an epic drama.

Robinett's subsequent departure from the field is disappointing because, although he had yet to create a significant body of work, there was evidence of both a serious concern for the use of literature as a means to explore the human potential, and a growing skill at developing logical plots with consistent and believable characters.

—Don D'Ammassa

---

**ROBINSON, Frank M(alcolm).** American. Born in Chicago, Illinois, 9 August 1926. Educated at Beloit College, Wisconsin B.S. in physics in 1950 (Phi Beta Kappa); Northwestern University, Evanston, Illinois, M.S. in journalism 1955. Served as radar technician in the United States Navy, 1944–45, 1950–51. Office boy, Ziff-Davis Publishing Company, 1944; assistant editor, *Family Weekly*, 1955–56, and *Science Digest*, 1956–59; editor, *Rogue*, 1959–65; managing editor, *Cavalier*, 1965–66; editor, *Censorship Today*, 1967; staff writer, *Playboy*, 1969–73. Since 1973, freelance writer. Agent: Curtis Brown, 10 Astor Place, New York, New York 10003, U.S.A.

SCIENCE-FICTION PUBLICATIONS

Novels

*The Power.* Philadelphia, Lippincott, 1956; London, Eyre and Spottiswoode, 1957.
*The Glass Inferno,* with Thomas N. Scortia. New York, Doubleday, 1974; London, Hodder and Stoughton, 1975.
*The Prometheus Crisis,* with Thomas N. Scortia. New York, Doubleday, 1975; London, Hodder and Stoughton, 1976.
*The Nightmare Factor,* with Thomas N. Scortia. New York, Doubleday, and London, Hodder and Stoughton, 1978.
*The Gold Crew,* with Thomas N. Scortia. New York, Warner, 1980; London, Panther, 1983.
*The Great Divide,* with John Levin. New York, Rawson Wade, 1982.
*Blow-Out!,* with Thomas N. Scortia. New York, Watts, 1987; London, Severn House, 1989.
*The Dark Beyond the Stars.* New York, Tor, 1991.

Short Stories

*A Life in the Day of . . . and Other Short Stories.* New York, Bantam, 1981.

Uncollected Short Stories

"The Girls from Earth," in *Out of This World 10,* edited by Amabel Williams-Ellis. London, Blackie, 1973.
"Situation Thirty," in *Combat SF,* edited by Gordon R. Dickson, New York, Ace, 1981.
"The Oceans Are Wide," in *Starships,* edited by Isaac Asimov, Martin H. Greenberg, and Charles G. Waugh. New York, Fawcett, 1983.

OTHER PUBLICATIONS

Other

Editor, with Earl Kemp, *The Truth about Vietnam.* San Diego, Greenleaf, 1966.
Editor, with Nat Lehrman, *Sex, American Style.* Chicago, Playboy Press, 1971.

*

Frank M. Robinson comments:

I have no particular statement to make about my own variety of science fiction except that I like to read and write science fiction based upon extrapolations of current trends in the physical sciences, psychology, cultural anthropology, politics, etc. Conversely, I have little interest in the type of fantasy that has come to dominate the field in recent years.

* * *

Despite his background in physical science, Frank M. Robinson's stories are most often based on psychology or cultural anthropology. One such story, "The Fire and the Sword," is concerned with the reactions of Earthmen to a "perfect" alien society. Robinson chose this story to represent his work in the anthology *SF: Author's Choice 4* (edited by Harry Harrison, 1974). He worked entertaining variations on time travel in "Untitled Story," and produced a short novel of headlong action in "The Hunting Season." "The Night Shift" is a clever short fantasy, and "The Oceans Are Wide" a short novel telling of a young boy's harsh passage to maturity in the warped society on board a generation-ship carrying colonists to a distant planetary system. Behind the editor's inappropriate title of "Dead End Kids of Space" was an entertaining story of the adventures of a survey team on a planet with a very confusing and unpredictable culture. Another light-hearted story with an anthropological basis was "The Santa Claus Planet" concerning a society in which the giving of gifts had been elevated into a ritual with decidedly sinister overtones. In another vein entirely, "Dream Street" was a deceptively simple story of a boy on the run from an orphanage, and of his longing to become a spaceman.

His first novel *The Power,* was published by Lippincott as part of a short-lived series of "novels of menace." It lived up to its billing admirably. The story concerns a navy-subsidized research team studying human endurance and survival characteristics. Results of an anonymous questionnaire suggest that one of the team members is a superman with an assortment of psychic powers, and the one team member who takes these results seriously promptly dies under mysterious circumstances. He leaves an uncompleted letter for team chairman William Tanner: "I want to tell you about Adam Hart. . . ." In his review of the book, Damon Knight characterized Robinson as "a gifted and sensitive writer" but found fault with his logic and with an anti-scientific tone to the book. Most readers and critics, on the other hand, found Tanner's nightmare battle against Adam Hart hair-raising and compulsively readable.

After the publication of *The Power,* Robinson temporarily gave up fiction writing and took a succession of editorial jobs. Occasionally another story would appear. "East Wind, West Wind" is a grim story of an inspector for Air Central, monitoring air quality in a smog-bound future Los Angeles in which all forms of air pollution, from cigarette smoking to internal combustion engines, are outlawed.

The collection, *A Life in the Day of . . . and Other Short Stories,* includes five of Robinson's stories from the 1950's and four later stories. The book is a reminder of just how good (and how underrated) Robinson's short fiction is, and is equally valuable for the extensive autobiographical commentary, which gives a vivid picture of the science-fiction field in the 1950's and 1960's.

In 1973, Robinson began a very successful collaboration with Thomas N. Scortia. The team produced a series of best-selling "disaster" novels, some of which are borderline science fiction. The first of these was *The Glass Inferno,* a story of a fire in a modern high-rise building. (Together with a similar book, *The Tower* by Richard Martin Stern, this was the basis for the popular film *The Towering Inferno*). *The Prometheus Crisis* is about a reactor failure in a nuclear power plant, *The Nightmare Factor,* covert biological warfare. Even when not concerned with science-fiction ideas, these books exhibit the science-fiction writer's careful analysis of processes, both physical and mental. This attention to expository detail is not allowed to interfere with the pace of the story, and serves to enhance the realistic tone.

*The Great Divide,* a collaboration with John Levin, is a political thriller set in the late 1980's. The Second Constitutional Convention and a renewed oil crisis provide an unscrupulous California governor with the tools for a coup that would split the country into two warring camps. The efforts of a vice-presidential aide and a small group of friends to uncover and stop this scheme make a tense and uncomfortably convincing narrative.

—R.E. Briney

**ROBINSON, Kim Stanley.** American. Born in Waukegan, Illinois, 23 March 1952. Educated at the University of California, San Diego, B.A. in literature, 1974, Ph.D. 1982; Boston University, M.A. in English 1975. Married Lisa Howland Nowell in 1982. Visiting lecturer, University of California, in Davis, 1982–84, 1985, and in San Diego, 1982, 1985. Recipient: World Fantasy award, 1983; *Locus* award, 1985. Address: c/o Tor Books, 49 West 24th Street, 9th floor, New York, New York 10010, U.S.A.

### Science-Fiction Publications

Novels (series: Orange County)

*The Wild Shore* (Orange County). New York, Ace, 1984; London, Futura, 1985.
*Icehenge*. New York, Ace, 1984; London, Futura, 1985.
*The Memory of Whiteness*. New York, Tor, 1985; London, Macdonald, 1986.
*Green Mars*, with *A Meeting with Medusa*, by Arthur C. Clarke. New York, Tor, 1988.
*The Blind Geometer*. New Castle, Virginia, Cheap Street, 1986; with *Return from Rainbow Bridge*, and *The New Atlantis*, by Ursula Le Guin, New York, Tor, 1989.
*The Gold Coast* (Orange County). New York, St. Martin's Press, and London, Macdonald, 1988.
*Pacific Edge* (Orange County). New York, Tor, and London, Unwin Hyman, 1990.
*A Short, Sharp Shock*. Shingletown, California, Siesing, 1990.

Short Stories

*The Planet on the Table*. New York, Tor, 1986; London, Futura, 1987.
*Escape from Kathmandu*. Eugene, Oregon, Axolotl Press, 1987; London, Unwin Hyman, 1990.
*Remaking History*. New York, Tor, 1991.

### Other Publications

Other

*The Novels of Philip K. Dick*. Ann Arbor, Michigan, UMI Research Press, 1984.

* * *

Kim Stanley Robinson quickly established a reputation as a promising young science-fiction author in the late 1970's and early 1980's with a series of remarkably well written stories. Robinson attended the Clarion SF Writers Workshop in 1975, and most of his early fiction appeared in Damon Knight's *Orbit*, and later in Terry Carr's *Universe*, the two anthology series that represented the literary cutting-edge of science fiction in the 1970's and early 1980's. By the early- to mid-1980's, Robinson's stories were perennially nominated for the major SF awards.

With the publication of his first novel, *The Wild Shore*, published as the first novel in Terry Carr's revived *Ace Specials* series, Robinson established himself as a major new author. The book earned a Nebula nomination, won the Philip K. Dick Special award, and was voted Best First Novel in the *Locus* poll. The book turned out to be the first novel in the Orange County trilogy, a series set in Orange County, California, where Robinson grew up. The trilogy was completed with *The Gold Coast* and *Pacific Edge*. The books are all set in the mid-21st century, but represent three very different futures, the first post-holocaust, the second a projected dystopia, and the third utopian.

In *The Wild Shore*, Robinson used a relatively pastoral, post-nuclear-war Southern California as background to a heart-warming and a sense-of-wonder-filled coming-of-age story. Robinson evokes a sense of wonder reminiscent of Mark Twain's *The Adventures of Huckleberry Finn* as his young protagonist discovers that his world is filled with danger and intrigue. In *The Gold Coast*, Robinson presents an over-crowded, urban Orange County dominated by defense contractors and designer drugs. Both novels are dominated by fine characterization and sense of place.

In *Pacific Edge*, Robinson presents his personal vision of a practical utopia. It is set in the small town of El Modena, some years after the establishment of a new world order based on a unique mix of ecology awareness, appropriate technologies, personal freedom, institutionalized community responsibility, and cultural tolerance. The general ambience of El Modena seems like a college campus with everyone matured by about a decade. Everyone in the novel is at heart an intellectual, no matter what their vocation, with a love of learning and a penchant for introspection. The most important aspect of *Pacific Edge*, however, is Robinson's new world order, which features a fascinating mix of individual freedom, environmental protection, and both capitalist and socialist economic principles. Robinson's town of El Modena functions as a cooperatively-owned corporation in which everyone is both owner and worker. Physical as well as intellectual fitness is a common interest, and most residents exhibit competency to do (and pride in doing) virtually any job. It could be seen as a more humanist, more left-wing version of Bruce Sterling's future corporation in *Islands in the Net*. Robinson has made a creditable attempt to merge the best concepts of the 1960's, 1970's, and 1980's in designing this new society.

In virtually all of Robinson's fiction, setting is of primary importance, with characterization playing a strong but secondary role. His novels and stories seldom rely on strong or fast-paced plots for their effectiveness. Robinson's most common milieus include, in addition to Orange County, the colonized Solar System (especially Mars), the Himalayas, and present or near-future America.

Robinson's second and third novels, which appeared soon after *The Wild Shore*, took place in his Solar System milieu, and further established his ability to handle hard SF concepts and themes. *Icehenge*, a complex, ambitious novel that incorporated two excellent stories published earlier—"On the North Pole of Pluto" (1980) and "To Leave a Mark" (1982)—featured a society of long-lived humans with limited memories, and a mystery regarding how a human-made monument of ice could be found on Pluto, on what was, according to official history, the first human visit to that planet. *The Memory of Whiteness*, expanded from Robinson's very first story—"In Pierson's Orchestra" (1976)—is set more than a millennium into humanity's solar-system culture, and uses music as a subject and as a metaphor for various cosmological themes. Both novels include perception versus reality themes reminiscent of Philip K. Dick.

Robinson's best work, however, has remained his shorter fiction, particularly stories of novelette to novella length. Four of his best stories were collected together to form a novel, *Escape From Kathmandu*, including "Escape From Kathmandu" (1986), "Mother Goddess of the World" (1987), and "The True Nature of Shangri-La" (1989) along with "The Kingdom Underground," in its first publication. These stories of American expatriates George and Fred and their wild adventures in the Himalayas are both hilarious and at times profound.

Another of Robinson's notable shorter works to be published in book form is *A Short, Sharp Shock*, a uniquely strange novella-length fantasy. The story begins with the protagonist waking to find himself under water in a stormy night-time sea, the first of what will be a continuing series of short, sharp shocks. The story moves along lines that are both unexpected and surreal. There are the treefolk who have small fruit trees growing from their shoulders, the evil, spine kings who often capture and horribly torture treefolk, the peaceful tribe who live in huge snail shells, which they drag around the beach to live nearest whomever they like most at the time, the solitary guide whose sole job is to help travelers across a long stretch where the narrow ridge of land exists only at low tide, the mysterious mirror that appears to transfer anything going through it into parallel dimensions and might have something to do with how the protagonist got to this world—all are part of an emotionally engaging series of intensely vivid, yet surreal, and dreamlike, experiences.

Most of Robinson's other short fiction has been collected in two anthologies, *The Planet on the Table* and *Remaking History*. Many have milieu and themes in common with various of his novels. Mountain climbing is central to several stories, including two set on Earth, "Ridge Running" (1984) and "The Return from Rainbow Bridge" (1987), and two set on Mars, "Exploring Fossil Canyon" (1982) and *Green Mars*. *Green Mars* is a particularly spectacular novella about climbing Olympus Mons on a partially terraformed Mars, and it was nominated for both the Nebula and Hugo awards. Several other works are near-future SF with similar themes to his Orange County novels, including "Stone Eggs" (1983), an eerie story set in the desert southwest, "Down and Out in the Year 2000" (1986), a highly memorable dystopian vision of a degenerated Washington, D.C., "Before I Wake" (1989), a story of Dickian complexity where dreams and reality mix, and "A History of the 20th Century, With Illustrations" (1991), a nearly plot-free, touching and intellectual plea for world sanity.

Other of Robinson's most memorable stories strike out into unique areas. "Venice Drowned" (1981) is set in a future where the Italian city is mostly under water. "Black Air," winner of the 1983 World Fantasy award, told from the point of view of a boy who survived the fall of the Spanish Armada, is set in the past, as is "The Lucky Strike" (1984), which gives an alternative ending to World War II. "Mercurial" (1984) is a murder mystery set on a Mercury inhabited by rich esthetes. "The Blind Geometer" (1987) features a blind mathematician unintentionally caught up in international intrigue, and was one of the best SF stories of the 1980's, as well as one of the few Robinson stories, along with "Mercurial," centered around a strong plot. "The Lunatics" (1988) is a highly original, hard SF story of miners tunneling under the surface of the Moon. "Glacier" (1988) is a superior but mostly overlooked story about a near-future ice age that has the bad luck to appear during one of the hottest summers on record, when everyone is worrying about the Greenhouse Effect.

Kim Stanley Robinson has clearly established himself as one of the most important SF authors of the 1980's, and possibly the most versatile, with superior work ranging from a transcendental, hard science sense of wonder to near-future social commentary, from contemporary humor to serious speculation on important philosophical issues. His next series of novels will return to his Mars milieu, and be called *Red Mars, Green Mars*, and *Blue Mars*.

—D. Douglas Fratz

---

**ROBINSON, Spider.** American. Born in New York City, 24 November 1948. Educated at the State University of New York, Stony Brook, B.A. 1972; New York State University College. Plattsburgh. Married Jeanne Rubbicco in 1975; one daughter. Realty editor, *Long Island Review*, Syosset, New York, 1972– 73. Since 1973, freelance writer: reviewer, *Galaxy*, 1974–77, *Destinies*, 1977–79, and *Analog*, 1978–80. Chairman of the Executive Council, Writers Federation of Nova Scotia, 1981–83. Instructor, Clarion SF Writers Workshop, Michigan State University, 1989. Recipient: John W. Campbell award, 1974; *Locus* award, for criticism, 1976, for fiction, 1977; Hugo award, 1977, 1978, 1983; Nebula award, 1977; Skylark award, 1977; Pat Terry award (Australia), 1977; Canada Council grant, 1983, and Senior Arts grant, 1984. Lives in Vancouver, British Columbia, Canada. Agent: Eleanor Wood, Spectrum Literary Agency, 111 Eighth Avenue, Suite 1503, New York, New York 10011, U.S.A.

### Science-Fiction Publications

Novels (Series: Callahan's Place; Lady Sally's Mouse; Stardance)

*Telempath*. New York, Berkley, 1976; London, Macdonald and Jane's, 1978.
*Stardance*, with Jeanne Robinson. New York, Dial Press, and London, Sidgwick and Jackson, 1979.
*Mindkiller*. New York, Holt Rinehart, 1982; London, Sphere, 1985.
*Night of Power*. New York, Baen, 1985.
*Callahan's Secret*. New York, Ace, 1986.
*Callahan and Company* (omnibus). Phantasia Press, 1987.
*Callahan's Lady* (Lady Sally's Mouse). New York, Ace, 1989.
*Time Pressure*. New York, Ace, 1987.
*Copyright Violation* (novella). Eugene, Oregon, Pulphouse, 1990.
*Starseed* (Stardance), with Jeanne Robinson. New York, Ace, 1991.

Short Stories

*Callahan's Crosstime Saloon*. New York, Ace, 1977.
*Antinomy*. New York, Dell, 1980.
*Time Travelers Strictly Cash*. New York, Ace, 1981.
*Melancholy Elephants*. Toronto, Penguin, 1984; New York, Tor, 1985.

### Other Publications

Other

Editor, *The Best of All Possible Worlds*. New York, Ace, 1980.

*

Spider Robinson comments:

I write "science fiction for people who don't read that crap." The ones who need to most . . .

* * *

With 13 books to his credit, Spider Robinson has established himself as an important SF writer and critic. He has won a number of major awards for his fiction, which typically combines two often incompatible themes, technological optimism and a critique of technological society. However, his storytelling is often marred by a coarse and sentimental didacticism, and his style by sophomoric wordplay, and he displays a distressing fondness for powerful leader fantasies.

Robinson's themes and style were established in his early SF stories, such as those collected in *Callahan's Crosstime Saloon*, a book about the unusual clientele of a Long Island tavern. The collection is a true symposium: the gruff but kindly barkeep Callahan presides over a series of dialogues and encounters that move from social disintegration to restored community in the final story, which takes place on New Year's Eve. This pattern also appears in the apocalyptic *Telempath:* there the remnant population of a post-catastrophe United States is threatened by powerful aliens and by conflict between technophiles and a naturalist cult, but the story ends in a love-feast of multiple marriages, restored filial relations, and administrative merger. In the other apocalyptic novel, *Stardance*, the final vision is of death and difference transcended, with human flesh become incorruptible and polymorphous sexual-spiritual communion among humanity's elect and the plasmoid, angelic aliens.

In more recent fictions, this master-myth crosses into self-parody. *Mindkiller* sports a professor whose life has disintegrated; he is restored by joining a conspiracy to change the world through "mindwiping" technology. In *Time Pressure*, the hermit-hippie Sam is not only brought somewhat forcibly into communal consciousness, he is also literally raised from the dead. In Russell Grant, *Night of Power* gives us a "wannabe soul brother," a white expatriate who finds fulfillment in his unlikely adoption by the charismatic leader of an African-American insurrectionist movement. At its most ludicrous (and sexist), the "communion of saints" becomes in *Callahan's Lady* the workers and clientele of an upscale Brooklyn whorehouse.

The first-person narrator plays a similar role in most of Robinson's fictions. Jake, frame-narrator of *Callahan's Crosstime Saloon*, is nursing a spiritual wound—he was responsible for his wife's and daughter's deaths in an auto accident—but it is he who articulates the redemptive (*cross*-time) nature of Callahan's place. In *Telempath*, Isham Stone has been nurtured on hatred, violence, and revenge, and early in the novel loses an arm and attempts to murder his father; yet, it is Isham who evolves the ability to communicate with the aliens and who makes peace between the two factions of humanity. Charlie Armstead of *Stardance* is similarly wounded. An embittered dancer whose career was destroyed when his hip was damaged by a gunman's bullet, he works as a video specialist with the dancer Shara Drummond. This leads to communication with the alien entity that threatens Earth, and later to his dance company's transcendence of a corrupt and polluted planet, union with the aliens, and reunion with Shara.

The theme of the disabled narrator, redeemed through the shared experience of pain, is underlined in "The Law of Conservation of Pain." In that story, a time traveler interferes with the early life of a blues singer. Rather than destroying her talent by obliterating the universe in which she suffered and was scarred, his interference creates a universe in which her songs of joy are as wrenching as her songs of pain ever were. The trope of the conservation laws makes joy and pain, like matter and energy, metonyms of the same reality. Still, we do not generally feel grateful toward those who afflict us. Curiously, however, the dual narrator of *Mindkiller* (English professor Norman/cat burglar Joe) comes to accept violence and a strong leader, beyond good and evil, as necessary to social progress, even though that individual has been directly responsible for most of Norman/Joe's personal misery. As Maureen of *Callahan's Lady* shows, it is easy to confuse satisfaction of the revenge appetite with the warm feelings aroused by friends and home.

As a stylist, Robinson is quite word-conscious, perhaps excessively so. A hallmark of his writings is the pun, from the "Punday night" contests in *Callahan's Crosstime Saloon* to the "abominable multi-level puns" swapped by Raoul and Charlie at the conclusion of *Stardance*. Especially in *Telempath*, the function of the pun is to call into question the ability of language to express any external reality. Another facet of Robinson's densely woven style is a heavy use of allusion, especially to SF writers, situations, and language, but also to jazz and popular songs, and in *Stardance* to the traditions of modern dance and space colonization literature. Also, except in *Night of Power*, which does not use a first-person narrator, Robinson devotes a high proportion of text to dialogue and internal monologue (and in *Telempath* to documents), often reducing narration to mere stage direction. Such a style, more lyric than narrative, is appropriate for Robinson's SF, with its poetic vision of a secular "communion of saints."

The lyric quality of Robinson's SF is his means of fusing social critique with technological optimism, two themes that do not easily join in the hard SF universe, governed as it is by the logic of science. In *Telempath, Stardance*, and *Night of Power*, we view a world literally poisoned by the effects of modern technical society: pollution, social injustice, overpopulation, war, crime, and madness. In *Callahan's Crosstime Saloon*, redemption from this world is allotted to those who chance upon Callahan's refuge and are able to share in its feast of love and empathy. In the two apocalyptic novels, redemption is communal: a remnant of humanity moves onto a new evolutionary plane of physical, intellectual, and spiritual fusion, partly through fortunate alien encounters, but mostly because some human beings make benign use of the most advanced technologies. Furthermore, such redemption obliterates the oppositions, including that between technology and nature, which seem to structure human experience.

The lyricism is nearly absent from *Mindkiller*, a more conventional SF mystery novel that seems to yield to the totalitarian temptations inherent in the "fusion" or "communion" motif. Through a series of reversals, it asks us to accept its apparent villain, a sinister practitioner of mind control, as really a benevolent scientist who wishes only to save the world. Promoting the theme that great ends justify any means, it urges the amorality of technology and of the visionary leader, and it seems naively unrealistic about the ends of power. When Norman's identity is restored at the end, he characterizes the technology as "mindfill" instead of "mindkill," but he and the other enthusiasts of mental surgery seem little more than puppets mouthing a new party line. In *Time Pressure*, the story's "continuation" in the past, the theme of mind control is even more problematic. Sam is a paranoid loner, but he has the good sense to recognize that mindrape is not a healthy erotics of communication—until he is shot to death and no longer has a choice.

Robinson's myth of the future is one in which human initiative and technological advancement play an active part, aided at times by superior entities from outside normal time or space. In many of his fictions, Robinson portrays humankind as moving toward a mystical fusion of individual identity with something greater than the self. In other stories he imagines individual consciousness as atomistically alone, transcending this condition only through forced submission to a strong leader or even a puppet master. If *Mindkiller, Night of Power, Time Pressure*, and *Callahan's Lady* represent Robinson's matured vision of humanity, an originally hopeful thematics of redemption has yielded to a bleaker one of reciprocal violence and the will to power.

—John P. Brennan

---

**ROCKLYNNE, Ross** (Ross Louis Rocklin). American. Born in Cincinnati, Ohio, 21 February 1913. Educated at schools in Cincinnati. Married Frances Rosenthal in 1941 (divorced 1947); two sons. Worked as a story analyst for Warner Brothers and a literary agency, sewing machines salesman and repairman, cab driver, lumberjack, sales clerk, and building manager. *Died in October 1988.*

SCIENCE-FICTION PUBLICATIONS

Short Stories

*The Men and the Mirror.* New York, Ace, 1973.
*The Sun Destroyers.* New York, Ace, 1973.

Uncollected Short Stories

"The Doom that Came to Blagham," in *Witchcraft and Sorcery 10* (Alhambra, California), 1974.
"Emptying the Place," in *Fantastic* (New York), April 1975.
"They Fly So High," in *Amazing Science Fiction Anthology: The Wild Years 1946–55*, edited by Martin H. Greenberg. Lake Geneva, Wisconsin, TSR, 1987.

* * *

Ross Rocklynne was one of the important authors of magazine science fiction's middle years. He published his first story in *Astounding* in 1935, and for some 15 years was a regular contributor to a variety of science-fiction magazines. His work was of sufficiently high quality that L. Sprague de Camp wanted to include him as one of the 20 or so leading writers in the field for his *Science-Fiction Handbook* (1953). Both the key early anthologies of science fiction featured Ross Rocklynne stories: "Quietus" was in the Healy and McComas *Adventures in Time and Space* (1946), and "Jackdaw" was in the Groff Conklin *The Best of Science Fiction* (1946). From 1950, Rocklynne's appearances were more sporadic.

Although he wrote some short novels, Rocklynne concentrated on shorter works. It is possible that his avoidance of the longer lengths had made his name less well known than it should be. Usually a careful craftsman, he wrote many types of science fiction: competent space operas, time-travel stories, effective mood pieces, scientific puzzle stories, detective stories, and yarns spun around the Big Idea. Typical of the latter was "The Moth" (*Astounding*, 1939). Here—in 14 pages—he presented what John Campbell called "a wholly new idea for a spaceship drive" and for good measure threw in a fairly sophisticated picture of competing corporations.

Rocklynne also wrote a series of stories about a character named Hallmeyer. They are unfortunately largely forgotten today. Dealing with a "Bureau of Transmitted Egos," they are early examples of reshaping human beings to live on alien worlds. More than that, Hallmeyer was a person who *cared*. The stories have an atmosphere of compassion, of questioning basic values, of sadness. (For example, see "Task to Lahri," *Planet*, Summer 1942.) Indeed, there is an elegiac quality that pervades many of Rocklynne's better stories. The experimental side of Rocklynne appears most notably in his *Darkness* stories (1940 to 1951). They are concerned with the fates of sentient stars, and the writing is far removed from the usual styles of pulp fiction. The series was reworked as *The Sun Destroyers*.

Ross Rocklynne was never less than a capable storyteller. However, he tried to be more than that: he pushed himself instead of always taking the easy way. He was a major creator of the science fiction of the past, but he was also one of those who pointed the way ahead.

—Chad Oliver

---

**ROESSNER, Michaela.** American. Born in San Francisco, California. Educated at California College of Arts and Crafts, Oakland, B.F.A. in ceramics; Lone Mountain College, San Francisco, M.F.A. in painting. Married Richard C. Herman. Has worked as maskmaker, janitor, audio-visual technician, toy person for children's store, freelance office worker for arts and somatics organizations; and assistant editor, *Locus* magazine, 1980–81. Recipient: Crawford award, 1989; Campbell award, 1989. Agent: Merrillee Heifetz, Writers House, 21 West 26th Street, New York, New York 10010, U.S.A.

SCIENCE-FICTION PUBLICATIONS

Novel

*Walkabout Woman.* New York, Bantam, 1988.

* * *

If the setting of the first half of Michaela Roessner's debut novel were a faraway desert planet, then there would be no doubt that it is a science-fiction novel. But *Walkabout Woman* is set in the Australian Outback, and is undoubtedly a fantasy. Indeed, from the narrator's perspective it is a mainstream novel for two-thirds of its length. Such distinctions actually matter very little, but it serves, at least, to show the borderline Roessner treads in this novel.

The eponymous heroine of *Walkabout Woman* is Raba, a young Aboriginal woman who is a child when the novel opens. She has powers few of her tribe possess, and so she is taken on as an apprentice by the healing woman Djilbara. Their conversations reveal enormous detail about the tribal law and belief, beginning with why Raba's friend Huroo is believed to be of the Goanna clan: to Raba, he is clearly Emu. This is due to the clan of Huroo's true father, the evil Numada, and most of Raba's most serious problems are caused by him. The rest come from her explorations of the Dreamtime, that magical spirit world of the aboriginal peoples. There she finds great power, and great danger. Meanwhile, her abandoned body is found half-buried in the sand by a well-meaning missionary, and she is taken to the hospital. Having been dragged out of the Dreamtime like this, Raba finds herself seemingly caught between the two worlds, and she is pursued by the wraith-like Rainbow Serpents and other Dreamtime inhabitants.

During Raba's education, both in the missionary school, and with Djilbara, she learns about the role of women in Christian society. Roessner has researched deeply (there is a bibliography appended), and the secular life of the 1950's Aborigine is convincing and natural. The missionaries are well-intentioned but misguided; even the woman who recognises Raba's intelligence and tries to steer her towards studying "whitefella" medicine. They cannot come to terms with the nudity and casual sexuality of the young Aborigines. The Dreamtime aspects, presumably, are equally accurate, but to the genre reader, they feel like fantasy.

Raba must face Numada, for she knows his secret, and she has become Huroo's lover in secret (his official clan is taboo to her), after revealing his true parentage to him. Numada is the most powerful man in his tribe, and although Raba eventually escapes, it is at great personal cost. She finds herself in the mental hospital, trying to block out the pain, and eventually leaves her tribe behind and goes to the city, where she studies and becomes a professor of European history, seeking to deny her past. She succeeds, until a young Welsh woman comes seeking information on tribal customs. Raba's freak vulnerability and Gwyneth's obsessive probing lead to Raba's reluctant acquiescence. But Gwyneth has more disturbing aims—she believes that she can regain the ancient Welsh equivalent of the Dreaming, and she insists that Raba helps her. It is at this point that the novel becomes a true fantasy, as the two women battle.

Michaela Roessner goes deeper into the culture of the Aborigines than most fantasists, and gives her novel a strong handle on reality. It is not a light, cheerful novel; Raba is beset by tragedy and by torture, and the ending is only happy in relation to what goes immediately before. It is, perhaps, a relieved ending.

In contrast, Roessner's recent short story, "An Excerpt from the Confession of the Alchemist Edward Dee, Who Was Burnt in the City of Findias on the Planet Paracelsus, 1437 Post Imperial Colonial Period" (in *Full Spectrum 2*, New York, Doubleday, 1989), is closer to SF with its alternate worlds. The story questions whether knowledge prevents us from seeing things and whether the simpler mind is really more open.

*Walkabout Woman* gained plenty of attention, not least because of the author's spell working for *Locus*. The depth of her research suggests that she may never be prolific, but her books will be awaited with interest.

—Kev P. McVeigh

---

**ROGERS, Pat.** *See* **PORGES, Arthur.**

---

**ROHMER, Richard (H).** Canadian. Born in Hamilton, Ontario, 24 January 1924. Educated at Fort Erie High School, Ontario; Assumption College, University of Western Ontario, London, B.A. 1948; Osgoode Hall, Toronto; read law with Phelan O'Brien and Phelan: called to Ontario bar 1951, to Northwest Territories bar 1970; Queen's Counsel, 1961. Served in the Royal Canadian Air Force, 1942–45: Distinguished Flying Cross, 1945; in the Royal Canadian Naval Reserve, 1946–48; Royal Canadian Air Force Auxiliary, 1950–53; Wing Commander; Honorary Colonel of 411 Air Reserve Squadron, 1971; Senior Air Reserve Adviser to the Chief of the Defence Staff and the Commander of Air Command: Brigadier-General, 1975; Commander, Air Reserve Group, 1976; Chief of Reserves of the Canadian Armed Forces, 1978–81: Major General. Married Mary Olivier Whiteside; two daughters. Since 1951, lawyer: partner, Rohmer and Swayze; counsel, Frost and Redway, Toronto; currently, counsel, Macaulay Lipson and Joseph, Toronto, and Bellamy Besse Augaitis and Vandergust, Collingwood, Ontario. Chairman, Royal Commission on Book Publishing, 1971–72; counsel, Royal Commission on Metropolitan Toronto, 1975–77. Since 1978, chancellor, University of Windsor, Ontario. Recipient: Centennial Medal, 1967; Northwest Territories Commissioner's award for Public Service, 1972; Jubilee Medal, 1977; Foundation for the Advancement of Canadian Letters award, 1984. LL.D.: University of Windsor. Commander, Order of St. John; Commander, Order of Military Merit, 1978. Address: c/o Irwin Publishing, 1800 Steels Avenue West, Concord, Ontario L4K 2P3, Canada.

### SCIENCE-FICTION PUBLICATIONS

Novels (series: Separation)

*Ultimatum*. Toronto, Clarke Irwin, and New York, Pocket Books, 1973.
*Exxoneration*. Toronto, McClelland and Stewart, 1974.
*Exodus/UK*. Toronto, McClelland and Stewart, 1975.
*Separation*. Toronto, McClelland and Stewart, 1976.
*Balls!* Don Mills, Ontario, General, 1979.
*Periscope Red*. Don Mills, Ontario, General, and New York, Beaufort, 1980.
*Separation Two*. Don Mills, Ontario, Paperjacks, 1981.
*Triad*. Don Mills, Ontario, General, 1981; New York, Beaufort, 1982.
*Retaliation*. Don Mills, Ontario, General, 1982.
*Starmageddon*. Toronto, Irwin, 1986.

### OTHER PUBLICATIONS

Novels

*Rommel and Patton: A Novel*. Toronto, Irwin, 1986.
*Hour of the Fox*. New York, New American Library, 1988.

Verse

*Images*. Don Mills, Ontario, General, 1981.

Other

*The Green North: Mid-Canada*. Toronto, Maclean Hunter, 1970.
*The Arctic Imperative: An Overview of the Energy Crisis*. Toronto, McClelland and Stewart, 1973.
*E. P. Taylor* (biography). Toronto, McClelland and Stewart, 1978.
*Patton's Gap: An Account of the Battle of Normandy 1944*. Don Mills, Ontario, General, New York, Beaufort, and London, Arms and Armour Press, 1981.
*Massacre 747*. Don Mills, Ontario, Paperjacks, 1984, as *Massacre 007: The Story of the Korean Air Lines Flight 007*, Sevenoaks, Coronet, 1984.
*How to Write a Bestseller*. Toronto, McClelland and Stewart, 1984.
*Red Arctic*. Markham, Ontario, Fitzhenry and Whiteside, 1989.

*   *   *

Richard Rohmer's novels only qualify for the epithet "science fiction" by virtue of their settings, which are projections of the contemporary international policial, economic, and military arena. As tales of the near future, they are ephemeral works, their fictional prognostications soon invalidated by historical reality (*Exodus/UK*, published in 1975, is set in the late 1970's, but the events narrated therein bear little resemblance to the actual political developments of the latter part of that decade).

They perhaps fit more permanently, within the science-fiction framework, as alternative histories; nevertheless, their plots, characters, and narrative style have closer affinities with political thrillers than science fiction.

All the novels deal with various political and economic intrigues and are made convincing by Rohmer's personal knowledge of the worlds of the law, politics, and the military. His stories are particularly persuasive when they describe major global events, such as the bankruptcy of Britain, due to the withdrawal of Arab monies, in *Exodus/UK*; the events leading up to the annexation of Canada, in *Ultimatum*; the Canadian take-over of the two American banks, in *Retaliation*; the natural gas crisis, in *Balls!* But while the construction of such realistic scenarios is Rohmer's major strength, the presentation of his *dramatis personae*, within these settings, is his major weakness. His characters are wooden and heavily stereotyped, given unrealistic dialogue (often for the sake of explication), and are frequently limited by a somewhat sexist representation. The male-female relationships are handled without subtlety—hard-drinking men seducing attractive and ambitious women—and conform to clichéd soap opera conventions (e.g., in *Retaliation* Samantha Scott, described as a handsome woman, unlikely to turn heads, is transformed when she removes her glasses).

All of the novels follow a consistent pattern of narrative technique, characterisation, and plot development. The chief part of each story is the description of an event (e.g., an energy crisis, take-over bid, military exercise) in which the characters are largely embodiments of certain prevailing elements within our society—what E.M. Forster would call "flat characters," built around a single idea or quality (the military man, the captain of industry, the superpower leader, etc). Inserted into general stream of the plot are some gratuitous digressions in a sensational vein (such as the Prime Minister's plane crash in *Exodus/UK* and the kidnapping of Dr. Huber's daughter in *Retaliation*), which do nothing to develop the characters or the plot and, I suspect, exist in order to make the rather impersonal central themes more immediately exciting. Another technique Rohmer uses, to this end, is the alternation of different streams, in an attempt to create an episodic cliff-hanger effect. A number of the stories have sequels: *Ultimatum* is followed by *Exxoneration; Exodus/UK* is followed by *Separation* and *Separation Two; Periscope Red* is followed by *Triad*.

Rohmer's novels reflect some of the most powerful examples of social-Darwinism that occur in our society, particularly among the upper levels of international politics and multinational business, in which the balance of power shifts in vast, impersonal games of profit and loss. However, rather than questioning and analysing these games, Rohmer constructs his narratives in simple affirmation of his acute right-wing philosophies. At times his work reflects particularly Canadian concerns—such as the divisionalism in Canadian provinces and the threat of succession.

Rohmer is, on the one hand, a writer with an impressive imagination, has considerable experience in the areas about which he writes and presents imminently plausible projections of modern-day events, yet, on the other hand, he is very much limited by artificial and clumsy technique, awkward plots and blunty stereotyped characterisations. Nevertheless, his books are popular with his audience, all of them best-sellers in his native Canada.

—Mark Warwick Leahy

---

**ROSE, Lawrence W.** *See* **FEARN, John Russell.**

---

**ROSHWALD, Mordecai (Marceli).** American. Born in Drohobycz, Poland, 26 May 1921. Educated at Hebrew University, Jerusalem, M.A. 1942, Ph.D. in philosophy 1947. Served in the Israeli Army, 1950–51. Married Miriam Wyszynski in 1945; one son. Lecturer, Israel Institute of Public Administration, Tel-Aviv, 1947–51, and Hebrew University, 1951–55. Visiting Lecturer, Brooklyn College, Summer 1956. Visiting Professor, Israel Institute of Technology, Haifa, 1963–64, Spring 1978, Spring 1988, University of Bath, Spring 1966, and Simon Fraser University, Burnaby, British Columbia, Summer 1971, 1972–73. Recipient: McKnight Foundation Humanities award, 1962, 1963. Address: G-2 Glacier Drive, Nashua, New Hampshire 03062; or, Humanities Program, University of Minnesota, Minneapolis, Minnesota 55455, U.S.A.

### Science-Fiction Publications

#### Novels

*Level Seven*. London, Heinemann, 1959; New York, McGraw Hill, 1960.
*A Small Armageddon*. London, Heinemann, 1962; New York, New American Library, 1976.

#### Uncollected Short Stories

"The Politics of Ratology," in *The Nation* (New York), 17 September 1960.
"Awakening in Olympus," in *The Nation* (New York), 30 January 1967.

### Other Publications

#### Other

*Adam ve'Hinukho* (Man and Education). Tel-Aviv, Dvir, 1954.
*Humanism in Practice*. London, Watts, 1955.
*Moses, Leader, Prophet, Man*, with Miriam Roshwald. New York, Yoseloff, 1969.

*

Mordecai Roshwald comments:

I became involved in fiction writing through concern about the menace to humanity from nuclear armament, as well as out of a sense of disenchantment with some aspects of modern life. However, an involvement in this kind of writing creates a momentum of its own, as it releases half-hidden emotions and sentiments in the writer's mind. Thus, in a way, I have become a fiction writer, intent on not neglecting this kind of self-expression and public address, despite my regular academic commitments to teaching and scholarly research, as well as occasional journalistic writing. The diversity of my activity does not prevent me from looking for a common denominator, a philosophy common to these varied efforts. Indeed, I believe I have maintained a fairly consistent approach throughout the different modes of expression.

The science fiction I have written is very much coloured by social, political, and cultural concern. Indeed, science fiction is for me a *form* of expression rather than an objective in its own right. In this sense I would classify it with such books as Swift's *Gulliver's Travels* or Huxley's *Brave New World*, rather than with some modern stories dealing with inter-stellar warfare, monsters from distant planets, and the like (unless such stories are used as parables). Though my main success as a fiction writer was due to the success of *Level Seven*, classified as science fiction, I do not feel restricted to this literary form.

* * *

Mordecai Roshwald's first book, *Level Seven*, is perhaps the most chilling of all warnings about the new and unlimited dangers of thermonuclear war—such as Nevil Shute's *On the Beach*, Eugene Burdick and Harvey Wheeler's *Fail Safe*, Peter George's *Red Alert*, and others. The story begins as the Pushbutton Officer X-127 is taken down the one-way escalator 4000 feet to Level 7, the deepest in his country's shelter system and the control centre for its offensive weapons. The personnel on this level have numbers and opinions, but not names and faces; they have an atomic reactor for power, synthetic food for 500 years, and taped music for amusement. Marriage is permitted and plans are made for raising children to carry on life as troglodytes after the inevitable war. Finally the order comes (set off, we learn, by an accidental rocket firing), X-127 and his colleagues push all their buttons and the surface of the planet is destroyed. Gradually, as the radiation penetrates deeper, the other Levels and those of the enemy and the neutrals falls silent. Level 7 itself is flooded with radiation from its faulty reactor, and X-127 dies with the others, huddled in his bunk and dreaming of the sun. The terrifying effect of *Level Seven* depends on the absolute inevitability of its outcome. The feeble protests of X-117, a button-pusher who refuses to do his duty, only underscore the iron determinism of the system. If the story were recast in more mundane and conventional form, using real characters instead of numbered abstractions, much of its unique capacity to convince and frighten would probably be lost.

We see the other side of the coin in Roshwald's second novel, *A Small Armageddon*. In this peculiar tale, a group of officers of the American nuclear submarine *Polar Lion* hold a clandestine drinking party while the ship is on patrol. When the captain finds them, a scuffle takes place in which the captain is killed. The submarine proceeds to cruise the world, exacting tribute under threat of its missiles. It is finally destroyed in an exchange of fire with a Minuteman base which has been taken over by religious fanatics. Meanwhile neo-Nazis have captured missile bases in Germany, and the African state of Qunta-Qunta announces its own demands, backed by three hydrogen bombs that it has managed to buy or steal.

*Level Seven* depends on the notion that heads of state are irresponsible maniacs. Its abstract nature enables the reader to believe this, at least enough to give the story a profound impact. *A Small Armageddon* requires us to believe that malcontents and fanatics can easily gain control of nuclear weapons. It fails because of Roshwald's failure to make either people or situations even remotely credible. Submarine officers are not sophomores who wait till the captain is asleep to hold booze parties. Armed civilians cannot take over a functional missile base as bandits might a supermarket. *Level Seven* is an effective work produced by an author who cannot handle the demands of mainstream fiction; as such; the book is interesting as an SF boundary marker as well as for its own real and unique terror.

—E.R. Bishop

---

**ROTSLER, William.** Also writes as William Arrow; John Ryder Hall. American. Born in Los Angeles, California, 3 July 1926. Educated at Ventura Junior College, California, 1946; Los Angeles County Art Institute, 1947–50. Served in the United States Army, 1944–45. Married Marian Abney in 1953 (divorced 1958); one daughter. Rancher in Camarillo, California, 1942–44, 1946; sculptor, 1950–59. Since 1959, photographer and film maker: writer, producer, and director of commercials, documentaries, and industrial and feature films. Recipient: *Locus* award, for artwork, 1971, 1972, 1973; Hugo award, for artwork, 1975, 1977, 1979. Guest of honor, 31st World Science Fiction Convention, 1973. Agent: Richard Curtis Associates, Box 11J, 75 East End Avenue, New York, New York 10028, U.S.A.

### Science-Fiction Publications

Novels (series: Zandra)

*Patron of the Arts*. New York, Ballantine, 1974; Morley, Yorkshire, Elmfield Press, 1975.
*Futureworld* (novelization of screenplay; as John Ryder Hall). New York, Ballantine, 1976.
*Man, The Hunted Animal* (novelization of TV play; as William Arrow). New York, Ballantine, 1976.
*To the Land of the Electric Angel*. New York, Ballantine, 1976.
*Visions of Nowhere* (novelization of TV play; as William Arrow). New York, Ballantine, 1976.
*Zandra*. New York, Doubleday, 1978.
*Iron Man: Call My Killer . . . Modok*. New York, Pocket Books, 1979.
*Dr. Strange*. New York, Pocket Books, 1979.
*The Far Frontier*. Chicago, Playboy Press, 1980.
*Shiva Descending*, with Gregory Benford. New York, Avon, and London, Sphere, 1980.
*The Hidden Worlds of Zandra*. New York, Doubleday, 1983.

Short Stories

*Star Trek II Short Stories*. New York, Simon and Schuster, 1982.
*Star Trek III Short Stories*. New York, Wanderer, and London, Ravette, 1984.

### Other Publications

Novels

*Superstud*. Los Angeles, Holloway, 1975.
*Supermouth*. Los Angeles, Holloway, 1975.
*Supertongue and Other Turn Ons*. Los Angeles, Holloway, 1975.
*Sinbad and the Eye of the Tiger* (novelization of screenplay; as John Ryder Hall). New York, Pocket Books, 1977.
*Mr. Merlin 1–2* (novelizations of TV series). New York, Simon and Schuster, 2 vols., 1981; London, Beaver, 2 vols., 1982.

*Grease 2* (novelization of screenplay). New York, Simon and Schuster, and London, Sphere, 1982.
Joanie Loves Chachi:
*Secrets*. New York, Simon and Schuster, 1982.
*A Test of Hearts*. New York, Simon and Schuster, 1982.
*The Pirate Movie*. New York, Simon and Schuster, 1982.
*Distress Call*. New York, Simon and Schuster, 1982.
*Vice Squad*. New York, Pinnacle, 1982.
The A-Team (novelization of TV series):
*Defense Against Terror*. New York, Simon and Schuster, 1983.
*The Danger Maze*. New York, Simon and Schuster, 1983; London, Target, 1985.
*The Love Boat: Voyage of Love* (novelization of TV series). New York, Simon and Schuster, 1983.
*Magnum, P.I.: Maui Mystery* (novelization of TV series). New York, Simon and Schuster, 1983.
*The Vulcan Treasure*. New York, Simon and Schuster, 1983; London, Ravette, 1984.
*Staying Alive* (novelization of screenplay). New York, Simon and Schuster, 1983.
*It's Your Move* (novelization of TV series). New York, Pocket, 1984.
*Cavern of Horror* (for children; novelization of *Goonies* screenplay). New York, Wanderer, and London, Corgi, 1985.

Plays

Screenplays: *The Agony of Love*, 1966; *The Girl with Hungry Eyes*, 1966; *Four Kinds of Love*, 1967; *Suburban Pagans*, 1967; *Like It Is*, 1968; *Mantis in Lace (Lila)*, 1968; *A Taste of Hot Lead*, 1969; *Shannon's Women*, 1969; *The Godson*, 1969; *She Did What He Wanted*, 1970; *Midnight*, 1970.

Other

*Contemporary Erotic Cinema*. New York, Ballantine, 1973.

*

Theatrical Activities:
Director: **Films**—all his screenplays.
Actor: **Films**—*The Notorious Daughter of Fanny Hill*, 1966; *The Agony of Love*, 1966; *Shannon's Women*, 1969; *The Secret Sex Life of Romeo and Juliet*, 1970.

* * *

William Rotsler is one of the few SF writers who has also achieved fame as a cartoonist. His distinctive style of cartooning has proven popular for over 30 years, and he writes frequently on the arts for such monthlies as *Adam*. It is little wonder, then, that Rotsler's first novel, *Patron of the Arts*, is about the nature of the artistic process. Rotsler attempts in this novel to determine the social effects of a *Gesamstwerk*, an attempt at the total union of the arts through a synthesis of holography and electronic music. This novel succeeds to the extent that the ideas it contains are reflections of authentic experience, but Rotsler's extrapolative sense is not keen, and the novel can best be characterised as an interesting failure.

From his promising first novel, Rotsler's work quickly declined. Rotsler has tried a career as a commercial entertainer, but fails to provide that depth of characterisation and intellection that the best popular writers, such as Poul Anderson and Gordon Dickson, provide. His later novels are mere repetition of formulas without any distinctive presence. His favourite formula is that of the Ship of Fools, a cast of various racial and sexual types gathered together to face a perilous situation. Thus in *Zandra* the varied cast is drawn together after their cruiseship passes through the Bermuda Triangle into another dimension. In *Shiva Descending* (with Gregory Benford) the cast faces the familiar peril of a meteor about to destroy Earth. Rotsler and Benford mine this tired lode of apocalyptic fiction to little effect. Rotsler's worst novel, however, is *The Far Frontier*. In this work, Rotsler fulfills the worst fantasies of those mundane critics who insist that science fiction is nothing more than Western formulas transported to a wider setting. Rotsler has replied with a novel complete with interstellar Indians, space cows, and planet rustlers. Rarely does one read a novel where the writer rejoices in its trashy content; such, unfortunately, is the case with *The Far Frontier*.

Rotsler, then, after achieving promise as a first novelist, has reneged upon that promise with his later novels. He is less important for his writings than for his cartoons, which have the distinction and wit that his novels lack.

—Martin Morse Wooster

---

**ROUSSEAU, Victor** (Victor Rousseau Emanuel). Also wrote as H.M. Egbert. American. Born in London, in 1879. Lived in South Africa at the turn of the century; emigrated to the United States, and wrote for pulp magazines until 1941. *Died 5 April 1960.*

Science-Fiction Publications

Novels

*The Messiah of the Cylinder*. Chicago, McClurg, and London, Curtis Brown, 1917; as *The Apostle of the Cylinder*, London, Hodder and Stoughton, 1918.
*Draught of Eternity* (as H.M. Egbert). London, Long, 1924.
*The Sea Demons* (as H.M. Egbert). London, Long, 1924; as Victor Rousseau, Westport, Connecticut, Hyperion Press, 1976.

Other Publications

Novels

*Derwent's Horse*. London, Methuen, 1901.
*Wooden Spoil*. New York, Doran, 1919; London, Hodder and Stoughton, 1923.
*The Big Muskeg*. Cincinnati, Stewart Kidd, 1921; London, Hodder and Stoughton, 1923.
*The Lion's Jaw*. London, Hodder and Stoughton, 1923.
*The Home Trail*. London, Hodder and Stoughton, 1924.
*The Big Man of Bonne Chance*. London, Hodder and Stoughton, 1925.
*The Golden Horde*. London, Hodder and Stoughton, 1926.

Novels as H.M. Egbert

*Jacqueline of Golden River*. New York, Doubleday, 1920; London, Hodder and Stoughton, 1924.
*My Lady of the Nile*. London, Hodder and Stoughton, 1923.
*The Big Malopo*. London, Long, 1924.

*Eric of the Strong Heart.* London, Long, 1925.
*Mrs. Aladdin.* London, Long, 1925.
*Salted Diamonds.* London, Long, 1926.
*Winding Trails.* London, Long, 1927.

Novels as V.R. Emanuel

*The Story of John Paul.* London, Constable, 1923.
*Middle Years.* New York, Minton Balch, 1925.
*The Selmans.* New York, Dial Press, 1925.

Plays

Screenplays: *West of the Rainbow's End*, with Daisy Kent, 1926; *Wanderer of the West*, with Arthur Hoerl and W. Ray Johnston, 1927; *Prince of the Plains*, with Arthur Hoerl, 1927; *Lightnin' Shot*, with J.P. McGowan, 1928; *Trailin' Back*, with Arthur Hoerl and J.P. McGowan, 1928.

* * *

Victor Rousseau's stories spring out immediately and absorb the reader with global plots and bold valiance. Rousseau's rare talent is to combine medieval values and Louis L'Amour's style in the science-fiction context. The result provides sentimental satisfaction. The amusement in reading Rousseau is similar to the *Star Wars* experience in cinema. Both *The Messiah of the Cylinder* and *The Sea Demons* present strong heroes and execrable villains.

Even if the "daring sexual implications" that the promotion page of *The Sea Demons* promise are hard to find, there are enough imagination and activity in the macrocosmic plots to satisfy thrill-seeking readers. In *The Messiah of the Cylinder*, our hero (Arnold) and his foul antagonist are prep school mates. One of their school-mates, Herman Lagaroff, invents the 100-year time-lock cylinder that transports the two men (and the pristine maiden whom they both love) into the year 2017. The time forwarding is believably described, involving Arnold's tortuous arrival in the strange London of 2017: "I flung myself upon my face and prayed, with all my will, to die." The story of these books is similar to Wells's *A Modern Utopia* and *When the Sleeper Wakes*. The time travelers in Rousseau's work are propelled into a barbarous authoritarian nightmare, however, where "the dull and the base" are categorized by size of cranium. "The Prophet Wells," as he is referred to by Rousseau, would be aghast at the cold brutality of the rational society as it is portrayed in *The Messiah*. The triumphant ending in *The Messiah* includes the destruction and overthrow of the (fascist) government, the outlawing of divorce, and a return to a "ruling class bound to its traditions of public service." Where Wells asserts the final victory of reason, Rousseau longs for a futuristic theocracy. The priests would be happier than the scientists in Rousseau's future. Nonetheless, Rousseau exhibits a vivid technological imagination. He writes about solar power, plausible flying machines, and a communication network similar to the current and projected reality. The sinister government's effective propagandistic use of the media is a startling reminder of the current world situation.

The plot of *The Sea Demon* is commonplace, and the story is similar to *The Messiah*. The strange sea creatures who are struggling to take over the world are discovered by noble Captain Donald Paget. Gallantry overcoming the hideous threat is the main course: Donald "raised the girl in his arms, and felt one of the blubbery flippers on his hand . . . the stinging flippers sucked the blood from his face and hands . . . but Donald could not lose with Ida's life at stake." The battle to save the world intensifies to involve all governments and world resources. The story culminates in suicidal frenzy as the Queen Sea Beast dies of a broken heart and leaves the hordes without leadership, which we all know leads immediately to destruction.

The enduring impressions one gets of Rousseau are staunch traditionalism and faith in a well-ordered universe. Rousseau is good for a cheerful escape from heady ambiguity, and the pleasures of a frantic plot with the sugar-coated conclusion never in doubt.

—Peter Lynch

---

**RUCKER, Rudy** (Rudolph von Bitter Rucker). American. Born in Louisville, Kentucky, 22 March 1946. Educated at Swarthmore College, Pennsylvania, B.A. in mathematics 1967; Rutgers University, New Brunswick, New Jersey, M.A. 1969, Ph.D. 1973. Married Sylvia Bogsch in 1967; two daughters and one son. Assistant Professor, State University of New York, Geneseo, 1972–78; Alexander von Humboldt Foundation Research Grantee, University of Heidelberg, 1978–80; Associate Professor, Randolph-Macon Woman's College, Lynchburg, Virginia, 1980–82. Since 1982, freelance writer. Recipient: Philip K. Dick Memorial award, 1983. Agent: Susan Protter, 110 West 40th Street, New York, New York 10018. Address: 1324 Church Street, Lynchburg, Virginia 24504 U.S.A.

Science-Fiction Publications

Novels

*White Light.* London, Virgin, and New York, Ace, 1980.
*Spacetime Donuts.* New York, Ace, 1981.
*Software.* New York, Ace, 1982.
*The Sex Sphere.* New York, Ace, 1983.
*Master of Space and Time.* New York, Bluejay, 1984.
*The Secret of Life.* New York, Bluejay, 1985.
*All the Visions*, with *Space Baltics*, by Anselm Hollo. Mountain View, California, Ocean View, 1990.

Short Stories

*The Fifty-Seventh Franz Kafka.* New York, Ace, 1983.

Other Publications

Verse

*Light Fuse and Get Away.* Lynchburg, Virginia, Carp, 1983.

Other

*Geometry, Relativity, and the Fourth Dimension.* New York, Dover, and London, Constable, 1977.
*Infinity and the Mind: The Science and Philosophy of the Infinite.* Cambridge, Massachusetts, Birkhauser, and Brighton, Harvester, 1982.
*The Fourth Dimension: A Guided Tour of the Higher Universe.* Boston, Houghton Mifflin, 1985; as *The Fourth Dimension: And How To Get There*, London, Rider, 1985.
*Mind Tools: The Five Levels of Mathematical Reality.* New York, Houghton Mifflin, 1987; London, Penguin, 1988.

*Wetware*. New York, Avon, 1988; London, New English Library, 1989.

*Transreal!* Englewood, Colorado, WCS, 1991.

Editor, *Speculations on the Fourth Dimension: Selected Writings of Charles H. Hinton*. New York, Dover, and London, Constable, 1980.

Editor, *Mathenauts: Tales of Mathematical Wonder*. New York, Arbor House, 1987; London, New English Library, 1989.

Editor, *The Hollow Earth: The Narrative of Mason Algiers Reynolds of Virginia*. New York, Morrow, 1990.

*

Rudy Rucker comments:

An unusual thing about my work is that I write popular speculative mathematics books as well as fiction. To some degree the fiction serves as a laboratory for thought-experiments related to my scientific and philosophical investigations.

Another aspect of my fiction is that much of it is, on a higher level, autobiographical. I call the device of writing about one's life in SF terms *transrealism*. Taken in sequence, *Secret of Life, White Light*, and *Sex Sphere* make up a transrealist trilogy.

My non-fiction has largely been devoted to expanding the range of things that people are able to think and talk about. Infinity and higher dimensions are of particular interest to me.

* * *

In his works of science fiction and science fact, Rudy Rucker extrapolates new physical and psychological modes of existence from current possibilities. He pursues these extrapolations by exploring how the mind can manipulate the physical universe and hence distort our commonsense perceptions of the world. The results of these distortions are a renewed sense of wonder about the external world and an enhancement of the internal world through increased self awareness.

Rucker frequently takes his hero or heroes—and vicariously, of course, the reader—on a mental journey toward some higher plane of reality. Sometimes this journey involves altering our world by imagining a concept from theoretical physics into an everyday reality. In *Master of Space and Time*, Fletcher and Harry physically occupy Hilbert space and, in the process, allow an alternate version of Harry to escape into our world. This inversion of Harry's affable, disordered personality—Gerry Herber, a figment of Harry's imagination run wild—unleashes a reign of terror that preys upon the weakest elements of society. Herber threatens to eradicate the independent thought and action that made him a physical reality in the first place. Furthermore, Fletcher and Harry are themselves the product of Alwin Bitter's imagination. Bitter's preoccupation with Hilbert space willed them into existence and manipulated their experiment, and, like Gerry Herber, they threaten the balance of the physical world. Similarly, through the imagination, a young Alwin Bitter in *The Sex Sphere* achieves first the transformation of the city of Heidelberg into a degraded carnival of sexual activity and then a return to normalcy. A hypersphere trapped in three-dimensional space and the others it spawns have varacious sexual appetites and an intense aversion to human females. The emotional ties that bind Bitter to a normal life become increasingly precarious. When they reach a breaking point, he wills into existence a world in which sexual gratification becomes completely divorced from human involvement. There are no females, only sex spheres. Bitter's wife reestablishes ties with him, and he wills the sex spheres and his experiences in Germany away. In both of these novels, Rucker imagines for us a world transformed by an idea and infinite possibilities for the recursion of this transformation.

In addition to theoretical concepts, machines are also the catalysts for the journeys Rucker's heroes take. The possibilities opened up by computers form the basis for several of Rucker's novels, and like concepts, physical objects can alter everyday reality in unexpected ways. In *Infinity and the Mind*, Rucker suggests that computers may one day become self-replicating and through natural selection mimic the intuition and subtlety of human thought. Further, he speculates that because of more favorable environmental conditions on the moon, computers may eventually form their own separate society there. This speculation forms the basis of the novel *Software* in which an old man strives for immortality and a young man for his connection to the rest of the human race. In *Software*, computers have achieved a rough parity with humans, and Rucker explores that delicate balance as humans fend off the computer's efforts to "eat their brains" and thus deprive them of their humanity. In *Spacetime Donuts*, the balance has shifted in favor of computers. They control most aspects of human activity, from dispensing food—a tasteless concoction called "dream food"—to plugging into the human consciousness every night and supplying mankind with dreams. Computers provide immediate gratification of all human needs, and men are little more than useless appendages of one large computer that rules the state. The novel explores one man's journey back to his own humanity with the help of theoretical physics and the revolution caused by that journey.

While the journeys prompted by ideas and technology threaten Rucker's heroes and their worlds, each journey ends in an affirmation of humanity. People become more aware and more open to their husbands, wives, lovers, children; people realize the best in themselves; people die because they are old and because death is the way the human race replenishes itself. This human affirmation brings a restoration of normalcy and with it an enhanced sense of wonder about the everyday world. This sense of wonder is what science fiction is all about.

—Terri Paul

---

**RUPPERT, Chester.** *See* **PHILLIPS, Rog.**

---

**RUSS, Joanna.** American. Born in New York City, 22 February 1937. Educated at Cornell University, Ithaca, New York, B.A. 1957; Yale University School of Drama, New Haven, Connecticut, M.F.A. 1960. Married Albert Amateau in 1963 (divorced 1967). Lecturer in Speech, Queensborough Community College, New York, 1966–67; Instructor, 1967–70, and Assistant Professor of English, 1970–72, Cornell University; Assistant Professor of English, State University of New York, Binghamton, 1972–73, 1974–75, and University of Colorado, Boulder, 1975–77. Associate Professor, 1977–84, and since 1984, Professor of English, University of Washington, Seattle. Occasional book reviewer, *Fantasy and Science Fiction*, 1966–79. Recipient: Nebula award, 1972, 1983; National Endowment for the Humanities Fellowship, 1974; Hugo award, 1983; *Locus* award, 1983. Agent: Ellen Levine Literary Agency, 15 East 26th Street, Suite 1801, New York, New York 10010. Address: Department of English, University of Washington, Seattle, Washington 98195, U.S.A.

### Science-Fiction Publications

#### Novels

*Picnic on Paradise.* New York, Ace, 1968; London, Macdonald, 1969.
*And Chaos Died.* New York, Ace, 1970.
*The Female Man.* New York, Bantam, 1975; London, Star, 1977.
*We Who Are About to . . . .* New York, Dell, 1977; London, Women's Press, 1987.
*Kittatinny: A Tale of Magic* (for children). New York, Daughters, 1978.
*The Two of Them.* New York, Berkley, 1978; London, Women's Press, 1986.
*On Strike Against God.* New York, Out and Out, 1980; London, Women's Press, 1987.
*Extra (Ordinary) People.* New York, St. Martin's Press, 1984; London, Women's Press, 1985.
*Souls,* with *Houston, Houston, Do You Read?,* by James Tiptree, Jr. New York, Tor, 1989.

#### Short Stories

*Alyx.* Boston, Gregg Press, 1976.
*The Adventures of Alyx.* New York, Pocket Books, 1983; London, Women's Press, 1985.
*The Zanzibar Cat.* Sauk City, Wisconsin, Arkham House, 1983.
*The Hidden Side of the Moon.* New York, St. Martin's Press, 1987; London, Women's Press, 1989.

### Other Publications

#### Play

*Window Dressing,* in *The New Woman's Theatre,* edited by Honor Moore. New York, Random House, 1977.

#### Other

*How to Suppress Women's Writing.* Austin, University of Texas Press, 1983; London, Women's Press, 1984.
*Magic Mommas, Trembling Sisters, Puritans and Perverts: Feminist Essays.* Trumansburg, New York, Crossing Press, 1985.

* * *

During the 1960's, Joanna Russ emerged as one of the most talented and provocative writers of science fiction's New Wave. While Russ identifies herself primarily as a feminist, she is equally well known for her experimental way of handling the conventional materials and narrative strategies of science fiction. Since Russ is opposed to all social fixities and intellectual givens, her major effort as a science-fiction writer has been to explore alternate realities and create new myths, especially ones that depict women as complex human subjects.

Russ's apprentice work is feminist only obliquely. Ostensibly, she aims at an interesting mix of historic fantasy and the supernatural, a combination she continues to use in her later work. The initial run of stories exploits the theme of the after-life to fresh effect. "Nor Custom Stale" (in *Fantasy and Science Fiction* September 1959) her first story, is untypically set in the future. It describes a bourgeois couple who live stubbornly immured in a future-tech "House" while catastrophic ages pass unnoticed outside; domestic monotony preserves them in a living death. Several of the stories are set in the 19th century, an era Russ understands but dislikes. "Mr. Wilde's Second Chance" (in *Fantasy and Science Fiction* September 1966) is a wry account of the dead poet's renunciation of an opportunity to live a conventionally tasteful second life. In "There Is Another Shore . . .," a revenant young woman, a kind of female Keats, returns to her deathplace in Rome to taste "the fullness of life" in romantic adventure. The ironic promise of this story—that if life for the 19th-century woman was death, death was liberation—is also the germ for "My Dear Emily," whose sober young heroine is passionately emancipated when she becomes a vampire. Part of the wit of such stories is their literary allusiveness; "My Dear Emily" condenses the romantic plot of *Wuthering Heights.*

With her first Alyx stories, Russ introduces a character new to science fiction, an adventuress whose daring and cunning issue from her womanly strength. Set in ancient Phoenicia, these stories launch her on a career as a soldier of fortune. In her natural setting, Alyx is of necessity an outlaw sensibility—a rationalist in a world of superstitious mystique, an imaginist in a world of empty, brutal pragmatism: in short, Russ implies, the ancestor of the intelligent modern woman. *Picnic on Paradise,* also build around Alyx, casts her again as an outlaw, here a ruthlessly sensible, martially skilled Trans-Temp agent abstracted from Tyre to a future world wasted by advanced capitalist war. Alyx is Russ's *agent provocateur*: neither Amazon nor androgyne, she foils both old and new notions of the feminine ideal. At the same time, her unromantic heroics are designed to satirize the "he-man ethos" of Sword and Sorcery. For all its modesty in plot and narrative strategy, *Picnic on Paradise* may be Russ's most inventive novel.

It was closely followed by another ground-breaking novel of the future and several increasingly accomplished shorter fantasies. *And Chaos Died* is at once a penetrating social critique and a lyrical celebration of a psionic near-utopia. Russ maroons her hero on a pastoral planet where he is drawn into an egalitarian community and taught psi-powers. What is really new in the novel is its style: the magic arbitrariness of the narrator's experience is rendered by a stream-of-expanding-consciousness technique that registers his initial nausea, then his growing joy, and finally his disgust when he is returned to a dystopic earth wholly given over to violence and mental imperialism. In the novelette "The Second Inquisition," Russ makes a poignantly funny story of one of her central concerns, a young girl's need for a worthy feminine model to counteract her social training in self-extinction. The tutelary genius in this case is a Trans-Temp agent from a non-sexist future world. The heroine of "The Zanzibar Cat" is yet another Alyx-like subversive ironist, a medieval miller's daughter who faces down a lord of Fantasyland. By the end of the tale, the humble milleress has grown into the mother of all meaning, the author. The archaic setting of "The Zanzibar Cat" and the Hellenistic background of "Poor Man, Beggar Man," a story that splits the historic Alexander into ego and ghostly alter ego, testify to Russ's continuing interest in unwritten history.

With "When It Changed" and "Nobody's Home," Russ reached a new level of achievement. These visions of an emancipated future for women on the wistfully named Whileaway are thorough reconstructions of the standard manless-world story. They are utopian, but only in a special sense: the particular virulence of male-dominated culture is no more, yet life remains unpredictably anguishing and rewarding.

*The Female Man*, a reconsideration of Whileawayan possibilities, has become an underground classic in both science-fiction and feminist circles. The book is built around the digressive journal of a present-day woman who encounters three other selves: the victim of an altered past even more oppressive of women than our own, an ambassador from a Whileawayan future, and an intermediary figure from a world split by gender war into Manland and Womanland. Each is, in her way, an Everywoman. Janet is Russ's ultimate heroine, "the Might-be of our dreams," the goal of feminine evolution. The way to Janet lies through Jael, or Alice Reasoner, the sex warrior based on Alyx; Jael knows that liberation must be won at hard cost. Joanna, the sometime narrator, and Jeanine are both confused products of a culture which invalidates their every aspiration. These four life histories are super-imposed on one another to create an anti-novel: narrative with dense novelistic details is interspersed with meditation, reverie, and fragments of the mythology and history of Whileaway. What holds all this together is impassioned articulation, a style as sensitive as ever to the bizarre complexities of women's lives, but here honed to laser precision by rage.

Russ distinguishes herself in *The Female Man* as radical intelligencer and stylist. Her next novel, *We Who Are About to . . .*, is a study of an hallucinating woman dying alone on an emptied planet. For all its eerie fascination, the book remains rather private and untransformed. In *The Two of Them*, Russ returns to an earlier mode of the politically and socially informed adventure. The Trans-Temp heroine of this novel has escaped from the stultifying world of America in the 1950's to become an agent in the future. Sent to a sexist society that owes something to the Arabian Nights and something to the Islamic world of today, she rescues a girl from a harem, discovering in the process the depth of her commitment to the child: ". . . it'll take longer than one woman's lifetime," she realizes, to free herself. Russ's own commitment to the liberation of the young has borne fruit in two recent short stories ("My Boat," "How Dorothy Kept Away the Spring") and *Kittatinny*, a fantasy written expressly for young girls.

*Extra (Ordinary) People* evinces both a growing technical mastery and an increasingly subtle feminist consciousness in a series of tales about diverse female liberators. A wry, formally inventive book, *Extra (Ordinary) People* is comprised of five narratives, the first four centered on the extramundane adventures of these wise women and the last a romp of a parody—a plot outline for a lesbian historical romance. As a casual linking device, a fragment of a tutorial introduces each tale to a native future "schoolkid." Repeating this structure, an ironic teaching and learning motif recurs in the stories proper: several of the heroine-mentors are isolated in dangerously ignorant, sexist societies of the past and future, and their often comic, always poignant reports are relayed as knowing letters home. Indeed, all of the stories present lessons in "the usual confusion and mess" of human sexuality. In the initial tale, the Hugo award-winning novella "Souls," for instance, a telepathic genius of a 12th-century abbess challenges the brutal sexual code of Viking invaders. In "The Mystery of the Young Gentleman" and "What Did You Do in the Revolution, Grandma?," lesbians in male disguise traverse sexual boundaries, demystifying their own "outlaw" sexuality and defamiliarizing orthodox sexual behavior as they go. Rendering from the inside the extraordinary sentience of her heroines as they struggle to endure or elude the meshes of simplistic alternate realities, Russ creates a fiction both immediate and ironically layered—a work of and about science fiction. *Extra (Ordinary) People* should keep Russ at the experimental forefront of the field.

—Carol L. Snyder

---

**RUSSELL, Eric Frank.** British. Born in Camberley, Surrey, 6 January 1905; grew up in Egypt. Served in the King's Regiment, 1922–26, and in the Royal Air Force, 1941–45. Married Ellen Russell in 1930; one daughter. Worked as a telephonist, quantity surveyor, and draughtsman. Founding member, British Interplanetary Society. Recipient: Hugo award, 1955. *Died 28 February 1978.*

## Science-Fiction Publications

### Novels

*Sinister Barrier.* Kingswood, Surrey, World's Work, 1943; Reading, Pennsylvania, Fantasy Press, 1948.
*Dreadful Sanctuary.* Reading, Pennsylvania, Fantasy Press, 1951; London, Museum Press, 1953; revised edition, New York, Lancer, 1963; London, New English Library, 1967.
*Sentinels from Space.* New York, Bouregy, 1953; London, Museum Press, 1954.
*Three to Conquer.* New York, Avalon, 1956; London, Dobson, 1957.
*Wasp.* New York, Avalon, 1957; London, Dobson, 1958.
*The Space Willies.* New York, Ace, 1958; revised edition as *Next of Kin*, London, Dobson, 1959.
*The Great Explosion.* London, Dobson, and New York, Torquil, 1962.
*With a Strange Device.* London, Dobson, 1964; as *The Mind Warpers*, New York, Lancer, 1965.

### Short Stories

*Deep Space.* Reading, Pennsylvania, Fantasy Press, 1954; London, Eyre and Spottiswoode, 1956.
*Men, Martians, and Machines.* London, Dobson, and New York, Roy, 1956.
*Six Worlds Yonder.* New York, Ace, 1958.
*Far Stars.* London, Dobson, 1961.
*Dark Tides.* London, Dobson, 1962.
*Somewhere a Voice.* London, Dobson, 1965; New York, Ace, 1966.
*Like Nothing on Earth.* London, Dobson, 1975.
*The Best of Eric Frank Russell*, edited by Alan Dean Foster. New York, Ballantine, 1978.

## Other Publications

### Other

*Great World Mysteries.* London, Dobson, and New York, Roy, 1957.
*The Rabble Rousers.* Evanston, Illinois, Regency, 1963.

* * *

Eric Frank Russell will always be remembered as the author of *Sinister Barrier*, the story that helped John W. Campbell launch the magazine *Unknown* in 1939. Boosted as "the greatest imaginative novel in two decades," it established the British writer at the centre of the international science-fiction scene where he remained a popular figure for more than 30 years. It also drew attention to the abundance of plot material in the much-maligned works of Charles Fort, whose philosophy of scepticism Russell upheld consistently on behalf of the Fortean Society.

The novel relies on the notion that the Earth belongs to an alien race that feeds on the human misery it causes. With consummate skill, goaded by Campbell, Russell presented it as a mystery story in the tradition of the detective pulps he had studied in preparing to write for the American market. His taut, racy style had first attracted attention in *Astounding Stories* in 1937, when "The Saga of Pelican West" showed the influence of Stanley G. Weinbaum, which affected many writers at that time. His contributions to the British *Tales of Wonder* and *Fantasy* also revealed a refreshing touch of humor coupled with a vigorous approach that was rare in science fiction. Typical examples were "Vampire from the Void," set in his Liverpool habitat, and "I, Spy!" concerning a Martian visitant that could simulate any form of terrestrial life. His amusing tales of Jay Score, the robot space-pilot, and his crewmen were collected in *Men, Martians, and Machines*. War service curtailed his writing, but "Metamorphosite," a story about a galactic empire, and *Dreadful Sanctuary* returned him to front-rank status. A fast-moving tale about a secret society which sabotaged the first attempts at space-travel, *Dreadful Sanctuary* seriously considers mankind's irrational ways while posing the question "How do you know you're sane?"

All through the 1950's Russell's lucid narratives delighted readers. He broke new ground with "First Person Singular" by adapting the Adam and Eve legend to an interstellar setting; in other stories he revealed an unsuspected flair for emotional themes and moral issues such as racial intolerance. "And There Were None" postulates the effect of passive resistance on planetary invaders, which later became the theme of his satirical novel *The Great Explosion. Three to Conquer* reflected the interest in *psionics* fostered by Campbell. "Allamagoosa" (Hugo) is a clever piece of nonsense. *Sentinels from Space*, in which a highly evolved species keeps a watch over lesser beings, derives something from Olaf Stapledon, with whom Russell maintained friendly contact after introducing him to American science fiction. *Wasp* is an action-thriller relating the escapades of a secret agent preparing the way for a Terran invasion of the Sirian Empire. Simplest of all Russell's novels is *With a Strange Device*, almost a straight mystery story about a conspiracy to sabotage a new defensive weapon. Almost as intriguing as any of his fiction, too, is his collection *Great World Mysteries* in which he delved into some of the enigmas that have baffled scientists over the past century or more.

—Walter Gillings

---

**RYMAN, Geoff.** British. Born in Canada. Moved to London in mid-1970's. Recipient: World Fantasy award, 1986; Arthur C. Clarke award, 1990; British Science Fiction award, 1990. Agent: Maggie Noach, 21 Redan Street, London, W14 0AB, England. Address: c/o HarperCollins Publishers, 77–85 Fulham Palace Road, London W6 8JB, England.

SCIENCE-FICTION PUBLICATIONS

Novels

*The Warrior Who Carried Life*. London, and Boston, Allen and Unwin, 1985.

*The Unconquered Country: A Life History* (novella). London, and Boston, Allen and Unwin, 1986.

*The Child Garden*. London, Unwin Hyman, 1989; New York, St. Martin's Press, 1990.

* * *

The heroines in the novels of Geoff Ryman (there are no heroes) suffer appallingly at the hands of the rulers of the worlds they inhabit, and have great anger as a result. But they also show inordinate tenderness for their partners, and through this love they finally transcend the pain their wounds inflict. This is the centre of all Ryman's work: the redemption human beings can achieve through love of other human beings. This central theme is played out against a background of other common themes—impersonal and tyrannical central governments, cultures that are recognisably oriental, and environments that are almost entirely bio-engineered—which are staggeringly different despite their commonality.

His first novel, *The Warrior Who Carried Life*, at once parodies and enriches the sword-and-sorcery fantasy genre. Cal Cara Kerig's family is mutilated and murdered by imperial troops. She joins a secret women's magic group, which demands that initiates take another form for a year. Much to the bewilderment of the women, who only use the stories of magic to exert power over one another, she actually transmogrifies into a fully armed and armoured warrior, and sets out to kill the prince who ordered the destruction of her family. Ryman adds extraordinary texture to this simple story with his vivid symbolic imagery and lucid prose.

The setting of *The Unconquered Country* could not be more different. Despite its utterly fantastic description—where houses are grown, treated as part of the family, and have to be tied down to stop them wandering off, and where women sell the use of their wombs for the growth of weapons—the country described is unmistakably Cambodia under the Khmer Rouge. But it is more than Cambodia, or else there would be no point in the symbolic representation of the way of life. The unconquered country could be any small nation that suffers more from the depredations of the nation supposedly protecting it than it does from the purported invaders. Caught between the proverbial rock and a hard place, it shows its ability to survive by absorbing what is done to it. The heroine is Third child, and through her eyes we see death breathed from the skies by sharks; living advertisement characters (to some of which she gives birth, and she beats another one to death). Her husband first rescues her from selling her body parts, then dies and is reincarnated as a crow. It would be far too easy to expend more words than the book contains on even a partial exegesis, and the only real recommendation can be to read this wonderfully dense story.

*The Child Garden* might be considered Ryman's first full-length novel. It is certainly longer than the other two put together. But there is no padding. Ryman's own description—"it's about two dykes putting on an opera in a Marxist/Leninist future London"—while indicative of the man's modesty, is further evidence of his ability to say no more than is necessary for his own ends.

Where the other novels are fantasies, *The Child Garden* is science fiction. Set in a future sub-tropical London protected from the rising seas and rivers by bio-engineered coral reefs, where people photosynthesise, and where all knowledge is imparted by genetically altered viruses, it is again a story of a young woman who is orphaned by the action of the state; she finds comfort in the love of another woman, and transcends her suffering to enhance an essentially ungrateful world.

The plot is taken from Dante's Divine Comedy, even as the plot of *The Warrior Who Carried Life* was taken from the epic of Gilgamesh. It becomes obvious that Ryman takes myth as the source of his work: the ancient mythic power of both Gilgamesh and the Divine Comedy is irrefutable, but there is no real difference between them and the 20th-century myth of the killing fields of Cambodia. Equally, in a lecture about the film of *The Wizard of Oz*, Ryman has claimed that, because the film was produced with many different writers and directors, it is a non-attributable mythic outpouring of early 20th-century consciousness. It is certainly nothing to do with L. Frank Baum's book, he maintains, and it is significant that it is the film, not the book, that has achieved classic status. It is no surprise, then, that his forthcoming novel, *Was*, is an account of what happened to Dorothy after she got home from Oz.

Ryman's other recurrent theme is of how it is not possible for anyone to intervene between audience and work of art to make the art easy to understand. In his first published short story, "The Diary of a Translator," he makes it clear that the only real way to learn from literature is to suffer through it oneself. In *The Child Garden*, Rolfa tells Milena, who can read music because she has been infected with the appropriate virus, "you haven't *learned* how to read music. If you haven't learned it, it isn't yours." In a recent story, "The History of Science Fiction," published in the September 1991 issue of *Science Fiction Nexus*, he explores yet another avenue of this theme, with an almost cyberpunk relish in the virtual reality he creates.

Ryman claims that, after *Was* is published, he is all written out. Given that he is not a prolific writer—three novels and less than a dozen short stories in 15 years—it is likely that his next novel is a long way off. Nevertheless, given the originality and the depth of what has appeared so far, it is certain that his next work is awaited with bated breath.

—Paul Brazier

# S

**SABE, Quien.** *See* **BATES, Harry.**

---

**SABERHAGEN, Fred (Thomas)** American. Born in Chicago, Illinois, 18 May 1930. Educated at Wright Junior College, Chicago, 1956–57. Served in the United States Air Force, 1951–55. Married Joan Dorothy Spicci in 1968; one daughter and two sons. Electronics technician, Motorola Inc., Chicago, 1956–62; assistant editor, *Encyclopaedia Britannica*, 1967–73. Freelance writer, 1962–67, and since 1973. Agent: Eleanor Wood, Spectrum Literary Agency, 111 Eighth Avenue, Suite 1502, New York, New York 10011, U.S.A.

SCIENCE-FICTION PUBLICATIONS

Novels (series: Berserker; Chup; Lost Swords)

*The Golden People*. New York, Ace, 1964.
*The Water of Thought*. New York, Ace, 1965; complete edition, Los Angeles, Pinnacle, 1981.
*The Empire of the East* (Chup). New York, Ace, 1979; London, Macdonald, 1984.
*The Broken Lands*. New York, Ace, 1968.
*The Black Mountains*. New York, Ace, 1971.
*Changeling Earth*. New York, DAW, 1973; as *Ardneh's World*, New York, Baen, 1988.
*Brother Assassin*. New York, Ballantine, 1969; as *Brother Berserker*, London, Macdonald, 1969.
*Berserker's Planet*. New York, DAW, and London, Futura, 1975.
*Specimens*. New York, Popular Library, 1976
*The Veils of Azlaroc*. New York, Ace, 1978.
*Love Conquers All*. New York, Ace, 1979.
*The Mask of the Sun*. New York, Ace, 1979.
*Berserker Man*. New York, Ace, 1979; London, Gollancz, 1988.
*Coils*, with Roger Zelazny. New York, Tor, 1980; London, Penguin, 1984.
*Octagon*. New York, Ace, 1981; London, Sinclair Browne, 1984.
Swords:
*The First [Second, Third] Book of Swords*. New York, Tor, 3 vols., 1983–84; London, Futura, 1985–86; as *The First Book of Lost Swords: Woundhealer's Story, The Second Book of Lost Swords: Sight-Blinder's Story*, and *The Third Book of Lost Swords: Stonecutter's Story*, New York, Tor, 1986–88; London, Futura, vols. 2 and 3, 1989.
*The Fourth Book of Lost Swords: Farslayer's Story*. New York, Tor, 1989.
*The Fifth Book of Lost Swords: Coinspinner's Story*. New York, Tor, 1989.
*The Sixth Book of Lost Swords: Mindsword's Story*. New York, Tor, 1991.
*A Century of Progress*. New York, Tor, 1983.
*The Berserker Throne*. New York, Simon and Schuster, 1985.
*Berserker: Blue Death*. New York, Tor, 1985; London, Gollancz, 1990.
*The Frankenstein Papers*. New York, Baen, 1986.
*Pyramids*. New York, Baen, 1987.
*The Berserker Attack*. New York, Waldenbooks, 1987.
*After the Fact*. New York, Baen, 1988.
*The White Bull*. New York, Baen, 1988.
*The Black Throne*, with Roger Zelazny. New York, Baen, 1990.

Short Stories

*Berserker*. New York, Ballantine, 1967.
*The Book of Saberhagen*. New York, DAW, 1975.
*The Ultimate Enemy* (Berserker). New York, Ace, 1979; London, Gollancz, 1990.
*The Berserker Wars*. New York, Tor, 1981.
*Earth Descended* (Berserker). New York, Tor, 1982.
*Saberhagen: My Best*. New York, Baen, 1987.

OTHER PUBLICATIONS

Novels

*The Dracula Tape*. New York, Warner, 1975.
*The Holmes-Dracula File*. New York, Ace, 1978.
*An Old Friend of the Family*. New York, Ace, 1979.
*Thorn*. New York, Ace, 1980.
*A Matter of Taste*. New York, Ace, 1980.
*Dominion*. New York, Tor, 1982.

Other

Editor, *A Spadeful of Spacetime*. New York, Ace, 1981.
Editor, with Joan Saberhagen, *Pawn to Infinity*. New York, Ace, 1982.
Editor, with Martin H. Greenberg, *Machines that Kill*. New York, Ace, 1984.
Editor, *Berserker Base*. New York, Tor, 1985.

* * *

For three decades, Fred Saberhagen's principal theme has been Life's War with Death across the evolutionary gradient: all his battles are wonder-wars. This is the very substance of his first and greatest success, the Berserker series. The berserkers are self-programming, self-replicating, robotic spacecraft set by their "long-dead masters to destroy anything that lived." Fighting these ineradicable foes unites all life forms in the galaxy, and, ironically, stimulates progress that might not otherwise have occurred without the machines' challenge. The berserkers are computerized demons, high-tech symbols of utter Evil.

This "divergent" series is a novelty for being organized around a common enemy instead of a continuing hero. Its premise, which originated in games theory, is not unique (see Theodore

Sturgeon's 1948 novella "There Is No Defence"). But Saberhagen has made it so completely his own that "his murderous mechanisms are the recognized standard in the field." (For the author's own account, see "The Berserker Story" in *Algol*, Summer, 1977.) Indeed, the berserker universe became so popular that Saberhagen "franchised" it to other authors in the collection *Berserker Base*.

A more recent success is his Swords series. Instead of characters, these stories are united by props—12 divinely forged weapons with fabulous powers to harm or even heal. Saberhagen created the material to serve as a computer game module, and, unfortunately, it reads like one despite much ingenuity in plot perils and a laudable realism in the low-tech setting.

The Swords series follows up Saberhagen's excellent science fantasy trilogy *The Empire of the East*. This lively variation on the usual "world where magic works" translates scientific laws into spells and back again, yielding such curiosities as a djinn technologist and valkyrie robots. Unlike commonplace technophobic fantasies, science is the liberating force in *The Empire of the East*, freeing Earth from "the old Dark Mystery" just as rationality cut cruel divinities down to size in the Swords books.

Saberhagen's scientific imagination can see a story in a Foucault pendulum ("Brother Berserker"), a black hole ("The Face of the Deep"), Paleolithic rituals (*The Water of Thought*) or a squash seed ("Pressure"). He also draws inspiration from gaming (*Octagon*), the arts ("Young Girl at an Open Half-Door"), and history (directly as in "Wings out of Shadow" or with time travel and alternatives, as in *A Century of Progress*, *Pyramids*, and *After the Fact*.) *The Mask of the Sun* combines history with gaming. His anthologies *Pawn to Infinity* and *A Spadeful of Spacetime* express his enthusiasms for chess and archeology.

Saberhagen has retold myths (*The White Bull*, taken from the Minotaur) and literary classics, including "The Knight's Tale" ("In the Temple of Mars"), *Moby-Dick* (*Berserker: Blue Death*), *Doctor Faustus* ("Some Events in the Templar Radiant"), and *Frankenstein* (*The Frankenstein Papers*). He can turn literary creators into literary characters: Dante Gabriel Rossetti in *The Veils of Azlaroc* and Edgar Allan Poe in *The Black Throne*.

Saberhagen's Dracula pastiches are his best efforts in this area. He presents the Count as exotic rather than monstrous and makes him a force for rough justice. Placing this epitome of Gothic horror in solidly realistic versions of Renaissance Italy, Victorian London, contemporary Chicago, or the American Southwest intensifies the impact.

Saberhagen is especially deft at blending the factual and legendary aspects of a subject and then infusing the result with theological significance. "Stone Place" recreates Don John of Austria, Philip II of Spain, and the Battle of Lepanto in a way G.K. Chesterton himself would have applauded. "Brother Berserker" brings St. Francis of Assisi, Galileo, and the mystical theories of Pierre Teilhard de Chardin together to beautiful effect.

Saberhagen's stated goal is "to impose new coordinates on the human condition," but the functions he plots there are traditional Western Christian ones. (Sandra Miesel's afterwords to *Berserker Man* and *The First Book of Swords* explore the religious and mythic resonances of Saberhagen's work.)

Initially, Saberhagen's style was awkward, but he has learned to make a virtue of plainness, allowing the innate power of the story to carry itself. Plot schematics occasionally hobble his natural flair for narration, as in *Love Conquers All*, which is too polemical to effectively satirize the sexual revolution. Rigid correspondences spoil his Orpheus tale, "Starsong," while arbitrariness and unresolved endings mar the Swords series.

Perhaps Saberhagen's greatest strength is the sheer, unsentimental conviction he brings to his writing. Because he believes, he can make his readers share his belief. His best characterizations are those that ought to have been the most difficult: Brother Jovann, his St. Francis; Johann Karlsen, his Don John; and Draffut the Beast-Lord, a godlike dog. *Berserker Man*'s hero Michel is attractive both as a child and as a hero despite carrying a heavy load of metaphysics and Arthuriana on his young shoulders.

Saberhagen's gift for dramatizing familiar ideas with compelling thoroughness—and fresh angles—has made him a solid presence in the SF field.

—Sandra Miesel

---

**ST. CLAIR, Margaret (née Neeley).** Has also written as Idris Seabright. American. Born in Hutchinson, Kansas, 17 February 1911. Educated at the University of California, Berkeley, M.A. 1933 (Phi Beta Kappa). Married Eric St. Clair in 1932. Horticulturist, St. Clair Rare Bulb Gardens, El Sobrante, California, 1938–41. Since 1945, full-time writer. Agent: Julie Fallowfield, McIntosh and Otis, 475 Fifth Avenue, New York, New York 10017. Address: 43951 Malo Pass Court, Manchester, California 95459, U.S.A.

SCIENCE-FICTION PUBLICATIONS

Novels

*Agent of the Unknown*. New York, Ace, 1956.
*The Green Queen*. New York, Ace, 1956.
*The Games of Neith*. New York, Ace, 1960.
*Sign of the Labrys*. New York, Bantam, and London, Corgi, 1963.
*Message from the Eocene*. New York, Ace, 1964.
*The Dolphins of Altair*. New York, Dell, 1967.
*The Shadow People*. New York, Dell, 1969.
*The Dancers of Noyo*. New York, Ace, 1973.

Short Stories

*Three Worlds of Futurity*. New York, Ace, 1964.
*Change the Sky and Other Stories*. New York, Ace, 1974.
*The Best of Margaret St. Clair*, edited by Martin H. Greenberg. Chicago, Academy, 1985.

*

Margaret St. Clair comments:

It would take me days to write adequately about my work. So I shall only say that I think I am better at short fiction than at novels—the short story is more philosophical—and that I like my amusing stories better than the frightening ones, and prefer both classes to what I call "uplift."

I am not a natural writer. Writing is painful and difficult for me.

* * *

Margaret St. Clair is an example of a woman writer who did not have to disguise her sex in order to be successful as a writer in a male-dominated field. She was able to write in a natural "female voice" at a time when some women writers of science fiction were outdoing the men in tough-flavored style, and, particularly in her fantasy short stories (generally written as by Idris Seabright), to introduce some sensitive characterization, including portrayals of housewives, single mothers, and young children, into a field which was highly technologically oriented. In common with other writing in the 1950's, St. Clair's fiction was oriented toward adventurous episodes, but she had a penchant for tackling controversial themes and for using gadgetry and environments symbolically.

Most of St. Clair's short fiction was published during the 1950's. Some of her astonishing output of approximately 130 stories may be found in *Three Worlds of Futurity* and *Change the Sky and Other Stories*; both are representative of her work. Other individual stories are found in anthologies: "Short in the Chest" (in Greenberg and Olander's *Science Fiction of the 50's*, 1979), featuring Marine Major Sonya Briggs and a "philosophical robot" psychologist called a "huxley," is remarkable for its portrayal of women and its grappling with questions of sexuality. "New Ritual" (in Boucher's *The Best from Fantasy and Science Fiction*, 1954), also featuring a female protagonist, gives a futuristic twist to the plight of the dissatisfied housewife as a deep freeze turns everything from apricots to an inattentive husband into more desirable items. "Child of Void" (in Conklin's *Invaders of Earth*, 1952) shows a lonely boy grappling with the unknown in the form of a luminous egg which presents children with alluring visions of those things they most desire.

St. Clair's novels, not as consistently well-crafted as her shorter work, are usually adventures and may be relied upon to convey a message. *Agent of the Unknown* is set on the synthetic pleasure plantoid Fyon. An appealing non-conformist with a drinking problem finds purpose in life when he rescues from the edge of the sea a small but awe-inspiring "Weeping Doll," the creation of the master craftsman Vulcan. The protagonist muses, "Sometimes I think everything in our world is synthetic, even happiness." While "Vulcan's Weeping Doll" passively changes in one world, *The Green Queen* and *The Games of Neith*, both feature heroines as active characters who are chosen to inspire or lead their respective societies toward change. Histrionic talents, intelligence, and physical beauty are attributes possessed by the Green Queen, who lives in a post-holocaust society ripe for revolution, "a place where ten percent of the population monopolized eighty percent of the dwelling space and fifty percent of the unpolluted food, and where everybody, Uppers and Lowers alike, was always terribly afraid of damage from the omnipresent radioactive elements. . . ." In *The Games of Neith*, Anassa, Priestess to the Goddess of Neith, possesses similar traits, and guides her seafaring society, which is threatening to return to the worship of primitive gods, to a new future. Anassa's relationship with Ehr'li Wan, a physics professor, is an excellent early example of a man and a woman in science fiction working in an equal part against evil forces.

*The Shadow People* is a striking work. Although the quality of the prose is uneven and the thrust of the narrative is excessively cheerless, an underworld of zombie-like people is memorably portrayed as scuttling through a rat-and-fungus-infested underworld in a hallucinatory, hopeless future. *Sign of the Labrys* portrays another dark underworld, this time inhabited by the survivors of a devastating plague who cower in damp caverns hacked out of rock until the hero, Sam Sewell, brings them awareness of an open, habitable world above ground. *Message from the Eocene* introduces Tharg, an ancient being of alien origin, who desperately attempts to overcome his condition of existing (for century upon century) as a disembodied sentient force so that he may convey a message to mankind. He eventually makes contact with a modern woman whose gift of mental sensitivity to unusual phenomena is sensitively portrayed.

St. Clair's best novel, *The Dolphins of Altair*, is a moving work critical of man's disregard for the ecosystems of Earth. Members of a well-drawn, intelligent dolphin society conspire with a few enlightened humans to preserve the world for an unusual new future. *The Dancers of Noyo*, like *Agent of the Unknown*, relies upon a male protagonist to hold together a tale of the future. A quest for personal identity is set against a world dominated by powerful androids.

St. Clair's best work is tightly written shorter fiction which introduced unusual protagonists to the pages of science-fiction magazines. While some of her longer works suffer from over-ambitious exploration of diverse themes, the best of her novels are those most concerned with an individual's experience with the extraordinary, or a group's commitment to a visionary future.

—Rosemary Herbert

---

**ST. JOHN, Philip.** *See* **del REY, Lester.**

---

**ST. PAUL, Sterner.** *See* **MEEK, S.P.**

---

**SALLIS, James.** American. Born in Helena, Arkansas, 21 December 1944. Attended Tulane University, New Orleans, 1962–64. Married Jane Rose in 1964; one son. Worked as a college instructor and publisher's reader; editor, *New Worlds*, London, 1969–70; now a full-time writer. Address: c/o Meredith Bernstein, 470 West End Avenue, New York, New York 10023, U.S.A.

SCIENCE-FICTION PUBLICATIONS

Short Stories

*A Few Last Words.* London, Hart Davis, 1969; New York, Macmillan, 1970.

Uncollected Short Stories

"This One," in *If* (New York), January 1970.
"Front and Centaur," in *New Worlds* (London), March 1970.
"Binaries" and "Only the Words Are Different," in *Orbit 9*, edited by Damon Knight. New York, Putnam, 1971.
"Mensuration," in *Quark 2*, edited by Samuel R. Delany and Marilyn Hacker. New York, Paperback Library, 1971.
"Field," in *Quark 3*, edited by Samuel R. Delany and Marilyn Hacker. New York, Paperback Library, 1971.
"The Fly at Ciron," in *Fantasy and Science Fiction* (New York), December 1971.
"At the Fitting Shop" and "53rd American Dream," in *Again, Dangerous Visions*, edited by Harlan Ellison. New York, Doubleday, 1972; London, Millington, 1976.
"Doucement, S'Il Vous Plait," in *Orbit 11*, edited by Damon Knight. New York, Putnam, 1973.
"Echo," in *The Berserkers*, edited by Roger Elwood. New York, Simon and Schuster, 1973.

"Delta Flight 281" and "The First Few Kinds of Truth," in *Alternities*, edited by David Gerrold. New York, Dell, 1974.
"My Friend Zarathustra," in *Orbit 13*, edited by Damon Knight. New York, Putnam, 1974.
"The Invasion of Dallas," in *Lone Star Universe*, edited by George W. Proctor and Steven Utley. Austin, Texas, Heidelberg, 1976.
"One Road to Damascus," in *2076: The American Tricentennial*, edited by Edward Bryant. New York, Pyramid, 1977.
"La Fin d'une Monde (Intérieure)," in *Fantastic* (New York), June 1977.
"Jackson," in *Fantastic* (New York), December 1977.
"Changes," in *Fantastic* (New York), April 1978.
"Exigency and Martin Heidegger," in *Amazing* (New York), November 1978.
"They Will Not Hush," with David Lunde, in *Whispers 2*, edited by Stuart David Schiff. New York, Doubleday, 1979.
"Miranda-Escobedo," in *100 Great Fantasy Short Stories*, edited by Isaac Asimov, Terry Carr, and Martin H. Greenberg. New York, Doubleday, 1984.
"Need," in *Isaac Asimov's Science Fiction Magazine* (New York), January 1985.
"Others," in *The Georgia Review*, Summer 1985.
"Attitude of the Earth toward Other Bodies," in *Full Spectrum 2*, edited by Lou Aronica. New York, Doubleday, 1989.

OTHER PUBLICATIONS

Other

*Down Home: Country-Western*. New York, Macmillan, 1971.
*The Guitar Players: One Instrument and Its Masters in American Music*. New York, Morrow, 1982.

Editor, *The War Book*. London, Hart Davis, 1969; New York, Dell, 1971.
Editor, *The Shores Beneath*. New York, Avon, 1970.
Editor, *Jazz Guitars: An Anthology*. New York, Morrow, 1984.

* * *

James Sallis's extraordinary fiction is distinguished by its honesty and meticulous artistry. With his highly imagistic stories, he has regularly displayed a finely honed mastery of sophisticated literary techniques and sharply etched psychological insights. Often the stories are clearly autobiographical, presenting painful indications of their author's personal difficulties, even his torments. They are not always easy to read, and it is sometimes hard to discern their intent or meaning, but they affect readers powerfully, at least those readers who demand more than thrill-seeking and fantastic adventures from the fiction they read. (It always sounds a bit pompous to score the escapist reader in such terms, but writers like Sallis, who employ quite subtle fictional devices, *do* demand more from their readers. In "My Friend Zarathustra," Sallis writes: "Yes—I mean what I say, and you must listen; must hear what's not said if you're to understand properly what is said.")

Many of his stories are moving portrayals of troubled or dazed individuals who are dissociated from their environments. In nearly every Sallis story the main character is helpless, or at least quite passive. Things are dreadfully confused in his private life or are being disrupted in the outside world. Sometimes nothing much is happening, but even then the character does not cope well. At the rare times when the character is able to act decisively, the action turns out to be futile or grotesque. (The disposal of the child in the brilliantly executed "Jim and Mary G." is a harrowing example of such futility and ugliness.) Usually the character is still helpless at the end of the story. In many stories, the protagonists are last seen merely waiting or going off into darkness or standing still as the world begins to disintegrate, literally or physically, around them. However Sallis dramatizes it, the main impression the reader receives from most of the stories is of humankind trapped in environments upon which they can have no effect, and for which they no longer have any effective responses or reactions. In "Faces, Hands: The Kettle of Stars" a courier is halted from his message-carrying mission and stranded in an intergalactic waiting room, where he contemplates art in the form of an also-waiting alien singer whose destiny is repulsive servitude on another planet, an injustice the courier perceives but cannot affect. The protagonist of "The History Makers" occupies himself with letters or music or sitting at a window while whole time-accelerated civilizations grow, decline, and fall nearby. The only movement he makes is to move away from a city's encroaching border. Nevertheless, he is able to speculate on the exigencies of time, as manifested in the slow progress of a beetle across sand or in a review of his own life or in the odd inverted timescale of the cities. In "A Few Last Words" a man attempts to decide what to do as a doomed city more or less empties before his eyes.

In such stories the sense of dissociation is pronounced both in the relationship of character to setting and in the character's own "inner space," the phrase emphasized by interpreters of the new wave of science fiction as its primary subject matter. Sallis's characters, even at their most articulate, are often in danger of breaking up themselves in just about the same way the setting is crumbling around them. In one of his most effective and painful stories, "Binaries," the narrator-writer (who perceives his immediate environment as being regularly broken up and moved away) is in a state of dissociation with himself as a person and as a writer:

> Someone has written a collection of short stories and published them under my name; they have even put my photograph on the back cover. I received a copy in the morning post. Anonymous, no return address, postmarked Grnd Cntrl Stn. The stories reveal my deepest secrets. Only one person could have written them. Or had reason to. My attorney is investigating the possibility of a lawsuit against the publisher but, as the work was copyrighted in my own name, there seems little we can do. The publisher expressed to my attorney his desire to meet the author, his admiration for the book.

The passage's poignancy, its precise delineation of the character's troubled emotions, and—incidentally—its wrenching irony, are all hallmarks of the fiction of James Sallis.

Sallis also has an appealing knack for humorous, especially surrealistic, writing, which he uses in stories like "Kazoo," "The Creation of Bennie Good," and "Miranda-Escobedo." It is worth noting, however, that, even in these works, with their clever improvisations, sly allusions, and superb word-play, the sense of psychological and emotional dissociation generally remains, as dazed or momentarily baffled characters and even ghost-cops are disoriented by their absurd environments.

Sallis started publishing science fiction in the 1960's, a time when the field was being rattled by a number of literary experimenters who came to be dubbed, for better or for worse, the "new wave" of science fiction. He served some time as an editor of the British magazine *New Worlds*, the SF publication that became most associated with the new wave because it dared to publish the works of adventuresome writers during a period when many other SF markets were resisting anything that did not correspond with accepted approaches to the genre. Now that the new furore has somewhat subsided, upheld in print only by a few still petulant writers, it is clear that the contributions of the new wavers are legitimate literary extensions of established science-fiction traditions, and that Sallis's stories are among the best writings to emerge from the phenomenon. In recent years James Sallis, never prolific, has published few stories, but the ones that have been published exhibit the same care for literary details and intellectual concerns as the earlier stories. One recent story, "Changes," ranks with the best of his fiction.

—Robert Thurston

---

**SALMONSON, Jessica Amanda.** American. Born in Seattle, Washington, 6 January 1950. Editor for *Windhaven* magazine, 1977–79, and *Fantasy and Terror,* since 1973. Recipient: World Fantasy award, for anthology, 1980; Lambda award, for anthology, 1990. Agent: Susan Lee Cohen, Riverside Agency, 2673 Broadway, Number 132, New York, New York 10025. Address P.O. Box 20610, Seattle, Washington 98102, U.S.A.

### Science-Fiction Publications

#### Novels

*Tragedy of the Moisty Morning* (chapbook). Seattle, Angst World Library, 1978.
*Tomoe Gozen.* New York, Ace, 1981.
*The Golden Naginata.* New York, Ace, 1982.
*The Swordswoman.* New York, Tor, 1982.
*Thousand Shrine Warrior.* New York, Berkley, 1984.
*Ou Lu Khen and the Beautiful Madwoman.* New York, Berkley, 1985.

#### Short Stories

*Hag's Tapestry.* Runcorn, Cheshire, Haunted Library, 1984.
*A Silver Thread of Madness.* New York, Ace, 1989.
*John Collier and Fredric Brown Went Quarrelling Through My Head.* Buffalo, New York, Ganley, 1989.

### Other Publications

#### Other

*The Encyclopedia of Amazons: Women Warriors from Antiquity to the Present Era.* New York, Paragon House, 1991.

Editor, *Amazons!* New York, DAW, 1979.
Editor, *Amazons II!* New York, DAW, 1982.
Editor, *Heroic Visions.* New York, Ace, 1983.
Editor, *Tales by Moonlight.* Chicago, Garcia, 1983.
Editor, *The Haunted Wherry and Other Rare Ghost Stories.* Madison, Wisconsin, Strange Company, 1985.
Editor, *The Faded Garden: The Collected Ghost Stories of Hildegarde Hawthorne.* Madison, Wisconsin, Strange Company, 1985.
Editor, *Heroic Visions II.* New York, Ace, 1986.
Editor, *The Supernatural Tales of Fitz-James O'Brien: Volume I, Macabre Tales.* New York, Doubleday, 2 vols., 1988.
Editor, *Tales by Moonlight II.* New York, Tor, 1989.
Editor, *What Did Miss Darrington See? An Anthology of Feminist Supernatural Fiction.* New York, Feminist Press, 1989.
Editor, with Isabelle D. Waugh and Charles G. Waugh, *Wife or Spinster: Stories by 19th Century Women.* Camden, Maine, Yankee Books, 1991.

*

Manuscript Collection: University of Oregon, Eugene.

Jessica Amanda Salmonson comments:

I am drawn to fantastic and supernatural fiction as an art. I have faith in fantastic fiction because there are or have been such writers as Bruno Shulz, Kafka, Poe, Gogol, Garcia Marquez and Baudelaire who have made the fantastic and the macabre sing with purpose and beauty. In the self-consciously trashy world of mass-market F/SF paperbacks, my presumptions about what fantasy can be and should be causes a significant number of my fellow professionals (I rarely consider them peers) to scoff. This tends to be a field where even the authors are narrowly read, are put off by fine writing, are proud to write without elegance to immature tastes, and very often do not even know who a Shulz or a Gogol ever were. I remember a writers conference at which I was stunned to discover I was the only fantasist who had read Tasso and Spenser or even William Morris. These were people illiterate in their own field, let alone outside their field, and their heroes were for the most part pulpsters who didn't even transcend pulp. They were people who thought Poe and Baudelaire starved because they couldn't cut it in the professional world, whereas L. Ron Hubbard was a genius, measured, of course, in dollar signs.

Of late, I've found myself sauntering away from the genre publishing arena, because it is so discouraging to see one's soul issued in a biodegradable format and marketed amidst innumerable short-term "monthly releases" which consist of some of the worst and most predictable writers outside of the romance field. My feeling is that either I'm *not* just another crappy fantasy writer, and therefore oughtn't be marketed amidst this great swamp of mediocrity and inferiority; or I am indeed no better than the rest, deserve no better company, and therefore shouldn't be writing these books at all, since there is presently no shortage of other people far happier to be writing to low industry standards.

I have no sense that publishers reward authors for striving for artistry, intelligence, and elegance. A snappy, easy read is the word of the day. Something that is easily "packaged." That categorizes well. Were I willing to write an endless series with a rubbishy formula, I'd be signed to a five-book contract at once. But serious books are sold cheaply one by one to whiny editors afraid they'll lose their jobs if they lose money on even one book that's too original. I can't reduce myself to the task required. So I've not finished a new novel in a few years, because it gives me the creeps every time I think of how it would invariably be marketed, and I recall the horrid company my books have had to share. I do continue to write short stories (my real love) for it is an area less fully commercialized in the worst sense, although the "shared world" anthologies have certainly made huge inroads in trashing up short story art.

My most recent book-length work to appear (and other works in progress) is nonfiction, though on very unusual topics: mysticism and mythology. It almost qualifies as the Fantastic, and one work-in-progress, *Everyday Life in Amazonia,* draws as much upon the world-building techniques of science fiction as it does from logical extension of the mythological record. It was so heartwarming to have my most recent title appear in a lovely hardcover and trade paperback from quality publishers, and find myself in a catalogue alongside translations of South American poets and studies of Kafka or Djuna Barnes. That felt so much more rewarding and inspiring than to find one's heartfelt and quirky fantasy novels peddled alongside quickly written, all-alike books aimed at supermarket racks rather than bookstores. I am *not* inherently an elitist, but do feel out of place and disappointed when surrounded by people whose measures of success are not predicated upon any critical faculty or artistic intent and ability.

I do have other fantasy novels in progress, but tinker with them seldomly. Unlike Robert Silverberg, I never made any elaborate statement of "leaving" the genre only to come mincing back, as I knew I loved fantastic literature too much to really stop writing it forever. But stage by stage, I dropped my membership with professional organizations for which I felt no real kinship, allowed my subscriptions to purportedly "essential" professional journals lapse, and stopped attending conferences. I quietly withdrew into intense research on peculiar nonfiction topics, and if anyone has missed me, I was too holed up to notice.

I probably won't return to the genre with full force until and unless I discover a publisher whose taste in books I could generally and honestly admire and whose authors I would feel pride to stand among. If that proves too utopian a requirement in a dreary and archly commercial area of publishing, then my next few books will probably continue to be nonfiction and/or non-genre. I continue to feel fantasy is potentially among the highest artforms when approached as art, but the current market requirements do not allow for such work to be rewarded. And at present it just does not feel like a success to have a publisher buy a book of mine because they consider it suited to a line of perfectly dreadful books.

* * *

Jessica Amanda Salmonson is best known as one of the most enthusiastic proponents of Amazonian fantasy, a subgenre of sword-and-sorcery fiction involving strong and independent female warriors that has been nurtured and inspired by sometimes radical feminist politics. She has played a major role as author, editor, critic, and political theorist in helping the fantasy genre develop.

Salmonson became active in science-fiction fandom in the 1970's, when she became involved in the editing and production of small fiction magazines with titles like *Windhaven: A Matriarchal Magazine* and *Fantasy and Terror*, which specialized in publishing amateur fantasy fiction of various types. Some of the fiction published in those magazines was of reasonably high quality, but it was unable to find paying markets. A growing market for fantasy novels had already begun, with markets having been created for high fantasy by the popularization of Tolkien, for heroic fantasy by the rediscovery of Robert E. Howard, and (to a much lesser degree) for dark fantasy in the Lovecraft tradition—a popular market for supernatural horror had to wait for Stephen King—but very few markets for short fantasy fiction existed. Of the dozens of amateur magazines dedicated to fantasy fiction, many specialized in specific types and styles and subgenres, and a few specialized in female-warrior heroic fantasy.

Salmonson stepped into the ranks of the professionals with her 1979 anthology, *Amazons!*, an original anthology featuring 13 stories with sword-wielding heroines, along with an introduction by Salmonson about actual women warriors throughout history and a recommended reading list by Susan Wood. The volume contains early stories from writers who would become major writers in the coming decade, including C.J. Cherryh, Megan Lindholm, Tanith Lee, and Elizabeth Lynn. These four, plus Charles R. Saunders, the only male author in the book, contribute the strongest stories. The other authors include Janrae Frank, T.J. Morgan, Janet Fox, Josephine Saxon, Margaret St. Clair, and Michelle Belling, most of whom Salmonson knew through fandom. There is also a story by Andre Norton that was probably included mostly in homage of her pioneering efforts in popularizing strong female fantasy protagonists, and a story by Emily Brontë, edited by Joanna Russ. It is unfortunate indeed that Russ was unable to contribute a story herself to this seminal volume, since her tales of Alyx, including *Picnic on Paradise* in 1968, are among the strongest genre antecedents to amazonian fantasy. (Among the strongest pulp-SF influences is C.L. Moore's *Jirel of Joiry.*)

*Amazons!* was not the first feminist-theme science fiction or fantasy anthology. It was immediately preceded by Pamela Sargent's three highly acclaimed *Women of Wonder* anthologies, as well as by Virginia Kidd's equally lauded *Millennial Women* and Alice Laurance's *Cassandra Rising.* But the high quality of the fiction, Salmonson's strong editorial presence in the volume, and the timeliness of the theme, led to *Amazons!* winning the World Fantasy award. A new fantasy subgenre was officially recognized, and Salmonson was acknowledged as one of its principle promoters.

A second volume in the series, *Amazons II!*, appeared in 1982. It also features a number of authors of significant talent, including Tanith Lee (the only repeat), Phyllis Ann Karr, Lillian Stewart Carl, Ardath Mayhar, Lee Killough, and Jo Clayton, along with several male authors such as F.M. Busby and George R. R. Martin. But none of the stories seems to match the best of the first volume. And instead of a manifesto or feminist tract, something that could have created some new level of controversy for added interest, Salmonson's introduction once again reviewed a litany of historical fighting women. *Amazons II!* received little critical or popular attention, and no more volumes in the series ever appeared.

But neither Amazonian fiction nor Jessica Salmonson were finished. Before *Amazons II!* appeared, Salmonson's first novel was published, *Tomoe Gozen*, the first in a saga that would include two more novels, *The Golden Naginata* and *Thousand Shrine Warrior.* All three books are set in an alternate-world Japan where the myths of our Japan are reality, and tell the adventures of a female Samurai, Tomoe Gozen. The latter volumes in the series drift away from violent action and supernatural menaces toward more concern with character and philosophy. Salmonson's lucid prose and imaginative setting, her characters and themes, led the series to be well regarded as a unique and interesting heroic fantasy.

The trend toward less violence and more characterization continued in Salmonson's only other novel to return to Oriental legendry, *Ou Lu Khen and the Beautiful Madwoman.* In this novel, Salmonson tells the story of a young Chinese man who has fallen in love with a madwoman, and charts his quest to find a solution to her condition so they can marry.

Salmonson also had another early sword-and-sorcery novel published. *The Swordswoman* once again involves an alternate world where swords and sorcery prevail, but this time the setting is a more traditional European fantasy world. The characters are of our world and find themselves able to travel to Endsworld through the use of a magic crystal. It is a well-written but unoriginal novel.

Salmonson also published two other anthology series of two volumes each. *Heroic Visions* and *Heroic Visions II* cover the broader subgenre of sword-and-sorcery fantasy, and are two of the best collections of that type of short fiction. The first volume includes two near-masterpieces, Fritz Leiber's "The Curse of the Smalls and the Stars" and Michael Bishop's "The Monkey's Bride," as well as good stories by Jane Yolen, Robert Silverberg, Joanna Russ, and others. The second volume includes fine tales by Keith Roberts, Bishop, Ellen Kushner, and Avram Davidson, as well as one of Salmonson's own stories, "The Lingering Minstrel." The other series of anthologies edited by Salmonson, *Tales by Moonlight* and *Tales by Moonlight II*, feature original horror short stories.

Salmonson's other projects have included collecting the forgotten fantasy fiction of notable female authors in *The Faded Garden: The Collected Ghost Stories of Hildegarde Hawthorne* and *What Did Miss Darrington See? An Anthology of Feminist Supernatural Fiction.* She has also written essays on fantasy fiction for many of the semi-professional SF critical journals, including *THRUST* and *Fantasy Review*, as well as numerous amateur SF and feminist magazines.

—D. Douglas Fratz

---

**SARBAN.** Pseudonym for John W. Wall. British *Died in 1989.*

SCIENCE-FICTION PUBLICATIONS

Novel

*The Sound of His Horn.* London, Davies, 1952; New York, Ballantine, 1960.

Short Stories

*Ringstones and Other Curious Tales.* London, Davies, and New York, Coward McCann, 1951.
*The Doll Maker and Other Tales of the Uncanny.* London, Davies, 1953; *The Doll Maker* published separately, New York, Ballantine, 1960.

* * *

The only true science-fiction novel to appear under the Sarban byline was *The Sound of His Horn*, a novel that evokes a mood of gloom and horror as well as anything that has ever been written. Kingsley Amis pointed out that it is one of the few novels ever to suggest a rural rather than urban dystopia, a future after Germany has won World War II and the other races of the world are viewed as little better than lower animals. Alan Querdilion wanders into an electrified fence while escaping from a German POW camp and finds himself somehow projected into a world where the Germans have already been victorious. After a brief period where he is the guest of a German landholder, he is set loose as prey for his host's periodic hunts.

Two other short novels appeared, both of which have been published as horror novels though the subject matter is such that they could as well be considered fantasies. In *The Doll Maker*, a young girl is compelled to become a tutor at mysterious Brackenbine Hall, and soon falls under the influence of Niall Sterne, a peculiar, reclusive man who roams the forests and exists only, it seems, for his collection of extremely lifelike dolls. In due course, the heroine learns of Sterne's connection with several past deaths, and comes to believe that he can transfer human souls into the dolls he creates. *The Doll Maker* also brilliantly creates a mood of despair and awakening horror. Sarban's skill at drawing the reader into his book is probably at its best, however, in *Ringstones.* A young woman is employed to tutor two young children at a remote estate, but soon becomes enmeshed in magic and the struggle to maintain her own personality and view of reality when faced with a form of existence that she had formerly considered only a dream. *Ringstones* is a haunting novel that is far more worthwhile than the hundreds of modern gothics which it in many ways resembles.

Sarban also created several excellent shorter pieces, although they are extremely hard to locate. The most noteworthy of these are probably "Calmahain" and "Capra." In the former, two young children allow their fantasy world to become so real that it overflows into the real world and adults begin to experience elements of the fantasy. In the latter, a vicious lover's triangle at a costume party has unexpected results when the real god Pan makes an entry.

The most striking element in the small body of fiction Sarban produced before his death is obviously the evocation of a weird atmosphere, the quiet construction of a world where things aren't as safe and logical as its characters would like to believe. The quality of the prose is also of note. Although couched in a very formal style, Sarban's words flow easily, drawing the reader along. There is never any hint that this was an amateur writing as a hobby; the competent hand of the professional is obvious. With only three slim volumes to his name, Sarban will remain a unique and significant writer.

—Don D'Ammassa

---

**SARGENT, Pamela.** American. Born in Ithaca, New York, 20 March 1948. Educated at the State University of New York, Binghamton, B.A. in philosophy 1968, M.A. 1970. Model and sales clerk, 1965–66; factory worker, Endicott Coil Company, 1966; sales clerk, Towne Distributors, 1966; typist, Harpur College, Binghamton, New York, 1966–67; office worker, Webster Paper Company, Albany, New York, 1969; teaching assistant in philosophy, State University of New York, Binghamton, 1969–71. Since 1971, freelance writer and editor. Agent: Joseph Elder Agency, 150 West 87th Street, New York, New York 10024. Address: Box 486, Johnson City, New York 13790, U.S.A.

SCIENCE-FICTION PUBLICATIONS

Novels (series: Earthminds; Venus)

*Cloned Lives.* New York, Fawcett, 1976; London, Fontana, 1981.
*The Sudden Star.* New York, Fawcett, 1979; as *The White Death*, London, Fontana, 1980.
*Watchstar* (Earthminds). New York, Pocket Books, 1980.
*The Golden Space.* New York, Simon and Schuster, 1982.
*The Alien Upstairs.* New York, Doubleday, 1983.
*Earthseed* (for children). New York, Harper, 1983; London, Collins, 1984.
*Eye of the Comet* (for children; Earthminds). New York, Harper, 1984.
*Homesmind* (for children; Earthminds). New York, Harper, 1984.
*Venus of Dreams.* New York, Bantam, 1986; London, Bantam, 1989.
*The Shore of Women.* New York, Crown, 1986; London, Chatto and Windus, 1987.
*Alien Child* (for children). New York, Harper, 1988.
*Venus of Shadows.* New York, Doubleday, 1988; London, Bantam, 1990.

Short Stories

*Starshadows.* New York, Ace, 1977.
*The Best of Pamela Sargent,* edited by Martin H. Greenberg. Chicago, Academy, 1987.

OTHER PUBLICATIONS

Other

*The Mountain Cage.* New Castle, Virginia, Cheap Street, 1983.

Editor, *Women of Wonder: Science-Fiction Stories by Women about Women.* New York, Random House, 1975; London, Penguin, 1978.
Editor, *More Women of Wonder: Science-Fiction Novelettes by Women about Women.* New York, Random House, 1976; London, Penguin, 1979.
Editor, *Bio-Futures: Science Fiction Stories about Biological Metamorphosis.* New York, Random House, 1976.
Editor, *The New Women of Wonder: Science-Fiction Novelettes by Women about Women.* New York, Random House, 1978.
Editor, with Ian Watson, *Afterlives: Stories about Life after Death.* New York, Random House, 1986.

*

Bibliography: *The Work of Pamela Sargent* by Jeffrey M. Elliot, San Bernardino, California, Borgo Press, 1990.

Manuscript Collection: David Paskow Science Fiction Collection, Temple University, Philadelphia.

* * *

In the two decades that Pamela Sargent has been writing SF, she has developed a reputation not so much for spinning yarns as for telling real stories, stories of the inner lives of human beings caught in unusual circumstances and stories of our species as it is and as it might be. Her fiction features action, adventure, and ideas, but its main focus is always character. She is a feminist and futurist for whom biotechnology, cybernetics, space travel, alien encounters, environmental degradation, and nuclear war provide new scenarios in which believable characters act out their life dramas.

In her novels for young adults, the central figure is always a 15-year-old girl coming of age in a world very different from ours. Although simpler in language and form than her adult fictions, these books offer pentrating psychological portraits of gifted and courageous young women. The heroines of the *Watchstar* trilogy (*Watchstar, Eye of the Comet,* and *Homesmind*) live on a far future earth inhabited by technologically primitive villagers who possess telepathic and telekinetic powers. Daiya, Lydee, and Anra question the conservative world views of their culture and seek to discover the secrets of their world and of the Comet Dwellers, the descendants of humans who long ago left earth. The fate of the planet is in the hands of these young visionaries. *Earthseed,* which is reminiscent of Panshin's *Rite of Passage* and a host of other spaceship-as-world novels, depicts the trials of a cohort of space-born humans nurtured and raised by an intelligent spacecraft they call "Ship." They must learn outdoor survival skills that include orienteering and conflict resolution. *Alien Child* is the story of a girl raised on post-nuclear earth by a furry alien who has come to study a race that committed global suicide. These novels display a refreshing faith in the energy, flexibility, and hopefulness of youth. (For a more detailed discussion see my article "Pamela Sargent's Science Fiction for Young Adults: Celebrations of Change," *Science-Fiction Studies 16,* July 1989.)

In Sargent's novels for adults, her protagonists face technologically and politically complicated worlds that are clear and often frightening extrapolations of the one we inhabit. Perhaps the most overtly hopeful (and certainly one of the richest) is the first, *Cloned Lives,* in which Sargent explores the social and psychological traumas of the world's first five clones. Although each clone has a chapter, the central figure is Kyra, the lone female. The Swenson clones are raised as siblings, but their kinship status—one the world has never before seen—is in question throughout the book. Kyra functions alternately as the male clones' mother, sister, and lover. When she perfects techniques that make immortality a possibility, she assumes a life-giving role that would be the envy of Eve. The impact of biological engineering on the life span is also the subject of *The Golden Space.* Here, immortality is a mixed blessing, and fear of life sometimes overshadows fear of death.

*The Sudden Star* and *The Alien Upstairs* are set in dismal not-so-distant alternate presents made possible by environmental rape and pillage. In *The Sudden Star,* crop failures, plagues, and institutional collapse make life almost unbearable in what used to be the United States. The human race blames the appearance of a bright star in 2000 A.D. for their troubles, "forgetting," as one character puts it, "that the heavens are vast and the stars unknowing of earth." Sameness and deprivation also pervade *The Alien Upstairs,* but in this case, the protagonist's life is given a little spice by the arrival of a mysterious neighbor whom she believes to be an alien. He turns out to be the immortal tool of unknown alien powers, and Sarah's adventures with him put human history in a cosmic perspective for both her and us.

Without question, Sargent's masterpiece to date is *The Shore of Women.* This feminist dystopian nuclear holocaust novel depicts an earth ruled by women from fortified enclaves who have banished men, the destroyers of the world, to the forests. Homosexuality is the norm for both groups, and procreation is accomplished through artificial insemination (the sperm is collected from electronically deluded males who believe that they are having sex with women). The principal characters, Birana and Arvil, recreate (at least for a time) heterosexual love during a series of life-threatening adventures. Both same and opposite sex liaisons are celebrated, as individuals, couples, and friends struggle to establish loving relationships in a world in which woman-made institutions are as corrupt as the man-made institutions of our own. The novel's multiple narrative perspectives, lyrical eroticism, and intellectual depth should make it a classic of intelligent SF.

The first two volumes of Sargent's Venus Trilogy, *Venus of Dreams* and *Venus of Shadows,* are the beginning and middle of a transgenerational saga of terraforming Venus (*Child of Venus* is in progress). It is not surprising, given Sargent's preoccupation with individuals (especially women) struggling against brittle and damaging social structures, that the colonists of Venus discover that, to earth's nominally Muslim rulers, terraformation means not only making Venus environmentally earthlike, but politically and socially earthlike as well. Descendants of a women's commune in the Midwest, the novels' protagonists must deal with the limitations of life as female residents of a colony ruled from afar by ruthless partriarchs.

It is a pity that Pamela Sargent's books have had such a hard time staying in print, for they offer unique and important glimpses into what being human is and will be like, as, for good or ill, we take uncertain control of the planetary environment and of our own evolutionary future.

—Thomas J. Morrissey

---

**SAWTRELLE, William Carter.** *See* **PHILLIPS, Rog.**

---

**SAXON, Richard.** Pseudonym for Joseph Lawrence Morrissey; also writes as Henry Richards. American. Born in 1905.

### Science-Fiction Publications

Novels

*City of the Hidden Eyes* (as J.L. Morrissey). London, Consul, 1964.
*Cosmic Crusade.* London, Consul, 1964; New York, Arcadia House, 1966.
*Future for Sale.* London, Consul, 1964; New York, Arcadia House, 1965.
*The Hour of the Phoenix.* London, Consul, 1964; as Henry Richards, New York, Arcadia House, 1965.
*The Stars Came Down.* London, Consul, 1964; New York, Arcadia House, 1967.

* * *

Richard Saxon's career was begun and ended in a single year. Although none of his novels was exceptional enough to attract any particular interest, they are not as unprepossessing as their poor success might indicate.

For the most part, Saxon eschewed melodrama in a period when action and suspense were the main attractions for most genre devotees. The protagonists of *Future for Sale* invent a time machine with which they travel to both the past and the future, but with considerable less liveliness than in, for example, Wells's *The Time Machine.* In the past, one character relives a poignant moment in his own life; in the future, he discovers that a scientific dictatorship has been created which provides mankind with all of its material wants but which exacts in payment an irresistible drive for conformity. Far from leading a revolt, the hero returns to our own time, where a quarreling mob destroys the time machine utterly.

*The Stars Came Down* is also more reflective than active. Humanity's first trip to the stars is over, and the returnees discover that a new civilization has evolved on Earth during the relative five millennia that have passed since their departure. For the most part, the latter half of the novel consists of a quiet discourse on the nature of Utopian society.

*The Hour of the Phoenix* is Saxon's most lively novel. The drive into space is cut short as a new astronomical object appears, destined to destroy our world in the near future. The usual occurs, mobs riot, order breaks down into chaos, and through it all a small group attempts to make plans to allow humanity to carry on elsewhere in space. The waning chapters are a bit sentimental, and this is in balance no more than a very lightweight imitation of Wylie and Balmer's *When Worlds Collide.*

*Cosmic Crusade* has another conventional plot, this time weighted with excessive ruminative discourses. An underground society slowly awakens to the reality of its existence and prepares to emerge onto the surface of its world. Once more, we are warned against the decay that inevitably accompanies conformity to the exclusion of individuality.

On balance, Saxon is a slightly above-average writer whose talents might have developed had he remained active. The small body of essentially minor work which he produced are reasonable entertainments, but neither original enough nor well-written enough to survive through the years.

—Don D'Ammassa

---

**SAXTON, Josephine (née Howard).** British. Born in Halifax, Yorkshire, 11 June 1935. Educated at Clare Hall County Secondary School, Halifax. Married 1) Geoffrey Banks in 1958, one son; 2) Colin Saxton in 1962 (divorced 1983), one son and one daughter. Agent: Maxine Jakubowski, 95 Finchley Lane, London N.W. 4. Address: 12 Plymouth Place, Leamington Spa, Warwickshire, CV31 IHN, England.

### Science-Fiction Publications

Novels (series: Jane Saint)

*The Hieros Gamos of Sam and An Smith.* New York, Doubleday, 1969.
*Vector for Seven; or, The Weltanshauung of Mrs. Amelia Mortimer and Friends.* New York, Doubleday, 1971.
*Group Feast.* New York, Doubleday, 1971.
*The Travails of Jane Saint.* London, Virgin, 1981.
*Queen of the States.* London, Women's Press, 1986.
*Jane Saint and the Backlash: The Further Travails of Jane Saint,* with *The Consciousness Machine.* London, Women's Press, 1989.

Short Stories

*The Power of Time.* London, Chatto and Windus, 1985.
*The Travails of Jane Saint and Other Stories.* London, Women's Press, 1986.

### Other Publications

Short Stories

*Little Tours of Hell: Tall Tales of Food and Holidays.* London, Pandora Press, 1986.

* * *

In the late 1960's and early 1970's when her work first appeared, Josephine Saxton's idiosyncratic, iconoclastic fiction fitted well with the New Wave sensibilities of the time. But as the New Wave spent itself in the mid-1970's, so Saxton's work seemed to fall out of favour, and it virtually disappeared from view until the feminist writing of the mid-1980's heralded a much deserved rediscovery. Yet her writing has not changed significantly during the intervening years to suit such apparently different camps so neatly. In fact, her writing seems to attract descriptions such as "New Wave," "feminist," or even "science fiction" more because there is no other way of categorising it than because it really belongs within such narrow bands. In *Jane Saint and the Backlash*, she manages to bring together one of her earliest stories, "The Consciousness Machine," with some of her most recent work, and the ideas and interests that drive them are the same in both. Most obviously, a long-time interest in Jungian psychology litters her work with archetypes. She makes little pretence of creating fully rounded characters, rather she peoples her books with figureheads representing attitudes and characteristics, and as often as not she isolates these figures in a barren landscape such as the wasteland of her first novel, *The Hieros Gamos of Sam and An Smith*, or the dreamscape in which Jane Saint has her carefully orchestrated encounters.

Certainly there is something of New Wave experimentalism in the dramatic isolation and the polemical or parable-like intent of her fiction, just as the polemic does carry a powerful feminist message. But these characteristics no more consign her work exclusively to these camps than the sight of a flying saucer in *Vector for Seven* or the aliens in *Queen of the States* make her stories unequivocally science fiction. Josephine Saxton writes stories that belong in one exclusive but highly entertaining genre: the Josephine Saxton story. The science-fiction trappings are usually there more to serve as a sign of the character's mental state than as a description of objective reality; one of the abiding elements in her work is a questioning of the differences between objective and subjective reality.

Other common features of this private genre are: journeys to be undertaken; the patient detailing of everyday life, how people dress, their hygiene, and above all how they cook and what they eat; and the progression from being alone, the absurdity of isolation and mutual distrust, to the achievement of togetherness, a mutually supportive social unit. Yet for all the seriousness of these concerns—and her feminism in particular is a strongly held position that comes through in everything she writes—Saxton is also a very funny writer. Serious points are made through absurdity.

Her first published story, "The Wall," is typical of all her work: a great wall lies across a barren landscape. This is no painstaking delineation of a place we instantly recognise, it is more a vague dreamscape, vast and empty, in which her characters, when they belatedly enter the scene, can be effectively and cruelly isolated. What's more, the wall's symbolic weight far outstrips a simple description of the scene—Saxton has always been more prodigal in her use of symbolism than most other science-fiction writers. It is far from being her best story, but it does stake out the territory she has occupied, to some extent, ever since.

Her first three novels further develop these characteristics. In *The Hieros Gamos of Sam and An Smith* (the title is from the Greek for "holy marriage"), a boy wandering in a depopulated landscape finds and cares for a newborn baby girl. In *Vector for Seven*, a disparate group of characters wander through a surreal landscape until their initial mistrust is replaced with unity. In *Group Feast*, a 24-hour party takes place in a house with a seemingly limitless number of rooms, giving Saxton the opportunity to dwell in perceptive and witty detail on material possessions and food, while Cora's artificial relationship with her servants is destroyed, and she is forced in the end to abandon it all.

Though demonstrating a growing ability and confidence, these books had little commercial success, and were followed by silence punctuated only by a few short stories, often more science fictional than her novels. Their dark humour tends to rely on inversion; thus in "Elouise and the Doctors of the Planet Pergamon," Elouise is healthy on a planet where everyone is legally obliged to be diseased, while in "Gordon's Women," Gordon believes he has a harem of perfect female automata not knowing that they are in fact alive.

Her more recent work, *The Travails of Jane Saint*, describes a quest through a typically surreal landscape in which a series of bizarre and ludicrous encounters with demon-like Zilp, Merleau-Ponty the talking dog, Simone de Beauvoir as a fairground sideshow, and others explore aspects of feminist consciousness until, as so often in Saxton's work, the lonely Jane Saint has been reunited with family and friends, and in this union succeeds in changing the world. The sequel, *Jane Saint and the Backlash*, retraces the journey slightly less successfully as a counterpoint to political apathy and the rise of the "new man."

Saxton's most successful novel, however, is *Queen of the States*, a vivid, multi-layered work that constantly forces us to examine our assumptions of reality. Is Magdalen really being examined by aliens, is she really Queen of America, how can her lover conjured up by the aliens become the doctor of her husband's mistress? And as reality is questioned, so are other assumptions. The book has a powerful underlying feminist message, yet, as in *Jane Saint*, the husband is no villain, and both he and Dr. Murgatroyd, the figures of authority and the establishment, can come through in the end if they accept their fantasies.

But perhaps we should leave it to one more short story to encapsulate the Saxton credo. "The Message" resolutely avoids the fantastic, though it does display all the familiar Saxton hallmarks, most notably the journey format. We follow an old woman walking home from a hospital, seeing the urban landscape as it has changed from the days of her youth, and coming to terms with both her age and her surroundings in typical Saxton fashion by finding unity with others along the way, an old man who lives alone, a bunch of young Rastafarians.

—Paul Kincaid

---

**SCARBOROUGH, Elizabeth (Ann).** American. Born in Kansas City, Missouri, 23 March 1947. Educated at Bethany Hospital School of Nursing, R.N.; University of Alaska, Fairbanks. Served as a nurse during Vietnam War. United States Army, Nurse Corps: Captain. Married Richard G. Kacsur in 1975 (divorced 1981). Surgical nurse, St. David's Hospital, Austin, Texas. Lives in Port Townsend, Washington. Recipient: Nebula award, 1989. Agent: Merrilee Heifetz, 21 West 26th Street, New York, New York 10010. Address: c/o Doubleday, 666 Fifth Avenue, New York, New York 10103, U.S.A.

Science-Fiction Publications

Novels (series: Songkiller)

*Song of Sorcery*. New York, Bantam, 1982.
*The Unicorn Creed*. New York, Bantam, 1983.
*Bronwyn's Bane*. New York, Bantam, 1983; London, 1987.
*The Harem of Aman Akbar; or, The Djinn Decanted*. New York, Bantam, 1984.
*The Christening Quest*. New York, Bantam, 1985.
*The Drastic Dragon of Draco, Texas*. New York, Bantam, 1986.
*The Goldcamp Vampire; or, The Sanguinary Sourdough*. New York, Bantam, 1987.
*Songs from the Seashell Archives*. New York, Bantam, 2 vols., 1987–88.
*The Healer's War*. New York, Doubleday, 1988.

*Nothing Sacred*. New York, Doubleday, 1991.
*Phantom Banjo* (Songkiller). New York, Bantam, 1991.
*Picking the Ballad's Bones* (Songkiller). New York, Bantam, 1991.

OTHER PUBLICATIONS

Other

*An Interview with a Vietnam Nurse*. New York, Bantam, 1989.

*

Elizabeth Ann Scarborough comments:
My earliest books were intended to be light, humorous, and entertaining, which I hope they were. I changed directions at the urging of my publisher, Lou Aronica at Bantam, to write *The Healer's War*, loosely based on my experiences in Vietnam. Since then, my work has been more of a blending of social science fiction, fantasy, political satire, and humor (particularly in the Songkiller Saga).

* * *

Elizabeth Scarborough made her debut with a traditional, light-hearted fantasy adventure called *Song of Sorcery*. Structurally, the book is a gentle version of the quest story, the protagonist is Maggie Brown, a good if somewhat disorganized witch, who sets out to find her half sister, meeting unicorns, dragons, and other magical creatures along the way. The sequel, *The Unicorn Creed*, continued Maggie's adventures, now in company with a minstrel and a unicorn, the latter of whom has difficulty relating to the growing intimacy between his companions. Even though the menace this time is an evil sorcerer, the overall tone is good natured, enlivened by Scarborough's refreshingly clear prose and a cast of amusing, interesting characters.

*Bronwyn's Bane* shares the same setting but a different pair of central characters. One is Bronwyn, a precocious but uncooperative princess who is cursed never to tell the truth, the other the daughter of Maggie and her minstrel husband. Together they experience an inventive and highly amusing series of adventures: they stop a war and survive various dangers, all of which is enlivened by the princess's curse, leading to some hilarious situations. Bronwyn's child must be rescued in *The Christening Quest*, the fourth book in the series, but although the story is well-paced and enjoyable, Scarborough seemed to be tiring of this setting. Her gift for light humor remains intact, but is less evident.

*The Harem of Aman Akar* was Scarborough's first non-series novel, an Arabian Nights adventure filled with djinn, evil emirs, and high adventure. Once again, the protagonist is a woman, one of Aman's wives who sets out to free him from a humiliating curse inflicted by a rival. Like most of Scarborough's female characters, Rasa is a strong-willed woman who refuses to allow society to define her place in its structure.

Scarborough's gradual drift away from fantasy to more serious and realistic themes was first visible in *The Drastic Dragon of Draco, Texas*. Set in the old west, the story involves the mysterious appearance of a fire-breathing dragon. Although there are still flashes of humor, it's a far more serious novel in most ways than those that preceded it. In *The Goldcamp Vampire*, set against the background of the Yukon gold rush, an adventurous young woman finds more than she bargained for when the suave foreigner courting her turns out to be a vampire, and she is blamed by the local people for one of his bloodthirsty attacks. As with the previous book, the serious tone is leavened by humor, but there was a clear evolution toward more serious themes.

Scarborough's first major novel, *The Healer's War*, was a complete change of pace, drawn from her experiences as an army nurse who served a tour of duty in Vietnam. Winner of the Nebula award as best novel of the year, it follows the experiences of Lieutenant Kitty McCulley, a nurse transferred to Vietnam who quickly discovers that there are undercurrents far deeper than she had ever experienced previously. After being presented with a magical amulet by a Vietnamese civilian, she becomes emotionally involved with the plight of the victims, both military and civilian, on both sides of the conflict, and eventually responds to a compulsion that she considers superior to the one imposed by her government. The novel reveals a depth of characterization only hinted at in earlier works, and carries a powerful emotional impact.

Although the book is to a certain extent a war novel, it is written from an unusual perspective, and deals more with the human effects of armed conflict and disruption rather than with the physical elements. At times bitter, the story is noticeably missing the lighter hand of her previous work, because levity would have been out of place with this theme.

Scarborough's first true science-fiction novel was *Nothing Sacred*, another story of armed conflict, this time set in a century in the future. The world has become a troubled place; the unemployed in America have little choice but to enlist in the military and be sent to fight in foreign wars. The protagonist is a woman taken prisoner and assigned to a camp in Tibet, where time seems to flow differently and the concerns of the outside world are less compelling. At least that's true until a nuclear conflict erupts, and they find themselves struggling to survive.

Most recently, Scarborough has returned to light fantasy with the Songkiller Saga, the first two titles of which are *Phantom Banjo* and *Picking the Ballad's Bones*. The series is a frequently amusing blend of ghosts, contemporary settings, magic, and the like. These seem to represent a change of pace from her more serious novels, but she has indicated that her future works will continue the diversity already demonstrated.

—Don D'Ammassa

---

**SCHACHNER, Nat(han).** Also wrote as Chan Corbett; Walter Glamis. American. Born in New York City, 16 January 1895. Educated at the City College of New York, B.S. 1915; New York University, J.D. 1919. Served in the United States Army chemical warfare service, 1917–18. Married Helen Lichtenstein in 1919; one daughter. Chemist, New York City Department of Health, 1915–17; admitted to the New York Bar, 1919; practicing lawyer, New York, 1919–33; freelance writer from 1933; editorial consultant, American Jewish Committee, 1945–51; director of public relations, National Council of Jewish Women, 1954–55. President, American Rocket Society, 1933. *Died 2 October 1955.*

SCIENCE-FICTION PUBLICATIONS

Novel

*Space Lawyer*. New York, Gnome Press, 1953.

Uncollected Short Stories (series: Past, Present, and Future)

"The Tower of Evil," with Leo Zagat, in *Wonder Stories Quarterly* (New York), Summer 1930.
"In 20,000 A.D.," with Leo Zagat, in *Wonder Stories* (New York), September 1930.
"Back to 20,000 A.D.," with Leo Zagat, in *Wonder Stories* (New York), March 1931.
"The Emperor of the Stars," with Leo Zagat, in *Wonder Stories* (New York), April 1931.
"The Menace from Andromeda," with Leo Zagat, in *Amazing* (New York), April 1931.
"The Death-Cloud," with Leo Zagat, in *Astounding* (New York), May 1931.
"The Revolt of the Machines," with Leo Zagat, in *Astounding* (New York), July 1931.
"Venus Mines, Incorporated," with Leo Zagat, in *Wonder Stories* (New York), August 1931.
"Exiles of the Moon," with Leo Zagat, in *Wonder Stories* (New York), September 1931.
"Pirates of the Gorm," in *Astounding* (New York), May 1932.
"Slaves of Mercury," in *Astounding* (New York), September 1932.
"Emissaries of Space," in *Wonder Stories Quarterly* (New York), Fall 1932.
"The Time Express," in *Wonder Stories* (New York), December 1932.
"The Memory of the Atoms," with R. Lacher, in *Wonder Stories* (New York), January 1933.
"The Eternal Dictator," in *Wonder Stories* (New York), February 1933.
"The Robot Technocrat," in *Wonder Stories* (New York), March 1933.
"The Revolt of the Scientists," in *Wonder Stories* (New York), April, May, June 1933.
"The Orange God" (as Walter Glamis), and "Fire Imps of Vesuvius," in *Astounding* (New York), October 1933.
"Ancestral Voices," in *Astounding* (New York), December 1933.
"Redmask of the Outlands," in *Astounding* (New York), January 1934.
"The Time Imposter," in *Astounding* (New York), March 1934.
"He from Procyon," in *Astounding* (New York), April 1934.
"The 100th Generation," in *Astounding* (New York), May 1934.
"The Living Equation," in *Astounding* (New York), September 1934.
"The Great Thirst," in *Astounding* (New York), November 1934.
"Mind of the World," in *Astounding* (New York), March 1935.
"The Orb of Probability," in *Astounding* (New York), June 1935.
"The Son of Redmask," in *Astounding* (New York), August 1935.
"World Gone Mad," in *Amazing* (New York), October 1935.
"I Am Not God," in *Astounding* (New York), October, November 1935.
"The Isotope Men," in *Astounding* (New York), January 1936.
"Entropy," in *Astounding* (New York), March 1936.
"Reverse Universe," in *Astounding* (New York), June 1936.
"Pacifica," in *Astounding* (New York), July 1936.
"The Return of the Murians," in *Astounding* (New York), August 1936.
"The Saphrophyte Men of Venus," in *Astounding* (New York), October 1936.
"The Eternal Wanderer," in *Astounding* (New York), November 1936.
"Infra Universe," in *Astounding* (New York), December 1936, January 1937.
"Beyond Which Limits," in *Astounding* (New York), February 1937.
"Earthspin," in *Astounding* (New York), June 1937.
"Sterile Planet," in *Astounding* (New York), July 1937.
"Crystallized Thought," in *Astounding* (New York), August 1937.
"Lost in the Dimensions," in *Astounding* (New York), November 1937.
"City of the Rocket Horde," in *Astounding* (New York), December 1937.
"Negative Space," in *Astounding* (New York), April 1938.
"Island of the Individualists" (Past), in *Astounding* (New York), May 1938.
"The Sun World of Soldus," in *Astounding* (New York), October 1938.
"Simultaneous Worlds," in *Astounding* (New York), November 1938.
"Palooka from Jupiter," in *Astounding* (New York), February 1939.
"Worlds Don't Care," in *Astounding* (New York), April 1939.
"When the Future Dies," in *Astounding* (New York), June 1939.
"City under the Sea," in *Fantastic Adventures* (New York), September 1939.
"City of the Corporate Mind" (Past), in *Astounding* (New York), December 1939.
"Cold," in *Astounding* (New York), March 1940.
"Space Double," in *Astounding* (New York), May 1940.
"Master Gerald of Cambray," in *Unknown Worlds* (New York), June 1940.
"Runaway Cargo," in *Astounding* (New York), October 1940.
"The Return of Circe," in *Fantastic Adventures* (New York), August 1941.
"Beyond All Weapons," in *Astounding* (New York), November 1941.
"Eight Who Came Back," in *Fantastic Adventures* (New York), November 1941.
"The Ultimate Metal," in *The Best of Science Fiction*, edited by Groff Conklin. New York, Crown, 1946.
"Stratosphere Towers," in *Astounding* (New York), August 1954.
"Past, Present and Future," in *Before the Golden Age*, edited by Isaac Asimov. New York, Doubleday, and London, Robson, 1974.
"The Shining One," in *Visions of Tomorrow*, edited by Roger Elwood. New York, Pocket Books, 1976.
"City of the Cosmic Rays" (Past), in *Astounding Science Fiction July 1939*, by John W. Campbell, edited by Martin H. Greenberg. Carbondale, Southern Illinois University Press, 1981.

Uncollected Short Stories as Chan Corbett

"When the Sun Dies," in *Astounding* (New York), March 1935.
"Intra-Planetary," in *Astounding* (New York), October 1935.
"Ecce Homo," in *Astounding* (New York), June 1936.
"The Thought Web of Minipar," in *Astounding* (New York), November 1936.
"Beyond Infinity," in *Astounding* (New York), January 1937.
"Nova in Messier 33," in *Astounding* (New York), May 1937.
"When Time Stood Still," in *Astounding* (New York), June 1937.

OTHER PUBLICATIONS

Novels

*By the Dim Lamps.* New York, Stokes, 1941.
*The King's Messenger.* Philadelphia, Lippincott, 1942.
*The Sun Shines West.* New York, Appleton Century, 1943.

*The Wanderer: A Novel of Dante and Beatrice*. New York, Appleton Century, 1944; London, Melrose, 1948.

Other

*Aaron Burr*. New York, Stokes, 1937.
*The Medieval Universities*. New York, Stokes, and London, Allen and Unwin, 1938.
*Alexander Hamilton*. New York, Appleton Century, 1946.
*The Price of Liberty: A History of the American Jewish Committee*. New York, American Jewish Committee, 1948.
*Thomas Jefferson*. New York, Appleton Century Crofts, 1951.
*Alexander Hamilton, Nation Builder*. New York, McGraw Hill, 1952.
*The Founding Fathers*. New York, Putnam, 1954.

* * *

Nat Schachner was attracted for a time to the vigorous, young genre of pulp-magazine science fiction, where he left an impression with his liberal ideas and earnest inventiveness. Schachner worked first as a chemist, spent a number of years in law practice, published hundreds of pieces of short fiction in the pulps (science, detective, mystery, western, and adventure stories), and wrote several scholarly books on history. During the Nazi threat before and during World War II, he defended human liberties vigorously in all his writings—both pulp fiction and scholarly. Schachner's total commitment to the life of letters and to humanitarian values makes him a true 20th-century representative of the Romantics whom he said he loved as a child. He represents the writer as hero; and the heroic vigor of the science-fiction genre during the time that he was active in it corresponds well with his later American Revolutionary history. Schachner's hopeful ideas for progress through clever technology and rationality had their roots both in the 18th-century Enlightenment of Thomas Jefferson and in the pulp-fiction world of the early *Astounding*.

The first dozen or so of Schachner's science-fiction stories were written in collaboration with Arthur Leo Zagat, but it was with the "thought variant" stories of the F. Orlin Tremaine *Astounding* that the inventive lawyer began to hit his stride as a writer who would extrapolate into the future his liberal ideas about the present and eventually about the past. The first thought variant story was Schachner's "Ancestral Voices," and new idea stories followed rapidly for the rest of the decade. In his book on the science-fiction pulp magazines, Paul Carter calls Schachner the earliest of the "anti-Nazi Paul Reveres" whose speculative fictions increasingly explored the opportunities for sociological themes that could be related to current events. A rather stiff and primitive story called "The Eternal Wanderer" contains a crude courtroom scene about interplanetary law that anticipates Schachner's only science-fiction book *Space Lawyer* (made out of two later stories, "Old Fireball" and "Jurisdiction").

Schachner's best writing and most memorable contribution to letters is undoubtedly his historical work, and he properly gave up work for the pulps in order to pursue that research. But one cannot help thinking that his thought variant extrapolations were both inspired by his knowledge of the Enlightenment and contributed greatly to his understanding of it. One of his more carefully written and sophisticated fictions, "Past, Present, and Future," performs just that balancing between a nostalgia for the heroic and glorious lost past on the one hand and an awareness of the challenges in the present on the other that creates the ironic complexity of mind that is necessary for true liberal thinking. Schachner was a hero among writers not only for the vast amount of work that he got done but also for how he did it—less an artist than a propagandist for democracy.

—Donald M. Hassler

---

**SCHENCK, Hilbert.** American. Born in Boston, Massachusetts, 12 February 1926. Educated at Williams College, Williamstown, Massachusetts, B.A. in physics 1950; Stanford University, California, M.S. in mechanical engineering 1952. Served as an electronic technician in the United States Navy, 1944–46. Married 1) Mary Low Taylor in 1950; 2) Anne Thompson in 1983; six children. Test engineer, Pratt & Whitney Aircraft, East Hartford, Connecticut, 1952–56; Assistant Professor to Professor, Clarkson College, Potsdam, New York, 1956–66; Professor, 1966–83, and director, Scuba Safety Project, 1968–80, University of Rhode Island, Kingston. Agent: Virginia Kidd, Box 278, Milford, Pennsylvania 18337, U.S.A.

Science-Fiction Publications

Novels

*At the Eye of the Ocean*. New York, Pocket Books, 1980.
*A Rose for Armageddon*. New York, Pocket Books, 1982; London, Allison and Busby, 1984.
*Chrono-Sequence*. New York, Tor, 1988.
*Steam Bird*. New York, Tor, 1988.

Short Stories

*Wave Rider*. New York, Pocket Books, 1980.

Other Publications

Other

*Shallow Water Diving for Pleasure and Profit*, with Henry Kendall. Cambridge, Maryland, Cornell Maritime Press, 1950.
*Underwater Photography*, with Henry Kendall. Cambridge, Maryland, Cornell Maritime Press, 1954.
*Shallow Water Diving and Spearfishing*, with Henry Kendall. Cambridge, Maryland, Cornell Maritime Press, 1954.
*Skin Diver's and Spearfisherman's Guide to American Waters*. Cambridge, Maryland, Cornell Maritime Press, 1955.
*Heat Transfer*. Englewood Cliffs, New Jersey, Prentice Hall, 1959.
*Thermodynamics*, with R. Kenyon. New York, Ronald Press, 1961.
*An Introduction to the Engineering Research Project*. New York, McGraw Hill, 1962.
*Fortran Methods in Heat Flow*. New York, Ronald Press, 1963.
*Theories of Engineering Experimentation*. New York, McGraw Hill, 1963; 3rd edition, 1978.

Editor, *Introduction to Ocean Engineering*. New York, McGraw Hill, 1975.

*

Hilbert Schenck comments:

My stories have been mainly concerned with the technology of ocean exploration, but also may contain fantasy elements. My first two novels are concerned both with the ocean and the area of Cape Cod, Mass. My novel *Steam Bird*, serialized last year in *F & SF* departs from these topics and is concerned with the flight of a nuclear-propelled aircraft, a project on which I worked in the 1950's at Pratt & Whitney Aircraft. Most recently, I have been fooling around with the idea of recursive fiction, that is, fiction that is concerned with its own creation. My two most recent fictions in *Analog* are attempts to push the idea of recursion as far as it seems possible to go, although several other of my stories have recursive elements. My two Cape Cod novels represent attempts to introduce classic SF themes (the idea of the superman and the idea of time travel) into a regional fiction setting. A third novel adds a third basic SF theme, visitation from another world, into the Cape Cod geographic and historic situation.

* * *

Hilbert Schenck's first science-fiction sale was "Tomorrow's Weather," a post-nuclear-war story about a meteorologist who plots the spread of radioactivity, published in *Fantasy and Science Fiction*, April 1953. Except for occasional bits of verse, this competent but forgettable story was his sole appearance for over two decades. It wasn't until 1977 that he began writing in earnest, producing a series of skillfully crafted short stories and novels, many reflecting his oceanographic background and his familiarity with the Cape Cod area of Massachusetts.

"Three Days at the End of the World" features an oceanographer who suspects that a biological weapon of unprecedented magnitude has been inadvertently lost at sea, threatening the entire biosphere. The protagonist and his allies must solve the problem, simultaneously thwarting a set of malevolent government agents, common villains in his fiction. This story was followed shortly by "The Morphology of the Kirkham Wreck," a far more ambitious and satisfying story. Set several decades in the past, it follows the efforts of a group of men to rescue the passengers and crew of a grounded ship. The protagonist is able to slip back through time and affect the situation slightly, increasing the chances of success, a subtle touch of fantasy in what is otherwise an excellent sea adventure tale.

"The Battle of the Abaco Reefs" is set after the world has broken up into scores of tiny states. The governor of California makes an alliance with Fidel Castro to invade and conquer the Bahamas, and is thwarted by the island nation's desperate and cleverly conceived defensive system. The main attraction in this very fine story is the interaction of the characters and forces, and while Schenck makes use of the plot to criticize the role of government, his political statements are unobtrusive and don't interfere with the flow of the story.

Two more sea stories followed, "Wave Rider" and "Buoyant Ascent," the first the story of a high-tech trimaran and an effort to break a world sailing record, the second concerned with attempts to rescue the crew of a sunken submarine. Although the plots of each are intense and well-constructed, Schenck fails to people either of these with the well-realized characters that made the previous stories so memorable.

Schenck's first novel, *At the Eye of the Ocean*, was markedly superior to any of his shorter fiction. Set in New England just prior to the Civil War, it features a sea captain who uses his ship to ferry runaway slaves to Canada, aided by his psychic ability to detect the moods of the ocean. At the same time, he is obsessed with his vision of the eye of the ocean, a mystical place whose existence is known to him alone.

*A Rose for Armageddon* is also set in Cape Cod, in the near future when the collapsing world economy seems to be headed directly toward universal anarchy. A research group strives to perfect a computer program of unprecedented scope, one which may provide critical insights into the nature of human civilization. But two of the scientists find something else on the island they are studying, a place where they can travel back through time to a simpler and more satisfying world.

"Hurricane Claude" (in *Fantasy and Science Fiction*, April 1983) is an interesting examination of weather control, the possibility of short-circuiting a hurricane. It is the best of three short stories that appeared in the early 1980's. They were followed by *Steam Bird*, which was quite different from anything Schenck had written before. *Steam Bird* is set in an alternate version of the present where technology took a slightly different direction. The story is set aboard a nuclear-powered bomber, one which, having taken off, has no place to land, and its presence in the sky suddenly sets off an international crisis.

"Send Me a Kiss by Wire" (in *Fantasy and Science Fiction*, April 1985) is the narrative of an unexpected encounter with a giant squid, a story that captures the mysterious and wondrous qualities of the undersea world very effectively. An unsavory real estate development deal is thwarted by a device that broadcasts depression and anxiety in "A Down East Storm."

Schenck's most recent novel is *Chrono-Sequence.* While in London, a college professor buys an antique journal, which seems to have originated in Nantucket, a place with a special meaning in her youth. Almost immediately, mysterious attempts are made to steal the book from her, a situation made even more disturbing when she reads the journal and discovers mention of the arrival of alien intelligences on the Earth, creatures that may have perished in the ocean near Nantucket. She returns there, only to discover a strong possibility that the aliens still live in some fashion, and that their presence has been subtly influencing the lives of anyone in the area who is sensitive to their emanations. The novel, a combination of historical novel, SF, and mystery, is easily the best work Schenck has produced to date.

In general, Schenck employs finely-rounded characters in intricately detailed settings, and the fantastic elements, while crucial to the plot, are understated. He has a superb ear for dialogue as well, which contributes to his ability to draw readers completely into the worlds he creates.

—Don D'Ammassa

---

**SCHMIDT, Stanley (Albert).** American. Born in Cincinnati, Ohio, 7 March 1944. Educated at the University of Cincinnati, B.S. in physics 1966 (Phi Beta Kappa); Case Western Reserve University, Cleveland, M.A. 1968, Ph.D. 1969. Married Joyce Tokarz in 1979. Assistant Professor of Physics, Heidelberg College, Tiffin, Ohio, 1969–78. Since 1978, editor, *Analog*, New York. Agent: Scott Meredith Literary Agency, 845 Third Avenue, New York, New York 10022. Address: c/o Analog, 380 Lexington Avenue, New York, New York 10017, U.S.A.

SCIENCE-FICTION PUBLICATIONS

Novels (series: Lifeboat Earth)

*Newton and the Quasi-Apple.* New York, Doubleday, 1975.
*The Sins of the Fathers* (Lifeboat Earth). New York, Berkley, 1976.

*Lifeboat Earth*. New York, Berkley, 1978.
*Tweediloop*. New York, Tor, 1986.

OTHER PUBLICATIONS

Other

Editor, *Analog's Golden Anniversary Anthology*. New York, Davis, 1981.
Editor, *Analog: Reader's Choice*. New York, Davis, 1982.
Editor, *Analog's Children of the Future*. New York, Davis, 1982.
Editor, *Analog's Lighter Side*. New York, Davis, 1982.
Editor, *Analog: Writer's Choice*. New York, Davis, 1983.
Editor, *Analog's War and Peace*. New York, Davis, 1983.
Editor, *Aliens from Analog*. New York, Davis, 1983.
Editor, *From Mind to Mind*. New York, Davis, 1984.
Editor, *Analog's Expanding Universe*. New York, Davis, 1986.
Editor, *Unknown*. New York, Baen, 1988.
Editor, with Martin H. Greenberg, *Unknown Worlds: Tales from Beyond*. New York, Galahad, 1988.
Editor, *Analog Essays on Science*. New York, Wiley, 1990.
Editor, with others, *Writing Science Fiction and Fantasy*. New York, St. Martin's Press, 1991.

*

Stanley Schmidt comments:

In most of my fiction I try to tell entertaining, thought-provoking stories about people in situations which are directly shaped by scientific or technological changes, with neither the human nor the technical parts of the foundation slighted in favor of the other. I am disturbed by the recent tendency to apply the term "science fiction" indiscriminately to a wide range of things which have little or nothing to do with science. Writers who think they can write meaningfully about the future of humanity without giving careful thought to *both* human nature and technology, and the ways they interact, are kidding themselves. And we need to try to anticipate not only those developments which science already knows are possible, but the wildest surprises we can imagine which present knowledge cannot definitely rule out. We have already had to rebuild our picture of the universe at least twice in this century alone; we dare not assume that we will never have to do it again.

Perhaps the best examples to date of the kinds of thing I try to do are *The Sins of the Fathers* and *Lifeboat Earth*, which together are sometimes referred to as the "Kyyra" or "Lifeboat Earth" series.

* * *

Stanley Schmidt seems to be one of the final products of the John Campbell influence on science fiction, although it is probably too early in Schmidt's career to tell definitely. His three novels to date, however, as well as the short story versions of them that appeared in *Analog*, all show the Campbell marks of hard science extrapolation, of positive-thinking, problem-solving approaches to thorny human and social problems, and of two-dimensional human beings compared to a sense of rounded sublimity for whole planets and even galaxies. *The Sins of the Fathers* and *Lifeboat Earth* begin what will no doubt be a series in which galactic history unfolds much like Campbell taught the young Asimov to attempt sublime galactic history four decades ago. The first novel narrates a segment from the history of the planet Ymrek in which the natives seem more interesting than the human emissaries to the planet. Even if Schmidt had not told us that correspondence and ideas from Campbell influenced him, the effects of that influence are apparent in all three novels.

Schmidt is best when he begins to suggest the unresolved and, perhaps, unresolvable tensions that underlie the problems that must be resolutely solved by technology and engineering techniques; these interesting tensions lurking beneath the Campbell-like scenarios are almost exclusively associated with the alien species of the latter two novels. Although Ymrek is an interesting alien extrapolation, its natives are not nearly as symbolically (or scientifically) suggestive as the Kyyra who were originally from nearer the center of our galaxy and who literally set in motion all the action in *The Sins of the Fathers* and its sequel, *Lifeboat Earth*. The more suggestive passages appear in the first book of the series when the Kyyra seem to symbolize the dilemmas of maturation. We must destroy our pasts and even our gods to atone for our mistakes—almost Christian and yet more universal symbolism of the dying god.

The strength related to this symbolic suggestiveness is the detailed elaboration of the aliens themselves—his departure from Campbell. Without the concrete detail to make them credible, the Kyyra could suggest nothing. In fact, as Beldan conducts his human visitor on a tour of the immense Kyyra spaceship orbiting the earth, and explains to her the language and the customs of his people, the reader is reminded of the tours through Walden Two. These aliens are an advanced culture with a kind of social engineering that B.F. Skinner would admire. The Campbell positivism is not unlike Skinner's hopes for managing behaviour, and it is to Schmidt's credit that while the parallels are developed in his narrative, the dilemmas are lurking just beneath the surface that Campbell may not have noticed. We can anticipate, perhaps, more development of the Kyyra in future Schmidt stories; and we can wonder if their utopian, problem-solving traits will prevail or if the tragic implications in the death of their god will haunt Schmidt more.

—Donald M. Hassler

---

**SCHMITZ, James H(enry).** American. Born to American parents in Hamburg, Germany, 15 October 1911. Educated at Realgymnasium Obersekunda. Served in the United States Army Air Force during World War II. Married Betty Mae Chapman in 1957. Worked for International Harvester Company, in Germany, 1932–39; built automobile trailers in the United States after the war. Full-time writer, from 1961. Recipient: Invisible Little Man award, 1973. *Died.*

SCIENCE-FICTION PUBLICATIONS

Novels (series: Telzey Amberdon)

*A Tale of Two Clocks*. New York, Torquil, 1962; as *Legacy*, New York, Ace, 1979.
*The Universe Against Her* (Telzey). New York, Ace, 1964.
*The Witches of Karres*. Philadelphia, Chilton, 1966.
*The Demon Breed*. New York, Ace, 1968; London, Futura, 1974.
*The Eternal Frontiers*. New York, Putnam, 1973; London, Sidgwick and Jackson, 1974.
*The Lion Game* (Telzey). New York, DAW, 1973; London, Sidgwick and Jackson, 1976.

Short Stories

*Agent of Vega.* New York, Gnome Press, 1960.
*A Nice Day for Screaming and Other Tales of the Hub.* Philadelphia, Chilton, 1965.
*A Pride of Monsters.* New York, Macmillan, 1970.
*The Telzey Toy.* New York, DAW, 1973; London, Sidgwick and Jackson, 1976.

*

Bibliography: *James H. Schmitz: A Bibliography* by Mark Owings, Baltimore, Croatan House, 1973.

* * *

James H. Schmitz was a craftsmanlike writer who was a steady contributor to science-fiction magazines for over 20 years. The best of his shorter works are collected in *A Nice Day for Screaming* and *A Pride of Monsters.* In the first work, the stories repeat a consistent theme that the universe is stranger than we can imagine, and that unexpected discoveries will meet us at every turn. Although the stories are set in the far future, humans (and others) continually encounter both creatures and behaviors they could not have foreseen, from the alien automated service-station for spaceships of the title story to an alien so intelligent it keeps humans for pets in "The Winds of Time." But aliens can be surprised too, as "The Other Likeness" shows: agents genetically engineered to resemble humans become so much like us that they begin to sympathize with humans against their masters. There are new machines, too, like the fear broadcaster of "The Tangled Web" or the half-men, half-machines of "The Machmen." And there are some things so strange yet so intelligent they can conceal their very existence from humans, like the forest-sized organism in "Balanced Ecology."

*A Pride of Monsters* collects stories that attempt to rejuvenate the idea of "the monster" through tales of future encounters with alien life-forms. In "Lion Loose," Detective Bad-News Quillan, a favorite character of Schmitz's, meets a rug-sized creature with the ability to pass through solid matter, but it is not nearly so dangerous as the radiation creature of "The Searcher," which endangers a pair of private detectives working undercover against interstellar hijackers. "The Pork Chop Tree" is an alien plant whose very presence is addictive, a less forthright menance than the plant of "Greenface," a story that is unusual (for Schmitz) in being set in the present.

In his longer works, Schmitz often showed a close cooperation between man and alien. The alien may be a machine, like the robot spaceships of the four thematically connected stories of *Agent of Vega*, or mutated animals, like the intelligent giant otters of *The Demon Breed*, who help to repel a threat to human civilization. The "aliens" may even be other humans, as in *The Eternal Frontiers*, in which the Swimmers have diverged so far from normal humanity as to be almost a different species. Rather than forming a close relationship, though, the two groups are keen competitors. And of course, there are aliens that, like those in *A Pride of Monsters*, are threats to humanity, ones such as the plasmoids in *A Tale of Two Clocks.*

A second theme that Schmitz frequently used is that of supranormal mental powers: Telzey, a telepathic teen-aged girl, is the central character in a number of stories. Telepathy (and various other kinds of mental powers, chiefly psychokinesis) is central to Schmitz's most celebrated work, *The Witches of Karres.* The book is a fast-moving, episodic adventure story of an ordinary human, Captain Pausert, who becomes entangled with three psychically endowed girls. Its account of the wakening of telepowers in Pausert draws on familiar science-fiction recipes, mixing appropriately evil villains with nick-of-time escapes, and spicing the whole with an entertaining sense of humor.

—Walter E. Meyers

---

**SCORTIA, Thomas N(icholas).** Also wrote as Scott Nichols. American. Born in Alton, Illinois, 29 August 1926. Educated at Washington University, St. Louis, A.B. 1949, graduate work 1950. Served in the United States Army Infantry, 1944–46, and chemical corps, 1951–53. Married Irene Baron in 1960 (divorced 1968); one adopted son. Senior chemist, Union Starch and Refining Company, Granite City, Illinois, 1954–57; director of research, Chromalloy, Edwardsville, Illinois, 1957–60; group leader, Celanese Corporation, Asheville, North Carolina, 1960–61; section head, United Technology Corporation, Sunnyvale, California, 1961–70. Full-time writer and lecturer, from 1970: author of comics *Targos, Creepy* magazine, May 1972, and *Galactic Prime*, both illustrated by Jack Katz. *Died in 1976.*

SCIENCE-FICTION PUBLICATIONS

Novels

*What Mad Oracle?* Evanston, Illinois, Regency, 1961.
*Artery of Fire.* New York, Doubleday, 1972.
*Earthwreck!* New York, Fawcett, 1974; London, Coronet, 1975.
*The Glass Inferno*, with Frank M. Robinson. New York, Doubleday, 1974; London, Hodder and Stoughton, 1975.
*The Prometheus Crisis*, with Frank M. Robinson. New York, Doubleday, 1975; London, Hodder and Stoughton, 1976.
*The Nightmare Factor*, with Frank M. Robinson. New York, Doubleday, and London, Hodder and Stoughton, 1978.
*The Gold Crew*, with Frank M. Robinson. New York, Warner, 1980; London, Panther, 1983.
*Blow-Out!*, with Frank M. Robinson. New York, Franklin Watts, 1987.

Short Stories

*Caution! Inflammable!* New York, Doubleday, 1975.
*The Best of Thomas N. Scortia*, edited by George Zebrowski. New York, Doubleday, 1981.

Uncollected Short Stories

"Fulfillment," in *Science Fiction Stories*, May 1957.
"Cat o' Nine Tales," in *Future* (New York), Summer 1957.
"Gag Rule," in *Science Fiction Stories*, July 1957.
"Genius Loci," in *Science Fiction Stories*, 1957.
"Cassandra" (as Scott Nichols), in *Science Fiction Quarterly* (Holyoke, Massachusetts), August 1957.
"The Lonely Stars," in *Future* (New York), Fall 1957.
"Insane Planet," in *Fantastic Universe* (Chicago), February 1958.
"The Avengers," in *Science Fiction Stories*, September 1958.
"The Bomb in the Bathtub," in *Fourth Galaxy Reader*, edited by H.L. Gold. New York, Doubleday, 1959.
"The Renegade," in *Future* (New York), April 1959.
"Alien Night," in *Get Out of My Sky.* New York, Crest, 1960.
"Caliban," with Jim Harmon, in *Future* (New York), April 1960.

"The Destroyer," in *Fantastic* (New York), June 1965.
"Broken Image," in *Fantastic* (New York), November 1966.
"Wipeout," in *Swank*, February 1967.
"Superiority Complex," in *Analog* (New York), December 1968.
"Morality," in *Fantastic* (New York), December 1969.
"Judas Fish," in *The Year 2000*, edited by Harry Harrison. New York, Doubleday, 1970, London, Faber, 1971.
"The Good and Faithful," in *Two Views of Wonder*, edited by Scortia and Chelsea Quinn Yarbro. New York, Ballantine, 1973.
"Final Exam," in *The Other Side of Tomorrow*, edited by Roger Elwood. New York, Random House, 1973.
"The Tower," in *Children of Infinity*, edited by Roger Elwood. New York, Watts, 1973.
"Who Is Sylvia?," with Chelsea Quinn Yarbro, in *Vampires, Werewolves, and Other Monsters*, edited by Roger Elwood. Philadelphia, Curtis, 1974.
"Blood Brother," in *Future Kin*, edited by Roger Elwood. New York, Doubleday, 1974.
"The Armageddon Tapes 1–4," in *Continum 1–4*, edited by Roger Elwood. New York, Putnam, 4 vols., 1974–75.
"The Worm," in *Beware More Beasts*. New York, Manor, 1975.
"Someday I'll Find You," in *Odyssey* (New York), April 1976.

OTHER PUBLICATIONS

Plays

Screenplays: *Endangered Species*, with Dalton Trumbo, 1976; *Darker Than You Think*, 1979.

Other

Editor, *Strange Bedfellows*. New York, Random House, 1972.
Editor, with Chelsea Quinn Yarbo, *Two View of Wonder*. New York, Ballantine, 1973.
Editor, with George Zebrowski, *Human-Machines: An Anthology of Stories about Cyborgs*. New York, Random House, 1975; London, Hale, 1977.

* * *

Thomas N. Scortia's first published story, "The Prodigy," immediately established him as an accomplished storyteller. Detailing a violent conflict with a paranormal child, the story reaches one of the few unguessable resolutions of the theme. "The Shores of Night" is a vision of a solar-system-wide civilization straining for the stars; here are the sounds and colors of change, as the human spirit readies itself with a new strength. Scortia writes with a virtuosity comparable to Bester's, with the high emotional content of a Lem in depicting "cruel miracles" at their most intense. This story belongs, to borrow the words of C.S. Lewis, "to those works of science fiction which are actual additions to life; they give, like certain rare dreams, sensations we never had before, and enlarge our conception of the range of possible experience." The work belongs to the period of Scortia's greatest attachment to the ideals of space travel. The story's success lies in its melding of personal loss with a haunting series of pictorial images.

His first novel, *What Mad Oracle?*, is based on Scortia's experience as a physico-chemist in the aerospace industry. It is a powerful story of engineers and corporations confronting the realities of American business and politics in the 1950's. SF in the sense that it shows the human impact of science and technology, the novel has a historical interest for SF readers.

As Scortia's involvement in aerospace increased, his SF production diminished; but stories continued to appear throughout the 1960's. One of the most notable is "Broken Image," depicting a future earth's attempts to have an ethical influence on an alien culture. Seldom has the theme of the saviour been given such a strong presentation. "The Destroyer" was an in-depth return to the theme of "The Prodigy," but this time the note was one of compassion. By 1970 Scortia was writing full time. The great success of this period is "The Weariest River," hailed by P.S. Miller and others as an instant classic on the theme of immortality, containing an original twist of great power; and *Artery of Fire*, a tense, taut novel of conflict over the building of an immense power system (the central image of the story is as strikingly original as that of Niven's *Ringworld*). John W. Campbell had turned down the novella version because he could not accept Scortia's prediction that fusion power would not be available by 1973 (appearing in 1960, the novella makes a striking contrast to "The Shores of Night" of four years before, prefiguring Scortia's critical approach to the products of technology).

Also appearing in the early 1970's was the novel *Earthwreck!* (the title was changed from *Endangered Species* without Scortia's consent), a strongly characterized story of human survival in space after an atomic war has devastated the earth. With the SF veteran Frank M. Robinson, Scortia wrote several disaster novels. These bestsellers earned the authors an international reputation, considerable monetary reward, and the often unfair scorn of the SF community. *The Prometheus Crisis* is of interest to SF readers because, in its depiction of a severe nuclear accident, the story is the legitimate descendant of such pioneering stories as Heinlein's "Blowups Happen" and del Rey's *Nerves.* There is a strong cautionary tone in all of Scortia's later work; it is the warning of the once idealistic, Campbell-influenced aerospace scientist who dreamed of space travel and found that human beings have a penchant for perverting any worthwhile project, from high-rise dwellings to atomic power plants.

Scortia's popular success outside the SF world is part of the continuing science fictionalization of our civilization, in the sense that many of the prophetic suggestions made by SF in the first half of this century, positive and negative, have become commonplace in the second half. That a veteran SF writer should take part in this infusion of what once would have been science-fiction themes and ideas into the body of popular fiction is not surprising. Scortia's special success lies in his genuine emotional and dramatic appeal to the general reader, and in showing how the real world has turned out to be more complex and full of human failure, darker than the idealistic SF on which he grew up had forseen. That human beings *can* do something is no longer enough; the problem is whether they will, or should.

Thomas N. Scortia's life might have been a science-fiction story, as written in some alternate dimension. He came to maturity in the 1950's, full of feeling and intellect, overflowing with the wonder of human possibilities as pictured in Campbell's *Astounding*, only to learn that human beings don't always do their best for worthy dreams. One might say that Scortia's views were modified by the kind of satirical SF which Gold published in *Galaxy* (Gold himself was a Campbell writer who extended his master's approach to SF to include the "soft" social sciences). Scortia's stories of the 1950's and 1960's are powerful streams of thought and feeling, combined with rigorous speculation, flowing out of his critical but compassionate disappointment with the world. Even in his 50's, it was hard to think of Scortia as anything but a young man with his crowning work still to come. His work in aerospace enabled humanity to send probes into the outer solar system, while at the same time he was struggling in his fiction to understand the failing, often partly rational inner space of human nature. *Blow-Out!*, written with Frank M. Robinson, a well-received novel about the construction of a tunnel for high-speed trains across the United States, was published in the year after Scortia's death.

—George Zebrowski

---

**SCOT, Chesman.** *See* **BULMER, Kenneth.**

---

**SEABRIGHT, John.** *See* **TUBB, E.C.**

---

**SEARLS, Hank** (Henry Hunt Searls, Jr.). American. Born in San Francisco, California, 10 August 1922. Educated at the University of California, Berkeley, 1940; United States Naval Academy, Annapolis, Maryland, B.S. 1944. Married Berna Ann Cooper; three children. Served in the United States Navy, 1941–54: Lieutenant Commander. Writer for Hughes Aircraft, Culver City, California, 1955–56, Douglas Aircraft, Santa Monica, California, 1956–57, and Warner Brothers, Burbank, California, 1959. Since 1959, freelance writer. Agent: Scott Meredith Literary Agency, 845 Third Avenue, New York, New York 10022, U.S.A.

Science-Fiction Publications

Novels

*The Big X.* New York, Harper, and London, Heinemann, 1959.
*The Crowded Sky.* New York, Harper, and London, Heinemann, 1960.
*The Astronaut.* London, Penguin, 1960; New York, Pocket Books, 1962.
*The Pilgrim Project.* New York, McGraw Hill, 1964; London, W.H. Allen, 1965.
*The Penetrators.* N.P., 1965; New York, Berkley, 1988.
*The Hero Ship.* Cleveland, World, and London, W.H. Allen, 1969.
*Overboard.* New York, Norton, and London, Raven, 1977.

Other Publications

Novels

*Pentagon.* New York, Geis, 1971.
*Never Kill a Cop.* New York, Pocket Books, 1977.
*Jaws 2* (novelization of screenplay). Universal City, California, MCA, and London, Pan, 1978.
*Firewind.* New York, Doubleday, 1981; London, Sphere, 1982.
*Sounding.* New York, Ballantine, 1982.
*Blood Song.* New York, Villard, 1984.
*Jaws: The Revenge.* New York, Berkley, and London, Futura, 1987.
*Kataki.* New York, McGraw Hill, 1987; London, Hale, 1988.
*The Adventures of Mike Blair: A Dime Detective Book.* New York, Mysterious Press, 1988.
*Altitude Zero.* New York, Norton, 1991.

Play

Television Play: *Wheels*, with Millard Lampwell (from novel by Arthur Hailey), 1978.

Other

*The Lost Prince: Young Joe, The Forgotten Kennedy.* Cleveland, World, 1969.

*   *   *

Hank Searls's stories revolve around the emerging space program, astronauts and their families, and whatever political machinations are most likely to create problems. His realistic contemporary fiction is built on timeliness, as each novel has foreshadowed a stage in man's actual venture into space.

*The Big X* explores some potential problems, both technical and human, of manned orbital space flight. Norco's X-F18, the experimental rocket-like ship of the title, must reach a speed of Mach 8 and prove maneuverable for Norco Aircraft to land the government contract for construction of the first manned spacecraft. Mitch Westerly, the test pilot for the Big X, knows he will probably be chosen as the first man in space if his testing is successful. But the test schedule grows tense as a psychopathic chief of operations orders more and more telemetering equipment mounted in the cockpit, despite Mitch's protests that the additional weight has made the ship unstable. The suspense of the impending Mach 8 test flight builds as Mitch must decide whether to push the plane beyond its limits, at the expense of the girl he wants to marry, and possibly his life, in order to provide telemetric data necessary to the space program. Besides an inside view of the politics of the aircraft industry, there is much authentic-sounding shop talk, as well as a love story with the turmoil surrounding the personal lives of men such as Mitch.

A story of our race for the moon, *The Pilgrim Project* begins as a routine orbital flight is mysteriously ordered to abort prematurely. Except for the commander, even the men aboard do not know that a top secret plan must be put into effect immediately to land an American on the moon ahead of the Russians. The reader remains in a sustained sense of urgency and intrigue as NASA officials, Congressmen, the President, the media, and the astronauts themselves unravel clues about a plan so secret that even the man who originated it does not know it is about to be carried out. The tempo accelerates even more when it is discovered that the Russian moon shot carries a civilian cosmonaut, and the American astronauts are quickly switched to include the civilian Steve Lawrence in order to prove our equally peaceful intentions. When the Pilgrim Project is finally revealed, all concerned must re-evaluate their psychological and moral attitudes about what appears to be a heroic but suicidal one-way flight to the moon. Both Russians and Americans launch, and the race is neck and neck all the way. Several subplots weave throughout the story, providing continuous action.

It is clear that Hank Searls knows his way around both the technical and the human aspects of the space program, and if his stories have not retained their impact, it is only a matter of timing. The fictional Big X barely preceded North American's X-15, untested in free flight at the time, and *The Pilgrim Project* preceded the actual moon landing by less than five years. Still, Searls has incorporated enough human drama into his stories that these after-the-fact elements detract only negligibly for the modern reader.

—Myra Barnes

---

**SELBY, Curt.** *See* **PISERCHIA, Doris.**

---

**SELLINGS, Arthur.** Pseudonym for Robert Arthur Ley; also wrote as Martin Luther. British. Born in 1921. Worked in Customs and as an antiquarian book dealer. *Died 24 September 1968.*

SCIENCE-FICTION PUBLICATIONS

Novels

*Telepath.* New York, Ballantine, 1962; as *The Silent Speakers,* London, Dobson, 1963.
*The Uncensored Man.* London, Dobson, 1964; New York, Berkley, 1967.
*The Quy Effect.* London, Dobson, 1966; New York, Berkley, 1967.
*Intermind* (as Martin Luther). New York, Banner, 1967; London, Dobson, 1969.
*The Power of X.* London, Dobson, 1968; New York, Berkley, 1970.
*Junk Day.* London, Dobson, 1970.

Short Stories

*Time Transfer and Other Stories.* London, Joseph, 1956.
*The Long Eureka.* London, Dobson, 1968.

Uncollected Short Stories

"The Trial," in *New Writings in SF 15,* edited by John Carnell. London, Dobson, 1969.
"The Legend and the Chemistry," in *Fantasy and Science Fiction* (New York), January 1969.
"The Dodgers," in *Fantastic* (New York), April 1969.
"The Last Time Around," in *If* (New York), November 1970.

* * *

Arthur Sellings was interested in how people react to the unknown, whether in outer space or on their own planet. He believed man is slowly evolving but that his essential self, with its present weaknesses and strengths, will endure—even if in unrecognizable forms. Thus his works explore man's inner space, his adaptability, his sense of responsibility, his psychological reactions (to holocaust, time travel, alien confrontation, genetic engineering), and his psychological potentialities (to control bodily shape, change reality, span dimensions, read thoughts). Notable among his short stories are "The Well-Trained Heroes," which deals with a special task force trained to predict and reduce urban tensions by becoming scapegoats; "Homecoming," wherein a disturbed space explorer discovers he has spent centuries in suspended animation and now resides amid aliens; "Verbal Agreement," about a cosmic salesman who learns, through poetry, to adapt a telepathic society to his needs; and "Start in Life," which records the robot training of five-year-old survivors of a starship plague.

Sellings's stories and novels focus on a well-developed central figure who must come to terms with the unexpected, while in the background large military complexes and political groups vie for power. In *The Power of X,* a conspiracy novel, an art dealer learns that other dimensions may be ones of time, not space, as he explores the dangers of "plying," a modern duplicating process that perfectly reproduces originals whether Old Masters or a living president. *The Quy Effect* depicts an aging inventor's struggle to perfect and publicize anti-gravity power, while *Intermind* focuses on a secret agent injected with a dead spy's memory. In *Telepath,* young strangers, suddenly intimate due to unsuspected telepathic powers, combat the destiny of their life form until they gradually understand and communicate to others this mutant power which can transform man's future, opening up the potentiality for preserving racial memories through generations in space. The intriguing and suspenseful *The Uncensored Man* focuses on a nuclear physicist's contact with another dimension, one where racial memories and the minds of earth's dead have accumulated and developed and now seek to reveal to man the power in his genes and in his physical and chemical heritage. The novel includes disappearing bodies, sympathetic, multi-personality beings warning of man's self-destructive blindness, and a hero who develops a full range of psi powers to protect the future of two dimensions. In Sellings's finest work, *Junk Day,* a cynical, gripping, post-holocaust tale of survival, a traumatized artist joins forces with a wary novitiate to tackle the junkman, a tough lower-class bully who, in a ruined world, is king of the London junkpile. The junkman's protection racket helps reunite dispersed humanity, while destroying the basic values that, from the artist's view, make life valuable. Ultimately, his power is confirmed by overbearing scientists who set themselves up as gods of the new order, reconditioning and transforming those who fail to meet their interpretation of the ideal citizen.

Sellings's works have interesting themes, careful characterization, sensory detail, and satisfying suspense, all handled with discipline and restraint. Frequently, a central character is an artist whose special power of perception, temperament, and intuitive insight raise him above the limitations of those around him. Sellings's typical pattern is for such a character, confronted with the unusual, first to doubt his sanity, but then rationally confirm his perceptions, and ultimately learn to deal with new powers or concepts, and understand and accept the responsibilities they entail.

—Gina Macdonald

---

**SENARENS, Luis P(hilip).** Also wrote as Captain Howard. American. Born in Brooklyn, New York, 24 April 1865. Educated at St. John's College, Brooklyn; law degree. Married in 1895; one son and one daughter. Freelance writer from age 16: editor, Frank Tousey publications, from 1904, and scenario writer from 1911; editor, *Moving Picture Stories Weekly,* from 1913; retired in 1923. *Died in 1939.*

SCIENCE-FICTION PUBLICATIONS

Novels (series: Frank Reade, Jr.)

*Frank Reade, Jr. and His Steam Wonder.* New York, Tousey, 1884.
*Frank Reade, Jr. and His Electric Boat.* New York, Tousey, 1884.
*Frank Reade, Jr. and His Adventures with His Latest Invention.* New York, Tousey, 1884.
*Frank Reade, Jr. and His Airship.* New York, Tousey, 1884.
*Frank Reade, Jr.'s Marvel; or, Above and Below Water.* New York, Tousey, 1884.
*Frank Reade, Jr. in the Clouds.* New York, Tousey, 1885.
*Frank Reade, Jr.'s Great Electric Tricycle and What He Did for Charity.* New York, Tousey, 1885.
*Frank Reade, Jr., and His Airship in Africa.* New York, Tousey, 1885.
*Across the Continent on Wings; or, Frank Reade, Jr.'s Greatest Flight.* New York, Tousey, 1886.
*Frank Reade, Jr. Exploring Mexico in His New Airship.* New York, Tousey, 1886.
*The Electric Man; or, Frank Reade, Jr. in Australia.* New York, Tousey, 1887.
*The Electric Horse; or, Frank Reade, Jr. and His Father in Search of the Lost Treasure of the Peruvians.* New York, Tousey, 1888.
*Frank Reade, Jr.'s Race Through the Clouds.* New York, Tousey, 1888.
*Frank Reade, Jr. and His Electric Team; or, In Search of a Missing Man.* New York, Tousey, 1888.
*Frank Reade, Jr.'s Search for a Sunken Ship; or, Working for the Government.* New York, Tousey, 1889.
*Frank Reade, Jr. in the Far West; or, The Search for a Lost Gold Mine.* New York, Tousey, 1890.
*Frank Reade, Jr. and His Queen Clipper of the Clouds.* New York, Tousey, 1890.
*Frank Reade, Jr. and His Monitor of the Deep; or, Helping a Friend in Need.* New York, Tousey, 1890.
*Frank Reade, Jr. Exploring a River of Mystery.* New York, Tousey, 1890.
*Frank Reade, Jr. and His Electric Air Yacht; or, The Great Inventor among the Aztecs.* New York, Tousey, 1891.
*Frank Reade, Jr. in a Sea of Sand and His Discovery of a Lost People.* New York, Tousey, 1891.
*Frank Reade, Jr. and His Greyhound of the Air; or, The Search for the Mountain of Gold.* New York, Tousey, 1891.
*From Pole to Pole; or, Frank Reade, Jr.'s Strange Submarine Voyage.* New York, Tousey, 1891.
*Frank Reade, Jr. and His Electric Coach; or, The Search for the Isle of Diamonds.* New York, Tousey, 1891.
*Frank Reade, Jr. and His Airship in Asia; or, A Flight Across the Steppes.* New York, Tousey, 1892.
*Frank Reade, Jr. and His Electric Ice Boat; or, Lost in the Land of Crimson Snow.* New York, Tousey, 1892.
*Frank Reade, Jr.'s Electric Cyclone; or, Thrilling Adventures in No Man's Land.* New York, Tousey, 1892.
*Frank Reade, Jr. with His New Steam Man; or, The Young Inventor's Trip to the Far West.* New York, Tousey, 1892.
*Frank Reade, Jr. with His New Steam Man in No Man's Land; or, On a Mysterious Trail.* New York, Tousey, 1892.
*Frank Reade, Jr. with His New Steam Man in Central America.* New York, Tousey, 1892.
*Frank Reade, Jr. with His New Steam Man in Texas; or, Chasing the Train Robbers.* New York, Tousey, 1892.
*Frank Reade, Jr. with His New Steam Man in Mexico; or, Hot Work Among the Greasers.* New York, Tousey, 1892.
*Frank Reade, Jr. with His New Steam Man Chasing a Gang of "Rustlers"; or, Wild Adventures in Montana.* New York, Tousey, 1892.
*Frank Reade, Jr. and His New Steam Horse; or, The Search for a Million Dollars.* New York, Tousey, 1892.
*Frank Reade, Jr. with His New Steam Horse among the Cowboys; or, The League of the Plains.* New York, Tousey, 1892.
*Frank Reade, Jr. with His New Steam Horse in the Great American Desert; or, The Sandy Trail of Death.* New York, Tousey, 1892.
*Frank Reade, Jr. with His New Steam Horse and the Mystery of the Underground Ranch.* New York, Tousey, 1892.
*Frank Reade, Jr. with His New Steam Horse in Search of an Ancient Mine.* New York, Tousey, 1892.
*Frank Reade, Jr. with His New Steam Horse in the North-West; or, Wild Adventures among the Blackfeet.* New York, Tousey, 1892.
*Frank Reade, Jr.'s Electric Air Canoe; or, The Search for the Valley of Diamonds.* New York, Tousey, 1892.
*Frank Reade, Jr.'s New Electric Submarine Boat "The Explorer"; or, To the North Pole under the Ice.* New York, Tousey, 1893.
*Frank Reade, Jr.'s New Electric Van; or, Hunting Wild Animals in the Jungles of India.* New York, Tousey, 1893.
*Frank Reade, Jr.'s "White Cruiser" of the Clouds; or, The Search for the Dog-Faced Men.* New York, Tousey, 1893.
*Frank Reade, Jr.'s Deep Sea Diver the "Tortoise"; or, The Search for a Sunken Island.* New York, Tousey, 1893.
*Frank Reade, Jr.'s New Electric Terror the "Thunderer"; or, The Search for the Tartar's Captive.* New York, Tousey, 1893.
*Frank Reade, Jr. and His Air-Ship.* New York, Tousey, 1893.
*Frank Reade, Jr.'s Latest Air Wonder the "Kite"; or, A Six Weeks' Flight Over the Andes.* New York, Tousey, 1893.
*Frank Reade, Jr.'s New Electric Invention the "Warrior"; or, Fighting the Apaches in Arizona.* New York, Tousey, 1893.
*Frank Reade, Jr.'s "Sea Serpent"; or, The Search for Sunken Gold.* New York, Tousey, 1893.
*Fighting the Slave Hunters; or, Frank Reade, Jr. in Central Africa.* New York, Tousey, 1893.
*Around the World Under Water; or, The Wonderful Cruise of a Submarine Boat.* New York, Tousey, 1893.
*Lost in the Land of Fire; or, Across the Pampas in the Electric Turret.* New York, Tousey, 1893.
*Six Weeks in the Great Whirlpool; or, Strange Adventures in a Submarine Boat.* New York, Tousey, 1893.
*Chased Across the Sahara; or, The Bedouins' Captive.* New York, Tousey, 1893.
*The Mystic Brand; or, Frank Reade, Jr. and His Overland Stage upon the Staked Plains.* New York, Tousey, 1893.
*Frank Reade, Jr. and His New Torpedo Boat; or, At War with the Brazilian Rebels.* New York, Tousey, 1893.
*Frank Reade, Jr. and His Magnetic Gun-Carriage; or, Working for the U.S. Mail.* New York, Tousey, 1893.
*Frank Reade, Jr. and His Engine of the Clouds; or, Chased Around the World in the Sky.* New York, Tousey, 1893.
*The Sunken Pirate; or, Frank Reade, Jr. in Search of Treasure at the Bottom of the Sea.* New York, Tousey, 1893.
*Frank Reade, Jr. and His Electric Air-Boat; or, Hunting Wild Beasts for a Circus.* New York, Tousey, 1893.
*The Black Range; or, Frank Reade, Jr. among the Cowboys with His New Electric Caravan.* New York, Tousey, 1894.
*From Zone to Zone; or, The Wonderful Trip of Frank Reade, Jr. with His Latest Air-Ship.* New York, Tousey, 1894.
*Frank Reade, Jr. and His Electric Prairie Schooner; or, Fighting the Mexican Horse Thieves.* New York, Tousey, 1894.
*Frank Reade, Jr. and His Electric Cruiser of the Lakes; or, A Journey Through Africa by Water.* New York, Tousey, 1894.

*Adrift in Africa; or, Frank Reade, Jr. among the Ivory Hunters with His New Electric Wagon.* New York, Tousey, 1894.
*Six Weeks in the Clouds; or, Frank Reade, Jr.'s Air-Ship, The Thunderbolt of the Skies.* New York, Tousey, 1894.
*Frank Reade, Jr.'s Electric Air Racer; or, Around the Globe in Thirty Days.* New York, Tousey, 1894.
*Frank Reade, Jr. and His Flying Ice Ship; or, Driven Adrift in the Frozen Sky.* New York, Tousey, 1894.
*Frank Reade, Jr. and His Electric Sea Engine; or, Hunting for a Sunken Diamond Mine.* New York, Tousey, 1894.
*Frank Reade, Jr. Exploring a Submarine Mountain; or, Lost at the Bottom of the Sea.* New York, Tousey, 1894.
*Frank Reade, Jr.'s Electric Buckboard; or, Thrilling Adventures in North Australia.* New York, Tousey, 1894.
*Frank Reade, Jr.'s Search for the Sea Serpent; or, Six Thousand Miles under the Sea.* New York, Tousey, 1894.
*Frank Reade, Jr.'s Desert Explorer; or, The Underground City of the Sahara.* New York, Tousey, 1894.
*Frank Reade, Jr.'s New Electric Air-Ship the "Zephyr"; or, From North to South Around the Globe.* New York, Tousey, 1894.
*Across the Frozen Sea; or, Frank Reade, Jr.'s Electric Snow Cutter.* New York, Tousey, 1894.
*Lost in the Great Atlantic Valley; or, Frank Reade, Jr. and His Submarine Wonder the "Dart."* New York, Tousey, 1894.
*Frank Reade, Jr. and His New Electric Air-Ship the "Eclipse"; or, Fighting the Chinese Pirates.* New York, Tousey, 1894.
*Frank Reade, Jr.'s Clipper of the Prairie; or, Fighting the Apaches in the Far Southwest.* New York, Tousey, 1894.
*Under the Amazon for a Thousand Miles; or, Frank Reade, Jr.'s Wonderful Trip.* New York, Tousey, 1894.
*Frank Reade, Jr.'s Search for the Silver Whale; or, Under the Ocean in the Electric "Dolphin."* New York, Tousey, 1894.
*Frank Reade, Jr.'s Catamaran of the Air; or, Wild and Wonderful Adventures in North Australia.* New York, Tousey, 1894.
*Frank Reade, Jr.'s Search for a Lost Man in His Latest Air Wonder.* New York, Tousey, 1894.
*Frank Reade, Jr. in Central India; or, The Search for the Lost Savants.* New York, Tousey, 1894.
*The Missing Island; or, Frank Reade, Jr.'s Wonderful Trip under the Deep Sea.* New York, Tousey, 1894.
*Over the Andes with Frank Reade, Jr. in His New Air-Ship; or, Wild Adventures in Peru.* New York, Tousey, 1894.
*Frank Reade, Jr.'s Prairie Whirlwind; or, The Mystery of the Hidden Canyon.* New York, Tousey, 1894.
*Under the Yellow Sea; or, Frank Reade, Jr.'s Search for the Cave of Pearls with His New Submarine Cruiser.* New York, Tousey, 1894.
*Around the Horizon for Ten Thousand Miles; or, Frank Reade, Jr.'s Most Wonderful Trip with His Air-Ship.* New York, Tousey, 1894.
*Frank Reade, Jr.'s "Sky Scraper"; or, North and South Around the World.* New York, Tousey, 1894.
*Under the Equator from Ecuador to Borneo; or, Frank Reade, Jr.'s Greatest Submarine Voyage.* New York, Tousey, 1894.
*From Coast to Coast; or, Frank Reade, Jr.'s Trip Across Africa in His Electric "Boomerang."* New York, Tousey, 1894.
*Frank Reade, Jr. and His Electric Car; or, Outwitting a Desperate Gang.* New York, Tousey, 1894.
*Lost in the Mountains of the Moon; or, Frank Reade, Jr.'s Great Trip with His New Air-Ship, the "Scud."* New York, Tousey, 1894.
*100 Miles Below the Surface of the Sea; or, The Marvelous Trip of Frank Reade, Jr.'s "Hardshell" Submarine Boat.* New York, Tousey, 1894.
*Abandoned in Alaska; or, Frank Reade, Jr.'s Thrilling Search for a Lost Gold Claim with His New Electric Wagon.* New York, Tousey, 1894.
*Around the Arctic Circle; or, Frank Reade, Jr.'s Most Famous Trip with His Air-Ship, The "Orbit."* New York, Tousey, 1894.
*Under Four Oceans; or, Frank Reade, Jr.'s Submarine Chase of a "Sea Devil."* New York, Tousey, 1894.
*From the Nile to the Niger; or, Frank Reade, Jr. Lost in the Soudan with His "Overland Omnibus."* New York, Tousey, 1894.
*The Chase of a Comet; or, Frank Reade, Jr.'s Most Wonderful Aerial Trip with His New Air-Ship, the "Flash."* New York, Tousey, 1894.
*Lost in the Great Undertow; or, Frank Reade, Jr.'s Submarine Cruise in the Gulf Stream.* New York, Tousey, 1894.
*From Tropic to Tropic; or, Frank Reade, Jr.'s Latest Tour with His Bicycle Car.* New York, Tousey, 1894.
*To the End of the Earth in an Air-Ship; or, Frank Reade, Jr.'s Great Mid-Air Flight.* New York, Tousey, 1894.
*The Underground Sea; or, Frank Reade, Jr.'s Subterranean Cruise in His Submarine Boat.* New York, Tousey, 1894.
*The Mysterious Mirage; or, Frank Reade, Jr.'s Desert Search for a Secret City with His New Overland Chaise.* New York, Tousey, 1894.
*The Electric Island; or, Frank Reade, Jr.'s Search for the Greatest Wonder on Earth with His Air-Ship, the "Flight."* New York, Tousey, 1894.
*For Six Weeks Buried in a Deep Sea Cave; or, Frank Reade, Jr.'s Great Submarine Search.* New York, Tousey, 1894.
*The Galleon's Gold; or, Frank Reade, Jr.'s Deep Sea Search.* New York, Tousey, 1894.
*Across Australia with Frank Reade, Jr. in His New Electric Car; or, Wonderful Adventures in the Antipodes.* New York, Tousey, 1894.
*Frank Reade, Jr.'s Greatest Flying Machine; or, Fighting the Terror of the Coast.* New York, Tousey, 1894.
*On the Great Meridian with Frank Reade, Jr. in His New Air-Ship; or, A Twenty-Five Thousand Mile Trip in Mid-Air.* New York, Tousey, 1895.
*Under the Indian Ocean with Frank Reade, Jr.; or, A Cruise in a Submarine Boat.* New York, Tousey, 1895.
*Astray in the Selvas; or, The Wild Experiences of Frank Reade, Jr., Barney and Pomp, in South America with the Electric Car.* New York, Tousey, 1895.
*Lost in a Comet's Tail; or, Frank Reade, Jr.'s Strange Adventure with His New Air-Ship.* New York, Tousey, 1895.
*Six Sunken Pirates; or, Frank Reade, Jr.'s Marvelous Adventures in the Deep Sea.* New York, Tousey, 1895.
*Beyond the Gold Coast; or, Frank Reade, Jr.'s Overland Trip with His Electric Phaeton.* New York, Tousey, 1895.
*Latitude 90; or, Frank Reade, Jr.'s Most Wonderful Mid-Air Flight.* New York, Tousey, 1895.
*Afloat in a Sunken Forest; or, With Frank Reade, Jr. on a Submarine Cruise.* New York, Tousey, 1895.
*Across the Desert of Fire; or, Frank Reade, Jr.'s Marvelous Trip to a Strange Country.* New York, Tousey, 1895.
*Over Two Continents; or, Frank Reade, Jr.'s Long Distance Flight with His New Air-Ship.* New York, Tousey, 1895.
*The Coral Labyrinth; or, Lost with Frank Reade, Jr. in a Deep Sea Cave.* New York, Tousey, 1895.
*Along the Orinoco; or, With Frank Reade, Jr. in Venezuela.* New York, Tousey, 1895.
*Across the Earth; or, Frank Reade, Jr.'s Latest Trip with His New Air-Ship.* New York, Tousey, 1895.
*1,000 Fathoms Deep; or, With Frank Reade, Jr. in the Sea of Gold.* New York, Tousey, 1895.
*The Island in the Air; or, Frank Reade, Jr.'s Trip to the Tropics.* New York, Tousey, 1895.

*In the Wild Man's Land; or, With Frank Reade, Jr. in the Heart of Australia.* New York, Tousey, 1895.
*The Sunken Isthmus; or, With Frank Reade, Jr. in the Yucatan Channel, with His New Submarine Yacht, the "Sea Diver."* New York, Tousey, 1895.
*The Lost Caravan; or, Frank Reade, Jr. on the Staked Plains with His "Electric Racer."* New York, Tousey, 1895.
*The Transient Lake; or, Frank Reade, Jr.'s Adventures in a Mysterious Country with His New Air-Ship, the "Spectre."* New York, Tousey, 1895.
*The Weird Island; or, Frank Reade, Jr.'s Strange Submarine Search for a Deep Sea Wonder.* New York, Tousey, 1895.
*The Abandoned Country; or, Frank Reade, Jr. Exploring a New Continent.* New York, Tousey, 1895.
*Over the Steppes; or, Adrift in Asia with Frank Reade, Jr.* New York, Tousey, 1895.
*The Unknown Sea; or, Frank Reade, Jr.'s Under-Water Cruise.* New York, Tousey, 1895.
*In the Black Zone; or, Frank Reade, Jr.'s Quest for the Mountain of Ivory.* New York, Tousey, 1895.
*The Lost Navigators; or, Frank Reade, Jr.'s Mid-Air Search with His New Air-Ship, the "Sky Flyer."* New York, Tousey, 1895.
*The Magic Island; or, Frank Reade, Jr.'s Deep Sea Trip of Mystery.* New York, Tousey, 1895.
*Through the Tropics; or, Frank Reade, Jr.'s Adventures in the Gran Chaco.* New York, Tousey, 1895.
*In White Latitudes; or, Frank Reade, Jr.'s Ten Thousand Mile Flight over the Frozen North.* New York, Tousey, 1895.
*Below the Sahara; or, Frank Reade, Jr. Exploring an Underground River, with His Submarine Boat.* New York, Tousey, 1895.
*The Black Mogul; or, Through India with Frank Reade, Jr. Abroad His "Electric Boomer."* New York, Tousey, 1895.
*The Missing Planet; or, Frank Reade, Jr.'s Quest for a Fallen Star with His New Air-Ship, "The Zenith."* New York, Tousey, 1895.
*The Black Squadron; or, Frank Reade, Jr. in the Indian Ocean with His Submarine Boat, the "Rocket."* New York, Tousey, 1895.
*The Prairie Pirates; or, Frank Reade, Jr.'s Trip to Texas with His Electric Vehicle, the "Detective."* New York, Tousey, 1895.
*Over the Orient; or, Frank Reade, Jr.'s Travels in Turkey with His New Air-Ship.* New York, Tousey, 1895.
*The Black Whirlpool; or, Frank Reade, Jr.'s Deep Sea Search for a Lost Ship.* New York, Tousey, 1895.
*The Silent City; or, Frank Reade, Jr.'s Visit to a Strange People with His New Electric "Flyer."* New York, Tousey, 1895.
*The White Desert; or, Frank Reade, Jr.'s Trip to the Land of Tombs.* New York, Tousey, 1895.
*Under the Gulf of Guinea; or, Frank Reade, Jr. Exploring the Sunken Reef of Gold with His New Submarine Boat.* New York, Tousey, 1895.
*The Yellow Khan; or, Frank Reade, Jr. among the Thugs in Central India.* New York, Tousey, 1895.
*Frank Reade, Jr. in Japan, with His War Cruiser of the Clouds.* New York, Tousey, 1895.
*Frank Reade, Jr. in Cuba; or, Helping the Patriots with His Latest Air-Ship.* New York, Tousey, 1895.
*Chasing a Pirate; or, Frank Reade, Jr. on a Desperate Cruise.* New York, Tousey, 1895.
*In the Land of Fire; or, Frank Reade, Jr. among the Head Hunters.* New York, Tousey, 1895.
*7,000 Miles Underground; or, Frank Reade, Jr. Exploring a Volcano.* New York, Tousey, 1895.
*The Demon of the Clouds; or, Frank Reade, Jr. and the Ghosts of Phantom Island.* New York, Tousey, 1895.
*The Cloud City; or, Frank Reade, Jr.'s Most Wonderful Discovery.* New York, Tousey, 1895.
*The White Atoll; or, Frank Reade, Jr. in the South Pacific.* New York, Tousey, 1895.
*The Monarch of the Moon; or, Frank Reade, Jr.'s Exploits in Africa with His Electric "Thunderer."* New York, Tousey, 1895.
*37 Bags of Gold; or, Frank Reade, Jr. Hunting for a Lost Steamer.* New York, Tousey, 1895.
*The Lost Lake; or, Frank Reade, Jr.'s Trip to Alaska.* New York, Tousey, 1895.
*The Caribs' Cave; or, Frank Reade, Jr.'s Submarine Search for the Reef of Pearls.* New York, Tousey, 1895.
*The Desert of Death; or, Frank Reade, Jr. Exploring an Unknown Land.* New York, Tousey, 1895.
*A Trip to the Sea of the Sun; or, With Frank Reade, Jr. on a Perilous Cruise.* New York, Tousey, 1895.
*The Black Lagoon; or, Frank Reade, Jr.'s Submarine Search for a Sunken City in Russia.* New York, Tousey, 1896.
*The Mysterious Brand; or, Frank Reade, Jr. Solving a Mexican Mystery.* New York, Tousey, 1896.
*Across the Milky Way; or, Frank Reade, Jr.'s Great Astronomical Trip with His Air-Ship, "The Shooting Star."* New York, Tousey, 1896.
*Under the Great Lakes; or, Frank Reade, Jr.'s Latest Submarine Cruise.* New York, Tousey, 1896.
*The Magic Mine; or, Frank Reade, Jr.'s Trip up the Yukon with His Electric Combination Traveller.* New York, Tousey, 1896.
*Across Arabia; or, Frank Reade, Jr.'s Search for the Forty Thieves.* New York, Tousey, 1896.
*The Silver Sea; or, Frank Reade, Jr.'s Submarine Cruise in Unknown Waters.* New York, Tousey, 1896.
*In the Tundras; or, Frank Reade, Jr.'s Latest Trip Through Northern Asia.* New York, Tousey, 1896.
*The Circuit of Cancer; or, Frank Reade, Jr.'s Novel Trip Around the World with His New Air-Ship, the "Flight."* New York, Tousey, 1896.
*The Sacred Sea; or, Frank Reade, Jr.'s Submarine Exploits among the Dervishes of India.* New York, Tousey, 1896.
*The Land of Dunes; or, With Frank Reade, Jr. in the Desert of Gobi.* New York, Tousey, 1896.
*Six Days under Havana Harbor; or, Frank Reade, Jr.'s Secret Service Work for Uncle Sam.* New York, Tousey, 1896.
*The Sinking Star; or, Frank Reade, Jr.'s Trip into Space with His New Air-Ship "Saturn."* New York, Tousey, 1896.
*In the Gran Chaco; or, Frank Reade, Jr. in Search of a Missing Man.* New York, Tousey, 1896.
*The Lost Oasis; or, Frank Reade, Jr. in the Australian Desert.* New York, Tousey, 1896.
*The Isle of Hearts; or, Frank Reade, Jr. in a Strange Sea with His Submarine Boat.* New York, Tousey, 1896.
*Jack Wright and Frank Reade, Jr., the Two Young Inventors; or, Brains Against Brains.* New York, Tousey, 1896.

Novels (series: Jack Wright)

*Jack Wright, the Boy Inventor; or, Hunting for a Sunken Treasure.* New York, Tousey, 1891.
*Jack Wright and His Electric Turtle; or, Chasing the Pirates of the Spanish Main.* New York, Tousey, 1891.
*Jack Wright's Submarine Catamaran; or, The Phantom Ship of the Yellow Sea.* New York, Tousey, 1891.
*Jack Wright and his Ocean Racer; or, Around the World in Twenty Days.* New York, Tousey, 1891.
*Jack Wright and His Electric Canoe; or, Working the Revenue Service.* New York, Tousey, 1891.

*Jack Wright's Air and Water Cutter; or, Wonderful Adventures on the Wing and Afloat*. New York, Tousey, 1891.
*Jack Wright and His Magnetic Motor; or, The Golden City of the Sierras*. New York, Tousey, 1891.
*Jack Wright, the Boy Inventor, and His Under-Water Iron-clad; or, The Treasure of the Sandy Sea*. New York, Tousey, 1892.
*Jack Wright and His Electric Deer; or, Fighting the Bandits of the Black Hills*. New York, Tousey, 1892.
*Jack Wright and His Prairie Engine; or, Among the Bushmen of Australia*. New York, Tousey, 1892.
*Jack Wright and His Electric Air Schooner; or, The Mystery of a Magic Mine*. New York, Tousey, 1892.
*Jack Wright and His Electric Sea-Motor; or, The Search for a Drifting Wreck*. New York, Tousey, 1892.
*Jack Wright and His Ocean Sleuth-Hound; or, Tracking an Underwater Treasure*. New York, Tousey, 1892.
*Jack Wright and His Dandy of the Deep; or, Driven Afloat in the Sea of Fire*. New York, Tousey, 1892.
*Jack Wright and His Electric Torpedo Ram; or, The Sunken City of the Atlantic*. New York, Tousey, 1892.
*Jack Wright and His Deep Sea Monitor; or, Searching for a Ton of Gold*. New York, Tousey, 1892.
*Jack Wright, the Boy Inventor, Exploring Central Asia in His Magnetic Hurricane*. New York, Tousey, 1892.
*Jack Wright and His Ocean Plunger; or, The Harpoon Hunters of the Arctic*. New York, Tousey, 1892.
*Jack Wright and His Electric "Sea-Ghost"; or, A Strange Under-Water Journey*. New York, Tousey, 1892.
*Jack Wright, the Boy Inventor, and His Deep Sea Diving Bell; or, The Buccaneers of the Gold Coast*. New York, Tousey, 1892.
*Jack Wright, the Boy Inventor, and His Electric Tricycle-Boat; or, The Treasure of the Sun-Worshippers*. New York, Tousey, 1892.
*Jack Wright and His Undersea Wrecking Raft; or, The Mystery of a Scuttled Ship*. New York, Tousey, 1892.
*Jack Wright and His Terror of the Seas; or, Fighting for a Sunken Fortune*. New York, Tousey, 1892.
*Jack Wright and His Electric Diving Boat; or, Lost under the Ocean*. New York, Tousey, 1892.
*Jack Wright and His Submarine Yacht; or, The Fortune Hunters of the Red Sea*. New York, Tousey, 1892.
*Jack Wright and His Electric Gunboat; or, The Search for a Stolen Girl*. New York, Tousey, 1893.
*Jack Wright and His Electric Sea Launch; or, A Desperate Cruise for Life*. New York, Tousey, 1893.
*Jack Wright and His Electric Bicycle-Boat; or, Searching for Captain Kidd's Gold*. New York, Tousey, 1893.
*Jack Wright and His Electric Side-Wheel Boat; or, Fighting the Brigands of the Coral Isles*. New York, Tousey, 1893.
*Jack Wright's Wonder of the Waves; or, The Flying Dutchman of the Pacific*. New York, Tousey, 1893.
*Jack Wright and His Electric Exploring Ship; or, A Cruise Around Greenland*. New York, Tousey, 1893.
*Jack Wright and His Electric Man-of-War; or, Fighting the Sea Robbers of the Frozen Coast*. New York, Tousey, 1893.
*Jack Wright and His Submarine Torpedo-Tug; or, Winning a Government Reward*. New York, Tousey, 1893.
*Jack Wright and His Electric Sea-Demon; or, Daring Adventures under the Ocean*. New York, Tousey, 1893.
*Jack Wright and His Electric "Whale"; or, The Treasure Trove of the Polar Sea*. New York, Tousey, 1893.
*Jack Wright and His Electric Marine "Rover"; or, 50,000 Miles in Ocean Perils*. New York, Tousey, 1893.
*Jack Wright and His Electric Deep Sea Cutter; or, Searching for a Pirate's Treasure*. New York, Tousey, 1893.
*Jack Wright and His Electric Monarch of the Ocean; or, Cruising for a Million in Gold*. New York, Tousey, 1893.
*Jack Wright and His Electric Devil-Fish; or, Fighting the Smugglers of Alaska*. New York, Tousey, 1893.
*Jack Wright and His Electric Demon of the Plains; or, Wild Adventures among the Cowboys*. New York, Tousey, 1893.
*Jack Wright and His Electric Balloon Ship; or, 30,000 Leagues above the Earth*. New York, Tousey, 1893.
*Jack Wright and His Electric Locomotive; or, The Lost Mine of Death Valley*. New York, Tousey, 1893.
*Jack Wright and His Iron-Clad Air-Motor; or, Searching for a Lost Explorer*. New York, Tousey, 1893.
*Jack Wright and His Electric Tricycle; or, Fighting the Stranglers of the Crimson Desert*. New York, Tousey, 1893.
*Jack Wright and His Electric Dynamo Boat; or, The Mystery of a Buried Sea*. New York, Tousey, 1893.
*Jack Wright and His Flying Torpedo; or, The Black Demons of Dismal Swamp*. New York, Tousey, 1893.
*Jack Wright and His Prairie Privateer; or, Fighting the Western Road-Agents*. New York, Tousey, 1893.
*Jack Wright and His Naval Cruiser; or, Fighting the Pirates of the Pacific*. New York, Tousey, 1893.
*Jack Wright, the Boy Inventor, and His Whaleback Privateer; or, Cruising in the Behring Sea*. New York, Tousey, 1893.
*Jack Wright and His Electric Phantom Boat; or, Chasing the Outlaws of the Ocean*. New York, Tousey, 1893.
*Jack Wright and His Winged Gunboat; or, A Voyage to an Unknown Land*. New York, Tousey, 1894.
*Jack Wright and His Electric Flyer; or, Racing in the Clouds for a Boy's Life*. New York, Tousey, 1894.
*Jack Wright, the Boy Inventor's Electric Sledge Boat; or, Wild Adventures in Alaska*. New York, Tousey, 1894.
*Jack Wright and His Electric Express Wagon; or, Wiping Out the Outlaws of Deadwood*. New York, Tousey, 1894.
*Jack Wright and His Submarine Explorer; or, A Cruise at the Bottom of the Ocean*. New York, Tousey, 1894.
*Jack Wright and His Demon of the Air; or, A Perilous Trip in the Clouds*. New York, Tousey, 1894.
*Jack Wright and His Electric Ripper; or, Searching for a Treasure in the Jungle*. New York, Tousey, 1894.
*Jack Wright and His King of the Sea; or, Diving for Old Spanish Gold*. New York, Tousey, 1894.
*Jack Wright and His Electric Balloons; or, Cruising in the Clouds for a Mountain Treasure*. New York, Tousey, 1894.
*Jack Wright and His Imp of the Ocean; or, The Wreckers of Whirlpool Reef*. New York, Tousey, 1894.
*Jack Wright and His Electric Cab; or, Around the Globe on Wheels*. New York, Tousey, 1894.
*Jack Wright and His Flying Phantom; or, Searching for a Lost Balloonist*. New York, Tousey, 1894.
*Jack Wright and His Submarine Warship; or, Chasing the Demons of the Sea of Gold*. New York, Tousey, 1894.
*Jack Wright and His Prairie Yacht; or, Fighting the Indians of the Sea of Grass*. New York, Tousey, 1894.
*Jack Wright and His Electric Air Rocket; or, The Boy Exile of Siberia*. New York, Tousey, 1894.
*Jack Wright and His Submarine Destroyer; or, Warring Against the Japanese Pirates*. New York, Tousey, 1894.
*Jack Wright and His Electric Battery Diver; or, A Two Months' Cruise under Water*. New York, Tousey, 1894.
*Jack Wright and His Electric Stage; or, Leagued Against the James Boys*. New York, Tousey, 1894.
*Jack Wright and His Wheel of the Wind; or, The Jewels of the Volcano Dwellers*. New York, Tousey, 1894.
*Jack Wright and the Head-Hunters of the African Coast; or, The Electric Pirate Chaser*. New York, Tousey, 1894.
*3,000 Pounds of Gold; or, Jack Wright and His Electric Bat, Fighting the Cliff-Dwellers of the Sierras*. New York, Tousey, 1894.

*Jack Wright and the Wild Boy of the Woods; or, Exposing a Strange Mystery with the Electric Cart.* New York, Tousey, 1894.
*Jack Wright among the Demons of the Ocean with His Electric Sea-Fighter.* New York, Tousey, 1894.
*Jack Wright, the Wizard of Wrightstown and His Electric Dragon; or, A Wild Race to Save a Fortune.* New York, Tousey, 1894.
*Jack Wright's Electric Land-Clipper; or, Exploring the Mysterious Gobi Desert.* New York, Tousey, 1894.
*Skull and Crossbones; or, Jack Wright's Diving-Bell and the Pirates.* New York, Tousey, 1895.
*Jack Wright, the Boy Inventor, and His Phantom Frigate; or, Fighting the Coast Wreckers of the Gulf.* New York, Tousey, 1895.
*Jack Wright and His Air-Ship on Wheels; or, A Perilous Journey to Cape Farewell.* New York, Tousey, 1895.
*Jack Wright and His Electric Roadster in the Desert of Death; or, Chasing the Australian Brigand.* New York, Tousey, 1895.
*Jack Wright's Ocean Marvel; or, The Mystery of a Frozen Island.* New York, Tousey, 1895.
*Jack Wright and His Electric Soaring Machine; or, A Daring Flight Through Miles of Peril.* New York, Tousey, 1895.
*Jack Wright and His Electric Battery Car; or, Beating the Express Train Robbers.* New York, Tousey, 1895.
*Jack Wright and His Electric Sea Horse; or, Seven Weeks in Ocean Perils.* New York, Tousey, 1895.
*Jack Wright and His Electric Balloon Boat; or, A Dangerous Voyage above the Clouds.* New York, Tousey, 1895.
*In the Jungles of India; or, Jack Wright as a Wild Animal Hunter.* New York, Tousey, 1895.
*50,000 Leagues under the Sea; or, Jack Wright's Most Dangerous Voyage.* New York, Tousey, 1895.
*Jack Wright, the Boy Inventor, Working for the Union Pacific Railroad; or, Over the Continent on the "Electric."* New York, Tousey, 1895.
*Over the South Pole; or, Jack Wright's Search for a Lost Explorer with His Flying Boat.* New York, Tousey, 1895.
*Jack Wright and His Electric Air Monitor; or, The Scourge of the Pacific.* New York, Tousey, 1895.
*The Boy Lion Fighter; or, Jack Wright in the Swamps of Africa.* New York, Tousey, 1895.
*Jack Wright and His Electric Submarine Ranger; or, Afloat among the Cannibals of the Deep.* New York, Tousey, 1895.
*The Demon of the Sky; or, Jack Wright's $10,000 Wager.* New York, Tousey, 1895.
*Adrift in the Land of Snow; or, Jack Wright and His Sledge-Boat on Wheels.* New York, Tousey, 1896.
*The Floating Terror; or, Jack Wright Fighting the Buccaneers of the Venezuelan Coast.* New York, Tousey, 1896.
*Lost in the Polar Circle; or, Jack Wright and His Aerial Explorer.* New York, Tousey, 1896.
*Jack Wright, the Boy Inventor, and the Smugglers of the Border Lakes; or, The Second Cruise of the Whaleback "Comet."* New York, Tousey, 1896.
*The Fatal Blue Diamond; or, Jack Wright among the Demon Worshippers with His Electric Motor.* New York, Tousey, 1896.
*Running the Blockade; or, Jack Wright Helping the Cuban Filibusters.* New York, Tousey, 1896.
*Jack Wright and Frank Reade, Jr., the Two Young Inventors; or, Brains Against Brains.* New York, Tousey, 1896.
*The Flying Avenger; or, Jack Wright Fighting for Cuba.* New York, Tousey, 1896.
*Jack Wright and His New Electric Horse; or, A Perilous Trip over Two Continents.* New York, Tousey, 1896.
*Over the Sahara Desert; or, Jack Wright Fighting the Slave Hunters.* New York, Tousey, 1896.
*Diving for a Million; or, Jack Wright and His Electric Ocean Liner.* New York, Tousey, 1896.

Uncollected Serials (all published in *Happy Days*, New York)

"Young Frank Reade and His Electric Air Ship; or, a 10,000 Mile Search for a Missing Man," 14 October–2 December 1899; "Jack Wright, the Boy Inventor, and His Electric Flying Machine; or, A Record Trip Around the World," 29 March–19 April 1902; "Jack Wright and His Marvel of the Sea; or, Among the Demons of the Deep," 1 June–5 July 1902; "Jack Wright and His Ship of the Desert; or, Adventures in the Sea of Sand," 26 July–16 August 1902; "Jack Wright and His King of the Clouds; or, Around the World on Wings," 16 August–6 September 1902; "Jack Wright and His Submarine Boat; or, Working for the Navy," 20 September–11 October 1902; "Jack Wright and His Red Terror; or, Fighting the Bushmen of Australia," 1–22 November 1902; "Jack Wright and His Tandem Balloons; or, Hunting Wild Beasts in India," 29 November–27 December 1902; "Jack Wright and His Queen of the Deep; or, Exploring Submarine Caves," 10–31 January 1903; "Jack Wright and His Wonder of the Prairie; or, Perils among the Cowboys," 28 February–21 March 1903; "Jack Wright and His Flying Ice Boat; or, Adrift in the Polar Regions," 28 March–18 April 1903; "Jack Wright's Floating Terror; or, Fighting the Pirates," 25 April–16 May 1903; "Jack Wright's Electric Prairie Car; or, Hot Times with the Broncho Busters," 23 May–13 June 1903; "Jack Wright's Sky Scraper; or, After the Lost Balloonists," 20 June–11 July 1903; "Jack Wright's Sea Demon; or, Running the Blockade," 18 July–8 August 1903; "Jack Wright's Rapid Transit; or, Trailing the Cattle Punchers," 29 August–19 September 1903; "Jack Wright's Queen of the Air; or, After the Cliff Dwellers' Gold," 6–27 February 1904; "Jack Wright's King of the Plains; or, Calling Down the Cowboys," 3–24 December 1904.

Uncollected Short Story

"Frank Reade's Christmas in the Air," in *Muldoon's Christmas.* New York, Tousey, 1889.

### Other Publications

Novels

*Young Sleuths in Demijohn City; or, Waltzing William's Dancing School.* New York, Tousey, 1894.
*Young Sleuths on the Stage; or, An Act Not on the Bills.* New York, Tousey, 1894.

Novels as Police Captain Howard

*A.D.T.; or, The Messenger Boy Detective.* New York, Champion, 1882.
*The Girl Detective.* New York, Champion, 1882.
*The Mystery of One Night.* New York, Champion, 1882.
*Young Vidocq.* New York, Champion, 1882.

Other

*How to Become a Naval Cadet.* New York, Tousey, 1891.
*How to Become a West Point Military Cadet.* New York, Tousey, 1891.

* * *

During his lifetime, Luis P. Senarens was referred to as "the American Jules Verne" and a comparison of the work of both writers indicates the similarity. Senarens was writing stories of airships suspended by helicopter blades ("helices") three years before the *Albatross* took off in *Robur le Conquérant* (*Clipper of the Clouds*) in 1886. His epic serial *Frank Reade, Jr. and His Queen Clipper of the Clouds* leaned heavily on Verne. Even the illustrations were identical, with three of those in Senarens's story also used in Verne's *Maitre du Monde* (*Master of the World*). Senarens's story is basically a long air voyage hampered by the presence of several malcontents and a lunatic scientist intent on seizing Frank's vessel.

Frank Reade, boy inventor, was created by Harry Enton, who put himself through medical school writing dime novels and storypaper serials. The steam-driven robot in *The Steam Man of the Plains* (1876) is mainly a device for transporting Frank and his cousin, Charley Gorse, to the far West. The story is a tongue-in-cheek yarn of encounters with outlaws and Indians, named "Motzer-Ponum" and "Sholum Alarkum." Out west, Frank meets the comic Irishman, Barney Shea. Barney and the black man, Pomp (introduced in a later story), became regular members of the cast. The plot may be improbable, but the steam man (borrowed from Edward S. Ellis's 1865 *Steam Man of the Prairies*) is engaging and novel for its day. We are told just enough about how it works to make it plausible. Senarens seemed to take the stories more seriously than Enton when he stepped in with the fifth serial. He introduced Frank Reade, Jr., but kept Frank, Sr., and eventually gave Jr. a wife. No stylist, he often wrote in the choppy manner peculiar to writers paid by the line. Without the aid of a typewriter, he wrote fast, kept the plot moving, and the characters in hot water. In formula fiction the fascination is in the variation on the basic themes. A new airship, surpassing any effort of the imagination; a new type of submarine; electrified equipment to drive off enemies; aluminum bullet-proof armor; pneumatic revolvers; damsels in distress; gentlemen unjustly accused of murder; a race against time; evil men determined to steal the invention; the pranks of comic relief companions, forever quarrelling; the wonderfully strange foreign lands; the deadly beauty of an undersea cavern or ice-locked vessel. Along the way a bit of social comment: does the U.S. government protect citizens abroad? Do the workshops in Readestown provide enough jobs for the community?

Senarens himself claimed authorship of most of the Frank Reade stories and all of the companion series about Jack Wright, who lived in Wrightstown and whose specialty was inventing submarines. His adventures were novelettes cut from the same pattern as the Frank Reades. In 1894, the two raced each other around the world for $10,000. Jack's submarine won by 15 minutes because Frank set down his airship to save a girl on a runaway horse. The stories ended in 1904 when public sentiment decided the ideas were too bizarre and Senarens ran out of ideas, though they lived on in reprints.

Senarens's contribution to science fiction is in his early and imaginative use of so many scientific marvels harnessed for popular consumption to a mass market. Had it not been for the wonders of Senarens there might have been no Tom Swift.

—J. Randolph Cox

---

**SERLING, (Edward) Rod(man).** American. Born in Syracuse, New York, 25 December 1924. Educated at Antioch College, Yellow Springs, Ohio, B.A. 1950. Served as a paratrooper in the United States Army during World War II. Married Carolyn Kramer in 1948; two daughters. Writer, WLW-Radio, 1946–48, and WKRC-TV, 1948–53, both Cincinnati; freelance writer from 1953; producer of television series *The Twilight Zone*, 1959–64, and *Night Gallery*, from 1969; taught at Antioch College, 1950's, and Ithaca College, New York, 1970's. President, National Academy of Television Arts and Sciences, 1965–66; member of the council, Writers Guild of America West, 1965–67. Recipient: Emmy award, for television plays, 1955, 1957, 1959; Sylvania award, 1955, 1956; Christopher award, 1956, 1971; Peabody award, 1957; Hugo award, for TV writing, 1960, 1961, 1962. D.H.L.: Emerson College, Boston, 1971; Alfred University, New York, 1972; Litt. D.: Ithaca College, 1972. *Died 28 June 1975.*

### Science-Fiction Publications

#### Short Stories

*Stories from the Twilight Zone.* New York, Bantam, 1960.
*More Stories from the Twilight Zone.* New York, Bantam, 1961.
*New Stories from the Twilight Zone.* New York, Bantam, 1962.
*From the Twilight Zone* (selection). New York, Doubleday, 1962.
*Night Gallery.* New York, Bantam, 1971.
*Night Gallery 2.* New York, Bantam, 1972.
*Rod Serling's Night Gallery Reader*, edited by Martin H. Greenberg, Carol Serling, and Charles G. Waugh. New York, Dembner, 1987.

### Other Publications

#### Novel

*Requiem for a Heavyweight* (novelization of screenplay). New York, Bantam, and London, Corgi, 1962.

#### Short Stories

*The Season To Be Wary.* Boston, Little Brown, 1967.

#### Plays

*Requiem for a Heavyweight* (televised, 1956). Included in *Patterns*, 1957; (revised version, produced New York, 1979).
*Patterns: Four Television Plays* (includes *Patterns, The Rack, Requiem for a Heavyweight, Old MacDonald Had a Curve*). New York, Simon and Schuster, 1957.
*The Killing Season* (produced New York, 1968).
*The Lonely*, in *Writing for Television*, edited by Max Wylie. New York, Cowles, 1970.
*A Storm in Summer*, in *Camera Two: Two Plays for Television*. Toronto, Holt Rinehart, 1972.

Screenplays: *Patterns*, 1956; *Saddle the Wind*, with Thomas Thompson, 1958; *Requiem for a Heavyweight*, 1962; *The Yellow Canary*, 1963; *Seven Days in May*, 1964; *Assault on a Queen*, 1966; *Planet of the Apes*, with Michael Wilson, 1968; *A Time for Predators*, 1971.

Television Plays: *Patterns*, 1955; *Requiem for a Heavyweight*, 1956; *Forbidden Area*, from the novel by Pat Frank, 1956; *The Comedian*, 1957; *The Doomsday Flight*, 1966; *The Movie Maker*, with Steve Bochko, 1967; *The Man*, 1971; *The Rack*; *Old MacDonald Had a Curve*; *Line of Duty*; *The Lonely*; *A Storm in Summer*; and other plays for *U.S. Steel Hour*, *Playhouse 90*,

*Hallmark Hall of Fame*, *Suspense*, *Twilight Zone*, *Night Gallery*, and *Danger* series.

*

Critical Study: *Rod Serling: The Dreams and Nightmares of Life in the Twilight Zone* (biography) by Joel Engel, Chicago, Contemporary Books, 1989.

*   *   *

One of the handful of scriptwriters who consistently produced quality drama during American television's "golden age" of the 1950's, Rod Serling demonstrated an interest in science-fiction themes as early as 1956, when he adapted Pat Frank's novels *Fobiden Area* for television. Later, as one of the few writers to be given relative artistic control over a TV series, he turned again to science fiction and fantasy with *The Twilight Zone*, an anthology series which began in 1959. *The Twilight Zone* is often cited as one of the first serious attempts to bring intelligent fantastic stories to television, and, in addition to the large number of scripts that Serling himself wrote for the series, he elicited scripts from major writers within the science fiction and fantasy field, including Richard Matheson, Charles Beaumont, and Ray Bradbury. A later TV series, *Night Gallery*, retained a few science-fiction stories but tended more toward fantasy and the supernatural. Serling also wrote the filmscripts for *Seven Days in May* and the hugely successful *Planet of the Apes*.

Serling adapted several of his *Twilight Zone* episodes as short stories. These often reveal the constraints of writing for television, and Serling for the most part made no effort to take advantage of the new form to develop or expand upon his initial scripts. The characters tend to be exaggerated stereotypes, easily recognizable in a half-hour TV format; the style is often precious or portentous, reflecting Serling's own opening and closing narrations for the original shows; and the fantastic elements are kept elementary and at times even simplistic. With their moralistic lessons and often sentimental tone, the tales work more as fables than as serious attempts at character or idea development.

Serling's attitude toward technology, for example, is decidedly ambiguous. When he writes of robots, he is unabashedly sentimental, as in "The Mighty Casey," which concerns a robot pitcher who nearly saves the Brooklyn Dodgers until he gets a mechanical heart which makes him too kind to strike out batters (the story is an odd combination of *Damn Yankees* and *The Wizard of Oz*), or "The Lonely," which concerns a prisoner sentenced to a lonely asteroid who finds companionship in a female robot brought by a kindly spaceship captain (a variation on a story by Ray Bradbury, who seems to be Serling's most consistent influence, even cropping up as a character name in a couple of Serling's stories). But in some stories mechanical contrivances become evil presences with minds of their own—a slot machine bent on destroying a compulsive gambler in "The Fever" or household appliances and a vengeful automobile in "A Thing about Machines." The implicit technophobia of "A Thing about Machines," however, is undercut by the almost pathological hostility of the victim who is the central character. Other stories also reflect technophobia in their concern with escape into a simpler past life ("A Stop at Willoughby," "Walking Distance"). The relatively few that deal with the familiar science-fiction theme of alien presences, such as "Mr. Dingle, The Strong" or "The Monsters Are Due on Maple Street," treat them as little more than background for stories essentially concerned with character relations.

Not surprisingly, the major strength in Serling's writing is the convincing dialogue and his ability to sketch recognizable characters quickly—both skills well-suited to TV writing. His exposition is weak and at times even cloying, his themes and plots derivative. He is most likely to be remembered for his powerful non-science fiction dramas, such as *Patterns* or *Requiem for a Heavyweight*, and for his contribution in bringing serious, character-oriented fantastic tales—however familiar such tales may have been to veteran readers—to the television screen.

—Gary K. Wolfe

---

**SERVISS, Garrett P(utnam).** American. Born in Sharon Springs, New York, 24 March 1851. Educated at Cornell University, Ithaca, New York, B.S. 1872; Columbia University, New York, LL. B. 1874. Married Henrietta Gros le Blond in 1907. Editorial writer, New York *Sun*, to 1892; then lecturer on travel, history, and astronomy, and writer. *Died 25 May 1929.*

SCIENCE-FICTION PUBLICATIONS

Novels

*The Moon Metal.* New York, Harper, 1900.
*A Columbus of Space.* New York and London, Appleton, 1911.
*The Second Deluge.* New York, McBride Nast, and London, Richards, 1912.
*Edison's Conquest of Mars.* Los Angeles, Carcosa House, 1947; abridged edition, as *Invasion of Mars*, Reseda, California, Powell, 1969.

OTHER PUBLICATIONS

Other

*Astronomy with an Opera-Glass.* New York, Appleton, 1888.
*Wonders of the Lunar Worlds; or, A Trip to the Moon.* New York, Urania, 1892.
*Napoleon Bonaparte* (lecture). Philadelphia, Morris, 1901.
*Other Worlds: Their Nature, Possibilities, and Habitability in the Light of the Latest Discoveries.* New York, Appleton, 1901.
*Pleasures of the Telescope.* New York, Appleton, 1901; London, Hirschfeld, 1902.
*The Heavens Without a Telescope*, with Leon Barritt. New York, Barritt, 1906.
*Planet Tables, Moon Phases, and the Sun's Daily Position*, with Leon Barritt. New York, Barritt, 1906.
*The Barritt-Serviss Star and Planet Finder, Northern Hemisphere*, with Leon Barritt. New York, Barritt, 1906.
*The Moon.* New York, Appleton, 1907; as *The Story of the Moon*, 1928.
*Astronomy with the Naked Eye.* New York, Harper, 1908.
*Curiosities of the Sky.* New York, Harper, 1909.
*Round the Year with the Stars.* New York, Harper, 1910.
*Eloquence: Counsel on the Art of Public Speaking.* New York, Harper, 1912.
*Astronomy in a Nutshell.* New York, Putnam, 1912.
*The Einstein Theory of Relativity.* New York, Fadman, 1923.

*Riding Through Space: The Earth's Scenic Voyage.* Springfield, Ohio, Corwell, 1923.

* * *

Most of the writings of Garrett P. Serviss were never read, or even suspected, by the generation that lauded his small but significant contribution to science fiction. As a staff writer for the New York *Sun*, and later for a newspaper syndicate, he produced many columns of popular science material, much of which was unsigned. Having made his name as the popular astronomer of his day, he wrote for several leading magazines on subjects ranging from "Facts and Fancies about Mars" to the Shakespeare-Bacon controversy. A series of articles (*Astronomy with an Opera-Glass*) in *Popular Science Monthly* was extended to become the first of a small library of works including such titles as *Other Worlds* and *Curiosities of the Sky.*

His first novel was serialised in 1898 in the New York *Evening Journal*, and was evidently designed to exploit the public interest engendered by H.G. Wells's *The War of the Worlds. Edison's Conquest of Mars* was in the nature of a sequel to the Wells classic, though it went far beyond the limits of imaginative conception that even the Master had essayed in a single story. The Martians, too, were rather more human than Wells's monstrous marauders; and they had no chance to launch a second invasion before the great American inventor had organised a counter-attack on Mars in a whole fleet of spaceships armed with deadly disintegrators. Though hurriedly written in a bombastic style, the story was remarkably inventive for its time, anticipating many of the devices that became the substance of later science fiction. No less remarkable is the fact that it was exhumed and published in hardcover only in 1947, having become legendary among fans who admired the author's subsequent stories.

One that attained classic status was *A Columbus of Space*, the tale of a voyage to Venus in an atomic-powered spaceship. Even more notable is *The Second Deluge*, in which a cosmic collision results in a universal flood. The story of how a latter-day Noah saved the human race from extinction proved so popular that it was twice reprinted by *Amazing*, where one reader found it so convincing that he wrote in asking for the plans of Cosmo Versál's ark so that he might save his family from the impending disaster. *The Moon Metal* concerned a mysterious metal originating in the lunar crater Tycho which replaced gold when this became as plentiful as iron. "The Sky Pirate" dared to predict air travel at 140 miles an hour in the year 1936; and "The Moon Maiden," the least of all his works, marked the last appearance of Serviss, in *Argosy*, the magazine that pioneered science fiction long before the advent of the specialist pulps.

—Walter Gillings

---

**SHARKEY, Jack.** (John Michael Sharkey). Also writes as Rick Abbot; Mark Chandler; Monk Ferris; Mike Johnson. American. Born in Chicago, Illinois, 6 May 1931. Educated at St. Mary's College, Winona, Minnesota, B.A. in English 1953. Served in the United States Army, 1955–56. Married Patricia Walsh in 1962; three daughters and one son. Since 1952, professional writer: assistant editor, *Playboy*, Chicago, 1963–64; editor, *Aim*, later *Good Hands*, for Allstate Insurance, Northbrook, Illinois, 1964–75. Recipient: American Association of Industrial Editors prize, 1967; Inland Theatre League award, for play, 1984. Agent: (plays) Samuel French, 45 West 25th Street, New York, New York 10010. Address: 24276 Ponchartrain Lane, El Toro, California 92630, U.S.A.

SCIENCE-FICTION PUBLICATIONS

Novels

*The Secret Martians.* New York, Ace, 1960.
*Ultimatum in 2050 A.D.* New York, Ace, 1965.

Uncollected Short Stories (series: Jerry Norcriss)

"The Captain of His Soul" and "The Obvious Solution," in *Fantastic* (New York), March 1959.
"The Arm of Enmord," in *Fantastic* (New York), April 1959.
"Queen of the Green Sun," in *Fantastic* (New York), May 1959.
"Bedside Monster," in *Fantastic* (New York), June 1959.
"The Kink-Remover," in *Fantastic* (New York), July 1959.
"Let X = Alligators," in *Fantastic* (New York), August 1959.
"Dolce al Fine," in *Amazing* (New York), August 1959.
"The Blackbird," in *Fantastic* (New York), September 1959.
"Ship Ahoy!," in *Fantastic* (New York), October 1959.
"Minor Detail," in *Amazing* (New York), November 1959.
"The Man Who Was Pale," in *Fantastic* (New York), December 1959.
"Multum in Parvo," in *The Year's Best S-F 5*, edited by Judith Merril. New York, Simon and Schuster, 1960; London, Mayflower, 1966.
"Old Friends Are the Best" in *Amazing* (New York), March 1960.
"The Dope on Mars," in *Galaxy* (New York), August 1960.
"The Crispin Affair," in *Fantastic* (New York), July, August 1960.
"The Business, As Usual," in *Galaxy* (New York), August 1960.
"Squeeze," in *Fantastic* (New York), September 1960.
"Status Quaint," in *Fantastic* (New York), October 1960.
"According to the Plan," in *Fantastic* (New York), January 1961.
"The Contact Point," in *If* (New York), January 1961.
"A Thread in Time," in *Fantastic* (New York), February 1961.
"Night Caller," in *Fantastic* (New York), March 1961.
"The Flying Tuskers of Kiniik-Kinaak," in *If* (New York), May 1961.
"Are You Now or Have You Ever Been?," in *Fantastic* (New York), May 1961.
"One Small Drawback," in *Fantastic* (New York), August 1961.
"Arcturus Times Three" (Norcriss), in *Galaxy* (New York), October 1961.
"Robotum Delenda Est!," in *Fantastic* (New York), March 1962.
"Big Baby" (Norcriss), in *Galaxy* (New York), April 1962.
"Double or Nothing," in *Fantastic* (New York), May 1962.
"Behind the Door," in *Fantastic* (New York), August 1962.
"A Matter of Protocol" (Norcriss), in *Galaxy* (New York), August 1962.
"It's Magic, You Dope!," in *Fantastic* (New York), November, December 1962.
"The Final Ingredient," in *Triple W*, edited by Rod Serling. New York, Bantam, 1963.
"The Leech," in *Fantastic* (New York), January 1963.
"The Smart Ones," in *Amazing* (New York), February 1963.
"The Trouble with Tweenity," in *Fantastic* (New York), July 1963.
"Collector's Item," in *Fantasy and Science Fiction* (New York), September 1963.
"The Aftertime," in *Fantastic* (New York), November 1963.

"The Creature Inside" (Norcriss), in *Worlds of Tomorrow* (New York), December 1963.
"The Awakening," in *Galaxy* (New York), February 1964.
"The Orginorg Way," in *Fantastic* (New York), February 1964.
"Survival of the Fittest," in *Fantasy and Science Fiction* (New York), March 1964.
"At the Feelies," in *Galaxy* (New York), April 1964.
"Illusion," in *Fantastic* (New York), June 1964.
"The Venus Charm," in *Fantastic* (New York), July 1964.
"Weetl," in *If* (New York), June 1964.
"Footnote to an Old Story," in *Fantastic* (New York), August 1964.
"The Colony That Failed" (Norcriss), in *Galaxy* (New York), August 1964.
"Hear and Obey," in *Fantastic* (New York), September 1964.
"The Grooves," in *Fantastic* (New York), October 1964.
"Breakthrough," in *Fantasy and Science Fiction* (New York), November 1964.
"The Seminarian," in *Amazing* (New York), November 1964.
"To Each His Own," in *The 6 Fingers of Time and 5 Other Science Fiction Novelets*. New York, Macfadden, 1965.
"The Twerlik," in *10th Annual Edition of the Year's Best SF*, edited by Judith Merril. New York, Delacorte Press, 1965; London, Mayflower, 1967.
"Trade-In," in *Best from Fantasy and Science Fiction 14*, edited by Avram Davidson. New York, Doubleday, 1965; London, Panther, 1967.
"Blue Boy," in *Amazing* (New York), January 1965.
"Look Out Below," in *Fantastic* (New York), March 1965.
"Essentials Only," in *Fantasy and Science Fiction* (New York), March 1965.
"The Trouble with Hyperspace," in *Fantastic* (New York), April 1965.
"The Glorious Fourth," in *Fantasy and Science Fiction* (New York), October 1965.
"Matrix Goose," in *Galaxy* (New York), August 1967.
"Life Cycle," in *If* (New York), September 1970.
"Conversation with a Bug," and "The Pool," in *From the "S" File*. Chicago, Playboy Press, 1971.
"Rate of Exchange," in *Galaxy* (New York), May 1971.
"Deadly Shade of Blue," in *Alfred Hitchcock's Tales to Fill You with Fear and Trembling*, edited by Eleanor Sullivan. New York, Dial Press, 1980.
"No Harm Done," in *Science Fiction from A to Z*, edited by Isaac Asimov, Martin H. Greenberg, and Charles G. Waugh. Boston, Houghton Mifflin, 1982.

### Other Publications

#### Novels

*Murder, Maestro, Please*. New York and London, Abelard Schuman, 1960.
*Death for Auld Lang Syne*. New York, Holt Rinehart, 1962; London, Joseph, 1963.
*The Addams Family*. New York, Pyramid, 1965.

#### Plays

*Here Lies Jeremy Troy* (produced New York, 1965). New York, French, 1969.
*M is for Million*. New York, French, 1971.
*How Green Was My Brownie*. New York, French, 1972.
*Kiss or Make Up*. New York, French, 1972.
*Meanwhile, Back on the Couch....* New York, French, 1973.
*A Gentleman and a Scoundrel*. New York, French, 1973.
*Roomies*. New York, French, 1974.
*Spinoff*. New York, French, 1974.
*Who's on First?* (produced Mount Prospect, Illinois, 1975). New York, French, 1975.
*What a Spot!*, with Dave Reiser. New York, French, 1975.
*Saving Grace*. New York, French, 1976.
*Take a Number, Darling*. New York, French, 1976.
*The Creature Creeps!* New York, French, 1977.
*Dream Lover*. New York, French, 1977.
*Hope for the Best*, with Dave Reiser. New York, French, 1977.
*Rich Is Better*. New York, French, 1977.
*The Murder Room*. New York, French, 1977.
*Pushover*, with Ken Easton. New York, French, 1977.
*Once Is Enough*. New York, French, 1977.
*The Clone People* (as Mike Johnson). New York, French, 1978.
*Missing Link*. New York, French, 1978.
*Turnabout*, with Ken Easton. New York, French, 1978.
*Not the Count of Monte Cristo?*, with Dave Reiser. New York, French, 1978.
*Turkey in the Straw*. New York, French, 1979.
*Operetta!*, with Dave Reiser. New York, French, 1979.
*My Son the Astronaut*. New York, French, 1980.
*Par for the Corpse*. New York, French, 1980.
*Honestly Now!* New York, French, 1981.
*The Return of the Maniac* (as Mike Johnson). New York, French, 1981.
*Slow Down, Sweet Chariot*, with Dave Reiser. New York, French, 1982.
*Woman Overboard*, with Dave Reiser. New York, French, 1982.
*Your Flake or Mine?* New York, French, 1982.
*The Picture of Dorian Gray*, with Dave Reiser, from the novel by Oscar Wilde. New York, French, 1982.
*The Saloonkeeper's Daughter*, with Dave Reiser. New York, French, 1982.
*The Second Lady*. New York, French, 1983.
*And on the Sixth Day*, with Dave Reiser. New York, French, 1984.

Other Plays: *Double Exposure*; *And Then I Wrote*, with Mel Buttorff; *The Well Dressed Liar*, with George Abbott; *My Husband the Wife* (lyrics only, with Dave Reiser), book by Ira and Brady Rubin, music by Dave Reiser; *Jekyll Hydes Again!*, with Dave Reiser; *Don't Tell Mother!* (as Monk Harris); *This Must Be the Place!* (as Monk Harris); *Let's Murder Marsha!* (as Monk Harris); *The Great All-American Disaster Musical*, with Tim Kelly; *Money, Power, Murder, Lust, Revenge and Marvelous Clothes*, with Tim Kelly; *A Fine Monster You Are!* (as Monk Harris); *Bone-Chiller* (as Monk Harris); *One Toe in the Grave*; *Zingo!*, with Dave Reiser; *Class Musical!* (as R. Abbot); *Love with a Twist*, with Dave Reiser; *The Woman in White*, with Tim Kelly; *Cinderella Meets the Wolfman!*, with Tim Kelly; *Sherlock Holmes and the Giant Rat of Sumatra*, with Tim Kelly; *The Three-and-a-Half Muskateers*, with Tim Kelly; *Time and Time Again!*, with Tim Kelly; *The Bride of Brackenloch!* (as R. Abbot); *Hamlet, Cha-Cha-Cha!* (as Monk Harris); *Nell of the Ozarks*; *While the Lights Were Out*; *Coping*, with Dave Reiser; *The Pinchpenny Phantom of the Opera*, with Dave Reiser; *Allocating Annie*; *Oh, Fudge!*; *100 Lunches*, with Leo Sears; *Oh, No! A Nuclear Musical!*, with Cenarth Fox; *The Perfect Murder* (as Mike Johnson); *The Premature Corpse* (as Mike Johnson); *The Swan Song* (as Mike Johnson); *I Shot my Rich Aunt* (as Mark Chandler); *Sorry! Wrong Chimney!*, with Leo Sears; *Doctor Death* (as Mark Chandler); *I Take This Man*; as Rick Abbot—*Dracula: The Musical?*; *Beauty and the Beast*; *Really*; *June Groom*; *Play On!*; *But Why Bump Off Barnaby?*; *A Turn for the Nurse*—all published New York, French.

Other

*Audition Pieces and Classroom Exercises.* New York, French, n.d.

*

Jack Sharkey comments:

I enjoy writing imaginative fiction and stage plays because of the marvelous "elbow room" it allows me when plotting; unconfined by anything—even the force of gravity!—I can tell stories occurring in situations Polti never dreamed of, I can fly like a bird at the touch of the typewriter-key, and set my characters on any planet in the known or unknown universe without the bother of paying for rocket fuel!

* * *

Jack Sharkey started publishing science fiction in 1959, but produced little fiction of any kind after 1965. In that span of time, Sharkey sold about 50 stories and seven novels.

Sharkey's best-known series featured Jerry Norcriss, Space Zoologist. These stories were typical SF puzzle stories where Norcriss would "merge" minds with an alien organism in order to solve the environmental puzzle and save a star colony. Two novels which were serialized but never published in book form are "The Crispin Affair," a thrilling space opera, and "It's Magic, You Dope!," a wildly funny fantasy in the mode of Pratt and de Camp's *The Incomplete Enchanter.*

Sharkey's two SF novels published in book form are complete opposites. *The Secret Martians* is a first-person account of the mystery of the missing Space Scouts and the discovery of the ancient Martian civilization. The action is fast paced and laced with humor. *Ultimatum in 2050 A.D.* is the grim story, with overtones of *Logan's Run*, of revolt against an Earth Society where all its citizens are completely programmed. Sharkey's works are enjoyable, well written, and unfortunately completely out-of-print.

—George Kelley

---

**SHAVER, Richard S(harpe).** Also wrote as Wes Amherst; Edwin Benson; Peter Dexter; Richard Dorset; Richard English; G.H. Irwin; Paul Lohrman; Frank Patton; Stan Raycraft. American. Born in 1907. Little is known of his life: probably a welder who lived in Pennsylvania. *Died 5 November 1975.*

SCIENCE-FICTION PUBLICATIONS

Short Stories

*I Remember Lemuria, and The Return of Sathanas.* Evanston Illinois, Venture, 1948.

Uncollected Short Stories (series: Red Dwarf)

"The Tale of the Red Dwarf," in *Fantastic Adventures* (New York), May 1947.
"Daughter of Night" (Dwarf), in *Amazing* (New York), December 1948.
"The Cyclops," in *Amazing* (New York), January 1949.
"The Cyclopeans," in *Fantastic Adventures* (New York), June 1949.
"Exiles of the Elfmounds," in *Amazing* (New York), July 1949.
"Erdis Cliff" (Dwarf), in *Amazing* (New York), September 1949.
"Where No Foot Walks" (as G.H. Irwin), and "The Fall of Lemuria," in *Other Worlds* (Evanston, Indiana), November 1949.
"Battle in Eternity," with Chester S. Geier, in *Amazing* (New York), November 1949.
"When the Moon Bounced" (as Frank Patton), and "Pillars of Delight" (as Stan Raycraft), in *Amazing* (New York), December 1949.
"Sons of the Serpent" (as Wes Amherst) in *Other Worlds* (Evanston, Indiana), January 1950.
"The Gamin" (as Peter Dexter), "Mahai's Wife" (as Edwin Benson), and "Lady," in *Other Worlds* (Evanston, Indiana), March 1950.
"The World of the Lost" (as Paul Lohrman), in *Fantastic Adventures* (New York), March 1950.
"We Dance for the Dom," in *Amazing* (New York), July 1950.
"The Palace of Darkness" (as Peter Dexter), in *Other Worlds* (Evanston, Indiana), September 1950.
"Glass Woman of Venus" (as G.H. Irwin) in *Other Worlds* (Evanston, Indiana), January 1951.
"Green Man's Grief," in *Future* (New York), January 1951.
"Yelisen," in *Other Worlds* (Evanston, Indiana), December 1951.
"Of Stegner's Folly," in *If* (New York), March 1952.
"The Sun Smiths," in *Other Worlds* (Evanston, Indiana), July, August, October 1952.
"Beyond the Barrier," in *Other Worlds* (Evanston, Indiana), November, December 1952, January, February 1953.
"The Dark Goddess," in *Imagination* (Evanston, Illinois) February 1953.
"Paradise Planet," in *Imagination* (Evanston, Illinois) Spring 1953.
"She Was Sitting in the Dark" (as Richard Dorset), in *Science Stories* (Evanston, Illinois), December 1953.
"The Dream Makers," in *Fantastic* (New York), July 1958.
"The Heart of the Game" (as Richard English), in *Orbit 1*, edited by Damon Knight. New York, Putnam, and London, Whiting and Wheaton, 1966.

* * *

If Richard S. Shaver is discussed today, it is usually as a curiosity in the history of science fiction, or as an early example of that dim area where fiction shades into UFO's and ancient astronauts. This is to some extent justified but not altogether fair. Although "The Shaver Mystery" series was presented for the most part as fact, it is far more akin to the science fiction of its time, both in execution and in sources, than most realize; and, taken as fiction, the stories do have intrinsic interest and merit.

During Shaver's writing career, spanning three decades, his stories and "non-fiction" explications were published in a number of magazines, primarily under his longtime editor and advocate, Ray Palmer, at first in science-fiction magazines such as *Amazing Stories* and *Other Worlds*, and later in "occult" publications such as *Hidden World.* A letter from Shaver (*Amazing*, December 1944) described the underground races called the "dero" and "tero" who had taught him the precatastrophe language of "Mantong." Then, at Palmer's request, Shaver sent a 10,000 word manuscript from which Palmer wrote a 31,000 word story, "I Remember Lemuria!" Constructed for high drama and written in colorful and traditional pulp style, it told the story of "Mutan Mion of ancient Lemuria," and fully outlined the background and dogma of the Shaver Mystery. The Atlans and Titans, Shaver reports, had been immortal giants of advanced technology; then the sun began to age and give off "heavy metal radiation," causing aging and death. Most fled the earth for a planet with a younger sun, but others burrowed beneath the ground seeking protection from the poisonous rays. These are the dero and tero Shaver claimed to have met in the caves—struggling remnants of a once-great civilization. Of these two warring factions, the dero are by far the more interesting; Shaver has developed the quintessential conspiracy theory. Whenever anything goes wrong, the degenerate dero, crazed by the sun's rays and using the almost-magical machines left by the Elder Races, are responsible. Against this depravity, the tero fight valiantly but often in vain, sometimes aided by sensitive surface men like Richard Shaver.

This is fairly basic stuff, at least in its psychological appeal both as archetype and as wish fulfillment, especially for *Amazing* with its younger and less demanding readership. What made it controversial was that, after the first story, the series was presented as fact. It is debatable whether Palmer believed this; it is probable that he saw it mainly as a way to increase circulation, at least at first. Shaver, however, apparently believed completely in his visit to the caves, in the voices that spoke to him from underground, and in what those voices told him. In the May 1978 *Science Fiction Review*, Palmer announced that the eight years Shaver spent "in the caves" were actually spent in the Ypsilanti State Hospital as a paranoid schizophrenic. This sheds light on the style as well as the content of Shaver's writing: besides adventure-writing devices and techniques, Shaver's style is marked by "schizophrenese" characteristics such as disjointed sentences and, more importantly, word-dismantling and "clang associations."

But it would be wrong to dismiss these writings as only psychotic ravings, or even as Shaver's ravings hammered into salable fiction by Palmer. For one thing, Shaver himself wrote for other magazines under a number of pseudonyms, including house names. Beyond that, the stories show an eclectic range of clearly literary influences. These include the lush fiction of A. Merritt, Wells's Morlocks and Eloi, and the fictional world view of H.P. Lovecraft, from whose novel *At the Mountains of Madness* Shaver probably got the term "Elder Race." Harry Warner, Jr. (in *All Our Yesterdays*) mentions a possible influence from E.R. Eddison, "whom Shaver once identified as his literary idol" and *A Reader's Guide to Science Fiction* demonstrates patterning, perhaps conscious, after the planetary romances of Edgar Rice Burroughs. Possible sources in occult non-fiction include Charles Fort, the Theosophy of Mme. Blavatsky, and James Churchward's Mu series, which Shaver mentions in his first letter to Palmer. Shaver also mentions Edith Hamilton's writings on mythology—which his own works explain and correct. The Bible, especially the Edenic theme, is also an important source.

What results is an odd but fascinating blend of high adventure, outrageous "science," and elusive but striking systems of cosmic speculation. If the characters are sometimes flat, if the plots too often seem "boy meets girl, boy beats dero, boy wins girl"—and this is not always the case—the sheer wealth and strangeness of the concepts Shaver develops more than compensate for that. There is a kind of Stapledonian scope to Shaver, a sense of epic, and mythic, panoramas; the races, societies, and technologies with which he populates his universe are varied and often impressive. The appeal of Richard Shaver to the reader then and now is, as Palmer said, "one thing only, his unusual imagination. His strange sense of the unusual, his feeling for emotion, his sense of the beautiful and his sense of the outré." For that reason Shaver's writings, shrouded in controversy and now largely neglected, are worthy of new attention.

—Bernadette Bosky

---

**SHAW, Bob** (Robert Shaw). British. Born in Belfast, Northern Ireland, 31 December 1931. Educated at Technical High School, Belfast, 1944–46. Married Sarah Gourley in 1954; two daughters and one son. Prior to 1960, worked in the steel and aircraft industries and as a cab driver; assistant publicity officer, 1960–66, and press officer, 1969–73, Short Brothers, and Harland, aircraft manufacturers, Belfast; journalist, Belfast *Telegraph*, 1966–69; publicity officer, Vickers Shipbuilding Group, 1973– 75. Recipient: British Science Fiction Association award, 1975; Hugo award, for criticism, 1979, 1980. Agent: Carnell Literary Agency, Danes Croft, Goose Lane, Little Hallingbury, Hertfordshire CM22 7RG. Address: 66 Knutsford Road, Grappenhall, Warrington, Cheshire WA4 2PB, England.

### Science-Fiction Publications

Novels (series: Orbitsville)

*Night Walk*. New York, Banner, 1967; London, New English Library, 1970.
*The Two-Timers*. New York, Ace, 1968; London, Gollancz, 1969.
*Shadow of Heaven*. New York, Avon, 1969; abridged edition, London, New English Library, 1970; revised edition, London, Corgi, 1978; revised edition, London, Gollancz, 1991.
*The Palace of Eternity*. New York, Ace, 1969; London, Gollancz, 1970.
*One Million Tomorrows*. New York, Ace, 1970; London, Gollancz, 1971.
*Ground Zero Man*. New York, Avon, 1971; London, Corgi, 1976; revised edition, as *The Peace Machine*, London, Gollancz, 1985.
*Other Days, Other Eyes*. New York, Ace, and London, Gollancz, 1972.
*Orbitsville*. London, Gollancz, and New York, Ace, 1975.
*A Wreath of Stars*. London, Gollancz, 1976; New York, Doubleday, 1977.
*Medusa's Children*. London, Gollancz, 1977; New York, Doubleday, 1979.
*Who Goes Here?* London, Gollancz, 1977; New York, Ace, 1978; with *The Giaconda Caper*, New York, VGSF, 1988.
*Ship of Strangers*. London, Gollancz, 1978; New York, Ace, 1979.
*Vertigo*. London, Gollancz, 1978; New York, Ace, 1979.
*Dagger of the Mind*. London, Gollancz, 1979; New York, Ace, 1982.
*Galactic Tours*, illustrated by David Hardy. New York and London, Proteus, 1981.
*The Ceres Solution*. London, Gollancz, 1981; New York, DAW, 1984.
*Orbitsville Departure*. London, Gollancz, 1983; New York, DAW, 1985.
*Fire Pattern*. London, Gollancz, 1984; New York, DAW, 1986.
*The Ragged Astronauts*. London, Gollancz, 1986; New York, Baen, 1987.
*The Wooden Spaceships*. London, Gollancz, 1987; New York, Baen, 1988.

*Killer Planet* (for children). London, Gollancz, 1989.
*The Fugitive Worlds*. London, Gollancz, 1989; New York, Baen, 1990.
*Orbitsville Judgement*. London, Gollancz, 1990.

Short Stories

*The Enchanted Duplicator*, with Walt Willis. Privately printed, 1954.
*Tomorrow Lies in Ambush*. London, Gollancz, and New York, Ace, 1973.
*Cosmic Kaleidoscope*. London, Gollancz, 1976; New York, Doubleday, 1977.
*A Better Mantrap*. London, Gollancz, 1982.
*Dark Night in Toyland*. London, Gollancz, 1989.

OTHER PUBLICATIONS

Other

*The Best of the Bushel*. Epsom, Surrey, Paranoid-Inca Press, 1979.
*The Eastercon Speeches*. Epsom, Surrey, Paranoid-Inca Press, 1979.

*

Manuscript Collection: Science Fiction Foundation, North East London Polytechnic.

Critical Study: *Bob Shaw* by Brian M. Stableford (includes bibliography by Mike Ashley), n. p., British Science Fiction Association, 1981.

Bob Shaw comments:

It is very difficult, if not impossible, for an author to write objectively about his own work, but I sum up my output by saying that I write science fiction for people who don't read a great deal of science fiction. This doesn't mean that I curb my imagination. I'm quite prepared to deal with the most fantastic concepts, but I try to do it in such a way that the ideas can be appreciated by any reader. The technique involves a minimal use of in-group jargon and a very firm emphasis on relating every fictional event to real characters of a kind that the reader can immediately recognise and identify or empathise with. The universe is wonderful, but only when there is somebody there to wonder at it. Humour also plays an important role in my work, partly because I feel that science fiction shouldn't become too gloomy and portentous, mainly because one of the things we need most these days is a good laugh.

* * *

Bob Shaw has reached an uneasy status within science fiction. The quality of his work is recognised, yet he is treated with the same easy acceptance and lack of critical attention as a much more journeyman writer. The problem, perhaps, is that he works so resolutely within the heartland of science fiction—an area occupied by relatively few British science-fiction writers—and most of his work has the fairly straightforward structure of a mystery story. Despite his undoubted achievements, this seems to smack of a lack of ambition. And this impression is not helped by the way he seems unable to leave his most workmanlike fiction alone. In particular *Shadow of Heaven*, perhaps his weakest novel, has been revised some four times; yet, even in 1991, the latest revision may pad out the thin story but cannot disguise the weakness of the plot or the poverty of characterisation.

Even when he writes a novel of undoubted power and originality, such as *Orbitsville*, its strength is somewhat dissipated by two belated sequels that really add little to the awesome vision of the original. The first book took his characters to a massive Dyson sphere that completely enclosed a sun. It is a book with similarities to Larry Niven's *Ringworld*, and original publication was in fact delayed for a while to avoid too close a comparison, but it is a far better novel than Niven's. Shaw is at his best when pitching his characters against the effects of impersonal science, and he is able to convey the size of this alien artefact with vivid, yet beautifully controlled and effective, prose, and it is made the more powerful by the reality of his characters, whose all too human beliefs and problems provide a scale against which the alienness of the sphere is best seen. It seems unnecessary icing on the cake to go on and introduce the original builders of the sphere into later novels.

In all of Bob Shaw's work, in fact, it is in the human scale that he is best. Though his work frequently follows the formula of hard science fiction, he rarely fails to make his characters believable and three-dimensional. Thus, in perhaps his best and most famous short story, "Light of Other Days," which introduced one of the few really original concepts in the history of science fiction, "slow glass," he made it clear that humanity must be pre-eminent over any new technical device. "Slow glass" was a substance that could slow down the passage of light, sometimes for a matter of moments, sometimes for years. In this story, a murder has been committed in the presence of "slow glass" and at some future date the crime itself may be revealed to witnesses. But a judge is faced with making a decision on the case now. It is a story that certainly satisfies all the usual hard SF demands for original ideas, yet in doing so, Shaw has also written one of the most humane stories in the genre.

Shaw's writing is always crisp and matter-of-fact, but, there are times when he attempts something transcendent to unexpectedly good effect. This is best demonstrated by *The Palace of Eternity*, which takes its hero beyond death to a messianic rebirth while still keeping the novel tightly and entertainingly structured around a conflict between human and alien, and between artistry and technology. In *A Wreath of Stars*, one of his most underrated novels, an anti-neutrino planet passes through the Earth and leaves in its wake reports of ghosts underground and tantalising glimpses of another form of life. These books disguise with vivid and often highly original SF trappings a much more deeply felt report on what it feels like to be human in the face of the unknown and the unknowable. This is why *Orbitsville* works best without the introduction of the aliens, since their appearance removes a substantial part of the mystery.

It was the human scale, however, that helped to make his most ambitious work to date so successful. The *Ragged Astronauts* trilogy is massive in scope, involving planet-wide adventures, other worlds, and more. Yet, by concentrating on character, and setting it all within a non-technological world, he manages to ensure that it is a humane and very accessible story. The human inhabitants of Land are threatened by the poisonous ptertha, which have suddenly become more than usually dangerous. As the threat increases, the only hope of survival lies in escape to the twin world of Overland. But the people of Land have no metals, and so, in a spectacular *coup de theatre*, Shaw takes them from one planet to the other by way of hot-air balloons. It is a daring idea carried off with great panache, and the writing displays all the delight of someone decking out a very high-tech SF adventure with determinedly low-tech paraphernalia. And, in a touch typical of Shaw, he manages to set these very science-fictional events as a backdrop to a story of dynastic troubles, human values, and romance. It is a scale he manages to sustain throughout the trilogy, which builds up to exactly the sort of climactic transcendence that is a feature of his very best work.

Shaw is a writer capable of soaring heights, but also of abysmal depths, and one sometimes gets the impression that he cannot tell one from the other. Nevertheless, for his ability to provide the most stimulating and inventive hard science fiction with a genuine human face, he deserves a level of appreciation far higher than he has ever achieved.

—Paul Kincaid

---

**SHAW, Brian.** *See* **TUBB, E.C.**

---

**SHAW, Bryan.** *See* **FEARN, John Russell.**

---

**SHAWN, Frank S.** *See* **GOULART, Ron.**

---

**SHECKLEY, Robert.** American. Born in New York City, 16 July 1928. Educated at New York University, B.A. 1951. Served in the United States Army, 1946–48. Married to Jay Rothbell. Fiction editor, *Omni*, 1980–82; Visiting Scholar, Massachusetts Institute of Technology, Cambridge, 1982. Recipient: Jupiter award, 1973. Address: c/o Bantam Books, 666 Fifth Avenue, New York, New York 10103, U.S.A.

SCIENCE-FICTION PUBLICATIONS

Novels

*Immortality Delivered.* New York, Avalon, 1958; revised edition, as *Immortality Inc.*, New York, Bantam, 1959; London, Gollancz, 1963.
*The Status Civilization.* New York, New American Library, 1960; London, New English Library, 1967.
*Journey Beyond Tomorrow.* New York, New American Library, 1962; London, Gollancz, 1964; as *Journey of Joenes*, London, Sphere, 1978.
*The 10th Victim.* New York, Ballantine, and London, Mayflower, 1966.
*Mindswap.* New York, Delacorte Press, and London, Gollancz, 1966.
*Dimension of Miracles.* New York, Dell, 1968; London, Gollancz, 1969.
*Options.* New York, Pyramid, 1975; London, Pan, 1977.
*Crompton Divided.* New York, Holt Rinehart, 1978; as *The Alchemical Marriage of Alistair Crompton*, London, Joseph, 1978.
*Dramocles.* New York, Holt Rinehart, 1983; London, New English Library, 1984.
*Victim Prime.* New York, New American Library, and London, Methuen, 1987.
*Hunter/Victim.* New York, New American Library, and London, Methuen, 1988.
*On the Planet of Bottled Brains*, with Harry Harrison. New York, Avon, 1990; as *Bill, the Galactic Hero on the Planet of Bottled Brains*, London, Gollancz, 1990.
*Bring Me the Head of Prince Charming*, with Roger Zelazny. New York, Bantam, 1991.

Short Stories

*Untouched by Human Hands; 13 Stories. New York, Ballantine, 1954; London, Joseph, 1955.*
*Citizen in Space.* New York, Ballantine, 1955; London, New English Library, 1969.
*Pilgrimage to Earth.* New York, Bantam, 1957; London, Corgi, 1959.
*Store of Infinity.* New York, Bantam, 1960.
*Notions: Unlimited.* New York, Bantam, 1960.
*Shards of Space.* New York, Bantam, and London, Corgi, 1962.
*The People Trap.* New York, Dell, 1968; London, Gollancz, 1969.
*Can You Feel Anything When I Do This?* New York, Doubleday, 1971; London, Gollancz, 1972; as *The Same to You Doubled and Other Stories*, London, Pan, 1974.
*The Robert Sheckley Omnibus*, edited by Robert Conquest. London, Gollancz, 1973.
*The Robot Who Looked Like Me.* London, Sphere, 1978.
*The Wonderful World of Robert Sheckley.* New York, Bantam, 1979; London, Sphere, 1980.
*Is THAT What People Do? The Selected Short Stories of Robert Sheckley.* New York, Holt Rinehart, 1984.

OTHER PUBLICATIONS

Novels

*Calibre .50.* New York, Bantam, 1961.
*Dead Run.* New York, Bantam, 1961.
*Live Gold.* New York, Bantam, 1962.
*The Man in the Water.* Evanston, Illinois, Regency, 1962.
*White Death.* New York, Bantam, 1963.
*The Game of X.* New York, Delacorte Press, 1965; London, Cape, 1966.
*Time Limit.* New York, Bantam, and London, New English Library, 1967.

Plays

Television Plays: 15 scripts for *Captain Video*, 1950's; *Murder Club*, from his own story, 1961 (UK).

Radio Play: 60 scripts for *Beyond the Green Door*, 1960's.

Other

*Futuropolis: Impossible Cities in Science Fiction and Fantasy.* New York, A and W, 1978; London, Big O, 1979.

Editor, *After the Fall: An Anthology.* New York, Ace, and London, Sphere, 1980.

* * *

Robert Sheckley is, if we must find a category for him, a metaphysical wit and satirist. His major theme, manifested in dozens of superb stories and novels, is that in an infinite universe "reality" is infinitely variegated, depending upon one's environmental or psychological framework. While some writers would regard this as a nihilistic nightmare, for Sheckley, it offers an opportunity for unbounded imaginative romping—precisely the sort of freedom that SF so eagerly welcomes. "The quest for non-ordinary reality is something more than curiosity and wishful thinking," Sheckley once said in a rare public address ("The Search for the Marvellous," delivered at the Institute of Contemporary Arts, London, 1975); "We are too crowded in our everyday lives by replicas of ourselves and by the repetitious artifacts of our days and nights. But we do not quite believe in this prosaic world. Continually we are reminded of the strangeness of birth and death, the vastness of time and space, the unknowability of ourselves." These somber thoughts Sheckley clothes with highly imaginative and entertaining plots. For example, in *Dimension of Miracles*, Carmody is brought to the galactic center for a prize he has won in the Intergalactic Sweepstakes. The prize is a sentient being in a gaily wrapped box that takes Carmody on a wild-goose chase through the universe in search of Earth (the Prize Committee does not know the co-ordinates for returning Carmody). Each episode makes it clear that the universe is such that one cannot go home again anyway, just as one cannot step into the same river twice. Carmody's search for home is also a search for self, and on this matter he has quite a bit to learn—such as the fact that the shapes of objects and creatures are a function of environment. What is evil or ugly in one environment may well appear benevolent and lovely when transferred to another.

This idea of the universe as protean and magical serves as a satirical ploy for Sheckley. In "The Petrified World" (*Is THAT What People Do?*, original title, "Dreamworld," from *The People Trap*) Lanigan, whose real world is one in which objects are continually changing shape and color, suffers from a recurring nightmare: he keeps finding himself on a world where change is largely imperceptible. "The pavement never once yielded beneath his feet. Over there was the First National City Bank. It had been there yesterday . . . but, worse, it would be there without fail tomorrow, and the day after that . . . grotesquely devoid of possibilities. It would never become a tomb, an airplane . . ." Lanigan finally becomes trapped in his nightmare—the nightmare that, Sheckley is suggesting, is our nightmare.

No matter how absurd and wildly episodic Sheckley's plots sometimes become, the metaphysician is always lurking in the wings, cueing us with tidbits of cosmic wisdom which are themselves refreshing. For example, *Mindswap* introduces us to a universe in which people can change bodies like garments. Marvin Flynn gets swindled out of his body by the notorious body-pirate Ze Kraggash, whose ruling philosophy is, "If a man cannot retain control of his own body, then he deserves to lose it." During the galaxy-wide search Flynn begins to realize just how indeterminate bodies really are and how useless it is to attach any lasting importance to them. "The acceptance of indeterminacy was the beginning of wisdom," a hermit on some alien world tells him. And after he chases Ze Kraggash into the Twisted World, he attains ultimate wisdom: "Nothing is permanent except our illusions."

Perhaps Sheckley's most dramatic rendering of the indeterminacy of selfhood is "Slaves of Time." Like the solipsistic nightmare world of Robert Heinlen's "All You Zombies," this story (omitted, unfortunately, from *Is THAT What People Do?*) depicts some of the uncannily paradoxical things that can happen if one engages in some serious time traveling. Gleister builds a time machine and goes into the future. Because nature "can tolerate a paradox but abhors a vacuum," it instantaneously creates another Gleister to take the first Gleister's place. This new Gleister, identical to the other, but on a different reality-track, also builds a time machine and travels into the future. The inevitable, grim result: an endless stream of Gleisters, each following his own reality-track. "It is strange," Gleister/Mingus says at one point where all the Gleister manifestations convene, "that all of us are one person, yet we represent widely different viewpoints." And Gleister/Ergon replies,"It's not so strange. . . . One person is many people even under normal circumstances."

*Options* offers yet another treatise on reality vs. illusion and mind-as-universe—embedded, but not too deeply, beneath a slapstick surface. Tom Mishkin, an intergalactic trader ("Frozen South African lobster tails, tennis shoes, air conditioners") finds himself stranded somewhere in the Lesser Megellanic Cloud, in need of a hard-to-get spare part for his ship. He is directed to Harmonia, a bizarre would where, as is almost always the case in Sheckley's cosmos, nothing is quite the way it seems. Mishkin and a mealy-mouthed robot set off on a mock-pilgrimage across Harmonia in search of the elusive spare part. To be sure, Harmonia is Tom Mishkin's disorderly mind strewn across an external milieu like an overstuffed closet that had burst open. Monsters pause in their deadly assaults to discuss metaphysical issues with him; carnival men entertain him; he meets poker players who think they are inside their hotel room in Manhatten (and very likely are). In one of the final episodes we get the sense that Mishkin is "really" just a little earth boy who has been engaged in a daydream that would make Walter Mitty's look dreary ("Tommy! Stop playing now!" "I'm not playing, Mom. This is real." . . . "Put down that broom and come into the house at once." "It's not a broom, it's a spaceship. Anyhow, my robot says . . ." "And bring that old radio in with you").

Many of Sheckley's works explore to some degree the nature of selfhood. The early, masterful tale, "Shape" (*Untouched by Human Hands; 13 Stories*) is about a team of alien space explorers who possess the ability to change shape at will, but whose society has forbidden them to do so (shapes were assigned and had to be rigorously maintained). No wonder, then, that when they land on a strange planet called Earth, they are so awed by the multitude of shapes, that they cannot bring themselves to return home; instead they joyfully assume the shapes of trees, rocks, animals, humans. And in *Crompton Divided*, Alistair Crompton, because of his multiple personality, is forced to undergo "Cleavage"—separation of the personalities, which are then placed in separate bodies and shipped, unknown to the main personality, to remote planets. Crompton, now mild-mannered but totally devoid of spunk, learns what has happened to him and, after raising sufficient funds by embezzling rare and exotic perfumes from his company, embarks on a galaxy-wide search for his lost selves. That this is yet another indictment of society for the pressures it exerts upon us to be consistent, predictable, content citizens is clear from the following passage:

On all sides of him, the envious Crompton saw people with all their marvelous complexities and contradictions constantly bursting out of the stereotypes that society tried to force on them. He observed prostitutes who were not good-hearted, army sergeants who detested brutality, wealthy men who never gave a cent to charity. Irishmen who hated talking, Italians who could not carry a tune. . . . Most of the human race seemed to live lives of a wonderful and unpredictable richness, erupting into sudden passions and strange calms, saying one thing and meaning another.

For Sheckley, to be fully human means to house a repertoire of selves, willing and able to assume different roles, changing our minds when we want to. The only danger is that one can get carried away with the ability to manipulate reality and start trying to play God, conquering and subjugating with no regard for the well-being—the selfhood—of others. Such is the circumstance we encounter in Sheckley's novel, *Dramocles.* "Travelling between realities," the power-hungry Otho tells his son Dramocles, ruler of Glorm, is "the way to life everlasting." Despite Otho's efforts to persuade him that the lives of mere mortals are irrelevant "when the rewards of godhood are within your grasp," Dramocles manages to resist.

Unlike the young man in Sheckley's "The Language of Love" who learned to express his deepest romantic feelings with such precision that his sweetheart quickly lost interest in him, Dramocles discovers that too much of a good thing can rob one of one's very humanity.

—Fred D. White

---

**SHEFFIELD, Charles.** Also writes as James Kirkwood. Born in England. Educated at St. John's College, Cambridge, B.A. and M.A. in mathematics, Ph.D. in theoretical physics. Formerly president of the American Astronautical Society; formerly president, Science Fiction Writers of America; currently chief scientist and board member, Earth Satellite Corporation. Address: 2848 Aquarius Avenue, Silver Springs, Maryland 20906, U.S.A.

SCIENCE-FICTION PUBLICATIONS

Novels (series: Proteus; Heritage Universe)

*Sight of Proteus.* New York, Ace, 1978; London, Sidgwick and Jackson, 1980.
*The Web Between the Worlds.* New York, Ace, 1979; London, Sidgwick and Jackson, 1980.
*Between the Strokes of Night.* New York, Baen, 1985.
*The Nimrod Hunt.* New York, Baen, 1986.
*Trader's World.* New York, Del Rey, 1988; London, New English Library, 1989.
*Proteus Unbound.* New York, Del Rey, and London, Hodder and Stoughton, 1989.
*Summertide* (Heritage). New York, Del Rey, and London, Gollancz, 1990.
*Divergence* (Heritage). New York, Del Rey, and London, Gollancz, 1991.

Short Stories

*Vectors.* New York, Ace, 1980.
*Hidden Variables.* New York, Ace, 1981.
*The McAndrew Chronicles.* New York, Tor, 1983.

OTHER PUBLICATIONS

Novels

*The Selkie,* with David F. Bischoff. New York, Macmillan, 1982.
*My Brother's Keeper.* New York, Ace, 1982.

Short Stories

*Erasmus Magister.* New York, Ace, 1982.

Other

*Earthwatch: A Survey of the World from Space.* London, Sidgwick and Jackson, and New York, Macmillan, 1981.
*Man on Earth.* London, Sidgwick and Jackson, and New York, Macmillan, 1983.
*Space Careers,* with Carol Rosin. New York, Morrow, 1984.

Editor, with John L. McLucas, *Commercial Operations in Space 1980–2000.* San Diego, American Astronautical Society, 1981.

Author of some 50 technical papers since 1965.

* * *

Although Charles Sheffield only began writing science fiction in the late 1970's, he has already achieved some popularity as a writer of hard science fiction. To date, most of Sheffield's prolific output—almost a book a year—falls into four subsets.

His first novel, *Sight of Proteus,* is at the center of a "form-change" subset. Combining biological feedback hardware with real-time computer programming, form-change enables human beings of the late 22nd century to reshape their bodies. And while most people explore only the cosmetic aspects of this technology, Robert Capman is at work diligently, but illegally, modifying the human body for space travel. Naturally, this brings him into conflict with Behrooz Wolf, the man in charge of seeking out illegal form-changes.

In the sequel, *Proteus Unbound,* Sheffield expands the scope from Earth to the solar system. The problem: normally reliable form-change equipment is breaking down at an alarming rate. Wolf once again finds the solution, just in time to save the solar system from a megalomaniac bent on destroying it.

Loosely connected to the form-change novels is *The Web Between the Worlds.* Set in the middle of the 21st century, it details the construction of Earth's first "Beanstalk," a cable thousands of miles long, anchored at the equator, ballasted at the other end by an asteroid, up and down which people and material can move—in other words, a "space elevator" similar to the one in Arthur C. Clarke's *The Fountains of Paradise.* More closely connected to the form-change novels is *The McAndrew Chronicles,* five short stories featuring Arthur Morton McAndrew, the system's foremost authority on power kernels (Kerr-Newman black holes) and the inventor of the McAndrew balanced drive.

Three works published in 1982 comprise a second subset of Sheffield's *oeuvre.* Not really science fiction, though they include SF ideas, these works are historical, horror, and espionage fiction, respectively.

The novellas in *Erasmus Magister* take place during 1776–1778 and are based on the life of Erasmus Darwin, physician and botanist, grandfather of Charles Darwin, and a figure near the top of Sheffield's personal pantheon of great scientists. In *The Selkie,* a novel that Sheffield wrote in collaboration with David Bischoff, an American hydrology expert in the late 20th century is studying tidal caves along the Scottish coast. When his wife joins him, she is seduced by one of the legendary race of seal-people who live in the caves. In *My Brother's Keeper,* medical research a century from now has just discovered a method to allow nerve regeneration, good news to twins nearly killed in a ghastly helicopter accident, who wind up in one body sharing parts of their two brains. At first the dominant personality is the concert pianist twin, but it turns out the other twin is a spy of some sort. Complications ensue.

A third subset is filled by three post-nuclear-holocaust SF novels. The holocaust in *Between the Strokes of Night* is absolutely catastrophic, the only survivors those few fortunate enough to be off planet. The holocaust in *Trader's World* is less catastrophic; so 50 years later the various remnants are gradually being unified via commercial transactions negotiated by the Traders, a group one reviewer called "a pragmatic version of the United Nations." The holocaust in *The Nimrod Hunt* is in the far-distant past; in the meantime humanity has made contact with various alien species.

The final subset includes Sheffield's most recent novels, *Summertide* and *Divergence*, Books One and Two of *The Heritage Universe.* Here Sheffield indulges his penchant for macroengineering, object-building on a truly gigantic scale. It's the 63rd century and the three known space-going species—human, Cecropian, Zardalu—have discovered, scattered throughout the galaxy, 1,236 massive artifacts left by a mysterious race they name the Builders. In *Summertide,* members of various species converge on the planetary doublet Opal and Quake just in time for a cataclysmic event that occurs once every 350,000 years. In *Divergence*, the same group winds up on a new artifact thousands of light years away, where they are tested for a chance to meet the fabled Builders.

But though Sheffield's *oeuvre* can be divided into these four subsets, each single work also shares noticeable family resemblances with the others. This is even true of *Vectors* and *Hidden Variables,* two short story collections that do not fit easily into any one of the subsets just discussed.

Details vary, but a similar optimistic vision of technology's future shows up throughout Sheffield's work. Beanstalks—not rockets—will help humanity colonize near-planetary space. Arks (i.e., generation starships) will gradually expand the sphere of human colonization. And eventually human ingenuity will discover faster-than-light travel. Before that, fusion power will yield to power kernels, asteroids will be mined, matter at the fringe of the solar system will be harvested, and various other forms of large- and small-scale engineering will be perfected.

Though flourishing as early as the 18th century and as late as the end of this universe, Sheffield's protagonists all resemble each other. They are male, early middle-aged, independent, confident, persistent, and courageous. And, like their author, many not only are expert specialists but also excel at both theoretical studies and practical applications.

The same themes show up again and again in a Sheffield work. Brain power is important because it leads to knowledge—and knowledge leads to survival in a universe hostile to ignorance. The most important activity is finding and facing the hardest problem available; and Sheffield's protagonists frequently solve these problems by indirect means, what he calls the ability to "think around corners." Sheffield values unflagging curiosity and the concomitant desire to explore the unknown. He also insists that negotiation is a much better method than war for handling conflict. Finally, love finds a place in his fictional universes.

Reviewers who are hard SF aficionados use words like imaginative, believable, intriguing, tantalizing, and compelling to describe Sheffield's work. Less sympathetic reviewers use different words: plodding, implausible, talky, nebulous, and inconclusive. As Sheffield himself, who sprinkles his work with Latin quotations and literary allusions, might say, "*De gustibus non est disputandum*": if SF adventure with a strong technological bent suits your tastes, you will probably like his work; if it does not, you will probably not like his work—but you might be surprised. Sheffield has not yet brought his writerly skills up to the brilliance of his ideas, and may never, but the gap is narrowing. Especially interesting lately, by the way, are his aliens and a move away from single protagonists to an ensemble of main characters.

—Todd H. Sammons

---

**SHELLEY, Mary (Wollstonecraft).** British. Born in Somers Town, London, 30 August 1797. Married Percy Bysshe Shelley in 1816 (died 1822); two sons and one daughter. Lived in Dundee, 1812, 1813–14, then returned to London; eloped to Europe with Shelley, 1814; writer from 1816; after Shelley's death lived in Genoa with the Leigh Hunts, 1822–23, then returned to England; travelled in Germany, 1840–41, and Italy, 1842–43. *Died 1 February 1851.*

### Science-Fiction Publications

Novels

*Frankenstein; or, The Modern Prometheus.* London, Lackington Hughes, 1818; revised edition, London, Colburn and Bentley, 1831; edited by M.K. Joseph, London and New York, Oxford University Press, 1969; 1818 edition edited by James Rieger, Indianapolis, Bobbs-Merrill, 1974.

*The Last Man.* London, H. Colburn, 1826; revised edition, edited by Hugh J. Luke, Lincoln, University of Nebraska Press, 1965; with new introduction by Brian W. Aldiss, London, Hogarth Press, 1985.

### Other Publications

Novels

*Valperga; or, The Life and Adventures of Castruccio, Prince of Lucca.* London, Whittaker, 1823.

*The Fortunes of Perkin Warbeck: A Romance.* London, Colburn and Bentley, 1830; Philadelphia, Carey, 1834.

*Lodore.* New York, Wallis and Newell, and London, R. Bentley, 1835.

*Falkner.* London, Saunders and Otley, and New York, Harper, 1837.

*Mathilda*, edited by Elizabeth Nitchie. Chapel Hill, University of North Carolina Press, 1959.

Short Stories

*Mary Shelley: Collected Tales and Stories,* edited by Charles E. Robinson. Baltimore, Maryland, Johns Hopkins University Press, 1976.

Plays

*Proserpine and Midas: Mythological Dramas,* edited by A. Koszul. London, H. Milford, 1922.

Verse

*The Choice: A Poem on Shelley's Death,* edited by H. Buxton Forman. London, privately printed, 1876.

Other

*History of a Six Weeks' Tour Through a Part of France, Switzerland, Germany and Holland*, with Percy Bysshe Shelley. London, Hookham and Ollier, 1817; abridged edition, as *Shelley's Visits to France, etc.*, edited by C.I. Elton, London, Bliss Sands, 1894.
*Rambles in Germany and Italy in 1840, 1842, and 1843*. London, Moxon, 2 vols., 1844.
*Shelley and Mary: A Collection of Letters and Documents of a Biographical Character*. London, privately printed, 3 vols., 1882.
*Letters of Mary Wollstonecraft Shelley, Mostly Unpublished*, edited by Henry H. Harper. Boston, Bibliophile Society, 1918.
*My Best Mary: The Selected Letters of Mary Wollstonecraft Shelley*, edited by Muriel Spark and Derek Stanford. New York, Roy, and London, Wingate, 1953.
*The Letters of Mary Wollstonecraft Shelley*, edited by Betty T. Bennett. Baltimore, Maryland, Johns Hopkins University Press, 3 vols., 1980–88.
*The Journals of Mary Shelley 1814–44*, edited by Paula R. Feldman and Diana Scott-Kilvert. Oxford, Clarendon Press, and New York, Oxford University Press, 2 vols., 1987.
*The Mary Shelley Reader* (contains *Frankenstein, Mathilda*, tales and stories, essays and reviews, and letters), edited by Betty T. Bennett and Charles E. Robinson. New York, Oxford University Press, 1990.

Editor, *Posthumous Poems*, by Percy Bysshe Shelley. London, Hunt, 1824.
Editor, *The Poetical Works of Percy Bysshe Shelley*. London, Moxon, 4 vols., 1839.
Editor, *Essays, Letters from Abroad, Translations, and Fragments*, by Percy Bysshe Shelley. London, Moxon, and Philadelphia, Lea and Blanchard, 2 vols., 1840.

*

Bibliography: *Mary Shelley: An Annotated Bibliography* by William H. Lyles, New York, Garland, 1975.

Critical Studies (selection): *Child of Light: A Reassessment of Mary Wollstonecraft Shelley* by Muriel Spark, Hadleigh, Essex, Tower Bridge, 1951, revised edition, as *Mary Shelley: A Biography*, New York, Dutton, 1987, London, Constable, 1988; *Mary Shelley: Author of Frankenstein* by Elizabeth Nitchie, New Brunswick, New Jersey, Rutgers University Press, 1953; *Mary Shelley* by Eileen Bigland, New York, Appleton Century, and London, Cassell, 1959; *Mary Shelley dans son oeuvre* by Jean de Palaccio, Paris, Klincksieck, 1969; *Mary Shelley* by William A. Walling, New York, Twayne, 1972; *Ariel Like a Harpy: Shelley, Mary, and Frankenstein* by Christopher Small, London, Gollancz, 1972, as *Mary Shelley's Frankenstein: Tracing the Myth*, Pittsburg, University of Pittsburg Press, 1973; *Shelley's Mary: A Life* by Margaret Leighton, New York, Farrar Straus, 1973; *Daughter of Earth and Water: A Biography of Mary Wollstonecraft Shelley* by Noel B. Gerson, New York, Morrow, 1973; *Mary Shelley's Monster: The Story of Frankenstein* by Martin Tropp, Boston, Houghton Mifflin, 1976; *Moon in Eclipse: A Life of Mary Shelley* by Jane Dunn, London, Weidenfeld and Nicolson, and New York, St. Martin's Press, 1978; *The Endurance of Frankenstein: Essays on Mary Shelley's Novel* edited by George Levine and U.C. Knoepflmacher, Berkeley, University of California Press, 1979; *Frankenstein's Creation: The Book, the Monster, and Human Reality* by David Ketterer, Victoria, British Columbia, University of Victoria Press, 1979; *The Lonely Muse: A Critical Biography of Mary Shelley* by Bonnie Rayford Neumann, Salzburg, Institut für Anglistik und Amerikanistik, 1979; *The Influence of William Godwin on the Novels of Mary Shelley* by Katherine Richardson Powers, New York, Arno Press, 1980; *The Frankenstein Catalog* by Donald F. Glut, Jefferson, North Carolina, McFarland, 1984; *Scientific Attitudes in Mary Shelley's Frankenstein* by S.H. Vasbinder, Ann Arbor, Michigan, U.M.I. Research Press, 1984; *Mary Shelley and Frankenstein: The Fate of Androgyny* by William Veeder, Chicago, University of Chicago Press, 1986; *The Monster in the Mirror: Gender and the Sentimental/Gothic Myth in Frankenstein* by Mary K. Patterson Thornburg, Ann Arbor, Michigan, U.M.I. Research Press, 1987; *Mary Shelley: Her Life, Her Fiction, Her Monsters* by Ann K. Mellor, New York and London, Routledge, 1988; *Mary Shelley: Romance and Reality* by Emily W. Sunstein, Boston, Little Brown, 1989; *The Godwins and the Shelleys: The Biography of a Family* by William St. Clair, New York, Norton, and London, Faber, 1989; *Approaches to Teaching Shelley's Frankenstein* edited by Stephen C. Behrendt, New York, M.L.A., 1990; *Hideous Progenies: Dramatizations of Frankenstein from Mary Shelley to the Present* by Steven Earl Forry, Philadelphia, University of Pennsylvania Press, 1990.

* * *

The theme of *Frankenstein; or, The Modern Prometheus* is startling, and may be simply expressed. A scientist rejects received past theories, turns to research, and patches together a human body from parts of corpses, in which he manages to instill life. The experiment goes wrong, bringing death and destruction to the scientist and his family.

This theme has troubled or amused the world for over a century and a half. The name of the scientist, Victor Frankenstein, has become synonymous with the irresponsible application of science and technology. And the myth was created some years before the term "scientist" was coined.

It is this theme—its far-sightedness and continued relevance—that qualifies *Frankenstein* as the first true work of science fiction, and Mary Shelley as its founding spirit. For the first time, man takes over God's work without supernatural aid.

So much for theme. The plot of the novel, the manner in which the theme unfolds, is the basis for most scholarly discussion. While the theme has been used over and over, on the stage and in movies and TV plays, the plot was disregarded until lately, and its undercurrents with it. Most people are familiar with Boris Karloff's make-up as Frankenstein's unnamed "monster." The plot, the development of a complex story of guilt and revenge, has proved more resistant to translation into other media.

Biographical details help our understanding of the writings of most authors. In the case of *Frankenstein* and Mary Shelley, they appear indispensable. It is the work of a young author, which is perhaps why the education of the creature plays such an important role. Mary Wollstonecraft Godwin was the daughter of two famous political philosophers, Mary Wollstonecraft and William Godwin, both of whom also published novels. She was 18 and still unmarried when, in June of 1816, she began to write her first and most famous novel. Significantly, as its inwardness perhaps shows, it originated in a horrid dream. The dreamer awoke and began to write: "It was on a dreary night of November, that I beheld the accomplishment of my toils. . . ."

She was at that time living in Switzerland with the poet Percy Bysshe Shelley, a married man, father of two children. Before the book could be published, her half-sister, Fanny Imlay, had committed suicide, as had Shelley's wife, Harriet. Death and insecurity surrounded her. Her mother had died in childbirth, while her father practically disowned her when she eloped with Shelley.

For a long while, the horror element of the novel obscured the fact that it deals with questions of parent-child relationships, families, the role of women, and the usages of power—all subjects of great importance to the youthful Mary Shelley. Victor's poor creature, disowned by its creator, shunned by mankind, embodies many of the teenage girl's own orphaned feelings of sorrow and rage.

As the story develops, our sympathies are cunningly transposed from Victor to his "daemon," as he sometimes calls it. If Victor is the Prometheus of the title, the god appointed to bring knowledge to humanity, then his forlorn creature must be *us*, upon whom injustice is heaped. Together, Victor and his creation, locked in a struggle to the death, represent a modern dilemma: art as opposed to science, instinct as opposed to intellect, even male as opposed to female (Victor usurps female power to bring forth living beings).

These polarities gain in subtlety as the doppelganger theme intensifies in the later chapters of the book. The creature's dire threat to Victor, "I will be with you on your wedding night," achieves new emphasis if the two of them are one. It is Victor who calls himself "the slave of my creature," not vice versa. It is Victor who admits to his father that he is the murderer: "William, Justine, and Henry—they all died by my hands." The final pursuit is as much between allies as enemies; between them, Victor and the daemon have destroyed all the women in the novel.

This uneasy sense of a double life is expressed in Mary Shelley's Journals. She speaks of herself as one who, "entirely and despotically engrossed by their own feelings, leads—as it were—an *internal* life quite different from the outward and apparent one." Victor shuns society, his monster craves it: thus are dramatized the two sides of their author, who simultaneously conceals and reveals her inner feelings. The issues raised in the novel *Frankenstein* still divert or torment us. It is an exemplar of what SF should and can be.

The terrible solitudes of the novel are lacking in the crowded *Frankenstein* movies, replete with their villains and hunchbacks. No such claptrap exists in the text—only the majestic desolations of the Alps, the *mer de glace*, the polar ice. This note of profound isolation is sounded again in Mary Shelley's other SF novel, *The Last Man.* This more prolix work concerns a plague which, arriving from the East, wipes out all mankind, until only Lionel Verney is left to tell the tale.

As is related in the introduction to the Hogarth edition of this novel, its author was merely extrapolating from an actual pandemic which scourged much of the world during the 1820's. But, more deeply, the book reflects Mary Shelley's darkened circumstances. By 1826, her husband had drowned; three of her children had died; she had suffered a serious miscarriage from which she almost died. Her famous friend, Lord Byron, had died while fighting the Greek cause for liberty. She was alone, impoverished in London, with a small son to support.

*The Last Man* never secured, and will never secure, the audience accorded its brilliant, mysterious predecessor. Nevertheless, it yields many pleasures and insights to a sympathetic reader. The theme itself is apocalyptic, made no less important by the dawn of the nuclear age. This threnody of the last survivor of a world-wide catastrophe was used in the movie *On the Beach* (1959), from Nevil Shute's novel of the same name, and more recently in a New Zealand film, *The Quiet Earth*, directed by Geoff Murphy (1985).

—Brian W. Aldiss

---

**SHEPARD, Lucius.** Recipient: Clarion award, 1984; *Locus* award, 1985; John W. Campbell award, 1985; Science Fiction Chronicle award, 1985; Nebula award, 1986; World Fantasy award, 1988. Address: c/o Arkham House, Box 546, Sauk City, Wisconsin 53583, U.S.A.

### Science-Fiction Publications

#### Novels

*Green Eyes.* New York, Ace, 1984; London, Chatto and Windus, 1986.
*Life During Wartime.* New York, Bantam, 1987; London, Grafton, 1988.
*The Father of Stones* (novella). Baltimore, Maryland, Washington Science Fiction Association, 1988.
*The Scalehunter's Beautiful Daughter* (novella). Willimant, Connecticut, Ziesing, 1988.
*Kalimantan.* London, Century, 1990.

#### Short Stories

*The Jaguar Hunter.* Worcester Park, Surrey, Kerosina, 1987; Sauk City, Wisconsin, Arkham House, 1988.
*Nantucket Slayrides: Three Short Novels*, with Robert Frazier. Nantucket, Massachusetts, Eel Grass Press, 1989.
*The Ends of the Earth: 14 Stories.* Sauk City, Wisconsin, Arkham House, 1991.

* * *

Lucius Shepard's first published short story, "The Taylorville Reconstruction," appeared in Terry Carr's prestigious anthology of original fiction, *Universe 13*, in 1983. In the years since, Shepard has produced more award-nominated and award-winning stories than any other writer of science fiction or fantasy. From novels like *Green Eyes* and *Life During Wartime* to shorter works such as "Solitario's Eyes," "A Traveller's Tale," "The Man Who Painted the Dragon Griaule," "Life of Buddha," and "Father of Stones," he has been a prolific, one-man literary renaissance, a creator of high art on a scale rarely seen before in science fiction. There is no way to do justice in this brief space to the many fine stories Shepard has written. Readers are best referred to his two superb short story collections, *The Jaguar Hunter* and *The Ends of the Earth*, and, of course, to the novels.

It is possible, however, to zero in on a number of Shepard's basic settings, themes, and characters, because his work is remarkably of a piece. The majority of his stories take place in the present or near future and are set on or near the Caribbean or the Gulf of Mexico. Most walk the border between fantasy and science fiction and many involve some form of possession. "Solitario's Eyes," for example, takes place somewhere on the Caribbean coast and details the strange relationship between an army officer of upper-class Castilian heritage, his beautiful Indian wife, and the native healer she seeks out during her pregnancy and then seduces. Her son, when born, appears to share some strange physical and psychic bond with the healer (since murdered by the army officer) and with his blind, possibly magical horse. In *Green Eyes*, a scientific experiment in resurrecting the dead, set in the bayou country of Louisiana, goes awry, and leads its participants into a dark universe of perversion, murder, and voodoo. Both "Salvador" and "A Traveller's Tale" take place in the snake-infested swamps and forests of Central America and both involve spirit possession. In the former story, an American soldier, stuck in an early 1990's Vietnam-like military campaign, is taken over by a native spirit seeking revenge against gringos. In the latter story, an American is possessed by an alien who, half insane, has been haunting the swampy site of her spaceship's crash for centuries. Among Shepard's more recent stories, "The Ends of the Earth" involves an American writer who becomes involved in an ancient Mayan game that temporarily transforms its participants into monstrous warriors. Through magic, dreams, drugs, or poorly understood science, Shepard's characters are often translated to other worlds. This happens to the protagonists of *Green Eyes,* "The Ends of the Earth" and, most recently, *Kalimantan.* The latter, set in the jungles of Borneo, features a native drug that gives those who take it the power to both change reality and, ultimately, escape it. Drugs feature prominently in Shepard's work, from the strung-out, hallucinating, government-drugged American soldiers of *Life During Wartime* to the entire pathetic cast of "Life of Buddha."

Shepard's characters tend to be drifters, dreamers, and drug addicts, men and women with no real place to go and no real purpose, victims of poverty, government-sponsored insanity and corruption, or their own irrational urges. Few, if any, can be called heroes. David Mingolla, the American GI caught in a nightmare war in Central America in *Life During Wartime*, maintains a certain degree of innocence, but it's all relative. Even he does things that, in our world, would be considered monstrous. Ray Kingsley, the writer-protagonist of "The Ends of the Earth," is in some sense the good guy in his magical contest with the charlatan Konwicki for the love of the woman Odille, but he's driven by hatred, and the sublimated need for revenge against the last woman who hurt him. MacKinnon, who experiments with native drugs in *Kalimantan* and dreams of saving the Borneo wilderness from developers is, nonetheless, corrupted by his own insecurities. He, like many of Shepard's other protagonists, falls victim to strange events and powers he never fully understands. When Shepard's characters accomplish things—create works of art, make scientific discoveries, make babies—they usually do it almost in spite of themselves, and their creations are frequently two-edged swords.

Somewhat different from Shepard's other published fictions are "The Man Who Painted the Dragon Griaule" and two other works set in the same universe, *The Scalehunter's Beautiful Daughter* and *The Father of Stones.* With a Central-European ambience much like that of Ursula K. Le Guin's *Orsinian Tales*, "Griaule" is the story of a man who attempts to paint a 6,000-foot long, living but dormant dragon: not a picture of the dragon, it must be understood, but the body of the dragon itself. All three novellas have been nominated for awards and have made various best of the year lists.

Jungles and swamps, whether found along the coast of Central America, in the bayou country of Louisiana, or in the upland wilds of Borneo, are a central image for Lucius Shepard, a symbol, perhaps, of the moral morass that his characters consistently find themselves in. The center will not hold. Nothing and no one can be trusted, not even the soggy ground beneath one's feet. The universe of Lucius Shepard is an uncomfortable one, lacking in absolutes. Although his politics are clearly leftist, as demonstrated by the anti-military and anti-American government sentiments of *Life During Wartime*, "Salvador," and other stories, there's something of the despairing conservative about him as well. This is demonstrated, perhaps, by his frequent reuse of themes and motifs borrowed from two of the darkest writers of the century, Joseph Conrad and, oddly enough, H.P. Lovecraft. Few writers of science fiction or fantasy give us so black a vision.

—Michael M. Levy

---

**SHERMAN, Michael.** *See* **LOWNDES, Robert A.W.**

---

**SHERMAN, Peter Michael.** *See* **LOWNDES, Robert A.W.**

---

**SHERRED, T(homas) L.** American. Born 27 August 1915. Attended Wayne State University, Detroit, Michigan. Production line engineer; for many years worked in the Packard toolroom, Detroit; later worked in technical writing and advertising. *Died 16 April 1985.*

SCIENCE-FICTION PUBLICATIONS

Novels

*Alien Island.* New York, Ballantine, 1970.
*Alien Main*, with Lloyd Biggle, Jr. New York, Doubleday, 1985.

Short Stories

*First Person, Peculiar.* New York, Ballantine, 1972.

Uncollected Short Story

"Bounty," in *Again, Dangerous Visions*, edited by Harlan Ellison. New York, Doubleday, 1972.

*

Manuscript Collection: Spenser Research Library, University of Kansas, Lawrence.

* * *

T.L. Sherred's science fiction output was small but of excellent quality. The reason for this, as Sherred explained to Harlan Ellison in the introduction to "Bounty" in *Again, Dangerous Visions*, was ". . . I didn't write very much because I was too busy making a living; I only wrote when I got in a hole and needed cash. When I got the cash, of course, I had pulled out of the hole and didn't write anymore . . ."

Sherred's most famous story is "E for Effort" published in *Astounding* (1947). Sherred takes ordinary people and elevates them to positions of great power. In "E for Effort" Ed Lefko is confronted by a television set that can look in on any scene in history. The implications, as developed by Sherred, are enormous. In "Eye for Iniquity" Sherred's main character can create ten-dollar bills out of thin air. "Cue for Quiet" presents us with a pipefitter who discovers that if he wishes hard enough, he can burst the noisy televisions, radios, and jukeboxes that annoy him. These stories are all included in Sherred's only short story collection, *First Person, Peculiar.*

Sherred's only solo novel, *Alien Island*, is a story of first contact. An alien commercial operation called the Regan Group opens relations with Earth by going through an ordinary laborer named Ken Jordan, a sometime alcoholic. By sharing minds with the Captain of the alien vessel, Jordan becomes changed, improved. The narrator of the novel is Dana Iverson, an American spy whose mission is to find out what Jordan and the aliens are planning. Jordan buys a Canadian island near Detroit and sets up a trading base: alien gold and other precious substances in return for Earth's luxury goods. Dana finds out what the Regan group is planning, yet finds their way of life attractive and joins them rather than reporting back to her superiors. The ending is bitter but appropriate.

—George Kelley

---

**SHERWOOD, Nelson.** *See* **BLUMER, Kenneth.**

---

**SHIEL, M(atthew) P(hipps).** Also wrote as Gordon Holmes. British. Born on Montserrat Island, West Indies, 21 July 1865. Educated at Harrison College, Barbados; King's College, London; St. Bartholomew's Hospital Medical School, London. Married 1) Carolina García Gomez in 1898 (died), two daughters; 2) Mrs. Gerald Jewson c. 1918. Taught mathematics at a school in Derbyshire, two years. Granted Civil List pension, 1938. *Died 14 February 1947.*

SCIENCE-FICTION PUBLICATIONS

Novels

*The Yellow Danger.* London, Richards, 1898; New York, Fenno, 1899.
*The Purple Cloud.* London, Chatto and Windus, 1901; revised edition, London, Gollancz, 1929; New York, Vanguard Press, 1930.
*The Lord of the Sea.* London, Richards, and New York, Stokes, 1901; revised edition, New York, Knopf, 1924; London, Gollancz, 1929.
*The Yellow Wave.* London, Ward Lock, 1905.
*The Isle of Lies.* London Laurie, 1909.
*This Knot of Life.* London, Everett, 1909.
*The Dragon.* London, Richards, 1913; New York, Clode, 1914; as *The Yellow Peril*, London, Gollancz, 1929.
*This Above All.* New York, Vanguard Press, 1933; as *Above All Else*, London, Cole, 1943.
*The Young Men Are Coming!* London, Allen and Unwin, and New York, Vanguard Press, 1937.

Short Stories

*Shapes in the Fire.* London, Lane, and Boston, Roberts, 1896.
*The Pale Ape and Other Pulses.* London, Laurie, 1911.
*The Invisible Voices*, with John Gawsworth. London, Richards, 1935; New York, Vanguard Press, 1936.
*The Best Short Stories of M.P. Shiel*, edited by John Gawsworth. London, Gollancz, 1948.

OTHER PUBLICATIONS

Novels

*The Rajah's Sapphire.* London, Ward Lock, 1896.
*Contraband of War.* London, Richards, 1899; revised edition, London, Pearson, 1914; Ridgewood, New Jersey, Gregg Press, 1968.
*Cold Steel.* London, Richards, 1899; New York, Brentano's, 1900; revised edition, London, Gollancz, and New York, Vanguard Press, 1929.
*The Man-Stealers.* London, Hutchinson, and Philadelphia, Lippincott, 1900; revised edition, Hutchinson, 1927.
*The Weird o' It.* London, Richards, 1902.
*Unto the Third Generation.* London, Chatto and Windus, 1903.
*The Evil That Men Do.* London, Ward Lock, 1904.
*The Lost Viol.* New York, Clode, 1905; London, Ward Lock, 1908.
*The Last Miracle.* London, Laurie, 1907; revised edition, London, Gollancz, 1929.
*The White Wedding.* London, Laurie, 1908.
*Children of the Wind.* London, Laurie, 1923.
*Dr. Krasinski's Secret.* New York, Vanguard Press, 1929; London, Jarrolds, 1930.
*The Black Box.* New York, Vanguard Press, 1930; London, Richards, 1931.
*Say Au R'Voir but Not Goodbye.* London, Benn, 1933.

Novels as Gordon Holmes (with Louis Tracy)

*An American Emperor.* New York, Putnam, and London, Pearson, 1897.
*The Late Tenant.* New York, Clode, 1906; London, Cassell, 1907.
*By Force of Circumstances.* New York, Clode, 1909; London, Mills and Boon, 1910.
*The House of Silence.* New York, Clode, 1911; as *The Silent House*, London, Nash, 1911.

Short Stories

*Prince Zaleski.* London, Lane, and Boston, Roberts, 1895.
*How the Old Woman Got Home.* London, Richards, 1927; New York, Vanguard Press, 1928.
*Here Comes the Lady.* London, Richards, 1928.
*Xélucha and Others.* Sauk City, Wisconsin, Arkham House, 1975.
*Prince Zaleski and Cummings King Monk.* Sauk City, Wisconsin, Arkham House, 1977.

Verse

(*Poems*), edited by John Gawsworth. London, Richards, 1936.

Other

*Science, Life, and Literature.* London, Williams and Norgate, 1950.
*The New King.* Cleveland, Ohio, Reynolds Morse Foundation, 1980.

Translator, *The Hungarian Revolution: An Eyewitness's Account,* by Charles Henry Schmitt. London, Worker's Socialist Federation, 1919.

*

Bibliography: *The Works of M.P. Shiel: A Study in Bibliography* by A. Reynolds Morse, Los Angeles, Fantasy, 1948.

* * *

Certainly one of the most idiosyncratic writers of the scientific romance, M.P. Shiel is primarily remembered today for a single novel, *The Purple Cloud*, and for his role in popularizing the racist theme of "the Yellow Peril," a phrase that he is sometimes credited with coining. A capable stylist whose fine attention to detail can make the most unlikely fantasies persuasive, Shiel also aspired to aesthetic and social theory in his 31 novels and several short stories, and seemed strongly influenced both by social Darwinism and the theories of the American social philosopher Henry George.

Shiel's first major work in a tradition historically allied with science fiction was the "future war" narrative *The Yellow Danger*, which portrayed the conquest by Japan and China of all Europe except for England, which successfully retaliates using biological weapons and finally comes to rule the world itself. Focusing more on the character of the opposing leaders than on technological marvels, the novel is disturbing in its racist implications, although it should be noted that this attitude was considerably muted in *The Yellow Wave*, a novel on a similar theme published seven years later. A more successful, if bizarre, novel is *The Lord of the Sea,* which has also been attacked for its racism, this time in the form of anti-Semitism. But Shiel's attitudes toward Jews in the novel are actually quite complex. Following a series of pogroms and anti-Semitic laws in Europe, England inherits a wave of Jewish immigrants, and quickly gains prosperity from this influx of skilled labor. A rapacious Jewish landlord is opposed by the hero—himself Jewish—and frames him for a murder. After escaping from prison and gaining great wealth, the hero constructs a series of enormous floating fortresses, making himself "Lord of the Sea" and forcing nations to participate in a complex land-reform scheme that ushers in an era of social progress. Later, as regent of England, he enacts a series of anti-Jewish laws forcing many Jews to emigrate to Palestine, where he joins them (after his betrayal and fall in England) as nothing less than the Messiah, who turns the new Israel into a powerful and prosperous nation! While Shiel does fall victim to several Jewish stereotypes common to his time, he also speaks in this novel of the Jewish "genius for righteousness," and makes a Jew the first major exemplar of his "overman" theme, drawn in part from Nietzsche. This theme returns prominently in *The Isle of Lies*, which concerns an archaeologist who raises his son in isolation to be superintelligent; upon discovering the true nature of humanity, the son embarks on a doomed idealistic scheme to improve the world.

Shiel's masterpiece, *The Purple Cloud*, deals with a more fundamental issue: the nature of the human psyche itself. Following the suggestion of an American millionaire that he write a novel about Robert Peary and his family returning from the North Pole to a dead world, Shiel commented that he "left out 'the family,' and 'Peary,' too, and wrote this." After committing murder to gain a position on a polar expedition, Adam Jeffson reaches the pole only to return to a world depopulated by a poisonous volcanic gas. Over the next few decades, Jeffson struggles with the "black" and "white" forces of his nature, sometimes collecting great works of art for his "palace," sometimes madly setting fire to the great cities of Europe. When he finds another survivor—a girl whose mind is a virtual *tabula rasa* from having lived alone in a dungeon her whole life (she was born just as the gas was dissipating)—he feels a strange impulse to kill and eat her. But her companionship seems to restore a kind of moral balance in Jeffson, and with her he sets out to start the race anew. Although the novel may not quite deserve the lavish praise heaped on it by H.G. Wells, Hugh Walpole, and Arthur Machen, it is a strangely powerful and moving novel, and remains one of the most widely-read "last man" novels, far outpacing in popularity its ancestor and probable influence, Mary Shelley's *The Last Man* (1826).

Late in his career, Shiel returned to fantastic literature with *This Above All*, a fantasy about Biblical figures surviving into the modern world, and a number of short stories. One of these stories, "How Life Climbs," became the genesis of the novel *The Young Men Are Coming!*, which concerns a scientist abducted by aliens and given a rejuvenating serum. Returning to earth, he forms a radical social movement called the Young Men, which gains such influence that the government assumes totalitarian powers to suppress it. In an odd conclusion that pits establishment religion against extraterrestrial science, the scientist stages a duel with an evangelist, each trying to summon a storm to prove the validity of their belief. The evangelist fails, of course, but the scientist's aliens produce a storm that nearly destroys the world.

Shiel undoubtedly deserves greater attention than he has generally received, not only as the author of one of science fiction's true masterworks, but as a participant in the debates regarding social Darwinism and economic reform which so preoccupied his contemporaries. At times visionary, at times intolerant, at times simply megalomaniacal, Shiel is among the more stimulating and provocative figures of British imaginative literature of the first half of this century.

—Gary K. Wolfe

---

**SHIRAS, Wilmar H(ouse).** Also wrote as Jane Howes. American. Born in Boston, Massachusetts, 23 September 1908. Educated at Holy Names College, Oakland, California; University of California, Berkeley, M.A. 1956. Married Russell Shiras in 1927; three daughters and two sons. *Died 23 December 1990.*

SCIENCE-FICTION PUBLICATIONS

Short Stories

*Children of the Atom.* New York, Gnome Press, 1953; London, Boardman, 1954.

Uncollected Short Stories

"Backward, Turn Backward," in *New Worlds of Fantasy 2*, edited by Terry Carr. New York, Ace, 1970.
"Shadow-Led," in *Fantastic* (New York), October 1971.

"Reality," in *Fantastic* (New York), February 1972.
"Bird-Song," in *Fantastic* (New York), April 1973.

OTHER PUBLICATIONS

Other

*Slow Dawning* (as June Howes). St. Louis, Herder, 1946.

*

Wilmar H. Shiras commented:

"In Hiding" grew out of my wondering whether very high-I.Q. children would have problems; the rest of the book deals with other such children and their problems.

* * *

Wilmar H. Shiras's total literary output is far from copious, and even of the total number of works, not all have been science fiction. In fact, she is known almost entirely for a single volume, *Children of the Atom.* Though it reveals serious shortcomings and limitations, its virtues are even greater.

*Children of the Atom* originated in three stories published in *Astounding;* the author added two further stories, collecting the five into an episodic work that experienced a considerable vogue in the 1950's. ("In Hiding," the first story in the cycle, has been anthologized no fewer than a dozen times.) The basic premise of the stories, questionable even in 1948 and now recognized as an absurdity, is that an accident in a nuclear industrial plant will produce a uniform mutation in the offspring of all workers in the plant. Specifically, all children born to women pregnant at the time of the accident, or conceived by workers present at the accident, will be of genius-grade intelligence and of highly creative temperament. The author postulates, further, that all of the workers exposed to the accident will die within approximately two years, but that their children will be perfect. Shiras's main concern is the problems of adjustment and development of these children in later years. Her major adult protagonists are a group of sympathetic educators and psychologists who discover the existence of these children (who are "in hiding"), and the existence of a network of communication among them. The author assumes that these mentally superior children will be automatically outcasts. The boys, with their inclination to study science, will not fit into a society that emphasizes athletics and violent competition; the girls, inclined toward art, will be similarly excluded from a society that emphasizes prettiness and socialization. Thus, the children, in order to survive, hide their superiority beneath a veneer of assumed ordinariness.

Although the author's notions of mutation were quickly seen as absurd, her portrayal of the "superior" children—hyperintellectual adolescents, the boys frequently myopic and unathletic, the girls similarly not adept at the sex-role dictates of the day—struck a strong responsive chord in the typical science-fiction readers of the period. Both Marion Zimmer Bradley and Barry Malzberg, in notes published with a 1978 reissue of the book, comment upon the sense of identity felt by the original readers with the youngsters in the book. It is this uncanny identification of reader with character that gave the book its popularity in the 1950's. In later years, the reading of science fiction gained a far greater acceptance in schools, *aficionados* ceased to be automatic outcasts, and this sense of identity became weakened, although it did not cease altogether.

In its later segments the novel shows unfortunate tendencies to degenerate into piously one-sided theological argumentation, and at the end the adult sponsors of the brilliant children are told by the children themselves that it will be best to terminate their experimental community and disperse themselves among the general populace. This ending, too, has proved controversial among readers of the book, many of them indicating that they see in it a surrender to the very standards of mediocrity and conformism which the children had earlier sought to escape. Shiras produced other short works of science fiction between long intervals. These have been uniformly pleasant, low-keyed, generally concerned with children, and have received little attention from readers.

—Richard A. Lupoff

---

**SHIRLEY, John (Patrick).** American. Born in Houston, Texas, 10 February 1953. High school education. Married Alexandra Allinne in 1982 (separated); twin sons. Has had various jobs including fruit picker, dancer, and office worker; regularly performs as lead singer with rock bands. Agent: Lori Perkins, 301 West 53rd Street, New York, New York 10019, U.S.A.

SCIENCE-FICTION PUBLICATIONS

Novels (series: Eclipse)

*Transmaniacon.* New York, Zebra, 1979.
*Dracula in Love.* New York, Zebra, 1979.
*Three-Ring Psychus.* New York, Zebra, 1980.
*City Come A-Walkin'.* New York, Dell, 1981.
*Cellars.* New York, Avon, 1982; London, Sphere, 1983.
A Song Called Youth:
*Eclipse.* New York, Bluejay, 1985; London, Methuen, 1986.
*Eclipse Penumbra.* New York, Popular Library, 1988.
*Eclipse Corona.* New York, Popular Library, 1990.
*A Splendid Chaos.* New York, Watts, 1988; London, Mandarin, 1989.
*In Darkness Waiting.* New York, New American Library, 1988.

Short Stories

*Heatseeker.* Los Angeles, California, Scream Press, 1989; London, Grafton, 1990.

OTHER PUBLICATIONS

Novels

*The Brigade.* New York, Avon, 1982; London, Sphere, 1983.
*Kamus of Kadizhar: The Black Hole of Carcosa.* New York, St. Martin's Press, 1988.

Plays

Screenplays: *Video Girl; The Other Side of Evil.*

*

John Shirley comments:

My early stories show that I was enamored of the surrealists; surrealist and expressionist painting influenced me more than writers. Although there was a political iconoclasm intrinsic to my writing, I've never sided with any particular political philosophy; I feel that the major political and economic theories have all been satirized even-handedly in my fiction. My newest novel, *Eclipse*—easily my most significant book—is essentially a political thriller set in the year 2020, when a non-nuclear world war has ravaged Europe, making it possible for an opportunistic cabal of genuine fascists to take over, through nationalistic puppets, one country after another. Essentially, Europe becomes a massive police state, and the heroes of *Eclipse* are the resistance. They're not Communists, particularly—that is, some are, some aren't. Nor are they radicals. They're simply the resistance to fascism. It happens I really and honestly believe that a resurgence of racism on a vast scale is about to transform Europe, due to the myopic and xenophobic reaction of European natives to the influx of third world immigrants, and also due to other sociological factors. *Eclipse* is a kind of warning novel about it, and an attempt to redefine the cultural backdrop of the near-future. The landscapes of bizarrities typical of much of my earlier writing, the attempt to realize abstractions in physical description—these are missing from *Eclipse*, at least in explicit manifestation. *Eclipse* is real life, contemporary life, seen through a science fiction lens. I've also given a much greater emphasis to characterization than ever before.

* * *

Of the writers herded together as "cyberpunks," John Shirley is perhaps one of the few to enjoy the label. Shirley already had participated in the punk scene as a rock musician, and also had made a reputation as an unusually vivid, uncomfortable writer. He liked the idea of fusing high-tech concepts with the visceral images he had been using to attack readers' preconceptions. And so, for a time, he was known as the most intense and disturbing of the cyberpunks. Actually, Shirley's work always has been distinctive for its stern insistence that people need to open themselves to new possibilities, enlivened by stunning imaginative riffs. Under whatever label, he has produced a striking, powerful body of fiction.

In his early novels, such as *Dracula in Love* and *City Come A-Walkin'*, Shirley's main character suffers because he is empty of purpose. He is attracted to an unchanging (but vicious) force trying to preserve itself; however, he winds up on the side of an amoral, stability-shattering entity that plots to destroy that stifling "father" power. The novels' action is morally equivocal at best, with huge numbers of people being vividly mutilated and/or slaughtered. The central character is never sure he is doing the right thing, and Shirley offers the possibility that his thirst for freedom might actually be a craving for oblivion (in madness or death). *Transmaniacon* (his first novel) is probably the most successful of Shirley's early novels in demonstrating hatred of a status quo, thanks to its fierce images of bizarre obsessions; that novel's conclusion explicitly links escape from constraints with mortal danger, but Shirley's hero gladly makes that choice. Also memorable is *Three-Ring Psychus* set after some people have been given psychic powers that let them transcend some physical limits; Shirley's characters discover that the change has given them new possibilities for growth, but that some of the possibilities threaten the survival of human consciousness. The book ends with determined uncertainty.

Reading these novels is unsettling as much for the manner of their telling as for their content. The stories refuse to let a reader sink into them as comfortable escapist fiction. The action lurches along. The characters let moral qualms interrupt what the reader expects to be a smooth, exciting flow of action. On the other hand, what might be key personal decisions are summarized in an offhand manner. Shirley began experimenting with less jarring narrative techniques when he turned away from science fiction briefly to write a mainstream suspense thriller (*The Brigade*), a horror fantasy in the vein of Stephen King, and various pseudonymous action novels for paperback series (such as the "Traveler" series of post-World War III adventures, which are notable for Shirley's wholesale bloodletting and his bitter, witty contempt for the military-political thinking that caused the nuclear war). Having returned to the science-fiction novel, he stated his intention "to write with crystaline realism about *this* world, but I'm still trying to make my readers question their assumptions. I'm spending a great deal more time investigating character, and controlling tone, the overall quality of writing."

Shirley's major work during this period and his clearest contribution to cyberpunk fiction is the trilogy *A Song Called Youth—Eclipse, Eclipse Penumbra*, and *Eclipse Corona.* This near-future story is set during and immediately after World War III, but it focuses on the struggle between new waves of fascists and a conglomeration of resistance fighters. Shirley describes how the seductiveness of fascism and the weight of inertia can be overcome by technology-enhanced idealism. Overall, the trilogy shows some of Shirley's limitations. The characters are vivid but are developed as people just enough to perform their roles in the action; also, the action itself feels rather prefunctory in the later books, with the heroes triumphing neatly as if evil and incompetence are synonymous. But Shirley's strengths are abundant. The scientific, political, and *social* extrapolation is detailed, startling, and plausible; in particular, the glimpses of mass media are grotesque enough to be quite plausible. And at each moment and during each scene the action and characters are convincing because of Shirley's grasp of sensory detail.

Unfortunately, the publication of the trilogy was less than successful. Shirley's early novels were inexpensive paperbacks that flicker in and out of print, and he was pleased that *A Song Called Youth* would be in the more substantial trade paperback format. But the original publisher failed after *Eclipse* appeared, and the later two books were published in mass market paperbacks by a company that did not promote them.

As a matter of fact, Shirley's only hardcover novel to date is *A Splendid Chaos*, which resembles his earlier fiction in using mental powers to threaten his characters with physical mutation in order to force them to enlarge their thinking. The splatterpunk novel, *In Darkness Waiting*, suggests grimmer prospects, as people converge on a slaughterhouse to be put through a kind of psychic meat grinder. Otherwise, he has published a satirical novel, *Kamus of Kadizhar: The Black Hole of Carcosa*, and has another horror novel awaiting publication.

Shirley's short stories, collected in *Heatseeker*, also deserve attention. Though Shirley's novels present his message more fully, some of his short stories are more successful at giving a burst of plausible argument and stunning imagery that take reality apart and put it together again inside out. In particular, "The Almost Empty Rooms" plays with the idea of free will in a wry story of World War III seen as a frolic of event-animals whose cells are human beings. Another outstanding story, "What Cindy Saw," seems to begin as a study of mental illness, then becomes a surrealistic look at modern life, but it ends by affirming the existence of a nightmarish world under the surface of normal reality. Two very recent, uncollected stories are worth noting, too. "The Prince" (in *When The Music's Over*) tries to find a non-violent solution to social injustice, though the prospects for real reform remain uncertain. In "A Walk Through Beruit" (in *Newer York* edited by Lawrence Watt-Evans, New York, Roc, 1991), Shirley returns to the milieu of *A Song Called Youth* to show a young musician coming to terms with himself, deciding not to commit suicide, and making as much of a personal commitment as is possible in our fragmented, confused society. Throughout his short fiction, Shirley demonstrates that he not only has an imagination that can take reality apart and put it together again inside out, but he also has a challenging but positive personal vision to share once he has our attention.

At the moment, Shirley is disenchanted with writing SF and intends to turn to screenplays. It may not be easy to break away. Like the characters in his fiction, he may feel compelled to leave familiar territory to run the risks of freedom. In any event, he has produced enough lively, gutsy fiction to make a mark, to force readers to live more alertly and authentically.

—Joe Sanders

---

**SHUTE, Nevil** (Nevil Shute Norway). British. Born in Ealing, London, 17 January 1899. Educated at Dragon School, Oxford; Shrewsbury School, Oxford; Royal Military Academy, Woolwich, London; Balliol College, Oxford, 1919–22, E.A. in engineering 1922. Served as a private in the Suffolk Regiment, British Army, 1918; commissioned in the Royal Naval Volunteer Reserve, 1940: Lieutenant Commander; retired 1945. Married Frances Mary Heaton in 1931; two daughters. Calculator, de Havilland Aircraft Company, 1923–24; chief calculator, 1924–28, and deputy chief engineer, 1928–30, on the construction of Rigid Airship R. 100 for the Airship Guarantee Company: twice flew Atlantic in R. 100, 1930; managing director, Yorkshire Aeroplane Club Ltd., 1927–30; founder and joint managing director, Airspeed Ltd., airplane constructors, 1931–38. Lived in Australia after 1950. Fellow, Royal Aeronautical Society, 1934. *Died 12 January 1960.*

SCIENCE-FICTION PUBLICATIONS

Novels

*What Happened to the Corbetts.* London, Heinemann, 1939; as *Ordeal*, New York, Morrow, 1939.
*An Old Captivity.* London, Heinemann, and New York, Morrow, 1940.
*No Highway.* London, Heinemann, and New York, Morrow, 1948.
*In the Wet.* London, Heinemann, and New York, Morrow, 1953.
*On the Beach.* London, Heinemann, and New York, Morrow, 1957.
*The Rainbow and the Rose.* London, Heinemann, and New York, Morrow, 1958.

OTHER PUBLICATIONS

Novels

*Marazan.* London, Cassell, 1926.
*So Disdained.* London, Cassell, 1928; as *Mysterious Aviator*, Boston, Houghton Mifflin, 1928.
*Lonely Road.* London, Cassell, and New York, Morrow, 1932.
*Ruined City.* London, Cassell, 1938; as *Kindling*, New York, Morrow, 1938.
*Landfall: A Channel Story.* London, Heinemann, and New York, Morrow, 1940.
*Pied Piper.* New York, Morrow, 1941; London, Heinemann, 1942.
*Pastoral.* London, Heinemann, and New York, Morrow, 1944.
*Most Secret.* London, Heinemann, and New York, Morrow, 1945.
*The Chequer Board.* London, Heinemann, and New York, Morrow, 1947.
*A Town Like Alice.* London, Heinemann, 1950; as *The Legacy*, New York, Morrow, 1950.
*Round the Bend.* London, Heinemann, and New York, Morrow, 1951.
*The Far Country.* London, Heinemann, and New York, Morrow, 1952.
*Requiem for a Wren.* London, Heinemann, 1955; as *The Breaking Wave*, New York, Morrow, 1955.
*Beyond the Black Stump.* London, Heinemann, and New York, Morrow, 1956.
*Trustee from the Toolroom.* London, Heinemann, and New York, Morrow, 1960.
*Stephen Morris.* London, Heinemann, and New York, Morrow, 1961.

Play

*Vinland the Good* (screenplay). London, Heinemann, and New York, Morrow, 1946.

Other

*Slide Rule: The Autobiography of an Engineer.* London, Heinemann, and New York, Morrow, 1954.

*

Manuscript Collection: National Library of Australia, Canberra.

Critical Study: *Nevil Shute (Nevil Shute Norway)* by Julian Smith, Boston, Twayne, 1976.

* * *

The popular author of 22 novels, the majority based on his experiences as an aeronautical engineer and aviator in both world wars, Nevil Shute is best known for his futuristic novel *On the Beach.* Shute's quiet, understated style, his fascination with machinery, entrepreneurship, and exploration, and his highly plausible personalities make him a good story-teller. Many of his novels are set in Australia, where he finally settled, and all contain superb technical details.

The title of *On the Beach* comes from a line in T.S. Eliot's "The Hollow Men": "In this last of meeting places/We grope together/And avoid speech/Gathered on this beach . . . This is the way the world ends/Not with a bang but a whimper." The quote, which begins the book, is most apt, for the central characters are all "gathered" on the Australian coast two years or so after the end of World War III. It is just after Christmas 1963, the entire northern hemisphere has been destroyed by a series of nuclear exchanges not really planned by any participant, and the deadly radiation produced by the cobalt bombs is creeping southward ineluctably. The characters indeed "grope together and avoid speech" about their imminent ends, while also obsessively practicing various forms of denial as the invisible death approaches. In the eight months that the novel covers, we watch the world end with "a whimper," and the effect is horrific.

The main characters are Dwight Towers, the captain of *USS Scorpion*, an American nuclear submarine stranded in Melbourne, the world's southernmost major city; Commander Peter Holmes, the Australian liaison with the *Scorpion;* his wife Mary, a *hausfrau* with a new baby; Moira Davidson, a party girl who dates Dwight Towers but is frustrated by his memories of his dead wife and children in Connecticut; and John Osborne, a scientist who works with the Australian government measuring radiation but whose real love is his Ferrari and car racing. These characters, gathered together by the interactions of their jobs and social lives, try desperately to maintain a normal life and hope for reprieve from death by radiation sickness, but the pitiless logic of Shute's premise leaves them helpless before their fate. Shute's artistry lies in his skillful analysis of defense and denial mechanisms, as Captain Towers follows navy rules to the letter, even though the U.S. Navy no longer exists; as Peter and Mary plant a garden that can never be harvested; and as each of the other characters copes with the certainty of knowing the date and circumstance of his or her impending death. The premise is artful in projecting a future very close to the present in time (the book was written in 1957 and set in 1962–63) and virtually identical in every other way, so we can see ourselves in these very normal people coping with nuclear holocaust. It is a very painful book to read, the discomfort coming from the shocking possibility, even likelihood, of the premise and the recognition of the true horror of nuclear catastrophe: not a personal end, nor even the deaths of many millions, but an end to entire cultures and then to human life itself.

Shute's other works have science-fiction elements but are not science fiction per se. For example, *No Highway* is a projection, a prediction of the dangers of metal fatigue as a potential and previously unconsidered cause of air disasters. In it, a metal fatigue expert finds himself aboard a plane that meets the criteria for disaster he had been unsuccessfully trying to convince others of. This book was published just before a Comet jet crash in real life—due to metal fatigue.

*An Old Captivity* is a modern romance including a Viking parallel universe; it gives a sense of other worlds and other realities, but historical rather than futuristic. On an archeological aerial survey in Greenland, the hazardous environment of ice floes and fog strains the nerves of Donald Ross, a seaplane pilot helping photograph Viking ruins. Already weakened by an addiction to sleeping pills, he begins to dream of Erik the Red, Leif Erikson, and the latter's fabled trip to Cape Cod, the Norsemen's "Vinland the Good." His drifting dream fantasies seem more real than his present life, and he becomes convinced that Alix, his employer's daughter, is in fact a reincarnation of Hekja, a Celtic slave girl that Ross, named Haki a thousand years earlier, loved and settled down with in the New World. Physical proof of Haki and Hekja's existence found by Ross and the Lockwoods on a trip to the Massachusetts coast lends substance to these incredible illusions. The adventure is an odd combination: historic detail about Celts and Vikings, both real and speculative, dream fantasy, Eskimo superstition, and makeshift psychoanalysis, set against a realistic delineation of the day-to-day particulars of aviation.

The dream vision technique allows Shute to build the novel on his strengths, his precise knowledge of aviation and his sensitivity to a modern love story, while indulging his taste for far-distant history. The modern characters and the Viking vision combine neatly and credibly in the eerie empty setting of Greenland, a place of stark landscapes where normality seems suspended. A flashback technique used in other Shute works here ameliorates the fantastic with the realistic "frame": a much older Ross recounting his dream experience to a psychiatrist on a stalled train.

*In the Wet* seems at first glance to be either a simple love story between a part aborigine Australian pilot and an English girl, both in the service of the English Queen, but is instead a deceptively simple projection into the near future (the 1980's seen from the 1950's). It postulates the British Labour party and the monarchy on a collision course that would lead all the royal heirs (Prince Charles included) to decline succession to the throne, and that would therefore require drastic measures to save the kingdom and the empire. Following the example of Australia (as Britain did with the secret ballot and the women's vote), a few far-sighted supporters of the monarchy act to limit the negative effects of working-class greed by revising the voting system to one of multiple votes, with extra votes added to a person's single vote according to level of education, property ownership, broadening travel, contribution to the nation, and so forth. The novel also toys with the idea of dream-reality, so that one is at first not sure whether the story is the hallucination of an opium-crazed outbacker dying of appendicitis, or whether the outbacker and the priest who comforts him are a bad dream of the pilot while suffering from food poisoning. The reality turns out to be just as fantastic: a fever-induced vision of reincarnation.

Shute's forte is to reduce the historical and the romantic to life-sized dimensions, to capture the excitement of the humdrum and the ordinariness of the historic, to pursue the effects of change on the common man—all in an artfully casual style. His works reflect an old-fashioned sense of goodness; they involve characters with a strong sense of purpose, of decency, of right, characters who enjoy being caught up in the unfolding of great enterprises. For Shute, both the past and the future are "made by plain and simple people like ourselves, doing the best . . . [they] can with each job as it comes along." Shute suggests domesticity as a powerful civilizing force that might well spur men to dreams and action. His men are industrious, competent and driven, his women are supportive, sometimes domestic but sometimes also competent in the world of men, so that they can ultimately save men from shortsightedness or from personal limitations. Shute's contribution to science fiction is not so much in following the central conventions of the genre as in using science-fiction elements in what otherwise would be conventional novels. His excellence in creating character and *milieu* in an appealing style bring quality and dignity to the science-fiction genre.

—Andrew F. Macdonald

---

**SHWARTZ, Susan (Martha).** Has also written as Gordon Kendall. American. Born in Youngstown, Ohio, 31 December 1949. Educated at Mount Holyoke College, Massachusetts, 1968–72, B.A. in English; Harvard University, Cambridge, Massachusetts, 1972–73, M.A. in English 1973, Ph.D. in English 1977. Summer study, Trinity College, Oxford, 1970, 1971. Post-doctoral fellow, Dartmouth College, New Hampshire, 1978. Teaching fellow, Harvard University, 1974–77; Assistant Professor of English, Ithaca College, New York, 1977–80; senior writer/researcher, Deutsch, Shea and Evans, New York, 1981–82; information coordinator, BEA Associates, New York, 1983–87; financial editor, Donaldson, Lufkin and Jenrette, New York, 1987–88. Financial writer/editor and assistant vice-president, Prudential Securities, New York, since 1988. Recipient: National Endowment for the Humanities grant, 1978. Agent: Richard Curtis Associates, 171 East 74th Street, New York, New York 10022. Address: One Station Square, Number 306, Forest Hills, New York 11375, U.S.A.

SCIENCE-FICTION PUBLICATIONS

Novels (series: Byzantium's Heirs)

*Byzantium's Crown.* New York, Warner, 1987; London, Pan, 1988.
*The Woman of Flowers.* (Byzantium's Heirs). New York, Warner, 1987; London, Pan, 1989.
*Queensblade* (Byzantium's Heirs). New York, Warner, 1988.
*Silk Roads and Shadows.* New York, Tor, 1988; London, Pan, 1989.
*Heritage of Flight.* New York, Tor, 1989.
*Imperial Lady: A Fantasy of Han China,* with Andre Norton. New York, Tor, 1989.

OTHER PUBLICATIONS

Novel

*White Wing,* (as Gordon Kendall) with Shariann N. Lewitt. New York, Tor, 1985; London, Sphere, 1986.

Other

Editor, *Hecate's Cauldron.* New York, DAW, 1982.
Editor, *Habitats* (science fiction anthology). New York, DAW, 1984.
Editor, *Moonsinger's Friends: An Anthology in Honor of Andre Norton.* New York, Bluejay, 1985; London, Severn House, 1986.
Editor, *Arabesques: More Tales of the Arabian Nights.* New York, Avon, 1988.
Editor, *Arabesques II.* New York, Avon, 1989.

*

Susan Shwartz comments:

For me, one world and one vision of that world have never been enough. I've spent a lifetime looking over my shoulder, into a mirror, or glancing quickly down a sidestreet for glimpses of the other worlds that I sense surround us all. As a writer, editor, critic, scholar, and businesswoman, I've spent most of my career building bridges (and occasionally burning them behind me); I look forward to spending the rest of my productive life linking unlikelinesses—Wall Street and academia, military science fiction and feminism, fantasy and Realpolitik, life as a New York City chauvinist and travel to as many places as funds, suitcases, and available transport will manage.

As a scholar, I was a medievalist and an Arthurian scholar. These fields enabled me to create a peephole into the "alternative" worlds of the Middle Ages and to move their literature forward into our own time. My forthcoming novel, *The Harlot and the Grail* (New York, Tor, 1992), is, essentially, a version of Wagner's redaction of Wolfram von Eschenbach's 13th-century work *Parzival*—from the standpoint of a sorceress who betrays the harlot, apostate Jew, and penitent. Writing this book compelled me to build a bridge between my own love of opera and my distrust of Richard Wagner, between my career as a writer of fiction and the career as a teacher and scholar that I left when I moved to New York.

Because of that desire to enter strange new worlds, I've come to specialize in exotic places, mostly Turkey and Central Asia, and all the way into Han and T'ang Dynasty China. In a way, this is quite conventionally medieval: traders, mercenaries, crusaders, and adventurers all tended to look East—first to Byzantium, starting point for four of my novels, thereafter to parts East . . . all the way out onto the steppes and to Ch'ang-an. Several of my anthologies are also set in this milieu.

At the same time, I write or attempt to write military science fiction that examines the ethical issues that worry me most—the ones considered to be almost unthinkable. *White Wing*, written in collaboration with S.N. Lewitt, examines the questions of Diaspora, refugees, and survival of a planetary holocaust from the point of view of the survivors; *Heritage of Flight* deals with genocide, from the standpoint of the people who committed it and who seek re-entry into the human race. The work I've done for Jerry Pournelle's War World shared universe enables me to examine questions of survival in a Hobbesian environment.

As a writer of short fiction, I try quite deliberately to be all over the map—from alternative history featuring a T.E. Lawrence who survived his 1935 motorcycle accident to a "President" George McGovern; from an insecure classicist to a temporary worker to a desert priestess to a cat with a gift for healing; to a boy with an aversion to Zero-G and doctrinaire ideologies; a werewolf who dreams of meeting God; an explorer pilot with the sniffles; a cantor on contract to a space station; or a heartsick lord of the Wild Hunt during nuclear winter.

I don't try to write strange things. I'm a story-teller who simply tries to throw up bridges of words, cemented by thoughts and some rather vivid dreams.

These fragments, as T.S. Eliot says in *The Waste Land*, have I shored against my ruins. For me, they provide all the colors of life and as much entertainment as I can safely handle.

* * *

Octavia Butler's cover blurb for *Heritage of Flight* says, "This novel reminds one that SF is a literature of ideas and not all those ideas are shiny and metallic." Indeed, Susan Shwartz lives up to her name (*schwarz*—black); all of her writing having some dark element either directly conveyed (as in *Heritage of Flight*) or creeping about in the background (as in her Heirs of Byzantium trilogy). Do not confuse her intent, however. She is not a pessimist, but she is able to see the gloomy side of things and lay it into her writing.

Steeped in centuries of English literature and tradition, Shwartz has quickly gained attention in the SF and fantasy fields with her somewhat controversial writing. She has been described as a feminist and as "having her own agenda," but whatever the label attributed to her, she most certainly has well-developed female characters, strong women who are able to carry their men through when they need help, yet are passionate enough to enjoy being loved and cared for at other times.

In *Heritage of Flight*, an almost documentary-style book set in the future, a galaxies-wide war is destroying the populations of entire planets; mankind is engaged in a most spectacular Civil War. In a *Battlestar Galactica*-type scenario ("a ragtag band of survivors in a ragtag fleet of spaceships"), a group of Alliance (North) civilians and warriors engage in a deep space battle with the Secessionists (South). As the battleship is destroyed, the personnel carrier "jumps" (much like the *Star Trek* warp drive) and escapes to a planet called Cynthia. There, the civilians and most of the crew are, for all intents and purposes, marooned as part of a bureaucrat's "Project Seedcorn," for "racial survival" in case the rest of the human race doesn't make it.

Unfortunately, the planet-bound humans were not informed of the alien lifeforms on the planet . . . a lifeform that is fatally dangerous to the humans and their survival. Pauli Yeager must "convince her people to commit a heinous crime or watch their children die." And when they commit the horrible crime, *Völkermord*, Pauli shoulders the entire burden.

In the Heirs to Byzantium trilogy, Shwartz examines the darkness of the human psyche: dreams, nightmares, guilt, terror, incest, dark magic. Marric, rightful Emperor of Byzantium, has had his power usurped by a black magician. And he spends the better part of three books fighting that darkness alongside his sister Alexa and his lover Stephana (who, in the fashion of *Conan*, returns from beyond the dark wall of death to fight with her love). And even though Marric is the central figure of the story, Stephana, Alexa, and the evil Irene are the characters who are best remembered.

—Daryl F. Mallett

---

**SILVA, Joseph.** *See* **GOULART, Ron.**

---

**SILVERBERG, Robert.** Also writes as Walker Chapman; Ivar Jorgenson; Calvin M. Knox; David Osborne; Robert Randall; Lee Sebastian. American. Born in New York City, 15 January 1935. Educated at Columbia University, New York, A.B. 1956. Married Barbara H. Brown in 1956. Full-time writer: associate editor, *Amazing*, January 1969 issue, and associate editor, *Fantastic*, February–April 1969 issues. President, Science Fiction Writers of America, 1967–68. Recipient: Hugo award, 1956, 1969; Nebula award, for story, 1969, 1971, 1974, for novel, 1971, for novella, 1985; Jupiter award, 1973; Prix Apollo, 1976; *Locus* award, 1981. Guest of Honor, 28th World Science Fiction Convention, 1970. Agent: Ralph Vicinanza, 432 Park Avenue South, Room 1205, New York, New York 10016, U.S.A.

SCIENCE-FICTION PUBLICATIONS

Novels (series: Majipoor; Nidor)

*Revolt on Alpha C* (for children). New York, Crowell, 1955.
*The 13th Immortal*. New York, Ace, 1957.
*Master of Life and Death*. New York, Ace, 1957; London, Sidgwick and Jackson, 1977.
*The Shrouded Planet* (Nidor; as Robert Randall, with Randall Garrett). New York, Gnome Press, 1957; London, Mayflower, 1964.
*Invaders from Earth*. New York, Ace, 1958; London, Sidgwick and Jackson, 1977.
*Invincible Barriers* (as David Osborne). New York, Avalon, 1958.
*Stepsons of Terra*. New York, Ace, 1958.
*Aliens from Space* (as David Osborne). New York, Avalon, 1958.
*Starhaven* (as Ivar Jorgenson). New York, Avalon, 1958.
*Starman's Quest* (for children). New York, Gnome Press, 1959.
*The Dawning Light* (Nidor; as Robert Randall, with Randall Garrett). New York, Gnome Press, 1959; London, Mayflower, 1964.
*The Planet Killers*. New York, Ace, 1959.
*Lost Race of Mars* (for children). Philadelphia, Winston, 1960.
*Collision Course*. New York, Avalon, 1961.
*The Seed of Earth*. New York, Ace, 1962; London, Hamlyn, 1978.
*Recalled to Life*. New York, Lancer, 1962; revised edition, New York, Doubleday, 1972; London Gollancz, 1974.
*The Silent Invaders*. New York, Ace, 1963; London, Dobson, 1975.
*Regan's Planet*. New York, Pyramid, 1964.
*Time of the Great Freeze* (for children). New York, Holt Rinehart, 1964.
*A Pair from Space*. New York, Belmont, 1965.
*Conquerors from the Darkness* (for children). New York, Holt Rinehart, 1965.
*The Gate of Worlds* (for children). New York, Holt Rinehart, 1967; London, Gollancz, 1978.
*To Open the Sky*. New York, Ballantine, 1967; London, Sphere, 1970.
*Thorns*. New York, Ballantine, 1967; London, Rapp and Whiting, 1969.
*Those Who Watch*. New York, New American Library, 1967; London, New English Library, 1977.
*The Time-Hoppers*. New York, Doubleday, 1967; London, Sidgwick and Jackson, 1968.
*Planet of Death*. New York, Holt Rinehart, 1967.
*Hawksbill Station*. New York, Doubleday, 1968; as *The Anvil of Time*, London, Sidgwick and Jackson, 1969.
*The Masks of Time*. New York, Ballantine, 1968; as *Vornan-19*, London, Sidgwick and Jackson, 1970.
*Up the Line*. New York, Ballantine, 1969; London, Gollancz, 1987.
*Nightwings*. New York, Avon, 1969; London, Sidgwick and Jackson, 1972.
*Across a Billion Years* (for children). New York, Dial Press, 1969; London, Gollancz, 1977.
*The Man in the Maze* (for children). New York, Avon, and London, Sidgwick and Jackson, 1969.
*Three Survived* (for children). New York, Holt Rinehart, 1969.
*To Live Again*. New York, Doubleday, 1969; London, Sidgwick and Jackson, 1975.
*World's Fair 1992* (for children). Chicago, Follett, 1970.
*Downward to the Earth*. New York, Doubleday, 1970; London, Gollancz, 1977.
*Tower of Glass*. New York, Scribner, 1970; London, Panther, 1976.
*A Robert Silverberg Omnibus*. London, Sidgwick and Jackson, 1970.
*The World Inside*. New York, Doubleday, 1971; London, Millington, 1976.
*A Time of Changes*. New York, Doubleday, 1971; London, Gollancz, 1973.
*Son of Man*. New York, Ballantine, 1971; London, Panther, 1979.
*The Book of Skulls*. New York, Scribner, 1971; London, Gollancz, 1978.
*Dying Inside*. New York, Scribner, 1972; London, Sidgwick and Jackson, 1974.
*The Second Trip*. New York, Doubleday, 1972; London, Gollancz, 1979.
*The Stochastic Man*. New York, Harper, 1975; London, Gollancz, 1976.
*Shadrach in the Furnace*. Indianapolis, Bobbs Merrill, 1976; London, Gollancz, 1977.
*Lord Valentine's Castle* (Majipoor). New York, Harper, and London, Gollancz, 1980.
*The Desert of Stolen Dreams*. Columbia, Pennsylvania, Underwood Miller, 1981.
*A Robert Silverberg Omnibus*. New York, Harper, 1981.
*Majipoor Chronicles*. New York, Arbor House, and London, Gollancz, 1982.

*Valentine Pontifex*. New York, Arbor House, 1983; London, Gollancz, 1984.
*Lord of Darkness*. New York, Arbor House, and London, Gollancz, 1983.
*The Conglomeroid Cocktail Party*. New York, Arbor House, 1984; London, Gollancz, 1985.
*Tom O'Bedlam*. New York, Fine, 1985; London, Gollancz, 1986.
*Sailing to Byzantium*. Columbia, Pennsylvania, Underwood Miller, 1985.
*Star of the Gypsies*. New York, Fine, 1986; London, Gollancz, 1987.
*Project Pendulum* (for children). New York, Walker, 1987; London, Hutchinson, 1989.
*At Winter's End*. New York, Warner, and London, Gollancz, 1988.
*The Secret Sharer* (novella). Los Angeles, California, Underwood Miller, 1988.
*The Mutant Season*, with Karen Haber. New York, Doubleday, 1989.
*Time Gate*, with Bill Fawcett. New York, Baen, 1989.
*The Queen of Springtime*. London, Gollancz, 1989.
*The New Springtime*. New York, Warner, 1990.
*Nightfall*, with Isaac Asimov. New York, Doubleday, and London, Gollancz, 1990.
*The Man in the Maze*. London, Gollancz, 1990.
*Letters from Atlantis* (for children). New York, Atheneum, 1990.
*In Another Country*, with *Vintage Season* by C.L. Moore. New York, Tor, 1990.
*The Face of the Waters*. New York, Bantam, and London, Grafton, 1991.

Novels as Calvin M. Knox

*Lest We Forget Thee, Earth*. New York, Ace, 1958.
*The Plot Against Earth*. New York, Ace, 1959.
*One of Our Asteroids Is Missing*. New York, Ace, 1964.

Short Stories

*Next Stop the Stars*. New York, Ace, 1962; London, Dobson, 1979.
*Godling, Go Home!* New York, Belmont, 1964.
*To Worlds Beyond*. Philadelphia, Chilton, 1965; London, Sphere, 1969.
*Needle in a Timestack*. New York, Ballantine, 1966; London, Sphere, 1967; revised edition, Sphere, 1979.
*To Open the Sky*. New York, Ballantine, 1967.
*The Calibrated Alligator* (for children). New York, Holt Rinehart, 1969.
*Dimension Thirteen*. New York, Ballantine, 1969.
*Parsecs and Parables*. New York, Doubleday, 1970; London, Hale, 1973.
*The Cube Root of Uncertainty*. New York, Macmillan, 1970.
*Moonferns and Starsongs*. New York, Ballantine, 1971.
*The Reality Trip and Other Implausibilities*. New York, Ballantine, 1972.
*Valley Beyond Time*. New York, Dell, 1973.
*Unfamiliar Territory*. New York, Scribner, 1973; London, Gollancz, 1975.
*Earth's Other Shadow*. New York, New American Library, 1973; London, Millington, 1977.
*Born with the Dead* (three novellas). New York, Random House, 1974; London, Gollancz, 1975.
*Sundance and Other Science Fiction Stories*. Nashville, Nelson, 1974; London, Abelard Schuman, 1975.
*Sunrise on Mercury* (for children). Nashville, Nelson, 1975; London, Gollancz, 1983.
*The Feast of St. Dionysus*. New York, Scribner, 1975; London, Gollancz, 1976.
*The Shores of Tomorrow*. Nashville, Nelson, 1976.
*The Best of Robert Silverberg*. New York, Pocket Books, 1976; London, Sidgwick and Jackson, 1977.
*Capricorn Games*. New York, Random House, 1976; London, Gollancz, 1978.
*The Songs of Summer and Other Stories*. London, Gollancz, 1979.
*World of a Thousand Colors*. New York, Arbor House, 1982.
*Beyond the Safe Zone: Collected Short Fiction*. New York, Fine, 1986.

Other Publications

Novels

*Gilgamesh the King*. New York, Arbor House, 1984; London, Gollancz, 1985.
*To the Land of the Living*. London, Gollancz, 1989; Norwalk, Connecticut, Easton Press, 1990.

Other

*Treasures Beneath the Sea* (for children). Racine, Wisconsin, Whitman, 1960.
*First American into Space*. Derby, Connecticut, Monarch, 1961.
*Lost Cities and Vanished Civilizations* (for children). Philadelphia, Chilton, 1962.
*The Fabulous Rockefellers*. Derby, Connecticut, Monarch, 1963.
*Sunken History: The Story of Underwater Archaeology* (for children). Philadelphia, Chilton, 1963.
*15 Battles That Changed the World*. New York, Putnam, 1963.
*Home of the Red Man: Indian North America Before Columbus* (for children). Greenwich, Connecticut, New York Graphic Society, 1963.
*Empires in the Dust*. Philadelphia, Chilton, 1963.
*The Great Doctors* (for children). New York, Putnam, 1964.
*Akhnaten, The Rebel Pharaoh*. Philadelphia, Chilton, 1964.
*The Man Who Found Nineveh: The Story of Austen Henry Layard* (for children). New York, Holt Rinehart, 1964; Kingswood, Surrey, World's Work, 1968.
*Man Before Adam*. Philadelphia, Macrae Smith, 1964.
*The Loneliest Continent* (as Walker Chapman). Greenwich, Connecticut, New York Graphic Society, 1965; London, Jarrolds, 1967.
*Scientists and Scoundrels: A Book of Hoaxes*. New York, Crowell, 1965.
*The World of Coral* (for children). New York, Duell, 1965.
*The Mask of Akhnaten* (for children). New York, Macmillan, 1965.
*Socrates* (for children). New York, Putnam, 1965.
*The Old Ones: Indians of the American Southwest*. Greenwich, Connecticut, New York Graphic Society, 1965.
*Men Who Mastered the Atom*. New York, Putnam, 1965.
*The Great Wall of China*. Philadelphia, Chilton, 1965.
*Niels Bohr, the Man Who Mapped the Atom* (for children). Philadelphia, Macrae Smith, 1965.
*Forgotten by Time: A Book of Living Fossils* (for children). New York, Crowell, 1966.
*Frontiers of Archaeology*. Philadelphia, Chilton, 1966.

*Kublai Kahn, Lord of Xanadu* (for children; as Walker Chapman). Indianapolis, Bobbs Merrill, 1966.
*The Long Rampart: The Story of the Great Wall of China*. Philadelphia, Chilton, 1966.
*Rivers* (for children; as Lee Sebastian). New York, Holt Rinehart, 1966.
*Bridges*. Philadelphia, Macrae Smith, 1966.
*To the Rock of Darius: The Story of Henry Rawlinson* (for children). New York, Holt Rinehart, 1966.
*The Dawn of Medicine*. New York, Putnam, 1967.
*The Adventures of Nat Palmer, Antarctic Explorer*. New York, McGraw Hill, 1967.
*The Auk, the Dodo, and the Oryx*. New York, Crowell, 1967; Kingswood, Surrey, World's Work, 1969.
*The Golden Dream: Seekers of El Dorado*. Indianapolis, Bobbs Merrill, 1967.
*Men Against Time: Salvage Archaeology in the United States*. New York, Macmillan, 1967.
*The Morning of Mankind*. Greenwich, Connecticut, New York Graphic Society, 1967; Kingswood, Surrey, World's Work, 1970.
*The World of the Rain Forest*. New York, Meredith Press, 1967.
*Light for the World: Edison and the Power Industry*. Princeton, New Jersey, Van Nostrand, 1967.
*Four Men Who Changed the Universe* (for children). New York, Putnam, 1968.
*Ghost Towns of the American West*. New York, Crowell, 1968.
*Mound Builders of Ancient America*. Greenwich, Connecticut, New York Graphic Society, 1968.
*The South Pole* (for children; as Lee Sebastian). New York, Holt Rinehart, 1968.
*Stormy Voyager: The Story of Charles Wilkes*. Philadelphia, Lippincott, 1968.
*The World of the Ocean Depths*. New York, Meredith Press, 1968; Kingswood, Surrey, World's Work, 1970.
*Bruce of the Blue Nile* (for children). New York, Holt Rinehart, 1969.
*The Challenge of Climate: Man and His Environment*. New York, Meredith Press, 1969; Kingswood, Surrey, World's Work, 1971.
*Vanishing Giants: The Story of the Sequoias*. New York, Simon and Schuster, 1969.
*Wonders of Ancient Chinese Science*. New York, Hawthorn, 1969.
*The World of Space*. New York, Meredith Press, 1969.
*If I Forget Thee, O Jerusalem: American Jews and the State of Israel*. New York, Morrow, 1970.
*Mammoths, Mastodons, and Man*. New York, McGraw Hill, 1970; Kingswood, Surrey, World's Work, 1972.
*The Pueblo Revolt*. New York, Weybright and Talley, 1970.
*The Seven Wonders of the Ancient World* (for children). New York, Crowell Collier, 1970.
*Before the Sphinx*. New York, Nelson, 1971.
*Clocks for the Ages: How Scientists Date the Past*. New York, Macmillan, 1971.
*To the Western Shore: Growth of the United States 1776–1853*. New York, Doubleday, 1971.
*Into Space*, with Arthur C. Clarke. New York, Harper, 1971.
*John Muir: Prophet among the Glaciers*. New York, Putnam, 1972.
*The Longest Voyage: Circumnavigation in the Age of Discovery*. Indianapolis, Bobbs Merrill, 1972.
*The Realm of Prester John*. New York, Doubleday, 1972.
*The World Within the Ocean Wave*. New York, Weybright and Talley, 1972.
*The World Within the Tide Pool*. New York, Weybright and Talley, 1972.
*Drug Themes in Science Fiction*. Rockville, Maryland, National Institute on Drug Abuse, 1974.

Editor, *Great Adventures in Archaeology*. New York, Dial Press, 1964; London, Hale, 1966.
Editor, *Earthmen and Strangers*. New York, Duell, 1966.
Editor (as Walker Chapman), *Antarctic Conquest*. Indianapolis, Bobbs Merrill, 1966.
Editor, *Voyagers in Time*. New York, Meredith Press, 1967.
Editor, *Men and Machines*. New York, Meredith Press, 1968.
Editor, *Mind to Mind*. New York, Meredith Press, 1968.
Editor, *Tomorrow's Worlds*. New York, Meredith Press, 1969.
Editor, *Dark Stars*. New York, Ballantine, 1969; London, Ballantine, 1971.
Editor, *Three for Tomorrow*. New York, Meredith Press, 1969; London, Gollancz, 1970.
Editor, *The Mirror of Infinity: A Critics' Anthology of Science Fiction*. New York, Harper, 1970; London, Sidgwick and Jackson, 1971.
Editor, *Science Fiction Hall of Fame 1*. New York, Doubleday, 1970; London, Gollancz, 1971.
Editor, *The Ends of Time*. New York, Hawthorn, 1970.
Editor, *Great Short Novels of Science Fiction*. New York, Ballantine, 1970; London, Pan, 1971.
Editor, *Worlds of Maybe*. New York, Nelson, 1970.
Editor, *Alpha 1–9*. New York, Ballantine, 5 vols., 1970–74; New York, Berkley, 4 vols., 1975–78.
Editor, *Four Futures*. New York, Hawthorn, 1971.
Editor, *The Science Fiction Bestiary*. New York, Nelson, 1971.
Editor, *To the Stars*. New York, Hawthorn, 1971.
Editor, *New Dimensions 1–12* (vols. 11 and 12 edited with Marta Randall). New York, Doubleday, 3 vols., 1971–73; New York, New American Library, 1 vol., 1974; New York, Harper, 6 vols., 1975–80; New York, Pocket Books, 2 vols., 1980–81; *5–7* published London, Gollancz, 3 vols., 1976–77.
Editor, *The Day the Sun Stood Still*. Nashville, Nelson, 1972.
Editor, *Invaders from Space*. New York, Hawthorn, 1972.
Editor, *Beyond Control*. Nashville, Nelson, 1972; London, Sidgwick and Jackson, 1973.
Editor, *Deep Space*. Nashville, Nelson, 1973; London, Abelard Schuman, 1976.
Editor, *Chains of the Sea*. Nashville, Nelson, 1973.
Editor, *No Mind of Man*. New York, Hawthorn, 1973.
Editor, *Other Dimensions*. New York, Hawthorn, 1973.
Editor, *Three Trips in Time and Space*. New York, Hawthorn, 1973.
Editor, *Mutants*. Nashville, Nelson, 1974; London, Abelard Schuman, 1976.
Editor, *Threads of Time*. Nashville, Nelson, 1974; London, Millington, 1975.
Editor, *Infinite Jests*. Radnor, Pennsylvania, Chilton, 1974.
Editor, *Windows into Tomorrow*. New York, Hawthorn, 1974.
Editor, with Roger Elwood, *Epoch*. New York, Berkley, 1975.
Editor, *Explorers of Space*. Nashville, Nelson, 1975.
Editor, *The New Atlantis*. New York, Hawthorn, 1975.
Editor, *Strange Gifts*. Nashville, Nelson, 1975.
Editor, *The Aliens*. Nashville, Nelson, 1976.
Editor, *The Crystal Ship*. Nashville, Nelson, 1976; London, Millington, 1980.
Editor, *Triax*. Los Angeles, Pinnacle, 1977; London, Fontana, 1979.
Editor, *Trips in Time*. Nashville, Nelson, 1977; London, Hale, 1979.
Editor, *Earth Is the Strangest Planet*. Nashville, Nelson, 1977.
Editor, *Galactic Dreamers*. New York, Random House, 1977.

Editor, *The Infinite Web*. New York, Dial Press, 1977.
Editor, *The Androids Are Coming*. New York, Elsevier Nelson, 1979.
Editor, *Lost Worlds, Unknown Horizons*. New York, Elsevier Nelson, 1979.
Editor, *The Edge of Space*. New York, Elsevier Nelson, 1979.
Editor, with Martin H. Greenberg and Joseph D. Olander, *Car Sinister*. New York, Avon, 1979.
Editor, with Martin H. Greenberg and Joseph D. Olander, *Dawn of Time: Prehistory Through Science Fiction*. New York, Elsevier Nelson, 1979.
Editor, *The Best of New Dimensions*. New York, Simon and Schuster, 1979.
Editor, with Martin H. Greenberg, *The Arbor House Treasury of Modern Science Fiction*. New York, Arbor House, 1980; as *Great Science Fiction of the 20th Century*, New York, Avenel, 1987.
Editor, with Martin H. Greenberg, *The Arbor House Treasury of Great Science Fiction Short Novels*. New York, Arbor House, 1980; as *Worlds Imagined*, New York, Avenel, 1989.
Editor, with Martin H. Greenberg and Charles G. Waugh, *The Science Fictional Dinosaur*. New York, Avon, 1982.
Editor, *The Best of Randall Garrett*. New York, Pocket Books, 1982.
Editor, with Martin H. Greenberg, *The Arbor House Treasury of Science Fiction Masterpieces*. New York, Arbor House, 1983; as *Great Tales of Science Fiction*, New York, Galahad, 1985.
Editor, with Martin H. Greenberg, *Fantasy Hall of Fame*. New York, Arbor House, 1983; as *The Mammoth Book of Fantasy All-Time Greats*, London, Robinson, 1988.
Editor, *The Nebula Awards 18*. New York, Arbor House, 1983.
Editor, with Martin H. Greenberg, *The Time Travelers: A Science Fiction Quartet*. New York, Fine, 1985.
Editor, with Martin H. Greenberg and Charles G. Waugh, *Neanderthals*. New York, New American Library, 1987.
Editor, *Robert Silverberg's Worlds of Wonder*. New York, Warner, 1987; London, Gollancz, 1988.
Editor, with Karen Haber, *Universe 1*. New York, Doubleday, 1990.
Editor, with Martin H. Greenberg, *The Horror Hall of Fame*. New York, Carroll and Graf, 1991.

*

Bibliography: in *Fantasy and Science Fiction* (New York), April 1974.

Manuscript Collection: Syracuse University, New York.

Critical Studies: "Robert Silverberg Issue" of *SF Commentary* (Melbourne), March 1977; *Robert Silverberg* by Thomas D. Clareson, Mercer Island, Washington, Starmont House, 1983.

* * *

Robert Silverberg's most personal anthology is *Worlds of Wonder.* In the series of classic science-fiction stories he chooses, Silverberg's narration of why these particular stories influenced him go beyond the goal of a mere writing manual and center on Silverberg's development as a writer. One of the stories that affected Silverberg so powerfully was C.L. Moore's "Vintage Season." In a brilliant marketing coup, Tor Books issued Silverberg's wonderful sequel, "In Another Country," with the C.L. Moore classic as *Tor SF Double #18.* Silverberg's story of the aftermath of "Vintage Season" is as moving and innovative as the story that inspired the sequel. "In Another Country" is Silverberg at his best.

However, a novelization of another science-fiction classic wasn't as successful. *Nightfall* by Isaac Asimov and Robert Silverberg is less than the sum of its parts. Asimov's classic story of the planet Kalgash—a planet that has never seen night—and the clash between science and religion is one of the best known science-fiction stories ever written. The process of turning a tight, taut classic story into a long novel hasn't produced a classic novel.

More successful is *Letters from Atlantis,* in which Silverberg captures the grandeur of that mysterious empire. Roy Colton, a 21st-century researcher, writes the letters based on his experiences in the past. Time travel for Colton is accomplished by sending his mind back in time to occupy a host body—an Atlantean prince. Silverberg's story both explores the mysteries of Atlantis and manages deftly to explore the ethics of being a voyeur without preaching. No science-fiction writer writes about time travel with more verve than Silverberg.

Silverberg's recent major science-fiction novels include *At Winter's End* and its sequel *The New Springtime.* The Long Winter, lasting 700 years, finally ends, and Koshmar, leader of a small band of humans, emerges from the underground cocoon where they've lived for centuries. There, amid the ancient ruins of Earth's superscience civilization, a new struggle for life begins *At Winter's End. The New Springtime* begins 40 years after the end of the Long Winter as the humans clash with the insectoids called the hijk for Earth's dominance. Few novels of the very far future are successful, yet *At Winter's End* and *The New Springtime* feature some of Silverberg's strongest writing in his long career.

Silverberg's writing career spans five decades. A prolific writer, Silverberg's writing style and themes have changed as he matured and gained the skills of a master storyteller. In his revealing autobiographical essay, "Sounding Brass, Tinkling Cymbal"(in *Hell's Cartographers*), Silverberg admits to producing over a million words per year of published material in his apprenticeship years 1955–59. Much of this was hackwork; stories like "Slaves of the Star Giants" and "Secret of the Green Invaders" and novels like *The Planet Killers* and *Stepsons of Terra.* Yet some of the stories were outstanding, like the dark "Road to Nightfall" and the clever "Translation Error," giving notice of the superb stories Silverberg was about to produce.

The late 1950's saw the decline and sudden contraction of the number of science-fiction magazines coupled with the declining market for science-fiction novels. Silverberg responded by shifting his main writing emphasis from SF to juvenile non-fiction, where he achieved critical acclaim for excellent works like *Treasures Beneath the Sea, Empires in the Dust,* and *Lost Cities and Vanished Civilizations.* Much of the research for these books would find itself transformed in Silverberg's future science fiction. He also produced over a hundred soft-core pornopaperbacks, most under the Don Elliot/Eliot pseudonym. Yet Silverberg did not entirely abandon the SF field during the 1960's. Frederik Pohl, then editor of *Galaxy, If,* and *Worlds of Tomorrow,* invited Silverberg to write whatever he wanted. Silverberg, intrigued by the open offer, submitted his now classic "To See the Invisible Man" (1962). Silverberg's narrator is punished by a future society for his crime of "coldness" by being completely ignored by everyone in that society for one year, even though the society is benign. "To See the Invisible Man" shows a shunned man in turn shunning a society; this is a sophisticated story light-years from Silverberg's earlier primitive action adventures like "Battle for the Thousand Stars."

The end of this transition period saw Silverberg begin to emerge as a powerful short-story writer. With "Flies," written for Harlan Ellison's *Dangerous Visions,* Silverberg breaks new ground. An alien race restores a dead starship pilot named Cassiday and enhances his powers. Sent back to Earth as a kind of transmitter for the aliens, Cassiday commits hideous acts of violence, since he is incapable of emotion. The aliens, realizing their mistake, return Cassiday to their world and give him back his conscience, providing the means of self-torture. The story deals with major moral and religious themes, themes Silverberg will expand on in his major novels. Silverberg won his first Nebula award for "Passengers," a horror story of humans dominated by parasitic aliens called Passengers who ride their host humans and utterly control them. "Passengers" explores the question of free will versus determinism, a major theme of later novels like *The Stochastic Man* and *Shadrach in the Furnace.*

Like the explosion of writing in Silverberg's early period, the years 1969–76 produced a similar flood of works; the difference was in the quality. *Nightwings* presents Silverberg's vision of the far future. Earth is a ruined planet, with the Americas sunk beneath the seas. Yet its superscience, which produces genetically engineered Flyers, coexists with a medieval political structure. Tomis the Watcher is a beautifully realized character who narrates this powerful story of hope, renewal, and redemption. In *Tower of Glass*, Silverberg's dark vision returns. The 23rd-century Earth is ruled by Simeon Krug, inventor of the android. His quest is to contact an alien race by building a mammoth tower of glass to send signals deep into space. At the same time, the androids are organizing to be granted person status instead of being considered property. The book abounds with racial, religious, and moral themes, yet the conclusion is very bitter. (About the time *Tower of Glass* was written, Silverberg suffered a fire in his house that destroyed part of his New York City home and left him depressed.)

*A Time of Changes*, which won a Nebula award, is a book misinterpreted as a vehicle for advocating the use of psychedelic drugs, because of the dreamlike quality of many sections of the book where the characters use a Sumaran drug, which allows a person to link minds with another person. *Son of Man* is a strange blend of Olaf Stapledon and David Lindsay's *A Voyage to Acturus* that results in a surreal plot that goes nowhere. But the characters Silverberg creates in Clay, Hanmer, and Ninameen remain unforgettable.

*The World Inside* presents some of Silverberg's more controversial solutions to overpopulation. Silverberg creates a world of gigantic living units, a thousand stories high, containing 800,000 people each. It is a unique future society that encourages sexual experimentation, encourages bearing children, encourages an anti-privacy culture. Contrast this to the situation Silverberg presents in *The Book of Skulls*, where a student finds a manuscript in the rare books of a university library that promises immortality. This launches a quest in what Barry N. Malzberg calls Silverberg's finest novel. Yet most critics consider *Dying Inside* Silverberg's best book. David Selig is a compelling character: he's 40 years old and writes term papers for college students to make enough money to survive. He also has the power to listen to other people's thoughts. As a young man, he considered his power a curse, but now Selig finds he is gradually losing his power to receive the thoughts of others. Silverberg creates a complex, sympathetic character whose plight—although strange and bizarre—becomes realistic and emotional through the exploration of the themes of loss, old age, racism, and change. In *Dying Inside*, Silverberg's powers as a novelist are most completely realized.

In 1976, *The Best of Robert Silverberg* appeared along with Silverberg's announcement that he was withdrawing from the SF field. Silverberg complained critics ignored his work and the science-fiction publishers failed to reward SF writers to the extent writers in other fields were rewarded. At the same time, SF writers like Harlan Ellison, Barry N. Malzberg, and Kurt Vonnegut were announcing their flight from the science-fiction ghetto. Ellison and Vonnegut fought to remove the SF label from their new works and reprints. Yet Silverberg did not withdraw from the SF field completely; in the years 1976–79, he edited *New Directions*, an original SF anthology series, as well as numerous SF theme reprint anthologies—from 1966 to 1981 Silverberg edited over 60 SF anthologies.

As early as 1979, rumors abounded that Silverberg was working on a "big book." Times had changed in publishing by the early 1980's: science fiction and fantasy, often ignored and ill-funded lines, became much more popular with the success of *Star Wars* and the *Star Trek* movies. Silverberg received critical acclaim and a six-figure advance for *Lord Valentine's Castle*, where he set up a huge planet called Majipoor with 20 million human and alien beings. Valentine's quest is one of identity. He is a wandering juggler who is actually a king dethroned by treachery, robbing him of his memory. The book lacks suspense: we know early on Valentine's quest will be successful, but Silverberg holds our interest for over 500 pages with adventures on Majipoor that are a delight. The planet becomes the star of the book. But the light fantasy of *Lord Valentine's Castle* gives way to the darker stories in *Majipoor Chronicles*, where Silverberg explores in more detail his mammoth planet. "The Desert of Stolen Dreams" gives us a lesson in Majipoorean guilt when the main character faces the death of a companion. "The Soul-Painter and the Shapeshifter" shows us a love affair between Majipoor's humans and aliens. The other stories fill out Silverberg's marvellous creation with a detailed history and philosophy of Majipoor. This culminates in *Valentine Pontifex* where Valentine's promotion from Coronal to Pontifex brings him up against an awesome challenge: the Metamorphs, shape-shifting natives of Majipoor, have broken the thousand years of peace with an attempt to dominate the planet. The fate of the planet is in Valentine's hands and this volume of the Majipoor saga is the most satisfying.

*The Conglomeroid Cocktail Party* contains some of Silverberg's finest short stories. "The Pope of the Chimps" is a revealing study of religion as an experimental group of chimps begin to worship humans. "The Changeling" is a clever twist on alternate reality themes. "Gianni" is a marvelous time-travel story where scientists bring 18th-century musical prodigy Giovanni Pergolesi, who died at the age of 26, back to the future with deterministic results.

Silverberg's fantasies, *Gilgamesh the King* and its sequel, *To the Land of the Living*, take us back to the ancient civilizations of 5000 years ago when the Sumerian god-king grew to maturity and reigned over an empire. With a blend of myth and magic, Silverberg presents quests where Helen of Troy and even Picasso can be found. The Gilgamesh books are Silverberg at his most playful.

Silverberg is a giant in the field of science fiction, a prolific writer whose long career has produced classic novels and award-winning short stories. The impressive fact that Silverberg continues to produce first-rate, sophisticated work only adds to his stature.

—George Kelley

---

**SIMAK, Clifford D(onald).** American. Born in Millville, Wisconsin, 3 August 1904. Attended the University of Wisconsin, Madison. Married Kay Kuchenberg in 1929; one son and one daughter. Reporter, 1924–76, news editor, 1949–62, and editor of Science Reading Series, 1962–76, Minneapolis *Star* and

*Tribune.* Recipient: International Fantasy award, 1953; Hugo award, for story, 1959, 1981, for novel, 1964; First Fandom Hall of Fame award, 1973; Grand Master Nebula award, 1976, and Nebula award, 1980; Jupiter award, 1978; *Locus* award, 1981; Bram Stoker Life Achievement award, 1988. Guest of Honor, 29th World Science Fiction Convention, 1971. *Died 25 April 1988.*

### Science-Fiction Publications

#### Novels

*Cosmic Engineers.* New York, Gnome Press, 1950; London, Magnum, 1982.
*Time and Again.* New York, Simon and Schuster, 1951; London, Heinemann, 1955; as *First He Died*, New York, Dell, 1953.
*Empire.* New York, Galaxy, 1951.
*Ring Around the Sun.* New York, Simon and Schuster, 1953; London, Consul, 1960.
*Time Is the Simplest Thing.* New York, Doubleday, 1961; London, Gollancz, 1962.
*The Trouble with Tycho.* New York, Ace, 1961.
*They Walked Like Men.* New York, Doubleday, 1962; London, Gollancz, 1963.
*Way Station.* New York, Doubleday, 1963; London, Gollancz, 1964.
*All Flesh Is Grass.* New York, Doubleday, 1965; London, Gollancz, 1966.
*Why Call Them Back from Heaven?* New York, Doubleday, and London, Gollancz, 1967.
*The Werewolf Principle.* New York, Putnam, 1967; London, Gollancz, 1968.
*The Goblin Reservation.* New York, Putnam, 1968; London, Rapp and Whiting, 1969.
*Out of Their Minds.* New York, Putnam, 1970; London, Sidgwick and Jackson, 1972.
*Destiny Doll.* New York, Putnam, 1971; London, Sidgwick and Jackson, 1972.
*A Choice of Gods.* New York, Putnam, 1972; London, Sidgwick and Jackson, 1973.
*Cemetery World.* New York, Putnam, 1973; London, Sidgwick and Jackson, 1975.
*Our Children's Children.* New York, Putnam, 1974; London, Sidgwick and Jackson, 1975.
*Enchanted Pilgrimage.* New York, Berkley, 1975; London, Sidgwick and Jackson, 1976.
*Shakespeare's Planet.* New York, Berkley, 1976; London, Sidgwick and Jackson, 1977.
*A Heritage of Stars.* New York, Berkley, 1977; London, Sidgwick and Jackson, 1978.
*Mastodonia.* New York, Ballantine, 1978; as *Catface*, London, Sidgwick and Jackson, 1978.
*The Visitors.* New York, Ballantine, 1980; London, Sidgwick and Jackson, 1981.
*Project Pope.* New York, Ballantine, and London, Sidgwick and Jackson, 1981.
*Special Deliverance.* New York, Ballantine, 1982; London, Severn House, 1983.
*Where the Evil Dwells.* New York, Ballantine, 1982; London, Severn House, 1984.
*Highway of Eternity.* New York, Ballantine, 1986; London, Severn House, 1987.
*Off-Planet.* London, Methuen, 1988.

#### Short Stories

*The Creator.* Los Angeles, Crawford, 1946.
*City.* New York, Gnome Press, 1952; London, Weidenfeld and Nicolson, 1954.
*Strangers in the Universe.* New York, Simon and Schuster, 1956; abridged edition, London, Faber, 1958.
*The Worlds of Clifford Simak.* New York, Simon and Schuster, 1960; abridged edition, as *Aliens for Neighbours*, London, Faber, 1961; abridged edition, as *Other Worlds of Clifford Simak*, New York, Avon, 1962.
*All the Traps of Earth.* New York, Doubleday, 1962; as *All the Traps of Earth* and *The Night of the Puudly*, London, New English Library, 2 vols., 1964.
*Worlds Without End.* New York, Belmont, 1964; London, Jenkins, 1965.
*Best Science Fiction Stories of Clifford Simak.* London, Faber, 1967.
*So Bright the Vision.* New York, Ace, 1968; London, Severn House, 1986.
*The Best of Clifford D. Simak*, edited by Angus Wells. London, Sidgwick and Jackson, 1975.
*Skirmish: The Great Short Fiction of Clifford D. Simak.* New York, Putnam, 1977.
*The Marathon Photograph and Other Stories*, edited by Francis Lyall. London, Severn House, 1986.
*Brothers and Other Stories.* London, Severn House, 1986.
*The Autumn Land and Other Stories*, edited by Francis Lyall. London, Mandarin, 1990.

### Other Publications

#### Novel

*The Fellowship of the Talisman.* New York, Ballantine, 1978; London, Sidgwick and Jackson, 1980.

#### Other

*The Solar System: Our New Front Yard* (for children). New York, St. Martin's Press, 1963.
*Trilobite, Dinosaur, and Man: The Earth's Story.* New York, St. Martin's Press, and London, Macmillan, 1966.
*Wonder and Glory: The Story of the Universe.* New York, St. Martin's Press, 1969.
*Prehistoric Man.* New York, St. Martin's Press, 1971.

Editor, *From Atoms to Infinity: Readings in Modern Science.* New York, Harper, 1965.
Editor, *The March of Science* (for children). New York, Harper, 1971.
Editor, *Nebula Award Stories 6.* New York, Doubleday, 1971.
Editor, *The Best of Astounding.* New York, Baronet, 1978.

*

Bibliography: *The Electric Bibliograph 1: Clifford D. Simak* by Mark Owings, Baltimore, Alice and Jay Haldeman, 1971.

* * *

Readers of science fiction lost a treasure when Clifford Simak died in 1988. This gentle, friendly man poured more pleasure onto the printed page than many writers have been able to muster. Simak was drawn early in his life to the world of journalism, where he worked on a number of newspapers, ending up at the *Minneapolis Star* and *Tribune* for 36 years. Among other duties, he was news editor and author of a science column, which led to a Minneapolis Academy of Science award for Distinguished Service to Science in 1967. This interest prompted his writing of several non-fiction works: *Prehistoric Man*; *The Solar System*; *Trilobite, Dinosaur, and Man*.

Simak's interest in science led him to *Amazing Stories* in 1927, possibly luring him into writing, for a 1931 *Wonder Stories* issue, his first attempt at science fiction: "World of the Red Sun." This work and some others used the standard devices of pulp magazines of the day, often trite and repetitive. But Simak lost interest in this sort of writing until John Campbell's influence elevated the standards of science-fiction writing in *Astounding* and other magazines.

Shaped by his boyhood on a farm in Wisconsin, Simak was moralistic in outlook and pastoral in temperament, feeling that man should be a harmonious element in the entire natural scheme of things, that his goals and standards must be only a part of the great scheme of all possibilities. Accordingly, his writing increasingly involved non-human figures—friendly, but not man. These intelligent beings often had special qualities man lacked: levitation, prescience, telekinesis. Such beings stressed both Simak's belief in man and his conviction that man could become an elevated being. Yarns like "Census," "Huddling Place," and "Desertion"—which ultimately grew into *City*—contrasted humans and aliens to make the point that man could be a shining figure if he *would*. *City* is still regarded by many readers as Simak's most interesting and stimulating product, winning the International Fantasy award in 1952.

An elegant term describes this unusual man. Clifford Simak was an adoxographer, a person who chooses lowly and ordinary ideas and makes them grand. The people in *Cosmic Engineers*, for example, seem like one's neighbors; they chatter along in slang as they finger mysterious controls and machinery while navigating their "Space Pup" out by Pluto. This may seem rather hum-drum—except that they become masters of the entire universe.

Rainbows are wonderful and exciting, especially after a violent rain storm, but they are actually quite commonplace, the products of light passing through moisture. Or are they? *Highway of Eternity* reveals them to be entities, the most ancient of races, who let themselves be seen in welcoming and promising situations.

In "The Big Front Yard," creatures from all over the universe swim out on the "lawn," trading a wide range of wonderful objects—machines, devices, and exotic things whose purpose can only be guessed. For this "ordinary" novelette, Simak won the Hugo award in 1959. Other honors have included a Hugo award for *Way Station* and the Nebula Grand Master award of the Science Fiction Writers of America.

It is not possible, however, to consider just the optimistic side of Simak without acknowledging other elements in his works. Man is often portrayed by him in less than flattering terms. To be realistic, humans are frequently not very nice beings. Simak more than suggests this in *They Walked Like Men*, where humans are likened to dogs. *City*'s robot Jenkins thinks that dogs had known how to talk long before they were given tongues to talk, or contact lenses to read. And later, the story "Aesop" reveals that the dogs have forgotten men entirely; Jenkins says man is a forgotten fireside tale. Granted, man has done it to himself. He has taken the long sleep in special supportive tombs, or is shipped off to Jupiter, deserting Earth. But in stories like "Wayside," or in *The Goblin Reservation*, and *All Flesh Is Grass*, the aliens—bowling ball forms, purple flowers, floating metal cylinders—romp the landscapes. Roles appear to have been switched when creatures in *A Heritage of Stars* seem human to onlookers. And to Asa Steels, the Catface of *Mastondonia* "looks sort of like a human being".

In a sense, one might say that Simak is really concerned with either pantheism or polytheism. Non-human life often has admirable qualities. Man frequently comes off poorly with respect to godly virtues—like patience, kindness, forbearance, and forgiveness in his daily living. *Time and Again*, a brotherhood of sapients, whatever their form, exemplifies and illustrates Simak's leaning away from mankind. Certainly, though, man's choice, in "Desertion," of the planet Jupiter for an abode, demanding as it did drastic transformation of his entire being for survival, lends a certain emphasis to man's dissatisfaction with himself. It meant conversion into a "Loper" in that incredible environment, surrounded by a perfumed purple atmosphere, bedazzled by beauties that human eyes could never comprehend, equipped with unthinkable powers. Why would man remain, under such circumstances, an animal with two feeble legs, a mockery of a brain, and other frailties that human flesh is heir to? Why would he *not* embrace godhood? As Simak frames it:

"I can't go back," said Towser.
"Neither can I," said Fowler.
"They would turn me back into a dog," said Towser.
"And me," said Fowler, "back into a man."

—Robert H. Wilcox

---

**SINCLAIR, Upton.** Also wrote as Frederick Garrison. American. Born in Baltimore, Maryland, 20 September 1878; moved with his family to New York City, 1888. Educated at the City College of New York, 1893–97, A.B. 1897; Columbia University, New York, 1897–1901. Married 1) Meta H. Fuller in 1900 (divorced 1911); 2) Mary Craig Kimbrough in 1913 (died 1961); 3) Mary Elizabeth Willis in 1961 (died 1967). Writer from 1893; wrote Clif Faraday stories (as Ensign Clarke Fitch) and Mark Mallory stories (as Lieutenant Frederick Garrison) for various boys' weeklies, 1897–98; founded socialist community, Helicon Home Colony, Englewood, New Jersey, 1906-07; Socialist candidate for Congress, from New Jersey, 1906; settled in Pasadena, California, 1915; Socialist candidate for Congress, 1920, and for the United States Senate, 1922, and for Governor of California, 1926, 1930; moved to Buckeye, Arizona, 1953. Recipient: Pulitzer prize, 1943; American Newspaper Guild award, 1962. *Died 25 November 1968.*

SCIENCE-FICTION PUBLICATIONS

Novels

*Prince Hagen*. Boston, Page, and London, Chatto and Windus, 1903.

*The Industrial Republic*. New York, Doubleday, and London, Heinemann, 1907.

*They Call Me Carpenter*. New York, Boni and Liveright, and London, Laurie, 1922.

*The Millennium: A Comedy of the Year 2000*. Girard, Kansas, Haldeman Julius, 1924; London, Laurie, 1929.

*Roman Holiday*. New York, Farrar and Rinehart, and London, Laurie, 1931.

*Our Lady*. Emmaus, Pennsylvania, Rodale Press, and London, Laurie, 1938.

Uncollected Short Story

"Author's Adventure," in *The Fantastic Pulps*, edited by Peter Haining. New York, St. Martin's Press, 1975.

OTHER PUBLICATIONS

Novels

*Springtime and Harvest: A Romance*. New York, Sinclair Press, 1901; as *King Midas*, New York and London, Funk and Wagnalls, 1901.
*The Journal of Arthur Stirling*. New York, Appleton, and London, Heinemann, 1903.
*Manassas*. New York and London, Macmillan, 1904; as *Theirs Be the Guilt*, New York, Twayne, 1959.
*The Jungle*. New York, Doubleday Page, and London, Heinemann, 1906; as *The Lost First Edition of Upton Sinclair's The Jungle*, edited by Gene DeGruson, Memphis, Tennessee, Peachtree, 1988.
*A Captain of Industry*. Girard, Kansas, Appeal to Reason, and London, Heinemann, 1906.
*The Metropolis*. New York, Moffat Yard, and London, Laurie, 1908.
*The Moneychangers*. New York, Dodge, and London, Long, 1908.
*Samuel the Seeker*. New York, Dodge, and London, Long, 1910.
*Love's Pilgrimage*. New York, Kennerley, 1911; London, Heinemann, 1912.
*Sylvia*. Philadelphia, Winston, 1913; London, Long, 1914.
*Damaged Goods*. Philadelphia, Winston, and London, Hutchinson, 1913.
*Sylvia's Marriage*. Philadelphia, Winston, 1914; London, Laurie, 1915.
*King Coal*. New York, Macmillan, and London, Laurie, 1917.
*Jimmie Higgins*. London, Hutchinson, 1918; New York, Boni and Liveright, 1919.
*The Spy*. London, Laurie, 1919; as *100%: The Story of a Patriot*, privately printed, 1920; excerpt, as *Peter Gudge Becomes a Secret Agent*, Moscow, State Publishing House, 1930.
*Oil!* New York, Boni, and London, Laurie, 1927.
*Boston*. New York, Boni, 1928; London, Laurie, 1929; abridged edition, as *August 22nd*, New York, Universal, 1965; Bath, Chivers, 1971.
*Mountain City*. New York, Boni, 1929; London, Laurie, 1930.
*The Wet Parade*. New York, Farrar and Rinehart, and London, Laurie, 1931.
*Co-op: A Novel of Living Together*. New York, Farrar and Rinehart, and London, Laurie, 1936.
*The Gnomobile*. New York, Farrar and Rinehart, and London, Laurie, 1936.
*Little Steel*. New York, Farrar and Rinehart, and London, Laurie, 1938.
*Marie Antoinette*. New York, Vanguard Press, and London, Laurie, 1939; as *Marie and Her Lover*, Girard, Kansas, Haldeman Julius, 1948.
*World's End*. New York, Viking Press, and London, Laurie, 1940.
*Between Two Worlds*. New York, Viking Press, and London, Laurie, 1941.
*Dragon's Teeth*. New York, Viking Press, and London, Laurie, 1942.
*Wide Is the Gate*. New York, Viking Press, and London, Laurie, 1943.
*Presidential Agent*. New York, Viking Press, 1944; London, Laurie, 1945.
*Dragon Harvest*. New York, Viking Press, and London, Laurie, 1945.
*A World to Win*. New York, Viking Press, 1946; London, Laurie, 1947.
*Presidential Mission*. New York, Viking Press, 1947; London, Laurie, 1948.
*One Clear Call*. New York, Viking Press, 1948; London, Laurie, 1949.
*O Shepherd, Speak!* New York, Viking Press, 1949; London, Laurie, 1950.
*Another Pamela; or, Virtue Still Rewarded*. New York, Viking Press, and London, Laurie, 1950.
*The Return of Lanny Budd*. New York, Viking Press, and London, Laurie, 1953.
*What Didymus Did*. London, Wingate, 1954; as *It Happened to Didymus*, New York, Sagamore Press, 1958.
*The Cup of Fury*. Great Neck, New York, Channel Press, 1956; London, Arco, 1957.
*Affectionately Eve*. New York, Twayne, 1961.
*The Coal War: A Sequel to King Coal*. Boulder, Colorado, Associated University Press, 1976.

Plays

*Prince Hagen*, adaptation of his own novel (produced San Francisco, 1909). Privately printed, 1909.
*Plays of Protest* (includes *Prince Hagen, The Naturewoman, The Machine, The Second-Story Man*). New York, Kennerley, 1912.
*Hell: A Verse Drama and Photo-Play*. Privately printed, 1923.
*The Pot Boiler*. Girard, Kansas, Haldeman Julius, 1924.
*Singing Jailbirds* (produced London, 1930). Privately printed, 1924.
*Bill Porter*. Privately printed, 1924.
*Wally for Queen! The Private Life of Royalty*. Privately printed, 1936.
*A Giant's Strength*. Girard, Kansas, Haldeman Julius, and London, Laurie, 1948.
*The Enemy Had It Too*. New York, Viking Press, 1950.
*Three Plays* (includes *The Second-Story Man, John D., The Indignant Subscriber*). Moscow, Progress, 1965.

Verse

*Songs of Our Nation* (as Frederick Garrison). New York, Marks Music, 1941.

Other

*The Toy and the Man*. Westwood, Massachusetts, Ariel Press, 1904.
*Our Bourgeois Literature*. Chicago, Kerr, 1905.
*Colony Customs*. Englewood, New Jersey, Sinclair, 1906.
*The Helicon Home Colony*. Englewood, New Jersey, Constitution, 1906.
*A Home Colony: A Prospectus*. New York, Jungle, 1906.
*What Life Means to Me*. Girard, Kansas, Appeal to Reason, 1906.
*The Overman*. New York, Doubleday, 1907.
*Good Health and How We Won It*, with Michael Williams. New York, Stokes, 1909; as *Strength and Health*, 1910; as *The Art of Health*, London, Health and Strength, 1909.
*War: A Manifesto Against It*. Girard, Kansas, Appeal to Reason, New York, Wilshire, and London, Clarion Press, 1909.
*Four Letters About "Love's Pilgrimage."* Privately printed, 1911.

*The Fasting Cure*. New York, Kennerley, and London, Heinemann, 1911.

*The Sinclair-Astor Letters: Famous Correspondence Between Socialist and Millionaire*. Girard, Kansas, Appeal to Reason, 1914.

*The Social Problem as Seen from the Viewpoint of Trade Unionism, Capital, and Socialism*, with others. New York, Industrial Economics Department of the National Civic Federation, 1914.

*Upton Sinclair: Biographical and Critical Opinions*. Privately printed, 1917.

*The Profits of Religion*. Privately printed, 1918; London, Laurie, 1936.

*Russia: A Challenge*. Girard, Kansas, Appeal to Reason, 1919.

*The High Cost of Living* (address). Girard, Kansas, People's Press, 1919.

*The Brass Check*. London, Laurie, 1919; Pasadena, California, privately printed, 1920; excerpt, as *The Associated Press and Labor*, privately printed, 1920.

*Press-titution*. Girard, Kansas, Appeal to Reason, 1920.

*The Crimes of the "Times": A Test of Newspaper Decency*. Privately printed, 1921.

*Mind and Body*. New York, Macmillan, 1921; revised edition, Girard, Kansas, Haldeman Julius, 4 vols., 1950.

*The Book of Life*. Pasadena, California, Sinclair Paine, 1922; London, Laurie, 1934.

*Love and Society*. Pasadena, California, Sinclair Paine, 1922; revised edition, Girard, Kansas, Haldeman Julius, 4 vols., n.d.

*The McNeal-Sinclair Debate on Socialism*. Girard, Kansas, Haldeman Julius, 1921.

*The Goose-Step: A Study of American Education*. Privately printed, 1922; revised edition, n.d.; London, Laurie, 1923.

*Biographical Letter and Critical Opinions*. Privately printed, 1922.

*The Goslings*. Privately printed, 1924; London, Laurie, 1930; excerpt, as *The Schools of Los Angeles*, privately printed, 1924.

*Mammonart*. Privately printed, 1925; London, Laurie, 1934.

*Letters to Judd*. Privately printed, 1926; revised edition, as *This World of 1949 and What to Do about It*, Girard, Kansas, Haldeman Julius, 1949.

*The Spokesman's Secretary*. Privately printed, 1926.

*Money Writes!* New York, Boni, 1927; London, Laurie, 1931.

*The Pulitzer Prize and "Special Pleading."* Privately printed, 1929.

*Mental Radio*. New York, Boni, and London, Laurie, 1930; revised edition, Springfield, Illinois, Thomas, 1962.

*Socialism and Culture*. Girard, Kansas, Haldeman Julius, 1931.

*Upton Sinclair on "Comrade" Kautsky*. Moscow, Co-operative Publishing Society of Foreign Workers in the USSR, 1931.

*American Outpost*. New York, Farrar and Rinehart, 1932; as *Candid Reminiscences: My First Thirty Years*, London, Laurie, 1932.

*I, Governor of California, and How I Ended Poverty*. New York, Farrar and Rinehart, and London, Laurie, 1933.

*Upton Sinclair Presents William Fox*. Privately printed, 1933.

*The Way Out—What Lies Ahead for America?* New York, Farrar and Rinehart, and London, Laurie, 1933; revised edition, as *Limbo on the Loose: A Midsummer Night's Dream*, Girard, Kansas, Haldeman Julius, 1948.

*EPIC Plan for California*. New York, Farrar and Rinehart, 1934.

*EPIC Answers: How to End Poverty in California*. Los Angeles, End Poverty League, 1934.

*Immediate EPIC*. Los Angeles, End Poverty League, 1934.

*The Lie Factory Starts*. Los Angeles, End Poverty League, 1934.

*An Upton Sinclair Anthology*, edited by I.O. Evans. New York, Farrar and Rinehart, and London, Laurie, 1934; revised edition, Culver City, California, Murray and Gee, 1947.

*Upton Sinclair's Last Will and Testament*. Los Angeles, End Poverty League, 1934.

*We, People of America, and How We Ended Poverty: A True Story of the Future*. Pasadena, California, National EPIC League, 1934.

*Depression Island*. Pasadena, California, privately printed, and London, Laurie, 1935.

*I, Candidate for Governor, and How I Got Licked*. New York, Farrar and Rinehart, 1935; as *How I Got Licked and Why*, London, Laurie, 1935.

*What God Means to Me: An Attempt at a Working Religion*. New York, Farrar and Rinehart, and London, Laurie, 1936.

*The Flivver King*. Girard, Kansas, Haldeman Julius, 1937; London, Laurie, 1938.

*No Pasoran! (They Shall Not Pass)*. New York, Labor Press, and London, Laurie, 1937.

*Terror in Russia: Two Views*, with Eugene Lyons. New York, Richard R. Smith, 1938.

*Upton Sinclair on the Soviet Union*. New York, Weekly Masses, 1938.

*Expect No Peace!* Girard, Kansas, Haldeman Julius, 1939.

*Telling the World*. London, Laurie, 1939.

*What Can Be Done about America's Economic Troubles?* Girard, Kansas, Haldeman Julius, 1939.

*Your Million Dollars*. Privately printed, 1939; as *Letters to a Millionaire*, London, Laurie, 1939.

*Is the American Form of Capitalism Essential to the American Form of Democracy?* Girard, Kansas, Haldeman Julius, 1940.

*Peace or War in America?* Girard, Kansas, Haldeman Julius, 1940.

*Index to the Lanny Budd Story*, with others. New York, Viking Press, 1943.

*To Solve the German Problem—A Free State?* Privately printed, 1943.

*A Personal Jesus: Portrait and Interpretation*. New York, Evans, 1952; London, Allen and Unwin, 1954; as *Secret Life of Jesus*, Philadelphia, Mercury, 1962.

*Radio Liberation Speech to the Peoples of the Soviet Union*. New York, American Committee for Liberation from Bolshevism, 1955.

*My Lifetime in Letters*. Columbia, University of Missouri Press, 1960.

*The Autobiography of Upton Sinclair*. New York, Harcourt Brace, 1962; London, Allen and Unwin, 1963.

*Upton Sinclair: Four Unpublished Letters*. San Francisco, California, Artichoke Press, 1984.

Editor, *The Cry for Justice: An Anthology of the Literature of Social Protest*. Philadelpha, Winston, 1915.

*

Bibliography: *Upton Sinclair: An Annotated Checklist* by Ronald Gottesman, Kent, Ohio, Kent State University Press, 1973.

Critical Studies: *This Is Upton Sinclair* by James Harte Lambert, Emmaus, Pennsylvania, Rodale Press, 1938; *The Literary Manuscripts of Upton Sinclair* by Ronald Gottesman and Charles L. P. Silet, Columbus, Ohio State University Press, 1972; *Upton Sinclair* by Jon A. Yoder, New York, Ungar, 1975; *Upton Sinclair, American Rebel* by Leon Harris, New York, Crowell, 1975; *Critics on Upton Sinclair* edited by Abraham Blinderman, Coral

Gables, Florida, University of Miami Press, 1975; *Upton Sinclair* by William A. Bloodworth, Boston, Twayne, 1977.

* * *

Upton Sinclair is best known as a socialist muckraking novelist, and has a spectacular history as a much-admired and much-traduced political crusader. However, as an "Economic Scientist," he has experimented in both science fiction and fantasy, especially of the time-travel variety. Since his talents are journalistic and narrative rather than evocative of character and subtle human relations, his SF drama is less skilful than his novels are.

One group of novels takes America into a possible alternative world, consequent upon Sinclair being elected Governor of California and his EPIC programme being adopted by the USA. *I, Governor of California, and How I Ended Poverty* is fiction only in the sense that it projects a political campaign into the immediate future, emphasising the virtues and values of the co-operative movement that defeats the Depression. *We, People of America, and How We Ended Poverty* expands the canvas and the time-scale, but is still more argument than fiction. *Co-op* is a genuine fiction, but leaves the reader to debate whether President Roosevelt will or will not embrace the Co-operative Commonwealth ideal. That ideal is interesting in itself, uniting patriotism with socialist and collectivist principles, but the protagonists of the novel are more typical than individually memorable.

Genuinely science-fiction and fantasy novels are *The Millennium: A Comedy of the Year 2000*, a satirical parable on the need for socialism combined with social justice, and the rather stiffly Utopian *The Industrial Republic.* More striking juxtapositions of modern American assumptions with those of very different societies make *Prince Hagen* still interesting; the avaricious Nibelung ruler is impressed by the superior chicanery and greed of "Christian" American capitalism. In *Roman Holiday*, a rich young American playboy, in the delirium following a motor-racing accident, finds himself back in patrician Rome, which tells him a great deal about his 20th-century life-style and society. *They Call Me Carpenter* also uses a rich and idle American as principal observer: laid out after a scuffle with "patriotic" demonstrators against the film *The Cabinet of Dr. Caligari*, he sees Christ step down from a cathedral window; inevitably "Carpenter" loves His fellow men, but is forced to denounce the press, the society's privileged, and especially the church that has deserted the revolutionary doctrines of its supposed Founder (the novel stops short of the crucifixion which its logic seems to entail). Sinclair's other major time-travel fantasy, *Our Lady*, is excellent in both research and the basic contrast between the mother of Jesus and the modern Californian Catholic world to which she is translated. Both her reaction to the ball-game where she first appears and her total alienation from any element of Roman Catholic faith that theoretically invokes her mingle comedy, pathos, and a genuine reverence for human spiritual exploration; even the exorcism climax has an obsessive power lacking in most of Sinclair's endings.

Most of Sinclair's immense number of novels were written too quickly, and stumble into structural faults as well as psychological shallowness. Yet the best of his writing carries immense compassion for human suffering and frustration, and the force and courage of his defence of human relations against capitalist priorities is worth the loss of many graces. Although genuinely convinced that all good art is primarily propaganda, Sinclair avoids portraying all capitalists or playboys as fools or ogres, and often relishes the sudden understanding that can spring up between characters socially alien to each other. In his drama there is genuine development between the versions of the "noble savage" girl in *The Naturewoman (Plays of Protest)* and *The Enemy Had It Too*, where the unspoiled maiden kills the sophisticated gangster by the use of flirtation and curare! Nonetheless, the exploration of Great Issues does not suit the stage, and mixing the world-disaster (or last-men) theme with the return-from-Mars, the noble savage, the satiric portrait, and the all-aboard-the-Ark themes makes even the latter too overloaded. It is for such novels as *Our Lady* that Sinclair most deserves the fantasy reader's attention.

—Norman Talbot

---

**SIODMAK, Curt** (Kurt Siodmak). American. Born in Dresden, Germany, 10 August 1902; brother of the film director Robert Siodmak. Educated at the University of Zurich, Ph.D. 1927. Married Henrietta De Perrot in 1931; one son. Railroad engineer and factory worker; film writer and director: worked for Gaumont British, 1931–37, and in the United States after 1937. Recipient: Bundespreis, for film, 1964. *Died in 1988.*

SCIENCE-FICTION PUBLICATIONS

Novels (series: Cory)

*F.P.1. Antwortet Nicht.* Berlin, Keils, 1931; translated by H. W. Farrell as *F.P.1. Does Not Reply*, Boston, Little Brown, 1933; as *F.P.1 Fails to Reply*, London, Collins, 1933.
*Donovan's Brain* (Cory). New York, Knopf, 1943; London, Chapman and Hall, 1944.
*Skyport.* New York, Crown, 1959.
*Hauser's Memory* (Cory). New York, Putnam, 1968; London, Jenkins, 1969.
*The Third Ear.* New York, Putnam, 1971.
*City in the Sky.* New York, Putnam, 1974; London, Barrie and Jenkins, 1975.

OTHER PUBLICATIONS

Novels

*Schluss in Tonfilmatelier.* Berlin, Scherl, 1930.
*Stadt Hinter Nebeln.* Salzburg, Berglund, 1931.
*Die Madonna aus der Markusstrasse.* Leipzig, Goldmann, 1932.
*Rache im Ather.* Leipzig, Goldmann, 1932.
*Bis ans Ende der Welt.* Leipzig, Goldmann, 1933.
*Die Macht im Dunkeln.* Zurich, Morgarten, 1937.
*Whomsoever I Shall Kiss.* New York, Crown, 1952.
*For Kings Only.* New York, Crown, 1961.

Plays

Screenplays: *Menschen am Sonntag (People on Sunday)* (documentary), with Billy Wilder, 1929; *Le Bal*, 1931; *Der Mann der Seinen Mörder Sucht (Looking for His Murderer)*, 1931; *F.P.1 Antwortet Nicht*, 1933; *Girls Will Be Boys*, with Clifford Grey and Roger Burford, 1934; *I Give My Heart*, with others, 1935; *The Tunnel (Transatlantic Tunnel)*, with L. DuGarde Peach and Clemence Dane, 1935; *It's a Bet*, with Frank Miller and L. DuGarde Peach, 1935; *Non-Stop New York*, with others, 1937; *Her Jungle Love*, with others, 1938; *The Invisible Man Returns*, with Lester Cole and Joe May, 1940; *The Ape*, with Richard

Carroll, 1940; *Black Friday*, with Eric Taylor, 1940; *The Wolf Man*, with Gordon Kann, 1940; *The Invisible Woman*, with others, 1941; *Pacific Blackout*, with others, 1941; *Aloma of the South Seas*, with others, 1941; *Midnight Angel*, with others, 1941; *London Blackout Murders*, 1942; *The Invisible Agent*, 1942; *I Walked with a Zombie*, with Ardel Wray and Inez Wallace, 1943; *Frankenstein Meets the Wolf Man*, 1943; *The Mantrap*, 1943; *Son of Dracula*, with Eric Taylor, 1943; *False Faces*, 1943; *The Purple "V,"* with Bertram Millhauser, 1943; *House of Frankenstein*, with Edward T. Lowe, 1944; *The Climax*, with Lynn Starling, 1944; *Frisco Sal*, with Gerald Geraghty, 1945; *Shady Lady*, with others, 1945; *The Return of Monte Cristo*, with others, 1946; *The Beast with Five Fingers*, with Harold Goldman, 1947; *Berlin Express*, with Harold Medford, 1948; *Tarzan's Magic Fountain*, with Harry Chandlee, 1949; *Four Days Leave*, with others, 1950; *Bride of the Gorilla*, 1951; *The Magnetic Monster*, with Ivan Tors, 1953; *Riders to the Stars*, 1954; *Creature with the Atom Brain*, 1955; *Earth vs. Flying Saucers*, with George Worthing Yates and Raymond Marcus, 1956; *Curucu, Beast of the Amazon*, 1956; *Love Slaves of the Amazon*, 1957; *The Devil's Messenger*, 1962; *Lightship*, 1963; *Ski Fever*, with Robert Joseph, 1967.

Television Plays: *13 Demon Street* series, 1959 (Sweden).

*

Theatrical Activities:
Director: **Films**—*Bride of the Gorilla*, 1951; *The Magnetic Monster*, 1953; *Curucu, Beast of the Amazon*, 1956; *Love Slaves of the Amazon*, 1957; *Ski Fever*, 1967.

* * *

As a novelist, screenwriter, and film director, Curt Siodmak had a long career, first in Germany and then in Hollywood, popularizing for the mass audience basic and extremely banal science-fiction motifs originated long before by other writers: an airfield floating in mid-ocean, the building of a trans-Atlantic tunnel or a spaceport, experiments with artificially induced telepathy or genetic manipulation all provide formulaic grist for some very melodramatic mills. Siodmak's protagonists in his novels and films are either Frankensteinian mad scientists in the grand pulp tradition or strong-willed and far-sighted entrepreneurial over-reachers in the Faustian/Ayn Rand mold. Indeed, perhaps the only redeeming feature of Siodmak's early German science-fiction work of the 1930's is that the films based on his novels (three versions of *F.P.1 Does Not Reply* and two versions of *Transatlantic Tunnel*) used some impressive special effects. Not even that much can be said for most of the movies based on his Hollywood screenplays in the 1940's, which were invariably low-budget programmers, that attempted to milk tried-and-true monster-movie formulas that had long been dried out.

Siodmak is best known, however, within both the science-fiction field and the mainstream of literary and cinematic popular culture, as the creator of *Donovan's Brain*, which has itself been adapted three times for the movies, with varying degrees of success: *The Lady and the Monster* (1947, with Erich von Stroheim), *Donovan's Brain* (1953, with Lew Ayres), and *The Brain* (1963, with Peter Van Eyck). In all of its manifestations, the story has held up durably and has retained to a certain extent its queasy fascination. The reclusive scientist-physician Patrick Cory extracts the still-living brain of the powerful industrialist Warren Horace Donovan after an airplane crash had mangled the tycoon's elderly body. Despite the stereotypical warnings of his devoted wife and an alcoholic colleague, Cory establishes telepathic contact with the disembodied brain, which, nurtured by chemicals, is growing daily in size and telepathic power. The brain quickly takes control of Cory's body, forcing it to wreak vengeance on Donovan's enemies. What gives Siodmak's novel its inherent power is not only its central theme of physical possession caused by unchecked and thus finally destructive scientific research, but also the first-person narration from Cory's panicky point of view. Unfortunately, the story eventually degenerates into unduly complicated histrionics detailing Donovan's desire to pay off an old debt by intruding on a murder investigation involving the heir of one of Donovan's early business partners. By plunging Donovan and his hapless, progressively will-less surrogate into such a desultory and pointless subplot so late in the proceedings, Siodmak conveniently sidesteps the more somber medical, legal, and metaphysical implications of his initially intriguing concept.

Siodmak's later novels continued his career-long tendency to graft mainstream genres onto science-fiction settings. Thus, *City in the Sky* is a kind of *Grand Hotel* in orbit, mixed in with political intrigue and prison-escape heroics, while *Skyport* is like a space-age *Fountainhead.* A bit more interesting to the genuine science-fiction enthusiast are *The Third Ear*, which concerns the chemically created cultivation of ESP abilities, and *Hauser's Memory*, Siodmak's belated sequel to *Donovan's Brain*, with the intrepid Cory again blazing new scientific trails, transplanting a German chemist's overactive, revenge-minded RNA onto another ill-fated human guinea pig. Despite the pseudo-scientific trappings, both books are relatively straightforward espionage thrillers, demonstrating again that Siodmak's talents lie in welding worn-out science-fiction themes with other conventional, pop-cultural formulas.

—Kenneth Jurkiewicz

---

**SKY, Kathleen.** American. Born in Alhambra, California, 5 August 1943. Married Stephen Goldin, *q.v.*, in 1972 (divorced 1982). Children's barber, Bullock's Department Store, Pasadena, California, 1964–71; volunteer worker for the Humane Society, Pasadena, 1972; film extra. Since 1968, freelance writer. Agent: Joseph Elder Agency, P.O. Box 298, Warwick, New York 10990, U.S.A.

SCIENCE-FICTION PUBLICATIONS

Novels

*Birthright*. Toronto, Laser, 1975.
*Ice Prison*. Toronto, Laser, 1976.
*Vulcan!* New York, Bantam, 1978; London, Corgi, 1984.
*Death's Angel*. New York, Bantam, 1980.
*Witchdame*. New York, Berkley, 1985.

Uncollected Short Stories

"One Ordinary Day, with Box," in *Generation*, edited by David Gerrold and Stephen Goldin. New York, Dell, 1972.
"Lament of the Keeku Bird," in *The Alien Condition*, edited by Stephen Goldin. New York, Ballantine, 1973.
"Door to Malequar," in *Vertex* (Los Angeles), June 1975.
"A Daisychain for Pav," in *Odyssey* (New York), Summer 1976.
"Motherbreast," in *Cassandra Rising*, edited by Alice Laurance. New York, Doubleday, 1978.

"Painting the Roses Red," with Stephen Goldin, in *Science Fiction Times*, May 1980.

"The Devil Behind the Leaves," with Stephen Goldin, in *Fantasy Book* (Pasadena, California), October 1981.

OTHER PUBLICATIONS

Other

*The Business of Being a Writer*, with Stephen Goldin. New York, Harper, 1982.

*

Kathleen Sky comments:

It's difficult to analyze my fiction on the basis of past output because I know that my best work still lies ahead of me. Nevertheless, I recognize some themes in my books that will continue to appear. Just as blacks and Chicanos need strong positive images in their literature, I feel that the increasing number of women who read science fiction will require strong female characters to give them a positive self-image. It's easy to write a strong woman as a bitch, but much harder to write her as a loving, caring person (the "mother" aspect). Nevertheless, I try. In my forthcoming fantasy series, *The Witchdame Trilogy*, I have a strong character, Princess Elizabeth, who eventually becomes the queen of her realm and consequently a strong mother figure. In my novel *Shalom*, there are several strong women, most notably Judith, who eventually becomes a mother figure to her entire planet.

In writing about strong women, I find I need strong male characters to match them. It's no use liberating only one gender; men and women need to share their strengths equally. I feel that everyone is psychologically bisexual—that is, each human being has both masculine and feminine components to his personality. Only by bringing out *all* the strengths, masculine and feminine, can people truly become liberated from the stereotypes of the past. Because of this, I reject the role of the traditional feminist. Too many of the radical women writers tend to view men as an enemy to be overcome. In doing so, they are doing more harm to themselves than to their supposed enemies. I view men and women as but two halves of a single race. If one side loses, we all do; only by having both sides succeed can humanity be the victor.

* * *

Kathleen Sky is good at understanding a special variety of emotion: the grief of a creature coerced by its own nature into a task both valuable to others and costly to itself. One could say it is a woman's grief—Sky makes it into the grief of a tired little man, or a green alien, or a Vulcan. Sky has the visibly struggling competence of a new writer, but also a depth of emotional perception which is already formed. The plight of her characters is both cleverly illustrated and deeply felt.

"One Ordinary Day, with Box," her first story, functions with the simplicity of a parable. A little old man travels from place to place with a big black box. To those who reach inside, the box gives what they need, but not what they want. The disparity between imagined want and true need runs like a moral lesson through this quick, effective tale, but the emotional focus is finally on the old man himself. Scorned by the people that the box has frustrated and insulted, he goes off alone, and at last reaches into the box himself. He is given another box. His need, the box implies, is to continue his thankless task, his unappreciated giving.

Sometimes the task is change itself. In the somewhat overwritten but surprisingly moving "Lament of the Keeku Bird," Sky details the painful process of an alien initiation ritual, a menopause by violence in which a female creature makes a ceremonial journey that wears off her sexuality. The writing task is difficult—Sky narrates in the first person present from the alien's point of view and thus must develop landscape, species, and personality all indirectly. The development is coherent and interesting; Sky manages not only to establish a believable extraterrestrial world but also to show the beginnings of personal change, the openings of thought in what was at first a thoughtless breeding animal. The mingling of grief and triumph at the end is consistent with Sky's awareness of the inner price to be paid for anything of value.

This awareness is carried into Sky's Star Trek novel, *Vulcan!* Enough young science-fiction writers have written Star Trek continuations that it may become a set exercise for entering the craft. As such it provides a useful device of classification: *Trek to Madworld* by Sky's former husband, Stephen Goldin, is whimsical and extravagant; Sky's version has a deeper concentration on personality, and is in effect a serious consideration of what it means to be a Vulcan or to love one. The fan's potential delight in this can be easily imagined, and Sky does well in capturing Spock's angular appeal, his passionless speech, his promise of intensities withheld. Her portrayal of Katalya Tremain, the scientist who tries to hate Vulcans in order to avoid loving them, is less consistent, but the book as a whole works. Sky transmits both Spock's calm appreciation of the powers he has and his regret at his limitations. He helps Tremain to change but cannot change himself. His last request to the women is that she help him to rediscover his childhood imagination and thus find a way out of his box of logical competence.

Sky's style is as yet unremarkable; she chooses the nearest words to communicate what she envisions—the view from inside a sensitive mind looking at a landscape both alien and alienating, where endurance is a value and change expensive. This view is one that lends itself to science fiction, to making new landscapes and locating characters in them emotionally as well as sensually. Sky's work is not an investigation into science or ideas, but into experience, and she succeeds, even in her career's outset, in making the experiences both strange and believable.

—Karen G. Way

---

**SLADEK, John (Thomas).** Also writes as Thom Demijohn; Cassandra Knye; Richard A. Tilms; James Vogh. American. Born in Waverly, Iowa, 15 December 1937. Educated at College of St. Thomas, St. Paul, Minnesota, 1955–56; University of Minnesota, Minneapolis, 1956–59. Married in 1970, one child. Engineering assistant, University of Minnesota, 1959–61; technical writer, Technical Publications Inc., St. Louis Park, Minnesota, 1961–62; switchman, Great Northern Railway, Minneapolis, 1962–63; draftsman, New York, 1964–65. Editor, with Pamela A. Zoline, *Ronald Reagan: The Magazine of Poetry*, London, 1968. Recipient: British Science Fiction Association award, 1984. Agent: Richard Curtis Associates, 171 East 74th Street, New York, New York 10021, U.S.A.; or, A.P. Watt Ltd., 10 John Street, London WC1N 2DR, England.

SCIENCE-FICTION PUBLICATIONS

Novels (series: Roderick)

*The Reproductive System.* London, Gollancz, 1968; New York, Avon, 1974; as *Mechanism*, New York, Ace, 1969.
*The Müller-Fokker Effect.* London, Hutchinson, 1970; New York, Morrow, 1971.
*Roderick; or, The Education of a Young Machine.* London, Granada, 1980; abridged edition, New York, Pocket Books, 1982.
*Roderick at Random; or, Further Education of a Young Machine.* London, Granada, 1983; New York, Carroll and Graf, 1988.
*Tik-Tok.* London, Gollancz, 1983.

Short Stories

*The Steam-Driven Boy and Other Strangers.* London, Panther, 1973.
*Keep the Giraffe Burning.* London, Panther, 1977.
*The Best of John Sladek.* New York, Pocket Books, 1981.
*Alien Accounts.* London, Panther, 1982.
*The Lunatics of Terra.* London, Gollancz, 1984.

OTHER PUBLICATIONS

Novels

*The House That Fear Built* (as Cassandra Knye, with Thomas M. Disch). New York, Paperback Library, 1966.
*The Castle and the Key* (as Cassandra Knye). New York, Paperback Library, 1967.
*Black Alice* (as Thom Demijohn, with Thomas M. Disch). New York, Doubleday, 1968; London, W.H. Allen, 1969.
*Black Aura.* London, Cape, 1974; New York, Walker, 1979.
*Invisible Green.* London, Gollancz, 1977; New York, Walker, 1979.
*Red Noise.* New Castle, Virginia, Cheap Street, 1982.
*The Book of Clues.* London, Corgi, 1984.
*Bugs.* London, Macmillan, 1989.
*Blood and Gingerbread.* New Castle, Virginia, Cheap Street, 1990.

Other

*The New Apocrypha: A Guide to Strange Science and Occult Beliefs.* London, Hart Davis MacGibbon, 1973; New York, Stein and Day, 1974.
*Arachne Rising: The Thirteenth Sign of the Zodiac* (as James Vogh). London, Hart Davis MacGibbon, 1977.
*The Cosmic Factor* (as James Vogh). London, Hart Davis MacGibbon, 1978.
*Judgement of Jupiter* (as Richard A. Tilms). London, New English Library, 1980.
*Using XyWrite II.* Berkeley, California, Osborne McGraw Hill, 1987.

*

Manuscript Collection: Texas A & M University, College Station.

John Sladek comments:

Most of my novels and short stories are set in the near future, in a recognizable America in which technology has either solved all of our problems or failed to solve any of them, or something else entirely has happened. Something else entirely is always happening in science fiction, I understand. My work is usually called satire or black humor, but it also reflects my preoccupation with certain themes.

I am endlessly fascinated by machines which can mimic or displace human beings. So a number of my characters are robots (such as "The Steam-Driven Boy") or computers or cyborgs, or selfreplicating machines (as in *Mechanism*). This theme informs *Roderick; or, The Education of a Young Machine*, first of a two-part novel which attempts to cover the entire "life" history of a robot learning machine, and efforts to assimilate him into human society.

A parallel concern is with dehumanizing processes—ways in which governments and other institutions, mistakenly modelled on machines, attempt to reduce their citizens or members to mechanical components. This is the argument of three novellas, "Masterson and the Clerks," "The Communicants," and "The Great Wall of Mexico," and of at least a dozen short stories, and it creeps into the novels, too. It seems almost as though machines, evolving rapidly towards a kind of mimetic humanity, are meeting humans on the way down.

People do of course escape the process of robotization, and one escape route is madness, another recurring theme. Most of the stories in *Keep the Giraffe Burning* seem to deal with mad people (as well as bad, sad, and silly people) and how they succeed at their madness. As the title indicates, these stories are steeped in Surrealism; they are meant to blur the border between dream and reality.

That border is blurred by science fiction all the time. Science fiction, it seems to me, constitutes the right brain hemisphere of contemporary fiction (the dreaming part). My work, if it isn't buried in the hypothalamus or the hippocampus or something, is probably somewhere near the lobotomy scars.

* * *

John Sladek ranks high among the relatively small number of authors who use science fiction as a vehicle for satire. Sladek's writing defies easy classification, inviting comparisons not only with other science-fiction authors but also with writers of traditional fiction. In the field of science fiction, his early work was associated with the British New Wave, and his novels have often been likened to those of Kurt Vonnegut, Jr. But Sladek himself uses allusion and direct quotes to link his fiction with major British authors such as Samuel Butler and Tobias Smollett. It would perhaps be most accurate (and complimentary) to compare his best fiction with the mordant satires of American life written by Nathanael West.

Sladek published his first science-fiction story, appropriately enough, in Harlan Ellison's provocative anthology *Dangerous Visions* (1967). "The Happy Breed" introduces a theme that recurs throughout Sladek's subsequent writing: the folly of trusting technology to create Utopia. His first novel, *The Reproductive System* (published in the United States as *Mechanism*), explores the related theme of technology run amuck. It is a comic-satiric fusion of Mary Shelley's *Frankenstein* and Jack Williamson's "With Folded Hands." At the same time, the writing reflects a conscious debt to Butler's satiric Utopian novel *Erewhon.* In Sladek's novel, a failing industry, acting on the correct belief that the government will support "a project that is utterly, hopelessly useless," develops a machine that reproduces itself. The rest of the novel recounts the disasters that result when the machine begins growing out of control and threatens to destroy civilization. The story reaches an apparently happy ending when the machine is brought under control and seems destined to transform earth into a Utopia, but the same warning expressed in "The Happy Breed" lurks beneath the surface of *The Reproductive System.* Sladek's satire works on a number of levels, for the "self-reproducing machine" at the heart of the tale suggests a wide range of human inventions and institutions that are created and grow larger to no useful purpose.

*The Müller-Fokker Effect,* Sladek's second science-fiction novel, is not only his funniest but also his most stylistically innovative work. The narrative proceeds as a series of comic events precipitated when a rich businessman instigates the kidnapping of the father of a family that he has been secretly observing. The kidnapped man's personality is subsequently recorded and transferred onto computer tapes. The plot revolves around the search for these tapes, which have been accidentally sold as army surplus. The novel paints a dark picture of an America dehumanized by the intertwined goals of profit and personal happiness. Sladek's specific targets include the military mind, popular journalists, evangelists, and Big Business. But above all, the novel satirizes the power of television in modern society, particularly its role in creating the delusion of a country without flaws or problems. The amoral businessman at the center of the story operates on the assumption that "reality was televised . . . and the advantage of televised reality was that one could tune out any ghosts of unpleasantness." This capacity not just of one man but rather of a whole society for self-deception serves as the basic theme of *The Müller-Fokker Effect.*

Sladek's writing is more consciously literary than much science fiction. The Roderick books represent an ambitious attempt to wed the conventions of science fiction to those of the mainstream picaresque novel. Early in his career, Sladek wrote several short stories that deal with robots seeking ways to understand and become part of human society (collected in *The Steam-Driven Boy and Other Strangers*). He develops this theme in *Roderick at Random; or, Further Education of a Young Machine,* which present the adventures of an intelligent robot in an absurd America. Television plays a major role also in these novels, providing Roderick his image of America as it provides America with an image of itself.

The titles contain unmistakable allusions to Smollett's *The Adventures of Roderick Random* (1748). The reference is particularly apt, since Smollett is generally regarded as the father of the English satirical novel. Smollett adapted the conventions of the picaresque novel for satiric purpose, and his *Roderick Random* combines high adventure with a fierce attack on the dreadful conditions existing at that time in the British navy. But Sladek's two novels, in addition to satirizing American values, also contain numerous references to other science fiction, especially the robot novels of Isaac Asimov. The *Roderick* novels implicitly parody the well-known "three laws of robotics" on which Asimov based many of his stories. The two *Roderick* novels, much like their 18th-century model, proceed as sequences of comic episodes. Specific episodes are often hilarious; however, the satire, perhaps because it ranges more widely and has a less clear focus, is less effective than that found in Sladek's first two novels.

Despite its comic and satiric power, Sladek's fiction has never achieved broad popularity among American readers of science fiction. Perhaps three factors have contributed to this relative obscurity. First, his novels tend toward a pessimistic assessment of human nature and American culture. Second, appreciation of his artfulness requires knowledge of both science fiction and a broad spectrum of mainstream literature. *Roderick,* for example, begins with two quotes: one from *Erewhon* and the other from the play *Dinner at Eight.* This linkage of high and low culture typifies Sladek's fiction. Finally, the recurring object of Sladek's wit has been the very fascination with technology that provides the inspiration for the genre of science fiction.

—Dennis M. Kratz

---

**SLOANE, William M(illigan, III).** Also wrote as William Milligan. American. Born in Plymouth, Massachusetts, 15 August 1906. Educated at Hill School, graduated, 1925; Princeton University, New Jersey, A.B. 1929 (Phi Beta Kappa). Married Julie Hawkins in 1930; one son and two daughters. Publisher: in play department, 1929–31, and editorial department, 1931, Longmans Green and Company; manager, Fitzgerald Publishing Company, 1932–37; associate editor, Farrar and Rinehart, 1937–38; manager of the trade department, 1939–46, and vice-president, 1944–46, Henry Holt and Company; president, William Sloane Associates, 1946–52; editorial director, Funk and Wagnalls Company and Wilfred Funk Inc., 1952–55; director, Rutgers University Press, 1955–74. Director, Council on Books in Wartime; chairman of the Editorial Committee, Armed Services Editions, 1943–44; staff member, Bread Loaf Writers Conference, 1946–72. President, Association of American University Presses, 1969–70. *Died 25 September 1974.*

### Science-Fiction Publications

#### Novels

*To Walk the Night.* New York, Farrar and Rinehart, 1937; London, Barker, 1938; revised edition, New York, Dodd Mead, 1954.

*The Edge of Running Water.* New York, Farrar and Rinehart, 1939; London, Methuen, 1940; as *The Unquiet Corpse,* New York, Dell, 1946.

*The Rim of Morning* (includes *To Walk the Night* and *The Edge of Running Water*). New York, Dodd Mead, 1964.

#### Uncollected Short Story

"Let Nothing You Dismay," in *Stories for Tomorrow,* edited by William M. Sloane. New York, Funk and Wagnalls, 1954; London, Eyre and Spottiswoode, 1955.

### Other Publications

#### Plays

*Back Home: A Ghost Play.* New York, Longman, 1931.

*Runner in the Snow: A Play of the Supernatural,* adaptation of the story "I Saw a Woman Turn Into a Wolf" by W.B. Seabrook. Boston, Baker, 1931.

*Digging Up the Dirt,* adaptation of a play by Bert J. Norton. New York, Longman, 1931.

*Crystal Clear.* New York, Longman, 1932.

*Ballots for Bill: A Light-Hearted Comedy of Politics,* with William Ellis Jones. New York, Fitzgerald, 1933.

*The Silence of God: A Play for Christmas.* Boston, Baker, 1933.

*Art for Art's Sake.* Boston, Baker, 1934.

*The Invisible Clue* (as William Milligan). New York, Fitzgerald, 1934.

*Gold Stars for Glory.* Boston, Baker, 1935.

Other

Editor, *Space, Space, Space*. New York, Watts, 1953.
Editor, *Stories for Tomorrow*. New York, Funk and Wagnalls, 1954; London, Eyre and Spottiswoode, 1955.

* * *

William M. Sloane had an extremely brief career as a science-fiction writer, completing two novels and a single short story, but those two novels have probably won him a permanent place in the history of the genre. He blended science and horror with consummate skill, and his calm, smooth-paced novels are more successful at developing suspense and tension than most of the lurid thrillers that reach the bestseller lists.

*To Walk the Night* uses a plot device so standard, so familiar, that it has long since become a cliché avoided even by the less inventive film makers, but in the hands of a writer with Sloane's talent, it is transformed into an entirely new vehicle. Two young men make a surprise visit to an old friend, and arrive just in time to see his body mysteriously incinerated as if from within. Although they are unable to explain the peculiar nature of his death, they are freed by the authorities. But one of them has become infatuated with the unexpected widow of his late friend. The perceptive reader will realize fairly soon that the mysterious death resulted from the scientist's researches into the nature of reality. Sloane leaves myriad hints of other oddities as well, the widow's awkwardness in familiar human situations, the disappearance of a young girl with virtually no intelligence, the mystery of yet another death, this time clearly suicide. Despite the fact that the reader has a clear idea what comprises the general nature of the mystery, the details provide the true suspense, and the climactic confrontation is one of the most effective scenes in the genre.

*The Edge of Running Water* broke no new ground either, and moves even further toward the supernatural, while still retaining the scientific rationale of its mystery. Although the characters are not as well drawn in this story of a man convinced he can develop a machine that will enable him to communicate with the dead, the element of suspense is just as expertly handled. There is little overt action, even though one character is eventually killed and another destroyed, propelled into another universe, but the reader's attention is unlikely to waver despite this fact.

Both novels have been published as mysteries, which they are, as horror stories, which they are, and science fiction, which they also are. Sloane's sole foray into more conventional science fiction, "Let Nothing You Dismay," is singularly unremarkable, a pedestrian examination of human refugees adjusting to a new world after the death of Earth. He was at his best at greater length, using a familiar setting and coloring it with a series of hints of something totally unfamiliar. His style was highly advanced for his time, and both novels are free of archaic anomalies and outdated prose. It seems clear that had Sloane chosen to pursue his career as a genre writer, he would have become one of the dominant forces within it.

—Don D'Ammassa

---

**SLONCZEWSKI, Joan (Lyn).** American. Born in Hyde Park, New York, 14 August 1956. Educated at Bryn Mawr College, Pennsylvania, A.B. 1977; Yale University, New Haven, Connecticut, Ph.D. in molecular biophysics and biochemistry. Married Michael J. Barich in 1977; two sons. Postdoctoral fellow, University of Pennsylvania, Philadelphia, 1982–84; Visiting Professor, Princeton University, 1990–91. Associate Professor, Kenyon College, Gambier, Ohio, since 1984. Recipient: John Campbell award, 1986. Agent: Valerie Smith, Route 44–55, R.R. Box 160, Modena, New York 12548. Address: Biology Department, Kenyon College, Gambier, Ohio 43022, U.S.A.

Science-Fiction Publications

Novels

*Still Forms on Foxfield*. New York, Ballantine, 1980.
*A Door into Ocean*. New York, Arbor House, 1986; London, Women's Press, 1987.
*The Wall Around Eden*. New York, Morrow, 1989; London, Women's Press, 1991.

*

Joan Slonczewski comments:

My work addresses the question: What does it mean to be a human being? What do we seek and desire most? Do women and men, and individuals of varied genetic and cultural backgrounds, share the same quest; or do they differ? The great apes share 99% of our genes; are they human, too? Is all life sacred, even that of rock-eating bacteria? When we meet our cousins from the stars, are they sacred, too? Anyone who asks these questions will find a friend in my books.

* * *

Although not a prolific writer, Joan Slonczewski has already made her mark on science fiction with three novels. The initially modest success of *Still Forms on Foxfield* was bolstered by the critical appreciation of *A Door Into Ocean*, which received the John W. Campbell Memorial award for best novel of 1986. *The Wall Around Eden* is a shorter work that appeals to younger audiences.

Slonczewski's fiction is characterized by details of daily life infused with Quaker principles, practices, and belief structures, by a deep commitment to pacifist philosophy, and a questioning of the contemporary cultural assumption that violence is necessary for creativity and progress. This latter theme recurs in all three novels; protagonists who are members of Quaker communities or pacifist societies struggle against a virtual expectation that non-violence leads to static, and therefore, undesirable, cultures. In *Still Forms on Foxfield*, Allison struggles at length with the violence of the United Nations Interplanetary culture, which is explained to her as a necessary part of all successful human cultures. Her rejection of this equation becomes the catalyst for rejection of UNI.

Biological speculation is added to the social experimentation in Slonczewski's novels. Her background includes a degree from Bryn Mawr, studies in biology and chemistry, graduate work at Yale in molecular biophysics, and continuing work in microbiology as an Assistant Professor in Biology at Kenyon College. Her career obviously provides material for the variations in human and alien biologies and ecologies so important to her fiction. All of her works relate human and alien communities. The reader, along with the characters, is misdirected into seeing aliens as hostile, but they are shown in mostly positive contexts as reader and characters become simultaneously familiar with them. Attention to both character and setting round out these scientific and philosophic speculations as her characters live their dilemmas on interpersonal and social levels.

*Still Forms on Foxfield* takes place on the planet Foxfield, named after the founder of Quakerism, George Fox. The narrative details the struggles of Allison and a human-alien symbiotic culture to resist totalitarian initiatives from off-planet humans. Foxfield has been isolated for at least a century by the breakdown of a disintegrating intergalactic culture from which the original colonists were fleeing. This narrative begins with re-establishment of contact between Foxfielders and the United Nations Intergalactic, a longed-for contact that is fraught with difficulties. Foxfielders have survived on a planet with a greater gravitational pull and few of the trace elements needed to keep them healthy by establishing a tolerant, beneficial symbiosis with the aliens they originally found on the planet. As they confront the re-establishment of relations with the UNI, the importance of consensus decision-making, as opposed to the majority-rule of UNI, is seminal. It seems that without the persistence of an early Foxfielder, these aliens, the Commensuals, would never have been recognized as sentient. They look like plants and talk with scent and gesture. Having sustained a viable symbiosis, the Foxfielders must decide whether to abandon it and the Commensuals for the questionable advantages of UNI, with its violence and destructive impulses.

In *A Door into Ocean*, pacificism is also a more powerful force than militarism in the hands of the Shorans. This is by far the most complex of Slonczewski's novels. It contrasts a militaristic, human culture with a pacifistic, alien one. Shora and Valedon both orbit the same sun, but Valedon, under the rule of the intergalactic, totalitarian Patriarch, has the traditional hierarchic structure, two sexes and stereotypical sex roles. Shorans, on the other hand, are all genetically but not functionally female. They reproduce parthenogenically only with the help of doctors as, even if there were male Shorans, the females have lost the ability to "be seeded" by males. They also have no established hierarchies and no central government; the groups inhabit islands of roots that float atop a water-covered planet in which they have established an ecological stability. *A Door into Ocean* is remarkable for several reasons, including the careful character development and multiple viewpoints, whereas alien cultures are usually introduced by one human mediator-character in science-fiction novels. Slonczewski here uses an adult, human, ruling-class female from Valedon whose fiancee will eventually head the military expedition that is supposed to subdue the Shorans. Berenice's loyalties are initially mixed as she struggles between the privileges of primacy in a hierarchical culture and the disadvantages of being female in a patriarchy.

*The Wall Around Eden* takes place on earth many decades after a nuclear holocaust has destroyed most life on earth. Any remaining humans have survived only because they were forcibly placed in protective domes by more powerful aliens. The work is tantalizing for its misdirection. Most humans believe that the aliens were responsible for the initial destruction and that they are lab animals, kept only for their research value. They believe that the periodic, colorful light-shows seen in the outside sky are the result of aliens attempting to destroy the ozone layer and that they have to fight the aliens in order to regain the earth and any freedom of movement. Some have even started revolutionary, violent movements against the aliens, though these have had very little success. It is only after another decade, as the protagonist, Isabel, grows to adulthood, that the aliens' benevolence is understood. They are in fact rebuilding the ozone layer and preserving as many humans as possible until the planet can again sustain human life.

Slonczewski has received little critical attention for her work, although several conference papers have included *A Door into Ocean* in their discussions of feminist SF. Perhaps this neglect is because she is creating new worlds with each book, thus far resisting the lure of the sequel that publishers find so attractive. Each of her novels is an entity in itself, and while readers might want her to explore a particular future or a particular world, the craft with which each individual work has been conceived more than compensates for the small number of works.

—Janice M. Bogstad

---

**SMITH, Clark Ashton.** American. Born 13 January 1893. Left school at 14. Married in 1954. Writer and artist: regular contributor to *Weird Tales* in the early 1930's; ceased writing in 1936. *Died 14 August 1961.*

### Science-Fiction Publications

#### Short Stories

*The Immortals of Mercury.* New York, Stellar, 1932.
*Tales of Science and Sorcery.* Sauk City, Wisconsin, Arkham House, 1964; London, Panther, 1976.
*Other Dimensions.* Sauk City, Wisconsin, Arkham House, 1970; London, Panther, 2 vols., 1977.

### Other Publications

#### Short Stories

*The Double Shadow and Other Fantasies.* Privately printed, 1933.
*The White Sybil.* Everett, Pennsylvania, Fantasy, 1935(?).
*Out of Space and Time* (includes verse). Sauk City, Wisconsin, Arkham House, 1942; London, Spearman, 1971.
*Lost Worlds.* Sauk City, Wisconsin, Arkham House, 1944; London, Spearman, 1971.
*Genius Loci.* Sauk City, Wisconsin, Arkham House, 1948; London, Spearman, 1972.
*The Abominations of Yondo.* Sauk City, Wisconsin, Arkham House, 1960; London, Spearman, 1972.
*Zothique, Hyperborea, Xiccarph, Poseidonis* (selections), edited by Lin Carter. New York, Ballantine, 4 vols., 1970–73.
*The Mortuary.* Glendale, California, Squires, 1971.
*Prince Alcouz and the Magician.* Glendale, California, Squires, 1977.
*The City of the Singing Flame*, edited by Donald Sidney-Fryer. New York, Pocket Books, 1981.
*The Monster of the Prophecy*, edited by Donald Sidney-Fryer. New York, Pocket Books, 1983.
*A Rendezvous in Averoigne: Best Fantastic Tales of Clark Ashton Smith.* Sauk City, Wisconsin, 1988.

#### Verse

*The Star-Treader and Other Poems.* San Francisco, Robertson, 1912.
*Odes and Sonnets.* San Francisco, Book Club of California, 1918.
*Ebony and Crystal: Poems in Verse and Prose.* Privately printed, 1923.
*Sandalwood.* Privately printed, 1925.

*Nero and Other Poems.* Lakeport, California, Futile Press, 1937.
*The Dark Chateau and Other Poems.* Sauk City, Wisconsin, Arkham House, 1951.
*Spells and Philtres.* Sauk City, Wisconsin, Arkham House, 1958.
*Poems in Prose.* Sauk City, Wisconsin, Arkham House, 1964.
*Grotesques and Fantastiques.* Saddle River, New Jersey, Gerry de la Ree, 1973.
*Klarkash-ton and Monstro Lieriv*, with Virgil Finlay. Saddle River, New Jersey, Gerry de la Ree, 1974.
*Fugitive Poems.* Privately printed, 4 vols., 1974–75.
*Nostalgia of the Unknown: The Complete Prose Poetry*, edited by Marc and Susan Michaud. West Warwick, Rhode Island, Necronomicon Press, 1988.

Other

*Planets and Dimensions: Collected Essays*, edited by Charles K. Wolfe. Baltimore, Mirage Press, 1973.
*The Black Book of Clark Ashton Smith.* Sauk City, Wisconsin, Arkham House, 1979.
*Clark Ashton Smith: Letters to H.P. Lovecraft*, edited by Steve Behrends. West Warwick, Rhode Island, Necronomicon Press, 1987.
*The Dweller in the Gulf*, edited by Steve Behrends. West Warwick, Rhode Island, Necronomicon Press, 1987.
*Mother of Toads.* West Warwick, Rhode Island, Necronomicon Press, 1987.
*The Vaults of Yoh-Vombis*, edited by Steve Behrends. West Warwick, Rhode Island, Necronomicon Press, 1988.
*Strange Shadows: The Uncollected Fiction and Essays of Clark Ashton Smith*, edited by Steve Behrends, Donald Sidney-Fryer, and Rah Hoffman. New York, and London, Greenwood, 1989.
*The Hashish-Eater; or, The Apocalypse of Evil.* West Warwick, Rhode Island, Necronomicon Press, 1989.
*The Devil's Notebook: Collected Epigrams and Pensées of Clark Ashton Smith*, edited by Don Herron. San Bernardino, California, Borgo Press, 1990.

*

Bibliography: *The Tales of Clark Ashton Smith: A Bibliography* by G.L. Cockcroft, Melling, New Zealand, Cockcroft, 1952; *Emperor of Dreams: A Clark Ashton Smith Bibliography* by Donald Sidney-Fryer and others, West Kingston, Rhode Island, Grant, 1978.

Critical Studies: *In Memoriam Clark Ashton Smith* edited by Jack L. Chalker, Baltimore, Anthem, 1963; *The Last of the Great Romantic Poets* by Donald Sidney-Fryer, Albuquerque, Silver Scarab Press, 1973; *The Fantastic Art of Clark Ashton Smith* by Dennis Rickard, Baltimore, Mirage Press, 1973.

* * *

Clark Ashton Smith was a contributor to the early science-fiction and fantasy pulp magazines whose output, despite its unevenness, became a seminal influence on modern science fiction. Jack Vance, Harlan Ellison, Theodore Sturgeon, Fritz Leiber, H.P. Lovecraft, Robert E. Howard, and Ray Bradbury, among others, were influenced by his work.

Smith's earliest short stories—he wrote no novels—are the primitive interplanetary narratives common in the pulp magazines. Of these, "Marooned in Andromeda" and "The Amazing Planet" are typical. They recount the adventures of the crew of the space ship *Alcoyne* on distant worlds, and are odysseys of perilous adventure distinguished only by Smith's exotic language and bizarre imagination.

Smith, also a poet, was concerned mainly with the poetry of death and the alien. His protagonists are decidedly unheroic, being either misfits or rogues who seek other worlds because they do not fit into their own. In "The Monster of the Prophecy," the suicidal poet Theophilus Alvor agreeably becomes the instrument through which the Antarean wizard Vizaphmal assumes control of his world. This lack of virtue does not prevent Alvor from finding true love in the arms of an Antarean woman. Similarly, the renegade and thief Datu Buang lives out his life in peace after assassinating an evil ruler with the aid of his consort in "As It Is Written."

The search for a better reality is the predominant theme in Smith. In his haunting classic, "The City of the Singing Flame," the author Giles Angarth discovers the gateway to another dimension where the Singing Flame lures the unwary into its fires. Angarth finds himself finally drawn to the flame and discovers it is the entrance to still another, better, reality beyond.

Those stories set wholly on other worlds, in which he gives his poetic vision free rein, are considered Smith's best. Among these are the sardonic tales of the world of Xiccarph and those set on the continent of Zothique in the last days of Earth. In "The Maze of Maal Dweb," the hunter Tiglari seeks his kidnapped lover in the stronghold of Xiccarph's tyrant, Maal Dweb, but falls victim to the tyrant's powers. Maal Dweb, on the other hand, is the protagonist of "The Flower-Women." It is a peculiarity of Smith's fiction that the amoral flourish and the good become the victims of ironic fates. Like Tiglari, the hero of "The Demon of the Flower" ultimately fails to rescue the woman he loves from the plant ruler of his world. The tales of Zothique, although set in Earth's distant future, are closer to fantasy. In these, Smith's macabre poetic vision is at its highest. "Xeethra" is a poignant story of a goatherd who partakes of strange fruit and imagines himself the ruler of a distant land. He goes in search of that land, only to find it in ruins. "The Last Hieroglyph" is an ironic tale of an astrologer, Nushain, who reads in the stars that he must go on a journey which will fulfill his destiny. At the voyage's end, he meets his end. "The Weaver in the Vault" relates the weird doom of two individuals who desecrate a tomb. Hope and futility are expertly balanced in "The Isle of the Torturers."

Despite the weird trappings of his stories, Smith's work cannot be rightfully labeled as horror stories. He was a fatalist who delighted in spinning phantasms, not terror. With rare exceptions ("Master of the Asteroid" and "The Dweller in the Gulf"), his work is too remote from reality to evoke a convincing mood of horror and his imaginings thus fascinate instead of terrify. The power of Smith's writing, and the reason for its widespread influence, lay in the fact that Smith shared with many of his protagonists a yearning for a reality *truer* than the one he knew, and he discovered a language that enabled him to express his unique vision.

—Will Murray

---

**SMITH, Cordwainer.** Pseudonym for Paul Myron Anthony Linebarger; also wrote as Felix C. Forrest; Carmichael Smith. American. Born in Milwaukee, Wisconsin, 11 July 1913. Educated at schools in Honolulu, Shanghai, and Baden Baden; University of Nanking, 1930; North China Union Language School,

1931; George Washington University, Washington, D.C., A. B. 1933 (Phi Beta Kappa); Oxford University, 1933; American University, Washington, D.C., 1934; University of Chicago, 1935; Johns Hopkins University, Baltimore, M.A. 1935; Ph.D. 1936; University of Michigan, Ann Arbor, 1937, 1939; Washington School of Psychiatry, certificate in psychiatry 1955; Universidad Interamericana, 1959–60. Served in the United States Army Intelligence Service, 1942–66: helped found Office of War Information, served in Chungking, 1942–46, and as consultant to British Forces in Malaya, 1950, and to 8th Army, Korea, 1950–52: Lieutenant Colonel. Married 1) Margaret Snow in 1936 (divorced 1949), two daughters; 2) Genevieve Cecilia Collins in 1950. Instructor, Harvard University, Cambridge, Massachusetts, 1936–37; Instructor, then Associate Professor, Duke University, Durham, North Carolina, 1937–46; Professor of Asiatic Politics, Johns Hopkins University School of Advanced International Studies, Washington, D.C., 1946–66. Visiting Professor, University of Pennsylvania, Philadelphia, 1955–56, and Australian National University, Canberra, 1957. President, American Peace Society. *Died 6 August 1966.*

SCIENCE FICTION PUBLICATIONS

Novels (series: Instrumentality in all books)

*The Planet Buyer.* New York, Pyramid, 1964.
*The Underpeople.* New York, Pyramid, 1968.
*Norstrilia* (omnibus). New York, Ballantine, 1975; London, Gollancz, 1988.
*The Rediscovery of Man.* London, Gollancz, 1988.

Short Stories (series: Instrumentality)

*You Will Never Be the Same.* Evanston, Illinois, Regency, 1963.
*Space Lords* (Instrumentality). New York, Pyramid, 1965; London, Sidgwick and Jackson, 1969.
*Quest of the Three Worlds.* New York, Ace, 1966; London, Gollancz, 1989.
*Under Old Earth and Other Explorations.* London, Panther, 1970.
*Stardreamer.* New York, Beagle, 1971.
*The Best of Cordwainer Smith,* edited by J.J. Pierce. New York, Doubleday, 1975.
*The Instrumentality of Mankind.* New York, Ballantine, 1979; London, Gollancz, 1988.

OTHER PUBLICATIONS

Novels

*Ria* (as Felix C. Forrest). New York, Duell, 1947.
*Carola* (as Felix C. Forrest). New York, Duell, 1948.
*Atomsk* (as Carmichael Smith). New York, Duell, 1949.

Other as P.M.A. Linebarger

*The Political Doctrines of Sun Yat-Sen.* Baltimore, Johns Hopkins University Press, 1937.
*Government in Republican China.* New York, McGraw Hill, 1938.
*The China of Chiang Kai-shek.* Boston, World Peace Foundation, 1941.
*Psychological Warfare.* Washington, D.C., Infantry Journal Press, 1948; revised edition, Washington, D.C., Combat Forces Press, 1954.
*Far Eastern Governments and Politics,* with Djang Chu and Ardath W. Burks. New York, Van Nostrand, 1952.

Editor, *The Gospel of Chung Shan,* by Paul Linebarger. Privately printed, 1932.
Editor, *The Ocean Men,* by Paul Linebarger. Washington, D.C., Mid-Nation, 1937.

*

Critical Studies: *Exploring Cordwainer Smith* (includes bibliography) edited by Andrew Porter, New York, Algol Press, 1975; *Concordance to Cordwainer Smith* by Anthony Lewis, Jr., Cambridge, Massachusetts, NESFA Press, 1984.

* * *

Paul Linebarger, who wrote science fiction under the name Cordwainer Smith, certainly stands as one of the most unusual and imaginative writers of fantastic literature of this century. Though his total output of fiction is relatively small, Smith's reputation and influence have grown consistently since his death in 1966. Virtually his entire science fiction output was in print in book form by early 1979, and the theme that ties most of these stories together—a future galactic civilization called the Instrumentality of Mankind—has emerged as one of the most striking and detailed future history constructs in all of science fiction. His non-science-fiction novels *Ria* and *Carola* also reveal the strength of imagination, idiosyncratic style, and sensitivity to character that make his better-known work stand out.

Smith was a Christian, a romantic, and a shrewd political theorist who had written under his own name an internationally influential text on psychological warfare. All of these strains come together in his fiction, giving it a complexity and depth of meaning that are sometimes confusing to readers encountering one of his stories for the first time. The first of his mature stories to be published (his first science-fiction story, "War No. 81-Q," had appeared when he was only 15), "Scanners Live in Vain," appeared in 1950, and clearly implied a more detailed imaginary universe than the story itself explained. Set early in the history of the Instrumentality, the tale concerns a threat posed to the guild of "scanners"—humans mechanically restructured to survive in space—by the discovery of a new and safer means of space travel. In a characteristically bizarre Smith touch, the new method depends on lining the spaceships with oysters to insulate the passengers from harm. Clearly, this odd version of a technological breakthrough represented an event of historical importance to this future world, but the nature of that world itself remained unclear.

During the next decade and a half, Smith gradually filled in some of the gaps. Following a series of disastrous wars that nearly reduced Earth to barbarism, humanity gradually recovers its vitality, aided by a powerful family called the Vomacts, descended from the daughters of a Nazi scientist who were placed in suspended animation in orbit and who returned following the wars ("Mark Elf" and "The Queen of the Afternoon"). The Vomacts help give rise to the universal government called the Instrumentality, which initially explores space with the aid of scanners, briefly replaces these with the oyster-shell ships, and in turn replaces these with ships powered by massive photonic sails ("The Lady Who Sailed *The Soul,*" "Think Blue, Count Two"). Finally, a near-instantaneous form of space travel, called planoforming, is discovered ("The Colonel Came Back from the

Nothing-at-All," "The Burning of the Brain"), but planoforming ships are subject to attacks by hideous, incorporeal outer-space "dragons" and must be protected by telepathic technicians called pinlighters, sometimes assisted by telepathic cats ("The Game of Rat and Dragon"). As the Instrumentality grows increasingly powerful and decadent—offering humans near-immortality through a life-extending drug called stroon—its economy comes to depend on a slave class of converted animals called underpeople. Aided by a few heroic underpeople and the sympathetic Jestocost family, the underpeople finally attain civil rights ("The Dead Lady of Clown Town," "Under Old Earth," "The Ballad of Lost C'Mell"), and a renaissance of humanism, the Rediscovery of Man, set in ("Alpha Ralpha Boulevard," *Norstrilia*). In the far distant future, civilization finally seems to be achieving some kind of stability (*Quest of the Three Worlds*), but the actual conclusion of the history of the Instrumentality, if planned by Smith, was not completed during his lifetime.

Although there is an abundance of political and social satire in Smith's work—the Instrumentality is clearly not a simple utopia—what stands out most are the memorable characters of near-mythic proportions, the romantic legends he weaves, and the oddly nostalgic style, reminiscent of oral history or folktales, in which he writes. Smith has a unique ability to make a romance between a man and a cat convincing ("The Game of Rat and Dragon") or to make an unconsummated romance between a servant girl and a lord as powerful as a medieval legend ("The Ballad of Lost C'Mell"). Occasionally, he turns to actual legends for his source material; "The Dead Lady of Clown Town" is a retelling of the Joan of Arc legend, with Joan made into an underperson converted from a dog. In other cases, he turns to literary culture for his sources; "Drunkboat" is essentially a tour de force on themes from Arthur Rimbaud. "Golden the Ship Was—Oh! Oh! Oh!" is at once a satire on the bureaucracy of war and a retelling of the Trojan horse story—with the horse becoming a 90-million-mile-long decoy spaceship used to frighten an enemy while the second-level bureaucrats drop poisonous bombs. Other of his stories are supposedly based on Chinese narrative techniques, and occasionally he deliberately plays games with the reader, such as working anagrammatic references to the Kennedy-Oswald assassinations into *Quest of the Three Worlds.*

One wonders, at times, whether Smith's curious style and unusual way of structuring stories is due to his great sophistication or to his ingenuousness as a writer. *Norstrilia* does not stand up as well as do many of the short stories, partly because the narrative tends to ramble, partly because the style seems to grow self-conscious over such an extended narrative. But Smith's short fiction includes some of science fiction's finest stories, but demonstrates that an author need not abandon sensitive insights into love and ethics in order to create imaginary universes of great imagination.

—Gary K. Wolfe

---

**SMITH, Doc.** *See* **SMITH, E.E.**

---

**SMITH, E(dward) E(lmer)** ("Doc" Smith). American. Born in Sheboygan, Wisconsin, 1 May 1890. Educated at the University of Idaho, Moscow; George Washington University, Washington, D.C., Ph.D. in food chemistry 1919. Served in an explosives arsenal during World War II. Married Jeanne Craig MacDougall; one daughter and one son. Worked as ranch hand, lumberjack, silver miner, and surveyor, before becoming chemist, specializing in food mixes: manager of General Mix Division of J.W. Allen and Company, 1945–57. Recipient: First Fandom Hall of Fame award (as "Doc" Smith), 1964. Guest of Honor, 2nd World Science Fiction Convention, 1940. *Died 31 August 1965.*

### Science Fiction Publications

Novels (series: Lensman; Lord Tedric; Skylark)

*The Skylark of Space*, with Mrs. Lee Hawkins Garby. Providence, Rhode Island, Buffalo, 1946; revised edition, New York, Pyramid, 1958; London, Digit, 1959.
*Spacehounds of IPC.* Reading, Pennsylvania, Fantasy Press, 1947; London, Panther, 1974.
*Skylark Three.* Reading, Pennsylvania, Fantasy Press, 1948; London, Panther, 1974.
The History of Civilization (Lensman):
*Triplanetary.* Reading, Pennsylvania, Fantasy Press, 1948; London, Boardman, 1954.
*First Lensman.* Reading, Pennsylvania, Fantasy Press, 1950; London, Boardman, 1955.
*Galactic Patrol.* Reading, Pennsylvania, Fantasy Press, 1950; London, W.H. Allen, 1971.
*Gray Lensman.* Reading, Pennsylvania, Fantasy Press, 1951; London, W.H. Allen, 1971.
*Second Stage Lensman.* Reading, Pennsylvania, Fantasy Press, 1953; London, W.H. Allen, 1972.
*Children of the Lens.* Reading, Pennsylvania, Fantasy Press, 1954; London, W.H. Allen, 1972.
*Skylark of Valeron.* Reading, Pennsylvania, Fantasy Press, 1949.
*The Vortex Blaster* (Lensman). New York, Gnome Press, 1960; as *Masters of the Vortex*, New York, Pyramid, 1968; London, W.H. Allen, 1972.
*The Galaxy Primes.* New York, Ace, 1965; London, Panther, 1975.
*Subspace Explorers.* New York, Canaveral Press, 1965; London, Panther, 1975.
*Skylark DuQuesne.* New York, Pyramid, 1966; London, Panther, 1974.
*Masters of Space.* London, Futura, 1976.
*Lord Tedric*, with Gordon Eklund. New York, Baronet, 1978.
*Lord Tedric: Alien Worlds.* London, Wright, 1978.
*Space Pirates*, with Gordon Eklund. New York, Baronet, 1979; as *Lord Tedric: The Space Pirates*, London, Wingate, 1979.
*Lord Tedric: The Black Knight of the Iron Sphere.* London, Star, 1979.
*Lord Tedric: Alien Realms.* London, Star, 1980.
*Subspace Encounter*, edited by Lloyd Arthur Eshbach. New York, Berkley, 1983.

Short Stories

*The Best of E.E. ("Doc") Smith.* London, Futura, 1975.

OTHER PUBLICATIONS

Other

*What Does This Convention Mean? A Speech Delivered at the Chicago 1940 World's Science Fiction Convention.* Privately printed, 1941.
*Galactic Roamer* (interview with Thomas Sheridan). West Warwick, Rhode Island, Necronomicon Press, 1977.

*

Critical Study: *The Universes of E.E. Smith* by Ron Ellik and Bill Evans, Chicago, Advent, 1966.

* * *

Determining the place of Edward E. "Doc" Smith in the history of science fiction is about as difficult as locating an electron. His career spans the history of science fiction in the 20th century. He began writing *The Skylark of Space* in 1915; today, other writers continue to use his characters and created universes as a basis for novels "by" E. E. Smith. All but five of his 17 books remain in print, and many have been translated into foreign languages such as Japanese and Vietnamese. Brian Aldiss considers Smith's *The Skylark of Space* as the starting point of the "trillion-year spree" that is modern science fiction. Yet he is dismissed by most recent critics in the field as an outdated writer of space operas whose style is awkward at best, whose plots are simplistic, and whose science is gadgetry and speculation.

He is best known for two multi-novel sagas, the Skylark series (four volumes and over 230,000 words in its final form) and the Lensman series (seven volumes and 500,000 words). Most of his works first appeared in the popular pulp science-fiction magazines. *The Skylark of Space* appeared as a serial in Hugo Gernsback's *Amazing Stories*, as did *Triplanetary.* The Lensman series is identified with John Campbell's *Astounding Science Fiction*, though *Galactic Patrol* appeared in *Astounding Stories* before Campbell's tenure. Other novels and stories appeared in *Comet Stories, Astonishing Stories, Other Worlds, Universe*, and *Worlds of If.* Beyond his 16 novels, he wrote only eight short stories or novelettes and three short articles, most of which are reprinted in *The Best of E.E. "Doc" Smith.*

Some of the themes and styles that Smith first articulated in *The Skylark of Space* remained a consistent part of his fictional armory: revolutionary innovations in basic science, engineering of those innovations into powerful technology with incredible speed, colorful descriptions of space battles, the whole intergalactic universe as the field of play, fundamental conflicts between good and evil, the interaction of human beings with alien races, and a "humanity first" philosophy. In *The Skylark of Space* (written between 1915 and 1920, first published in 1928), the young scientific genius Richard Seaton accidentally discovers an unknown metal in his laboratory that makes space travel possible; but the discovery is noticed by Seaton's amoral colleague, Marc DuQuesne. Seaton and his millionaire friend Martin Reynolds quickly use the discovery to build a spaceship, the "Skylark" of the title, but so does DuQuesne, who uses his ship to kidnap Seaton's fiance Dorothy Vaneman and her friend Margaret Spencer. The two sides set off on an intergalactic journey that takes them through two more novels *(Skylark Three*, and *Skylark of Valeron)*, three technological transformations of the original "Skylark"—the final "Skylark of Valeron" is as big as a small planet, and has alliances with several alien but human-minded races against powerful and physically monstrous aliens, and space battles too numerous to count. The final conflict with DuQuesne and an evil race of disembodied intelligences ends in triumph, with the universe at peace and the forces of evil sent off in a prison of force to the ends of the universe.

Thirty years later, in the last novel Smith completed before his death, he returned to the Skylark saga precisely at the point he had left it. In *Skylark DuQuesne (Worlds of If*, 1965; in book form in 1966), DuQuesne and the intelligences escape, humanity is again threatened by the alien Fenachrone and Chlorans, and "Blackie" DuQuesne becomes the hero. He defeats the aliens, finds his amoral soul-mate in the physicist Stephanie de Marigny, and finally flees "sissy" humanity to become colonist and emperor of a new civilization "on the rim of this universe." There is so little in this final Skylark episode of the thematic and attitudinal changes Smith demonstrated in his other novels between 1935 and 1965 that one wonders if it had in fact been drafted in the 1930's.

The conflicts in the original Skylark series are between male individuals: the female characters serve mainly as quest objects (though in the final novel Dorothy and Margaret fight beside their husbands), and the alien races as foils for the conflict between Seaton and DuQuesne. In *Spacehounds of IPC* and *Triplanetary*, however, Smith begins to envision an *organized* fight against evil. Though the action of both novels is restricted to the solar system, the Inter-Planetary Corporation and the Triplanetary Service are preliminary studies for the Galactic Patrol: humanity-centered organizations that pit good people against the forces of evil. In *Spacehounds of IPC*, the good guys become involved in wars between good and bad alien races on Jupiter and Saturn and their moons, while the criminals in *Triplanetary* are human.

The plot of the original Skylark series seems unplanned: the chance meeting and coincidence are its principal narrative devices. When Smith published *Galactic Patrol* in 1937–1938, however, he had conceived the entire plot of the Lensman series in advance. The narrative frame transcends all normal time and space in a conflict between two races of almost pure intelligence: the Eddorians, who came into "our" universe "from some horribly different plenum" and whose sole motivation is the lust for power, and the Arisians, whose only interest is knowledge but who unwillingly become the opponents of the Eddorians. The Arisians keep their existence unknown to the Eddorians and establish a billion-year plan that culminates in two individuals: Kimball Kinnison and Clarissa MacDougall. Kim's father Roderick had, a century or two after our own time, helped to found the Galactic Patrol, whose symbol and source of power was the *lens*, a telepathic jewel given to Patrol members by the Arisians—each lens uniquely linked to the mind of its owner.

The four novels of the original series *(Galactic Patrol, Gray Lensman, Second Stage Lensman*, and *Children of the Lens)* form a continuous narrative. In a series of suspenseful investigations, individual conflicts, and space battles whose scope and magnificence grow ever grander, Kim and his Patrol allies, the physically monstrous but "humanly" good aliens Worsel of Velantia, Tregonsee of Rigel IV, and Nadreck of Palain VII, slowly learn to use the powers bred into their genetic lines by the Arisians; level by level, they fight their way up the Eddorian hierarchy of evil. The final conflict is reserved, however, for the children of Kim and Clarissa: Christopher, Karen, Kathryn, Camilla and Constance. The climax of the Arisians' breeding plan, they are able to merge their minds into The Unit, a single entity through which the Arisians are finally able to confront and destroy the Eddorians and make both the First and Second galaxies safe for Civilization.

All of the themes and narrative devices of the Skylark series, good and bad, are carried on in the Lensman series, but put at the service of an encompassing and remarkably coherent plot structure. New to the Lensman series is telepathy: the power of mind, which becomes the central force of the later series. The "lens" is initially an enabling device, but the Children are able to do without the lens. The importance of the female characters is also new: though much of the rhetoric and the conversational interactions remain bound in the sexist conventions of the 1930's and 1940's, Clarissa and her daughters here play roles as important as those of Kim and his son.

When the Lensman series was published in book form, Smith rewrote *Triplanetary* with a long historical introduction linking its events to the billion-year history of the Lensman series, and followed it with *First Lensman* (one of the two Smith novels to appear only in book form), in which Virgil Samms, the hero of *Triplanetary*, learns of the Arisians and acquires the first lens. The series is usually taken to include also *The Vortex Blaster*, a weak novel sewn together out of shorter stories that had appeared in magazines in 1941–1942, and 1952, and vaguely set in the early years of the Galactic Patrol.

The new themes of telepathy and the cooperative interaction of male and female characters appear again in the novels that Smith wrote in his post-Lensman period. In *The Galaxy Primes* (1959 in *Amazing Stories*) the "primes" are super-telepaths in a galaxy of telepathic potential who use their power to establish a galactic government; the subplot in this novel, poorly integrated with the main plot, is the growing love between Cleander Garlock and Belle Bellamy, two "primes" whose personalities are originally in bitter conflict. In *Subspace Explorers* (originally a novelette in *Analog Science Fact/Science Fiction* in 1960), by contrast, two pairs of telepaths fall in love instantly because of their mental contact; the plot, however, is like *Spacehounds of IPC* in that a disaster sends the heroes into a different space from which they must return with difficulty. A subplot introduces the theme of "enlightened self-interest" as a governing philosophy. Its sequel *Subspace Encounter* (edited and published in 1983 after Smith's death) combines the telepathic theme with the kind of galactic conflict familiar from Smith's earlier novels. Both *The Galaxy Primes* and *Subspace Encounter* conclude with suggestions of an Arisia-like force behind the events.

Smith's penultimate novel, *Masters of Space* (in the magazine *Worlds of If*, 1961–1962), was in fact his completion of a novel by his fan and friend E. Everett Evans in which telepathic robots finally re-encounter the humans who had created them centuries before; robots and humans combine to defeat a race of evil aliens. Its collaborative nature points to what has happened since Smith's death. David Kyle and William Ellern have continued the Lensman series (four novels between 1977 and 1983). Stephen Goldin took a novelette, "Imperial Stars," that Smith had published in 1964 shortly before his death, and used it as a basis for a series, "The Family D'Alembert," which came to ten novels between 1976 and 1985. The Family consists of interstellar circus performers who are actually secret agents of the galactic emperor. The D'Alembert series, like Smith's original story, follows the trend so obvious in science fiction of the 1970's and 1980's of placing sword-and-sorcery stories in a science-fiction context, as did the Lord Tedric series, three novels by Gordon Eklund (1978–79) based on two short stories Smith had published in 1953–54.

Smith's achievement as a science-fiction writer is considerable and his impact is lasting. Those who criticize his style, his plots, his characterization, and his pseudo-science are correct enough, as far as they go. But his imagination was as far-reaching as the universe itself, and his ideal of a galactic civilization where human and alien, male and female, worked together for the common good is as attractive as it is unrealizable. The fact remains that Smith's novels are not only immensely readable and enjoyable, but they can be reread with growing pleasure. They are as much fantasy as they are science fiction in the narrow sense of the word—and that, perhaps, is one source of their continuing influence in a period when more than half of the science-fiction novels published are of the sword-and-sorcery brand.

—Bruce A. Beatie

---

**SMITH, Evelyn E.** Also writes as Delphine C. Lyons. American. Born in 1937. Editor, writer, and crossword puzzle compiler. Address: P.O. Box 226, Ansonia Station, New York, New York 10023, U.S.A.

SCIENCE-FICTION PUBLICATIONS

Novels

*The Perfect Planet.* New York, Avalon, 1962.
*Flower of Evil.* New York, Pyramid, 1965.
*House of Four Widows.* New York, Lancer, 1965.
*The Depths of Yesterday.* New York, Lancer, 1966.
*Valley of Shadows* (as Delphine C. Lyons). New York, Lancer, 1968.
*Phantom at Lost Lake.* New York, Prestige, 1970.
*Unpopular Planet.* New York, Dell, 1975.
*The Copy Shop.* New York, Doubleday, 1985.

Uncollected Short Stories

"Nightmare on the Nose," in *Fantastic Universe* (Chicago), November 1953.
"Baxbr Daxbr," in *Time to Come*, edited by August Derleth. New York, Farrar Straus, 1954.
"Not Fit for Children" and "Tea Tray in the Sky," in *Second Galaxy Reader of Science Fiction*, edited by H. L. Gold. New York, Crown, 1954; London, Grayson, 1955.
"Call Me Wizard," in *Beyond* (New York), January 1954.
"The Agony of the Leaves," in *Beyond* (New York), July 1954.
"At Last I've Found You," in *Fantasy and Science Fiction* (New York), October 1954.
"Collector's Item," in *Galaxy* (New York), December 1954.
"The Laminated Woman," in *Fantastic Universe* (Chicago), December 1954.
"Helpfully Yours," in *Galaxy* (New York), February 1955.
"The Big Jump," in *Fantastic Universe* (Chicago), March 1955.
"Man's Best Friend," in *Galaxy* (New York), April 1955.
"The Princess and the Physicist," in *Galaxy* (New York), June 1955.
"The Faithful Friend," in *Fantasy and Science Fiction* (New York), June 1955.
"Dragon Lady," in *Beyond* (New York), June 1955.
"The Doorway," in *Fantastic Universe* (Chicago), September 1955.
"Jack of No Trades," in *Galaxy* (New York), October 1955.
"Floyd and the Eumenides," in *Fantastic Universe* (Chicago), December 1955.
"The Captains's Mate," in *Fantasy and Science Fiction* (New York), March 1956.
"The Venus Trap," in *Galaxy* (New York), June 1956.
"Mr. Replogle's Dream," in *Fantastic Universe* (Chicago), December 1956.
"Woman's Touch," in *Super Science Fiction* (New York), February 1957.
"The Ignoble Savages," in *Galaxy* (New York), March 1957.
"The Lady from Aldebaran," in *Fantastic Universe* (Chicago), March 1957.

"The 4D Bargain," in *Saturn* (Holyoke, Massachusetts), May 1957.
"Outcast of Mars," in *Fantasy and Science Fiction* (New York), May 1957.
"The Man Outside," in *Galaxy* (New York), August 1957.
"The Weegil," in *Super Science Fiction* (New York), December 1957.
"The Vilbar Party," in *The Third Galaxy Reader*, edited by H. L. Gold. New York, Doubleday, 1958.
"The Blue Tower," in *Galaxy* (New York), February 1958.
"My Fair Planet," in *Galaxy* (New York), March 1958.
"Two Suns of Morcali," in *Fantastic Universe* (Chicago), July 1958.
"Once a Greech," in *Worlds That Couldn't Be and 8 Other SF Novelets*, edited by H.L. Gold. New York, Doubleday, 1959.
"The People Upstairs," in *Fantastic Universe* (Chicago), March 1959.
"The Alternate Host," in *Fantastic Universe* (Chicago), September 1959.
"Send Her Victorious," in *Fantasy and Science Fiction* (New York), February 1960.
"The Hardest Bargain," in *Mind Partner and 8 Other Novelets from Galaxy*, edited by H.L. Gold. New York, Doubleday, 1961.
"Sentry of the Sky," in *Galaxy* (New York), February 1961.
"Robert E. Lee at Moscow," in *Fantasy and Science Fiction* (New York), October 1961.
"Softly While You're Sleeping," in *The Best from Fantasy and Science Fiction 11*, edited by Robert P. Mills. New York, Doubleday, 1962.
"They Also Serve," in *Fantasy and Science Fiction* (New York), September 1962.
"The Last of the Spode," in *17 × Infinity*, edited by Groff Conklin. New York, Dell, 1963.
"The Martian and the Magician," in *Fifty Short Science Fiction Tales*, edited by Isaac Asimov and Groff Conklin. New York, Macmillan, 1963.
"Little Gregory," in *Fantasy and Science Fiction* (New York), February 1964.
"Calliope and Gherkin and the Yankee Doodle Thing," in *The Best from Fantasy and Science Fiction 19*, edited by Edward L. Ferman. New York, Doubleday, 1971.
"A Day in the Suburbs," in *Sociology Through Science Fiction*, edited by John W. Milstead and others. New York, St. Martin's Press, 1974.
"Gerda," in *Dragon Tales*, edited by Isaac Asimov, Martin H. Greenberg, and Charles G. Waugh. New York, Fawcett, 1982.
"The Most Sentimental Man," in *Last Man on Earth*, edited by Isaac Asimov, Martin H. Greenberg, and Charles G. Waugh. New York, Fawcett, 1982.
"The Good Husband" and "Weather Prediction," in *100 Great Fantasy Short Short Stories*, edited by Isaac Asimov, Terry Carr, and Martin H. Greenberg. New York, Doubleday, 1984.
"Teragram," in *Young Witches and Warlocks*, edited by Isaac Asimov, Martin H. Greenberg, and Charles G. Waugh. New York, Harper and Row, 1987.

OTHER PUBLICATIONS

Novels

*Miss Melville Regrets.* New York, Fine, 1987.
*Miss Melville Returns.* New York, Fine, 1988.
*Miss Melville's Revenge.* New York, Fine, 1989.

Other as Delphine C. Lyons

*The Armchair Shopper's Guide.* New York, Essandess, 1968.
*The Whole World Catalog.* New York, Quadrangle, 1973.

* * *

Although Evelyn E. Smith's individual works of SF vary greatly in style, mood, and focus, it is possible to characterize her work as making a wry statement about human nature. Here is an author who is optimistic in spite of herself; even in those works which focus on post-nuclear holocaust worlds, humanity has survived and—whether or not its representatives are honorable or otherwise admirable—they do possess the ability to meet wild challenges and to survive their own foibles.

Smith's comments on human nature range from sharp and ironical to light and ludicrous. Her first story, "The Last of the Spode," is a terse portrayal of three Britishers who, by a twist of fate, seem to be the sole survivors of nuclear holocaust. A "correct" professor and a young chap join a figure of British womanhood in an afternoon tea at the end of the world. As the Spode teapot is poured out, they reveal their chief concern as to whether or not their tea supply will last them to the end of their days. "No point in anything, really," the young chap remarks. "We must face the facts, lad," the professor says and then adds, in a gem of understatement, "pity about the Bodleian, though." "The Hardest Bargain" envisions another post-holocaust future, in which the American populace is weakened with hunger and racial debility. Presidential advisor Dr. Livingston, who believes that "the thinking man is the despairing man," urges President Buchbinder to accept extraterrestrial aid in decontaminating the lands, but when the earthlings fail to keep their bargain to pay the extraterrestrial Foma in famous works of art, the Foma reveals his true identity as a pied piper to the robots which are so desperately needed by human society. "Not Fit for Children" is representative of Smith's more lighthearted stories. Here a group of alien children pose as war-dancing "natives" on an asteroid-like space ship which is visited regularly by human tourists. In payment for their antics, the children receive coins which are melted down by their disbelieving elders into metal which is needed to repair their space ship.

Most of Smith's short stories appeared during the 1950's; just as they varied in seriousness of theme as well as sophistication of writing technique, her novels represent the extremes of the author's abilities. *The Perfect Planet* shares the wry ironic tone of so many of her shorter works, as the author tells an amusing but insubstantial tale of two astronauts, one male and one female, who land on a planet populated by vain health enthusiasts who foist their obsession with slim, perfect physiques upon the slightly pudgy, space-weary duo. While the book does have some impact as a critique of mindless conformity, sadly the astronauts, who start out as rebellious to the ways of this world, come to have a fondness for the pampered inhabitants of "the perfumed planet." The initially gutsy female astronaut Moodie comes to value herself as an alluring female using charm, artifice, and cosmetics to enhance her self-worth while the captain learns to be protective of his changed space partner. *Unpopular Planet* is also preoccupied with questions of sexual identity. While it, too, features some portrayals of women which would not please feminists—the hero's partner is a female who is fully mature sexually although mentally and chronologically she is but three years old—such characterization is used with more sophisticated satirical purpose. An aspiring musician, Nicholas Piggot, careens perplexedly yet enthusiastically through a series of picaresque adventures observed by blue dragons. They turn out not to be the result of drunken fancy but to be "real" beings from another dimension who have a particular genetic purpose in store for the hero, who rises from life as an unknown in subterranean Manhattan to become father of a new future.

—Rosemary Herbert

---

**SMITH, George H(enry).** Also writes as M.J. Deer; Jan Hudson; Jerry Jason; Clancy O'Brien; Hal Stryker; Diana Summers. American. Born in Vicksburg, Mississippi, 27 October 1922. Educated at the University of Southern California, Los Angeles, B.A. 1950. Served in the United States Navy, 1942–45. Married M. Jane Deer in 1950. Since 1950, freelance writer. Address: 4113 West 180th Street, Torrance, California 90504, U.S.A.

SCIENCE-FICTION PUBLICATIONS

Novels (series: Annwn)

*Satan's Daughter.* New York, Epic, 1961.
*1976: Year of Terror.* New York, Epic, 1961.
*Scourge of the Blood Cult.* New York, Epic, 1961.
*The Coming of the Rats.* New York, Pike, 1961; London, Digit, 1964.
*Doomsday Wing.* Derby, Connecticut, Monarch, 1963.
*The Unending Night.* Derby, Connecticut, Monarch, 1964.
*The Forgotten Planet.* New York, Avalon, 1965.
*The Psycho Makers* (as Jerry Jason). New York, Tempo, 1965.
*The Four Day Weekend.* New York, Belmont, 1966.
*Druids' World* (Annwn). New York, Avalon, 1967.
*Kar Kaballa* (Annwn). New York, Ace, 1969.
*Witch Queen of Lochlann* (Annwn). New York, New American Library, 1969; London, Hale, 1981.
*The Second War of the Worlds* (Annwn). New York, DAW, 1976.
*The Island Snatchers* (Annwn). New York, DAW, 1978.
*NYPD 2025* (as Hal Stryker). New York, Pinnacle, 1985.

OTHER PUBLICATIONS

Novels

*A Place Called Hell* (as M.J. Deer, with M. Jane Deer Smith). New York, France, 1963.
*Flames of Desire* (as M.J. Deer, with M. Jane Deer Smith). New York, France, 1963.
*The Devil's Breed.* Chicago, Playboy Press, 1979.
*The Rogues.* Chicago, Playboy Press, 1980.
*The Firebrands.* Chicago, Playboy Press, 1980.
*A Rebel's Pleasure.* New York, Dell, 1986.

Novels as Diana Summers

*Wild Is the Heart.* Chicago, Playboy Press, 1978.
*Love's Wicked Ways.* Chicago, Playboy Press, 1978.
*Fallen Angel.* Chicago, Playboy Press, 1981.
*Louisiana.* New York, Dell, 1984.
*The Emperor's Lady.* New York, Charter, 1984.

Other

*Who Is Ronald Reagan?* New York, Pyramid, 1968.
*Martin Luther King, Jr.* New York, Lancer, 1971.

Other as Jan Hudson

*Hell's Angels.* San Diego, Greenleaf, 1965; London, New English Library, 1967; as *The New Barbarians*, New English Library, 1973.
*The People in the Saucers.* San Diego, Greenleaf, 1967.
*Bikers at War.* London, New English Library, 1976.

*

George H. Smith comments (1981):

Science fiction was my first love in writing, and I've done it off and on for the last 25 years. Five of my novels are set in the imaginary Celtic other world called Annwn. I am currently committed to a series of historical novels so it will be some time before I get back to science fiction, but when I do I hope to continue the Annwn series.

* * *

The career of George H. Smith as a writer of science fiction is a peculiar one. Since most of his early novels were written for small paperback houses specializing in lurid action and violent sex, there is a certain crudity about them that masks his positive values as a writer. It was not until the 1970's that Smith began to sell novels to the more prestigious paperback houses, and the quality of his novels seems to have improved proportionately.

The early novels made use of a standard set of characters. The typical male protagonist was an indecisive man who had some insight into the future and realized that a significant change was coming to the world, but who was unable to communicate this to those around him. Typically, he spends the first half of each novel infatuated with a woman obviously unsuited for him, gradually awakening to the fact that some third character is actually the person with whom he wishes to spend his life. This is the pattern of *The Coming of the Rats*, for example; the hero finally convinces his totally impractical girlfriend to accompany him to a remote cave as nuclear war hovers just over the horizon. In the aftermath, the rats of the title challenge man for supremacy with predictable results. The pattern repeats itself in *Doomsday Wing*, also about a nuclear war, this time threatening to extinguish all life on Earth, and *The Unending Night*, wherein runaway nuclear reactors knock Mars out of its orbit, and threaten to pull our own planet away from the warmth of the sun. In the former, the dedicated military man cannot convince his ambitious wife of the importance of serving his country, and in the latter a hyper-liberated woman is convinced that the best thing that can happen to the human race is for it to descend to a primitive culture. The scientist hero of the latter is thoroughly enamored of her until she proves insane. This basic arrangement of characters also appears in *The Four Day Weekend*, involving a plot by secret aliens to take over the world by reprogramming the computers that direct our motor vehicles. Although there is some amusing satire here, it is rather silly most of the time, possibly the worst of Smith's novels.

Surprisingly enough, one of his better novels was published by a softcore pornography publisher. *1976: Year of Terror* is set in a future America in which the Libertarian Party has seized power by assassination and clever plotting by the head of the Federal Security Police. Opposed to him is a secret agent intent on finding the missing vice-president and restoring democratic rule to the country. This anticipates a number of thrillers along similar lines, and is fairly well written.

Somewhere along the line, Smith became interested in mythology and druidism. It crops up first in *Druids' World*, a fairly dull novel, then to much better effect in *Witch Queen of Lochlann*, written in the mode of the stories made famous by *Unknown* magazine. Duffus January is a magician of sorts who undertakes to restore the rightful queen to the throne of Lochlann, a Welsh alternate world where magic works. A low-key sword-and-sorcery tale, this seems to have set the stage for a major series of novels. *Kar Kaballa* is named for the king of the Gogs, a barbaric nation of nomads whose existence is barely noted by their neighbors, the civilized inhabitants of Avalon, a nation comparable to 19th-century England in our universe. Dylan MacBride, a young adventurer, is convinced that the imminent freezing of the channel between Avalon and the northern regions will result in a massive invasion, but he is unable to convince anyone in authority of the seriousness of the threat. Despondent, he seems doomed to failure when he encounters a man from our own universe who plans to sell Gatling guns to the alternate world. Smith went on to chronicle the Martian invasion of his alternate world in *The Second War of the Worlds*, an entertaining novel throughout, and a magical plot to destroy civilization in *The Island Snatchers*, the weakest in the series. These latter books are far better than his earlier efforts, with more complex characters, a quieter and more careful style, and more significant care taken in establishing settings, mood, and suspense.

Smith seems to have abandoned the field of science fiction since the late 1970's; his only novel in recent years is *NYPD 2025*, written under the pseudonym Hal Stryker. This fast-paced story of an android policeman battling heavily armed criminals in the not-too-distant future was supposed to be a continuing series, cut short when the publisher went out of business. It should also be noted that although his shorter fiction is generally unmemorable, he wrote one interesting tale at that length. "In the Imagicon" (in *Nebula Award Stories 2*, edited by Brian Aldiss and Harry Harrison, New York, Doubleday, and London, Gollancz, 1987) is set in a future where a machine allows people to create a mental world of their own choosing.

—Don D'Ammassa

---

**SMITH, George O(liver).** American. Born in Chicago, Illinois, 9 April 1911. Attended the University of Chicago, 1929–30. Served as an editorial engineer, National Defense Research Council, 1944–45. Married 1) Helen Kunzler in 1936 (divorced 1948), one daughter and one son; 2) Dona Louise Stebbins in 1949 (died 1974), one son. Radio Serviceman, Chicago, 1932–35; radio engineer: General Household, 1935–38, Wells-Gardiner, 1938–40, Philco, 1940–42, 1946–51, Crosley, 1942–44; manager, Emerson Radio components engineering, 1951–57; analyst, ITT Defense Communications, 1959–74. Reviewer, *Space Science Fiction. Died.*

SCIENCE-FICTION PUBLICATIONS

Novels

*Pattern for Conquest: An Interplanetary Adventure.* New York, Gnome Press, 1949; London, Clerke and Cockeran, 1951.
*Nomad.* Philadelphia, Prime Press, 1950.
*Operation Interstellar.* Chicago, Century, 1950.
*Hellflower.* New York, Abelard Press, 1953; London, Lane, 1955.
*Highways in Hiding.* New York, Gnome Press, 1956; abridged edition, as *The Space Plague*, New York, Avon, 1957.
*Troubled Star.* New York, Avalon, 1957.
*Fire in the Heavens.* New York, Avalon, 1958.
*The Path of Unreason.* New York, Gnome Press, 1958.
*Lost in Space.* New York, Avalon, 1959.
*The Fourth "R".* New York, Ballantine, 1959; as *The Brain Machine*, New York, Lancer, 1968.

Short Stories

*Venus Equilateral.* Philadelphia, Prime Press, 1947; enlarged edition, London, Futura, 2 vols., 1975; and as *The Complete Venus Equilateral*, New York, Ballantine, 1976.
*Worlds of George O.* New York, Bantam, 1982.

OTHER PUBLICATIONS

Other

*Mathematics, The Language of Science* (for children). New York, Putnam, 1961.
*Scientists' Nightmares.* New York, Putnam, 1972.

* * *

When one mentions "the golden age of science fiction," several stereotypes come to mind, including bug-eyed aliens who act like humans, humans who act like supermen, mysterious gadgets and even more mysterious ray guns. Fortunately, much of the science fiction written during this period did not employ such stereotypes. A few became classics. Many more, while certainly not classics, have to be considered as good, solid science fiction.

One such work is George O. Smith's *Highways in Hiding.* Although it might be classified as a science-fiction mystery, it moves fast enough and has enough action to keep your attention. In fact, it is difficult to put down. The characterizations are only adequate, but the plot is well thought out, involving psychic phenomena, a mysterious disease, and a baffling disappearance. There is a political message here, too, which is common in Smith's works: the fruits of science should be for all and not just the elite. *The Fourth "R"* is another Smith work which makes use of this underlying idea. This time it is the Holden Electromechanical Educator which promises to be mankind's salvation. However, Jimmy Holden's parents, who developed the device, are murdered by an unscrupulous business associate who wishes the device to further his own aims. Because Jimmy's parents had used the device on him, he is no ordinary five-year-old, but practically an adult trapped in a child's body, and his adventures protecting the device make a very clever work.

*Fire in the Heavens, Nomad, Hellflower*, and *Troubled Star* are less interesting. The first has a lot of science but not much plot: the sun is about to go nova and a young scientist who doesn't believe in the Law of Conservation of Energy or in neutrinos must save the day. The plot of *Hellflower* is a little worn, though suspenseful. Space pilot Farradyne crashes his ship, killing 33 people. He is banished to the Venusian fungus field until a federal agent gives him a chance to prove himself anew by becoming an undercover agent and helping to break the hellflower smuggling ring. *Troubled Star* may not have been intended as a tongue-in-cheek stab at 1950's science fiction, but I take it as such. Dusty Britton of the space patrol has so many TV followers that, when a group of aliens plan to make Sol into a three-day variable beacon, they approach Dusty to be their spokesman. In *Nomad* humans are made out to be monsters who use sub-science life forms for vivisections and who annihilate the "10th" planet of the solar system with little provocation. It is a particularly frightening projection of the future of mankind.

No discussion of Smith's works would be complete without mentioning *Venus Equilateral.* Venus Equilateral Relay Station is a manned satellite circling the sun at the orbit of Venus, but 60 degrees ahead of that planet. Its purpose is to relay radio transmissions among the inhabited planets whenever the sun interferes with direct transmission. The stories mostly concern technical problems and their solution by the station's scientists. Most of the problems are archaic by today's standards, but the stories are of interest, at least from a historical perspective. Many of the stereotypes of golden-age science fiction are found here.

—Paul Swank

---

**SMITH, Thorne.** American. Born in 1893. *Died in 1934.*

SCIENCE-FICTION PUBLICATIONS

Novels (series: Topper)

*Topper: An Improbable Adventure.* New York, McBride, and London, Holden, 1926.
*Topper: A Ribald Adventure.* New York, Grosset and Dunlap, 1926.
*The Stray Lamb.* New York, Cosmopolitan, 1929; London, Heinemann, 1930.
*The Night Life of the Gods.* New York, Doubleday, 1931; London, Barker, 1934.
*Turnabout.* New York, Doubleday, 1931; London, Barker, 1933.
*Topper Takes a Trip.* New York, Doubleday, 1932; London, Barker, 1935.
*The Jovial Ghosts: The Misadventures of Topper.* London, Barker, 1933.
*Skin and Bones.* New York, Doubleday, 1933; London, Barker, 1936.
*Rain in the Doorway.* New York, Doubleday, 1933; London, Barker, 1936.
*The Glorious Pool.* New York, Doubleday, 1934; London, Barker, 1935.
*The Passionate Witch* (completed by Norman Matson). New York, Doubleday, 1941; London, Barker, 1942.

OTHER PUBLICATIONS

Novels

*Dream's End.* New York, McBride, 1927; London, Jarrolds, 1928.
*Did She Fall?* New York, Cosmopolitan, 1930; London, Barker, 1936.
*The Bishop's Jaegers.* New York, Doubleday, 1932; London, Barker, 1934.

Other

*Lazy Bear Lane.* New York, Doubleday, 1931.
*Thorne Smith: His Life and Times,* with Roland Young and others. New York, Doubleday, 1934.

* * *

There is a scene in *Free Live Free* by Gene Wolfe set in a lunatic asylum in which a doctor and a visitor talk to each other at cross-purposes the whole time. It was an homage to Thorne Smith, amplified even further by Wolfe's *There Are Doors,* a book that echoes in many ways Thorne Smith's *Rain in the Doorway.*

Thorne Smith was one of the finest of all American comic writers who reacted to the puritanism of America between the wars with a series of outrageous novels in which the whole purpose of life was shown to revolve around sex and alcohol. In a typical Thorne Smith novel an unhappy middle-aged man learns how to escape the imprisonment of a shrewish wife or a dull job by some miracle that introduces him to the pleasures of loose women and booze.

In several of his stories the fantastic element is limited to one instance of almost wish-fulfilment magic that sets up the misadventures to follow. The pool in *The Glorious Pool,* for instance, exists simply to transform Rex Pebble and his middle-aged mistress Spray Summers into youths again, while *The Night Life of the Gods* endows its hero, Hunter Hawk, with the ability to transform statues into living people mostly to allow the spree with Bacchus and Venus, which personify the twin elements of his vision of personal liberty.

However, where the needs of the story dictate, Smith could be quite rigorous in his working out of the effects of his miracle. What's more, much of his work sits squarely within the tradition of fantastic literature. *Skin and Bones,* perhaps the most science-fictional of his books, is a comic counterpoint to *The Invisible Man.* Quintus Bland is experimenting to discover a fluoroscopic camera film but the result renders him invisible save for his skeleton, and it is this near-invisibility that is the key to the story. Using Bland's inability to control the transformations, Smith creates some hilarious set-pieces, as when a barber unwinds the hot towels from around his customer's face to reveal a grinning skull, or as Bland is introduced to the pleasures of a brothel.

In *Turnabout,* on the other hand, Smith tapped into a theme that had already been used to humorous effect in F. Anstey's *Vice Versa,* and that was to surface again only a few years later in the work of another humourist, *Laughing Gas* by P.G. Wodehouse. However, in Smith's book the two souls that are swapped are not man and boy, but man and woman. Inevitably, this is an excuse for much sexual innuendo and by-play, though it also allows Smith to make fun of each sex's narrow-minded disregard of the other. Thus when Sally and Tim first face each other in their new bodies, there is the following exchange: " 'You leave that man alone,' cried Sally furiously. 'Keep your hands off him and be careful what you do with my body. First thing you know you'll be presenting me with a nameless child. I could never bear that.' 'You won't have to bear it,' he said slowly. 'I'd have to bear it. Wouldn't that be awful?' " This exchange is typical of Smith's comic practice in that it turns upon a pun, though more usually the puns and misunderstandings were used to develop conversations in which both participants fail entirely to interpret the other person aright. Such a technique was used to excellent effect, for instance, in *Rain in the Doorway,* in which the put-upon hero escapes the rain by going through a door that takes him into another world, a ludicrously run department store of which he finds himself to be one of the partners. Of course in this world there is a liberality of attitude on many things, but particularly sex and drink, which means that by the time Mr. Hector Owen returns to his own world, he has acquired the skills he needs to escape the more transcendent greyness of his life of which the initial rain is no more than a symbol.

Smith's skills are limited: his male characters are either dull people who need to learn how to have fun or else expansive adventurers who have already learned the lessons of booze and sex; his females are either domineering and shrewish, or else jolly, sexy, and eager to initiate the hero into the pleasures of the world. His view of life was limited also; in the post-World War I America of prohibition and puritanism in which he wrote, he only saw the one route by which to transform and fulfil the lives of his characters. Nevertheless, he had a unique gift for comedy, especially for comic dialogue, and at their best his books are excellent examples of their type. Most typical, perhaps, is his best-known work, *The Jovial Ghosts*, which was filmed as *Topper* and launched a series of popular films in the 1930's. Cosmo Topper begins the book as a repressed, upright member of staid society, but by the time the ghosts of George and Marion Kerby have introduced him, willing or no, to a host of activities that Topper regards as sinful, his repression has cracked and he is no longer able to sustain the old staidness. It is a straightforward, undemanding novel, hardly shocking though it must have seemed so at the time it was written, but like so much of Smith's work it is very funny.

—Paul Kincaid

---

**SOHL, Jerry** (Gerald Allan Sohl). Also writes as Nathan Butler; Roberta Jean Mountjoy; Sean Mei Sullivan. American. Born in Los Angeles, California, 2 December 1913. Attended Central College, Chicago, 1933–34. Served in the United States Army Air Force, 1942–45: Sergeant. Married Jean Gordon in 1942; one son and two daughters. Reporter, telegraph editor, photographer, and feature writer, Bloomington *Daily Pantagraph*, Illinois, 1945–58. Since 1958, freelance writer: staff writer for *Star Trek*, *Alfred Hitchcock Presents*, and *The New Breed*; also concert pianist. Agent: Joseph Elder Agency, 150 West 87th Street, New York, New York 10024. Address: P.O. Box 1336, Thousand Oaks, California 91360, U.S.A.

SCIENCE-FICTION PUBLICATIONS

Novels

*The Haploids*. New York, Rinehart, 1952.
*Costigan's Needle*. New York, Rinehart, 1953; London, Grayson, 1955.
*The Transcendent Man*. New York, Rinehart, 1953.
*The Altered Ego*. New York, Rinehart, 1954.
*Point Ultimate*. New York, Rinehart, 1955.
*The Mars Monopoly*. New York, Ace, 1956; London, Satellite, 1958.
*The Time Dissolver*. New York, Avon, 1957; London, Sphere, 1967.
*The Odious Ones*. New York, Rinehart, 1959; London, Consul, 1961.
*One Against Herculum*. New York, Ace, 1959.
*Night Slaves*. New York, Fawcett, 1965.
*The Anomaly*. New York, Curtis, 1971.
*I, Aleppo*. Toronto, Laser, 1976.
*Death Sleep*. New York, Fawcett, 1983.

OTHER PUBLICATIONS

Novels

*Prelude to Peril*. New York, Rinehart, 1957.
*The Lemon Eaters*. New York, Simon and Schuster, and London, Cassell, 1967.
*The Spun Sugar Hole*. New York, Simon and Schuster, 1971.
*The Resurrection of Frank Borchard*. New York, Simon and Schuster, 1973.
*Supermanchu, Master of Kung Fu* (as Sean Mei Sullivan). New York, Ballantine, 1974.
*Night Wind* (as Roberta Jean Mountjoy). New York, Coward McCann, 1981.
*Black Thunder* (as Roberta Jean Mountjoy). New York, Berkley, 1983.

Novels as Nathan Butler

*Dr. Josh*. New York, Fawcett, 1973.
*Mamelle*. New York, Fawcett, 1974.
*Blow-Dry*. New York, Fawcett, 1976.
*Mamelle, The Goddess*. New York, Fawcett, 1977.
*Kaheesh*. New York, Fawcett, 1983.

Plays

Screenplays: *Twelve Hours to Kill*, 1960; Monster of Terror *(Die Monster, Die!)*, 1965; *Frankenstein Conquers the World*, with Kaoru Mabuchi and Reuben Bercovitch, 1966.

Television Plays: *The Corbomite Maneuver* (*Star Trek* series), 1966; *Night Slaves*, from his own novel, 1970; and episodes for *Naked City, Route 66, M-Squad, G.E. Theater, Markham, Border Patrol, The Twilight Zone, The Invaders, The Outer Limits, Target: The Corrupters, Man from Atlantis*, and *The Next Step Beyond* series.

Other

*Underhanded Chess*. New York, Hawthorn, 1973.
*Underhanded Bridge*. New York, Hawthorn, 1975.

*

Manuscript Collection: University of Wyoming, Laramie.

Jerry Sohl comments:

The corpus of my science-fiction work reflects, I believe, rather accurately what was fashionable in the genre from 1950 to 1970, moving from gimmick as story to people as story. Although superior to what it was prior to 1970, today's science fiction is often too abstruse to be understood.

While I continue to write science fiction now and then, my interest has shifted to mainstream and I am at the moment at work on a super-suspense novel entitled *The Pacem Complex* as well as novels I can only describe as *avant-garde*, one entitled *Mortal Coils* and the other *The Gold Triskelion*.

* * *

Like many fans-turned-writers, Jerry Sohl reveals an appreciative understanding of the surface structures of science-fiction narratives but often fails at deeper levels of conceptualization and extrapolation. Although Sohl has contributed little of originality to the genre, he is in many ways a representative popular writer of the 1950's, skilled in generating an initial sense of mystery and wonder, but often confusing or even absurd in his resolutions.

Most of his novels and stories deal with familiar science-fiction themes. *The Transcendent Man*, for example, borrows a premise from Charles Fort via earlier treatments by Eric Frank Russel, L. Ron Hubbard, and others: the idea that humanity's intelligence and civilization are the creations of a vastly superior race of invisible aliens who feed off the emotional energy generated by catastrophes such as war and plagues. Although these aliens, called the Capellans in this novel, might serve as an interesting metaphor for the paradoxical quality in human nature that somehow accounts for both creative and destructive impulses, Sohl develops the story into little more than an adventure narrative concerning one supernormal human who discovers the alien secret and, in the end, singlehandedly takes on the task of maintaining civilization. *Point Ultimate*, Sohl's contribution to the literature of dystopia, concerns a world conquered by communists who seem to come right out of the nightmares of Joe McCarthy, and quickly descends into a welter of germ warfare, gypsies, underground railways, and secret Martian colonies. *The Altered Ego* involves the somewhat more intriguing notion of a society which has learned how to resurrect important citizens after death, but soon becomes a familiar tale of chases and conspiracies.

Sohl's more successful novels are those in which the science-fiction element is kept fairly simple or relegated to the background. *The Time Dissolver* is an intriguing amnesia mystery for most of its length, with the protagonist and his wife awaking one morning to find that their memories from 1946 to 1957 have disappeared—and that, consequently, they do not even know each other. The carefully wrought details of the investigation into the missing years of their lives provide a suspenseful narrative, and the rather weak explanation concerning a memory-dissolving machine does not interfere greatly with the overall impact of the novel. *Costigan's Needle*, an exploration of the parallel-universe theme, is perhaps Sohl's best novel: an account of a group of people who pass into a parallel world through a needle-shaped machine invented by a Chicago scientist, only to find themselves trapped in the other world and forced to spend years redesigning the technology that will enable them to build another machine (which, it turns out, will only enable them to enter another of an apparently infinite series of parallel worlds). Understandably, the people choose not to abandon this new world that they have created with their own hands. Although the characters in the novel are a familiar assortment of popular fiction stereotypes, the exploration of the problems inherent in trying to recreate a sophisticated technology from raw materials is well-handled.

Sohl has had relatively little influence on the genre, although one of his novels, *Night Slaves*—concerning a community dominated by alien visitors—provided the basis for a television movie. A writer with undeniable skill in constructing suspenseful situations, and one who enjoyed some popularity during the 1950's, his works in retrospect seem weakened by inadequate conceptualization of the scientific and social ideas he dealt with.

—Gary K. Wolfe

---

**SOMTOW, S.P.** *See* **SUCHARITKUL, Somtow.**

---

**SPINRAD, Norman (Richard).** American. Born in New York City, 15 September 1940. Educated at the City College of the City University of New York, B.S. 1961. Since 1963, full-time writer. President, Science Fiction Writers of America, 1980–81. Recipient: Prix Apollo, 1974; Jupiter award, 1975. Address: c/o Bantam Books, 666 Fifth Avenue, New York, New York 10019, U.S.A.

### Science-Fiction Publications

#### Novels

*The Solarians*. New York, Paperback Library, 1966; London, Sphere, 1979.
*Agent of Chaos*. New York, Belmont, 1967; London; Corgi, 1981.
*The Men in the Jungle*. New York, Doubleday, 1967; London, Sphere, 1972.
*Bug Jack Barron*. New York, Walker, 1969; London, Macdonald, 1970.
*The Iron Dream*. New York, Avon, 1972; London, Panther, 1974.
*Riding the Torch*. New York, Dell, 1978.
*A World Between*. New York, Pocket Books, 1979; London, Arrow, 1980.
*Songs from the Stars*. New York, Simon and Schuster, 1980; London, Sidgwick and Jackson, 1981.
*The Void Captain's Tale*. New York, Pocket Books, 1983; London, Panther, 1984.
*Child of Fortune*. New York, Bantam, 1985.
*The Mind Game*. New York, Bantam, 1985.
*Little Heroes*. New York, Bantam, 1987; London, Grafton, 1989.
*Russian Spring*. New York, Bantam, 1991.

#### Short Stories

*The Last Hurrah of the Golden Horde*. New York, Doubleday, 1970; London, Macdonald, 1971.
*No Direction Home*. New York, Pocket Books, 1975; London, Millington, 1976.
*The Star-Spangled Future*. New York, Ace, 1979.
*Other Americas* (four novellas). New York, Bantam, 1988.

### Other Publications

#### Novel

*Passing Through the Flame*. New York, Putnam, 1975.

#### Plays

Television Plays: for *Star Trek* series.

#### Other

*Fragments of America*. North Hollywood, California, Now Library Press, 1970.

*Experiment Perilous: Three Essays on Science Fiction*, edited by Andrew Porter. New York, Algol Press, 1976.
*Staying Alive: A Writer's Guide*. Norfolk, Virginia, Donning, 1983.
*Science Fiction in the Real World* (essays). Carbondale, Southern Illinois University Press, 1990.

Editor, *The New Tomorrows*. New York, Belmont, 1971.
Editor, *Modern Science Fiction*. New York, Doubleday, 1974.

*

Bibliography: *Le Livre d'Or de Norman Spinrad* by Patrice Duvic, Paris, Presses Pocket, n.d.

* * *

In Spinrad's 1969 classic "The Big Flash," the Pentagon wants to end "the war in Asia" quickly and victoriously, but is stymied by a public opinion that recoils from the use of tactical nukes. So the psy-warriors create a heavy-metal band, The Four Horsemen, whose every song is a high-pitched plea, complete with war video montage and a subliminal "DO IT," for the orgasmic fulfillment of nuclear destruction. The media blitz is a bit too effective, however, reaching the monitors of ICBM and SLBM officers and triggering nuclear holocaust.

"The Big Flash" is like an embryo enfolding the techniques and concerns of Spinrad's later fictions: multiple viewpoints, the order/chaos dialectic, the sex-violence connection, the 1960's trinity of sex, drugs, and rock and roll, and affectionate satire of the modes of popular culture. As he makes clear in his recent book of essays, *Science Fiction in the Real World*, Norman Spinrad regards the 1960's as a time of crucial cultural innovation, both in SF and in the larger world. So his imagined futures are ones in which representative characters work out the unfinished business of that watershed era.

The Order/Chaos dialectic (in which Chaos disrupts Order only to generate a new Order) is central to most of Spinrad's plots: action itself results from the irruption of wildcards or random factors. In *Agent of Chaos*, the random factor is the secret Brotherhood of Assassins, so devoted to Chaos that it is the custodian of a long-term plot to subvert the Hegemony of Man, a council that rules the solar system in peace and prosperity. In the imaginary sociologist Gregor Markowitz's paradoxical thermodynamics of culture and society, entropy or Chaos is the truly liberating and creative power of the universe, while the existing Order equates to sterility, repression, and just plain boredom. In *Bug Jack Barron*, it is the interactive TV talk show host Jack Barron, whose career is at least superficially devoted to undermining the pretensions of the powerful. In *A World Between*, the "order" of the human worlds is the Pink and Blue War, a struggle for dominance between radical lesbian Femocrats and male-chauvinist Transcendental Scientists; the random factor seems to be the utopian psychosexual balance on Pacifica, the planet over which the two sides are contending. In this novel, Chaos is not mere disorder, but rather a dynamic equilibrium opposed to the stasis of either male or female domination.

The doctrines of Gregor Markowitz are again alluded to in the near-futuristic world of *Little Heroes*, in which the Chaos/Order contrast closely parallels Julia Kristeva's opposition of the Semiotic and the Symbolic. Glorianna O'Toole, the Crazy Lady of Rock and Roll, is the wildcard who helps undermine the mega-corporation that has come to dominate popular music through demographic targeting, statistical analysis, and predictability. She does it by recouping the raw erotic power of rock's imagery and language.

Order and Chaos contend for control through the mass media in more than one of Spinrad's fictions, where the electronic "web" or "net" is often the primary reality. In the story "Prime Time," people retire into a kind of suspended animation, "Total Television Heaven," in which they can re-view, participate in, and interact through over one hundred channels of action-adventures, soaps, porn flicks, and old home movies. Unfortunately for the male viewpoint character, the diversity of this internal CATV system begins to pall, and his connection is broken. In *The Mind Game*, the Transformationalists (modeled upon the Scientology cult) use their media savvy to stop Jack Weller from exposing them, planting stories and images that quickly become quotidian reality.

Using the electronic media to manipulate, to mystify, and to manufacture reality, is not, for Spinrad, a practice to be simplistically denounced. The potential of the "web" is a fact of life; decrying its misuse will not make it go away, and, anyway, it enhances the individual and enriches culture. In *Songs from the Stars*, Sunshine Sue, leader of the Word of Mouth communications guild in post-holocaust Aquaria, is willing to cooperate with the "Black Scientists" of Space Systems, Inc., because their secret space shuttle project might enable her to obtain use of the inactive Big Ear satellite and link the scattered remnants of humanity. The satellite itself might be solar-powered and thus only a "gray" technology, but to get to it, Sue must compromise by depending on machines that burn hydrocarbons or use nuclear-generated electricity. The "clear blue Way" and "white science" of Aquaria are already compromised by reliance on infiltrated Spacer technology, so the prospective merger of white and black at the novel's end amounts to a recognition more than an alteration. In *Bug Jack Barron*, the power of the TV celebrity and of electronic communication technology is ultimately used to expose the political corruption, racism and murders that underlie Benedict Howards' immortality technology. And, in *Little Heroes*, the media corporation's own hardware and software are used to undermine its control. Thus whether communications technology is benign or malign depends crucially upon the morality of its owners and users.

In most of his fiction, Spinrad sedulously avoids using the consistently omniscient or unitary limited narrator, and only rarely does he adopt the first-person narrator. While most of his novels and stories do not shift viewpoint as frequently and as rapidly as "The Big Flash," (which accelerates the shifting to mimic the rhythms of sexual intercourse), it is clear that Spinrad finds the single-consciousness narrator suspiciously privileged. (The major departures from this preference—*The Iron Dream, The Void Captain's Tale, The Mind Game*, and *Child of Fortune*—are all principled exceptions.) This restriction works particularly well in *Songs from the Stars*, where the two main viewpoint characters, Sunshine Sue and Clear Blue Lou, begin with different perspectives on the proper relationship of "Black Science" to the Aquarian Way. In the final chapter, by which time they have come to agree on how to handle the alien signals received at the space station, their viewpoints are subtly merged, so that narrative technique reflects the developing relationship between the characters.

The viewpoint also shifts back and forth between Vanderling and Fraden in *The Men in the Jungle*, reflecting not only the physical distance between the two, but also the moral distance. In *Bug Jack Barron*, the multiple viewpoints perhaps reflect the split-screen technique used on Barron's TV interview show; if that reading is valid, it underlines one reason for careful separation of multiple viewpoints—the multiplexed array of them made available (or necessary) through electronic media technology. In any case, such is the explicit meaning of viewpoint switching in *Little Heroes*, a narrative in which individuals actually internalize the multiple viewpoint, depending upon the extent to which they "plug in, turn on, tune out." Or, as Spinrad puts it in *Science Fiction in the Real World*, commenting on John Shirley's *Eclipse*, "Electronic amplification and consciousness-altering drugs have *already* changed the parameters of the human sensorium, and altered, thereby, our perceptual and psychic definitions of what it means to be human."

Nostalgia for the 1960's counterculture has a bad name these days; our new cultural commissars seem to consider it a particularly nasty form of "political correctness." Spinrad, however, has (unlike the title character of *Bug Jack Barron*), kept the faith, so to speak, though not sentimentally or uncritically. *Child of Fortune*, while formally a SF *bildungsroman* and thematically a meditation on the storyteller's art, is also a critical celebration of hippiedom. Moussa's escape from the lotus-eating life of the Bloomenkinder ("Flower Children") is a rejection of drug-induced nirvana, but not of all consciousness-enhancement. And the street life of the Gypsy Jokers is one of energy and enterprise rather than vagrant beggary. *Little Heroes* is in one sense a paean to 1960's rock and roll; as a story in which the rockers and the computer hackers seize the "software" to return it to the people, it is indeed a 1960's fantasy, but one based on the entertainment technology of the eighties.

Graphic portrayal of human sexual encounters has long been a characteristic of Spinrad's fiction, but the role of sex has changed over the years, as Spinrad has become more sensitive in his treatment of women. In the early *Agent of Chaos*, not one woman appears, even as the object of a male gaze. (Perhaps this is a feature of male-dominated SF that Spinrad parodies in *The Iron Dream*, another female-free novel.) In *Bug Jack Barron, The Men in the Jungle* and *The Mind Game*, and in many pre-1980 short stories, women appear only as objects of male desire and are seemingly valued according to their skill in fellation. In the earlier fictions sex and violence seem to substitute one for another, but with *Songs from the Stars* this changes, as the consciousness of a female character often becomes the viewpoint of narration (a viewpoint from which sexual descriptions, for whatever reason, tend to emphasize emotional response and setting rather than engorgement and penetration). The whole of *Child of Fortune* is told by a first person feminine narrator convincingly different from Spinrad's masculine viewpoint characters. While *Little Heroes* returns to the multiple viewpoint mode dropped for *The Void Captain's Tale* and *Child of Fortune*, viewpoint is pretty evenly parceled out among male and female characters, and only one female viewpoint, that of Cyborg Sally, offers graphic detail in sexual description. The novel also plays up the sex-violence connection, especially in the fantasies of "streetie" Paco Monaco; Paco, however, adopts a gentler sexual mode under the benign influence of the consciousness-enhancing Zap, a fine hairnet of charged wires that symbolizes the web or network of electronic culture.

The topic of sex in Spinrad's fiction demands a look at the strange world of *The Void Captain's Tale.* In the Second Starfaring Age (also the setting of *Child of Fortune*), humanity travels about the galaxy in Void Ships, vessels that use an alien technology to "jump" timelessly the great interstellar distances that would take lifetimes to cross at even relativistic velocities. The technology has one peculiarity: it requires that a human female, the Jump Pilot, be wired into the guidance system. Her role is ultimately self-destructive, for she will end up like the drug and charge addicts spotted here and there in Spinrad's fiction. Her reward for becoming thus wasted is that in each Jump she experiences a transcendent orgasm, a momentary fusion with the "Great and Only."

The plot of *The Void Captain's Tale* depends from an inadvertant social gaffe, when the captain, Genro Kane Gupta, becomes acquainted with his pilot, Dominique Alia Wu. It thickens when Genro, fascinated with the "platform orgasm" experience of pilots, becomes sexually involved with Dominique. It climaxes when the captain, succumbing to the pilot's mad entreaties, gives her the ultimate charge—a jump without destination coordinates, a Blind Jump. This has negative consequences—a pilot is dead, a ship's crew and passengers are likely marooned to die—but it is said to give the pilot the ultimate peak experience as she dies. (And we have gotten another, very different take on the theme of "The Big Flash.") *The Void Captain's Tale* is a haunting, melancholy romance, multi-layered in the texture of its meanings, seeming to mean more than it can possibly say, not least because it is a male confession of inability to plumb the sexual experience of the human female.

In *The Iron Dream*, Spinrad gave Adolf Hitler the worst punishment he could dream up. He created an alternate universe in which Hitler was no longer an almost successful Madman Who Conquered the World. He made him into a penniless emigrant and hack SF writer, the leaden-prosed composer of a sick racist fantasy overladen with violent phallic symbols, *Lord of the Swastika*, and inflicted upon him a vacuous critical essay written by an English professor. Critically aware of the turbulent unconscious of science fiction, street- and book-smart Spinrad has crafted a shelf of SF that rivals anyone's for inventiveness, zestful prose, and hipness.

—John P. Brennan

---

**SPRAGUE, Carter.** *See* **MERWIN, Sam, Jr.**

---

**SPRINGER, Nancy (Connor).** American. Born in Montclair, New Jersey, 5 July 1948. Educated at Gettysburg College, Pennsylvania, 1966–1970, B.A. Married Joel Springer in 1969; one daughter and one son. Library clerk, St. Joseph's College, Emmitsburg, Maryland, 1969; teacher, Delone Catholic High School, McSherrytown, Pennsylvania, 1970–71; teacher's aide, Hoffman Home for Children, Littlestown, Pennsylvania, 1972–73. Teacher, York College and Franklin and Marshall College, since 1986. Communications instructor, Bradley Academy for the Visual Arts, since 1990. Since 1972, writer. Address: c/o Atheneum Publishers, 866 Third Avenue, New York, New York 10022, U.S.A.

### Science-Fiction Publications

Novels (series: Isle; Sea King)

*The Book of Suns* (Isle). New York, Pocket Books, 1977; revised edition, as *The Silver Sun*, New York, Pocket Books, 1980; Glasgow, Drew, 1984.

*The White Hart* (Isle). New York, Pocket Books, 1979; Glasgow, Drew, 1984.

*The Sable Moon* (Isle). New York, Pocket Books, 1981; Glasgow, Drew, 1985.

*The Black Beast* (Isle). New York, Pocket Books, 1982; Glasgow, Drew, 1985.

*The Book of Vale* (includes *The Black Beast* and *The Golden Swan*). New York, Doubleday, 1984.

*The Golden Swan* (Isle). New York, Timescape, 1983; Glasgow, Drew, 1985.

*Wings of Flame*. New York, Tor, 1985; London, Arrow, 1986.
*Chains of Gold*. New York, Arbor House, 1986; London, Macdonald, 1987.
Sea King trilogy:
*Madbond*. New York, Tor, 1987; London, Futura, 1988.
*Mindbond*. New York, Tor, 1987; London, Futura, 1989.
*Godbond*. New York, Tor, 1988; London, Futura, 1990.
*The Hex Witch of Seldom*. New York, Baen, 1988.
*Apocalypse*. Novato, California, Underwood Miller, 1989.

Short Stories

*Chance: And Other Gestures of the Hand of Fate* (includes poetry). New York, Baen, 1987.

OTHER PUBLICATIONS

Novels for children

*A Horse to Love*. New York, Harper and Row, 1987.
*Not on a White Horse*. New York, Atheneum, 1988.
*They're All Named Wildfire*. New York, Atheneum, 1989.
*Red Wizard*. New York, Atheneum, 1990.
*Colt*. New York, Dial, 1991.
*The Friendship Song*. New York, Atheneum, 1992.

*

Nancy Springer comments:

Fiction writing for me is an advanced form of gossip without the hurtful effects that might occur if I speculated on paper (or on the porches with the neighbors) about actual living individuals. I contemplate imaginary people instead, but the fascination with human personality and behavior is the same. For that matter, so is the yen for story, narrative, with a thrill of shock or a pang of emotion at its core.

For me, at least, fiction writing has always started with those two things: people (fictional characters), and a tendency never to let the literal truth get in the way of a good story. Ideally, the story should grow out of the characters themselves, like a tree springing up in a flower garden.

Writing fantasy involves the same fascination in a more complicated form: the characters often are aspects of the human psyche, acting out their conflicts on a dream-landscape straight out of what Jung called the "collective unconscious." Looking for political realism? Don't look in my books. Armies and princes exist in the kingdoms of the psyche merely as matrix for the archetypical story. When writing fantasy, really I am writing about myself and all others like me.

* * *

Nancy Springer is a gifted fantasist whose work consistently improves, growing stronger and more subtle with each new publication, and whose range is expanding in both audience and excitement. She is a horse lover, with horses (as well as imaginary animals) and riding horses representing a rich thread through much of her work. The quest theme is central to her writing. While the quest is never a mere journey, the novels can certainly be read on one level as exciting, fast-paced adventure gently touched with magic and myth, and peopled by believable characters with realistic flaws and strengths. Her later works develop strong female characters, who come into their strength/self-knowledge through the fear and trials of the quest. Springer uses the quest to explore the consequences of vision, the relative and subjective view of choices made, and life's contrasts (good-evil, light-dark, intentions-outcome), and further as vehicle for the testing and nurturing of relationships and interpersonal bonds, those between lovers, parents and children, brothers and friends.

Springer's first published novels, aimed at young adults, are set in her imaginary world of Isle. *The White Hart* and *The Silver Sun* (based on *The Book of Suns*), are adequate conventional fantasy but suffer from several serious flaws. They are derivative of fantasy classics, mired in fantastical jargon, and so overly burdened with (Celtic) mythological components that both characterization and world building are slighted. However, even these weakest of her works provide well-paced quest adventures. They also introduce us to her fresh, appealing depiction of real and imaginary animals.

Each new addition to the series, *The Sable Moon, The Black Beast, The Golden Swan*, shows Springer's continuing growth as a storyteller, her refined use of language (with fantastical jargon no longer interrupting the story flow), her use of mythological elements enriching the story rather than bogging it down, and her characters—people with human frailties as well as strength. The series does a good job of illuminating the tension between good and evil. The use of imaginary animals, especially unicorns and swans, as relative indicators of social and cultural good/evil is particularly well done.

*Wings of Flame* and *Chains of Gold* are Springer's more romantic fantasies. They present outwardly different, yet equally strong female characters. *Wings* offers vibrantly detailed romantic fantasy with magic winning the day over superstition. *Chains* is triumphant and compelling fantasy showcasing Springer's growth as a writer, especially her world building, vivid characterization, and subtle touch with magic and fantasy elements. She takes the Druidic ritual virgin sacrifice made to ensure fertility (here the virgin is both male and female) and gives it a modern twist. The sacrificial winterking, Arlen, and bride, Cerilla, fall in love, refusing their ritual destiny. This is the story of their flight through a world whose landscape is of both dreams and nightmares, of their relationship and personal growth, and of their relationship with the ghost of their savior. The book is notable for the character of Cerilla, her interactions with the Oracle and Goddess, her maturation, and her growth to self-knowledge and strength.

The Sea King trilogy, *Madbond, Mindbond, Godbond*, is a strong fantasy with "real" people in a well-developed imaginary world. The books explore relationships, those between choices and consequences and those between people, and the relativity of good and evil. Again the quest is the mechanism employed as both illumination and catalyst. The trilogy is a pleasure to read, gracefully written and resonating with poetic imagery.

Springer's repertoire includes both short fiction and poetry, collected in *Chance: And Other Gestures of the Hand of Fate*, and contemporary fantasy, *The Hex Witch of Seldom*. The short fiction takes traditional themes (the princess and the peasant) and standard fantastic subjects (living forest, wizards/gods) and gives them provocative twists resulting in subtle, original fantasy. *Chance* is an excellent introduction to Springer's work, allowing a taste of her style, poetic imagery, fantastic landscapes and believable characters that will make fans of its readers. In *Hex*, the wonderfully drawn, misfit, young woman comes of age during her struggle with the forces of good and evil against a backdrop of fantastic elements and characters (witch, magical black stallion) wedded with regional folklore (Pennsylvania Dutch).

Springer's recent work has branched out to include material aimed at children, featuring authentically presented horses. *A Horse to Love, Not on a White Horse*, and *They're all Named Wildfire* are compelling and realistic stories featuring female characters whose relationship with and responsibility for horses allows them to grow, gain confidence, and recognize their own strength. *Red Wizard*, a fantasy for children, is not quite as strong as the material written for the young adult audience, but it does contain some interesting ideas, imagery, and witty puns.

*Apocalypse* is Springer's most exciting work to date. It vibrates with powerful imagery, contrasts, and the sophisticated use of cultural idiom. The setting is a grim, economically depressed mining town juxtaposed against pagan natural beauty, seductive magic, and the horrific supernatural. The main characters include the "Four Horsewomen of the Apocalypse," the female catalyst, Joanie, and an outsider male, Barry. These characters carry all the cultural shorthand of their stereotype but are fully developed people with weaknesses and strengths, good and evil traits. Joanie and Barry are particularly poignant characters, both having physical defects, both tormented as outsiders, whose innate goodness ultimately triumphs. It is the complicity of the community in the tormenting, its lack of tolerance, its narrow-mindedness that is shown as true evil, more so than the nightmarish visions and plagues provided courtesy of the devil. The reworking of a myth through the lens of popular culture, *Apocalypse* presents the classic struggle between good and evil with much of the focus on the gray areas, not merely the black and white.

—Catherine M. Currier

---

**SPRUILL, Steven.** American. Born in Battle Creek, Michigan, 20 April 1946. Educated at Andrews University, Berrien Springs, Michigan, B.A. in biology 1968; Catholic University of America, Washington, D.C., M.A. in psychology 1979, Ph.D. in clinical psychology 1981. Married Nancy Lyon in 1969. Biological technician, Hazleton Laboratories, Falls Church, Virginia, 1969–73; psychology intern, Veterans Administration Hospital, Washington, D.C., 1978–79, and Mt. Vernon Community Health Center, Alexandria, Virginia, 1979–80. Since 1981, full-time writer. Agent: Al Zuckerman, 21 West 26th Street, New York, New York 10010, U.S.A.

SCIENCE-FICTION PUBLICATIONS

Novels (series: Elias Kane)

*Keepers of the Gate*. New York, Doubleday, and London, Hale, 1977.
*The Psychopath Plague* (Kane). New York, Doubleday, and London, Hale, 1978.
*Hellstone*. New York, Playboy, 1980.
*The Imperator Plot* (Kane). New York, Doubleday, 1983.
*The Genesis Shield*. New York, Tor, 1985.
*Paradox Planet* (Kane). New York, Doubleday, 1988.
*Painkiller*. New York, St. Martin's Press, 1990.

*

Steven Spruill comments:

My purpose in writing is primarily to entertain the reader and produce an emotional experience in the process. I believe people read in order to feel. Consequently, I consider it extremely important to write in the technical sense in such a way that the reader feels him or herself to *be* the viewpoint character, wanting what that character wants, fearing what he or she fears, and sensing along with the character. In the process of writing this way I feel it is quite important for the author to remain as nearly invisible as possible.

In addition, I prefer the extraordinay to the ordinary (which is all too readily available to us in real life) when I structure the plots of my novels. Consequently, most of my novels are concerned with the bizarre, the complicated, the strange, and the psychological, hopefully made clear through "simple" writing, and engaging through the hopes, needs, fears, and, in general, the emotional journey of the characters through their rather baroque plots and landscapes. I might sum up my position as a writer by naming the two other authors I most admire—Bob Shaw and Ken Follett.

* * *

Three of Spruill's novels are science fiction only by the broadest definition. *Hellstone* is a horror story about the Loch Ness monster, but a pre-publication reviewer was right in suggesting that readers are bored for much of the early pages and only "mildly chilled" by what actually happens. *The Genesis Shield* is a mildly successful application of biological and psychological themes to a heating up of the Cold War. *Painkiller*, the latest novel, achieved some popularity as Literary Guild and Doubleday Book Club selections, but it is a somewhat disappointing medical thriller that, despite an attractive doctor-heroine and an interesting mystery, is a dull and even expected letdown.

Spruill's first novel, *Keepers of the Gate* is not, as a pre-publication reviewer suggested, uninspired and routine, but a space opera that reads well and is a promise of future excellence. Two long short stories, "Prime Culture" (in *Aries 1*, edited by John Grant, Newton Abbot, Devon, David and Charles, 1979) and "The Janus Equation" (in *Binary Star 4*, New York, Dell, 1980), are competent but not especially noteworthy.

On the other hand, despite several less than enthusiastic reviews, the Elias Kane novels, *The Psychopath Plague, The Imperator Plot*, and *Paradox Planet*, which bear a superficial resemblance to Asimov's Elijah Baley series, are well-plotted, well-written, and entertaining. Elias, former Navy lieutenant, is highly intelligent, possessed of eidetic memory, and has spent years in various educational institutions studying, among other things, psychology, criminology, physics, and biology. A superman he is not, for he makes the kind of errors caused by human fallibility and emotion, a touch that obviously draws heavily on Spruill's background as clinical psychologist.

In *The Psychopath Plague*, Elias, aided by the Cephantine Pendrake, locates the source of the widening contamination that causes people to be seized by a compulsion to kill or maim anyone who happens to be nearby, pinpoints the criminals, and wins his true love Elizabeth, the million-credit reward, and the gratitude of the Imperator, who rules Earth and the nine, sometimes rebellious, colonies. In *The Imperator Plot*, three years of happiness with Elizabeth end when Elias is summoned by the Imperator to head the investigation of an assassination plot. Unfortunately, the assassin strikes first, Elizabeth dies saving Elias, and the Imperator, his body destroyed, is saved only because his personal physician, Martha Reik, quickly attaches his uninjured head to an advanced life support system. In *Paradox Planet*, under orders from Imperator Briana, Kane, Pendrake, and Martha thwart a rebellion on the heavy-gravity planet Cassiodorus, source of the beta-steel needed for Imperial dreadnoughts. A sequel seems inevitable in view of the escape of rebel dreadnaughts. Kane's willingness to continue serving the Imperator is ensured when he learns that he has fathered her soon-to-be born son. In all three, the extent of the real plot is uncovered only after a long series of harrowing experiences and sidetracks, during which Elias learns much about himself and humanity.

What lifts these novels from the ordinary is often at first reading almost unnoticeable. Thus, in *The Psychopath Plague* only further reflection shows parallels between a seemingly insignificant conversation about the difference between perception and reality, between the human being's belief that his or her thoughts can control behavior and the view of all other intelligent creatures in the galaxy that this belief is irrational and that it is really environment, physical, mental, and emotional, that controls all behavior, including that of humanity. Since the attack on Earth is alien, partly physical and partly through the tremendous mental powers of the innocent-appearing invaders, it is a nice touch that this discussion is conducted with a friendly alien not yet identified as part of the problem.

In *The Imperator Plot*, the significance of the demands of the bodiless head for a new body, for a way to experience the pleasure of eating, even the desire for a human touch on its forehead, is not at first obvious. Only later do certain questions arise: How would the Imperator deprived of all sensation accept the situation? What would be the effect on his behavior? How does it affect his Ornyl bodyguard? An integral part of the solution is Elias's own experience of a temporary total sensory deprivation and his subsequent understanding of both self and the Ornyl. A similar understanding of the physiological make-up of the sauroids is essential to solving the problem in *Paradox Planet.*

Spruill's human characters are well-developed and believable, their actions made plausible by the motivations established early on. He also has an inventive turn of mind where aliens are concerned, and some of his creations are most interesting. Pendrake, the Cephantine, is an orange-skinned giant of enormous strength from a species known for its inability to permit violence or death, empathetic with all plant and animal life, and respected as incapable of uttering a falsehood; his absolute loyalty to Elias, who has gambled him out of slavery, is a major ingredient in the successful investigations. The musal trees control the humanoid Krythians and the illusory, comical, penguin-like traders, the Chirpones, who actually carry out their plot against humanity. The Moitans, "fish-people," are an advanced technological civilization. The Ornyls, humanoid giant insects, are fierce warriors; their binding to their chosen masters is irrevocable and complete. The sauroids of Cassiodorus are essential to the rebels' ability to live on that planet. In every case—except, perhaps, for the S'uniphs, who are nearly mindless anyway—the behavior of these aliens is consistent with the internal psychology established for them when they first appear on the scene.

Spruill writes well, invents interesting plots, and uses his own technical knowledge effectively. Critics have complained, with some justification, of inaccuracies in his understanding of hard science. They have not, however, been able to fault the inventiveness and clarity of his behavioral science constructions. In this latter respect, Spruill—even in his less successful work—is a talented writer, deserving of continued attention, no little praise, and genuine anticipation of his work to come.

—Arthur O. Lewis

---

**STABLEFORD, Brian M(ichael).** Also writes as Brian Craig. British. Born in Shipley, Yorkshire, 25 July 1948. Educated at Manchester Grammar School; University of York, B.A. (honours) in biology 1969, D. Phil, in sociology 1979. Married Vivien Owen in 1973; one son and one daughter. Lecturer in Sociology, University of Reading, Berkshire, 1976 and since 1977. Recipient: J. Lloyd Eaton award, 1987. Address: 113 St. Peter's Road, Reading, Berkshire RG6 1PG, England.

SCIENCE-FICTION PUBLICATIONS

Novels (series: Asgard; Daedalus; Dies Irae; Hooded Swan)

*Cradle of the Sun*. New York, Ace, and London, Sidgwick and Jackson, 1969.
*The Blind Worm*. New York, Ace, and London, Sidgwick and Jackson, 1970.
*The Days of Glory* (Dies Irae). New York, Ace, and Manchester, Five Star, 1971.
*In the Kingdom of the Beasts* (Dies Irae). New York, Ace, 1971; London, Quartet, 1974.
*Day of Wrath* (Dies Irae). New York, Ace, 1971; London, Quartet, 1974.
*To Challenge Chaos*. New York, DAW, 1972.
*Halcyon Drift* (Swan). New York, DAW, 1972; London, Dent, 1974.
*Rhapsody in Black* (Swan). New York, DAW, 1973; London, Dent, 1975.
*Promised Land* (Swan). New York, DAW, 1974; London, Dent, 1975.
*The Paradise Game* (Swan). New York, DAW, 1974; London, Dent, 1976.
*The Fenris Device* (Swan). New York, DAW, 1974; London, Pan, 1978.
*Swan Song*. New York, DAW, 1975; London, Pan, 1978.
*Man in a Cage*. New York, Day, 1975.
*The Face of Heaven*. London, Quartet, 1976.
*The Mind-Riders*. New York, DAW, 1976; as *The Mind Riders*, London, Fontana, 1977.
*The Florians* (Daedalus). New York, DAW, 1976; London, Hamlyn, 1978.
*Critical Threshold* (Daedalus). New York, DAW, 1977; London, Hamlyn, 1979.
*The Realms of Tartarus*. New York, DAW, 1977.
*Wildeblood's Empire* (Daedalus). New York, DAW, 1977; London, Hamlyn, 1979.
*The City of the Sun* (Daedalus). New York, DAW, 1978; London, Hamlyn, 1980.
*The Last Days of the Edge of the World* (for children). London, Hutchinson, 1978; New York, Berkley, 1985.
*Balance of Power* (Daedalus). New York, DAW, 1979; London, Hamlyn, 1984.
*The Walking Shadow*. London, Fontana, 1979; New York, Carroll and Graf, 1989.
*The Paradox of Sets* (Daedalus). New York, DAW, 1979.
*Optiman*. New York, DAW, 1980; as *War Games*, London, Pan, 1981.
*The Castaways of Tanagar*. New York, DAW, 1981.
*Journey to the Center* (Asgard). New York, DAW, 1982; revised as *Journey to the Centre*, London, New English Library, 1987.
*The Gates of Eden*. New York, DAW, 1983; London, New English Library, 1990.
*The Empire of Fear*. London, Simon and Schuster, 1988.
*The Centre Cannot Hold* (Asgard). London, New England Library, 1990.
*Invaders from the Centre* (Asgard). London, New England Library, 1990.

Novels as Brian Craig

*Zaragoz.* Brighton, West Sussex, Games Workshop, 1989.
*Plague Daemon.* Brighton, West Sussex, Games Workshop, 1990.
*Storm Warriors.* Brighton, West Sussex, Games Workshop, 1991.

Short Stories

*Sexual Chemistry: Sardonic Tales of the Genetic Revolution.* London, Simon and Schuster, 1991.

OTHER PUBLICATIONS

Novel

*The Werewolves of London.* London, Simon and Schuster, 1990.

Other

*The Mysteries of Modern Science.* London, Routledge, 1977; Totowa, New Jersey, Littlefield Adams, 1980.
*A Clash of Symbols: The Triumph of James Blish.* San Bernardino, California, Borgo Press, 1979.
*Masters of Science-Fiction: Essays on Science-Fiction Authors.* San Bernardino, California, Borgo Press, 1981.
*Bob Shaw.* N.p., British Science Fiction Association, 1981.
*The Science in Science Fiction,* with Peter Nicholls and David Langford. London, Joseph, 1982; New York, Knopf, 1983.
*Future Man: Brave New World or Genetic Nightmare?* London, Granada, and New York, Crown, 1984.
*The Third Millennium: A History of the World AD 2000-3000,* with David Langford. London, Sidgwick and Jackson, and New York, Knopf, 1985.
*Scientific Romance in Britain, 1870-1950.* London, Fourth Estate, and New York, St. Martin's Press, 1985.
*The Sociology of Science Fiction.* San Bernardino, California, Borgo Press, 1987.
*The Way to Write Science Fiction.* London, Elm Tree, 1989.

Editor, *The Dedalus Book of Decadence (Moral Ruins).* Sawtry, Cambridgeshire, Dedalus, 1990.
Editor, *Tales of the Wandering Jew.* Sawtry, Cambridgeshire, Dedalus, 1991.

* * *

Brian Stableford would have made a mark on the SF world even if he had not become a writer of fiction. *Scientific Romance in Britain* and *The Sociology of Science Fiction* are among the small number of books by British critics that have made a significant addition to our understanding of SF, and he has played a significant role in the production of some of the most important works of SF reference: he was, for instance, a major contributor to Peter Nicholls's *The Science Fiction Encyclopedia,* F.N. Magill's *Survey of Science Fiction Literature* and Neil Barron's *Anatomy of Wonder* (1987), for the 3rd edition of which he wrote some 180 pages. He has not only published critical articles in numerous journals, but also hundreds of perceptive reviews of SF books, including around 90 in *Foundation* alone.

Few people in the SF world have quite such an extensive knowledge of the field, including some of its obscurest corners. This knowledge has had a clear influence on his considerable fictional output, although not always a beneficial one. Throughout his years at university, both as a student and as an academic (in the Department of Sociology at the University of Reading), he was able to turn out fairly routine novels with remarkable facility, using his knowledge to play variations on rather familiar themes. Indeed, even in very recent years, after his decision to leave university life and become a full-time writer, his work has occasionally been no more than competent, as witness the series of fantasy novels (the Orfeo series, beginning with *Zaragoz*) and short stories published by Games Workshop under the pseudonym "Brian Craig," which are linked into GW's role-playing fantasy games.

Because of this visible presence of what could be regarded as hack work, critics have tended to underestimate his fiction, some of which do not take sufficient account of the original elements in his various space operas. The series known variously as the "Hooded Swan" (after the spaceship) or "Star Pilot Grainger" (after the "hero") has features that set it on a level above the run-of-the-mill space opera published by DAW in the 1970's. The six missions offer some complex scientific puzzles, in which Stableford draws upon his earlier biological training. And there is also the complex figure of the narrator Grainger: a large part of the interest in the narrative is picking out, from Grainger's actions and from the reactions of his friends, how false that proposed self-image is. Grainger is indeed central to the purpose of the series, which Stableford explains in a recent autobiographical piece in *Foundation* (no. 50, Autumn 1990): "I decided that although I would deploy all the promised clichés I would do my best to subvert—or at least to pervert—every one. I further resolved that this would be the first space opera series in which the hero would not only never shoot anybody but would not even hit anybody (and, if invited to fight, would always politely decline to do it)." If it was the first, it was not the last: this same character trait is found in the narrator of the three Centre novels. As for the hero in the Daedalus books, he subverts one of the basic premises of SF: a woolly liberal, he tries to solve puzzles, but he usually finds them beyond solution.

Critics have also unjustly neglected *The Walking Shadow,* the most ambitious and successful of Stableford's early novels: indeed, neglect by critics and publishers were behind Stableford's decision to abandon writing fiction, in 1981. *The Walking Shadow* is one of those rare attempts to equal the vision of Wells's *The Time Machine* or Stapledon's *Last and First Men:* a story of involuntary time-travellers whose journey takes in the whole history of humanity from the present to its end—its closing sentences are: "Herdsman's descendents, in time, became extinct, and there was no human life in the universe. Meanwhile . . ." There are flaws in the novel, notably the tendency to inject passages of scientific lecture: but as a scientific and historical vision, it stands on its own in the SF of the 1970's. It is the first to deal squarely and critically with Lovelock's "Gaia" hypothesis, and foreshadows the ambitious work of such 1980's writers as Bear and Simmons.

Stableford returned to fiction writing with "And He Not Busy Being Born . . ." (in *Interzone 16,* Summer 1986). Short stories were a very minor part of his output in the 1970's, but he has published much more extensively since 1986, and with considerable success: "The Magic Bullet" topped the *Interzone* readers' poll in 1989. Most of these stories have had near-contemporary settings, and have been concerned with the effects of biotechnological innovation, going back to the classic "What if. . . ?" story premise: these have been collected in Stableford's only volume of short fiction, *Sexual Chemistry.* Several have ignored one of the most basic of the so-called rules of writing fiction, being prose narratives almost totally deprived of dialogue: like "Sexual Chemistry" itself, historical accounts of scientific and sociological change. Yet they work as stories, they distance Stableford from the pulp style of his earlier fiction, and establish him as one of the few British writers today writing stories in the classic SF mode about the effects of scientific change.

Stableford is a science-fiction writer with an interest in hard science, and a sceptical and materialist view of the world, a man who has "never been able to understand how anyone finds the concept of God remotely plausible." On the surface, then, he appears an unlikely person to embark on a series of what he calls "metaphysical fantasies": a long novel about vampires, *The Empire of Fear*, and a trilogy on werewolves, of which only the first volume, *The Werewolves of London*, has so far appeared. But these fantasies are in a sense scientific. Stableford has imagined a scientific basis for vampirism, and realises that if immortal vampires existed, then the entire history of the world would have been quite different: the vampires would inevitably have become rulers. The novel is thus an alternative history novel, set in 17th-century London and Africa. He has worked out the problems with considerable ingenuity, and clearly taken much more trouble with the construction and the writing than with some of his earlier novels. Imagining a scientifically plausible world with werewolves, of course, involves changing most of the basic premises of science as well as history, and this as yet unfinished project looks like it could be the most ambitious and imaginative he has undertaken. The "new" SF career which Stableford began in 1986 is far too early to assess, but it would seem that he has already gained the status which eluded him in the 1970's, of being one of the leading British writers of serious speculative fiction.

—Edward James

---

**STALLMAN, Robert.** American. Born in 1930. *Died in August 1980.*

SCIENCE-FICTION PUBLICATIONS

Novels (series: The Beast)

The Book of the Beast:
*The Orphan.* New York, Pocket Books, 1980; London, Granada, 1981.
*The Captive.* New York, Pocket Books, 1981; London, Granada, 1982.
*The Beast.* New York, Pocket Books, 1982; as *The Book of the Beast*, London, Granada, 1982.

* * *

Robert Stallman's exquisite fantasy novel *The Orphan* was published in March 1980. By August 1980 he was dead of cancer at fifty. He had completed two more volumes of the series, published posthumously, *The Captive* and *The Beast.* The vanguard novel, *The Orphan*, would have been enough: it was so good that it was nominated for a Hugo award in 1981—a great honor because it was the only work of fiction that Stallman wrote.

Summarized very superficially, the three volumes of the Book of the Beast narrate the four-year maturation process of an other-worldly creature and the mate who will finally join him in love. *The Orphan* begins in mid-1930's south-western Michigan at the farm of Catherine and Martin Nordmeyer, where the "Beast" appears for the first time and "shifts" into the person of Robert Lee Burney, a boy of about five. Robert is adopted by the kindly Nordmeyers. So begins the kinship of the Beast and the matriarchal line of Aunt Cat as the six major episodes of the three volumes unfold. With Aunt Cat and her husband Martin, Robert/Beast begin to mature. But the idyllic summer months end in tragedy when drifters terrorize the Nordmeyers and Martin is killed by an errant shotgun blast, even as the Beast, shifting from Robert's five-year-old person to its physically and mentally superhuman self, intervenes to save the family. Witnessing the connection between the Beast and Robert, Aunt Cat, driven insane with grief at the loss of Martin, hounds it until it flees and arrives in Illinois as early teen-aged Charles Cahill to live with Grandmother Stumway, Aunt Cat's mother. Charles goes to school for the year, at the end of which the Beast, in a fit of springtime lust, is discovered coupling, as Charles, with a cow. He shifts to Beast and flees to Chicago. *The Orphan* is a stunning work.

In *The Captive*, the beast joined with the person of Barry Golden, falls in love with Rene, daughter of Aunt Cat. Rene's alcoholic husband, William Hegel, nearly succeeds in killing Barry in a car/train wreck. Shifted into Beast, however, Barry/Beast survive, only to be held in captivity in an open cage by a farmer. Escaped and reunited with Rene (divorced from William), Barry, Rene and her daughter Mina move to Arizona. All is not finally well until Barry/Beast rescue kidnapped Rene and Mina from William and his American-Nazi training cell mustered in the mountains. In *The Beast*, the Beast's female partner-to-be saves the life of George (Bo) Beaumont from cancer. Bo is the father of Charles Cahill of *The Orphan.* Bo believes Charles is dead in his early teens. Charles is dead, provisionally. But the Beast can make Charles live if Bo wishes, though Bo must relinquish the life of a woman he loves in exchange. Bo chooses Charles's life. The two beasts finally get together in a mystical marriage, leaving Bo reunited with his resurrected son, and Barry, also permanently resurrected, with Rene and Mina.

The adventure of the Beast in *The Orphan* is a pristine metaphor. The successor volumes, *The Captive* and *The Beast*, provide ethers, metaphysics, transcendence, and substantial explanation. Ironically, they are lesser in quality than *The Orphan* just because their purpose is to finish its story and to explain its vision. Aesthetic considerations aside, the three volumes together are an initiation story, a tale of a Beast's quest that tells us, thereby, about human quests. It is full of lovely natural-state settings and objects plucked from contexts by the super senses of the Beast to convey a feeling of seeing the essence of the landscapes, the flora, the animals—indeed the very furniture and trinkets in the Nordmeyer farm house. It evokes many wonderful traditional motifs. Principally there is the shape-shifter tale such as that about the bear-man in the ancient Icelandic Grettissaga, and reused by Tolkien in the Beorn character of *The Hobbit.* We may also remember R.L. Stevenson's *The Strange Case of Dr. Jekyll and Mr. Hyde*, or think of Robert Silverberg's sinister tale "Passengers." It recalls "beauty and the beast" stories. It erects an occult universe and, in the relationship of the Beast to its "persons," reinterprets notions of the golem and zombie. The basic narrative gives the reader humor, cleverness, and, best of all and mostly, unposturing clarity.

In a telephone interview, Mrs. Stallman has spoken of her husband's interest in the Jungian notion of a collective unconscious. The suggestion is helpful in an attempt to explain what a meaning of the story might be. Surely the elegance of the tale is rooted in the daring simple obviousness of its theme. The theme is a progress that beings, "there is a Beast in all of us. . . ." It feels and tastes things more sensually. It is physically stronger. It is smarter. Its appetites are keener—for food, for sex, for beauty. It loves music. It is the foundation of our emotions. It is the source of our creative drive. In the story the Beast might be the novelist himself—is, in fact, when he is personed with writer Barry Golden. The Beast is always trying to fit itself into the human world. It participates in virtually all of our meaningful existence. But it is not us. It is not human. It can be a guiltless maverick to our human ideas of order and morality. It is amoral, yet innocent. It is heedlessly curious, willing to learn what may be fatally dangerous for humans to know. Therefore, it is a mistake to imagine that humanity and Beast are an identity—or even a unity. People are always human. Beasts are only Beasts.

—John R. Pfeiffer

---

**STAPLEDON, (William) Olaf.** British. Born near Wallasey, Cheshire, 10 May 1886. Educated at Abbotsholme School; Balliol College, Oxford, M.A. 1909; University of Liverpool, Ph.D. 1925. Served in the Friends' Ambulance Unit in France, 1916–19. Married Agnes Zena Miller in 1919; one son and one daughter. Assistant headmaster, Manchester Grammar School, 1910; worked for Alfred Holt and Company, shippers, Liverpool and Port Said, 1911; Lecturer in History and English, Workers' Educational Association, University of Liverpool, 1912–15; after World War I, Lecturer in Philosophy and Psychology, University of Liverpool. *Died 6 September 1950.*

### Science-Fiction Publications

Novels

*Last and First Men: A Story of the Near and Far Future.* London, Methuen, 1930; New York, Cape and Smith, 1931.
*Last Men in London.* London, Methuen, 1932; Boston, Gregg Press, 1976.
*Odd John: A Story Between Jest and Earnest.* London, Methuen, 1935; New York, Dutton, 1936.
*Star Maker.* London, Methuen, 1937; as *The Star Maker*, New York, Berkley, 1961.
*Darkness and the Light.* London, Methuen, 1942; Westport, Connecticut, Hyperion Press, 1974.
*Sirius: A Fantasy of Love and Discord.* London, Secker and Warburg, 1944; included in *To the End of Time*, 1953.
*Death into Life.* London, Methuen, 1946.
*The Flames.* London, Secker and Warburg, 1947.
*Worlds of Wonder* (includes *The Flames; Death into Life; Old Man in New World*). Los Angeles, Fantasy, 1949.
*A Man Divided.* London, Methuen, 1950.
*To the End of Time: The Best of Olaf Stapledon*, edited by Basil Davenport. New York, Funk and Wagnalls, 1953.
*Nebula Maker.* Hayes, Middlesex, Bran's Head, 1976; New York, Dodd Mead, 1982.
*Nebula Maker and Four Encounters.* New York, Dodd Mead, 1983.

Short Stories

*Old Man in New World.* London, Allen and Unwin, 1944.
*Four Encounters.* Hayes, Middlesex, Bran's Head, 1976.
*Far Future Calling: Uncollected Science Fiction and Fantasies*, edited by Sam Moskowitz. Philadelphia, Trainer, 1980.

### Other Publications

Verse

*Latter-Day Psalms.* Liverpool, Young, 1914.

Other

*A Modern Theory of Ethics: A Study of the Relations of Ethics and Psychology.* London, Methuen, and New York, Dutton, 1929.
*Waking World.* London, Methuen, 1934.
*New Hope for Britain.* London, Methuen, 1939.
*Saints and Revolutionaries.* London, Heinemann, 1939.
*Philosophy and Living.* London, Penguin, 2 vols., 1939.
*Beyond the "Isms".* London, Secker and Warburg, 1942.
*The Seven Pillars of Peace.* London, Common Wealth, 1944.
*Youth and Tomorrow.* London, St. Botolph, 1946.
*The Opening of the Eyes*, edited by Agnes Z. Stapledon. London, Methuen, 1954.
*Talking Across the World: The Love Letters of Olaf Stapledon and Agnes Miller 1913-1919*, edited by Robert Crossley. Hanover, New Hampshire, University Press of New England, 1987.

*

Bibliography: *Olaf Stapledon: A Bibliography* by Harvey J. Satty and Curtis C. Smith, Westport, Connecticut, Greenwood Press, 1984.

Critical Studies: *Olaf Stapledon* by Patrick A. McCarthy, Boston, Hall, 1982; *Olaf Stapledon, A Man Divided* by Leslie A. Fiedler, New York and Oxford, Oxford University Press, 1983; *The Legacy of Olaf Stapledon: Critical Essays and an Unpublished Manuscript* edited by Patrick A. McCarthy, Martin H. Greenberg, and Charles Elkin, New York, Greenwood, 1989.

* * *

An appreciation of Olaf Stapledon's science fiction demands some mention of his overt discussions of philosophy, the chief subject of his work in adult education. The publication of his "study of the relations of ethics and psychology," *A Modern Theory of Ethics* (1929), preceded by a year his first novel, *Last and First Men.* In *Ethics*, he is much concerned with the psychological "moods" that, transcending mental routines of daily life, may colour an individual's perception of and actions within the social milieu, and in face of a seemingly indifferent cosmos. These are moods of "moral zeal," "disillusion," and "ecstasy," the last implying awareness that, although failure to attain the good may induce bleak disillusion, nothing is eternally lost in a universe of excellence. Such a "beyond good and evil" holistic and synthesizing perspective may only be achieved in conditions of psychological, and maybe physical, extremity. In a later popular philosophical exposition, *Philosophy and Living*, Stapledon developed the concept of "individuality within community" (a single menage or an entire culture) as defining the human arena where such a potentially liberating and motivating dialectic can operate.

When Penguin Books in 1938 published a paperback edition of *Last and First Men*, it did so under its non-fiction label, a decision indicative of the degree to which Stapledon's fiction is a mythicizing of his agnostic/quasi-religious speculations. The two-billion-year time-span of this novel sees the appearance, eclipse, and resurgence of 18 species of human: great-brained, miniaturized, winged, furry, or telepathic, as determined by responses to such changing conditions as energy depletion, vulcanism, glaciation, planetary invasion, and terraforming. The long, retrospective history is told by one of the Last Men on Neptune at a time when stellar catastrophe is about to put an end to humans (save possibly for seed dispersed through the void). "But," says Stapledon's Neptunian mouthpiece, "when he is done he will not be as nothing, not as though he had never been; for he is eternally a beauty in the eternal form of things." Throughout the course of human's existence, Stapledon depicts achievement and failure as equally parts of the cosmic pattern—the "ecstasy" perspective. By removing us from contemporary preoccupations, Stapledon makes us more sensitively aware of their significance, as we view them in the light of the fates and actions of beings from whom we are bizarrely distant, yet with whom we have a kinship in consciousness of selfhood—beings who are subject to the caprices of external nature and to limitations of their own physical and psychic structuring.

In *Last and First Men*, the dialectical interplay of "moods" is related less to personalized beings than to races as a whole. Described as each race is in graphic physical and psychological detail, it acts within the narrative almost as a prototypical entity, as a personality ultimately existing in relation to the cosmic community. This fictive method is developed more thoroughly in *Star Maker*, a myth of cosmic creation. The first-person narrator moves from the status of observer to that of participant, as his consciousness is expanded until in cosmic awareness it is "awakened to a degree thrice removed beyond the self-consciousness of human beings" and "the life of [his] body was itself the life of myriads of infinitely diverse worlds and myriads of infinitely diverse individual creatures . . ." Yet even so, at the book's end, the entire epic of creation having taken place in dream-vision within a single clock-stroke, there is confrontation of the "I," now surrogate for humanity and for all creation, with that "dread mystery, compelling adoration": namely, the cold, yet ecstatically, contemplative Star Maker.

Dichotomy and confrontation are signified by several of the titles of fictions in which Stapledon projects his "mood" dialectic onto estranged individuals: for example, *Darkness and the Light, Old Man in New World*, the semi-autobiographical *A Man Divided*, and *Odd John: A Story Between Jest and Earnest.* John is a mutation in the direction of a different humanity, alienated not only by a duality in his own nature but by a gap between that and the contemporary human race, whose ethic he defies in episodes of theft, murder, and incest. Telepathically assembling his scattered peers, he occupies with them an oceanic island, and with them commits suicide in the face of invasion by threatened mankind. The theme of individual consciousness seeking community is repeated in a late novel, *Sirius: A Fantasy of Love and Discord*, where the protagonists are Sirius, an experimentally bred large-brained dog, and Plexy, the woman he loves, both tragically half-divorced from the social and sexual norms of their race. Sirius's only release is in death; but what Stapledon calls the Sirius-Plexy "bright gem of community" is in cosmic perspective a high achievement, an ecstatic synthesis.

*Sirius* is considered by many to be Stapledon's finest work; but undoubtedly the two "cosmic histories" are what have most influentially impacted on genre writing and critical thought. Brian Aldiss has called *Last and First Men* "the one great grey holy book of science fiction"; and Stanislaw Lem has commented on its demonstration of relativity in "all norms, legal codes, dogmas, and values." In his own day, Stapledon's influence is explicit in Wells's *Star-Begotten;* and it provoked ideological/theological reaction in C.S. Lewis's interplanetary novels. The occurrence of the term "Stapledonian" in contemporary criticism suggests a pervading influence, not only in extending concepts of life in an ambiguous space-time universe, but in denoting an existential angst. In his unfinished *The Opening of the Eyes*, Stapledon wrote of his preference for at least a pragmatically-imagined transcendence, without which he was "no more than a reflex animal and the world is dust."

—K.V. Bailey

---

**STASHEFF, Christopher.** American. Born in Mt. Vernon, New York, in January 1944. Educated at the University of Michigan, Ann Arbor, B.A. 1965, M.A. 1966; University of Nebraska, Lincoln, Ph.D. in theater 1972. Married Mary Miller in 1973; three daughters and one son. Instructor, 1972–77, and since 1977, Assistant Professor of Speech and Theater, Montclair State College, New Jersey. Agent: Blassingame-Spectrum Corporation, 111 Eighth Avenue, Suite 1501, New York, New York 10011, U.S.A.

### Science-Fiction Publications

Novels (series: Warlock)

*The Warlock in Spite of Himself.* New York, Ace, 1969.
*King Kobold* (Warlock). New York, Ace, 1971; revised edition, as *King Kobold Revived*, 1984.
*A Wizard in Bedlam.* New York, Doubleday, 1979; London, Mayflower, 1982.
*The Warlock Unlocked.* New York, Ace, 1982; London, Panther, 1984.
*Escape Velocity* (Warlock). New York, Ace, 1983.
*The Warlock Enraged.* New York, Ace, 1985.
*Her Majesty's Wizard.* New York, Ballantine, 1986.
*The Warlock Is Missing.* New York, Ace, 1986.
*The Warlock Wandering.* New York, Ace, 1986.
*The Warlock Heretical.* New York, Ace, 1987.
*The Warlock's Companion.* New York, Ace, 1988.
*The Warlock Insane.* New York, Ace, 1989.
*The Warlock Rock.* New York, Ace, 1990.
*A Company of Stars.* New York, Ballantine, 1991.

### Other Publications

Plays

*The Three-Legged Man* (produced Lincoln, Nebraska, 1970).
*Cotton-Eye Joe* (produced Lincoln, Nebraska, 1970).
*Joey Win* (produced Lincoln, Nebraska, 1971).

*

Christopher Stasheff comments:

I'm not concerned with the novel as an end in itself, but as a means towards the end of trying to awaken the audience to an awareness of the issues I consider important, and to convey some vital facts and a few opinions. I'm also trying to reverse some trends I discern in popular literature, which I believe to be detrimental to us as people and as society. But none of this will do any good if no one reads it; so, first and foremost, I try to entertain.

* * *

Christopher Stasheff wrote a wild and ribald mixture of science fiction and fantasy with his first novel, the fabulous *The Warlock in Spite of Himself.* Rodney d'Armond, who renames himself Rod Gallowglass, and his goofy robot steed, Fess, arrive on Gramarye, a planet where magic works. Their mission is to bring democracy to this feudal society. They find themselves kidnapped by elves, encounter ghosts and goblins, and meet other legendary creatures. Gallowglass falls in love with a lovely witch and saves Gramarye's feudalism. All of this is told in a bold swashbuckling style with great humor. *The Warlock in Spite of Himself* is more than a successful blending of science fiction and sword-and-sorcery; it is wonderful entertainment. Readers agree, which led Stasheff to write ten more volumes in the Warlock series.

The original sequel to *The Warlock in Spite of Himself, King Kobold*, received negative reviews, chiefly from Lester del Rey who was book reviewer for *Worlds of If.* When Stasheff's publishers wanted to re-release the book, Stasheff insisted on rewriting the book to take into account del Rey's criticisms. The rewritten book, *King Kobold Revived*, is better than the original 1971 edition. Rod Gallowglass has to save Gramarye from an evil band of time-travelling Neanderthals who are the latest weapon in the transtemporal wars. To defeat them, Gallowglass needs the assistance of a power witch and a clever wizard; however, the plot revolves around their reluctance to get involved and Gallowglass's attempts to recruit them.

*The Warlock Unlocked* carries the story farther: Gramarye is still threatened by sinister time-travellers, and Rod Gallowglass is its main defender. The plot centers around the attempt to cause a rift between the Church and the State. Rod Gallowglass is cunningly trapped and sent with his family to an alternate world. There he must defeat wicked elves and monsters before he can return to Gramarye and save it from ruin.

*Escape Velocity* is a "prequel" to the Warlock series and answers some of the questions about Gramayre's origin—technically it should be read as the first book in the series. Unfortunately, it is one of the weaker books in the series because much of the action takes place on decadent Earth, and the lead characters, Dar and Samantha, tend to deliver speeches on sociopolitics rather than engage in the glib dialog Stasheff is famous for.

*The Warlock Is Missing* is one of the stronger books in the series. While the Warlock is busy having adventures told in *The Warlock Wandering*, his children are lured by a unicorn into adventures of their own as they search for their father. Although the usual monsters are defeated and the predictable formula of helping the King is maintained, the change of pace makes *The Warlock Is Missing* pure entertainment.

Unfortunately, the rest of the series never matches the flare and fun of these titles. *The Warlock's Companion* is the dull story of Fess, the Warlock's cybernetic steed. *The Warlock Insane* has Rod Gallowglass tormented by hallucinations. In regaining his sanity in magical Granclarte, the Warlock aids a knight called Beaubras in rescuing Lady Haugheur from the High Dudgeon. The standard kobolds, ogres, and harpies are around to fight, but all of this is told without suspense or tension.

The latest book in the Warlock series, *The Warlock Rock*, features mysterious, musical crystals whose rock and roll threatens Gramarye. Clearly, Stasheff has tired of the series and is just going through the motions at this point.

Another sign of this is his recent shared world project in *The Siege of Arista* edited by Bill Fawcett where Stasheff's story, "Papa Don't 'Low," tells the story of a marine, Pepe Stuart, injured in battle against the insectoids called the Hothri. He becomes a quartermaster who takes his job seriously as he rejects defective munitions being produced by the private sector. Papa and his girl-friend Alice discover a conspiracy to produce defective weapons so the humans will lose in their battles with the Hothri. Not surprisingly, a story about quality control fails to generate much excitement.

Stasheff's other non-Warlock fantasy, *Her Majesty's Wizard*, is the story of graduate student Matt Mantrell who finds himself in an alternate universe where England isn't an island but attached to the continent. Of course, magic works, but the entire adventure is a clumsy, ponderous clone of Piers Anthony's Xanth series.

Christopher Stasheff wrote a classic with *The Warlock in Spite of Himself*, but none of the books in the Warlock series nor any of his non-series work comes close to that book's originality and zest.

—George Kelley

---

**STATTEN, Vargo.** *See* **FEARN, John Russell.**

---

**STEBER, A.R.** *See* **PALMER, Raymond A.; PHILLIPS, Rog.**

---

**STEELE, Morris J.** *See* **PALMER, Raymond A.**

---

**STEFFANSON, Con.** *See* **GOULART, Ron.**

---

**STEPHENSON, Andrew M(ichael).** British. Born in Maracaibo, Venezuela, 8 October 1946. Educated at Rottingdean Pre-Preparatory School, Sussex, 1956–60; Stowe School, Buckinghamshire, 1960–65; City University, London, B.Sc. (honours) in electrical and electronic engineering 1969. Design engineer, Plessey Telecommunications Research, Taplow, Buckinghamshire, 1969–76. European Representative, Science Fiction Writers of America, 1976–78. Lives in High Wycombe, Buckinghamshire. Agent: Frances Collin, Frances Collin Literary Agency, 110 West 40th Street, New York, New York 10018, U.S.A.

SCIENCE-FICTION PUBLICATIONS

Novels

*Nightwatch.* London, Futura, 1977; New York, Dell, 1979.
*The Wall of Years.* London, Futura, 1979; New York, Dell, 1980.

Uncollected Short Stories

"Holding Action," in *Analog* (New York), 1971.
"The Giant Killers," in *Andromeda 1*, edited by Peter Weston.

London, Futura, 1976; New York, St. Martin's Press, 1979.

*

Andrew M. Stephenson comments:

The notion of making any sort of introductory statement on my work repels me: it feels as though I am being required to define what I wrote about, whereas the work itself is sufficient definition. All I will say is that I am content to be described (where relevant) as a writer of science fiction, provided my works are judged on their *individual* merits, not as samples of "science fiction," whatever that may be.

* * *

Andrew M. Stephenson began his career in SF as an illustrator. "The Giant Killers," like *Nightwatch*, is highly technophilic, but at the same time possesses a deep concern and sensitivity for human and animal suffering. Whereas in the short story, man is seen at war against himself, in the novel he is seen pitted against an alien intruder. It is a competent if unoriginal novel about semi-sentient machines and their creator, set mainly on the moon.

A much lengthier and far more successful novel is *The Wall of Years*, moulding together two traditional SF themes—time travel and parallel worlds—into a story that is both convincing and compelling. Experiments into parallel worlds reveal that there are nearby worlds of possibility and that the majority of these are engaged in warfare. The bonds that separate the worlds break and they begin to intermingle. As the world falls into chaos, some humans escape into the future of the 26th century where they set about trying to stabilise their own history (in this alternate world). The protagonist, Jerlan Nilssen, goes back to the time of Alfred the Great to ensure that history is not changed by an outside agency that might wish to see the future city destroyed. Stephenson ties the plot threads together tightly and portrays with some accuracy the clash between modern and ninth-century world views. As before, there is a marked sensitivity in his characterisation, though the writing itself shows a much greater assurance. The crudity of the dark ages is well drawn as Stephenson informs us of the laws of necessity that governed behaviour in those times. By comparison, the world of the 21st century (the time of the break-up of reality, where parallel worlds begin to impose upon one another) is not so well focused and hints that Stephenson would probably feel more at home writing historical fiction. However, the absence of further novels during the 1980's and early 1990's suggests that we may, unfortunately, have seen the last of this promising British writer.

—David Wingrove

---

**STERLING, Brett.** *See* **HAMILTON, Edmond.**

---

**STERLING, Bruce.** American. Born in Brownsville, Texas, 14 April 1954. Educated at the University of Texas, Austin, 1972–76, B.A. in journalism 1976. Married Nancy Baxter in 1979; one daughter. Agent: Merrilee Heifetz, Writers House, 21 West 26th Street, New York, New York 10010. Address: 4525 Speedway, Austin, Texas 78751, U.S.A.

SCIENCE-FICTION PUBLICATIONS

Novels

*Involution Ocean.* New York, Jove, 1977; London, New English Library, 1980.
*The Artificial Kid.* New York, Harper, 1980; London, Penguin, 1985.
*Schismatrix.* New York, Arbor House, 1985; London, Penguin, 1986.
*Islands in the Net.* New York, Arbor House, and London, Century, 1988.
*The Difference Engine*, with William Gibson. London, Gollancz, 1990; New York, Bantam, 1991.

Short Stories

*Crystal Express.* Sauk City, Wisconsin, Arkham House, 1989; London, Century, 1990.

OTHER PUBLICATIONS

Other

Editor, *Mirrorshades: The Cyberpunk Anthology.* New York, Arbor House, 1986; London, Paladin, 1988.

* * *

Besides building an impressive body of his own work, Sterling has helped shape modern SF as the spokesman for the cyberpunk movement. Sterling was ambivalent about this role. Although he shared movement concerns, he was uneasy about seeing diverse people lumped together into a sub-genre, and he is pleased that by now the movement writers have gone off in their separate directions.

Sterling's own self-assurance can be seen in the deft construction and coolly precise style of even his very early writing. He always has seemed to believe in himself. Actually, even in his first publications (*Involution Ocean* and *The Artificial Kid*), Sterling began exploring the very nature of self-control as his protagonists gain experience and self-knowledge within bizarre future societies. Each character must adjust to so many unsettling situations that it would be comforting if he could find someone else who has found a way to interpret experience and act effectively. Instead, the young narrators see that older people generally drift toward death because they have tried different beliefs and roles until no faith is convincing enough to hold their attention. The few old men who do manage to cling to one purpose do so with a foolish fanaticism that also leads to death. At first, Sterling's protagonists escape confusion by using drugs (*Involution Ocean*) or edited versions of experience (*The Artificial Kid*) to give themselves an illusion of controlled action pursuing significant goals. When events strip them of their illusions, they must begin to explore the notion of commitment. They come to realize how much any belief depends on lies or contrivance, but they also recognize that humans cannot long exist without belief.

From the beginning of his career, Sterling was grappling with a major human concern: Believing in a set of values gives consciousness a center but narrows it; how can one gain the focus that faith makes possible without the accompanying destructiveness? Sterling considers this repeatedly in his series of short stories describing the struggle between the Shapers (who have restructured people through biosciences) and the Mechs (who augment human powers through mechanical means). Those movements, the factions they spawn, and the sub-factions *they* produce all attempt to dominate the race after most of humanity has abandoned Earth and begun to spread through space. In form, the stories give glimpses of events that readers must strain to interpret and connect. In substance, the stories focus on characters who attempt to find something that they can confidently assert in their confusing milieu. Conclusions tend to be somewhat equivocal, as in the award nominee "Swarm," which challenges readers' comfortable assumption that humanity equals exploring and intelligence equals mastery. With wit and ironic ambiguity, Sterling describes the multiplicity of beliefs that develop as human consciousness is fragmented.

The Shaper series, occupying the first section of Sterling's collection *Crystal Express*, concludes with *Schismatrix.* This novel shows one man trying out many identities and beliefs. Although the book explains the complex future history into which the Shaper stories fit, a reader (like Sterling's hero) is challenged to grasp nuances and adapt to them rapidly, avoiding both confusion and staleness. No one faith finally satisfies Sterling's protagonist. The important thing is that his wide sympathy and flexibility eventually make him a fit companion for a Presence that has observed humanity's development but disdains the idea of taking part in its unrestricted evolution even if that might lead to godlike consciousness and power.

His central subject is the wonder of the human response to experience, the fascinating ways people liberate or limit themselves.

This concern is, in fact, at the heart of cyberpunk SF. Sterling is fascinated by the changes in human life made possible by new technologies, especially as they could increase the range of choices for individuals. He also sees, though, how we ignore possibilities and avoid choices. Cyberpunk, according to Sterling's preface to *Mirrorshades: The Cyberpunk Anthology*, represents "an unholy alliance of the technical world and the world of organized dissent—the underground world of pop culture, visionary fluidity, and street-level anarchy." In a fluid situation, it is foolish to cling to *any* established formulas, especially when they become establishment. However, though government is a handy symbol for the denial of freedom, cyberpunks like Sterling see the real problem as individuals' determined avoidance of vision or responsibility. Consequently, cyberpunk fiction is insistent in showing what technology can do for people, and it is downright rude in showing what people can do for themselves if they continue to deny responsibility.

Of the movement writers, Sterling has been one of the more radical in extrapolating changes but one of the coolest in describing human reactions. In *Islands in the Net*, for example, his most recent solo novel, Sterling integrates enough ideas for ten books in a near-future, corporation-dominated world; then he sets up innocent, idealistic Laura Webster, described by Roger Zelazny as a "high-tech Candide," and sends her tumbling through an avalanche of events. Laura is the perfect receptor for the manic strangeness swirling around her. All she wants is to preserve the humane, democratic values of her corporation/family. But to do so she must use the Net, the communications network that ties everyone in the world together, like it or not. Sterling delicately suggests but leaves unresolved the question whether the Net itself is a tool for freedom or repression—and whether decent, likeable people like Laura can learn to see the difference.

Sterling's most recent major publication is his collaboration with William Gibson, *The Difference Engine*, which shows contemporary issues "with the amps turned up" by describing how mechanical calculating machines could have changed Victorian England so that human values might have become extinct by our times. He currently is working on a non-fiction study of a 1990 federal crackdown on computer hackers.

Listing Sterling's consistent concerns in fiction and non-fiction should not suggest that he always preaches the same message or that he subordinates storytelling to ideology. He is committed to using SF to analyze and influence social trends, but he recognizes that the best way to do that is by involving readers in memorable fiction. And Sterling's combination of intellectual excitement and human sympathy make his work some of the most memorable contemporary SF.

—Joe Sanders

---

**STEVENS, Francis.** Pseudonym for Gertrude Barrows Bennett. American. Born in Minneapolis, Minnesota, 18 September 1884. Widow; one daughter. Disappeared in September 1939.

SCIENCE-FICTION PUBLICATIONS

Novels

*The Heads of Cerberus.* Reading, Pennsylvania, Polaris Press, 1952.
*Claimed!* New York, Avalon, 1966.
*The Citadel of Fear.* New York, Paperback Library, 1970.

Uncollected Short Stories

"The Nightmare," in *All-Story* (New York), 14 April 1917.
"Behind the Curtain," in *All-Story* (New York), 7 September 1918.
"The Elf Trap," in *Argosy* (New York), 5 July 1919.
"Serapion," in *Argosy* (New York), 19 June–10 July 1920.
"Sunfire," in *Weird Tales* (Chicago), July–August, September 1923.
"Friend Island," in *Under the Moons of Mars*, edited by Sam Moskowitz. New York, Harper, 1970.
"Unseen—Unfeared," in *Horrors Unknown*, edited by Sam Moskowitz. New York, Walker, 1971.

* * *

The body of writing for which the name Francis Stevens is remembered was published during a span of little more than six years (1917–23), and was probably written in an even shorter period. Gertrude Barrows Bennett, the woman who used the pseudonym Francis Stevens, wrote under pressure of economic necessity, and stopped when the immediate need for extra income was removed. Through the years those readers who have fallen under the spell of her remarkable fantasies have had cause to regret not only the premature cessation of her fiction-writing, but also the fact that some already-completed work remained unpublished (and is now presumed to be lost).

Francis Stevens wrote mainly for *All-Story* and *Argosy* magazines during the same period in which the first of A. Merritt's fantasies were published. It has been said that some readers thought Francis Stevens was a pen-name of Merritt's. The conjecture could just as easily have gone the other way, for when Stevens's first major novel, *The Citadel of Fear*, appeared, Merritt had published only a few short works. Merritt was, in fact, a great admirer of Stevens's work, and was instrumental in having several of her stories reprinted during the 1940's. Although the first part of *The Citadel of Fear,* which takes place in the lost city of Tlapallan in an uncharted corner of Mexico, is superficially similar to Merritt's work, Stevens replaced Merritt's romantic/tragic outlook with a much more down-to-earth viewpoint. The story, while forfeiting none of its appeal as an exotic lost-race adventure, is told with liveliness and humor, to which the hints of darker things form an effective counterpoint. In the latter two-thirds of the novel, the very real and concrete evil of Tlapallan reappears in the quiet American countryside, and a succession of mysterious events builds up to a climactic confrontation between supernatural forces.

The second of Francis Stevens's three major works, *The Heads of Cerberus,* was serialized in *The Thrill Book* in 1919. Like *The Citadel of Fear* the novel opens with an episode of Merrittesque fantasy, involving a substance called the Dust of Purgatory which transports people into the strange alternate world of Ulithia. But once the main characters have passed through Ulithia and find themselves in a future Philadelphia in the year 2118, the novel becomes political and social satire of a high order. The two parts of the novel fit somewhat oddly together, but each is so good in itself that one is willing to accept the discontinuity between them. In the introduction to the Polaris Press edition, P. Schuyler Miller is quoted as saying that the novel "can be read as perhaps the first work of fantasy to envisage the parallel-time-track concept, with an added variation that so far as I know has not been reused since"—the idea that time moves at different rates in the alternate tracks.

The third of Stevens's important works is *Claimed!* Here the focus of attention is a carved oblong box found on a volcanic island in the Atlantic. The box comes into the possession of millionaire Jesse Robinson, whose creed is, "What I want, I get— and what I get, I keep." The novel tells, in a straightforward narrative without any of the subplots or sidetrips evident in earlier works, of the attempts at recovery of the box by the supernatural being who had created it many thousands of years in the past.

Three novels by Francis Stevens have so far appeared only in magazine form. Her first work was the short novel "The Nightmare," of which Stevens herself said that its only merit was "a rather grotesque originality." "Serapion" is a grim and powerful story of psychic possession which stands up well in comparison to more recent works on the same theme. "Sunfire" was a return to both the lost-race fantasy and the light-hearted narrative style of earlier works.

Of Stevens's short works, "Friend Island" is notable for its background of a future world when women are the dominant gender, but the story itself is little more than an extended joke. (It is probably nothing more than coincidence that the byline "Francis Stevens" appeared on a story called "The Curious Experience of Thomas Dunbar" in the March 1904 issue of *Argosy.*)

—R.E. Briney

---

**STEWART, George R(ippey).** American. Born in Sewickley, Pennsylvania, 31 May 1895. Educated at Pasadena High School, California; Princeton University, New Jersey, A.B. 1917 (Phi Beta Kappa); University of California, Berkeley, M.A. 1920; Columbia University, New York, Ph.D. 1922. Served in the United States Army Ambulance Service, 1917–19; civilian technician, United States Navy, 1944. Married Theodosia Burton in 1924; one daughter and one son. Instructor, University of Michigan, Ann Arbor, 1922–23. Member of the English Department from 1923, Professor of English, 1942–62, then Emeritus, University of California. Taught at the University of Michigan, summer 1926, Duke University, Durham, North Carolina, summer 1939; Fellow in Creative Writing, Princeton University, 1942–43; Fulbright Professor, University of Athens, 1952–53. Recipient: International Fantasy award, 1951; American Association for State and Local History award, 1963; Hillman award, 1969. L.H.D.: University of California, 1963. *Died 22 August 1980.*

SCIENCE-FICTION PUBLICATIONS

Novel

*Earth Abides.* New York, Random House, 1949; London, Gollancz, 1950.

OTHER PUBLICATIONS

Novels

*East of the Giants.* New York, Holt, 1938; London, Harrap, 1939.
*Doctor's Oral.* New York, Random House, 1939.
*Storm.* New York, Random House, 1941; London, Hutchinson, 1942.
*Fire.* New York, Random House, 1948; London, Gollancz, 1951.
*Sheep Rock.* New York, Random House, 1951.
*The Years of the City.* New York, Random House, 1955.

Other

*The Technique of English Verse.* New York, Holt, 1930.
*Bret Harte, Argonaut and Exile.* Boston, Houghton Mifflin, 1931.
*A Bibliography of the Writings of Bret Harte in the Magazines and Newspapers of California 1857–1871.* Berkeley, University of California Press, 1933.
*Ordeal by Hunger: The Story of the Donner Party.* New York, Holt, and London, Cape, 1936; revised edition, Boston, Houghton Mifflin, 1960.
*English Composition.* New York, Holt, 2 vols., 1936.
*John Phoenix, Esq.* New York, Holt, 1937.
*Take your Bible in One Hand: The Life of William Henry Thomes.* San Francisco, Colt Press, 1939.
*Names on the Land.* New York, Random House, 1945; revised edition, Boston, Houghton Mifflin, 1958, 1967.
*Man: An Autobiography.* New York, Random House, 1946; London, Cassell, 1948.
*The Year of the Oath: The Fight for Academic Freedom at the University of California,* with others. New York, Doubleday, 1950.
*U.S. 40.* Boston, Houghton Mifflin, 1953.
*American Ways of Life.* New York, Doubleday, 1954.
*To California by Covered Wagon* (for children). New York, Random House, 1954; as *The Pioneers Go West,* 1987.
*N.A. 1: The North-South Continental Highway.* Boston, Houghton Mifflin, 1957.
*Pickett's Charge.* Boston, Houghton Mifflin, 1959.
*Donner Pass and Those Who Crossed It.* San Francisco, California Historical Society, 1960.
*The California Trail.* New York, McGraw Hill, 1962; London, Eyre and Spottiswoode, 1964.

*Committee of Vigilance: Revolution in San Francisco 1851.* Boston, Houghton Mifflin, 1964.
*This California*, photographs by Michael Bry. Berkeley, California, Diablo Press, 1965.
*Good Lives.* Boston, Houghton Mifflin, 1967.
*The Department of English of the University of California on the Berkeley Campus.* Berkeley, University of California, 1968.
*Not So Rich as You Think.* Boston, Houghton Mifflin, 1968.
*American Place-Names.* New York, Oxford University Press, 1970.
*Names on the Globe.* New York, Oxford University Press, 1975.
*American Given Names: Their Origin and History in the Context of the English Language.* New York, Oxford University Press, 1979.

Editor, *The Luck of Roaring Camp and Selected Stories and Poems*, by Bret Harte. New York, Macmillan, 1928.
Editor, *Map of the Emigrant Road from Independence, Missouri, to St. Francisco*, by T.H. Jefferson. San Francisco, California Historical Society, 1945.
Editor, *The Opening of the California Trail*, by Moses Shallenberger. Berkeley, University of California Press, 1953.

*

Manuscript Collection: Bancroft Library, University of California, Berkeley.

Critical Study: *George R. Stewart* by John Caldwell, Boise, Idaho, Boise State University, 1981.

* * *

In 1951, George R. Stewart received the first of the International Fantasy awards for *Earth Abides*, the only one of his novels to fall into the SF genre. He is also the author of non-fiction works which, like his novels, all touch on some aspect of American history or culture.

*Earth Abides* inverts the famous story of Ishi, the last wild Indian in North America, a story recently retold by Theodora Kroeber in *Ishi in Two Worlds* (1962). Ishi, the last member of the Yahi, a tribe of California Indians long thought to be extinct, emerged from his Stone Age world to live in the early 20th-century world of trolley cars and electric lights. He was rescued by an anthropologist at the University of California, and taken to live in its Museum of Anthropology, then located in San Francisco, where he passed his remaining years. He showed the anthropologists the native Yahi way of making and hunting with a bow and arrow, and of making fire. With these lessons Ishi paid his way and enjoyed the fruits of civilization, which for him were mainly glue (for the easier feathering of arrows) and matches. His name in Yahi means "man."

The hero of *Earth Abides* is named Ish, which in Hebrew also means "man." Ish is one of a very few to survive a pandemic disease to see civilization collapse and his descendants return to the life of Stone Age hunters like that of Ishi. Ish is the last of the civilised Americans as Ishi is the last of the aboriginal Americans. Naked, hungry, and weakened by snake bite, the real Ishi stumbled into industrial America on 29 August 1911. The last of the Yahi, he wandered down from his native hills into the corral of a slaughter-house near Oroville, California. There he fell exhausted, was jailed as a "wild man," was finally recognised for what he was, and taken to the museum in San Francisco. Weakened by snake bite, the fictional Ish stumbles out of the same hills into a dead civilization, its populace almost wiped out by some deadly virus. He had been studying the ecology of the Sacramento Valley, Ishi's tribal home, for a master's degree at the University of California. Throughout the novel, Ish watches with ecological detachment the transformation of a world emptied of men.

He returns to his home in a suburb of San Francisco, overlooking the Golden Gate bridge. The few survivors he gathers around him facetiously call themselves the "Tribe." Everybody forages in stores for food and other goods, trying to maintain the old way of life under new conditions. One couple brings home a bridge lamp and a fancy radio set, even though no electricity is available. Even Ish, the only one to think about the future, teaches spelling and arithmatic, although the world is so depopulated it cannot sustain occupational specialties based on literacy. At last Ish realises the futility of his classroom lessons and school is dismissed. He then teaches the children a game, which he knows will have to become a way of life once there are no more store goods to scavenge: he teaches them how to make and use the bow and arrow, and how to make fire without matches, the same technology he knew from his study of anthropology to have been the basis for successful living by our pre-civilized ancestors.

In time, the tribe departs the crumbling ruins of San Francisco. By then Ish is an old man and the tribe, now skilled hunters, sets out to cross the bridge to new lands. Crossing the bridge, Ish slows to a stop. Before he dies, he reflects on the course of human history and the fate of his grandchildren and others of their generation, who squat in a half circle around him. "They were very young in age, at least by comparison with him, and in the cycle of mankind they were many thousands of years younger than he. He was the last of the old; they were the first of the new. But whether the new would follow the course which the old had followed, that he did not know." But the moral of the novel is certain. Inverting the story of Ishi, Stewart dramatises the humanistic fact that man is man, be he civilised or tribal; that a Stone Age culture is just as valid a setting for being human as is an industrial culture.

—Leon Stover

---

**STEWART, Will.** *See* **WILLIAMSON, Jack.**

---

**STINE, G(eorge) Harry.** Also writes as Lee Correy. American. Born in Philadelphia, Pennsylvania, 26 March 1928. Educated at University of Colorado, Colorado Springs (editor, *The Window*, 1948–49), 1946–50; Colorado College, Colorado Springs, B.A. in physics 1952. Married Barbara Ann Kauth in 1952; two daughters and one son. Chief of the Propulsion Branch, Controls and Instruments Section, 1952–55, and chief of Range Operations division and Navy flight safety engineer, 1955–57, White Sands Proving Ground, New Mexico; design specialist, Martin Company, Denver, 1957; president and chief engineer, Model Missiles, Denver, 1957–59; vice-president and chief engineer, MicroDynamics, Broomfield, Colorado, 1959; design engineer, Stanley Aviation, Denver, 1959–60; assistant director of research, Huyck Corporation, Stamford, Connecticut, 1960–65; freelance consultant, 1965–73; marketing manager, Flow Technology, Phoenix, 1973–76. Since 1976, freelance consultant and writer. Editor, *Missile Away!*, 1953–57; columnist ("Conquest of Space"), *Mechanix Illustrated*, 1956–57; editor, *The Model Rocketeer*, 1957–64 and 1976–78; senior editor, *Aviation/Space*, 1982–84. Since 1980, columnist ("The Alternate View"), *Analog;* since 1985, principal writer, Space Report, Metavision-KAET, Los Angeles; since 1987, president, Enterprise Institute, Inc., Phoenix. Founder and past president, National Association of Rocketry; associate fellow, American Institute of Aeronautics and Astronautics. Agent: Richard C. Curtis, Richard C. Curtis Associates, 171 East 74th Street, New York, New York 10021. Address: 616 West Frier Drive, Phoenix, Arizona 85021, U.S.A.

SCIENCE-FICTION PUBLICATIONS

Novels as G. Harry Stine (series: Warbots in all books)

*Warbots*. New York, Pinnacle, 1988.
*Operation Steel Band*. New York, Windsor, 1988.
*The Bastaard Revolution*. New York, Windsor, 1988.
*Sierra Madre*. New York, Pinnacle, 1988.
*Operation High Dragon*. New York, Windsor, 1989.
*The Lost Battalion*. New York, Windsor, 1989.
*Operation Iron Fist*. New York, Windsor, 1989.
*Force of Arms*. New York, Windsor, 1990.
*Blood Siege*. New York, Pinnacle, 1990.
*Guts and Glory*. New York, Pinnacle, 1991.

Novels as Lee Correy

*Starship Through Space* (for children). New York, Holt Rinehart, 1954.
*Contraband Rocket*. New York, Ace, 1955.
*Rocket Man* (for children). New York, Holt Rinehart, 1955.
*Star Driver*. New York, Ballantine, 1980.
*Shuttle Down*. New York, Ballantine, 1981.
*Space Doctor*. New York, Ballantine, 1981.
*The Abode of Life*. New York, Pocket Books, 1982.
*Manna*. New York, DAW, 1984.
*A Matter of Metalaw*. New York, DAW, 1986.

OTHER PUBLICATIONS as G. Harry Stine

Other

*Rocket Power and Space Flight*. New York, Holt Rinehart, 1957.
*Earth Satellites and the Race for Space Superiority*. New York, Ace, 1957.
*Man and the Space Frontier*. New York, Knopf, 1962.
*Handbook of Model Rocketry*. Chicago, Follett, 1965; revised edition, 1967, 1970, 1976, 1983.
*The Third Industrial Revolution*. New York, Putnam, 1975.
*Shuttle into Space: A Ride in America's Space Transportation System* (for children). Chicago, Follett, 1978.
*The Space Enterprise*. New York, Ace, 1980.
*Space Power*. New York, Ace, 1981.
*Confrontation in Space*. Englewood Cliffs, New Jersey, Prentice Hall, 1981.
*The Hopeful Future*. New York, Macmillan, 1983.
*The Silicon Gods*. New York, Dell, 1984.
*Handbook for Space Colonists*. New York, Holt Rinehart, 1985.
*The Untold Story of the Computer Revolution*. New York, Arbor House, 1985.
*On the Frontiers of Science: Strange Machines You Can Build*. Atheneum, 1985, as *Weird and Wonderful Machines You Can Build*, Largo, Florida, Top of the Mountain, 1991.
*The Corporate Survivors*. New York, Amacon, 1986.
*ICBM: The Making of the Weapon that Changed the World*. New York, Orion, 1991.

*

G. Harry Stine comments:

Since 1951, I've written "hard" science fiction because that's the sort of story I like to read. I was influenced at an early and impressionable age by one Robert Anson Heinlein who, in 1950, was kind enough to take me under his wing and coach me. But John W. Campbell, Willy Ley, Dan Cole, and Herman Kahn must also share the blame for what I've become. Much of the background for my SF novels came from consulting work for NASA, the Department of Energy, or the Hudson Institute, for example. Or from careful and continual reading, reading, reading of scientific journals, reports, books, magazines, and papers to keep up with our growing knowledge of a universe that's becoming stranger every day. Often I've written an SF novel rather than present the same material in a science-fact book because (a) it made a better fiction piece, and (b) nobody would believe it as a science-fact work! ("Shuttle Down" is an example of this.) Incidentally, I've used the pseudonym "Lee Correy" to tag my SF in order to separate it from my science-fact writing, a differentiation that's getting more difficult to determine every day. Although I've written some "far out" science fiction, I'm just not interested in "swords and sorcery" fairy tales masquerading as "science fiction." (People are free to write and read what they want, but I wish they'd start referring to SF for what it is, and it isn't science fiction!) I don't write "literature" or to change the world; I try to write entertainment as Heinlein taught me. I find lots of story material in the potentials and problems of the next hundred years which come down to: How do we learn to handle wealth and power in a universe where we're largely in control of the forces of nature? I've never written a downside doomsday story and probably never will. I have enormous faith in the ability of human beings to make the world a better place for their children. I would have enjoyed being a member of John Herschel's Analytical Society at Cambridge, England, whose members promised one another to "do their best to leave the world wiser than they found it."

* * *

Even the most cursory exposure to the science fiction of Lee Correy (the pseudonym for G. Harry Stine) demonstrates his assumption that space travel and other technological advances are of paramount importance to the future of the human race. Many of his novels and stories deal with space travel not just as a plot element, but as the focus of the entire plot.

*Contraband Rocket* suggests that if the government is not willing to exert time and money conquering space, then perhaps private industry will do so instead. The idea that a collection of idealists could refurbish an old rocket for a moon flight has become unbelievable in view of the sophisticated knowledge we now possess, but this early novel exudes the optimistic self-confidence of its time. Other novels, particularly *Star Driver* and *Space Doctor*, returned to this idea, but take into consideration the realities of modern technology.

In *Star Driver*, a small company develops a working anti-gravity unit and mounts it on commercial aircraft in order to make a dramatic presentation of the potential of the device, as well as enabling them to avoid government regulation. Unfortunately, the plot is slowed by episodes of polemics as Correy restates his arguments. *Space Doctor* is far more successful. An orbital construction project is underway to create a new power source for the earth. Its completion will be an economic boon for the companies financing the project. To reduce their expenses and the possible loss of lives, they hire a doctor to head an orbiting hospital outfitted to handle emergencies as they arise. Correy has much better control of the plot here; lectures on the advantages of an active space program still exist, but are far less intrusive.

The government is itself sponsoring space travel in *Shuttle Down*, in which an aborted space flight results in a shuttle stuck on Easter Island, faced with physical and political problems before it can be removed. The protagonists have to deal with terrorists, spies, Russian naval maneuvers, and various problems of supply and manpower before everything can be resolved. Correy seems to have lost faith in established governments in *Manna*, however, which features a libertarian Utopia in Africa with a large-scale manned space program. This new society attracts unfriendly attention from the rest of the world because of its unconventional government. Alien invasion is the theme of *A Matter of Metalaw*, with an interstellar society's equilibrium challenged by a race of genetically altered beings.

In 1988, under his own name—G. Harry Stine—he turned his attention to an adventure series with *Warbots*, which has now spawned several sequels. A special military force consisting of technicians and specially equipped robots is dispatched in each to another trouble spot to battle terrorists, rebels, and other villains. Although exceptionally well-written considering the genre, they tend to be repetitive and uninteresting.

For the most part, Correy's short stories deal with the mechanics of space exploration. In "The Test Stand," a man's view of his own career is revised when he is nearly killed preventing an accident during a test firing. The importance of the human factor in even the most sophisticated aspects of space flight is demonstrated in "Coffin Run," in which a substitute pilot must be retrained quickly despite the objections of his superiors. Neither story descends into overt lecturing, but Correy is clearly attempting to humanize the space program.

Correy's best-known short story is "The Easy Way Out." Alien invaders land in a remote part of the world and set out to discover how susceptible the planet is to invasion. They encounter a number of animals and rate each on a Ferocity Index, eventually retreating in utter terror when they witness the bullying of a pet wolverine by a pair of human children. Although the basic concept is amusing, the assumption that a sophisticated space-travelling species would be so easily fooled is not particularly credible. Less ambitious but far more effective is "Something in the Sky." A test missile veers from its intended target and strikes some invisible object in space. Without melodrama, and in just a few words, Correy conveys an effective mood of mystery and wonder.

—Don D'Ammassa

---

**STIRLING, S(tephen) M(ichael).** Canadian. Born in Metz, France, 30 September 1953. Educated at Carleton University, Ottawa, Ontario, B.A. in history and English 1976, LL.B. 1979. Married Janet Cathryn Moore in 1988. Address: 50 Cornwall Street, Number 803, Toronto, Ontario M5A 4K5, Canada.

SCIENCE-FICTION PUBLICATIONS

Novels (series: Fifth Millennium, Draka)

*Snowbrother* (Fifth Millennium). New York, New American Library, 1985.
*The Sharpest Edge* (Fifth Millennium), with Shirley Meier. New York, New American Library, 1986.
*Marching Through Georgia* (Draka). New York, Baen, 1988.
*The Cage*, with Shirley Meier. New York, Baen, 1989.
*Under the Yoke* (Draka). New York, Baen, 1989.
*Man-Kzin Wars II*, with Larry Niven, Dean Inge, and Jerry Pournelle. New York, Baen, 1989.
*Man-Kzin Wars III*, with Larry Niven, Dean Inge, and Jerry Pournelle. New York, Baen, 1990.
*The Stone Dogs* (Draka). New York, Baen, 1990.
*The Forge*, with David Drake. New York, Baen, 1991.
*Go Tell the Spartans*, with Jerry Pournelle. New York, Baen, 1991.

OTHER PUBLICATIONS

Other

Editor, with Frank McSherran, Jr., *Fantastic Civil War II*. New York, Baen, 1990.

*

S.M. Stirling comments:

My work to date has included both fantasy—the Fifth Millennium series that began with *Snowbrother*—and science fiction. The SF includes the Draka books, which are alternate history set in a universe where the loyalists went to South Africa instead of Canada in the 1780's, after the American Revolution. I've also collaborated with Dave Drake and Jerry Pournelle. In both fantasy and SF, I try for a gritty realist style, besides a good plot, a densely realized background, and characters who arise organically from it. SF and fantasy are—or should be—literatures of possibility, and I want to show people who are not like us as they react to different surroundings.

* * *

What distinguishes S.M. Stirling from the majority of science-fiction writers is not that more than half of his books give us a very visual description of the field of battle, but that he seems to find it necessary to go into extremely gory details. His first science-fiction novel, *Marching Through Georgia*, is a fast-paced and brilliantly written account of an alternative universe after the American Revolution. Dispossessed loyalists end up in South Africa, in the company of other refugees, where they create a nation of serfs and slaves dominated by an aristocracy (themselves). They gain control of the whole of Africa and part of Asia; by the time World War II breaks out and Hitler comes to power, they have formed an alliance with their original enemies, the United States. In order to understand this complex novel, the reader is supplied with a map of the world as it stands in this dystopia. The only problem is that the more interesting are such maps, the more frustrating is the writer's insistence in concentrating on only a small portion of this new world. Nothing is said about how and when Free Australia, the Empire of Brazil, or the Republic of Grand Columbia have come into existence. Ironically, Great Britain seems to have escaped this dividing (and simplification) of the geographical and political into only a few countries.

Stirling attempts to maintain a balance by having an American reporter take over the description and the coverage of the Eurasian war of 1942. The need for an alliance between the United States and the Domination of the Draka, to defeat the Nazis, is emphasized in spite of the abhorrence that the reporter feels towards Drakan policies and their feudal system. In fact, Stirling manages to make the Drakan view of the world nearly palpable in comparison with the Nazis'. Stirling has acquired the reputation of being a controversial right-wing writer in science fiction, and consequently sets himself considerably apart from the humanistic tendencies of new Canadian science fiction. The alternate history in *Marching Through Georgia* is compelling reading for its re-creation of another timeline, complete with documents that are presented as official papers or history textbooks.

Unfortunately, the same cannot be said of his second SF novel, *Under the Yoke*, which takes place in the same universe and starts after the end of the Eurasian Wars. The greatest part of the book is filled with battle descriptions that have nothing to do with science fiction. Stirling's pitiful attempt at turning this second novel into a pot boiler makes him write in gory and unnecessary detail about physical torture that has more to do with the description of sadism than with the progression of the plot or the setting of an atmosphere. Perhaps the author wants his readers to react against the unhealthy hegemony of the Draka; however, one gets a distinct impression that lack of imagination was replaced by a succession of fillers.

*The Stone Dogs* takes place within the same dystopia, and returns more reliably to the science-fiction genre. The book entertains us with a vision of the two main powers (the United States and the Domination of the Draka) gaining new scientific knowledge in genetics, computer science, and electronics, in order to bring their endless struggle into space. Although Stirling does manage to recapture the style and ideas that made *Marching Through Georgia* a success, *The Stone Dogs* is marred by lurid descriptions of sex: sexual scenes are described not as such but through the device of overt voyeurism. *The Stone Dogs* is still a much better novel than *Under the Yoke.* It is filled with the description of the Drakan society and their mores and customs while not overburdening us with endless battle fire. At times even, Stirling goes into the details and psychology of an alternate society operating under a totally different philosophy from ours. Nevertheless, Stirling cannot resist dedicating the entire half of a 40-page appendix to a detailed description of the paraphernalia of weaponry. This is a small price to pay for keeping it out of the main body of the novel.

—Henry Leperlier

---

**STOCKTON, Frank R.** (Francis Richard Stockton). American. Born in Philadelphia, Pennsylvania, 5 April 1834. Educated at Zane Street School, 1840–48, and Central High School, 1848–52, both in Philadelphia. Married Marian Edwards Tuttle in 1860. Apprenticed as a wood-engraver in 1852, and worked as an engraver until 1870. Assistant editor, *Hearth and Home*, 1868–73, and *St. Nicholas* magazine, 1873–78, both New York. Regular contributor to *Scribner's Magazine. Died 20 April 1902.*

## Science-Fiction Publications

### Novels

*The Great War Syndicate.* New York, Collier, and London, Longman, 1889.
*The Great Stone of Sardis.* New York and London, Harper, 1898.

### Short Stories

*The Science Fiction of Frank R. Stockton*, edited by Richard Gid Powers. Boston, Gregg Press, 1976.

## Other Publications

### Novels

*The Late Mrs. Null.* New York, Scribner, and London, Sampson Low, 1886.
*The Hundredth Man.* New York, Century, and London, Sampson Low, 1887.
*The Stories of the Three Burglars.* New York, Dodd Mead, and London, Sampson Low, 1890.
*The Merry Chanter.* New York, Century, and London, Sampson Low, 1890.
*Ardis Claverden.* New York, Dodd Mead, and London, Sampson Low, 1890.
*The House of Martha.* Boston, Houghton Mifflin, and London, Osgood, 1891.
*The Squirrel Inn.* New York, Century, and London, Sampson Low, 1891.
*Pomona's Travels.* New York, Scribner, and London, Cassell, 1894.
*The Adventures of Captain Horn.* New York, Scribner, and London, Cassell, 1895.
*Mrs. Cliff's Yacht.* New York, Scribner, and London, Cassell, 1896.
*The Girl at Cobhurst.* New York, Scribner, and London, Cassell, 1898.
*The Novels and Stories.* New York, Scribner, 23 vols., 1899–1904.
*A Bicycle in Cathay.* New York, Harper, 1900.
*The Captain's Toll Gate*, edited by Marian E. Stockton. New York, Appleton, and London, Cassell, 1903.

### Short Stories

*Rudder Grange.* New York, Scribner, 1879, Edinburgh, Douglas, 1883.
*The Lady or the Tiger? and Other Stories.* New York, Scribner, and Edinburgh, Douglas, 1884.
*The Transferred Ghost.* New York, Scribner, 1884.
*The Casting Away of Mrs. Lecks and Mrs. Aleshine.* New York, Century, and London, Sampson Low, 1886.
*The Christmas Wreck and Other Stories.* New York, Scribner, 1886; as *A Borrowed Month and Other Stories*, Edinburgh, Douglas, 1887.
*The Dusantes.* New York, Century, and London, Sampson Low, 1888.
*Amos Kilbright, His Adscititious Experiences, with Other Stories.* New York, Scribner, and London, Unwin, 1888.
*The Rudder Grangers Abroad.* New York, Scribner, and London, Sampson Low, 1891.

*The Watchmaker's Wife and Other Stories.* New York, Scribner, 1893; as *The Shadrach and Other Stories.* London, W.H. Allen, 1893.
*A Chosen Few.* New York, Scribner, 1895.
*A Story-Teller's Pack.* New York, Scribner, and London, Cassell, 1897.
*The Associate Hermits.* New York and London, Harper, 1898.
*The Vizier of the Two-Horned Alexander.* New York, Century, and London, Cassell, 1899.
*Afield and Afloat.* New York, Scribner, and London, Cassell, 1901.
*John Gayther's Garden.* New York, Scribner, and London, Cassell, 1903.
*The Magic Egg and Other Stories.* New York, Scribner, 1907.
*Stories of New Jersey.* New Brunswick, New Jersey, Rutgers University Press, 1961.

Other (for children)

*Ting-a-Ling.* Boston, Hurd and Stoughton, 1870; London, Ward and Downey, 1889.
*Roundabout Rambles in Lands of Fact and Fancy.* New York, Scribner, 1872.
*What Might Have Been Expected.* New York, Dodd Mead, 1874; London, Routledge, 1875.
*Tales Out of School.* New York, Scribner, 1875.
*A Jolly Friendship.* New York, Scribner, and London, Kegan Paul, 1880.
*The Floating Prince and Other Fairy Tales.* New York, Scribner, and London, Ward and Downey, 1881.
*Ting-a-Ling Tales.* New York, Scribner, 1882.
*The Story of Viteau.* New York, Scribner, and London, Sampson Low, 1884.
*The Bee-Man of Orn and Other Fanciful Tales.* New York, Scribner, 1887; London, Sampson Low, 1888.
*The Queen's Museum.* New York, Scribner, 1887.
*Personally Conducted.* New York, Scribner, and London, Sampson Low, 1889.
*The Clocks of Rondaine and Other Stories.* New York, Scribner, and London, Sampson Low, 1892.
*Fanciful Tales,* edited by Julia E. Langworthy. New York, Scribner, 1894.
*Captain Chap; or, The Rolling Stones.* Philadelphia, Lippincott, and London, Nimmo, 1896; as *The Young Master of Hyson Hall,* Lippincott, 1899.
*New Jersey, from the Discovery of the Scheyichbi to Recent Times.* New York, Appleton, 1896; as *Stories of New Jersey,* New York, American Book Company, 1896.
*The Buccaneers and Pirates of Our Coasts.* New York, Macmillan, 1898.
*Kate Bonnet.* New York, Appleton, and London, Cassell, 1902.
*Stories of the Spanish Main.* New York, Macmillan, 1913.
*The Poor Count's Christmas.* New York, Stokes, 1927.
*The Fairy Tales of Frank R. Stockton,* edited by Jack Zipes. New York, Signet, 1990.

*

Critical Study: *Frank R. Stockton* by Martin I.J. Griffin, Philadelphia, University of Pennsylvania Press, 1939 (includes bibliography).

* * *

Frank R. Stockton's science fiction has been neglected in histories of the field, perhaps because his literary reputation has suffered such eclipse in this century (he was highly praised during his life-time), and because science fiction was only a small part of his literary output. Except in his two important novels, *The Great War Syndicate* and *The Great Stone of Sardis,* his science fiction was light and humorous popular magazine fiction. A recent collection, *The Science Fiction of Frank R. Stockton,* assembles all his SF stories (and *The Great Stone of Sardis*), and the introduction by Richard Gid Powers is notable for its disdain for his lack of "seriousness."

Most of Stockton's SF stories have a similar plot: a gentleman amateur wins fame and fortune and gets the girl by means of an invention. This is true in "My Terminal Moraine," *The Great Stone of Sardis,* "My Translatophone," and, to a certain extent, "A Tale of Negative Gravity." The remainder are fantasies laced with contemporary science: "The Water Devil" concerns the trans-Atlantic cable and a ship whose cargo is electricity; "Amos Kilbright" is a ghost story; "The Knife That Killed Po Hancy" is a Jekyll and Hyde story concerning blood transfusions. Powers points out that *The Great Stone of Sardis* (the stone is a great diamond at the earth's core) combines Jules Verne's books *Journey to the Center of the Earth* and *The Adventures of Captain Hatteras* in a novel of polar exploration (Clewes, the amateur scientist/hero is first to reach the North Pole) and geological theory (Clewes invents an "Artesian Ray" to explore the interior of the earth). Clewes's adventures (set in 1947) are a significant contribution to the development of the "wonders of science" novel.

Stockton's major novel, however, is *The Great War Syndicate.* Although not mentioned in I.F. Clarke's *Voices Prophesying War,* Stockton's novel of a war between the United States and England, fought using such new technology as an ultimate weapon (a disintegrator), is perhaps the most important SF novel in the "future war" tradition between *The Battle of Dorking* (1871) and *The War of the Worlds* (1898). World peace, capitalism, and the English language are enforced by an Anglo-American syndicate using the threat of ultimate destruction. The novel surpasses its many contemporaries, which characteristically dealt with politics, military tactics, and unimaginative technology (with minor innovations such as a new gun which would cause tactics to change) and were warnings clothed in fictional attributes. *The Great War Syndicate* is a true science-fiction vision of a new world created by a war to end war and a weapon to end war, the archetype of that naive hope which led to the building and use of the first atomic bombs and the "pax Americana."

That Stockton's immediate followers in this mode were for the most part popular hacks (e.g., George Griffith) has not enhanced his reputation as progenitor. However, despite its failings as a novel (principally a lack of adequate characterization), *The Great War Syndicate* repays serious examination.

—David G. Hartwell

---

**STORM, Eric.** *See* **TUBB, E.C.**

---

**STRATFORD, H. Philip.** *See* **BULMER, Kenneth.**

---

**STRATTON, Thomas.** *See* **COULSON, Robert; DE WEESE, Gene.**

---

**STRETE, Craig (Kee).** American. Born in Fort Wayne, Indiana, 6 May 1950; son of a Cherokee Indian father. Educated at Wright State University, Dayton, Ohio, B.A. in theatre arts 1974; University of California, Irvine, M.F.A. 1978. Married to Countess Irmgard Margaretha Christina Von Dam. Since 1980, foreign rights and international acquisitions editor, De Knipscheer, Amsterdam, and Rogner & Bernhard, Munich. Editor, *Red Planet Earth*, 1974–75; managing editor, *East West Players Newsletter*, 1984–85. Co-founder and director, Society of Ethnic Literature in Translation. Agent: (novels) Kirby McCauley Ltd., 432 Park Avenue South, Suite 1509, New York, New York 10016. Address: c/o Doubleday, 666 Fifth Avenue, New York, New York 10103, U.S.A.

SCIENCE-FICTION PUBLICATIONS

Novels

*Death in the Spirit House.* New York, Doubleday, 1988.
*Death Chants.* New York, Doubleday, 1988.

Short Stories

*Als Al het Andere Faalt.* Amsterdam, Knipscheer, 1976; expanded edition, as *If All Else Fails*, New York, Doubleday, 1980.
*The Bleeding Man and Other Science Fiction Stories* (for children). New York, Greenwillow, 1977.
*Dreams That Burn in the Night.* New York, Doubleday, 1982.

OTHER PUBLICATIONS

Novel

*Burn Down the Night.* New York, Warner, 1982.

Plays

*Paint Your Face on a Drowning in the River* (produced Los Angeles, 1984).
*A Sunday Visit with Great Grandfather, and The Arrow That Kills with Love* (produced New York, 1984).

Screenplays: *Killing Moves*, 1975; *Honor Code*, 1976; *Blodets Röst*, 1978; *Sous les toits de nuit*, 1978.

Television Plays (under pseudonyms): for *Streets of San Francisco, Baretta*, and *McCloud* series.

Verse

*In Geronimo's Doodkist.* Amsterdam, Knipscheer, 1978.
*Dark Journey.* Amsterdam, Knipscheer, 1979.

Other (for children)

*Paint Your Face on a Drowning in the River.* New York, Greenwillow, 1978.
*Oom Coyote en de Bisonpizza.* Amsterdam, Knipscheer, 1978.
*When Grandfather Journeys into Winter.* New York, Greenwillow, 1979.
*Spiegel je gezicht.* Amsterdam, Knipscheer, 1979.
*Twee Spionnen in het Huis van de Liefde.* Amsterdam, Knipscheer, 1981.
*Met de Pijn die het Liefheeft en Haat.* Amsterdam, Knipscheer, 1983.
*Big Thunder Magic.* New York, Greenwillow, 1990.

* * *

Craig Strete has the flamboyance of R.A. Lafferty and Norman Spinrad, combining flights of fantasy with intense social criticism. He capitalizes on his Indian heritage in theme, motif, humor, plot, story-telling technique, and subjects of social criticism, leaning heavily on the mythic to generate a feeling of universality. His works are relatively short and indicate fascination with the sound and rhythm of sentences, giving the poetic effect of the native American oral tradition. Exaggeration, word play, and comic, low-key dialogue are characteristic. Because he often omits transitions, becomes pyrotechnical, and demands close attention, Strete is not to be read rapidly.

Strete's recurrent theme is society's attempt to mold human beings into productive working parts of the white man's big world machine. What does not work is thrown out (the old man of "Time Deer"), or put to better use, providing blood for transfusions ("Bleeding Man") or adding color to movies ("A Horse of a Different Technicolor"). "Bleeding Man," his most conventionally narrated work, is most illustrative of the clash that occurs when emotionless bureaucracy meets the supernatural. On one level, it is a parable of the policy of first making war with Indians and then studying them. "Time Deer" similarly contrasts values. "A Horse of a Different Technicolor," a horror story of mind control, and "Why Has the Virgin Mary Never Entered the Wigwam of Standing Bear?" attack materialism and forced conformity, using television as a metaphor for the regimented spectator/consumer life. In fact, the stories published in *The Bleeding Man* frequently refer to cultural conflict and genocide.

Strete's novels for children, published under the name Craig Kee Strete, though not science fiction, should be taken into account as contributing to understanding the more complex stories. In *Paint Your Face on a Drowning River* Old Cat tells his grandson, who is about to leave the reservation, about his early life. The story is part of "Time Deer" and prophetic of the young man's life in the white world.

—Mary S. Weinkauf

---

**STURGEON, Theodore (Hamilton).** Also wrote as Frederick R. Ewing; Ellery Queen. American. Born Edward Hamilton Waldo in Staten Island, New York, 26 February 1918; name changed on adoption, 1929. Attended Overbrook High School, Philadelphia. Married 1) Dorothy Fillingame in 1940, two daughters; 2) Mary Mair in 1949; 3) Marion Sturgeon in 1951, four children; 4) Wina Golden in 1969, one son. Salesman in early 1930's; seaman, 1935–38; hotel manager, West Indies, 1940–41; assistant chief steward for United States Army, 1941; bulldozer operator, Puerto Rico, 1942–43; advertising copy editor, 1944; literary agent, 1946–47; circulation staff member, *Fortune* and *Time*, New York, 1948–49; story editor, *Tales of To-*

*morrow*, 1950; feature editor, 1961–64, and contributing editor, 1972– 74, *If*, New York; television writer, 1966–75. Book reviewer, *Venture*, 1957–58, *Galaxy*, 1972–74, and *New York Times*, 1974–75; columnist, *National Review*, New York, 1961–73. Recipient: *Argosy* prize, 1947; International Fantasy award, 1954; Nebula award, 1970; Hugo award, 1971. Guest of Honor, 20th World Science Fiction Convention, 1962; World Fantasy Convention Life Achievement award, 1985. *Died 8 May 1985.*

### Science-Fiction Publications

#### Novels

*The Dreaming Jewels*. New York, Greenberg, 1950; London, Nova, 1955; as *The Synthetic Man*, New York, Pyramid, 1957.
*More Than Human*. New York, Farrar Straus, 1953; London, Gollancz, 1954.
*The Cosmic Rape*. New York, Dell, 1958; as *To Marry Medusa*, New York, Baen, 1986.
*Venus Plus X*. New York, Pyramid, 1960; London, Gollancz, 1969.
*Voyage to the Bottom of the Sea* (novelization of screenplay). New York, Pyramid, 1961.
*. . . and My Fear Is Great; Baby Is Three*. New York, Universal, 1965.
*Godbody*. New York, Fine, 1986.
*The Widget, the Wadget, and Boff*, with *The Ugly Little Boy* by Isaac Asimov (for children). New York, Tor, 1989.

#### Short Stories

*It*. Philadelphia, Prime Press, 1948.
*Without Sorcery*. Philadelphia, Prime Press, 1948.
*E Pluribus Unicorn*. New York, Abelard Press, 1953; London, Abelard Schuman, 1960.
*Caviar*. New York, Ballantine, 1955; London, Sidgwick and Jackson, 1968.
*A Way Home*. New York, Funk and Wagnalls, and London, Mayflower, 1955.
*Thunder and Roses*. London, Joseph, 1957.
*A Touch of Strange*. New York, Doubleday, 1958; London, Hamlyn, 1978.
*Aliens 4*. New York, Avon, 1959.
*Beyond*. New York, Avon, 1960.
*Not Without Sorcery*. New York, Ballantine, 1961.
*Sturgeon in Orbit*. New York, Pyramid, 1964; London, Gollancz, 1970.
*The Joyous Invasions*. London, Gollancz, 1965.
*Starshine*. New York, Pyramid, 1966; London, Gollancz, 1968.
*Sturgeon Is Alive and Well*. New York, Putnam, 1971.
*The Worlds of Theodore Sturgeon*. New York, Ace, 1972.
*To Here and the Easel*. London, Gollancz, 1973.
*Case and the Dreamer*. New York, New American Library, 1973; London, Pan, 1974.
*Visions and Venturers*. New York, Dell, 1978; London, Gollancz, 1979.
*Maturity*. Minneapolis, Science Fiction Society, 1979.
*The Golden Helix*. New York, Doubleday, 1979.
*The Stars Are the Styx*. New York, Dell, 1979.
*Slow Sculpture*. New York, Pocket Books, 1982.
*Alien Cargo*. New York, Bluejay, 1984.
*A Touch of Sturgeon*, edited by David Pringle. London, Simon and Schuster, 1987.

### Other Publications

#### Novels

*I, Libertine* (as Frederick R. Ewing). New York, Ballantine, 1956.
*The King and Four Queens*. New York, Dell, 1956.
*Some of Your Blood*. New York, Ballantine, 1961; London, Sphere, 1967.
*The Player on the Other Side* (as Ellery Queen). New York, Random House, 1963.
*The Rare Breed*. New York, Fawcett, 1966.

#### Short Stories

*Sturgeon's West*. New York, Doubleday, 1973.

#### Plays

*It Should Be Beautiful* (produced Woodstock, New York, 1963?).
*Psychosis: Unclassified*, adaptation of his novel *Some of Your Blood* (produced 1977).

Radio Plays: *Incident at Switchpath*, 1950; *The Stars Are the Styx*, 1953; *Mr. Costello Here*, 1956; *Saucer of Loneliness*, 1957; *The Girl Had Guts, The Skills of Xanadu*, and *Affair with a Green Monkey*, all in the 1960's; *More Than Human*, 1967.

Television Plays: *Mewhu's Jet* and *The Adoptive Ultimate*, from fiction by Stanley Weinbaum (*Beyond Tomorrow* series), *They Came to Bagdad*, from the novel by Agatha Christie (*Playhouse 90* series), *Ordeal in Space*, from story by Robert Heinlein, and *The Sound Machine*, from story by Roald Dahl (both *CBS Stage 14* series)—all 1950's; *Dead Dames Don't Dial* (*Schlitz Playhouse* series), 1959; *Shore Leave*, 1966, and *Amok Time*, 1967 (both *Star Trek* series); *Killdozer!*, with Ed MacKillop, from the story by Sturgeon, 1974; *The Pylon Express* (*Land of the Lost* series), 1975–76.

#### Other

Editor, *New Soviet Science Fiction*. London, Collier Macmillan, 1980.

Comic Books: wrote *Iron Munro* (2 issues), 1940; *How to Build Boats*, 1940; *It*, 1972; *Killdozer!*, 1974; *Microcosmic God*, 1976.

*

Bibliography: *Theodore Sturgeon: A Primary and Secondary Bibliography* by Lahna F. Diskin, Boston, Hall, 1980.

Critical Studies: *Theodore Sturgeon* by Lucy Menger, New York, Ungar, 1981; *Theodore Sturgeon* by Lahna F. Diskin, Mercer Island, Washington, Starmont House, 1981.

* * *

In Kurt Vonnegut's fictional universe, Kilgore Trout writes SF stories pregnant with emotion and philosophy, but relegated to the unread pages of pornographic magazines, while he ekes out a living with odd jobs. Trout's most likely model is Theodore Sturgeon, whose much-anthologized stories have made him probably the best *loved* of all SF writers. Inclined toward magic and fantasy, unashamedly romantic and psychologically penetrating, Sturgeon commonly writes about the yearning for wholeness that characterizes love in a disjointed, repressive society. This emotional edge and his mastery of styles, using a classically restrained vocabulary, make him second only to Heinlein as a contemporary model for other SF writers. Bradbury and Delany acknowledge their debt openly; others, like Vonnegut, are more indirect. Beside extensive writing outside SF, Sturgeon's fantasies fill over a dozen volumes of stories and several novels, plus the novelization of the movie, *Voyage to the Bottom of the Sea.*

Of his earliest work, *It* and "Killdozer" concern menaces whose life and terrestrial origins are in question. The latter is a compelling metaphor of machine malevolence. Another horror story, extraordinarily sensuous, is "Bianca's Hands" which tells of an idiot with beautiful hands that work without conscious direction, eventually strangling her lover. Other early stories include "Shottle Bop," about a mysterious shop selling talents people inevitably misuse, and "Microcosmic God" in which a misanthropic scientist drives the evolution of a race of tiny creatures who propitiate him with remarkable inventions. "Maturity" concerns a charming self-educated polymath whose perpetual youthful irresponsibility stems from a glandular defect; when it is corrected medically, he ripens and dies. The maturing of a society is the subject of "Thunder and Roses" in which a beautiful entertainer, dying from radiation sickness, persuades the men at a key military base in an America crippled by nuclear attack to spare their enemy and the human race.

Sturgeon's first novel, *The Dreaming Jewels,* is a mad melodrama of circus freaks and humanoid products of living crystals. Its few poetic moments cannot overcome simplistic conflicts among telepathic cardboard characters, but elements in it look forward to *More Than Human*, which won the International Fantasy award. In *Baby Is Three* a boy finds out in a marathon psychiatric session why he tried to kill his foster mother. With the analyst's vocabulary and his own repressed memories, he discovers his role as the central ganglion of a multi-person form, or gestalt, whose other members are also children with parapsychological powers complementing his own. Actually killing off the governess in the middle section of the novel, Sturgeon begins it with the youthful outcasts and an older "idiot" coalescing into the gestalt's "first draft," and ends it with the addition of a moral component who binds the entity to homo sapiens while he opens the door to the superior race, homo gestalt. Written in a vivid, impressionistic style, this parable of social organization and psychological integration became for many readers the one SF classic. Completing this parapsychological trilogy, *The Cosmic Rape* finds another outcast repelling a group-mind invasion by uniting Earth's mental forces over the galaxy-spanning alien being. In the process, he breaks through his isolation and finds himself, while healing the fragmentation of the individualistic human race.

Featuring magic and wish-fulfillment, aliens and ESP, Sturgeon's stories exploit the most peripheral of science-fiction content. In "Saucer of Loneliness" a girl learns from a miniature flying saucer that someone is lonelier than she is. Though it brings tribulations, it sustains her through them, finally bringing the love of the narrator, who saves her from suicide. "The World Well Lost" appears to concern a pair of aliens, "loverbirds" from Dirnadu, a planet closed to mankind. It is really about the love between two human space crewmen, which literally "cannot speak its name," and which taints the entire human race from the perspective of the aliens, whose gender differences are more pronounced. Apparent homosexuality also surfaces in "Affair with a Green Monkey," in which a slightly built young man is rescued from thugs by a pompously "well-adjusted" psychologist. Overbearingly tolerant, the host throws his wife and his guest together, and a platonic affair develops. Its consummation is prevented not by the guest's being gay but by his being an alien, far too well-endowed sexually for interspecies sex. But what may seem merely a dirty joke is in fact a sensitive plea for understanding, tolerance, and tenderness.

Closer to hard science fiction, "Bulkhead" (originally "Who?") tells of an astronaut kept company by the childish half of his artificially split personality, supposedly beyond a bulkhead which actually separates him from the vacuum of space. More utopian is the far-future pastoral world of "The Skills of Xanadu" where people are integrated by means of "belts" that virtually transcend technology, freeing them to realize their (and our) potential. Three other tales show the variety of Sturgeon's production in the 1950's. In "The Girl Had Guts" a symbiotic alien saves human lives by becoming a false digestive system, vomited out in times of peril. Marooned on Mars, a man disguises from himself, with lyrical impressions and memories, his impending death as the first human to take this next evolutionary step into an alien environment ("The Man Who Lost the Sea"). The comic elegy "Like Young" suggests that fun-loving otters have already inherited the earth from a doomed human race.

Never avoiding controversy, Sturgeon anticipated by a decade Le Guin's Gethenians in *Venux Plus X.* In alternating chapters, suburbanites talk about sexual variety and stereotypes, and a downed aviator with macho hangups fails to be integrated into a utopian society of surgically created bisexuals. Flirting with another taboo, *Some of Your Blood* takes the vampire theme seriously, probing its causes in a fictional case history of a man's bizarre need. Like these novels, Sturgeon's later stories tend to be talky, as well as controversial. "When You Care, When You Love" extends love to one's own creation, a cloned replica of a lost beloved. "If All Men Were Brothers, Would You Want One to Marry Your Sister?" posits a world in which keeping sex in the family is the "healthy" rule, not a frequently broken proscription. In perhaps his best story about healing, "Slow Sculpture" compares it to raising bonsai plants (Hugo and Nebula awards). His more recent work is less successful. A case in point is "Case and the Dreamer"; ambitious but diffused, it is about an astronaut and his lover, resurrected by an indrawn human race to explore the universe for it, in the company of a clownish "god" (the dreamer) with whom their ship's computer has fallen in love.

Sturgeon equates science with wisdom, not with hardware and limitations. Moving even when they are talky, his fantasies are wrought from emotional experiences his readers recognize as theirs, but which his skill with words can distance artistically. As unselfishly giving and fiscally irresponsible as the protagonist of "Maturity," Sturgeon never profited much financially from his writing. But he turned his suffering into beauty, encapsulating in fiction the longing for alternatives that characterizes many people's fascination with science fiction and fantasy.

—David N. Samuelson

---

**STRYKER, Hal.** *See* **SMITH, George H.**

---

**SUCHARITKUL, Somtow.** Also writes as S.P. Somtow. Born in Bangkok, Thailand, in 1952; grew up in Europe. Educated at Eton College, Cambridge University, B.A., M.A. Conductor and composer: director, Bangkok Opera Society, 1977–78, and Asian Composer's Conference-Festival, Bangkok, 1978; compositions include *Gongula 3* and *Star Maker—An Anthology of Universes.* Recipient: John W. Campbell award, 1981; *Locus* award, 1982. Address: c/o Tor Books, 49 West 24th Street, Ninth Floor, New York, New York 10010, U.S.A.

SCIENCE-FICTION PUBLICATIONS

Novels (series: Inquestor)

*Starship and Haiku.* New York, Pocket Books, 1981.
Inquestor:
*Light on the Sound.* New York, Pocket Books, 1982.
*The Throne of Madness.* New York, Pocket Books, 1983.
*Utopia Hunters.* New York, Pocket Books, 1984.
*The Darkling Wind.* New York, Bantam, 1985.
*V: The Alien Swordmaster* (as S.P. Somtow). London, Pinnacle, 1985; as Sucharitkul, New York, New American Library, 1986.
*The Fallen Country* (for children). New York, Bantam, 1986.
*The Shattered Horses* (as S.P. Somtow). New York, Tor, 1986.
*Forgetting Places* (as S.P. Somtow). New York, St. Martin's Press, 1987.
*Symphony of Tenor* (for children). New York, Tor, 1988.
*Aquila and the Iron Horse* (as S.P. Somtow). New York, Ballantine, 1988.
*Aquila and the Sphinx* (as S.P. Somtow). New York, Ballantine, 1988.
*Moondance* (as S.P. Somtow). New York, Tor, 1989; London, Gollancz, 1991.

Short Stories

*Mallworld.* Norfolk, Virginia, Donning, 1981.
*Fire from the Wine-Dark Sea.* Norfolk, Virginia, Donning, 1983.
*The Aquiliad.* New York, Pocket Books, 1983.

OTHER PUBLICATIONS

Novel

*Vampire Junction* (as S.P. Somtow). Norfolk, Virginia, Donning, 1984; London, Macdonald, 1986.

* * *

The works of Somtow Sucharitkul have been aptly described, at their best, as droll, witty, cosmic, symbolic, mythopoetic, startlingly original, inventive, and masterful, but, at their worst, as cryptic, obscure, unrestrained, convoluted and ponderous pulp. They echo the familiar, either historical (featuring Romans, Olmecs, lost tribes of Israel, samurai) or present (the threat of nuclear holocaust, lab-born plagues, the slaughter of whales), or pseudo-mythic (Bigfoot, flying saucers, and vampires), but also partake of the alien and the bizarre (sentient suns, cities in the heads of monstrous snakes, a Throne of Madness, a Utopia of the dead, a dust sculpturess, a web-dancer, and a rainbow king). Sucharitkul, an active contributor to the *Fantasy Review* under his pen name S.P. Somtow, is at his best exploring sentient cultures grudgingly forced to face the common bonds that link them despite appearance, tradition, and culture, whether they be earthlings and lizards (*The Alien Swordmaster*), Windbringers and Inquestors (*Light on the Sound, The Throne of Madness, Utopia Hunters, The Darkling Wind*), Selespridons and humans (*Mallworld*), Romans and American Indians (*The Aquiliad*) or whales and Japanese (*Starship and Haiku*). His works, whether set eons in the future or in an alternate antiquity, show benevolence and compassion devolving into a mass blood lust until salvation comes from some unexpected quarter, some unknown hero who spearheads a resistance, engages in a strategic game of life and death with thousands of lives or thousands of planets at stake, and proves his/her mettle defending old-fashioned values of goodness, justice and family. Often it is the very young or the very old in Sucharitkul's works who are the most perceptive and the most attuned to the pain and the tragedy of other sentient beings.

*Light on the Sound*, the first of the Inquestor series, introduces those vigilant guardians of the Dispersal of Man, the anti-Utopian, omnipotent, immortal, absentminded, despotic Inquestors, and exposes their hypocrisy. Inquestors believe the human race "fallen" and the burden of decision-making for all humanity theirs by default; however, their behavior proves them not just elitists but sadistic tyrants. Because they need the disembodied brains of a whale-like sentient race (Windbringers) to power their faster-than-light vehicles, they have developed a race of deaf and blind humans genetically designed to be impervious to the beauty of light and sound which the Windbringers marshal as their only defense. However, a sighted throwback, the girl Darktouch, sees their beauty and, empowered by a sympathetic Inquestor heretic (Davaryush) who dreams of Utopia and doubts the Inquestor "mission," precipitates the fight to save both races. The suspenseful and gripping *The Throne of Madness* continues the story without a pause for recapitulation. This book follows the progress of a young Inquestor (Kelver), a peasant boy selected and trained by the heretic Inquestor Davaryush in preparation for the monumental task of countering Inquestor despotism, cruelty and madness. Kelver begins his preparation by crossing the galaxy and pursuing the required Inquestor quest for an understanding of murder, hatred, war and compassion. In so doing, he, along with two other fledgling Inquestors, experiences numerous wonders that prepare him to assume his planet's throne and then, hopefully, to overthrow the Inquest itself. *Utopia Hunters* provides the history of the Inquest through a series of ornate and moving linked tales told a young "lightweaver," Jenjen, by an ancient Inquestor who believes she will become a great artist. As these stories trace the life of the Inquestor who tells them from his pre-Inquestor youth to his guilt-ridden present, they reveal the sadness, anguish, and madness that afflict beings who tyrannize and destroy worlds in order to fulfill their own single-minded vision. Chosen to fashion a great lightsculpture celebrating the Inquest's crusade against utopias, Jenjen gradually learns to overcome her fear of darkness and to see in her own conflicts and creations the dark that is a texture in every light, a dark that threatens the Inquest but that nonetheless could save it. Her growth as an artist and her changing view of Inquestors help her finally understand the need to destroy false utopias that blind man to truth and that make him a slave to false hopes. The final tale of the destruction of flaming phoenixes that will rise no more sums up the paradoxes of dark and light. *The Darkling Wind* concludes the galactic chronicle of the decline and fall of the Inquestors with a complex "spectacle" of death and destruction, stalemates and endings that lead ultimately to the self-destruction of Mother Vara, the creator of the Inquest, the approach of what the sole surviving Inquestor views as the "dark ages," and the beginning of an "egalitarian" human system. An appendix debates the textual authenticity of the supposed sources of this history: mystic drawings and emblems on a deck of Inquestor cards. This tetralogy, with its metaphorical complexity, its paradoxes, its exploration of the lights and darks that make up socio-political systems, and its rejection as delusion the idea of the compassionate sacrifice of individuals for abstract ideals, represents Sucharitkul's story-telling at its best.

*Fire from the Wine-Dark Sea* contains two interviews, a musical piece, two poems and ten carefully constructed short stories, including "Darktouch," about an expedition to a long-dead Earth, two early Inquestor stories depicting rebellions against cruel Inquestor rulers who rely on live power sources, and a precursor of *Starship and Haiku*, entitled "The Last Line of the Haiku." The latter is a compact, intriguing piece in which Japanese culture dominates a post-disaster world. *Starship and Haiku* expands its premise, juxtaposing the modern and the ancient, the technological and the artistic in a story of a dying earth 40 years hence: its land and seas polluted by nuclear radiation, its inhabitants diseased and mutated. Therein, the Japanese prove to be the offspring of whales, who contact them telepathically through Ryoko, the daughter of the Minister of Survival (Sucharitkul draws parallels between the two cultures). Spurred on by a madman, the Minister of Ending, many commit mass *seppuku* for having waged genocide not just against an intelligent species but against their own ancestors. However, Ryoko and her lover ensure that a hybrid race (whale and human) survives in space to carry life to the stars.

*The Alien Swordmaster* (one of the *V* series) also reflects Sucharitkul's interest in Japan, with its man-eating alien villainness named after a fastidious 11th-century Japanese authoress, Lady Murasaki, and its focus on an alien attraction to martial arts, pre-Meiji isolation, and ancient Japanese feudal traditions.

The idea of alternative worlds delights Sucharitkul, though he is not always careful to work out the particular details that would make them fully credible. "Sunsteps," for example, examines the world of Montezuma's Empire at a technologically advanced stage of development, and the ramifications of Aztec scientists' inevitable discovery of a rational, scientific explanation of the sun's power; how sun-worship somehow survived modern advances is never explained. In *The Aquiliad*, the invention of steam power helps the Romans extend their empire to America, from which, assisted by a wily, aged Indian chief, they hope to dominate China as well. However, they get into trouble and must be rescued by a time patrol. An evil time-traveller, pre-columbian genetic engineering, flying saucers, Bigfoot, the lost tribes of Israel, and cops helping Olmecs are only a few of the unusual twists of this sprawling plot. The narrator, a dim-witted general favored by Nero, continually clashes with the aged Indian, whose Latin word play is the wittiest part of a novel dominated by annoyingly verbose and stilted prose. *The Shattered Horses*, in turn, provides an unromantic view of the bitter aftermath of the Trojan War. Astyanax, son of Hector, narrates this rambling tour of the ancient world, the story of his maturation as he discovers reality deceptive, squalid and ignoble. As he tells of his escape from the Greeks (a slave mistakenly killed in his stead), his claim to Troy's throne, his witnessing the revenge of Orestes and Electra against their mother for the murder of their father, his reabduction of Helen from Menelaos, and the reenactment of the Trojan War, this time with Orestes demanding Helen's return, he paints a world in which individual heroism has given way to technology and discipline and the simple has become distressingly complex.

Though not an alternative world, *Vampire Junction* further demonstrates Sucharitkul's fascination with rewriting history as its narrator, the jaded, millionaire vampire, Timmy Valentine, recounts his experiences as a child slave singing for a Sybil when Pompei fell, as a victim of Bluebeard's rage at the martyrdom of Joan of Arc, and as the center of pursuit of a 19th-century Cambridge undergraduate cabal, self-named The Gods of Chaos. In our age Valentine and his vampire friends thrive on Manhattan's teenage rock scene, sucking the blood of vacuous groupies, Hollywood production companies, Jungian psychoanalysts, and rock concert audiences, until pursued to a snowbound Idaho town, where the vampire-hunting Gods of Chaos make a final stand against them.

*Mallworld* is a delightful series of bizarre glimpses of the inhabitants of a futuristic "shopping mall" world, stocked with exotic goods from throughout the solar system. This world is being investigated by a superior alien race, the Selespridons, who are fascinated by the strength of the human spirit and appalled by human barbarism and bad taste. This book depicts a world of the unexpectedly familiar transformed: St. Betty Crocker, St. Martin Luther King Kong, a nude female Pope, babies custom-designed at Storkways, Inc., suicide parlors featuring death by vampire, a megacredit card system that permits the shopping spree of the century, and the Bible belt, a mixture of Amish, Buddhist, and Hare Krishna, and the center of that ancient art, reading. Yet amid this modern insanity, man struggles to create, to free his body and soul, to achieve human dignity, love and understanding, and so touches the heart of jaded aliens that they cannot escape man's pull.

In sum, Sucharitkul creates worlds and languages, customs and cultures in narratives that are gripping, moving, well-crafted set pieces, with dense prose and metaphorical overtones, though at times his attempts at complex poetic diction and epic scope distract and obscure. At his best he is a wildly imaginative mythmaker, projecting topsy-turvy worlds that somehow remain human, entertaining, and compelling. He offers an Eastern perspective on art and nature, and a humanistic concern for man and his world.

—Gina Macdonald

---

**SUTTON, Andrew.** *See* **TUBB, E.C.**

---

**SUTTON, Jeff and Jean.** American. **SUTTON, Jeff(erson Howard):** Born in Los Angeles, California, 25 July 1913. Educated at San Diego State College, B.A. 1954, M.A. 1956. Served in the United States Marine Corps, 1941–45: Technical Sergeant. Married Eugenia Geneva Hansen in 1941; one son and one daughter. Photographer, International News Photos, Los Angeles, 1937–40; reporter, photographer, public relations writer for General Dynamics Astronautics; freelance writer and editorial consultant to aerospace industries from 1960. *Died 31 January 1979.* **SUTTON, Jean** (Eugenia Geneva Sutton, née Hansen): Born in Denmark, Wisconsin, 5 July 1916. Educated at the University of Wisconsin, Madison, 1934–37; University of California, Los Angeles, B.A. in economics 1940; San Diego State University, M.A. in education 1959. Personnel worker, U.S. Steel, Los Angeles, 1940–41; construction company timekeeper, San Diego, 1942–45; lathe operator, Douglas Aircraft, Santa Monica, California, and social worker in Los Angeles; executive secretary, San Diego City Council, 1949–52; administrative assistant, San Diego State College, 1953–55; social studies teacher, San Diego county high schools, 1958–71. Consultant assistant, from 1971. Agent: Scott Meredith Literary Agency, 845 Third Avenue, New York, New York 10022. Address: 4325 Beverly Drive, La Mesa, California 92041, U.S.A.

SCIENCE-FICTION PUBLICATIONS

Novels by Jeff Sutton

*First on the Moon.* New York, Ace, 1958.
*Bombs in Orbit.* New York, Ace, 1959.
*Spacehive.* New York, Ace, 1960.
*The Atom Conspiracy.* New York, Avalon, 1963.
*Apollo at Go* (for children). New York, Putnam, 1963; London, Mayflower, 1964.
*The Missile Lords.* New York, Putnam, 1963; London, Sidgwick and Jackson, 1964.
*Beyond Apollo* (for children). New York, Putnam, 1966; London, Gollancz, 1967.
*H-Bomb over America.* New York, Ace, 1967.
*The Man Who Saw Tomorrow.* New York, Ace, 1968.
*Whisper from the Stars.* New York, Dell, 1970.
*Alton's Unguessable.* New York, Ace, 1970.
*The Mindlocked Man.* New York, DAW, 1972.
*Cassady.* New York, St. Martin's Press, 1979; London, Hale, 1981.

Novels by Jeff and Jean Sutton (for children)

*The River.* New York, Belmont, 1966.
*The Beyond.* New York, Putnam, 1968.
*The Programmed Man.* New York, Putnam, 1968.
*Lord of the Stars.* New York, Putnam, 1969.
*Alien from the Stars.* New York, Putnam, 1970.
*The Boy Who Had the Power.* New York, Putnam, 1971.

*

Manuscript Collection: San Diego State University, California.

* * *

Jeff Sutton's first novel, *First on the Moon*, was considered promising because its technological detailing seemed authentic, perhaps owing to the author's engineering background. His second novel, *Bombs in Orbit*, again elicited some praise for its handling of technological details and for what appeared to be an increased skill in manipulating plot and creating suspense. However, the next two novels, *Spacehive* and *The Atom Conspiracy*, aroused substantial critical misgivings. No one doubted Sutton's ability to describe technological processes, current and extrapolated, and to suggest thereby verisimilitude. But plotting and characterization seemed more and more throwbacks to 1930's space opera; further, Sutton's style increasingly manifested an embarrassing fondness for cliché.

*The Atom Conspiracy* aptly illustrates Sutton's limitations. Its portrait of the Empire of Earth in 2449 when research in the atom is outlawed because of previous nuclear catastrophes, and a World Government is directed by an elite Council of Six who possess the highest IQ, is neither original nor convincing. The world looks and society functions very much the way they do today, and the Council of Six appear no better or worse than anyone with normal IQ. For reasons not entirely clear the Empire also looks with disdain upon anyone with ESP powers. The novel's hero, Max Krull, a government agent and a secret ESPer, is sent to investigate the circumstances behind the death by nuclear burning of a long-missing man. Most of the action, consisting of conventional intrigue, flight and chase, confrontations with supposedly all-powerful figures, and a gingerly touch of sex, is designed to keep Max from being where it was foretold he would be regardless of anything done to prevent it. Finally, Sutton's use of ESP owes more to a need for narrative gimmicks than a desire to investigate seriously an important topic.

Sutton's next novel, *Apollo at Go*, was written for the juvenile market. Buoyed by the novel's positive acceptance, Sutton turned out seven additional children's SF novels, most of which were written in collaboration with his wife Jean. (Several more Jeff Sutton adult SF novels were published but none made any stir.) Unfortunately, after initial acceptance and subsequent tinkering to find other effective ways of attracting young readers, the Suttons never realized the one unqualified success that would establish them as significant authors of SF. Still, their children's SF is as good as the representative Nourse or Lightner juvenile, and superior to a typical Hugh Walters story. *The Programmed Man, Lord of the Stars*, and *Alien from the Stars*, in particular, are all action-packed, quick-moving novels. Considered as a whole, then, Jeff Sutton's SF, whether intended for adults or children, has fallen short of the first rank. Although always solid in its depiction of technological process and procedures and usually adequately grounded in its scientific speculation, his fiction never moved beyond the merely competent and predictable to achieve originality and literary distinction.

—Francis J. Molson

---

**SWANN, Thomas Burnett.** American. Born in Tampa, Florida, 12 October 1928. Educated at Duke University, B.A. (Phi Beta Kappa) 1950; University of Tennessee, M.A. 1955; University of Florida, Ph.D. 1960. Taught at Florida Southern College, Wesleyan College (Macon, Georgia), and Florida Atlantic University. *Died 5 May 1976.*

SCIENCE-FICTION PUBLICATIONS

Novels (series: Minotaur; Rome)

*Day of the Minotaur.* New York, Ace 1966; St. Albans, Mayflower, 1975.
*The Weirwoods.* New York, Ace, 1967.
*Moondust.* New York, Ace, 1968.
*The Dolphin and the Deep.* New York, Ace, 1968.
*Where Is the Bird of Fire?* New York, Ace, 1970.
*The Goat Without Horns.* New York, Ballantine, 1971.
*The Forest of Forever* (Minotaur). New York, Ace, 1971; St. Albans, Mayflower, 1975.
*Wolfwinter.* New York, Ballantine, 1972.
*Green Phoenix.* New York, DAW, 1972.
*How Are the Mighty Fallen.* New York, DAW, 1974.
*The Not-World.* New York, DAW, 1975.
*The Tournament of Thorns.* New York, Ace, 1976.
*Lady of the Bees* (Rome). New York, Ace, 1976.
*Will-o-the-Wisp.* London, Corgi, 1976.
*The Gods Abide.* New York, DAW, 1976.
*The Minikins of Yam.* New York, DAW, 1976.
*Cry Silver Bells* (Minotaur). New York, DAW, 1977.
*Queens Walk in the Dusk* (Rome). Forest Park, Georgia, Heritage Press, 1977.

OTHER PUBLICATIONS

Other

*Ernest Dawson*. New York, Twayne, 1965.
*A.A. Milne*. New York, Twayne, 1971.
*The Heroine or the Horse: Leading Ladies in Republic's Films*. South Brunswick, New Jersey, Barnes, 1977.

*

Bibliography: *Thomas Burnett Swann: A Brief Critical Biography and Annotated Bibliography* by Robert A. Collins, Boca Raton, Florida Atlantic University, 1979.

* * *

A scholar as well as a fantasist, Thomas Burnett Swann wrote fiction that reflects his abiding interest in the western cultural tradition, particularly ancient history and mythology. Although his fiction has sometimes been criticized as overly sentimental, in fact criticism of basic western values forms a major element of his work. Swann makes striking and often radical changes whenever he employs inherited material, refashioning myths and legends to criticize the underlying values of the tradition from which they sprang. Two recurring distinctions play important roles in Swann's development of this philosophic dimension of his fiction. The first distinction involves the bestial and the human. In his myth-based fiction he often uses legendary "Beasts" such as minotaurs and fauns as his central characters, and his positive portrayal of these creatures contrasts with the often villainous behavior of the human characters. The second distinction presents female virtues as preferable to male virtues, and this is linked with the human/beast dichotomy in several novels.

Classical legend provides the basis for several novels that rank among Swann's best work. *Day of the Minotaur* and two "prequels," *The Forest of Forever* and *Cry Silver Bells*, offer Swann's version of the myth of the minotaur. As in most of his novels, Swann draws obvious moral distinctions between his good and evil characters. In this respect, several of his novels resemble heroic fantasy, although in every other way his work stands in stark opposition to that particular subgenre. Swann's presentation, like John Gardner's in his novel *Grendel* (1971), inverts the traditional view of the monster as evil. In the Minotaur trilogy, the humans represent evil. Swann emphasizes the competitive nature of the human characters, the Achaeans. They are cruel, callous, and obsessed with military conquest. On the other hand, the so-called Beasts, such as Zoe the Dryad and Eunostos the Minotaur, reflect in their behavior the ideal of balance. Unlike the humans, who exploit nature to fulfill their own desires, the Beasts take only what they need and seek to live in harmony with the natural world. The overall mood of both the entire trilogy and the individual novels that comprise it is sadness. The advance of human civilization dooms both the Beasts and the moral ideal that they symbolize.

Swann builds several other novels based on classical mythology around this dichotomy. Two of the most powerful connect the beast-human tension with a second symbolic distinction, the male and the female. *Lady of the Bees*, an expansion of *Where Is the Bird of Fire?*, is part of a trilogy based on the legendary founding of Rome. It portrays the victory of Romulus over Remus and his Dryad lover Mellonia as the conquest of aggression and assertion over the ideal of intuitive knowledge and harmony with nature. Swann's later fiction tends to emphasize the tension generated by these conflicting values. Another novel in the Rome trilogy, *Queens Walk in the Dusk*, further emphasizes Swann's preference for feminine values of harmony and balance over male concerns for domination and conquest. A tragic novel, *Queens Walk in the Dusk* offers a striking and sympathetic portrait of Dido, the Carthaginian queen abandoned by Aeneas.

Swann develops the distinction between male and female values perhaps most clearly in *The Minikins of Yam*. This novel, set in ancient Egypt, pits a worshipper of the female Isis against a priest of Ra, the male god of reason. Here, the goddess prevails, and the novel ends happily.

Swann extended his criticism of unbalanced, conquest-oriented values to the Judaeo-Christian tradition. *How Are the Mighty Fallen* is a Biblical fantasy that celebrates the love of Jonathan and David, who secretly worship the mother goddess Ashtoreth. The counterpoint is offered by the vindictive Yahweh, his prophet Samuel (a bitter old man who turns King Saul against Jonathan), and Saul himself.

A later novel, *The Gods Abide*, focuses on the efforts of Ashtoreth to protect her creatures from Yahweh, the vengeful "desert king" who pursues all who oppose his rule. The distinction between the feminine Ashtoreth and the masculine Yahweh reflects a larger principle present in several of the novels discussed above: Swann champions a feminine vision of engagement and empathetic knowledge over the masculine ideal of competitive rationality and military conquest. Indeed, Ashtoreth states explicitly the theme that runs through many of Swann's novels when she blames the destruction of joy and beauty on Yahweh's aggressive values. She even prophesies the perversion of Christ's feminine message of harmony by the masculine vision of Paul, by whom "the love he taught was turned into Law."

The three qualities that characterize Swann's fiction help explain not only the praise his work has received but also his relative obscurity. First, the majority of his novels and stories articulate an almost gentle vision. Few battles and little violence occur, but the stories emphasize relationships among characters. The landscapes reflect the same gentle vision, particularly the almost Edenic world of the Beasts that Swann employs as a contrast to the destructive world of human violence and ambition. Second, Swann's language is both graceful and highly literary, reflecting in particular a fondness for literary allusion that is perhaps a reflection of his academic training. Third, his best fiction is intellectually provocative, an aspect of his writing that the other two qualities have caused many readers to miss. He proposes a value system based on harmony with nature and sympathy that offers a stark contrast to the "heroic" code that dominates the more widely read fantasies of the sword-and-sorcery subgenre. *Lady of the Bees* and *How Are the Mighty Fallen*, both of which reflect all three aspects of Swann's unusual art with particular clarity, offer excellent introductions to his work.

—Dennis M. Kratz

---

**SWANWICK, Michael.** American. Born in Schenectady, New York, 18 November 1950. Educated at The College of William and Mary, 1968–72, B.A. Married Marianne Catherine Porter in 1980; one son. Information analyst for National Solar Heating and Cooling Information Center 1977–80. Since 1980, full-time writer. Recipient: Theodore Sturgeon Memorial award, 1990. Agent: Virginia Kidd Agency, Box 278, 538 East Hartford Street, Milford, Pennsylvania 18337. Address: 457 Lexington Avenue, Philadelphia, Pennsylvania 19128, U.S.A.

SCIENCE-FICTION PUBLICATIONS

Novels

*In the Drift.* New York, Berkley, 1985; London, Century, 1989.
*Vacuum Flowers.* New York, Arbor House, 1987; London, Simon and Schuster, 1988.
*Griffin's Egg* (novella). London, Legend, 1990.
*Stations of the Tide.* New York, Morrow, 1991.

Short Stories

*Gravity's Angels: 13 Stories.* Sauk City, Wisconsin, Arkham House, 1991.

Uncollected Short Stories

"Mummer Kiss," in *Universe 11*, edited by Terry Carr. New York, Doubleday, 1979–83.
"Ginungagap," in *Triquarterly*, Fall 1980.
"The Feast of St. Janis," in *Best Science Fiction Stories of the Year*, edited by Gardner Dozois. New York, Dutton, 1981.
" 'Til Human Voices Wake Us," in *Proteus: Voices for the 80's*, edited by Richard S. McEnroe. New York, Ace, 1981.
"Touring," with Jack Dann and Gardner Dozois, in *Penthouse*, April 1981.
"Walden Three," in *New Dimensions 12*, edited by Marta Randall and Robert Silverberg. New York, Timescape, 1981.
"Snow Job," with Gardner Dozois, in *High Times*, April 1982.
"Virgin Territory," with Jack Dann and Gardner Dozois, in *Penthouse*, March 1984.
"When the Music's Over," in *Light Years and Dark*, edited by Michael Bishop. New York, Berkley, 1984.
"Afternoon at Schrafft's," with Jack Dann and Gardner Dozois, in *Amazing*, March 1984.
"The Golden Apples of the Sun," with Jack Dann and Gardner Dozois, in *Penthouse*, March 1984.
"Ice Age," in *Amazing*, January 1984.
"Marrow Death," in *Isaac Asimov's Science Fiction Magazine*, December 1984.
"Trojan Horse," in *Omni*, December 1984.
"The Man Who Met Picasso," in *Omni Book of Science Fiction*, edited by Ellen Datlow. New York, Zebra, 1985.
"Anyone Here from Utah?" in *Isaac Asimov's Science Fiction Magazine*, May 1985.
"Dogfight," with William Gibson, in *Omni*, July 1985.
"The Gods of Mars," with Jack Dann and Gardner Dozois, in *Omni*, March 1985.
"The Overcoat," in *Omni*, May 1988.
"The Dragon Line," in *Terry's Universe*, edited by Beth Meacham. New York, Tor, 1988.
"The Edge of the World," in *Full Spectrum 2*, edited by Lou Aronica. New York, Doubleday, 1989.
"Snow Angels," in *Omni*, March 1989.

*

Michael Swanwick comments:

My father was an engineer, and in the normal course of things, I probably would have become one as well. But I was lured away from the engineering by science, and then lured away from science by literature. Science fiction allows me to keep faith with my past as well as the future.

The works themselves range from hard science fiction to stone fantasy, with stops at all stations in between, and are written at whatever length serves them best. There is much about them that seems obvious to me, much that cuts close to the bone. But I'm neither a confessional writer nor a ventriloquist. Stories must speak for themselves or not at all.

* * *

Michael Swanwick distinguished himself in the early 1980's as the author of several highly acclaimed short stories, the best of which was "Mummer's Kiss." The story is set in an alternate present, where the Three Mile Island's disaster did, in fact, result in a meltdown, and North America subsequently has become a fragmented and often bizarre place to live. Philadelphia and its environs have become a kind of free state governed by the mummers organization, a place where physical mutation and short life spans are the order of the day, and life itself is a precious but all too fragile property. The protagonist is initially outlawed by the mummers, and later rises to prominence within the organization. The story and a later sequel, "Marrow Death," were incorporated into Swanwick's first novel, *In the Drift*, which follows the development of the resulting society through an entire generation. Although the episodic nature and shifting viewpoint occasionally make for abrupt and disconcerting transitions, for the most part the novel is a cohesive entity and maintains reader interest throughout.

Swanwick is not, however, a predictable author. The fact that one novel is a fairly linear narrative does not always mean that the same will be true of the next. The publication of *Vacuum Flowers* resulted in Swanwick's being associated with the cyberpunk writers, an informal and not particularly accurate label for those who wish to explore the interface between humanity and the machine, specifically computers and artificial enhancement of human senses. The cyberpunk movement is associated with a blend of high-tech jargon, experimental writing styles, and a somewhat jaded world view. Although *Vacuum Flowers* does meet these criteria in general, it would be a mistake to apply a simplistic label to Swanwick's work, since he continues to change styles and subject matter at will.

The novel is set in a future where the asteroids have been colonized, offering a relatively safe haven for certain criminal elements. There, a fugitive seeks a safe haven from which to establish a new base of operations; her profession is a criminal one in a future where implants can change everything, including personalities. A pyrotechnic writing style and a colorful cast of characters contribute to the remarkable novel, but it has been quickly overshadowed by Swanwick's latest novel.

*Stations of the Tide* is a novel whose overall atmosphere is so unique that it is very difficult to adequately describe. Comparisons are not readily available. There are touches of the otherworldliness of Jack Vance at his best, or the powerful grasp of language of Gene Wolfe, but the overall product is undeniably Michael Swanwick's. The planet Miranda has been colonized by humans, but its unstable ecology is such that all of the land areas are in danger of being flooded by a maritime upheaval previously unexperienced. Travel between the planets is impractical in traditional terms, so evacuation is not an option. At the same time, a messianic religion has arisen under the leadership of a cult figure with enormous charismatic appeal.

Gregorian, the cult leader and one time criminal, has stolen proscribed technology and taken it into the hinterlands. The authorities on Earth send an agent to recover it. This is accomplished by a kind of matter transmission/duplication, so that their agent can function on Miranda, although his present body and personality will have to remain, never to return to the home world. Once arrived, he sets off in pursuit of Gregorian, but soon finds himself in a phantasmagorical web of intrigue, betrayal, misplaced loyalties, and mass delusion. Eventually he begins to question not only the motivations of his allies on Miranda, but the purposes for which he was dispatched in the first case. A stunningly realized blend of nightmare and adventure, *Stations of the Tide* is superior in almost every way to either of Swanwick's earlier novels.

Swanwick's three dozen or so short stories should not be overlooked either. "Til Human Voices Wake Us," his very first publication, is an exciting story of human courage in the face of disaster. "Ginungagap" demonstrates the difficulty of communicating with truly alien beings. The world of art and the creative urge are described in "The Man Who Met Picasso," and the religious urge is examined on the brink of a nuclear war in "Covenant of Souls." Other stories of particular note are "Dogfight," written in collaboration with William Gibson, "Trojan Horse," "The Golden Apples of the Sun," one of Swanwick's rare outright fantasies, "The Overcoat," and "The Edge of the World."

Swanwick has continuously demonstrated his willingness to experiment with new forms, new themes, and new ways to use language to create situations and characters. Throughout this experimentation, he has never lost sight of the basic values of good writing, an interesting story, polished narrative technique, and respect for the reader. He will be one of the major new voices in the field for a long time to come.

—Don D'Ammassa

---

**SZILARD, Leo.** American. Born in Budapest, Hungary, 11 February 1898; emigrated to the United States, 1937; naturalized, 1943. Educated at the Budapest Institute of Technology; University of Berlin, D. Phil. 1922. Married Gertrud Weiss in 1951. Staff member, University of Berlin, 1925–32; research worker in nuclear physics, St. Bartholomew's Hospital, London, and Clarendon Laboratory, Oxford, 1934–38; staff member at Columbia University, New York, 1939–42, and, with Enrico Fermi, University of Chicago, 1942–46: devised chain reaction system with Fermi; resident fellow, Salk Institute of Biological Studies, La Jolla, California, 1964. Recipient: Atoms for Peace prize, 1959. *Died 30 May 1964.*

SCIENCE-FICTION PUBLICATIONS

Short Stories

*The Voice of the Dolphins and Other Stories.* New York, Simon and Schuster, and London, Gollancz, 1961.

OTHER PUBLICATIONS

Other

*The Collected Works of Leo Szilard,* edited by Bernard T. Feld and Gertrud Weiss Szilard. Cambridge, Massachusetts Institute of Technology, 1972.

*Leo Szilard: His Version of the Facts: Selected Recollections and Correspondence,* edited by Spencer R. Weart and Gertrud Weiss Szilard. Cambridge, Massachusetts Institute of Technology Press, 1978.

*

Critical Studies: *Toward a Liveable World: Leo Szilard and the Crusade for Nuclear Arms Control* edited by Helen S. Hawkins, G. Allen Greb, and Gertrud Weiss Szilard, Cambridge, Massachusetts Institute of Technology Press, 1987; *Genius in the Shadows: A Biography of Leo Szilard, the Man Behind the Bomb* by William Lanouette and Bela Silard, New York, Scribner, 1989.

* * *

Leo Szilard will always be remembered more for his involvement with the atomic bomb than for his literary achievements. His sole work of science fiction, *The Voice of the Dolphins and Other Stories,* is of interest more because it is written by a famous physicist than for any particular merit. All the stories are told in dry, lecture-tour manner, rather like the crudest efforts of the Gernsback era. Szilard was a vigorous thinker but he showed no interest in character development or plot. Instead, he merely presented ideas. The title story concerns efforts by dolphins to control the human race, using scientific organizations as fronts. They do fairly well for a while. All this is told in straight exposition, as a "non-fact" history. Some of the political predictions have turned out to be uncannily on the mark, others way off. "My Trial as a War Criminal" concerns the possible guilt of the early atomic bomb scientists. The others are less important. "Report on 'Grand Central Terminal' " has future extraterrestrial archeologists puzzling over pay toilets.

—Darrell Schweitzer

---

# T

**TAINE, John.** Pseudonym for Eric Temple Bell. American. Born in Aberdeen, Scotland, 7 February 1883. Educated at the University of London, 1902; Stanford University, California, A.B. 1904 (Phi Beta Kappa); University of Washington, Seattle, A.M. 1908; Columbia University, New York, Ph.D. 1912. Married Jessie Lillian Brown in 1910; one child. Professor of Mathematics, University of Washington, 1912–26, and California Institute of Technology, Pasadena, 1927–53. Vice president, American Mathematical Society, 1926; president, Mathematical Association of America, 1931–33. Recipient: Bocher prize, for academic work, 1920–24. Vice president, American Academy of Arts and Sciences, 1930; Member, National Academy of Sciences. *Died 21 December 1960.*

SCIENCE-FICTION PUBLICATIONS

Novels

*The Purple Sapphire.* New York, Dutton, 1924.
*Quayle's Invention.* New York, Dutton, 1927.
*The Gold Tooth.* New York, Dutton, 1927.
*Green Fire.* New York, Dutton, 1928.
*The Greatest Adventure.* New York, Dutton, 1929.
*The Iron Star.* New York, Dutton, 1930.
*Before the Dawn.* Baltimore, Williams and Wilkins, 1934.
*The Time Stream.* Providence, Rhode Island, Buffalo, 1946.
*The Forbidden Garden.* Reading, Pennsylvania, Fantasy Press, 1947.
*The Cosmic Geoids, and One Other.* Los Angeles, Fantasy, 1949.
*Seeds of Life.* Reading, Pennsylvania, Fantasy Press, 1951; London, Rich and Cowan, 1955.
*The Crystal Horde.* Reading, Pennsylvania, Fantasy Press, 1952; as *White Lily,* in *Seeds of Life, and White Lily,* New York, Dover, 1966.
*G.O.G. 666.* Reading, Pennsylvania, Fantasy Press, 1954; London, Rich and Cowan, 1955.

Uncollected Short Stories

"Twelve Eighty-Seven," in *Astounding* (New York), May 1935.
"Tomorrow," in *Marvel* (New York), April–May 1939.
"The Ultimate Catalyst," in *My Best Science Fiction Story,* edited by Leo Margulies and O.J. Friend. New York, Merlin Press, 1949.

OTHER PUBLICATIONS

Verse

*Recreations* (as J.T.). Boston, Gorham Press, 1915.
*The Singer* (as J.T.). Boston, Gorham Press, 1916.

Other as Eric Temple Bell

*The Cyclotomic Quinary Quintic.* New York, Columbia University, 1912.
*An Arithmetic Theory of Certain Numerical Functions.* Seattle, University of Washington, 1915.
*Algebraic Arithmetic.* New York, American Mathematical Society, 1927.
*Debunking Science.* Seattle, University of Washington Book Store, 1930.
*The Queen of the Sciences.* Baltimore, Williams and Wilkins, 1931.
*Numerology.* Baltimore, Williams and Wilkins, 1933.
*The Handmaiden of the Sciences.* Baltimore, Williams and Wilkins, and London, Baillière, 1937.
*Men of Mathematics.* New York, Simon and Schuster, and London, Gollancz, 1937.
*Man and His Lifebelts.* Baltimore, Williams and Wilkins, 1938.
*The Development of Mathematics.* New York, McGraw Hill, 1940; revised edition, 1945.
*The Magic of Numbers.* New York, McGraw Hill, 1946.
*Mathematics, Queen and Servant of Science.* New York, McGraw Hill, 1951; London, Bell, 1952.
*The Last Problem.* New York, Simon and Schuster, 1961; London, Gollancz, 1962.

* * *

John Taine was the pseudonym used by the prominent research mathematician Eric Temple Bell in his science-fiction novels. Taine was a respected science-fiction novelist during the 1920's who turned to the pulp SF magazines with the Depression. His best work blended theoretical inquiry into the unknown with high adventure in the H. Rider Haggard tradition, and he combined sound science with a rare storytelling ability.

The major preoccupation in Taine's handful of novels is that of technological disaster. In almost all his work, scientific inquiry into the unknown precipitates an impending cataclysm. These disasters can be man-made, as in *Seeds of Life,* natural, as in *The Iron Star,* or accidental, as the monsters created in *White Lily.* In *The Greatest Adventure* and *The Purple Sapphire* unknown cataclysms in remote antiquity have their effect on the modern world. *The Time Stream* links the destruction of a future world with the great San Francisco earthquake.

Taine's novels invariably focus on individuals who band together to quest into the unknown. Often, he teams a scientist with an adventurer. On one level his narratives function as scientific mystery stories in which inexplicable phenomena screen a hidden truth. Taine slowly—in *White Lily,* ponderously—reveals the solution through his close-mouthed scientist characters. At times complete and final answers are withheld in order to maintain a sense of wonder and mystery. This is particularly true in *The Greatest Adventure* and *The Purple Sapphire,* both of which concern survivals of ancient super-civilizations of Earth's past. In *The Greatest Adventure* an Antarctic expedition uncovers the remnants of such a civilization. Under the ice is a city which had entombed itself alive rather than allow the possibility of escape to the mutated creatures spawned when they discovered the secret of life. The expedition inadvertently activates the menace. Taine concentrates on the biological nightmares, and neither explores nor identifies the ancient civilization, but this enhances the power of the novel. On the other hand, this reserve limits the otherwise excellent *The Purple Sapphire.* Three seekers of fortune discover a fantastic city in the heart of Central Asia where a degraded theocracy guards its technological marvels against the day its true inhabitants return. They do not return, and the three successfully rescue the kidnapped daughter of a British General but lose the secret of transmuting matter.

Genetic mutation is a theme Taine finds fascinating. Two novels, *Seeds of Life* and *G.O.G. 666*, deal with the consequences of human genetic tampering. *Seeds of Life* chronicles the brief career of a dissolute research scientist, Neils Bork, who becomes a superman when exposed to radiation. Bork, who considers human life beneath contempt, masterminds a fiendish plan to eradicate all humans, but is stymied when he regresses and falls in love with the woman he has chosen as the instrument of annihilation. A similar figure is Gog, the hulking travesty of a man whom plant geneticist Dr. Clive Chase encounters in his investigation of a Soviet plan to liberate its workers from drudgery in *G.O.G. 666.* Gog is the keystone of the plan, and he hides a secret darker than that of Neils Bork. *G.O.G. 666* is somewhat marred by its Cold War preoccupations. *White Lily* also depicts Russia in an uncomplimentary light. In China, two despicable Russian agents foment revolution. Against this bloody backdrop, a U.S. soldier has unwittingly introduced silicon-based life forms on Earth, which run unchecked.

Considered to be his greatest work, *The Time Stream* is a complex excursion into the dynamics of time travel and cyclical universes. The Time Stream is the medium by which ten individuals from the future send their minds back to 20th-century San Francisco. There they live new lives in an attempt to determine if a scientifically forbidden marriage will result in the destruction of their world. Although somewhat confusing in its narrative structure, *The Time Stream* is nevertheless a compelling example of imaginative writing. Of his other works, *The Iron Star*, a novel of a destructive asteroid, and "The Ultimate Catalyst" are noteworthy.

—Will Murray

---

**TALL, Stephen.** Pseudonym for Compton Newby Crook. American. Born in Rossville, Tennessee, 14 June 1908. Educated at George Peabody College (now Vanderbilt University), Nashville, B.S. 1932, M.A. 1933; Johns Hopkins University, Baltimore; Arizona State University, Tempe. Served as an intelligence officer in the Office of Strategic Services, 1943–45: Captain. Married Lucy Beverly Courtney; three children. Science teacher, Appalachian State University, Boone, North Carolina; Middle Tennessee State University, Murfreesboro; Tennessee Polytechnic Institute; Western Reserve University, Cleveland; College of William and Mary, Williamsburg, Virginia; and Episcopal Academy, Philadelphia, 1933–39. Instructor, then Professor of Biology and Department Chairman, 1939–73, and from 1973, Professor Emeritus, Towson State University, Baltimore. Ranger and naturalist with the National Park Service, eight summers. Recipient: National Science Foundation grants for ecological study. *Died 15 June 1981.*

Science-Fiction Publications

Novels

*The Ramsgate Paradox.* New York, Berkley, 1976.
*The People Beyond the Wall.* New York, DAW, 1980.

Short Stories

*The Stardust Voyages.* New York, Berkley, 1975.

Uncollected Short Stories

"Lights on Precipice Peak," in *Galaxy* (New York), October 1955.
"Allison, Carmichael, and Tattersall," in *Galaxy* (New York), April 1970.
"The Angry Mountain," in *Fantasy and Science Fiction* (New York), June 1970.
"Talk with the Animals," in *Analog* (New York), September 1970.
"The Mad Scientist and the FBI," in *Galaxy* (New York), December 1970.
"This Is My Country," in *Galaxy* (New York), February 1971.
"Space Bounce," in *If* (New York), October 1973.
"Chlorophyll," in *Fantasy and Science Fiction* (New York), June 1976.
"The Rock and the Pool," in *Galaxy* (New York), December 1976.
"The Man Who Saved the Sun," in *Fantasy and Science Fiction* (New York), January 1977.
"The King is Dead, Long Live the Queen!," in *Amazing* (New York), January 1978.
"Home Is the Hunter," in *Analog* (New York), August 1979.
"The Merry Men of Methane," in *Fantasy and Science Fiction* (New York), May 1980.
"The Hot and Cold Running Waterfall," in *Fantasy Annual 4*, edited by Terry Carr. New York, Pocket Books, 1981.

*

Stephen Tall commented:

(1981) I was born in Tennessee near the Big River, the Mississippi, the son of a country doctor and a cultured, sensitive mother. The levees, the cotton fields, the cypress swamps, and the cane breaks were my first playgrounds. And in our home books and good reading always had status. Respect for knowledge and how it is acquired was instilled early.

I have always been a biologist writing fiction, not the other way around. I write because I like to tell a good story, and because the mechanics of good writing are pleasing to me. My stories are about what I know, and about what I have concern for. They have always reflected my awareness of and interest in the living world other than man. I wrote stories based on ecology before the word was generally familiar. I regard science fiction as almost the ideal medium for expressing ecological concerns: any species, any race, anywhere.

* * *

Approximately half of Stephen Tall's science fiction concerns the crew of the interstellar exploration ship *Stardust:* six short stories collected as *The Stardust Voyages* and one of two novels, *The Ramsgate Paradox.* A crew of 400 staffs the ship as it makes its way from one star system to another, but for all practical purposes there are only three characters. Roscoe Kissinger is the obligatory hero, not too long on brains but courageous to a fault. Equally necessary is Lindy Peterson, the attractive female scientist whose major role seems to be to require rescue by Roscoe. Finally we have Pegleg Williams, the best friend, comic relief, and jack of all trades. There is also an elderly woman whose psychic abilities manifest themselves in cryptic paintings.

There is no doubt that the entire series is built around stereotypes, but the adventures themselves enjoy considerable popularity. Perhaps the best known is "The Bear with a Knot on His Tail," in which the star Mizar is about to explode, and our heroes arrive to carry off significant records and frozen germ plasma of the local intelligent species. The most interesting story in the series is the first, "Seventy Light-Years from Sol" (later retitled "A Star Called Cyrene"). This time the crew lands on a planet inhabited by two distinct races. The first consists of featureless varicolored cubes who can teleport from one location to another, and do so frequently in order to escape the predations of a species of carnivorous wheels. But now the cubes face a new threat, invasion from a nearby island of formless blobs, against which they have no defense. Human policy is to avoid taking sides in local squabbles, but the crew decides that offering advice is not interference. This strange twist of logic seems not to present any problems for the characters or the author, and the story is well written enough to overcome the logical shortcomings. These two stories set the pattern for subsequent adventures, in which the protagonists meet and overcome a variety of menaces ranging from a manifestation of ancient Greek gods to mutated giant crabs. The latter appear in "The Invaders," another above-average story flawed by problems of internal logic.

A non-series story of note is "Allison, Carmichael, and Tattersall," which seems to have been influenced by the Arcot, Morey, and Wade stories of John W. Campbell Jr. Indeed, Tall's fiction would not be out of place in the 1930's pulp magazines, although the quality of the writing is considerably higher. This was also the beginning of a truncated series, and is a satisfying light adventure story marred by over-reliance on coincidence.

*The Ramsgate Paradox* is distinguished from the shorter stories only by length, making no serious effort to add substantial depth to the characters. The second novel, *The People Beyond the Wall*, is also a return to a tradition largely abandoned in the genre, the Utopian novel. A pair of adventurers set off to explore an area of glacier in the Antarctic and find themselves in a hidden land where people have returned to a pastoral existence unmarred by organized strife. Although this is probably the most ambitious work Tall produced during his career, it falls prey to the usual internal problems of Utopian literature; the plot slows to a crawl as various aspects of the totally sane but rather dull society are revealed. Tall seemed to lose control entirely in the waning chapters, jumping years forward in time, introducing new characters for no real purpose. The first half of the novel was, however, a definite break with the formula stories Tall had been writing previously, and seems to indicate his writing would have moved into new areas had he lived longer.

—Don D'Ammassa

---

**TARR, Judith.** American. Born in Augusta, Maine, 30 January 1955. Educated at Mount Holyoke College, 1972–76, A.B.; Cambridge University, 1976–78, B.A. in classics, 1978; M.A. in classics, 1983; Yale University, 1978–79, M.A. in medieval studies, 1979; Yale University, 1981–88, Ph.D. in medieval studies, 1988. Teacher of Latin, Edward Little High School, Auburn, Maine, 1979–81. Visiting lecturer in liberal studies and visiting writer, Wesleyan University, Middletown, Connecticut, since 1989. Visiting Assistant Professor of classics, Wesleyan University, since 1990. Recipient: Crawford Memorial award, 1987; Mary Lyon award, Mt. Holyoke College, 1989. Agent: Jane Butler, 212 Third Street, Milford, Pennsylvania 18337. Address: 94 Foster Street, Number 3, New Haven, Connecticut 06511, U.S.A.

SCIENCE-FICTION PUBLICATIONS

Novels (series: Avaryan Rising; The Hound and the Falcon)

The Hound and the Falcon:
*The Isle of Glass.* New York, Bluejay, 1985; London, Bantam, 1986.
*The Golden Horn.* New York, Bluejay, 1985; London, Bantam, 1986.
*The Hounds of God.* New York, Bluejay, 1986; London, Bantam, 1987.
Avaryan Rising:
*The Hall of the Mountain King.* New York, Tor, 1986.
*The Lady of Han-Gilen.* New York, Tor, 1987.
*A Fall of Princes.* New York, Tor, 1988.
*A Wind in Cairo.* New York, Bantam, 1989; London, 1990.
*Ars Magica.* New York, Bantam, 1989.
*Alamut.* New York, Doubleday, 1989.
*The Dagger and the Cross: A Novel of the Crusades.* New York, Doubleday, 1991.

*

Judith Tarr comments:

It is usually, and casually, assumed that a woman who writes books with slightly frilly covers and the label "Fantasy" on the spine, must write a particular kind of book: i.e., Female Fantasy—elves, dragons, unicorns, cuddly animals. It is further assumed that if these books are set in the Middle Ages, or in fact in any preindustrial setting, they must necessarily be Generic Medieval.

I have a deplorable tendency to Do Things to assumptions and conventions. The three books labeled Trilogy by their publisher and given by me the corporate appellation *The Hound and the Falcon* were conceived originally as science fiction of a particular kind: the Psi Mutant variation with a spice of the Immortal Race, but transported into a historical setting, with terms of the time applied to the characters. Hence, elves, daemons, Jinn. *The Isle of Glass* is the least historically precise of the five books in that universe (not a cycle as such, and not a trilogy in the current sense of one long book chopped into several parts: each book stands on its own)—I essentially made it up as I went along. With *The Golden Horn* I discovered the joys of writing historical fiction with SF/fantasy characters, as I was then taking a graduate course in Byzantine history and I much prefer writing novels to writing term papers. I tossed a pair of my odd people into Constantinople during the Fourth Crusade, to see what they would do. With *The Hounds of God* I returned to Western Europe and a form of dénouement. *Alamut* and *The Dagger and the Cross* take place some decades before *The Isle of Glass* and are a melding of historical novel, medieval romance, and SF/fantasy. With these books and with the entirely separate fantasy, *A Wind in Cairo*, I was able to take advantage of a lifelong fascination with the Crusades. *Ars Magica*, in its turn, is the mutated off-spring of a course paper on a medieval pope, Pope Sylvester II to be exact. It's not really a novel but a collection of three somewhat loosely related novellas; someday I'd like to write a fourth to round them off.

The so-called "High Fantasy" which has so far appeared as the three volumes of Avaryan Rising was actually, originally conceived as related to the historical material—it's the other side of my childhood science-fantasy mega-epic. No elves there, no dragons, and the riding animals are horned but as antelopes, not as unicorns (it is, after all, an alien world). Nor is it medieval. In the time-honored fashion of SF, which mines history for all the gold it contains, these books are a melange of Alexander the Great, the ancient Near and Middle East, and Imperial China. Magic works in this universe. Maybe. If it is actually magic. And not . . .

But that would be telling.

* * *

Judith Tarr's critically heralded debut in 1985 with *The Isle of Glass*, the first in her The Hound and the Falcon trilogy, marked her as one of the strongest voices in the tradition of SF's scholar-writers.

Like J.R.R. Tolkien and C.S. Lewis, Tarr is a medieval scholar. Her formidable academic background and grounding in the history, theology, and arts of several medieval cultures contribute to the rich texture and deeply realized backgrounds of her books. At the same time, this medievalist's training—which is the scholar's equivalent of planet-building since the medievalist must recreate a "reading" of a culture from the ground up—enables Tarr to excel at world building in her Avaryan trilogy. Just as the medievalist must confront the Other in the form of the people and cultures she studies, Tarr confronts the Other in the form of the long-lived, almost inhumanly talented, and supernaturally gifted creatures who move among human beings in The Hound and the Falcon trilogy and subsequently in *Alamut* and *Ars Magica.* Thought patterns alien from those of humans also occur in *Avaryan Rising*, especially in the magical system, which is intricate and ruthless: the familiar of Gerbert, the mage-pope of *Ars Magica*, shows a similar outlook composed of equal loyalty to her chosen human, an almost frightening indifference to outsiders, and a highly feline interest in playing with people and passing events.

An accomplished horsewoman, Tarr's love of horses gets full play in *A Wind in Cairo*, which shows the transformation of a spoiled Arab princeling, punished for raping a mage's daughter, into a horse owned by another young woman.

Tarr's characters, especially her female characters, tend to be rebels. Alf, in The Hound and the Falcon books, spends much of his long life rebelling against his talents, his vocations as priest and mage, and his love for the intractable and dazzling Thea. Elian, in *The Lady of Han-Gilen*, becomes a woman warrior: Zamaniyah, who becomes a fighter in deference to her father, fights for the right to choose her own life.

Tarr's shift in focus Eastward, begun in *A Wind In Cairo*, continues in the Crusade novels *Alamut* and *The Dagger and The Cross.* Tarr, like many Crusaders who looked East, has become fascinated with Muslim culture, the intricacies of which find a home in her own style. She portrays its splendors richly and intelligently at a time in our own history when this type of understanding is necessary.

Though Tarr is primarily known for her novels, she has produced some fine short fiction. Recently, she has expanded her range to take part in two shared worlds, Andre Norton's *Witch World* and Jerry Pournelle's *War World*, which, along with "Parity" (in *Pulphouse*), may mark yet another expansion into hard science fiction.

—Susan Shwartz

---

**TATE, Peter.** British. Journalist. Address: Pinetree Lodge, 3 Seaway Avenue, Friars Cliff, Christchurch, Dorset 8H23 4EU, England.

SCIENCE-FICTION PUBLICATIONS

Novels

*The Thinking Seat.* New York, Doubleday, 1969; London, Faber, 1970.
*Gardens One to Five.* New York, Doubleday, 1971; as *Gardens, 1, 2, 3, 4, 5*, London, Faber, 1971.
*Country Love and Poison Rain.* New York, Doubleday, 1973.
*Moon on an Iron Meadow.* New York, Doubleday, 1974.
*Faces in the Flames.* New York, Doubleday, 1976.
*Greencomber.* New York, Doubleday, 1979.

Short Stories

*Seagulls Under Glass.* New York, Doubleday, 1975.

* * *

Although Peter Tate can be a futurist, an allegorist, and a fantasist, in his major work he is a realist who uses current trends in natural and social science as well as technology for conveying his values. His concept of science fiction is a "work styled in protest at a particular facet of . . . technology and using research to qualify that protest" (introduction to "The Post-Mortem People" in *Seagulls Under Glass*). Unlike futurists who project their characters onto other planets, eons removed from the present, Tate remains on a familiar earth only a few years distanced from the copyright date. He chooses recognizable settings (Waukegan, Zimbabwe, New Forest) and with them creates an illusion that his scientific and technological projections have already left the laboratory and are threatening the balance in man and nature. Likewise, he interweaves imagined crises with references to current headlines (Che Guevara, Vorster, Kent State, Mozambique), thus enabling the reader to fuse fabrication with newspaper fact. Sobering is his recognition that heroes sometimes die. Tate further asserts the realness of his fictions by overlapping characters and plots. Simeon and Tomorrow Julie star in *The Thinking Seat, Moon on an Iron Meadow*, and *Faces in the Flames;* Scarlatti and Prinz counter each other in *Gardens One to Five* and *Faces in the Flames.* Famous Gogan slips in and out of *The Thinking Seat, Gardens One to Five* and *Faces in the Flames;* and Shem of *Gardens One to Five* is a memory in *Faces in the Flames.* Even more interesting than overlapping is Tate's technique of using fiction to authenticate fiction, as in *Moon on an Iron Meadow* where he returns to the buildings, people, and atmosphere created 50 years before by his mentor Ray Bradbury in *Something Wicked This Way Comes.*

Many of Tate's plots are compelling in their fast-paced intrigue ("Skyhammer"); their allegorical assessment of social and political forces (*Gardens One to Five*); or their subtle ambivalence between realism and fantasy (*Greencomber*). A few are bizarre.

In "Mars Pastorale" a defenseless poppy seed invades a defenseless human's throat; in "Post-Mortem People" licensed ghouls stalk dying men for healthy body parts; in "The Gloom Pattern"—whose science, says Tate, is "bunkum"—a youngster is sucked up from his earthly existence on an "ecstasy beam" when he craves a sad man's happiness. Tate's humor surfaces in the provocative "Same Autumn in a Different Park." In this parody of the Adam-Eve story, Addison springs from the side of Tina who with the help of "molecular rejig" turns into an apple which is eaten by the new Adam.

Tate sees the world as essentially good; but it has been contaminated by ignorance, indifference, misguided heroics, self-serving, and malice. As in Bradbury's *Something Wicked This Way Comes*, the spirit of evil is pervasive and its confrontation inevitable. It periodically erupts in such "bodies" as the United Nations, desalination plants, canisters of biological weapons, defoliants, contaminated rabbits, atom bombs, church "Prinzes," and Hitlerian megalomaniacs. Once this force is loose, balance between good and evil can be restored only by a figure who embodies the spirit of pristine Christianity: "the time of authenticity on the lake shores of Nazareth before two thousand years of controversy and schism and compromise and commerce had muddied the waters beyond perception" (*Faces in the Flames*). Simeon, along with Shem, Nelso Ojukwe (*Faces in the Flames*), Greencomber, and Adams ("Mainchance"), insist on rational, willed self-involvement—even to the point of death—against any sort of manipulation of humans. Like the Galilean, all of these heroes provoke action in the quiescent; by the force of their integrity, they transform Judases and self-deceivers into disciples. A developing theme from *The Thinking Seat* to *Greencomber* is individual and social transformation effected by altruistic love.

Tate enjoys language. He puns, makes memorable metaphors, and sometimes achieves a mesmerizing lyricism. His use of myth is haunting: blood is the price for exaltation; life consciously saved counterbalances that which is wantonly taken; love dispels enslaving myths created by malevolent scientists. At times he mistakes clichés for original expression, or reaches too far for an apt comparison. But Tate is a stimulating writer who structures complex materials into convincing fictions.

—Rosemary Coleman

---

**TEMPLE, William F(rederick).** British. Born in Woolwich, London, 9 March 1914. Educated at Gordon School, London, 1919–27; Woolwich Polytechnic, London, 1928–30. Served in the Royal Artillery, 1940–46. Married Joan Streeton in 1939; one daughter and one son. Head clerk, Stock Exchange, London, 1930–50. Editor, British Interplanetary Society *Bulletin. Died 15 July 1989.*

SCIENCE-FICTION PUBLICATIONS

Novels (series: Martin Magnus)

*Four-Sided Triangle*. London, Long, 1949; New York, Fell, 1951.
*Martin Magnus, Planet Rover* (for children). London, Muller, 1955.
*Martin Magnus on Venus* (for children). London, Muller, 1955.
*Martin Magnus on Mars* (for children). London, Muller, 1956.
*The Automated Goliath, The Three Sons of Amara*. New York, Ace, 1962.
*Battle on Venus*. New York, Ace, 1963.
*Shoot at the Moon*. New York, Simon and Schuster, and London, Whiting and Wheaton, 1966.
*The Fleshpots of Sansato*. London, Macdonald, 1968.

Uncollected Short Stories

"The Kosso," in *Thrills*. London, Philip Allan, 1935.
"Lunar Lilliput," in *Tales of Wonder 2* (Kingswood, Surrey), 1938.
"Mr. Craddock's Amazing Experience," in *Amazing* (New York), February 1939.
"Experiment in Genius," in *Tales of Wonder* (Kingswood, Surrey), Summer 1940.
"The Monster on the Border," in *Super Science* (Kokomo, Indiana), November 1940.
"The Three Pylons," in *New Worlds 1* (London), 1946.
"Miracle Town," in *Thrilling Wonder Stories* (New York), October 1948.
"The Brain Beast," in *Super Science* (Kokomo, Indiana), July 1949.
"For Each Man Kills," in *Amazing* (New York), March 1950.
"Martian's Fancy," in *New Worlds* (London), Summer 1950.
"Wisher Take All," in *Other Worlds* (Evanston, Indiana), July 1950.
"The Bone of Contention," in *Thrilling Wonder Stories* (New York), October 1950.
"Forget-Me-Not," in *The Best Science Fiction Stories 1951*, edited by E.F. Bleiler and T.E. Dikty. New York, Fell, 1951.
"Conditioned Reflex," in *Other Worlds* (Evanston, Indiana), January 1951.
"You Can't See Me," in *Fantastic Adventures* (New York), June 1951.
"Double Trouble," in *Science Fantasy* (Bournemouth), Winter 1951.
"A Date to Remember," in *Invaders of Earth*, edited by Groff Conklin. New York, Vanguard Press, 1952; London, Weidenfeld and Nicolson, 1953.
"The Two Shadows," in *The Best Science-Fiction Stories 1952*, edited by E.F. Bleiler and T.E. Dikty. New York, Fell, 1952; London, Grayson, 1953.
"Counter-Transference," in *The Best Science-Fiction Stories 1953*, edited by E.F. Bleiler and T.E. Dikty. New York, Fell, 1953; London, Grayson, 1955.
"Way of Escape," in *Science Fiction Adventures in Dimension*, edited by Groff Conklin. New York, Vanguard Press, 1953; London, Grayson, 1955.
"Immortal's Playthings," in *Authentic* (London), January 1953.
"Field of Battle," in *Other Worlds* (Evanston, Indiana), February 1953.
"Mind Within Mind," in *Authentic* (London), May 1953.
"Limbo," in *Nebula* (Glasgow), Summer 1953.
"Pawn in Revolt," in *Nebula* (Glasgow), Autumn 1953.
"Destiny Is My Enemy," in *Nebula* (Glasgow), September 1953.
"Moon Wreck," in *Boy's Own Paper* (London), November 1953.
"Explorers of Mars," in *Authentic Book of Space*, edited by Herbert J. Campbell. London, Panther, 1954.
"Pilot's Hands," in *Nebula* (Glasgow), February 1954.
"Errand of Mercy," in *Authentic* (London), March 1954.
"Space Saboteur," in *Boy's Own Paper* (London), March 1954.
"Eternity," in *Science Fantasy* (Bournemouth), February 1955.
"Man in a Maze," in *Authentic* (London), February 1955.
"The Lonely," in *Imagination* (Evanston, Illinois), July 1955.
"Better Than We Know," in *Science Fiction Quarterly* (Holyoke, Massachusetts), August 1955.
"Mansion of Love," in *Nebula* (Glasgow), September 1955.

"Uncle Buno," in *Science Fantasy* (Bournemouth), November 1955.
32 stories, in *Rocket* (London), April to November 1956.
"The Girl from Mars," in *Heiress* (London), September 1956.
"Outside Position," in *Nebula* (Glasgow), November 1956.
"A Date to Remember," in *Nebula* (Glasgow), July 1957.
"Against Goliath," in *Nebula* (Glasgow), August 1957.
"Brief Encounter," in *Nebula* (Glasgow), October 1957.
"War Against Darkness," in *Nebula* (Glasgow), June 1958.
"The Different Complexion," in *New Worlds* (London), October 1958.
"Imbalance," in *Nebula* (Glasgow), May 1959.
"Magic Ingredient," in *Science Fantasy* (Bournemouth), December 1959.
"The Whispering Gallery," in *Zacherley's Midnight Snacks*, edited by Zacherley. New York, Ballantine, 1960.
" 'L' Is for Lash," in *Amazing* (New York), July 1960.
"Sitting Duck," in *New Worlds* (London), November 1960.
"The Unknown," in *Amazing* (New York), March 1961.
"A Trek to Na-Abiza," in *Science Fiction Adventures* (London), July 1961.
"Beyond the Line," in *Fantastic* (New York), September 1964.
"A Niche in Time," in *World's Best Science Fiction 1965*, edited by Donald A. Wollheim and Terry Carr. New York, Ace, 1965.
"The Legend of Ernie Deacon," in *Analog* (New York), March 1965.
"Coco-Talk," in *New Writings in SF7*, edited by John Carnell. London, Dobson, 1966; New York, Bantam, 1971.
"Echo," in *Famous Science Fiction* (New York), Winter 1967.
"The Year Dot," in *If* (New York), January 1969.
"When in Doubt—Destroy!," in *Vision of Tomorrow* (New castle upon Tyne), August 1969.
"The Undiscovered Country," in *A Sea of Space*, edited by William F. Nolan. New York, Bantam, 1970.
"Life of the Party," in *Vision of Tomorrow* (Newcastle upon Tyne), February 1970.
"The Impatient Dreamers," in *Vision of Tomorrow* (Newcastle upon Tyne), June 1970.
"The Unpicker," in *Androids, Time Machines, and Blue Giraffes*, edited by Roger Elwood and Vic Ghidalia. Chicago, Follett, 1973.
"The Man Who Wasn't There," in *Amazing* (New York), November 1978.
"The Smile of the Sphinx," in *The Best Animal Stories of Science Fiction and Fantasy*, edited by Donald J. Sobol. New York, Warne, 1979.
"The Green Car," in *The Thirteen Crimes of Science Fiction*, edited by Isaac Asimov, Martin H. Greenberg, and Charles G. Waugh. New York, Doubleday, 1979.
"The Four-Sided Triangle," in *Amazing Science Fiction Anthology: The War Years 1936–45*, edited by Martin H. Greenberg. Lake Geneva, Wisconsin, TSR, 1987.

OTHER PUBLICATIONS

Novel

*The Dangerous Edge*. London, Long, 1951.

Other

*The True Book about Space Travel*. London, Muller, 1954; as *The Prentice-Hall Book about Space Travel*, New York, Prentice Hall, 1955.

*

William F. Temple commented:

(1981) I've read SF since childhood. At first, uncritically: I didn't notice it was only two-dimensional, i.e., lacked depth, especially in characterization. Then critically: I decided to try to add that third dimension in my writing. Then despairingly: Nobody noticed that I had. Then cynically: Nobody wanted it, anyway. They preferred their robots. Then uncaringly: I don't bother to write it any more.

* * *

Most critics would agree that the golden age of modern science fiction occurred in the 1930's, when such visionary editors as John Campbell encouraged and developed the writers who were to become almost legendary figures in the field. While Asimov, van Vogt, and others were honing their skills in the United States, William F. Temple was drawn to science fiction in England. Temple's interest, like that of his counterparts across the sea, was fostered by his companionship with Arthur C. Clarke, John Wyndham, and John Christopher. In the early days of science fiction there seemed to work among such individuals a kind of cross current which stimulated and sustained them in the creation of materials at which conventional critics of the day looked askance. Only the hardy survived those pioneering times to bring forth such books as *Childhood's End* and *No Blade of Grass*. That Temple was of durable stuff was demonstrated by what he went through to turn out what was perhaps his most notable work, *Four-Sided Triangle*. While serving in Africa with the Eighth Army in World War II, Temple converted what had been a short story into novel length. Despite the novel's publication delay, its survival qualities could not be extinguished. In a fascinating variation of the trite, a woman selects one of the two suitors who vie for her. The man who loses uses a matter-copying device to create an "exact" duplicate of her—which loads the novel's plot structure engrossingly.

Some readers may find Temple's work a bit stuffy at times, but his plots employ interesting contrasts and conflicts: a group of explorers investigates the alien topography of the Moon, but the real territory to be mapped is the unknown personality of warring party members. His story ideas are usually quite interesting, as in a short story like "A Date to Remember." This yarn seems almost banal in some ways—a wife about to bring forth a child, rainy night, success/failure conflict of two old school chums. Then we discover the central idea, that Martians have long "passed" as Earthlings, struggling to civilize the inhabitants of Earth while disguised as Byron, Pasteur, Haydn, and others throughout the centuries.

—Robert H. Wilcox

---

**TENN, William.** Pseudonym for Philip Klass. American. Born in Des Moines, Iowa, 8 November 1919. Educated at Iowa State University, Ames, B.S. 1941. Served in the United States Army during World War II. Consulting editor, *Fantasy and*

*Science Fiction*, New York, 1958. Since 1966, member of the Department of English, Pennsylvania State University, University Park. Address: Department of English, Pennsylvania State University, University Park, Pennsylvania 16802, U.S.A.

SCIENCE-FICTION PUBLICATIONS

Novels

*Of Men and Monsters.* New York, Ballantine, 1968; London, Pan, 1971.
*A Lamp for Medusa.* New York, Belmont, 1968.

Short Stories

*Of All Possible Worlds.* New York, Ballantine, 1955; enlarged edition, London, Joseph, 1956.
*The Human Angle.* New York, Ballantine, 1956.
*Time in Advance.* New York, Bantam, 1958; London, Gollancz, 1963.
*The Seven Sexes.* New York, Ballantine, 1968.
*The Square Root of Man.* New York, Ballantine, 1968; London, Pan, 1971.
*The Wooden Star.* New York, Ballantine, 1968; London, Pan, 1971.

Uncollected Short Stories

"On Venus, Have We Got a Rabbi," in *The Best Science Fiction of the Year 4*, edited by Terry Carr. New York, Ballantine, and London, Gollancz, 1975.
"Bernie the Faust," in *Dark Sins, Dark Dreams*, edited by Barry N. Malzberg and Bill Pronzini. New York, Doubleday, 1978.
"There Were People on Bikini," in *The Best of Omni Science Fiction 5*, edited by Don Myrus. New York, Omni, 1983.
"My Mother Was a Witch," in *Witches*, edited by Isaac Asimov, Martin H. Greenberg, and Charles G. Waugh. New York, New American Library, 1984.
"The Human Angle," in *100 Great Fantasy Short Stories*, edited by Isaac Asimov, and Terry Carr, Martin H. Greenberg. New York, Doubleday, 1984.
"Eastward Ho!" in *Beyond Armageddon*, edited by Walter M. Miller, Jr. and Martin H. Greenberg. New York, Fine, 1985.
"Mistress Sary," in *Young Witches and Warlocks*, edited by Isaac Asimov, Martin H. Greenberg, and Charles G. Waugh. New York, Harper and Row, 1987.

OTHER PUBLICATIONS

Other

Editor, *Children of Wonder.* New York, Simon and Schuster, 1953; as *Outsiders*, New York, Permabooks, 1954.
Editor, with Donald E. Westlake, *Once Against the Law.* New York, Macmillan, 1968.

* * *

"The incredible William Tenn," as he has been dubbed by Brian Aldiss, started a whole school of comic and satiric science fiction in the 1940's. Tenn quickly perfected a way of looking at things, at once funny, bitter, and serious, that made him the natural heir to the nearly silent tradition of Swift and Voltaire. Sheckley, Pohl, Ellison, Russell, Goulart, Knight, Kagan, Eisenberg, Brown, Lafferty, and Malzberg have all echoed Tenn's work at one time or another. A serious humorist, Tenn has had a double problem. The science-fiction genre has always made it difficult to tell serious writers from entertainers, through the manner of publications and because the entertainers often claim to be serious, or have it claimed for them; also, satirists and funny men have rarely risen high in the genre (in terms of awards and sales). Tenn was a pioneer whose example was imitated by writers who developed in different ways, but who also became known for the angle opened up by Tenn, thus diffusing the effect he might have had if his plumage had not been confused with that of imitators. Tenn imitations might have been more acceptable to some editors of the 1950's because they were watered-down versions of Tenn-like material—less serious and not so critical of the world and human nature. Tenn's stories are always a bit disturbing at some level, even when they are breathlessly readable, amusing, or cute.

An outgoing but sensitive man, Tenn fell silent by the end of the 1960's, even as his work was gathered into an impressive, though editorially flawed, six-volume set from Ballantine. One suspects that neglect made him feel that perhaps his work was not worthy. He went on to become an excellent college teacher, leaving behind a body of work sufficient to secure the reputation of any major writer in this field, and a name often confused with another Klass in various reference works. He published one story in the 1970's, "On Venus, Have We Got a Rabbi," which Damon Knight called "the great story he was talking about in the fifties." It was well received, garnering award nominations and appearing in a best of the year collection. There have been recent signs that he will soon have several works, including a new novel, to offer his readers. Tenn was also the editor of *Children of Wonder*, a pioneering theme anthology which was notable for its variety of stories and non-parochial choice of authors. Two incisive essays, "The Fiction in Science Fiction" (*Science Fiction Adventures*, March 1954) and "Jazz Then, Musicology Now" (*Fantasy and Science Fiction*, May 1972), are both required reading for anyone who cares about the ideals of literate science fiction, if not its practice.

Notable stories from Tenn's first two decades include "Brooklyn Project," which Fritz Leiber has called a "Marvelously cynical" time-travel story, and "Firewater!," one of the most sophisticated stories ever published by John W. Campbell, with its unforgettable lament by Larry for the loss of what he was and what he cannot be as humanity struggles to keep its sanity before the seemingly superior aliens who have taken up residence on earth. The story should have taken all the awards. "Generation of Noah" is one of the finest atomic threat stories ever written. "Of All Possible Worlds," "Wednesday's Child" (a fascinating sequel to the much reprinted classic "Child's Play"), "Time Waits for Winthrop," "Eastward Ho!," and "The Malted Milk Monster" all drew honorable mentions in Judith Merril's best of the year collections, while "Bernie the Faust" took pride of place as the first story in the 1964 collection. "Time Waits for Winthrop" shows a remarkable use of exotic ideas, among them fairly advanced biological concepts, another feature of Tenn's stories that makes them unusual for the 1950's. "The Discovery of Morniel Mathaway" shows an understanding of the creative process that is usually beyond most SF writers. Jacques Sadoul has called it "the most beautiful example of a temporal paradox offered by science fiction." "The Custodian," with its plea for the blending of art and utility, and "Down among the Dead Men," with its clever use of offstage space opera to heighten a pathetic predicament, both manage to do what few SF stories can do—move us emotionally and intellectually on a mature level.

Tenn is always a master of situations, which at first prod and intrigue, then provoke curiosity, make us laugh a bit, then explode into some thoughtful irony or observation. Once you catch on to a Tenn situation, you can't stop reading. The satirical tones of irony, mockery, slapstick, and occasional bitterness do wonders for genre materials, precisely because Tenn joins these materials to human experience outside the insular worlds of SF wish-fulfillment and power fantasy. The science-fiction materials are all there, strong and clear, but just as you're about to accept the story at its face value Tenn hits you with something real and painful. He's a very sly writer, inserting polished, precise narratives into our minds through unexpected channels. Many of his stories have the effect of blossoming into a single line of great beauty and illumination; but always the aesthetic fires are banked by irony and, above all, eloquent wit, behind which sits the ultimate authority of an author who has something to say, who sometimes seems to believe with Oscar Wilde that eloquence and wit alone can make the scales fall from human eyes. One senses an author laughing and crying at the same time, exhibiting intellect and dramatic talent within the confines of a narrow genre.

Tenn's two long works are the novel *Of Men and Monsters* and the short novel *A Lamp for Medusa.* The second work is easily worthy of having appeared in *Unknown Worlds.* Funny, atmospheric, and wonderfully paced, this neglected work has seen only a shabby book appearance. It is not surprising, given Tenn's tendencies, that is recalls the poise of the *Unknown Worlds* tradition, since that magazine was the only sizable market for humorous work of the early 1940's, and Tenn's only antecedent within the SF genre.

*Of Men and Monsters*, a story of humanity living in the walls of the houses of giant aliens who have occupied the earth, is a vivid, energetically paced story which best embodies one of Tenn's main points: that humanity is not what it thinks itself to be, that implicit in our biological history is a nature not of our making; we may glimpse it, even understand it at time, but it may be a while before we can remake ourselves, if ever. In his awareness of biological and anthropological complexities, Tenn has at the center of his work the most thoroughgoing of science-fiction methods: the collision of the possible with the actual, with the actual displaying fantastic holding power. Eric the Eye, the Lilliputian viewpoint character of the novel, learns that his society is not what he thought it was, that its rites of passage are a sham, and finally that human beings are not what he thought they were either; since change seems unlikely on a radical scale, he accepts this human nature and joins the plan to make of it something pervasive and influential. Eric becomes part of the reverse invasion of human vermin as they begin the infestation of the great alien starships. The story is very vivid, the characters charming (Eric meets Rachel Esthersdaughter, one of the nicest nice Jewish girls in all science fiction). The death of Eric's uncle is shatteringly presented. There are great wonder and awesome confrontation, sharply realized. Most importantly, there is an anthropological sophistication in the depiction of social systems; the aliens are properly terrifying, puzzling, and *other.* Tenn's tendency to romance, compassion, and brief, hard-bitten sentimentality shows through his bitterness just enough to be believable. The novel may be compared to Daniel Galouye's *Dark Universe* and Thomas M. Disch's *The Genocides.*

It is regrettable that Tenn stopped his development in the 1960's, when it was clear that the continuous practice of his craft, coupled with his acute and constant rethinking of the nature of fiction and science fiction, would certainly have produced a mighty progress over his very worthy body of work. Now that he seems poised at the start of his most mature period, it remains to be seen whether he will continue the main line suggested by his previous work, or whether his silence is a sign that he has been developing a new direction. He can do anything he wants, except hack work ("I have no talent for it," he has said). Few writers have ever suggested so much promise at the start of their sixth decade. Tenn belongs to the great generation of Asimov, Heinlein and Clarke. He is the most perfect example of the failure of the awards system within the science-fiction community, and an obvious candidate for the Grand Master Nebula award. His work is a clear example that SF can be literature, that it can provoke us to see, feel, and think. Tenn belongs to that unbroken chain of sayers who expose our delusions and foibles, our willful blindness and stupidity, and who ultimately stand against death and the amnesia of generations. "Tenn is another artist," Damon Knight has written, "who won't stop till he's had the last word."

—George Zebrowski

---

**TENNANT, Emma (Christina).** Also writes as Catherine Aydy. British. Born in London, 20 October 1937. Educated at St. Paul's Girls' School, London. Has one son and two daughters. Travel correspondent, *Queen*, London, 1963; features editor, *Vogue*, London, 1966; editor, *Bananas*, London, 1975–78. Since 1982, general editor, *In Verse*, London; since 1985, editor, Lives of Modern Women series, Viking, publishers, London. Fellow, Royal Society of Literature, 1982. Agent: Sheil Land, 43 Doughty Street, London WC1N 2LF. Address: c/o Faber and Faber Ltd., 3 Queen Square, London WC1N 3AU, England.

Science-Fiction Publications

Novels

*The Time of the Crack.* London, Cape, 1973; as *The Crack*, London, Penguin, 1978.
*The Last of the Country House Murders.* London, Cape, 1974; New York, Nelson, 1976.
*Hotel de Dream.* London, Gollancz, 1976.
*Queen of Stones.* London, Cape, 1982.
*Two Women of London: The Strange Case of Ms. Jekyll and Mrs. Hyde.* London, Faber, 1989.

Other Publications

Novels

*The Colour of Rain* (as Catherine Aydy). London, Weidenfeld and Nicolson, 1964.
*The Bad Sister.* London, Gollancz, and New York, Coward McCann, 1978.
*Wild Nights.* London, Cape, 1979; New York, Harcourt Brace, 1980.
*Alice Fell.* London, Cape, 1980.
*Woman Beware Woman.* London, Cape, 1983; as *The Half-Mother*, Boston, Little Brown, 1985.
*Black Marina.* London, Faber, 1985.
*The Adventures of Robina, by Herself.* London, Faber, 1986; New York, Persea, 1987.
*The House of Hospitalities.* London, Viking, 1987.
*A Wedding of Cousins.* New York, Viking, 1988.
*The Magic Drum.* London, Viking, 1989.
*Sisters and Strangers: A Moral Tale.* London, Grafton, 1990.

Other (for children)

*The Boggart.* London, Granada, 1980.
*The Search for Treasure Island.* London, Penguin, 1981.
*The Ghost Child.* London, Heinemann, 1984.

Other

Editor, *Bananas.* London, Quartet-Blond and Briggs, 1977.
Editor, *Saturday Night Reader.* London, W.H. Allen, 1979.

* * *

Emma Tennant writes in the school of science fiction established by J.G. Ballard, John Sladek, and Michael Moorcock. In *The Crack* (also known as *The Time of the Crack*), a massive fissure tears London apart. Part disaster novel in the Ballard tradition, part psychological novel, *The Crack* follows the motivations of the characters to "get to the other side" of the crack. The book features one of Tennant's famous characters: Baba, a Playboy Club bunny. The book pokes fun at many groups who try to cope with the catastrophe in a desperate attempt to maintain their power: the rich, the psychiatrists, the environmentalists, and the class system itself. Allegorical aspects of Tennant's work attack the decadence of modern society and the paranoia and fanaticism she sees in contemporary life.

In *Two Women of London* Tennant retells Robert Louis Stevenson's *The Strange Case of Dr. Jekyll and Mr. Hyde* with a woman protagonist who lives two separate lives by taking a drug that allows her to become another person. Clearly, Tennant is attacking the lifestyle choices women in England suffer at the hands of advantage and social class—and their destructive impacts on women's beliefs and behaviors.

Tennant is capable of writing bitingly sarcastic social commentaries like *The House of Hospitalities* and *A Wedding of Cousins* but her work takes on an added dimension when she mixes social commentary with science fictional elements. In *Wild Nights* a child watches as his uncles and aunts turn themselves into rabbits and birds. The novel is a comment on the fear of growing up but also has a surreal, occult flavor that transcends Tennant's text.

One of Tennant's best known and widely praised books is her genre blending *The Last of the Country House Murders.* This sly, clever novel is a mystery novel in the Agatha Christie tradition but written in the style of J.G. Ballard. The setting is a futuristic England burdened by massive overpopulation. The "body in the library" type of murder is impossible because the population pressures have destroyed privacy and space. The owner of the last existing manor house, Jules Tanner, is to be murdered publicly as part of Woodiscombe Manor's conversion into a tourist attraction. The Government selects a detective to interview assassins, plant clues, and in general design a murder worthy of the rich foreign tourists and the mass audience who will witness the murder. *The Last of the Country House Murders* is wickedly funny and mocks the "bread and circuses" mentality of contemporary governments who manage reality instead of solving basic economic and social problems.

Other weapons in Tennant's arsenal are parody and pastiche. Tennant takes on militant feminist guerrillas in *The Bad Sister* and the court of Queen Elizabeth II in *The Adventures of Robina, by Herself.* The invasion of Grenada and the U.S. Marines are at the heart of *Black Marina.* Tennant's books can be stark, as in *Woman Beware Woman*, where a murdered novelist's family finds itself part of a vengeance plot; or they can be wildly inventive, as in *Hotel de Dream* where fictional characters try to kill the novelist who created them to prevent the conclusion she's about to write for them.

Emma Tennant is a writer of extraordinary range whose works use science fictional elements in consistently original and innovative ways.

—George Kelley

---

**TENNESHAW, S.M.** *See* **GARRETT, Randall; Silverberg, Robert.**

---

**TEVIS, Walter (Stone).** American. Born in San Francisco, California, 28 February 1928. Educated at the University of Kentucky, Lexington, M.A. 1956; University of Iowa, Iowa City, M.F.A. 1961. Served in the United States Navy. Divorced; one son and one daughter. Worked for Kentucky highway department in 1950's and early 1960's; after 1965, Professor of English, Ohio University, Athens. *Died 9 August 1984.*

SCIENCE-FICTION PUBLICATIONS

Novels

*The Man Who Fell to Earth.* New York, Fawcett, and London, Muller, 1963.
*Mockingbird.* New York, Doubleday, and London, Hodder and Stoughton, 1980.
*The Steps of the Sun.* New York, Doubleday, 1983; London, Gollancz, 1984.

Short Stories

*Far from Home.* New York, Doubleday, 1981; London, Gollancz, 1983.

OTHER PUBLICATIONS

Novels

*The Hustler.* New York, Harper, 1959; London, Joseph, 1960.
*The Queen's Gambit.* New York, Random House, and London, Heinemann, 1983.
*The Color of Money.* New York, Warner, 1984; London, Severn House, 1985.

*

Walter Tevis commented:

(1981) I suppose I write disguised autobiographies. The idea, as far as I know, is to move other people. I feel alienated from other people sometimes; when I was younger the feeling was stronger than it is now. My major characters are alienated, by virtue of being pool players, from Mars, robots, the only people alive who can read, or alcoholics. I like to write about people under psychological stress, and when I write I am very serious about it.

* * *

Thomas Jerome Newton, in Walter Tevis's *The Man Who Fell to Earth*, is an emissary from the dying planet of Anthea, sent to prepare a refuge and transportation for its last few survivors. We never learn his real name. By introducing advanced Anthean technology Newton amasses the necessary millions of dollars, but attracts the attentions of the FBI who imprison and interrogate him, blinding him in the process. Eventually released, he abandons his project and dwindles into perpetual alcoholic exile. Earth, though they colonised it in the first place, is no place for Antheans.

Walter Tevis's novel is the classic refutation of the alien invasion theme in SF. He reduces the interplanetary war to a case of depression, the story of the loneliest man in the world. Newton could save mankind, but he represents a threat to the American economy. He is disabled, not by military might or scientific ingenuity, but by smothering bureaucracy. Seeing Newton decrepit and drunk in a bar, Nathan Bryce, his only human confidant, reflects that he "certainly would not have been the first means of possible salvation to get the official treatment." Christ, it seems, was an Anthean too. The failure of Newton's mission is a slow, pathetic crucifixion. Bryce remembers Thoreau's dictum: "quiet desperation" is the mood of the novel, an unobtrusive tragedy in an unostentatious style that conceals irony, bitterness, and ultimately cold fury. "I worked very hard to become an imitation human being. . . ." Newton says. "And of course I succeeded."

*Mockingbird* is altogether less original and distinctive. In a future America run and serviced by robots, human faculties, emotions, and even social urges have been eroded. The senior robot, Bob Spofforth (Mark Nine), is an interesting figure of moral ambivalence, sexless and immortal, but plagued by human dreams that slipped in under his mental programming. As in Bradbury's *Fahrenheit 451*, literacy is suppressed but the hero learns to read and is emboldened to further rebellion when he meets a woman less obedient to convention than he is. The book is efficiently plotted and written, but suffers from too much formula and too little variation.

Tevis's only collection, *Far from Home*, divides neatly into six competent but routine novelty stories, mostly from *Galaxy* at the end of the 1960's, and seven more searching pieces from 1979–80, including four previously unpublished highly Freudian self-examinations. These latter fictions demand to be read with a sympathy for their author which they do not altogether repay, but it seems that in its primary therapeutic purpose Tevis's writing finally, if precariously, succeeded. *The Steps of the Sun* tells how a big, rich, glum, impotent American restores himself and his impoverished nation by an illegal venture into space. In Tevis's quaintly benevolent cosmos, Ben Belson swiftly finds not only "safe" uranium but also a perfect analgesic and a sentient planet that mothers him through his self-induced psychological crisis. What is hard is bringing these gifts back to Earth, whose authorities treat the returning explorer with all the suspicion and hostility they showed to the extra-terrestrial benefactor in *The Man Who Fell to Earth.* Whereas Thomas Jerome Newton is last seen drunk and defeated, Ben Belson's life on the run culminates in a period of stringent purification in a bleak, utopian China before a final symbolic tableau in which he and his wife switch on all the lights of a New York dark for 30 years and more. *The Steps of the Sun* annoys those who insist on reading science fiction literally, but as a fantasy quest through a damaged psyche it is effective and affecting. It ended Tevis's melancholy career on a hopeful note.

—Colin Greenland

---

**THANET, Neil.** *See* **FANTHORPE, R. Lionel.**

---

**THOMAS, Cogswell.** *See* **COGSWELL, Theodore R.; THOMAS, Ted.**

---

**THOMAS, D(onald) M(ichael).** British. Born in Redruth, Cornwall, 27 January 1935. Educated at Redruth Grammar School; University High School, Melbourne; New College, Oxford, B.A. (honours) in English, 1958, M.A. Served in the British Army (national service), 1953–54. Has two sons and one daughter. Teacher, Teignmouth Grammar School, Devon, 1959–63; Senior Lecturer in English, Hereford College of Education, 1964–78. Visiting Lecturer in English, Hamline University, St. Paul, Minnesota, 1967; Creative Writing teacher, American University, Washington, D.C., 1982. Recipient: Richard Hillary Memorial prize, 1960; Cholmondeley award, 1978; *Guardian*–Gollancz Fantasy Novel prize, 1979; Los Angeles *Times* prize, 1981; Silver Pen award, 1982. Address: The Coach House, Rashleigh Vale, Cornwall TR1 1TJ, England.

SCIENCE-FICTION PUBLICATIONS

Verse

*Penguin Modern Poets 11*, with D.M. Black and Peter Redgrove. London, Penguin, 1968.
*Two Voices.* London, Cape Goliard Press, and New York, Grossman, 1968.

OTHER PUBLICATIONS

Novels

*The Flute-Player.* London, Gollancz, and New York, Dutton, 1979.
*Birthstone.* London, Gollancz, 1980.
*The White Hotel.* London, Gollancz, and New York, Viking Press, 1981.
*Ararat.* London, Gollancz, and New York, Viking Press, 1983.
*Swallow.* London, Gollancz, and New York, Viking Press, 1984.
*Sphinx.* London, Gollancz, 1986; New York, Viking Press, 1987.
*Summit.* London, Gollancz, 1987; New York, Viking Press, 1988.
*Lying Together.* London, Gollancz, and New York, Viking Press, 1990.

Plays

*The White Hotel*, adaptation of his own novel (produced Edinburgh, 1984).

Radio Plays: *You Will Hear Thunder*, 1981; *Boris Godunov*, from play by Pushkin, 1984.

Verse

*Personal and Possessive.* London, Outposts, 1964.
*The Lover's Horoscope: Kinetic Poem.* Laramie, Wyoming, Purple Sage, 1970.
*Logan Stone.* London, Cape Goliard Press, and New York, Grossman, 1971.
*The Shaft.* Gillingham, Kent, Arc, 1973.
*Lilith-Prints.* Cardiff, Second Aeon, 1974.
*Symphony in Moscow.* Richmond, Surrey, Keepsake Press, 1974.
*Love and Other Deaths.* London, Elek, 1975.
*The Rock.* Knotting, Bedfordshire, Sceptre Press, 1975.
*Orpheus in Hell.* Knotting, Bedfordshire, Sceptre Press, 1977.
*The Honeymoon Voyage.* London, Secker and Warburg, 1978.
*Dreaming in Bronze.* Secker and Warburg, 1981.
*Selected Poems.* London, Secker and Warburg, and New York, Viking Press, 1983.
*News from the Front,* with Sylvia Kantaris. Todmorden, Lancashire, Arc, 1983.

Other

*The Devil and the Floral Dance* (for children). London, Robson, 1978.
*Memories and Hallucinations* (memoir). London, Gollancz, and New York, Viking Press, 1988.

Editor, *The Granite Kingdom: Poems of Cornwall.* Truro, Cornwall, Barton, 1970.
Editor, *Poetry in Crosslight.* London, Longman, 1975.
Editor, *Songs from the Earth: Selected Poems of John Harris, Cornish Miner, 1820–84.* Padstow, Cornwall, Lodenek Press, 1977.

Translator, *Requiem, and Poem Without a Hero,* by Anna Akhmatova. London, Elek, and Athens, Ohio University Press, 1976.
Translator, *Way of All the Earth,* by Anna Akhmatova. London, Secker and Warburg, and Athens, Ohio University Press, 1979.
Translator, *Invisible Threads,* by Evtushenko. New York, Macmillan, 1981.
Translator, *The Bronze Horseman and Other Poems,* by Pushkin. London, Secker and Warburg, and New York, Viking Press, 1982.
Translator, *A Dove in Santiago,* by Evtushenko. London, Secker and Warburg, 1982; New York, Viking Press, 1983.
Translator, *You Will Hear Thunder,* by Anna Akhmatova. London, Secker and Warburg, and Athens, Ohio University Press-Swallow Press, 1985.

*

D.M. Thomas comments:

Most of my science-fiction poetry is collected in one publication, *Penguin Modern Poets 11* (1968). Since then I have remained interested in the mythic aspect of SF, but have moved away from "pure" SF into other areas of myth.

* * *

D.M. Thomas's SF writing is largely restricted to his earlier poetry, published from the mid-1960's through the 1970's. Since that time he has turned increasingly to fiction, and he has gained considerable attention, especially for *The White Hotel, Ararat,* and its sequel, *Swallow.* Thomas's work in these forms is unified by common themes, particularly by the emotional and psychological structures that link sex, love, death, and artistic creation.

Thomas's SF poetry is often narrative, relying on SF settings and tropes to explore the emotional tangles that might arise in these placements with effective imagery, striking metaphors, and evocative language and tone. Poems like "Missionary," "A Dead Planet," and "The Strait" tell the stories we identify with science fiction—alien contacts and troubles with androids. Other poems show Thomas moving confidently across a variety of forms: from the vocative lyrics of "Fire Victims" and "Elegy for an Android" to striking dramatic monologues reminiscent of Browning like "Tithonus" and "Hera's Spring." The poet can produce both the traditional dialogue "A Conversation upon the Shadow" and visually stimulating concrete poems like "Symbiosis" and "Mercury." In most of these, Thomas demonstrates his skill at reworking the mythic inspirations supplied by science-fiction stories. The most striking examples of this latter strategy are "The Strait," based on Bradbury's *Marionettes Inc.*, and "Hera's Spring," arising in response to Clarke's *The City and the Stars.* The former work poignantly captures the painful emotions aroused when a living woman must be replaced by an android duplicate. In "Hera's Spring" the motherly speaker tries to allay the sudden sense of loss and sorrow that a newly reminded Jeserac faces when he realizes the hundreds of lives he has lived before his present existence.

Thomas often relies on the myths of SF to emphasize isolation and alienation, love, sex, and violence, concerns especially apparent in his formally innovative, tabular poem "Hospital of Transplanted Hearts." In its multiple possibilities for reading and interpretation, this work seems to anticipate Calvino's *Castle of the Crossed Destinies.* In "The Head-Rape" Thomas explores the need for personal mental seclusion, especially in the complex and powerfully charged atmosphere of sexual violence—here as brutalization, but in "A Conversation upon the Shadow" as part of intimacy and love.

These themes continued to fascinate Thomas, and his later work often returns to them, often published in *New Worlds.* Indeed, pieces appearing in this periodical reveal Thomas's progression from poetry within the genre to work belonging more in the mainstream. Long and extremely complex poems like *Two Voices* and "Computer 70: Dreams and Love Poems" still rely on technology and estranged settings to examine love and sorrow; and the former is particularly evocative of a post-holocaust survivor's experience balanced by the reflections of a woman who is both the unwilling human and the mythic earth mother. "Mr. Black's Poems of Innocence" marks the first of Thomas's incursions into the social sciences for his estranging material, and the poem is a masterpiece of parody mixed with serious, if fictionalized, psychotherapy. A mute schizophrenic suffers operant conditioning therapy, but between his outward, verbal answers we read his inner figurative musings. These center on a fantasy of his own entrapment and isolation, first associated with being a trapped sweep in a labyrinthine chimney, and then with passages from Rider Haggard's *King Solomon's Mines.* This latter material is especially important because it returns in yet another guise in Thomas's novel, *Swallow,* where once again the writer feels compelled to rework the figures of desire, greed, and death.

Although Thomas published several more pieces in *New Worlds,* these were increasingly removed from the usual settings and tropes marking SF. With the series that appeared in September 1979 ("Primitive Behavior," "A Letter From Marina," "Fathers, Sons and Lovers," and "The Woman to Freud"), he seemed to have given up the technological side of SF altogether. Here, we find material anticipating that in *The White Hotel*—for example, in the next to last poem cited, a historical fictionalization of the letter preceding the suicide of one of Freud's disciples, and in the last the sexual fantasy about a hysteria victim and Freud's son, which becomes the first section of the "Don Giovanni" section in the novel. Throughout his work, Thomas shows the potentiality of science fiction's myths for poetic expression.

—Len Hatfield

---

**THOMAS, K.** *See* **FEARN, John Russell.**

---

**THOMAS, Ted** (Theodore L. Thomas). Also wrote as Leonard Lockhard; Cogswell Thomas. American. Born in New York City, 13 April 1920. Educated at Massachusetts Institute of Technology, S.B. 1947; Georgetown University, Washington, D.C., J.D. 1953. Served in the United States Army, 1943–46: 1st Lieutenant. Married Virginia Kent Paton in 1947; two daughters and one son. Chemical engineer, American Cyanamid Company, Stamford, Connecticut, 1947–50. Patent lawyer, in Washington, D.C., 1950–55, and from 1955, for Armstrong Cork Company, Lancaster, Pennsylvania. Columnist ("Science for Everybody"), Stamford *Advocate*, 1949–79, and columnist ("The Science Springboard"), *Fantasy and Science Fiction*, New York, 1964–67. Chairman, Lancaster Zoning Board of Adjustments, 1966–70, and Lancaster Narcotics and Dangerous Drugs Committee, 1970–71. *Died.*

Science-Fiction Publications

Novels

*The Clone*, with Kate Wilhelm. New York, Berkley, 1965; London, Hale, 1968.
*Year of the Cloud*, with Kate Wilhelm. New York, Doubleday, 1970.

Uncollected Short Stories

"The Revisitor," in *Space Science Fiction* (New York), September 1952.
"The Fatal Third," in *Planet* (New York), November 1953.
"The Penultimate Weapon," in *Future* (New York), January 1954.
"The Disciplinarian," in *Blue Book* (Chicago), October 1954.
"Trial Without Combat," in *Future 28* (New York), 1955.
"The Far Look," in *SF: 57*, edited by Judith Merril. Philadelphia, Gnome Press, 1957.
"The Disappearing Man," in *Science Fiction Stories*, July 1957.
"Mars Trial," in *Future* (New York), Summer 1957.
"Twice-Told Tales," in *Super Science Fiction* (New York), August 1957.
"The Attractive Nuisance," in *Science Fiction Quarterly* (Holyoke, Massachusetts), August 1957.
"Just Rub a Lamp," in *Science Fiction Stories*, September 1957.
"The Sound of the Wind," in *Science Fiction Stories*, June 1958.
"The Law School," in *Analog* (New York), June 1958.
"The Back of a Hand," in *Future* (New York), June 1958.
"The Destroyer," in *Science Fiction Stories*, September 1958.
"Satellite Passage," in *SF: 59*, edited by Judith Merril. Philadelphia, Gnome Press, 1959.
"The Good Work," in *If* (New York), February 1959.
"Broken Tool," in *Analog* (New York), July 1959.
"New Model Spaceman," in *Future* (New York), August 1959.
"The Sound of Screaming," in *Amazing* (New York), October 1960.
"The Crackpot," in *Analog* (New York), November 1960.
"The Flames of Life," in *Amazing* (New York), December 1960.
"The Moon v. Nansen," in *New Worlds* (London), February 1961.
"Passage to Malish," in *Fantastic* (New York), August 1961.
"Day of Succession," in *A Century of Science Fiction*, edited by Damon Knight. New York, Simon and Schuster, 1962; London, Gollancz, 1963.
"The Spy," in *If* (New York), May 1962.
"Test," in *Best from Fantasy and Science Fiction 12*, edited by Avram Davidson. New York, Doubleday, 1963.
"The Weather Man," in *Analog 2*, edited by John W. Campbell, Jr. New York, Doubleday, 1964.
"The Soft Woman," in *Fantastic* (New York), February 1964.
"The Lonely Man," in *The Eighth Galaxy Reader*, edited by Frederik Pohl. New York, Doubleday, 1965.
"Manfire," in *Worlds of Tomorrow* (New York), January 1965.
"Lunar Landing," in *Fantasy and Science Fiction* (New York), September 1965.
"December 28th," in *The Playboy Book of Science Fiction and Fantasy*. New York, Paperback Library, 1966.
"The Doctor," in *Orbit 2*, edited by Damon Knight. New York, Putnam, 1967.
"The Being in the Tank," in *Galaxy* (New York), August 1967.
"The Other Culture," in *Analog* (New York), January 1969.
"Welcome, Centaurians," in *Galaxy* (New York), January 1969.
"The Weather on the Sun," in *Orbit 8*, edited by Damon Knight. New York, Putnam, 1970.
"The Intruder," in *A Pocketful of Stars*, edited by Damon Knight. New York, Doubleday, 1971; London, Gollancz, 1972.
"The Tour," in *Fantasy and Science Fiction* (New York), March 1971.
"The Swan Song of Dame Horse," in *Analog* (New York), March 1971.
"Motion Day at the Courthouse," in *Analog* (New York), October 1971.
"Paradise Regained" (as Cogswell Thomas, with Theodore R. Cogswell), in *Saving Worlds*, edited by Roger Elwood and Virginia Kidd. New York, Doubleday, 1973.
"Early Bird," with Theodore R. Cogswell, in *Astounding*, edited by Harry Harrison. New York, Random House, 1973; London, Sidgwick and Jackson, 1974.
"The Rescuers," in *Fantasy and Science Fiction* (New York), September 1974.
"Players at Null-G," with Theodore R. Cogswell and Algis Budrys, in *Fantasy and Science Fiction* (New York), July 1975.
"The Family Man," in *Fantasy and Science Fiction* (New York), March 1978.
"Ceramic Incident," in *The Analog Anthology 1*, edited by Stanley Schmidt. New York, Davis, 1980.
"The Innocents' Refuge," in *Travels Through Time*, edited by Isaac Asimov, Martin H. Greenberg, and Charles G. Waugh. Milwaukee, Raintree, 1981.

Uncollected Short Stories as Leonard Lockhard (series: Patent Attorney in all stories)

"Improbable Profession" (with Charles L. Harness), September 1952, "That Professional Look" (with Charles L. Harness),

January 1954, "The Curious Profession," April 1956, "The Professional Touch," February 1959, "The Lagging Profession," January 1961, "The Professional Approach," September 1962, and "Professional Dilemma," October 1964, all in *Astounding* (New York). "The Magnificent Profession," in *Fantastic Universe* (Chicago), November 1955.

* * *

Over a period of more then two decades, Ted Thomas produced a small but steady stream of short stories of unusually high calibre. Although he did not produce a novel that was solely his own work, he collaborated with Kate Wilhelm twice at novel length, and in each case the end product has been of superior quality. *The Clone*, for example, based on a short story of the same name by Thomas alone, is one of the most frightening and plausible tales of biochemistry gone wild. An amorphous creature is spawned in the sewers of a major city, able to absorb virtually any other organic structure—including people—upon contact.

*Year of the Cloud* deals with the theme of world disaster. The Earth passes through a strange interstellar cloud that has catastrophic effects on the planet. Tidal waves and volcanic activity are only short-term problems. The oceans turn into a gelatin-like substance and water is in short supply everywhere. The disaster is seen through the eyes of a number of characters, some of whom are working to reverse the effects of the cloud. But the cloud eventually proves to be a mixed blessing in this story, which combines scientific investigation with straightforward adventure.

Thomas himself is best known for his short stories, including those set against a background where the Weather Control Board controls the Earth because of its ability to affect the lifestyles and commercial undertakings of everyone on Earth. In "The Weather Man" a section of Australia refuses to abide by their authority and is threatened with a drought as a consequence. In "The Weather on the Sun" the efficacy of the government is endangered when the nature of the sun begins to alter, with unpredictable effects on the weather of our own planet.

"Satellite Passage" is a poignant tale of the near passage of two manned satellites, one from the United States and one from the Soviet Union. As the time of passage nears, there is considerable worry by the Americans that the Russians will commit some overt act of violence, but ultimately there is an accident in space and a Soviet cosmonaut is rescued by the Americans. Thomas also portrays the effects of a prolonged stay by a team of two men on the moon in "The Far Look." After experiencing a number of near disasters, the returning men possess a difference in demeanor that is quite noticeable.

Thomas assumed that H.G. Wells was correct about the Martians in "Day of Succession." When a ruthless general begins destroying the inhabitants of landing space vessels without warning, the authorities remove him from authority. The next capsule unleashes a technological onslaught against which human armies cannot stand, and the general assassinates the president in order to resume his program of eradication. A criminal is sentenced to be hanged each year in "December 28th," then brought back to life and allowed to recover in time for his next execution.

Thomas's use of irony is perhaps best illustrated in "The Doctor." A physician is stranded in prehistoric times when an accident destroys his time machine. He attempts to help the local residents by using his medical skills, but his attempts to extract teeth, set bones, etc. are viewed as hostile acts, as his intentions are totally misunderstood. Similarly, in "The Tour" a scientist realizes that visiting politicians do not understand his policy of using drugs to treat incurable murderers, and he subsequently commits murder himself in order to protect his program.

Thomas collaborated several times with Theodore Cogswell, most notably with "Early Bird," a humorous tale of a human space pilot whose ship becomes transformed when it arrives on a most peculiar planet, evolving in a strange merge of mechanical and organic development, and in "Paradise Regained," in which political exiles decide to terraform the planet upon which they have been confined. "The Players at Null-G," written with Cogswell and Algis Budrys, is a humorous spoof of the time-travel story.

—Don D'Ammassa

---

**THOMSON, Edward.** *See* **TUBB, E.C.**

---

**THORPE, Trebor.** *See* **FANTHORPE, R. Lionel.**

---

**THURSTON, Robert (Donald).** American. Born in Lockport, New York, 28 October 1936. Educated at the University of Buffalo, now State University of New York, B.A. in English 1959, M.A. 1967. Served in the United States Army Air Defense Command, 1960–62. Married 1) Joan K. Sullivan in 1964 (died, 1980), one son; 2) Rosemary E. Fox in 1982. Reporter, *Union-Sun and Journal*, Lockport, 1959–60; Assistant Professor, Alliance College, Cambridge Springs, Pennsylvania, 1967–68; manager, Glen Art Book Store, Williamsville, New York, 1968–71. Recipient: Clarion Workshop award, 1970. Address: 86 Ceder Street, Ridgefield Park, New Jersey 07660, U.S.A.

SCIENCE-FICTION PUBLICATIONS

Novels (series: Battlestar Galactica)

*Alicia II.* New York, Berkley, 1978.
*Battlestar Galactica*, with Glen A. Larson. New York, Berkley, and London, Futura, 1978.
*Battlestar Galactica 2: The Cylon Death Machine*, with Glen A. Larson. New York, Berkley, 1979.
*Battlestar Galactica 3: The Tombs of Kobol*, with Glen A. Larson. New York, Berkley, 1979.
*Battlestar Galactica 4: The Young Warriors*, with Glen A. Larson. New York, Berkley, 1980.
*A Set of Wheels.* New York, Berkley, 1983.
*Battlestar Galactica 11: The Nightmare Machine*, with Glen A. Larson. New York, Berkley, 1984.
*Q Colony.* New York, Berkley, 1985.
*Battlestar Galactica 12: Die, Chameleon!* with Glen A. Larson. New York, Berkley, 1986.
*Apollo's War*, with Glen A. Larson. New York, Berkley, 1987.
*Surrender the Galactica*, with Glen A. Larson. New York, Ace, 1988.
*Robot Jox.* New York, Avon, 1989.

*Isaac Asimov's Robot City: Robots and Aliens.* New York, Ace, 1990.

Uncollected Short Stories

"Stop Me Before I Tell More," in *Orbit 9*, edited by Damon Knight. New York, Putnam, 1971.
"Wheels," "Anaconda," and "The Last Desperate Hour," in *Clarion*, edited by Robin Scott Wilson. New York, New American Library, 1971.
"Get FDR!," "Punchline," and "The Good Life," in *Clarion 2*, edited by Robin Scott Wilson. New York, New American Library, 1972.
"Goodbye Shelley, Shirley, Charlotte, Charlene," in *Orbit 11*, edited by Damon Knight. New York, Putnam, 1972.
"Carolyn's Laughter," in *Fantasy and Science Fiction* (New York), January 1972.
"She/Her," in *Infinity 5*, edited by Robert Hoskins. New York, Lancer, 1973.
"Up Against the Wall," in *School and Society Through Science Fiction*, edited by Martin H. Greenberg and Joseph D. Olander. New York, Random House, 1974.
"Soundtrack: The Making of a Thoroughbred," in *Fantastic* (New York), May 1974.
"Under Siege," in *Fantasy and Science Fiction* (New York), July 1974.
"Searching the Ruins," in *Amazing* (New York), August 1974.
"The Hippie-Dip File," in *Social Problems Through Science Fiction*, edited by Martin H. Greenberg and others. New York, St. Martin's Press, 1975.
"Theodora and Theodora," in *New Dimensions 5*, edited by Robert Silverberg. New York, Harper, 1975.
"Jack and Betty," in *Orbit 16*, edited by Damon Knight. New York, Harper, 1975.
"Dream by Number," in *Fantasy and Science Fiction* (New York), September 1975.
"The Haunted Writing-Manual," in *Fantastic* (New York), October 1975.
"Groups," in *Fantastic* (New York), February 1976.
"If That's Paradise, Toss Me an Apple," in *Amazing* (New York), March 1976.
"One Magic Ring, Used," in *Fantastic* (New York), May 1976.
"Parker Frightened on a Tightrope," in *Fantastic* (New York), November 1976.
"Aliens," in *Fantasy and Science Fiction* (New York), December 1976.
"The Kingmakers," in *New Voices in Science Fiction*, edited by George R.R. Martin. New York, Macmillan, 1977.
"The Mars Ship," in *Fantasy and Science Fiction* (New York), June 1977.
"Wheels Westward," in *Cosmos* (New York), November 1977.
"What Johnny Did on His Summer Vacation," with Joe Haldeman, in *Rod Serling's Other Worlds*. New York, Bantam, 1978.
"The Bulldog Nutcracker," in *Chrysalis 2*, edited by Roy Torgeson. New York, Kensington, 1978.
"Seedplanter," in *Chrysalis 3*, edited by Roy Torgeson. New York, Kensington, 1978.
"Vibrations," in *Chrysalis 4*, edited by Roy Torgeson. New York, Kensington, 1979.
"The Oonaa Woman," in *The Berkley Showcase 3*, edited by Victoria Schochet and John W. Silbersack. New York, Berkley, 1981.
"Alternate 51: Bliss," in *The Berkley Showcase 4*, edited by Victoria Schochet and John W. Silbersack. New York, Berkley, 1981.
"The Wanda Lake Number," in *Light Years and Dark*, edited by Michael Bishop. New York, Berkley, 1984.
"The Fire at Sarah Siddons," in *Isaac Asimov's Science Fiction Magazine* (New York), August 1984.
"Was That House There Yesterday?" in *Universe 16*, edited by Terry Carr. New York, Doubleday, 1986.

OTHER PUBLICATIONS

Novels

*Rugger 1: For the Silverfish.* New York, Avon, 1985.
*Rugger 2: In Justice's Prison.* New York, Avon, 1985.

*  *  *

Robert Thurston established himself as a significant new writer in the science-fiction genre on the basis of his short fiction and has only recently turned to original novels, some of which develop themes presented earlier in short form.

One of Thurston's earliest short stories, "Carolyn's Laughter," hovered around the border between science fiction and the supernatural. A young man is troubled by memories of his first wife, now deceased, and eventually resorts to a computer medium in a half-hearted effort to contact her spirit. Carolyn had agreed to have her organs used in transplants, and there is some evidence that she may have reached across the borderline between life and death in an effort to reclaim the parts of her body that survived. This theme recurs in another story, "The Fire at Sarah Siddons," in which a man's life is completely dominated by a message he receives from his dead wife.

Both stories are well plotted, but the outstanding quality of these and most of Thurston's short fiction is the detailed and convincing development of characters. "Under Siege," for example, works only because of its fine characterization. Within the context of a racist police state, a white liberal with a black wife is plagued by the constant silent presence of a black man. The growing tensions among the three are superbly handled, and the story might well have attracted much serious attention if it had been published in mainstream markets.

Time travel is ostensibly the subject of "The Kingmakers," in which a man travels through the past to write a biography of a pivotal figure, but the four visits he makes, spaced widely apart in the lifespan of both men, cause tensions and contrasts that are the main focus of the story. Thurston's short stories run the gamut from comic to surreal, occasionally strongly plot oriented but more frequently concerned with character and theme. Doppelgangers show up frequently, with inexplicable duplicate women in "Goodbye Shelley, Shirley, Charlotte, Charlene," a host of people with no apparent pasts in "Searching the Ruins," and two virtually identical wives in "Theodora and Theodora." Some of his stories deal with controversial themes, such as "Aliens," wherein a human male is used as a sex object by non-humanoid aliens, and "The Oonaa Woman," also quite explicitly sexual in subject matter.

Thurston's first novel, *Alicia II*, was uneven. As might be expected, Thurston did a remarkable job of developing his characters as human beings. Voss Geraghty callously accepts the society he lives in, one which classifies people early in their lives, designating some as "rejects" whose bodies will be confiscated in young adulthood to become the home of non-rejects. But Geraghty's new body was sabotaged by its former owner, and cannot function sexually. Following this blow to his view of the world, he must then re-examine much of what he believes about his own society. Unfortunately, the setting of the novel is unconvincing, and the long delay before the advent of organized resistance to its system is not particularly credible.

*A Set of Wheels* was a bit of a disappointment after the promise of Thurston's first novel. In the not too distant future, a young man becomes involved in a love affair with an illegal automobile. The setting is brutal and dirty, a world of clandestine repair shops, police nearly as corrupt as the people they hunt, love tainted by mistrust and self-interest. Thurston uses unconventional dialogue, perhaps to emphasize the depersonalization of his future, but it also serves to flatten his characters as well.

*Q Colony* uses "The Oonaa Woman" as its opening and proceeds from there to provide the history of a failed human research colony on an alien world. It is easily Thurston's most successful full-length effort. He has carefully avoided the stereotyped characters common in the field, and the result is a mixture of the admirable and the reprehensible. Oonaa and humans can interbreed, providing an effective device for examining the collision of differing cultures and value systems.

Thurston's recent efforts have been primarily novelizations, including episodes of the "Battlestar Galactica" television program and the film, *Robot Jox.* He has also contributed an episode to the multi-authored "Robot City" series, set in the universe of Isaac Asimov's classic robot stories.

—Don D'Ammassa

---

**TILLEY, Patrick.** British. Born in Southend, Essex, 4 July 1928. Educated at Royal Grammar School, Newcastle upon Tyne; King's College of Art, University of Durham. Married in 1951; two sons and one daughter. Graphic designer and illustrator, 1954–68, then full-time writer. Creative adviser, *Oh, What a Lovely War!*, 1969; technical/historical adviser, *A Bridge Too Far*, 1977. Agent: Peters, Fraser and Dunlop, Fifth Floor, The Chambers, Chelsea Harbour, London SW10 OXF, England; or, Stirling Lord Literistic, Inc., 1 Madison Avenue, New York, New York 10010, U.S.A.

SCIENCE-FICTION PUBLICATIONS

Novels (series: Amtrak Wars)

*Fade-Out.* London, Hodder and Stoughton, and New York, Morrow, 1975.
The Amtrak Wars:
*Cloud Warrior.* London, Sphere, 1983; New York, Macmillan, 1984.
*First Family.* London, Sphere, 1985; New York, Baen, 1986.
*Iron Master.* London, Sphere, 1987; New York, Baen, 1988.
*Blood River.* London, Sphere, 1988.
*Death-Bringer.* London, Sphere, 1989.
*Earth-Thunder.* London, Sphere, 1990.
*Xan.* London, Grafton, 1986.

OTHER PUBLICATIONS

Novels

*Whatever Happened to the Likely Lads?* (novelization of TV series). London, BBC, 1973.
*Mission.* London, Joseph, and Boston, Little Brown, 1981.

Plays

Screenplays: *Wuthering Heights*, 1970; *People That Time Forgot*, 1977; *The Legacy*, 1977.

Television Plays: *Crane* series (3 episodes), 1959.

Other

*Dark Visions: An Illustrated Guide to the Amtrak Wars.* London, Sphere, 1988.

*

Patrick Tilley comments:

(1985) The books I write are designed primarily as entertainment but they are, essentially, about the human condition. For me, the elements of a story should go together like a Swiss watch. The plot has to have a logical basis; the story should not insult the reader's intelligence. A writer's job is to communicate with his readers as simply and effectively as possible. He should not make them reach for a dictionary, or try to impress other writers with the quality of his prose.

(1991) Although I am widely perceived as a science-fiction writer, my stories are not about spaceships or bug-eyed monsters. They are about ordinary people in extraordinary situations. The keynote is plausibility. I'm told I have a gift for making fantastic ideas seem quite logical and totally believable.

* * *

One of the hallmarks of writers of stature is that they can take a standard plot and do something novel with it, something that makes it stand out among a crowd of similar stories. Perhaps one of the oldest, most overdone situations in science fiction is the invasion of Earth by aliens in flying saucers, and almost as hoary a plot is the first contact story. So it is particularly interesting that Patrick Tilley's debut novel, *Fade-Out*, is in fact a melding of both of these into a novel that should have been derivative and uninspired. The result was quite the contrary.

Borrowing from the film *The Day the Earth Stood Still*, Tilley has his aliens cut off all power to human machinery during their landing. Soon the government of the United States must cope with a mysterious vehicle and its inhabitants who either cannot or will not communicate, but who possess abilities far beyond those of the human race. The novel covers several months of tentative and then increasingly strident attempts by the government to regain control of the situation. Tilley has done in this novel much the same thing that Michael Crichton did for the space plague in *The Andromeda Strain*, that is, examine the situation in incredible detail, and portray the unfolding events in such convincing fashion that the reader is convinced that this really is the way things would happen.

Tilley's second novel, *Mission*, on the other hand, was further from the mainstream of science fiction, although it also is pervaded by a sense of absolute conviction about the sequence of events, the details of official reaction, and the manner in which the characters react to the situation. A dead body is discovered bearing the same wounds as those of Jesus when he died on the cross. But shortly after the body is declared officially dead, there are signs of life. The medical staff is understandably amazed, but their investigation is cut short when their patient mysteriously disappears from the hospital. The protagonist finds his life disrupted even further when his missing patient reappears, apparently quite healthy, and identifies himself as Jesus. At this point, readers might dismiss the novel as an allegorical religious fantasy, but Tilley has more surprises in store. "Jesus" is actually an alien from another universe, using a human body from our far past, travelling through time because, to his/its perceptions, all times are simultaneous and it is an act of will to move from one to the other. In fact, the protagonist ends up travelling back through time himself in what is a very strange adventure novel, more ambitious than *Fade-Out*, and in some ways more interesting, but less successful as entertainment.

Tilley's most noteworthy science-fiction work is the Amtrak Wars series. Once again, Tilley uses a standard genre theme as background, in this case the primitive civilization existing following a nuclear holocaust. The culture is tribal, and the hero, one of the Wingmen, is captured in the first volume by his enemy, the Mutes. His sojourn as a prisoner exposes him to life among the Mutes and, rather than continuing to view them as enemies, he begins to accept them as fellow human beings. Peace suddenly becomes more desirable than continued conflict. His personal goal becomes the resolution of the internecine conflict. Unfortunately, things don't go quite that smoothly, and as the series progresses and we see more of his world, including a resurgent Samurai class in Japan, the inevitability of conflict seems less and less avoidable.

*Xan* was far less successful and in fact has not been reprinted in the United States. A family vacationing in a remote area begins to fear that a demonic force is seeking to possess one of their number. In actuality, alien beings who drift through the universe are the culprits. Although not as satisfying as Tilley's other work, *Xan* still contains some memorable scenes.

—Don D'Ammassa

---

**TIPTREE, James, Jr.** Pseudonym for Alice Sheldon, née Bradley. American. Born in Chicago, Illinois, in 1916. Educated at Sarah Lawrence College, Bronxville, New York; University of California, Berkeley; George Washington University, Washington, D.C., Ph.D. in psychology 1967. Served in the United States Army Air Force, 1942–46. Married 1) William Davey in 1934 (divorced, 1938); 2) Huntington Denton Sheldon in 1945. Worked as an art critic, for the Central Intelligence Agency, in personal business, and as college teacher and experimental psychologist. Recipient: Nebula award, 1973, 1976, 1977; Hugo award, 1974, 1977; *Locus* award, 1984. *Died 19 May 1987.*

SCIENCE-FICTION PUBLICATIONS

Novels

*Up the Walls of the World.* New York, Berkley, and London, Gollancz, 1978.
*Brightness Falls from the Air.* New York, Tor, 1985; London, Sphere, 1986.

Short Stories

*Ten Thousand Light-Years from Home.* New York, Ace, 1973; London, Eyre Methuen, 1975.
*Warm Worlds and Otherwise.* New York, Ballantine, 1975.
*Star Songs of an Old Primate.* New York, Ballantine, 1978.
*Out of the Everywhere and Other Extraordinary Visions.* New York, Ballantine, 1981.
*Byte Beautiful.* New York, Doubleday, 1985.
*The Starry Rift.* New York, Tor, 1986.
*Tales of the Quintana Roo.* Sauk City, Wisconsin, Arkham House, 1986.
*Crown of Stars.* New York, Tor, 1988; London, Sphere, 1990.
*Her Smoke Rose Up Forever: The Great Years of James Tiptree, Jr.* Sauk City, Wisconsin, Arkham House, 1990.

*

Critical Study: *The Fiction of James Tiptree, Jr.* by Gardner Dozois, New York, Algol Press, 1977.

* * *

Although her writing career began late in life and was regrettably brief (1968–1987), Alice Sheldon managed to turn out several stories and novels whose vivid, elegiac style won her universal acclaim among science fiction readers and several nominations, awards, and multiple awards. Her greatest success was achieved in the 1970's with a series of stories illuminating and lamenting the great gulf of sensibility and human objectives existing between the sexes. These included "Love Is the Plan, the Plan Is Death," "The Women Men Don't See," "The Girl Who Was Plugged In," "Houston, Houston, Do You Read?" and "The Screwfly Solution." Typically James Tiptree Jr. (her successful pseudonymous disguise through 1977) develops a tale around the protagonist's agonizing re-appraisal of the nature of human existence disclosed in a horrid epiphany. In "Love Is the Plan, The Plan Is Death," the mating game of an alien species is revealed to resemble more that of the praying mantis than that of humankind. In "The Women Men Don't See," a presumptuous man discovers that the woman he has been protecting is more at home with alien creatures than with him. And in "Houston, Houston, Do You Read?," Tiptree's most celebrated tale, astronauts from the male-dominated culture of the N.A.S.A. Space Center pass through a time warp to find a future Earth populated entirely by female clones who not only reject male companionship but even deny them continued existence: hence the heavy double-entendre of the title: 1) "Houston can you hear us astronauts?"; 2) "N.A.S.A. are you listening to us women?" These latter two stories are fraught with mystery of all kinds—disguised motives, muffled, sinister conversations, depths of fear, regret, and remorse, and an overall atmospheric gloom as uniformly developed and as finely crafted as the best writing of Edgar Allan Poe. Both stories won both Nebula and Hugo awards.

This is not to say that Sheldon-Tiptree was in any sense an imitator of Poe or of any other writer of gothic fiction; on the contrary, she used gothicism to develop her own brand of tough-minded yet oddly optimistic story in which humans fight a losing battle with entropy but fight bravely and with a ferocity not found elsewhere in the animal kingdom. One is reminded of the famous struggle for survival of Scott's expeditionary force or of Guillaumet's famous pronouncement in Antoine de St. Exupery's *Wind, Sand, and Stars:* "I swear that what I went through no animal would have gone through." This characteristic Tiptree effect is enlarged by grotesque humor on occasion. In "The Screwfly Solution," which consists entirely of the desperate epistles of what may be the last woman on Earth, the protagonist suggests that she has seen in an angelic alien invader, "A real-estate agent." Her attempts to buoy her spirits as she witnesses the entire set of Earth males turn homicidal provides that sort of comic effect which ultimately deepens the story's horrific impact.

Neither of Tiptree's two novels, *Up the Walls of the World* and *Brightness Falls from the Air*, has the power of her best stories and novellae; it is as if the Tiptree effect does not grow by extension but rather is attenuated thereby.

Tiptree was a woman of uncommon strength, a world traveller, an artist-photographer, a person of great wit and erudition who was heard to say of all art, "If you can't laugh at it, what good is it," and at the same time one who when she deemed the time had come could end the life of her desperately sick husband and then her own. These biographical details are cited to illustrate Tiptree's mature, implacable, existential pragmatism, a character trait found in her heroes and heroines at their best. Although her life is over there may still appear as-yet-unpublished stories. It would be surprising if these were to show any radical shift of sensibility from her other work. For, as she told an interviewer once, she came to writing with her opinions and her outlook on life largely complete. Her debt to feminist thought of the 1960's and 1970's is great, and her interest to feminist critics now and in the future is understandable; yet continued reading may prove her to be less a feminist writing about women than a philosopher of the human condition who refused even in the vast fields of science fiction to fake information not found in her own hormonal data base. Ironically her writing was for the years of her greatest success seen by many to arise of necessity from a masculine sensibility even as that very writing called into question such vapid and outworn gender distinctions. Science fiction poet Dick Allen, saw the task of 20th-century science fiction as the search for a definition of humankind which could exist in the light of 20th-century knowledge; clearly Tiptree's work has added much to that quest.

—Thom Dunn

---

**TOLKIEN, J(ohn) R(onald) R(euel).** British. Born in Bloemfontein, Orange Free State, South Africa, 3 January 1892; came to England, 1895. Educated at King Edward VI's School, Birmingham, 1900–02, 1903–11; St. Philip's School, Birmingham, 1902–03; Exeter College, Oxford (open classical exhibitioner; Skeat prize, 1914), 1911–15, B.A. (honours), 1915, M.A. 1919. Served in the Lancashire Fusiliers, 1915–18: lieutenant. Married Edith Mary Bratt in 1916 (died 1971); three sons and one daughter. Assistant, Oxford English Dictionary, 1919–20; Reader in English, 1920–23, and Professor of the English language, 1924–25, University of Leeds, Yorkshire; at Oxford University: Rawlinson and Bosworth Professor of Anglo-Saxon, 1925–45; fellow, Pembroke College, 1926–45; Leverhulme research fellow, 1934–36; Merton Professor of English language and literature, 1945–59; honorary fellow, Exeter College, 1963, and Merton College, 1973. Andrew Lang lecturer, University of St. Andrews, Fife, 1939; W.P. Ker lecturer, University of Glasgow, 1953; lived in Bournemouth, Dorset, 1968–71, and Oxford, 1971–73. Artist: one-man show: Ashmolean Museum, Oxford, 1977. Recipient: International Fantasy award, 1957; Royal Society of Literature Benson medal, 1966; Foreign Book prize (France), 1973; World Science Fiction Convention Gandalf award, 1974; Hugo award, 1978. D.Litt.: University College, Dublin, 1954; University of Nottingham, 1970; Oxford University, 1972; Dr. en Phil et Lettres: Liège, 1954; honorary degree: University of Edinburgh, 1973. Fellow, Royal Society of Literature, 1957. C.B.E. (Commander, Order of the British Empire), 1972. *Died 2 September 1973.*

SCIENCE-FICTION PUBLICATIONS

Novels (series: Lord of the Rings)

*The Hobbit; or, There and Back Again*, illustrated by the author. London, Allen and Unwin, 1937; Boston, Houghton Mifflin, 1938; revised edition, 1951; revised edition, 1966; *The Annotated Hobbit*, edited by Douglas A. Anderson, London, Unwin Hyman, and Boston, Houghton Mifflin, 1989.

*The Lord of the Rings*:

*The Fellowship of the Ring*. London, Allen and Unwin, and Boston, Houghton Mifflin, 1954; revised edition, Allen and Unwin, 1966; Houghton Mifflin, 1967.

*The Two Towers*. London, Allen and Unwin, 1954; Boston, Houghton Mifflin, 1955; revised edition, Allen and Unwin, 1966; Houghton Mifflin, 1967.

*The Return of the King*. London, Allen and Unwin, 1955; Boston, Houghton Mifflin, 1956; revised edition, Allen and Unwin, 1966; Houghton Mifflin, 1967.

*The Silmarillion*, edited by Christopher Tolkien. London, Allen and Unwin, and Boston, Houghton Mifflin, 1977.

Short Stories

*Unfinished Tales of Númenór and Middle-Earth*, edited by Christopher Tolkien. London, Allen and Unwin, and Boston, Houghton Mifflin, 1980.

OTHER PUBLICATIONS

Novels

*Farmer Giles of Ham*, illustrated by Pauline Baynes. London, Allen and Unwin, 1949; Boston, Houghton Mifflin, 1950.

*Smith of Wootton Major*, illustrated by Pauline Baynes. London, Allen and Unwin, and Boston, Houghton Mifflin, 1967.

*The Father Christmas Letters*, edited by Baillie Tolkien, illustrated by the author. London, Allen and Unwin, and Boston, Houghton Mifflin, 1976.

*Mr. Bliss*, illustrated by the author. London, Allen and Unwin, 1982.

Play

*The Homecoming of Beorhtnoth Beorhthelm's Son* (broadcast, 1954). Included in *The Tolkien Reader*, 1966; in *Tree and Leaf, Smith of Wootton Major, The Homecoming of Beorhtnoth Beorhthelm's Son*, 1975.

Radio Play: *The Homecoming of Beorhthnoth Beorhthelm's Son*, 1954.

Verse

*Songs for the Philologists*, with others. Privately printed, 1936.

*The Adventures of Tom Bombadil and Other Verses from the Red Book*, illustrated by Pauline Baynes. London, Allen and Unwin, 1962; Boston, Houghton Mifflin, 1963.

*The Road Goes Ever On: A Song Cycle*, music by Donald Swann. Boston, Houghton Mifflin, 1967; London, Allen and Unwin, 1968; revised edition, Houghton Mifflin, 1978.

*Bilbo's Last Song*, illustrated by Pauline Baynes. London, Allen and Unwin, and Boston, Houghton Mifflin, 1974.

*Poems and Stories*. London, Allen and Unwin, 1980.

Other

*A Middle English Vocabulary.* Oxford, Clarendon Press, and New York, Oxford University Press, 1922.
*Beowulf: The Monsters and the Critics.* London, Oxford University Press, 1937.
*Tree and Leaf* (includes short story "Leaf by Niggle" and essay "On Fairy-Stories"). London, Allen and Unwin, 1964; Boston, Houghton Mifflin, 1965; revised edition, London, Unwin Hyman, 1988.
*The Tolkien Reader.* New York, Ballantine, 1966.
*Tree and Leaf, Smith of Wootton Major, The Homecoming of Beorhtnoth Beorhthelm's Son.* London, Allen and Unwin, 1975.
*Pictures.* London, Allen and Unwin, and Boston, Houghton Mifflin, 1979.
*The Letters of J.R.R. Tolkien,* edited by Humphrey Carpenter. London, Allen and Unwin, and Boston, Houghton Mifflin, 1981.
*Finn and Hengest: The Fragment and the Episode,* edited by Alan Bliss. London, Allen and Unwin, and Boston, Houghton Mifflin, 1983.
*The Monsters and the Critics and Other Essays,* edited by Christopher Tolkien. London, Allen and Unwin, 1983; Boston, Houghton Mifflin, 1984.
*The History of Middle-Earth,* edited by Christopher Tolkien:
*The Book of Lost Tales 1–2.* London, Allen and Unwin, 2 vols., 1983–84; Boston, Houghton Mifflin, 2 vols., 1984.
*The Lays of Beleriand.* London, Allen and Unwin, and Boston, Houghton Mifflin, 1985.
*The Shaping of Middle-Earth.* London, Allen and Unwin, and Boston, Houghton Mifflin, 1986.
*The Lost Road and Other Writings.* London, Unwin Hyman, and Boston, Houghton Mifflin, 1987.
*The Return of the Shadow.* London, Unwin Hyman, 1988; Boston, Houghton Mifflin, 1989.
*The Treason of Isengard.* London, Unwin Hyman, and Boston, Houghton Mifflin, 1989.

Editor, with E.V. Gordon, *Sir Gawain and the Green Knight.* Oxford, Clarendon Press, and New York, Oxford University Press, 1925.
Editor, *Ancrene Wisse.* London, Oxford University Press, 1962; New York, Oxford University Press, 1963.

Translator, *Sir Gawain and the Green Knight, Pearl, and Sir Orfeo,* edited by Christopher Tolkien. London, Allen and Unwin, and Boston, Houghton Mifflin, 1975.
Translator, *The Old English Exodus,* edited by Joan Turville-Petre. Oxford, Clarendon Press, 1981.

*

Bibliography: *Tolkien Criticism: An Annotated Checklist* by Richard C. West, Kent, Ohio, Kent State University Press, 1970; revised edition, 1981.

Manuscript Collections: Wade Collection, Wheaton College, Illinois; Marquette University, Milwaukee.

Critical Studies (selection): *Master of Middle-Earth: The Fiction of J.R.R. Tolkien* by Paul Kocher, Boston, Houghton Mifflin, 1972, London, Thames and Hudson, 1973; *Tolkien's World,* London, Thames and Hudson, and Boston, Houghton Mifflin, 1974, and *Tolkien and the Silmarils,* Thames and Hudson, 1981, both by Randel Helms; *J.R.R. Tolkien: A Biography* (includes bibliography) by Humphrey Carpenter, London, Allen and Unwin, and Boston, Houghton Mifflin, 1977; *The Mythology of Middle-Earth* by Ruth S. Noel, London, Thames and Hudson, and Boston, Houghton Mifflin, 1977; *The Complete Guide to Middle-Earth* by Robert Foster, London, Allen and Unwin, and New York, Ballantine, 1978; *Tolkien's Art: A Mythology for England* by Jane C. Nitzche, London, Macmillan, 1979; *Tolkien: New Critical Perspectives* edited by Neil D. Isaacs and Rose A. Zimbardo, Lexington, University Press of Kentucky, 1981; *The Road to Middle-Earth* by T.A. Shippey, London, Allen and Unwin, 1982, Boston, Houghton Mifflin, 1983; *J.R.R. Tolkien: This Far Land* edited by Robert Giddings, London, Vision, 1983; *The Song of Middle-Earth; J.R.R. Tolkien's Themes, Symbols, and Myths* by David Harvey, London, Allen and Unwin, 1985; *The Magical World of the Inklings: J.R.R. Tolkien, C.S. Lewis, Charles Williams, Owen Barfield* by Gareth Knight, Shaftesbury, Element, 1990; *A Tolkien Thesaurus* by Richard E. Blackwelder, New York, Garland, 1990.

* * *

J.R.R. Tolkien's *The Hobbit,* now a classic of the genre, introduces the reader to hobbits and their culture in Middle-Earth. As the tale develops, we are to meet characters that step into Bilbo's adventure out of folk legend and fairy story: a wizard, dwarfs bent upon revenge and the recovery of a fabulous treasure, trolls, goblins, elves both magical and dangerous, a bear-man changeling, and above all the great dragon Smaug. Much of the story's success depends upon the way in which Tolkien introduces us to the character of Bilbo Baggins, the hobbit whose uneventful life as a comfortable bachelor at Bag End is forever upset by the intervention of Gandalf the wizard who leads Thorin Oakenshield and his company of dwarfs to Bilbo's door with the promise that Bilbo will prove to be a daring and resourceful burglar, and just the person needed to win back the treasure of the dwarfs from Smaug. Bilbo is an unwilling adventurer who loves his comfortable hobbit hole and his reputation as a respectable member of a community of innocent, good-natured burghers. Tolkien manages successfully the difficult task of keeping the comic dimensions of Bilbo's character pleasantly in focus while at the same time developing the equally endearing qualities of good humor, humility, moral courage, and a temperate mind.

In the course of the action, two things are happening. The first is the discovery of the shape, constitution, and nature of Middle-Earth and its wondrous if sometimes menacing inhabitants. Tolkien opens a prospect of unexplored territory in fairyland, and rarely misses an opportunity to enrich the reader's imagination with new and permanent boundary markers. The second is that, in the course of the action, Bilbo comes to discover his limitations but also his own powers and his place in the wide world. Tolkien has shaped the action of Bilbo's quest as correlative to the experience of growing up. His adventures remind us of the solicitude of a wise parent: be yourself, trust your instincts for good, overcome your belittling fears, be generous and brave always, be courteous, especially in strange company or in foreign lands, be resourceful, and the world will discover your worth and praise your accomplishments, and you will be numbered with the mighty and powerful.

Since Bilbo's initiation into life is one of the substructures shaping this narrative, part of his learning experience comes from rubbing elbows with creatures of other kinds and species. He learns about the special virtues, powers, and shortcomings of dwarfs, elves, orcs, goblins, wizards, and men. He learns a bit of the history and lore of Middle-Earth and of the polite conventions that make common action possible between variant races and species. In learning these things, Bilbo comes to understand himself better as a hobbit and to see his place and that of his kind in the great scheme of things, although the full revelation of that place awaits *The Lord of the Rings.* Bilbo learns to his surprise, discomfort, and eventual satisfaction that he has a role to play in life and in the great adventures of the wide world—even of the wild world.

Tolkien made a revision of *The Hobbit* after he had completed the trilogy *The Lord of the Rings.* The revision was a major one, raising the tone and characterization considerably above the original child's story level to the threshold of the legendary, making it more consistent with the great sequel to which, in a way, it gave birth. Tolkien also made some adjustments in the details of the original story so as to bring them into line with the more serious mythology of the trilogy.

In the end, the greatness of the trilogy has to be assessed on the basis of what Tolkien attempted. The trilogy is, of course, fantasy, an extension of the fairy-story elements of *The Hobbit* into the heroic tradition. Some critics have called it "high fantasy," others myth, still others saga, legend, even science fiction and "super science fiction." Tolkien himself described the trilogy as "feigned history," and as such it is best understood. Feigned history is imagined history, which is not at all the same thing as imaginary history.

The appearance of *Unfinished Tales of Númenór and Middle-Earth* and *The History of Middle-Earth* throws new light on Christopher Tolkien's extraordinary contributions as editor of *The Silmarillion* and offers sufficient background evidence that *The Silmarillion* continued to mature in Tolkien's mind as much after the writing of *The Lord of the Rings* as before. Although the published *The Silmarillion* is unfinished and not the work the author hoped to produce, what we have is incomparable. *The Silmarillion* is best read as the scripture and legendary history of the elves. Nor is it presumed that the history was all given in the same voice, style, or at the same moment. All three of the major branches of the elves (Vanyar, Noldor, Teleri) seem to have their temperaments represented in the various books: the Vanyar in "Ainulindale," the Teleri in "Valaquenta," and the Noldor in "Quenta Silmarillion." As such, *The Silmarillion* is Tolkien's elvish scripture, a feigned sacred writing: the revelation, lore, and practice from which we are to surmise those myths and legends grew that gave birth eventually to the hobbit records of the last war against Sauron in *The Lord of the Rings.* The feigned history of *The Lord of the Rings* which includes its own epic-heroic-legendary transformation now ultimately rests upon the elvish revelations of *The Silmarillion.* If the gods be absent from *The Lord of the Rings,* as many critics once complained (even though gods are very much felt), they are present and immanent in *The Silmarillion.*

Clearly, *The Silmarillion* is the foundation of Tolkien's Middle-Earth and everything in it. He began writing parts of the Silmaril mythos before he went off to World War I, declaring to his future wife and to friends that his intention was to create a mythology for England. *The Silmarillion* was to be an English epic fit to rival Homer and Virgil, the stated ambition of every major English poet since Spenser. As the other poets, Tolkien rests his epic claims on language, but in his case it is not merely the narrative language but the languages of the subtexts of Middle-Earth. In the case of *The Silmarillion,* especially elvish. More than any work of its type, *The Silmarillion* grew out of language, both received and invented.

Tolkien's genius for naming grew directly out of his interest in developing imaginary languages spoken by beings all the more imaginary for dwelling in the world of faerie. Tolkien's world is the backward extension of the one we know from romance, legend, folklore, and fairy tale. Thus the revelation at the beginning of "Ainulindale" that the elvish name for Eru, the creator, was Iluvatar is revelation indeed, but perhaps more of elvishness than divinity. Tolkien is at his best when working at the roots of words and at the heart of languages wherein the inquiring mind discovers itself reflected in its most basic operations. Thus, the Tolkien power of name-giving is reflexive, revealing both the thing named and the namer—here the elves—but it stirs hidden responses in the receptive reader to the universal sense of the power of names, when they are the right names. And Tolkien is almost infallibly right in his naming, perhaps because his inspirations come from an understanding of the nature and practice of language similar to that which a scientist might develop after long study of the secrets of nature. Inventing names is Tolkien's chief (but not only) method of activating the power of language structures to both quicken the imagination and convey the assurance that existence follows upon the name, as indeed in Tolkien's world it truly does.

We cannot separate Tolkien's interest in and experiments with languages both real and imagined from his vision of faerie, a vision that grew with his exploration of its imaginative potential. Tolkien revealed that the vision was in his words "a gift," and it remained for him all his life a hobby and a pastime, bound up with both his scholarship as an Oxford don and his parenting of his own children. Many of the key episodes that anchored *The Silmarillion* in Tolkien's imagination were visions, visual images, which Tolkien felt he was obliged to find the explanation of. He always held that Middle-Earth was a world discovered rather than dreamed up. It was to be found in the logic of cause and effect: an imagined language extended itself necessarily to ethology, and thence to geology, geography, botany, zoology and so on, producing the coherent infrastructures of a realized secondary world suited to the imagination.

No critical estimate of Tolkien and *The Silmarillion* would be worth producing without a word on style. Thanks to the publication of some of the earlier drafts of Silmarillion materials, we can assess the process by which Tolkien's mature style developed. How fortunate literature has been that Tolkien's elvish mythology did not enjoy an early success. The early drafts are discovered to be stylistically mannered, artificial in the bad sense, and feebly imitative of 19th-century aesthetic models. As Tolkien's imagination expanded so did the range of his style. Finally, he found the proper voices for his elves in *The Silmarillion,* which contains elements of the most lyrical prose ever written in English. *The Silmarillion* is, moreover, rich in sustained, inspired story-telling, in mythic and epic elements that range from the literature of revelation to the tragic beauty of elvin history in Middle-Earth, an accounting of a species exiled by fate and by choice from felicity. In addition to numerous instances in the published version of *The Silmarillion,* readers should not overlook two jewels of heroic and tragic narrative reaching that rarest of all literary achievements, the sublime, in the stories of Tuor and Turin, both found in *Unfinished Tales.*

*The Lord of the Rings* and *The Silmarillion* are not merely great fantasy; they are great literature. Tolkien will continue to interest scholars and students who have already begun the exhaustive study of his work, its sources, inspirations, and its elements. There is little doubt that Tolkien will eventually take his place somewhere in the neo-romantic movement which followed the aestheticism and decadence of the late 19th century. He has already been placed in the tradition of writers like Rider Haggard and William Morris, and the influences of the Eddas, the Kalevala, Anglo-Saxon, and Middle English romance have already been noted and will doubtless yield more secrets in the future. Nor should we ignore the influence of the Inklings and their interest in Tolkien's work during the long, difficult years before recognition came. Other students will consider the relation or at least the parallels to contemporary writers of fantasy like Mervyn Peake and Austin Tappan Wright. In the end, it may be that Tolkien will be understood best when linked and compared to James Joyce, an unlikely pairing, perhaps, but one that is full of telling comparisons and contrasts.

—Donald L. Lawler

---

**TORRO, Pel.** *See* **FANTHORPE, R. Lionel.**

---

**TRENT, Olaf.** *See* **FANTHORPE, R. Lionel.**

---

**TRIMBLE, Louis (Preston).** Also wrote as Stuart Brock; Gerry Travis. American. Born in Seattle, Washington, 2 March 1917. Educated at Eastern Washington State College, Cheney, B.A. 1950, Ed.M. 1953; University of Washington, Seattle, 1952–53, 1955, 1956–57; University of Pennsylvania, Philadelphia, 1955–56. Served as an editor in the United States Army Corps of Engineers Architects Division. Married 1) Renee Eddy in 1938 (died, 1951), one daughter; 2) Jacquelyn Whitney in 1952; 3) Mary Todd in 1974. English teacher, Bonners Ferry High School, Idaho, 1946–47; instructor in Spanish and English, Eastern Washington State College, 1950–54; Instructor, 1956–59, Assistant Professor, 1959–65, Associate Professor, 1965–76, and Professor of Humanities and Social Studies, 1976–80, University of Washington. Participated in English as a Second Language Seminars in Yugoslavia, 1972–74, 1976. Member of the Executive Board, Western Writers of America, 1963–64. *Died 9 March 1988.*

### Science-Fiction Publications

#### Novels

*Anthropol.* New York, Ace, 1968.
*The Noblest Experiment in the Galaxy.* New York, Ace, 1970.
*Guardians of the Gate*, with Jacqueline Trimble. New York, Ace, 1972.
*The City Machine.* New York, DAW, 1972.
*The Wandering Variables.* New York, DAW, 1972.
*The Bodelan Way.* New York, DAW, 1974.

### Other Publications

#### Novels

*Fit to Kill.* New York, Phoenix Press, 1941.
*Date for Murder.* New York, Phoenix Press, 1942.
*Tragedy in Turquoise.* New York, Phoenix Press, 1942.
*Design for Dying.* New York, Phoenix Press, 1945.
*Murder Trouble.* New York, Phoenix Press, 1945; London, Wells Gardner, 1949.
*Give Up the Body.* Seattle, Superior, 1946.
*You Can't Kill a Corpse.* New York, Phoenix Press, 1946.
*Valley of Violence.* Philadelphia, Macrae Smith, 1948; London, Corgi, 1951.
*The Case of the Blank Cartridge.* New York, Phoenix Press, 1949.
*The Tide Can't Wait.* New York, Bouregy, 1949; London, Wright and Brown, 1959.
*Gunsmoke Justice.* Philadelphia, Macrae Smith, 1950; London, Corgi, 1951.
*Blonds Are Skin Deep.* New York, Lion, 1950.
*Gaptown Law.* Philadelphia, Macrae Smith, 1950.
*Fighting Cowman.* New York, Popular, 1952; Manchester, World Distributors, 1956.
*Crossfire.* New York, Avalon, 1953.
*Bullets on Bunchgrass.* New York, Avalon, 1954.
*Stab in the Dark.* New York, Ace, 1956.
*The Virgin Victim.* New York, Mercury, 1956.
*Nothing to Lose But My Life.* New York, Ace, 1957.
*Mountain Ambush.* New York, Avalon, 1958.
*The Smell of Trouble.* New York, Ace, 1958.
*Cargo for the Styx.* New York, Ace, 1959.
*The Corpse Without a Country.* New York, Ace, 1959.
*Obit Deferred.* New York, Ace, 1959.
*Til Death Do Us Part.* New York, Ace, 1959.
*The Duchess of Skid Row.* New York, Ace, 1960.
*Girl on a Slay Ride.* New York, Avon, 1960.
*Love Me and Die.* New York, Ace, 1960.
*Deadman and Canyon.* New York, Ace, 1961.
*Montana Gun.* New York, Hillman, 1961; London, White Lion, 1972.
*The Surfside Caper.* New York, Ace, 1961.
*Siege at High Meadow.* New York, Ace, 1962; Bath, Chivers, 1992.
*The Dead and the Deadly.* New York, Ace, 1963.
*The Man from Colorado.* New York, Ace, 1963.
*Wild Horse Range.* New York, Ace, 1963.
*Trouble at Gunsight.* New York, Ace, 1964.
*The Desperate Deputy of Cougar Hill.* New York, Ace, 1965; London, Severn House, 1979.
*The Holdout in the Diablos.* New York, Ace, 1965.
*Showdown in the Cayuse.* New York, Ace, 1966.
*Standoff at Massacre Buttes.* New York, Ace, 1967.
*Marshal of Sangaree.* New York, Ace, 1968.
*West to the Pecos.* New York, Ace, 1968.
*The Hostile Peaks.* New York, Ace, 1969; London, Severn House, 1979.
*Trouble Valley.* New York, Ace, 1970; London, Severn House, 1979.
*The Lonesome Mountains.* New York, Ace, 1970.
*The Ragbag Army.* New York, Ace, 1971.

#### Novels as Gerry Travis

*Tarnished Love.* New York, Phoenix Press, 1942.
*A Lovely Mask for Murder.* New York, Avalon, 1956.
*The Big Bite.* New York, Avalon, 1957.

#### Novels as Stuart Brock

*Death Is My Lover.* New York, Mill, 1948.
*Just Around the Coroner.* New York, Mill, 1948.
*Railtown Sheriff.* New York, Bouregy, 1949; London, Barker, 1959.
*Bring Back Her Body.* New York, Ace, 1953.
*Double-Cross Ranch.* New York, Avalon, 1954; London, Barker, 1957.
*Action at Boundary Peak.* New York, Avalon, 1955.
*Whispering Canyon.* New York, Avalon, 1955.
*Forbidden Range.* New York, Avalon, 1956.
*Killer's Choice.* New York, Graphic, 1956.

Other

*Sports of the World*. Los Angeles, Golden West, 1938.
*Working Papers in English for Science and Technology*, with Robert Bley-Vroman and Larry Selinker. Seattle, University of Washington, 1972.
*New Horizons: A Reader in Scientific and Technical English*, (and *Teachers' Guide*), with others. Zagreb, Skolska Knjiga, 2 vols., 1975.
*Course Materials for Non-Native Speakers Planning to Enter U.S. Universities to Study Science or Technology*, with Mary Todd Trimble. San Francisco, Pacific American Institute, 1977.
*English for Multinational Business*, with Mary Todd Trimble. Washington, D.C., International Communication Agency, 1978.
*English for Science and Technology: A Discourse Approach*. Cambridge and New York, Cambridge University Press, 1985.

Editor, *Criteria for Highway Benefit Analysis*. Seattle, University of Washington-National Academy of Sciences, 3 vols., 1964–65; revised edition, with Robert G. Hennes, Washington, D.C., National Highway Research Board, 1966–67.
Editor, *Incorporation of Shelter into Apartments and Office Buildings*. Washington, D.C., Office of Civil Defense, 1965.
Editor, with Karl Drobnic and Mary Todd Trimble, *English for Specific Purposes: Scientific and Technical English*. Corvalis, Oregon State University Press, 1978.

*

Bibliography: in *English for Academic and Technical Purposes: Studies in Honor of Louis Trimble* edited by Larry Selinker and others, Rowley, Massachusetts, Newbury House, 1981.

Manuscript Collections: University of Oregon Library, Eugene; University of Wyoming, Laramie.

Louis Trimble commented:

The basic purpose of my science fiction is to entertain while at the same time commenting on some of the unchanging characteristics of humans. I have chosen one of the least complicated ways of showing this—by setting my books several thousand years in the future, when "earth-originated" people have spread throughout the galaxy, colonizing. In some cases they conquered and at times displaced native peoples; in others living harmoniously with them or mixing (when possible). By using this galaxy and this time period in all of my books, I hope to show that in several thousand years there has been little change in political attitudes, social attitudes, and—in fact—the way people act and think.

* * *

Louis Trimble made his debut as a science-fiction novelist in 1968 with the publication of *Anthropol.* Trimble has mastered one form of the futuristic novel, the lyrical fantasy, quite handily. Especially entertaining are *The Wandering Variables, The City Machine*, and *The Bodelan Way*, books which share a motif of whimsical fantasy underpinning the rather standard fare of futuristic gadgetry and intergalactic conflict. In each the setting reminds one of the more familiar works of C.S. Lewis and Jules Verne; there are botanical wildernesses, shimmering islands, stark winter steppes, deep pools, and medieval valleys.

The lyrical tone is a result of the presence of fantastic goddesses, women of divine birth or superior knowledge, who accompany kind-hearted and competent, if somewhat insecure, males on their adventures. Because Trimble's novels transpire under this divine feminine sanction, the gratuitous violence typical of so much popular science fiction is diminished, and in its place has come the spirit of romance. His books move from loss to reacquisition, from discord to harmony, from problem to solution.

However, Trimble often achieves the effect of romance at the expense of sound narrative construction. There is frequently too much fortuitous coincidence in his books, too many miraculous rescues of the protagonists, too little real threat of failure or death. We are too rarely awe-struck by what happens and too often left incredulous. Neither are his romances of the heart or of the head: his problems tend to be created and resolved by machines rather than by human experience. The problem for Trimble's characters is always to escape physical threat or to build a new city or to return to a familiar planet. Thus only rarely, as in the final scenes of *The Bodelan Way* and *Guardians of the Gate*, does the solution involve the emotional or intellectual growth we demand of first-rate fiction. There is altogether too little development of Trimble's characters and too little engagement of our deeper human sympathies in his situations. Another difficulty arises from the fact that Trimble's novels sometimes cannot sustain their futurism through an entire narrative. In particular, *The Wandering Variables* and *The City Machine* retain their futurism only through the initial phase of exposition before finding their true subject in earth's Middle Ages. At the center of these books are dirt floors, oxdrawn carts, and bellicose medieval clans. Consequently, one feels that in these books science fiction is more peripheral than central, more a vehicle to Trimble's real interest, which is in the past rather than the future.

Nevertheless, through more than 50 books Trimble developed a prose style which is elaborate yet efficient, and vividly descriptive yet never excessive. Like so many others, his narratives are fastpaced and full of action, yet one does not have the sensation that their pace and action are purely an exploitation of commercial appeal. More often, one feels that though Trimble's novels may fall short of the very best, his concern with the remote future is sincere and his imagination sufficient to include the human condition in that future. For young readers initiating themselves into the worlds of futuristic literature, Trimble's works are fine preparation for the more distant and rewarding vision of Lewis and others like him.

—Marvin W. Hunt

---

**TROUT, Kilgore.** *See* **FARMER, Philip Jose.**

---

**TUBB, E(dwin) C(harles).** British. Also writes as Chuck Adams; Stuart Allen; Anthony Armstrong; Ted Bain; Alice Beecham; Anthony Blake; L.T. Bronson; Raymond L. Burton; Morley Carpenter; Julian Carey; Jud Cary; Julian Cary; J.F. Clarkson; Norman Dale; Robert D. Ennis; James Evans; James S. Farrow; James R. Fenner; R.H. Godfrey; Charles S. Graham; Charles Grey; Volsted Gridban; Alan Guthrie; D.W.R. Hill; George Holt; Gill Hunt; Alan (or Allan) Innes; E.F. Jackson; Gordon Kent; Gregory Kern; King Lang; Mike Lantry; P. Lawrence; Chet Lawson; Nigel Lloyd; Robert Lloyd; Frank T. Lomas; Ron Lowam; Arthur Maclean; Carl Maddox; Philip Martyn; John Mason; Carl Moulton; L.C. Powers; M.L. Powers;

Edward Richards; Paul Schofield; John Seabright; Brian Shaw; Roy Sheldon; John Stevens; Eric Storm; Andrew Sutton; Edward Thomson; Ken Wainwright; Frank Weight; Douglas West; Eric Wilding; Frank Winnard. British. Born in London, 15 October 1919. Married Iris Kathleen Smith in 1944; two daughters. Has worked as a welfare officer, catering manager, and printing machine salesman. Editor, *Authentic Science Fiction*, London, 1956–57, and *Eye and Vector*, 1958–60. Recipient: Cytricon award, 1955; Eurocon award, 1972. Guest of Honor, World Science Fiction Convention, Heidelberg, 1970. Agent: Carnell Literary Agency, Danescroft, Goose Lane, Little Hallingbury, Bishop's Stortford, Herts. CM22 7RG. Address: 67 Houston Road, London SE23 2RL, England.

SCIENCE-FICTION PUBLICATIONS

Novels (series: Dumarest; Space 1999)

*Saturn Patrol* (as King Lang). London, Curtis, 1951.
*Planetfall* (as Gill Hunt). London, Curtis, 1951.
*Argentis* (as Brian Shaw). London, Curtis, 1952.
*Alien Impact*. London, Hamilton, 1952.
*Atom War on Mars*. London, Panther, 1952.
*The Mutants Rebel*. London, Panther, 1953.
*Venusian Adventure*. London, Comyns, 1953.
*Alien Life*. London, Paladin, 1954.
*The Living World* (as Carl Maddox). London, Pearson, 1954.
*World at Bay*. London, Panther, 1954.
*The Metal Eater* (as Roy Sheldon). London, Panther, 1954.
*Journey to Mars*. London, Scion, 1954.
*Menace from the Past* (as Carl Maddox). London, Pearson, 1954.
*City of No Return*. London, Scion, 1954.
*The Stellar Legion*. London, Scion, 1954.
*The Hell Planet*. London, Scion, 1954.
*The Resurrected Man*. London, Scion, 1954.
*Alien Dust*. London, Boardman, 1955; New York, Avalon, 1957.
*The Space-Born*. New York, Ace, 1956; London, Digit, 1961.
*Touch of Evil* (as Arthur Maclean). London, Fleetway, 1959.
*Moon Base*. London, Jenkins, and New York, Ace, 1964.
*Death Is a Dream*. London, Hart Davis, and New York, Ace, 1967.
*The Winds of Gath* (Dumarest). New York, Ace, 1967; as *Gath*, London, Hart Davis, 1968.
*C.O.D. Mars*. New York, Ace, 1968.
*Derai* (Dumarest). New York, Ace, 1968; London, Arrow, 1973.
*S.T.A.R. Flight*. New York, Paperback Library, 1969; London, Hale, 1980.
*Toyman* (Dumarest). New York, Ace, 1969; London, Arrow, 1973.
*Escape into Space*. London, Sidgwick and Jackson, 1969.
*Kalin* (Dumarest). New York, Ace, 1969; London, Arrow, 1973.
*The Jester at Scar* (Dumarest). New York, Ace, 1970; London, Arrow, 1977.
*Lallia* (Dumarest). New York, Ace, 1971; London, Arrow, 1977.
*Technos* (Dumarest). New York, Ace, 1972; London, Arrow, 1977.
*Century of the Manikin*. New York, DAW, 1972 London, Millington, 1975.
*Mayenne* (Dumarest). New York, DAW, 1973; London, Arrow, 1977.
*Veruchia* (Dumarest). New York, Ace, 1973; London, Arrow, 1977.
*Jondelle* (Dumarest). New York, DAW, 1973; London, Arrow, 1977.
*Zenya* (Dumarest). New York, DAW, 1974; London, Arrow, 1978.
*Breakaway* (Space 1999; novelization of TV series). London, Futura, and New York, Pocket Books, 1975.
*Eloise* (Dumarest). New York, DAW, 1975; London, Arrow, 1978.
*Eye of the Zodiac* (Dumarest). New York, DAW, 1975; London, Arrow, 1978.
*Collision Course* (Space 1999; novelization of TV series). London, Futura, 1975; New York, Pocket Books, 1976.
*Jack of Swords* (Dumarest). New York, DAW, 1976; London, Arrow, 1979.
*Alien Seed* (Space 1999; novelization of TV series). New York, Pocket Books, and London, Barker, 1976.
*Spectrum of a Forgotten Sun* (Dumarest). New York, DAW, 1976; London, Arrow, 1980.
*Rogue Planet* (Space 1999; novelization of TV series). New York, Pocket Books, and London, Futura,1976.
*Earthfall* (Space 1999; novelization of TV series). London, Futura, 1977.
*Haven of Darkness* (Dumarest). New York, DAW, 1977; London, Arrow, 1980.
*Prison of Night* (Dumarest). New York, DAW, 1977; London, Arrow, 1980.
*The Primitive*. London, Futura, 1977.
*Incident on Ath* (Dumarest). New York, DAW, 1978.
*The Quillian Sector* (Dumarest). New York, DAW, 1978; London, Arrow, 1982.
*Stellar Assignment*. London, Hale, 1979.
*Web of Sand* (Dumarest). New York, DAW, 1979; London, Arrow, 1983.
*Death Wears a White Face*. London, Hale, 1979.
*Iduna's Universe* (Dumarest). New York, DAW, 1979; London, Arrow, 1985.
*The Luck Machine*. London, Dobson, 1980.
*The Terra Data* (Dumarest). New York, DAW, 1980; London, Arrow, 1985.
*Pawn of the Omphalos*. New York, Fawcett, 1980.
*World of Promise*. New York, DAW, 1980; London, Arrow, 1985.
*Nectar of Heaven*. New York, DAW, 1981; London, Arrow, 1985.
*Earth Is Heaven* (Dumarest). New York, DAW, 1982.
*The Coming Event*. New York, DAW, 1982.
*Stardeath*. New York, Ballantine, 1983.
*Melome* (Dumarest). New York, DAW, 1983.
*Angado* (Dumarest). New York, DAW, 1984.
*Symbol of Terra*. New York, New American Library, 1984.
*The Temple of Truth*. New York, DAW, 1985.

Novels as Volsted Gridban

*Alien Universe*. London, Scion, 1952.
*Reverse Universe*. London, Scion, 1952.
*Planetoid Disposals Ltd*. London, Milestone, 1953.
*De Bracy's Drug*. London, Scion, 1953.
*Fugitive of Time*. London, Milestone, 1953.

Novels as Charles Grey

*The Wall*. London, Milestone, 1953.
*Dynasty of Doom*. London, Milestone, 1953.
*Tormented City*. London, Milestone, 1953.

*Space Hunger*. London, Milestone, 1953.
*I Fight for Mars*. London, Milestone, 1953.
*The Extra Man*. London, Milestone, 1954.
*The Hand of Havoc*. London, Merit, 1954.
*Enterprise 2115*. London, Merit, 1954; as *The Mechanical Monarch (as E.C. Tubb), New York, Ace, 1958.*

Novels as Gregory Kern (series: Cap Kennedy in all books)

*Galaxy of the Lost*. New York, DAW, 1973; London, Mews, 1976.
*Slave Ship from Sergan*. New York, DAW, 1973; London Mews, 1976.
*Monster of Metelaze*. New York, DAW, 1973.
*Enemy Within the Skull*. New York, DAW, 1974.
*Jewel of Jarhen*. New York, DAW, 1974; London, Mews, 1976.
*Seetee Alert!* New York, DAW, 1974; London, Mews, 1976.
*The Gholan Gate*. New York, DAW, 1974.
*The Eater of Worlds*. New York, DAW, 1974.
*Earth Enslaved*. New York, DAW, 1974.
*Planet of Dread*. New York, DAW, 1974.
*Spawn of Laban*. New York, DAW, 1974.
*The Genetic Buccaneer*. New York, DAW, 1974.
*A World Aflame*. New York, DAW, 1974.
*The Ghosts of Epidoris*. New York, DAW, 1975.
*Mimics of Dephene*. New York, DAW, 1975.
*Beyond the Galactic Lens*. New York, DAW, 1975.
*Das Kosmiche Duelle*. Bergisch Gladbach, Germany, Bastei, 1976.
*The Galactiad*. New York, DAW, 1983.

Novels as Edward Thomson (series: Atilus in all books)

*Atilus the Slave*. London, Futura, 1975.
*Atilus the Gladiator*. London, Futura, 1975.
*Gladiator*. London, Futura, 1978.

Short Stories

*Ten from Tomorrow*. London, Hart Davis, 1966.
*A Scatter of Stardust*. New York, Ace, 1972; London, Dobson, 1976.

Uncollected Short Stories

"No Short Cuts," in *New Worlds 10* (London), Summer 1951.
"Greek Gift," in *New Worlds 11* (London), Autumn 1951.
"Grounded," in *Science Fantasy* (Bournemouth), Winter 1951.
"Third Party," in *New Worlds 14* (London), March 1952.
"Alien Impact," in *Authentic* (London), May 1952.
"First Effort" (as L.T. Bronson), in *Worlds of Fantasy* (London), September 1952.
"Heroes Don't Cry" (as Gordon Kent), in *New Worlds 19* (London), January 1953.
"Dark Solution," in *Nebula* (Glasgow), Spring 1953.
"Confessional," in *Science Fantasy* (Bournemouth), Spring 1953.
"Freight," in *Nebula* (Glasgow), Summer 1953.
"Lone Wolf" (as Eric Storm), in *Authentic* (London), August 1953.
"The Pilot," in *Nebula* (Glasgow), Autumn 1953.
"The Troublemaker," in *Nebula* (Glasgow), September 1953.
"Conversation Piece," in *Authentic* (London), October 1953.
"Subtle Victory," in *Authentic* (London), November 1953.
"Tea Party," in *Nebula* (Glasgow), December 1953.
"The Inevitable Conflict," in *Vargo Statten's Science Fiction Magazine* (Luton, Bedfordshire), January 1954.
"Test Piece" (as Morley Carpenter), in *Vargo Statten's Science Fiction Magazine* (Luton, Bedfordshire), February 1954.
"Emancipation," in *Nebula* (Glasgow), February 1954.
"Sword of Tormain" (as Eric Storm), in *Planet* (New York), March 1954.
"Episode," in *Nebula* (Glasgow), April 1954.
"Death Deferred," in *Authentic* (London), May 1954.
"Tomorrow," in *Science Fantasy* (Bournemouth), May 1954.
"Illusion" (as Anthony Armstrong) and "Forbidden Fruit," in *Vargo Statten's Science Fiction Magazine* (Luton, Bedfordshire), May 1954.
"Occupational Hazard," in *Science Fantasy* (Bournemouth), July 1954.
"Project One," in *Nebula* (Glasgow), August 1954.
"Logic," in *Authentic* (London), September 1954.
"Homeward Bound" (as Anthony Armstrong), in *British Science Fiction Magazine* (Luton, Bedfordshire), September 1954.
"Hidden Treasure of Kalin," in *Authentic* (London), October 1954.
"Closing Time," in *Nebula* (Glasgow), October 1954.
"Into Thy Hands," in *New Worlds 29* (London), November 1954.
"Star Haven," in *Authentic* (London), December 1954.
"The Robbers," in *New Worlds 30* (London), December 1954.
"The Enemy Within Us," in *Science Fantasy* (Bournemouth), December 1954.
"Death-Wish" (as Eric Wilding) and "Nonentity," in *Authentic* (London), February 1955.
"School for Beginners," in *New Worlds 32* (London), February 1955.
"Lover, Where Art Thou?" (as Alice Beecham) and "Murder Most Innocent," in *Authentic* (London), March 1955.
"Snowflake," in *Flying Review*, March 1955.
"The Veterans" (as Norman Dale), in *New Worlds 33* (London), March 1955.
"Poor Henry," in *Science Fantasy* (Bournemouth), April 1955.
"Forgetfulness" (as Phillip Martyn) and "No Place for Tears" (as R.H. Godfrey), in *New Worlds 34* (London), April 1955.
"Agent," in *Science Fantasy* (Bournemouth), June 1955.
"Ethical Assassin," in *Authentic* (London), June 1955.
"Perac," in *New Worlds 37* (London), July 1955.
"Decision," in *Authentic* (London), August 1955.
"See No Evil," in *New Worlds 38* (London), August 1955.
"One Every Minute," in *Authentic* (London), September 1955.
"Planetbound," in *Nebula* (Glasgow), September 1955.
"The Predators," in *Science Fantasy* (Bournemouth), September 1955.
"That Zamboni," in *Authentic* (London), October 1955.
"Unwanted Eden" (as Eric Wilding) and "The Shell Game," in *Authentic* (London), November 1955.
"Quis Custodiet," in *Nebula* (Glasgow), November 1955.
"Venus for Never," in *Authentic* (London), December 1955.
"Prime Essential" (as Frank Weight) and "Lawyer at Large," in *New Worlds 42* (London), December 1955.
"Mistake on Mars," in *Authentic* (London), January 1956.
"Investment," in *Nebula* (Glasgow), January 1956.
"When He Died" (as Anthony Blake), in *Authentic* (London), February 1956.
"Asteroids," in *Authentic* (London), February 1956.
"The Moron" (as John Seabright) and "Dying to Live," in *Nebula* (Glasgow), March 1956.
"Man in Between" (as Carl Moulton) and "A Woman's Work," in *Authentic* (London), March 1956.
"Tailor Made" (as Anthony Blake), in *Authentic* (London), March 1956.
"Time to Kill," in *Galaxy* (New York), April 1956.

"The Letter" (as Alice Beecham) and "Secret Weapon" (as Frank T. Lomas), in *Authentic* (London), April 1956.
"Like a Diamond" (as Alice Beecham), in *Authentic* (London), June 1956.
"Into the Empty Dark," in *Nebula* (Glasgow), July 1956.
"Wishful Thinking" (as Carl Moulton), in *Authentic* (London), July 1956.
"Reluctant Farmer," in *Nebula* (Glasgow), November 1956.
"Mistaken Identity" (as D.W.R. Hill), in *Science Fantasy* (Bournemouth), December 1956.
"YOU Go," in *Galaxy* (New York), December 1956.
"Special Pleading" (as Phillip Martyn) and "A Fine Day for Dying," in *Science Fantasy* (Bournemouth), February 1957.
"Man of Imagination," in *Nebula* (Glasgow), March 1957.
"The Devil's Dictionary" (as Edward Richards), "The Ancient Alchemist" (as John Mason), "The Artists' Model" (as Robert D. Ennis), "The Witch of Peronia" (as L.C. Powers), "The Dolmen" (as Raymond L. Burton), and "Snake Vengeance" (as Andrew Sutton), all in *Supernatural Stories*, April 1957.
"Ad Infinitum," in *Science Fantasy* (Bournemouth), June 1957.
"Sentimental Journey," in *Nebula* (Glasgow), August 1957.
"Food for Friendship," in *Authentic* (London), August 1957.
"Second from the Sun" (as Ron Lowam) and "Linda" (as James Evans), in *Authentic* (London), September 1957.
"Pride of Possession" (as Ron Lowam), in *Authentic* (London), October 1957.
"Training Aid," in *Nebula* (Glasgow), January 1958.
"Requiem for a Harvey," in *New Worlds 68* (London), February 1958.
"The Touch of Reality," in *Nebula* (Glasgow), March 1958.
"The Wanton Jade," in *Nebula* (Glasgow), May 1958.
"The Beatific Smile," in *Nebula* (Glasgow), June 1958.
"Way Out" (as Robert Lloyd), "Conflagration" (as Stuart Allen), and "Talk Not at All," in *Nebula* (Glasgow), August 1958.
"Sell Me a Dream" (as Stuart Allen) and "Wallpaper War," in *Nebula* (Glasgow), November 1958.
"Beware?," in *Science Fantasy* (Bournemouth), December 1958.
"Somebody Wants You," in *Science Fantasy* (Bournemouth), August 1959.
"Galactic Destiny," in *Science Fiction Adventures* (London), October 1959.
"The Window," in *Science Fantasy* (Bournemouth), November 1959.
"Good-By, Gloria" (as Ted Bain) and "Orange," in *If* (New York), November 1959.
"Man of War," in *New Worlds 93* (London), April 1960.
"Too Bad!," in *Science Fantasy* (Bournemouth), April 1960.
"Grit," in *Science Fiction Adventures* (London), May 1960.
"Iron Head," in *Science Fiction Adventures* (London), September 1960.
"Memories Are Important," in *New Worlds 99* (London), October 1960.
"Umbrella in the Sky," in *Science Fiction Adventures* (London), January 1961.
"Gigolo," in *New Worlds 104* (London), March 1961.
"Jackpot," in *New Worlds 107* (London), June 1961.
"The Seekers," in *New Writings in SF6*, edited by E.H. Carnell. London, Dobson, 1965; New York, Bantam, 1971.
"The Life Buyer," in *New Worlds 149* (London), April 1965.
"An Answer for Augustus," in *Tangent*, September 1965.
"Boomerang," in *Science Fantasy* (Bournemouth), September 1965.
"State of Mind," in *Science Fantasy* (Bournemouth), October 1965.
"As Others See Us," in *Science Fantasy* (Bournemouth), December 1965.
"In Vino Veritas," in *Science Fantasy* (Bournemouth), January 1966.
"Sing Me No Sorrows," in *Science Fantasy* (Bournemouth), February 1966.
"Secret Weapon," in *New Worlds 162* (London), May 1966.
"Quarry," in *Vision of Tomorrow* (Sydney), December 1969.
"Trojan Horse," in *Vision of Tomorrow* (Sydney), January 1970.
"Full-Five," in *Vision of Tomorrow* (Sydney), March 1970.
"A Matter of Survival," in *Vision of Tomorrow* (Sydney), June 1970.
"Spawn of Jupiter," in *Vision of Tomorrow* (Sydney), August 1970.
"The Winner," in *New Writing in Horror and the Supernatural I*, edited by David Sutton. London, Sphere, 1971.
"Mistaken Identity," in *Space 1*, edited by Richard Davis. London, Abelard Schuman, 1973.
"Death God's Doom," in *Witchcraft and Sorcery* (Alhambra, California), Winter 1973.
"Lazarus," in *Beyond This Horizon*, edited by Christopher Carrell. Sunderland, Ceolfrith Press, 1974.
"Made to Be Broken," in *New Writings in SF 23*, edited by Kenneth Bulmer. London, Sidgwick and Jackson, 1974.
"Face to Infinity," in *New Writings in SF 28*, edited by Kenneth Bulmer. London, Dobson, 1976.
"Random Sample," in *New Writings in SF 29*, edited by Kenneth Bulmer. London, Sidgwick and Jackson, 1976.
"Block-Buster," in *Diversifier* (Oroville, California), July 1976.
"Read Me This Riddle," in *New Writings in SF 30*, edited by Kenneth Bulmer. London, Corgi, 1978.
"The Captain's Dog," in *The Androids Are Coming*, edited by Robert Silverberg. New York, Elsevier Nelson, 1979.
"Blood in the Mist," in *Heroic Fantasy*, edited by Gerald W. Page and Hank Reinhardt. New York, DAW, 1979.

Uncollected Short Stories as Charles Grey

"Intrigue on Io," in *Tales of Tomorrow* (London), September 1952.
"There's No Tomorrow," in *Worlds of Fantasy* (London), September 1952.
"Helping Hand," in *Wonders of the Spaceways* (London), December 1952.
"Honour Bright," in *Futuristic* (London), August 1953.
"Visiting Celebrity," in *Futuristic* (London), November 1953.
"Museum Piece," in *Futuristic* (London), Spring 1954.
"Accolade," in *New Writings in SF 23*, edited by Kenneth Bulmer. London, Sidgwick and Jackson, 1974.

Uncollected Short Stories as George Holt

"Emergency Exit," in *British Science Fiction Magazine* (Luton, Bedfordshire), September 1954.
"Skin Deep," in *British Science Fiction Magazine* (Luton, Bedfordshire), December 1954.
"Oversight," in *British Science Fiction Magazine* (Luton, Bedfordshire), March 1955.
"Brutus," in *Authentic* (London), April 1955.
"Kalgan the Golden," in *British Space Fiction Magazine* (Luton, Bedfordshire), August 1955.
"Lost Property," in British Space Fiction Magazine (Luton, Bedfordshire), December 1955.
"The Answer," in *British Space Fiction Magazine* (Luton, Bedfordshire), February 1956.

Uncollected Short Stories as Julian Carey or Julian Cary

"Repair Job," May 1955, "Blow the Man Down," October 1955, "Cure for Dreamers," April 1956, "The Give-Away Worlds," August 1956, and "Combination Calamitous," January 1957, all in *Authentic* (London).

Uncollected Short Stories as Alan Guthrie

"Samson," in *New Worlds 35* (London), May 1955.
"No Space for Me," in *New Worlds 37* (London), July 1955.
"Dear Ghost," in *Science Fantasy* (Bournemouth), September 1955.
"The Pensioners," in *New Worlds 43* (London), January 1956.
"Emergency Call," in *New Worlds 45* (London), March 1956.
"Breathing Space," in *Science Fantasy* (Bournemouth), August 1956.
"Thirty-Seven Times," in *New Worlds 55* (London), January 1957.
"The Greater Ideal," in *New Worlds 56* (London), February 1957.

Uncollected Short Stories as Douglas West

"The Dogs of Hanooie," in *Science Fantasy* (Bournemouth), September 1955.
"Number Thirteen," in *Authentic* (London), May 1956.
"Point of View," in *Authentic* (London), July 1956.
"Reward for a Hero," in *Authentic* (London), September 1956.
"Legal Eagle," in *Authentic* (London), December 1956.
"Dead Weight," in *Authentic* (London), March 1957.

Uncollected Short Stories as Ken Wainwright

"Sleeve of Care," February 1956, "The Big Secret," June 1956, "Enemy of the State," November 1956, and "Grzdle," June 1957, all in *Authentic* (London).

Uncollected Short Stories as Frank Winnard

"First Impression," February 1956, "Misplaced Person," July 1956, and "Melly and the Martian," January 1957, all in *Authentic* (London).

Uncollected Short Stories as Alan (or Allan) Innes

"The Long Journey," March 1956, "The Dilettantes," April 1956, "The Spice of Danger," May 1956, "We, The Brave," January 1957, all in *Authentic* (London).

Uncollected Short Stories as Nigel Lloyd

"Upstairs," March 1957, "The Honest Philosopher," April 1957, "Eve No Adam,"May 1957, "There's Only One Winner," June 1957, "Patient of Promise," July 1957, all in *Authentic* (London).

OTHER PUBLICATIONS

Novels

*The Fighting Fury* (as Paul Schofield). London, Spencer, 1955.
*Assignment New York* (as Mike Lantry). London, Spencer, 1955.
*Comanche Capture* (as E.F. Jackson). London, Spencer, 1955.
*Sands of Destiny* (as Jud Cary). London, September, 1955.
*Men of the Long Rifle* (as J.F. Clarkson). London, Spencer, 1955.
*Scourge of the South* (as M.L. Powers). London, Spencer, 1956.
*Vengeance Trail* (as James S. Farrow). London, Spencer, 1956.
*Quest for Quantrell* (as John Stevens). London, Spencer, 1956.
*Trail Blazers* (as Chuck Adams). London, Spencer, 1956.
*Drums of the Prairie* (as P. Lawrence). London, Spencer, 1956.
*Men of the West* (as Chet Lawson). London, Spencer, 1956.
*Wagon Trail* (as Charles S. Graham). London, Spencer, 1957.
*Colt Vengeance* (as James R. Fenner). London, Spencer, 1957.
*Target Death*. London, Micron, 1961.
*Lucky Strike*. London, Fleetway, 1961.
*Calculated Risk*. London, Fleetway, 1961.
*Too Tough to Handle*. London, Fleetway, 1962.
*The Dead Keep Faith*. London, Fleetway, 1962.
*The Spark of Anger*. London, Fleetway, 1962.
*Full Impact*. London, Fleetway, 1962.
*I Vow Vengeance*. London, Fleetway, 1962.
*Gunflash*. London, Fleetway, 1962.
*Hit Back*. London, Fleetway, 1962.
*One Must Die*. London, Fleetway, 1962.
*Suicide Squad*. London, Fleetway, 1962.
*Airbourne Commando*. London, Fleetway, 1963.
*No Higher Stakes*. London, Fleetway, 1963.
*Penalty of Fear*. London, Fleetway, 1963.

*

Bibliography: in *Science Fiction Collector 7*, February 1980.

* * *

The quantity of E.C. Tubb's output can be gauged by the fact that he has used nearly 60 pseudonyms. Since 1951 he has been turning out novels and stories on a monthly basis, occasionally editing on the side; Michael Ashley in *The History of the Science Fiction Magazine* calls Tubb "an inspired fiction machine." His popularity, well established in England, is now sizable in America as well. He is quick to turn ideas into stories set out in hard, clear prose, and many of his plots have been repeated by younger writers, not always with as much success.

Tubb writes of a hostile universe where men seek to dominate each other, and nowhere is it as hostile or extensive as in the Dumarest saga. Stretching now to a score of novels, the long quest of Earl Dumarest for his lost Earth is an effective device for creating science-fiction adventure. Reticent, grim, dressed in grey, and quick with a knife, Dumarest travels from planet to planet pursued by the Cyclan, cold zealots whose emotions have been surgically removed and who are psychically linked to an organic computer of a million embalmed brains. They want Dumarest because he has the secret to another kind of psychic linking, and Dumarest wants his mythical Earth because it is his own home. In effect the books form a 20-novel chase sequence. Some aspects become repetitive—for example, the description of Low and High travelling (frozen vs. time-accelerated) is transferred almost verbatim from book to book. And in each story Dumarest is injured in ghastly detail, which he stoically endures until advanced medicine repairs him. But the planets are different—vivid landscapes and weathers similar only in their exoticism and their environmental exacerbation of the baser emotions. There is also range in the interpersonal plots. Sometimes Dumarest finds friends, sometimes only enemies; sometimes the lush women (all of whom desire him) have to be taught a lesson, and sometimes they do not; and in *Jondelle*, with creditable devotion, Dumarest defends a child. All this escapes being ludicrous through the stolid understatement in Tubb's competent style, and through the character of Dumarest himself, who is so determined and so quiet that he remains something of an enigma even after repeated adventures. That he has no sense of humor can be attributed to the desperate situations his author devises for him, situations in which genuine heroism can only consist of bleak courage and violent action.

Violence is important to Tubb; his interest in it is conscious and explicitly defended, not only in the Dumarest series but in novels like *Century of the Manikin* as well. The "manikins" are people who have been conditioned to believe violence is wrong. They live on a decadent, drug-controlled Earth where sex is so free that the only secret pleasure is violent. It takes a 20th-century woman, thawed out from cryogenic sleep, to tell them that men need weapons and honest fighting in order to be truly masculine and alive. Like almost every woman in Tubb's books, she finds male combat sexually exciting. But violence is not Tubb's only theme, however much it motivates his characters. His plots cover the full range of traditional science fiction, from first-contact riddles like "Random Sample," to sad tales of awakening computers like "J Is for Jeanne," and even to mood pieces like "The Last Day of Summer," where a man waits for the Bureau of Euthanasia. Tubb can also play with concepts of time and space; in *S.T.A.R. Flight* the instantaneous transport Gates of the dictatorial Kaltich are a puzzle to be solved, rather bloodily, by Earth's resistance organization.

E.C. Tubb is a good candidate for the theory that science fiction is essentially conservative. Against varying backgrounds of unexplained technology, Tubb talks about the most basic human passions. And however many suns are in the sky, the framework for ethical decision remains the same. For Tubb, the old values matter in the new places—matter more, since the strangeness isolates the grasping nature of men in plainer sight. Dumarest appears as an appropriate alter-ego for a man whose prose is lean and unsentimental. Tubb works in a highly colored imaginative landscape, but like Dumarest he does his job quickly and then moves on, convictions unchanged, to the next world.

—Karen G. Way

---

**TUCKER, (Arthur) Wilson ("Bob").** American. Born in Deer Creek, Illinois, 23 November 1914. Educated at Normal High School, Illinois. Married 1) Mary Jan Joestine in 1937 (divorced 1942); 2) Fern Delores Brookes in 1953; one daughter and four sons. Motion picture projectionist, 1933–72, and electrician for 20th Century Fox and the University of Illinois at Urbana and at Normal. Publisher of many fan magazines: *The Planetoid*, 1932, *Science Fiction News Letter, D'Journal, Le Zombie*, 1938–75, *Fantasy and Weird Fiction*, 1938–39, *Yearbook of Science, Fanewscard Weekly, Fanzine Yearbook*, 1941–45, *Fapa Variety.* President, National Fantasy Fan Federation, 1942–43. Recipient: Hugo award, 1970; John W. Campbell Memorial award, 1976. Guest of Honor, 25th World Science Fiction Convention, 1967. Agent: Curtis Brown, 10 Astor Place, New York, New York 10003, U.S.A.

SCIENCE-FICTION PUBLICATIONS

Novels

*The City in the Sea.* New York, Rinehart, 1951; London, Nova, 1955.
*The Long Loud Silence.* New York, Rinehart, 1952; London, Lane, 1953; revised edition, New York, Lancer, 1970.
*The Time Masters.* New York, Rinehart, 1953; revised edition, New York, Doubleday, 1971; London, Gollancz, 1973.
*Wild Talent.* New York, Rinehart, 1954; London, Joseph, 1955; as *Man from Tomorrow*, New York, Bantam, 1955.
*Time Bomb.* New York, Rinehart, 1955; as *Tomorrow Plus X*, New York, Avon, 1957.
*The Lincoln Hunters.* New York, Rinehart, 1958; London, Phoenix House, 1961.
*To the Tombaugh Station.* New York, Ace, 1960.
*The Year of the Quiet Sun.* New York, Ace, 1970; London, Hale, 1971.
*Ice and Iron.* New York, Doubleday, 1974; revised edition, New York, Ballantine, and London, Gollancz, 1975.
*Resurrection Days.* New York, Pocket Books, 1981.

Short Stories

*The Science-Fiction Subtreasury.* New York, Rinehart, 1954; as *Time: X*, New York, Bantam, 1955.
*The Best of Wilson Tucker.* New York, Pocket Books, 1982.

OTHER PUBLICATIONS

Novels

*The Chinese Doll.* New York, Rinehart, 1946; London, Cassell, 1948.
*To Keep or Kill.* New York, Rinehart, 1947; London, Cassell, 1950.
*The Dove.* New York, Rinehart, 1948; London, Cassell, 1950.
*The Stalking Man.* New York, Rinehart, 1949; London, Cassell, 1950.
*Red Herring.* New York, Rinehart, 1951; London, Cassell, 1953.
*The Man in My Grave.* New York, Rinehart, 1956; London, Macdonald, 1958.
*The Hired Target.* New York, Ace, 1957.
*Last Stop.* New York, Doubleday, 1963; London, Hale, 1965.
*A Procession of the Damned.* New York, Doubleday, 1965; London, Hale, 1967.
*The Warlock.* New York, Doubleday, 1967; London, Hale, 1968.
*This Witch.* New York, Doubleday, 1971; London, Gollancz, 1972.
*The Neo-Fan's Guide to Science Fiction Fandom.* Privately printed, 1955.

*

Wilson Tucker comments (1985):

I write to entertain an editor, his readers, and myself, in that order. If I fail to entertain the editor, there will be no readers; if I fail to entertain the readers my own livelihood will be reduced accordingly. Some critics have said that my books may paint a bleak picture for humanity but that I always offer hope and sunshine for the future. That's news to me. I had always believed that I was writing adventure and offering entertainment, nothing more.

* * *

Wilson Tucker's stories have the modesty of realistic black-and-white films. His casts are small, his scale intimate, and his settings familiar. He develops his plots and characters using human actions and reactions. He prefers concrete imagery to abstract verbiage: he tells by showing. In *The Year of the Quiet Sun*, for example, shots of the same swimming pool in four different years give instant summaries of intervening events at the site. Indeed, the cinematic flow of Tucker's narratives may reflect his 40 years' experience as a motion picture projectionist.

Tucker's style is economical and unadorned. He understates so much that careless readers sometimes miss the full implications of his text, such as clues to the hero's race in *The Year of the Quiet Sun* or the practice of cannibalism in *The Long Loud Silence.* He actually had to revise the ending of *Ice and Iron* after its initial publication to supply additional explanations. Characterization is his strongest gift. His heroes are marked by a certain ornery ordinariness and a stubborn integrity that the critic Bruce Gillespie calls "the ability neither to give in to the world nor to push it around" (*SF Commentary 43*, 1976). These heroes crave simplicity and distrust institutions. They wield their talents—anything from telepathy to acting to survival skills—without bravado. They establish prickly, often unsatisfactory relationships with heroines as stubborn as themselves. Tucker sensibly combines appreciation of feminine charms with respect for feminine strength.

Historical, not physical, sciences have been Tucker's major inspiration. His personal enthusiasm for history and archeology fuels the well-researched vitality of *The Lincoln Hunters* and *The Year of the Quiet Sun.* The human dimensions of time travel have seldom been better portrayed in SF, for instance in the chief Lincoln-hunter's joy at meeting people from past eras: "They were living *now* and he was among them." Although he does plot with time paradoxes, Tucker always makes time travel a means rather than an end in itself. In *The Lincoln Hunters* it enables the author to place his hero in two radically different environments—a sterile, repressive future and a burgeoning, liberal past—and then generates a eucatastrophe to leave him in the happier world. Tucker keeps restating the proposition that life itself is a kind of time machine operating at the maximum rate of one second per second.

A poignant version of temporal translation is achieved through extreme longevity in *The Time Masters.* A marooned extraterrestrial who had been Gilgamesh in ancient Sumer waits thousands of years while the mayfly lives of ordinary humans flicker out around him before he finds an alternative to both loneliness and escape. The hero of *The Time Masters* reappears in a minor role in *Time Bomb*, a novel in which mechanical time travel changes history by eliminating a McCarthy-like villain in his larval stage. This premise is inverted in Tucker's finest work, *The Year of the Quiet Sun*, when data gleaned from temporal research preserve a villain and trigger a catastrophic world race war. Every element in this honest, solidly built book meshes securely and unobtrusively to present a close-up of Armageddon.

Tucker thriftily incorporated the same research on Biblical archeology and the Dead Sea Scrolls used for *The Year of the Quiet Sun* into his mystery novel, *This Witch.* He prefers doing mysteries because he finds them easier and more fun to write than SF, but his dual careers cross-fertilize each other. He often uses SF elements (even facts about SF fandom) in his mysteries and employs mystery/thriller conventions in his SF. (Compare the espionage apparatus and psychic elements in *Wild Talent* and *The Warlock.*) The clearest instance of Tucker's debt to the hard-boiled mystery styles of the 1940's is *The Long Loud Silence.* Its protagonist is a mono-maniac scrambling for survival in a plague-devasted eastern United States. Although the unrelenting brutality of this novel cost it popular acceptance on its initial publication, it remains a chilling reflection of Cold War attitudes.

Yet despite the grimness that underlies much of his professional work, Tucker has been one of SF fandom's favorite humorists—in person and in print—for half a century. His close friend Robert Bloch calls him "a legend in his own time." Tucker's chief handicap as a writer is an excess of humility—even after a score of novels he still refuses to think of himself as a professional writer. But the author of *The Year of the Quiet Sun* need stand in awe of no one.

—Sandra Miesel

---

**TUREK, Ian Francis.** *See* **BINDER, Eando.**

---

**TUREK, Ione Frances.** *See* **BINDER, Eando.**

---

**TURNER, George (Reginald).** Australian. Born in Melbourne, Victoria, 8 October 1916. Educated in Victoria state schools; at University High School, Melbourne. Served in the Australian Imperial Forces, 1939–45. Employment officer, Commonwealth Employment Service, Melbourne, 1945–49, and Wangaratta, Victoria, 1949–50; textile technician, Bruck Mills, Wangaratta, 1951–64; senior employment officer, Volkswagen Ltd., Melbourne, 1964–67; beer transferrer, Carlton and United Breweries, Melbourne, 1970–77. Since 1970, science fiction reviewer, Melbourne *Age.* Recipient: Miles Franklin award, 1963; Commonwealth Literary Fund award, 1968; Ditmar award, 1984; Arthur C. Clarke award, 1988. Agent: Cherry Weiner Literary Agency, 28 Kipling Way, Manalapan, New Jersey 07726, U.S.A. Address: 4/296 Inkerman Street, East St. Kilda, Victoria 3183, Australia.

### Science-Fiction Publications

Novels (series: Ethical Culture)

*Beloved Son* (Ethical Culture). London, Faber, 1978; New York, Pocket Books, 1979.
*Vaneglory* (Ethical Culture). London, Faber, 1981.
*Yesterday's Men* (Ethical Culture). London, Faber, 1983.
*The Sea and Summer.* London, Faber, 1987; as *Drowning Towers*, New York, Arbor House, 1987.
*Brain Child.* New York, Morrow, 1991.

Short Stories

*A Pursuit of Miracles.* Adelaide, Aphelion, 1990.

### Other Publications

Novels

*Young Man of Talent.* London, Cassell, 1959; as *Scobie*, New York, Simon and Schuster, 1959.

*A Stranger and Afraid.* London, Cassell, 1961.
*The Cupboard under the Stairs.* London, Cassell, 1962.
*A Waste of Shame.* Melbourne and London, Cassell, 1965.
*The Lame Dog Man.* Melbourne, Cassell, 1967; London, Cassell, 1968.
*Transit of Cassidy.* Melbourne, Nelson, 1978; London, Hamish Hamilton, 1979.

Other

*In the Heart or in the Head* (autobiography). Melbourne, Norstrilia Press, 1984.
*Off-Cuts* (memoirs). Perth, Western Australia, Swancon, 1986.

Editor, *The View from the Edge.* Melbourne, Norstrilia Press, 1977.

*

George Turner comments:

Since it is my personal view (admittedly shared by few contemporary SF writers) that SF long ago lost its way among erotica, exotica, wishdreams, metaphysical guesswork, "mind-blowing" conceptions, and plain bad writing, I prefer to maintain a low key in my own work. To this end I have concentrated on simple, staple SF ideas, mostly those which have become conventions in the genre, injected without background or discussion into stories on the understanding that readers know all they need about such things. So in *Beloved Son* I used only the everyday ingredients of the genre—genetic manipulation, telepathy, the nature of World War III, the politics of renaissance—in order to rethink them and point out that all is not as obvious as conventional SF usage would have the readers believe.

My work will always be concerned with how human beings behave—as all fiction ultimately must be. Super-heroes, super-intelligences, and unlikely worlds created for melodrama or the spelling out of doubtful metaphors for the future of man do not interest me. My SF method remains the same as for my mainstream novels—set characters in motion in a speculative situation and let them work out their destinies with a minimum of auctorial interference.

* * *

A well-known and prize-winning mainstream novelist of the 1960's, George Turner has earned a reputation as Australia's most rigorous and astute science-fiction critic and reviewer. (He claims, with justification, that his "thirty-year apprenticeship" in the writer's craft has given him "the critical confidence to stand in awe of no-one but Shakespeare and Tolstoy.") His autobiography, *In the Heart or in the Head*, shows his lifelong commitment to literature, expounds his view of the history and shortcomings of the SF genre, and acts as a model for literary criticism in its engrossing blend of the personal and the critical, the subjective and the objective.

Turner's career as SF writer began late in life with the three novels of his Ethical Culture series: *Beloved Son, Vaneglory*, and *Yesterday's Men* (which, though linked, do not form a trilogy). Each book is set in the post-holocaust reconstructed world of the 21st century. The Collapse of 1992 (caused by genetic interference with food-crops, worsened by the spread of mutated-disease epidemics, and climaxed by hysterical nuclear bombing) has left the world's population greatly reduced, but within half a century a new world has emerged. Built on the Ethic of Non-Interference, the new culture relies upon an imprinted fear of the greed, obscenity, and cruelty of the past, and many of these old-world ills have genuinely been overcome—but only through fear and ignorance, not intellectual resolve.

Old social problems soon emerge, for dissent against the new order grows. But new problems also arise: experiments in cloning lead to attempts to tinker with human genetic stock (in *Beloved Son*), and further manipulations take place after the discovery of mutant humans with a lifespan of centuries (*Vaneglory*). *Yesterday's Men* draws the series to an intellectually satisfying close when the new society finally seeks to learn the truth about the "barbarians" of the 20th century . . . and discovers that human nature has not (and possibly cannot) change.

Ostensibly, the three novels are about the abuses and consequences of supposed "progress" in the biological sciences, but they are more centrally concerned with the pitfalls of romantic idealism and utopian thinking. The emblem of this sad, depleted future is the Security Headquarters building: "Plain, ugly, efficient and temporary, it was uncompromisingly an administrative block. Like this entire civilization, it was there only to serve a passing purpose and be torn down. It symbolized with repellent neatness a world with an immutable past and a hopefully solid future but only a ramshackle, disposable present."

The compelling wisdom of Turner's novels lies in his ability to see with this kind of clarity: to perceive the shabby present amid the rosy dreams of the future. Such qualities have attracted charges of dourness, cynicism, and pessimism, but these accusations miss the point of the novels' achievement. The books may be forthright and uncompromising in their judgements of man and society, but they are also honest—bluntly, harshly honest. To use a phrase from *Beloved Son*, they deal with "the unholy competence of man," demonstrating that man's wisdom is less than his ability, and that the human talent for self-delusion and naive dreaming can be disastrous in its consequences.

These qualities are best illustrated in Turner's masterpiece, *The Sea and Summer* (titled *Drowning Towers* in the U.S.A.). This is a *realist* SF novel; it deals with the everyday lives and interpersonal tensions of characters living in Melbourne under the Greenhouse Effect. The city is drowning, and so is the Australian economy and social structure. Those who still have a job and a home are the Sweet; the Swill are the unemployed and homeless, the helpless flotsam and jetsam of the world ruined by neglect. Curiously, *The Sea and Summer* does not offer a pessimistic vision: a narrative framing device establishes that the world *has* survived its upheavals, and, more importantly, the novel's blunt (some critics say *pugnacious*) tone suggests that the battle for a better future has not been lost.

*The Sea and Summer* is a major work of 20th-century literature, and breaks important new ground as science fiction. George Turner's contribution to the SF field deserves more attention than it has received.

—Van Ikin

---

**TURTLEDOVE, Harry.** American. Agent: Scott Meredith, 845 Third Avenue, New York, New York 10022, U.S.A.

SCIENCE-FICTION PUBLICATIONS

Novels

*Agent of Byzantium.* New York, Congdon and Weed, 1987; London, New English Library, 1988.

*Noninterference.* New York, Ballantine, 1988.
*A Different Flesh.* New York, Congdon and Weed, 1988.

Short Stories

*Kaleidoscope.* New York, Ballantine, 1990.

OTHER PUBLICATIONS

Novels

*An Emperor for the Legion.* New York, Ballantine, 1987.
*The Legion of Videssos.* New York, Ballantine, 1987.
*The Misplaced Legion.* New York, Ballantine, 1987.
*Swords of the Legion.* New York, Ballantine, 1987.
*A World of Difference.* New York, Ballantine, 1990.
*Krispos of Videssos.* New York, Ballantine, 1991.
*Krispos Rising.* New York, Ballantine, 1991.

Other

*The Chronicle of Theophanes: An English Translation of Anni Mundi 6095-6305 (A.D. 602-813).* Philadelphia, University of Pennsylvania Press, 1982.

* * *

Harry Turtledove is a Byzantine historian who has published scholarly translations and studies of historians of the Eastern empire. His fiction, appropriately for an historian, is divided into three categories: straight SF, alternative history, and fantasy. The bulk of his straight SF and his alternate histories share a common thread: the working out of the effect, over a fairly long period of time, of a particular act or a particular change in conditions. Perhaps it is this which constitutes an overlap in the classes "SF" and "Alternate Histories."

By far his most satisfying book is *Agent of Byzantium*, which supposes a single event at the beginning of the seventh century to have been different. It is, moreover, a difference that seems intuitively a quite possible "might-have been." The supposition is that, when, as a young merchant, Mohammed met and conversed with a Nestorian priest, he was converted to the Christian superstition instead of going off to found one of his own. By the early 14th century, when Turtledove's story takes place, the changes consequent upon this single change have been immense. The violent eruption of enthusiasm that shattered the Persian, amputated the Byzantine, and established the Arab empires has never happened. Consequently, the first two remain, locked in inconclusive but interminable rivalry; and this scenario is the background to the adventures of Basil Argyros, first an army officer and later a secret agent of the Byzantine empire.

Turtledove effectively conveys the cool calculation, the labyrinthine bureaucracy, and the superstitious turmoil of that strange polity. At the same time, Basil—a character who is well drawn and fairly sympathetic—has some good knockabout adventures. He is involved in the introduction into the empire of the telescope, of gunpowder, of distillation and of printing (it is not made clear who invented the first two of these, or even exactly where). He himself discovers vaccination: truly a full and exciting life, but each separate event is made credible enough. The narrative carries the reader along; and if we are not deeply saddened by the death from smallpox of Basil's family, we at least believe that he was.

*A Different Flesh* makes a much larger initial change and spans a longer period of time. It is supposed that, when the Europeans discovered America, they found, not Amerindians and buffaloes, but *Homo Erectus* and a pleistocene fauna. Perhaps this is rather a lot to swallow, but the book is highly entertaining. In one section, Samuel Pepys tells how he came to think of evolution. The style is not quite Sam's, and it may not hold up to re-consideration; but the idea is engaging and the presentation full of humour. In another, set about 1800, the presence of sub-men makes it much easier to abolish negro slavery.

Turtledove's main "straight" SF treatment of the theme of significant initial change is *Noninterference.* Here, the one significant act is the cure, by terrestrial observers, of an amiable native queen who is dying of cancer. This kindly act is strictly contrary to the non-interference rule by which the explorers are supposed to be bound. What they had not forseen is that the cure, which would have been quite specific to the particular disease if applied to a human being, has the effect of completely arresting the normal aging processes in an extra-terrestrial. When another exploring party arrives centuries later, they find the good queen still going strong and treated as a divinity. Again, the single change is a lot to swallow, but the consequences are worked out with considerable ingenuity.

Turtledove has also produced the Videssos Cycle, a fantasy series in which some cohorts of one of Caesar's legions are magically translated from Gaul to a world of wizards and whatnots, where they manage rather well for themselves. As with his other books, the writing is smooth and the action brisk.

In all three of his fictional fields, Harry Turtledove provides lively enjoyment and ideas which, if not always watertight, are presented with enough vigor to produce a temporary suspension of disbelief. He does not aim for the highest achievements of literature: he does not try to modify our ways of thinking, or to produce prose which enriches and stays in the mind; but where he aims, he hits. He is an entertainer, and a successful one.

—M. Hammerton

---

**TUTTLE, Lisa.** American. Born in Houston, Texas, 16 September 1952. Educated at Syracuse University, New York, B.A. in English 1973. Editor of the fan magazine *Mathom*, 1968–70; television columnist, Austin American Statesman, Texas, 1976–79. Recipient: John W. Campbell Award, 1974; Nebula Award, 1982. Agent: Howard Morhaim, 175 Fifth Avenue, Room 709, New York, New York 10010, U.S.A.; or, A. P. Watt Ltd., 20 John Street, London WC1N 2DL, England.

SCIENCE-FICTION PUBLICATIONS

Novels

*Windhaven*, with George R. R. Martin. New York, Pocket Books, 1981; London, New English Library, 1982.
*Familiar Spirit.* New York, Berkley, and London, New English Library, 1983.

Uncollected Short Stories

"Stranger in the House," in *Clarion 2*, edited by Robin Scott Wilson. New York, New American Library, 1972.
"Till Human Voices Wake Us . . . ," in *Clarion 3*, edited by Robin Scott Wilson. New York, New American Library, 1973.

"I Have Heard the Mermaids," in *Survival from Infinity*, edited by Roger Elwood. New York, Watts, 1974.
"Changelings," in *Best SF 75*, edited by Harry Harrison and Brian Aldiss. Indianapolis, Bobbs Merrill, and London, Weidenfeld and Nicolson, 1976.
"Woman Waiting," in *Lone Star Universe*, edited by George W. Proctor and Steven Utley, Austin, Texas, Heidelberg, 1976.
"Stone Circle," in *Amazing* (New York), March 1976.
"Mrs. T," in *Amazing* (New York), September 1976.
"Tom Sawyer's Sub-Orbital Escapade," with Steven Utley, in *Ascents of Wonder*, edited by David Gerrold and Stephen Goldin. New York, Popular Library, 1977.
"The Family Monkey," in *New Voices in Science Fiction*, edited by George R. R. Martin. New York, Macmillan, 1977.
"Flies by Night," with Steven Utley, in *SF Choice 77*, edited by Mike Ashley. London, Quartet, 1977.
"Kin to Kaspar Hauser," in *Galazy* (New York), April 1977.
"Sangre," in *Fantastic* (New York), June 1977.
"The Horse Lord," in *The Year's Best Horror Stories 6*, edited by Gerald W. Page. New York, DAW, 1978.
"A Mother's Heart: A True Bear Story," in *Isaac Asimov's Science Fiction Magazine* (New York), January-February 1978.
"Uncoiling," with Steven Utley, in *Fantastic* (New York), April 1978.
"The Hollow Man," in *New Voices 2*, edited by George R. R. Martin. New York, Harcourt Brace, 1979.
"In the Arcade," in *The Year's Best Horror Stories 7*, edited by Gerald W. Page. New York, DAW, 1979.
"The Birds of the Moon," in *Fantastic* (New York), January 1979.
"Sun City," in *New Terrors I*, edited by Ramsey Campbell. London, Pan, 1980.
"Where the Stones Grow," in *Dark Forces*, edited by Kirby McCauley. New York, Viking Press, 1980.
"Bug House," in *Fantasy and Science Fiction* (New York), June 1980.
"The Other Mother," in *Fantasy and Science Fiction* (New York), December 1980.
"A Spaceship Built of Stone," in *The 1981 Annual World's Best SF*, edited by Donald A. Wollheim. New York, DAW, 1981.
"Need," in *Shadows 4*, edited by Charles L. Grant. New York, Doubleday, 1981.
"Dollburger," in *Horrors*, edited by Charles L. Grant. New York, Berkley, 1981.
"The Bone Flute," in *Fantasy and Science Fiction* (New York), May 1981.
"Treading the Maze," in *Fantasy and Science Fiction* (New York), November 1981.
"A Friend in Need," in *The Year's Best Fantasy Stories 8*, edited by Arthur W. Saha. New York, DAW, 1982.
"Wives," in *The Best from Fantasy and Science Fiction 24*, edited by Edward l. Ferman. New York, Doubleday, 1982.
"The Memory of Wood," in *Fantasy and Science Fiction* (New York), September 1982.
"The Nest," in *Fantasy and Science Fiction* (New York), April 1983.
"The Cure," in *Light Years and Dark*, edited by Michael Bishop. New York, Berkley, 1984.
"Redcap," in *Fantasy and Science Fiction* (New York), September 1984.
"Children of the Centaur," in *Amazing* (New York), September 1984.
"The Other King," in *Isaac Asimov's Science Fiction Magazine* (New York), December 1984.
"No Regrets," in *Fantasy and Science Fiction* (New York), May 1985.
"Flying to Byzantium," in *Twilight Zone* (New York), May 1985.
"From Another Country," "Riding the Nightmare," and "The Dragon's Bride," in *Night Visions 3*, edited by George R.R. Martin. Niles, Illinois, Dark Harvest, 1986.
"Jamie's Grave," in *Shadows 10*, edited by Charles L. Grant. New York, Doubleday, 1987.
"The Colonization of Edwin Beal," in *Fantasy and Science Fiction*, October 1987.
"The Wound," in *Other Edens*, edited by Robert Holdstock and Christopher Evans. London, Unwin Hyman, 1987.
"A Birthday," in *Tales from the Forbidden Planet*, edited by Roz Kavany. London, Titan, 1987.
"Memories of the Body," in *Interzone*, Winter 1987.
"The Other Room," in *Masters of Darkness II*, edited by Dennis Etchison. New York, Tor, 1988.
"The Spirit Cabinet," in *Women of Darkness*, edited by Kathryn Ptacek. New York, Tor, 1988.
"A Friend in Need," in *What Did Miss Darrington See?: An Anthology of Feminist Supernatural Fiction*, edited by Jessica Amanda Salmonson. New York, Feminist Press, 1989.
"Skin Deep," in *Dark Fantasies*, edited by Chris Morgan. London, Legend, 1989.
"In Translation," in *Zenith*, edited by David S. Garnett. London, Sphere, 1989.
"The Walled Garden," in *Hidden Turnings*, edited by Diana Wynne Jones. London, Metheun, 1989.
"Heart's Desire," in *Other Edens 3*, edited by Robert Holdstock and Christopher Evans. London, Unwin Hyman, 1989.
"Dead Television," in *Zenith 2*, edited by David S. Garnett. London, Orbit, 1990.
"Husbands," in *Alien Sex*, edited by Ellen Datlow. New York, Dutton, 1990.
"Lizard Lust," in *Interzone*, September 1990.
"To Be of Use," in *Interzone*, December 1990.

OTHER PUBLICATIONS

Novel

*Angela's Rainbow*. Limpsfield, Surrey, Dragon's World, 1983.

Other

*Catwitch* (for children). Limpsfield, Surrey, Dragon's World, and New York, Doubleday, 1983.
*Children's Literary Houses*, with Rosalind Ashe. Limpsfield, Surrey, Dragon's World, 1984.

* * *

George R. R. Martin has called Lisa Tuttle's writing "distinctive, delightful," and Ted White attributed to her "a reputation for strong stories which deal with human responses to the unusual."

Tuttle has called her first story, "Stranger in the House," a "going home story." A young woman returns home and attempts to regain her childhood. This is a theme writers such as Bradbury and Ellison have used to produce stories of ineffable sadness, but Tuttle goes a step further to produce a work of genuine horror, catching an aspect of our desire to relive the past that few writers seem to understand. It was a fitting start. Tuttle quickly revealed herself as a writer of interesting variety and skill.

It's just as important that she's revealed herself as a writer of highly original horror fiction. "Changelings," for example, is a nicely extrapolated sociological vignette about a society that employs surgery to cure anti-social behavior; in it, a father is betrayed by his pre-school-age child. "Flies by Night," written with Steven Utley, is a psychological study of a woman who longs to turn into a fly. "Stone Circle" is a complex character study set in a near-future welfare state. "In the Arcade" depicts a future where racism is offered as a sideshow attraction. "Sangre" and "The Horse Lord" are almost, but not quite, conventional, the first juxtaposing the story of a woman's affair with her stepfather with a tale of vampirism, the other telling of a family that encounters Indian superstition that turns out to be justified—again, parents are betrayed by their children.

In "The Family Monkey" a rural Texas couple saves an alien from a crashed spaceship and adopts it as a servant. The story is simple and straightforward: the alien is saved, becomes a sort of family retainer, is discovered years later by its own people, and leaves. The story acquires a remarkable depth, however, because Tuttle's interest lies not with the plot, or even the alien, but with character relationships. Relationship provides the focus of most of her work, in fact. "The Hollow Man," set in the near future, concerns a woman whose husband commits suicide. She has him brought back to life through new medical techniques only to discover the flesh has been revived, but nothing else. Cold and indifferent, the husband lacks even the interest necessary to kill himself. The tragedy of the ending is classically inevitable, and quite powerful.

Little of Tuttle's fiction takes place away from the Earth. In "Wives," one of the few set on another planet, aliens are permitted by their Earthman conquerers to exist only so long as they pretend to be the humans' wives. "The Birds of the Moon" is set on Earth, but tells about a woman whose astronaut husband has been to the moon. The voyage has changed him, and his wife hallucinates about beings—strange, ugly birds—which live on the moon. As with many of Tuttle's stories, the line between hallucination and reality is impossible to discern, particularly in man-woman relationships. In "Flies by Night" the woman who longs to be a fly is captured by men who have become spiders—or so she believes.

As striking as such images are in a writter of Tuttle's talent, they never dominate her stories; neither, for that matter, does her interest in relationships. If anything, they seem to provide a focus for what appears to be a still-emerging concern for the nature of her characters' humanity. In "Bug House" a young woman, visiting an aunt who lives in a lonely isolated house, finds her aunt sick and the house overrun by insects. When the aunt dies, it is apparently as the victim of a strange young man whose connection with her, the house, the insects, becomes apparent only when it's too late. As in "Stone Circle" sex is treated as a numbing, enslaving element.

"Flying to Byzantium," another "going home" story, is about a writer elevated from a drab, lonely life by the modest success of a fantasy novel. At a science-fiction convention, she finds herself forced, through a confrontation with her readers, back into her hated, previous existence. The story permits some cogent observations on the problems of being a writer in the 1980's, and its last paragraph is as powerful as the idea itself. But the story fails to satisfy, possibly because the matter-of-fact style in which most of it is written fails to deliver the emotional impact it demands. "Need" is a far more successful story in which a young woman's fears and insecurities lead her into a situation that neatly brings a twist to the conventional ghost story plot—but in a way that is emotional and satisfying: few writers other than Tuttle could have pulled it off.

*Windhaven*, written with George R. R. Martin, is not typical Tuttle fiction, but it would be wrong to call it typical Martin, either. It's a superb collaborative effort set on a planet whose inhabitants, descendants of the survivors of a spaceship wreck, are dependent on the skills of messengers who travel on artificial wings, similar to hang gliders. It's good, solid science fiction, carefully crafted. It makes the most of Martin's eye for the exotic and of his ability to plot, and of Tuttle's graceful style and sensitivity to people.

Tuttle's first solo novel, *Familiar Spirit*, is more in line with her short fiction. A commercial horror novel, it is well written, carefully plotted, and marked with Tuttle's customary vivid characterization. Its weakness lies in an unsatisfying formula ending. Even so, it's head and shoulders above all but a handful of the horror novels of its decade. While *Familiar Spirit* makes fewer demands on her talent than such shorter works as "The Family Monkey" or "The Hollow Man," her skills and the several themes she has been developing, seem to demand the longer form.

—Gerald W. Page

---

**TWAIN, Mark.** Pseudonym for Samuel Langhorne Clemens. American. Born in Florida, Missouri, 30 November 1835; grew up in Hannibal, Missouri. Married Olivia Langdon in 1870 (died, 1904); one son and three daughters. Printer's apprentice from age 12; helped brother with Hannibal newspapers, 1850–52; worked in St. Louis, New York, Philadelphia, Keokuk, Iowa, and Cincinnati, 1853–57; river pilot's apprentice, on the Mississippi, 1857: licensed as a pilot, 1859; went to Nevada as secretary to his brother, then in the service of the governor, and also worked as a goldminer, 1861; staff member, *Territorial Enterprise*, Virginia City, Nevada, 1862–64; moved to San Francisco, 1864; writer from 1867, lecturer from 1868; editor, *Buffalo Express*, New York, 1868–71; moved to Hartford, Connecticut, and became associated with the Charles L. Webster Publishing Company, 1884: went bankrupt, 1894 (last debts paid, 1898). M.A.: Yale University, New Haven, Connecticut, 1888; Litt.D.: Yale University, 1901; Oxford University, 1907; LL.D.: University of Missouri, Columbia, 1902. *Died 21 April 1910.*

SCIENCE-FICTION PUBLICATIONS

Novel

*A Connecticut Yankee in King Arthur's Court.* New York, Webster, and London, Chatto and Windus, 1889.

Short Stories

*The Science Fiction of Mark Twain*, edited by David Ketterer. Hamden, Connecticut, Shoe String Press, 1984.

OTHER PUBLICATIONS

Novels

*The Innocents Abroad; or, The New Pilgrims' Progress.* Hartford, Connecticut, American Publishing Company, 1869; London, Routledge, 2 vols., 1872.
*The Innocents at Home.* London, Routledge, 1872.
*The Gilded Age: A Tale of Today*, with Charles Dudley Warner. Hartford, Connecticut, American Publishing Company, 1873; London, Routledge, 3 vols., 1874; *The Adventures of Colonel Sellers, Being Twain's Share of "The Gilded Age,"* edited by

Charles Neider, New York, Doubleday, 1965; London, Chatto and Windus, 1966.
*The Adventures of Tom Sawyer.* London, Chatto and Windus, and Hartford, Connecticut, American Publishing Company, 1876.
*A Tramp Abroad.* Hartford, Connecticut, American Publishing Company, and London, Chatto and Windus, 1880.
*The Prince and the Pauper.* London, Chatto and Windus, and Boston, Osgood, 1881.
*The Adventures of Huckleberry Finn (Tom Sawyer's Companion).* London, Chatto and Windus, 1884; New York, Webster, 1885; edited by Charles Neider, New York, Doubleday, 1985.
*The American Claimant.* New York, Webster, and London, Chatto and Windus, 1892.
*Pudd'nhead Wilson: A Tale.* London, Chatto and Windus, 1894; as *The Tragedy of Pudd'nhead Wilson*, Hartford, Connecticut, American Publishing Company, 1894.
*Personal Recollections of Joan of Arc. . . .* New York, Harper, and London, Chatto and Windus, 1896.
*A Double Barrelled Detective Story.* New York, Harper, and London, Chatto and Windus, 1902.
*Extracts from Adam's Diary.* New York, and London, Harper, 1904.
*Eve's Diary.* New York and London, Harper, 1906.
*A Horse's Tale.* New York and London, Harper, 1907.
*Simon Wheeler, Detective*, edited by Franklin R. Rogers. New York, New York Public Library, 1963.
*The Complete Novels*, edited by Charles Neider. New York, Doubleday, 2 vols., 1964.
*Mississippi Writings* (Library of America). New York, Literary Classics of the United States, and London, Cambridge University Press, 1982.

Short Stories

*The Celebrated Jumping Frog of Calaveras County and Other Sketches*, edited by John Paul. New York, Webb, 1867.
*A True Story and the Recent Carnival of Crime.* Boston, Osgood, 1877.
*Date 1601: Conversation as It Was by the Social Fireside in the Time of the Tudors.* Privately printed, 1880; as *1601 . . .*, edited by Franklin J. Meine, Chicago, privately printed, 1939.
*The Stolen White Elephant Etc.* London, Chatto and Windus, and Boston, Osgood, 1882.
*Merry Tales.* New York, Webster, 1892.
*The £1,000,000 Bank-Note and Other New Stories.* New York, Webster, and London, Chatto and Windus, 1893.
*Tom Sawyer Abroad.* New York, Webster, and London, Chatto and Windus, 1894.
*Tom Sawyer Abroad, Tom Sawyer, Detective, and Other Stories.* New York, Harper, 1896; as *Tom Sawyer, Detective, as Told by Huck Finn, and Other Tales.* London, Chatto and Windus, 1897.
*The Man That Corrupted Hadleyburg and Other Stories and Essays.* New York, Harper, and London, Chatto and Windus, 1900.
*A Dog's Tale.* London, National Anti-Vivisection Society, and New York, Harper, 1904.
*The $30,000 Bequest and Other Stories.* New York, Harper, 1906; London, Harper, 1907.
*Extract from Captain Stormfield's Visit to Heaven.* New York and London, Harper, 1909; revised edition, as *Report from Paradise*, edited by Dixon Wecter, New York, Harper, 1952.
*The Mysterious Stranger: A Romance.* New York, Harper, 1916; London, Harper, 1917.
*The Curious Republic of Gondour and Other Whimsical Sketches.* New York, Boni and Liveright, 1919.
*The Mysterious Stranger and Other Stories.* New York and London, Harper, 1922.
*The Adventures of Thomas Jefferson Snodgrass*, edited by Charles Honce. Chicago, Covici, 1928.
*A Boy's Adventure.* Privately printed, 1928.
*Jim Smiley and His Jumping Frog*, edited by Albert Bigelow Paine. Chicago, Pocahontas Press, 1940.
*A Murder, A Mystery, and a Marriage.* Privately printed, 1945.
*The Complete Short Stories*, edited by Charles Neider. New York, Hanover House, 1957.
*The Complete Humorous Sketches and Tales*, edited by Charles Neider. New York, Doubleday, 1961.
*Mark Twain's Satires and Burlesques*, edited by Franklin R. Rogers. Berkeley, University of California Press, 1967.
*Mark Twain's Mysterious Stranger Manuscripts*, edited by William M. Gibson. Berkeley, University of California Press, 1969.
*Mark Twain's Hannibal, Huck, and Tom*, edited by Walter Blair. Berkeley, University of California Press, 1969.
*Early Tales and Sketches*, edited by Edgar M. Branch and Robert H. Hirst. Berkeley, University of California Press, 2 vols., 1979–81.
*Wapping Alice.* Berkeley, California, Friends of the Bancroft Library, 1981.
*Huck Finn and Tom Sawyer among the Indians and Other Unfinished Stories*, edited by Dahlia Armon and Walter Blair. Berkeley, University of California Press, 1989.
*Goldminers and Guttersnipes: Tales of California*, edited by Ken Chowder. San Francisco, Chronicle Books, 1991.

Plays

*Colonel Sellers as a Scientist*, with William Dean Howells, adaptation of the novel *The Gilded Age* by Twain and Charles Dudley Warner (produced New Brunswick, New Jersey, and New York, 1887). Published in *The Complete Plays of William Dean Howells*, edited by Walter J. Meserve, New York, New York University Press, 1960.
*Ah Sin*, with Bret Harte, edited by Frederick Anderson (produced Washington, D.C., 1877), San Francisco, Book Club of California, 1961.
*The Quaker City Holy Land Excursion: An Unfinished Play.* Privately printed, 1927.

Verse

*On the Poetry of Mark Twain, with Selections from His Verse*, edited by Arthur L. Scott. Urbana, University of Illinois Press, 1966.

Other

*Mark Twain's (Burlesque) Autobiography and First Romance.* New York, Sheldon, 1871.
*Memoranda: From the Galaxy.* Toronto, Canadian News and Publishing Company, 1871.
*Roughing It.* London, Routledge, and Hartford, Connecticut, American Publishing Company, 1872.
*A Curious Dream and Other Sketches.* London, Routledge, 1872.
*Screamers: A Gathering of Scraps of Humour, Delicious Bits, and Short Stories.* London, Hotten, 1872.
*Sketches.* New York, American News Company, 1874.
*Sketches, New and Old.* Hartford, Connecticut, American Publishing Company, 1875.
*Old Times on the Mississippi.* Toronto, Belford, 1876.

*Punch, Brothers, Punch! and Other Sketches.* New York, Slote Woodman, 1878.

*An Idle Excursion.* Toronto, Belford, 1878.

*A Curious Experience.* Toronto, Gibson, 1881.

*Life on the Mississippi.* London, Chatto and Windus, and Boston, Osgood, 1883.

*Facts for Mark Twain's Memory Builder.* New York, Webster, 1891.

*How to Tell a Story and Other Essays.* New York, Harper, 1897; revised edition, 1900.

*Following the Equator: A Journey Around the World.* Hartford, Connecticut, American Publishing Company, 1897; as *More Tramps Abroad*, London, Chatto and Windus, 1897.

*The Writings of Mark Twain.* Hartford, Connecticut, American Publishing Company, and London, Chatto and Windus, 25 vols., 1899–1907.

*The Pains of Lowly Life.* London, London Anti-Vivisection Society, 1900.

*English as She Is Taught.* Boston, Mutual, 1900; revised edition, New York, Century, 1901.

*To the Person Sitting in Darkness.* New York, Anti-Imperialist League, 1901.

*Edmund Burke on Croker, and Tammany* (lecture). New York, Economist Press, 1901.

*My Debut as a Literary Person, with Other Essays and Stories.* Hartford, Connecticut, American Publishing Company, 1903.

*Mark Twain on vivisection.* New York, New York Anti-Vivisection Society, 1905(?).

*King Leopold's Soliloquy: A Defense of His Congo Rule.* Boston, Warren, 1905; revised edition, 1906; London, Unwin, 1907.

*Editorial Wild Oats.* New York, Harper, 1905.

*What Is Man?* (published anonymously). New York, DeVinne Press, 1906; as Mark Twain, London, Watts, 1910.

*Mark Twain on Spelling* (lecture). New York, Simplified Spelling Board, 1906.

*The Writings of Mark Twain* (Hillcrest Edition). New York and London, Harper, 25 vols., 1906–07.

*Christian Science, with Notes Containing Corrections to Date.* New York and London, Harper, 1907.

*Is Shakespeare Dead? From My Autobiography.* New York and London, Harper, 1909.

*Mark Twain's Speeches*, edited by F.A. Nast. New York and London, Harper, 1910; revised edition, 1923.

*Queen Victoria's Jubilee.* Privately printed, 1910.

*Letter to the California Pioneers.* Oakland, California, Dewitt and Snelling, 1911.

*What Is Man? and Other Essays.* New York, Harper, 1917; London, Chatto and Windus, 1919.

*Mark Twain's Letters, Arranged with Comment*, edited by Albert Bigelow Paine. New York, Harper, 2 vols., 1917; shortened version, as *Letters*, London, Chatto and Windus, 1920.

*Moments with Mark Twain*, edited by Albert Bigelow Paine. New York, Harper, 1920.

*The Writings of Mark Twain* (Definitive Edition), edited by Albert Bigelow Paine. New York, Gabriel Wells, 37 vols., 1922–25.

*Europe and Elsewhere.* New York and London, Harper, 1923.

*Mark Twain's Autobiography*, edited by Albert Bigelow Paine. New York and London, Harper, 2 vols., 1924.

*Sketches of the Sixties by Bret Harte and Mark Twain . . . from "The Californian," 1864–67.* San Francisco, John Howell, 1926; as *California Sketches*, New York, Dover, 1991.

*The Suppressed Chapter of "Following the Equator.* Privately printed, 1928.

*A Letter from Mark Twain to His Publisher, Chatto and Windus.* San Francisco, Penguin Press, 1929.

*Mark Twain the Letter Writer*, edited by Cyril Clemens. Boston, Meador, 1932.

*Mark Twain's Works.* New York, Harper, 23 vols., 1933.

*The Family Mark Twain.* New York, Harper, 1935.

*The Mark Twain Omnibus*, edited by Max J. Herzberg. New York, Harper, 1935.

*Representative Selections*, edited by Fred L. Patee. New York, American Book Company, 1935.

*Mark Twain's Notebook*, edited by Albert Bigelow Paine. New York, Harper, 1935.

*Letters from the Sandwich Islands, Written for the "Sacramento Union,"* edited by G. Ezra Dane. San Francisco, Grabhorn Press, 1937; London, Oxford University Press, 1938.

*The Washoe Giant in San Francisco, Being Heretofore Uncollected Sketches . . .*, edited by Franklin Walker. San Francisco, George Fields, 1938.

*Mark Twain's Western Years, Together with Hitherto Unreprinted Clemens Western Items*, by Ivan Benson. Stanford, California, Stanford University, 1938.

*Letters from Honolulu Written for the "Sacramento Union,"* edited by Thomas Nickerson. Honolulu, Thomas Nickerson, 1939.

*Mark Twain in Eruption: Hitherto Unpublished Pages about Men and Events*, edited by Bernard De Voto. New York, Harper, 1940.

*Travels with Mr. Brown, Being Heretofore Uncollected Sketches Written for the San Francisco "Alta California" in 1866 and 1867*, edited by Franklin Walker and G. Ezra Dane. New York, Knopf, 1940.

*Republican Letters*, edited by Cyril Clemens. Webster Groves, Missouri, International Mark Twain Society, 1941.

*Letters to Will Brown . . .*, edited by Theodore Hornberger. Austin, University of Texas, 1941.

*Letters in the "Muscatine Journal,"* edited by Edgar M. Branch. Chicago, Mark Twain Association of America, 1942.

*Washington in 1868*, edited by Cyril Clemens. Webster Groves, Missouri, International Mark Twain Society, and London, Laurie, 1943.

*Mark Twain, Business Man*, edited by Samuel Charles Webster. Boston, Little Brown, 1946.

*The Letters of Quintus Curtius Snodgrass*, edited by Ernest E. Leisy. Dallas, Southern Methodist University Press, 1946.

*The Portable Mark Twain*, edited by Bernard De Voto. New York, Viking Press, 1946; London, Penguin, 1977.

*Mark Twain in Three Moods: Three New Items of Twainiana*, edited by Dixon Wecter. San Marino, California, Friends of the Huntington Library, 1948.

*The Love Letters of Mark Twain*, edited by Dixon Wecter. New York, Harper, 1949.

*Mark Twain to Mrs. Fairbanks*, edited by Dixon Wecter. San Marino, California, Huntington Library, 1949.

*Mark Twain to Uncle Remus 1881–1885*, edited by Thomas H. English. Atlanta, Emory University Library, 1953.

*Twins of Genius* (letters to George Washington Cable), edited by Guy A. Cardwell. East Lansing, Michigan State College Press, 1953.

*Mark Twain of the "Enterprise" . . .*, edited by Henry Nash Smith and Frederick Anderson. Berkeley, University of California Press, 1957.

*Traveling with Innocents Abroad: Mark Twain's Original Reports from Europe and the Holy Land*, edited by Daniel Morley McKeithan. Norman, University of Oklahoma Press, 1958.

*The Autobiography of Mark Twain*, edited by Charles Neider. New York, Doubleday, 1959.

*The Art, Humor, and Humanity of Mark Twain*, edited by Minnie M. Brashear and Robert M. Rodney. Norman, University of Oklahoma Press, 1959.

*Mark Twain and the Government*, edited by Svend Petersen. Caldwell, Idaho, Caxton Printers, 1960.

*Mark Twain-Howells Letters: The Correspondence of Samuel L. Clemens and William Dean Howells 1872–1910*, edited by Henry Nash Smith and William M. Gibson. Cambridge, Massachusetts, Harvard University Press, 2 vols., 1960; abridged edition, as *Selected Mark Twain-Howells Letters*, 1967.

*Your Personal Mark Twain....* New York, International Publishers, 1960.

*Life as I Find It: Essays, Sketches, Tales, and Other Material*, edited by Charles Neider. New York, Doubleday, 1961.

*The Travels of Mark Twain*, edited by Charles Neider. New York, Doubleday, 1961.

*Contributions to "The Galaxy," 1868–1871*, edited by Bruce R. McElderry. Gainesville, Florida, Scholars Facsimiles and Reprints, 1961.

*Mark Twain on the Art of Writing*, edited by Martin B. Fried. Buffalo, Salisbury Club, 1961.

*Letters to Mary*, edited by Lewis Leary. New York, Columbia University Press, 1961.

*The Pattern for Mark Twain's "Roughing It": Letters from Nevada by Samuel and Orion Clemens, 1861–1862*, edited by Franklin R. Rogers. Berkeley, University of California Press, 1961.

*Letters from the Earth*, edited by Bernard De Voto. New York, Harper, 1962.

*Mark Twain on the Damned Human Race*, edited by Janet Smith. New York, Hill and Wang, 1962.

*Selected Shorter Writings*, edited by Walter Blair. Boston, Houghton Mifflin, 1962.

*The Complete Essays*, edited by Charles Neider. New York, Doubleday, 1963.

*Mark Twain's San Francisco*, edited by Bernard Taper. New York, McGraw Hill, 1963.

*The Forgotten Writings of Mark Twain*, edited by Henry Duskus. New York, Citadel Press, 1963.

*General Grant by Matthew Arnold, with a Rejoinder by Mark Twain* (lecture), edited by John Y. Simon. Carbondale, Southern Illinois University Press, 1966.

*Letters from Hawaii*, edited by A. Grove Day. New York, Appleton Century Crofts, 1966; London, Chatto and Windus, 1967.

*Which Was the Dream? and Other Symbolic Writings of the Later Years*, edited by John S. Tuckey. Berkeley, University of California Press, 1967.

*The Complete Travel Books*, edited by Charles Neider. New York, Doubleday, 1967.

*Letters to His Publishers, 1867–1894*, edited by Hamlin Hill. Berkeley, University of California Press, 1967.

*Clemens of the "Call": Mark Twain in California*, edited by Edgar M. Branch. Berkeley, University of California Press, 1969.

*Correspondence with Henry Huttleston Rogers, 1893–1909*, edited by Lewis Leary. Berkeley, University of California Press, 1969.

*Man Is the Only Animal That Blushes—or Needs to: The Wisdom of Mark Twain*, edited by Michael Joseph. Los Angeles, Stanyan Books, 1970.

*Mark Twain's Quarrel with Heaven: Captain Stormfield's Visit to Heaven and Other Sketches*, edited by Roy B. Browne. New Haven, Connecticut, College and University Press, 1970.

*Everybody's Mark Twain*, edited by Caroline Thomas Harnsberger. South Brunswick, New Jersey, A.S. Barnes, and London, Yoseloff, 1972.

*Fables of Man*, edited by John S. Tuckey. Berkeley, University of California Press, 1972.

*A Pen Warmed Up In Hell: Mark Twain in Protest*, edited by Frederick Anderson. New York, Harper, 1972.

*The Choice Humorous Works of Mark Twain*. London, Chatto and Windus, 1973.

*Mark Twain's Notebooks and Journals*, edited by Frederick Anderson and others. Berkeley, University of California Press, 1975 (and later volumes).

*Letters from the Sandwich Islands*, edited by Joan Abramson. Norfolk Island, Australia, Island Heritage, 1975.

*Mark Twain Speaking*, edited by Paul Fatout. Iowa City, University of Iowa Press, 1976.

*The Mammoth Cod, and Address to the Stomach Club*. Milwaukee, Maledicta, 1976.

*The Comic Mark Twain Reader*, edited by Charles Neider. New York, Doubleday, 1977.

*Mark Twain Speaks for Himself*, edited by Paul Fatout. West Lafayette, Indiana, Purdue University Press, 1978.

*The Devil's Race-Track: Mark Twain's Great Dark Writings: The Best from "Which Was the Dream" and "Fables of Man,"* edited by John S. Tuckey. Berkeley, University of California Press, 1980.

*The Selected Letters of Mark Twain*, edited by Charles Neider. New York, Harper, 1982.

*Mark Twain's Letters*, edited by Edgar M. Branch, Michael B. Frank, and Kenneth M. Sanderson. Berkeley, University of California Press, 1987.

*The Outrageous Mark Twain*, edited by Charles Neider. New York, Doubleday, 1987.

*Mark Twain's Aquarium: The Samuel Clemens Angelfish Correspondence*. Athens, University of Georgia Press, 1991.

Translator, *Slovenly Peter (Der Struwwelpeter)*. New York, Limited Editions Club, 1935.

*

Bibliography: *A Bibliography of the Works of Mark Twain, Samuel Langhorne Clemens* by Merle Johnson, New York, Harper, revised edition, 1935; in *Bibliography of American Literature 2* by Jacob Blanck, New Haven, Connecticut, Yale University Press, 1957; *Mark Twain: A Reference Guide* by Thomas Asa Tenney, Boston, Hall, 1977; *Mark Twain International: A Bibliography and Interpretation of His World-wide Popularity* edited by Robert H. Rodney, Westport, Connecticut, Greenwood Press, 1982.

Critical Studies (selection): *Mark Twain: A Biography* by Albert Bigelow Paine, New York, Harper, 3 vols., 1912, abridged edition, as *A Short Life of Mark Twain*, 1920; *Mark Twain: The Man and His Work* by Edward Wagenknecht, New Haven, Connecticut, Yale University Press, 1935, revised edition, Norman, University of Oklahoma Press, 1961, 1967; *Mark Twain: Man and Legend* by De Lancey Ferguson, Indianapolis, Bobbs Merrill, 1943; *A Casebook on Mark Twain's Wound* edited by Lewis Leary, New York, Crowell, 1962; *Discussions of Mark Twain* edited by Guy A. Cardwell, Boston, Heath, 1963; *Mr. Clemens and Mark Twain: A Biography* by Justin Kaplan, New York, Simon and Schuster, 1966, London, Cape, 1967; *Mark Twain: The Fate of Humor* by James M. Cox, Princeton, New Jersey, Princeton University Press, 1966; *The Art of Mark Twain* by William M. Gibson, New York, Oxford University Press, 1976; *Mark Twain: A Collection of Criticism* edited by Dean Morgan Schmitter, New York, McGraw Hill, 1976; *Mark Twain* by Robert Keith Miller, New York, Ungar, 1983; *The Authentic Mark Twain: A Literary Biography of Samuel L. Clemens* by Everett Emerson, Philadelphia, University of Pennsylvania

Press, 1984; *The Making of Mark Twain: A Biography* by John Lauber, Boston, Houghton Mifflin, 1985; *Mark Twain and Science* by Sherwood Cummings, Baton Rouge, Louisiana State University Press, 1989; *Mark Twain: The Bachelor Years* by Margaret Sanborn, New York, Doubleday, 1990; *The Inventions of Mark Twain* by John Lauber, New York, Hill and Wang, 1990.

* * *

Although Mark Twain's science-fiction works are frequently labeled as mimetic fiction (in which what occurs can be explained as dreams rather than actual time travel resulting from scientific extrapolation), his dystopic creations and employment of the ideology of science within or preceding the dream structures qualifies some of his works as science fiction. In other works his use of alternate settings and actual scientific extrapolation outside of the dream/reality contexts appears, particularly in his shorter and sometimes incomplete stories.

*Report from Paradise, The Mysterious Stranger*, and *Letters from the Earth* are fantasy rather than science fiction: satires on man's place in the universe in which science is used neither as a tool to create the condition of the stories nor as a thematic consideration within them. Twain's fascination with comets, particularly Halley's comet, is evidenced in "Captain Stormfield's Visit to Heaven," "A Letter from a Comet," and "A Curious Pleasure Excursion." The interstellar travel included in each is either in or on a comet rather than in any kind of man-made space vessel and relegates these writings as fantasy.

Several of Twain's shorter works, "Mental Telegraphy," "Mental Telegraphy Again," and "My Platonic Sweetheart" focus on parapsychology—in which Twain professed a firm belief—thus excluding them from his science-fiction works. Two other stories that have been classified as science fiction by some are "Earthquake Almanac" and "Petrified Man." However, both depend on natural phenomena rather than on extrapolated science, social or physical.

Twain does extrapolate on technology of his time, predicting long distance telephone service in "The Loves of Alonzo Fitz Clarence and Rosannah Ethelton," and long distance balloon flight in *Tom Sawyer Abroad* and in the incomplete manuscripts of "A Murder, A Mystery, and a Marriage," and "The Mysterious Balloonist." "The Comedy of Those Extraordinary Twins," neither extrapolative nor predictive, is based on the Tocci Twins. Physical science extrapolation is used in "Sold to Satan" where Satan is made of radium and Twain predicts the isolation of various elements by Madame Curie, and in the incomplete "Shackleford's Ghost" where a man becomes invisible after taking a potion created after numerous experiments by the local scientist.

Two works containing alternate settings, "The Curious Republic of Gondour" and "History 1,000 Years from Now," are seeming utopias. In "Curious Republic" weighted universal suffrage has developed; education, common sense, and, to a lesser extent, money earn the citizens extra votes. In the incomplete manuscript "History," society has evolved from a democracy to a monarchy. Three incomplete works by Twain employ alternate settings: "The Generation Iceberg," "The Secret History of Eddypus, The World-Empire," and "3000 Years among the Microbes." In "3000" Twain satirizes the human condition. By having a wizard accidently turn a man into a cholera microbe instead of a bird, Twain adopts a distancing from reality that has been a science-fiction technique used by many writers to allow for social criticism without immediately alienating the reader. The setting is the diseased body of a tramp within which millions of microbes live and where nations have their own languages, customs, and governments, all patterned after nations existing during the early 20th century. The microbes are not described as aliens; instead they look, act, talk, and think precisely as man does. This setting allows Twain to comment on his favorite themes: the stupidity of government officials, the hypocrisy of organized religions, the prejudices evident in class systems, the problem of the lie—here related to the tall tale. The microbe tells his friends about the real world and they compliment him on his poetic inspiration—with one exception he is flatly not believed.

Unlike Hank of *A Connecticut Yankee in King Arthur's Court*, the microbe does not introduce new technology to the society. Instead the society is ahead of his time, having a device that records thoughts and images and condenses them to perfectly understandable encapsulations of facts and meanings. Notably, a religious scientist reveals to the microbe a world view akin to Twain's by expounding on the absurdity of man's false sense of superiority. Technology is celebrated when a microscope is used to discover that on every level of organism the cycle of life is the same; thereby enforcing the moral treatise of the absurdity of man's presumptious superiority.

In "The Secret History of Eddypus, the World-Empire," Twain presents a 29th-century dystopia ruled by the Christian Science church that is comparable to the late 18th-century lifestyle, dominated by religious persecution, arrogance, and misinformation. He presents no new technology, scientific inquiry having been effectively stopped by the church. He shows the absurdities of organized religion, which perpetuates the status quo, encourages a distinct disrespect for truth, and consistently and with a vengence destroys knowledge for fear that it would abrogate the power of the church. The narrator has begun to write a history of the world, all such references having been destroyed by the church and replaced by the church's version. The history is a humorous mish-mash of erroneous facts until the 19th-century section, which contains an accurate delineation of scientific discoveries and their effects, focusing on evolution, both biological and societal, in which he identifies circumstances and environment as those factors which chart the course of the world.

In "The Generation Iceberg" Twain speculates on the type of society that would evolve in a group totally isolated. This fascination with isolated groups and the effect of their exposure to technology is also evident in "A Murder, A Mystery, and A Marriage" as well as *A Connecticut Yankee in King Arthur's Court.*

"From the 'London Times' of 1904," "The Great Dark," and *A Connecticut Yankee in King Arthur's Court* all reflect the increasing cynicism of Twain's later years. In the confusion of dream and reality accompanied by alteration of time and space, Twain creates different worlds for his protagonists to struggle in. These dystopias present Twain's perception of the unchanging human condition; man as a petty being, always willing to prey on his fellowman.

The comic relief in *Connecticut Yankee* (a literary burlesque of Malory's *Morte Darthur*) erupts through Twain's satire of the age of chivalry whose precepts had been adopted by the Old South, a frequent target of Twain's social criticism in his mainstream works. But primarily Twain investigates the effects of industrialization on a pre-industrial society, a matter of public concern both in relation to the United States and to our foreign policy at the time. In this view, Twain attacked Social Darwinism: the establishment of an industrialized, capitalistic society where the common man was once again suppressed by the financial power of a few individuals who had gained their power through that technological revolution.

Hank, the protagonist of *Connecticut Yankee*, a 19th-century common working man, rises to power in King Arthur's Court through creative use of his technical skills and scientific knowledge. By introducing industrialization, Hank attempts to change the economic, political, and intellectual structures of a nation of oppressed people, but his failure results not so much through the powers of the church and state as through his own weakness. He succumbs to one of the primary evils of capitalism (according to Twain): once Hank gains power, he becomes self-absorbed. The megalomanic Hank instigates a civil war (purportedly in the name of creating a viable civilization for the common man) which results in the ultimate destruction of all that he has established. What makes *Connecticut Yankee* science fiction is not just the question of whether Hank actually experiences time travel and suspended animation or whether he dreams it. Instead it is Twain's questioning of the effects of technology, his concentration on the idea of technology in another time and space.

The problem of dream versus reality occurs again in "The Great Dark." Whereas in *Connecticut Yankee* the protagonist goes back in time to a setting already familiar to the reader, in "The Great Dark" Twain concentrates on establishing a setting in which circumstance, not time, is important. Presenting a tiny world as seen through a microscope, Twain creates a whole watery universe filled with monsters, destruction, and suffering for his protagonist to attempt to survive in. Like Hank, Mr. Edwards returns to the present no longer accepting it as real, finding his other existence to have all the qualities of reality and his present that of the dream. This exploration of dream versus reality is closely linked with temporal/spatial relationships so that time and setting become an integral part of what makes these works science fiction. In *Connecticut Yankee*, science, or at least technology, is a thematic consideration, whereas in "The Great Dark" technology is used only as a tool to create the setting in which the characters must question temporal/spatial relationships. Twain embarks on another approach to science in "From the 'London Times' of 1904." Instead of employing a thematic consideration of technology as in *Connecticut Yankee* or using an already existing scientific instrument to create the circumstances of the story as in "The Great Dark," Twain invents the telectroscope (television) to use in conjunction with his usual exploration of thought and visual transference in temporal/spatial relationships.

In these works, Twain, as an early writer of science fiction, presents three different approaches still frequently used in the genre. Additionally, through his social criticism, Twain is one of the first mainstream writers to present dystopias rather than utopias to show by comparison rather than by contrast the inequities of the social institutions he questions: religion, government, taxes, prejudice, slavery, censorship, and politics. Yet his dark view of man is made bearable through his caustic humor. He invokes our laughter even as we accept with humility his accusations of our greed, jealousy, lack of common sense, thirst for power, cruelty, and ultimately the smallness of mind of the human beast.

—Jane B. Weedman

---

# U

**UTLEY, Steven.** American. Born in 1948. Address: c/o Heidelberg Publishers, 1003 Brown Building, Austin, Texas 78701, U.S.A.

SCIENCE-FICTION PUBLICATIONS

Uncollected Short Stories

"The Unkindest Cut of All," in *Perry Rhodan 20.* New York, Ace, 1972.
"Parrot Phrase," in *Perry Rhodan 24.* New York, Ace, 1973.
"The Queen and I," in *Perry Rhodan 31.* New York, Ace, 1973.
"Crash Cameron and the Slime Beast," in *Vertex* (Los Angeles), June 1973.
"The Reason Why," in *Vertex* (Los Angeles), December 1973.
"Hung Like an Elephant," with Joe Pumilia, and "Womb, with a View," in *Alternities*, edited by David Gerrold, New York, Dell, 1974.
"Sport," in *Best SF 1973*, edited by Harry Harrison and Brian Aldiss. New York, Putnam, and London, Sphere, 1974.
"Deeper Than Death," in *Vertex* (Los Angeles), April 1974.
"Act of Mercy," in *Galaxy* (New York), July 1974.
"Big Black Whole" and "Time and Variance," in *Galaxy* (New York), August 1974.
"Amber Eyes," in *Galaxy* (New York), December 1974.
"The Great Red Spot," with Joe Pumilia, and "Dear Mom, I Don't Like It Here," in *Vertex* (Los Angeles), February 1975.
"Caring for Your Edaphosaurus," in *Vertex* (Los Angeles), August 1975.
"The Other Half," in *Galaxy* (New York), September 1975.
"Custer's Last Jump," with Howard Waldrop, in *Universe 6*, edited by Terry Carr. New York, Doubleday, 1976; London, Dobson, 1978.
"Predators," in *The Ides of Tomorrow*, edited by Terry Carr. Boston, Little Brown, 1976.
"Ghost Seas," in *Lone Star Universe*, edited by George W. Proctor and Steven Utley. Austin, Texas, Heidelberg, 1976.
"Sic Transit . . . ?," with Howard Waldrop, in *Stellar 2*, edited by Judy-Lynn del Rey. New York, Ballantine, 1976.
"Getting Away," in *Galaxy* (New York), January 1976.
"Larval Stage," in *Galaxy* (New York), July 1976.
"Ocean," in *Fantastic* (New York), August 1976.
"The Man at the Bottom of the Sea," in *Galaxy* (New York), October 1976.
"The Thirteenth Labor," in *Stellar 3*, edited by Judy-Lynn del Rey. New York, Ballantine, 1977.
"Black as the Pit, from Pole to Pole" with Howard Waldrop, in *New Dimensions 7*, edited by Robert Silverberg. New York, Harper, and London, Gollancz, 1977.
"Sidhe," in *More Devil's Kisses*, edited by Linda Lovecraft. London, Corgi, 1977.
"In Brightest Day, In Darkest Night," in *Fantastic* (New York), February 1977.
"Passport for a Phoenix," in *Galaxy* (New York), April 1977.
"Spectator Sport," in *Amazing* (New York), July 1977.
"The Maw," in *Fantasy and Science Fiction* (New York), July 1977.
"Flies by Night," with Lisa Tuttle, in *SF Choice 77*, edited by Mike Ashley. London, Quartet, 1977.
"Tom Sawyer's Sub-Orbital Escapade," with Lisa Tuttle, in *Ascents of Wonder*, edited by David Gerrold and Stephen Goldin. New York, Popular Library, 1977.
"Losing Streak," in *Fantasy and Science Fiction* (New York), January 1977.
"Our Vanishing Triceratops," with Joe Pumilia, in *Amazing* (New York), March 1977.
"Time and Hagakure," in *Asimov's Choice: Black Holes and Bug-Eyed Monsters*, edited by George H. Scithers. New York, Dale, 1978.
"Deviation from a Theme," in *The Rivals of King Kong*, edited by Michel Parry. London, Corgi, 1978.
"Uncoiling," with Lisa Tuttle, in *Fantastic* (New York), April 1978.
"Personal Column," in *Sex in the 21st Century*, edited by Michel Parry and Milton Subotsky. London, Panther, 1979.
"The Man Who Ran Up the Clock," in *Fantastic* (New York), January 1979.
"Leaves," in *Amazing* (New York), February 1979.
"Genocide Man," in *Fantasy and Science Fiction* (New York), April 1979.
"Upstart," in *The Best from Fantasy and Science Fiction 23*, edited by Edward L. Ferman. New York, Doubleday, 1980.

OTHER PUBLICATIONS

Other

Editor, with George W. Proctor, *Lone Star Universe: Speculative Fiction from Texas.* Austin, Texas, Heidelberg, 1976.

*

Steven Utley comments:

I don't have much to say, meaningful or otherwise, about my stories. I did, of course, think rather highly of some of my own work when I wrote it. I was possessed of considerable enthusiasm for what I was about. Disenchantment with the SF field, when it set in, set in hard, and now time has made all the difference. Anymore, I view my having been a writer as just a phase, like puberty, into which I entered at one point in my life and from which I emerged, not exactly unscathed, at a subsequent point. I've done some writing since the, ah, divorce, but I no longer *think* of myself as a writer, only as someone who every now and then misses the actual grueling work of sitting in front of the typewriter for hours on end. Most of my energy goes into other pursuits which are quite unrelated to SF and, more to the point, quite satisfying.

* * *

After a self-enforced hiatus of eight years, Steven Utley, who published nearly 60 short SF, fantasy, or horror stories from 1972 to 1981, began writing and publishing again in the late 1980's. His "retirement" stemmed from disillusionment with science fiction and an emotionally satisfying commitment to other pursuits, especially listening to and collecting swing-era music and writing and drawing an outrageously satiric comic strip called "The Huggybunnies."

In the first seven years of his career (1972–1979), Utley established a reputation as a prolific author of short stories and novelettes, either alone or in collaboration with a number of other Texas-based writers, most notably Howard Waldrop and Lisa Tuttle. With George W. Proctor, he edited a volume of SF and fantasy by Texans, *Lone Star Universe*, whose publication Harlan Ellison hailed as a "watershed event." Working solely at less-than-novel length, Utley produced fiction either competent but conventional ("Genocide Man") or both bleak and moving ("Getting Away"). At his best, his angst leavened with humor, angry wit, or local color, he created chilling horror stories ("Ghost Seas"), scathingly funny satires ("Upstart"), marvelous pastiches ("Black as the Pit, from Pole to Pole," with Waldrop), and evocative and melancholy science fiction ("The Man at the Bottom of the Sea").

"Custer's Last Jump," with Waldrop, first secured wide notice for Utley's talents. In frontier America, the Oglala Sioux, flying Krupp monoplanes, defeat George Armstrong Custer's 7th Calvary and its airborne auxiliary, the 505th Balloon Infantry. Related in earnest textbook prose, this off-the-wall tour de force concludes with a "Suggested Reading" list as wacky and authentic-seeming as the "historical" matter before it, a bibliographic fillip probably inspired by Farmer's convolute appendices in the mock-biography *Tarzan Alive* (1972).

A second Utley-Waldrop collaboration, "Black as the Pit, from Pole to Pole," pays homage to Farmer (again), Mary Shelley, Poe, Verne, Burroughs, and others. Its hero is that quintessential symbol of alienation, the Frankenstein monster, and its setting is the perilous hollow interior of the earth. Although its disparate elements do not always mesh convincingly, sheer narrative *chutzpah* often disguises the fact.

Among Utley's solo efforts, "Upstart" is a blunt and hilarious satire of SF's spacefarer-as-superhero ethos, perhaps the last word on this indefatigable idiocy. "Ghost Seas" invokes the desolate West Texas landscape in the service of a terrifying tale of avarice and revenge. "Time and Hagakure" presents the son of a Japanese kamikaze pilot trying to preserve his sanity by mediating, through time, the salvation of his doomed father. "Getting Away" exploits Utley's deep-seated interest in dinosaurs, which gives his protagonist a means of psychological escape from a disheartening future. And his final early-period story "The Beasts of Love" dissects a foundering marriage, with an impact as profound as that of Richard Matheson's classic 1950 story "Born of Man and Woman."

The strongest apparent influences on Utley while writing these early stories were Ray Bradbury's October landscapes, the ironic pessimism of Robert Silverberg's *Tower of Glass* and *Dying Inside*, the pop-culture eclecticism of Philip José Farmer, and the manic-depressive black humor of Barry N. Malzberg, whose approach Utley affectionaly parodied in "Losing Streak." Working to discover his own voice and méteir, he seemed close to a personal breakthrough when he simply abandoned the game, remarking, "Disenchantment with the SF field, when it set in, set in hard."

In 1989, Utley returned with a technically adroit revision of an older story, "My Wife," published in *Isaac Asimov's Science Fiction Magazine*, a character study of a rich monomaniac with a disturbing set of reasons for reversing the suicide of his wife. Showing a more confident grasp of the storyteller's art than ever before, "My Wife" signaled the resurgence of Utley's career. His next story, "The Tall Grass," also published in *Isaac Asimov's Science Fiction Magazine*, was a first-person time-travel story recalling Theodore Sturgeon's "The Man Who Lost the Sea" and the ruin-pocked South Pacific landscapes of J.G. Ballard, without seeming derivative. (In fact, "The Tall Grass," is a near-perfect example of the doomed-protagonist SF story.) "Where or When" (in *Asimov's*) and "Look Away," (forthcoming in *Fantasy and Science Fiction*), both from 1991, reveal Utley's intense interest in the American Civil War; the former misdirects two time-tourists bound for London, 1851, into a battle in Virginia, 1864, while the latter dilates on the manifest destiny of a triumphant Confederacy and the would-be Napoleon set on creating a vast new slave empire in Latin America.

More stories will surely follow, including "The Glowing Cloud," a novella about the eruption of Mount Pelée. As a result, Utley's once constricted reputation can only grow.

—Michael Bishop

---

# V

**VANCE, Gerald.** *See* **GARRETT, Randall; PHILLIPS, Rog.**

---

**VANCE, Jack** (John Holbrook Vance). Also writes as John Holbrook Vance; Peter Held; Ellery Queen; Alan Wade. American. Born in San Francisco, California, 28 August 1916. Educated at the University of California, Berkeley, B.A. 1942. Married Norma Ingold in 1946; one son. Self-employed writer. Recipient: Mystery Writers of America Edgar Allan Poe award, 1960; Hugo award, 1963, 1967; Nebula award, 1966; Jupiter award, 1974; World Fantasy Convention Life Achievement award, 1984. Agent: Ralph Vicinanza Ltd., 432 Park Avenue South, Suite 1205, New York, New York 10016. Address: 6383 Valley View Road, Oakland, California 94611, U.S.A.

SCIENCE-FICTION PUBLICATIONS

Novels (series: Alastor; Big Planet; Cadwal Chronicles; Dying Earth; Durdane; Keith Gersen; Demon Princes; Lyonesse; Tschai/Planet of Adventure)

*The Space Pirate.* New York, Toby Press, 1953; abridged edition as *The Five Gold Bands*, New York, Ace, 1963; London, Granada, 1980.
*Vandals of the Void* (for children). Philadelphia, Winston, 1953.
*To Live Forever.* New York, Ballantine, 1956; London, Sphere, 1976.
*Big Planet.* New York, Avalon, 1957; London, Coronet, 1977.
*The Languages of Pao.* New York, Avalon, 1958; London, Coronet, 1989.
*Slaves of the Klau.* New York, Ace, 1958.
*The Dragon Masters.* New York, Ace, 1963; London, Dobson, 1965.
*The Houses of Iszm, Son of the Tree.* New York, Ace, 1964; *Son of the Tree* published separately, London, Mayflower, 1974.
*The Star King* (Gersen). New York, Berkley, 1964; London, Dobson, 1966.
*The Killing Machine* (Gersen). New York, Berkley, 1964; London, Dobson, 1967.
*Monsters in Orbit.* New York, Ace, 1965; London, Dobson, 1977.
*Space Opera.* New York, Pyramid, 1965; London, Coronet, 1982.
*The Blue World.* New York, Ballantine, 1966; London, Mayflower, 1976.
*The Brains of Earth.* New York, Ace, 1966; London, Dobson, 1975; as *Nopalgarth*, New York, DAW, 1980; London, Panther, 1984.
*The Palace of Love* (Gersen). New York, Berkley, 1967; London, Dobson, 1968.
*City of the Chasch* (Tschai). New York, Ace, 1968; London, Dobson, 1975; as *Chasch*, New York, Bluejay, 1986.
*Emphyrio.* New York, Doubleday, 1969.
*Servants of the Wankh* (Tschai). New York, Ace, 1969; London, Dobson, 1975; as *Wankh*, New York, Bluejay, 1986.
*The Dirdir* (Tschai). New York, Ace, 1969; London, Dobson, 1975.
*The Pnume* (Tschai). New York, Ace, 1970; London, Dobson, 1975.
*The Anome* (Durdane). New York, Dell, 1973; London, Hodder and Stoughton, 1975; as *The Faceless Man*, New York, Ace, 1978; London, Gollancz, 1987.
*The Brave Free Men* (Durdane). New York, Dell, 1973; London, Hodder and Stoughton, 1975.
*Trullion: Alastor 2262.* New York, Ballantine, 1973; London, Mayflower, 1979.
*The Asutra* (Durdane). New York, Dell, 1974; London, Hodder and Stoughton, 1975.
*The Gray Prince.* Indianapolis, Bobbs Merrill, 1974; London, Coronet, 1976.
*Marune: Alastor 933.* New York, Ballantine, 1975; London, Coronet, 1978.
*Showboat World* (Big Planet). New York, Pyramid, 1975; London, Coronet, 1977.
*Maske: Thaery.* New York, Berkley, 1976; London, Fontana, 1978.
*Wyst: Alastor 1716.* New York, DAW, 1978.
*The Face* (Gersen). New York, DAW, 1979; London, Dobson, 1980.
*The Book of Dreams* (Gersen). New York, DAW, 1981; London, Coronet, 1982.
*Cugel's Saga* (Dying Earth). New York, Pocket Books, 1983; London, Panther, 1985.
*Rhialto the Marvellous* (Dying Earth). New York, Baen, and London, Panther, 1984.
*Strange Notions.* Columbia, Pennsylvania, Underwood Miller, 1985.
*The Dark Ocean.* Columbia, Pennsylvania, Underwood Miller, 1985.
*Light from a Lone Star.* Cambridge, Massachusetts, Nesfa Press, 1985.
*Araminta Station* (Cadwal). Los Angeles, Underwood Miller, 1987; London, New English Library, 1988.
*Ecce and Old Earth* (Cadwal). New York, St. Martin's Press, 1991.

Short Stories (series: Dying Earth)

*The Dying Earth.* New York, Curl, 1950; London, Mayflower, 1972.
*Future Tense.* New York, Ballantine, 1964; as *Dust of Far Suns*, New York, DAW, 1981.
*The World Between and Other Stories.* New York, Ace, 1965; as *The Moon Moth and Other Stories*, London, Dobson, 1976.
*The Eyes of the Overworld* (Dying Earth). New York, Ace, 1966; London, Mayflower, 1972.
*The Many Worlds of Magnus Ridolph.* New York, Ace, 1966; London, Dobson, 1977; as *The Complete Magnus Ridolph*, San Francisco, Underwood Miller, 1984.
*The Last Castle.* New York, Ace, 1967.

*Eight Fantasms and Magics.* New York, Macmillan, 1969; as *Fantasms and Magics*, London, Mayflower, 1978.
*The Worlds of Jack Vance.* New York, Ace, 1973.
*The Best of Jack Vance.* New York, Pocket Books, 1976.
*Green Magic.* San Francisco, Underwood Miller, 1979.
*The Bagful of Dreams.* San Francisco, Underwood Miller, 1979.
*The Seventeen Virgins.* San Francisco, Underwood Miller, 1979.
*Galactic Effectuator.* Columbia, Pennsylvania, Underwood Miller, 1980; London, Coronet, 1983.
*The Narrow Land.* New York, DAW, 1982; London, Coronet, 1984.
*Lost Moons.* Columbia, Pennsylvania, Underwood Miller, 1982.
*The Augmented Agent*, edited by Steven Owen Godersky. San Francisco, Underwood Miller, 1986; London, New English Library, 1989.
*The Dark Side of the Moon.* San Francisco, Underwood Miller, 1986; London, New English Library, 1989.
*Chateau d'If and Other Stories.* Lancaster, Pennsylvania, Underwood Miller, 1990; London, New English Library, 1989.

OTHER PUBLICATIONS

Novels (Lyonesse series)

*Suldrum's Garden.* New York, Berkley, 1983; London, Granada, 1984.
*The Green Pearl.* San Francisco, Underwood Miller, 1985; London, Grafton, 1986.
*Madouc.* Los Angeles, Underwood Miller, 1989; London, Grafton, 1990.

Novels as John Holbrook Vance

*Isle of Peril* (as Alan Wade). New York, Curl, 1957; as *Bird Isle*, Los Angeles, Underwood Miller, 1988.
*Take My Face* (as Peter Held). New York, Curl, 1957; as Jack Vance, Los Angeles, Underwood Miller, 1988.
*The Man in the Cage.* New York, Random House, 1960; London, Boardman, 1961.
*The Fox Valley Murders.* Indianapolis, Bobbs Merrill, 1966; London, Hale, 1967.
*The Pleasant Grove Murders.* Indianapolis, Bobbs Merrill, 1967; London, Hale, 1968.
*The Deadly Isles.* Indianapolis, Bobbs Merrill, 1969; London, Hale, 1970.
*Bad Ronald.* New York, Ballantine, 1973.
*The House on Lily Street.* San Francisco, Underwood Miller, 1979.
*The View from Chickweed's Window.* San Francisco, Underwood Miller, 1979.

Novels as Ellery Queen

*The Four Johns.* New York, Pocket Books, 1964; as *Four Men Called John*, London, Gollancz, 1976.
*A Room to Die In.* New York, Pocket Books, 1965.
*The Madman Theory.* New York, Pocket Books, 1966.

Plays

Television Plays: *Captain Video* (6 episodes), 1952-53.

*

Bibliography: *Fantasms: A Bibliography of the Literature of Jack Vance* by Daniel J.H. Levack and Tim Underwood, San Francisco, Underwood Miller, 1978.

Manuscript Collection: Mugar Memorial Library, Boston University.

Critical Studies: *Jack Vance, Science Fiction Stylist* by Richard Tiedman, Wabash, Indiana, Coulson, 1965; *Jack Vance* edited by Tim Underwood and Chuck Miller, New York, Taplinger, 1980; *Demon Prince: The Dissonant Worlds of Jack Vance* by Jack Rawlins. San Bernardino, Borgo Press, 1986.

* * *

Jack Vance has been called "a gaudily painted coelacanth," who "swashbuckled on a million imaginary worlds." Unfortunately, Vance is generally viewed as a writer of SF not far removed from fantasy more interested in effect than thought. Yet if analyzed closely, Vance's works often unexpectedly subvert the genre they appear to typify. Most noticeable about Vance's writing is his imaginative fecundity in constructing exotic yet plausible societies, many often in the same novel. For instance, in *Big Planet* the characters travel through at least eight different societies—yet cover only a thousand of the planet's 40 thousand miles. This strength becomes a weakness when characters (and readers) who have just grown familiar with one society are plunged into yet another.

Only recently revealing a loose internal connectedness, Vance's galaxy is predominately human. Aliens, if encountered, never exist with humans in amity. In *Nopalgarth* (published first as *The Brains of Earth*), when humans and Xaxan must unite to throw off telepathic parasites, the hero muses that "there could never be a comaraderie [sic]." More often, both species can only exist in a master and slave relationship, as in *The Dragon Masters*, where the dragons and humans employ the genetically manipulated descendants of each other as their soldiery. Perhaps the best-known of Vance's aliens occur in his most successful series, The Planet of Adventure, in which the hero must liberate humans from the four alien races who have molded and enslaved them.

Vance lavishes his inventiveness on these societies, providing languages, epigraphs, footnotes, and appendices. His much-praised style (estimable only perhaps in comparison to what passes for it in the genre) results from his desire to describe these communities as fully as possible. Overlooked under its rococo flourishes is the depth of their presentation, particularly their economic bases. *The Houses of Iszm* describes an attempt to break a monopoly for cheap housing; *Emphyrio* details how an aristocracy's restraint of trade keeps a society at a feudal level; *Wyst: Alastor 1716* shows how a society that denigrates labor becomes static.

Vance's societies are never altruistic. When a character uses the word trust, another will ask, "What word is that?" A guidebook advises: "NOTHING IS FREE except the air you breathe." This distancing reveals an undervalued aspect of Vance's style: its humor, produced by the contrast of the heated descriptions with the dispassionate, almost juridical tone. *Space Opera*, his funniest novel, deflates the usual connotations of its title; a director is warned not to adapt *Fidelio* completely to alien understanding: "their sex play is a matter of spraying the intended mate with a viscous liquid. I doubt if you wish to carry similitude to quite this extent."

Vance usually endorses the typical *Analog* virtues of freedom and independence, as his title *The Brave Free Men* indicates. The hero of *The Dragon Masters* argues that the sacerdotes might not be as gentle as they appear: "We do not know that they are pacifists. We do know that they are men." Yet Vance at times plays with these conventions. In *Servants of the Wankh*, the aliens must be rescued from the tyranny their human servants have placed them under.

Vance, of course, does write space opera, most notably in the Demon Princes series, a tale of galactic-wide revenge, and the Planet of Adventure series, both however weakened by the facelessness of the main characters. The paradigmatic Vance plot is the SF *bildungsroman*, familiar from Heinlein's juveniles. His heroes soon come to an epiphany in which they realize, in characteristic rhetoric, they have "to wrench sense from archaic nonsense; to strike the sigil of human will upon elemental chaos; to affirm the shining brilliance of one soul alone but alive among five trillion flaccid gray corpuscles." Yet Vance realizes the danger in such a position, and his villains are not far removed from his heroes; as one of the Demon Princes tells Kirth Gersen, "You are a monomaniac; I am the same." What separates them is the heroes's realistic sense of their place in the universe, both temporally and spatially. Vance's villain "lived in the present, certain only of his own ego; the past was a record, the future an amorphous blot waiting for shape." While his heroes may call themselves "vagabonds" and comment on their "picaresque" adventures, their balanced sense of purpose gives them their reality.

Vance often fools the expectations of readers used to the conventional SF plot of hero-conquering through technological or personal force. In *Space Opera*, the prison planet is named Skylark, a dig at E.E. "Doc" Smith. In *The Languages of Pao*, Vance's justly celebrated elaboration of the Whorf-Sapir linguistic hypothesis, a false rumor is spread about the young hero's return: "He trained a corps of metal-clad warriors impervious to fire, steel or power; the mission of his life was to avenge his father's death." Instead, the warriors rebel against the hero, and he must use language to gain his goal. Vance's most complete subversion occurs in the Durdane trilogy, where the young hero, after defeating an alien invasion, leads an unnecessary war of liberation on their home planet: "The spaceship which they had taken with such grim determination—it actually had come to take them back to Durdane. Small wonder the resistance had been so scant!" This seems Vance's answer to the accusation of mindless swashbuckling.

*Araminta Station*, like many recent works by veteran SF writers, is long, but not inflated. All his trademarks are present, including a mystery to be solved (Vance is one of the few writers to win the Edgar as well as the Hugo and Nebula awards). This refreshingly youthful work contains a characteristic scene when the hero contemplates the universe: "I looked up at the sky and felt a sudden openness—as if my mind were aware of the whole galaxy. At the same time I felt all the millions and billions of people who had spread through the stars. Their lives, or the people, seemed to give off a whir or a hum, really a soft slow music." This sense of wonder at the possibilities of an infinite universe, and of the humanity which inhabits it, is what propels and informs all of Vance's work, and makes him an important writer.

—William Laskowski, Jr.

---

**VAN LHIN, Eric.** *See* **del REY, Lester.**

---

**VAN SCYOC, Sydney J(oyce).** American. Born in Mt. Vernon, Indiana, 27 July 1939. Educated at Florida State University, Tallahassee; University of Hawaii, Honolulu; Chabot College, Hayward, California; California State University, Hayward. Married Jim R. Van Scyoc in 1957; one daughter and one son. Since 1962, freelance writer. Secretary, 1975–77, and president, 1977–79, Starr King Unitarian Church, Hayward. Agent: Howard Morhaim Literary Agency, 501 Fifth Avenue, New York, New York 10017. Address: 2636 East Avenue, Hayward, California 94541, U.S.A.

SCIENCE-FICTION PUBLICATIONS

Novels (series: Darkchild)

*Saltflower*. New York, Avon, 1971.
*Assignment: Nor'Dyren*. New York, Avon, 1973.
*Starmother*. New York, Berkley, 1976.
*Cloudcry*. New York, Berkley, 1977.
*Sunwaifs*. New York, Berkley, 1981.
*Darkchild*. New York, Berkley, 1982; London, Penguin, 1984.
*Bluesong* (Darkchild). New York, Berkley, 1983; London, Penguin, 1984.
*Starsilk* (Darkchild). New York, Berkley, 1984.
*Drowntide*. New York, Berkley, and London, Futura, 1987.
*Feather Stroke*. New York, Avon, 1989.
*Deepwater Dreams*. New York, Avon, 1991.

Uncollected Short Stories

"Shatter the Wall," in *Galaxy* (New York), February 1962.
"Bimmie Says," in *Galaxy* (New York), October 1962.
"Pollony Undiverted," in *Galaxy* (New York), February 1963.
"Zack with His Scar," in *Fantasy and Science Fiction* (New York), March 1963.
"Cornie on the Walls," in *Fantastic* (New York), August 1963.
"Soft and Soupy Whispers," in *Galaxy* (New York), April 1964.
"One Man's Dream," in *Fantasy and Science Fiction* (New York), November 1964.
"The Dead Ones," in *Worlds of Tomorrow* (New York), January 1965.
"A Visit to Cleveland General," in *World's Best Science Fiction 1969*, edited by Donald A. Wollheim and Terry Carr. New York, Ace, and London, Gollancz, 1969.
"Unidentified Fallen Object," in *Fantasy and Science Fiction* (New York), January 1969.
"Little Blue Hawk," in *Galaxy* (New York), May 1969.
"Summons to the Medicmat," in *Worlds of Tomorrow* (New York), Spring 1971.
"Noepti-Noe," in *Galaxy* (New York), November 1972.
"When Petals Fall," in *Two Views of Wonder*, edited by Thomas M. Scortia and Chelsea Quinn Yarbro. New York, Ballantine, 1973.
"Mnarra Mobilis," in *The Best from If 2*. New York, Award, 1974.
"Skyveil," in *Galaxy* (New York), April 1974.
"Aberrant," in *Analog* (New York), June 1974.
"Sweet Sister, Green Brother," in *The Best from Galaxy 3*, edited by James Baen. New York, Award, 1975.

"Deathsong," in *The 1975 Annual World's Best SF*, edited by Donald A. Wollheim and Arthur W. Saha. New York, DAW, 1975; Morley, Yorkshire, Elmfield Press, 1976.
"Nightfire," in *Cassandra Rising*, edited by Alice Laurance. New York, Doubleday, 1978.
"Mountain Wings," in *Isaac Asimov's Science Fiction Magazine* (New York), November 1979.
"Darkmorning," in *Isaac Asimov's Science Fiction Magazine* (New York), March 1980.
"Stonefoal," in *Isaac Asimov's Science Fiction Magazine* (New York), August 1980.
"Laughing Man," in *Isaac Asimov's Science Fiction Magazine* (New York), November 1980.
"Bluewater Dreams," in *Isaac Asimov's Science Fiction Magazine* (New York), March 1981.
"The Teaching," in *Isaac Asimov's Science Fiction Magazine* (New York), April 1982.
"Fire-Caller," in *Isaac Asimov's Space of Her Own*, edited by Shawna McCarthy. New York, Davis, 1983.
"Meadows of Light," in *Isaac Asimov's Science Fiction Magazine* (New York), December 1985.

*

Manuscript Collection: California State University, Fullerton.

Sydney J. Van Scyoc comments:

My earlier short fiction was set on Earth in the not-too-distant future and dealt primarily with individuals struggling against an increasingly dehumanizing technological society. I took several years off from writing in the mid-1960's, while my children were very young. Soon after I began writing again, I found my focus had shifted to short fiction set on other planets and dealt primarily with communities struggling against inexplicable alien environments. I am increasingly intrigued now by the genetic and social changes which I believe will overtake the human race once we begin to colonize other planets. I prefer not to deal in much detail with the inevitable technological changes we will see. Instead I like to set my fiction on isolated worlds inhabited by a relatively small human population. My personal orientation is increasingly pantheistic, and in my longer fiction I am attempting to deal with the spiritual relationship of human to environment.

* * *

Sydney J. Van Scyoc's early stories are set on earth not very far in the future and show the dehumanization of persons in an advanced technological society. The dehumanization is primarily apparent in the characters's lack of personal freedom and conscious choice in such stories as "Pollony Undiverted," "Soft and Soupy Whispers," and the chilling "A Visit to Cleveland General." "Nightfire" is an unusual story in which a stalemated war in North America has confined 12 million noncombatants as virtual hostages in orbit above the earth for 41 years. The protagonist, Corneil Rothler, in a carefully planned coup d'etat ruthlessly engineers a truce alone.

A major shift in her work becomes apparent in the long short story "Little Blue Hawk," set in the 21st century; this story focuses on the personal and social costs of human genetic engineering. Van Scyoc's interest in the relationship of human with alien species and an alien ecology appears in "Noepti-Noe," "Sweet Sister, Green Brother," and "Aberrant." These stories emphasize the interdependence and unity of all life forms.

Van Scyoc's impressive first novel, *Saltflower*, takes the basic premise of a dying race seeding earth to generate a transpecies who will be able to reproduce and be viable. The novel is set on earth in the year 2024, and follows the adventures of one of the "transracial" children, Hadley Greer, who is under surveillance by the U.S. government agency SIBling. Most of the action takes place at the Purification Colony's headquarters near Salt Lake City. The Purification Colony is a cult headed by a psychotic leader, Dr. Braith. The novel deftly blends government intrigue, and burgling, religious fanaticism, mysterious murders, and credible alien consciousness, reactions, and biology.

*Assignment: Nor'Dyren* is an anti-utopian novel with strong satiric elements. It begins on earth in the not-too-distant future with a maintenance sub-engineer, Tollan Bailey, attempting to get a job in the huge company CalMega. Only a few people are employed; the rest live comfortable, futile lives without realizing the social controls that narrow their existence. Bailey wins a trip to the planet Nor'Dyren inhabited by three humanoid species whose rigid social roles and asexual inter-species marriage are leading to a breakdown of the moneyless economy and culture. The Gonnegon are the thinkers and administrators, the Allegon serve, and the Berregon manufacture. The novel follows Bailey's attempts to understand the culture and his maturation. He is an appealing character, particularly in his enchantment with trying to repair machines on Nor'Dyren and help the aliens. The anthropologist Laarica Johns, sent to aid him in his legal battle, discovers the reason for the de-evolution on Nor'Dyren with the help of Patt, a rebellious Berregon. The satire of earth bureaucracy, rigid social and sexual roles, and crippling cultural assumptions both on earth and Nor'Dyren is effective. The novel is an impassioned plea for a humane culture in which persons can be free to develop their capacities and make ethical choices.

*Starmother* presents the pathos of ostracized human mutants on a colony world, a race of aliens, the dirads, and the testing of the young protagonist, Jahna Swiss, a cadet of the Service Corps from the planet Peace. The novel alternates the points of view of Jahna, Zuniin, an alienated social outcast, and a young mother, Piety, who is a victim of the superstition and fanaticism of the puritanical human colonists, known as The First Fathers, on the planet Nelding. The alien planet, the various social groups, and species are vividly realized. Suspense is generated by the attempt of Zuniin to kill Jahna out of insane jealousy and xenophobia. Jahna's ethical dilemma and her final commitment to the mutant children enrich the novel. Van Scyoc contrasts the civilization of Peace, Jahna's planet, with Nelding, showing the deficiencies of rigid social roles, fanatic religion, and superstition which make life almost unbearable on the unlovely Nelding.

*Cloudcry* is an expansion and development of the short story "Deathsong." Around the core of the earlier story of an encounter with still-powerful alien artifacts resembling flutes by members of two humanoid races on an alien planet, Van Scyoc has added the framestory of the human space adventurer Verron's search for the man-leopards of the planet Rumar and the complication of a deadly space disease called bloodblossom. Verrons is exiled on the quarantine plant, Selmarii, along with another human, Sadler Wells, and a sentient bird-man alien because they have the disease. Aleida, one of the descendants of the ancient race, has psionic powers and heightens them with a crystal which focuses solar energy. The radiation from the light dancer's flute cures the bloodblossom disease. Verrons leaves the abandoned isolation planet haunted by the prospect of Aleida and a new race of powerful light dancers who do not share humane values. *Cloudcry*, like Van Scyoc's other novels, is distinguished by vivid imagery and sensuous detail, particularly when she portrays non-human perceptions and consciousness.

*Sunwaifs* continues the author's focus on humans struggling to adapt on uncongenial planets. The sunwaifs are six children born with paranormal mutant abilities, resulting from unusual solar activity during their conception on the harsh planet Destiny. In two alternating points of view over 14 years, the reader follows their development and deepening relationship with the planet. The adaptation of the other humans is aided by the mutant teenagers's increasing understanding of the planet ecology. The climax and resolution of personal and social difficulties comes from an ecological pantheism based on cooperation with natural forces. This hopeful ending promises further enrichment of all intelligent life on the planet Destiny.

Two short stories, "Mountain Wings" and "Darkmorning," set on the harsh planet Brakrath, show the promising direction of Van Scyoc's imagination. This promise is brilliantly fulfilled in the following three novels, set primarily on the same planet. The trilogy, *Darkchild, Bluesong,* and *Starsilk,* forms a major achievement demonstrating her strengths as a science-fiction writer: invention of believable alien environments and psychologies which are truly strange, powerful new myths, and striking relationships of humans and aliens with action plots and memorable characters. Perhaps the finest invention is the sentient starsilk which appears in each novel. The starsilk can form a symbiotic relationship with various sentient beings, providing the occasion for effective poetic description; various types of consciousness are presented which have been a strength of Van Scyoc's style for some years. Also notable is the sun goddess myth, which functions to explain the harnessing of solar energy and is the basis for the testing of characters in all three novels. The individual works fit together in a satisfying whole with an epic sweep encompassing several planets, but each novel can be enjoyed independently as good adventure science fiction.

Her strengths as a writer are evident in two recent novels. *Drowntide* features two credible human cultures on a far planet in the future; each has adapted differently to the presence of sentient whales. The main character's primary conflict involves accepting his real identity and his real people in a kind of *bildungs roman* journey. There are striking descriptions of the sea and humans communicating with and riding intelligent whales. *Feather Stroke* demonstrates Van Scyoc's continuing antipathy to aristocracies, established religions, and priesthoods that limit freedom of thought and produce tyranny. The "simple folk" have a peaceful, democratic, equalitarian way of life that is beautiful in its utopian simplicity and productivity. The author's interest in sun myths is again shown but in a demonic, masculine way with the priesthood of the sun and the evil antagonist of the novel, Narkin, a firemaster, who must be destroyed. While sharing with the previous novel the theme of finding one's identity, this novel is more engrossing with greater suspense and conflict as Dara, the main character, learns to project her consciousness and perceptions into birds; the descriptions of flight are lyrical.

—Diane Parkin-Speer

---

**van VOGT, A(lfred) E(lton).** American. Born near Winnipeg, Manitoba, Canada, 26 April 1912. Educated in schools in Manitoba, graduated 1928; University of Ottawa; University of California, Los Angeles. Served in the Department of National Defense, Ottawa, 1939–41. Married Lydia I. Brayman (second marriage) in 1979. Census clerk, Ottawa, 1931–32; western representative, Maclean Trade Papers, Winnipeg, 1936–39. Managing director, Hubbard Dianetic Research Foundation of California, Los Angeles, 1950–53; co-owner, Hubbard Dianetic Center, Los Angeles, 1953–61, and president, California Association of Dianetic Auditors, 1958–81. Recipient: Manuscripters Literature award, 1948; Count Dracula Society Ann Radcliffe award, 1968; Academy of Science Fiction, Fantasy, and Horror Films award, 1979. B.A.: Golden Gate College, Los Angeles. Guest of Honor, 4th World Science Fiction Convention, 1946, European Science Fiction Convention, 1978 and Metz Festival, France, 1985. Address: c/o DAW Books, 375 Hudson Street, New York, New York 10014, U.S.A.

SCIENCE-FICTION PUBLICATIONS

Novels (series: Clane; Gilbert Gosseyn; Weapon Shop)

*Slan.* Sauk City, Wisconsin, Arkham House, 1946; revised edition, New York, Simon and Schuster, 1951; London, Weidenfeld and Nicholson, 1953.

*The Weapon Makers* (Weapon Shop). Providence, Rhode Island, Hadley, 1947; revised edition, New York, Greenberg, 1952; London, Weidenfeld and Nicolson, 1954; as *One Against Eternity*, New York, Ace, 1955.

*The Book of Ptath.* Reading, Pennsylvania, Fantasy Press, 1947; as *Two Hundred Million A.D.*, New York, Paperback Library, 1964.

*The World of A* (Gosseyn). New York, Simon and Schuster, 1948; revised edition, as *The World of Null-A*, London, Dobson, 1969; New York, Berkley, 1970.

*The Voyage of the Space Beagle.* New York, Simon and Schuster, 1950; London, Grayson, 1951; as *Mission: Interplanetary*, New York, New American Library, 1952.

*The House That Stood Still.* New York, Greenberg, 1950; London, Weidenfeld and Nicolson, 1953; revised edition, as *The Mating Cry*, New York, Galaxy, 1960; as *Undercover Aliens*, London, Panther, 1976.

*The Weapon Shops of Isher.* New York, Greenberg, 1951; London, Weidenfeld and Nicolson, 1952.

*The Mixed Men.* New York, Gnome Press, 1952; as *Mission to the Stars*, New York, Berkley, 1955; London, Digit, 1960.

*The Universe Maker.* New York, Ace, 1953; in *The Universe Maker, and The Proxy Intelligence*, London, Sidgwick and Jackson, 1976.

*Planets for Sale*, with E. Mayne Hull. New York, Fell, 1954; London, Panther, 1978.

*The Pawns of Null-A* (Gosseyn). New York, Ace, 1956; London, Digit, 1960; as *The Players of Null-A*, New York, Berkley, 1966.

*Empire of the Atom* (Clane). Chicago, Shasta, 1957; London, New English Library, 1975.

*The Mind Cage.* New York, Simon and Schuster, 1957; London, Panther, 1960.

*Triad* (omnibus). New York, Simon and Schuster, 1959.

*The War Against the Rull.* New York, Simon and Schuster, 1959; London, Panther, 1961.

*Siege of the Unseen.* New York, Ace, 1959; as *The Three Eyes of Evil*, with *Earth's Last Fortress*, London, Sidgwick and Jackson, 1973.

*The Wizard of Linn* (Clane). New York, Ace, 1962; London, New English Library, 1976.

*The Beast.* New York, Doubleday, 1963; as *Moonbeast*, London, Panther, 1969.

*Rogue Ship.* New York, Doubleday, 1965; London, Dobson, 1967.

*The Winged Man*, with E. Mayne Hull. New York, Doubleday, 1966; London, Sidgwick and Jackson, 1967.

*A Van Vogt Omnibus 1-2.* London, Sidgwick and Jackson, 2 vols., 1967–71.

*The Silkie.* New York, Ace, 1969; London, New English Library, 1973.

*Quest for the Future.* New York, Ace, 1970; London, Sidgwick and Jackson, 1971.

*Children of Tomorrow*. New York, Ace, 1970; London, Sidgwick and Jackson, 1972.
*The Battle of Forever*. New York, Ace, 1971; London, Sidgwick and Jackson, 1972.
*The Darkness on Diamondia*. New York, Ace, 1972; London, Sidgwick and Jackson, 1974.
*Future Glitter*. New York, Ace, 1973; London, Sidgwick and Jackson, 1976; as *Tyranopolis*, London, Sphere, 1977.
*The Secret Galactics*. Englewood Cliffs, New Jersey, Prentice Hall, 1974; London, Sidgwick and Jackson, 1975; as *Earth Factor X*, New York, DAW, 1976.
*The Man with a Thousand Names*. New York, DAW, 1974; London, Sidgwick and Jackson, 1975.
*The Anarchistic Colossus*. New York, Ace, 1977; London, Sidgwick and Jackson, 1978.
*Supermind*. New York, DAW, 1977; London, Sidgwick and Jackson, 1978.
*Renaissance*. New York, Pocket Books, 1979.
*Cosmic Encounter*. New York, Doubleday, 1980; London, New English Library, 1981.
*Computerworld*. New York, DAW, 1983; London, New English Library, 1986; as *Computer Eye*, Beverly Hills, California, Morrison Raven Hill, 1985.
*Null-A Three* (Gosseyn). New York, DAW, and London, Sphere, 1985.

Short Stories

*Out of the Unknown*, with E. Mayne Hull, Los Angeles, Fantasy, 1948; London, New English Library, 1970; expanded edition, Reseda, California, Powell, 1969; as *The Sea Thing and Other Stories*, London, Sidgwick and Jackson, 1970.
*Masters of Time*. Reading, Pennsylvania, Fantasy Press, 1950; as *Earth's Last Fortress*, New York, Ace, 1960; *The Changeling* published separately, New York, Macfadden Bartell, 1967; in *The Three Eyes of Evil, and Earth's Last Fortress*, London, Sidgwick and Jackson, 1973.
*Away and Beyond*. New York, Pellegrini and Cudahy, 1952; London, Panther, 1963.
*Destination: Universe!* New York, Pellegrini and Cudahy, 1952; London, Weidenfeld and Nicolson, 1953.
*The Twisted Men*. New York, Ace, 1964.
*Monsters*. New York, Paperback Library, 1965; London, Corgi, 1970; as *The Blal*, New York, Zebra, 1976.
*The Far-Out Worlds of A.E. van Vogt*. New York, Ace, 1968; London, Sidgwick and Jackson, 1973; expanded edition, as *The Worlds of A.E. van Vogt*, Ace, 1974.
*More Than Superhuman*. New York, Dell, 1971; London, New English Library, 1975.
*The Proxy Intelligence and Other Mind Benders*. New York, Paperback Library, 1971.
*M33 in Andromeda*. New York, Paperback Library, 1971.
*The Book of van Vogt*. New York, DAW, 1972; as *Lost: Fifty Suns*, DAW, 1979; London, New English Library, 1980.
*The Best of A.E. van Vogt*. London, Sphere, 1974; New York, Pocket Books, 1976.
*The Gryb*. New York, Zebra, 1976; London, New English Library, 1980.
*Pendulum*. New York, DAW, 1978; London, New English Library, 1982.

Other Publications

Novel

*The Violent Man*. New York, Farrar Straus, 1962.

Other

*The Hypnotism Handbook*, with Charles Edward Cooke. Los Angeles, Griffin, 1956.
*The Money Personality*. West Nyack, New York, Parker, 1972; Wellingborough, Northamptonshire, Thorsons, 1975; as *Unlock Your Money Personality*, Beverly Hills, California, Morrison Raven Hill, 1983.
*Reflections of A.E. van Vogt*. Lakemont, Georgia, Fictioneer, 1975.

* * *

In the stories of A.E. van Vogt all things are possible, for saying makes them so. It seems of little moment that any event logically follow the preceding one or that one character dominate the action. For readers expecting tightly structured plots, careful characterization, polished prose style, and a logical extrapolation, van Vogt affords a field day for criticism. (For a classic lambasting on such matters see Demon Knight's "Cosmic Jerry-builder: A.E. van Vogt" in *In Search of Wonder*.) But for the reader willing to submit his reason to another's wide-ranging imagination van Vogt is a "good read."

Van Vogt's canon offers a melange of intriguing situations spiced with telepathy, teleportation, shape control, inner and outer space, mass consciousness, time shifts, technological wonders beyond count. Humans, super-creatures, androids, and aliens perform an intricate dance of adventure on a cosmic stage, existing in past, present, and future time, out-of-time and space as we know them, and often out-of-phase with each other. Incidents bombard us, with little transition to ease the pace. Disconcerting as this can be, it does have the trade-off value of keeping one in continual suspense. In "Complication in the Science Fiction Story" (in *Of Worlds Beyond*, edited by Lloyd Arthur Eshbach, Reading, Pennsylvania, Fantasy Press, 1947; London, Dobson, 1965), van Vogt explained his method of writing scenes in 800-word blocks, the first one to introduce both scene and story purpose. As the main plot develops logically in succeeding scenes, van Vogt adds a secondary plot and minor plot threads deriving from "theme science and atmosphere." While one may question the success of the logical development, there is no argument about van Vogt's ability to handle the minor threads skillfully to induce a sense of mystery, wonder, and suspense.

Since van Vogt writes both short stories and novels, often combining the former to create the latter, a mixed sampling of these modes makes a valid introduction to his characters, situations, and techniques. One especially notices van Vogt's emphasis on superior beings, well exemplified in *The Mixed Men*, a novel combining three short stories. In the earliest story of this group, "The Storm," we meet three super-creatures: the Dellian robots, physically and mentally advanced over man; the non-Dellian robots, higher in creativity; and the Mixed Men of human form but with double brains. Another superhuman, Gilbert Gosseyn of *The World of Null-A*, also has the extra brain, in addition possessing the ability to evade death, thus becoming a more godlike entity than Captain Maltby of the Mixed Men.

Van Vogt's catalog of aliens ranges from BEM's to intelligent forms fearsome in appearance but cooperative in action, once accepted by men. In *The Voyage of the Space Beagle*, four aliens appear; the catlike Coeurl, the Ixtl, the Riim folk (a colony-psyche), and the anabis. All four pose grave problems to the expedition whose aim is "to explore limits of deep space and contact alien life forms." By contrast, two sympathetic aliens aid men in *The War Against the Rull*. For mutual survival they contribute their telepathetic ability and energy-conducting bodies respectively. The inimical Rull in turn infiltrates human society, using its capability to assume human form. This minor theme of replication appears in many van Vogt tales, starting with "Vault of the Beast" (1940), with the ultimate example being the title character of *The Silkie*, which can shift from fish to bullet-like spaceship to human form to innumerable other shapes for its own purposes and protection.

These aliens often educate man about his own nature. In *The Replicators*, a harmless alien assumes the form of its first human contact, an ex-Marine full of anger and aggressiveness. The resultant trouble is predictable. A more gentle lesson comes from the super-intelligent, catlike creature in "The Cataaaaa." On assignment to study man on earth the Cat does so from the stage of a carnival freak show. The title, linking the Cat with the spontaneous awed exclamation of the carnival crowd, spotlights the human response. The Cat's response comes in the final act of his study when he communicates to one man the conclusion that the basic human characteristic is self-dramatisation. This may well be the most agreeable comment van Vogt can offer about humans. All too often the enemy turns out to be one of our own. In the power struggle that runs as a major theme throughout van Vogt's stories, the specific enemy is often the trusted man-in-charge. Morlake of "The Earth Killers" tracks down the destroyers of civilization, only to find them racists headed by a power-driven ex-senator pretending to be the altruistic guardian of the people.

Critics note in van Vogt a predilection for the power of monarchy, such as held by the Isher empire in *The Weapon Shops of Isher* and the House of Linn in *Empire of the Atom.* More notable is van Vogt's sense of the drama inherent in all authoritarian systems. Finding authority operating all around us, he exploits the emotional possibilities in such situations as the struggle of the "dynasties" in *Rogue Ship*, the parent-child confrontations in *Children of Tomorrow*, and the professional friction aboard the *Space Beagle.* However, van Vogt always supplies an antithesis to authoritarianism. Most intriguing are those single characters who perform this duty, those superior beings motivated by a sense of mission and possessing a gift or a powerful idea to be manipulated for benefit of all. The combination is varied: Lesley Craig and "toti-potency" in *Masters of Time*; Elliot Grosvenor and "Nexialism" on the *Space Beagle;* Robert Hedrock and the Weapon Shops opposing Isher power; Gilbert Gosseyn with Null-A training (here van Vogt gives a nod to Alfred Korzybski's *Theory of General Semantics*); and others. A natural extension of this balance is a recognition of the cyclic nature of human society in the character of Morton Cargill of *The Universe Maker.* The most famous "saviour" of human values and idealism is Johnny Cross of *Slan*, the novel usually considered van Vogt's most outstanding. A member of a mutant group hated and persecuted by the majority, the slan Johnny Cross is a telepath, superior both in intelligence and physique to ordinary men. From childhood his training points toward the end of bringing slans and normal men closer together in harmony. He must contend not only with John Petty, the human chief of the secret police, but also with Kier Gray, the head of the government and a slan passing as a normal human.

*Slan* epitomizes van Vogt's major thematic issues: the tenacity of the life force whatever its form, the need of cooperative effort for mutual survival, and an overwhelming optimism that a consciousness shared with all life forms can work only to a mutual benefit. For the new reader approaching van Vogt, *Slan* provides a satisfactory entry into van Vogt's provocative and imaginative worlds.

For the seasoned reader of van Vogt, *Computerworld* over 35 years later addresses these major issues in the context of a very contemporary concern: computerized control. In the near-future of 2094 the omnipresent, multiform computer has relieved humans of all onerous labor but has sapped them of moral energy. Through Eye-O ports it tracks human activity, registering data for identification and correcting aberrant behaviour with weapons of graduated power. Questions arise. Who will control this force? How can the spiritual sense necessary for humanness exist in the strictly logical environment of the machine? The protagonist-computer asks the key question: "How does a human differ from a machine?" Only when it develops a "sense of self" comes the recognition that uniqueness requires cooperative understanding for coexistence, that recognition being a basic van Vogtian theme.

This requirement for cooperative understanding for coexistence finds one of its most complete treatments in van Vogt's three-part series featuring the Gilbert Gosseyns. The series is noted not only for its content but also for the dramatic events spurring van Vogt's revisions and writing of sequels (see van Vogt's personal introduction to the first two novels *in re* scathing reviews and reader discontent) and for the time span between the first and last volumes. The span suggests the original philosophical ideas and plot lines fermented some 40 years in the author's mind, urging logical completion.

The Gosseyn story of three duplicate bodies, each with an extra brain, able to share memories, objectives, and communication with each other over light years of space, takes the reader to a universe of 2560. This world is filled with various human civilizations, many engaged in interstellar and/or galactic power struggles. The Gosseyns serve as models of Null-A or non-Aristotelian way of thought. In other words, they seek to shift each group from seeing problems as either/or situations to using multi-valued maps of reality, in accordance with Alfred Korzybski's theory of general semantics (see his 1933 book, *Science and Sanity*). A reader can find testimony to van Vogt's reliance on *General Semantics* not only in the above-mentioned introduction but also in the many epigraphs to chapters of the novels, especially in *The Players of Null-A.*

In the Null-A novels, van Vogt uses many of the aspects of space opera: space ships, interplanetary travel, alien forms with human responses, extrasensory perception, ability to traverse time and space. Van Vogt also combines some of the characteristics of spy thrillers and mystery stories: interstellar power struggles, conspiracies to seize control of solar system, leaks of pertinent information bringing about adverse results. More important is the pervasive thought running through all three novels: with a shift in human reasoning from the restricted Aristotelian pattern to a Null-A pattern a better world would result. Near the end of *Null-A Three*, the authorial voice breaks into the narrative to offer readers a thought worthy of deep consideration: "The very heart of a system of absolute power modified to include democratic procedures."

—Hazel Pierce

---

**VARDRE, Leslie.** *See* **DAVIES, L.P.**

---

**VARLEY, John.** Also writes as Herb Boehm. American. Born in Austin, Texas, in 1947. Attended Michigan State University, East Lansing, 1966. Married Anet Mconel; three sons. Since 1973, freelance writer. Recipient: *Locus* award, 1977, 1979 (twice), 1981, 1982 (twice); Jupiter award, 1978; Nebula award, 1979, 1984; Hugo award, 1984; Prix Apollo, 1979; Science Fiction Chronicle award, 1985. Lives in Eugene, Oregon. Agent: Kirby McCauley Ltd., 432 Park Avenue South, New York, New York 10016, U.S.A.

### Science-Fiction Publications

Novels (series: Cirocco Jones)

*The Ophiuchi Hotline*. New York, Dial Press, 1977; London, Sidgwick and Jackson, 1978.
*Titan* (Jones). New York, Berkley, and London, Sidgwick and Jackson, 1979.
*Wizard* (Jones). New York, Berkley, 1980; London, Futura, 1981.
*Millennium*. New York, Berkley, 1983; London, Sphere, 1985.
*Demon* (Jones). New York, Putnam, 1984; London, Futura, 1985.
*Picnic on Nearside* (novelette). New York, Berkley, 1984.
*Press Enter* (novella), with *Hawksbill Station*, by Robert Silverberg. New York, Tor, 1990.

Short Stories

*The Persistence of Vision*. New York, Dial Press, 1978; as *In the Hall of the Martian Kings*, London, Sidgwick and Jackson, 1978.
*The Barbie Murders and Other Stories*. New York, Berkley, 1980; London, Futura, 1983.
*Blue Champagne*. Niles, Illinois, Dark Harvest, 1986.

### Other Publications

Plays

Screenplays: *Galaxy*, 1978; *Millennium*, 1983.

*

Manuscript Collection: Special Collections, Temple University, Philadelphia.

* * *

Although John Varley has produced relatively few novels, he merits consideration for his inventiveness. His first novel, *The Ophiuchi Hotline*, takes place in a time in the future after mysterious invaders have come to our solar system and done away with human technology. This novel exhibits an environmentalist's bias in that the Invaders have abolished earth's industrial-technical system to save whales and dolphins who, as some have long suspected, outclass humans in their intellectual potentiality. Yet someone out there wants humankind to survive, for, over the decades, a "hotline" to a mysterious presence in another part of the universe continues to feed the remaining people information vital to their survival. Part of the story revolves around the attempt to discover who these "good Samaritans" are. For a short novel, *The Ophiuchi Hotline* certainly does not lack action; in fact, so much goes on that the plot at times becomes confusing.

Varley exhibits better control over his enthusiasm for inventing new worlds and improbable beings in his series consisting of *Wizard, Titan*, and *Demon* which chronicles the adventures of a displaced earth women, Cirocco Jones, sometimes-NASA-spaceship-pilot and adventurer. Not content simply to send her to another planet—in this case Saturn—to struggle against aliens, Varley turns the planet itself into a sentient being, the quasi-goddess Gaea. The trilogy follows Jones's transformation from friendly adventurer learning about Gaea's whimsical personality, to an alcoholic "wizard" in Gaea's employ, and finally to the only adversary who can vanquish the "goddess"-gone-mad and save the many lifeforms that populate this fascinating ring world. In this series we are asked to consider space opera from a moderately feminist point of view. At least that seems to be the perspective Varley wants his readers to take, for most of his major characters are either completely female or oddly bisexual. In some ways his focus on lesbian relationships is gratuitous; ultimately, the romantic couplings and jealousies add little to the trilogy's sense of entertainment which, in fact, is derived from the familiar quest-adventure motif found so frequently in science fiction.

*Millennium* considers an equally odd topic, human catastrophes. It seems that for as long as people have been mass-murdering each other or having accidents involving large numbers of people, a group of time travelers have been snagging the victims and whisking them through a time port to the far-future. These time travelers stand close to the end of life on earth; these kidnapping efforts represent their attempt to perpetuate life at a time millions of years beyond their immediate destruction. Varley combines and makes interesting twists on catastrophe/Bermuda Triangle themes, theories concerning the nature of time, and an old-fashioned love story between future alien and 20th-century deadbeat. The results entertain because *Millennium* resists the standard clichés of time travel and end-of-the-world tales.

Varley's short stories concern themselves with the same topics that he raises in his novels: speculations of the quality of life in the future, cloning, the nature of the alien "personality," to name a few. Like his novels, these stories are entertaining, and, like his novels, they also demand a certain degree of patient toleration on the part of their reader. Varley likes to pack his writing with action, gadgets, and many characters. Frequently the reader must untangle some of the snarls this type of writing inevitably creates. Although such roughness can irritate, Varley is a writer worth reading: he entertains because he isn't afraid to take risks with his plots, characters, or inventive view of the future. Furthermore, he takes fresh and timely perspectives on old chestnuts: love, war, the environment, and a human's place in the universe.

—Melissa E. Barth

---

**VERRILL, A(lpheus) Hyatt.** Also wrote as Ray Ainsbury. American. Born in New Haven, Connecticut, 23 July 1871. Educated at Yale University School of Fine Arts, New Haven; studied zoology with his father. Married 1) Kathryn L. McCarthy in 1892, four children; 2) Lida Ruth Shaw in 1944. Natural history illustrator for *Webster's International Dictionary*, 1896, and for *Clarendon Dictionary;* invented the autochrome process of photography, 1920; explorer and archaeologist: lived in Domenica, 1903–06, British Guiana, 1913–17, and Panama, 1917–21, and made expeditions to Central and South America, the West Indies, and Mexico, to 1950; did undersea excavation in the West Indies, 1933–34; established the Anhlarka experimental gardens and natural science museum, Florida, 1940; established shell business, Lake Worth, Florida, 1944. *Died 14 November 1954.*

### Science-Fiction Publications

Novels

*Uncle Abner's Legacy*. New York, Holt, 1915.
*The Golden City* (for children). New York, Duffield, 1916.
*The Trial of the Cloven Foot* (for children). New York, Dutton, 1918.
*The Trial of the White Indians* (for children). New York, Dutton, 1920.
*The Boy Adventures in the Land of the Monkey Men* (for children). New York, Putnam, 1923.
*The Bridge of Light*. Reading, Pennsylvania, Fantasy Press, 1950.
*When the Moon Ran Wild* (as Ray Ainsbury). London. Consul, 1962.

Uncollected Short Stories

"Through the Crater's Rim," in *Amazing* (New York), December 1926.
"The Man Who Could Vanish," in *Amazing* (New York), January 1927.
"The Plague of the Living Dead," in *Amazing* (New York), April 1927.
"The Voice from the Inner World," in *Amazing* (New York), July 1927.
"The Ultra-Elixir of Youth," in *Amazing* (New York), August 1927.
"The Astounding Discoveries of Doctor Mentiroso," in *Amazing* (New York), November 1927.
"The Psychological Solution," in *Amazing* (New York), January 1928.
"The King of the Monkey Men," in *Amazing Stories Quarterly* (New York), Spring 1928.
"The World of the Giant Ants," in *Amazing Stories Quarterly* (New York), Fall 1928.
"Into the Green Prism," in *Amazing* (New York), March 1929.
"Death From the Skies," in *Amazing* (New York), October 1929.
"Vampires of the Desert," in *Amazing* (New York), December 1929.
"Beyond the Green Prism," in *Amazing* (New York), January 1930.
"The Feathered Detective," in *Amazing* (New York), April 1930.
"The Non-Gravitational Vortex," in *Amazing* (New York), June 1930.
"Monsters of the Ray," in *Amazing Stories Quarterly* (New York), Summer 1930.
"A Visit to Suari," in *Amazing* (New York), July 1930.
"The Dirigibles of Death," in *Amazing Stories Quarterly* (New York), Winter 1930.
"The Treasures of the Golden God," in *Amazing* (New York), January 1933.
"The Death Drum," in *Amazing* (New York), May 1933.
"Through the Andes," in *Amazing* (New York), September 1934.
"The Inner World," in *Amazing* (New York), June 1935.
"The Mummy of Ret-Seh," in *Fantastic Adventures* (New York), May 1939.
"Beyond the Pole," in *The Gernsback Awards 1, 1926*, edited by Forrest J. Ackerman. London, Turret, 1982.
"The Exterminator," in *Caught in the Organ Draft*, edited by Isaac Asimov, Martin H. Greenberg, and Charles G. Waugh, New York, Farrar Straus, 1983.

### Other Publications

Novels (for children)

*The American Crusoe*. New York, Dodd Mead, 1914.
*The Cruise of the Cormorant*. New York, Holt, 1915.
*In Morgan's Wake*. New York, Holt, 1915.
*Marooned in the Forest*. New York, Harper, 1916.
*Jungle Chums*. New York, Holt, 1916.
*The Boy Adventurers in the Forbidden Land [in the Land of El Dorando, in the Unknown Land]*. New York, Putnam, 3 vols., 1922–24.
*The Deep Sea Hunters [in the Frozen Sea, in the South Seas]*. New York, Appleton, 3 vols., 1922–24.
*The Radio Detectives [in the Jungle, Southward Bound, under the Sea]*. New York, Appleton, 4 vols. 1922.
*Bartons Mills: A Saga of the Pioneers*. New York, Appleton, 1932.
*The Incas' Treasure House*. Boston, Page, 1932; London, Harrap, 1936.
*Before the Conquerors*. New York, Dodd Mead, 1935.
*The Treasure of the Bloody Gut*. New York, Putnam, 1937.

Other

*Gasoline Engines: Their Operation, Use and Care*. New York, Henley, 1912.
*Knots, Splices, and Rope Work*. New York, Henley, 1912; revised edition, 1917, 1922.
*Harper's Book for Young Naturalists [Gardeners]*. New York, Harper, 2 vols., 1913–14.
*Harper's Wireless [Aircraft, Gasoline Engine] Book*. New York, Harper, 3 vols., 1913–14.
*Cuba Past and Present*. New York, Dodd Mead, 1914; revised edition, 1920.
*South and Central American Trade Conditions of Today*. New York, Dodd Mead, 1914; revised edition, 1919.
*Porto Rico Past and Present*. New York, Dodd Mead, 1914.
*Pets for Pleasure and Profit*. New York, Scribner, 1915.
*The Boys' Outdoor Vacation Book*. New York, Dodd Mead, 1915.
*The Amateur Carpenter*. New York, Dodd Mead, 1915.
*The Boy Collector's Handbook*. New York, McBride, 1915.
*Isles of Spice and Palm*. New York, Appleton, 1915.
*A-B-C of Automobile Driving*. New York, Harper, 1916.
*The Real Story of the Whaler*. New York, Appleton, 1916.
*The Ocean and Its Mysteries*. New York, Duffield, 1916.
*The Book of the Motor Boat [Sailboat]*. New York, Appleton, 2 vols., 1916.
*The Book of the West Indies*. New York, Dutton, 1917.
*The Book of Camping*. New York, Knopf, 1917.
*How to Operate a Motor Car*. Philadelphia, McKay, 1918.
*Getting Together with Latin America*. New York, Dutton, 1918.
*Islands and Their Mysteries*. New York, Duffield, 1920; London, Melrose, 1922.
*Panama, Past and Present*. New York, Dodd Mead, 1921.
*The Boys' Book of Whalers [Carpentry, Buccaneers]*. New York, Dodd Mead, 3 vols., 1922–23.
*Radio for Amateurs*. New York, Dodd Mead, and London, Heinemann, 1922.
*Rivers and Their Mysteries*. New York, Duffield, 1922.
*The Home Radio*. New York, Harper, 1922; revised edition, 1924; revised edition, as *The Home Radio Up to Date*, with E.E. Verrill, 1927.
*In the Wake of the Buccaneers*. New York, Century, and London, Parsons, 1923.

*The Real Story of the Pirate.* New York, Appleton, 1923.
*Smugglers and Smuggling.* New York, Duffield, and London, Allen and Unwin, 1924.
*Love Stories of Some Famous Pirates.* London, Collins, 1924.
*Panama [Cuba, Jamaica, West Indies] of Today.* New York, Dodd Mead, 4 vols., 1927–31.
*The American Indian.* New York, Appleton, 1927.
*Old Civilization of the New World.* Indianapolis, Bobbs Merrill, and London, Williams and Norgate, 1929.
*Thirty Years in the Jungle.* London, Lane, 1929.
*Great Conquerors of South and Central America.* New York, Appleton, 1929.
*Lost Treasure.* New York, Appleton, 1930.
*Gasoline-Engine Book for Boys.* New York, Harper, 1930.
*Under Peruvian Skies.* London, Hurst and Blackett, 1930.
*Secret Treasure.* New York, Appleton, 1931.
*The Inquisition.* New York, Appleton, 1931.
*Romantic and Historic Maine [Florida, Virginia].* New York, Dodd Mead, 3 vols., 1933–35.
*Our Indians.* New York, Putnam, 1935.
*They Found Gold.* New York and London, Putnam, 1936; as *Carib Gold*, London, Collins, 1939.
*The Heart of Old New England.* New York, Dodd Mead, 1936.
*Along New England Shores.* New York, Putnam, 1936.
*Sea Shells [Insects, Reptiles, Birds, Fish, Animals] and Their Stories.* Boston, Page, and London, Harrap, 6 vols., 1936-39.
*My Jungle Trails.* Boston, Page, and London, Harrap, 1937.
*Foods America Gave the World.* Boston, Page, 1937.
*Minerals, Metals and Gems.* Boston, Page, 1939.
*Wonder Plants and Plant Wonders.* New York, Appleton Century, 1939.
*Perfumes and Spices.* Boston, Page, 1940.
*Wonder Creatures of the Sea.* New York, Appleton Century, 1940.
*Strange Prehistoric Animals and Their Stories.* Boston, Page, 1948.
*The Strange Story of Our Earth.* Boston, Page, 1952.
*America's Ancient Civilization*, (with R. Verrill). New York and London, Putnam, 1954.

* * *

A. Hyatt Verrill was one of the more distinguished writers who helped in the development of *Amazing Stories* during its early years, and who continued to contribute to it until the mid-1930's. Many of his stories are set in the South American jungles with which he was so familiar, or deal with ancient civilisations whose cultures he studied for more than half a century. But he did not limit himself to such themes, drawing on astronomy, biology, optics, atomic physics, and fourth-dimension theory for ideas which he developed with equal facility.

The magazine was only six months old when his first offering, "Beyond the Pole," dealing with a race of intelligent crustaceans discovered in the Antarctic, appeared late in 1926. It compared favourably with the stories of Wells and Verne, which almost monopolised those early issues, while the editor, Hugo Gernsback, contrived to nurture new writers to displace them. Some of Verrill's longer stories went to fill out the inch-thick *Amazing Stories Quarterly;* "The World of the Giant Ants" was remarkable for its engrossing narrative combined with an enlightening insight into its subject. Even more fascinating was "Into the Green Prism," with its sequel, "Beyond the Green Prism," which sought to dispel the storm of controversy over the scientific fallacies it raised. "The Astounding Discoveries of Doctor Mentiroso" began the endless argument in the readers' columns over the time-travel theme. "Death from the Skies" was about a bombardment of Earth by the Martians, and *The Bridge of Light* took readers to a hidden city where the Mayas still thrived. Verrill's flights of imagination reached their peak in 1931 with "Monsters of the Ray" and *When the Moon Ran Wild;* but his later contributions, such as "The Death Drum" and "Through the Andes," were pure adventure tales which reflected the gradual decline of *Amazing.*

—Walter Gillings

---

**VINGE, Joan (Carol) D(ennison).** American Born in Baltimore, Maryland, 2 April 1948. Educated at San Diego State University, California, B.A. in anthropology 1971. Married 1) Vernor Vinge, *q.v.*, in 1972 (divorced 1979); 2) the publisher James R. Frenkel in 1980. Salvage archaeologist, San Diego County, 1971. Recipient: Hugo award, 1978, 1981; *Locus* award, 1981. Agent: Merrilee Heifetz, Writers House Inc., 21 West 26th Street, New York, New York 10010. Address: 26 Douglas Road, Chappaqua, New York 10514, U.S.A.

### Science-Fiction Publications

Novels (series: Cat; Heaven Belt; Snow Queen)

*The Outcasts of Heaven Belt.* New York, New American Library, 1978; London, Futura, 1981.
*The Snow Queen.* New York, Dial Press, and London, Sidgwick and Jackson, 1980.
*Psion* (Cat; for children). New York, Delacorte Press, 1982; London, Futura, 1983.
*Return of the Jedi Storybook* (novelization of screenplay; for children). New York, Random House, and London, Futura, 1983.
*The Dune Storybook* (novelization of screenplay). New York, Putnam, 1984; London, Sphere, 1984.
*World's End* (Snow Queen). New York, Bluejay, 1984; London, Futura, 1985.
*Ladyhawke* (novelization of screenplay). New York, New American Library, 1985; London, Piccolo, 1985.
*Catspaw.* New York, Warner, 1988; as *Cat's Paw*, London Gollancz, 1989.
*Heaven Chronicles* (includes "Legacy" and *The Outcasts of Heaven Belt*). New York, Warner, 1991.
*The Summer Queen* (Snow Queen). New York, Warner, 1991.

Short Stories

*Fireship.* New York, Dell, 1978; as *Fireship, and Mother and Child*, London, Sidgwick and Jackson, 1981.
*Eyes of Amber and Other Stories.* New York, New American Library, 1979; London, Futura, 1981.
*Phoenix in the Ashes.* New York, Bluejay, 1985; London, Futura, 1986.

### Other Publications

Novels (novelizations of screenplays)

*Mad Max: Beyond the Thunderdome.* New York, Warner, and London, W.H. Allen, 1985.

*Return to Oz*. New York, Ballantine, and London, Purnell, 1985.
*Santa Claus*. New York, Berkley, and London, Sphere, 1985.
*Willow* (novelization of screenplay). New York, Random House, 1988.

Other

*Tarzan, King of Apes* (for children). New York, Random House, 1983.
*The "Santa Claus—The Movie" Storybook* (for children). New York, Grosset and Dunlap, 1985.

*

Manuscript Collection: Elizabeth Charter Science Fiction Collection, San Diego University.

Critical Study: *Suzy Charnas, Joan Vinge, and Octavia Butler* by Richard Law, with others, San Bernardino, California, Borgo Press, 1986.

Joan D. Vinge comments:

(1981) Because I have a degree in anthropology, I tend to write anthropological science fiction, with an emphasis on the interaction of different cultures (human and alien) and of individual people to their surroundings. The importance of communication across barriers of alienness often becomes a theme in my stories. Mythology and music also influence my work; my novel *The Snow Queen* was in large part inspired by Robert Graves's *The White Goddess.* I have written several stories with a "hard" science background, thanks to the borrowed expertise of my husband, who is a mathematician and also a science-fiction writer; however, I've written other stories which I hope cover a wide range of moods and styles, I feel as if I'm just beginning to explore the infinite possibilities of the future.

* * *

Though her output has been fairly small for a major writer, there is no question about the importance of Joan D. Vinge's work. Her stories are not only interesting and entertaining, they are original, richly detailed, and thought-provoking as well. Influenced strongly by the work of Andre Norton, her stories often feature strong female, alien, or half-breed characters, who, when placed in difficult circumstances, grow measurably by working through their problems positively and constructively. Other common Vinge themes are: the difficulty of loving, understanding, and communicating, the role of free women, and the appreciation of individuals and cultures that are not the norm. Her work is influenced by mythology, music, legend, and the fairy tale. Vinge works slowly and carefully, creating physical and social works that are complex and informative. This is no doubt due to her background as an anthropologist.

While each of her stories has its own virtues, Vinge's reputation rests on (a few) exceptional works, some of which are interrelated. Of particular interest are: "Eyes of Amber," "Fireship," "Legacy", *The Outcasts of Heaven Belt, The Snow Queen, World's End, Psion*, and *Catspaw.*

Set on Titan, "Eyes of Amber" is, according to Richard Law (in *Suzy McKee Charnas, Joan Vinge, Octavia Butler*), a fairy tale in design, sharing its motifs of "sibling rivalry, benevolent mother, rescue device, and ultimate exaltation of the ill-treated heroine." The story's heroine is Lady T'uupieh, a chiropteran who has been dispossessed of her lands and must live as an outcast. As leader of a band of outlaws, she eventually kills Klovhiri, the wicked nobleman who brought about her downfall. She succeeds by means of an Earth probe, which she regards as a demon. Through it, she carries on a relationship with a young rock musician, who also has superb linguistic abilities, named Shannon Wyler. Because of what essentially becomes an inter-species "love affair," he begins to wean her away from the values of her culture towards our own. Set on Mars, "Fireship" explores the behavior of a composite personality named Ethan Ring (a cyborg produced when a low-intellect lab assistant is surgically altered so that he can be connected to a massive computer). Ring matches wits with a shiek, Khorran Kabir, who controls most of the wealth on Earth after World III. Kabir has had his own consciousness transferred into a computer. While notable as a study of communications with and understanding other forms of life, "Fireship" is also richly comic.

"Legacy" and *The Outcasts of Heaven Belt* are related by being set in the same world and by sharing a character. The Heaven Belt, made up of thousands of asteroids, planetoids, and planets, and populated by the descendants of Earth colonists, has been wasted by civil war, leaving two feuding societies. "Legacy" is the story of two lonely people, Chaim Dartagnan, a "media man" who loses his job but regains his integrity, and Mythili Fukinuki, a sterilized space pilot, who also loses her job. Estranged from one another after an initial attraction, they are reconciled by Wadie Abdhiamal, a government negotiator, who arranges rights to a dead prospector's ship for them so they can forge careers as salvagers. Through their adventures, they learn self-respect, realize their inter-dependence, and fall in love. *The Outcasts of Heaven Belt*, set in the same world, uses Abdhiamal as a principal character. It focuses primarily, however, upon Betha Torgussen, the captain of the *Ranger*, a spaceship from the planet Morningside, several light years away. Morningside, itself endangered and unaware of the civil war, has sent the *Ranger* to bargain for resources. Because of its fusion reactor, the ship becomes the target of both colonies, but after several attempts to capture it fail, an alliance is struck that benefits all parties. Against this background is set a love story, focusing on Betha and Wadie and exploring the concept of the multiple-marriage family unit. While both "Legacy" and *The Outcasts of Heaven Belt* are well-crafted and entertaining, neither reaches the excellence of *The Snow Queen.*

This novel counterposes two plots to explore one of literature's great and recurring themes—renewal. The most evident story follows the development of young, Moon Dawntreader, as she fulfills her destiny by becoming the new queen of the planet Tiamat. Unknown to Moon, she is one of several clones of the reigning queen, Arienrhod, and because of how she has been raised, Moon is opposite to Arienrhod in both values and philosophies. Moon represents good. Arienrhod's story is one of Machiavelian manipulation. She wants desperately to continue to rule, and schemes and plots to assure it. She not only lengthens her own life by using the blood of intelligent sea creatures (mers) but clones herself as well. As Richar Law writes in *Suzy McKee Charnas, Joan Vinge, Octavia Butler*, "Arienrhod perceives that evil is inherent, takes license from it, and pursuing her lusts marshals the evil in her world." Taken together, Moon and Arienrhod represent most of the dialectical pairs that frame all our lives: good and evil, youth and age, innocence and experience. But the fact that Moon succeeds Arienrhod when the old queen dies and that her name links her to a perpetual cycle symbolized by the moon-trinity, New, Full, and Old, suggests a renewal theme. Arienrhod, like evil in most fantastic literature, falls of her own weight, but is succeeded by her genetic self who is morally opposite.

*World's End* is related to *The Snow Queen* by virtue of taking up the story BZ Gundhalinu, a character in the latter novel, after he has left Tiamat and become a maladjusted police inspector on a planet called Number Four. Out of his own sense of guilt, BZ feels compelled to travel into the bizarre and grotesque landscape of *World's End* to find his two stupid and greedy brothers and a demented female. The story is Vinge's exploration of the "heart of darkness." In wandering through both the physical wasteland of *World's End* and his own psychological wasteland, BZ searches for his sanity and saves soul. This, like *The Snow Queen*, is a renewal story.

*Psion* is a coming-of-age novel, in which an adolescent, half-breed named Cat is initiated into the adult world. Influenced by the work of Andre Norton, Cat resembles many of her characters: disenfranchised, isolated, scorned and both physically and mentally different from those around him. An orphan who grew up in a city actually lying beneath another city, Cat is symbolically born into the adult world when the woman who had "mothered" him dies. During his adventures, Cat learns about trust and friendship, falls in love with another psion named Jule, undergoes mind-rape by a criminal named Rubiy who lusts after him, learns how to use his psionic powers, and kills Rubiy. Ironically, the killing leaves Cat unable to use his psionic powers, and Jule's love for Siebeling, the director of the research center, leaves him alone once more. Despite these setbacks, however, Cat has undergone an initiation into manhood that has taught him how to survive and permitted him to mature.

*Catspaw* continues Cat's adventures a few years later. It is a novel rich in detail, suspense, and characters. Essentially a "palace-intrigue," Cat finds himself hired to bodyguard Lady Elnear, a member of Jule's powerful corporate family, the tamings. He learns eventually, of course, that he is the cats-paw.

Pushed to test himself against the manipulations and politics of gigantic corporations headquartered on Earth, Cat regains the use of his psionic powers by means of "drug patches," solves the mystery of who is trying to kill Lady Elnear, and learns even more about himself and the adult world. In particular, he learns about the enormous difficulty of interpersonal communications. Vinge is superb in examining the erotic invasion of another individual's mind in an act of real love, the effects of a simbiotic, mental link-up, and the psionic intrusion into a bio-electronic system that functions like a collective consciousness. By the end of the novel, Cat has reached another level of maturation. As Anne Hudson Jones indicated in the first edition of this volume, Vinge's "is a major talent."

—Carl B. Yoke

---

**VINGE, Vernor (Steffen).** American. Born in Waukesha, Wisconsin, 2 October 1944. Educated at Michigan State University, East Lansing, B.S 1966; University of California, San Diego, M.A. 1968, Ph.D. 1971. Married Joan Carol Dennison (i.e., Joan D. Vinge, *q.v.*), in 1972 (divorced 1979). Assistant Professor, 1972–78, and since 1978, Associate Professor of Mathematics, San Diego State University. Address: Department of Mathematics, San Diego State University, San Diego, California 92182, U.S.A.

SCIENCE-FICTION PUBLICATIONS

Novels

*Grimm's World.* New York, Berkley, 1969; London, Hamlyn, 1978.
*The Wilting.* New York, DAW, and London, Dobson, 1976.
*True Names* in *Binary Star 5.* New York, Dell, 1981.
*The Peace War.* New York, Bluejay, 1984.
*Marooned in Realtime.* New York, Bluejay, 1986.

Short Stories

*True Names and Other Dangers.* New York, Baen, 1987.
*Threats and Other Promises.* New York, Baen, 1988.

* * *

Vernor Vinge is not a prolific writer but his significance is considerably greater than the size of his output because of the high quality of much of his work. Especially in his best stories, most of which are collected in *True Names and Other Dangers* and *Threats and Other Promises,* Vinge deals with extreme social situations, with crises within a society or with intercultural conflict. Much of his work is permeated with a melancholy awareness of the evanescence of all human institutions. Typically, Vinge's characters are faced with some personal problem arising out of social change. They furnish the best possible solution given the initial conditions, but it is never more than a half-solution, and they must live with their failure as well as their success.

Vinge's first two novels, both set on other planets, move in the characteristic Vinge pattern. *Grimm's World,* set on a retrogressed colony planet now climbing back to high technology, centers on intrigues and struggles of a native-born superwoman whose only intellectual equals are two visitors from a higher interstellar culture. The novel focuses our greatest sympathy not on the superhumans but on the ordinary people caught up in their machinations. The various cultures of this largely archipelagic, metal-poor world, and especially its alternative technologies, are described in fascinating elaboration. *The Witling* has many of the same story elements (covert interplanetary visitors, an emotionally crippled woman genius, a person of ordinary capacity caught up in all this, a pet with psionic powers), but the combination is less successful. For one thing, much of the exposition is taken up with a brilliantly logical but never quite believable development of a world where practically everyone has an inborn ability to teleport. The title (which Vinge uses to mean approximately "half-wit") is a pun: at first it is applied in scorn to Pelio, the native hero who lacks his race's usual teleportational ability, but by the end it applies with more justification to the genius heroine. In a typical Vinge twist-of-the-knife ending, she suffers brain damage that both impairs her intellect and renders her a more balanced, happier person, a suitable partner for the love-stricken Pelio.

In his next two novels, Vinges returns to Earth. The widely acclaimed *True Names* features a computer net perceived by its users as a magical realm, and centers on a struggle by hobbyist "wizards" against a bloated Federal bureaucracy on the one hand, and against the mysterious malevolent Mailman on the other. The same loving elaboration applied to teleportation in the *The Witling* is here put to a more plausible initial premise (the "magic" computer net), with brilliant results. As in previous novels, *True Names* features superhumans, but this time they attain that status largely by computer interface, rather than solely on the basis of their inborn talents. The love affair, within the "magical" realm where youth can be eternal, between the young hero and the old heroine (so ancient she had actually worked as a keypunch operator!) recalls, probably intentionally, a similar relationship in Heinlein's "Magic Incorporated." The technological innovation put to scrutiny in *The Peace War* is the stasis field, described in a few throw-away lines in Heinlein's *Beyond This Horizon* and perhaps best used before *The Peace*

*War* in Niven's Known Space series. Vinge finds a variety of new applications for the idea, using it as an offensive weapon, a shield, a prison, and a time machine. In a combination of previous superman notions, *The Peace War's* main viewpoint character is a genius even unassisted, and something unprecedented when interfaced with computers. Like *Grimm's World, The Peace War* depicts an elaborate sociological situation growing out of its basic assumptions (chiefly use of the stasis field, progress in genetic engineering and electronics, and the deliberate suppression of high-powered machinery). As in *True Names*, there is a romance blighted by age disparity—this time between a woman Air Force captain, newly emerged from stasis, and her one-time lover, who has aged throughout the 50 years since she was entrapped.

Both *True Names* and *The Peace War* show a considerable mellowing in tone over Vinge's previous work, which had been powerful and effective, but generally so bleak in outlook that it was made bearable only by the sparsity of the author's production. True, most of the human race is wiped out offstage in *The Peace War*, and the threat of bureaucracy is not entirely gone by the end of *True Names*, but life does now seem to be dealing Vinge viewpoint characters somewhat better cards. At the very least, the author is demonstrating his control of a wider range of approaches. The steady accumulation of quality work will indeed earn him a major reputation with the passing of years.

—Patrick L. McGuire

---

**VONNEGUT, Kurt, Jr.** American. Born in Indianapolis, Indiana, 11 November 1922. Educated at Cornell University, Ithaca, New York, 1940–42; Carnegie Institute, Pittsburgh, 1943; University of Chicago, 1945–47. Served in the United States Army Infantry, 1942–45; Purple Heart. Married 1) Jane Marie Cox in 1945 (divorced 1979), one son and two daughters; 2) Jill Krementz in 1979, one daughter. Police reporter, Chicago City News Bureau, 1946; worked in public relations for the General Electric Company, Schenectady, New York, 1947–50. Since 1950, freelance writer. Since 1965, teacher, Hopefield School, Sandwich, Massachusetts. Visiting Lecturer, Writers Workshop, University of Iowa, Iowa City, 1965–67, and Harvard University, Cambridge, Massachusetts, 1970–71; Visiting Professor, City University of New York, 1973–74. Recipient: Guggenheim Fellowship, 1967; American Academy grant, 1970. M.A.: University of Chicago, 1971; Litt. D.: Hobart and William Smith Colleges, Geneva, New York, 1974. Member, American Academy, 1973. Agent: Donald C. Farber, 99 Park Avenue, New York, New York 10016, U.S.A.

### Science-Fiction Publications

#### Novels

*Player Piano.* New York, Scribner, 1952; London, Macmillian, 1953; as *Utopia 14*, New York, Bantam, 1954.
*The Sirens of Titan.* New York, Dell, 1959; London, Gollancz, 1962.
*Cat's Cradle.* New York, Holt Rinehart, and London, Gollancz, 1963.
*Slaughterhouse-Five; or, The Children's Crusade.* New York, Delacorte Press, 1969; London, Cape, 1970.
*Galápagos.* New York, Delacorte Press, and London, Cape, 1985.
*Bluebeard.* New York, Delacorte Press, 1987; London, Cape, 1988.
*Hocus Pocus; or, What's the Hurry, Son?* New York, Putnam, and London, Cape, 1990.

#### Short Stories

*Canary in a Cat House.* New York, Fawcett, 1961.
*Welcome to the Monkey House: A Collection of Short Works.* New York, Delacorte Press, 1968; London, Cape, 1969.

### Other Publications

#### Novels

*Mother Night.* New York, Fawcett, 1962; London, Cape, 1968.
*God Bless You, Mr. Rosewater; or, Pearls Before Swine.* New York, Holt Rinehart, and London, Cape, 1965.
*Breakfast of Champions; or, Goodbye, Blue Monday.* New York, Delacorte Press, and London, Cape, 1973.
*Slapstick; or, Lonesome No More!* New York, Delacorte Press, and London, Cape, 1976.
*Jailbird.* New York, Delacorte Press, and London, Cape, 1979.
*Deadeye Dick.* New York, Delacorte Press, 1982; London, Cape, 1983.

#### Plays

*Happy Birthday, Wanda June* (as *Penelope*, produced Cape Cod, Massachusetts, 1960; revised version, as *Happy Birthday, Wanda June*, produced New York, 1970; London, 1977). New York, Delacorte Press, 1970; London, Cape, 1973.
*The Very First Christmas Morning*, in *Better Homes and Gardens* (Des Moines, Iowa), December 1962.
*Between Time and Timbuktu; or, Prometheus-5: A Space Fantasy* (televised, 1972; produced New York, 1976). New York, Delacorte Press, 1972; London, Panther, 1975.
*Fortitude*, in *Wampeters, Foma, and Granfalloons* 1974.
*Timesteps* (produced Edinburgh, 1979).
*God Bless You, Mr. Rosewater*, adaptation of his own novel (produced New York, 1979).

Television Plays: "Auf Wiedersehen," with Valentine Davies, 1958; *Between Time and Timbuktu*, 1972.

#### Other

*Wampeters, Foma and Granfalloons: Opinions.* New York, Delacorte Press, 1974; London, Cape, 1975.
*Sun Moon Star.* New York, Harper, and London, Hutchinson, 1980.
*Palm Sunday: An Autobiographical Collage.* New York, Delacorte Press, and London, Cape, 1981.
*Fates Worse Than Death: An Autobiographical Collage of the 1980's.* Nottingham, Spokesman, 1980(?); New York, Putnam, 1991.
*Nothing Is Lost Save Honor: Two Essays.* Jackson, Mississippi, Nouveau Press, 1984.
*Who Am I this Time?* Minneapolis, Minnesota, Redpath Press, 1987.
*Conversations with Kurt Vonnegut* (interviews), edited by William Rodney Allen. Jackson, University of Mississippi Press, 1988.

*

Bibliography: *Kurt Vonnegut, Jr.: A Descriptive Bibliography and Annotated Secondary Checklist* by Asa B. Pieratt, Jr., and Jerome Klinkowitz, Hamden, Connecticut, Shoe String Press, 1974; *Kurt Vonnegut: A Comprehensive Bibliography* by Asa B. Pieratt, Jr., Julie Huffman-Klinkowitz, and Jerome Klinkowitz, Hamden, Connecticut, Archon, 1987.

Critical Studies: *Kurt Vonnegut, Jr.* by Peter J. Reed, New York, Warner, 1972; *Kurt Vonnegut: Fantasist of Fire and Ice* by David H. Goldsmith, Bowling Green, Ohio, Popular Press, 1972; *The Vonnegut Statement* edited by Jerome Klinkowitz and John Somer, New York, Delacorte Press, 1973, London, Panther, 1975, *Vonnegut in America: An introduction to the Life and Work of Kurt Vonnegut* edited by Klinkowitz and Donald L. Lawler, New York, Delacorte Press, 1977, and *Kurt Vonnegut* by Klinkowitz, London, Methuen, 1982; *Kurt Vonnegut, Jr.* by Stanley Schatt, Boston, Twayne, 1976; *Kurt Vonnegut* by James Lundquist, New York, Ungar, 1977; *Vonnegut: A Preface to His Novels* by Richard Giannone, Port Washington, New York, Kennikat Press, 1977; *Kurt Vonnegut: The Gospel from Outer Space* by Clark Mayo, San Bernardino, California, Borgo Press, 1977; *Vonnegut's Duty-Dance with Death: Theme and Structure in Slaughterhouse-Five* by Monica Loeb, Umeå, Sweden, Umeå Studies in the Humanities, 1979.

* * *

What is Kurt Vonnegut's relationship to SF? It would be misleading to say that he began as a SF writer and later drifted away from the "lodge." Vonnegut never identified with the "lodge," and he has continued to use SF as a mine of metaphors for his sad, zany chronicles of the disintegration of middle American culture. The bizarre post-holocaust scene of *Cat's Cradle* shrinks in *Deadeye Dick* to the depopulation of Midland City by a neutron bomb, but the weirdness of Vonnegut's fiction is characteristically SF.

One way to go wrong is to take straight Eliot Rosewater's much-quoted drunken speech (in *God Bless You, Mr. Rosewater*) to a SF writer's convention ("I love you sons of bitches. . . . You're all I read any more. . . . You're the only ones with guts enough to really care about the future. . . ."). Eliot is compassionate and humane, to be sure, but he is also a drunken lunatic. And even Eliot admits that SF writers can't "write for sour apples," while claiming that Kilgore Trout, the dean of hacks, is "the greatest writer alive today."

Another way to go wrong is to misread Vonnegut's remark that, since writing *Player Piano*, he has "been a sore-headed occupant of a file drawer labeled 'science fiction,' " and that he wants out, "particularly since so many serious critics regularly mistake the drawer for a urinal." The urinal mistake is not Vonnegut's: he attributes it to critics who didn't take enough science courses in college, and he goes on to provide a clear-headed and sympathetic account of the SF writer's "lodge" and the SF branch of the publishing industry.

Perhaps the best approach to mapping Vonnegut's SF connection is to consider Donald Lawler's analysis of *The Sirens of Titan.* Lawler claims that the "narrative shell" of *Sirens* is "space opera," and that it serves Vonnegut as "an enabling form of satire." Lawler is right to see the satirical punch of the novel as arising from its SF form and content; however, the SF form opposite to the "shaggy dog story" Lawler finds in the novel is the apocalypse, the kind of SF story that portrays a catastrophic transformation of the human scene in order to reveal the purpose of human history.

One of the most ambitious of SF's apocalyptic fictions is Arthur C. Clarke's *Childhood's End,* published five years before *The Sirens of Titan.* In 1978, Vonnegut called Clarke's novel one of SF's few masterpieces. ("All of the others were written by me," he said.) *Childhood's End* portrays the end of human evolution on earth, revealing that the latent destiny of humankind is to transform its last generation into a collective immaterial entity that will soar away from earth and join the Overmind, a godlike union of similar "racial" consciousnesses that is gradually taking over the universe. Compared to Clarke's grandiose concept, the apocalyptic revelation of *Sirens* is a shaggy dog indeed, for its plot discloses that 50 thousand years of human history have had one trivial purpose: to ensure the delivery of a repair part to the spacecraft of an alien courier stranded on Titan. Not only that, the courier discovers that the message he has spent his being to carry from one end of the galaxy to the other is merely "Greetings."

The foregoing illustrates one way in which Vonnegut uses SF conventions—by writing against them, often to the point of parody. SF stories, whether they end well or badly for their protagonists, generally embody a romantic concept of human purpose. Immanent or extrinsic, fated or born of the human struggle with nature, the destiny of humankind is noble and meaningful: to dominate and make sense of the universe. The *Sirens of Titan* uses SF motifs to counter this tradition. Its hero, Malachi Constant ("the eternal pilgrim") learns, along with Winston Niles Rumfoord and the rest of mankind, that the "outward push" is pointless, that there is no meaning to the universe, and that there is no god but "God the Utterly Indifferent."

Another indicator of Vonnegut's relationship to SF is, of course, the feckless SF writer Kilgore Trout, who appears regularly in Vonnegut's fiction. Promised his freedom in *Breakfast of Champions* (which was supposed to be Vonnegut's final novel), he was pressed into service again for *Jailbird* and revived anonymously for *Hocus Pocus.* In *Galápagos*, he appears briefly to his son, the million-year-old narrator. Trout knows and cares little about science, writes terribly, and has earned neither critical nor popular acclaim: his books can be found, remaindered and misleading titled, only in pornographic bookstores. His fate as a SF writer is far worse than that of the late Theodore Sturgeon, but his name is almost certainly a wicked parody of Sturgeon's.

Trout, however, is clearly also an alter ego of Vonnegut. His novel *2BRO2B*, so admired by Eliot Rosewater, appears to involve the situation of *Player Piano*, Vonnegut's first novel, with the addition of Ethical Suicide Parlors for population control, themselves an appurtenance of the *Playboy* story "Welcome to the Monkey House" (written about the same time as *God Bless You, Mr. Rosewater*). Trout may be partly a foul-smelling old hack, but he is also a lovable eccentric whose fictions are based on big, imaginative concepts like that of Sturgeon's *The Cosmic Rape*, which saw its title parodied and its plot inverted in Vonnegut's notorious "The Big Space Fuck," published in *Again, Dangerous Visions* (edited by Harlan Ellison, New York, Doubleday, 1972; London, Millington, 1976).

Kilgore Trout is perhaps Vonnegut's chief SF metaphor—the writer whose vision outstrips his knowledge and his craft. In that his condition is Sturgeon's—but also Vonnegut's, and any writer's. Perhaps he also represents any writer's (and any reader's) fear of becoming an old, derelict failure—or of actually being one already. Perhaps he embodies some nagging fear of his creator that what he has created might just possibly be a bunch of worthless, second-rate SF.

Vonnegut's SF (many of the early stories, *Player Piano, The Sirens of Titan, Cat's Cradle, Slaughterhouse-Five*, and *Galápagos*) is not second-rate. *Player Piano*, perhaps, has suffered unfair competition from the major dystopian novels of its time: *1984, Fahrenheit 451*, and *The Space Merchants*, all of which have similar plots involving the rebellion of an insider against an oppressive social order. But, like the others, the story of Paul Proteus has a unique target—automated production—and, like the others, it presents a plausible vision of post-industrial society. *The Sirens of Titan* is not only the parody of apocalyptic SF discussed above: published at the beginning of the age of space, it is a satirical critique of a society obsessed with technological accomplishments that lead to little more than "empty heroics, low comedy, and pointless death."

*Cat's Cradle*, with its story that counterpoints the careless disposal of a doomsday weapon with the history of a harmless cult religion, is perhaps even stronger in its denunciation of the follies of technological society. The discoverer of Ice-Nine, the substance that destroys the planet by freezing all its water, irresponsibly leaves the fatal chunk to his three less-than-normal offspring. Dr. Felix Hoenikker was already the "father of the A-Bomb," a scientist who would play with any dangerous research idea suggested by the military sources of his funding. Contrasted with him is the playful Bokonon, inventor of a religion he acknowledges to be lies and illusions (or a fiction), but knows will relieve the miserable lives of the inhabitants of his poor Caribbean island. Bokonon is a holy fool who has created a warm extended family; Hoenikker is a man of reason who has neglected his children. The dreams of reason prove more dangerous than the illusions of religion.

*Slaughterhouse-Five* is the perfect marriage of Vonnegut's SF with his more "mundane" themes. "Billy Pilgrim has come unstuck in time." Unlike the purposeful time travelers of SF convention (but much like the Winston Niles Rumfoord of *Sirens*, jerked around by the chrono-synclastic infundibulum), this unlikely hero lives all the moments of his life simultaneously, including his P.O.W. captivity in Dresden during the firebombing, and his captivity in an exhibit on the planet Tralfamador. From this perspective, optometrist Billy sees that the universe is mechanically preordained, and that the solution is to live only the happy moments. Billy, of course, is regarded as a harmless lunatic (especially since he is a devoted fan of SF writer Kilgore Trout). However, it is not the holy fools and lunatic dreamers who run the death camps and firebomb Dresden: a different kind of madman has polluted the stream of reason that trickles so weakly in a Billy, a Bokonon, and an Eliot Rosewater.

With *Slaughterhouse-Five*, Vonnegut's fiction becomes more personal, and the line begins to blur between fictional narrative and autobiographical essay. The auctorial voice becomes more direct, and hard to distinguish from those of first-person narrators who are clearly, unlike Trout, projections of Vonnegut. In the much-maligned *Breakfast of Champions*, the author-narrator actually appears in a cocktail lounge occupied by several of the novel's characters, and, at its conclusion, he confronts a pathetic Kilgore Trout. Though he tries to dismiss Trout, however, Vonnegut's SF roots will not disappear so easily. In *Slapstick*, he employs a Troutian conceit (telepathic intelligence-boosting between twins) and a vague post-holocaust setting to articulate the idea of artificial extended families as an antidote for the rootlessness of contemporary Americans. In *Deadeye Dick*, a freak neutron bomb accident is a metaphor for the demolition of the rich cultural matrix of a place much like the Indianapolis of Vonnegut's youth.

Vonnegut's most recent novels continue to address audiences familiar with SF conventions. *Galápagos*, Vonnegut's answer to Swift's *Voyage to the Land of the Houyhnhms*, Wells's *Time Machine*, and Stewart's *Earth Abides*, takes the post-holocaust fiction into new territories of rational absurdity. Its million-year old narrator (the ghost of Kilgore Trout's son) unfolds for us the saga of how the human species was saved (sort of) when a plague rendered virtually all women permanently sterile. By chance, a small, motley group ends up stranded in the Galápagos Archipelago and is unafflicted by the plague. Their descendants, we are told, evolve into creatures who can digest seaweed and swim with flippers, whose brains are not of the big, dangerous sort possessed by their ancestors—and who do not know they are going to die. Most of the story's actual events take place in the 20th century, and those events would seem to justify the conclusion that humanity's curious devolution would not be such a bad outcome.

While *Bluebeard*, the story of the Armenian-American minimalist painter who appeared briefly in *Breakfast of Champions*, is not explicitly connected with Vonnegut's SF, the same cannot be said of *Hocus Pocus*. The involute saga of Eugene Debs Hartke, Vietnam hero, fired college teacher, prison warden, and TB victim, is narrated in the year 2001. Several other allusions to Arthur C. Clarke suggest that we are to take the story as another of Vonnegut's peeks at the contrast between our millennial pretensions and our cultural and economic decay. The novel plays promiscuously with elements of Vonnegut's fictional cosmos and the often depressing world of our daily newspapers and the detritus of our popular culture, and the effects often seem inexplicable. Why, for instance, is an ostentatious vulgarian clearly modeled on Malcolm Forbes given the name Arthur *K.* Clarke? The answer might be found in the text of the anonymous "Protocols of the Elders of Tralfamadore" stowed in Hartke's footlocker, a Troutian big-concept story that reveals the origin of life and religion in a conspiracy of superhuman aliens. Or it might not.

Vonnegut has been writing about two things since the beginning—the loss of old Indianapolis, a symbol of middle America, and its way of life (noble in spite of racism, pretentiousness, and abuse and neglect of the poor); and what seems to be replacing it (a racist, pretentious, exploitative vulgarity). Vonnegut, by his own admission not a member of the "lodge" and not a reader of SF pulps as a youngster, may not be a "licensed" SF writer. Yet he remains an ornament to SF, for without the SF devices that shape his fictions, he could not have made them what they are. If his chronicle of contemporary America's endless Great Depression has enduring value, it is largely due to Vonnegut's quirky dialect of the language of SF.

—John P. Brennan

---

**WAINWRIGHT, Ken.** *See* **TUBB, E.C.**

---

**WALDROP, Howard.** American. Born in Houston, Mississippi, 15 September 1946. Educated at Arlington High School, Texas, 1962–65; University of Texas, Arlington, 1965–70, 1972–74. Served as an information specialist in the United States Army, 1970–72. Linotype operator, Arlington *Daily News*, 1965–68; advertising copywriter, Lindell-Keyes, Dallas, 1972; auditory research subject, Dynastat Inc., Austin, 1975–80. Recipient: Nebula award, 1980; World Fantasy award, 1981. Agent: Joseph Elder Agency, P.O. Box 298, Warwick, New York 10990. Address: P.O. Box 49335, Austin, Texas 78765, U.S.A.

SCIENCE-FICTION PUBLICATIONS

Novels

*The Texas-Israeli War: 1999*, with Jake Saunders. New York, Ballantine, 1974.
*Them Bones*. New York, Ace, 1984; London, Century, 1989.
*A Dozen Tough Jobs* (novella). Shingletown, California, Zeising, 1989.

Short Stories

*Howard Who?* New York, Doubleday, 1986.
*All about Strange Monsters of the Recent Past*. Kansas City, Missouri, Ursus, 1987.
*Night of the Cooters*. Kansas City, Missouri, Ursus, 1990.

Uncollected Short Stories

"Lunchbox," in *Analog* (New York), May 1972.
"Mono no Aware," in *Haunt of Horror* (New York), August 1973.
"A Voice and Bitter Weeping," with Jake Saunders, in *The Best from Galaxy 2*. New York, Award, 1974.
"My Sweet Lady Jo," in *Universe 4*, edited by Terry Carr. New York, Random House, 1974.
"Time and Variance," in *Vertex* (Los Angeles), August 1974.
"Sic Transit. . . ?" with Steve Utley, in *Stellar 2*, edited by Judy-Lynn del Rey. New York, Ballantine, 1976.
"Sun Up!," with Al Jackson, in *Faster Than Light*, edited by Jack Dann and George Zebrowski. New York, Harper, 1976.
"Custer's Last Jump," with Steve Utley, in *Universe 6*, edited by Terry Carr. New York, Doubleday, 1976; London, Dobson, 1978.
"Unsleeping Beauty and the Beast," in *Lone Star Universe*, edited by George W. Proctor and Steve Utley. Austin, Texas, Heidelberg, 1976.
"Men of Greywater Station," with George R.R. Martin, in *Songs of Stars and Shadows*, by Martin. New York, Pocket Books, 1977.
"Black as the Pit, From Pole to Pole," with Steve Utley, in *New Dimensions 7*, edited by Robert Silverberg. New York, Harper, and London, Gollancz, 1977.
"Billy Big-Eyes," in *Berkley Showcase 1*, edited by Victoria Schochet and John W. Silbersack. New York, Berkley, 1980.
"Fair Game," in *Afterlives: An Anthology of Stories about Life after Death*, edited by Pamela Sargent and Ian Watson. New York, Vintage, 1986.
"Flying Saucer Rock and Roll," in *Omni*, January 1985.
"French Scenes," in *Synergy: New Science Fiction*, edited by George Zebrowski. San Diego, Harcourt Brace Jovanovich, 1987.
"Hoover's Men," in *Omni*, October 1988.
"The Lions Are Asleep This Night," in *Omni*, August 1986.
"Night of the Cooters," in *Omni*, April 1987.
"Do Ya, Do Ya, Wanna Dance?" in *The Year's Best Science Fiction*, edited by Gardner Dozois. New York, St. Martin's Press, 1989.
"The Passing of the Western," in *Razored Saddles*, edited by Joe R. Lansdale and Pat LoBrutto. Arlington Heights, Illinois, Dark Harvest, 1989.

* * *

The thing about Howard Waldrop is that the myths are true: he really does talk about his stories for a long time before writing them just in time to read at a convention; he did withdraw stories from high-payers and sell them cheaper (but for good reasons). That's the man, or a fraction of him. The published fiction is something else again. If any writer in this book can be called unique, for any reason, then it should be Howard Waldrop.

For 20 years Waldrop has used his sense of the absurd coupled with a mastery of the techniques of pastiche to produce some of the most off-beat stories of any period. In addition, he has both an encyclopaedic knowledge of all sorts of things, notably the 1950's films and rock'n'roll, and an obsession with research, which result in his stories being packed with little gems that most readers will miss. (It doesn't matter, you've almost certainly picked up things everyone else has missed, that's a small part of the fun.) For example, his story for the *Wild Cards* anthology, "30 Minutes Over Broadway," about the comic hero character Jetboy's last flight, was reprinted with notes—nine pages of them—on a 36-page story! They take in obscure technical terms, obscure film references, and even a double allusion through the references in a Silverberg novel. Howard says he missed a lot more out of this list, and he's never done it with any other story.

Often, of course, these little references become the focus of the story. "Ike at the Mike" (in *Howard Who?*) has rising young politician E. Aron Presley attending the farewell performance of legendary jazz clarinetist Dwight Eisenhower, with George S. Patton on the drums. And in "Save a Place in the Lifeboat for Me" (in *Howard Who?*), all the great comedians come back to try to save Buddy Holly and the Big Bopper and Richie Valens. Believe me, nobody has done Groucho so well.

Those stories, and dozens like them, gave Waldrop a major reputation, and not a few award nominations, and eventually Terry Carr asked him to write a novel for the revived Ace Specials. Waldrop had co-written *The Texas-Israeli War: 1999* with Jake Saunders, early in his career, but it's not worth what you'd probably have to pay for it now. The original story, "A Voice and Bitter Weeping," works well, telling how Israeli mercenaries help Texas fight off the other 49 states over oil, but like many of Waldrop's ideas it's really a conceit, a notion, and it doesn't carry a plot beyond a few thousand words. Not so *Them Bones*, which takes three time-travel strands and braids them carefully. First an archaeological dig in the 1920's finds all kinds of disturbing anachronisms; second, 21st-century time traveller Madison Yazoo Leake meets Greek-speaking Amerindians and traders from an Islamic old world after Carthage defeated Rome. It gets further from the mainstream as it goes, and it is rivetting fun. *Them Bones* stood out even in the exalted company of the Ace Specials.

But it is still his only novel, although he's been thinking about writing *I, John Mandeville* for 20 years. Howard Waldrop is a major writer, primarily on the strength of his short stories, and he's getting better. His first real classic was probably "The Ugly Chickens" (in *Howard Who?*), which sends a young ornithologist off searching for the last surviving dodoes, in Mississippi. It won the Nebula award, and might be selected as the prime example of Waldrop's tightly trimmed prose conjuring up real visions of distorted (or plain warped) reality alongside ordinary people. The balance of tragedy and comedy sways either way through the story, and is only restored with the final line.

Mississippi is also the setting for Howard's other book-length story, the novella *A Dozen Tough Jobs*, which purports to be a re-telling of the labours of Hercules. The work-parole ex-con Houlka Lee is assigned by the vicious plantation owner who takes him on. This is really the story of the narrator, a young black kid called I.O. Lace, coming of age, and it is a story about racism and slavery. The story reads very simply, far simpler than most of Waldrop's work, and this led some critics to consider it slight and lightweight. The allusions are still there, the rural pictures are still as perfect as in "The Ugly Chickens," and the characters are warm and human.

But Waldrop can make you believe in all his reality changes, however much you know it ain't necessarily so. That is the genius that some writers bring into our lives. And I haven't even mentioned the (mostly) true, and very funny, story "Flying Saucer Rock'n'Roll."

—Kev P. McVeigh

---

**WALLACE, (Richard Horatio) Edgar.** British. Born in Greenwich, London, 1 April 1875. Educated at St. Peter's School, London, Board School, Camberwell, London, to age 12. Served in the Royal West Kent Regiment in England, 1893–96, and in the Medical Staff Corps in South Africa, 1896–99: bought his discharge, 1899; served in the Lincoln's Inn branch of the Special Constabulary, and as a special interrogator for the War Office, during World War I. Married 1) Ivy Caldecott in 1901 (divorced 1919), two daughters and two sons; 2) Violet King in 1921, one daughter. Worked in a printing firm, shoe shop, rubber factory, and as a merchant seaman, plasterer, and milk delivery boy, in London, 1886–91; South African correspondent for Reuter's, 1899–1902, and the London *Daily Mail*, 1900–02; editor, *Rand Daily News*, Johannesburg, 1902–03; returned to London: reporter, *Daily Mail*, 1903–07, and *Standard*, 1910; racing editor, and later editor, *The Week-End*, later *The Week-End Racing Supplement*, 1910–12; racing editor and special writer, *Evening News*, 1910–12; founded *Bibury's Weekly* and *R.E. Walton's Weekly*, both racing papers; editor, *Ideas* and *The Story Journal*, 1913; writer, and later editor, *Town Topics*, 1913–16; regular contributor to the *Birmingham Post*, and *Thomson's Weekly News*, Dundee; racing columnist, *The Star*, 1927–32, and *Daily Mail*, 1930–32; drama critic, *Morning Post*, 1928; founder, *The Bucks Mail*, 1930; editor, *Sunday News*, 1931. Chairman of the board of directors, and film writer/director, British Lion Film Corporation. Chairman, Press Club, London, 1923–24. *Died 10 February 1932.*

SCIENCE-FICTION PUBLICATIONS

Novels

*1925: The Story of a Fatal Peace*. London, Newnes, 1915.
*The Green Rust*. London, Ward Lock, 1919; Boston, Small Maynard, 1920.
*Captains of Souls*. Boston, Small Maynard, 1922; London, Long, 1923.
*The Day of Uniting*. London, Hodder and Stoughton, 1926; New York, Mystery League, 1930.
*Planetoid 127* (includes *The Sweizer Pump*). London, Readers Library, 1929.

OTHER PUBLICATIONS

Novels

*The Four Just Men*. London, Tallis Press, 1905; revised edition, 1906; revised edition, Sheffield, Weekly Telegraph, 1908; Boston, Small Maynard, 1920.
*Angel Esquire*. Bristol, Arrowsmith, 1908; Boston, Small Maynard, 1920.
*The Council of Justice*. London, Ward Lock, 1908.
*The Duke in the Suburbs*. London, Ward Lock, 1909.
*Captain Tatham of Tatham Island*. London, Gale and Polden, 1909; revised edition, as *The Island of Galloping Gold*, London, Newnes, 1916; as *Eve's Island*, Newnes, 1926.
*The Nine Bears*. London, Ward Lock, 1910; as *Silinski, Master Criminal*, Cleveland, World, 1930; as *The Cheaters*, London, Digit, 1964.
*The Other Man*. New York, Dodd Mead, 1911.
*Private Selby*. London, Ward Lock, 1912.
*The Fourth Plague*. London, Ward Lock, 1913; New York, Doubleday, 1930.
*Grey Timothy*. London, Ward Lock, 1913, as *Pallard the Punter*, 1914.
*The River of Stars*. London, Ward Lock, 1913.
*The Man Who Bought London*. London, Ward Lock, 1915.
*The Melody of Death*. Bristol, Arrowsmith, 1915; New York, Dial Press, 1927.
*The Clue of the Twisted Candle*. Boston, Small Maynard, 1916; London, Newnes, 1917.
*A Debt Discharged*. London, Ward Lock, 1916.
*The Tomb of Ts'in*. London, Ward Lock, 1916.
*The Just Men of Cordova*. London, Ward Lock, 1917.
*Kate Plus Ten*. Boston, Small Maynard, 1917; London, Ward Lock, 1919.
*The Secret House*. London, Ward Lock, 1917; Boston, Small Maynard, 1919.
*Down under Donovan*. London, Ward Lock, 1918.

*The Man Who Knew.* Boston, Small Maynard, 1918; London, Newnes, 1919.
*Those Folk of Bulboro.* London, Ward Lock, 1918.
*The Daffodil Mystery.* London, Ward Lock, 1920; as *The Daffodil Murder*, Boston, Small Maynard, 1921.
*Jack o'Judgment.* London, Ward Lock, 1920; Boston, Small Maynard, 1921.
*The Book of All Power.* London, Ward Lock, 1921.
*The Angel of Terror.* Boston, Small Maynard, and London, Hodder and Stoughton, 1922; as *The Destroying Angel*, in *Street and Smith's Detective Story Magazine*, 1922.
*The Crimson Circle.* London, Hodder and Stoughton, 1922; New York, Doubleday, 1929.
*The Flying Fifty-Five.* London, Hutchinson, 1922.
*Mr. Justuce Maxell.* London, Ward Lock, 1922.
*The Valley of Ghosts.* London, Odhams Press, 1922; Boston, Small Maynard, 1923.
*The Books of Bart.* London, Ward Lock, 1923.
*The Clue of the New Pin.* Boston, Small Maynard, and London, Hodder and Stoughton, 1923.
*The Green Archer.* London, Hodder and Stoughton, 1923; Boston, Small Maynard, 1924.
*The Missing Million.* London, Long, 1923; as *The Missing Millions*, Boston, Small Maynard, 1925.
*The Dark Eyes of London.* London, Ward Lock, 1924; New York, Doubleday, 1929.
*Double Dan.* London, Hodder and Stoughton, 1924; as *Diana of Kara-Kara*, Boston, Small Maynard, 1924.
*The Face in the Night.* London, Long, 1924; New York, Doubleday, 1929.
*Room 13.* London, Long, 1924.
*Flat 2.* New York, Garden City Publishing Company, 1924; revised edition, London, Long, 1927.
*The Sinister Man.* London, Hodder and Stoughton, 1924; Boston, Small Maynard, 1925.
*The Three Oak Mystery.* London, Ward Lock, 1924.
*Blue Hand.* London, Ward Lock, 1925; Boston, Small Maynard, 1926.
*The Black Avons.* London, Gill, 1925; as *How They Fared in the Times of the Tudors, Roundhead and Cavalier, From Waterloo to the Mutiny*, and *Europe in the Melting Pot*, 4 vols., 1925.
*The Daughters of the Night.* London, Newnes, 1925.
*The Fellowship of the Frog.* London, Ward Lock, 1925; New York, Doubleday, 1928.
*The Gaunt Stranger.* London, Hodder and Stoughton, 1925; as *The Ringer*, New York, Doubleday, 1926.
*The Hairy Arm.* Boston, Small Maynard, 1925; as *The Avenger*, London, Long, 1926.
*A King by Night.* London, Long, 1925; New York, Doubleday, 1926.
*The Strange Countess.* London, Hodder and Stoughton, 1925; Boston, Small Maynard, 1926.
*The Three Just Men.* London, Hodder and Stoughton, 1925; New York, Doubleday, 1930.
*The Man from Morocco.* London, Long, 1925; as *The Black*, New York, Doubleday, 1930.
*Barbara on Her Own.* London, Newnes, 1926.
*The Black Abbot.* London, Hodder and Stoughton, 1926; New York, Doubleday, 1927.
*The Door with Seven Locks.* London, Hodder and Stoughton, and New York, Doubleday, 1926.
*The Joker.* London, Hodder and Stoughton, 1926; as *The Colossus*, New York, Doubleday, 1932.
*The Million Dollar Story.* London, Newnes, 1926.
*The Northing Tramp.* London, Hodder and Stoughton, 1926; New York, Doubleday, 1929; as *The Tramp*, London, Pan, 1965.
*Penelope of the Polyantha.* London, Hodder and Stoughton, 1926.
*The Square Emerald.* London, Hodder and Stoughton, 1926; as *The Girl from Scotland Yard*, New York, Doubleday, 1927.
*The Terrible People.* London, Hodder and Stoughton, and New York, Doubleday, 1926.
*We Shall See!* London, Hodder and Stoughton, 1926; as *The Gaol Breaker*, New York, Doubleday, 1931.
*The Yellow Snake.* London, Hodder and Stoughton, 1926.
*Big Foot.* London, Long, 1927.
*The Feathered Serpent.* London, Hodder and Stoughton, 1927; New York, Doubleday, 1928.
*Number Six.* London, Newnes, 1927.
*The Forger.* London, Hodder and Stoughton, 1927; as *The Clever One*, New York, Doubleday, 1928.
*The Hand of Power.* London, Long, 1927; New York, Mystery League, 1930.
*The Man Who Was Nobody.* London, Ward Lock, 1927.
*The Ringer* (novelization of stage play). London, Hodder and Stoughton, 1927.
*The Squeaker.* London, Hodder and Stoughton, 1927; as *The Squealer*, New York, Doubleday, 1928.
*Terror Keep.* London, Hodder and Stoughton, and New York, Doubleday, 1927.
*The Traitor's Gate.* London, Hodder and Stoughton, and New York, Doubleday, 1927.
*The Double.* London, Hodder and Stoughton, and New York, Doubleday, 1928.
*The Thief in the Night.* London, Readers Library, 1928; augmented edition, London, Digit, 1962.
*The Flying Squad.* London, Hodder and Stoughton, 1928; New York, Doubleday, 1929.
*The Gunner.* London, Long, 1928; as *Gunman's Bluff*, New York, Doubleday, 1929.
*The Twister.* London, Long, 1928; New York, Doubleday, 1929.
*The Golden Hades.* London, Collins, 1929.
*The Green Ribbon.* London, Hutchinson, 1929; New York, Doubleday, 1930.
*The India-Rubber Men.* London, Hodder and Stoughton, 1929; New York, Doubleday, 1930.
*The Terror.* London, Detective Story Club, 1929; augmented edition, London, Digit, 1962.
*The Calendar.* London, Collins, 1930; New York, Doubleday, 1931.
*The Clue of the Silver Key.* London, Hodder and Stoughton, 1930; as *The Silver Key*, New York, Doubleday, 1930.
*The Lady of Ascot.* London, Hutchinson, 1930.
*White Face.* London, Hodder and Stoughton, 1930; New York, Doubleday, 1931.
*On the Spot.* London, Long, and New York, Doubleday, 1931.
*The Coat of Arms.* London, Hutchinson, 1931; as *The Arranways Mystery*, New York, Doubleday, 1932.
*The Devil Man.* London, Collins, and New York, Doubleday, 1931; as *The Life and Death of Charles Peace, 1932.*
*The Man at the Carlton.* London, Hodder and Stoughton, 1931; New York, Doubleday, 1932.
*The Frightened Lady.* London, Hodder and Stoughton, 1932; New York, Doubleday, 1933.
*When the Gangs Came to London.* London, Long, and New York, Doubleday, 1932.
*The Road to London*, edited by Jack Adrian. London, Kimber, 1986.

Short Stories

*Smithy.* London, Tallis Press, 1905; revised edition, as *Smithy, Not to Mention Nobby Clark and Spud Murphy*, London, Newnes, 1914.
*Smithy Abroad: Barrack Room Sketches.* London, Hulton, 1909.
*Sanders of the River.* London, Ward Lock, 1911; New York, Doubleday, 1930.
*The People of the River.* London, Ward Lock, 1912.
*Smithy's Friend Nobby.* London, Town Topics, 1914; as *Nobby*, London, Newnes, 1916.
*The Admirable Carfew.* London, Ward Lock, 1914.
*Bosambo of the River.* London, Ward Lock, 1914.
*Bones, Being Further Adventures in Mr. Commissioner Sanders' Country.* London, Ward Lock, 1915.
*Smithy and the Hun.* London, Pearson, 1915.
*The Keepers of the King's Peace.* London, Ward Lock, 1917.
*Lieutenant Bones.* London, Ward Lock, 1918.
*Tam o'the Scouts.* London, Newnes, 1918; as *Tam of the Scouts*, Boston, Small Maynard, 1919; as *Tam*, Newnes, 1919.
*The Fighting Scouts.* London, Pearson, 1919.
*The Adventures of Heine.* London, Ward Lock, 1919.
*Bones in London.* London, Ward Lock, 1921.
*The Law of the Four Just Men.* London, Hodder and Stoughton, 1921; as *Again the Three Just Men*, New York, Doubleday, 1933.
*Sandi, the King-Maker.* London, Ward Lock, 1922.
*Bones of the River.* London, Newnes, 1923.
*Chick.* London, Ward Lock, 1923.
*Educated Evans.* London, Webster, 1924.
*The Mind of Mr. J.G. Reeder.* London, Hodder and Stoughton, 1925; as *The Murder Book of Mr. J.G. Reeder*, New York, Doubleday, 1929.
*More Educated Evans.* London, Webster, 1926.
*Sanders.* London, Hodder and Stoughton, 1926; as *Mr. Commissioner Sanders*, New York, Doubleday, 1930.
*The Brigand.* London, Hodder and Stoughton, 1927.
*Good Evans!* London, Webster, 1927; as *The Educated Man—Good Evans!*, London, Collins, 1929.
*The Mixer.* London, Long, 1927.
*Again Sanders.* London, Hodder and Stoughton, 1928; New York, Doubleday, 1929.
*Again the Three Just Men.* London, Hodder and Stoughton, 1928; as *The Law of the Three Just Men*, New York, Doubleday, 1931; as *Again the Three*, London, Pan, 1968.
*Elegant Edward.* London, Readers Library, 1928.
*The Orator.* London, Hutchinson, 1928.
*Again the Ringer.* London, Hodder and Stoughton, 1929; as *The Ringer Returns*, New York, Doubleday, 1931.
*Four Square Jane.* London, Readers Library, 1929.
*The Big Four.* London, Readers Library, 1929.
*The Black.* London, Readers Library, 1929; augmented edition, London, Digit, 1962.
*The Ghost of Down Hill* (includes *The Queen of Sheba's Belt*). London, Readers Library, 1929.
*The Cat Burglar.* London, Newnes, 1929.
*Circumstantial Evidence.* London, Newnes, 1929; Cleveland, World, 1934.
*Fighting Snub Reilly.* London, Newnes, 1929; Cleveland, World, 1934.
*The Governor of Chi-Foo.* London, Newnes, 1929; Cleveland, World, 1934.
*The Little Green Man.* London, Collins, 1929.
*The Prison-Breakers.* London, Newnes, 1929.
*Forty-Eight Short Stories.* London, Newnes, 1929.
*For Information Received.* London, Newnes, 1929.
*The Lady of Little Hell.* London, Newnes, 1929.
*The Lone House Mystery.* London, Collins, 1929.
*Red Aces.* London, Hodder and Stoughton, 1929; New York, Doubleday, 1930.
*The Reporter.* London, Readers Library, 1929.
*Circumstantial Evidence.* London, Newnes, 1929; Cleveland, World, 1934.
*Fighting Snub Reilly.* London, Newnes, 1929; Cleveland, World, 1934.
*The Governor of Chi-Foo.* London, Newnes, 1929; Cleveland, World, 1934.
*The Iron Grip.* London, Readers Library, 1930.
*Killer Kay.* London, Newnes, 1930.
*The Stretelli Case and Other Mystery Stories* (omnibus). Cleveland, World, 1930.
*The Lady Called Nita.* London, Newnes, 1930.
*Mrs. William Jones and Bill.* London, Newnes, 1930.
*The Guv'nor and Other Stories.* London, Collins, 1932; as *Mr. Reeder Returns*, New York, Doubleday, 1932; as *The Guv'nor and Mr. J.G. Reeder Returns*, Collins, 2 vols., 1933–34.
*Sergeant Sir Peter.* London, Chapman and Hall, 1932; as *Sergeant Dunn C.I.D.*, London, Digit, 1962.
*The Steward.* London, Collins, 1932.
*The Last Adventure.* London, Hutchinson, 1934.
*The Woman from the East and Other Stories.* London, Hutchinson, 1934.
*Nig-Nog* (omnibus). Cleveland, World, 1934.
*The Undisclosed Client.* London, Digit, 1962.
*The Man Who Married His Cook and Other Stories.* London, White Lion, 1976.
*Unexpected Endings.* Oxford, Edgar Wallace Society, 1979.
*Two Stories, and The Seventh Man.* Oxford, Edgar Wallace Society, 1981.
*The "Sooper and Others,"* edited by Jack Adrian. London, Dent, 1984.
*The Death Room: Strange and Startling Stories*, edited by Jack Adrian. London, Kimber, 1986.

Plays

*An African Millionaire* (produced South Africa, 1904). London, Davis Poynter, 1972.
*The Four Just Men* (produced Colchester, 1906).
*The Forest of Happy Dreams* (produced London, 1910; New York, 1914). Published in *One-act Play Parade*, London, Hodder and Stoughton, 1935.
*Dolly Cutting Herself* (sketch; produced London, 1911).
Sketches, in *Hullo, Ragtime* (produced London, 1912).
Sketches, in *Hullo, Tango!* (produced London, 1912).
*Hello, Exchange!* (sketch; produced London, 1913; as *The Switchboard*, produced New York, 1915).
*The Manager's Dream* (sketch; produced London, 1913).
*Business as Usual* (one act; produced London, 1914).
*The Centibarbe* (one act; produced London, 1914?).
*The Future Lady Shelbourne* (one act; produced London, 1914?).
*Kate Plus Ten* (one act; produced London, 1919?).
*The Whirligig* (revue), with Wal Pink and Albert de Courville, music by Frederick Chappelle (produced London, 1919; as *Pins and Needles*, produced New York, 1922).
*M'Lady* (produced London, 1921).
*The Whirl of the World* (revue), with Albert de Courville and William K. Wells, music by Frederick Chappelle (produced London, 1924).
*The Looking Glass* (revue), with Albert de Courville, music by Frederick Chappelle (produced London, 1924).

*The Ringer*, adaptation of his own novel *The Gaunt Stranger* (produced London, 1926). London, Hodder and Stoughton, and New York, French, 1929.
*The Mystery of Room 45* (one act; produced London, 1926).
*The Terror*, adaptation of his own novel *Terror Keep* (produced Brighton and London, 1927). London, Hodder and Stoughton, 1929.
*Double Dan*, adaptation of his own novel (produced Blackpool and London, 1926).
*A Perfect Gentleman* (one act; produced London, 1927).
*The Yellow Mask*, music by Vernon Duke, lyrics by Desmond Carter (produced Birmingham, 1927; London, 1928).
*The Flying Squad*, adaptation of his own novel (produced Oxford and London, 1928). London, Hodder and Stoughton, 1929.
*The Man Who Changed His Name* (produced London, 1928; New York, 1932). London, Hodder and Stoughton, 1929.
*The Squeaker*, adaptation of his own novel (produced London, 1928; as *Sign of the Leopard*, produced New York, 1928). London, Hodder and Stoughton, 1929.
*The Lad* (produced Wimbledon, 1928; London, 1929).
*Persons Unknown* (produced London, 1929).
*The Calendar* (also director: produced Manchester and London, 1929). London, French, 1932.
*On the Spot* (produced London and New York, 1930).
*The Mouthpiece* (produced London, 1930).
*Smoky Cell* (produced London, 1930).
*Charles III*, adaptation of a play by Curt Götz (produced London, 1931).
*The Old Man* (produced London, 1931).
*The Case of the Frightened Lady* (produced London, 1931). London, French, 1932; as *Criminal at Large* (produced New York, 1932), New York, French, 1934.
*The Green Pack* (produced London, 1932). London, French, 1933.
*The Frog* (adaptation by Ian Hay of *The Fellowship of the Frog*; produced London, 1936.
*The Sun Never Sets* (musical, based on Sanders stories; produced London, 1938).
*Number Six* (adaptation of novel; produced London, 1939).

Screenplays: *Nurse and Martyr*, 1915; *The Ringer*, 1928; *Valley of the Ghosts*, 1928; *The Forger*, 1928; *Red Aces*, 1929, *The Squeaker*, 1930; *Should a Doctor Tell?*, 1930; *The Hound of the Baskervilles*, with V. Gareth Gundrey, 1931; *The Old Man*, 1931; *King Kong*, with others, 1933; and over 160 films based on Edgar Wallace material.

Verse

*The Mission That Failed! A Tale of the Raid and Other Poems.* Cape Town, Maskew Miller, 1898.
*Nicholson's Nek.* Cape Town, Eastern Press, 1900.
*War! and Other Poems.* Cape Town, Eastern Press, 1900.
*Poems for the Period: Nicholson's Nek.* Cape Town, Eastern Press, 1900.
*Writ in Barracks.* London, Methuen, 1900.

Other

*Unofficial Despatches.* London, Hutchinson, 1901.
*Famous Scottish Regiments.* London, Newnes, 1914.
*Fieldmarshall Sir John French and His Campaigns.* London, Newnes, 1914.
*Heroes All: Gallant Deeds of War.* London, Newnes, 1914.
*The Standard History of the War.* London, Newnes, 4 vols., 1914–16.
*War of the Nations.* London, Newnes, vols 2–11, 1914–19.
*Kitchener's Army and the Territorial Forces: The Full Story of a Great Achievement.* London, Newnes, 6 parts, 1915.
*The Real Shell-Man: The Story of Chetwynd of Chilwell.* London, Waddington, 1919.
*People: A Short Autobiography.* London, Hodder and Stoughton, 1926; New York, Doubleday, 1929.
*This England.* London, Hodder and Stoughton, 1927.
*My Hollywood Diary.* London, Hutchinson, 1932.
*A Fragment of Medieval Life.* St. Peter Port, Guernsey, Toucan Press, 1977(?).

Ghostwriter: *The Story of My Life*, by Evelyn Thaw, London, Long, 1914.

Recording: *The Man in the Ditch*, Columbia, 1929.

*

Bibliography: *The British Bibliography of Edgar Wallace* by W.O.G. Lofts and Derek Adley, London, Baker, 1969; *A Guide to the First Editions of Edgar Wallace* by Charles Kiddle, Motcombe, Dorset, Ivory Head Press, 1981.

Critical Studies: *Edgar Wallace—Each Way* by Robert G. Curtis, London, Long, 1932; *Edgar Wallace* by Ethel V. Wallace, London, Hutchinson, 1932; *Edgar Wallace: The Biography of a Phenomenon* by Margaret Lane, London, Heinemann, 1938, New York, Doubleday, 1939, revised edition, London, Hamish Hamilton, 1964.

Theatrical Activities:
Director: **Plays**—*The Calendar*, Manchester and London, 1929; *Brothers* by Herbert Ashton, Jr., London, 1929. **Films**—*Red Aces*, 1929, *The Squeaker*, 1930.

* * *

As the best-known and most prolific British writer of thrillers of the early 20th century, Edgar Wallace possessed a fertile imagination. While he is still considered to be primarily a writer of thrillers, readers of early science fiction and fantasy have found nuggets in his prose that anticipate many recurring themes in that genre. During his lifetime, his works were packaged as mysteries or thrillers by his publishers.

Edgar Wallace's most enduring contribution to literature is the long series of short stories about Commissioner Sanders, "Sanders of the River." Based on first-hand observation in Africa at the turn of the century, they are splendid examples of their author's undoubted talent as a storyteller. Wallace's Africa is a plausible world viewed through the prism of romance and fantasy.

Wallace soon returned to the genre of the thriller and mystery, but his search for new plots and situations brought him to write a sort of "embryonic" science fiction on occasion. One of the more obvious science-fiction themes found in Wallace's work is the future war. At least two of his early novels belong to that category of works that predict a war between Britain and a great Continental power, or the invasion of Britain by a nation on the European Continent. One was published before World War I while the other appeared during its early stages. In *Private Selby*, the emphasis is on the military and political, with a liberal helping of romance, while in *1925: The Story of a Fatal Peace*, there is a technological element—a submarine detector activated by the sound of propellers. The story itself takes place ten years into the future from its date of publication. Blatantly propagandistic, it suggests the consequences for Britain if Germany is not totally beaten in World War I. During the Festival of Schleswig-Holstein in 1925, the Germans attempt to invade Britain in the very transport that had brought British veterans to the German Festival. In retrospect (or mere hindsight), there seems a remarkable correspondence between events in his work and the actual situations in World War I.

In *The Green Rust*, Germany is once again the enemy as a scientist schemes to infest the world's grain crop with bacteria in order to put his nation in the dominant position in the world order. *The Day of Uniting* shares its theme of world destruction with an earlier novel by one of Wallace's contemporaries, Sir Arthur Conan Doyle. The emphasis in both *The Day of Uniting* and *The Poison Belt* is less on the fact of destruction than on the effect the knowledge of impending doom has on the characters. In Wallace's novel, there is a view of science by a non-scientist that adds the comic and human touch to the story of the moral dilemma that is posed—should the people be told what is in store for them or be protected from needless panic? Wallace's title refers to the official day of the proclamation that families be reunited before the end of the world.

The "sound strainer" invented by Professor Colson in *Planetoid 127* is a device by which he communicates with his alter ego on the planet Vulcan. Vulcan rotates about the sun directly opposite from the earth, and thus this story has been referred to as an early example of the "twin world" theme. Wallace describes the communication device in imprecise terms as a thing of "instruments, of wires that spun across the room like the web of a spider, of strange machines which seemed to be endowed with perpetual motion." The dominant theme here of the mis-use of scientific knowledge is a common one in early science fiction.

*Captains of Souls* is something of a tour de force for Wallace. Its theme of the transfer of the souls of two men, Ambrose Sault and Robert Morelle, allowed the author to explore character development to a depth he seldom found time for in his fast-paced thrillers.

The continued popularity of the film *King Kong* has sometimes obscured the fact that Wallace was in Hollywood for its inception. Although he died before its production, the fact that his was the germ of the idea behind it suggests he still had a store of fantastic ideas to be tapped. Popular and prolific, Wallace probably never thought of himself as a writer of science fiction. He was primarily a storyteller whose search for material was as boundless as his sense of what the public would enjoy.

—J. Randolph Cox

---

**WALLACE, F(loyd) L.** American. Lives in California.

### Science-Fiction Publications

Novel

*Address: Centauri.* New York, Gnome Press, 1955.

Uncollected Short Stories

"Hideaway," in *Astounding* (New York), February 1951.
"Student Body," in *Crossroads in Time*, edited by Groff Conklin. New York, Permabooks, 1953.
"Worlds in Balance," in *Science Fiction Plus* (Philadelphia), May 1953.
"The Music Master," in *Imagination* (Evanston, Illinois), November 1953.
"The Seasoned Traveler," in *Universe* (Evanston, Illinois), December 1953.
"Forget Me Nearly," in *Galaxy* (New York), June 1954.
"The Man Who Was Six," in *Galaxy* (New York), September 1954.
"Simple Psiman," in *Startlin* (New York), Fall 1954.
"The Impossible Voyage Home," in *Science Fiction Adventures in Mutation*, edited by Groff Conklin. New York, Vanguard Press, 1955.
"The Assistant Self," in *Fantastic Universe* (Chicago), March 1956.
"Little Thing for the House," in *Astounding* (New York), July 1956.
"The Nevada Virus," in *Venture* (Concord, New Hampshire), September 1957.
"End as a World," in *The Third Galaxy Reader*, edited by H.L. Gold. New York, Doubleday, 1958.
"Tangle Hold," in *5 Galaxy Short Novels*, edited by H.L. Gold. New York, Doubleday, 1958.
"Mezzerow Loves Company," in *World That Couldn't Be and 8 Other SF Novelets*, edited by H.L. Gold. New York, Doubleday, 1959.
"Delay in Transit," in *Bodyguard and 4 Other Short SF Novels from Galaxy*, edited by H.L. Gold. New York, Doubleday, 1960.
"Second Landing," in *Amazing* (New York), January 1960.
"Privates All," in *Fantasy and Science Fiction* (New York), September 1961.
"Accidental Flight," in *Time Waits for Winthrop and Four Other Short Novels*, edited by Frederick Pohl. New York, Doubleday, 1962.
"Bolden's Pets," in *Great Science Fiction about Doctors*, edited by Groff Conklin and Noah D. Fabricant. New York, Macmillan, 1963.
"Big Ancestor," in *Five-Odd*, edited by Groff Conklin. New York, Pyramid, 1964.
"Growing Season," in *Frozen Planet and 4 Other SF Novellas*. New York, Macfadden, 1966.
"The Deadly Ones," in *Flying Saucers*, edited by Isaac Asimov, Martin H. Greenberg, and Charles G. Waugh. New York, Fawcett, 1982.

### Other Publications

Novels

*Three Times a Victim.* New York, Ace, 1957.
*Wired for Scandal.* New York, Ace, 1959.

* * *

Still a hazy figure in the history of science fiction, F.L. Wallace was one of the field's most outstanding and least appreciated writers during the 1950's. His only SF novel, *Address: Centauri*, is a minor work that was an expansion of his very good story "Accidental Flight" (*Galaxy*, 1952). Wallace's other SF stories are of high quality, characterized by a depth and a thoroughness uncommon to the field in the 1950's. Among his most noteworthy stories are "Delay in Transit"; "Big Ancestor," a powerful commentary on the human race and its future direction; "Student Body," which features one of the very best descriptions and development of an alien life form in all of science fiction; "Bolden's Pets," wherein Wallace brilliantly employs the unique concept of *positive* parasitism; "Mezzerow Loves Company"; "Tangle Hold"; and "The Impossible Voyage Home."

—Martin H. Greenberg

---

**WALLACE, Ian.** Pseudonym for John Wallace Pritchard. American. Born in Chicago, Illinois, 4 December 1912. Educated at the University of Michigan, Ann Arbor, B.A. in English 1934, M.A. in educational psychology 1939, graduate study 1949–51; Wayne University, now Wayne State University, Detroit, education certificate 1936, Ed. D. 1957. Served as a clinical psychologist in the United States Army during World War II: Captain. Married Elizabeth Paul in 1938; two sons. Psychology technician, clinical psychologist, department head, administrative assistant, director, and divisional director, Board of Education, Detroit, 1934–74; now retired. Part-time lecturer in education, Wayne State University, 1955–74. Lives in Asheville, North Carolina. Address: c/o DAW Books, 375 Hudson Street, New York, New York 10014, U.S.A.

SCIENCE-FICTION PUBLICATIONS

Novels (series: Croyd; St. Cyr and U. Tuli)

*Croyd.* New York, Putnam, 1967.
*Dr. Orpheus* (Croyd). New York, Putnam, 1968.
*Deathstar Voyage* (St. Cyr). New York, Putnam, 1969; London, Dobson, 1972.
*The Purloined Prince* (St. Cyr). New York, McCall, 1971.
*Pan Sagittarius.* New York, Putnam, 1973.
*A Voyage to Dari* (Croyd). New York, DAW, 1974.
*The World Asunder.* New York, DAW, 1976; London, Dobson, 1978.
*The Sign of the Mute Medusa* (St. Cyr). New York, Popular Library, 1977.
*Z-Sting* (Croyd). New York, DAW, 1978.
*Heller's Leap.* New York, DAW, 1979.
*The Lucifer Comet.* New York, DAW, 1980.
*The Rape of the Sun.* New York, DAW, 1982.
*Megalomania.* New York, DAW, 1989.

OTHER PUBLICATIONS as John Wallace Pritchard

Novel

*Every Crazy Wind.* New York, Dodd Mead, 1952.

Other

*Frank Cody, A Realist in Education*, with others. New York, Macmillan, 1943.
*Off to Work*, with Paul H. Voelker. Pittsburgh, Stanwix House, 1962.

Author-editor-publisher of numerous Detroit Board of Education textbooks and teaching guides, 1942–74.

*

Ian Wallace comments:

I aim my books at well-educated or self-educated minds. For them, I try to write pleasurable, frequently startling, coherently designed stories, taking advantage of fantasy to enlarge their scope, but disciplining the tales with logic and with scientific and philosophic theory. I try to portray humans living at the highest levels of their humanity, entailing many-sided intelligence, emotion intelligently guided and expressed, and human fellow-feeling for all the different kinds of humans (including some weird-bodied instances on other planets); that, for me, is both a moral issue and a taste preference.

* * *

Ian Wallace is best known for his two science-fiction series: the Croyd series of space operas and the St. Cyr futuristic detective series. The first book in the Croyd series is the most well known. Croyd is a humanoid with psychic powers that the rulers of the human Galaxy put to use as a secret agent. But, in *Croyd*, Croyd finds his body invaded by a gnurl—an alien agent—whose mission is to destroy the Galaxy. Croyd finds his identity transferred into the body of a female human. Croyd has two missions: to regain possession of his own superior body and to stop the destruction of the Galaxy before it's too late.

*Dr. Orpheus* features Croyd's powers of travelling "uptime" and "downtime" to defeat both a human agent who is attempting to weaken humanity with a drug called Anagonon—its effects make users unquestioning slaves—and the alien race behind the plot who see humanity as the ideal mammalian food-sources to implant their eggs. Only Croyd's time-travelling powers, which take him to ancient Greece to discover a vital clue, foil the plot within a plot.

*A Voyage to Dari* is the most ambitious of the Croyd novels; Wallace almost attempts too much. With the loss of his powers, Croyd still attempts to deal with a political confrontation modeled on India and colonial Britain. Added to the mix is a space-dwelling alien who adopts medieval imagery as its mental universe. Although the plot is sometimes muddled, the sheer alienness of the action makes reading *A Voyage to Dari* compulsive.

*Z-Sting* begins with Croyd in old age. He has eliminated war with his Comcord system. When a nation on the planet reaches a certain discord quotient, the Comcord system would trigger Z-sting: the offending nation would be surrounded and isolated from the rest of the world. But something has gone wrong with the system, and Croyd, with the help of his great-granddaughter, discovers a monstrous plot that threatens the whole human order.

In *Megalomania*, Croyd finds a threat to the galaxy from within its own government. Croyd is the leader of Sol Galaxy. His first minister, Dino Trigg, lusts for Croyd's position. When Croyd easily beats Trigg in the galactic elections, Trigg devises a plot to destroy Sol Galaxy with the Magellanic Clouds, which he will use to form a new galaxy. The scope of this space opera is cosmic and the action leaves the reader breathless.

The St. Cyr series lacks the galaxy-spanning scale of the Croyd books, but makes up for that with clever detection and careful plotting. *Deathstar Voyage* introduces Claudine St. Cyr, a 25th-century policewoman, whose mission is to bodyguard the king of Ligeria from the assassins plotting to kill him. The action takes place on a huge starship called *Eiland*, whose atomic pile is threatening to explode because of sabotage. St. Cyr's must identify the assassins, solve several bizarre murders, and solve the crisis of the *Eiland* before everything blows up. Wallace concocts a spellbinding mystery in *Deathstar Voyage. The Purloined Prince* is a delicious mystery in which St. Cyr is threatened with death for most of the book, but she has the grit to continue her investigation and solve the mystery.

*The Sign of the Mute Medusa* is a less flamboyant book. St. Cyr investigates a series of disappearances that might be murders in a domed city on Planet Turquoise. Much is made of the political struggle of the Haves—the ruling class—and the Have-nots—the rebels. The plotting is ingenious but the political sub-plots are heavy handed and diminish the book's enjoyment. The first two St. Cyr books are entertaining because of Wallace's light touch and sense of fun. But *The Sign of the Mute Medusa* is too slight to carry Wallace's ponderous political message.

The best St. Cyr is *Heller's Leap*, in which Claudine solves the murder of Klaus Heller, a survivor of a journey through a black hole. The bonus is that Wallace brings Croyd into the action to help St. Cyr solve the mystery and prevent the destruction of a planet. This union of Wallace's two most famous characters makes *Heller's Leap* one of his best novels.

Wallace's non-series books vary in quality. In *The World Asunder*, long philosophical speeches replace action. *The Rape of the Sun* starts promisingly with aliens who steal our Solar System as a present to their Princess, but then gets bogged down in pseudo-profound dialogue. The best of Wallace's non-series books is *The Lucifer Comet*, in which a battle between Good and Evil avoids the mind-deadening dialogues of many of Wallace's books and concentrates on the characters of Prometheus and Lucifer. Wallace's novels blend Van Vogtian plotting with E.E. Smith's comic scale to produce space operas with action as vast as the galaxies.

—George Kelley

---

**WALTERS, Hugh.** Pseudonym for Walter Llewellyn Hughes. British. Born in Bilston, Staffordshire, 15 June 1910. Educated at St. Martin's School; Bilston Central School; Dudley Grammar School, 1923–26; Wednesbury College, 1939–41; Wolverhampton Polytechnic, 1941–43. Married 1) Doris Higgins in 1933, one son and one daughter; 2) Susan Hughes in 1977. Since 1954, managing director, Bransteds Ltd., engineers, and chairman, Walter Hughes Ltd., furnishings. Justice of the Peace, 1947–74. Agent: John Farquharson Ltd., 162–168 Regent Street, London W1R 5TB, England.

SCIENCE-FICTION PUBLICATIONS

Novels (for children; series: Chris Godfrey in all books)

*Blast off at Woomera.* London, Faber, 1957; as *Blast-Off at 0300*, New York, Criterion, 1958.
*The Domes of Pico.* London, Faber, 1958; as *Menace from the Moon*, New York, Criterion, 1959.
*Operation Columbus.* London, Faber, 1960; as *First on the Moon*, New York, Criterion, 1961.
*Moon Base One.* London, Faber, 1961; as *Outpost on the Moon*, New York, Criterion, 1962.
*Expedition Venus.* London, Faber, 1962; New York, Criterion, 1963.
*Destination Mars.* London, Faber, 1963; New York, Criterion, 1964.
*Terror by Satellite.* London, Faber, and New York, Criterion, 1964.
*Mission to Mercury.* London, Faber, and New York, Criterion, 1965.
*Journey to Jupiter.* London, Faber, 1965; New York, Criterion, 1966.
*Spaceship to Saturn.* London, Faber, and New York, Criterion, 1967.
*The Mohole Mystery.* London, Faber, 1968; as *The Mohole Menace*, New York, Criterion, 1969.
*Nearly Neptune.* London, Faber, 1969; as *Neptune One Is Missing*, New York, Washburn, 1969.
*First Contact?* London, Faber, 1971; Nashville, Nelson, 1973.
*Passage to Pluto.* London, Faber, and Nashville, Nelson, 1973.
*Tony Hale, Space Detective.* London, Faber, 1973.
*Murder on Mars.* London, Faber, 1975.
*Boy Astronaut.* London, Abelard Schuman, 1977.
*The Caves of Drach.* London, Faber, 1977.
*The Last Disaster.* London, Faber, 1978.
*The Blue Aura.* London, Faber, 1979.
*First Family on the Moon.* London, Abelard Schuman, 1979.
*The Dark Triangle.* London, Faber, 1981.
*School on the Moon.* London, Abelard Schuman, 1981.
*P-K, (photokinesis).* London, Severn House, 1986.

*

Hugh Walters comments (1981):

All my books are for young people in the 9–11 and 11– 16 age groups. I believe that books for this readership should 1) entertain, which is the primary object; 2) educate painlessly (astronomy, mathematics, geology, etc.); 3) inspire the young people of today to become the scientists and technicians of tomorrow.

* * *

Hugh Walters has devoted his entire writing career to children's SF, and the results have been mixed. At first, his novels were welcomed as filling a void in SF publishing, being praised as the way SF should be written for children. Gradually critical opinion shifted as Walter's fiction came to be seen as repetitive, formula-bound, and even carelessly written; and the attention it received from the review media in both SF and children's literature virtually ceased. In the face of critical neglect and sometimes even open scorn, the wonder is that Walter's novels continue to be published and have retained popularity for as long as they have. Obviously, his publishers are satisfied that the young audience Walters writes for does read and enjoy his novels and, ignoring adult disapproval, even puts pressure upon librarians to keep his books in circulation and order new titles as they appear. This phenomenon is readily understood once it is perceived that Walter's fiction is the result of his attempt to wed the formulas and expectations of boy's series books and SF. In other words, Walter's SF manifests both the strengths and weaknesses of children's series fiction writing.

On one hand, Walters's SF celebrates the exploits of youthful, dashing, and resourceful protagonists that boys chaffing under the dullness of their routine-filled lives enthusiastically identify with. In *Operation Columbus*, Chris Godfrey, hero of Walters's SF, is the first person on the moon and he also magnanimously saves the life of his young Russian rival, Serge Smyslov, who had previously disabled Chris's space craft. Chris then pilots the Russian space ship safely to earth in spite of not being familiar with the controls. In *Terror by Satellite*, Tony Hale, who appears in some of the Godfrey books, is the remaining link between earth and the Observatory, the space satellite taken over by its crazed commander, Hendriks, who threatens to destroy earth; through his skill in electronics Tony proves indispensable as Chris successfully retakes control of the Observatory. Walters is clearly a knowledgeable author of children's books, and is careful to balance Chris, the public-school boy born to privilege and noblesse oblige, with Tony, the son of lower-class shop-keeping parents. In this way, many different kinds of young readers may be able to identify with Walter's protagonists. Further, although he does emphasize action and the various dangers of space exploration—emphases obviously intended to capture the attention of young readers—Walters does not neglect space technology and weaponry. Described in detail, these are usually up-to-date or plausibly extrapolated so that youngsters looking for "nuts and bolts SF" are readily satisfied.

On the other hand, Walters's SF exhibits the weaknesses characteristic of most series fiction: conventional, two-dimensional characterization, repetitive and predictable plotting, and dull, pedestrian writing. As a result of these weaknesses, Walters has been denied major status. At the same time, however, it would be unfair to dismiss Walters as just another author of series SF, another Victor Appleton II or John Blaine. For, in view of his strengths, it is clear that Walter's work is definitely a cut or two above typical series SF.

—Francis J. Molson

---

**WATERLOO, Stanley.** American. Born in St. Clair County, Michigan, 21 May 1846. Educated at the University of Michigan, Ann Arbor, A.B. 1869. Married Anna C. Kitten in 1874. Journalist and editor: reporter in Chicago, 1870–71; co-owner, St. Louis *Journal*, 1872; editor, St. Louis *Republic Chronicle* and *Globe-Democrat;* founded St. Paul *Day;* writer, Chicago *Tribune;* editor-in-chief, Chicago *Mail;* editor, Washington *Critic and Capitol.* A.M.: University of Michigan, 1898. *Died 11 October 1913.*

SCIENCE-FICTION PUBLICATIONS

Novels

*The Story of Ab: A Tale in the Time of the Cave Men.* Chicago, Way and Williams, 1897.
*Armageddon.* Chicago, Rand McNally, 1898.
*A Son of the Ages.* New York, Doubleday, and London, Curtis Brown, 1914.

Short Stories

*The Wolf's Long Howl.* Chicago, Stone, 1899.

OTHER PUBLICATIONS

Novels

*A Man and a Woman.* Chicago, Schulte, 1892; London, Redway, 1896.
*An Odd Situation.* Chicago, Morrill Higgins, 1893; London, Black, 1896.
*The Launching of a Man.* Chicago, Rand McNally, 1899.
*The Seekers.* Chicago, Stone, 1900.
*The Cassowary.* Chicago, Monarch, 1906.

Other

*How It Looks.* New York, Brentano's, 1888.
*Honest Money.* Chicago, Equitable, 1895.
*These Are My Jewels* (for children). Chicago, Coolidge and Waterloo, 1902.

Editor, with John Wesley Hanson, Jr., *Famous American Men and Women.* Chicago, Wabash, 1896; as *Eminent Sons and Daughters of Columbia,* Chicago International, 1896; as *Our Living Leaders,* Chicago, Monarch, 1896.
Editor, *The Parties and the Men; or, Political Issues of 1896.* Chicago, Conkey, 1896.
Editor, *The Story of a Strange Career.* New York, Appleton, 1902.

* * *

In discussing Stanley Waterloo's novels, it is necessary to differentiate between the conception and the execution of the works. *The Story of Ab* is an early realistic novel of prehistoric man. Jack London admitted plagiarizing it for his *Before Adam,* and Waterloo's novel predated even H.G. Wells's splendid "A Story of the Stone Age" by some months. (Lang's still earlier "The Romance of the First Radical" differs from both works in being based in anthropology, not archeology, and being primarily a vehicle for social comment.) Similarly, *Armageddon* was probably the first of the fictional attempts to presage World War I with its weaponry and fabric of alliances. Writers as fine as Wells and Shiel (and many of lesser note) again followed in Waterloo's footsteps. On the other hand, Waterloo's execution (with a few brief exceptions) ranged from poor to worse. Both these novels as well as mainstream novels by Waterloo show signs of hasty construction and a basic lack of writing talent.

*The Story of Ab* is a serious attempt at the biography of a Stone Age (perhaps Neanderthal) man, told through significant incidents. Ab does many of the things that prehistoric heroes have done in more recent fiction: he hunts mammoths, domesticates dogs, slays a sabre-toothed tiger, invents the bow, and wages the first war. He does *not* tame fire. Waterloo claims to have based his novel on the best contemporary scientific opinion. Fire had been used by men long before the rise of Ab's subspecies, and Waterloo refused to take artistic license with scientific fact. While our knowledge of prehistory has greatly increased in the years since the book was published, Waterloo's obvious care keeps the novel from being too badly dated. Indeed, Waterloo's picture of the Clam People combing tide flats for food and scuttling deeper in the water when danger threatens anticipates that drawn by Elaine Morgan in her 1972 treatise *The Descent of Woman.* However, the incidents of Ab's life are only incidents. Some of them are spun into short skeins, but there is no connected purpose controlling the action of the novel. In general, chapters stand or fall on their own merits. There is little preparation for later events and almost no character development.

*Armageddon* is also rich in exciting material: the creation of the first airship, the building of a sea-level canal through Nicaragua, the greatest sea battle of all time, and, for that matter, a romance between parties of widely differing social positions. Waterloo's failure to make any of this material interesting results from a combination of flaws. First, characters are not fully realized. Second, matters of large moment are trivialized by their handling. For instance, the novel's description of the international political situation descends beneath the level of national stereotype to the anthropomorphization of nations *as* national stereotypes. Third, the gritty details that could create the illusion of reality in a fictional world are absent. From the evidence of the novel, Waterloo simply did not know enough about the gadgetry of the present to be able to describe realistically the gadgetry of his future.

Waterloo was imaginative and capable of good research. His writing, however, was generally pedestrian and invariably hasty. *The Story of Ab* remains readable, especially for younger people; *Armageddon* is at most of historical interest.

—David A. Drake

---

**WATKINS, William Jon.** American. Born in Coaldale, Pennsylvania, 19 July 1942. Educated at Neshaminy High School, Langehorne, Pennsylvania; Rutgers University, New Brunswick, New Jersey, B.S. 1964, M. Ed. 1965. Married Sandra Lee Preno in 1961; three children. Instructor, Delaware Valley College, Doyleston, Pennsylvania, 1965–68; high school teacher, Asbury Park, New Jersey, 1968–69. Instructor, 1969–70, Assistant Professor, 1970–71, and since 1971, Associate Professor of Humanities, Brookdale Community College, Lincroft, New Jersey. Recipient: Per Se award, for play, 1970. Address: 1406 Garven Avenue, Ocean, New Jersey 07712, U.S.A.

SCIENCE-FICTION PUBLICATIONS

Novels

*Ecodeath*, with Gene Snyder. New York, Doubleday, 1972.
*Clickwhistle*. New York, Doubleday, 1973.
*The God Machine*. New York, Doubleday, and London, Angus and Robertson, 1973.
*The Litany of Sh'reev*, with Gene Snyder. New York, Doubleday, 1976.
*What Rough Beast*. Chicago, Playboy Press, 1980.
*The Centrifugal Rickshaw Dancer*. New York, Warner, 1985.
*Going To See the End of the Sky*. New York, Popular Library, 1986.
*The Last Deathship off Antares*. New York, Popular Library, 1989.

OTHER PUBLICATIONS

Plays

*The Judas Wheel* (produced Warrensburg, Missouri, 1970). New York, Smith, 1969.
*A Kind of a Hole*. Elgin, Illinois, Performance, 1974.

Verse

*Five Poems*. Chula Vista, California, Word Press, 1968.

Other

*A Fair Advantage* (for children). Englewood Cliffs, New Jersey, Prentice Hall, 1975.
*Tracker*, with Tom Brown, Jr. Englewood Cliffs, New Jersey, Prentice Hall, 1978.
*The Psychic Experiment Book*. Englewood Cliffs, New Jersey, Prentice Hall, 1980.
*The Psychic Diet Book*. Asbury Park, New Jersey, Grappling Press, 1980.
*Suburban Wilderness*. New York, Putnam, 1981.
*Who's Who in New Jersey Wrestling*. Asbury Park, New Jersey, Grappling Press, 1981.

* * *

William Jon Watkins's novels, two of which were written with Gene Snyder, show man as a corrupt evil-doer who creates his own doomsday crises in which he barely avoids the total extinction of human life on Earth.

In *Ecodeath*, Earth is about to die from water pollution. Two characters, Watkins and Snyder, start out as opponents but soon pool forces in order to rescue humankind. They use teleportation and finally link their mindpower to transport a small group of survivors to a pollution-free parallel earth of the future by telekinesis. Humankind survives because Watkins realizes that time implies parallel worlds existing simultaneously in infinity.

In *Clickwhistle*, extraterrestrial beings take possession of the minds of killer whales to send computerized commands to atomic missiles stored in submarines. Dr. Pearson, a dolphin authority, defeats the aliens with the help of dolphins, but other human beings are either evil-doers or slaves of dark political powers. Intrigue and betrayal run rampant while Orcas and dolphins battle. Earth is saved when dolphins triumph, but humans will forever live in fear of political bosses.

*The God Machine* shows perpetual and total warfare between a totalitarian worldwide state machine of Orwell's *Nineteen Eighty-Four* type and a highly technological underground opponent. Sophisticated weapons and tactics improve with the need to accelerate extermination. A reduction machine, the "micronizer," is central to several plot twists. Ecological negligence is the trademark of the status quo. An unbreathable atmosphere makes the use of masks and air filters universal. Neither side is a definite winner in the end.

In *The Litany of Sh'reev*, Sh'reev uses mental powers to heal and save lives while a chronic state of revolutionary wars wrecks civilization. Empire is run by the will of an absolute and totalitarian ruler who destroys extant royal families to seize their wealth. The revolutionaries are ESPers who reject the increase of oppression. Sh'reev gets his spiritual power from Tao techniques. His mind fuses with those of the sick and dying in a state called Sh'aela. Eternal Return in its Eastern version provides further existences for Sh'reev.

The central action of *What Rough Beast* is the hunt for one huge, extraterrestrial, telekinetic, furry humanoid female who lands on Earth in order to help humans acquire her talents. Corporation mentality as the villainous hunter is aided by an almost sentient computer, Slic 1000, and his offspring Tad. There is an ironical twist when corporational man, dominated by a rigid mentality, becomes a dehumanized animal backbiting other corporate members in the struggle for power and rewards while the computers become humanized. The hero and savior is Lth, the alien furry female whose telepathic abilities merge with Tad in order to confer superhuman status upon humans. Humankind is saved when sentient microcomputers become an implanted standard stabilizing device in human brains.

Although Watkins's novels are simply constructed and appropriate for juvenile audiences, they deal with the vital issue of human's chances of survival. In each instance, they bring a catastrophic end upon themselves and an environment they can neither preserve nor duplicate, and avoid self-annihilation by the slightest margin. Watkins implies that humankind, part angel but mostly beast, is on a cyclical course and will probably repeat its past mistakes. In *What Rough Beast*, Watkins introduces two new solutions to the "scorpion syndrome," man against himself. One is Lth's Superwoman mentality; the other is brain microcomputer implantation. In both cases, Watkins suggests that man cannot be his own master.

—Eric A. Fontaine

---

**WATSON, Ian.** British. Born in North Shields, Northumberland, 20 April 1943. Educated at Tynemouth School, 1948–59; Balliol College, Oxford, 1960–65, B.A. (honours) in English 1963, B.Litt. 1965, M.A. 1966. Married Judith Jackson in 1962; one daughter. Lecturer, University College, Dar es Salaam, Tanzania, 1965–67, and Tokyo University of Education, 1967–70; Lecturer, 1970–75, and Senior Lecturer in Complementary Studies, 1975–76, Birmingham Polytechnic Art and Design Centre; features editor and regular contributor, *Foundation*, London, 1975–90; Writer-in-Residence, Nene College, Northampton, 1984. Since 1983, European Editor, *Science Fiction Writers of America Bulletin*. Recipient: Prix Apollo (France), 1975; Orbit award, 1976; British Science Fiction Association award, 1978; Southern Arts Association bursary, 1978. Address: Daisy Cottage, Moreton Pinkney, near Daventry, Northamptonshire, NN11 6SQ England.

SCIENCE-FICTION PUBLICATIONS

Novels (series: Yaleen)

*The Embedding*. London, Gollancz, 1973; New York, Scribner, 1975.
*The Jonah Kit*. London, Gollancz, 1975; New York, Scribner, 1976.
*The Martin Inca*. London, Gollancz, and New York, Scribner, 1977.
*Alien Embassy*. London, Gollancz, 1977; New York, Ace, 1978.
*Miracle Visitors*. London, Gollancz, and New York, Ace, 1978.
*God's World*. London, Gollancz, 1979; New York, Carroll and Graf, 1990.
*The Gardens of Delight*. London, Gollancz, 1980; New York, Pocket Books, 1982.
*Under Heaven's Bridge*, with Michael Bishop. London, Gollancz, 1981; New York, Ace, 1982.
*Deathhunter*. London, Gollancz, 1981; New York, St. Martin's Press, 1986.
*Chekhov's Journey*. London, Gollancz, 1983; New York, Carroll and Graf, 1989.
*Converts*. London, Granada, 1984; New York, St. Martin's Press, 1985.
Black Current trilogy (Yaleen):
*The Book of the River*. London, Gollancz, 1984; New York, DAW, 1986.
*The Book of the Stars*. London, Gollancz, 1985.
*The Book of Being*. London, Gollancz, 1985; New York, DAW, 1986.
*Queenmagic, Kingmagic*. London, Gollancz, and New York, St. Martin's Press, 1986.
*The Power*. London, Headline, 1987.
*The Fire Worm*. London, Gollancz, 1988.
*Whores of Babylon*. London, Paladin, 1988.
*The Flies of Memory*. London, Gollancz, 1990.
*Inquisitor*. Brighton, West Sussex, Games Workshop, 1990.
*Nanoware Time*, with *The Persistance of Vision*, by John Varley. New York, Tor, 1991.

Short Stories

*The Very Slow Time Machine*. London, Gollancz, and New York, Ace, 1979.
*Sunstroke and Other Stories*. London, Gollancz, 1982.
*Slow Birds and Other Stories*. London, Gollancz, 1985.
*The Book of Ian Watson* (includes non-fiction). Willimantic, Connecticut, Ziesing, 1985.
*Evil Water and Other Stories*. London, Gollancz, 1987.
*Salvage Rites and Other Stories*. London, Gollancz, 1989.
*Stalin's Teardrops*. Brighton, West Sussex, Games Workshop, 1991.

OTHER PUBLICATIONS

Novel

*Meat*. London, Headline, 1988.

Other

*Japan: A Cat's Eye View* (for children). Osaka, Bunken, 1969.

Editor, *Pictures at an Exhibition: A Science Fiction Anthology*. Cardiff, Greystoke Mobray, 1981; San Bernardino, California, Borgo Press, 1987.
Editor, with Pamela Sargent, *Afterlives: Stories about Life after Death*. New York, Vintage, 1986.

Manuscript Collection: Science Fiction Foundation, North-East London Polytechnic.

Ian Watson comments:

My books are all primarily about the relationship between reality and consciousness (testing out this theme variously by way of linguistics, speculation about cetacean intelligence, evolution, novel life forms, the UFO mythos, etc.) and whether any kind of ultimate understanding of the nature of reality and the reason for life and the universe may or may not be arrived at. Intersecting this is frequently—particularly in my earlier books—a strong socio-political underpinning to events. A dialectic of history and transcendence is at work. I regard my fiction as a research programme, in fictional form, into the nature of existence and the nature of knowledge.

* * *

Ian Watson's fiction often explores the nature of reality as it is perceived by humans: how our minds work, what we believe we know about the universe and how that belief stands up in practice, how we deal with our mortality. His approach is often highly sophisticated, intelligent, and metaphysical, sometimes so original in concept and execution that casual readers become confused or alienated from his work. It is unfortunate that even as his critical success has grown, his commercial viability appears to have declined in the United States.

Watson's debut novel was *The Embedding*, which examined the role of language in shaping our existence and the callous manner in which we make use of other human beings for our own purposes. A group of children has been deliberately exposed only to an artificial language; yet, aliens are willing to trade technology for human brains, which may be the key to a transcendent experience. Virtually every party in this novel intends to sacrifice the welfare of others in return for some perceived advantage. Having presented his observations, Watson leaves it to the reader to draw conclusions.

*The Jonah Kit* is thematically similar. The universe is defined by our perception of it, and if we change what we believe to be true, the truth itself alters. A Soviet experiment that involves the imprinting of human intelligence in whales takes an unexpected twist when they appear to have become a link with another form of intelligence. A mysterious virus inadvertently brought back from Mars is the catalyst for dramatic changes in *The Martian Inca*, raising the question of what it means to be a human being.

*Alien Embassy* presents an innovative way around the lightspeed limit. Humanity reaches the stars by means of psychic projection, gathering information, contacting other intelligent species, and transforming human society to what appears to be a near Utopia. The appearance is deceiving, however. Information is "managed" by a few for the assumed good of the many. There is a new caste system, censorship of ideas, conflict where there should have been cooperation. This atmosphere of repression becomes crucial when it appears that humanity itself may be on the brink of a transformation. Perhaps the most accessible of Watson's early novels, it is also a thoughtful work that raises and examines important questions.

*Miracle Visitors* uses the UFO phenomenon as the springboard for another examination of multiple realities. The novel also contains some very humorous sequences, although as with its predecessors, the central focus is always serious. *The Gardens of Delight* is an intellectual puzzle set within a standard SF plot framework. A starship lands on a bizarre world, which one crew member recognizes as that of the famous Bosch painting. *Under Heaven's Bridge*, written in collaboration with Michael Bishop, deals with efforts to establish communication with a species facing imminent destruction, and raises the question of just what is meant by "intelligence."

*Deathhunter* is set in a society that views death as an experience to be met willingly. The protagonist has helped many people end their lives, but he questions his own life experience when involved in an atempt to capture death literally personified. *Chekhov's Journey* is less impressive, but still an interesting story. A Russian stage crew uses hypnosis to help an actor identify with Chekhov, convincing him that he is the writer's reincarnation, but what "Chekhov" remembers is a radically different past than the one in the history books.

The Black Current trilogy, *The Book of the River*, *The Book of the Stars*, and *The Book of Being*, is Watson's most ambitious and most successful work to date. The opening volume is set on a world divided by a river into two rival societies, one repressive and male-dominated, the other less autocratic, dominated by women. Intercourse between the two societies is limited because the river is occupied by an enigmatic alien intelligence that drives men insane if they venture into its reach. The trilogy, which involves the battle between two omnipotent intelligences whose conflict threatens the entire universe, is much more obviously adventurous than Watson's other novels, but retains a serious examination of the nature of the universe.

*Queenmagic, Kingmagic* also plays with realities, this time in the context of fantasy, a world whose natural laws are based on the game of chess. An amusing and cleverly constructed entertainment, it retains echoes of Watson's continuing interest in the nature of the universe.

Watson has also proven to be a skillful and prolific short story writer. One of his earliest stories, "The Very Slow Time Machine," is a unique look at time paradoxes. "Thy Milk Like Blood" raises a number of ethical questions in a new context, as does "The Roentgen Refugees." Other outstanding stories include "Returning Home," "Slow Birds," "We Remember Babylon," "On the Dream Channel Panel," and the "Emir's Clock." Watson has also dabbled in the supernatural, most notably with the story "Salvage Rites."

—Don D'Ammassa

---

**WEBB, Ron.** *See* **WEBB, Sharon.**

---

**WEBB, Sharon.** Also writes as Ron Webb. American. Born in Tampa, Florida, 29 February 1936. Attended Tampa public schools; Florida Southern College, Lakeland, 1953–56; Miami-Dade College School of Nursing, 1970–72. Married Bryan Webb in 1956; three children. Freelance writer, 1959–65; registered nurse, Baptist Hospital, Miami 1972–73, and in Blairsville, Georgia, 1973–81. Since 1979, freelance writer. Agent: Merrilee Heifetz, Writers House, Inc., 21 West 26th Street, New York, New York 10010. Address: Route 2, Box 2600, Blairsville, Georgia 30512, U.S.A.

Science-Fiction Publications

Novels (series: Kurt Kraus in Earth Song trilogy)

Earth Song trilogy:
*Earthchild*. New York, Atheneum, 1982.
*Earth Song*. New York, Atheneum, 1983.
*Ram Song*. New York, Atheneum, 1984.
*The Adventures of Terra Tarkington*. New York, Bantam, 1985.

Uncollected Short Stories

"Atomic Reaction" (as Ron Webb), in *Fantasy and Science Fiction*, May 1963.
"The Girl with the 100 Proof Eyes" (as Ron Webb), in *Fantasy and Science Fiction*, July 1964.
"Hitch on the Bull Run," in *Isaac Asimov's Science Fiction Magazine* (New York), June 1979.
"Sharing Time in the Gallery," in *Isaac Asimov's Science Fiction Magazine* (New York), November 1979.
"Miss Nottworthy and the Aliens," in *Other Worlds*, edited by Roy Torgeson. New York, Zebra, 1979.
"Itch on the Bull Run," in *Space Mail 1*, edited by Isaac Asimov, Martin H. Greenberg, and Joseph D. Olander. New York, Fawcett, 1980.
"The Cathedral in Dying Time," in *Chrysalis 8*, edited by Roy Torgeson. New York, Doubleday, 1980.
"Transference," in *Isaac Asimov's Science Fiction Magazine* (New York), July 1980.
"Rare Bird," in *Isaac Asimov's Science Fiction Magazine* (New York), September 1980.
"Variation on a Theme from Beethoven," in *1981 Annual World's Best SF*, edited by Donald A. Wollheim. New York, DAW, 1981.
"The Dust of Creeds Outworn," in *Isaac Asimov's Science Fiction Magazine* (New York), February 1981.
"Sand," in *Isaac Asimov's Science Fiction Magazine* (New York), March 1981.

"Twitch on the Bull Run," in *Isaac Asimov's Science Fiction Magazine* (New York), April 1981.
"Bridges," in *Isaac Asimov's Science Fiction Magazine* (New York), May 1981.
"Bitch on the Bull Run," in *Isaac Asimov's Science Fiction Magazine* (New York), June 1981.
"Reliquary for an Old Soul," in *Isaac Asimov's Science Fiction Magazine* (New York), September 1981.
"Our Man in Vulnerable," in *Isaac Asimov's Science Fiction Magazine* (New York), October 1981.
"Niche on the Bull Run," and "Switch on the Bull Run," in *Space Mail 2*, edited by Isaac Asimov, Martin H. Greenberg, and Charles G. Waugh. New York, Fawcett, 1982.
"Slow Virus," in *Parsec* (Russellville, Alabama), June 1982.
"Threshold," in *Amazing* (New York), November 1982.
"The Syncopated Man," in *Amazing* (New York), March 1983.
"Shadows from a Small Template," in *Isaac Asimov's Space of Her Own*, edited by Shawna McCarthy. New York, Davis, 1983; London, Hale, 1984.
"With Gl-oon'sha, Dreams Come," in *Amazing* (New York), January 1984.
"Misplaced Friends," in *Softalk* (North Hollywood, California), February and March 1984.
"A Demon in Rosewood," in *Shadows 8*, edited by Charles L. Grant. New York, Doubleday, 1985.
"The Thing That Goes Burp in the Night," in *Dragons and Dreams: A Collection of New Fantasy and Science Fiction Stories*, edited by Jane Yolen, Martin H. Greenberg, and Charles G. Waugh. New York, Harper and Row, 1986.

OTHER PUBLICATIONS

Novels

*Pestis 18*. New York, Tor, 1987.
*The Halflife*. New York, Tor, 1990.

Other

*R.N.* New York, Zebra, 1982.

*

Manuscript Collection: University of Georgia, Athens.

Sharon Webb comments:

The sciences I studied in nursing school gave me the confidence to write something that I had loved since childhood: science fiction. Thirty stories and three SF books later, I can look back and see that this "tool" of science, while useful to the genre, is not essential to the writing of it. The real tool of SF is the use of metaphor to describe the human condition, and it is this, I believe, that explains the seductiveness of science fiction for the reader.

* * *

Sharon Webb's first publication in a science-fiction magazine was a short poem called "Atomic Reaction" in the May 1963 issue of *The Magazine of Fantasy and Science Fiction*, during the short but potent editorial reign of Avram Davidson. Her first science-fiction short story, "The Girl with the 100 Proof Eyes" appeared in the July 1964 issue of the same magazine. Both bore the pseudonym Ron Webb. She also sold some suspense stories under that name. But it was not until the publication in 1979 of "Hitch on the Bull Run," the first of her Terra Tarkington stories in *Isaac Asimov's Science Fiction Magazine*, that her SF career can really be said to have been launched.

These stories, collected and novelized in *The Adventures of Terra Tarkington*, concern the escapades of a member of the Interstellar Nurses Corps whose assignment, far from the human-populated portions of the galaxy, involves her with strange lifeforms and stranger circumstances, including a political struggle between the intelligence agencies of competing galactic powers. The stories are deftly plotted and written, filled with delightfully outrageous ideas and characters, and stand among the most enjoyable of science-fiction humor series. Like much of her fiction, they draw on Webb's long experience as a registered nurse for background.

Not all of Webb's fiction is humorous, however. Also in 1979, *Asimov*'s published "Sharing Time in the Gallery," the story of a petty crook who attempts to sell fake paintings to extra-terrestrial art collectors. It is an effective example of the biter bit story, with a nice edge to its point of view. With the 1980 publication of "Variation on a Theme from Beethoven," she established herself as a writer of considerable serious ability.

It was this story that formed the basis for her first novel-length work, *Earthchild*, the beginning of the Earth Song trilogy, which continued with *Earth Song* and *Ram Song*. Although published ostensibly as juveniles, these novels, as with many so-called young adult science-fiction works, concern themselves with distinctly adult ideas.

In the relatively near future, a process is discovered that can endow humans with apparent immortality, barring violent death. But, the recipient must be treated while still in his mid-teens, thus robbing adults of the process's benefits. Many of the potential immortals must face a personal sacrifice; the price of prolonging life is the complete loss of artistic creativity. The novel concerns 15-year-old Kurt Kraus, a budding musician who arrives at orchestra rehearsal one day only to learn that the Mouat-Gari process has already secretly been administered to the world's population. His immortality is assured. His career as a musician is ended.

Webb paints a frightening picture of a world in which adults are faced with the knowledge that they will die while children never will. Incidents of child abuse increase. Mobs mindlessly attack and inflict horrible deaths on children. At last, for their own protection, children have to be isolated from the general adult population. But the future has begun, and a very changed one it is for humankind.

Kurt becomes a leader of the society that emerges from these changes and begins to realize what the loss of art means to humanity. The only solution to that problem lies in yet another change. From now on, youngsters who show the promise of creativity will be given a choice: they may opt for immortality or they may choose a short, natural life-span, with the ability to express their creativity. Whichever their choice, there is no turning back. In *Ram Song*, set some ten thousand years in the future, the conflicts that arise are those of evolution and the nature of the universe itself.

Two main interests govern Webb's choices of story ideas and themes: her lifelong career in medicine (she is a registered nurse), and her love of music (she plays guitar). Her stories usually draw on physical settings familiar to her, either her native Tampa, Florida, or the environs of Chattanooga, Tennessee, Atlanta, or the Blue Ridge Mountains of Georgia where she and her husband now live. Even the rather outre settings of the Bull Run stories are often only satiric extrapolations of the sorts of hospital environments she worked in for so many years.

Her latest two books are not science-fiction novels, but medical thrillers. *Pestis 18* deals with a terrorist threat to release a deadly experimental virus. It's a tautly plotted and written story. Her most recent novel, *The Halflife*, though also ostensibly a medical thriller, contains a sufficiency of science-fictional touches to warrant discussion here. It concerns a government experiment to implant constructed personalities in the subconscious of certain subjects when they are teenagers. Years later it is hoped these personalities (unsuspected even by their hosts) can be activated and used as couriers by the CIA. The experiment goes wrong when it turns out that some of the subjects are victims of Multiple Personality Syndrome. These subjects integrate the constructed personality into their library of identities with dangerous results, at least one of them becoming a murderer. One of the subjects is a trance medium, and it is the relationship between her spirit contact and the constructed personality that gives rise to conflict. The novel explores its ideas deftly and interestingly but never once falters in maintaining its pace or suspense.

One of Webb's outstanding tools as a writer is her style. On the surface, it is simply a pleasing, unobtrusive style that does its job without drawing much attention to itself. But on closer examination, it is remarkable for the way in which it serves such a range of technical needs. Science fiction can boast far too many styles that are much flashier than hers, but few are more practical in serving the requirements of both writer and reader.

—Gerald W. Page

---

**WEIGHT, Frank.** *See* **TUBB, E.C.**

---

**WEINBAUM, Stanley G(rauman).** American. Born in Louisville, Kentucky, in 1902. Educated at public schools in Milwaukee; University of Wisconsin, Madison, B. Chem. Engr. 1923. Married Margaret Weinbaum. Worked as movie theater manager. *Died 14 December 1935.*

SCIENCE-FICTION PUBLICATIONS

Novels

*The New Adam.* Chicago, Ziff Davis, 1939; London, Sphere, 1974.
*The Black Flame.* Reading, Pennsylvania, Fantasy Press, 1948.
*The Dark Other.* Los Angeles, Fantasy, 1950.

Short Stories

*Dawn of Flame.* New York, Ruppert, 1936.
*A Martian Odyssey and Others.* Reading, Pennsylvania, Fantasy Press, 1949.
*The Red Peri.* Reading, Pennsylvania, Fantasy Press, 1952.
*The Best of Stanley G. Weinbaum.* New York, Ballantine, 1974; London, Sphere, 1977.

*

Critical Study: *After Ten Years: A Tribute to Stanley G. Weinbaum* edited by Gerry de la Ree and Sam Moskowitz, Westwood, New Jersey, de la Ree, 1945.

* * *

It is now formulaic to include the term "tragic death" with each mention of the name Stanley G. Weinbaum. His total career as a writer lasted from the publication of "A Martian Odyssey" in the July 1934 issue of *Wonder Stories* to his death in December 1935. Almost every critic who discusses the early years of pulp science fiction singles out Weinbaum as a unique voice who never had the chance to develop fully his powers as a writer. While one can never know just how far these powers would have in fact developed, a number of conclusions can be drawn, based on the short stories published during Weinbaum's career and a number of stories published after his death.

With his very first story, Weinbaum managed to break a number of standard formulae in pulp fiction. "A Martian Odyssey" not only attempted to portray aliens as creatures unlike man but went so far as to present one such creature in a highly sympathetic light. Weinbaum seems to have been one of the first, if not the first, to realize that aliens may differ from humans in not only their outer appearance but their inner thought processes as well. His invention of the bib-bird-like creature Tweel in "A Martian Odyssey" stands as a major step in the genre because it undertakes the difficult task of describing the actions of a creature that clearly thinks differently. Given its non-human nature, Weinbaum uses a human character's interaction with Tweel to bring out the alien's basic nature. While both the human character and the reader begin the story amused at the weird actions of Tweel, this amusement is changed to admiration and respect by the end of the story. Tweel first grasps the possibility of communication between alien and human, and is able to make use of the human language while the human character gives up any chance of comprehending Tweel's. Tweel shows the greater understanding of the other aliens on Mars, and looks more at home on Mars, even though he too is an explorer from another planet. In other words, with Tweel readers were given an alternative to the murderous aliens of H.G. Wells, and many writers were soon imitating Weinbaum.

But Weinbaum's stories were not successful simply because he had invented a new attitude toward aliens. In the stories that followed (all in *Wonder Stories*), Weinbaum continued to emphasize the fact that his aliens lived by systems of logic that were different from man's, and it is the fact that these different systems were both strange *and* internally consistent that won him a wide audience. The care with which Weinbaum created new aliens and described their alienness was unique to the pulp fiction of its time. Thus, even in a story such as "Paradise Planet," in which alien forms on Venus do menace humans, the threat originates in the nature of life on Venus and not in some anthropomorphic desire to rape and pillage humanity.

As *Wonder Stories* continued to publish stories by Weinbaum almost monthly, a second reason for his popularity became apparent: his stories contained a good deal of humor. This humor was often achieved at the expense of human character and human science. Thus in a series of stories based on a delightfully "mad" scientist named Professor Haskel van Manderpootz ("The Worlds of If," "The Ideal," and "The Point of View"), inventions constantly appear that seem to have no other reason for existence than the fact that they constantly complicate the life of Dixon Wells, a young and somewhat love-sick romantic.

Weinbaum's treatment of aliens and his use of humor, however, did not free him from all of the pulp formulas. In "Pygmalion's Spectacles," for example, Weinbaum refuses to bring the story to its logical, tragic conclusion. A young man, while wearing spectacles that allow the wearer to take full part in an illusion, falls in love with a dream woman. When the dream ends and he must take off the glasses, he remains in love with the woman. Weinbaum, however, begs the whole issue of illusion and reality when at the end of the story a living counterpart of the dream woman is produced. Given the strength with which Weinbaum evokes the dream world and the sadness that the hero undergoes with its loss, one feels that "Pygmalion's Spectacles" could have been a better story. Weinbaum's ties to pulp fiction can also be seen in *The Black Flame*, which contains two versions of the same story. The first version, "Dawn of Flame," is a competent but uninspired story of the innocent young man who meets the exotic and erotic immortal woman. Reminiscent of H. Rider Haggard's *She*, the story contains some powerfully sexual scenes but basically remains a formula story. In the second version, "The Black Flame," however, Weinbaum rewrites the story and adds the paraphernalia of a pulp story complete with happy ending. The mixture of these two separate traditions was less than successful, and "The Black Flame" seems to be constantly struggling to make up its mind as to exactly what it wants to be.

On those occasions when Weinbaum does completely overcome his pulp environment, however, the fiction he produces is both sensitive and moving. In "The Adoptive Ultimate," he refuses to opt for the happy ending, and in *The New Adam*, Weinbaum takes the stock superman character and turns him into a sympathetic character who is alone in a world of mere humans. Because of the first-person narration, the reader is able to see a side of such a character that rarely was portrayed before Weinbaum's treatment, and never so carefully or intimately. Lester del Rey calls the hero of *The New Adam* "a rather helpless failure," but such a characterization refuses to take into account what caused that failure, what it was in the nature of being a superman that led to it. And it is Weinbaum's investigation of exactly these questions in a sympathetic and painstaking manner that makes the novel so readable.

Works like *The New Adam* are rare in science fiction. Too often they are ignored when they do appear, and such was particularly true during the great age of the pulps. Weinbaum is remembered best for his aliens and the strange worlds he created for his stories in *Wonder Stories.* Thus, "A Martian Odyssey" remains Stanley Weinbaum's best known work. While such stories have had a significant effect on the direction science fiction was to take in the 1940's, *The New Adam* deserves far more notice than it has received to date.

—Stephen H. Goldman

---

**WEINER, Andrew.** Canadian/British. Born in London, England, 17 June 1949. Educated at University of Sussex, 1967–70, B.A. in social psychology; London School of Economics, 1972–73, M.Sc. in social psychology. Married Barbara Moses in 1973; one son. Copywriter, Ogilvy and Mather, London, 1970–72. Lecturer in psychology, Dawson College, Montreal, Canada, 1975–77. Since 1977, freelance writer. Agent: Richard Curtis, 171 East 74th Street, New York, New York 10021, U.S.A. Address: 26 Summerhill Gardens, Toronto, Ontario M47 1B4, Canada.

SCIENCE-FICTION PUBLICATIONS

Novel

*Station Gehenna.* New York, Congdon and Weed, 1987.

Short Stories

*Distant Signals and Other Stories.* Victoria, British Columbia, Porcepic Books, 1989.

*

Andrew Weiner comments:

I suppose I am primarily a short-story writer, having published only one novel in almost two decades (I recently completed a second novel which is now with my agent). I grew up reading mainly short SF in preference to novels, and even now I think there are very few good SF novels being written and published.

I write in a number of modes: experimental, humorous, apocalyptic. Sometimes these overlap. In a sense all my stories, however apparently conventional in form, are experiments, since I'm never sure how they're going to turn out or even, in many cases, why I am writing them at all.

I think that what I write is less "science fiction" than a more or less skillful imitation of the "real" thing. Actually, I think this is probably true of almost every writer of my generation (e.g., post-1945), but some of us are more aware of it than others. I am personally unable to take aliens, distant planets, faster-than-light spaceships, mental powers, etc. *seriously*, although they can serve as convenient props. In this I place myself in a line of descent from Dick, Aldiss, Ballard, Sheckley, and Malzberg, as well as such "mainstream" writers of SF as Vonnegut and Walter Tevis. For want of a better word, I would call this self-conscious imitation of "real" SF "postmodern."

Actually I rarely write about outer space (the whole idea gives me vertigo) or the far future. I do, however, make heavy use of aliens, usually a metaphor for exploring the human mind.

* * *

While Andrew Weiner is not new to science-fiction readers, his name has only recently come to prominence. After publishing stories in various magazines, Weiner published a science-fiction thriller, *Station Gehenna*, which tells the story of a team on the planet Gehenna that tries to "terraform" the hostile planet into a hospitable one. Special agent Victor Lewin finds evidence that a murder has been committed, and the novel, part of the "Isaac Asimov presents" series, owes much to the whodunnit genre.

Weiner's first collection of short stories, *Distant Signals*, was published by the Canadian Porcepic Press and as such belongs to the new sophisticated school of Canadian science fiction with the likes of Candas Jane Dorsey and Elisabeth Vonarburg. The opening work, "The News from D Street," is one of Weiner's best stories, with many overtones of film noir. An agent is asked to find a missing person, and in typical film noir fashion we do not learn the agent's name until the fifth page. Only gradually do the science-fiction elements come into the story, in the same way that missing clues come slowly together to a private investigator in a film. The more information we get about the surroundings, the less they seem to make sense, and we have to wait until the end of the story when as in a thriller we are given the solution we had been suspecting for several pages.

"Klein's Machine," from the same collection, could not be more different in style, setting, and technique. Philip Herbert Klein is a 23-year-old on a bus, his eyes blank and "the remains of a bright green crushed flower in his left hand." Unable either to answer any questions or to remember how he found himself on a bus with a one-way ticket from New York to San Francisco, Klein is stopped in Ohio and transferred to a state mental hospital. The "patient," according to a psychiatrist's report, while "suffering a classical dissociative reaction of amnesia coupled with fugue state," claims to have been "travelling in time." We are then shown Klein's own diary, in which he gives an account of his secret experiments with a time travel machine and his successful attempts at making a hamster travel through time and return. However, Klein cannot remember anything about his own trip into the future, so with the help of sodium pentathol, he is induced into reliving his travel experience into a future society where there are only machines and everything is in the hands of a computer because "the people have gone now, all gone away to other worlds." The reader is left to decide for himself whether Klein has really traveled in time. In "Empire of the Sun," Weiner turns to poetic prose that might deter readers in search of an easy-to-follow plot. A succession of tableaux that should be read as a film script, the story becomes clear only after several readings.

Weiner's penchant for ambiguity, for a blurring of the divide between reality and imagination, finds its highest expression in the title story, "Distant Signals." A faded movie star, Vance Macoby, is hired by mysterious investors to act again in a TV series that was cancelled after six episodes in 1961. The investors want Macoby to shoot new episodes of the series in which the character played by Macoby is an amnesiac gunslinger who wanders from town to town in search of his lost identity. Weiner has written a perfect blend of film noir and comedy while teaching us a lesson about our own place in the universe.

—Henry Leperlier

---

**WELLMAN, Manly Wade.** Also wrote as Gans T. Field; Levi Crow; Gabriel Barclay; John Cotten; Hampton Wells; Wade Wells; Manuel Fernez. American. Born in Kamundongo, Angola, 21 May 1903; brother of the writer Paul I. Wellman. Educated at Wichita State University, Kansas, A.B. 1926; Columbia University, New York, B.Lit. 1927. Married Frances Obrist in 1930; one son. Reporter and feature writer, Wichita *Beacon*, 1927–30, and *Eagle*, 1930–34; assistant project supervisor, WPA Writers Project, New York, 1936–38; Instructor of Creative Writing, Elon College, North Carolina, 1962–70, and University of North Carolina evening college, Chapel Hill, 1963–73. Recipient: Ellery Queen award, 1946; Mystery Writers of America award, 1955; World Fantasy award, 1975, 1980; H.P. Lovecraft award, 1975; British Fantasy award, 1984. *Died 5 April 1986.*

SCIENCE-FICTION PUBLICATIONS

Novels

*The Invading Asteroid.* New York, Stellar, 1932.
*Romance in Black* (as Gans T. Field). London, Utopian, 1946.
*Sojarr of Titan.* New York, Crestwood, 1949.
*The Beasts from Beyond.* Manchester, World, 1950.
*Devil's Planet.* Manchester, World, 1951.
*Twice in Time* (revised edition). New York, Avalon, 1957; original edition, New York, Baen, 1988.
*Giants from Eternity.* New York, Avalon, 1959.
*The Dark Destroyers.* New York, Avalon, 1959.
*Island in the Sky.* New York, Avalon, 1961.
*The Solar Invasion.* New York, Popular Library, 1969(?).
*Sherlock Holmes's War of the Worlds,* with Wade Wellman. New York, Warner, 1975.
*The Beyonders.* New York, Warner, 1977.
*The Old Gods Waken.* New York, Doubleday, 1979.
*After Dark.* New York, Doubleday, 1980.
*The Lost and the Lurking.* New York, Doubleday, 1981.
*The Hanging Stones.* New York, Doubleday, 1982.
*What Dreams May Come.* New York, Doubleday, 1983.
*The Voice of the Mountain.* New York, Doubleday, 1984.
*The School of Darkness.* New York, Doubleday, 1985.
*Cahena: A Dream of the Past.* New York, Doubleday, 1986.

Short Stories

*Who Fears the Devil?* Sauk City, Wisconsin, Arkham House, 1963.
*A True Story of the Revolting and Bloody Crimes of Sergeant Stanlas, U.S.A.* Wichita, Kansas, Four Ducks Press, 1964.
*Worse Things Waiting.* Chapel Hill, North Carolina, Carcosa, 1973.
*Lonely Vigils.* Chapel Hill, North Carolina, Carcosa, 1981.
*Valley So Low: Southern Mountain Stories.* New York, Doubleday, 1987.
*John the Balladeer.* New York, Baen, 1988.

OTHER PUBLICATIONS

Novels

*A Double Life* (novelization of screenplay). Chicago, Century, 1947.
*Find My Killer.* New York, Farrar Straus, 1947; London, Sampson Low, 1948.
*Fort Sun Dance.* New York, Dell, and London, Corgi, 1955.
*Candle of the Wicked.* New York, Putnam, 1960.
*Not at These Hands.* New York, Putnam, 1962.

Novels (for children)

*The Sleuth Patrol.* New York, Nelson, 1947.
*The Mystery of Lost Valley.* New York, Nelson, 1948.
*The Raiders of Beaver Lake.* New York, Nelson, 1950.
*The Haunts of Drowning Creek.* New York, Holiday House, 1951.
*Wild Dogs of Drowning Creek.* New York, Holiday House, 1952.
*The Last Mammoth.* New York, Holiday House, 1953.
*Gray Riders: Jeb Stuart and His Men.* New York, Aladdin, 1954.
*Rebel Mail Runner.* New York, Holiday House, 1954.
*Flag on the Levee.* New York, Washburn, 1955.
*To Unknown Lands.* New York, Holiday House, 1956.
*Young Squire Morgan.* New York, Washburn, 1956.
*Lights over Skeleton Ridge.* New York, Washburn, 1957.
*The Ghost Battalion.* New York, Washburn, 1958.
*Ride, Rebels!* New York, Washburn, 1959.
*Appomattox Road.* New York, Washburn, 1960.
*Third String Center.* New York, Washburn, 1960.
*Rifles at Ramsour's Mill.* New York, Washburn, 1961.
*Battle for King's Mountain.* New York, Washburn, 1962.
*Clash on the Catawba.* New York, Washburn, 1962.
*The River Pirates.* New York, Washburn, 1963.

*Settlement on Shocco.* Winston-Salem, North Carolina, Blair, 1963.
*The South Fork Rangers.* New York, Washburn, 1963.
*The Master of Scare Hollow.* New York, Washburn, 1964.
*The Great Riverboat Race.* New York, Washburn, 1965.
*Mystery at Bear Paw Gap.* New York, Washburn, 1965.
*Battle at Bear Paw Gap.* New York, Washburn, 1966.
*The Specter of Bear Paw Gap.* New York, Washburn, 1966.
*Jamestown Adventure.* New York, Washburn, 1967.
*Brave Horse: The Story of Janus.* Williamsburg, Virginia, Colonial Williamsburg, 1968.
*Carolina Pirate.* New York, Washburn, 1968.
*Frontier Reporter.* New York, Washburn, 1969.
*Mountain Feud.* New York, Washburn, 1969.
*Napoleon of the West: A Story of the Aaron Burr Conspiracy.* New York, Washburn, 1970.
*Fast Break Five.* New York, Washburn, 1971.

Play

*Many Are the Hearts.* Raleigh, North Carolina Confederate Centennial Commission, 1961.

Other

*Giant in Gray: A Biography of Wade Hampton of South Carolina.* New York, Scribner, 1949.
*Dead and Gone: Classic Crimes of North Carolina.* Chapel Hill, University of North Carolina Press, 1954.
*Rebel Boast: First at Bethel—Last at Appomattox.* New York, Holt, 1956.
*Fastest on the River.* New York, Holt, 1957.
*The Life and Times of Sir Archie,* with Elizabeth Amis Blanchard. Chapel Hill, University of North Carolina Press, 1958.
*The County of Warren, North Carolina, 1586–1917.* Chapel Hill, University of North Carolina Press, 1959.
*They Took Their Stand: The Founders of the Confederacy.* New York, Putnam, 1959.
*The Rebel Songster,* with Frances Wellman. New York, Heritage House, 1959.
*Harpers Ferry, Prize of War.* Charlotte, North Carolina, McNally and Loftin, 1960.
*The County of Gaston,* with Robert F. Cope. Gastonia, North Carolina, Gaston County Historical Society, 1961.
*The County of Moore 1847–1947.* Southern Pines, North Carolina, Moore County Historical Association, 1962.
*Winston-Salem in History: The Founders.* Winston-Salem, North Carolina, Blair, 1966.
*The Kingdom of Madison: A Southern Mountain Fastness and Its People.* Chapel Hill, University of North Carolina Press, 1973.
*The Story of Moore County.* Southern Pines, North Carolina, Moore County Historical Association, 1974.

*

Manly Wade Wellman commented:

I came to America from an African wilderness, but with strong family heritage and association in the American west and south. I began by wanting to write of the fantastic, the imaginative. I wrote in other fields, too, but now I've returned to that first love. A writer must find himself out all alone, must understand himself, use himself in all he writes. More than by years or ability or reputation, your life is measured by the work you do. You pave your road by your writing, and travel it always into new wonders and perils and joys and sorrows. You find and use things out of sight and sound of all others. It's part of you, like the blood in your veins, the breath in your nostrils.

I look back on more than half a century of writing, and hope to keep on until they say the last words over me.

* * *

The bulk of Manly Wade Wellman's writing has been outside the science-fiction field. A popular writer during the heyday of the SF pulps, he is best known today as a fantasy author and for his fiction and nonfiction work in the field of Southern regionalism.

Wellman began selling SF as early as 1927 with "Back to the Beast" in *Weird Tales.* In 1930, he turned to writing as a full-time profession, and in 1934, moved to New York in order to be closer to his markets. After "Outlaws on Callisto" made the cover of the April 1936 *Astounding Stories,* Wellman became a client of the noted agent, Julius Schwartz, under whose direction he became part of the Better Publications stable. There Wellman became a regular contributor to *Thrilling Wonder Stories* and *Startling Stories.* These popular pulps, aimed at an adolescent readership, were well suited to Wellman's brisk, simple narrative style, and the bulk of his SF appeared in these and similar pulps. Most of his SF books are reprints of his earlier work, although recently he had begun to write fantasy.

Wellman's first book publication was *The Invading Asteroid.* It set the tone for the sort of space opera Wellman was to become known for. He created a consistent futuristic setting of the 30th century, and utilized this for some 16 of his stories. Wellman's 30th century was pretty much the same as the 20th, with the addition of interplanetary travel and extraterrestrials. Nonetheless, so well-liked was Wellman's future world that fans cried "plagiarism" when Nelson Bond used certain of these elements for a story of his own, and Wellman had to explain that Bond had done so with his permission.

*Sojarr of Titan* is a "Tarzan of outer space" pastiche written at editor Leo Margulies's request. *The Beasts from Beyond* made use of the idea of invasion at the intersection point of bubble universes that Wellman returned to in *The Beyonders.* Devil's Planet, part of his 30th-century series, is a murder mystery set on Mars that teams a human and an android as detectives, and appears to be the archetype of Asimov's *Caves of Steel. Twice in Time* is a novel of a man who travels through time to become Leonardo da Vinci. It is Wellman's most important SF work and remains a superior time-travel novel. The 1988 Baen Books edition restores the original and superior text of the 1940 magazine version of *Twice in Time*—it also includes "The Timeless Tomorrow," an excellent novelette about Nostradamus. *The Dark Destroyers* has Earthmen throwing off the yoke of extraterrestrial conquest. In *Giants from Eternity,* Pasteur, Darwin, Newton, Edison, and Curie are brought back to life to combat an alien growth that threatens to engulf the earth. In *Island in the Sky* a future gladiator rebels against a technological dictatorship that holds Earth in thrall. A final reprint from the pulp days, *The Solar Invasion* is Wellman's one fling at writing a Captain Future episode.

During the 1960's, Wellman collaborated with his son, Wade Wellman, for a series of droll pastiches that placed Doyle's Sherlock Holmes and Watson alongside Professor Challenger in the London of Wells's *War of the Worlds.* These were expanded and collected as *Sherlock Holmes's War of the Worlds,* a book that ranks among the best of the Holmes pastiches. *The Beyonders* is a routine novel of invasion by creatures from another dimension, with the saving charm of its Southern mountain setting.

While even the best of Wellman's SF seems naive and badly dated to modern readers, the same is not true for his fantasy writing, which remains some of the finest in the genre. The best of his short fantasy fiction has been collected in *Who Fears the Devil?, Worse Things Waiting, Lonely Vigils, Valley So Low*, and *John the Balladeer. Worse Things Waiting* collects the best of Wellman's fantasy/horror short fiction from the pulp era, while *Lonely Vigils* collects the cases of three occult investigators, Judge Pursuivant, Professor Enderby, and John Thunstone, whose separate series originally appeared in *Weird Tales* and *Strange Stories. Valley So Low* collects the best of his Southern mountain fantasy stories, all written during the last 15 years of his career. *Who Fears the Devil?* collects the adventures of a wandering balladeer, named simply "John," who confronts supernatural evil in the Southern Appalachians. The stories originally appeared in *The Magazine of Fantasy and Science Fiction* during the 1950's. Wellman revised the stories, not for the better, for their book publication. The original versions are presented in *John the Balladeer*, in addition to the six new John stories Wellman wrote later in life.

When Warner rejected a proposed sequel to *The Beyonders*, Wellman revived John and rewrote his SF outline into the fantasy novel, *The Old Gods Waken.* This was the first in a series of fantasy novels written for Doubleday. John also stars in *After Dark, The Lost and the Lurking, The Hanging Stones*, and *The Voice of the Mountain.* Delving further into his back pages, Wellman reintroduced Judge Pursuivant in *The Hanging Stones*, then brought back John Thunstone as the hero of *What Dreams May Come* and *The School of Darkness.* Wellman, however, was far better with short fiction, and these later novels suffer from paucity of content and tiresome padding. *Cahena*, his final novel, is a historical fantasy/adventure set during the Islamic conquest of Northern Africa. Wellman had worked on it for years, but the novel he considered would be his magnum opus was a bust. His monument is his short fantasy/horror fiction, the best of which can stand proudly with the best in this genre, while his John stories remain true classics of American fantasy.

—Karl Edward Wagner

---

**WELLS, H(erbert) G(eorge).** Brtish. Born in Bromley, Kent, 21 September 1866. Educated at Mr. Morley's Bromley Academy until age 13: certificate in book-keeping; apprentice draper, Rodgers and Denyer, Windsor, 1880; pupil-teacher at a school in Wookey, Somerset, 1880; apprentice chemist in Midhurst, Sussex, 1880–81; apprentice draper, Hyde's Southsea Drapery Emporium, Hampshire, 1881–83; student/assistant, Midhurst Grammar School, 1883–84; studied at Normal School (now Imperial College) of Science, London (editor, *Science School Journal*), 1884–87; teacher, Holt Academy, Wrexham, Wales, 1887–88, and at Henley House School, Kilburn, London, 1889; B.Sc. (honours) in zoology 1890, and D.Sc. 1943, University of London. Married 1) his cousin Isabel Mary Wells in 1891 (separated 1894; divorced 1895); 2) Amy Catherine Robbins in 1895 (died 1927), two sons; had one daughter by Amber Reeves, and one son by Rebecca West, the writer Anthony West. Tutor, University Tutorial College, London, 1890–93; full-time writer from 1893; theatre critic, *Pall Mall Gazatte*, London, 1895; member of the Fabian Society, 1903–08; Labour candidate for Parliament, for the University of London, 1922, 1923; lived mainly in France, 1924–33. International president, PEN, 1934–46, D. Lit: University of London, 1936. Honorary fellow, Imperial College of Science and Technology, London. *Died 13 August 1946.*

SCIENCE-FICTION PUBLICATIONS

Novels

*The Time Machine: An Invention.* London, Heinemann, and New York, Holt, 1895; as *The Definitive Time Machine: A Critical Edition*, edited by Harry M. Geduld, Bloomington, Indiana University Press, 1987.
*The Island of Doctor Moreau.* London, Heinemann, and New York, Stone and Kimball, 1896.
*The Invisible Man: A Grotesque Romance.* London, Pearson, and New York, Arnold, 1897.
*The War of the Worlds.* London, Heinemann, and New York, Harper, 1898.
*When the Sleeper Wakes.* London and New York, Harper, 1899; revised edition, as *The Sleeper Wakes*, London, Nelson, 1910.
*The First Men in the Moon.* London, Newnes, and Indianapolis, Bowen Merrill, 1901.
*The Food of the Gods, and How It Came to Earth.* London, Macmillan, and New York, Scribner, 1904.
*A Modern Utopia.* London, Chapman and Hall, and New York, Scribner, 1905.
*In the Days of the Comet.* London, Macmillan, and New York, Century, 1906.
*The War in the Air, and Particularly How Mr. Bert Smallways Fared While It Lasted.* London, Bell, and New York, Macmillan, 1908.
*The World Set Free: A Story of Mankind.* London, Macmillan, and New York, Dutton, 1914.
*Men Like Gods.* London, Cassell, and New York, Macmillan, 1923.
*The Shape of Things to Come: The Ultimate Resolution.* London, Hutchinson, and New York, Macmillan, 1933; revised edition, as *Things to Come* (film story), London, Cresset Press, and New York, Macmillan, 1935.
*The Croquet Player.* London, Chatto and Windus, 1936; New York, Viking Press, 1937.
*Star Begotten: A Biological Fantasia.* London, Chatto and Windus, and New York, Viking Press, 1937.
*The Holy Terror.* London, Joseph, and New York, Simon and Schuster, 1939.

Short Stories

*The Stolen Bacillus and Other Incidents.* London, Methuen, 1895.
*The Plattner Story and Others.* London, Methuen, 1897.
*Thirty Strange Stories.* New York, Arnold, 1897.
*Tales of Space and Time.* London, Harper, and New York, Doubleday, 1899.
*Twelve Stories and a Dream.* London, Macmillan, 1903; New York, Scribner, 1905.
*The Country of the Blind and Other Stories.* London, Nelson, 1911; revised edition of *The Country of the Blind*, London, Golden Cockerel Press, 1939.
*The Door in the Wall and Other Stories.* New York, Kennerley, 1911; London, Richards, 1915.
*The Short Stories of H.G. Wells.* London, Benn, 1927; New York, Doubleday, 1929.
*28 Science Fiction Stories.* New York, Dover, 1952.
*Selected Short Stories.* London, Penguin, 1958.
*Best Science Fiction Stories of H.G. Wells.* New York, Dover, 1966.
*The Complete Short Stories of H.G. Wells.* London, Black, and New York, St. Martin's Press, 1987.

### Other Publications

#### Novels

*The Wonderful Visit.* London, Dent, and New York, Macmillan, 1895.
*The Wheels of Chance.* London, Dent, and New York, Macmillan, 1896.
*Love and Mr. Lewisham.* London, Harper, and New York, Stokes, 1900.
*The Sea Lady: A Tissue of Moonshine.* London, Methuen, and New York, Appleton, 1902.
*Kipps.* London, Macmillan, and New York, Scribner, 1905.
*Tono-Bungay.* New York, Duffield, 1908; London, Macmillan, 1909.
*Ann Veronica.* London, Unwin, and New York, Harper, 1909.
*The History of Mr. Polly.* London, Nelson, and New York, Duffield, 1910.
*The New Machiavelli.* London, Lane, and New York, Duffield, 1911.
*Marriage.* London, Macmillan, and New York, Duffield, 1912.
*The Passionate Friends.* London, Macmillan, and New York, Harper, 1913.
*The Wife of Sir Isaac Harman.* London and New York, Macmillan, 1914.
*Boon* (as Reginald Bliss). London, Unwin, and New York, Doran, 1915.
*Bealby.* London, Methuen, and New York, Macmillan, 1915.
*The Research Magnificent.* London and New York, Macmillan, 1915.
*Mr. Britling Sees It Through.* London, Cassell, and New York, Macmillan, 1916.
*The Soul of a Bishop.* London, Cassell, and New York, Macmillan, 1917.
*Joan and Peter.* London, Cassell, and New York, Macmillan, 1918.
*The Undying Fire.* London, Cassell, and New York, Macmillan, 1919.
*The Secret Places of the Heart.* London, Cassell, and New York, Macmillan, 1922.
*The Dream.* London, Cape, and New York, Macmillan, 1924.
*Christina Alberta's Father.* London, Cape, and New York, Macmillan, 1925.
*The World of William Clissold.* London, Benn, 3 vols., and New York, Doran, 2 vols., 1926.
*Meanwhile: The Picture of a Lady.* London, Benn, and New York, Doran, 1927.
*Mr. Blettsworthy on Rampole Island.* London, Benn, and New York, Doubleday, 1928.
*The King Who Was a King: The Book of a Film.* London, Benn, and New York, Doubleday, 1929.
*The Autocracy of Mr. Parham.* London, Heinemann, and New York, Doubleday, 1930.
*The Bulpington of Blup.* London, Hutchinson, 1932; New York, Macmillan, 1933.
*Man Who Could Work Miracles* (film story). London, Cresset Press, and New York, Macmillan, 1936.
*Brynhild.* London, Methuen, and New York, Scribner, 1937.
*The Camford Visitation.* London, Methuen, 1937.
*Apropos of Dolores.* London, Cape, and New York, Scribner, 1938.
*The Brothers.* London, Chatto and Windus, and New York, Viking Press, 1938.
*The Holy Terror.* London, Joseph, and New York, Simon and Schuster, 1939.
*Babes in the Darkling Wood.* London, Secker and Warburg, and New York, Alliance, 1940.
*All Aboard for Ararat.* London, Secker and Warburg, 1940; New York, Alliance, 1941.
*You Can't Be Too Careful: A Sample of Life 1901–1951.* London, Secker and Warburg, 1941; New York, Putnam, 1942.
*The Wealth of Mr. Waddy,* edited by Harris Wilson. Carbondale, Southern Illinois University Press, 1969.

#### Short Stories

*Select Conversations with an Uncle (Now Extinct) and Two Other Reminiscences.* London, Lane, and New York, Merriman, 1895.
*A Cure for Love.* New York, Scott, 1899.
*The Vacant Country.* New York, Kent, 1899.
*Tales of the Unexpected [of Life and Adventure, of Wonder],* edited by J.D. Beresford. London, Collins, 3 vols., 1922–23.
*The Valley of Spiders.* London, Collins, 1964.
*The Cone.* London, Collins, 1965.
*The Man with the Nose and Other Uncollected Short Stories,* edited by J.R. Hammond. London, Athlone Press, 1984.

#### Plays

*Kipps,* with Rudolf Besier, adaptation of the novel by Wells (produced London, 1912).
*The Wonderful Visit,* with St. John Ervine, adaptation of the novel by Wells (produced London, 1921).
*Hoopdriver's Holiday,* adaptation of his novel *The Wheels of Chance,* edited by Michael Timko. Lafayette, Indiana, Purdue University English Department, 1964.

Screenplays: *H.G. Wells Comedies (Bluebottles, The Tonic, Daydreams),* with Frank Wells, 1928; *Things to Come,* 1936; *The Man Who Could Work Miracles,* 1936.

#### Other

*Text-Book of Biology.* London, Clive, 2 vols., 1893.
*Honours Physiography,* with R.A. Gregory. London, Hughes, 1893.
*Certain Personal Matters: A Collection of Material, Mainly Autobiographical.* London, Lawrence and Bullen, 1897.
*Anticipations of the Reaction of Mechanical and Scientific Progress upon Human Life and Thought.* London, Chapman and Hall, 1901; New York, Harper, 1902.
*The Discovery of the Future* (lecture). London, Unwin, 1902; New York, Huebsch, 1913; revised edition, London, Cape, 1925.
*Mankind in the Making.* London, Chapman and Hall, 1903; New York, Scribner, 1904.
*The Future in America: A Search after Realities.* London, Chapman and Hall, and New York, Harper, 1906.
*Faults of the Fabian* (lecture). Privately printed, 1906.
*Socialism and the Family.* London, Fifield, 1906; Boston, Ball, 1908.
*Reconstruction of the Fabian Society.* Privately printed, 1906.
*This Misery of Boots.* London, Fabian Society, 1907; Boston, Ball, 1908.
*Will Socialism Destroy the Home?* London, Independent Labour Party, 1907.
*New Worlds for Old.* London, Constable, and New York, Macmillan, 1908; revised edition, London, Constable, 1914.
*First and Last Things: A Confession of Faith and Rule of Life.* London, Constable, and New York, Putnam, 1908; revised edition, London, Cassell, 1917; London, Watts, 1929.
*Floor Games* (for children). London, Palmer, 1911; Boston, Small Maynard, 1912.

*The Labour Unrest.* London, Associated Newspapers, 1912.
*War and Common Sense.* London, Associated Newspapers, 1913.
*Liberalism and Its Party.* London, Good, 1913.
*Little Wars* (children's games). London, Palmer, and Boston, Small Maynard, 1913.
*An Englishman Looks at the World, Being a Series of Unrestrained Remarks upon Contemporary Matters.* London, Cassell, 1914; as *Social Forces in England and America*, New York, Harper, 1914.
*The War That Will End War.* London, Palmer, and New York, Duffield, 1914; reprinted in part as *The War and Socialism*, London, Clarion Press, 1915.
*The Peace of the World.* London, Daily Chronicle, 1915.
*What Is Coming? A Forecast of Things after the War.* London, Cassell, and New York, Macmillan, 1916.
*The Elements of Reconstruction.* London, Nisbet, 1916.
*War and the Future.* London, Cassell, 1917; as *Italy, France, and Britain at War*, New York, Macmillan, 1917.
*God the Invisible King.* London, Cassell, and New York, Macmillan, 1917.
*A Reasonable Man's Peace.* London, Daily News, 1917.
*In the Fourth Year: Anticipations of a World Peace.* London, Chatto and Windus, and New York, Macmillan, 1918; abridged edition, as *Anticipations of a World Peace*, Chatto and Windus, 1918.
*British Nationalism and the League of Nations.* London, League of Nations Union, 1918.
*History Is One.* Boston, Ginn, 1919.
*The Outline of History, Being a Plain History of Life and Mankind.* London, Newnes, 2 vols., and New York, Macmillan, 2 vols., 1920 (and later revisions).
*Russia in the Shadows.* London, Hodder and Stoughton, 1920; New York, Doran, 1921.
*The Salvaging of Civilisation.* London, Cassell, and New York, Macmillan, 1921.
*The New Teaching of History, with a Reply to Some Recent Criticisms of "The Outline of History."* London, Cassell, 1921.
*Washington and Hope of Peace.* London, Collins, 1922; as *Washington and the Riddle of Peace*, New York, Macmillan, 1922.
*The World, Its Debts, and the Rich Men.* London, Finer, 1922.
*A Short History of the World.* London, Cassell, and New York, Macmillan, 1922; revised edition, London, Penguin, 1946.
*Socialism and the Scientific Motive* (lecture). Privately printed, 1923.
*The Story of a Great Schoolmaster, Being a Plain Account of the Life and Ideas of Sanderson of Oundle.* London, Chatto and Windus, and New York, Macmillan, 1924.
*The P.R. Parliament.* London, Proportional Representation Society, 1924.
*A Year of Prophesying.* London, Unwin, 1924; New York, Macmillan, 1925.
*Works* (Atlantic Edition). London, Unwin, and New York, Scribner, 28 vols., 1924.
*A Forecast of the World's Affairs.* New York, Encyclopaedia Britannica, 1925.
*Works* (Essex Edition). London, Benn, 24 vols., 1926–27.
*Mr. Belloc Objects to "The Outline of History."* London, Watts, 1926.
*Democracy under Revision* (lecture). London, Hogarth Press, and New York, Doran, 1927.
*Wells' Social Anticipations*, edited by H.W. Laidler. New York, Vanguard Press, 1927.
*In Memory of Amy Catherine Wells.* Privately printed, 1927.
*The Way the World Is Going: Guesses and Forecasts of the Years Ahead.* London, Benn, 1928; New York, Doubleday, 1929.
*The Open Conspiracy: Blue Prints for a World Revolution.* London, Gollancz, and New York, Doubleday, 1928; revised edition, London, Hogarth Press, 1930; revised edition, as *What Are We to Do with Our Lives?*, London, Heinemann, and New York, Doubleday, 1931.
*The Common Sense of World Peace* (lecture). London, Hogarth Press, 1929.
*Imperialism and the Open Conspiracy.* London, Faber, 1929.
*The Adventures of Tommy* (for children). London, Harrap, and New York, Stokes, 1929.
*The Science of Life: A Summary of Contemporary Knowledge about Life and Its Possibilities*, with Julian Huxley and G.P. Wells. London, Amalgamated Press, 3 vols., 1930; New York, Doubleday, 4 vols., 1931; revised edition, as *Science of Life Series*, London, Cassell, 9 vols., 1934–37.
*The Problem of the Troublesome Collaborator.* Privately printed, 1930.
*Settlement of the Trouble Between Mr. Thring and Mr. Wells: A Footnote to The Problem of the Troublesome Collaborator.* Privately printed, 1930.
*The Way to World Peace.* London, Benn, 1930.
*The Work, Wealth, and Happiness of Mankind.* New York, Doubleday, 2 vols., 1931; London, Heinemann, 1 vol., 1932; revised edition, Heinemann, 1934; as *The Outline of Man's Work and Wealth*, Doubleday, 1936.
*After Democracy: Addresses and Papers on the Present World Situation.* London, Watts, 1932.
*What Should Be Done—Now.* New York, Day, 1932.
*Experiment in Autobiography: Discoveries and Conclusions of a Very Ordinary Brain (since 1866).* London, Gollancz-Cresset Press, 2 vols., and New York, Macmillan, 1 vol., 1934.
*Stalin-Wells Talk: The Verbatim Record, and A Discussion*, with others. London, New Statesman and Nation, 1934.
*The New America: The New World.* London, Cresset Press, and New York, Macmillan, 1935.
*The Anatomy of Frustration: A Modern Synthesis.* London, Cresset Press, and New York, Macmillan, 1936.
*The Idea of a World Encyclopaedia.* London, Hogarth Press, 1936.
*World Brain.* London, Methuen, and New York, Doubleday, 1938.
*Travels of a Republican Radical in Search of Hot Water.* London, Penguin, 1939.
*The Fate of Homo Sapiens: An Unemotional Statement of the Things That Are Happening to Him Now and of the Immediate Possibilities Confronting Him.* London, Secker and Warburg, 1939; as *The Fate of Man*, New York, Alliance, 1939.
*The New World Order, Whether It Is Obtainable, How It Can Be Obtained, and What Sort of World a World at Peace Will Have to Be.* London, Secker and Warburg, and New York, Knopf, 1940.
*The Rights of Man; or, What Are We Fighting For?* London, Penguin, 1940.
*The Common Sense of War and Peace: World Revolution or War Unending?* London, Penguin, 1940.
*The Pocket History of the World.* New York, Pocket Books, 1941.
*Guide to the New World: A Handbook of Constructive World Revolution.* London, Gollancz, 1941.
*The Outlook for Homo Sapiens* (revised versions of *The Fate of Homo Sapiens* and *The New World Order*). London, Secker and Warburg, 1942.
*Science and the World-Mind.* London, New Europe, 1942.

*Phoenix: A Summary of the Inescapable Conditions of World Reorganization*. London, Secker and Warburg, 1942; Girard, Kansas, Haldeman Julius, n.d.

*A Thesis on the Quality of Illusion in the Continuity of Individual Life of the Higher Metazoa, with Particular Reference to the Species Homo Sapiens*. Privately printed, 1942.

*The Conquest of Time*. London, Watts, 1942.

*The New Rights of Man*. Girard, Kansas, Haldeman Julius, 1942.

*Crux Ansata: An Indictment of the Roman Catholic Church*. London, Penguin, 1943; New York, Agora, 1944.

*The Mosley Outrage*. London, Daily Worker, 1943.

*'42 to '44: A Contemporary Memoir upon Human Behavior During the Crisis of the World Revolution*. London, Secker and Warburg, 1944.

*Marxism vs. Liberalism* (interview with Stalin). New York, Century, 1945.

*The Happy Turning: A Dream of Life*. London, Heinemann, 1945.

*Mind at the End of Its Tether*. London, Heinemann, 1945.

*Mind at the End of Its Tether, and The Happy Turning*. New York, Didier, 1945.

*The Desert Daisy* (for children), edited by Gordon N. Ray. Urbana, University of Illinois Press, 1957.

*Henry James and H.G. Wells: A Record of Their Friendship, Their Debate on the Art of Fiction, and Their Quarrel*, edited by Leon Edel and Gordon N. Ray. Urbana, University of Illinois Press, and London, Hart Davis, 1958.

*Arnold Bennett and H.G. Wells: A Record of a Personal and Literary Friendship*, edited by Harris Wilson. London, Hart Davis, 1960.

*George Gissing and H.G. Wells: Their Friendship and Correspondence*, edited by Royal A. Gettman. London, Hart Davis, 1961.

*Journalism and Prophecy 1893–1946*, edited W. Warren Wagar. Boston, Houghton Mifflin, 1964; revised edition, London, Bodley Head, 1965.

*Early Writings in Science and Science Fiction*, edited by Robert M. Philmus and David Y. Hughes. Berkeley, University of California Press, 1975.

*H.G. Wells's Literary Criticism*, edited by Patrick Parrinder and Robert M. Philmus. Brighton, Harvester Press, 1980.

*H.G. Wells in Love*, edited by G.P. Wells. London, Faber, 1984.

*The Discovery of the Future, with The Common-Sense of World Peace and The Human Adventure*, edited by Patrick Parrinder. London, PNL, 1989.

Editor, with G.R.S. Taylor and Frances Evelyn Warwick, *The Great State: Essays in Construction*. London, Harper, 1912; as *Socialism and the Great State*, New York, Harper, 1914.

*

Bibliography: *H.G. Wells: A Comprehensive Bibliography*, London, H.G. Wells Society, 1966, revised editions, 1968, 1986; *Herbert George Wells: An Annotated Bibliography of His Works* by J.R. Hammond, New York, Garland, 1977; *H.G. Wells: A Reference Guide* by William J. Scheick and J. Randolf Cox, Boston, 1988.

Manuscript Collection: University of Illinois, Urbana.

Critical Studies (selection): *The World of H.G. Wells* by Van Wyck Brooks, New York, Mitchell Kennerley, and London, T. Fisher Unwin, 1915; *H.G. Wells: A Biography*, London, Longman, 1951; *The Early H.G. Wells: A Study of the Scientific Romances* by Bernard Bergonzi, Manchester, Manchester University Press, 1961, and *H.G. Wells: A Collection of Critical Essays* edited by Bergonzi, Englewood Cliffs, New Jersey, Prentice Hall, 1976; *H.G. Wells: An Outline* by F.K. Chaplin, London, P.R. Macmillan, 1961; *H.G. Wells and the World State* by W. Warren Wagar, New Haven, Connecticut, Yale University Press, 1961; *The Life and Thought of H.G. Wells* by Julius Kagarlitsky (translated by Moura Budberg), London, Sidgwick and Jackson, 1966; *H.G. Wells* by Richard Hauer Costa, New York, Twayne, 1967, revised edition, 1985; *H.G. Wells: His Turbulent Life and Times* by Lovat Dickson, London, Macmillan, 1969; essay in *A Soviet Heretic* by Yevgeny Zamyatin (translated by Mirra Ginsburg), Chicago, University of Chicago Press, 1970; *H.G. Wells* by Patrick Parrinder, Edinburgh, Oliver and Boyd, 1970, New York, Capricorn, 1977, and *H.G. Wells: The Critical Heritage* edited by Parrinder, London, Routledge, 1972; *The Time Traveller: The Life of H.G. Wells* by Norman and Jeanne Mackenzie, London, Weidenfeld and Nicolson, 1973, as *H.G. Wells: A Biography*, New York, Simon and Schuster, 1973; *H.G. Wells: Critic of Progress* by Jack Williamson, Baltimore, Mirage Press, 1973; *H.G. Wells and Rebecca West* by Gordon N. Ray, New Haven, Connecticut, Yale University Press, and London, Macmillan, 1974; *The Scientific Romances of H.G. Wells* by Stephen Gill, Cornwall, Ontario, Vesta, 1975; *Anatomies of Egotism: A Reading of the Last Novels of H.G. Wells* by Robert Bloom, Lincoln, University of Nebraska Press, 1977; *H.G. Wells and Modern Science Fiction* edited by Darko Suvin and Robert M. Philmus, Lewisburg, Pennsylvania, Buckness University Press, 1977; *H.G. Wells: A Pictorial Biography* by Frank Wells, London, Jupiter, 1977; *The H.G. Wells Scrapbook* edited by Peter Haining, London, New English Library, 1978; *Who's Who in H.G. Wells* by Brian Ash, London, Elm Tree, 1979; *H.G. Wells, Discoverer of the Future: The Influence of Science on His Thought* by Roslynn D. Haynes, New York, New York University Press, and London, Macmillan, 1980; *H.G. Wells: Interviews and Recollections* edited by J.R. Hammond, London, Macmillan, 1980; *The Science Fiction of H.G. Wells: A Concise Guide* by P.H. Niles, Clifton Park, New York, Auriga, 1980; *The Science Fiction of H.G. Wells* by Frank McConnell, New York, Oxford University Press, 1981; *H.G. Wells and the Culminating Ape: Biological Themes and Imaginative Obsessions* by Peter Kemp, London, Macmillan, and New York, St. Martin's Press, 1982; *The Logic of Fantasy: H.G. Wells and Science Fiction* by John Huntington, New York, Columbia University Press, 1982; *H.G. Wells* by Robert Crossley, Mercer Island, Washington, Starmont House, 1984; *H.G. Wells: Aspects of a Life* by Anthony West, London, Hutchinson, and New York, Random House, 1984; *H.G. Wells* by John Batchelor, London, Cambridge University Press, 1985; *H.G. Wells: Desperately Mortal: A Biography* by David C. Smith, New Haven, Connecticut, Yale University Press, 1986; *H.G. Wells: Reality and Beyond* edited by Michael Mullin, Champaign, Illinois, Public Library, 1986; *The Prophetic Soul: A Reading of Things To Come* by Leon Stover, Jefferson, North Carolina, and London, McFarland, 1987; *H.G. Wells* by Michael Draper, London, Macmillan, and New York, St. Martin's Press, 1987; *Bennett, Wells, and Conrad: Narrative in Transition* by Linda R. Anderson, London, Macmillan, and New York, St. Martin's Press, 1988; *H.G. Wells* by Christopher Martin, Hove, Wayland, 1988; *H.G. Wells under Revision* edited by Patrick Parrinder and Christopher Rolfe, Selinsgrove, Pennsylvania, and London, Susquehanna University Presses, 1990; *H.G. Wells* by Brian Murray, New York, Continuum, 1990.

* * *

Bernard Bergonzi, in his monograph *The Early H.G. Wells*, notes somewhat caustically that if Wells had died in 1900, like his young American friend Stephen Crane, "he would be remembered primarily as a literary artist." The 45 years of ardent "pamphleteering" that followed would not have occurred, and Wells's place in the firmament of high culture would have been more secure, unshadowed by the embarrassment of his crusades for public enlightenment, or even by his sometimes awkward attempts after 1900 to write mainstream fiction. From the perspective of literary criticism as it is practiced in the second half of the 20th century, Bergonzi's judgment is hard to fault. What Wells produced between 1894 and 1901, from the earliest short stories in *The Pall Mall Budget* to *The First Men in the Moon*, was not only the most imaginative and artistically satisfying science fiction of any novelist of his generation, but also the best writing of his long career. None of the mainstream novels, sociological tracts, prophetic manifestos, collections of journalism, or encyclopedic surveys of science and history that Wells published after 1900 bears comparison, as art, with his early science fiction. Most of his later science fiction also suffers when measured against the standards he set for himself between 1894 and 1901.

Fortunately for his literary soul, Wells did more than enough in his salad days to win admission to the ranks of the immortals. From 1894 to 1901 his output of fantasy and science fiction (chiefly the latter) came to six novels and more than 30 short stories; most of these captured immediate public and critical acclaim. *The Time Machine*, the first of the novels, is a profound dystopian parable and the archetype of all time-travel stories in 20th-century science fiction. *The Island of Doctor Moreau* retells the Frankenstein tale, with dark satirical touches reminiscent of Swift. *The Invisible Man: A Grotesque Romance* furnishes the model for every later warning in science fiction of the Faustian potentiality for human self-destruction in the powers of science. *The War of the Worlds* is the first great story of interplanetary conflict, and *When the Sleeper Wakes* inspired Zamyatin's *We* and Huxley's *Brave New World.* In *The First Men in the Moon*, Wells produced a masterful fantasia on the theme of biological engineering and one of the first credible accounts of space travel.

Several of the short stories have the same archetypal quality as the early novels. The deadliness of nature disclosed by modern science, which has supplied the raw material for a huge literature of disaster in our century, was a subject thoroughly exploited by Wells in his early stories, and in a few others written just after 1901. Apart from *The War of the Worlds*, which can also be read as a Darwinian fairy-tale, there were stories of man-eating orchids and cephalopods, giant birds and spiders, world-conquering ant hordes, and, in "The Star," an astrophysical disaster story of classical discipline, which seems almost to have been carved in ice. In "A Story of the Stone Age," Wells was among the first writers to make imaginative use of modern anthropology. "The New Accelerator" and "A Dream of Armageddon" carry further the admonitions in *The Invisible Man* on the perils of science and technology. "You know the silly way of the ingenious sort of men who make these things," the dreamer tells the narrator in "A Dream of Armageddon," recalling the weapons research in his nightmare of future life. "They turn 'em out as beavers build dams, and with no more sense of the rivers they're going to divert and the lands they're going to flood!"

The flow of science fiction from Wells's pen did not stop in 1901, but time sapped his creative powers and eroded his craftsmanship. He grew careless. Between 1902 and 1914 he wrote six fantasy and science-fiction novels and a dozen stories. From 1914 until his death another five science-fiction novels made their appearance, three filmscripts, and several works located in a literary no-man's-land halfway between speculative and mainstream fiction. In his later work some of the warnings and anxieties of the first novels emerge again, and new ground is broken as well. What chiefly distinguishes Wells's science fiction after 1901 is its heightened political consciousness. Scenarios of global war fought with diabolical weapons alternate with visions of a technocratic worldwide utopia. Wells foresaw tank warfare in 1903 ("The Land Ironclads"), massive bombardment of cities by aircraft in 1908 (*The War in the Air*), and atomic bombs in 1914 (*The World Set Free*). He satirized fascism in *The Autocracy of Mr. Parham* and turned it to his advantage in *The Holy Terror.* His three major utopian novels, *A Modern Utopia, Men Like Gods*, and *The Shape of Things to Come*, are landmarks in that extraordinarily difficult genre.

Writing in 1934, Wells took stock of the "incurable habit with literary critics to lament some lost artistry and innocence in my early work and to accuse me of having become polemical in my later years." In his defense, he observed—quite correctly—that his work had always been concerned with contemporary issues and with "life in the mass." So far, so true. But Wells could not bring himself to admit the decline of imagination and technique that overtook his later fiction. The success of such eminently polemical writers of science fiction as George Orwell and Walter M. Miller, Jr., who have as many axes to grind as Wells at his worst, suffices to show that Wells did not go wrong by abandoning "pure" literature for "pamphleteering." He merely let impatience and irritability diminish the effectiveness of his art. But the size of his achievement remains formidable. Wells's best work is superb, and grandly paradigmatic. No other early writer of science fiction opened so many pathways. He is also a singularly universal figure. One may wonder if even one significant writer in the genre anywhere in the world in this century has missed reading H.G. Wells. Quite simply, he is to science fiction what Albert Einstein is to modern physics, or Pablo Picasso to modern art.

—W. Warren Wagar

---

**WELLS, John J.** *See* **BRADLEY, Marion Zimmer; COULSON, Juanita.**

---

**WERNHEIM, John.** *See* **FEARN, John Russell.**

---

**WEST, Douglas.** *See* **TUBB, E.C.**

---

**WHEATLEY, Dennis (Yates).** British. Born in London, 8 January 1897. Educated at Dulwich College, London, 1908; H.M.S. Worcester, 1909–13; privately in Germany, 1913. Married 1) Nancy Robinson in 1923 (divorced 1931), one son; 2) Joan Gwendoline Johnstone in 1931. Served in the Royal Field Artillery, City of London Brigade, 1914–17; 36th Ulster Division, 1917–19 (invalided out); recommissioned in Royal Air Force Volunteer Reserve, 1939; member, National Recruiting

Panel, 1940–41; member, Joint Planning Staff of War Cabinet, 1941–44; Wing Commander, 1944–45; United States Army Bronze Star. Joined his father's wine business, Wheatley & Son, London, 1914; worked in the business, 1919–26; sole owner, 1926–31. Editor, Dennis Wheatley's Library of the Occult, Sphere Books, London, from 1973 (over 40 volumes). Received Livery of Vintners' Company, 1918, and Distillers' Company, 1922. Fellow, Royal Society of Arts, and Royal Society of Literature. *Died 11 November 1977.*

### Science-Fiction Publications

#### Novels

*Such Power Is Dangerous*. London, Hutchinson, 1933.
*Black August*. London, Hutchinson, and New York, Dutton, 1934.
*The Fabulous Valley*. London, Hutchinson, 1934.
*They Found Atlantis*. London, Hutchinson, and Philadelphia, Lippincott, 1936.
*The Secret War*. London, Hutchinson, 1937.
*Uncharted Seas*. London, Hutchinson, 1938.
*Sixty Days to Live*. London, Hutchinson, 1939.
*The Man Who Missed the War*. London, Hutchinson, 1945.
*Star of Ill-Omen*. London, Hutchinson, 1952.

### Other Publications

#### Novels

*The Forbidden Territory*. London, Hutchinson, and New York, Dutton, 1933.
*The Devil Rides Out*. London, Hutchinson, 1935; New York, Bantam, 1967.
*The Eunuch of Stamboul*. London, Hutchinson, and Boston, Little Brown, 1935.
*Murder Off Miami*. London, Hutchinson, 1936; as *File on Bolitho Blane*, New York, Morrow, 1936.
*Contraband*. London, Hutchinson, 1936.
*Who Killed Robert Prentice?* London, Hutchinson, 1937; as *File on Robert Prentice*, New York, Greenberg, 1937.
*The Malinsay Massacre*. London, Hutchinson, 1938; New York, Rutledge Press, 1981.
*The Golden Spaniard*. London, Hutchinson, 1938.
*The Quest of Julian Day*. London, Hutchinson, 1939.
*Herewith the Clues!* London, Hutchinson, 1939.
*The Scarlet Imposter*. London, Hutchinson, 1940; New York, Macmillan, 1942.
*Three Inquisitive People*. London, Hutchinson, 1940.
*Faked Passports*. London, Hutchinson, 1940; New York, Macmillan, 1943.
*The Black Baroness*. London, Hutchinson, 1940; New York, Macmillan, 1942.
*Strange Conflict*. London, Hutchinson, 1941.
*The Sword of Fate*. London, Hutchinson, 1941; New York, Macmillan, 1944.
*"V" for Vengeance*. London, Hutchinson, and New York, Macmillan, 1942.
*Codeword—Golden Fleece*. London, Hutchinson, 1946.
*Come into My Parlour*. London, Hutchinson, 1946.
*The Launching of Roger Brook*. London, Hutchinson, 1947; New York, Ballantine, 1973.
*The Shadow of Tyburn Tree*. London, Hutchinson, 1948; New York, Ballantine, 1973.
*The Haunting of Toby Jugg*. London, Hutchinson, 1948; New York, Ballantine, 1974.
*The Rising Storm*. London, Hutchinson, 1949.
*The Second Seal*. London, Hutchinson, 1950.
*The Man Who Killed the King*. London, Hutchinson, 1951; New York, Putnam, 1965.
*To the Devil—A Daughter*. London, Hutchinson, 1953; New York, Bantam, 1968.
*Curtain of Fear*. London, Hutchinson, 1953.
*The Island Where Time Stands Still*. London, Hutchinson, 1954.
*The Dark Secret of Josephine*. London, Hutchinson, 1955.
*The Ka of Gifford Hillary*. London, Hutchinson, 1956; New York, Ballantine, 1973.
*The Prisoner in the Mask*. London, Hutchinson, 1957.
*Traitors' Gate*. London, Hutchinson, 1958.
*The Rape of Venice*. London, Hutchinson, 1959.
*The Satanist*. London, Hutchinson, 1960; New York, Bantam, 1967.
*Vendetta in Spain*. London, Hutchinson, 1961.
*Mayhem in Greece*. London, Hutchinson, 1962.
*The Sultan's Daughter*. London, Hutchinson, 1963.
*Bill for the Use of a Body*. London, Hutchinson, 1964.
*They Used Dark Forces*. London, Hutchinson, 1964.
*Dangerous Inheritance*. London, Hutchinson, 1965.
*The Wanton Princess*. London, Hutchinson, 1966.
*Unholy Crusade*. London, Hutchinson, 1967.
*The White Witch of the South Seas*. London, Hutchinson, 1968.
*Evil in a Mask*. London, Hutchinson, 1969.
*Gateway to Hell*. London, Hutchinson, 1970; New York, Ballantine, 1973.
*The Ravishing of Lady Mary Ware*. London, Hutchinson, 1971.
*The Strange Story of Linda Lee*. London, Hutchinson, 1972.
*The Irish Witch*. London, Hutchinson, 1973.
*Desperate Measures*. London, Hutchinson, 1974.

#### Short Stories

*Mediterranean Nights*. London, Hutchinson, 1942; revised edition, London, Arrow, 1963.
*Gunmen, Gallants, and Ghosts*. London, Hutchinson, 1943; revised edition, London, Arrow, 1963.

#### Play

Screenplay: *An Englishman's Home* (*Madmen of Europe*), with others, 1939.

#### Other

*Old Rowley: A Private Life of Charles II*. London, Hutchinson, 1933; as *A Private Life of Charles II*, 1938.
*Red Eagle: A Life of Marshal Voroshilov*. London, Hutchinson, 1937.
*Invasion* (war game). London, Hutchinson, 1938.
*Blockade* (war game). London, Hutchinson, 1939.
*Total War*. London, Hutchinson, 1941.
*The Seven Ages of Justerini's*. London, Riddle Books, 1949; revised edition, as *1749–1965: The Eight Ages of Justerini's*, Aylesbury, Buckinghamshire, Dolphin, 1965.
*Alibi* (war game). London, Geographia, 1951.
*Stranger Than Fiction*. London, Hutchinson, 1959.
*Saturdays with Bricks and Other Days under Shell-Fire*. London, Hutchinson, 1961.
*The Devil and All His Works*. London, Hutchinson, and New York, American Heritage Press, 1971.

*The Time Has Come: The Memoirs of Dennis Wheatley.* London, Arrow, 1981.
*The Young Man Said 1897–1914.* London, Hutchinson, 1977.
*Officer and Temporary Gentleman 1914–1919.* London, Hutchinson, 1978.
*Drink and Ink 1919–1977,* edited by Anthony Lejeune. London, Hutchinson, 1979.
*The Deception Planners: My Secret War,* edited by Anthony Lejeune. London, Hutchinson, 1980.

Editor, *A Century of Horror Stories.* London, Hutchinson, 1935; Freeport, New York, Books for Libraries, 1971; selection as *Quiver of Horror* and *Shafts of Fear,* London, Arrow, 2 vols., 1965; as *Tales of Strange Doings* and *Tales of Strange Happenings,* Hutchinson, 2 vols., 1968.
Editor, *A Century of Spy Stories.* London, Hutchinson, 1938.
Editor, *Uncanny Tales.* London, Sphere, 2 vols., 1974.

*

Bibliography: *Fyra Decennier med Dennis Wheatley: En Biografi & Bibliografi* by Iwan Hedman and Jan Alexandersson, privately printed, 1963; revised edition, Strägnäs, Sweden, DAST, 1973.

* * *

In 1940, a critic for the *Times Literary Supplement* referred to Dennis Wheatley as the "Prince of Thriller Writers," and the phrase became an advertising slogan for his publishers for the next 30 years. Although he produced over 60 books in his lifetime, he was neither as prolific nor as imaginative as Edgar Wallace with whom he might be compared. Little of his work appeared in the United States. His contributions to the field of high adventure and espionage have not survived him, but his novels of the occult and of Black Magic still retain an appeal for many readers.

Wheatley's novels and short stories fall into at least six recognizable categories: the straight adventure stories, the stories of Black Magic, and four groups with continuing characters. The stories about Gregory Sallust, Julian Day, and the Duke de Richleau are set in contemporary times (although Wheatley tried to fill in the gaps in his characters' lives by writing stories of their youth), but the Roger Brook series takes place in the 18th and early 19th centuries. Wheatley had little difficulty moving his characters between realistic adventures and situations of fantasy, so that most of his heroes spend some of their time fighting the supernatural. Only a handful of his novels can be considered science fiction and those contain very traditional science-fiction themes. He did not set out to break any new ground.

A consistent theme is the discovery of a group of Satanists in contemporary Britain and the theory that the Nazis owed what success they enjoyed during World War II to their use of supernatural forces. *The Devil Rides Out* (a part of the Duke de Richleau series) is considered his best work; certainly it is his best supernatural novel. (Wheatley himself considered *The Second Seal,* a thriller set in World War II, to be his best novel.) In *The Devil Rides Out,* Wheatley created the formula he would repeat throughout most of his writing career and made the supernatural a plausible element in his fiction.

In too many of his other Black Magic novels, *Strange Conflict, They Used Dark Forces, Gateway to Hell,* and *The Haunting of Toby Jugg,* for example, he made the mistake of describing the dark powers in such detail that his characters never seem to be in real jeopardy, and the reader is never really frightened. He never learned that actual malevolence is never as convincing as the suggestion that the supernatural might be possible. For all their bluster, Wheatley's diabolists too often are merely gangsters in fancy dress. By contrast, the ghost hunter stories collected in *Gunmen, Gallants, and Ghosts* more successfully evoke true shudders.

Wheatley's more traditional science-fiction novels rely on lost-race themes or Wellsian views of the future of Britain. The future in Wheatley's fiction is not one filled with optimism. *Black August* deals with a Communist revolution in Britain, *Sixty Days to Live* is another story of the possibility of the world being destroyed by a comet, while the menace of flying saucers is the focus of *Star of Ill-Omen.* In fact, there is more menace than science in a Wheatley science-fiction novel.

It was part of Wheatley's plan that each novel he wrote should give the reader his money's worth. Thus, his 300- to 400-page books include not only such incidents as might be found in Alexandre Dumas (Wheatley's primary literary inspiration) but his own political and social philosophy. By his own hand, he is revealed as a monarchist, a racist, and a chauvinist, but during his lifetime, his readers either shared his views or skipped those sections. Largely because of the sentiments they contain, the majority of his novels now seem dated.

The best of his work contains vividly portrayed heroes, magnificently grotesque villains, and stories of intrigue, logically plotted and paced to keep the reader turning the pages to learn what will happen next. The best of his Black Magic novels deserve their continuing readership and even those that are seldom read today may someday serve as primary sources in a study of popular taste during the middle of the 20th century.

—J. Randolph Cox

---

**WHITE, James.** British. Born in Belfast, Northern Ireland, 7 April 1928. Educated at St. John's Primary School, 1935–41, and St. Joseph's Secondary Technical School, 1942–43, both Belfast. Married Margaret Sarah Martin in 1955; one daughter and two sons. Salesman and manager in several tailoring stores, Belfast, 1943–65. Technical clerk, 1965–66, publicity assistant, 1966–68, and publicity officer, 1968–84, Shorts Aircraft, Belfast. Patron, Irish Science Fiction Association, 1974; council member, British Science Fiction Association, 1975. Recipient: Europa award, 1972. Agent: Pamela Buckmaster, Carnell Literary Agency, Danescroft, Goose Lane, Little Hallingbury, Bishop's Stortford, Hertfordshire CM22 7RG, England. Address: 2 West Drive, Portstewart BT55 7ND, Northern Ireland.

SCIENCE-FICTION PUBLICATIONS

Novels (series: Sector General)

*The Secret Visitors.* New York, Ace, 1957; London, Digit, 1961.
*Second Ending.* New York, Ace, 1962.
*Star Surgeon* (Sector). New York, Ballantine, 1963; London, Corgi, 1967.
*Escape Orbit.* New York, Ace, 1965; as *Open Prison,* London, New English Library, 1965.
*The Watch Below.* New York, Ballantine, and London, Whiting and Wheaton, 1966.
*All Judgment Fled.* London, Rapp and Whiting, 1968; New York, Walker, 1969.

*Tomorrow Is Too Far*. New York, Ballantine, and London, Joseph, 1971.
*Dark Inferno*. London, Joseph, 1972; as *Lifeboat*, New York, Ballantine, 1972.
*The Dream Millennium*. London, Joseph, and New York, Ballantine, 1974.
*Underkill*. London, Corgi, 1979.
*Ambulance Ship* (Sector). New York, Ballantine, 1979; London, Corgi, 1980.
*Star Healer* (Sector). New York, Ballantine, 1985; London, Futura, 1987.
*Code Blue—Emergency* (Sector). New York, Ballantine, 1987; London, Severn House, 1990.
*Federation World*. New York, Ballantine, 1988; London, Futura, 1990.

Short Stories (series: Sector General)

*Hospital Station* (Sector). New York, Ballantine, 1962; London, Corgi, 1967.
*Deadly Litter*. New York, Ballantine, 1964; London, Corgi, 1968.
*The Aliens Among Us*. New York, Ballantine, 1969; London, Corgi, 1970.
*Major Operation* (Sector). New York, Ballantine, 1971.
*Monsters and Medics*. London, Corgi, and New York, Ballantine, 1977.
*Future Past*. New York, Ballantine, 1982.
*Sector General*. New York, Ballantine, 1983.

*

James White comments:

I have always felt that the best stories are those in which ordinary people are faced with extraordinary situations, and my early attraction to science fiction, both as a very young reader and later as a writer, was that it was the only genre which allowed ordinary people to be faced with truly extraordinary situations. My favourite of these is the one in which Earth-human characters make first contact with an extraterrestrial species. The attempts to understand the behaviour and thought processes of the aliens frequently illuminate the human condition as well, and the problem of learning to understand and adapt to a totally alien viewpoint places in proper perspective the very minor differences of skin pigmentation and politics which bedevil our own culture.

* * *

One of the most memorable of James White's many intriguing settings is to be found in *The Watch Below*: a colony survives for several generations trapped inside the hull of a tanker torpedoed during World War II. In their effort to keep themselves sane, one of the things the first generation does is to attempt to recall every story any of them has ever read. One survivor has read a few works in the relatively new genre of science fiction. He particularly remembers a Doc Smith novel with a character "who was a winged dragon with scales, claws, four extensible eyes, and a lot of other visually horrifying features and who was more human than some of the human characters." Now, since *The Watch Below* is a "first contact" story, there are reasons of plot for this introduction of this tribute to the idea of interspecific brotherhood. But beyond this, the tradition of the fraternity of all intelligent life which first took firm hold in magazine SF in the mid-1930's is one which has had a marked impact on White himself as an author.

Most of White's stories involve extraterrestrials, and these beings are a varied lot indeed, including creatures indistinguishable from terrestrials in *The Secret Visitors*, aquatic life-forms in *The Watch Below*, chlorine-breathers in *Open Prison*, and giant caterpillar-like tree-dwellers in *All Judgment Fled*. All these varieties together, and others besides, can be found at once in *Hospital Station* and the other books in White's series about Sector Twelve General Hospital, a multi-environmental hospital in deep space with staff and patients from a diverse galactic culture. Indeed, as an author White is quite fond of the field of medicine, perhaps seeing in it a paradigm of the cooperation and fellowship which should embrace all intelligent beings. Even outside the Sector General series, physicians are important characters in *The Secret Visitors, The Watch Below, All Judgment Fled*, and *Underkill*.

But soldiers figure almost as prominently as doctors in White's work. One section of *Hospital Station* is given over to the hero's realization that the Monitor Corps performs a necessary police function. White is not happy about this fact of life. Indeed, in at least three different books characters are relieved to have it turn out that the life-forms they were forced to kill are only animals, and not intelligent beings after all. And beyond such justified violence, White's work also depicts some conflicts based on honest misunderstanding, and others stemming from deliberate selfishness and greed. But with one exception, the accent in White's work is not on the existence of such abominations but on the possibility of doing something about them. White's stories almost always close with harmony restored, or at least with such a restoration anticipated. This stubborn optimism has been one of White's trademarks.

A second trademark, already alluded to, is his inventiveness regarding environments. If his most brilliant achievement in this area is the sunken tanker in *The Watch Below*, other instances are almost equally imaginative—the prison planet of *Open Prison*, the alien starship overrun with laboratory animals in *All Judgment Fled*, the energy-poor world of the "powerdown" in *Underkill*, and others.

White's work does have its defects. His human characters are too much alike, and sometimes their actions are inadequately motivated. Often White's extra-terrestrials have incongruously human—indeed, Western—psychologies, whatever their external forms. White's fascinating environments are also sometimes a little too visibly contrived. Until fairly recently, the single most serious accusation that could be brought against White was his utopianism, his seeming belief that no group of intelligent beings could willfully persist in wrongdoing once they had had the right path pointed out to them. White, however, effectively countered any such accusation with *Underkill*, a novel presumably growing out of White's experience of the civil unrest in his home of Northern Ireland. In this novel, extra-terrestrials—playing as it were the part of an Old-Testament Yahweh—find mankind so depraved (particularly by the ethnic and sectarian hatreds that lead to terrorism) that they see no solution but to destroy all the earth's population save for a chosen remnant of ten million, and to start over with those. Unlike other White books, *Underkill* is charged with a bitterness and forcefulness reminiscent of Jonathan Swift. However, after this aberration, White's next several books went back with no obvious difficulty to the seeming utopianism of the Sector General series. This return to a familiar path could have been based on commercial considerations, since *Underkill* failed to find an American publisher. (Presumably its bitterness was judged to be unviable in an American market that was beginning to emerge from the gloom of much Vietnam-era SF.) In any case, *Underkill* makes it clear that in his other books, White is presenting a view of human relations as they ought to be, not as he actually takes them to be. White is not naive—merely hopeful.

—Patrick L. McGuire

---

**WHITE, Ted** (Theodore Edward White). Also writes as Ron Archer; Norman Edwards. American. Born in Washington, D.C., 4 February 1938. Educated in public schools in Falls Church, Virginia. Married 1) Sylvia Dees in 1958; 2) Robin Postal in 1966; one child. Head of foreign department, Scott Meredith Literary Agency, 1963; assistant editor, 1963–67, and associate editor, 1967–68, *Fantasy and Science Fiction;* associate editor, Lancer Books, 1966; managing editor, 1969, and editor, 1970–78, *Amazing* and *Fantastic;* co-editor, *Void* fan magazine, 1959–68; editor, *Heavy Metal*, New York, 1979–81. Recipient: Hugo award, for criticism, 1968. Agent: Henry Morrison Inc., 320 McLain Street, Bedford Hills, New York 10705, U.S.A.

SCIENCE-FICTION PUBLICATIONS

Novels

*Invasion from 2500* (as Norman Edwards, with Terry Carr). Derby, Connecticut, Monarch, 1964.
*Android Avenger*. New York, Ace, 1965.
*Phoenix Prime*. New York, Lancer, 1966.
*The Sorceress of Qar*. New York, Lancer, 1966.
*The Jewels of Elsewhen*. New York, Belmont, 1967.
*Lost in Space* (novelization of TV play; as Ron Archer, with Dave Van Arnam). New York, Pyramid, 1967.
*Secret of the Marauder Satellite*. Philadelphia, Westminster Press, 1967.
*Sideslip*, with Dave Van Arnam. New York, Pyramid, 1968.
*Captain America: The Great Gold Steal*. New York, Bantam, 1968.
*The Spawn of the Death Machine*. New York, Paperback Library, 1968.
*No Time Like Tomorrow* (for children). New York, Crown, 1969.
*By Furies Possessed*. New York, New American Library, 1970.
*Star Wolf!* New York, Lancer, 1971.
*Trouble on Project Ceres* (for children). Philadelphia, Westminster Press, 1971.
*Forbidden World*, with David F. Bischoff. New York, Popular Library, 1978.

OTHER PUBLICATIONS

Other

Editor, *The Best from Amazing Stories*. New York, Manor, 1973; London, Hale, 1976.
Editor, *The Best from Fantastic*. New York, Manor, 1973; London, Hale, 1976.

* * *

Ted White, like many writers of his generation, first achieved prominence as a fan. He was responsible for what was recognised as the first fanzine devoted exclusively to comics in 1953; his fanzine *Void* helped advance both his own career and that of Gregory Benford.

White's career as a novelist was relatively short. His novels tend to be all of a type, in that they usually deal with supermen with neuroses. Thus, *The Spawn of the Death Machine*, a novel much better than its title suggests, concerns an android in a post-apocalyptic future who wanders about determining the limits of his powers. In *Phoenix Prime*, the cab-driver Maximillan Quest learns that he is an incomplete superman and is rushed to another dimension to fight a cosmic war. White's novels are essentially imitative, at times reminding one of Heinlein, at other times of Van Vogt; while his work is competent, he has not achieved any writing of the first rank, save for certain sections of the fascinating failure, *The Jewels of Elsewhen*, White's favorite among his own works.

White's distinction is as an editor, more than as a writer. White was editor of *Amazing Stories* and *Fantastic Science Fiction* for some ten years; he returned the magazines to a policy of publishing original fiction, and developed some of the talented young writers of the 1970's.

—Martin Morse Wooster

---

**WHITEFORD, Wynne (Noel).** Australian. Born in East Melbourne, Australia, 23 December 1915. Educated at Royal Melbourne Institute of Technology, 1939–41; Melbourne University, 1948–50. Married Laurel Miriam Fairey in 1949 (died 1978). Proprietor, Wynray Studios, Prahran, Victoria, 1933–35; aircraft assembler, Commonwealth Aircraft Corporation, Fisherman's Bend, Victoria, 1939–43. Reporter, *Australian Motor Sports*, then technical editor, *Australian Motor Manual*, Melbourne, 1953–57. Lived in New York and London, 1957–60. Editor of newsletter and organizer of trade displays, Soil Conservation Authority of Victoria, 1961–65. President, Eastern Writers Group, 1962–85, 1991. Editor, *Zest* anthologies, Melbourne, 1989 and 1990. Recipient: Epicurean and Cultural Society Short Story award, 1987; Ditmar award, 1990. Agent: Cherry Weiner, 28 Kipling Way, Manalapan, New Jersey 07726, U.S.A. Address: "Illalangi", 3 Stringybark Road, Eltham, Victoria 3095, Australia.

SCIENCE-FICTION PUBLICATIONS

Novels

*Breathing Space Only*. St. Kilda, Victoria, Void Publications, 1980; New York, Berkley, 1986.
*Sapphire Road*. St. Kilda, Victoria, Cory and Collins, 1982; New York, Berkley, 1986.
*Thor's Hammer*. St. Kilda, Victoria, Cory and Collins, 1983; New York, Berkley, 1985.
*The Hyades Contact*. New York, Berkley, 1987.
*Lake of the Sun*. New York, Berkley, 1989.
*The Specialist*. New York, Berkley, 1990.

*

Wynne Whiteford comments:

My work has been mostly of the type described as "hard" science fiction. It is generally set in near-future environments extrapolated from present-day trends.

Until a few years ago, I had written fiction only in my spare time. I had my first three novels published in Australia in 1980, 1982, and 1983. I then took extended leave from Leader Newspapers, for whom I was working at the time, and took copies of these novels to New York publishers. Berkley accepted the three and asked for more. Returning to Australia, I came to an arrangement with Leader Newspapers to work three days a week (later two) at their busiest times of the week, leaving myself more time for writing. After selling another novel in the U.S.A., I switched to full-time writing of fiction. Early experience in engineering plants has given me, I think, a solid basis for realistic mechanical descriptions. My wife Laurel, to whom I was married for 27 years, was a psychologist, and this gave me an interest in studying people, their motives, reactions, characteristics, etc., which has been very helpful. I now share a house with historical novelist Gwayne Naug in bushland. It has taken me a long time to work out a smooth technique in writing fiction. If I write fast, the story flows out naturally, but I forget to make some points along the way. If I write slowly and carefully, the narrative seems to creak with changes of mood and tempo. Now, I build a story slowly, by notes in files, then write one draft, *fast*, straight through from beginning to end, directly onto the machine. For the final draft, I use two IBM Selectrics, on desks reachable from a single swivel chair, one to try out doubtful sentences before committing them to the "clean" draft—saves a lot of retyping.

* * *

Wynne Whiteford's emergence in the 1980's as Australia's most reliable producer of SF thrillers, of old-fashioned "good reads," marks the third and most productive phase of a writing career that, in hindsight, goes back surprisingly far, to the brief flirtation during the 1930's and the frequent publication of short stories in the 1950's. The major phase was sparked off by the excitement of the WorldCon in Melbourne.

The first of Whiteford's novels, *Breathing Space Only*, was greeted with some enthusiasm. It employs an identifiable local scene, the Kosciusko region, and is set not unbelievably two or three hundred years hence as a last outpost of civilization above the smog of the plains below, in which are burning opencast coal fields. If one goes to this high country in summer one may easily get the feeling of being happily placed above the dull heat of the less fortunate Australians below; in Whiteford's future time, those unfortunates are known as Perms (Permissives), ridden by disease and divided into warring tribes. The upland scientific community is somewhat paranoid, and when an attempt is made to contact them by a returning starship's satellite they observe radio silence. A small group risks establishing contact and, after executing a dangerous mission into Perm territory, three of them have the opportunity of leaving Earth and attaining immortality. In this novel, the idea of humans modified into huge four-armed creatures (tetrabrachs) is first proposed; it is used again in Whiteford's later novels.

*Sapphire Road* is set further in the future than *Breathing Space Only*, although it could be part of the same history. Action is divided between Earth and Alcenar, one of the colonized planets of Alpha Centaurus. On Earth, following some dim catastrophe, power has devolved to the southern hemisphere. The watchword is "Stability" and progress is slow. The hero, industrialist Max Vanmore, has to cope with the murder of his family in central Australia before embarking in quest of sapphires on the distant planet. He races in his Indian friend Rajendra Naryan's ship in competition with his clandestine enemy, Captain Kranzen of the National Stability Council, who commands a military vessel. The plot is in outline not unlike one of Bob Shaw's thrillers, although the exposition is managed somewhat clumsily. To compensate, there is a memorable character, Bianca Baru, one of several notable humans in Whiteford's work whose physical modification causes mingled attraction and repulsion to the Earth-normal types. A giant from the high-gravity planet Chiron, Bianca accompanies Vanmore and Naryan to Alcenar.

*Thor's Hammer* gives the hero, Kingston Hannam, two unusual female companions in the tradition of Bianca. Hannam has been given a mission to find a fellow-employee, Slade Anton, who has disappeared after making a threat. Anton suggested that he might hurl an asteroid at the earth, since he believes that the future lies exclusively with the colony planets. Anton's former girl friend, Gail Busentil, has a "domehead" appearance: she is a superwoman with computer-enhanced brainpower and surgically increased height and breasts; the other woman helper, Yetta, is a dwarf. The denizens of Ceres are over-sized and another leading character, Yetta's partner in prospecting, Des Marston, has had his legs amputated in an accident. One begins to get the impression that the author thinks the future will be a paradise for freaks. Certainly, with such talents as his helpers command, Hannam has to exhibit little intelligence to perform his mission.

In *The Hyades Contact* we have a long-delayed completion to a story of first contact with a superior cat-like species which began in three chapters presented first as short stories in *Void* collections of 1978 and 1979. These chapters register effectively the shock of encountering fast-moving, highly-intelligent carnivores who have superior technology, the Kesrii. After failing to outmanoeuvre them in space, the humans are settled on a colony planet, which they call Terranova. The colonists divide between those who wish to go back to the home planets and those who wish to settle. The principal hero, Connor, is one of the latter; he marries a doctor, Zella, and their baby is rendered super-intelligent, thanks to the child-birth help of a female Kesrii. Much of the interest of the story lies in the growth of the colony as relatively primitive energy sources are developed to ensure its continued viability. When a second colony is discovered, of greyish eight-armed "droms," also dumped on the planet by the Kesrii, the encounter proves disastrous: they murder one of the humans but are in turn destroyed (*War of the Worlds* style) by his micro-organisms. The humans come to accept that they are a second-rate species, but unlike the droms they at least have a future. Whitefordian freaks in this novel include Nordstrom, over 200 years old, who has a cybernetic body; Sven, a squat giantess from a heavy planet; and Dr. Voll, who has been adapted to life on a space station and needs an exoskeleton to survive in Earth gravity: basically he is a brain with a very small body.

Whiteford's two most recent novels are both set mainly on Mars, but they do not share quite the same history. *Lake of the Sun* is a relatively simple but satisfying story of first contact: the main complication is that, when Earthmen meet Martians, they find there are two Martian races. The *ashti* are cyclopian, having one large eye; the *vora* have two eyes, larger than the Terran ones, although they share a remote Terran ancestry. (The Terrans themselves have already begun to adapt their bodies to their altered circumstances.) Ancient and modern humans meet after the subterranean denizens of Mars hear the explosions of colonists testing for minerals near the surface. Whiteford develops his thriller plot in a natural and convincing fashion: the conclusion is guardedly optimistic and sounds a warning heard also in Robert L. Forward's cheela books, that an encounter with a race that has developed superior technology might take away "our" future. *The Specialist*, set later in the colonists' future on Mars (it begins in 2095), ignores the idea of surviving Martian races and substitutes that of genetically engineered superhuman races. Whiteford's hero does not seem to look back to Robert Sheckley's famous "Specialist": the alienated humanoids in the book, giant Siamese twins and tetrabrachs and clones, leave

Lance Garrith behind when they go space-voyaging. Lance, a generalist when considered as a top Earth newscaster, is allowed to survive as a specialist for his reporting skills after he has inconveniently penetrated the secret society of new people that has been able to develop on the margins of the apparently closed bubble-city life of Mars but would have found Earth inimical to them long before their plans could have matured. This novel is a splendid showcase for the author's own specialty: presenting close encounters with giants, grotesques, and aliens (especially women).

—Michael J. Tolley

---

**WILDER, Cherry.** Pseudonym for Cherry Barbara Grimm, née Lockett. New Zealander. Born in Auckland, 3 September 1930. Educated at Canterbury University College, Christchurch, B.A. 1952. Married 1) A.J. Anderson in 1952; 2) H.K.F. Grimm in 1963, two daughters. Lived in Australia, 1954–76: high school teacher, editorial assistant, theatre director; regular reviewer from Sydney *Morning Herald* and *The Australian*, 1964–74. Recipient: Australia Council grant, 1973, 1975. Address: 19 Egelsbacher Strasse, 6070 Langen/Hessen, Germany.

Science-Fiction Publications

Novels (series: Torin)

*The Luck of Brin's Five* (for children; Torin). New York, Atheneum, 1977; London, Angus and Robertson, 1979.
*The Nearest Fire* (for children; Torin). New York, Atheneum, 1980.
*Second Nature.* New York, Pocket Books, 1982; London, Allen and Unwin, 1986.
*The Tapestry Warriors* (for children; Torin). New York, Atheneum, 1983.

Other Publications

Novels (series: Hylor)

Hylor series:
*A Princess of the Chameln.* New York, Atheneum, 1984; London, Unwin, 1985.
*Yorath the Wolf.* New York, Atheneum, 1984; London, Unwin, 1986.
*The Summer's King.* New York, Atheneum, 1985; London, Unwin, 1987.
*Cruel Designs.* London, Piatkus, 1988.

*

Manuscript Collection: de Grummond Collection, University of Southern Mississippi, Hattiesburg.

* * *

Cherry Wilder's first novel, *The Luck of Brin's Five*, describes the first encounter on the planet Torin with a visitor from Earth. The narrator was 12 years "shown" when this happened; he is a marsupial humanoid, who reckons his age not from birth but from the date of leaving the maternal pouch. Readers will readily associate marsupials (such as koalas and kangaroos) with Australia. But the marsupial civilization of Torin is not the only unconventionality that can be traced to Wilder's origins "down under," a description informally applied to New Zealand and Australia in relation to Britain and the United States.

Anglo-Celts first settled "down under" little more than 200 years ago, and even today, derive their culture chiefly from the northern hemisphere. Thus, they are paradoxically aware of their own surroundings as familiar and natural, and yet at the same time exotic and "wrong" (with Christmas in summer and Easter in autumn). This sense both of wrongness and of being very distant in space from one's cultural origins is the imaginative core of *Second Nature*, Wilder's novel about the somewhat mutated descendants of some Earth people whose spaceship crashlanded on the planet Rhomary 265 years earlier. The pioneer and frontier legends of the United States are well known, and unconsciously influence a lot of science fiction. Instead, in *Second Nature*, the characteristic myths of Australian history have inspired the plot, which is essentially about the lost becoming found. A second spaceship from Earth has gone astray and broken apart above Rhomary; the survivors, in their emergency capsules, are unaware of the marooned human settlers already on Rhomary, with their fruitless longing for Earth ships to arrive. A gigantic marine species, "the Vail," is one of three non-human intelligent life-forms so far encountered on Rhomary, and the Vail, too, has become lost—mourned as extinct, in consequence of a ten-year drought. Rhomary's deserts and droughts, the waiting for ships from "Home," the wanderers lost in the bush, and even the inland sea (which Australian explorers believed in but never found) correspond closely to Anglo-Celtic Australian legends.

On Rhomary, as on Torin, the local customs and extraordinary surroundings are richly present, yet illuminated as if in passing, without delaying the plot and the interweaving subplots. Local fauna on Rhomary include "parmels," which are like camels, but six-legged and with extendible flaps on either side. This kind of detail, and Wilder's skilfully ample-seeming prose, cause her readers to feel welcome and cared-for, nerving them, in all her novels, to assimilate a wealth of strangeness and a sometimes daunting number of characters and relationships.

*Second Nature* describes only two physical skirmishes and its only villain is prejudice, resulting from religious bigotry. By contrast, Wilder's completed trilogies about Torin and Hylor, which are marketed as "juveniles," have conflicts and a villain in every volume. *A Princess of the Chameln* is the first novel about the "Rulers of Hylor." Invaders from Mel'Nir threaten the ruling houses of the Chameln lands, and the princess Aidris flees into exile and works incognita in the stables of neighbouring Athron as a "kedran," or female soldier. Battles against the armies of Mel'Nir are seen from Aidris's viewpoint. But the sequel, *Yorath the Wolf*, is told by a Mel'Nir prince, also in exile, and thought to have been killed at birth. The third novel, *The Summer's King*, tells of King Sharn, who is Aidris's co-ruler.

Behind Hylor's troubles lurks a villainous magician—for this is a fantasy world, where magical trees recognize virgins and where the fairy or "Light" people are genuinely terrifying. But in the Torin trilogy, too, where people have only psychic powers, the opponent of Torin's villains is popularly known as Magician and Great Diviner, as well as Maker of Engines. In contrast to conventional tales, like that of Merlin versus Morgan Le Fay, Hylor's villain (Rosmer) and the villains of Torin (the Great Elder and the Juran) are male; the good magicians (Guenna in Hylor, Nantgeeb in Torin) are female. Moreover, both Torin and Hylor follow an undemanding religion centred on a Great Mother or Goddess, and one of Rosmer's villainies is to invent a religion with a male god, which vilifies women as "half-made."

Wilder's approach always suggests that more remains to be told. The Torin trilogy begins, in *The Luck of Brin's Five*, with the viewpoint of a bush weaver, Dorn Brinroyan, who describes the traditional five-member family in Torin's marsupial humanoid civilization: three adults of mating age, one elderly person ("the ancient") and one person with an abnormality ("the luck"). But in the second novel, *The Nearest Fire*, the narrator, Yolo Harn, is a miner who reveals that town dwellers consider pair-marriages normal, and, moreover, have no fear of "fire-metal-magic" and no knowledge of other traditions that Dorn considered universal. Yolo is an "omor," the sturdiest and most muscular class of the species—females with special training and diet, who are medically rendered sterile. A third and equally youthful viewpoint is given in *The Tapestry Warriors*, where Rovan Wentroy, a "grandee," or member of the ruling class, reveals that the children of grandees are alienated from their elders in a way unknown among weavers and "townees."

Torin's strong females are matched by the "kedrans" and "sword lilies" of Hylor and by the brawny sailor lasses on Rhomary, while male brutality is markedly absent. This is made up for, however, in Wilder's horror novel, *Cruel Designs*, set in 20th-century Germany, where a house of evil influence and *jugendstil* design brings out the worst in the abusive father of a family who rents it. Indeed, Wilder's chillingly effective recent horror stories, such as "Anzac Day," "The House on Cemetery Street," and "The Gingerbread House," may well empower critical attention for her earlier work, where the combination of such original matter with so mild a manner seems often to have struck commentators dumb—groping in vain for a recognized context.

—Yvonne Rousseau

---

**WILDING, Eric.** *See* **TUBB, E.C.**

---

**WILEY, John.** *See* **PHILLIPS, Rog.**

---

**WILHELM, Kate (Gertrude, née Meredith).** American. Born in Toledo, Ohio, 8 June 1928. Married 1) Joseph B. Wilhelm in 1947 (divorced 1962), two sons; 2) Damon Knight, *q.v.*, in 1963, one son. Co-Director, Milford Science Fiction Writers Conference, 1963–72; Lecturer, Clarion Science Fiction Writers Conference, since 1968, and Tulane University, New Orleans, 1971. Recipient: Nebula award, 1968, 1986, 1987; Hugo award, 1977; Jupiter award, 1977; *Locus* award, 1977. Agent: Brandt and Brandt, 1501 Broadway, New York, New York 10036. Address: 1645 Horn Lane, Eugene, Oregon 97404, U.S.A.

SCIENCE-FICTION PUBLICATIONS

Novels

*The Clone*, with Ted Thomas. New York, Berkley, 1965; London, Hale, 1968.
*The Nevermore Affair*. New York, Doubleday, 1966.
*The Killer Thing*. New York, Doubleday, 1967; as *The Killing Thing*, London, Jenkins, 1967.
*Let the Fire Fall*. New York, Doubleday, 1969; London, Panther, 1972.
*Year of the Cloud*, with Ted Thomas. New York, Doubleday, 1970.
*Abyss*. New York, Doubleday, 1971.
*Margaret and I*. Boston, Little Brown, 1971.
*The Clewiston Test*. New York, Farrar Straus, 1976; London, Hutchinson, 1977.
*Where Late the Sweet Birds Sang*. New York, Harper, 1976; London, Arrow, 1977.
*Juniper Time*. New York, Harper, 1979; London, Hutchinson, 1980.
*A Sense of Shadow*. Boston, Houghton Mifflin, 1981.
*Oh, Susannah!* Boston, Houghton Mifflin, 1982.
*Welcome, Chaos*. Boston, Houghton Mifflin, 1983; London, Gollancz, 1986.
*Huysman's Pets*. New York, Bluejay, and London, Gollancz, 1986.
*Crazy Time*. New York, St. Martin's Press, 1988.
*The Dark Door*. New York, St. Martin's Press, 1988; London, Gollancz, 1990.
*Cambio Bay*. New York, St. Martin's Press, 1990; London, Hale, 1991.
*Sweet, Sweet Poison*. New York, St. Martin's Press, 1990; London, Hale, 1991.

Short Stories

*The Mile-Long Spaceship*. New York, Berkley, 1963; as *Andover and the Android*, London, Dobson, 1966.
*The Downstairs Room*. New York, Doubleday, 1968.
*The Infinity Box*. New York, Harper, 1975; London, Arrow, 1979.
*Somerset Dreams and Other Fictions*. New York, Harper, 1978; London, Hutchinson, 1979.
*Listen, Listen*. Boston, Houghton Mifflin, 1981.
*Children of the Wind*. New York, St. Martin's Press, 1989.

OTHER PUBLICATIONS

Novels

*More Bitter Than Death*. New York, Simon and Schuster, 1963; London, Hale, 1965.
*City of Cain*. Boston, Little Brown, 1974; London, Gollancz, 1975.
*Fault Lines*. New York, Harper, 1977; London, Hutchinson, 1978.
*The Hamlet Trap*. New York, St. Martin's Press, 1987; London, Gollancz, 1988.
*Smart House: A Charlie and Constance Mystery*. New York, St. Martin's Press, and London, Gollancz, 1989.
*Death Qualifier: A Mystery of Chaos*. New York, St. Martin's Press, 1991.

Other

*Better Than One*, with Damon Knight. Cambridge, Massachusetts, NESFA Press, 1980.

Editor, *Nebula Award Stories 9*. London, Gollancz, 1974; New York, Harper, 1975.

Editor, *Clarion SF.* New York, Berkley, 1977.

*

Manuscript Collection: Syracuse University, New York.

* * *

Kate Wilhelm has said that about half of her published work is science fiction, though much of the rest contains elements of fantasy. Her first novel was a mystery; later works such as *Margaret and I* and *Fault Lines* are novels of contemporary life, though *Margaret and I* makes use of a speculative element by portraying the protagonist's subconscious as a separate character. Wilhelm is primarily a writer who skillfully uses genre elements—suspenseful plots, scientific or technological notions, and slick prose—to produce fiction as satisfying and as well-rounded as any being written today.

Wilhelm's technique, in most of her work, is to introduce a character or set of characters in a commonplace setting, then to reveal the unusual or uncommon elements of the story through the thoughts and actions of the people in it. Her characters are some of the most fully realized people to be found in science fiction. Her style is the smooth, almost slick manner of so much women's magazine fiction, complete with the details of domestic and everyday life; this manner of telling her stories makes the contrast and tension between the usual and the unusual even more striking. This technique can be seen in Wilhelm's first novel, *More Bitter Than Death.* A young couple, Eve and Grant, return to Grant's home, where the body of Grant's murdered mother has been found. Eve must come to terms with her husband, who is one of those suspected of the murder, and Grant must deal with long-suppressed feelings about his home and family. The problems raised here are resolved by the book's conclusion, though in her later work Wilhelm's characters find answers more difficult to come by, life more complex, and reconciliations more problematic. The problem Eve and Grant face, that of having to understand the past and to reconcile it with their future hopes in the midst of unusual events, is present in Wilhelm's later work, and is especially prominent in her science fiction. These same problems are depicted movingly in the novella "Somerset Dreams," ostensibly a story about dream research in a dying town.

In two early science-fiction novels, Wilhelm writes about standard science-fiction themes. In *The Killer Thing*, a computerized robot which is trying to kill all life must be destroyed; in *Let the Fire Fall*, an alien landing on Earth and the rise of a new religion are shown. *The Killer Thing* shows Wilhelm's mastery of the technique of suspense. Though it is set in the familiar future of colonized planets so common in SF, the book shows the author's concern with the moral issues raised by space travel and human greed. *Let the Fire Fall* begins in the familiar, almost cozy, environs of a small American city. This novel is written in an uncharacteristically breezy style; the author's strong opinions about organized religion and cults are not concealed, and the new religion is much like some rather disturbing present-day cults. These books, and early pieces such as "The Mile-Long Spaceship" and "Stranger in the House," are better than average stories, but it is in later works that Wilhelm shows her real strengths.

Wilhelm, unlike many writers, is a master of both the novel and shorter forms of fiction. Her short story "Baby, You Were Great" shows a world where it is possible, through brain-implanted electrodes, to live a celebrity's life vicariously and to feel all her emotions as well. Her Nebula award-winning "The Planners" concerns biological research, and "The Funeral" depicts a rigid future society. But these stories are not simply intellectual adventures comfortably removed from us in time. "The Planners" shows a scientist who does not fully comprehend the moral and ethical implications of his research, "The Funeral" reveals the crippling constraints in which adults often place children, and "Baby, You Were Great" takes place in a world uncomfortably like our own. Her recent stories "Forever Yours, Anna" and "The Girl Who Fell into the Sky," which share this sense of familiarity and strangeness, were both honored with the Nebula award.

Wilhelm's work gains much of its strength by showing us life as it is lived, as so many works of science fiction do not. Her stories are easily accessible, but they are not escapist entertainments which one can read and then put aside; the issues she raises are present in our lives. She is a concerned writer, but she does not moralize and she does not lapse into despair. Many of her works, notably *City of Cain*, a novel about a plot to build an underground city where experiments will be conducted on survivors of atomic and environmental disasters, show the dangers of excessive power thoughtlessly used. One especially strong novella, "The Infinity Box," shows the corrupting influence of power from the inside; the story is made more disturbing by the fact that the protagonist is a likeable, intelligent, and sympathetic man who is altered and changed simply by having the power to enter another person's mind. *Where Late the Sweet Birds Sang* (Hugo award) has been called the best treatment of cloning in science fiction by many critics. But the novel is also about the often destructive strategies human beings can employ in order to survive, and it shows the author's concern with the damage we have done to the earth, a common theme in her work.

Wilhelm's abilities are at their height in *The Clewiston Test* and *Juniper Time. The Clewiston Test* is both a feminist novel and a psychological thriller which presents issues in the context of a suspenseful story. The isolation of the protagonist, Anne Clewiston, who is recovering from a serious accident, is symbolic of the isolation felt by so many women; the scientific project in the novel is used as a plot device to illuminate the personal conflicts of the characters, as well as to present issues about human experimentation. *Juniper Time* tells the story of two people, Jean Brighton and Arthur Cluny, who are the children of astronauts. The two grow up in a drought-plagued world in which the dream of space exploration, the goal to which their fathers had devoted themselves, has died. The conflicts in the book reflect our own predicament; we must live with our technology, however uneasily, and cannot turn back, but we must conserve what is valuable of the past, and keep future hopes from being perverted to unworthy and short-sighted ends.

*Welcome, Chaos* also unites many of Wilhelm's concerns and techniques, and deals with the dilemmas that immortality might raise. In an earlier novella, "April Fool's Day Forever," the author also dealt with immortality; there, the price of endless life turned out to be the loss of the bond with the collective unconscious and all creative forces. In *Welcome, Chaos*, Wilhelm, in the context of a thriller, asks difficult questions: What if the serum that makes immortality possible kills half of those people who are exposed to it? Should such a serum be limited to only a few? How will its protection against the effects of radiation affect the nuclear balance of terror? It is to Wilhelm's credit that she attempts to give answers, however tentative, to these questions.

In her science fiction, Kate Wilhelm holds a mirror to our world, and in her work we can see the dilemmas present in our uneasy, late-20th-century lives.

—Pamela Sargent

**WILLIAMS, John A(lfred).** Also writes as J. Dennis Gregory. American. Born in Jackson, Mississippi, 5 December 1925. Educated at Central High School, Syracuse, New York; Syracuse University, A.B. 1950. Served in the United States Navy, 1943–46. Married 1) Carolyn Clopton in 1947 (divorced), two sons; 2) Lorrain Isaac in 1965, one son. Member of the public relations department, Doug Johnson Associates, Syracuse, 1952–54, and Arthur P. Jacobs Company; staff member, CBS, Hollywood and New York, 1954–55; publicity director, Comet Press Books, New York, 1955–56; publisher and editor, *Negro Market Newsletter*, New York, 1956–57; staff member, Abelard-Schuman, publishers, New York, 1957–58; director of information, American Committee on Africa, New York, 1958; European correspondent, *Ebony* and *Jet* magazines, 1958–59; announcer, WOV Radio, New York, 1959; Africa correspondent, *Newsweek*, New York, 1964–65. Regents Lecturer, University of California, Santa Barbara, 1972; Distinguished Professor of English, La-Guardia Community College, City University of New York, 1973–75; Visiting Professor, University of Hawaii, Summer 1974, and Boston University, 1978–79. Since 1979, Professor of English and journalism, Rutgers University, New Brunswick, New Jersey. Member of the Editorial Board, *Audience*, Boston, 1970–72; contributing editor, *American Journal*, New York, 1972. Recipient: American Academy grant, 1962; Syracuse University Outstanding Achievement award, 1970; National Endowment for the Arts grant, 1977; Before Columbus Foundation award, 1983. Litt.D.: Southeastern Massachusetts University, North Dartmouth, 1978. Address: 693 Forest Avenue, Teaneck, New Jersey 07666, U.S.A.

SCIENCE-FICTION PUBLICATIONS

Novels

*The Man Who Cried I Am.* Boston, Little Brown, 1967; London, Eyre and Spottiswoode, 1968.
*Sons of Darkness, Sons of Light: A Novel of Some Probability.* Boston, Little Brown, 1969; London, Eyre and Spottiswoode, 1970.
*Captain Blackman.* New York, Doubleday, 1972.

OTHER PUBLICATIONS

Novels

*The Angry Ones.* New York, Ace, 1960; as *One for New York*, Chatham, New Jersey, Chatham Bookseller, 1975.
*Night Song.* New York, Farrar Straus, 1961; London, Collins, 1962.
*Sissie.* New York, Farrar Straus, 1963; as *Journey Out of Anger*, London, Eyre and Spottiswoode, 1968.
*Mothersill and the Foxes.* New York, Doubleday, 1975.
*The Junior Bachelor Society.* New York, Doubleday, 1976.
*! Click Song.* Boston, Houghton Mifflin, 1982.
*The Berhama Account.* New York, New Horizon Press, 1985.
*Jacob's Ladder.* New York, Thunder's Mouth Press, 1987.

Other

*Africa: Her History, Lands, and People.* New York, Cooper Square, 1962.
*The Protectors* (on narcotics agents; as J. Dennis Gregory), with Harry J. Anslinger. New York, Farrar Straus, 1964.
*This Is My Country, Too.* New York, New American Library, 1964; London, New English Library, 1966.
*The Most Native of Sons: A Bibliography of Richard Wright.* New York, Doubleday, 1970.
*The King God Didn't Save: Reflections on the Life and Death of Martin Luther King, Jr.* New York, Coward McCann, 1970; London, Eyre and Spottiswoode, 1971.
*Flashbacks: A Twenty-Year Diary of Article Writing.* New York, Doubleday, 1973.
*Minorities in the City.* New York, Harper, 1975.
*If I Stop I'll Die: The Comedy and Tragedy of Richard Pryor.* New York, Thunder's Mouth Press, 1991.

Editor, *The Angry Black.* New York, Lancer, 1962.
Editor, *Beyond the Angry Black.* New York, Cooper Square, 1967.
Editor, with Charles F. Harris, *Amistad I* and *II.* New York, Knopf, 2 vols., 1970–71.
Editor, with Gilbert H. Muller, *Introduction to Literature.* New York, McGraw Hill, 1985.

*

Manuscript Collection: Syracuse University, New York; University of Rochester, New York.

Critical Study: *The Evolution of a Black Writer: John A. Williams* by Earl Cash, New York, Third Press, 1974.

* * *

Three of the nine novels by John A. Williams are revolutionary fiction, or "awful warning" stories. He writes at a high level of prestige in the mainstream of American fiction. His principal characters are African Americans. The three novels in question present a progress of plots and themes from warning story to virtually apocalyptic race revolution triumph. In every case, the science-fictionally extraordinary events of these works are actual and real, but Williams also always stops short of describing in much detail either their process or their completion. Perhaps he regards the events he predicts as obscene and believes they should not be described (for example, the "King Alfred" plan of *The Man Who Cried I Am*); or perhaps the stories are more effective as warnings when details are left to readers' imaginations. Because they are novels of character, they are especially effective in depicting the meaning of radical social and political changes on the lives of individuals.

The books present protagonists who are victims of a national racist conspiracy, ones who are *agents provocateur* in violent revolutionary acts, and protagonists who overthrow a racist Caucasian U.S. government. These novels are about a fictional revolutionary intervention in the history of racial discrimination against Africans in Europe and America. As such, they belong to a body of works that depict extraordinary events or racial revolutions in whole nations, especially the United States, that either preserve racist governments or change forever the political and economic structures of the Euro-American nations. Notable examples are Raymond Patterson's poem, "After the Thousand-Day Rebellion" (*Transatlantic Monthly*, Winter/Spring 1972), George Samuel Schuyler's *Black No More* (1931), William Melvin Kelley's *A Different Drummer* (1959), Ronald Fair's *Many Thousand Gone* (1965), and Sam Greenlee's *The Spook Who Sat by the Door* (1969).

*The Man Who Cried I Am* is the most celebrated of all of Williams's novels. Its hero is the rising African American writer Max Reddick, World War II veteran, who, in the pre-civil rights era, laboriously works his way up through jobs as a journalist to recognition as a great contemporary novelist, much like James

Baldwin or Ralph Ellison. Meanwhile, his several relationships with women are never completely happy ones—a microcosm of the situation of his race, his personal life is nearly hopelessly unsettled. Moreover, he has contracted a progressive rectal cancer, baldly symbolic of the metaphoric "ass-reaming" non-white peoples, especially Africans, have received historically from Europeans and Americans. The tragedy of Reddick's personal health is parallelled and ultimately overshadowed by the threat of genocide to the African American population when he learns of a scheme by the U.S. leaders that would put the Nazi extermination of six million Jews in the shade—to kill 22 million African Americans. The plan is called "King Alfred," and included as stage one is the legal process of detention of this massive population. Indeed, Williams's novel was a long way from being merely fictional. Title II, "Emergency Detention," of the McCarran "Internal Security Act of [September 23] 1950" (co-sponsored by Richard Nixon, among others) provided the enabling legislation for such mass incarceration, at the U.S. president's order. The Title II sections of the act were repealed on September 25, 1971, four years after the publication of *The Man Who Cried I Am.*

The second of Williams's three speculative novels of revolution, *sons of darkness, sons of light* [lower case letters deliberate], *A Novel of Some Probability*, he called a "pot-boiler." It is nevertheless a well-made novel about the character, Eugene Browning, possessor of a Ph.D. in political science, with a lovely wife and two children. He works in the New York-based Institute for Racial Justice. He is locally effective, but racial justice on a national scale is nowhere in prospect. Therefore, Browning hires a mafia hit of a white New York policeman who has escaped penalty for the flagrant murder, during an arrest process, of a sixteen-year-old black youth. Simultaneously, and not connected to Browning except as inspiration, a secret movement of African Americans, armed with weapons and explosives, seals off and takes over Manhattan. The novel ends as they present fair and equitable demands for minorities. The reader is sure they will not be met because they require immense social and economic change. The reader knows, therefore, that the take-over of New York will be re-enacted in all the major cities of the United States in a national race war.

*Captain Blackman* was dismissed by a few critics as minor Williams fiction because its nearly two-hundred-year-old principal character, Abraham Blackman, "doesn't develop." Williams, however, had a revolutionary political agenda in writing it. Employing the device of the fabulously long-lived protagonist, used by Henry James in *The Sense of the Past* (1916) and Virginia Woolf in *Orlando* (1929), to dramatize the connection of historical events to the present, Williams has "Blackman" enlisted as a soldier in all the American wars from the Revolutionary War to the Vietnam conflict. The culturally psychotic treatment of black soldiers in war after war repeats itself. Pathetically eager to die for America and its promises of equality in all the earlier wars, black soldiers by the 1970's have left patriotism behind in favor of a plan for revolution that uses "fish," blacks that can pass for Caucasian, located in key positions in the U.S. nuclear defense system. These people capture and nullify America's nuclear retaliation capability. The United States will be helpless if its enemies attack. The novel is satirical and angry. It predicts the certain end of white America's political and economic dominance of its African American population.

—John Pfeiffer

---

**WILLIAMS, Paul O(sborne).** American. Born in Chatham, New Jersey, 17 January 1935. Educated at Principia College, Elsah, Illinois, B.A. 1956; University of Pennsylvania, Philadelphia, M.A. 1958, Ph.D. 1962. Married 1) Nancy Ellis in 1961 (divorced 1984), one daughter and one son; 2) Kerry Lynn Blau in 1985. Instructor, 1961–62, and Assistant Professor of English, 1962–64, Duke University, Durham, North Carolina. Assistant Professor, 1964–68, Associate Professor, 1968–77, Professor of English, 1977–81, and since 1981, Cornelius and Muriel Wood Professor of Humanities, Principia College. Member, Board of Trustees, Village of Elsah, 1969–75; president, Greater St. Louis Historical Association, 1975, and Thoreau Society, 1977; director, Elsah Museum, 1981–84. Recipient: John W. Campbell award, 1983. Address: c/o Historic Elsah Foundation, Box 117, Elsah, Illinois 62028, U.S.A.

### Science-Fiction Publications

Novels (series: Pelbar)

Pelbar series:
- *The Breaking of Northwall.* New York, Ballantine, 1981; London, Futura, 1985.
- *The Ends of the Circle.* New York, Ballantine, 1981; London, Futura, 1986.
- *The Dome in the Forest.* New York, Ballantine, 1981.
- *The Fall of the Shell.* New York, Ballantine, 1982.
- *An Ambush of Shadows.* New York, Ballantine, 1983.
- *The Song of the Axe.* New York, Ballantine, 1984.

*The Sword of Forbearance.* New York, Ballantine, 1985.
*The Gifts of the Gorboduc Vandal.* New York, Ballantine, 1989.

### Other Publications

Other

*Elsah: A Historic Guidebook*, with Charles B. Hosmer. Elsah, Illinois, Historic Elsah Foundation, 1967.
*The McNair Family of Elsah, Illinois: Uncommon Common Men.* Elsah, Illinois, Historic Elsah Foundation, 1982.
*Frederick Oakes Sylvester: The Artist's Encounter with Elsah.* Elsah, Illinois, Historic Elsah Foundation, 1986.

* * *

The Pelbar cycle consists of six novels based on the hypothesis that a nuclear war occurred in the late 20th/early 21st century. Focusing on the land area of Urstadge (the United States and southwestern Canada), Paul O. Williams surmises that despite the devastation, isolated groups of people survived. His series, set about 1000 years after the devastation, explores these groups of people when they are large and stable enough to be expanding beyond their borders.

The cycle is rich in detail about political systems, languages, games, architecture, dress, food, weaponry, technology, music, art, education. Williams's societies are influenced by his knowledge of Native Americans, especially in the Mississippi River valley; his scholarship in 19th-century American romanticism, especially Thoreau; his Christian Science religion which offers strong female models; his reading of western expeditions, particularly that of Lewis and Clark; and his clear love for the immensity of the land, the endurance of nature and its patterns, and the symbolism and power of the Mississippi River, a feature he has watched from the limestone cliffs just north of St. Louis where he has lived for many years.

The cycle depicts humankind moving toward unity as the individual societies realize the advantages of open trade, exchange of knowledge and skills, and their common historical and religious foundations. The impetus for the move toward unification comes from the Pelbar, people living in three elaborately designed stone cities along the Heart River (Mississippi). Individual novels echo the cycle's movement from fragmentation to federation by depicting journeys by psychological and physical discovery by young protagonists. Each protagonist's search culminates not only in a return home and a new or renewed marriage but also in a treaty or agreement with other societies.

The cyclic nature of these novels is evident in a number of ways but most clearly in its open-endedness; although certain individuals or social groups reach agreements about the sharing of responsibilities, land, or resources, there is always the potential for separation and renewed isolation. Underneath the movement toward unity is the potential for injustice, tyranny, and destruction. How these conflicting desires for unity and for power are handled by individuals is the real focus of the series. The solutions affect the married couple (Williams's ideal for human fulfillment and social unity) and the nature of individual societies. Unification in the cycle requires the combined skills of different heroes—the visionary, the inventor/technician, the diplomat, the social leader, the rebel, the explorer, the military strategist, the warrior.

*The Breaking of Northwall*, besides providing background, recounts the influences that lead the people of Northwall, the northernmost Pelbar city, to share knowledge and to intermarry with the other two valley tribes of the valley, the Sentani and the Shumai. The external tribes are hunters and nomads; the Pelbar offer these intelligent, honorable peoples a high level of culture and a settled existence. *The Ends of the Circle* tells of the personal quest of Ahroe, a young Pelbar wife, for Stel, her husband who has fled West to escape the severe domination of Ahroe's family. In Pelbar society, women are the administrators and men are laborers. The adventures of both Ahroe and Stel lead them to an increased understanding of human love and hate, men and women, social order and change. *The Dome in the Forest* is an account of the emergence of a small group of "the ancients" from a sealed dome where they have perpetuated themselves through several generations for over 1000 years. Even more isolated than the Pelbar, they bring with them advanced technology and reason but lack the social skills, emotions, and intuitions of their rescue party composed of Pelbar, Sentani, and Shumai.

*The Fall of the Shell* turns to the third and most conservative Pelbar city where twin adolescent boys defy the harsh rule and are punished severely. One twin is imprisoned in the city and contemplates the architectural and social structure of his society; the other escapes to journey south on the river and return with great knowledge of new societies. By different routes, the twins learn the basic human virtues of love, forbearance, kindness, and goodwill. *An Ambush of Shadows* depicts the strained marriage of Ahroe and Stel as she goes to the Heart River Federation Convention as a diplomat and he travels north to seek contact with new societies. *The Song of the Axe*, the only novel to use non-Pelbars as protagonists, recounts a journey that began at the end of *The Dome in the Forest.* Tor, a Shumai axeman, and his nephew, Tristal, travel far into the northwest. Although Tor, a man of intuition and vision, chooses not to return to the Heart, he helps shape his nephew so that he does return with the combined skill of the diplomat and the explorer.

*The Fall of the Shell* best exemplifies the themes and structure of the cycle. The concept that each society is in artifact and that its design determines its strengths and weaknesses is universal in the cycle. Williams uses the nautilus shell and the Mississippi River as symbols of the beauty, limitations, and potentiality of human society. The river/highway gives access to a variety of human societies and greater knowledge of the single religion that underlies all of the Urstadge societies. The shell is rich in ambiguity for a shell can house mature life as a society shelters its citizens, but it may also inhibit life and have to be cracked open.

—Elizabeth Cummins Cogell

---

**WILLIAMS, Robert Moore.** American. Born in Farmington, Missouri, 19 June 1907. Educated at the University of Missouri Columbia, B.A. in journalism. Married Margaret Jelley in 1938 (divorced 1952); one daughter. Full-time writer, 1937–72. *Died in 1977.*

SCIENCE-FICTION PUBLICATIONS

Novels (series: Jongor; Zanthar)

*The Chaos Fighters.* New York, Ace, 1955.
*Conquest of the Space Sea.* New York, Ace, 1955.
*Doomsday Eve.* New York, Ace, 1957.
*The Blue Atom.* New York, Ace, 1958.
*World of the Masterminds.* New York, Ace, 1960.
*The Day They H-Bombed Los Angeles.* New York, Ace, 1961.
*The Darkness Before Tomorrow.* New York, Ace, 1962.
*King of the Fourth Planet.* New York, Ace, 1962.
*Walk Up the Sky.* New York, Avalon, 1962.
*The Star Wasps.* New York, Ace, 1963.
*Flight From Yesterday.* New York, Ace, 1963.
*The Lunar Eye.* New York, Ace, 1964.
*The Second Atlantis.* New York, Ace, 1965.
*Vigilante—21st Century.* New York, Lancer, 1967.
*Zanthar of the Many Worlds.* New York, Lancer, 1967.
*Zanthar of the Edge of Never.* New York, Lancer, 1968.
*The Bell from Infinity.* New York, Lancer, 1968.
*Zanthar at Moon's Madness.* New York, Lancer, 1968.
*Zanthar at Trip's End.* New York, Lancer, 1968.
*Beachhead Planet.* New York, Dell, and London, Sidgwick and Jackson, 1970.
*Jongor of Lost Land.* New York, Popular Library, 1970.
*Return of Jongor.* New York, Popular Library, 1970.
*Jongor Fights Back.* New York, Popular Library, 1970.
*Now Comes Tomorrow.* New York, Curtis, and London, Sidgwick and Jackson, 1971.

Short Stories

*The Void Beyond and Other Stories.* New York, Ace, 1958.
*To the End of Time.* New York, Ace, 1960.
*When Two Worlds Meet.* New York, Curtis, 1970.

Uncollected Short Story

"Now Comes Tomorrow," in *Science Fiction Special 6.* London, Sidgwick and Jackson, 1973.

OTHER PUBLICATIONS

Other

*Love Is Forever, We Are for Tonight* (autobiography). New York, Curtis, 1970.

* * *

During the editorship of Ray Palmer in the 1940's, *Amazing Stories* and *Fantastic Adventures* were juvenile action pulps principally written by a stable of writers under their own bylines and an assortment of house names. Robert Moore Williams was part of this stable, producing scores of stories, including a few under the name Russell Storm. (It is not clear which stories he wrote under house names, but it's probable that most of the stories published prior to 1951 under the name E.K. Jarvis are his.) Even today, Williams is largely associated with these magazines and their juvenile policy, but the truth is he was one of only a handful of writers of those years who were able to cut across policy boundaries and sell stories to almost all the existing science-fiction magazines. He appeared often, for example, in both *Thrilling Wonder* and *Startling,* and also in John Campbell's *Astounding* (Campbell thought enough of his talents to mention him in his essay for Lloyd Eshbach's *Of Worlds Beyond*). In fact, of these writers, Williams is unique in sustaining a continuous career as an SF writer through to the 1970's.

Although Williams wrote almost 200 stories, it is possible from one of his collections to get a good feel for his approaches and talent. The stories in *When Two Worlds Meet* are linked through a common background of Earthman conflict although the background details of Mars and the Martians are inconsistent. The title story tells of an Earthman who tries to learn the secret behind a "god weapon" that allows one race to subjugate another. "Aurochs Came Walking" concerns a shaman's crystal ball that turns out to be a control device for a machine built by ancient Martians. In "The Sound of Bugles," Martians show an Earthman the secret of creating such resources as food and housing from pure thought. The weakest story in the book is probably "When the Spoilers Came," marred by an unconvincing and rather sentimental resolution, something not especially common in the fiction of Williams whose romantic streak more often manifested itself as a mildly ironic cynicism. "The Final Frontier," in which a dying Martian wields strange powers to thwart exploitative Earthmen, is only technically better. The best story in the book is "On Pain of Death," a suspense story about a group of Earthmen trapped in a strange prison that may be either a particularly efficient machine or a test of their worthiness to live.

Again and again, Williams's fiction deals with machines that bestow godlike powers, or ordinary humans who possess a special rapport with machines or elemental energies. In "The Night the General Left Us," a mathematician's love of machines is returned by a model rocket that attacks a general who orders the man arrested. "The Smallness Beyond Thought" deals with an eccentric hermit whose ability to grow food without water is related to his ability to sense the flow of electromagnetic and less familiar forms of energy.

It should not be assumed that Williams is playing with the traditional science-fiction theme of the superman. Rather, his work expresses a basically mystical view of the world. This is borne out by "The Grove of God" (*Other Worlds,* 1956), whose editor described it as too taboo-breaking for other magazines. An expedition of space explorers from Earth lands on a planet where they discover god-like humans living in a primitive paradise. They discover that the planet is actually Earth, to which they have returned through some sort of application of Lorenz-Fitzgerald principle that none of the scientists seems to have been aware of. The narrative is as awkward and downright clumsy as the idea, something surprising in the work of a professional as experienced as Williams. Ironically, another story by him in that issue ("The Steogar" as by Russell Storm) deals more effectively with similar material: a research scientist at a government installation acquires godlike abilities through the agency of a miraculous invention.

Williams turned to novels for the growing paperback markets in 1955 with *The Chaos Fighters.* During the next decade and a half Williams produced almost 30 books. By and large they were not too different from the mass of his magazine fiction and they abound with such concepts as aliens trying to control human destiny, Earthman exploiting alien planets, and humans with miraculous powers. Williams did manage, in *The Day They H-Bombed Los Angeles* and *The Second Atlantis,* to find interesting ways to destroy Southern California. The Jongor series consist of Burroughs-like lost-land stories, and the Zanthar series are about a super scientist who seems as interested in the occult as in physics. The last, appropriately called *Zanthar at Trip's End,* has him coping with a machine that blows the souls out of people's bodies.

The strangest of Williams's books, however, is a slim volume titled *Love Is Forever, We Are for Tonight.* Although it's called science fiction on one cover and a "strange and fantastic novel of a man trapped in an inner world of fear and evil" on the other, the book is autobiography with no pretense of being fiction. It begins with some fairly evocative description of his childhood and youth but soon focuses on Williams's interest in and experiences with such things as dianetics, hallucinogenic gases, and communes (in the 1950's). The style reminds one of Ray Palmer's in his editorials for *Other Worlds,* but Palmer's delightful flamboyance and self-directed humor are missing and missed. The book is often vague and evasive, but some facts about the man crop up and the portions dealing with dianetics, while not particularly revealing, might hold interest for anyone curious about the impact of that cult on the SF field.

Williams doesn't seem to have very often probed deeply into any of his ideas or themes, and this makes some of his work, while perfectly readable on the surface, seem disturbingly incomplete. His best work tends to be stories of adventure and suspense, such as "On Pain of Death," and stories about determined human beings trying to survive, such as "Last Ship Out," where two disfigured survivors of atomic war try to battle their way on board a spaceship bound for Mars. The story is slight but compact and straightforward and very readable. It satisfies more than the ponderous "Grove of God," reminding us that Williams is more likely to be at his best writing about people and situations than about ideas.

—Gerald W. Page

---

**WILLIAMSON, Jack** (John Stewart Williamson). Also wrote as Will Stewart. American. Born in Bisbee, Arizona, 29 April 1908. Educated at Richland High School, New Mexico; West Texas State University, Canyon, 1928–30; University of New Mexico, Albuquerque, 1931–32; Eastern New Mexico University, Portales, B.A. (summa cum laude), M.A. 1957; University of Colorado, Boulder, Ph.D. 1964. Weather forecaster in the United States Army, 1942–45: Staff Sargeant. Married Blanche Slaten Harp in 1947; two step-children. Writer from 1928; wire editor, Portales *News Tribune,* 1947; created comic strip *Beyond*

*Mars*, New York *Sunday News*, 1952–55; Instructor in English, New Mexico Military Institute, Roswell, 1958–60, and University of Colorado, 1960; Professor of English, Eastern New Mexico University, 1960–77, now retired. President, Science Fiction Writers of America, 1978–80. Recipient: Pilgrim award, 1973; Grand Master Nebula award, 1975; Hugo award, for non-fiction, 1985. Guest of Honor, 35th World Science Fiction Convention, 1977. Agent: Eleanor Wood, 111 Eighth Avenue, Suite 1501, New York, New York 10011. Address: Box 761, Portales, New Mexico 88130, U.S.A.

## Science-Fiction Publications

Novels (series: Cuckoo's Saga; Jim Eden; Legion of Space; Seetee; Starchild)

*The Girl from Mars*, with Miles J. Breuer. New York, Stellar, 1929.
*The Legion of Space*. Reading, Pennsylvania, Fantasy Press, 1947; London, Sphere, 1977.
*The Humanoids*. New York, Simon and Schuster, 1949; London, Museum Press, 1953.
*The Green Girl*. New York, Avon, 1950.
*The Cometeers* (Legion). Reading, Pennsylvania, Fantasy Press, 1950; London, Sphere, 1977; expanded section published as *One Against the Legion*, New York, Pyramid, 1967; London, Sphere, 1977.
*Seetee Shock* (as Will Stewart). New York, Simon and Schuster, 1950; Kingswood, Surrey, World's Work, 1954.
*Seetee Ship* (as Will Stewart). New York, Gnome Press, 1951.
*Dragon's Island*. New York, Simon and Schuster, 1951; London, Museum Press, 1954; as *The Not-Men*, New York, Belmont, 1968.
*The Legend of Time*. Reading, Pennsylvania, Fantasy Press, 1952; as *The Legion of Time* and *After World's End*, London, Digit, 2 vols., 1961; New York, Bluejay, 1985.
*Undersea Quest* (Eden), with Frederik Pohl. New York, Gnome Press, 1954; London, Dobson, 1966.
*Dome Around America*. New York, Ace, 1955; London, Faber, 1964.
*Star Bridge*, with James E. Gunn. New York, Gnome Press, 1955; London, Sidgwick and Jackson, 1978.
*Undersea Fleet* (Eden), with Frederik Pohl. New York, Gnome Press, 1956; London, Dobson, 1968.
*Undersea City* (Eden), with Frederik Pohl. Hicksville, New York, Gnome Press, 1958; London, Dobson, 1968.
*The Trial of Terra*. New York, Ace, 1962.
*The Starchild Trilogy*, with Frederik Pohl. New York, Doubleday, 1977; London, Penguin, 1980.
  *The Reefs of Space*. New York, Ballantine, 1964; London, Dobson, 1965.
  *Starchild*. New York, Ballantine, 1965; London, Dobson, 1966.
  *Rogue Star*. New York, Ballantine, 1969; London, Dobson, 1972.
*Bright New Universe*. New York, Ace, 1967; London, Sidgwick and Jackson, 1969.
*Trapped in Space* (for children). New York, Doubleday, 1968.
*The Moon Children*. New York, Putnam, 1972; Morley, Yorkshire, Elmfield Press, 1975.
*Farthest Star* (Cuckoo's Saga), with Frederik Pohl. New York, Ballantine, 1975; London, Pan, 1976.
*The Power of Blackness*. New York, Berkley, 1976; London, Sphere, 1978.
*Brother to Demons, Brother to God*. Indianapolis, Bobbs Merrill, 1979; London, Sphere, 1981.
*The Humanoid Touch*. New York, Holt Rinehart, 1980; London, Sphere, 1982.
*The Birth of a New Republic*, with Miles J. Breuer. New Orleans, P.D.A., 1981.
*Manseed*. New York, Ballantine, 1982; London, Sphere, 1986.
*The Queen of the Legion*. New York, Pocket Books, 1983; London, Sphere, 1984.
*Wall Around a Star* (Cuckoo's Saga), with Frederik Pohl. New York, Ballantine, 1983.
*Lifeburst*. New York, Ballantine, 1984; London, Sphere, 1987.
*Firechild*. New York, Bluejay, 1986; London, Methuen, 1988.
*Land's End*, with Frederik Pohl. New York, Tor, 1988.
*Mazeway*. Norwalk, Connecticut, Easton Press, and London, Mandarin, 1990.
*The Singers of Time*, with Frederik Pohl. New York, Doubleday, 1990.

Short Stories

*Lady in Danger*. London, Utopian, 1945(?).
*The Pandora Effect*. New York, Ace, 1969.
*People Machines*. New York, Ace, 1971.
*The Early Williamson*. New York, Doubleday, 1975; London, Sphere, 1978.
*Dreadful Sleep*. Chicago, Weinberg, 1977.
*The Best of Jack Williamson*. New York, Ballantine, 1978.
*The Alien Intelligence*. New Orleans, P.D.A., 1980.

## Other Publications

Novels

*Darker Than You Think*. Reading, Pennsylvania, Fantasy Press, 1948; London, Sphere, 1976.
*Golden Blood*. New York, Lancer, 1964.
*The Reign of Wizardry*. New York, Lancer, 1964.

Other

*Teaching Science Fiction*. Privately printed, 1972.
*H.G. Wells, Critic of Progress*. Baltimore, Mirage Press, 1973.
*Wonder's Child: My Life in Science Fiction*. New York, Bluejay, 1984.
*Medea: Harlan's World*, with others, edited by Harlan Ellison. Huntington Woods, Michigan, Phantasia Press, 1985.
*Leigh Brackett: American Writer*, with John L. Carr. Polk City, Iowa, Drum, 1986.
*Beyond Mars* (comic strips; with Lee Elias). El Cajon, California, Blackthorne, 2 vols., 1987–88.

Editor, *Teaching Science Fiction for Tomorrow*. Philadelphia, Owlswick Press, 1980.

*

Bibliography: *Jack Williamson: A Primary and Secondary Bibliography* by Robert E. Myers, Boston, Hall, 1980.

Manuscript Collection: Golden Library, Eastern New Mexico University, Portales.

Critical Study: *Jack Williamson: An Interview* by Larry McCaffrey, Dallas, Texas, Northouse, 1988.

Jack Williamson comments:

I began writing at 20, hardly half-educated but dazzled with visions of science and intoxicated with science fiction as a device for exploring the possible. In all the years since, the known universe has vastly expanded and science fiction has grown as fast. Now at 83 I'm still held by the unfolding of science and still excited about science fiction. As a career, it has been rewarding. Though in the first few decades the pay in money was meager, there were always rich compensations in the satisfactions of creating, in the fine friendships, in the opportunities to observe the explosions of scientific knowledge and the human impacts of science and technology. The writers and readers of science fiction form a special community, still tiny when I first discovered it, inhabited by the most able and interesting people I have known. Belonging to it has been a privilege.

* * *

Williamson's early life was spent in a covered wagon on one of the last frontiers, that of rural New Mexico. His first story, "The Metal Man" (1928), resulted from reading one of the first numbers of *Amazing Stories.* In a crude but enthusiastic way, it established one of Williamson's *leitmotifs:* the interface between man and machine, as the hero becomes a technological object, a "person-machine." After several early novels that have never been published in book form (e.g., "The Stone from the Green Star") Williamson first earned a reputation as a master of space opera with *The Legion of Space* (1934). This novel put Williamson in the same rank with such galaxy-conquerors as John W. Campbell and E.E. "Doc" Smith; but the novel resembles those of his contemporaries only in its exuberance. Unlike Campbell and Smith, Williamson was not espousing either technocracy, as Campbell did, or the joys of physics unchecked by any intellectual bound, as Smith did. Williamson is neither pro- nor anti-technology; while there is a great deal of gimcrack physics scattered throughout the text, the central device that allows the heros to conquer their foes, AKKA, can be activated only by a few scraps and an act of will; its operation is never explained. *The Legion of Space* is important because it is the first sign that SF was moving away from the epic of technocracy; although it is what Alexei Panshin would call a lost-race novel of space (much of the action is standard lost-race adventure transported to the jungle-covered moon of Jupiter, Titan), it is still an advance over other, duller works of the time and can still be read with pleasure. Its sequels are better written but less entertaining. Williamson was one of the few writers of the 1930's who could write with equal facility for the *Astounding* of F. Orlin Tremaine and the *Astounding* of John Campbell. It is generally forgotten that *One Against the Legion* was published in Campbell's *Astounding.* Campbell prodded Williamson to excellence in much the same way as he prodded other writers; Williamson's best work dates from this period, and the only novel that Williamson produced after 1948 that achieves excellence is a result of a Campbell-inspired fragment of 1941.

Williamson's three great works deal with the same theme: the eternal tension of society. Man, Aristotle teaches, is a social animal; it is the degree to which an individual must participate in society without abandoning free will that Williamson seeks to find in *Darker Than You Think, The Humanoids,* and *Star Bridge.*

*Darker Than You Think* is a result of the two years Williamson spent in psychoanalysis in the late 1930's. Ostensibly, it concerns a war between lycanthropy and humanity for dominance; but the werewolves are seen as agents of freedom, creatures that put the lie to scientific and psychoanalytic explanations with mystical truth that transcends attempts at rationalization. But freedom, in this novel, requires a price, a sum of dependence, of eternal vigilance. It is as if the werewolves were organised anarchists, determined to preserve absolute liberty with a new order. Added to this, Williamson has produced what is the best explanation of lycanthropy extent (it depends on probablistic physics, a theme deepened in *The Humanoids*). *Darker Than You Think* is an excellent thriller as well, being the finest novel of the occult produced by a science-fiction writer.

Williamson continued his search for controlling agents in his best work, *The Humanoids.* In two ancillary works designed to match each other as thesis and antithesis, "With Folded Hands" and "The Equalizer," Williamson ruminated on the use and abuse of technology. The former introduces a classic dystopian theme, that of robots following a categorical imperative to its logical limit; the latter shows that technology can preserve as well as destroy free will. But these two novellas are two halves of a larger whole; they cannot be read apart, and consequently they lose some of their artistic impact. Only in *The Humanoids* does Williamson attempt a synthesis; and he does this by relying on the old Campbellian warhorse, that of psionic power, as Williamson combines metaphysics with particle physics and the laws of probability to produce a new unified field theory. It is hard for the modern reader to accept psionics with the willingness of those in the late 1940's; but Williamson transcends mere reciting of psionic power to examine the epistemological foundations behind that power. Williamson also examines the fate of those who have accepted the humanoid categorical imperative, producing an examination of the middle ground between the two cultures of pure technocracy and pure mysticism that still retains its impact. *The Humanoids* is Williamson's best novel, a classic dystopia and the single best work on robot instrumentalities outside the work of Isaac Asimov.

Williamson began a rapid decline after *The Humanoids;* for the next dozen years, he produced works only in collaboration. These collaborations with Frederik Pohl are minor entertainments; the earlier novels such as *Undersea City* are competent juveniles, but rapidly decline to reach a nadir with *Starchild*, the worst novel of either author. Williamson's other "collaboration" is not one at all, but is instead the completion of a Williamson fragment by James Gunn. This novel, *Star Bridge,* is Williamson's last important work, an examination of the processes of political change no less searching than his examination of psychoanalysis in *Darker Than You Think* and of technology in *The Humanoids.* The dialectic between individual and society here is less distinct; the chief representative of individualism is an assassin who does not know what he stands for, the society a corporate state whose internal dynamic has been spent.

After *Star Bridge,* Williamson began a creative drought which lasted 27 years. During this period Williamson's only important work was non-fiction; he began an academic career in the late 1950's, his dissertation forming part of *H.G. Wells, Critic of Progress.* Williamson's novels during this period returned to stories that would have achieved minor billing in *Planet Stories;* such a work as *The Power of Blackness* suffers from a black hero so characterless that Williamson can find no other descriptive qualities for him than the color of his skin. By the 1980's, Williamson was reduced to writing unneeded sequels to his major works; *The Humanoid Touch* is a minor, darker pastiche of *The Humanoids,* while *The Queen of the Legion* is a frothy conceit lacking in the force of its predecessors.

*Manseed* marked a new phase in Williamson's career. This tale of a latent superman struggling to discover the limits of his powers, while seriously flawed, marked a new seriousness in Williamson's career. Williamson followed *Manseed* with a collaboration with Frederik Pohl, *Wall Around a Star,* one of the few novels to use linguistics as the scientific base for its intricate plot.

*Lifeburst* is his most important novel since *The Humanoids.* In *Lifeburst,* Williamson returns to his eternal theme—in relations between man and the world. *Lifeburst* is a surprisingly dark exploration of galactic power politics, with the power struggles between clans used as a metaphor for sexual and social tension. Gritty and imaginative, *Lifeburst* is to Williamson what *Capriccio* was to Richard Strauss: an autumnal masterpiece that ensures that Williamson, unlike most writers of his generation, remains a major force in science fiction in his fifth decade as a professional writer.

—Martin Morse Wooster

---

**WILLIS, Connie** (Constance E. Willis). American. Born in Denver, Colorado, 31 December 1945. Educated at the University of Northern Colorado, Greeley, B.A. in English and elementary education 1967. Married Courtney W. Willis in 1967; one daughter. Teacher in elementary and junior high schools, Branford, Connecticut, 1967–69; substitute teacher, Woodland Park, Colorado, 1974–81. Since 1982, full-time writer. Recipient: National Endowment for the Arts grant, 1982; Nebula award, 1982 (twice), 1988, 1989; Hugo award, 1982, 1988; John W. Campbell award, 1988. Agent: Ralph Vicinanza, 111 8th Avenue, Suite 1501, New York, New York 10011. Address: 1716 13th Avenue, Greeley, Colorado 80631, U.S.A.

SCIENCE-FICTION PUBLICATIONS

Novels

*Water Witch,* with Cynthia Felice. New York, Ace, 1982.
*Lincoln's Dreams.* New York, Bantam, 1987; London, Grafton, 1988.
*Light Raid,* with Cynthia Felice. New York, Ace, 1989.

Short Stories

*Fire Watch.* New York, Bluejay, 1985.

*

Connie Willis comments:

I love the short story. People are constantly telling me how the short story is dying and how it is economically impossible to make a career out of writing short stories, but I still love the short story, and I've been writing them for 20 years. I think I like the variety of moods, styles, and themes I can explore in the short story, which I have always felt was the most successful form of science fiction. It is necessary to work with only a few characters, to create worlds with only a few words and hints of background, and to make everything in the story do double duty. It's an exciting challenge. I have written everything from screwball comedies to mysteries to fairy tales and have found to my delight that science fiction welcomes them all.

I have always been fascinated by the problem of time and our place in it, and science fiction has allowed me to explore that theme in a variety of ways. I have written stories that involve the impact of the past on the present and on the future and on the far-reaching and sometimes devastating effects time travel would have on us. My story "Fire Watch" and my new novel *Doomsday Book* concern a history department at Oxford that has time travel at its disposal. Time travel can be a wonderful aid to history, but the lessons to be learned are not always simple or painless ones. The theme of time is one of endless possibilities and I find the stories unfolding one after the other as if I hadn't even begun.

* * *

Despite her comparatively infrequent publications, Connie Willis has established a reputation as one of the most reliably skillful writers in the genre, particularly at shorter length. She is also one of the least predictable, ranging from science fiction to fantasy to horror. It is in science fiction, however, that her talents are best displayed, as Hugo and Nebula awards attest. Her first novel, *Water Witch,* written in collaboration with Cynthia Felice, was an interesting but not outstanding story of a shrew and not particularly honest con artist on a planet where water is in short supply. Although it made little impression when it appeared, the publication of the collection *Fire Watch* three years later corrected the situation.

The title story concerns a man who travels back through time to the London Blitz as part of his training to study history. He becomes involved with the effort to save an historic cathedral from destruction, waiting on the roof during each air raid to extinguish incendiary bombs before they can do any great damage. He becomes involved emotionally with his fellow defenders and ultimately learns more about himself than he does about the Blitz. In "A Letter from the Clearys," Willis illustrates the strongest point of her fiction, her ability to create utterly convincing characters, in this case a young woman struggling for mental equilibrium in the aftermath of a nuclear war.

"The Sidon in the Mirror" is set in a small mining colony on the surface of a burnt out star. The reader is exposed to the unravelling of the various relationships among the staff and patrons of a bordello catering to the miners. Rather than dwell on grotesqueries, however, Willis forces our attention to the human characters that exist beneath the facade. "The Curse of Kings" is somewhat more conventional. Archaeologists on a primitive world uncover a fabulous treasure, but a mysterious and fatal illness begins to claim members of their party.

Her skill at the shorter form continues to improve with experience. "Daisy, in the Sun" involves the survival of consciousness following the extinction of our sun. "Blued Moon" is untypical of her work, a quite funny tale of what happens when the disposal of industrial waste affects the laws of probability. "Samaritan" is set in a future where most of the organized churches have combined into one ecumenical body. A minister and his assistant differ when their orangutan servant apparently requests baptism. Predictably, many members of the congregation are appalled at the idea of accepting an "animal" as a member, and the minister himself is torn between conflicting emotions. More recently, her "The Swartzchild Radius" has won her a host of new fans, and "The Last of the Winnebagos" is one of the most poignant stories of the near future ever to appear in the field.

Two solo novels have also appeared. *Lincoln's Dreams* is not properly science fiction at all, but this haunting tale of a woman who shares the dreams of the Civil War period has definite fantastic overtones. *Light Raid* is more definitely science fiction, however. North America is split into warring factions, and phantasmagorical attacks are frequently launched through the skies of one city-state or another. The protagonist is a young woman who seeks to clear her parents' name, after some mysterious organization brands them as traitors.

Willis has also written some unusually effective traditional ghost stories, most notably "The Service for the Burial of the Dead," "Distress Call," and "Substitution Trick." The versatility, strong grasp of the complexity of the human character, and highly accessible style mark her as one of the premier stylists in the genre.

—Don D'Ammassa

---

**WILSON, Colin (Henry).** British. Born in Leicester, 26 June 1931. Educated at Gateway Secondary Technical School, Leicester, 1942–47. Served in the Royal Air Force, 1949–50. Married 1) Dorothy Betty Troop in 1951 (marriage dissolved), one son; 2) Pamela Joy Stewart in 1973, two sons and one daughter. Laboratory assistant, Gateway School, 1948–49; tax collector, Leicester and Rugby, 1949–50; labourer and hospital porter in London, 1951–53; salesman for the magazines *Paris Review* and *Merlin*, Paris, 1953. Since 1954, full-time writer. British Council Lecturer in Germany, 1957; Writer-in-Residence, Hollins College, Virginia, 1966–67; Visiting Professor, University of Washington, Seattle, 1968; Professor, Institute of the Mediterranean (Dowling College, New York), Mallorca, 1969; Visiting Professor, Rutgers University, New Brunswick, New Jersey, 1974. Agent: David Bolt Associates, 12 Heath Drive, Send, Surrey, GU23 7EP. Address: Tetherdown, Trewallock Lane, Gorran Haven, Cornwall PL26 6NT, England.

### Science-Fiction Publications

Novels (series: Spider World)

*The Mind Parasites*. London, Barker, and Sauk City, Wisconsin, Arkham House, 1967.
*The Philosopher's Stone*. London, Barker, 1969; New York, Crown, 1971.
*The Space Vampires*. London, Hart Davis MacGibbon, and New York, Random House, 1976.
Spider World series:
*The Tower*. London, Grafton, 1987; New York, Ace, 1989.
*The Delta*. London, Grafton, 1987; New York, Ace, 1990.
*The Fortress*. New York, Ace, 1987.
*The Magician from Siberia*. London, Hale, 1988.
*The Desert*. New York, Ace, 1988.

Short Stories

*The Return of the Lloigor*. London, Village Press, 1974.

Uncollected Short Story

"Timeslip," in *Aries 1*, edited by John Grant. Newton Abbot, Devon, David and Charles, 1979.

### Other Publications

Novels

*Ritual in the Dark*. London, Gollancz, and Boston, Houghton Mifflin, 1960.
*Adrift in Soho*. London, Gollancz, and Boston, Houghton Mifflin, 1961.
*The World of Violence*. London, Gollancz, 1963; as *The Violent World of Hugh Greene*, Boston, Houghton Mifflin, 1963.
*Man Without a Shadow: The Diary of an Existentialist*. London, Barker, 1963; as *The Sex Diary of Gerard Sorme*, New York, Dial Press, 1963; as *The Sex Diary of a Metaphysician*, Berkeley, California, Ronin Press, 1988.
*Necessary Doubt*. London, Barker, and New York, Simon and Schuster, 1964.
*The Glass Cage: An Unconventional Detective Story*. London, Barker, 1966; New York, Random House, 1967.
*The Killer*. London, New English Library, 1970; as *Lingard*, New York, Crown, 1970.
*The God of the Labyrinth*. London, Hart Davis, 1970; as *The Hedonists*, New York, New American Library, 1971.
*The Black Room*. London, Weidenfeld and Nicolson, 1971; New York, Pyramid, 1975.
*The Schoolgirl Murder Case*. London, Hart Davis MacGibbon, and New York, Crown, 1974.
*The Janus Murder Case*. London, Granada, 1984.
*Personality Surgeon*. San Francisco, Mercury House, 1986; London, New English Library, 1987.

Plays

*Viennese Interlude* (produced Scarborough, Yorkshire, and London, 1960).
*Strindberg* (as *Pictures in a Bath of Acid*, produced Leeds, Yorkshire, 1971; as *Strindberg: A Fool's Decision*, produced London, 1975). London, Calder and Boyars, 1970; New York, Random House, 1971.
*Mysteries* (produced Cardiff, 1979).
*Mozart's Journey to Prague* (produced London, 1991).

Other

*The Outsider*. London, Gollancz, and Boston, Houghton Mifflin, 1956.
*Religion and the Rebel*. London, Gollancz, and Boston, Houghton Mifflin, 1957.
*The Age of Defeat*. London, Gollancz, 1959; as *The Stature of Man*, Boston, Houghton Mifflin, 1959.
*Encyclopaedia of Murder*, with Patricia Pitman. London, Barker, 1961; New York, Putnam, 1962.
*The Strength to Dream: Literature and the Imagination*. London, Gollancz, and Boston, Houghton Mifflin, 1962.
*Origins of the Sexual Impulse*. London, Barker, and New York, Putnam, 1963.
*Rasputin and the Fall of the Romanovs*. London, Barker, and New York, Farrar Straus, 1964.
*Brandy of the Damned: Discoveries of a Musical Eclectic*. London, Baker, 1964; as *Chords and Discords: Purely Personal Opinions on Music*, New York, Crown, 1966; augmented edition, as *Colin Wilson on Music*, London, Pan, 1967.
*Beyond the Outsider: The Philosophy of the Future*. London, Barker, and Boston, Houghton Mifflin, 1965.
*Eagle and Earwig* (essays). London, Barker, 1965.
*Introduction to the New Existentialism*. London, Hutchinson, 1966; Boston, Houghton Mifflin, 1967; as *The New Existentialism*, London, Wildwood House, 1980.
*Sex and the Intelligent Teenager*. London, Arrow, 1966; New York, Pyramid, 1968.
*Voyage to a Beginning* (autobiography). London, Cecil and Amelia Woolf, 1966; New York, Crown, 1969.
*Bernard Shaw: A Reassessment*. London, Hutchinson, and New York, Atheneum, 1969.
*A Casebook of Murder*. London, Frewin, 1969; New York, Cowles, 1970.
*Poetry and Mysticism*. San Francisco, City Lights, 1969; London, Hutchinson, 1970.

*The Strange Genius of David Lindsay*, with E.H. Visiak and J.B. Pick. London, Barker, 1970; as *The Haunted Man*, San Bernardino, California, Borgo Press, 1979.

*The Occult*. New York, Random House, and London, Hodder and Stoughton, 1971.

*New Pathways in Psychology: Maslow and the Post-Freudian Revolution*. New York, Taplinger, and London, Gollancz, 1972.

*Order of Assassins: The Psychology of Murder*. London, Hart Davis, 1972.

*L'Amour: The Ways of Love*, photographs by Piero Rimaldi. New York, Crown, 1972.

*Strange Powers*. London, Latimer New Dimensions, 1973; New York, Random House, 1975.

*Tree by Tolkien*. London, Covent Garden Press-Inca, 1973; Santa Barbara, California, Capra Press, 1974.

*Hermann Hesse*. London, Village Press, and Philadelphia, Leaves of Grass Press, 1974.

*Wilhelm Reich*. London, Village Press, and Philadelphia, Leaves of Grass Press, 1974.

*Jorge Luis Borges*. London, Village Press, and Philadelphia, Leaves of Grass Press, 1974.

*A Book of Booze*. London, Gollancz, 1974.

*The Unexplained*. Lake Oswego, Oregon, Lost Pleiade Press, 1975.

*Mysterious Powers*. London, Aldus, and Danbury, Connecticut, Danbury Press, 1975; as *They Had Strange Powers*, New York, Doubleday, 1975; revised edition, as *Mysteries of the Mind*, with Stuart Holroyd, Aldus, 1978.

*The Craft of the Novel*. London, Gollancz, 1975.

*Enigmas and Mysteries*. Danbury, Connecticut, Danbury Press, and London, Aldus, 1976.

*The Geller Phenomenon*. London, Aldus, 1976.

*Mysteries: An Investigation into the Occult, the Paranormal, and the Supernatural*. London, Hodder and Stoughton, 1978; New York, Putnam, 1980.

*Science Fiction as Existentialism*. Hayes, Middlesex, Bran's Head, 1978.

*The Laurel and Hardy Theory of Consciousness*. San Francisco, Brigg, 1979.

*The Search for the Real Arthur*, with *King Arthur Country in Cornwall*, by Brenda Duxbury and Michael Williams. Bodmin, Cornwall, Bossiney, 1979.

*Starseekers*. London, Hodder and Stoughton, 1980; New York, Doubleday, 1981.

*The War Against Sleep: The Philosophy of Gurdjieff*. Wellingborough, Northamptonshire, Aquarian Press, and York Beach, Maine, Weiser, 1980.

*Frankenstein's Castle*. Sevenoaks, Kent, Ashgrove Press, 1980; Salem, New Hampshire, Salem House, 1982.

*Anti-Sartre, with an Essay on Camus*. San Bernardino, California, Borgo Press, 1981.

*The Quest for Wilhelm Reich*. London, Granada, and New York, Doubleday, 1981.

*Witches*. Limpsfield, Surrey, Dragon's World, 1981; New York, A and W, 1982.

*Poltergeist! A Study in Destructive Haunting*. London, New English Library, 1981; New York, Putnam, 1982.

*Access to Inner Worlds: The Story of Brad Absetz*. London, Rider, 1983.

*Encyclopaedia of Modern Murder 1962–1982*, with Donald Seaman. London, Barker, 1983; New York, Putnam, 1985.

*Psychic Detectives: The Story of Psychometry and the Paranormal in Crime Detection*. London, Pan, 1984.

*A Criminal History of Mankind*. London, Granada, and New York, Putnam, 1984.

*Lord of the Underworld: Jung and the Twentieth Century*. Wellingborough, Northamptonshire, Aquarian Press, 1984.

*The Essential Colin Wilson*. London, Harrap, 1985.

*Existential Essays*, edited by Howard F. Dossor. Bath, Ashgrove Press, 1985.

*Afterlife*. London, Harrap, 1985; New York, Doubleday, 1987.

*The Bicameral Critic*, edited by Howard F. Dossor. Bath, Avon, Ashgrove Press, and New Hampshire, Salem House, 1985.

*Rudolf Steiner: The Man and His Vision*. Wellingborough, Northamptonshire, Aquarian Press, 1985.

*Scandal! An Encyclopaedia*, with Donald Seaman. London, Weidenfeld and Nicolson, and New York, Stein and Day, 1986.

*Poetry and Mysticism*. San Francisco, City Lights, 1986.

*The Philosopher's Stone*. Los Angeles, Tarcher, 1986.

*The Craft of the Novel*. Bath, Avon, Ashgrove Press, 1986.

*Alister Crowley: The Nature of the Beast*. Wellingborough, Northamptonshire, Aquarian Press, 1987.

*An Essay on the "New" Existentialism*. Nottingham, Pauper's Press, and San Bernardino, California, Borgo Press, 1987.

*The Musician as "Outsider."* Nottingham, Pauper's Press, 1987.

*The Encyclopedia of Unsolved Mysteries*, with Damon Wilson. London, Harrap, 1987; Chicago, Contemporary Books, 1988.

*Jack the Ripper: Summing Up and Verdict*, with Robin Odell, edited by Joe Gaute. London, and New York, Bantam, 1987.

*Beyond the Occult*. London, Corgi, 1988; New York, Carroll and Graf, 1989.

*Existentially Speaking*. San Bernardino, California, Borgo Press, 1989.

*Autobiographical Reflections*. Nottingham, Pauper's Press, 1988.

*The Mammoth Book of True Crime*, edited by Howard Dossor. London, Robinson, and New York, Carroll and Graf, 1988.

*The Decline and Fall of Leftism*. Nottingham, Pauper's Press, 1989; San Bernardino, California, Borgo Press, 1990.

*The Mammoth Book of True Crime 2*, edited by Damon Wilson. London, Robinson, and New York, Carroll and Graf, 1990.

*The Misfits: A Study of Sexual Outsiders*. London, Grafton, 1988; New York, Carroll and Graf, 1989.

*Lord Halifax's Ghost Book*. London, Bellew, 1989.

*Written in Blood: A History of Forensic Detection*. London, Equation, 1989; as *Written in Blood: Detectives and Detection*, New York, Warner, 1991.

*Music, Nature, and the Romantic Outsider*. San Bernardino, California, Borgo Press, 1990.

*The Serial Killers*, with Donald Seaman. New York, Carroll and Graf, 1990.

Editor, *Colin Wilson's Men of Mystery*. London, W.H. Allen, 1977.

Editor, *Dark Dimensions: A Celebration of the Occult*. New York, Everest House, 1978.

Editor, with John Grant, *The Book of Time*. Newton Abbot, Devon, David and Charles, 1980.

Editor, with John Grant, *The Directory of Possibilities*. Exeter, Webb and Bower, and New York, Rutledge Press, 1981.

Editor, with Ronald Duncan, *Marx Refuted*. Bath, Avon, Ashgrove, 1987.

Editor, with Christopher Evans, *The Book of Great Mysteries*. London, Robinson, 1986; New York, Dorset, 1990.

*

Manuscript Collection: University of Texas, Austin.

Critical Studies: *The Angry Decade* by Kenneth Allsop, London, Owen, 1958; *The World of Colin Wilson* by Sidney Campion, London, Muller, 1963; "The Novels of Colin Wilson" by R.H.W. Dillard, in *Hollins Critic* (Hollins College, Virginia), October 1967; *Colin Wilson* by John A. Weigel, New York, Twayne, 1975; *Colin Wilson: The Outsider and Beyond* by Clifford P. Bendau, San Bernardino, California, Borgo Press, 1979; *The Novels of Colin Wilson* by Nicolas Tredell, London, Vision Press, 1982; *An Odyssey of Freedom: Four Themes in Colin Wilson's Novels* by K. Gunnar Bergstrom, Uppsala, Sweden, University of Uppsala, 1983; *Colin Wilson* (essays and interview) by John Moorhouse and Paul Newman, edited by Colin Stanley, Nottingham, Pauper's Press, 1989, San Bernardino, California, Borgo Press, 1990; *Colin Wilson: The Man and His Mind* by Howard Dossor, Shaftsbury, Element, 1990.

Colin Wilson comments:

I would prefer to describe my three SF novels *The Mind Parasites, The Philosopher's Stone* and *The Space Vampires* as philosophical fiction, and feel that it is a pity that such a classification does not yet exist. When it finally does, we shall have a new type of fiction, designed to explore the same field as philosophy, and to appeal to the reader's intelligence. After all, we agree that philosophy is an "adventure of ideas" that can open breathtaking vistas to the human mind; why should these vistas not provide the excitement in works of fiction?

*The Mind Parasites* was written as a result of a challenge by H.P. Lovecraft's friend and publisher August Derleth. I had remarked in an interview that I thought Lovecraft an appalling stylist, and Derleth challenged me to see if I could do better. I took over much of the Lovecraft "Cthulhu" machinery, but used the novel to explore a theme that has always been central to my work since my first book *The Outsider*: that there is something basically wrong with human beings, something that Christian theologians had in mind when they talked of original sin. As machines, we are hopelessly inefficient. None of us ever lives up to our full potentialities. Yet it also seems to me that what is wrong is not seriously wrong. It is due to the strange woodenness of human consciousness, its almost hypnotic fixity. You could compare this mechanical defect to a clock whose hands are loose, so that it is useless as a clock—yet all it requires is for someone to tighten the hands. So, in *The Mind Parasites*, I developed a myth of some invisible parasites that live in the human mind, draining our vitality, keeping us permanently below our proper level. On a plot level, the central question of the book is: how could we combat parasites who are in the mind, so that they knew what we are thinking even as we think it?

In *The Philosopher's Stone*, I was again concerned with the problem of the invisible blocks to human evolution, but this time I accepted Shaw's challenge to write a parable about longevity—his belief that, if we could simply be galvanised by a sense of necessity, we would find it perfectly natural to live to be at least 300. Stravinsky had once made the interesting remark that rats fed on a diet of ecstasy live far longer. It struck me that if we could find some way of widening man's narrow consciousness, so that he can see the distant horizons that allure every poet, we would experience such a sense of enthusiasm and purpose that our lives would automatically be extended far beyond the present range. In the novel, a scientist accidentally discovers a brain operation that will unblock the hidden powers of the mind (at that time, I was toying with the idea that the secret of inspiration lay in the pre-frontal lobes, whereas I was later inclined to place it in the right brain). But even when this new freedom has been achieved by one or two people, they realise that some force seems to be actively opposed to the evolution of human consciousness. And once again I drew upon Lovecraft for my invisible monsters—the "Ancient Old Ones" who prefer human beings to remain hypnotised, and who symbolise original sin.

*The Space Vampires* is probably my best SF novel as science fiction. Its basic idea is the perception that some people seem to drain your energy, leaving you exhausted, while others seem to impart vitality. I am convinced that this is so, and that we actually feed on one another's energies far more than we realise. In the novel, aliens who have been found in the asteroid belt in a state of suspended animation are brought back to Earth; when awakened, they prove to be energy-vampires who live by sucking human vitality. The interesting logistic problem is that they can also transfer themselves into the bodies of their victims, so that the hunters are faced with an interesting problem in detection: how would you track down a criminal who can move from body to body?

The novel has the dubious distinction of having inspired one of the worst movies ever made, *Life Force.* It should have been a masterpiece, written by Dan O'Bannon (of *Alien*) and directed by Tobe Hooper. But the film makers seem to have been inspired to overkill by the 30 million dollars they had to spend on it, and neglected the story-line (without which any film is bound to be a flop) for spectacular special effects, thus demonstrating once again that low-budget movies (like *Alien*) have a better start in life than movies that are born with a silver spoon in their mouths.

My greatest regret is that the flop led to the cancellation of a sequel, *Return of the Space Vampires,* which I planned to write with my old friend A.E. Van Vogt . . .

*Spider World* is fantasy rather than science fiction, and was planned in three large volumes. Planned casually as a collaboration with a friend, and designed as an 80-thousand-word novel, it startled me by going its own way and quickly developing into a 200,000-word "first part" (beginning with *The Desert* and ending with *The Delta*). The second "volume" of *Spider World* is entitled *The Magician*, and its first half, consisting of *The Assassins* and *The Living Dead* is due out in England in the autumn of 1991, to be followed by the second half, *Shadowland;* these will be succeeded by a third volume, *New Earth*, at present also planned in three parts. In its finished form, the total work should be about twice as long as Tolkien's *Lord of the Rings.*

The theme of the first part—an earth of the future, taken over by giant spiders who breed human beings for food—soon transformed itself into my basic obsession, a study of precisely what is wrong with human beings: what is it that means that we are at our best under crisis, and that happiness—lack of crisis, challenge—bores us and causes us to degenerate? I am still hoping to live long enough to pin down the answer, and express it with such clarity that the human race will suddenly wake up to its basic potentialities. Never addicted to what Shaw called "the modest cough of the minor poet," I become increasingly aware as I grow older that my fundamental ambition is to be the least pessimistic writer who has ever lived.

* * *

Colin Wilson is an enormously energetic and eclectic writer whose works include non-fiction and fiction of many classes. For his worldview he acknowledges a seminal and continuing influence of Bernard Shaw, whose long science-fantasy play *Back to Methuselah* is a sort of mainspring for Wilson's science-fiction novels.

In the preface to *The Mind Parasites* Wilson remarks that the work is his first attempt at fantasy and likely his last. It was not. Several more have followed. In *The Mind Parasites,* Professor Gilbert Austin discovers a counter-life entity competing with humanity for life energy from the wellspring of creation.

Throughout history the parasites have masked from men mankind's own true powers—which are enormous, even godlike. Austin and his cohorts turn the tide of battle in favor of man, after themselves becoming considerably advanced in this "natural" power. Similarly, in *The Philosopher's Stone*, Howard Lester seeks and finds the answer to the problem of death. The power of the will to live has been blocked by the "Old Ones," a superspecies millions of years old that caused and then intercepted the evolution of man. Long asleep, the Old Ones may soon awaken. Lester hopes to lead men to confront them as "Masters" where they once served the Old Ones as slaves. *The Space Vampires* streamlines in style and strategy a similar tale. Spaceship Commander Carlsen discovers a gigantic interstellar craft carrying perverted aliens from the star-system Rigel. These creatures cheat death by absorbing life energy from host species such as humanity. Fortunately for mankind, sane Rigelians catch up with the vampire Rigelians just in time. Carlsen acts as a medium for the saviours, and in the process learns wholesome means by which mankind can be "immortal."

There are an enthusiam and bright-eyed bombast about these tales that make it not unrewarding to read them as parodies of science fiction. This may account for a number of the elements common in the three works, though one need not forego taking them seriously as well. Each is furnished with a preface acknowledging a debt to H.P. Lovecraft or August Derleth. Each manifests considerable erudition exhibiting Wilson's encyclopaedic knowledge of the occult as well as the arts and history, anthropology, and science: ancient mythologies are found to have considerable basis in fact. Each story presents an intellectual power fantasy. The hero, in whom a panoply of parapsychological abilities is emerging, seems torn between visions of mankind as mean, gullible, and cowardly and man with a destiny of vaulting grandeur. These heroes, after lifting the yoke of mental slavery from both themselves and humanity, win a form of personal transcendence, a step in the direction of joining the advanced intelligent life that lives throughout the universe.

In the four books of the Spider World series, *The Desert, The Tower, The Fortress*, and *The Delta*, Wilson wrote a science-fiction children's book, and thanks his three children for helping to form the guidelines. Mostly worthy of the warm reviews it received, in its compromise for children readers, the series eschews detailed description and analyses of the sexual behavior of its characters. Otherwise it imagines, as in earlier works, a universe imbued with a Shavian life force engaged in creative evolution. In the not-too-distant future, a vegetable embodiment of the life force comes to earth, and causes a riot in the evolution of earth's flora and fauna. Much of the human species has escaped to Alpha Centauri. Remaining behind is Niall, a young man with special mental powers, to encounter and neutralize the species of now fully sentient giant spiders that has enslaved most of the remaining humans. Humanity has another chance to solve what Wilson contends is its abiding problem: Man must learn to control his own mind so that the control he so easily exerts over the material world can avoid yet another catastrophe like those that fill human history.

Of these novels the Spider World series is a respectable reprise of the earlier works. *The Space Vampires (Life Force)* is the shortest and slickest. *The Philosopher's Stone* bogs us down and seems precisely repetitive of *The Mind Parasites* whose patient narrative, nicely deployed scenic hyperboles, and wonderful message were Wilson's first, and best attempt after all.

—John R. Pfeiffer

---

**WILSON, F(rancis) Paul.** American. Born in Jersey City, New Jersey, 17 May 1946. Married Mary Murphy in 1969; two daughters. Since 1974, physician, Cedar Bridge Medical Group, Bricktown, New Jersey. Recipient: Prometheus award, 1979. Agent: Albert Zuckerman, Writers House, 21 West 26th Street, New York, New York 10010, U.S.A.

SCIENCE-FICTION PUBLICATIONS

Novels (series: LaNague Federation)

*Healer* (LaNague). New York, Doubleday, 1976; London, Sidgwick and Jackson, 1977.
*Wheels Within Wheels* (LaNague). New York, Doubleday, 1979; London, Sidgwick and Jackson, 1980.
*An Enemy of the State* (LaNague). New York, Doubleday, 1980.
*The Keep*. New York, Morrow, 1981; London, New English Library, 1982.
*Dydeetown World* (LaNague). New York, Baen, 1989.
*Reborn*. Arlington Heights, Illinois, Dark Harvest, and London, New English Library, 1990.
*The Tery* (LaNague). New York, Baen, 1990.
*Reprisal*. Arlington Heights, Illinois, Dark Harvest, 1991.

Short Stories

*Soft and Others*. New York, Tor, 1989.
*Ad Statum Perspicuum*. Eugene, Oregon, Pulphouse, 1990.

OTHER PUBLICATIONS

Novels

*The Tomb*. Binghamton, New York, Whispers Press, 1984; London, New English Library, 1985.
*The Touch*. New York, Putnam, and London, New English Library, 1986.
*Black Wind*. New York, Tor, 1988; London, Joseph, 1989.
*Midnight Mass* (novella). Eugene, Oregon, Axolotl Press, 1990.

*

F. Paul Wilson comments:

I spent the 1970's writing science fiction, spent the 1980's writing horror of a cosmic sort (with occasional side trips back into SF). I'm not sure what the 1990's will bring, but I feel I've said most of what I have to say in the field of supernatural horror. Maybe it's time to move closer to home, come down to street level, to the here-and-now. The new novel *SIBS* is, I believe, a sign post on the road I'm traveling. We'll see where it takes me.

* * *

F. Paul Wilson's first stories were relatively undistinguished formula pieces for *Analog* magazine, but he quickly distinguished himself with a few outstanding works, most notably "Pard" and "Lipidleggin'." "Pard" deals with the symbiotic relationship between a human and an alien, immortal and with unique mental powers that allow them to fulfill a unique role in human history. This story was later incorporated into Wilson's first novel, *Healer*, in which the paired intelligences must deal with an interstellar psionic plague that drives entire populations into madness.

A natural catastrophe would be bad enough, but the plague is actually a weapon wielded by another consciousness, against which even the Healer may find his abilities inadequate. The larger-than-life nature of the character makes identification difficult, but Wilson keeps the plot moving so quickly, the flaw is largely invisible.

Wilson's second novel, *Wheels Within Wheels*, is a combination of scientific puzzle with conventional mystery. An alien race incapable of violent acts or conscious lies admits to having murdered a human being, but will not explain the circumstances. Twenty years later, the victim's daughter arrives to investigate. The alien culture is fascinating and the resolution is both plausible and clever, but the story's pacing is slow at times. *An Enemy of the State*, set against the same interstellar civilization, is more in the mold of his early magazine stories, a fairly routine interplanetary political thriller with lots of overt action, occasionally interspersed with short but somewhat obtrusive observations by the author. Again, a single human being must take command of the destiny of the entire race. At about the same time, Wilson produced *The Tery*, pitting some physically unprepossessing aliens against a fanatical human religious cult with predictable but very engaging results. One of Wilson's better stories, it was originally published as a novella in Dell's short lived "Binary Star" series, later reprinted as an independent novel.

In 1981, Wilson's *The Keep* catapulted him into the public eye. Marketed as a horror novel, it is all of that and arguably SF as well; certainly, it is not easily classifiable. Nazi soldiers occupy an ancient castle during World War II, where they inadvertently free an ageless evil presence that has been imprisoned there. When it begins to slay members of their party, they resort to using a Jewish academic and his daughter in an attempt to determine the nature of the menace they face. The internal tensions among the Nazi officers is particularly well handled, and the story succeeds on a number of levels. On the surface, *The Keep* is a vampire novel, but Wilson turns the theme around. The monster is only one aspect of a duality that involves an ageless warrior who has lived secretly among the human race. Now the two must meet again in what may be the last battle between them. The popularity of the novel resulted in a mediocre though occasionally interesting film version, and it certainly established his reputation. Almost ten years later, Wilson would write a sequel of sorts, *Reborn*, also marketed as horror but even more clearly science fiction. An aging scientist has died and mysteriously leaves his entire fortune to a young man whom he seemed never to have known. The recipient investigates to satisfy his own curiosity, and learns that he is the result of an illegal experiment in cloning. Although there are horrific elements, the fantastic elements are held at arms length, and the book could as easily have been marketed as science fiction.

Having established himself as a horror writer of some importance, most of Wilson's novels during the past several years have been in that field. A shipload of hideous creatures menaces modern America in *The Tomb*. The horror is less overt in *The Touch*, and almost non-existent in traditional terms in the thoughtful *Black Wind*. Another straight science-fiction novel, *Dydeetown World*, also appeared during this period, an interesting tour of strange culture, written in the style of a traditional private investigator story, but with some unique twists and turns. It is also one of Wilson's rare forays into humor, although the whimsy is always subservient to the plot. The novel, though aimed at an adult audience, gained considerable acclaim as a book for younger readers.

Wilson continued to write short fiction in both the horror and SF genres during the latter 1980's. One of his more interesting is a horror novella, "Midnight Mass," set in a world where vampires have taken control, a theme Richard Matheson examined earlier in *I Am Legend*. Other short stories worth noting include "Kids," "Soft," "Traps," "Cuts," and "The Last One Mo Once Golden Revival." The best of his short fiction has been collected in *Soft and Others*.

Wilson has stated in print that he doesn't wish to be labelled as a writer in any particular genre, that he wishes to be free to use styles, themes, and subject matter that appeal to him, rather than those that fit a particular market. Certainly he has proven to be capable of wide ranging styles; *Dydeetown World, Black Wind*, and *The Keep* read like the works of three entirely different writers. The one thing they all have in common is strong narrative techniques and a sense that the author genuinely admires his protagonists.

—Don D'Ammassa

---

**WILSON, Gabriel.** *See* **CUMMINGS, Ray.**

---

**WILSON, Richard.** American. Born in Huntington Station, New York, 23 September 1920. Educated at Brooklyn College, 1935–36; University of Chicago, 1947–48. Served in the United States Army Signal Corps and Air Force, 1942–46. Married 1) Jessica Gould in 1941 (divorced 1944); 2) Doris Owens in 1950 (divorced 1967); 3) Frances Daniels in 1967 (divorced 1982); one son and one step-daughter. Reporter, copyreader, and assistant drama critic, Fairchild Publications, New York, 1941–42; Chief of Bureau, Transradio Press, Chicago, Washington, D.C. and New York, 1946–51; reporter, and deputy to the North American editor, Reuters, New York, 1951–64; director, Syracuse University News Bureau, New York, 1964–80, and university editor, 1980–82. Recipient: Nebula award, 1968. *Died in 1987(?).*

SCIENCE-FICTION PUBLICATIONS

Novels

*The Girls from Planet 5.* New York, Ballantine, 1955; London, Hale, 1968.
*And Then the Town Took Off.* New York, Ace, 1960.
*30-Day Wonder.* New York, Ballantine, 1960; London, Icon, 1963.

Short Stories

*Those Idiots from Earth.* New York, Ballantine, 1957.
*Time Out for Tomorrow.* New York, Ballantine, 1962; London, Mayflower, 1967.
*The Kid from Ozone Park and Other Stories.* Polk City, Iowa, Drumm, 1987.

Uncollected Short Stories (series: Harry Protagonist)

"Friend of the Family," in *Star 2* (Derby, Connecticut), 1953.
"The Enemy," in *Infinity* (New York), October 1957.
"Man Working," in *Star* (Derby, Connecticut), November 1958.
"Frostbite," in *Future* (New York), February 1959.
"The Carson Effect," in *The Year's Best S-F 10*, edited by Judith Merril. New York, Delacorte Press, 1965.
"Box," in *New Worlds* (London), February 1965.

"The Eight Billion," in *Fantasy and Science Fiction* (New York), July 1965.

"Watchers in the Glade," in *The Ninth Galaxy Reader*, edited by Frederik Pohl. New York, Doubleday, and London, Gollancz, 1966.

"Deserter," in *Impulse* (Bournemouth), March 1966.

"Inside Out," in *Impulse* (Bournemouth), December 1966.

"Green Eyes," in *Impulse* (Bournemouth), January 1967.

"The Evil Ones," in *If* (New York), February 1967.

"9-9-99," in *Galaxy* (New York), August 1967.

"The South Waterford Rumble Club," in *Galaxy* (New York), December 1967.

"Mother to the World," in *Orbit 3*, edited by Damon Knight. New York, Putnam, 1968.

"See Me Not," in *World's Best Science Fiction 1968*, edited by Donald A. Wollheim and Terry Carr. New York, Ace, and London, Gollancz, 1968.

"Harry Protagonist, Undersec for Overpop," in *Magazine of Horror* (New York), December 1969.

"A Man Spekith," in *World's Best Science Fiction 1970*, edited by Donald A. Wollheim and Terry Carr. New York, Ace, and London, Gollancz, 1970.

"If a Man Answers," in *If* (New York), January 1970.

"Have It Your Own Way," in *The Most Thrilling Science Fiction Ever Told* (New York), Winter 1970.

"The Day They Had the War," in *Fantasy and Science Fiction* (New York), June 1971.

"The Far King," in *Asimov's Choice: Comets and Computers*, edited by George H. Scithers. New York, Davis, 1978.

"Harry Protagonist, Brain-Drainer," in *100 Great Science Fiction Short-Short Stories*, edited by Isaac Asimov, Martin H. Greenberg, and Joseph D. Olander. New York, Doubleday, and London, Robson, 1978.

"The Story Writer," in *The 1980 Annual World's Best SF*, edited by Donald A. Wollheim. New York, DAW, 1980.

"Gone Past," in *Destinies* (New York), Fall 1980.

"The Nineteenth Century Spaceship," in *Last Wave* (New York), August 1984.

"Lark Thou Never Wert," in *Pandora* (Tampa, Florida), December 1984.

OTHER PUBLICATIONS

Plays

*Jack and Jill* (produced Syracuse, New York, 1965).

*Another Time*, in *Modern Radio Production*. Belmont, California, Wadsworth, 1985.

Radio Play: *Inside Story* (*X Minus One* series), 1955.

Other

*Syracuse University: The Critical Years* (vol. 3 of university history). Syracuse, New York, Syracuse University, 1984.

*

Manuscript Collection: Bird Library, Syracuse University, New York.

* * *

Richard Wilson's career as a writer breaks quite nicely into two stages. In his early years, Wilson was a satirical humorist in the mode of Henry Kuttner and Robert Sheckley, whose stories were frequently infused with a grim humor and a sharp eye for humanity's foibles. The three novels written at this time are cases in point. *The Girls from Planet 5* takes a pair of old stand-by plots and fuses them, with delighted results. America has become a matriarchy, where only one state still upholds the macho ideal—Texas, naturally. Into this strife-ridden world come invaders from another world, but invaders who are actually beautiful women. Frustrated by their loss of preeminence, the Texan patriarchs are not willing to become a minor backwater in an increasingly female universe. Aliens appear again in *And Then the Town Took Off*, a shorter novel that details the effect upon the citizens of Superior, Ohio, when their city uproots itself from Earth and rises into space to become a separate planet. This rollicking escapade pokes amusing if unconscious fun at James Blish's famous "Cities in Flight" series. The third and best of the novels is *30-Day Wonder*, which takes what should be an ideal situation and turns it completely around. The Monolithians are alien visitors who express their determination to obey scrupulously all human laws and regulations, and ensure that all humans in their vicinity will do the same. The effect on rush-hour traffic of several automobiles sedately travelling well within the speed limit is just the beginning of an increasingly taxing month of the human race.

Although most of Wilson's early short stories, such as "Those Idiots from Earth," were satirical or actively funny, his most well-known story of that period was very serious. The heroine of "Love" is a blind human girl living on Mars, who is in love with one of the despised Martian natives. When her father forbids her to have anything further to do with him, she runs off for one last meeting, and together they discover an ancient artifact that may well cure her sight. It is a touching tale told somewhat awkwardly, but effective.

The awkwardness left during the years that followed, and several of Wilson's more recent works are outstanding. "Mother to the World" won a Nebula award for its tender, effective portrayal of the last man on Earth and the last woman, a gentle but retarded individual whose tolerance and flexibility overcome the horrors of their situation. Wilson returned to the last man theme in "A Man Spekith," in which a disc jockey and a computer remain in orbit, looking down over the corpse of the earth. "See Me Not" is one of the few recent treatments of invisibility that contains any novelty. "The Carson Effect" portrays a wave of philanthropy on the eve of the last day of the world, an ending that is miscalculated and never happens, much to the consternation of those who have given away their fortunes. "The Story Writer" is a complex, engrossing story that contains enough complexity for a brace of novels. An aging successful pulp writer sits in flea markets, writing stories for people as a whim, until he finds himself a character in one of his own stories, the tale of the meeting of our own race and another that has reached us through another plane of existence in their flight from a ravaged homeworld. The last few stories to appear by Wilson before his death employed a rich, witty style that demonstrated his continued growth as a writer. It is unfortunate that we will never know how much further he would have progressed.

—Don D'Ammassa

---

**WILSON, Robert Anton.** American. Born in Brooklyn, New York, 18 January 1932. Educated at Brooklyn Polytechnic Institute; New York University, Paideia University, B.S., M.A. 1978, Ph.D. 1981. Married Arlen Riley in 1959; four children.

Engineering aide, Ebasco Inc., New York, 1950–56; salesman, Doubleday Publishers, 1957; copywriter, Popular Club, Passaic, New Jersey, 1959–62; sales manager, Antioch Bookplate, Yellow Springs, Ohio, 1962–65; astrology columnist, *National Mirror*, and editor, *Jaguar*, 1965; associate editor, *Playboy*, Chicago, 1965–71. Agent: Al Zuckerman, Writers House, 21 West 26th Street, New York, New York 10010, U.S.A.

SCIENCE-FICTION PUBLICATIONS

Novels (series: Illuminatus; Schrödinger's Cat)

*Illuminatus! The Eye in the Pyramid, The Golden Apple, Leviathan*, with Robert Shea. New York, Dell, 3 vols., 1975; London, Sphere, 3 vols., 1976; one vol. edition, Dell, 1984.
*Schrödinger's Cat Trilogy*. New York, Dell, 1988.
*The Universe Next Door*. New York, Pocket Books, 1979; London, Sphere, 1980.
*The Trick Top Hat*. New York, Pocket Books, 1980; London, Sphere, 1981.
*Homing Pigeons*. New York, Pocket Books, 1981; London, Sphere, 1982.
*Masks of the Illuminati*. New York, Pocket Books, and London, Sphere, 1981.
The Historical Illuminatus Chronicles:
*The Earth Will Shake*. Los Angeles, Tarcher, 1982.
*The Widow's Son*. New York, Bluejay, 1985.
*Nature's God*. New York, Roc, 1991.

OTHER PUBLICATIONS

Novel

*The Sex Magicians*. Los Angeles, Jaundice Press, 1974.

Plays

*Illuminatus!* (produced Liverpool, 1976; London, 1977; Seattle, 1978).
*Wilhelm Reich in Hell* (produced Dublin, 1985).

Other

*Playboy's Book of Forbidden Words*. Chicago, Playboy Press, 1972.
*Sex and Drugs*. Chicago, Playboy Press, 1973; London, Mayflower, 1975.
*The Book of the Breast*. Chicago, Playboy Press, 1974.
*Cosmic Trigger: Final Secret of the Illuminati*. Berkeley, California, And/Or Press, 1977; London, Abacus, 1979.
*Neuropolitics*, with Timothy Leary. Culver City, California, Peace Press, 1977.
*The Illuminati Papers*. Berkeley, California, And/Or Press, 1980; London, Sphere, 1982.
*Right Where You Are Sitting Now: Further Tales of the Illuminati*. Berkeley, California, And/Or Press, 1982.
*Prometheus Rising*. Santa Monica, California, Falcon Press, 1983.
*The New Inquisition: Irrational Rationalism and the Citadel of Science*. Phoenix, Arizona, Falcon Press, 1988.
*Coincidance: A Head Test*. Phoenix, Arizona, Falcon Press, 1989.
*Quantum Psychology*. Phoenix, Arizona, Falcon Press, 1990.

*

Robert Anton Wilson comments:

I define my writing as guerilla ontology—that is, a literary expression of the discoveries of physical relativity (Einstein), cultural relativity (anthropology), neurological relativity (Korzybski, Leary) and the new head-spaces opened to us by psychedelics, bio-feedback, scientific study of yoga, etc. Each of my books presents not one map of reality, but several; the humor, the suspense, and the philosophical meaning (if any) derive from the search for the one reality, never quite found, which will synthesize or include all the alternative reality-tunnels presented. As in quantum physics, the isolated observer or omniscient narrator does not exist in my world; it is a participatory universe in which each entity projects/creates its own surrounding experiential continuum.

* * *

Games of all sorts and at all levels abound throughout Robert Anton Wilson's books. Those most typical in this respect are perhaps *Masks of the Illuminati*, whose overall structure is that of a detective story (the most formal sort of literary game, and here played with strict attention to the rules) and whose subject is the mind-game played on an innocent seeking occult knowledge. And Wilson would solemnly assure us that the book is part of the mind-game he is playing with his readers, Operation Mindfuck, to lead them to some level of further awareness.

Some readers will find that last level, Wilson's philosophical pretensions, spoils the books for them. But insofar as he's serious about anything, Wilson is serious about bringing home to people the limits that their own viewpoints impose on them and the possibility of transcending those limits. To this end Wilson makes a mockery of all political viewpoints (including the anarchism he himself espouses) and in *Prometheus Rising* tries to give some structure to a course of self-liberation. *Prometheus Rising* and *Quantum Psychology* are practical handbooks of his peculiar philosophy, although *The Illuminati Papers* and *Coincidance* may be more easily accessible to the casual reader. Perhaps the "Transcendental Agnosticism" that has come to Wilson from drinking too deep of too many springs of ultimate wisdom, from hearing too many Ultimate Truths contradict each other; perhaps it's too much a product of the late 1960's to appeal to the True Believers who infest more recent decades. But happily Wilson doesn't seem to have noticed and continues to pillory our "normal primate behaviour." He is especially funny concerning scientific dogmatism in *The New Inquisition* and *The Widow's Son*.

And if you want to just sit back, forget the message and look at the scenery, Wilson will keep you happily entertained, stealing from any source that pleases him, Joyce, Lovecraft, Tolkien, or "Elephant Doody Comix" and throwing up the lunatic touches of characterisation that make the patchwork structures of his novels shine.

Wilson's viewpoint is determinedly optimistic, as his essays on Buckminster Fuller and on the conquest of stupidity show. Yet there is in his novels alongside the jugglers and buffoons a sense of pain and tragedy that isn't diminished by its futility. To quote Wilson's own motto: "It isn't true unless it makes you laugh, but you don't understand it until it makes you cry."

The best sampler works for those who want to explore Wilson's fiction are *Masks of the Illuminati* and *The Earth Will Shake; Illuminatus!* and *Schrödinger's Cat* may be a little heavy.

—Michael Cule

---

**WILSON, Robert Charles.** Canadian. Born in 1953. Lives in Vancouver, British Columbia. Address: c/o Doubleday, 666 Fifth Avenue, New York, New York 10103, U.S.A.

SCIENCE-FICTION PUBLICATIONS

Novels

*A Hidden Place.* New York, Bantam, 1986; London, Orbit, 1990.
*Memory Wire.* New York, Bantam, 1988; London, Orbit, 1990.
*Gypsies.* New York, Doubleday, 1989; London, Orbit, 1990.
*The Divide.* New York, Doubleday, and London, Orbit, 1990.
*A Bridge of Years.* New York, Doubleday, 1991.

* * *

Robert Charles Wilson is an extraordinarily gifted writer with a deep understanding of the importance of love, in all its forms, in human relationships. For these reasons he has often been compared to Theodore Sturgeon. Although he has published a number of short stories, his strength comes out mainly in his novels. *A Hidden Place*, his first novel, hallmarked him as a significantly talented writer. Travis Fisher, after his mother's death, moves into his aunt's house in a small prairie town, Haute Montagne, during the Great Depression. There, with his new found sweetheart, Nancy Wilcox, he falls under the spell of Anna Blaise, a strange and mysteriously radiant woman. Anna Blaise is from another universe and only half present, for she must be reunited with her "male part," Bone, in order to return home. In the meantime, Bone, an amnesiac hobo travelling on the railroads, is becoming distantly aware of his true nature. All the protagonists in *A Hidden Place* are estranged persons. Travis is estranged from his family, Nancy from her own town, Anna and Bone from each other and from their world while all the inhabitants of Haute Montagne strive to belong and conserve their position in the small community and not fall into the rejection that is Nancy and Travers' lot. However, *A Hidden Place* is not a nostalgic novel, for Wilson manages to keep it paced and have its plot progressing briskly while combining romance and suspense without falling into the trap of an ordinary love story.

Wilson's second novel, *Memory Wire*, is an incursion into the world of cyberpunk. It is a slight departure from the usually realistic and contemporary setting that Wilson tends to lay out at the beginning of all his other novels. *Memory Wire* catapults us into the next century right from the beginning when volunteers are employed to function as human video-recorders by TV news networks after having been dotted with implants. Once again, Wilson deals with the theme of alienation, the inescapable condition of the main characters: Keller is the all seeing angel who is transformed into an unfeeling being for the main purpose of forgetting his past. Teresa, contrary to Keller, is trying to recapture her past through "oneiriltihs," extraterrestrial dreaming jewels discovered in the Amazone that enable one to remember one's past extremely accurately. All this makes up for a tense thriller in which love, described in a touching and delicate way, occupies a central place.

*Gypsies*, Wilson's third novel, is an excellent book slightly marred by the apparent determination of its author to explain all scientific events with words that have more to do with magic and fantasy than science fiction. It tells of siblings with the ability to travel between parallel universes who, up till now, have been living most of their lives in our reality/universe. Since they are the products of genetic research and government funding from another universe, it is puzzling, if not irritating, to find a constant reference to magic, spells, and words usually more associated with pure fantasy rather than science fiction. It is quite possible that Wilson, whose science fiction relies much more on "soft sciences" (such as psychology and sociology), feels uncomfortable with the use of scientific terminology in *Gypsies;* nevertheless, it is a science-fiction novel that deals with human suffering: in an attempt to prevent them from using their powers and therefore to protect them from their former masters, two of the protagonists were often beat up by their parents, and this has left permanent scars that are explored movingly in the novel. As in many of his works, Wilson does not shy away from going deep into his characters' psyche and for this purpose often puts them into realistic situations, even if it is to escape the science-fiction atmosphere for a while; in fact, this departure makes the return to the science-fiction aspect of the story all the more alluring and compelling. A good example is to be found in Karen's painful and truthful phone conversations with her estranged and "normal" husband. *The Divide*, set in Toronto, presents John Shaw, who has been transformed by U.S. research into a super being gifted with hyper sensory organs and intelligence. The project has been dropped, but now John Shaw's health is deteriorating, and Benjamin, his alternate persona, is taking control of John's mind. His split personality will kill him unless he finds a way of fusing his two minds. The novel is reminiscent of *A Hidden Place* with its theme of split personalities and inner reconciliation. In *The Divide*, Wilson engages in a bolder description of love while succeeding in writing a melancholic story about the search for oneself.

It is quite possible that Wilson will be one the few writers of the 1980's that will survive his own era. His treatment of contemporary themes such as alienation and the loss of identity puts him in the same league with many science fiction and mainstream writers who have managed to resist the passage of time.

—Henry Leperlier

---

**WINGRAVE, Anthony.** *See* **WRIGHT, S. Fowler.**

---

**WINGROVE, David (John).** British. Born in London, England, 1 September 1954. Educated at Battersea Grammar School, 1965–71; University of Kent, Canterbury, 1979–84, First Class Honours Degree, English and American literature. Common law wife, Susan Oudôt; three daughters. Worked in banking, 1971–79. Membership secretary, British Science Fiction Association, 1976–77. Editor, *Vector* magazine, 1977–79. Recipient: Science Fiction Achievement award (Hugo), 1987. Agent: Hilary Rubinstein, A.P. Watt, 20 John Street, London WC1N 2DR, England.

SCIENCE-FICTION PUBLICATIONS

Novels (series: Chung Kuo)

*Chung Kuo: The Middle Kingdom.* London, New English Library, 1989; New York, Delacorte, 1990.
*Chung Kuo: The Broken Wheel.* London, New English Library, 1990; New York, Delacorte, 1991.
*Chung Kuo: The White Mountain.* London, New English Library, 1991; New York, Delacorte, 1992.

OTHER PUBLICATIONS

Other

*Apertures: A Study of the Writings of Brian W. Aldiss*, with Brian Griffin. Westport, Connecticut, Greenwood Press, 1984.
*Trillion Year Spree: The History of Science Fiction*, with Brian Aldiss. London, Gollancz, and New York, Atheneum, 1986.

Editor, *The Science Fiction Source Book.* London, Longman, and New York, Van Nostrand Reinhold, 1984.
Editor, *The Science Fiction Film Source Book.* London, Longman, 1985.

*

David Wingrove comments:

If writing about the future is to have any prodromic significance, it must—in its themes and subject matter—address what is happening to our world right now. Over-population, the destruction of the eco-system, and man's tendency to seek rigid authoritarian solutions to the problems he creates are symptoms of a world seriously out of balance. In my eight-volume novel, *Chung Kuo*, I seek to illuminate some of these matters in an involving and, I hope, entertaining manner. If the sequence is about anything, it is about the search for balance—for a system of behaviour that can accommodate peacefully and healthily all the people we are.

* * *

David Wingrove's *Chung Kuo* is a large work which, on publication of the final volume, will portray 60 years of a future history of the human race. From a short story written in 1983, *Chung Kuo* expanded in intermediate stages (to one novel, then two novels) before attaining a form that satisfied the author—an eight-volume novel of which three volumes have thus far appeared.

The world of *Chung Kuo* is a world in stasis. The Han—or Chinese—utterly dominate the globe, and Earth's population inhabit vast, continent-spanning Cities, 300 levels high and completely cut off from the outside. There are seven great regional Cities, each ruled by its T'ang, and together these absolute rulers constitute the Council of the Seven. *Chung Kuo*'s society is rigidly stratified, its governing apparatus strictly authoritarian, and the Seven see their task as maintaining this state of affairs, thus resisting change.

But the very existence of *Chung Kuo* is based on a huge lie: that the ancient Chinese defeated the Roman Empire and went on to conquer the world. The founders of *Chung Kuo* devoted immense effort in fabricating a complex alternative history and erasing the truth, which was that in the mid-21st century the Western nations collapsed into chaos and war and were subjugated by a resurgent China led by a ruthless tyrant, Tsao Ch'un, at the cost of billions of lives and the obliteration of entire cultures. Tsao Ch'un was himself overthrown by his seven ministers who went on to establish their own power as the Council of the Seven and to complete the global hegemony of Chung Kuo. And Humanity was physically confined within the Cities, and mentally imprisoned by the strictures and codes of Han culture, by its imposed homogeneity.

Volume one, *The Middle Kingdom*, begins over a century later, with Earth's population more than 34 billion and rising, with demands that the 114-year-old Edict of Technological Control be moderated, and with undercurrents of political opposition to the rule of the Seven. Chung Kuo is ripe for change.

Change is one of David Wingrove's main themes and is continually shadowed by its corollary, the search for balance. This duality is openly stated in the prologue of *The Middle Kingdom*:

> Uncharacteristically, Li Shai Tung put his hands to his face. He had been having dreams. Dreams in which he saw the Cities burning. Dreams in which old friends were dead—brutally murdered in their beds, their children's bodies torn and bloodied on the nursery floor.
>
> In his dreams he saw the darkness bubble up into the bright-lit levels. Saw the whole edifice slide down into the mire of chaos. Saw it clearly as he saw his hands, now, before his face.
>
> Yet it was more than dreams. It was what would happen—unless they acted.
>
> Li Shai Tung, T'ang, Ruler of City Europe, one of the Seven, shuddered.

Li Shai Tung's resistance to change brings him (and by extension, the Seven) into conflict with its proponents. First are the Dispersionists, a political faction led by Berdichev, Wyatt, and Lehmann, wealthy businessmen in City Europe. After six years of confrontation, both overt and covert, Wyatt and Lehmann are dead, Berdichev has fled to Mars, and the Dispersionists are a spent force. But the rulers have not come through unharmed: by the end of *The Middle Kingdom*, four of the Seven are dead, replaced by young, inexperienced heirs, and Li Shai Tung's elder son has been assassinated.

Other opponents to the rule of the Seven come to the fore. In volume two, *The Broken Wheel*, revolutionaries called the *Ping Tiao* carry out acts of sabotage and terrorism against the state. But when, at the start of volume three, *The White Mountain*, they help to destroy a major fortress/barracks in City Europe, killing thousands of innocents, the backlash from the T'ang's security forces almost wipes them out. Soon after, another revolutionary group, the *Yu*, rises to prominence and by the end of *The White Mountain* has established a reputation for moral discrimination by assassinating only those responsible for corruption or murder.

David Wingrove's vast story of a world undergoing catastrophic change is also a story of movers, shakers, and victims, and of ambiguity and contradiction. Even though Li Shai Tung, and later his younger son, Li Yuan, are absolute rulers, they are not archetypal monstrous tyrants. Both display dignity and compassion, qualities somewhat lacking in the Dispersionists and particularly in one of their main allies, Howard DeVore, a major in the T'ang's security forces. DeVore later emerges as the Seven's leading adversary, conducting a shadowy, almost secret war against the entire edifice of *Chung Kuo*, and becoming a personification of change—or at least its dark, masculine, Yang aspect.

This dark aspect of change resonates strongly with the very character of *Chung Kuo*: it is a society where yin and yang are severely out of balance, where the latter dominates the former and contributes to the atmosphere of wrongness and oppression, to the sense that a gentler aspect of human nature is missing.

Given the large cast of characters introduced in the first three volumes of *Chung Kuo*, and the devious (and often overlapping) intrigues in which they are involved, it is no surprise that the author chose to adopt a clear, straightforward prose style. Nothing is obscured, and with the open use of metaphor and leitmotif Wingrove has reached levels of meaning seldom encountered in science fiction. But before all matters of connotation comes the story itself, and through clarity of expression David Wingrove has thus far created a highly readable, genuinely enjoyable epic rich in symbolism.

—Michael Cobley

---

**WINIKI, Ephraim.** *See* **FEARN, John Russell.**

---

**WINNARD, Frank.** *See* **TUBB, E.C.**

---

**WINTER, H.G.** *See* **BATES, Harry.**

---

**WODHAMS, Jack.** Also writes as Trudy Rose. Australian. Born in Dagenham, Essex, England, 3 September 1931; emigrated to Australia in 1955. Has worked as a weighing-machine mechanic, brush salesman, a porter in mental hospital, taxi and truck driver, bartender, welder, and magician's assistant. Currently mailvan driver, Brisbane, Guest of Honor, Melbourne Science Fiction Convention, 1968. Address: P.O. Box 48, Caboolture, Queensland 4510, Australia.

SCIENCE-FICTION PUBLICATIONS

Novels

*The Authentic Touch.* New York, Curtis, 1971.
*Looking for Blücher.* St. Kilda, Victoria, Void, 1980.
*Ryn.* St. Kilda, Victoria, Cory and Collins, 1982.

Short Stories

*Future War.* St. Kilda, Victoria, Cory and Collins, 1982.

Uncollected Short Stories

"The Pearly Gates of Hell," in *Analog* (New York), September 1967.
"The Cure-All Merchant," in *Analog* (New York), November 1967.
"The Helmet of Hades," in *New Writings in SF 11*, edited by John Carnell. London, Corgi, 1968.
"The God Pedlars," in *Analog* (New York), February 1968.
"Handyman," in *Analog* (New York), April 1968.
"The Fuglemen of Recall," in *Analog* (New York), August 1968.
"Homespinner," in *Galaxy* (New York), October 1968.
"Try Again," in *Amazing* (New York), November 1968.
"Split Personality," in *Analog* (New York), November 1968.
"The Form Master," in *Analog* (New York), December 1968.
"Hey but No Presto," in *Analog* (New York), April 1969.
"A Run of Deuces," in *Fantasy and Science Fiction* (New York), June 1969.
"The Empty Balloon," in *Analog* (New York), July 1969.
"Androtomy and the Scion," in *Analog* (New York), August 1969.
"Anchor Man," in *Vision of Tomorrow* (Newcastle upon Tyne), August 1969.
"Star Hunger," in *Galaxy* (New York), August 1969.
"The Visitors," in *Analog* (New York), September 1969.
"Undercover Weapon," in *Vision of Tomorrow* (Newcastle upon Tyne), December 1969.
"There Is a Crooked Man," in *Analog 7*, edited by John W. Campbell, Jr. New York, Doubleday, 1970.
"The Ill Wind," in *Vision of Tomorrow* (Newcastle upon Tyne), January 1970.
"On Greatgrandfather's Knee," in *Vision of Tomorrow* (Newcastle upon Tyne), February 1970.
"Dali, for Instance," in *Analog* (New York), February 1970.
"Wrong Rabbit," in *Analog* (New York), March 1970.
"Zwoppover," in *Vision of Tomorrow* (Newcastle upon Tyne), April 1970.
"Beau Farscon Regrets," in *Analog* (New York), July 1970.
"Top Billing," in *Analog* (New York), September 1970.
"Enemy by Proxy," in *Amazing* (New York), November 1970.
"Big Time Operator," in *Analog* (New York), December 1970.
"Sprog," in *Analog* (New York), January 1971.
"The Pickle Barrel," in *Analog* (New York), February 1971.
"The Amazon," in *Man* (Sydney), August, 1971.
"You Don't Know What It's Like," in *Man* (Sydney), August 1971.
"Knight Arrant," in *Analog* (New York), September 1971.
"Foundling's Father," in *Analog* (New York), December 1971.
"Stormy Bellwether," in *Analog* (New York), January 1972.
"Budnip," in *Analog* (New York), August 1972.
"Lien Low," in *Void 1* (St. Kilda, Victoria), 1975.
"The 200-1 Asset," in *Void 2* (St. Kilda, Victoria), 1975.
"Squawman," in *Void 3* (St. Kilda, Victoria), 1976.
"The Masque Behind the Face," in *Void 4* (St. Kilda, Victoria), 1976.
"The Giveaway," in *Void 5* (St. Kilda, Victoria), 1977.
"The Butterfly Must Die," in *Envisaged Worlds*, edited by Paul Collins. St. Kilda, Victoria, Void 1978.
"Jade Elm," in *Other Worlds*, edited by Paul Collins. St. Kilda, Victoria, Void, 1978.
"One Clay Foot," and "Pin a Medal for a Winkle" (as Trudy Rose), in *Alien Worlds*, edited by Paul Collins. St. Kilda, Victoria, Void, 1979.
"Whosa Whatsa?," in *The Seven Deadly Sins of Science Fiction*, edited by Isaac Asimov, Martin H. Greenberg, and Charles G. Waugh. New York, Fawcett, 1980.
"Armstrong," and "Vandal" (as Trudy Rose), in *Distant Worlds*, edited by Paul Collins. St. Kilda, Victoria, Cory and Collins, 1981.
"Mostly Meantime," in *Analog* (New York), February 1981.
"Counter Espionage," in *Omega Science Digest* (Sydney), July/August 1981.
"Freeway," in *Amazing* (New York), November 1981.
"To Catch a Thief," in *Omega Science Digest* (Sydney), January/February 1982.
"The Making of a Gaffa," in *Rigel* (Richmond, California), Spring 1982.

"Telepathetique," in *Fantasy Book* (Pasadena, California), May 1982.
"Death of an Echo," in *Omega Science Digest* (Sydney), July/August 1982.
"Premonition," in *Twilight Zone* (New York), September 1982.
"The Hide," in *Future Worlds*, edited by Paul Collins. St. Kilda, Victoria, Cory and Collins, 1983.
"Gauntlet's World," in *Rigel* (Richmond, California), Summer 1983.
"The Maroon Is Rue," in *Fantasy Book* (Pasadena, California), August 1983.
"Station 2152," in *Analog* (New York), August 1986.
"Picaper," in *Analog* (New York), mid-December 1986.
"Roadbreakers," in *Analog* (New York), June 1988.
"The Token Pole," in *Analog* (New York), February 1990.

*

Jack Wodhams comments:

Why do I write SF? I write SF because it is a genre that isn't a genre. Someone selecting a romance can anticipate heartthrob; a western a shootout; a whodunnit clues to a killer. SF abides by no such predictable format. SF permits its writer to explore where that writer will, be it *20,000 Leagues Under the Sea*, or what it would be like to be an Invisible Man, or how it might feel to voyage in space, to discover other worlds, to encounter other sentient beings.

Past, present, future. Techniques, methods, inventions, laws, societies, ways of life. To a high degree an SF writer may declare the rules of the tale she or he would unfold. When a reader picks up a collection of SF short stories, it is with the certain knowledge that no two will match in time, place, or circumstance. Each will carry its own distinct thought, idea, aspect, that cannot beforehand be pre-emptively presumed.

SF is simply the most interesting, beguiling, stimulating literature to exercise the mind. It certainly provides grand exercise for the mind of a writer.

* * *

It is well known that science fiction tends to emphasise content at the expense of style, but the positive influence this has had on narrative techniques is not always appreciated. Writers have been encouraged to create methods better adapted to its needs than traditional story-telling procedures. Jack Wodhams is one such writer. The way his stories are constructed could have been evolved in traditional short-story writing. Smooth, effortless, controlled, a typical Wodhams story moves irresistibly ahead, mostly carried by dialog with a minimum of description and explanation. Indeed, when the author intrudes to fill in background or discuss principles, the pace slows or falters. There may be a firm single viewpoint, or a focus of action on a continuing situation if it is required. Often there are frequent scene changes as the action unfolds through related events. Characters tend to be no more than voices whose conversation shows what is happening, details of motivation unknown and irrelevant. The effect at its best is of the story happening, not being reported. It has much in common with modern film scripts, but it emerged naturally in science fiction as the field matured and a sophisticated readership developed.

Wodham's stories usually grow out of an original scientific premise, often a revaluation of a familiar speculation. They may bring out new objects or snags or turn a familiar argument around, often for a surprise ending. Some are in the venerable "dangerous invention" tradition. Thus "Stormy Bellwether" devastatingly sets out the bad news about person-to-person television. "The Fuglemen of Recall" has criminal exploitation of a memory recording and transfer process. "The Empty Balloon" looks at a "mind-reading" device working on sub-vocalised verbal thinking, an uncomfortable possibility, with a spy plot. In "Androtomy and the Scion" a cloned duplicate brain, in rapport with the original, gives the forces of evil new powers for coercion. "Split Personality" has an even more macabre atrocity, a felon physically dissected into living left and right halves for use as a better form of radio for an interstellar expedition.

Two examples of encounter with nonhumans with incomprehensible powers and purposes, viewed with an individual eye, are in "Freeway" and "Gauntlet's World." "Mostly Meantime" imagines a problem of time in interstellar communications, with a series of messages between Earth and Antares through centuries with the changing circumstances at both ends. "The Butterfly must Die" visualises a different kind of possible world disaster and threat to civilisation in a paper and film-eating microbe striking at recorded information. "The Making of a Gaffa," set on an extrasolar planet settled by man but fragmented into nationalities, suggests how an effective international peacekeeping organisation might work: it is distasteful but feasible.

The author's awareness of the social implications of radical new techniques, their value for oppression by ever-ready authority or for private anti-social acts, shows in many other stories. Thus "Whosa Whatsa" explores the utter ruin of traditional legal assumptions and conventions implicit in human sex reversal, and its impact on adultery, divorce, custody, and inheritance. "The Form Master" brings out the weakness of the coming world data bank, including its use for fraud by selective use of false input. In "Sprog" the inventor of a system of predicting future events cannot get a hearing and ends up exploiting the gullible as an ordinary fortune-teller. In "The Cure-All Merchant" behavior modification drugs have been refined into effective specifics for all problems, but a practitioner treats patients just as well by suggestion. One group of stories deals with the hazards and misuses of matter-transmission systems. "There Is a Crooked Man" shows future crime and detection in action. In "Wrong Rabbit" communication is accidentally opened with another world. "Top Billing" looks at duplication of people transmitted. "Hey but No Presto" shows a future form of hijacking. Among the stories of the interstellar future, "Star Hunger" is an excellent look at the need to reach the stars, the drive for habitable new worlds, and the danger of failure.

Wodham's first two novels are similar, though episodic and with more complexity of detail. *The Authentic Touch* uses the setting of a planet settled with re-creations of past epochs for jaded tourists of an opulent future, which tends to get out of control through too much realism. *Looking for Blücher* has a thin framing device to link up a series of shared hallucinatory adventures—easy stuff to write no doubt, but not very satisfactory reading. It is really a disappointing waste of effort. *Ryn* does not seem to qualify as science fiction despite a vague gesture at rationalising its theme of reincarnation of metempsychosis. But it is a strongly unified work, strictly following the logic of its premises, and a compelling study of a victim of circumstances trying to cope with his narrowly restricted situation: as an infant with full consciousness and memory of a previous adult life in another milieu.

A few stories look with unstated but implicit contempt and loathing at a pervasive theme in science fiction, war in the future. Some of the common ideas are examined, bringing out their absurdity as well as obscenity. Four of these are collected in *Future War*, two of note. In "Pet," there is a dehumanised military caste isolated from its sponsoring society. The fighter who accidentally captures a civilian insists on keeping it as a pet. In "Butcher Mackinson," only the handicapped are drafted to work in the mechanised war, partly a sort of inverted eugenics.

In "One Clay Foot," war in space is depersonalised and fought at great distances. Here, as in some of the other stories, the fighters may come to think that the real enemy is the service organisation, or other units, or their superiors. The characters in these stories have a total ethical vacuity and no sense of any meaning underlying the conflict, but we may draw our own conclusions.

Perhaps because Wodhams' writing is so typical of *Analog* in particular, where so many of his stories have appeared, and more generally of the magazines of the period, he does not seem distinctive, despite his considerable originality and individuality.

—Graham Stone

---

**WOLF, Gary K.** American. Born in Berwyn, Illinois, 24 January 1941. Educated at the University of Illinois, Urbana, B.S. 1963. M.S. 1969. Served in the United States Air Force, in Vietnam, 1963–69: Major. Vice-president and creative director, Crosson Austin Wolf, advertising and public relations, Amherst, New Hampshire. President, Cry Wolf! Inc., writing consultants, Harvard, Massachusetts. Agent: William Reiss, John Hawkins and Associates, 71 West 23rd Street, Suite 1600, New York, New York 10010. Address: c/o Cry Wolf! Inc., Box 436, Harvard, Massachusetts 01451, U.S.A.

SCIENCE-FICTION PUBLICATIONS

Novels

*Killerbowl.* New York, Doubleday, 1975; London, Sphere, 1976.
*A Generation Removed.* New York, Doubleday, 1977.
*The Resurrectionist.* New York, Doubleday, 1979.

Uncollected Short Stories

"Love Story," in *Worlds of Tomorrow* (New York), Winter 1970.
"Dissolve," in *Orbit 11*, edited by Damon Knight. New York, Putnam, 1973.
"Therapy," in *Orbit 13*, edited by Damon Knight. New York, Putnam, 1974.
"The Bridge Builder," in *Orbit 14*, edited by Damon Knight. New York, Harper, 1974.
"Slammer," in *Fantasy and Science Fiction* (New York), March 1974.
"Dr. Rivet and Supercon Sal," in *Fantasy and Science Fiction* (New York), January 1976.

OTHER PUBLICATIONS

Novels

*Who Censored Roger Rabbit?* New York, St. Martin's Press, 1981.
*Who P-P-P-Plugged Roger Rabbit?* New York, Villard, 1991.

* * *

Gary K. Wolf primarily known as the author of *Who Censored Roger Rabbit?*, the hilarious hard-boiled detective pastiche that was the source for the enormously successful fantasy motion picture *Who Framed Roger Rabbit?* (1988). The Touchstone film, which was produced by Steven Spielberg and directed by Robert Zemeckis, differs significantly from the original, but many of the movies' funniest bits come directly from the novel. Although not science fiction and thus beyond the scope of this essay, *Who Censored Roger Rabbit?* is far and away Wolf's best full-length work. Appearing in 1981, it was also, for a decade at least, the author's farewell to science fiction and fantasy, as no other genre fiction has appeared under his name since. Wolf has recently finished a sequel, entitled *Who P-P-P-Plugged Roger Rabbit?*

Wolf began his genre-writing career in the early 1970's as the author of a number of serious and often experimental short stories, several of which appeared in Damon Knight's highly regarded *Orbit* original anthology series. His first published SF work, "Love Story," opens with a marriage ceremony, during which the couple involved are required to relive briefly their pasts. Their civilization at first seems typically dystopian—conception occurs artificially, each fetus is properly programmed, children are raised in state facilities—yet Wolf cleverly reverses the situation, making it clear that the children are both well cared for and happy. We briefly tour a culture where there is no excess population, where everyone is content and virtually immortal. Our protagonists grow to adulthood, fall in love, and live together. Eventually they decide to have children and, their twin babies born artificially, they prepare for marriage. "Love Story" ends with a jolt. The priest at the ceremony hands them each a wafer. Eucharist-like, symbolic of their love, poisoned. They give up immortality to provide space for their babies.

"Dissolve" argues that television, because of its documentary-like quality and its oversimplification of moral problems, is drastically distorting our view of reality. The story jumps montage-like between a TV talk-show discussion of the problem, a number of typical television programs, and a young couple living in a bombed out TV studio after an atomic war. The girl is dying from radiation sickness, but the boy, immersed in the simplistic television mind set, seems to think that he can save her by making a video-tape in which she is cured. A grim story, it is very effective and even more believable today than it was in 1973. Equally powerful is "The Bridge Builder," a gripping story set in a world where the main transportation system is the Bridge, a matter transmitter. The protagonist builds bridges, repairs them, and is, in fact, fatally addicted to their use.

In "Therapy" Wolf began to show the talent for madcap humor that was to blossom in *Who Censored Roger Rabbit?* "Therapy" is a slight, funny piece about a computer marriage counselor, one of its less successful cases, and a robot elevator that thinks it's the computer's mother. "Slammer" and "Dr. Rivet and Supercon Sal" are both wildly comic tales reminiscent of Ron Goulart. The first concerns a prissy momma's boy who, mistakenly arrested for breaking into his own car and interred in a city reserved entirely for criminals, decides to stay there and become one. The second details the adventures of two shysters out to make a fast buck. He's a failure with people, but can do anything with machines. She's just the reverse. Their partner in crime is a rogue robot kitchenette. The story ends with one of the most hilarious chase scenes in recent fiction.

Wolf's science-fiction novels, as a rule, are not of the same quality as his short fiction. *Killerbowl*, the best of them, is set in the world of street football, a cross between our current sport and guerilla warfare. The playing field covers several square city blocks, knives, clubs, and rifles are routinely issued, and the millions of fans keep statistics not only on touchdowns but also on kills. T.R. Mann, a veteran quarterback, has been marked for assassination because he isn't bloody enough. The novel is effective, but seems derivative of William Harrison's well-known story "Roller Ball Murder" (1973). Less successful are *A Generation Removed*, which involves a near-future American where only those under 20 can hold political office and where those over 55 are "euthed," and *The Resurrectionist*, which details the adventures of a Bridge (see "The Bridge Builder") who must rescue a defector lost in the lines during transmission. Both novels suffer from weaknesses of plot, characterization, and style. All three books involve basically the same character motivation: a competent, middle-aged protagonist, while working for the System, discovers it to be corrupt and, finding himself in jeopardy, sets out vigilante-style to destroy it.

Wolf is a talented but uneven writer who has produced his best science fiction at the shorter lengths, most notably in such slightly experimental stories as "Dissolve" and "The Bridge Builder," and in the broad comedy of "Slammer" and "Dr. Rivet." Wolf's talent for broad, often slapstick humor has best shown itself in *Who Censored Roger Rabbit?*

—Michael M. Levy

---

**WOLFE, Bernard.** American. Born in New Haven, Connecticut, 28 September 1915. Educated at Yale University, New Haven, 1931–36, B.A. 1935 (Phi Beta Kappa). Married Dolores Michaels in 1964. Taught at Bryn Mawr College, Pennsylvania, 1936; Trotsky's secretary, Mexico, 1937; served in the United States Merchant Marine, 1937–39; editor, *Mechanix Illustrated*, New York, 1944–45; ghostwriter for Billy Rose's syndicated column, "Pitching Horseshoes," 1947–50; taught creative writing, University of California, Los Angeles, 1966–68. Screenwriter, Universal-International Productions, and Tony Curtis Productions, Hollywood. *Died 27 October 1985.*

SCIENCE-FICTION PUBLICATIONS

Novel

*Limbo.* New York, Random House, 1952; abridged edition, as *Limbo 90*, London, Secker and Warburg, 1953.

Uncollected Short Stories

"Self Portrait," in *The Robot and the Man*, edited by Martin H. Greenberg. New York, Gnome Press, 1953.

"The Never Ending Penny," in *The Year's Best S-F 6*, edited by Judith Merril. New York, Simon and Schuster, 1961; London, Mayflower, 1963.

"The Dot and Dash Bird," in *The Playboy Book of Science Fiction and Fantasy*, edited by Ray Russell. Chicago, Playboy Press, 1966; London, Souvenir Press, 1967.

"The Biscuit Position" and "The Girl with the Rapid Eye Movements," in *Again, Dangerous Visions*, edited by Harlan Ellison. New York, Doubleday, 1972; London, Millington, 1976.

OTHER PUBLICATIONS

Novels

*Really the Blues*, with Mezz Mezzrow. New York, Random House, 1946; London, Musicians Press, 1947.

*The Late Risers: Their Masquerade.* New York, Random House, 1954; London, Consul, 1962; as *Everything Happens at Night*, New York, New American Library, 1963.

*In Deep.* New York, Knopf, 1957; London, Secker and Warburg, 1958.

*The Great Prince Died.* New York, Scribner, and London, Cape, 1959; as *Trotsky Dead*, Los Angeles, Wollstonecraft, 1975.

*The Magic of Their Singing.* New York, Scribner, 1961.

*Come On Out, Daddy.* New York, Scribner, 1963.

*Memoirs of a Not Altogether Shy Pornographer.* New York, Doubleday, 1972.

*Logan's Gone.* Los Angeles, Nash, 1974.

*Lies.* Los Angeles, Wollstonecraft, 1975.

Short Stories

*Move Up, Dress Up, Drink Up, Burn Up.* New York, Doubleday, 1968.

Plays

Television Plays: *Assassin!*, 1955; *The Ghost Writer*, 1955; *The Five Who Shook the Mighty*, 1956.

Other

*Full Disclosure*, edited by Annette Welles. Los Angeles, Wollstonecraft, 1975.

*Julie: The Life and Times of John Garfield.* Los Angeles, Wollstonecraft, 1976.

Translator, with Alice Backer, *The Plot*, by Egon Hostovsky. London, Cassell, 1961.

*

Critical Study: *Bernard Wolfe* by Carolyn Geduld, New York, Twayne, 1972.

* * *

A lifelong enemy of science fiction, to judge from his comments in Harlan Ellison's *Again, Dangerous Visions*, Bernard Wolfe wrote a few science-fiction stories and a celebrated dystopian novel. The stories are tightly written, but *Limbo* is a masterpiece.

Zany, action-packed, *Limbo* is formally and conceptually complex and unremittingly analytical, both politically and psychologically. Most effectively of Wolfe's novels, it argues Dr. Edmund Bergler's acceptance of ambivalence opposition to "pseudo-aggression." Alongside Korzybskian semantics, cybernetics, and various technological fantasies (van Vogt is cited by name in the Afterword), Bergler's neo-Freudian theories are entertained in an entertaining manner. Besides its Dantesque associations, the novel's title signifies voluntary amputation, the absurdist idea for literal "disarmament" Dr. Martine left behind in a journal when he deserted World War III's automated carnage. Self-exiled among the relatively primitive Mandunji for 18 years, he has perfected their traditional cure for evil spirits, lobotomy. When civilization invades his island in 1990, Martine feels compelled to return to the mainland, where he finds the postwar "Inland Strip" and its great power rival, the "East Union," have taken his gallows humor seriously.

As in Plato's *Republic*, the state is the individual writ large; only Martine, as its unwitting begetter, can end this travesty, after he comes to know himself. Others are little more than extensions of him, for or against the prosthetic limbs that are more dangerous than their originals. Tom, son of his loins, is the ultimate pacifist, a basket case, and a spokesman for the Anti-Pros. Children of Martine's thought are his former colleague, now President Helder (hero) and the charismatic Theo (god) whose wartime amputation by Martine started the whole chain of ideas. Performing a social lobotomy, Martine removes both party "heads," returning with Theo to his tropical island. There, his healthy native son, Rambo (for Arthur Rimbaud), is leading a similar revolution against single-minded solutions.

Not a prediction of 1990, *Limbo* is a metaphorical extension of a literal malaise, most dangerous among the technologically sophisticated whose dependence on their tools blinds them to their own responsibility. Self-amputation is no answer to the human dilemma, rather a symptom of it. This central absurdity is the most important of many estranging devices integrated into a thoroughly modernist novel; its vision of wholeness and balance is both its form and its substance. Wolfe does not simply arouse anxiety about the uncontrollable, or appease it with an appeal to contemplate the artwork. *Limbo* locates the trouble's source in the individual, whose recognition of the problem is the necessary first step toward its solution.

This therapy may not have worked for Wolfe, whose subsequent novels belabored Berglerian analysis without winning much of an audience. Nor has post-1952 American society been self-evidently more able to laugh at and accept its ambivalence. The book's acceptance in SF circles is marginal; reviewed at arm's length, it has often been ignored in historical studies of the genre. Though its direct influence is questionable, *Limbo* is still a harbinger of more stylish, sexy, complex novels to come. On its literary merits, *Limbo* is the "great American dystopia."

—David N. Samuelson

---

**WOLFE, Gene (Rodman).** American. Born in Brooklyn, New York, 7 May 1931. Educated at Texas A and M University, College Station, 1949, 1952; University of Houston, B.S. 1956; Miami University. Served in the United States Army, 1952–54. Married Rosemary Frances Dietsch in 1956; two sons and two daughters. Project engineer, Procter and Gamble, 1956–72; senior editor, *Plant Engineering*, Barrington, Illinois, 1972–84. Recipient: Nebula award, 1973, 1982; Rhysling award, for verse, 1978; *Locus* award, 1982, 1987; World Fantasy award, 1982; British Science Fiction Association award, 1982; British Fantasy award, 1983; John W. Campbell Memorial award, 1984. Agent: Virginia Kidd, Box 278, Milford, Pennsylvania 18337. Address: P.O. Box 69, Barrington, Illinois 60010, U.S.A.

SCIENCE-FICTION PUBLICATIONS

Novels (series: Book of the New Sun; Latro)

*Operation ARES.* New York, Berkley, 1970; London, Dobson, 1977.
*The Shadow of the Torturer* (New Sun). New York, Simon and Schuster, 1980.
*The Claw of the Conciliator* (New Sun). New York, Simon and Schuster, 1981.
*The Sword of the Lictor* (New Sun). New York, Simon and Schuster, and London, Sidgwick and Jackson, 1982.
*The Citadel of the Autarch* (New Sun). New York, Simon and Schuster, and London, Sidgwick and Jackson, 1983.
*Free Live Free.* New York, Tor, and London, Gollancz, 1985.
*Soldier of the Mist* (Latro). New York, Tor, and London, Gollancz, 1986.
*The Urth of the New Sun.* New York, Tor, and London, Gollancz, 1987.
*There Are Doors.* New York, Tor, 1988; London, Gollancz, 1989.
*Soldier of Arete* (Latro). New York, Tor, 1989; London, New English Library, 1990.
*Castleview.* New York, Tor, 1990; London, New English Library, 1991.

Short Stories

*The Fifth Head of Cerberus.* New York, Scribner, 1972.
*The Island of Doctor Death and Other Stories and Other Stories.* New York, Pocket Books, 1980.
*Gene Wolfe's Book of Days.* New York, Doubleday, 1981; London, Arrow, 1985.
*Storeys from the Old Hotel.* Worcester Park, Surrey, Kerosina, 1988.
*Endangered Species.* New York, Tor, 1989; London, Orbit, 1990.

OTHER PUBLICATIONS

Novels

*Peace.* New York, Harper, 1975; London, Chatto and Windus, 1985.
*The Devil in a Forest* (for children). Chicago, Follett, 1976; London, Panther, 1985.
*The Castle of the Otter.* Willimantic, Connecticut, Ziesing, 1982.
*The Wolfe Archipelago.* Willimantic, Connecticut, Ziesing, 1983.
*Plan[e]t Engineering.* Cambridge, Massachusetts, NESFA Press, 1984.

Verse

*For Rosemary.* Worcester Park, Surrey, Kerosina, 1988.

Other

*Bibliomen: Twenty Chapters Waiting for a Book.* New Castle, Virginia, Cheap Street, 1984.
*The Boy Who Hooked the Sun.* New Castle, Virginia, Cheap Street, 1985.
*Empires of Foliage and Flower.* New Castle, Virginia, Cheap Street, 1987.
*Pandora by Holly Hollander.* New York, Tor, 1990.

*

Bibliography: in *The Castle of the Otter*, 1982.

Manuscript Collection: Merril Collection, Toronto Public Library, Canada.

Gene Wolfe comments:

I am frequently called an *Orbit* writer, by which the callers appear to mean an obscurantist. I do not feel the term is justified.

I try to bring pleasure to my readers on more than one level; but that, I think, is a characteristic of virtually all good fiction. I avoid private symbolism, and usually provide more than enough clues for such small puzzles as I set. If I show a man lying when it is to his advantage to lie, I assume that my reader is intelligent enough to see that the man in question is a liar—and so on.

My heroes are often boys or young men trying to find a place in the world (Tacky Babcock in "The Island of Doctor Death and Other Stories," Mark in *The Devil in a Forest*, Number Five in *The Fifth Head of Cerberus* and so on); perhaps despite a conscious conviction to the contrary, I feel that the most adventurous years are between 10 and 30. But I have written about old women too, and young ones, aliens, and middle-aged men. Recently I wrote a story—"The War Beneath the Tree"—in which the chief character was an automated teddy bear.

I think I am still at least as much a reader as a writer. I like Proust, Chesterton, Dickens (I've done a Dickens story: "Our Neighbor by David Copperfield"), Washington Irving, Lewis Carroll (not just *Alice*), Kipling, Maugham, Wells, John Fowles, R.A. Lafferty, Ursula K. Le Guin, Kate Wilhelm, Jorge Luis Borges, Tolkien, and C.S. Lewis. If you like half or more of those writers (for example, Maugham as far as the 'h') you should probably try me. Trembling, I throw myself on the mercy of the court.

* * *

Gene Wolfe's witty and entertaining short stories first began to appear in the late 1960's, but it wasn't until the beginning of the 1970's that he began to be recognized as a major talent in the field. An early novel, *Operation ARES*, provided glimpses of what was to come, but this story of Earth invaded by the Martian colonists is not in the same class as his subsequent works.

*The Fifth Head of Cerberus* is a collection consisting of the title story and two others. Had Wolfe stopped writing at this point in his career, he would probably still be regarded as one of the most interesting writers of the 1970's. The three tales are set on a world colonized by humans, but it is possible that the world was once rumored to have been home to an alien species capable of perfectly mimicking other lifeforms to a point where they lost their own identity. The question then arises, who conquered whom? The title story is one of the most moving tales the field has ever produced, and features a young boy searching for his own identity.

The Severian books (Book of the New Sun) began to appear shortly thereafter, and Wolfe was acknowledged immediately as a superior stylist with a gift for narrative, evocative settings, and innovative concepts rivalled by few of his contemporaries. *The Shadow of the Torturer* introduces Severian, member of the torturers' guild, who violates the rules of that organization and is exiled to a remote post, pursued by his enemies but emboldened by what he believes to be the proper course of action. Volumes could be written examining the intricacies of the subsequent three volumes, *The Claw of the Conciliator, The Citadel of the Autarch*, and *The Sword of the Lictor*, which concludes with Severian undergoing a transformation as he reaches the heart of this far-future society. Unexpectedly, Wolfe later wrote one further volume, *The Urth of the New Sun*, which continues Severian's adventures in his new role, a work that had no difficulty maintaining the high standards of the first four.

Although Wolfe adopted much of the lyricism and plot devices of fantasy in the Severian books, they remain science fiction, with each "magical" device extrapolated from known science. But in his subsequent novels, Wolfe moved straightforwardly into fantasy settings. *Soldier of the Mist* and its sequel, *Soldier of Arete*, are set in Ancient Greece, where a mercenary soldier is afflicted with recurrent amnesia, which is balanced by his newfound ability to see and communicate with the supernatural world of ghosts, spirits, and gods that surround him.

Wolfe uses contemporary settings for his other fantasies, *Free Live Free, There Are Doors*, and *Castleview*. The last of these is a haunting suspense story set in a small town from which, under the right conditions, a magical castle is invisible. Murder, mysterious apparitions, and closely held secrets mark the path to a stunning climax.

Although Wolfe has proven himself a masterful novelist, his short stories should not be overlooked. Well over a hundred have appeared, many already classics of the genre, and a very large proportion are significant award contenders or winners. "The Island of Dr. Death" features a man who finds fictional characters affecting his life. "The Death of Doctor Island" is set in a psychological clinic, where a decision must be made about the relative worth of the patients. A blind boy with paranormal powers creates imaginary beings to help him escape malevolent government agents in "The Eyeflash Miracles."

An international agreement to turn prisoners into slaves is the basis for "How the Whip Came Back," and the destruction of American society by pollution provides the setting for an unusual love affair in "Seven American Nights." Many of Wolfe's short pieces are fantasy, most notably "The Cabin on the Coast" and "War Beneath the Tree." And many of his short stories play with bizarre images: animated houses (in "Many Mansions"), an automobile giving birth (in "Car Sinister"), robotic spoofs of Sherlock Holmes (in "The Rubber Band" and others), car shows as an alternative to conflict (in "How I Lost the Second World War"), and an odd deformity (in "The Headless Man"). He also handles more conventional themes skillfully, such as time travel in "Against the Lafayette Escadrille," murder in space in "Cherry Jubilee," and the struggle to survive in a strange environment in "Eyebem."

What separates his fiction from scores of superficially similar works is his extraordinary gift for prose, as well as a ceaselessly inventive imagination and a powerful insight into the strengths and foibles of the human character. Wolfe consistently entertains his readers; at the same time he makes them think about the moral and philosophical issues he raises. It is a tribute to Wolfe's uniqueness that, despite his popularity, there has been no serious attempt to imitate his achievements.

—Don D'Ammassa

---

**WOLLHEIM, Donald A(llen).** Also wrote as David Grinnell. American. Born in New York City, 1 October 1914. Educated at New York University, B.A. Married Elsie Balter in 1943; one daughter. Editor, *Stirring Science Stories*, 1941–42, *Cosmic Stories*, 1941, *Out of This World Adventures*, 1950, *10 Story Fantasy*, 1951; editor, Avon Books, 1947–52, and Ace Books, 1952–67; editorial consultant, *Saturn*, 1957–58. Publisher and editor, DAW Books, from 1971. Recipient: Hugo award, for editing, 1964, and Special award, 1975; 33rd World Science Fiction Convention award, 1975; World Fantasy award, 1981; British Fantasy award, 1984. *Died in 1990.*

SCIENCE-FICTION PUBLICATIONS

Novels (for children: series: Mike Mars)

*The Secret of Saturn's Rings [The Martian Moons, The Ninth Planet].* Philadelphia, Winston, 3 vols., 1954–59.
*One Against the Moon.* Cleveland, World, 1956.
*Mike Mars, Astronaut [at Cape Canaveral (at Cape Kennedy), Flies the X-15, in Orbit, Flies the Dyna-Soar, South Pole Spaceman, and the Mystery Satellite, Around the Moon].* New York, Doubleday, 8 vols., 1961–64.

Novels as David Grinnell (series: Ajax Calkins)

*Across Time.* New York, Avalon, 1957.
*Edge of Time.* New York, Avalon, 1958.
*The Martian Missile.* New York, Avalon, 1959.
*Destiny's Orbit* (Calkins). New York, Avalon, 1961.
*Destination: Saturn* (Calkins), with Lin Carter. New York, Avalon, 1967.
*To Venus! To Venus!.* New York, Ace, 1970.

Short Stories

*Two Dozen Dragon Eggs.* Reseda, California, Powell, 1969; London, Dobson, 1977.
*The Men from Ariel.* Cambridge, Massachusetts, NESFA Press, 1982.

OTHER PUBLICATIONS

Other

*Lee de Forest: Advancing the Electronic Age* (for children). Chicago, Encyclopaedia Britannica Press, 1962.
*The Universe Makers: Science Fiction Today.* New York, Harper, 1971; London, Gollancz, 1972.
*Up There and Other Strange Directions.* Cambridge, Massachusetts, NESFA, 1988.

Editor, *The Pocket Book of Science Fiction.* New York, Pocket Books, 1943.
Editor, *Portable Novels of Science.* New York, Viking Press, 1945.
Editor, *Avon Bedside Companion: A Treasury of Tales for the Sophisticated.* New York, Avon, 1947.
Editor, *Avon Detective Mysteries 3.* New York, Avon, 1947.
Editor, *Avon Fantasy Reader 1–18.* New York, Avon, 18 vols., 1947–51.
Editor, *Avon Western Reader 3–4.* New York, Avon, 2 vols., 1947.
Editor, *Where the Girls Were Different and Other Stories,* by Erskine Caldwell. New York, Avon, 1948.
Editor, *Yesterday's Love and Eleven Other Stories,* by James T. Farrell. New York, Avon, 1948.
Editor, *Yvedtte and Other Stories,* by Maupassant. New York, Avon, 1949.
Editor, *Avon Book of New Stories of the Great Wild West.* New York, Avon, 1949.
Editor, *The Fox Woman and Other Stories,* by A. Merritt. New York, Avon, 1949.
Editor, *The Girl with the Hungry Eyes and Other Stories.* New York, Avon, 1949.
Editor, *A Hell of a Good Time and Other Stories,* by James T. Farrell. New York, Avon, 1950.
Editor, *The Avon All-American Fiction Reader.* New York, Avon, 1951.
Editor, *Avon Science-Fiction Reader 1–3.* New York, Avon, 3 vols., 1951–52.
Editor, *Flight into Space.* New York, Fell, 1950; London, Cherry Tree, 1951.
Editor, *Every Boy's Book of Science-Fiction.* New York, Fell, 1951.
Editor, *Giant Mystery Reader.* New York, Avon, 1951.
Editor, *Hollywood Bedside Reader.* New York, Avon, 1951.
Editor, *Let's Go Naked.* New York, Pyramid, 1952.
Editor, *Prize Science Fiction.* New York, McBride, 1953; as *Prize Stories of Space and Time,* London, Weidenfeld and Nicolson, 1953.
Editor, *Adventures in the Far Future.* New York, Ace, 1954.
Editor, *Tales of Outer Space.* New York, Ace, 1954.
Editor, *The Ultimate Invader and Other Science-Fiction.* New York, Ace, 1954.
Editor, *Adventures on Other Planets.* New York, Ace, 1955.
Editor, *Terror in the Modern Vein.* New York, Hanover House, 1955; abridged edition, as *Terror [and More Terror] in the Modern Vein,* London, Digit, 2 vols., 1961.
Editor, *The End of the World.* New York, Ace, 1956.
Editor, *The Earth in Peril.* New York, Ace, 1957.
Editor, *Men on the Moon.* New York, Ace, 1958.
Editor, *The Hidden Planet.* New York, Ace, 1959.
Editor, *The Macabre Reader.* New York, Ace, 1959; London, Digit, 1960.
Editor, *More Macabre.* New York, Ace, 1961.
Editor, *More Adventures on Other Planets.* New York, Ace, 1963.
Editor, *Swordsmen in the Sky.* New York, Ace, 1964.
Editor, with Terry Carr, *World's Best Science Fiction 1965* [to *1971*]. New York, Ace, 1965–71; *1968* to *1971* vols. published London, Gollancz, 4 vols., 1969–71; first 4 vols. published as *World's Best Science Fiction: First [*to *Fourth*] *Series,* Ace, 1970.
Editor, *Operation Phantasy: The Best from the Phantagraph.* Rego Park, New York, Phantagraph Press, 1967.
Editor, with George Ernsberger, *The Avon Fantasy Reader* [and *2nd Reader*]. New York, Avon, 2 vols., 1969.
Editor, *A Quintet of Sixes.* New York, Ace, 1969.
Editor, *Ace Science Fiction Reader.* New York, Ace, 1971; as *A Trilogy of the Future,* London, Sidgwick and Jackson, 1972.
Editor, *The 1972* [to *1990*] *Annual World's Best SF* (first 4 and last 9 vols. edited with Arthur W. Saha). New York, DAW, 19 vols., 1972–1990; first 8 vols. published as *Wollheim's World's Best SF 1–8,* 8 vols., 1977–85; 1974–1975 vols. published as *The World's Best Short Stories 1–2,* Morley, Yorkshire, Elmfield Press, 1975–76; *World's Best SF 4–6,* London, Dobson, 3 vols., 1979–81.
Editor, *The Best from the Rest of the World: European Science Fiction.* New York, Doubleday, 1976.
Editor, *The DAW Science Fiction Reader.* New York, DAW, 1976.

*

Manuscript Collections: Syracuse University, New York; University of Wyoming, Laramie (includes correspondence).

* * *

Although Donald A. Wollheim made his first sale while still in his teens ("The Man from Ariel," *Wonder Stories,* January 1934) and wrote about 20 volumes of science fiction, his greatest impact on science fiction has been in capacities other than that of author. Wollheim was one of the pioneering fan publishers in the 1930's, founded the influential Fantasy Amateur Press Association (which still exists), and was a founding member of the original Futurian Society. The Futurians, founded in New York in 1938, were an odd combination of science-fiction club, radical political movement, communal residential society, and literary mutual aid association. At one point, Futurians controlled no fewer than seven science-fiction pulp magazines—*Stirring Science Stories* and *Cosmic Stories* edited by Wollheim, *Super Science Stories* and *Astonishing* edited by Frederik Pohl, and *Future, Science Fiction*, and *Science Fiction Quarterly* edited by Robert A.W. Lowndes.

Since the Futurians numbered among their membership such young talents as James Blish, Damon Knight, Isaac Asimov, Judith Merril, and Richard Wilson, in addition to the three editors, there was a constant flow of material into the magazines. Wollheim's *Stirring* was the most interesting of the seven, divided into science-fiction and fantasy sections. Wollheim later edited *The Pocket Book of Science Fiction* (1943), generally regarded as the first significant science-fiction anthology, and helped A.A. Wyn in the creation of Ace Books in 1952. At Ace, Wollheim was known for his keen choices and successful mixture of commercially popular and artistically valid works. Besides publishing many important new SF writers, he was responsible for publication of the first mass-market editions of Tolkien's *The Lord of the Rings* and of many of the science-fiction works of Edgar Rice Burroughs. In 1972, Wollheim left Ace to create DAW books, the first mass publisher devoted entirely to science fiction. At DAW, Wollheim continued his formula of mixing pulp-style adventure series with significant works.

Notwithstanding the greater importance of Wollheim's work as editor and publisher, his own production of fiction was substantial. In the 1950's, he wrote three juvenile novels in the "Secret of. . . ." series; all are set in the intermediate-near future and deal with the exploration of the solar system. In the 1960's, Wollheim produced eight novels featuring the juvenile hero Mike Mars; these are set even closer in the future than the previous series. Among Wollheim's other novels, many readers have found amusement in *Destiny's Orbit* and its sequel *Destination: Saturn.* These amusing space opera-comedies feature Ajax Calkins, introduced in a series of short stories written by Wollheim under the pseudonym Martin Pearson. Also of interest is the novel *Edge of Time*, regarded by many as the definitive (although far from the first) treatment of the macro micro-universe theme.

A good collection of Wollheim's shorter fiction is *Two Dozen Dragon Eggs.* The short stories tend toward extreme simplicity of plot and minimal characterization, concentrating on a mix of atmosphere and "idea." "The Rag Thing" and "Mimic," probably Wollheim's two best stories, are both included in this collection. Wollheim's short critical volume, *The Universe Makers: Science Fiction Today*, is one of the most cohesive and convincing statements of philosophy to date in the context of science fiction.

His own works remain for the most part out of print, and apparently of only passing significance. His contribution as an editor and publisher, however, will continue to affect literature both within and beyond the science-fiction field. He was responsible for the publication of early works—in many cases, first novels—by authors as diverse as Ursula K. Le Guin, Robert Silverberg, Roger Zelazny, Marion Zimmer Bradley, and Thomas M. Disch. He was a major force in the popularization of science fiction to a mass audience between the 1950's and 1980's.

—Richard A. Lupoff

---

**WOODCOTT, Keith.** *See* **BRUNNER, John.**

---

**WOODS, Lawrence.** *See* **LOWNDES, Robert A.W.**

---

**WORTH, Peter.** *See* **PHILLIPS, Rog.**

---

**WRIGHT, Austin Tappan.** American. Born in Hanover, New Hampshire, 20 August 1883. Educated at Harvard University, Cambridge, Massachusetts, A.B. 1905, LL.B. 1908. Corporation and admiralty lawyer: practiced with firm of Brandeis Dunbar and Nutter, Boston, 1908–16; Professor of Law, University of California, Berkeley, 1916–24, and University of Pennsylvania, Philadelphia, 1924–31. *Died 18 September 1931.*

SCIENCE-FICTION PUBLICATIONS

Novel

*Islandia.* New York, Farrar and Rinehart, 1942.

*

Critical Studies: *An Introduction to Islandia* by Basil Davenport, New York Farrar and Rinehart, 1942; *The Islandian World of Austin Wright* by Lawrence Clark Powell, privately printed, 1957.

* * *

The reputation of Austin Tappan Wright rests on only one work, but it is safe to say there is nothing quite like *Islandia* in all of literature. If one can make a fine semantic distinction between science fiction and speculative fiction, Wright's novel is more the latter than the former. His "speculation" is in the area of geography and, spinning off that, sociology and cultural anthropology.

Islandia is a nation located on the southern half of the Karain subcontinent in the southern hemisphere. It is civilized but isolationist, and for it Wright has created the most detailed and in-depth of all fictional cultures. There are discernible elements of Japan, Madagascar, Indonesia, and India, but the sum total is curiously more Western than Eastern, more homely than exotic. Islandia is revealed to the reader in all its richness by the action of the novel, which takes place in the early part of this century. The country has decided to end its isolation from the rest of the world, and a few representatives of other governments are allowed in. One of these is a young American diplomat, John Lang; we learn about Islandia through his eyes as he travels the country and becomes acquainted and involved with her people.

The novel is peripherally a remarkable portrait of the nationalistic power plays that were occurring at the turn of the century, and a fine character sketch of an intelligent, moral young American confronted with values different from his own. But it is

Islandia and the wonderful cast of characters with which it is peopled that is Wright's most notable achievement.

—Baird Searles

---

**WRIGHT, Kenneth.** *See* **del REY, Lester.**

---

**WRIGHT S(ydney) Fowler.** Also wrote as Sydney Fowler; Alan Seymour; Anthony Wingrave. British. Born 6 January 1874. Educated at King Edward's School, Birmingham. Married 1) Nellie Ashbarry in 1895 (died 1918), three sons and three daughters; 2) Truda Hancock in 1920, one son and three daughters. Accountant in Birmingham from 1895. Editor, *Poetry* (later *Poetry and the Play*) magazine, Birmingham, 1920–32. *Died 25 February 1965.*

SCIENCE-FICTION PUBLICATIONS

Novels

*The Amphibians: A Romance of 500,000 Years Hence.* London, Merton Press, 1925.
*Deluge.* London, Fowler Wright, 1927; New York, Cosmopolitan, 1928.
*The Island of Captain Sparrow.* London, Gollancz, and New York, Cosmopolitan, 1928.
*The World Below* (includes *The Amphibians*). London, Collins, 1929; New York, Longman, 1930; *The World Below* published as *The Dwellers,* London, Panther, 1954.
*Dawn.* New York, Cosmopolitan, 1929; London, Harrap, 1930.
*Dream; or, The Simian Maid.* London, Harrap, 1931.
*Beyond the Rim.* London, Jarrolds, 1932.
*Prelude in Prague: A Story of the War of 1938.* London, Newnes, 1935; as *The War of 1938,* New York, Putnam, 1936.
*The Vengeance of Gwa* (as Anthony Wingrave). London, Butterworth, 1935.
*Four Days War.* London, Hale, 1936.
*Megiddo's Ridge.* London, Hale, 1937.
*The Hidden Tribe.* London, Hale, 1938.
*The Adventure of Wyndham Smith.* London, Jenkins, 1938.
*The Screaming Lake.* London, Hale, 1939.
*The Adventure in the Blue Room* (as Sydney Fowler). London, Rich and Cowan, 1945.
*Spiders' War.* New York, Abelard Press, 1954.

Short Stories

*The New Gods Lead* (as Sydney Fowler). London, Jarrolds, 1932.
*The Witchfinder.* London, Books of Today, 1945.
*Justice, and The Rat.* London, Books of Today, 1945(?).
*The Throne of Saturn.* Sauk City, Wisconsin, Arkham House, 1949; London, Heinemann, 1951.

OTHER PUBLICATIONS

Novels

*Elfin.* London, Harrap, and New York, Longman, 1930.
*Seven Thousand in Israel.* London, Jarrolds, 1931.
*Red Ike,* with J.M. Denwood. London, Hutchinson, 1931; as *Under the Brutchstone,* New York, Coward McCann, 1931.
*Lord's Right in Languedoc.* London, Jarrolds, 1933.
*Power.* London, Jarrolds, 1933.
*David.* London, Butterworth, 1934.
*Ordeal of Barata.* London, Jenkins, 1939.
*The Siege of Malta: Founded on an Unfinished Romance by Sir Walter Scott.* London, Muller, 1942.

Novels as Sydney Fowler

*The King Against Anne Bickerton.* London, Harrap, 1930; as *The Case of Anne Bickerton,* New York, Boni, 1930; as *Rex V. Anne Bickerton,* London, Penguin, 1947.
*The Bell Street Murders.* London, Harrap, and New York, Macaulay, 1931.
*By Saturday.* London, Lane, 1931.
*The Hanging of Constance Hillier.* London, Jarrolds, 1931; New York, Macaulay, 1932.
*Crime & Co.* New York, Macaulay, 1931; as *The Hand-Print Mystery,* London, Jarrolds, 1932.
*Arresting Delia.* London, Jarrolds, and New York, Macaulay, 1933.
*The Secret of the Screen.* London, Jarrolds, 1933.
*Who Else But She?* London, Jarrolds, 1934.
*Three Witnesses.* London, Butterworth, 1935.
*The Attic Murder.* London, Butterworth, 1936.
*Was Murder Done?* London, Butterworth, 1936.
*Post-Mortem Evidence.* London, Butterworth, 1936.
*Four Callers in Razor Street.* London, Jenkins, 1937.
*The Jordans Murder.* London, Jenkins, 1938; New York, Curl, 1939.
*The Murder in Bethnal Square.* London, Jenkins, 1938.
*The Wills of Jane Kanwhistle.* London, Jenkins, 1939.
*The Rissole Mystery.* London, Rich and Cowan, 1941.
*A Bout with the Mildew Gang.* London, Eyre and Spottiswoode, 1941.
*Second Bout with the Mildew Gang.* London, Eyre and Spottiswoode, 1942.
*Dinner in New York.* London, Eyre and Spottiswoode, 1943.
*The End of the Mildew Gang.* London, Eyre and Spottiswoode, 1944.
*Too Much for Mr. Jellipot.* London, Eyre and Spottiswoode, 1945.
*Who Murdered Reynard?* London, Rich and Cowan, 1947.
*With Cause Enough?* London, Harvill Press, 1954.

Verse

*Scenes from the Morte d'Arthur* (as Alan Seymour). London, Erskine MacDonald, 1919.
*Some Songs of Bilitis.* Birmingham, Poetry, 1921.
*The Song of Songs and Other Poems.* London, Merton Press, 1925; New York, Cosmopolitan, 1929.
*The Ballad of Elaine.* London, Merton Press, 1926.
*The Riding of Lancelot: A Narrative Poem.* London, Fowler Wright, 1929.

Other

*Police and Public: A Political Pamphlet.* London, Fowler Wright, 1929.
*The Life of Walter Scott: A Biography.* London, Poetry League, 1932; New York, Haskell House, 1971.
*Should We Surrender Colonies?* London, Readers' Library, 1939.

Editor, *Voices on the Wind: An Anthology of Contemporary Verse.* London, Merton Press, 3 vols., 1922–24.
Editor, *Poets of Merseyside: An Anthology of Present-Day Liverpool Poetry.* London, Merton Press, 1923.
Editor, with R. Crompton Rhodes, *Poems: Chosen by Boys and Girls.* Oxford, Blackwell, 4 vols., 1923–24.
Editor, *Birmingham Poetry 1923–24.* London, Merton Press, 1924.
Editor, *From Overseas: An Anthology of Contemporary Dominion and Colonial Verse.* London, Merton Press, 1924.
Editor, *Some Yorkshire Poets.* London, Merton Press, 1924.
Editor, *A Somerset Anthology of Modern Verse 1924.* London, Merton Press, 1924.
Editor, *The County Series* (verse anthologies). London, Fowler Wright, 13 vols., 1927–30.
Editor, *The Last Days of Pompeii: A Redaction*, by Edward Bulwer-Lytton. London, Vision Press, 1948.

Translator, *The Inferno*, by Dante. London, Fowler Wright, 1928.
Translator, *Marguerite de Valois*, by Dumas Père. London, Temple, 1947.
Translator, *The Purgatorio*, by Dante. Edinburgh, Oliver and Boyd, 1954.

* * *

S. Fowler Wright escaped being an accountant and poetry magazine editor with tales of fantasy, adventure, detection, and disaster. This prolific and versatile author began writing fantasy at 50.

His early novels reflect the influence of H.G. Wells. Wright, however, had such a pessimistic view of man's devolution that most human beings and their social customs vanish with dramatic flourishes. *The World Below* features a time-machine trip 500,000 years ahead to encounter Amphibians, delicate, web-footed, and cerebral, and Dwellers, gigantic seekers of knowledge through scientific investigation. The hero is most like the lizard-like Killers, who boil and eat victims. Much of the conversation between him and his amphibian companion reveals man's mistreatment of other living things, while many of the adventures show how close he is to bestiality when he throws reason aside in panic.

In *Beyond the Rim* descendants of British Puritans live in an Antarctic theocracy, raided occasionally by the Anabaptist horde from the volcanic hell nearby. The explorers include two strong women, one of whom remains while the other and her lover return home, but never to tell the real story. Similarly, in *The Island of Captain Sparrow* Charlton Fogle is shipwrecked where a pirate established a kingdom for his men and their women. Already present were a race of satyrs, providing meat, and a tribe of handsome natives decimated by disease brought by the outsiders. Charlton and Marcelle, intended for Sparrow's ugly, vicious heir, fall in love. At the book's spectacular climax the giant rokas, birds used for agricultural work, turn on the pirates, leaving the young lovers and the last native child to start over.

*Deluge* narrates a cataclysmic flood in which a hero and two heroines survive the barbarity to which most civilized people descend and found a new order. Martin Webster and Claire Arlington are among the few who adapt to living with nature. Because she is the kind of woman men put on a pedestal, Helen Webster also survives with her children. Some men—a murderer among them—become humane while others degenerate into ravaging, rapacious beasts who must be exterminated. At the end of this engrossing novel, Wright surprises his readers by allowing Martin to have both women. What's more—with noble psychological struggles—the women love each other. In *Dawn*, its sequel, Wright goes back in time to introduce new characters and repeat the flood's horrors. Defeat of the threatening gang and escape from another flood promise a future.

In *Dream* and its sequel, *Spiders' War*, Marguerite Leinster enjoys dangerous adventures with the help of a psychologist-magician. In the first she dreams of an ape-girl fighting off the river rats that challenge human supremacy. In *Spiders' War* she goes into a future where the threat to divided humanity stalks in the form of giant spiders. Her man, a scholar of 20th-century history, is also a warrior-leader. Together they organize three hostile groups against the intelligent monsters. *The Vengeance of Gwa* contrasts similar groups, ranging from starving barbarism to bored perfection, in a tale of an evil queen and her well-deserved end.

*Prelude in Prague, Four Days War*, and *Megiddo's Ridge* form a trilogy dealing with an ugly near-future in which Germany conquers Europe, by the use of a freezing gas, air raids, and political terrorism. In this apocalyptic disaster culminating in the destruction of the powerful forces of Von Teufel, Wright creates and kills a large cast of interesting characters, including a double agent and a woman pilot. He also vents anger at British underestimation of Germany, lack of preparation for war, and callousness about highway moralities. As in *Deluge* he warns readers that, while they vegetate, their neighbors hover a step from savagery.

In addition, Wright produced numerous short stories—light fantasy, medieval romance, mystery, and satire. Among the best are "Justice" and "Original Sin," a short version of *The Adventure of Wyndham Smith.* Society can be so perfect that only mass suicide can abolish boredom. So often does Wright annihilate mankind that it is not surprising that the heroine of his last story, "The Better Choice," prefers to remain a cat.

—Mary S. Weinkauf

---

**WYLIE, Philip (Gordon).** Also wrote as Leatrice Homesley. American. Born in Beverly, Massachusetts, 12 May 1902. Educated at Montclair High School, New Jersey; Princeton University, New Jersey, 1920–23. Member of the Board, Office of Facts and Figures, 1942; with Bureau of Personnel, United States Army Air Force, 1945. Married 1) Sally Ondeck in 1928 (divorced 1937), one daughter; 2) Frederica Ballard in 1938. Staff member, *The New Yorker*, 1925–27; advertising manager, Cosmopolitan Book Corporation, 1927–28; screenwriter, Paramount Pictures, 1931–33, and MGM, 1936–37; editor, Farrar and Rinehart, publishers, New York, 1944. Member of the Council, Authors Guild, 1945. Consultant to the Federal Civil Defense Administration, 1949–71. Recipient: Freedom Foundation Gold Medal, 1953; Hyman Memorial Trophy, 1959. D.Litt.: University of Miami; Florida State University, Tallahassee. *Died 26 October 1971.*

### SCIENCE-FICTION PUBLICATIONS

Novels

*Gladiator*. New York, Knopf, 1930.
*The Murderer Invisible*. New York, Farrar and Rinehart, 1931.
*The Savage Gentleman*. New York, Farrar and Rinehart, 1932.
*When Worlds Collide*, with Edwin Balmer. New York, Stokes, and London, Paul, 1933.
*After Worlds Collide*, with Edwin Balmer. New York, Stokes, and London, Paul, 1934.
*Finnley Wrenn: A Novel in a New Manner*. New York, Farrar and Rinehart, 1934.
*The Disappearance*. New York, Rinehart, and London, Gollancz, 1951.
*Tomorrow!* New York, Rinehart, 1954.
*Triumph*. New York, Doubleday, 1963.
*Los Angeles: A.D. 2017* (novelization of TV play). New York, Popular Library, 1971.
*The End of the Dream*. New York, Doubleday, 1972; Morley, Yorkshire, Elmfield Press, 1975.

Short Stories

*Night unto Night*. New York, Farrar and Rinehart, 1944.
*Three to Be Read*. New York, Rinehart, 1952; *Experiment in Crime* and *The Smuggled Atom Bomb* published separately, New York, Avon, 2 vols., 1956.
*The Answer*. New York, Rinehart, and London, Muller, 1956.

Uncollected Short Story

"Jungle Journey (The Paradise Crater)," in *Masterpieces of Science Fiction*, edited by Sam Maskowitz. Cleveland, World, 1967.

### OTHER PUBLICATIONS

Novels

*Heavy Laden*. New York, Knopf, 1928.
*Babes and Sucklings*. New York, Knopf, 1929; as *The Party*, New York, Popular Library, 1966(?).
*Blondy's Boy Friend* (as Leatrice Homesley). New York, Chelsea House, 1930.
*Footprint of Cinderella*. New York, Farrar and Rinehart, 1931; as *9 Rittenhouse Square*, New York, Popular Library, 1959.
*Five Fatal Words*, with Edwin Balmer. New York, Long and Smith, 1932; London, Paul, 1933.
*The Golden Hoard*, with Edwin Balmer. New York, Stokes, 1934.
*As They Reveled*. New York, Farrar and Rinehart, 1936.
*Too Much of Everything*. New York, Farrar and Rinehart, and London, Chapman and Hall, 1936.
*The Shield of Silence*, with Edwin Balmer. New York, Stokes, 1936; London, Collins, 1937.
*An April Afternoon*. New York, Farrar and Rinehart, 1938.
*Danger Mansion*. Los Angeles, Bantam, 1941.
*The Other Horseman*. New York, Farrar and Rinehart, 1942.
*Corpses at Indian Stones*. New York, Farrar and Rinehart, 1943.
*Opus 21*. New York, Rinehart, 1949; London, Consul, 1962.
*They Were Both Naked*. New York, Doubleday, 1965.
*Autumn Romance*. New York, Lancer, 1965.
*A Resourceful Lady*. New York, Popular Library, 1966.
*The Spy Who Spoke Porpoise*. New York, Doubleday, 1969.

Short Stories

*The Big Ones Get Away!* New York, Farrar and Rinehart, 1940.
*Salt Water Daffy*. New York, Farrar and Rinehart, 1941.
*Fish and Tin Fish: Crunch and Des Strike Back*. New York, Farrar and Rinehart, 1944.
*Fifth Mystery Book*, with others. New York, Farrar and Rinehart, 1944.
*Selected Short Stories*. New York, Editions for the Armed Services, 1946.
*Crunch and Des: Stories of Florida Fishing*. New York, Rinehart, 1948.
*The Best of Crunch and Des*. New York, Rinehart, 1954.
*Treasure Cruise and Other Crunch and Des Stories*. New York, Rinehart, 1956.

Plays

Screenplays: *Island of Lost Souls*, with Waldemar Young, 1932; *The Invisible Man*, with R.C. Sherriff, 1933; *Murders in the Zoo*, 1933; *The King of the Jungle*, with Fred Niblo, Jr., 1933; *Death in Paradise Canyon*, with Saul Elkins and Norman Foster, 1936.

Other

*The Army Way: A Thousand Pointers for New Soldiers*, with William W. Muir. New York, Farrar and Rinehart, 1940.
*Generation of Vipers*. New York, Farrar and Rinehart, 1942; revised edition, Rinehart, and London, Muller, 1955.
*An Essay on Morals*. New York, Rinehart, 1947.
*Denizens of the Deep: True Tales of Deep-Sea Fishing*. New York, Rinehart, 1953.
*The Innocent Ambassadors*. New York, Rinehart, 1957; London, Muller, 1958.
*The Lerner Marine Laboratory at Bimini, Bahamas*. New York, American Museum of Natural History, 1960.
*The Magic Animal*. New York, Doubleday, 1968.
*Sons and Daughters of Mom*. New York, Doubleday, 1971.

*

Manuscript Collection: Princeton University, New Jersey.

Critical Study: *Philip Wylie* by Truman Frederick Keefer, Boston, Twayne, 1977.

* * *

Philip Wylie's science fiction represents only a small portion of his profile output of magazine stories, novels, polemics, and screenplays. Wylie consciously and carefully placed himself in the "popular" market where his strongly moralistic and iconoclastic eye could not only observe and criticise but where his work would be read by large numbers. For, unlike the satirist, Wylie passionately believed that his pen could contribute to the sweeping away of cant and the creation of a modern and sane society.

*Gladiator* was accepted for publication in 1928 but Wylie's publishers held it for two years until he had produced two non-science-fiction works. In it and in *The Murderer Invisible* he set the pattern for his ventures in the science-fiction idiom. In both novels, the scientific projections (a genetically produced superman and an invisible man) are put in place quickly and without fuss as in H.G. Wells's novels, and the real stress lies on what the innovation can reveal about human nature and human society. Hugo Danner, the superman in *Gladiator*, observes the futility of human greed and of things like fraternity parties, football games, and the stock market. Through Hugo, Wylie poses the problem of what could be done to improve the lot of man even by a superman if the masses would not change themselves. In *The Murderer Invisible*, moral issues emerge because a scientist, William Carpenter, seriously wronged in a previous career on the commodities market, develops invisibility with intentions of a fair revenge and further use for the good of mankind. But he becomes a megalomaniac and attempts to take over the world for its own good. In these novels Wylie keeps calling his characters back to reckonings of conscience and analyses of the society which they are trying to change. These real and central concerns of his work were continued in *The Savage Gentleman*, a novel about a child educated away from mankind which offers a Tarzan-like variation on the single-man-against-society theme of the earlier novels.

Wylie's most optimistic venture into SF comes in two novels written in collaboration with Edwin Balmer, *When Worlds Collide* and *After Worlds Collide.* In these cosmic disaster stories two planets, a gas giant with an Earthlike planet in orbit about it, enter the solar system and destroy the earth when the gas giant brushes against it. *When Worlds Collide* chronicles the discovery of the threat and the desperate efforts of a group of scientists to build rockets to get them onto Bronson Beta, the smaller of the invaders. Several parties succeed and the second novel deals with their survival on Bronson Beta, their discovery of a high civilisation there, and the conflicts between the American party and a Japanese-Chinese-Soviet party which has also survived. These novels contain a good deal of Wylie's most careful scientific prognostication in astronomy, earth physics, and in the prediction of human behaviour in times of extreme crisis, although the extrapolations about rocketry and interplanetary travel are considerably flawed.

Time spent in Hollywood, war work, and the pursuit of other kinds of writing leave a gap in Wylie's SF output until the publication of *The Disappearance.* The simple but very elegant premise of this novel is a world in which all of the women disappear in an instant from the world of men and all of the men disappear from the world of the women. Although no real explanation is offered for this split in the stream of reality, the device is a perfect instrument for some very carefully considered opinions on the roles of the sexes, particularly in modern America. Wylie cleverly sets a great deal of the novel in a family unit very much like his own which lives in Miami and has all the domestic complications that society tends to produce. On one level the novel is fascinating because chapters taking place in exactly the same surroundings trace the varied collapse of the two worlds, the men having an all-out atomic war and a return to savagery while the women struggle with technological collapse. But in addition to the outward struggle there runs through the book some very serious contemplation of the double standard and the fragility of male-female relationships.

Wylie's next three SF works deal in various ways with his deep concern for the dangers of nuclear war, a phenomenon about which he was particularly well informed because of his activities in civil defence organisation. *Tomorrow!* is a detailed portrait of a nuclear attack on an American city and the civil defence response. He is heavily critical of the failure of face and prepare for this inevitability, and his realistically detailed picture of the carnage is both blunt and sobering. *The Answer* is a brief allegory in which both the Americans and the Russians bring down an angel in their bomb tests. The angel was carrying the message "Love one another" to mankind. *Triumph* paints the most horrible picture of holocaust, in which virtually the only survivors in the northern hemisphere are 14 people in a supershelter prepared by a farsighted millionaire.

Wylie's posthumous legacy to mankind, *The End of the Dream*, is his prediction of the pollution death of the world. Like John Brunner's novel of the same year, *The Sheep Look Up, The End of the Dream* ties together projections of man's mistreatment of the environment to foresee mass deaths from air pollution in the cities, a rice blight which leaves most of the world starving, and a particularly horrible mutation of an ocean leech which sucks the life from millions. *The End of the Dream* is a fitting culmination of Wylie's career, for it combines his anger against human foolishness with his obvious desire to warn and thus influence the future positively. From *Gladiator* to *The End of the Dream* Philip Wylie has used the science-fiction mode and the style of the popular writer to reach and caution the widest possible audience in his life-long crusade to save man from his own foolishness and blinkered views.

—Peter A. Brigg

---

**WYNDHAM, John.** Pseudonym for John Wyndham Parkes Lucas Beynon Harris; also wrote as John Beynon; Johnson Harris. British. Born in Knowle, Warwickshire, 10 July 1903. Educated at Bedales School, Petersfield, Hampshire; also read for the Bar. Served in the Royal Signals during World War II. Married Grace Wilson in 1963. *Died 11 March 1969.*

### Science-Fiction Publications

#### Novels

*The Secret People* (as John Beynon). London, Newnes, 1935; as John Wyndham, New York, Fawcett, 1973.
*Planet Plane* (as John Beynon). London, Newnes, 1936; revised edition, as *Stowaway to Mars*, London, Nova, 1953.
*The Day of the Triffids*. New York, Doubleday, and London, Joseph, 1951; as *Revolt of the Triffids*, New York, Popular Library, 1952.
*The Kraken Wakes*. London, Joseph, 1953; as *Out of the Deeps*, New York, Ballantine, 1953.
*Re-Birth*. New York, Ballantine, 1955; as *The Chrysalids*, London, Joseph, 1955.
*The Midwich Cuckoos*. London, Joseph, 1957; New York, Ballantine, 1958; as *Village of the Damned*, Ballantine, 1960.
*The Outward Urge* (as John Wyndham and Lucas Parkes). London, Joseph, and New York, Ballantine, 1959.
*Trouble with Lichen*. London, Joseph, and New York, Ballantine, 1960.
*Chocky*. New York, Ballantine, and London, Joseph, 1968.
*Web*. London, Joseph, 1979.

#### Short Stories

*Jizzle*. London, Dobson, 1954.
*The Seeds of Time*. London, Joseph, 1956.
*Tales of Gooseflesh and Laughter*. New York, Ballantine, 1956.
*Consider Her Ways and Others*. London, Joseph, 1961.
*The Infinite Moment*. New York, Ballantine, 1961.
*The Best of John Wyndham*. London, Sphere, 1973; as *The Man from Beyond and Other Stories*. London, Joseph, 1975.

Short Stories as John Beynon

*Sleepers of Mars.* London, Coronet, 1973.
*Wanderers of Time.* London, Coronet, 1973.
*Exiles on Asperus.* London, Severn House, 1979.

OTHER PUBLICATIONS

Novels

*Foul Play Suspected* (as John Beynon). London, Newnes, 1935.
*Love in Time* (as Johnson Harris). London, Utopian, 1946.

Verse

*'Melia Ann: A Fantasy of the W.I.* Taunton, Somerset, Wessex Press, 1953.

* * *

Beginning in 1930, J.B. Harris published—primarily in the United States and under several pseudonyms—a great many short stories and several novels. Eventually it was the novel *The Day of the Triffids* that, in 1951, brought Harris wide public recognition and permanently affixed to him the pseudonym under which he had published it: John Wyndham. Wyndham is justifiably considered to be the truest disciple of H.G. Wells in English literature. He himself said that of all science fiction he was most influenced by two of Wells's novels, *The Time Machine* and *War of the Worlds.* Indeed, Wyndham more than once dealt with themes raised in those novels, such as displacement in time and invasion from outerspace, though Wells's influence on Wyndham was not restricted to thematic borrowing.

Wyndham loved to write about perfectly familiar things, some everyday occurrence, and let the fantastic element help him uncover unprecedented and unforeseen possibilities in that daily routine. Only one of his novels, *The Outward Urge*, deals with other worlds. In his other novels and stories the action is set on Earth and in time frames not all that distant from ours. Nor does he burden us with technical minutiae. Being a firm opponent of the Jules Verne school of science fiction, resurrected and modernized in the U.S. by Hugo Gernsback, Wyndham uses technical—and other—detail only insofar as he or any other writer needs it: for the sake of credibility, realism, authenticity. In addition Wyndham has the ability—decidedly not within any other writer's reach—to compel us to suspend disbelief by being true to human character. Damon Knight correctly observed that Wyndham achieved his objective with down-to-earth means, that is, making us believe the most unbelievable things simply because they happened to people whom we all knew well. Wyndham's imagination is very tactile, sequential, logical. He follows the Wellsian method of the "single premise." In each of his books there is, then, one fantastic assumption; something in the world has changed and all subsequent changes follow as a consequence. Wyndham has the inventiveness to illustrate with many examples the impact of an event on all realms of life. All this causes Wyndham's fantasy novels to be part of the basic current of literature. He has no use for space opera; instead he practices a special kind of "realism in fantasy." One of his tasks has been the exploration of possibilities created by application of science-fiction motifs to various types of short stories. That is the guiding principle behind the collection *The Seeds of Time.* Here again there can be no doubt about the influence of H.G. Wells.

The influence of Wells also determined the basic theme of Wyndham's writings. He is usually concerned with some catastrophe, cosmic or social, which results in the discovery of hitherto hidden dangers in daily life, in the revelation of character under novel circumstances, in the disclosure of defects in the society. In searching for his "single fantastic premise" Wyndham displays a degree of imagination which belies his ostensibly traditional manner. In *The Day of the Triffids,* which remains Wyndham's best-known novel, he showed his greatest originality. The novel deals with the disintegration of the social order under the impact of two events—a rain of meteors which has blinded most of the human race, and the appearance of mobile carnivorous plants. In two other novels Wyndham writes about the invasion of Earth by beings from other planets. In the first of these, *The Kraken Wakes*, invaders from space who can exist only under conditions of enormous pressure, establish a bridgehead deep under the ocean. In an attempt to wipe out the human race, they melt down the polar ice caps; the resulting flooding of the continents almost brings about the desired end. All this occurs under Cold War conditions, with mutual suspicion between the great powers preventing them from joining forces against the invaders. In the final analysis the catastrophe is caused by human divisiveness. In *The Midwich Cuckoos* the subject matter is not so much invasion as a kind of "penetration" from space. Here the non-earthlings isolate the village of Midwich and a few other places on Earth from their surroundings and put their inhabitants to sleep. Nine months later there appear in those localities children of non-earthly origin who are evidently destined to become the rulers of all mankind. Their intellectual and spiritual superiority is such that the earthlings submit without protest, even to the point of taking actions clearly detrimental to themselves. What makes these children from outer space so superior is their capacity to communicate constantly with each other by telepathy. Thus, while remaining individual beings, they form at the same time a formidable collective force. Anything learned by one becomes immediately part of everyone's knowledge. And the group also has the ability to channel everyone's will in one direction. Eventually the extra-planetary colony becomes so dangerous to Earth that it must be destroyed.

Telepathy is rather common theme in Wyndham's fiction. It serves as a means of demonstrating its relationship to various forms of collectivism. The collectivism of the non-earthlings in *The Midwich Cuckoos*, for instance, reminds one of a fascist order. *The Chrysalids* provides an example of another sort of collectivist order. *The Chrysalids* takes place many centuries after a devastating nuclear war. Enclaves of life are cut off from one another by vast areas of radioactive contamination. Random mutations are occurring. As a result people, animals, and plants become so grotesquely disfigured that their hideousness exceeds even that which Wells anticipated in *The Island of Doctor Moreau.* These circumstances have given rise to puritanical communities seeking salvation by suppressing anything "different." Should anything new turn out to be superior to the old, these puritans are all the more eager to suppress it. They are convinced that they themselves represent the only kind of perfection possible, and at the very thought that elsewhere there might live people of a different color, they fly into a rage. Nevertheless, life, movement, progress win out even here. These horrible, monstrous families produce children similar to those who tried to control Midwich. They differ in one respect, though; they hate cruelty. According to Wyndham these children who feel themselves to be members of one single family will not merely rebuild the old world: they will build a new and better one. *Trouble with Lichen* is the least interesting of Wyndham's novels. Taking the theme of Shaw's *Back to Methuselah,* he discusses the possibilities a vastly extended life expectancy could open for mankind.

—Julius Kagarlitsky

---

# Y

**YARBRO, Chelsea Quinn.** Also writes as Terry Nelson Bonner; Vanessa Pryor. American. Born in Berkeley, California, 15 September 1942. Attended San Francisco State College, 1960–63. Married Donald P. Simpson in 1969 (divorced 1982). Theatre manager and playwright, Mirthmakers Children's Theatre, San Francisco, 1961–64; children's counsellor, 1963; cartographer, C.E. Erickson and Associates, Oakland, California, 1963–70; composer; card and palm reader, 1974–78. Secretary, Science Fiction Writers of America, 1970–72; president, Horror Writers of America, 1988–89. Lives in Berkeley. Agent: Ellen Levine Literary Agency, 15 East 26th Street, Suite 1801, New York, New York 10010, U.S.A.

Science-Fiction Publications

Novels

*Time of the Fourth Horseman.* New York, Doubleday, 1976; London, Sidgwick and Jackson, 1980.
*False Dawn.* New York, Doubleday, 1978; London, Sidgwick and Jackson, 1979.
*Hyacinths.* New York, Doubleday, 1983.
*Nomads* (novelization of screenplay). New York, Bantam, 1984.

Short Stories

*Cautionary Tales.* New York, Doubleday, 1978; expanded edition, New York, Warner, and London, Sidgwick and Jackson, 1980.
*On Saint Hubert's Thing.* New Castle, Virginia, Cheap Street, 1982.
*Signs and Portents.* Santa Cruz, California, Dream Press, 1984.

Other Publications

Novels

*Ogilvie, Tallant, and Moon.* New York, Putnam, 1976; as *Bad Medicine*, New York, Berkley, 1990.
*Hôtel Transylvania: A Novel of Forbidden Love.* New York, St. Martin's Press, 1978; London, New English Library, 1981.
*Music When Sweet Voices Die.* New York, Putnam, 1979; as *False Notes*, New York, Berkley, 1990.
*The Palace.* New York, St. Martin's Press, 1979; London, New English Library, 1981.
*Blood Games.* New York, St. Martin's Press, 1980.
*Ariosto.* New York, Pocket Books, 1980.
*Dead and Buried* (novelization of screenplay). New York, Warner, and London, Star, 1980.
*Sins of Omission.* New York, New American Library, 1980.
*Path of the Eclipse.* New York, St. Martin's Press, 1981.
*Tempting Fate.* New York, St. Martin's Press, 1982.
*A Taste of Wine* (as Vanessa Pryor). New York, Pocket Books, 1982.
*The Godforsaken.* New York, Warner, 1983.
*The Making of Australia 5: The Outback* (as Terry Nelson Bonner). New York, Dell, 1983.
*A Mortal Glamour.* New York, Bantam, 1985.
*To the High Redoubt.* New York, Warner, 1985.
*A Baroque Fable.* New York, Berkley, 1986.
*A Flame in Byzantium.* New York, Tor, 1987.
*Firecode.* New York, Popular Library, 1987.
*Taji's Syndrome.* New York, Popular Library, 1988.
*Crusader's Torch.* New York, Tor, 1988.
*Beastnights.* New York, Popular Library, 1989.
*A Candle for D'Artagnan.* New York, Tor, 1989.
*The Law in Charity.* New York, Doubleday, 1989.
*Out of the House of Life.* New York, Tor, 1990.

Short Stories

*The Saint-Germain Chronicles.* New York, Pocket Books, 1983.

Other

*Messages from Michael on the Nature of the Evolution of the Human Soul.* Chicago, Playboy Press, 1979.
*Locadio's Apprentice* (for children). New York, Harper, 1984.
*Four Horses for Tishtry* (for children). New York, Harper, 1985.
*Floating Illusions* (for children). New York, Harper, 1986.
*More Messages from Michael.* New York, Berkley, 1986.
*Michael's People.* New York, Berkley, 1988.

Editor, with Thomas N. Scortia, *Two Views of Wonder.* New York, Ballantine, 1973.

*

Chelsea Quinn Yarbro comments:

My work, for the most part, has to do with some aspect of love and survival, though that should be interpreted in its broadest sense. Music has very much influenced me, not only as subject matter, but structurally as well. Since I make my living as a writer, I do, in a pragmatic sense, write for money. However, I regard writing as an art, and feel that within certain realistic limitations a part of my responsibility is to maintain and protect the integrity of my work.

* * *

Chelsea Quinn Yarbro has written well-received works in a wide range of popular genres, including not only science fiction and fantasy but also mysteries and most recently a historical novel set in the American west. Her science-fiction novels tend to combine elements of the medical thriller with those of the "disaster" novel. In these works she employs stark language to explore dire consequences of scientific or technological developments. Yarbro is best known, however, for elaborate fantasy narratives that blend aspects of the historical romance with the horror novel. Both types of fiction reflect her fascination with the darker aspects of human nature.

The danger of tampering with the natural order, even with noble intentions, provides the common theme of Yarbro's best science fiction. A collection of her early short stories, for example, is aptly titled *Cautionary Tales. Time of the Fourth Horseman*, her first published science-fiction novel, could itself be described as a cautionary narrative. A secret project sponsored by the government is attempting to ease severe overpopulation by fostering the controlled re-emergence of such diseases as cholera, polio and diphtheria. But these efforts result in the unforeseen outbreak of a new form of polio that is particularly virulent and highly contagious. The novel recounts the discovery of this ill-conceived plan by a young physician, Dr. Natalie Lebbreau, whose husband is in charge of the research and whose son is among its first casualties. *Time of the Fourth Horseman* reflects two of Yarbro's strengths as a novelist: her ability to create sympathetic characters and her skill in fashioning a compelling plot.

Yarbro's next science-fiction novel, *False Dawn*, contains several of the same elements: ecological disaster, a strong heroine, and a struggle for survival against overwhelming odds. *False Dawn* depicts an even bleaker future in which the earth has been devastated by a series of natural and human-caused disasters. The narrative centers on two individuals: Thea, a mutant woman, and Evan Montague, the deposed (and reformed) leader of a gang of marauding "pirates." Paired by chance, the two wander through the ravaged wilderness of the western United States in search of a rumored oasis. Yarbro balances the story of their struggles against both human enemies and nature with the slow growth of a warm and mutually respectful love between the two protagonists. On one level, the novel has a disturbing ending, as the lovers' hope of a refuge proves futile. But their concern for and commitment to each other soften the harshness of the conclusion. Yarbro's powerful but restrained depiction of the horrors of this future, joined with her treatment of a love that survives in a brutal world, makes this an excellent introduction to her science fiction.

Yarbro's other science-fiction novels repeat the basic concerns and themes of the first two books. *Hyacinths*, for example, postulates a future in which artificially induced dreams serve as the major source of mass entertainment. In this work disaster results from the government's attempt to use these dreams for propaganda. *Taji's Syndrome* returns to the medical subject matter of her first novel. Genetic tampering leads to the emergence of a new disease that almost always proves fatal but leaves its rare survivors with psychokinetic powers. Moral issues are both less clearly defined and more important in *Taji's Syndrome* than in *Time of the Fourth Horseman.* The action centers on powerful interests with two opposed purposes, one wishing to eradicate the disease and the other (lured by the new powers of the survivors) wishing to foster its spread.

In the field of fantasy, Yarbro has proved particularly adept as a writer of horror novels. *The Godforsaken* combines the horror theme of lycanthropy with the human atrocities of the Spanish Inquisition. She has also written several strong horror novels set in the contemporary world, among them *Sins of Omission* and *Nomads.* But her reputation as a fantasist rests most solidly on her novels about vampirism, especially her series based on the exploits of the vampire Francois Rgoczy, Count of Saint Germain. While the writing in her science fiction is generally controlled and even austere, in her historical horror-fantasies, Yarbro employs far more elaborate language and provides lengthy, detailed descriptions of the time and places in which they are set.

Yarbro's Saint Germain series invites comparison with the vampire novels of Ann Rice and Fred Saberhagen. Saint Germain emerges as a noble, sympathetic character, an alien to be engaged and understood rather than a monster to be feared and destroyed. The villains of the various novels that comprise the series are the human characters. In *Hôtel Transylvania*, the novel that introduces Saint Germain, the villain is the leader of a satanic cult who would destroy the count's lover. Other villains include Savanarola (*The Palace*), a priestess of the goddess Kali (*Path of the Eclipse*), and even Joseph McCarthy (*The Saint-Germain Chronicles*).

More recently, Yarbro has begun a new vampire series featuring Atta Olivia Clemens, who was Saint Germain's lover in Imperial Rome in *Blood Games.* Strong and intelligent, Olivia calls to mind not only Saint Germain but also characters such as Thea and Dr. Lebbreau from Yarbro's science-fiction novels. *A Flame in Byzantium*, the first novel in the projected series, involves Olivia in the court intrigues of Constantinople. *Crusader's Torch* requires her to travel from Tyre to Rome during the Crusades. These more recent novels, however, seem more historical romances about a vampire than fantastic fictions that make use of historical settings. The early novels in the St. Germain series, particularly *Hôtel Transylvania* and *Path of the Eclipse*, offer more compelling examples of Yarbro's skill as a writer of horrific fantasy.

In an epilogue to *Hôtel Transylvania*, Yarbro has written that the vampire reflects "a generally ambivalent attitude about immortality" and speaks "to some hidden part of ourselves." That ambivalence permeates her vampire fantasies, much as an ambivalence about science and technology, particularly when they are controlled by political purposes, is central to her science fiction. Yarbro's ability to explore such dark themes in novels that successfully blend elements of other popular genres (such as the medical thriller and the historical romance) has earned her a reputation as a writer of consistently entertaining and occasionally superior science fiction and fantasy.

—Dennis M. Kratz

---

**YEP, Laurence (Michael).** American. Born in San Francisco, California, 14 June 1948. Educated at Marquette University, Milwaukee (Dretzka award, 1968), 1966–68; University of California, Santa Cruz, B.A. in English 1970; State University of New York, Buffalo, 1970–75, Ph.D. in English 1975. Part-time English teacher, Foothill College, Mountain View, California, 1975, and San Jose City College, California, 1975–76; Professor, University of California, Berkeley, 1987–88. Recipient: Book-of-the-Month-Club fellowship, 1970; International Reading Association award, 1976; National Council for the Social Studies Woodson award, 1976; Boston *Globe-Horn Book* award, 1977; Women's International League for Peace and Freedom Jane Addams award, 1978. Agent: Maureen Walters, Curtis Brown, 10 Astor Place, New York, New York 10003. Address: 593 11th Avenue, San Francisco, California 94118, U.S.A.

SCIENCE-FICTION PUBLICATIONS

Novels

*Sweetwater* (for children). New York, Harper, 1973; London, Faber, 1976.
*Seademons*. New York, Harper, 1977.

*Shadow Lord* (Star Trek). New York, Pocket Books, 1985; Bath, Chivers, 1987.
*Monster Makers, Inc.* New York, Arbor House, 1986.

OTHER PUBLICATIONS

Novels (for children)

*Dragonwings.* New York, Harper, 1975.
*Child of the Owl.* New York, Harper, 1977.
*Sea Glass.* New York, Harper, 1979.
*The Mark Twain Murders.* New York, Four Winds Press, 1982.
*Kind Hearts and Gentle Monsters.* New York, Harper, 1982.
*Dragon of the Lost Sea.* New York, Harper, 1982.
*Liar, Liar.* New York, Morrow, 1983.
*The Serpent's Children.* New York, Harper, 1984.
*The Tom Sawyer Fires.* New York, Morrow, 1984.
*Dragon Steel.* New York, Harper, 1985.
*Mountain Light.* New York, Harper, 1985.
*The Curse of the Squirrel,* illustrated by Dirk Zimmer. New York, Random House, 1987.
*The Lost Garden.* Englewood Cliffs, New Jersey, Silver Burdett Press, 1990.
*Dragon Cauldron.* New York, Harper Collins, 1991.
*The Star Fisher.* New York, Morrow, 1991.

Plays

*Pay the Chinaman, and Fairy Bones* (produced San Francisco, 1987).
*Dragonwings* (adapted from the novel; produced Berkeley, 1991).

Other

*The Rainbow People* (retelling), illustrated by David Wiesner. New York, Harper, 1989.
*A Lesson Plan Book for Dragonwings.* Jefferson City, Missouri, 1990.
*When the Bomb Dropped: The Story of Hiroshima.* New York, Random House, 1990.

*

Laurence Yep comments:

Growing up as a Chinese in America, I felt much like Ralph Ellison's "invisible man": without form and without shape. In my studies and in my teaching, I pursued the psychological figure of the Stranger, both in the American classics and in the works of popular culture. In writing science-fiction stories about aliens and alienated heroes, I was also unconsciously seeking my own identity. I've used the results to good effect in my children's books on Chinese-Americans. When I'm having problems with a historical novel, I still find it useful to do a science-fiction story on a similar theme.

* * *

Laurence Yep is making his mark as a writer of realism as well as SF fantasy for adults and children. In his children's novels depicting Chinese-American experience in San Francisco, *Dragonwings, Child of the Owl,* and *Sea Glass,* Yep, himself Chinese-American, has deliberately and effectively sought to combat racial stereotyping, and these novels have been praised because they have repaired some of the harm inflicted by racist persistence in describing Chinese or Chinese-Americans as characters resembling Charlie Chan or Fu Manchu, or playing the seemingly omnipresent houseboy, gardener, or launderer. The impact of these novels largely derives from the author's frank, sympathetic rendering of the painful clash between an old generation of Chinese in America who, while mindful of the opportunities their new home provides, still cherish the folkways of their mother country and a young generation, convinced of the importance of change and the necessity of becoming American, who are tempted to deny the value of their ancestral past. It is surely not coincidental that a similar clash is the thematic center of *Sweetwater,* a most distinguished children's SF novel.

Set on Harmony some centuries in the future, *Sweetwater* describes the efforts of the Silkies, descendants of the Anglic starship crew who had brought the first colonists and then been forced to remain, to maintain their own distinctive society—one lived in harmony with the sea which dominates their lives—and resist the blandishments of the descendants of the first colonists, who are enamored of the latest technology. The Silkies are led by Captain Inigo Priest whose son, Tyree, is both the narrator and moral center of the novel. His several ethical choices, making up a great part of the plot, encapsulate the novel's focus upon the conflict between tradition and the necessity of change and growth. The most prominent element is the setting created for Harmony, in particular, its ecology. Not knowing that the planet is subject to cyclic flooding, the settlers, aided by the Argans, an indigenous race resembling spiders, build on the flood plain. When the waters rise, the settlement, Old Sion, is abandoned by all except the Silkies who struggle to wrest a livelihood from the sea. *Sweetwater* also concerns the development of an artist, a relatively rare topic in children's fiction of any kind, as Tyree senses within himself a gift for music which his parents disdain. Secretly abetted by Amadeus, an old Argan (the many references to music and the Old Testament contribute to the allusive richness of the novel), Tyree gradually internalizes the expressive nature of music and its centrality in any life that aspires for wholeness. Both thematic complexity and verbal richness, then, make *Sweetwater* superior SF.

A subsequent SF novel, *Seademons,* describes Fancyfree, a world colonized by the Folk, other descendants of the Anglics. Unlike the Silkies, the Folk do not live in harmony with the Seadeamons, intelligent life-forms native to Fancyfree, until catastrophe forces them to. Like *Sweetwater, Seademons* dramatizes a clash between tradition and change, and its most prominent element too is the sea-dominant setting. Also *Seademons,* a densely written and poetically evocative novel like *Sweetwater,* effectively incorporates Celtic lore into its plot. Yep also has written *Shadow Lord,* a volume in the Star Trek series; two young adult novels; and *Dragon of the Lost Sea,* a retelling of a Chinese legend. The merit of the last, in particular its witty interplay between a young boy and the ancient dragon, suggests that Yep, in spite of his desire for versatility, writes most distinctively whenever he focuses on the clash between generations and their conflicting values and draws upon his Chinese-American heritage.

—Francis J. Molson

---

**YERMAKOV, Nicholas.** *See* **HAWKE, Simon.**

---

**YOLEN, Jane (Hyatt).** American. Born in New York City, 11 February 1939. Educated at Staples High School, Westport, Connecticut, graduated 1956; Smith College, Northampton, Massachusetts, B.A. 1960; New School for Social Research, New York; University of Massachusetts, Amherst, 1975–78, M.Ed. 1976. Married David W. Stemple in 1962; one daughter and two sons. Staff member, *This Week* magazine and *Saturday Review*, New York, 1960–61; assistant editor, Gold Medal Books, New York, 1961–62; associate editor, Rutledge Books, New York, 1962–63; assistant editor, Alfred A. Knopf Juvenile Books, New York, 1963–65; Lecturer in Education, Smith College, 1979–84. Columnist ("Children's Bookfare"), *Daily Hampshire Gazette*, Northampton, Massachusetts, 1972–80. Massachusetts delegate, Democratic National Convention, Miami, 1972. Member of the Board of Directors, Society of Children's Book Writers since 1974, and Children's Literature Association, 1977–79; president, Science-Fiction Writers of America, 1986–88. Recipient: Society of Children's Book Writers Golden Kite award, 1974; Christopher award, 1978; University of Minnesota Kerlan award, 1988. LL.D.: College of Our Lady of the Elms, Chicopee, Massachusetts, 1980. Agent: Marilyn Marlow, Curtis Brown, 10 Astor Place, New York, New York 10003. Address: 31 School Street, Box 27, Hatfield, Massachusetts 01038, U.S.A.

### Science-Fiction Publications

#### Novels

*Cards of Grief.* New York, Ace, 1984; London, Futura, 1986.
*Sister Light, Sister Dark.* New York, Tor, 1988; London, Futura, 1989.
*White Jenna.* New York, Tor, 1989.

#### Short Stories

*Tales of Wonder.* New York, Schocken, 1983; London, Futura, 1987.
*Merlin's Booke.* New York, Steeldragon Press, 1986.

### Other Publications

#### Fiction (for children)

*The Witch Who Wasn't.* New York, Macmillan, and London, Collier Macmillan, 1964.
*Gwinellen, The Princess Who Could Not Sleep.* New York, Macmillan, 1965.
*Trust a City Kid,* with Anne Huston. New York, Lothrop, 1966; London, Dent, 1967.
*Isabel's Noel.* New York, Funk and Wagnalls, 1967.
*The Emperor and the Kite.* Cleveland, World, 1967; London, Macdonald, 1969.
*The Minstrel and the Mountain.* Cleveland, World, and Edinburgh, Oliver and Boyd, 1968.
*Greyling.* Cleveland, World, 1968; London, Bodley Head, 1969.
*The Longest Name on the Block.* New York, Funk and Wagnalls, 1968.
*The Wizard of Washington Square.* New York, World, 1969.
*The Inway Investigators; or, The Mystery at McCracken's Place.* New York, Seabury Press, 1969.
*The Seventh Mandarin.* New York, Seabury Press, and London, Macmillan, 1970.
*Hobo Toad and the Motorcycle Gang.* New York, World, 1970.
*The Bird of Time.* New York, Crowell, 1971.
*The Girl Who Loved the Wind.* New York, Crowell, 1972; London, Collins, 1973.
*The Girl Who Cried Flowers and Other Tales.* New York, Crowell, 1974.
*Rainbow Rider.* New York, Crowell, 1974; London, Collins, 1975.
*The Adventures of Eeka Mouse.* Middletown, Connecticut, Xerox, 1974.
*The Boy Who Had Wings.* New York, Crowell, 1974.
*The Magic Three of Solatia.* New York, Crowell, 1974.
*The Little Spotted Fish.* New York, Seabury Press, 1975.
*The Transfigured Hart.* New York, Crowell, 1975.
*The Moon Ribbon and Other Tales.* New York, Crowell, 1976; London, Dent, 1977.
*Milkweed Days.* New York, Crowell, 1976.
*The Sultan's Perfect Tree.* New York, Parents' Magazine Press, 1977.
*The Seeing Stick.* New York, Crowell, 1977.
*The Lady and the Merman.* Easthampton, Massachusetts, Pennyroyal Press, 1977.
*The Hundredth Dove and Other Tales.* New York, Crowell, 1977; London, Dent, 1979.
*The Giants' Farm.* New York, Seabury Press, 1977.
*Hannah Dreaming.* Springfield, Massachusetts, Springfield Museum of Fine Arts, 1977.
*The Mermaid's Three Wisdoms.* New York, Collins World, 1978.
*No Bath Tonight.* New York, Crowell, 1978.
*The Simple Prince.* New York, Parents' Magazine Press, 1978.
*Spider Jane.* New York, Coward McCann, 1978.
*Dream Weaver.* New York, Collins, 1979.
*The Giants Go Camping.* New York, Seabury Press, 1979.
*Spider Jane on the Move.* New York, Coward McCann, 1980.
*Mice on Ice.* New York, Dutton, 1980.
*Commander Toad in Space.* New York, Coward McCann, 1980.
*The Robot and Rebecca.* New York, Random House, 1980.
*Shirlick Holmes and the Case of the Wandering Wardrobe.* New York, Coward McCann, 1981.
*Uncle Lemon's Spring.* New York, Dutton, 1981.
*The Boy Who Spoke Chimp.* New York, Knopf, 1981.
*Brothers of the Wind.* New York, Philomel, 1981.
*The Gift of Sarah Barker.* New York, Viking Press, 1981.
*The Acorn Quest.* New York, Crowell, 1981.
*The Robot and Rebecca and the Missing Owser.* New York, Knopf, 1981.
*Sleeping Ugly.* New York, Coward McCann, 1981.
*Dragon's Blood.* New York, Delacorte Press, 1982; London, MacRae, 1983.
*Commander Toad and the Planet of the Grapes.* New York, Coward McCann, 1982.
*Neptune Rising: Songs and Tales of the Undersea Folk.* New York, Philomel, 1982.
*Commander Toad and the Big Black Hole.* New York, Coward McCann, 1983.
*Heart's Blood.* New York, Delacorte Press, and London, MacRae, 1984.
*Children of the Wolf.* New York, Viking Kestrel, 1984.
*The Stone Silenus.* New York, Philomel, 1984.
*Commander Toad and the Dis-Asteroid.* New York, Coward McCann, 1985.
*Dragonfield and Other Stories.* New York, Ace, 1985.
*Commander Toad and the Intergalactic Spy.* New York, Coward McCann, 1986.
*A Sending of Dragons.* New York, Delacorte Press, and London, MacRae, 1987.

*Piggins*. San Diego, Harcourt Brace, 1987; London, Piccadilly Press, 1988.
*Owl Moon*. New York, Philomel, 1987.
*Commander Toad and the Space Pirates*. New York, Putnam, 1987.
*Picnic with Piggins*. San Diego, Harcourt Brace, 1988.
*The Devil's Arithmetic*. New York, Viking Kestrel, 1988.
*Piggins and the Royal Wedding*. San Diego, Harcourt Brace, 1989.
*Dove Isabeau*. San Diego, Harcourt Brace, 1989.
*The Faery Flag: Stories and Poems of Fantasy and the Supernatural*. New York, Orchard, 1989.
*Baby Bear's Bedtime Book*. San Diego, Harcourt Brace, 1990.
*Dinosaur Dances*. New York, Putnam, 1990.
*The Dragon's Boy*. New York, Harper and Row, 1990.
*Elfabet: An ABC of Elves*. Boston, Little Brown, 1990.
*Sky Dogs*. San Diego, Harcourt Brace, 1990.
*All Those Secrets of the World*. Boston, Little Brown, 1991.
*Grandad Bill's Song*. New York, Philomel, 1991.
*Greyling*. New York, Philomel, 1991.
*Letting Swift River Go*. Boston, Little Brown, 1991.
*Wings*. San Diego, Harcourt Brace, 1991.
*Wizard's Hall*. San Diego, Harcourt Brace, 1991.

Play

*Robin Hood*, music by Barbara Green (produced Boston, 1967).

Verse

*See This Little Line?* New York, McKay, 1963.
*It All Depends*. New York, Funk and Wagnalls, 1969.
*An Invitation to the Butterfly Ball: A Counting Rhyme*. New York, Parents' Magazine Press, 1976; Kingswood, Surrey, World's Work, 1978.
*All in the Woodland Early: An ABC Book*, music by the author. Cleveland, Collins, 1979.
*How Beastly! A Menagerie of Nonsense Poems*. New York, Collins, 1980.
*Dragon Night and Other Lullabies*. New York, Methuen, 1980; London, Methuen, 1981.
*Ring of Earth: A Child's Book of Seasons*. San Diego, Harcourt Brace, 1986.
*The Three Bear Rhyme Book*. San Diego, Harcourt Brace, 1987.
*Best Witches: Poems for Halloween*. New York, Putnam, 1989.
*Bird Watch*. New York, Philomel, 1990.

Other

*Pirates in Petticoats*. New York, McKay, 1963.
*World on a String: The Story of Kites*. Cleveland, World, 1968.
*Friend: The Story of George Fox and the Quakers*. New York, Seabury Press, 1972.
*The Wizard Islands*. New York, Crowell, 1973.
*Writing Books for Children*. Boston, The Writer, 1973; revised edition, 1983.
*Ring Out! A Book of Bells*. New York, Seabury Press, 1974; London, Evans, 1978.
*Simple Gifts: The Story of the Shakers*. New York, Viking Press, 1976.
*Touch Magic: Fantasy, Faerie, and Folklore in the Literature of Childhood*. New York, Philomel, 1981.
*The Sleeping Beauty* (retelling). New York, Knopf, 1986.
*Guide to Writing for Children*. Boston, The Writer, 1989.
*Tam Lin: An Old Ballad* (retelling). San Diego, Harcourt Brace, 1990.
*Hark! A Christmas Sampler*. New York, Putnam, 1991.

Editor, *The Fireside Song Book of Birds and Beasts*, music by Barbara Green. New York, Simon and Schuster, 1972.
Editor, *Zoo 2000: Twelve Stories of Science Fiction and Fantasy Beasts*. New York, Seabury Press, 1973; London, Gollancz, 1975.
Editor, *Rounds about Rounds*, music by Barbara Green, illustrated by Gail Gibbons. New York, Watts, 1977; London, Watts, 1978.
Editor, *Shape Shifters: Fantasy and Science Fiction Tales about Humans Who Can Change Their Shapes*. New York, Seabury Press, 1978.
Editor, *The Lullaby Songbook*, music arranged by Adam Stemple, illustrated by Charles Mikolaycak. San Diego, Harcourt Brace, 1986.
Editor, with Martin H. Greenberg and Charles G. Waugh, *Dragons and Dreams: A Collection of New Fantasy and Science Fiction Stories*. New York, Harper, 1986.
Editor, *Favorite Folktales from Around the World*. New York, Pantheon, 1986.
Editor, with Martin H. Greenberg and Charles G. Waugh, *Spaceships and Spells*. New York, Harper, 1987.
Editor, with Martin H. Greenberg, *Werewolves*. New York, Harper, 1988.
Editor, with Martin H. Greenberg, *Things That Go Bump in the Night*. New York, Harper, 1989.
Editor, *The Lap-Time Song and Play Book*. San Diego, Harcourt Brace, 1989.
Editor, with Martin H. Greenberg, *Vampires*. New York, Harper Collins, 1991.
Editor, *2041 A.D.: Twelve Stories about the Future by Today's Top Science Fiction Writers*. New York, Delacorte Press, 1991.

*

Manuscript Collection: Kerlan Collection, University of Minnesota, Minneapolis.

* * *

Jane Yolen is first and foremost a storyteller. When one reads her works, the words transcend the eye and settle on the ear, as in her retelling of the ancient Scottish ballad of *Tam Lin*. Her choice and placement of words, her polished prose, maintains the rhythm of the ballad while rendering it in narrative text. Though *Tam Lin* is a picture book, Yolen accomplishes the same quality of a story being told, rather than read, in her adult works.

Yolen is not only an accomplished storyteller but an acknowledged authority on folklore. In her book of essays *Touch Magic: Fantasy, Faerie, and Folklore in the Literature of Childhood*, she posits that "These four functions of myth and folklore should establish the listening to and learning of the old tales as being among the most basic elements of our education: creating a landscape of allusion, enabling us to understand our own and other cultures from the inside out, providing an adaptable tool of therapy, and stating in symbolic or metaphoric terms the abstract truths of our common human existence." Combining her creativity with the solid grounding in folklore, Yolen is able to devise stories that resonate to our deepest understanding of myth while being set in worlds of her own creation.

Versatility is a hallmark of Yolen's work, and she has written more than 100 books ranging across genres and levels of appeal. Among her strongest works are those that are science fiction or fantasy. Her adult companion books *Sister Light, Sister Dark* and *White Jenna* share an interesting structure. The books are comprised of "The Myth," a terse, polished, and formal presentation that foreshadows the action; "The Legend," an account closer to the action but removed to the level of a tale told over time and passed from listener to listener; and "The Story," the actual unfolding of the tale. Sections called "The History" are from the writings of an imagined historian/folklorist and reveal the battles that rage in academia over interpretation of history and myth. Yolen's structure provides a tongue-in-cheek deflation of such behaviors.

A group of strong mountain women, outcasts from neighboring villages because they were deformed or because the village had too many females, has evolved into a society scattered across the landscape in mountain fortresses called Hames. They are united in their belief in The Book of Light by the Great Alta. Each light sister has a dark sister, visible only when there is light, called from the dark at maturity. *Sister Light, Sister Dark* tells of Jenna, a baby who came to Selden Hame under unusual circumstances and who as she reached maturity seemed to be the fulfillment of a prophecy foretelling the coming of a leader known by various names—the Anna, the White One, etc. Jenna's meeting with Carum, an exiled prince, her slaying of two evil brothers, and the destruction of Nill's Hame provide adventurous and thought-provoking reading.

*White Jenna* continues the saga, with Jenna setting out to warn the Hames of coming destruction. She meets Sorrel, one of the Grenna, and becomes "cocooned in time in the circle." In this underworld she meets Alta, named for the Goddess, and learns that "Time has come for the world to turn." Jenna's part in this is to fulfill the prophecy, overcoming evil. The setting and action are original while incorporating archetypes from our world.

Yolen's first book assembled directly for adults is *Tales of Wonder*, a collection of short stories that exemplifies the wide range of the author's talents. Some are witty, such as "Boris Chernevsky's Hands," some inexpressibly sad, as "Names." The collection contains the story "The Cards of Grief," which was later expanded into a novel, though other stories are complete in themselves and are reminiscent of traditional folk and fairy tale, as in "The Girl Who Loved the Wind." In the introductory essay, which recounts her process of creation, Yolen writes, "I would *like* to believe that there is that of faerie in each of us, a little trickle or stream that, if we could but tap it, would lead us back to the great wellspring of magic we share with every human being, every creature—and the world." Such a sentiment underlies the power of Jane Yolen's writing and explains her ability to reach the reader in many forms.

For her acclaimed young adult fantasy series, The Pit Dragon Trilogy, Yolen created an austere world, Austar IV. Once a penal colony, it is now a harsh world of masters and slaves. Its economy is based on gambling on the fighting pit dragons. *Dragon's Blood* begins the chronicle with Jakkin, a young bonder, stealing a dragon's egg and raising the young dragon to be a fighter in the pits. His success results in his attaining the status of master. In *Heart's Blood*, the story develops much more complexity. Jakkin and his love, Akki, become enmeshed in a rebel plot to overthrow the government. When it all turns sour, Jakkin and Akki are saved only by Heart's Blood's sacrifice of her life, resulting in their new ability to communicate on the level of a dragon. *A Sending of Dragons* completes the cycle, with Jakkin and Akki captured by a race of people who are also able to communicate by mind-sending. Yolen explores many moral complexities within the plot, such as the true meaning of freedom, the possibility of good going awry through venal desires, and one's responsibility for others.

Venturing onto the worn pathway of the tales of King Arthur, Yolen breaks her own trail in *The Dragon's Boy*. For the reader steeped in the lore King Arthur, *The Dragon's Boy* will be a splendid uncovering of clues to characters and ideas as the story unfolds in a new setting, and as Yolen plays with language and ideas in clever ways.

All of Yolen's work is saturated with her knowledge, her wit, and her belief in the importance of story. In her own words, "Knowing that . . . magic has consequences, whether it is the magic of wonder, the magic of language, or the magic of challenging a waiting mind, . . . it is up to the artist, the writer, the storyteller to reach out and touch that awesome magic. Touch magic—and pass it on."

—M. Jean Greenlaw

---

**YOUNG, Robert F(ranklin).** American. Born in Silver Creek, New York, 8 June 1915. Served in the United States Army during World War II. Married Regina M. Sadusky in 1941; one daughter. Inspector in a non-ferrous foundry. *Died in 1986.*

SCIENCE-FICTION PUBLICATIONS

Novels

*La Quête de la Sainte Grille*. Paris, Opta, 1975.
*Starfinder*. New York, Pocket Books, 1980.
*The Last Yggdrasill*. New York, Ballantine, 1982.
*Eridahn*. New York, Ballantine, 1983.
*The Vizier's Second Daughter*. New York, DAW, 1985.

Short Stories

*The Worlds of Robert F. Young*. New York, Simon and Schuster, 1965; London, Gollancz, 1966.
*A Glass of Stars*. Jacksonville, Illinois, Harris Wolfe, 1968.
*Le Pays d'esprit*. Paris, Oswald, 1982.

Uncollected Short Stories

"Pithecanthropus Astralis," in *Venture* (Concord, New Hampshire), August 1969.
"The Ogress," in *The Future Is Now*, edited by William F. Nolan. Los Angeles, Sherbourne Press, 1970.
"Reflections," in *Galaxy* (New York), March 1970.
"To Touch a Star," in *If* (New York), April 1970.
"A Ship Will Come," in *Worlds of Fantasy* (New York), Winter 1970.
"Genesis 500," in *Analog* (New York), February 1972.
"The Hand," in *Galaxy* (New York), March 1972.
"Whom the Gods Love," in *If* (New York), December 1972.
"The Years," in *Best SF 1972*, edited by Harry Harrison and Brian Aldiss. New York, Putnam, 1973; as *The Year's Best Science Fiction 6*, London, Sphere, 1973.
"Remnants of Things Past," in *Fantasy and Science Fiction* (New York), April 1973.
"Girl Saturday," in *Galaxy* (New York), May 1973.
"The Adventures of the Last Earthman in Search of Love," in *Amazing* (New York), June 1973.
"The Giantess," in *Fantasy and Science Fiction* (New York), July 1973.
"Ghosts," in *Best Science Fiction Stories of the Year*, edited by Lester del Rey. New York, Dutton, 1974.

"No Deposit, No Refill," in *Amazing* (New York), February 1974.
"The Star of Stars," in *Fantasy and Science Fiction* (New York), March 1974.
"Tinkerboy," in *Galaxy* (New York), May 1974.
"New Route to the Indies," in *Amazing* (New York), August 1974.
"Spacetrack," in *Fantasy and Science Fiction* (New York), September 1974.
"Hex Factor," in *Fantasy and Science Fiction* (New York), November 1974.
"The Decayed Leg Bone," in *Amazing* (New York), December 1974.
"Perchance to Dream," in *Fantastic* (New York), February 1975.
"Techmech," in *Fantastic* (New York), June 1975.
"Lord of Rays," in *Amazing* (New York), July 1975.
"The Curious Case of Henry Dickens," in *Fantasy and Science Fiction* (New York), August 1975.
"Shakespeare of the Apes," in *Fantasy and Science Fiction* (New York), December, 1975.
"Clay Suburb," in *The Best Science Fiction of the Year 5*, edited by Terry Carr. New York, Ballantine, and London, Gollancz, 1976.
"Above This Race of Men," in *Amazing* (New York), January 1976.
"Ghur R'Hut Urr," in *Amazing* (New York), June 1976.
"PRNDLL," in *Fantasy and Science Fiction* (New York), June 1976.
"Milton Inglorious," in *Fantasy and Science Fiction* (New York), September 1976.
"The Day the Limited Was Late," in *Fantasy and Science Fiction* (New York), March 1977.
"Fleuve Red," in *Fantastic* (New York), September 1977.
"The Space Roc," in *Amazing* (New York), January 1978.
"The Journal of Nathaniel Worth," in *Fantastic* (New York), July 1978.
"The Winning of Gloria Grandonwheels," in *Amazing* (New York), August 1978.
"Hologirl," in *Fantasy and Science Fiction* (New York), August 1978.
"Crutch," in *Amazing* (New York), November 1978.
"The First Mars Mission," in *Fantasy and Science Fiction* (New York), May 1979.
"Project Hi-Rise," in *The Best from Fantasy and Science Fiction 23*, edited by Edward L. Ferman. New York, Doubleday, 1980.
"The Tents of Kedar," in *Fantasy and Science Fiction* (New York), December 1980.
"Yours,—Guy," in *Shadows 4*, edited by Charles L. Grant. New York, Doubleday, 1981.
"The Summer of the Fallen Star," in *Fantasy and Science Fiction* (New York), April 1981.
"Invitation to the Waltz," in *Fantasy and Science Fiction* (New York), March 1982.
"Dark Space," in *Isaac Asimov's Science Fiction Magazine* (New York), March 1982.
"Earthscape," in *Isaac Asimov's Science Fiction Magazine* (New York), May 1982.
"Universes," in *Isaac Asimov's Science Fiction Magazine* (New York), August 1982.
"The Moon of Advanced Learning," in *Isaac Asimov's Science Fiction Magazine* (New York), October 1982.
"Glimpses," in *Isaac Asimov's Science Fiction Magazine* (New York), February 1983.
"The Lost Earthman," in *Fantasy and Science Fiction* (New York), November 1983.
"The Princess of Akkir," in *Isaac Asimov's Science Fiction Magazine* (New York), March 1984.
"Divine Wind," in *Fantasy and Science Fiction* (New York), April 1984.
"Glass Houses," in *Fantasy and Science Fiction* (New York), November 1984.
"Findokin's Way," in *Isaac Asimov's Science Fiction Magazine* (New York), November 1984.
"Mars Child," in *Amazing* (New York), January 1985.
"A Drink in Darkness," in *Fantastic Stories: Tales of the Weird and Wondrous*, edited by Martin H. Greenberg and Patrick L. Price. Lake Geneva, Wisconsin, TSR, 1987.

*

Robert F. Young commented:

(1985) My books and stories deal with a variety of subjects. My motive in writing most of them stems in part from a fascination for science fiction dating from the long-ago years when I discovered Edgar Rice Burroughs and H.G. Wells, and in part from the genre's capability of providing a writer with the opportunity to make the impossible seem possible.

* * *

In an introductory essay to Robert F. Young's *A Glass of Stars*, Fritz Leiber remarks: "And I say that the field to which Robert F. Young has many times proven his claim is that of romantic love. The magic potion of which he is master creator is the love philter." It could be further noted that the potion is not meant merely for the characters in his stories, but to captivate the audience that reads them. Young's realm is the realm of boy meets girl, not in some bygone era but on other worlds or in a future mired in the sins of our own time, crass commercialism and the violation of the environment. Almost always Young surveys his domain with the force of his sense of humor, inserting it at the proper junctures so as not to allow "boy meets girl" to become soap opera. Young skillfully weaves his plots in such a manner that the reader can only smile at the fact that the man and woman are together, living happily ever after, in the end.

An especially fine example of Young's plot-twisting talent is the story "L'Arc de Jeanne," which takes place on the planet Ciel Bleu, near the key city of Fleur du Sud. This is a planet committed to the Psycho-Phenomenalist Church. We find it under attack by the forces of the evil tyrant O'Riordan. All that stands in the way of conquest is a young maiden who rides a "magnificent black stallion" and is armed with what appears to be a magic bow and arrow. O'Riordan wants the maiden captured, and sends a computer-selected young man guaranteed to be irresistible to the maiden, to win her affection. The story evolves in such a manner that Young's Joan of Arc must burn at the stake, yet Young manages the plot so that the story ends happily.

Young's conservation concerns show forth in "To Fell a Tree." A young treeman has the task of felling a glorious 1000-foot tree, a job his company has been hired to do by a rather greedy village. The tree is so enormous that he must live in the tree for a number of days in order to bring it down. While in the tree he meets a dryad, the spirit of the tree, who is seen slowly dying as the tree is cut down, a tree the sap of which looks just like blood. Young's talent as a weaver of words is revealed in this story, along with his passionate concern for nature's living forms.

Young, a shrewd commentator on the crassness of commercialism, had a special fondness for the crudities of the automotive world. In "Romance in a Twenty-First-Century Used-Car-Lot," the auto industry has managed to miniaturize cars sufficiently so that they can be worn as clothing, and then convinced the public that not wearing them is obscene. Those who don't wear cars are called nudists and consigned to a nudist colony. "It wasn't hard to do," Howard Highways tells Arabella Grille, "because people had been wearing their cars unconsciously all along." Then there is Emily ("Emily and the Bards Sublime"), an assistant curator of a museum. She is extremely fond of the android poets, especially Lord Tennyson. One day she is told that the poets must go to make room for a display of 20th-century art, cars, that is. Mr. Brandon tells her she will be taking over the new exhibit; "Mr. Brandon handed her the big book he was carrying. '*An Analysis of the Chrome Motif in Twentieth Century Art.* Read it religiously, Miss Meredith. It's the most important book of our century.' "

However, Young's first love was romance, and he was willing to go to, or to manipulate, the ends of time to bring his loved ones together. "The Dandelion Girl," "The Girl Who Made Time Stop," and "Mine Eyes Have Seen the Glory" are all examples of first-rate stories that entail clever use of the intricacies of time as the fourth dimension. Young's gift as a story teller is brought out in these tales, for by the end of each story the reader has been moved to believe in the possibility of romantic love even when it entails bending the known laws of physics.

In *Starfinder*, Young also makes much use of the intricacies of time travel. The book deals with giant creatures—space whales—who can dive into the past, spaceships constructed from the carcases of these creatures, and one man's relationship to both the spacecraft and one of the creatures. Young takes full advantage of the paradoxes of time travel as he spins yet another story of romance across the eons. The reader should be forewarned, however, that Young's romanticism takes something of a rather sexist turn in its portrayal of one of the most important female characters and the planet she helps rule. Several segments of *Starfinder* were first published in short-story versions over a number of years.

—Mitchell Aboulafia

---

# Z

**ZACHARY, Hugh.** *See* **HUGHES, Zach.**

---

**ZAGAT, Arthur Leo.** American. Born in New York City, in 1895. Educated at City College of New York, B.A.; Bordeaux University; Fordham University Law School, New York, LL.D. Served in the United States Army during World War I, and with the Office of War Information during World War II. Married Ruth Zagat; one daughter. Founded Writers Workshop at New York University. Member of the Council, Authors League of America. *Died 3 April 1949.*

SCIENCE-FICTION PUBLICATIONS

Novel

*Seven Out of Time.* Reading, Pennsylvania, Fantasy Press, 1949.

Uncollected Short Stories

"The Tower of Evil," with Nat Schachner, in *Wonder Stories Quarterly* (New York), Summer 1930.
"In 20,000 A.D.," with Nat Schachner, in *Wonder Stories* (New York), September 1930.
"Back to 20,000 A.D.," with Nat Schachner, in *Wonder Stories* (New York), March 1931.
"The Emperor of the Stars," with Nat Schachner, in *Wonder Stories* (New York), April 1931.
"The Menace from Andromeda," with Nat Schachner, in *Amazing* (New York), April 1931.
"The Death-Cloud," with Nat Schachner, in *Astounding* (New York), May 1931.
"The Revolt of the Machines," with Nat Schachner, in *Astounding* (New York), July 1931.
"Venus Mines Incorporated," with Nat Schachner, in *Wonder Stories* (New York), August 1931.
"Exiles of the Moon," with Nat Schachner, in *Wonder Stories* (New York), September 1931.
"The Great Dome on Mercury," in *Astounding* (New York), April 1932.
"When the Sleepers Woke," in *Astounding* (New York), November 1932.
"The Living Flame," in *Astounding* (New York), February 1934.
"Spoor of the Bat," in *Astounding* (New York), July 1934.
"Beyond the Spectrum," in *Astounding* (New York), August 1934.
"The Land Where Time Stood Still," in *Thrilling Wonder Stories* (New York), August 1936.
"Flight of the Silver Eagle," in *Thrilling Wonder Stories* (New York), April 1937.
"Lost in Time," in *Thrilling Wonder Stories* (New York), June 1937.
"The Cavern of the Shining Pool," in *Thrilling Wonder Stories* (New York), October 1937.
"Island in the Sky," in *Argosy* (New York), 17 December 1937.
"The Green Ray," in *Thrilling Wonder Stories* (New York), August 1938.
"Tomorrow," in *Argosy* (New York), 27 May 1939.
"Children of Tomorrow," in *Argosy* (New York), 17 June 1939.
"Bright Flag of Tomorrow," in *Argosy* (New York), 9 September 1939.
"Thunder Tomorrow," in *Argosy* (New York), 16 March 1940.
"Sunrise Tomorrow," in *Argosy* (New York), 8–15 June 1940.
"The Long Road to Tomorrow," in *Argosy* (New York), 1–22 March 1941.
"The Two Moons of Tranquillia," in *Weird Tales* (New York), January 1943.
"Jungle Interlude," in *Argosy* (New York), February 1943.
"Sunward Flight," in *Super Science* (Kokomo, Indiana), February 1943.
"Venus Station," in *Science Fiction Stories* (New York), April 1943.
"The Lanson Screen," in *Best of Science Fiction*, edited by Groff Conklin. New York, Crown, 1946.
"Slaves of the Lamp," in *Astounding* (New York), August, September 1946.
"Grim Rendezvous," in *Thrilling Wonder Stories* (New York), December 1946.
"The Faceless Men," in *Thrilling Wonder Stories* (New York), April 1948.
"No Escape from Destiny," in *Startling* (New York), May 1948.
"Drink We Deep," in *Fantastic Novels* (New York), January 1951.

* * *

Arthur Leo Zagat is essentially an early 1930's figure, to be seen in the context of science fiction broadening, diversifying, and acquiring a definite character as more magazines emerged.

His relatively small science-fiction output reflected a personal interest in futuristic ideas; as with many others of the time whose overall output was trivial hack work, he showed originality and vision in science fiction. Every cliché began as an inspiration. Though his stories ranged over a variety of themes, his main contribution was to space flight. This was then something predicted for the indefinite future, but it was a vision that excited that generation as no other. The spectacular progress of aviation had made a profound impression, clearly made obvious the pace of technological change, and raised imagination from the ground.

Interplanetary travel had a long literary tradition, but, aside from its use as a springboard to introduce a Utopia or a reflection on man's follies, its emphasis had always been on the initial problems to be solved. By the time SF was firmly established, readers had gone over that ground many times and were ready to go beyond it. Early 1930's science fiction tried to imagine regular traffic between worlds, and settled into a picture analogous to ocean shipping as it had been in earlier times when it was more hazardous and maritime countries more remote and diverse. Zagat helped build up the image of a dangerous yet established trade, of interplanetary shipping lines and business rivalries, of a rough spaceport district analogous to the traditional waterfront, of a rough frontier class of spacemen, with occasional piracy and clashes with natives, or a well-disciplined space service to keep order.

Inevitably this led to the repetitive action stories Tucker aptly tagged space opera. It tended to trivialise space flight by glossing over the problems, though it popularised the concept. Its rather optimistic view had a strong appeal in its time. Zagat's stories such as "The Great Dome on Mercury," "Spoor of the Bat," and "The Cavern of the Shining Pool" were good entertainment, and added to the movement's repertory of expectations. World-scale conflict of East and West, another standard theme, was exploited in "The Death-Cloud," "The Green Ray," and "Flight of the Silver Eagle," dated, but showing what then seemed good probabilities: a world shrunk by better communications, conflict mainly airborn, death-rays and other devices.

And there are many other themes, all fairly new and treated originally—unearthlike life, the amorphous "The Menace from Andromeda," logically evolved; a nonhuman intelligent race in "The Emperor of the Stars" sympathetically treated without humanising it; invisible subterranean beings in "Beyond the Spectrum"; machine intelligence in "The Revolt of the Machines"; the world depopulated and left to a few chance survivors in "When the Sleepers Woke"; big business replacing traditional state power in "Exiles of the Moon" and "Lost in Time"; glimpses of future custom and folklore, even sport, in "Sunward Flight"; dangerous inventions in "The Lanson Screen," the defensive shield that became a deadly prison.

Zagat's only book, *Seven Out of Time*, drew on elements he had used before and clearly suffers from spinning out the suspense in a six-part serial. The early chapters with their missing-person plot and eery touches contrast with the strange remote world of millions of years hence, where the group of dehumanised monsters evolved from us try to recover the insights and motivations they have lost by studying their kidnapped people of our own and earlier times. Dated and plausable only as symbolic fantasy even in 1939, it has merit for the message it presents even today.

The volume of science fiction still appearing in the general fiction magazines through the 1930's is generally overlooked, but it was considerable and, though mostly less original, it has interest. *Seven Out of Time* first ran in *Argosy* which had a long history of including science fiction on its merits. Perhaps a better novel serialised there, never made a book, is "Drink We Deep," though hampered by its use of the primitive diary-letter form. This mystery with seemingly supernatural elements developed into a wild extravaganza of early science-fiction fancies, with size-change to bring the leading characters from everyday America into a miniature people's realm under a lake, with scientific marvels and a possible menace to the human world, plot elements reminiscent of Burroughs or Merritt, and some memorable scenes. The 1939–41 series of six tales beginning with "Tomorrow" was discontinued without resolution, perhaps because its background of a future America enslaved by the Yellow Peril came to be less a stock theme than an uncomfortable possibility. But its treatment with a group of children growing into Noble Savages in a wilderness retreat to lead revolt was an unusual concept.

Zagat's first works were written with Nat Schachner, whose role cannot be distinguished. The writing is conventional, the human interest elementary, with characterisation going little beyond stock figures. But it is competent, good of its kind in its time, and it has conviction.

—Graham Stone

---

**ZAHN, Timothy.** American. Born in Chicago, Illinois, 1 September 1951. Educated at Michigan State University, East Lansing, 1969–73, B.A. in physics 1973; University of Illinois, Urbana, 1973–79, M.S. in physics 1975. Married Anna L. Zahn in 1979; one son. Since 1980, full-time writer. Recipient: Hugo award, 1984. Agent: Russell Galen, Scott Meredith Literary Agency, 845 Third Avenue, New York, New York 10022. Address: 2014 Vawter Street, Apt. 2, Urbana, Illinois 61801, U.S.A.

SCIENCE-FICTION PUBLICATIONS

Novels (series: Blackcollar; Cobra)

*The Blackcollar.* New York, DAW, 1983.
*A Coming of Age.* New York, Bluejay, 1985.
*Cobra.* New York, Baen, 1985.
*Spinneret.* New York, Bluejay, 1985.
*Cobra Strike.* New York, Baen, 1986.
*The Backlash Mission* (Blackcollar). New York, DAW, 1986.
*Triplet.* New York, Baen, 1987.
*Cobra Bargain.* New York, Baen, 1988.
*Deadman Switch.* New York, Baen, 1988.
*Warhorse.* New York, Baen, 1990.
*Heir to the Empire.* New York, Bantam, 1991.

Short Stories

*Cascade Point and Other Stories.* New York, Bluejay, 1986.
*Time Bomb and Zahndry Others.* New York, Baen, 1988.

*

Timothy Zahn comments:

There are as many definitions of "science fiction" as there are writers, readers, and critics; but to me the important word here is "fiction," and fiction means telling a story. I enjoy speculating in my stories—playing the "if-then" game—and when I can make a point about humanity or society as well I feel I am helping, in a small way, to fulfill the promise of depth and richness that science fiction has always offered its readers. But the basic story *must* be worth reading; must hold the readers' attention and firmly draw them into the world the writer has created. Otherwise any message is likely to be lost, or never read at all.

The number-one goal in my writing, therefore, is to entertain my audience—to entertain with high adventure, as in *The Blackcollar*; to entertain with details of an unusual society, as in *A Coming of Age*; to entertain with scientific-puzzle stories, as in many of my shorter stories. But the entertainment must be there. Always. It's part of the job.

*   *   *

Timothy Zahn started his career primarily as a short story writer for *Analog* magazine during the early 1980's. Although most of his early stories are entertaining, they are also largely formulaic. His blend of sound extrapolation of scientific principles and well-paced, convincing plots began to mark his work as unusual in such stories as "Between a Rock and a High Place," an exceptional story of a disastrous accident in space, "The Cassandra," and "When Johnny Comes Marching Home." The most noteworthy of these, and still his best single shorter work, is "Cascade Point," which won the Hugo award. It deals with a strange phenomenon associated with travel at faster-than-light speeds during which human beings are able to see alternate versions of themselves.

His first novel, *The Blackcollar*, also demonstrates another of his recurring concerns—technological augmentation of the human body and the role of the professional soldier in society. Earth has been subjugated by alien conquerors despite the best efforts of the elite Blackcollar units to defend humanity. A generation later, one man learns that some of these supersoldiers have survived, and he sets out to use them to overthrow the invaders. Their limited success is plausible, and the story as a whole is convincing and fast-moving entertainment. Zahn returns to this setting for a sequel, *The Backlash Mission*. The secret to the success of the Blackcollars is their use of a secret drug. The secret of its manufacture has been lost, but there is a rumored storehouse deep in alien territory. Although the fast-paced action of the first novel is repeated here, the results are less satisfactory, essentially only reprising the original story.

*A Coming of Age* is more ambitious and successful. A colony world has recovered from near chaos when new born children begin demonstrating telekinetic abilities, which thankfully disappear as they grow older. A well-constructed mystery story is superimposed over this background, but the real focus of the novel is the exploration of the implications of the society that resulted from these unusual conditions.

The plight of the returned soldier during peacetime is examined in some of Zahn's earliest stories, and two of these are incorporated into the first of the *Cobra* series. Jonny Moreau has had powerful weapons surgically implanted in his body, and his deadly abilities create an artificial barrier between himself and his neighbors, until a new alien menace, the Troft, alters the situation. Moreau returns in *Cobra Strike*, a generation later, although the novel is more concerned with one of his sons. Humans and the Troft have become reconciled to one another, but they are both threatened by the appearance of a new race. The third in the series, *Cobra Bargain*, returns to an examination of anti-military sentiment, balanced by a renewed danger of warfare, and embellished by the battle for and against the inclusion of women in the all-male Cobra forces.

*Spinneret* concerns the discovery of remnants of the technology of a vanished alien race, a more sophisticated novel than those preceding it. One strain of the plot is the obvious mystery surrounding the artifacts, while the primary conflict is among various human and alien interests, which attempt to gain power through control of knowledge. Zahn blurs the borders between science fiction and fantasy with *Triplet*. A newly discovered planet contains gates leading to two other worlds; in one of the worlds there exists a technology so sophisticated that it is indistinguishable from magic, and in the other, magic itself holds sway. *Triplet* is an ambitious work that makes some interesting contrasts, but it suffers from the inconsistency of atmosphere required by the plot.

The questions of ethics raised in *Deadman Switch* give an already excellent hard science-fiction novel an extra dimension. A resource-rich string of moons that has been unapproachable for generations proves attainable only at the cost of two human lives, one to penetrate the system, one to allow departure. As a consequence, condemned criminals are used as sacrifices to expediency by a civilization intent upon exploiting the situation. The ethical problem becomes the primary focus when one of the criminals is discovered to be innocent.

*Warhorse*, an expansion of two early short stories, presents a similar conflict. Humanity's expansion to the stars causes contact with the Tampies, a star-travelling species that has used bioengineering to breed living spaceships. Both species feel that they are destined to shape the future for all life in the universe, and the massive differences in cultural outlook inevitably lead to conflict. *Warhorse* and *Deadman Switch* are both serious and thoughtful novels as well as fast-paced adventure stories.

Although Zahn has shifted his emphasis to novels, he still writes occasional short stories. Among the most interesting are "Evidence of Things Not Seen" and "The Hand That Rocks the Casket." His most recent project is a trilogy of novels set in the years following the events of the "Star Wars" movies, of which only the first, *Heir to the Empire*, has appeared. Although necessarily restricted by the requirements of character and setting, Zahn has done an admirable job of capturing the pace and feel of the films, and introduces an interesting and suitably malevolent new villain.

—Don D'Ammassa

---

**ZEBROWSKI, George.** American. Born in Villach, Austria, 28 December 1945. Attended the State University of New York, Binghamton, 1964–69. Copy editor, Binghamton *Evening Press*, 1967; filtration plant operator, New York, 1969–70; lecturer in science fiction, State University of New York, Binghamton, Spring 1971; editor, *SFWA Bulletin*, 1970–75, and 1983–1991; general editor and consultant, Crown, publishers, New York, 1983–85. Freelance writer, editor, and lecturer. Agent: Joseph Elder Agency, 150 West 87th Street, New York, New York 10024. Address: Box 486, Johnson City, New York 13790, U.S.A.

SCIENCE-FICTION PUBLICATIONS

Novels (series: Omega Point)

*The Omega Point.* New York, Ace, 1972; London, New English Library, 1974.
*The Star Web.* Toronto, Laser, 1975.
*Ashes and Stars.* New York, Ace, 1977; London, New English Library, 1978.
*Macrolife.* New York, Harper, 1979; London, Futura, 1980.
*The Omega Point Trilogy* (includes *The Omega Point* and *Ashes and Stars*, both revised, and *Mirror of Minds*). New York, Ace, 1983.
*Sunspacer* (for children). New York, Harper, 1984.
*The Stars Will Speak* (for children). New York, Harper, 1985.
*Stranger Suns.* Norwalk, Connecticut, Easton Press, 1991.

Short Stories

*The Monadic Universe and Other Stories.* New York, Ace, 1977; augmented edition, 1985.
*A Silent Shout.* Tulsa, Educational Development Corporation, 1979.
*The Firebird.* Tulsa, Educational Development Corporation, 1979.

Uncollected Short Stories

"Dark, Dark, the Dead Star," with Jack Dann, in *If* (New York), July–August 1970.
"Listen, Love," with Jack Dann, in *New Worlds Quarterly 2*, edited by Michael Moorcock. London, Sphere, and New York, Berkley, 1971.
"Traps," with Jack Dann, in *Coming Through*, edited by Nina C. Woessner and William D. Sheldon. Boston, Allyn and Bacon, 1972.
"Fountain of Force," with Grant Carrington, in *Inifinity 4*, edited by Robert Hoskins. New York, Lancer, 1972.
"OD," with Jack Dann, in *Omega*, edited by Roger Elwood. New York, Walker, 1974.
"Adrift in Space" (for children), in *Adrift in Space and Other Stories*, edited by Roger Elwood. Minneapolis, Lerner, 1974.
"Darkness of Day," with Pamela Sargent, in *Continuum 3*, edited by Roger Elwood. New York, Berkley, 1974.
"Thirty-Three and One Third," with Jack Dann, in *Long Night of Waiting and Other Stories*, edited by Roger Elwood. Nashville, Aurora, 1974.
"The Flower That Missed the Morning" (for children), with Jack Dann, in *The Killer Plants and Other Stories*, edited by Roger Elwood. Minneapolis, Lerner, 1974.
"Journey to Another Star" (for children), in *Journey to Another Star and Other Stories*, edited by Roger Elwood. Nashville, Aurora, 1974.
"The Iron Butterfly" (for children), in *Current Science*, 20 February 1974.
"Faces Forward," with Jack Dann, and "Weapons," with Pamela Sargent, in *Dystopian Visions*, edited by Roger Elwood. Englewood Cliffs, Prentice Hall, 1975.
"Yellowhead," with Jack Dann, in *New Constellations*, edited by Thomas M. Disch and Charles Naylor. New York, Harper, 1976.
"Transfigured Night," in *Immortal*, edited by Jack Dann. New York, Harper, 1978.
"Fire of Spring," in *Chillers*, July 1981.
"Earth Around His Bones," in *Chillers*, September 1981.
"The Alternate," in *Chillers*, November 1981.
"The Falling," with Pamela Sargent, in *Isaac Asimov's Science Fiction Magazine* (New York), March 1983.
"The Sea of Evening," in *Isaac Asimov's Science Fiction Magazine* (New York), July 1983.
"The Eichmann Variations," in *Light Years and Dark*, edited by Michael Bishop. New York, Berkley, 1984.
"The City of Thought and Steel," in *Isaac Asimov's Science Fiction Magazine* (New York), March 1984.
"Gödel's Doom," in *Mathenauts: Tales of Mathematical Wonder*, edited by Rudy Rucker. New York, Arbor House, 1987.
"The Idea Trap," in *Universe 16*, edited by Terry Carr. New York, Doubleday, 1986.
"Foundation's Conscience," in *Foundation's Friends: Stories in Honor of Isaac Asimov*, edited by Martin H. Greenberg. New York, Tor, 1989.

Other Publications

Other

*Perfecting Visions, Slaying Cynics: The Life and Times of George Zebrowski*, with Jeffrey M. Elliot. San Bernardino, California, Borgo Press, 1989.

Editor, *Tomorrow Today*. Santa Cruz, California, Unity Press, 1975.
Editor, with Thomas N. Scortia, *Human-Machines: An Anthology of Stories about Cyborgs*. New York, Random House, 1975; London, Hale, 1977.
Editor, with Jack Dann, *Faster Than Light: An Anthology of Stories about Interstellar Travel*. New York, Harper, 1976.
Editor, *The Best of Thomas N. Scortia*. New York, Doubleday, 1981.
Editor, with Isaac Asimov and Martin H. Greenberg, *Creations: The Quest for Origins in Story and Science*. New York, Crown, 1983; London, Harrap, 1984.
Editor, *Nebula Awards [20–22]*. San Diego, California, Harcourt Brace, 1985–88.
Editor, *Synergy [1–4]*. San Diego, California, Harcourt Brace, 1987–89.

*

Bibliography: *The Work of George Zebrowski: An Annotated Bibliography and Guide* by Jeffrey M. Elliot, San Bernardino, California, Borgo Press, 1986, 1990.

Manuscript Collection: Paskow Science Fiction Collection, Temple University, Philadelphia.

George Zebrowski comments:

I have been described as a "hard SF writer with literary intent"—which makes me sound like a difficult person about to commit a crime of some sort. What "literary" means in this description, I believe, is that I pay attention to the writerly virtues of style, characterization, and lucid storytelling, as much as I do to what makes a work science fiction—its scientific facts, speculative ideas, and philosophical considerations. Nothing wrong with that; I wouldn't think much of any hard SF writer who deliberately leaves all that out.

James Blish, a favorite writer of mine, once said that SF should be hard (thoroughgoing) all the way through—in its ideas and literary virtues, which seems to me to be beyond argument as a prescription. It's the ideal I started with as a writer.

The knowledge of what one does as an SF writer can be clearly stated, but not easily practiced. One writes fiction that deals with the human impact of possible future changes in science and technology. Even if you remove science and technology, you still have "the human impact of possible future change." You might remove future, since many SF works are set in the present or past, but you can still substitute "imaginary but plausible" here and not violate the spirit of SF. The "human impact" makes it literature; the "plausible imaginary changes" makes it SF. How well the literary and science-fictional conceits come out depends on the ambition and skill of the writer.

* * *

Like Olaf Stapledon, George Zebrowski paints his fictive vistas with the brush of eons, adding and subtracting galaxies with a single great stroke. Not for him are the crabbed miniatures of most science-fiction novelists, whose collective vision barely extends over the next hill. Zebrowski is concerned with the "big picture," the long-term fate of humankind, the end (and the beginning) of things, the how and where, and particularly the *why* of life, the universe, and everything. Where so many of his compatriots are now producing western, mystery, and mainstream novels with SF trappings, in sequel upon sequel, this author continues to write brilliant science fiction that could be presented in no other conceivable way.

Beginning life as a Polish refugee born into the turmoil of post-Nazi Europe, Zebrowski grew up in the South Bronx, even then a wasteland of broken dreams and deadened hopes. He began reading science fiction at an early age, and was writing his first stories in the 1960's. By 1970, he had published "The Water Sculptor," the first of about 50 shorter works that quickly earned him the reputation of a rising SF star. His first novel, *The Omega Point*, later expanded into *The Omega Point Trilogy*, provided an initial showcase for Zebrowski's cosmic visions of man and the universe. These early fictions pale, however, before the sweep and impact of the writer's two major novels, *Macrolife* and *Stranger Suns*, which would ensure him a place in the SF hall of fame even if he never wrote another word.

Zebrowski had written the first drafts of *Macrolife* as early as 1964, although the book was not completed until 15 years later. In a near-future Earth, the discovery of bulerite (named for the Bulero family) has revolutionized architecture and economics. Lightweight, versatile, stronger than steel, bulerite has enabled the construction of huge cityplexes, and facilitated the exploration of near-Earth space, with the subsequent colonization of Mars, the asteroids, and several of the larger moons in the Solar System. Unknown to the Buleros, bulerite is inherently unstable, and as structures made of the element begin to disintegrate or explode, they pull civilization down with it. Three of the Buleros—Richard, Sam, and Janet—escape to Asterome, a hollowed-out, ten-mile-long asteroid in Earth orbit, along with other scattered refugees from the devastated planet below. Earth is enveloped in an impenetrable cloud, with no hope of any life surviving the incessant lightning storms raging over its surface.

Asterome represents the first stage of macrolife, a self-sufficient, self-contained structure that will eventually spread intelligent life to every part of the universe. Eventually, Asterome leaves the Solar System, traveling to nearby stars, and using the raw materials from their planets to construct new macrolife globes as its own compartments become crowded, or as social divisions develop among the populace. The flexibility of this arrangement, and the gradual lengthening of life-spans, enable humanity to grow literally without limits, to avoid frictions that might lead to war, to develop intellectually and emotionally in ways never before contemplated. Eventually, an alien macrolife unit is located, one of many such structures traversing the galaxy, and contact is made, to the mutual benefit of both races. The mental links between these groups seem to promise another stage of development of mankind.

Eventually, a hundred billion years later, all intelligence has merged into one group mind. But the universe is winding down toward ultimate nullity, when all matter will collapse into the final explosion. John Bulero, a clone of Samuel Bolero, suddenly finds his consciousness reconstituted for some ultimate decision. Is there something more? the intelligences ask. Can anything survive the final debacle? The answers to these questions lead Bulero to the third level of macrolife, a consciousness so powerful that it can create its own universes, and can transcend time and space itself.

Zebrowski's newest novel, *Stranger Suns*, also represents 15 years of effort, an earlier draft having been published in very abridged form in 1975. Juan Obrion and his three companions discover an abandoned alien spaceship buried deep in the Antarctic ice. The ship admits them, then abruptly takes off for an unknown destination. The explorers discover matter-replicators within the ship that solve immediate problems of food and water supply, but no sign of the race that had constructed the vessel. They determine that the aliens have built a network of way stations within the suns of both our galaxy and its neighbors; these sophisticated facilities are also old and abandoned, as are the surface structures found on a barren planet at the end of the chain. Eventually Juan and his friends determine that a set of black panels in the ship's bowels connect directly through hyperspace to similar panels on two other vessels left within the Solar System, one buried in the Amazon jungle, the other on the Moon, and to other alien vessels and facilities, enabling instantaneous movement through tremendous distances.

However, nothing in Zebrowski's works is ever quite what it seems, because the very act of moving back and forth through the portals alters either the viewer or the viewed in ways that are sometimes subtly, sometimes grossly, skewed from the original. Eye color may be changed, or the outcome of a football game—or the fundamental history of the world as Obrion has known it. Why did the alien race develop this alternate mode of transportation? Why have all their facilities been abandoned? Where have they gone? How can mankind use these structures to ensure its survival? The answers to these questions lead Obrion and company on a strange odyssey beyond the universe to an existence outside time and space as we know it.

Both of these books tell us that we must rise from the mud of our mundane existences and lift our faces to the stars, our sole natural destiny if the race is to survive the wars and chances of planet-bound existence. Life on Earth is inherently flawed, the author implies; by creating a world on the edge of collapse, we have imperiled our own future existence. In Zebrowski's cosmos, limited or unlimited, Earth (the soil) is Hell, the stars (the universe) are Heaven, and humans can become either god or devil, savior or destroyer, as they so choose.

—Robert Reginald

---

**ZEIGFRIED, Karl.** *See* **FANTHORPE, R. Lionel.**

---

**ZELAZNY, Roger (Joseph).** Also writes as Harrison Denmark. American. Born in Cleveland, Ohio, 13 May 1937. Educated at Noble School, 1943–49, Shore Junior High School, 1949–52, and Euclid Senior High School, 1952–55, all Euclid, Ohio; Western Reserve University, Cleveland (Foster Poetry award, 1957, 1959), 1955–59, B.A. in English 1959; Columbia University, New York, 1959–60, M.A. 1962. Served in the Ohio National Guard, 1960–63, and the United States Army Reserve, 1963–66. Married 1) Sharon Steberl in 1964 (divorced 1966); 2) Judith Callahan in 1966, two sons and one daughter. Claims representative, Cleveland, 1963–65, and claims specialist, Baltimore, 1965–69, Social Security Administration. Since 1969, freelance writer and lecturer. Secretary-Treasurer, Science Fiction Writers of America, 1967–68. Recipient: Nebula award, 1965 (twice), 1975; Hugo award, for novel, 1966, 1968, for story, 1976, 1982; Prix Apollo, 1972; American Library Association award, 1976; *Locus* award, 1984, 1986. Guest of Honor, 32nd World Science Fiction Convention, 1974, and Australian National Science Fiction Convention, 1978. Agent: Pimlico Agency, 155 East 77th Street, Suite 1A, New York, New York 10021. Address: 1045 Stagecoach Road, Santa Fe, New Mexico 87501, U.S.A.

SCIENCE-FICTION PUBLICATIONS

Novels (series: Amber)

*This Immortal.* New York, Ace, 1966; London, Hart Davis, 1967.

*The Dream Master.* New York, Ace, 1966; London, Hart Davis, 1968.
*Lord of Light.* New York, Doubleday, 1967; London, Faber, 1968.
*Isle of the Dead.* New York, Ace, 1969; London, Rapp and Whiting, 1970.
*Creatures of Light and Darkness.* New York, Doubleday, 1969; London, Faber, 1970.
*Damnation Alley.* New York, Putnam, 1969; London, Faber, 1971.
*Nine Princes in Amber.* New York, Doubleday, 1970; London, Faber, 1972.
*Jack of Shadows.* New York, Walker, 1971; London, Faber, 1973.
*The Guns of Avalon* (Amber). New York, Doubleday, 1972; London, Faber, 1974.
*Today We Choose Faces.* New York, New American Library, 1973; London, Millington, 1974.
*To Die in Italbar.* New York, Doubleday, 1973; London, Faber, 1975.
*Sign of the Unicorn* (Amber). New York, Doubleday, 1975; London, Faber, 1977.
*Doorways in the Sand.* New York, Harper, 1976; London, W.H. Allen, 1977.
*The Hand of Oberon* (Amber). New York, Doubleday, 1976; London, Faber, 1978.
*Bridge of Ashes.* New York, New American Library, 1976.
*Deus Irae*, with Philip K. Dick. New York, Doubleday, 1976; London, Gollancz, 1977.
*The Courts of Chaos* (Amber). New York, Doubleday, 1978; London, Faber, 1980.
*The Chronicles of Amber* (omnibus). New York, Doubleday, 2 vols., 1979.
*The Bells of Shoredan.* Columbia, Pennsylvania, Underwood Miller, 1979.
*Roadmarks.* New York, Ballantine, 1979; London, Futura, 1981.
*Changeling.* New York, Ace, 1980.
*Madwand.* Huntington Woods, Michigan, Phantasia Press, 1981.
*Coils*, with Fred Saberhagen. New York, Tor, 1980; London, Penguin, 1984.
*The Changing Land.* New York, Ballantine, 1981.
*Eye of the Cat.* New York, Pocket Books, 1982; London, Sphere, 1984.
*Dilvish, The Damned.* New York, Ballantine, 1982.
*Trumps of Doom* (Amber). New York, Arbor House, 1985; London, Sphere, 1986.
*Blood of Amber.* New York, Arbor House, 1986; London, Sphere, 1987.
*A Dark Traveling* (for children). New York, Walker, 1987; London, Hutchinson, 1989.
*Sign of Chaos* (Amber). New York, Arbor House, 1987; London, Sphere, 1988.
*Knight of Shadows* (Amber). New York, Morrow, 1989.
*The Black Thorne*, with Fred Saberhagan. New York, Baen, 1990.
*The Mask of Lohi*, with Thomas T. Thomas. New York, Baen, 1990.
*Bring Me the Head of Prince Charming.* New York, Bantam, 1991.
*Prince of Chaos.* New York, Morrow, 1991.

Short Stories

*Four for Tomorrow.* New York, Ace, 1967; as *A Rose for Ecclesiastes*, London, Hart Davis, 1969.
*The Doors of His Face, the Lamps of His Mouth, and Other Stories.* New York, Doubleday, 1971; London, Faber, 1973.
*My Name Is Legion.* New York, Ballantine, 1976; London, Faber, 1979.
*The Last Defender of Camelot.* New York, Pocket Books, 1980.
*Unicorn Variations.* New York, Pocket Books, 1983.
*Frost and Fire.* New York, Morrow, 1989.

OTHER PUBLICATIONS

Verse

*Poems.* N.p., Discon, 1974.
*When Pussywillows Lost in the Catyard Bloomed.* Carlton, Australia, Nostrilia Press, 1980.
*To Spin Is Miracle Cat.* Columbia, Pennsylvania, Underwood Miller, 1982.

Other

*The Authorized Illustrated Book of Roger Zelazny*, illustrated by Gray Morrow. New York, Baronet, 1978.
*Roger Zelazny's Visual Guide to Castle Amber*, with Neil Randall. New York, Avon, 1988.

Editor, *Nebula Award Stories 3.* New York, Doubleday, and London, Gollancz, 1968.

*

Bibliography: *Roger Zelazny: A Primary and Secondary Bibliography* by Joseph L. Sanders, Boston, Hall, 1980; *Amber Dreams: A Roger Zelazny Bibliography* by Daniel J.H. Levack, Columbia, Pennsylvania, Underwood Miller, 1983.

Manuscript Collections: George Arents Research Library, Syracuse University, New York; Special Collections, University of Maryland, Baltimore.

Critical Studies: *A Reader's Guide to Roger Zelazny* by Carl B. Yoke, West Linn, Oregon, Starmont House, 1979; *Roger Zelazny* by Theodore Krulik, New York, Unger, 1986.

Roger Zelazny comments:

My earlier writing involved considerable use of mythological materials. I have, however, attempted to diversify over the years. I write both fantasy and science fiction, as well as mixtures of the two. My objectives vary from book to book, but in general I begin with character in mind rather than plot. Among my personal favorites are the *Lord of Light* and *Doorways in the Sand.*

* * *

A writer who constantly challenges himself, Roger Zelazny is difficult to categorize. He has successfully written both fantasy and "hardcore" science fiction, his work has been both light and serious in tone, he is adept at all lengths, he has tackled most of the standard science-fiction themes. Even his style has changed since he published his first short story in 1962—from one that was highly mythic and richly poetic to one that is more controlled, economical, and precise. Yet despite the wide variation in tone, content, and style of his work, there are definite and consistent characteristics in his writing. Certain themes recur; certain kinds of characters reappear. Perhaps it is in his characterization that the threads which link his works are most easily seen.

Zelazny's ability to create believable characters is probably his single most important contribution to science fiction. Even though his protagonists usually possess some ability or talent which makes them "larger-than-life," they remain entirely credible. They prize their self-reliance, personal integrity, and individualism. They must develop their own unique abilities and talents. And, since growth is a result of experience, the psychological growth of the characters is directly linked to their adventures. Frequently, Zelazny's stories begin with his protagonist disillusioned, alienated, or geographically isolated, and, whatever the circumstances, the specific conditions of his situation set him off on some kind of quest. In addition to attaining some physical objective, however, Zelazny's heroes are also set off unconsciously on a psychological quest—which is to achieve a metamorphosis of a personality, to raise their level of consciousness. If successful, this new maturity brings the disparate elements of their personalities into harmony, gives them a broader and deeper knowledge of themselves and the worlds in which they live, and creates the possibility for love. Of Zelazny's best works, the Amber novels, both series, "A Rose for Ecclesiastes," and "The Doors of His Face, the Lamps of His Mouth" use protagonists who achieve metamorphosis in the course of the story, while *Lord of Light* and *This Immortal* tells stories which could not happen until after their protagonists have achieved this growth.

Zelazny's recurrent themes are integrally related to the psychological quests of his heroes. Vanity, greed, power, guilt, and revenge block metamorphosis and must be overcome before it can occur. Immortality permits a character to achieve a fuller realization of his capabilities. Zelazny recognizes that as long as a healthy person lives, psychological growth will continue. Love and fertility, in all their possible forms, are the positive benefits of metamorphosis. Self-reliance, personal integrity, and individualism are the keys to achieving it. Renewal, or restoration, which appears so frequently in Zelazny's stories, is an encompassing theme which signals both physical and psychological success.

Zelazny's most important works are the stories "A Rose for Ecclesiastes," "The Doors of His Face, The Lamps of His Mouth," "Home Is the Hangman," "Permafrost," and "24 Views of Mt. Fuji, by Hokusai," and the novels *This Immortal, The Dream Master, Lord of Light*, and the ten Amber books. "A Rose for Ecclesiastes" and "The Doors of His Face, The Lamps of His Mouth" are renewal stories, and both Gallinger, the conceited Earth poet, and Carlton Davits, the bankrupt baitman, must overcome their vanity in order to achieve personality metamorphosis. Each does, and in the process Gallinger saves the Martians from racial suicide and restores fertility to the planet, whilst Davits brings both his and his ex-wife's personalities into harmony and creates a healthy relationship. "Home Is the Hangman," one of Zelazny's "no-name detective" stories, presents a unique twist on the metamorphosis motif. In it, the Hangman, a combination telefactor and computer, returns to Earth after many years in space to show its teachers that it has overcome the neurosis they created for it. The anthropomorphic machine has successfully integrated the elements of its personality, while, ironically, one of its teachers, Jessie Brockden, is so overpowered by guilt that he believes that the machine has returned to kill him.

This immortal presents a protagonist, Conrad Nomikos, who has already achieved maturity by the time the story begins, so the focus of the story shifts from achieving metamorphosis to the role of the hero in restoring the irradiated Earth. A revolutionary group believes that the Vegans, a superior alien culture, are about to begin a wholesale exploitation of the planet, when in truth they are testing Conrad's worth to inherit and subsequently restore it.

*The Dream Master* presents the only instance in Zelazny's writing where a protagonist fails to achieve metamorphosis. Because his particular personality fault, once again pride, continues to dominate, Dr. Charles Render, a neuroparticipation therapist, is ultimately drawn into the madness of one of his patients. His vanity has prevented him from seeing the limits of his abilities. In one of Zelazny's more interesting attempts to expand a novel through the use of myth, he links Render to the Scandinavian *ragnarok* and Eileen, his patient, to Arthurian legend. The *ragnarok* represents Render's view of the world and signifies the psychologically deterministic course of his life. The Arthurian material characterizes Eileen's chivalric and highly idealized view of the world. Though the concept is ingenious, the use of symbolic mythic sequences tends to confuse meaning for the perceptive reader rather than clarify it. In addition to illustrating the dangers inherent in allusion, it also illustrates the danger of assuming that Zelazny is attempting to translate whole bodies of myth into science fiction.

*Lord of Light*, undoubtedly Zelazny's best novel, also treats renewal—in this case the renewal of a society. By the time the story begins, Sam, the protagonist, has long since passed on to a higher state of consciousness. The world of Urath is ruled by colonists who have virtually become gods. They patterned the new after the Hindu culture that they left behind on Earth, and they have achieved virtual immortality because they have the technology for body transfer. Unfortunately, their power has corrupted them. They exploit the masses, their own descendants, and refuse to let them share their technological benefits. Society is repressive and stagnant, and Sam sets out to change it. Of course, he accomplishes his reform mission.

Both sets of Amber novels treat the physical and psychological sides of renewal—the restoration of the land and the metamorphosis of personality. In the first series, Corwin, the protagonist, journeys from youthful and romantic idealism to pragmatism in the course of his adventures to keep the universe from being absorbed back into chaos. In the process, he learns that the most important reason for living is psychologically healthy human relationships.

Both the first and second Amber series dramatize Zelazny's form and chaos philosophy and stress how man should relate to these basic forces of the universe. The second series, Merlin's Story, probes the relationship between these forces in great detail. Corwin's son, Merlin, must reestablish a balance between Form and Chaos while he achieves his own destiny—to become the King of Chaos. Maintaining a balance between the principal generators of reality, the Pattern, for Form, and the Logrus, for Chaos, would not seem to be much of a challenge except that both have become sentient and are consciously playing against each other for advantage. Set against this is the bildungsroman of Merlin's education for kingship, complete with his transformation.

The Amber novels are not only a major fantasy work, they are also an excellent window on Zelazny's talents. Criticized by some who feel that he has not achieved the stature projected for him when he broke into the field more than 20 years ago, Zelazny has, perhaps more than any other writer, brought the techniques, style, and language of mainstream literature to science fiction and fantasy. There is no question about his stature. He is a major author who has written several major works, but his greatest contribution in the end may be that he has brought characters who are psychologically credible, who are sympathetic, who have depth and scope, to a literature famous for its cardboard figures.

Zelazny's stories of the early 1980's showed two interesting lines of development. In *Changeling, Madwand*, and *Eye of the*

*Cat*, he consciously used Jungian imagery and concepts to shape his stories, much as he did earlier in "The Doors of His Face, the Lamps of His Mouth." Such usage reinforces the renewal theme, which pervades his work and which is evident in these stories, especially in the personality growth of his characters. This technique is very similar to what he did in his early writing with mythology.

His work during this period also leans strongly towards fantasy, but it is fantasy that has been hedged. That is, he takes great care to treat the worlds of these stories as if they were simply governed by physical laws different from our own. Magic, supernatural events, and other motifs and devices usually left unexplained in fantasy are treated as if they were a normal part of another reality in these worlds. In *Changeling* and *Madwand*, for instance, magic is a skill. There are different forms of it, there are rules to govern its use, and there are various degrees of adeptness in its practice. In short, Zelazny provides means for his characters to tap into and use the basic forces that govern their story worlds. Though these forces are different from our own, he implies that lying beneath all sets is something common. In these works, Zelazny is probing the question of reality and offering differing scenarios as possibilities.

In addition to the second Amber series, Zelazny's most recent work includes two award-winning works, "Permafrost" and "24 Views of Mt. Fuji, by Hokusai." Both of these stories explore male-female relationships that have gone bad.

In "Permafrost," a man returns to an ice cave where his female friend perished, to clean up evidence of her demise and to claim a treasure in rare crystals. While he did not murder her, he chose to grab a bag of the crystals rather than save her. He discovers that she has not died. Rather, she has become part of the permafrost that girds the planet and acquired special abilities that permit her to arrange a most fitting revenge for him.

In "24 Views of Mt. Fuji, by Hokusai," a dying Japanese-American woman goes on a quest to discover herself and to rid the world of her husband who has transferred his being into an enormous data-net. She chooses her humanity over virtual electronic immortality when she realizes that the potential of such an existence has changed her husband into a megalomaniac. Behind these broken romances is yet another exploration of reality. Both the woman merged with the permafrost and the husband whose being has been transferred to a data-net pose questions about the reality of our identities.

Both of these stories show the hand of a master craftsman. Their writing is lean and precise, their worlds are original, and their themes continue Zelazny's investigation of imagined alternatives to our own concept of reality. *Prince of Chaos*, the final novel of Merlin's Story, makes a particular point of examining the limits of reason and discusses, at various times, the validity of other means of knowing.

—Carl B. Yoke

---

**ZETFORD, Tully.** *See* **BULMER, Kenneth.**

---

**ZINDELL, David.** Address: c/o Donald I. Fine Inc, 19 West 21st Street, New York, New York 10010, U.S.A.

SCIENCE-FICTION PUBLICATIONS

Novel

*Neverness.* New York, Fine, 1988; London, Grafton, 1989.

* * *

In common with writers such as Karen Joy Fowler and Robert (Touzalin) Reed, David Zindell first properly came to public attention through the L. Ron Hubbard Writers of the Future contest, where he was one of the quarterly winners with his story "Shanidar." However, it was with *Neverness*, his first and so far only novel, that he achieved wider fame, including being shortlisted for the 1988 Arthur C. Clarke award in the United Kingdom.

As a debut novel, it is in many respects a remarkable *tour de force*, a complex mixture of fantasy and science fiction, drawing on the author's knowledge of mathematics and anthropology to create a strange and exotic society. Focussing on Mallory Ringness, a wayward novitiate in the semi-mystical Order of Pilots (reminiscent of the Knights Templar), the first part of the novel follows his quest to discover the Solid State Entity, a vast galactic brain composed of planet-sized biocomputers. That he so quickly achieves what others, more capable, have failed to do is clearly the major flaw of the novel, as is the rapidity with which what might have been the climax of another fictional work is disposed of, in the first third of the book. Nevertheless, Zindell manages to create a very real sense of what the Entity is, and how Ringness had achieved the impossible in his manipulation, as a Pilot, of the laws of space and time, leaving the reader with the temporary sense of having grasped the most arcane intricacies of mathematical calculation.

Ironically, considering that this section of the novel is so soon dismissed, it is undoubtedly the confrontation with the Solid State Entity, rather than Ringness's subsequent exploration of his own world, which remains in the reader's mind. The remainder of the novel is devoted to a search for the key to immortality, Ringness's death and subsequent resurrection as a human biocomputer, akin to the entity he discovered, and to the retrieval of knowledge lost by his culture. Yet somehow the impetus of the early part of the novel is rarely recaptured, except perhaps in Zindell's descriptions of the ice city of Neverness, one of the more remarkable imaginary cities in recent SF and fantasy literature.

Whether Zindell is a slow writer, or whether he has written himself out remains to be seen. Should the latter possibility prove to be so, *Neverness* will still stand as a remarkable if flawed achievement.

—Maureen Speller

---

**ZOLINE, Pamela.** American. Born in Chicago, Illinois, in 1941. Educated at the Slade School of Fine Art, London. Artist and illustrator; group show, Young Contemporaries, 1966. Lives in Colorado. Address: c/o Coffee House Press, 27 North Fourth Street, Suite 400, Minneapolis, Minnesota 55401, U.S.A.

SCIENCE-FICTION PUBLICATIONS

Short Stories

*Busy About the Tree of Life and Other Stories.* London, Women's Press, 1988; as *The Heat Death of the Universe*, Kingston, New York, McPherson, 1988.

OTHER PUBLICATIONS

Novel

*Annika and the Wolves: A Fairy Tale.* Minneapolis, Minnesota, Coffee House Press, 1985.

* * *

Pamela Zoline, while highly regarded within the SF field, remains obscure. This situation is due not only to a low profile, but also a low output: the five stories collected in *Busy About the Tree of Life* were written over a period of 20 years. More remains unpublished, such as the extracts from a novel reportedly in Harlan Ellison's final *Dangerous Visions* anthology.

Zoline has never been a full-time writer; Brian Aldiss and Harry Harrison stated in their introduction to *Decade: the 1960's* that she was "primarily an artist." In this capacity she illustrated for the magazine *New Worlds* in the late 1960's, including the serial of Thomas M. Disch's *Camp Concentration.* Recently she has been working with her husband on designing a "radical mountain community" in Telluride, Colorado, where they live, and also has been composing "a real-time, interactive Computer Opera, *The Life and Death of Harry Houdini.* She describes herself as "neither a writer who paints nor a painter who writes."

Her first story, "The Heat Death of the Universe," published in 1967, was instantly acclaimed as one of the best of the New Wave fictions. Brian Aldiss described it as "superlative" in the first edition of *Billion Year Spree.*

"The Heat Death of the Universe" is, like Zoline's illustrations for *Camp Concentration*, a collage, incorporating dictionary definitions of concepts as diverse as ontology, love, and entropy. It also shows Zoline's fascination with lists, not only in the numbering of each paragraph (there are 54 in all) but in passages where the protagonist, a young housewife named Sarah Boyle, suddenly gets the urge to buy one of every cleaning product in the local supermarket, which she does "deliberately and with a careful ecstasy."

"The Heat Death of the Universe" describes American suburbia from an alien perspective. The theme of the trapped housewife has seldom been presented so bizarrely: Sarah responds to domestic tedium by imagining a household organized on Dada principles, or writing comments about the Nitrogen cycle on the lid of the diaper bin (in "Blushing Pink Nitetime lipstick"). She is, however, a metaphor, a microcosm of the universe itself, for as with the process of entropy the universe tends towards maximum disorder, so Sarah, exhausted after a children's party, breaks down into chaos. The heat death of the universe takes place in a Californian kitchen, as physics and sociology collide in one of the most elegantly written stories in the SF canon.

Zoline's second story, "The Holland of the Mind," published in 1969, again used collage techniques for a psychological investigation, this time into the failure of a marriage. A young American couple vacation in Holland; their increasing alienation is reflected by extracts from travel guides, art histories, particularly on Rembrandt and Vermeer, phrasebooks, even instructions for artificial respiration.

"Sheep," first published in 1981, is a longer, more experimental piece, with not only the familiar samples, from such sources as recipe books and husbandry manuals, but also a long, typographically distinct essay on "The Virtues of Wool," which initially appears to have had all the vowels coloured in by a child (as the author explains, clothes moths have eaten holes in the fabric of the text). The rest of "Sheep" is equally zany, as a spy narrative meets cowboys meets the pastoral, all occurring within the context of a sleepless night, in which a woman counts 259 sheep.

"Instructions for Exiting This Building in Case of Fire" is the most political of Zoline's published tales, concentrating upon her recurrent theme of children. The story is concerned with an entirely novel way of preventing war, in which the children of prominent politicians throughout the world are kidnapped and resettled in enemy territory: "Russian, American and Chinese children have been scattered over the planet like grains of rice; in Northern Ireland such is the nature of the horrid conflict that Catholic and Protestant babies have been exchanged and reworked so that they are often living down the street from their biological natural parents."

Five stories is a small oeuvre in terms of SF, where authors' bibliographies can include hundreds of items. Yet few writers can claim to have such a consistently high standard, precisely because Zoline has not wasted her words. She has not published in quantity, yet should her one book be measured in the SF quality scales, it would prove weightier than a pile of trilogies and decalogies.

—Lucy Sussex

# FOREIGN-LANGUAGE APPENDIX

**ABE, Kobo** (1924– ). Japanese. *The Face of Another*, 1966; *Inter Ice Age Four*, 1970; *The Box Man*, 1975; *Secret Rendezvous*, 1979; *The Ark Sakura*, 1988.

* * *

To understand the science fiction of Kobo Abe and to place it in perspective, it is necessary to note that science fiction is but a part of his work. Even so, his creations often are just as much science fiction as the works of Stanislaw Lem, who is accepted as a major writer of modern SF. The works of Abe and Lem have some similar qualities, though Abe is more inclined to psychological and introspective treatments than is Lem.

As a medical school graduate, Abe had the technical knowledge and experience to do outstanding work in some aspects of SF. Another key to Abe's work, besides his psychological approach, is his propensity for experimental literary techniques, combining his familiarity with European—especially French—20th-century trends, along with the characteristic Japanese awareness of more than a thousand years of indigenous cultural tradition.

One important example of the above factors is his novel *The Face of Another*, which appeared also in 1967 as a motion picture. This work is not mainstream SF, but has technological content, the methods by which a realistic mask is substituted for a horribly disfigured face. The mask has been a major resource of Japanese drama for centuries. In this book, the hero compares himself to the monsters of television, and the film is filled with the organ-laden laboratories of the Frankenstein tradition.

*The Face of Another* can be grouped with those SF novels that have as an important concern alienation, or related questions as to what does or does not constitute humanity ("humanness"). The very word alienation comes from a Latin root meaning "other." Abe himself is in some ways alienated in Japan. He was brought up in Manchuria, then under Japanese influence or control, but not a part of the homeland. Certainly the mask of this novel is a form of "otherness." Alternatively it may be viewed as an insulation of the real *person* from others. (The word *person* derives from the Greek word for mask, and a much-favored classic Japanese dramatic form, the *No* drama, uses masks for the chief characters, as did some classic Greek drama.)

Related to the foregoing concepts is Abe's novel *The Box Man*. The title characters are insulated by being semi-encased in cardboard boxes. The novel reads somewhat like a stage play, reflecting Abe's preference for plays over novels as a medium. He is in fact known as well, or better, for his plays than for his novels in Japan. In *The Box Man*, as these strangely packaged characters move about, other men are suspicious of them, and even shoot at them. The feeling of alienation accumulates as a wounded boxman is hospitalized and receives the unloving care of a disdainful nurse. The reader is left to wonder if the injured person is a criminal or some sort of misfit. The dramatic action, sparse in itself, is amplified by the insertion of news flashes, and is varied by movements back and forth in time. The author encourages the reader to wonder if the "different" persons are really different. He leaves much uncertainty in this eerie analog of modern life.

More alienation and despair appear in *The Ark Sakura*, Abe's first novel in eight years. It features a plump narrator called Mole who fails in his design for escape from nuclear holocaust. The "ark" is actually a vast, deserted quarry. Mole plans that it will be a refuge, and he sells tickets to the people who he hopes will help him harmoniously to operate the refuge. Everything goes wrong, however, as the crew defy his authority and prevent his plans from being carried out. Add to this impasse some troublesome intruders, and poor Mole winds up trapped in the huge toilet, a major symbol of this novel. A lovelier symbol is the *sakura* of the title, which means cherry blossom. The Japanese are always mindful that this is a wonderful flower, but blooms ever so briefly.

*The Ark Sakura* and Abe's novel *Secret Rendezvous* resemble Lem's novel, *Memoirs Found in a Bathtub*. In all three books, the scene is an enormous, appalling structure full of confusion and ambiguity. The situation in all three is thought-provoking and replete with symbols and analogs, but not convincing as narratives. To the authors, it is sometimes more worthwhile to challenge or mystify the reader than to tell a story. Where Lem's locale for *Memoirs* is an immense Pentagon-like warren of military stereotypes, *Secret Rendezvous* is set in a huge hospital, to which the narrator's wife has been taken. Whether her hospitalization is a mistake or indeed a device for a rendezvous is uncertain. As the narrator tries to locate her, he is drawn into the bizarre society of the hospital. He encounters many amazing devices that monitor the life of the denizens. The final prospect is that the secret rendezvous may mean his death.

The greatest SF opus of Abe is *Inter Ice Age Four*, in which the forthcoming inundation of the Earth by melting polar ice caps is to be dealt with by modifying embryos to produce gill-breathers. Important in predicting the disaster here is computer technology, and we are told that the computers have also discerned Communism as the shape of things to come. However, according to a leading character, Communism *would* fit the predictions of a machine; it neglects free will. The computers also are described as scanning a human mind completely, then engaging in dialogue with the "individual" stored in their data banks. When this dialogue with the "data bank ghost" is extended to the mind of a newly dead person, one sees an old Japanese concept in action: the 11th-century novel, *Tale of Genji*, includes an interview with the spirit of the dead Lady Rokujo, and the modern film Rashomon also has an interview with a deceased person, through a medium.

Abe's philosophy of present-future relationships is especially significant. *Inter Ice Age Four* comments that the future is not to be judged by us, but rather it sits in judgment on the present. It gives a verdict of guilty, says Abe, and the people of the present, confident of their microcosm, are to be scorned. The author's vision here may have been enhanced by his sense of alienation from his immediate present. Also monumental in his work is an eager confrontation with the great borderlines between life and death, between illusion and reality, and between the inner and outer worlds of human beings.

—Frank H. Tucker

---

**ANDREVON, Jean-Pierre** (1937– ). French. "Observation of Quadragnes," in *View from Another Shore*, edited by Franz Rottensteiner, 1973; "The Time of the Big Sleep," in *A Shocking Thing*, edited by Damon Knight, 1974.

* * *

Jean-Pierre Andrevon is perhaps the best-known French SF writer. He quickly became the most prolific contributor to the main Parisian SF monthly, *Fiction*, both as a critic and short-story writer, introducing political views in both fields, to the delight of progressive readers and the (very vocal) fury of the more conventional ones. He was one of the first to explode the taboos of sex ("Observation of Quadragnes") as well as death (*Le Reflux de la Nuit*), to strip the glamour from war on the earth ("Retour à Broux") as well as in space (*La Guerre des Gruulls*), and to denounce the excesses of technology. In his anthologies—the 3 volumes of *Retour à la Terre* (whose title clearly express the intention of re-focusing SF on the problems of our world), the two volumes of *Compagnons en Terre Etrangère*—he rallied round him a whole school of young writers who shared his preoccupation with imminent perils (pollution, overpopulation, the misuse of nuclear energy, social and international conflicts).

Andrevon should not, however, be considered as a pure son of the protest movement of 1968: contrary to many of his followers who tended to reduce their SF to ideological tracts, and whose readership consequently dwindled very fast, he never forgot that he was expected to tell stories, and to tell them well. In his first novel, *Les Hommes-Machines contre Gandahar*—a sort of *Great Dictator* of the future, with a strange time-controlling creature thrown in as game-master—the libertarian message and the appeal of mystery and adventure were already cleverly blended. Putting to use both his sense of everyday dialogue (to the inclusion of slang and vulgarisms) and the eye of the painter that he also is, he unites truly poetic visions with the most implacable realism, which he sometimes tempers with fantasy and humour, as in *L'Immeuble d'en face* and *Hôpital Nord* (both recently published in collaboration with Philippe Cousin, a disciple with a strong personality of his own).

Though he has kept exploring his main obsessions (death and sex in *Il Faudra Bien Se Réoudre à Mourir Seul*) and concerns (the follies of mankind and the endangered future of the planet in *Paysages de Mort* and *Dans les Décors Truqués;* more particularly the nuclear peril in *Neutron*), Andrevon has achieved a great diversity of themes and approaches: his latest anthology, *L'Oreille contre les Murs*, is an attempt to launch a modern fantastic school; *Le Travail du Furet à l'Intérieur du Poulailler*, though about overpopulation, is in the form a thriller; *Le Désert du Monde* and *Cauchemar . . . Cauchemars* have something of Philip K. Dick's interplay of reality and illusion; *Le Fée et le Géomètre* shows that writing for young people does not entail self-censorship of one's convictions.

The latter book is indeed one of Andrevon's finest expressions of his ideology, which has shifted from Trotskyist marxism to ecology—harmony between various social groups being now subject in his opinion to saner relationships between man and his environment. The main short-coming that he has been reproached with is that, because of the huge gap between his views of the ideal future and the present evils he denounces, he has failed to imagine any acceptable transition: in his novel *Le Temps des Grandes Chasses* an idyllic society emerges only after world-wide disaster; and in *Le Monde Enfin* our planet finds beauty and balance again at the cost of the disappearance of humanity!

Yet, by the abundance and variety of his production, his rich characterization, and the wide resources of his style as well as by the warning function he often gives his fiction, Andrevon's stature in French SF can be compared to John Brunner's in the United Kingdom.

—George W. Barlow

---

**BARJAVEL, René** (1911– ). French. *Ashes, Ashes*, 1967; *Future Times Three*, 1970; *The Ice People*, 1970; *The Immortals*, 1974.

* * *

René Barjavel's science-fiction work contrasts pastoral utopias full of love with war-torn dystopias full of distrust. Although *Le Diable l'Emporte, Colomb de la Lune*, and *L'Homme Forte* have not been translated, *Ashes, Ashes, Future Times Three, The Ice People*, and *The Immortals*, available in English, are passionately anti-war, erotic, and satiric, relating vividly penned horrors and sentimental romance.

Although Barjavel is a screenwriter, journalist, and writer of romantic novels, *Future Times Three* is typical science fiction, dealing with the paradoxes and dangers of time travel. Playful escapades in the near future and malicious forays into the 19th century echo Wells's *Invisible Man*, and the specialized races of 100,000 A.D. follow Stapledon. Exploring the future, mathematician and physicist brood over questions of God and causality. This episodic novel declares—like Faust—that man cannot safely extend beyond God.

In traveling to 2052, St. Menoux learns the fate of the survivors of *Ashes, Ashes*, in which some inexplicable sunspot phenomenon cuts off electricity and the world goes mad. Fire and bloodshed purge a decadent technological society on the verge of all-out war. As in the earlier novel, the pure love of two young people provides hope. The heroes, however, are ruthless killers who fight their way into the country to found a pastoral society where books and inventions are forbidden.

One of the numerous Swiftian sallies of *Ashes, Ashes* explains the system of freezing ancestors. In *The Ice People* South Pole explorers find two gorgeous bodies from 900,000 years earlier, obviously remnants of a vastly advanced society destroyed by atomic holocaust. Unfrozen, Elea transmits her memories of her perfect love with Paikan and her selection as the mate to be preserved for the mastermind, Coban. This Romeo and Juliet tale is set against political turmoil of past and present. Only a coalition of scientists and students might save the world, though Elea and Paikan are destroyed.

Using the actual backdrop and leaders of his own time, *The Immortals* examines the frightening long-range political effects of a drug that defeats death and disease. Since immortality is contagious, all those involved in research have been isolated on an Aleutian paradise. They are, however, human time bombs doomed to annihilation by world powers when scientists learn there is nowhere for man in space. Although pessimistic, Barjavel didactically asserts the values of love and peace.

—Mary S. Weinkauf

---

**BELYAEV, Aleksandr** (1884–1942). Russian. *The Amphibian*, n.d.; *The Struggle in Space*, 1965; *Professor Dowell's Head*, 1980.

* * *

Aleksandr Belyaev's first SF stories were published in adventure journals in 1925 and his first book in 1926. He wrote about 30 SF stories, about 20 novels, and a dozen articles or prefaces (e.g., to Jack London's novels), which make him the first penetrating Russian SF critic. He used the breathtaking

Vernean adventure plot or the current detective-thriller-SF (from Wells, London, Renard, Burroughs, or A. Tolstoy) with an isolated and romantically alienated hero, either a scientist with humanistic ideals, a biologically modified man who is a naive child of nature (Ichthyander in his most popular novel, *The Amphibian*, or Ariel in the novel of the same title), or quite openly an artist (such as Presto in the two variant novels *The Man Who Lost His Face* and *The Man Who Found His Face*). This bearer of the novum and of the desire for freedom is opposed to and hounded by the cruel power of wicked scientists and financiers; most interestingly, he is at the center of an extreme situation or novum validated by a bold scientific technique. This is usually biological adaptation, including the changing use of the senses, and, most prominently, a sundering of brain from body as in *Professor Dowell's Head* (much superior to Renard's *New Bodies for Old*) or various, often humorous and folktale-like, scientific inventions in the "Professor Wagner" cycle. Such works are imbued with an aching lyricism and a vibrant humanistic vehemence. But often Belyaev's hero triumphs thanks to an essentially fairytale metamorphosis that allows him to vanquish physical gravity and social injustice. The black-and-white opposition of his threatened hero to a grotesque capitalist environment becomes then a form of escapism into a wicked Ruritania.

In the late 1920's and early 1930's Belyaev's SF was interrupted by a campaign against the genre. From 1934 he largely shifted his focus to short-range technological anticipation and (more interestingly) to interplanetary work and struggles, domesticating the notions of Tsiolkovsky and early Soviet rocket experimenters. For all his shortcomings, Belyaev's basic concern with human metamorphosis striving for freedom and the external resistance and inner anxieties it provokes have not only made of him at least the equal of any interwar German, French, or United States SF writer, and a lasting influence in Russia, but also an author who remains of interest today.

—Darko Suvin

---

**BORGES, Jorge Luis** (1899–1986). Argentine. *Labyrinths*, 1962; *Fictions*, 1965; *The Aleph and Other Stories 1933–1969*, 1970; *The Book of Sand* (stories), 1977; *Borges: A Reader*, 1981.

* * *

Despite being an assiduous reader of Thomas More, Jonathan Swift, H.G. Wells, and C.S. Lewis, Borges had a natural disdain for SF. His opinion of it is clearly stated in a review, published in the Argentine literary magazine *Sur* (March 1936), of *The Domestic Statue*, a novel by his collaborator and long-time friend Adolfo Bioy Casares:

> I suspect that a general scrutiny of fantastic literature would reveal that it is not very fantastic. I have visited many utopias—from the eponymous one of More to *Brave New World*—and I have not yet found a single one that exceeds the cozy limits of satire or sermon and describes in detail an imaginary country, with its geography, its history, its religion, its language, its literature, its music, its government, its metaphysical and theological controversy . . . in short, its encyclopaedia; all of it organically coherent, of course, and (I know I'm very demanding) with no reference whatsoever to the horrible injustices suffered by the artillery Captain Alfred Dreyfus. Of Wells's (and even Swift's) imaginary theories, we know that there is in each of them only one fantastic element; of the *One Thousand and One Nights*, that a good part of its marvel is involuntary because 13th-century Egyptians believed in talismans and in exorcisms. In short, I wouldn't be surprised if the Universal Library of Fantastic Literature did not contain more than a volume by Lewis Carroll, a couple of Disney films, a poem by Coleridge and (because of the absent-mindedness of its author) Manuel Gálvez's *Opera omnia* (my translation).

Borges implicitly uses the term "fantastic" to cover SF, and thinks that true SF should compete with God's creation. To honor its foundation, it should build perfect self-sufficient universes, like ours, but without our reality mixing in. Not only is he deeply unsatisfied with all he has read; he chooses to refer to it as "not very fantastic." Still, by refusing its premises, he actually sets forth a program for himself, to be achieved four years later, in his short story "Tlön, Uqbar, Orbis Tertius" (*Sur*, May 1940). In it, he positively describes a visionary universe that is beyond satire, and shows its imaginary geography, history, and religion, its language, literature, and government, and its metaphysical and theological realities. Furthermore, the door to its amazing, uncanny reality is a misleading encyclopaedia he and Bioy Casares discover one afternoon, a reprint of the *Encyclopaedia Britannica* of 1902.

Tlön-Uqbar is a society that exists only in and around ideas; it conceives things as a series of mental processes. The story, as we now know thanks to Emir Rodriguez Monegal's biography of the Argentinian, was inspired by C.S. Lewis's *Out of the Silent Planet* (1938). Interestingly enough, however, this is not another distant planet one could travel to in a spaceship; it's an alternative reality parallel to ours. Borges the idealist places his fictitious community, not in the future, but "in the memory (if not in the hopes or fears) of all my readers" (*Labyrinths*). That is, it "exists" in a nonspatial dimension. The reader never gets references to modern technology, old myths, or 19th- or 20th-century science. Neither can the text be understood as a description of a utopia, or an anti-utopia.

A fascinating discussion of Borges and SF can be found in Stanislaw Lem's essay "Unitas Oppositorum: The Prose of Jorge Luis Borges" (1971; in *Microworlds*, 1984), in which the Polish writer analyzes the Argentinian's antipathy for technology and for progressive, utopian futures, thanks to his love affair with the past. Strictly speaking, Borges never wrote SF. Although very notorious are the innumerable stories and essays in which he dealt with time ("The Cyclic Night," 1940; "The Secret Miracle," 1944; "The Flower of Coleridge," 1945; and especially "New Refutation of Time," 1947), one gets the impression that for him science and art were incompatible.

I know of only three pieces in which Borges wrote about the future. The first and most self-conscious one is the story "Utopia of a Tired Man" (*The Book of Sand*). Its main character is said to have been born in Buenos Aires in 1897, two years before Borges. His name is Eudoro Acevedo, which was the maiden name of Borges's mother. He is 70 years old, teaches American and English literature, and writes imaginary tales. As in Wells's *The Time Machine*, he travels in the future. How? We don't know, since we first see him already wandering through unknown geographies that look like Oklahoma, Texas, and the Argentinian pampas. Once more, this fact evidences Borges's disdain for SF: he is interested in the adventure, not in the mechanistic manouvers that explain the voyage. After a long walk, Acevedo meets a tall, anonymous individual and enters his house. The dialogue between them makes up the entire story, and it offers some epistemological clues valuable for an understanding of our time. About the act of reading, for instance, the anonymous man says that the citizens of the future re-read, never read, because the classics are the only important thing. Printing has been abolished, since it tends to multiply unnecessary texts. Among Acevedo's other discoveries are the absence of cities, governments, dates, statistics, poverty and wealth, and the fact that the world has fallen back on Latin. It's quite clear that the narration is a comment on today, as seen from a future perspective. Borges uses a lucid epigraph by Quevedo that helps for understanding its implications: "He called it *Utopia*, a Greek word meaning *there is no such place.*"

The second piece by Borges dealing with future events has the same limitation. Figuring as the epilogue to the Spanish edition of his *Complete Works* (Emecé, 1974), it is an entry for Borges himself in the so-called *Encyclopaedia Sudamericana*, to appear in 2074, in Santiago, Chile. The ingeniousness of such a profile lies in its encapsulating all the writer's biographical data, with the exception, of course, of the date of his death. The third and final item is the poem "The Web" (in *The New Yorker*, 2 June 1986). It asks which city is the author doomed to die in, at what time, and when. The last lines read: "These questions are/ disgressions that stem not from fear/but from impatient hope./ They form part of that fateful web/of cause and effect/that no man can foresee,/nor any god." Again, the future is not the main concern here; what matters is the randomness of fate. Nothing in tomorrow interests Borges, except the details that could affect him in a personal, introspective way.

—Ilan Stavans

---

**BOULLE, Pierre** (1912– ). French. *Planet of the Apes*, 1963 (as *The Monkey Planet*, 1964); *Garden on the Moon*, 1964; *Time Out of Mind and Other Stories*, 1966; *Because It Is Absurd* (stories), 1971; *Desperate Games*, 1973; *The Marvelous Palace and Other Stories*, 1977; *The Good Leviathan*, 1979; *The Whale of the Victoria Cross*, 1983; *Trouble in Paradise*, 1985.

* * *

Like the venerable minister-priest of the Religion of Doubt who is the narrator of the six "*histoires perides*" that make up *The Marvelous Palace and Other Stories*, Pierre Boulle has viewed his main function throughout his prolific and varied career as his duty "to arouse curiosity by the prospect of an enigma." In Boulle's wryly laconic fables, the enigmatic takes many forms: in *The Good Leviathan*, an oil supertanker capable of miraculous cures; in *The Whale of the Victoria Cross*, another kind of good leviathan, one that sacrifices itself to save its friends on the British fleet during the Falklands conflict; in "The Heart of the Galaxy" (*Because It is Absurd*), a message from the stars, engendered by an immense expenditure of energy, which—much to the consternation of the scientists on earth who decipher it—turns out to be an advertising slogan; in *Desperate Games*, a world government of Nobel Prize-winning scientists who cure all of mankind's social ills but must devise destructive war games to prevent the universal ennui that sets in when man is left with nothing to struggle against. Boulle's style is too arch and his stance too knowing for his science-fiction tales to be called cautionary, just as his espionage stories set in the Far East are too coolly ironic to be labeled merely escapist thrillers: even a casual reader must have anticipated that the astronaut escaping from *Planet of the Apes*—undoubtedly Boulle's best-known SF work and the basis for the popular film series—was returning to an Earth in which a similar evolutionary movement had taken its inevitable course.

Most recently, Boulle's double-edged, deadpan observance of man's social and political foibles has even taken him to the Throne of Heaven itself. When Boulle, in *Trouble in Paradise*, has the Virgin Mary coming back to Earth to help patch up a quarrel between the bickering members of the Holy Trinity, only to become a media celebrity and prime minister of France, her eventual triumphant ascension back to Paradise as Supreme Goddess could be construed as either a pro- or anti-feminist statement. In all of Boulle's work, however, the tone may be cynical or obscure but it is rarely morose, since Boulle remains detached from the delusions, vanities, and follies of technocratic man confronting the remorselessness of an implacable Nature and the unchangingness of his own proud and enigmatic heart.

—Kenneth Jurkiewicz

---

**BOYE, Karin** (1900–41). Swedish. *Kallocain*, 1966.

* * *

Karin Boye was a distinguished Swedish poet and a disciple of the radical French pacifist Henri Barbusse. She committed suicide a year after the publication of *Kallocain* in 1940. She was one of those intellectuals horrified by the rise of Nazism, and she returned disappointed from a journey to the Soviet Union, a country she had considered a hope for the future. Her anxieties and her experiences with Nazism and Stalinism are clearly reflected in her novel, one of the few dystopias written by a woman. Her work uncannily anticipates many of the black features that Orwell made known in *Nineteen Eighty-Four*, in particular the total surveillance of citizens by spy-lenses in their private homes, the concept of a thought police and thought crime, and the thoroughgoing division of the world into two big states, which are so antagonistic to each other that they deny their enemy the common human ancestry. Leo Kall, a chemist and inventor of the epynomous truth serum Kallocain, is a citizen of the "world state" in the 21st century—a "fellow soldier," for the country's organization is thoroughly militaristic. The police are omnipresent, and citizens are urged to denounce their friends and relatives and to join in communal "hate sessions." The fear of spies is so great that even simple geographical data are treated as secrets of state. Leo Kall is deeply distrustful of his immediate superior Edo Rissen, one of the few human beings who has kept their individualism, and he suspects that his wife is unfaithful to him. Knowing very well that under the influence of his new drug all are equally guilty, Kall decides to attack and to denounce Rissen, who is promptly sentenced. In the end the "world state" is invaded by the "universal state," which is, we may assume, different only by name, and Kall serves his new masters with equal zeal. The psychological conflicts of the hero are depicted powerfully, and the novel reflects a deep fear of the rise of totalitarianism and an all-powerful state that inexorably crushes the individual.

—Franz Rottensteiner

---

**BRYUSOV, Valery** (1873–1924). Russian. *The Republic of the Southern Cross and Other Stories,* 1918.

* * *

Valery Bryusov, from a rich merchant family, became a leader of Russian Symbolist poetry, publishing a dozen books of formidably erudite and polished verse, as well as stories, plays, brilliant verse translations from many languages (including the complete poetry of Poe), and interesting criticism of poetry. His esoteric disdain for the multitude changed after the 1904–05 revolution into a growing acceptance of social responsibility and sympathy for the revolutionary destruction of the "ugly and shameful" captialist order. He thus became one of the few prominent non-Marxists to take an active part in Soviet cultural life, and in 1920 even joined the Communist party.

Bryusov had a long-standing interest in a "scientific poetry" akin to SF. Two of his major preoccupations were more obviously SF. From the 1890's he was haunted by the fall of world civilization, envisioned as a giant symbolic city. In his play *Youth* (1904) a revolt of youth shatters the glass dome that bars the city from sunshine and open space; the revolt both seeks liberation and exposes the city to the risk of death. (See also his story "The Last Martyrs".) Written after the defeat of the 1905 revolution, his Poesque story "The Republic of the Southern Cross" is frankly dystopian: an enclosed industrial city on the South Pole falls prey to an epidemic leading the afflicted to do the opposite from what they wish to do; a resolute bourgeois minority fighting for order is overwhelmed by the brutalized inhabitants. Raskolnikov's dream at the end of *Crime and Punishment* blends here with a parable on the great social convulsions of our century. Bryusov's second SF theme is one of cosmic contacts, treated both in his poetry and in a number of unfinished stories and plays, and influenced by the utopian philosopher Fyodorov and his disciple Tsiolkovsky, by Poe, Wells, and most of all Flammarion; such influences often involved a cometary world. His old theme of catastrophe and a distant presentiment of a possible new world lent themselves well to the widespread post-1917 equation of the social revolution with man's leap into interplanetary space. Bryusov thus became the link between, on the one hand, the tradition of Russian utopianism, 19th-century European SF, and philosophic speculation leading from Leibniz to Spengler, and, on the other, early Soviet "Cosmist" poetry and SF. Bryusov's peculiar double horizon, embracing both dystopia and utopia is his greatest strength: he clearly managed to influence both Zamyatin and Mayakovsky, and, through them as well as directly, most prewar Russian SF.

—Darko Suvin

---

**BULGAKOV, Mikhail** (1891–1940). Russian. *The Master and Margarita,* 1967; *Heart of a Dog,* 1968; *Diaboliad and Other Stories,* 1972.

* * *

"The stars will remain when the shadows of our presence and our deeds have vanished from the earth. There is no man who does not know that. Why, then, will we not turn our eyes towards the stars?" This is the leitmotiv of Mikhail Bulgakov's science fiction: the nature of a true relationship between a Kantian universe and a human existence of thought and action.

Bulgakov's early science-fiction stories established an allegoric parallel between scientific discovery and social revolution, using every technique from slapstick comedy to black humor and horror, to show the absurdity and danger of trying to impose human purposes on reality. In "The Fatal Eggs" (*Diaboliad*), based on H.G. Wells's *The Food of the Gods,* mammoth artificially hatched serpents almost devour Moscow. In "The Crimson Island"—"Jules Verne translated into Aesopian"—an involuted rebellion results in nothing but a drunken revel and a telegram to the West: "Go (indecipherable) your (indecipherable) mother."

The novella *Heart of a Dog* exhibits Bulgakov's characteristic literary method: a fantastic realism that is a combination of grotesque action and a naturalistic background, with a satiric intent, serving a philosophical idea. It concerns a Moscow professor who transforms a dog into a man in a rejuvenation experiment. The identification of professor and Lenin, rejuvenation and revolution is implicit. Within a week, the new creation has a vocabulary of "every known Russian swearword"; he can't button his fly, eats toothpaste, and has fleas. He is immediately made a Commissar. His mature virtues include greed, viciousness, and "cosmic stupidity." Disgusted, the professor curses the attempt to substitute the artificial for the authentic, whether dog for man or dogma for life, and reverses the experiment.

Bulgakov's science-fiction plays range from burlesque to near-tragedy, but all deal with the ontological theme. In *Bliss* a wondrous future utopia is revealed to be inadequate and boring compared to the mystery of reality and the adventure of living. In *Ivan Vasilievich* Ivan the Terrible's farcical misadventures in modern Moscow revolve around a confusion of definitions and roles with actualities. The best of the type, however, both in character development and seriousness of thought, is the tragicomedy *Adam and Eve.* In a war-devastated Leningrad, a few surviving men and one woman must choose between reality and ideology, represented by the pacifist Yefrosimov, whose anti-gas invention saved them, and Adam Krasovsky, who wants to risk annihilation for the sake of Communism. In the end, Eve chooses Yefrosimov for her mate because, as she tells Adam, "the forest and the singing of the birds, and the rainbow, this is real, but you with your frenzied cries are unreal."

*The Master and Margarita* is Bulgakov's masterpiece of indefinable genre and indeterminate meaning, wherein Satan visits Moscow, punishing evil, driving rationalists insane, and "putting the fear of God" into atheists. In it, the science-fiction theme converges with all of Bulgakov's other themes, styles, and techniques, and is fully realized. In *The Master and Margarita,* reality is infinite, eternal, and transcendent; time and space are relative; man is immortal. Living according to the demands of universal truth is a moral duty for which man is held accountable. "Cowardice is the worst sin of all" for a character like Pontius Pilate whose "mind is too closed" and whose life is too cramped." Yet man's denial and betrayal of reality cannot alter it. "All will be as it should," the devil promises; "that is how the world is made."

By his science-fiction model of a surreal method to present a multi-dimensional universe, and by the example of his artistic courage, Bulgakov obliged Russian writers to contemplate "the shadows of man's presence" from the perspective of the stars and therefore "to a complete truth of thought and word."

—Jana I. Tuzar

---

**BUZZATI, Dino** (1906–72). Italian. *The Tartar Steppe*, 1952; *Larger Than Life*, 1962; *Catastrophe* (stories), 1965; *Restless Nights* (stories), 1983.

* * *

Although Dino Buzzati became first widely known with his novel *The Tartar Steppe*, his real strength is in his short stories—concise, absurd, wonderful fables and parables of modern existence, often fantasies. Buzzati has frequently been compared to Kafka, and although there is a certain similarity in the mysteries both writers touch upon, their differences are quite marked, both in style and rhythm and their manner of storytelling.

Actually, Buzzati is much more a fantasist than Kafka, showing the influences of E.T.A. Hoffmann and Gogol, as well as of fairy and folk tales. Often his stories are allegorical. This is marked in his brief novel *The Secret of the Old Forest*, which revolves around the conflict between nature and civilization; the spirits of an old forest, untouched by human hands for centuries, wage a war against the greedy owner who starts exploiting the old trees. The absurdity of existence and the vanity of human ambitions is the subject of Buzzati's best novel, *The Tartar Steppe.* Isolated in a lonely fortress at the border of a big desert, engaging in senseless military drill, the commander of the small forces garrisoned in the fort spends his whole life waiting for an invasion that never comes, and when rumors seem to indicate that the dreaded onslaught of the Tartars may come, he is already an old man, falls ill and dies. An obsessive concern with military duties and a senseless waiting for an event that may never come is turned into a parable of the futility of human existence when all aspirations for transcendent meaning are destroyed by accidental death. Compared to this puzzling and disturbing novel, Buzzati's only SF novel proper, *Larger Than Life*, is an uninspired computer story; a big computer is programmed with the personality of a woman, and this mawkish story is not better than countless other SF novels of big computers.

Generally, Buzzati's few genuine SF stories tend to be weak and unoriginal, lacking the power of his fantastic stories. There are a few tales of time travel, the atomic bomb, the end of the world, and flying saucers. Much more impressive are his stories that blend the everyday and the fantastic in an intricate, inseparable manner, and are told with the economy and eye for factual details of the journalist that Buzzati was. Buzzati declared: ". . . fantasy should be as close as possible to journalism. The right word is not 'banalising,' although in fact a little of this is involved. Rather, I mean that the effectiveness of a fantastic story will depend on its being told in the most simple and practical terms." Something that would have been applauded by Edmund Wilson. By quite simple means, in elegantly turned stories, Buzzati manages to convey alternatively a sense of wonder, horror, the absurdity of existence, the bewildering complexity of modern society, and the inexplicable workings of fate. Strive as they might, his characters have a particular destiny waiting for them from which they cannot escape. Often their whole efforts prove to be in vain, and a long wait or a long search turns out ultimately to be a waste of their lives, as in "The Colomber" or "The Walls of Anagoor." Buzzati's most impressive story is probably "The Slaying of the Dragon"—the story of a hunt for a murderous monster, turned upside down. There the human hunters show only base motives, vanity and greed, while the dragon alone exhibits courage, compassion, and dignity. "Seven Floors" is another parable of modern existence, the story of a hospital, which the patients enter in perfectly good health at the seventh floor, and are gradually moved down to the basement where they arrive terminally ill.

Buzzati's stories are characterized by a search for meaning; they express the existential fears of modern man and interpret the anxieties of modern civilization, explore the labyrinthic existence of cities and the threats of machinery. Their dreamlike mood is often underpinned by an ironical sense of humor, and they exhibit a deep feeling for his fellow-sufferers. They show the absurdity of existence, but the hope for salvation is nevertheless a redeeming feature in them; for all their sometimes ferocious criticism of human beings they do not condemn but leave open an avenue of hope.

—Franz Rottensteiner

---

**CALVINO, Italo** (1923–1985). Italian. *Cosmicomics* (stories), 1968; *T Zero*, 1969 (as *Time and the Hunter*, 1970); *The Watchers and Other Stories*, 1971; *Invisible Cities*, 1974; *The Castle of Crossed Destinies*, 1977.

* * *

Italo Calvino is perhaps better known as a writer of fantasy/surreal/experimental fiction than as the creator of science fiction. Yet at some points these two branches of fiction intersect with interesting results. His first science-fiction work, *Cosmicomics*, considers the origin of the universe, the development of life, and the advance of human consciousness and technology—all from the perspective of the "cell/narrator," Qfwfq, who has been present as an observer in one form or another from the beginning of time. This collection of vignettes pre-dates Douglas Adams's *Hitchhiker's Guide to the Galaxy* by many years and takes the same wry perspective on the struggle to survive on the planet Earth and in the universe. Calvino uses the science-fiction format as his vehicle for observing human foibles, in much the same way that any writer of science fiction places "human" protagonists in alternate universes and times to explore how any creature, human or otherwise, handles challenges.

*T Zero* considers the meaning of time, space, motion, and values. In this episodic series Calvino investigates such polarities as unity and multiplicity, past and present, chaos and order, probability and certainty. As in most of his work, Calvino experiments as much with narrative form as an expression of observed "reality" as he does with creating entertaining characters and plots.

Calvino also makes use of arcane subjects in order to explore the nature of the universe. For example, he patterns the events in *The Castle of Crossed Destinies* on the array of cards in the Tarot pack. The cards and the things they stand for shift meaning as he sets them in different time frames: one grouping shows us such figures as Faust, Parsifal, and Oedipus from the perspective of a medieval castle; another examines them as they would manifest themselves in a more modern setting.

Stylistically similar is *Invisible Cities*, in which an imaginary Marco Polo meets with an improbable Kublai Khan to describe the cities of his empire. Each chapter explores a different city in this imaginary world and provides accompanying dialogues between Polo and the Khan.

Calvino is rewarding to read, for his work not only challenges our assumptions about time, ethics, and perception but also forces us to re-examine the comfortable methods we generally employ to avoid dealing with paradox. He explores these topics thematically at the same time that he makes conscious efforts to extend and distort the boundaries of conventional fiction. His fiction has as much to do with the structure and nature of fiction itself as it does with characters and plot. For this reason, Calvino can be grouped with such writers of fantasy as Jorge Luis Borges, Umberto Eco, Donald Barthelme, and Robert Coover, all of whom want their readers to be aware of what it means to be a *reader*, a participant in their fictions.

—Melissa E. Barth

---

**CAPEK, Karel** (1890–1938). Czech. Fiction—*Krakatit*, 1925 (as *An Atomic Fantasy*, 1948); *The Absolute at Large*, 1927; *War with the Newts*, 1937. Plays—*R.U.R. (Rossum's Universal Robots)*, 1923; *And So Ad Infinitivum (The Life of the Insects)*, 1923 (as *The Insect Play*, 1923; as *The World We Live In*, 1933); *The Makropoulos Secret*, 1925; *Adam the Creator*, 1929; *Power and Glory*, 1937.

* * *

Karel Capek was a prolific author of stories, essays, novels, travelogues, plays, and newspaper articles. The word "robot" was coined by his brother Josef (his collaborator in some works), but its blend of psycho-physiology and politics expresses precisely Karel's preoccupation with contemporary inhumanity, opposing Natural Man to Unnatural Pseudo-Man, a manlike, reasoning, but unfeeling being associated with capitalist technology and the social extremes of upper-class tycoon and working-class multitude. Capek's heroes range from small employees and craftsmen to doctors and deviant scientists, and his most stubborn values arise from peasant confidence in traditional things and relationships. In the plays, this is openly expressed by his small people and ideological arbiters, such as Nana in *R.U.R.* or Kristina in *The Makropoulos Secret*, while in the novels it is implied by key actions such as the final return to normality in *Krakatit* and *The Absolute at Large.* Yet Capek was also spellbound and terrified by the workers's world of factories and the power of capitalists (e.g., Bondy from both the latter novel and *War with the Newts*).

In Capek's first SF phase, after World War I, the tension between the little people (the audience he was writing for) and the catastrophic forces of technology and violence is largely vitiated by the ambiguity between a menace to man and to the middle class: does it arise from aliens created by the large industry, its capitalists and engineers, or from the workers? The robots of *R.U.R.*, synthetic androids outwardly like men, are mass-produced to be "workers with the minimum amount of requirements," i.e. without the non-exploitable emotions. In their first story, "System" (1908), the Capeks had shown a workers's revolt in such circumstances; the machine-men of *R.U.R.* are technological stand-ins for workers (and for Wells's Morlocks) but also, simultaneously, inhuman aliens "without history." Their creation doesn't lead to Domin's engineering utopia with Nietzschean supermen but to genocidal revolt. Yet during the play they grow more like a new human order than like inhuman aliens, more workers than machines; reacquiring feelings, they usher in a new cycle of creation. This oscillation, parallel to one between psychological and collective drama, has dated *R.U.R.* This holds even more strongly for *Adam the Creator* and *The Makropoulos Secret* (about the elixir of longevity). In *And So Ad Infinitivum* the flighty erotics of upperclass "golden youth," the acquisitive sentimentalities of the petty bourgeoisie, and the militarism and deathlust racism of incipient fascism are personified as insects in a bitter satire, Capek's best stage play.

Capek's SF strength lies in his novels. *The Absolute at Large* presents another supposedly utopian but destructive invention: the Absolute or God, mass-produced as a by-product of atomic fission in "karburators" that supply cheap energy. The novel passes in sarcastic review its abuses by church and state, corporations and individuals, academics and journalists: both the economy and personal relations collapse. Absolutized sectarian and national fanaticism lead to the "Greatest War," which peters out only when all "atomotors" have been destroyed along with most people. Yet it isn't clear why the Absolute, a "mystical Communism," must bend itself to capitalist economy and competitive psychology, or work disparately in things (overpopulation of industrial goods only) and in people (destructiveness matching the overpopulation). The power unleashed is simply a chaotic magnification of acquisitive economics and psychology. This makes for brilliant if spotty social satire, in which the little people outlast the highminded idea, but hardly for consistent SF.

In *Krakatit* the naive genius who pierces the secret of atomic fission finds a parallel "destructive chemistry" in Dostoevskian fevered nightmares, dissociations of memory, and explosive human encounters, and develops from "value-free" science to painful recognition of the primacy and dangers of human relationships. Capek integrated here popular literature—detection mystery and epic adventure from Homer through the folktale to pulp thrillers—into poetic and committed modern SF. The love and heroism of sensational melodrama and the counter-creation of the mad-scientist tradition are balanced by a sympathetic, suffering, and relatively complex hero, who rejects a series of erotic-cum-political temptations—not only the established class and new personal power but also the idyllic retreat. He is left with a resolve to achieve useful warmth instead of destructive explosions, and emerges from the fog of yearning into the clarity of moderation. Though the novel doesn't quite fuse realism and allegory, ethical moderation and folktale certainties, it largely succeeds in transcending the opposition between scientific progress and human happiness. For the first and last time in Capek's SF, a believable hero fights back successfully at destructive forces within himself and society.

Capek's second phase comprises some minor, marginally SF stories, *War with the Newts*, and one play. The rise of Nazism dispelled his illusions of the little man's instinctual rightness and the relativity of truth. Instead of satirizing the intellect, he wrote sharply against irrationalism, "be it the cult of will, of the soil, of the subconscious, of the mass instincts, or of the violence of the powerful." The pseudo-human becomes clearly evil when the Salamanders's become analogous to the Nazi aggressors. Their rise is interwoven with a satire on the illusion industries which screen biological and social reality from mankind—the exotic and juvenile adventure romance, sensational tabloid newspaper, Hollywood movies, pseudo-scientific polls and interviews in newspapers. Scientists and academics are as timid and ideologically limited as the public at large, but the real villains are the capitalists who finance the menace through the Salamander Syndicate—an industrial utopianism satirized in the minutes of its meeting. The Salamanders, who began as exotic pets, become an "extremely cheap labor force" parallel to the transformation of competitive merchant-buccaneering into a global exploitative corporation aiming at a new Atlantis—which will end as Atlantis did. An appendix on the Salamanders's sexual life shows that their "Collective Male" horde is capable of politics and technics but not of real sociability: the Syndicate is the greatest illusion of them all. Progressing to a powerful alternate society, learning well mankind's combination of slavery and stock-market, aggression and ideological propaganda, they begin their assault. Capek's satire is here most bitter, topical, and precise. Startlingly, even his beloved small people are found guilty of complacency as continents crumble around them.

The satire of literary, journalistic, and essayistic forms of this novel is also a critique of SF. The history of the Salamanders echoes Wells's *Island of Dr. Moreau*, Conan Doyle's *Lost World*, and the animal fable; the global overview latches onto Wells's later SF and Anatole France's *Penguin Island;* it ends with Wellsian havoc-wreaking aliens—but also with an open question, much superior to ordinary SF: "No cosmic catastrophes, nothing but state, official, economic, and other causes . . . ." The menace could have been stopped—if people had organized to fight it, if "All the industries. All the banks. All the different states" had not financed "this End of the World." Such writing makes of Capek not only the pioneer of all anti-fascist and anti-militarist SF but also (together with Zamyatin) the most significant SF writer between the World Wars. True, *War with the Newts* didn't quite manage to overcome this ambiguity: the Salamanders are at the beginning a wronged inferior race and yet grow into an embodiment of both the Nazis and robotized masses. Russia, moreover, is presented as a Tsarist state: Capek couldn't deal with socialism or any positive radical novelty. He dealt in catastrophes, and concentrated his fire almost entirely on bourgeois society. Conversely, such a love-hate relationship led the Communist bureaucracy in Czechoslovakia to neglect him in the early 1950's, though he has since been rehabilitated.

Capek's evolution is not simple. One of his best works, *Krakatit*, is early, and his final SF play, *Power and Glory*—a critique of fascism, militarism, and subservient medicine—is second-rate. But in a few works he left a precious heritage. He—rather than Burroughs or Gernsback—is the missing link between Wells and a literature which will be both entertaining (which means popular) and cognitively (which means also formally) avant garde. He infused the legacy of the adventure novel and melodramatic thriller, French and British SF, and German fantasy with the prospects of modern poetry, painting, and movies as well as with an eager and constant interest in societal relationships, in natural and physical sciences, and above all in the richly humorous and idiomatic language of the street and the little people. In that way, he is the most "American" of the often elitest European SF writers. And yet he is also not only intensely Czech, but a "European local patriot" for whom Europe meant culture and humanism; when they were betrayed, the Salamanders—read fascists—had arrived.

—Darko Suvin

---

**ENDE, Michael** (1930?– ). German. *The Neverending Story*, 1983.

* * *

Considered first and foremost a young-adult storyteller, Michael Ende, the son of a Surrealist painter, is a supporter of "escapist" literature. His celebrated *The Neverending Story*, first published in German in 1979, is a metaliterary narrative deeply akin to the art of the Argentinian novelist Julio Cortázar. Ende's books have been translated into numerous languages, yet he is best known as the author of this unique and fascinating tale. His SF affinities are dubious. A promoter of what Roger Caillois and Tzvetan Tordorov refer to as "the fantastic," a genre that enjoys disrupting the natural course of things without introducing horror, Ende dislikes using technological or scientific tools or references in his work. Instead, he adapts ancient myths and allegories to capture his audience's imagination and address their collective unconscious.

Unlike some of the SF adventures of Aldous Huxley, Stanislaw Lem, or Ray Bradbury, Ende's are not located in the future but in another, parallel dimension—one similar to that of Lewis Carroll's 1871 *Through the Looking Glass.* Thus, his intention is not to write parables about the forthcoming human condition but fabulous sagas. Not without reason, Ende has been honored with the Hans Christian Andersen award.

His narrative tales in *Der Spiegel im Spieleg: Ein Labyrinth* are a tribute to Jorge Luis Borges and Franz Kafka. Similar to a situation in Kafka's *The Trial*, one of Ende's many characters awaits with enduring patience the opening of a door that will mysteriously offer the clue to the secrets of his own earthly existence. Another simply dreams of having wings and, upon waking, finds that the hope has become real. The book's title and content make use of two of Borges's favorite metaphors: mirrors are the key to understanding "Tlön, Uqbar, Orbis Tertius," and labyrinths are at the center of "The Garden of Forking Paths" (*Ficciones*, 1944).

With its references to philosophical and individual Time, Ende's 1973 novel *Momo*, which won the Deutscher Jugendbuchpreis, is influenced by H.G. Wells and Henri Bergson. It tells the story of a young hero who battles an ever-powering group of enemies, the grey-suited business men who negotiate with Time and take away happiness from people. It's a delicious moral story about courage and the triumph of good over evil.

But Ende owes his success to Bastian Bathazar Bux, the ten- or eleven-year-old protagonist of *The Neverending Story* who voraciously reads a book called "The Never-Ending Story" in which he himself is one of the major characters. After stealing "The Never-Ending Story," Bastian Balthazar Bux, whose mother is dead and whose father is a fearful castigator, hides himself in the attic of his day-school. In the segments pertaining to his own reality, Ende uses red-colored ink; in those dealing with the imaginary tale about the kingdom of Fantasia, he uses green; and a unifying red prevails when the protagonist joins Atreyu, a fantastic hero, in combating the spreading of Nothingness in the geographies of Fantasia and the sudden, fatal sickness of the Child Empress. *The Neverending Story* could be considered SF only if one agrees to place *Alice in Wonderland* and *The Wizard of Oz* in the same category. An admirer of *One Thousand and One Nights*, Jules Verne, the Renaissance chivalry novel, the "Niebelungenlied" and other Germanic medieval sagas, Ende makes every possible effort to reject science. In fact, he could be considered an anti-SF author in that he makes sure his fabulous tales do not contain elements within the realm of future possibility.

—Ilan Stavans

---

**FRANKE, Herbert W.** (1927– ). Austrian. *The Orchid Cage*, 1973; *Zone Null*, 1974.

* * *

Writer, scientist, spelunker, computer expert, and academic, Herbert W. Franke writes novels, short stories, and science books for laymen about computers, information science and the potentialities of psychological manipulation through electronic sensory stimulation. His earlier novels emphasized dominant military-industrial systems allied to conformist drug cultures, radioactive desolations, decadent game-satiated mass cultures, entrapment in plastic environments, and the definition of enforced "superiority" as conformity to one man's monomaniacal obsessions. Some of the novels of the late 1970's and early 1980's portray superman-obsessed leaders who use electronic simulations to test and delude their trainees (*Schule für Übermenschen*). From *Glasfalle* to *Kälte des Weltraums* tyrants are a continuing thread, but the later novels allow their heroes more freedom. Although Franke portrays enforced "superiority" harshly, a hero may submit voluntarily to the training school rigors in the beginning to survive a tyrant in the end (*Schule für Übermenschen*). His analysis of scientists's responsibility for the state of affairs continues in *Keine Spur vom Leben* and *Tod eines Unsterblichen.* Most striking is the development of the entertainment park theme in *The Orchid Cage* through *Zone Null* and *Sirius Transit* (1979). There the dominant personality is a "Star" who manipulates the masses by faking the conquest of a distant planet. Two recent works: *Endzeit* (1985) and *Dea Alba* (1988), revolve around the ambiguities of computer interpreted data. A sound cassette accompanies *Dea Alba* to reflect the descriptions of strange sensory effects on a crew investigating a far distant planet, effects which entice two crew members away from their compatriots and transform their physical natures. *Endzeit*'s hero is expected to solve Earth's loss-of-water/energy problem by data manipulation. Both novels have quasi-religious endings with the rain storm after arid millennia (1985) or matter transformation (1988). Though some characters show a modest development, the novels are often ironic in outline and analytical in the disclosure of unifying social, psychological and electronic systems. With the basic themes of heroes who question, critical encounters with a deadening status quo and analyses of the psychological potentialities of advanced technology, Franke continues to plumb the long term problems of both individual and species survival.

—Alice Carol Gaar

---

**GAIL, Otto** (1896–1956). German. "The Stone from the Moon," in *Science Wonder Quarterly*, Spring 1930; *By Rocket to the Moon* (for children), 1931; *The Shot into Infinity*, 1975.

* * *

Otto Gail, the German popular science and science-fiction writer, was closely associated with rocketry pioneers such as Hermann Oberth, and influential in development of realistic depiction of space travel in Anglo-American and even Soviet SF. All three of Gail's science-fiction novels were translated into English.

Until the appearance of *The Shot into Infinity* in *Wonder Stories Quarterly* in 1929 there was little technical realism in Anglo-American SF devoted to the conquest of space. Victorian devices like anti-gravity were still common, and even when rockets were used they tended to be built by precocious inventors right in their back yards. Gail, also the author of a 1928 nonfiction work of popularization, *With Rocket Ships into Space*, was familiar with the work of Oberth and other theorists. And if he did not *fully* realize the logistical problems of the Space Age, he was certainly aware space travel would be a massive undertaking. *The Shot into Infinity* mixes Vernean SF with romantic melodrama. August Korf, the hero, has been working on a multi-stage liquid-fuel rocket—a project that has languished for lack of funding (partly due to his own stubbornness: he is too proud to appeal to the world for help). A rival has stolen his earlier plans for a solid-fuel craft, and sent an astronaut to the Moon. Alas, solid fuel proves inadequate, and the luckless pilot is trapped in lunar orbit. So naturally Korf speeds completion of his *Geryon* to attempt a rescue, and of course the dying pilot turns out to be his former true love, who was impatient with his caution and wanted to go herself. Amid the melodrama, there remain realistic scenes of acceleration, stage separation, space walks, and the like. Too, there is the sense that reality is unforgiving, as in Tom Godwin's later "The Cold Equations," and, above all, a sense of mission: space travel as a cause. *The Shot into Infinity* is ancestor to such later works as Robert A. Heinlein's "The Man Who Sold the Moon" and Arthur C. Clarke's *Prelude to Space.*

"The Stone from the Moon" is less interesting; although it features a space station, the plot centers on an occult Lost Atlantis theme. *By Rocket to the Moon* is strictly juvenile. Despite the earlier influence of Konstantin Tsiolkovsky, Gail's work seems to have had some impact on Soviet SF through translations. Aleksandr Belyaev tries to go *The Shot into Infinity* one better with *A Leap into Nothingness* (1933), with even more attention to logistics and outdoes "The Stone from the Moon" with the space station in *KETStar* (1936).

—John J. Pierce

---

**JESCHKE, Wolfgang** (1936– ). German. "A Little More Than Twelve Minutes," in *New Writings in SF,* edited by Kenneth Bulmer, 1975; "The King and the Dollmaker," in *The Best from the Rest of the World: European Science Fiction*, edited by Donald A. Wollheim, 1976; *The Last Day of Creation*, 1982; "The Land of Osiris," in *Isaac Asimov's Science Fiction Magazine*, March 1985; *Midas*, 1990.

* * *

Although Wolfgang Jeschke's output is small—so far two SF novels, more than a dozen longer tales and short stories, a number of poems, and most recently some radio dramas—he ranks among Germany's most important SF writers, but is much better known as editor (since 1972) of Wilhelm Heyne's successful SF line—the largest in Europe.

As a writer, he is almost the exact opposite of somebody like H.W. Franke (generally considered to be the most important SF writer in Germany), who is more interested in content than in the manner of expressing it, and who has turned a style severe and austere into a virtue. Jeschke is a more natural writer, interested in a tale well told, rich in background, narrative turns, and incident. Mood and stylistic qualities are often more important than plot, subject matter, or theme. Consequently, many of his stories are variations on well-known SF themes or build upon previous SF. His first professionally published story, "Der Türmer," is typical of this: a sentient and telepathic plant on a far planet comes into contact with a lonely human being, striving like the humans to conquer space and to spread its seeds on other planets. One of Jeschke's favorite topics is time-travel and its paradoxes, as in one of his earliest stories, "Supernova," later revised as "The Gap in the Mountain"—an earthman is caught in a time-loop. Similarly in "A Little More Than Twelve

Minutes" time travelers from the future wait for the building of the first time machine so that they can return home. Sometimes Jeschke's stories contain mythical allusions or provide SF versions of classical tales, as in "Sirens on the Shore." His imminent death is made bearable for a dying spaceman by aliens that project his inmost longings into his mind. This character of wish-fulfillment is also evident in "The Gate of Night," in which the after-effects of an atomic war are undone by mutants who create another reality track, thus giving mankind another chance. Other early stories feature a horrible new disease, the transplantation of human memories into robot bodies or the long voyage to the stars by human beings who have forgotten their origins and purpose. These are well-written but not terribly original, old-fashioned and slight stories. Of quite a different order is the long story "The King and the Dollmaker," another time-travel tale, but this time a virtuoso performance, so complex and well-constructed a story that it can stand beside the best time-travel stories, a tour de force that turns artifice into a high art, although this was recognized (upon its appearance in Donald A. Wollheim's *The Best from the Rest of the World*) only by perceptive critics like Michael Bishop.

Jeschke's newer stories are both more substantial in content and more experimental in form. "Heike the Heretic's Writings" is a skilful arrangement of real and fictitious newspaper reports, essays, speeches of politicians, news, and quotations from books, all relating to the current political state of the world, while "The Land of Osiris" offers a journey through a post-atomic Africa, and a contact with an alien visitor.

Jeschke's first novel, *The Last Day of Creation*, again turns back to time-travel. The book starts with the discovery of a series of mysterious artifacts that are both a spoof on Erich von Däniken's ancient astronauts theories and the saintly traditions of the Roman Catholic Church. The discoveries are taken by the American authorities to mean that their project is viable: to travel back into the past in order to change the present, to steal the Arab oil from under the noses of the sheikhs. But from the beginning, everything goes wrong, the time troops arrive in little groups, spaced years apart, and are already awaited by superior and better-equipped enemy forces. They are not even all from the same future but from alternate futures, and they are soon stranded in the past, for no return is possible, and all that is left to them is fighting for their bare survival in the jungles of the Mediterranean (then not yet a sea), with only dim prospects of a golden Atlantis in the Bermudas ahead. Jeschke's novel is both an engaging fast-paced adventure story and a narrative with deeper meanings, satiric both of the current situation of the world and other SF stories depicting attempts to improve history by time-travel.

Jeschke's second SF novel, *Midas*, might be described as a German contribution to cyberpunk SF; MIDAS (Molecular Integrating and Digital Assembling System) allows the reconstruction and electronical storing of human beings who then appear as irritating factors in the world-wide information nets. *Midas* is one of those novels in which it is more interesting to journey than to arrive, in this instance through a run-down world shaken by civil wars and local strife, from Sri Lanka to the High Tec countries. It takes the form of a thriller in which plots and counterplots proliferate, but in which there is no final resolution and cannot be one. Giant airships, propelled by genetically engineered animal muscles, are among the most vivid images of a novel that is more remarkable for its gloomy futuristic setting than for its plot or characters, and the dense atmospheric effect of the novel continues to haunt the reader long after the ramifications of the plot have been forgotten.

—Franz Rottensteiner

---

**JEURY, Michel** (1934– ). French. *Chronolysis*, 1980.

* * *

When *Le Temps Incertain* (*Chronolysis*) appeared in 1973, a new author arrived in French science fiction and established himself immediately at his peak. Michel Jeury was neither a young writer nor a newcomer. Born in 1934, he had already published in 1960 (under the pseudonym of Albert Higon) *Aux Etoiles du Destin* and *La Machine du Pouvoir*, which attempted a synthesis between the French tradition of the *roman d'anticipation* and recent American science fiction. Then for more than ten years Jeury was silent. Of humble, peasant background, which had already placed him apart in the social universe of science fiction, he spent many difficult years and had nearly ceased writing entirely. This origin, these difficulties, these uncertainties on the order of the world, are essential to the understanding of his work.

In *Chronolysis* two futures, the one dominated by a multinational fascist HKH, the other more human and asserted by intelligent computers, the Phords, dispute our present, which will decide their existence. Both futures have use of the weapon *chronolyse*, which permits sending agents into the past, or rather projecting their personality there. But the chronolitic drug is not as certain as a machine, because it acts upon the mind. Robert Holzach thus enters into a universe of uncertainty where the past, the present, the future, and the possible encounter each other and are superimposed, alternatively. He's a man hunted to the depths of his own psyche. So well is this done that the novel has the characteristics of a realistic nightmare, without becoming hallucinatory.

Jeury is so remarkable for creating the social fabric of a period that he specializes both in economic problems and the hesitations of the real, as well as an anguish that is sometimes precise, other times diffuse. Therefore, certain commentators relate Jeury to Philip K. Dick. But one can also discern in the *principe d'incertitude* the influence of Robbe-Grillet. If this is the case, Jeury brings to the *nouveau roman* a simplicity of writing and an almost prophetic content which it ordinarily lacks. In reality, Jeury invents—and does not cease to explore in his major works—a personal world that is somber, even pessimistic, controlled by vast social machines, by informational networks, by the omnipresence of tyranny, by the image, the falsification of the real for the benefit of the dominant groups.

In this universe where nothing is ever exactly as it seems, the central character, a little man, flees, tries to survive and even bring about a better world, a utopia like that in *La Fête du changement*, perhaps Jeury's most brilliant novel but a utopia without rules.

The result defies all analytic description. If *Chronolysis* and its successors have known an instant success, it is in the dissolution of the framework of the real and in joining the philosophic themes then developed by Lyotard, Deleuze, and Guttari, whom Jeury probably hadn't yet read.

The little man hunted is evidently Jeury himself, perceiving the crushing of his social group by the great forces fighting among themselves for absolute supremacy.

One finds again these preoccupations, this obsession, in his later works, notably in *Soleil chaud, poisson des profondeurs* and in *Les Animaux de Justice.* But with *Les Yeux Geants* the writer was to go further yet, describing the encounter between a society in crisis in the beginning of the 21st century and an absolute strangeness, an extra-terrestrial who manifests himself always in an elusive manner. The novel is a long progression towards the discovery of the other as indicated by the last sentence: "the ending of this story can never be written with human words." In this terrain, Jeury has surpassed, in my judgment, Stapledon, Clarke, and Lem. He borders on the frontier of mysticism without ever letting himself be taken into its pitfalls, and shows that it is a question at the same time of a mediated perception and a social phenomenon. He has thus profoundly renewed science fiction; too much perhaps for its habitual public.

The other side of the coin is that the narrowness of the French quest for science-fiction works of high quality limits Jeury to producing more commercial work, where he is less comfortable. His skill even in describing problematic unknown universes in dissolution prevents him from producing simple and manichaean works which please the larger public. And that is precisely because his characters, without being anti-heroes, cannot and will not dominate the conflicts that confront them. If science fiction is a literature obsessed by theory, Jeury introduces to it, exaggerated by the taste of the majority, doubt.

The drama, and I weigh my words, is that Jeury, as with so many other writers of breadth, might find himself prevented from writing what he is and obliged to turn away from and devalue his talent. This would be an immense loss for French literature and for world-wide science fiction. The reader will profit from consulting my preface to the *Livre d'or de Michel Jeury* (Presses-Pocket, 1982) where I develop the ideas briefly sketched here on the sense, the importance, and the genesis of Jeury's work.

—Gérard Klein (translated by Ann K. Smith)

---

**KAFKA, Franz** (1883–1924). Czech. *The Castle*, 1930; *The Trial*, 1937; *The Basic Kafka*, 1979.

* * *

Albert Einstein could not read Kafka. He handed back a novel of Kafka's Thomas Mann had lent him, confessing he had been unable to finish it, saying, "The human mind isn't that complex." Something of Einstein's bafflement has been felt by every honest critic approaching Kafka's work. It speaks for itself. It is plain, unadorned. It holds no mystery. Kafka hides nothing. "As Gregor Samsa awoke one morning from uneasy dreams he found himself transformed in his bed into a gigantic insect." Nothing could be more transparent, anticipated even.

The quoted sentence opens the story "Metamorphosis," a favourite with science-fiction readers. Yet the question must be asked, Is Franz Kafka a science-fiction writer? The answer has to be that such a question diminishes him. He is one of the great writers of the 20th century, eternally readable, eternally astonishing. Among the shelves of books of criticism on his work, there is no critic rash enough to claim him for SF.

And yet with Kafka there are always qualifications. There was a long-prevailing fashion within the SF field—promoted by John W. Campbell—to regard the universe as a large wiring diagram that could be rapidly scrutinized and solved—possessed—within a generation. His writers in his magazine wrote as if this were so. Their world picture has dated badly.

The opposing view is that the universe, now revealed as so full of anomalies, is ultimately unfathomable to the human mind, which is a subordinate part of the whole. Of this view (not at all defeatist, but rather quietist), Kafka is king. His two great novels, *The Trial* and *The Castle*—unfinished at his premature death—both present their central character with problems to which no solution appears possible.

Not that these novels are allegories. Nor are they religious, though religious intensity is certainly there. They seem rather to be Symbolist novels, the equivalent in prose of a Max Ernst painting. ("The symbol *is* what it represents; the allegory represents what, in itself, it is *not*"—Eric Heller, in *The World of Franz Kafka*, edited by J.P. Stern, 1980). Perhaps it would be safest to say that Kafka achieved a new kind of fiction for modern man, as SF has scarcely managed to do. He was dedicated, as Proust was dedicated, to the written word to a remarkable degree; they were not commercial authors.

The inexplicable has much to do with it. In *The Trial*, K is inexplicably under arrest for a crime he cannot determine. In *The Castle*, K arrives at a village where he believes a job awaits him; inexplicably, nobody can confirm this. Against these monstrous dilemmas, K brings determination and logic. Ever and again, new complications arise.

Both *The Trial* and *The Castle*, among the greatest novels of the century, contain a great deal of wit, or more precisely black humour. Charles Dickens was one of the Kafka's models. The pure fantasy stories are also humorous and owe something to the Jewish tradition. For instance, "Investigations of a Dog" is as written by a dog. A certain sly native masochism appears in "In the Penal Settlement" and some of the shorter stories; in "The Vulture," a man suffers a vulture to mutilate his feet, before finally drowning it in his own blood.

A Czech born in Prague, Kafka wrote in German, mainly for himself and his circle of friends, among whom Max Brod was responsible for saving the manuscripts Kafka wanted burnt. The Mitteleuropean complexion of the work has led critics to see in it predictive qualities, foreseeing the complexities of oppression Hitler's Third Reich was to inflict on Czechs and, more particularly, Jews. One of Kafka's unconsumated loves was for Milena Jesenska, who was to die in the Ravensbruck concentration camp in 1944, 20 years after Kafka's death in a sanitorium.

The paradox of Kafka's art and his life is well expressed in Pietro Citati's biography: "All the people who met Franz Kafka in his youth or maturity had the impression that he was surrounded by a 'wall of glass.' There he stayed, behind that very transparent glass, walking gracefully, gesticulating, speaking. . . . The more he participated in the destiny and sufferings of others, the more he excluded himself from the game."

Almost everything Kafka wrote is worth reading and re-reading. His *Diaries* (2 vols., 1948) are recommended, and also his restrainedly crushing "Letter to His Father"—that father, a prosperous Jewish merchant, being a source of his son's misery and inspiration alike. "You, so tremendously the authoritative man, did not keep the commandments you imposed on me."

—Brian W. Aldiss

---

**KELLERMANN, Bernhard** (1879–1951). German. *The Tunnel*, 1915.

* * *

Bernhard Kellermann's only science-fiction novel, *The Tunnel*, was influential in development of a school of SF better known in the Soviet Union than in the West. "Industrial science fiction," as it was later christened by Soviet critics, goes beyond the strict invention-adventure format of Jules Verne as represented in both the *voyages extraordinaires* and the juvenile SF (dime novels, Tom Swift, etc.) that imitated them: vast engineering projects change both the face of the world and ordinary people's lives. But no more than in straight Vernean SF is there any fundamental change in society. Early examples include André Lauries's *New York to Brest in Seven Hours* (1888, France), involving construction of a transatlantic oil pipeline, and Luigi Motta's *The Submarine Tunnel* (1912, Italy), which anticipates the project in Kellermann's novel.

*The Tunnel* was undoubtedly the most popular of these; it was translated into English within a year, and was still remembered fondly enough two decades later to inspire three movie versions, *The Tunnel* (1933, in simultaneous French and German versions) and *Transatlantic Tunnel* (1935, Britain). Even the novel reads like a cross between Verne and Cecil B. DeMille. Mac Allan, the hero, is an idealistic engineering genius typical of invention SF. But realization of his dream requires billions of dollars and entire armies of workers—and costs thousands of lives. Kellermann realizes the scale of logistics for such a project, from an artificial Niagara to provide electric power to a new city to house workers. Although gigantic boring machines do the basic tunneling work, the toll on human life is great—and the project is nearly doomed by an explosion that kills nearly 3,000 and leads to strikes and riots. Despite being made a scapegoat for the disaster and being sent to jail (his wife and child already having been killed by rioters), Allan eventually redeems himself and completes the tunnel. Through it all, there are no basic moral or social questions: Western civilization is united by the ideals of science and engineering; there are no wars or serious international disputes. Even the scientific imagination is short-sighted: the possibility of *air* travel across the Atlantic is curtly dismissed.

Kellermann's collected works were translated in 1930 in the Soviet Union, where his sympathy for the Bolshevik Revolution struck a responsive chord. *The Tunnel* undoubtedly helped inspire Aleksandr Kazantsev's *Arctic Bridge* (1946), involving a similar project across the Arctic Ocean, as well as such industrial SF novels as Aleksandr Belyaev's *Under the Arctic Sky* (1938), Grigori Adamov's *The Banishment of the Lord* (1946), Vladimir Nemtsov's *Golden Bottom* (1948) and Kazantsev's *Northern Jetty* (1952), devoted to Siberian development and similar projects.

—John J. Pierce

---

**KLEIN, Gérard** (1937– ). French. *The Day Before Tomorrow*, 1972; *Star Masters' Gambit*, 1973; *The Overlords of War*, 1973.

* * *

Science fiction has flourished in the land of Jules Verne. And clearly the most important figure in French SF since Verne is Gérard Klein. Klein is one of the very few French SF authors (aside from Verne) to have multiple works translated into English. Despite this "privilege," however, these translations give little sense of Klein's real accomplishment. For not only is he a highly sophisticated novelist (the purely space-opera packaging DAW Books has given to his translated work gives little hint of this), but a fine short-story writer and a perceptive critic as well. What is more, he is the genre's premier editor in France, whose groundbreaking *Ailleurs et demain* has, virtually by itself, set the course for postwar development of SF in that country. Only traces of this accomplishment exist in English. Klein deserves a massive translation effort in order to bring his criticism and editorial commentary to light, thus allowing him to take his rightful place beside Gernsback and Campbell and Aldiss as one of the shapers of SF.

Born in 1937, Klein holds advanced degrees in economics and in psychology. He works (and continues to work) for various French think tanks, engaged in projecting future social trends. Given this background, Klein tends to see his SF (and SF in general) as an extension of this activity: specifically, as an instrument for investigating problems at the level of the structures that are seen to govern the development of human civilization. Klein's social-scientist approach is unwavering, but over the years his emphasis has shifted. The young "romantic" intellectual of the mid 1950's soon experienced, in succession, the Algerian War, the events of May 1968, the consumer conservatism of the Giscard 1970's, and finally the techno-socialism of François Mitterand. Correspondingly, his approach to socioeconomic structures in his SF extrapolations has evolved from a more classic Marxist analysis, to a flirtation with 1970's anarcho-ecolo-leftism, and finally to a fascination with the Mitterand "technorevolution," the latter seen in his recent willingness to publish writers like Benford and Forward. Constant in these changes in method and emphasis, however, is an abiding sense of the limits of human nature: a metaphysical stand that commentators have variously labeled "gnostic," or "stoic," but that, closer to French intellectual tradition, seems to partake rather of Pascal's terror of the infinite.

Klein's first work of SF was a story published in the magazine *Fiction* in 1956. Initially intended to be the French-language version of *The Magazine of Fantasy and Science Fiction*, this magazine rapidly shifted emphasis to admit new French writers. And Klein's work—both stories and critical articles—was to become one of the major forces in directing the policies of this journal toward the creation of a reborn French SF. At the same time Klein published his first novel, *Starmaster's Gambit*, in 1958, in Gallimard's Rayon fantastique series. This was followed by the publication, in close succession, of five more novels in ostensible space-opera format. All these were produced for *Fleuve noir* anticipation—an openly pulpish line that, with garish covers, claimed to be purveying "American" fare to its avid French reading public. These novels are: *Chirurgiens d'une planète* (Surgeons of a Planet), 1960; *Les Voiliers du soleil* (Schooners of the Sun), 1961; *Le long voyage* (The Long Voyage), 1964; *Les Tueurs de temps* (English translation *The Mote in Time's Eye*, 1975), 1965; and *Le Sceptre du hasard* (The Scepter of Chance), 1986. The pseudonym Klein used for the five novels (Gilles d'Argyre—argentum = silver = money) implies at the very least an ironic detachment from the commercial space-opera formula. And indeed, on careful reading, the novels reveal a highly self-conscious use of these conventions. What otherwise would be mindless action-adventure becomes the stuff of philosophical tales in the tradition of Voltaire. And the aggregate of these tales forms something like an epic of the rational mind in the face of a purely material universe: a saga whose implications are, beyond parody and satire, potentially tragic in a Pascalian sense.

The time travel theme, which Klein begins to cultivate in *The Mote in God's Eye*, becomes in his hands, more than a clever "gambit," a genuinely Cartesian device, where "time" is essentially mind, and "travel" the adjustment of an inner/rational realm to spatiotemporal *res extensa.* It is this theme that gives rise to two novels generally considered to be Klein's finest: *Le Temps n'a pas d'odeur* (English translation *The Day Before Tomorrow*, 1972), 1963; and *Les Seigneurs de la guerre* (English translation *The Overlords of War*, 1973), 1970.

This latter novel—which John Brunner thought enough of to translate into English—is a full-blown cosmic epic. Here Georges Corson, a mercenary fighting future battles, finds himself transported to Aergistal, a nexus beyond conventional spacetime where a race of "overlords," through control of time, create a backdrop or theater where classic battles are fought and refought. Aergistal is a "laboratory" where experiments in warfare are carried out for complex and paradoxical ends. The overlords's "goals" are three: to eradicate war, to understand war, and finally to preserve war. The need to make war, they explain, is rooted in human existence, and they remain, despite their mastery, the product of that nature. What they seek, in this rhythm of eradicating and preserving, is the structure of warfare. And this they need, for, as with Pascal's mankind, they still see Aergistal having a frontier existence, on the border between Reason and the Exterior, menace from the void of infinite nonrational space. Corson is given the choice between the three options: extirpate, know, preserve. But, however much he feels for the endless suffering caused by this cycle, he cannot dismantle the structure by choosing. For he too realizes that, in this universe, mankind seems destined to live at the borderline. Klein has often been compared to Stapledon. But this novel, with its almost gnostic sense of world limitations and cosmic imperfection, seems closer to the vision of works like Clarke's *Childhood's End* and Lem's *Solaris.*

In 1969, Klein launched for the publisher Robert Laffont the SF series *Ailleurs et demain.* This is a crucial moment for French SF, for it is Klein's carefully directed publishing program—in this "luxury" trade paperback series with distinctive metallized silver and gold covers—that systematically introduced key American texts to the French reader. Klein was right on top of the American new wave, and published in rapid succession: Heinlein's *Stranger in a Strange Land*, Herbert's *Dune*, Le Guin's *Left Hand of Darkness*, Delany's *Nova*, and Spinrad's *Bug Jack Barron.* Most central however was the visionary publication of Dick's *Ubik* in 1970, and its companion work *A Maze of Death* in 1972. Through these novels, Dick's influence on French SF in the 1970's was to be pervasive, spawning such "Dickian" French masterpieces as Michel Jeury's *Le Temps incertain* and Andre Ruellan's *Tunnel*, both published in turn by Klein in his series. In 1990, *Ailleurs et demain* published a 20-year retrospective volume. The list of distinguished French writers published here has grown immensely. And the list of Anglo-Saxon authors published reveals that Klein has kept close to the pulse of SF development. The direction in the 1980's has, true to the U.S. scene, followed two distinct paths: on one hand that of the "harder" technocrats—Benford, Brin, Forward, Bear; and on the other that of a renewed social consciousness—Shepard, Sargent. Klein's inspired selection of texts, coupled with the insightful and provocative introductions he writes for many of these volumes, offers as close to a "classic" SF collection as any nation possesses.

Klein's fictional output has, alas, diminished since he assumed near-full-time editing duties, and many regret this. Klein however has never ceased writing criticism. And it is perhaps, in the end, as a critic and theoretician that he has made his most distinctive contribution to SF. In 1977, Klein published the expanded version of his essay, "Malaise dans la science-fiction" (an edited version was published in English in *Science-Fiction Studies*, March 1977). This is a major socioeconomic analysis of the genre that has as much if not more bearing on French SF (indeed on the condition of the literary intellectual in France in general) as it does on the Anglo-Saxon novels it specifically targets.

Klein's essays in redefining SF culminate in the figure, not of Heinlein, but of Lewis Carroll. Carroll is the master of the mind-world interface, of the proto-surrealist search for lateral or alternate, rather than expanded, universes. And by claiming Carroll as model for SF creation—an SF that, in accordance with the inward retreat of Cartesian doubt, seeks its models not in expansionist space opera but in the inner journeys of symbolist and surrealist poets—Klein effectively sets the generic direction for SF in France. Klein's vision—where inward retreat from the material world can eventually fuel the need, within the mind-space of this retreat, to improve upon Descartes and not merely eradicate but actually annihilate that world over and over again—effectively describes the dynamic of numerous works of French SF in the 1970's and 1980's.

—George Slusser

---

**KOMATSU, Sakyo** (1931– ). Japanese. *Japan Sinks*, 1976 (as *The Death of the Dragon*, 1978).

* * *

Sakyo Komatsu has written widely in science fiction, other types of fiction, and non-fiction. He was characterized in the early 1970's, when a number of his major works were published and his fame spread, as one of the "Big Five" of Japanese SF writers, the others being Yasutaka Tsutsui, Shin'ichi Hoshi, Ryu Mitsuse, and Taku Mayumura. That grouping left aside Kobo Abe, who exceeded the "Big Five" in national fame, but is by no means an SF specialist, having produced much mainstream literature.

Komatsu himself is not at all a tightly specialized SF writer. He is sometimes called the Robert Heinlein of Japan, while Hoshi is contrastingly referred to as Japan's Ray Bradbury. Like Heinlein, Komatsu gives much thought to political and international problems, but is less inclined to specify a *correct* solution to the problems. Both writers have had a diversified cultural, technical, and occupational background. For Komatsu, this diversified experience contributes to his ability to present natural and realistic narratives, and it contributed most notably to his great success with *Japan Sinks.*

One may also say that Komatsu resembles Isaac Asimov in his continuing output of non-fiction and fiction other than SF. His non-fiction often gets into futurology, as in *Future Technology and Human Society*, co-authored with Hidetoshi Kato (1983), which explores the way in which our dreams of today may be realized in the future. His *The Dead Space of Japanese Civilization* (1977) is a critical examination of Japanese culture. Komatsu's critical writings include a piece of SF criticism in English, "H.G. Wells and Japanese Science Fiction," found in a book he wrote with Judith Merril, Tetsu Yano, and Robert Philmus, *H.G. Wells and Modern Science Fiction* (1977). His book of thoughtful essays on history and criticism, *The Pleasure of Reading and Narrating* was published in 1985. He has also written numerous mysteries, detective stories, and travel books—these last help to account for his impressive physical descriptions.

His story "Fukurokoji" (Blind Alley) is a summary of his futurology, and is included in his book, *Hoshi Goroshi* (Star Killer)—a title drawn from another very original story in that volume. In the same book are his skilled narratives of the birth and death of our moon, "Kaigo" (Conjunction) and "Wareta Kagami" (The Broken Mirror). The title story of another collection, *Chi ni wa Heiwa* (Peace on Earth) was nominated for the Naoki Prize, while a short-short-story therein, "Koppu Ippai no Senso" (A Full Cup of War) deals with the development and hazards of nuclear war. The story "Hokusai no Sekai" (The World of Hokusai) was one of the first Japanese SF stories to appear in Russian for Soviet readers.

*Japan Sinks* (1973) appeared in English in 1976 and has greatly enlarged Komatsu's fame, selling over four million copies in Japan, with renditions in a number of languages. It led to a motion picture, which has been widely exhibited in Japan and abroad. By the 1980's Komatsu was referred to in publications as "Mr. Submersion" and as "the man who sank Japan." In this novel he makes plausible, with abundant data from geology and physics, what would otherwise be regarded as highly fantastic, the submergence of virtually the entire Japanese archipelago as the result of sliding plates, earthquakes, and terrific volcanic action. The loss of Japan in a mere year or so of time is the fantastic element here. The same process extending over millions of years would not be so questionable—nor might it take much of a narrative.

Komatsu has called this novel a fable, and it surely can be read as a caution against insularity in Japan or any nation. On the question of the surviving Japanese people and their culture after their land disappears, Komatsu says that beyond ethnocentric national nationalism is a better, enriched identity, that even after a diaspora one's own language and customs can be kept, while enhanced by a global blending. He also considers the often problematic question of how peoples in distress may interact with the nations to which they call for help.

*At the End of the Endless Stream* (1966) uses a panoramic treatment of the development of the universe and our species, and it shares to some extent the question posed in *Japan Sinks* of how man may fare if dislodged from his historic environment. Another theme here is the possibility of changing human evolutionary potential for the better.

*Goodbye Jupiter* (1982) is mainstream, technical SF featuring a mammoth project to use Jupiter as a sort of secondary sun, so that the outer planets may become habitable. This was a best seller, won high acclaim in Japan, and appeared as a film with the title "Bye-bye, Jupiter."

A sequel of sorts to *Japan Sinks* is *Shuto Shoshitsu*, translatable as *Tokyo Disappears*, or more literally *The Disappearance of the Capital.* This was published as a two-volume book in 1985 by Tokuma Shoten after having been serialized 1982–83 by newspapers all over Japan. In this narrative, vast storms and other catastrophic phenomena of nature cut off Tokyo completely from the rest of Japan. One has to consider that Tokyo looms much larger in Japan than do many capitals in other countries. Thus its disappearance represents to the Japanese a much greater catastrophe than the loss of Washington or Rome would constitute in the United States or Italy, for example. The situation here enables Komatsu to ruminate on modern vulnerability with regard to collapse of telecommunications and computer networks, and to consider at length how a society and its economy might proceed to survive such a disaster.

Indeed catastrophes and near-catastrophes are a leading theme in Komatsu's SF. He can be compared therefore with many other SF authors who have considered the "end of civilization as we know it," the destruction of our planet, or the end of the human race. All such themes give the writer a fine opportunity to deal with the essence of nationhood, humanity, and destiny. Komatsu deals superbly with such challenges.

—Frank H. Tucker

---

**LASSWITZ, Kurd** (1848–1910). German. *Two Planets*, 1971.

* * *

During his lifetime German professor Kurd Lasswitz was known not only for philosophical and scientific writings but also for short stories, speculative novels, and essays on the writing of science fiction. Some 40 years after this death Willy Ley's translations into English of several Lasswitz short stories introduced him to a wider readership. *Fantasy and Science Fiction* published three: "When the Devil Took the Professor" (January 1953); "Aladdin's Lamp" (May 1953); and "Psychotomy" (July 1954). In 1958 Clifton Fadiman included "The Universal Library" in his *Fantasia Mathematica.* In 1971 the 1897 Lasswitz novel *Auf Zwei Planeten* appeared in an abridged English translation as *Two Planets.*

The short stories illustrate Lasswitz's ability to combine physics, metaphysics, philosophy, mathematics, all flavored with wry humor, into intriguing speculative fiction. In "When the Devil Took the Professor" Lasswitz presents a professor talking to a group of amusingly stereotypical people, a talk that develops a Faustian situation in which the professor and the devil verbally spar over the speed of light, the power of reason, the nature of infinity, and the devil's "lot to make all the mistakes in the universe." In the other stories Lasswitz takes a more satiric look at contemporary 19th-century scientific and philosophical ideas. Even writers are not safe from criticism, as Lasswitz refers to those "superfluous volumes" in "The Universal Library." Ironically, in all four of the above-mentioned stories Professor Lasswitz features a professor as the protagonist.

In the literature of space travel Kurd Lasswitz's *Two Planets* merits notice, particularly for its acknowledged impact upon a generation of German scientist-engineers. After the initial 1897 publication, translations fostered audiences throughout Europe. Lasswitz's thousand-page novel (abridged in the English translation) focuses on the conflict of values when intellectually and ethically superior but physically similar Martians ("Nume") invade Earth ("Ba").

Three explorers accidentally discover the Martian land station at Earth's North Pole. Their balloon runs afoul of the "abaric" or anti-gravity field used to propel craft to a solar-powered, ring-shaped satellite. Despite this peaceful contact a subsequent misunderstanding between Martians and the crew of an English warship precipitates military reactions from Earth, soon nullified by superior Martian weapons utilizing repulsion rather than destruction. Ensuing events admit no victory for Earth. The Martians reduce Earth to protectorate status and institute a stringent system of education. Ironically they in turn suffer a re-awakening of the corrupting urge to power. Only through such efforts as those of La, a Nume, and the explorer Saltner does compromise occur. Offering a microcosmic solution for the macrocosmic problem, these two fulfill destiny, or "reason within timeless will," by becoming one with love: "To follow destiny is freedom; to satisfy it is dignity."

Even as the novel gains philosophical complexity, it suffers weak plotting and characterization. Its great strength lies in description and exposition. In detail Lasswitz describes the Martian utopia as a society accommodating freedom of the individual moral will. His scientific and technological exposition of establishment of space stations, utilization of solar energy, synthetic food, and the healthy balance of scientific and humanitarian concerns prophetically foreshadows contemporary interests.

—Hazel Pierce

---

**LEM, Stanislaw** (1921– ). Polish. *Solaris*, 1971; *Memoirs Found in a Bathtub*, 1973; *The Invincible*, 1973; *The Investigation*, 1974; *The Cyberiad*, 1974; *The Futurological Congress*, 1974; *The Star Diaries*, 1976 (as *Memoirs of a Space Traveller*, 1982); *Mortal Engines*, 1977; *The Chain of Chance*, 1978; *Tales of Pirx the Pilot*, 1979 (as *More Tales*, 1982); *A Perfect Vacuum*, 1979; *Return from the Stars*, 1980; *The Cosmic Carnival*, 1981; *Imaginary Magnitude*, 1984; *His Master's Voice*, 1984; *Hospital of the Transfiguration*, 1988; *Eden*, 1989.

* * *

Stanislaw Lem's linguistic and intellectual versatility, his humanism, his scientific accuracy, and his serious commitment to philosophical questions of science and of society make him one of the most respected and innovative of modern science-fiction writers. Critical of much science fiction as "hopeless" pulp, "empty games" dominated by "charlatans," Lem takes the genre seriously as an intellectual tool to investigate man's limits and potentials, to satirize his governments, his pretensions, his militancy, his illusions and delusions, and his failure of imagination. His attack encompasses East and West: Marxist and Capitalist, the scientist, the tourist, the bureaucrat, the technician, the researcher, the theoretician. In *Microworlds: Writings on Science Fiction and Fantasy* (1984), Lem criticizes writers for squandering the potential of science fiction, resorting to clichéd patterns and devices and rehashing old tales instead of initiating experiments and evolving processes of discovery to heighten human awareness and to challenge the intellect. These last mentioned goals he has made his own. He has been compared to both Swift and Voltaire for his dark wit, his serous vision, and his controversial ideas. His cynicism, his sense of man's alienation and of his absurdity in the face of the incomprehensible, his understanding of the limits of theories and interpretations (too often more reflective of their individual creator than of any reality), his fear of a scientific obsession with trivia undermining any possibility of understanding and discovery, his willingness to face the human condition, explore and criticize it, and his special perspective as a Polish scholar/scientist/social critic lend his writings significance and distinction. Generally lacking conventional plots, his works are an organic blend of learned disquisitions, real science, and philosophic questions on the nature of man and his universe within a semi-fictive or imaginative mode. They praise man's resourcefulness and decry his arrogance. Lem's particular models act as metaphors evolving universals—to both profit and delight.

Unlike those writers whose anthropomorphism he attacks as banal and absurd, Lem treats the alien as truly unknown and unknowable, with man limited by nature and experience, the alien beyond human reason and human understanding in manifestation, laws, purposes and essence, and man's persistent but failed efforts to translate the unknowable into human terms doomed to reflect only man himself. In *Solaris*, confronted with a possible sentient, colloidal ocean whose teeming diversity contradicts scientific "laws" and whose materializations bring to life their deepest obsessions, scientists collect reams of frustrating and contradictory data, write volumes of theories, and even develop an anti-field to exorcise the psychic mirrors this sentient creates, but remain stymied by alien phenomena whose essence remains forever mysterious. Their observations, theories, and methodology ultimately serve only to reveal themselves and their needs, some of which are too deeply shameful to be shared; yet they deny even these, preferring false hopes to an admission of existential absurdity (as in Kelvin's rejection and attempted murder of Rheya, an innocent "neutrino" ocean creation, an exact duplicate of his lost love, who become tragically more human with continued contact).

In *The Invincible* the nature of the alien also remains elusive, but as man measures his limits against that alien, he discovers more about his own nature. Therein an unmanned ship probing and measuring a new planet reveals "undefinable formations," an inexplicable black cloud, cybernetic insects, war machines, and other puzzling signs of mayhem. These lead to numerous theories about hidden civilizations and human migrations—all nonsense—and eventually force the human observers to recognize their vincibility; their specialists can study and their destructive machines attack, but man remains impotent, more in tune with the frailty and absurdity of a befuddled robot than with the dark, inscrutable configuration that defies interpretation. The main character, Rohan, stands in "numbed awe," and concludes that "not everywhere has everything been intended for us." In *Return from the Stars*, the central figure, Hal Bregg, tells his girlfriend about an inexplicable incident on a dusty planetoid, one "like nothing. We have no referents. No analogies." In turn, Doctor Digoras in *Memoirs of a Space Traveller* finds himself the subject of an experiment he thought he was conducting, and stands helpless, "without a chance of understanding" before two amorphous fungoids.

*Eden* begins as a fairly straightforward adventure—a resourceful and intelligent spaceship crew crash-landed on a beautiful and previously unexplored planet whose advanced civilization, though obviously alien, seems readily comprehensible. When, however, direct contact is finally made with a native (a "doubler"), all theories and all known "facts" thus far recorded prove fallacious as once again Lem shows man narrowly seeing only his own patterns reflected in alien data. Eden proves a dystopia, characterized by genetic engineering run amuck and by an Orweillian form of disinformation and double-think so extreme that it has literally made some facets of "reality" (like a central controller) unthinkable. Yet human intervention would prove futile and destructive. The stories of Ijon Tichy and Pilot Pirx confirm Lem's theme: man stands alone, alienated from his universe, misunderstanding his fellow creatures, destructively tampering with the unknowable, redeemed only when he shows respect for other life forms and gains insight into his own nature.

Related to Lem's image of man projecting the familiar onto the alien is his focus on man's obsession with theorizing and hypothesizing, seeking a pattern amid the random chance of myriad realities. Confronted with chaos, his characters regularly declare, as does the nuclear physicist in *The Invincible*, "All this must mean something." *Philosophy of Change* and *Summa technologiae* (philosophical essays that provide keys to his views) establish his absurdist attitudes toward man's search for meaning amid meaninglessness. The former denounces structuralism and questions why different ages and cultures respond differently to different works of literature while the latter explores the outermost limits of future possibilities from the genetic remodeling of man to the total reconstruction of reality.

In both *The Investigation* and *The Chain of Chance* private investigators try to unravel bizarre mysteries, in the former resurrection of corpses, in the latter a series of deaths on Italian highways and disappearances at an Italian seaside resort. Deductive reasoning, causal arguments, and the laws of probability imposed on a chain of coincidences seemingly explain the inexplicable, but in fact do not; man imposes significance where in reality there may be none.

In this same vein, *His Master's Voice* delineates man's attempts to interpret as some sort of stellar code, a pulsating stream of life-promoting neutrino radiation. Twenty-five thousand specialists advance divergent hypotheses to decode the so-called message, with explanations ranging from a technological gift from a dying civilization to a formula for the ultimate weapon; all are convincingly detailed, but reveal more about the theorists than the reality. The penetrating description of the formulation of scientific theories and their social impact, the moral responsibility of the scientist and the limits of his knowledge, the controversy and the conspiracies are the heart of the novel, but the role of chance and the problem of communication (between worlds, societies, and individuals) are also central. Franz Rottensteiner describes Lem's universe as "a giant Rorscharsh test"—an apt phrase, for in this book even the final theory, that communication with alien worlds is impossible, may well be only a reflection of Lem's narrator's own limitations. Lem's final image is of men "like snails, each stuck to his own leaf."

*Hospital of the Transfiguration*, Lem's first novel, initiates concerns found in later works: the inhumanity, insanity, cruelty, and corruption of military governments and bureaucracies. A young doctor hopes employment in a provincial Polish insane asylum will provide "a kind of extraterrestrial observatory" from the safety of which he can observe the madness of the Third Reich; instead, the abuses doctors inflict on patients prove only a foretaste of the madness observed firsthand when Nazis turn the asylum into an SS hospital.

*Memoirs Found in a Bathtub* continues the focus on militarism and global destruction first introduced in Lem's early "social realism": *Astronauts, The Magellan Nebula*, and "Sesame." It postulates the mysterious disintegration of all paper except for a record of what happened in the "Third Pentagon" after an American revolution. These memoirs expose a bureaucratic, Dantesque hell in which intelligence gathering and surveillance are turned inward as the Pentagon invents functions, and nameless characters are caught in a senseless maze filled with double and triple agents, secret codes, loyalty tests, polygraph "mittens," sewage espionage filters, and "Seminars on Applied Agony." The military bureaucrats even invent an Antibuilding, the supposed headquarters of the opposition, though Lem's descriptions could apply equally to Moscow's Ministry of Defense, KGB centers, or the American Air Defense headquarters in the Rocky Mountains.

The reminiscences of Ijon Tichy, tourist of the universe and protagonist of *The Star Diaries, The Futurological Congress*, and *Memoirs of a Space Traveller*, point up the ridiculousness of human institutions and doctrines in a more comic vein. Tichy is average and mundane, yet his outrageous adventures, recorded in a free-wheeling, episodic diary, tilt at scientists and scientific laws, concepts of progress and nature, repression, jargon, bureaucratese, and even "unaccommodated man" with delightful informality and gusto. In the seventh Voyage Tichy gets caught in a time warp and splits into multiple selves, while in the fourth he finds his cultural assumptions about personal identity challenged. In *The Futurological Congress* he encounters revolution and chemical warfare, drug therapy and psychemization, and a "pitifully empty" world that changes grass to cheese without the cow. In *Space Traveller* "Phools" consent to their own destruction, a scientist discovers that the mechanical beings he has created are as real as he, and Tichy realizes that eternal life without body or social contact is eternal hell.

*Mortal Engines* and *The Cyberiad* are serio-comic robot "fairy tales," satiric parodies of human avarice, cruelty, and stupidity. In them man figures only as a monster, a cosmic joke, a "paleface," but in fact the robots themselves are contemptible mirrors of human frailty and human fallibility. Throughout the stories, whether of a robotic "Sleeping Beauty," a pirate drowned in a paper sea of trivial information, soldiers plugged together for greater efficiency, or a tyrant ironically saved by his greed and suspicion but ultimately trapped in a dream about dreaming, two robot constructors tackle complex engineering problems and perform experiments that go awry. "The Mask," a powerful story of a robot programmed to kill the man she has come to love, verges on pathos, "The Dragons of Probability" toys with the laws of probability and the properties of subatomic particles, and "How Trurl's Own Perfection Led to No Good" involves a simulated world sadistically tormented by its builder. Here and elsewhere Lem tackles the question of artificial intelligence, suggesting that consciousness deserves respect but brings pain, error, and vice. In this whole set of witty, amusing works Lem finds a touch "of dry, mischievous Voltairean misanthropy" and "the despair and anger by the conduct of mankind" that motivates "the great humorists."

*Tales of Pirx the Pilot* also deals with man versus machines to question not only man's institutions and philosophies but even the value of his biological make-up. Astronaut Pirx is tough and courageous though unheroic, prosaic and bumbling but irresistible. His training mission teaches him the inadequacy of textbook knowledge and the importance of sheer guts, and his first mission shows the limits of technology and the need for close observation; each problem proves more difficult than the last, and his last adventure involves deciphering the final acts of a long dead crew from the encoded memories of a psychically wounded robot. In contrast, Hal Bregg of *Return from the Stars* is a worn-out astronaut, returning home after harrowing adventures only to find himself overpowered by changes on earth which make it alien and intimidating. He finds aggressions medically neutralized sophisticated robots in charge, social customs incomprehensible, and risk and challenge lost concepts; yet he learns to assert his humanity and to find love and meaning and a new life. Lem himself rejects this book as "primitive" and "false" in its treatment of eliminating social evils.

Clearly Lem enjoys variety and experimentation. His *Imaginary Magnitude* consists of introductions to nonexistent books, while *A Perfect Vacuum* has clever reviews of nonexistent books, including a review of Lem's reviews. *Dialogues* (1957) examines the potentials of cybernetics through Socratic dialogues, while *Provocation* (1981), which Lem describes as "a kind of science fiction," reviews a fictitious German historical text on "The Final Solutions Considered as Redemption," in which an historian/anthropologist hypothesizes about the role of mass death as a persistent cultural phenomenon.

*The Cosmic Carnival* provides a good panoramic selection of Lem's best, his range from realism to fantasy, from comedy to tragedy, from the technological to the poetic. Lem is fond of situations that lend themselves to multiple interpretations, dialectics that leave the final reality ambiguous. Mirrors, masks, and multiple levels add to the confusion and to the depth of his message. Double and triple puns, intentional ambiguities, codes, neologisms, cybernetic and futuristic jargon, and carefully selected proper names add to the fun and the potential possible interpretations. However, what is most important to him is science fiction as a laboratory for exploring new cognitive approaches, of thinking what has not yet been thought, of opening man's vision of himself—his potentials and his inescapable limitations—dark and surreal though it be.

—Gina Macdonald

---

**MAUROIS, André** (1885–1967). French. *The Next Chapter: The War Against the Moon*, 1927; *Voyage to the Island of the Articoles*, 1928; *A Private Universe* (stories), 1932; *The Thought-Reading Machine*, 1938; *The Weigher of Souls, and the Earth Dwellers*, 1963.

* * *

The scores of diverse books published by André Maurois show the varied experience and interests of the man. His family business of cloth manufacturing claimed his attention in early life, and World War I also delayed his full-time devotion to writing, thus helping to carry out the advice of his mentor, Emile Chartier, that he should experience the real world amply before turning to a life of literary creativity. Certainly his novels and short stories evince a mastery of human nature and profound understanding of the French and English character. His careful analysis and biographies of Percy and Mary Shelley, Charles Dickens, Honoré de Balzac, and other authors contributed further to this impression, as did his many works of history and commentary on modern affairs.

Maurois gave only a fraction of his literary attention to science fiction, and his typical works in this genre are novellas. In these, as always with Maurois, we see reflections of the universal curiosity to which he himself gives major credit for his successes. Always also there is the readiness to interpret discerningly. In *The Thought-Reading Machine* a professor makes a machine to detect the passing thoughts of the targeted persons, but Maurois discerns that transient thoughts are of quite limited value. In *Voyage to the Island of the Articoles* the author imagines a South Sea island society, but he is also satirizing the purblindness of his European contemporaries. Maurois's close acquaintance with H.G. Wells and with even more innovation-minded Frenchmen of his time did not prevent him from warning against rapid changes in society. He also warned of the destructiveness of then undeveloped "ray" and atomic weapons. *The Next Chapter* contemplates wars of genocidal scope—with 30 million deaths in 1947 alone. Equally imaginative, for 1927, is his description of the marshalling of the media to shape and control public opinion on a grand scale. The author's historical works show that he knew how this opinion-moulding had worked in the propaganda for the wars before 1927. The ambitious re-casting of national opinion is shown as the benevolent but arbitrary project of the powerful magnates who control the media of the world, and Maurois envisions unforeseen, even catastrophic, effects from this tampering with the outlook of the masses.

In quality, the science fiction of Maurois can be ranked among the early classics, with impressive insights into human affairs.

—Frank H. Tucker

---

**MAYAKOVSKY, Vladimir** (1893–1930). Russian. *The Bedbug* (play), 1960; *The Bathhouse*, in *Complete Plays*, 1968.

* * *

Vladimir Mayakovsky, the futurist poet and playwright, is one of the brightest stars in the great constellation of modern Russian literature. His paradoxical fusion of lyrical tenderness and oratorical violence marks a decisive change and renewal. Some of his works—even though, or perhaps because, only partly SF—are most representative of the embattled utopianism of the Soviet structure of feeling 1917–30. In poems such as "About It," "150,000,000," and "The Fifth International," in short propagandist pieces such as *Before and Now*, in film scenarios, and most clearly in his three post-revolutionary plays, the mainspring of Mayakovsky's creation was the tension between anticipatory utopianism and recalcitrant reality. An admirer of Wells and London, Mayakovsky wrote his witty masterpiece *Mystery Buffo* to celebrate the first anniversary of the October revolution, envisaging it as a second cleansing Flood in which the working classes, inspired by a poetic vision from the future, get successively rid of their masters, devils, heaven, and (in the 1921 version) economic chaos, and finally achieve a Terrestrial Paradise of reconciliation with Things around them. The revolution is thus both political and cosmic, it is an irreversible and eschatological, irreverent and mysterious, earthy and tender return to direct relationships of men with a no longer alien universe. No wonder that Mayakovsky's two later plays become satirical protests against the threatening separation of the classless heavens from the Earth. The future heavens of the sun-lit Commune remain the constant horizon of Mayakovsky's imaginative experiments, and it is by its values that the grotesque tendencies of petty-bourgeois restoration in *The Bedbug* or of bureaucratic degeneration in *The Bathhouse* are savaged. Indeed, in the second part of both plays, the future—though too vaguely imagined from scenic purposes—irrupts into the play. In *The Bedbug* it absorbs and quarantines the petty "bedbugus normalis" in its bestiary. In *The Bathhouse* the newly proclaimed Soviet Five-Year-Plan slogan of "Time forward!" materializes into the invention of a time machine that communicates with and leaps into the future, sweeping along the productive and the downtrodden characters but spewing out the bureaucrats. The victory over time was for Mayakovsky a matter of central political, cosmic, and personal importance: intrigued by Fyodorov and by Einstein's theory of relativity, he firmly expected it to make immortality possible for men. His suicide in 1930 cut him off in the middle of a fierce fight against the bureaucrats whom he envisaged as holding time back and who engineered the failure of Meyerhold's production of *The Bathhouse.*

—Darko Suvin

---

**NESVADBA, Josef** (1926– ). Czech. "The Last Secret Weapon of the Third Reich," in *The Year's Best S-F10*, edited by Judith Merril, 1965; "Mordair," in *Czech and Slovak Short Stories*, 1967; "The Planet Circè," in *New Writing from Czechoslovakia*, edited by George Theiner, 1969; "Vampire Ltd.," in *Other Worlds, Other Seas*, edited by Darko Suvin, 1970; *In the Footsteps of the Abominable Snowman* (stories), 1970 (as *The*

*Lost Face*, 1971); "Captain Nemo's Last Adventure," in *View from Another Shore*, edited by Franz Rottensteiner, 1973.

* * *

Josef Nesvadba is a practicing psychiatrist. Almost all of his stories are introverted, brooding, and hauntingly effective probings of humanist morality and the "small people" that inhabit the real world of modern, Soviet-dominated Czechoslovakia. Those stories which have appeared in English show his penchant for intellectual and psychological questions; Nesvadba's tales are rarely "upbeat" as they dig beneath appearances, peel away affectations, and discover a universality in man that transcends the hated memories of the Nazis, the heavy presence of Soviet power, and the occasionally wistful reflections about Britons and somewhat distant Americans.

One major collection has appeared in translation, *In the Footsteps of the Abmoninable Snowman.* The best in this assortment is "The Death of an Apeman," a wry retelling of the Tarzan story with a typical twist: the nobleman (German, not English) must commit suicide once he has learned what "civilized" men are like. "Expedition in the Opposite Direction" tells of time travel gone afoul, especially when one's sense of *déjà vu* cannot prevent the inevitable; "The Trial Nobody Ever Heard Of" focuses on petty scientists and their academic wars extrapolated by analogy into the Nazi murderers and their callous inhumanity; "The Lost Face" suggests that even plastic surgery cannot change essentials; "The Chemical Formula of Destiny" examines the uniqueness of genius; "Inventor of His Own Undoing" asks what would happen if everyone worked for fun; "Doctor Moreau's Other Island" grumpily predicts man's inevitable degeneracy; and the title story is a moving tale of wanderlust, perhaps indicative of Nesvadba's sense of isolation.

Other stories that have appeared in English include "Mordair," which suggests a cheap and inhumane solution to fuel costs; "Vampire Ltd.," a beautifully crafted tale of the soul-sucking qualities of the modern automobile; "Captain Nemo's Last Adventure," one of Nesvadba's best, showing the wanderlust and the eternal search for "The Fundamental Question of Life" and its "Final Answer"; "The Planet Circè," which examines the dangers of total indolence and complete satisfaction of childhood desires; and "The Last Secret Weapon of the Third Reich," which recalls the nightmare of the Nazi ability to pit Czech against Czech.

Nesvadba writes with great dexterity, and his stories deserve wider attention in the West. He represents a brand of science fiction quite distinct from either the Russian variety, which sometimes smothers good writing in the cocoon of socialistic theorizing, or from the American-British science fiction, which tends to focus on disasters (man-made or natural) or how heroes with mechanical know-how can undo cosmic evils. Nesvadba is a clear descendent in Czech literature of Hašek and perhaps Polacek, but not Capek. The zest of Capek's furious and ironic humor does not appear in Nesvadba's writing. The vision is narrowed, and Capek's wide-ranging internationalism has been replaced by a poignant sadness, an inner reflection of the fate of the Czech nation.

—John Scarborough

---

**RENARD, Maurice** (1875–1939). French. *New Bodies for Old*, 1923; *Blind Circle*, with Albert Jean, 1928; *The Hands of Orlac*, 1929; *The Flight of the Aerofix*, 1932.

* * *

Maurice Renard is considered a pioneer of French SF and one of the most important SF writers of the period 1910–30. His first novel, a wildly impressionist fantasy akin to Wells's *The Island of Dr. Moreau*, albeit with more overt sexuality that sometimes rises to strange ecstasies, was *New Bodies for Old*, in which the brain of the hero is transplanted into a bull by one of the proverbial mad scientists of science fiction; the novel ends with an even more fantastic identity change that brings to mind demoniac possession. A similar grafting experiment on a more modest scale (a pianist is given the hands of a criminal), but with hardly less gruesome consequences, appears in the more glib and weaker *The Hands of Orlac*, which is probably better known since it was filmed twice. In *L'Homme Truqué*, finally, a giant is given a pair of electric eyes which turns the world into a nightmarish vision. *Un Homme Chez les Microbes* is an elegant and sophisticated treatment of the journey into a microscopic world, a theme often mishandled in American SF by Ray Cummings. Renard's most ambitious novel, however, is *Le Pé ril Bleu*, an almost surrealist work with strong Fortean overtones. It introduces a strange civilization of ethereol lifeforms, the Oniweig, living on top of our atmosphere and fishing for objects in the air as we might fish the deep seas. They abduct humans and experiment with them, returning them to the surface of Earth only as a rain of picked bones and skeletons. Another SF novel is *Le Maître de la Lumière*, a fantastic mystery novel about duplicated bodies. His short stories tend towards the mystical and fantastic; a common theme is the relativity of perception, and their favorite device a distortion of perspective: time and space, other dimensions, mirrors, and changed sense organs figure prominently in them, and he is fond of joining together opposites, cold reason as well as feverish dreams.

—Franz Rottensteiner

---

**SERNINE, Daniel** (1955– ). Canadian. *Those Who Watch Over the Earth*, 1990; *Argus Steps In*, 1990.

* * *

Daniel Sernine is an extremely prolific writer and one of a handful who has taken the plunge and decided to be a full-time author in Québec. This he has been able to manage quite well, for Sernine writes all sorts of fiction, horror, fantastic, science fiction, and juvenile fiction.

He was one of the founders of the science-fiction magazine *Requiem* which, with *Imagine*, is an essential element in the successful establishment and development of a distinctly "Québécois" brand of science fiction. *Requiem*, later changed into *Solaris*, has been the most important source and inspiration for a typically Québécois (French-Canadian being a totally disused term in Québec in spite of a few works by writers from outside Québec) school of criticism. Daniel Sernine, along with Québécois writers such as Denis Côté and Suzanne Martel among others, has been keen to provide the young Québécois public with a science fiction literature it could identify with.

The series of Argus books is a successful example. The first two of them have been published in English translations: *Those Who Watch Over the Earth* and *Argus Steps In.* The series revolves around two youngsters, Marc and Carl, who have joined an organization, Argus, the purpose of which is to save earth from destroying itself. Argus is run by the Eryméens, extraterrestrials, whose pacific and political aims are the common thread to all the novels. In the second book two more heros are added, Cynthia and Francis. It is written in the shape of a whoddunit with a good dose of general documentary information.

Sernine's short stories have appeared in numerous anthologies of Québécois science fiction and contribute to his very strong presence on the Québec scene. His major work however is the novel *Les Méandres du temps,* which helped give Sernine the stature he deserved and showed his detractors that he had the ability to write long works and present us with heroes devoid of naiveness. At the time of its publication, *Les Méandres du temps* was one of the longest science-fiction novels published in Québec. It tells the story of Nicolas, a young telepath who accepts, under his adoptive father's pressure, to participate in a scientific experiment designed to test his unusual powers.

Similarly to the Eryméens in the Argus series, Nicolas is spotted by the Eryméens for his abilities; but more interestingly his past is linked with his future and his true origins that are not entirely terrestrial. Sernine does not shy away from difficult romantic and risqué scenes and shows real skill in their treatment.

Like the heroes of Charles Robert Wilson, another Canadian, Sernine's protagonists are endowed with telepathic and telekinetic powers. This emphasizes the involuntary (and perhaps unavoidable) similarities between the French-Canadian and English-Canadian schools of science fiction: an emphasis on the "soft" sciences such as psychology and the powers of the mind. Also, Sernine, like many of his Canadian contemporaries, concerns himself with the search for a better world.

Sernine's characters in *Les Méandres du temps* are put in very similar situations to the ones experienced by Marc and Cynthia in the Argus series. However, the comparison stops there. Sernine has managed to give a more complex psychology than the simplistic idealism that is the norm of juvenile fiction.

—Henry Leperlier

---

**STRUGATSKY, Boris** (1933– ), and **Arkady** (1925– ). Soviet. *Far Rainbow*, 1967; *Hard to Be a God*, 1973; *The Final Circle of Paradise*, 1976; *Monday Begins on Saturday*, 1977; *Roadside Picnic*, 1977; *Prisoners of Power*, 1977; *Tale of the Troika*, 1977; *Definitely Maybe*, 1978; *Noon: 22nd Century* (stories), 1978; *The Ugly Swans*, 1978; *Far Rainbow and The Second Invasion from Mars*, 1979; *The Snail on the Slope*, 1980; *Beetle in the Anthill*, 1980; *Space Apprentice*, 1981; *Escape Attempt*, 1982; *Aliens, Travelers and Other Strangers*, 1984.

* * *

Boris and Arkady Strugatsky, a Japanese/English specialist and translator, and a computer mathematician, astronomer, and astrophysicist, are the best known Russian science-fiction writers outside the Soviet Union. Widely translated, they have successfully merged science fiction with fable and fantasy to create future worlds that reflect our own. They bring to the genre linguistic versatility and wit (though some of their more masterly dialogues do not translate easily), an ability to make even minor fictive characters fully believable, a visual sense that makes descriptions of absurdities, heroism, and worlds in chaos live on in the mind's eye long after details of plot have faded away, and a political satire characterized by allegorical indirection. They rarely have their characters engage in full-fledged debate; instead, their technique is reminiscent of that of Spenser's *Fairie Queene* in its "kaleidoscopic" exploration of moral and social issues through enchanted lands reflective of ideas, values, theories, and mind sets, lands where the individual is tested, his values questioned, his potential explored. At times, there is a complex layering effect of meaning within meaning; at other times, what Westerners take as imaginative creativity (especially descriptions of complex bureaucracies) for Soviets is a thinly disguised description of an ongoing reality. For this reason some of the Strugatskys's works have been circulated only through the underground Soviet *samizdat.* (However, as of *ca.* 1989 all of their works have been available in the huge print runs usual for them.) The very Russian nature of the Strugatskys's characters and situations open up for Westerners a mind and a world that has for too long been closed.

The Strugatskys' early cycle—the triology *The Country of Crimson Clouds* (about a flight to Venus), *A Voyage to Amaltheia, The Space Apprentice*, and the short stories in *Six Matches* and *Noon: 22nd Century*—is an optimistic "future history" on or near Earth, a not quite systematic series with interlocking characters progressing through the next two centuries. For example, Leonid Gorbovsky, Captain of the spaceship Tariel in *Noon*, a kindly, intelligent man, ironical witty and human, a laconic expert whose actions reflect his high ethical values, makes the key decision in *Far Rainbow*, one that assures his own death, but he is later resurrected in "The Kid." Amid vivid, variegated surroundings, the young explorers and scientists in this adventure-packed series take action leading to ethical choice. In this first idyllic cycle, except for some surviving problems with egotism and with capitalism, conflicts take place between man and nature, "between the good and the better." The societies depicted, based on friendship, community, equality, shared property, and shared values, have overcome modern worries about overpopulation, pollution, and mechanical dehumanization, but still face human problems of man's limitations and failures, torments of conscience, boredom, and unhappiness. *Noon: 22nd Century* cleverly juxtaposes space travellers adjusting to utopia with four maturing indigenous youths questioning this future world, as they are taught to value work and teachers and to feel contempt for aggression and "sportsmanship." Some of these early tales focus on human frailty; the short stories of *Aliens, Travelers and Other Strangers* spoof the complications caused by a greedy time-travelling art collector or make wry comments on the space hero cult, while *Space Apprentice* focuses on the adventures of a galactic hitchhiker who sees greed, ambition, and jealousy dividing workers and threatening the security of communities and who finally sacrifices his life for knowledge. It is such frailty that darkens the somewhat aseptically bright horizons.

The dialectics of innocence and experience, of utopian ethics and historical destructiveness provide the Strugatskys's main tension in their second phase (1962–65). In *Escape Attempt* a tourist hunting holiday leads to a brutal planet where barbaric masters force enslaved masses, made subhuman by cruel abuse, to test out alien weaponry, machinery that moves endlessly across a frozen wasteland. Communication and assistance prove impossible due to divergent *a priori* premises, and even attack proves futile. This interest in utopian ethics tested through inhuman and apparently irresistible destruction continues in the Strugatskys' first masterpieces, *Far Rainbow* and *Hard to Be a God.* All three books involve a theme the Strugatskys explore throughout their canon, that of interference in the history of an alien planet, and of the moral, logical, and social problems arising therefrom. On the small planet Far Rainbow, a physical Black Wave, unintentionally produced by a joyous community of experimenting creators, destroys them in a clear historical parable. Setting in opposition the selfish and the self-sacrificing, the novel focuses on the decisions involved in the final 24 hours before destruction: whether to rely on cold logic and preserve the knowledge stored on the planet or to act humanely and irrationally and save the children, the biological future. Almost all remaining heroes of the first cycle die here; only the children, and the mysterious deathless man-robot Kamill (a lonely and powerless Reason, which has purposefully reduced its human frailties), survive. *Hard to Be a God*, a very successful and highly popular SF version of the historical novel, faces the conflict between utopia and militant philistinism, stupidity, and social entropy; the result is rich and subtle. The hero is an emissary from classless Earth to a feudal planet, instructed to observe without interfering. However, the Earth historians' projection of progress turns out to be wrong; organized obscurantism is killing off intellectuals and destroying all human values, and even the agent interveners find themselves seduced by the violence of their milieu. The planet triggers readers' memories of human history as the worst excesses of the medieval, the fascist, and the Stalinist merge (ignorance, superstitious hatred of intelligence, violence, and oppression; a militant church, stormtroopers and bandits), and revolt simply leads to more calamity. Outside interference would introduce a new benevolent dictatorship, but the Earthling "gods" are trapped in a dilemma—their humanism and ethical sense compel them to reduce suffering and to save those they love and respect, yet in so doing they will introduce weapons that will be misused, and will push the planet's progress forward so rapidly that its inhabitants will be deprived of their own history, a history that would humanize them and that would form the dark base for their brighter future.

A cautionary tale, *The Final Circle of Paradise* (originally *Predatory Things of Our Age!)* at first seems to return to the anticipatory universe of the first cycle as it delineates an apparent utopia: democratic, peaceful, unified, and abundantly wealthy. However, this "utopia" proves a spiritually regressive dystopia, wherein humanity, freed from historic problems, becomes endangered by too much ease and a new hedonism summed up in "slug," a mysterious addictive substance that provides instant pleasures but that destroys thought, that creates an aversion to books, culture, and art of any sort, and that binds man in a dehumanizing cycle of self-gratification. As fanatics rampage against museums, the protagonist, a Soviet cosmonaut turned UN agent, flushes out demoralizing pleasure centers and seeks to overcome them through education and conflict. The ending is left open, the outcome uncertain, the warning clear.

Running into increasing political pressures, the Strugatskys opted in their third phase (1965–68) for parables with more pronounced satirical overtones, ones characterized by a formal mastery of technique and an interest in sociological confusions. The protagonists provide a privileged point of view, often a naive glance at a disharmonious world with monopolized information channels. A follow-up to the invasion recorded in H.G. Wells's *War of the Worlds, The Second Invasion from Mars* lampoons capitalism as selling man's soul (and body) for short-term profit. In his diary of the Martian invasion, the protagonist, a philistine busybody, happily records his submission to the new Martian bosses, who enslave and conquer by using local traitors, economic corruption, misinformation, and capitalistic business practices, instead of heat rays and gases. Renewable human body fluids (much prized by Martians) become big business, and only the active opposition of the strongly independent can possibly keep the human race from becoming—for economic gain—the Martians' dumb, complacent sheep. The work is infused with details that relate the action directly to Soviet society: long shopping lines, farmers touted for productivity, incomprehensible news reports of new wheat deals, ill-will toward returning POWs, alcoholism, persecution of the press, sleek black KGB Volgas, and the self-serving rationalizations of privileged party bosses. However, the use of names out of Greek mythology to add another layer of meaning is unconvincing.

In the two interlocked stories of *The Snail on the Slope* protagonists painfully struggle to understand a fantastic and symbolic forest seen indistinctly from inside and outside. The "Kandid" narrator's stream of consciousness is replete with rural idioms, as infuriatingly repetitive and monotonous as the life whose flavor they convey: a "vegetable way of life," bereft of history and subject to unknown destructive forces, a dearth of information and the impossibility of generalizing. The "Pepper" narrator views the forest from the perspective of the Kafkaesque bureaucracy supposedly managing it. The two protagonists come to stand for the alternatives of modern intellectuals faced with power: accommodation versus refusal. A culmination of the Strugatskys' escape from politics into ethics, the novel is among their most interesting creations, and the Kandid part a gem of contemporary Russian literature. The jargonate nonsense of Directorate communications, images of blindfolded men seeking a lost classified machine whose sight is forbidden, and descriptions of meaningless and contradictory processes and inexplicable political maneuverings—an historical accumulation of absurdities—are set off against an incomprehensible, chaotic forest of organic anomalies (faceless men, disappearing villages, mermaids, Amazonian Maidens, "Swampings," "Harrowings," and "deadlings"); in other words, annihilation for the sake of control contends with the inexplicable and frightening chaos of Nature. The Strugatskys compare man's journey toward knowledge to that of a snail climbing Mount Fugi—limited, uncertain, myopic.

*The Ugly [Nasty] Swans*, only recently published in the U.S.S.R., merges a real past/present (a feudal system, quarreling police factions, paramilitary Fascists, an ingrown bureaucracy) and a fantastic future (multiplying "rainmen," sudden metamorphoses, reborn children, a mysterious "Voice" from the fog, whiskey turned to water) in its depiction of a Shchedrinian satiric city whose persistent rainfall signifies the end of a morally corrupt society. The setting is the West, but the capital is Moscow, and unrelenting fog obscures all. Mutant "lepers," midwives of the "New," prove sinister pied-pipers, helping children evolve to a higher, more just intelligence and leading them from a limited, corrupt past to a transformed future. Contradictions and metamorphoses are the essence of this novel, whose title is a counterproject to Hans Christian Andersen's optimistic fairy tale. As in the former novel, the puzzles are left unsolved; all we can infer from the final exodus of the children, through the hardboiled, polemical vernacular and the ambiguous protagonist (a politically suspect writer who embodies a spirit of opposition), is that our species is doomed. Stanislaw Lem believes *Ugly Swans* is about the Jewish diaspora—but, if so, "we are all Jews," as a Russian poet remarked.

*Monday Begins on Saturday* and its sequel, *Tale of the Troika*, are linked by a shared main character, but the first is "fairy tales of junior scientists" while the second is more darkly satiric. The Strugatskys' updating of folktale to embody the "magic" of modern alienated sciences and society results in a loose picaresque work ranging from fabulistic fun to the Goyaesque horrors of charlatanism and bureaucratic power. *Monday* deals primarily with the misuse and abuse of science by incompetents, profiteerers, and immovable bureaucrats. Science is reduced to magic tricks. The director of the Scientific Institute for Magic, studying human happiness, has split into a present scientist and a future administrator who lives backward in time; the demagogic charlatan Vybegallo plans a happy Universal Consumer but his homunculus is destroyed just short of consuming the universe. This work also spoofs both Soviet and Western SF, with their utopias, their time machines, and their robot wars. *Troika* shows a bureaucratic triumvirate "rationalizing" a country of unexplained phenomena. The Troika's semiliterate jargon and fossilized pseudo-democratic slogans, its incompetent quid pro quos and malapropisms, make for wildly hilarious black humor. Somewhat uneven, this is perhaps the Strugatskys' weightiest experiment.

The post-1968 novels can be thought of as their fourth phase, somber and uneven, often of adolescent heroics amid increasing alienation and desperation. *Prisoners of Power* is a very good adventure wherein the utopian protagonist, a Terran explorer marooned on a planet wasted by nuclear holocaust and hence beset by genetic degeneration, fights a Nazi-style military dictatorship and its new persuasion technologies. However, to change this world, with its Cold War rivalries and brinkmanship strategies, he too must change, experience its cruelties and ignorance, unravel its mysteries. The masterly depiction of various social strata bereft of history, the insights into both oligarchy and underground politics, and the pessimistic vision of terrible methods employed for the best of motives undercut the idea of a superhero and a happy ending. In *Beetle in the Anthill* the choice is again between ethics and survival; a space explorer is suspected of being programmed by aliens to destroy the human race. The racy mystery, told by a confused Terran security officer, ends with the security chief, an ex-space hero, murdering the suspect—just in case. *Hotel "To the Lost Climber"*, *Kid from Hell*, and *Space Mowgli* are entertaining lightweights. The first is a mystery with a SF twist involving alien robots with strange powers. In the second, humane interference in a grotesque war between equally violent societies produces a limited peace, but failure to truly change a trained killer from one of the societies, after prolonged intellectual and emotional contact, suggests conflict is inevitable, people cannot be changed, peace is doomed. In the third, a "wolfchild" tale, contact with a humanoid—modified for survival and raised to manhood by an incomprehensible alien life form—raises false hopes of bridging the gulf between human and alien. The most challenging work of this period is *Roadside Picnic*, simultaneously a "first contact" SF story, folktale, utopian quest, and psychological novel, with a rich array of viewpoints and vernaculars. In it Earthlings seek meaning (and power) amid the strange and dangerous discarded trash of unknown and indifferent cosmic travelers, trash that causes extreme deviations from statistical norms, incomprehensible causal connections, mutations, and wildly divergent theorizing. The story centers on one of the blackmarketeers, "Red" Schuhart, a daring rogue who penetrates the alien Zones to steal artifacts and to perhaps find knowledge/salvation but whose attainment (at great sacrifice) of an alien Golden Ball said to grant all wishes produces only an ineffective wish for general happiness. The alien influence is catalytic, showing up man as greedy and ignorant, ingenious and courageous. Through Dr. Pilman, a senior physicist, the Strugatskys suggest an absurdist universe upon which man imposes unrealistic theories that fit his preconceptions. In *Definitely Maybe*, a farcical but chilling fragmented parable verging on the supernatural, an unknown force disrupts (in peculiar ways) the lives, work, and happiness of the world's leading scientists, whose groping hypotheses blame a supercivilization and/or the universal laws of nature for holding human advancement in check and for controlling destiny. Critics suggest a subtext about KGB harassment and dissident choices. The somber prevails, but the tough-minded clarity of relationships and a glimmer of utopian brightness persist.

Through a series of letters, memoranda, interrogations, and reports, *The Time Wanderers* traces the attribution of a series of unexplained events (disorder in the world of whales, mass phobias like "fukamiphobia", statistical anomalies, the sudden development of new talents and extraordinary abilities, the unexplained disappearance and reappearance of people, conflicting interpretations of alien encounters) to alien "Wanderers" who cross through time, testing human beings for those with a hidden potential ("the third impulse") and a tolerance of others that will allow transformation to a higher consciousness. In fact, all that is inexplicable is blamed, perhaps erroneously, on "The Wanderers" though, as one character puts it, there "are no answers and never will be." There is a 400-million year old giant Silurian mollusk with a poisonous biofield, Embryophores from which emerge quasibiological creatures, an Institute of Eccentrics, and double mentograms (two or more independent consciousnesses in one body), but the central questions posed through all the oddities are whether any being has the right to interfere in the lives and evolutions of others and whether man is doomed to a mental schism between xenophobes fearful of alien contact and more kindly, more tolerant humans who see in aliens their own pains and joys.

Some of their latest long novels, notably *Lame Destiny* incorporating *The Ugly Swan*), *The Doomed City* (one of their peaks;), and the *Bulgakovian Burdened by Evil* (not SF) have not yet been translated into English. They will add significantly to the Strugatskys' reputation.

The Strugatskys's work is at the heart of Soviet SF; its polemic acted as an aesthetic and ideological icebreaker. From static utopian brightness in a near future they have moved through a return to the complex dynamics of history to an unresolvable tension between the necessity of utopian ethics and the inhuman inscrutable powers of anti-utopian stasis. There are deficiencies in their vision: the junction of ethics with either politics and philosophy has remained unclear, the localization of events has been erratic; the socio-philosophic criticism has sometimes fitted only loosely into the SF framework. Their writing is at times obscure, at times consciously illogical and untidy. Nonetheless, half a dozen of their works approach major literature. Their later phases are a legitimate continuation of the Gogal vein and of the great Soviet tradition of Ilf and Petrov or Olesha, at the borders of SF and satirical fantasy, as in Mayakovsky's late plays, Lem, Kafka, or Carroll. The Strugatskys's work has some of George Orwell's fascination with language—a mimicry of bureaucratic and fanatic jargon, irony and parody, colloquialisms and neologisms. Their satire of officialese is masterful, as is their control of conversational idiom. They are polemical at the deepest level of wordcraft and vision, making untenable what they termed the "fiery banalities" of the genre.

The Strugatskys's works are full of humor, irony, exciting action, and a clear sense of historical inevitability. They infuse scientific and technological elements with typically Russian ones, from dachas to central committees. They mix historical realities and future settings (and often seem indifferent to the precise motivation of their story's framework). In *Escape Attempt*, for example, a central character turns out to be an escapee from a Nazi concentration camp flung into a "better" future by sheer will power, only to find history a blind alley. The Strugatskys introduce characters *in medias res* and leave readers gradually to work out relationships. The main characters are complex, introspective—at times contradictory—in nature; they are changed by events, and grow and evolve with experience.

Within the Russian tradition, the best of the later Strugatskys reads like an updating of Shchedrin's fabulistic chronicle of "Foolsville." However, their hero and ideal reader is the contemporary scientific and cultural intellectual, the reader of Voznesensky and Voltaire, Wiener, and Wells. The Strugatskys's argue the value of education in their works and praise young scientist-citizen-activists who are inner-directed by and toward "constant cognition of the unknown." However, they deplore man's failure to live up to his potential, and are cynical about the possibility of a progress bound by perverse strictures of power and prejudice. They warn against pat solutions and the enemy within man himself. Ultimately, through indirection, they seek to both "profit and delight." The Strugatskys's ethics of cognition springs from a confluence of utopianism and modern philosophy of science. With all its oscillations from bright to somber horizons, such a confluence transcends Russian borders, explains their international following, and marks their rightful place in world SF and literature.

—Gina Macdonald and Darko Suvin

---

**TOLSTOY, Alexey** (1882–1945). Russian. *The Deathbox*, 1934 (as *The Garin Death Ray*, 1955); *Aelita*, 1957.

* * *

Alexey Tolstoy published two collections of poetry before he turned away from both verse and Symbolism to stories and novels in the tradition of 19th-century Realism. He emigrated to Germany after the Bolshevik revolution, but returned to Russia in 1923 and became a leading and privileged exponent of the official Socialist Realism, especially in a number of historical novels.

Tolstoy became the first classic writer of Russian SF by giving the fast-developing genre the accolade of literary quality and respectability, much as his model Wells did. In *Aelita* this blend is enriched with a lyrical component, the love of Los, the inventor of the rocketship, for the Martian princess Aelita. Los, the creative intellectual, with his vacillations and individualist concerns, is contrasted to but also allied with Gusev, a shrewd man of the people and fearless fighter who leads the revolt of Martian workers (the Martians are descendants of the Atlantans) against the decadent dictatorship of the Engineers' Council. If the standard adventure and romance were taken over from Wells and pulp SF (e.g., Benoit's *Atlantis* and Burroughs's *A Princess of the Moon*) or indeed from theosophy, the politics are diametrically opposed to Lasswitz's and Bogdanov's idea of a Martian benevolent technocracy. Yet if the workers' uprising led by a Red Army man was a clear parable for the times, such as could have been shared by all Soviet SF from Mayakovsky to Zamyatin, the dejected and somewhat hasty return which has Los listening at the end to the desperate wireless calls of his beloved is clearly of a Wellsian gloom (*The First Men in the Moon*). But this ambiguity, which sometimes strains the plot mechanics, makes also for an encompassing of differing attitudes and levels that follows Bogdanov by envisaging the price as well as the necessity of an activist happiness. This is achieved by plastic characterization, differentiated language, and consistent verisimilitude.

Tolstoy's second novel, *The Deathbox* (four versions from 1926 to 1937), is a retreat to the "catastrophe" novel: Vernean adventures and Chestertonian detections and conspiracies revolve around a well-drawn amoral scientist who beats the capitalist industry kings at their own game but comes to grief when faced with popular revolt. It moves fast if jerkily; as Tolstoy had training in engineering, its science is believable (atomic disintegration of a transuranium element is posited as well as something resembling lasers), and it remains a prototype of the anti-imperialist and antifascist satire-thriller melodrama, always a vigorous strand in Russian SF. The two novels, as well as the stories "Blue Cities" and "The League of the Five" and several plays (including an adaptation of Capek's *R.U.R.*), blended SF adventures (interplanetary flight, the revolt of machines, or global struggle for a new scientific invention) with a utopian pathos arising from revolutionary social perspectives in a way calculated to please almost all segments of the reading public. This blend was to remain the basic Soviet SF tradition until Yefremov, and indeed through the end of the 1960's.

—Darko Suvin

---

**TSIOLKOVSKY, Konstantin** (1857–1935). Russian. *Beyond the Planet Earth*, 1960; *The Call of the Cosmos* (miscellany), 1963.

* * *

Konstantin Tsiolkovsky lost most of his hearing as a boy, and grew up a lonely eccentric. He became a provincial teacher, writing scientific papers all the while—particularly on aeronautics (from balloons to jet aircraft) and interplanetary travel. A self-made mathematician, he often rediscovered already known hypotheses; yet he also created the theory of rocket flight for interplanetary space (formula for attaining cosmic velocities). Disregarded before the revolution, he was elected to the Socialist Academy in 1918 and given a pension in 1921, when he devoted himself entirely to writing. His SF tales *On the Moon* and *Beyond the Planet Earth* and his anticipatory fictionalized essays bordering on SF, *Dreams of Earth and Heaven: The Effects of Universal Gravitation*, as well as some other anticipatory essays, are collected in *The Call of the Cosmos*, while other essays are collected in *Life in Interstellar Environment;* a number of utopian visions, notably *Sorrow and Genius*, have been relatively slighted.

The deep-seated obsession in all of Tsiolkovsky's writings is liberation from earthly and indeed universal gravity. The cosmic alternative—on rocket spaceships, satellite stations, asteroids, or space colonies—is accompanied by diverse aspects of bliss: perpetual Spring, physical ease and health, utopian-socialist democracy, unheard-of technological achievements, "heavenly life without sorrow," and finally immortality—possibly for individuals and certainly for the human species moving from sun to sun through billions of years. When touching on such a cluster of beatific desires Tsiolkovsky's clear but very pedestrian style rises to passages of a naive poetry, e.g., in descriptions of life-forms on the low-gravity Moon. This is also what makes for the peculiar hybrid genre of these writings, oscillating between fantastic idea and scientific (or popularizing) prose, with the stories just on this and the essays just on that side of an imaginary halfway house. Visionary essays seem the primary form of his expression, while the tales are primarily an attempt at reaching a wider readership. Thus even their clumsy plots and non-existent characterizatoin are an interesting testimonial to the genesis of one kind of SF, the "literature of ideas" (in Tsiolkovsky, this embraces also speculations on "etheric" beings, on a photonic phase of mankind and universe, on reversing entropy).

The main literary influences on Tsiolkovsky seem to have been the eccentric Russian philosopher of cosmic utopianism and this-worldly resurrection N.F. Fyodorov, Verne, and Flammarion. In his turn, he stands behind all Soviet writings on cosmic travel, in fiction from Tolstoy and Belyaev to Yefremov and Altov, and in science from Oberth and others down to the Sputnik and Vostok constructors. He remains one of the great pioneers of modern SF, particularly important for his refusal to discriminate between utopia and science.

—Darko Suvin

---

**VARSHAVSKY, Ilya** (1909– ). Russian. "In Man's Own Image," in *Russian Science Fiction 1968*, edited by Robert Magidoff, 1968; "Out in Space," in *Last Door to Aiya*, edited by Mirra Ginsburg, 1968; "A Raid Takes Place at Midnight," in *Russian Science Fiction 1969*, edited by Robert Magidoff, 1969; "Preliminary Research," in *The Ultimate Threshold*, edited by Mirra Ginsburg, 1970; "Biocurrents, Biocurrents," "Lectures on Parapsychology," "The Noneaters," and "Somp," in *Other Worlds, Other Seas*, edited by Darko Suvin, 1970; "Robby," in *Path into the Unknown*, 1973; "Escape," in *Best SF 1973*, edited by Harry Harrison and Brian Aldiss, 1974.

* * *

Ilya Varshavsky's main interests are thinking machines, space travel, and advanced medical and mechanical technology. His attitude toward science is generally humorous or ironic, but at times bitingly satiric or questioning. He expresses nostalgia for the beauty and spirit of the 20th century.

Varshavsky's machines are subject not only to the laws of mathematical logic but to those of self-organization, which demand that robots eventually develop the impulses and drives of humans. For example, when confronted with "death," they are impelled to reproduce themselves ("Homunculus"); rather than harm their robot children, they choose a life of frustration ("Conflict"); thoughts of soccer and redheads can subvert them ("The Duel"); like any vocabulary-gifted human, they can develop into pompous, abusive, tricky, intellectually perverse beings ("Robby"). Of interest to Varshavsky is the relationship between language and humanness, as well as the obstacles to a robot's thinking processes posed by connotation, non-objective reality, and accidental characteristics.

Varshavsky uses space travel to examine his ideas on closed-circuit systems (animal organisms in "The Noneaters"; time in "The Trap"); the effects of man on other life forms ("Lilac Planet"; "The Noneaters"); the continuity of human qualities, from petty to heroic ("The Return"). He twits simpleton-scientists ("Somp"; "Lectures on Parapsychology"; "A Raid Takes Place at Midnight"); castigates those who sell their minds to blind projects ("Preliminary Research"); and satirizes science-fiction writers who do anything for a plot. He questions both means and ends of psycho-scientists ("Escape") and ponders the human complications of organ transplants ("Plot for a Novel").

—Rosemary Coleman

---

**VERCORS.** Pseudonym for Jean Bruller (1902–91). French. *You Shall Know Them*, 1953 (as *Borderline*, 1954; as *The Murder of the Missing Link*, 1955); *The Insurgents*, 1956; *Sylva*, 1962.

* * *

Although never really considered a genre writer, Vercors contributed two interesting and well-crafted novels to the field. *Sylva* is a poetic fantasy about a fox that changes magically into a human woman before the eyes of a hunter. The man falls in love with this wereperson, but the peculiarities of her origin provide rather unusual stresses in their married life. *Sylva* bears more than a passing resemblance to David Garnett's fantasy *Lady into Fox*, though with a more coherent plot. There are traces of satire as well, much in the tradition of John Collier's *His Monkey Wife* or Mikhail Bulgakov's *Heart of a Dog*. But Vercors is less a humorist than a novelist, and his novel portrays a touching love story that transcends the gimmick that might otherwise seem central to the story.

At the same time, *Sylva* reflects the concerns mentioned in his more significant novel, *You Shall Know Them*. We are told in the latter that "all man's troubles arise from the fact that we do not know what we are and do not agree on what we want to be." The relevance to the lady into fox theme is obvious, but the statement has equal validity when applied to the latter novel. A thoughtful man becomes aware of the existence of a sub-human race on Earth, the legendary missing link in our own evolutionary climb. Concerned about their exploitation by the rest of humanity, he embarks on a bizarre course to determine their legal humanity. He sires a child which he then kills, confessing himself a murderer and surrendering to the authorities. The stage is hereby set for a precedent-setting murder trial, for if the protagonist is indeed guilty of murder, then the sub-humans must be considered our equals and be protected by the law. If they are not to be considered as human, then he has not in fact committed anything worse than cruelty to animals. In conception, this is one of the finest novels in the genre, establishing and examining a genuine ethical question with ruthless realism. At the same time, it is a well-balanced, craftily written tale that should appeal to all readers. Indeed, the novel has been marketed as a mystery, which in at least one sense it is. But it is also that most rare of creations, a novel of science fiction that tells us something about ourselves and our society.

Only one other of Vercors's novels can truly be said to be science fiction. *The Insurgents* chronicles one man's search for physical immortality, and the perils and prices inherent in both the search and the attainment. Thematically, it is remarkably similar to Aldous Huxley's *After Many a Summer*, and in some ways is more effectively handled.

—Don D'Ammassa

---

**VERNE, Jules** (1828–1905). French. *Five Weeks in a Balloon*, 1869; *From the Earth to the Moon*, 1869, complete version, 1873 (as *The American Gun Club*, 1874; as *The Baltimore Gun Club*, 1874) (sequels: *All Around the Moon*, 1876; *The Purchase of the North Pole*, 1890); *A Journey to the Centre of the Earth*, 1871; *Twenty Thousand Leagues under the Sea*, 1872; *Doctor Ox and Other Stories*, 1874; *A Floating City, and The Blockade Runners*, 1874; *From the Clouds to the Mountains*, 1874 (as *Dr. Ox's Experiment*, n.d.); *The Mysterious Island: Shipwrecked in the Air* (as *Dropped from the Clouds*), *Abandoned*, *The Secret of the Island*, 3 vols., 1874–75; *The Voyages and Adventures of Captain Hatteras: The English at the North Pole, The Field of Ice*, 2 vols., 1874–76; *Hector Servadoc*, 1877 (as *To the Sun*, 1878; as *Off on a Comet*, 1957; as *Homeward Bound*, 1965; as *Anomalous Phenomena*, 1965); *The Begum's Fortune*, 1879 (as *500 Millions of the Begum*, 1879); *The Steam House; The Demon of Cawnpore, Tigers and Traitors*, 2 vols., 1881; *The Clipper of* *the Clouds*, 1887 (as *Robur the Conqueror*, 1887; as *A Trip Around the World in a Flying Machine*, 1887) (sequel: *Master of the World*, n.d.); *Adventures of a Chinaman in China*, 1889; *The Winter amid the Ice and Other Stories*, 1890; *The Castle of the Carpathians*, 1893; *The Floating Island*, 1896 (as *Propeller Island*, 1961); *For the Flag*, 1897 (as *Facing the Flag*, 1897); *An Antarctic Mystery*, 1898 (as *The Mystery of Arthur Gordon Pym*, 1960); *The Chase of the Golden Meteor*, 1909 (as *Hunt for the Meteor*, 1965); *The Master of the World*, 1914; *The Lottery Ticket, and The Begum's Fortune*, 1919; *The Barsac Mission; The City in the Sahara, Into the Niger Bend*, 2 vols., 1960; *Village in the Treetops*, 1964.

* * *

The key biographical fact in Jules Verne's life, for the understanding of his *voyages extraordinaires*, is his induction, at the height of his fame, into the French Legion of Honor by none other than Ferdinand de Lesseps, builder of the Suez Canal and a disciple of Henri Saint-Simon. Saint-Simon is the pre-Marxist patriarch of socialism, whose disciples coined the very word for "socialism," and who meant by it what we mean by the word "technocracy." They worshipped industrial production as a world-wide process, not merely the international proletarian worker as in later Marxism, and their slogan was "The whole world belongs to mankind." Their romantic globalism is captured in Verne's most famous novel, *Around the World in Eighty Days.* The Saint-Simonians were apostles of world transport and a world-industrial civilization, to which the Suez Canal was a programmatic contribution.

Their view was that the industrial revolution would make for the socialist revolution, replacing the feudalistic love of war with peaceful production, and Catholic theology with science; thereby uniting mankind in universal association for the exploitation of nature, instead of being divided for the exploitation of nature, instead of being divided for the exploitation of man by man. Verne's great novelization of this doctrinal thesis is *From the Earth to the Moon.*

Verne wrote this novel during the fourth year of the American Civil War. As a Saint-Simonian socialist, he pondered on American wartime technology, wondering how it might be converted to peacetime industry. How redirect these destructive energies into a creative project? His answer, as the war concluded, was symbolically to melt down its entire arsenal of cannons in the casting of the *Columbiad* for the peaceful colonization of space and the development of interplanetary travel. But the moonshot is not America's project alone.

While a civilian spinoff of her military technology, the Baltimore Gun Club that initiated the project raises funds for it from a world-wide subscription. All humanity is drawn into it with a collective enthusiasm. The Gun Club itself is internationalized on the model of the Council of Newton—the name Saint-Simon gave the brain center of his technocratic council of world direction—as it calls upon scientific talent wherever it is to be found, including the world's astronomers to track the moon capsule in flight. Moreover, the Gun Club's council of directors wins to its purpose the happy collaboration of the American work force, organized on a gigantic scale as one national workshop of united interests. This is a harbinger of Saint-Simon's prophecy: "All men shall work; they will regard themselves as laborers attached to one workshop and whose efforts will be directed by the supreme Council of Newton.

In its exalted atmosphere of class collaboration between captains of industry and the proletarian workers, all this in the service of man's harmonious conquest of nature, the novel is a technocratic hymn to the partnership of knowledge and work, science and labor. The arts of war are again translated into peaceful production in Verne's model mining community, Coal City, in *Black Diamonds.* Coal City is a veritable military colony, where its miners live and work together inside the mine itself, a huge underground cavern lit by the promethian light of electricity. Here they live with and for their work, under the direction of their chief engineer, a former army engineer, together constituting "a peaceful army of labor" that toils in harmony and collective joy. With their division of labor modeled after that of the armed forces, they are able to realize the ideals of fraternity and equality. All are united in "one big family with the same interests."

So, too, in *The Mysterious Island.* The scientifically versatile army engineer, Capt. Cyrus Harding, leads the survivors of a balloon crash to salvation through endurance and their zeal for hard work, epitomizing the Saint-Simonian motto, "Down with idlers." The island is a microcosm of the socialist utopia, the well-regulated and fraternal cooperation of humanity in the exploitation of the globe in the light of scientific knowledge. At the end of the novel, Capt. Nemo appears, and gives them his blessing after they have proved themselves by their readiness for labor. "You love this island," he says on his deathbed in his submarine. "You have changed it by your efforts and it is truly yours."

Capt. Nemo's all-electric submarine is itself a miniature Saint-Simonian world, with its crew of international sailors who speak a universal synthetic language. Observing their grim and robotlike round of tireless work under Capt. Nemo's direction, Ned Land in *Twenty Thousand Leagues Under the Sea* suspects that they, too, are "run by electricity." Their work, however, is not peaceful production; it is making war for peace, the business of sinking British ships, punishing them for their nation's world-dividing colonial wars. In this Capt. Nemo is like the hero of *Robur the Conqueror* and *The Master of the World.* He does his vengeance by smiting the world's warships from out of the sky in his airplane, *The Terro*, by way of enforcing the union of nations and a cooperative oneness in the "economic and political ways of the world." For the whole world belongs to mankind.

—Leon Stover

---

**VONARBURG, Elisabeth** (1947– ). Canadian. *The Silent City*, 1988.

* * *

Elisabeth Vonarburg has long been a very well-known participant on the Canadian science-fiction scene. She has been one of the founding members of the very serious Magazine *Solaris*, in which she published many of her short stories. She has been a prime mover in the establishment of a French Canadian school of science fiction and its blossoming into a unique Québécois independent current of culture. If many of her short stories are unavailable in English translations, we are lucky enough to have an English version of her major work, *The Silent City.*

*The Silent City* is an original and important work in the field of international science fiction for its treatment of androgyny. Like much Canadian science fiction, *The Silent City* takes place in a post-cataclysmic world. Scientists have taken refuge in an enclosed city to isolate and protect themselves from the barbaric humans who continue to exist outside and whose genes, altered through the effects of radiation, have a detrimental effect on their life expectancy and general physical health. One of the most damning consequences is an inability to produce more than one boy for nine girls.

In the city, a crazy scientist named Paul decides to create a new super race that should be endowed with the powers of self-regeneration and self-healing tending to immortality. He succeeds in creating Elisa who, after his death, will continue his project. She manages to transmit one of her most extraordinary powers: the faculty to transform herself into a man and vice-versa. Elisa can become a man and then experience all that a man goes through, including sexual desire and intercourse. What is important is that as a man she can remember the feelings she had as a woman and turning herself back into a woman again she is not the woman she was before her transformation. She manages to create several new generations of offspring from her own genes capable of metamorphosis at will.

Vonarburg appears extremely concerned with the equality of the sexes and sees it coming through a bisexual integration, if not physical (as it is described with finesse in the novel), at least sensual and psychological. Contrary to much of contemporary science fiction, in *The Silent City* technology is dependent on the psychologies of the characters. Technological gadgets are reduced to a minimum and the working of all medical procedures is barely sufficient to make it credible. As much of Vonarburg seems at ease in the dual male/female aspect of our personalities, she seems to be unwilling to give a fully complete description of the actual working of the "City" and its everyday working when she feels that they are not relevant to the story. There is a lot of space for at least two other novels: one that could tell us about the genesis of the "City," another that could fill up the unsatisfactory ending: one is not quite sure that the main protagonists will be able to fulfill their destiny. The children are not compelled to become a fusion of the two sexes. Rather, they are encouraged to explore the two personalities, female and male, and then choose what they think is their real self. Such a process does not seek to do away with the differences between the sexes: on the contrary, it furthers the existing distinctions while creating a natural desire for empathy.

One of the most promising aspects and, at the same time most frustrating, is that *The Silent City* poses as many questions as it attempts to resolve. The sexual difference between men and women leads in the novel to the desire of each group to dominate the other rather than to seek any sort of accommodation. This confrontation is resolved through an effort to accept that everyone is capable, to a certain extent, of acquiring some traits of the other sex. What is lacking, however, is a description of the process that will eventually lead to it rather than fanciful wishful thinking on the part of the protagonists.

Vonarburg shows us that our bisexuality is a key to inner knowledge and that all of us could benefit from some empathy with the other sex. If only for that reason, *The Silent City* is a unique work that will, hopefully, spawn other works of exploration in the same subject.

—Henry Leperlier

---

**WITKIEWICZ, Stanislaw** (1885–1939). Wrote as Witkacy. Polish. *Insatiability*, 1977; plays—*The Madman and the Nun and Other Plays*, 1968; *The Cuttlefish*, in *Treasury of the Theatre 2*, edited by Bernard F. Dukore and John Gassner, 1969; *Tropical Madness: Four Plays*, 1972.

* * *

Labelled old-fashioned by his peers but *avant-garde* and prophetic by modern critics, a precursor of the Theater of the Absurd, a forewarner of Hitler-like aberrations and Red Chinese power, Stanislaw Witkiewicz defies categorization. At times parodying Shakespeare, Ibsen, Chekhov, Stendhal, or Strindberg, Witkacy combines the wit and urbanity of an Oscar Wilde with the dramatic sensitivity and the sense of the absurd of a Samuel Beckett, the artistic perception of unity in fragmentation of a Picasso with the Renaissance conception of individual discord, disintegration, lunacy, and crisis as microcosmic reflections of the world at large. In both novels and plays he paints horrifying images of anti-utopias, characterized by exploding violence, the destruction of the individual, and the emergence of a totalitarian state of insect-like automatons. These mechanized men in mass are summed up most graphically in "the mobile yellow wall," a solid block of completely depersonalized Chinese soldiers who encircle Poland in *Insatiability.* The way "They" destroy art, language, creativity, and individuality, and harness man's sexual energies to produce a neutral social machine, bland, boring, and bogged down in mindless bureaucratic red tape and senseless cruelty, is Orwellian in conception. So too is his emphasis on fear tactics and collective madness. He envisions the destruction of contemporary civilization by mechanization and egalitarian levelling, with clone-like technocrats the wave of the future, a "dusk of mechanized grayness," not physical dissolution only but psychological too. The title of one of his plays destroyed during World War II sums up his final vision: *The End of the World.*

In a childhood play, *Cockroaches*, a preview of his adult concerns, an army of identical gray insects from America invades a city, while in *The Cuttlefish*, a Renaissance pope, a modern artist, and a potential dictator debate ethical, political, and artistic relativity. In *The Mother*, the individuals are bloodsuckers, ultimately trapped in a room with no exits, dominated by a giant tube used by the mechanized workers of the State to suck out life. In *The Crazy Locomotive*, set against a hurtling cinematic backdrop, the machine that will supposedly carry man to higher knowledge ends up in a headlong collision, death, and a pile of human and mechanical debris with "no help possible." They suggests a vast conspiracy, a dread and secret menace that bans art and crushes artists. In *The Madman and the Nun* the authorities, represented by a Freudian psychologist, imprison the artist, imposing physical and psychological restraints on his humanity, but at the end are forced to question their own sanity and the sanity of all systems which limit the individual. *The Water Hen* ends in revolution, with grenades exploding, heaps of corpses in the street, advocates of community property "banging away in fine style," and thinking man resigned to his fate, playing out a card hand amid chaos, the final call a "Pass." *The Shoemakers* envisions revolution after revolution—capitalism overturned by a fascist coup followed by a worker's rebellion in turn overthrown by nameless, identical technocrats who annihilate freedom and uniqueness and make boredom the ultimate reality.

Like his plays, Witkacy's novels are a kaleidoscopic mixture of the erotic, the philosophical, and the apocalyptic. They follow the adventures and musings of an artist who struggles against domination, but who ultimately fails, partly due to his own weakness, partly due to the disintegration of society around him, partly due to historical inevitability. *Farewell to Autumn* (1927), set in an unspecified future world, concentrates on a period of change, with metaphorical winter coming, an old regime failing, and "the amorphous anthill" dominating. As a bourgeois democratic revolution is followed by the reign of "Levellers," the artist hero seeks escape in cocaine and sex and faraway places, but finally succumbs to the horror of the new system: petty regimentation, a drab daily routine, and futile, fatal boredom. In a number of his works, Witkacy focuses on the debilitating power of drugs that paralyze those individuals who might have stood against the State. In "Sluts and Butterflies" he portrays whites, in the face of the vitality of primities, resorting to pills as substitutes for real feelings; "Mother" includes a cocaine party, a sign of social decadence and a refusal to face facts; *Insatiability* predicts the Chinese use of a very special pill (and accompanying mystic pseudo-philosophy) to pacify and lull the European enemy populace, and thereby to effect the takeover of Russia and then Poland. Witkacy's most famous novel, *Insatiability* is a black comedy of chaos and loss, with the hero seeking personal identity in a world where identity is slowly but definitely being annihilated. The government has become a sport, news reporting false, women dominant, sexuality absurd, madness the norm. The Chinese, "flawless, fearless machines," threaten Poland and all of Western culture, first with painless palliatives, then with the possibility of crossbreeding to produce an Oriental-Occidental hybrid that is totally deindividualized. In this work, as is true throughout Witkacy's canon, sexual perversions, emasculated males and destructive, insatiable females are harbingers of totalitarian sterility, and images of the insect world sum up collective society. At their victory banquet the Chinese serve rats' tails in a bedbug sauce; Witkacy's childhood nightmare is realized; the world is in chains, and lunacy prevails. The fate of the individual and of society follow parallel courses; decapitation of victors and victims occurs after the human mind has already become extinct.

Witkacy's tone is mocking, irreverent, ironic. He depicts man baffled by an inexplicable universe, waging a hopeless battle for identity and control. Images of imprisonment, restraint, confinement are played off against those of stifled creativity. His characters are oversexed misfits, the lunatic fringe (the bastions of sanity in a world gone mad)—neurotic artists, criminals, demonic women, and mathematical geniuses, indulging in self-gratification, seeking thrills and oblivion, but sometimes making a last frenzied stand before being engulfed by historical inevitability. His works are full of fake deaths and resurrected corpses, as fantasy and psychological realism meet in a symbolic, metaphorical world of the grotesque. His style is an incredibly varied hodge-podge of forms: a new language of insults and obscenities, allusions, puns, jokes in mock Russian, parody, polemic, digression, political and philosophical argument, buffoonery, free-for-alls, cabaret routines, accelerated and decelerated tempos, anti-climaxes, sight gags, masks, and disclosures and exposures; although the triple puns, multiple connotations, and amazing manipulation of sound and meaning are lost in translation, his style remains impressively versatile. His future includes a Ministry of the Mechanization of Culture, a Department of Metaphysical Absurdity, a Commissariat of Sexual Nonsense, a Council for the production of Handmade Crap, and an organization of Vigilant Youth. Characters split in two, corpses prove dummies or return unscathed, the aging process is eliminated, and time and space are confused.

His works are not science fiction as we generally envision it; but they are science fiction in the sense of fantastic creations that project political worlds that could well (and in some cases did) evolve in the very near future.

—Gina Macdonald

---

**YEFREMOV, Ivan** (1907–72). Russian. *A Meeting over Tuscarora* (stories), 1946; *Stories*, 1954; *Andromeda*, 1959.

* * *

Ivan Yefremov, with degrees in geology and biology, was Professor of Paleontology at the Paleontological Institute in Moscow. His first book of stories was *A Meeting over Tuscarora*, hovering between folk legends, sea and historical romance, scientific popularization, and SF. His first "cosmic" novella was "Stellar Ships" (*Stories*), but it is *Andromeda* which is his breakthrough, the bearer of the post-Stalinist "thaw" in SF, and the supreme achievement of its first phase (1957–63). *Andromeda* achieved this position after a long and acrimonious public debate, unheard of in the USSR since the enthronement of dogmatic literary policy and the Stalinist purges of the 1930's. Against violent ideological opposition, this debate resulted in 1957–58 in the victory of the new wave, which wanted to build upon the pristine Soviet tradition, in abeyance since the Leninist 1920's. The opinion of "warm stream" critics, and of the thousands of readers who wrote to the author, newspapers, and periodicals, that this was a liberating turning-point in Soviet SF, finally prevailed.

*Andromeda* creatively revived the classical utopian and socialist vision, which looks forward to a unified, affluent, humanist, classless, and stateless world. The novel is situated in year 408 of the Era of the Great Ring, when mankind has established communicational contact with inhabitants of distant constellations who pass information to each other through a ring of inhabited systems. The Earth itself is administered—by analogy with the associative centers of the human brain—by an Astronautic Council and an Economic Council which tallies all plans with existing possibilities; their specialized research academies correspond to man's sensory centers. Within this framework of the body politic, Yefremov concentrates on new ethical relationships of disalienated men. For all the theatrical loftiness of his characters, whose emotions are rarely less than sublime, they can learn through painful mistakes and failures, as distinct from the desperado and superman clichés of "socialist realism" or much American SF after Gernsback.

The novel's strong narrative sweep full of action, from fist-fights to encounters with electrical predators and a robot-spaceship from the Andromeda nebula, is imbued with the joy and romance of cognition. Yefremov's strong anthropocentric bent places the highest value on creativity, a simultaneous adventure of deed, thought, and feeling, resulting in physical and ethical beauty. Even his title indicates not only a constellation but also the chained Greek beauty rescued from a monster (here, class egotism and violence, personified in the novel as a bull, and often bearing hallmarks of Stalinism) by a flying hero endowed with superior science. Astronautics thus don't evolve into a new uncritical cult, but are claimed as a humanist discipline, in one of the most significant fusions of physical sciences, social sciences, ethics, and art established as the norm for Yefremov's new people. Such a connection is embodied even in the compositional oscillation between cosmic and terrestrial chapters, where the "astronautic" Erg-Nisa subplot is finally integrated with the "earthly" Darr-Veda subplot by means of the creative beauty of science united to art (Mven-Chara and Renn-Evda). Furthermore, this future is not the arrested, pseudo-perfect end of history—that weak point of optimistic utopianism. Freed from economic and power worries, people must still redeem time through a dialectics of personal creativity and societal teamwork mediated by functional beauty, shown in Dar's listening to the "Cosmic Symphony in F-minor, Color Tone 4.75 $\mu$." Creativity is always countered by entropy, and self-realization paid for in effort and suffering. In fact, several very interesting approaches to a Marxist "optimistic tragedy" can be found in Andromeda, e.g., in Mven's "happy Fall"; the failed and destructive "null-space" experiment finally leads to great advances. Significantly, the accent on beauty and responsible freedom places at the center of the novel female heroines, interacting with the heroes and contributing to the emotional motivation of new utopian ethics—in contrast to SF in the United States during those times.

True, *Andromeda* has somewhat dated. In a number of places its dialogue, motivation, and rhythm flag, and it falls back on melodrama and preaching. Yefremov's characters tend to be plaster-of-Paris statuesque, and his incidents often exploit the quantitatively grandiose: Mven blows up a satellite and half a mountain, Veda loses the greatest anthropological find ever; Erg is manly, Nisa is pure. One feels in *Andromeda* the presence of an unsophisticated reader, who is, as Yefremov wrote, "still attracted to the externals, decorations, and theatrical effects of the genre," and the presence of the erotic, philosophic, and literary taboos of the cultural context. Yefremov's epistemology is a naive anthropocentrism: the 19th-century view of man as subject and the universe as object of a cognition that is ever expanding, if necessary through a basic social change yet without major existential consequences. Doubt and the menace of entropy are only external enemies—e.g., the electric predators of a far-off planet; if any epistemological opaqueness ever becomes internalized in a man, then he is a melodramatic villain, such as Pour Hyss.

Yefremov's ideology is thus receptive only to a certain romantically codified range of creativity. His limitations are more clearly manifested in his later works. In *The Heart of the Serpent* Terrans meeting a fluorine-based mankind put an end to its loneliness by promising to transmute fluorine into oxygen. This story—an avowed counterblast to Leinster's "First Contact" with its aggressive and acquisitive presuppositions—might be a legitimate pacifist-socialist allegory for changing US capitalist meritocrats into Russian socialist ones, yet it is curiously ethnocentric. Yefremov's last SF novel, *The Hour of the Bull*, demonstrates this even more clearly. Though he took from Lem and the Strugatskys the device of showing heroes (and heroines) facing anti-utopia, his old preachiness reaches monumental proportions; and the fascist regime of Tormans seems nearer to US pulp SF of the 1930's and 1940's, or indeed to the weirdnesses of Lindsay (from whom the planet's name is taken), than to either the reactionary capitalism or Maoism which Yefremov declared he wanted to hit in one fell swoop. Such parochial views preclude a full development of imaginative SF vistas.

Yet any discussion of such vistas in Soviet SF was made possible by Yefremov's pioneering effort. *Andromeda* has polyphonic scope and a large number of protagonists; it is Tolstoian rather than Flaubertain. Not limited to the consciousness of one central hero, it is one of the first utopias in world literature which successfully shows new characters creating, and being created by, a new society, i.e., the personal working out of a collective utopia (analogous to what Scott did for the historical novel). Yefremov's unfolding the narration as if the anticipated future was already a normative present unites the classic "looking backward" of utopian anticipations with the modern Einsteinian conception of different coordinate systems with autonomous norms: 20th-century science and the age-old Russian folk dreams of a just and happy society meet in his novel. This meeting made it a nodal point of the Russian and socialist SF tradition, and enabled it to usher in the second Golden Age of Soviet SF—an age which closed with the 1960's.

—Darko Suvin

---

**ZAMYATIN, Yevgeny** (1884–1937). Russian *We*, 1924.

* * *

Yevgeny Zamyatin wrote some 40 books of fiction, fables, plays, and essays. After the October Revolution he became a prominent figure in key literary groups, but from 1921 he incurred much critical disfavor, eventually culminating in a campaign of vilification, especially after *We* was published in an émigré journal. He died in Paris shunned both by Soviet officialdom and right-wing émigrés.

As all post-revolutionary Russian SF, *We* (written in 1920) deals with the relation of the new Heavens and the old Earth. It incorporates significant features of Zamyatin's novella satirizing life-crushing bourgeois respectability and clerical philistinism written in England during World War I (sex coupons, Taylorite "table of compulsory salvation" through minutely regulated daily occupations). In *We* the Revolution, sunlike principle of life and movement, is opposed to Entropy, principle of dogmatic evil and death. Zamyatin thought of himself as a utopian, more revolutionary than the latter-day Bolsheviks. He is thus not primarily anti-Soviet—even though the increasingly dogmatic high priest of Soviet letters thought so. Extrapolating the repressive possibilities of every strong state and technocratic set-up, including the socialist ones, Zamyatin describes a Unique State 12 centuries hence having for its leader "the Benefactor" (a prototype for Orwell), where art is a public utilitarian service, and science a guide for linear, undeviating happiness. Zamyatin's sarcasm against abstract utopian prescriptions takes on Dostoevskian and Shchedrinian overtones against the totally rationalized city. The only irrational element left is people, like the narrator, the mathematician and rocketship builder D-503, and the temptress from the underground movement who for a moment makes of him a deviant. But man has a built-in instinct for slavery, the rebellion fails, and all the citizen "Numbers" are subjected to brain surgery removing the possibility of harmful imagination.

A practicing scientist committed to the scientific method, Zamyatin could not seriously blame it for the deformation of life. How was it then that a certain rationalism, claiming to be scientific, became harmful? Zamyatin could answer this only in mythical terms: the victory of any lofty ideal causes it to turn repressive. To the extent that *We* equates Leninist communism with institutionalized Christianity and models it fable on an inevitable Fall from Eden ending in ironical crucifixion, it has a strong anti-utopian streak. Instead of motivations, it advances through powerful recurring images, unable to reconcile rationalism and irrationalism, science and art (including the art of love). Zamyatin's political ideology conflicts here with his experimental approach: a meaningful exploration would have to be conducted in terms of the least alienating utopia imaginable—one in which there is no misuse of natural sciences by a dogmatic science of man.

Yet the basic values of *We* imply a stubborn vision of a classless new moral world free from all social alienations, a vision common to Anarchism and libertarian Marxism. Zamyatin confronts absolutistic control—extrapolated from both tsarist-bourgeois and early socialist state practices—with a utopian-socialist norm.

As he wrote: "We do not turn to those who reject the present in the name of a return to the past, nor to those hopelessly stupefied by the present, but to those who can see the far-off tomorrow—and in the name of tomorrow, in the name of man, we judge the present." His novel brought to SF the realization that the new world cannot be a static changeless paradise of a new religion—albeit of steel, mathematics, and interplanetary flights. The materialist utopia must subject itself to a constant scrutiny; its values are for Zamyatin centered in an ever-developing human personality and expressed in irreducible and subversive erotic passion. For all its resolute one-sidedness, the uses of Zamyatin's bitter and paradoxical warning in a dialectical utopianism seem obvious.

The expressionistic language of *We*, manipulated for speed and economy ("a high voltage of every word"), helps to subsume the protagonist's defeat under the novel's concern for the integrity of man's knowledge (science) and practice (love and art). By sensitively subjecting the deformities it describes to the experimental examination and hyperbolic magnification of SF, Zamyatin's method makes it possible to identify and cope with them. In his own vocabulary, the protagonist's defeat is of the day but not necessarily of the epoch. The defeat in the novel *We* is not the defeat of the novel itself, but an exasperated shocking of the reader into thought and action. Zamyatin's encyclopedic knowledge embraced the SF tradition before and after Wells, from the utopias through the planetary and underground novels to the anticipations of Odoevsky, About, Bellamy, Morris, Lasswitz, Willbrandt, Jack London, and most notably Anatole France. *We* is thus a document of an acute clash between the "cold" and the "warm" utopia: it probably fails to attain full consistency because of the one-sided assumptions, but Zamyatin remains a heretic socialist.

Zamyatin also wrote the SF story "A Story about the Most Important Thing," interleaving developments on three levels—an episode of the Russian civil war, the death of a caterpillar, and four people on a dying "star" (planet, asteroid?) rushing toward destruction on Earth. Its lyrical investigation of the kinds of love and death that are "the most important thing" doesn't quite come off, but presents an interesting literary experiment.

—Darko Suvin

---

# TITLE INDEX

The following list includes the titles of all novels and short stories (designated "s") cited as science-fiction publications. The name(s) in parenthesis after the title is meant to direct the reader to the appropriate entry where full publication information is given. The term "series" indicates a recurring distinctive word or phrase (or name) in the titles of the entrant's books; the term "trans" is used to refer to the appendix on foreign-language writers whose works are available in translation. Series characters (noted in the fiction lists) are also listed here, even if their names do not appear in specific titles of works.

Odyssey to Earthdeath (Kelley), 1968
Of Alien Bondage (Offutt, as Cleve), 1982
Of All Possible Worlds (s Tenn), 1955
Of Earth Foretold (Bulmer), 1961
Of Godlike Power (Reynolds), 1966
Of Man and Mantra (Anthony), 1986
Of Men and Monsters (Tenn), 1968
Of Other Worlds (s Lewis), 1966
Of Space/Time and the River (Benford), 1985
Of the Fall (McAuley), 1989
Of Time and Stars (s Clarke), 1972
Off Center (s D. Knight), 1965
Off on a Comet (Verne, trans), 1957
Off-Planet (Simak), 1988
Off-Worlders (Baxter), 1966
Ogre, Ogre (Anthony), 1982
Oh, Susannah! (Wilhelm), 1982
Old Captivity (Shute), 1940
Old Die Rich (s Gold), 1955
Old Funny Stuff (Effinger), 1989
Old Gods Waken (Wellman), 1979
Old Man in New World (s Stapledon), 1944
Old Nathan (Drake), 1991
Old Tin Sorrows (Cook), 1989
Ole Doc Methuselah (s Hubbard), 1970.
O'Leary series (Laumer), from 1966
Olga Romanoff (Griffith), 1894
Omega Cage (Reaves), 1988
Omega Man (Matheson), 1971
Omega Point series (Zebrowski), from 1972
Omega Worm (Rankine, as Mason), 1976
Omen of Kregen (Bulmer, as Akers), 1985
Omha Abides (MacApp), 1968
Omicron Invasion (Goldin), 1984
Omnibus of Time (s Farley), 1950
Omnivore (Anthony), 1968
On a Pale Horse (Anthony), 1984
On a Planet Alien (Malzberg), 1974
On Saint Hubert's Thing (s Yarbro), 1982
On Stranger Tides (Powers), 1987
On Strike Against God (Russ), 1980
On the Beach (Shute), 1957
On the Flip Side (Fisk), 1983
On the Planet of Bottled Brians (Sheckley), 1990
On the Red World (Kelley), 1979
On the Run (Dickson), 1979
On the Seas of Destiny (Emerson), 1989
On the Symb-Socket Circuit (Bulmer), 1972
On Wheels (Jakes), 1973
On Wings of Song (Disch), 1979
Once Departed (Reynolds), 1970
Once There Was a Giant (s Laumer), 1971
One Against Eternity (van Vogt), 1955
One Against Herculum (Sohl), 1959
One Against the Moon (Wollheim), 1956
One Hundred and Two H-Bombs (s Disch), 1966
One in Three Hundred (McIntosh), 1954
One is One (Rankine), 1968
One Million Centuries (Lupoff), 1967
One Million Tomorrows (Shaw), 1970
One of Our Asteroids Is Missing (Silverberg, as Knox), 1964
One Side Laughing (s D. Knight), 1991
One Step from Earth (s H. Harrison), 1970
One Winter in Eden (s Bishop), 1984
One-Eyed Mystic, The Man Who Fell Up (Dent, as Robeson), 1982
Only Begotten Daughter (Morrow), 1990
Open Prison (J. White), 1965
Operation ARES (G. Wolfe), 1970
Operation Chaos (Anderson), 1971
Operation Columbus (Walters), 1960
Operation High Dragon (Correy, as Stine), 1989
Operation Interstellar (G. O. Smith), 1950
Operation Iron Fist (Correy, as Stine), 1989
Operation Nuke (Caidin), ), 1974
Operation: Outer Space (Leinster), 1954
Operation Steel Band (Correy, as Stine), 1988
Operation Terror (Leinster), 1962
Operation Time Search (Norton), 1967
Operation Umanaq (Rankine), 1973
Operation Venus (Fearn), 1950
Ophiuchi Hotline (Varley), 1977
Opium General (s Moorcock), 1984
Optiman (Stableford), 1980
Options (Sheckley), 1975
Or All the Seas with Oysters (s Davidson), 1962
ORA CLE (O'Donnell), 1984
Oracle of the Thousand Hands (Malzberg), 1968
Orange County series (K. Robinson), from 1984
Orbit One (Fanthorpe, as Muller), 1962
Orbit Unlimited (s Anderson), 1961
Orbitsville series (Shaw), from 1975
Orchid Cage (Franke, trans), 1973
Orc's Opal (Anthony), 1990
Ordeal (Shute), 1939
Ordeal in Otherwhere (Norton), 1964
Organ Bank Farm (Boyd), 1970
Orion series (Bova), from 1984
Orion Shall Rise (Anderson), 1984
Orn (Anthony), 1971
Orphan (Stallman), 1980
Orphan Star (A. Foster), 1977
Orphans of the Sky (s Heinlein), 1963
Orvis (Hoover), 1987
Ossian's Ride (F. Hoyle), 1959
Other Americas (s Spinrad), 1988
Other Days, Other Eyes (Shaw), 1972
Other Dimensions (s C.A. Smith), 1970
Other Eyes Watching (Fearn, as Cross), 1946
Other Foot (D. Knight), 1966
Other Half of the Planet (Capon), 1952
Other Half of the Sun (Capon), 1950
Other Human Race (Piper), 1964
Other Log of Phileas Fogg (Farmer), 1973
Other Passenger (s Cross), 1944
Other Place (s Priestley), 1953
Other Side of Green Hills (Cross), 1947
Other Side of Here (Leinster), 1955
Other Side of Nowhere (Leinster), 1964
Other Side of the Sky (s Clarke), 1958
Other Side of Time (Laumer), 1965
Other Sky (s Laumer), 1968
Other Time (Reynolds), 1984
Other Times, Other Worlds (s J. MacDonald), 1978
Other Voices (Greenland), 1988
Other World (Dent, as Robeson), 1968
Ou Lu Khen and the Beautiful Madwoman (Salmonson), 1985
Our Children's Children (Simak), 1974
Our Friends from Frolix 8 (Dick), 1970
Our Lady (Sinclair), 1938
Out (Meltzer), 1969
Out from Ganymede (s Malzberg, as O'Donnell), 1974
Out of Bounds (s Merril), 1960.

People Beyond the Wall (Tall), 1980
People Machines (s Williamson), 1971
People Maker (D. Knight), 1959
People Minus X (Gallun), 1957
People of the Abyss (England), 1965
People of the Comet (Hall), 1948
People of the Mist (Haggard), 1894
People of the Talisman (Brackett), 1964
People of the Wind (Anderson), 1973
People Trap (s Sheckley), 1968
Perchance to Dream (Reynolds), 1977
Peregrine (Anderson), 1978
Perelandra (Lewis), 1943
Perfect Lover (Priest), 1977
Perfect Planet (Evelyn Smith), 1962
Perfect Vacuum (Lem, trans), 1979
Peril Ahead (Creasey), 1946
Peril from Space (Bulmer, as Maras), 1955
Peril of the Starmen (Neville), 1967
Peril on Mars (P. Moore), 1958
Perilous Country (Creasey), 1949
Perilous Dreams (s Norton), 1976
Perilous Galaxy (Fanthorpe, as Muller), 1962
Perilous Seas (Dave Duncan), 1991
Peripheral Vision (s Fowler), 1990
Periscope Red (Rohmer), 1980
Perry's Planet (Jack Haldeman), 1980
Persistence of Vision (s Varley), 1978
Personal Demon (Bischoff), 1985
Petrified Planet (Fearn, as Statten), 1951
Phaeton Condition (Rankine, as Mason), 1973
Phantastes (G. MacDonald), 1858
Phantom Banjo (Scarborough), 1991
Phantom City (Dent, as Robeson), 1966
Phantom Crusader (s Fanthorpe, as Brett), 1963
Phantom Ones (Fanthorpe, as Torro), 1961
Phantom series (Goulart, as Shawn), from 1973
Phantom Universe (Garnett), 1975
Pharaoh's Ghost, The Time Terror (Dent, as Robeson), 1981
Phase IV (Malzberg), 1973
Phase Two (W. and L. Richmond), 1980
Phaze Doubt (Anthony), 1990
Phenomena X (Fanthorpe, as Muller), 1966
Philosopher's Stone (C. Wilson), 1969
Phobos, The Robot Planet (Capon), 1955
Phoenix (Cowper), 1968
Phoenix in the Ashes (s J. Vinge), 1985
Phoenix of Megaron (Rankine), 1976
Phoenix Prime (T. White), 1966
Phoenix Ship (W. and L. Richmond), 1969
Phoenix Without Ashes (Ellison, Bryant), 1975
Phthor (Anthony), 1975
Phule's Company (Asprin), 1990
Picking the Ballad's Bones (Scarborough), 1991
Pickle Creature (Pinkwater), 1979
Picnic on Nearside (Varley), 1984
Picnic on Paradise (Russ), 1968
Piece of Martin Cann (Janifer), 1968
Pig Ignorant (Fisk), 1991
Pilgrim Project (Searls), 1964
Pilgrimage (s Henderson), 1961
Pilgrimage to Earth (s Sheckley), 1957
Pillars of Eternity (Bayley), 1982
Pimpernel Plot (Hawke), 1984
Pink of Fading Neon (s Blaylock), 1986
Pioneer 1990 (Fearn, as Statten), 1953
Pioneers (Mann), 1988
Pirate Isle, The Speaking Stone (Dent, as Robeson), 1983
Pirate of the Pacific (Dent, as Robeson), 1967
Pirate's Ghost (Dent, as Robeson), 1971
Pirates of Thunder (Chalker), 1987
Pirates of Venus (E. Burroughs), 1934
Pirates of Zan (Leinster), 1959
Pitman's Progress (Rankine, as Mason), 1976
Pixilated Peeress (de Camp), 1991
P-K (photokinesis) (Walters), 1986
Place of Silver Silence (Mayhar), 1988
Plague Daemon (Stableford, as Craig), 1990
Plague from Space (H. Harrison), 1965
Plague of Demons (Laumer), 1965
Plague of Pythons (Pohl), 1965
Plague of Silence (Creasey), 1958
Plague of Sound (Goulart, as Steffanson), 1974
Plague Ship (Norton, as North), 1956
Plains (Murnane), 1982
Planet Buyer (C. Smith), 1964
Planet Called Krishna (de Camp), 1966
Planet Called Treason (Card), 1979
Planet Called Utopia (McIntosh), 1979
Planet Explorer (Leinster), 1957
Planet for Texans (Piper), 1958
Planet in Peril (Christopher), 1959
Planet Killers (Silverberg), 1959
Planet Mappers (E. Evans), 1955
Planet Murderer (Offutt, as Cleve), 1984
Planet of Death (Silverberg), 1967
Planet of Death (F. and G. Hoyle), 1982
Planet of Dread (Tubb, as Kern), 1974
Planet of Exile (Le Guin), 1966
Planet of Fear (P. Moore), 1977
Planet of Fire (P. Moore), 1969
Planet of Flowers (Norwood), 1984
Planet of Judgment (Joe Haldeman), 1977
Planet of Light (R. Jones), 1953
Planet of No Return (Anderson), 1957
Planet of No Return (H. Harrison), 1981
Planet of Peril (Kline), 1929
Planet of the Apes (Boulle, trans), 1963
Planet of the Apes series (Effinger), from 1974
Planet of the Damned (H. Harrison), 1962
Planet of the Double Sun (N. Jones), 1967
Planet of the Dreamers (J. MacDonald), 1953
Planet of the Voles (Platt), 1977
Planet of Treachery (Goldin), 1982
Planet of Whispers (Kelly), 1984
Planet of Your Own (Brunner), 1966
Planet of Youth (Colblentz), 1952
Planet on the Table (s K. Robinson), 1986
Planet Patrol (Dorman), 1978
Planet Pirate series (McCaffrey), from 1990
Planet Plane (Wyndham, as Beynon), 1936
Planet Poachers (Lightner), 1965
Planet Run (Laumer, Dickson), 1967
Planet Savers (Bradley), 1962
Planet Seekers (Fanthorpe, as E. Barton), 1964
Planet Story (H. Harrison), 1979
Planet Strappers (Gallun), 1961
Planet Wizard (Jakes), 1969
Planetary Agent X (Reynolds), 1965
Planeteers (s Campbell), 1966
Planetfall (Cover), 1988
Planetfall (Caidin), 1974
Planetfall (Tubb, as Hunt), 1951
Planetoid 127 (E. Wallace), 1929

Siege of Faltara (Darnay), 1978
Siege of the Unseen (van Vogt), 1959
Siege of Wonder (Geston), 1976
Siege Perilous (Fairman, as del Rey), 1966
Sierra Madre (Stine), 1988
Sight-Blinder's Story (Saberhagen), 1987
Sigma Curve (Barnwell), 1981
Sign of Chaos (Zelazny), 1987
Sign of the Burning Hart (Keller), 1938
Sign of the Labrys (St. Clair), 1963
Sign of the Mute Medusa (I. Wallace), 1977
Sign of the Unicorn (Zelazny), 1975
Signs and Portents (s Yarbro), 1984
Signs and Wonders (s Beresford), 1921
Silence Is Deadly (Biggle), 1977
Silent City (Vonarburg, trans), 1988
Silent Invaders (Silverberg), 1963
Silent Multitude (Compton), 1966
Silent Shout (s Zebrowski), 1979
Silent Sky (s Biggle), 1979
Silent Speakers (Sellings), 1963
Silent Voice (Hodder-Williams), 1977
Silicon Man (Platt), 1991
Silistra series (Morris), from 1977
Silk Roads and Shadows (Shwartz), 1988
Silkie (van Vogt), 1969
Silmarillion (Tolkien), 1977
Silver Eggheads (Leiber), 1962
Silver Locusts (s Bradbury), 1951
Silver Metal Lover (Lee), 1982
Silver Mountain (Friesner), 1986
Silver on the Tree (S. Cooper), 1977
Silver Spike (Cook), 1989
Silver Sun (Springer), 1980
Silver Thread of Madness (s Salmonson), 1989
Silverthorn (Feist), 1985
Sime/Gen series (Lichtenberg), from 1974
Simulacra (Dick), 1964
Simulacron-3 (Galouye), 1964
Sin in Space (Kornbluth and Merril, as Judd), 1961
Sinbad: The Thirteenth Voyage (Lafferty), 1989
Sinful Ones (s Leiber), 1953
Singers of Time (Pohl, Williamson), 1991
Singing Citadel (s Moorcock), 1970
Singing Stones (J. Coulson), 1968
Single Combat (Ing), 1983
Sinister Barrier (Russell), 1943
Sinister Ray (s Dent), 1987
Sins of the Fathers (Schmidt), 1976
Sioux Spaceman (Norton), 1960
Sipstrassi series (Gemmell), from 1987
Sir Gibbie (G. MacDonald), 1879
Sirens of Titan (Vonnegut), 1959
Sirian Experiments (Lessing), 1981
Sirius (Stapledon), 1944
Siscoe, Nick and Ross Block series (Hailblum), from 1984
Sister Light, Sister Dark (Yolen), 1988
SIVA! (W. and L. Richmond), 1979
Six Gates from Limbo (McIntosh), 1968
Six Weeks in the Great Whirlpool (Senarens), 1893
Six Worlds Yonder (s Russell), 1958
Six-Gun Planet (Jakes), 1970
Six-Gun Solution (Hawke), 1991
Sixth Column (Heinlein), 1949
Sixty Days to Live (Wheatley), 1939
Skaith series (Brackett), from 1976
Skeleton-in-Waiting (Dickinson), 1989
Skies Discrowned (Powers), 1976
Skin and Bones (s T. Smith), 1933
Sky Breaker (G. Jones, as Halam), 1990
Sky Is Falling, Badge of Infamy (del Rey), 1963
Sky is Filled with Ships (Meredith), 1969
Skyclimber (Gallun), 1981
Skyfall (H. Harrison), 1976
Skylark series (E. E. Smith), from 1946
Skylords series (Brosnan), from 1988
Skynappers (Brunner), 1960
Skyport (Siodmak), 1959
Skyripper (Drake), 1983
Skyrocket Steele (Goulart), 1980
Skyship (Brosnan), 1981
Slan (van Vogt), 1946
Slaughterhouse-Five (Vonnegut), 1969
Slave Planet (Janifer), 1963
Slave Ship (Pohl), 1957
Slave Ship from Sergan (Tubb, as Kern), 1973
Slavers of Space (Brunner), 1960
Slaves of Heaven (E. Cooper), 1974
Slaves of Ijax (Fearn), 1948
Slaves of Sleep (Hubbard), 1948
Slaves of Spiegel (Pinkwater), 1982
Slaves of the Klau (Vance), 1958
Slaves of the Spectrum (Bulmer, as Kent), 1954
Slaves of the Volcano God (Gardner), 1989
Sleep! (Creasey), 1964
Sleep Eaters (Lymington), 1973
Sleep Has His House (Kavan), 1948
Sleeper Wakes (Wells), 1910
Sleepers of Mars (s Wyndham, as Beynon), 1973
Sleepside Story (Bear), 1988
Sleepwalker's World (Dickson), 1971
Slippery (s Lafferty), 1985
Slipt (A. Foster), 1984
Slitherers (Fearn), 1984
Slow Birds (s Watson), 1985
Slow Fall to Dawn (Leigh), 1981
Slow Freight (Busby), 1991
Slow Sculpture (s Sturgeon), 1982
Small Armageddon (Roshwald), 1962
Small Assassin (s Bradbury), 1962
Small Changes (s Clement), 1969
Smile on the Void (S. Gordon), 1981
Smog (Creasey), 1970
Smoke Ring (Niven), 1987
Smuggled Atom Bomb (Wylie), 1956
Smuggler's Gold (Cherryh), 1988
Snail on the Slope (Strugatsky, trans), 1980
Snake in His Bosom (s Lafferty), 1983
Snarkout Boys series (Pinkwater), from 1982
Sneak Preview (Bloch), 1971
Snoggle (Priestley), 1971
Snow Queen series (J. Vinge), from 1980
Snowbrother (Stirling), 1985
Snows of Ganymede (Anderson), 1958
Snow-White Soliloquies (MacLeod), 1970
So Bright the Vision (s Simak), 1968
So Close to Home (s Blish), 1961
So Dark a Heritage (Long), 1966
So Long, and Thanks for All the Fish (Adams), 1984
Sodom and Gomorrah Business (Malzberg), 1974
Soft (s F. Wilson), 1989
Soft Come the Dragons (s Koontz), 1970
Soft Machine (Burroughs), 1961
Soft Targets (Ing), 1979

Warlord of Mars (E. Burroughs), 1919
Warlord of the Air (Moorcock), 1971
Warlords of Antares (Bulmer, as Akers), 1988
Warlord's World (Anvil), 1975
Warm Worlds and Otherwise (s Tiptree), 1975
Warrior (Drake), 1991
Warrior of Llarn. (Fox), 1964
Warrior of Mars (Fearn), 1950
Warrior of Scorpio (Bulmer, as Akers), 1973
Warrior Who Carried Life (Ryman), 1985
Warrior Woman (Bradley), 1985
Warrior's Apprentice (Bujold), 1986
Warriors of Dawn (M. Foster), 1975
Warriors of Day (Blish), 1953
Warriors of Mars (Moorcock, as Bradbury), 1965
Warriors of the Storm (Chalker), 1987
Wasp (Russell), 1957
Watch Below (J. White), 1966
Watchers (s Calvino, trans), 1971
Watchers of the Dark (Biggle), 1966
Watchers of the Forest (s Fanthorpe), 1958
Watching World (Fanthorpe), 1966
Watchstar (Sargent), 1980
Water King's Laughter (Friesner), 1989
Water of the Wondrous Isles (W. Morris), 1897
Water of Thought (Saberhagen), 1965
Water Witch (Felice, Willis), 1982
Waters of Centaurus (R. Brown), 1970
Waters of Lethe (Keller), 1937
Wave Rider (s Schenck), 1980
Wave Without a Shore (Cherryh), 1981
Waves (M. Foster), 1980
Way Back (Chandler), 1976
Way Down the Hill (Powers), 1986
Way Home (s Sturgeon), 1955
Way of the Gods (s Kuttner), 1954
Way of the Pilgrim (Dickson), 1987
Way Station (Simak), 1963
Waylander (Gemmell), 1986
We (Zamyatin, trans), 1924
We All Died at Breakaway Station (Meredith), 1969
We Can Build You (Dick), 1972
We Claim These Stars (Anderson), 1959
We Could Do Worse (Benford), 1988
We, in Some Strange Power's Employ, Move on a Rigorous Line (Delany), 1990
We, The Venusians (Rackham), 1965
We Who Are About to . . . . (Russ), 1977
Wealth of the Void (Fearn, as Statten), 1954
Weapon from Beyond (Hamilton), 1967
Weapon Shop series (van Vogt), from 1947
Weathermakers (Bova), 1967
Weathermonger (Dickinson), 1968
Web (Wyndham), 1979
Web Between the Worlds (Sheffield), 1979
Web of Angels (Ford), 1980
Web of Darkness (Bradley), 1984
Web of Everywhere (Brunner), 1974
Web of Light (Bradley), 1982
Web of Sand (Tubb), 1979
Web of the Chozen (Chalker), 1978
Web of the Magi (s Cowper), 1980
Web of Time (Harding), 1979
Weeping May Tarry (del Rey, R. Jones), 1978
Weeping Sky (Harding), 1977
Weighed and Wanting (G. MacDonald), 1882
Weigher of Souls, and The Earth Dwellers (Maurois, trans), 1963
Weird Tales of Terror and Detection (s Heard), 1946
Weirwoods (Swann), 1967
Weisman Experiment (Rankine), 1969
Welcome, Chaos (Wilhelm), 1983
Welcome to Mars (Blish), 1967
Welcome to Moonbase (Bova), 1987
Welcome to the Monkey House (s Vonnegut), 1968
Well at the World's End: A Tale (W. Morris), 1896
Well of Darkness (Garrett), 1983
Well of Shiuan (Cherryh), 1978
Well of the Worlds (Kuttner and C.L. Moore, as Padgett), 1953
Well World series (Chalker), from 1977
Wempires (Pinkwater), 1991
Werewolf among Us (Koontz), 1973
Werewolf at Large (s Fanthorpe), 1960
Werewolf Principle (Simak), 1967
Werewolves of Kregen (Bulmer, as Akers), 1985
West, Julian series (Reynolds), 1973
West of Eden series (H. Harrison), from 1984
West of Honor (Pournelle), 1976
West of January (Dave Duncan), 1989
West of the Sun (Pangborn), 1953
Westlin Wind (de Lint), 1989
Westminster Disaster (F. and G. Hoyle), 1978
Whale of the Victoria Cross (Boulle, trans), 1983
What Did I Do Tomorrow? (Davies), 1972
What Dreams May Come (Wellman), 1983
What Dreams May Come. . . (Beresford), 1941
What Entropy Means to Me (Effinger), 1972
What Happened to the Corbetts (Shute), 1939
What Mad Oracle? (Scortia), 1961
What Mad Universe (F. Brown), 1949
What Rough Beast (Watkins), 1980
What Strange Stars and Skies (s Davidson), 1965
Whatever Became of Aunt Margaret? (DeWeese), 1990
What's Become of Screwloose? and Other Inquiries (s Goulart), 1971
What's It Like Out There (s Hamilton), 1974
What's Mine's Mine (G. MacDonald), 1886
Wheel in Space (P. Moore), 1956
Wheel of Stars (Norton), 1983
Wheel of the Winds (Engh), 1988
Wheelie in the Stars (Fisk), 1976
Wheels of If (s deCamp), 1948
Wheels Within Wheels (F. Wilson), 1979
Wheelworld (H. Harrison), 1981
When Chaugnar Walks (s Long), 1978
When Gravity Fails (Effinger), 1987
When Harlie Was One (Gerrold), 1972
When the Birds Fly South (Colblentz), 1945
When the Dream Dies (Chandler), 1981
When the Kissing Had to Stop (FitzGibbon), 1960
When the Moon Ran Wild (Verrill, as Ainsbury), 1962
When the Sky Burned (Bova), 1973
When the Sleeper Wakes (Wells), 1899
When the Star Kings Die (Jakes), 1967
When the Tripods Came (Christopher), 1988
When the Waker Sleeps (Goulart), 1975
When the World Shook (Haggard), 1919
When They Come from Space (Clifton), 1962
When Trouble Beckons (McQuay), 1981
When Two Worlds Meet (s R. Williams), 1970
When Worlds Collide (Wylie), 1933
Whenabouts of Burr (Kurland), 1975

Where Eternity Ends (s Binder), 1950
Where is the Bird of Fire (Swann), 1970
Where Late the Sweet Birds Sang (Wilhelm), 1976
Where No Stars Guide (Kippax), 1975
Where No Sun Shines (Kelley), 1979
Where the Evil Dwells (Simak), 1982
Where Time Winds Blow (Holdstock), 1982
Whetted Bronze (Bulmer, as Norvil), 1978
Whiff of Madness (Goulart), 1976
Whipping Star (F. Herbert), 1970
Whirligig of Time (Biggle), 1979
Whirlpool of Stars (Bulmer, as Zetford), 1974
Whirlwind of Death (s Fanthorpe), 1960
Whisker of Hercules, The Man Who Was Scared (Dent, as Robeson), 1981
Whisper from the Stars (Jeff Sutton), 1970
White Bull (Saberhagen), 1988
White Death (Sargent), 1980
White Dragon (McCaffrey), 1978
White Fang Goes Dingo (s Disch), 1971
White Hart (Springer), 1979
White Hotel (D. Thomas), 1981
White Jenna (Yolen), 1989
White Light (Rucker), 1980
White Mountain (Wingrove), 1991
White Mountains (Christopher), 1967
White Plague (F. Herbert), 1982
White Rose (Cook), 1985
White Serpent (Lee), 1988
White Widows (Merwin), 1953
Who? (Budrys), 1958
Who Can Replace a Man? (s Aldiss), 1966
Who Fears the Devil? (s Wellman), 1963
Who Goes Here? (Shaw), 1977
Who Goes There? (s Campbell), 1948
Who Is Lewis Pindar? (Davies), 1966
Who Made Stevie Crye? (Bishop), 1984
Who Needs Enemies? (s A. Foster), 1984
Who Needs Men? (E. Cooper), 1972
Whole Man (Brunner), 1964
Whores of Babylon (Watson), 1988
Why Call Them Back from Heaven (Simak), 1967
Why I Want to Fuck Ronald Reagan (s Ballard), 1968
Wicked Cyborg (Goulart), 1978
Widget, the Wadget, and Boff (Sturgeon), 1989
Widow's Son (R.A. Wilson), 1985
Wielding a Red Sword (Anthony), 1986
Wiggin, Ender series (Card), from 1985
Wild Alien Tamer (Resnick), 1983
Wild Boys (Burroughs), 1971
Wild Card (Bryant), 1986
Wild Country (Ing), 1985
Wild Jack (Christopher), 1974
Wild Ones (Chandler), 1985
Wild Seed (Butler), 1980
Wild Shore (K. Robinson), 1984
Wild Talent (Tucker), 1954
Wildeblood's Empire (Stableford), 1977
Wildings of Westron (Lake), 1977
Wildsmith (Goulart), 1972
Wilfrid Cumbermede (G. MacDonald), 1872
Wilk Are Among Us (Hailblum), 1975
Will-o-the-Wisp (Swann), 1976
Willow (Drew), 1988
Wind from a Burning Woman (s Bear), 1983
Wind from Bukhara (Engh), 1989
Wind from Nowhere (Ballard), 1962
Wind from the Abyss (Morris), 1978
Wind from the North (O'Neill), 1934
Wind from the Sun (s Clarke), 1972
Wind in Cairo (Tarr), 1989
Wind in the Door (L'Engle), 1973
Wind of Liberty (Bulmer), 1962
Wind series (Meluch), from 1981
Wind Whales of Ishmael (Farmer), 1971
Windhaven (Martin, Tuttle), 1980
Windhover Tapes series (Norwood), from 1982
Windows (Compton), 1979
Windows of Forever (Morressy), 1975
Winds of Altair (Bova), 1973
Winds of Change (s Asimov), 1983
Winds of Gath (Tubb), 1967
Winds of Limbo (Moorcock), 1969
Winds of Time (Oliver), 1957
Wind's Twelve Quarters (s Le Guin), 1975
Wine of the Dreamers (J. MacDonald), 1951
Wine of Violence (Morrow), 1981
Winged Man (van Vogt), 1966
Wingman (Pinkwater), 1975
Wings (Pratchett), 1990
Wings of Flame (Springer), 1985
Wings of Peace (Creasey), 1948
Winners (s Anderson), 1981
Winter amid the Ice (s Verne, trans), 1890
Winter of the World (Anderson), 1975
Winterlong (Hand), 1990
Winter's Children (Coney), 1974
Winter's Youth (Gloag), 1934
Winterwood and Other Hauntings (s Roberts), 1989
Wisdom's Daughter (Haggard), 1923
Wise Woman: A Parable (G. MacDonald), 1875
Wishbringer (Gardner), 1988
Witch of Kregen (Bulmer, as Akers), 1985
Witch of the Dark Gate (Jakes), 1972
Witch Queen of Lochlann (G. H. Smith), 1969
Witch Tree (Long), 1971
Witchdame (Sky), 1985
Witches of Karres (Schmitz), 1966
Witchfinder (s S. Wright), 1945
Witching Hour (s Gunn), 1970
Witch's Welcome (Broxon, as Skaldaspillir), 1979
Witchwood Cradle (Friesner), 1987
With a Finger in My I (s Gerrold), 1972
With a Strange Device (Russell), 1964
With a Tangled Skein (Anthony), 1985
With Friends Like These (s A. Foster), 1977
With Mercy Toward None (Cook), 1985
Without Sorcery (s Sturgeon), 1948
Witling (V. Vinge), 1976
Wizard (Varley), 1980
Wizard Crystal (Pinkwater), 1973
Wizard in Bedlam (Stasheff), 1979
Wizard of Anharitte (Kapp), 1975
Wizard of Lemuria (L. Carter), 1965
Wizard of Linn (van Vogt), 1962
Wizard of Starship Poseidon (Bulmer), 1963
Wizard of Venus (s E. Burroughs), 1970
Wizard series (Hawke), from 1987
Wizard Spawn (Cherryh), 1989
Wizards of Senchuria (Bulmer), 1969
Wizenbeak (Gilliland), 1986
Wolf and Iron (Dickson), 1990
Wolf Hollow Bubbles (s Keller), 1934(?)
Wolf in Shadow (Gemmell), 1987

# NOTES
# ON
# ADVISERS
# AND
# CONTRIBUTORS

**ABOULAFIA, Mitchell.** Professor of Philosophy and the Humanities, University of Houston, Clear Lake City. Author of *The Self-Winding Circle: A Study of Hegel's System*, 1982, and *The Mediating Self: Mead, Sartre, and Self-Determination*, 1986. **Essay:** Robert F. Young.

**ALDISS, Brian.** See his own entry. **Essays:** Franz Kafka; Mary Shelley.

**ARBUR, Rosemarie.** Associate Professor of English, Lehigh University, Bethlehem, Pennsylvania. Author of *Leigh Brackett, Marion Zimmer Bradley, Anne McCaffrey: A Primary and Secondary Bibliography*, 1982, *Computer-Assisted Preparation of Texts*, 1982, *Marion Zimmer Bradley: A Reader's Guide*, 1985, and of articles in journals and collections. **Essay:** Leigh Brackett.

**BAILEY, K.V.** Freelance writer. Author of *The Listening Schools*, 1957, *The Earth Is Your Spaceship*, 1959, *Education and Heritage*, 1976, *Other Worlds and Alderney*, 1982, and articles in journals and anthologies. **Essays:** James P. Blaylock; Olaf Stapledon.

**BARBOUR, Douglas.** Professor of English, University of Alberta, Edmonton; poetry editor, *Canadian Forum.* Author of several books of poetry, including *Visible Visions: The Selected Poems*, 1984, and *Worlds Out of Words: The SF Novels of Samuel R. Delany*, 1979, and articles on Delany, Tolkien, and Zelazny. **Essay:** Barry N. Malzberg.

**BARLOW, George W.** Teacher of English in Grenoble, France. Author of short stories and essays in French science-fiction magazines; editor and translator of *Le Livre d'Or de John Brunner*, 1979, *Le Livre d'Or d'Arthur Clarke*, 1981, and *Le Livre d'Or de Harry Harrison*, 1985. **Essay:** Jean-Pierre Andrevon (foreign-language).

**BARNES, Myra.** Teacher. Author of *Linguistics and Language in Science Fiction-Fantasy*, 1975. **Essay:** Hank Searls.

**BARR, Marleen S.** Assistant Professor of English, Virginia Polytechnic Institute and State University, Blacksburg. Author of *Alien to Femininity: Women and Contemporary Science Fiction*, forthcoming. Editor of *Future Females: A Critical Anthology*, 1981, *Women and Utopia: Critical Interpretations* (with Nicholas Smith), 1983, and the feminist SF issue of *Women's Studies International Forum*, June 1984. **Essays:** Suzy McKee Charnas; Zoë Fairbairns.

**BARRETT, David V.** Special projects editor, *Computer Weekly.* Council member, Science Fiction Foundation. Editor of *Vector*, 1985–89. Author of *Computer User Satisfaction Survey*, vol. 1, 1990, and of numerous short stories, and critical articles in newspapers and magazines. Editor of *Digital Dreams*, 1990. **Essays:** Brian Aldiss; Rachel Pollack.

**BARTH, Melissa E.** Professor of English, Appalachian State University, Boone, North Carolina. Author of *A Reader's Guide to Stephen R. Donaldson, A Reader's Guide to Orson Scott Card*, (forthcoming), and of essays on numerous contemporary American and British authors, book reviews, biographical essays, and several textbooks. **Essays:** Italo Calvino (foreign-language); John Varley.

**BARTTER, Martha A.** **Essays:** Lois McMaster Bujold; M.J. Engh.

**BEATIE, Bruce A.** Professor of German and comparative literature, Cleveland State University, Ohio. **Essay:** E.E. Smith.

**BISHOP, E.R.** Associate Professor of Mathematics, Acadia University, Wolfville, Nova Scotia. **Essays:** Paul Park; Mordecai Roshwald.

**BISHOP, Michael.** See his own entry. **Essay:** Steven Utley.

**BLACKFORD, Russell.** Federal labour relations representative, for Australian universities. Author of *The Tempting of the Witch King* (a fantasy novel), 1983, SF and fantasy stories, and regular articles in *Science Fiction: A Review of Speculative Literature.* Co-editor of *Urban Fantasies* (forthcoming). **Essays:** John Calvin Batchelor; William S. Burroughs.

**BLANSFIELD, Karen Charmaine.** Freelance writer. Author of reviews in *Mid-American Review* and *San Francisco Chronicle.* Has taught at East Carolina University, Greenville, North Carolina, and University of Delaware, Newark; former assistant editor of the journal *Teaching English in the Two-Year College.* **Essay:** E.C. Large.

**BOGSTAD, Janice M.** Librarian, McIntyre Library, University of Wisconsin-Eau Claire. Author of *An Introduction to Fantasy and Science Fiction* (with F.J. Lemoine), 1985, and of articles and book reviews in journals. Former editor of the magazine *Janus.* **Essays:** Gene DeWeese; Ru Emerson; Carol Emshwiller; M.A. Foster; Ardath Mayhar; R.M. Meluch; Joan Slonczewski.

**BOSKY, Bernadette.** Teacher of literature and composition; P.h.D. candidate, Duke University, Durham, North Carolina. Author of articles on numerous topics, including studies of LeGuin, Peter Straub, and Stephen King. **Essays:** Philip K. Dick; David A. Drake; Suzette Haden Elgin; Joe R. Lansdale; Rebecca Ore; Tim Powers; Richard S. Shaver.

**BRAZIER, Paul.** **Essays:** Samuel R. Delany; Harry Harrison; Geoff Ryman.

**BRENNAN, John P.** Associate Professor of English, and Director of Graduate Studies, Indiana University-Purdue University, Fort Wayne. Author of articles on Le Guin, Kornbluth, Orwell, and Pohl. **Essays:** John Brunner; James P. Hogan; L. Ron Hubbard; Spider Robinson; Norman Spinrad; Kurt Vonnegut, Jr.

**BRIGG, Peter A.** Associate Professor of English, University of Guelph, Ontario. Author of *J.G. Ballard*, 1985, and articles in *Arthur C. Clarke*, 1977, *Ursula K. Le Guin*, 1979, *Survey of Science Fiction Literature*, 1979, and in several periodicals including *Mosaic, Science-Fiction Studies, Extrapolation*, and *Foundation.* **Essays:** Phyllis Gotlieb; Guy Gavriel Kay; Lester del Rey; Philip Wylie.

**BRINEY, R.E.** Professor of computer science and Chairman of the Computer Science Department, Salem State College, Massachusetts; editor, *Rohmer Review;* a founder, Advent publishers. Author of *SF Bibliographies* (with Edward Wood), 1972, essays in *The Mystery Writer's Art*, 1971, *The Conan Grimoire*, 1971, and *The Mystery Story*, 1976, and of articles and bibliographies in journals. Editor of *Master of Villainy: A Biography of Sax Rohmer*, 1972; co-editor of *Multiplying Villainies: Selected Mystery Criticism* by Anthony Boucher, 1973; contributing editor of *Encyclopedia of Mystery and Detection*, 1976, and *Encyclopedia* *of Frontier and Western Fiction*, 1983. Contributing editor of the journal *Views and Reviews*, 1972–75; member of the editorial board, Mystery Library, 1975–80, and Collection of Mystery Classics (Bantam Books), 1985. **Essays:** Juanita Coulson; Robert Coulson; August Derleth; Henry Kuttner; Rog Phillips; Frank M. Robinson; Francis Stevens.

**BRIZZI, Mary T.** Associate Professor of English, Kent State University, Ohio. Associate editor, *Extrapolation*, 1978–85. Author of *Philip José Farmer: A Reader's Guide*, 1980, *Anne McCaffrey: A Reader's Guide*, 1986, and fiction and poetry under the name Mary A. Turzillo. **Essays:** Philip José Farmer; H.F. Heard; Anne McCaffrey.

**BRUNNER, John.** See his own entry. **Essay:** Rudyard Kipling.

**BURGESS, Scott.** Freelance writer. **Essay:** Stephen Leigh.

**BUTRYM, Alexander J.** Associate Professor of English, Seton Hall University, South Orange, New Jersey; director of the program to train teachers of technical writing, Fund for the Improvement of Post-Secondary Education. Author of "For Suffering Humanity: Ethics of Scientists in SF," in *The Transcendent Adventure*, edited by Robert Reilly, 1984. **Essay:** Sam J. Lundwall.

**CARTER, Gay E.** Reference/Documents Librarian, University of Houston, Clear Lake City. **Essays:** Phyllis Eisenstein; Vonda N. McIntyre.

**CARTER, Steven R.** Teacher in San Juan, Puerto Rico. Author of articles on mystery fiction, black literature, and science fiction in *Dimensions of Detective Fiction, Popular Culture Association Newsletter*, and *Armchair Detective*. **Essay:** Ayn Rand.

**CHAPMAN, Edgar L.** Associate Professor of English and foreign languages, Bradley University, Peoria, Illinois. Author of *The Magic Labyrinth of Philip José Farmer*, 1984, and articles on numerous science-fiction writers, and a forthcoming book on Robert Silverberg. **Essays:** John Crowley; Mike McQuay.

**CHAUVETTE, Cathy.** Program Coordinator, Fairfax County Public Library, Virginia. Author of book reviews for *School Library Journal*, and other articles. **Essay:** Tanith Lee.

**COBLEY, Michael.** Freelance writer. Author of short stories, and articles in various science-fiction magazines. **Essay:** David Wingrove.

**COGELL, Elizabeth Cummins.** Assistant Professor of English, University of Missouri, Rolla; member of the editorial board, *Extrapolation*. Author of *Ursula K. Le Guin: A Primary and Secondary Bibliography*, 1983, and an article on Darko Suvin in *Essays in Arts and Sciences*, August 1980. **Essay:** Paul O. Williams.

**COLBERT, Robert E.** Associate Professor of English, Louisiana State University, Shreveport. Author of articles on Brian Aldiss's criticism, James Blish's criticism, Stanley Elkin, Saul Bellow, F.R. Leavis, and Ford Madox Ford, and of conference papers on Doris Lessing's SF and on C.M. Kornbluth's satire. **Essay:** Russell M. Griffin.

**COLEMAN, Rosemary.** Associate Professor of literature, Illinois Benedictine College, Lisle. **Essays:** Peter Tate; Ilya Varshavsky (foreign-language).

**COUGHLAN, Gary.** Teacher. **Essay:** Patrick Moore.

**COWPER, Richard.** See his own entry. **Essay:** George Orwell.

**COX, F. Brett.** Graduate student, English Department, Duke University, Durham, North Carolina. Author of several critical essays. **Essays:** John Kessel; Jack McDevitt; James Morrow.

**COX, J. Randolph.** Reference and Documents Librarian, and Associate Professor, St. Olaf College, Northfield, Minnesota; reviewer of popular culture for *Choice*. Author of *Man of Magic and Mystery: A Guide to the Works of Walter B. Gibson*, 1989, *Masters of Mystery and Detective Fiction*, 1989, and bibliographies and studies of John Buchan, M.R. James, the Nick Carter authors, George Harmon Coxe, and others for *Dime Novel Roundup, Baker Street Journal, English Literature in Transition, Armchair Detective*, and other journals; contributor of the dime novel sections to *Mystery, Detective and Espionage Magazines*, 1983, and *Detective and Mystery Fiction: An International Bibliography of Secondary Sources*, 1985. Editor of *H.G. Wells: A Reference Guide*, with William J. Scheick, 1989. **Essays:** Ron Goulart; Luis P. Senarens; Edgar Wallace; Dennis Wheatley.

**CULE, Michael.** Actor. Appeared in the stage and TV versions of *The Hitch-Hiker's Guide to the Galaxy*. **Essays:** Jack L. Chalker; David Eddings; Randall Garrett; David Langford; Robert Anton Wilson.

**CUSHING, Charles.** Adult Services Librarian, Hamilton Public Library, Ontario. **Essay:** Charles L. Harness.

**CURRIER, Catherine M.** Automation Manager/Coordinator of Technical Services, Murphy Library, University of Wisconsin-La Crosse; assistant editor, *New Moon*. Author of papers on science-fiction issues. **Essays:** Douglas Adams; John M. Ford; Nancy Springer.

**D'AMMASSA, Don.** Assistant vice-president, Data Processing, Taunton Silversmiths; book reviewer for *Science Fiction Chronicle* since 1986; book reviewer for *Mystery Science* since 1989. Past editor of *Mythologies*. Author of *Blood Beast*, 1988, and numerous short stories and articles. **Essays:** Piers Anthony; Isaac Asimov; Steven Barnes; William Barnwell; Neal Barrett; Barrington John Bayley; Gregory Benford; Alfred Bester; David F. Bischoff; Robert Bloch; J.F. Bone; Ben Bova; Mildred Downey Broxon; Edward Bryant; David R. Bunch; Anthony Burgess; Paul Capon; Terry Carr; Rob Chilson; D.G. Compton; Glen Cook; Alfred Coppel; Brian C. Daley; Arsen Darney; L. Sprague de Camp; Samuel R. Delany; Peter Dickinson; Wayland Drew; Dave Duncan; Larry Eisenberg; Christopher Evans; Mick Farren; William R. Forstchen; Esther M. Friesner; H.B. Fyfe; Craig Shaw Gardner; Stephen Goldin; Lisa Goldstein; Rex Gordon; Stuart Gordon; William Greenleaf; Isadore Haiblum; Jack C. Haldeman; Simon Hawke; James Herbert; Philip E. High; Christopher Hodder-Williams; Robert Holdstock; Fred and Geoffrey Hoyle; Barry Hughart; James Patrick Kelly; Lee Killough; Damon Knight; Brad Linaweaver; Barry Longyear; Richard Lupoff; Laurence Manning; Richard M. McKenna; George R.R. Martin; Dean McLaughlin; Thomas F. Monteleone; Michael Moorcock; C.L. Moore; Dan Morgan; John Morressy; Janet Morris; Ed Naha; Ray Nelson; Alan E. Nourse; Doris Piserchia; Jerry Pournelle; Terry Pratchett; Paul Preuss; Christopher Priest; John Rackham; Francis G. Rayer; Robert Reed; Mike Resnick; Stephen Robinett; Sarban; Richard Saxon; Elizabeth Ann Scarborough; Hilbert Schenck; William M. Sloane; George H. Smith; G. Harry Stine; Michael Swanwick; Stephen Tall; Ted Thomas; Robert Thurston; Patrick Tilley; Vercors (foreign-language); Ian Watson; Connie Willis; F. Paul Wilson; Gene Wolfe; Timothy Zahn.

**DRAKE, David. A.** See his own entry. **Essays:** Arthur Porges; Stanley Waterloo.

**DUNN, Thomas P.** Professor of English, Miami University, Oxford, Ohio; member of the editorial board, *Extrapolation.* Author of various articles on science fiction. Editor, with Richard D. Erlich, *The Mechanical God: Machines in Science Fiction*, 1982, and *Clockwork Worlds: Mechanized Environments in SF*, 1983. **Essays:** C.J. Cherryh; H.M. Hoover; Kevin O' Donnell, Jr.; James Tiptree, Jr.

**EDWARDS, Karren C.** Teacher. **Essay:** Fenton Ash.

**EDWARDS, Malcolm.** Administrator, Science Fiction Foundation, London, and editor, *Foundation*, London. Editor of *Vector*, 1972–74; SF editor for Gollancz publishers, 1976–77.

**EGGELING, John.** SF bibliographer.

**EISENSTEIN, Alex.** Author of several SF short stories with Phyllis Eisenstein. **Essay:** C.M. Kornbluth.

**ELKINS, Charles.** Associate Professor of English, Director of the Humanities Program, and Associate Dean for College Programs, Florida International University, Miami; co-editor, *Science Fiction Studies.* Author of a chapter in *Isaac Asimov*, 1977, and of essays in *Survey of Science Fiction Literature*, 1979, and periodicals.

**FEELEY, Gregory.** Freelance writer and critic. Author of a forthcoming biography of James Blish, *Alchemy under Pressure.* **Essays:** Jack Dann; Felix C. Gotschalk; Donald Kingsbury.

**FONTAINE, Eric A.** Freelance writer, author of articles on French and Latin American literature. **Essay:** William Jon Watkins.

**FRANE, Jeff.** Freelance writer. Author of *Fritz Leiber*, 1980. Co-editor of *A Fantasy Reader*, 1981. **Essay:** Elizabeth A. Lynn.

**FRATZ, D. Douglas.** Publisher and editor, *Quantum*, previously *Thrust*, since 1973. Scientist, Chemical Specialties Manufacturers Association, since 1980. Author of various book reviews and articles in *Thrust/Quantum, Fantasy Review*, and *The Washington Post*, and numerous papers in scientific journals and chemical industry trade magazines. **Essays:** Elizabeth Hand; Michael E. Kube-McDowell; Charles Platt; Kim Stanley Robinson; Jessica A. Salmonson.

**GAAR, Alice Carol.** Associate University Librarian, Florida State University Library, Tallahassee. Co-author of *Deutsche Stunden*, 1964, and author of articles in *Robert A. Heinlein*, 1978, *Quarber Merkur, Science Fiction Studies*, and *SForum*, and reviews, and poems. **Essay:** Herbert W. Franke (foreign-language).

**GARNER, John V.** High school language director. **Essay:** Mark S. Geston.

**GILLINGS, Walter.** Editor and publisher of British science fiction from the 1930's; editor of *Tales of Wonder, Scientifiction, Fantasy Review, Science Fantasy*, and *Cosmos Science-Fantasy Review;* associate editor of Utopian Publications, and founding director of Nova Publications. Died in 1979. **Essays:** S.P. Meek; Bob Olsen; Eric Frank Russell; Garrett P. Serviss; A. Hyatt Verrill.

**GOLDMAN, Stephen H.** Associate Professor of English, University of Kansas, Lawrence. Author of articles in *Survey of Science Fiction*, and *Science-Fiction Studies.* **Essays:** Tom Godwin; James E. Gunn; Daniel Keyes; Stanley G. Weinbaum.

**GOUGH, John.** Lecturer in mathematics education, Victoria College, Malven. Author of writing manuals, and numerous articles on children's literature, teaching, and mathematics education. **Essays:** Susan Cooper; George MacDonald.

**GREENBERG, Martin H.** Professor of Regional Analysis, University of Wisconsin, Green Bay; series co-editor of Alternatives (Southern Illinois University Press) and Writers of the Twenty-First Century (Taplinger). Co-author of *Index to Stories in Thematic Anthologies of Science Fiction*, 1978. Editor of more than 100 anthologies and single-author collections. **Essays:** Christopher Anvil; Chan Davis; F.L. Wallace.

**GREENLAND, Colin.** See his own entry. **Essays:** Mervyn Peake; Walter Tevis.

**GREENLAW, M. Jean.** Regents Professor of Education, University of North Texas, Denton. **Essay:** Jane Yolen.

**HALL, Hal W.** Head, Special Formats Division, Texas A and M University, College Station. Compiler of *Science Fiction Book Review Index 1923–73, 1974–79*, and annual volumes since 1980, and of the annual *Science Fiction and Fantasy Research Index.* Guest editor of *Science Fiction Collections*, 1983.

**HAMMERTON, M.** Professor Emeritus of psychology, University of Newcastle. Author of *Statistics for the Human Sciences*, 1975, and over 50 technical papers in various psychological journals, and papers on other subjects, including science-fiction writers. **Essays:** Harry Turtledove; Robert L. Forward.

**HARBOTTLE, Philip J.** Local government officer. Author of *The Multi-Man* (on John Russell Fearn), 1968, *Vultures of the Void* (with Stephen Holland), 1991, *British Science Fiction Paperbacks* (with Holland), 1991, and *The Work of John Russell Fearn*, forthcoming. Research consultant and contributor, *The Visual Encyclopaedia of Science Fiction*, 1977. Editor, *The Best of E.E. "Doc" Smith*, 1975. **Essay:** John Russell Fearn.

**HARDING, Lee.** See his own entry.

**HARTWELL, David G.** Consulting editor, Tor Books and William Morrow, New York. Author of *Age of Wonders: Exploring the World of Science Fiction*, 1985. Editor of (with Kathryn Kramer), *Spirits of Christmas*, 1989. Former SF editor for Signet-New American Library, Berkley-Putnam, and Timescape-Pocket Books. **Essays:** Peter George; Frank R. Stockton.

**HASSLER, Donald M.** Professor of English, Kent State University, Kent, Ohio; editor, *Extrapolation.* President, Science Fiction Research Association, 1985–86. Author of *The Comedian as the Letter D: Erasmus Darwin's Comic Materialism*, 1973, *Erasmus Darwin*, 1974, *Comic Tones in Science Fiction: The Art of Compromise with Nature*, 1982, and *Hal Clement*, 1982. Editor of *Patterns of the Fantastic*, 2 vols., 1983–84, and co-editor, *Death and the Serpent: Immortality in Science Fiction and Fantasy*, 1985, and *Isaac Asimov*, 1990. **Essays:** Harry Bates; James

Blish; Hal Clement; Raymond Z. Gallun; David H. Keller; Norman L. Knight; Murray Leinster; Nat Schachner; Stanley Schmidt.

**HATFIELD, Len.** Instructor in English, Indiana University, Bloomington; book review editor, *Victorian Studies.* Author of articles on Yeats and May Sinclair, and reviews for *Fantasy Review.* Assistant editor, *College English*, 1982–84. **Essay:** D.M. Thomas.

**HECHT, Sharon-Ilona.** Technical editor for a NASA contractor. **Essay:** M.K. Joseph.

**HERBERT, Rosemary.** Reference Librarian, Harvard University, Cambridge, Massachusetts; Instructor, The Experimental College, Tufts University, Massachusetts. Author of a book of photographs, and a collection of interviews of mystery writers, forthcoming. **Essays:** Arthur Conan Doyle; Ursula K. Le Guin; Margaret St. Clair; Evelyn E. Smith.

**HILLS, Norman L.** Director of Data Processing, Servi Share, Inc. Author of articles on Harness and Leiber. **Essays:** Lawrence Durrell; Fritz Leiber.

**HOLM, Janis Butler.** Assistant Professor of English, Ohio University, Athens. Author of articles on literary theory, textual bibliography, Tudor cultural history, and women's studies. **Essay:** Sheila MacLeod.

**HUGHES, Terry.** Freelance writer. **Essay:** Lee Hoffman.

**HULL, Elizabeth Anne.** Associate Professor of English, William Rainey Harper College, Palatine, Illinois; North American Secretary of World SF, and editor of *World SF Newsletter.* Author of essays in *Clockwork Worlds, Extrapolation, Essays in Arts and Sciences, Destinies*, and *Starlog Science Fiction Yearbook;* contributor to *Locus, Science Fiction Chronicle*, and *Fantasy Review.* **Essays:** Lloyd Biggle, Jr.; Robert A. Heinlein; Judith Merril.

**HUNT, Marvin W.** Graduate student in English, University of North Carolina, Chapel Hill. Author of a travel narrative, "The Road to Key West," in the Winston-Salem *Journal*, December 1984. **Essays:** Paul W. Fairman; Tom Purdom; Louis Trimble.

**IKIN, Van.** Lecturer in English, University of Western Australia, Nedlands; editor of *Science Fiction: A Review of Speculative Literature*, SF columnist for the *Sydney Morning Herald.* Editor of *Australian Science Fiction*, 1982, and *Glass Reptile Breakout and Other Australian Speculative Stories*, 1990. **Essays:** John Baxter; Frank Bryning; Terry Dowling; Lee Harding; George Turner.

**JAKUBOWSKI, Maxim.** Publisher, writer, and owner of Murder One crime bookshop, London. Series editor of Blue Murder crime imprint; editor of *New Crimes, The Detective Directory* (forthcoming), and many other books on crime fiction, science fiction, fantasy, film, and music. Contributor of reviews and articles to many journals and newspapers including *The Times, Time Out,* and *The Observer.*

**JAMES, Edward.** Senior Lecturer of history, Co-director, Centre for Medieval Studies, University of York. Editor, *Foundation.* Author of *The Merovingian Archaeology of South-West Gaul*, 2 vols., 1977, *The Origins of France*, 1982, *Gregory of Tours: Life of the Fathers*, 1985, *The Franks*, 1988, and numerous articles on various subjects, including the history of science fiction and reviews of science fiction. Editor, *Visigothic Spain*, 1980, and *The Profession of Science Fiction*, with Maxim Jakubowski, 1991. **Essays:** Christine Brooke-Rose; John Gribbin; Gwyneth Jones; Ian McDonald; Brain Stableford.

**JONES, Anne Hudson.** Associate Professor of literature and medicine, Institute for the Medical Humanities, University of Texas Medical Branch, Galveston; editor-in-chief of the journal *Literature and Medicine*, and member of the editorial board, *Medical Heritage.* Author of several articles on feminist science fiction, and on literature and medical ethics. Editor of *Literature and Medicine: Images of Healers*, 1983. **Essay:** Katherine MacLean.

**JURKIEWICZ, Kenneth.** Assistant Professor of English, Central Michigan University, Mount Pleasant. Author of articles on space movies, Ramsey Campbell, and Saki. **Essays:** Pierre Boulle (foreign-language); Curt Siodmak.

**KAGARLITSKY, Julius.** Freelance critic; member of the editorial board, Library of Modern SF. Author of *The Life and Thought of H.G. Wells*, 1966, *What Does It Mean, SF?* 1974, *Western Theatre of the 18th Century in the Eyes of Russian Critics*, 1976, *Shakespeare and Voltaire*, 1980, *Theatre for All Ages*, 1986. Editor of a 15-volume edition of works by Wells, 1964. Former Professor at the State Theatrical Institute, Moscow. **Essay:** John Wyndham.

**KELLEY, George.** Professor of business administration, Erie Community College-City Campus, Buffalo, New York. Contributor to *Twentieth-Century Crime and Mystery Writers, Twentieth-Century Western Writers, Mass Market Publishing in America,* and *Poison Pen.* **Essays:** Michael Bishop; Mark Clifton; John Creasey; Miriam Allen deFord; Gardner Dozois; Cynthia Felice; Jane Gaskell; M. John Harrison; Joe L. Hensley; Trevor Hoyle; Zach Hughes; Dean Ing; K.W. Jeter; Leo P. Kelley; Crawford Kilian; William Kotzwinkle; Milton Lesser; Jack Sharkey; T.L. Sherred; Robert Silverberg; Christopher Stasheff; Emma Tennant; Ian Wallace.

**KETTERER, David.** Professor of English, Concordia University, Montreal. Author of *New Worlds for Old: The Apocalyptic Imagination, Science Fiction, and American Literature*, 1974, *The Rationale of Deception in Poe*, 1979, *Frankenstein's Creation: The Book, The Monster, and Human Reality*, 1979, and *Imprisoned in a Tesseract: The Life and Work of James Blish*, forthcoming. Editor of *The Science Fiction of Mark Twain*, 1984.

**KINCAID, Paul.** Reviews editor, *Vector*, 1985–90. Co-ordinator, British Science Fiction Association, 1986–89. Author of *Keith Roberts*, 1983, and of short stories, and reviews in various journals, including *The Times Literary Supplement, Vector*, and *Foundation.* **Essays:** John Brosnan; Karen J. Fowler; Keith Roberts; Josephine Saxton; Bob Shaw; Thorne Smith.

**KLEIN, Gérard.** See his entry in the foreign-language appendix. Editor, Editions Robert Laffont, Paris, and consultant economist. Author of novels (*Le Gambit des Etoiles*, 1958, *Les Seigneurs de la Guerre*, 1971), short stories (*Les Perles du Temps*, 1958, *La Loi du Talion*, 1973, *Histoires comme si . . .*, 1985), and the critical book *Malaise dans la science-fiction américaine*, 1979. **Essay:** Michel Jeury (foreign-language).

**KOHLER, Vince.** Staff writer and SF reviewer, *The Oregonian*, Portland. **Essay:** John Kippax.

**KRATZ, Dennis M.** Professor of arts and humanities, University of Texas, Dallas. Author of *Mocking Epic: Waltharius, Alexandreis and the Problem of Christian Heroism*, 1980, *Waltharius and Ruodlieb*, 1984, *The Romances of Alexander*, 1991, and numerous articles on fantasy, science fiction, and medieval literature. **Essays:** Lin Carter; John Sladek; Thomas B. Swann; Chelsea Quinn Yarbo.

**LAKE, David.** See his own entry. **Essays:** Russell Hoban; C.S. Lewis.

**LASKOWSKI, William, Jr.** Assistant Professor of English, Jamestown College, North Dakota. **Essays:** Larry Niven; Jack Vance.

**LAWLER, Donald L.** Professor of English, East Carolina University, Greenville, North Carolina; editor of *Victorians Institute Journal.* Co-author of *Vonnegut in America*, 1977, and author of *Approaches to Science Fiction*, 1978, and articles on 19th- and 20th-century British and American writers. Contributing editor of *Survey of Science Fiction Literature*, 1979, consulting editor of *Survey of Modern Fantasy Literature*, 5 vols., 1983, and editor of a forthcoming edition of Wilde's *The Picture of Dorian Gray.* **Essays:** Anthony Boucher; Avram Davidson; David Gerrold; Otis Adelbert Kline; Kris Neville; J.R.R. Tolkien.

**LAWSON, John I.** Reference Librarian, Fairfax County Public Library, Virginia. Author of various articles and reviews. **Essay:** Alan Dean Foster.

**LEAHY, Mark Warwick.** Graduate student, University of Adelaide, South Australia. **Essays:** Sylvia Engdahl; Richard Rohmer.

**LEPERLIER, Henry D.** Journalist, *LA*, Ireland; translator, teacher, and broadcaster. Ph.D. candidate in comparative literature, University of Sherbrooke, Quebec. Author of numerous articles and reviews. **Essays:** Candace Jane Dorsey; Daniel Sernine (foreign-language); S.M. Stirling; Elisabeth Vonarburg (foreign-language); Andrew Weiner; Robert Charles Wilson.

**LEVY, Michael M.** Professor of English, University of Wisconsin-Stout, Menomonie; contributing editor of *Science Fiction and Fantasy Book Review Annual.* Author of *Natalie Babbitt*, 1991, and articles on *Paradise Lost* and *Doctor Who*, and reviews for *Fantasy Review.* **Essays:** Warren Norwood; Philip Francis Nowlan; Lucius Shepard; Gary K. Wolf.

**LEWIS, Arthur O.** Professor Emeritus of English, Pennsylvania State University, University Park; member of the advisory board, *Alternative Futures.* Author of many books; those on SF-related topics include *Of Men and Machines*, 1963, *American Utopias: Selected Short Fiction*, 1971, and *Utopian Literature in the Pennsylvania State University Libraries: A Selected Bibliography*, 1984. Editor of *Utopian Literature*, 41 vols., 1971, and the SF issue, 1976, and Utopian Studies issue, 1981, of *Journal of General Education.* **Essays:** Ernest Callenbach; Joseph O'Neill; Marge Piercy; Steven Spruill.

**LOWENKOPF, Shelly.** Adjunct Professor, Professional Writing Program, University of Southern California, Los Angeles. Author of more than 40 books (fiction and non-fiction), and of numerous essays and reviews. Former director, Dell Publishing, California Office, and former editor-in-chief, American Bibliographical Center-Clio Press and Ross-Erikson Inc. **Essays:** A. Bertram Chandler; Madeleine L'Engle.

**LUNAN, Duncan.** Freelance writer, lecturer, and critic. Author of *Man and the Stars*, 1974 (in USA as *Interstellar Contact*), *New Worlds for Old*, 1979, and *Man and the Planets*, 1983 (all non-fiction), many articles and papers, and 24 short stories. **Essays:** Charles Chilton; Joe Haldeman; Naomi Mitchison.

**LUPOFF, Richard A.** See his own entry. **Essays:** Edwin L. Arnold; Robert Asprin; Eando Binder; Edgar Rice Burroughs; Orson Scott Card; Stanton A. Coblentz; George Allan England; Hugo Gernsback; H.L. Gold; Michael Kurland; Frank Belknap Long; Sam Merwin; Raymond A. Palmer; Wilmar H. Shiras; Donald A. Wollheim.

**LYNCH, Peter.** Freelance writer, Houston. **Essays:** Gordon Eklund; Victor Rousseau.

**MACDONALD, Andrew.** Academic Director of Intensive English and English as a Second Language, Loyola University, New Orleans. Author of articles on Jonson, Shakespeare, English as a second language, SF, and popular culture. **Essays:** Martin Caidin (with Gina Macdonald); Doris Lessing; Neville Shute.

**MACDONALD, Gina.** Assistant Professor of English, Loyola University, New Orleans. Author of articles on Shakespeare, Robert Greene, English as a second language, popular culture, and SF. **Essays:** Kingsley Amis; Martin Caidin (with Andrew Macdonald); William Golding; Frank Herbert; Robert Hoskins; Aldous Huxley; Stanislaw Lem (foreign-language); Thomas Pynchon; John Rankine; Arthur Sellings; Somtow Sucharitkul; Boris and Arkady Strugatsky (foreign-language; with Darko Suvin); Stanislaw Witkiewicz (foreign-language).

**MACRAE, Cathi.** Young Adult Librarian, Boulder Public Library, Colorado. Author of *Presenting Young Adult Fantasy*, forthcoming, young adult book review column in *Wilson Library Bulletin*, and other articles. **Essays:** R.A. MacAvoy; Patricia McKillip.

**MALLETT, Darryl F.** Assistant to curator, J. Lloyd Eaton Collection, University of California, Riverside; senior assistant editor, Borgo Press, San Bernardino, California. **Essays:** Greg Bear; David Brin; Susan Shwartz.

**MANOUSOS, Anthony.** Member of the Department of English, Carleton College, Northfield, Minnesota. Author of articles in *Dictionary of American Science Fiction Writers*, and on D.H. Lawrence and Swift. **Essay:** L.P. Davies.

**McGUIRE, Patrick L.** Civil servant, U.S. Federal government. Author of *Red Stars: Political Aspects of Soviet Science Fiction*, 1985, and articles on Joe Haldeman, the Strugatskys, C.J. Cherryh, and Poul Anderson. Consulting editor, *Survey of Science Fiction Literature*, 1979; translator of works of Soviet SF. **Essays:** Keith Laumer, Vernor Vinge; James White.

**McVEIGH, Kev P.** Co-ordinator, British Science Fiction Association; editor, *Vector*, since 1989. **Essays:** Storm Constantine; Leigh Kennedy; Judith Moffet; Pat Murphy; Michaela Roessner; Howard Waldrop.

**MEYERING, Sheryl L.** Assistant Professor of English, Southern Illinois University, Edwardsville. Author of *Charlotte Perkins Gilman: The Woman and Her Work*, 1989, *Sylvia Plath: A Reference Guide*, 1990, *Studies in the Short Fiction of Willa Cather*, forthcoming, and various articles and reviews. **Essay:** Charlotte Perkins Gilman.

**MEYERS, Walter E.** Professor of English, North Carolina State University, Raleigh; member of the editorial board, *Science Fiction Studies.* Author of *Aliens and Linguists*, 1980. Consulting editor, *Survey of Science Fiction Literature*, 1979. **Essays:** T.J. Bass; Rosel George Brown; H. Rider Haggard; Ward Moore; James H. Schmitz.

**MIESEL, Sandra.** Freelance writer; Ph.D. candidate in history, Indiana University, Bloomington. Author of *Myth, Symbol, and Religion in Lord of the Rings*, 1973, *Against Time's Arrow: The High Crusade of Poul Anderson*, 1979, *Dreamrider*, 1982, *Shaman*, 1989, and of articles in *Amazing, SF Monthly, Isaac Asimov's Science Fiction Magazine*, and other periodicals. Editor of story collections and anthologies. **Essays:** Poul Anderson; Gordon R. Dickson; Alexis A. Gilliland; Zenna Henderson; R.A. Lafferty; Fred Saberhagen; Wilson Tucker.

**MILLER, Richard W.** Associate Professor of Philosophy, University of Missouri, Rolla. **Essay:** H. Beam Piper.

**MOLSON, Francis J.** Professor of English, Central Michigan University, Mount Pleasant. Author of chapters on SF for children in *Anatomy of Wonder, The Art and Aesthetics of Fantasy*, and *The Science Fiction Reference Book*, and of articles on Le Guin, Emily Dickinson, Frances Hodgson Burnett, and other writers. **Essays:** Monica Hughes; Alexander Key; Alice Lightner; Jeff and Jean Sutton; Hugh Walters; Laurence Yep.

**MONTGOMERIE, Lee.** Freelance writer. Past contributor to *Foundation.* **Essay:** W.E. Johns.

**MORRISSEY, Thomas J.** Professor of English, State University of New York College at Plattsburgh. Author of various critical essays and poetry. **Essay:** Pamela Sargent.

**MURRAY, Will.** Editorial Director of Odyssey Publications and freelance writer. Author or co-author of *The Man Behind Doc Savage*, 1974, *The Duende History of The Shadow Magazine*, 1979, and *The Assassin's Handbook*, articles in *Starlog, Lovecraft Studies, Crypt of Cthulhu, Xenophile, Etchings and Odysseys*, and fiction in *Ellery Queen's Mystery Magazine, Eldritch Tales*, and other magazines. Past editor of the magazines *Duende* and *Skullduggery.* **Essays:** Lester Dent; Clark Ashton Smith; John Taine.

**NELLIS, Marilyn K.** Assistant Professor, Liberal Studies Center, Clarkson University, Potsdam, New York. **Essay:** James Kahn.

**NICHOLS, Ian.** English teacher, Churchlands Senior High, Australia. *Analyzing the Trooper in Heinlein*, 1986, *Moorcock and the New Wave*, 1987, *Conan the Messiah*, 1985, and *Mythology and Samuel R. Delany*, 1988. **Essays:** A.A. Attanasio; Raymond E. Feist.

**OLIVER, Chad.** See his own entry. **Essays:** Edmond Hamilton; Ross Rocklynne.

**ORODENKER, Richard.** Associate Professor of English, Peirce Junior College, Philadelphia. Author of criticism and fiction in *North American Review, Benzene, Studies in Short Fiction*, and other publications. **Essay:** F.M. Busby.

**PAGE, Gerald W.** Writer and editor. Author of many SF and fantasy stories since 1963. Editor of the anthologies *Year's Best Horror Stories 4–7, Nameless Places*, and *Heroic Fantasy* (with Hank Reinhardt); former editor of *Witchcraft and Sorcery Magazine* and consultant editor of *Amazing.* **Essays:** Nelson S. Bond; Charles L. Fontenay; Gardner F. Fox; Neil R. Jones; Raymond F. Jones; Lisa Tuttle; Sharon Webb; Robert Moore Williams.

**PARKIN-SPEER, Diane.** Professor of English, Southwest Texas State University, San Marcos. Author of articles in 16th- and 17th-century English literature, history of ideas, and the relation of law and literature. **Essays:** Alexei Panshin; Sydney J. Van Scyoc.

**PATTEN, Frederick.** Catalog librarian in an aerospace technical library. Author of the guide to comic books in *Magazines for Libraries*, and of reviews of SF in *Library Journal, Science Fiction, Locus*, and other publications. Publisher and co-editor of *Delap's F & SF Review*, 1975-77. **Essay:** C.C. MacApp.

**PAUL, Terri.** Senior Scientific Programmer, McDonnell Douglas Technical Services Company, Houston. Author of articles on Pohl, women in SF, time travel, and technical writing. **Essay:** Rudy Rucker.

**PERKINS, Michael.** Freelance writer. Arts Program Director, Woodstock Guild, New York. Author of *Evil Companions* (novel), 1968, *Down Here* (stories), 1969, *The Secret Record* (criticism), 1976, and *The Persistence of Desire* (poetry), 1977. Editor of *Ulster Arts* magazine, 1977-79, and former editor for Tompkins Square Press and Croton Press. **Essays:** Thomas M. Disch; David Meltzer.

**PFEIFFER, John R.** Professor of English, Central Michigan University, Mount Pleasant; bibliographer, *Shaw Annual.* Author of *Fantasy and Science Fiction: A Critical Guide*, 1971, and essays on Brunner, Le Guin, Huxley, Morris, and others; co-author of a chapter on the modern period in *Anatomy of Wonder*, 1976 (revised, 1981, 1987). Special editor of "GBS and Science Fiction" issue of *Shaw Review.* **Essays:** Octavia Butler; John Christopher; Robert Stallman; John A. Williams; Colin Wilson.

**PHILLIPS, Gene.** Librarian. Author of fantasy stories. **Essays:** Kenneth Bulmer; Alan Dean Foster; Colin Kapp; Emil Petaja; Bob Shaw.

**PHILMUS, Robert M.** Professor of English, Concordia University, Montreal; editor, *Science-Fiction Studies.* Author of *Into the Unknown: The Evolution of Science Fiction from Francis Godwin to H.G. Wells*, 1970 (2nd edition 1983), and a chapter on early SF in *Anatomy of Wonder*, 1976 (revised 1981). Co-editor of *H.G. Wells: Early Writings in Science and Science Fiction*, 1975, *H.G. Wells and Modern Science Fiction*, 1977, and *H.G. Wells's Literary Criticism*, 1980.

**PIERCE, Hazel.** Professor Emeritus of English, Kearney State College, Nebraska; member of the editorial board, *Platte Valley Review.* Author of *Philip K. Dick*, 1982, *A Literary Symbiosis: Science Fiction/Fantasy/Mystery*, 1983, and essays on Asimov, Bradbury, and Dick in *Writers of the 21st Century* volumes, and on Blake and Byron. **Essays:** George Alec Effinger; Kurd Lasswitz (foreign-language); Phillip Mann; A.E. van Vogt.

**PIERCE, John J.** Associate editor, Private Label magazine. Author of essays on Cordwainer Smith. Editor of *The Best of Cordwainer Smith*, 1975, *Norstrilia*, 1975, *The Best of Murray Leinster*, 1978, and *The Best of Raymond Z. Gallun*, 1978. Former editor of *Galaxy*, and of the fanzines *Renaissance* and *Tension, Apprehension, and Dissension.* **Essays:** Otto Gail (foreign-language); Bernhard Kellermann (foreign-language).

**PRATT, Nick.** Freelance photographer; also book reviewer. **Essay:** R.W. Mackelworth.

**PRIEST, Christopher.** See his own entry.

**PRONZINI, Bill.** Author of 50 novels, 3 nonfiction books, 4 collections, and several hundred stories, articles, and essays. Editor of numerous thematic anthologies. **Essays:** Arthur K. Barnes; Charles Beaumont; Cleve Cartmill; Edward D. Hoch; Even Hunter.

**QUINN, Joseph A.** Associate Professor of English, University of Windsor, Ontario. Author of articles and reviews in *Chesterton Review, University of Windsor Review, Christianity and Literature,* and *Alternative Futures.* **Essays:** Constantine FitzGibbon; Alun Llewellyn.

**RABKIN, Eric S.** Professor of English and Arthur F. Thurnau Professor, University of Michigan, Ann Arbor. Author of *The Fantastic in Literature*, 1976, *Science Fiction: History, Science, Vision* (with Robert Scholes), 1977, *Arthur C. Clarke*, 1979, *Teaching Writing that Works* (with Macklin Smith), 1990, and others. Co-editor of *The End of the World*, 1983, and others. **Essay:** Arthur C. Clarke.

**REGINALD, R.** Professor, California State University, San Bernardino; publisher, Borgo Press. Author of numerous books, and of over 100 articles. Editor of SF reprint series. **Essays:** Arthur B. Cover; R. Lionel Fanthorpe; Katherine Kurtz; Bruce McAllister; William F. Nolan; Michael Reaves; George Zebrowski.

**REILLY, Robert.** Professor of English, Rider College, Lawrenceville, New Jersey. Author of *The Transcendent Adventure: Studies of Religion in Science Fiction/Fantasy*, 1984, and articles on Ray Bradbury, Silverberg, and Zelazney. **Essays:** D.F. Jones; Vincent King.

**RIES, Lawrence R.** Assistant Director of the University Without Walls, Skidmore College, Saratoga Springs, New York. Author of *Wolf Masks: Violence in Contemporary Poetry*, 1977. **Essay:** Sterling E. Lanier.

**ROTTENSTEINER, Franz.** Freelance editor, translator, and literary agent. Editor of Suhrkamp's Fantastic Library series (12–24 annual vols.). Author of *The Science Fiction Book*, 1975, and *The Fantasy Book*, 1978. Editor of *View from Another Shore: European SF*, 1973, *The Slaying of the Dragon: Modern Tales of the Playful Imagination*, 1984, and *Microworlds*, by Lem, 1984, and numerous anthologies in German. **Essays:** Karin Boye (foreign-language); Dino Buzzati (foreign-language); Wyman Guin; Wolfgang Jeschke (foreign-language); Maurice Renard (foreign-language).

**ROUSSEAU, Yvonne.** Freelance writer and editor. Joint editor of *Australian Science Fiction Review*, 1986–91. Author of *The Murders at Hanging Rock*, 1980, and of several short stories. **Essay:** Cherry Wilder.

**RUDDICK, Nicholas.** Associate Professor of English, University of Regina, Canada; Science fiction division head, International Association for the Fantastic in the Arts, since 1988. Author of *Christopher Priest*, 1989, *British Science Fiction: A Chronology 1478–1990*, forthcoming, and numerous articles on British and American poetry and fiction. Editor of *State of the Fantastic*, forthcoming. **Essays:** J.G. Ballard; Iain Banks.

**RUSS, Joanna.** See her own entry. **Essay:** H.P. Lovecraft.

**SAMMONS, Todd.** Associate Professor of English, University of Hawaii, Manoa. Author of numerous articles and reviews of science fiction. **Essays:** Julian May; Charles Sheffield.

**SAMUELSON, David N.** Professor of English, California State University, Long Beach; member of the editorial board, *Science Fiction Studies* and *Survey of Science Fiction Literature.* Author of *Visions of Tomorrow: Six Voyages from Outer to Inner Space*, 1974, *Arthur C. Clarke: A Primary and Secondary Bibliography*, 1984, and essays and reviews in newspapers and journals. **Essays:** John Boyd; Max Ehrlich; Howard Fast; Walter M. Miller, Jr.; Theodore Sturgeon; Bernard Wolfe.

**SANDERS, Joe.** Professor of English, Lakeland Community College, Mentor, Ohio; associate editor of *The Year's Scholarship in Science Fiction, Fantasy, and Horror Literature* since 1980. Author of *Roger Zelazny: A Primary and Secondary Bibliography*, nine essays in *Survey of Fantasy Literature*, 1983, and an article on Richard Condon in *Extrapolation*, 1984. **Essays:** John Shirley; Bruce Sterling.

**SARGENT, Pamela.** See her own entry. **Essay:** Kate Wilhelm.

**SATTY, Harvey J.** President of the Olaf Stapledon Society. Author of *Olaf Stapledon: A Bibliography* (with Curtis C. Smith), 1984. **Essay:** John Gloag.

**SCARBOROUGH, John.** Professor of classics and ancient history, and the history of pharmacy and medicine, University of Wisconsin, Madison. Author of *Roman Medicine*, 1969, *Facets of Hellenic Life*, 1976, "Medicine in Science Fiction," in *The Science Fiction Encyclopedia*, 1979, *Pharmacy's Ancient Heritage*, 1985, *Greek and Latin Origins of Medical Terminologies*, 1992, and articles on Rider Haggard, Wyndham, Lem, Anthony, and von Däniken. Editor of *Symposium on Byzantine Medicine*, 1984, and *Folklore and Folk Medicines*, 1987. **Essay:** Josef Nesvadba (foreign-language).

**SCHLOBIN, Roger C.** Professor of English, Purdue University North Central Campus, Westville, Indiana; editor for Starmont publishers. President, International Association for the Fantastic in the Arts, 1983–85. Author of *A Research Guide to Science Fiction Studies* (with Marshall B. Tymn and L.W. Currey), 1977, *The Year's Scholarship in Science Fiction and Fantasy* (with Tymn), 1979, *The Literature of Fantasy* (bibliography), 1979, *Andre Norton: A Primary and Secondary Bibliography*, 1980, and *Urania's Daughters: A Checklist of Women Science Fiction Writers 1697–1982*, 1983. **Essays:** Lord Dunsany; Andre Norton.

**SCHOLES, Robert.** Professor of English, Brown University, Providence, Rhode Island; general editor, Masters of Science Fiction series. Author of *The Fabulators*, 1969, *Structural Fabulation*, 1975, and *Science Fiction History; Science, Vision* (with Eric S. Rabkin), 1977.

**SCHUYLER, William M., Jr.** Professor of Philosophy, University of Louisville, Kentucky. Author of articles and chapters on philosophy and SF. **Essay:** Diane Duane.

**SCHWEITZER, Darrell.** Freelance writer; assistant editor, *Amazing*, SF critic, Philadelphia *Inquirer.* Author of *The Dream Quest of H.P. Lovecraft*, 1978, *We Are All Legends* (stories), 1981, *The Shattered Goddess* (novel), 1982, *Tom O'Bedlam's Night Out* (stories), 1985, and a forthcoming study of Lord

Dunsany. Editor of *Essays Lovecraftian*, 1976, *Science Fiction Voices 1*, 1979, *Discovering Modern Horror Fiction*, 1985, and *Exploring Fantasy Worlds*, 1985. **Essay:** Leo Szilard.

**SEARLES, Baird.** Owner and manager, The Science Fiction Shop, New York; film columnist, *Amazing*, and book columnist, *Isaac Asimov's Science Fiction Magazine.* Author or co-author of a study of Heinlein, *The Science Fiction Quiz Book*, 1974, *A Reader's Guide to Science Fiction [Fantasy]*, 2 vols., 1979–82, and many reviews. **Essays:** A. Merritt; Austin Tappan Wright.

**SEIDEL, Kathryn Lee.** Associate Professor of English, University of Central Florida. Author of *The Southern Belle in American Fiction: Her Rise and Fall*, 1985, and articles on Russ, Piercy, Le Guin, Zora Neale Hurston, and others. Editor, *Zora in Florida*, 1991. **Essay:** Dean R. Koontz.

**SHWARTZ, Susan.** See her own entry. **Essays:** Marion Zimmer Bradley; Jayge Carr; Jacqueline Lichtenberg; Judith Tarr.

**SLUSSER, George.** Professor, Center for Bibliographical Studies and Research, Eaton Program for Science Fiction and Fantasy Studies, University of California, Riverside. **Essay:** Gérard Klein (foreign-language).

**SMITH, Curtis C.** Professor of Literature, University of Houston, Clear Lake City. Author of *Olaf Stapledon: A Bibliography* (with Harvey J. Satty), 1984. Editor of *Twentieth-Century Science-Fiction Writers*, 1981 (2nd edition 1986). **Essays:** Laurence M. Janifer; Philip Latham; Jack London; Robert A.W. Lowndes; Mack Reynolds.

**SNYDER, Carol L.** Associate Professor of Humanities, University of Houston, Clear Lake City. **Essay:** Joanna Russ.

**SNYDER, Judith.** Teacher and freelance writer. **Essay:** Gertrude Friedberg.

**SPELLER, Maureen.** Student of comparative literature and philosophy, Canterbury College. Co-ordinator, British Science Fiction Association, 1989–91, and editor of *Malnor* (BSFA Newsletter), 1986–90. Author of reviews in *Vector* and other journals. Editor of *The Gate*, 1989. **Essays:** Eric Brown; Charles de Lint; David Gemmell; David Zindell.

**STABLEFORD, Brian M.** See his own entry.

**STAPLES, Katherine.** Translator of works by Henri Rousseau and of *Les Illuminations* by Rimbaud. **Essay:** J.T. McIntosh.

**STAVANS, Ilan.** Assistant Professor of Latin American Letters, Baruch College, The City University of New York. Author of *Talia y el cielo*, 1989, *Prontuario*, 1991, *Imagining Columbus: The Literary Voyage*, 1992, and of fiction and criticism in *The New York Times, Diario 16, Science-Fiction Studies*, and other journals and newspapers. **Essays:** Jorge Luis Borges (foreign-language); Michael Ende (foreign-language).

**STEPHENSEN-PAYNE, Philippa.** Freelance writer. **Essay:** Nicholas Fisk.

**STONE, Graham.** Bookseller. Author of *Australian Science Fiction Index 1925–1967*, 1968 (supplement 1976), *Index to British Science Fiction Magazines 1934–1953*, 1980, and *Notes on Australian Science Fiction*, 1991. **Essays:** Christopher Blayre; Erle Cox; Ray Cummings; Lloyd Arthur Eshbach; P. Schuyler Miller; Jack Wodhams; Arthur Leo Zagat.

**STOVER, Leon.** Professor of Anthropology, Illinois Institute of Technology, Chicago. Author of the novels *Stonehenge*, with Harry Harrison, 1972 (revised as *Stonehenge: Where Atlantis Died*, 1983) and *The Shaving of Karl Marx*, 1982, and several works of non-fiction, including *La Science-Fiction Amèricaine*, 1972, *The Cultural Ecology of Chinese Civilization*, 1973, *Stonehenge: The Indo-European Heritage*, with Bruce Kraig, 1978 (British edition: *Stonehenge and the Origins of Europe)*, and *The Prophetic Soul: A Reading of H.G. Wells's "Things to Come"*, forthcoming. **Essays:** John W. Campbell, Jr.; George R. Stewart; Jules Verne (foreign-language).

**SULLIVAN, C.W., III.** Professor of English, and Director of Graduate Studies, East Carolina University, Greenville, North Carolina; editor of *Children's Folklore Newsletter;* vice-president, International Association for the Fantastic in the Arts. Author of *Welsh Celtic Myth in Modern Fantasy*, 1989, and of articles and reviews in various journals and anthologies. Editor of *As Tomorrow Becomes Today*, 1974. **Essays:** E.R. Eddison; Harlan Ellison; Pat Frank; John Norman; Andrew J. Offutt; Kit Reed.

**SUSSEX, Lucy.** Researcher, Department of English, University of Melbourne. Author of *The Peace Garden* (children's novel), 1989, and *My Lady Tongue and Other Tales* (short stories), 1990. Editor of *The Fortunes of Mary Fortune*, 1989. **Essays:** Katherine Burdekin; Pamela Zoline.

**SUVIN, Darko.** Professor of English and comparative literature, McGill University, Montreal. Author of *Russian Science Fiction 1956–1974: A Bibliography*, 1976, *Metamorphoses of Science Fiction*, 1979, *Victorian Science Fiction in the UK: The Discourses of Knowledge and of Power*, 1983, *To Brecht and Beyond*, 1984, *The Long March*, 1987, *Positions and Presuppositions in Science Fiction*, 1988, and *Azmizana Arkadija*, 1990. Editor of *Other Worlds, Other Seas*, 1970, *Science Fiction Studies* (with R.D. Mullen), 2 vols., 1976–78, and *H.G. Wells and Modern Science Fiction* (with Robert M. Philmus), 1977. **Essays:** Edward Bellamy; Aleksandr Belyaev (foreign-language); Valery Bryusov (foreign-language); Samuel Butler; Karel Capek (foreign-language); Robert Cromie; George Griffith; C.J. Cutcliffe Hyne; Vladimir Mayakovsky (foreign-language); Boris and Arkady Strugatsky (foreign-language; with Gina Macdonald); Alexey Tolstoy (foreign-language); Konstantin Tsiolkovsky (foreign-language); Ivan Yefremov (foreign-language); Yevgeny Zamyatin (foreign-language).

**SWANK, Paul.** Assistant Professor of educational psychology, University of Houston, University Park. **Essays:** Fletcher Pratt; George O. Smith.

**TALBOT, Norman.** Professor of English, University of Newcastle, New South Wales; managing editor, Nimrod Publications. Author of several books of poetry, the most recent being *The Kelly Haiku*, and works of literary criticism. Editor of anthologies of poetry, criticism, and prose. **Essays:** William Morris; Upton Sinclair.

**THURSTON, Robert.** See his own entry. **Essays:** Richard C. Meredith; James Sallis.

**TOLLEY, Michael J.** Reader in English, University of Adelaide, South Australia; editorial adviser, *Blake Studies.* Author of 20 essays on Blake and reviews for *SF and F Book Review* and *Fantasy Review*, mainly on Australian writing. Co-editor of *William Blake's Designs for Edward Young's Night Thoughts*, 2 vols., 1980 and *The Stellar Gauge: Essays on Science Fiction Writers*, 1980. **Essays:** Mark Adlard; Damien Broderick; Angela

Carter; Michael G. Coney; Michael Frayn; Joseph Green; Lindsay Gutteridge; David Lake; John D. MacDonald; Gerald Murnane; Kit Pedler and Gerry Davis; Wynne Whiteford.

**TUCK, Donald H.** Bibliographer and industrial manager. Author of *A Handbook of Science Fiction and Fantasy*, 1954 (revised edition, 2 vols., 1959), and *The Encyclopedia of Science Fiction and Fantasy*, 3 vols., 1974–83.

**TUCKER, Frank H.** Professor Emeritus of history, Colorado College, Colorado Springs. Author of *The White Conscience*, 1969, a chapter in *Robert A. Heinlein*, 1978, *The Frontier Spirit and Progress*, 1980, and articles in *Russian Affairs, Japanese Affairs, Intellect*, and *Extrapolation.* **Essays:** Kobo Abe (foreign-language); Sakyo Komatsu (foreign-language); André Maurois (foreign-language).

**TURNER, George.** See his own entry. **Essays:** J.D. Beresford; M. Barnard Eldershaw.

**TUTTLE, Lisa.** See her own entry. **Essay:** Tom Reamy.

**TUZAR, Jana I.** Doctoral student, University of Chicago. **Essay:** Mikhail Bulgakov (foreign-language).

**TYMN, Marshall B.** Professor of English, Eastern Michigan University, Ypsilanti; director of the National Workshop on Teaching Science Fiction; editor of the Contributions to the Study of Science Fiction and Fantasy series. Author of *Thomas Cole's Poetry*, 1972, *A Research Guide to Science Fiction Studies* (with Roger C. Schlobin and L.W. Currey), 1977, *Index to Stories in Thematic Anthologies of Science Fiction*, 1978, *American Fantasy and Science Fiction* (bibliography), 1979, *Fantasy [Horror] Literature: A Core Collection and Reference Guide*, and numerous articles, essays, and bibliographies. Editor of the annual bibliography *The Year's Scholarship in Science Fiction, Fantasy, and Horror Literature*, and of *Thomas Cole: Collected Essays and Prose Sketches*, 1980.

**UTLEY, Stevens.** See his own entry. **Essay:** Ralph Milne Farley.

**VARDEMAN, Robert E.** Freelance writer; president of the Cenotaph Corporation. Editor, *SFWA Forum*, 1978–79; vice-president, SFWA, 1979–80. Author of more than 90 books, including *Sandcats of Rhyl*, 1978, *Colors of Chaos*, 1988, and *Space Vectors*, 1990, and of short stories in various science-fiction and horror anthologies. **Essay:** George W. Proctor.

**WAGAR, W. Warren.** Professor of history, State University of New York, Binghamton; member of the editorial board, *Futures Research Quarterly*, and *Utopian Studies*; vice-president, H.G. Wells Society. Author of *H.G. Wells and the World State*, 1961, *The City of Man*, 1963, *Building the City of Man*, 1971, *Good Tidings: The Belief in Progress from Darwin to Marcuse*, 1972, *Books in World History*, 1973, *World Views: A Study in Comparative History*, 1977, *Terminal Visions: The Literature of Last Things*, 1982, and *A Short History of the Future*, 1989. Editor of *H.G. Wells: Journalism and Prophesy*, 1964, *European Intellectual History since Darwin and Marx*, 1967, *Science, Faith, and Man*, 1968, *The Idea of Progress since the Renaissance*, 1969, *History and the Idea of Mankind*, 1971, and *The Secular Mind: Transformations of Faith in Modern Europe*, 1982. **Essay:** H.G. Wells.

**WAGNER, Karl Edward.** Freelance writer, editor of *Carcosa.* Author of *Darkness Weaves*, 1970; *Death Angel's Shadow*, 1973, *Bloodstone*, 1975, *Dark Crusade*, 1976, *Legion from the Shadows*, 1976, *Night Winds*, 1978, *The Road of Kings*, 1978, *In a Lonely Place*, 1983, *Killer* (with David A. Drake), 1985, *The Book of Kane*, 1985, and *Why Not You and I?*, 1987. Editor of *The Year's Best Horror Stories 8–20, Echoes of Valor 1-3, Intensive Scare*, and the authorized Conan series. **Essay:** Manly Wade Wellman.

**WATSON, Ian.** See his own entry. **Essay:** David I. Masson.

**WAY, Douglas E.** Retired businessman. **Essays:** J.U. Giesy; Austin Hall and Homer Eon Flint.

**WAY, Karen G.** Teaching Assistant, Department of English, Rutgers University, New Brunswick, New Jersey. Past editor of *Lovejoy's Guidance Digest.* **Essays:** Jonathan Fast; J.B. Priestley; Walt and Leigh Richmond; Kathleen Sky; E.C. Tubb.

**WEEDMAN, Jane B.** Assistant Professor of English, Texas Tech University, Lubbock. Author of *Samuel R. Delany*, 1982, and articles on Delany, James White, and E.E. Smith. Editor of *Women Worldwalkers: New Dimensions of Science Fiction and Fantasy*, forthcoming. **Essays:** Anna Kavan; Mark Twain.

**WEINKAUF, Mary S.** Professor of English and Head of the Department, Dakota Wesleyan University, Mitchell, South Dakota. Author of *Early Poems by a Late Beginner*, 1976, *Lew Archer, Humanist Priest*, 1985, forthcoming studies of S. Fowler Wright and Ngaio Marsh, and of articles and reviews in *Fantasy and Science Fiction Book Review, SFRA Newsletter, Extrapolation, Studies in English Literature, Texas Quarterly*, and other periodicals. **Essays:** René Barjavel (foreign-language); William Dean Howells; Craig Strete; S. Fowler Wright.

**WELCH, Dennis M.** Associate Professor of English and humanities, Virginia Polytechnic and State University, Blacksburg. Author of articles on Tennyson, science and literature, Sturgeon, Blake, and Shelley. **Essay:** Theodore R. Cogswell.

**WHITE, Fred D.** Assistant Professor of English, University of Santa Clara, California. Author of *Composition: Art and Craft* (forthcoming), and articles in *San Jose Studies, Arizona Quarterly, Journal of English Teaching Techniques, The Writing Instructor*, and other publications. **Essay:** Robert Sheckley.

**WILCOX, Robert H.** Professor Emeritus, Glendale College, Arizona. Former consulting editor, *Amazing*, and editor-in-chief, Industrial Publications, New York. **Essays:** Fredric Brown; Louis Charbonneau; Frederick Pohl; Clifford D. Simak; William F. Temple.

**WILDER, Cherry.** See her own entry. **Essays:** Colin Greenland; Ira Levin.

**WINGROVE, David.** See his own entry. **Essays:** Richard Cowper; Christopher Evans; David Garnett; Mary Gentle; Gary Kilworth; Paul McAuley; Andrew M. Stephenson.

**WOLFE, Gary K.** Professor of humanities, Roosevelt University, Chicago. Author of *The Known and the Unknown: The Iconography of Science Fiction*, 1979, *Elements of Research*, 1979, *David Lindsay*, 1982, *Critical Terms for Science Fiction and Fantasy*, 1986, and articles and reviews for books and periodicals.

**Essays:** Sharon Baker; Ray Bradbury; Edmund Cooper; John Keir Cross; Jack Finney; William Hope Hodgson; Nigel Kneale; David Lindsay; John Lymington; Richard Matheson; Chad Oliver; Daniel M. Pinkwater; Rod Serling; M.P. Shiel; Cordwainer Smith; Jerry Sohl.

**WOLFE, Gene.** See his own entry. **Essay:** Algis Budrys.

**WOOSTER, Martin Morse.** Washington Editor, *Reason.* Author of articles in *Esquire, Wall Street Journal, Chicago Tribune, Fantasy Review*, Toronto *Star*, Boston *Globe*, and other publications. **Essays:** Reginald Bretnor; William Rotsler; Ted White; Jack Williamson.

**WYGANT, Alice Chambers.** Reference Librarian, Moody Medical Library, Galveston, Texas. Died. **Essay:** Sonya Dorman.

**YOKE, Carl B.** Assistant to the associate vice-president for the Extended University, and Associate Professor of English, Kent State University, Ohio; associate editor of *Extrapolation.* Author of *A Reader's Guide to Roger Zelazny and Andre Norton: Proponents of Individualism* (forthcoming), and articles on Jakes, Galouye, Crichton, Joan Vinge, Maine, Kuttner, C.L. Moore, Merritt, Moorcock, and other SF and fantasy writers. Co-editor of *Death and the Serpent: Immortality in Science Fiction and Fantasy*, 1985. **Essays:** Michael Crichton; Daniel F. Galouye; John Jakes; Charles Eric Maine; Joan D. Vinge; Roger Zelazny.

**ZAKI, Hoda M.** Assistant Professor of political science, Hampton University, Virginia. Reviewer for *Hypatia: A Journal of Feminist Philosophy*, Hampton and Newport News *Daily Press*, and the National Women's Studies Association's *Newsletter.* **Essay:** Marta Randall.

**ZEBROWSKI, George.** See his own entry. **Essays:** David Duncan; Edgar Pangborn; Thomas N. Scortia; William Tenn.